Now and Forever

DANIELLE STEEL

SPHERE BOOKS LIMITED
30/32 Gray's Inn Road, London WC1X 8JL

First published in Great Britain by
Sphere Books Ltd 1979

Published by arrangement with
Dell Publishing Co., Inc.

TRADE MARK

Set in 10 on 11 pt Plantin

Printed in Great Britain by
C. Nicholls & Company Ltd
The Philips Park Press, Manchester

To special people,
for a special time,
with special love:

Susan Alan
Beatrice Baer
Melba Beals
Frances Brauer
Lillian Oksman
Consuelo Smith
Patricia Tuttle

To Claude-Eric
for giving me so much,
especially writing.

To Dan for lessons learned
and shared.
For everything !

And to Beatrix
for being wonderful
and always loving.

D.S.

'There are three kinds of souls,
three kinds of prayers.
One: I am a bow in your hands, Lord.
Draw me lest I rot.
Two: Do not overdraw me, Lord.
I shall break.
Three: Overdraw me, and who cares
if I break!

Choose!'

From 'Report to Greco'
by Nicos Kazantzakis

CHAPTER I

The weather was magnificent. A clear blue sunny day, with sharply etched white clouds in the sky. The perfect Indian summer. And so hot. The heat made everything slow and sensual. And it was so totally unlike San Francisco. That was the best part. Ian sat at a small pink marble table, his usual seat, in a patch of sunlight at Enrico's restaurant on Broadway. The traffic whizzed by while lunch-hour couples strolled. The heat felt delicious.

Under the table, Ian swung one long leg easily over the other. Three daisies bobbed in a glass, and the bread was fresh and soft to the touch. The almost too thin, graceful fingers tore one slice of bread carefully away from the others. Two young girls watched him and giggled. He wasn't 'cute', he was sexy. Even they knew it. And beautiful. Handsome. Elegant. He had class. Tall, thin, blond, blue-eyed, with high cheek-bones and endless legs, hands that one noticed, a face one hated to stop looking at . . . a body one watched. Ian Clarke was a beautiful man. And he knew it, in an offhand sort of way. He knew it. His wife knew it. So what? She was beautiful too. It wasn't something they really cared about. But other people did. Other people loved to watch them, in that hungry way one stares at exceptionally good-looking people, wanting to know what they're saying, where they're going, who they know, what they eat . . . as though some of it might rub off. It never does. One has to be born with it. Or spend a great deal of money to fake it. Ian didn't fake it. He had it.

The woman in the large natural straw hat and pink dress had noticed it too. She stared at him through the mesh of the straw. She watched his hands with the bread, his mouth as he drank. She could even see the blond hair on his arms as he rolled up his sleeves in the sun. She was several tables away, but she saw. Just as she had seen him there before. But he never saw her. Why would he? She saw everything, and then she stopped watching. Ian didn't know she was alive. He was busy with the rest of the view.

Life was incredibly good. Ripe and golden and easy. His for the plucking. He had worked on the third chapter of his novel all morning, and now the characters were coming to life, just like the people wandering along Broadway . . . strolling, laughing, playing games. His characters were already that real to him. He knew them intimately. He was their father, their creator, their friend. And they were his friends. It was such a good feeling, starting a book. It populated his life. All those new faces, new heads. He could feel them in his hands as he rat-tat-tapped on the typewriter keys. Even the keyboard felt good to his touch.

He had it all, a city he loved, a new novel at last, and a wife he still laughed and played with and loved making love to. Seven years and everything about her still felt good to him: her laughter, her smile, the look in her eyes, the way she sat naked in his studio, perched in the old wicker rocking chair, drinking root beer and reading his work. Everything felt good, and better now, with the novel beginning to blossom. It was a magical day. And Jessie was coming home. It had been a productive three weeks, but he was suddenly lonely and horny as hell . . . Jessie.

Ian closed his eyes and blotted out the sounds of traffic drifting by . . . Jessie . . . of the graceful legs, the blonde hair like fine satin, the green eyes with gold specks . . . eating peanut butter and apricot jam on raisin bread at two in the morning, asking him what he thought of the spring line for her shop . . . 'I mean honestly, Ian, tell me the truth, do you hate the spring things, or are they okay? From a man's point of view . . . be honest . . .' As though it really mattered, from a man's point of view. Those big green eyes searching his face as though asking him if she were okay, if he loved her, if . . . he did.

Sipping his gin and tonic, he thought of her, and felt indebted to her again. It gave him a tiny pinched feeling somewhere in the pit of his stomach. But that was part of it: he did owe her a lot. She had weathered a lot. Teaching jobs that had paid him a pittance, substitute teaching that had paid less, a job in a bookstore, which she had hated because she felt it demeaned him. So he had quit. He had even had a brief fling with journalism, after his first novel had bombed. And then her inheritance had solved so many of their problems. Theirs, but not necessarily his.

'You know, Mrs. Clarke, one of these days you're going to get sick and tired of being married to a starving writer.' He had watched her face intently as she'd shaken her head and smiled in the sunlight of a summer day three years before . . .

'You don't look like you're starving to me.' She patted his stomach, and then kissed him gently on the lips. 'I love you, Ian.'

'You must be crazy. But I love you too.' It had been a rough summer for him. He hadn't made a dime in eight months. But Jessie had her money, of course. Dammit.

'Why am I crazy? Because I respect your work? Because I think you're a good husband, even if you're not working on Madison Avenue anymore? So what, Ian? Who gives a damn about Madison Avenue? Do you? Do you miss it so much, or are you just going to use it to torment yourself for the rest of your life?' There was a faint tinge of bitterness in her voice, mixed with anger. 'Why can't you just enjoy what you are?'

'And what's that?'

'A writer. And a good one.'

'Who says?'

'The critics "says," that's who says.'

'My royalties don't says.'

'Fuck your royalties.' She looked so serious that he had to laugh.

'I'd have a tough time trying—they're not big enough to tickle, let alone fuck.'

'Oh, shut up . . . creep . . . sometimes you make me so mad.' A smile began to warm her face again and he leaned over and kissed her. She ran a finger slowly up the inside of his thigh, watching him with that quiet smile of hers, and he tingled all over . . .

He still remembered it. Perfectly.

'Evil woman, I adore you. Come on, let's go home.' They had left the beach hand in hand, like two kids, sharing their own private smile. They hadn't even waited until they'd gotten home. A few miles later, Ian had spotted a narrow creek a little distance from the road, and they had parked there and made love under the trees, near the creek, with the summer sounds all around them. He still remembered lying on the soft earth with her afterward, wearing only their shirts and letting their toes play with the pebbles and grass. He still remembered thinking that he would never quite understand what bound her to him . . . why? And what bound him to her? The questions one never asks of marriage . . . why, for your money, darling, why else? No one in his right mind ever asked those questions. But sometimes he was so tempted to. He sometimes feared that what bound him to her was her faith in his writing. He didn't want to think it was that, but that was certainly part of it.

All those nights of argument and coffee and wine in his studio. She was always so goddam sure. When he needed her to be. That was the best part.

'I know you'll make it, Ian. That's all. I just know you will.' So goddam sure. That's why she had made him quit his job on Madison Avenue, because she was so sure. Or was it because she'd wanted to make him dependent on her? Sometimes he wondered about that too.

'But *how* do you know, dammit? How can you possibly know I'll make it? It's a dream, Jessie. A fantasy. The great American novel. Do you know how many absolute zeroes are out there writing crap, thinking "this is it"?'

'Who gives a damn? That's not you.'

'Maybe it is.' She had thrown a glass of wine at him once when he'd said that, and it made him laugh. They had wound up making love on the thick fur rug while he dripped wine from his chin to her breasts and they laughed together.

It was all part of why he had to write a good one now. Had to. For her. For himself. He had to this time. Six years of writing had produced one disastrous novel and one beautiful book of fables that the critics had hailed as a classic. It had sold less than seven hundred copies. The novel hadn't even done *that* 'well'. But this one was going to be different. He knew it. It was his brainchild against hers, Lady J.

Lady J was Jessie's boutique. And Jessie had made it a smash. The right touches, the right flair, the right line at the right time. She was one of those people who casts a spell on whatever they touch. A candle, a scarf, a jewel, a flash of colour, a hint of a smile, a glow of warmth, a dash of pizzazz, a dollop of style. A barrel of style. Jessie had been born with it. She oozed it. Stark naked and with her eyes closed, she had style.

Like the way she flew into his studio at lunchtime, her blonde mane flying, a smile in her eyes, a kiss on his neck, and suddenly one fabulous salmon rose dropped across his papers. One perfect rose, or one brilliant yellow tulip in a crystal vase next to his coffee cup, a few slices of prosciutto, some cantaloupe, a thin sliver of Brie . . . *The New York Times* . . . or *Le Figaro*. She just had it. A gift for transforming everything she touched into something more, something better.

Thinking of her made Ian smile again as he watched the people at the other tables. If Jessie had been there she would have worn something faintly outrageous, a sundress that exposed her back but covered her arms, or something totally covered up but with a slit that gave passersby just the quickest flash of leg, or an unbearably beautiful hat that would only allow them to catch a glimpse of one striking green eye, while the other flirted, then hid. Thinking of her like that drew his attention to the woman in the straw hat a few tables away. He hadn't seen her before. And he thought she was definitely worth seeing. On a hot, sunny afternoon, with two gin and tonics under his belt. He could barely see her face. Only the point of her chin.

She had slender arms and pretty hands with no rings. He watched her sip something frothy through a straw. He felt a familiar stirring as he thought of his wife and watched the girl in the hat. It was a damn shame Jessie wasn't home. It was a day to go to the beach, and swim, and sweat, and get covered with sand, and rub your hands all over each other, oozing suntan oil. The way the woman in the straw hat moved her mouth on the straw in her drink bothered him. It made him want Jessie. Now.

His cannelloni arrived, but it had been a poor choice. Too creamy, too hot, and too much. He should have ordered a salad. And he was loath to order coffee after his few bites of lunch. It was too easy a day to be hard on yourself. It was so much easier just to let yourself go, or your mind, at least. That was harmless. He was having a good time. He always did at Enrico's. He could relax there, watch strangers, meet writers he knew, and admire the women.

For no reason in particular, he let the waiter bring him a third drink. He rarely drank anything other than white wine, but the gin was cool and pleasant. And a third drink wouldn't kill him. There was something about hot days in a usually cool climate . . . you went a bit mad.

The crowd at Enrico's ebbed and flowed, crowding the sidewalk for tables, shunning the red booths indoors. Businessmen freed their necks of ties, models preened, artists scribbled, street musicians played, poets joked. Even the traffic noises were dimmed by the music and the voices. It reminded him of the last day of school. And the topless bars were silent on either side of the restaurant, their neon doused until nightfall. This was much better than neon. It was real. It was young and alive and had the spice of a game.

The girl in the hat never revealed her face as Ian left, but she watched him, and then silently shrugged, and signalled for the check. She could always come back, or maybe . . . what the hell . . .

Ian was thinking of her on his way to the car, slightly tipsy but not so much that it showed. He was dreaming up verses to 'Ode to a Faceless Beauty'. He laughed to himself as he slid behind the wheel of Jessie's car, wishing he were sliding into Jessie. He was unbearably horny.

He was driving Jessie's little red Morgan. And thoroughly enjoying it. It had been a damn handsome gift, he reflected, as he pulled out the choke. A damn handsome gift. For a damn handsome woman. He had bought it for her with his advance for the fables. The whole cheque for the car. Madness. But she had adored it. And he adored her.

He swung back onto Broadway and stopped at a light, passing Enrico's again on his way home, just as a whisper of pink brushed past his right eye. The hat swirled on one finger now as her face looked up toward the sky, her behind undulating freely as she walked in high-heeled white sandals. The pink dress tugged at her hips, but not blatantly, and her red hair framed her face in loose curls. She looked pretty in pink, and so goddam sexy. So round and so ripe and so young . . . twenty-two? . . . twenty-three? He felt the same hunger again in his loins as he watched her. Her copper hair reflected the sun. He wanted to touch it. To tear the hat from her hand and run away, to see if she'd follow him. He wanted to play, and he had no one to play with.

He drove slowly past her, and she looked up, and then her face flushed and she looked away, as though she hadn't expected to see him again and now it changed everything. She turned her head and looked at him again, the surprise replaced by a slow smile and a barely visible shrug. Destiny. Today had been the day after all. She had dressed for it. And now she was glad. She seemed unwilling to go, under the heat of his gaze. He hadn't driven on. He simply sat there, while she stood at the corner and watched him. She was not as young as he'd thought. Twenty-six . . . twenty-seven? But still fresh. Fresh enough, after three gin and tonics and not a great deal of food.

Her eyes searched his face, clawing a little, but carefully, and then, as he watched, she approached, showing the full bosom in sharp contrast to the girlish shape of her arms.

'Do I know you?' She stood holding her hat, one ankle suddenly crossing the other; it made her hipbones jut forward, and Ian's trousers were instantly too tight.

'No. I don't think so.'

'You've been staring.'

'Yes . . . I'm sorry. I . . . I liked your hat. I noticed it at lunch.' Her face eased and he returned her smile, disappointed, though. She was older than Jessie, perhaps even a year or two older than he. Made up to look exquisite at a thirty-foot distance, at twenty feet the illusion was shattered. And the red hair showed a thin line of black roots. But he *had* been staring, she was right.

'I'm really awfully sorry. Do you need a lift?' Why not? She couldn't be headed far off his path; probably to an office a few blocks away.

'Yeah, sure. Thanks. It's too hot to walk.' She smiled again, and struggled with the handle on the door. Ian released it for her from within, and she pounced onto the seat, displaying a comforting amount of cleavage. That much was real.

'Where can I take you?'

She paused for a moment and then smiled. 'Market and Tenth. Is that out of your way?'

'No, that's fine. I'm not in a hurry.' But he was surprised at the address. It was an odd place to work, a bad place to live.

'Did you take the day off?' She was looking at him questioningly.

'Sort of. I work at home.' He wasn't usually that expansive, but she made him uncomfortable, made him feel as though he should talk. She wore a heavy perfume, and her skirt had slipped well up her thighs. Ian was hungry. But for Jessie. And she was still ten hours away.

'What do you do?' For an odd moment he wanted to say he was a gigolo, kept by his wife. He argued the point in his head as he frowned.

'I'm a writer.' The answer was curt.

'Don't you like it?'

'I love it. What made you ask that?' This time he was surprised.

'The way you started to frown. You're a nice-looking guy when you smile.'

'Thank you.'

'*De nada.* You also drive a nice-looking car.' Her eyes had sized up the scene. The well-cut St. Tropez shirt, the

Gucci shoes with no socks. She didn't know they were Gucci, but she knew they were expensive. 'What is this? An MG?'

'No. A Morgan.' *And it's my wife's . . .* the words stuck in his throat. 'What do you do?' Tit for tat.

'Right now I wait table at the Condor, but I wanted to see what the neighbourhood looks like in the daylight. That's why I came down here for lunch. It's a whole different crowd. And at this time of day they're a lot more sober than they are when we get them later.'

The Condor was not known for its decorous clientele. It was the home of the 'Original Topless', and Ian assumed that the woman waited on tables half nude. She shrugged and then let her face grow soft in a smile. She looked almost pretty again, but there was a sadness somewhere in her eyes. A kind of regret, haunting and distant. She glanced at him oddly once or twice. And again Ian found that she had made him uncomfortable.

'You live at Market and Tenth?' It was something to say.

'Yeah. In a hotel. You?' That one was a bitch to answer. What could he say? But she filled the pause for him. 'Let me guess. Pacific Heights?' The brightness in her eyes was gone now, and the question sounded brittle and accusing.

'What makes you say that?' He tried to sound amused and look mock-hurt, but it didn't come off. He looked at her as they stopped in a snarl of Montgomery Street traffic. She could have been someone's secretary, or a girl doing a bit part in a movie. She didn't look cheap. She looked tired. And sad.

'Sweetheart, you smell of Pacific Heights. It's all over you.'

'Don't let fragrances fool you. As in "all that glitters" . . .' They laughed lightly together and he played with the choke as the traffic jam eased. He turned the car onto Market.

'Married?'

He nodded.

'Too bad. The good ones always are.'

'Is that a deterrent?' It was an insane thing to have said, but he was more curious than serious, and the gin and tonics had taken their toll.

'Sometimes I go for married guys, sometimes I don't. Depends on the guy. In your case . . . who knows? I like you.'

'I'm flattered. You're a nice-looking woman, as you put it. What's your name?'

'Margaret. Maggie.'

'That's a nice name.' She smiled at him again. 'Is this it, Maggie?' It was the only hotel on the block, and it was no beauty.

'Yeah, this is it. Home sweet home. Beautiful, ain't it?' She tried to cover her embarrassment with flippancy, and he found himself feeling sorry for her. The hotel looked bleak and depressing.

'Want to come up for a drink?'

He knew from the look in her eyes that she'd be hurt if he didn't. And, hell, he was in no shape to go home and work. And he still had nine and a half hours to kill before driving out to the airport. But he also knew what might happen if he accepted Maggie's invitation. And letting that happen seemed like a rotten thing to do to Jessie the day she was coming home. He had held out for three weeks. Why not one more afternoon? . . .

But this girl looked so lonely, so unloved, and the gin and the sun were spinning in his brain. He knew he didn't want to go back to the house. Nothing in it was his, not really his, except five file drawers of his writing and the new Olivetti typewriter Jessie had given him. The gigolo king. Jessie's consort.

'Sure. I've got time for a drink. As long as you make it coffee. What'll I do with the car?'

'I think you can park it in front of the door. It's a white zone, they won't tow you away.'

He parked the car in front of the hotel, and Maggie carefully watched the back of the car as he pulled in to the kerb. It was an easy plate to remember. It spelled what she thought was his name. Jessie.

CHAPTER II

Jessica heard the landing gear grind out of the plane's belly and smiled. Her seat belt was in place, her overhead light was out, and she felt her heart begin to beat faster as the plane circled the runway for the last time. She had a clear view of the lights below.

She looked at her watch. She knew him so well. Right now he would be frantically looking for a parking space in the airport garage, terrified that he was late and might miss her at the gate. He'd find a space then, and run like hell for the terminal, and would be panting and smiling, nerves jangled, when he reached her. But he'd get there in time. He always did. It made coming home something special.

She felt as though she had been away for a year, but she'd bought such good things. The spring line would be lovely. Soft pastels, gentle wools cut on the bias, creamy plaids, silk shirts with full sleeves, and some marvellous suedes. She could never resist the suedes. It would be a great spring at the boutique. The goodies she had ordered wouldn't begin to arrive for another three or four months, but she was already excited thinking about them. She had them all memorized. The spring line was set. She liked to plan ahead like that. Liked knowing what was coming. Liked knowing that she had her life, and her work, all mapped out. Some people might find that boring, but it never bothered Jessie.

She and Ian were planning a trip to Carmel in October. Thanksgiving would be spent with friends. Maybe Christmas skiing at Lake Tahoe, and then a quick hop to Mexico for some sun after the New Year. And then the spring line would start to come in. It was all perfectly planned. Like her trips, like her meals, like her wardrobe. She had what it took to make plans—a business that worked, a husband she loved and could always count on, and reliable people around her. Very little was variable, and she liked it that way. She wondered if that was why she had never wanted a baby: it would be a variable. Something she couldn't totally plan. She didn't know how it would look or act, or exactly when it might be born, or what she would do with it once she had it. The idea of a baby unnerved her. And life was so much simpler like this. Just Jessie and Ian. Alone. And that way there were no rivals for Ian's affection. Jessie didn't like to compete, not for Ian. He was all she had now.

The wheels touched the runway, and she closed her eyes . . . Ian . . . she had longed for him over the past weeks. The days had been full and the nights busy, yet she had usually called him when she'd reached the hotel in the evening. But she hadn't been able to reach out and touch him, or be held. She hadn't been able to laugh into his eyes, or tickle his feet, or stand next to him under the shower, chasing drops of water past the freckles on his back with her tongue. She stretched her long legs ahead of her as she waited for the plane to come to a halt.

It was hard to be patient. She wanted the trip to be over. She wanted to run out and see him. Right now. There had never been other men. It was hard to believe, but there hadn't. She had given it some thought, once or twice, but it had never seemed worth it. Ian was so much better than anyone else, in her eyes. Sexier and smarter and kinder and more loving. Ian understood so well what she needed, and fulfilled so many needs. In the seven years they'd been married, she had lost track of most of her close women friends in New York, and hadn't replaced them with others in San Francisco. She didn't need women friends, a confidante, a 'best' friend. She had Ian. He was her best friend, her lover, even her brother, now that Jake was dead. And so what if now and then Ian had a 'fling'? It didn't happen often, and he was discreet. It didn't bother her. Men did those things when they had to, when their wives were away. He didn't use it, or flaunt it, or grind it into her heart. She just suspected that he did it. That was all. She understood. As long as she didn't have to know. She assumed, which was different from knowing.

Her parents had had a marriage like that, and they had been happy for years. Watching them, Jessie had understood about the things you didn't talk about, didn't hurt each other with, didn't use. A good marriage relied on consideration, and sometimes keeping your mouth shut and just letting the other guy be was consideration . . . love. Her parents were dead now; they hadn't been young when she'd been born. Her mother had been in her late thirties, her father just past forty-five. And Jessie had been four when Jake was born. But marrying late, they had respected each other more than most couples did. They were not inclined to make changes in each other. It had taught Jessie a lot.

But they were all gone now. It had already been three years. Almost exactly. Her parents had died within months of each other. Jake had died a year before that, in Vietnam, at the crest of his twenties. Gone. Jessica was the only one left. But she had Ian. Thank God there was Ian. It sent little tremors up her spine when she thought of it that way . . . what would she do without Ian? Die . . . the way her father had done without her mother . . . die . . . she couldn't live without Ian. He was her all now. He held her late at night when she was afraid. He made her laugh when something touched too deep and made her sad. He remembered the moments that mattered, knew the things that she loved, understood her private language, laughed at all her worst jokes. He knew. She was his woman, and his little girl. That was what she needed. Ian. So what did it matter if there were occasional indiscretions she didn't really know about? As long as he was there when it counted. And he always was.

She heard the doors slide open; the people began to press into the aisles. The five-hour flight was over. It was time to go home. Jessie brushed the creases from her slacks with one hand and reached for her coat with the other. It was a bright orange suede that she wore over beige suede pants and a print silk shirt in shades of caramel. Her green eyes glowed in her suntanned face, and her blonde hair swung thick and free past her shoulders. Ian loved her in orange, and she had bought the coat in New

York. She smiled to herself, thinking how he'd love it—almost as much as the Pierre Cardin blazer she'd brought him. It was fun to spoil Ian.

Three businessmen and a gaggle of women pressed out before her, but she was tall enough to see over the chattering women's heads. He was there at the gate, and she waved as he grinned broadly, waving back, and then he moved swiftly toward her, gently weaving his way through the people ahead of her. Then he had reached her and was taking her in his arms.

'It's about time you came home . . . and looking like that, you'll be lucky if I don't rape you right here.' He looked so pleased. And then he kissed her. She was home.

'Go ahead. Rape me. I dare you.' But they stood where they were, drinking each other in, saying it all with their eyes. Jessie couldn't keep a smile from her lips, or her hands from his face. 'You feel so good.' She loved the softness and spiced lemon smell of his skin.

'Jessie, if you knew how I missed you . . .' She nodded, knowing. She had missed him at least as much.

'How's the book?'

'Nice.' They spoke in the brief banalities of those who know each other better than well. They didn't need many words. 'Really nice.' He picked up her large brown leather tote from the floor where she'd dropped it to kiss him. 'Come on, sexy lady, let's go home.' She looped her arm into his, and together they walked in long even strides, her hair brushing his shoulder, her every move a complement to his.

'I brought you a present.'

He smiled. She always did.

'Bought yourself one too, I see. That's some coat.'

'Do you like it? Or is it awful? I was afraid it was a little too loud.' It was a burnt caramel bordering on flame.

'On you it looks good. Everything does.'

'Jesus, you're being nice to me! What did you do? Smash up the car?'

'Now, is that a nice thing to say? I ask you. Is that nice?'

'Did you?' But she was laughing and so was he.

'No, I traded it for a Honda motorcycle. I thought you might like that better.'

'What a nice thought! Gee, darling, I'm just thrilled. Now come on, tell the truth. How bad is the car?'

'Bad? I'll have you know that it happens to be not only in impeccable condition, but clean, a condition it was *not* in when you left. That poor little car was filthy!'

'Yeah, I know.' She hung her head and he grinned.

'You're a disgrace, Mrs. Clarke, but I love you.' He kissed the tip of her nose and she slid her arms around his neck.

'Guess what?'

'How many guesses do I get?'

'One.'

'You love me?'

'You guessed it!' She giggled and kissed his neck.

'What do I get as a prize for guessing?'

'Me.'

'Terrific. I'll take it.'

'Boy, I'm glad to be home.' She heaved a small sigh and stood in the circle of his arms as they waited for her bags to appear on the turntable. He could see the relief in her eyes. She hated going away, hated flying, was afraid to die, was afraid he'd die in a car wreck while she was gone. Ever since her parents and her brother . . . so many terrors. It wasn't as if they had died violently. Her mother had just been old. Old enough. Sixty-eight. And her father in his seventies. He had died of grief less than a year later. But Jessie hadn't been ready for the double loss and it was incredible to see what it had done to her. She had never fully recovered from her brother's death, but after her parents . . . At times Ian wondered if she'd make it. The terrors, the hysteria, the nightmares. She felt so alone and so frightened. At times she wasn't even someone he knew. She was suddenly so dependent on him, so unlike the old Jessie. And it seemed as though she wanted to be sure he was equally dependent on her . . . That was when he had let her talk him into quitting his job and writing full-time. She could afford it. But in some ways he wasn't sure *he* could. It suited both of them though, most of the time. And supporting him made Jessie feel more secure. He really *was* all she had now.

She looked up at him again and smiled.

'Just wait till I get you home, Mrs. Clarke.'

'Lech.'

'Yep. And you love it.'

'Yes. I do.'

People were watching them, but they didn't notice. They gave people something pretty to look at, something to smile at, to feel good about, to wish for. And something to enjoy as well. They were two beautiful people who had it all. That usually aroused an interesting medley of emotions in those who watched them.

They walked to the garage to reclaim the Morgan and Jessie grinned with pride when she saw it.

'Christ, it looks good. What did you do to it?'

'Have it washed. You should try it sometime. You'll love the effect.'

'Oh, shut up.' She swung at him playfully, and he ducked, catching her arm as she laughed.

'Before you beat me up, Amazon, get in the car.' He slapped her on the behind and unlocked the door.

'Don't call me an Amazon, you miserable creep! Masher!'

'Masher? Did I hear you call me a masher?' He looked shocked and walked back to where she stood. 'Lady, how dare you call me a name like that?' And with that he swung her off her feet and slid her onto the seat of the car. 'There. And let me tell you, with a broad your size, that's no mean feat!'

'Ian, you're a shit.' But he knew she wasn't sensitive about her height. They both liked it. 'Besides, I think I'm shrinking.'

'Oh? Down to six-one now, are you?' He chuckled as he finished strapping her bag to the luggage rack in the back. He still had the top down on the car, and she was watching him with a smile.

'Go to hell. You know perfectly well I'm only five-eleven, but I measured myself the other day and I was only five-ten-and-a-half.'

'You must have been sitting down.'

He slid in beside her and turned to look into her eyes. 'Hello, Mrs. Clarke. Welcome home.'

'Hello, my love. It's so good to be back.' They shared a long smile as he started the car, and she shrugged out of the new coat and rolled up the sleeves of her blouse. 'Was it hot here today? It still feels warm now.'

'It was boiling and gorgeous and sunny. And if it's anything like that tomorrow, you can call the boutique and tell them you're snowed in in Chicago. We're going to the beach.'

'Snowed in, in September? You're crazy. And, darling, I really can't.' But she liked the idea and he knew it,

'Oh, yes you can. I'll kidnap you if I have to.'

'Maybe I could go in late.'

'Now you've got the idea.' He smiled victoriously as he pulled the choke.

'Was it really that nice today?'

'Nicer. And it would have been better yet if you had been home. I got crocked at lunch at Enrico's, and I didn't know what to do with myself all day.'

'I'm sure you found something.' But there was no malice in her tone, and no expression on his face.

'Nah. Nothing much.'

CHAPTER III

'Jessie, you are without a doubt the most beautiful woman I know.'

'It's entirely mutual.' She lay on her stomach, smiling up at him, the scent of their bodies heavy in the air, their hair tousled. They had not been awake very long. Only long enough to make love.

'It can't be mutual, silly. I'm not a beautiful woman.'

'No, but you're a magnificent man.'

'And you are adorably corny. You must live with a writer.' She smiled again and he ran a finger gently up her spine.

'You're going to get into trouble again, darling, if you do that.' She accepted a puff on the cigarette they shared, and exhaled over his head before sitting up to kiss him again.

'What time are we going to the beach, Jessie, my love?'

'Who said we were going to the beach? Jesus, darling, I have to get to the shop. I've been gone for three weeks.'

'So be gone for another day. You said you were going to the beach with me today.' He looked faintly like a pouting boy.

'I did not.'

'You most certainly did. Well, almost. I told you I'd kidnap you, and you seemed to like the idea.' She laughed, running a hand through his hair. He was impossible. A great big boy. But such a beautiful boy. She could never resist him.

'You know something?'

'What?' He looked pleased as he gazed down into her face. She was beautiful in the morning.

'You're a pain in the ass, that's what. I have to work. How can I go to the beach?'

'Easy. You call the girls, tell them you can't come in till tomorrow, and off we go. Simple. How can you waste a day like this, for Chrissake?'

'By making a living.'

Those were the comments he didn't like. They implied that he didn't make a living.

'How about if I go in this morning and cut the day short?'

'Yeah. And leave the boutique just as the fog comes in. Jessica, you're a party pooper. Yep. Party pooper. A-1.' But she was already on her way to make coffee, and answered him over her shoulder as she walked naked into the kitchen.

'I promise I'll leave the shop by one. How's that?'

'Better than nothing. Christ, I love your ass. And you lost weight.' She smiled and blew him a kiss.

'One o'clock, I promise. And we can have lunch here.'

'Does that mean what I think it does?' He was smiling again and she nodded. 'Then I'll pick you up at twelve-thirty.'

'That's a deal.'

Lady J nestled on the ground floor of a well-tended Victorian house just off Union Street. The house was painted yellow with white trim, and a small brass plaque on the door was engraved with LADY J. Jessie had had a broad picture window put in, and she did the window display herself twice a month. It was simple and effective, and as she pulled the Morgan into the driveway she looked up to see what they'd done with the display while she was gone. A brown tweed skirt, a camel-coloured stock shirt, amber beads, a trim knit hat, and a little fox jacket draped over a green velvet chair. It looked pretty damn good, and it was the right look for fall . . . though not for Indian summer. But that didn't matter. No one bought for Indian summer. They bought for fall.

The things she had ordered in New York flashed through her mind as she pulled her briefcase out of the car and ran up the few steps to their door. It was open; the girls had known she'd be in early.

'Well, look who's home! Zina! Jessie's back!' A tiny, fine-featured Oriental girl clapped her hands and jumped to her feet, running toward Jessie with a look of delight. 'You look fantastic!' The two were a striking pair. Jessie's fair, lanky beauty was in sharp contrast to the Japanese girl's delicate grace. Her hair was shiny and black and hung in a well-shaped slant from the nape of her neck towards the point of her chin.

'Kat! You cut your hair!' Jessie was momentarily taken aback. Only a month before the girl's hair had hung to her waist—when she hadn't worn it in a tight knot high on her head. Her name was Katsuko, which meant peace.

'I got sick of wearing it up. How do you like it?' She pirouetted swiftly on one foot and let her hair swing around her head as she smiled. She was dressed in black, as she often was, and it accented her litheness. It was her catlike grace that had given her the nickname Jessie used.

'I love it. Very chic.' They smiled at each other and were rapidly interrupted by a war cry of glee.

'Hallelujah! You're home!' It was Zina. Auburn-haired, brown-eyed, sensual, and Southern. She was buxom where the other two were elegantly small-breasted, and she had a mouth that said she loved laughter and men. Her hair danced close to her head in a small halo of curls, and she had great, sexy legs. Men dissolved when she moved, and she loved to tease. 'Did you see what Kat did to her hair?' She said 'hair' as though it would go on forever. 'I'd have cried for a year.' She smiled, letting her mouth slide over the words. She made each one a caress. 'How was New York?'

'Beautiful, wonderful, terrible, ugly, and hot. I had a ball. And wait till you see what I bought!'

'What kind of colours?' For a girl who almost always wore white or black, Kat had a flair for hot colours. She knew how to buy them, mix them, contrast them, blend them. Everything except wear them.

'It's all pastel, and it's so beautiful, you'll die.' Jessica strutted the thick beige carpeting of Lady J. It felt good to be back in her domain. 'Who did the window? It looks great.'

'Zina.' Kat was quick to single out her friend for praise. 'Isn't that a nice touch with the green chair for contrast?'

'It's terrific. And I see nothing's changed around here. You two are still as tight as Siamese twins. Did we make any money while I was gone?' She sat in her favourite beige leather chair, a deep one that allowed her plenty of room for her legs. It was the chair men usually sat in while they waited.

'We made lots of money. For the first two weeks anyway. This week's been slow; the weather's been too good.' Kat was quick with the report, and the last of it reminded Jessie that she had only four hours in which to work before Ian would come to spirit her away to the beach.

Zina handed her a cup of black coffee as she looked around. What she saw was the fall line she had bought, mostly in Europe, five months before, and against the beige and brown wools and leathers of the shop's subtle decor it showed up well. Two walls were mirrored and there was a jungle of plants in each corner. More greenery dripped from the ceiling, highlighted by subtle lighting.

'How's that Danish line doing?' The Danes had gone heavy on red—skirts, sweaters, three different styles of blazers, and a marvellous wrap-around coat in a deep cherry red that, in its own way, made a woman feel as exotic and sexy as fur would have. It was a great coat. Jessie had ordered one for herself.

'The Danish stuff is doing fine,' Zina intervened with her New Orleans drawl. 'How's Ian? We haven't seen him in weeks.' He had turned up once to cash a cheque, the day after Jessie had left.

'He's working on the new book.' Zina smiled warmly and nodded. She liked him. Kat was never as sure. She helped with the account books, so she knew how much of Jessica's profits he spent. But Zina had been in the shop much longer, and she had come to know Ian and appreciate him. Kat was newer, and still wore the brittle mantle of New York over her heart. She had been a sportswear buyer there until she'd tired of the pressure and decided to move to San Francisco. She had landed the job at Lady J within a week of her arrival, and she felt as lucky to be there as Jessie did having her in the shop. She knew the business. Totally.

The three women spent a half hour chatting over coffee while Katsuko showed Jessie some clippings of articles mentioning the boutique that had appeared in the papers. They had two new customers who had practically bought out the shop. And they talked easily of what Jessie had lined up for the fall. She wanted to set up a fashion show before she left for Carmel in October. Kat could get started on ideas for that.

The shop was alive with her presence, and together they made a powerful threesome. All three had something to offer. It showed in the fact that the boutique hadn't suffered while she'd been gone. She couldn't afford to have it do that, and she wouldn't have tolerated it, either. Both of the girls knew that, and they cherished their jobs. She paid well, they got marvellous clothes at a discount, and she was a reasonable woman to work for, which was rare. Kat had worked for three bitches in a row in New York, and Zina had escaped a long line of horny men who wanted her to type, take shorthand, and screw, not necessarily in that order. Jessica expected long hours and hard work, but she put in the same herself, and often more. She had made Lady J a success, and she expected them to help her maintain it. It wasn't a difficult task. She infused fresh life into it every season, and her clientele loved it. Lady J was as solid as a rock. Just like Jessica herself, and everything around her.

'And now, you two, I'd better dig through my mail. How bad is it?'

'Not too bad. Zina answered the dingy stuff. The letters from Texas from women who were here in March and wonder if the little yellow turtleneck is still on sale. That kind of stuff . . . she answered them all.'

'Zina, I love you.'

'At your service.' She swept a deep curtsy and the bright green halter she wore over white trousers bobbed with the weight of her breasts. But the other two had stopped teasing her long ago. Each was content with herself, and all three had good reason to be.

Jessie wandered into her small office three steps up in the back and looked around, pleased. Her plants were thriving, her mail was neatly divided and stacked, her bills had been paid. She saw at a glance that all was in order. Now all she had to do was sift through it. She was halfway through reading her mail when Zina appeared in the doorway, looking puzzled.

'There's a man here to see you, Jessie. He says it's urgent.' She looked almost worried. He was not one of their usual customers, and he hadn't come there to buy.

'To see me? What about?'

'He didn't say. But he asked me to give you his card.'

Zina extended the small rectangle of stiff white paper, and Jessie looked into her eyes.

'Something wrong?' Zina shrugged ignorance and Jessie read the name: 'William Houghton. Inspector. San Francisco Police.' She didn't understand and looked back at Zina for clues. 'Did anything happen while I was gone? Did we get robbed?' And Christ, wouldn't it be like them not to worry her at first, but wait and tell her an hour or two later!

'No, Jessie. Honest. Nothing happened. I don't have any idea what this is about.' The drawl sounded childish when Zina was worried.

'Neither do I. Why don't you bring him in here? I'd better talk to him.'

William Houghton appeared, following Zina with some interest. The fit of her white slacks over her trim hips was in sharp contrast to the fullness in her halter. The inspector looked hungry.

'Inspector Houghton?' Jessie stood to her full height, and Houghton seemed impressed. The three were an interesting group; Katsuko had not missed his thorough gaze either. 'I'm Jessica Clarke.'

'I'd like to speak to you alone for a minute, if that'll be all right.'

'That's fine. May I offer you a cup of coffee?' The door closed behind Zina, and he shook his head as Jessie indicated a chair near her desk and then sat back down in her own. She swivelled to face him. 'What can I do for you, Inspector? Miss Nelson said it was urgent.'

'Yes. It is. Is that your Morgan outside?' Jessie nodded, feeling queasy under the sharp look in his eyes. She was wondering if Ian had forgotten to pay his tickets again. She had had to fish him out of jail once before, for a neat little fine of two hundred dollars. In San Francisco, they didn't fool around. You paid your tickets or they took you to jail. Do not pass Go, and do not collect two hundred dollars.

'Yes, that's my car. My name's on the plates.' She smiled pleasantly and hoped that her hand didn't shake while she lit another cigarette. It was absurd. She hadn't done anything wrong, but there was something about the man, about the word 'Police', that produced instant guilt. Panic. Terror.

'Were you driving it yesterday?'

'No, I was in New York on business. I flew back last night.' As though she had to prove that she was out of town, and for a legitimate reason. This was crazy. If only Ian were here. He handled things so much better than she did.

'Who else drives your car!' Not 'does anyone else?', but 'who else?'

'My husband does.' Something sank in the pit of her stomach when she mentioned Ian.

'Did he drive it yesterday?' Inspector Houghton lit a cigarette of his own and looked her over, as if assessing her.

'I don't know for certain. He has his own car, but he was driving mine when he picked me up at the airport. I could call him and ask.' Houghton nodded and Jessica waited.

'Who else drives the car? A brother? A friend? Boyfriend?' His eyes dug into hers on the last word, and at last she felt anger.

'I'm a married woman, Inspector. And no one else drives the car. Just my husband and I.' She had gotten the point across, but something in Houghton's face told her it was not a victory.

'The car is registered to your business? You have commercial plates, and the address on the registration is this store.' Store! Boutique, you asshole, boutique! 'I assume you own this place?'

'That's correct. Inspector, what is this about?' She exhaled lengthily and watched the smoke as she felt her hand shake slightly. Something was wrong.

'I'd like to speak to your husband. Would you give me the address of his office, please?' He instantly took out a pen and waited, holding it poised over the back of one of his cards.

'Is this about parking tickets? I know my husband . . .

well, he's forgetful.' She smiled for Houghton's benefit, but it didn't take.

'No, this is not about parking tickets. Your husband's business address?' The eyes were like ice.

'He works at our home. It's only six blocks from here. On Vallejo.' She wanted to offer to go with him, but she didn't dare. She scribbled the address on one of her own cards and handed it to him.

'Thank you. I'll be in touch.' But what the fuck about, dammit? She wanted to know. But he stood up and reached for the door.

'Inspector, I'd appreciate it very much if you'd tell me what this is about. I—' He looked at her oddly again, with that searching look of his that asked questions but did not answer them.

'Mrs. Clarke, I'm not entirely sure myself. When I am, I'll let you know.'

'Thank you.' Thank you? Thank you for what? Shit.

But he was already gone, and as she walked back into the main room of the boutique, she saw him get into an olive green sedan and drive off. There was another man at the wheel. They travelled in pairs. The antenna on the back of the car swung crazily as they drove toward Vallejo.

'What was that all about?' Katsuko's face was serious, and Zina looked upset.

'I wish to hell I knew. He just asked me who drives the car and then said he wanted to talk to Ian. Goddammit, I'll bet he hasn't been paying his parking tickets again.' But it didn't feel like that, and Houghton had said it wasn't that—or was it? Jesus. Some welcome home.

She went back to her office and dialled their home number. It was busy. And then Trish Barclay walked into the shop and Jessie got tied up with nonsense like the fur jacket in the window, which Trish bought. She was one of their better customers, and Jessie had to keep up the façade, at least for a while. It was twenty-five minutes later when she got back to the phone to call Ian. This time there was no answer.

It was ridiculous! He had to be there. He had been

there when she'd left for the boutique. And the line had been busy when she'd called . . . the police had been on their way over. Christ, maybe it was serious. Maybe he had had an accident with the car and hadn't told her. Maybe someone had been hurt. But he'd have said something. Ian wouldn't just let something like that happen and not tell her. The phone rang endlessly, and no one answered. Maybe he was on his way over. It was a little after eleven.

But Nick Morris needed something 'fabulous' for his wife's birthday; he'd forgotten, and he had to have at least four hundred dollars' worth of goodies for her by noon. She was a raving bitch and she wasn't worth it, but Jessie gave him a hand. She liked Nick, and before he left the store weighted down with their shiny brown and yellow boxes, Barbara Fuller had walked in, and Holly Jenkins, and then Joan Wilcox, and . . . it was noon. And she hadn't heard from Ian. She tried the phone again and began to panic. No answer. Maybe this time he *was* on his way over. He had said he'd pick her up at twelve-thirty.

At one o'clock he hadn't shown up and she was near tears. It had been a horrible morning. People, pressures, deliveries, problems. Welcome home. And no Ian. And that asshole Houghton making her nervous with his mysterious inquiries about the car. She took refuge in her office as Zina went out to lunch. She needed to be alone for a minute. To think. To catch her breath. To get up the courage to do what she didn't want to do. But she had to know. It would be an easy way of finding out, after all. Hell, all she had to do was call down there, ask if they had an Ian Powers Clarke, and heave a sigh of relief when they said no. Or grab her chequebook and run down there and get him out if he was in the can for parking violations again. No big deal. But it took another swallow of coffee, and yet another cigarette, before she could bring her hand to the phone.

Information gave her the number. Hall of Justice. City Prison. This was ridiculous. She felt foolish, and grinned thinking of what Ian would say if she were calling the jail when he walked in. He'd make fun of her for a week.

A voice barked into her ear at the other end. 'City Prison. Palmer here.' Jesus. Now what? Okay, you called, so ask the man, dummy.

"I . . . I was wondering if you have a . . . a Mr. Ian Clarke, Ian Powers Clarke, down there, Sergeant. On parking violations.'

'What's the spelling?' The desk sergeant was not amused. Parking violations were serious business.

'Clarke. With an 'E' at the end. Ian. I-A-N C-L-A-R-K-E.' She took another drag on her cigarette while she waited, and Katsuko stuck her head in the door with an inquiry about lunch. Jessica shook her head vehemently and motioned to close the door. Her nerves had begun to fray hours ago, with the arrival of Inspector Houghton.

The voice came back on the phone after an interminable pause.

'Clarke. Yeah. We got him.' Well, bully for you. Jessica heaved a small sigh of relief. It was disagreeable, but not the end of the world. And at least now she knew, and she could have him out in half an hour. She wondered how many tickets he hadn't paid this time. But this time she was going to let him have a piece of her mind. He had scared the shit out of her. And that was probably what Houghton had wanted to do. He had, too, by not admitting that the problem was parking violations. Bastard.

'We booked him an hour ago. They're talking to him now.'

'About parking tickets?' How ridiculous. Enough was enough. And Jessica had had more than enough already.

'No, lady. Not about parking tickets. About three counts of rape and a charge of assault.' Jessie thought she could feel the ceiling pressing down on her head as the walls rushed in to squeeze the breath out of her lungs.

'What?'

'Three counts of rape. And a charge of assault.'

'My God. Can I talk to him?' Her hands shook so hard it took both of them to hold the phone, and she felt her breakfast rise in her throat.

'No. He can talk to his lawyer, and you can see him

tomorrow. Between eleven and two. Bail hasn't been set. The arraignment's on Thursday.' The desk sergeant hung up on her then, and she was holding the dead receiver in her hand, with a blank look in her eyes and tears beginning to stream down her face, when Katsuko opened the door and held out a sandwich. It took her a moment to absorb what she saw.

'My God. What happened?' She stopped in her tracks and stared into the bedlam of Jessica's eyes. Jessica never came apart, never cried, never wavered, never . . . At least they never saw that side of her at the shop.

'I don't know what happened. But there's been this incredible, horrible, most ridiculous fucking mistake!' She was shouting and she picked up the sandwich Kat had brought in and threw it across the room. Three counts of rape. And one count of assault. What in hell was going on?

CHAPTER IV

'Jessie? Where are you going?'

She brushed past Zina, returning from lunch, as she rushed out the door.

'Just make believe I never got back from New York. I'm going home. But don't call me.' She yanked open the door of her car and got in.

'Are you sick?' Zina was calling from the top of the steps, but Jessica just shook her head, pulled the choke, turned on the ignition, and roared into reverse.

Zina walked into the boutique bewildered, but Katsuko could tell her nothing more than what she had seen. Jessie was upset, but Kat didn't know why. It had something to do with the policeman's visit that morning. The two girls were worried, but she had told them not to call her at home, and the afternoon at the boutique was too busy for them to have time to speculate. Katsuko figured it had something to do with Ian, but she didn't know what. Zina was left in the dark.

When she got home, Jessica grabbed for the phone with one hand and her address book with the other. A cup half filled with coffee sat on the kitchen table. Ian had been in the middle of his breakfast when they'd taken him away, and something in Jessie's heart told her that Houghton had been the one who had taken Ian away. She wondered if the neighbours had seen it.

A stack of pages from the new book lay near the coffee. Nothing else. No note or message to her. He must have been shocked. And obviously it was an insane accusation. They had the wrong man. In a few hours the nightmare would be over, and he would be home. Her sanity had returned. Now all they needed was an attorney. She simply wouldn't allow herself to panic.

Her address book yielded the name she wanted, and she was in luck; he was free when she called, and not out to lunch as she'd feared he would be. He was a man she and Ian respected, an attorney with a good reputation, senior partner of his firm. Philip Wald.

'But Jessica, I don't do criminal work.'

'What difference does that make?'

'Quite a lot, I'm afraid. What you want is a good criminal defence attorney.'

'But he didn't do it, for Chrissake. We just need someone to straighten things out and get him out of this mess.'

'Have you spoken to him?'

'No, they wouldn't let me. Look, Philip, please. Just go down there and talk to them. Talk to Ian. This whole thing is absurd.' At the other end of the phone, there was silence.

'I can do that. But I can't take the case. It wouldn't be fair to either of you.'

'What case? This is just a matter of misidentification.'

'Do you know what it's based on?'

'Something to do with my car.'

'Did they have your licence plate?'

'Yes.'

'Well, yes, then they might have transposed the numbers or letters.' She didn't say anything, but it was hard to transpose the spelling of 'Jessie' and come up with the wrong name. That was the only thing that bothered her. The tie-in with her car. 'I'll tell you what. I'll go down and see him, find out what's going on, and I'll give you some names of defence attorneys. Get in touch with them, and whoever you settle on, tell him I'll give him a call later and fill him in on what I know. And tell them I told you to call.'

She sighed deeply. 'Thank you, Philip. That helps.'

He gave her the names and promised to come by the house as soon as he'd seen Ian. And she settled down with Ian's cold coffee to phone Philip's friends. Criminal defence attorneys all. The calls were not cheering.

The first one was out of town. The second one was in court for at least the next week and could not be disturbed with a new case. The third was too tied up to talk to her. The fourth was out. But the fifth spent some time with her on the phone. Jessie hated his voice.

'Does he have a previous record?'

'No. Of course not. Only parking violations.'

'Drugs? Any problems with drugs?'

'None.'

'Is he a drinker?'

'No, only wine at social occasions.' Christ, the man already thought Ian had done it. That much was clear.

'Did he know this woman before . . . ah . . . was he previously acquainted with her?'

'I don't know anything about the woman. And I assume that this is all a mistake.'

'What makes you think so?'

Bastard. Jessie already hated him.

'I know my husband.'

'Did she identify him?'

'I don't know. Mr. Wald can tell you all that when he comes back from seeing Ian.' At the jail . . . oh Jesus . . . Ian was in jail and it was for real, and this goddam lawyer was asking her stupid questions about whether or not Ian knew the woman who was accusing him of rape. Who cared? She just wanted him home, dammit. Now. Didn't anyone understand that? Her chest got tight and it was hard to breathe as she attempted to keep her voice calm to hide the rising panic pumping at her insides.

'Well, young lady, I'll tell you. You and your husband have a pile of trouble on your hands. But it's an interesting case.' Oh, for Chrissake. 'I'd be willing to handle the matter for you. But there is the question of my fee. Payable in advance.'

'In advance?' She was shocked.

'Yes. You'll find that most of my colleagues, if not all, handle matters the same way. I really have to collect before I get into a case, because once I appear in Superior Court for your husband, I then become the attorney of record, and legally I'm locked into the case, whether you pay the fee or not. And if your husband goes to prison, you just may not pay up. Do you have any assets?'

Ian go to prison? Fuck you, mister.

'Yes, we have assets.' She could hardly unclench her teeth.

'What kind of assets?'

'I can assure you that I could manage your fee.'

'Well, I like to be sure. My fee for this would be fifteen thousand dollars.'

'What? In advance?'

'I'd want half of that before the arraignment. I believe you said that's on Thursday. And half immediately after.'

'But there's no way I could possibly turn my assets into cash in two days.'

'Then I'm afraid there's no way I could possibly handle the case.'

'Thank you.' She wanted to tell him to get fucked. But by then she was beginning to panic again. Who in God's name would help her?

The sixth person whose name Philip had given her turned out to be human. His name was Martin Schwartz.

'Sounds like you've got yourself one hell of a problem, or at least your husband does. Do you think he did it?' It was an interesting question, and she liked him for even assuming there was some doubt. She hesitated for only a moment. The man deserved a thoughtful answer.

'No, I don't. And not just because I'm his wife. I don't believe he could do something like that. It isn't in him, and he doesn't need to.'

'All right, I'll accept that. But people do strange things, Mrs. Clarke. For your own sake, be prepared to accept that. Your husband may have a side to him you don't even know.'

It was possible. Anything was possible. But she didn't believe it. She couldn't.

'I'd like to talk to Philip Wald after he sees him,' Schwartz went on.

'I'd appreciate it if you would. There's something called an arraignment scheduled for Thursday. We're going to need legal counsel by then, and Philip doesn't feel he's qualified to take the case.' The case . . . the case . . . the case . . . she already hated the word.

'Philip's a good man.'

'I know. Mr. Schwartz . . . I hate to bring this up, but . . .'

'My fee?'

'Your fee.' She heaved a deep sigh and felt a knot tighten in her stomach.

'We can discuss that. I'll try to be reasonable.'

'I'll tell you frankly, the man I spoke to before you asked for fifteen thousand dollars by Thursday. I couldn't even begin to swing that.'

'Do you have any assets?' Oh Christ, not that again.

'Yes, I have assets.' Her tone was suddenly disagreeable. 'I have a business, a house, and a car. And my husband also has a car. But we can't just sell the house, or my business, in two days.'

It interested him the way she said 'my business', not 'our'. He wondered what 'his' business was, if any.

'I wasn't expecting you to liquidate your assets on the spot, Mrs. Clarke.' His tone was calm but firm. Something about him soothed her. 'But I was thinking that you may need some collateral for the bail—if they make the charges stick, which remains to be seen. Bail can run pretty high. We'll worry about that later. As for my fee, I think two thousand dollars up to trial would be reasonable. And if it goes to trial, an additional five thousand dollars. But that won't be for a couple of months, and if you're a friend of Philip's, I won't worry.' It struck her then that people who weren't 'friends of Philip's' were in a world of trouble. She felt suddenly grateful. 'How does that sound to you?'

She nodded silently to herself, aghast but relieved. It was certainly better than the fee she had heard a few moments before. It would clean out her savings account, but at least she could manage the two thousand. They could worry about the other five later, if it came to that. She'd sell the Morgan if she had to, and without thinking twice. Ian's ass was on the line, and she needed him one hell of a lot more than she needed the Morgan. And there was always her mother's jewellery. But that was sacred. Even for Ian.

'We can manage.'

'Fine. When can I see you?'

'Anytime you like.'

'Then I'd like to see you tomorrow in my office. I'll talk to Wald this afternoon, and get up to see Mr. Clarke in the morning. Can you be in my office at ten-thirty?'

'Yes.'

'Good. I'll get the police reports and see what the score is there. All right?'

'Wonderful. I suddenly feel as though a thousand-pound weight is off my back. I'll tell you, I've been totally frantic. I'm way out of my league. Police, bail, counts of this and counts of that, arraignments . . . I don't know what the hell is going on. I don't even know what the hell happened.'

'Well, we're going to find out. So you just relax.'

'Thank you, Mr. Schwartz. Thank you very much.'

'See you in the morning.'

They hung up and Jessica was suddenly in tears again. He had been nice to her. Finally someone had been decent to her in all this. From police inspectors who would tell her nothing, to desk sergeants who announced the charges and hung up in her ear, to attorneys who wanted fifteen thousand dollars in cash on their desks in forty-eight hours, to . . . Martin Schwartz, a human being. And according to Philip Wald, Schwartz was a competent lawyer. It had been an incredible day. And oh God, where was Ian? The tears burned a hot damp path down her face again. It felt as though they had been coming all day. And she had to pull herself together. Wald would be there soon.

Philip Wald arrived at five-thirty. His face wore an expression of grave concern and his eyes were tired.

'Did you see him?' Jessie could feel her eyes burn again and had to fight back the tears.

'I did.'

'How is he?'

'He's all right. Shaken, but all right. He was very concerned about how you are.'

'Did you tell him I'm fine?' Her hands were shaking violently again and the coffee she'd been drinking all day had only made matters worse. She looked a far cry from 'fine'.

'I told him you were very upset, which is certainly natural, under the circumstances. Jessica, let's sit down.' She didn't like the way he said it, but maybe he was just tired. They'd all had a long day. An endless day.

'I spoke to Martin Schwartz,' she said. 'I think he'll take the case. And he said he'd call you this afternoon.'

'Good. I think you'll both like him. He's a very fine attorney, and also a very nice man.'

Jessica led Philip into the living room, where he took a seat on the long white couch facing the view. Jessica chose a soft beige suede chair next to an old brass table she and Ian had found in Italy on their honeymoon. She took a deep breath, sighed, and let her feet slide into the rug. It was a warm, pleasant room that always gave her solace. A place she could come home to and unwind in . . . except now. Now she felt as though nothing would ever be all right again, and as though it had been years since she had known the comfort of Ian's arms, or seen the light in his eyes.

Almost instinctively, her eyes went to a small portrait of him that she had done years before. It hung over the fireplace and smiled at her gently. It was agonizing. Where was he? She was suddenly and painfully reminded of the feeling she had had looking at Jake's high-school pictures when she'd gone through his things after they'd gotten the telegram from the Navy. That smile after it's all over.

'Jessica?' She glanced up with a shocked expression, and Philip looked pained. She seemed distraught, confused, as though her mind were wandering. He had seen her staring at the small oil portrait, and for a moment she had worn the bereft expression of a grieving widow . . . the face that simply does not understand, the eyes that are drowning in pain. What a ghastly business. He looked at the view for a moment, and then back at her, hoping she might have composed herself. But there was nothing to compose. Her manner was in total control; it was the expression in her eyes that told the rest of the story. He wasn't at all sure how much she was ready to hear now, but he had to tell her. All of it.

'Jessica, you've got trouble.' She smiled tiredly and brushed a stray tear away from her cheek.

'That sounds like the understatement of the year. What else is new?' Philip ignored the feeble attempt at humour and went on. He wanted to get it over with.

'I really don't think he did it. But he admits to having slept with the woman yesterday afternoon. That is to say, he . . . he had intercourse with her.' He concentrated on his right knee, trying to run the distasteful words into one long unintelligible syllable.

'I see.' But she didn't really see. What was there to see? Ian had made love to someone. And the someone was accusing him of rape. Why couldn't she feel something? There was this incredible numbness that just sat on her like a giant hat. No anger, no anything, just numb. And maybe pity for Ian. But why was she numb? Maybe because she had to hear it from Philip, a relative stranger. Her cigarette burned through the filter and went dead in her hand, and still she waited for him to go on.

'He says that he had too much to drink yesterday at lunch, and you were due home last night. Something about your being away for several weeks, and his being a man—I'll spare you that. He noticed this girl in the restaurant, and after a few drinks she didn't look bad.'

'He picked her up?' She felt as though someone else were speaking her words for her. She could hear them, but she couldn't feel her mouth move. Nothing seemed to be functioning. Not her mind, not her heart, not her mouth. She almost laughed hysterically, wondering what would happen if she had to go to the bathroom; surely she would pee all over the suede chair and not even know she was doing it. She felt as if she had overdosed on Novocain.

'No, he didn't pick her up. He left the restaurant to go home and work on his book, but he drove past Enrico's again on his way, and she just happened to be standing at the corner when he stopped for a light. And just for the hell of it, he offered her a lift. She didn't look like much when she got in, she was quite a bit older than he had thought. She claims thirty on the police report, but he says she's at least thirty-seven or -eight. She gave him the address of a hotel on Market where she claimed she lived, and Ian says he felt sorry for her when she invited him up for a drink. So he went up with her, had a drink—there was half a bottle of bourbon in her room—and he says it went to his head, and he . . . they had intercourse.' Wald cleared his throat, looked away, and went on. Jessica's face showed no expression; the cigarette filter was still in her hand. 'And he says that was it. To put it bluntly, he put on his pants and went home. He had a shower, took a nap, made a sandwich, and came out to meet your plane, That's the whole story. Ian's story.' But she could hear in his voice that there was more.

'It sounds fairly tawdry, Philip. But it does not sound like rape. What are they basing the charges on?'

'Her story. And you've got to remember, Jessica, how

sensitive an issue rape is these days. For years women cried rape, and men made damaging statements about those women in court. Private investigators uncovered the supposedly startling fact that the plaintiff was not a virgin, and instantly the men were exonerated, the cases dismissed, and the women disgraced. For many reasons, it doesn't work like that anymore. No matter what really happened. Now the police and the courts are more cautious, more inclined to believe the women, and give the victim a much fairer deal. It's a damn good thing too, and about time . . . except once in a while, some woman comes along with an axe to grind, tells a lie, and some decent guy takes a bad fall. Just like some decent women used to get hurt the way things were before, now some decent guys get it in the . . . ahem . . . where it hurts.'

Jessica couldn't suppress a smile. Philip was so utterly, totally proper. She was sure he made love to his wife with his Brooks Brothers boxer shorts on.

'Frankly, Jessica, I think that what happened here is that Ian fell into the hands of a sick, unhappy woman. She slept with him, and then called it rape. Ian says she was seductive in her manner and claimed to be a waitress in a topless bar, which is not the case. But she could have been playing a very sick psychological game with him. And God knows how often she's done this before, in subtle ways, with threats, accusations. Apparently, though, she's never gone to the police before. I think you're going to have a hell of a time proving she's lying. Certainly not without a trial. Rape is hard to prove, but it's also hard to prove that it wasn't rape. If she's insisting it was, then the district attorney has to prosecute. And apparently the inspector on the case believes this woman's story. So we're stuck. If they've decided they want Ian's head, for whatever reasons, it'll have to go to a jury.'

They were both silent for a long time, and then Philip sighed and spoke again.

'I read the police reports, and the woman claims that he picked her up and she asked him to take her back to her office. She's a secretary at a hotel on Van Ness. Instead, he took her to this hotel on Market where they . . .

where they had that last drink. Given that part of the story, he's damn lucky they didn't hit him with a charge of kidnap as well. In any case, he allegedly forced her into both normal intercourse, and . . . unnatural acts. That's where the second and third counts of rape come in, and the one charge of assault. Though I assume they'll drop the assault—there's no medical proof of it.' Somehow Philip sounded horrifyingly matter-of-fact about the details, and Jessica was beginning to feel sick. She felt as though she were swimming in molasses, as though everything around her was slow and thick and unreal. She wanted to scrape the words off her skin with a knife. 'Unnatural acts.' What unnatural acts?

'For Chrissake, Philip, what do you mean by 'unnatural'? Ian is perfectly normal in bed.' Philip blushed. Jessie didn't. This was no time to be prim.

'Oral copulation, and sodomy. They are felonies, you know.' Jessica pursed her lips and looked fierce. Oral copulation hardly seemed unnatural.

'There was no clear evidence of the sodomy, but I don't think they'll drop it. Again, it's her word against his, and they're listening, and unfortunately, before I got down there, Ian admitted to the inspector on the case that he had had intercourse with the woman. He didn't confess to the oral copulation or the sodomy, but he shouldn't have admitted to intercourse at all. Damn shame that he did.'

'Will it hurt the case?'

'Probably not. We can have the tape withheld in court on the grounds that he was distraught at the time. Martin will take care of it.'

Jessica sat with her eyes closed for a moment, not believing the weight of it all.

'Why is she doing this to us, Philip? What can she possibly want from him? Money? Hell, if that's what she wants, I'll give it to her, what*ever* she wants. I just can't believe this is really happening.' She opened her eyes and looked at him again, feeling the now familiar wave of confusion and unreality sweep over her again.

'I know this is very hard on you, Jessica. But you have an excellent attorney now. Put your faith in him; he'll do a good job for you. One thing you absolutely must not do though, under any circumstances, is offer this woman money. The police won't drop the case now, even if she does, and you'll be compounding a felony and God knows what else if you try to bribe her. And I'm serious—the police seem to be taking a special interest in this. It isn't often that they get their hands on a Pacific Heights rape case, and I get the feeling that some of them think it's about time the upper class got theirs. Sergeant Houghton, the inspector on this case, made some very nasty cracks about "certain kinds of people who think they can get away with anything they want at the expense of certain other people of lesser means." It isn't a pretty inference, but if that's how he's thinking, he ought to be treated with kid gloves. I got the feeling that he doesn't like how Ian looks, or what he saw of you. I almost wonder if he doesn't think you're a couple of sickoes doing whatever amuses you for kicks. Who knows what he thinks—I'm just giving you my impression—but I want you to be very careful, Jessica. And whatever you do, don't pay this woman off. You'll be hurting Ian, and yourself, if you try to do that. If she wants money, if she calls you . . . let her talk. You can testify to it later. But don't give her a dime!' He was emphatic on the last point, and then ran a hand through his hair.

'I hate to have to tell you all this, Jessica. Ian was sick about it. But obviously you have to know what went on. It isn't very pretty, though, and I must say you're taking it remarkably well.'

But the tears welled up again at that, and she wanted to beg him not to be nice to her, not to congratulate her on how well she was taking it. She could handle the rough stuff, but she knew that if anyone put his arms around her, sympathized, cared . . . or if Ian should walk in the door just then . . . she would sob until she died.

'Thank you, Philip.' He thought her voice sounded oddly cold, as though she were warding him off. 'At least it's obviously not rape, and that's bound to be made clear in court. If Martin Schwartz is any good.'

'Yes, but . . . Jessie, it's going to be ugly. You have

to be prepared for that.' His eyes sought hers and she nodded.

'I understand that.' But she didn't. Not really. It hadn't even begun to sink in yet. How could it? Nothing had sunk in since eleven o'clock that morning. She was in shock. She only knew two things, and she didn't even understand those two things: that Ian was gone, that she couldn't see him, feel him, hear him, touch him; that he had slept with another woman. She had to face that now too. Publicly. The rest would sink in later.

There wasn't much more Philip could do, and he didn't know Jessica well enough to offer her any comfort. Only Ian knew Jessica that well. And Jessie made Philip nervous. She remained so calm. He was grateful that she was subdued, but it made him feel cold toward her, and confused. He found himself wondering what she was really thinking. He thought of his own wife and how she might react to something like this, or his sister, any of the women he knew. Jessie was a different breed of cat entirely. Too poised for his taste—and yet there was something shattering about her eyes. Like two broken windows. They were the only hint that all was not well within.

'Is there any chance he can call me? I thought you had a right to make one phone call from jail.' He had before, when they had busted him for his tickets.

'Yes. But I gather that he didn't want to call you, Jessica.'

'He didn't?' She seemed to recede still further into her own reserve.

'No. He said he wasn't sure how you'd feel. Said something about maybe this would be the last straw.'

'Asshole.' Philip looked away, and in a few moments took his leave. It had been an excessively unpleasant day. He found himself feeling grateful that he didn't practise criminal law. He couldn't stomach it. He didn't envy Martin Schwartz this case, however much money he made on it.

Jessie sat in the living room long after Philip had left. She was waiting for the sound of the phone . . . or of

Ian's key in the door. This couldn't be happening. Not really. He would come home. He always did. She tried to pretend that the house wasn't quiet. She sang little songs and talked to herself. He couldn't leave her alone . . . no! . . . she sometimes heard her mother's voice late in the night . . . and Jake's . . . and Daddy's . . . but never Ian's . . . never Ian . . . never . . . He would call, he had to. He couldn't leave her alone, scared like that, he wouldn't do that to her, he had promised he never would, and Ian never broke his promises . . . but he had. He had broken a promise now. She remembered it as she sat on the floor in the hall, in the dark, late into the night. That way she would hear his key sooner when he came home. He would come home, but he had broken a promise. He had slept with another woman, and now he was making her face it. She couldn't ignore it anymore. She hated her . . . hated her . . . hated . . . her, but not him. Oh God . . . maybe Ian didn't love her anymore . . . maybe he was in love with the other woman . . . maybe . . . why didn't he call, dammit? Why didn't he . . . why had he . . . the tears ran down her face like hot summer rain as she lay on the smooth wood floor in the hall and waited for Ian. She lay on the floor until morning. The phone never rang.

CHAPTER V

The offices of Schwartz, Drewes, and Jonas were located in the Bank of America Building on California Street, an excellent address. Jessica rode to the forty-fourth floor looking prim, sleek, and tired. She wore a large pair of dark glasses and a sombre navy blue suit. It was an outfit reserved for business meetings and funerals. This was a little bit of both. It was ten-twenty-five. She was five minutes early, but Martin Schwartz was waiting.

A secretary led her down a long carpeted corridor with a sweeping view of the bay. His offices took up one corner on the north side of the building. It was evidently a large, prosperous firm.

Martin Schwartz's office boasted two walls of glass, but the decor was Spartan and chill. He rose from behind his desk, a man of medium height with a full head of grey hair. He wore glasses, and he was frowning.

'Mrs. Clarke?' The secretary had announced her, but he would have known her anyway. She looked the way he had expected her to—wealthy, elegant. But she was younger than he had expected, and more composed than he had dared to hope.

'Yes. How do you do?' She held out a hand, and he took in her full height. She was a striking young woman. He mentally made a pair of her and the unshaven, tired, but still handsome young man he had seen in the city prison that morning. They must look quite something together. They would also look good in court. Maybe too good—too beautiful, too young. He didn't like the looks of this case.

'Won't you sit down?' She nodded, slid into a chair across from his desk, and declined his offer of coffee.

'You've seen Ian?'

'I have. And Sergeant Houghton. And the assistant district attorney assigned to the case. And I spoke to Philip Wald for over an hour last night. Now I want to talk to you, and then we'll see what kind of a case we really have here.' He attempted a smile and shuffled some papers on his desk. 'Mrs. Clarke, have you ever been into drugs?'

'No. And neither has Ian. Nothing more than a few joints once in a while. But I don't think we've smoked any grass in over a year. Neither of us ever liked it much. And we don't drink anything more exotic than wine.'

'Let's not jump ahead of ourselves. I want to get back to drugs. Are any of your friends in that scene?'

'Not that I know of.'

'Would anything of that nature be likely to turn up in an investigation of you or Mr. Clarke?'

'No, I'm sure that nothing would.'

'Good.' He looked only slightly relieved.

'What makes you ask?'

'Oh, some of the angles that I sense Houghton might be working on. He made some disagreeable remarks about your shop. Some girl in there who looks like a belly dancer, apparently, and an 'exotic' Oriental he mentioned. Also the fact that your husband is a writer, and you know the kind of fantasies people have about that. Houghton is a man with a vivid imagination, a typical lower-middle-class mind, and a strong dislike for anything that comes from your part of town.'

'I suspected as much. He came to talk to me at the shop before he arrested Ian. And the 'bellydancer' he's having fantasies about is a young lady who has the misfortune to wear a size 38 bra with a D cup. She happens to go to church twice a week.' Jessica was not smiling. But Martin Schwartz was.

'She sounds delightful.' He forced a smile out of her, with some effort.

'And if Sergeant Houghton thinks we look like we have too much money, he happens to be mistaken about that too. But what he does see can be explained by the fact that my parents and my brother died several years ago. I inherited what they had. My brother had no wife and children to leave anything to, and there were no other brothers or sisters.'

'I see.' And then after a brief pause he looked up at her again. 'It must be lonely with no family.' She nodded silently and kept her eyes on the view.

'I have Ian.'

'Any children?' She shook her head, and he began to understand something. The reason she was not angry, why she so desperately wanted her husband home, without a single word of criticism about the charges. The reason for the almost frightening urgency he had sensed in her voice on the phone, and again now in his office. The 'I have Ian' said it all. He suddenly knew that as far as Jessica Clarke was concerned, that was *all* she had.

'I take it there's no chance they might drop the charges?'

'None. Politically, they can't. The victim in this case is making such a stink. She wants his ass, if you'll pardon the expression. And I think it's reasonable to expect that they'll be prying fairly heavily into your lives. Can you weather it?' She nodded, and he didn't tell her that Ian was afraid she couldn't stand the pressure. 'Is there anything I should know? Any indiscretions on your part? Problems with the marriage? Sexual . . . well, "exoticisms," shall we say, orgies you may have gone to, whatever?'

She shook her head again, looking annoyed.

'I'm sorry I have to ask, but it'll all come out anyway. It's best to be candid now. And of course we'll want our own investigation of the girl. I have a very good man. Mrs. Clarke, we're going to do our damnedest for Ian.'

He smiled at her again, and for a moment she felt as though she were living a dream. This man was not real, he wasn't asking her if she'd ever gone to orgies, or been into drugs . . . Ian wasn't really in jail . . . this man was a friend of her father's and it was all a big game. She felt him staring at her then, and she had to return to the pretence that this was reality. Worse yet, to the reality that Ian was in jail.

'Can we get Ian out of jail before the trial?'

'I hope so. But that will most likely depend on you. If the charges were a little less severe, we might have been able to get him released on his own recognizance—in other words, with no bail to pay. But on charges of this nature, I'm almost certain the judge will insist on bail being posted, despite the fact that Ian has no previous record. And his getting out will depend on whether or not you can put up the bail. They're talking about setting it at twenty-five thousand dollars. That's pretty steep, and it means you'd either have to put twenty-five thousand dollars in cash in the keeping of the court until the trial is over, or pay twenty-five hundred to a bailbondsman and give him collateral to cover his bond. Either way, it's a stiff fee. But we'll see about getting it down to something more reasonable.'

Jessica heaved a deep sigh and absentmindedly took off

her dark glasses. What he saw then shocked him. Two deep purple trenches lay beneath her eyes, which were bloodshot and swollen and filled with terror. He was looking at a woman with the eyes of a child. The poise was all a front. He had been so sure she was the balls in the outfit, but maybe not, maybe not. Maybe she was only the bucks, and Ian was her lifeline. It made him feel better, somehow, about Ian. He was in better shape than she was, that was for sure.

Schwartz forced his mind back to the question of bail as Jessica's eyes continued to watch him. She seemed unaware of how much she had just shown him.

'Do you think you'll be able to meet the bail, Mrs. Clarke?' She looked tiredly into his eyes and shrugged slightly.

'I suppose I can put up my business.' But she knew that she couldn't pay the bailbondsman's fee if she handed Schwartz the two-thousand-dollar cheque in her bag. And she had no choice. They needed a lawyer before they could even begin to worry about a bailbondsman. She'd have to get a loan on the car. Or on . . . something. What the hell. It didn't matter now. Nothing did. She'd even put up the house if she had to. But what if . . . she had to know. 'What if we can't quite meet the bail right away?'

'There's no credit there, Mrs. Clarke. You pay the full bailbondsman's fee and put up satisfactory collateral or they simply don't let Ian out of jail.'

'Until when?'

'After the trial.'

'God. Then I don't have much choice, do I?'

'In what sense?'

'We'll just put up whatever we have to.'

He nodded, sorry for her. It was rare that he felt anything stir in his heart for a client, and had she ranted and whined and cried, she would have annoyed him. Instead she had won his respect—and his pity. Neither of them deserved this kind of trouble. It made him wonder again what the real story was with the rape charges. He felt in his gut that it had not been a rape. But the question was, could that be proven?

He spent another ten minutes explaining the arraignment procedures: a simple appearance in court to put the charges on record, establish the bail, and set a date for Ian's next appearance in court, at a preliminary hearing. The victim would not be at the arraignment. Jessica was relieved.

'Is there a number, Mrs. Clarke, where I can reach you today if I need you?' She nodded and scribbled the number of the boutique. It was the first time she'd thought of going in.

'I'll be there after I see Ian. I'm going over to see him now. And Mr. Schwartz, please call me Jessica, or Jessie. It sounds like we're going to be seeing a lot of each other.'

'Yes, we will. And I want you back in my office on Friday. Both of you, if you've managed to get Ian out on bail.' The 'if' sent a shiver down her spine. 'No, actually, make it Monday. In case you do get him out, you two will deserve a little time off. And then we'll get down to work in earnest. We don't have much time.'

'How much time?' It was like asking a doctor how long you had to live.

'We'll have a better idea of that after the arraignment. But the trial will probably come up in about two months.'

'Before Christmas?' She reminded him again of an overgrown child as she asked.

'Before Christmas. Unless we get a continuance for some reason. But your husband told me this morning that he wants to get this over with as quickly as possible, so you could put it behind you and forget it.'

Forget it? she thought. Who would ever forget it?

He stood up and held out a hand, removing his glasses for a moment. 'Jessica, try to relax. Leave the worrying to me for a while.'

'I'll do my best.' She stood up too, shook his hand, and he was once again taken aback by her height. 'Thank you, Martin, for everything. Any message for Ian?' She paused in the doorway.

'Tell him I said he's a lucky man.' His eyes warmed her and she smiled at the compliment and slipped out the door.

Martin Schwartz sat down, swivelled his chair to face the view, chewed on his glasses, and shook his head. This was going to be a bitch of a case. He was sure Ian hadn't done it, but they both would be a real problem in court. Young, happy, beautiful, and rich. The jury would resent his screwing around on a woman like Jessie; the women in court would hate Jessie; the men in court would dislike Ian because they wouldn't believe that writing was work. And they looked as if they had too much money, no matter how sensible the explanation of Jessie's inheritance was. He just didn't like the looks of this case. And the victim was obviously a strange woman, maybe a sick one. His only hope was that they'd find out enough on her to destroy her. It was an ugly game to play, but it was Ian's only chance.

CHAPTER VI

Jessica stopped in the lobby to call the boutique. Zina's voice was concerned when she heard her.

'Jessie, are you all right?' They had finally tried her at home at ten-thirty that morning, but she had already gone out.

'I'm fine.' But Zina didn't like the sound of her voice. 'Everything okay at your end?'

'Sure, we're okay. Are you coming in?'

'After lunch. See ya later.' She hung up before Zina could ask more questions and went to reclaim the Morgan from the garage. She was off to the Hall of Justice to see Ian.

She was two thousand dollars poorer, but now she felt better. She had left the cheque in a blue envelope with the secretary at the front desk. The first part of Martin

Schwartz's fee. She had been as good as her word. Now there were a hundred and eighty-one dollars left in their joint savings account, but Ian had an attorney. What a price they were going to pay for one piece of ass!

She tried not to let herself think as she drove across town. She wasn't so much angry as confused. What had happened? Who was this woman? Why was she doing this to them? What did she have against Ian? After speaking to Martin, Jessie was more certain than ever that Ian had done nothing wrong—except pick the wrong woman for an afternoon of delight. Oh Jesus, had he picked the wrong woman!

She found a parking space on Bryant Street, across from a long strip of neon-lit bailbondsmen's offices. She found herself wondering which one she'd be haggling with by the next afternoon. They all looked so sleazy; she wouldn't have wanted to enter any of those places to get in out of the cold, let alone to do business. She walked quickly into the Hall of Justice, where a metal detector checked her out while a guard rifled through her handbag. She had to stop for a pass for the jail, show her driver's licence, and identify herself as Ian's wife. There was a crowd of people standing in line, but the line moved forward quickly.

It was a shaggy, dishevelled-looking lot of humanity, and she was strikingly out of place. Her height set her apart from the rest of the women and most of the men, and the navy blue suit looked absurd. There were white women in imitation leather pants wearing fake leopard jackets, beehive hairstyles, and floppy white sandals. Black men in puce satin, and black girls in what looked like cheap satin nightgowns or pyjamas. It was an interesting crowd, but for a movie, not for a life. She couldn't help wondering if the woman Ian had slept with looked like one of these. She hoped not—not that it mattered at this point. Her knees were already quaking, and she didn't know what she'd say to him. What could she say?

Her hand trembled as she pressed the elevator button for the sixth floor. There was an alternating sensation of sinking and rising in her stomach as she wondered what the jail would be like. She had seen it briefly the one time she had bailed him out, but there had never been time for a visit, thank God. She'd just gone down and gotten him. This time it was all so different.

The elevator let her out on the sixth floor, and all she knew was that she wanted to see Ian. Suddenly she knew she could crawl through any amount of fear and anger, over a thousand puce satin pimps, just to get to Ian.

The visitors waited in single file outside an iron door and a guard let them into the room beyond in groups of five or six. They made their exit through another door at the far side of the room. But it seemed to Jessie that they were being swallowed up, never to be seen again.

A moment later, Jessica was inside. The room was hot and stuffy, windowless and fluorescent-lit. There were long glass panes in the interior walls with little shelves on either side holding telephones. She realised then that she would see him through a window. She hadn't thought about that. What could you say on a phone?

His face appeared in a far window as she wondered which one to go to, and he stood there, watching her as she felt tears burn her eyes. She couldn't let herself cry . . . couldn't . . . couldn't . . . couldn't! She walked slowly toward the phone, feeling a vice tighten around her heart and her legs turn to straw, but she was walking, one foot after the other, and he couldn't see her hands tremble as she waved hesitantly. And then suddenly she was facing him, and she had the phone in her hand. They watched each other briefly in silence. And then he spoke first.

'Are you okay?'

'I'm fine. How are you?'

He was silent again for a moment and then nodded with a small, crooked smile.

'Terrific.' But the smile faded quickly. 'Oh baby, I'm so sorry to put you through this. It's all so crazy and so goddam . . . I think all I want to tell you, Jess, is that I love you, and I don't know how this whole fucking mess happened. I wasn't sure how you'd take it.'

'What did you think? That I'd run away? Have I ever done that?' She looked so hurt he wanted to turn away. It was hard to look at her. Very hard.

'No, but this isn't exactly your run-of-the-mill problem, like a thirty-dollar overdraft at the bank. I mean this is . . . Jesus, what can I say, Jessie?' She gave him a tiny smile in answer.

'You already said it. And I love you too. That's all that matters. We'll get this thing straightened out.'

'Yeah . . . but . . . Jess, it doesn't sound like it's going to be easy. That woman is sticking to the accusations, and this cop, Houghton, he acts like he thinks he's got the local hotshot rapist on his hands.'

'Adorable, isn't he?'

'He talked to you?' Ian looked surprised.

'Just before he went to the house to see you.' Ian looked pale.

'Did he tell you what it was about?' She shook her head and looked away. 'Oh, Jess . . . what an incredible horror show to put you through. I just can't believe it.'

'Neither can I. But we'll survive it.' She gave him her best brave girl smile. 'What do you think of Martin?'

'Schwartz? I like him. But that's going to cost you a pretty penny, isn't it?' Jessie tried to look noncommittal and started to say something, but he cut her off. 'How much?' There was a look of bitterness in his eyes for a moment.

'That's not important.'

'Maybe not to you, Jessie, but it is to me. How much?'

'Two thousand now, and another five if it goes to trial.' There was no avoiding that look in his eyes. She had had to tell him.

'Are you kidding?'

Jessie shook her head in reply.

'The man I spoke to before him wanted fifteen thousand, in cash, and by the end of this week.'

'Jesus Christ, Jessica . . . that's insanity. But I'll pay you back for Schwartz.'

'You're boring me, sweetheart.'

'I love you, Jess.' They exchanged a long tender look and Jessica felt the hot coals behind her eyes again.

'How come you didn't call me last night?' She didn't tell him that she had lain on the floor all night, waiting, frightened, almost hysterical, but too tired to move. She had felt as though her body were paralysed while her mind was racing.

'How could I call you, Jess? What could I say?' That you love me . . . 'I think I was in shock. I just kept sitting here, stunned. I couldn't understand it.'

Then why did you screw her, damn you? But the flash of anger left her eyes again as soon as she looked up at him. He was as unhappy as she was. More so.

'Why do you suppose she accused you of . . . of . . .'

'Rape?' He said it as if it were a death sentence. 'I don't know. Maybe she's sick or crazy, or pissed off at someone, or maybe she wanted money. What the hell do I know? I was a fool to do that anyway. Jessie, I—' He looked away and then back into her eyes with tears hovering in the corners of his own. 'How are we going to live with this? How are you going to live with it, Jessie? Without hating me? And . . . I just don't see . . .'

'Stop it!' She spat the words into the phone in a whisper. 'Stop it right now! We'll see this thing through and it'll be over and straightened out and we'll never have to think about it again.'

'But won't you? I mean honestly, Jessie, won't you? Every time you look at me, won't you hate me a little bit for her, and for the money this'll cost you, and . . . fuck.' He ran a hand through his hair and reached into his pocket for a cigarette. Jessie watched him and then suddenly noticed his pants. He was wearing white cotton hospital pyjama bottoms.

'Good God, what happened to your pants? Didn't they give you time to get dressed?' Her eyes grew wide as she envisioned Sergeant Houghton dragging him out of the house bare-assed and in handcuffs.

'Adorable, aren't they? They took my pants down to the lab to test them for sperm.' It was all so goddam tawdry, so ugly, so . . . 'I'm going to need some pants for court tomorrow morning, by the way.' And then he grew pensive for a moment and took a long drag on his cigarette. 'I just don't understand it. You know, if she wanted money, all she had to do was call and blackmail me. I told her I was married.' How nice . . . and then for no reason she could fathom, she looked at Ian, at his wrinkled white cotton pyjamas, at the boyish face and rumpled blond hair, at the madhouse of people around her, and she started to laugh.

'Are you okay?' He looked suddenly frightened. What if she got hysterical? But she didn't look hysterical, she looked genuinely amused.

'You know something nutty? I'm fine. And I love you, and this is ridiculous, dammit, so will you please come home—and you know what else? You look cute in pyjamas.' It was the same laughter he had heard a million times at two in the morning when she'd teased him about walking around the house reading his work, stark naked, and with a pencil behind each ear. It was the laughter of splashing water at each other in the shower, of tickling him when he got into bed. It was Jessie, and it suddenly made him smile, as he hadn't smiled since this whole nightmare had begun.

'Lady, you are absolutely screwy, but I adore you. Will you please get me out of this shithouse so I can come home and—' He stopped on the word and looked suddenly pale.

'Rape me? Why not?' And then they grinned again, but quietly. She was okay now. She had Ian right in front of her, she knew she was loved and safe and protected. With Ian suddenly gone and that incredible silence, it had been as though he were dead. But he wasn't dead. He was alive. He would always be alive, and he was all hers. Suddenly she wanted to dance, standing there in the jail in the midst of pimps and thieves, she wanted to dance. She had Ian back.

'Mr. Clarke, how come I love you so much?'

'Because you happen to be mentally retarded, but I love you that way. Hey, lady, could you be serious for a moment?' His face showed that he meant it, but Jessie still had laughter in her tired, bloodshot eyes.

'What?'

'I meant what I said about paying you back. I will.'

'Don't worry about it.'

'But I will. I think it's time I went back to some kind of job anyway. It doesn't work like this, Jess, and you know it too.'

'Yes, it does. What do you mean, "it doesn't work"?' She looked frightened again.

'I mean I don't like being kept, even if it is for the supposed benefit of my writing career. It's lousy for my ego, and worse for our marriage.'

'Bullshit.'

'No bullshit. I'm serious. But this isn't the time or the place to talk about it. I just want you to know, though, that whatever money you put out on this, you're getting back. Is that clear?' She looked evasive, and Ian's voice got louder in her ear. 'I mean it, Jessie. Don't fuck around with me on this. You're not paying for it.'

'Okay.' She looked at him pointedly, and at the same moment a guard tapped her on the shoulder. The visit was over. And they had so much left to say.

'Take it easy, sweetheart. I'll see you in court tomorrow.' He had seen the stricken look on her face.

'Can you call me tonight?'

He shook his head. 'No, they won't let me now.'

'Oh.' But I need to hear you . . . I need you, Ian . . . I . . .

'Get yourself a good night's sleep before the court thing tomorrow. Promise?' She nodded, looking like a child, and he smiled at her. 'I love you so much, Jess. Will you please take care, for me?'

She nodded again. 'And you too? Ian . . . I . . . I'd die without you.'

'Don't think like that. Now go on, I'll see you tomorrow. And Jess . . . thank you. For everything.'

'I love you.'

'I love you too.'

On the last words, the phones suddenly went dead in their hands, and she waved at him as she followed the flock of visitors into the elevator. She was alone with them again now. Ian was gone. But it was different this time.

She felt full of the way he looked and sounded, of the colour of his hair, and even the smell of his skin. He was vivid again now. He was still with her.

CHAPTER VII

Zina and Katsuko were both busy with customers when Jessica walked in, and she had a moment to compose herself in her office before joining them. It was crazy, really. Guess where I've been? To visit Ian in jail. From city prison to Lady J in one swift leap. Madness.

The girls were helping a couple of women who wanted dresses for Palm Springs. They were overweight, overdressed, overbearing, and not overly friendly. And Jessica found it nearly impossible to work. She kept thinking of Ian, of the jail, of Martin Schwartz, of Inspector Houghton. The inspector's eyes seem to haunt her.

'And what does your husband do?' One of the women asked her, while looking over a rack of their new velvet skirts. They were a rich Bordeaux colour with black satin trim. Copies of St. Laurent.

'My husband? He rapes . . . I mean, writes!' The women found it hilarious, and even Zina and Kat had to laugh. Jessica laughed through tears in her eyes.

'My husband used to be that way too—before he took up golf.' The second woman found the interlude delightful and settled on two skirts and a blouse while the first woman went back to the slacks.

It was a long day, but it saved her from talking to Zina and Kat. It was almost five before they sat down for a round of hot coffee.

'Jess, is everything okay now?'

'Much better. We had a few problems, but everything will be worked out by tomorrow.' At least then he'd be home, and they could work it out together. Just so he came home!

'We were worried as hell about you. I'm glad everything's fine.' Zina seemed satisfied, but Katsuko continued to search Jessie's eyes. Something didn't sit right.

'You look like shit, Jessica Clarke.'

'Flattery, flattery. It's just this grim suit.' She looked around, wondering if she should change into something from the shop's fall line just to pick up her sagging spirits. But it was late, and she was tired, and she didn't have the energy to get into or out of anything. It would only be another ten or fifteen minutes before Zina locked the doors for the night.

Jessica stood up, stretched, and was aware of the ache in her back and neck from the long crazy night she'd spent on the floor. Not to mention the tension of the day. She was arching her back gingerly, trying to ease out the kinks, when a woman walked into the boutique. Jessie, Kat, and Zina quickly glanced at each other, deciding who would stand up and be helpful, but it was Jessie who turned toward the woman with a smile. The woman looked pleasant, and it did Jessie good to deal with the clients. It kept her mind off herself.

'May I help you?'

'Do you mind if I browse? I heard about the boutique from a friend, and you have some lovely things in the window.'

'Thank you. Let me know if you need any help.'

Jessica and the woman exchanged an easy smile, and the customer began to look through the sportswear. She was elegant, somewhere in her mid- to late thirties, maybe even forty, but it was hard to tell. She wore a trim, simple black pantsuit, a cream linen blouse, a small bright scarf at her neck, and a healthy amount of obviously expensive gold jewellery—a handsome bracelet, a nice chain, several very solid looking rings—and a striking pair of onyx-diamond earrings that had caught Jessie's attention when she'd walked into the shop. The woman spelled money. But her face showed warmth, and something else—as though she enjoyed the pretty things she was wearing, but understood that there were other things in her life that mattered more.

Jessie watched her as she moved from rack to rack. She looked content, happy. And she had a kind of grace that made her easy to watch. The face was young, the hair ash blonde streaked with grey. In an odd way she reminded Jessie of a Siamese cat, particularly the pale china blue of her eyes. Something about her made you want to know more.

'Did you have anything special in mind? We have some new things in the back.' The woman smiled at Jessie and shrugged.

'I should be shot for this, but what about that suede coat over there? Have you got it in an eight?' She looked guilty, like a small child buying more bubble gum than she was supposed to, but she also looked as though she were having a good time. And as though she could afford one hell of a lot of bubble gum, or anything else.

'I'll take a look.' Jessica disappeared into the stockroom, wondering if they did have the coat in a smaller size.

They didn't. But they had a similar one that sold for forty dollars more. Jessica removed the price tag and took the coat out to the woman. It was a warm cinnamon colour with a soft clinging shape. It was actually a better-looking coat than the first one, and the woman noticed that instantly.

'Damn. I was hoping I'd hate it.'

'It's a hard coat to hate. And it looks well on you.'

They watched the woman swirling gracefully in the brown suede coat. It suited her marvellously, and she knew it. It was a pleasure to see clothes on someone like that. But then, she could have worn the rug and looked fabulous.

'How much is it?'

'Three hundred and ten.' Zina and Kat exchanged a quizzical glance, but they knew enough not to question the price aloud. Jessie always had a method to her madness, and she was usually right. Maybe this was someone special Jessie had been hoping to lure into the shop. She certainly looked like someone one ought to recognize. And the woman did not look overwhelmed by the price of the coat.

'Does it have matching pants?'

'It did, but they're gone.'

'That's too bad.' But she managed to casually collect three sweaters, a blouse, and a suede skirt to go with the coat before she decided that she'd done enough damage for one day. It was a beautiful sale for the shop, and an easy one. She pulled out her chequebook, encased in emerald green suede, and looked up at Jessie with a smile. 'And if you see me back here in less than a week, throw me out the door.'

'Do I have to?' Jessie looked mock-regretful.

'That's an order, not a request!'

'What a pity.' The two women laughed and the shopper filled out her cheque. It was for well over five hundred dollars. But she hardly looked worried. Her name was Astrid Bonner, and her address was on Vallejo, only a block from Jessie's home.

'We're almost neighbours, Mrs. Bonner.' Jessie told her her address, and Astrid Bonner looked up with a smile.

'I know that house! It's the little blue and white one, I'll bet, with all those fabulous bright flowers out front!'

'You can see us for miles!'

'Don't apologise; you do wonders for the area! And you have a little red sports car?' Jessie pointed out the window.

'That's me.' They laughed together and Zina quietly locked the doors. It was a quarter to six. 'Would you like a drink?' They kept a bottle of Johnnie Walker in the back. Some of their customers stayed late to chat. It was another nice touch.

'I'd love to, but I won't. You probably want to get home.' Jessie smiled and Katsuko put Mrs. Bonner's purchases in two large shiny brown boxes filled with yellow and orange tissue paper and tied them with plaid ribbons.

'Do you own the shop?'

Jessie nodded.

'You have some beautiful things. And I needed that coat like another hole in my head. But . . . no will power. It's my worst problem.'

'Sometimes a splurge is good for the soul.'

Astrid Bonner nodded quietly at the remark and the two women exchanged a long glance. Jessie felt very comfortable with her. She was sorry Astrid Bonner wouldn't stay for the drink; Jessie had nothing to rush home for, and she would have liked to talk to her. She wondered which of the houses on the next block was hers. And then she had an idea.

'Can I give you a lift home, by the way? I'm leaving now.' It would also spare her the questions that Zina and Kat might have saved to hurl at her after hours. She couldn't face that yet. And Astrid Bonner would give her safe passage. She still hadn't told them she wouldn't be in the following morning, while she went to the arraignment.

'A lift would be terrific. Thank you. I usually walk when I'm this close to home, but with these two boxes . . . delightful.' She smiled and looked even younger. Jessie wondered how old she really was.

Jessica picked up her coat, grabbed her bag, and waved at the other two. 'Good night, ladies. See you sometime tomorrow. I won't be in in the morning.' The four smiled at one another, Jessie unlocked the door for Astrid, Zina locked it again behind them, and they were on their way. No questions, no answers, no lies. Jessie was enormously relieved. She hadn't realized how she had been dreading that all afternoon.

She unlocked the car and Astrid slid in, the boxes tall on her lap, and they headed for home.

'The shop must keep you busy.'

'It does, but I love it. And I'm Jessica Clarke, by the way. I just realized that I haven't introduced myself. I'm sorry.' They exchanged another smile, and the evening breeze rustled through Astrid Bonner's freshly done hair. 'Would you like me to put the top up?'

'Of course not.' She laughed suddenly and looked at Jessie. 'I'm not that old and stuffy, for God's sake. And I must say, I envy you that shop. I used to work on a magazine in New York. That was ten years ago, and I still miss fashion in any form.'

'We came out from New York too. Six years ago. What brought you here?'

'My husband. Well, no actually it was a business trip. Then I met my husband out here—and never went back.' She looked pleased at the memory.

'Never? Are they still expecting you back?' The two women laughed in the soft twilight.

'No, I returned for all of three weeks. Gave them notice and that was that. I was the career-woman sort, never going to marry, all of that . . . and then I met Tom. And bingo, end of the career.'

'Did you ever regret it?' It was an outrageously personal thing to ask, but she seemed to invite one to feel at ease with her. And Jessie did.

'No. Never. Tom changed everything.' Jessica found herself wanting to say 'how awful' and then wondering why. After all, Ian had changed things for her too, but not like that; he hadn't cost her a career, hadn't forced her to leave New York. She had wanted to move to San Francisco, but she couldn't conceive of giving up Lady J.

'No, I never regretted it for a moment. Tom was a remarkable man. He died last year.'

'Oh. I'm sorry. Do you have children?'

Astrid laughed and shook her head. 'No, Tom was fifty-eight when I married him. We had a splendid ten years—alone. It was like a honeymoon.' Jessie was reminded of her life with Ian, and smiled.

'We feel sort of the same way. Children might interfere with so much.'

'Not if that's what you want. But we both thought we were too old. I was thirty-two when I married him, and I just wasn't the motherly type. We never regretted it. Except that life is awfully quiet now.'

So Astrid was forty-two. Jessie was surprised.

'Why don't you take a job?' she said.

'What could I possibly get a job doing? I worked for *Vogue*, but there's nothing like that out here. And even *Vogue* wouldn't want me anymore, not after ten years. You get rusty, and I've gotten about as rusty as you can get. And besides, I have no intention of moving back to New York. Ever.'

'Get something in a field related to fashion.'

'Like what?'

'A boutique.'

'Which brings us back to where we started, my dear. I'm green with envy over yours.'

'Don't be too envious. It has its problems.'

'And its rewards, I'll bet. Do you go back to New York often?'

'I came back two days ago.' And yesterday my husband got arrested for rape. It was on the tip of her tongue to say it, but Astrid would have been horrified. Anyone would have been. She sighed deeply, forgetting for a moment that she was not alone.

'Was the trip as bad as all that?' Astrid asked, smiling.

'What trip?'

'The trip to New York. You said you just got back from New York two days ago, and then you sighed as though your best friend had died.'

'I'm sorry. It's been a long day.' She tried to smile, but suddenly everything felt heavy again; the nightmare had rushed back to overwhelm her. There was a moment's pause, and then Astrid looked at her over the brown boxes on her lap.

'Is anything wrong?' It was a deep, searching look, and hard to meet it with a lie.

'Nothing that won't be smoothed out soon.'

'Anything I can do to help?' What a nice woman, they were total strangers and she was asking Jessie about her problems. Jessie smiled and slowed at the corner.

'No, everything's okay really. And you already did help. You finished my day with a nice dollop of sunshine. Now, which house is it?'

Astrid smiled and pointed. 'That one. And you were an angel to drive me home.'

It was a sombre brick mansion with black shutters and white trim and politely carved hedges around it. Jessie wanted to whistle. She and Ian had noticed the house often and had wondered who lived there. They had suspected the owners travelled a lot, because the house often looked closed.

'Mrs. Bonner, I'd like to return the compliment on the house. We've envied you this one for years.'

'I'm flattered. And call me Astrid. But your house looks like so much more fun, Jessica. This one is awfully . . . well . . .' She giggled. 'Grown-up, I suppose is the right word. Tom already had it when we married, and he had some beautiful things. You'll have to come over for coffee sometime. Or a drink.'

'I'd love it.'

'Then how about right now?'

'I . . . I'd love to, but to tell you the truth, I'm just beat. It's been a very hectic couple of days since I got back, and I ran myself ragged for three weeks in New York. Would a rain check be possible?'

'With pleasure. Thanks again for the ride.' She let herself out of the car, and waved as she climbed the steps to her house. Jessie waved back. That was some house! And she was pleased with having met Astrid Bonner. A delightful woman.

Jessica drove into her own driveway, thinking of Astrid and what she had said. It sounded as though she had given up a lot for her husband. And she looked happy about it.

Jessie walked into the dark house, kicked off her shoes, and sat down on the couch without turning on the lights. She was reviewing the day. It had been unbelievable. Everything from the meeting with Martin Schwartz, to emptying her savings into his pockets, to seeing Ian in jail, to the civilised exchanges with Astrid Bonner . . . when would life become real again?

She thought about making herself a drink, but she couldn't get up the energy to move. Her mind raced, but her body had turned to stone. The machinery just wouldn't move anymore. But her mind . . . her mind . . . she kept thinking about the visit to Ian. She was home again now. Alone, where he had always waited for her at night. The house was so unbearably quiet . . . the way Jake's apartment had been when she'd gone back to it . . . after he died . . . why did she keep thinking of Jake now? Why did she keep comparing him to Ian? Ian wasn't dead. And he would be home tomorrow—wouldn't he? He would. But what if . . . she just couldn't stop. The doorbell rang and she didn't even hear it until finally the insistent buzzer yanked her attention off the merry-go-round of her thoughts. It required her last ounce of energy to get up and answer the door.

She stood in her stocking feet in the darkness of the front hall and spoke through the door. She was too tired even to try to guess who it was.

'Who is it?' Her voice barely penetrated through to the opposite side. But he heard her. He looked over his shoulder at his companion and nodded. The second man walked slowly back toward the green car.

'Police.'

Jessie's heart flew into trip-hammer action at the sound of the word, and she leaned trembling against the wall. Now what?

'Yes?'

'It's Inspector Houghton. I want to speak to Mrs. Clarke.' But he already knew it was she. And on the other side of the door, Jessica was tempted to tell him that Mrs. Clarke was not at home. But her car was plainly visible out front, and he'd just hang around waiting. There was no escaping them anymore. They owned her life, and Ian's.

Jessie slowly unlocked the door and stood silently in the dark hall. Even without shoes, she stood about an inch taller than the inspector. Their eyes held for a long moment. All the hatred she could not feel for Ian's betrayal she lavished on Inspector Houghton. He was easy to hate.

'Good evening. May I come in?' Jessie stood to one side, flicked on the lights, and then preceded him into the living room. She stood in the centre of the room, facing him, and did not invite him to sit down.

'Well, Inspector? What now?' Her tone hid nothing.

'I thought we could have a little chat.'

'Oh? Is that usual?' she was frightened, but she was even more afraid to show it. What if he wanted to rape her? A real rape this time. What if . . . oh God . . . where was Ian?

'This is perfectly usual, Mrs. Clarke.'

They seemed to circle each other with their eyes, enemies from birth. A python and his prey. She didn't like her role. She feared him, but would not show it. He found her beautiful, but he didn't let that show either. He hated Ian for a number of reasons. That showed.

'Mind if I sit down?' Yes. Very much.

'Not at all.' She waved him to the couch and sat down in her usual chair.

'Lovely house you have, Mrs. Clarke. Have you lived here long?' He glanced around, seeming to take in all the details, while she fantasized about telling him to go fuck himself and scratching his eyes out. But now she knew that wasn't real. You might hate cops, but you didn't let your hostilities show. She was innocent, Ian was innocent, but she was terrified.

'Inspector, is this a formal interrogation or a social call? Our attorney told me today that I don't have to speak to anyone unless he's present.' She was watching the brown double-knit leg and the maroon sock, wondering if he was going to try to rape her. He was wearing a shiny mustard-coloured tie. She was beginning to feel nauseated, and suddenly panicked, wondering if she had taken the pill that morning. And then suddenly she looked at him and knew she'd kill him if he tried. She'd have to.

'No, you don't have to speak to anyone unless your attorney is presnt, Mrs. Clarke, but I have a few questions, and I thought it would be more pleasant for you to answer them here.' Big favour.

'I think I'd rather answer them in court.' But they both knew she didn't have to answer anything in court. She was the defendant's wife. Legally, she didn't have to testify.

'Suit yourself.' He stood up to leave and then stopped at the bar. 'You a drinker, too?' The question infuriated her.

'No, and neither is my husband.'

'Yeah, that's what I thought. He claims he was ripped

when he took the victim to the hotel. I figured he was lying, though. He doesn't look like a drinker.' Jessie's heart sank and her eyes filled with hatred. This sonofabitch was trying to trap her.

'Inspector, I'm asking you to leave. Now.'

Houghton turned to her then and searched her eyes with a look of feigned kindness. But his own eyes returned the anger of Jessie's. His voice was barely audible as he stood a foot away from her.

'What are you doing with a weak-kneed punk like him?'

'Get out of my house!' Her voice was as low as his and her whole body was trembling.

'What'll you do when he goes to the joint? Find another gigolo sweetheart like him? Believe me, sister, don't sweat it. They're a dime a dozen.'

'*Get out*!' The words were like two fists in his face, and he turned on his heel and walked to the door. He paused for a moment and looked back at her.

'See ya.'

The door closed behind him, and for the first time in her life Jessica wanted to kill.

He was back at ten that night, with two plainclothesmen and a search warrant, to look for weapons and drugs. This time Houghton was straight-faced and businesslike, and he avoided her eyes for the entire hour they were there, digging into closets and drawers, unfolding her underwear, dumping her handbags on the bed, pouring out soap flakes, and spreading Ian's clothes and papers all over the living room.

They found nothing, and Jessie said nothing about it to Ian. Ever. It took her four and a half hours to get everything put away, and another two hours to stop sobbing. Her fears had been justified. They had raped her. Not in the way she had feared, but in another way. Photographs of her mother lay strewn all over her desk, her birth-control pills lay dumped out in the kitchen, half of them gone, to be tested at the lab. Her whole life was spread all over the house. It was her war now too. And she was ready to fight. That night had changed everything. Now they were *her* enemy too, not just Ian's.

And for the first time in seven years, Ian was not there to defend her. Not only that, but it was he who had put her face to face with this enemy. He had brought this down around her ears as well as his own. And she was helpless. It was Ian's fault. Now he was the enemy too.

CHAPTER VIII

Jessica waited with Martin Schwartz in the back rows of the courtroom until after ten. The docket was heavily overscheduled, and the court was running late. The procedures Jessie watched looked very dull. Most of the charges were rattled off by number, bails were arbitrarily set, and new faces were brought in. Ian finally arrived through a door leading in from the jail, accompanied by a guard on each side.

Martin walked to the front of the room, and the charges were, mercifully, read off by number, not description. Ian was asked if he understood what he was accused of, and he answered, gravely, in the affirmative.

The bail was set at twenty-five thousand dollars. Martin asked to have it reduced and the judge pondered the question while a female assistant D.A. jumped to her feet and objected. She felt that the matter before the court warranted a heavier bail. But the judge didn't agree. He lowered it to fifteen thousand, smacked his gavel, and had another man brought in. The preliminary hearing had been set for two weeks hence.

'Now what do we do?' Jessica whispered to Martin as he came back to her seat. Ian had already left the court and was back in the jail.

'Now you scare up fifteen hundred bucks to pay to a bailbondsman, and give him something worth fifteen thousand in collateral.'

'How do I do that?'

'Come on. I'll take you over myself.'

But Jesus . . . fifteen thousand? Now it suddenly hit her. Fifteen thousand. It was enormous. Could anything be worth that much money? Yes. Ian.

They went down to the lobby and across the street to one of a long row of neon-lit bail offices. They didn't look like nice places, and the one they walked into was no better than the rest. It reeked of cigar smoke, the ash-trays were full to overflowing, and two men were asleep on a couch, apparently waiting. A woman with teased yellow hair asked them their business and Martin explained. She called the jail and made a note of the charges while looking lengthily at Jessie. Jessie tried not to flinch.

'You'll have to put up the collateral. Do you own your own home?'

Jessie nodded, and explained the mortgage. 'And I own my own business as well.' She gave the woman the name and address of the boutique, the address of the house, and the name of the bank where they had their mortgage.

'What do you think your business is worth? What is it, anyway? A dress shop?' Jessie nodded, feeling degraded somehow, though she was not quite sure why. Maybe it was because the woman now knew what the charges were.

'Yes, it's a dress shop. And we have a fairly large inventory.' Why did she want to impress this idiot woman? But then she knew that it was because the woman held the key to Ian's bail. Martin Schwartz was standing to one side, watching the proceedings.

'We'll have to call your bank. Come back at four o'clock.'

'And then can you bail him?' Oh God, please, can you bail him? The panic was coming back in her throat again, thick and sweet and bitter, like bile.

'We'll bail him depending on what your bank says about the house and the shop,' she said flatly. 'Do you use the same bank for both?' Jessie nodded, looking grey. 'Good. That'll save time. Bring the fifteen hundred with you when you come back. In cash.'

'In cash?'

'Cash or a bank cheque. No personal cheques.'

'Thank you.'

They went back to the street and Jessie took a long breath of fresh air. It felt like years since she'd had any. She breathed again and looked at Martin.

'What happens to people who don't have the money?'

'They don't bail.'

'And then what?'

'They stay in custody till after the verdict.'

'Even if they're innocent? They stay in jail all that time?'

'You don't know if they're innocent until after the trial.'

'What the hell ever happened to "innocent until proven guilty"?'

He shrugged and looked away, remaining silent. It had depressed him to be in the bail office. He rarely went to bailbondsmen with clients. But Ian had asked him to and he had promised. It seemed odd to treat such a tall, independent-looking woman as though she were frail and helpless. But he suspected that Ian was right: beneath the coat of armour, she hid a terrifying vulnerability. He wondered if that armour would crack before this was over. That was all they needed.

'What do poor people do about lawyers?' Jesus. He had enough headaches without playing social worker.

'They get public defenders, Jessica. And we have plenty to think about ourselves right now, without worrying about poor people, don't you think? Why don't you just get yourself to the bank and get this over with?'

'Okay. I'm sorry.'

'Don't be. The system is lousy, and I know it. But it's not set up for the comfort of the poor. Just be grateful that you're not one of them right now, and let it go at that.'

'That's hard to do, Martin.'

He shook his head and gave her a small smile. 'Are you going to the bank?'

'Yes, sir.'

'Good. Do you want me to come with you?'

'Of course not. Is baby-sitting service always part of the deal, or did Ian strong-arm you into that?'

'I . . . no . . . oh, for Chrissake. Just go to the bank. And let me know when you get him out. Or before that, if there's anything I can do.'

How about lending us fifteen thousand bucks, baby? She smiled, said good-bye, and walked slowly to her car. She still didn't have any idea of how she'd come up with the money. And what the hell would she tell the bank? The truth. And she'd beg them if she had to. Fifteen thousand . . . it looked like the top of Mount Everest.

After six cigarettes and half an hour of agonizing conversation with the bank manager, Jessica took out a personal loan for fifteen hundred dollars against the car. And they assured her that all would be in order when the bail office called. There was a look of astonishment on the bank manager's face throughout the conversation, and he tried desperately to conceal it. Unsuccessfully. And Jessica had not even told him what the charges were, only that Ian was in jail. She prayed that the bail office wouldn't tell them the charges either, and that if they did he would keep his mouth shut. He had already sworn to her that he would see that everything remained confidential. And at least she had the fifteen hundred dollars . . . she had it . . . she had it! And her house and the business were worth ten times the collateral that she needed. But somehow she still didn't feel that it was enough. What if they still wouldn't let Ian out? And then she thought of it. The safe-deposit box.

'Mrs. Clarke?'

She didn't answer. She just sat there.

'Mrs. Clarke? Was there something else?'

'Sorry. Oh . . . I . . . was just thinking of something. Yes, I . . . I think I'd like to get into my vault today.'

'Do you have the key with you?'

She nodded. She kept it on her key chain. She reached into her bag and handed it to him.

'I'll have Miss Lopez open the box for you.'

Jessie followed him pensively, and then found herself following Miss Lopez, whom she did not know. And then she was standing in front of her safe-deposit box and Miss

Lopez was looking at her, holding the box. It was a large one.

'Would you like to go into a room with this?'

'I . . . I . . . yes. Thank you.' She shouldn't have done it. She didn't need it. It was a mistake . . . no . . . but what if the house and Lady J weren't enough? She knew she wasn't making sense now. She was panicking. But it was better to be sure . . . to be . . . for Ian. But it was all so painful. And now she had to face it alone.

Miss Lopez left her in a small, sterile room with a brown Formica desk and a black vinyl chair. On the wall hung an ugly print of Venice that looked as though it had been cut from the top of a candy box. And she was alone with the box. Jessie opened it carefully and took out three large brown leather boxes and two faded red suede jewellery cases. There was another, smaller box at the bottom, in faded blue. The blue box was filled with Jake's few treasures. The studs Father had given him on his twenty-first birthday, his school ring, his Navy ring. Junk, mostly, but very Jake.

The brown leather boxes contained the real treasures. Letters her parents had written to each other over the years. Letters they had exchanged while her father was in the service during the war. Poems her mother had written to her father. Photographs. Locks of her hair and Jake's. Treasures. All the things that had mattered. Now, all the things that hurt most.

She opened the blue box first and smiled through a veil of tears as she saw Jake's trinkets lying helter-skelter on the beige chamois. It still held the faintest hint of Jake's smell. She remembered teasing him about the high-school ring. She had told him it was hideous, and he had been so damn proud of it. And now there it was. She slipped it on her finger. It was much too big for her. It would have been too big for Ian too. Jake had been almost six foot five.

She turned to the brown boxes then. She knew their touch so well. They were engraved with her parents' initials, tiny gold letters in the lower right-hand corners. Each box identical. They were a family tradition. In the first box she found a picture of the four of them taken one Easter. She had been eleven or twelve; Jake had been seven. It was really more than she could face. She closed the box quietly and turned to what she had come for.

The red suede jewellery cases. It was incredible, really. She was actually going to take her mother's jewellery with her. It was so precious to her, so sacred, so much still her mother's that Jessie had worn none of it in all these years. And now she was willing to leave it in the hands of strangers. For Ian.

She carefully unfolded the cases and looked at the long row of rings. A ruby in an old setting that had been her grandmother's. Two handsome jade rings her father had brought back from the Far East. The emerald ring her mother had wanted so much and had gotten for her fiftieth birthday. The diamond engagement ring . . . and her wedding ring, her 'real' one, the worn, thin gold band she had always worn, always preferred to the emerald-and-diamond one Jessie's father had bought to match the emerald ring. There were two simple gold chain bracelets. A gold watch with tiny diamonds carefully set around the face. And a large handsome sapphire brooch with diamonds set around it that had also been Jessie's grandmother's.

The second case held three strands of perfectly matched pearls, pearl earrings, and a small pair of diamond earrings that she and Jake had bought her together the year before she'd died. It was all there. Jessie's stomach turned over as she looked at it. She knew she wouldn't really be able to leave it with the bailbondsman, but at least she had it if she needed it. Two days before she wouldn't have considered such a thing, but now . . .

She put the rest of the boxes back into the metal vault and left the room almost two hours after she had entered it. The bank was almost ready to close.

When she went back to Bryant Street the woman was eating a dripping cheeseburger over the afternoon paper. 'Got the money?' She looked up and spoke to Jessica with her mouth full.

Jessica nodded. 'Did you talk to the bank about the collateral?' She had had enough, and wading through the private agony that safe-deposit box represented had topped it off. She wanted the nightmare to end. Now.

'What bank?' The woman's face wore an unexpectedly blank expression, and Jessie clenched her hands to keep from screaming.

'The California Union Trust Bank. I wanted to bail my husband out tonight.'

'What were the charges?' For Chrissake, what was this woman trying to *do* to her? She remembered that Jessica was due back with some money—how could she have forgotten the rest? Or was she playing a game? Well, if she was, fuck her.

'The charges were rape and assault.' She almost shouted the words.

'Did you own any property?' Oh, shit.

'For God's sake, we went through all that this morning, and you were going to call my bank about my business and our mortgage. I was here with our attorney, filled out papers, and . . .'

'Okay. What's your name?'

'Clarke. With an "E." '

'Yeah. Here it is.' She pulled out the form with two greasy fingers. 'Can't bail him now, though.'

'Why not?' Jessie's stomach turned over again.

'Too late to call the bank.'

'Shit. Now what?'

'Come back in the morning.' Sure, while Ian sat in jail for another night. Wonderful. Tears of frustration choked her throat, but there was nothing she could do except go home and come back in the morning.

'You want to talk to the boss?'

Jessie's face lit up.

'Now?'

'Yeah. He's here. In the back.'

'Fabulous. Tell him I'm here.' Oh God, please . . . please let him be human . . . please . . .

The man emerged from the back room picking his teeth with a dirty finger that boasted a small gold ring with a large pink diamond. He had a beer can in his other hand. He was wearing jeans and a T-shirt, and had a lot of curly black hair on his arms and at the neck of the shirt; his hair was almost an Afro. And he wasn't much older than Jessie. He grinned when he saw her, gave a last stab at his teeth, then removed his hand from his mouth and extended it for her to shake. She shook it, but with difficulty.

'How do you do. I'm Jessica Clarke.'

'Barry York. What can I do you for?'

'I'm trying to bail my husband.'

'From what? What are the charges? Hey . . . wait a minute. Let's go in my office. You want a beer?' Actually, she did. But not with him. She was hot and tired and thirsty and fed up and scared, but she didn't want to drink anything with Barry York, not even water.

'No thanks.'

'Coffee?'

'No, really. I'm fine, but thanks.' He was trying to be decent. One had to give him credit for that. He led her into a small, dingy office with pictures of nude women on the walls, sat down in a swivel chair, put a green eye-shade on his head, switched on a stereo, and grinned at her.

'We don't see many people like you, Mrs. Clarke.'

'I . . . no . . . thank you.'

'So what's with the old man? What's the beef? Drunk driving?'

'No, rape.' Barry whistled lengthily while Jessie stared at his stomach. At least he was honest about what he thought. 'That's a bitch. What's the bail?'

'Fifteen thousand.'

'Bad news.'

'Well, that's why I'm here.' Good news for you, Barry, baby; maybe you can even buy yourself a gold toothpick after this, with a diamond tip. 'I spoke to the young lady out there earlier today, and she was to call my bank, and . . .'

'And?' His face hardened slightly.

'She forgot.'

Barry shook his head. 'She didn't forget. We don't do bonds that high.'

'You don't?'

He shook his head again. 'Not usually.' Jessica thought she was going to cry. 'I guess she just didn't want to tell you.'

'So I lost a day, and my husband is still in jail, and my bank is expecting to hear from you, and . . . now what, Mr. York? What the hell do I do now?'

'How about some dinner?' He turned the stereo down and patted her hand. His breath smelled like pastrami and garlic. He stank.

Jessica simply looked at him and stood up. 'You know, my attorney must be all wrong about this place, Mr. York. And I have every intention of telling him just that.'

'Who's your attorney?'

'Martin Schwartz. He was here with me this morning.'

'Look, Mrs. . . . what's your name again?'

'Clarke.'

'Mrs. Clarke. Why don't you sit down and we'll talk a little business.'

'Now or after dinner? Or after we listen to a few more records?'

He smiled. 'You like the records? I thought that was a nice touch.'

He turned the stereo up again and Jessie didn't know whether to laugh, cry, or scream. It was obvious that she'd never get Ian out of jail. Not at this rate. 'You want to have dinner?'

'Yes, Mr. York. With my husband. What are the chances of your getting my husband out of jail so I can have dinner with him?'

'Tonight? No way. I've got to talk to your bank first.'

'That's exactly where I left it at twelve-thirty this afternoon.'

'Yeah, well, I'm sorry. And I'll take care of it myself in the morning, but I can't do anything after banking hours, not on a bond the size of the one you're talking about. What are you putting up as collateral?'

'My business and/or my house. That's up to you. I'm willing to put up either one or both. Or I was. But I have another idea.' It was crazy, it was stupid, it was immoral, it was wrong, but she was so goddam fed up, she had to. She reached into her bag and pulled out the two cases with her mother's jewellery in them. 'What about these?'

Barry York sat down very quietly and didn't say a word for almost ten minutes.

'Nice.'

'Better than that. The emerald and the diamond rings are very fine stones. And the sapphire brooch is worth a great deal of money. So are the pearls.'

'Yeah. Probably so. But the problem is I don't know nothing until I take them to a jeweller. I still can't get the old man out tonight.' The old man . . . asshole. 'Very nice jewellery, though. Where'd you get it?'

We stole it. 'It's my mother's.'

'She know the old man's in the can?'

'Hardly, Mr. York. She's dead.'

'Oh, I'm sorry. Listen, I'll take this to the appraiser first thing tomorrow morning. I'll call your bank. We'll get the old man out by noon. Swear, if the stuff is good. I can't do anything before that. But by noon, if everything is in order. Do you have my fee?'

Yes, darling, in pennies. 'Yes.'

'Okay, then we're all set.'

'Mr. York, why can't you just take all the jewellery tonight and let him come home? He won't go anywhere, and we'll get all this financial nonsense straightened out tomorrow. If your assistant had called the bank when she said she would . . .'

He was shaking his head, picking his teeth again and holding up his other hand. 'I'd like to. But I can't. That's all. I can't. My business is at stake. I'll take care of it first thing in the morning. I swear. Be here at ten-thirty and we'll get everything done.'

'Fine.' She rose to her feet, feeling as though the weight of the world were resting on her shoulders. She folded up the two suede cases and put them back in her bag.

'You're not leaving me those?'

'Nope. That was just if I could get him out tonight. I thought you'd recognize their value. Otherwise, I'd much rather put up my house and the business.'

'Okay. Yeah.' But he didn't look pleased. 'That's a hell of a big bond, you know.' She nodded tiredly.

'Don't worry. It's a nice house and a good business, and he's a decent man. He won't run away on you. You won't lose a dime.'

'You'd be surprised who runs away.'

'I'll see you at ten-thirty, Mr. York.' She held out a hand and he shook it, smiling again.

'You sure about dinner? You look tired. Maybe some food would do you good. A little wine, a little dancing . . . hell, enjoy yourself a little before the old man gets home. And look at it this way, if he got busted for rape, you gotta know he wasn't just out with the boys.'

'Good night, Mr. York.'

She walked quietly out of the door, out to her car, and drove home.

She was asleep on the couch half an hour later, and she didn't wake up until nine the next morning. When she did, she felt as though she had died the night before. And she had a terrifying case of the shakes.

It was all beginning to take its toll. The ever deepening circles under her eyes now looked irreparable, the eyes themselves seemed to be shrinking, and she noticed that she was beginning to lose weight. She smoked six cigarettes, drank two cups of coffee, played with a piece of toast, and called the boutique and told them to forget about her again today. She arrived back at Yorktowne Bonding at ten-thirty. On the dot.

There were two new people at the desk—a girl with dyed black hair the colour of military boots who was snapping bubble gum, and a bearded young man with a Mexican accent. This time Jessie asked for Mr. York right away.

'He's expecting me.' The two clerks looked up as though they had never heard the words before.

He appeared two minutes later in dirty white shorts and

a navy blue T-shirt, carrying a copy of *Playboy* and a tennis racket.

'You play?' Oh, Jesus.

'Sometimes. Did you talk to the bank?'

He smiled, looking pleased. 'Come into my office. Coffee?'

'No, thanks.' She was beginning to feel as though the nightmare would never end. She would simply spend the rest of her life ricocheting among the Inspector Houghtons and Barry Yorks, the courtroom and jails, the banks and . . . it was endless. Just when it seemed about to end, there would be another false door. There was no way out. She was almost sure of it now. And Ian was only a myth anyway. Someone she had made up and never known. The keeper of the Holy Grail.

'You know, you look tired. Do you eat right?'

'I eat splendidly. But my husband is in jail, Mr. York, and I would very much like to get him out. What are the chances of that, in the immediate future?'

'Excellent.' He beamed. 'I talked to the bank and everything's in order. You put up the house and agree to a lien on your earnings at the boutique if he defaults. And we keep the emerald ring and sapphire brooch for you.'

'What?' He had made it sound as if he were ordering lunch for her, but he had caught her attention with the mention of her mother's jewellery. 'I don't think you understood, Mr. York. The house and the business are all I'm putting up. I told you last night that I was only offering my mother's jewellery if I could get him out then, without your calling the bank and all. Sort of a guarantee.'

'Yeah. Well, I'd feel better with that same guarantee now.'

'Well, I wouldn't.'

'How would your husband feel staying in jail?'

'Mr. York, isn't there a law against bailbondsmen taking too much as collateral?' Martin had told her about it.

'Are you accusing me of being dishonest?' Oh, God, she was going to blow it . . . oh no . . .

'No. Look, please . . .'

'Look, baby, I'm not gonna do business with some broad

who calls me dishonest. I do you a favour and stick my ass out on a limb for your old man on a fifteen-thousand-dollar bond, and you call me a thief. I mean, look, I don't gotta take that shit from no one.'

'I'm sorry.' The tears were burning her eyes again. She was beginning to wonder if she'd live through this. And then he looked over at her and shrugged.

'All right. I'll tell you what. We'll just keep the ring. You can take the brooch. Does that sound any better?'

'Fine.' It sounded stinking, but she didn't care anymore. It didn't matter. It didn't even matter if Ian ran away and they took the house and the business and the car and the emerald ring. Nothing mattered.

York managed to make the forms take twice as long as necessary, and to slide a hand across her breast as he reached for another pen. She looked up into his face and he smiled and told her she'd be beautiful if she ate right, and how he'd had a tall girlfriend in high school. A girl named Mona. Jessica just nodded and went on signing her name. Finally all the paperwork was done. He bit the end off a long thin cigar and picked up the phone to notify the jail.

'I'll have Bernice take you across the street, Jessica.' He had decided to call her by her first name. 'And listen, if you ever need any help, just call. I'll keep in touch.' She prayed that he wouldn't, and shook his hand before leaving his office. She felt as though she would stumble on the way out. She had reached her limit. Days ago.

By the time Barry York had delegated the gum-chewing clerk to take Jessie across the street to bail Ian, it was almost noon. To Jessie it felt like the middle of the night. She was confused and exhausted and everything was beginning to blur. She was living in an unreal world filled with evil, leering people.

The woman he'd called Bernice took charge of the papers, shuffled them for a moment, and then walked across the street with Jessie and into the Hall of Justice. She slipped the sheaf of papers Jessie and Barry York had signed into a slot in a window on the second floor, and then turned to look at Jessica for a moment.

'You going to stick by your old man?'

'I beg your pardon?'

'You going to stay with your husband?'

'Yes . . . of course . . . why?' She was feeling confused again. And why was this woman asking her that?

'That's a hell of a beef, sister. And what's a good-looking chick like you want with a loser like him? He's going to cost you a bundle on this one.' She shook her head and snapped her gum twice.

'He's worth it.'

The girl shrugged and waved at the bank of elevators. 'You can go up to the jail now. We're all through.' No, lady, *I'm* all through. That's different. The clerk departed with a last snap of her gum and headed down a stairway.

Jessica reached the jail a few moments later and had to ring a small buzzer to bring a guard to the door.

'Yeah? It's not visiting time yet.'

'I'm here to bail out my husband.'

'What's his name?'

'Ian Clarke.' You know, the famous rapist. 'Yorktowne Bonding just called about it.'

'I'll check.' Check? Check what? With the house, the business, and Mom's emerald ring on the line, you're going to check, mister? Well, screw you. And Yorktowne Bonding . . . and Inspector Houghton . . . and . . . Ian too? She wasn't really sure anymore. She didn't know what she felt. She was angry at him, but not for what he had done, only for not being there when she needed him so badly.

She waited at the door for almost half an hour, stupefied, dazed, leaning against the wall and hardly knowing why. What if she never saw him again? But suddenly the door opened and he stood there facing her. He was unshaven, bedraggled, filthy, and exhausted. But he was free. Everything she owned was riding on him now. And he was free. She sank slowly towards him with an unfamiliar whimpering sound, and he led her gently into the elevator.

"It's all right, baby . . . it's all right. Everything's going to be all right, Jess . . . sshhh . . .' It was Ian. Actually, really, honestly Ian. And he held her so gently and almost carried her down to the car. She couldn't take any more and he knew it. He didn't know all the details of what had been happening, but when he saw the bail papers and noticed the mention of her mother's emerald ring, he understood much more than she could tell him.

'It's okay, baby . . . everything's going to be fine.'

She clutched him blindly as they stood beside the car, the tears streaming down her cheeks, her face in a rictus of shock and despair, the same little squeaking noises escaping from her between sobs.

'Jessie . . . baby . . . I love you.' He held her tightly, and then quietly drove her home.

CHAPTER IX

'What are you doing today, darling?'

Jessie poured Ian a second cup of coffee at breakfast and glanced at the clock. It was almost nine and she hadn't been to the boutique for two days. She felt as though she had been gone for a month, existing in a kind of twilight zone all her own. A never-ending nightmare, but it was over now. Ian was home. She had spent most of the day before asleep in his arms. And he looked like Ian again. Clean, shaven, a little more rested. He was wearing grey slacks and a wine-coloured turtleneck. Every time she looked at him she wanted to touch him to make sure he was real.

'Are you going to write today?'

'I don't know yet. I think I might just spend the day feeling good.' But he didn't ask her to play hookey with him. He knew she had to work. She had done enough for him in the past few days. He couldn't ask for more.

'I wish I could stay home with you.' She looked at him wistfully over her coffee and he patted her hand.

'I'll pick you up for lunch.'

'I have an idea. Why don't you hang around the boutique today?'

He watched her eyes and knew what she was thinking.

She had been like that for months after Jake had died. That terror that if he left her sight, he'd vanish.

'You wouldn't get any work done, my love. But I'll be around. I'll be right here most of the time.' But what about the rest of the time? She reached over and held his hand. Nothing was said. There was nothing to say. 'I thought maybe I'd talk to a couple of people about work.'

'No!' She pulled back her hand and her eyes darted fire. 'No, Ian! Please.'

'Jessica, be reasonable. Have you thought of what this disaster is costing us? Costing *you*, to be more exact? And this is as good a time as any to get a job. Nothing exotic, just something to bring a little money in.'

'And what happens when you have to start making court appearances? And during the trial? Just how much good do you think you'll be to anyone then?' She held tightly to his hand again and he saw the pain in her eyes. It was going to take months for the desperation to pass.

'Well, what exactly do you expect me to do, Jess?'

'Finish the book.'

'And let you pick up the tab for this mess?'

She nodded. 'We can straighten it out later, if you want to. But I don't really give a damn, Ian. What does it matter who signs the cheques?'

'It matters to me.' It always has mattered, always will matter. But he knew, too, that he'd never be able to concentrate on anything while this was hanging over his head. The trial . . . the trial . . . it was all he could think of. While she had slept all those hours the previous afternoon, it had kept running through his mind . . . the trial. He was in no frame of mind to get a job. 'We'll see.'

'I love you.' There were tears in her eyes again, and he tweaked the end of her nose.

'If you get dewy-eyed on me once more, Mrs. Clarke, I'm going to drag you back to bed and really give you something to cry about.' She laughed in response and poured some more coffee.

'I just can't believe you're home. It was so incredibly awful while you were gone . . . it was . . . it was like . . .' The words caught in her throat.

'It was probably like peace and quiet for a change, and you were too silly to enjoy it. Hell, you didn't think I'd stay down there forever, did you? I mean, even for a writer that kind of living research gets stale after a while.'

'Jerk.' But she was smiling now; she had nothing to fear.

'Want me to drive you to work?'

'As a matter of fact, I'd love it.' She beamed as she put the cups in the sink and grabbed her orange suede coat off the back of a chair. She was wearing it over well-tailored jeans and a beige cashmere sweater. She looked like Jessie again—everywhere except around the eyes. She slid the dark glasses into place and smiled at him. 'I think I'd better hang on to these for a couple of days. I still look like I've been on a two-week drunk.'

'You look beautiful and I love you.' He pinched her behind as they headed out the front door, and she leaned backward to kiss him haphazardly over one shoulder. 'You even smell nice.'

'Nothing but the best. Eau de Mille Pieds.' She said it with a broad grin and he groaned.

'Oh, for Chrissake.' It was one of their oldest jokes. Water of a thousand feet.

She pointed out Astrid's house to him on their way to the boutique, and told him about her visit to the shop.

'She seems like a nice woman. Very quiet and pleasant.'

'Hell, I'd be quiet and pleasant too, with that kind of money.'

'Ian!' But she grinned at him and ran a hand through his hair. It felt so good to be sitting next to him again, to be looking at his profile as he drove, to feel the skin on his neck with her mouth as she kissed him. She had awakened a dozen times during the night to make sure he was still there.

'I'll come by for you around twelve. Okay?'

She looked at him for a moment before nodding. 'You'll be here? For sure?'

'Oh, baby . . . I'll be here. Promise.' He took her in his arms and she held him so tightly that it hurt. He knew she was thinking of the day he'd been arrested and hadn't shown up for lunch. 'Be a big girl.' She grinned and hopped out of the car and blew him a last kiss before running up the steps of the shop.

Ian lit a cigarette as he drove away, and glanced over to look at the ships on the bay. It was a beautiful day. Indian summer was passing, and it was not as warm as it had been a few days before, but the sky was a bright blue and there was a gentle breeze. It made him think back to that day five days before. It felt like five years before. He still couldn't understand it.

He paused at a stop sign, and another thought came to mind. The emerald ring Jessie had put up as bail. It still astounded him. He knew how she felt about her mother's things. She wouldn't even wear them. They were sacred, the last relics of a long-demolished shrine. And that ring meant more to her than any of the other pieces. He had watched her slip it on her finger once while her hand trembled out of control. She had put the ring back in the case, and never gone to the vault again. And now she had turned it over to a bailbondsman, for him. It told him something that nothing else ever had. It was crazy, but he felt as though he loved her more than he had before all this had begun, and maybe Jessie had learned something too. Maybe they knew what they had now. Maybe they'd take better care of it. He knew one thing. His days of discreet interludes were over. Forever. All of a sudden he had a wife. More of a wife than he had ever known he had. What more could he want? A child, perhaps, but he had resigned himself to the absence of children. He was happy enough with just Jessie.

'Morning, ladies.' Jessie strolled into the store with a quiet smile on her face. And Katsuko looked up from the desk.

'Well, look who's here. And on a Saturday, yet. We were beginning to think you'd found a better job.'

'No such luck.'

'Is everything okay?'

'Yes. Everything's okay.' Jessica nodded slowly and Katsuko knew that it was. Jessie was herself again.

'I'm glad.' Katsuko handed her a cup of coffee and Jessie perched on the corner of the chrome-and-glass desk.

'Where's Zina?'

'In the back, checking the stock. Mrs. Bonner came back looking for you yesterday. She bought one of the new wine velvet skirts.'

'It must have looked great on her. Did she try it with the cream satin shirt?'

'Yup. Bought them both, and the new green velvet pant-suit. That lady must have money burning holes in her pockets.' Yeah. And loneliness burning holes in her heart. Jessie had had a taste of it now. She knew.

'She'll be back,' Katsuko added.

'I hope so. Even if she doesn't buy. I like her. Anything taking shape for the fashion show?'

'I had a few ideas yesterday, Jessie, I made some notes and left them on your desk.'

'I'll go take a look.' She stretched lazily and wandered towards her office, carrying her coffee. It was a slow morning, and she felt as if she had come back after a very long absence, a long illness maybe. She felt slow and careful and frail. And everything looked suddenly different. The shop looked so sweet, the two girls so pretty . . . Ian so beautiful . . . the sky so blue . . . everything seemed better and more.

She read her mail, paid some bills, changed the window, and discussed the fashion show with Katsuko while Zina waited on customers. The morning sped by, and Ian was there five minutes before noon. With an armload of roses. The delicate salmon ones Jessie loved best.

'Ian! They're fabulous!' There were about three dozen, and she could see an awkward square lump in his jacket pocket. He was spoiling her and she loved it. He smiled at her and headed toward her office.

'Can I see you for a minute, Mrs. Clarke?'

'Yes, sir. For three dozen roses you can see me for several weeks!' The two girls laughed and Jessie followed Ian into her office. He closed the door gently and grinned at her.

'Have a nice morning?'

'You brought me back to this secluded spot to ask me if

I had a nice morning?' He was grinning and she was starting to giggle. 'Come on, tell the truth. Is it bigger than a breadbox?'

'What?'

'The surprise you bought me, of course.'

'What surprise? I buy you roses and you want more! You greedy spoiled miserable . . .' But he was looking too pleased with himself to convince even Jessie. 'Oh . . . here.' He pulled the box out of his pocket and grinned from ear to ear. It was a solid chunk of gold bracelet; inside it was engraved ALL MY LOVE, IAN. He had literally stood over the jewellers all morning while they did the engraving. It was no time to spend money, but he'd known that she needed something like that, and it had suddenly come to him as he'd sat down to work. It was a beautiful bracelet, and the proportions were just right for her hand. It had cost him the last of his private savings.

'Oh, darling . . . it's beautiful.' She slipped it onto her wrist and it held there. 'Wow. It's just perfect! Oh Ian . . . you're crazy!'

'I happen to be madly in love with you.'

'I'm beginning to think you struck oil, too. You spent a fortune this morning.' But there was no edge to her voice, only pleasure, and Ian shrugged. 'Wait till I show the girls!' She planted a kiss on the corner of his mouth, opened the door, and bumped into Zina, who was walking past to the stockroom. 'Look at my bracelet!'

'My, my! Does that mean you're engaged to the handsome man with the roses?' She giggled and winked at Ian.

'Oh, shut up. Isn't it super?'

'It's gorgeous. And all I want to know is where you find another one like him.'

'Try Central Casting.' Ian looked over Jessie's shoulder with a grin.

'I might just do that.' Zina disappeared into the stockroom, and, with a look of victory, Jessie showed her new bracelet to Katsuko. A few minutes later, she and Ian were on their way out the door to lunch.

'Boy, I love my bracelet!' She was like a child with a new toy, and held up her arm to look at it in the sunlight.

'Darling, it's just gorgeous! And how did you get them to engrave it so fast?'

'At gunpoint, of course. How else?'

'Oh, for Chrissake . . . you know, you really have a lot of class.'

'For a rapist.' But he was smiling when he said it.

'Ian!'

'Yes, my love?' He kissed her and she laughed as she got into the car. He had more style than any man she knew.

They went to the movies that night, and slept late on Sunday morning. It was another warm blue day, with puffy, pasted-on-looking clouds that rolled along high in the sky, looking like painted scenery.

'Want to go to the beach, Mrs. Clarke?' He stretched lazily on his side of the bed and then reached over and kissed her. She liked the feel of his beard stubble against her cheek. It was rough but it didn't quite hurt.

'I'd love to. What time is it?'

'Almost noon.'

'You're lying. It must be nine.'

'I am not. Open your eyes and take a look.'

'I can't. I'm still asleep.'

But he nibbled her neck and made her laugh and her eyes flew open.

'Stop that!'

'I will not. Get up and make me breakfast.'

'Slave driver. Haven't you ever heard of women's lib?' She lay on her back sleepily and yawned.

'What's that?'

'Women's lib. It says husbands have to cook breakfast on Sunday . . . but . . . on the other hand.' She looked at her bracelet again with a broad smile. 'It doesn't say you have to give your wife such gorgeous jewellery. So maybe I'll make you breakfast.'

'Beulah Big Heart, don't knock yourself out.'

'I won't. Fried eggs okay?' She lit a cigarette and sat up.

'I have a better idea.'

'The Fairmont for brunch?' She grinned at him and flashed the bracelet again.

'No. I'll help. You're too busy waving your bracelet at me to make us a decent breakfast anyway. How about a smoked-oyster-and-cheese omelette?' He looked enchanted with the combination and Jessie made a terrible face.

'Yerchk! Can we skip the smoked oysters?'

'Why not skip the cheese?'

'How about skipping the omelette?'

'The Fairmont for breakfast, then?'

'Ian, you're crazy . . . but I love you.' She nibbled at his thigh and he ran a hand down the smoothness of her spine.

It was another hour before they got out of bed. Even their lovemaking was different now. There was an odd combination of desperation and gratitude, of 'Oh God, I love you' mixed with 'Let's pretend everything's better than normal'. It wasn't, but the pretence helped. A little. Their motors were still racing a little too fast.

'Are we or are we not going to the beach today?' He sat up in bed, his blond hair tousled like a boy's.

'Sounds fine to me, but I still haven't been fed yet.'

'Aww . . . poor baby. You didn't want my smoked-oyster omelette.'

She tugged at a lock of his hair. 'I prefer what I got instead.'

'Shame on you.'

She stuck out her tongue at him, got out of bed, and headed for the kitchen.

'Where are you going bare-assed like that?'

'To the kitchen, to make breakfast. Any objection?'

'Nope. Need a voyeur on hand?'

A minute later she heard the garden door slam and then saw him reappear in the kitchen, wearing a blanket around his waist and carrying a mixed bouquet of her petunias.

'For the lady of the house.'

'Sorry, she's out. Can I have them instead?' She kissed him gently and took the flowers from his hand and set them down on the drainboard as he took her into his arms and let the blanket fall to the floor.

'Darling, I happen to love you madly, but if you don't

stop, the bacon will burn and we'll never get to the beach.'

'Do you care?' They were both smiling and the bacon was splattering furiously while the eggs began to bubble.

'No. But we might as well eat while it's ready. Damn.' He patted her behind and she turned off the flame and served scrambled eggs, bacon, toast, orange juice and coffee. Still naked, they sat down to breakfast.

They didn't get to the beach until almost three, but it was still a beautiful day and the sun stayed warm until six. They had a fish dinner in Sausalito on the way home, and he bought her a silly little dog made out of seashells.

'I love it. Now I feel like a tourist.'

'I thought you should have something really expensive to remember this evening with.' They were in high spirits as they crossed the bridge going home, but his words struck her oddly. Suddenly they were buying souvenirs and clutching at memories.

'Hey, sweetheart, how's the book coming?'

'Better than I want to admit. Don't ask me yet.'

'For real?'

'For real.'

She looked at him, pleased. He looked almost proud of himself and a little bit afraid to be.

'Have you sent any of it to your agent yet?'

'No, I want to wait till I finish a few more chapters before I do that. But I think this one is good. Maybe even very good.' He said it with a solemnity that touched her. He hadn't sounded like that about his work in years. Not since the fables, and they had been very good. Not very profitable, but definitely good. The critics had certainly agreed, even if the public hadn't.

On the way home, they stopped outside the yacht club near the bridge and turned off the lights and the motor. It was nice to sit and watch the water lap at a small lip of beach while the foghorns bleated softly in the distance. They were both oddly tired, as though each day were an endless journey. Their few days of trauma had taken a heavy toll. She noticed it in the heavy way he slept now, and she herself felt tired all the time, no matter how happy she was again. There was a new passion, too. A new need, a new hunger for each other, as though they must stock up for a long empty winter. They had rough times ahead. This was just the beginning.

'Want to go out for an ice cream cone?' There was a restless look around his eyes.

'Honestly? No. I'm bushed.'

'Yeah. Me too. And I want to do some reading tonight. The chapter I just finished.'

'Can I read some too?'

'Sure.' He looked pleased as he started the car and headed for home. It was funny how neither of them wanted to go home. The stop near the yacht club, the offer of an ice cream cone—what was the lurking demon they feared at home? Jessica wondered; but she knew who her private demon was. Inspector Houghton. She constantly expected him to jump out at her and take Ian back into custody. She had thought about it all day at the beach, wondering if he would spring from behind a dune and try to spirit Ian away. She hadn't said anything to Ian. Neither of them ever spoke of his arrest now. It was all either of them could think of, and the only thing they wouldn't talk about.

He was stretched out in front of the fire reading his manuscript when she decided that she had to remind him. She hated to bring it up, but somebody had to.

'Don't forget about tomorrow, love.' She said it softly, regretfully.

'Huh?' He had been deep into his work.

'I said don't forget about tomorrow.'

'What's tomorrow?' He looked blank.

'We have a ten o'clock appointment with Martin Schwartz.' She tried to make it sound like a double appointment with the hairdresser, but it didn't come off like that. Ian looked up at her and didn't say a word. His eyes said it all.

CHAPTER X

The meeting with Martin Schwartz was sobering. Sitting there with him, having to discuss the charges, they couldn't hide from it anymore. Jessica felt sick as she sat and listened. It was real now. She even felt sick thinking of the security she had put up. It came home to her now. She had put everything on the line. The house. The shop's profits. Even the emerald ring. Everything . . . Jesus . . . and what if Ian panicked and ran? What if . . . my God . . . she'd lose it all. She looked at him, feeling a lump rise in her throat, and tried to concentrate on what was being said. She almost couldn't hear. She just kept thinking of the fact that she needed one man so desperately that she had given all for him. And now what would happen?

Martin explained the preliminary hearing to them, and they agreed to hire an investigator to see what could be learned of the 'victim'. Plenty, they hoped, and all of it unsavoury. They were not going to be kind to Miss Margaret Burton. Destroying her was Ian's only way out.

'There's got to be a reason for it though, Ian. Think about it. Carefully. Did you rough her up in some way? Sexually? Verbally? Humiliate her? Hurt her?' Martin looked at Ian pointedly, and Jessie looked away. She hated the uncomfortable look on Ian's face. 'Ian?' And then Martin looked at her. 'Jessie, maybe you ought to let us have this out alone for a few moments.'

'Sure.' It was a relief to leave the room. Ian didn't look up as she left. They were down to the nitty-gritty now. Of who had done what to whom, where, how, for how long, and how often. He died thinking of what Jessie would hear in court at the trial.

She wandered the carpeted halls, looking at prints on the wall, smoking, alone with her own thoughts, until she found a small love seat placed near a window with the same splendid view as the one from Martin's office. She had a lot to think about.

A secretary came to get her half an hour later and escorted her back to Martin's office. Ian looked harassed and Martin was scowling. Jessie tried to make light of it. 'Did I miss all the good parts?' But her smile was forced and they didn't try to return it.

'According to Ian, there were no "good" parts. It must have something to do with a personal grudge.'

'Against Ian? Why? Did you know her?' She turned to her husband with a look of surprise. She had understood that the woman was a stranger to him.

'No. I didn't know her. But Martin means that she was out to hurt someone, anyone, maybe just a man, and I came along at the wrong time.'

'You can say that again.'

'I just hope we can prove it, Ian. Green ought to come up with something on her.'

'He'd better, at twenty bucks an hour.' Ian frowned again and looked at Jessie, as she nodded almost imperceptibly. This was no time to get tight with money. They'd find it wherever they had to, but they couldn't skimp on this.

Martin explained the preliminary to them once more to make sure it was clear. It was a sort of mini-trial at which the plaintiff/victim and the defendant would state their sides of the story, and the judge would decide if the matter should be dropped, or go on to a higher court for an ultimate decision—in this case, to trial. Martin held out no hope that the matter would be dropped. The opposing stories were equally vehement, the circumstances cloudy. No judge would take it upon himself to decide a case like that at the preliminary state. It didn't help that the woman had maintained the same job for years and was respected where she worked. And there were certain psychological aspects of the case that made Martin Schwartz exceedingly uncomfortable: the fact that Ian was being virtually supported by his wife and hadn't had a successful book in a number of years, though he'd been writing for almost six, could have produced a certain resentment against women; at least, a good prosecutor could make it look that way. The investigator would be out to talk to Ian that afternoon or the following morning.

Jessie and Ian rode down in the elevator in silence, and Jessie finally spoke as they reached the street.

'Well, babe, what do you think?'

'Nothing good. Sounds like if we don't dig up some dirt on her, she's got me by the balls. And according to Schwartz, the courts frown on that kind of character assassination these days. But in this case, it's our only hope. It's her version against mine, and of course the medical testimony too, but that sounds pretty weak. They can tell that there was intercourse, but no one can tell if it was rape. The assault charge has already been dropped. Now we're just down to the nitty-gritty and my "sexual aberrations". ' Jessica nodded and said nothing.

It was a quiet drive to the boutique. She was thinking about the hearing with dread. She didn't want to see that woman, but there was no way to escape it. She had to see her, had to listen, had to hold up her end, if only for Ian's sake, no matter how ugly the whole thing got.

'Want me to leave you the car, love? I can walk home.' Ian prepared to get out after he drove her to the shop.

'No, darling, I . . . actually, come to think of it, I'm going to need it today. Does that louse you up?' She was trying to sound pleasant, but she had just had a thought. She needed the car today, and there were no maybe's about it, whether it loused him up or not.

'No sweat. I've got the Swedish sex bomb if I need it.' He was referring to his Volvo, and she grinned.

'Want to come in for a cup of coffee?' But neither of them felt talkative. The morning's interview had left them feeling pensive and distant from each other.

'No, I'll let you get to work. I want to spend a little time by myself.' It was pointless to ask him if he was upset. They both were.

'Okay, love. I'll see you later.' At the door to the boutique they parted with a quick kiss.

She rapidly took refuge in her office and made an appointment for one-thirty. It was the only thing she could think of. Ian would be crushed, but what choice did she have? And he was in no position to object.

'Well, what do you think?' She hated the man's looks and resented him already. He was fat and oily and sly.

'Not bad. Pretty slinky little number. How's it look under the hood?'

'Impeccable.' He was examining the little red Morgan as if it were a piece of meat in a supermarket or a hooker in a bordello. Jessie's skin crawled; this felt like selling their child into white slavery. To this fat nauseating man.

'You in a hurry to sell her?'

'No. Just curious about the price I might get for it.'

'Why do you want to sell her? Need the bread?' He looked Jessie over carefully.

'No. I need a larger car.' But it was all very painful. She still remembered her astonishment and delight the day Ian had driven up in the Morgan and handed her the keys, with a broad grin on his face. Victory. And now it would be like selling her heart. Or his.

'Tell you what, I'll make you an offer.'

'How much?'

'Four thousand . . . nah . . . maybe, as a favour to you, forty-five hundred.' The dealer looked her over and waited.

'That's ridiculous. My husband paid seven for it, and it's in better condition now than when he bought it.'

'Best I can do. And I think it's the best you'll get on short notice. It needs a little work.' It didn't, and they both knew it, but he was right about the short notice. A Morgan was a beautiful car, but very few people wanted to own one, or could afford to.

'I'll let you know. Thank you for your time.' Without further comment she got back in the car and drove off. Damn. What a miserable thing to even consider. But she had the rest of Schwartz's fee to pay, and now the investigator, the business and the house were already tied up by Yorktowne Bonding, and she already had a loan out on the car. She'd be lucky if the bank would even let her sell it. But they knew her well enough. They just might let her. And despite Ian's flourish about going out and getting a job, he had done nothing. He was knee deep in the book and going nowhere except to his studio with a pencil stuck behind his ear. Artistic, but hardly lucrative at this point. And even if he did get a job, how much money could he make in the month or two before the trial, waiting on tables or tending bar while he wrote at night? Maybe the book would sell. There was always that to hope for. But Jessie knew from experience that that took time, and too often they had teased themselves with that slim hope. She knew better now. It would have to be the Morgan. Sooner or later.

She kept to herself for the rest of the day, and it was a pleasant surprise when Astrid Bonner walked into the shop shortly before five. She might bring relief from the day's tensions.

'Well, Jessica, you certainly are hard to get hold of!' But she was in high spirits. She had just bought a new topaz ring, a handsome piece of work, thirty-two carats' worth encased in a small fortune in gold, and she 'hadn't been able to resist it'. On anyone else it would have been vulgar; on Astrid it had style. But it made Jessie's heart ache again over the Morgan. The topaz with the narrow diamond baguettes had probably cost Astrid twice the amount she needed so badly.

'Life has been pretty crazy ever since I got back from New York. And that's some ring, Astrid!'

'If I get tired of it, I can always use it as a doorknob. I can't quite decide if it's gorgeous or ghastly, and I know no one will ever tell me the truth.'

'It's gorgeous.'

'Truth?' She looked at Jessie teasingly.

'So much so I've been green with envy since you walked in.'

'Goody! It really was a shockingly self-indulgent thing to do. Amazing what a little ennui will do to a girl.' She laughed coquettishly and Jessie smiled. Such simple problems. Ennui.

'Want a lift home, or did you come to do some shopping?'

'No shopping, and I have the car, thanks. I came by on my way home to invite you and your husband to dinner.' The girls had told her that Jessie was married.

'What a sweet thought. We'd love it. When do you want us?'

'How about tomorrow?'

'You're on.' They exchanged a smile of pleasure and Astrid walked comfortably around Jessie's small, cheerful office.

'You know, Jessica, I'm falling in love with this place. I might have to con you out of it one of these days.' She laughed mischievously and watched Jessica's eyes.

'Don't waste your energies conning me. I might just give it to you. Right about now, I might even gift wrap it!'

'You're making me drool.'

'Spare your saliva. Can I talk you into a drink? I don't know about you, but I could use a stiff one.'

'Still those problems you mentioned the other day?'

'More or less.'

'Which means mind my own business. Fair enough.' She smiled easily; she didn't know that Jessica had spent the day trying to forget that Barry York had a lien on her business. It made Jessica sick to think about it, and all the while Ian was out of touch with the world, working on that bloody book night and day. Jesus. She needed someone to talk to. And why did he have to start tuning out right now? He always got that way when he was into a book. But now?

'I have an idea, Jessica.'

Jessie looked up, startled. For a moment she had totally forgotten Astrid.

'How about having that drink at my place?'

'You know what? I'd love that. You're sure it's not too much trouble?'

'It's no trouble; it would be fun. Come on, let's get going.'

Jessie bid a rapid good night to the girls and found herself relieved to leave the boutique. It hadn't used to be like that. She used to feel good just walking in the door in the morning, and pleased with herself and her life as she walked out at night. Now she hated to think of the place. It was shocking how things could change in so little time.

Jessie followed Astrid home in her car. The older woman was driving a two-year-old black Jaguar sedan. It was perfect for her, as sleek and elegant as she was. This woman was surrounded by beautiful things. Including her home.

It was a breathtaking mixture of delicate French and English antiques, Louis XV, Louis XVI, Hepplewhite, Sheraton. But none of it was overwhelming. There was an airy quality to the house. Lots of yellow and white, delicate organdy curtains, eggshell silks, and, upstairs, bright flowered prints and a magnificent collection of paintings. Two Chagalls, a Picasso, a Renoir, and a Monet that lent a summer night's mood to the dining room.

'Astrid, this is fabulous!'

'I must admit, I love it. Tom had such marvellous things. And they're happy things to live with. We bought a few pieces together, but most of it was already his. I picked out the Monet, though.'

'It's a beauty.' Astrid looked proud. She had every right to.

Even the glasses she poured the Scotch into were lovely—paper-thin crystal, with a rainbow hue to them as they were held up to the late afternoon light. And there was an overpowering view of the Golden Gate Bridge and the bay from the library upstairs, where they settled down with their drinks.

'God, what a magnificent house. I don't know what to say.' It was splendid. The library was wood-panelled and lined with old books. There was a portrait of a serious-looking man on one wall, and a Cezanne over the small brown marble fireplace. The portrait was of Tom. Jessie could easily see them together, despite the broad difference in age. There was a warm light in his eyes; one sensed approaching laughter. As she looked at the portrait, Jessie suddenly realized how lonely Astrid must be now.

'He was a fine-looking man.'

'Yes, and we suited each other so well. Losing him has been an awful blow. But we were lucky. Ten years is a lot, when they're ten years like the ones we had.' But Jessie could tell that Astrid still hadn't decided what to do with her life. She was floating—into dress shops and jewellers, into furriers, off on trips. She had nothing to anchor her. She had the house, the money, the paintings, the clothes . . . but no longer the man. And he was the key. Without Tom none of it really meant anything. Jessie could imagine what that might be like. It gave her chills thinking of it.

'What's your husband like, Jessica?'

Jessie smiled. 'Terrific. He's a writer. And he . . . well, he's my best friend. I think he's crazy and wonderful and brilliant and handsome. He's the only person I can really talk to. He's someone very special.'

'That says it all, doesn't it?' There was a gentle light in Astrid's eyes as she spoke, and Jessie suddenly felt guilty. How could she so blatantly rave about Ian to this woman who had lost the man who meant every bit as much to her as Ian meant to Jessie?

'No, don't look like that, Jessica. I know what you're thinking, and you're wrong. You should feel that way. You should say it with just exactly that wonderful victorious look on your face. That's how I felt about Tom. Cherish it, flaunt it, enjoy it, don't ever apologise for it, and certainly not to me.'

Jessica nodded pensively over her drink, and then looked up at Astrid.

'We're having some nasty problems right now.'

'With each other?' Astrid was surprised. It didn't show in Jessica's face. Something did, but not trouble with her husband—she had looked too happy when she described him. Maybe money problems. Young people had those. There was something, though. It surfaced at unexpected moments. A whisper of fear, almost terror. Sickness, perhaps? The loss of a breast? Astrid wondered, but didn't want to pry.

'I guess you might call this a crisis. Maybe even a

big one. But the problem isn't with each other, not in that sense.' She looked out at the bay and fell silent.

'I'm sure you'll work it out.' Astrid knew Jessie didn't want to talk about it.

'I hope so.'

Their talk turned unexpectedly to business then, to how the shop was run and what sort of clients Jessie had. Astrid made her laugh telling her some of the stories from her days at *Vogue* in New York. It was almost seven before Jessie got up to go home. And she hated to leave.

'See you tomorrow. At seven-thirty?'

'We'll be here with bells on. I can't wait to show Ian the house.' And then she had a thought. 'Astrid, do you like the ballet?'

'I adore it.'

'Want to come see the Joffrey with us next week?'

'No . . . I . . .' There was a moment of sadness in her eyes.

'Come on, don't be a drag. Ian would love to take us both. God, what that would do to his ego!' She laughed, and Astrid seemed to hesitate. Then she nodded with a small girl's grin.

'I can't resist. I hate to be the fifth wheel—I went through that after Tom died, and it's the loneliest thing in the world. It's actually much easier to be alone. But I'd love to go with you, if Ian won't mind.'

They left each other like two new school friends who have the good fortune to find that they live across the street from each other. And Jessie ran home to tell Ian about the house.

He was going to love it, and Astrid. She reminded Jessie of herself, as she would have liked to be. All the poise in the world, and so gentle, so open and sunny. She might be uncertain about the course her life would take, but she had long since come to terms with herself, and it showed. She radiated loving and peace, no longer grabbing at life like Jessie. But Jessie didn't really envy her. She still had Ian, and Astrid no longer had Tom. And, as she drove home, Jessica found herself speeding the car into the driveway, anxious to see Ian, not just his portrait.

As she approached their front door she saw a man walking away from the house toward an unfamiliar car parked in the driveway. He gave her a long examining glance and then nodded. And Jessie felt terror wash over her. Police . . . the police were back . . . what were they doing now? The terror reached her eyes as she stood there, rooted to the spot. The nightmare was back again. At least he wasn't Inspector Houghton. And where was Ian? She wanted to scream, but she couldn't. The neighbours might hear.

'I'm Harvey Green. Mrs. Clarke?' She nodded and stood there, still eyeing him with horror. 'I'm the investigator Martin Schwartz referred to your case.'

'Oh, I see. Have you spoken to my husband?' She suddenly felt the cool breeze on her face, but it would take a while for her heart to stop pounding.

'Yes, I've spoken to him.'

'Is there anything you want me to add?' Other than money . . .

'No. We have everything under control. I'll be in touch.' He made a gesture of mock salute toward his colourless hair and walked on toward his car. It was beige or pale blue, Jessie wasn't even sure in the twilight. Maybe it was white. Or light green. Like him, it was totally nondescript. He had unpleasant eyes and a forgettable face. He would blend well in a crowd. He looked ageless, and his clothes would have been out of style in any decade. He was perfect for his role.

'Darling, I'm home!' But her voice had a nervous lilt to it now, as his did when he spoke. 'Darling? . . . We've been invited to dinner tomorrow.' Not that either of them cared. Suddenly Harvey Green seemed much more of the present than Astrid.

'Invited? By whom?' Ian was pouring himself a drink in the kitchen. And not the usual white wine either. It was bourbon or Scotch, which he rarely drank, except when they had guests from back east.

'That new customer I met at the shop. Astrid Bonner. She's lovely; I think you'll like her.'

'Who?'

'You know. I told you. The widow who lives in the brick palazzo on the corner.'

'All right.' He tried to muster a smile, but it was rough going. 'Did you see Green on your way in?'

She nodded. 'I thought he was a cop. I jumped about four feet in the air.'

'So did I. Fun, isn't it, living like this?'

She tried to pass over the remark and sat down in her usual chair.

'Could you make me one too?'

'Scotch and water?'

'Why not?' It would be her third.

'Okay. That must be some place the widow's got herself.' But he didn't sound as though he really cared. He dropped ice cubes in another glass.

'You'll see it tomorrow. And Ian . . . I invited her to join us at the ballet. Do you mind?' It was a moment and two sips before he looked into her eyes and answered, and when he did, she didn't like what she saw.

'Baby, at this point, I really don't give a damn.'

They tried to make love that night after dinner, and for the first time since they'd met, Ian couldn't. He didn't give a damn about that either. It felt like the beginning of the end.

CHAPTER XI

'Are you dressed yet?' Jessica could hear Ian rattling around in the room where he worked, and she had just finished brushing her hair. She was wearing white silk slacks and a turquoise crocheted sweater, and she still wasn't sure if she looked right. Astrid was liable to be wearing something fabulous, and it sounded as though Ian had stayed submerged in the studio. 'Ian! Are you ready?' The rattling stopped and she heard footsteps.

'More or less.' He smiled at her from the bedroom

doorway, and she looked into his eyes as she walked towards him.

'Mr. Clarke, you look absolutely beautiful.'

'So do you.' He was wearing the new dark blue Cardin blazer she'd brought him from New York, a cream-coloured shirt, and a wine-coloured paisley tie with beige gabardine slacks she had found in France. They sculpted his long graceful legs.

'You look terribly proper and terribly handsome, and I think I'm terribly in love with you, darling.'

He swept her a neat bow and put his arms around her as she reached him.

'In that case, how about if we stay home instead?' He had a mischievous gleam in his eyes.

'Ian, don't you touch me! Astrid would be so disappointed if we didn't make it. And you'll love her.'

'Promises, promises.' But he offered her his arm as she picked up the white silk jacket she'd left on the chair in the hall. He was going to the dinner to humour her. He had other things on his mind.

They walked the half block to the brick house on the corner, and it was the first night there had been a chill in the air. Autumn was coming, in its own gentle fashion. San Francisco in the fall was nothing like that season in New York. It was part of the reason they'd both fallen in love with San Francisco in the first place. They loved the easy, temperate weather.

Jessica rang the bell, and they waited. For a moment there was no answer.

'Maybe she's decided she doesn't want us.'

'Oh, shut up. You just want to go home and work on your book.' But she smiled at him and then they heard footsteps.

The door opened a second later and there was Astrid, resplendent in a floor-length black knit dress and a long rope of pearls. Her hair was loosely swept up in the back and her eyes sparkled as she led them inside. She looked even more beautiful than Jessica had found her before. And Ian was obviously stunned. He had been expecting a middle-aged widow, and had agreed to the evening mostly as a concession to Jessie. He had had no hint of this vision in black with the Dresden-doll waist and long, elegantly arched neck—and that face. He liked the face. And the look in her eyes. This was no dowager. This was a woman.

The two women embraced, and Ian stood back for a moment, watching them, intrigued by the older woman he did not yet know, and by the formidable home he was beginning to glimpse over her shoulder. It was impossible not to stare, whether he looked at her or at the house.

'And this is Ian.' He obeyed the summons, feeling like a small boy being introduced by his mother—'Say good evening to the nice lady, darling'—and held out his hand.

'How do you do.' He was suddenly glad he had worn the new Cardin jacket and tie. This was not going to be just any old dinner. And she was probably a roaring snob. She had to be, in a setup like that. And widowed, yet. Nouveau riche as all hell . . . but somehow a murmuring suspicion told him that that wasn't the case either. She didn't have the dead-fish eyes of a snob, or the over-worked eyebrows. She had nice eyes, in a nice face. She looked like a person.

Astrid laughed gaily as she led them upstairs to the library, and Ian and Jessica exchanged glances as they passed delicate sketches and etching on the stairs . . . Picasso . . . Renoir . . . Renoir again . . . Manet . . . Klimt . . . Goya . . . Cassatt . . . He wanted to whistle, and Jessie grinned at him like a conspirator who had assisted in getting him into the neighbourhood haunted house. He raised both eyebrows and she stuck out her tongue. Astrid was ahead of them and already down the hall. He wanted to whisper, and Jessie wanted to giggle, but they couldn't. Not till they got home. But she was thoroughly enjoying the look on his face; it made her feel suddenly mischievous. She pinched him delicately on the behind as she passed in front of him to enter the library.

Astrid had a plate of hors d'oeuvres waiting for them and a handsome pâté. A fire roared in the grate. Ian accepted a slice of pâté on a slim piece of toast and then laughed into Astrid's eyes.

'Mrs. Bonner, I don't know how to say this, and I feel about fourteen years old, but I am overwhelmed by your home.' And my hostess. He smiled the ingenuous smile that Jessie loved, and Astrid laughed with him.

'I'm delighted, that's a lovely compliment, but calling me "Mrs. Bonner" isn't. You may feel fourteen, but you make me feel about four hundred. Try "Astrid" '—she threw up both hands impishly—'or I may have to kick you out. And not "Aunt Astrid" either, God forbid.' All three of them laughed, and she slid out of her shoes and tucked her legs under her in a large comfortable chair. 'But I really am glad you like the house. It's embarrassing sometimes, now that Tom isn't here anymore. I love it so much, but I occasionally feel that I never quite grew into it all. I mean, it's so . . . so . . . well, as though it should be my mother's and I'm just house-sitting. I mean, really, me? In all this? How ridiculous!' Except that it wasn't ridiculous at all. It suited her perfectly. Ian wondered if she knew how perfectly, or if she meant what she had just said. He imagined Tom had built the place around her, right down to the paintings and the view.

'It suits you very well, you know.' Ian was watching her eyes, and Jessie was watching the exchange.

'Yes, it does, in some ways, and not in others. It frightens people away sometimes. The lifestyle does. The opulence. The . . . I guess you could call it an aura. A lot of it is Tom, and some of it is just . . . oh . . . things.' She waved vaguely around the room, encompassing rapidly a fortune in art objects. Things. 'And some of it is me.' Ian liked the fact that she conceded the point. 'People expect you to be a lot when you live like this. Sometimes they expect me to be something I'm not, or they don't stick around long enough to see what I am. I told you, Jessie, I'd trade you for your jewel of a house any day. But . . .' She grinned like a cat stretching lazily in the sun. '. . . This isn't a bad place to live, either.'

'Looks like a damn nice place to live, if you ask me, Mrs. . . . Astrid.' They exchanged a quick burst of laughter over the slip. 'But I doubt if you'd trade us for our "jewel", once you plugged in the hair drver and the washing machine blew, or when the plumbing fell through to the basement. Our place has a few kinks.'

'That does sound like fun.' It was clear that nothing like that happened here, and Jessie was grinning broadly, remembering the last time all the fuses had blown, and Ian had refused to deal with it; they had spent the rest of the evening by candlelight—until he wanted to work, and needed the electric typewriter. He looked up sheepishly, knowing what she was thinking.

'Well, children? Do you want a tour of the place?' Astrid interrupted their thoughts. Jessie hadn't seen the whole thing, and Ian nodded quickly.

She tiptoed barefoot along the carpeted hall, flipping switches under brass sconces, opening doors, turning on more lights. There were three bedrooms upstairs. Hers in bright, flowery yellow prints with a large four-poster bed and the same splendid view of the bay. She had a small mirrored boudoir and a white marble bath, which was repeated in pale green across the hall, to go with a quietly elegant bedroom full of small French Provincial antiques.

'My mother sleeps here when she comes to the city, and this suits her perfectly. You'll know what I mean when you see her. She's very lively and little and funny, and she likes lots of flowers everywhere.'

'Does she live in the East?' Ian was curious, and remembered only that Jessie had told him Astrid had originally come from New York.

'No, Mother lives on a ranch out here, of all things. She bought it a few years ago, and she's having a great time with it. Much to our astonishment, it actually agrees with her. We thought she'd be bored in six months, but she's not. She's very independent, and she rides a lot and loves to play cowboy. At seventy-two, if you please. She reminds one a bit of Colette.'

It made Jessie smile to think of a tiny white-haired woman in cowboy gear ensconced in the delicately appointed room. But if she was anything like Astrid, she could pull it off. With cowboy boots custom-made by Gucci and a hat by Adolfo.

The bedroom next to Astrid's was more sombre, and

had apparently belonged to her husband. Jessie and Ian exchanged a rapid, casual glance . . . they had had separate bedrooms? But Jessie remembered the difference in age. There was a small, elegant study next to his room, rich in red leathers, with a handsome old desk covered with pictures of Astrid.

Astrid passed quickly through the room and went back out to the hall, closing the door of the green guest room as Jessie and Ian followed.

'It's a magnificent house.' Jessie sighed. It was the sort of place that made you want to appear for the next dinner invitation with everything you owned in your arms. You wanted to stay there forever. Now they both understood why she didn't close the house and find something smaller. It told a tale of people who cared—about beauty, about each other, and about living well.

'And you saw the downstairs. It's not very exciting, but it's pretty.' Jessie wondered why there was no trace of servants. One expected at least a white-aproned maid, or a butler, but she seemed to live alone.

'Do you both like crab? I really should have called to ask, but I forgot.' She looked faintly embarrassed.

'We love crab!' Jessie answered for them both.

'Oh, good! Seems that every time I order it for friends, and forget to ask beforehand, it turns out that someone is allergic to it or something. I love it.'

It was an unusual feast. Astrid piled a mountain of dismembered cracked crabs on a vast plate in the centre of the dining-room table, set out a huge carafe of white wine, added a salad and hot rolls, and invited her guests to dig in. She rolled up the sleeves of her black knit dress, invited Ian to take off his jacket, and sat there like a child, vying for the claws with whoever saw them first.

'Ian, you're a fiend. I saw that one first, and you know it!' She rapped him gently on the knuckles with the claw as she removed it, giggling and sipping her wine. She was right—she did look like a young girl whose mother was out for the evening and had let her have her friends over for dinner 'as long as you're all good.' She was delightful, and both Jessie and Ian fell in love with her.

It was an easy-going evening; they looked like three people with no problems at all—just expensive taste, and a liking for pleasure. It was after midnight when Ian stood up and held out a hand to Jessie.

'Astrid, I could stay here till four in the morning, but I have to get up tomorrow and work on the book, and if Jessie doesn't get enough sleep, she turns into a monster.' But it was obvious that they all shared regret that the evening was over. 'You'll come to the ballet with us next week?'

'With pleasure. And I'll have you know that Jessie said I would love you, and she was obviously one-hundred-percent right. I can't think of two peoplie I'd rather be a fifth wheel with.'

'Good. Because you're not. Fifth wheel, my ass.' They all laughed, and Astrid hugged them both as they left, as though she had known them for years. They felt as though she had, as Astrid stood barefoot in the doorway, waving before closing the shiny black door with its brass lion-head knocker.

'Christ, Jess, what a nice evening. And what a marvellous woman. She's amazing.'

'Isn't she? But she must be lonely as hell. There's something about the way she invites people into her life, as though she has a lot of leftover loving and no one to give it to most of the time.' Jessie yawned on the last words and Ian nodded. Talking over the evening was always the best part. She could no longer remember when Ian hadn't been around to share secrets, and opinions, and questions. He had been with her forever.

'What do you suppose her husband was like, Jess? I suspect he wasn't as much fun as she is.'

'What makes you say that?' His comment surprised her; there was nothing to suggest that Tom Bonner had been less amusing than his wife. And then Jessica laughed as she guessed what Ian meant. 'The separate bedrooms?' He grinned sheepishly and she pinched him. 'You're a creep.'

'I am not. And let me tell you, madam, I don't care if I live to be ninety, you'll never get me out of our bedroom . . . or our bed!' He looked adamant and very pleased with himself as he held her closer on the short walk home.

'Is that a promise, Mr. Clarke?'

'In writing, if you'd like, Mrs. Clarke.'

'I may just hold you to that.' They paused for a moment and kissed before walking the last few steps toward their home. 'I'm glad you liked Astrid, love. I really enjoy her. I'd like to get to know her better. She's a good person to talk to. You know, I . . . well, I almost wanted to tell her what's happening to us. We started to talk the other day, and . . .' Jessie shrugged; it was hard to put into words, and Ian was beginning to scowl. 'She just kind of makes me want to tell her the truth.' Ian stopped walking and looked at her.

'Did you?'

'No.'

'Good. Because I think you're kidding yourself, Jess. She's a nice woman, but no one is going to understand what's happening to us right now. No one. How do you tell someone you have a trial pending on charges of rape? Do us both a big favour, babe, and don't talk about it. We've got to hope this whole mess will blow over and we can forget it. If we tell people, it could haunt us for years.'

'That's what I decided. And, hey, come on . . . trust me a little, will you please? I'm not stupid. I know it would be hard for most people to handle.'

'So don't ask them to.'

Jessica didn't answer, and Ian walked ahead of her to open the door to the house. For the first time Jessie could remember, their chosen separateness from the rest of the world, almost like a secret society, now felt like lonely isolation. She couldn't talk to anyone but Ian. He had forbidden it. In the past it had always been a matter of choice.

Jessie followed him inside and left her jacket in the front hall.

'Want a cup of tea before bed, love?' She put a kettle of water on and heard him go into his studio.

'No, thanks.'

She stood in the doorway of his studio for a moment and smiled at him as he sat at his desk. He had a snifter of cognac beside him and a small stack of papers on the desk in front of him. He loosened his tie and sat back and looked at his wife.

'Hello, beautiful lady.'

'Hi.' They exchanged the subtlest of smiles for a moment and Jessie cocked her head to one side. 'You planning to work?'

'Just for a little while.'

She nodded and went to take the kettle off the stove; it was whistling fiercely. She made a cup of tea, turned off the rest of the lights, and walked quietly into the bedroom. She knew that Ian wouldn't come to bed for hours. He couldn't. He couldn't try to make love to her tonight. Not after last night. The sour taste of failure had stayed with them. Like the rest of what was happening to them, it was new, and painful, and raw.

Their evening at the ballet with Astrid was as great a success as the dinner at her home. They picked her up just in time to make the curtain, and Jessie had prepared a late supper that was waiting for them at home. Steak tartare, cold asparagus, a variety of cheeses and French bread, and a home-made fudge cake. Off to the side, was a large bowl of fresh strawberries and whipped cream, a huge crystal bowl filled with Viennese style *Schlag*, for the berries or the cake. It was a feast, and her audience approved.

'Dear girl, is there anything you can't do?'

'Plenty.' But Jessie was pleased at the compliment.

'Don't believe her. She can do anything.' Ian seconded the compliment with a kiss as he poured a round of Bordeaux. Chateau Margaux '55. It felt like an occasion, and he had brought out one of his favourite wines.

By now the three were a trio, telling jokes, sharing

stories, and feeling at ease. They were well into their second bottle of wine when Astrid stood up and glanced at the clock.

'Good God, children, it's two o'clock. Not that I have anything to do tomorrow, but you do. I feel very guilty keeping you up.' Ian and Jessica exchanged a sharp glance: they did have to be up early the next morning. But Astrid did not see the look. She was hunting for her bag.

'Don't be silly. Evenings like this are a gift for us.' Jessie smiled at her friend.

'They couldn't be as much so as they are for me. You have no idea how I've loved this. And what are you up to tomorrow, Jessica? Can I tempt you with lunch at the Villa Taverna?'

'I . . . I'm sorry, Astrid, but I can't make lunch tomorrow.' Another look flashed its way to Ian. 'We have to go to a business meeting in the morning and I don't know what time we'll be through.'

'Then why don't all three of us go to lunch?' She had found her handbag and was ready to leave. 'You can call me when you're through with your meeting.'

'Astrid, we'd better make it another day, much as I hate to.' Ian was regretful but firm.

'I think you're both mean.' But now she sensed something between them, a tension that hadn't been there before. Something was just a wee bit off balance, but she couldn't tell what, and she found herself remembering the problem Jessica had hinted at when they had first met. There had never been any mention of it again, and Astrid had gone on assuming that Jessie meant a money problem. It was hard to believe, but it obviously couldn't be anything else. Not health, not problems with the marriage certainly—there was too much hugging, touching, kissing, quick pats on the back, rapid squeezes as they stood side by side—there was much too much of that for anyone to believe the marriage was in trouble.

'Maybe we can all go to a movie this weekend.' Ian looked at the two women and tried to make light of the too-quiet moment. 'Not as classy as the ballet, but there's a new French thriller on Union. Anyone interested?'

'Oh, let's!' Jessie clapped her hands and looked at Astrid, who grinned and put on a cautious look.

'Only if you absolutely swear to buy me a gallon of popcorn.'

'I swear.' Ian solemnly held up a hand in a formal oath.

'Cross your heart?'

'Cross my heart.' He did, and the three of them started to laugh. 'You sure drive a hard bargain.'

'I have to. I'm addicted to popcorn. With butter!' She looked at him sternly and he gave her a brotherly hug. Astrid returned the hug and leaned over to give Jessie a kiss on the cheek. 'And now I shall bid you both good night. And let you get some sleep. I'm really sorry it got so late.'

'Don't be. We aren't.'

Jessica followed her to the door, and Astrid left with a curious feeling. Almost an eerie sensation. There was nothing she could see or touch or be absolutely sure of, but something seemed to hang in the air, just over their heads—like a hunk of concrete.

The preliminary hearing was scheduled for the next morning.

CHAPTER XII

Jessica walked into the miniature courtroom with Ian's hand held tightly in hers. She wore the navy blue suit and dark glasses again, and Ian looked tired and pale. He hadn't gotten much sleep, and he had a headache from his share of the wine the night before. The three of them had knocked off both bottles of Margaux.

Martin Schwartz was waiting for them in the courtroom. He was going through a file on a small desk at the side of the room, and he motioned to them to join him outside.

'I'm going to ask for a closed hearing. I thought you

should know, so you wouldn't be surprised.' He looked terribly professional, and they both felt confused. Ian spoke up first, with a worried frown.

'What's a closed hearing?'

'I think the victim may speak more openly if there are no observers in court. Just you, her, the assistant D.A., the judge, and myself. It's a sensible precaution. If she brings friends, she'll want them to think she's as pure as the proverbial driven snow. And she may react badly to having Jessica there.' For no reason she could understand, Jessica flinched involuntarily at the sound of her own name.

'Look, if I can take it, so can she.' Jessie was unbearably nervous, and she dreaded seeing the woman. She wanted to be anywhere but there. Every fibre of her being shrieked at the prospect of what lay ahead. The enemy. So much to face in one human being. Ian's infidelity, her own inadequacy, the threat to their future, the memory of the almost unscalable mountain of trying to bail him. All of it wrapped up in that one woman.

Martin could see how tense they both were. He pitied them, and he accurately suspected what was at the root of Jessie's nerves: Margaret Burton.

'Just trust me, Jessie. I think a closed hearing will be best for all concerned. We should be getting under way in a few minutes. Why don't you two go for a walk down the hall? Just stay close enough, and I'll come out and signal when the judge is ready to start.' Ian nodded tersely and Martin strode back inside. Ian's arm felt as if it had a lead weight hanging from it. Jessie.

They had nothing to say as they paced the length of the hall, turned at the far end, and came back again. Jessica found her mind drifting to memories of other marble halls . . . City Hall, where she and Ian had gotten their marriage licence . . . waiting outside the principal's office in high school . . . the funeral parlour in Boston when Jake had died . . . and then, one by one, her parents.

'Jessie?'

'Huh?' She was frowning oddly as she looked at him, as though she had difficulty coming back to the present.

'Are you okay?' He looked worried; she had been squeezing his arm too tightly and walking faster and faster as they paced the hall. He had had to shake her arm to catch her attention.

'Yeah. I'm okay. Just thinking.'

'Well, stop thinking. Everything's going to be fine. Relax.' She started to say something, and he could tell from the look in her eyes that it wasn't going to be pleasant. She was much too nervous to be cautious or kind.

'I'm . . . I'm sorry . . . this is just such a weird day. Doesn't it seem weird to you? Or is it just me?' She began to wonder if she were going crazy.

'No, it doesn't seem weird. Shitty, yes, but not weird.' He tried to smile, but she wasn't looking at him. She was looking off into the distance, dreamy-eyed again. She was beginning to frighten him. 'Look, dammit, if you don't pull yourself together right now, I'm going to send you home.'

'Why? So I don't see her?'

'Is that what you're worried about, for Chrissake? Seeing her? Is that all? Jesus. My ass is on the line, and you're worried about seeing her. Who gives a shit about her? What if they revoke my bail?'

'They won't.'

'How the hell do you know?'

'I . . . I . . . oh, Ian, I don't know. They just can't, that's all. Why would they?' She hadn't even thought of that. Now it was one more thing to worry about.

'Why *wouldn't* they?'

'Well, maybe if I'd seduced Inspector Houghton, or Barry York, our beloved bailbondsman, maybe they wouldn't. But since I didn't, maybe they will.' Her tone was bitter and scared.

'Go home, Jessica.'

'Go to hell.'

And then Ian stopped talking and looked past her. Time seemed to stop as Jessica too turned to look. It was Margaret Burton.

She was wearing the same hat. But with a polite little beige suit. She was even wearing white gloves. The clothes were cheap, but they were tidy-looking, and very proper. She looked very dull. Like the stereotype of a school-teacher or a librarian, somebody terribly serious and asexual. Her hair was pulled back in a tight knot at her neck, scarcely visible under the hat. The black roots were nowhere to be seen. She was wearing no makeup and her shoes were low-heeled and dowdy. It was obvious that a woman like this could only be made love to at gunpoint.

Ian said nothing, but looked for a long moment, then turned away. Jessica was staring, with a look of hatred on her face that Ian had never seen. She was rooted to the spot.

'Jess . . . come on, baby. Please.' He took her elbow and tried to propel her back down the hall, but she wouldn't move. Margaret Burton disappeared into the courtroom without ever having shown a sign of having seen them. And Jessica still wouldn't move. Inspector Houghton followed quickly on Miss Burton's heels, and Martin Schwartz came out and beckoned to Ian, while Jessie simply stood and stared.

'Look, Jessie, just sit down on that bench for a few minutes. I'll be back as soon as I can.' She was in terrible shape, and he had enough to worry about.

'Ian?' She turned and looked at him with a stricken expression in her eyes, and he felt his guts turn to sand. 'I just don't understand anything anymore.' There weren't even tears in her eyes. Only pain.

'Neither do I. But I've got to go inside now. Will you be okay out here, or do you want to go home?' He wasn't sure he trusted her alone. The look in her eyes was getting to be all too familiar.

'I'll be here.'

That wasn't what he had asked her, but he didn't have time to argue. He disappeared inside the courtroom, and Jessie sat alone on the cold marble bench. She watched people come and go. Ordinary-looking people. Men with attaché cases. Women with tissues clutched in their hands. Small bedraggled children in shoes that were worn through at the heel and pants that were too short for their skinny legs. Bailiffs, lawyers, judges, victims, defendants, witnesses . . . people. They came and went while Jessie sat and thought of Margaret Burton. Who was she? Why had she done it? Why Ian? She had looked so goddamned proud, so self-righteous as she had walked into the courtroom. The courtroom . . .

Suddenly her eyes were rivetted to the door. It was of dark, highly polished wood with brass knobs and two tiny glass windows, like eyes, looking out . . . looking out . . . looking in . . . inside . . . she had to be there . . . inside . . . to see her . . . to listen . . . to find out why . . . she had to.

A small sign hung crookedly from one of the doorknobs—CLOSED—and a grey-uniformed bailiff stood slightly off to one side, looking uninterestedly at passersby. Jessica stood to her full height, smoothed her skirt, and suddenly felt very calm. She fixed a small smile in place. There was the tiniest of tremors in the corner of her right eye, the convulsions of a butterfly, but who would notice? She looked very much in command, and smiled curtly at the bailiff as she strode to the door and put a hand on the knob.

'Sorry, ma'am. Courtroom's closed.'

'Yes. I know.' She looked almost pleased at his news, as though she were responsible and was comforted to learn that her orders had been carried out. 'I'm sitting in on the case.'

'An attorney?' He started to step aside. The tremor in her eye now felt as though it would tear off the lid.

She nodded quietly. 'Yes.' Oh, Jesus. No. What if he asked for credentials? Or went inside to talk to the judge? Instead he held open the door for her with a smile, and Jessie walked sedately into the room. The whole scene had been typically Jessica. No one ever questioned her. But what now? What if the judge stopped the proceedings? What if he threw her out? What if . . .

The judge was small and undistinguished, with glasses and blond-grey hair. He looked up momentarily, unimpressed by the new arrival, and directed a raised eyebrow at Martin Schwartz. After a sharp glance at Jessica,

Schwartz nodded reluctantly, then threw a rapid look at the assistant district attorney, who shrugged. She was in.

Inspector Houghton was seated near the bench, making some sort of statement. The room was wood-panelled, with leather-covered seats in the front row, and straight-backed chairs behind them. It was hardly larger than Martin Schwartz's office, but there was an aura of tremendous tension in the air. Ian and Martin sat together at a desk, slightly to the left. And only a few feet away sat Miss Burton and the assistant district attorney, who, much to Jessie's chagrin, was a woman. Young, tough-looking, with oversprayed hair and an abundance of powder on too fleshy cheeks. She wore a matronly green dress and a sedate string of pearls, and at the corners of her mouth the hard edges of anger had formed. She exuded righteous indignation for her client.

The young attorney turned to look at Jessica, and Jessie figured her to be about her own age, somewhere in her early thirties. The two women exchanged a look of ice. But Jessica saw contempt in the other woman's face as well, and then she understood what this was going to be. A class war. Big, nasty, college grad, preppie Pacific Heights Ian had raped poor little lower-class, abused, misunderstood secretary, who was going to be defended by clean, tough, pure, devoted middle-class young attorney. Jesus. That was all they needed. Jessica suddenly wondered if she had worn the wrong thing. But even in slacks and a shirt, Jessica had the kind of style those women would hate. How insane even to have to consider what she was wearing.

Miss Burton hadn't seen Jessica come in, or had shown no sign of it, at any rate. Nor had Ian. She slipped quietly into a straight-backed chair behind him, and then suddenly, as though he had been slapped, he raised his head and spun around in his seat, a look of shock on his face when he saw her there behind him. He started to shake his head, and then leaned toward her as though to say something, but Jessica's eyes were steely. She squeezed his shoulder briefly, and he averted his gaze: it was pointless to argue. But as he turned away, his broad shoulders seemed to sag.

Inspector Houghton rose from the seat from which he'd been addressing the judge, thanked the court, and returned to a chair on the other side of Margaret Burton. Now what? Jessica's heart pounded. Suddenly she wasn't so sure she wanted to be there. What would she hear? Could she take it? What if she fell apart? Went crazy . . . screamed . . .

'Miss Burton, take the stand, please.'

As Margaret Burton slowly left her seat Jessica's heart seemed hell-bent on freeing itself from her body. A pulse thundered at her temple and she wondered if she'd faint as she stared down at her trembling hands. The oath was administered to Miss Burton, and Jessica looked up, her whole body trembling now. *Why her*? She was so plain, so ugly, so . . . cheap. But no, she wasn't really ugly. There was something about her, a grace to the hands folded over her knees, the vestige of prettiness in a face now grown too hard to be arresting. Something . . . maybe. Jessie wondered how Ian felt, sitting just in front of her. He seemed a thousand miles away. Margaret Burton seemed much, much closer. Jessica felt as though she could see every pore, every hair, the slightly flared nostrils, the weave of the dreary beige suit. She had a wild urge to run up and touch her, slap her maybe, shake her into telling the truth. Tell them what happened, damn you! The truth! Jessica's breath caught and she coughed, trying to clear her head.

'Miss Burton, would you please explain what happened on the day in question, from the moment you first saw Mr. Clarke. Tell us simply, in your own words. This is not a trial. This is merely a preliminary hearing, to determine if this matter deserves further attention from the court.'

The judge spoke as though he were reading an orange-juice label—words he had spoken a thousand times before and no longer heard. But it was all the invitation Margaret Burton needed. She cleared her throat with a small look of importance and the tiniest of smiles. Inspector

Houghton frowned as he watched her, and the prosecuting attorney seemed to be keeping an eye on the judge.

'Miss Burton?' The judge looked off into space as he spoke, and everyone waited.

'Yes, sir. Your honour.' Jessica felt that the 'victim' didn't look sufficiently distraught. Victorious, maybe, but not distraught. Not violated. Pleased? That was crazy. Why should she be pleased? But Jessie could not put aside that impression as she stared at the woman who claimed her husband had raped her. And then the recital began.

'I had lunch at Enrico's, and afterward I started walking up Broadway.' She had a flat, unpleasant voice. A little too high. A little too loud. She would have nagged well. And she sounded too loud to be hurt. Hurt inside. Jessica wondered if the judge was listening to more than just the words. He didn't look it.

'I was walking up Broadway,' she went on, 'and he offered me a ride.'

'Did he threaten you, or just offer a ride?'

She shook her head, almost regretfully. 'No, he didn't threaten. Not really.'

'What do you mean, "not really"?'

'Well, I think he might have gotten mad if I'd turned down the ride, but it was kind of a hot day, and I couldn't see a bus for blocks, and I was late getting back to the office, and . . .' She looked up at the judge and his face was blank. 'Anyway, I told him where I worked.' She stopped for a moment, looked down at her hands, and sighed. Jessie wanted to wring her neck. That pathetic little sigh. She dug her hand into Ian's shoulder without thinking, and he jumped, and turned to look at her with a worried face. She forced a tiny smile and he patted her hand before looking back at Margaret Burton.

'Go on.' The judge was prodding her. She seemed to have lost the thread of her tale.

'I'm sorry, your honour. He . . . he didn't take me back to my office, and . . . well, I know I was crazy to accept the ride. It was just such a pretty day, and he looked like a nice man. I thought . . . I never realised . . .' Unexpectedly, a small tear glided from one eye and then the other; Jessie's grip on Ian's shoulder became almost unbearable. He reached for her hand and gently held it until she nervously pulled it away.

'Please go on, Miss . . . Miss Burton.' He checked the name on the papers on his desk, took a swallow of water, and looked up. Jessie was reminded that this hearing was no more than daily routine to him; he seemed totally separate from the drama that absorbed the rest of them.

'I . . . he took me . . . to a hotel.'

'You went with him?' But there was no judgment in the voice; it was only a question.

'I thought he was taking me back to my office.' She sounded strident and angry suddenly. The tears were gone.

'And when you saw that he hadn't taken you back to your office, why didn't you leave then?'

'I . . . I don't know. I just thought it would . . . he only wanted to have a drink, he said, and he wasn't unpleasant, just silly. I thought he was harmless and it would be easier to go along with it—with the drink, I mean—and then . . .'

'Was there a bar in the hotel when you went inside?' She shook her head. 'A desk clerk? Did anyone see you go in? Could you have called for help? I don't believe Mr. Clarke held a gun on you, or anything of the sort, did he?'

She flushed and shook her head reluctantly.

'Well, did anyone see you?'

'No.' The word was barely audible. 'There was no one there. It looked like . . . like sort of an apartment hotel.'

'Do you remember where it was?'

She shook her head again, and Jessica felt Ian stir restlessly in front of her, and when she looked there was anger on his face. At last. He looked alive again, instead of buried under grief and disbelief.

'Could you tell us the location of the hotel, Miss Burton?'

Again, the negative shake of the head. 'No. I . . . I

was so upset I . . . I just didn't look. But he . . . he . . .' Suddenly her face was transformed again. The eyes lit up and almost glowed with such hatred and fury that for an instant Jessie almost believed her, and she saw Ian go suddenly very still. 'He took my life and threw it away! He ruined it! He . . .' She sobbed for a moment, and then took a deep breath as the glitter left her eyes. 'As we went inside, he just grabbed me, and dragged me into an elevator and up to a room, and . . .' Her silence said it all, as she hung her head in defeat.

'Do you remember what room?'

'No.' She didn't look up.

'Would you recognise the room again?'

'No. I don't think so.' No? Why not? Jessie couldn't imagine not remembering a room you'd been raped in. It would be engraved on your mind forever.

'Would you recognise the hotel?'

'I'm not sure. I don't think so, though.' She still had not looked up, and Jessie doubted her story still further—and then realised what had been happening: if she was doubting the story, then at some point she must have believed it might be true. In that one burst of tears and fury, the woman had convinced them all. Or come damn close to it. Even Jessica. Almost. She turned to look at Ian and saw him watching her, his eyes bright with tears. He knew what was happening too. Jessica reached for his hand again, this time quietly and with strength. She wanted to kiss him, hold him, tell him it would be all right, but now she wasn't so sure. She was sure of only one thing—of how much she hated Margaret Burton.

Martin Schwartz was looking none too happy either. If the Burton woman claimed not to remember where the hotel was, they had lost the last shred of hope of finding a witness who had seen them there. Ian couldn't place the hotel either. He had been just drunk enough that his memory was blurred, and the address he thought he remembered had turned out to be wrong. It was a warehouse. There were plenty of small sleazy residential hotels in the area, and Martin had sent Ian into dozens of lobbies before the preliminary hearing: Nothing looked familiar. So it was going to remain a case of his word against hers, with no one to corroborate either side. Schwartz was liking the looks of the case less and less. She was a damn unpleasant witness. Erratic, emotional, one moment hard as a rock, the next heart-wringing and tearful. The judge would ship them off to trial for sure, if for no other reason than to avoid dealing with the issue himself.

'All right, Miss Burton,' the judge said, fingering a pencil and gazing at the opposite wall, 'what happened in that room you don't remember?' His tone was dry and uninterested.

'What happened?'

'What did Mr. Clarke do after he dragged you into that room? You did say he dragged you?'

She nodded.

'And he wasn't using a weapon?' She shook her head, and finally looked up at her audience.

'No. Only . . . only his hand. He slapped me several times and told me he'd kill me if I didn't do what he wanted.'

'And what was that?'

'I . . . he . . . he forced me to . . . to have . . . oral copulation with him . . . to do . . . to, well . . . to do it to him.' My, how painful you make it sound . . . Jessica wanted to slap her again.

'And you did?'

'I did.'

'And then? Did he . . . did Mr. Clarke have an orgasm?'

She nodded.

'Please answer the question.'

'Yes.'

'And then?'

'Then he sodomised me.' She said it in a dull, flat voice, and Jessie could feel Ian flinch. She herself felt increasingly uncomfortable. She had anticipated drama, not this slow, drawn-out recital. Christ, how humiliating it all was. How dry and ugly and awful. The words, the acts, the thoughts, all so old and dreary.

'Did he climax again?'

'I . . . I don't know.' She had the grace to blush.

'Did you?' Her eyes flew open then and Houghton and the young district attorney watched tensely.

'I? But how could I? He . . . I . . . he raped me.'

'Some women enjoy that, Miss Burton, in spite of themselves. Did you?'

'Of course not!'

'You did not climax, then?' Jessica was beginning to enjoy the other woman's discomfiture.

'No, of course not! No!' She almost shouted it, looking hot and angry and nervous.

'All right. And then what?' The judge looked terribly bored and unimpressed by Miss Burton's indignation.

'Then he raped me again.'

'How?'

'He . . . he just raped me. You know . . . the usual way this time.' Jessica almost wanted to laugh. A 'usual rape'!

'Did he hurt you?'

'Yes, of course he did.'

'Very much?'

But she was looking down again, distant and pensive and sad. It was at those moments that one should feel sorry for her. And for a tiny flash of a second, Jessica wondered about her own reactions. At any other time, the story she was hearing would have touched her. Maybe even very much. But now . . . how could she let it touch her? She didn't believe the woman. But what did the judge think? There had been no answer to his last question.

'Miss Burton, I asked if Mr. Clarke hurt you very much.'

'Yes. Very much. I . . . he . . . he didn't care about me. He just . . . he just . . .' The tears flowed slowly down her face and it was as though she were talking about someone else, not Ian, not a total stranger who had raped her. Why would he care about her if he were raping her? 'He didn't care if I got pregnant, or . . . or anything. He just . . . just left.' And now the tears turned to anger again. 'I know this type, they play with poor girls like me! Girls with no money, no fancy family, and then they . . . they do what he did . . . they leave . . .' Her voice sank back to a whisper then as she looked blindly into her lap. 'He left, and went back to her.'

'Who?' The judge looked confused, and Miss Burton looked up again, with a slightly dazed look on her face. 'Who did he go back to?'

'His wife.' She said it very plainly, but without looking at Jessica.

'Miss Burton, did you know Mr. Clarke from somewhere, from before this? Had you ever been romantically involved with him before?' So the judge had also picked up on that—a faint suggestion that Ian was not a stranger after all.

'No. Never.'

'Then how did you know about his wife?'

'He looked married. And anyway, he told me.'

'I see. And he just left you at the hotel afterward?' She nodded again. 'What did you do then? Call the police? Go to a doctor? Call a cab?'

'No. I walked for a while. I felt confused. And then I went home and washed up. I felt awful.' Now she was believable again.

'Did you see a doctor?'

'After I called the police.'

'And when did you do that? It wasn't immediately, was it?'

'No.'

'Why not?'

'I was scared. I had to think about it.'

'And you're sure of your story, now, Miss Burton? This is the whole truth? The story you originally told the police was a little different from this, wasn't it?'

'I don't know what I told them then. I was confused. But this is the truth now.'

'You're under oath now, Miss Burton, so I hope this is the truth.'

'It is.' She nodded expressionlessly, her eyes dead.

'There's nothing you want to change?'

'No.'

'And you're certain that this was not a misunderstanding, an afternoon fling that went sour?' And then suddenly the hatred blazed up in her eyes again, and she squeezed them tightly shut.

'He ruined my life.' She hissed the words into the silent room.

'All right, Miss Burton. Thank you. Mr. Schwartz, any questions?'

'Only a few, Your Honour. And I'll be quick. Miss Burton, has anything similar ever happened to you before?'

'What do you mean?'

'I mean, have you ever been raped, even in fun, as a sort of game, by a lover, a boyfriend, a husband?'

'Of course not.' She looked incensed.

'Have you ever been married?'

'No.'

'Engaged?'

'No.' Again there was no hesitation.

'No broken engagements?'

'No.'

'Any serious, broken-off loves?'

'None.'

'A boyfriend now?'

'No.'

'Thank you, Miss Burton. What about romantic interludes? Have you ever picked up a stranger before?'

'No.'

'Then you agree that you picked up Mr. Clarke?'

'No! I . . . he offered me a ride, and . . .'

'And you accepted, even though you didn't know him. Does that seem wise to you, in a city like San Francisco?' His tone was politely concerned, and Margaret Burton looked angry and confused.

'No, I . . . it . . . no, I've never picked anyone up before. And I just thought that . . . he looked like he was okay.'

'What do you mean by okay, Miss Burton? He was drunk, wasn't he?'

'A little tiddly maybe, but not bombed. And he looked, well . . . like a nice guy.'

'You mean rich? Or fancy? Or what? Like a Harvard grad?'

'I don't know. He just looked clean-cut.'

'And handsome? Do you think he's handsome?'

'I don't know.' She was looking at her lap.

'Did you think he'd get involved with you, maybe? Fall in love? That's a fair assumption. You're a nice-looking woman, why not? A hot summer day, a good-looking guy, a lonely woman . . . how old are you, Miss Burton?'

'Thirty-one.' But she'd fumbled.

'You told the police thirty. Isn't it more like thirty-eight? Isn't it just possible that—'

'Objection!' The district attorney was on her feet, her face furious, and the judge nodded.

'Sustained. Mr. Schwartz, this is not a trial, and you might as well save the pressure tactics for later. Miss Burton, you don't have to answer that. Are you almost through, Mr. Schwartz?'

'Almost, Your Honour. Miss Burton, what were you wearing on the day of your encounter with Mr. Clarke?'

'What was I wearing?' She looked nervous and confused. He had been pelting her with difficult questions. 'I . . . I don't know . . . I . . .'

'Was it something like what you have on now? A suit? Or something lighter, more revealing? Something sexy, maybe?' The prosecuting attorney was frowning fiercely again, and Jessica was beginning to enjoy the situation. She liked Martin's style. Even Ian looked intrigued, almost pleased.

'I . . . I don't know. I guess I must have worn a summer dress.'

'Like what? Something low-cut?'

'No. I don't wear things like that.'

'Are you sure, Miss Burton? Mr. Clarke says you were wearing a very short, low-cut pink dress, with a hat—were you wearing that same hat? It's a very nice hat.'

Suddenly she was torn between the compliment and the implication.

'I don't wear pink.'

'But the hat is pink, isn't it?'

'It's more a kind of neutral colour, more like beige.' But there was a pinkish cast to it. That was obvious to all.

'I see. And what about the dress? Did that have a kind of beige cast to it too?'

'I don't know.'

'All right. Do you go to Enrico's often?'

'No, I've been just a couple of times. But I've walked by it.'

'Had you seen Mr. Clarke there before?'

'No. I don't remember seeing him.' She was regaining her composure. These questions were easy.

'Why did you tell him you were a topless waitress on Broadway?'

'I never told him that.' Now she was angry again, and Martin nodded, looking almost preoccupied.

'All right, thank you, Miss Burton. Thank you, Your Honour.'

The judge looked questioningly at the assistant district attorney, who shook her head. She had nothing to add. He indicated that Margaret Burton could step down, then spoke the words Jessica had dreaded. 'Mr. Clarke, please take the stand.'

Ian and Margaret Burton passed inches from each other, their faces without expression. Only moments before, she had said that he had ruined her life, yet now she looked right through him. Jessica felt more confused than ever by the woman.

The oath was administered, and the judge looked over his glasses at Ian.

'Mr. Clarke, would you please give us your account of what happened?' The judge looked excessively bored as Ian launched into his version of that day's events. The lunch, the drinks, picking her up, the seductive way she was dressed, her story about being a topless waitress, the drive to Market Street to an address she had given him but which he could no longer remember. And finally her invitation to her room, where they had had a drink and made love.

'Whose room was it?'

'I don't know. I assumed it was hers. But it was kind of empty. I don't know. I'd had a lot to drink at lunch. and I wasn't thinking very clearly.'

'But clearly enough to go upstairs with Miss Burton?'

Ian flushed. He felt like an errant schoolboy called to the principal's office . . . *Ian, did you look up Maggie's dress? Tsk, tsk, tsk!* But it wasn't like that at all. The stakes were too high for this to be child's play.

'My wife was away, and had been for three weeks.' Jessie's heart was pounding again. Was it supposed to be her fault, then? Was that the implication? Was that what he thought, what he wanted her to feel? She was responsible for his feelings of inadequacy?

'And what happened after it was all over?'

'I left.'

'Just like that? Did you intend to see Miss Burton again?' Ian shook his head.

'No. I didn't intend to see her again. I felt guilty as hell for what had already happened.' Martin was frowning at his answer and Jessie cringed. The judge had picked up on it too.

'Guilty?'

'I mean, because of my wife. I don't usually do that sort of thing.'

'What sort of thing, Mr. Clarke? Rape?'

'No, for God's sake, I didn't rape her!' He had bellowed his denial and small beads of sweat were glistening on his forehead. 'I mean, I felt guilty for cheating on my wife.'

'But you did force Miss Burton upstairs at the hotel?'

'I did not. She took me upstairs. It was her room, not mine. She invited me up.'

'What for?'

'A drink. And probably for exactly what she got.'

'Then why do you suppose she claims you raped her?'

'I don't know.' Ian looked blank and exhausted, and the judge shook his head and looked around the room.

'Ladies and gentlemen, neither do I. The purpose of this hearing is to determine if there was a misunderstanding afoot, if the problem is one that can be simply resolved here and now, to determine in effect if a rape did take place, and if the case merits further judicial attention. It is my job to decide to dismiss the action or send it on to a higher court to be tried. In order for me to make the decision to dismiss the action, I have to feel quite certain that this was clearly not a rape.

'In the event that I am unable to decide, that the matter is not clear, then I have no choice but to send it on to a higher court, and possibly to a jury, to decide. And it would appear that this is no simple matter before us now. The stories of the two parties are widely divergent. Miss Burton says rape, Mr. Clarke says not. There is no evidence in either direction. So I am afraid this matter will have to be handled by a higher court, and presumably given a jury trial. We cannot simply dismiss the matter. Serious allegations have been made. I move that the matter be referred to Superior Court, and that Mr. Clarke be arraigned in Superior Court two weeks from today, in the court of Judge Simon Warberg. Court is dismissed.' And without further ado, he got up and walked out of the room. Jessica and Ian rose and looked at each other in confusion as Martin shuffled papers for a moment. Margaret Burton was whisked away by Inspector Houghton.

'Now what?' Jessica spoke to Ian in a whisper.

'You heard the man, Jess—we go to trial.'

'Yeah.' She looked for a last moment at the retreating back of the Burton woman, fresh hatred filling her soul for this woman who was inexplicably destroying their lives. She knew no more now than she had three hours ago. Why?

'Well, Martin?' Jessica turned to Martin now. He looked very serious. 'What do you think?'

'We'll discuss it in my office, but I smell one thing I don't like. I can't be sure, but I had a case like this once years ago. Crazy case with a crazy plaintiff. It had to do with vengeance. Not against the guy she said had raped her, but against someone who actually had raped her in her late teens. She had waited twenty-two years to get revenge against an innocent man. I can't tell you why, it's just a gut feeling, but this reminds me of that case.' He had spoken in a barely audible whisper. Jessica leaned toward him to hear, and was intrigued by his idea. She had had a strange feeling about the Burton woman too. Ian still looked too shaken to react to much of anything. He looked at Jessie then with irritation in his eyes.

'I told you to wait outside.'

'I couldn't.'

'Yeah. I had a feeling you'd wind up in here. Fun, wasn't it?' He sounded bitter and tired. They were the only people left in the courtroom, and he looked around as though he'd just waked up from a bad dream. It had been a gruelling session, and even Jessica felt as though she had aged five years in the course of the morning.

'When will the trial be?' she asked Martin. She didn't quite know what to say to Ian: there was so much to say; too much.

'In six weeks. You heard the judge say that the Superior Court arraignment is in two. The trial will be four weeks after that. And we're going to have to do some very fast work.' Martin was wearing a look of intense sobriety, and Jessica found herself aching to ask how that other client had come out, the one who had been accused of rape by the woman seeking revenge, but she was afraid to know. Ian hadn't asked the question either, and Martin hadn't volunteered the information. 'I want Green on the case night and day, and I want you both available for meetings whenever I call you.' His voice was stern.

'We'll be available.' Jessie spoke first, trying to keep the tears out of her voice. 'We'll win, won't we, Martin?' She was still whispering, but she wasn't sure why. It was no longer necessary.

'I think it'll be a tight one. It's her word against yours, Ian. But yes, we ought to win.' He didn't sound sure enough for Jessie, though, and the full weight of the situation settled on her heart again. How had it all happened? Where had it all started? Was it really just a matter of her having been in New York for too long? Had he just been horny? Was it bad luck? Was the Burton woman some kind of lunatic who'd been gunning for anyone, or had Ian been singled out? Whose fault was it? And when would it all go away?

'Will they revoke Ian's bail?' That had been her constant terror. And Ian's.

'They can, but they won't. There's no reason to, as long as he keeps making his court appearances, and the judge didn't mention it. Just don't either of you go off on any trips, just now. No business trips, no disappearing acts, no visits back east to your family. Stick around; I'll be needing you. All right?'

They nodded solemnly and he walked them slowly from the courtroom as Jessie thought of what he'd said. Family? What family? As old and frail as Ian's parents were, they would be the last people to turn to. She and Ian had already agreed on that. His parents were so proper and so gentle, and much too old to understand any of this. He was their only child, and truly it would have killed them. Besides, why tell them? It would all work out. It had to.

Ian and Jessie shook hands with Martin and he left them outside the courtroom. It had been an endless morning.

'Do we have a minute to stop at the john?' Jessica looked at Ian nervously. She felt strange and uncomfortable with him, as though someone had just told them he had cancer. She wasn't sure whether to cry or to offer encouragement, or just to run away and hide. She wasn't even sure what she felt yet.

'Sure. I think it's down the hall. I have to go too.' Conversation was awkward between them. It was going to be hard to find the way back. But as they walked along the hall, he stopped her suddenly and turned to face her, holding her arm. 'Jessie, I don't know what to say. I didn't do it, but I'm almost beginning to wonder if that even matters. I can't stand seeing what this is doing to you. I was a total ass for a couple of hours, and you're the one who's paying the price.'

She smiled tiredly in answer. 'And what about you? You're enjoying this maybe? Baby, we're in it now, and we just have to keep on walking till we're through it. That's all. And for Chrissake, don't give up now.' She was looking at him with a gentleness he hadn't seen all day. She slid her arms around him as they stood in the long marble hall, and he folded her into his arms without saying a word. He needed her desperately, and she knew it.

'Come on, hot stuff, I have to pee.' Her voice was gruff and sexy, and he smiled at her as they walked on down the hall, hand in hand. There was something very special between them. Always had been, always would be—if they could just survive what was happening to them now.

'I'll be back in a second.' She pecked a gentle kiss at his neck, squeezed his hand, and disappeared into the ladies' room.

Inside, she let herself into one of the booths and bolted the door. There were women on either side of her. A pair of red platform shoes and navy slacks on her left, slim ankles and simple black pumps on her right. Jessica straightened her stockings, smoothed down her skirt, and unbolted the door at the same moment that the black pumps emerged to her right. She cast a casual glance in that direction as she headed toward the sink, only to find herself rooted to the floor, staring into Margaret Burton's face—staring down at it, actually, with the difference in their height—the pale pink hat only slightly obscuring her view of the enemy's face.

Margaret Burton stood very still and stared back at her, as Jessica felt her insides turn cold. She was right there in front of her . . . within reach . . . grab her . . . hit her . . . kill her . . . but she couldn't move. There was only the sound of a sharp intake of breath as the Burton woman came to her senses and ran toward the door, the hat flying gently to Jessica's feet. It had taken only a few seconds, but it seemed hours, days, years . . .

and she was gone, as Jessie stood there helpless, tears starting down her face. She stooped down very slowly and picked up the hat before walking slowly toward the door. She could hear someone knocking nervously, frantically. It was Ian. He had seen Margaret Burton fly through the door as he'd come out of the men's room across the hall. And suddenly he was terrified. What had happened? What had Jessica done?

She emerged silently, the hat in her hand, tears on her face.

'What happened?'

Jessica only shook her head, clutching the hat.

'Did she do anything?'

She shook her head again.

'Did you?'

And again, a silent no.

'Oh, babe.' He pulled her into his arms, and took the hat from her hand, tossing it onto a nearby bench. 'Let's get the hell out of here and go home.' In fact, he was going to get her out of town. To hell with what Martin said, they needed to get away. Carmel, maybe. Anywhere. He wondered how long Jessica could take the pressure. How long he could. The hat seemed to look at him accusingly from the bench as he held his wife in his arms, and he shuddered. It was the hat she had worn that day at Enrico's. That day . . . the day he'd be paying for for years, one way or another. He kept an arm around Jessica's shoulders and walked her slowly toward the elevator. He wanted to pour his soul into hers, but he wasn't even sure he had enough for himself anymore, let alone for anyone else. He wanted the horror to be over, and it was only beginning.

When the elevator came she walked silently into it. Her eyes were soldered to the doors, and he wanted to shake her. He was watching her slip away again: he had seen this mask before.

The elevator spat them out into the chaos of the lobby. It was filled with police and inspectors, private lawyers and assistant district attorneys, and people waiting in line to get passes to the jail. Ian and Jessica melted into the sea of swarming people. And here and there was an ordinary, untroubled face, someone in the building to pay a parking ticket, or fill out a car-registration form. But they were so few that they blended in with the rest, which was why neither Jessica nor Ian saw Astrid, on her way to get a new sticker for the one that had fallen off her plates at the car wash. They were only a few feet away and never saw her. But she saw them, and was stricken by the expression on their faces. They passed six feet away, and she let them go. It was the same look she had worn when the doctors had told her just how sick Tom really was.

CHAPTER XIII

The following morning, Ian made up his mind. Jessica had to get away. They both did. And when she was making breakfast, he even went to the trouble of clearing it with Martin over the phone. Martin agreed, and Ian announced it to Jessie as a *fait accompli.*

'We're doing what?' She looked at him incredulously as she stood barefoot in her robe in the kitchen.

'We're leaving for Carmel in half an hour.' This time he smiled when he said it. 'Pack your gear, my love.'

'You're crazy. Martin said—'

'—to send him a postcard.' Ian smiled victoriously as Jessica chuckled.

'And just when did he say that?'

'Just now.'

'You called him?' She still looked dubious, but amused.

'I just hung up. So, my beloved—' he approached her slowly, with a wisp of a smile—'get your beautiful ass moving before we waste the day.'

'You're a nut.' He kissed her and she smiled up at him with her eyes closed. 'But such a nice nut.'

They reached Carmel in two hours with Ian at the wheel of the Morgan. The air was cooler than it had been for weeks, and it was brilliantly sunny all the way down. They put the top down on the Morgan and arrived wind-blown and happier. It was almost as though the constant sweep of wind on the highway had cleared the worry from their minds. The trip hadn't been such a bad idea after all, and after the first fifty miles, Jessie had stopped imagining that Inspector Houghton was following them. She was constantly haunted by him, but maybe now it would stop. It was just that he seemed omnipotent. He would go away and then could come back again, with a search warrant, a gun, a friend, a look in his eye . . . a twist of his mouth . . . he terrified her, and she didn't dare tell Ian how much. She never mentioned him. She had also been worried about the expense of the trip, but Ian had insisted that he had enough left in his account to cover it. She had been ordered to mind her own business and warned that they were going economy all the way, no deluxe accommodations this time. She felt guilty, doubting his assurances, but she was obsessed with their finances now, and the upcoming staggering expense of the trial. And Ian was so strange about money, maybe because he had never had any. He had a way of buying her fabulous presents and creating magnificent moments when they were plainly out of funds. He would take the last of what he had and throw it out the window in style. In the past, this trait had amused her. Right now it did not.

But she was grateful for the trip to Carmel. She knew how much she needed it. Her nerves had been on the raw edge of disaster. And she knew that Ian's had been too, no matter how hard he'd tried to cover up.

Astrid had told them about a little hotel where she had stayed the previous spring that she'd insisted was a bargain. So they forfeited the deluxe delights of the familiar Del Monte for the cosy plaid and pine atmosphere of L'Auberge. It was run by a middle-aged French couple, and among its other pleasures, it boasted 'Café Complet' in bed in the morning. The Café Complet consisted of home-made croissants and brioches, with bowls of steaming *café au lait*.

They walked to the beach and canvassed the shops, and on Saturday took a picnic out to the edge of a cliff overlooking the sea.

'More wine, love?'

Ian nodded and pushed a long strand of blonde hair from her eyes. They were lying side by side, and she was looking up at the sky while he rested on one elbow and looked down at her. He smoothed her face with his hand and kissed her gently on the lips, the eyes, the tip of the nose.

'If you do that, I'll never sit up to get you your wine, my love.' He smiled again and she blew him a kiss.

'You know something, Ian?'

'What?'

'You make me very happy.' His face clouded as she said it, and she caught his chin in her hand and forced him to look at her. 'I mean it. You do.'

'How can you say that now?'

'Because now is no different from any other time, Ian. You do beautiful things to me. You give me what I need, and I need a lot. Sometimes you pay a price for that. And okay, so it's hard now, but this'll be over soon. It won't go on forever. All in all I think we're damn lucky.' She sat up and faced him, and finally he looked away.

'Lucky, eh? I guess that's one way to look at it.' He sounded bitter, and she reached for his hand.

'You don't feel lucky anymore?'

'I do. But do you, Jessie, really? Be honest.' He looked back at her with an unfamiliar look in his eyes, a kind of openness that frightened her: as though he were questioning everything. Her. Himself. Them. Life. Everything.

'Yes, I feel lucky.' Her voice was a whisper in the brisk wind of the sunny October day.

'Jessica, my love, I was unfaithful to you. I made love to another woman. A neurotic tramp, but still another woman. You've been supporting me for almost six years. I am not a successful writer. And I'm about to go on trial for rape, I may go to prison, and even if I don't, this is going to be the ugliest thing we've ever lived through.

And you feel lucky? How do you manage that little feat?'

She looked down at her hands for a long time, and then back up into his face. 'Ian, I don't care if you made love to another woman. I don't like it, but it doesn't matter. It doesn't change anything. Not for me. Don't *you* let it change anything. I don't suppose it was the first time, but I don't want to know. That's not the point. The point is, so what? So you made love to someone, so what? So you jacked off, so what? *I don't care*. Does that make any sense to you? I don't care. I care about you, about us, about our marriage, about your career. And I don't "support" you. Lady J supports us both. We're lucky to have it, and one of these days you're going to sell a book and a movie and another book and a pile of brilliant work, and make a fortune. So what's the problem?'

'Jessica, you're crazy.' He was smiling at her, but his eyes still looked serious.

'No, I'm not. And I mean it. You make me happy. You make me glow, you make me care, you make me know I'm loved, you're always there for me. You know who I am and what I am and why I am better than I do even. Ian, that's so rare. I look at other people and they never seem to have what we have.' Her eyes were fiery now, and the colour of jade.

'I don't know what to say, Jessie . . . I love you. And I need you too. Not just to support me while I write. I need . . . oh, hell—' he smiled, more to himself than to her— 'I need you sitting bare-assed and solemn-faced at two in the morning, telling me why my fourth chapter isn't working. I need the way you fly in the door at night with that look of "Oh, wow!" on your face . . . the way you know, the way you . . . respect me, even when I don't respect myself.'

'Oh, Ian.' She slid into his arms again and closed her eyes as he held her.

'I need you a lot, babe. But . . . something's going to have to change.'

Her eyes opened slowly. He had just said something important. She knew it from the change in the way he held her more than from the words.

'What do you mean?'

'I don't know yet. But something's got to change, after we survive this holocaust we're going to walk through in the next couple of months.'

'Like what, dammit? Change what?' Her voice was unexpectedly shrill, and she sat back from him a little so she could read his eyes.

'Take it easy, Jessie. I just think it's about time for an overhaul. I don't know, maybe it's time I shelved my fancy ideas about a writing career. Something. We can't go on exactly like this, though. In some ways it doesn't work.'

'Why not?'

'Because I feel kept. You pay the bills, or most of them, and I can't live with that anymore. Do you know what it feels like to have no income? To feel guilty every time you dig into the kitty, the "joint account", so-called, to buy a couple of T-shirts? Do you have any idea how it feels to have you footing the bill for this disaster now? To have you pick up the tab on my alleged "rape"? Jesus, Jessie, it chokes me. It's killing me. Why the hell do you think I've been impotent lately? Because I'm so thrilled with myself for how I'm running my life?'

'You can't really take that seriously. You're under an incredible amount of strain right now.' She wanted to brush it aside, but he wasn't going to let her.

'That's right. I am under a lot of strain. But part of that strain is because we haven't got things set up the way they should be. Did you ever wonder what would happen if you didn't have Lady J, or if your parents hadn't left you some money?'

'I'd be working for someone else, and you'd be working in advertising and hating it. Doesn't that sound like fun?'

'No. But what if you weren't working at all, and I were working at something else?'

'Like what?' Her face seemed to freeze on the words.

'I don't know like what. I haven't figured that out yet.'

'Ian, you're out of your mind. I've never seen you work as hard on a book as you are on this one now, I've never heard you sound so sure about anything you've written. And now you want to quit?'

'I didn't say that. Not yet. But maybe. What I'm saying is: What would happen to you, to us, to our marriage, if you didn't support us, Jessie, if *I* did? What if we just kept your money as a nest egg, as an investment?'

'And what would I do all day? Needlepoint? Play bridge?'

'No. I was thinking of something else. Maybe for later.' There was something soft and distant in his eyes as he spoke.

'What's the something else?'

'Like . . . well . . . like what if we finally had children —after this whole mess is over, I mean. We haven't talked about that for a long time. Not since before . . .' She knew what he meant by 'before'. Before things had changed. Before her parents had died. Before she'd inherited their money . . . before. That one word said it all. They both knew. 'Jessie . . . baby, I want to take care of you. Besides, you've earned it.'

'Why?'

'What do you mean, "why"?' He looked momentarily confused.

'I mean why should we scramble everything up now? Why should you suddenly take on the whole burden? I love working; it's not a burden for me. It's fun.'

'Can't kids be fun too?'

'I didn't say they weren't.' Her face was as tight as a drum.

'But?'

'Oh, for Chrissake, Ian, why do we have to get into that now?' That one hadn't come up in years.

'I didn't say now. We're just talking what if's.'

'That's ridiculous. It's like playing games.' She turned away and suddenly felt Ian's hand on her arm. Hard.

'It's not like playing games. I'm serious, Jessie. I've turned myself into a fucking gigolo in the last six years. I'm a failure as a writer, and I just balled some two-bit tramp and got falsely accused of rape. I'm trying to figure out what means something in my life and what doesn't, and what needs changing. And maybe part of what needs changing is us. Not even maybe. I know it does. Now are you going to listen, and talk to me, or aren't you?'

She sat silent, looking at him. But she knew she had no choice. He let go of her arm and poured two more glasses of wine. 'I'm sorry. But this is important to me, Jess.'

'Okay. I'll try.' She took the glass of wine and sighed deeply as she looked up at the sky. 'All this because I told you that you make me happy? *Oy vey* . . . I should have kept my mouth shut!' She smiled back at him, and he kissed her again.

'I know. I'm a bastard. But Jessie . . . I want to make it work with us. I want to make it better. I don't want to go screwing other women, or hating myself or . . . it matters. It really matters. And I'm glad I make you happy, and you make me happy too. Very happy. But we can do better, I know we can. I've got to feel like your husband, like a man, like I carry the weight, or most of it at least, even if it means selling the house and living someplace where I can pay our rent. But I *need* to do things like that for you. I'm tired of having you "take care" of me. And I don't mean to sound ungrateful, Jess, but . . . I just need to, dammit.'

'Okay. But why? Why now? Because of that idiot woman? Margaret Burton? Because of her, you have to give up writing and move us into some shack in the Mission where you can pay the rent?' She was getting bitchy now and he didn't like it. The comment hadn't missed its mark.

'No, sweetheart. Margaret Burton is just a symptom, just like the hundred or two hundred pieces of ass before her. Is that how you want to play this, Jessie? Shitty, or straight? Take your pick. I'm willing to play either way.'

She polished off the rest of her wine at a gulp and shrugged. 'I just don't get the point.'

'Maybe that is the point. Just like when I talk about having a child. You don't get the point of that either, do you? Doesn't that mean anything to you at all, Jessie?'

She shook her head solemnly, looking down, avoiding his eyes.

'I just don't understand that. Why? Look at me, dammit. This is important to me. To both of us.' But when she looked up, he was surprised.

'It scares me.'

'A baby?' She had never admitted that to him before. Usually she'd gotten nasty about it and closed the subject rapidly. It made him feel tender toward her to hear that. Scared?

'It scares you physically?' He reached for her hand gently and held it.

'No. It . . . I'd have to share you, Ian, and I . . . I can't.' Tears swam in her eyes and her chin trembled as she looked at him. 'I really can't share you, Ian. I can't, not ever. You're all I have. You're . . .'

'Oh, baby . . .' He took her in his arms and rocked her gently, tears stinging his own eyes. 'What a crazy thing to think. A baby's not like that. It would never be. We're special. A baby would be something more, not less.'

'Yes, but it would be yours. Real family.' And then he understood. He had his parents, of course, but they were so remote and so old. He hardly ever saw them. But a baby would be so present, so real.

'You're my real family, silly. You'll always be my real family.' How often had he told her that, after her parents had died? A thousand times? Ten thousand? It was strange to think back to those days. She had been so fiercely independent and sure of herself when he'd married her. But she had loved both her parents and adored her brother; just hearing her speak of them was like hearing reminiscences of very dear friends who had had a marvellous time together. And spending time with them was an extraordinary experience—four exceedingly handsome people, with lightning minds and quick laughter and immeasurable style. They'd been quite something. And when they were gone, part of her went too. Not an obvious part. She still had as much spirit, as much life, as much style, but suddenly in her soul she was an orphan.

She had loved Ian before, but she hadn't needed him in the same way. Then she'd become like a frightened child lost in a war zone, stricken, scared, wandering from the burnt shell of one memory to another. Lost and alone. The attempted suicide had come after Jake. And it had left her different. Dependent. It was Ian who had led her to safety again after that. That was when she had started calling him 'real family'. Where before their closeness had been a loosely woven, sparkling mesh, suddenly there was nothing loose about it, and over the years it had all gotten too goddam tight. And now there wasn't even room in her heart for a child. He had known that for a long time, but he had thought that eventually the panic would ebb. It hadn't, now he was sure of it. Her own needs were still too intense, and probably always would be. It was a bitter thing for him to accept.

'Oh, God, Ian, I love you so much and I'm so scared . . . I'm so fucking scared.' He felt her in his arms again, his mind pulled back to her, away from his own thoughts. She took a deep breath and held tightly to him as he slowly stroked her hair, thinking of what he now understood and had to accept. Had to. Nothing was ever going to change. Oh, some things would, and he was going to see about making those changes, but she was never going to stand on her own two feet again, not entirely, not enough for them both to reach out to a child.

'I'm scared too, Jess. But it's going to be okay.'

'How can it be okay if you're going to change everything after we get through this? You want me to sell the shop, have a baby, and you're going to stop writing and get a job and make us move and . . . oh, Ian! It sounds horrible!' She sobbed in his arms again and he laughed softly as he held her. Maybe she was all he needed. Maybe it wasn't even normal for a man to want a child as much as he did. Maybe it was just an ego trip. He brushed the thoughts from his mind.

'Jesus, did I say I was going to change all that? It does sound pretty heavy. Maybe we should just pick a couple of things, like I'll have a baby, and you get a job, and . . . I'm sorry, babe, I didn't mean to hit you with ten thousand things at once. I just know that something needs fixing.'

'But all that?'

'No, probably not all that. And not unless you agree with me. It wouldn't work otherwise. We've both got to want it.'

'But you make it sound like our life will never be the same again.'

'Maybe it won't, Jessie. Maybe it shouldn't be. Did you ever think of that?'

'No.'

'And you're not going to, either, huh? Look at you, hunched over like an Indian squaw, trying not to hear anything I'm telling you, with an ant crawling up your arm . . .' He waited. It took half a second. She leapt to her feet with a scream.

'A what?'

'Oh . . . tsk . . . how could I forget? That's right, you're afraid of ants.' He brushed her sleeve lightly as he stood up next to her and she punched him in the chest.

'Goddam you, Ian Clarke! We're having a serious talk and how can you do that to me! There was no ant on me, was there? *Was there*?"

'Would I lie to you?'

'I hate you!' She was still trembling with a jumble of emotions, terror and fury and fear because of the ant, and the much more real emotions of moments before. He'd invented the ant to lighten the mood.

It was a reprieve. Ian was good at them.

'What do you mean, you hate me? You said I made you happy.' He looked all innocence as he put his arms around her.

'Don't touch me!' But she was limp in his arms and trying hard to conceal a smile. 'You know—' her voice was soft again now—'sometimes I wonder if you really love me.'

'Sometimes everyone wonders stuff like that, Jess. You can't have the kind of ironclad guarantees you want, sweetheart. I love you just as much as your mother and father did, just as much as Jake did, just as much as . . .

anyone. But I'm not them. I'm me, your husband, a man, just like you're my wife, not my mother. And maybe one day you'll get sick of me and walk off into the sunset with someone else. Mothers aren't supposed to do that to their kids, but wives do that sometimes. I have to accept that.'

'Are you trying to tell me something?' She was suddenly stiff in his arms.

'No, silly, only that I love you. And that I can only be and do so much. I think I'm trying to tell you not to be so insecure and not to worry so much. Sometimes I think that's why you put up with so much shit from me, and pay the bills and all the rest, because that way you know you've got me. But I'll tell you a secret—that way you don't got me. As it so happens you've got me, but for all the other reasons.'

'Like what?' She was smiling again.

'Oh . . . like the beautiful way you sew.'

'Sew? I can't sew.' She looked at him strangely and then started to laugh.

'You can't?'

'Nope.'

'I'll teach you.'

'You're adorable.'

'Come to think of it, lady, so are you. Which reminds me. Reach into my pocket.' Her eyebrows lifted with interest and she grinned mischievously at him.

'A surprise for me?'

'No, my laundry bill.'

'Creep.' But she slipped her hand carefully into his jacket pocket as they talked, her eyes sparkling with excitement. It was easy to find the little square box. She pulled it out with a grin and held it clutched in her hand.

'Aren't you going to open it?'

'This is the best part.' She giggled again and he grinned at her.

'It's not the Hope diamond, I promise.'

'It's not?'

'Oh, for Chrissake . . .' And then she suddenly snapped open the box. And he watched.

'Oh . . . it's . . . oh, Ian! You nut!' She gave a whoop

of laughter and looked at it again. 'How in God's name did you get it?'

'I saw it, and I knew you had to have it.'

She laughed again and started to put it on. It was a thin gold chain with a gold pendant shaped like a lima bean. The thing she had hated most in the world as a child.

'Good God, I never thought I'd see the day when I'd wear one of the bloody things. And in gold, yet.' She laughed again, kissed him, and tucked in her chin to look down at the small gold nugget on its chain.

'Actually, it looks very elegant. If you didn't know what it was, you'd never guess. I had a choice between a kidney bean, a lima bean, and some other kind of bean. They're done by the same very fancy designer, I'll have you know.'

'And you just saw it in a window?'

'Yep. And I figured that if you have faith as a mustard seed, you can move mountains and all that stuff. So hell, if you have faith like a lima bean, you can probably move half the world.'

'Which half?'

'Any half, sexy lady. Come on, let's go back to the hotel.'

'Lima beans . . . sweetheart, you're crazy. May I ask how large a portion of your fortune this sensational lima bean cost you?' She had noticed that it was eighteen-carat gold and that the box was from a very extravagant store.

'You most certainly may not. How can you ask such a thing?'

'Curiosity.'

'Well, don't be so curious. And do me a favour. Don't eat it.' She laughed again and bit his neck as she reached over for the rest of the wine.

'Sweetheart, there is one thing you can bet on. I ain't never gonna eat lima beans. Not even a gold one.' And then they both burst into laughter, because that was exactly what she had told him the first time he had cooked dinner for her at his place eight years before.

He had fixed roast pork, mashed potatoes, and lima

beans. She had devoured the meat and potatoes, but he had found her rapidly shovelling lima beans into her handbag when he'd come back from the kitchen with the glass of water she'd requested, and she had looked at him, thrown up her hands, burst into laughter and said, 'Ian, I ain't never gonna eat lima beans. Not even if they're solid gold.' And this one was indeed solid gold. For the tiniest of moments, her stomach felt queasy at the thought of the expense. But that was Ian. They were going down the tubes in style. With picnics and passion and gold.

The mood for the rest of the weekend was sheer holiday spirit. Jessica flashed her gold lima bean at every possible opportunity, and they teased and hugged and kissed. L'Auberge restored their love life to what it had always been. They had dinner by candlelight in their room—a feast of fried chicken from a nearby take-out place, devoured with a small bottle of champagne they had bought on the way back to the hotel. They giggled like children and played like honeymooners, and the threats of the morning were forgotten. Everything was forgotten except Ian and Jessie. They were the only people who mattered.

The only sorrow, and it was a hidden one, was Ian's hope of a child, now put away. Insanely, desperately, he had wanted to father a child, now, before the trial, before . . . what if . . . who knew what was coming? A year from then he could be in prison or dead. It wasn't a cheerful way to look at things, but the realities were beginning to frighten him. And the possibilities were even more terrifying when he let himself think of them. A baby would be a fresh blade of grass springing from ashes. But now that he understood how panicked Jessie still was, the subject was closed. His books were his children. He would simply work that much harder on the new book.

On Sunday, Jessie bought Ian a Sherlock Holmes hat and a corncob pipe. They shared a banana split for lunch, then rented a tandem bike and rode around near the hotel, laughing at their lack of precision. Jessica collapsed when faced with a hill.

'What do you mean, "no"? Come on, Jessie, *push!*"

'The hell I will. You push. I'll walk.'

'Stinkpot.'

'Look at that hill. Who do you think I am? Tarzan?'

'Well, look at your legs, for Chrissake. They're long enough to run up that hill carrying me, let alone bicycling.'

'You, sir, are a creep.'

'Hey . . . look at the spider on your leg.'

'I . . . what? . . . Aaaahh . . . Ian! Where?' But he was laughing at her, and when she looked up she knew. 'Ian Clarke, if you do that to me one more time, I'll . . .' She was spluttering and he was laughing harder than ever. 'I'll . . .' She hit him a walloping blow on the shoulder, knocking him off the bicycle and into the tall grass next to the path. But he reached out and grabbed her as she stood laughing at him, and pulled her down beside him. 'Ian, not here! There are probably snakes in here! Ian! Dammit! Stop that!'

'No snakes. I swear.' He was reaching into her blouse with a leer that made her giggle.

'Ian . . . I mean it—no! Ian . . .' She forgot about the snakes almost immediately.

CHAPTER XIV

'Well, how did you like my favourite hideaway in Carmel?' With a smile, Astrid poked her head in the door of Jessica's office.

'We adored it. Come on in. How about some coffee?'

Jessie's smile said it all. The two days in Carmel had been a peaceful island in a troubled sea.

'I'll skip the coffee, thanks. I'm on my way downtown to talk to Tom's attorneys. Maybe I'll stop by again on my way home.' Jessica showed her the gold lima bean, gave her a brief, expurgated account of the weekend, and blew Astrid a kiss as she left. For the rest of the day, Lady J was a madhouse.

There were deliveries, new clients, old customers who wanted something new but needed it altered 'right now', invoices that got misplaced, and two shipments that Jessie needed desperately never showed up at all. And Katsuko couldn't help, because she was swamped with details for the fashion show. So Zina juggled the customers while Jessie tried to untangle the problems. And the bills. The next two weeks were more of the same.

Harvey Green appeared twice at the boutique to discuss minor things with Jessie, things about Ian's habits and her own, but she had little to tell him. Neither did Ian. They led a simple life and had nothing to hide. The two girls in the boutique still didn't know what was happening, and the weeks since Jessie's frantic and erratic disappearances from the shop had been too hectic for questions. They assumed that the problem, whatever it was, had blown over. And Astrid was careful not to pry.

Ian was lost in his new book, and the two subsequent court appearances went smoothly. As Martin had predicted the bail was not revoked: there was never even a suggestion of it. Jessica joined Ian both times in court, but there was nothing to see. He would walk to the front of the courtroom with Martin, they would mumble for a few moments in front of the judge, and then they could all leave. By now it seemed like an ordinary part of their everyday lives; they had other things to think about. Jessie was worried about part of the fall line that hadn't moved, another shipment that had never shown up, and the money that was draining from her bank account. Ian was troubled by chapter nine, and incoherent about anything else. That was what their real life was about, not mechanical appearances before a bored judge.

It was a month later when Harvey Green came up with the first part of his bill. Eighteen hundred dollars. The statement arrived at the boutique, as she had requested, and Jessica gasped when she opened it. She felt almost sick. Eighteen hundred dollars. For nothing. He hadn't unearthed a damn thing, except the name of a man Margaret Burton had gone to dinner with twice and never slept with. Peggy Burton appeared to be clean. Her co-workers thought her a decent woman, not very sociable, but reliable and pleasant to work with. Several mentioned that she was occasionally distant and moody. She had no torrid love affairs in her past, no drug problems, no drinking habits to speak of. She had never returned to any hotel on Market Street in all the time Green had been tailing her, nor had she had any men into her apartment at any time since the surveillance had begun. She went home alone every night after work; had gone to three movies in a month, again alone; and an attempt to pick her up on the bus had totally failed. An assistant of Green's had made eyes at her for several blocks, got an encouraging look in response, he said, and had then received a firm 'No, thanks, buster' when he'd invited her out for a drink. He had said she'd even looked pissed at him for asking. At worst, she was confused. At best . . . she was the second best thing to the Virgin Mary, and Ian's case would look very flimsy in court. They had to find something. But they hadn't. And now Harvey Green wanted eighteen hundred dollars. And they couldn't even let him go. Martin had said the Burton woman would have to be watched right up until the trial, possibly even during the trial, although both he and Green admitted that the police had probably told her to behave herself. The prosecution didn't want their case shot down by a random piece of ass Miss Margaret Burton might indulge herself with a few weeks before the trial.

Green hadn't even been able to come up with any dirt on her past. She had been married once, at the age of eighteen, and the marriage had been annulled a few months later. But he didn't know why, or who she had married. Nothing. And there was no record of it, which was probably why she hadn't admitted to it at the preliminary hearing. (What he knew he had learned from a woman Margaret Burton worked with.) What Jessie was paying for was a clean bill of health on the woman.

Jessie sat at her desk, staring at Green's bill, and opened

the rest of her mail. A statement from Martin for the five thousand they still owed, and nine statements from New York for her purchases for the spring line. Ian's bill for his physical two months before, still due, for two hundred and forty-two dollars, and her own chest X ray for forty, as well as a seventy-four-dollar bill from a record store where she'd splurged before she'd gone to New York. As she sat there, she wondered what had ever made her think that seventy-four dollars for records wasn't so awful. She could still remember saying that to Ian at the time. Yeah . . . not so awful if you haven't found yourself with ten thousand dollars in legal bills in the meantime . . . and the florist . . . and the cleaner's . . . and the drugstore . . . she could feel her stomach constrict as she tried not to add up the amounts. She reached for the phone, looked at the card in her address book, and called.

She phoned the bank before going to the appointment, and she was lucky, more or less. Based on the previous performance of her account, the bank was willing to leave her loan uncovered by collateral. She could sell it. She had been secretly hoping that they wouldn't let her. But now she had no choice.

She sold the Morgan at two in the afternoon. For fifty-two hundred dollars. The guy gave her 'a deal'. She deposited the cheque in the bank before closing, and sent a cheque of her own to Martin Schwartz for five thousand dollars. He was paid. It was taken care of. She could breathe now. For weeks she had had nightmares about something happening to her and nobody being able to help Ian with the bills . . . horrible fantasies of Ian begging Katsuko for the money, and being refused because she wanted the money to buy kimonos for the shop, while Barry York threatened to drag Ian back to jail. Now they were saved. The legal fees were paid. If something happened to her, Ian had his attorney.

She then borrowed eighteen hundred dollars from Lady J's business account to pay Green his fee. She was back at her desk at three-thirty—with a splitting headache. Astrid showed up at four-thirty.

'You're not looking too happy, Lady J. Anything wrong?'

Astrid was the only one who called her that, and it made her smile tiredly.

'Would you believe *everything's* wrong?'

'No, I wouldn't. But—anything special you want to tell me?' Astrid sipped the coffee Zina had poured for her and Jessie sighed and shook her head.

'Nothing much to tell. Not unless you have about six hundred spare hours to listen, and I don't have that much spare time to tell you anyway. How was your day?'

'Better than yours. But I didn't take any chances. I got up at eleven and spent the afternoon having my hair done.' Jesus. How could she tell her? How could Astrid possibly understand?

'Maybe that's where I went wrong. I washed my hair myself last night.' She grinned lopsidedly at her friend, but Astrid didn't smile. She was worried. Jessie had been looking tired and troubled for weeks, and there was nothing she could say.

'Why don't you call it a day, and go home to your gorgeous young husband? Hell, Jessica, if I had him around, wild horses couldn't keep me here.'

'You know something? I think you're right.' It was the first real smile Jessica had produced all day. 'Are you heading home? I could use a ride.'

'Where's your baby?'

'The Morgan?' She tried to stall. She didn't want to lie, but . . . Astrid nodded, and Jessie felt a pain in her heart.

'I . . . it's in the shop.'

'No problem. I'll give you a ride.'

Ian watched Astrid drop her off from the window in his studio, and he looked puzzled. It was time to take a break anyway—he'd been working straight through since seven that morning. He opened the door for Jessie before she got out her key.

'What's with the car? Did you leave it at the boutique?'

'Yes . . . I . . .' She looked up and she could almost

feel the colour draining from her face. She had to tell him. 'Ian, I . . . I sold it.' She winced at the look on his face. Everything stopped.

'*You did what*?' It was worse than she had feared.

'I sold it. Darling, I had to. Everything else is tied up. And we needed almost seven thousand bucks in the next two weeks for Martin's fee, and the first half of Green's bill, and Green is going to hit us with another one in two weeks. There was nothing else I could do.' She reached out to touch him and he brushed her hand away.

'You could have asked me, at least! Asked me, said something—for God's sake, Jessica, don't you consult me on *anything* anymore? I gave you that car as a gift. It meant something to me!' He strode across the room and grabbed for the Scotch. He poured some into a glass while she watched.

'Don't you think it meant something to *me*?' Her voice was trembling, but he didn't hear, and she watched while he swallowed the half glass of Scotch neat. 'Darling, I'm so . . . I just couldn't see any other . . .' She fell silent, with tears in her eyes. She remembered so well the day he had driven it home for her. Now . . .

He swallowed the last of his drink and pulled on his jacket.

'Where are you going?'

'Out.' His face looked like grey marble.

'Ian, please, don't do anything crazy.' She was frightened at the look in his eyes, but he only stood there and shook his head.

'I don't have to do anything crazy. I already did.' The door slammed behind him a moment later.

He came back at midnight, silent and subdued, and Jessica didn't ask him where he'd been. She was afraid to: maybe Inspector Houghton would be paying them another visit. But she hated herself for the thought when she watched Ian take off his shoes. Two small hills of sand poured out of them, and she looked at his face. He looked better. They had always done that together—gone to the beach at night to talk things out, or think, or just walk quietly together. He had taken her there when Jake had died. To their beach. Always together. Now she was afraid even to reach out and touch him, but she wanted to, needed to. He looked at her silently and walked into the bathroom and closed the door. Jessie turned out the lights and wiped two tears from her face. She felt the funny gold lima bean at her throat and tried to make herself smile, but she couldn't. They were past laughing at lima beans now, past laughing at anything, and who knew—one day she might sell the lima bean too. She hated herself as she lay in the dark.

She heard the bathroom door open, then Ian's soft footsteps, and then she felt the bed dip on the far side. He sat there for what seemed like a long time, smoking a cigarette. He leaned against the headboard and stretched his legs. She knew all his movements without looking, and she lay very still, wanting him to think she was sleeping. She didn't know what to say to him.

'I have something for you, Jess.' His voice was gruff and low in the stillness of the room.

'Like a punch in the mouth?'

He laughed and put a hand on her hip as she lay on her side with her back to him.

'No, dummy. Turn around.' She shook her head like a child, and then peeked over her shoulder.

'You're not mad at me, Ian?'

'No, I'm mad at me. There was nothing else you could do. I know that. I just hate myself for getting us in this spot, and I'd rather have sold a lot of things than the Morgan.'

She nodded, still at a loss for words. 'I'm so sorry.'

'Me too.' He leaned over and kissed her gently on the mouth and then put something light and sandy in her hand. 'Here. I found it in the dark.' It was a perfect sand dollar, a milky white shell with a tiny fossil imprint at its heart.

'Oh, darling, it's beautiful.' She smiled up at him, holding it in the flattened palm of her hand.

'I love you.' And then with a slow, gentle smile he

pulled her into his arms and let his lips follow an exquisite path to her thighs.

The next two weeks spun past them crazily. Hours at the shop, long lunches at home, violent arguments about who wasn't watering the plants, and then passionate making up and making love and making out, and insomnia, and oversleeping, and forgetting to eat and then eating too much, and constant indigestion, and terror about the bills followed by spending huge amounts of money on a Gucci wallet for Ian or a suede skirt from another store for Jessie, when she could have gotten it at cost from her own, and baubles and junk and garbage, and all of it charged, of course, as though the day of reckoning would never come. Utter madness. None of it made any sense. Jessie felt for weeks as though she were ricocheting off walls, never to be stationary again. Ian had the impression he was drowning.

It was the day before the trial when everything finally stopped. Jessie had made arrangements at the shop to take a week off, two if things turned out that way. She left the boutique early and went for a long walk before going home to Ian. She found him sitting pensively in a chair, staring at the view. It was the first time she had seen him not working furiously on the new novel. That was all he seemed to do now, when he wasn't spending money, or silently and urgently taking her body. They talked less than they ever had. Even meals were either silent disasters or frantic and frenzied—never normal.

But that night they lit a fire together, and talked until dark. She felt as though she hadn't seen him in months. At last she was talking to Ian again, the man she loved, her husband, her lover, her friend. She had missed his friendship most of all in these endless lonely weeks. It was the first time they really hadn't been able to reach out to each other and help. Now they shared a quiet dinner, sitting on the floor in front of the fire. Their peacefulness made the trial seem less terrifying. And the reality of it had worn off in the weeks since Ian had been released from jail. Jail had been reality. Fighting her way upstream to bail had been reality. Leaving her mother's emerald ring had been reality. But what was the trial? Merely a formality. A verbal exchange between two paid performers, theirs and the State's, with a black-robed umpire looking on, and somewhere in the background a woman no one knew named Margaret Burton. A week, maybe two weeks, and then it would be over. That was the only reality.

She rolled over on her back on the rug in front of the fire and smiled up at him sleepily as he bent to kiss her. It was a long, haunting kiss that brought back the gentleness they had lost and made her body beg to respond, and in a few minutes they were hungrily making love. It was one of those rare nights when souls and bodies blended and ignited and burned on for hours. They said little, but they made love again and again. It was almost dawn when Ian deposited Jessica sleepily in their bed.

'I love you, Jessie. Get some sleep now. Tomorrow will be a long day.' He whispered the words, and she smiled at his voice as she drifted off to sleep. A long day? Oh . . . that's right . . . the fashion show . . . or was it that they were going back to the beach? . . . She couldn't remember . . . a picnic? Was that it?

'I love you too . . .' Her voice drifted off as she fell asleep at his side, her arms wrapped around him like a small child's. He stroked her arm gently as he lay beside her, smoking a cigarette, and then he looked down into her face, but he wasn't smiling. Nor was he sleepy. He loved Jessica more than ever, but there were too many other things crowding his mind.

He spent the rest of the night in a lonely vigil. Watching his wife, thinking his own thoughts, listening to her breathe and murmur, wondering what would come next.

The next morning he was going on trial for rape.

CHAPTER XV

The courtroom at City Hall was a far cry from the small room where the preliminary hearing had been held. This one looked like a courtroom in the movies. Gold leaf, wood panelling, long rows of chairs, the judge's bench set up high on a platform, and the American flag in plain view of all. The room was full of people, and a woman was calling names one by one. She stopped when she had twelve. They were selecting the jury.

Ian sat with Martin at the front of the room, at the desk assigned to the defence. A few feet away sat a different assistant district attorney, with Inspector Houghton at his side. Margaret Burton was nowhere in sight.

The twelve jurors took their seats, and the judge explained the nature of the trial. A few of the women looked surprised and cast glances at Ian, and one man shook his head. Martin made rapid notes and watched the prospective jurors closely. He had the right to excuse ten people from the jury, and the assistant D.A. could do the same. The faces looked innocuous, like those of people you'd see on a bus.

Martin had told Ian and Jessie earlier that morning about the nature of the jury he wanted. No 'old maids' who would be shocked at the accusation of rape, or who might identify with the victim; yet perhaps they might try to hang on to some staunch middle-class housewives who might condemn Burton for allowing Ian to pick her up. Young people might be in sympathy with Ian, yet they might resent the way the couple looked, too comfortable for their age. They were walking a delicate line.

Jessie watched the twelve men and women from her seat in the front row, searching their faces and that of the judge. But just as Martin stood up to question the first prospective juror, the judge called a recess for lunch.

It was a slow process; it was the end of the second day

before the jury had been picked. They had been interrogated by both attorneys as to their feelings about rape, had been questioned about their jobs and their mates, their habits and the number of children they had. Martin had explained that fathers of women Miss Burton's age would not be a good idea either; they'd feel too protective of the victim. One had to consider so many things, and some base was inevitably left uncovered. There were a couple of people on the jury even now who did not meet with Martin's full approval, but he had used up his challenges, and now they had to hope for the best. Martin had set up an easy bantering style with the jurors, and now and then someone had laughed at a foolish answer or a joke.

Finally the jury was set. Five men, three retired and two young, and seven women, five in their middle years and comfortably married, two young and single. That had been a stroke of good fortune. They hoped it would counterbalance two of the retired men Martin did not like. But on the whole, he was reasonably satisfied, and Ian and Jessie assumed he was right.

As they all left the courtroom at the end of the second day, Jessie felt as though she could have recited the jurors' life stories in her sleep, listed their occupations and those of their mates. She would have known their faces in a crowd of thousands, and would remember them for a lifetime if she never saw them again after that day.

Their first shock came on the third day. The quiet male assistant district attorney who had replaced the irritating female D.A. of the preliminary hearing did not appear in court. He had developed acute appendicitis during the night, it was reported to the court, and had been operated on early that morning for a perforated appendix. He was resting comfortably at Mt. Zion Hospital, which Jessica found to be small consolation. This news was reported to the judge by one of the sick man's colleagues, who happened to be trying a case in the adjoining courtroom. But His Honour was assured that a replacement had been chosen and would arrive at any moment. Jessie's and Ian's hearts sank. The woman from the preliminary hearing would be back on the case. It had seemed immeasurable good luck when she hadn't appeared at the opening of the trial, and now . . .

Martin bent to whisper something in Ian's ear as the judge called a short recess while they waited for the new assistant D.A. to arrive. Everyone stood up, the judge left the courtroom, and there was a stretching and shuffling toward the halls. It was still early, and even a cup of coffee from one of the machines in the hall would taste good. It was something to do. Jessica could feel depression weighing on her shoulders as she held her small Styrofoam cup of steaming, malevolent-looking coffee. All she could think of was that damned D.A. and how badly her presence might hurt their case. She glanced at Ian, but he said nothing. And Martin had vanished somewhere.

He had told them not to discuss the case in the hall during recesses or lunch, and suddenly it was difficult to find banalities with which to break the silence. So they kept silent, standing close together with the look of refugees waiting for a train to arrive, but not really understanding what was happening to them.

'More coffee?'

'Hm?' Her thoughts had been in limbo.

'Coffee. Do you want more coffee?' Ian tried it again. But she only shook her head with a vague attempt at a smile. 'Don't worry so much, Jess. It'll be okay.'

'I know.' Words. All words. With no meaning behind them. Nothing had any meaning anymore. Everything was confusing, impossible to understand. What were they doing there? Why were they standing around like awkward mourners at a funeral? Jessica crushed out a cigarette on the marble floor and looked up at the ceiling. It was ornate and beautiful and she hated it. It was too fancy. Too elaborate. It reminded her of where she was. City Hall. The trial. She lit another cigarette.

'You just put one out, Jess.' His voice was soft and sad. He knew what was happening too.

'Huh?' She squinted at him through the flame from her lighter.

'Nothing. Shall we go back?'

'Sure. Why not?' She tried a flip smile as she tossed the empty Styrofoam cup into a large metal ashtray filled with sand.

They walked back into the courtroom side by side, but not touching. Ian walked slowly toward the desk that set him and Martin apart from everyone else. And Jessica followed him with her eyes, watching him, watching Martin rapidly scratch out notes on a long yellow legal pad. The perfect lawyer, the image caught in a pool of sunlight splashed bravely across the inlaid marble floor. She stared at the light for a minute, thinking of nothing, only wishing herself somewhere else, and then absentmindedly she looked across at the desk reserved for the assistant D.A.

There she sat. Matilda Howard-Spencer, tall, lean; everything about her seemed sharp. She had a narrow head with blunt-cut short blonde hair, and long thin agile hands that seemed ready to point accusing fingers. She wore a sober grey suit and a pale grey silk shirt, and her eyes almost matched her suit. Slate grey, and just as hard. Long, skinny legs, and the only piece of jewellery she wore was a thin gold band. She was married to Judge Spencer, whose name she had incorporated into hers, and she was the holy terror of the D.A.'s office. Her best cases were rapes. Neither Ian nor Jessie knew any of that, but Martin did, and he had wanted to cry as he'd watched her walk into the courtroom. She had the delicacy and charm of a hatchet delivered bull's-eye to the balls. He had tried another case against her once, and he hadn't won. Nobody had. His client had committed suicide nine days into the trial. He probably would have anyway, but still . . . Matilda, darling Matilda. And all Ian and Jessie knew was what they saw and what they felt.

Ian saw a woman who made him nervous as she seemed to stalk within an invisible cage around her desk. Jessie saw a woman carved in ice, and sensed something that filled her with fear. Now it wasn't a game. It was a full-scale war. Just the way the woman looked at Ian told her that. She glared across at him once, and then through him several times, as though he were not a person to acknowledge, and considerably less than a man. She spoke to Houghton in a rapid flow of words, and he nodded several times, then got up and walked away. It was very clear who was in command. Jessica cursed the man with the appendix. This woman was one piece of luck they didn't need.

'All rise . . .' The judge was back in his seat, and tension filled the air. He showed obvious pleasure at the new addition to the scene, and acknowledged her presence with a respectful greeting. Terrific.

Matilda Howard-Spencer made a few quick, friendly remarks to the jury, all of which they seemed to respond to. She could inspire confidence as well as fear. Her voice and manner exuded authority, and belied her age: she must be no older than forty-two or -three. She was someone you could count on, someone who would take care of business, take care of you, see that things worked. This was a woman who could fight a war, lead an army, and still manage to see that the children took Latin as well as algebra. But she had no children. She had been married for less than two years. The law was her lover. Her husband was only her friend, and he was a man well into his sixties.

The sparring began with one of the least interesting of witnesses. The medical examiner took the stand and said nothing damaging to Ian, nothing helpful to Margaret Burton. He testified only that he had examined her, that there had been intercourse, but that nothing more than that could be ascertained. Despite Matilda Howard-Spencer's best urging, he stuck to his assertion that there was no evidence that force had been used. Martin's objections to her near-badgering were rapidly quelled, but the testimony was too colourless to make much difference. It all seemed very boring to Jessica, and after an hour she settled her attention on the middle red nylon stripe in the flag. It was something to stare at as she tried to float away from where she was . . . those words droning on endlessly . . . 'infamous crime against nature' . . . sodomy . . . rape . . . intercourse . . . rectum . . . vagina . . .

sperm . . . it was like a child's guide to fantasy. All those terrible words you looked up in the dictionary when you were fourteen, and were titillated by. Now she had a chance to try each one on for size. Vagina. The prosecutor seemed fond of that one. And rape. She said it with a capital letter 'R'.

The day ended at last, and they went home as silently as they had throughout the week. It was exhausting just being there, keeping up the front for those watchers in the jury box, for anyone who might be paying attention. If you frowned, the jury might think you were mad—mad at Ian—or upset. Upset? No, darling, of course not! If you smiled, it meant you took the proceedings too lightly. If you wore the wrong thing, you looked rich. Something too cheerful, and you looked flip. Sexy in court? At a rape trial? God forbid. Vagina? Where? No, of course I don't have one. It wasn't even frightening anymore, just exhausting. And that damned woman was relentless, squeezing every last thought and word out of the witnesses. And Martin was such a fucking gentleman. But what did it matter anymore? If they could just stay awake and keep turning up in court, soon it would be over. Soon . . . but it seemed as though it had just begun. There were lifetimes to go. They hardly said a word over dinner that night, and Jessica was fast asleep in her bathrobe before Ian came out of the shower. It was just as well; he was too tired to say anything. And what was there to say?

She stretched sleepily in the car the next morning and smiled tiredly at the early morning light on the buildings.

'What are you smiling at, Jess?'

'A crazy thought. I was just thinking that this is like when we used to go to work together in New York.' She looked thoughtful, but he didn't smile.

'Not exactly.'

'No. Do we have time to stop for a quick cup of coffee on the way?' They hadn't had time for breakfast, and it was already late.

'We'd better just settle for coffee out of the machine up there, Jess. I don't want to be late. They can hold me in contempt for that, and pull my bail.' Jesus. And all for a cup of coffee.

'Okay, love.' She touched his shoulder gently and lit a fresh cigarette. The only place she didn't smoke now was in court.

She slipped her hand inside his arm as they walked up the steps of City Hall, and everything seemed bright and shiny and new. It was that kind of morning, no matter what horrors were happening to their life. It almost seemed as though God didn't know. He went right on with the sunlight and pretty days.

They reached the hall outside the courtroom with three minutes to spare, and Jessica hurried for the coffee machine.

'Want some?' He started to answer no, but then nodded yes. How much worse could his heartburn get, and what did it matter? He took the cup from her hand; it was so shaky she almost spilled the coffee.

'Baby, it's going to take a year to put us back together after this.'

'You mean my adorable quivers?' He smiled back into her face.

'Have you seen mine?' He held out a hand and they both laughed.

'Occupational hazard, I guess.'

'For a rapist?' She had tried to sound flip, but he didn't.

'Okay, Ian, knock it off.' It ended the brief conversation between them, and Jessica noticed a flurry of activity near an unmarked door. There were people coming and going. Four men, a woman, the sound of voices, as though someone of importance were arriving.

The activity caught Jessie's attention, but it was Ian who looked strange, his head cocked to one side, listening intently. She wanted to ask him what was happening, but she wasn't sure she should. He seemed so totally absorbed by the sounds and the voices. Then there was the quick slam of a door, and a woman in a plain white wool dress rounded the corner. Jessica gasped. It was Margaret Burton.

Ian's mouth opened and then closed, but none of them

moved. Jessica stood, transfixed, feeling shaken and cold, her eyes driving into Margaret Burton, who had come to a rapid halt, taken one short step backward, and then stopped with an expression of astonishment on her face as the three of them stood there. It seemed as though the entire building had fallen silent, and they were the only three people left in the world. Nothing moved . . . except Margaret Burton's face. Slowly, ever so slowly, like a wax mask melting in the sun, her face moulded into an incredible smile. It was a rictus of victory, for only Ian to see. Jessica watched her, horrified, and then, as though her body moved of its own accord, she lurched wildly forward and swung at the Burton woman with the handbag held clenched in her hand.

'Why? Why, dammit, why?' It was a piercing wail of pain from Jessica's heart. The woman fell back a step, looking startled, as though waked from a dream, while at the same moment Ian leaped forward to grab Jessie. Something terrible could have happened. She had murder in her eyes. And that cry of 'Why?' was echoed again and again through the halls as Margaret Burton fled, her heels tapping a haunting staccato in the marble corridor as Jessie sobbed in Ian's arms.

A fleet of men rapidly came running, then turned away as they saw only Ian and Jessie standing there. There was no brawl to dispel, nothing more than a husband and wife fighting, and a wife having herself a good cry. But Martin had heard the sounds too, and for some reason, as he had been about to enter the court, something had told him to follow the sounds. And then seeing Margaret Burton hurry into a door near the court, he knew that something had happened. He found Jessie trembling on a bench, with Ian trying to soothe her.

'Is she all right?'

Ian looked grim in response and didn't answer.

'What happened?'

'Nothing. She . . . we just . . . had an unexpected encounter with the illustrious Miss Burton.'

'Did she do anything to Jessie?' Martin prayed that she had. It would be the best thing that had happened to their case.

'She smiled.' Jessie stopped sobbing long enough to explain.

'She smiled?' Martin was puzzled.

'Yes. Like someone who has just killed someone else, and is glad.'

'Now, Jess . . .' Ian tried to pacify her, but he knew she was right. That was exactly how Margaret Burton had looked, but they were the only ones who had seen it.

'You know damn well that's what she looked like.' She tried to explain it to Martin, but he made no comment.

'Are you all right now?' She nodded slowly and took a deep breath.

'I'm okay.'

'Good. Because we should get into court. We don't want to be late.'

Jessica rose unsteadily, with both men watching her worriedly. She took another deep breath and closed her eyes. What a hideous morning.

'Jessie . . .'

'No. Now just let me alone, and I'll be fine.' She had known what Ian was going to say. He wanted her to go home.

As they walked into court, she felt a few heads turn, and wondered who had heard her shrieks as the Burton woman had fled down the hall. It rapidly became clear who had. They were less than three feet into the courtroom before Inspector Houghton was standing belligerently in front of them, with an angry look on his face that was directed at Jessie.

'If you ever do that again, I'll have you arrested, and his bail pulled so fast both your heads will swim.' Ian looked agonised and Jessica gaped as Martin stepped in front of them.

'Do what, exactly, Inspector?'

'Threaten Miss Burton.'

'Jessica, did you threaten Miss Burton?' Martin looked at her as a father would, asking his five-year-old if she had poured Mommy's perfume down the toilet.

'No. I . . . I screamed . . .'

'What did you scream?'

'I don't know.'

'She said "why?" That's all she said,' Ian filled in for her.

'That doesn't sound like a threat to me, Inspector. Does it to you? As a matter of fact, I heard Mrs. Clarke shouting that word all the way down the hall, which was what drew me to the scene.'

'I consider that a threat.' I consider you an asshole. Jessie was dying to say it.

'Where I come from, Inspector, "why" is a question, not a threat. Unless our asking that kind of question threatens you.' And then, without another word, Houghton turned on his heel and returned to the chair next to Matilda Howard-Spencer. But he was looking none too pleased, and neither was Ian. Jessie could feel him shaking next to her.

'I'm going to kill that sonofabitch before this is over.' But the look on Martin's face stopped both of them. It was terrifying.

'No, dammit, you're going to sit here and look like Mr. and Mrs. America if it kills *you*. And right now. Is that clear? Both of you? Jessica, that means you too. Smile, beautiful, smile. Bullshit. Better than that. And take her arm, Ian. Jesus, all we need is for the jury to think there's trouble. There isn't. Yet. Just remember that.' And with that, he walked toward the desk at the front of the room with a look of solemnity but not of concern. He smiled in the direction of the prosecutor, and took in the room with a benevolent air. Jessie and Ian didn't do quite as well, though they tried. And they still had the Burton woman's testimony to live through. But remarkably, after that demonic smile, hearing her talk wasn't as bad as they had feared.

She told the now-familiar tale as she sat primly on the witness stand. The white dress looked terribly pure, overwhelmingly ladylike. She sat so demurely that her legs might have been soldered together just before she'd come into court, and Jessica noticed that her hair was now tinted more brown than red. If she was wearing makeup, you couldn't see it, and if she had a bosom, she had done remarkable things to make it disappear. She seemed to have no figure at all.

'Ms. Burton, would you care to tell us what happened?' The assistant district attorney was wearing an extremely sombre black dress, a perfect contrast to the witness's white one. It was like something out of a 'B' movie.

The recitation that followed sounded very familiar indeed. At the end of her client's story, the prosecutor asked, 'Had anything like this ever happened to you before?'

The witness hung her head and barely seemed able to whisper. 'No.' It was a gentle sound, like a leaf falling to earth, and Jessie felt her nails dig into her palms. It was the first time in her life she had ever hated anyone that much. And sitting there, watching her, having to listen to her, made her want to kill the woman.

'How did you feel after he left you there in that sleazy hotel?' Oh, Jesus.

'Like I wanted to kill myself. I thought about it for a while. That was why it took me so long to call the police.' What a performance! It almost required a standing ovation and a chorus of bravos. But it was far from amusing. Jessie knew Margaret Burton was winning over the jury with her demure little airs.

What could Martin do now? If he tore her to shreds, the jury would hate him. Cross-examining her was going to be like roller skating through a mine field.

After more than an hour of testimony, Matilda Howard-Spencer had finished her questioning, and it was Martin's turn to begin. Jessica felt her stomach rise and then rapidly fall. She wanted to hold on to Ian. She couldn't stand it anymore. But she had to. And she wondered what he was feeling as he sat isolated from the world. The accused. The rapist. Jessica shuddered.

'Ms. Burton, why did you smile at Mr. Clarke this morning outside the court?' Martin's first question shocked everyone in the courtroom, even Jessie. The jury looked stunned, while Houghton smoulded and whispered something to the prosecutor.

'Smile? . . . I . . . why . . . I didn't . . . I didn't smile at him!' She was blushing and looked absolutely furious, nothing like the virgin of a moment before.

'Then what did you do?'

'I . . . nothing, dammit . . . I . . . I mean . . . oh, I don't know what I did . . .' Here came the virgin again, and helplessness to boot. 'I was just so shocked to see him there, and his wife called me a name. She . . .'

'Did she? What did she call you?' Martin looked vastly amused, and Jessie wondered if he really was. It was hard to tell with him; she was learning that more each day. 'Go on, Miss Burton, don't be shy. Tell us what she called you. But do remember that you are under oath.' He smiled at her and assumed an attitude of waiting.

'I don't remember what she called me.'

'You don't? Well, if it was such a traumatic encounter, wouldn't you remember what she'd called you?'

'Objection, Your Honour!' Matilda Howard-Spencer was on her feet and looking annoyed. Very.

'Sustained.'

'All right. But just one minor point . . . isn't it true that you leered at Mr. Clarke, almost as though . . .'

'*Objection!*' The D.A.'s voice could have shattered concrete, as Martin smiled angelically. He had got his point across.

'Sustained.'

'Sorry, Your Honour.' But it was a good beginning. And the rest of the story droned on after that. How she had been debased, abused, used, humiliated, violated. The words were getting to be almost laughable. 'What exactly did you expect from Mr. Clarke?'

'What do you mean?' The witness looked haughty, but confused.

'Well, did you think he'd propose marriage in that hotel room, or whip an engagement ring out of his pocket, or . . . well, what did you expect?'

'I don't know. I . . . he . . . I thought he just wanted to have a drink. He was a little drunk anyway.'

'Did you find him attractive?'

'Of course not.'

'Then why did you want to have a drink with him?'

'Because . . . oh, I don't know. Because I thought he was a gentleman.' She looked delighted with her response, as though that said it all.

'Aha. That was it, eh? A gentleman. Would a gentleman take you to a hotel on Market Street?'

'No.'

'Did Mr. Clarke take you to a hotel on Market Street . . . or did you take him?' She flushed furiously, and then hid her face in her hands, muttering something no one could hear, until the judge admonished her to speak up.

'I didn't take him anywhere.'

'But you went with him. Even though you did not find him attractive. Did you particularly want to have that drink with him?'

'No.'

'Then what did you want to do?' Ouch. The question almost made Jessie smile. Beautiful.

'I wanted . . . I wanted . . . to be friends.'

'Friends?' Martin looked even more amused. She was making a fool of herself.

'Not, not friends. Oh, I don't know. I wanted to go back to work.'

'Then why would you agree to go and have a drink with him?'

'I don't know.'

'Were you horny?'

'Objection!'

'Rephrase your question, Mr. Schwartz.'

'How long had it been since you'd had intercourse, Miss Burton?'

'Do I have to answer that, Your Honour?' She looked pleadingly at the judge, but he nodded assent.

'Yes. You do.'

'I don't know.'

'Give us an idea.' Martin was insistent.

'I don't know.' Her voice was shrinking.

'Roughly. A long time? Not so long? A month . . . two months . . . a week? A few days?'

'No.'

'No? What do you mean by no?' Martin was beginning to look annoyed.

'I mean no, not a few days.'

'Then how long? Answer the question.'

'A while.' The judge glared at her, and Martin started moving closer. 'All right, a long time,' she said finally. 'Maybe a year.'

'Maybe longer?'

'Maybe.'

'Was it with anyone special the last time?'

'I . . . I don't remember . . . I . . . yes!' She almost shouted the last word.

'Someone who hurt you in some way, Miss Burton? Someone who didn't love you as much as he should have, someone who . . .' His voice was so soft it would have lulled a baby to sleep, and then the assistant district attorney jumped to her feet and broke the spell.

'Objection!'

It took two more hours to finish Martin's questioning, and Jessica felt as though she were going to melt into a small invisible blur by the time it was over. She couldn't even begin to imagine what Margaret Burton felt like as she was led, crying, from the stand. She was assisted by Inspector Houghton while Matilda Howard-Spencer rearranged her papers. Jessica had the impression that the austere prosecutor was interested in the case, not the victim.

The judge called a recess and dismissed them until Monday. For a moment they all stood numbly in the courtroom; it was only lunchtime, but Jessie wanted to climb into bed and sleep for a year. She had never been so tired in her life. Spent. And Ian looked five years older than he had that morning.

When they emerged from the courtroom with Martin behind them, Margaret Burton was nowhere to be seen. She had been escorted out through the judge's chambers, and Martin guessed that she would be taken out some more discreet exit, to avoid another encounter like the one that morning. He had a feeling that Houghton didn't quite trust the woman either, and didn't want any more trouble than he already had.

As they walked out into the sunshine, Jessie felt as though she hadn't seen it for years. Friday. It was Friday. The end of an interminable week, and now two whole days to themselves. Two and a half days. And all she wanted was to go home and forget this rococo hell-hole where their lives seemed to be coming to an end at the hands of a mad-woman. It was like a Greek play, really . . . the jury could play the chorus.

'What are you thinking?' Ian was still worried about her after the morning's outburst. Now more than ever. The testimony had been grim.

'I don't know. I'm not sure I can think anymore. I was just drifting.'

'Well, let's drift on home. Shall we?' He guided her quietly toward the car, and opened the door for her, and she felt two hundred years old as she slid onto the seat of the Volvo. But it was familiar, it was home. She needed that right now more than anything. She wanted to scrub the whole morning out of her soul.

'What do you think, love?' She looked at him through a haze of cigarette smoke as he drove slowly home.

'What do you mean?' He tried to evade her question.

'I mean, how do you think it's going? Did Martin say anything?'

'Not much. He plays it pretty close to the vest.'

She nodded again. He hadn't said much as they'd left except that he wanted to see them in his office on Saturday. 'But I guess everything's going okay.' Sure it was. It had to be.

'It looks okay to me too.' Okay? Christ, it looked horrible. But it was supposed to. Wasn't it?

'I like Martin's style.'

'So do I.'

They both still thought they would win, but now they were beginning to realize the price they'd have to pay. Not in money, not in cars, but in flesh, guts, and souls.

CHAPTER XVI

On Saturday morning, Ian went down to Martin's office to discuss his testimony on the stand the following week. Jessica stayed home with a migraine. As a favour, Martin came to see her at the house that evening, to discuss her own testimony.

And on Sunday afternoon, Astrid called, as the pair sat zombielike in chairs, watching old movies on television.

'Hello, children. How about a spaghetti dinner at my place tonight?' For once Jessie was short with her friend.

'I'm sorry, Astrid, we just can't.'

'Oh, you two. Busy, busy, busy. I've tried to reach you all week, and you haven't been in the shop.' Shit.

'I know. I had some work to do here, and I'm helping Ian . . . edit his book.'

'That sounds like fun.'

'Yeah. Sort of.' But her voice didn't carry the lie well. 'I'll give you a call sometime next week. But thanks for the invitation.' They blew kisses and hung up, and Jessica marvelled at the fact that no one knew what was happening. It seemed remarkable that the newspapers hadn't picked it up, but she had finally realized that what was happening to them was in no way extraordinary. There were a dozen cases like it every day. It was new to them, but not to the news business. And there were far juicier cases than theirs to pick from—except, of course, for the Pacific Heights angle, and Jessie's exclusive boutique. It would destroy her business if it came out. But there didn't seem to be any danger of that. No members of the press had appeared thus far, and there had been no interest shown at all. It was something to be grateful for. And she was. And Martin had promised that if some stray reporter did happen through, he'd call the paper and ask for their discretion. He felt sure that they'd co-operate with him. They had before.

Jessie felt bad about having cut Astrid short. They hadn't

seen her in a while, and they hadn't seen their other friends in two months now. It would have been hard to face anyone. It was getting harder even to face Astrid. And it would have been impossible to confront the girls in the shop this week. Jessie had no intention of going near the place. She was afraid they'd read too much in her face. For the same reasons, Ian had been staying away from everyone he knew since the arrest. And he was content to lose himself in his book. The characters he'd invented kept him company.

And meanwhile, the bills continued to mount. Zina dropped off Jessie's mail every day during the trial, and most of it was bills, including Harvey Green's second bill, for another nine hundred dollars. And once again for nothing. It had been 'in case' money—in case Margaret Burton had done something she shouldn't have, in case something had turned up, in case . . . but nothing had. He had managed to come up with absolutely nothing. Until Sunday night, right after Jessie talked to Astrid.

The phone rang, and it was Martin. He and Green wanted to come right over. She woke Ian, and they were waiting, tensely, when the two men arrived. They were dying to know what Green had found out.

What he had was a photograph. Of Margaret Burton's husband from the rapidly annulled marriage of almost twenty years before. The photograph could have been of Ian. The man in the picture was tall, blond, blue-eyed with laughter in his face. He was standing next to an MG; it was of a much earlier vintage than the Morgan, but there was still a great deal of resemblance between the cars as well as the men. If you squinted, even a little, it looked like Ian and the Morgan. The man's hair was shorter than Ian's, his face was a little longer, the car was black instead of red . . . the details were off, but not by much. It was a shock just looking at the photograph. It told the entire story. Now they knew the why. And Martin's first suspicion had been right. It must have been revenge.

The four of them sat in the living room in total silence. Green had got the photograph from a cousin of Miss Burton's, a last-minute lead he'd decided to follow, just on a hunch. A damn good hunch, as it had turned out.

Schwartz heaved a sigh of what sounded like relief and leaned back in his chair. 'Well, now we know. The cousin will testify?' But Green shook his head.

'Says she'll take the Fifth, or lie. She doesn't want to get involved. She said that Burton would kill her. You know, this woman, the cousin I mean, almost sounds as though she's afraid of the Burton woman. Said she's the most vindictive person she's ever known. You gonna subpoena her?'

'Not if she's going to take the Fifth on us. Did she tell you why the Burton woman annulled the marriage?' Martin was pensively chewing on a pencil as he asked the questions, while Ian and Jessica listened silently. Ian still held the photograph in his hand, and it made him exceedingly nervous. The likeness was startling.

'Peggy Burton didn't annul the marriage. The husband did.'

Martin raised his eyebrows quickly. 'Oh?'

'The cousin thinks Margaret was pregnant—just a guess,' Green went on. 'She had just graduated from high school and was working in this guy's father's office, a law firm. Hillman and Knowles, no less.' Ian looked up and Martin whistled. 'She married Knowles's son. A kid named Jed Knowles. He was only in law school at the time, and was spending the summer working in his father's office. He's the kid in the picture.' Green waved vaguely at the snapshot still resting in Ian's hand.

'Anyway, they got married in a big hurry, but very quietly, at the end of the summer. And the father made a real stink that nothing be made public, no announcement of the marriage, no nothing. The Burton girl's parents were both living in the Midwest, so she didn't have any family out here except the cousin, who isn't even sure if they ever lived together. They just got married, and the next thing she remembers is that Margaret was in the hospital for a couple of weeks. She thinks she might have had a complicated abortion, miscarriage, something. Knowles had the marriage annulled right after that, and Margaret was out of a husband, out of a job, and maybe out of a baby. She had kind of a nervous breakdown, it sounds like, and spent three months in a Catholic retreat house. I went back to check out the retreat house, but it was torn down twelve years ago, and the sisters of that order are now located in Kansas, Montreal, Boston, and Dublin. Not very likely we'd find any records on it, and if we did they'd be privileged anyway.'

'What about the Knowles boy? Did you check him out?'

'Yeah.' Green didn't look pleased. 'He married some debutante, with a big splash and a lot of noise, at the Thanksgiving of that year. Parties, showers, announcements in all the papers. The clippings at the *Chronicle* said that they'd been engaged for over a year, which was obviously why Papa Knowles didn't want any publicity when sonny boy married the Burton girl.'

'Did you talk to Knowles?'

Green nodded unhappily. 'He and his bride crashed in a two-engine plane seventeen months later. The father died of a heart attack this summer, and his mother is travelling in Europe, no one seems to know where.'

'Terrific.' Martin scowled and started to gnaw on his pencil again. 'Any brothers and sisters? Friends who might know what happened? Anyone?'

'Its a dead end, Martin. No brothers and sisters. And who'd remember now, among his friends? Jed Knowles has been dead for eighteen years. That's a hell of a long time.'

'Yeah. A long time to carry a grudge. Shit. We have it all wrapped up, and we don't have a fucking goddam thing. Nothing.'

'What do you mean, nothing?' It was the first time Ian had spoken since seeing the photograph. He had been listening closely to the other men's exchange. 'It sounds like we've got everything.'

'Yes.' Martin rubbed his eyes slowly with one hand and then opened them again. 'And nothing we can use in court. It's all guesswork. That's all it is. What we have here is undoubtedly the truth, and the full psychological explanation of why Margaret Burton has accused you of rape. You look just like some rich man's son who got her pregnant, married her, probably made her have an abortion, and then ditched her and married his high society girlfriend a few weeks later. Miss Burton met the handsome prince and then he shat on her. Back to Cinderella again. And she's been out to get him for twenty years. Which is probably why she hasn't tried to hit you two for money. She doesn't want money. She wants revenge. She probably got a little money out of it the first time. Money is too easy for some people.' Jessica rolled her eyes at the remark and Ian gestured to her to keep still.

'The point is, she'd rather see you go to prison than hit you for bucks. In her mind, you're just another Jed Knowles, and you're going to take it for him. You look like him to a frightening degree, your car looks like his, you probably even sound like him, for all we know. And she probably spotted you at Enrico's months ago. You're a regular. She may well have set you up from beginning to end. But the problem is, that we can't prove that in court.' He turned back to Green. 'You're sure the cousin won't testify willingly?'

'Positive.' Green was curt and emphatic. Martin shook his head.

'Wonderful. And that, Ian, is why we can't prove a goddam thing in court. Because a hostile witness who takes the Fifth Amendment would ruin you faster than never having her on the stand at all. And besides, even if she took the stand, we couldn't prove any of this. All we could prove is that Burton married Knowles, and shortly thereafter Knowles had the marriage annulled. The rest is pure conjecture, hearsay, guesswork. That doesn't hold up in court, Ian, not without solid proof. The prosecution would have the whole theory thrown out of court in ten minutes. You and I now know what probably happened, but we could never prove that to the jury, not without someone to testify that she was pregnant when Knowles married her, that she did have an abortion, that she did have a nervous breakdown, that someone heard her swear to take revenge. And how're you going to prove all that, even if the cousin did take the stand? What we have here, I'm afraid, is the truth, and no way to prove it.'

Jessica felt tears burning her eyes as she listened, and

Ian was paler than she'd ever seen him. He looked almost grey.

'So what do we do now?'

'We give it a try, and we pray. I'll call Burton for redirect and see how much she'll admit to. And how much they'll let us get away with. But it won't be much, Ian. Don't count on anything.'

Green left a few moments later with a quiet handshake in the hall for Martin, and a shake of the head: 'I'm sorry.' Martin nodded, and left a few moments later.

The trial continued on Monday, and Martin recalled Margaret Burton to the stand. Had she been married to Jed Knowles? Yes. For how long? Two and a half months. Ten weeks? Yes, Ten weeks. Was it true that she had to marry him because she was pregnant? Absolutely not. Did she have a nervous breakdown . . . objection! . . . over-ruled! . . . did she have a nervous breakdown after the marriage was annulled? No. Never. Didn't the defendant bear a striking resemblance to Mr. Knowles? No. Not that she had noticed. Had Mr. Knowles remarried almost immediately after . . . objection! Sustained, with an admonition to the jury to disregard the previous line of questioning. The judge warned Martin about asking irrelevant questions and badgering the witness, and Jessica noticed that Margaret Burton was silent and pale but totally poised. Almost too much so. She found herself praying that the woman would lose control, would disintegrate on the stand and scream and shriek and destroy herself by admitting that she had wanted to destroy Ian because he looked like Jed Knowles. But Margaret Burton did none of those things. She was excused from the stand. And Jessica never saw her again.

Late that afternoon Martin asked Ian to drum up two friends to attest to his character and morals. Like Jessie's testimony it was going to be considered biased, but character witnesses never hurt. Ian agreed to ask a couple of people, but there was a look of despair in his eyes that it killed Jessica to watch. As though Margaret Burton had already won. She had simply slipped away. Dropped her bomb and left, leaving them with a photograph as explanation.

Ian hated having to explain to anyone what was happening, and in recent years he had not been as close to his friends as he once had. His writing seemed to devour more and more of his time, his energy, his devotion. He wanted to finish another book, to sell it, to 'make it', before he went back to hanging around bars with old buddies; he needed to do something, be something, build something first. He was tired of explaining about rejections, and agents, and rewrites. So he stopped explaining. He stopped seeing them. And the rest of the time he spent with Jessie. She had a way of making herself an exclusive. She didn't like sharing the time he could spare from the studio.

That night, he called a writer he knew and a classmate from college, a stockbroker who had also moved to the West. They were stunned about the charges, sympathetic, and anxious to help. Neither of them was overly fond of Jessie, but they felt bad for both of them. The writer felt that Jessie wanted too much of Ian, that she was too clinging and didn't leave him enough space to write in. The college friend had always thought Jessie too headstrong. She wasn't their kind of woman.

But the two men made pleasant, clean-cut appearances on the stand. The writer, wearing tweeds, testified that he had recently won an award and published three stories in *The New Yorker* and a hardcover novel. He was respectable, as writers went. And he spoke well on the stand. The college friend made an equally pleasing impression in a different vein. Solid, upper-middle-class, respectable family man, 'known Ian for years,' hip hip, tut tut, rah rah. They both did what they could, which wasn't much.

On Tuesday afternoon the judge dismissed them all early, and Ian and Jessie came home to relax.

'How are you holding up, babe? I can't say either of us looks like much lately.' He smiled ruefully and opened the icebox. 'Want a beer?'

'Make it a case.' She kicked off her shoes and stretched. 'Jesus, I'm sick of that shit. It just goes on and on and on and . . . and I feel like I haven't sat down and talked to you for a year.' She took the beer from him and went to lie down on the couch. 'Besides which, I'm running out of polite clothes to wear.' She was wearing an ugly brown tweed suit that she had had since her college days in the East.

'Fuck it. Go in wearing a bikini tomorrow. By now the jury deserves something to look at.'

'You know, I thought the trial would be a lot more dramatic. It's funny that it isn't.'

'The case isn't all that dramatic. Her word against mine as to who screwed whom and why, where, and for what. By now, I don't even feel uncomfortable with you there, listening to the testimony.' Now that Margaret Burton was no longer in court.

'It doesn't bother me much either, except I want to laugh every time someone says "an infamous crime against nature". It seems so overdone.' They laughed easily for the first time in a long time. As they relaxed in the familiar charm of their living room, the trial seemed like a bad joke. Somebody else's bad joke.

'Want to go to a movie, Jessie?'

'You know something? I'd love to.' The tension was beginning to drain away. They had decided that they had it made, even without solid proof that Margaret Burton was a freak looking for revenge on a man who had been dead for almost twenty years. So what? Ian was innocent. In the end, it was as simple as that. 'Want to take Astrid with us, darling?'

'Sure. Why not?' He smiled and leaned over to kiss her. 'But don't call her for another half hour.' Jessie returned the smile and ran a finger slowly up his arm.

Astrid was delighted with the invitation and the three went to a movie that had them in tears, they all laughed so hard. It was just what Jessie and Ian needed.

'I was beginning to think I'd never see you two again. It's been weeks! What have you been up to? Still working on the book?' They nodded in unison, changed the subject, and went out for coffee.

It was a pleasant evening that did them all good. And Astrid felt better now that she had seen them. Ian looked haggard and Jessica looked tired, but they looked happy again. Maybe whatever problem had been bothering them had been worked out.

Astrid reported having been in the boutique almost every day, and the fashion show had been a smash. Katsuko had done a great job. Astrid had even bought four or five things from the show, which Jessie told her was silly.

'That's ridiculous. Don't buy anymore when I'm not there. I'll give you a discount when I'm in. Wholesale at least. And on some things I can sell to you at cost.'

'That's crazy, Jessica. Why should you sell things any cheaper to me? You might as well share the wealth!' She threw her arms wide in a flash of jewellery and the three of them laughed.

They drove her home in the Volvo, and when she asked about the Morgan, Jessica claimed that the engine had needed too much work. They all agreed that it was a shame.

'What a fabulous evening!' Jessica slid into bed with a smile, and Ian yawned, nodding happily. 'I'm glad we went out.'

'So am I.'

She rubbed his back for him and they chatted about nothing in particular; it was the kind of talk they had always shared late at night. Casual mentions of the movie, thoughts about Astrid, Jessie noticed a small bruise on his leg and asked him how he'd got it, he told her never to cut her hair. Night talk. As though nothing untoward had ever happened to them. For once they even got some sleep, which was remarkable since Ian was to take the stand the next day.

CHAPTER XVII

Ian's testimony under direct examination lasted two hours. The jury looked a little more interested than they had in the previous days, but not much. And it was only during the last half hour that they actually seemed to wake up. It was Matilda Howard-Spencer's turn to question him. She seemed to pace in front of Ian, as though thinking of something else, while all eyes in the courtroom stayed on her, particularly Ian's. And at last she stopped, directly in front of him, crossed her arms, and tilted her head to one side.

'You're from the East?' The question surprised him, as did the friendly look on her face.

'Yes. New York.'

'Where did you go to college?'

'Yale.'

'Good school.' She smiled at him, and he returned the smile. 'I tried to get into their law school, but I'm afraid I didn't quite make it.' She had gone to Stanford instead, but Ian couldn't know that, and was suddenly baffled as to whether he was supposed to offer sympathy, silence, or a smile. 'Did you do any graduate work?' She didn't call him Ian, and she didn't call him Mr. Clarke. She talked to him as though she knew him, or honestly wanted to. An interested dinner partner at a pleasant soirée.

'Yes. I got my master's.'

'Where did you do that?' She tilted her head again with an expression of interest. This was not at all the line of questioning Martin had prepared him for. This was lots easier to deal with.

'I went to Columbia. School of journalism.'

'And then?'

'I went into advertising.'

'With whom?' He named a big firm in New York.

'Well, we certainly all know who they are.' She smiled at him again, and looked pensively out the window.

'Did you go out with anybody special in college?' Aha, here it came, but she still sounded gently inquiring.

'A few people.'

'Like who?'

'Just girls.'

'From neighbouring schools? Who? How about some names?' This was ridiculous. Ian couldn't see the reason for it.

'Viveca Harreford. Maddie Whelan. Fifi Estabrook.' She wouldn't know them. Why ask?

'Estabrook? As in Estabrook and Lloyd? They're the biggest stockbrokers on Wall Street, aren't they?' She actually looked pleased for him, as though he had done something wonderful.

'I wouldn't know.' Her remark had made him uncomfortable. Of course they were the Estabrooks of Estabrook and Lloyd, but that wasn't why he'd gone out with Fifi, for Chrissake.

'And it seems to me that Maddie Whelan has kind of a familiar ring too. Something tells me she was somebody important. Let's see, Whelan . . . oh, I know, the department store in Phoenix, isn't it?' Ian was actually blushing, but Matilda Howard-Spencer was still smiling angelically, seeming to enjoy the social pleasantries.

'I can't remember.'

'Sure you can. Anyone else?'

'Not that I can recall.' This was a ridiculous line of questioning, and he couldn't see where she was going, except making him look like a fool. Was it really as simple as that?

'All right. When did you first meet your wife?'

'About eight years ago. In New York.'

'And she has a lot of money, doesn't she?' The prosecutor's tone was almost embarrassed, as if she'd asked an indiscreet question.

'Objection!' Martin was livid; he knew exactly where she was going, whether Ian did or not. But Ian was beginning to; he had been led right into her trap.

'Sustained. Rephrase the question.'

'Sorry, Your Honour. All right, then, I understand that your wife has a wonderfully successful boutique here in San Francisco. Did she have one in New York too?'

'No. When I met her, she was the fashion co-ordinator and stylist at the ad agency where I worked.'

'She did that for fun?' Now there was an edge to her tone.

'No. For money.' Ian was getting annoyed.

'But she didn't have to work, did she?'

'I never asked.'

'And she doesn't have to work now, does she?'

'I don't . . .' He looked to Martin for help, but there was none forthcoming.

'Answer the question. Does she have to work now, or is her income sufficient to support her, and you, in a very luxurious style?'

'Not luxurious, no.' Christ. Jessie and Martin cringed simultaneously. What an answer. But the questions were coming at him like gumballs from a machine, and there was no time to dodge them.

'But her income is adequate to support you both?'

'Yes.' He was very pale now. And very angry.

'Do you work?'

'Yes.' But he said it too softly, and she smiled.

'I'm sorry, I didn't hear your answer. Do you work?'

'Yes!'

'At a job?'

'No. At home. But it's work. I'm a writer.' Poor, poor Ian. Jessie wanted to run up and hold him. Why did he have to go through all that? The bitch.

'Do you sell much of what you write?'

'Enough.'

'Enough for what? Enough to support yourself on?'

'Not at the moment.' There was no hiding from her.

'Does that make you angry?' The question was almost a caress. The woman was a viper.

'No, it doesn't make me angry. It's just one of the facts of life, for the moment. Jessica understands.'

'But you do cheat on her. Does she understand that?'

'Objection!'

'Overruled!'

'Does she understand that?'

'I don't cheat on her.'

'Come, come. You yourself claim that you willingly went to bed with Ms. Burton. Is that a normal occurrence in your life?'

'No.'

'This was the first time?'

His eyes were glued to his knees. 'I can't remember.'

'You're under oath; answer the question.' Her voice slithered like a cobra threatening to strike.

'No.'

'What?'

'No. This was not the first time.'

'Do you cheat on your wife often?'

'No.'

'How often?'

'I don't know.'

'And what kind of woman do you use—your own kind, or other kinds, "lesser" women, lower-class women, whores, poor girls, whatever?'

'Objection!'

'Overruled!'

'I don't "use" anyone.'

'I see. Would you cheat on your wife with Fifi Estabrook, or is she a nice girl?'

'I haven't seen her in years. Ten, eleven years. I wasn't married when I went out with her.'

'I mean, would you cheat on your wife with someone *like* her, or do you just sleep with "cheap" women, women you aren't liable to run across in your own social circle? It could be embarrassing, after all. It might be a lot simpler just to keep your playing as far from home as possible.'

'I do.' Oh, God. No, Ian . . . no . . . Martin was staring at the wall, trying to let nothing show on his face, and Jessie had sensed that disaster was near.

'I see. You do sleep with "cheap" women, to keep it as far as possible from home? Did you consider Ms. Burton a "cheap" woman?'

'No.' But he had, and his 'no' was a weak one.

'She wasn't of your social set, though, was she?'

'I don't know.'

'Was she?' The words closed in on him now.

'No.'

'Did you think she'd call the police?'

'No.' And then as an afterthought, he looked up, panic-stricken, and added 'She had no reason to'. But it was too late. The damage was done.

She excused Ian from the stand with the proviso that she might want to recall him later. But she had all but killed him as it was.

Ian left the stand quietly and sat down heavily next to Martin. And five minutes later, the judge called a recess for lunch.

They left the courtroom slowly, with Ian shaking his head and looking sombre until the threesome reached the street.

'I really blew it.' Jessie had never seen him look worse.

'You couldn't help it. That's how she works. The woman is lethal.' Martin heaved a sigh and gave them a small, wintry smile. 'But the jury sees that too. And the jury's not all that lily pure either.' There was no point making Ian feel even worse, but Martin was worried. The cheating didn't bother him nearly as much as the class conflict. 'I'm going to put Jessica on the stand this afternoon. At least this way, it'll be over with.'

'Yeah, she can massacre us both on the same day.' Ian looked tired and beaten, and Jessica looked tense.

'Don't be an ass.'

'You consider yourself a match for her?' Ian looked sarcastic and bitter.

'Why not?'

'I'll tell you why not. Because if you pit yourself against her, Ian'll lose,' Martin was quick to interject. 'You have to be the gentlest, sweetest, calmest wife in the world. You come on like a hellion, and she'll break you in two right on the stand. We went over everything this weekend. You know what you have to do.' Jessica nodded sombrely, and

Ian sighed. Martin had gone over everything with him too, but that damn woman hadn't asked any of the right questions. And God only knew what she'd ask Jessie. 'All right?'

'All right.' Jessica smiled softly, and they dropped Martin off near City Hall. He had to go back to his office, and they had decided to go home to unwind. Jessica wanted a little time to take care of Ian. He needed it after the morning, and it kept her mind off what she'd have to say that afternoon.

When they got home, she made him lie down on the couch, took off his shoes, loosened his tie, and ran a soft hand through his hair. He lay there for a few minutes, just looking at her.

'Jess . . .' He didn't even know how to say it, but she knew.

'None of that. Just lie there and relax. I'll go make some lunch.' For once he didn't argue; he was too tired to do anything more than just lie there.

When she came back with a covered bowl of steaming soup and a plate piled high with sandwiches, he was asleep. He had the exhausted look of tragedy. The pale rumpled look one got when someone has died, when a child is terribly ill, when one's business has failed. Those times when schedules were disrupted, and one was suddenly at home, in seldom-worn clothes, looking terribly tired and afraid. She stood looking down at him for a moment and felt a wave of pity for him rush up inside her. Why did she feel so protective of him? Why did she feel as though he couldn't cope with it all, but she could? Why wasn't she angry? Why didn't she look like that now? She had when he was in jail, but he was here now, she could touch him and hold him and take care of him. The rest wasn't real. It was awful, but it wouldn't last. It would hurt, and it would rock him and humiliate him and do all sorts of grim things, but it wouldn't kill him. And it wouldn't take him away. As she sat quietly next to him and lifted his hand onto her lap, she knew that nothing would ever take him away from her. No Margaret Burton, no district attorney, no court, not even a jail. Margaret Burton would fade, Matilda Howard-Spencer would go on to some other case, as would Martin and the judge, and it would all be over. It was just a question of keeping themselves afloat until the storm passed. And she needed Ian too desperately to let anything, even her own feelings, jeopardize what they had. She wouldn't let herself get angry. She couldn't afford to.

There was the briefest flash of bitterness as she looked out over the bay and thought of her father. He wouldn't have done something like this, and he wouldn't have let her mother go through it, either. He'd have protected his wife more than Ian was protecting her. But that was her father. And this was Ian. Comparisons served no purpose now. She had Ian. It was as simple as that. She demanded a lot of him, so she had to give a lot too. She was willing. And right now it was her turn to give.

Looking down at him, as he slept there on her grey skirt, he looked like a very tired little boy. She smoothed his hair off his forehead and took a deep breath, thinking of that afternoon. It was her turn now. And she wasn't going to lose. She had decided that after the disastrous morning. The case was going to be won. And that was that. It was insane that it had gone this far. But it was not going much further. Jessie had had enough.

Ian woke shortly before two and looked up in surprise.

'Did I fall asleep?'

'No. I hit you on the head with my shoe and you fainted.'

He smiled at her and yawned into her skirt. 'You smell delicious. Did you know that every single item of clothing you own smells of your perfume?'

'Want some soup?' She was smiling at the compliment. He'd gotten them into one hell of a mess, but one thing was certain, and that was how much she loved him. Not just needed him, loved him. How could she be angry? How dare she ask for his left arm when fate had already taken his right? They had suffered enough. Now it was time to finish it.

'Christ, you look determined. What've you been up to?'

'I haven't been up to a thing. Do you want soup?' She

eyed him alluringly as she held a Limoges cup in one hand and her mother's best soup ladle in the other.

'My, so fancy.' He sat up and kissed her and looked at the tray. 'You know something, Jessica, you're the most remarkable woman I know. And the best.' She wanted to tease him and ask if she was better than Fifi Estabrook, but she didn't dare. She suspected that the wounds of the morning were still raw.

'For you, milord, nothing but the best.' She carefully poured the asparagus soup into the cup and added two neat little roast-beef sandwiches to the plate. There was a fresh salad too.

'You're the only woman I know who can make a sandwich lunch look like a dinner party.'

'I just love you.' She put her arms around his neck and nibbled his ear, and then stretched and stood up.

'Aren't you going to eat?'

'I already did.' She was lying, but she couldn't have eaten a thing before going on the stand in less than an hour. She looked at her watch and headed for the bedroom. 'I'll straighten out my face. We have to leave in ten minutes.' He waved happily from the midst of his lunch and she disappeared into the bedroom.

'Ready?' He walked into the bedroom five minutes later, tightening his tie and glancing at his ruffled hair in the mirror. 'Good lord, I look like I've been sleeping all day.'

'As a matter of fact, darling, you do.' And she was pleased. The brief hour of sleep had done him good. The time they'd spent at home had done them both good. Jessie felt stronger than she had in weeks. Margaret Burton wasn't going to touch them. How could she? Jessie had decided to ignore her, to rob her of her powers. And it was as though Ian sensed the rebirth in his wife.

'You know something? I feel better. I was really beat after this morning.' And he hated to think of what Jessie would have to go through that afternoon, but she seemed ready for it. 'You changed?'

'I thought this looked more appropriate.' It was a wonderfully ladylike dress, the kind she might wear to a tea. It was a soft grey silk with full feminine sleeves, and a belt of the same fabric. The whole line of the dress was gentle and easy, and without being fancy, it screamed 'class'. 'As long as they're going to bill us as being so upper-class, we might as well look decent. I'm so sick of those fucking tweed skirts, I'm going to burn them all on the front steps the day this is over.'

'You look gorgeous.'

'Too dressed up?'

'Perfect.'

'Good.' She slipped on quiet black kid pumps, clipped pearl earrings on her ears, picked up her bag, and headed for the closet to get out her black coat. Ian truly did think she looked gorgeous. He was so damn proud of her. Not just of how she looked, but of how she was taking this.

Martin was not quite as pleased, though, when they walked into the courtroom. He noticed Jessica's black coat and the glimpse of grey silk. It was just what he didn't want. Everything about her looked expensive. It was as though she had set out to prove everything Matilda Howard-Spencer had suggested. Jesus. Where were their heads? Crazy kids, they didn't realise what was happening. They had an unnerving assurance about them as they took their seats, as though they had arranged everything and there was nothing more to worry about. It was a bad time for them to make a show of strength, however subtle. And yet, maybe it was just as well that they felt a little more confident. They had both looked so beaten after the morning.

This new look of confidence underlined the bond between them. One was always aware of that, of them as a pair, not just Ian or Jessie, but both. It was frightening to think what would happen to them both if someone tried to sever that bond. If they lost.

Jessica looked remarkably calm as she walked up to the witness stand. The grey dress moved gracefully with her, the full sleeves gentling her impressive stature. She took the oath and looked at Ian for one tiny instant before turning her attention to Martin.

His questions built up a picture of a devoted couple

and of a wife who respected her husband too much to doubt that he was telling the truth. He was pleased with Jessica's quiet, dignified manner, and when he relinquished his witness to the prosecutor, he had to repress a smile. He would have liked to see these two women roll up their sleeves and stalk each other around the room. They were evenly matched. At least he hoped so.

With Jessica, Matilda Howard-Spencer was not going to waste time. 'Tell us, Mrs. Clarke, were you aware that your husband had cheated on you before this?'

'Indirectly.'

'What do you mean by that?' The attorney looked puzzled.

'I mean that I assumed that was a possibility, but that it was nothing serious.'

'I see. Just a little lighthearted fun?' She was back on that track again, but Jessie had seen it coming.

'No. Nothing like that. Ian isn't flip about anything. He's a sensitive man. But I travel quite a bit. And what happens, happens.'

'Does it happen to you as well?' Now the attorney's eyes were glittering again. Gotcha!

'No, it does not.'

'You're under oath, Mrs. Clarke.'

'I'm aware of that. The answer is no.'

She looked surprised. 'But you don't mind if your husband fools around?'

'Not necessarily. It depends on the circumstances.' Jessica looked every inch a lady, and Ian was incredibly proud of her.

'And these particular circumstances, Mrs. Clarke, how do you feel about them?'

'Confident.'

'Confident?' Jessica's interrogator looked taken aback, and Martin fidgeted. 'How can you be confident, and what about?'

'I'm confident that the truth about this matter will come out, and that my husband will be acquitted.' Martin watched the jury. They liked her. But they had to like Ian too. And more than that, they had to believe him.

'I admire your optimism. Are you footing the bill for the expense of this?'

'No, not really.' Ian almost cringed. She was lying under oath. 'My husband made a very wise investment after he sold his last book. He put the investment in my care, and we decided to sell it to cover the expense of the trial. So I can't say I'm footing the bill.' Bravo! The Morgan! And she was telling the truth! He wanted to jump up and hug her.

'Would you say that you have a good marriage?'

'Yes.'

'Very good?'

'Extremely good.' Jessica smiled.

'But your husband does sleep with other women?'

'Presumably.'

'Did he tell you about Margaret Burton?'

'No.'

'Did he tell you about any of his women?'

'No. And I don't think there were very many.'

'Did you encourage him to sleep around?'

'No.'

'But as long as they were little nobodies, you didn't care, is that it?'

'Objection!'

'Sustained. Leading the witness.'

'Sorry, Your Honour.' She turned back to Jessica. 'Has your husband ever been violent with you?'

'No.'

'Never?'

'No.'

'Does he drink a great deal?'

'No.'

'Does he have problems about his manhood, because you pay the bills?' What a question!

'No.'

'Do you love him very much?'

'Yes.'

'Do you protect him?'

'What do you mean?'

'I mean, do you shield him from unpleasantness?'

'Of course, I'd do anything I had to to shield him from unpleasantness. I'm his wife.'

Matilda Howard-Spencer's face settled into a satisfied smile. 'Including lie in court to protect him?'

'No!'

'The witness is excused.'

The assistant district attorney turned on her heel and went back to her seat as Jessica sat gaping on the witness stand. That damned woman had done it again.

CHAPTER XVIII

Everyone was back in their seats the next morning for the two attorney's summations to the jury. Ian and Jessica were pleased by Martin's comments and his style in addressing the jury, and they felt that he created a real wave of sympathy for the defence. Everything was in control. Then Matilda Howard-Spencer stood up, and the assistant district attorney was demonic. She painted a portrait of a wronged, distraught, heartbroken, brutally abused woman—hard-working, clean-living Peggy Burton. She also made a strong case that men like Ian Clarke shouldn't be allowed to dally where they wished, use whom they wanted, rape whom they chose, only to toss the women away and go home to the wives who supported them, who would 'do anything to protect them', as Jessie herself had said. Martin objected and was sustained. He explained later that it was rare to have to object to a closing argument, but that this woman breathed fire at the mere mention of Ian's name. And Jessie was still steaming when the court adjourned for lunch.

'Did you hear what that bitch said?' Her voice was loud and strident and Martin and Ian quelled her rapidly with a look.

'Keep your voice down, Jess,' Ian pleaded. It wouldn't pay to antagonize anyone now, least of all the jury, who were filtering past them on their way out to lunch. He had seen two of them look at Jess as she'd started to talk.

'I don't give a damn. That woman . . .'

'Shut up.' And then he put an arm around her and gave her a squeeze. 'Bigmouth. But I love you anyway.' She sighed loudly and then smiled.

'Damn, that aggravated me.'

'Okay, me too. Now let's forget about this crap for a while, and go get some lunch. Deal? No talk about the case?'

'Okay.' But she said it grudgingly as they walked down the hall.

'No "okay", I want a solemn promise. I refuse to have my lunch wrecked by this. Just make believe we're on the jury and can't discuss it.'

'You really think they stick to that?' He shrugged indifferently and pulled a lock of his wife's hair.

'I don't care what they do. Just tell me if I have that promise from you. No talking about the case. Right?'

'Right. I promise. You nag, you.'

'That's me. Your basic nagging husband.' He seemed very nervous as they ran down the stairs to the street, yet in surprisingly good spirits.

They went home for lunch and Jessie glanced at the mail while Ian rifled through *Publishers Weekly* and then went on to read the paper over the sandwiches she had made.

'You're terrific company today.' She was munching a turkey sandwich and flicked at the centre of his paper with a grin.

'Huh?'

'I said your fly is open.'

'What?' He looked down and then made a face. 'Oh, for Chrissake.'

'Well, talk to me, dammit, I'm lonely.'

'I read the paper for five minutes and you get lonely?'

'Yup. Want some wine with lunch?'

'No, I'll pass. Do we have any Cokes?'

'I'll go check.' She went to look, and he was reading

the paper again when she came back with the cold can of Coca-Cola. 'Now listen, you . . .'

'Shh . . .' He waved at her impatiently and went on reading. There was something about his face, about the look in his eyes as he read. He looked shocked.

'What is it?' He ignored her, finished the article, and finally looked up with an expression of defeat.

'Read that.' He pointed to the first four columns on page two, and Jessie's heart turned over as she read the headline: RAPE—IT'S TIME TO GET TOUGH. The article reported on a criminal justice committee meeting held the day before to discuss current punishment of rapists. There was talk in the article of stiffer sentences, no probation, suggestions for making it easier and less humiliating to report rape. It made anyone accused of rape sound as though he should be hanged without further ado. Jessie put down the paper and stared at Ian. It was bad luck to have that in the paper on the day the jury would be going out to deliberate.

'Do you think it'll have any effect, Ian? The judge told them not to be influenced by . . .'

'Oh, bullshit, Jessica. If I say something to you and someone else tells you to unhear it, will you have heard it or not? Will you remember it or not? They're only human, for Chrissake. Of course they're influenced by what they hear. So are you, so am I, so's the judge.' He ran a hand through his hair and pushed his lunch away. Jessica folded the paper and threw it onto the counter.

'Okay, so maybe they read the paper today, maybe not. But there isn't a damn thing we can do about it. So why not just let it pass, darling? Just forget about it. Can we try to do that? You're the one who made me promise not to discuss the case, remember?' She smiled gently at him. His eyes looked like sapphires, dark and bright and troubled.

'Yes, but Jessie . . . for God's . . . all right. You're right. I'm sorry.' But it was a tense meal after that, and neither of them finished their sandwiches.

They were silent on the drive down to City Hall, and Jessica heard her heels echo on the marble floors as they walked in. Her heart seemed to be pounding with equal force and in tune to the echo, like a death knell.

The judge addressed the jury for less than half an hour, and they filed out silently to be locked into a room across the hall while a bailiff stood guard outside.

'Now what, gentlemen?' Martin and Ian had joined Jessie at her seat.

'Now we wait. The judge will call a recess if they haven't come to a decision by five. Then they'll come back in the morning.'

'And that's it?' Jessie looked surprised.

'Yes, that's it.' How strange. It was all over. Almost. All that droning and boredom mixed with tension and sudden drama. And then it's over. The two teams have done their debating, the judge makes a little speech to the jury, they go lock themselves in a room, talk to each other, pick a verdict, everyone goes home, and the trial is over. It was weird somehow. Like a game. Or a dance. All terribly organized and ritualistic. A tribal rite. The thought made her want to laugh, but Ian and Martin were looking so serious. She smiled up at her husband, and their attorney looked at her with worried eyes. She really didn't understand. And he wasn't sure Ian did either. Maybe it was just as well.

'What do you think, Martin?' Ian turned to him with the question, but Martin had the feeling that he was asking more for Jessie's benefit than his own.

'I don't know. Did you see this morning's papers?' Ian's face sobered further.

'Yes. At lunch. That doesn't help, does it?'

The lawyer shook his head.

'Well, at least we put on a good show.'

'It would have been a better show if Green could have come up with something solid about Burton and Jed Knowles. I just know that that was the crux of this.' Martin shook his head angrily, and Ian patted his shoulder.

'Will she be coming back for the verdict?' Jessie was curious.

'No. She won't be back in court.'

'Bitch.' It was a small, low word, from the pit of her gut.

'Jessie!' Ian was quick to silence her, but she wouldn't be silenced.

'Well? She fucks up our life, blasts us practically into bankruptcy, not to mention what she's done to our nerves, and then she just walks off into the sunset. What do you expect me to feel toward her? Gratitude?'

'No, but there's no point . . .'

'Why not?' Jessie was getting loud again, and Ian knew how nervous she was. 'Martin, can't we sue her after we win the case?'

'Yes, I suppose so, but what would you get out of it? She doesn't have anything.'

'Then we'll sue the state.' She hadn't thought of that before.

'Look, why don't you two go for a walk down the hall?' He gave Ian a pointed look and Ian nodded. 'It may be a while before the jury comes in, probably will be. Just stay close; don't leave the building.' Jessie nodded and stood up, reaching for Ian's hand. Martin left them and went back to the desk. It was terrifying the way Jessica would not accept the possibility that they might lose.

'I wish we could go for a drink.' She walked slowly into the hall and leaned against the wall while Ian lit their cigarettes. Her legs were shaking and she wondered how long she could keep up the front of Madam Cool. She wanted to sink to the floor and clutch Ian's knees in desperation. It had to go all right. Had to . . . had to . . . she wanted to pound on the door to the jury room . . . to . . .

'It'll all be over soon, Jess. Just hang in there.'

'Yeah.' She smiled a half-smile and linked her arm in his as they started to walk down the corridor.

They were silent for a long time, and Jessie let her mind travel as it chose, wandering and darting, floating between thoughts as she smoked, and walked, and held on to Ian. It took almost an hour, but her brain finally stopped whirling, probably from exhaustion. She felt lonely and tired and sad, but she no longer felt as if she were going at the wrong speed. It was something, anyway.

She decided to call the boutique, just to see how things were going. It was an odd time to call, but she suddenly wanted to touch base with something familiar, to know that the world hadn't simply shrunk to one endless corridor in which she and Ian were condemned to walk their lives away in terrified silence. She missed the bustle of the boutique. The trivia. The faces.

The girls told her what was happening and she felt better. It was like going to the movies with Astrid. Normalcy. It diminished the proportions of what was happening to them to something she could bear for a while longer.

By four o'clock Ian had relaxed too, and they were playing word games. At four-thirty they started trading old jokes.

'What's grey and has four legs and a trunk?'

'An elephant?' She was already giggling.

'No, dummy, a mouse going on vacation.' Ian grinned, pleased with his joke. They were like second-graders sent out to the hall.

'Okay, smartass. How can you tell if your pants have fallen down?' She came back at him quickly and he started to laugh, but then they saw Martin beckon them urgently from the end of the hall. The jokes were suddenly over. Ian stood up first and looked into Jessica's face. She felt pale as terror swept over her. Pale and hollow, as though her frame might break. It was happening now. No more games to make believe it would never happen . . . it was here. Oh God . . . no!

'Jessie, no panicking!' He could see the look on her face, and took her swiftly into his arms and held her as tightly as he could. 'I love you. That's all. I love you. Just know that, and that nothing will ever change that, and that you're fine, you're always fine. Got that?' She nodded, but her chin was trembling as he looked at her. 'You're fine. And I love you.'

'You're fine, and you love you . . . I mean me . . .' She laughed a watery laugh and he held her tight again.

'You're fine, silly. Not I'm fine.'

'You're not fine?' She was better now. She always was when he held her.

'Oh Jessie . . . I'll tell you one thing. I wish to hell my pants had never fallen down.' They both laughed and then he pulled away from her again. 'Everything's gonna be okay. Now let's go.'

'I love you, darling. I wish you knew how much I love you.' Tears blinded her as she walked along at his side, quickly, trying to tell him too much in too little time.

'You're here. That tells me everything. Now stop being so dramatic, and get the mascara off your face.' She giggled nervously again and ran her hands over her cheeks. There were black streaks on her palms when she stopped.

'I must look terrific.'

'Gorgeous.'

And then they were there. The door to the courtroom.

'Okay?' He looked at her long and hard as they stood facing each other. The bailiff watched them and then turned away.

'Okay.' She nodded quietly and they smiled into each other's eyes.

They walked into the courtroom and the jury was already seated; the judge was back at his bench. The defendant was asked to rise, and Jessica almost rose from her seat with him and had to remind herself not to. She kept silently repeating to herself. 'Okay . . . okay . . . okay . . .' Her fingers dug into the seat of her chair and she closed her eyes, waiting. It would be okay, it was just so horrible waiting. She thought it must be like having a bullet pulled out of your arm. It wouldn't kill you, but God it was so awful getting it out.

The foreman was asked to read off the verdict, and she held her breath, wishing she were standing next to Ian. This was it.

'How does the jury find the defendant on the charge of sodomy, an infamous crime against nature?' They were starting at the least of the charges, and working their way up . . . she waited.

'Guilty, Your Honour.' Her eyes flew open and she saw Ian flinch, as though the tip of a whip had struck his face. But he didn't turn around to look at her.

'And on the charge of forcible oral copulation?'

'Guilty, Your Honour.'

'And on the charge of forcible rape?'

'Guilty, Your Honour.'

Jessica sat there stunned. Ian hadn't moved.

Martin looked toward her, and she felt the tears begin to pour down her face as the jury was dismissed and left the room. Ian sat down now and she went toward him. His eyes were blank when she looked into his face. She couldn't think of anything to say, and two lone tears crept down his face toward his chin.

CHAPTER XIX

'I didn't do it, Jessie. I don't care about the rest, but you have to know that. I didn't rape her.'

'I know.' It was barely a whisper, and she clung to his hand as the assistant district attorney snappily asked that the defendant be taken into custody, pending sentencing.

It was all over in five minutes. They led him away, and Jessica stood alone in the courtroom, clinging to Martin. She was alone in the world, clinging to a man she hardly knew. Ian was gone now. She was gone. Everything was gone. It was as though someone had taken a hammer to her life and shattered it. And she couldn't tell what was mirror and what was glass, what was Ian and what was Jessie.

She couldn't move, she couldn't speak, she could hardly breathe, and Martin led her slowly and carefully from the courtroom. This great, tall, healthy-looking young woman had suddenly become a zombie. It was as though there were no insides left to Jessie, and her whole being was deflating. Her eyes stayed glued to the door Ian had passed through when they'd taken him away, as if by staring hard enough she could make him come back through that door. Martin had no idea how to handle her. He had never been left alone with a client in this kind of condition. He wondered if he should call his secretary, or his wife. The court was deserted now except for the bailiff who was waiting to lock up. The judge had looked at her regretfully when he'd left the bench, but Jessie hadn't noticed. She hadn't even seen Houghton leave, shortly after Ian. It was just as well. And all she could hear was the echo of the word that kept ringing through her head again and again and again. Guilty . . . guilty . . . guilty . . .

'Jessie, I'll take you home.' He led her gently by the arm and was grateful that she followed him. He wasn't entirely certain that she knew who he was or where they were going, but he was glad that she didn't fight him. And then she stopped and looked at him vaguely.

'No, I . . . I'll wait for Ian here. I . . . I want . . . need . . . I need Ian.' She stood beside the middle-aged attorney and cried like a child, her face hidden in her hands, her shoulders shaking. Martin Schwartz sat her down on a chair in the hall, handed her a handkerchief, and patted her shoulder. She was holding Ian's wallet and watch and car keys in her hand like treasures she had been bequeathed. Ian had left with empty pockets and dry eyes. In handcuffs.

'What . . . what . . . will they do . . . to him now?' She was stammering through her tears. 'Can . . . can . . . he come home?' Martin knew she was too close to hysterics now to be told anything even approaching the truth. He just patted her shoulder again and helped her to her feet.

'Let's just get you home first. And then I want to go down and see Ian.' He thought it would comfort her, but he had only excited her again.

'Me too. I want to see Ian too.'

'Not tonight, Jessica. We're going home.' It was the right tone to take. She got to her feet, took his arm, and followed him out of the building. Walking with her was like walking a mechanical rag doll.

'Martin?'

'Yes?' They were out in the fresh air now, and she took a deep breath as he turned to her.

'Can we app—appeal?' She was calmer again. She seemed to be floating in and out of rationality, but she knew what was happening.

'We'll talk about it.'

'Now. I want to talk about it now.' Standing on the steps

of City Hall, frantic and hysterical, at six o'clock at night. It was hard to believe that this broken woman was the confident, sophisticated Jessica Clarke.

'No, Jessica, not now. I want to talk to Ian first. And I want to get you home. Ian will be very upset if I don't get you home.' Oh, Jesus. And she was going to make it difficult every inch of the way. Just getting her to the car was taking forever.

'I want to see Ian.' She stood at the top of the steps like a pouting child, irrational again. 'I . . . I need Ian . . .' And the tears began to flow again. It made it easier to get her into the car. Until she remembered that she had to drive the Volvo home. It was Ian's.

'I'll have it brought to you tomorrow, Jessica. Just give me the garage stub.' She handed it to him, and he turned the ignition in the new chocolate brown Mercedes. He kept a close watch on her as he drove her home. She looked frighteningly vague and dishevelled, and he wondered if he should call her doctor for her when he got her home. He asked her about it and she objected vehemently. 'What about a friend? Is there someone you want me to call?' He hated to leave her alone, but she only shook her head, mute, with an odd look in her eyes. She was thinking of the jury . . . of Margaret Burton . . . of Inspector Houghton . . . she wanted to kill them all . . . they had stolen Ian . . .

'Jessica? *Jessica*?' She turned to look at him blankly. They were in front of the house on Vallejo.

'Oh.' She nodded silently again and opened the door carefully on her side. 'I . . . will you see Ian now?'

'Yes. Is there anything you want me to tell him?' She nodded quickly and tried to speak normally.

'Just that . . . that . . .' But she couldn't speak through her tears.

'I'll give him your love.' She nodded gratefully and looked into his eyes with an air of being almost herself again. The hysterical vagueness seemed to be fading. What he saw now was shock, and grief. 'Jessica, I'm . . . I'm terribly sorry.'

'I know.' She turned away then, closed the door, and walked slowly toward her house. She moved like a very old woman, and the long brown Mercedes pulled slowly away. It felt wrong to watch her. It seemed kinder to let her grieve in private. But he would never forget the way she looked, walking slowly up the brick walk, her head bent, her hair tangled, with Ian's things cradled in her hands. It was an unbearable sight.

She heard the car pull away and looked at their flower beds blankly as she approached the house. Was this the house where she had come for lunch with Ian that day? Was this the house where they lived? She looked up at it as though she had never seen it before, and stopped as though she couldn't walk any further. She lifted one foot slowly then and mounted the small step. But the other foot was too heavy to lift. She couldn't. She didn't want to. She couldn't go in that house. Not without Ian. Not alone . . . not . . . like this . . .

'Oh God, *no*!' She sank to her knees on the front step and sobbed with her head bowed and her hands full of what had been in Ian's pockets. A voice called her name and she didn't turn. It wasn't Ian. Why bother to answer . . . it wasn't Ian . . . he was gone now. Everyone was gone. She felt as though he had died in the courtroom—or maybe she had. She wasn't quite sure. The voice called her name again, and she felt as if she was sinking through the brick. The contents of her handbag lay strewn on the step, the knit of her skirt had snagged on the brick, and her hair covered her face like a pale widow's veil.

'Jessie! Jessica?'

She heard the rapid footsteps behind her, but couldn't turn around. She didn't have the strength. It was all over.

'Jessie . . . darling, what's wrong?'

It was Astrid. Jessica turned to look into her face, and the tears continued to flow.

'What happened? Tell me! Everything will be all right. Just take it easy.' She smoothed Jessie's hair like a child's, and wiped the tears from her face as they continued to come. 'Is it Ian? Tell me, darling, is it Ian?'

Jessie nodded with a distraught look of grief on her face, and Astrid felt her heart stop . . . oh no, not Ian . . . not like Tom. No!

'He was convicted of rape.' The words came out as though from someone else's mouth, and Astrid looked as if she'd been slapped. 'He's in jail.'

'Good lord, Jessica, no!' But it was true. She knew it as Jessica nodded and let her friend gently take her inside and put her to bed. The pills Astrid gave her put her out almost instantly. Astrid still carried them—ever since Tom.

It was three-thirty in the morning when Jessie woke up. The house was quiet. She could hear the clock tick. It was dark in the bedroom, but there were lights on in the living room. She listened for Ian's sounds—the typewriter, his chair squeaking back on the studio floor. She sat up in bed, listening, hearing nothing, and her head swam. Then she remembered the pills. And Astrid. And how it had all begun. She sat up in bed and reached for her cigarettes with a trembling hand. She was still wearing her sweater and stockings and slip. Her jacket and skirt were neatly draped over a chair. She couldn't remember getting into bed. All she could remember was the sound of Astrid's voice, cooing gently, saying things she didn't really understand as she drifted off to sleep. But there had been someone there . . . someone . . . now there was no one. She was alone.

She lay there smoking in the darkness of the bedroom, dry-eyed, faintly nauseated and still slowed from the pills, and suddenly she reached for the phone. She got the number from information and called.

'City Prison. Langdorf here.'

'I'd like to speak to Ian Clarke, please.'

'He work here!' The desk sergeant sounded surprised.

'No. He was taken into custody yesterday. After a trial.' She didn't volunteer the nature of the conviction. And she was surprised at the steadiness of her own voice. She didn't feel steady, but she knew that if she could make herself sound calm, they might give her what she wanted. All she had to do was sound terribly calm and put a little authority into her voice and . . .

'He'd be in the county jail, lady, not here. And you can't talk to him anyway.'

'I see. Do you have the number there?' She thought of telling them it was an emergency, but decided not to. She was afraid to lie to them. The desk sergeant at the city prison gave her the number of the county jail in the Hall of Justice, and she dialled quickly. But it didn't work. They told her that she could visit her husband the day after tomorrow, and he wasn't allowed to get phone calls. Then they hung up on her.

She shrugged one shoulder and flicked on a lamp. It was cold in the room. Jessie pulled a bathrobe over her sweater and slip and padded out to the living room in stocking feet. She stood in the middle of the room and looked around. The room was faintly messy, but not very, just enough to remind her . . . impressions in the softness of the couch, a mark where the back of a head had pressed into a cushion, the book he'd been reading last weekend . . . his loafers under the chair . . . his . . . she felt a sob rise and stick in her throat and she turned and walked into the kitchen for something to drink . . . tea . . . coffee . . . Coke . . . something . . . her mouth was dry and her head felt fuzzy, but everything else was so clear. She found the plates from lunch in the sink, and the newspaper on the counter where she had thrown it, the article on rape folded out. It was as though he had just been in the room, as though he had taken a walk around the block, as though . . . she sat down at the kitchen table, dropped her head, and cried.

The studio was as bad. Worse. Dark and empty and lonely. It looked as though it expected his presence but had been stood up. It needed him to come alive. Ian was the room's living soul. And hers. Jessie's soul. She needed him more than his studio did. She found herself moving from one foot to the other, like a disturbed child, standing in doorways, smoothing her hand over his books, or his shirts, holding his loafers close to her and jumping when a shadow cast an odd light. She was alone. In the house, in the night, in the world. With no one to help her, or take care of her, or give a damn about her, or . . . she opened her mouth to scream, but no sound came. She simply sank slowly to the floor, with the loafers in her arms, and waited. But no one came. She was alone.

CHAPTER XX

It was nine-thirty in the morning and she was sitting in the bathtub trying to fight a wave of hysteria when the doorbell rang. It was all right. All right. Everything was going to be all right. She'd stay in the bath for a little while and then she'd have a cup of tea, and some breakfast, and get dressed, and go to the boutique. Or maybe she'd stay in bed all day. Or . . . but it was all right. First the hot bath, and then . . . but she couldn't call Ian. She couldn't talk to him. She needed to talk to him. She took another deep breath and then listened. It sounded like the doorbell, or maybe that was just the running water playing games with her ears. but it wasn't. The bell went on ringing. But she didn't have to answer it. All she had to do was keep breathing and stay calm, and let the warm water relax her. Ian had shown her how to stay calm like that, and not get hysterical, when . . . when her mother . . . and Jake . . . but the doorbell. She jumped out of the tub suddenly, grabbed a towel, and ran for the door. What if it was Ian? She had his keys. What if . . . she ran to the front door, dripping water along the way, a half smile on her mouth, her eyes suddenly bright and large, the towel covering her torso inadequately. She pulled the door open without remembering to ask who was there, and then jumped back, startled. Too surprised to close the door again. She simply stood there, fear pounding in her heart.

'Good morning. I wouldn't make a habit of opening the door like that if I were you.' She looked down quickly and tightened the towel. The caller was Inspector Houghton.

'I . . . how do you. What can I do for you?' She pulled herself to her full height and stood regally in the doorway in spite of the towel.

'Nothing. I just thought I'd see how you are.' He wore the ironic look of victory in his eyes, the look that she had missed the day before. It made her want to scratch his eyes out.

'I'm fine.' You filthy bastard. 'Was there anything else?'

'Got any coffee ready, Mrs. Clarke?' From him the formalities were almost abusive.

'As a matter of fact, no, Inspector Houghton, I don't. And I have to get to work shortly. If you have business to discuss with me, I suggest you go buy yourself a cup of coffee on Union Street, and see me in my office in an hour.'

'Feisty, aren't you? You must have had a nasty shock yesterday, though.'

She closed her eyes, fighting the wave of nausea that rose to her throat. The man was sadistic. But she couldn't faint now. Couldn't. She heard Ian's voice saying 'Okay?' with that special way of his, and she nodded imperceptibly and thought 'Okay'.

'Yes, it was a shock. Do you enjoy that, Inspector? Seeing other people unhappy, I mean.'

'I don't see it that way.' He pulled out a pack of cigarettes and offered her one. She shook her head. He was enjoying this, all right.

'I guess not. Miss Burton must have been pleased.'

'Very.' He smiled at her through the cigarette smoke and she had to fight herself not to slap him or flail at him. That took more control than not getting sick.

'And what happens to you now?' So that's what this was all about.

'What do you mean?'

'Any plans?'

'Yes, work. And seeing my husband tomorrow. And dinner with friends next week, and . . .'

He smiled again, but did not look amused.

'If he goes to prison, it could wreak havoc with your marriage, Mrs. Clarke.' His voice was almost gentle.

'Possibly. Almost anything can wreak havoc with a marriage, if you let it. Depends on how good your marriage is, and how hard you want to work at keeping it that way.'

'And how good is yours?'

'Excellent. And from the bottom of my heart, Inspector Houghton, I thank you for your concern. I'll be sure to mention it to both my husband and our attorney. I know Mr. Clarke will be deeply touched. You know, you're really a very sensitive man, Inspector—or is it just that you have a particular fondness for marriage counselling?'

His eyes blazed back into hers, but it was too late; he had walked right into it. He had come to her house, rung the bell, and made his own mistakes that morning.

'You know, as a matter of fact, I think I might even call your superior to tell him what a marvellously thoughtful man you are. Imagine caring about how my marriage is.'

He slipped the cigarette pack back into his pocket and his smile was long since gone.

'All right, I get the point.'

'Do you? My, how quick you are, Inspector.'

'Bitch.' He said it through clenched teeth.

'I beg your pardon?'

'I said "bitch" and you can tell *that* to my superior too. But if I were you, baby, I wouldn't bother to call. You've got enough problems, and you ain't gonna see your old man around here for a long time. You'd better get used to it, sister. You and that little literary punk of yours are through. So when you get tired of sitting here by yourself in the dark, start looking around. There's better out there than what you got stuck with.'

'Oh, really? And I suppose you're a prime example?' She was trembling with fury now and her voice was rising to match his.

'Pick who you want, but you'll be out looking. I give you two months to be down at Jerry's with the rest of them.'

'Get out of here, Inspector. And if you ever set foot near this house again, with or without a search warrant, I'll call the judge, the mayor, and the fire department. Or I may not call a goddam living soul. I may just take aim at you out of my window.'

'Have a gun, do you?' He raised an eyebrow with interest.

'Not yet, but I will. Apparently I need one.'

He opened his mouth to say something and she took one graceful step backward and slammed the door in his face. Tactically, it was a poor move, but it made her feel better.

For a moment. When she walked back into the house, she threw up in the kitchen. It took her two hours to stop shaking.

Astrid arrived at eleven. She had flowers with her, and a roast chicken she'd bought for Jessie to pick on, and a bag full of fruit. And a small vial of yellow pills. But after twenty minutes of persistently ringing the doorbell there was still no answer; Astrid knew Jessie was there because she had called the boutique to make sure. Finally she began to worry seriously and knocked on the kitchen windows with her rings. Jessie peered cautiously between the curtains and then jumped half a foot when she saw Astrid. She had thought it was Houghton again.

'Good Lord, child, I thought something had happened. Why didn't you answer the door? Worried about press?'

'No, there's no problem with that. It's . . . oh . . . I don't know.' And then there were tears in her eyes again and she was standing there looking like an overgrown child and telling Astrid about the visit from Houghton. 'I just can't take it. He's so . . . so evil, and so happy about what happened. And he said that our . . . our marriage . . .' She was crying too hard to go on and Astrid made her sit down.

'Why don't you come and stay with me for a little while, Jessica? You could have the guest room and get away from here for a few days.'

'No!' Jessie sprang to her feet and started pacing the room, touching chairs as she sped past, or picking something up and then putting it down again. It was a series of odd little staccato gestures, but Astrid recognised them. She had reacted the same way when Tom had died.

'No. Thank you, Astrid, but I want to be here. With . . . with . . .' She faltered, not quite sure of what she wanted to say.

'With Ian's things. I know. But maybe that's not such a good idea. And is it worth the price of being heckled by people like that policeman? And what if there are others who show up the same way? Do you want to have to deal with that?'

'I won't open the door.'

'You can't live like that, Jessica. Ian won't want you to.'

'Yes, he will. Honest. Really . . . I . . . oh, God, Astrid, I'm going crazy, I can't . . . I don't know how without Ian.'

'But you're not without Ian. You'll see him. I still don't understand what happened, but maybe you can work it out. He's not gone, Jessica. He's not dead, for God's sake. Stop acting like he is.'

'But he's not here.' Her voice had a pitiful sound. 'I need him here. I'll go crazy without him, I'll . . . I'll . . .'

'No, you won't. Not unless you *want* to go crazy, or make yourself do so. Take yourself in hand, Jessica, and sit down. Right now. Come on, sit down.' Jessica had been popping in and out of chairs like a jack-in-the-box for the past five minutes. Her voice was rising to a desperate pitch. 'Have you had breakfast?' Jessica shook her head and started to say that she didn't want any, but Astrid held up her hand and vanished into the kitchen. She emerged five minutes later with toast, jelly, the fresh fruit she had brought, and a cup of steaming tea. 'Would you rather have coffee?' Jessie shook her head and closed her eyes for a moment.

'I just don't believe this is happening, Astrid.'

'Don't think about it yet. You can't make sense of it, so don't try. When can you see Ian?' Jessie's eyes opened and she sighed at the question.

'Tomorrow.'

'All right. Then all you have to do is try and stay calm till tomorrow. You can do that, can't you?'

Jessica nodded, but she wasn't quite sure. That meant a day, and a night, and a morning. And the night would be the worst. Full of ghosts and voices and echoes and terrors. She had twenty-four hours to survive until she saw Ian.

But there was one thing she did want to do. Now. Before she saw Ian. And that was to talk to Martin about an appeal. He was in his office when she called, and he sounded subdued.

'Are you all right, Jessica?'

'I'm okay. How's Ian?' Her voice caught on the words, and at the other end Martin frowned. He was remembering how she had looked the night before when he'd dropped her off.

'He's holding up. He was awfully shocked, though.'

'I can imagine.' She said it softly with a distracted smile. Shocked. They both were. 'Martin, I called because I wanted to ask you something now, right away, before I see Ian tomorrow.'

'What?'

'I want to know what we can do about an appeal, how we do it, do you do it, all of that.' And how the hell do we pay for it? That was another thing.

'Well, we can talk about that after the sentencing, Jessica. If he gets probation, then there isn't much point in pressing for an appeal, except as a matter of record, to clear Ian of the felony. He might want to do that. But I think you should wait till after the sentencing to make a decision. There's a limited time in which to file an appeal, but you'll still have plenty of time then.'

'How soon is the sentencing?'

'Four weeks from tomorrow.'

'But why wait till after that?'

'Because, Jessie, you don't know what's going to happen. If they send him home on probation, Ian may not want to spend his last dime, or yours, on an appeal. It's not as if he's in a delicate position professionally where it can hurt him to have that on his record. All right, it can hurt him,' he reconsidered, 'but not that badly in his profession. And if he's free, what do you care?'

'What do you mean, *if* he's free?' Jessie was feeling confused again.

'All right, the alternative is, if they don't give him probation, they'll send him to prison. In that case, you may well want to appeal. But all an appeal is going to do for you, Jessica, is get you a new trial. You'll have to go through the whole ordeal again. There isn't a shred of evidence we didn't submit. Nothing would change. So you'd be going through it all again, maybe to no avail. I think right now our push should be for probation. And we can worry about an appeal after we see what happens with that. All right?'

Jessica reluctantly agreed, and hung up. What did he mean, 'if' they set Ian free? What was the 'if'?

CHAPTER XXI

'Okay?'

'Okay.' She smiled and instinctively her hand went to the gold lima bean at her throat, and played with it for a moment as she looked at him. She had survived the twenty-four hours, and Houghton had not returned. 'I love you, Ian.'

'Darling, I love you too. Are you really all right?' He looked so worried about her.

'I'm fine. What about you?'

His eyes told their own tale. He was in county jail this time, and he was wearing the filthy overalls they had given him. They had stuffed his clothes in a shopping bag and returned them to Martin. He had sent them back to Jessie the evening before, along with the Volvo. After that she had taken the two pills Astrid had left her.

'Martin says they might give you probation.' But they both remembered the article they had read the day of the trial. It had been in favour of abolishing probation on rape cases. The public mood was not lenient just now.

'We'll see, Jessie, but don't count on it. We'll give it a try.' He smiled and Jessie fought back tears. What would happen if he didn't get probation? She hadn't even begun to face that yet. Later. Another 'later', like the trial, and the verdict. 'Have you been behaving yourself? No panic, no freakies?' He knew her too well.

'I've been fine. And Astrid's been taking care of me like a child.' She didn't tell him about Houghton. Or the night of semicraziness that she had had to fill with pills just to survive. She had crawled through that night as if it were a mine field.

'Is she here with you now?' He looked around but didn't see her.

'Yes, but she waited downstairs. She was afraid you'd feel awkward. And she figured we'd want to talk.'

'Tell her I love her. And I'm glad you're not here alone. Jessie, I've been worried sick over you. Promise me you won't do anything crazy. Please. Promise.' His eyes pleaded with her.

'I promise. Honest, darling. I'm okay.' But she didn't look it. They both looked like hell. Ravaged, shocked, exhausted, and in Ian's case two days' growth of beard didn't help.

For half an hour they exchanged the disjointed banalities of people still in shock. Jessie stayed busy trying not to cry, and she managed not to until she rejoined Astrid downstairs. They were tears of anger and pain.

'They have him up there in a goddam cage like an animal!' And that damn woman was probably in her office, doing her job, living her life. She had got her revenge and now she could be happy. While Ian rotted in jail, and Jessie went crazy alone at night.

Astrid took her home, cooked her dinner, and waited until she was half asleep. It was an easier night for Jessie, mostly because she was too exhausted to torture herself thinking, to wander. She simply slept. And Astrid was back early the next morning with fresh strawberries, a copy of *The New York Times* and a brand new *Women's Wear Daily* as though that still mattered.

'Lady, what would I do without you?'

'Sleep later, probably. But I was up so I thought I'd come over.' Jessie shook her head and hugged her friend as she poured two cups of tea. It was going to be a long haul, and Astrid was a godsend. It would be another twenty-seven days until the sentencing. And God only knew what would happen after that.

Jessie had the shop to think of too, but she wasn't ready to face that yet. She managed it with increasingly rare phone calls and a great deal of faith in Katsuko. Astrid took her along to her own appointment with the hairdresser, more to keep an eye on her than anything else. Jessie could only see Ian twice a week, and there was a frightening aimlessness about her in the meantime. She'd start to say things and then forget them, take objects out of her handbag and then forget why she'd brought them out; she would listen to Astrid talk and look right through her as though she couldn't see or hear her. She wasn't making a great deal of sense. She looked the way she felt, like a lost child far from home hanging desperately to a new mother. Astrid. But without Ian nothing made any sense. Least of all living. And with no contact, it was hard to remind herself that he still existed. Astrid was just trying to keep her afloat until the next time she could see him.

There had been a small article on the back page of the paper the day after the verdict. But no one had called, only the two friends who had appeared for Ian in court. They were shocked by the news. Astrid took the calls and Jessica dropped them each a note. She didn't want to talk to anyone now.

On Monday she went back to work, and Zina and Katsuko were subdued. Kat had spotted the article, but hadn't mentioned it on the phone; she had wanted to wait until she could say something to Jessie in person. And she had known from the sound of her voice on the phone that Jessie didn't want them to know. It was a painful moment when she and Astrid walked into the shop. She read the knowledge at once in their faces, and Zina instantly had tears in her eyes. Jessie hugged them both.

Now the two girls knew why Houghton had come to the shop, why Jessie had been so frantic, why the Morgan was gone. They finally understood.

'Jessie, is there anything we can do?' Katsuko spoke for both of them.

'Only one thing. Don't talk about it after this. There's nothing I can say right now. Talking doesn't help.'

'How's Ian?'

'He's surviving. That's about the best you can say.'

'Do you have any idea what'll happen?' She shook her head and sat down quietly in her usual chair.

'Nope. No idea at all. Does that answer everybody's questions?' She looked at the two women's faces, and she already felt tired.

'Do you need any help at home, Jessie?' Zina had finally spoken up. 'It must be lonely. And I don't live very far.'

'Thanks, love. I'll let you know.' She gave the girl a

squeeze as she headed toward her office with Astrid at her heels. The last thing she wanted was to spend evenings with Zina commiserating. It would be worse than the terrors of being alone. She turned at the door to her office with a serious look on her face. 'One thing, though. I'm not going to be around much for the next few weeks. I have things to do for Ian. People to see about the sentencing, and just a hell of a lot on my mind. I'll be here whenever I can, but you two count on carrying the ball for me. Like you've been doing. Okay?' Katsuko saluted and Jessie smiled. 'Couple of nuts. It's nice to be back.'

'What if I pitch in and help?' Astrid was looking at her with interest as she sat down at her desk.

'To tell you the truth, I need you more everywhere but the shop. Kat has this place under control. The real problem is me. Mornings, evenings, late nights . . . you know.' Astrid did know. She had seen Jessie's face at eight-thirty in the morning, and had heard her voice at two. It told a perfect tale of what the nights were like. The terror that daylight would never come again. That Ian would never come home. That the world would swallow her up and never spit her out. That Houghton would break down the door and rape her. Real fears and unreal fears, demons of her own making and men who weren't worthy of the name —all tangled together in her mind.

'Any idea what time you'll be through work? I'll pick you up. We can have dinner at my place tonight, if you feel up to it.'

'You're too good to me.' And it was amazing, considering how short a time they'd known each other. But Astrid knew what it was like. She had a healthy respect for what Jessica was going through.

Most of Jessica's efforts went toward Ian's sentencing. Twice she saw the probation officer detailed to the case, and she hounded Martin night and day. What was he doing? What did he have in mind? Had he spoken to the probation officer? What were the man's impressions? Should Martin talk to the man's superiors? She even went to speak to the judge one day at lunchtime. He was sympathetic, but didn't want to be pressured about the sentencing. Jessie had the distinct impression that had she been a little less ladylike the judge might have been a little less kind in his reception. As it was, he was not overly welcoming. She also collected letters from a number of discreet friends, testifying to Ian's good character. She even got a letter from his agent, hoping to show that Ian had to be free to complete the new book, and that going to prison would destroy his career.

Thanksgiving came and went like any other day. Or at least Jessica tried to ensure that it did. She treated it like any day when she wasn't working. She wouldn't allow herself to think of past Thanksgivings. She refused to let it be festive in any way. That would have been too much for her. She spent it with Astrid, and Ian spent it in jail. There was no visiting at the county jail on Thanksgiving Day. He ate stale chicken sandwiches and read a letter from Jessie. She ate steak with Astrid, who went out of her way to ignore the holiday this year, sacrificing a long weekend at the ranch with her mother. But the sacrifice was well worth it. She was worried about Jessie, who always seemed to move about in a haze now, stopping and starting, jangled, at one extreme or the other: fuzzy and full of pills, or wild from too much coffee.

And she worked night and day. Figuring out what to do for the sentencing, and suddenly pouring her energy back into Lady J, as she hadn't in years. She worked on Saturdays again. At home she did anything, everything—cleaned the basement, straightened out the garage, redid her closets, tidied the studio—anything, trying not to think. And maybe, maybe, if she did everything perfectly, maybe at the end of the month, he'd come home. Maybe they'd give him probation, maybe . . . she moved like a whirling dervish, but she had to; the pounding of her mind was deafening her. And constantly there was fear. She never escaped it. Sheer, raw, endless terror. Beyond human proportions. But she wasn't human anymore. She barely ate, she hardly slept. She wouldn't allow herself to feel. She didn't dare to be human. Humans fell apart. And that was what scared her most. Falling apart. Like Humpty-Dumpty. And all the king's horses and all the king's men . . . that was what she was afraid of. Ian knew it, but he couldn't stop her now. He couldn't touch her, hold her, feel her, make her feel. He couldn't do anything except watch her through the window and talk to her on the phone at the jail as she played nervously with the cord and snapped her earring absentmindedly.

And he continued to look steadily worse—unshaven, unwashed, ill fed, and with dark circles under his eyes that seemed to get darker each time she saw him.

'Don't you sleep in here?' There was a raw edge to her voice now. It was higher, shriller, scareder. He pitied her, but he couldn't help her now. They both knew it, and he wondered how long it would take her to hate him for it. For failing her. He was terrified that a day would come when he couldn't keep the boogey man from the door for her, and then she would turn on him. Jessie expected a lot. Because she needed so much.

'I sleep now and then.' He tried to smile. Tried not to think. 'What about you? Looks like a lot of makeup under your eyes, my love. Am I right?'

'Are you ever wrong?' She smiled back and shrugged, snapping the earring again. She had lost twelve pounds, but she was sleeping a little better. She just didn't look it. But the new red pills helped. They were better than the yellow ones, or even the little blue ones Astrid had let her graduate to after that. They were the same kind, only stronger. The red ones were something else. She didn't discuss it with Ian. He would have been difficult about it. And she was careful. But the pills were the best part of her day. The two bright moments with Ian were the only livable parts of her week, and in between she had to get through the days. The pills did that for her. And Astrid doled them out one by one, refusing to leave the bottle with her.

Ian would have been frantic if he had known. She had promised him solemnly, after Jake had died—no more pills. He had stood at her side all night while they'd pumped her stomach, and afterward she had promised. She thought about that sometimes when she took the pills. But she had to. She really had to. Or she'd die anyway. One way or another. She worried about things like jumping out a window, without wanting to. About little demons seizing her and making her do things she didn't want to. She couldn't talk to customers in the shop anymore. She stayed in the back office because she was afraid of what she'd say. She was no longer in control. Of anything. Jessica was not in her own driver's seat. No one was.

The four weeks between the verdict and the sentencing ground by like a permanent nightmare, but the sentencing finally came. The plea for probation was heard by the judge, and this time Jessie stood beside Ian as they waited. It was less frightening now, though, and she kept touching his hand, his face. It was the first time in a month that she had touched him. He smelled terrible and his nails were long. They had given him an electric razor at the jail and it had torn his face apart. But it was Ian. It was, at last the touch of the familiar in a world that had become totally unfamiliar to her. Now she could stand next to him. Be his. She almost forgot the seriousness of the sentencing. But the courtroom formalities brought her back. The bailiff, the court reporter, the flag. It was the same courtroom, the same judge. And it was all very real now.

Ian was not granted probation. The judge felt that the charges were too serious. And Martin explained later that with the political climate what it was, the judge could hardly have done otherwise. Ian was given a sentence of four years to life in state prison, and he would have to serve at least a fourth of his minimum sentence: one year.

The bailiff led him away, and this time Jessie did not cry.

CHAPTER XXII

Three days later, Ian was moved from county jail to state prison. He went, like all male prisoners in Northern California, to the California Medical Facility in Vacaville for 'evaluation'.

Jessica drove there two days later with Astrid, in the black Jaguar, and with two yellow pills under her belt. Astrid said these were the last she would give her, but she always said that. Jessica knew she felt sorry for her.

Except for the gun tower peering over the main gate and the metal detector that searched them for weapons, the prison at Vacaville looked innocuous. Inside, a gift shop sold ugly items made in the prison, and the front desk might have been the entrance to a hospital. Everything was chrome and glass and linoleum. But outside, it looked like a modern garage. For people.

They asked to see Ian, filled out various forms, and were invited to sit in the waiting room or wander in the lobby. Ten minutes later a guard appeared to unlock a door to an inner courtyard. He instructed them to pass through the courtyard and go through yet another door, which they would find unlocked.

The inmates in the courtyard wore blue jeans, T-shirts, and an assortment of shoes, everything from boots to sneakers, and Astrid raised an eyebrow at Jessica. It didn't look like a prison. Everyone was casually playing with the soda machines or talking to girlfriends. It looked like a high school at recess, with here and there the exception of a sober face or a watery-eyed mother.

What she saw gave Jessie some hope. She could visit Ian somewhere in the courtyard, could touch him again, laugh, hold hands. It was madness to be regressing to that after seven years of marriage, but it would be an improvement over the doggie-in-the-window visits at the county jail.

As it turned out, there was no improvement. Ian was months away from visits in the courtyard, if he stayed in that institution at all. There was always Folsom or San Quentin to worry about now. Anything was possible. And for the time being they were faced once again with more visits through a glass window, talking over a phone. Jessica felt a surging desire to smash the receiver through the window as she tried to smile into his face. She longed for the touch of his face, the feel of his arms, the smell of his hair. And instead all she had in her hands was a blue plastic phone. Next to her there was a pink one, and further down a yellow. Someone with a sense of humour had installed pastel-coloured princess-style phones all the way down the line. Like a nursery, with a glass window. And you could talk to the darling babies on the phone. What she needed was her husband, not a phone pal.

But he looked better—thinner, but at least clean. He had even shaved in the hope of a visit. They fell into some of their old jokes, and Astrid shared the phone with Jessica now and then. It was all so strange, sitting there, making conversation with a wall of glass between the two women and Ian. The strain told in his eyes, and the humour they inflicted on each other always had a bitter edge.

'This is quite a harem. For a rapist.' He grinned nervously at his own bad joke.

'Maybe they'll think you're a pimp.' Their laughter sounded like tinsel rustling.

The reality was that he was there. For at least a year. Jessie wondered how long she could take it. But maybe she didn't have to. Maybe neither of them did. She wanted to talk to him about an appeal.

'Did you talk to Martin about it?'

'Yes. And there won't be an appeal.' He answered her solemnly, but with certainty in his voice.

'*What?*' Jessie's voice was suddenly shrill.

'You heard me. I know what I'm doing, Jess. Nothing would change next time around. Martin feels the same way. For another five or ten thousand bucks, we'd sink ourselves further into debt, and when the second trial rolled around, we'd have nothing different to say. The suspicions we have about her husband are inadmissible on the flimsy evidence we have. All we've got is an old photograph and a lot of fancy ideas. No one will testify. There's nothing to hang our hats on except blind hope. We did that once, but we didn't have any choice. We're not going through that again. A new trial would come out the same goddam way, and it'll just make these people mad. Martin thinks I'm better off living through this, just being a nice guy, and they'll probably give me an early parole. Anyway, I've made my decision, and I'm right.'

'Who says you're right, dammit, and why didn't anyone ask me?'

'Because we're talking about my time in here, not yours. It's my decision.'

'But it affects my life too.' Her eyes filled with tears. She wanted an appeal, another chance, something, anything. She couldn't accept just waiting around until he got paroled. There was talk of changing the California laws to bring in a determinate sentence, but who had time to wait for that? And even then, Martin had once said that Ian might have to do a couple of years. Two years? Jesus. How would she survive? She could barely speak as she held the phone in her hand.

'Jessie, trust me. It has to be this way. There's no point.'

'We could sell something. The house. Anything.'

'And we might lose again. Then what? Let's just grit our teeth and get through this. Please, Jessie—please, please try. I can't do anything for you right now except love you. You've got to be strong. And it won't be for long. It probably won't be more than a year.' He tried to sound cheerful about it, for her sake.

'What if it's more than a year?'

'We'll worry about it then.' The tears spilled down her face in answer. How could they have decided this without talking to her? And why weren't they willing to try again? Maybe they could win . . . maybe . . . she looked up to see Ian exchanging a look with Astrid and shaking his head. 'Baby, you have to pull yourself together.'

'What for?'

'For me.'

'I'm okay.'

He shook his head and looked at her. 'I wish to hell you were.' Thank God she had Astrid.

They talked on for a while, about the other men there, about some tests they'd put him through, about his hopes of being kept there rather than sent on to another prison. Vacaville at least seemed civilised, and he expected that he could work on his book after he'd been there for a while and had calmed down. Jessie told herself that it made her feel better to know that he was still interested in the book. At least he was still alive mentally, spiritually. But she found that she didn't really care. What about her? After the outburst over the appeal, she felt even lonelier. She tried to pump life into her smile, but it hurt so much not to be able to reach out to him or be held in his arms.

He watched her face for a long moment and wished only that he could touch her. Even he didn't have enough words anymore, and too often they fell silent.

'How's the shop?'

'Okay. Great, really. Business is booming.' But it was a lie. Business was far from booming. It was the worst it had been in all the years since she'd opened Lady J. But what could she tell him, what was there to say without voicing agonising recriminations, and accusations, and cries of outrage and despair? What was left? There was always the truth that business was lousy and he should have been home working to help pay the bills . . . the truth that he shouldn't be in prison . . . the truth that he looked terrible and his haircut made him look old and tired . . . the truth that she even worried now that he'd become a homosexual in jail—or worse, that someone would kill him . . . the truth that she didn't know how to pay the bills anymore and was afraid that she couldn't survive the nights alone . . . the truth that she wanted to die . . . the truth that he never should have balled

Margaret Burton . . . the truth that he was a sonofabitch and she was beginning to hate him because he wasn't there anymore . . . he was gone. But she couldn't tell him the truth. There was too much of it now, and she knew it would kill him.

He was talking again; she had to look up and focus her attention.

'Jess, I want you to do something for me when you get home today. Get the book Xeroxed, put the copy in the bank, and send me the original. I'm getting special permission to work on it, and by the time the manuscript gets here, I'll have the paperwork squared away at this end. Don't forget, though. Try and get it out to me today.' There was summer in his eyes again as he spoke, but Astrid wondered at the look on Jessica's face. Jessie was stunned. He had just been sentenced to prison and he was worried about his book?

The visit was called to a close after little more than an hour. There was a frantic flurry of good-byes on the phone, cheery farewells from Astrid, a few last verbal hugs from Ian, and a moment of panic that Jessie thought would close her throat. She couldn't even kiss him good-bye. But what if she needed to hold him? Didn't they understand that all she had in the world was Ian? What if . . .

She watched him walk away slowly, reluctant to leave, but a big boyish smile hung on his face, while she tried to smile too. But she was running on an empty tank now, and secretly she was glad the visit was over. It cost her more each time she saw him now. It was even harder here than it had been in county jail. She wanted to throw a fist through the glass, to scream, to . . . anything, but she gave him a last smile, and numbly followed Astrid back to the car.

'Do you have any more of those magical little pills, fairy godmother?'

'No, I don't. I didn't bring them.' Astrid said nothing more, but touched her arm gently and gave her a hug before unlocking the car. There was nothing more she could say. And she left Jessie the dignity of not seeing her tears as they drove home in silence, the radio purring softly between them.

'Want me to drop you off at home, so you can relax for a while?' She smiled as they came to a stop on Broadway where the freeway poured them back into the city traffic. Two blocks later they drove past Enrico's.

'Nope. And that's where it all began.'

'What?' Astrid hadn't noticed, and she turned to see Jessie staring at the tables clustered on the sidewalk under the heaters. It was cold now, but a few hardy souls still sat outside.

'Enrico's. That's where he met her. I wonder what she's doing now.' There was a haunted look on Jessica's face, and she spoke almost dreamily.

'Jessie, don't think of that.'

'Why not?'

'Because there's no point now. It's over. Now you have to look ahead to the other end. You just have to trot on through the tunnel, and before you know it . . .'

'Oh, bullshit! You make it sound like a fairy tale, for Chrissake. Just what do you think it feels like to look at your husband through a glass window, not to be able to touch him, or . . . oh, God. I'm sorry. I just can't stand it, Astrid. I can't accept it, I don't want this happening to my life, I don't want to be alone. I need him.' She ended softly, with tears thick in her throat.

'And you still have him. In all the ways that matter. Okay, so he's behind a window, but he won't be there forever. What do you suppose it felt like when I looked down at Tom in that stinking box? He would never talk to me again, hold me again, need me again, love me again. Ever, Jessie. Ever. With you and Ian, it's only an intermission. The only thing you don't have is his presence in the house every night. You have all the rest.'

But that was what she needed. His presence. What 'rest' was there? She couldn't remember anymore. Was there a 'rest'? Had there ever been?

'And you've got to stop taking those pills, Jessie.' Astrid's tone brought her back again. They were a few blocks from her house now.

'Why? They don't do any harm. They just . . . they just help, that's all.'

'They won't in a while. They'll just depress you more, if they aren't doing that already. And if you don't watch out you'll get so dependent on them that you'll have a real problem. I did, and it was a bitch to get rid of. I spent weeks down at Mother's ranch trying to "kick", as it were. Do yourself a big favour—give 'em up now.' Jessie brushed off the suggestion and pulled a comb out of her bag.

'Yeah. Maybe I'll just go straight to the shop.'

'Why don't you at least go home for five minutes to unwind first? How would that be?' Lousy. Painful.

'Okay. If you'll come in for coffee.' She didn't want to be alone there. 'I have to pick up Ian's book and get it Xeroxed for him. He wants to start working again.' Astrid noticed the strained tone in her voice. Could she be jealous? It seemed almost impossible. But these days, anything was possible with Jessie.

'At least they'll let him work on the book.'

'Apparently.' Jessie shrugged as Astrid pulled into the driveway.

'It'll do him good.'

Jessie shrugged again and got out.

There was a look of slight disorder in the front hall, of jackets and coats tried on and discarded before her visit to Ian that morning. Astrid noticed Ian's coats crammed to one side of the closet and the now predominantly female clutter here and there. He had only been gone for five weeks, yet it was beginning to look like a woman's house. She wondered if Jessie had noticed the change.

'Coffee or tea?'

'Coffee, thanks.' Astrid smiled and settled into a chair to look at the view. 'Want any help?' Jessica shook her head and Astrid tried to relax. It was difficult to be with Jessica now. There was obviously so much pain, and so little one could do to help. Except be there. 'What are you doing for Christmas?'

Jessica appeared with two flowered cups and laughed hollowly. 'Who knows? Maybe I'll hang myself this year instead of a stocking.'

'Jessica, that's not funny.'

'Is anything anymore?'

Astrid sighed deeply and set down the cup Jessie had given her.

'Jessie, you have to stop feeling so sorry for yourself. Somehow, somewhere, you're going to have to find something to hang on to. For your own sake, not just for his. The shop, a group of people, me, a church, whatever it is you need, but you just have to grab on to something. You can't live like this. Not only will your marriage not survive, but, much worse, *you* won't.' That was what had been frightening Ian: Astrid knew that. Once or twice he had looked at her, and she had understood.

'This isn't forever, you know. You'll get back what you had before. It isn't over.'

'Isn't it? How do you know that? I don't even know that. I don't even know at this point what the hell we had, or if it's worth wanting back.' She was shocked at her own words but she couldn't stop herself now. She gripped her shaking hands together. 'What did we have? Me supporting Ian, and him hating me for it, so much that he had to go out and screw a bunch of other women to feel like a man. Pretty portrait of a marriage, isn't it, Astrid? Just what every little girl dreams of.'

'Is that how you feel about it now?' Astrid watched the hurt on Jessica's face and her heart went out to her. 'From what I've seen, there's a lot more to your marriage than that.' They had looked so young and so happy when she'd met them, but she realised now that there was a lot she didn't know. There had to be. She met Jessica's eyes now and ached for her. Jessica had a lot to find out in the next months.

'I don't know, Astrid. I feel as though I did everything wrong before, and I want to make it right now. But it's too late. He's gone. And I don't care what you say, it feels in my gut like he's never coming home again. I play games with myself, I listen for his footsteps, I wander around his studio—and then we go up and see him there, like an ape in a cage. Astrid, he's my husband, and they have him locked up like an animal!' Tears and confusion flooded her eyes.

'Is that what really bothers you, Jessie?'

She looked irate at the question. 'Of course it is! What do you think?'

'I think that bothers you, but I think other things bother you just as much. I think you're afraid everything will change. He'll change. He wants his book now, and that frightens you.'

'It does not frighten me. It annoys me.' At least that was honest. She had admitted it.

'Why does it annoy you?'

'Because I sit here by myself, going crazy, dealing with reality, and what does he want to do? Doodle around on his book, like nothing ever happened. And . . . oh . . . I don't know, Astrid, it's so complicated. I don't understand anything anymore. It's all making me crazy. I can't take it. I *just can't take it.*'

'You can take it, and so can Ian. You've already gone through the worst part. The trial must have been hell.' Jessie nodded soberly.

'Yeah, but this is worse. This goes on forever.'

'Of course not. And Jessie, you can take a lot more than you think. So can Ian.' As she said the words, she hoped she was right.

'How can you be so sure? Remember how he looked today, Astrid? How long do you think he can take all that? He's spoiled, spoiled rotten, and used to a comfortable life with civilised people. Now he's in there. We don't see what it's really like, but what do you think will happen when some guy pulls a knife on him, or some jerk wants to make love to him? Then what? Are you really sure he can handle it, Astrid?' Her voice was rising to an hysterical pitch. 'And you know what the real joke of this whole mess is? That he's in there because of me. Not because of Margaret Burton. Because of me. Because I castrated him so completely that he needed her to prove something. I did it. I might as well have put the handcuffs on him myself.'

The tragedy of it was that Astrid knew she believed that. She went to her and tried to put her arms around her as Jessica sobbed.

'Jessica, no . . . no, baby. You know . . .'

'I know. It's true! I know it. And he knows it. And the fucking woman even knew it. You should have seen how she looked at me in court. God knows what he told her. But I looked at her with hatred, and she looked at me with . . . pity. Dammit, Astrid, please give me some of those pills.' She looked up at Astrid with a ravaged face, but her friend shook her head.

'I can't.'

'Why not? I need them.'

'You need to think right now. Clearly. Not in a fogged state. What you just told me is totally crazy, and a lot of what you're thinking is probably pretty crazy. You might as well get it all straightened out in your head now, and have done with it. Pills won't help.'

'They'll get me through it.' She was begging now.

'No they won't. You've lost all perspective about what happened, and they'll only make it worse. And I can tell you one thing for sure. If you don't straighten out your thinking now, it will only get worse, and you won't have a marriage left when Ian comes out. You'll eventually wind up hating him, maybe even as much as you hate yourself right now, if that's possible. You owe yourself some serious thinking, Jessica.'

'So you're going to see that I get it, is that it?' Jessica's voice was bitter now.

'No, I can't do that. I can't force you to think. But I won't give you anything to cloud your thinking anymore either. I can't do that, Jessica. I just can't.' Jessica felt an almost irresistible urge to stand up and hit her, and then she knew that she must be going crazy. Wanting to hit Astrid was very crazy. But also very real. She wanted those goddam pills.

'You'll have to face it sooner or later anyway.' And then suddenly there were tears in Jessie's eyes again.

'But what if I go crazy? I mean really crazy?'

'Why should you?'

'Because I can't handle it. I just can't handle it.'

Astrid felt out of her depth and wondered how her mother had stood her when she had been in similar shape after Tom's death. It gave her an idea.

'Jessie, why don't you come down to the ranch with me at Christmas? Mother would love it, and it would do you good.'

Jessica shook her head even before Astrid had finished her sentence.

'I can't.'

'Why not?'

'I have to spend Christmas with Ian.' She looked mournful at the thought.

'You don't "have" to.'

'All right, I want to.' Christmas without Ian? No way.

'Even with the window between you?' Jessica nodded. 'Why, for God's sake? As a penance to absolve you of the guilt you're heaping on your own head? Jessica, don't be ridiculous. Ian would probably love to know that you're doing something pleasant, like going down to the ranch.' Jessica didn't answer, and after a pause, Astrid said what she had really been thinking. 'Or would you rather torture him by letting him see how much you can suffer on Christmas?'

Jessica's eyes flew wide open again on that one.

'Jesus, you make it sound like I'm trying to punch him.'

'Maybe you are. I think you just can't decide right now who you hate more—him or yourself. And I think you've both had enough punishment, Ian at the hands of the State, and you at your own. Can't you start to be good to yourself now, Jessica? And maybe then you'll be able to be good to him.' There was more truth in Astrid's words than Jessie was ready for.

'You *can* take care of you, Jessie. And Ian will take care of you, even at a distance. Your friends will help.

But most of all, you have to see that you're much more capable than you know.'

'How do you know?'

'I know. You're scared and you have a right to be. But if you'd just calm down a little, and take stock of yourself, *kindly*, you'd be a lot less scared. But you're going to have to stop running to do that.'

'And stop taking pills?'

Astrid nodded, and Jessie remained silent. She wasn't ready to do that yet. She knew it without even trying.

But she did try. Astrid left without giving her any, and Jessica went to the bank with Ian's manuscript—with trembling hands and trembling knees, but without taking another pill. From there she went to the post office, and from there on to the shop. She lasted at Lady J for less than an hour, and then she came home to pace. She spent the night huddled in a chair in the living room, nauseated, trembling, wide-eyed, and wearing a sweater of Ian's. It still had the smell of his cologne on it, and she could feel him with her. She could sense him watching her as she sat in front of the fireplace. She kept seeing faces in the fire—Ian's, her mother's, Jake's, her father's. They came to her late in the night. And then she thought she heard strange sounds in the garage. She wanted to scream but couldn't. She wanted pills but didn't have any. She never went to bed that night, and at seven in the morning she called the doctor. He gave her everything she wanted.

CHAPTER XXIII

At Christmas, Astrid spent three weeks at the ranch with her mother. Jessica was swamped at the boutique. She was falling into a routine now with her visits to Ian. She drove up two weekday mornings and on Sundays. She was putting four hundred miles a week on his car, and the Volvo wasn't going to take the wear much longer.

She almost wondered if she and the car would die together, simply keel over at the side of the road and die. In the Volvo's case it would be from old age; in Jessie's, from strain and exhaustion. That and too many pills. But she functioned well with them now. Most people still couldn't tell. And Ian hadn't yet confronted her about them. She assumed that he simply didn't want to see what was happening. It was fine with her.

She couldn't send him a Christmas present this year. He was allowed to receive only money, so she sent him a cheque. And forgot to buy Christmas presents for the two girls in the shop. All she thought about was putting gas in the car, surviving the visits with Ian on the opposite side of the glass window, and getting her prescriptions refilled. Nothing else seemed to matter. And whatever energy she had left she spent figuring out the bills. She was making some headway with them, and she would wake up in the morning figuring out how to cover this, if she borrowed from that, if she didn't pay that until . . . she was hoping that Christmas profits would put her back in the black. But Lady J was having its own problems. Something was off, and she couldn't bring herself to care as much as she'd used to. Lady J was only a vehicle now, not a joy. It was a means of paying bills, and a place to go in the daytime. She could hide in the little office in the back of the shop and juggle those bills. She rarely came out to see customers now. After a few minutes, the now familiar rising wave of panic would seize her throat and she'd have to excuse herself . . . a yellow pill . . . a blue one . . . a quick sip of Scotch . . . something . . . anything to kill the panic. It was easier just to sit in the back and let the girls handle the customers. She was too busy anyway. With the bills. And with trying not to think. It took a lot of effort not to think, especially late at night or early in the morning. Suddenly, for the first time in years, she had perfect recall of her mother's voice, her father's laughter. She had forgotten them for so long, and now they were back. They said things . . . about each other . . . about her . . . about Ian . . . and they were right. They wanted her to think.

Jake even said something once. But she didn't want to think. It wasn't time yet. She didn't have to . . . didn't want to . . . couldn't . . . they couldn't make her . . . they . . .

Christmas did not fall on a visiting day, so she couldn't spend it with Ian after all. She spent it alone, with three red pills and two yellow ones. She didn't wake up until four the next afternoon, and then she could go back to the shop. She wanted to mark some things down for a sale. They had lost money at Christmas and she had to make it up. A good fat sale would really do it. She would send out little cards to their best customers. It would bring them in droves—she hoped.

She worked on the books straight through New Year's, and finally remembered to give Zina and Kat cheques instead of the Christmas presents she had overlooked. Jessie had gotten three presents, and a poem from Ian. Astrid had given her a simple and lovely gold bracelet, and Zina and Kat had given her small, thoughtful things. A homemade potpourri in a pretty French jar from Zina, and a small line drawing in a silver frame from Katsuko. And she had read the poem from Ian over and over on Christmas Eve. It was quickly dog-eared as it lay on her nightstand.

She had taken it with her to the office, and now carried it in her bag, to bring out and read during the day. She knew it by heart the day after she'd gotten it.

Katsuko and Zina wondered what she did in her office all the time now. She would emerge for coffee, or to look for something in the stockroom, but she rarely spoke to them, and never joked anymore. Gone were the days of cosy gossip and the easy camaraderie the three had shared. It was as though Jessie had vanished when Ian did. She would appear at the door of her small office at the end of the day, sometimes with a pencil stuck in her hair, a distracted look, a small packet of bills in one hand, and sometimes with eyes that were bloodshot and swollen. She was quicker to snap at people now, quicker to lose patience over trivial matters. And there was always that dead look in her eyes. The look that said she lay awake at night. The look that said she was more frightened than she wanted them to know. And the unmistakable glaze from the pills.

Only the days when she visited Ian were a little different. She was alive then. Something sparkled behind the wall she had built between herself and the rest of the world. Something different would happen in her eyes then, but she would share it with no one. Not even with Astrid, who was spending more and more time at the shop, and getting to know Zina and Katsuko. In a sense, Astrid had replaced Jessie. She had the kind of easy-going ways that Jessie had had before. She enjoyed the shop, the people, the clothes, the girls. She had time to talk and laugh. She had new ideas. She loved the place, and it showed. The girls had grown fond of her. She even came in on the days when Jessie was with Ian.

'You know, sometimes I think I sit here just so I know when she gets back. I worry about her making that drive.'

'So do we.' Katsuko shook her head.

'She told me the other day that she just does it on "automatic pilot".' Zina's words weren't much comfort. 'She says that sometimes she doesn't even remember where she is or what she's doing until she sees that sign.'

'Terrific.' Astrid took a sip of coffee and shook her head.

'Grim, isn't it? I wonder how long she'll hold up. She can't just keep plodding on like that. She has to go somewhere, see people, smile occasionally, sleep.' And sober up. Katsuko didn't say it, but they all thought it. 'She doesn't even look like the same woman anymore. I wonder how he's doing.'

'A little better than she is, actually. But I haven't seen him for a while. I think he's less afraid.'

'Is that what it is with her?' Zina looked stunned. 'I thought she was just exhausted.'

'That too. But it's fear.' Astrid sounded hesitant to discuss it.

'And pressure. Lady J has been giving her a rough time lately.'

'Oh? Looks busy enough.'

Katsuko shook her head, reluctant to say more. She had taken calls lately from people Jessie owed money to. For the first time the business was in trouble, and there was no money to fall back on. Jessie had bled every last cent of their spare money for Ian. So now Lady J was paying Ian's price too.

Jessie walked into the shop then, and the conversation came to a halt. She looked haggard and thin but there was something brighter in her eyes, that indefinable something that Ian poured back into her soul. Life.

'Well, ladies, how has life been treating you all today? Are you spending all your money here again, Astrid?' Jessie sat down and took a sip of someone's cold coffee. The small yellow pill she slipped into her mouth at the same time was barely noticeable. But Astrid noticed.

'Nope. Not spending a dime today. Just dropped by for some coffee and company. How's Ian?'

'Fine, I guess. Full of the book. How was business today?' She didn't seem to want to talk about Ian. She rarely spoke of anything important to her anymore. Even to Astrid.

'It was pretty quiet today.' Katsuko filled her in on business while Zina watched the slight trembling of Jessie's hand.

'Terrific. A dead business, and a dead car. The Volvo just breathed its last.' She sounded unconcerned, as though it really didn't matter because she had twelve other cars at home.

'On your way home?'

'Naturally. I hitched a ride with two kids in Berkeley. In a 1952 Studebaker truck. It was pink with green trim and they called it the Watermelon. It drove like one too.' She tried to make light of it while the three women watched her.

'So where's the car?'

'At a service station in Berkeley. The owner offered me seventy-five bucks for it, and agreed to drop the towing charge.'

'Did you sell it?' Even Katsuko looked stunned.

'Nope. I can't. It's Ian's. But I guess I will. That car

has had it.' And so have I. She didn't say it, but they all heard it in her voice. 'Easy come, easy go. I'll pick up something cheap for my trips up to Ian.' But with what? Where would the money come from for that?

'I'll drive you.' Astrid's voice was quiet and strangely calm. Jessica looked up at her and nodded. There was no point in protesting. She needed help and she knew it, and not just with the drive.

Astrid drove Jessica up to see Ian three times a week from then on. It saved Jessie the trouble of waiting to take the two yellow pills when she got there. This way she could take two in the morning, and another two after she saw him. Sometimes she even threw in a green-and-black one. Every little bit helped.

And Astrid could no longer talk to her. There was no use even trying. All she could do was stand by and be there when the roof finally came down. If it did, when it did, wherever and however. Jessica was heading for a stone wall as fast as she could. Nothing less was going to stop her. And Ian couldn't reach her either. Astrid saw that clearly now. He couldn't face what was happening to Jessie, because he couldn't help. If he couldn't help, he wouldn't see. And each time Jessie appeared, looking more tortured, more exhausted, more brittle, more rooted in pain and draped in bravado, it would only hurt Ian more. He would feel greater guilt, greater indebtedness, greater pain of his own. Their eyes rarely met now. They simply talked. He about the book, she about the boutique. Never about the past or the future or the realities of the present. They never spoke of feelings, but only threw out 'I love you' at regular intervals, like punctuation. It was grisly to watch, and Astrid hated the visits. She wanted to shake them both, to speak out, to stop what she was seeing. Instead they just went on dying quietly on opposite sides of the glass wall, in their own private hells, Ian with his guilt and Jessica with hers, and each of them with their blindness about themselves and about each other. While Astrid watched, mute and horrified.

If only they could have held each other, then they might

have been real. But they couldn't, and they weren't. Astrid knew that as she watched them. She could see it in Jessie's eyes now. There was constant pain, but there was also the look of a child who does not understand. Her husband was gone, but what was a husband, and where had he gone? The pills had allowed her to submerge herself in a sea of vagueness, and she rarely came to the surface anymore. She was very close to drowning, and Astrid wasn't entirely sure if Ian hadn't already drowned. Astrid could have done without the visits. But they were all locked into their roles now. Husband, wife, and friend.

January bled into February and then limped into March. The boutique had a two-week sale that brought scarcely any business. Everyone was busy or away or feeling poor. The last of their winter line hadn't done well at all; the economy was weak, and luxuries were going with it. Lady J was not a boutique to supply ordinary needs. It catered to a select clientele of the internationally chic. And her clients' husbands were telling them to lay off. The market was bad. They were no longer amused by a 'little' sweater and a 'nothing' skirt that cost them *in toto* close to two hundred dollars.

'Christ, what are we going to do with all this junk?' Jessie paced the floor, opening a fresh pack of cigarettes. She had seen Ian that morning. Once again through the window. Still through the window. Forever through the window. She had visions of finally getting to touch him again when they were both ninety-seven years old. She didn't even dream of his coming home anymore. Just of being able to touch him.

'We're going to have a real problem, Jessie, when the spring line comes in.' Katsuko looked around pensively.

'Yeah, the bastards. It was due in last week and it's late.' She swept into the stockroom to see what was there. She was annoyed much of the time now. The pain was showing itself differently. It wasn't enough now to hide: it was taking more to silence her inner voices.

'You know, I've been thinking.' Katsuko had followed her into the stockroom and was watching her.

'Was it painful?' Jessie looked up, smiled awkwardly, and then shrugged. 'Sorry. What were you thinking, Kat?' That sounded like the old Jessie. But it was rare now.

'About next fall's line. Are you going to New York one of these days?' On what? A broomstick?

'I don't know yet.'

'What'll we do for a fall line if you don't?' Katsuko was worried. There was almost no money for a new line, and there were still unpaid bills all over Jessie's desk.

'I don't know, Kat. I'll see.'

She walked into her office and slammed the door, her mouth in a small set line. Zina and Kat exchanged a glance. Zina answered the phone when it rang. It was for Jessie. From some record store. She buzzed Jessie's office and watched her pick up the phone. The light on the phone Zina had answered went out only a few moments later.

And in her office Jessie's hands were trembling as she toyed with a pencil on her desk. It had been another one of those calls. They were sure it was an oversight, undoubtedly she had forgotten to send them a cheque for the amount that was due . . . at least these had been polite. The doctor's office had called yesterday and he had threatened to sue. For fifty dollars? A doctor was going to sue her for fifty dollars? . . . And a dentist for ninety-eight . . . and there was still a liquor store bill for Ian's wine for a hundred and forty-five . . . and she owed the cleaner's twenty-six and the drugstore thirty-three and the phone bill was forty-one . . . and I. Magnin . . . and Ian's old tennis club . . . and new plants for the shop and the electricians' bill when the lights had gotten screwed up over Christmas . . . and a plumbing bill for the house . . . and on and on and on it went, and the Volvo was gone, and Lady J was going down the tubes, and Ian was in prison, and everything just kept getting worse instead of better. There was almost a satisfaction in it, like playing a game of 'how bad can things get?' And meanwhile Astrid was buying sweaters from her at cost, and 'amusing' gold bracelets at Shreve's, and having her hair done every three days at twenty-five bucks a crack. And now there was the fall line to think about. Three hundred bucks' worth of plane fare, and a hotel bill, not to mention the cost of what she bought. It would sink her further into debt, but she didn't have much choice. Without a fall line, she might as well close up Lady J on Labour Day. But it was getting to the point where she was afraid to walk into the bank to cash a cheque. She was always sure that she'd be stopped on the way out and ushered to the manager. How long would they put up with the overdrafts, the problems, the bullshit? And how long would she?

As she was trying to figure out how expensive the trip to New York would be, the intercom buzzed to let her know she had a call. She picked up the phone absent-mindedly, without finding out from Zina who it was.

'Hi, gorgeous, how's about some tennis?' The voice was jovial and already sounded sweaty.

'Who is this?' She suspected an obscene phone caller and was thinking of hanging up as the man on the other end took a large swallow of something, presumably beer.

'Barry. And how've ya been?'

'Barry who?' She recoiled from the phone as though from a snake. This was no one she knew.

'Barry York. You know. Yorktowne Bonding.'

'What?' She sat up as though someone had slapped her.

'I said . . .'

'I know what you said. And you're calling me to play tennis?'

'Yeah. You don't play?' He sounded surprised, like a small boy who's just been severely disappointed.

'Mr. York, do I understand you correctly? You want to play tennis with me?'

'Yeah. So?' He belched softly into the phone.

'Are you drunk?'

'Of course not. Are you?'

'No, I'm not. And I don't understand why you called me.' Her voice was straight out of the Arctic Circle, long-distance.

'Well, you're a good-looking woman, I was going to

play tennis, and I figured maybe you'd want to play. No big deal. You don't dig tennis, we can go have dinner somewhere.'

'Are you out of your mind? What in God's name makes you think I have any desire whatsoever to play tennis, play hopscotch, have dinner, or do anything else with you?'

'Well, listen to the red-hot mama. Sing it, sweetheart. What's to get so excited about?'

'I happen to be a married woman.' She was shouting and Zina and Kat could hear her tone from the other side of the door. They wondered who had called. Kat raised an eyebrow, and Zina went to help a client. Inside, the conversation continued.

'Yeah, so you happen to be a married woman. And your old man happens to be sitting on his ass in the joint. Which is too bad, but which leaves you out here with the rest of us human beings who like to play tennis, play hopscotch, eat dinner, and get laid.' Now she felt genuinely nauseated. She was remembering his thick black hair and the smell of him, and the ugly ring with the pink stone in it. It was incredible. That man, that hideous pig of a man, that absolute total stranger was calling her and talking about 'getting laid'. She sat there pale and trembling with tears starting to sting her eyelids again. It was funny. She knew that somewhere in all this it was funny. But it didn't make her want to laugh. It made her want to cry, want to go home, want to . . . this was what Ian had left her. The Barry Yorks of the world, and people calling about the cheques she had 'forgotten' to send and that she would continue to forget for at least another six or seven or nine or ten weeks or maybe even years. To the point that she was afraid to walk into the florist now for so much as a bunch of daisies, because she probably owed him money too. She owed everyone money. And now this animal on the phone wanted to get laid.

'I . . . Mr. . . . I'm . . .' She fought the tears out of her voice and swallowed hard.

'Whatsa matter, sweetheart, married women in Pacific Heights don't get horny, or you already got a boyfriend?'

Jessica sat looking at the phone, her chin trembling,

her hand shaking, tears streaming down her face, and her lower lip pouting as if she were a child whose best doll had just been smashed to bits. It had finally all hit her. This was what had happened to her life. She shook her head slowly, and gently hung up the phone.

CHAPTER XXIV

'See you later, ladies.' She picked up her bag, and started out of the shop. It was early April, and a beautiful warm Friday morning. Spring seemed to be everywhere.

'Where are you going, Jessie?' Zina and Kat looked up surprised.

'To see Ian. I have some other things to do tomorrow, so I thought I'd go up today.'

'Give him our love.' She smiled at the two girls and left the shop quietly. She had been very quiet again lately. Oddly so. The irritability seemed to be passing, ever since the call from Barry York. That had been three weeks ago. She had never told Ian. But the degradation showed in her face.

York, Houghton, people calling for bills, it didn't really matter. It was her own fault. She had done it all to herself. The great Jessica Clarke. The all-powerful, all-knowing, all-paying Mrs. Jessica Clarke, and her wonderful husband Mr. Jessica Clarke. She saw it all now. The sleepless nights were beginning to pay off. She couldn't run away from it anymore. She was beginning to think, to remember, to understand. She heard it now like old tapes played back in the dark of night. She had nothing else to do but remember . . . incidents, moments, trivia, voices. Not her mother's voice now. Not Jake's. But her own, and Ian's. 'Fables, darling? Do they sell?' As though that were the only thing that mattered. He had blurted out half a dozen reasons, explanations—as though he owed her any—and the fables had been beautiful. But it didn't matter, she had killed them before they'd been born. With one line. 'Do they sell?' Who cared if they sold? It was probably why he had bought her the Morgan with his publisher's advance. It was the loudest way he could think of to answer.

And other times.

'The opera, sweetheart? Why the opera? It's so expensive.'

'But we enjoy it. Don't you, Jessie? I thought you did.'

'Yeah, but—oh, what the hell. I'll take it out of the house money.'

'Oh, is that it?' There had been a long pause. 'I already bought the tickets, Jess. With "my" money.' But he had decided not to go in the end. He had decided to work at the last minute. He hadn't gone all that season.

Tiny moments, minute phrases that slashed into hearts with the blow of a machete, leaving scars on a life, on a marriage, on a man. Why? When she needed him so much? Or was that it? That she needed him, and she knew he didn't need her in the same way?

'But he needed me too.' Her voice sounded loud in the solitude of the car. She couldn't allow Astrid to chauffeur her three times a week, so she now rented a compact to go up and see him. Another expense she could ill afford. But as she drove along, she wondered. Why the barbs? The small digs over the years? To clip his wings so he never flew away? Because if he had flown away, she couldn't have survived. And the joke of it was that he had flown anyway. For one afternoon, and maybe a thousand afternoons before that, but for one afternoon that had cost them everything. He had needed a woman who didn't shoot off her mouth, didn't cut him down. Someone who didn't need him, didn't love him, didn't hurt him.

It was crazy, really. Whatever she had done, she had done out of the fear of losing him. And now look at where they were. She was so engrossed in her thoughts that she almost missed the turnoff, and she was still pensive as she waited for him to appear at the window.

Even after Ian arrived, she seemed to have her mind

more on the past than the present. And he seemed wrapped up in his own thoughts too. She looked up at him and tried to smile. She had a splitting headache and she was tired. She kept seeing her own reflection in the glass window that stood between them. It made her feel as if she were talking to herself.

'You're not very chatty today, Mr. Clarke. Anything wrong?'

'No, just thinking about the book, I guess. I'm getting to the point where it's hard to relate to much else. I'm all wrapped up in it.' He noticed an odd flash in her eyes as he finished speaking, and started to tell her about the book. She let him ramble on for a few minutes and then interrupted.

'You know something? You're amazing. I come all the way up here to find out how you are, and to talk to you about what's happening in my life. And you talk to me about the book.'

'What's wrong with that?' He looked puzzled as he watched her from the other side of the glass. 'You tell me about Lady J.'

'That's different, Ian. That's real, for Chrissake.' She was sounding shrill, and it irritated him.

'Well, the book is real to me.'

'So real that you can't even take an hour of your precious time to talk to me? Hell, you've been sitting there like a zombie for the last hour, telling me about the goddam book. And every time I start to tell you about me, you fade out.'

'That's not true, Jess.' He looked upset and reached for a cigarette. 'The book is just going really well and I wanted to tell you about it. I don't think I've ever hit such a good writing spell, that's all.' He knew he'd said the wrong thing as soon as the words were out of his mouth. The look on her face was incredible. 'Jessie, what the hell is wrong with you? You look like someone just shoved a hot poker up your ass.'

'Yeah, or slapped my face, maybe. Jesus Christ, you sit there and you tell me how brilliantly your writing is going, how you've never "hit such a good writing spell", like you're on some kind of fucking vacation in there. Do you know what's happening in *my* life?' She took a deep breath and he felt as if poison were pouring at him through the phone. She had lost control and she wasn't about to stop now.

'You really want to know what's happening to me while you're having such a "good writing spell"? Well, I'll tell you, darling. Lady J is going broke, people are calling me up day and night telling me to pay our bills and threatening to sue me. Your car fell apart, my nerves have had it, I have nightmares about Inspector Houghton every night, and the bailbondsman called me up for a date three weeks ago. He figured I needed to get laid. And maybe the sonofabitch is right, but not by him. I haven't so much as touched your hand in I don't know how many months, and I'm going goddam crazy. My whole stinking life is on the rocks, and you're having a good writing spell! And you know what else is terrific, *darling*—' she dripped venom in his ear, and others in the room watched as he sat there incredulous. She wasn't keeping any secrets from anyone.

'What's absolutely marvellous, Ian my love, is that I drove all the way up here today blaming myself for the nine-thousandth time for everything I've done wrong in our marriage, about the pressures I've put on you, about the rotten things I've said. Do you realise that by now I've replayed every lousy scene in our marriage, everything I've ever done wrong that made you even want to go to bed with a piece of shit like Margaret Burton? I've been blaming myself ever since it happened. I've even blamed myself for supporting your writing career, thinking that I stole your manhood. And while I'm crucifying myself, you know what you're doing? Having the best writing spell in your life. Well, you know what? You make me sick. While you sit up here in this glorified writers' colony they call a prison, my whole life is coming apart and you're not doing a goddam thing about it, sweetheart. Nothing. And I'll tell you something else, I'm sick to death of that puking window, of having to twist around like a pretzel just to see you and not a reflection of myself. I'm sick of getting sweaty hands and sweaty ears and a sweaty brain just talking to you on the goddam phone here . . . I'm sick to death of the whole goddam mess!' She was shouting so loudly that the whole room was watching now, but neither of them noticed. It had been building for months.

'And I suppose you think I enjoy it here?'

'Yes, I think you enjoy it here. A colony for gigolo writers.'

'That's right, sweetheart. That's what this is. And that's all I do here, is write. I never think about my wife, and how I got here, and why, and of that damn woman, or of the trial. I never have to shove my way out of getting laid by some guy with the hots for me.

'Listen, lady, if you think this is my idea of living, you can shove it right up your ass. But I'll tell you something else. If you think our marriage is my idea of living you can put that in the same place. I thought we had a marriage. I thought we had something. Well, guess what, Mrs. Clarke? We didn't have a fucking thing. Nothing. No kids, no honesty, and two half-assed careers. Two half-assed people, the way I see it now. And you've spent most of the last six years trying not to grow up and playing cripple after you lost your parents. Not only that, but making me feel guilty for God knows what, so I'd stick around and hold your hand. And I was dumb enough to swallow all that because I was stupid enough to love you and I wanted to have my writing career too. Well, the combo, such as it was, was a lousy one, Lady Bountiful. And you can have it. I happen to need a wife, not a banker or a neurotic child. Maybe that's why I'm happy right now, believe it or not, as stinking as this place happens to be. I'm writing and you're not supporting me. How's that for a shocker, baby? You're not picking up the tab and I don't owe you one thing except for the fact that you held my hand every inch of the way during the trial and you were marvellous. But I'm going to pay you back for the bills on that eventually. And if your idea now is to make me suffer as much as possible, to make me feel as guilty as possible over how fucked up you can get, how bad the bills are, and how fast my car can fall apart, then fuck you. I can't do anything about anything in here. All I can do is give a damn about you, be grateful you come to see me, and finish my fucking book. And if you don't dig seeing me, do me a big favour and don't come anymore. I can live without it.'

Jessica felt the all-too-familiar surge of panic clutch at her chest as she watched his face. But this time it was worse. They had never said things like this to each other. And she couldn't stop now. She could still feel the bile frothing up in her soul.

'Why don't you want me to come see you, darling? Did you find another sweetheart in here? Is that it, angel? Does the big he-man have another he-man to love?' Ian stood up and looked as if were going to hit her, right through the glass window, much to the fascination of the now silent crowd on both sides of the glass.

'Is that it, darling? Have you gone gay!'

'You make me sick.'

'Oh, that's right, I forgot. You don't like "infamous crimes against nature". Or do you?' She looked intolerably sweet as she raised her eyebrows, and her heart pounded violently in her chest. 'Maybe you did rape that woman after all.'

'Lady, if I weren't in here I'd put my fist right through your face.' He towered over her, with the veil of glass between them, the phones still in their hands, and slowly Jessica rose to face him. She knew that the moment had come and she couldn't believe it. She still couldn't stop.

'Put your fist through my face?' Their voices were soft now. He had spoken to her with the measured tone of a man who is almost finished, and she was speaking in the silvery whisper of a viper about to strike the last blow. 'Put your fist through my face?' She repeated the words again with a smile. 'But why now, darling? You never had the balls to before. Did you, love?'

He answered her in less than a whisper, and her heart almost stopped when she saw the look in his eyes.

'No, Jess, I didn't. But I don't have anything to lose now. I've already lost it. And that makes everything a lot easier.' He smiled a small, strange smile that chilled her, looked at her thoughtfully for a brief moment, put down the phone, and walked out. He never looked back once, and she felt her mouth open in astonishment. What had he just said? She wanted him to come back, so she could ask him again, so that . . . what did he mean, 'that makes everything a lot easier'? What did . . . the sonofabitch . . . he was walking out on her, he had no right to, he couldn't, he . . . and what had she done? What had she said? She sank into her seat as though she were in shock, and slowly the babble of voices around her returned to normal. Ian had long since disappeared through the far door, was no longer visible. She had been wrong. He did have the balls. And he had done just what she had always feared most. He had walked out on her.

The front bumper of the rented car brushed the hedges in front of the house as she pulled into the driveway. She put her head down on the wheel and felt the breath catch in her throat. There was a sob lodged there somewhere, but it was stuck, it wouldn't come out. The weight of her head set off the horn, and the sound felt like it was blowing off the top of her head. It felt good. She wouldn't take her head off the steering wheel. She just stayed there until two men passing by came rushing into the driveway on foot. They knocked on the window and she turned her face slowly to one side, looked at them, and laughed, a high-pitched hysterical giggle. The men looked at each other questioningly, opened the car door, and gently eased Jessie's body back on the seat. She looked from one to the other, laughed hysterically again, and then the laughter snagged on a sob. It wrenched itself from her throat and became a long, sad, lonely wail. She shook her head slowly and said one word over and over between sobs: 'Ian'.

'Lady, are you drunk?' The older man of the two looked hot and uncomfortable. He had thought she was hurt, or sick, with her head down on the steering wheel like that, and making such a racket with the horn. But here she was, drunk, or crazy, or stoned. He hadn't bargained on that. The younger man looked at her, shrugged his shoulders, and grinned.

Jessie shook her head slowly from side to side and said the only word she could focus on: 'Ian'.

'Sister, you stoned?' She didn't answer and the younger man shrugged again and grinned. 'Must be good stuff.'

'Ian.'

'Who's Ian? Your boyfriend?'

Another blind shake of the head.

The two men looked at each other again and closed the door of the car. At least the horn wasn't blaring anymore, and she wouldn't sober up for hours. They walked away, the younger one amused, the older one less so.

'You sure she's stoned? She looks kind of mixed up to me. I mean like mixed-up sick. Kinda crazy.'

'Stoned crazy.' The younger man laughed, slapped his belly, and put his arm around his friend just as Astrid drove by and noticed them walking out of the driveway, laughing and looking pleased with themselves. She stopped the car and frowned as a ripple of fear ran up her spine. They didn't look like police, but . . . they noticed her watching them and the younger man waved while the older one smiled. Astrid couldn't understand what was happening, but they slid into a red sedan and seemed to be taking their time. There was nothing furtive or rapid about their movements, and Astrid noticed Jessie in her rented car now. Everything was all right. Astrid honked. But Jessie didn't turn around. She honked again, and once more, and the two men broke into raucous laughter.

'Not you too, sister. The woman in that car is so loaded we had to peel her off the steering wheel just to get her off the horn.' They waved vaguely toward Jessie's driveway, started their car, and pulled out of the parking space as Astrid hopped out of her car and ran into the driveway.

Jessie was still sitting there, crying and sobbing and holding her single word in her mouth. 'Ian.' Astrid wasn't so sure she was stoned. A little maybe, but not as much as she looked. In shock maybe. Something had snapped.

'Jessica?' She slid an arm around her and spoke gently

as Jessie slumped slightly in the seat. 'Hi, Jessie, it's me, Astrid.' Jessica looked at her and nodded. The two men were gone now. Everyone was gone. Even Ian.

'Ian.' She said it more clearly now.

'What about Ian?'

'Ian.'

Astrid wiped her face gently with a handkerchief.

'Tell me about Ian.' Astrid's heart was pounding and she was trying to keep her mind clear and watch Jessica's eyes. She didn't think it was an overdose of pills. More like an overdose of trouble. Jessie had finally had enough.

'What about Ian, love? Tell me. Was he sick today?'

Jessica shook her head. At least he wasn't hurt. Astrid had thought of that first, with tales of prison horrors from the newspapers instantly coursing through her head. But Jessica had motioned no.

'Was something wrong?'

Jessica took a deep breath and nodded. She took another deep breath and leaned back against the seat a little.

'We . . . we had . . . a fight.' The words were barely intelligible, but Astrid nodded.

'What about?'

Jessica shrugged, looking confused again. 'Ian.'

'What did you fight about, Jessie?'

'I . . . I don't . . . know.'

'Do you remember?'

Jessica shrugged again and closed her eyes. 'About . . . everything . . . I think. We both . . . said . . . terrible things. Over.'

'Over what?' But she thought she knew.

'Over. All over.'

'What's all over, Jessie?' Her voice was so gentle, and the tears poured down Jessica's face with fresh force.

'Our marriage is . . . all . . . over . . .' She shook her head dumbly and closed her eyes again. 'Ian . . .'

'It's not all over, Jessie. Just take it easy, now. You two probably just had a lot to get off your chests. You've been through a lot of rough times together lately. A lot of shocks. It had to come out.' But Jessica shook her head.

'No, it's over. I . . . I was so awful to him. I've always . . . been awful to him. I . . .' But then she couldn't speak anymore.

'Why don't we go inside so you can lie down for a while.' Jessica shook her head and wouldn't move, and Astrid fought to get her attention. 'Jessie, listen to me for a minute. I want to take you somewhere.' The girl's eyes flew open in terror. 'Someplace very nice, you'll like it. We'll go together.'

'A hospital?'

Astrid smiled for the first time in five minutes. 'No, silly. My mother's ranch. I think it would do you a lot of good, and . . .'

Jessica shook her head stubbornly. 'No . . . I . . .'

'What? Why not?'

'Ian.'

'Nonsense. I'm going to take you down there, and you'll have a good rest. I think you've really had enough for a while. Don't you?'

Jessica nodded mutely with her eyes closed again.

'Jessie, did you take a lot of pills today?'

She started to shake her head and then stopped and shrugged.

'How many? Tell me.'

'I don't know . . . not sure.'

'Just give me a rough idea. Two? Four? Six? Ten?' She prayed it wouldn't be that many.

'Eight . . . I don't know . . . seven . . . nine . . .' Jesus.

'Are they in your bag?' Jessica nodded. And Astrid gently took her handbag from the seat. 'I'm going to take them, Jessie, okay?' Jessica smiled then for the first time and took a long deep breath. She almost looked like herself again.

'Do I . . . have a choice?' The two women laughed, one fuzzily and the other nervously, and Jessica let her friend help her inside. She wasn't so much stoned as wrung out. She let herself slide slowly into a chair in the living room and didn't even move as she listened to the sounds of Astrid bustling around the bedroom and bathroom. It was going to be so good to be away from it all, even from the sight of Ian behind the glass window. She knew then that she would never see him there again. She'd work the rest out later, but she already knew that. She heaved a deep sigh and went to sleep in the chair until Astrid woke her and led her out to the Jaguar.

Her bags had been packed, the house was locked up, and Jessie felt as though she were a small child again, well taken care of and greatly loved.

'What about the car?'

'The one you rented?' It still sat crookedly in the driveway. Jessica nodded. 'I'll have someone pick it up later. Don't worry about it.' Jessica didn't. It was part of the bliss of having money. Having 'someone pick it up later'. Anonymous faces and hands to do menial tasks. 'And I called the girls at the shop and told them you were going away with me. You can call them yourself tomorrow and give them instructions.'

'Who'll . . . who'll . . . you know, well, run it?' Everything was still jumbled in Jessica's head, and Astrid smiled and patted her cheek gently.

'I will. And I can hardly wait. What a treat, a vacation for you and a job for me.' Jessica smiled and looked more like herself again.

'And the fall line?'

Astrid raised an eyebrow in surprise as she started the car.

'You must be sobering up. I'll send Katsuko, with your permission. I'll take care of the finances of it, and you can pay me back later.' Jessica shook her head and looked back at her friend. The brief nap had sobered her.

'I can't pay you back later, Astrid. Lady J is fighting just to survive. That's one of the reasons nobody's gone to New York yet.'

'Would Lady J accept a loan from me?'

Jessica smiled. 'I don't know, but her mother might. Can I give it some thought?'

'Sure. After Katsuko gets back. I have news for you. You're not allowed to make any decisions for the next two weeks. None. Not even what you eat for breakfast. That's part of the ground rules of this little vacation of yours. I'll advance the money for the fall line, and we'll work it out later. I need a tax write-off anyway.'

'I . . . but . . .'

'Shut up.'

'You know something?' Jessie looked at her with a small smile and tired, swollen eyes. 'Maybe I will. I need the fall line or the shop will fold anyway. What the hell. Was Katsuko happy about going?'

'What do you think?' The two women smiled again and Astrid pulled up in front of her own house. 'Can you make it up my stairs?' Jessica nodded, and slowly followed Astrid into the house. 'I just need a few things; I'll only be gone overnight. I want to be at work tomorrow.' She glowed at the words. And fifteen minutes later they were back in the car and heading for the freeway. Jessie still felt as though a bomb had hit her life, now everything was moving too quickly.

The words with Ian came back to her as they drove along in silence. She had closed her eyes and Astrid thought she was sleeping. But she was wide awake. Too much so. And more awake than she had been in a long time. She needed another pill, and Astrid had flushed them all down the toilet, back at the house. All of them. The red ones, the blue ones, the yellow ones, the black-and-green ones. There was nothing left. Except her own head, pounding with Ian's words . . . and his face . . . and . . . why had they done that to each other? Why the venom, the hatred, the anger? It didn't make sense to her. Nothing did. Maybe they'd always hated each other. Maybe even the good times had been a lie. It was so hard to figure it all out now. And it was too late anyway. Looking for the answers was like searching for your grandmother's silver thimble in the rubble of your home after it had burned to the ground. Together, she and Ian had set fire to their marriage, and from opposite sides of a pane of glass had watched it burn, fanning the flames, refusing to leave until the last beam was gone.

CHAPTER XXV

Astrid touched her shoulder again and she woke up, frightened and confused about where she was. The pills had really worn off now and she felt jangled.

'Take it easy, Jessie. You're at the ranch. It's almost midnight, and everything's fine.' Jessica stretched and looked around. It was dark but stars shone overhead. There was a fresh smell in the air, and she could hear the whinny of horses somewhere in the distance. And just to their right was a large stone house with bright yellow shutters. The house was well lit and a door stood open.

Astrid had slipped inside for a moment with her mother before waking Jessie. Her mother was not shocked or even surprised. She had been through crises before, with Astrid, with friends, with family years before. Things happened to people, they were shaken for a while, but most of them survived. A few didn't, but most did. And the ranch was a good place to recover.

'Come on, sleepyhead, my mother has some hot chocolate and sandwiches waiting, and I don't know about you, but I'm starved.' Astrid stood next to the open car and Jessica ran a comb through her hair with a rueful grin.

'How's she fixed for pills?'

'She's not.' Astrid looked searchingly at Jessie. 'Is it bad?'

Jessica nodded and then shrugged.

'But I'll live. Hot chocolate, huh? How does that compare to Seconal?' Astrid made a face at her and got her suitcase out of the trunk.

'I went through the same thing after Tom. I arrived here and my mother threw everything out. All the pills. And I was a lot less good-natured about it than you were this afternoon.'

'I was just too stoned to react. You were lucky. And here, let me carry that.' She reached for the suitcase and

Astrid gave it up to her. 'Ian always says that an Amazon like me . . .' And then she stopped and let her voice trail off. Astrid watched the bowed head as she quietly walked toward the house. She was glad she had brought her, and only sorry she hadn't done it before. She wondered just how serious the fight with Ian had been. Something told her this was for real, but it was impossible to tell.

Their shoes crunched on the gravel walk that led to the house, and the smell of fresh grass and flowers was everywhere. Jessie noticed that the place looked cheerful even in the dark. There was an array of multicoloured flowers all around the stone building and in great profusion near the door. She smiled as she walked past them and up the single step.

'Watch your head!' Astrid called out as she almost hit it against the doorway, and the two women arrived in the front hall side by side. There was a small upright piano there, painted bright red, a long mirror, a number of bronze spittoons, and a wall of exotic and colourful hats. Just beyond were pine floors and hooked rugs, comfortable couches and a rocking chair by the fire. There were warm-looking oil paintings and a long wall of books. It was an odd combination of good modern, delightful Victorian, simply enjoyable, and pleasantly old, but it worked. Plants and an old Victrola painted red like the piano, some first-edition books, and a very handsome modern couch covered in a pale oatmeal fabric. Old lace granny curtains hung at the windows, and a large tiled stove stood in one corner. The room looked happy and warm, with a surprising element of chic.

'Good evening.'

Jessica turned at the sound of a voice and saw a tiny woman standing in the kitchen doorway. She had the same blonde-grey hair as her daughter and cornflower blue eyes that sparkled and laughed. The simple words 'good evening' sounded as though they amused her. She walked slowly toward Jessica and held out a hand. 'It is very nice indeed to have you here, my dear. I take it Astrid has warned you that I'm a querulous old woman and the ranch is dull as dishwater. But I'm delighted you've come down.' The light in her eyes danced like flame.

'I warned her of no such thing, Mother. I raved about the place, so you'd better be on your best behaviour.'

'Good God, how awful. Now I shall have to put away all my pornographic books and cancel the dancing boys, shall I? How distressing.' She clasped her hands as though greatly disturbed and then burst forth with a youthful giggle. She gestured comfortably toward the couch and the two women followed her to seats near the fire. The promised hot chocolate was waiting in a Limoges china service patterned with delicate flowers.

'That's pretty, Mother. Is it new?' Astrid poured herself a cup of hot chocolate and looked at the china.

'No, dear. It's very old—1880, I believe.' The two women exchanged a teasing glance. One could easily see that they were not only mother and daughter, but also friends. Jessica felt a pang of envy as she watched, but also the glow of reflected warmth.

'I meant, is it new to you?' Astrid took a sip of the warm chocolate.

'Oh, that's what you meant! Yes, as a matter of fact it is.'

'Wretch, and you knew I'd notice and you used it tonight just to show it off.' But she looked pleased at the implied compliment, and her mother laughed.

'You're absolutely right! Pretty, isn't it?'

'Very.' The two women's eyes danced happily, and Jessica smiled, taking in the scene. She was surprised at the youthful appearance of Astrid's mother. And at the elegance that had stayed with her despite the passing of years and life on the ranch. She was wearing well-cut grey gabardine slacks and a very handsome silk blouse that Jessie knew must have come from Paris. It was in very flattering blues that picked up the colour of her eyes. She wore it with pearls and several large and elegant gold rings, one with a rather large diamond set in it. She looked more New York or Connecticut than ranch. Jessie almost laughed aloud remembering the image Astrid had portrayed of her months before, in cowboy gear. That was hardly the picture Jessie was seeing.

'You came at the right time, Jessica. The countryside is so lush and lovely at this time of year. Soft and green and almost furry-looking. I bought the ranch at this time of year, and that's probably why I succumbed. Land is so seductive in the spring.'

Jessica laughed. 'I didn't exactly plan it this way, Mrs. Williams. But my husband went to prison and I turned into a junkie on sleeping pills and tranquillisers and you see, I tried very hard to have a nervous breakdown and we had this awful fight this morning and . . .' she laughed again and shook her head. 'I didn't plan it at all. And you're very kind to have me down here on such short notice.'

'No problem at all.' She smiled, but her eyes took in everything. She noticed that Jessica was eating nothing and only sipping at her hot chocolate. She was smoking her second cigarette in the moments since the two women had arrived. She suspected that Jessica had acquired the same problem Astrid had had after Tom's death. Pills. 'Just make yourself at home, my dear, and stay as long as you like.'

'I may stay forever.'

'Of course not. You'll be bored in a week.' The old woman's eyes twinkled again and Astrid laughed.

'You're not bored here, Mother.'

'Oh yes, I am, but then I go to Paris or New York or Los Angeles, or come up to visit you in that dreadful mausoleum of yours . . .'

'Mother!'

'It is and you know it. A very handsome mausoleum, but nonetheless . . . you know what I think. I told you last year that I thought you ought to sell it and get a new house. Something smaller and younger and more cheerful. I'm not even old enough to live there. I told Tom that when he was alive, and I can't imagine why I shouldn't tell you now.'

'Jessica has the sort of place you would adore.'

'Oh? A grass hut in Tahiti, no doubt.' All three women

laughed and Jessica made an attempt at eating a sandwich. Her stomach was doing somersaults, but she hoped that if she ate something her hands might cease trembling. She suspected that she was in for a rough couple of days, but at least the company would be good. She was already in love with Astrid's outspoken mother.

'She lives in that marvellous blue-and-white house in the next block from us. The one with all the flowers out front.'

'I do remember it more or less. Pretty, but a bit small, isn't it?'

'Very,' Jessica said between bites. The sandwich was cream cheese and ham with fresh watercress and paper-thin slices of tomato.

'I can't bear the city anymore myself. Except for a visit. But after a while, I'm glad to come home. The symphonies bore me, the people overdress, the restaurants are mediocre, the traffic is appalling. Here, I ride in the morning, walk in the woods, and life feels like an adventure every day. I'm too old for the city. Do you ride?' Her manner was so brisk that it was hard to believe she was past fifty-five; Jessica knew she was in fact seventy-two. She smiled at the question.

'I haven't ridden in years, but I'd like to.'

'Then you may. Do whatever you want, whenever you want. I make breakfast at seven, but you don't have to get up. Lunch is a free-lance proposition, and dinner's at eight. I don't like country hours. It's embarrassing to eat dinner at five or six. And I don't get hungry till later anyway. And by the way, my daughter introduced me as Mrs. Williams, but my name is Bethanie. I prefer it.' She was peppery as all hell, but the blue eyes were gentle and the mouth always looked close to laughter.

'That's a beautiful name.'

'It'll do. And now, ladies, I bid you good night. I want to ride early in the morning.' She smiled warmly at her guest, kissed her daughter on the top of her head, and walked briskly up the stairs to her bedroom, having assured Jessica that Astrid would give her a choice of rooms. There were three to choose from, and they were all quite ready for guests. People came to visit Bethanie often, Astrid explained. It was a rare week when no one stayed at the ranch. Friends from Europe included her in their elaborate itineraries, other friends flew out to the Coast from New York and rented cars to drive down to see her, and she had a few friends in Los Angeles. And of course Astrid.

'Astrid, this is simply fabulous.' Jessica was still a bit overwhelmed by it all. The house, the mother, the hospitality, the openness of it all, and the peppery warmth of her hostess. 'And your mother is remarkable.' Astrid smiled, pleased.

'I think Tom married me just so he wouldn't lose track of her. He adored her, and she him.' Astrid smiled again, pleased at the look on Jessica's face.

'I can see why he loved her. Ian would fall head over heels for her.' Her tone changed as she said it, and she seemed to drift off. It was a moment before her attention returned to Astrid.

'I think it'll do you good to be down here, Jessie.'

Jessica nodded slowly. 'It sounds corny, but I feel better already. A little shaky—' she held up a hand to show the trembling fingers, and grinned sheepishly—'but better nonetheless. It's such a relief not to have to go through another night alone in that house. You know, it's crazy. I'm a grown woman. I don't know why it gets to me so badly, but it's just awful, Astrid. I almost hope the damn place burns to the ground while I'm gone.'

'Don't say that.'

'I mean it. I've come to hate that house. As happy as I once was there, I think I detest it twice as much now. And the studio—it's like a reminder of all my worst failings.'

'Do you honestly feel that you've failed, Jessica?'

Jessica nodded slowly but firmly.

'Single-handedly?'

'Almost.'

'I hope you come to realise how absurd that is.'

'You know what hurts the worst? The fact that I thought we had a fantastic marriage. The best. And now . . . it all looks so different. He swallowed his resentments, I did things my way. He cheated on me and didn't tell me; I guessed but didn't want to *know*. It's all so jumbled. I'm going to need time to sort it out.'

'You can stay down here as long as you like. Mother will never get tired of you.'

'Maybe not, but I wouldn't want to abuse her hospitality. I think if I stay a week, I'll be not only lucky, but eternally grateful.' Astrid only smiled over her hot chocolate. People had a way of saying they'd stay for a few days or a week and of still being there five weeks later. Bethanie didn't mind, as long as they didn't get in her hair. She had her own schedule, her friends, her gardening, her books, her projects. She liked to go her own way and let other people go theirs, which was part of her charm and her great success as a hostess. She was exceedingly independent and she had a healthy respect for people's solitude, including her own.

Astrid showed Jessica the choice of available rooms, and Jessie settled on a small, cosy, pink room with an old-fashioned quilt on the bed and copper pots hanging over the fireplace. It had a high slanted ceiling, high enough so she wouldn't bump her head when she got out of bed. There was a lovely bay window with a window seat, and a rocking chair by the fireplace. Jessica heaved a deep sigh and sat on the bed.

'You know, Astrid, I may never go home.' It was said between a smile and a yawn.

'Good night, puss. Get some sleep. I'll see you at breakfast.' Jessica nodded and yawned again. She waved as Astrid closed the door, and then called a last sleepy 'Thanks.'

She would have to write to Ian in the morning, to tell him where she was. To tell him something. But she'd worry about that tomorrow. For the moment she was a world and a half away from all her problems. The boutique, Ian, bills, that unbearable window in Vacaville. None of it was real anymore. She was home now. That was how it felt, and she smiled at the thought as she lit the kindling and put a log on the fire before slipping into her nightgown. Ten minutes later she was asleep. For the first time in four months, without any pills.

There was a knock on Jessie's door moments after she had closed her eyes. But when she opened them, sunlight was streaming in between the white organdie curtains, and a fat calico cat yawned sleepily in a patch of sunlight on her bed. The clock said ten-fifteen.

'Jessie? Are you up?' Astrid poked her head in the door. She was carrying an enormous white wicker tray laden with goodies.

'Oh no! Breakfast in bed! Astrid, you'll spoil me forever!' The two women laughed and Jessie sat up in bed, her blonde hair falling over her shoulders in a tumult of loose curls. She looked like a young girl and surprisingly rested now.

'You're looking awfully healthy this morning, madam.'

'And hungry as hell. I slept like a log. Wow!' She was faced with waffles, bacon, two fried eggs and a steaming mug of hot coffee, all of it served on delicate flowered china. There was a vase in the corner of the tray with one yellow rose in it. 'I feel like it's my birthday or something.'

'So do I! I can hardly wait to get to the shop!' Astrid giggled and slid into the rocking chair while Jessie went to town on the breakfast. 'I should have let you sleep a while longer, but I wanted to get back to the city. And Mother decided you needed breakfast in bed on your first day.'

'I'm embarrassed. But not too embarrassed to eat all this.' She chuckled and dived into the waffles. 'I'm starving.'

'You should be. You didn't have any dinner.'

'What's your mother up to this morning?'

'God knows. She went riding at eight, came back to change, and just drove off a few minutes ago. She goes her own way, and doesn't invite questions.'

Jessica smiled and sat back in the bed with a mouthful of waffle. 'You know, I should feel guilty as hell, sitting here like this with Ian where he is, but for the first time in five months, I don't. I just feel good. Fabulous, as a matter of fact.' And relieved. It was such a relief not to *have* to do anything. Not to have to be at the shop, or on the way to see Ian, or opening bills, or taking phone calls. She was in another world now. She was free. 'I feel so super, Astrid.' She grinned, stretched, and yawned, with a splendid breakfast under her belt, and the sun streaming across her bed.

'Then just enjoy it. You needed something like this. I wanted to bring you down here over Christmas. Remember?' Jessica nodded regretfully, remembering what she had done instead. She had blotted out Christmas with a handful of pills.

'If I'd only known.'

She stroked the calico cat and it licked her finger as Astrid sat in the rocking chair, quietly rocking and watching her friend. With one good night of sleep she already looked better. But there was still a lot to resolve. She didn't envy Jessica the task ahead of her.

'Why don't you stay down for a couple of days, Astrid?'

Astrid let out a whoop and shook her head. 'And miss all the fun of running the boutique? You're crazy. You couldn't keep me down here if you tied me to a gatepost. This'll be the most fun I've had in years!'

'Astrid, you're nutty, but I love you. If it weren't for you, I couldn't sit around down here like a lady of leisure. So go have a good old time with Lady J. She's all yours!' And then Jessie looked wistful. 'I almost wish I really never had to go back.'

'Do you want to sell me Lady J?' Something in Astrid's voice made Jessica look up.

'Are you serious?'

'Very. Maybe even a partnership, if you don't want to sell out completely. But I've given it a lot of thought. I just never knew how to broach it to you.'

'Like you just did, I guess. But I've never thought of it. It might be an idea. Let me mull it over. And see how you enjoy it while I'm gone. You may hate the place by next weekend.'

But Astrid could tell from the sound of her voice that Jessica had no intention of giving up Lady J. There was still that pride of ownership in her voice. Lady J was hers, no matter how out of sorts with it she was at the moment.

'Were you really serious about sending Katsuko to New York, by the way?' Jessie was still stunned by all that had happened in a mere twenty-four hours.

'I was. I told her to plan on leaving tomorrow. That way you can give her any instructions you want. We can square the finances of it later. Much later. So don't go adding that to your pile of worries. What about the fall line? Any thoughts, orders, requests, caveats, whatever?'

'None. I trust her implicitly. She has a better buying sense than I do, and she's been in retailing for long enough to know what she's doing. After the season we just had, I'm not sure I'm fit to buy for the place anymore.'

'Everyone can have an off season.'

'Yeah. All the way around.' Jessie smiled and Astrid looked back at her friend with warmth in her eyes.

'Well, I'd best be getting my fanny in gear. I have a long drive ahead. Any messages for the home front?'

'Yeah. One.' Jessica grinned, then threw back her head and laughed. 'Good-bye.'

'Jerk. Have a good time down here. This place put me back together once.'

'And you look damn good to me.' Jessie climbed lazily out of bed, stretched again, and gave Astrid a last hug. 'Have a safe trip and give the girls my love.'

She watched her leave and waved from the bedroom window. Jessie was alone in the house now except for the cat, which was parading slowly across the window-seat. There were country sounds from outside, and a delicious silence all around her in the airy, sun-filled house. She wandered barefoot down the long upstairs hall, peeking into rooms, opening books, pirouetting here and there, looking at paintings, chasing the cat, and then went downstairs to do more of the same. She was free! Free! For the first time in seven years, ten years, fifty years, forever, she was free. Of burdens, responsibilities, and terrors. The day before she had hit rock bottom. The last support of her decaying foundation had come tumbling, roaring down . . . and she hadn't fallen with it. Astrid had held her up, and taken her away.

But the best part of all was that she hadn't cracked. She would remember all her life that moment when two strangers had pulled her back from the steering wheel where she was pressing on the horn. She had decided to let herself go crazy then, just slide into a pool of oblivion, never to return to the land of the ugly and dying and evil, the land of the 'living'. But she hadn't gone crazy at all. She had hurt. More than she had ever hurt in her life. But she hadn't gone crazy. And here she was, wandering around a delightful house in the country, barefoot, in her nightgown, with a huge breakfast in her stomach and a smile on her face.

And the amazing thing was that she didn't need Ian. Without him, the roof hadn't fallen in. It was a new idea to Jessie, and she didn't quite know what to do with it yet. It changed everything.

CHAPTER XXVI

It was late in the afternoon of her first day on the ranch that Jessica decided to sit down and write to Ian. She wanted to let him know where she was. She still felt she had to check in. But it was hard to explain to him why she was there. Having kept up the front for so long, it was difficult to tell him just what kind of shape she'd been in behind the façade. She had blown it the day before, but now she had to sit down and tell him quietly. It turned every 'fine' she had ever told him into a lie. And most of them had been lies. She hadn't been willing to admit to herself how far from fine she was, and now she had to do both—admit it to herself and to him. She had no more accusations to level at him, but no explanations she wanted to give either.

Words didn't come easily. What could you say? I love you, darling, but I also hate you . . . I've always been afraid to lose you, but now I'm not sure anymore . . . get lost . . . she grinned at the thought, but then tried to get serious. Where to begin? And there were questions. So many questions. Suddenly she wondered how many other women there had been. And why. Because she was inadequate, or because he was hungry, or because he needed to prove something, or . . . why? Her parents had never asked each other questions, but they had been wrong, or at least, wrong for her. She had followed their example, but now she wanted answers, or thought she did. But she recognised the possibility that the answers she sought were her own. Did she love Ian? Or only need him? Did she need him, or only someone? And how do you ask seven years of questions in half a page of letter . . . do you respect me? Why? How can you? She wasn't sure if she loved or respected him or herself at this point.

She wanted to take the easy way out and simply tell him about Mrs. Williams and the ranch, but that seemed dishonest. And so it took her two hours to write the letter. It was one page long. She told him that yesterday had shown her she needed a rest. Astrid had come up with a marvellous suggestion, her mother's ranch.

It is precisely the kind of place where I can finally relax, come to my senses, breathe again, and be myself. Myself being, these days, an odd combination of who I used to be, who I have been catapulted into being during the past six months, and who I am becoming. It all frightens me more than a little. But even that is changing somewhat, Ian. I am tired of always being so frightened. It must have been a great burden on you all this time, my constant fears. But I am growing now. Perhaps 'up'; I don't know yet. Keep at the book, you're right, and I'm sorry for yesterday. I will regret all our lives that we have borne all of this with such dignity and self-control. Perhaps if we had screamed, shrieked, kicked, yelled, and torn at our hair on the courtroom floor instead—perhaps we'd both be in better shape now. It has to come out sooner or later. I'm working on that now. Right? Well, darling. I love you. J.

She hesitated lengthily with the letter in her hands, and then folded it carefully and put it into an envelope. There was much she had not said. She just didn't want to say it yet. And she carefully inscribed his name on the envelope. But not her own. She wondered if he would think the lack of a return address was an oversight. It wasn't.

Jessica joined Astrid's mother in the living room for an after-dinner drink.

'You have no idea how happy you've made Astrid, my dear. She needs something to do. Lately all she's done is spend money. That's not healthy. The constant acquisition of meaningless possessions, just to pass the time. She doesn't enjoy it, she just does it to fill a void. But your boutique will fill that void in a far better way.'

'I met her through the boutique, as a matter of fact. She just walked in one day, and we liked each other. And she's been so good to me. I hope she really enjoys the shop this week. I'm relieved to be away from it.'

'Astrid mentioned that you'd had a hard time of late.'

Jessie nodded, subdued.

'You'll grow from it in the end. But how disagreeable life can be while one grows!' She laughed over her Campari, and Jessie smiled. 'I've always had a passionate dislike for character-building situations. But in the end, they turn out to be worthwhile, I suppose.'

'I'm not sure I'd call my situation worthwhile. I suspect it's going to be the end of my marriage.' There was a look of overwhelming sorrow in Jessica's eyes, but she was almost certain that she knew her mind now. She simply hadn't wanted to admit it to herself before this.

'Is that what you want now, child? Freedom from your marriage?' She was sitting quietly by the fire, watching Jessica's face intently.

'No, not my freedom, really. I've never had problems about my "freedom". I love being married. But I think we've reached a time when we're simply destroying each other, and it will only get worse. In looking back now, I wonder if we didn't always destroy each other. But it's different now. I see it. And there's no excuse for letting it continue once you see.'

'I suppose you'll have to take the matter in hand, then. How does your husband feel about it?' Jessie paused for a moment.

'I don't know. He's . . . he's in prison right now.' She couldn't think of anyone else she would have told, and she didn't know that Astrid had already told her mother, only that Bethanie appeared to take the news in her stride. 'And we've had to visit each other under such strained conditions that it's been difficult to talk. It's even hard to think. You feel obliged to be so staunch and brave and noble, that you don't dare admit even to yourself, let alone each other, that you've just plain had it.'

'Have you "had it"?' She smiled gently, but Jessie did not return the smile as she nodded. 'It must be very hard for you, Jessica. Considering the guilt attached to leaving someone who's in a difficult situation.'

'I think that's why I haven't allowed myself to think. Not past a certain point. Because I didn't dare "betray" him, even in my thoughts. And because I wanted to think of myself as noble and long-suffering. And because I was . . . scared to. I was afraid that if I let go, I'd never find my way back again.'

'The funny thing is that one always does. We are all so much tougher than we think.'

'I guess I'm beginning to understand now. It's taken me a terribly long time. But yesterday everything fell apart. Ian and I had an all-out fight where we both went for the jugular with everything we said, and I just let myself go afterward. I almost tempted the fates to break me. And . . .' She raised her hands palm up with a philosophical shrug. 'Here I am. Still in one piece.'

'That surprises you?' The old woman was amused.

'Very much.'

'You've never been through crises before?'

'Yes. My parents died. And my brother was killed in

Vietnam. But . . . I had Ian. Ian buffered everything, Ian played ten thousand roles and wore a million different hats for me.'

'That's a lot to ask of anyone.'

'Not a lot. It's too much. Which is probably why he's in prison.'

'I see. You blame yourself?'

'In a way.'

'Jessica, why can't you let Ian have the right to his own mistakes? Whatever got him into prison, no matter how closely it relates to you—doesn't he have a right to own that mistake, whatever it was?'

'It was rape.'

'I see. And you committed the rape for him.' Jessica giggled nervously.

'No, of course not. I . . .'

'You what?'

'Well, I made him unhappy. Put a lot of pressure on him, paid the bills, robbed him of his manhood . . .'

'You did all that for him?' The older woman smiled and Jessica smiled too. 'Don't you suppose he could have said no?' Jessica thought about it and then nodded.

'Maybe he couldn't say no, though. Maybe he was afraid to.'

'Ah, but then it's not your responsibility, is it? Why must you wear so much guilt? Do you like it?' The younger woman shook her head and looked away.

'No. And the absurd thing is that he didn't commit the rape. I know that. But the key to the whole thing is why he was in a position even to be accused of rape. And I can't absolve myself.'

'Can you absolve the woman, whoever she was?'

'Of course, I . . .' And then Jessica looked up, stunned. She had forgiven Margaret Burton. Somewhere along the line, she had forgiven her. The war with Margaret Burton was over. It was one less weight on her heart. 'I'd never thought of that before, not lately.'

'I see. I'm intrigued to know how you robbed him of his manhood, by the way.'

'I supported him.'

'He didn't work?' There was no judgment in Bethanie's voice, only a question.

'He worked very hard. He's a writer.'

'Published?'

'Several times. A novel, a book of fables, several articles, poems.'

'Is he any good?'

'Very—he's just not very successful financially. Yet. But he will be.' The pride in her voice surprised her, but not Bethanie.

'Then how dreadful of you to encourage him. What a shocking thing to do.' Bethanie smiled as she sipped her Campari.

'No, I . . . it's just that I think he hates me for having "kept" him.'

'He probably does. But he probably loves you for it too. There are two sides to every medal, you know, Jessica. I'm sure he knows that too. But I'm still not quite clear about why you want to get out of the marriage.'

'I didn't say that. I just said that I thought the marriage would end.'

'All by itself? With no one to help it along? My dear, how extraordinary!' The two women laughed and then Bethanie waited. She was adept with her questions. Astrid had know she would be, and had purposely not warned Jessica. Bethanie made one think.

Jessica looked up after a long pause and found the core of Bethanie's eyes. She looked right into them. 'I think the marriage already has ended. All by itself. No one killed it. We just let it die. Neither of us was brave enough to kill it, or save it. We just used it for our own purposes, and then let it expire. Like a library card in a town you no longer live in.'

'Was it a good library?'

'Excellent. At the time.'

'Then don't throw the card away. You might want to go back, and you can have the card renewed.'

'I don't think I'd want to.'

'He makes you unhappy, then?'

'Worse. I'd destroy him.'

'Oh, for God's sake, child. How incredibly boring of you—you're being noble. Do stop thinking of him, and think of yourself. I'm sure that's all he's doing. At least I hope so.'

'But what if I'm not good for him and never was good for him, and . . . what if I hate the life I lead now, waiting for him?' Now they were getting to the root of it. 'What if I'm afraid that I only used him, and I'm not even sure if I love him anymore? Maybe I just need someone, and not specifically Ian.'

'Then you have some things to think out. Have you seen other men since he's been gone?'

'No, of course not.'

'Why not?' Jessica looked shocked and Bethanie laughed. 'Don't look at me like that, my dear. I may be ancient, but I'm not dead yet. I tell Astrid the same thing. I don't know what's wrong with your generation. You're all supposed to be so liberated, but you're all terribly prim and proper. It could just be that you need to be loved. You don't have to sell yourself on a street corner, but you might find a pleasant friend.'

'I don't think I could do that, and stay with Ian.'

'Then maybe you ought to leave him for a while, and see what you want. Perhaps he *is* a part of your past. The main thing is not to waste your present. I never have, and that's why I'm a happy old woman.'

'And not an "old" woman.'

Bethanie made a face at the compliment. 'Flattery won't do at all! I seem extremely old to me, each time I look in the mirror, but at least I've enjoyed myself on the way. And I'm not saying that I've been a libertine. I haven't. I'm merely saying that I didn't lock myself in a closet and then find myself hating someone for what I chose to do to myself. That's what you're doing right now. You're punishing your husband for something he can't help, and it sounds to me as though he's been punished enough, and unjustly at that. What you have to think about, and with great seriousness, is whether or not you can accept what happened. If you can, then perhaps it'll all work itself out. But if you're going to try to get restitution from him for the rest of your lives, then you might as well give up now. You can only make someone feel guilty for so long. A man won't take much of that, and the backlash from him will be rather nasty.'

'It already has been.' Jessica was thinking back to the argument in Vacaville as she looked dreamily into the fire.

'No man can take that for very long. Nor any woman. Who wants to feel guilty eternally? You make mistakes, you say you're sorry, you pay a price, and that's about it. You can't ask him to pay and pay and pay again. He'll end up hating you for it, Jessica. And maybe you're not just making him suffer for the present. Maybe you're just using this as an opportunity to collect an old debt. I may be wrong, but we all do that at times.'

Jessica nodded soberly. It was exactly what she had been doing. Making him pay for the past, for his weaknesses and her own. For her insecurities and uncertainty. She was thinking it out when Bethanie's voice gently prodded into her thoughts again.

'Maybe you should tell me to mind my own business.'

Jessica smiled and sat back in her chair again. 'No, I think you're probably right. I haven't been looking at any of this with much perspective. And you make a great deal of sense. More than I want to admit, but still . . .'

'You're a good sport to listen, child.' The two women smiled at each other again and the older woman rose to her feet and stretched delicately, her diamond rings sparkling in the firelight. She was wearing black slacks and a blue cashmere sweater the colour of her eyes, and as Jessica watched her, she found herself thinking again what a beauty the woman must have been in her youth. She was still remarkably pretty in a womanly way, with a gentle veil of femininity softening whatever she did or said. She was actually even lovelier than her daughter. Softer, warmer, prettier—or perhaps it was just that she was more alive.

'You know, if you'll forgive me, Jessica, I think I'll go up to bed. I want to ride early in the morning and I won't ask you to join me. I rise at such uncivilized hours.' Laughter danced in her eyes as she bent to kiss Jessica's forehead, and Jessie quickly lifted her arms to hug her.

'Mrs. Williams, I love you. And you're the first person who's made sense to me in a very long time.'

'In that case, my dear, do me the honour of not calling me "Mrs. Williams". I abhor it. Couldn't you possibly settle for "Bethanie", or "Aunt Beth" if you prefer? My friends' children still call me that, and some of Astrid's friends.'

'Aunt Beth. It sounds lovely.' And suddenly Jessica felt as though she had a new mother. Family. It had been so long since she'd had any, other than Ian. Aunt Beth. She smiled and felt a warm glow in her soul.

'Good night, dear. Sleep well. I'll see you in the morning.'

They exchanged another hug, and Jessica went upstairs half an hour later, still thinking about some of the things Bethanie had said. About punishing Ian ... it made her wonder. Just how angry at Ian was she? And why? Because he had cheated on her? Or because he was in prison now and no longer around to protect her? Because he had gotten "caught" sleeping with Margaret Burton? Would it have mattered as much if she hadn't been forced to confront it? Or was it other things? The books that didn't sell, the money that only she made, his passion for his writing? She just wasn't sure.

Breakfast was waiting for Jessica when she came down the next morning. A happy little note signed 'Aunt Beth' told her there were brioches being kept warm in the oven, crisp slices of bacon, and a beautiful bowl of fresh strawberries. The note suggested that they drive over the hills in the Jeep that afternoon.

They did, and they had a marvellous time. Aunt Beth told her stories about the 'ghastly' people who had lived at the ranch before and had left the main house in 'barbarous condition'.

'I daresay the man was a first cousin of Attila the Hun, and their children were simply frightful!'

Jessica hadn't laughed as easily or as simply in years, and as they tooled over the hills in the Jeep, it dawned on her how well she was doing without pills. No tranquillisers, no sleeping pills, nothing. She was surviving with Aunt Beth's company, a lot of sunshine, and much laughter. They cooked dinner together that night, burned the hollandaise for the asparagus, underdid the roast, and laughed together at each new mistake. It was more like having a roommate her own age than being the guest of a friend's mother.

'You know, my first husband always said I'd poison him one day if he wasn't careful. I was a terrible cook then—not that I'm much better now. I'm not at all sure these asparagus are cooked.' She crunched carefully on one of the stems, but seemed satisfied with what she found.

'Were you married twice?'

'No. Three times. My first husband died when I was in my early twenties, which was a great shame. He was a lovely boy. Died in a hunting accident two years after we were married. And then I had a rather enjoyable time for a while—' she sparkled a bit and then went on—'and married Astrid's father when I was thirty. I had Astrid when I was thirty-two. And her father died when she was fourteen. And my third husband was sweet, but dreadfully boring. I divorced him five years ago, and life has been far more interesting since.' She examined another asparagus stalk and ate it as Jessica laughed.

'Aunt Beth, you're a riot. What was the last one like!'

'Dead, mostly, except no one had told him yet. Old people can be so painfully dull. It was really quite embarrassing to divorce him. The poor man was dreadfully shocked. But he got over it. I visit him when I'm in New York. He's still just as boring, poor thing.' She smiled angelically and Jessica dissolved in another fit of laughter. Aunt Beth wasn't nearly as flighty as she liked to make herself sound, but she certainly hadn't led a dull life either.

'And now? No more husbands?' They were friends now. She could ask.

'At my age? Don't be ridiculous. Who would want an old woman? I'm perfectly content as I am, because I enjoyed my life when I was younger. There's nothing worse than an old woman pretending that she isn't. Or a young woman pretending she's old. You and Astrid do a fine job of that.'

'I didn't use to do it.'

'Neither did she, when Tom was alive. It's time she found

herself someone else and burned down that tomb of a mansion. I think it's appalling.'

'But it's so pretty, Aunt Beth. More than pretty.'

'Cemeteries are pretty too, but I wouldn't dream of living in one—until I had no other option. As long as one has the option, one ought to use it. But she's getting there. I think your shop might do her some good. Why don't you sell it to her?'

'And then what would *I* do?'

'Something different. How long have you had the shop?'

'Six years this summer.'

'That's long enough for anything. Why not try something else?' Long enough for a marriage, too?

'Ian wanted me to stay home and have a child. At least that's what he was saying recently. A few years ago he was perfectly happy with things as they were.'

'Maybe you've just found one of the answers you've been looking for.'

'Such as?' Jessica didn't understand.

'That a few years ago he was "perfectly happy with things as they were". How much has changed in those few years? Maybe you forgot to make changes Jessica. To grow.'

'We grew . . .' But how? She wasn't really sure they had.

'I take it you didn't want children.'

'No, it's not that I didn't want any, it's that it wasn't time yet. It was too soon and we were happy alone.'

'There's nothing wrong with not having children.' Aunt Beth looked at her very directly. A little too directly. 'Astrid has never wanted any either. Said it wasn't for her, and I think she was quite right. I don't think she's ever regretted it. Besides, Tom was really a bit past that when they married. Your husband is a young man, isn't he, Jessica?'

She nodded.

'And he wants children. Well, my dear, you can always stay on the pill and tell him you're trying, can't you?' The older woman's eyes hunted Jessie's. Jessica averted her gaze slightly and looked thoughtful.

'I wouldn't do that.'

'Oh, you wouldn't, would you? That's good.' And then Jessica's eyes snapped back to Aunt Beth's.

'But I've thought of it.'

'Of course you have. I'm sure a lot of women have. A lot of them have probably done more than thought of it. Sensible in some cases, I imagine. It seems a pity to have to be that dishonest. You know, I was never that sure I wanted children. And Astrid was a little bit of a surprise.' Aunt Beth almost blushed, but not quite. It was more a softening of her eyes as she looked backward in time and seemed to forget Jessica for a moment. 'But I really grew quite fond of her. She was very sweet when she was small. And simply horrid for a few years after that. But still sweet in an endearing sort of way. I actually enjoyed her very much.' She made Astrid sound more like an adventure than a person, and Jessica smiled, watching her face. 'She was very good to me when her father died. I thought the world had come to an end, except for Astrid.' Jessie almost envied her as she listened. She made it sound as though life were less lonely because of Astrid, instead of more so.

'I've always been, well, afraid, I guess. Afraid of having children, because I thought it would put an obstacle between me and Ian. I thought it would make me lonely.' Bethanie smiled and shook her head.

'No, Jessica. Not if your husband loves you. Then he'll only love you that much more because of the child. It's an additional bond between you, an extension of both of you, a blending of what you love most and hate most and need most and laugh at most, of the two of you. It's a very lovely thing. I can think of a good many reasons to fear having children, but that shouldn't be one of them. Can't you love more than one person?'

It was a good question, and Jessica decided to be honest.

'I don't think so, Aunt Beth. Not anymore. I haven't loved anyone but Ian in a long time. So I guess I can't imagine him loving someone besides me—even a child. I know it must sound selfish, but it's how I feel.'

'It doesn't sound selfish. It sounds frightened, but not really selfish.'

'Maybe one day I'll change my mind.'

'Why? Because you think you ought to? Or because you

want to? Or so you can punish your husband some more?' Aunt Beth didn't pull any punches. 'Take my advice, Jessica. Unless you really want a child, don't bother. They're a terrible nuisance, and even harder on the furniture than cats.' She said it with a straight face as she stroked the calico cat sitting on her lap. Jessica laughed in surprise at the remark. 'As pets go, I much prefer horses. You can leave them outside without feeling guilty.' She looked up with another of her saintly smiles, and Jessica grinned. 'Don't always take me seriously. And having children is really a matter of one's own choice. Whatever you do, don't be pressured by what other people think or say—except your husband. And my, my, aren't you lucky to have me stomping about where angels fear to tread?'

The two women laughed then and moved on to other subjects. But it amazed Jessica to realise the depth of the topics they discussed. She was finding herself revealing secrets and feelings to Aunt Beth that before she would have shared only with Ian. She seemed to be constantly showing Aunt Beth one piece or another of her soul, pulling it out to exhibit, dusting it off, questioning; but she was beginning to feel whole again.

The days were delightful and relaxing on the ranch, filled with fresh air and pleasant mornings spent on horseback in solitary canters over the hills or in idle walks. And the evenings flew by with Aunt Beth to laugh with. Jessica found herself taking naps in the afternoon, reading Jane Austen for the first time since high school, and making small idle sketches in a notebook. She had even made a few secret sketches that could be worked into an informal portrait of Aunt Beth. She was feeling shy about asking her new friend to sit for a portrait. But it was the first one she had wanted to paint since Ian's, years before. Aunt Beth's face would lend itself well to that sort of thing, and it would make a nice gift for Astrid—who appeared, much to Jessica's chagrin, two weeks later.

'You mean I have to come home now?' Astrid looked tired but happy, and Jessica had the sinking feeling she'd had as a child when her mother had arrived too early to fetch her home from a birthday party.

'Don't you dare come home, Jessica Clarke! I came down to see how Mother was doing.'

'We're having a great time.'

'Good. Then don't stop now. I'll be miserable when you come back to the city and take away my toy.' She filled Jessie in on Katsuko's trip to New York, and the spring line was doing better than Jessie had dared to hope. It seemed years since she had bought those pastels, years since she'd come home and Ian had been arrested, centuries since the trial. The shock of it all was finally beginning to fade. The scars barely showed. She had gained five pounds and looked rested. Astrid brought her a letter from Ian, which she didn't open until later.

> ... I can't believe it, Jess. Can't believe I'd say those things to you. Maybe this disaster is finally taking its toll. Are you all right? Your silence is strange now, your absence stranger. And I find that I don't really know what I want: you to reappear, or for that damn window between us to disappear. I know how you hate it, darling. I hate it as much. But we can overcome it. And how is the vacation? Doing wonders, I'm sure. You've really earned it. I suppose that's why I'm not hearing from you. You're 'busy resting'. Just as well, probably. As usual, I'm all wrapped up in the book. It's going unbelievably well, and I'm hoping that ...

The rest was all about the book. She tore the letter in half and threw it into the fire.

Aunt Beth quizzed her about the letter later, after Astrid had gone to bed. There was a kind of conspiracy between them now that excluded even Astrid.

'Oh, he says that he loves me and the book is going well, all in the same breath.' She tried to sound blithe and only succeeded in sounding a trifle less bitter.

'Aha! So you're jealous of his work!' Aunt Beth's eyes sparkled. Now she saw something she had not seen before, not clearly, anyway. It was all coming into focus.

'I am not jealous of his work. How ridiculous!'

'I quite agree. But why do you begrudge him his writing? What would happen, Jessica, if you no longer had to support him? You'd have no control over him then, would you? What if he actually did get successful? Then what would you do?'

'I'd be delighted for him.' But it didn't sound convincing, even to Jessica.

'Would you? Do you think you could handle it? Or are you much too jealous even to try?'

'How absurd.' She didn't like the sound of Beth's theory.

'Yes, it is absurd. But I don't think you know that yet, Jessica. The fact is that he either loves you or he doesn't. If he doesn't you couldn't keep him. And if he does, you probably can't lose him. And if you insist on supporting him forever, my dear, he'll wind up finding someone he can support, who lets him feel like a man. Someone who might even give him children. Mark my words.'

Jessica fell silent and they went up to bed. But Aunt Beth's words had hit home. Ian had said the same thing to her himself, in his own way. In Carmel, he had told her that things would have to change. Well, they were going to. But not in the way Ian had in mind.

CHAPTER XXVII

'Good morning, Aunt Beth . . . Astrid.' There was a look of determination on Jessica's face as she sat down to breakfast with them. That expression was new to her friends.

'Good heavens, child, what are you doing up at this hour?' She had rarely risen before ten since she'd been on the ranch, and Aunt Beth was surprised.

'Well.' She looked carefully at Astrid, knowing how disappointed she would be. 'I want to enjoy my last day. I've decided to go home with you tonight, Astrid.' Her friend's face fell at the words.

'Oh no, Jessie! Why?'

'Because I have things to do in town, and I've been lazy for long enough, love. Besides, If I don't go back now, I probably never will.' She tried to make her tone light as she helped herself to some cinnamon toast, but she knew that the words were a blow to Astrid. And she felt bad about leaving the ranch too. Only Aunt Beth looked unruffled by the news.

'Did you tell Mother before you told me, Jessie?' Astrid had noticed the look on her mother's face.

'She did not.' Aunt Beth was quick to answer. 'But I felt it coming last night. And Jessica, I think you're probably right to go back now. Don't look like that, Astrid, it will give you wrinkles. What did you think? That she'd never go back to her own shop? Don't be foolish. Are either of you going to ride with me this morning?' She buttered her toast matter-of-factly, and Astrid cleared the frown from her brow the way a child smoothes messages out of the sand. Her mother was right about Jessie going back, of course. But she had enjoyed Lady J even more than she had thought she would.

Jessie had been watching her face and now looked almost remorseful. 'I'm really sorry, love. I hate to do it to you.' The two younger women fell silent and Aunt Beth shook her head.

'How tedious you both are. I'm going riding. You're quite welcome to mope here. One feeling ridiculously guilty, the other feeling childishly deprived, and both of you making fools of yourselves. I'm surprised either of you has time for such nonsense.' Jessica and Astrid laughed then, and decided to ride with their more sensible elder.

It was a pleasant ride and an enjoyable day, and Jessie left Aunt Beth with regret. She vowed to come back as soon as she could, and struggled for the words to tell her how much the two weeks had meant.

'They restored me.'

'You restored yourself. Now don't waste it by going back to the city and doing something foolish.'

So she knew. It was astonishing. There was nothing you could hide from her.

'I won't approve if you do something stupid, child. And I'm not at all sure I like the look in your eye.'

'Now, Mother.' Astrid saw Jessie's discomfort, and

Bethanie did not pursue the matter after the interruption. She simply gave them a bag of apples, a tin of home-made cookies, and some sandwiches.

'That ought to keep you two well fed till you get home.' Her expression softened again and she put a gentle arm around Jessica's waist. 'Come back soon. I shall miss you, you know.' There was a soft hug about the waist, a warmth in the eyes, and Jessica bent her head to kiss her on the cheek.

'I'll be back soon.'

'Good. And Astrid, dear, drive safely.'

She waved at them from the doorway, until the sleek black Jaguar had turned a corner and sped out of sight.

'You know, I really hate to leave here. The last two weeks have been the best I've had in years.'

'I always feel like that when I leave.'

'How come you don't just move down here, Astrid? I would if she were my mother, and it's such beautiful country.' Jessie settled back in her seat for the long drive, musing over the two precious weeks, and the last few moments of conversation with Aunt Beth.

'Good Lord, Jessica, I'd die of boredom down here. Wouldn't you, after a while?'

Jessica shook her head slowly, a small, thoughtful frown between her eyes. 'No, I don't think I'd be bored. I never even thought of that.'

'Well, I have. In spite of my mother. There's nothing to do here except ride, read, take walks. I still need the insanity of the city.'

'I don't. I almost hate to go back.'

'Then you should have stayed.' For the tiniest moment, the spoiled child was back in Astrid's voice.

'I couldn't stay, Astrid. I have to get back. But I feel like a rat taking the shop back, if you can call it that. You really gave me the most marvellous vacation.' Astrid smiled back at Jessie's words.

'Don't feel bad. The two weeks were a lovely gift.' Astrid sighed gently and followed the serene country road. The sun had just set over the hills, and there was a smell of flowers in the air. In a distant field they could see horses in the twilight.

Jessie took a long look around the now familiar countryside, and sank back in her seat with a small private smile. She'd be back. She had to come back. She was leaving a piece of her soul here, and a new friend.

'You know something, Mrs. Bonner?'

Astrid grinned in response. 'What, Mrs. Clarke?'

'I adore your mother.'

'So do I.' The two women smiled, and Astrid stole a glance at Jessie. 'Was she good to you? Or did she give you a hard time? She can be very tough, and I was a little bit afraid she'd indulge herself with you. Did she?'

'Not really. Honest, but not tough. And never mean. Just straightforward. Sometimes painfully so. But she was generally right. And she made me think a lot. She saved my life. Hell, I'm not even a junkie anymore!' Jessica laughed and bit into one of the apples. 'Want an apple?'

'No, thanks. And I'm glad it worked out. How did Ian sound in the letter I brought you, by the way? I meant to ask, and I forgot.' Jessica's face set at the question, but Astrid had her eyes on the road and didn't see.

'That's why I'm going back.'

'Something wrong?' Astrid stole a quick look at Jessica.

'No. He's fine.' But her voice was strangely cold.

'You're going back to see him, Jessie?' Astrid was a trifle confused.

'No. To see Martin.'

'Martin? Ian's lawyer? Then something is wrong!'

'No, not . . . not like that.' And then she turned her face away and watched the hills drift past the window. 'I'm going back to get a divorce.'

'You're what?' She slowed down the car and turned to face Jessie, stunned. 'Jessica, no! You don't want that! Do you?'

Jessica nodded, holding the apple core in her trembling hand. 'Yes. I do.' They did not speak for the next hundred miles. Astrid couldn't think of anything to say.

Martin was free to see her when Jessie called him the next morning. She went right down to his office and was shown down the painfully familiar corridor. It seemed that she was never there for anything except the high points of drama in her life.

As usual, he was sitting at his desk with his glasses pushed up on his head and the standard frown on his face. She hadn't seen him since December.

'Well, Jessica, how have you been?' He looked her over as he stood up and held out his hand. It still gave her a sinking feeling to see him. In his own way, he was as painful a reminder to her as Inspector Houghton was. He was part of an era. But the era was finally coming to a close.

'I've been fine, thank you.'

'You look very well.' So much so it surprised him. 'Have a seat. And tell me, what brings you here? I had a letter from Ian last week. He sounds like he's weathering it.' A flash of something passed through Martin's eyes. Regret? Sorrow? Guilt? Or maybe Jessie only wished it. Why hadn't he been able to keep Ian free? Why hadn't he talked him into an appeal and then won? If he had, she wouldn't be in his office now. Or maybe she would.

'Yes, I think he's surviving.'

'He mentioned that he thinks he might be selling his book. Said he was waiting to hear more from his agent.'

'Oh.' That was news. 'I hope he does sell it. That would do a lot for him.' Especially now. But that was all Ian wanted anyway. Another book, and this time a big one, a hot seller. He wouldn't need her if he had a book. Wouldn't even miss her.

'So? You still haven't told me what brings you here.' The amenities were now officially over. Jessica took a small breath and looked him in the eyes.

'What brings me here, Martin, is a divorce.' But nothing registered on his face.

'A divorce?'

'Yes. I want to divorce Ian.' Something inside her trembled at the words, turned over and gasped, and tried to clutch at the old familiar branch. But she wouldn't let it. It didn't matter if she fell into a bottomless pit now; she had to do this. And she knew now that she would survive the bottomless pit. She had already been there.

'Jessica, are you tired of waiting for him? Or is there someone else?' The questions seemed indiscreet, but perhaps he had to know.

'No. Neither, really. Well, maybe a little tired of waiting. But only because I don't think we'll have a marriage left when he gets out. So what is there to wait for?'

'Did you have a marriage before?' He had always wondered, had never been quite sure. It had looked as if they had a strong bond and a firm commitment, but you never knew from the outside.

Jessica nodded at his question, and then looked away, her hands clenched in her lap.

'I thought we had a marriage. But . . . I told myself a lot of fairy tales then.'

'Such as?' She wondered why they had to get into all of this now.

'Such as I thought we were happy. That was a lie, among other lies. Ian was never really happy with me. Too many things got in the way. My shop, his work, other things. He'd never have gone off with that woman if he'd been happy.'

'Do you really believe that?'

'I don't know. I didn't at first. But now I begin to see what I didn't give him. Self-respect, for starters. And my time . . . my faith, maybe. I mean real faith that he could make a big success of another book.'

'You didn't respect him?'

'I'm not absolutely sure. I needed him, but I don't know if I respected him. And I never wanted him to know how much I needed him. I always wanted him to think he was the one who needed me. Pretty, isn't it?'

'No. But it's not unusual either. So why the divorce? Why not just clean up the picture and stick to what you've got? It's still better than most, and you're lucky—you see the mistakes; most don't. Does Ian see it as clearly as you do?'

'I have no idea.'

'You haven't spoken to him about this?' He looked shocked as she shook her head. 'He doesn't know you want a divorce?' She shook her head again and then looked up at him squarely.

'No, he doesn't. And . . . Martin, this is just the way I want it. It's too late to "clean up the picture". I've given it a lot of thought, and I know this is the right way. We have no children, and, well . . . this is as good a time as any.'

He nodded, chewing on the stem of his glasses.

'I can understand your thinking, Jessica, and you're a young woman. It may prove to be quite a burden to be married to a man who was sent to prison for rape. Maybe you should be free now to start another life.'

'I think so.' But why did it feel like such a betrayal of Ian? Such a rotten thing to do . . . but she had to. Had to. She wanted this for herself. She had decided. But she kept hearing Aunt Beth's words, just before she'd left the ranch the night before: 'I won't approve if you do something stupid.' But this wasn't stupid. It was right. But what was Ian going to say? . . . And why should she care now? Except that she did. She did, dammit.

'Would it affect your decision in any way if he sold this new book, Jessica?' She thought about it for a moment and then shook her head.

'No, it wouldn't. Because nothing would change. He'd come home, bitter about the time he's spent in prison, and even more bitter against me, because I'd just be supporting him all over again eventually, and nothing would have changed. Book advances don't last long, unless the book is a success.'

'You don't think he's capable of writing a success?' The tone of Martin's voice filled her with shame, and she lowered her eyes again.

'I didn't mean that. And that's not the point anyway. Everything would still be the same. I'd still have the shop, the bank account . . . no, Martin. This is what I want. I'm absolutely sure.'

'Well, Jessica, you're old enough to make your own decisions. When are you going to tell Ian?'

'I thought I'd write to him tonight. And—' she hesitated, but she had to ask him—'I was hoping you'd go up to see him.'

'To break the news?' Martin looked very tired as he asked. She nodded slowly. 'Frankly, Jessica, I don't normally handle domestic affairs. Marital law, as you know, is not my speciality.' And this was going to be a mess. But Ian was his client. And his client's wife was sitting opposite him, looking at him as though it were his fault that she was getting the divorce, as though he had cost her her marriage. And why the hell did he always feel guilty if things didn't work out just right?

'Oh well, I suppose I could handle this for you. Will it be a complicated sort of affair?'

'No. Terribly simple. The shop is mine. The house belongs to both of us, and I'll sell it if he wants, and put his share of the money in an account for him. That's all there is. I get custody of the plants, and he gets his file cabinets in his studio. End of a marriage.' The only thing she had left out was the furniture, and neither of them cared, except for the few pieces that were her parents', which were obviously hers. So simple. So miserably simple after seven years.

'You make it sound very quick and easy.' But he was dubious, and sad for them both.

'Maybe quick, but no, not very easy. Will you go up and see him soon?'

'By the end of the week. Will you be going up to see him yourself?' She shook her head carefully. She had seen Ian for the last time . . . on that godawful day when he had gotten up and walked away and she had watched him from behind a window, holding a dead phone in her hands. Her eyes filled with tears at the memory, and Martin Schwartz looked away. He hated this kind of thing. It seemed so wasteful.

Jessica looked up at Martin, holding back the tears. Her voice was barely a whisper. 'No, Martin, I won't see him anymore.'

He told her that she would be divorced in six months.

In September. A year after he had been arrested, a year after the end of their marriage had begun.

There was a letter from Ian waiting when she stopped by the house for her mail on her way to the boutique. It was only a brief note. And a poem. She read it with wide, sad eyes, and then tore it carefully in half and threw it away. But it had stuck in her mind somehow. Like a satin thorn. It was the last letter from Ian she opened. The poem decided her.

You are the explosive celebration
of my sunbursts
every morning,
You are the whisper
in my late
late nights,
You are the symphony in my sunsets,
You are the splendour and the glory
of the dawning
of my life.

The dawning of his life was past, with her, at least. But she felt as though she had singlehandedly killed the sunrise. Cancelled it. Sent it away. Made it cry. Broken something sacred. Him, and herself, and the thing that was both of them. The thing she now believed had never been at all. But she knew she had to do what she was doing.

CHAPTER XXVIII

The boutique was in beautiful shape. There were new displays all over the main room, and the window looked like a vision of spring. Astrid had done it herself. And the pastels and creams and delicate shades Jessie had bought in New York more than six months before looked good on display. There were two new plants in her office, with bright yellow flowers in full bloom, and there was a neat, crisp air to the shop that she had almost forgotten. She had been gone for only two weeks, but Lady J had been reborn, just as she had been. It looked the way it had when Jessie had first opened it, in the days when she'd been madly in love with it and had put her heart and soul into its birth. Now it showed the signs of Astrid's fresh enthusiasm and love. She hadn't changed anything radically, she had just pulled it together. Even Katsuko and Zina looked happier.

'How was the vacation?' Katsuko looked up, delighted to see her, but she didn't need to ask. Jessie looked like Jessie again, only better.

'It was exactly what I needed. And look at this place! It looks like you painted it or something. So cheerful and pretty.'

'That's just the new line. It looks pretty damn good.'

'How's it selling?'

'Like hotcakes. And wait till you see what I picked up for fall. Everything's orange or red. Lots of black, and some marvellous silver knits for the opera.' The browns of the winter before were already forgotten. Next year it would be red. Bright, busy, alive, maybe that was a good sign for her new life . . . new life. Jesus. She didn't want to think about it yet. And there would be so many people to tell . . . to explain to . . . to . . .

Jessica settled down in her office, looked around with pleasure, and enjoyed the feeling of having come home. It softened the burden of the morning, the meeting with Martin. She tried to keep it out of her mind. She would write to Ian tonight. For the last time. She didn't want to get into a long exchange of letters with him. He was too good at it. The letters would be . . . too much. They could work everything out through their lawyer. The less they said to each other, even by letter, the better. She had made up her mind. It was done now, and it was for the best. Now she had to look ahead and steel herself not to look back at the years with Ian. They were over now. A part of her past, like out-of-date fashions. Jessica and Ian were 'passé'.

'Jessie? Got a minute?' Zina's curly head poked in the door, and Jessie looked up and smiled. She felt older, quieter, but no longer tired. And she felt strong. For the first time in months, the nights alone did not terrify her. The house was no longer haunted. Her life was no longer infested by ghosts. Her first night back in the house had actually been peaceful. Finally.

She forced her attention back to Zina, still hovering in the doorway. 'Sure, Zina. I've got lots of time.' The slower pace of the country was still with her. She didn't feel harried yet, and she loved it.

'You're lookin' good.' Zina sat in the chair next to Jessie's desk and looked slightly uncomfortable. She asked a few questions about Jessie's vacation, and seemed to hesitate each time there was a pause. Finally, Jessie had had enough.

'Okay, lady, what's on your mind?'

'I don't know what to say, Jessie, but . . .' She looked up and suddenly Jessie sensed it. The hard months had taken their toll on everyone, not only on her. And she was almost surprised that neither of them had done it before. They probably hadn't because they were too loyal. She took a long breath and looked into Zina's eyes.

'You're quitting?'

Zina nodded. 'I'm getting married.' She said it almost apologetically.

'You are?' Jessie hadn't even known that Zina had a boyfriend. She hadn't had one the last time they'd talked . . . but when had that been? Last month? Two months ago? More like six. Since then she'd been too busy with her own problems to inquire or to care.

'I'm getting married in three weeks.'

'Zina, that's lovely news! What are you looking so sorry about, dummy?' Jessie smiled broadly and Zina looked overwhelmingly relieved.

'I just feel bad about leaving you. We're moving to Memphis.'

Jessica laughed. It sounded like a horrible fate, but she knew Zina didn't think so, and now that the news was out, Zina looked ecstatic.

'I met him at a Christmas Eve party, and oh . . . Jessie! He's the most beautiful man, in all possible ways! And I love him! And we're going to have lots of babies!' She grinned contentedly and Jessica jumped up and gave her a hug. 'And look at my ring!' She was pure Southern belle as she flashed the tiniest of diamonds.

'Were you wearing that before I went on vacation?' Jessica was beginning to wonder just how much she'd been missing.

'No. He gave it to me last week. But I didn't want to write and tell you, so I waited till you got back.' And Astrid had forbidden all potentially disturbing communications to Jessie. Like news of the creditors who kept calling about the bills she still hadn't paid. 'It's such a pretty little ring, isn't it?'

'It's gorgeous. And you're crazy, but I love you, and I'm so happy for you!' And then a flash of pain struck through to her core. Zina was getting married, she was getting divorced. You come, you go, you start, you end, you try, you lose, and maybe later you get another try, a fresh start, and this time win. Maybe. Or maybe it didn't really matter. She hoped Zina would win on the first try.

'I feel so bad giving you such short notice, Jess. But we just decided. Honest.' She almost hung her head, but the smile was too big to hide.

'Stop apologising, for heaven's sake! I'm just glad I came home. Where's the wedding?'

'In New Orleans, or my mother would kill me. I'm flying home in two weeks, and she's already going crazy over the wedding. We didn't give her much notice either. She called me four times last night, and you should have heard Daddy!' They both giggled, and Jessica started to think.

'Do you need a dress?'

'I'm going to wear my great-grandmother's.'

'But you need a trousseau. Right? And a going-away dress, and . . .'

'Oh, Jessie, yes, but . . . no . . . I can't let you do that . . .'

'Mind your own business, or I'll fire you!' She waggled a finger at Zina and they both started to laugh again. Jessie flung open her office door and marched Zina into the main room of the shop and stopped in front of a startled Katsuko.

'Kat, we have a new customer. VIP. This is Miss Nelson, and she needs a trousseau.' Katsuko looked up in astonishment, then understood and joined in their giggles and smiles. She was relieved that it had gone well. She had been worried for Zina. For the last couple of months it had been frightening to tangle with Jessie. But she was all right now. They could all tell. And now she was bubbling on about Zina's trousseau.

'It's going to be perfect with all the spring colours. Kat, give her anything she wants at ten percent under cost, and I'll give her her going-away suit as a wedding present. And as a matter of fact . . . don't I know just the one!' A gleam had come into her eyes, and she walked into the stockroom and came out with a creamy beige silk suit from Paris. It had a mid-calf skirt and a jacket that would subtly conceal Zina's oversized chest. She pulled out a mint green silk blouse to go with it, and Zina practically drooled.

'With dressy beige sandals, and a hat . . . Zina, you're going to look unbelievable!' Even Katsuko's eyes glowed at the outfit Jessie held up in her hand. Zina looked shocked.

'Jessie, no! You can't! Not that one!' She spoke in a whisper. The suit sold for over four hundred dollars.

'Yes, that one.' Her voice was gentle now. 'Unless there's another one you like better.' Zina shook her head solemnly and Jessica gave her a warm hug, and with a smile and a last wink at Zina she walked back into her office. It had been a startling morning, and now she had another startling idea.

She reached Astrid at the hairdresser.

'Is something wrong?' Maybe Jessie had hated the window display, or didn't like what she'd done with the stock. She was worried as she stood there dripping hair-setting lotion on her new suede Gucci shoes.

'No, silly, nothing's wrong. Want a job?'

'Are you kidding?'

'No. Zina just quit. She's getting married. And I may be crazy, because with you in the shop there'd be three of us capable of running this joint, but if you don't mind being the overqualified low man on the totem pole for a while, the job's all yours.'

'Jessie! I'll take it!' She grinned broadly and forgot about what she was doing to her shoes.

'Then you're hired. Want to go to lunch?'

'I'll be right over. No, I can't, dammit, my hair is still wet . . . oh . . . shit.' They both laughed and Astrid's smile seemed to broaden by the minute. 'I'll be there in an hour. And Jessie . . . thanks. I love you.' They both hung up with happy smiles and Jessica was glad she had called.

The four of them closed the doors to Lady J promptly at five instead of at five-thirty, and Jessica brought out a bottle of champagne she had ordered that afternoon. Zina had decided to leave a week earlier than planned now that Jessie had Astrid to take her place. They finished the bottle in half an hour, and Astrid drove Jessica home.

'Want to come home with me for a drink? I still haven't celebrated my new job.'

Jessie smiled, but shook her head. She was beginning to feel the effects of the day . . . which had begun with seeing Martin about the divorce. It was odd how she kept forgetting that. The morning seemed light years behind her. She wished the divorce were already behind her too.

'No thanks, love. Not tonight.'

'Afraid to fraternise with the help?' Jessie laughed at the thought.

'No, silly, I'm pooped and I'm already half crocked from the champagne, and . . . I've got a letter to write.' Astrid's face sobered as she listened.

'To Ian?' Jessica nodded gravely, the laughter totally gone from her eyes now.

'Yes. To Ian.'

Astrid patted her hand and Jessie slid quietly out of

the car with a wave. She unlocked the door and stood in the sunlit front hall for a moment. It was so quiet. So unbearably quiet. Not frightening anymore. Only empty. Who would take care of her now? It was odd to realise that no one knew what time she came home or went out, or where she was. No one knew and no one cared. Well, there was Astrid, but no one to report to, explain to, rush home for, do errands for, wake up for, set the alarm for, buy food for . . . an overwhelming sensation of emptiness engulfed her. Tears slid down her face as she looked around the house that had once been their home. It was a shell now. A hall of memories. Someplace to come back to at night after work. Like everything else, it had suddenly been catapulted into the past. It was all moving so quickly. People were going and changing and moving away, new people were taking their places . . . Zina getting married . . . Astrid in the shop . . . Ian gone . . . and in six months she'd be divorced. Jessica sat down on the chair in the front hall, her coat still on, her handbag slung on her shoulder, as she tasted the word aloud. Divorced.

It was almost midnight before she licked the stamp on the letter. She felt a hundred years old. She had forced Ian out of her life, and she would stand by her decision. But now she had no one except herself.

CHAPTER XXIX

'Well, look at you! What are you up to tonight?'

Astrid looked embarrassed as she buttoned the mink coat. It was May, but still chilly at night, and the fur coat looked good on her.

Jessie had just locked the doors to the shop. The arrangement was working out well. She, Katsuko, and Astrid got along like sisters. They made a powerful team, almost too much so, but they liked it, and the boutique was doing much better. Calls from creditors were getting rare. You could see the relief in Jessica's face.

'All right, nosey-body—' Astrid looked at Jessica watching her with amusement—'I happen to have a date.' She said it like a sixteen-year-old, with a faint blush on her cheeks, and Jessica burst out laughing.

'And you already look guilty as hell. Who's the guy?'

'Some idiot I met through a friend.' She looked almost pained.

'How old is he?' Jessie was suspicious of Astrid's passion for men over sixty. She was still looking for Tom.

'He's forty-five.' With a virginal expression, she finished buttoning the coat.

'At least he's a decent age. For a change.'

'Thank you, Aunt Jessie.' The two women laughed and Jessica pulled a comb out of her handbag.

'As a matter of fact, I have a date too.' She looked up with a small smile.

'Oh? With whom?' The tables were turned now, and Astrid looked as though she enjoyed it. But Jessie had been going out a good deal in the past weeks. With young men, with old ones, with a photographer, a banker, even with a law student once. But never with writers. And she never talked about Ian anymore. The subject was forbidden and mention of Ian met with silence or black looks.

'I'm going out with a friend of a friend from New York. He's just in San Francisco for a week. But what the hell, why not? He sounded decent on the phone. A little bit of a Mr. New York Smoothie, but at least he seemed halfway intelligent. He had a nice quick sense of humour on the phone. I just hope he behaves himself.' Jessica sighed softly as she put her comb back in her bag. Her hair hung well past her shoulders in a sheet of satiny blonde.

'*You* should worry about how he behaves? Big as you are, you can always beat him up.'

'I gave that up when I was nine.'

'How come?'

'I met a kid who was bigger than I was, and it hurt.' She grinned and propped her feet up on the desk.

'Want a ride home, Jessie?'

'No thanks, love. He's picking me up here. I thought I'd show him the action at Jerry's.' Astrid nodded, but Jerry's wasn't her style. It was a local 'in' bar, full of secretaries and ad men looking to get laid. It made her feel lonely. She was having dinner at L'Etoile. That was much more her style. It would have been Jessie's style too, if she'd let it. But she was still seeking her own level. A new level. Any level. Jessie knew Jerry's wasn't for her, but the action gave her something to watch as she listened to the hustles being carried on at the bar.

'See you tomorrow.'

Jessie waved good night, and Astrid passed a young man on the steps. He was slightly taller than Jessie and had dark bushy hair. He was wearing a grey turtleneck sweater and jeans. Nice-looking, but too 'fuzzy', Astrid decided, as she smiled and walked past. She wondered how Jessie stood them; they all looked the same, no matter what colour their hair, or how they dressed, they looked hungry and horny and bored. Astrid was suddenly glad she was no longer thirty. Thirty-year-old men had so far to go. With a sigh, she slipped into the Jaguar and turned on the ignition. She wondered how Ian was doing. She had wanted to write to him for a month, but she hadn't dared. Jessica might have considered it treason. Astrid saw the letters torn in half before they were opened when she emptied the wastebasket in the office they now shared. Jessie could be unyielding when she decided to be. And she had decided to be. The door to the shop opened and Astrid saw the young man go inside.

'Hi, Mario. I'm Jessie.' She assumed he was the young man she was waiting for, and offered him her hand. He ignored it with a casual smile.

'I take it you work here.' No greeting, no introduction, no handshake, no hello. He was just looking the place over. And her with it. Okay, sweetheart, if that's how it is.

'Yes. I work here.' She decided not to tell him she owned it.

'Yeah. I think I just passed your boss on the stairs. An old chick in a fur coat. Ready to go?' Jessie was already bristling. Astrid was not an 'old chick', and she was her friend.

He seemed bored with the action at Jerry's, but he had four glasses of red wine anyway. He explained that he was a playwright, or was trying to be, and he tutored English, maths, and Italian on the side. He had grown up in New York, in a tough neighbourhood on the West Side. At least that's how he put it. But Jessie wondered. He looked more like middle-class West Side than tough anything. Or maybe even the suburbs. And now he had grown up to be unwashed, unfriendly, and rude. It made her wonder about the friends who'd given him her name. People she knew through business, but still . . . how could they send her this?

'Well, how's New York? I haven't been back in a while.'

'Yeah? How long?'

'Almost eight months.'

'It's still there. I went to a great cocaine party last week in St. Mark's Place. How's the action out here?'

'Cocaine? I wouldn't know.' She sipped her wine.

'Not your thing?' He continued to look bored while working hard at looking cynical. Big-city kid in the provinces. Jessie was wishing he would drop dead on the spot. Or disappear, at least.

'You don't dig cocaine?' He pursued the point.

'No. But this is a nice city. It's a good place to live.'

'It looks dull as shit.' She looked up and smiled brightly, hoping to disappoint him. Mario the playwright was turning out to be an A-1 pain in the ass.

'Well, Mario, it's not as exciting as West Side New York, but we do have our fun spots.'

'I hear it's an intellectual wasteland.' So are you, darling.

'Depends on who you talk to. There are some writers out here. Good ones. Very good ones.' She was thinking of Ian and wanted to cram him down this jerk's throat. Ian was quality. Ian was charming. Ian was brilliant. Ian was beautiful. What was she doing out with this pig? This boor? This . . .

'Yeah? Like who?'

'What?' Her mind had wandered away from Mario to Ian.

'You said there are some good writers out here. And I said like who. You mean science-fiction writers?' He said it with utter distaste and that cynical smile that made Jessica want to plant the wineglass in his teeth.

'No, not just science-fiction writers. I mean like fiction, straight fiction, nonfiction.' She started reeling off names, and realised that they were all friends of Ian's. Mario listened, but offered no comment. Jessica was fuming.

'You know what knocks me out?' No. But tell me quick, I'll find one.

'What?'

'That a bright woman like you sells dresses in some shop. I don't know, I figured you were doing something creative.'

'Like writing?'

'Writing, painting, sculpture, something meaningful. What kind of existence is that, selling dresses for old broads in fur coats?'

'Well, you know how it is. One does what one can.' Jessie tried to keep her lip from curling as she smiled. 'What sort of play are you writing?'

'New theatre. An all-female cast, in the nude. There's a really great scene taking shape now for the second act. A homosexual love scene after a woman gives birth.'

'Sounds like fun.' Her tone went over his head. 'Hungry yet?' And she still had dinner to look forward to with him. She was considering pleading a violent attack of bubonic plague. Anything to get away from him. But she'd live through it. She'd been through it before. More often than she wanted to admit.

'Yeah. I could dig a good meal.' She made several suggestions and he settled on Mexican, because good Mexican food was rare in New York. At least he had that much sense. She took him to a small restaurant on Lombard Street. The company stank, but at least the food was good.

After dinner she yawned loudly several times and hoped he'd take the hint, but he didn't. He wanted to see some 'night life', if there was any. There was, but she wasn't going for it. Not tonight and not with him. She suggested a coffeehouse on Union Street, close to home. She'd have a quick cappuccino and ditch him. She needed the coffee anyway. She had drunk three or four glasses of wine at dinner. But Mario had had at least twice that, after his earlier consumption at Jerry's. He was beginning to slur his words.

They settled down in the coffeehouse, he with an Irish coffee and she with a frothy cappuccino, and he eyed her squintingly over the top of his glass.

'You're not a bad-looking chick.' He made it sound like a chemical analysis. Your blood type is O positive.

'Thank you.'

'Where do you live, anyway?'

'Just up a hill or two from here.' She drank the sweet milk foam on the top of her coffee and busied herself looking evasive. One thing she was not planning to share with Mario was her address. She'd had more than enough already.

'Big hills?'

'Medium. Why?'

''Cause I don't want to walk any big motherfucking hills, sister, that's why. I'm piss-eyed tired. And just a wee bit drunk.' He made a pinch with his fingers and smiled leeringly. It almost made Jessie sick to look at him.

'No problem, Mario. We can take a cab and I'll be happy to drop you off wherever you're staying.'

'What do you mean "wherever I'm staying"?' There was a small spark of anger in his eyes, smouldering in confusion.

'You're a smart boy. What did it sound like?'

'It sounded for a minute there like you were being a prissy pain in the ass. I assume that I'm staying with you.' For a moment she wanted to tell him she was married, but she wouldn't solve it that way. Besides, then how could she explain going out to dinner with him?

'Mario—' she smiled sweetly at him—'you assumed wrong. We don't do things that way out in the provinces. Or I don't, anyway.'

'What's that supposed to mean?' He sat slumped in his chair now, with a disagreeable expression on his face.

'It means thank you for a lovely evening.' She started buttoning her jacket and stood up with a wistful look in her eyes. But he leaned across the table and grabbed her arm. His grip on her wrist was surprisingly painful.

'Listen, bitch, we had dinner, didn't we? I mean what the fuck do you think . . .' There was a look on his face that she never wanted to see again, and suddenly the earlier conversation with Astrid flashed into her mind . . . 'If he misbehaves, you can hit him' . . . and she wrenched her arm free, and something in the set of her face told him not to press the point.

'I don't know what you think, mister. But I know what I think. And I think you'll be extremely sorry if you touch me again. Good night.' She was gone before he could react again, and it was the waiters who bore the brunt of his anger as he swept his arm across the table, knocking the cups and glasses to the floor. It took two waiters to convince him that what he wanted was some air.

Jessica was almost home by then. As she walked quietly up the last hill to the house, the night air was soft on her face, and she felt surprisingly peaceful. It had been a rotten evening, but she was rid of him. And she would never have to see him again. Men like that made her flesh crawl, but at least she knew how to handle them. And herself. At first, such evenings had terrified her. But she had dated all types by now—all the creeps in creepdom. The good ones were either married or off hiding somewhere. And what was left were all the same. They drank too much, they laughed too hard or not at all, they were pompous or neurotic or borderline gay, they were into drugs or group sex, or wanted to talk about how they hadn't had an erection in four years because of what their ex-wives had done to them. She was beginning to wonder if she wouldn't be happier staying home by herself. The libertine life wasn't much fun.

'How was last night?' Jessie asked Astrid first, as she came into the shop the next morning. She was hoping to quell Astrid's questions that way. She had no desire to talk about Mario.

'It was a nice evening, actually. I sort of liked it.' She looked happy and relaxed and almost surprised. Unlike Jessie, she didn't really expect to have a good time on a date. It made her easier to please.

'How was your evening? I think I passed your young man on the steps on my way out.'

'I think you did too. Damn shame you didn't trip him up on your way.'

'That bad, huh?' Astrid looked sympathetic, which hurt more.

'Actually, considerably worse. He was the pits.' In Astrid's opinion, he had looked it. 'Well, back to the drawing board.'

Jessie managed a thin smile as she sifted quickly through the mail, sorting out the letters from the bills. She paused only for a moment to look at a long plain white envelope before tearing it in half and dropping the pieces in the wastebasket. Another letter from Ian. It hurt Astrid every time she saw Jessie do that. It seemed so unkind, such a waste. She wondered if Ian knew, or suspected, that Jessie wasn't reading his letters. She wondered what he was saying in the letters.

'Don't look like that, Astrid.' Jessica's voice broke into her thoughts.

'Like what?'

'Like I tear your heart out every time I throw out his letters.' She had continued sorting the mail, looking almost indifferent. But not quite. Astrid saw her hands tremble just a trifle.

'But why do you do that?'

'Because we have nothing to say to each other anymore. I don't want to hear it, read it, or open any doors.

It would be misleading. I don't want to get suckered into any kind of dialogue with him.'

'But shouldn't you give him a chance to say what he thinks? This way seems so unfair.' Astrid's eyes were almost pleading, and Jessica looked back at the mail as she answered.

'It doesn't matter. I don't give a damn what he says. I've made up my mind. He could only make things harder now. He couldn't change anything.'

'You're that sure you want the divorce?'

Jessica looked up before she answered and fixed Astrid's eyes with her own. 'Yes. I'm that sure.' In spite of the Marios, in spite of the loneliness and the emptiness, she was still sure divorce was the right thing. But that didn't mean it didn't hurt.

Two customers walked into the shop at that moment and spared Jessica any further discussion. Katsuko was out, and Astrid had to offer to help. Jessica walked into her office and gently closed the door. Astrid knew what that meant. The subject was closed. It always was.

It was a busy day after that, a busy week, a busy month. The shop was in fine shape now, and people were buying for summer.

They had occasional postcards from Zina, who was already pregnant, and Katsuko had decided to grow her hair long again. Life had returned to trivial details: who was going to Europe, what the new hemline would be, whether or not to paint the front of the shop, planting new geraniums in Katsuko's tiny garden apartment. Jessie never ceased to feel gratitude for the trivia. The orchestration in her life had been so sombre for so long; now it was Mozart and Vivaldi again. Simple and easy and light. And having made the decision to get the divorce, there were no big decisions left.

It was almost as if the horror story had never happened. Her mother's emerald ring was safely back in the bank. The ownership on the house and the shop were free and clear again. The shop was back on its feet. But there had been changes. A lot more than she wanted to admit. And she had changed. She was more independent, less frightened, more mature. Life was moving along.

They were all having coffee in the boutique one morning when Jessie got to her feet and started going through some of the racks.

'Planning to knock five or ten inches off your height?' Astrid smiled as she watched Jessie go through the size eights.

'Oh, shut up.' She looked over her shoulder with a grin, and then knit her brow. 'Kat, what size does Zina usually wear?'

'Oh, Jesus. That's a tough one. A size four on the hips, and about a fourteen up top.'

'Terrific. So in a smock shape, what size would you say?'

'An eight.'

'That's what I was looking at.' She cast a victorious glance at Astrid. 'I thought maybe we should send her a present. That kid she married doesn't have much money, and she's going to be hard to fit now that she's pregnant. What do you think of these?' She pulled out three tent-shaped dresses from the spring line, in ice cream colours and easy shapes.

'Super!' Kat instantly approved, and Astrid looked touched.

'What a sweet thing to do.'

Jessie looked almost embarrassed as she smiled and handed them to Katsuko.

'Ahh . . . bullshit.' All three of them laughed and Jessie sat back down to her coffee. 'Send those out to her today, okay, Kat? Do you suppose we ought to send her something for the baby?' She didn't know why, but she wanted to celebrate Zina's baby. As though he, or she, were someone special.

'Not yet. It isn't due for months. Besides, that's bad luck.' Astrid looked slightly uncomfortable. 'What's with all the interest in maternity goodies?'

'I've decided that if I'm never going to be a mother, I might as well enjoy being an aunt. Besides, I figured that if I started buttering her up early, she might make me godmother.' Astrid laughed, and Katsuko carefully folded the dresses into a box full of yellow tissue paper. She glanced quickly at Jessie, but Jessie got up and walked away. She felt lonely suddenly. Lonely for a child for the first time in her life. And why now? She decided that it was just because she was ready to love somebody again.

'She's going to adore them, Jessie. And who says you're never going to be a mother?' Katsuko was intrigued. It was the first time Jessie had talked openly about children. Katsuko had always suspected that Jessie must have come to some decision about children, but it was rare for her to open up about anything personal. She was not one of those women who discussed her sex life and her dearest dreams in the office. But Jessie seemed to be in an unusually chatty mood. And she didn't have Ian to confide in anymore. She often seemed hungry for someone to talk to these days. She sat down once more before she replied.

'*I* say I'm never going to be a mother. I mean, Jesus, have you seen what's out there these days? If I've been seeing any kind of standard sampling, I wouldn't think of propagating the breed. They ought to be considering how to stamp it out!' The other two women laughed and Jessie finished her coffee. 'Halfwits, no wits, nitwits, and dimwits. Not to mention the ones who've blitzed out their brains on acid, the sonsofbitches cheating on their wives, and the ones with no sense of humour. You expect me to marry one of those darlings and have a kid, maybe?' And then her face grew serious. 'Besides, I'm too old.'

'Don't be ridiculous.' Astrid spoke up first.

'I'm not. I'm being honest. By the time I got around to having a child, I'd be thirty-four, thirty-five maybe. That's too old. You should do it at Zina's age. How old is she? Twenty-six? Twenty-seven?' Katsuko nodded pensively and then asked Jessie a question that hit hard.

'Jessie . . . are you sorry now that you didn't have children with Ian?' There was a long pause before she answered, and Astrid was afraid she'd lose her temper, or her cool, but she didn't.

'I don't know. Maybe I am. Maybe I can only say that because I've never been within miles of a kid. But it seems sad—worse than sad, wasted, empty—to live so many years with a man and have nothing. Some books, some plants, a few pieces of furniture, a burnt-out car. But nothing real, nothing lasting, nothing that says "We were", even if we aren't anymore, that says "I loved you", even if I don't love you anymore.' There were tears in her eyes as she shrugged gently and stood up. She avoided their eyes and looked busy as she headed back to her little office. 'Anyway, so it goes. Back to work, ladies. And don't forget to send the dresses to Zina right away, Kat.' They didn't see her again until lunchtime, and neither Astrid nor Katsuko dared comment on the conversation.

But they were all basically happy. Jessie was restless and sick of the men she was going out with, but she wasn't unhappy. There were no traumas, no crises in her life anymore. And Astrid was still seeing the same man she had been seeing earlier that spring. And enjoying it more than she wanted to admit. He took her to the theatre a lot, collected the work of unknown young sculptors, and had a small house in Mendocino that Astrid finally admitted she'd been to. She was spending weekends there, which was why Jessie never heard from her anymore between Friday and Monday.

Jessica was busy too; she was working Saturdays at Lady J, and there were always new men. The trouble was that there were never 'old' men, men she had known long enough to feel comfortable with. It was always a birthday party, never old galoshes. She got bored with the constant explanations. Yes, I ski. Yes, I play tennis. No, I don't like to hike. Yes, I drive a car. No, I'm not allergic to shellfish. I prefer hard mattresses, wear a size eight narrow shoe, a size ten dress, am five feet ten and a half, like rings, love earrings, hate rubies, love emeralds . . . all of the above, none of the above. It was like constantly applying for a new job.

She was having trouble sleeping again, but she had stayed away from pills ever since her stay at the ranch. She knew they weren't the solution, and someday . . . someday . . . someone would come along, and she'd want him to stay. Maybe. Or maybe not. She had even considered the possibility that no one would come along again. No one she could love. It was a horrible thought, but she did admit it as a possibility. It was what had made her suddenly and almost cruelly regret never having had children. She had always thought she had the option. Now her options were gone.

But maybe it didn't matter if she never had children, or loved another man, or . . . maybe it didn't matter at all. She wondered if she had already fulfilled her destiny. Seven years with Ian, an explosion at the end, a boutique, and a few friends. Maybe that was it. There was a sameness to her life now, a blandness and lack of purpose that made her wonder. All she had to do was get up, go to work, stay at the shop all day, close it at five-thirty, go home and change, go out to dinner, say good night, go to bed. And the next day it would all start all over again. She was tired, but she wasn't depressed. She wasn't happy, but at least she wasn't frightened or lonely. She wasn't anything. She was numb.

Ian had sent a message, via Martin, not to sell the house; he'd buy her half eventually if he had to, but he didn't want the house to go. So she went on living there, but now it was just a house. She kept it tidy, it suited her needs, it was comfortable, and it was familiar. But she had put all of Ian's things in the studio and locked it. And the house had lost half its personality when she'd done that. It was just a house now. Lady J was just a shop. She was just another soon-to-be divorcee on the market.

'Morning, madam. Want a date?' Astrid was carrying lily of the valley as she walked into the shop, and she dropped a clump of it next to Jessie's coffee cup.

'Jesus, don't you look happy for this time of the morning.' Jessica attempted a smile and winced, regretting the last half bottle of white wine the night before. But it pleased even Jessie to see Astrid like that, wearing her hair down much of the time now, and with a happy light in her eyes.

'Okay, Miss Sunshine. What kind of date?' She tried

another smile and meant it. It was impossible not to smile at Astrid.

'A date with a man.' She looked almost girlish.

'I should hope so. You mean a blind date?'

'No, I don't think he's blind, Jessica. He's only thirty-nine.' The two women laughed and Jessica shrugged.

'Okay, why not? What's he like?'

'Very sweet, and a little bit "not too tall".' Astrid looked cautiously at Jess. 'Does that matter?'

'Will I have to stoop over to talk to him?'

Astrid giggled and shook her head. 'No. And he's really very nice. He's divorced.'

'Isn't everyone?' It constantly amazed Jessie to realise how many marriages failed. She hadn't been that aware of it before she'd filed for divorce herself. It had always seemed that everyone she knew was married. And now everyone she knew was divorced.

They had dinner as a foursome that Thursday night, and Astrid's beau was delightful. He was elegant, amusing, and good-looking. In fact, he was the first man Jessie had met in a long time who actually appealed to her. He had the same kind of graceful looks as Ian, but with silver hair and a well-trimmed narrow rim of beard. He had travelled extensively, was knowledgeable in art and music, was very funny as he told of some of his exploits, and he was wonderful with Astrid. Jessica wholeheartedly approved, but what pleased her most about the evening was seeing Astrid's happiness. She had really found the perfect man for her.

Jessie's date for the evening was pleasant, kind, and unbearably boring. Divorced with three children, he worked in the trust department of a bank. He was also five feet seven, and Jessie had worn heels. She stood almost a head taller than he. But when Astrid suggested dancing, Jessie didn't have the heart to argue. At least this one didn't wrestle her at the door. He shook her hand, told her he'd call her while she made a mental note not to hold her breath waiting, and he went home alone. She was sure that by the next morning she wouldn't even remember his name. Why bother?

She took off her clothes and went to bed, but it was two hours later when she finally fell asleep. She felt as if she had just closed her eyes when the phone rang the next morning. It was Martin Schwartz.

'Jessie?'

'No. Veronica Lake.' Her voice was husky and she was still half asleep.

'I'm sorry, I woke you.'

'That's okay, I have to get to work anyway.'

'I have something for you.'

'My divorce?' She sat up in bed and reached for her cigarettes. She wasn't sure she was prepared for that kind of news.

'No. That won't be for another four months. I have something else. A cheque.'

'What in hell for?' It was all very confusing.

'Ten thousand dollars.'

'Jesus. But why? And from whom?'

'From your husband's publisher, Jessica. He sold the book.'

'Oh.' She exhaled carefully and frowned. 'Well, put it in his account, Martin. It's not mine, for Chrissake.'

'Yes, it is. He endorsed it to you.'

'Well, unendorse it, dammit. I don't want it.' Her hands were shaking now, and so was her voice.

'He says it's to reimburse you for my trial fee, and Green's fee, and a number of other things.'

'That's ridiculous. Just tell him I don't want it. I paid those bills, and he doesn't owe me anything.'

'Jessica . . . he signed it over to you.'

'I don't give a damn. Cross it out. Tear it up. Do whatever you want with it, but *I don't want it!*' Her voice was rising nervously.

'Can't you do it for him? It seems to mean so much to him. I think it's a question of integrity with him. He really seems to feel that he owes this to you.'

'Well, he's wrong.'

'Maybe I'm wrong.' Martin could feel a thin film of sweat veiling his brow. 'Maybe he just wants to give it to you as a gift.'

'Maybe so. But whatever the case, Martin, I will not accept the cheque.' Martin's voice had been pleading and she shook her head vehemently as she stubbed out her cigarette. 'Look. It's simple. He doesn't owe me anything. I don't want anything. I won't accept anything. I'm glad he sold the book, and I think that's just wonderful for him. Now he should keep the money and leave me alone. He's going to need money when he gets out anyway. Now that's it, Martin. I don't want it. Period. Okay?'

'Okay.' He sounded defeated and they hung up. At her end, she was trembling; at his he sat looking out at the view, wondering how to tell Ian. His eyes had been so alive when he'd talked about paying Jessie back. And now Martin had to tell him this.

Jessie's day was off to a bad start. She burned her coffee, and her shower ran cold. She stubbed her foot on the bed, and the newspaper boy forgot to leave her the morning paper. She looked fierce by the time she got to the shop. Astrid looked at her sheepishly.

'All right, all right. I know. You hated him.'

'Hated who?' Jessica looked suddenly blank.

'The guy we introduced you to at dinner last night. I never realised he was that dull.'

'Well, he is, but that's not what I'm mad about, so forget it.' And then she looked up and saw Astrid's face, hurt and confused, like a child's. 'Oh, hell, Astrid, I'm sorry. I'm just in a stinking lousy mood. Everything has already gone wrong today. Schwartz called this morning.'

'What about?' Astrid's face instantly turned worried.

'Ian sold his book.'

'What's wrong with that?' The worry turned to confusion again.

'Nothing. Except he's trying to give me the money, and I don't want it, and it's a pain in the ass, that's all.' She poured herself a cup of coffee and sat down. But Astrid's face was grave now.

'Now you know how he used to feel. Taking your money.'

'What does that mean?'

'Just what it sounded like. Sometimes it's easier to give than it is to take.'

'You sound like your mother.'

'I could do worse.'

Jessie nodded and walked into her office. She stayed there until lunchtime.

Astrid knocked on the closed door at twelve-thirty. A smile was struggling to escape her serious face . . . wait till Jessie saw it! She forced her features back into an expression of official business and looked almost sombre when Jessie opened the door.

'What's up?'

'We have a problem, Jessica.'

'Can't you take care of it? I'm just checking the invoices.'

'I'm sorry, Jessica, but I simply can't handle this.'

'Terrific.' Jessie threw her pen on the desk behind her and walked into the main room. Astrid watched her nervously. She had signed for it. Maybe Jessie would kill her, but she didn't care. She owed that much to Ian.

Jessie looked around. There was no one in the shop but Katsuko, busy on the phone. 'So? Who's here? What's the problem?' She was beginning to look extremely annoyed.

'It's a delivery, Jessie. Outside. They made a big fuss about not unloading inside. Said something about not having to do anything more than make sidewalk deliveries, muttered about the waybill, and drove off.'

'Damn them! We hassled that out with them last month, and I told them that if . . .' She yanked open the door and stalked outside, her eyes blazing, checking the sidewalk for their delivery. And then she saw it. Parked in the driveway where Astrid's Jaguar had been a little while earlier.

It was a sleek little racing green Morgan with black trim and red leather seats. The top was down. It was a beauty, and in even better condition than her old Morgan had been. Jessica looked stunned for a moment, and then looked at Astrid and started to cry. She knew it was from Ian.

CHAPTER XXX

With Astrid badgering her day and night, she decided to keep it. 'As a favour to him.' She wouldn't admit how much she loved it, and she still wouldn't open his letters.

In June she decided to take a five-day vacation and go down to visit Aunt Beth at the ranch.

'Hell, Astrid, I've earned it. It'll do me good.' She was vaguely embarrassed about going but she wasn't sure why.

'Don't make excuses to me. I'm taking three weeks off in July.' Astrid was flying to Europe with her beau, but she was loath to discuss it. She kept her affairs very private, even from Jessie. Jessie wondered if maybe she was afraid things would fall through.

Jessica left early on a Wednesday afternoon in the Morgan, in high spirits, her hair flying out behind her. Aunt Beth had been delighted to hear she was coming.

'Well, well, you have a new car, I see. Very pretty.' She had heard Jessica drive up on the gravel, and had come out to meet her. The sun was setting over the hills.

'It was a present from Ian. He sold his book.'

'Very handsome present. And how are you, dear?' She hugged Jessica fondly, and the younger woman bent to kiss her cheek. Their hands found each other and held tightly. They were equally pleased to see each other.

'I couldn't be better, Aunt Beth. And you look wonderful!'

'Older by the hour. And meaner too, I've been told.' They chuckled happily and walked into the house arm in arm.

The house looked the same as it had two months before, and Jessica let a sigh escape her as she looked around.

'I feel like I'm home.' She looked at Aunt Beth from across the room, and found her own face being carefully searched by the other woman's piercing blue eyes.

'How have you really been, Jessica? Astrid says very little, and your letters tell me even less. I've wondered how things worked out. Cup of tea?' Jessica nodded and Aunt Beth poured her a cup of Earl Grey.

'I've been fine. I filed for a divorce when I went back, but I told you that in my first letter.'

Aunt Beth nodded expressionlessly, waiting for more. 'Do you regret it?'

Jessica hesitated for only a split second before answering and then shook her head. 'No, I don't. But I regret the past a great deal of the time, more than I like to admit. I seem to find myself hashing it over, reliving it, thinking back to "if only" this and "if only" that. It seems so pointless.' She looked sad as she set down the cup of tea and looked up at Aunt Beth.

'It is pointless, my dear. And there is nothing more painful than looking back at happy times that no longer are. Or just simply old times. Do you hear from him?'

'Yes, in a way.' Jessica tried to look vague.

'What does that mean?'

'It means he writes to me and I tear his letters up and throw them away.' Aunt Beth raised an eyebrow.

'Before or after you read them?'

'Before. I don't open them.' She felt foolish and averted her eyes from the old woman's.

'Are you afraid of his letters, Jessica?'

To Aunt Beth she could tell the truth. She nodded slowly.

'Yes. I'm afraid of recriminations and pleas and poems and words that are perfectly designed to sound the way he knows I want to hear them. It's too late for that. It's over. Done with. I did the right thing, and I won't hash it over with him. I've seen other people do that, and there's no point. He'd only make me feel guilty.'

'You do that to yourself. But you know, you make me wonder. If he weren't in prison, would you still be pressing for this divorce?'

'I don't know. Maybe eventually it would have come to this anyway.'

'But aren't you rather taking advantage of his situation, Jessica? If he were free, he could force you to discuss it with him. Now all he can do is write, and you won't give him the courtesy of reading his letters. I'm not sure if that's rude, or cowardly, or simply unkind.' They were harsh words, but her eyes said she meant them. 'And I also don't understand about the car. You said he gave you the new car. You accepted that . . . but not his letters?' Jessica flinched at the inference.

'That's Astrid's fault. She said that I owed it to him to keep it. He wanted to pay me back the money I put out for the trial, and I wouldn't accept the cheque from our attorney. So Ian had him buy me the car. And I assume he kept the rest of the money.'

'And you didn't thank him for the car?' She sounded every bit a mother. What? No thank-you note to your hostess? Jessica almost laughed.

'No, I didn't.'

'I see. And what now?'

'Nothing. The divorce will be final in three months. And that'll be that.'

'And you'll never see him again?' Aunt Beth looked doubtful, but Jessica shook her head firmly. 'I think you'll regret it, Jessica. One needs to say good-bye. If you don't, in a satisfactory way, you never quite get all the splinters out of your soul. It might trouble you more like this. You can't really wash seven years out of your life without saying good-bye. Or can you? Well, you seem to have made up your mind, in any event.' She sat watching Jessica's bent head as the younger woman played with the calico cat. 'You have made up your mind, haven't you?' She was determined to get at the truth, if only for Jessie's sake.

'I . . . yes, well . . . oh, damn. I don't know, Aunt Beth. Sometimes I just don't know. I've made up my mind, and I'll go through with it, but now and then, I . . . oh, I suppose it's just regret.'

'Maybe not, child. Maybe it's doubt. Maybe you don't really want to divorce him.'

'I do . . . but . . . but I miss him so awfully. I miss the way we know each other. He's the only person in the whole world who really knows me. And I know him just as well. I miss that. And I miss what we used to dream, what I thought we once were, what I wanted him to be. Maybe I didn't even know him, though. Maybe I only think I did. Maybe he cheated on me all the time. Maybe that woman was his girlfriend, and she accused him of rape because she was mad about something else. Maybe he hated me for paying the bills, or maybe that's why he stayed married to me. I just don't know anything anymore. Except that I miss him. But it could just be that what I'm missing never even existed.'

'Why don't you ask him? Don't you think he'd tell you the truth now? Or is it that you're afraid he might indeed tell you the truth?'

'Maybe that. Maybe the truth is something I'd never want to hear.'

'So you'll keep tearing up letters and make sure you never do. And what'll you do when he gets out? Move to another town and change your name?' Jessica laughed at the preposterous suggestion.

'Maybe by then he won't want to talk to me either.' But she didn't sound as though she believed it.

'Don't count on it. But more important, Jessica, do you realize what you're saying? You're saying that the man probably never loved you, that there was nothing about you he loved except your ability to pay his bills. Isn't that it?'

'Maybe.' But her eyes grew sullen. She had had enough of the painful probing. 'What difference does it make now?'

'All the difference in the world. It means the difference between knowing you were loved, and thinking you were used. And what if he did use you, if he loved you too? Didn't you use him too, Jessica? Most people who love each other do, and not necessarily in a bad way. It's part of the arrangement, to fulfil each other's needs—financial, emotional, whatever.'

'I never thought of it that way. And the funny thing is

that I always thought I was using him. Ian's not afraid to be alone. I always was. I felt so lost without my family after they all died. I had no one except Ian. I could make all the decisions in the world, do anything I wanted, be proud of myself . . . as long as I had Ian. He kept me propped up so I could go on fooling the world, and myself, that I was such tough stuff. I used him for that, but I never thought he knew it.' She looked almost ashamed to admit it.

'And what if he did know it? So what? It's no sin to have weaknesses, or to use the strength of the person you love. As long as you don't use it unkindly. And what about now? Are you stronger?'

'Stronger than I thought.'

'And happy?' That was the crux of it.

She hesitated and then shook her head. 'No. I'm not. My life is so . . . so empty, Aunt Beth. So dead. Sometimes I feel as if I have nothing to live for. For what? For myself? To get dressed up every morning and changed at six o'clock at night? To go out with some idiot stranger with bad breath and no soul? To water my plants? What am I living for? A boutique I don't give a damn about anymore? . . . What?' Aunt Beth waved a hand and she stopped.

'I can't bear it, Jessica. You sound just the way Astrid used to. And it's all nonsense. You have everything to live for, with or without young men with bad breath. But at your age, above all you have *yourself* to live for. You have it all ahead of you. You have youth. And look at me, I still find things to live for, many things, and not just begrudgingly. I thoroughly enjoy my life, even at my age.'

'Then I envy you. I wake up in the morning and I honestly wonder why sometimes. The rest of the time I just keep moving like a robot. But what in hell do I have?'

'You have what you are.'

'And what's that? A thirty-one-year-old divorced woman who owns a boutique, half a house, several plants, and a sports car. I have no children, no husband, no family, no one who loves me and no one to love. Jesus, why bother?' There were hot tears filling her eyes as she continued.

'Then find someone to love, Jessica. Haven't you tried?

Other than the soulless ones with bad breath.' Aunt Beth's eyes twinkled and Jessica laughed tearfully and then shrugged.

'You should see what's around. They're awful.' The tears started to creep down her cheeks now. 'They're really just awful. And ... no one knows me.' She closed her eyes tightly on the last words, and bent her head.

'That's what Astrid used to say, Jessica, and now look at her.' Aunt Beth walked around the back of Jessica's chair and gently stroked her hair. 'She's flapping around like a schoolgirl, pretending to be "discreet", and having a marvellous time. She's about as discreet as the sunrise. But I'm glad for her. She's finally happy. She's found someone, and so will you, my dear. It takes time.'

'How much time?' Jessie felt twelve years old again, asking the impossible of an all-knowing parent.

'That's up to you.'

'But *how*? *How*?' Jessie turned in her seat to look up at Aunt Beth. 'They're all so awful. Young men who think they're terrific and want to go to bed with you and every woman on the street, who want to leave their track shoes on the dining-room table, and their drug stash in your house. They make you feel like a parking meter. They put a dime in and come around later ... maybe ... if they remember where they parked you. They make me feel like a nameless nothing. And the older men aren't much better; they're all out proving they're macho and pretending to love women's lib because it's expected ... but Ian never was ... oh, hell. It all bores me to tears. Everything does. The people I know bore me, and the people I don't know bore me. And ...' She knew she was whining, but she didn't sound bored as much as she sounded frantic.

'Jessie, darling, *you* bore *me*. With garbage like that. All right, you need a change. Let's agree on that much. Then why not leave San Francisco for a while? Have you thought of that?' Jessie nodded sorrowfully, and Aunt Beth gave her the look she reserved only for very spoiled children. 'Are you thinking of going back to New York?'

'No ... I don't know. That would be worse. Maybe the mountains or the beach, or the country. Something like that. Aunt Beth, I'm so tired of people.' She sat back with a sigh, dried her face, and stretched her legs. Aunt Beth was looking annoyed.

'Oh, shut up. Do you know what your problem is, Jessica? You're spoiled rotten. You had a husband who adored you and made you feel like a woman, and a very loved woman at that, and you had a boutique you enjoyed, and a home that you both shared and seemed to have enjoyed too. Well, by your own choice, you no longer have the husband, and you've squeezed all you can from that shop, and maybe the house has served its usefulness too. So get rid of it. All of it. And start afresh. I did when I got my divorce, and I was sixty-seven. Jessica, if I can do it, so can you. I came out from the East, bought this ranch, met new people, and I've had a wonderful time since. And if in five years it begins to bore me, then I'll close up shop, sell, and do something else, if I'm still alive. But if I *am* alive, then I'll *be* alive. Not living here half dead and no longer interested in what I'm doing. So, what are you going to do now? It's time you did *something*!' The old woman's eyes blazed.

'I've been thinking of getting rid of the shop, but I can't sell the house. It's half Ian's.'

'Then why not rent it?'

It was a thought. The idea had never occurred to her before. And she was a little bit shocked at what she had just said. Sell the shop? When had she thought of that? Or had she been thinking of it all along? The words had just slipped out.

'I'll have to think it all out.'

'This is a good place to do it, Jessica. I'm glad you came down.'

'So am I. I'd be lost without you.' She went to her side and gave her a hug. Aunt Beth was becoming a mainstay to her.

'Are you hungry yet?'

'I'm getting that way.'

'Good. We can burn dinner together.'

They made hamburgers and artichokes with hollandaise sauce, a favourite of Aunt Beth's, and this time they neither burned nor curdled the sauce. It was a delightful meal and they sat up until almost midnight, speaking of easier subjects than those they had covered before dinner.

Jessica stretched out on the bed in her now familiar pink room and watched the fire glow and flicker as the old calico cat settled down next to her. It was good to be back. It really did feel like home. This was one place she was not tired of.

Aunt Beth was out riding when Jessie arose the next morning, and there was a note in the kitchen explaining which horse she could ride if she chose to. She had learned the terrain well enough the time before to handle a ride in the hills on her own now.

Shortly after eleven, she set off on a pleasant chestnut mare. She wore a wide-brimmed straw hat and had tucked a book and an apple into a small saddlebag. She felt like being alone for a while, and this was a perfect way to do it. After a half hour's ride, she found a small stream and tied the horse to the limb of a tree. The mare didn't seem to object, and Jessie took off her boots and went wading. She laughed as she sang songs to herself and unbuttoned her cuffs to roll up her sleeves. She felt freer than she had in as long as she could remember. It was then that she saw the man watching her.

She looked up with a start and he smiled an apology. It was frightening to suddenly see someone in what she thought was her own private wilderness, but he was tall and very well dressed in a fawn-coloured riding habit. He spoke gently, and with a British accent.

'I'm sorry. I meant to say something earlier, but you looked so happy, I hated to spoil your fun.' She was suddenly glad she hadn't taken off her shirt, which she had been considering.

'Am I trespassing?' She stood barefoot in the stream, one sleeve rolled up, and her hair loosely tied in a knot on top of her head. To him, she looked like a vision. A golden-haired Greek goddess in modern riding dress. One didn't see many women like that—not here in the 'provinces'. Lost on a hillside, barefoot in a stream. It was like a scene in an eighteenth-century painting, and it made him want to walk down and touch her. Kiss her perhaps. The thought made him smile again as she watched him.

'No, I fear I'm the trespasser. I came out for a ride this morning, and I'm not very familiar with the territory, property boundaries and the like. I daresay I'm intruding.' The accent was pure public-school English. Eton, perhaps. The alleged 'intruder' was every inch a gentleman. And as she looked at him, it struck her how much he resembled Ian. He was taller, a little broader, but the face . . . the eyes . . . the tilt of the head . . . his hair was very blonde, blonder than Jessie's. But still there was something of Ian about him, enough to haunt her. She looked away from him and sat down to put on her boots, carefully rolling her sleeves down first. While the unknown man continued to watch her with a small smile.

'You needn't leave because of me. I have to get home now in any case. But tell me, do you live here?' She shook her head slowly, unpinned her hair, and looked up at him. He was very good-looking.

'No, I'm a houseguest.'

'Really? So am I.' He mentioned the name of the people he was staying with, but she didn't recall having heard Aunt Beth mention them. 'Will you be down here long?'

'A few days. Then I'll have to get back.'

'To?' He was very inquisitive. Almost annoyingly so, except that he was so damned good-looking.

'San Francisco. I live there.' She had avoided the next question, and now it was her turn. Why not? 'And you?' The idea of questioning him amused her.

'I live in Los Angeles. But I'll be moving to San Francisco within the month, actually.' She almost giggled as she listened to him. He sounded like all the imitations she'd ever heard of stuffy Englishmen. He was *sooo* British, standing there on a hilltop in his impeccable riding habit and flicking a riding crop across his palm. He was really quite something.

'Did I say something funny?'

'No, sir.' With a half smile, she started up the hill toward him. Her horse was tied quite close to where he stood.

'My firm is transferring me to San Francisco. I came out

from London three years ago, and I've had enough of L.A.'

'You'll like San Francisco; it's a wonderful town.' It was a totally mad conversation between two strangers in the middle of nowhere; they were behaving as though they were on Fifth Avenue, or Union Street, or the Faubourg St. Honoré. She burst into laughter as she found herself standing next to him.

'I seem to have a way of amusing you without intending to.'

She smiled again and shrugged gently. 'Lots of things do that.'

'I see.' He held out a hand to her then and looked rather solemn, but the smile still danced in his eyes. 'How do you do? I'm Geoffrey Bates.'

'Hello. I'm Jessica Clarke.' Standing under the tree, they shook hands and she smiled at him again. At close range, he didn't look quite so much like Ian. But he was very pretty in his own right, Mr. Geoffrey Bates from London. And he was thinking how much he liked the way she looked when she smiled. And she seemed as though she did that a lot.

He hesitated for a moment before asking her the next question, but he finally gave in. He wanted to know.

'Where are you staying, by the way?' By the way? It made Jessica smile again and then laugh.

'With the mother of a friend.' She was vague, and he smiled as he raised an eyebrow.

'And you won't tell me who? I promise not to disgrace you and appear uninvited to dinner.'

She laughed back and felt silly, but the Englishman's face had grown serious. He had just realized that she might well be travelling with a man. That would be awkward. He had looked at her left hand almost instantly and been relieved to see it bare of rings, especially plain gold ones. But he hadn't looked closely enough to see the little worn ridge or the slightly paler strip where she had worn her wedding band for seven years before removing it a few months before.

'I'm staying with Mrs. Bethanie Williams.'

'I believe I've heard someone mention her name.' He looked enormously relieved. 'Leg up?' She was standing next to her horse as he asked, and she turned to him with a look of amusement.

'Hardly. But should I say yes?' She thought she saw him blush as she swung easily into the saddle. It was a foolish question to ask someone as tall as she was, but then she noticed his height. He was at least four or five inches taller than Ian . . . six five? Six six? Not even Ian was that tall . . . 'not even' . . . why did she still think of him that way? As though he were the ultimate man. The paragon of perfection to which all other men would always be compared, in her mind.

'May I call you at Mrs. Williams'?' Jessica nodded, cautious again. This was certainly an unusual way to meet a man, and she really had no idea who or what he was.

'I won't be here for very long.'

'Then I'll have to call you soon, won't I?' Persistent bastard, aren't you? She smiled again, wondering. But he didn't look like a bastard. He looked like a nice man. Somewhere in his mid-thirties, with gentle grey eyes and soft silky hair. And the clothes he wore looked expensive. He was also wearing a small gold ring on the smallest finger of his right hand; she thought she could see a crest etched into the gold, but she didn't want to stare. Everything about him looked formal and elegant. With his jodhpurs we was wearing polished black boots and a soft blue shirt with a stock. His fawn-coloured tweed jacket hung from a branch and he looked a bit odd in the rugged setting, but at the same time incredibly beautiful. Better and better as she watched him. Which was precisely how he felt about her, although Jessica had begun to wonder how dishevelled her hair looked.

'Nice to meet you.' She prepared to ride off with a smile and a wave.

'You didn't answer my question.' He held her horse's bridle as he watched Jessica's eyes. She knew what he meant. And she liked his style.

'Yes. You can call me.' He stepped back in silence and, with a dazzling smile, swept her a bow. She liked that about him too. His smile. And she laughed to herself as she rode off towards the ranch.

CHAPTER XXXI

'Have a nice ride, dear?'

'Very. And I met a very strange man.'

'Really? Who?' Aunt Beth looked intrigued. Strange men were few and far between around the ranch, except an odd foreman here and there.

'He's someone's houseguest, and terribly British. But he's also very nice-looking.'

Aunt Beth smiled at the look on her face. 'Well, well. A tall, dark, handsome stranger on my ranch? Good heavens! Where is he? And how old?'

Jessica giggled. 'I saw him first. And besides, he's not dark. He's blonde, and a lot taller than I am.'

'Then he's yours, my dear. I never did like tall men.'

'I adore them.'

Aunt Beth looked over the top of her reading glasses with careful solemnity. 'You haven't much choice.' They both laughed again and enjoyed a blazing sunset over the hills.

It was another peaceful evening, and Jessica was up at seven the next day. She had a craving to wander, but this time not on the chestnut mare. She made herself a cup of coffee—for once up before Aunt Beth was—and took off as quietly as she could in the Morgan. She had never driven much around there, and she had been itching to explore.

The sun was high in the sky when she found it. And it was in very sad shape. But it was a beauty. It looked as though someone had lost it in the tall grass and then tired of looking for it, decades before. And now there it sat, alone and unloved, with a FOR RENT sign listing badly to one side just beyond the front steps. It was a small but perfectly proportioned Victorian house. She tried the front door, but it was locked. And Jessica found herself sitting on the front steps fanning her face with her large-brimmed straw hat, smiling. She wasn't sure why, but she felt good. And incredibly happy.

She drove home at fifty on the dusty country road and strode into the house with a grin. Aunt Beth was checking her mail and looked up, surprised.

'Well, where have you been? You left awfully early.' There was mischief in the old woman's blue eyes, and delighted suspicion.

'Wait till you hear what I've found!'

'Another man on my land? And this time a Frenchman! I knew it. Dear girl, you're having delusions from the sun.' Aunt Beth clucked sympathetically and Jessica burst into laughter and tossed her hat high in the air.

'No, not a man! Aunt Beth, it's a house! An incredible, beautiful, marvellous, Victorian house! And I'm madly in love with it.'

'Oh God, Jessie, not the one I think it is? The old Wheeling house out on the North Road?' She knew exactly which one.

'I haven't the vaguest idea, I just know that I love it.'

'And you've bought it, and your decorator is due in from New York first thing tomorrow morning.' Aunt Beth refused to be serious.

'No. I mean it. It's lovely. Did you ever stand back and look at it? I did, for an hour this morning, and I sat on the front steps for almost as long. What's it like inside? It was locked, dammit. I even tried all the windows.'

'God only knows what it looks like inside. No one's lived in it for almost fifteen years. Actually, it used to be very lovely, but it hasn't much land, so no one will buy it. You could probably get more land with it now, though, because the Parkers behind there just decided that they want to sell off a very nice parcel. Almost forty acres, if I remember correctly. But as far as I know, the Wheeling place just sits there empty. Year after year. The realty people showed it to me when I came down to buy the ranch, but I had no interest in the place. Too much house, too little land, and I wanted something more modern. Why on earth would you want a Victorian house out in the middle of nowhere?'

'But Aunt Beth, it's so beautiful!' Jessica looked young and romantic as she smiled at her friend.

'Ah, the illusions of youth. Maybe you have to be young

and in love to want a house like that. I wanted something more practical-looking. But I can see why you liked it.' She was noticing the brightness in her young friend's green eyes. 'Jessica, what exactly do you have in mind?' Her voice was quiet and serious now.

'I don't know yet. But I'm thinking. About a lot of different things. Maybe they're all crazy ideas, but something's brewing.' Jessica looked decidedly pleased with herself. It had been a marvellous morning, and something wonderful had happened in her head or her heart, she wasn't sure which, but she felt alive and excited and brand new again. It was crazy, really. A Bible passage that she had once learned in Sunday school had come to mind as she sat looking at the house. 'Behold, old things are passed away. All things are become new.' She had kept thinking of that, and she knew it was true. All the old things were drifting out of her life . . . even the horror of the trial . . . even Ian . . .

'Well, Jessie, let me know what you come up with when everything's "brewed". Or before that, if I can help.'

'Not just yet. But maybe later.' Aunt Beth nodded and went back to her mail and Jessie headed up the stairs, humming to herself. And then she stopped and looked back at Aunt Beth. 'How would I go about seeing the inside of that house?'

'Call the realtors. They'll be thrilled. I don't suppose they get to show the place more than once every five years. Just look them up in the book. Hoover County Realty. Terribly original name.' Aunt Beth was beginning to wonder . . . but she couldn't take Jessie seriously. This must be a passing fancy, a mood. But it would keep Jessie amused. Just thinking of something other than her own boredom would do her good. One thing was certain—she hadn't looked bored when she'd come in. Not that morning. And certainly not the evening before.

Geoffrey Bates telephoned that afternoon while Jessie was out, and he called again around five, just when she got back. He politely inquired if he could 'come around' for a drink, or bring her over to meet the people where he was staying. Jessie opted to have him for drinks at Aunt Beth's. And she was in high spirits.

He was terribly charming, very amusing, very proper, and quite taken with Aunt Beth, which pleased Jessie. But he was even more taken with Jessie, which pleased Beth. He looked even more splendid than Jessie had warned, in a blazer and ivory gabardine slacks, a Wedgewood blue shirt, and a navy ascot at his neck. Terribly elegant, but also very appealing. And they made a spectacular couple, both tall and blonde, with a natural grace. They would have turned heads anywhere, just as they looked sitting easily in the living room at the ranch.

'I rode the hills in search of you today, Jessica, and all in vain. Where were you hiding?'

'In a house with a bathtub four feet deep and a kitchen straight out of a museum.'

'Playing Goldilocks, I presume. Did the three bears come home before you left, and how was the porridge?'

'Delightful.' She laughed at him and blushed slightly when he reached for her hand. But he held it for only a second.

'I thought you were an apparition yesterday on the hills. You looked like a goddess.'

'Aunt Beth accused me of delusions from the sun.'

'Yes, but she didn't think she'd seen a god, at least.' Aunt Beth cut him down to size just to see how he'd take it, but he took it well. He was very gracious, and left them shortly before dinner, having invited them both to join him at his hosts' for lunch the next day. Aunt Beth excused herself on the grounds that she would have business to attend to on the ranch, but Jessica accepted with pleasure. He drove off in a chocolate brown Porsche, and Jessica looked up with a girlish gleam in her eyes.

'Well, what do you think?'

'Too tall by far.' Aunt Beth tried to look stern, but instantly failed as her face broke into a grin. 'But otherwise, I heartily approve. He's perfectly lovely, Jessica! Simply lovely.' Aunt Beth sounded almost as excited as Jessie herself felt. She was trying to fight it, but with difficulty.

'He is nice, isn't he?' She looked dreamy for a moment and then pirouetted on one foot. 'But he's not as nice as my house.'

'Jessica, you confuse me! I'm too old for such games! What house? And how dare you compare a man like that to a house?'

'Easily, because I'm mean. And I'm talking about *my* house. The one I rented today, for the whole summer!'

Aunt Beth's face grew serious at the news. 'You rented the Wheeling house for the summer, Jessica?'

'Yes. And if I like it, I'll stay longer. Aunt Beth, I'm happy down here, and you were right, it is time for a change.'

'Yes, child. But to something like this? This is a life for an old woman, not for you. You can't lock yourself up in the country. Who will you talk to? What will you do?'

'I'll talk to you, and I'll start to paint again. I haven't done that in years, and I love it. I might even paint you.'

'Jessica, Jessica! Always so flighty! You worry me at times. Last time you leapt to your feet and ran home to get a divorce, and now what are you doing? Please, dear, think this over with care.'

'I have, and I am, and I will. I only rented it for the summer. And we'll see after that. It's not a permanent move. I'll try it. The only permanent decision I've come to is to sell the shop.'

'Good God, you have been busy. Are you sure about all this?' Aunt Beth was more than slightly taken aback. She'd suggested selling the shop, but she hadn't thought Jessica would take her seriously. What had she done?'

'I'm absolutely sure. I'm going to sell Lady J to Astrid, or offer it to her, anyway, when I go back.'

'And she'll buy it. You can be sure of that, Jessica. I can't say I'm sorry. I think it would be good for her. But won't you be sorry? The boutique seems to mean a lot to you, dear.'

'It did, but it's a part of the past now. A part I have to get rid of. I don't think I'll regret it.'

'I hope not.' There was a change in the air again; they both sensed it. But for the first time in a long time, Jessie felt alive, and not in the least bored.

'Is the house livable?'

'More or less, with a good scrub. A very good scrub.'

'What will you do about furniture?'

'Live in a sleeping bag.' She didn't look at all perturbed.

'Don't be ridiculous. I have some spare furniture out in the shed, and more in the attic. Help yourself. At least you'll be comfortable.'

'And happy.'

'Jessie ... I hope so. And please try not to do anything major too quickly. Take your time. Think. Weigh your decisions.'

'Is that what you do?'

Aunt Beth couldn't stifle her mirth at the question. 'No. But it's the sort of advice old women are supposed to give young girls. I always rush in and do what I want, and mend fences later. And to tell you the truth, I'll love having you down here for the summer.' The older woman smiled gently and Jessica grew pensive.

'And what if I stay after the summer?'

'Oh, I'll close my doors to you and shoot at you from the kitchen windows. What do you suppose I'd do? Be delighted, of course. But I won't encourage you to move down here for my sake. I don't even do that to Astrid.' But she didn't really think Jessie would move down; by the end of the summer she'd be tired of the lack of excitement ... and the Englishman who was moving to San Francisco looked very promising.

He came to take Jessie to lunch the next day, and she returned to Aunt Beth's in high spirits. She had liked his friends, and they had been delighted at the prospect of her moving down for the summer, and had extended an invitation to drop in on them anytime she liked. They were a couple in their fifties who invited friends up often from L.A. Geoffrey was among them ...

'I see I'm going to be spending a lot of time here this summer.' he'd said.

'Oh?'

'Yes, and it's a damn long drive down from San Francisco. You could have picked someplace closer for your summer haunt, Jessica.' She had not yet mentioned to him that she was thinking of moving down for good. She'd laughed up into his eyes as he'd handed her out of his car at Aunt Beth's. 'Speaking of which, Miss Clarke, when are you going back to the city?'

'Tomorrow.' But the 'Miss' Clarke had unnerved her ... Miss? It had sounded so strange. So ... so empty.

'I'm going back to L.A. tomorrow too. But as a matter of fact—' he'd looked down at her almost slyly, and definitely pleased with himself—'I'm planning to be in San Francisco on Wednesday. How about dinner?'

'I'd love it.'

'So would I.' He'd looked surprisingly serious as they'd walked towards the house, and he'd quietly slipped his hand around hers.

CHAPTER XXXII

Astrid was stunned by Jessica's offer, but she leapt at the idea. She had wanted to buy the boutique since the first time she'd seen it.

'But are you sure?'

'Positive. Take it. I'll give you an idea of what the inventory's worth, talk to my attorney, and we'll come up with a price.' She spoke to Philip Wald and two days later they set a price. Astrid didn't hesitate.

She asked her own attorneys to have the papers drawn up. Lady J would become hers for the sum of eighty-five thousand dollars. Both she and Jessie were pleased with the price. The only twinge Jessica felt was at the mention of Astrid's changing the name of the boutique to Lady A. At least it would sound almost the same to their clients. But it wouldn't be the same anymore. It would be Astrid's. The end of an era had finally come.

They were sitting in the back office discussing plans for the sale when Katsuko appeared in the doorway with a smile on her face.

'There's someone here to see you, Jessie. Someone very pretty to look at, I might add.'

'Oh?' She poked her head out of the door and saw

Geoffrey. 'Oh! Hello.' She beckoned him into the office, and introduced him to Astrid, explaining that Mrs. Williams was her mother.

'You know my mother?' Astrid was surprised. Her mother didn't know anyone like Geoffrey.

'I had the pleasure of meeting her this weekend, at the ranch.' Astrid's eyebrows shot up as she cast a look of surprise at Jessica, and Geoffrey added quickly, 'I was down there visiting friends.' And suddenly Astrid's face said that she understood why Jessica was planning to spend the summer down there, in her creaking rented Victorian house. Astrid almost wondered if that was why she was selling the shop. But she felt as though she had missed a piece of the story somehow. Had Jessica been keeping secrets? She looked over to see Geoffrey looking at Jessica warmly. And Astrid restrained the questions on the tip of her lips. How? When? What next? Did he . . . was he . . . would he . . . He broke into her thoughts with another blistering smile.

'May I invite you two lovely ladies to lunch?' He even managed gently to encompass Katsuko with a look of regret; he knew someone would have to stay home, to mind the store. His manners were impeccable. And Astrid liked that. She was almost tempted into lunch, out of curiosity, but she didn't want to do that to Jessie. But Jessica was quick to shake her head about lunch.

'Don't even tempt us, Geoffrey. We were just discussing some business matters, about the sale of the shop, and . . .'

'Oh, for heaven's sake, Jessica!' Astrid broke in on Jessie's conscientious protests. 'Don't be silly—we can talk business later. I have some errands to do anyway. I have to go downtown—' she looked sorrowfully at Geoffrey—'but you two go ahead and have a nice lunch. I'll meet you back here around two or two-thirty.'

'Make it two-thirty, Mrs. Bonner.' Geoffrey was quick to step in. And Jessica sat back and watched. She liked the way he dealt with things. He was used to wielding power and it showed. It made her feel safe, but not threatened. Now that she didn't need to be taken care of, his attentions were a luxury, not a life-giving plasma. She was enjoying the difference, and found herself wondering what it would have been like with Ian, had her needs not been so desperate, had she been more sure of herself. But she brushed the thought from her mind.

They had lunch nearby, in a garden restaurant on Union Street, and it was a very pleasant meal. He had a passion for horses, and flew his own plane, was planning a trip to Africa the following winter, and had gone to Cambridge, after Eton. And it was clear that he was very taken with Jessie. And every time he smiled that magnificent smile of his, she melted.

'I must say, Jessica, you look very different up here, in town.'

'It's amazing what a difference it makes when I comb my hair.' They both smiled at the memory of their first meeting. 'I even wear shoes around here.'

'Do you? How refreshing. Let me take a look.' He teasingly swept aside the tablecloth to glance at her feet, and saw a very handsome pair of cinnamon suede Gucci shoes. They were almost exactly the colour of the suede skirt she had on with a salmon silk blouse. The salmon shade was Ian's favourite colour, and she had had to force herself to put it on this morning. So what if it was Ian's favourite? That was no reason to give it up. She hadn't worn the blouse in months, as though by not doing so she were somehow renouncing him. Now it seemed foolish.

'I approve of your shoes. And by the way, that's a very handsome blouse.' She blushed at the compliment, mostly because it reminded her of Ian. There was something about Geoffrey . . .

'What were you just thinking?' He had glimpsed a shadow passing rapidly across her eyes.

'Nothing.'

'Shame on you, telling lies. Something serious crossed your mind. Something sad?" It had looked that way.

'Of course not.' She was embarrassed that he had seen so much. Too much. He was very observant.

'Have you never been married, Jessie? It seemed remarkable to have the good fortune to find a woman like you, free and unattached. Or am I making assumptions?' But he had wanted to know ever since he'd met her.

'You're making the right assumptions. I'm free and unattached. And yes, I was married.' His timing was amazing, as thought he had read her mind.

'Any children?' He raised an eyebrow with a curious air.

'No. None.'

'Good.'

'Good?' It was an odd thing to say. 'You don't like children, Geoffrey?'

'Very much. Other people's.' He smiled without embarrassment. 'In fact, I'm a perfectly marvellous uncle. But I'd make a perfectly terrible father.'

'What makes you say that?'

'I move about too much. I'm too selfish. When I love a woman, I detest sharing her in any major way, and if you're going to be a proper mother, you've got to spread yourself pretty thin between husband and offspring. Perhaps I'm too much a child myself, but I want to enjoy long romantic evenings, unexpected trips to Paris, skiing in Switzerland without three little runny-noses crying in the car . . . I can give you a thousand dreadful, horribly selfish reasons. But all of them honest. Does that shock you?' He didn't apologise for what he was saying, but he was willing to accept that she might not approve. He had long since stopped making excuses. In fact, he had seen to it that there was no longer a possibility of a 'slip'. He had made up his mind, and now there was no question of it.

'No, it doesn't shock me. I've always felt that way myself. In fact, exactly that way.'

'But?'

'What do you mean?'

'There was a "but" in your voice.' He said it very softly, and she smiled. 'Was there? I'm not sure. I used to have very definite ideas on the subject. But I don't know . . . I've changed a lot.'

'Changing is natural if you've gotten divorced. But suddenly you find you want children? I should think you'd want permanent freedom.'

'Not necessarily. And I haven't made any grandiose policy changes about children either. I've just started asking myself a lot of questions.'

'Actually, Jessie—' he held her hand gently as he said it —'I rather think you'd be happier without children. You seem very much like me. Determined, free; you enjoy what you do; I somehow can't imagine you chucking all that for a little squally person in diapers.' She grinned at the thought.

'God.'

'Quite.' They laughed for a moment, and took a sip of their wine as the second batch of lunch customers began to arrive. They had already been sitting there for almost two hours. It was odd to be talking to him about children all of a sudden. She got the feeling that the subject was important to him, and he wanted to get it out of the way early. And he certainly shared all the views she'd held dear for a decade.

Jessica stretched her legs and finished her wine, wondering if she should get back to the shop, and then suddenly thinking that she must be keeping him from appointments too. But the time together was so pleasant, it was hard to bring it to an end.

'I'm going to Paris on business next week, Jessica. Is there anything I can bring you?'

'What a lovely thought. Paris.' Her eyes danced at the idea. Paris.

'Let's see ... you could bring me ... the Louvre ... Sacré-Coeur . . . the Café Flore . . . the Brasserie Lipp . . . the Champs Elysées ... oh, and the entire Faubourg St. Honoré.' She giggled at the thought of it.

'That's what I like. A woman who knows what she wants. As a matter of fact, how about coming with me?'

'Are you kidding?'

'I certainly am not. I'll only be gone for three or four days. You could get away for that long, couldn't you?' Yes, but with a total stranger? God only knew who he was.

'I've been meaning to go to New York for the shop, but now I don't need to, and ... Paris ... ?' She didn't know what to say. After all those jerks who had crawled all over her, here was a perfectly heavenly man, and he wanted to take her to Paris.

'We don't ...' He looked awkward but sweet. 'We don't

have to share the same room. If you'd be more comfortable . . .'

'Geoffrey! You're an angel. And stop it, or I'll wind up doing it and neglecting all the things I ought to do here. I'm very touched that you'd ask, but I really can't.'

'Well, let's wait and see. You might change your mind.'

Wow. Geoffrey was really quite amazing. Paris? She almost wanted to say yes, but . . . why not? Why the hell not? Paris? . . . God, it would be gorgeous, but . . . dammit, why did she feel as if she'd be cheating on Ian? What difference did it make now? She was free. He wouldn't even know. She never saw him anymore anyway. But . . . somehow . . . he was there . . . with a look of pain in his eyes, as though he didn't want her to go. She tried to shake his face from her mind, and smiled at Geoffrey.

'Thank you for the offer.'

'I do wish you'd come. See what I mean about enjoying impromptu trips? I love that sort of thing! Not much fun if you have to drag along a nanny and four brats, or leave them at home and feel guilty. Being an uncle is really much simpler. Have you any nieces or nephews?' She shook her head quietly. 'Brothers or sisters?'

'No. I had a brother, but he died in the war.'

Geoffrey looked puzzled for a moment. 'The second one, or Korea? In either case, he must have been quite a bit older.'

'No. Vietnam.'

'Of course. How stupid of me. How awful. Were you very close?' His pressure on her hand grew a trifle stronger, as though to support her. His thoughtfulness pleased her a great deal.

'Yes. We were very close. It did awful things to me when he died.' It was the first time she had ever been able to say that. The last few months had freed her in more ways than she knew.

'I'm sorry.'

She nodded and smiled. 'And how many brothers and sisters do you have?'

'Two sisters, and a very stuffy brother. My sisters are quite mad. But very amusing.'

'Do you still spend much time in Europe?'

'Quite a bit. A few days here, a few days there. I enjoy it very much that way. By the way, Jessica, shouldn't I be taking you back to the shop for your meeting with Astrid?'

'Christ. I forgot all about it. You're right!' She looked at her watch regretfully, and smiled at him again. It had been a lovely few hours.

'I've been keeping you from your appointments too, I suspect.'

'Yes, I . . .' But laughter took the place of seriousness and he looked at her with a mischievous smile. 'No, I didn't have a single appointment. I came up here entirely to see you.' He sat back in his chair and laughed at himself, as though very pleased.

'You did?' Jessica looked astonished.

'I most certainly did. I hope you don't mind.'

'No. I'm just surprised.' Very surprised, and a little taken aback. What did that mean? He had come up to see her . . . and the suggestion of the trip to Paris . . . dammit. Was he going to be like everyone else and expect to exchange a meal for her body?

'Oh, the look on your face, Jessica!'

'What look?' There was laughter and embarrassment in her voice. What if he really had known what she'd been thinking? He seemed to do that a lot.

'Would you like to know what look?'

'Okay. See if you can guess.' She might as well brazen it out.

'Well, if I tell you that I have a room at the Huntington, will you feel any better?'

'Oh! You!' She swatted him with her napkin. 'I was not . . . !'

'You were too!'

'I was too!'

They both laughed, and he slipped a large bill onto the waiter's plate and got up to help Jessica into her jacket.

'I apologise for my thoughts.' Jessica hung her head with a grin.

'You certainly ought to.' But he gave her a friendly

hug on their way out and they laughed and teased all the way back to the shop. Astrid was waiting for them with a relaxed smile when they got in. It pleased her to see Jessie happy again, and with a man.

'I'll leave you now to your meetings and your business and your whatever-it-is-you-do. And Jessica, what time shall I fetch you?'

'From here?' She looked surprised. It was strange to be taken care of again, escorted and assisted, picked up and brought back. She had missed it for so long, and now she didn't quite know how to handle it again. It was like coming back to shoes after months of bare feet.

'Would you rather I meet you after work?'

'Either way.' She looked at him happily, and for a moment neither of them spoke. She had been about to offer him her car, but she couldn't quite do that. Not . . . not the Morgan. She felt rotten for not offering it, but she couldn't.

'Why don't I give you time to go home and relax? May I pick you up there?' Since he already knew that she was a little bit skittish, they both laughed, but she nodded.

'That'll be fine.'

'Say at seven? Dinner at eight.'

'Super.' And then suddenly she had a thought. He was almost at the door of the shop, and she quickly walked toward him. 'You don't know San Francisco very well, do you?'

'Not very. But I expect I can find my way around.' He looked amused at her concern.

'How would you like a tour at the end of the day?'

'With you?'

'Of course.'

'That's a splendid idea.'

'Great. Where will you be around five?'

'Anywhere you say.'

'All right. I'll pick you up outside the St. Francis Hotel at five. Okay?'

'Very much so.'

He gave her a quick salute and ran quickly down the steps of the shop as Jessica turned back to Astrid.

Somehow she had a hard time keeping her mind on what they were saying as they discussed the sale of Lady J.

'Right, Jessie?'

'Huh?' Astrid was grinning at her when she looked up. 'Oh, shit.'

'Don't tell me you're falling in love.'

'Nothing like it. But he's a very nice man. Isn't he?' She wanted Astrid's approval.

'He looks like it, Jessie.'

Jessica looked up at her friend and giggled like a schoolgirl. It seemed hours before they had their business settled, although both women were pleased with the results. Jessica got up jubilantly from her desk, pirouetted on one heel of the pretty Gucci shoes, and looked at her watch.

'And now, I have to go.' She picked up her bag, blew Astrid a kiss, and paused happily at the door for a moment. 'In fifteen minutes I have to pick up Ian.' With a rapid wave she was out the door and down the steps—without ever realising what she had said. Astrid shook her head and wondered if she'd ever get over him. More than that, she wondered how Ian was doing. She missed him. And thinking of him threw a damper on her excitement about Jessie's new friend.

Jessie was already backing out of the drive and on her way to meet Geoffrey.

CHAPTER XXXIII

'Am I late?' She looked worried as she pulled up in front of the St. Francis. She had run into unexpected traffic on the way downtown. But he looked happy and relaxed, like a man who is looking forward to seeing someone, not like a man who has been kept waiting.

'Oh, I've been here for hours.'

'Liar.'

'Heavens! What an outrageous thing to call a man!' But he looked delighted to see her, and allowed himself to lean over and give her a peck on the cheek. She liked the friendliness of it. The hugs before passion ever became an issue. The little touches of the hand, the quick kiss on the cheek. It made things less awesome that way. They were becoming friends. She was falling in like.

'Where are you taking me?'

'Everywhere.' She eyed him with pleasure as she drove up to Nob Hill.

'What a promise. Well, I know where we are now, anyway. That's my hotel.' She ignored him, and he grinned.

'This is Nob Hill.' And she pointed out Grace Cathedral, the Pacific Union Club, and three of the city's poshest hotels. From there they swooped down California Street to the Embarcadero, the Ferry Building, and a quick view of the docks. Up toward Ghirardelli Square and the Cannery, where she pointed out the honeycomb of boutiques right after they passed Fisherman's Wharf (where she had stopped and bought him a well-filled cup of fresh shrimp and a huge hunk of sourdough bread).

'What a tour. My dear, I'm overwhelmed.' And she was having a marvellous time as well.

From there, they went on to watch the old men playing boccie on the rim of the bay, and then up to the yacht basin and the St. Francis Yacht Club. This was followed by a sedate tour past blocks and blocks and blocks of elaborate mansions. After which they took refuge in Golden Gate Park. And her timing was perfect. It was just nearing sunset, and the light on the flowers and lawns was gold and pink and very lovely. It was Jessica's favourite time of day.

They walked past endless flower beds, and along curved walks, past little waterfalls, and around a small lake, until at last they reached the Japanese tea garden.

'Jessica, you give an extraordinarily good tour.'

'At your service, sir.' She swept him a formal curtsy,

and he put a quick arm around her shoulders. It had been a beautiful day and she was beginning to feel as though she really knew him.

She liked his reactions, his way of thinking, his sense of humour, and the gentle way he seemed to care about how she felt. And he seemed so much like her. He had the same kind of free and easy ways, the same craving for independence. He seemed to like his work, and he certainly didn't appear to be suffering financially. He really seemed the perfect companion. For a while, anyway. And he was nice to her. She had learned to be grateful for that, without leaning on him too heavily.

'What do you like to do more than anything in this world, Jessica?' They were sipping green tea and munching little Japanese cookies in the tea garden.

'More than anything else? Paint, I guess.'

'Really?' He seemed surprised. 'Are you good? Stupid question, but one always feels compelled to ask that, useless though it is. People who are any good insist that they're awful. And of course the bad ones tell you they're the best.'

'Now what do I say?' They both laughed and she shared the last cookie with him. 'I don't know if I'm any good or not, but I love it.'

'What sort of things do you paint?'

'It depends. People. Landscapes. Whatever. I work in watercolour or oils.'

'You'll have to show me sometime.' But he sounded indulgent and not as though he took her very seriously. He had a kind of placating, fatherly way about him sometimes, which made her feel like a little girl. It was odd that now that she had gotten used to being a grown-up, someone had appeared who would have let her go on being a child. But she wasn't sure she still wanted to be one.

When the tea garden closed, they walked slowly back to the car, and Geoffrey seemed to see it for the first time.

'You know, Jessica, it's really a beauty. These are almost collectors' items now. Where did you get it?'

'I'm not sure one should admit that sort of thing, but it was a gift.' She looked proud as she said it.

'Good lord, and a handsome one.' She nodded in silence and he cast her a glance without asking the question. But whoever had given her the car, he knew it was someone important in her life, and most likely her husband. Jessica was not the sort of woman to accept large gifts from just anyone. He already knew that much about her. She was a woman of breeding, and considerable style.

'Have you ever flown? I mean flown a plane yourself.' She laughed at the idea and shook her head. 'Want to try?'

'Are you serious?'

'Why not? We'll go up in my plane sometime. It's not hard flying at all. You could learn in no time.'

'What a funny idea.'

He was full of funny ideas, but she liked them. And she liked him.

They shared a wonderful evening. The food at L'Etoile was superb, the piano in the bar was gentle, and Geoffrey was delightful to be with. They shared a chateaubriand with truffles and béarnaise, white asparagus, hearts of palm with endive salad in a delicate mustard dressing, and a bottle of Mouton-Rothschild wine, 1952, 'a very good year,' he assured her in his clipped English way, but warmed by a smile produced just for her. He always managed to create an atmosphere of intimacy without making her feel uncomfortable.

And after dinner they danced at Alexis'. It was a far cry from the evening she'd spent there with the blind date Astrid had provided. Geoffrey danced beautifully. It was a thoroughly different evening from any she had spent in years. There was luxury and romance and excitement. She hated to go home and see it end. They both did.

They drove to her house in silence, and he kissed her gently at the door. It was the first time he had really kissed her, and it didn't send rockets off in her head, but it pulled threads all the way up her thighs. Geoffrey was a totally magnetic man. He pulled away from her slowly, with the tiniest of smiles tugging at one side of his mouth. 'You're an exquisite woman, Jessica.'

'Would you like to come in for a drink?' She wasn't sure if she wanted him to, and the way she said it told him so. She almost hoped he'd refuse. She didn't want to . . . not yet. But he was so appealing, and it had been such a long time.

'Are you sure you're not too tired? It's awfully late, young lady.' He looked so gentle, so thoughtful, so much like . . . like Geoffrey. She forced her thoughts back to the present and smiled into his eyes.

'I'm not too tired.' But she stiffened a little and he sensed it. He smiled at her back as she opened the door with her key. She had nothing to fear from him. He wanted much more than she could give in a night. He wasn't going to rush her. He already knew what he wanted, and what he wanted was for keeps.

She opened the door and turned on some lights, and he lit the candles as she poured cognac into two handsome snifters.

'Is cognac all right?'

'Perfect. And so is the view. This is quite a house.' But he wasn't surprised. He had expected something like this. 'And what a beautiful woman you are . . . taste . . . style . . . elegance . . . beauty . . . intelligence . . . a woman of a thousand virtues.'

'And a fat head, if you don't stop soon.' She handed him the snifter of cognac and sat down in her favourite chair. 'It's a nice view from here.'

'It is. I'll be looking for something like this in a few weeks.'

'Will you?' She couldn't resist a burst of laughter. 'Or did you make up that story about moving to San Francisco too?'

He smiled boyishly. 'No, that was true. Are houses like this hard to find?'

'You mean you want to buy?' She had assumed that he would rent.

'That depends.' He looked into her eyes and then into his cognac while she watched him.

'Maybe I'll rent you this place for the summer.' She was teasing, and he raised an eyebrow.

'Are you serious?'

'No.' Her eyes grew sad as she looked into the candle and spoke. 'You wouldn't be happy here, Geoffrey.' And she didn't want him in 'their' house. It would have made her uncomfortable.

'Are *you* happy here, Jessica?'

'I don't think of it that way.' She looked back into his eyes, and he was surprised at the pain he saw lurking there. It made her seem suddenly years older. 'To me, it's just a house now. A roof, a clump of rooms, an address. The rest is gone.'

'Then you should move out. Maybe we'll find a . . . I'll find . . . a larger place. Would you consider selling this?'

'No, just renting. It's not mine to sell.'

'I see.' He took another sip of his cognac and then smiled at her again. 'I should be going soon, Jessica, or you'll be terribly tired tomorrow. Are you busy for breakfast?'

'Not usually.' She laughed at the thought.

'Good. Then why don't we have breakfast somewhere amusing before I fly back to L.A. I can pick you up in a cab.' She loved the idea of breakfast with him. She would have preferred to cook it for him and sit naked at the kitchen table with him, or juggle strawberries and fresh cream on a tray in bed. But she almost wondered if one did that sort of thing with Geoffrey. He looked as if he might wear a dressing gown and silk pyjamas. But there was a definite sensuality about him too.

'What do you eat for breakfast?' It was a crazy question, but she wanted to know. It suddenly mattered to her. Everything did.

'What do I eat?' He seemed amused. 'Generally something light. Poached eggs, rye toast, tea.'

'That's all? Not even bacon? No waffles? No French toast? No papaya? Just poached eggs and rye toast? Yerghk.' He roared with laughter at her reaction and began to enjoy the game.

'And what do you eat for breakfast that's so much more exotic, my love?'

'Peanut butter and apricot jam on English muffins. Or cream cheese and guava jelly on bagels. Orange juice, bacon, omelettes, apple butter, banana fritters . . .' She let her imagination run wild.

'Every day?'

'Absolutely.' She tried to look solemn but had a hard time.

'I don't believe you.'

'Well, you're right . . . about most of it. But the peanut butter and cream cheese part was true. Do you like peanut butter?'

'Hardly. It tastes like wet cement.'

'Have you eaten a lot of that?' She looked across at him with interest.

'What?'

'Wet cement.'

'Certainly. Marvellous on thin wheat toast. Now, are you serious about joining me for breakfast tomorrow? I'm sure we can get you some peanut butter on croissants. Will that do?'

'Perfect.' She was starting to be Jessie now, and it amused him. He liked everything about her. She kicked off her shoes and curled her legs up in her chair. 'Geoffrey—' she tried to sound solemn—'do you read comic books?'

'Constantly. Particularly Superman.'

'What? No Batman comic books?'

'Oh yes, of course, but Superman has always been my favourite.' He stopped playing for a minute then and looked into his glass. 'Jessica . . . I like you. I like you very much.' He surprised her with the directness of his words, and she was touched by the way he said them. His style was an odd mixture of formality and warmth. She hadn't thought the combination was possible, but apparently it was.

'I like you too.'

They sat across from each other and he made no move

to approach her. He didn't want to rush her. She was a woman you got close to gradually, after much thought.

'You haven't said much about it, nothing in fact, but I somehow have the feeling that you've suffered a lot. A very great deal, even.'

'What makes you think that?'

'The things you don't say. The times you back off. The wall you run behind now and then. I won't hurt you, Jessica. I promise I'll try very hard not to.'

She didn't say anything, but only looked at him and wondered how often promises turned to lies. But she wanted him to prove her wrong, and he wanted to try.

CHAPTER XXXIV

'Well, how was your evening?' Astrid was already at the shop when Jessie got there the next day. Jessie wasn't getting in as early anymore. She didn't have to. Or want to.

'Delightful.' She beamed, even more enchanted with their breakfast at the Top of the Mark that morning, but she didn't feel like telling Astrid about it. 'Very, very nice.' She looked cryptic and pleased with herself.

'I'd say he's "very, very nice" too.'

'Now, Mother. Don't push.' The two women laughed, and Astrid held up a hand innocently in protest.

'Who needs to push? He sells himself all by himself. Are you in love with him, Jessie?' Astrid looked serious and so did Jessica.

'Honestly? No. But I like him. He's the nicest man I've met in a long time.'

'Then maybe the rest will come later. Give him a chance.' Jessica nodded and looked at the mail that was hers. She didn't like sharing the shop anymore. It was different now. And it was like prolonging the end. She wanted to say good-bye to Lady J and get out of town.

This was just like one more divorce. And there was another letter from Ian with the rest of her mail. She took it and set it apart from the rest. Astrid noticed, but she didn't say anything. This was the first time Jessie hadn't torn up one of his letters. She saw Astrid's look and shrugged as she poured herself a fresh cup of coffee.

'You know, I keep thinking that maybe I should drop him a note and thank him for the car. Seems like the least I could do. Your mother and I talked about it last weekend.'

'What did she say?'

'Nothing much.' Which only meant that Jessie wasn't telling.

In the end, she threw out the letter he had sent her.

They met with the lawyers for the next two afternoons, and everything was settled. On Saturday morning, Jessie went to three real-estate agents and listed the house as a summer rental. But she wanted careful screening of the tenants; she was leaving all her furniture there. And Ian's studio would be locked. She felt she owed him that.

It was almost midnight on Sunday when she sat down to write him a note about the car. In the end, she jotted down five or six lines, telling him how pleased she had been, how lovely it was, and that he hadn't had to do that. She wanted to cancel the debt between them. He didn't owe her anything. But it took her almost four hours to compose the short note.

Five days later the house had been rented from the fifteenth of July till the first of September, and she was almost ready to leave town. She hoped to be gone in a week. Geoffrey wanted to come up and see her again, and even invited her down to L.A. for a weekend, but she was too busy. She had found leads to two houses and an apartment for him, but she was tied up with her own affairs. There didn't seem to be room for Geoffrey just then, and she wanted him to stay away until she had closed the house, given up the shop, put away the past. She wanted to come to him 'clean' and new, if he would just give her the time. She had to do it that way. Be alone to sever the last cords by herself. It was harder this way, but he didn't belong in her life yet. She would see him in the country once she was settled.

She seldom went to the shop now, except to answer questions for Astrid. But now Astrid knew fairly well how everything worked, and Katsuko was a great help. She was staying on at Lady J. And Jessie just didn't want to be there anymore. Workmen were busy changing the sign, and cards were being sent to all their customers announcing the small change in the name. It still hurt, but Jessica told herself that all changes did, perhaps especially those for the better. She wouldn't regret it once she left town. But then what would she do? Yes, paint . . . but for how long? She wasn't ready to become another Grandma Moses. But something would turn up . . . something better. Geoffrey? Maybe he was the answer.

Jessica stopped in at the shop for the last time on a Friday afternoon. She was leaving two days later, on Sunday. She had put away all the small treasures she didn't want to share with her new tenants. And photographs of Ian. She had unearthed so much as she'd packed. Everything hurt now. It seemed as though every moment were filled with painful reminders of the past.

She slid the car into the driveway behind Astrid's car and walked quietly into the shop. It already looked different. Astrid had added a few things, and a lovely painting in what was now her office. It was all Astrid's now. And the money from the sale was all Jessie's. It was funny how little that meant to her now. Nine months before, seven months, six . . . she would have begged for one-tenth of that money . . . and now . . . it didn't matter. The bills were paid, Ian was gone, and what did she need? Nothing. She didn't know what to do with the money, and she didn't really care. It hadn't dawned on her yet that she had made a great deal of money selling the shop Later she would be pleased, but not yet. And she still felt as though she had sold her only child. To a good friend, but still . . . she had abandoned the only thing she had ever nurtured and helped to grow.

'Mail for you, madam.' Astrid handed it to her with

a smile. She looked happy these days, and even younger than she had when Jessie had met her. It was difficult to believe that she had just had a birthday and turned forty-three. And in July, Jessie would be thirty-two. Time was moving. Quickly.

'Thanks.' Jessie slid the letters into a pocket. She could look at them later. 'Well, I'm all packed and ready to go.'

'And already homesick.' Astrid had guessed. She took her out to lunch and they drank too much white wine, but Jessie felt better. It helped. She went home in a much better mood.

She opened the windows and sat in a patch of sunlight on the floor, looking around the living room she had sat in so often with Ian. She could see him sprawled out on the couch, listening to her talk about the shop, or telling her about something brilliant he'd said in a new chapter. That was what was missing—that excitement of sharing the things they loved doing. Of laughing and being two kids on a warm sunny day, or a cold winter afternoon while he lit the fire. A man like Geoffrey would spoil her, and take her to the best restaurants and hotels all over the world, but he wouldn't take a splinter out of her heel, or scratch her back just right where it itched . . . he wouldn't burp over a beer watching a horror movie in bed, or look like a boy when he woke up in the morning. He would look very handsome, and smell of the cologne he had worn to dinner that time . . . and he hadn't been there when Jake had died . . . or her parents . . . but Ian had. You couldn't replace that. Maybe you shouldn't even try.

She wondered as she stared out at the bay, and remembered the letters Astrid had handed her before lunch. She went back to them now, digging into her jacket pocket . . . she hoped . . . she didn't . . . and she did . . . and there was . . . a letter from Ian. Her eyes swept quickly across the lines. He had gotten her note about the car.

. . . I write these to myself now, wondering only for a moment if you read them. And then suddenly, a few quick nervous lines from you, but you kept the car.

That's all that mattered. I wanted you to have that more than you can know, Jess. Thanks for keeping it.

I assume that you don't open my letters . . . I know you. Rip, snap, gone.

She smiled at the image. And he was, of course, right.

But I seem to need to write them anyway, like whistling in the dark, or talking to myself. Who do you talk to now, Jessie? Who holds your hand? Who makes you laugh? Or holds you when you cry? You look such a mess when you cry, and God, how I miss that. I imagine you now, driving the new Morgan, and that note the other day . . . it sounded like something you'd write to your grandmother's best friend. 'Thank you, dear Mr. Clarke, for the perfectly lovely car. I needed one just that colour to go with my best skirt and my favourite gloves and hat.' Darling, I love you. I only hope that you'll be happier now. With whomever, whenever. You have a right to that. And I know you must need someone. Or do you have a right to that? My heart aches so at the thought, yet I can't see myself stamping my feet and raising hell. How could I possibly say anything after all this? Nothing except good luck . . . and I love you.

It does make me sad that now that the book has sold, and I have sat back and taken a look at my life, you're not here to enjoy the changes. I've grown up here. It's a tough school to learn in, but I've learned a lot about you, and myself. It isn't enough just to make money, Jessie. And I don't give a damn who pays the bills. I want to pay them, but I don't think I'd get an ulcer anymore every time you signed a cheque. Life is so much fuller and simpler than that, or it can be. In an odd way, my life is full now, yet so empty without you. Darling, impossible Jessie, I still love you. Go away, leave my mind, let me go in peace, or come back. Oh God, how I wish you'd do that. But you won't. I understand. I'm not angry. I only wonder if it would have been different if I hadn't walked out that day, leaving you there with the phone in your hand. I still

> see your face on that day . . . but no, it's not all because of that one stinking day. We're both paying for old, old sins now—because I still believe that we are both suffering this loss. Or are you free of it now? Maybe you don't care anymore. I can't tell you the empty feeling that gives me, but that's what will happen in time, I suppose. Neither of us will give a damn. Not something I look forward to. A lot of good years 'from dust to dust'. Gone. And I still see you and see you and see you. I touch your hair and smile into your eyes. Perhaps you can feel that now—my smile into your eyes as you go your own way. Go in peace, Jessie dearest, and watch out for lizards and ants. They won't bite you, I promise, but the neighbours might call the cops when you scream. Just keep the hair spray handy, and take it easy on yourself. Always, Ian.

She laughed through her tears as she read it . . . lizards and ants. The two things she had always feared most. Other than loneliness. But she had lived with that now, so maybe she could even get used to lizards and ants . . . but to life without Ian? That would be so much harder. She hadn't realised how much she had missed the sound of his voice until she read the letter. It was there. His words, his tone, his laughter, his hand rumpling her hair as he talked. The look he gave her that made her feel safe.

Without thinking, she got to her feet and went to the desk. There was still some paper there. She reached for a pen and wrote to him, telling him that she had sold the shop, and about the house near Aunt Bethanie's ranch. She described the house down to its tiniest detail as he had taught her to do when she had thought she wanted to write. She didn't have a knack for it, but she had learned how to write careful descriptions so that her reader could see all that she did. She wanted him to see the fading Victorian in all its possible splendour, now nestled in weeds. She was going to clean it up and make it pretty. That would keep her busy for a while. She gave him the address and mentioned that she had rented the house, but to a pleasant couple without children or pets. They'd keep it in good shape, and she was sure to tell him that the studio was locked. His file cabinets were safe. And she would try to stay safe from lizards and ants. It all flowed into the letter. It was like writing to a long-lost best friend. He had always been that. She put a stamp on the envelope and walked out to the mailbox on the corner, slipped it in, and then noticed Astrid driving home. She waved, and Astrid drove into the block and stopped at the corner.

'What are you up to tonight, Jessie? Want to have dinner?'

'You mean you're not busy for a change, Mrs. Bonner? I'm stunned.' Jessica laughed, feeling happier than she had in ages. She was actually looking forward to leaving. For the past weeks, she had almost wondered if she'd done the wrong thing. It was all so brutal, so final. But now she knew that she'd been right, and she was glad. She felt relieved, and as though she had just touched base with her soul. Ian still lived there. In her soul. Even now. Jessica tried to pry her thoughts from Ian as she smiled at Astrid.

'No smartass, I'm not busy. And I have a wild craving for spaghetti. How's the packing going?'

'All done. And spaghetti sounds great.'

They dined in the noise and chaos of Vanessi's, and moved on to a sidewalk café, for cappuccino after that. They watched the tourists beginning to appear, the first wave of summer, and the air was surprisingly warm.

'Well, love, how do you feel? Scared, miserable, or glad?'

'About leaving? All three. It's a little bit like leaving home forever . . .' Like leaving Ian—again. Packing up their private treasures and odds and ends had revived so many feelings. Feelings that were better left buried now. She would not unpack those boxes again, and she had separated her things from Ian's. It would be very easy now, if they ever sold the house. Their worldly goods were no longer in one heap.

'Well, that house of yours will keep you busy. Mother says it's a mess.'

'It is. But it won't be for long.' Jessica looked proud as

she said the words. She already loved the place. It was like a new friend.

'I'll try to get down to see it before we go away in July.'

'I'd love that.' Jessica smiled, feeling lighthearted and happy. A burden she couldn't quite identify had been lifted from her shoulders. She had felt its absence all evening. It was like no longer having a toothache or a cramp that she had lived with for months, not really aware of it yet subtly crippled by its presence.

'Jessica, you look happy now. You know, I felt terribly guilty for a while, for taking the shop away from you. I was afraid you'd hate me for it.' Astrid looked young and unsure as she looked into Jessie's face. But Jessica only smiled and shook her blonde mane.

'No. You don't need to worry about that.' She patted her friend's hand. 'You didn't take it away from me, Astrid. I sold it to you. I had to. To you, or to someone else, even if it hurt a little. And better to you. I'm glad it's yours now. I had outgrown it, I guess. I've changed a lot.'

Astrid nodded assent. 'I know you have. I hope it all works out.'

'Yeah, me too.' Her smile was almost rueful, and the two women finished their coffee. They were like two soldiers who have weathered the war together and now have nothing left to talk about except to make occasional guesses about the peace. Would it work? Jessie hoped so. Astrid wondered. They had both come a long way in the past months. And Astrid knew she had what she wanted now. Jessica wasn't yet quite as sure.

'Any news of Geoffrey this week, Jessie?'

'Yes. He called and said he'd come up to the country to see me next week.' He had been sensitive enough to know she needed to be left alone in the city.

'That'll do you good.'

Jessica nodded, but she didn't say more.

The doorbell rang at nine-fifteen the next morning. Her bags were packed and Jessica was washing the breakfast dishes for the last time, keeping one eye on the view. She wanted to remember it all, hang on for one last hour, and then leave. Quickly. She felt almost the way she had the morning she had left for college, old times packed away in mothballs and a new life ahead. She planned to come back, at least that was what she said, but would she? She wasn't really sure. She had the odd sensation that she was leaving for longer than a summer. Maybe forever.

The bell rang again and she dried her hands on her jeans and ran to the front door, throwing her hair back from her face, barefoot, her shirt buttoned but not quite far enough. She looked precisely the way she did when Ian loved her best. Pure Jessie.

'Who is it?' She stood beside the front door with a small smile on her face. She knew it was probably Astrid or Katsuko. One last good-bye. But this time she would laugh, not cry as they all had at the shop.

'It's Inspector Houghton.' Everything inside her turned to stone. With trembling hands, she unbolted the door and opened it. The party mood was suddenly gone, and for the first time in months, there was terror in her eyes again. It was amazing how quickly it could all come flooding back. Months of slowly rebuilding the foundations, and in as long as it took to ring a doorbell her life was a shambles again. Or that was how she felt.

'Yes?' Her eyes looked like greenish-grey slate and her face was set like a mask.

'Good morning. I ... uh ... this isn't an official call exactly. I ... I found your husband's pants in the property room the other day and I thought I'd drop them off and see how you were doing.'

'I see. Thank you.' He handed her a brown bag with an awkward smile. Jessie did not return the smile.

'Going on a trip?' His eyes glanced over the bags and boxes in the hall, and she looked over her shoulder and then quickly into his eyes. Bastard. What right did he have to be there now? Jessica nodded in answer to his question and looked down at her feet. It was a good time to end the war, to hold out a hand in peace, to go quietly. But she couldn't. He made her want to scream again, to pummel him, to scratch his face. She couldn't bear the sight of him. Terror and hatred swept over her like a tidal wave and she had the sudden urge to slither down the wall and crumple into a heap and cry. She felt as though she had been swept up in a hurricane and then cast aside by her own emotions. She looked up at him suddenly, with open pain in her eyes.

'Why did you come here today?' There was the look of a child who does not understand in her face, and he looked away and down at his hands.

'I thought you'd want your husband's . . .' His voice trailed off and his face grew hard. Coming to see her had been a dumb thing to do, and now he was sure of it. But he had just had that feeling for days now. Of wanting to see her. 'Your husband's pants were just lying around the property room. I thought . . .'

'Why? Why did you think? Is he liable to be coming home and needing them in the immediate future? Or aren't they wearing denims in prison anymore? I'm a little out of touch. I haven't been up there in a while.' She instantly regretted the words. His eyes showed interest and warmed again slightly.

'Oh?'

'I've been busy.' She looked away.

'Problems?' Vulture. And then she found his eyes again.

'Do you really give a damn?' She wouldn't let go of his eyes. She wanted to scratch them out.

'Maybe I do give a damn. Maybe . . . I'm sorry. You know, I always felt sorry for you through the whole case. You seemed to believe in him so much. You were wrong, though. You know that now, don't you?' She hated the tone of his voice.

'No. I wasn't wrong.'

'The jury said you were.' He looked so smug, the bastard, so sure of 'the system'. So sure of everything, including Ian's guilt. She wanted to hit him. The urge was almost overpowering now.

'The jury didn't make me wrong, Inspector Houghton.' She held tightly to the brown bag he had given her and clenched her fists.

'Are you . . . are you free now, Mrs. Clarke?'

'Does that mean, have I left my husband?' He nodded

and pulled a pack of cigarettes out of his coat pocket. 'Why?'

'Curious.' Horny.

'Is that why you came back here? Out of curiosity? To see if I'd left my husband? Would that make you happy?' She was boiling now. 'And why didn't you bring this to the shop?' She held out the brown bag with Ian's pants in it.

'I did. I was there yesterday. They told me that you don't work there anymore. True?' She nodded.

'I don't. So now what?' She looked him in the eye again and suddenly almost a year of fear vanished. He could try to do anything he wanted and she'd kill him. With pleasure. It was a relief to confront him. She looked at him again and six months of pain passed from her eyes to his. It was a naked vision he saw there, of a human being badly scarred, and he took a long drag on his cigarette and looked away.

'What time are you leaving on your trip? Have you got time for lunch?' Oh, Jesus. It was almost laughable, except that it still made her want to cry.

She shook her head slowly, looked down, and then slowly she looked up again as tears filled her eyes and slid down her cheeks. It was over now. The last of the anger and the horror and the terror and the pain slid slowly down her cheeks; the trial and the jury and the verdict and the arrest and Inspector Houghton all melted into silent tears, pouring slowly down her face. He couldn't bear to look at her. It was much worse than a slap in the face. He was sorry he had come. Very sorry.

She took a deep breath, but she did nothing about the tears. She needed them to wash all the filth away. 'I'm leaving this town to get away from a nightmare, Inspector. Not to celebrate it. Why would we possibly want to have lunch together? To talk about old times? To reminisce about the trial? To talk about my husband? To . . .' A sob caught in her throat and she leaned against the wall with her eyes closed, the paper bag still clutched in her hand. It was all rushing in on her again. He had brought it all back in a brown paper bag. She put a hand to her forehead, squeezed her eyes tightly shut, took a slow breath, and then opened her eyes again. He was gone. She heard the door of his car slam shut at that precise moment, and a moment later the green sedan pulled away. Inspector Houghton never looked back. She closed the front door slowly and sat down in the living room.

The trousers she pulled out of the bag had large holes carefully cut out of them at the crotch, where the police lab had tested the fabric for sperm. As she looked at them she remembered that first time she had seen Ian in jail, in the white pyjama bottoms. The pants were a great good-bye present.

But now she knew once again why she was leaving town. And she was glad. As long as she stayed it would all have stayed with her. In some form or other. She would always have wondered if Houghton might appear again. Sometime. Somewhere. Somehow. He was gone now. Forever. As was the nightmare. And the trial. All of it. Even Ian. But she had had to leave it all. There was no carving the good from the bad anymore. It was all bad, corrupt, venomous, cancerous. And suddenly she wasn't even angry at Ian anymore. Or at Inspector Houghton. She dried her face and looked around the room and realised something. It wasn't hers anymore. None of it was. Not the pants, not the problems, not the inspector, not even the bad memories. They no longer belonged to her. They belonged in the garbage with the trousers she held in her hand. She was leaving. She had left.

It was all behind her now. His papers in the studio. Her old check stubs filed in boxes in the basement. She was leaving all of that forever. What she was taking with her were the beautiful moments, the tender memories from long before, the portrait of Ian that she had painted when they were first married—she couldn't leave that with the new tenants—favourite books, cherished treasures. Only the good stuff. She had decided that was all she had room for anymore. To hell with Inspector Houghton. She was almost glad he had come. Now she knew she was free. Not wanting to be free, or trying to be free, or working at being free. But free.

CHAPTER XXXV

Leaving San Francisco was easier than she had thought it would be. She wouldn't let herself think. She just got on the highway and kept driving. No one had come to wave handkerchiefs or cry bitter tears and she was glad.

After Inspector Houghton's visit, she had had a cup of tea, finished the dishes, put on her shoes, checked the house and the windows one last time, and left.

The drive south was lovely, and she felt young and adventurous when she reached her decaying house on the old North Road. And she was touched when she went inside and saw what Aunt Beth had done. The house was spotlessly clean, and the sleeping bag she had left there earlier was unnecessary. There was a narrow bed in the bedroom with a bright patchwork quilt carefully folded at the foot. It was the one from her bedroom at Aunt Beth's. A young girl's Victorian desk stood in a corner, and two lamps made the room bright. The kitchen was stocked, and there were two rocking chairs and a large table in the living room, and a large easy chair by the fire. There were candles all around, and logs near the fire. She had everything she needed.

And dinner with Aunt Beth the next day was a jovial affair. She had spent the first night alone in the new house. She had wanted it that way, and had wandered from room to room like a child, not feeling lonely, only excited. It was like the beginning of an adventure. She felt reborn.

'Well, how do you like it? Are you ready to go home yet?' Aunt Beth chuckled with her over tea.

'Not on your life. I'm ready to stay here forever. And thanks to you, the house is as cosy as can be.'

'It'll take more than that to make it cosy, my dear.'

But what Jessica had sent in the two crates helped a bit. Photographs, planters, a little marble owl, a collection of treasured books, two bright paintings, and the portrait of

Ian. There were also blankets and brass candlesticks, and odds and ends that she loved. And she filled the house with plants and bright flowers. At the end of the week, she added to her old treasures with a few new ones she acquired at auction. Two low rough-hewn tables, and an oval hooked rug. She put them in the living room and stood back, looking pleased. It looked more like home every day. She had sent books in the trunks, and her painting things were set up in a corner, but she hadn't had time to paint anything yet. She was too busy with the house.

The foreman's son from Aunt Beth's spent the week-end pulling weeds and mowing the lawn, and they had even discovered a crumbling gazebo far out in the back. And now she wanted a swing. Two of them. One to hang from a tall tree near the gazebo, where she could swing high and watch the sunset on the hills, and another to sit in front of the house, the kind on which young couples sat and whispered 'I love you's' on warm summer nights, creaking slowly back and forth, sure that they were unique in the world.

The letter from Ian came on Saturday morning. She had been in her new house for six days.

And there you are, funny girl, with dust in your hair and a smudge on your nose, grinning with pride at the order you're making from chaos. I can see you now, barefoot and happy, with a cornstalk in your teeth. Or wearing your Guccis and hating it? What's it like? I can see the house perfectly now, though I can't imagine you happy in a sleeping bag on the floor. Don't tell me you've gotten that rugged! But it sounds lovely, Jessie, and it will do you good. Though I was shocked to hear about the shop. Won't you miss it? Sounds like a hell of a good price, though. What'll you do with that pile of bucks? At this end, I'm hearing news about the making of a movie from the book. Don't hold your breath; I'm not. Those things never happen. They just get talked about. Though on the other hand, I never thought you'd sell the shop. How does that feel? Painful, I'll bet, but maybe a relief? Time to do other things. Travel, paint, clean up that palace you've saddled yourself with for the summer—or longer? I heard something in the tone of your last letter. It sounds like love for the house, and the country around it, and Aunt Beth. She must be a remarkable woman. And how are the ants and the lizards so far? Staying away? Or all wearing your best hair spray and loving it?

She chuckled as she read; once she had tried to kill a lizard in their hotel room in Florida with her hair spray. They had asphyxiated themselves out of the room, but the lizard had loved it.

She finished reading the letter and went to sit at the large table Aunt Beth had provided. She wanted to tell him about the things Aunt Beth had put in the house, and the goodies she'd found at auction. It didn't seem fair to let him think she was sleeping on the floor.

The correspondence got under way as simply as that, and without the determination of their halt in communication. She didn't think about it, she just wrote to him to give him the news. It was harmless, and she was pleased for him about the movie. Maybe this time it would happen. She hoped so, for him.

She was surprised at the length of her response. It covered six tightly written pages, and it was almost dark when she sealed the envelope and put on the stamp. She cooked dinner on the old stove, went to bed early, and got up very early the next morning. She drove into town, mailed the letter, and stopped at Aunt Beth's for a cup of coffee. But Aunt Beth was out riding.

The afternoon was quiet and pretty. Jessie did some sketches while sitting dangling her feet on her front porch. She felt like Huck Finn's older sister, in overalls and a red T-shirt and bare feet. The sun was bright on her face and it was a beautiful day, and her hair looked like spun gold looped up in loose curls at the top of her head.

'Good afternoon, mademoiselle.' Jessica jumped, the sketch pad flying from her hands. She had thought there was no one anywhere near the house. But when she looked up, she laughed. It was Geoffrey.

'My God, you scared me to death!' But she hopped

lightly from the porch as he picked up her pad and looked at it with surprise.

'Great Scott, you *can* draw! But much more interesting than that, you're exquisite and I adore you!' He folded her into a great warm hug, and she smiled up at him from her bare feet in the tall grass around the house. They hadn't quite gotten up all the weeds yet. 'Jessica, you look perfectly beautiful!'

'Like this?' She laughed at him, but she was slow to leave his embrace. She was just beginning to realise how much she'd missed him.

'Yes, I adore you like that. The first time I saw you, you were barefoot and had your hair looped up like that. I told you, you looked just like a Greek goddess.'

'Heavens!'

'Well, aren't you going to give me the grand tour, after you've kept me at arm's length all this time?'

'Of course, of course!' She laughed delightedly, and pointed majestically toward the house. 'Won't you come in?'

'In a moment.' But first he drew her into his arms for a long tender kiss. 'Now I'm ready to see the house.' She laughed at him, and then stopped and took a long look at him.

'No, you're not.'

'I'm not?' He looked confused. 'Why not?'

'First take off your tie.'

'Now?'

'Absolutely.'

'Before we go inside?' She nodded insistently, and, smiling at her, he took off the navy blue tie dotted with white, which she correctly guessed was from Dior.

'It's a lovely tie, but you don't need it here. And I promise, I won't tell a soul you took it off.'

'Promise?'

'Solemnly.' She held up a hand and he kissed it. The feeling in the centre of her palm was delicious.

'Oh, that was nice.'

'You're a tease. All right, then, will this do?' She looked him over again but shook her head. 'What?'

'Take your jacket off.'

'You're impossible.' But he slipped out of it, dropped it over his arm, and swept her a bow. 'Satisfied, milady?'

'Quite.' She imitated his accent and he laughed as, at last, he followed her inside.

She took him around room by room, holding her breath a little, afraid he might hate it. And she wanted him to love it. It was important to her. The house meant so much to her. It was symbolic of so much in her that had changed. And it was still a little bare, but she liked it that way. She had room to grow in, and to collect new things. She felt freer here than she had in San Francisco. Here, it was all new and fresh.

'Well, what do you think?'

'Not exactly overdecorated, is it?' She smiled as he chuckled, but she wanted him to like it, not make fun of it. 'All right, Jessica, don't look so sensitive. It's lovely, and it ought to be great fun for a summer.' But what about for a life? She hadn't said anything to him yet about staying there, but she wasn't quite sure yet either, so there was no point. And it didn't really matter. If he fell in love with her, he could fly down to see her in his plane. It would give her the weeks alone to paint and walk and think and spend time with Aunt Beth, and the weekends with him.

'What on earth are you thinking about?' She jumped as he broke into her thoughts. 'You had the most outrageous little smile on your face.'

'Did I?' But she couldn't tell him what she had in mind. It had to grow slowly, she couldn't sketch it all out for him ahead of time.

'You did, and I love your little house. It's sweet.' But he made it sound silly, and she was disappointed. He meant well, but he just didn't understand.

'Would you like a cup of tea?' It was a hot day, but he seemed to like hot tea whatever the weather. That or Scotch. Or martinis. She already knew.

'Love some. And then, Jessica my love, I have a surprise for you.'

'Do you? I love surprises! Give it to me now.' She

looked like a little kid again as she plonked down on the couch and waited.

'Not now. But I thought we'd do something special tonight.'

'Like what?' She wanted to do something special too, and it showed in her smile, but he let it pass.

'I want to take you down to Los Angeles; there's a party at the consulate. I thought you might rather enjoy it.'

'In Los Angeles?' But why Los Angeles? She wanted to stay in the country.

'It's going to be quite a nice party. Of course, if you'd rather not . . .' But the way he said it didn't leave her much choice.

'No, no . . . I'd love to . . . but I just thought . . .'

'Well, what would we do here? I thought it would be much nicer to run down to the city for a bit. And I want to introduce you to some of my friends.' He said it so nicely that she felt badly about her reluctance. It was just that she had wanted to share a quiet evening with him in the new house. But there would be other times. Lots of them.

'All right. It sounds terrific.' She was going to get into the spirit of it. 'What sort of party is it?'

'White tie. Late dinner. And there ought to be quite a lot of important people there.'

'*White* tie? But that means tails!'

'As a rule, yes!'

'But Geoffrey, what in hell can I wear? I don't have anything here. Just a lot of country stuff.'

'I thought that might be the case.'

'So what'll I do?' She looked horrified. White tie? Christ. She hadn't even seen white tie since all those ridiculous deb balls her mother had made her go to fifteen years ago. And she had nothing even remotely possible to wear. Everything dressy was still in San Francisco.

'Jessica, if you won't be too cross at me, I took the liberty of . . .' He looked more nervous than she had ever seen him. He knew she had exquisite taste and he was terrified of what he had done. 'I hope you won't be angry, but I just thought that under the circumstances . . . admittedly, I . . .'

'What on earth is going on?' She was half amused, half frightened.

'I bought you a dress.'

'You did what?' She was dumbfounded.

'I know, it was a ridiculous thing to do, but I just assumed that you probably didn't have anything here and . . .' But she was laughing at him. She wasn't angry. 'You're not cross?'

'How could I be cross? No one's ever done that for me before.' Certainly not a man she barely knew. What an amazing man he was turning out to be! 'That was a lovely thing to do.' She hugged him and laughed again. 'Can I see it?'

'Of course.' He bolted toward the door and returned five minutes later, as he had parked a little distance away. He had wanted to surprise her when he arrived, and the Porsche didn't lend itself well to surprises. But he was back with an enormous box in his arms, and a large bag that seemed to hold several smaller boxes.

'What on earth did you do?'

'I went shopping.' He looked pleased with himself now. He dumped all of it on the couch and stood back with a breathless look of pleasure.

Jessica slowly pulled open the large box and gasped. The fabric was the most delicate she'd ever seen. It was a silk crepe, the lightest imaginable. It seemed to float through her fingers, and it was a warm ivory, which would set off her dark tan to perfection. When she took the dress out of the box, it seemed to clasp at one shoulder and leave the other bare. And when she saw the label it explained the design and the fabric. Geoffrey had bought her a couture dress, which must have cost him at least two thousand dollars.

'My God, Geoffrey!' She was speechless.

'You hate it.'

'Are you kidding? It's magnificent. But how could you buy me that?'

'Do you like it, dammit?' He couldn't make head or tail out of what she was saying, and it made him nervous, waiting to find out.

'Of course I like it. I love it. But I can't accept it. That's a terribly expensive dress.'

'So? You need it for tonight.' She laughed at the logic.

'Not exactly. That's like wearing a new car.' And a Rolls, yet.

'If you like it, I want you to wear it. Will it fit?' She considered not even trying it, but she was dying to know how it looked, how it felt. Just for a moment.

'I'll try it. But I won't keep it. Absolutely not.'

'Nonsense.'

But she went to try it on, and when she came back she was smiling. And the vision he saw made him smile too.

'Good heavens, you're beautiful, Jessica. I've never seen anyone look like that in a dress.' It looked as though it had been made for her. 'Wait, you have to try it with these.' He dived into the bag of goodies and came out with a shoebox. Little ivory satin strands of sandals on delicate heels. Again, a perfect fit. Geoffrey certainly knew how to shop. A little silver and white beaded bag. All put together, it was dazzling. And they were equally overwhelmed. He with looking at her, and she to be wearing it all. She was used to good clothes, but these were extravagantly beautiful. And outrageously expensive.

'Well, it's settled, then.' He looked decisive, and pleased. 'Where's my tea?'

'You don't expect me to serve tea in this, do you?'

'No. Take it off.'

'Yes, love, and I'm going to keep it off. It's so pretty, but I just can't.'

'You can and you will, and I won't discuss it. That's all.'

'Geoffrey, I . . .'

'Quiet.' He silenced her with a kiss, and she had the feeling that the entire matter had been taken out of her hands. When he wanted to be, he was very forceful. 'Now get me my tea.'

'You're impossible.' She took off the dress and got him the tea, but in the end he won. At six o'clock she got out of the tub, did her makeup and her hair, and slipped into the dress. She felt faintly as though she were prostituting herself. A two-thousand-dollar dress was no small gift. Somehow he made it seem like a scarf or a hankie, but this was no hankie. As she slipped the dress over her head, she practically drooled.

And so did he when he saw her twenty minutes later in her new bedroom doorway. The house certainly wasn't used to this sort of grandiose coming and going in its halls. Geoffrey had gone to his friends' house to change, and had come back looking impeccable in white tie and tails. His shirt front was perfectly starched. Nothing on him appeared to move. He looked like someone in a 1932 movie. And Jessica smiled when she saw him.

'You look beautiful, sir.'

'Madam, you have no idea how extraordinary you look.'

'I must say, this all feels pretty super. But I feel like Cinderella. Are you sure I won't turn into a pumpkin at midnight?' She was still more than a little embarrassed by the extravagance of it all, but for some reason she had let herself be swept away on the tide of his insistence. And she had to admit, it was fun.

'Are you ready to go, darling?' The 'darling' was new, but she didn't mind it. She could get used to it. She supposed that she could get used to a lot of things if she tried.

'Yes, sir.' She looked down at her bare hands then and wished she had both jewellery and gloves. At any event as formal as this one obviously was going to be, it seemed as though long white kid opera gloves were in order, and jewellery . . . jewellery . . . she thought of something as they started to leave. 'Wait a second, Geoffrey.' She had brought it with her, and she had totally forgotten it. She had hidden it, for safety's sake. But it would be perfect.

'Something wrong?'

'No, no.' She smiled mysteriously and ran back into the bedroom, where she bent down carefully to look for a tiny package tied in the underside of the bed. It had been the only place she could think of. But she had wanted to bring it with her. She didn't know why, but she had wanted to. She quickly took the box from its hiding place and then opened it, pulling the soft suede jewel case out of the box, and then spilling the gem into her hand. It was more beautiful than ever, and for a moment her heart stopped as she saw it. It brought back so many painful memories, but so many nice ones as well. She could remember seeing it on her mother's hand . . . and then taking it out for Ian . . . putting it back when the trial was all over. It was her mother's emerald ring. She had never brought herself to wear it, just as a piece of jewellery, a thing, a bauble. But tonight was a night to wear it, as a thing of beauty and pride, as something special that had been given to her. Tonight it signified a new beginning to her life. It was perfect. And tears came to her eyes as she slipped it on. She felt her mother approve.

'Jessica, what are you doing? We've got quite a drive to L.A.—do hurry up.'

She smiled to herself as she slipped it on her hand. It was exactly what she needed. She also had on a pair of pearl earrings that Ian had given her years ago. They were the only jewellery she had brought, except for the ring, which she really hadn't planned to wear. She caught a last glimpse in the mirror, and smiled to herself as she rushed out to join Geoffrey. 'Coming!'

'Everything all right?'

'Wonderful.'

'Ready?'

'Yes, sir.'

'Oh, and by the way, I forgot to give you these.'

'These' were two more boxes, a long thin flat one and a small cube.

'More? Geoffrey, you're crazy! What are you doing?' It was like Christmas. And why was he doing this? She didn't even want presents, but he looked so hurt when she baulked that she started to open the packages. No man had ever done this to her before.

As she began with the long thin box, Geoffrey suddenly exclaimed.

'Jessica, how lovely. What an extraordinarily fine piece of jewellery.' He was admiring her mother's ring, and with a trembling hand, she held it up for him to see. 'It means a great deal to you, doesn't it?' She nodded, and then, after a pause, his voice softened. 'Was it your engagement ring for when you were married?'

'No.' She looked at him solemnly. 'It was my mother's.'

'Was? . . . Is she . . .' So that was why she never spoke of her family. She had told him about the brother, but she had never mentioned her parents. Now he understood.

'Yes, she and my father died only a few months apart. It's a long time ago now, I suppose, though it doesn't really feel like it. But I've never . . . I've never worn the ring, like tonight.'

'I'm honoured that you'd wear it with me.' He pulled her face gently toward him with the tip of one finger, and kissed her ever so carefully. It made her whole body tingle. And then he stood back and smiled. 'Go on. Finish opening your things.' She had forgotten the boxes, and she went back to them now.

The long thin box yielded the gloves she had thought of as she was dressing. It was as though he read her mind. Again.

'You think of everything!' They made her laugh, but she was delighted as she slid one into place. 'How did you know all my sizes?'

'A lady should never ask a question like that, Jessica. It implies I have too much knowledge of women.'

'Aha!' The idea amused her. And she went on to the next box. This one was small enough to fit into the palm of her hand. Geoffrey was watching her with interest as she tore off the paper and got to the small navy blue leather box. It had a snap holding it closed and she flicked it open and gasped. 'Jesus. Geoffrey! No!' He couldn't tell if she was angry or pleased, but he quietly took the box from her and took them out, holding the diamond teardrops to her ears.

'They're just what you need. Put them on.' It was a

quiet order, but Jessica took one step backward and looked at him.

'Geoffrey, I can't. I really can't.' Diamonds? She hardly knew him. And the earrings were not terribly small. They were heavenly, but not at all something she could accept. 'Geoffrey, I'm sorry.'

'Don't be silly. Just try them for tonight. If you don't like them, you can give them back.'

'But imagine if I lost one.'

'Jessica, they're yours.' But silently she shook her head and stood firm.

'Please.' He looked so woebegone that she felt sorry for him, but she couldn't take diamonds from this man . . . she had already accepted the outfit she was wearing, which was far too expensive a gift as it was. But diamonds? Who in heaven's name was he? No matter who, she knew who *she* was, and what she could and could not do. This she could not. No. But he was looking at her so sadly that she finally wavered for an instant. 'Just try them on.'

'All right, Geoffrey, but I won't wear them tonight and I won't keep them. You save them. And maybe someday . . .' She tried to make him feel better about them as she reached up to take off one of her own earrings, and then she remembered that she was wearing Ian's pearls.

The pearls were much less grandiose than the diamonds, but she loved them. She tried on one of Geoffrey's sparkling teardrops and it looked dazzling on her left ear . . . but on the right ear sat the pretty little pearl from the man who had loved her . . . from Ian . . .

'You don't like them.' He sounded crushed.

'I love them. But not for right now.'

'You looked just now as though something had made you terribly sad.'

'Don't be ridiculous.' She smiled, and handed him back the earring, and then leaned up to kiss him chastely on the cheek. 'No man has ever been as good to me, Geoffrey. I don't quite know what to do with it all.'

'Sit back and enjoy it. Now. We're off.' He didn't press

the point about the earrings, and they left them carefully hidden in her desk drawer. She felt relieved not to be wearing them. Geoffrey had been right. Taking off Ian's pearls would have made her sad. She wasn't quite ready to yet. It would come in time. She still clung to some of their souvenirs. Like his portrait, which now hung over the fireplace.

The party was like something in a multimillion-dollar movie. Gallons of champagne, platoons of liveried butlers, and armies of black-uniformed maids. Every two feet of inlaid marble floor space seemed to be covered by the looming shadow of an immense crystal chandelier. And pillars and columns and Aubusson rugs and Louis XV furniture, and a fortune in diamonds and emeralds and sapphires, and hundreds of minks. It was the kind of party you read about but couldn't even faintly imagine going to. And there she was, with Geoffrey. Almost everyone there was either British or famous or both. And Geoffrey seemed to know everyone. Movie stars whom Jessie had only read of in the papers ran up to greet him, promised to call him, or left lipstick on his cheeks. Ambassadors cornered him over the pâté, or urged Jessie to dance. Businessmen and diplomats, socialites and politicians, movie stars and celebrities of dubious fame. Everyone was there. It was the kind of party people worked years to get invited to. And there she was, with Geoffrey, who turned out to be not "Mr.", but "Sir".

'Why didn't you tell me?'

'Why? It's silly. Don't you think so?'

'No. And it's part of your name.'

'So now you know. Does it matter?' He looked amused, and she shook her head. 'All right, then. Now how about dancing with me, Lady Jessica?'

'Yes, sir. Your Majesty. Your Grace. Your Lordship.'

'Oh, shut up.'

The party went on until two and they stayed till the end. It was almost four when they got back to the little Victorian house tucked into the hills.

'Now I know I'm Cinderella.'

'But did you have fun?'

'I had a fabulous evening.' She had felt a tiny bit as though he had put her on display, like a pretty new doll, but he had introduced her to everyone, and how could she complain? How many dates give you two-thousand-dollar evening dresses and diamond earrings? What an evening. She looked down at her mother's ring again as they got out of the car. She was glad she had worn it. Not just because it was an emerald, but because it had been her mother's.

'You looked radiant tonight, Jessica. I was so proud of you.'

'It was just the dress.'

'Bullshit.'

'What?' She gave a tired little crow of laughter and looked at him with amusement. '*Sir* Geoffrey said "bull-shit"? I didn't think you said things like that!'

'I do, and I say lots of things you don't know about, my dear.'

'That sounds intriguing.' They exchanged a glance of mutual interest in front of her house. 'I don't know whether to offer you brandy, coffee, tea, or aspirin. Which'll it be?'

'We can figure that out inside.' She glided up the steps with the grace of a butterfly in the magnificent white dress. Even at the end of the evening, she looked like a vision, and seemed scarcely tired. She pleased him enormously. In fact, he had decided not to wait a great deal longer. She was everything he wanted, and it was time for him. He had been waiting for Jessie for a long, long time. He knew that she wasn't quite ready, but she would be very quickly. He would help her sweep the cobwebs from her present. Now and then he saw old ghosts haunting her eyes, but it was time she left them. He needed her. And she had done beautifully at the party. Everyone said so.

'Do you go to things like that often?' She stifled a yawn as she slipped out of the sandals he had given her.

'Fairly. Did you really enjoy it?'

'What woman wouldn't, for heaven's sake? Geoffrey . . . excuse me, *Sir* Geoffrey—' she grinned—'that's like being queen for a day. And everyone in the whole world was there. I must say, I was very impressed.'

'So were they.'

'About what?'

'About you. You were the most beautiful woman there.' But she knew that wasn't true, and more than half the attention she'd got had been over the dress. He had equipped her well for her debut, even down to the virginal white dress. But some of the great beauties of the world had been at that party. She was hardly stiff competition. She just wasn't that kind of woman. Not the sort who drips diamonds ear to ear while dragging chinchilla behind her, in the latest Givenchy dress. Those women were in the big leagues.

'Thank you.' It seemed simpler not to argue. 'Tea?'

'Not really.' He was looking at her pensively, a little distracted.

'Would you like me to light a fire?' She felt like sitting with him and talking, as she'd used to do with . . . no! She couldn't let herself do that.

'Who's that?' He waved to the boyish face over the fireplace, and Jessica smiled. 'Your brother?'

'No. Someone else.'

'Mr. Clarke?' She nodded, sober-faced now. 'You still keep his portrait up?'

'I painted it.'

'That's not much of a reason. Do you still see him?' Somehow he had thought she didn't, though they had never discussed it.

'No. Not anymore.'

'That's for the best.' And then he did something that made Jessica's heart stop. Very quietly, without asking, without saying a word, he lifted the portrait from where it hung and set it gently down on the floor near her desk, facing the wall. 'I think this is a good time to put that away, darling, don't you?' But there was no question in his voice and for a moment she was too stunned to speak. She wanted it up. She liked it. She had brought it specially from San Francisco. Or was he right? Was there no place for that anymore? There shouldn't have been, and they both knew it.

'Don't you want tea?' She couldn't think of anything else to say, and her voice was only a croak.

'No.' With a gentle smile he shook his head and walked slowly toward her. He stopped in front of her and kissed her longingly. It stirred the very tip of her soul. She needed him now. He was stripping her of something she had needed to survive. And now she was beginning to need him. He couldn't take Ian from her, but he was going to, and she was letting him. They stood together, their mouths hungrily discovering each other, and ever so gently he unclasped the hook at the shoulder of her dress. As it gave, the dress fell loosely to her waist, and he lowered his mouth slowly to her breasts, as her whole body seemed to reach out to him—but something inside her said no.

'Geoffrey . . . Geoffrey . . .' He went on kissing her, and the dress fell slowly away from her. All that exquisite silk crepe lying heaped at her feet as carefully, relentlessly he undressed her. She fumbled at the hard white starched shirt front, and got nowhere. All she could reach of him was the bulge in his trousers, but even his zipper seemed to resist her. And in a moment she stood there, naked before him, and he was still fully dressed in white tie and tails.

'My God, Jessica, how beautiful you are, my love . . . beautiful, beautiful, elegant little bird . . .' He led her slowly into her bedroom, speaking loving words to her all the way, and she followed him, as though in a trance, until he laid her carefully on her bed and slowly slipped off his jacket as she waited. He seemed to purr at her, and she felt she was under his spell. He had the jacket off now, but the starched white front was still in place. It made him look like a surgeon, and as she turned her head on the pillow, something pinched her ear. She was still wearing her earrings, and she reached up to take them off and felt the pearls fall into her hand. The pearls . . . Ian's pearls . . . and here was this man undressing in front of her. He had undressed her. She was naked and he was going to be, and he had taken Ian's portrait off the wall . . .

'No!' She sat bolt upright on the bed and stared at him as though he had just thrown cold water in her face.

'Jessica?'

'No!'

He sat down next to her and folded her into his arms, but she fought free of them, still clutching the pearl earrings in her hand. 'Don't be afraid, darling. I'll be gentle, I promise.'

'No, no!' There were tears welling up in her throat now and she jumped past him, pulling at Aunt Beth's quilt at the foot of the bed and covering herself with it. What was wrong with her, though? For a moment she thought she was crazy. Only a few minutes before she had wanted him so desperately, or had thought she did. And now she knew that she didn't. She couldn't. Now she knew everything.

'Jessica, what in hell is going on?' She was cowering near the window, with tears running down on her face.

'I can't go to bed with you. I'm sorry . . . I . . .'

'But what happened? A moment ago . . .' For once, he looked totally baffled. This had never happened to him. Not like this.

'I know. I'm sorry. It must seem crazy, it's just that . . .'

'That what, dammit?' He stood in front of her, and he was looking very unnerved by the experience. His jacket lay strangely on the floor, as though it had been thrown there. 'What happened to you?'

'I just can't.'

'But, darling, I love you.' He walked to her again and tried to put his arms around her, but she wouldn't let him.

'You don't love me.' It was something she could sense, not something she could explain. And more importantly, she didn't love him. She wanted to love him. She knew she *should* love him. She knew that he was the kind of man women are supposed to love, and beg to marry. But she didn't, and she couldn't, and she knew she never would.

'What do you mean I don't love you? Goddammit, Jessica, I want to marry you. What sort of game do you think I've been playing? You're not the sort of woman one makes a mistress of. Do you think I'd have taken you to that party tonight if I weren't serious? Don't be absurd.'

'But you don't know me.' It was a plaintive wail from the corner.

'I know enough.'

'No, you don't. You don't know anything.'

'Breeding shows.' Oh, Jesus.

'But what about my soul? What I think, what I feel, what I am, what I need?'

'We'll learn that about each other.'

'Afterward?' She looked horrified.

'Some people do it that way.'

'But I don't.'

'You don't know what the devil you do. And if you have a brain at all, you'll marry a man who tells you what to do and when to do it. You'll be much happier that way.'

'No, that's just it. I used to want that, Geoffrey, but I don't anymore. I want to give as well as take, I want to be the grown-up as well as the child. I don't want to be pushed around and shown off and dressed up. That's what you did tonight. I know you meant well, but I was nothing more than a Barbie doll, and that's all I ever would be. No! How could you!'

'I'm sorry if I offended you.' He stooped down and picked up his jacket. He was beginning to wonder about her; it was almost as though she were a bit mad.

But suddenly she didn't feel mad at all. She felt good, and she knew she was doing the right thing. Maybe no one else would think so, but she knew it.

'You don't even want children.' It was a ridiculous accusation to be making at five o'clock in the morning, standing wrapped in a quilt, talking to a man in white tie and tails.

'And you do want children?'

'Maybe.'

'Nonsense. The whole thing is nonsense, Jessica. But I'm not going to stand here and argue with you. You know where I stand. I love you and I want to marry you. When you come to your senses in the morning, give me a call.' He looked at her pointedly, shook his head, walked to the corner, kissed the top of her head, and patted her shoulder. 'Good night, darling. You'll feel better in the morning.'

She didn't say a word as he left, but when he was gone she packed all of his gifts into the large white box he had brought; in the morning she would send it all over to the house where he was staying. Maybe it was an insane thing to do, but she was so sure of it. She had never been so sure of anything in her life. She had put the pearl earrings down on her night table, and now she wasn't even sleepy. She stood happy and naked in her living room, drinking steaming black coffee, as the sun rose over the hills. The portrait was back on the wall.

CHAPTER XXXVI

'And how's your young man?' She and Aunt Beth were drinking iced tea after a long ride, and Jessica had been unusually quiet.

'What young man?' But she wasn't fooling anyone.

'I see. Are we going to play cat and mouse, or has he fallen out of the running?' Aunt Beth's eyes searched hers and Jessie ventured a smile. Cat and mouse, indeed.

'Your point. Fallen out of the running.'

'Any special reason?' For once she was surprised. 'I saw a rather spectacular photograph of you two, at some very posh party in L.A.'

'Where in hell did you see that?' Jessica was not pleased.

'My, my. He must have fallen into considerable disfavour! I saw the photograph in the L.A. paper. Something about a consulate party, wasn't it? Quite a number of illustrious people seemed to be hovering around you too.'

'I didn't notice.' Jessie sounded gloomy.

'I'm impressed.' And so was Jessie. But not pleasantly so. She was wondering who else had seen the picture. There was no point in being linked with Geoffrey now. Oh, well—like everything else, the gossip would die down eventually. And it was probably much harder on Geoffrey. He had to live with all those people. She didn't. 'Did he do something dastardly, or was he simply a bore, or should I mind my own business?'

'Of course not. No, I just couldn't, that's the only way to put it. I wanted to make myself love him. But I couldn't. He was perfect. He had everything. He did everything. He was everything. But . . . I . . . I can't explain it, Aunt Beth. I had the feeling he was going to try to make me into what he wanted.'

'That's a disagreeable feeling.'

'I kept feeling that he was checking me out, like a quarterhouse. I felt so . . . so lonely with him. Isn't that crazy? And there was no reason to.' She told her about the dress and the diamond earrings. 'I should have been thrilled. But I wasn't. It frightened me. It was too much . . . I don't know. We were such strangers.'

'Anyone will be a stranger at first.' Jessica nodded pensively and finished her iced tea. 'He seemed nice enough, but if that special ingredient isn't there, that special magic . . . there's really no point.' It made Jessica think back to that night.

'I'm afraid I didn't back off very elegantly. I went bananas.' She smiled at the memory, and the older woman laughed.

'Probably did him good. He was awfully proper.'

'He certainly was. And he was wearing white tie and tails while I freaked out and practically started throwing things. I sent back all his goodies the next day.'

'Did you hurl them through the window?' Beth looked

greatly amused, and almost hoped that she had. Men needed excitement.

'No.' She blushed for a moment. 'I had one of your ranch hands take them over.'

'So that's what they do with their afternoons.'

'I'm sorry.'

'Don't be. I'm sure whoever it was enjoyed the whole thing immensely.'

They sat quietly for a moment with their iced teas, and Jessica was frowning.

'You know what bothered me too?'

'I'm anxious to hear.'

'Stop teasing—I'm serious.' But she enjoyed the banter with her friend. 'He didn't want children.'

'Neither do you. What bothered you about that?'

'That's a good question, but something's been happening. I don't think the idea of children frightens me so much anymore. I keep thinking that . . . I don't know, I'm too old anyway, but I keep thinking that . . .' She knew she wasn't too old, but she wanted someone to tell her so.

'You want a baby?' Beth was stunned. 'Do you mean that?'

'I don't know.'

'Well, it's certainly not too late at your age. You're not even thirty-two yet. But I must say, I'm surprised.'

'Why?'

'Because your fear of it ran so deep. I didn't think you'd ever be sure enough of yourself to weather the competition. What if you had a beautiful daughter? Could you bear that? Think about it. That can be very painful for a mother.'

'And probably very rewarding. Doesn't that sound corny? I feel like an ass. It's been bothering me for a while, but I haven't had the courage to tell anyone. Everyone is so sure that I am what I am. Career woman, city slicker, child hater, now gay divorcee. Even when you stop being the same person, it seems as though no one will let you take the old labels off.'

'Then burn them. You certainly have, though. You got

rid of your husband, the shop, the city. There's not much left to change.' She said it ruefully, but with affection. 'And to hell with other people's labels. There's plenty we can't change, but if there are things you want to change and can, go ahead and enjoy it.'

'Imagine having a baby . . .' She sat there, smiling, enjoying the thought.

'You imagine it. I can't even remember it, and I'm not sure I'd want to. I never felt very romantic on the subject, but I love Astrid very much.'

'You know, it's as though I've lived several chapters of my life one way, and now I'm ready to move on. Not to throw the past out the window, but just to go on. Like a journey. We've been long enough in the same country; after a while you have to move on. I think that's what happened. I've just moved on to different places, different needs. I feel new again, Aunt Beth. The only sad thing is that I have no one to share it with.'

'You could have had Geoffrey. Just think what you missed!' But Aunt Beth didn't think she'd missed anything either. There hadn't been enough fire in the man, enough daring and wild dreams. He was travelling a well-charted course. If nothing else, it would have been very boring. She knew Jessie had done the right thing. She wondered only at the violence of Jessie's reaction. 'Something else has been bothering you lately too, hasn't it?'

'I'm not sure what you mean.'

'Yes, you are. Quite sure. You're not only quite sure of what I mean, but you're quite sure of the rest. In fact, I daresay that was the problem with Geoffrey, wasn't it? It had damned little to do with him after all.' Jessica was laughing, but she wouldn't say anything.

'You know me too well.'

'Yes, and you're finally beginning to know yourself too. And I'm glad. But now what are you going to do about it?'

'I was thinking of going away for a couple of days.'

'You don't want permission from me, do you?' Aunt Beth was laughing, and Jessica shook her head.

She began the drive at six the next morning as the sun peeked its nose over Aunt Beth's hill. She had a long way to go. Six hours, maybe seven, and she wanted to be there in time. She had worn a light shirt for the ride, and a skirt, which was cooler than pants. She had a Thermos full of iced coffee, a sandwich, a bag full of apples, and some nuts and cookies in a tin that the foreman's boy had brought her a few days before. She was fully equipped. And determined. And also afraid. They had exchanged letters two and three times a week for two months now. But letters were very different. It had been four months since she'd seen his face. Four months since he'd turned his back and walked out on her after they had both thrown rocks they should never have picked up. And so much had changed now. They were both cautious in their letters. Careful, afraid, and yet joyful. Bursts of fun would turn up on every page, silly remarks, casual references, foolishness, and then caution again, as though each was afraid to show too much to the other. They kept to safe subjects. Her house, and his book. There was still no news on the movie contract, but the book was due out in the fall. She was excited for him. As excited as he was about her house. He was careful always to call it "hers", and it was. For the moment.

They were separate people now, no longer woven together of a single cloth. They had been blasted apart by what had happened to them, by what they had done to each other, by what neither could any longer pretend. She wondered if there was a way to come back after something like that. Maybe not, but she had to know. Now, before they waited any longer. What if he expected never to see her again? He sounded as though he had almost accepted it. He never asked for a visit. But he was going to get one. She wanted to see him, to look into his face and see what was there, not just hear the echo of his voice in the letters.

She drove up to the familiar building at one-thirty that afternoon. They checked her through, searched her handbag, and she went inside and wrote her name on a form at the desk. She took a seat and waited an endless half hour, her eyes restlessly darting between the wall clock and the door. Her heart was pounding now. She was here. And she was terrified. Why had she come? What would she say? Maybe he didn't even want to see her, maybe that was why he hadn't mentioned her coming for a visit. It was madness to have come here . . . insanity . . . stupid . . .

'Visit for Clarke . . . visit for Ian Clarke.' The guard's voice droned his name and Jessica jumped from her seat, fighting to keep her pace normal as she walked toward the uniformed man who stood sentry at the door to the visiting area. It was a different door from the one she had passed through before, and as she looked beyond she realised that Ian was in a different section now. Maybe there would be no glass window between them.

The guard unlocked the door, checked her wrist for the stamp they'd impressed on the back of her hand at the main gate, and stood aside to let her through. The door led out to a lawn dotted with benches and framed with flower beds, and there were no apparent boundaries, only a long strip of healthy-looking lawn beyond. She crossed the threshold slowly and saw couples wandering down walks on either side of the lawn. And then she saw Ian, at the far end, standing there, watching her, stunned. It was like a scene in a movie, and her feet felt like lead.

She just stood there and so did he, until a broad smile began to take over his face. He looked like a tall, gangly boy, watching her and grinning, his eyes damp, but no more so than her own. It was crazy—half a block of lawn between them and neither of them moved . . . she had to . . . she had come here to see him, to talk to him, not just to stand there and gape at him with a smile on her face. She walked slowly along the walk, and he began to walk toward her too, the smile on his face spreading further, and then suddenly, finally, at last, she was in his arms. It was Ian. The Ian she knew. It smelled like Ian, it felt like Ian, her chin fit in the same place on his shoulder. She was home.

'What happened? You run out of hair spray, or did the lizards get to be too much for you?'

'Both. I came up so you could save me.' She was having a hard time fighting back tears, but so was he, and still their smiles were like bright sunshine in a summer shower.

'Jessie, you're crazy.' He held her tightly and she laughed.

'I think I must be.' She was clinging to him tightly. He felt so damn good. She put a hand on his head and felt the silk of his hair. She would have known it blindfolded in a room full of men. It was Ian. 'Jesus, you feel good.' She pulled away from him just to look at him. He looked fabulous. Skinny, a little tired, a little suntanned, and totally overwhelmed. Fabulous. He pulled her close again and nestled her head on his shoulder.

'Oh, baby, I couldn't believe it when you started writing. I'd given up hope.'

'I know. I'm a shit.' She felt bad suddenly for the long months of silence; now, looking right into his face, she could see how much they must have hurt him. But she had had to. 'I'm a super-shit.'

'Yeah, but such a beautiful super-shit. You look wonderful, Jessie. You've even gained a little weight.' He held her at arm's length again and looked her over. He didn't want to let go. He was afraid she'd vanish again. He wanted to hold on to her, to make sure she was real. And back. And his. But maybe . . . maybe she had only come back to visit . . . to say hello . . . or good-bye. His eyes suddenly showed the pain of what he was thinking, and Jessica wondered what was on his mind. But she didn't know what to say. Not yet.

'Country life is making me fat.'

'And happy, from the sound of your letters.' He pulled her close to him again, and then pinched her nose. 'Let's go sit down. My knees are shaking so bad, I can hardly stand up.' She laughed at him and wiped the tears from her cheeks.

'*You're* shaking! I was afraid you wouldn't see me!'

'And pass up the chance to make the other guys drool? Don't be ridiculous.' He noticed then that she was wearing the gold lima bean, and he quietly took her hand in his.

They found a bench to one side of the lawn and sat down, still holding hands. He had one arm around her, and her hand was trembling in his. And then the words began to rush out. She couldn't hold back anymore. The dam had finally given way.

'Ian, I love you. It's all so lousy without you.' It sounded so corny, but that was what she had come to tell him. She was sure of it now. She knew what she wanted. And now it was a question of want more than need. She still needed him, but differently. Now she knew how much she wanted him.

'Your life doesn't sound lousy, baby. It sounds good. The country, the house . . . but . . .' He looked at her with gratitude rushing over his face. '. . . I'm glad if it's lousy, even if it's only a little bit lousy. Oh Jess . . . I'm so glad.' He pulled her back into his arms.

'Do you still love me a little?' She was wearing her little-girl voice. It was so long since anyone had heard that, so long since he had. But what if he didn't want her anymore? Then what would she do? Go back to the Geoffreys of the world and the fuzzy-haired idiot playwrights from New York? And the emptiness of a house and a gazebo and a swing and a world made for Ian . . . but without him? What was there to go back to? Staring at his portrait? Thinking of his voice? Wearing the pearl earrings he'd given her?

'Hey, lady, you're drifting. What were you thinking?'

'About you.' She looked him square in the eyes. She needed to know. 'Ian, do you still love me?'

'More than I can ever tell you, babe. What do you think? Jessie, I love you more than I ever did. But you wanted the divorce, and it seemed fair. I couldn't ask you to live through all this.' He gestured vaguely to the prison behind him. It brought worry to her eyes.

'What about you? Are you surviving it?' She pulled away to look at him again. He looked a lot thinner. Healthy, but much thinner.

'I'm making it a lot better than I thought I would.

Ever since I finished the book. They're letting me teach in the school now, and I'm due . . .' He seemed to hesitate, looked at something over her head, and took a deep breath. 'I'm due for an early hearing in September. They might let me go. In fact, it's almost certain they will. Through some kind of miracle, they've knocked out the famous California indeterminate sentence since I've been here, and as a first-time offender my time could be pretty much up, if they're amenable. So it looks like I could be coming home pretty soon.'

'How soon could it be?'

'Maybe six weeks. Maybe three or four months. Six months at worst. But that's not the point, Jess. What about all the rest of it? What about us? My being in prison wasn't our only problem.'

'But so much has changed.' He knew it was true. He had heard it in her letters, knew it from what she'd done, and now he could see it in her face. She was more woman than she had ever been before. But something magical also told him that she was still his. Part of her was. Part of her belonged only to Jessie now, but he liked it that way. She had been that way long, long ago. But she was better now. Richer, fuller, stronger. She was whole. And if she still wanted him now, they would really have something. And he had grown a lot too.

'I think a lot has changed, Jess, but some of it hasn't and some of it won't. And maybe it's more than you want to mess with. You could do a lot better.' He looked at her, wondering about the photograph he'd seen in the paper. He had seen the same article Beth had. And if she could have Sir Geoffrey Whatnot, why the hell did she still want him?

'Ian, I like what I've got. If I've still got it. And I couldn't do better. I don't want to do better. You're everything I want.'

'I don't have any money.'

'So?'

'Look, I got a ten-thousand-dollar advance for the book, and half of that went for your new car. And the other five thousand won't go very far when I get out. You'll be stuck supporting me again. And baby, I have to write. I really know that. It's something I have to do, even if I have to wait table in some dive to support myself in the meantime. There's no way I'll give up writing, though, to be "respectable".' He looked rueful but firm. And Jessie looked impatient.

'Who gives a damn about "respectable"? I made a fortune selling the shop to Astrid. What the hell difference does it make now who earns what doing what, for what . . . so what, dummy? What do you think I'll do with that money now? Wear it? We could do such nice things with it.' She was thinking of the house. And other things.

'Like what?' He smiled at the sound of her voice and held her closer.

'All kinds of things. Buy the house in the country, fix it up a little. Go to Europe . . . have a baby . . .' She turned her face and smiled at him, nose to nose.

'What did you say?'

'You heard me.'

'I'm not so sure I did. Are you serious?'

'I think so.' She smiled mysteriously and kissed him.

'What brought that on?'

'A simple process, darling. I've grown up since I saw you last. And it's just something I've been thinking about lately. And I realised something else. I don't just want "a baby". I want *your* baby. Our baby. Ian . . . I just want you, with kids, without kids, with money, without . . . I don't know how else to tell you. I love you.' Two huge tears slid down her face and she looked at him so intensely that he wanted to hold her forever.

He threw his arms around her and held her to him with a huge smile on his face. 'You know what's going to happen, Jess? Any minute, some asshole with a flashlight is going to walk up to me, it's going to be two in the morning, and I'm going to wake up, holding my pillow. Because this can't be real. I've dreamed it too often. It's not happening. I want it to be, but . . . tell me it's for real.'

'It's for real . . . but you're breaking my left arm.'

'Sorry.' He pulled away from her for a moment and

they both laughed. 'Sweetheart, I love you. I don't even care if you want a baby anymore. I love you, in that ramshackle empty house you got yourself, or in a palace, or wherever. And aside from that, I happen to think you're nuts. I don't know what made you come back, but I'm so damn glad you did.'

'So am I.' She threw her arms around him again, nibbled his ear, and then bit him. 'I love you,' she whispered it in his ear, and he pinched her. It had been so long since he'd even touched her, held her, felt her. Even pinching and biting felt good. It was all such a luxury now. 'Christ, Ian, what's the matter with you?'

'What do you mean?' He looked suddenly worried.

'You didn't even yell when I pinched you. You always yell when I pinch you. Don't you love me anymore?' But her eyes were dancing as they hadn't in years. Maybe as they never had before, Ian thought.

'You came up here for me to yell at you?'

'Sure. And so I could yell at you. And hug you and kiss you, and beg you to get the hell out of here and come home, for Chrissake. So will you please, dammit? Will you!' Jesus. Twelve hours ago, she hadn't even been sure he still wanted her. But he did! Thank God he did!

'I will, I will. What's your hurry? What do you have, snakes in that place? Spiders? That's why you want me, right? The exterminator—I know your type.'

'Bullshit. No spiders, no snakes, but . . .' She grinned.

'Aha!'

'Ants. I walked into the kitchen the other night to make a peanut-butter sandwich, and I screamed so loud, I . . . what are you laughing at? Goddam you, what are you laughing at?' And then suddenly she was laughing too, and he had his arms around her and he was kissing her again, and they were both laughing through their tears. The war was over.

And eight weeks later, he was home.

And Don't Miss

THE PROMISE
by Danielle Steel
Based on a screenplay by Garry Michael White

THE PROMISE IS FOREVER

For Michael and Nancy, the carefree days of innocence were drawing to an end, bringing love's hardest test.

HE was the handsome heir to the mighty Hillyard business empire.

SHE was just twenty-one, beautiful – and an orphan from nowhere.

That fateful day after graduation, they sealed a bond for the years to come – a vow of love that would have to prove itself in the face of terrible tragedy, doubt and despair . . .

THEY PROMISED NEVER TO SAY 'GOOD-BYE'

NOW AN UNFORGETTABLE FILM STARRING KATHLEEN QUINLAN AND STEPHEN COLLINS

ROMANCE   0 7221 8129 9   85p

Info... Sports Almanac

With Year in Review Commentary from ESPN anchors and analysts:

David Aldridge
on Pro Basketball

Chris Berman
on Pro Football

Al Bernstein
on Boxing

John Clayton
on Pro Football

Linda Cohn
on Women's Golf

Lee Corso
on College Football

Steve Cyphers
on College Sports

Rece Davis
on Auto Racing

Mike Durbin
on Bowling

Jack Edwards
on College Hockey
Olympics and
International Sports

Rich Eisen
on the Top 40 Moments

Chris Fowler
on College Basketball and
College Football

Hank Goldberg
on Horse Racing

Mimi Griffin
on Women's College Basketball

Steve Levy
on Pro Hockey

Bob Ley
on Soccer

Kenny Mayne
on the Top 20 Personalities

Sal Paolantonio
on Tennis

Dan Patrick
on the Top 20 Personalities

Karl Ravech
on Ballparks and Arenas
and Baseball

Dave Ryan
on College Baseball

Stuart Scott
on the Top 40 Moments

Bob Stevens
on Business

Mike Tirico
on Golf

Dick Vitale
on College Basketball

The Champions of 1998

Auto Racing

NASCAR Circuit
- Daytona 500 ... Dale Earnhardt
- Winston 500 ... Dale Jarrett
- Coca-Cola 600 ... Jeff Gordon
- Southern 500 ... Jeff Gordon

CART Circuit
- U.S. 500 ... Greg Moore
- PPG Cup Championship ... Alex Zanardi

Indy Racing League Circuit
- Indianapolis 500 ... Eddie Cheever Jr.
- Points Championship ... Kenny Brack

Formula One Circuit
- World Driving Championship ... Mika Hakkinen, 90 pts
- (through Oct. 31) Michael Schumacher, 86 pts

Baseball

World Series ... New York def. San Diego, 4-0
- MVP ... Scott Brosius, NY, 3B

All-Star Game ... AL 13, NL 8 in Colorado
- MVP ... Roberto Alomar, Baltimore, 2B

College World Series ... USC 21, Arizona St. 14
- MVP ... Wes Rachels, USC, 2B

College Basketball

Men's NCAA Final Four
- Championship ... Kentucky 78, Utah 69
- MVP ... Jeff Sheppard, Kentucky, G

Women's NCAA Final Four
- Championship ... Tennessee 93, La. Tech 75
- MVP ... Chamique Holdsclaw, Tennessee, F

Pro Basketball

NBA Finals ... Chicago def. Utah 4 games to 2
- MVP ... Michael Jordan, Chicago, G

Eastern Final ... Chicago def. Indiana 4 games to 3

Western Final ... Utah def. LA Lakers 4 games to 0

All-Star Game ... East 135, West 114 in New York
- MVP ... Michael Jordan, Chicago, G

Bowling

Men's Major Championships
- PBA National ... Pete Weber
- Tournament of Champions ... Dennis Horan Jr.
- ABC Masters ... Mike Aulby
- BPAA U.S. Open ... Walter Ray Williams Jr.

Women's Major Championships
- Sam's Town Invitational (1997) ... Kim Adler
- WIBC Queens ... Lynda Norry
- BPAA U.S. Open ... Aleta Sill
- AMF Gold Cup ... Dana Miller-Mackie

College Football (1997)

National Champions
- AP ... Michigan (12-0)
- ESPN/USA Today Coaches' ... Nebraska (13-0)

Major Bowls
- Orange ... Nebraska 42, Tennesse 17
- Rose ... Michigan 21, Washington St. 16
- Sugar ... Florida St. 31, Ohio St. 14
- Fiesta ... Kansas St. 35, Syracuse 18

Heisman Trophy .Charles Woodson, Michigan, DB/WR

Pro Football (1997)

Super Bowl XXXII ... Denver 31, Green Bay 24
- MVP ... Terrell Davis, Denver, RB

AFC Championship ... Denver 24, Pittsburgh 21

NFC Championship ... Green Bay 23, San Francisco 10

Pro Bowl ... AFC 29, NFC 24
- MVP ... Warren Moon, Seattle, QB

CFL Grey Cup Final ... Toronto 47, Saskatchewan 23
- MVP ... Doug Flutie, Toronto, QB

Golf

Men's Major Championships
- Masters ... Mark O'Meara
- U.S. Open ... Lee Janzen
- British Open ... Mark O'Meara
- PGA Championship ... Vijay Singh

Seniors Major Championships
- The Tradition ... Gil Morgan
- PGA Seniors ... Hale Irwin
- U.S. Senior Open ... Hale Irwin
- Senior Players Championship ... Gil Morgan

Women's Major Championships
- Nabisco Dinah Shore ... Pat Hurst
- LPGA Championship ... Se Ri Pak
- U.S. Women's Open ... Se Ri Pak
- du Maurier Classic ... Brandie Burton

National Team Competition
- Solheim Cup ... United States 16, Europe 12

Hockey

Stanley Cup ... Detroit def. Washington 4 games to 0
- MVP ... Steve Yzerman, Detroit, C

Western Final ... Detroit def. Dallas 4 games to 2

Eastern Final ... Washington def. Buffalo 4 games to 2

All-Star Game .. North America 8, World 7 in Vancouver
- MVP ... Teemu Selanne, World, RW

NCAA Div. 1 Final .. Michigan 3, Boston College 2 (OT)
- MVP ... Marty Turco, Michigan, G

Horse Racing

Triple Crown Champions
- Kentucky Derby ... Real Quiet (Kent Desormeaux)
- Preakness ... Real Quiet (Kent Desormeaux)
- Belmont ... Victory Gallop (Gary Stevens)

Harness Racing
- Hambletonian ... Muscles Yankee (John Campbell)
- Little Brown Jug ... Shady Character (Ron Pierce)

Soccer

- World Cup ... France 3, Brazil 0
  - MVP ... Ronaldo, Brazil, F
- CONCACAF Gold Cup ... Mexico
- MLS Champ. Game ... Chicago 2, D.C. United 0
  - MVP ... Peter Nowak, Chicago, M

Tennis

Men's Grand Slam Championships
- Australian Open ... Petr Korda
- French Open ... Carlos Moya
- Wimbledon ... Pete Sampras
- U.S. Open ... Patrick Rafter

Women's Grand Slam Championships
- Australian Open ... Martina Hingis
- French Open ... Arantxa Sanchez Vicario
- Wimbledon ... Jana Novotna
- U.S. Open ... Lindsay Davenport

National Team Competition
- Davis Cup (1997) ... Sweden 5, United States 0
- Fed Cup (Women) ... Spain 3, Switzerland 2

Miscellaneous Champions

Little League World Series ... Toms River, NJ

Tour de France ... Marco Pantani (ITA)

Iditarod ... Jeff King

THE 1999 ESPN INFORMATION PLEASE® SPORTS ALMANAC

Gerry Brown
Michael Morrison
EDITORS

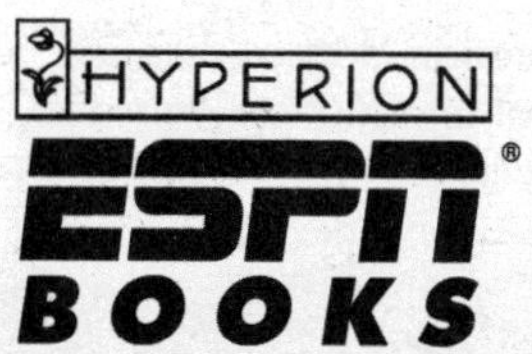

Editors
Gerry Brown, Michael Morrison
Assistant Editor
John Gettings
Reporters
Kevin Foley, Bill Magrath
Production Editor
Elaine Rho
Database/Production Manager
Susan Hyde
Graphics
Meghan Toczko
Technical Support
Karl DeBisschop
Fact Checking
Larry Schwartz

Printed in the United States of America.

Comments and suggestions from readers are invited. Because of the many letters received, however, it is not possible to respond personally to every correspondent. Nevertheless, all letters are welcome and each will be carefully considered. The **1999 ESPN Information Please Sports Almanac** does not rule on bets or wagers. Address all correspondence to: Sports, Information Please LLC, 31 St. James Avenue, Boston, MA 02116.
Email: ipsa@infoplease.com.

ISBN 0-7868-8366-9

FIRST EDITION

10 9 8 7 6 5 4 3 2 1

Usually when we tell people what we do for a living, the response is, "Wow. What a great job." or "That's every guy's dream." And for the most part, they're right. Editing the sports almanac is without a doubt a fun job to have, and while dealing with mind-numbing amounts of numbers and statistics can make us feel like accountants at times (not that there's anything wrong with that— for all you accountants out there), all we need to do is think of something that the almanac's founder, Mike Meserole, said once.

Mike said something along the lines of "Yeah, there's a lot of numbers to deal with, but all the numbers in this book have life to them."

So in that vein, when you pour over the amazing amount of facts and figures in this book, keep Mike's words in the back of your mind. And consider that each and every number represents a great game, race, season or career in the life of an athlete.

All of sports' great numbers can be found in here. And this year, we were lucky enough to add what could go down as one of the greatest of all time. So where were you when Mark McGwire hit No. 70? You know it's a big deal if it can be associated with the "Where were you when..." question. For example, "Where were you when Buster knocked out Tyson?" (p. 917, 921), or "Where were you when Dwight Clark made 'The Catch' for San Francisco?" (p. 248). And then of course there's the whole Buckner thing that we'd rather not get into.

Putting a project like this together every year takes the hard work and dedication of countless people. First and foremost, we'd like to thank Assistant Editor John Gettings. His knowledge and love of sports made him a perfect match for the job. Thanks for fitting right in and making our lives easier and more fun. Thanks to reporters Kevin (Go Terps!) Foley and Bill Magrath for their tenacity and thoroughness in chasing down all those hard-to-find facts and figures.

Thanks also to the Information Please production team, beginning with Production Editor Elaine Rho. Elaine was our secret weapon this year and amazed us with her expertise so much that we began to take it for granted. Thanks also to Susan Hyde for keeping the book on schedule and keeping the editors in line. Thanks to our web team of Paul Evenson, Ben Snowden, and of course Meghan Toczko for a great job on the book's graphics.

Thanks to the technical staff of Boris Goldowsky, Jim Dubinsky, Kate Wrigley, Christian DelPrete and Karl DeBisschop who helped us in ways that we don't even understand. We just feel safe in knowing they play for our team.

Thanks as well go out to our other Information Please cohorts, Liz Kubik, Jim Bryant, Scott Beatty, Borgna Brunner, Pam Greene and Nicole Guest, who were all instrumental in putting the book in your hands and on the web.

This almanac marks the second year in our growing relationship with ESPN. We'd like to thank our ace-in-the-hole at ESPN and fellow Red Sox fan Sharyn Taymor. Special thanks also go out to ESPN's Vince Doria, Howie Schwab, Russell Baxter and the entire "Inside the Numbers" team led by coordinating producer Matthew Ipsan.

Our relationship with ESPN has given us the luxury of being able to call upon some of the best personalities in sports journalism to write the almanac's essays. There are too many to thank in this little space but for a complete list, turn back to page one. With a lineup like that, how can you go wrong?

Getting all of this information on paper and then onto the bookshelves is no easy task but our team made it look that way. For that, we thank Gretchen Young and Jennifer Morgan at Hyperion, Jim Murphy at Mail-Well Graphics and Arlene Gioia at Digital Fine Color.

Outside assistance was graciously provided by the incomparable Carolyn McMahon at the Associated Press, Michael Shulman at Archive Photos, Barbara Zidovsky at Nielsen Media Research, Mike Woitalla at Soccer America and Larry Schwartz. We'd also like to thank Italian bobsledder Giacomo Conti, Peggy Lawton, and whoever invented the Pocket Vortex. All kept us loose and in good spirits, even through the stressful times.

And finally, we've got to give a hearty thanks to the book's former editors Mike Meserole and John Hassan for being there for us both as mentors and friends. Mes gave birth to the Information Please Sports Almanac 10 years ago and John took over before being snatched up by ESPN, The Magazine. We hope this edition makes you both proud.

Gerry Brown and Michael Morrison
Boston
October 26, 1998

Major League Cities & Teams

As of Oct. 31, 1998, there were 129 major league teams playing or scheduled to play baseball, basketball, NFL football, hockey and soccer in 49 cities in the United States and Canada. Listed below are the cities and the teams that play there.

Anaheim
AL Angels
NHL Mighty Ducks of Anaheim

Atlanta
NL Braves
NBA Hawks
NFL Falcons

Baltimore
AL Orioles
NFL Ravens

Boston
AL Red Sox
NBA Celtics
NFL N.E. Patriots (Foxboro)
NHL Bruins
MLS N.E. Revolution (Foxboro)

Buffalo
NFL Bills (Orchard Park)
NHL Sabres

Calgary
NHL Flames

Charlotte
NBA Hornets
NFL Carolina Panthers

Chicago
AL White Sox
NL Cubs
NBA Bulls
NFL Bears
NHL Blackhawks
MLS Fire

Cincinnati
NL Reds
NFL Bengals

Cleveland
AL Indians
NBA Cavaliers
NFL Browns

Columbus
MLS Crew

Dallas
AL Texas Rangers (Arlington)
NBA Mavericks
NFL Cowboys (Irving)
NHL Stars
MLS Burn

Denver
NL Colorado Rockies
NBA Nuggets
NFL Broncos
NHL Colorado Avalanche
MLS Colorado Rapids

Detroit
AL Tigers
NBA Pistons (Auburn Hills)
NFL Lions (Pontiac)
NHL Red Wings

East Rutherford
NBA New Jersey Nets
NFL New York Giants
NFL New York Jets
NHL New Jersey Devils
MLS NY/NJ Metrostars

Edmonton
NHL Oilers

Green Bay
NFL Packers

Greensboro
NHL Carolina Hurricanes

Houston
NL Astros
NBA Rockets

Indianapolis
NBA Pacers
NFL Colts

Jacksonville
NFL Jaguars

Kansas City
AL Royals
NFL Chiefs
MLS Wizards

Los Angeles
NL Dodgers
NBA Clippers
NBA Lakers (Inglewood)
NHL Kings (Inglewood)
MLS Galaxy (Pasadena)

Miami
NL Florida Marlins
NBA Heat
NFL Dolphins
NHL Florida Panthers (Sunrise)
MLS Fusion

Milwaukee
NL Brewers
NBA Bucks

Minneapolis
AL Minn. Twins
NBA Minn. Timberwolves
NFL Minn. Vikings

Montreal
NL Expos
NHL Canadiens

Nashville
NFL Tennessee Oilers
NHL Predators

New Orleans
NFL Saints

New York
AL Yankees
NL Mets
NBA Knicks
NHL Rangers
NHL N.Y. Islanders (Uniondale)

Oakland
AL Athletics
NBA Golden St. Warriors
NFL Raiders

Orlando
NBA Magic

Ottawa
NHL Senators (Kanata)

Philadelphia
NL Phillies
NBA 76ers
NFL Eagles
NHL Flyers

Phoenix
NBA Suns
NFL Arizona Cardinals (Tempe)
NL Arizona Diamondbacks
NHL Coyotes

Pittsburgh
NL Pirates
NFL Steelers
NHL Penguins

Portland
NBA Trail Blazers

Sacramento
NBA Kings

St. Louis
NL Cardinals
NFL Rams
NHL Blues

Salt Lake City
NBA Utah Jazz

San Antonio
NBA Spurs

San Diego
NL Padres
NFL Chargers

San Francisco
NL Giants
NFL 49ers

San Jose
NHL Sharks
MLS Clash

Seattle
AL Mariners
NBA SuperSonics
NFL Seahawks

Tampa
NFL T.B. Buccaneers
NHL T.B. Lightning
AL T.B. Devil Rays
MLS T.B. Mutiny

Toronto
AL Blue Jays
NBA Raptors
NHL Maple Leafs

Vancouver
NBA Grizzlies
NHL Canucks

Washington
NBA Wizards
NFL Redskins (Raljon, Md.)
NHL Capitals
MLS D.C. United

Updates

Chicago Fire midfielder and MLS Cup '98 MVP **Peter Nowak** hoists the Rothenberg Trophy after his team's victory over the defending champion D.C. United.

AP/Wide World Photos

Mike Psyched

Mike Tyson regained his boxing license and is looking forward to a quick return to the ring.

A down and out Mike Tyson, $13 million in debt to the IRS, was allowed to get back to doing what he does best when the exiled former heavyweight champion was reinstated by the Nevada Athletic Commission on Oct. 19, 1998.

The humbled and repentant Iron Mike was accompanied at his final hearing by two famous supporters. Magic Johnson and Muhammad Ali both appeared to speak in the fallen champ's behalf and it may have swayed the commissioners.

Tyson, who had his license to box revoked 15 months previous after inexplicably biting the ears of reigning champion Evander Holyfield in their 1997 heavyweight title fight, won a split decision as the Commission voted 4-1 to return Tyson's license.

A medical panel from Boston's Massachusetts General Hospital had examined Tyson and said in their report that while he had his problems, a repeat performance of his disqualification loss to Holyfield was highly unlikely and that he was "fit" to return to the ring.

Tyson's handlers, which now apparently include the fallen talk-show host Johnson, say that while the 32-year-old Tyson could be back in the ring before the end of the year, they will bring him along slowly.

"I'll be the closest guy to him," said Johnson who is set to replace Don King as Tyson's promoter. "Making all the decisions."

"We're going to be bringing Mike along very slowly," Johnson said. "Don't be looking for him to be fighting these champions."

Speaking of "these champions," Holyfield and Lennox Lewis seemed on the verge of signing for a much-anticipated unification bout. Holyfield, the WBA and IBF champion, and Lewis, the WBC champ, would most likely fight in late February or early March of 1999. Holyfield is expected to get $20 million for the fight and Lewis will get $8 million.

The final potential snag in Tyson's return to prizefighting seemed about to go away as well. Two men who

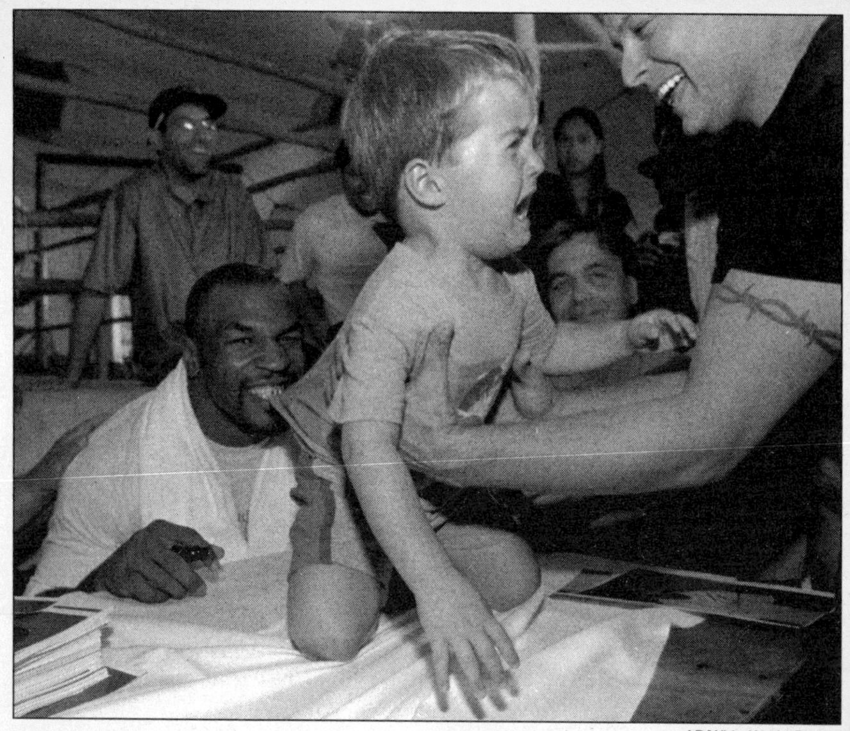

AP/Wide World Photos

Returning heavyweight **Mike Tyson** shows he can still intimidate, putting a scare into 2-year-old Florin Bouros of Tempe, Ariz. at a public workout in Phoenix.

accused Tyson of assaulting them in an Aug. 31 traffic dispute were ready to agree to a financial settlement to end the matter. If the case went to trial and Tyson was found guilty of the two assault charges, he could return to prison for up to 10 years for each charge.

Pro Basketball

NBA Lockout— The NBA owners, who forced the NBA lockout that as of Oct. 26, 1998 had led to the cancellation of the entire preseason and the first two weeks of the regular season, got a huge victory in their ongoing battle with the players' union when arbitrator John Feerick decided in their favor on Oct. 19.

Feerick, dean of Fordham Law School, ruled that the owners were not compelled to pay the 224 players who filed a grievance claiming that all players with guaranteed contracts should be paid during the lockout. The two sides are fighting over several issues but primarily the dispute is about how much money the owners will devote to player salaries.

The owners say that salaries have gotten out of control and they are now outpacing revenues. They want a new agreement that will limit payroll costs. The players' union had vowed to oppose any deal that includes a "hard" salary cap. The previous deal included the so-called "Larry Bird exception" which allowed teams to exceed the salary cap to resign their own free agents.

The bargaining position of the owners was significantly strengthened with Feerick's decision. They have large amounts of money already saved and the owners will still get the money from the NBA's new television contract while the players must make do with what little money is in the union's fund.

"The players will not back down," union director Billy Hunter said. "The sooner the owners realize this and end the lockout, the quicker we can avoid enormous damage to the sport of basketball."

The players met in Las Vegas to decide what their best course of action was. A potential ace-in-the-hole for the players could be a decertification of the union. Decertification would mean that a court injunction, if granted, would end the lockout and the owners would open camps and impose new work rules.

If the new rules were more restrictive than the old ones, which is what the owners want, then the players could file an antitrust suit against the league. Players with long-term contracts could very well benefit from decertification since they would begin to draw their salaries soon. However, free agents and players who have been in the league less than three years would be forced to play under the new rules until the antitrust suit was settled, which could be several years.

Soccer

The Chicago Fire, in their first year as a franchise, beat the two-time defending champion D.C. United 2-0 in the MLS Cup at the Rose Bowl on Oct. 25. The Fire got two assists from Polish midfielder Peter Nowak and their defense, including goalkeeper Zach Thornton, shut down the potent United offense to win the 1998 MLS championship.

"This is a very special day for me because I've never won a championship," said Nowak who set up goalscorers Jerzy Podbrozny and Diego Gutierrez 16 minutes apart in the first half.

United coach Bruce Arena complained about the officiating following his team's loss in the title match.

"I'm very disappointed with a couple of controversial calls in the game," said Arena. "It's hard for me to believe we are not champions. The breaks went their way. A couple of breaks go our way and maybe we're champions again.

"It seemed like we weren't given a chance in some way to defend our championship, with the number of cards dealt against us."

Fire coach Bob Bradley, a former assistant under Arena at the University of Virginia and then with the United, agreed with his former boss that the United got burned.

"Bruce is right on those issues. The Fire ended up getting breaks and that helped determine the game," Bradley said.

Among the controversial plays was the no-call by referee Kevin Terry on an early tackle of D.C. midfielder and season MVP Marco Etcheverry by Lubos Kubik in the Chicago penalty box. Arena contended that his team should have been awarded a penalty kick.

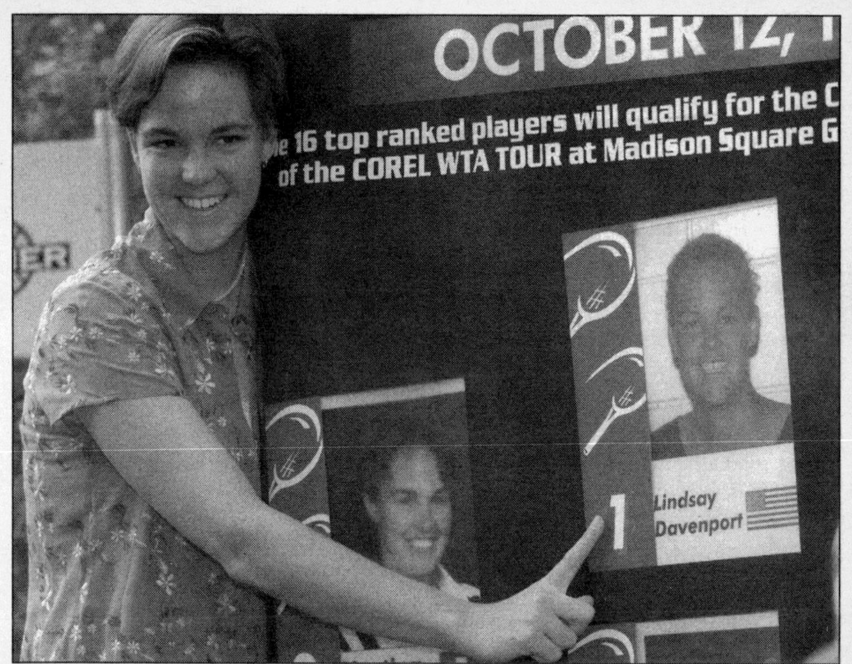
OCTOBER 12,
16 top ranked players will qualify for the C
of the COREL WTA TOUR at Madison Square G
1
Lindsay
Davenport

AP/Wide World Photos

Tennis player **Lindsay Davenport** points out her new spot on the world ranking table at the European Championships in Kloten, Switzerland. Davenport is just the third American-born woman to be ranked No. 1.

Arena will soon have bigger things to worry about because two days after the MLS Cup he was named the new head coach of the U.S. National Team, replacing the departed Steve Sampson. The 47-year-old Arena reportedly signed a four-year deal worth more than $500,000 per year.

Tennis

On October 12, Lindsay Davenport became just the third American-born woman (Tracy Austin, Chris Evert) to top the world rankings when she was elevated to No. 1, replacing Swiss teenager Martina Hingis. Hingis had been No. 1 for 80 straight weeks dating back to March 31, 1997.

Davenport then celebrated her new ranking by successfully defending her singles title at the European Championships, beating No. 5 Venus Williams in straight sets to give her five titles in her last seven events.

Golf

Mark O'Meara happily took home the PGA of America Player of the Year Award in October, knowing he may not get to take home the Player of the Year Award voted on by tour players.

That's because David Duval is having the best calendar year of golf in almost two decades. He has won four tournaments already in 1998 and is the tour's top money winner with a record $2,470,498 and counting. Not bad for someone who won his first PGA tournament on Oct. 12, 1997.

The voting could come down to the Tour Championship. If Duval successfully defends his title, he'll get the nod from the players.

It looks like Casey Martin, the Nike Tour golfer who sued for the right to use a motorized cart during tournaments, will not finish in the top 25 of Nike Tour money leaders. That means he won't get an exemption to the finals, and he'll have to play the second stage of the PGA Tour Qualifying tournament in November. Only the top 35 finishers in the tournament win PGA Tour cards. We may not see Martin, or his cart, on the PGA Tour until 2000.

Se Ri Pak cooled down with the weather this fall, while Annika Sorenstam heated things up in the race for Player of the Year honors.

Sorenstam, the LPGA's leading money winner and No. 1 ranked golfer, didn't win her first tournament in 1998 until June, but has played solid golf and racked up four titles and four second-place finishes.

Health issues ruled the Senior Tour headlines in October.

Players thoughts were with Chi-Chi Rodriguez, who had successful angioplasty surgery and also needed to be treated for angina late in the season. And, tragically, a week before Arnold Palmer was to make his return to the Tour after radiation treatments for prostate cancer, his family announced that his wife Winnie is battling ovarian cancer.

Horse racing

Skip Away injured his right-front ankle during the Jockey Gold Cup in Belmont, N.Y. on Oct. 10, and finished in third place, snapping his nine-race winning streak.

Silver Charm and Awesome Again will be waiting at the Breeders Cup on Nov. 7, when Skip Away looks to become the sport's first $10 million winner. A third-place finish will earn $480,000 and would push Skip Away into eight-figures and an insurmountable lead in the Horse of the Year race.

Auto racing

Jeff Gordon saw his streak of consecutive top-five NASCAR finishes snapped at 17 races (one short of the record) with a seventh-place showing at the rain-shortened Dura Lube/Kmart 500 in Phoenix.

No matter. Gordon is almost assured of winning his third Winston Cup Series championship in 1998. Despite gaining 29 points on Gordon, Mark Martin still trails the points leader 4,963 to 4,634, a difference of 329 points.

All Gordon needs to do to win the title is start the season's final two races, the ACDelco 400 and the NAPA 500. With a finish of 40th or better at the ACDelco 400 on Nov. 1, Gordon will capture the title with one race to spare.

The Formula One championship will be determined at the Japanese Grand Prix on Nov. 1 in Suzuka, Japan. Finland's Mika Hakkinen, who's won seven times in 1998, has a four-point lead on two-time champion Michael Schumacher. Hakkinen needs to finish no-less-than second to secure his first Formula One title. ■

TENNIS

Late 1998 Tournament Results

Men's Tour

Finals	Tournament	Winner	Earnings	Loser	Score
Oct. 4	Mallorca Open	Gustavo Kuerten	$64,000	C. Moya	67(5) 62 63
Oct. 4	Toulouse Open	Jan Siemerink	54,000	G. Rusedski	64 64
Oct. 4	Grand Slam Cup (Munich)	Marcelo Rios	1,300,000	A. Agassi	64 26 76(1) 57 63
Oct. 11	Swiss Indoors (Basel)	Tim Henman	137,000	A. Agassi	64 63 36 64
Oct. 11	Int'l Championship of Sicily	Mariano Puerta	45,000	F. Squillari	63 62
Oct. 18	Heineken Open (Singapore)	Marcelo Rios	107,000	M. Woodforde	64 62
Oct. 18	CA Tennis Trophy (Vienna)	Pete Sampras	125,400	K. Kucera	63 76(3) 61
Oct. 25	Czech Indoors (Ostrava)	Andre Agassi	137,000	J. Kroslak	62 36 63
Oct. 25	Lyon Grand Prix	Alex Corretja	101,500	T. Hass	26 76(6) 61

Remaining Events (10): Eurocard Open (Nov. 1); Mexican Open (Nov. 1); Paris Open (Nov. 8); Colombian Open (Nov. 8); Kremlin Cup (Nov. 15); Chevrolet Cup (Nov. 15); Stockholm Open (Nov. 15); ATP Tour Doubles Championship (Nov. 22); ATP Tour World Championship (Nov. 29); Davis Cup Final (Nov. 29).

Women's Tour

Finals	Tournament	Winner	Earnings	Loser	Score
Oct. 4	Grand Slam Cup (Munich)	Venus Williams	$800,000	P. Schnyder	62 36 62
Oct. 11	Porsche Grand Prix (Filderstadt)	Sandrine Testud	79,000	L. Davenport	75 63
Oct. 18	European Championships (Zurich)	Lindsay Davenport	150,000	V. Williams	75 63
Oct. 25	Kremlin Cup (Moscow)	Mary Pierce	165,000	M. Seles	76(2), 63

Remaining Events (6): Bell Challenge (Nov. 1); Seat Luxembourg Open (Nov. 1); Sparkassen Cup (Nov. 8); Advanta Championships (Nov. 15); Volvo Women's Open (Nov. 22); WTA Tour Chase Championships (Nov. 29).

GOLF

Late 1998 Tournament Results

PGA Tour

Last Rd	Tournament	Winner	Earnings	Runner-Up
Oct. 11	Michelob Championship	David Duval (268)	$342,000	P. Tataurangi (271)
Oct. 18	Las Vegas International	Jim Furyk (335)	360,000	M. Calcavecchia (336)
Oct. 25	National Car Rental Classic	John Huston (272)	360,000	D. Love III (273)

Remaining Events (8): The Tour Championship (Oct. 29-Nov. 1); Sarazen World Open (Nov. 5-8); Shark Shootout (Nov. 12-15); Skins Game (Nov. 28-29); JC Penney Classic (Dec. 3-6); Presidents Cup (Dec. 11-13); Three-Tour Challenge (Dec. 19-20); Diners Club Matches (Dec. 31-Jan. 3).

European PGA Tour

Last Rd	Tournament	Winner	Earnings	Runner-Up
Oct. 11	Alfred Dunhill Cup	South Africa (3-0)	$300,000	Spain
Oct. 18	Open Novotel Perrier	Jarmo Sandelin/ Olle Karlsson (329)	35,000 (each)	R. Boxall/ D. Cooper (332)

Remaining Events (3): Volvo Masters (Oct. 29-Nov. 1); Sarazen World Open (Nov. 5-8); World Cup of Golf (Nov. 19-22).

Senior PGA Tour

Last Rd	Tournament	Winner	Earnings	Runner-Up
Oct. 11	The TransAmerica	Jim Colbert (205)	$150,000	D. Lundstrom (206)
Oct. 18	Raley's Gold Rush	Dana Quigley (203)	150,000	J. Morgan (206)
Oct. 25	Maui Kaanapali Classic	Jay Sigel (201)	150,000	H. Baiocchi & L. Laoretti (203)

Remaining Events (5): Ralph's Senior Classic (Oct. 30-Nov. 1); Senior Tour Championship (Nov. 5-8); Senior Match Play (Nov. 13-15); Lexus Challenge (Dec. 19-20); Three-Tour Challenge (Dec. 19-20).

LPGA Tour

Last Rd	Tournament	Winner	Earnings	Runner-Up
Oct. 11	LPGA Tournament of Champions	Kelli Robbins (276)	$122,000	J. Inkster (280)
Oct. 25	World Championship of Golf	Juli Inkster (275)	137,000	A. Sorenstam (278)

Remaining Events (5): Nichirei International (Oct. 30-Nov.1); Japan Classic (Nov. 6-8); Tour Championship (Nov. 19-22); JC Penney Classic (Dec. 3-6); Three-Tour Challenge (Dec. 19-20).

Team Competition

Alfred Dunhill Cup

at St. Andrews, Scotland (Oct. 8-11)

South Africa def. Spain, 3-0

Semifinals (Spain def. United States, 2-1): John Daly (USA) def. Miguel Angel Jiménez (SPA), 73-75; Santiago Luna (SPA) def. Tiger Woods (USA), 71-72; José Maria Olazábal (SPA) def. Mark O'Meara (USA), 72-76.

Semifinals (South Africa def. Australia, 2-1): David Frost (S.AFR) def. Craig Perry (AUS), 72-78; Retief Goosen (S.AFR) def. Stuart Appleby (AUS), 71-74; Steve Elkington (AUS) def. Ernie Els (S.AFR), 72-73.

Finals (South Africa def. Spain, 3-0): Retief Goosen (S.AFR) def. Santiago Luna (SPA), 72-73; David Frost (S.AFR) def. Miguel Angel Jiménez (SPA), 76-78; Ernie Els (S.AFR) def. José Maria Olazábal (SPA), 75-77.

THOROUGHBRED RACING

Late 1998 Major Stakes Races

Date	Race	Location	Miles	Winner	Jockey	Purse
Sept. 26	Vosburgh Stakes	Belmont	7 F	Affirmed Success	Jorge Chavez	$250,000
Sept. 26	Queen Elizabeth II Stakes	Ascot	1 (T)	Desert Prince	Olivier Peslier	£320,000
Sept. 27	Super Derby	Louisiana Downs	1¼	Arch	Corey Nakatani	500,000
Oct. 4	L'Arc De Triomphe	Longchamp	1⅛ (T)	Sagamix	Olivier Peslier	1,250,000
Oct. 10	Jockey Club Gold Cup	Belmont	1¼	Wagon Limit	Robbie Davis	1,000,000
Oct. 10	Champagne Stakes	Belmont	1 1/16	The Groom Is Red	Corey Nakatani	400,000
Oct. 10	Beldame Stakes	Belmont	1 1/16	Sharp Cat	Corey Nakatani	400,000
Oct. 10	Frizette Stakes	Belmont	1 1/16	Confessional	Jerry Bailey	400,000
Oct. 10	Turf Classic Invitational	Belmont	1½ (T)	Buck's Boy	Shane Sellers	500,000
Oct. 17	Goodwood Breeders Cup	Santa Anita	1⅛	Silver Charm	Gary Stevens	446,000
Oct. 17	Spinster Stakes	Keeneland	1⅛	Banshee Breeze	Robbie Albarado	551,500
Oct. 18	Canadian International	Woodbine	1½ (T)	Royal Anthem	Gary Stevens	1,050,000
Oct. 24	TC of America Stakes	Keeneland	6 F	Bourbon Belle	Willie Martinez	100,000
Oct. 24	Empire Classic	Belmont	1⅛	Mellow Roll	Jerry Bailey	250,000
Oct. 25	Oak Tree's Turf Champ.	Santa Anita	1 (T)	Sapphire Ring	Gary Stevens	100,000

HARNESS RACING

Late 1998 Major Stakes Races

	Race	Raceway	Winner	Driver	Purse
Oct. 9	Kentucky Futurity	Lexington	Trade Balance*	David Wade	$331,340
Oct. 16	Messenger Pace	Ladbroke	Fit For Life†	John Campbell	484,224

* By winning the Kentucky Futurity, Trade Balance spoiled Shady Character's bid to become the ninth pacer in history to win the Triple Crown.

† By winning the Messenger Pace, Fit For Life spoiled Muscles Yankee's bid for the first Trotting Triple Crown since Super Bowl in 1972.

STEEPLECHASE RACING

Late 1998 Major Stakes Races

Date	Race	Location	Miles	Winner	Jockey	Purse
Oct. 24	BC Grand National	Far Hills, NJ	2⅝	Flat Top	Bitsy Patterson	$150,000

AUTO RACING

Late 1998 Results

NASCAR

Date	Event	Location	Winner	Avg.mph	Earnings	Pole	Qual.mph
Oct. 17	Pepsi 400*	Daytona	Jeff Gordon (8)	144.549	$184,325	B. Labonte	193.611
Oct. 25	Dura-Lube 500	Phoenix	Rusty Wallace (6)	108.211	78,005	K. Schrader	131.234

* The Pepsi 400 was rescheduled from July 4 after wildfires in Central Florida spread dangerously close to the race track grounds.

Note: The Dura-Lube 500 was shortened from 312 laps to 257 due to rain.

Winning Cars: CHEVY MONTE CARLO (1)— Gordon; FORD THUNDERBIRD (1)—Wallace.

Remaining Races (2): AC-Delco 400 in Rockingham (Nov. 1); NAPA 500 in Atlanta (Nov. 8).

NHRA

Date		Event	Winner	Time	MPH	2nd Place	Time	MPH
Oct. 11	Pennzoil Nationals	Top Fuel	Joe Amato	4.648	318.92	K. Bernstein	4.696	315.12
		Funny Car	Al Hofmann	5.172	280.43	C. Pedregon	16.584	64.88
		Pro Stock	Warren Johnson	6.901	199.20	K. Johnson	6.964	198.50
Oct. 17	Parts America	Top Fuel	Cory McClenathan	6.298	279.93	K. Bernstein	9.454	315.12
		Funny Car	Ron Capps	5.111	285.53	A. Hoffman	8.160	104.28
		Pro Stock	Warren Johnson	6.943	197.67	J. Coughlin	6.951	197.71
Oct. 25	Revell Nationals	Top Fuel	Gary Scelzi	4.653	300.00	M. Dunn	8.582	84.53
		Funny Car	John Force	4.860	320.17	D. Skuza	4.915	311.95
		Pro Stock	Warren Johnson	6.950	199.02	J. Yates	7.961	128.36

Remaining Events (2): Matco Tools Supernationals in Houston, Tex. (Oct. 29-Nov. 1); Winston Finals in Pomona, Cal. (Nov. 12-15).

BOWLING

1998 Fall Tour Results

PBA

Final	Event	Winner	Earnings	Final	Runner-Up
Sept. 20	Japan Cup	Parker Bohn III	$50,000	238-226	Steve Jones
Oct. 7	National Finance Championship	Brian Voss	20,000	265-257	Walter Ray Williams Jr.
Oct. 14	Long Island Open	Walter Ray Williams Jr.*	19,000	214-188	Robert Smith
Oct. 21	Rochester Open	Norm Duke	18,000	213-211	Steve Hoskins

* The Long Island Open was Williams' 27th career PBA title moving him into third place all-time behind Earl Anthony (41) and Mark Roth (34).

Remaining Events See PBA fall schedule on page 771.

Senior PBA

Final	Event	Winner	Earnings	Final	Runner-Up
Sept. 17	Greater Sebring Open	Ron Winger	$8,000	246-193	Johnny Petraglia
Sept. 24	Naples Senior Open*	Pete Couture	8,000	236-223	Mike Durbin
Oct. 8	Jackson Senior Open	Steve Neff	8,000	217-214	Gary Dickinson

* Because of Hurricane Georges, play was suspended after the ninth game in the only round of match play and Couture was declared the winner. It was the first time in PBA history a tournament was shortened.

Remaining Events See SPBA fall schedule on page 771.

PWBA

Final	Event	Winner	Earnings	Final	Runner-Up
Sept. 17	Visionary Classic	Marianne DiRupo	$10,000	196-186	Liz Johnson
Sept. 24	Track Triton Open	Wendy Macpherson	11,000	227-193	Carolyn Dorin-Ballard
Oct. 1	Columbia 300 Delaware Open	Carol Gianotti-Block	11,000	204-171	Anne Marie Duggan
Oct. 7	Storm Three Rivers Open	Carol Gianotti-Block	11,000	258-201	Kim Canady
Oct. 15	AMF Gold Cup	Dana Miller-Mackie	28,000	278-170	Dede Davidson
Oct. 22	Brunswick World Open	Carolyn Dorin-Ballard	25,000	227-203	Dede Davidson

Remaining Events See PWBA fall schedule on page 771.

SOCCER

Major League Soccer

Western Conference Finals
Best-of-three

Chicago Fire beat Los Angeles Galaxy, 2 games to 0.

Date	Result	Site
Oct. 10	Fire, 1-0	at Los Angeles
Oct. 16	Fire, 2-1 (SO)	at Chicago

Eastern Conference Finals
Best-of-three

D.C. United beat Columbus Crew, 2 games to 1.

Date	Result	Site
Oct. 11	United, 2-0	at Wash., D.C.
Oct. 18	Crew, 4-2	at Columbus
Oct. 21	United, 3-0	at Wash., D.C.

MLS Cup '98

Chicago Fire 2, D.C. United 0

Oct. 25 at Rose Bowl, Pasadena, Calif.
Attendance: 51,350

	1	2	Final
Washington D.C.	0	0	– **0**
Chicago	2	0	– **2**

Scoring Summary

1st Half: CHI– Jerzy Podbrozny (Peter Nowak, Ante Razov) 29th minute; CHI–Diego Gutierrez (Nowak), 45th.

MVP: Peter Nowak, Chicago, M

DC–Total Shots: 22 (Roy Lassiter 6, Marco Etcheverry 6); Shots on Goal: 8 (Lassiter 3); Fouls: 8 (Lassiter 2, Tony Sanneh 2, Etcheverry 2); Offside: 1; Corner Kicks: 12; Saves: Tom Presthus 1; Cautions: Sanneh (25th), Etcheverry (33rd).

CHI–Total Shots: 10 (Podbrozny 2, Razov 2, Gutierrez 2); Shots on Goal: 4 (Podbrozny 2); Fouls: 27 (Podbrozny 5); Offside: 5; Corner Kicks: 3; Saves: Zach Thornton 8; Cautions: Razov (31st), Gutierrez (50th), Jesse Marsch (60th).

MLS Annual Awards

MVP: Marco Etcheverry, D.C. United
Coach of the Year: Bob Bradley, Chicago
Goalkeeper of the Year: Zach Thornton, Chi.
Defender of the Year: Lubos Kubik, Chicago
Rookie of the Year: Ben Olsen, D.C. United
Fair Play Individual: Thomas Dooley, Columbus
Fair Play Team: Kansas City Wizards

All MLS Team

G– Zach Thornton, Chicago
D– Robin Fraser, Los Angeles
D– Thomas Dooley, Columbus
D– Eddie Pope, D.C. United
D– Lubos Kubik, Chicago
M– Chris Armas, Chicago
M– Mauricio Cienfuegos, L. Angeles
M– Peter Nowak, Chicago
M– Marco Etcheverry, D.C. United
F– Cobi Jones, Los Angeles
F– Stern John, Columbus

Olympics

Winter Games

Year	No.	Host City	Dates
2002	XIX	Salt Lake City, Utah	Feb. 8-24

Summer Games

Year	No.	Host City	Dates
2000	XXVII	Sydney, Australia	Sept. 16-Oct. 1
2004	XXVIII	Athens, Greece	Aug. 13-29

All-Star Games

Baseball

Year	Site	Date
1999	Fenway Park, Boston	July 13
2000	Pro Player Stadium, Miami	TBD

NBA Basketball

Year	Site	Date
1999	First Union Center, Philadelphia	Feb. 14
2000	New Oakland Coliseum, Oakland	Feb. 13

NFL Pro Bowl

Year	Site	Date
1999	Aloha Stadium, Honolulu	Feb. 7
2000	Aloha Stadium, Honolulu	Feb. 6
2001	Aloha Stadium, Honolulu	Feb. 4

NHL Hockey

Year	Site	Date
1999	Ice Palace, Tampa Bay	Jan. 24
2000	Air Canada Center, Toronto	Feb. 6

Auto Racing

The Daytona 500 stock car race is usually held on the Sunday before the third Monday in February, while the Indianapolis 500 is usually held on the Sunday of Memorial Day weekend in May. The following dates are tentative.

Year	Daytona 500	Indianapolis 500
1999	Feb. 14	May 23
2000	Feb. 19	May 28
2001	Feb. 18	May 20

NCAA Basketball

Men's Final Four

Year	Site	Date
1999	Tropicana Field, St. Petersburg	March 27-29
2000	RCA Dome, Indianapolis	April 1-3
2001	Metrodome, Minneapolis	Mar. 31-Apr. 2
2002	Georgia Dome, Atlanta	Mar. 30-Apr. 1
2003	Louisiana Superdome, New Orleans	April 5-7

Women's Final Four

Year	Site	Date
1999	San Jose Arena, San Jose	March 26-28
2000	First Union Center, Philadelphia	Mar. 31-Apr. 2
2001	Kiel Center, St. Louis	Mar. 30-Apr. 1
2002	Alamodome, San Antonio	March 29-31

NFL Football

Super Bowl

No.	Site	Date
XXXIII	Pro Player Stadium, Miami	Jan. 31, 1999
XXXIV	Georgia Dome, Atlanta	Jan. 30, 2000
XXXV	Raymond James Stadium, Tampa	Jan. 28, 2001

Golf

The Masters

Year	Site	Date
1999	Augusta National Ga	April 8-11
2000	Augusta National Ga.	April 6-9

U.S. Open

Year	Site	Date
1999	Pinehurst CC, Pinehurst, N.C.	June 17-20
2000	Pebble Beach (Calif.) Golf Links.	June 15-18
2001	Southern Hills, Tulsa, Okla.	June 14-17

U.S. Women's Open

Year	Site	Date
1999	Old Waverly GC, West Point, Miss.	June 3-6
2000	Merit Club, Libertyville, Ill.	July 20-23

U.S. Senior Open

Year	Site	Date
1999	Des Moines GC, W. Des Moines, Iowa	July 5-11
2000	Saucon Valley GC, Bethlehem, Pa.	TBA

PGA Championship

Year	Site	Date
1999	Medinah CC, Medinah, Ill.	Aug. 12-15
2000	Valhalla GC, Louisville, Ky.	Aug. 17-20
2001	Atlanta Athletic Club, Duluth, Ga.	TBD
2002	Hazeltine National CC, Chaska, Minn.	TBD
2003	Oak Hill CC, Rochester, N.Y.	TBD

British Open

Year	Site	Date
1999	Carnoustie, Scotland	July 15-18
2000	St. Andrews, England	July 20-23
2001	TBD	July 19-22

Ryder Cup

Year	Site	Date
1999	The Country Club, Brookline, Mass.	Sept. 24-26
2001	The Belfrey, England	Sept. 28-30
2003	Oakland Hills CC, Bloomfield Hills, Mich.	TBD
2005	Ireland	TBD
2007	Valhalla GC, Louisville, Ky.	TBD

Horse Racing

Triple Crown

The Kentucky Derby is always held at Churchill Downs in Louisville on the first Saturday in May, followed two weeks later by the Preakness Stakes at Pimlico Race Course in Baltimore and three weeks after that by the Belmont Stakes at Belmont Park in Elmont, N.Y.

Year	Ky Derby	Preakness	Belmont
1999	May 1	May 15	June 5
2000	May 6	May 20	June 10
2001	May 5	May 19	June 9

Tennis

U.S. Open

Usually held from the last Monday in August through the second Sunday in September, with Labor Day weekend the midway point in the tournament.

Year	Site	Date
1999	Arthur Ashe Stadium, NYC	Aug. 30-Sept. 12
2000	Arthur Ashe Stadium, NYC	Aug. 28-Sept. 10
2001	Arthur Ashe Stadium, NYC.	Aug. 26-Sept. 9

Personalities

How familiar is this sight? **Michael Jordan** blows past another defender (in this case Reggie Miller) on his way to another two points and yet another Bulls' championship.

AP/Wide World Photos

Top 20 Personalities of 1998

SportsCenter's prime-time anchors pick their prime-time personalities from the past year.

by
Dan Patrick and Kenny Mayne

When Kenny and I were first asked to choose our top 20 list of sports individuals for 1998, we knew we were in for a tough task. The hard part wasn't trying to come up with 20 individuals to write about, rather it was narrowing the list down to such a small amount. In fact, 1998 was such a banner a year in sports that we easily could have picked over 100 people to grace these pages.

So here it is— our list of people that, as paid employees in the sports world, made our jobs more enjoyable, and more importantly as fans, captured our hearts and surpassed our wildest imaginations.

By the way, Kenny and I flipped a coin to see who got to go first. I won. So let's get to it.

Dan Patrick and Kenny Mayne are the co-anchors of ESPN's 11 pm *SportsCenter*.

Marion Jones

Move over Michael. The women's sports world has an MJ of its own. Coincidentally, this one was also a star basketball player at North Carolina, but unlike Jordan, Marion Jones has found being a two-sport star a bit more to her liking. Like her basketball counterpart, however, Jones seemed to do just about anything she wanted in 1998.

She is currently the world's top-ranked woman in the 100-meters, the 200-meters and the long jump. At the time of this writing, Jones had 16 consecutive wins in the 100. During a 12 month span in 1997-98, she had participated in 37 events and she recorded . . . you guessed it . . . 37 wins. Her presence in the women's track world alone is making the retirement of track legend Jackie Joyner-Kersee just a little easier to swallow.

Archive Photos

Twenty-year-old **Se Ri Pak** acknowledges the gallery after finishing the second round of the U.S. Women's Open on July 3. She went on to beat Jenny Chuasiriporn on the 92nd hole for her second major win of the year.

Dominik Hasek

The Dominator's performance in the Czech Republic's semifinal round victory over Canada in February's Olympic Winter Games is reason enough for him to be included in this list. Hasek was brilliant at Nagano and got the Buffalo Sabres one series short of the Stanley Cup Finals. Throw in his fourth Vezina Trophy in the last five years and his second NHL Most Valuable Player Award and you've got the world's best goaltender.

Se Ri Pak

At the age of 18, Pak turned professional in her native Korea. In the 14 events she played in, she won six and was runner-up seven times. Now consider this. She started playing golf when she was 14. You won't see any Tiger-like commercials of Pak winning tournaments as a 5-year-old. This year, Pak burst onto the LPGA Tour at the ripe old age of 20. In fact, "burst" may be an understatement.

Having already won the McDonald's LPGA Championship, Pak became the first woman under the age of 21 to win two majors in one season by thwarting gutsy amateur Jenny Chuasiriporn on the 20th extra hole of the U.S. Women's Open. It was just the kind of suspense that women's golf needs. And Pak is just the kind of champion that women's golf needs. Why shouldn't she be? After all, she's been playing for six whole years.

Brian Habib, Tony Jones, Tom Nalen, Mark Schlereth and **Gary Zimmerman**

I know what you're thinking. Who? Individually, the names don't exactly strike fear into the hearts of anyone, but put them all together and they become one of the best offensive lines in football—an immovable, impenetrable force and the engine of the car that drove the Denver Broncos to the AFC's first Super Bowl win in 13 years. They were much-maligned all season. Too small, too slow, too this, too that. Experts predicted that they would be manhandled in the big game by the Packers' Reggie White, Santana Dotson and the massive Gilbert Brown. They weren't. John Elway got the much-deserved press and Terrell Davis got the touchdowns and the MVP award, but they really ought to buy a few rounds for their protectors up front. Their grit, tenacity, toughness and skill level is what really put the Broncos over the top in 1998.

Michael Jordan

This guy again, huh? Basically, Jordan could be at or near the top of this list every year. What more needs to be said? Six world championships, six MVP trophies, 10 scoring titles—you've heard it all before. But this year was a special one for Michael because it may very well be his last.

If he does make last year's championship-winning shot his last and ride off into the proverbial sunset with coach Phil Jackson, he'll be one of those rare players that had the luxury of leaving the game as its best player. Mario Lemieux did it in hockey last year. This year it could be Jordan's turn. Here's a scary thought. Even if he does retire, he'll still be the most important figure in sports into the next millennium.

Pat Summitt

Don't bother asking her team for the time of day at the Big Dance. They're out of your league. Summitt gets more from her team in the NCAA Tournament than any other coach, winning 61 of her 72 career tournament games. She guided Tennessee to an undefeated season and capped it off with the team's unprecedented third straight national title. It was the sixth time in her 23 seasons coaching the Vols that her season ended with a national championship.

Mark O'Meara

Who wasn't convinced that either David Duval or Fred Couples had the Masters wrapped up going into 18 on Sunday? Apparently O'Meara, who calmly drained a 20-foot birdie putt on the tournament's 72nd hole at Augusta to win his first major tournament and set the pace for his most remarkable year of golf as a professional. He added his second major, the British Open, three months later. He proved the PGA Tour veterans aren't ready to give up the game just yet to golf's next generation.

Jeff Gordon

In 1997, he produced the greatest money-making season in NASCAR history, becoming the first $6 million man. And in 1998, he's threatening his own mark. How's this for dominating? There are close to 70 drivers on the NASCAR circuit. Through 29 official events, Gordon had won ten, finished in second six more times and has finished out of the top 10 just five times. He's the guy everyone in the business

AP/Wide World Photos

Mark McGwire (r) blows a trademark Sammy Sosa kiss to the Chicago slugger after Sosa walked in the seventh inning on August 19. Both hit their 48th home run in the game. There would be more.

wrongly thinks they need to hate. He's the brash young kid with the great looks, the one with the beautiful wife and the one who, despite racing against the best stock car drivers in the world, has turned the NASCAR circuit into his own playground. Don't hate him for that. Admire him for being one of the leaders in taking his sport to previously unattained levels of popularity.

Sammy Sosa

Holy Cow! Harry would have loved watching Sosa's enthusiasm for the game and explosive power shine through this summer. Sosa refused to sit quietly in the shadow of Mark McGwire. His jump from 36 homers in 1997 to 66 in 1998 was the fourth largest power surge in baseball history. He became a more disciplined hitter at the plate, and he gave Chicago's baseball fans a reason to love the Cubs in August and September.

Mark McGwire

All McGwire did this year was take the most hallowed, recognizable record in all of sports and make a mockery of it. Seventy home runs. Let me say that again. Seventy home runs. OK, so maybe expansion has diluted the overall pitching talent in the league, maybe the balls are wound just a little tighter than they used to be, and maybe the ballparks have become a bit more hitter-friendly (though McGwire all but put that argument to rest by averaging 423 feet per homer, making the size of the ballparks largely irrelevant). His accomplishment is one of the most amazing I've ever witnessed. But possibly even more impressive than his titanic blasts was the way he handled himself during the media frenzy that surrounded the final days of the chase. While taking the entire country for a ride in August and September, sometimes even bumping Bill and Monica off the front page, he managed to stay true to his family, his friends, his teammates and his fans. He showed the utmost respect for the game, the record and the man who once held it.

Thanks Dan. We agree on most, but not all things.

Randall Cunningham

Is it possible that a quarterback can be in violation of that "one voice in the huddle" rule? Cunningham tested the question during his time in Philadelphia, when he spoke of himself so often in third person. The complaints from teammates were long—like his throwing motion. And he was done. I wondered what happened to that college freshman I knew—the one that possessed a blend of cockiness and warmth that won over friends and teammates.

Now it's Minnesota's good fortune that the genuine Randall Cunningham has resurfaced. And whatever the football result, it's Randall's too.

Mo Vaughn

It's opening day at Fenway and the distractions are many for Mo. An off-season incident, a contract impasse—but the question put to him regards neither.

"Will you play some wiffle ball in September to help out some kids?"

Six months later, apologetic for being ten minutes late to the game, Mo contributes in a way his .337 batting average and 40 home runs can't. Maybe it was coincidence, maybe it was the chemotherapy, but maybe it was Mo's touch. When you're 11 years old and you have cancer, and you ask that spending time with Mo be your medicine, why would any other cures stand out when by October, the cancer had gone into remission?

Larry Bird

These spare words aren't for Bird's entrance into the Hall of Fame. That was a given. And what's a guy doing in the top 20 personalities list when he's spent his career deflecting attention?

It's for the way he put his second imprint on the game. First year back: coach of the year, and a play or two shy of making it to the NBA Finals. His work ethic as a player would have been enough. Nothing else was required of him. But now he's giving us another look at his brand of basketball which never needed an encore to begin with.

Andre Agassi

So when is it time to give it up? How about when you're ranked so low that people thought you already had? Andre Agassi opened the season 122nd in the world. And the critics were ready to agree with him about image being everything.

But some people just couldn't distinguish between an old ad campaign and a new image of a guy who worked himself from the fringe back into the top 10.

So when is it time to pick it up again?

Shawon Dunston

For what children in general, and his in particular, mean to him, it was wonderful to see Mark McGwire and his son share in the record. But mostly, children see their fathers struggle and that's why another father-son celebration stood out.

Dunston didn't have his best year. He hit just .222. But in a late season game that mattered, his pinch-hit three-run home run helped the Giants close in on the wild-card. And as he rounded third, in what he'd later call "the greatest play of my career," his 5-year-old bat-boy son, Shawon Jr. was waiting at home plate. And fathers and sons who had it tough elsewhere were in on the hug.

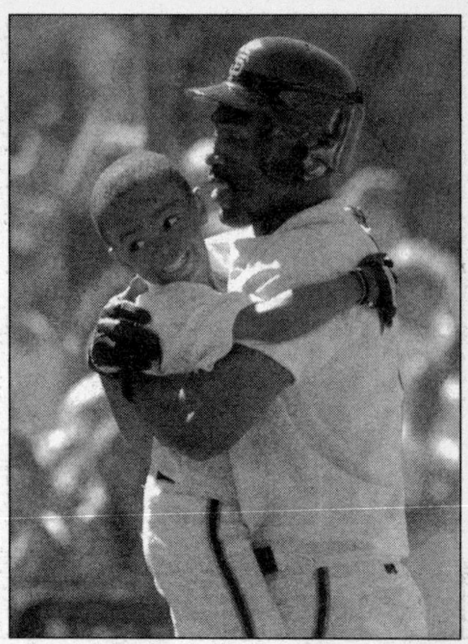

AP/Wide World Photos

San Francisco Giants' **Shawon Dunston** is embraced by his five-year-old son, Shawon Jr., after belting a pinch-hit three-run home run to lead the Giants to a much-needed win over the New York Mets on August 27.

Gary Stevens

He'd rated Victory Gallop just right and won the Belmont by a nose over Real Quiet. But his words after the event were just as measured as his ride. Stevens had just spoiled the Triple Crown for jockey Kent Desormeaux. Only a year before, Stevens himself suffered the same loss when his horse Silver Charm was passed late in the Belmont. And so, celebration for his win was tempered by empathy for his rival. Nothing about revenge. A lot about understanding. And Stevens won a whole lot of respect in addition to a horse race.

Anna Kournikova

Let the woman who hasn't made mention of tight NFL uniforms cast the first stone. OK, she's not really in the elite yet, but remember, this is a list of top 20 personalities. Pictures speak a thousand words and any publicity is good publicity. With that in mind, Kournikova did more for tennis' market share in one year than any number of men's five-set multiple-tie-break grand slams could possibly do. And she's pretty good at tennis too. So don't sweat the sexism thing. Sex is popular.

The Maris Family

Here's hoping it really works that way—that Roger Maris took in the whole thing through some kind of heavenly broadcast. The family he left behind carried on with the same kind of dignity he'd displayed back when it was villainous, not heroic, to hit for the record.

His kids were honest. Of course they didn't want the record broken. But as it became clear it would fall, they handled things like we imagine their father would. And while McGwire's gesture of pointing up to the

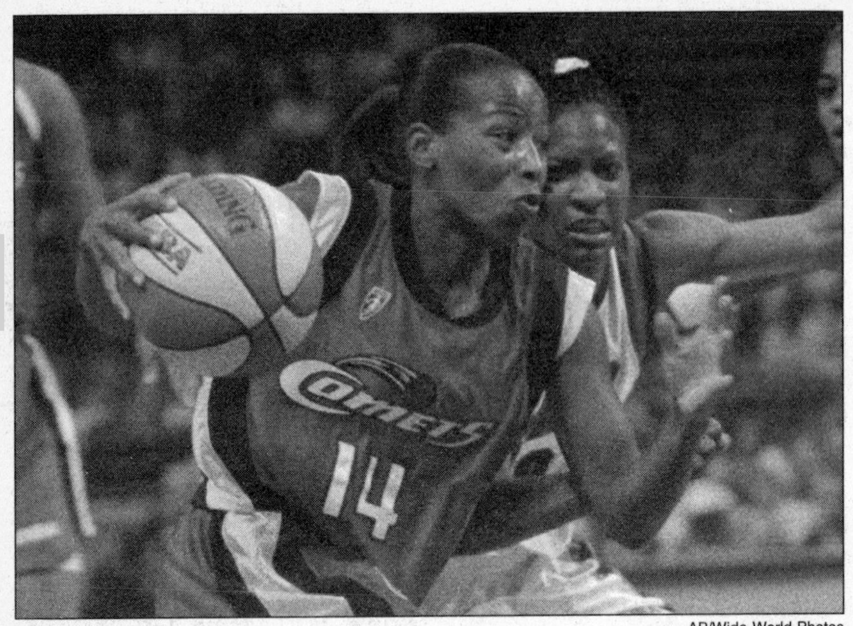

AP/Wide World Photos

Houston star **Cynthia Cooper** drives to the hoop during the Comets' playoff win over the Charlotte Sting on August 22. The Comets won their second straight WNBA title while "Coop" grabbed her second straight MVP award.

sky was classy, it may have been unnecessary. Roger Maris had already been reflected down here.

Cynthia Cooper

Cynthia Cooper has a book deal. She's got a story to tell. And it could be about last season when she won the league and title series MVPs for her WNBA-champion Houston Comets at age 35. Or it could be about the year before when she did the exact same thing.

But that's just basketball.

Her coach calls her "the most resilient person" he's ever seen. That's a product of her upbringing. She saw her single mother raise eight children in a tough part of Los Angeles. Cooper didn't even play the game until her junior year in high school . . . and then got a full ride to USC. Apparently she's a quick study . . . and now she has a platform to teach.

The Yankees

Without one serious MVP candidate, the Yankees won an American League record 114 games. The work was spread around. Six pitchers won at least ten games. Ten batters hit 10 or more home runs.

And then there was the day when the team contributed toward the common goal like they never had before. ESPN's Harold Reynolds was about to conduct an interview for reaction to the news that Darryl Strawberry had cancer. In Reynolds' background were the New York Yankees. Solemn. Defiant. Gathered around each other as one. ■

Moments

Phillip Ozersky of St. Louis had quite a moment on Sept. 27, 1998 when he caught Mark McGwire's 70th and final home run of the season.

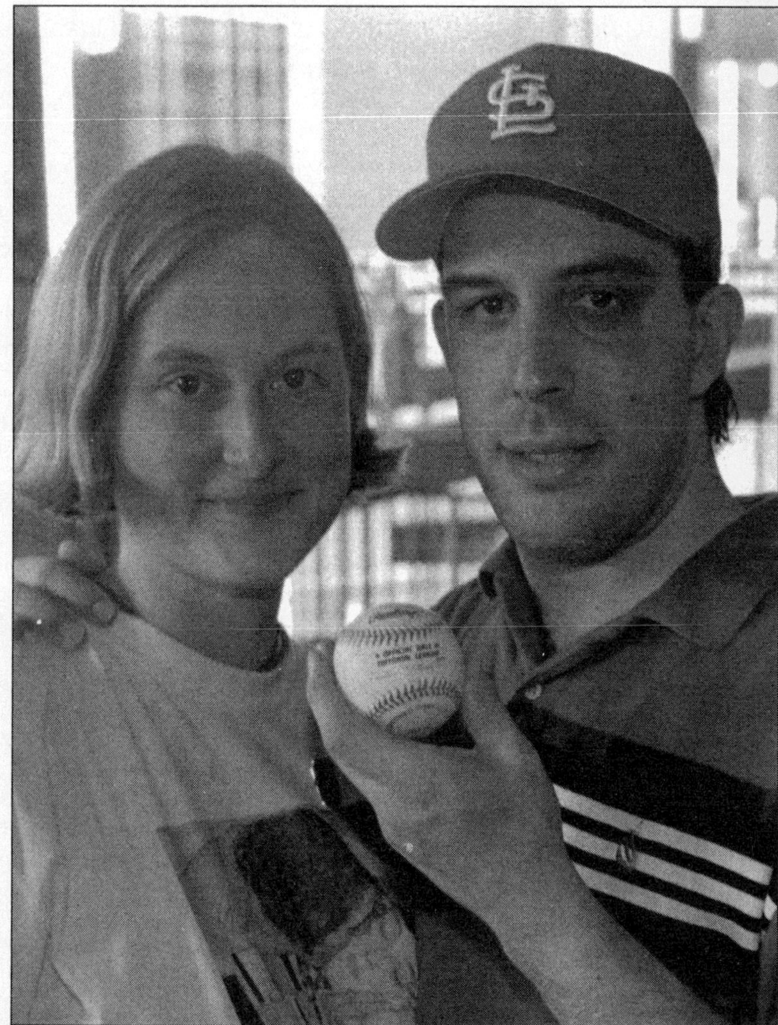

AP/Wide World Photos

Top 40 Moments

Rich and Stuart show Mark and Sammy what a 1-2 punch is all about as they deliver the magic moments of 1998.

by
Rich Eisen and Stuart Scott

If you were with us last year you may have noticed that Stuart went first and scooped up most of the biggest moments before I had a chance. This time around, Stuart was magnanimous enough to allow me to choose my top 20 moments before he got to name his. But as you'll see, because I'm such a nice guy, I let him do all the Michael Jordan stuff. You know, that whole North Carolina connection. In return, he agreed not to mention the Chris Webber Timeout incident to me, on air and off, for at least one full year.

Anyway, here goes.

20. Game 163

The Giants and Cubs capped off baseball's best year ever with a one-game playoff, at Wrigley Field, one of the greatest theaters in the sport. The hometown Cubs won and put Sammy Sosa, one of the greatest sluggers of all time, into the playoffs, in which, unfortunately, he didn't homer. The last out: future Hall-of-Famer Joe Carter, author of one of the greatest post-season moments of all time, popped out to Mark Grace, the only current Cub who had previously been to the playoffs. What a season.

19. The 1998 Belmont Stakes

Boy, did we almost have a Triple Crown winner for the first time since Affirmed in 1978. Real Quiet came real close. But Victory Gallop charged from well behind in the stretch to nose out Real Quiet in a photo finish to win the Belmont Stakes. It wasn't meant to be. Even if Real Quiet and jockey Kent Desormeaux had held off Victory Gallop down the stretch, the horse would have been disqualified for bumping Victory Gallop in the wild finish.

18. McGwire's 55th Home Run

Why not his 31st? Why not his 12th for that matter? The reason this home

---

Rich Eisen and **Stuart Scott** are anchor/reporters on ESPN's *SportsCenter.*

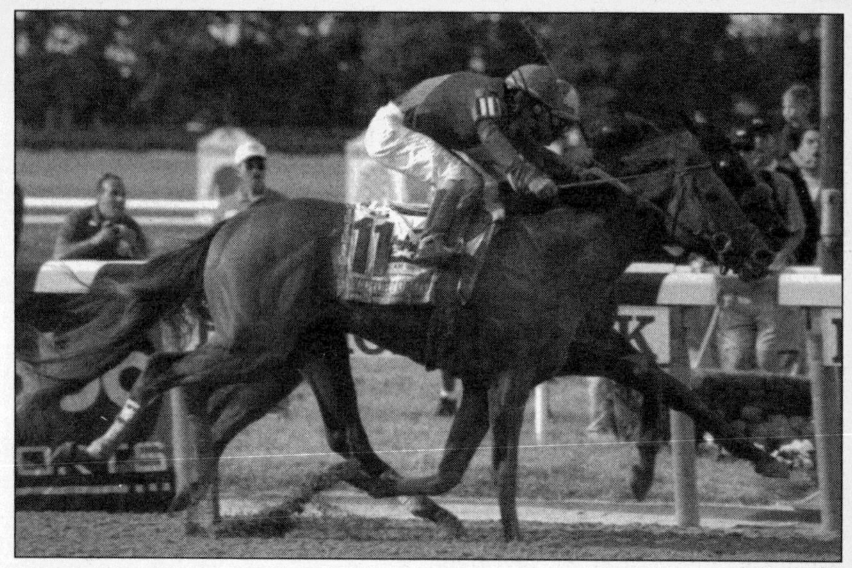

Archive Photos

The Belmont Stakes provided moments of incredible excitement in 1998. **Real Quiet** (#11) narrowly missed horse racing's first Triple Crown in 20 years, getting nosed out at the wire by **Victory Gallop** in a wild finish.

run, the one he hit off of Atlanta's Dennis Martinez on Aug. 30, makes the list is because of its length: 501 feet, the SHORTEST of all his 500-foot-plus home runs. When you begin categorizing home runs in terms of the shortest of his moon shots, you know you're in the midst of watching something special.

17. NLCS Game 5

A playoff game in which three players hit home runs to put their team ahead? In which Kevin Brown and Greg Maddux came out of the bullpen? In which 58,988 fans were screaming for virtually every pitch, every hit? In which the Braves scored six times in the eighth inning to stave off elimination? No question, this was the best playoff game of the baseball postseason.

16. Jeff Gordon Wins Four Straight Races

July 26: The Pennsylvania 500
August 1: The Brickyard 400
August 9: The Bud at the Glen
August 16: The Pepsi 400

Jeff Gordon had the pole for only one of those races, the one in Watkins Glen. No matter. Gordon won them all. That tied a modern-era NASCAR Winston Cup Series record, held by Cale Yarborough, Darrell Waltrip, Dale Earnhardt, Harry Gant, Bill Elliott and Mark Martin, the last driver to win four in a row in 1993. It almost didn't happen. At the Pepsi 400, Gordon took the lead for the first time in the race with three laps to go. By the way, Martin broke up the streak the next week, winning the Goody's 500. Gordon, however, won the next two races after that. He's good.

15. McGwire's 50th Home Run

After Big Mac belted this one on Aug. 20 at Shea Stadium, it was the first time all season that he showed outward emotion while trotting around the bases. He pumped his fist after touching first. The homer gave him 50 for three straight years, No one—not even the Babe—had ever done that. Plus, it gave all the Maris chase questions an air of legitimacy. It was McGwire himself who had always said that the only way he had a shot to break the record was to have 50 by Sept. 1. He beat that deadline by 11 days.

14. Farewell Tom

The reason why the coaches took half the title away from Michigan: to give it to Tom Osborne, the retiring legendary coach at Nebraska. In a way, it was the mother of all gold watches. Osborne's Cornhuskers also finished the season undefeated by whipping Tennessee and eventual No. 1 overall draft pick Peyton Manning in the Orange Bowl, sight of many memorable Osborne moments. Final score on this night: Nebraska 42, Tennessee 17. It was a typical Osborne team effort. The quarterback, Scott Frost, completed 9 of 12 passes for 125 yards, but ran for three touchdowns. Ahman Green, the leader of the Husker rushing attack, rushed for an Orange Bowl-record 206 yards and two touchdowns. And the defense battered Manning. Osborne finished his career with a record of 255-49-3, including 60-3 in the last five years.

13. Jeff Van Gundy and Alonzo Mourning

You've heard of people attached at the hip? How about attached at the ankle? Would you believe the Knicks and Heat had another donnybrook in the playoffs? What year is it, you ask? Well, at the tail end of Game 4, with a Knicks victory a foregone conclusion, Alonzo Mourning tried to take a swipe at Larry Johnson. Lots of pushing and shoving broke out, but the one making most of the contact was Knicks coach Jeff Van Gundy who was trying to break up the mess . . . by hanging onto Zo's ankle (see photo p. 347) and not letting go. The sight of a stunned Mourning trying to shake Van Gundy off his ankle—like someone trying to flick a mosquito off his arm—was one of the more, shall we say, comical moments of the season. Certainly one that we'll remember for some time. Not the type of memory the NBA would call fannnn-tastic, but, hey, it's better than a lockout!

12. This Bud's For You

It only took baseball five and a half years to remove the "acting" label from Bud Selig's figurehead title, but on July 9, 1998, five years, nine months and 30 days after the owners fired Fay Vincent, Selig became official commissioner of Major League Baseball. Selig has a lot to work on, but at least baseball HAS a commissioner now, and with the addition of Paul Beeston and Sandy Alderson to the executive branch of baseball, the sport may have a fighting chance of doing something right.

AP/Wide World Photos

In a year filled with great moments in baseball, New York Yankees pitcher **David Wells** made his mark, throwing just the 15th perfect game in history.

11. "Pacer"

NCAA tournament . . . first round . . . Midwest Regional. Mississippi, the fourth seed, had its hands full with 13th-seeded Valparaiso all game. But now the Rebels seemed to have the Crusaders down and virtually out. The Rebels led by two points with 4.5 seconds left and had Ansu Sesay at the free-throw line. He missed both. With 2.5 seconds remaining, Valpo's Jamie Sykes threw a long pass from the baseline past midcourt to Bill Jenkins, who touched it to Bryce Drew, the 1997 Mid-Continent Conference Player of the Year and son of Valparaiso coach Homer Drew. It was a set play. A play Coach Drew dubbed "Pacer." Off-balance, pressured, Drew hit nothing but net and Cinderella advanced . . . all the way to the Round of 16. Long live Valpo!

10. David Wells' Perfect Game

Now with all these baseball stories cracking my top 20, this must mean two things: either baseball had its best regular season ever, or Stuart left me all the baseball stories because he knows it's my favorite sport. Well, it's both. And one of the crowning moments of the baseball season was an event that helped give it that imprimatur of best regular season ever: only the 15th perfect game in the history of the sport, thrown by, of all people, the free-spirited David Wells. Wells had a history of not performing up to his potential. Why, even two starts before his perfect game, Wells imploded in the Texas heat, giving up seven runs in 2⅔ innings. Afterwards, Joe Torre publicly questioned his work ethic, wondering if Wells didn't need to lose weight. He sat down with Torre and two starts later, on May 17, 1998, Wells faced 27 Minnesota Twins and set them all down in order. In front of 49,280 at Yankee Stadium, most of them young children on hand for "Beanie Baby Day," Wells was, for one day, perfect.

9. Mark O'Major

Mark O'Meara came into 1998 best known as Tiger Woods' most famous neighbor...after Ken Griffey Jr. O'Meara was known as the king of the B's, the man who won at Pebble Beach and a couple of other PGA tournaments, but a major?? Hah! Over the previous two years, O'Meara inherited the label of being the best player to never win a major. Who knew he'd wear it like a crown? After an opening round 74, O'Meara stuck around the top of the leaderboard at the Masters. In round two he shot a 70. In round three a 68. And then, in the final round, when everyone was paying attention to the battle between David Duval and Fred Couples, guess who snuck in there? O'Meara stuck birdie putts on 15, 17 and then 18 to shoot a 5-under par-67 to win the green jacket which was fittingly placed on his shoulders by his buddy, Tiger. And what better way to follow up a Masters win than by clutching the Claret Jug? O'Meara went out and won the British Open at Royal Birkdale in exciting fashion, in the distinctive British Open four-hole playoff. He beat the virtually unknown, yet inspired fellow American, Brian Watts to complete the unique American double-play.

8. Iran Beats USA

Team USA finished in 32nd place at this year's World Cup. That's only because there is no 33rd place. After a Cup opening loss to Germany, the Americans had one chance to stave off virtual elimination from advancing to the second round. Beat Iran. However, the Iranians were inspired to beat the Great Satan. In a taut contest that rivaled any major American sports playoff game in terms of intensity, the Americans had no luck at all. Their shots hit more wood than Paul Bunyan's axe. Only a late goal avoided Team USA the embarrassment of being shutout by Iran. USA Soccer was left in shambles, but this game was truly one of the best watches of the year.

7. Michigan Beats Washington St. in the Rose Bowl

After decades upon decades of heartache and pain, the Michigan Wolverines finally won a national championship in football. Only to have the ESPN/USA Today Coaches' poll steal half of it away. But that's a different story. Before 101,219 fans, the Heisman Trophy winner, Charles Woodson, went mano-a-mano with the eventual No. 2 pick in the NFL draft, the gun-slinging Ryan Leaf. It would be the last college game for both players. Michigan led by eight with 11 minutes left. Leaf led the charge and the game came down to the last second on the Michigan 26-yard line, with time running out on Washington State before Leaf could spike the ball to stop the clock. While Cougar fans complained about that call, Michigan fans

AP/Wide World Photos

American **Ernie Stewart** stands dejected as jubilant Iranian players celebrate their win over the United States in the World Cup.

were still steaming over the lack of an offensive pass interference call that led to Leaf being down that far in Wolverine territory anyway. Final Score: Michigan 21, Washington State 16.

6. Tom's River #1

The boys from Tom's River, N.J. did the Garden State and the other 49 states proud, winning the Little League World Series and becoming the first American team to do so since 1993. It was an exhilarating ride for the Jersey kids. It began with an 11-inning, three-hour, 11-minute game (the longest in Little League World Series history) against Jenison, Mich. and ended with a nail-biting 12-9 win over the Far East in the Championship Game that featured 11 home runs. Tom's River shortstop Chris Cardone hit two of them, prompting his manager Mike Gaynor to tell him, "You're my Bucky Dent." Cardone's response? "Who's Bucky Dent?" Oh, man, even I'm feeling old.

5. The Dominator Wins Gold

Take your pick. Dominik Hasek's 20-save, shutout performance in the Gold Medal win over Russia or his semifinal stoning of Canada in the most exciting shootout you'll ever see. His on-his-back, arm-flipping desperation save on Eric Lindros alone was easily the most amazing sequence I've ever seen in ice hockey. Either way, Hasek finished the six-game tournament with a 5-1-0 record, two shutouts, a 0.97 GAA, and a .961 save percentage. It was easily the defining Olympic hockey moment of the year, unless it's Team USA trashing its Olympic Village room.

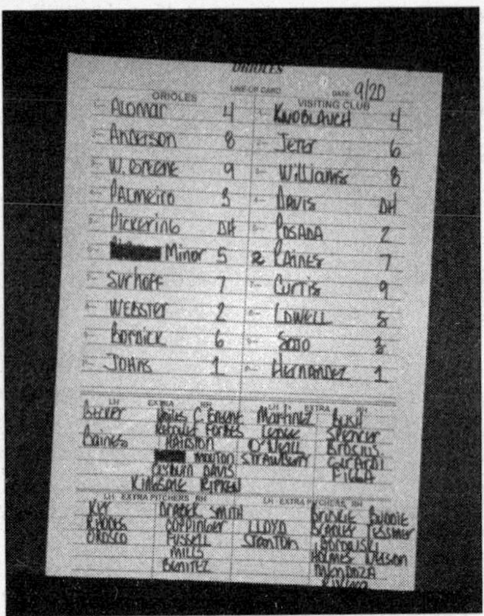

AP/Wide World Sports

The lineup card from the Sept. 20 Baltimore Orioles game with the New York Yankees illustrates a moment that was huge, not because someone did something, but because someone didn't.

4. 20-year-old Kerry Wood Strikes Out His Age

May 6, 1998. 9 IP, 1 H, 0 ER, 0 BB, 20 Ks. Possibly the most dominating pitching line you will ever see. And that hit looks like a line drive here, but in actuality, it was a trickling infield dribbler from Ricky Gutierrez that hit off the glove of third baseman Kevin Orie. Wood struck out the side in the first, fifth, seventh and eighth innings and struck out eight of the last nine Astros he faced to tie Roger Clemens' all-time record for most Ks in a game. It was the first clear-cut sign, before Sammy Sosa went on his home run binge, that the Cubs had something special going in 1998.

3. Cal Sits Down

Alright, yet another baseball moment, another one that helped crown the '98 season baseball's best ever. Cal Ripken Jr., after 2,632 consecutive games played, SAT HIMSELF DOWN. He said he thought it was time. He said he wanted to do it in Baltimore, on the last day of the home schedule, Sept. 20, 1998, because he wanted to share the moment with the fans. And boy did he ever. He signed autographs from the field in between innings. He visited the bullpen during the game and shook hands with fans. And, when the whole night was over, after listening to and answering all the questions, with a flight to Toronto to catch, Cal stood in the parking lot and, as usual, signed more autographs and chatted with the fans.

2. Vlady's Return

It had been a year and five days since Vladimir Konstantinov nearly lost his life in a limousine accident, an accident that occurred on the way home from a team celebration of the Red Wings' first Stanley Cup in nearly a half-century. In the days since, he staved off death, sparked hopes around the globe and worked at rehabilitating his debilitated body. In one of the sweetest sports stories you'll ever witness, one year and five days after his near-death experience, Konstantinov celebrated the second of back-to-back Stanley Cups with his teammates, on the ice in the MCI Center in Washington, D.C.

1. McGwire's 62nd Home Run

The timing couldn't have been more perfect. In the first game after he hit number 61, with the whole world watching, with Sammy Sosa, his colleague, companion and friend in the outfield, with the Maris family children in attendance, with his own son in the dugout, Mark McGwire stepped up to the plate in his second at-bat and belted it. Into a crevice between the stands and the wall. No money-grubbing memorabilia freak had the ball. Just a humble 22-year-old member of the Cardinals grounds crew, who couldn't have been more happy to return the ball to McGwire. For free. Everything was perfect.

My share of the 20-greatest sports moments of 1998 starts with McGwire's record breaking 62nd . . . oh . . . wait a second . . . Rich already got that one . . . that's the trouble with going second. Rich already picked over the good ones. Good thing. There are so many other phat ones. Why should I complain. I got first dibs last year and left Rich with things like- . . . Coaching Comebacks.

Here goes.

20. This One's Personal

OK. Just like last year, I've got a personal moment to share. I'll get it out of the way before I get down to business. On the links . . . at the Jimmy V golf tournament in August. There's a hole-in-one tournament for some of the celebrities. It's about 165 yards. Talk about sticky, intense pressure . . . along with a huge gallery . . . nobody really important watching . . . just Michael Jordan and Charles Barkley. I pull out a 6-iron and—I'll be honest—I'm not so much concerned with hitting the green as I am with just getting it up in the air. No ground balls, no whiffs, no crazy slices. If you've never hit a golf ball with hundreds of eyes on you, then you do not know pressure. As I'm standing over the ball, I almost say out-loud, "just breathe . . . don't think . . . breathe . . . now . . . keep your head behind the ball . . . swing easy" *Ssscchhakk!!* The sweetest sound I've ever heard. Straight up (sure it curved slightly right and landed on the right fringe) but it was no worse than anyone else's shot. One swing. One moment. My moment. Money.

19. The Other Three-peat

A three-peat for the "three Meeks." Actually Tennessee's three-peat national championship was just a three-peat for All-Galaxy Chamique Holdsclaw. Tamika Catchings and Semeka Randall were the newcomers on Pat Summitt's team this year. All three will be back next year. Anybody gonna bet against them taking four in a row?

18. She's No Tiger

It'd be too easy and too simple to call golfer Se Ri Pak a "women's Tiger Woods." After all, Tiger only won one major. Pak won two—two straight. Her latest major win was at an epic U.S. Women's Open. Pak took the title on the second hole of sudden-death after a dramatic 18-hole playoff against amateur—and fellow rising star—Jenny Chuasiriporn. Did I mention Pak was a rookie on the LPGA Tour?

17. Mr. Smith Goes To Lexington

Rick Pitino won a national title at Kentucky. Rick Pitino left. The UK basketball coaching duties were picked up by Tubby Smith. The irony was lost on no one that Smith, an African-American, was taking over a program made great by Adolph Rupp, who refused to recruit African-Americans. Smith didn't become Kentucky's "black" coach, he became Kentucky's national championship-winning coach.

16. Football Futures

The future of the NFL went 1-2 in the draft. They were two high-priced, big-time, "pin-your-hopes-and-dreams -on-this-kid" quarterbacks. Peyton Manning and Ryan Leaf. They said Manning was the more polished quarterback, that he had completed more passes in college than Ryan Leaf had even attempted. They said Leaf had the stronger arm. Truth is, Leaf is more polished than people think and Manning's arm is stronger than people think. It shows you can't always believe what you read.

15. France 3, Brazil 0

The biggest sporting event in the world took place on their home stage and everybody thought mighty Brazil would win another trophy. But talk about a phat party on the Champs-D'Elysses. France wins the World Cup.

14. Jana's Turn

The year's biggest tennis moment didn't belong to Martina Hingis. It wasn't one of the young guns, Venus or Serena Williams, or Anna Kournikova. It wasn't the sentimental choice, Monica Seles. It wasn't the fast-rising Lindsay Davenport. It belonged to Jana Novotna and her Wimbledon moment. Her first grand slam singles title.

13. Tara vs. Michelle

They were the two best figure skaters in the world. Everybody knew it. They both had been world champions before. It came down to Tara Lipinski and Michelle Kwan for the Olympic Gold Medal. And Lipinski, who after the preliminaries was in danger of not even making the finals, took home the gold.

AP/Wide World Photos

Injured UConn star **Nykesha Sales** took part in one of the more controversial moments of the year when she scored this pre-arranged, uncontested basket to give her the school scoring record.

12. Garrison Downs Jets

Week one in the NFL. What in the world were the Jets doing taking the 49ers to overtime? What was Glenn Foley doing throwing for over 400 yards? What were the Jets doing backing the Niners up on their own 2-yard line in OT??? Obviously, New York was just watching because Garrison Hearst broke bad with a 98-yard overtime touchdown run. Steve Sabol, president of NFL Films, called it the most dramatic run in NFL history.

11. Ruben's Tribute

On Feb. 19, University of Cincinnati basketball star Ruben Patterson lost his mother. Almost anyone else would've been too distraught to do ANYTHING that day. Go to work, to class, to even function. Patterson wanted to pay a tribute to his mom. He figured the best way to do that was to play that night's Bearcats game as scheduled. It was the most touching 32 points scored all year.

10. The Most Talked About Two Points of the Year

No matter how you feel about it, the two points that put Nykesha Sales atop UConn's all-time scoring list created more water cooler debates than anything except the Clinton scandal. Yes, she was hurt. Yes, it was a gimme. But don't blame her. She didn't ask for it, and as a youngster, how could she say no to her coach who wanted to do it for her?? Maybe you think Geno Auriemma's decision was wrong. His motives, however, were not.

9. About Time for Elway

Now for our "finally" segment. The winningest quarterback in NFL history, the guy with the most fourth-quarter comebacks, the guy destined for the Hall of Fame, finally got a Super Bowl ring. Winning made it easier for John Elway to admit what he'd been untruthful about all these years. The absence of a Super Bowl win really did hurt.

8. Every Dog Has His Daytona

Another entry that falls under the heading of "finally." After a record-tying seven Winston Cup Championships, after more wins at the Daytona International Speedway than anybody else, but no Daytona 500 checkered flags to show for it, Dale Earnhardt finally won NASCAR's most coveted trophy. He then showed that "The Intimidator" is just a little kid, doing impromptu donuts in the infield after the race.

7. Keeping Up With Jones

No one had even come close to Flo Jo's 100-meter mark, that is until Marion Jones came along. Jones quickly established herself as one of the top female athletes in the world by winning the world championship in the 100. Later she also set a personal best with a 10.65-second hundred. She was faster than anybody . . . since Flo Jo.

6. A Big Loss

We remembered Florence Griffith Joyner for her beauty, brains (understanding that her sport needed flair to get attention) and her speed. The sports world lost a gem when Flo Jo passed away. The Olympic gold medalist crushed world records in the 100 and 200 ten years ago. Those records still stood at the time of her death.

5. Locked Out

More NBA, or lack thereof. David Stern, generally regarded as the best commissioner in pro sports, met just as worthy an opponent in Billy Hunter, president of the NBA Players Association. They're two powerful, smart, stubborn men and when neither backs down, you have an NBA lockout that cancelled regular season games for the first time in league history.

4. Mailman Braves Ring

From Jordan and his Bulls to the most, uh . . . "interesting" Bull and his NBA Finals power forward opponent. Dennis Rodman, you'd expect to see in a pro wrestling ring. Karl Malone, you wouldn't. But for all the critics, Karl is a grown man, a former MVP, very respected and he doesn't care what people think. He likes wrestling. He understands its entertainment value and just wanted to do it.

AP/Wide World Photos

Karl Malone chose to enter the world of professional wrestling (temporarily, at least) providing us with one of the more surreal sports moments of the year. Above, Malone, who is not used to choking when it comes to sports, gets abused by **Hollywood Hulk Hogan**.

3. Jordan Does It Once Again

If it weren't so unreal, the repetitiveness of Michael Jordan would become boring. But it is unreal. Just when you thought he couldn't top his Game 5 from '97, when he was sick and led the Bulls to victory, along comes MJ in Game 6 of the '98 Finals. Scottie Pippen's back was in severe distress. Pip, courageously played on, but it was MJ who strapped the team on his back, scored 45 points, stole the ball from Karl Malone late, held his pose after shaking Byron Russell out of his high-tops and hit the game-winning shot. MJ . . . the best ever.

2. McGwire Ties Maris

If McGwire's 62nd and 70th were special, you can't leave out his 61st. Big Mac's son Matthew showed up just before the game, gave dad a big hug and watched. Also watching from the stands was McGwire's dad, who turned 61 years old that same day. Number 61 on dad's 61st birthday.

1. Don't Forget About Sammy

If McGwire's 62nd counts, Sammy Sosa's has to as well. Actually, we have to put Sosa's 61st and 62nd together because he hit them on the same day. So what if Bud Selig didn't show up even though he lived just 90 miles away. So what if baseball dropped the ball when they didn't specially mark Sosa's balls like they did McGwire's. It was still a special moment for a special ballplayer. Yes, Sammy Sosa has been "bery, bery" good for baseball. ■

Calendar

On April 20, 1998, Australian-born wheelchair racer **Louise Sauvage** (l) lunges across the finish line ahead of seven-time winner **Jean Driscoll** in what is the closest finish in the Boston Marathon's 102-year history. Both racers recorded an official time of 1:41:19.

AP/Wide World Photos

NOV '97

Sun	Mon	Tue	Wed	Thu	Fri	Sat
						1
2	3	4	5	6	7	8
9	10	11	12	13	14	15
16	17	18	19	20	21	22
23/30	24	25	26	27	28	29

Sizzling/Sad Starts

On November 25, Tim Hardaway and the Miami Heat beat the Lakers, 103-86 for their first blemish of the 1997-98 season after 11 consecutive wins. Conversely, the Denver Nuggets lost their first 12 games of the season before finally beating the Minnesota Timberwolves, 95-84 on November 28. Below are the best and worst starts in NBA history.

	Most Wins
Washington Capitols, 1948-49	15
Houston Rockets, 1993-94	15
Boston Celtics, 1957-58	14
Chicago Bulls, 1996-97	12
Seattle SuperSonics, 1982-83	12

	Most Losses
Miami Heat, 1988-89	17
L.A. Clippers, 1994-95	16
Philadelphia 76ers, 1972-73	15
Cleveland Cavaliers, 1970-71	15
Denver Nuggets, 1949-50	15

Consecutive PGA Wins

David Duval won the Tour Championship on November 2 for his third consecutive PGA tournament victory. Duval would have to keep his streak going well into the 1998 season, however, if he wanted to break Byron Nelson's astonishing mark of 11 consecutive tour victories.

	Consecutive PGA Wins
Byron Nelson, 1945	11
Ben Hogan, 1948	6
Jackie Burke Jr., 1952	4
Byron Nelson, 1945	4
Ben Hogan, 1953	4
Accomplished by 31 players	3

1 **Former Celtic great Larry Bird** earns the first win of his NBA coaching career as the Indiana Pacers beat the Golden St. Warriors, 96-83.

Boston University football players don generic white jerseys with no logo in a 45-7 loss to UConn in protest to the school's decision to drop its football program after the season.

2 **David Duval cards** a final round 68 at the Tour Championship to win his third consecutive PGA Tour victory, the first three of his career. Tiger Woods ties for 12th but takes home $97,600 which boosts him over the $2 million mark for the season.

Kenyan John Kagwe wins the 28th New York City Marathon in 2:08:12 despite stopping twice to tie his shoes.

3 **Red Sox shortstop** Nomar Garciaparra earns all 28 first-place votes to become the 13th unanimous American League Rookie of the Year.

4 **Phillies' third baseman** Scott Rolen unanimously wins the National League Rookie of the Year Award, making it only the third time that both rookie winners are chosen by unanimous selection.

5 **Davey Johnson** resigns as manager of the American League East champion Baltimore Orioles amidst recent conflicts with club owner Peter Angelos. Later in the day, he is voted AL Manager of the Year.

Milwaukee Brewers become the first major league team this century to switch leagues, moving from the AL Central to the NL Central beginning in 1998.

6 **Dusty Baker** is crowned NL Manager of the Year for the second time after leading the surprising San Francisco Giants to the NL West title.

8 **Skip Away edges** Deputy Commander by ¾ of a length to win the $4 million Breeders' Cup Classic at Hollywood Park. Other Breeders' Cup winners include turf horse Chief Bearhart, juvenile Favorite Trick, Spinning World, Ajina, Elmhurst, and Countess Diana.

Top-ranked Nebraska runs its record to 9-0 with a stunning 45-38 OT win over Missouri, highlighted by receiver Scott Davison's miracle game-tying catch off the foot of teammate Shevin Wiggins with no time left in regulation.

Heavyweight Evander Holyfield floors Michael Moorer twice in the seventh round and then finally puts him away at the end of the eighth to capture his second heavyweight championship belt. The WBA and IBF champ now needs just the WBC title, held by Lennox Lewis, to unify the division.

Washington Capital Phil Housley becomes the second American-born player and the fifth defenseman in NHL history to accumulate 1,000 points in a career.

9 **USA soccer** cruises to a 3-0 victory over Canada to clinch a berth in the 1998 World Cup in France.

Chris Simon of the Washington Capitals is suspended for three games by the NHL for uttering a racial remark directed at Edmonton forward Mike Grier.

10 **Toronto ace Roger Clemens** wins the American League Cy Young award, becoming the first AL pitcher to win four in a career.

11 **Florida Marlins** begin to cut payroll and dismantle their world championship team, trading left fielder Moises Alou to the Houston Astros for three minor leaguers.

Montreal Expo Pedro Martinez earns 25 of 28 first-place votes to win the National League Cy Young award, outdistancing four-time winner Greg Maddux, 134 points to 75. He is the first Expo and the first Dominican to win the award.

AP/Wide World Photos

Vancouver's **Mark Messier** shows his emotions on Nov. 25 while watching a tribute to him at his first return to Madison Square Garden since becoming a free agent. The popular former captain of the Rangers spent six seasons in New York and in 1994 led them to their first Stanley Cup since 1940.

NBC and Turner Broadcasting sign new contracts with the NBA, whereby they retain television rights to the NBA until 2002. The two networks commit to paying a combined $2.64 billion over the next four years, a 140 percent increase over the deal about to expire.

12 Seattle's Ken Griffey Jr. unanimously wins his first American League MVP award, outpolling first basemen Tino Martinez and Frank Thomas.

13 Iron Mike Keenan returns to the coaching ranks, replacing Vancouver Canucks coach Tom Renney one day after the team ends a 10-game losing streak.

Colorado outfielder Larry Walker becomes the first Rockies player to win the National League MVP award and the first Canadian in either league to take home the prize.

16 Jeff Gordon races to a 17th place finish at the NAPA 500 on nearly bald tires to win his second NASCAR Winston Cup points championship. Needing to finish in the top 18 to win the title, a pre-race accident forces him to use his backup car.

Doug Flutie leads the Toronto Argonauts to a 47-23 pounding of the Saskatchewan Rough Riders for their second consecutive CFL Grey Cup win. Flutie, the game and league MVP, throws for three touchdowns and runs for another.

18 Youth and pitching are the hot commodities at the Major League Baseball expansion draft as the Tampa Bay Devil Rays and Arizona Diamondbacks spurn high-priced veteran free agents for youngsters. Tampa Bay selects Florida Marlins 23-year-old LHP Tony Saunders with the first overall pick.

Boston Red Sox acquire NL Cy Young award winner Pedro Martinez from the Montreal Expos for pitching prospects Carl Pavano and Tony Armas Jr.

20 St. Louis Rams release oft-troubled running back Lawrence Phillips amidst a myriad of on and off-the-field problems.

Dallas Maverick A.C. Green plays in his 907th consecutive NBA game, passing Randy Smith as the league's all-time iron man. Green still has a way to go to catch Ron Boone's record of 1,041 straight games played. Boone's streak was tallied in eight seasons in the ABA followed by five in the NBA.

Isiah Thomas resigns as general manager of the 1-9 Toronto Raptors to join NBC Sports.

22 Michigan ends its regular season as it normally does, beating up on Ohio State 20-14. Also, Florida ruins Florida State's hopes for a national title with a 32-29 victory.

Heavyweight George Foreman loses a controversial majority decision to Shannon Briggs. The 48-year-old announces his retirement immediately after the fight.

23 Annika Sorenstam wins the LPGA Tour Championship in Las Vegas on the third playoff hole to give her a record $1,236,789 in winnings for the season.

25 The Los Angeles Lakers, playing without center Shaquille O'Neal, lose their first game of the season, 103-86 to the Miami Heat, after beginning the season with 11 straight wins.

29 Grambling legend Eddie Robinson coaches the last game of his 56-year career, a 30-7 loss to rival Southern University in the Bayou Classic.

Swedes Jonas Bjorkman and Nicklas Kulti pound Americans Todd Martin and Jonathan Stark, 6-4, 6-4, 6-4 to clinch the Davis Cup title for Sweden for the sixth time in history and second time in four years.

DEC '97

Sun	Mon	Tue	Wed	Thu	Fri	Sat
	1	2	3	4	5	6
7	8	9	10	11	12	13
14	15	16	17	18	19	20
21	22	23	24	25	26	27
28	29	30	31			

Title Hoarders

Although the Chicago Bulls have ruled the headlines as the NBA's current dynasty, many wildly successful programs at the collegiate level have gone relatively unnoticed. On Dec. 7, the North Carolina women's soccer team won their 9th NCAA championship in the last 10 years. Few other teams have been so successful, but a handful of NCAA sports have been dominated recently. Below is a ranking of the most national titles won in the past 10 seasons (through Dec. '97).

Titles	Sport	School
10	Women's Outdoor Track	LSU
9	Women's Soccer	N. Carolina
9	Coed Rifle	W. Virginia
9	Men's Indoor Track	Arkansas
7	Women's Indoor Track	LSU
6	Women's X-Country	Villanova
6	Women's Swimming	Stanford
6	Men's Outdoor Track	Arkansas
6	Wrestling	Iowa

San Francisco T(h)REAT

On Dec. 15, Joe Montana returned to San Francisco to have his number retired. The former Notre Dame standout teamed with Jerry Rice to form one of the greatest touchdown combinations in league history. Remarkably, the Montana-to-Rice tandem is not the top combination in NFL history or even in the 49ers' record books. Below is a list of the most prolific TD tandems in league history as of Dec. '97.

TDs	Quarterback	Receiver
79	Dan Marino	Mark Clayton
75	Steve Young	Jerry Rice
65	Jim Kelly	Andre Reed
63	Johnny Unitas	Raymond Berry
56	Jay Hadel	Lance Alworth
55	Joe Montana	Jerry Rice

1 Warrior guard Latrell Sprewell attacks head coach P.J. Carlesimo during practice and is suspended for ten games.

Bleacher-bomber Matt Williams is traded from Cleveland to the expansion Arizona Diamondbacks for third baseman Travis Fryman. The power-hitter also signs a five-year, $45 million contract extension, which places him seventh on baseball's salary list.

2 San Francisco 49ers owner and chairman, Eddie DeBartolo Jr., resigns from his position after reports surface that he is involved in a gambling conspiracy.

The MCI Center opens in Washington, D.C. as the hometown Wizards post a 95-78 win over the Seattle Supersonics. The arena is equipped with a restaurant overlooking the floor, a complete sports museum and a full size practice court.

NFL badboy Lawrence Phillips signs a two-year deal with the Miami Dolphins. The troubled running back resurfaces after being waived by the St. Louis Rams following numerous discipline problems.

4 The NBA suspends Golden State guard Latrell Sprewell for a year, pending a hearing, just one day after the Warriors waive his contract.

Chicago White Sox hire Jerry Manuel as their new manager after his successful 1997 campaign as the Florida Marlins bench coach.

Former Redskins quarterback Doug Williams replaces college football's all-time winningest coach, Eddie Robinson, at Grambling State University. Williams, the 1988 Super Bowl MVP, once played for Robinson, who leaves the school after 57 years.

5 Stevin Smith and Isaac Burton Jr. plead guilty to conspiracy charges after they admit to receiving bribes to fix four Arizona State basketball games.

6 Senior Chris McCoy leads the Naval Academy to a 39-7 victory over Army to end a five-game losing streak versus the Cadets. The star quarterback tallies 208 rushing yards, 74 passing yards and scores four touchdowns in the rout.

7 North Carolina women's soccer team wins their 15th NCAA title with a 2-0 decision over the University of Connecticut.

Nick Price posts a final round 68 to win the Million Dollar Challenge over Davis Love III and Ernie Els.

Super Bowl Champion Green Bay Packers clinch their third consecutive NFC Central title with a 17-6 win over the Tampa Bay Buccaneers.

8 The Cleveland Indians sign free agent outfielder Kenny Lofton and pitcher Dwight Gooden. The same day, Lofton, who was traded by the Indians in 1996 for Marquis Grissom, saw his trade counterpart shipped to Milwaukee in a five-player deal that brought three pitchers, including Ben McDonald, to Cleveland.

9 University of Michigan wrestler Jeff Reese collapses and dies during a workout as he attempts to make weight for the season opener by exercising in a rubber suit.

10 Coaching legend Tom Osborne announces that he will retire from the University of Nebraska at the end of the season, ending his 25 years with the football program. Osborne will leave Lincoln as college football's winningest active coach with a win percentage of .836 and three national championships.

11 Holdout Paul Kariya signs a two-year deal with the Mighty Ducks of Anaheim that will pay him a record $8.5 million in his second year.

AP/Wide World Photos

Latrell Sprewell addresses the media on Dec. 9, 1997 in Oakland, Calif. and explains his reasons for choking Golden State Warriors coach P.J. Carlesimo. His agent **Arn Tellem** (c) and lawyer **Johnnie Cochran** (r) look on.

12 $75 million is the price tag on National League Cy Young award winner Pedro Martinez, who agrees to a six-year deal with the Boston Red Sox.

13 And the Heisman goes to... Michigan defensive back Charles Woodson, who not only becomes the first primarily defensive player to win the 67-year old award, but spoils Peyton Manning's perfectly planned senior season.

14 MVP Seth George scores twice as UCLA outshoots Virginia 2-0 to win their third NCAA men's soccer championship.

Preseason cellar-pick New York Giants clinch the NFC East title with a 30-10 win over division rival Washington Redskins.

15 The dismantling Florida Marlins make their fifth major move of the offseason by unloading pitching ace Kevin Brown to the San Diego Padres for three prospects.

Joe Montana returns to San Francisco to have his number retired, while his favorite wide receiver, Jerry Rice, returns from "season-ending" knee surgery to catch a touchdown pass. Rice re-injures his knee in the game, ending his season for a second time.

17 John Robinson is fired as coach of USC after he fails to maintain a winning program following the Trojans' Rose Bowl victory two years ago.

Flyers center Eric Lindros matches the contract of the Ducks' Paul Kariya by receiving a contract revision that will pay him $8.5 million next season.

18 Sixers swingman Jerry Stackhouse is traded to the Pistons in an attempt to rebuild Philadelphia's backcourt chemistry. Philadelphia receives Aaron McKie and Theo Ratliff in the deal which also sends center Eric Montross to Motown.

19 Home run hitter Cecil Fielder leaves the Yankees for the sunshine of Anaheim, signing a one-year contract with the Angels.

21 Barry Sanders becomes the third man in NFL history to rush for 2,000 yards in a season. The Lions' running back gains 184 yards in the final game of the year to finish with 2,053, joining Eric Dickerson (2,105 in 1984) and O.J. Simpson (2,003 in 1973) in the record books.

Knicks' Patrick Ewing has season-ending surgery on his wrist following a hard foul by Milwaukee's Andrew Lang the night before.

22 It might be an outstanding record for Prairie View A&M, but the 3-13 Indianapolis Colts want nothing to do with it as they fire head coach Lindy Infante.

23 Penn St. running back Curtis Enis announces he will not play in the Citrus Bowl because he lied to his coach about an agent purchasing a suit for him.

Bulls' guru Phil Jackson wins his 500th career game, reaching the plateau faster than any other coach in NBA history.

27 New York Giants collapse and allow the Vikings to score nine points in the final 90 seconds as Minnesota steals the wild card game 23-22.

Barry Sanders and Brett Favre each receive eighteen votes and a share of the NFL's MVP award.

28 Patriots' defense holds down the fort in Foxboro as New England defeats Miami for the third time this season and the second in only six days, as they move to the AFC Divisional playoff game with a 17-3 win.

30 Tiger Woods and Martina Hingis are named as the Associated Press Male and Female Athletes of the Year.

JAN '98

Sun	Mon	Tue	Wed	Thu	Fri	Sat
				1	2	3
4	5	6	7	8	9	10
11	12	13	14	15	16	17
18	19	20	21	22	23	24
25	26	27	28	29	30	31

Rocky Mountain Low

The Denver Nuggets tied the NBA single season record for consecutive losses when they dropped their 23rd straight contest at Phoenix on Jan. 23. The Nuggets were able to avoid total infamy by beating the Clippers on Jan. 24, ending the streak one game short of the overall record. It was not enough, however, to save Allan Bristow's job. The Nuggets vice president of basketball operations would get the boot in early February with the team's record at 4-42. Below is a ranking of the league's longest losing streaks.

24: Cleveland Cavaliers, 3/19/82–11/5/82 (19 games in 1981-82, five games in 1982-83)

23: Vancouver Grizzlies, 2/16/96–4/3/96

23: Denver Nuggets, 12/9/97–1/23/98

21: Detroit Pistons, 3/7/80–10/22/80 (14 games in 1979-80, seven games in 1980-81)

20: L.A. Clippers, 4/18/94–12/5/94 (four games in 1993-94, 16 games in 1994-95)

20: Dallas Mavericks, 11/13/93–12/22/93

20: New York Knicks, 3/23/85–11/9/85 (12 games in 1984-85, eight games in 1985-86)

Against All Odds

The Denver Broncos were 11-point underdogs heading into Super Bowl XXXII. Their seven-point victory was the third biggest upset in the big game's history.

Spread	
18 pts	NY Jets over favorite Baltimore (Super Bowl III), 16-7
12 pts	Kansas City over favorite Minnesota (Super Bowl IV), 23-7
11 pts	**Denver over favorite Green Bay, (Super Bowl XXXII), 31-24**
7 pts	NY Giants over favorite Buffalo (Super Bowl XXV), 20-19

1 **The Michigan Wolverines** end a perfect 12–0 campaign defeating #8 Washington State 21-16 in the Rose Bowl. Blowouts headline the other games as Georgia knocks off unranked Wisconsin at the Outback bowl, the "Mack Brown-less" North Carolina Tarheels suffocate Virginia Tech at the Gator Bowl, and #4 Florida State handles #10 Ohio State at the Sugar.

2 **Split polls result** in NCAA football co-champions as Nebraska routs #3 Tennessee 42-17 in the Orange Bowl. The Cornhuskers' impressive performance earns them first place in the coaches' poll while Michigan is tops with the media.

Ryan Leaf, Washington State's field general and quarterback, announces that he will forego his final year of eligibility and enter the NFL Draft.

3 **A crowd of 24,597 shows up** in Knoxville to watch the #1 Tennessee Lady Vols defeat the #3 UConn Huskies 84-69, setting a collegiate women's basketball attendance record.

5 **The fifth time is the charm** for retired Dodgers pitcher Don Sutton, who is elected to Baseball's Hall of Fame by receiving 386 votes from the media. Former Cincinnati Reds' first baseman Tony Perez falls 34 votes shy of the honor.

Defensive Coordinator Wade Phillips is named the Bills' head coach just one week after Marv Levy retires.

6 **The 4-12 Oakland Raiders** release head coach Joe Bugel following his first season after posting the franchise's worst record since 1962.

Six months in jail is the sentence handed down to former heavyweight boxer Tommy Morrison following a drunk-driving accident which injured three people.

Billionaire Tom Hicks buys the Texas Rangers from a group led by Texas Governor George W. Bush for $250 million.

Michigan head coach Lloyd Carr is named Division I coach of the year by the American Football Coaches Association.

8 **Figure skater Todd Eldredge** wins his fifth U.S. national figure skating title and Michael Weiss and Scott Davis round out the Olympic qualifiers.

Marshall wide receiver Randy Moss, who caught a record 26 touchdown passes, will forego his final two years of college and enter the NFL draft. Texas' NCAA rushing and scoring leader Ricky Williams will return to the Longhorns for his final year.

9 **Heisman Trophy winner Charles Woodson** announces he will turn pro and forego his final season with the Michigan Wolverines.

10 **Michelle Kwan, Tara Lipinski** and Nicole Bobek finish 1-2-3 at the US national figure skating championships. It's Kwan's second title, while Lipinski and Bobek are also former winners.

11 **Casey Martin rides to victory** at the Lakeland (Fla.) Classic with a final round 69. The 25-year-old golfer, who is suing the PGA Tour because they will not allow him to use a golf cart for his congenital leg disability, uses the cart during the Nike Tour event.

12 **The NFL returns to CBS** for the record price of $4 billion. The eight year deal gives the network rights to the AFC and marks the first time since 1965 that NBC will not be a part of the NFL.

The shake-up gets underway in Dallas as coach Barry Switzer resigns under pressure from owner Jerry Jones.

One-time Saint top dog Jim Mora leaves NBC to become the head coach of the struggling 3–13 Indianapolis Colts.

Archive Photos

The crowd at the 1998 U.S. Figure Skating Championships in Philadelphia is dazzled by the precision of 1996 national champion **Michelle Kwan**, who records 15 perfect 6.0's in her two performances, making her the gold-medal-favorite at next month's Olympic Winter Games.

13 Completing the NFL's mega television deal, ESPN and ABC pay $600 and $550 million a year, respectively, for their weekly primetime NFL games.

15 Fox Sports signs John Madden to a five-year contract extension worth $8 million a year.

17 Swimmer Jenny Thompson caps off a strong United States effort in the World Championships with a silver medal in the 800 meter freestyle relay to add to her four golds.

18 Robert Parish's '00' is raised to the rafters in Boston as the Celtics' great has his number retired during halftime of the Pacers 103-96 win, marking Larry Bird's return to Beantown.

North America conquers the World in the NHL All-Star game. MVP Teemu Selanne records a hat trick for the World team, but the Americans rally on Mark Messier's goal to win 8-7.

It is showtime in Lake Buena Vista, Florida as MVP Shalonda Enis scores 15 points to lead the West team to a 102-73 ABL All-Star game victory. The weekend is highlighted by a blindfolded jam by Sylvia Crawley in the inaugural dunk contest.

19 Legendary play-by-play man Chick Hearn broadcasts his 3,000th consecutive Los Angeles Laker game. The play-by-play announcer has only missed two games in 38 years, one because he was delayed at the Bob Hope Classic Golf Tournament and the other due to bad weather.

Mike Tyson is hungry to get back into the ring, but the former heavyweight champ announces at a press conference that he will only be a referee in Wrestlemania XIV.

20 Washington Wizard Chris Webber is arrested and charged with assault, resisting arrest, possession of marijuana, driving under the influence of marijuana and other traffic violations during a routine speeding stop.

21 The golfing world mourns the loss of three-time Senior PGA Tour winner Larry Gilbert, who dies at the age of 55 from lung cancer.

22 Oakland Raiders hire Philadelphia Eagles offensive coordinator Jon Gruden as head coach. The 34-year-old Gruden, the third head coach for the Raiders in as many seasons, becomes the youngest head coach in the NFL.

24 The Denver Nuggets end their 23-game losing streak with a 99-81 road win over the Los Angeles Clippers.

25 Denver Broncos pull the upset and beat the heavily-favored Green Bay Packers, 31-24, in Super Bowl XXXII, becoming the first AFC team to win the NFL championship since 1984. Bronco Terrell Davis, despite missing most of the second quarter with a migraine, rushes for 157 yards and a record three touchdowns, earning MVP honors.

27 Goalkeeper Jorge Campos, perhaps the most popular player in Major League Soccer, is traded from the Los Angeles Galaxy to the Chicago Fire in a four-player deal.

31 Martina Hingis retains her Australian Open championship, dispatching challenger Conchita Martinez, 6-3, 6-3, making her the youngest player in 110 years to successfully defend a Grand Slam title.

FEB '98

Sun	Mon	Tue	Wed	Thu	Fri	Sat
1	2	3	4	5	6	7
8	9	10	11	12	13	14
15	16	17	18	19	20	21
22	23	24	25	26	27	28

A Little Help from my Friends

FEB 24–Nykesha Sales's record-breaking shot isn't the first time in sports history achievements have been made under questionable circumstances:

9/27/97 – Randy Johnson of the Seattle Mariners, normally a starter, replaces pitcher Omar Olivares at the start of the fifth inning with the Mariners ahead, 7-2, in order to win his 20th game and become the first Seattle pitcher to reach the milestone. He responds with two shutout innings and is awarded the win.

3/20/96 – Anthony Bowie of the Orlando Magic needs one more assist for his first career triple-double and calls a timeout with 2.7 seconds left and his team ahead by a comfortable margin. Detroit Pistons coach Doug Collins is furious about the ploy and orders his team off the floor. With no defenders on the court, Bowie passes the ball for his 10th assist and the tainted triple-double.

4/24/94 – David Robinson of the San Antonio Spurs scores 71 points against the Los Angeles Clippers on the final day of the NBA regular season to win the scoring title. Robinson's effort gave him an average of 29.787 per game to edge Shaquille O'Neal's 29.346. Coach John Lucas and his players later acknowledge that aside from trying to beat the Los Angeles Clippers it was their collective goal to help Robinson take the scoring title.

9/19/68 – Detroit Tigers pitcher Denny McLain serves up three straight fastballs over the middle of the plate to Mickey Mantle who hits the third one for his 535th home run, moving him past Jimmie Foxx and into third place on the career homer list.

1 **Game MVP Warren Moon rallies** the AFC, which trailed by 14 points at halftime, for a touchdown with 1:49 left and defeats the NFC, 29-24, in the NFL Pro Bowl.

Casey Martin's suit against the PGA Tour for the right to use a golf cart under the Americans With Disabilities Act opens in Martin's hometown of Eugene, Ore.

2 **Head Coach Doug Collins is fired** by the Detroit Pistons after a 21-24 start and is replaced by assistant Alvin Gentry.

3 **A group led by novelist Tom Clancy** makes a preliminary offer to buy the Minnesota Vikings for $200 million.

Yankees GM Bob Watson, the only minority general manager in the major leagues, resigns and is replaced by his assistant Brian Cashman.

American sprinter Maurice Greene follows through on his bold prediction and breaks his own world indoor record in the 60-meter-run (6.39 seconds) in Madrid.

The Rhode Island Rams' mascot is ejected after a fracas breaks out at mid-court between it and the Hawk from St. Joseph's just seconds after the Ram tossed an inner tube around the Philly fowl.

4 **A blockbuster three-team deal is inked** in MLS, sending the league's all-time leading scorer Washington D.C.'s Raul Diaz Arce to New England, while Revolution star Alexi Lalas is shipped to the New York/New Jersey Metrostars. In return Washington gets draft picks, including New England's #1 in 1999.

5 **Antawn Jamison scores 35 points and rips** down 11 rebounds powering #2 North Carolina past #1 Duke, 97-73. The Tarheels are 6-0 all-time in #1 vs. #2 games.

6 **Minnesota second baseman** Chuck Knoblauch is dealt to the Yankees for $3 million and four New York prospects, ending months of rumors and scenarios.

7 **Opening ceremonies** are held in Nagano, Japan, the site of the 18th Olympic Winter Games.

The NHL breaks its regular season action so players can travel to Nagano and represent their nations' teams at the Olympics.

8 **Michael Jordan scores** a game-high 23 points and brings home his third career MVP trophy in possibly his last NBA All-Star game as his East team defeats the West team, 135-114.

Charlotte Hornets power forward Anthony Mason and his cousin are released on $20,000 bail after being charged with statutory rape and sexual abuse of two girls over the weekend.

9 **Boston University's Nick Gillis scores** at 5:51 of overtime, sparking the Terriers to a 2-1 victory over Harvard in the title game of the 46th Beanpot College Hockey Tournament.

10 **"The miracle on turf" stuns soccer fans** in America and horrifies them in Brazil as the U.S. upsets the Brazilians 1-0 in the CONCACAF Gold Cup.

11 **U.S. Magistrate Judge Thomas Coffin** in Oregon awards golf's newest cult hero, Casey Martin, the right to keep his motorized golf cart.

Jonny Moseley ends the U.S. medal drought in Nagano, winning a gold in the freestyle skiing men's moguls.

Tiger Woods wins two awards and shares a third, Male Athlete of the Year, with Ken Griffey Jr. at ESPN's annual ESPY Awards Show in New York.

Archive Photos

Closing ceremony fireworks light up the evening sky over **Minami Park** as the world says "sayonara" to Nagano, Japan which played host to the final Olympic Games of the 20th century.

12 Cowboys owner Jerry Jones names former Steelers offensive coordinator Chan Gailey head coach of "America's Team" after interviewing several candidates.

15 Legendary driver Dale Earnhardt, like John Elway three weeks earlier, rips the proverbial albatross from around his neck, winning his first Daytona 500 in 20 tries.

Golfer John Huston sizzles in the Pacific sun, firing a 28-under-par 260 at the final Hawaiian Open (to be replaced by the Sony Classic in Hawaii in 1999) and breaking a PGA record for shots under par.

16 Goalie Patrick Roy makes 30 saves and Keith Primeau scores two goals, helping Canada avenge its World Cup embarrassment by defeating the United States 4-1 in the first round of the Olympic ice hockey tournament.

Toronto point guard Damon Stoudamire, Walt Williams and Carlos Rogers are sent to Portland in exchange for Kenny Anderson, Gary Trent and Alvin Williams, two first-round draft picks and a second-round choice.

17 Minnesota Vikings re-sign DT John Randle to a five-year, $32.5 million contract, making him the highest paid defensive player in league history.

18 "The biggest waste of time. Ever," says Keith Tkachuk after America's hockey "Dream Team" is eliminated from the quarterfinal round with a 4-1 loss to the Czech Republic, making it five straight medalless games for the U.S. since "The Miracle on Ice."

Norwegian cross country skier Bjorn Dählie wins his second gold medal at Nagano, (10k and 40k relay) giving him a Winter Olympic record seven career golds and 11 medals overall.

19 The New York Rangers hire 64-year-old John Muckler one day after axing head coach Colin Campbell.

20 Czech goalie Dominik Hasek gets in the way of Canada's trip to the gold medal game. The Czechs beat the tournament favorites in a shootout, 1-0, after the game ends tied after one overtime.

Fifteen-year-old Tara Lipinski edges teammate Michelle Kwan and becomes the youngest woman ever to win the Olympic gold medal in figure skating.

22 Despite having the least amount of NHL players of any team in the medal round (11), the Czech Republic finishes it's amazing run in Nagano, defeating Russia 1-0 in the gold medal final.

Closing ceremonies are held in Nagano, bringing the 18th Winter Games to a close.

24 Forward Nykesha Sales becomes Connecticut's all-time women's basketball scoring leader after the coaches arrange a deal which allows her to score an uncontested basket at the beginning of UConn's season finale against Villanova. Sales ruptured her right Achilles' tendon in the previous game, seemingly ending her career two points short of the record.

25 After a seven-year saga the New York Islanders sale to New York Sports Ventures is completed for $195 million.

26 The battle for All-Star Sergei Fedorov ends when the Detroit Red Wings match a Carolina offer which could pay the restricted free agent $28 million in salary and bonuses by July 1.

Chinese swimmer Hu Xiaowen, 18, breaks the women's 100-meter individual medley world record set in 1992 with a time of 1:00.60 in Beijing.

MAR '98

Sun	Mon	Tue	Wed	Thu	Fri	Sat
1	2	3	4	5	6	7
8	9	10	11	12	13	14
15	16	17	18	19	20	21
22	23	24	25	26	27	28
29	30	31				

Dust in the Tournament

Kansas coach Roy Williams has led the Jayhawks to the NCAA men's basketball tournament every year this decade. But despite never being seeded lower than fourth (and grabbing the #1 spot four times), Kansas has never put together a 6-0 run to win it all.

Season	Seed	W-L	Finish	Spoiler
1989-90	#2	1-1	2nd Round	UCLA
1990-91	#3	5-1	Championship Game	Duke
1991-92	#1	1-1	2nd Round	UTEP
1992-93	#2	4-1	Final Four	N. Carolina
1993-94	#4	2-1	Regional Semifinals	Purdue
1994-95	#1	2-1	Regional Semifinals	Virginia
1995-96	#2	3-1	Regional Finals	Syracuse
1996-97	#1	2-1	Regional Semifinals	Arizona
1997-98	#1	1-1	2nd Round	URI

Number One S(w)eeds

When Chile's Marcelo Rios broke Pete Sampras' streak of 102 weeks atop the ATP Tour rankings, it ended the tour's third longest streak since it started the rankings system on Aug. 23, 1973. The two longest streaks in tour history were both broken by Swedish-born players.

Wks	Dates	No.1	Defeated by
160	7/74 – 8/77	Jimmy Connors	Bjorn Borg
157	9/85 – 9/88	Ivan Lendl	Mats Wilander
102	4/96 – 3/98	Pete Sampras	Marcelo Rios

The Rich Get Richer

Tennessee women's basketball star Chamique Holdsclaw, who in three years has won three national championships, surpassed 2,000 points and 1,000 rebounds, had her freshman scoring record of 583 points (16.2 per game) shattered in 1998 by teammate Tamika Catchings who scored 711 points (18.2) for the Lady Vols.

1 Venus Williams wins her first WTA title by defeating Joannette Kruger 6-3, 6-2 at the IGA Tennis Classic in Oklahoma City.

3 Red Sox first baseman Mo Vaughn is found not guilty of drunken driving by a Massachusetts jury after a two-day trial and three hours of deliberation.

The Tennessee Oilers announce a deal that will allow the team to move from the Liberty Bowl in Memphis to Vanderbilt's stadium in Nashville in time for the 1998 season.

4 Latrell Sprewell is a Golden State Warrior again after an arbitrator cuts his NBA-imposed suspension by five months and reinstates his contract that is designed to pay him $17.3 million over the next two seasons.

5 Mike Tyson files a $100 million lawsuit seeking to end his relationship with promoter Don King.

9 The struggling Philadelphia Flyers name Roger Neilson coach and demote Wayne Cashman to assistant.

10 AL Rookie of the Year Nomar Garciaparra signs a five-year $23.25 million contract with the Boston Red Sox.

One day after a standoff with local law officials, Chicago Bears defensive end Alonzo Spellman is found outside his hospital "running around" without a shirt or shoes in freezing weather. Spellman is reportedly concerned about rumors that he is being traded.

11 New York Islanders GM Mike Milbury fires coach Rick Bowness and names himself head coach in an attempt to get the team into the playoffs for the first time since 1994.

Pete Rose gives an impromptu motivational speech to a Cincinnati Reds farm team that includes his son, possibly violating his mandatory life banishment from baseball.

12 The NCAA men's basketball tournament opens and 14th-seeded Richmond grabs the Cinderella spotlight first with a 62-61 victory over #3 South Carolina.

In desperate need of a quarterback, the San Diego Chargers move up one spot in next month's draft, sending their 1998 first and third round picks and first in 1999 plus two players to Arizona for the Cardinals second overall pick and a shot at either Peyton Manning or Ryan Leaf.

13 Bryce Drew's buzzer-beating three pointer becomes the odds-on-favorite for play of the tournament as Valparaiso (13th seed) sends fourth-seeded Mississippi home early 70-69.

14 Jerome Davis, a world champion bull rider in 1995, is paralyzed from the neck down after a collision with a bull during a Professional Bull Riders' Cup Tour event in Fort Worth, Texas.

15 Valerie Still scores 25 points and is named playoff MVP as the Columbus Quest win their second straight American Basketball League championship in a row 86-81 over the Long Beach (Calif.) StingRays.

The first No. 1 seed in the NCAA men's basketball tournament falls, as Kansas loses a shocker to eighth-seeded Rhode Island which ends a streak of five straight Sweet Sixteen appearances for the Jayhawks.

16 Jeff King wins his third Iditarod Trail Sled Dog race, finishing the 1,100-mile course from Anchorage to Nome in nine days, five hours and 52 minutes.

18 Houston Rockets guard Clyde Drexler announces he will retire at the end of the basketball season and return to his alma mater Houston to coach its men's basketball team.

Archive Photos

Former heavyweight boxing champion **Mike Tyson** returns to the ring as a "special enforcer" at Wrestlemania XIV on March 29. As expected, pandemonium breaks out and Tyson is forced to serve as referee during the main event – never once taking his eyes off the ears of the wrestlers.

19 Baseball owners approve the sale of the Los Angeles Dodgers to media tycoon Rupert Murdoch for a reported $311 million, ending the era of family owned sports teams and getting Ted Turner really, really mad.

22 A 17-point, second half Kentucky rally leads to a 86-84 victory over Duke, securing the Wildcats the last spot in the Final Four with Stanford, Utah and North Carolina.

23 The NFL awards Cleveland an expansion team for the 1999 season.

Wil Cordero finds a new home in Chicago, signing a $1 million contract with the White Sox, four months after pleading guilty to assaulting his wife and being released by the Red Sox after the season.

25 NFL owners fail to approve instant replay at their annual meeting.

Running back Curtis Martin becomes a member of the NY Jets as the deadline passes and New England fails to match the Jets offer sheet.

26 The NFL all-time sack leader Reggie White addresses the Wisconsin legislature and delivers a memorable soliloquy in which he calls homosexuality a sin and stereotypes several ethnic groups.

Two members of Northwestern's 1995 basketball team are indicted on charges they conspired to fix three conference games for $4,000.

27 An NBA-record 62,046 pack into the Georgia Dome to witness what might be the last game in Atlanta for Michael Jordan. He responds by scoring 34 points to lead the Chicago Bulls to their eighth straight win. Eight thousand fans bought "video screen only" tickets that offered no actual view of the court.

28 Lennox Lewis knocks down Shannon Briggs three times and retains his World Boxing Council heavyweight title after the referee stops the fight in the fifth round.

29 Chamique Holdsclaw scores 25 points, has 10 rebounds and six assists, powering undefeated Tennessee past Louisiana Tech 93-75 and garnering the team its third straight NCAA women's basketball championship.

Pat Hurst captures the first major championship of her career, carding a 1-under-par 71 for a one-stroke triumph at the Nabisco Dinah Shore.

Chile's Marcelo Rios claims the world No. 1 ranking with a 7-5, 6-3, 6-4 win over Andre Agassi in the final of the Lipton Tennis Championships, ending Pete Sampras' 102 consecutive weeks in the top spot.

Playing without leading scorers Reggie Miller and Rik Smits, the Indiana Pacers set a modern era NBA record for fewest points in a game in a 74-55 loss to San Antonio.

30 Scott Padgett scores 17 points and Jeff Sheppard adds 16, helping Kentucky erase a 10-point deficit, the largest halftime hole any champion has ever overcome, and win its seventh national championship 78-69 over Utah.

Houston Rockets forward Charles Barkley receives a $10,000 fine from the NBA for calling referee Jack Nies "gutless" after a Mar. 27 Rockets loss to the Magic.

31 It's Opening Day in major league baseball and Mark McGwire and Ken Griffey Jr. continue their home run derby, blasting one a piece in their respective games. Expansion teams Arizona and Tampa Bay both lose their home openers.

APR '98

Sun	Mon	Tue	Wed	Thu	Fri	Sat
			1	2	3	4
5	6	7	8	9	10	11
12	13	14	15	16	17	18
19	20	21	22	23	24	25
26	27	28	29	30		

Major Accomplishment

Mark O'Meara won 14 PGA Tour events before winning his first tour major – the Masters Tournament in 1998. The following current PGA Tour players are still waiting for a victory in either the Masters, U.S. Open, British Open and/or the PGA Championship – golf's Grand Slam Events (through April 1998).

Player	Tour Victories	Best Major finish
Bruce Lietzke	13	T-4th, 1981 PGA
Wayne Levi	12	T-11th, 1984 Masters
Phil Mickelson	12	3rd, 1996 Masters & 1994 PGA
John Cook	10	2nd, 1992 British & T-2nd 1992 PGA
David Frost	10	T-5th, 1995 Masters
Mark McCumber	10	T-5th, 1987 PGA

The Original Dominators

Carolina Hurricanes goalie Trevor Kidd set a team record by not allowing a goal for 219 minutes and 21 seconds over a four-game stretch between March 31 and April 8. Buffalo Sabres defenseman Jason Woolley's power-play goal ended the streak with 3:28 left in the first period. Kidd's performance, although noteworthy, is still well short of the league record for a consecutive shutout sequence by a goaltender. Here are the top four in NHL history ranked by total minutes and seconds:

Time	Goalie	Team	Season
461:29	Alex Connell	Ottawa	1927-28*
343:05	George Hainsworth	Montreal	1928-29
324:40	Roy Worters	NY Americans	1930-31
309:21	Bill Durnan	Montreal	1948-49

*Forward passing was not permitted in the attacking zones in 1927-28.

2 Former UNLV men's basketball coach Jerry Tarkanian receives $2.5 million from the NCAA to settle a suit he filed in 1992, charging the NCAA with singling him out for punishment during his tenure at the school 1973-92.

The housekeeping staff at the White House breathes a collective sigh of relief after Olympic Committee officials announce that the men's hockey team will not be invited to a reception there to honor U.S. Olympians on April 29.

Kansas All-American Paul Pierce becomes the first underclassman in Roy Williams' 10-year tenure to leave early when the junior announces his eligibility for the NBA draft in June.

3 Michael Jordan scores 41 points in a victory over the Timberwolves and becomes the third player in NBA history to reach 29,000 career points.

4 An NCAA tournament-record crowd watches Josh Langfeld score at 17:51 of overtime, earning the Michigan Wolverines a 3-2 victory over Boston College and their record ninth men's hockey national championship.

5 Arizona Diamondbacks pitcher Andy Benes allows two runs over seven innings as Arizona holds off San Francisco 3-2 to pick up the franchise's first victory after five straight losses to open the season.

8 Carolina Hurricanes goalie Trevor Kidd's bid to become the first goalie since the 1948-49 season to record four straight shutouts is ruined by Jason Woolley's power-play goal in the first period during a 3-1 loss to the Sabres.

9 Kansas City Chiefs running back Marcus Allen, the NFL's all-time leader in rushing touchdowns, announces his retirement and his plans to join CBS as a studio analyst in the fall.

12 Mark O'Meara calmly strokes in an 18-foot birdie putt on the 72nd hole of the tournament, capturing his first Masters victory and his first major championship title after 18 years on the PGA Tour.

The New York Knicks think they have a victory over the Miami Heat after Allan Houston appears to bank in a shot with .2 seconds left, but the referees wave off the shot and Miami wins the controversial game 82-81.

Kentucky Derby favorite Lil's Lad will have to pull out of next month's Run for the Roses after doctors discover a chipped left ankle bone following Lad's loss in the Blue Grass Stakes.

13 A 500-pound beam falls in an empty Yankee Stadium crushing a seat and causing the Yankee's game that evening to be postponed. The ballpark is closed to fans until the entire 75-year-old structure can be inspected.

Seattle outfielder Ken Griffey Jr. hits career home runs 299 and 300 in a 6-5 loss at Cleveland and becomes the second-youngest player (Jimmy Foxx) to reach the 300 homer plateau.

14 Cardinals first baseman Mark McGwire smacks three home runs in a 15-5 victory over Arizona. It's the third three-homer game for McGwire in his career.

15 With the Stadium Ruth built still closed, the Yankees borrow Shea Stadium for an afternoon game against Anaheim (W, 6-3), and the Mets take the field later that night to beat the Cubs 2-1.

Bo Jackson and Jim McMahon highlight a class of 10 elected into the College Football Hall of Fame.

18 The Indianapolis Colts make Tennessee quarterback Peyton Manning the first overall pick at the 1998 NFL Draft.

AP/Wide World Photos

This wasn't left behind after the innovative "Concrete Giveaway Day" at **Yankee Stadium**. On the contrary, the team avoided a serious incident when this 500-pound supporting joint used to connect two beams fell hours before the more than 20,000 fans that were expected for an evening game against Anaheim filed into the stadium.

Prince Naseem Hamed remains undefeated and retains his WBO featherweight title for the 10th straight time, knocking out Wilfredo Vazquez in the seventh round.

19 **All-Pro defensive end Reggie White** announces his retirement from the NFL.

Kenyan Tegla Loroupe sets a new women's marathon record, racing to a time of 2:20:47 at the Rotterdam (Netherlands) Marathon.

20 **Moses Tanui wins the Boston Marathon** and becomes the eighth straight Kenyan to win the event. Fatuma Roba successfully defends her women's title.

Chicago Blackhawks center Brent Sutter announces his retirement from the NHL.

21 **All-Pro defensive end Reggie White** decides he doesn't want to retire, and says he will play one more season with the Packers.

Former PGA Tour deputy commissioner Tim Smith is named as the first commissioner of the National Thoroughbred Racing Association.

The World Boxing Association and World Boxing Council agree to consolidate their rules, paving the way for undisputed title bouts between holders of the two belts.

22 **PGA Tour all-time leading money winner** Greg Norman undergoes surgery on his left shoulder, sidelining him for the 1998 season.

The WNBA announces expansion teams will be awarded to Minneapolis and Orlando in 1999.

23 **White Sox outfielder Wil Cordero hits** the first pitch he sees for a home run in the majors since being convicted of assaulting his wife.

25 **Light heavyweight champion** Roy Jones Jr. continues his dominance in the ring, needing just over 10 minutes to knock out Virgil Hill in their title match in Mississippi.

26 **Winston Cup driver Bobby Labonte avoids** a crash at mile 125 in the DieHard 500 and speeds Team Pontiac to victory at Talladega Superspeedway for the first time in 15 years.

Stephon Marbury's 25 points helps the Minnesota Timberwolves erase nine years of frustration by winning the first playoff game in franchise history 98-93 over Seattle.

27 **Men's college basketball player of the year** Antawn Jamison announces he will forgo his senior year at North Carolina and enter the NBA draft.

Hall of Fame pitcher Juan Marichal is hospitalized after he was injured in an automobile accident in the Dominican Republic.

29 **The first ever lottery draw** for starting positions in the Kentucky Derby is drawn and redrawn after a mistake was made in reading one of the numbers midway through the first try.

30 **With 1.4 seconds left in a series-tying** 90-85 New York victory, Alonzo Mourning and Miami's Larry Johnson fire punches at each other. Truly memorable video of the fight shows Knicks head coach Jeff Van Gundy's attempt to stop the fight by holding on to Mourning's leg for dear life. See photo on page 347.

UCLA's men's basketball program is placed on three years probation by the NCAA for violating recruiting regulations and giving improper benefits to athletes. The Bruins remain eligible to compete in post-season play and can appear on television.

MAY '98

Sun	Mon	Tue	Wed	Thu	Fri	Sat
					1	2
3	4	5	6	7	8	9
10	11	12	13	14	15	16
17	18	19	20	21	22	23
24/31	25	26	27	28	29	30

20-Strikeout Club

Membership doubled in May when Cubs rookie Kerry Wood joined Roger Clemens as the only pitchers to strike out 20 batters in a game, a feat Clemens has done twice. When you study the pitch counts of each game, Wood's performance becomes even more impressive.

	Pitches	Balls/ Strikes	Hits	BB
Wood, 5/6/98	122	38/84	1	0
Clemens, 9/18/96	151	54/97	5	0
Clemens, 4/29/86	138	37/101	3	0

I Must Be in the Front Row

On May 25 President Bill Clinton became the first sitting president to take time off from running the country and other various "activities" to check out an NHL hockey game. The NHL becomes the last of the four major sports to get a visit from an "active" Commander in Chief. Here's when the other three major sports got their first visits:

NBA—February 5, 1978; Former Georgia governor Jimmy Carter takes in the All-Star Game at The Omni in Atlanta where the East beats the West 133-125.

NFL—August 3, 1966; Democratic president Lyndon Johnson attends a preseason game between the Washington Redskins and Baltimore Colts at RFK Stadium.

MLB—June 6, 1892; Republican president and North Bend, Ohio native Benjamin Harrison watches the Cincinnati Reds beat the host Washington Senators 7-4 in 11 innings.

2 Unheralded racehorse Real Quiet grabs the lead on the backstretch at Churchill Downs and holds off Victory Gallop to win the Kentucky Derby.

4 In the biggest financial judgment ever levied against the NCAA, a federal jury orders it to pay nearly $67 million in damages for restricting the earnings of some assistant coaches.

5 Atlanta Hawks center Dikembe Mutombo garners his record third straight NBA Defensive Player of the Year Award.

6 Cubs rookie pitcher Kerry Wood sets a National League record and ties a major league record by striking out 20 Houston Astros en route to a one-hit, 2-0 victory at Wrigley Field.

Phillies fan Robert Cotter, 87, sits behind the Philadelphia dugout as a guest of the team 69 years after pocketing a foul ball at a game in 1929 and landing a night in jail because of it. A day later a judge ruled that Cotter was acting on a natural impulse and set the modern-day precedent for fans being allowed to keep foul balls.

7 The IAAF announces women's pole vault and the hammer throw will be added to the 1999 World Championships and 2000 Olympics, meaning for the first time women will compete in the same number of field events as men.

8 Cardinals slugger Mark McGwire becomes the 26th and fastest major league baseball player to hit 400 home runs, after Big Mac rips one into the left field seats at Shea Stadium during his team's 9-2 loss to the Mets.

Sisters Venus and Serena Williams meet for the second time as professionals in the quarterfinals of the Italian Open, and Venus remains undefeated versus her younger sister, 6-4, 6-2.

10 St. Louis defenseman Chris Pronger collapses on the ice and is sent to a nearby hospital after being struck in the chest by a puck during a 6-1 loss at Detroit.

11 Top high school basketball prospect Al Harrington of St. Patrick High in Elizabeth, N.J. decides to enter the NBA draft.

12 Indiana Pacers first year coach Larry Bird is named NBA coach of the year and becomes the second coach ever to garner the rookie coach of the year and coach of the year awards in the same season.

Chicago Cubs 20-year-old Kerry Wood sets another major league record—this one for strikeouts in consecutive games—when he sets down 13 Arizona Diamondbacks in a 4-2 victory five days after his 20-punchout performance.

Former NY Giants star Lawrence Taylor spends 10 hours in jail after being rounded up with 51 other "dead-beat" dads who are behind on child support payments.

13 St. John's men's basketball coach Fran Fraschilla, who led the team to its first NCAA appearance in five years, is fired by the school for what it says are "fundamental differences."

Ryan Klesko's sixth inning home run helps the Atlanta Braves tie a major league record and set a National League record for consecutive games with at least one home run–25.

14 Legally-challenged Washington Wizards forward Chris Webber is traded to the Sacramento Kings for Mitch Richmond and Otis Thorpe.

Orioles ace Mike Mussina suffers a broken nose and a concussion after he is hit just above his right eye by a screaming line drive off the bat of Cleveland's Sandy Alomar Jr.

AP/Wide World Photos

Relief pitcher Graeme Lloyd (upper left) leads a brigade of **New York Yankees** towards the dugout of the **Baltimore Orioles** in an all-out AL East brawl on Aug. 19 at Yankee Stadium. The fight was ignited by Orioles relief pitcher Armando Benitez, who beaned Yankees batter Tino Martinez after Bernie Williams hit a three-run home run to give the Bronx Bombers a two-run lead en route to a 9-5 victory.

15 **LA Dodgers catcher Mike Piazza** is the centerpiece of a historic trade in Major League Baseball. Piazza and 3B Todd Zeile are sent to Florida in exchange for Gary Sheffield, Bobby Bonilla, Charles Johnson, Jim Eisenreich and a player to be named later.

16 **Real Quiet takes one more step closer** to winning the first Triple Crown in 20 years with a rousing victory at 123rd Preakness Stakes.

17 **New York Yankees pitcher David Wells** becomes the 15th player in Major League Baseball history to throw a perfect game, blanking the Twins 4-0 at Yankee Stadium.

LPGA rookie Se Ri Pak, 20, of South Korea wins her first major championship and becomes the youngest woman to win the LPGA Championship, firing a final round 68 at the DuPont Country Club in Wilmington, Del.

18 **The Tampa Bay Lightning's** 17-month long wait for an owner ends when Palm Beach, Fla. businessman Arthur L. Williams, a former CFL owner, buys the club and its arena lease for around $130 million.

Michael Jordan wins his fifth NBA Most Valuable Player Award.

Oakland A's third baseman Mike Blowers hits for the cycle in a 14-0 victory over the White Sox.

20 **Author Tom Clancy withdraws his bid** to buy the Minnesota Vikings after NFL owners question the reliability of his cash investment.

22 **For the second Friday in a row**, Mike Piazza is traded. This time the Marlins deal the all-star catcher to the Mets for three prospects.

24 **Eddie Cheever Jr. wins** the 82nd Indianapolis 500 after failing in eight previous attempts.

25 **President Clinton becomes the first** sitting president to attend an NHL game when he and Vice President Gore watch Washington defeat Buffalo 3-2 in overtime in Game 2 of the Eastern Conference finals at the MCI Center.

The Fresno State women's softball team captures its first NCAA title after failing in four previous national title game appearances.

26 **Seattle Supersonics coach George Karl** is fired after more than six seasons with the team and a regular season winning percentage of .719, which is a franchise record.

Western Athletic Conference officials announce that half of the conference's 16 teams will leave at the end of the 1998-99 school year.

27 **Major League Soccer signs Mexico's all-time** leading international scorer, Carlos Hermosillo, 33, to a two-year deal and assigns him to the Los Angeles Galaxy.

Colorado Avalanche head coach Marc Crawford shocks the Rocky Mountain State and announces he's quitting despite one year still remaining on his current contract.

29 **With charges of sexual assault still looming** over him in Toronto, NFL all-purpose back David Meggett is released by the New England Patriots.

30 **Oakland Raiders** 1998 second-round draft pick DT Leon Bender is found dead in his bathroom of what may have been a fatal epileptic seizure.

31 **Toni Kukoc scores 14 of his 21 points** in the third quarter, sparking host Chicago to an 88-83 victory over Indiana in Game 7 of the Eastern Conference finals.

JUNE '98

Sun	Mon	Tue	Wed	Thu	Fri	Sat
	1	2	3	4	5	6
7	8	9	10	11	12	13
14	15	16	17	18	19	20
21	22	23	24	25	26	27
28	29	30				

Sweeps Week

By knocking off Washington in four games, Detroit made it four NHL seasons in a row that the Stanley Cup Finals were a less-than-captivating four-game mini-series. Other than the NHL, only major league baseball has seen consecutive finals sweeps.

Year	Series—NHL (4)
1994-95	New Jersey Devils def. Detroit Red Wings
1995-96	Colorado Avalanche def. Florida Panthers
1996-97	Detroit Red Wings def. Philadelphia Flyers
1997-98	Detroit Red Wings def. Washington Capitals
Year	**Series—MLB (2)**
1927	New York Yankees def. Pittsburgh Pirates
1928	New York Yankees def. St. Louis Cardinals
Year	**Series—MLB (2)**
1938	New York Yankees def. Chicago Cubs
1939	New York Yankees def. Cincinnati Reds
	NBA (0)

JUNE-MANJI !!!

Sammy Sosa's 20 home runs in June helped him set the all-time major league record for most home runs hit in a 30-day stretch. Sosa clobbered 21 between May 25 and June 23. The following is a list of the players with the year they set or tied the mark for each month during the regular season.

March— (1) Darren Bragg, Sea; Frank Thomas, Chi-A, 1996.
April— (13) Ken Griffey Jr., Sea, 1997.
May— (16) Mickey Mantle, NY-A, 1956.
June— (20) Sammy Sosa, Chi-N, 1998
July— (15) Joe DiMaggio, NY-A, 1937; Hank Greenberg, Det., 1938; Joe Adcock, Mil., 1956; Juan Gonzalez, Tex., 1996; Albert Belle, Chi-A, 1998.
August— (18) Rudy York, NY-A, 1937.
September— (17) Babe Ruth, NY-A, 1927; Albert Belle, Cle., 1995.
October— (4) Ned Williamson, Chi-N, 1884; Gus Zernial, Chi-A, 1950; Mike Schmidt, Phi, 1980; George Brett, KC, 1985; Ron Kittle, Chi-A, 1985; Dave Parker, Cin, 1985; Wally Joyner, Cal, 1987.

1 Denver Broncos quarterback John Elway announces to the press he'll be back for his 16th NFL season at the age of 38 to defend his first league championship.

Fox cancels "Nomomania," as the Los Angeles Dodgers management removes pitcher Hideo Nomo, the 1995 NL Rookie of the Year, from the 40-man roster after his 2-7 start.

2 AL President Gene Budig witnesses his league's second ugly brawl in as many months as the Royals and Angels clash twice at Kauffman Stadium, bringing about 12 ejections.

University of Miami-FL third baseman Pat Burrell is selected first overall in baseball's major league draft.

3 Orlando Hernandez, the Yankees' rookie right-hander who defected from Cuba on a raft five months earlier to play baseball in the U.S., reaches the end of his journey, winning his major league debut 7-1 over the Tampa Bay Devil Rays in Yankee Stadium.

4 Washington forward Joe Juneau slaps a rebound past Sabres goalie Dominik Hasek in overtime and propels the Capitals into the Stanley Cup Finals for the first time in the team's 24-year history.

The New York Mets trade pitchers Dave Mlicki and Greg McMichael to Los Angeles for Hideo Nomo.

Former heavyweight champion Riddick Bowe will serve 18-24 months in prison after he pleads guilty to a charge of interstate domestic violence for threatening and then taking his wife and five children from their North Carolina home and driving them to Virginia.

5 The WBA title fight between Evander Holyfield and Henry Akinwande, scheduled for June 6, is cancelled after a doctor says Akinwande has tested positive for hepatitis B.

Mark McGwire sets a single-season Busch Stadium record with his 18th home run in St. Louis. Now look at the date again.

6 Real Quiet misses its opportunity to win the first Triple Crown in two decades by a nose, losing to Victory Gallop at the Belmont Stakes.

Arkansas wins its seventh consecutive men's title and Texas its first women's title since 1986 at the NCAA Outdoor Track and Field Championships in Buffalo.

USC wins its first college baseball World Series in 20 years by defeating Arizona St. by a Rose Bowl-like score of 21-14.

7 Carlos Moya completes "The Spanish Acquisition" at the French Open, defeating fellow countryman Alex Corretja to capture the men's singles title a day after fellow Spaniard Arantxa Sanchez Vicario won her third women's title.

Utah commits 26 turnovers en route to an NBA finals record 42-point loss to Chicago 96-54 in Game 3 of the teams' championship series.

10 World Cup '98 opens in France with defending champion Brazil defeating Scotland 2-1 and Norway and Morocco playing to a 2-2 draw.

A drunken riot erupts when fans at a World Cup opening day pageant assault police officers on the Champs-Elysees, injuring 34 officers.

11 After eight seasons at George Washington, coach Mike Jarvis climbs up into the Big East and fills the head coach vacancy at St. John's.

13 It takes less than nine minutes for WBC welterweight champion Oscar De La Hoya to knock out his number one challenger Patrick Charpentier and retain his title in El Paso, Texas.

Archive Photos

British soccer fans burn a Tunisian flag during a riot the day before the first-round World Cup match between England and Tunisia in Marseille, France on June 14. It was just one of many violent disturbances which drew attention away from the otherwise thrilling international tournament.

14 Michael Jordan scores 45 points, including the game winner with 5.2 seconds left to lead the Chicago Bulls to a 87-86 victory over Utah in Game 6, garnering the team its sixth title in eight seasons.

Tennessee Vols junior basketball player Chamique Holdsclaw is awarded the Honda Broderick Cup, which is awarded to the nation's top female athlete.

15 USA Soccer comes out firing in the second half of its first World Cup game against Germany, but it isn't enough as the Americans lose 2-0.

Stanford wins its fourth consecutive Director's Cup given to the country's best all-around sports program.

16 The Detroit Red Wings beat Washington 4-1 in game four of the Stanley Cup Finals and for the second straight year become NHL champions by sweeping their opponent.

17 Former Phoenix Suns head coach Paul Westphal is hired to replace George Karl in Seattle.

21 USA soccer misses another opportunity to gain respect in the international spotlight, losing to Iran 2-1 in the team's second first-round loss at the World Cup.

Golfer Lee Janzen rallies from seven strokes down to win his second U.S. Open title by beating Payne Stewart 280-281 after Stewart shoots a final round 74 on Sunday.

Two longtime members of the LA Dodgers' family—GM Fred Claire and manager Bill Russell—are fired and replaced by Tommy Lasorda and minor league manager Glenn Hoffman respectively.

Florida Panthers GM Bryan Murray announces the hiring of his brother Terry as the organization's fourth head coach.

22 Phil Jackson rides off on his motorcycle, signaling the end of his tenure with the Chicago Bulls which lasted nine seasons and ended with the team's sixth NBA title.

Lenny Wilkens joins John Wooden as the only two men elected to the Pro Basketball Hall of Fame as a player and a coach.

23 Aided by a controversial late penalty kick, Norway shocks Brazil 2-1 in World Cup action. It's Brazil's first World Cup loss since 1990.

24 University of Pacific seven-foot center Michael Olowokandi is chosen first overall by the LA Clippers at the NBA Draft in Toronto.

Neil O'Donnell's soap opera with the NY Jets ends when the team waives him after signing free agent Vinny Testaverde earlier in the day.

25 Sammy Sosa sets a major league record for home runs hit in one month by launching his 19th homer of June into the upper deck at Tiger Stadium.

Yugoslavia beats the U.S. 1-0 in their World Cup first-round game, sending the Americans home with a miserable 0-3 record.

A cement balcony collapses at the Russian National Freestyle Wrestling Competition in Nalchik, killing 22 spectators and injuring 39 more.

27 French Canadian teen Vincent Lecavalier is selected first overall at the NHL draft by the Tampa Bay Lightning.

29 NBA owners vote to impose a player lockout that takes effect at midnight.

U.S. national men's soccer team coach Steve Sampson resigns under heavy criticism after the team's World Cup performance.

JULY '98

Sun	Mon	Tue	Wed	Thu	Fri	Sat
			1	2	3	4
5	6	7	8	9	10	11
12	13	14	15	16	17	18
19	20	21	22	23	24	25
26	27	28	29	30	31	

The Mile-Stone Club

When Roger Clemens notched strikeout number 3,000 on July 5, he joined another exclusive baseball club. Only 10 other pitchers can say they've recorded 3,000 or more strikeouts. The following is a list of baseball's most popular hall-of-fame measuring sticks and how many players have matched or surpassed that mark in a career:

Milestone Clubs	# of Members
3,000 Strikeouts	11
500 Home Runs	15
300 Wins	20
3,000 Hits	21

King Floyd

A closer look at the career of Tim Floyd, the man who will inherit control of the decade's most successful sports franchise:

Full Name: Timothy Fitzpatrick Floyd
Born: February 25, 1954
College: Louisiana Tech, 1977

Coaching Career:
Iowa State Record: 81-49 (4 years)
Overall Record: 243-130 (12 years)
1994-98 Head Coach, Iowa State University
... 1st ISU coach to post three straight 20-win seasons
... 1997 Sweet 16 berth
... two NCAA 2nd round appearances
... 1996 Big Eight Coach of the Year
1988-94 Head Coach, Univ. of New Orleans
... two NCAA Tournament berths
... three NIT appearances
1986-88 Head Coach, Univ. of Idaho
1977-86 Asst. Coach, UTEP

Playing Experience
1976-77 Student assistant coach, Louisiana Tech
1975-76 Scholarship player, Louisiana Tech
1972-74 Walk-on, Southern Mississippi

Family Ties:
Floyd's father, the late Lee Floyd, was head men's basketball coach at Southern Mississippi for 14 years, recording a 246-147 overall mark.

2 Red McCombs, former San Antonio Spurs and Denver Nuggets owner is approved by the NFL as new owner of the Minnesota Vikings.

Utah Jazz coach Jerry Sloan signs a new three-year deal with the team.

3 Six-time NHL all star Brett Hull ends his 10-year stay in St. Louis, agreeing to a three-year $17 million contract with the Dallas Stars.

Prospect J.D. Drew ends his holdout and agrees to a four-year $7 million contract with the St. Louis Cardinals.

4 Jana Novotna wins her first Wimbledon women's singles title after a 6-4, 7-6 (7-2) victory over 16th-ranked Nathalie Tauziat.

5 Nobody is more surprised than 20-year-old amateur Jenny Chuasiriporn when she rolls in a 30-foot birdie putt at the final hole of the U.S. Open to force an 18-hole playoff with LPGA rookie Se Ri Pak.

Pete Sampras captures his fifth Wimbledon title in the last six years and his 11th grand slam victory overall after defeating 14th ranked Goran Ivanisevic in the men's singles final.

Roger Clemens strikes out Tampa Bay's Randy Winn for his 3,000th career strikeout, becoming the 11th player to reach the plateau.

6 Eighteen playoff holes aren't enough, and on the second hole of sudden death Se Ri Pak cards a birdie to capture the U.S. Women's Open and her second major of the year.

A reluctant Ken Griffey Jr. makes a last minute decision to enter baseball's Home Run Derby for the fans and wins the competition.

7 Orioles 2B Roberto Alomar becomes the second Alomar in as many years to win the All-Star Game MVP award after helping the American League to a 13-8 victory. Last year his brother Sandy Alomar Jr. won the award.

Brazil advances to the World Cup championship game, beating the Netherlands 4-2 in a shootout following a 1-1 draw in their semifinal contest.

Unrestricted NHL free agent goalie John Vanbiesbrouck signs a two-year, $11 million deal with the Philadelphia Flyers.

8 Legendary golfer Jack Nicklaus announces he will withdraw from next week's British Open, ending his streak of consecutive majors for which he's been eligible at 154 (41 years).

France ends the run of Croatia, the World Cup tournament Cinderella, with a 2-1 defeat in the semifinals.

9 Cardinals pitcher Todd Stottlemyre bats eighth, becoming the first pitcher to crack the starting lineup card anywhere but ninth in the order since Steve Carlton in 1979.

11 On the streets of Dublin, 189 bikers race during the prologue stage for the leader position for the 86th Tour de France.

12 Host country France upsets Brazil in the World Cup final 3-0 thanks to two goals from star midfielder Zinedine Zidane.

Mark McGwire hits two home runs in a 6-4 victory over Houston, giving him 40 home runs in the fewest at-bats (281) ever needed to reach that mark in major league history.

13 The NHL's ninth all-time leading scorer Ron Francis signs with the Carolina Hurricanes for $20.8 million over four years.

Archive Photos

In search of something more uncomfortable than a bicycle seat, **riders at the Tour de France** find refuge on the cold, hard French asphalt during a protest which delays the start of the 12th stage of the race. The protest was fueled by riders who thought they were being treated unfairly by race officials during a drug scandal that marred the entire race.

15 An Indiana jury finds the University of Notre Dame guilty of age discrimination and awards $86,000 in back pay to former assistant football coach Joe Moore.

Former NBC sportscaster Marv Albert is rehired by the Madison Square Garden Network to host a nightly wrap-up show and work radio broadcasts of New York Knicks games almost a year after pleading guilty to misdemeanor assault charges.

18 The 1998 Goodwill Games open in New York City.

19 At 41-years-old, golfer Mark O'Meara becomes the oldest player to ever win two major titles in the same year as he staves off Brian Watts in a four-hole playoff to win the British Open.

Three laps before the end of the race Alex Zanardi passes Michael Andretti to capture the Molson Indy Toronto, tying a CART series record with his fourth straight victory.

21 The Mighty Ducks of Anaheim name Craig Hartsburg as the team's third new head coach in the last 13 months.

Chinese gymnast Sang Lan crashes off the vault while practicing during the Goodwill Games and becomes paralyzed from the chest down.

22 San Francisco 49ers president Carmen Policy officially resigns from his post and immediately joins Al Lerner and Bernie Kosar as one of five groups seeking ownership of the Cleveland Browns expansion team in 1999.

A probe into which U.S. Olympic hockey players were responsible for trashed hotel rooms during the Winter Games in Nagano, Japan ends without discovering who did it.

23 Former Iowa State basketball coach Tim Floyd is named director of basketball operations for the defending champion Chicago Bulls.

25 San Diego rookie quarterback Ryan Leaf agrees to a contract which will pay him an NFL rookie record $11.15 million signing bonus.

26 Three spectators are killed when a tire from the car of Adrian Fernandez rockets over a 15-foot protective fence and into the stands during the 175th lap of the U.S. 500 at Michigan Speedway.

27 Olympic gold medalists and world champions Randy Barnes (shot put) and Dennis Mitchell (sprints) are suspended by the IAAF for positive drug tests.

Former Utah Jazz coach and current president Frank Layden makes his coaching debut with the WNBA's Utah Starzz, beating the Phoenix Mercury 90-80.

29 Suspended heavyweight Mike Tyson appears before the New Jersey Athletic Control Board at a hearing to decide whether he is emotionally fit to return to boxing and blurts out an obscenity during the proceedings.

A second rider protest nullifies the 17th stage of the Tour de France.

30 Latrell Sprewell's $30 million lawsuit against the NBA, which charges that the league's suspension of him was racially motivated and violated his right to make a living, is dismissed by a federal judge.

31 Randy Johnson's trade to Houston for two minor leaguers highlights a trading deadline flurry in baseball as Todd Stottlemyre, Royce Clayton, Juan Guzman, Ellis Burks, Carlos Perez and Todd Zeile all switch uniforms.

AUG '98

Sun	Mon	Tue	Wed	Thu	Fri	Sat
						1
2	3	4	5	6	7	8
9	10	11	12	13	14	15
16	17	18	19	20	21	22
23	24	25	26	27	28	29
30	31					

An American Tragedy

It was a heart-wrenching decision for Pat LaFontaine to make, and it was a difficult one for fans to accept, when the 15-year NHL veteran decided to take doctors' advice and retire at the age of 33. One of the league's greatest American-born players, here's where the five-time all-star's career numbers rank with other U.S.-born players.

Record	Rank	Career Total
Goals	2nd	468
Points	3rd	1,013
Assists	6th	545
Points (Season)	1st	148 (1992-93)

Gordon the Magnificent

NASCAR superstar Jeff Gordon had plenty to celebrate when his 27th birthday rolled around on Aug. 4. Three days earlier Gordon won his second Brickyard 400 title which was his 35th career Winston Cup victory. His birthday also fell right in the middle of his record-tying four-race win streak from July 26 to Aug. 16. The following table lists the top seven active leaders in Winston Cup victories and how many victories they had before turning 27. (Through Aug. 31, 1998).

Driver	Winston Cup Races	Career Wins	Before age 27
Darrell Waltrip	743	84	0
Dale Earnhardt	597	71	0
Rusty Wallace	448	47	0
Bill Elliot	537	40	0
Jeff Gordon	179	38	35
Mark Martin	380	27	0
Terry Labonte	597	20	0

Ages (Year of first Winston Cup victory): Waltrip – 28 (1975); Earnhardt – 27 (1979); Wallace – 29 (1986); Elliot – 28 (1983); Gordon – 22 (1994); Martin – 30 (1989); Labonte – 35 (1980).

2 **Italy's Marco Pantani wins** the Tour de France, becoming only the sixth rider to ever win it and the Giro of Italy in the same year.

The Cuban national baseball team captures its sixth consecutive world baseball championship title with a 7-1 victory over South Korea, extending its tournament winning streak to 41 games (since 1986).

Jeff Gordon becomes the first NASCAR driver to win two Brickyard 400s.

3 **Amateur golfer Matthew Scott becomes** the youngest person to make a hole-in-one when the 5-year-old aces the 86-yard, par-3 seventh hole at Fox Ridge Country Club in Indiana.

5 **Walt Disney Co. offers to pay** $600 million for exclusive U.S. broadcast rights to NHL hockey for five years, triple what Fox Sports and ESPN currently pay.

6 **Ohio St. garners the preseason** #1 ranking in the *USA Today*/ESPN Top 25 Coaches' Poll.

Commissioner David Stern and owners abruptly walk out of the first meeting of the NBA and the players union since the lockout.

Big East men's basketball officials announce it will scrap the two-division format next season.

8 **Minnesota DH Paul Molitor steals** his 500th base, making him the fifth major league player to reach that milestone and also collect 3,000 hits.

9 **Atlanta Braves righthander Dennis Martinez** earns his 244th career major league victory, breaking the record for Latin American pitchers, formerly held by Juan Marichal.

Yugoslavia wins the World Basketball Championships in Athens with a 64-62 victory over Russia.

10 **Despite a plea from John Elway,**, retired offensive lineman Gary Zimmerman tells coach Mike Shanahan he is not coming back for the 1998-99 season.

11 **Following the advice his doctors gave** him, NY Rangers center Pat LaFontaine announces his retirement from the NHL after 15 pro seasons.

The International Basketball League announces plans to form a new men's professional league which will begin its first 64-game season in November 1999.

12 **Seattle shortstop Alex Rodriguez**, 23, becomes the fourth-youngest player ever to reach 100 career home runs.

14 **For the first time this decade** a major league baseball game (Reds vs. Expos) features both teams with brothers in the starting lineup, Wilton and Vladimir Guerrero for Montreal and Aaron and Bret Boone for the Reds.

16 **Fiji-born golfer Vijay Singh shoots** a 2-under-par 68, to capture the PGA Tour's final major of the year, the PGA Championship, at Sahalee Country Club in Redmond, Wash.

NASCAR driver Jeff Gordon ties a Winston Cup record by winning his fourth consecutive race, the Pepsi 400 at Michigan Speedway. Mark Martin, whose father, stepmother, and half-sister died in a plane crash Aug. 9, finishes second.

NFL football returns to CBS after a 4½ year hiatus, as the network broadcasts a preseason game between San Francisco and Seattle.

Baltimore Orioles outfielder Eric Davis has his season-best 30-game hit streak snapped by the Cleveland Indians.

17 **Six months after the second round**, Phil Mickelson cards a 5-under-par 67 to win the El Nino-delayed PGA Tour Pebble Beach (Calif.) National Pro-Am.

AP/Wide World Photos

Hailey Simpson (392) tucks into her ivory-colored car and coasts to victory ahead of A.J. Sanders (411) and Spencer Thulin (371) at the **All-American Soap Box Derby** in Akron, Ohio on Aug. 8. Simpson, the pride and joy of Salem, Ore., turned the tide on her opponents early in the race, edging them out for the AASBD Stock Division title.

ABC television affiliates interrupt coverage of the 1998 American Bowl between the Patriots and Cowboys to bring viewers live coverage of President Clinton's address to the nation which followed his grand jury testimony earlier that day.

18 The Sacramento Kings announce the firing of head coach Eddie Jordan as well as assistant Mike Bratz and say that a search for their replacements is on.

20 Mark McGwire becomes the first major league baseball player in history to hit at least 50 home runs in three consecutive seasons, by launching #50 into the left field seats at Shea Stadium in the first game of a day-night doubleheader. He hits #51 in the nightcap.

Giants cornerback Jason Sehorn tears ligaments in his right knee while returning the opening kickoff in a preseason game against the Jets and is lost for the season.

23 Monica Seles needs just 76 minutes to beat Arantxa Sanchez Vicario in winning her fourth straight du Maurier Open in Montreal.

Running back Bill Hamilton rushes for an Arena Bowl-record 82 yards and three touchdowns, leading the Orlando Predators to a 62-31 victory over the Tampa Bay Storm.

26 The NHL's fifth-leading goal scorer Mike Gartner calls it quits after 19 seasons and five teams.

Hockey Hall of Famer Bobby Hull releases a statement denying comments he made in a story for *The Moscow Times* in which he allegedly said, among other things, "Hitler, for example, had some good ideas. He just went a little too far."

29 Baseball fans are shocked by the news that Mark McGwire was ejected in the first inning of the Cardinals-Braves game for arguing a called third strike, keeping his run at the record stalled at 54 home runs.

Indy Racing League driver Kenny Brack captures his third straight event, speeding to victory at the Indy 200 at Atlanta Motor Speedway.

Green Bay running back Dorsey Levens ends his training-camp holdout.

30 SMU golfer Hank Kuehne beats Tom McKnight 2 and 1 before a record crowd of 10,500 at Oak Hill C.C. in Rochester N.Y. to garner the 98th U.S. Amateur Championship.

Shortstop Todd Frazier goes 4-for-4, with a homer, scores three runs and earns the victory as a relief pitcher, sparking Toms River, N.J. to a 12-9 victory over Kashima, Japan at the Little League World Series.

NASCAR officials at the CMT 300 take tire samples from the cars of winner Jeff Gordon and runner-up Mark Martin after opposing teams charge the two drivers' crews with "soaking" tires to make them softer.

31 Just in time for the pennant chase, the Cleveland Indians obtain Seattle second baseman Joey Cora for David Bell.

Florida State defeats Texas A&M 23-14 in the Kickoff Classic.

The ubiquitous Mike Tyson is involved in an automobile accident where, reportedly, he has to be restrained by his bodyguards from pummeling the driver of the other car.

SEPT '98

Sun	Mon	Tue	Wed	Thu	Fri	Sat
		1	2	3	4	5
6	7	8	9	10	11	12
13	14	15	16	17	18	19
20	21	22	23	24	25	26
27	28	29	30			

Once In A Gr-eight While

When Lindsay Davenport and Patrick Rafter captured singles titles at the U.S. Open in September, it meant that for only the fifth time since the Grand Slam of tennis was recognized in 1925 (when the French Open was added) all eight singles titles (four men's, four women's) were won by different players.

1926 **Australian** — John Hawkes, Daphne Akhurst
French — Henri Cochet, Suzanne Lenglen
Wimbledon — Jean Borota, Kathleen Godfree
U.S. Open — Rene Lacoste, Molla Mallory

1948 **Australian** — Adrian Quist, Nancye Bolton
French — Frank Parker, Nelly Landry
Wimbledon — Bob Falkenburg, Louise Brough
U.S. Open — Pancho Gonzales, Margaret du Pont

1966 **Australian** — Roy Emerson, Margaret Smith
French — Tony Roche, Ann Jones
Wimbledon — Manuel Santana, Billie Jean King
U.S. Open — Fred Stolle, Maria Bueno

1990 **Australian** — Ivan Lendl, Steffi Graf
French — Andres Gomez, Monica Seles
Wimbledon — Stefan Edberg, Martina Navratilova
U.S. Open — Pete Sampras, Gabriela Sabatini

1998 **Australian** — Petr Korda, Martina Hingis
French — Carlos Moya, Arantxa Sanchez Vicario
Wimbledon — Pete Sampras, Jana Novotna
U.S. Open — Patrick Rafter, Lindsay Davenport

1 **Houston forward Sheryl Swoopes** scores 10 of her team's last 17 points, leading the Comets to a 80-71 victory and their second straight WNBA Championship.

Detroit Tigers coach Buddy Bell is fired and replaced by bench coach Larry Parrish.

2 **Future Hall of Fame receiver** Jerry Rice signs a new six-year, $36 million contract with the San Francisco 49ers.

4 **The New York Yankees record** their 100th victory of the season, quicker than any other American League team in history.

6 **Eight NFL starting quarterbacks** suffer injuries during their Week 1 games, including New Orleans' Billy Joe Hobert who is lost for the season.

7 **On his dad's 61st birthday**, Cardinals slugger Mark McGwire ties Roger Maris' 37-year old record for home runs in a season when he blasts #61 into the left-field seats at Busch Stadium in St. Louis.

Dario Franchitti wins his second consecutive CART race – the Vancouver Molson Indy, but Alex Zanardi's fourth-place finish secures him his second consecutive CART series championship.

8 **A ball hit by Mark McGwire** barely makes it over the left-field fence at Busch Stadium and becomes his 62nd and shortest home run of the season. The fourth-inning blast breaks the record for most home runs ever hit in a season, and it is done in the Cardinal's 144th game of the season.

NFL owners award the Cleveland expansion franchise to the group headed by Alfred Lerner, after the banker bids $530 million for the new Browns.

9 **The NBA lockout forces** the cancellation of a preseason game between the Miami Heat and an Israeli team to be held Oct. 12, marking the league's first game wiped out by a labor dispute.

Rupert Murdoch's BSkyB satellite company, which supplies pay TV worldwide, agrees to purchase England's Manchester United soccer team for a record $1 billion.

11 **Cubs outfielder Sammy Sosa** smacks his 61st and 62nd home runs in an 11-10, 10-inning victory at Wrigley Field, becoming the second man in baseball history (and this season) to reach that total.

12 **Lindsay Davenport captures** her first grand slam title by defeating defending champion Martina Hingis 6-3, 7-5 at the U.S. Open.

Country singer Garth Brooks takes batting practice with his childhood favorites, the Pittsburgh Pirates, and hits one home run from each side of the plate, becoming possibly the only country singer on the charts to do that.

13 **Patrick Rafter successfully defends** his U.S. Open men's singles championship against Mark Philippoussis.

14 **Marv Albert makes his return** to broadcasting, anchoring a 30-minute New York sports highlight show for the MSG cable network.

16 **Detroit Lions coach Bobby Ross** announces he's demoting QB Scott Mitchell to third string and is replacing him with 1998 second round pick Charlie Batch.

IOC President Juan Antonio Samaranch confirms that China is seriously considering a bid to host the 2008 Olympic Summer Games.

17 **Rick Adelman signs on** to coach the Sacramento Kings for the 1998-99 season.

18 **Norris Trophy winner Rob Blake** ends his five-day holdout and becomes the NHL's richest defenseman, inking a three-year $15.8 million deal.

AP/Wide World Photos

Word spreads fast when your hometown college wins its first football game in nine years. This sign appeared on Sept. 27, the morning after the **Prairie View A&M football team** won its first game since Oct. 28, 1989, mercifully ending college football's longest losing streak ever at 80 games.

Possibly signaling the end of a renowned career, Julio Cesar Chavez (101-3-2) refuses to answer the bell for the ninth round after being pummeled by Oscar De La Hoya, who defeats Chavez for the second time in his career.

U.S. Soccer star Mia Hamm scores her 100th career international goal and adds another, helping the U.S. defeat Russia 4-0 in the Nike U.S. Women's Cup series in Rochester, N.Y.

19 Pitted against the best and brightest at the $500,000 Woodward Stakes, Skip Away powers to victory, giving the thoroughbred its ninth victory in a row and seventh in 1998 against no losses.

Evander Holyfield successfully defends his heavyweight title, but only after going the distance with opponent Vaughn Bean and winning a unanimous decision.

20 Orioles third baseman Cal Ripken ends his consecutive games played streak at 2,632 games, sitting out the Orioles game against the New York Yankees at Camden Yards. Ripken's record streak began on May 30, 1982, the day after he watched the second game of a double-header against Toronto from the Orioles' dugout.

21 Just four days short of the 10th anniversary of her first gold medal at the 1988 Olympics in Seoul, track star Florence Griffith Joyner dies at her home in Mission Viejo, Calif. at the age of 38.

Evander Holyfield admits in an interview with the *Atlanta Journal-Constitution* to having fathered two children out of wedlock in the last year with two ex-girlfriends.

22 Two-time CART series champion Alex Zanardi announces he's bolting back to Formula One, signing a three-year deal with the London-based Williams Formula One team.

Hoping to erase the memories of one of the worst seasons in NBA history, the Denver Nuggets hire Mike D'Antoni, the team's director of player personnel, to coach next season.

NCAA bans Louisville's men's basketball team from postseason play for a year because of rules violations related to recruiting and financial aid benefits.

24 The NBA cancels 24 exhibition games due to the lockout.

Shady Character wins the Little Brown Jug, harness racing's second leg of the Pacing Triple Crown, in Delaware, Ohio.

25 The New York Yankees set a new American League record for victories in a season with 112, beating the Tampa Bay Devil Rays 6-1 at home.

26 Prairie View A&M's football team ends its NCAA-record 80-game losing streak with a 14-12 victory against Langston (Okla.) in Oklahoma City.

27 Mark McGwire hits two home runs in the Cardinals' season finale against Montreal, becoming the first player ever to hit 70 home runs in a season.

Chicago's Sammy Sosa doesn't hit a home run, but has his season extended one day when his Cubs and the San Francisco Giants finish the season tied and are forced to play a one-game playoff.

NASCAR veteran Ricky Rudd, nearly overcome by heat exhaustion, wins the NAPA 500 to extend his streak of years with at least one victory to 16.

28 Chicago Cubs starter Steve Trachsel pitches six innings of no-hit baseball, powering Chicago to a 5-3 victory over San Francisco and a wild card berth.

30 The Los Angeles Dodgers re-open the search for a new manager by re-assigning interim manager Glenn Hoffman to a new coaching position with the team.

OCT '98

Sun	Mon	Tue	Wed	Thu	Fri	Sat
				1	2	3
4	5	6	7	8	9	10
11	12	13	14	15	16	17
18	19	20	21	22	23	24
25	26	27	28	29	30	31

World Series Win Streaks

With their four-game sweep of the San Diego Padres, the New York Yankees' consecutive World Series game victory streak was extended to eight games. Although there are plenty of Yankees teams atop this list, the Cincinnati Reds hold the longest active streak.

Years	Teams	Consecutive Games Won
1927-28, 1932	New York Yankees	12
1938-39, 1941	New York Yankees	10
1975-76, 1990	Cincinnati Reds	9 (active)
1996, 98	New York Yankees	8 (active)

Cornerstones & stiffs

The Carolina Panthers hoped to build around Penn St. QB Kerry Collins after they chose him with the franchise's first pick in 1995. The dream ended on Oct. 13 when Collins was put on waivers after asking not to play. Here's how expansion teams in the 1990s have spent their first draft pick, and where those players are now.

NFL

Drafted, Year	Player	Current Team
Carolina, 1995	Kerry Collins, QB	New Orleans
Jacksonville, 1995	Tony Boselli, OT	same

NBA

Drafted, Year	Player	Current Team
Toronto, 1995	Damon Stoudamire, G	Portland
Vancouver, 1995	Bryant Reeves, C	same

NHL

Drafted, Year	Player	Current Team
San Jose, 1991	Pat Falloon, C	Edmonton
Ottawa, 1992	Alexi Yashin, C	same
Tampa Bay, 1992	Roman Hamrlik, D	Edmonton
Anaheim, 1993	Paul Kariya, LW	same
Florida, 1993	Rob Niedermayer, C	same

MLB

Drafted, Year	Player	Current Team
Colorado, 1993	Jamey Wright, P	same
Florida, 1993	Marc Valdes, P	Montreal
Arizona, 1996	Nick Bierbrodt, P	South Bend (A)
Tampa Bay, 1996	Paul Wilder, OF	Charleston (A)

2 Florida Marlins manager Jim Leyland exercises an out clause in his contract and announces he is leaving the team that he helped win the World Series in 1997.

Former Boston Celtics great Larry Bird is inducted into the Basketball Hall of Fame.

3 Former Cubs pitcher Greg Maddux and his Atlanta Braves shut down Chicago 6-2 in Game 3 of the National League Divisional Series, completing a sweep of the Cubs and improving their all-time NLDS record to 12-1 (since 1995).

Red Sox closer Tom Gordon blows his first save since April 14, giving up a game-winning two-run double to Cleveland's David Justice, propelling the Indians into the ALCS to face the Yankees.

Yankees outfielder Darryl Strawberry undergoes three hours of surgery to remove a cancerous tumor from his colon.

Canada's Peter Reid and Switzerland's Natascha Badmann win the 20th annual Ironman Triathlon in Hawaii.

4 The San Diego Padres beat Houston 6-1, sending them to the NLCS for the first time in 14 years.

Officials penalize the San Francisco 49ers 22 times in their 26-21 loss to Buffalo, tying a 54-year-old NFL record for penalties by one team in a football game.

5 The NBA cancels its remaining 114 preseason games due to the ongoing lockout.

Former Marlins manager Jim Leyland signs a three-year deal to manage the Colorado Rockies.

San Francisco 49ers owner Eddie DeBartolo pleads guilty to charges he concealed an alleged plot by former Louisiana Gov. Edwin Edwards to extort money from him in a casino licensing case.

6 Tampa Bay Lightning forward John Cullen's comeback is made official when his name is included in the team's opening night roster after 18 months of treatment for non-Hodgkins lymphoma.

7 Yankees second baseman Chuck Knoblauch argues with the first base umpire while the go-ahead run scores from first, in a 4-1 loss to Cleveland in the ALCS, qualifying Knoblauch for the exclusive postseason boner club, co-chaired by Bill Buckner and Fred Merkle.

8 Carolina Panthers quarterback Kerry Collins tells head coach Dom Capers he'd like to be benched for Sunday's game against Dallas.

9 U.S. Open champ Lindsay Davenport ends Martina Hingis' 18-month reign as women's tennis' No. 1 ranked player, after Hingis loses her quarterfinal match against Dominique van Roost in the Filderstadt Grand Prix.

11 David Duval continues his winning ways on the PGA Tour in 1998, capturing his fourth tournament title of the year at the Michelob Championship in Williamsburg, Va.

13 A report from the six-member medical team which studied boxer Mike Tyson as a condition set by the Nevada State Athletic Commission says the former champion needs regular psychotherapy and has problems controlling his anger but is "mentally fit to return to boxing."

The NBA cancels the first two weeks of the regular season. It's the first time in the league's 52-year history that games have been lost to a work stoppage.

After a four-game losing streak, San Diego Chargers coach Kevin Gilbride is fired and replaced by assistant coach June Jones.

AP/Wide World Photos

Florida Panthers center Rob Niedermayer (44) battles with Greg Johnson of the Nashville Predators for the first puck dropped in Predators' franchise history on Oct. 10 in Nashville Arena. The NHL will continue its expansion over the next two seasons, adding teams in Atlanta (1999), Columbus and Minneapolis (2000).

Tampa Bay Lightning GM Phil Esposito is fired by the team and his job title is given to coach Jacques Demers.

14 NLCS MVP Sterling Hitchcock and four relievers allow just four hits in a 5-0 Game 6 victory over Atlanta, sending the Padres to the World Series for just the second time in team history.

The New Orleans Saints claim former Panthers QB Kerry Collins 24 hours after Carolina put their former number-one draft pick on waivers.

15 Green Bay QB Brett Favre throws three interceptions for the third straight game, and Detroit gets 155 yards rushing from Barry Sanders, powering the Lions to a 27-20 upset victory.

The Detroit Tigers lift the "interim" title from manager Larry Parish's nameplate, signing him to a two-year deal.

16 Tennis star Venus Williams records a 127 mph serve – the fastest ever in women's tennis – against a stunned Mary Pierce at the European Championships.

17 Yankees 2B Chuck Knoblauch hits a game-tying three-run homer and Tino Martinez adds a grand slam, powering New York past San Diego 9-6 in Game 1 of the World Series.

Nearly five-touchdown underdog Temple rallies from a 17-point halftime deficit to shock 10th ranked and previously unbeaten Virgina Tech 28-24 in Div. 1 college football.

19 The Nevada State Athletic Commission reinstates the boxing license it stripped from Mike Tyson 15 months earlier.

Arbitrator John Feerick rules that NBA owners are not required to pay players during the lockout.

Former NY Giants linebacker Lawrence Taylor is arrested on charges of purchasing crack cocaine from an undercover police officer.

21 The New York Yankees capture their 24th World Series title and second in the last three years by completing a four-game sweep of the San Diego Padres.

Alpine skiier Katja Seizinger's team trainer tells a German newspaper that the Olympic champion will not race again this World Cup season and may end her career because of severe knee injuries she suffered in a crash in June.

22 The *Cincinnati Post* reports Reds owner Marge Schott has agreed in writing to sell her controlling interest in the team by the end of 1998.

Orange County medical examiners put to rest rumors of drug use by announcing that Florence Griffith Joyner died of asphyxiation, caused by an epileptic seizure she suffered on Sept. 21.

23 Davey Johnson is introduced as the new manager of the Los Angeles Dodgers.

Detroit Red Wings coach Scotty Bowman reappears behind his team's bench for the first time this season after recovering from angioplasty in July to clear a blocked artery and knee-replacement surgery in August.

Auburn football coach Terry Bowden quits after the Tigers win just one of their first six games. It's the team's worst start since 1952.

25 Denver place-kicker Jason Elam ties a 28-year-old NFL record when he boots a 63-yard field goal against the Jaguars in Mile High Stadium.

The expansion Chicago Fire upset two-time defending MLS Cup champion D.C. United 2-0 in Major League Soccer's championship game.

26 N.Y. Mets catcher Mike Piazza signs the richest contract in baseball history, a seven-year $91 million deal to stay in the Big Apple.

JANUARY

1 Major bowl games: Sugar (New Orleans); Rose (Pasadena)
2 Orange Bowl (Miami)
4 Fiesta Bowl, National Title Game (Tempe, Ariz.)
7 U.S. Figure Skating Champs. begin (Salt Lake City)
9 NCAA Convention begins (San Antonio)
9 NFL Playoffs (2): AFC/NFC semifinal games
10 NFL Playoffs (2): AFC/NFC semifinal games
14 Winter X Games begin (Crested Butte, Colo.)
17 NFL playoffs (2): AFC/NFC championship games
18 Australian Open Tennis begins (Melbourne)
23 NHL All-Star Game (Tampa Bay)
31 Super Bowl XXXIII (Miami)

FEBRUARY

7 NFL Pro Bowl (Honolulu)
8 Westminster Dog Show begins (New York City)
12 NBA All-Star Weekend begins (Philadelphia)†
14 Daytona 500 (Daytona Beach, Fla.)
15 ESPY Awards (New York City)
21 PBA National Championship begins (Toledo)

MARCH

5 NCAA Indoor Track & Field Champs. begin (Indianapolis)
6 Iditarod Trail Sled Dog race begins (Anchorage)
7 NCAA Men's and Women's Basketball Tournament Selections
12 NCAA Men's Division I Basketball tournament begins
12 NCAA Women's Division I Basketball tournament begins
14 NFL Annual Meeting begins (Phoenix)
18 NCAA Women's Div. I Swimming & Diving Champs. begin (Athens, Ga)
22 LPGA Dinah Shore Golf begins (Palm Springs, Calif.)
23 World Figure Skating Champs. begin (Helsinki, FIN)
25 NCAA Men's Div. I Swimming & Diving Championships begin (Indianapolis)
26 NCAA Women's Basketball Final Four begins (San Jose)
27 NCAA Men's Basketball Final Four begins (St. Petersburg, Fla.)
29 Davis Cup Tennis First Round begins (various sites)

APRIL

1 NCAA Division I Hockey Final Four begins (Anaheim)
6 Baseball Opening Day*
8 Masters Golf (Augusta, Ga.)
12 Women's Fed Cup Tennis First Round begins (various sites)
17 NFL Draft begins (New York City)
18 ABL Women's Basketball Finals begin
18 NHL Regular Season ends
19 Boston Marathon
21 NHL Stanley Cup Playoffs begin
21 NBA Regular Season ends
24 NBA Playoffs begin

MAY

1 Kentucky Derby (Louisville)
3 ABC Masters Bowling tournament begins (Syracuse, N.Y.)*
8 Stanley Cup Finals begin
15 Preakness Stakes (Baltimore)
16 NBA Draft Lottery
23 Indianapolis 500
24 French Open begins (Paris)
27 NCAA Women's Softball Champs. begin (Oklahoma City)
29 NCAA Men's Lacrosse Final Four begins (College Park, Md.)

* tentative dates
† barring a lockout

JUNE

2 NCAA Men's and Women's Track & Field Champs. begin (Boise, Idaho)
3 U.S. Open Women's Golf begins (West Point, Miss.)
5 Belmont Stakes (Belmont, N.Y.)
11 NCAA Div. I College World Series begins (Omaha, Neb.)
17 U.S. Open Golf begins (Pinehurst, N.C.)
19 WNBA Regular Season begins*
21 LPGA Championship begins (Wilmington, Del.)
21 Wimbledon Tennis begins
23 NBA Draft (TBD)
25 Summer X Games begin (San Francisco)
26 NHL Draft (Boston)

JULY

3 Tour de France Cycling begins
5 Senior U.S. Open Golf begins (Des Moines)
12 Davis Cup Tennis Second Round begin (various sites)
13 Baseball All-Star Game (Boston)
15 British Open Golf begins (Carnoustie, SCOT)
17 MLS All-Star Game (San Diego)
19 Women's Fed Cup Tennis Semifinals begin (various sites)
25 U.S. 500 (Brooklyn, Mich.)

AUGUST

5 Bass Masters Classic begins*
8 Players Championship Women's Bowling tournament begins*
12 PGA Championship begins (Medinah, Ill.)
14 All-American Soap Box Derby (Akron, Ohio)
22 Little League World Series begins (Williamsport, Pa.)*
25 U.S. Gymnastics Champs. begin (Sacramento, Calif.)
30 U.S. Open Tennis begins (Flushing Meadows, N.Y.)

SEPTEMBER

12 NFL Regular Season begins
13 Women's Fed Cup Tennis Finals begin
20 Davis Cup Semifinals begin (various sites).
21 Ryder Cup Men's Golf begins (Brookline, Mass.)
26 Baseball Regular Season ends
29 Baseball Playoffs begin*

OCTOBER

9 College Football: Oklahoma at Texas
10 AMF Gold Cup Women's Bowling tournament begins*
16 World Series begins (in city of NL champion)*
23 Ironman Triathlon Championship (Hawaii)
30 Sam's Town Invitational Women's Bowling tournament begins (Las Vegas)*

NOVEMBER

6 Breeders Cup Horse Racing (Lexington, Ky.)
7 New York City Marathon
14 MLS Cup Final (Foxboro, Mass.)
15 WTA Tour Tennis Championships begin
17 Tournament of Champions Men's Bowling tournament begins (Overland, Kan.)
20 College Football: Ohio St. at Michigan; Alabama at Auburn; UCLA at USC and Harvard at Yale
22 ATP Tour Tennis Championships begin
28 CFL Grey Cup (Vancouver)
29 Davis Cup Final begins

DECEMBER

3 National Finals Rodeo begin (Las Vegas)
3 NCAA Women's Soccer Final Four begins (San Jose)
4 College Football: Big 12 Championship Game (TBD); SEC Championship Game (Atlanta); Army vs. Navy (Philadelphia)
9 NCAA Men's Soccer Final Four (Charlotte, N.C.)
11 Heisman Trophy winner announced (New York City)
18 NCAA Div. I-AA Football Championship (Chattanooga, Tenn.)
27 NFL regular season ends

* tentative dates

Baseball

The number behind him says it all. **Mark McGwire** rounds the bases for the final time in 1998 after hitting No. 70 off Montreal rookie Carl Pavano.

AP/Wide World Photos

The Best Ever?

Let the arguments begin. In 1998, we may have seen the best team and the best season in baseball history.

by
Karl Ravech

It was exactly one year ago when I wrote the opening paragraph to summarize the 1997 baseball season and the last line referred to the sport of Major League Baseball as being "out of whack."

Somebody please whack me, or wake me up because what happened in 1998 had to be a dream. It seems virtually impossible that so many forces could come together at the exact same time and unfurl over the course of the entire season, each week seemingly topping the one before it until in the end, arguably one of the greatest teams of all time stamped an indelible exclamation point onto what the children of the baby-boom generation will remember as the greatest baseball season of all time.

That is not to suggest that those who remember seeing Babe Ruth circle the bases or Roger Maris blast 61 home runs in 1961 would not also concur. The 1998 baseball season began with more teams than ever before. Tampa Bay and Arizona gave us an even number of 30. Detractors of expansion suggested that more teams would lead to lower quality of pitching throughout the league and thus the game would become more like basketball than baseball, with scoring every 5.8 seconds. That didn't exactly happen. But Mark McGwire and Sammy Sosa did.

If McGwire and Sosa were trees in a forest, McGwire would be a redwood and Sosa an oak. Both men are as strong as wood and stood above the game like no two figures ever had. By Sept. 4, both men had broken Hack Wilson's National League record of 56 home runs in a season. Nine days later, Sosa blasted two against Milwaukee, tying him with McGwire at 62. At one point, they were tied at 65, and it was Sosa who reached 66 first. His lead lasted all of 45 minutes. McGwire ended the year by hitting

---

Karl Ravech is the host of ESPN's *Baseball Tonight.*

AP/Wide World Photos

World Series MVP **Scott Brosius** celebrates the Yankees' 3-0 victory on Oct. 21 in San Diego, completing a four-game sweep of the Padres. It was New York's all-time record 125th win of the season as they captured their 24th World Series Championship.

five home runs in his final three games for an unheard of total of 70. McGwire carried baseball on his back. Sosa carried the Cubs into the postseason.

Let the record show that Sosa had help in Chicago— namely 20-year-old rookie Kerry Wood, who on May 6, tied the major league record by striking out 20 Astros in one game. I told you it was the greatest season ever. The Cubs, thanks to a victory in a one-game playoff against the Giants, were joined in the N.L. playoffs by the Astros, Padres and Braves. The American League contingent consisted of the Rangers, Indians, Red Sox and Yankees.

In the end, none of the playoff series saw a deciding fifth or seventh game and the World Series simply belonged to the Yankees. As they had done throughout the entire season, breaking the A.L. regular-season record for wins with 114, they played near-perfect baseball. And perfect is an appropriate word to use, for on May 17, their ace David Wells pitched a perfect game against the Twins.

The World Series hero was third baseman Scott Brosius. His two home runs in game three rallied the Yankees to a come-from-behind win and symbolized what the '98 Yankees were all about—TEAM. Not one of the Yankees' regulars started the All-Star game.

Underneath the gold which glittered over the season, problems still remain with the game. Big market teams with revenue streams not shared with those

AP/Wide World Photos

Chicago slugger **Sammy Sosa** became a national hero both in the United States and his native Dominican Republic as his 66 home runs carried the Cubs into the playoffs for the first time since 1989.

in Montreal and Pittsburgh continue to underscore the need for some type of revenue sharing. Otherwise, there will be no teams in Montreal and Pittsburgh and what a shame it would be for fans in those cities to be on the outside looking in on a game that is as strong now as ever before. ■

Karl Ravech's Top Ten Highlights of the 1998 Baseball Season.

As host of ESPN's *Baseball Tonight*, I was privileged to provide the country with a nightly diary of the greatest baseball season I can remember. That being said, please disregard the numbers next to these events and consider each as monumental as the one before it.

10. **Opening Day**— The expansion Tampa Bay Devil Rays and Arizona Diamondbacks both play, and both lose. Mark McGwire hits a grand slam. Who knew then that he would hit more home runs than either expansion franchise would win games.

9. **The House that Ruth Built**— Thankfully no one is hurt when a large piece of Yankee Stadium (weighing approximately 500 pounds) falls some 100 feet onto some seats below. The Yankees are forced to play some home games at Shea Stadium, home of their city rival— the Mets.

8. **Kerry Wood**— The 20-year-old pitcher takes Chicago by storm, tying a major league record by

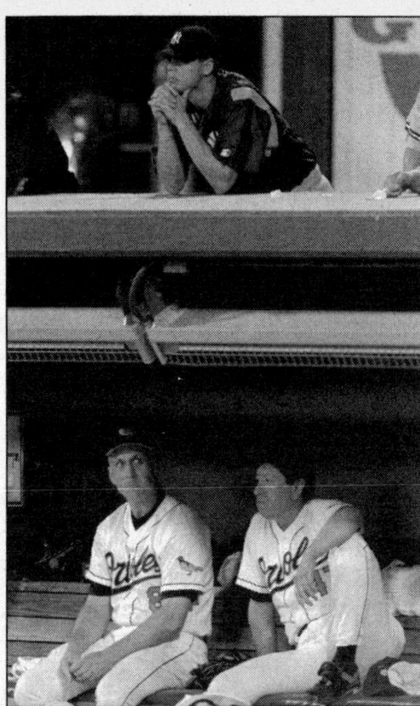

AP/Wide World Photos

Baltimore's **Cal Ripken Jr.** (l) sits as a spectator in the Orioles bullpen with reliever Jesse Orosco as his streak of 2,632 consecutive games played comes to an end.

striking out 20 Astros in a game. Towards the end of the season, his arm tires but he succeeds in waking up the Cubbies and helping to bring them to the postseason. Maybe next season, the promised land.

7. **Harry Caray**— The lovable legend of broadcasting passes away in 1998, leaving a void in Wrigley Field and the game that can not be filled. He brought to baseball a spirit and enthusiasm that will be missed not just by Cubs fans but all baseball fans alike. The man is gone but the legend lives on and for that we thank Harry and the Cubs.

6. **David Wells**— He pitches a perfect game on May 17 and, as rumor has it, celebrates by putting down 27 beers that night. A classic character cut from play-dough, he epitomizes the 1998 Yankees' "never-say-die" attitude. When he's between the lines, it's all business and no team went to work like the Yankees.

5. **Bud Selig**— The man who insisted he did not want to become the ninth commissioner of baseball finally cedes to the pressure of the owners. Or maybe he wanted it all along. In any event, he piloted the game through the '94 strike and in '98 was in the cockpit again as baseball celebrated a perfect flight. Along with Paul Beeston and other major appointments, the game now has its house in order and actually gets along with the Players' Association.

4. **The Umpires**— For some reason, many of them believe fans pay to see them do their jobs. Not true. Too often the men in blue were at the center of controversy and more often than not, they acted as the instigator, not the peacemaker. It is one of the biggest problems the game must address.

3. **Sammy Sosa**— The world fell in love with a guy that was once known as much for the gold around his neck and his penchant for striking out than anything else. In '98, he blasted 66 home runs and showed the world that pressure is only what you make of it. He made us laugh, he made McGwire laugh and his infectious smile meant that all was good again.

2. **The New York Yankees**— Give me a break. They raced out to 17 wins by the end of April and by the end of August had 98. They ended up with 114 for the regular season and 125 at the conclusion of their World Series sweep. The greatest team? It's impossible to compare them with teams from other decades but I'd wager George Steinbrenner's money on them anytime.

1. **Mark ·McGwire**— He hit four home runs in his first four games and rarely, if ever, appeared agitated by the media spotlight, which burned at 1,000 watts over the second half of the season. The biggest, strongest man in baseball reminded everyone that it's OK to cry and it's important to keep your feet on the ground. He hugged his son after he blasted No. 61 and we all felt better about the game and ourselves. Thank you Mark and thank you baseball for a season that will never be forgotten. ■

INSIDE THE NUMBERS

by

Craig Wachs, Jeff Bennett and Keith Lipscomb

M & M's

Compare the similarities to Roger Maris and his record-breaking year in 1961 and this past year of Mark McGwire. Also note that McGwire's record season was 13 years after Maris' death while Maris' season was 13 years after Babe Ruth's death. Hmmm.

	Maris	**McGwire**
Record HR	4th inning	4th inning
Opposing pitcher	Tracy Stallard (13 letters)	Steve Trachsel (13 letters)
October 1	60th HR	Birthday
Traded to St. Louis	11th year	11th year
Record HR caught by	Sal Durante, 19 Bus Driver	Tim Forneris, 22 Grounds Crew

PARTNERS IN CLOUT

This was indeed the most prolific season for home runs in the history of baseball. Take a look at the most round trippers hit by two teammates in one season. Three of the top five are from 1998.

Year	**Duo**	**Home runs**	**Break down**
1961	Maris/Mantle, Yankees	115	61/54
1927	Ruth/Gehrig, Yankees	107	60/47
1998	McGwire/Lankford, Cardinals	101	70/31
1998	Griffey Jr./A. Rodriguez, Mariners	98	56/42
1998	Sosa/H. Rodriguez, Cubs	97	66/31

THEN AND NOW

A whole lot has changed over the past 16 years since Cal Ripken Jr. began his record streak. To put things in perspective, Ripken's replacement Ryan Minor was eight years old when the streak began.

	5/30/82	**9/20/98**
President	Reagan	Clinton
Dow Jones Ind.	819.54	7895.66
No. 1 Song	Ebony and Ivory	I Don't Want to Miss a Thing
Commissioner	Bowie Kuhn	Bud Selig
Ripken's Salary	$64,000	$6.3 million

■

Final Major League Standings

Division champions (*) and Wild Card (†) winners are noted. Number of seasons listed after each manager refers to current tenure with club.

American League

East Division

	W	L	Pct	GB	Home	Road
*New York	114	48	.704	–	62-19	52-29
†Boston	92	70	.568	22	51-30	41-40
Toronto	88	74	.543	26	51-30	37-44
Baltimore	79	83	.488	35	42-39	37-44
Tampa Bay	63	99	.389	51	33-48	30-51

1998 Managers: NY– Joe Torre (3rd season); **Bos**– Jimy Williams (2nd); **Tor**– Tim Johnson (1st); **Bal**– Ray Miller (1st); **TB**–Larry Rothschild (1st).

1997 Standings: 1. Baltimore (98-64); 2. New York (96-66); 3. Detroit (79-83); 4. Boston (78-84); 5. Toronto (76-86). **Note:** Tampa Bay was an expansion team in 1998.

Central Division

	W	L	Pct	GB	Home	Road
*Cleveland	89	73	.549	–	46-35	43-38
Chicago	80	82	.494	9	44-37	36-45
Kansas City	72	89	.447	16½	29-51	43-38
Minnesota	70	92	.432	19	35-46	35-46
Detroit	65	97	.401	24	32-49	33-48

1998 Managers: Cle– Mike Hargrove (8th season); **Chi**– Jerry Manuel (1st); **KC**– Tony Muser (2nd); **Min**– Tom Kelly (13th); **Det**– replaced Buddy Bell (4th, 52-85) on Sept. 1 with Larry Parrish (13-12).

1997 Standings: 1. Cleveland (86-75); 2. Chicago (80-81); 3. Milwaukee (78-83); 4. Minnesota (68-94); 5. Kansas City (67-94).

West Division

	W	L	Pct	GB	Home	Road
*Texas	88	74	.543	–	48-33	40-41
Anaheim	85	77	.525	3	42-39	43-38
Seattle	76	85	.472	11½	42-39	34-46
Oakland	74	88	.457	14	39-42	35-46

1998 Managers: Tex– Johnny Oates (4th season); **Ana**– Terry Collins (2nd); **Sea**– Lou Piniella (6th); **Oak**– Art Howe (3rd).

1997 Standings: 1. Seattle (90-72); 2. Anaheim (84-78); 3. Texas (77-85); 4. Oakland (65-97).

National League

East Division

	W	L	Pct	GB	Home	Road
*Atlanta	106	56	.654	–	56-25	50-31
New York	88	74	.543	18	47-34	41-40
Philadelphia	75	87	.463	31	40-41	35-46
Montreal	65	97	.401	41	39-42	26-55
Florida	54	108	.333	52	31-50	23-58

1998 Managers: Atl– Bobby Cox (9th season); **NY**– Bobby Valentine (3rd); **Phi**– Jim Fregosi (8th); **Mon**– Felipe Alou (7th); **Fla**– Jim Leyland (2nd).

1997 Standings: 1. Atlanta (101-61); 2. Florida (92-70); 3. New York (88-74); 4. Montreal (78-84); 5. Philadelphia (68-94).

Central Division

	W	L	Pct	GB	Home	Road
*Houston	102	60	.630	–	55-26	47-34
†Chicago	90	73	.552	12½	51-31	39-42
St. Louis	83	79	.512	19	48-34	35-45
Cincinnati	77	85	.475	25	39-42	38-43
Milwaukee	74	88	.457	28	38-43	36-45
Pittsburgh	69	93	.426	33	40-40	29-53

1998 Managers: Hou– Larry Dierker (2nd season); **Chi**– Jim Riggleman (4th); **St.L**– Tony La Russa (3rd); **Cin**– Jack McKeon (2nd); **Mil**– Phil Garner (7th); **Pit**– Gene Lamont (2nd).

1997 Standings: 1. Houston (84-78); 2. Pittsburgh (79-83); 3. Cincinnati (76-86); 4. St. Louis (73-89); 5. Chicago (68-94). **Note:** Milwaukee moved to the National League in 1998, becoming the first team to switch leagues this century.

West Division

	W	L	Pct	GB	Home	Road
*San Diego	98	64	.605	–	54-27	44-37
San Francisco	89	74	.546	9½	49-32	28-16
Los Angeles	83	79	.512	15	48-33	35-46
Colorado	77	85	.475	21	42-39	35-46
Arizona	65	97	.401	33	34-47	31-50

1998 Managers: SD– Bruce Bochy (4th season); **SF**– Dusty Baker (6th); **LA**– replaced Bill Russell (3rd, 36-38) with Glenn Hoffman (47-41) on June 21; **Col**– Don Baylor (6th); **Ari**– Buck Showalter (1st).

1997 Standings: 1. San Francisco (90-72); 2. Los Angeles (88-74); 3. Colorado (83-79); 4. San Diego (76-86). **Note:** Arizona was an expansion team in 1998.

Wild Card Playoff Game

On September 28, 1998, the Chicago Cubs and San Francisco Giants, each with a regular-season record of 89-73, staged a playoff game to determine the winner of the National League wild card spot. It was the ninth time in baseball history that an extra game was needed as a tie-breaker, and the first time in history that a tiebreaker was needed to determine the wild card winner.

The game was played at Wrigley Field in Chicago due to a coin toss and the Cubs went on to defeat the Giants 5-3 to advance to the Division Series against Atlanta.

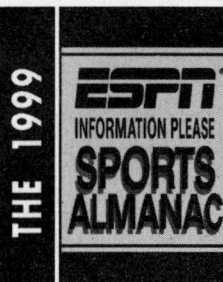

Seattle Mariners
Ken Griffey Jr.
Home Runs

Texas Rangers
Juan Gonzalez
RBI, Doubles

Oakland Athletics
Rickey Henderson
Stolen Bases, Walks

Toronto Blue Jays
Roger Clemens
ERA, Wins, Strikeouts

American League Leaders

Batting

	Bat	Gm	AB	R	H	Avg	TB	2B	3B	HR	RBI	BB	Int BB	SO	SB	Slg Pct	OBP
Bernie Williams, NY	S	128	499	101	169	**.339**	287	30	5	26	97	74	9	81	15	.575	.422
Mo Vaughn, Bos	L	154	609	107	205	**.337**	360	31	2	40	115	61	13	144	0	.591	.402
Albert Belle, Chi	R	163	609	113	200	**.328**	399	48	2	49	152	81	10	84	6	.655	.399
Eric Davis, Bal	R	131	452	81	148	**.327**	263	29	1	28	89	44	0	108	7	.582	.388
Derek Jeter, NY	R	149	626	127	203	**.324**	301	25	8	19	84	57	1	119	30	.481	.384
Nomar Garciaparra, Bos	R	143	304	111	195	**.323**	353	37	8	35	122	33	1	62	12	.584	.362
Edgar Martinez, Sea	R	154	556	86	179	**.322**	315	47	1	29	102	106	4	96	1	.567	.429
Ivan Rodriguez, Tex	R	145	579	88	186	**.321**	297	40	4	21	91	32	4	88	9	.513	.358
Tony Fernandez, Tor	S	138	486	71	156	**.321**	223	36	2	9	72	45	5	53	13	.459	.387
Juan Gonzalez, Tex	R	154	606	110	193	**.318**	382	50	2	45	157	46	9	126	2	.630	.366
Paul O'Neill, NY	L	152	602	95	191	**.317**	307	40	2	24	116	57	2	103	15	.510	.372
Todd Walker, Min	L	143	528	85	167	**.316**	250	41	3	12	62	47	9	65	19	.473	.372
Jose Offerman, KC	S	158	607	102	191	**.315**	266	28	13	7	66	89	1	96	45	.438	.403
Alex Rodriguez, Sea	R	161	686	123	213	**.310**	384	35	5	42	124	45	0	121	46	.560	.360
Hal Morris, KC	L	127	472	50	146	**.309**	180	27	2	1	40	32	6	52	1	.381	350

Home Runs

Griffey, Sea .56
Belle, Chi .49
Canseco, Tor .46
Gonzalez, Tex .45
Ramirez, Cle .45
Palmeiro, Bal .43
Rodriguez, Sea .42
Vaughn, Bos .40
Delgado, Tor .38
Garciaparra, Bos .35
Green, Tor .35

Triples

Offerman, KC .13
Damon, KC .10
Winn*, TB .9
Garciaparra, Bos .8
O'Leary, Bos .8
Jeter, NY .8
Durham, Chi .8
Anderson, Ana .7
McCracken, TB .7

On Base Pct.

Martinez, Sea .429
Williams, NY .422
Thome, Cle .413
Salmon, Ana .410
Offerman, KC .403
Vaughn, Bos .402
Belle, Chi .399

Runs Batted In

Gonzalez, Tex .157
Belle, Chi .152
Griffey, Sea .146
Ramirez, Cle .145
Rodriguez, Sea .124
Martinez, NY .123
Garciaparra, Bos .122
Palmeiro, Bal .121
Palmer, KC .119

Doubles

Gonzalez, Tex .50
Belle, Chi .48
Martinez, Sea .47
Valentin, Bos .44
Delgado, Tor .43
Edmonds, Ana .42
Clark, Tex .41
Grieve*, Oak .41
Anderson, Ana .41
Walker, Min .41

Slugging Pct.

Belle, Chi .655
Gonzalez, Tex .630
Griffey, Sea .611
Ramirez, Cle .599
Delgado, Tor .592
Vaughn, Bos .591
Garciaparra, Bos .584
Thome, Cle .584

Hits

Rodriguez, Sea .213
Vaughn, Bos .205
Jeter, NY .203
Belle, Chi .200
Garciaparra, Bos .195
Gonzalez, Tex .193
O'Neill, NY .191
Offerman, KC .191
Rodriguez, Tex .186

Runs

Jeter, NY .127
Durham, Chi .126
Rodriguez, Sea .123
Griffey, Sea .120
Knoblauch, NY .117
Edmonds, Ana .115
Belle, Chi .113
Valentin, Bos .113
Garciaparra, Bos .111
Cora, Sea-Cle .111

Walks

Henderson, Oak .118
Thomas, Chi .110
Martinez, Sea .106
Salmon, Ana .90
Offerman, KC .89
Thome, Cle .89
McLemore, Tex .89
Lofton, Cle .87

Stolen Bases

	SB	CS
Henderson, Oak	66	13
Lofton, Cle	54	10
Stewart, Tor	51	18
Rodriguez, Sea	46	13
Offerman, KC	45	12
Hunter, Det	42	12
Goodwin, Tex	38	20
Vizquel, Cle	37	12
Nixon, Min	37	7

Total Bases

Belle, Chi .399
Griffey, Sea .387
Rodriguez, Sea .384
Gonzalez, Tex .382
Vaughn, Bos .360
Garciaparra, Bos .353
Palmeiro, Bal .350
Ramirez, Cle .342
Green, Tor .321

Strikeouts

Canseco, Tor .159
Vaughn, Bos .144
Green, Tor .142
Thome, Cle .141
Delgado, Tor .139
Palmer, KC .134
Davis, Sea .134
Sorrento, TB .133

Pitching

	Arm	W	L	ERA	Gm	GS	CG	ShO	Sv	IP	H	R	ER	HR	HB	BB	SO	WP
Roger Clemens, Tor	R	20	6	**2.65**	33	33	5	3	0	234.2	169	78	69	11	7	88	271	6
Pedro Martinez, Bos	R	19	7	**2.89**	33	33	3	2	0	233.2	188	82	75	26	8	67	251	9
Kenny Rogers, Oak	L	16	8	**3.17**	34	34	7	1	0	238.2	215	96	84	19	7	67	138	5
Chuck Finley, Ana	L	11	9	**3.39**	34	34	1	1	0	223.1	210	97	84	20	6	109	212	8
David Wells, NY	L	18	4	**3.49**	30	30	8	5	0	214.1	195	86	83	29	0	29	163	2
Mike Mussina, Bal	R	13	10	**3.49**	29	29	4	2	0	206.1	189	85	80	22	4	41	175	10
Jamie Moyer, Sea	L	15	9	**3.53**	34	34	4	3	0	234.1	234	99	92	23	10	42	158	3
David Cone, NY	R	20	7	**3.55**	31	31	3	0	0	207.2	186	89	82	20	1	59	209	6
Rolando Arrojo*, TB	R	14	12	**3.56**	32	32	2	2	0	202.0	195	84	80	21	19	65	152	3
Bartolo Colon, Cle	R	14	9	**3.71**	31	31	6	2	0	204.0	205	91	84	15	3	79	158	4
Brian Moehler, Det	R	14	13	**3.90**	33	33	4	3	0	221.1	220	103	96	30	2	56	123	4
Bret Saberhagen, Bos	R	15	8	**3.96**	31	31	0	0	0	175.0	181	82	77	22	6	29	100	4
Jeff Fassero, Sea	L	13	12	**3.97**	32	32	7	0	0	224.2	223	115	99	33	10	66	176	12
Scott Erickson, Bal	R	16	13	**4.01**	36	36	11	2	0	251.1	284	125	112	23	13	69	186	4
Omar Olivares, Ana	R	9	9	**4.03**	37	26	1	0	0	183.0	189	92	82	19	5	91	112	5

Wins

Clemens, Tor.........20-6
Helling, Tex.........20-7
Cone, NY..........20-7
Martinez, Bos........19-7
Sele, Tex..........19-11
Wells, NY..........18-4
Wakefield, Bos.......17-8
Rogers, Oak.........16-8
Erickson, Bal.......16-13
Pettitte, NY.........16-11
Four tied with 15 each.

Appearances

Runyan, Det..........88
Quantrill, Tor..........82
Swindell, Min-Bos......81
Guardado, Min........79
Plesac, Tor...........78
Trombley, Min.........77
Groom, Oak..........75
Gordon, Bos..........73
Service, KC..........73

Complete Games

Erickson, Bal..........11
Wells, NY..............8
Rogers, Oak...........7
Fassero, Sea...........7
Colon, Cle.............6
Five tied with 5 each.

Losses

Candiotti, Oak......11-16
Guzman, Tor-Bal....10-16
Navarro, Chi........8-16
Sirotka, Chi........14-15
Thompson, Det......11-15
Saunders, TB........6-15
Rusch, KC..........6-15
Six tied with 14 each.

Innings

Erickson, Bal.......251.1
Rogers, Oak.......238.2
Clemens, Tor.......234.2
Moyer, Sea.......234.1
Belcher, KC.......234.0
Martinez, Bos......233.2
Fassero, Sea.......224.2
Finley, Ana........223.1
Thompson, Det.....222.0
Moehler, Det.......221.1
Helling, Tex........216.1
Pettitte, NY........216.1
Wakefield, Bos.....216.0

Shutouts

Wells, NY.............5
Clemens, Tor...........3
Moyer, Sea............3
Moehler, Det...........3
Eight tied with 2 each.

Saves

	SV	BS
Gordon, Bos	46	1
Percival, Ana	42	6
Wetteland, Tex	42	5
Jackson, Cle	40	5
Aguilera, Min	38	11
Rivera, NY	36	5
Montgomery, KC	36	5
Taylor, Oak	33	4
Jones, Det	28	4
Myers, Tor	28	6
Hernandez, TB	26	9

HRs Given Up

Belcher, KC..........37
Williams, Tor..........36
Nagy, Cle............34
Fassero, Sea..........33
Moehler, Det..........30
Wakefield, Bos........30
Candiotti, Oak........30
Burba, Cle...........30
Sirotka, Chi..........30
Navarro, Chi..........30

Wild Pitches

Navarro, Chi..........18
Stein, Oak...........15
Candiotti, Oak........14
Rapp, KC.............14
Fassero, Sea..........12

Strikeouts

Clemens, Tor.........271
Martinez, Bos........251
Johnson, Sea.........213
Finley, Ana..........212
Cone, NY...........209
Erickson, Bal.........186
Fassero, Sea.........176
Mussina, Bal.........175
Saunders, TB.........172
Guzman, Tor-Bal......168
Sele, Tex.............167

Walks

Saunders, TB.........111
Finley, Ana..........109
Rapp, KC............107
Guzman, Tor-Bal.......98
Olivares, Ana.........91

Opp. Batting Average

Clemens, Tor...... .198
Martinez, Bos...... .217
Irabu, NY......... .233
Cone, NY......... .237
Wells, NY......... .239
Guzman, Tor-Bal... .240

Team Leaders

Batting

Team	Avg	AB	R	H	HR	RBI	SB
Texas	.289	5672	940	1637	201	894	82
New York	.288	5643	965	1625	207	901	153
Boston	.280	5601	876	1568	205	827	72
Seattle	.276	5628	859	1553	234	822	115
Baltimore	.273	5565	817	1520	214	783	86
Anaheim	.272	5630	787	1530	147	739	94
Cleveland	.272	5616	850	1530	198	811	143
Chicago	.271	5585	861	1516	198	806	127
Minnesota	.266	5641	734	1499	115	691	112
Toronto	.266	5580	816	1482	221	776	184
Detroit	.264	5664	722	1494	165	691	121
Kansas City	.263	5543	715	1459	134	686	135
Tampa Bay	.261	5559	620	1450	111	579	120
Oakland	.257	5490	803	1413	149	755	131

Pitching

	ERA	W	Sv	CG	ShO	HR	BB	SO
New York	3.82	114	48	22	16	156	466	1080
Boston	4.19	92	53	5	8	168	504	1025
Toronto	4.29	88	47	10	11	169	587	1154
Tampa Bay	4.35	63	28	7	8	171	643	1008
Cleveland	4.45	89	47	9	4	171	563	1037
Anaheim	4.49	85	52	3	5	164	630	1091
Baltimore	4.73	79	37	16	10	169	535	1065
Minnesota	4.76	70	42	7	9	180	458	952
Oakland	4.83	74	39	12	4	179	529	922
Detroit	4.93	65	32	9	4	185	595	947
Seattle	4.95	76	31	17	7	196	528	1156
Texas	5.00	88	46	10	8	164	519	994
Kansas City	5.16	72	46	6	7	196	568	999
Chicago	5.24	80	42	8	4	211	580	911

St. Louis Cardinals
Mark McGwire
Home Runs, On Base Pct., Slugging Pct., Walks

Chicago Cubs
Sammy Sosa
RBI, Runs, Total Bases, Strikeouts

Chicago Cubs
Kerry Wood
Opp. Batting Average

Philadelphia Phillies
Curt Schilling
Complete Games, Innings, Strikeouts

National League Leaders

Batting

	Bat	Gm	AB	R	H	Avg	TB	2B	3B	HR	RBI	BB	Int BB	SO	SB	Slg Pct	OBP
Larry Walker, Col	L	130	454	113	165	**.363**	286	46	3	23	67	64	2	61	14	.630	.445
John Olerud, NY	L	160	557	91	197	**.354**	307	36	4	22	93	96	11	73	2	.551	.447
Dante Bichette, Col	R	161	662	97	219	**.331**	337	48	2	22	122	28	2	76	14	.509	.357
Mike Piazza, LA-Fla-NY	R	151	561	88	184	**.328**	320	38	1	32	111	58	14	80	1	.570	.390
Jason Kendall, Pit	R	149	535	95	175	**.327**	253	36	3	12	75	51	3	51	26	.473	.411
Craig Biggio, Hou	R	160	646	123	210	**.325**	325	51	2	20	88	64	6	113	50	.503	.403
Vladimir Guerrero, Mon	R	159	623	108	202	**.324**	367	37	7	38	109	42	13	95	11	.589	.371
Jeff Cirillo, Mil	R	156	604	97	194	**.321**	269	31	1	14	68	79	3	88	10	.445	.402
Tony Gwynn, SD	L	127	461	65	148	**.321**	231	35	0	16	69	35	6	18	3	.501	.364
Vinny Castilla, Col	R	162	645	108	206	**.319**	380	28	4	46	144	40	7	89	5	.589	.362
Brian Jordan, St.L	R	150	564	100	178	**.316**	301	34	7	25	91	40	1	66	17	.534	.368
Todd Helton*, Col	L	152	530	78	167	**.315**	281	37	1	25	98	53	5	54	3	.530	.380
Derek Bell, Hou	R	156	630	111	198	**.314**	309	41	2	22	108	51	0	126	13	.490	.364
Chipper Jones, Atl	S	160	601	123	188	**.313**	329	29	5	34	107	96	1	93	16	.547	.404
Bob Abreu, Phi	L	151	497	68	155	**.312**	247	29	6	17	74	84	14	133	19	.497	.409

Home Runs

McGwire, St.L 70
Sosa, Chi 66
Vaughn, SD 50
Castilla, Col 46
Galarraga, Atl 44
V. Guerrero, Mon 38
Alou, Hou 38
Burnitz, Mil 38
Bonds, SF 37
Bagwell, Hou 34
C. Jones, Atl 34
Lopez, Atl 34

Triples

Dellucci*, Ari 12
B. Larkin, Cin 10
Perez, Col 9
W. Guerrero, Mon 9
A. Jones, Atl 8
Garcia*, Ari 8
DeShields, St.L 8
Ten tied with 7 each.

On Base Pct.

McGwire, St.L 470
Olerud, NY 447
Walker, Col 445
Bonds, SF 438
Sheffield, Fla-LA 428
Bagwell, Hou 424
Kendall, Pit 411

Runs Batted In

Sosa, Chi 158
McGwire, St.L 147
Castilla, Col 144
Kent, SF 128
Burnitz, Mil 125
Alou, Hou 124
Bonds, SF 122
Bichette, Col 122
Galarraga, Atl 121

Doubles

Biggio, Hou 51
Bichette, Col 48
Young, Cin 48
Walker, Col 46
Rolen, Phi 45
Floyd, Fla 45
Bonds, SF 44
Fullmer*, Mon 44
Bell, Hou 41

Slugging Pct.

McGwire, St.L 752
Sosa, Chi 647
Walker, Col 630
Bonds, SF 609
Vaughn, SD 597
Galarraga, Atl 595
Castilla, Col 589
V. Guerrero, Mon 589
Alou, Hou 582

Hits

Bichette, Col 219
Biggio, Hou 210
Castilla, Col 206
V. Guerrero, Mon 202
Sosa, Chi 198
Bell, Hou 198
Vina, Mil 198
Olerud, NY 197
Cirillo, Mil 194

Runs

Sosa, Chi 134
McGwire, St.L 130
Bagwell, Hou 124
Biggio, Hou 123
C. Jones, Atl 123
Rolen, Phi 120
Bonds, SF 120
Walker, Col 113

Walks

McGwire, St.L 162
Bonds, SF 130
Bagwell, Hou 109
C. Jones, Atl 96
Olerud, NY 96
Sheffield, LA 95
Rolen, Phi 93
Grace, Chi 93
Lankford, St.L 86
Three tied with 84 each.

Stolen Bases

	SB	CS
Womack, Pit	58	8
Biggio, Hou	50	8
Young, LA	42	13
Renteria, Fla	41	22
Bonds, SF	28	12
Floyd, Fla	27	14
A. Jones, Atl	27	4
Lankford, St.L	26	5
B. Larkin, Cin	26	3
DeShields, St.L	26	10
Kendall, Pit	26	5

Total Bases

Sosa, Chi 416
McGwire, St.L 383
Castilla, Col 380
V. Guerrero, Mon 367
Vaughn, SD 342
Alou, Hou 340
Bichette, Col 337
Bonds, SF 336

Strikeouts

Sosa, Chi 171
Burnitz, Mil 158
McGwire, St.L 155
Lankford, St.L 151
Galarraga, Atl 146
Rolen, Phi 141
Hernandez, Chi 140

Pitching

	Arm	W	L	ERA	Gm	GS	CG	ShO	Sv	IP	H	R	ER	HR	HB	BB	SO	WP
Greg Maddux, Atl	R	18	9	**2.22**	34	34	9	5	0	251.0	201	75	62	13	7	45	204	4
Kevin Brown, SD	R	18	7	**2.38**	36	35	7	3	0	257.0	225	77	68	8	10	49	257	10
Al Leiter, NY	L	17	6	**2.47**	28	28	4	2	0	193.0	151	55	53	8	11	71	174	4
Tom Glavine, Atl	L	20	6	**2.47**	33	33	4	3	0	229.1	202	67	63	13	2	74	157	3
Omar Daal, Ari	L	8	12	**2.88**	33	23	3	1	0	162.2	146	60	52	12	3	51	132	0
John Smoltz, Atl	R	17	3	**2.90**	26	26	2	2	0	167.2	145	58	54	10	4	44	173	3
Dustin Hermanson, Mon	R	14	11	**3.13**	32	30	1	0	0	187.0	163	80	65	21	3	56	154	4
Pete Harnisch, Cin	R	14	7	**3.14**	32	32	2	1	0	209.0	176	79	73	24	6	64	157	4
Curt Schilling, Phi	R	15	14	**3.25**	35	35	15	2	0	268.2	236	101	97	23	6	61	300	12
Francisco Cordova, Pit	R	13	14	**3.31**	33	33	3	2	0	220.1	204	91	81	22	3	69	157	1
Andy Ashby, SD	R	17	9	**3.34**	33	33	5	1	0	226.2	223	90	84	23	7	58	151	7
Mike Hampton, Hou	L	11	7	**3.36**	32	32	1	1	0	211.2	227	92	79	18	5	81	137	4
Kerry Wood*, Chi	R	13	6	**3.40**	26	26	1	1	0	166.2	117	69	63	14	11	85	233	6
Rick Reed, NY	R	16	11	**3.48**	31	31	2	1	0	212.1	208	84	82	30	6	29	153	1
Shane Reynolds, Hou	R	19	8	**3.51**	35	35	3	1	0	233.1	257	99	91	25	2	53	209	5

Wins

Glavine, Atl 20-6
Reynolds, Hou 19-8
Tapani, Chi..........19-9
Maddux, Atl 18-9
Brown, SD............18-7
Leiter, NY 17-6
Smoltz, Atl 17-3
Ashby, SD............17-9
Millwood, Atl 17-8

Appearances

Beck, Chi 81
Nen, SF 78
McElroy, Col 78
Kline, Mon 78
Telford, Mon 77
Ligtenberg*, Atl........75
Cook, NY...............73
Shaw, Cin-LA..........73
Wickman, Mil 72

Complete Games

Schilling, Phi 15
Maddux, Atl.............9
Hernandez, Fla 9
Brown, SD 7
Perez, Mon-LA 7
Ashby, SD...............5
Neagle, Atl..............5
Five tied with four each.

Losses

Kile, Col 13-17
Blair, Ari-NY 5-16
Remlinger, Cin 8-15
Vazquez*, Mon 5-15
Eight tied with 14 each.

Innings

Schilling, Phi 268.2
Brown, SD 257.0
Maddux, Atl.........251.0
Perez, Mon-LA......241.0
Hernandez, Fla 234.1
Reynolds, Hou 233.1
Lima, Hou...........233.1
An Benes, Ari 231.1
Kile, Col 230.1
Glavine, Atl 229.1
Ashby, SD 226.2
Park, LA 220.2
Cordova, Pit........220.1

Shutouts

Maddux, Atl............5
Johnson, Hou 4
Brown, SD 3
Glavine, Atl 3
Nine tied with two each.

Saves

	SV	BS
Hoffman, SD	53	1
Beck, Chi	51	7
Shaw, Cin-LA	48	9
Nen, SF	40	5
Franco, NY	38	8
Urbina, Mon	34	4
Ligtenberg*, Atl.	30	4
Wagner, Hou.	30	5
Olson, Ari	30	4

HRs Given Up

Anderson, Ari 39
Astacio, Col...........39
Hernandez, Fla 37
Lima, Hou.............34
Blair, Ari-NY...........31
Vazquez*, Mon.........31
Reed, NY 30
Tapani, Chi 30
Gardner, SF 29
Hitchcock, SD 29

Wild Pitches

Schmidt, Pit 15
Nomo, LA-NY 13
Schilling, Phi 12
Kile, Col 12
Hershiser, SF 12
Remlinger, Cin.........11
Hitchcock, SD 11

Strikeouts

Schilling, Phi 300
Brown, SD 257
Wood*, Chi 233
Reynolds, Hou.........209
Maddux, Atl 204
Park, LA 191
Leiter, NY.............174
Smoltz, Atl 173
Astacio, Col...........170

Walks

Hamilton, SD.........106
Hernandez, Fla.......104
Park, LA 97
Kile, Col 96
Wright, Col 95
Nomo, LA-NY 94
Sanchez*, Fla 91
Remlinger, Cin.........87

Opp. Batting Average

Wood*, Chi....... .196
Leiter, NY......... .216
Maddux, Atl....... .220
Harnisch, Cin...... .228
Smoltz, Atl .... .231
Hermanson, Mon... .234
Brown, SD .... .235
Schilling, Phi ...... .236
Glavine, Atl .... .238

Team Leaders

Batting

	Avg	AB	R	H	HR	RBI	SB
Colorado	.291	5632	826	1640	183	791	67
Houston	.280	5641	874	1578	166	818	155
S. Francisco	.274	5628	845	1540	161	800	102
Atlanta	.272	5484	826	1489	215	794	98
Chicago	.264	5649	831	1494	212	788	65
Philadelphia	.264	5617	713	1482	126	672	97
Cincinnati	.262	5496	750	1441	138	723	95
Milwaukee	.260	5541	707	1439	152	673	81
New York	.259	5510	706	1425	136	671	62
St. Louis	.258	5593	810	1444	223	781	133
Pittsburgh	.254	5493	650	1395	107	613	159
San Diego	.253	5490	749	1390	167	715	79
Los Angeles	.252	5461	669	1374	159	630	137
Montreal	.249	5417	644	1348	147	602	91
Florida	.248	5558	667	1381	114	621	115
Arizona	.246	5491	665	1353	159	621	73

Pitching

	ERA	W	Sv	CG	ShO	HR	BB	SO
Atlanta	3.25	106	45	24	23	117	467	1232
Houston	3.50	102	44	12	11	147	465	1187
San Diego	3.63	98	59	14	11	139	501	1217
New York	3.77	88	46	9	16	152	532	1129
Los Angeles	3.81	83	79	16	10	135	587	1178
Pittsburgh	3.91	69	41	7	10	147	530	1112
S. Francisco	4.19	89	44	6	6	171	562	1089
St. Louis	4.32	83	44	6	10	151	558	972
Montreal	4.39	65	39	4	5	156	533	1017
Cincinnati	4.44	77	42	6	8	170	573	1098
Chicago	4.50	90	56	7	7	180	575	1207
Milwaukee	4.63	74	39	2	2	188	550	1063
Arizona	4.64	65	37	7	6	188	489	908
Philadelphia	4.64	75	32	21	11	188	544	1176
Colorado	5.00	77	36	9	5	174	562	951
Florida	5.20	54	24	11	3	182	715	1016

McGwire and Sosa pass Maris

St. Louis Cardinals first baseman Mark McGwire and Chicago Cubs right fielder Sammy Sosa both surpassed Major League Baseball's single season home run record in 1998. The record, set by New York Yankees right fielder Roger Maris when he hit 61 homers in 1961, stood for 37 years until McGwire finished the 1998 season with 70 home runs establishing a new milestone. Below is a chronological list of McGwire's and Sosa's home runs. McGwire's home runs are listed in **bold** type.

No.	Date	Hit by	Pitcher	Count	Dist. (ft.)
1	**Mar. 31**	**MM**	**Ramon Martinez, vs. LA**	**1-0**	**360**
2	**Apr. 2**	**MM**	**Frank Lankford, vs. LA**	**0-1**	**370**
3	**Apr. 3**	**MM**	**Mark Langston, vs. SD**	**3-2**	**370**
1	Apr. 4	SS	Marc Valdes, vs. Mon.	2-1	371
4	**Apr. 4**	**MM**	**Don Wengert, vs. SD**	**2-1**	**430**
2	Apr. 11	SS	Anthony Telford, at Mon.	1-2	350
5	**Apr. 14**	**MM**	**Jeff Suppan, vs. Ari.**	**1-2**	**420**
6	**Apr. 14**	**MM**	**Jeff Suppan, vs. Ari.**	**1-1**	**340**
7	**Apr. 14**	**MM**	**Barry Manuel, vs. Ari.**	**2-0**	**460**
3	Apr. 15	SS	Dennis Cook, at NYM	3-2	430
8	**Apr. 17**	**MM**	**Matt Whiteside, vs. Phi.**	**2-2**	**410**
9	**Apr. 21**	**MM**	**Trey Moore, at Mon.**	**0-0**	**440**
4	Apr. 23	SS	Dan Miceli, vs. SD	0-1	420
5	Apr. 24	SS	Ismael Valdes, at LA	3-1	430
10	**Apr. 25**	**MM**	**Jerry Spradlin, at Phi.**	**1-2**	**410**
6	Apr. 27	SS	Joey Hamilton, at SD	0-1	434
11	**Apr. 30**	**MM**	**Marc Pisciotta, at Cubs**	**2-1**	**380**
12	**May 1**	**MM**	**Rod Beck, at Cubs**	**1-2**	**360**
7	May 3	SS	Cliff Politte, vs. St.L	2-1	370
13	**May 8**	**MM**	**Rick Reed, at NYM**	**0-2**	**350**
14	**May 12**	**MM**	**Paul Wagner, vs. Mil.**	**1-2**	**527**
15	**May 14**	**MM**	**Kevin Millwood, vs. Atl.**	**1-1**	**380**
8	May 16	SS	Scott Sullivan, at Cin.	2-1	420
16	**May 16**	**MM**	**Livan Hernandez, vs. Fla.**	**1-0**	**550**
17	**May 18**	**MM**	**Jesus Sanchez, vs. Fla.**	**2-0**	**478**
18	**May 19**	**MM**	**Tyler Green, at Phi.**	**2-0**	**420**
19	**May 19**	**MM**	**Tyler Green, at Phi.**	**0-2**	**390**
20	**May 19**	**MM**	**Wayne Gomes, at Phi.**	**0-0**	**420**
9	May 22	SS	Greg Maddux, at Atl.	2-2	440
21	**May 22**	**MM**	**Mark Gardner, vs. SF**	**1-1**	**425**
22	**May 23**	**MM**	**Rich Rodriguez, vs. SF**	**1-0**	**370**
23	**May 23**	**MM**	**John Johnstone, vs. SF**	**2-2**	**480**
24	**May 24**	**MM**	**Robb Nen, vs. SF**	**2-2**	**390**
25	**May 25**	**MM**	**John Thomson, vs. Col.**	**2-2**	**430**
10	May 25	SS	Kevin Millwood, at Atl.	2-2	410
11	May 25	SS	Mike Cather, at Atl.	0-1	420
12	May 27	SS	Darrin Winston, vs. Phi.	1-2	460
13	May 27	SS	Wayne Gomes, vs. Phi.	0-0	400
26	**May 29**	**MM**	**Dan Miceli, at SD**	**0-1**	**388**
27	**May 30**	**MM**	**Andy Ashby, at SD**	**0-1**	**423**
14	June 1	SS	Ryan Dempster, vs. Fla.	1-0	430
15	June 1	SS	Oscar Henriquez, vs. Fla.	1-0	410
16	June 3	SS	Livan Hernandez, vs. Fla.	1-0	370
17	June 5	SS	Jim Parque, vs. WSox	1-2	370
28	**June 5**	**MM**	**Orel Hershiser, vs. SF**	**1-2**	**410**
18	June 6	SS	Carlos Castillo, vs. WSox	2-2	410
19	June 7	SS	James Baldwin, vs. WSox	3-2	380
29	**June 8**	**MM**	**Jason Bere, at WSox**	**0-0**	**360**
20	June 8	SS	LaTroy Hawkins, at Min.	0-2	340
30	**June 10**	**MM**	**Jim Parque, at WSox**	**1-0**	**410**
31	**June 12**	**MM**	**Andy Benes, at Ari.**	**1-0**	**450**
21	June 13	SS	Mark Portugal, at Phi.	0-1	350
22	June 15	SS	Cal Eldred, vs. Mil.	1-0	420
23	June 15	SS	Cal Eldred, vs. Mil.	2-1	410
24	June 15	SS	Cal Eldred, vs. Mil.	2-1	415
25	June 17	SS	Bronswell Patrick, vs. Mil.	2-2	430
32	**June 17**	**MM**	**Jose Lima, at Hou.**	**1-2**	**350**
33	**June 18**	**MM**	**Shane Reynolds, at Hou.**	**1-1**	**450**
26	June 19	SS	Carlton Loewer, vs. Phi.	2-2	380
27	June 19	SS	Carlton Loewer, vs. Phi.	1-0	380
28	June 20	SS	Matt Beech, vs. Phi.	3-2	366
29	June 20	SS	Toby Borland, vs. Phi.	2-0	500
30	June 21	SS	Tyler Green, vs. Phi.	2-2	380
34	**June 24**	**MM**	**Jaret Wright, at Cle.**	**1-1**	**430**
31	June 24	SS	Seth Greisinger, at Det.	0-2	390
35	**June 25**	**MM**	**Dave Burba, at Cle.**	**2-2**	**461**

No.	Date	Hit by	Pitcher	Count	Dist. (ft.)
32	June 25	SS	Brian Moehler, at Det.	1-0	400
36	**June 27**	**MM**	**Mike Trombley, at Min.**	**2-2**	**430**
33	June 30	SS	Alan Embree, vs. Ari.	3-2	364
37	**June 30**	**MM**	**Glendon Rusch, vs. KC**	**0-1**	**470**
34	July 9	SS	Jeff Juden, at Mil.	0-2	430
35	July 10	SS	Scott Karl, at Mil.	1-0	450
38	**July 11**	**MM**	**Billy Wagner, vs. Hou.**	**0-2**	**440**
39	**July 12**	**MM**	**Sean Bergman, vs. Hou.**	**0-0**	**400**
40	**July 12**	**MM**	**Scott Elarton, vs. Hou.**	**2-1**	**390**
41	**July 17**	**MM**	**Brian Bohanon, vs. LA**	**0-0**	**510**
36	July 17	SS	Kirt Ojala, at Fla.	2-1	440
42	**July 17**	**MM**	**Antonio Osuna, vs. LA**	**1-0**	**430**
43	**July 20**	**MM**	**Brian Boehringer, at SD**	**2-1**	**450**
37	July 22	SS	Miguel Batista, vs. Mon.	1-0	365
38	July 26	SS	Rick Reed, vs. NYM	2-2	420
44	**July 26**	**MM**	**John Thomson, at Col.**	**0-0**	**452**
39	July 27	SS	Willie Blair, at Ari.	1-1	350
40	July 27	SS	Alan Embree, at Ari.	0-0	420
45	**July 28**	**MM**	**Mike Myers, vs. Mil.**	**2-2**	**420**
41	July 28	SS	Bob Wolcott, at Ari.	3-1	400
42	July 31	SS	Jamey Wright, vs. Col.	3-2	380
43	Aug. 5	SS	Andy Benes, vs. Ari.	3-2	380
46	**Aug. 8**	**MM**	**Mark Clark, vs. Cubs**	**2-1**	**380**
44	Aug. 8	SS	Rich Croushore, at St.L	1-0	400
45	Aug. 10	SS	Russ Ortiz, at SF	3-1	370
46	Aug. 10	SS	Chris Brock, at SF	2-1	420
47	**Aug. 11**	**MM**	**Bobby Jones, vs. NYM**	**1-0**	**470**
47	Aug. 16	SS	Sean Bergman, at Hou.	0-1	360
48	Aug. 19	SS	Kent Bottenfield, vs. St.L	0-0	368
48	**Aug. 19**	**MM**	**Matt Karchner, at Cubs**	**3-1**	**398**
49	**Aug. 19**	**MM**	**Terry Mulholland, at Cubs**	**2-0**	**409**
50	**Aug. 20**	**MM**	**Rick Reed, at NYM**	**3-2**	**385**
51	**Aug. 20**	**MM**	**Willie Blair, at NYM**	**2-1**	**369**
49	Aug. 21	SS	Orel Hershiser, vs. SF	3-2	430
52	**Aug. 22**	**MM**	**Francisco Cordova, at Pit.**	**0-2**	**460**
50	Aug. 23	SS	Jose Lima, vs. Hou.	3-2	433
53	**Aug. 23**	**MM**	**Ricardo Rincon, at Pit.**	**2-2**	**390**
51	Aug. 23	SS	Jose Lima, vs. Hou.	1-0	388
52	Aug. 26	SS	Brett Tomko, at Cin.	1-1	440
54	**Aug. 26**	**MM**	**Justin Speier, vs. Fla.**	**0-1**	**510**
53	Aug. 28	SS	John Thomson, at Col.	1-2	414
54	Aug. 30	SS	Darryl Kile, at Col.	1-2	482
55	**Aug. 30**	**MM**	**Dennis Martinez, vs. Atl.**	**1-0**	**500**
55	Aug. 31	SS	Brett Tomko, vs. Cin.	0-1	364
56	**Sept. 1**	**MM**	**Livan Hernandez, at Fla.**	**1-1**	**450**
57	**Sept. 1**	**MM**	**Donn Pall, at Fla.**	**0-0**	**470**
56	Sept. 2	SS	Jason Bere, vs. Cin.	0-1	370
58	**Sept. 2**	**MM**	**Brian Edmondson, at Fla.**	**2-1**	**430**
59	**Sept. 2**	**MM**	**Robby Stanifer, at Fla.**	**0-0**	**458**
57	Sept. 4	SS	Jason Schmidt, at Pit.	2-0	400
60	**Sept. 5**	**MM**	**Dennis Reyes, vs. Cin.**	**2-0**	**380**
58	Sept. 5	SS	Sean Lawrence, at Pit.	3-1	405
61	**Sept. 7**	**MM**	**Mike Morgan, vs. Cubs**	**1-1**	**430**
62	**Sept. 8**	**MM**	**Steve Trachsel, vs. Cubs**	**0-0**	**341**
59	Sept. 11	SS	Bill Pulsipher, vs. Mil.	0-1	433
60	Sept. 12	SS	V. De Los Santos, vs. Mil.	3-2	390
61	Sept. 13	SS	Bronswell Patrick, vs. Mil.	0-1	480
62	Sept. 13	SS	Eric Plunk, vs. Mil.	2-1	480
63	**Sept. 15**	**MM**	**Jason Christiansen, vs. Pit.**	**1-0**	**385**
63	Sept. 16	SS	Brian Boehringer, vs. Mil.	1-0	434
64	**Sept. 18**	**MM**	**Rafael Roque, vs. Mil.**	**3-1**	**410**
65	**Sept. 20**	**MM**	**Scott Karl, vs. Mil.**	**2-1**	**420**
64	Sept. 23	SS	Rafael Roque, at Mil.	1-0	344
65	Sept. 23	SS	Rod Henderson, at Mil.	2-2	410
66	Sept. 25	SS	Jose Lima, at Hou.	0-1	420
66	**Sept. 25**	**MM**	**Shayne Bennett, vs. Mon.**	**1-2**	**380**
67	**Sept. 26**	**MM**	**Dustin Hermanson, vs. Mon.**	**0-0**	**400**
68	**Sept. 26**	**MM**	**Kirk Bullinger, vs. Mon.**	**1-1**	**440**
69	**Sept. 27**	**MM**	**Mike Thurman, vs. Mon.**	**1-1**	**377**
70	**Sept. 27**	**MM**	**Carl Pavano, vs. Mon.**	**0-0**	**370**

1998 All-Star Game

69th Baseball All-Star Game. **Date:** July 7 at Coors Field, Denver, Colo.; **Managers:** Mike Hargrove, Cleveland (AL) and Jim Leyland, Florida (NL); **Most Valuable Player:** 2B Roberto Alomar, Baltimore (AL): three hits, including solo home run.

American League

	AB	R	H	BI	BB	SO	Avg
Kenny Lofton, Cle, lf	3	0	1	0	1	0	.333
Darin Erstad, Ana, lf-cf	2	1	0	0	0	0	.000
Roberto Alomar, Bal, 2b	4	2	3	1	1	0	.750
Ray Durham, Chi, 2b	1	1	1	1	0	0	1.000
Ken Griffey Jr., Sea, cf	3	1	2	1	1	0	.667
Paul O'Neill, NY, lf	2	0	0	0	0	0	.000
Juan Gonzalez, Tex, rf	3	0	0	1	0	1	.000
Manny Ramirez, Cle, rf	1	0	0	1	0	0	.000
Jim Thome, Cle, 1b	2	1	0	0	2	1	.000
Rafael Palmeiro, Bal, 1b	2	1	2	1	0	0	1.000
Alex Rodriguez, Sea, ss	3	2	2	1	0	1	.667
Derek Jeter, NY, ss	1	0	0	0	0	1	.000
Omar Vizquel, Cle, ss	2	0	1	0	0	0	.000
Ivan Rodriguez, Tex, c	4	1	3	1	0	0	.750
Sandy Alomar Jr., Cle, c	1	0	1	1	0	0	1.000
Cal Ripken Jr., Bal, 3b	4	1	1	2	0	0	.250
Dean Palmer, KC, 3b	1	0	0	0	0	0	.000
Damion Easley, Det, 2b	1	1	1	0	0	0	1.000
Ben Grieve, Oak, rf	0	0	0	0	1	0	.000
Scott Brosius, NY, 3b	2	1	1	0	0	1	.500
TOTALS	43	13	19	11	6	5	

National League

	AB	R	H	BI	BB	SO	Avg
Craig Biggio, Hou, 2b	3	0	0	0	0	3	.000
Greg Vaughn, SD, lf	1	0	1	2	0	0	1.000
Tony Gwynn, SD, rf	2	0	1	2	0	0	.500
Devon White, Ari, cf	3	1	3	0	0	0	1.000
Mark McGwire, St.L, 1b	2	1	0	0	1	1	.000
Andres Galarraga, Atl, 1b	2	0	0	0	0	0	.000
Barry Bonds, SF, lf	2	1	1	3	1	0	.500
Dante Bichette, Col, lf-rf	2	0	0	0	0	1	.000
Chipper Jones, Atl, 3b	2	1	0	0	1	0	.000
Vinny Castilla, Col, 3b	2	0	0	0	0	0	.000
Mike Piazza, NY, c	3	0	1	0	0	0	.333
Javy Lopez, Atl, c	1	0	0	0	0	1	.000
Jason Kendall, Pit, c	1	0	1	0	0	0	1.000
Larry Walker, Col, cf-rf	1	1	0	0	1	0	.000
Moises Alou, Hou, rf-cf	3	1	1	0	0	2	.333
Walt Weiss, Atl, ss	3	1	2	1	0	0	.000
Edgar Renteria, Fla, ss	1	1	0	0	0	0	.000
Gary Sheffield, Fla, rf	1	0	0	0	0	0	.000
Fernando Vina, Mil, 2b	1	0	1	0	1	0	1.000
TOTALS	36	8	12	8	5	8	

	1	2	3	4	5	6	7	8	9		R	H	E
American League	0	0	0	4	1	3	1	1	3	–	**13**	19	2
National League	0	0	2	1	3	0	0	2	0	–	**8**	12	1

LOB— American 30, National 18. **2B**—Ripken (AL). **3B**— Bonds (NL). **HR**—A. Rodriguez (AL, off Ashby), R. Alomar (AL, off Hoffman), Bonds (NL, off Colon). **SB**—Lofton (AL, 2nd base off Maddux/Piazza), R. Alomar (AL, 3rd base off Urbina/Lopez), I. Rodriguez (AL, 2nd base off Urbina/Lopez), Brosius (AL, 2nd base of Nen/Lopez). **PB**—Lopez (NL).

AL Pitching	IP	H	R	ER	BB	SO	NP
David Wells, NY	2.0	0	0	0	1	1	23
Roger Clemens, Tor	1.0	2	2	2	1	1	26
Brad Radke, Min	1.0	2	1	1	1	1	20
Bartolo Colon, Cle (W)	1.0	2	3	3	1	1	26
Rolando Arrojo, TB	1.0	2	0	0	0	1	12
John Wetteland, Tex	1.0	0	0	0	0	1	7
Tom Gordon, Bos	1.0	3	2	1	1	0	19
Troy Percival, Ana	1.0	1	0	0	0	2	15
TOTALS	9.0	12	8	7	5	8	148

NL Pitching	IP	H	R	ER	BB	SO	NP
Greg Maddux, Atl	2.0	3	0	0	1	1	31
Tom Glavine, Atl	1.1	5	4	4	3	0	57
Kevin Brown, SD	0.2	0	0	0	0	1	8
Andy Ashby, SD	1.0	1	1	1	1	0	23
Ugueth Urbina, Mon (L)	1.0	3	3	3	1	2	35
Trevor Hoffman, SD	1.0	1	1	1	0	1	20
Jeff Shaw, LA	1.0	3	1	1	0	0	17
Robb Nen, SF	1.0	3	3	1	0	0	23
TOTALS	9.0	19	13	11	6	5	214

Umpires—Ed Montague (plate); Derryl Cousins (1b); Brian Gorman (2b); Rick Reed (3b); Rich Rieker (lf); Tim McClelland (rf). **Attendance**—51,267. **Time**— 3:38. **TV Rating**—13.3/25 share (NBC).

Home Attendance

Overall 1998 regular season attendance in Major League Baseball was 70,618,731 in 2,403 games for an average per game crowd of 29,388; numbers in parentheses indicate ranking in 1997; HD indicates home dates; Attendance based on tickets sold.

American League

	Attendance	HD	Average
1 Baltimore (1)	3,685,194	81	45,496
2 Cleveland (2)	3,467,299	81	42,806
3 New York (5)	2,949,734	80	36,872
4 Texas (4)	2,927,409	81	36,141
5 Seattle (3)	2,644,166	81	32,644
6 Anaheim (9)	2,519,210	80	31,101
7 Tampa Bay (NR)	2,506,023	81	30,939
8 Toronto (6)	2,454,303	81	30,300
9 Boston (7)	2,343,947	80	29,299
10 Kansas City (10)	1,494,875	79	18,922
11 Detroit (13)	1,409,391	79	17,840
12 Chicago (8)	1,391,146	79	17.609
13 Oakland (14)	1,232,339	79	15,599
14 Minnesota (12)	1,165,980	81	14,395
TOTALS	32,191,016	1,124	28,640

National League

	Attendance	HD	Average
1 Colorado (1)	3,789,347	81	46,782
2 Arizona (NR)	3,602,856	81	44,480
3 Atlanta (2)	3,361,350	81	41,498
4 St. Louis (4)	3,195,021	79	39,938
5 Los Angeles (3)	3,089,222	81	38.139
6 Chicago (6)	2,623,000	80	32,788
7 San Diego (7)	1,925,634	79	32,353
8 Houston (8)	2,450,451	80	30,631
9 New York (9)	2,287,942	77	29,714
10 San Francisco (11)	1,925,634	80	24,070
11 Milwaukee (NR)	1,811,548	79	22,931
12 Florida (5)	1,750,395	79	22,157
13 Cincinnati (10)	1,793,679	81	22,144
14 Philadelphia (13)	1,715,702	79	21,718
15 Pittsburgh (12)	1,560,950	80	19,512
16 Montreal (14)	914,717	81	11,293
TOTALS	38,427,715	1,279	30,045

AL Team by Team Statistics

At least 135 at bats or 40 innings pitched during the regular season, unless otherwise indicated. Players who competed for more than one AL team are listed with their final club. Players traded from the NL are listed with AL team only if they have 135 AB or 40 IP. Note that (*) indicates rookie and PTBN indicates player to be named.

Anaheim Angels

Batting (170 AB)	Avg	AB	R	H	HR	RBI	SB
Jim Edmonds	.307	599	115	184	25	91	7
Tim Salmon	.300	463	84	139	26	88	0
Darin Erstad	.296	537	84	159	19	82	20
Garret Anderson	.294	622	62	183	15	79	8
Gary DiSarcina	.287	551	73	158	3	56	11
Randy Velarde	.261	188	29	49	4	26	7
Matt Walbeck	.257	338	41	87	6	46	1
Charlie O'Brien	.257	175	13	45	4	18	0
Justin Baughman*	.255	196	24	50	1	20	10
Chad Kreuter	.250	252	27	63	2	33	1
Dave Hollins	.242	363	60	88	11	39	11
Phil Nevin	.228	237	27	54	8	27	0
Noberto Martin	.215	195	20	42	1	13	3

Acquired: C O'Brien from ChW for two minor leaguers (Jul. 30); P Fetters from Oak. for PTBN and cash (Aug. 10); C Kreuter from ChW for cash (Sept. 18).

Pitching (50 IP)	ERA	W-L	Gm	IP	BB	SO
Shigetoshi Hasegawa	3.14	8-3	61	97.1	32	73
Chuck Finley	3.39	11-9	34	223.1	109	212
Troy Percival	3.65	2-7	67	66.2	37	87
Omar Olivares	4.03	9-9	37	183.0	91	112
Rich DeLucia	4.27	2-6	61	71.2	46	73
Mike Fetters	4.30	2-8	60	58.2	25	43
Steve Sparks	4.34	9-4	22	128.2	58	90
Pep Harris	4.35	3-1	49	60.0	23	34
Jarrod Washburn*	4.62	6-3	15	74.0	27	48
Ken Hill	4.98	9-6	19	103.0	47	57
Jack McDowell	5.09	5-3	14	76.0	19	45
Allen Watson	6.04	6-7	28	92.1	34	64
Jason Dickson	6.05	10-10	27	122.0	41	61

Saves: Percival (42); Fetters and Hasegawa (5); DeLucia (3). **Complete games:** Finley, Olivares and Watson (1). **Shutouts:** Finley (1).

Baltimore Orioles

Batting (135 AB)	Avg	AB	R	H	HR	RBI	SB
Eric Davis	.327	452	81	148	28	89	7
Harold Baines	.300	293	40	88	9	57	0
Rafael Palmeiro	.296	619	98	183	43	121	11
Lenny Webster	.285	309	37	88	10	46	0
Roberto Alomar	.282	588	86	166	14	56	18
B.J. Surhoff	.279	573	79	160	22	92	9
Cal Ripken Jr.	.271	601	65	163	14	61	0
Jeffrey Hammonds	.269	171	36	46	6	28	7
Chris Hoiles	.262	267	36	70	15	56	0
Mike Bordick	.260	465	59	121	13	51	6
Joe Carter	.247	283	36	70	11	34	3
Brady Anderson	.236	479	84	113	18	51	21

Acquired: P Guzman from Tor. for P Nerio Rodriguez and minor leaguer (Jul. 31).
Traded: OF Carter to SF for minor leaguer (Jul. 23); OF Hammonds to Cin. for IF Willie Greene (Aug. 10).

Pitching (55 IP)	ERA	W-L	Gm	IP	BB	SO
Jesse Orosco	3.18	4-1	69	56.2	28	50
Mike Mussina	3.49	13-10	29	206.1	41	175
Arthur Rhodes	3.51	4-4	45	77.0	34	83
Alan Mills	3.74	3-4	72	77.0	50	57
Armando Benitez	3.82	5-6	71	68.1	39	87
Scott Erickson	4.01	16-13	36	251.1	69	186
Jimmy Key	4.20	6-3	25	79.1	23	53
Juan Guzman	4.35	10-16	33	211.0	98	168
Doug Johns	4.57	3-3	31	86.2	32	34
Sidney Ponson*	5.27	8-9	31	135.0	42	85
Doug Drabek	7.29	6-11	23	108.2	29	55

Saves: Benitez (22); Orosco (7); Rhodes (4); Mills (2); Johns and Ponson (1). **Complete games:** Erickson (11); Mussina (4); Guzman (2); Drabek (1). **Shutouts:** Mussina and Erickson (2).

Boston Red Sox

Batting (135 AB)	Avg	AB	R	H	HR	RBI	SB
Mo Vaughn	.337	609	107	205	40	115	0
Nomar Garciaparra	.323	604	111	195	35	122	12
Reggie Jefferson	.306	196	24	60	8	31	0
Damon Buford	.282	216	37	61	10	42	5
Darren Bragg	.279	409	51	114	8	57	5
Orlando Merced	.277	213	22	59	5	35	1
Scott Hatteberg	.276	359	46	99	12	43	0
Mike Benjamin	.272	349	46	95	4	39	3
Troy O'Leary	.270	611	95	165	23	83	2
Darren Lewis	.268	585	95	157	8	63	29
Mike Stanley	.256	497	74	127	29	79	3
Jason Varitek*	.253	221	31	56	7	33	2
John Valentin	.247	588	113	145	23	73	4
Chris Snopek	.204	137	19	28	1	6	3

Acquired: IF Stanley from Tor. for two minor leaguers (Jul. 30); OF Merced and P Swindell from Min. for three minor leaguers (Jul. 31); P Schourek from Hou. for cash (Aug. 6); IF Snopek from ChW for minor leaguer (Aug. 31).
Released: OF Merced (Aug. 31).

Pitching (40 IP)	ERA	W-L	Gm	IP	BB	SO
Jim Corsi	2.59	3-2	59	66.0	23	49
Tom Gordon	2.72	7-4	73	79.1	25	78
Pedro Martinez	2.89	19-7	33	233.2	67	251
Rich Garces	3.33	1-1	30	46.0	27	34
Greg Swindell	3.59	5-6	81	90.1	31	63
Bret Saberhagen	3.96	15-8	31	175.0	29	100
Derek Lowe	4.02	3-9	63	123.0	42	77
Pete Schourek	4.30	1-3	10	44.0	14	36
Tim Wakefield	4.58	17-8	36	216.0	79	146
Steve Avery	5.02	10-7	34	123.2	64	57
John Wasdin	5.25	6-4	47	96.0	27	59

Saves: Gordon (46); Lowe (4); Swindell (2); Garces (1). **Complete games:** Martinez (3); Wakefield (2). **Shutouts:** Martinez (2).

Chicago White Sox

Batting (135 AB)	Avg	AB	R	H	HR	RBI	SB
Albert Belle	.328	609	113	200	49	152	6
Mike Caruso*	.306	523	81	160	5	55	22
Ray Durham	.285	635	126	181	19	67	36
Magglio Ordonez*	.282	535	70	151	14	65	9
Jeff Abbott*	.279	244	33	68	12	41	3
Wil Cordero	.267	341	58	91	13	49	2
Frank Thomas	.265	585	109	155	29	109	7
Robin Ventura	.263	590	84	155	21	91	1
Greg Norton*	.237	299	38	71	9	36	3
Mike Cameron	.210	396	53	83	8	43	27

Waived: P Bere (Jul. 16).

Pitching (40 IP)	ERA	W-L	Gm	IP	BB	SO
Bob Howry*	3.15	0-3	44	54.1	19	51
Bill Simas	3.57	4-3	60	70.2	22	56
Keith Foulke	4.13	3-2	54	65.1	20	57
John Snyder*	4.80	7-2	15	86.1	23	52
Mike Sirotka	5.06	14-15	33	211.2	47	128
Jim Parque*	5.10	7-5	21	113.0	49	77
Carlos Castillo	5.11	6-4	54	100.1	35	64
James Baldwin	5.32	13-6	37	159.0	60	108
Scott Eyre	5.38	3-8	33	107.0	64	73
Jaime Navarro	6.36	8-16	37	172.2	77	71
Jason Bere	6.45	3-7	18	83.2	58	53
Tom Fordham*	6.75	1-2	29	48.0	42	23

Saves: Simas (18); Howry (9); Foulke and Navarro (1). **Complete games:** Sirotka (5); Snyder, Baldwin and Navarro (1). **Shutouts:** none.

Cleveland Indians

Batting (135 AB)	Avg	AB	R	H	HR	RBI	SB
Richie Sexson*	.310	174	28	54	11	35	1
Manny Ramirez	.294	571	108	168	45	145	5
Jim Thome	.293	440	89	129	30	85	1
Omar Vizquel	.288	576	86	166	2	50	37
Travis Fryman	.287	557	74	160	28	96	10
Mark Whiten	.283	226	31	64	6	29	2
Kenny Lofton	.282	600	101	169	12	64	54
David Justice	.280	540	94	151	21	88	9
Joey Cora	.276	602	111	166	6	32	15
Brian Giles	.269	350	56	94	16	66	10
Pat Borders	.238	160	12	38	0	6	0
Shawon Dunston	.237	156	26	37	3	12	9
Sandy Alomar	.235	409	45	96	6	44	0
Cecil Fielder	.233	416	49	97	17	68	0

Acquired: P Doug Jones from Mil. for P Plunk (Jul. 23); IF Cora from Sea. for IF David Bell (Aug. 31).
Traded: P Mesa, IF Dunston, P Al Morman to SF for P Steve Reed and OF Jacob Cruz (Jul. 23).
Claimed: IF Fielder off waivers from Ana. (Aug. 14).
Released: IF Fielder (Sept. 18).

Pitching (40 IP)	ERA	W-L	Gm	IP	BB	SO
Mike Jackson	1.55	1-1	69	64.0	13	55
Paul Shuey	3.00	5-4	43	51.0	25	58
Paul Assenmacher	3.26	2-5	69	47.0	19	43
Bartolo Colon	3.71	14-9	31	204.0	79	158
Dwight Gooden	3.76	8-6	23	134.0	51	83
Dave Burba	4.11	15-10	32	203.2	69	132
Jaret Wright	4.72	12-10	32	192.2	87	140
Eric Plunk	4.83	3-1	37	41.0	15	38
Jose Mesa	5.17	3-4	44	54.0	20	35
Charles Nagy	5.22	15-10	33	210.1	66	120
Chad Ogea	5.61	5-4	19	69.0	25	43

Saves: Jackson (40); Assenmacher (3); Shuey (2); Mesa (1). **Complete games:** Colon (6); Nagy (2); Wright (1). **Shutouts:** Colon (2); Wright (1).

Detroit Tigers

Batting (135 AB)	Avg	AB	R	H	HR	RBI	SB
Juan Encarnacion*	.329	164	30	54	7	21	7
Tony Clark	.291	602	84	175	34	103	3
Bobby Higginson	.284	612	92	174	25	85	3
Frank Catalanotto*	.282	213	23	60	6	25	3
Paul Bako*	.272	305	23	83	3	30	1
Damion Easley	.271	594	84	161	27	100	15
Luis Gonzalez	.267	547	84	146	23	71	12
Deivi Cruz	.260	454	52	118	5	45	3
Joe Randa	.254	460	56	117	9	50	8
Brian L. Hunter	.254	595	67	151	4	36	42
Gabe Alvarez*	.231	199	16	46	5	29	1
Geronimo Berroa	.225	191	23	43	1	13	1

Acquired: OF Berroa from Cle. for minor leaguer (Jun. 24).

Pitching (40 IP)	ERA	W-L	Gm	IP	BB	SO
Doug Brocail	2.73	5-2	60	62.2	18	55
Matt Anderson*	3.27	5-1	42	44.0	31	44
Sean Runyan*	3.58	1-4	88	50.1	28	39
Brian Moehler	3.90	14-13	33	221.1	56	123
Dean Crow*	3.94	2-2	32	45.2	16	18
Justin Thompson	4.05	11-15	34	222.0	79	149
Bryce Florie	4.80	8-9	42	133.0	59	97
Todd Jones	4.97	1-4	65	63.1	36	57
Seth Greisinger*	5.12	6-9	21	130.0	48	66
Doug Bochtler	6.15	0-2	51	67.1	42	45
Brian Powell*	6.35	3-8	18	83.2	36	46
A.J. Sager	6.52	4-2	31	59.1	23	23
Frank Castillo	6.83	3-9	27	116.0	44	81

Saves: Jones (28); Sager (2); Runyan and Castillo (1). **Complete games:** Thompson (5); Moehler (4). **Shutouts:** Moehler (3).

Kansas City Royals

Batting (135 AB)	Avg	AB	R	H	HR	RBI	SB
Jose Offerman	.315	607	102	191	7	66	45
Hal Morris	.309	472	50	146	1	40	1
Dean Palmer	.278	572	84	159	34	119	8
Shane Mack	.278	209	31	58	6	29	8
Johnny Damon	.277	642	104	178	18	66	26
Jeff King	.263	486	83	128	24	93	10
Mike Sweeney	.259	282	32	73	8	35	2
Terry Pendleton	.257	237	17	61	3	29	1
Jeff Conine	.256	309	30	79	8	43	3
Larry Sutton*	.245	310	29	76	5	42	3
Mendy Lopez*	.243	206	18	50	1	15	5
Jermaine Dye	.234	214	24	50	5	23	2
Sal Fasano	.227	216	21	49	8	31	1
Shane Halter	.221	204	17	45	2	13	2

Acquired: OF Mack and PTBN from Oak. for C Mike Macfarlane and cash (Apr. 8).
Traded: P Haney to ChC for cash (Sept. 12).

Pitching (40 IP)	ERA	W-L	Gm	IP	BB	SO
Ricky Bones	3.04	2-2	32	53.1	24	38
Scott Service	3.48	6-4	73	82.2	34	95
Tim Belcher	4.27	14-14	34	234.0	73	130
Jose Rosado	4.69	8-11	38	174.2	57	135
Matt Whisenant	4.90	2-1	70	60.2	33	45
Jeff Montgomery	4.98	2-5	56	56.0	22	54
Hipolito Pichardo	5.13	7-8	27	112.1	43	55
Pat Rapp	5.30	12-13	32	188.1	107	132
Glendon Rusch	5.88	6-15	29	154.2	50	94
Brian Barber	6.00	2-4	8	42.0	13	24
Brian Bevil	6.30	3-1	39	40.0	22	47
Jim Pittsley	6.59	1-1	39	68.1	37	44
Chris Haney	7.03	6-6	33	97.1	36	51

Saves: Montgomery (36); Service (4); Whisenant (2); Bones, Rosado, Pichardo and Rusch (1). **Complete games:** Belcher and Rosado (2); Rapp and Rusch (1). **Shutouts:** Rosado, Rapp and Rusch (1).

Minnesota Twins

Batting (135 AB)	Avg	AB	R	H	HR	RBI	SB
Todd Walker	.316	528	85	167	12	62	19
Otis Nixon	.297	448	71	133	1	20	37
Paul Molitor	.281	502	75	141	4	69	9
Matt Lawton	.278	557	91	155	21	77	16
David Ortiz*	.277	278	47	77	9	46	1
Ron Coomer	.276	529	54	146	15	72	2
Pat Meares	.260	543	56	141	9	70	7
Alex Ochoa	.257	249	35	64	2	25	6
Marty Cordova	.253	438	52	111	10	69	3
Brent Gates	.249	333	31	83	3	42	3
Terry Steinbach	.242	422	45	102	14	54	0
Denny Hocking	.202	198	32	40	3	15	2
Javier Valentin*	.198	162	11	32	3	18	0

Traded: P Morgan to ChC for cash and PTBN (Aug. 25).

Pitching (40 IP)	ERA	W-L	Gm	IP	BB	SO
Mike Morgan	3.49	4-2	18	98.0	24	50
Mike Trombley	3.63	6-5	77	96.2	41	89
Rick Aguilera	4.24	4-9	68	74.1	15	57
Brad Radke	4.30	12-14	32	213.2	43	146
Hector Carrasco	4.38	4-2	63	61.2	31	46
Eddie Guardado	4.52	3-1	79	65.2	28	53
Bob Tewksbury	4.79	7-13	26	148.1	20	60
LaTroy Hawkins	5.25	7-14	33	190.1	61	105
Eric Milton*	5.64	8-14	32	172.1	70	107
Dan Serafini	6.48	7-4	28	75.0	29	46
Frank Rodriguez	6.56	4-6	20	70.0	30	62

Saves: Aguilera (38); Trombley and Carrasco (1). **Complete games:** Radke (5); Tewksbury and Milton (1). **Shutouts:** Radke (1).

New York Yankees

Batting (135 AB)	Avg	AB	R	H	HR	RBI	SB
Bernie Williams	.339	499	101	169	26	97	15
Derek Jeter	.324	626	127	203	19	84	30
Paul O'Neill	.317	602	95	191	24	116	15
Scott Brosius	.300	530	86	159	19	98	11
Tim Raines	.290	321	53	93	5	47	8
Tino Martinez	.281	531	92	149	28	123	2
Joe Girardi	.276	254	31	70	3	31	2
Jorge Posada	.268	358	56	96	17	63	0
Chuck Knoblauch	.265	603	117	160	17	64	31
Darryl Strawberry	.247	295	44	73	24	57	8
Chad Curtis	.243	456	79	111	10	56	21
Luis Sojo	.231	147	16	34	0	14	1

Pitching (40 IP)	ERA	W-L	Gm	IP	BB	SO
Mariano Rivera	1.91	3-0	54	61.1	17	36
Orlando Hernandez*	3.13	12-4	21	141.0	52	131
Ramiro Mendoza	3.25	10-2	41	130.1	30	56
Darren Holmes	3.33	0-3	34	51.1	14	31
David Wells	3.49	18-4	30	214.1	29	163
David Cone	3.55	20-7	31	207.2	59	209
Jeff Nelson	3.79	5-3	45	40.1	22	35
Hideki Irabu	4.06	13-9	29	173.0	76	126
Andy Pettitte	4.24	16-11	33	216.1	87	146
Mike Stanton	5.47	4-1	67	79.0	26	69
Mike Buddie*	5.62	4-1	24	41.2	13	20

Saves: Rivera (36); Stanton (6); Nelson (3); Holmes (2); Mendoza (1). **Complete games:** Wells (8); Pettitte (5); Cone and Hernandez (3); Irabu (2); Mendoza (1). **Shutouts:** Wells (5); Hernandez, Mendoza and Irabu (1).

Oakland Athletics

Batting (135 AB)	Avg	AB	R	H	HR	RBI	SB
Jason Giambi	.295	562	92	166	27	110	2
Matt Stairs	.294	523	88	154	26	106	8
Ben Grieve*	.288	583	94	168	18	89	2
Bip Roberts	.268	295	45	79	1	24	16
Scott Spezio	.259	406	54	105	9	50	1
Ryan Christenson*	.257	370	56	95	5	40	5
Jason McDonald	.251	175	25	44	1	16	10
Mike Macfarlane	.243	218	29	53	7	34	1
Mike Blowers	.237	409	56	97	11	71	1
Rickey Henderson	.236	542	101	128	14	57	66
Miguel Tejada	.233	365	53	85	11	45	5
A.J. Hinch*	.231	337	34	78	9	35	3
Rafael Bournigal	.225	209	23	47	1	19	6
Ed Sprague	.222	469	57	104	20	58	1

Acquired: C Macfarlane and cash from KC for OF Shane Mack and PTBN (Apr. 8); IF Roberts from Det. for PTBN (Jun. 23); P Worrell from Cle. for IF Adam Robinson (Jul. 12); IF Sprague from Tor. for minor leaguer (Jul. 31).

Pitching (40 IP)	ERA	W-L	Gm	IP	BB	SO
Gil Heredia	2.74	3-3	8	42.2	3	27
Kenny Rogers	3.17	16-8	34	238.2	67	138
Billy Taylor	3.58	4-9	70	73.0	22	58
Buddy Groom	4.24	3-1	75	57.1	20	36
T.J. Mathews	4.58	7-4	66	72.2	29	53
Tom Candiotti	4.84	11-16	33	201.0	63	98
Jimmy Haynes	5.09	11-9	33	194.1	88	134
Mike Mohler	5.16	3-3	57	61.0	26	42
Tim Worrell	5.24	2-7	43	103.0	29	82
Mike Oquist	6.22	7-11	31	175.0	57	112
Blake Stein*	6.37	5-9	24	117.1	71	89

Saves: Taylor (33); Mathews (1). **Complete games:** Rogers (7); Candiotti (3); Haynes and Stein (1). **Shutouts:** Rogers, Haynes and Stein (1).

Seattle Mariners

Batting (135 AB)	Avg	AB	R	H	HR	RBI	SB
Edgar Martinez	.322	556	86	179	29	102	1
Alex Rodriguez	.310	686	123	213	42	124	46
David Segui	.305	522	79	159	19	84	3
Glenallen Hill	.290	259	37	75	12	33	1
Ken Griffey Jr.	.284	633	120	180	56	146	20
David Bell	.274	420	48	115	10	49	0
Russ Davis	.259	502	68	130	20	82	4
Dan Wilson	.252	325	39	82	9	44	2
Jay Buhner	.242	244	33	59	15	45	0
Shane Monahan*	.242	211	17	51	4	28	1
Rob Ducey	.240	217	30	52	5	23	4
Joe Oliver	.225	240	20	54	6	32	1

Acquired: IF Bell from Cle. for IF Joey Cora (Aug. 31).
Traded: P Johnson to Hou. for two minor leaguers and PTBN (Jul. 31).
Claimed: C Oliver off waivers from Det. (Jul. 24).
Waived: OF Hill (Jul. 6).

Pitching (40 IP)	ERA	W-L	Gm	IP	BB	SO
Mike Timlin	2.95	3-3	70	79.1	16	60
Jamie Moyer	3.53	15-9	34	234.1	42	158
Jeff Fassero	3.97	13-12	32	224.2	66	176
Randy Johnson	4.33	9-10	23	160.0	60	213
Heathcliff Slocumb	5.32	2-5	57	67.2	44	51
Bill Swift	5.85	11-9	29	144.2	51	77
Bob Wells	6.10	2-2	30	51.2	16	29
Ken Cloude	6.37	8-10	30	155.1	80	114
Paul Spoljaric	6.48	4-6	53	83.1	55	89
Bobby Ayala	7.29	1-10	62	75.1	26	68

Saves: Timlin (19); Ayala (8); Slocumb (3). **Complete games:** Fassero (7); Johnson (6); Moyer (4). **Shutouts:** Moyer (3); Johnson (2).

Tampa Bay Devil Rays

Batting (135 AB)	Avg	AB	R	H	HR	RBI	SB
Aaron Ledesma	.324	299	30	97	0	29	9
Quinton McCracken	.292	614	77	179	7	59	19
Bubba Trammell	.286	199	28	57	12	35	0
Fred McGriff	.284	564	73	160	19	81	7
Wade Boggs	.280	435	51	122	7	52	3
Randy Winn*	.278	338	51	94	1	17	26
Bobby Smith*	.276	370	44	102	11	55	5
Miguel Cairo*	.268	515	49	138	5	46	19
Dave Martinez	.256	309	31	79	3	20	8
Mike Kelly	.240	279	39	67	10	33	13
Mike DeFelice	.230	248	17	57	3	23	0
Rich Butler*	.226	217	25	49	7	20	4
Paul Sorrento	.225	435	40	98	17	57	2
Kevin Stocker	.208	336	37	70	6	25	5
John Flaherty	.207	304	21	63	3	24	0

Claimed: P Santana off waivers from Tex. (Apr. 27).

Pitching (40 IP)	ERA	W-L	Gm	IP	BB	SO
Albie Lopez	2.60	7-4	54	79.2	32	62
Jim Mecir	3.11	7-2	68	84.0	33	77
Rolando Arrojo*	3.56	14-12	32	202.0	65	152
Rick White	3.80	2-6	38	68.2	23	39
Esteban Yan*	3.86	5-4	64	88.2	41	77
Roberto Hernandez	4.04	2-6	67	71.1	41	55
Tony Saunders	4.12	6-15	31	192.1	111	172
Julio Santana	4.39	5-6	35	145.2	62	61
Wilson Alvarez	4.73	6-14	25	142.2	68	107
Bryan Rekar	4.98	2-8	16	86.2	21	55
Dennis Springer	5.45	3-11	29	115.2	60	46
Jason Johnson*	5.70	2-5	13	60.0	27	36

Saves: Hernandez (26); Lopez and Yan (1). **Complete games:** Arrojo and Saunders (2); Santana, Rekar and Springer (1). **Shutouts:** Arrojo (2).

Texas Rangers

Batting (200 AB)	Avg	AB	R	H	HR	RBI	SB
Roberto Kelly	.323	257	48	83	16	46	0
Ivan Rodriguez	.321	579	88	186	21	91	9
Juan Gonzalez	.318	606	110	193	45	157	2
Rusty Greer	.306	598	107	183	16	108	2
Will Clark	.305	554	98	169	23	102	1
Tom Goodwin	.290	520	102	151	2	33	38
Luis Alicea	.274	259	51	71	6	33	4
Fernando Tatis	.270	330	41	89	3	32	6
Lee Stevens	.265	344	52	91	20	59	0
Mark McLemore	.247	461	79	114	5	53	12
Kevin Elster	.232	297	33	69	8	37	0

Acquired: P Crabtree from Tor. for C Kevin Brown (Mar. 14); P Loaiza from Pit. for P Todd Van Poppel and minor leaguer (Jul. 17); IF Todd Zeile from Fla. for two minor leaguers (Jul. 31); P Stottlemyre and IF Royce Clayton from St.L for P Darren Oliver, IF Fernando Tatis and PTBN (Jul. 31). **Traded:** P Witt to St.L for PTBN (Jun. 22).

Pitching (60 IP)	ERA	W-L	Gm	IP	BB	SO
John Wetteland	2.03	3-1	63	62.0	14	72
Tim Crabtree	3.59	6-1	64	85.1	35	60
Aaron Sele	4.23	19-11	33	212.2	84	167
Todd Stottlemyre	4.33	5-4	10	60.1	30	57
Rick Helling	4.41	20-7	33	216.1	78	164
Danny Patterson	4.45	2-5	56	60.2	19	33
Eric Gunderson	5.19	0-3	68	67.2	19	41
John Burkett	5.68	9-13	32	195.0	46	131
Esteban Loaiza	5.90	3-6	14	79.1	22	55
Darren Oliver	6.53	6-7	19	103.1	43	58
Bobby Witt	7.66	5-4	14	69.1	33	30

Saves: Wetteland (42); Patterson (2); Hernandez and Cadaret (1). **Complete games:** Helling (4); Sele (3); Oliver (2); Loaiza (1). **Shutouts:** Sele and Helling (2).

Toronto Blue Jays

Batting (135 AB)	Avg	AB	R	H	HR	RBI	SB
Tony Fernandez	.321	486	71	156	9	72	13
Carlos Delgado	.292	530	94	155	38	115	3
Darrin Fletcher	.283	407	37	115	9	52	0
Shannon Stewart	.279	516	90	144	12	55	51
Shawn Green	.278	630	106	175	35	100	35
Craig Grebeck	.256	301	33	77	2	27	2
Jose Cruz Jr.	.253	352	55	89	11	42	11
Alex Gonzalez	.239	568	70	136	13	51	21
Jose Canseco	.237	583	98	138	46	107	29

Traded: P Myers to SD for minor leaguer and PTBN (Aug. 6). **Released:** P Hanson (Jun. 16).

Pitching (40 IP)	ERA	W-L	Gm	IP	BB	SO
Paul Quantrill	2.59	3-4	82	80.0	22	59
Roger Clemens	2.65	20-6	33	234.2	88	271
Kelvim Escobar	3.73	7-3	22	79.2	35	72
Dan Plesac	3.78	4-3	78	50.0	16	55
Chris Carpenter	4.37	12-7	33	175.0	61	136
Woody Williams	4.46	10-9	32	209.2	81	151
Randy Myers	4.46	3-4	41	42.1	19	32
Dave Stieb	4.83	1-2	19	50.1	17	27
Pat Hentgen	5.17	12-11	29	177.2	69	94
Bill Risley	5.27	3-4	44	54.2	34	42
Erik Hanson	6.24	0-3	11	49.0	29	21

Saves: Myers (28); Quantrill (7); Plesac (4); Steib (2). **Complete games:** Clemens (5); Carpenter and Williams (1). **Shutouts:** Clemens (3); Carpenter and Williams (1).

Players Who Played in Both Leagues in 1998

While all indivdual major league statistics count on career records, players cannot transfer their stats from one league to the other if they are traded during the regular season. Here are the combined stats for batters with 375 at bats and pitchers with 120 innings pitched, who played in both leagues in 1998.

Batters (375 AB)

	Avg	AB	R	H	HR	RBI	SB
David Bell	.273	429	48	117	10	49	0
ST.L	.222	9	0	2	0	0	0
CLE	.262	340	37	89	10	41	0
SEA	.325	80	11	26	0	8	0
Joe Carter	.260	388	51	101	18	63	4
BAL	.247	283	36	70	11	34	3
SF	.295	105	15	31	7	29	1
Royce Clayton	.251	541	89	136	9	53	24
ST.L	.234	355	59	83	4	29	19
TEX	.285	186	30	53	5	24	5
Willie Greene	.258	396	65	102	15	54	7
CIN	.270	356	57	96	14	49	6
BAL	.150	40	8	6	1	5	1
Glenallen Hill	.310	390	63	121	20	56	1
SEA	.290	259	37	75	12	33	1
CHI (NL)	.351	131	26	46	8	23	0
Greg Jefferies	.301	555	72	167	9	58	12
PHI	.294	483	65	142	8	48	11
ANA	.347	72	7	25	1	10	1
Fernando Tatis	.276	532	69	147	11	58	13
TEX	.270	330	41	89	3	32	6
ST.L	.287	202	28	58	8	26	7
Todd Zeile	.271	572	85	155	19	94	4
LA	.253	158	22	40	7	27	1
FLA	.291	234	37	68	6	39	2
TEX	.261	180	26	47	6	28	1

Pitchers (120 IP)

	ERA	W-L	Gm	IP	BB	SO
Jason Bere	5.65	6-9	27	127.1	78	84
CHI (AL)	6.45	3-7	18	83.2	58	53
CIN	4.12	3-2	9	43.2	20	31
Randy Johnson	3.28	19-11	34	244.1	86	329
SEA	4.33	9-10	23	160.0	60	213
HOU	1.28	10-1	11	84.1	26	116
Jeff Juden	5.80	8-14	32	178.1	84	148
MIL	5.53	7-11	24	138.1	66	109
ANA	6.75	1-3	8	40.0	18	39
Esteban Loaiza	5.16	9-11	35	171.0	52	108
PIT	4.52	6-5	21	91.2	30	53
TEX	5.90	3-6	14	79.1	22	55
Mike Morgan	4.18	4-3	23	120.2	39	60
MIN	3.49	4-2	18	98.0	24	50
CHI (NL)	7.15	0-1	5	22.2	15	10
Darren Oliver	5.73	10-11	29	160.1	66	87
TEX	6.53	6-7	19	103.1	43	58
ST.L	4.26	4-4	10	57.0	23	29
Pete Schourek	4.43	8-9	25	124.0	50	95
HOU	4.50	7-6	15	80.0	36	59
BOS	4.30	1-3	10	44.0	14	36
Todd Stottlemyre	3.74	14-13	33	221.2	81	204
ST.L	3.51	9-9	23	161.1	51	147
TEX	4.33	5-4	10	60.1	30	57

NL Team by Team Statistics

At least 135 at bats or 40 innings pitched during the regular season unless otherwise indicated. Players who competed for more than one NL team are listed with their final club. Players traded from the AL are listed with NL team only if they have 135 AB or 40 IP. Note that (*) indicates rookie and PTBN indicates player to be named.

Arizona Diamondbacks

Batting (150 AB)	**Avg**	**AB**	**R**	**H**	**HR**	**RBI**	**SB**
Damian Miller*	.286	168	17	48	3	14	1
Devon White	.279	563	84	157	22	85	22
Andy Fox	.277	502	67	139	9	44	14
Tony Batista	.273	293	46	80	18	41	1
Travis Lee*	.269	562	71	151	22	72	8
Matt Williams	.267	510	72	136	20	71	5
David Dellucci*	.260	416	43	108	5	51	3
Kelly Stinnett	.259	274	35	71	11	34	0
Jay Bell	.251	549	79	138	20	67	3
Bernard Gilkey	.233	365	41	85	5	33	9
Brent Brede	.226	212	23	48	2	17	1
Karim Garcia*	.222	333	39	74	9	43	5
Yamil Benitez	.199	206	17	41	9	30	2

Acquired: P Embree from Atl. for P Russ Springer (Jun. 23); OF Gilkey and minor leaguer from NYM for P Willie Blair, C Jorge Fabregas and cash (Jul. 31).
Claimed: P Telemaco off waivers from ChC (May 15); P Chouinard off waivers from Mil. (Jun. 13).
Sold: P Suppan to KC (Sept. 3).

Pitching (45 IP)	**ERA**	**W-L**	**Gm**	**IP**	**BB**	**SO**
Omar Daal	2.88	8-12	33	162.2	51	132
Gregg Olson	3.01	3-4	64	68.2	25	55
Amaury Telemaco	3.93	7-10	41	148.2	46	78
Andy Benes	3.97	14-13	34	231.1	74	164
Alan Embree	4.19	4-2	55	53.2	23	43
Brian Anderson	4.33	12-13	32	208.0	24	95
Clint Sodowsky	5.68	3-6	45	77.2	39	42
Jeff Suppan	6.68	1-7	13	66.0	21	39

Saves: Olson (30); Rodriguez (5); Embree (1). **Complete games:** Daal (3); Anderson (2); Benes and Suppan (1). **Shutouts:** Daal and Anderson (1).

Atlanta Braves

Batting (135 AB)	**Avg**	**AB**	**R**	**H**	**HR**	**RBI**	**SB**
Eddie Perez	.336	149	18	50	6	32	1
Chipper Jones	.313	601	123	188	34	107	16
Greg Colbrunn	.307	166	18	51	3	23	4
Gerald Williams	.305	266	46	81	10	44	11
Andres Galarraga	.305	555	103	169	44	121	7
Javy Lopez	.284	489	73	139	34	106	5
Walt Weiss	.280	347	64	97	0	27	7
Ozzie Guillen	.277	264	35	73	1	22	1
Ryan Klesko	.274	427	69	117	18	70	5
Andruw Jones	.271	582	89	158	31	90	27
Keith Lockhart	.257	366	50	94	9	37	2
Danny Bautista	.250	144	17	36	3	17	1
Michael Tucker	.244	414	54	101	13	46	8
Tony Graffanino	.211	289	32	61	5	22	1

Acquired: P Springer from Ari. for P Alan Embree (Jun. 23); IF Colbrunn from Col. for two minor leaguers (Jul. 30).
Claimed: IF Guillen off waivers from Bal. (May 6).

Pitching (40 IP)	**ERA**	**W-L**	**Gm**	**IP**	**BB**	**SO**
Greg Maddux	2.22	18-9	34	251.0	45	204
Tom Glavine	2.47	20-6	33	229.1	74	157
Kerry Ligtenberg*	2.71	3-2	75	73.0	24	79
John Smoltz	2.90	17-3	26	167.2	44	173
Denny Neagle	3.55	16-11	32	210.1	60	165
Mike Cather	3.92	2-2	36	41.1	12	33
Kevin Millwood	4.08	17-8	31	174.1	56	163
Russ Springer	4.10	5-4	48	52.2	30	56
Dennis Martinez	4.45	4-6	53	91.0	19	62

Saves: Ligtenberg (30); Martinez (2). **Complete games:** Maddux (9); Neagle (5); Glavine (4); Millwood (3); Smoltz (2); Martinez (1). **Shutouts:** Maddux (5); Glavine (3); Smoltz and Neagle (2); Millwood and Martinez (1).

Chicago Cubs

Batting (135 AB)	**Avg**	**AB**	**R**	**H**	**HR**	**RBI**	**SB**
Mark Grace	.309	595	92	184	17	89	4
Sammy Sosa	.308	643	134	198	66	158	18
Mickey Morandini	.296	582	93	172	8	53	13
Brant Brown	.291	347	56	101	14	48	4
Gary Gaetti	.281	434	60	122	19	70	1
Lance Johnson	.280	304	51	85	2	21	10
Tyler Houston	.255	255	26	65	9	33	2
Jose Hernandez	.254	488	76	124	23	75	4
Henry Rodriguez	.251	415	56	104	31	85	1
Manny Alexander	.227	264	34	60	5	25	4
Scott Servais	.222	325	35	72	7	36	1
Jeff Blauser	.219	361	49	79	4	26	2

Acquired: P Wengert from SD for P Ben VanRyn (May 5); P Heredia and minor leaguer from Fla. for IF Kevin Orie and two minor leaguers (Jul. 31).
Claimed: Gaetti off waivers from St.L (Aug. 19).

Pitching (40 IP)	**ERA**	**W-L**	**Gm**	**IP**	**BB**	**SO**
Terry Mulholland	2.89	6-5	70	112.0	39	72
Rod Beck	3.02	3-4	81	80.1	20	81
Kerry Wood*	3.40	13-6	26	166.2	85	233
Marc Pisciotta*	4.09	1-2	43	44.0	32	31
Terry Adams	4.33	7-7	63	72.2	41	73
Steve Trachsel	4.46	15-8	33	208.0	84	149
Mark Clark	4.84	9-14	33	213.2	48	161
Kevin Tapani	4.85	19-9	35	219.0	62	136
Felix Heredia	5.06	3-3	71	58.2	38	54
Don Wengert	5.26	1-5	31	63.1	28	46
Jeremi Gonzalez	5.32	7-7	20	110.0	41	70

Saves: Beck (51); Mulholland (3); Heredia (2); Adams and Wengert (1). **Complete games:** Clark and Tapani (2); Wood, Trachsel and Gonzalez (1). **Shutouts:** Tapani (2); Wood, Clark and Gonzalez (1).

Cincinnati Reds

Batting (180 AB)	**Avg**	**AB**	**R**	**H**	**HR**	**RBI**	**SB**
Dmitri Young	.310	536	81	166	14	83	2
Barry Larkin	.309	538	93	166	17	72	26
Aaron Boone	.282	181	24	51	2	28	6
Eddie Taubensee	.278	431	61	120	11	72	1
Sean Casey*	.272	302	44	82	7	52	1
Willie Greene	.270	356	57	96	14	49	6
Reggie Sanders	.268	481	83	129	14	59	20
Bret Boone	.266	583	76	155	24	95	6
Chris Stynes	.254	347	52	88	6	27	15
Paul Konerko*	.217	217	21	47	7	29	0

Acquired: P Hudek from NYM for IF Lenny Harris (Jul. 3); IF Konerko and P Reyes from LA for P Jeff Shaw (Jul. 4).
Traded: IF Greene to Bal. for OF Jeffrey Hammonds (Aug. 10).

Pitching (45 IP)	**ERA**	**W- L**	**Gm**	**IP**	**BB**	**SO**
John Hudek	3.09	5-6	58	64.0	47	68
Pete Harnisch	3.14	14-7	32	209.0	64	157
Stan Belinda	3.23	4-8	40	61.1	28	57
Danny Graves	3.32	2-1	62	81.1	28	44
Steve Parris	3.73	6-5	18	99.0	32	77
Gabe White	4.01	5-5	69	98.2	27	83
Jason Bere	4.12	3-2	9	43.2	20	31
Brett Tomko	4.44	13-12	34	210.2	64	162
Dennis Reyes*	4.54	3-5	19	67.1	47	77
Mike Remlinger	4.82	8-15	35	164.1	87	144
Scott Sullivan	5.21	5-5	67	102.0	36	86
Scott Winchester*	5.81	3-6	16	79.0	27	40

Saves: White (9); Graves (8); Belinda and Sullivan (1). **Complete games:** Harnisch (2); Parris, Tomko, Remlinger and Winchester (1). **Shutouts:** Harnisch, Parris and Remlinger (1).

Colorado Rockies

Batting (135 AB)	Avg	AB	R	H	HR	RBI	SB
Larry Walker	.363	454	113	165	23	67	14
Dante Bichette	.331	662	97	219	22	122	14
Vinny Castilla	.319	645	108	206	46	144	5
Todd Helton*	.315	530	78	167	25	97	3
Darryl Hamilton	.308	561	95	173	6	51	13
Jeff Reed	.290	259	43	75	9	39	0
Mike Lansing	.276	584	73	161	12	66	10
Neifi Perez	.274	647	80	177	9	59	5
Kirt Manwaring	.247	291	30	72	2	26	1
Curtis Goodwin	.245	159	27	39	1	6	5

Acquired: OF Hamilton and minor leaguer from SF for OF Ellis Burks (Jul. 31).

Pitching (40 IP)	ERA	W-L	Gm	IP	BB	SO
Dave Veres	2.83	3-1	63	76.1	27	74
Chuck McElroy	2.90	6-4	78	68.1	24	61
Mike DeJean	3.03	3-1	59	74.1	24	27
Jerry Dipoto	3.53	3-4	68	71.1	25	49
Curt Leskanic	4.40	6-4	66	75.2	40	55
John Thomson	4.81	8-11	26	161.0	49	106
Darryl Kile	5.20	13-17	36	230.1	96	158
Bobby M. Jones*	5.22	7-8	35	141.1	66	109
Mike Munoz	5.66	2-2	40	41.1	16	24
Jamey Wright	5.67	9-14	34	206.1	95	86
Pedro Astacio	6.23	13-14	35	209.1	74	170

Saves: Dipoto (19); Veres (8); Munoz (3); McElroy, DeJean and Leskanic (2). **Complete games:** Kile (4); Thomson (2); Jones and Wright (1). **Shutouts:** Kile (1).

Florida Marlins

Batting (135 AB)	Avg	AB	R	H	HR	RBI	SB
Dave Berg*	.313	182	18	57	2	21	3
Edgar Renteria	.282	517	79	146	3	31	41
Cliff Floyd	.282	588	85	166	22	90	27
Mark Kotsay*	.279	578	72	161	11	68	10
Todd Zeile	.276	392	59	108	13	66	3
John Cangelosi	.251	171	19	43	1	10	2
Todd Dunwoody*	.251	434	53	109	5	28	5
Craig Counsell	.251	335	43	84	4	40	3
Ryan Jackson*	.250	260	26	65	5	31	1
Derrek Lee*	.233	454	62	106	17	74	5
Kevin Orie	.219	379	47	83	8	38	2
Luis Castillo	.203	153	21	31	1	10	3
Gregg Zaun	.188	298	19	56	5	29	5

Acquired: IF Zeile and C Mike Piazza from LA for OF Gary Sheffield, OF Jim Eisenreich, C Charles Johnson, IF Bobby Bonilla and P Manuel Barrios (May 22); IF Orie and two minor leaguers from ChC for P Felix Heredia and minor leaguer (Jul. 31).
Traded: C Piazza to NYM for OF Preston Wilson and two minor leaguers (May 22); IF Zeile to Tex. for two minor leaguers (Jul. 31).
Claimed: P Edmondson off waivers from Atl. (Jun. 4).

Pitching (40 IP)	ERA	W-L	Gm	IP	BB	SO
Matt Mantei	2.96	3-4	42	54.2	23	63
Vic Darensbourg*	3.68	0-7	59	71.0	30	74
Brian Edmondson*	3.91	4-4	53	76.0	37	40
Antonio Alfonseca*	4.08	4-6	58	70.2	33	46
Kirt Ojala*	4.25	2-7	41	125.0	59	75
Jesus Sanchez*	4.47	7-9	35	173.0	91	137
Livan Hernandez	4.72	10-12	33	234.1	104	162
Brian Meadows*	5.21	11-13	31	174.1	46	88
Robby Stanifer	5.63	2-4	38	48.0	22	30
Rafael Medina*	6.01	2-6	12	67.1	52	49
Joe Fontenot*	6.33	0-7	8	42.2	20	24
Ryan Dempster*	7.08	1-5	14	54.2	38	35
Andy Larkin*	9.64	3-8	17	74.2	55	43

Saves: Mantei (9); Alfonseca (8); Darensbourg and Stanifer (1). **Complete games:** Hernandez (9); Ojala and Meadows (1). **Shutouts:** none.

Houston Astros

Batting (160 AB)	Avg	AB	R	H	HR	RBI	SB
Craig Biggio	.325	646	123	210	20	88	50
Sean Berry	.314	299	48	94	13	52	3
Derek Bell	.314	630	111	198	22	108	13
Moises Alou	.312	584	104	182	38	124	11
Jeff Bagwell	.304	540	124	164	34	111	19
Richard Hidalgo*	.303	211	31	64	7	35	3
Carl Everett	.296	467	72	138	15	76	14
Bill Spiers	.273	384	66	105	4	43	11
Brad Ausmus	.269	412	62	111	6	45	10
Ricky Gutierrez	.261	491	55	128	2	46	13
Tony Eusebio	.253	182	13	46	1	36	1

Acquired: P Powell from Fla. for minor leaguer (Jul. 6); P Johnson from Sea. for two minor leaguers and PTBN (Jul. 31).
Traded: P Schourek to Bos. for cash (Aug. 6).

Pitchers (55 IP)	ERA	W-L	Gm	IP	BB	SO
Randy Johnson	1.28	10-1	11	84.1	26	116
Billy Wagner	2.70	4-3	58	60.0	25	97
Doug Henry	3.04	8-2	59	71.0	35	59
Scott Elarton*	3.32	2-1	28	57.0	20	56
Jay Powell	3.33	7-7	62	70.1	37	62
Mike Hampton	3.36	11-7	32	211.2	81	137
Shane Reynolds	3.51	19-8	35	233.1	53	209
Jose Lima	3.70	16-8	33	233.1	32	169
Sean Bergman	3.72	12-9	31	172.0	42	100
C.J. Nitkowski	3.77	3-3	43	59.2	23	44
Pete Schourek	4.50	7-6	15	80.0	36	59

Saves: Wagner (30); Powell (7); Nitkowski (3); Henry and Elarton (2). **Complete games:** Johnson (4); Reynolds and Lima (3); Hampton and Bergman (1). **Shutouts:** Johnson (4); Hampton, Reynolds and Lima (1).

Los Angeles Dodgers

Batting (200 AB)	Avg	AB	R	H	HR	RBI	SB
Gary Sheffield	.302	437	73	132	22	85	22
Trenidad Hubbard	.298	208	29	62	7	18	9
Eric Karros	.296	507	59	150	23	87	7
Eric Young	.285	452	78	129	8	43	42
Raul Mondesi	.279	580	85	162	30	90	16
Mark Grudzielanek	.272	589	62	160	10	62	18
Jose Vizcaino	.262	237	30	62	3	29	7
Bobby Bonilla	.249	333	39	83	11	45	1
Roger Cedeno	.242	240	33	58	2	17	8
Matt Luke*	.236	237	34	56	12	34	2
Charles Johnson	.218	459	44	100	19	58	0
Juan Castro	.195	220	25	43	2	14	0

Acquired: OF Sheffield, OF Jim Eisenreich, C Johnson, IF Bonilla and P Manuel Barrios from Fla. for IF Todd Zeile and C Mike Piazza (May 22); P Mlicki and P Greg McMichael from NYM for P Hideo Nomo and P Brad Clontz (Jun. 4); P Shaw from Cin. for IF Paul Konerko and P Dennis Reyes (Jul. 4); P Bohanon from NYM for P McMichael (Jul. 10); P Perez, IF Grudzielanek and minor leaguer from Mon. for IF Wilton Guerrero and three minor leaguers (Jul. 31).
Purchased: OF Luke from Cle. (Jun. 20) after they released him (Jun. 8).

Pitching (55 IP)	ERA	W-L	Gm	IP	BB	SO
Jeff Shaw	2.12	3-8	73	85.0	19	55
Scott Radinsky	2.63	6-6	62	61.2	20	45
Brian Bohanon	2.67	7-11	39	151.2	57	111
Ramon Martinez	2.83	7-3	15	101.2	41	91
Antonio Osuna	3.06	7-1	54	64.2	32	72
Carlos Perez	3.59	11-14	34	241.0	63	128
Chan Ho Park	3.71	15-9	34	220.2	97	191
Ismael Valdes	3.98	11-10	27	174.0	66	122
Darren Dreifort	4.00	8-12	32	180.0	57	168
Dave Mlicki	4.57	8-7	30	181.1	63	117

Saves: Shaw (48); Radinsky (13); Osuna (6); Lankford (1). **Complete games:** Perez (7); Mlicki (3); Bohanon, Park and Valdes (2); Martinez and Dreifort (1). **Shutouts:** Perez and Valdes (2); Dreifort and Mlicki (1).

Milwaukee Brewers

Batting (135 AB)	Avg	AB	R	H	HR	RBI	SB
Jeff Cirillo	.321	604	97	194	14	68	10
Mark Loretta	.316	434	55	137	6	54	9
Fernando Vina	.311	637	101	198	7	45	22
Marquis Grissom	.271	542	57	147	10	60	13
Dave Nilsson	.269	309	39	83	12	56	2
Jeromy Burnitz	.263	609	92	160	38	125	7
Darrin Jackson	.240	204	20	49	4	20	1
Mike Matheny	.238	320	24	76	6	27	1
Marc Newfield	.237	186	15	44	3	25	0
Bobby Hughes*	.229	218	28	50	9	29	1
Geoff Jenkins*	.229	262	33	60	9	28	1
Jose Valentin	.224	428	65	96	16	49	10
Bob Hamelin	.219	146	15	32	7	22	0
John Jaha	.208	216	29	45	7	38	1

Acquired: P Eric Plunk from Cle. for P Jones (Jul. 23); P Pulsipher from NYM for minor leaguer (Jul. 31).
Claimed: P Weathers off waivers from Cin. (Jun. 24).
Traded: P Juden to Ana. for PTBN (Aug. 7).

Pitching (40 IP)	ERA	W-L	Gm	IP	BB	SO
Mike Myers	2.70	2-2	70	50.0	22	40
Bob Wickman	3.72	6-9	72	82.1	39	71
Chad Fox	3.95	1-4	49	57.0	20	64
Al Reyes	3.95	5-1	50	57.0	31	58
Steve Woodard*	4.18	10-12	34	165.2	33	135
Scott Karl	4.40	10-11	33	192.1	66	102
Bronswell Patrick*	4.69	4-1	32	78.2	29	49
Cal Eldred	4.80	4-8	23	133.0	61	86
Rafael Roque*	4.88	4-2	9	48.0	24	34
Dave Weathers	4.91	6-5	44	110.0	41	94
Brad Woodall*	4.96	7-9	31	138.0	47	85
Bill Pulsipher	5.10	3-4	26	72.1	31	51
Doug Jones	5.17	3-4	46	54.0	11	43
Jeff Juden	5.53	7-11	24	138.1	66	109
Paul Wagner	7.11	1-5	13	55.2	31	37

Saves: Wickman (25); Jones (12); Myers (1). **Complete games:** Juden (2). **Shutouts:** none.

New York Mets

Batting (135 AB)	Avg	AB	R	H	HR	RBI	SB
John Olerud	.354	557	91	197	22	93	2
Mike Piazza	.328	561	88	184	32	111	1
Jermaine Allensworth	.289	287	39	83	5	28	8
Edgardo Alfonzo	.278	557	94	155	17	78	8
Matt Franco	.273	161	20	44	1	13	0
Carlos Baerga	.266	511	46	136	7	53	0
Brian McRae	.264	552	79	146	21	79	20
Lenny Harris	.259	290	30	75	6	27	6
Butch Huskey	.252	369	43	93	13	59	7
Luis Lopez	.252	266	37	67	2	22	2
Rey Ordonez	.246	505	46	124	1	42	3
Tony Phillips	.223	188	25	42	3	14	1
Jorge Fabregas	.197	183	11	36	2	20	0

Acquired: C Piazza from Fla. for OF Preston Wilson and two minor leaguers (May 22); P Nomo and P Brad Clontz from LA for P Dave Mlicki and P Greg McMichael (Jun. 4); IF Harris from Cin. for P John Hudek (Jul. 3); P McMichael from LA for P Brian Bohanon (Jul. 10); OF Phillips from Tor. for minor leaguer (Jul. 31); P Blair, C Fabregas and cash from Ari. for OF Bernard Gilkey and minor leaguer (Jul. 31); OF Allensworth from KC for cash (Aug. 10).

Pitching (40 IP)	ERA	W-L	Gm	IP	BB	SO
Dennis Cook	2.38	8-4	73	68.0	27	79
Al Leiter	2.47	17-6	28	193.0	71	174
Turk Wendell	2.93	5-1	66	76.2	33	58
Rick Reed	3.48	16-11	31	212.1	29	153
John Franco	3.62	0-8	61	64.2	29	59
Armando Reynoso	3.82	7-3	11	68.1	32	40
Masato Yoshii*	3.93	6-8	29	171.2	53	117
Bobby Jones	4.05	9-9	30	195.1	53	115
Greg McMichael	4.10	5-4	64	68.0	35	55
Hideo Nomo	4.92	6-12	29	157.1	94	167
Willie Blair	4.98	5-16	34	175.1	61	92
Mel Rojas	6.05	5-2	50	58.0	30	41

Saves: Franco (38); Wendell (4); McMichael and Rojas (2); Cook (1). **Complete games:** Leiter (4); Nomo (3); Reed (2); Yoshii (1). **Shutouts:** Leiter (2); Reed (1).

Montreal Expos

Batting (135 AB)	Avg	AB	R	H	HR	RBI	SB
Vladimir Guerrero	.324	623	108	202	38	109	11
Rondell White	.300	357	54	107	17	58	16
Wilton Guerrero	.284	402	50	114	2	27	8
Orlando Cabrera*	.280	261	44	73	3	22	6
Brad Fullmer*	.273	505	58	138	13	73	6
Derrick May	.239	180	13	43	5	15	0
Shane Andrews	.238	492	48	117	25	69	1
Chris Widger	.233	417	36	97	15	53	6
Jose Vidro	.220	205	24	45	0	18	2
Terry Jones*	.217	212	30	46	1	15	16
F.P. Santangelo	.214	383	53	82	4	23	7
Ryan McGuire	.186	210	17	39	1	10	0

Acquired: IF Wilton Guerrero and three minor leaguers from LA for P Carlos Perez, IF Mark Grudzielanek and minor leaguer (Jul. 31).

Pitching (40 IP)	ERA	W-L	Gm	IP	BB	SO
Ugueth Urbina	1.30	6-3	64	69.1	33	94
Steve Kline	2.76	3-6	78	71.2	41	76
Dustin Hermanson	3.13	14-11	32	187.0	56	154
Mike Maddux	3.72	3-4	51	55.2	15	33
Miguel Batista	3.80	3-5	56	135.0	65	92
Anthony Telford	3.86	3-6	77	91.0	36	59
Carl Pavano*	4.21	6-9	24	134.2	43	83
Mike Thurman*	4.70	4-5	14	67.0	26	32
Trey Moore*	5.02	2-5	13	61.0	17	35
Shayne Bennett*	5.50	5-5	62	91.2	45	59
Javier Vazquez*	6.06	5-15	33	172.1	68	139

Saves: Urbina (34); Kline, Maddux, Telford and Bennett (1). **Complete games:** Hermanson (1). **Shutouts:** none.

Philadelphia Phillies

Batting (135 AB)	Avg	AB	R	H	HR	RBI	SB
Kevin Sefcik	.314	169	27	53	3	20	4
Bob Abreu	.312	497	68	155	17	74	19
Gregg Jefferies	.294	483	65	142	8	48	11
Scott Rolen	.290	601	120	174	31	110	14
Doug Glanville	.279	678	106	189	8	49	23
Kevin Jordan	.276	250	23	69	2	27	0
Rico Brogna	.265	565	77	150	20	104	7
Mike Lieberthal	.256	313	39	80	8	45	2
Mark Lewis	.249	518	52	129	9	54	3
Desi Relaford*	.245	494	45	121	5	41	9
Bobby Estalella*	.188	165	16	31	8	20	0

Traded: OF Jefferies to Ana. for minor leaguer (Aug. 28).
Claimed: P Byrd off waivers from Atl. (Aug. 15).

Pitchers (40 IP)	ERA	W-L	Gm	IP	BB	SO
Paul Byrd	2.68	5-2	9	57.0	18	39
Curt Schilling	3.25	15-14	35	268.2	61	300
Jerry Spradlin	3.53	4-4	69	81.2	20	76
Mark Leiter	3.55	7-5	69	88.2	47	84
Yorkis Perez	3.81	0-2	57	52.0	25	42
Wayne Gomes	4.24	9-6	71	93.1	35	86
Mark Portugal	4.44	10-5	26	166.1	32	104
Tyler Green	5.03	6-12	27	159.1	85	113
Matt Beech	5.15	3-9	21	117.0	63	113
Mike Grace	5.48	4-7	21	90.1	30	46
Carlton Loewer*	6.09	7-8	21	122.2	39	58
Ricky Bottalico	6.44	1-5	39	43.1	25	27

Saves: Leiter (23); Bottalico (6); Spradlin and Gomes (1). **Complete games:** Schilling (15); Portugal (3); Byrd (2); Loewer (1). **Shutouts:** Schilling (2); Byrd (1).

Pittsburgh Pirates

Batting (135 AB)	**Avg**	**AB**	**R**	**H**	**HR**	**RBI**	**SB**
Jason Kendall	.327	535	95	175	12	75	26
Adrian Brown*	.283	152	20	43	0	5	4
Tony Womack	.282	655	85	185	3	45	58
Kevin Young	.270	592	88	160	27	108	15
Jose Guillen	.267	573	60	153	14	84	3
Turner Ward	.262	282	33	74	9	46	5
Freddy Garcia	.256	172	27	44	9	26	0
Manny Martinez*	.250	180	21	45	6	24	0
Lou Collier*	.246	334	30	82	2	34	2
Al Martin	.239	440	57	105	12	47	20
Aramis Ramirez*	.235	251	23	59	6	24	0
Kevin Polcovich	.189	212	18	40	0	14	4
Doug Strange	.173	185	9	32	0	14	1

Acquired: P Van Poppel and minor leaguer from Tex. for P Loaiza (Jul. 17).

Pitching (45 IP)	**ERA**	**W-L**	**Gm**	**IP**	**BB**	**SO**
Mike Williams	1.94	4-2	37	51.0	16	59
Jason Christiansen	2.51	3-3	60	64.2	27	71
Ricardo Rincon	2.91	0-2	60	65.0	29	64
Jeff Tabaka	3.02	2-2	37	50.2	22	40
Francisco Cordova	3.31	13-14	33	220.1	69	157
Rich Loiselle	3.44	2-7	54	55.0	36	48
Chris Peters	3.47	8-10	39	148.0	55	103
Jason Schmidt	4.07	11-14	33	214.1	71	158
Jon Lieber	4.11	8-14	29	171.0	40	138
Jose Silva*	4.40	6-7	18	100.1	30	64
Esteban Loaiza	4.52	6-5	21	91.2	30	53
Todd Van Poppel	5.36	1-2	18	47.0	18	32
Elmer Dessens*	5.67	2-6	43	74.2	25	43

Saves: Loiselle (19); Rincon (14); Christiansen (6); Peters and Lieber (1). **Complete games:** Cordova (3); Lieber (2); Peters and Silva (1). **Shutouts:** Cordova (2).

St. Louis Cardinals

Batting (155 AB)	**Avg**	**AB**	**R**	**H**	**HR**	**RBI**	**SB**
Brian Jordan	.316	564	100	178	25	91	17
Mark McGwire	.299	509	130	152	70	147	1
Ray Lankford	.293	533	94	156	31	105	26
Delino DeShields	.290	420	74	122	7	44	26
Fernando Tatis	.287	202	28	58	8	26	7
Willie McGee	.253	269	27	68	3	34	7
John Mabry	.249	377	41	94	9	46	0
Eli Marrero*	.244	254	28	62	4	20	6
Ron Gant	.240	383	60	92	26	67	8
Royce Clayton	.234	355	59	83	4	29	19
Tom Lampkin	.231	216	25	50	6	28	3
Tom Pagnozzi	.219	160	7	35	1	10	0

Acquired: P Witt from Tex. for PTBN (Jun. 22); P Oliver, IF Tatis and PTBN from Tex. for P Stottlemyre and IF Clayton (Jul. 31);

Pitching (40 IP)	**ERA**	**W-L**	**Gm**	**IP**	**BB**	**SO**
Matt Morris	2.53	7-5	17	113.2	42	79
Juan Acevedo	2.56	8-3	50	98.1	29	56
Todd Stottlemyre	3.51	9-9	23	161.1	51	147
Curtis King*	3.53	2-0	36	51.0	20	28
Lance Painter	3.99	4-0	65	47.1	28	39
Donovan Osborne	4.09	5-4	14	83.2	22	60
John Frascatore	4.14	3-4	69	95.2	36	49
Darren Oliver	4.26	4-4	10	57.0	23	29
Jeff Brantley	4.44	0-5	48	50.2	18	48
Kent Bottenfield	4.44	4-6	44	133.2	57	98
Mike Busby*	4.50	5-2	26	46.0	15	33
Mark Petkovsek	4.77	7-4	48	105.2	36	55
Bobby Witt	4.94	2-5	17	47.1	20	28
Rich Croushore*	4.97	0-3	41	54.1	29	47
Kent Mercker	5.07	11-11	30	161.2	53	72
Manny Aybar	5.98	6-6	20	81.1	42	57

Saves: Acevedo (15); Brantley (14); Croushore (8); Bottenfield (4); King (2); Painter (1). **Complete games:** Stottlemyre (3); Morris (2); Osborne (1). **Shutouts:** Morris and Osborne (1).

San Diego Padres

Batting (135 AB)	**Avg**	**AB**	**R**	**H**	**HR**	**RBI**	**SB**
Tony Gwynn	.321	461	65	148	16	69	3
Wally Joyner	.298	439	58	131	12	80	1
Greg Vaughn	.272	573	112	156	50	119	11
Chris Gomez	.267	449	55	120	4	39	1
Quilvio Veras	.267	517	79	138	6	45	24
Jim Leyritz	.266	143	17	38	4	18	0
Carlos Hernandez	.262	390	34	102	9	52	2
Ken Caminiti	.252	452	87	114	29	82	6
Steve Finley	.249	619	92	154	14	67	12
Greg Myers	.246	171	19	42	4	20	0
Andy Sheets	.242	194	31	47	7	29	7
Mark Sweeney	.234	192	17	45	2	15	1
Ed Giovanola	.230	139	19	32	1	9	1
Ruben Rivera*	.209	172	31	36	6	29	5

Acquired: C Leyritz and minor leaguer from Bos. for P Carlos Reyes, P Dario Veras and C Mandy Romero (Jun. 21); P Bruske from LA for minor leaguer (Jul. 23).
Traded: P Smith to Bal. for P Eric Estes (Jun. 9); P Bruske and minor leaguer to NYY for two minor leaguers (Aug. 23).

Pitching (40 IP)	**ERA**	**W-L**	**Gm**	**IP**	**BB**	**SO**
Trevor Hoffman	1.48	4-2	66	73.0	21	86
Kevin Brown	2.38	18-7	36	257.0	49	257
Donne Wall	2.43	5-4	46	70.1	32	56
Dan Miceli	3.22	10-5	67	72.2	27	70
Andy Ashby	3.34	17-9	33	226.2	58	151
Jim Bruske	3.53	3-0	39	51.0	23	35
Sterling Hitchcock	3.93	9-7	39	176.1	48	158
Joey Hamilton	4.27	13-13	34	217.1	106	147
Brian Boehringer	4.36	5-2	56	76.1	45	67
Pete Smith	4.78	3-2	10	43.1	18	36
Mark Langston	5.86	4-6	22	81.1	41	56

Saves: Hoffman (53); Miceli (2); Wall, Bruske and Hitchcock (1). **Complete games:** Brown (7); Ashby (5); Hitchcock (2). **Shutouts:** Brown (3); Ashby and Hitchcock (1).

San Francisco Giants

Batting (135 AB)	**Avg**	**AB**	**R**	**H**	**HR**	**RBI**	**SB**
Marvin Benard	.322	286	41	92	3	36	11
Barry Bonds	.303	552	120	167	37	122	28
Jeff Kent	.297	526	94	156	31	128	9
Bill Mueller	.294	534	93	157	9	59	3
Ellis Burks	.292	504	76	147	21	76	11
Stan Javier	.290	417	63	121	4	49	21
Charlie Hayes	.286	329	39	94	12	62	2
Rey Sanchez	.285	316	44	90	2	30	0
Brent Mayne	.273	275	26	75	3	32	2
Rich Aurilia	.266	413	54	110	9	49	3
J.T. Snow	.248	435	65	108	15	79	1
Brian Johnson	.237	308	34	73	13	34	0

Acquired: P Jose Mesa, IF Shawon Dunston and P Al Morman from Cle. for P Reed and OF Jacob Cruz (Jul. 23); OF Burks from Col. for OF Darryl Hamilton and minor leaguer (Jul. 31).

Pitching (40 IP)	**ERA**	**W-L**	**Gm**	**IP**	**BB**	**SO**
Steve Reed	1.48	2-1	50	54.2	19	50
Robb Nen	1.52	7-7	78	88.2	25	110
John Johnstone	3.07	6-5	70	88.0	38	86
Rich Rodriguez	3.70	4-0	68	65.2	20	44
Julian Tavarez	3.80	5-3	60	85.1	36	52
Mark Gardner	4.33	13-6	33	212.0	65	151
Kirk Rueter	4.36	16-9	33	187.2	57	102
Orel Hershiser	4.41	11-10	34	202.0	85	126
Russ Ortiz*	4.99	4-4	22	88.1	46	75
Shawn Estes	5.06	7-12	25	149.1	80	136
Danny Darwin	5.51	8-10	33	148.2	49	81

Saves: Nen (40); Rodriguez (2); Reed and Tavarez (1). **Complete games:** Gardner (4); Rueter and Estes (1). **Shutouts:** Gardner (2); Estes (1).

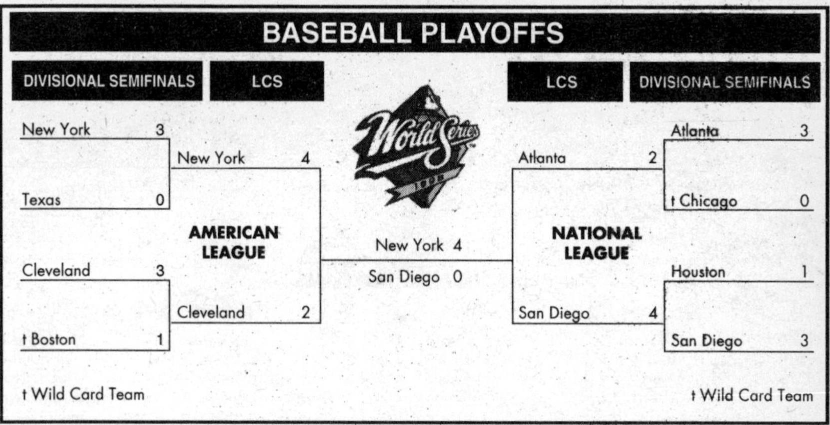

Divisional Series Summaries
AMERICAN LEAGUE

Yankees, 3-0

Date	Winner	Home Field
Sept. 29	Yankees, 2-0	at New York
Sept. 30	Yankees, 3-1	at New York
Oct. 2	Yankees, 4-0	at Texas

Game 1

Tuesday, Sept. 29, at New York

	1 2 3	4 5 6	7 8 9	R	H	E
Texas	0 0 0	0 0 0	0 0 0	0	5	0
New York	0 2 0	0 0 0	0 0 x	2	6	0

Win: Wells, NY (1-0). **Loss:** Stottlemyre, Tex. (0-1). **Save:** Rivera, NY (1).
2B: Texas— McLemore; New York— O'Neill, Curtis, Martinez. **RBI:** New York— Brosius.
Attendance: 57,362. **Time:** 3:02.

Game 2

Wednesday, Sept. 30, at New York

	1 2 3	4 5 6	7 8 9	R	H	E
Texas	0 0 0	0 1 0	0 0 0	1	5	0
New York	0 1 0	2 0 0	0 0 x	3	8	0

Win: Pettitte, NY (1-0). **Loss:** Helling, Tex. (0-1). **Save:** Rivera, NY (2).
2B: Texas— Gonzalez, Kelly; New York— O'Neill. **HR:** New York— Spencer (1), Brosius (1). **RBI:** Texas— Rodriguez; New York— Brosius 2, Spencer. **SB:** New York— Bush (1).
Attendance: 57,360. **Time:** 2:58.

Game 3

Friday, Oct. 2, at Texas

	1 2 3	4 5 6	7 8 9	R	H	E
New York	0 0 0	0 0 4	0 0 0	4	9	1
Texas	0 0 0	0 0 0	0 0 0	0	3	1

Win: Cone, NY (1-0). **Loss:** Sele, Tex. (0-1).
2B: New York— Martinez, Raines. **HR:** New York— O'Neill (1), Spencer (2). **RBI:** New York— Spencer 3, O'Neill. **SB:** New York— Curtis (1).
Attendance: 49,450. **Time:** 2:58.

Indians, 3-1

Date	Winner	Home Field
Sept. 29	Red Sox, 11-3	at Cleveland
Sept. 30	Indians, 9-5	at Cleveland
Oct. 2	Indians, 4-3	at Boston
Oct. 3	Indians, 2-1	at Boston

Game 1

Tuesday, Sept. 29, at Cleveland

	1 2 3	4 5 6	7 8 9	R	H	E
Boston	3 0 0	0 3 2	0 3 0	11	12	0
Cleveland	0 0 0	0 0 2	1 0 0	3	7	0

Win: Martinez, Bos. (1-0). **Loss:** Wright, Cle. (0-1).
2B: Boston— Vaughn; Cleveland— Alomar, Giles, Justice.
HR: Boston— Vaughn 2 (2), Garciaparra (1); Cleveland— Lofton (1), Thome (1). **RBI:** Boston— Vaughn 7, Garciaparra 4; Cleveland— Lofton 2, Thome.
Attendance: 45,185. **Time:** 3:16.

Game 2

Wednesday, Sept. 30, at Cleveland

	1 2 3	4 5 6	7 8 9	R	H	E
Boston	2 0 1	0 0 2	0 0 0	5	10	0
Cleveland	1 5 1	0 0 1	0 1 x	9	9	1

Win: Burba, Cle. (1-0). **Loss:** Wakefield, Bos. (0-1). **Save:** Jackson, Cle. (1).
2B: Boston— Garciaparra, Lewis; Cleveland— Alomar 2, Ramirez 2, Lofton, Justice. **HR:** Cleveland— Justice (1). **RBI:** Boston— Garciaparra 3, Varitek; Cleveland— Justice 4, Alomar 2, Lofton, Ramirez. **SB:** Boston— Lewis (1); Cleveland— Lofton (1).
Attendance: 45,229. **Time:** 3:25.

Game 3

Friday, Oct. 2, at Boston

	1 2 3	4 5 6	7 8 9	R	H	E
Cleveland	0 0 0	0 1 1	1 0 1	4	5	0
Boston	0 0 0	1 0 0	0 0 2	3	6	0

Win: Nagy, Cle. (1-0). **Loss:** Saberhagen, Bos. (0-1). **Save:** Jackson, Cle. (2).
HR: Cleveland— Ramirez 2 (2), Thome (2), Lofton (2); Boston— Garciaparra (2). **RBI:** Cleveland— Ramirez 2, Thome, Lofton; Boston— Garciaparra 3.
Attendance: 33,114. **Time:** 2:27.

Game 4

Saturday, Oct. 3, at Boston

	1 2 3	4 5 6	7 8 9	R H E
Cleveland	0 0 0	0 0 0	0 2 0	2 5 0
Boston	0 0 0	1 0 0	0 0 0	1 6 0

Win: Reed, Cle. (1-0). **Loss:** Gordon, Bos. (0-1). **Save:** Jackson, Cle. (3).
2B: Cleveland— Justice 2, Fryman; Boston— Lewis, Valentin, Vaughn. **HR:** Boston— Garciaparra (3). **RBI:** Cleveland— Justice 2; Boston— Garciaparra. **SB:** Cleveland— Fryman (1), Lofton (2).
Attendance: 33,537. **Time:** 3:00.

Playoff Series

The AL and NL League Championship Series began in 1969 with a Best of 5 format, then changed to Best of 7 in 1985. The '95 season was the first year for wild card teams and the new Best of 3 Divisional Series.

NATIONAL LEAGUE

Braves, 3-0

Date	Winner	Home Field
Sept. 30	Braves, 7-1	at Atlanta
Oct. 1	Braves, 2-1 (10 inn.)	at Atlanta
Oct. 3	Braves, 6-2	at Chicago

Game 1

Wednesday, Sept. 30, at Atlanta

	1 2 3	4 5 6	7 8 9	R H E
Chicago	0 0 0	0 0 0	0 1 0	1 5 1
Atlanta	0 2 0	0 0 1	4 0 x	7 8 0

Win: Smoltz, Atl. (1-0). **Loss:** Clark, Chi. (0-1).
2B: Chicago— Sosa. **HR:** Chicago— Houston (1); Atlanta— Tucker (1), Klesko (1). **RBI:** Chicago— Houston; Atlanta— Klesko 4, Tucker 2, A. Jones. **SB:** Atlanta— A. Jones (1).
Attendance: 45,598. **Time:** 2:34.

Game 2

Thursday, Oct. 1, at Atlanta

	1 2 3	4 5 6	7 8 9	10	R H E
Chicago	0 0 0	0 0 1	0 0 0	0	1 4 1
Atlanta	0 0 0	0 0 0	0 0 1	1	2 6 0

Win: Perez, Atl. (1-0). **Loss:** Mulholland, Chi. (0-1).
HR: Atlanta— Lopez (1). **RBI:** Chicago— Johnson; Atlanta— C. Jones, Lopez. **SB:** Chicago— Hill (1); Atlanta— Tucker (1).
Attendance: 51,713. **Time:** 2:47.

Game 3

Saturday, Oct. 3, at Chicago

	1 2 3	4 5 6	7 8 9	R H E
Atlanta	0 0 1	0 0 0	0 5 0	6 9 0
Chicago	0 0 0	0 0 0	0 2 0	2 8 2

Win: Maddux, Atl. (1-0). **Loss:** Wood, Chi. (0-1).
2B: Atlanta— Maddux, Bautista; Chicago— Rodriguez. **HR:** Atlanta— Perez (1). **RBI:** Atlanta— Perez 4, Williams; Chicago— Morandini, Grace. **SB:** Atlanta— A. Jones (2).
Attendance: 39,597. **Time:** 2:57.

Padres, 3-1

Date	Winner	Home Field
Sept. 29	Padres, 2-1	at Houston
Oct. 1	Astros, 5-4	at Houston
Oct. 3	Padres, 2-1	at San Diego
Oct. 4	Padres, 6-1	at San Diego

Game 1

Tuesday, Sept. 29, at Houston

	1 2 3	4 5 6	7 8 9	R H E
San Diego	0 0 0	0 0 1	0 1 0	2 9 1
Houston	0 0 0	0 0 0	0 0 1	1 4 0

Win: Brown, SD (1-0). **Loss:** Johnson, Hou. (0-1). **Save:** Hoffman (1).
2B: San Diego— Gwynn; Houston— Spiers. **HR:** San Diego— Vaughn (1). **RBI:** San Diego— Vaughn, Leyritz.
Attendance: 50,080. **Time:** 2:38.

Game 2

Thursday, Oct. 1, at Houston

	1 2 3	4 5 6	7 8 9	R H E
San Diego	0 0 0	0 0 2	0 0 2	4 8 1
Houston	1 0 2	0 0 0	0 1 1	5 11 1

Win: Wagner, Hou. (1-0). **Loss:** Miceli, SD (0-1).
2B: San Diego— Finley; Houston— Spiers 2, Eusebio. **HR:** San Diego— Leyritz (1); Houston— Bell (1). **RBI:** San Diego— Leyritz 2, Finley, Gwynn; Houston— Bagwell 3, Spiers, Bell. **SB:** Houston— Gutierrez (1).
Attendance: 45,550. **Time:** 2:53.

Game 3

Saturday, Oct. 3, at San Diego

	1 2 3	4 5 6	7 8 9	R H E
Houston	0 0 0	0 0 0	1 0 0	1 4 0
San Diego	0 0 0	0 0 1	1 0 x	2 3 0

Win: Miceli, SD (1-1). **Loss:** Elarton, Hou. (0-1). **Save:** Hoffman, SD (2).
HR: San Diego— Leyritz (2). **RBI:** Houston— Biggio; San Diego— Gwynn, Leyritz.
Attendance: 65,235. **Time:** 2:32.

Game 4

Sunday, Oct. 4, at San Diego

	1 2 3	4 5 6	7 8 9	R H E
Houston	0 0 0	1 0 0	0 0 0	1 3 1
San Diego	0 1 0	0 0 1	0 4 x	6 7 1

Win: Hitchcock, SD (1-0). **Loss:** Johnson, Hou. (0-2).
2B: Houston— Biggio; San Diego— Vaughn, Gwynn. **3B:** San Diego— Vander Wal. **HR:** San Diego— Leyritz (3), Joyner (1). **RBI:** Houston— Bagwell; San Diego— Vander Wal 2, Joyner 2, Leyritz.
Attendance: 64,898. **Time:** 2:39.

American League Championship Series

Yankees, 4-2

Date	Winner	Home Field
Oct. 6	Yankees, 7-2	at New York
Oct. 7	Indians, 4-1 (12 inn.)	at New York
Oct. 9	Indians, 6-1	at Cleveland
Oct. 10	Yankees, 4-1	at Cleveland
Oct. 11	Yankees, 5-3	at Cleveland
Oct. 13	Yankees. 9-5	at New York

Game 1

Tuesday, Oct. 6, at New York

	1 2 3	4 5 6	7 8 9	R	H	E
Cleveland	0 0 0	0 0 0	0 0 2	2	5	0
New York	5 0 0	0 0 1	1 0 x	7	11	0

Win: Wells, NY (2-0). **Loss:** Wright, Cle. (0-2).
2B: New York— O'Neill, Williams. **HR:** Cleveland— Ramirez (3); New York— Posada (1). **RBI:** Cleveland— Ramirez 2; New York— Williams 2, Posada 2, O'Neill, Brosius. **SB:** Cleveland— Vizquel (1); New York— Martinez (1), Jeter (1).
Attendance: 57,138. **Time:** 3:31.

Game 2

Wednesday, Oct. 7, at New York

	1 2 3 4 5 6 7 8 9	10	11	12	R	H	E
Cleveland	0 0 0 1 0 0 0 0 0	0	0	3	4	8	1
New York	0 0 0 0 0 0 1 0 0	0	0	0	1	7	1

Win: Burba, Cle. (2-0). **Loss:** Nelson, NY (0-1). **Save:** Jackson, Cle. (4).
2B: New York— Jeter, O'Neill, Brosius. **3B:** Cleveland— Vizquel. **HR:** Cleveland— Justice (2). **RBI:** Cleveland— Lofton 2, Justice; New York— Brosius. **SB:** New York— Jeter (2), Bush (2).
Attendance: 57,128. **Time:** 4:28.

Game 3

Friday, Oct. 9, at Cleveland

	1 2 3	4 5 6	7 8 9	R	H	E
New York	1 0 0	0 0 0	0 0 0	1	4	0
Cleveland	0 2 0	0 4 0	0 0 x	6	12	0

Win: Colon, Cle. (1-0). **Loss:** Pettitte, NY (1-1).
2B: Cleveland— Whiten, Ramirez. **HR:** Cleveland— Thome 2 (4), Ramirez (4), Whiten (1). **RBI:** New York— Williams; Cleveland— Thome 3, Ramirez, Whiten, Wilson.
Attendance: 44,904. **Time:** 2:53.

Most Valuable Player

David Wells, New York, P

ERA	W-L	IP	H	ER	BB	SO	HR
2.87	2-0	15.2	12	5	2	18	3

Game 4

Saturday, Oct. 10, at Cleveland

	1 2 3	4 5 6	7 8 9	R	H	E
New York	1 0 0	2 0 0	0 0 1	4	4	0
Cleveland	0 0 0	0 0 0	0 0 0	0	4	3

Win: Hernandez, NY (1-0). **Loss:** Gooden, Cle. (0-1).
2B: New York—Davis, Martinez; Cleveland— Lofton. **HR:** New York— O'Neill (2). **RBI:** New York— O'Neill, Davis, Martinez, Brosius. **SB:** New York— Martinez (2), O'Neill (1), Jeter (3), Williams (1); Cleveland— Vizquel 2 (3).
Attendance: 44,981. **Time:** 3:31.

Game 5

Sunday, Oct. 11, at Cleveland

	1 2 3	4 5 6	7 8 9	R	H	E
New York	3 1 0	1 0 0	0 0 0	5	6	0
Cleveland	2 0 0	0 0 1	0 0 0	3	8	0

Win: Wells, NY (3-0). **Loss:** Ogea, Bal. (0-1). **Save:** Rivera, NY (3).
HR: New York— Davis (1); Cleveland— Lofton (3), Thome (5). **RBI:** New York— Davis 3, Raines, O'Neill; Cleveland— Lofton, Ramirez, Thome. **SB:** New York— O'Neill (2); Cleveland— Vizquel (4), Fryman (2).
Attendance: 44,966. **Time:** 3:33.

Game 6

Tuesday, Oct. 13, at New York

	1 2 3	4 5 6	7 8 9	R	H	E
Cleveland	0 0 0	0 5 0	0 0 0	5	8	3
New York	2 1 3	0 0 3	0 0 x	9	11	1

Win: Cone, NY (2-0). **Loss:** Nagy, Cle. (1-1).
2B: New York— Knoblauch. **3B:** New York— Jeter. **HR:** Cleveland— Thome (6); New York— Brosius (2). **RBI:** Cleveland— Thome 4, Justice; New York— Brosius 3, Williams 2, Jeter 2, Davis. **SB:** Cleveland— Lofton (3).
Attendance: 57,142. **Time:** 3:31.

ALCS Composite Box Score

Cleveland Indians

	LCS vs. New York								Overall AL Playoffs							
Batting	**Avg**	**AB**	**R**	**H**	**HR**	**RBI**	**BB**	**SO**	**Avg**	**AB**	**R**	**H**	**HR**	**RBI**	**BB**	**SO**
Omar Vizquel, ss	.440	25	2	11	0	0	1	3	.300	40	3	12	0	0	2	3
Manny Ramirez, rf	.333	21	2	7	2	4	4	9	.343	35	4	12	4	7	5	13
Jim Thome, 1b	.304	23	4	7	4	8	1	8	.237	38	6	9	6	10	3	13
Mark Whiten, lf	.286	7	2	2	1	1	1	3	.286	7	2	2	1	1	1	3
Enrique Wilson, 2b	.214	14	2	3	0	1	1	3	.188	16	2	3	0	1	1	3
Kenny Lofton, cf	.185	27	2	5	1	3	1	7	.256	43	7	11	3	7	2	8
Travis Fryman, 3b	.174	23	2	4	0	0	1	5	.167	36	3	6	0	0	4	9
David Justice, lf-dh	.158	19	2	3	1	2	3	3	.229	35	4	8	2	8	3	4
Joey Cora, 2b	.143	7	1	1	0	0	2	1	.059	17	3	1	0	0	5	3
Brian Giles, lf	.083	12	0	1	0	0	1	3	.136	22	1	3	0	0	2	7
Sandy Alomar, c	.063	16	1	1	0	0	0	2	.138	29	3	4	0	2	1	6
Jeff Branson, ph	.000	1	0	0	0	0	0	0	.000	1	0	0	0	0	0	0
Einar Diaz, c	.000	4	0	0	0	0	0	1	.000	4	0	0	0	0	0	1
Richie Sexson, 1b	.000	6	0	0	0	0	0	3	.000	8	0	0	0	0	2	4
TOTALS	.220	205	20	45	9	19	16	51	.215	331	38	71	16	36	31	77

Pitching	ERA	W-L	SV	Gm	IP	H	BB	SO	ERA	W-L	Sv	Gm	IP	H	BB	SO
Paul Shuey	0.00	0-0	0	5	6.1	4	7	7	0.00	0-0	0	8	9.1	7	8	11
Paul Assenmacher	0.00	0-0	0	3	2.0	0	0	3	0.00	0-0	0	6	3.0	2	0	5
Steve Reed	0.00	0-0	0	3	1.2	0	1	0	11.57	1-0	0	5	2.1	1	2	1
Jim Poole	0.00	0-0	0	4	1.1	0	1	2	0.00	0.0	0	6	2.1	1	2	4
Mike Jackson	0.00	0-0	1	1	1.0	0	0	2	3.60	0-0	4	4	5.0	3	1	3
Bartolo Colon	1.00	1-0	0	1	9.0	4	4	3	1.23	1-0	0	2	14.2	9	7	6
Dave Burba	3.00	1-0	0	3	6.0	3	5	8	3.97	2-0	0	4	11.1	7	7	12
Charles Nagy	3.72	0-1	0	2	9.2	13	1	6	2.55	1-1	0	3	17.2	17	1	9
Dwight Gooden	5.79	0-1	0	1	4.2	3	3	3	9.00	0-1	0	2	5.0	4	5	4
Chad Ogea	8.10	0-1	0	2	6.2	9	5	4	8.10	0-1	0	2	6.2	9	5	4
Jaret Wright	8.10	0-1	0	2	6.2	7	8	4	9.82	0-2	0	3	11.0	14	10	10
Doug Jones	—	0-0	0	0	0.0	0	0	0	6.75	0-0	0	1	2.2	3	1	1
TOTALS	3.60	2-4	1	6	55.0	27	35	42	4.15	5-5	4	9	91.0	77	49	70

Wild Pitches— LCS (Burba 2, Shuey, Wright); OVERALL (Burba 2, Shuey, Wright). **Hit Batters—** LCS (Ogea 2); OVERALL (Ogea 2, Reed, Wright).

New York Yankees

	LCS vs Cleveland								Overall AL Playoffs							
Batting	**Avg**	**AB**	**R**	**H**	**HR**	**RBI**	**BB**	**SO**	**Avg**	**AB**	**R**	**H**	**HR**	**RBI**	**BB**	**SO**
Bernie Williams, cf	.381	21	4	8	0	5	7	4	.250	32	4	8	0	5	8	8
Scott Brosius, 3b	.300	20	2	6	1	6	2	4	.333	30	3	10	2	9	2	7
Chili Davis, dh	.286	14	2	4	1	5	2	3	.250	20	2	5	1	5	2	5
Paul O'Neill, rf	.280	25	6	7	1	3	3	4	.306	36	7	11	2	4	4	5
Joe Girardi, c.	.250	8	2	2	0	0	1	0	.333	15	2	5	0	0	1	1
Derek Jeter, ss	.200	25	3	5	0	2	2	5	.176	34	3	6	0	2	4	7
Chuck Knoblauch, 2b	.200	25	4	5	0	0	4	2	.167	36	4	6	0	0	4	6
Jorge Posada, c.	.182	11	1	2	1	2	4	2	.154	13	2	2	1	2	5	4
Tino Martinez, 1b	.105	19	1	2	0	1	6	8	.167	30	2	5	0	1	6	10
Tim Raines, lf	.100	10	0	1	0	1	2	5	.143	14	1	2	0	1	3	6
Shane Spencer, lf	.100	10	1	1	0	0	1	3	.250	16	4	4	2	4	1	4
Chad Curtis, lf	.000	4	0	0	0	0	1	2	.286	7	1	2	0	0	2	3
Ricky Ledee, lf	.000	5	0	0	0	0	0	0	.000	5	0	0	0	0	0	0
Homer Bush, pr-dh	—	0	1	0	0	0	0	0	—	0	1	0	0	0	0	0
TOTALS	.218	197	27	43	4	25	35	42	.229	288	36	66	8	33	42	66

Pitching	ERA	W-L	Sv	Gm	IP	H	BB	SO	ERA	W-L	Sv	Gm	IP	H	BB	SO
Orlando Hernandez	0.00	1-0	0	1	7.0	3	2	6	0.00	1-0	0	1	7.0	3	2	6
Mariano Rivera	0.00	0-0	1	4	5.2	0	1	5	0.00	0-0	3	7	9.0	1	2	7
Ramiro Mendoza	0.00	0-0	0	2	4.1	4	0	1	0.00	0-0	0	2	4.1	4	0	1
Mike Stanton	0.00	0-0	0	3	3.2	2	1	4	0.00	0-0	0	3	3.2	2	1	4
Graeme Lloyd	0.00	0-0	0	1	0.2	1	0	0	0.00	0-0	0	2	1.0	1	0	0
David Wells	2.87	2-0	0	2	15.2	12	2	18	1.90	3-0	0	3	23.2	17	3	27
David Cone	4.15	1-0	0	2	13.0	12	6	13	2.89	2-0	0	3	18.2	14	7	19
Andy Pettitte	11.57	0-1	0	1	4.2	8	3	1	5.40	1-1	0	2	11.2	11	3	9
Jeff Nelson	20.26	0-1	0	3	1.1	3	1	3	6.75	0-1	0	5	4.0	5	2	5
TOTALS	3.21	4-2	1	6	56.0	45	16	51	2.28	7-2	3	9	83.0	58	20	78

Wild Pitches— LCS (Wells); OVERALL (Wells). **Hit Batters—**LCS (Nelson 2, Wells 2, Hernandez); OVERALL (Nelson 2, Wells 2, Hernandez).

Score by Innings

	1	2	3	4	5	6	7	8	9	10	11	12		R	H	E
Cleveland	2	2	0	1	9	1	0	0	2	0	0	3	–	20	45	7
New York	12	2	3	3	0	4	2	0	1	0	0	0	–	27	43	2

DP: Cleveland 7, New York 5. **LOB:** Cleveland 39, New York 48. **2B:** Cleveland— Ramirez, Whiten, Lofton; New York— O'Neill (2), Williams, Brosius, Davis, Jeter, Knoblauch, Martinez. **3B:** Cleveland— Vizquel; New York— Jeter. **SB:** Cleveland— Vizquel (4), Fryman, Lofton; New York— Jeter (3), Martinez (2), O'Neill (2), Bush, Williams. **CS:** Cleveland— Vizquel; New York— Posada, Williams. **S:** New York— Jeter (2), Brosius. **SF:** Cleveland— Ramirez; New York— Martinez, Brosius, Davis. **HBP:** by Wells (Thome), by Nelson (Alomar).

Umpires: Jim Evans, Ted Hendry, John Shulock, Larry Young, Tim Welke, Jim McKean.

National League Championship Series

Padres, 4-2

Date	Winner	Home Field
Oct. 7	Padres, 3-2 (10 inn.)	at Atlanta
Oct. 8	Padres, 3-0	at Atlanta
Oct. 10	Padres, 4-1	at San Diego
Oct. 11	Braves, 8-3	at San Diego
Oct. 12	Braves, 7-6	at San Diego
Oct. 14	Padres, 5-0	at Atlanta

Game 1

Wednesday, Oct. 7, at Atlanta

	1 2 3	4 5 6	7 8 9 10	R H E
San Diego	0 0 0	0 1 0	0 1 0 1	3 7 0
Atlanta	0 0 1	0 0 0	0 0 1 0	2 8 3

Win: Hoffman, SD (1-0). **Loss:** Ligtenberg, Atl. (0-1). **Save:** Wall, SD (1).
2B: San Diego— Rivera; Atlanta— Tucker, Lockhart. **HR:** San Diego— Caminiti (1); Atlanta— A. Jones (1). **RBI:** San Diego— Gwynn, Leyritz, Caminiti; Atlanta— A. Jones 2, Galarraga. **SB:** San Diego— Finley (1).
Attendance: 42,117 . **Time:** 3:27.

Game 2

Thursday, Oct. 8, at Atlanta

	1 2 3	4 5 6	7 8 9	R H E
San Diego	0 0 0	0 0 1	0 0 2	3 11 0
Atlanta	0 0 0	0 0 0	0 0 0	0 3 1

Win: Brown, SD (2-0). **Loss:** Glavine, Atl. (0-1).
2B: San Diego— Veras, Gomez. **RBI:** San Diego— Veras, Finley, Joyner.
Attendance: 43,083. **Time:** 2:54.

Game 3

Saturday, Oct. 10, at San Diego

	1 2 3	4 5 6	7 8 9	R H E
Atlanta	0 0 1	0 0 0	0 0 0	1 8 2
San Diego	0 0 0	0 2 0	0 2 x	4 7 0

Win: Hitchcock, SD (2-0). **Loss:** Maddux, Atl. (1-1). **Save:** Hoffman (3).
2B: San Diego— Finley, Hernandez. **RBI:** Atlanta— Weiss; San Diego— Finley, Caminiti; **SB:** Atlanta— Weiss (1); San Diego— Rivera (1).
Attendance: 62,799. **Time:** 3:00.

Most Valuable Player

Sterling Hitchcock, San Diego, P

ERA	W-L	IP	H	ER	BB	SO	HR
0.90	2-0	10	5	1	8	14	0

Game 4

Sunday, Oct. 11, at San Diego

	1 2 3	4 5 6	7 8 9	R H E
Atlanta	0 0 0	1 0 1	6 0 0	8 12 0
San Diego	0 0 2	0 0 1	0 0 0	3 8 0

Win: Martinez, Atl. (1-0). **Loss:** Hamilton, SD (0-1).
2B: Atlanta— C. Jones; San Diego— Gwynn, Rivera. **3B:** Atlanta— Lockhart. **HR:** Atlanta— Lopez (2); Galarraga (1); San Diego— Leyritz (4). **RBI:** Atlanta— C. Jones, Klesko, Lopez, Guillen, Galarraga 4; San Diego— Gwynn, Leyritz 2.
Attendance: 65,042. **Time:** 2:58.

Game 5

Monday, Oct. 12, at San Diego

	1 2 3	4 5 6	7 8 9	R H E
Atlanta	0 0 0	1 0 1	0 5 0	7 14 1
San Diego	2 0 0	0 0 2	0 0 2	6 10 1

Win: Rocker, Atl. (1-0). **Loss:** Brown, SD (2-1). **Save:** Maddux, Atl. (1).
2B: Atlanta— Graffanino. **HR:** Atlanta— Tucker (2); San Diego— Caminiti (2), Vander Wal (1), G. Myers (1). **RBI:** Atlanta— Tucker 5, Graffanino; San Diego— Caminiti 2, Vander Wal 2, G. Myers 2. **SB:** Atlanta— A. Jones (3).
Attendance: 58,988. **Time:** 3:17.

Game 6

Wednesday, Oct. 14, at Atlanta

	1 2 3	4 5 6	7 8 9	R H E
San Diego	0 0 0	0 0 5	0 0 0	5 10 0
Atlanta	0 0 0	0 0 0	0 0 0	0 2 1

Win: Hitchcock, SD (3-0). **Loss:** Glavine, Atl. (0-2).
RBI: San Diego— Leyritz, Joyner, Veras. **SB:** Atlanta— Williams (1).
Attendance: 50,988. **Time:** 3:10.

NLCS Composite Box Score

San Diego Padres

	LCS vs Atlanta								Overall NL Playoffs							
Batting	**Avg**	**AB**	**R**	**H**	**HR**	**RBI**	**BB**	**SO**	**Avg**	**AB**	**R**	**H**	**HR**	**RBI**	**BB**	**SO**
Greg Myers, ph	1.000	1	1	1	1	2	1	0	1.000	1	1	1	1	2	0	0
Kevin Brown, p	.500	4	1	2	0	0	0	1	.286	7	1	2	0	0	0	3
John Vander Wal, lf	.429	7	1	3	1	2	0	2	.400	10	2	4	1	4	0	3
Steve Finley, cf	.333	21	3	7	0	2	0	2	.258	31	5	8	0	3	7	6
Carlos Hernandez, c	.333	18	2	6	0	0	1	5	.367	30	2	11	0	0	1	5
Wally Joyner, 1b	.313	16	3	5	0	2	4	3	.273	22	4	6	1	4	5	5
Ken Caminiti, 3b	.273	22	3	6	2	4	5	4	.222	36	5	8	2	4	6	7
Quilvio Veras, 2b	.250	24	2	6	0	2	5	7	.205	39	3	8	0	2	6	13
Greg Vaughn, lf-ph	.250	8	1	2	0	0	1	1	.304	23	3	7	1	1	1	5
Tony Gwynn, rf	.231	26	1	6	0	2	1	2	.220	41	2	9	0	4	1	4
Ruben Rivera, lf-ph-rf	.231	13	1	3	0	0	0	7	.158	19	1	3	0	0	0	10
Sterling Hitchcock, p	.200	5	1	1	0	0	0	0	.143	7	1	1	0	0	0	1
Jim Leyritz, ph-1b-c	.167	12	1	2	1	4	0	2	.273	22	4	6	4	9	0	4
Chris Gomez, ss	.150	20	2	3	0	0	2	5	.194	31	3	6	0	0	6	6
Joey Hamilton, p	.000	2	0	0	0	0	0	1	.000	2	0	0	0	0	0	1
Mark Sweeney, ph	.000	2	1	0	0	0	1	1	.000	3	1	0	0	0	2	1
Andy Sheets, ss-ph	.000	3	0	0	0	0	0	1	.000	3	0	0	0	0	0	1
Andy Ashby, p	.000	4	0	0	0	0	0	4	.000	5	0	0	0	0	0	4
George Arias, ph	—	0	0	0	0	0	0	0	.000	1	0	0	0	0	0	1
TOTALS	.255	208	24	53	5	20	27	48	.240	333	38	80	10	33	35	80

Pitching	ERA	W-L	Sv	Gm	IP	H	BB	SO	ERA	W-L	Sv	Gm	IP	H	BB	SO
Brian Boehringer	0.00	0-0	0	3	3	3	1	1	0.00	0-0	0	3	3	3	1	1
Mark Langston	0.00	0-0	0	3	1.1	1	0	1	0.00	0-0	0	3	7.1	1	0	1
Sterling Hitchcock	0.90	2-0	0	3	10	5	8	14	1.13	3-0	0	3	16	8	8	25
Andy Ashby	2.08	0-0	0	2	13	14	2	5	3.18	0-0	0	3	17	20	3	9
Trevor Hoffman	2.08	1-0	1	3	4.1	2	2	7	1.23	1-0	3	7	7.1	5	3	11
Kevin Brown	2.61	1-1	0	2	10.1	5	4	12	1.44	2-1	0	4	25.0	10	11	33
Donne Wall	3.00	0-0	1	3	3	3	4	4	4.50	0-0	1	4	4	5	4	6
Joey Hamilton	4.91	0-1	0	2	7.1	7	3	6	3.38	0-1	0	4	10.2	8	5	9
Randy Myers	13.50	0-0	0	4	2	3	2	3	13.50	0-0	0	4	2	3	2	3
Dan Miceli	13.50	0-0	0	3	.2	4	0	1	4.50	0-0	1	4	4.0	5	4	6
TOTALS	2.78	4-2	2	6	55	47	26	54	2.24	7-3	5	10	96.1	68	41	104

Wild Pitches— LCS (Hitchcock 2, Brown, R. Myers); OVERALL (Hitchcock 2, Brown, R. Myers). **Hit Batters—**LCS (none); OVERALL (none).

Atlanta Braves

	LCS vs San Diego								Overall NL Playoffs							
Batting	**Avg**	**AB**	**R**	**H**	**HR**	**RBI**	**BB**	**SO**	**Avg**	**AB**	**R**	**H**	**HR**	**RBI**	**BB**	**SO**
Eduardo Perez, c.	.750	4	0	3	0	0	0	0	.444	9	1	4	1	4	0	2
Ozzie Guillen, ph-ss	.417	12	1	5	0	1	0	1	.385	13	1	5	0	1	0	1
Michael Tucker, ph-rf	.385	13	1	5	1	5	2	5	.333	21	2	7	2	7	4	5
Greg Colbrunn, ph	.333	6	0	2	0	0	0	2	.250	8	0	2	0	0	0	2
Tony Graffanino, ph-2b	.333	3	2	1	0	1	2	1	.333	3	2	1	0	1	2	1
Javier Lopez, ph-c	.300	22	2	6	1	1	0	7	.296	27	3	8	2	2	1	8
Andruw Jones, ph-rf	.273	22	3	6	1	2	1	4	.194	31	5	6	1	3	4	6
Tom Glavine, p	.250	4	0	1	0	0	1	2	.200	5	0	1	0	0	1	2
Keith Lockhart, 2b-ph	.235	17	2	4	0	0	0	4	.276	29	4	8	0	0	1	4
Chipper Jones, 3b	.208	24	2	5	0	1	4	5	.206	34	4	7	0	2	8	8
Walt Weiss, ss	.200	15	0	3	0	1	2	5	.179	28	2	5	0	1	3	8
John Smoltz, p	.200	5	0	1	0	0	0	1	.286	7	0	2	0	0	1	2
Gerald Williams, lf-rf	.154	13	0	2	0	0	1	6	.200	15	1	3	0	1	1	7
Andres Galarraga, 1b	.095	21	1	2	1	4	6	6	.333	33	2	5	1	4	7	9
Ryan Klesko, ph-lf	.083	12	2	1	0	1	6	3	.174	23	3	4	1	5	6	6
Greg Maddux, p	.000	1	0	0	0	0	0	0	.200	5	1	1	0	0	0	1
Marty Malloy, pr-2b	.000	1	1	0	0	0	0	1	.000	1	1	0	0	0	0	1
Denny Neagle, p	.000	2	0	0	0	0	0	0	.000	2	0	0	0	0	0	0
Danny Bautista, pr-lf	.000	5	0	0	0	0	0	1	.143	7	0	1	0	0	0	1
John Rocker, p	—	0	1	0	0	0	1	0	—	0	1	0	0	0	1	0
TOTALS	.235	200	18	47	4	17	26	54	.233	301	33	70	8	31	40	74

Pitching	ERA	W-L	Sv	Gm	IP	H	BB	SO	ERA	W-L	Sv	Gm	IP	H	BB	SO
John Rocker	0.00	1-0	0	6	5.2	3	1	5	0.00	1-0	0	8	6	4	1	7
Dennis Martinez	0.00	1-0	0	4	3.1	1	1	0	0.00	1-0	0	4	3.1	1	1	0
Tom Glavine	2.31	0-2	0	2	11.2	13	9	8	1.93	0-2	0	3	18.2	16	10	16
Greg Maddux	3.00	0-1	1	2	6	5	3	4	2.77	1-1	1	3	13	12	3	8
Denny Neagle	3.52	0-0	0	2	7.2	8	2	9	3.52	0-0	0	2	7.2	8	2	9
John Smoltz	3.95	0-0	0	2	13.2	13	6	13	2.95	1-0	0	3	21.1	18	6	19
Rudy Seanez	6.00	0-0	0	4	3	2	1	4	4.50	0-0	0	5	4	2	1	4
Kerry Ligtenberg	7.36	0-1	0	4	3.2	3	2	5	3.86	0-1	0	7	7	4	6	8
Odalis Perez	54.00	0-0	0	2	.1	5	2	0	18.00	1-0	0	3	1	5	2	1
TOTALS	3.50	2-4	1	6	54	53	27	48	2.74	5-4	1	9	82	70	32	72

Wild Pitches— LCS (none); OVERALL (none). **Hit Batters—**LCS (Maddux); OVERALL (Maddux).

Score by Innings

	1	2	3	4	5	6	7	8	9	10		R	H	E
San Diego	2	0	2	0	3	9	0	3	4	1	–	24	53	1
Atlanta	0	0	2	2	0	2	6	5	1	0	–	18	47	8

DP: San Diego 6, Atlanta 6. **LOB:** San Diego 52, Atlanta 46. **2B:**. San Diego— Hernandez (2), Rivera (2), Finley, Gwynn, Veras; Atlanta— Graffanino, C. Jones, Lockhart, Tucker. **3B:** Atlanta— Lockhart. **SB:** San Diego— Finley, Rivera; Atlanta— Weiss, A. Jones, Williams. **CS:** San Diego— Veras; Atlanta— A. Jones. **S:** San Diego— Ashby, Gwynn; Atlanta— Maddux, E. Perez. **SF:** Atlanta— A. Jones. **PB:** Atlanta— Lopez. **Balk:** Atlanta— Ligtenberg.

Umpires: Terry Tata, Larry Poncino, Tom Hallion, Gregory Bonin, Gerald Davis, Steve Rippley.

WORLD SERIES

New York, 4-0

Date	Winner	Home Field
Oct. 17	Yankees, 9-6	at New York
Oct. 18	Yankees, 9-3	at New York
Oct. 20	Yankees, 5-4	at San Diego
Oct. 21	Yankees, 3-0	at San Diego

Most Valuable Player

Scott Brosius, New York, 3B

Avg.	AB	H	R	RBI	HR	E
.471	17	8	3	6	2	0

Game 1

Saturday, Oct. 17, at New York

	1 2 3	4 5 6	7 8 9		R	H	E
San Diego	0 0 0	0 1 0	0 2 0	–	3	10	1
New York	3 3 1	0 2 0	0 0 x	–	9	16	0

San Diego	AB	R	H	BB	SO
Veras, 2b	5	0	1	0	3
Gwynn, rf	4	0	1	1	0
Vaughn, dh	4	0	0	1	1
Caminiti, 3b	5	1	1	0	2
Joyner, 1b	2	0	0	1	0
Leyritz, ph-1b	1	0	0	0	1
Finley, cf	4	0	0	0	1
Vander Wal, lf	3	0	2	0	1
R. Rivera, ph-lf	1	1	1	0	0
G. Myers, c	3	0	0	0	1
Hernandez, ph-c	1	0	1	0	0
Gomez, ss	3	1	2	0	0
Sweeney, ph	1	0	1	0	0
Sheets, ss	0	0	0	0	0
TOTALS	37	3	10	3	10

New York	AB	R	H	BB	SO
Knoblauch, 2b	3	2	2	2	1
Jeter, ss	5	1	2	0	1
O'Neill, rf	5	1	1	0	0
Williams, cf	4	1	1	1	0
Davis, dh	3	1	1	2	2
Bush, pr-dh	0	0	0	0	0
Martinez, 1b	5	1	3	0	0
Brosius, 3b	5	1	3	0	1
Posada, c	4	1	1	1	0
Ledee, lf	3	0	2	1	0
TOTALS	37	9	16	7	5

San Diego	IP	H	ER	BB	SO
Ashby (L, 0-1)	2⅔	10	4	1	1
Boehringer	1⅔	4	2	1	2
Wall	2⅔	1	0	3	1
Miceli	1	1	0	2	1

New York	IP	H	ER	BB	SO
Hernandez (W, 1-0)	7	6	1	3	7
Stanton	⅔	3	2	0	1
Nelson	1⅓	1	0	0	2

2B: San Diego— Veras, Vander Wal, Caminiti, Rivera; New York— Ledee. **3B:** San Diego— Gomez. **HR:** New York— Williams (1), Posada (1). **RBI:** San Diego— Veras, Rivera, Sweeney; New York— Davis, Brosius, Jeter, Williams 2, Ledee, Posada 2. **SB:** New York— Knoblauch (1). **CS:** New York—Ledee
Attendance: 56,692. **Time:** 3:31.

Game 2

Sunday, Oct. 18, at New York

	1 2 3	4 5 6	7 8 9		R	H	E
San Diego	0 0 2	0 3 0	0 1 0	–	6	8	1
New York	0 2 0	0 0 0	7 0 x	–	9	9	1

San Diego	AB	R	H	BB	SO
Veras, 2b	4	1	1	1	0
Gwynn, rf	4	1	3	0	0
Vaughn, lf	4	3	2	0	0
Caminiti, 3b	3	0	0	1	2
Leyritz, dh	4	0	0	1	1
Joyner, 1b	3	0	0	1	1
Finley, cf	4	0	1	0	0
Hernandez, c	3	0	0	0	0
G. Myers, ph	1	0	0	0	1
Gomez, ss	3	1	1	0	0
Vander Wal, ph	1	0	0	0	1
TOTALS	34	6	8	3	7

New York	AB	R	H	BB	SO
Knoblauch, 2b	4	1	2	0	1
Jeter, ss	4	1	1	1	0
O'Neill, rf	5	0	0	0	1
Williams, cf	4	1	0	1	3
Davis, dh	3	2	1	1	0
Martinez, 1b	3	2	1	1	1
Brosius, 3b	4	0	1	0	1
Posada, c	3	1	1	1	1
Ledee, lf	3	1	2	1	0
TOTALS	33	9	9	6	8

San Diego	IP	H	ER	BB	SO
Brown	6⅓	6	4	3	5
Wall (L, 0-1, BS, 1)	0	2	2	0	0
Langston	⅔	1	3	2	0
Boehringer	⅓	0	0	1	1
Myers	⅔	0	0	0	2

New York	IP	H	ER	BB	SO
Wells (W, 1-0)	7	7	5	2	4
Nelson	⅔	1	0	1	1
Rivera (S, 1)	1⅓	0	0	0	2

2B: San Diego— Finley; New York— Ledee. **HR:** San Diego— Vaughn 2 (2), Gwynn (1); New York— Knoublach (1), Martinez (1). **RBI:** San Diego— Vaughn 3, Gwynn 2; New York— Ledee 2, Knoblauch 3, Martinez 4.
Attendance: 56,712. **Time:** 3:29.

Game 3

Tuesday, Oct. 20 at San Diego

	1 2 3	4 5 6	7 8 9		R	H	E
New York	0 0 0	0 0 0	2 3 0	–	5	9	1
San Diego	0 0 0	0 0 3	0 1 0	–	4	7	1

New York	**AB**	**R**	**H**	**BB**	**SO**
Knoblauch, 2b	4	0	1	1	0
Jeter, ss	4	0	1	1	1
O'Neill, rf	4	1	1	1	1
Williams, cf	4	0	0	0	2
Martinez, 1b	3	1	0	1	0
Brosius, 3b	4	2	3	0	0
Spencer, lf	3	1	1	0	2
Ledee, ph-lf	1	0	0	0	0
Girardi, c	2	0	0	0	1
Posada, ph-c	2	0	1	0	0
Cone, p	2	0	1	0	0
Davis, ph	1	0	0	0	0
Bush, pr	0	0	0	0	0
Lloyd, p	0	0	0	0	0
Mendoza, p	1	0	0	0	0
Rivera, p	0	0	0	0	0
TOTALS	35	5	9	4	8

San Diego	**AB**	**R**	**H**	**BB**	**SO**
Veras, 2b	3	2	1	1	0
Gwynn, rf	4	1	2	0	0
Rivera, pr-rf	0	0	0	0	0
Vaughn, lf	3	0	0	0	0
Caminiti, 3b	2	0	0	1	2
Joyner, 1b	3	0	0	1	0
Finley, cf	4	0	0	0	1
Leyritz, c	2	0	0	0	1
Hernandez, c	2	0	1	0	1
Vander Wal, pr	0	0	0	0	0
Gomez, ss	3	0	1	0	1
Hoffman, p	0	0	0	0	0
Sweeney, ph	1	0	1	0	0
Hitchcock, p	2	1	1	0	0
Hamilton, p	0	0	0	0	0
Myers, p	0	0	0	0	0
Sheets, ss	2	0	0	0	1
TOTALS	31	4	7	3	7

New York	**IP**	**H**	**ER**	**BB**	**SO**
Cone	6	2	2	3	4
Lloyd	⅓	0	0	0	0
Mendoza (W, 1-0)	1	2	1	0	1
Rivera (S, 2)	1⅔	3	0	0	2

San Diego	**IP**	**H**	**ER**	**BB**	**SO**
Hitchcock	6	7	1	1	7
Hamilton	1	0	0	1	1
Myers	0	0	1	1	0
Hoffman (L, 0-1, BS, 1)	2	2	2	1	0

2B: New York— Spencer; San Diego— Veras. **HR:** New York— Brosius 2 (2). **RBI:** New York— Brosius 4, Davis. San Diego— Gwynn, Caminiti, Vaughn. **SF:** San Diego— Gwynn, Caminiti, Vaughn. **SB:** San Diego— Finley (1).
Attendance: 64,667. **Time:** 3:14.

Game 4

Wednesday, Oct. 21, at San Diego

	1 2 3	4 5 6	7 8 9		R	H	E
New York	0 0 0	0 0 1	0 2 0	–	3	9	0
San Diego	0 0 0	0 0 0	0 0 0	–	0	7	0

New York	**AB**	**R**	**H**	**BB**	**SO**
Knoblauch, 2b	5	0	1	0	0
Jeter, ss	4	2	2	1	1
O'Neill, rf	5	1	2	0	0
Williams, cf	4	0	0	0	0
Martinez, 1b	2	0	1	2	1
Brosius, 3b	4	0	1	0	2
Ledee, lf	3	0	2	0	1
Girardi, c	4	0	0	0	1
Pettitte, p	2	0	0	0	2
Nelson, p	0	0	0	0	0
Rivera, p	1	0	0	0	0
TOTALS	34	3	9	3	8

San Diego	**AB**	**R**	**H**	**BB**	**SO**
Veras, 2b	3	0	0	1	1
Gwynn, rf	4	0	2	0	0
Vaughn, lf	4	0	0	0	1
Caminiti, 3b	4	0	1	0	1
Leyritz, 1b	3	0	0	1	0
Rivera, cf	4	0	3	0	0
Hernandez, c	4	0	0	0	0
Gomez, ss	2	0	0	1	0
Sweeney, ph	1	0	0	0	0
Brown, p	2	0	1	0	0
Vander Wal, ph	1	0	0	0	0
Miceli, p	0	0	0	0	0
Myers, p	0	0	0	0	0
TOTALS	32	0	7	3	5

New York	**IP**	**H**	**ER**	**BB**	**SO**
Pettitte (W, 1-0)	7⅓	5	0	3	4
Nelson	⅓	0	0	0	1
Rivera (S, 3)	1⅓	2	0	0	0

San Diego	**IP**	**H**	**ER**	**BB**	**SO**
Brown (L, 0-1)	8	8	3	3	8
Miceli	⅔	1	0	0	0
Myers	⅓	0	0	0	0

2B: New York— Ledee, O'Neill; San Diego— Rivera. **RBI:** New York— Williams, Brosius, Ledee. **S:** New York— Pettittee. **SF:** New York— Ledee.
Attendance: 65,427. **Time:** 2:58.

World Series Composite Box Score

San Diego Padres

	WS vs New York								Overall Playoffs							
Batting	**Avg**	**AB**	**R**	**H**	**HR**	**RBI**	**BB**	**SO**	**Avg**	**AB**	**R**	**H**	**HR**	**RBI**	**BB**	**SO**
Ruben Rivera, ph-lf-cf	.800	5	1	4	0	1	0	0	.292	24	2	7	0	1	0	10
Mark Sweeney, ph	.667	3	0	2	0	1	0	0	.333	6	1	2	0	1	2	1
Tony Gwynn, rf	.500	16	2	8	1	3	1	0	.298	57	4	17	1	7	2	4
Kevin Brown, p	.500	2	0	1	0	0	0	0	.333	9	1	3	0	0	0	3
Sterling Hitchcock, p	.500	2	1	1	0	0	0	0	.222	9	2	2	0	0	0	1
John Vander Wal, lf-ph	.400	5	0	2	0	0	0	2	.400	15	2	6	1	4	0	5
Chris Gomez, ss	.364	11	2	4	0	0	1	1	.238	42	5	10	0	0	7	7
Quilvio Veras, 2b	.200	15	3	3	0	1	3	4	.204	54	6	11	0	3	9	17
Carlos Hernandez, c-ph	.200	10	0	2	0	0	0	3	.325	40	2	13	0	0	1	8
Ken Caminiti, 3b	.143	14	1	2	0	1	2	7	.200	50	6	10	2	5	8	14
Greg Vaughn, lf-dh	.133	15	3	2	2	4	1	2	.237	38	6	9	3	5	2	7
Steve Finley, cf	.083	43	5	9	0	3	7	8	.083	12	0	1	0	0	0	2

Batting	WS vs New York Avg	AB	R	H	HR	RBI	BB	SO	Overall Playoffs Avg	AB	R	H	HR	RBI	BB	SO
Andy Sheets, ss	.000	2	0	0	0	0	0	1	.000	5	0	0	0	0	0	2
Greg Myers, ph-c	.000	4	0	0	0	0	0	2	.200	5	1	1	1	2	1	2
Wally Joyner, 1b	.000	8	0	0	0	0	3	1	.200	30	4	6	1	4	8	6
Jim Leyritz, ph-c-1b	.000	10	0	0	0	0	1	4	.188	32	4	6	4	9	1	8
George Arias, ph	—	0	0	0	0	0	0	0	.000	1	0	0	0	0	0	1
Andy Ashby, p	—	0	0	0	0	0	0	0	.000	5	0	0	0	0	0	4
Joey Hamilton, p	—	0	0	0	0	0	0	0	.000	2	0	0	0	0	0	1
TOTALS	.239	134	13	32	3	11	12	29	.239	436	46	104	13	41	41	103

Pitching	ERA	W-L	Sv	Gm	IP	H	BB	SO	ERA	W-L	Sv	Gm	IP	H	BB	SO
Dan Miceli	0.00	0-0	0	2	1.2	2	2	1	3.18	1-1	0	8	5.2	8	2	6
Joey Hamilton	0.00	0-0	0	1	1	0	1	1	3.09	0-1	0	5	11.2	8	6	10
Sterling Hitcock	1.50	0-0	0	1	6	7	1	7	1.23	3-0	0	4	22	15	9	32
Kevin Brown	4.40	0-1	0	2	14.1	14	6	13	2.52	2-2	0	6	39.1	24	17	46
Donne Wall	6.75	0-1	0	2	2.2	3	3	1	5.40	0-1	1	6	6.2	8	7	7
Brian Boehringer	9.00	0-0	0	2	2	4	2	3	3.60	0-0	0	5	5	7	3	4
Trevor Hoffman	9.00	0-1	0	1	2	2	1	0	2.89	1-1	3	8	9.1	7	4	11
Randy Myers	9.00	0-0	0	3	1	0	1	2	12.00	0-0	0	7	3.0	3	3	5
Andy Ashby	13.50	0-1	0	1	2.2	10	1	1	4.58	0-1	0	4	19.2	3	3	5
Mark Langston	40.50	0-0	0	1	.2	1	2	0	13.50	0-0	0	4	2.0	2	2	1
TOTALS	5.82	0-4	0	4	34	43	20	29	3.33	7-7	4	14	124.1	85	56	127

Wild Pitches—WS (Langston); OVERALL (Hitchcock 2, Langston, Brown , R. Myers). **Hit Batters**—WS (Boehringer); OVERALL (Brown 3, Ashby, Boehringer, Hitchcock). **Balk**—WS (none); OVERALL—(none).

New York Yankees

Batting	WS vs San Diego Avg	AB	R	H	HR	RBI	BB	SO	Overall Playoffs Avg	AB	R	H	HR	RBI	BB	SO
Ricky Ledee, lf-ph	.600	10	1	6	0	4	2	1	.400	15	1	6	0	4	2	1
David Cone, p	.500	2	0	1	0	0	0	0	—	0	0	0	0	0	0	0
Scott Brosius, 3b	.471	17	3	8	2	6	0	4	.383	47	6	18	4	15	2	11
Tino Martinez, 1b	.385	13	4	5	1	4	4	2	.233	43	6	10	1	5	10	12
Chuck Knoblauch, 2b	.375	16	3	6	1	3	3	2	.231	52	7	12	1	3	7	8
Derek Jeter, ss	.353	17	4	6	0	1	3	3	.235	51	7	12	0	3	7	10
Jorge Posada, c-ph	.333	9	2	3	1	2	2	2	.227	22	4	5	2	4	7	6
Shane Spencer, lf	.333	3	1	1	0	0	0	2	.263	19	5	5	2	4	1	6
Chili Davis, dh-ph	.286	7	3	2	0	2	3	2	.259	27	5	7	1	7	5	7
Paul O'Neill, rf	.211	19	3	4	0	0	1	2	.273	55	10	15	2	4	5	7
Bernie Williams, cf	.063	16	2	1	1	3	2	5	.188	48	6	9	1	8	10	13
Mariano Rivera, p	.000	1	0	0	0	0	0	0	—	0	0	0	0	0	0	0
Ramiro Mendoza, p	.000	1	0	0	0	0	0	0	—	0	0	0	0	0	0	0
Andy Pettitte, p	.000	2	0	0	0	0	0	2	—	0	0	0	0	0	0	0
Joe Girardi, c	.000	6	0	0	0	0	0	2	—	0	0	0	0	0	0	0
Tim Raines, ph	—	0	0	0	0	0	0	0	.143	14	1	2	0	1	3	6
Homer Bush, pr-dh	—	0	0	0	0	0	0	0	—	0	1	0	0	0	0	0
TOTALS	.309	139	26	43	6	25	20	29	.257	393	59	101	14	58	59	87

Pitching	ERA	W-L	Sv	Gm	IP	H	BB	SO	ERA	W-L	Sv	Gm	IP	H	BB	SO
Andy Pettitte	0.00	1-0	0	1	7.1	5	3	4	3.32	2-1	0	3	19	16	6	13
Mariano Rivera	0.00	0-0	3	3	4.1	5	0	4	0.00	0-0	6	10	13.1	6	2	11
Jeff Nelson	0.00	0-0	0	3	2.1	2	1	4	4.26	0-1	0	8	6.1	7	3	9
Graeme Lloyd	0.00	0-0	0	1	.1	0	0	0	0.00	0-0	0	3	1.1	1	0	0
Orlando Hernandez	1.29	1-0	0	1	7	6	3	7	0.64	2-0	0	2	14	9	5	13
David Cone	3.00	0-0	0	1	6	2	3	4	2.92	2-0	0	4	24.2	16	10	23
David Wells	6.43	1-0	0	1	7	7	2	4	2.93	4-0	0	4	30.2	24	5	31
Ramiro Mendoza	9.00	1-0	0	1	1	2	0	1	1.69	1-0	0	3	5.1	6	0	2
Mike Stanton	27.00	0-0	0	1	.2	3	0	1	4.15	0-0	0	4	4.1	5	1	5
TOTALS	2.75	4-0	3	4	36	32	12	29	2.42	11-2	6	13	119	90	32	107

Wild Pitches—WS (none); OVERALL (Wells). **Hit Batters**—WS (none); OVERALL (Wells 2, Nelson 2, Hernandez). **Balk**—WS (none); OVERALL—(none).

Score by Innings

	1	2	3	4	5	6	7	8	9	R	H	E
San Diego	0	0	2	0	4	3	0	4	0	—13	32	3
New York	3	5	1	0	2	1	9	5	0	—26	43	2

DP: New York 4, San Diego 5. **LOB:** San Diego 27, New York 34. **2B:** San Diego— Rivera (2), Veras (2), Vander Wal, Caminiti, Finley; New York— Ledee (3), Spencer, O'Neill. **3B:** San Diego— Gomez. **SB:** San Diego— Finley; New York— Knoblauch. **CS:** New York— Ledee. **S:** New York— Pettitte **SF:** San Diego— Caminiti, Vaughn; New York— Ledee. **IBB:** New York— off Langston (Williams), off Brown (Martinez 2); **PB:** San Diego—Leyritz.

Umpires: Richie Garcia (AL), Mark Hirschbeck (NL), Dale Scott (AL), Dana DeMuth (NL), Tim Tschida (AL), Jerry Crawford (NL).

COLLEGE

Final *Baseball America* Top 25

Final 1998 Division I Top 25, voted on by the editors of *Baseball America* and released after the NCAA College World Series. Given are final records (excluding ties) and winning percentage (including all postseason games); records in College World Series and team eliminated by (DNP indicates team did not play in tourney); head coach (career years and Division I record including 1998 postseason); preseason ranking and rank before start of CWS.

		Record	Pct	CWS Recap	Head Coach	Preseason Rank	Rank before CWS
1	USC	50-17	.746	5-1	Mike Gillespie (12 yrs: 484-267-2)	5	4
2	Arizona St.	41-23	.641	3-1 (USC)	Pat Murphy (14 yrs: 522-258-3)	6	7
3	Miami-FL	51-12	.810	1-2 (Long Beach)	Jim Morris (17 yrs: 753-319-1)	2	1
4	Louisiana St.	48-19	.716	2-2 (USC)	Skip Bertman (15 yrs: 733-267-1)	3	2
5	Florida	46-18	.719	0-2 (USC)	Andy Lopez (16 yrs: 577-343-5)	4	3
6	Stanford	42-14	.750	DNP	Mark Marquess (22 yrs: 895-467-4)	1	6
7	Florida St.	52-20	.722	0-2 (Long Beach)	Mike Martin (19 yrs: 1021-350-3)	25	5
8	Wichita St.	56-7	.889	DNP	Gene Stephenson (21 yrs: 1165-346-3)	19	8
9	Auburn	46-18	.719	DNP	Hal Baird (19 yrs: 692-355)	11	9
10	Long Beach St.	43-23	.652	2-2 (Ariz. St.)	Dave Snow (14 yrs: 572-298-4)	NR	11
11	Texas A&M	46-18	.719	DNP	Mark Johnson (14 yrs: 616-259-2)	NR	10
12	Alabama	46-18	.719	DNP	Jim Wells (9 yrs: 386-163)	7	12
13	CS-Fullerton	47-17	.734	DNP	Augie Garrido (30 yrs: 1228-563-7)	NR	13
14	Mississippi St.	42-23	.646	1-2 (USC)	Pat McMahon (6 yrs: 231-109)	21	14
15	Rice	46-17	.730	DNP	Wayne Graham (7 yrs: 277-140)	10	15
16	South Carolina	44-18	.710	DNP	Ray Tanner (10 yrs: 472-215-3)	15	16
17	Washington	41-17	.707	DNP	Ken Knutson (6 yrs: 226-132)	12	17
18	South Alabama	46-18	.689	DNP	Steve Kittrell (15 yrs: 603-321-1)	23	18
19	Georgia Tech	41-22	.651	DNP	Danny Hall (11 yrs: 423-217)	14	19
20	Tulane	48-15	.762	DNP	Rick Jones (10 yrs: 480-201-1)	NR	20
21	Clemson	43-16	.729	DNP	Jack Leggett (19 yrs: 623-375)	NR	21
22	Baylor	41-20	.672	DNP	Steve Smith (4 yrs: 130-98-1)	13	22
23	Illinois	41-21	.661	DNP	Richard Jones (32 yrs: 1022-578-5)	NR	23
24	North Carolina	42-23	.646	DNP	Mike Roberts (21 yrs: 780-428-3)	NR	24
25	Texas Tech	44-20	.688	DNP	Larry Hays (28 yrs: 1157-623-2)	8	25

College World Series

CWS Seeds: 1. Florida (46-16); **2.** Miami-FL (50-10); **3.** Florida St. (53-18); **4.** USC (44-16); **5.** LSU (46-17); **6.** Arizona St.(38-22); **7.** Long Beach St. (41-21); **8.** Mississippi St. (41-21).

Bracket One

May 29—Arizona St. 11 .... Florida St. 10
May 29—Miami-FL 3 .... Long Beach St. 1
May 31—Arizona St. 9 .... Miami-FL 2
May 31—Long Beach St. 7 .... Florida St. 4 (out)
June 2—Long Beach St. 6 .... Miami-FL 3 (out)
June 3—Arizona St. 14 .... Long Beach St. 4 (out)

Bracket Two

May 30—LSU 12 .... USC 10
May 30—Mississippi St. 14 .... Florida 13
June 1—LSU 10 .... Mississippi St. 8
June 1—USC 12 .... Florida 10, 11-inn (out)
June 2—USC 7 .... Mississippi St. 1 (out)
June 4—USC 5 .... LSU 4
June 5—USC 7 .... LSU 3 (out)

CWS Championship Game

Saturday, June 6, at Rosenblatt Stadium in Omaha.

	1 2 3	4 5 6	7 8 9		R	H	E
USC	3 5 1	0 0 2	3 2 5	—	21	23	1
Arizona St.	0 5 0	3 0 0	5 1 0	—	14	16	0

Win: USC– Jason Lane (9-2). **Loss:** Arizona St.– Ryan Mills (8-4). **Save:** USC– Jack Krawczyk (23) **Starters:** USC– Rick Currier; Arizona St.– Mills. **Strikeouts:** USC– Currier 3, Lane, Steve Immel, Mike Weibling, Krawczyk; Arizona St.– Mills, Aaron Kramer, Chad Pennington.

2B: USC– Morgan Ensberg, Wes Rachels, Jeremy Freitas, Mikel Moreno. **HR:** USC– Lane (14), Rachels (3), Brad Ticehurst (18), Robb Gorr 2 (16); Arizona St.– Andrew Beinbrink (12), Casey Myers (8), Jeff Phelps (5), Mike Collins (4). **SB:** USC– Ensberg (20), Freitas (4), Seth Davidson (17); Arizona St.– Moreno (27).

Attendance: 24,456. **Time** 3:59.

Most Outstanding Player

Wes Rachels, USC, 2B

Avg	AB	R	H	HR	RBI
.357	28	7	10	1	9

Annual Awards

Chosen by *Baseball America*, *Collegiate Baseball*, National Collegiate Baseball Writers Association and the American Baseball Coaches Association.

Players of the Year

Damon Thames, Rice .... ABCA
Jeff Austin, Stanford .... *BA*
Kevin Mench, Delaware .... *CB*
Brad Wilkerson, Florida .... NCBWA

Coaches of the Year

Pat Murphy, Arizona St. .... *BA*
Mike Batesole, Cal St.-Northridge .... *CB*
Mike Gillespie, USC .... ABCA, *CB*

Consensus All-America Team

NCAA Division I players cited most frequently by the following four selectors: the American Baseball Coaches Assn. (ABCA), *Baseball America*, *Collegiate Baseball*, and the National Collegiate Baseball Writers Assn. (NCBWA). Holdovers from the 1997 All-America first team are in **bold** type.

First Team

Pos		Cl	Avg	HR	RBI
C	Sammy Serrano, Stetson	Jr.	.457	13	68
1B	Eddy Furniss, Louisiana St.	Sr.	.398	25	67
2B	Jeff Pickler, Tennessee	Sr.	.445	7	61
SS	Damon Thames, Rice	Jr.	.422	26	113
3B	Paul Day, Long Beach St.	Jr.	.424	13	81
OF	Bubba Crosby, Rice	Jr.	.394	25	91
OF	Kevin Mench, Delaware	So.	.464	33	68
OF	Eric Valent, UCLA	Jr.	.336	30	73
UT	Brad Wilkerson, Florida	Jr.	.349	23	69

		Cl	W-L	Sv	ERA
P	Jack Krawcyzk, USC	Sr.	2-2	21	1.71
P	Josh Fogg, Florida	Jr.	7-2	13	2.05
P	Alex Santos, Miami	So.	14-1	0	2.45
P	Shane Wright, Texas Tech	Jr.	14-1	0	2.71
P	Seth Etherton, USC	Jr.	12-3	0	2.85
P	Jeff Austin, Stanford	Jr.	12-4	0	3.11
P	Jeff Weaver, Fresno St.	Jr.	10-4	1	3.98

Second Team

Pos		Cl	Avg	HR	RBI
C	Josh Bard, Texas Tech	So.	.389	16	67
1B	Carlos Pena, Northeastern	Jr.	.309	11	41
2B	Xavier Nady, California	Fr.	.404	15	70
SS	Brian Roberts, UNC	So.	.366	12	47
3B	Andrew Beinbrink, Arizona St.	Jr.	.321	9	77
OF	Jeff Ryan, Wichita St.	Jr.	.454	23	105
OF	James Matan, UNC-Charlotte	Sr.	.408	27	95
OF	Brian Cox, Florida St.	Sr.	.397	18	84
UT	Brandon Inge, Va. Commonwealth	Jr.	.343	9	42

		Cl	W-L	Sv	ERA
P	Mark Mulder, Michigan St.	Jr.	7-2	4	2.26
P	Mike Fischer, South Alabama	Jr.	11-1	0	2.31
P	Ryan Rupe, Texas A&M	Sr.	11-4	0	2.87
P	Ryan Mills, Arizona St.	Jr.	6-3	0	2.88
P	Chad Hutchin, Stanford	Jr.	8-4	0	5.76
P	Kip Wells, Baylor	Jr.	13-4	0	6.35

NCAA Division I Leaders

Batting

Average

(At least 75 AB)	Cl	Gm	AB	H	Avg
Pat Magness, Wichita St.	So.	60	224	104	.464
Sammy Serrano, Stetson	Jr.	62	245	112	.457
Ryan Fleming, Dayton	Sr.	40	156	71	.455
Kevin Mench, Delaware	So.	52	187	85	.455
Aaron Meyer, Dartmouth	So.	41	151	68	.450
Jeff Pickler, Tennessee	Sr.	55	245	109	.445
Muchie Dagliere, UMass	Sr.	38	151	67	.444
Tom Stoudt, Lafayette	Sr.	33	113	50	.442
Jeff Ryan, Wichita St.	Jr.	63	261	115	.441
Antonio Banks, Miss. Val. St.	So.	34	105	46	.438
Jon Palmieri, Wake Forest	Jr.	64	256	112	.438
Bob Osipower, Lafayette	So.	36	128	56	.438

Home Runs (per game)

(At least 15)	Cl	Gm	HR	Avg
Kevin Mench, Delaware	So.	52	33	0.63
Jason Hart, SW Mo. St.	Jr.	53	28	0.53
Eric Valent, UCLA	Jr.	57	30	0.53
Casey Kelley, Washington St.	Jr.	49	25	0.51
Ryan Fry, Missouri	Sr.	54	27	0.50
Jason Story, New Mexico St.	Sr.	46	23	0.50
Jason Sparks, Tulane	Jr.	62	30	0.48
Jeff Tidwell, Jacksonville St.	Sr.	54	25	0.46
Sonny Cortez, Tennessee	Sr.	52	24	0.46
Brad Cresse, LSU	So.	63	29	0.46
John Summers, Utah	Jr.	50	23	0.46

Runs Batted In

(At least 50)	Cl	Gm	RBI	Avg
Damon Thames, Rice	Jr.	63	115	1.83
Jason Story, New Mexico St.	Sr.	46	82	1.78
Jason Hart, SW Mo. St.	Jr.	53	91	1.72
Sonny Cortez, Tennessee	Sr.	52	87	1.67
Jeff Ryan, Wichita St.	Jr.	63	105	1.67
Pat Magness, Wichita St.	So.	60	100	1.67
Shayne Carnes, UAB	Sr.	53	87	1.64
Bo Robinson, UNC-Charlotte	Sr.	62	100	1.61
Lyle Overbay, Nevada	Jr.	53	85	1.60
Bubba Crosby, Rice	Jr.	58	91	1.57

Stolen Bases

(At least 25)	Cl	Gm	SB	SBA	Avg
Kalin Foulds, San Diego St.	Sr.	56	58	66	1.04
Brian Roberts, North Carolina	So.	65	63	76	0.97
Mike Curry, South Carolina	Jr.	62	60	69	0.97
Schuyler Doakes, Jackson St.	Sr.	50	45	49	0.90
Juan Pierre, South Alabama	Jr.	61	54	62	0.89
Jason Maule, Cen. Conn. St.	Jr.	43	37	42	0.86
Herbert Wheat, Howard	Sr.	46	39	42	0.85
Terrence Smalls, Citadel	Sr.	61	49	61	0.80
John Penatello, Iona	Sr.	48	38	45	0.79
Shawn Pearson, Old Dominion	So.	51	38	44	0.75

Pitching

Earned Run Avg.

(At least 50 inn.)	Cl	Gm	IP	ERA
Aaron Heilman, Notre Dame	Fr.	31	67.0	1.61
Bobby Castelli, Eastern Ill.	Jr.	29	54.2	1.65
Jay Krystofolski, Rhode Island	Jr.	11	68.0	1.72
Eric Gutshall, Yale	Sr.	19	73.2	1.83
Josh Fogg, Florida	Jr.	40	84.1	2.03
Kevin McGerry, St. John's-NY	Fr.	12	65.2	2.06
Brandon Emmanuel, Northwestern St.	Jr.	25	62.2	2.15
Mike Fischer, South Alabama	Jr.	20	124.2	2.31
Jason Parsons, UNC-Greensboro	Sr.	29	66.0	2.32
Nick Stocks, Florida St.	Fr.	17	76.2	2.35

Wins

	Cl	Gm	IP	W-L
Alex Santos, Miami-FL	So.	18	110.0	15-1
Shane Wright, Texas Tech	Jr.	21	152.2	14-1
Josh Bobbitt, Tulane	Sr.	18	116.2	13-1
Geoff Geary, Oklahoma	Sr.	20	123.1	13-1
Darryl Roque, Miami-FL	Jr.	20	84.1	13-2
Javier Pamus, San Jose St.	Sr.	21	115.2	13-3
Seth Etherton, USC	Sr.	18	136.2	13-3
Hayden Gliemmo, Auburn	Fr.	21	118.1	13-3
John Hendricks, Wake Forest	Jr.	27	143.1	13-4
Kip Wells, Baylor	Jr.	20	123.2	13-4
Chad Berryman, Va. Commonwealth	Sr.	19	113.1	13-4

Nine tied with 12 wins each

Strikeouts (per 9 inn.)

(At least 50 inn.)	Cl	IP	SO	Avg
Brian Wiley, Citadel	Jr.	101.2	159	14.1
Rick Currier, USC	Fr.	71.1	100	12.6
Monty Ward, Texas Tech	Jr.	108.1	151	12.5
Jody Fuller, Tenn.-Martin	Sr.	85.0	118	12.5
Chris Pine, Oregon St.	Jr.	75.1	104	12.4
Randy Keisler, LSU	Jr.	99.2	135	12.2
Josh Fogg, Florida	Jr.	84.1	114	12.2
Rickey Lewis, Mississippi Val. St.	Jr.	61.2	83	12.1

Four tied with 12.0 each

Saves

	Cl	IP	ERA	Saves
Jack Krawczyk, USC	Sr.	49.1	2.01	23
Josh Fogg, Florida	Jr.	84.1	2.03	13
Jarred Kingrey, Alabama	Sr.	83.2	2.47	13
Jason Arnold, Central Fla.	Fr.	35.1	2.04	12
Robbie Morrison, Miami-FL	Jr.	40.1	4.24	12
Marc Bluma, Wichita St.	Jr.	57.0	1.74	11
Brandon Inge, Va. Commonwealth	Jr.	43.0	2.09	11

Six tied with 10 each

Other College World Series

Participants' final records in parentheses.

NCAA Div. II

at Montgomery, Ala. (May 22-May 30)

Participants: Cen. Missouri St. (39-6); Tampa (42-14); Cal State Chico (35-15); West Georgia St. (41-15); Millersville, Pa. (37-14); St. Joseph's, Ind. (38-17); New Haven (29-9-1); Kennesaw St., Ga. (58-4).

Championship: Tampa def. Kennesaw St., 6-1.

NAIA

at Tulsa, Okla. (May 18-May 23)

Participants: Albertson, Idaho (51-7); St. Thomas, Fla. (53-12); Cumberland, Tenn. (50-12); Bellevue, Neb. (46-12); Oklahoma City (42-18); Point Park, Pa. (46-4-2) Indiana Tech., (44-18); Culver-Stockton, Mo. (39-15).

Championship: Albertson def. Indiana Tech., 6-3.

NCAA Div. III

at Salem, Va. (May 23-27)

Participants: Eastern Conn. St. (36-10); Wisc.-Oshkosh, (40-3); Aurora, Ill. (31-4); Cal Lutheran (28-13); Anderson, Ind. (34-13); Cortland St., N.Y (37-3); Montclair St., N.J. (31-9-1); N.C. Wesleyan (41-7).

Championship: Eastern Conn. St. def. Montclair St., 16-1.

NJCAA Div. I

at Grand Junction, Colo. (May 23-30)

Participants: Cowley, Kan. (50-8); Indian Hills, Iowa (49-9); Central Fla. (41-16); Brevard, N.C. (43-15); Meridian, Miss. (50-10); Grayson, Texas (46-17); DeKalb, Ga. (42-15); San Jacinto, Texas (44-13); Maple Woods, Mo. (47-11); Dixie, Utah (40-17).

Championship: Cowley def. San Jacinto, 15-11.

MLB Amateur Draft

First round selections at the 34th Amateur Draft held June 2-4, 1998. Selections 1-30 are first round picks and 31-41 are supplemental first round picks awarded for the loss of free agents while picks 42 and 43 are compensation for unsigned 1997 selections.

First Round

No	Team	Player	Pos
1	Philadelphia	Pat Burrell, Miami	3B
2	Oakland	Mark Mulder, Michigan St.	LHP
3	Chicago-NL	Corey Patterson, of Harrison HS-Kennesaw, Ga.	OF
4	Kansas City	Jeff Austin, Stanford	RHP
5	St. Louis	J.D. Drew, Florida St.	OF
6	Minnesota	Ryan Mills, Arizona St.	LHP
7	Cincinnati	Austin Kearns, Lafayette HS-Lexington, Ky.	RF
8	Toronto	Felipe Lopez, Lake Brantley HS-Altamonta Springs, Fla.	SS
9	San Diego	Sean Burroughs, Wilson HS-Long Beach, Calf.	3B
10	Texas	Carlos Pena, Northeastern	1B
11	Montreal	Josh McKinley, Malvern Prep, Downington, Pa.	SS
12	Boston	Adam Everett, South Carolina	SS
13	Milwaukee	J.M. Gold, North HS-Tom's River, N.J.	RHP
14	Detroit	Jeff Weaver, Fresno St.	RHP
15	Pittsburgh	Clint Johnston, Vanderbilt	LHP-OF
16	Chicago-AL	Kip Wells, Baylor	RHP
17	**a-**Houston	Brad Lidge, Notre Dame	RHP
18	Anaheim	Seth Etherton, USC	RHP
19	**b-**San Francisco	Tony Torcata, Woodland (Calif.) HS	SS-3B
20	Cleveland	C.C. Sabathia, Vallejo (Calif.) HS	LHP
21	New York Mets	Jason Tyner, Texas A&M	OF
22	Seattle	Matt Thorton, Grand Valley St.	LHP
23	Los Angeles	Bubba Crosby, Rice	OF
24	New York-AL	Andy Brown, Richmond (Ind.) HS	OF
25	San Francisco	Nate Bump, Penn St.	RHP
26	Baltimore	Rick Elder, Sprayberry HS Marietta, Ga.	OF
27	Florida	Chip Ambres, West Brook HS-Beaumont, Texas	OF
28	**c-**Colorado	Matt Roney, North HS-Edmond, Okla.	RHP
29	**d-**San Francisco	Arturo McDowell, Forest Hills HS-Jackson, Miss.	OF
30	**e-**Kansas City	Matt Burch, Virgina Commonwealth	RHP
31	Kansas City	Christopher George, Klein HS-Spring, Texas	LHP
32	St. Louis	Benjamin Diggins, Bradshaw HS-Dewey, Ariz.	OF
33	Montreal	Stephen Wilkerson, Florida	LHP
34	Detroit	Nathan Cornejo, Wellington (Kan.) HS	RHP
35	Chicago-AL	Aaron Rowand, California	OF
36	Colorado	Raphael Freeman, Dallas	OF
37	Houston	Michael Nannini, Green Valley HS-Henderson, Nev.	RHP
38	San Francisco	Christopher Jones, South Mecklenburg HS-Charlotte, N.C.	LHP
39	Baltimore	Mamon Tucker, Stephen F. Austin HS-Austin, Texas	OF
40	Colorado	Jeffrey Winchester, Rummel Boys HS-Metairie, La.	C
41	San Francisco	Jeffrey Urban, Ball St.	LHP
42	**f-**Philadelphia	Eric Valent, California	OF
43	**g-**New York-AL	Mark Prior, University HS-Bonita, Calif.	RHP

Acquired picks: **a**–from Colorado for signing Darryl Kile; **b**–from Houston for signing Doug Henry; **c**–from Atlanta for signing Andres Galarraga; **d**–from Tampa Bay for signing Roberto Hernandez; **e**–from Arizona for signing Jay Bell; **f**–for not signing 1997 pick J.D. Drew; **g**–for not signing 1997 pick Carlton Godwin.

Impressions of Omaha

by Dave Ryan

When sports fans think of the College World Series, images of a young, flame throwing Roger Clemens (University of Texas), a sweet swinging Will Clark (Mississippi State), or a running and gunning Barry Bonds (Arizona State) come to mind. As in the past, this year's event in Omaha featured some players that will be regulars on major league rosters for years to come. Miami's slugging third baseman Pat Burrell (Phillies first overall pick), Arizona State's graceful lefty Ryan Mills and USC's catcher Eric Munson (possible first overall selection in next year's draft) are just the beginning.

While it was thrilling to meet and watch these future major league all stars compete for the crown, covering the "other" players is what really stands out. These young men, who will never see a day in the big leagues, take batting practice, lift weights and work on drills year round with one goal in mind - to be in the joyous pileup at the mound that USC enjoyed this year by winning the CWS title. They all share the dream of what players call "making it to baseball heaven."

Our ESPN and espn2 telecasts were full of riveting human interest stories, perhaps none greater than that of Arizona State's 26-year-old outfielder Rudy "Pops" Arguelles. Just as he was entering his freshman year at Riverside Community College in 1990, his grandparents became ill, causing him to quit the game in order to make the family's ends meet. He worked four years at a rock quarry and packaging plant, married his high school sweetheart and they had a son together when he finally realized he had to get back to school. He had to tryout at his old school, and made it through four rounds of cuts, becoming the last player on the list to make the team. His college career really blossomed though when he transferred to ASU.

Upon arrival in Nebraska, he and wife Michelle were soon expecting their second child. After a ten minute conversation with Rudy, it was obvious how difficult and emotional his journey to Rosenblatt Stadium had been. His genuine and complete joy at just being there was something I'll never forget. It was real. It was honest. The "Rudy" character in the Notre Dame football movie has nothing on this guy!

Walking in the stands and patrolling the dugouts gave me a vantage point and relationship with the players, coaches, and fans which is unique to the College World Series. Players' parents were sometimes overjoyed, sometimes reluctant to talk about their sons, and sometimes so nervous that they had to watch the game alone on a concourse monitor. Others moved from seat to seat around the stadium to change the team's luck. And there were big league connections as well. We spoke with Minnesota Twins trainer Dick Martin (father of Florida infielder Ty), Florida Marlins hitting instructor Manuel Crespo (father of Miami infielder Manny), and Los Angeles Dodgers bullpen coach Mark Cresse, who had never seen his son play a college game in person due to the obvious schedule conflicts. As his son Brad was at the plate for LSU, we interviewed Mark. "I came here to see him hit one out of the park!", claimed the elder Cresse. It proved prophetic for on the next pitch, Brad went deep, and Mark went nuts. It was an amazing College World Series moment.

The college baseball fans in Omaha are unlike any I have seen or heard. For nine days, a near-capacity crowd jammed into Rosenblatt. With eye-popping variety in weather that ranged from 95 degrees to a crisp, October-like 45 degrees at night, the fans tolerated and cheered through it all. Some have been attending games since the CWS came to Omaha in the 1960's, not missing a game along the way. Others, like the left field "bleacher creatures," take a liking to a certain player each year. This year the chosen player was Mississippi State left fielder Rusty Thoms, who won them over by passing out old batting gloves and souvenir balls throughout the games.

"The Omaha fans are amazing," said Thoms. "They treat you like gold. This is one way I can give a little back." The fans realize how deeply ingrained this event is to their community, how crucial its success is to the city's livelihood. They embrace the teams and the history of the college game. Above all, they display a 100 percent real love for baseball. It's in their eyes, their voices, and as you can feel from walking the aisles during the College World Series, it is in their hearts. ■

Dave Ryan is an in-the-stands reporter for ESPN's college baseball coverage.

Minor League Triple-A Final Standings

International League

North Division	W	L	Pct	GB
Buffalo (Indians)	81	62	.566	—
Syracuse (Blue Jays)	80	62	.563	½
Pawtucket (Red Sox)	77	64	.546	3
Rochester (Orioles)	70	74	.486	11½
Ottawa (Expos)	69	74	.483	12
Scranton-WB (Phillies)	67	75	.472	13½
South Division	**W**	**L**	**Pct**	**GB**
Durham (Devil Rays)	80	64	.556	—
Norfolk (Mets)	70	72	.493	9
Charlotte (Marlins)	70	73	.490	9½
Richmond (Braves)	64	80	.444	16
West Division	**W**	**L**	**Pct**	**GB**
Louisville (Brewers)	77	67	.535	—
Indianapolis (Reds)	76	67	.531	½
Columbus (Yankees)	67	77	.465	10
Toledo (Tigers)	52	89	.369	23½

Playoffs

Division Finals (Best of Five)

Buffalo 3 ... Syracuse 0
Durham 3 ... Louisville 0

Championship (Best of Five)
Buffalo vs. Durham

Sept. 14	Buffalo, 9-6	at Buffalo
Sept. 15	Buffalo, 6-4	at Buffalo
Sept. 16	Durham, 9-8	at Durham
Sept. 17	Durham, 7-6	at Durham
Sept. 18	Buffalo, 3-1	at Durham

Buffalo wins series, 3-2

Pacific Coast League

American Conference

East Division	W	L	Pct	GB
New Orleans (Astros)	76	66	.535	—
Oklahoma (Rangers)	74	70	.514	3
Memphis (Cardinals)	74	70	.514	3
Nashville (Pirates)	67	76	.469	9½
Midwest Division	**W**	**L**	**Pct**	**GB**
Iowa (Cubs)	85	59	.590	—
Omaha (Royals)	79	64	.552	5½
Albuquerque (Dodgers)	61	82	.427	23½
Colorado Springs (Rockies)	55	89	.382	30

Pacific Conference

South Division	W	L	Pct	GB
Fresno (Giants)	81	62	.566	—
Salt Lake (Twins)	79	64	.552	2
Las Vegas (Padres)	70	72	.493	10½
Tucson (D'Backs)	57	85	.401	23½
West Division	**W**	**L**	**Pct**	**GB**
Calgary (White Sox)	81	62	.566	—
Tacoma (Mariners)	77	67	.535	4½
Edmonton (Athletics)	76	67	.531	5
Vancouver (Angels)	53	90	.371	28

Playoffs

Division Finals (Best of Five)

New Orleans 2* ... Iowa 1
Calgary 3 ... Fresno 2
*Series shortened by rain.

Championship (Best of Five)
New Orleans vs. Calgary

Sept. 15	New Orleans, 4-1	at Calgary
Sept. 16	Calgary, 12-8	at Calgary
Sept. 17	Calgary, 5-2	at New Orleans
Sept. 18	New Orleans, 8-1	at New Orleans
Sept. 19	New Orleans, 4-3	at New Orleans

New Orleans wins series, 3-2

1998 Minor League All-Star Team

As presented by *Baseball America* and covering all Minor League levels.

Pos.	Name, Team (Major Affiliate)
C	Michael Barrett, Harrisburg (Expos)
1B	Calvin Pickering, Bowie (Orioles)
2B	Ron Belliard, Louisville (Brewers)
3B	Eric Chavez*, Edmonton (Athletics)
SS	Pablo Ozuna, Peoria (Cardinals)
OF	Lance Berkman, New Orleans (Astros)
OF	Alex Escobar, Capital City (Mets)
OF	Gabe Kapler, Jacksonville (Tigers)
DH	Chris Hatcher, Omaha (Royals)
SP	Rich Ankiel, Prince William (Cardinals)
SP	Ryan Bradley, Columbus (Yankees)
SP	Bruce Chen, Richmond (Braves)
SP	Brad Penny, High Desert (D'Backs)
RP	Brent Stentz, New Britain (Twins)

*Player of the Year

Triple-A World Series

The Triple-A World Series was introduced in 1998 and will continue at least through the year 2000. Played between the champions of the International and Pacific Coast Leagues, it is the first time in history that there will be a single Triple-A champion on a continuing basis. All 1998 games were played at Cashman Field in Las Vegas.

New Orleans vs. Buffalo

(Best of Five)

Sept. 21 New Orleans, 7-2
Sept. 22 Buffalo, 9-2
Sept. 24 New Orleans, 3-2
Sept. 25 New Orleans, 12-6

New Orleans wins series, 3-1

MVP: Lance Berkman, OF, New Orleans

The World Series

The World Series began in 1903 when Pittsburgh of the older National League (founded in 1876) invited Boston of the American League (founded in 1901) to play a best-of-9 game series to determine which of the two league champions was the best. Boston was the surprise winner, 5 games to 3. The 1904 NL champion New York Giants refused to play Boston the following year, so there was no Series. Giants' owner John T. Brush and his manager John McGraw both despised AL president Ban Johnson and considered the junior circuit to be a minor league. By the following year, however, Brush and Johnson had smoothed out their differences and the Giants agreed to play Philadelphia in a best-of-7 game series. Since then the World Series has been a best-of-7 format, except from 1919-21 when it returned to best-of-9.

After surviving two world wars and an earthquake in 1989, the World Series was cancelled for only the second time in 1994 when the players went out on strike Aug. 12 to protest the owners' call for revenue sharing and a salary cap. On Sept. 14, with no hope of reaching a labor agreement to end the 34-day strike, the owners called off the remainder of the regular season and the entire postseason. The strike ended after 232 days on Mar. 31, 1995.

In the chart below, the National League teams are listed in CAPITAL letters. Also, each World Series champion's wins and losses are noted in parentheses after the Series score in games.

Multiple champions: New York Yankees (24); Philadelphia-Oakland A's and St. Louis Cardinals (9); Brooklyn-Los Angeles Dodgers (6); Boston Red Sox, Cincinnati Reds, New York-San Francisco Giants and Pittsburgh Pirates (5); Detroit Tigers (4); Baltimore Orioles, Boston-Milwaukee-Atlanta Braves and Washington Senators-Minnesota Twins (3); Chicago Cubs, Chicago White Sox, Cleveland Indians, New York Mets and Toronto Blue Jays (2).

Year	Winner	Manager	Series	Loser	Manager
1903	Boston Red Sox	Jimmy Collins	5-3 (LWLLWWWW)	PITTSBURGH	Fred Clarke
1904	Not held				
1905	NY GIANTS	John McGraw	4-1 (WLWWW)	Philadelphia A's	Connie Mack
1906	Chicago White Sox	Fielder Jones	4-2 (WLWLWW)	CHICAGO CUBS	Frank Chance
1907	CHICAGO CUBS	Frank Chance	4-0-1 (TWWWW)	Detroit	Hughie Jennings
1908	CHICAGO CUBS	Frank Chance	4-1 (WWLWW)	Detroit	Hughie Jennings
1909	PITTSBURGH	Fred Clarke	4-3 (WLWLWLW)	Detroit	Hughie Jennings
1910	Philadelphia A's	Connie Mack	4-1 (WWWLW)	CHICAGO CUBS	Frank Chance
1911	Philadelphia A's	Connie Mack	4-2 (LWWWLW)	NY GIANTS	John McGraw
1912	Boston Red Sox	Jake Stahl	4-3-1 (WTLWWLLW)	NY GIANTS	John McGraw
1913	Philadelphia A's	Connie Mack	4-1 (WLWWW)	NY GIANTS	John McGraw
1914	BOSTON BRAVES	George Stallings	4-0	Philadelphia A's	Connie Mack
1915	Boston Red Sox	Bill Carrigan	4-1 (LWWWW)	PHILA. PHILLIES	Pat Moran
1916	Boston Red Sox	Bill Carrigan	4-1 (WWLWW)	BROOKLYN	Wilbert Robinson
1917	Chicago White Sox	Pants Rowland	4-2 (WWLLWW)	NY GIANTS	John McGraw
1918	Boston Red Sox	Ed Barrow	4-2 (WLWWLW)	CHICAGO CUBS	Fred Mitchell
1919	CINCINNATI	Pat Moran	5-3 (WWLWWLLW)	Chicago White Sox	Kid Gleason
1920	Cleveland	Tris Speaker	5-2 (WLLWWWW)	BROOKLYN	Wilbert Robinson
1921	NY GIANTS	John McGraw	5-3 (LLWWLWWW)	NY Yankees	Miller Huggins
1922	NY GIANTS	John McGraw	4-0-1 (WTWWW)	NY Yankees	Miller Huggins
1923	NY Yankees	Miller Huggins	4-2 (LWLWWW)	NY GIANTS	John McGraw
1924	Washington	Bucky Harris	4-3 (LWLWLWW)	NY GIANTS	John McGraw
1925	PITTSBURGH	Bill McKechnie	4-3 (LWLLWWW)	Washington	Bucky Harris
1926	ST.L. CARDINALS	Rogers Hornsby	4-3 (LWWLLWW)	NY Yankees	Miller Huggins
1927	NY Yankees	Miller Huggins	4-0	PITTSBURGH	Donie Bush
1928	NY Yankees	Miller Huggins	4-0	ST.L. CARDINALS	Bill McKechnie
1929	Philadelphia A's	Connie Mack	4-1 (WWLWW)	CHICAGO CUBS	Joe McCarthy
1930	Philadelphia A's	Connie Mack	4-2 (WWLLWW)	ST.L. CARDINALS	Gabby Street
1931	ST.L. CARDINALS	Gabby Street	4-3 (LWWLWLW)	Philadelphia A's	Connie Mack
1932	NY Yankees	Joe McCarthy	4-0	CHICAGO CUBS	Charlie Grimm
1933	NY GIANTS	Bill Terry	4-1 (WWLWW)	Washington	Joe Cronin
1934	ST.L. CARDINALS	Frankie Frisch	4-3 (WLWLLWW)	Detroit	Mickey Cochrane
1935	Detroit	Mickey Cochrane	4-2 (LWWWLW)	CHICAGO CUBS	Charlie Grimm
1936	NY Yankees	Joe McCarthy	4-2 (LWWWLW)	NY GIANTS	Bill Terry
1937	NY Yankees	Joe McCarthy	4-1 (WWWLW)	NY GIANTS	Bill Terry
1938	NY Yankees	Joe McCarthy	4-0	CHICAGO CUBS	Gabby Hartnett
1939	NY Yankees	Joe McCarthy	4-0	CINCINNATI	Bill McKechnie
1940	CINCINNATI	Bill McKechnie	4-3 (LWLWLWW)	Detroit	Del Baker
1941	NY Yankees	Joe McCarthy	4-1 (WLWWW)	BKLN. DODGERS	Leo Durocher

Year	Winner	Manager	Series	Loser	Manager
1942	ST.L. CARDINALS	Billy Southworth	4-1 (LWWWW)	NY Yankees	Joe McCarthy
1943	NY Yankees	Joe McCarthy	4-1 (WLWWW)	ST.L. CARDINALS	Billy Southworth
1944	ST.L. CARDINALS	Billy Southworth	4-2 (LWLWWW)	St. Louis Browns	Luke Sewell
1945	Detroit	Steve O'Neill	4-3 (LWLWWLW)	CHICAGO CUBS	Charlie Grimm
1946	ST.L. CARDINALS	Eddie Dyer	4-3 (LWLWLWW)	Boston Red Sox	Joe Cronin
1947	NY Yankees	Bucky Harris	4-3 (WWLLWLW)	BKLN. DODGERS	Burt Shotton
1948	Cleveland	Lou Boudreau	4-2 (LWWWLW)	BOSTON BRAVES	Billy Southworth
1949	NY Yankees	Casey Stengel	4-1 (WLWWW)	BKLN. DODGERS	Burt Shotton
1950	NY Yankees	Casey Stengel	4-0	PHILA. PHILLIES	Eddie Sawyer
1951	NY Yankees	Casey Stengel	4-2 (LWLWWW)	NY GIANTS	Leo Durocher
1952	NY Yankees	Casey Stengel	4-3 (LWLWLWW)	BKLN. DODGERS	Charlie Dressen
1953	NY Yankees	Casey Stengel	4-2 (WWLLWW)	BKLN. DODGERS	Charlie Dressen
1954	NY GIANTS	Leo Durocher	4-0	Cleveland	Al Lopez
1955	BKLN. DODGERS	Walter Alston	4-3 (LLWWWLW)	NY Yankees	Casey Stengel
1956	NY Yankees	Casey Stengel	4-3 (LLWWWLW	BKLN. DODGERS	Walter Alston
1957	MILW. BRAVES	Fred Haney	4-3 (LWLWWLW)	NY Yankees	Casey Stengel
1958	NY Yankees	Casey Stengel	4-3 (LLWLWWW)	MILW. BRAVES	Fred Haney
1959	LA DODGERS	Walter Alston	4-2 (LWWWLW)	Chicago White Sox	Al Lopez
1960	PITTSBURGH	Danny Murtaugh	4-3 (WLLWWLW)	NY Yankees	Casey Stengel
1961	NY Yankees	Ralph Houk	4-1 (WLWWW)	CINCINNATI	Fred Hutchinson
1962	NY Yankees	Ralph Houk	4-3 (WLWLWLW)	SF GIANTS	Alvin Dark
1963	LA DODGERS	Walter Alston	4-0	NY Yankees	Ralph Houk
1964	ST.L. CARDINALS	Johnny Keane	4-3 (WLLWWLW)	NY Yankees	Yogi Berra
1965	LA DODGERS	Walter Alston	4-3 (LLWWWLW)	Minnesota	Sam Mele
1966	Baltimore	Hank Bauer	4-0	LA DODGERS	Walter Alston
1967	ST.L. CARDINALS	Red Schoendienst	4-3 (WLWWLLW)	Boston Red Sox	Dick Williams
1968	Detroit	Mayo Smith	4-3 (LWLLWWW)	ST.L. CARDINALS	Red Schoendienst
1969	NY METS	Gil Hodges	4-1 (LWWWW)	Baltimore	Earl Weaver
1970	Baltimore	Earl Weaver	4-1 (WWWLW)	CINCINNATI	Sparky Anderson
1971	PITTSBURGH	Danny Murtaugh	4-3 (LLWWWLW)	Baltimore	Earl Weaver
1972	Oakland A's	Dick Williams	4-3 (WWLWLLW)	CINCINNATI	Sparky Anderson
1973	Oakland A's	Dick Williams	4-3 (WLWLLWW)	NY METS	Yogi Berra
1974	Oakland A's	Alvin Dark	4-1 (WLWWW)	LA DODGERS	Walter Alston
1975	CINCINNATI	Sparky Anderson	4-3 (LWWLWLW)	Boston Red Sox	Darrell Johnson
1976	CINCINNATI	Sparky Anderson	4-0	NY Yankees	Billy Martin
1977	NY Yankees	Billy Martin	4-2 (WLWWLW)	LA DODGERS	Tommy Lasorda
1978	NY Yankees	Bob Lemon	4-2 (LLWWWW)	LA DODGERS	Tommy Lasorda
1979	PITTSBURGH	Chuck Tanner	4-3 (LWLLWWW)	Baltimore	Earl Weaver
1980	PHILA. PHILLIES	Dallas Green	4-2 (WWLLWW)	Kansas City	Jim Frey
1981	LA DODGERS	Tommy Lasorda	4-2 (LLWWWW)	NY Yankees	Bob Lemon
1982	ST.L. CARDINALS	Whitey Herzog	4-3 (LWWLLWW)	Milwaukee Brewers	Harvey Kuenn
1983	Baltimore	Joe Altobelli	4-1 (LWWWW)	PHILA. PHILLIES	Paul Owens
1984	Detroit	Sparky Anderson	4-1 (WLWWW)	SAN DIEGO	Dick Williams
1985	Kansas City	Dick Howser	4-3 (LLWLWWW)	ST.L. CARDINALS	Whitey Herzog
1986	NY METS	Davey Johnson	4-3 (LLWWLWW)	Boston Red Sox	John McNamara
1987	Minnesota	Tom Kelly	4-3 (WWLLLWW)	ST.L. CARDINALS	Whitey Herzog
1988	LA DODGERS	Tommy Lasorda	4-1 (WWLWW)	Oakland A's	Tony La Russa
1989	Oakland A's	Tony La Russa	4-0	SF GIANTS	Roger Craig
1990	CINCINNATI	Lou Piniella	4-0	Oakland A's	Tony La Russa
1991	Minnesota	Tom Kelly	4-3 (WWLLLWW)	ATLANTA BRAVES	Bobby Cox
1992	Toronto	Cito Gaston	4-2 (LWWWLW)	ATLANTA BRAVES	Bobby Cox
1993	Toronto	Cito Gaston	4-2 (WLWWLW)	PHILA. PHILLIES	Jim Fregosi
1994	Not held				
1995	ATLANTA BRAVES	Bobby Cox	4-2 (WWLWLW)	Cleveland	Mike Hargrove
1996	New York Yankees	Joe Torre	4-2 (LLWWWW)	ATLANTA BRAVES	Bobby Cox
1997	FLORIDA MARLINS	Jim Leyland	4-3 (WLWLWLW)	Cleveland	Mike Hargrove
1998	New York Yankees	Joe Torre	4-0	SAN DIEGO	Bruce Bochy

Most Valuable Players

Currently selected by media panel made up of representatives of CBS Sports, CBS Radio, AP, UPI, and World Series official scorers. Presented by *Sport* magazine from 1955-88 and by Major League Baseball since 1989. Winner who did not play for World Series champions is in **bold** type.

Multiple winners: Bob Gibson, Reggie Jackson and Sandy Koufax (2).

Year	Year	Year
1955 Johnny Podres, Bklyn, P	1960 **Bobby Richardson**, NY, 2B	1965 Sandy Koufax, LA, P
1956 Don Larsen, NY, P	1961 Whitey Ford, NY, P	1966 Frank Robinson, Bal., OF
1957 Lew Burdette, Mil., P	1962 Ralph Terry, NY, P	1967 Bob Gibson, St.L., P
1958 Bob Turley, NY, P	1963 Sandy Koufax, LA, P	1968 Mickey Lolich, Det., P
1959 Larry Sherry, LA, P	1964 Bob Gibson, St.L., P	1969 Donn Clendenon, NY, 1B

Year		Year		Year	
1970	Brooks Robinson, Bal., 3B	1981	Pedro Guerrero, LA, OF; Ron Cey, LA, 3B; & Steve Yeager, LA, C	1990	Jose Rijo, Cin., P
1971	Roberto Clemente, Pit., OF	1982	Darrell Porter, St.L., C	1991	Jack Morris, Min., P
1972	Gene Tenace, Oak., C	1983	Rick Dempsey, Bal., C	1992	Pat Borders, Tor., C
1973	Reggie Jackson, Oak., OF	1984	Alan Trammell, Det., SS	1993	Paul Molitor, Tor., DH/1B/3B
1974	Rollie Fingers, Oak., P	1985	Bret Saberhagen, KC, P	1994	Series not held.
1975	Pete Rose, Cin., 3B	1986	Ray Knight, NY, 3B	1995	Tom Glavine, Atl., P
1976	Johnny Bench, Cin., C	1987	Frank Viola, Min., P	1996	John Wetteland, NY, P
1977	Reggie Jackson, NY, OF	1988	Orel Hershiser, LA, P	1997	Livan Hernandez, Fla., P
1978	Bucky Dent, NY, SS	1989	Dave Stewart, Oak., P	1998	Scott Brosius, NY, 3B
1979	Willie Stargell, Pit., 1B				
1980	Mike Schmidt, Phi., 3B				

All-Time World Series Leaders

CAREER

World Series leaders through 1998. Years listed indicate number of World Series appearances.

Hitting

Games

	Yrs	Gm
Yogi Berra, NY Yankees	14	75
Mickey Mantle, NY Yankees	12	65
Elston Howard, NY Yankees-Boston	10	54
Hank Bauer, NY Yankees	9	53
Gil McDougald, NY Yankees	8	53

At Bats

	Yrs	AB
Yogi Berra, NY Yankees	14	259
Mickey Mantle, NY Yankees	12	230
Joe DiMaggio, NY Yankees	10	199
Frankie Frisch, NY Giants-St.L. Cards	8	197
Gil McDougald, NY Yankees	8	190

Batting Avg. (minimum 50 AB)

	AB	H	Avg
Pepper Martin, St.L. Cards	55	23	.418
Paul Molitor, Mil. Brewers-Tor. Blue Jays	55	23	.418
Lou Brock, St. Louis	87	34	.391
Marquis Grissom, Atl-Cle	77	30	.390
Thurman Munson, NY Yankees	67	25	.373
George Brett, Kansas City	51	19	.373
Hank Aaron, Milw. Braves	55	20	.364

Hits

	AB	H	Avg
Yogi Berra, NY Yankees	259	71	.274
Mickey Mantle, NY Yankees	230	59	.257
Frankie Frisch, NYG-St.L. Cards	197	58	.294
Joe DiMaggio, NY Yankees	199	54	.271
Hank Bauer, NY Yankees	188	46	.245
Pee Wee Reese, Brooklyn	169	46	.272

Runs

	Gm	R
Mickey Mantle, NY Yankees	65	42
Yogi Berra, NY Yankees	75	41
Babe Ruth, Boston Red Sox-NY Yankees	41	37
Lou Gehrig, NY Yankees	34	30
Joe DiMaggio, NY Yankees	51	27

Home Runs

	AB	HR
Mickey Mantle, NY Yankees	230	18
Babe Ruth, Boston Red Sox-NY Yankees	129	15
Yogi Berra, NY Yankees	259	12
Duke Snider, Brooklyn-LA	133	11
Lou Gehrig, NY Yankees	119	10
Reggie Jackson, Oakland-NY Yankees	98	10

Runs Batted In

	Gm	RBI
Mickey Mantle, NY Yankees	65	40
Yogi Berra, NY Yankees	75	39
Lou Gehrig, NY Yankees	34	35
Babe Ruth, Boston Red Sox-NY Yankees	41	33
Joe DiMaggio, NY Yankees	51	30

World Series Appearances

In the 94 years that the World Series has been contested, American League teams have won 55 championships while National League teams have won 39.

The following teams are ranked by number of appearances through the 1998 World Series; (*) indicates AL teams.

	App	W	L	Pct.	Last Series	Last Title
NY Yankees*	35	24	11	.686	1998	1998
Bklyn/LA Dodgers	18	6	12	.333	1988	1988
NY/SF Giants	16	5	11	.313	1989	1954
St.L. Cardinals	15	9	6	.600	1987	1982
Phi/KC/Oak.A's*	14	9	5	.643	1990	1989
Chicago Cubs	10	2	8	.200	1945	1908
Boston Red Sox*	9	5	4	.556	1986	1918
Cincinnati Reds	9	5	4	.556	1990	1990
Detroit Tigers*	9	4	5	.444	1984	1984
Bos/Mil/Atl.Braves	8	3	5	.375	1996	1995
Pittsburgh Pirates	7	5	2	.714	1979	1979
St.L/Bal.Orioles*	7	3	4	.429	1983	1983
Wash/Min.Twins*	6	3	3	.500	1991	1991
Cle.Indians*	5	2	3	.400	1997	1948
Phi.Phillies	5	1	4	.200	1993	1980
Chi.White Sox*	4	2	2	.500	1959	1917
NY Mets	3	2	1	.667	1986	1986
Tor. Blue Jays*	2	2	0	1.000	1993	1993
KC Royals*	2	1	1	.500	1985	1985
SD Padres	2	0	2	.000	1998	—
Fla. Marlins	1	1	0	1.000	1997	1997
Sea/Mil.Brewers*	1	0	1	.000	1982	—

Stolen Bases

	Gm	SB
Lou Brock, St. Louis	21	14
Eddie Collins, Phi. A's-Chisox	34	14
Frank Chance, Chi. Cubs	20	10
Davey Lopes, Los Angeles	23	10
Phil Rizzuto, NY Yankees	52	10

Total Bases

	Gm	TB
Mickey Mantle, NY Yankees	65	123
Yogi Berra, NY Yankees	75	117
Babe Ruth, Boston Red Sox-NY Yankees	41	96
Lou Gehrig, NY Yankees	34	87
Joe DiMaggio, NY Yankees	51	84

Slugging Pct. (minimum 50 AB)

	AB	Pct
Reggie Jackson, Oakland-NY Yankees	98	.755
Babe Ruth, Boston Red Sox-NY Yankees	129	.744
Lou Gehrig, NY Yankees	119	.731
Al Simmons, Phi. A's-Cincinnati	73	.658
Lou Brock, St. Louis	87	.655

Pitching

Games

	Yrs	Gm
Whitey Ford, NY Yankees	11	22
Rollie Fingers, Oakland	3	16
Allie Reynolds, NY Yankees	6	15
Bob Turley, NY Yankees	5	15
Clay Carroll, Cincinnati	3	14

Wins

	Gm	W-L
Whitey Ford, NY Yankees	22	10-8
Bob Gibson, St. Louis	9	7-2
Allie Reynolds, NY Yankees	15	7-2
Red Ruffing, NY Yankees	10	7-2
Lefty Gomez, NY Yankees	7	6-0
Chief Bender, Philadelphia A's	10	6-4
Waite Hoyt, NY Yankees-Phi. A's	12	6-4

ERA (minimum 25 IP)

	Gm	IP	ERA
Jack Billingham, Cincinnati	7	25.1	0.36
Harry Brecheen, St. Louis	7	32.2	0.83
Babe Ruth, Boston Red Sox	3	31.0	0.87
Sherry Smith, Brooklyn	3	30.1	0.89
Sandy Koufax, Los Angeles	8	57.0	0.95

Saves

	Gm	IP	Sv
Rollie Fingers, Oakland	16	33.1	6
Allie Reynolds, NY Yankees	15	77.1	4
Johnny Murphy, NY Yankees	8	16.1	4
John Wetteland, NY Yankees	5	4.1	4

Eight pitchers tied with 3 each.

Shutouts

	GS	CG	ShO
Christy Mathewson, NY Giants	11	10	4
Three Finger Brown, Chi. Cubs	7	5	3
Whitey Ford, NY Yankees	22	7	3

Seven pitchers tied with 2 each.

Innings Pitched

	Gm	IP
Whitey Ford, NY Yankees	22	146.0
Christy Mathewson, NY Giants	11	101.2
Red Ruffing, NY Yankees	10	85.2
Chief Bender, Philadelphia A's	10	85.0
Waite Hoyt, NY Yankees-Phi. A's	12	83.2

Complete Games

	GS	CG	W-L
Christy Mathewson, NY Giants	11	10	5-5
Chief Bender, Philadelphia A's	10	9	6-4
Bob Gibson, St. Louis	9	8	7-2
Whitey Ford, NY Yankees	22	7	10-8
Red Ruffing, NY Yankees	10	7	7-2

Strikeouts

	Gm	IP	SO
Whitey Ford, NY Yankees	22	146.0	94
Bob Gibson, St. Louis	9	81.0	92
Allie Reynolds, NY Yankees	15	77.1	62
Sandy Koufax, Los Angeles	8	57.0	61
Red Ruffing, NY Yankees	10	85.2	61

Bases on Balls

	Gm	IP	BB
Whitey Ford, NY Yankees	22	146.0	34
Allie Reynolds, NY Yankees	15	77.1	32
Art Nehf, NY Giants-Chi. Cubs	12	79.0	32
Jim Palmer, Baltimore	9	64.2	31
Bob Turley, NY Yankees	15	54.0	29

Losses

	Gm	W-L
Whitey Ford, NY Yankees	22	10-8
Christy Mathewson, NY Giants	11	5-5
Joe Bush, Phi. A's-Bosox-NY Yankees	9	2-5
Rube Marquard, NY Giants-Brooklyn	11	2-5
Eddie Plank, Philadelphia A's	7	2-5
Schoolboy Rowe, Detroit	8	2-5

League Championship Series

Division play came to the major leagues in 1969 when both the American and National Leagues expanded to 12 teams. With an East and West Division in each league, League Championship Series (LCS) became necessary to determine the NL and AL pennant winners. In 1994, teams were realigned into three divisions, the East, Central, and West with division winners and one wildcard team playing a best of five series to determine the LCS competitors. In the charts below, the East Division champions are noted by the letter E, the Central division champions by C and the West Division champions by W. A wildcard winner is noted by WC. Also, each playoff winner's wins and losses are noted in parentheses after the series score. The LCS changed from best-of-5 to best-of-7 in 1985. Each league's LCS was cancelled in 1994 due to the players' strike.

National League

Multiple champions: Cincinnati and LA Dodgers (5); Atlanta (4); NY Mets, Philadelphia and St. Louis (3); Pittsburgh and San Diego (2).

Year	Winner	Manager	Series	Loser	Manager
1969	E- New York	Gil Hodges	3-0	W- Atlanta	Lum Harris
1970	W- Cincinnati	Sparky Anderson	3-0	E- Pittsburgh	Danny Murtaugh
1971	E- Pittsburgh	Danny Murtaugh	3-1 (LWWW)	W- San Francisco	Charlie Fox
1972	W- Cincinnati	Sparky Anderson	3-2 (LWLWW)	E- Pittsburgh	Bill Virdon
1973	E- New York	Yogi Berra	3-2 (LWWLW)	W- Cincinnati	Sparky Anderson
1974	W- Los Angeles	Walter Alston	3-1 (WWLW)	E- Pittsburgh	Danny Murtaugh
1975	W- Cincinnati	Sparky Anderson	3-0	E- Pittsburgh	Danny Murtaugh
1976	W- Cincinnati	Sparky Anderson	3-0	E- Philadelphia	Danny Ozark
1977	W- Los Angeles	Tommy Lasorda	3-1 (LWWW)	E- Philadelphia	Danny Ozark
1978	W- Los Angeles	Tommy Lasorda	3-1 (WWLW)	E- Philadelphia	Danny Ozark
1979	E- Pittsburgh	Chuck Tanner	3-0	W- Cincinnati	John McNamara
1980	E- Philadelphia	Dallas Green	3-2 (WLLWW)	W- Houston	Bill Virdon
1981	W- Los Angeles	Tommy Lasorda	3-2 (WLLWW)	E- Montreal	Jim Fanning
1982	E- St. Louis	Whitey Herzog	3-0	W- Atlanta	Joe Torre
1983	E- Philadelphia	Paul Owens	3-1 (WLWW)	W- Los Angeles	Tommy Lasorda
1984	W- San Diego	Dick Williams	3-2 (LLWWW)	E- Chicago	Jim Frey
1985	E- St. Louis	Whitey Herzog	4-2 (LLWWWW)	W- Los Angeles	Tommy Lasorda
1986	E- New York	Davey Johnson	4-2 (LWWLWW)	W- Houston	Hal Lanier
1987	E- St. Louis	Whitey Herzog	4-3 (WLWLLWW)	W- San Francisco	Roger Craig
1988	W- Los Angeles	Tommy Lasorda	4-3 (LWLWWLW)	E- New York	Davey Johnson
1989	W- San Francisco	Roger Craig	4-1 (WLWWW)	E- Chicago	Don Zimmer

Year	Winner	Manager	Series	Loser	Manager
1990	W- Cincinnati	Lou Piniella	4-2 (LWWWLW)	E- Pittsburgh	Jim Leyland
1991	W- Atlanta	Bobby Cox	4-3 (LWWLLWW)	E- Pittsburgh	Jim Leyland
1992	W- Atlanta	Bobby Cox	4-3 (WWLWLLW)	E- Pittsburgh	Jim Leyland
1993	E- Philadelphia	Jim Fregosi	4-2 (WLLWWW)	W- Atlanta	Bobby Cox
1994	Not held				
1995	E- Atlanta	Bobby Cox	4-0	C- Cincinnati	Davey Johnson
1996	E- Atlanta	Bobby Cox	4-3 (WLLLWWW)	C- St. Louis	Tony LaRussa
1997	E-Florida	Jim Leyland	4-2 (WLWLWW)	E-Atlanta	Bobby Cox
1998	W-San Diego	Bruce Bochy	4-2 (WWWLLW)	E-Atlanta	Bobby Cox

NLCS Most Valuable Players

Winners who did not play for NLCS champions are in **bold** type.

Multiple winner: Steve Garvey (2).

Year	Year	Year
1977 Dusty Baker, LA, OF	1985 Ozzie Smith, St.L., SS	1992 John Smoltz, Atl., P
1978 Steve Garvey, LA, 1B	1986 **Mike Scott,** Hou., P	1993 Curt Schilling, Phi., P
1979 Willie Stargell, Pit., 1B	1987 **Jeff Leonard,** SF, OF	1994 LCS not held.
1980 Manny Trillo, Phi., 2B	1988 Orel Hershiser, LA, P	1995 Mike Devereaux, Atl., OF
1981 Burt Hooton, LA, P	1989 Will Clark, SF, 1B	1996 Javy Lopez, Atl., C
1982 Darrell Porter, St.L., C	1990 Rob Dibble, Cin., P	1997 Livan Hernandez, Fla., P
1983 Gary Matthews, Phi., OF	& Randy Myers, Cin., P	1998 Sterling Hitchcock, SD, P
1984 Steve Garvey, SD, 1B	1991 Steve Avery, Atl., P	

American League

Multiple champions: NY Yankees and Oakland (6); Baltimore (5); Boston, Cleveland, Kansas City, Minnesota and Toronto (2).

Year	Winner	Manager	Series	Loser	Manager
1969	E- Baltimore	Earl Weaver	3-0	W- Minnesota	Billy Martin
1970	E- Baltimore	Earl Weaver	3-0	W- Minnesota	Bill Rigney
1971	E- Baltimore	Earl Weaver	3-0	W- Oakland	Dick Williams
1972	W- Oakland	Dick Williams	3-2 (WWLLW)	E- Detroit	Billy Martin
1973	W- Oakland	Dick Williams	3-2 (LWWLW)	E- Baltimore	Earl Weaver
1974	W- Oakland	Alvin Dark	3-1 (LWWW)	E- Baltimore	Earl Weaver
1975	E- Boston	Darrell Johnson	3-0	W- Oakland	Alvin Dark
1976	E- New York	Billy Martin	3-2 (WLWLW)	W- Kansas City	Whitey Herzog
1977	E- New York	Billy Martin	3-2 (LWLWW)	W- Kansas City	Whitey Herzog
1978	E- New York	Bob Lemon	3-1 (WLWW)	W- Kansas City	Whitey Herzog
1979	E- Baltimore	Earl Weaver	3-1 (WWLW)	W- California	Jim Fregosi
1980	W- Kansas City	Jim Frey	3-0	E- New York	Dick Howser
1981	E- New York	Bob Lemon	3-0	W- Oakland	Billy Martin
1982	E- Milwaukee	Harvey Kuenn	3-2 (LLWWW)	W- California	Gene Mauch
1983	E- Baltimore	Joe Altobelli	3-1 (LWWW)	W- Chicago	Tony La Russa
1984	E- Detroit	Sparky Anderson	3-0	W- Kansas City	Dick Howser
1985	W- Kansas City	Dick Howser	4-3 (LLWLWWW)	E- Toronto	Bobby Cox
1986	E- Boston	John McNamara	4-3 (LWLLWWW)	W- California	Gene Mauch
1987	W- Minnesota	Tom Kelly	4-1 (WWLWW)	E- Detroit	Sparky Anderson
1988	W- Oakland	Tony La Russa	4-0	E- Boston	Joe Morgan
1989	W- Oakland	Tony La Russa	4-1 (WWLWW)	E- Toronto	Cito Gaston
1990	W- Oakland	Tony La Russa	4-0	E- Boston	Joe Morgan
1991	W- Minnesota	Tom Kelly	4-1 (WLWWW)	E- Toronto	Cito Gaston
1992	E- Toronto	Cito Gaston	4-2 (LWWWLW)	W- Oakland	Tony La Russa
1993	E- Toronto	Cito Gaston	4-2 (WWLLWW)	W- Chicago	Gene Lamont
1994	Not held				
1995	C- Cleveland	Mike Hargrove	4-2 (LWLWWW)	W- Seattle	Lou Piniella
1996	E- New York	Joe Torre	4-1 (WLWWW)	E- Baltimore	Davey Johnson
1997	C- Cleveland	Mike Hargrove	4-2 (LWWWLW)	E- Baltimore	Davey Johnson
1998	E- New York	Joe Torre	4-2 (WLLWWW)	C- Cleveland	Mike Hargrove

ALCS Most Valuable Players

Winner who did not play for ALCS champions is in **bold** type.

Multiple winner: Dave Stewart (2).

Year	Year	Year
1980 Frank White, KC, 2B	1987 Gary Gaetti, Min., 3B	1994 LCS not held.
1981 Graig Nettles, NY, 3B	1988 Dennis Eckersley, Oak., P	1995 Orel Hershiser, Cle., P
1982 **Fred Lynn,** Cal., OF	1989 Rickey Henderson, Oak., OF	1996 Bernie Williams, NY, OF
1983 Mike Boddicker, Bal., P	1990 Dave Stewart, Oak., P	1997 Marquis Grissom, Cle., OF
1984 Kirk Gibson, Det., OF	1991 Kirby Puckett, Min., OF	1998 David Wells, NY, P
1985 George Brett, KC, 3B	1992 Roberto Alomar, Tor., 2B	
1986 Marty Barrett, Bos., 2B	1993 Dave Stewart, Tor., P	

Other Playoffs

Seven times from 1946-80, playoffs were necessary to decide league or division championships when two teams tied for first place at the end of the regular season. In the strike year of 1981, there were playoffs between the first and second half-season champions in both leagues. In 1995, the 1994-95 players' strike shortened the regular season to 144 games. In 1998, the Chicago Cubs played the San Francisco Giants in a one game playoff to determine the NL Wild Card entry.

National League

Year	NL	W	L	Manager
1946	Brooklyn	96	58	Leo Durocher
	St. Louis	96	58	Eddie Dyer
	Playoff: (Best-of-3) St. Louis, 2-0			
	NL	**W**	**L**	**Manager**
1951	Brooklyn	96	58	Charlie Dressen
	New York	96	58	Leo Durocher
	Playoff: (Best-of-3) New York, 2-1 (WLW)			
	NL	**W**	**L**	**Manager**
1959	Milwaukee	86	68	Fred Haney
	Los Angeles	86	68	Walter Alston
	Playoff: (Best-of-3) Los Angeles, 2-0			
	NL	**W**	**L**	**Manager**
1962	Los Angeles	101	61	Walter Alston
	San Francisco	101	61	Alvin Dark
	Playoff: (Best-of-3) San Francisco, 2-1 (WLW)			

Year	NL West	W	L	Manager
1980	Houston	92	70	Bill Virdon
	Los Angeles	92	70	Tommy Lasorda
	Playoff: (1 game) Houston, 7-1 (at LA)			
	NL East	**W**	**L**	**Manager**
1981	(1st Half) Philadelphia	34	21	Dallas Green
	(2nd Half) Montreal	30	23	Jim Fanning
	Playoff: (Best-of-5) Montreal, 3-2 (WWLLW)			
	NL West	**W**	**L**	**Manager**
1981	(1st Half) Los Angeles	36	21	Tommy Lasorda
	(2nd Half) Houston	33	20	Bill Virdon
	Playoff: (Best-of-5) Los Angeles, 3-2 (LLWWW)			
	NL Wild Card	**W**	**L**	**Manager**
1998	Chicago	89	73	Jim Riggleman
	San Francisco	89	73	Dusty Baker
	Playoff: (1 game) Chicago, 5-3 (at Chi)			

American League

Year	AL	W	L	Manager
1948	Boston	96	58	Joe McCarthy
	Cleveland	96	58	Lou Boudreau
	Playoff: (1 game) Cleveland, 8-3 (at Boston)			
	AL East	**W**	**L**	**Manager**
1978	Boston	99	63	Don Zimmer
	New York	99	63	Bob Lemon
	Playoff: (1 game) New York, 5-4 (at Boston)			

Year	AL East	W	L	Manager
1981	(1st Half) N.Y.	34	22	Bob Lemon
	(2nd Half) Milw.	31	22	Buck Rodgers
	Playoff: (Best-of-5) New York, 3-2 (WWLLW)			
	AL West	**W**	**L**	**Manager**
	(1st Half) Oakland	37	23	Billy Martin
	(2nd Half) Kan.City	30	23	Jim Frey
	Playoff: (Best-of-5), Oakland, 3-0			
	AL West	**W**	**L**	**Manager**
1995	Seattle	78	66	Lou Piniella
	California	78	66	M. Lachemann
	Playoff: (1 game) Seattle, 9-1 (at Seattle)			

Regular Season League & Division Winners

Regular season National and American League pennant winners from 1900-68, as well as West and East divisional champions from 1969-93. In 1994, both leagues went to three divisions—West, Central and East. However, due to the 1994 players' strike that resulted in the cancelling of the season after games played on Aug. 11, division leaders at the time of the strike are not considered official champions by either league. Note that (*) indicates 1994 divisional champion is unofficial and that **GA** column indicates games ahead of the second place club. See National League Pennant Winners from 1876-99 for NL Pennant winners before 1900.

National League

Multiple pennant winners: Brooklyn-LA (19); New York-SF Giants (17); St. Louis (15); Chicago (10); Cincinnati and Pittsburgh (9); Boston-Milwaukee-Atlanta (8); Philadelphia (5); New York Mets (3); San Diego (2).

Multiple division winners: WEST—Los Angeles (8); Cincinnati (7); Atlanta (5); San Francisco (4); San Diego (3); Houston (2). CENTRAL—Cincinnati and Houston (2). EAST—Pittsburgh (9); Philadelphia (6); Atlanta and NY Mets (4); St. Louis (3); Chicago (2).

Year		W	L	Pct	GA
1900	Brooklyn	82	54	.603	4½
1901	Pittsburgh	90	49	.647	7½
1902	Pittsburgh	103	36	.741	27½
1903	Pittsburgh	91	49	.650	6½
1904	New York	106	47	.693	13
1905	New York	105	48	.686	9
1906	Chicago	116	36	.763	20
1907	Chicago	107	45	.704	17
1908	Chicago	99	55	.643	1
1909	Pittsburgh	110	42	.724	6½
1910	Chicago	104	50	.675	13
1911	New York	99	54	.647	7½
1912	New York	103	48	.682	10
1913	New York	101	51	.664	12½
1914	Boston	94	59	.614	10½
1915	Philadelphia	90	62	.592	7
1916	Brooklyn	94	60	.610	2½
1917	New York	98	56	.636	10
1918	Chicago	84	45	.651	10½
1919	Cincinnati	96	44	.686	9
1920	Brooklyn	93	61	.604	7

Year		W	L	Pct	GA
1921	New York	94	59	.614	4
1922	New York	93	61	.604	7
1923	New York	95	58	.621	4½
1924	New York	93	60	.608	1½
1925	Pittsburgh	95	58	.621	8½
1926	St. Louis	89	65	.578	2
1927	Pittsburgh	94	60	.610	1½
1928	St. Louis	95	59	.617	2
1929	Chicago	98	54	.645	10½
1930	St. Louis	92	62	.597	2
1931	St. Louis	101	53	.656	13
1932	Chicago	90	64	.584	4
1933	New York	91	61	.599	5
1934	St. Louis	95	58	.621	2
1935	Chicago	100	54	.649	4
1936	New York	92	62	.597	5
1937	New York	95	57	.625	3
1938	Chicago	89	63	.586	2
1939	Cincinnati	97	57	.630	4½
1940	Cincinnati	100	53	.654	12
1941	Brooklyn	100	54	.649	2½

Year		W	L	Pct	GA
1942	St. Louis	106	48	.688	2
1943	St. Louis	105	49	.682	18
1944	St. Louis	105	49	.682	14½
1945	Chicago	98	56	.636	3
1946	St. Louis†	98	58	.628	2
1947	Brooklyn	94	60	.610	5
1948	Boston	91	62	.595	6½
1949	Brooklyn	97	57	.630	1
1950	Philadelphia	91	63	.591	2
1951	New York†	98	59	.624	1
1952	Brooklyn	96	57	.627	4½
1953	Brooklyn	105	49	.682	13
1954	New York	97	57	.630	5
1955	Brooklyn	98	55	.641	13½
1956	Brooklyn	93	61	.604	1
1957	Milwaukee	95	59	.617	8
1958	Milwaukee	92	62	.597	8
1959	Los Angeles†	88	68	.564	2
1960	Pittsburgh	95	59	.617	7
1961	Cincinnati	93	61	.604	4
1962	San Francisco†	103	62	.624	1
1963	Los Angeles	99	63	.611	6
1964	St. Louis	93	69	.574	1
1965	Los Angeles	97	65	.599	2
1966	Los Angeles	95	67	.586	1½
1967	St. Louis	101	60	.627	10½
1968	St. Louis	97	65	.599	9
1969	West—Atlanta	93	69	.574	3
	East—N.Y. Mets	100	62	.617	8
1970	West—Cincinnati	102	60	.630	14½
	East—Pittsburgh	89	73	.549	5
1971	West—San Francisco	90	72	.556	1
	East—Pittsburgh	97	65	.599	7
1972	West—Cincinnati	95	59	.617	10½
	East—Pittsburgh	96	59	.619	11
1973	West—Cincinnati	99	63	.611	3½
	East—N.Y. Mets	82	79	.509	1½
1974	West—Los Angeles	102	60	.630	4
	East—Pittsburgh	88	74	.543	1½
1975	West—Cincinnati	108	54	.667	20
	East—Pittsburgh	92	69	.571	6½
1976	West—Cincinnati	102	60	.630	10
	East—Philadelphia	101	61	.623	9
1977	West—Los Angeles	98	64	.605	10
	East—Philadelphia	101	61	.623	5
1978	West—Los Angeles	95	67	.586	2½
	East—Philadelphia	90	72	.556	1½
1979	West—Cincinnati	90	71	.559	1½
	East—Pittsburgh	98	64	.605	2
1980	West—Houston †	93	70	.571	1
	East—Philadelphia	91	71	.562	1
1981	West—Los Angeles$	63	47	.573	—
	East—Montreal$	60	48	.556	—
1982	West—Atlanta	89	73	.549	1
	East—St. Louis	92	70	.568	3
1983	West—Los Angeles	91	71	.562	3
	East—Philadelphia	90	72	.556	6
1984	West—San Diego	92	70	.568	12
	East—Chicago	96	65	.596	6½
1985	West—Los Angeles	95	67	.586	5½
	East—St. Louis	101	61	.623	3
1986	West—Houston	96	66	.593	10
	East—N.Y. Mets	108	54	.667	21½
1987	West—San Francisco	90	72	.556	6
	East—St. Louis	95	67	.586	3
1988	West—Los Angeles	94	67	.584	7
	East—N.Y. Mets	100	60	.625	15
1989	West—San Francisco	92	70	.568	3
	East—Chicago	93	69	.574	6
1990	West—Cincinnati	91	71	.562	5
	East—Pittsburgh	95	67	.586	4
1991	West—Atlanta	94	68	.580	1
	East—Pittsburgh	98	64	.605	14
1992	West—Atlanta	98	64	.605	8
	East—Pittsburgh	96	66	.593	9
1993	West—Atlanta	104	58	.642	1
	East—Philadelphia	97	65	.599	3
1994	West—Los Angeles*	58	56	.509	3½
	Central—Cincinnati*	66	48	.579	½
	East—Montreal*	74	40	.649	6
1995	West—Los Angeles	78	66	.542	1
	Central—Cincinnati	85	59	.590	9
	East—Atlanta	90	54	.625	21
1996	West—San Diego	91	71	.562	1
	Central—St. Louis	88	74	.543	6
	East—Atlanta	96	66	.593	8
1997	West—San Francisco	90	72	.556	2
	Central—Houston	84	78	.519	5
	East—Atlanta	101	61	.623	9
1998	West—San Diego	98	64	.605	9½
	Central—Houston	102	60	.630	12½
	East—Atlanta	106	56	.654	18

†Regular season playoffs: 1946—St. Louis def. Brooklyn (2 games to 1); **1951**—New York def. Brooklyn (2 games to 1); **1959**—Los Angeles def. Milwaukee (2 games to none); **1962**—San Francisco def. Los Angeles (2 games to 1); **1980**–Houston def. Los Angeles (1 game, 7-1). **1981**—East: Montreal def. Philadelphia (3 games to 2) and West: Los Angeles def. Houston (3 games to 2).

$Divsional playoffs: 1981—East: Montreal def. Philadelphia (3 games to 2) and West: Los Angeles def. Houston (3 games to 2).

American League

Multiple pennant winners: NY Yankees (35); Philadelphia-Oakland A's (15); Boston (10); Detroit (9); Baltimore and Washington-Minnesota (6); Chicago (5); Cleveland (3); KC Royals and Toronto (2).

Multiple division winners: WEST—Oakland (10); Kansas City (6); Minnesota (4); California (3); Chicago and Texas (2). EAST—Baltimore (8); NY Yankees (7); Boston and Toronto (5); Detroit (3). CENTRAL—Cleveland (4).

Year		W	L	Pct	GA
1901	Chicago	83	53	.610	4
1902	Philadelphia	83	53	.610	5
1903	Boston	91	47	.659	14½
1904	Boston	95	59	.617	1½
1905	Philadelphia	92	56	.622	2
1906	Chicago	93	58	.616	3
1907	Detroit	92	58	.613	1½
1908	Detroit	90	63	.588	½
1909	Detroit	98	54	.645	3½
1910	Philadelphia	102	48	.680	14½
1911	Philadelphia	101	50	.669	13½
1912	Boston	105	47	.691	14
1913	Philadelphia	96	57	.627	6½
1914	Philadelphia	99	53	.651	8½
1915	Boston	101	50	.669	2½
1916	Boston	91	63	.591	2
1917	Chicago	100	54	.649	9
1918	Boston	75	51	.595	2½
1919	Chicago	88	52	.629	3½
1920	Cleveland	98	56	.636	2
1921	New York	98	55	.641	4½
1922	New York	94	60	.610	1
1923	New York	98	54	.645	16
1924	Washington	92	62	.597	2
1925	Washington	96	55	.636	8½
1926	New York	91	63	.591	3

Year		W	L	Pct	GA
1927	New York	110	44	.714	19
1928	New York	101	53	.656	2½
1929	Philadelphia	104	46	.693	18
1930	Philadelphia	102	52	.662	8
1931	Philadelphia	107	45	.704	13½
1932	New York	107	47	.695	13
1933	Washington	99	53	.651	7
1934	Detroit	101	53	.656	7
1935	Detroit	93	58	.616	3
1936	New York	102	51	.667	19½
1937	New York	102	52	.662	13
1938	New York	99	53	.651	9½
1939	New York	106	45	.702	17
1940	Detroit	90	64	.584	1
1941	New York	101	53	.656	17
1942	New York	103	51	.669	9
1943	New York	98	56	.636	13½
1944	St. Louis	89	65	.578	1
1945	Detroit	88	65	.575	1½
1946	Boston	104	50	.675	12
1947	New York	97	57	.630	12
1948	Cleveland†	97	58	.626	1
1949	New York	97	57	.630	1
1950	New York	98	56	.636	3
1951	New York	98	56	.636	5
1952	New York	95	59	.617	2
1953	New York	99	52	.656	8½
1954	Cleveland	111	43	.721	8
1955	New York	96	58	.623	3
1956	New York	97	57	.630	9
1957	New York	98	56	.636	8
1958	New York	92	62	.597	10
1959	Chicago	94	60	.610	5
1960	New York	97	57	.630	8
1961	New York	109	53	.673	8
1962	New York	96	66	.593	5
1963	New York	104	57	.646	10½
1964	New York	99	63	.611	1
1965	Minnesota	102	60	.630	7
1966	Baltimore	97	63	.606	9
1967	Boston	92	70	.568	1
1968	Detroit	103	59	.636	12
1969	West—Minnesota	97	65	.599	9
	East—Baltimore	109	53	.673	19
1970	West—Minnesota	98	64	.605	9
	East—Baltimore	108	54	.667	15
1971	West—Oakland	101	60	.627	16
	East—Baltimore	101	57	.639	12
1972	West—Oakland	93	62	.600	5½
	East—Detroit	86	70	.551	½
1973	West—Oakland	94	68	.580	6
	East—Baltimore	97	65	.599	8
1974	West—Oakland	90	72	.556	5
	East—Baltimore	91	71	.562	2
1975	West—Oakland	98	64	.605	7
	East—Boston	95	65	.594	4½
1976	West—Kansas City	90	72	.556	2½
	East—New York	97	62	.610	10½
1977	West—Kansas City	102	60	.630	8
	East—New York	100	62	.617	2½
1978	West—Kansas City	92	70	.568	5
	East—New York†	100	63	.613	1
1979	West—California	88	74	.543	3
	East—Baltimore	102	57	.642	8
1980	West—Kansas City	97	65	.599	14
	East—New York	103	59	.636	3
1981	West—Oakland$	64	45	.587	—
	East—New York$	59	48	.551	—
1982	West—California	93	69	.574	3
	East—Milwaukee	95	67	.586	1
1983	West—Chicago	99	63	.611	20
	East—Baltimore	98	64	.605	6
1984	West—Kansas City	84	78	.519	3
	East—Detroit	104	58	.642	15
1985	West—Kansas City	91	71	.562	1
	East—Toronto	99	62	.615	2
1986	West—California	92	70	.568	5
	East—Boston	95	66	.590	5½
1987	West—Minnesota	85	77	.525	2
	East—Detroit	98	64	.605	2
1988	West—Oakland	104	58	.642	13
	East—Boston	89	73	.549	1
1989	West—Oakland	99	63	.611	7
	East—Toronto	89	73	.549	2
1990	West—Oakland	103	59	.636	9
	East—Boston	88	74	.543	2
1991	West—Minnesota	95	67	.586	8
	East—Toronto	91	71	.562	7
1992	West—Oakland	96	66	.593	6
	East—Toronto	96	66	.593	4
1993	West—Chicago	94	68	.580	8
	East—Toronto	95	67	.586	7
1994	West—Texas*	52	62	.456	1
	Central—Chicago*	67	46	.593	1
	East—New York*	70	43	.619	6½
1995	West—Seattle†	79	66	.545	1
	Central—Cleveland	100	44	.694	30
	East—Boston	86	58	.597	7
1996	West—Texas	90	72	.556	4½
	Central—Cleveland	99	62	.615	14½
	East—New York	92	70	.568	4
1997	West—Seattle	90	72	.556	6
	Central—Cleveland	86	75	.534	6
	East—Baltimore	98	64	.605	2
1998	West—Texas	88	74	.543	3
	Central—Cleveland	89	73	.549	9
	East—New York	114	48	.704	22

†**Regular season playoffs: 1948**—Cleveland def. Boston, 8-3 (one game); **1978**—New York def. Boston, 5-4 (one game); **1995**—Seattle def. California, 9-1 (one game).
$**Divsional playoffs: 1981**—East: New York def. Milwaukee (3 games to 2) and West: Oakland def. Kansas City (3 games to none);

The All-Star Game

Baseball's first All-Star Game was held on July 6, 1933, before 47,595 at Comiskey Park in Chicago. From that year on, the All-Star Game has matched the best players in the American League against the best in the National. From 1959-62, two All-Star Games were played. The only year an All-Star Game wasn't played was 1945, when World War II travel restrictions made it necessary to cancel the meeting. The NL leads the series, 40-28-1. In the chart below, the American League is listed in **bold** type.

The All-Star Game MVP Award is named after Arch Ward, the *Chicago Tribune* sports editor who founded the game in 1933. First given at the two All-Star games in 1962, the name of the award was changed to the Commissioner's Trophy in 1970 and back to the Ward Memorial Award in 1985.

Muitiple winners: Gary Carter, Steve Garvey and Willie Mays (2).

Year		Host	AL Manager	NL Manager	MVP
1933	**American,** 4-2	Chicago (AL)	Connie Mack	John McGraw	No award
1934	**American,** 9-7	New York (NL)	Joe Cronin	Bill Terry	No award

Year		Host	AL Manager	NL Manager	MVP
1935	**American,** 4-1	Cleveland	Mickey Cochrane	Frankie Frisch	No award
1936	National, 4-3	Boston (NL)	Joe McCarthy	Charlie Grimm	No award
1937	**American,** 8-3	Washington	Joe McCarthy	Bill Terry	No award
1938	National, 4-1	Cincinnati	Joe McCarthy	Bill Terry	No award
1939	**American,** 3-1	New York (AL)	Joe McCarthy	Gabby Hartnett	No award
1940	National, 4-0	St. Louis (NL)	Joe Cronin	Bill McKechnie	No award
1941	**American,** 7-5	Detroit	Del Baker	Bill McKechnie	No award
1942	**American,** 3-1	New York (NL)	Joe McCarthy	Leo Durocher	No award
1943	**American,** 5-3	Philadelphia (AL)	Joe McCarthy	Billy Southworth	No award
1944	National, 7-1	Pittsburgh	Joe McCarthy	Billy Southworth	No award
1945	Not held				
1946	**American,** 12-0	Boston (AL)	Steve O'Neill	Charlie Grimm	No award
1947	**American,** 2-1	Chicago (NL)	Joe Cronin	Eddie Dyer	No award
1948	**American,** 5-2	St. Louis (AL)	Bucky Harris	Leo Durocher	No award
1949	**American,** 11-7	Brooklyn	Lou Boudreau	Billy Southworth	No award
1950	National, 4-3 (14)	Chicago (AL)	Casey Stengel	Burt Shotton	No award
1951	National, 8-3	Detroit	Casey Stengel	Eddie Sawyer	No award
1952	National, 3-2 (5, rain)	Philadelphia (NL)	Casey Stengel	Leo Durocher	No award
1953	National, 5-1	Cincinnati	Casey Stengel	Charlie Dressen	No award
1954	**American,** 11-9	Cleveland	Casey Stengel	Walter Alston	No award
1955	National, 6-5 (12)	Milwaukee	Al Lopez	Leo Durocher	No award
1956	National, 7-3	Washington	Casey Stengel	Walter Alston	No award
1957	**American,** 6-5	St. Louis	Casey Stengel	Walter Alston	No award
1958	**American,** 4-3	Baltimore	Casey Stengel	Fred Haney	No award
1959-a	National, 5-4	Pittsburgh	Casey Stengel	Fred Haney	No award
1959-b	**American,** 5-3	Los Angeles	Casey Stengel	Fred Haney	No award
1960-a	National, 5-3	Kansas City	Al Lopez	Walter Alston	No award
1960-b	National, 6-0	New York	Al Lopez	Walter Alston	No award
1961-a	National, 5-4 (10)	San Francisco	Paul Richards	Danny Murtaugh	No award
1961-b	TIE, 1-1 (9, rain)	Boston	Paul Richards	Danny Murtaugh	No award
1962-a	National, 3-1	Washington	Ralph Houk	Fred Hutchinson	Maury Wills, LA (NL), SS
1962-b	**American,** 9-4	Chicago (NL)	Ralph Houk	Fred Hutchinson	Leon Wagner, LA (AL), OF
1963	National, 5-3	Cleveland	Ralph Houk	Alvin Dark	Willie Mays, SF, OF
1964	National, 7-4	New York (NL)	Al Lopez	Walter Alston	Johnny Callison, Phi., OF
1965	National, 6-5	Minnesota	Al Lopez	Gene Mauch	Juan Marichal, SF, P
1966	National, 2-1 (10)	St. Louis	Sam Mele	Walter Alston	Brooks Robinson, Bal., 3B
1967	National, 2-1 (15)	California	Hank Bauer	Walter Alston	Tony Perez, Cin., 3B
1968	National, 1-0	Houston	Dick Williams	Red Schoendienst	Willie Mays, SF, OF
1969	National, 9-3	Washington	Mayo Smith	Red Schoendienst	Willie McCovey, SF, 1B
1970	National, 5-4 (12)	Cincinnati	Earl Weaver	Gil Hodges	Carl Yastrzemski, Bos., OF-1B
1971	**American,** 6-4	Detroit	Earl Weaver	Sparky Anderson	Frank Robinson, Bal., OF
1972	National, 4-3 (10)	Atlanta	Earl Weaver	Danny Murtaugh	Joe Morgan, Con., 2B
1973	National, 7-1	Kansas	Dick Williams	Sparky Anderson	Bobby Bonds, SF, OF
1974	National, 7-2	Pittsburgh	Dick Williams	Yogi Berra	Steve Garvey, LA, 1B
1975	National, 6-3	Milwaukee	Alvin Dark	Walter Alston	Bill Madlock, Chi. (NL), 3B & Jon Matlack, NY (NL), P
1976	National, 7-1	Philadelphia	Darrell Johnson	Sparky Anderson	George Foster, Cin., OF
1977	National, 7-5	New York (AL)	Billy Martin	Sparky Anderson	Don Sutton, LA, P
1978	National, 7-3	San Diego	Billy Martin	Tommy Lasorda	Steve Garvey, LA, 1B
1979	National, 7-6	Seattle	Bob Lemon	Tommy Lasorda	Dave Parker, Pit, OF
1980	National, 4-2	Los Angeles	Earl Weaver	Chuck Tanner	Ken Griffey, Cin., OF
1981	National, 5-4	Cleveland	Jim Frey	Dallas Green	Gary Carter, Mon., C
1982	National, 4-1	Montreal	Billy Martin	Tommy Lasorda	Dave Concepcion, Cin., SS
1983	**American,** 13-3	Chicago (AL)	Harvey Kuenn	Whitey Herzog	Fred Lynn, Cal., OF
1984	National, 3-1	San Francisco	Joe Altobelli	Paul Owens	Gary Carter, Mon., C
1985	National, 6-1	Minnesota	Sparky Anderson	Dick Williams	LaMarr Hoyt, SD, P
1986	**American,** 3-2	Houston	Dick Howser	Whitey Herzog	Roger Clemens, Bos., P
1987	National, 2-0 (13)	Oakland	John McNamara	Davey Johnson	Tim Raines, Mon., OF
1988	**American,** 2-1	Cincinnati	Tom Kelly	Whitey Herzog	Terry Steinbach, Oak., C
1989	**American,** 5-3	California	Tony La Russa	Tommy Lasorda	Bo Jackson, KC, OF
1990	**American,** 2-0	Chicago (NL)	Tony La Russa	Roger Craig	Julio Franco, Tex., 2B
1991	**American,** 4-2	Toronto	Tony La Russa	Lou Piniella	Cal Ripken Jr., Bal., SS
1992	**American,** 13-6	San Diego	Tom Kelly	Bobby Cox	Ken Griffey Jr., Sea., OF
1993	**American,** 9-3	Baltimore	Cito Gaston	Bobby Cox	Kirby Puckett, Min., OF
1994	National, 8-7 (10)	Pittsburgh	Cito Gaston	Jim Fregosi	Fred McGriff, Atl., 1B
1995	National, 3-2	Texas	Buck Showalter	Felipe Alou	Jeff Conine, Fla., PH
1996	National, 6-0	Philadelphia	Mike Hargrove	Bobby Cox	Mike Piazza, LA, C
1997	**American,** 3-1	Cleveland	Joe Torre	Bobby Cox	Sandy Alomar Jr., Cle., C
1998	**American**, 13-8	Colorado	Mike Hargrove	Jim Leyland	Roberto Alomar, Bal., 2B

Major League Franchise Origins

Here is what the current 30 teams in Major League Baseball have to show for the years they have put in as members of the National League (NL) and American League (AL). Pennants and World Series championships are since 1901.

National League

	1st Year	Pennants & World Series	Franchise Stops
Arizona Diamondbacks	1998	None	• Phoenix (1998–)
Atlanta Braves	1876	8 NL (1914,48,57-58,91-92,95,96) 3 WS (1914,57,95)	• Boston (1876-1952) Milwaukee (1953-65) Atlanta (1966–)
Chicago Cubs	1876	10 NL (1906-08,10,18,29,32,35,38,45) 2 WS (1907-08)	• Chicago (1876–)
Cincinnati Reds	1876	9 NL (1919,39-40,61,70,72,75-76,90) 5 WS (1919,40,75-76,90)	• Cincinnati (1876-80) Cincinnati (1890–)
Colorado Rockies	1993	None	• Denver (1993–)
Florida Marlins	1993	1 NL (1997) 1 WS (1997)	• Miami (1993–)
Houston Astros	1962	None	• Houston (1962–)
Los Angeles Dodgers	1890	18 NL (1916,20,41,47,49,52-53,55-56, 59,63, 65-66,74,77-78, 81,88) 6 WS (1955,59,63,65,81,88)	• Brooklyn (1890-1957) Los Angeles (1958–)
Milwaukee Brewers	1969	1 AL (1982)	• Seattle (1969) Milwaukee (1970–)
Montreal Expos	1969	None	• Montreal (1969–)
New York Mets	1962	3 NL (1969,73,86) 2 WS (1969,86)	• New York (1962–)
Philadelphia Phillies	1883	5 NL (1915,50,80,83,93) 1 WS (1980)	• Philadelphia (1883–)
Pittsburgh Pirates	1887	7 NL (1903,09,25,27,60,71,79) 5 WS (1909,25,60,71,79)	• Pittsburgh (1887–)
St. Louis Cardinals	1892	15 NL (1926,28,30-31,34,42-44,46,64, 67-68,82,85,87) 9 WS (1926,31,34,42,44,46,64,67,82)	• St. Louis (1892–)
San Diego Padres	1969	2 NL (1984,98)	• San Diego (1969–)
San Francisco Giants	1883	16 NL (1905,11-13,17,21-24,33,36-37,51, 54,62,89) 5 WS (1905,21-22,33,54)	• New York (1883-1957) San Francisco (1958–)

American League

	1st Year	Pennants & World Series	Franchise Stops
Anaheim Angels	1961	None	• Los Angeles (1961-65) Anaheim, CA (1966–)
Baltimore Orioles	1901	7 AL (1944,66,69-71,79,83) 3 WS (1966,70,83)	• Milwaukee (1901) St. Louis (1902-53) Baltimore (1954–)
Boston Red Sox	1901	9 AL (1903,12,15-16,18,46,67,75,86) 5 WS (1903,12,15-16,18)	• Boston (1901–)
Chicago White Sox	1901	4 AL (1906,17,19,59) 2 WS (1906,17)	• Chicago (1901–)
Cleveland Indians	1901	5 AL (1920,48,54,95,97) 2 WS (1920,48)	• Cleveland (1901–)
Detroit Tigers	1901	9 AL (1907-09,34-35,40,45,68,84) 4 WS (1935,45,68,84)	• Detroit (1901–)
Kansas City Royals	1969	2 AL (1980,85) 1 WS (1985)	• Kansas City (1969–)
Minnesota Twins	1901	6 AL (1924-25,33,65,87,91) 3 WS (1924,87,91)	• Washington, DC (1901-60) Bloomington, MN (1961-81) Minneapolis (1982–)
New York Yankees	1901	35 AL (1921-23,26-28,32,36-39,41-43,47, 49-53,55-58,60-64,76-78,81,96,98) 24 WS (1923,27-28,32,36-39,41,43,47, 49-53,56,58,61-62,77-78,96,98)	• Baltimore (1901-02) New York (1903–)
Oakland Athletics	1901	14 AL (1905,10-11,13-14,29-31,72-74, 88-90) 9 WS (1910-11,13,29-30,72-74,89)	• Philadelphia (1901-54) Kansas City (1955-67) Oakland (1968–)
Seattle Mariners	1977	None	• Seattle (1977–)
Tampa Bay Devil Rays	1998	None	• Tampa Bay (1998–)
Texas Rangers	1961	None	• Washington, DC (1961-71) Arlington, TX (1972–)
Toronto Blue Jays	1977	2 AL (1992-93) 2 WS (1992-93)	• Toronto (1977–)

The Growth of Major League Baseball

The National League (founded in 1876) and the American League (founded in 1901) were both eight-team circuits at the turn of the century and remained that way until expansion finally came to Major League Baseball in the 1960s. The AL added two teams in 1961 and the NL did the same a year later. Both leagues went to 12 teams and split into two divisions in 1969. The AL then grew by two more teams in 1977, but the NL didn't follow suit until adding its 13th and 14th clubs in 1993. The NL added two teams in 1998 when the expansion Arizona Diamondbacks entered the league and the Milwaukee Brewers moved over from the AL.

Expansion Timetable (Since 1901)

1961—Los Angeles Angels (now Anaheim) and Washington Senators (now Texas Rangers) join AL; **1962**—Houston Colt .45s (now Astros) and New York Mets join NL; **1969**—Kansas City Royals and Seattle Pilots (now Milwaukee Brewers) join AL, while Montreal Expos and San Diego Padres join NL; **1977**—Seattle Mariners and Toronto Blue Jays join AL; **1993**—Colorado Rockies and Florida Marlins join NL; **1998**—Arizona Diamondbacks join NL and Tampa Bay Devil Rays join AL.

City and Nickname Changes

National League

1953—Boston Braves move to Milwaukee; **1958**—Brooklyn Dodgers move to Los Angeles and New York Giants move to San Francisco; **1965**—Houston Colt .45s renamed Astros; **1966**—Milwaukee Braves move to Atlanta.

Other nicknames: Boston (Beaneaters and Doves through 1908, and Bees from 1936-40); **Brooklyn** (Superbas through 1926, then Robins from 1927-31; then Dodgers from 1932-57); **Cincinnati** (Red Legs from 1944-45, then Redlegs from 1954-60, then Reds since 1961); **Philadelphia** (Blue Jays from 1943-44).

American League

1902—Milwaukee Brewers move to St. Louis and become Browns; **1903**—Baltimore Orioles move to New York and become Highlanders; **1913**—NY Highlanders renamed Yankees; **1954**—St. Louis Browns move to Baltimore and become Orioles; **1955**—Philadelphia Athletics move to Kansas City; **1961**—Washington Senators move to Bloomington, Minn., and become Minnesota Twins; **1965**—LA Angels renamed California Angels; **1966**—California Angels move to Anaheim; **1968**—KC Athletics move to Oakland and become A's; **1970**—Seattle Pilots move to Milwaukee and become Brewers; **1972**—Washington Senators move to Arlington, Texas, and become Rangers; **1982**—Minnesota Twins move to Minneapolis; **1987**—Oakland A's renamed Athletics; **1997**—California Angels renamed Anaheim Angels.

Other nicknames: Boston (Pilgrims, Puritans, Plymouth Rocks and Somersets through 1906); **Cleveland** (Broncos, Blues, Naps and Molly McGuires through 1914); **Washington** (Senators through 1904, then Nationals from 1905-44, then Senators again from 1945-60).

National League Pennant Winners from 1876-99

Founded in 1876, the National League played 24 seasons before the turn of the century and its eventual rivalry with the younger American League.

Multiple winners: Boston (8); Chicago (6); Baltimore (3); Brooklyn, New York and Providence (2).

Year		Year		Year		Year	
1876	Chicago	1882	Chicago	1888	New York	1894	Baltimore
1877	Boston	1883	Boston	1889	New York	1895	Baltimore
1878	Boston	1884	Providence	1890	Brooklyn	1896	Baltimore
1879	Providence	1885	Chicago	1891	Boston	1897	Boston
1880	Chicago	1886	Chicago	1892	Boston	1898	Boston
1881	Chicago	1887	Detroit	1893	Boston	1899	Brooklyn

Champions of Leagues That No Longer Exist

A Special Baseball Records Committee appointed by the commissioner found in 1968 that four extinct leagues qualified for major league status—the American Association (1882-91), the Union Association (1884), the Players' League (1890) and the Federal League (1914-15). The first years of the American League (1900) and Federal League (1913) were not recognized.

American Association

Year	Champion	Manager	Year	Champion	Manager	Year	Champion	Manager
1882	Cincinnati	Pop Snyder	1886	St. Louis	Charlie Comiskey	1890	Louisville	Jack Chapman
1883	Philadelphia	Lew Simmons	1887	St. Louis	Charlie Comiskey	1891	Boston	Arthur Irwin
1884	New York	Jim Mutrie	1888	St. Louis	Charlie Comiskey			
1885	St. Louis	Charlie Comiskey	1889	Brooklyn	Bill McGunnigle			

Union Association

Year	Champion	Manager
1884	St. Louis	Henry Lucas

Players' League

Year	Champion	Manager
1890	Boston	King Kelly

Federal League

Year	Champion	Manager
1914	Indianapolis	Bill Phillips
1915	Chicago	Joe Tinker

Annual Batting Leaders (since 1900)

Batting Average

National League

Multiple winners: Tony Gwynn and Honus Wagner (8); Rogers Hornsby and Stan Musial (7); Roberto Clemente and Bill Madlock (4); Pete Rose and Paul Waner (3); Hank Aaron, Richie Ashburn, Jake Daubert, Tommy Davis, Ernie Lombardi, Willie McGee, Lefty O'Doul, Dave Parker and Edd Roush (2).

Year		Avg
1900	Honus Wagner, Pit	.381
1901	Jesse Burkett, St.L	.382
1902	Ginger Beaumont, Pit	.357
1903	Honus Wagner, Pit	.355
1904	Honus Wagner, Pit	.349
1905	Cy Seymour, Cin	.377
1906	Honus Wagner, Pit	.339
1907	Honus Wagner, Pit	.350
1908	Honus Wagner, Pit	.354
1909	Honus Wagner, Pit	.339
1910	Sherry Magee, Phi	.331
1911	Honus Wagner, Pit	.334
1912	Heinie Zimmerman, Chi	.372
1913	Jake Daubert, Bklyn	.350
1914	Jake Daubert, Bklyn	.329
1915	Larry Doyle, NY	.320
1916	Hal Chase, Cin	.339
1917	Edd Roush, Cin	.341
1918	Zack Wheat, Bklyn	.335
1919	Edd Roush, Cin	.321
1920	Rogers Hornsby, St.L	.370
1921	Rogers Hornsby, St.L	.397
1922	Rogers Hornsby, St.L	.401
1923	Rogers Hornsby, St.L	.384
1924	Rogers Hornsby, St.L	.424
1925	Rogers Hornsby, St.L	.403
1926	Bubbles Hargrave, Cin	.353
1927	Paul Waner, Pit	.380
1928	Rogers Hornsby, Bos	.387
1929	Lefty O'Doul, Phi	.398
1930	Bill Terry, NY	.401
1931	Chick Hafey, St.L	.349
1932	Lefty O'Doul, Bklyn	.368
1933	Chuck Klein, Phi	.368
1934	Paul Waner, Pit	.362
1935	Arky Vaughan, Pit	.385
1936	Paul Waner, Pit	.373
1937	Joe Medwick, St.L	.374
1938	Ernie Lombardi, Cin	.342
1939	Johnny Mize, St.L	.349
1940	Debs Garms, Pit	.355
1941	Pete Reiser, Bklyn	.343
1942	Ernie Lombardi, Bos	.330
1943	Stan Musial, St.L	.357
1944	Dixie Walker, Bklyn	.357
1945	Phil Cavarretta, Chi	.355
1946	Stan Musial, St.L	.365
1947	Harry Walker, St.L-Phi	.363
1948	Stan Musial, St.L	.376
1949	Jackie Robinson, Bklyn	.342
1950	Stan Musial, St.L	.346
1951	Stan Musial, St.L	.355
1952	Stan Musial, St.L	.336
1953	Carl Furillo, Bklyn	.344
1954	Willie Mays, NY	.345
1955	Richie Ashburn, Phi	.338
1956	Hank Aaron, Mil	.328
1957	Stan Musial, St.L	.351
1958	Richie Ashburn, Phi	.350
1959	Hank Aaron, Mil	.355
1960	Dick Groat, Pit	.325
1961	Roberto Clemente, Pit	.351
1962	Tommy Davis, LA	.346
1963	Tommy Davis, LA	.326
1964	Roberto Clemente, Pit	.339
1965	Roberto Clemente, Pit	.329
1966	Matty Alou, Pit	.342
1967	Roberto Clemente, Pit	.357
1968	Pete Rose, Cin	.335
1969	Pete Rose, Cin	.348
1970	Rico Carty, Atl	.366
1971	Joe Torre, St.L	.363
1972	Billy Williams, Chi	.333
1973	Pete Rose, Cin	.338
1974	Ralph Garr, Atl	.353
1975	Bill Madlock, Chi	.354
1976	Bill Madlock, Chi	.339
1977	Dave Parker, Pit	.338
1978	Dave Parker, Pit	.334
1979	Keith Hernandez, St.L	.344
1980	Bill Buckner, Chi	.324
1981	Bill Madlock, Pit	.341
1982	Al Oliver, Mon	.331
1983	Bill Madlock, Pit	.323
1984	Tony Gwynn, SD	.351
1985	Willie McGee, St.L	.353
1986	Tim Raines, Mon	.334
1987	Tony Gwynn, SD	.370
1988	Tony Gwynn, SD	.313
1989	Tony Gwynn, SD	.336
1990	Willie McGee, St.L	.335
1991	Terry Pendleton, Atl	.319
1992	Gary Sheffield, SD	.330
1993	Andres Galarraga, Col	.370
1994	Tony Gwynn, SD	.394
1995	Tony Gwynn, SD	.368
1996	Tony Gwynn, SD	.353
1997	Tony Gwynn, SD	.372
1998	Larry Walker, Col.	.363

American League

Multiple winners: Ty Cobb (12); Rod Carew (7); Ted Williams (6); Wade Boggs (5); Harry Heilmann (4); George Brett, Nap Lajoie, Tony Oliva and Carl Yastrzemski (3); Luke Appling, Joe DiMaggio, Ferris Fain, Jimmie Foxx, Edgar Martinez, Pete Runnels, Al Simmons, George Sisler and Mickey Vernon (2).

Year		Avg
1901	Nap Lajoie, Phi	.422
1902	Ed Delahanty, Wash	.376
1903	Nap Lajoie, Cle	.355
1904	Nap Lajoie, Cle	.381
1905	Elmer Flick, Cle	.306
1906	George Stone, St.L	.358
1907	Ty Cobb, Det	.350
1908	Ty Cobb, Det	.324
1909	Ty Cobb, Det	.377
1910	Ty Cobb, Det	.385
1911	Ty Cobb, Det	.420
1912	Ty Cobb, Det	.410
1913	Ty Cobb, Det	.390
1914	Ty Cobb, Det	.368
1915	Ty Cobb, Det	.369
1916	Tris Speaker, Cle	.386
1917	Ty Cobb, Det	.383
1918	Ty Cobb, Det	.382
1919	Ty Cobb, Det	.384
1920	George Sisler, St.L	.407
1921	Harry Heilmann, Det	.394
1922	George Sisler, St.L	.420
1923	Harry Heilmann, Det	.403
1924	Babe Ruth, NY	.378
1925	Harry Heilmann, Det	.393
1926	Heinie Manush, Det	.378
1927	Harry Heilmann, Det	.398
1928	Goose Goslin, Wash	.379
1929	Lew Fonseca, Cle	.369
1930	Al Simmons, Phi	.381
1931	Al Simmons, Phi	.390
1932	Dale Alexander, Det-Bos	.367
1933	Jimmie Foxx, Phi	.356
1934	Lou Gehrig, NY	.363
1935	Buddy Myer, Wash	.349
1936	Luke Appling, Chi	.388
1937	Charlie Gehringer, Det	.371
1938	Jimmie Foxx, Bos	.349
1939	Joe DiMaggio, NY	.381
1940	Joe DiMaggio, NY	.352
1941	Ted Williams, Bos	.406
1942	Ted Williams, Bos	.356
1943	Luke Appling, Chi	.328
1944	Lou Boudreau, Clev	.327
1945	Snuffy Stirnweiss, NY	.309
1946	Mickey Vernon, Wash	.353
1947	Ted Williams, Bos	.343
1948	Ted Williams, Bos	.369
1949	George Kell, Det	.343
1950	Billy Goodman, Bos	.354
1951	Ferris Fain, Phi	.344
1952	Ferris Fain, Phi	.327
1953	Mickey Vernon, Wash	.337
1954	Bobby Avila, Clev	.341
1955	Al Kaline, Det	.340
1956	Mickey Mantle, NY	.353
1957	Ted Williams, Bos	.388
1958	Ted Williams, Bos	.328
1959	Harvey Kuenn, Det	.353
1960	Pete Runnels, Bos	.320
1961	Norm Cash, Det	.361*
1962	Pete Runnels, Bos	.326
1963	Carl Yastrzemski, Bos	.321
1964	Tony Oliva, Min	.323
1965	Tony Oliva, Min	.321
1966	Frank Robinson, Bal	.316
1967	Carl Yastrzemski, Bos	.326
1968	Carl Yastrzemski, Bos	.301

Year		Avg
1969	Rod Carew, Min	.332
1970	Alex Johnson, Cal	.329
1971	Tony Oliva, Min	.337
1972	Rod Carew, Min	.318
1973	Rod Carew, Min	.350
1974	Rod Carew, Min	.364
1975	Rod Carew, Min	.359
1976	George Brett, KC	.333
1977	Rod Carew, Min	.388
1978	Rod Carew, Min	.333
1979	Fred Lynn, Bos	.333
1980	George Brett, KC	.390
1981	Carney Lansford, Bos	.336
1982	Willie Wilson, KC	.332
1983	Wade Boggs, Bos	.361
1984	Don Mattingly, NY	.343
1985	Wade Boggs, Bos	.368
1986	Wade Boggs, Bos	.357
1987	Wade Boggs, Bos	.363
1988	Wade Boggs, Bos	.366
1989	Kirby Puckett, Min	.339
1990	George Brett, KC	.329
1991	Julio Franco, Tex	.341
1992	Edgar Martinez, Sea	.343
1993	John Olerud, Tor	.363
1994	Paul O'Neill, NY	.359
1995	Edgar Martinez, Sea	.356
1996	Alex Rodriguez, Sea	.358
1997	Frank Thomas, Chi	.347
1998	Bernie Williams, NY	.339

*Norm Cash later admitted to using a corked bat the entire season. He played 16 other seasons and never hit better than .286.

Home Runs

National League

Multiple winners: Mike Schmidt (8); Ralph Kiner (7); Gavvy Cravath and Mel Ott (6); Hank Aaron, Chuck Klein, Willie Mays, Johnny Mize, Cy Williams and Hack Wilson (4); Willie McCovey (3); Ernie Banks, Johnny Bench, George Foster, Rogers Hornsby, Tim Jordan, Dave Kingman, Eddie Mathews, Dale Murphy, Bill Nicholson, Dave Robertson, Wildfire Schulte and Willie Stargell (2).

Year		HR
1900	Herman Long, Bos	12
1901	Sam Crawford, Cin	16
1902	Tommy Leach, Pit	6
1903	Jimmy Sheckard, Bklyn	9
1904	Harry Lumley, Bklyn	9
1905	Fred Odwell, Cin.	9
1906	Tim Jordan, Bklyn	12
1907	Dave Brain, Bos	10
1908	Tim Jordan, Bklyn	12
1909	Red Murray, NY	7
1910	Fred Beck, Bos	10
	& Wildfire Schulte, Chi	10
1911	Wildfire Schulte, Chi	21
1912	Heinie Zimmerman, Chi	14
1913	Gavvy Cravath, Phi	19
1914	Gavvy Cravath, Phi	19
1915	Gavvy Cravath, Phi	24
1916	Cy Williams, Chi	12
	& Dave Robertson, NY	12
1917	Gavvy Cravath, Phi	12
	& Dave Robertson, NY	12
1918	Gavvy Cravath, Phi	8
1919	Gavvy Cravath, Phi	12
1920	Cy Williams, Phi	15
1921	George Kelly, NY	23
1922	Rogers Hornsby, St.L	42
1923	Cy Williams, Phi	41
1924	Jack Fournier, Bklyn	27
1925	Rogers Hornsby, St.L	39
1926	Hack Wilson, Chi	21
1927	Cy Williams, Phi	30
	& Hack Wilson, Chi	30
1928	Jim Bottomley, St.L	31
	& Hack Wilson, Chi	31
1929	Chuck Klein, Phi	43
1930	Hack Wilson, Chi	56
1931	Chuck Klein, Phi	31
1932	Chuck Klein, Phi	38
	& Mel Ott, NY	38
1933	Chuck Klein, Phi	28
1934	Rip Collins, St.L	35
	& Mel Ott, NY	35
1935	Wally Berger, Bos	34
1936	Mel Ott, NY	33
1937	Joe Medwick, St.L	31
	& Mel Ott, NY	31
1938	Mel Ott, NY	36
1939	Johnny Mize, St.L	28
1940	Johnny Mize, St.L	43
1941	Dolf Camilli, Bklyn	34
1942	Mel Ott, NY	30
1943	Bill Nicholson, Chi	29
1944	Bill Nicholson, Chi	33
1945	Tommy Holmes, Bos	28
1946	Ralph Kiner, Pit	23
1947	Ralph Kiner, Pit	51
	& Johnny Mize, NY	51
1948	Ralph Kiner, Pit	40
	& Johnny Mize, NY	40
1949	Ralph Kiner, Pit	54
1950	Ralph Kiner, Pit	47
1951	Ralph Kiner, Pit	42
1952	Ralph Kiner, Pit	37
	& Hank Sauer, Chi	37
1953	Eddie Mathews, Mil	47
1954	Ted Kluszewski, Cin	49
1955	Willie Mays, NY	51
1956	Duke Snider, Bklyn	43
1957	Hank Aaron, Mil	44
1958	Ernie Banks, Chi	47
1959	Eddie Mathews, Mil	46
1960	Ernie Banks, Chi	41
1961	Orlando Cepeda, SF	46
1962	Willie Mays, SF	49
1963	Hank Aaron, Mil	44
	& Willie McCovey, SF	44
1964	Willie Mays, SF	47
1965	Willie Mays, SF	52
1966	Hank Aaron, Atl	44
1967	Hank Aaron, Atl	39
1968	Willie McCovey, SF	36
1969	Willie McCovey, SF	45
1970	Johnny Bench, Cin	45
1971	Willie Stargell, Pit	48
1972	Johnny Bench, Cin	40
1973	Willie Stargell, Pit	44
1974	Mike Schmidt, Phi	36
1975	Mike Schmidt, Phi	38
1976	Mike Schmidt, Phi	38
1977	George Foster, Cin	52
1978	George Foster, Cin	40
1979	Dave Kingman, Chi	48
1980	Mike Schmidt, Phi	48
1981	Mike Schmidt, Phi	31
1982	Dave Kingman, NY	37
1983	Mike Schmidt, Phi	40
1984	Dale Murphy, Atl	36
	& Mike Schmidt, Phi	36
1985	Dale Murphy, Atl	37
1986	Mike Schmidt, Phi	37
1987	Andre Dawson, Chi	49
1988	Darryl Strawberry, NY	39
1989	Kevin Mitchell, SF	47
1990	Ryne Sandberg, Chi	40
1991	Howard Johnson, NY	38
1992	Fred McGriff, SD	35
1993	Barry Bonds, SF	46
1994	Matt Williams, SF	43
1995	Dante Bichette, Col	40
1996	Andres Galarraga, Col	47
1997	Larry Walker, Col	49
1998	Mark McGwire, St.L	70

Note: In 1997 Mark McGwire hit 58 home runs but hit 34 of them in the AL with Oakland before getting traded to St. Louis.

American League

Multiple winners: Babe Ruth (12); Harmon Killebrew (6); Home Run Baker, Harry Davis, Jimmie Foxx, Hank Greenberg, Reggie Jackson, Mickey Mantle and Ted Williams (4); Lou Gehrig, Ken Griffey Jr. and Jim Rice (3); Dick Allen, Tony Armas, Jose Canseco, Joe DiMaggio, Larry Doby, Cecil Fielder, Juan Gonzalez, Mark McGwire, Wally Pipp, Al Rosen and Gorman Thomas (2).

Year		HR
1901	Nap Lajoie, Phi	14
1902	Socks Seybold, Phi	16
1903	Buck Freeman, Bos	13
1904	Harry Davis, Phi	10
1905	Harry Davis, Phi	8
1906	Harry Davis, Phi	12
1907	Harry Davis, Phi	8
1908	Sam Crawford, Det	7
1909	Ty Cobb, Det	9

Year		HR
1910	Jake Stahl, Bos	10
1911	Home Run Baker, Phi	11
1912	Home Run Baker, Phi	10
	& Tris Speaker, Bos	10
1913	Home Run Baker, Phi	12
1914	Home Run Baker, Phi	9
1915	Braggo Roth, Chi-Cle	7
1916	Wally Pipp, NY	12
1917	Wally Pipp, NY	9
1918	Babe Ruth, Bos	11
	& Tilly Walker, Phi	11
1919	Babe Ruth, Bos	29
1920	Babe Ruth, NY	54
1921	Babe Ruth, NY	59
1922	Ken Williams, St.L	39
1923	Babe Ruth, NY	41
1924	Babe Ruth, NY	46
1925	Bob Meusel, NY	33
1926	Babe Ruth, NY	47
1927	Babe Ruth, NY	60
1928	Babe Ruth, NY	54
1929	Babe Ruth, NY	46
1930	Babe Ruth, NY	49
1931	Lou Gehrig, NY	46
	& Babe Ruth, NY	46
1932	Jimmie Foxx, Phi	58
1933	Jimmie Foxx, Phi	48
1934	Lou Gehrig, NY	49
1935	Jimmie Foxx, Phi	36
	& Hank Greenberg, Det	36
1936	Lou Gehrig, NY	49
1937	Joe DiMaggio, NY	46
1938	Hank Greenberg, Det	58
1939	Jimmie Foxx, Bos	35
1940	Hank Greenberg, Det	41
1941	Ted Williams, Bos	37
1942	Ted Williams, Bos	36
1943	Rudy York, Det	34
1944	Nick Etten, NY	22
1945	Vern Stephens, St.L	24
1946	Hank Greenberg, Det	44
1947	Ted Williams, Bos	32
1948	Joe DiMaggio, NY	39
1949	Ted Williams, Bos	43
1950	Al Rosen, Cle	37
1951	Gus Zernial, Chi-Phi	33
1952	Larry Doby, Cle	32
1953	Al Rosen, Cle	43
1954	Larry Doby, Cle	32
1955	Mickey Mantle, NY	37
1956	Mickey Mantle, NY	52
1957	Roy Sievers, Wash	42
1958	Mickey Mantle, NY	42
1959	Rocky Colavito, Cle	42
	& Harmon Killebrew, Wash	42
1960	Mickey Mantle, NY	40
1961	Roger Maris, NY	61
1962	Harmon Killebrew, Min	48
1963	Harmon Killebrew, Min	45
1964	Harmon Killebrew, Min	49
1965	Tony Conigliaro, Bos	32
1966	Frank Robinson, Bal	49
1967	Harmon Killebrew, Min	44
	& Carl Yastrzemski, Bos	44
1968	Frank Howard, Wash	44
1969	Harmon Killebrew, Min	49
1970	Frank Howard, Wash	44
1971	Bill Melton, Chi	33
1972	Dick Allen, Chi	37
1973	Reggie Jackson, Oak	32
1974	Dick Allen, Chi	32
1975	Reggie Jackson, Oak	36
	& George Scott, Mil	36
1976	Graig Nettles, NY	32
1977	Jim Rice, Bos	39
1978	Jim Rice, Bos	46
1979	Gorman Thomas, Mil	45
1980	Reggie Jackson, NY	41
	& Ben Oglivie, Mil	41
1981	Tony Armas, Oak	22
	Dwight Evans, Bos	22
	Bobby Grich, Cal	22
	& Eddie Murray, Bal	22
1982	Reggie Jackson, Cal	39
	& Gorman Thomas, Mil	39
1983	Jim Rice, Bos	39
1984	Tony Armas, Bos	43
1985	Darrell Evans, Det	40
1986	Jesse Barfield, Tor	40
1987	Mark McGwire, Oak	49
1988	Jose Canseco, Oak	42
1989	Fred McGriff, Tor	36
1990	Cecil Fielder, Det	51
1991	Jose Canseco, Oak	44
	& Cecil Fielder, Det	44
1992	Juan Gonzalez, Tex	43
1993	Juan Gonzalez, Tex	46
1994	Ken Griffey Jr., Sea	40
1995	Albert Belle, Cle	50
1996	Mark McGwire, Oak	52
1997	Ken Griffey Jr., Sea	56
1998	Ken Griffey Jr., Sea	56

Note: In 1997 Mark McGwire hit 58 home runs but hit 24 of them in the NL with St. Louis after getting traded from Oakland.

Runs Batted In

National League

Multiple winners: Hank Aaron, Rogers Hornsby, Sherry Magee, Mike Schmidt and Honus Wagner (4); Johnny Bench, George Foster, Joe Medwick, Johnny Mize and Heinie Zimmerman (3); Ernie Banks, Jim Bottomley, Orlando Cepeda, Gavvy Cravath, Andres Galarraga, George Kelly, Chuck Klein, Willie McCovey, Dale Murphy, Stan Musial, Bill Nicholson and Hack Wilson (2).

Year		RBI
1900	Elmer Flick, Phi	110
1901	Honus Wagner, Pit	126
1902	Honus Wagner, Pit	91
1903	Sam Mertes, NY	104
1904	Bill Dahlen, NY	80
1905	Cy Seymour, Cin	121
1906	Jim Nealon, Pit	83
	& Harry Steinfeldt, Chi	83
1907	Sherry Magee, Phi	85
1908	Honus Wagner, Pit	109
1909	Honus Wagner, Pit	100
1910	Sherry Magee, Phi	123
1911	Wildfire Schulte, Chi	121
1912	Heinie Zimmerman, Chi	103
1913	Gavvy Cravath, Phi	128
1914	Sherry Magee, Phi	103
1915	Gavvy Cravath, Phi	115
1916	Heinie Zimmerman, Chi-NY	83
1917	Heinie Zimmerman, NY	102
1918	Sherry Magee, Cin	76
1919	Hy Myers, Bklyn	73
1920	Rogers Hornsby, St.L	94
	& George Kelly, NY	94
1921	Rogers Hornsby, St.L	126
1922	Rogers Hornsby, St.L	152
1923	Irish Meusel, NY	125
1924	George Kelly, NY	136
1925	Rogers Hornsby, St.L	143
1926	Jim Bottomley, St.L	120
1927	Paul Waner, Pit	131
1928	Jim Bottomley, St.L	136
1929	Hack Wilson, Chi	159
1930	Hack Wilson, Chi	190
1931	Chuck Klein, Phi	121
1932	Don Hurst, Phi	143
1933	Chuck Klein, Phi	120
1934	Mel Ott, NY	135
1935	Wally Berger, Bos	130
1936	Joe Medwick, St.L	138
1937	Joe Medwick, St.L	154
1938	Joe Medwick, St.L	122
1939	Frank McCormick, Cin	128
1940	Johnny Mize, St.L	137
1941	Dolph Camilli, Bklyn	120
1942	Johnny Mize, NY	110
1943	Bill Nicholson, Chi	128
1944	Bill Nicholson, Chi	122
1945	Dixie Walker, Bklyn	124
1946	Enos Slaughter, St.L	130
1947	Johnny Mize, NY	138
1948	Stan Musial, St.L	131
1949	Ralph Kiner, Pit	127
1950	Del Ennis, Phi	126
1951	Monte Irvin, NY	121
1952	Hank Sauer, Chi	121
1953	Roy Campanella, Bklyn	142
1954	Ted Kluszewski, Cin	141
1955	Duke Snider, Bklyn	136
1956	Stan Musial, St.L	109
1957	Hank Aaron, Mil	132
1958	Ernie Banks, Chi	129
1959	Ernie Banks, Chi	143
1960	Hank Aaron, Mil	126
1961	Orlando Cepeda, SF	142
1962	Tommy Davis, LA	153
1963	Hank Aaron, Mil	130
1964	Ken Boyer, St.L	119
1965	Deron Johnson, Cin	130
1966	Hank Aaron, Atl	127
1967	Orlando Cepeda, St.L	111
1968	Willie McCovey, SF	105
1969	Willie McCovey, SF	126
1970	Johnny Bench, Cin	148
1971	Joe Torre, St.L	137
1972	Johnny Bench, Cin	125
1973	Willie Stargell, Pit	119

Year		RBI
1974	Johnny Bench, Cin	129
1975	Greg Luzinski, Phi	120
1976	George Foster, Cin	121
1977	George Foster, Cin	149
1978	George Foster, Cin	120
1979	Dave Winfield, SD	118
1980	Mike Schmidt, Phi	121
1981	Mike Schmidt, Phi	91
1982	Dale Murphy, Atl	109
	& Al Oliver, Mon	109
1983	Dale Murphy, Atl	121
1984	Gary Carter, Mon	106
	& Mike Schmidt, Phi	106
1985	Dave Parker, Cin	125
1986	Mike Schmidt, Phi	119
1987	Andre Dawson, Chi	137
1988	Will Clark, SF	109
1989	Kevin Mitchell, SF	125
1990	Matt Williams, SF	122
1991	Howard Johnson, NY	117
1992	Darren Daulton, Phi	109
1993	Barry Bonds, SF	123
1994	Jeff Bagwell, Hou	116
1995	Dante Bichette, Col	128
1996	Andres Galarraga, Col	150
1997	Andres Galarraga, Col	140
1998	Sammy Sosa, Chi	158

American League

Multiple winners: Babe Ruth (6); Lou Gehrig (5); Ty Cobb, Hank Greenberg and Ted Williams (4); Albert Belle, Sam Crawford, Cecil Fielder, Jimmie Foxx, Jackie Jensen, Harmon Killebrew, Vern Stephens and Bobby Veach (3); Home Run Baker, Cecil Cooper, Harry Davis, Joe DiMaggio, Buck Freeman, Nap Lajoie, Roger Maris, Jim Rice, Al Rosen, and Bobby Veach (2).

Year		RBI
1901	Nap Lajoie, Phi	125
1902	Buck Freeman, Bos	121
1903	Buck Freeman, Bos	104
1904	Nap Lajoie, Cle	102
1905	Harry Davis, Phi	83
1906	Harry Davis, Phi	96
1907	Ty Cobb, Det	116
1908	Ty Cobb, Det	108
1909	Ty Cobb, Det	107
1910	Sam Crawford, Det	120
1911	Ty Cobb, Det	144
1912	Home Run Baker, Phi	133
1913	Home Run Baker, Phi	126
1914	Sam Crawford, Det	104
1915	Sam Crawford, Det	112
	& Bobby Veach, Det	112
1916	Del Pratt, St.L	103
1917	Bobby Veach, Det	103
1918	Bobby Veach, Det	78
1919	Babe Ruth, Bos	114
1920	Babe Ruth, NY	137
1921	Babe Ruth, NY	171
1922	Ken Williams, St.L	155
1923	Babe Ruth, NY	131
1924	Goose Goslin, Wash	129
1925	Bob Meusel, NY	138
1926	Babe Ruth, NY	145
1927	Lou Gehrig, NY	175
1928	Lou Gehrig, NY	142
	& Babe Ruth, NY	142
1929	Al Simmons, Phi	157
1930	Lou Gehrig, NY	174
1931	Lou Gehrig, NY	184
1932	Jimmie Foxx, Phi	169
1933	Jimmie Foxx, Phi	163
1934	Lou Gehrig, NY	165
1935	Hank Greenberg, Det	170
1936	Hal Trosky, Cle	162
1937	Hank Greenberg, Det	183
1938	Jimmie Foxx, Bos	175
1939	Ted Williams, Bos	145
1940	Hank Greenberg, Det	150
1941	Joe DiMaggio, NY	125
1942	Ted Williams, Bos	137
1943	Rudy York, Det	118
1944	Vern Stephens, St.L	109
1945	Nick Etten, NY	111
1946	Hank Greenberg, Det	127
1947	Ted Williams, Bos	114
1948	Joe DiMaggio, NY	155
1949	Ted Williams, Bos	159
	& Vern Stephens, Bos	159
1950	Walt Dropo, Bos	144
	& Vern Stephens, Bos	144
1951	Gus Zernial, Chi-Phi	129
1952	Al Rosen, Cle	105
1953	Al Rosen, Cle	145
1954	Larry Doby, Cle	126
1955	Ray Boone, Det	116
	& Jackie Jensen, Bos	116
1956	Mickey Mantle, NY	130
1957	Roy Sievers, Wash	114
1958	Jackie Jensen, Bos	122
1959	Jackie Jensen, Bos	112
1960	Roger Maris, NY	112
1961	Roger Maris, NY	142
1962	Harmon Killebrew, Min	126
1963	Dick Stuart, Bos	118
1964	Brooks Robinson, Bal	118
1965	Rocky Colavito, Cle	108
1966	Frank Robinson, Bal	122
1967	Carl Yastrzemski, Bos	121
1968	Ken Harrelson, Bos	109
1969	Harmon Killebrew, Min	140
1970	Frank Howard, Wash	126
1971	Harmon Killebrew, Min	119
1972	Dick Allen, Chi	113
1973	Reggie Jackson, Oak	117
1974	Jeff Burroughs, Tex	118
1975	George Scott, Mil	109
1976	Lee May, Bal	109
1977	Larry Hisle, Min	119
1978	Jim Rice, Bos	139
1979	Don Baylor, Cal	139
1980	Cecil Cooper, Mil	122
1981	Eddie Murray, Bal	78
1982	Hal McRae, KC	133
1983	Cecil Cooper, Mil	126
	& Jim Rice, Bos	126
1984	Tony Armas, Bos	123
1985	Don Mattingly, NY	145
1986	Joe Carter, Cle	121
1987	George Bell, Tor	134
1988	Jose Canseco, Oak	124
1989	Ruben Sierra, Tex	119
1990	Cecil Fielder, Det	132
1991	Cecil Fielder, Det	133
1992	Cecil Fielder, Det	124
1993	Albert Belle, Cle	129
1994	Kirby Puckett, Min	112
1995	Albert Belle, Cle	126
	& Mo Vaughn, Bos	126
1996	Albert Belle, Cle	148
1997	Ken Griffey Jr., Sea	147
1998	Juan Gonzalez, Tex	157

Batting Triple Crown Winners

Players who led either league in Batting Average, Home Runs and Runs Batted In over a single season.

National League

	Year	Avg	HR	RBI
Paul Hines, Providence	1878	.358	4	50
Hugh Duffy, Boston	1894	.438	18	145
Heinie Zimmerman, Chicago	1912	.372	14	103
Rogers Hornsby, St. Louis	1922	.401	42	152
Rogers Hornsby, St. Louis	1925	.403	39	143
Chuck Klein, Philadelphia	1933	.368	28	120
Joe Medwick, St. Louis	1937	.374	31*	154

*Tied for league lead in HRs with Mel Ott, NY.

American League

	Year	Avg	HR	RBI
Nap Lajoie, Philadelphia	1901	.422	14	125
Ty Cobb, Detroit	1909	.377	9	115
Jimmie Foxx, Philadelphia	1933	.356	48	163
Lou Gehrig, New York	1934	.363	49	165
Ted Williams, Boston	1942	.356	36	137
Ted Williams, Boston	1947	.343	32	114
Mickey Mantle, New York	1956	.353	52	130
Frank Robinson, Baltimore	1966	.316	49	122
Carl Yastrzemski, Boston	1967	.326	44*	121

*Tied for league lead in HRs with Harmon Killebrew, Min.

Stolen Bases

National League

Multiple winners: Max Carey (10); Lou Brock (8); Vince Coleman and Maury Wills (6); Honus Wagner (5); Bob Bescher, Kiki Cuyler, Willie Mays and Tim Raines (4); Bill Bruton, Frankie Frisch and Pepper Martin (3); George Burns, Frank Chance, Augie Galan, Marquis Grissom, Stan Hack, Sam Jethroe, Davey Lopes, Omar Moreno, Pete Reiser, Jackie Robinson and Tony Womack (2).

Year		SB
1900	Patsy Donovan, St.L	45
	& George Van Haltren, NY	45
1901	Honus Wagner, Pit	49
1902	Honus Wagner, Pit	42
1903	Frank Chance, Chi	67
	& Jimmy Sheckard, Bklyn	67
1904	Honus Wagner, Pit	53
1905	Art Devlin, NY	59
	& Billy Maloney, Chi	59
1906	Frank Chance, Chi	57
1907	Honus Wagner, Pit	61
1908	Honus Wagner, Pit	53
1909	Bob Bescher, Cin	54
1910	Bob Bescher, Cin	70
1911	Bob Bescher, Cin	81
1912	Bob Bescher, Cin	67
1913	Max Carey, Pit	61
1914	George Burns, NY	62
1915	Max Carey, Pit	36
1916	Max Carey, Pit	63
1917	Max Carey, Pit	46
1918	Max Carey, Pit	58
1919	George Burns, NY	40
1920	Max Carey, Pit	52
1921	Frankie Frisch, NY	49
1922	Max Carey, Pit	51
1923	Max Carey, Pit	51
1924	Max Carey, Pit	49
1925	Max Carey, Pit	46
1926	Kiki Cuyler, Pit	35
1927	Frankie Frisch, St.L	48
1928	Kiki Cuyler, Chi	37
1929	Kiki Cuyler, Chi	43
1930	Kiki Cuyler, Chi	37
1931	Frankie Frisch, St.L	28
1932	Chuck Klein, Phi	20
1933	Pepper Martin, St.L	26
1934	Pepper Martin, St.L	23
1935	Augie Galan, Chi	22
1936	Pepper Martin, St.L	23
1937	Augie Galan, Chi	23
1938	Stan Hack, Chi	16
1939	Stan Hack, Chi	17
	& Lee Handley, Pit	17
1940	Lonny Frey, Cin	22
1941	Danny Murtaugh, Phi	18
1942	Pete Reiser, Bklyn	20
1943	Arky Vaughan, Bklyn	20
1944	Johnny Barrett, Pit	28
1945	Red Schoendienst, St.L	26
1946	Pete Reiser, Bklyn	34
1947	Jackie Robinson, Bklyn	29
1948	Richie Ashburn, Phi	32
1949	Jackie Robinson, Bklyn	37
1950	Sam Jethroe, Bos	35
1951	Sam Jethroe, Bos	35
1952	Pee Wee Reese, Bklyn	30
1953	Bill Bruton, Mil	26
1954	Bill Bruton, Mil	34
1955	Bill Bruton, Mil	25
1956	Willie Mays, NY	40
1957	Willie Mays, NY	38
1958	Willie Mays, SF	31
1959	Willie Mays, SF	27
1960	Maury Wills, LA	50
1961	Maury Wills, LA	35
1962	Maury Wills, LA	104
1963	Maury Wills, LA	40
1964	Maury Wills, LA	53
1965	Maury Wills, LA	94
1966	Lou Brock, St.L	74
1967	Lou Brock, St.L	52
1968	Lou Brock, St.L	62
1969	Lou Brock, St.L	53
1970	Bobby Tolan, Cin	57
1971	Lou Brock, St.L	64
1972	Lou Brock, St.L	63
1973	Lou Brock, St.L	70
1974	Lou Brock, St.L	118
1975	Davey Lopes, LA	77
1976	Davey Lopes, LA	63
1977	Frank Taveras, Pit	70
1978	Omar Moreno, Pit	71
1979	Omar Moreno, Pit	77
1980	Ron LeFlore, Mon	97
1981	Tim Raines, Mon	71
1982	Tim Raines, Mon	78
1983	Tim Raines, Mon	90
1984	Tim Raines, Mon	75
1985	Vince Coleman, St.L	110
1986	Vince Coleman, St.L	107
1987	Vince Coleman, St.L	109
1988	Vince Coleman, St.L	81
1989	Vince Coleman, St.L	65
1990	Vince Coleman, St.L	77
1991	Marquis Grissom, Mon	76
1992	Marquis Grissom, Mon	78
1993	Chuck Carr, Fla	58
1994	Craig Biggio, Hou	39
1995	Quilvio Veras, Fla	56
1996	Eric Young, Col	53
1997	Tony Womack, Pit	60
1998	Tony Womack, Pit	58

30 Homers & 30 Stolen Bases in One Season

National League

	Year	Gm	HR	SB
Willie Mays, NY Giants	1956	152	36	40
Willie Mays, NY Giants	1957	152	35	38
Hank Aaron, Milwaukee	1963	161	44	31
Bobby Bonds, San Francisco	1969	158	32	45
Bobby Bonds, San Francisco	1973	160	39	43
Dale Murphy, Atlanta	1983	162	36	30
Eric Davis, Cincinnati	1987	129	37	50
Howard Johnson, NY Mets	1987	157	36	32
Darryl Strawberry, NY Mets	1987	154	39	36
Howard Johnson, NY Mets	1989	153	36	41
Ron Gant, Atlanta	1990	152	32	33
Barry Bonds, Pittsburgh	1990	151	33	52
Ron Gant, Atlanta	1991	154	32	34
Howard Johnson, NY Mets	1991	156	38	30
Barry Bonds, Pittsburgh	1992	140	34	39
Sammy Sosa, Chicago	1993	159	33	36
Barry Bonds, San Francisco	1995	144	33	31
Sammy Sosa, Chicago	1995	144	36	34
Barry Bonds, San Francisco	1996	158	42	40
Ellis Burks, Colorado	1996	156	40	32
Dante Bichette, Colorado	1996	159	31	31
Larry Walker, Colorado	1997	153	49	33
Barry Bonds, San Francisco	1997	159	40	37
Raul Mondesi, Los Angeles	1997	159	30	32
Jeff Bagwell, Houston	1997	162	43	31

American League

	Year	Gm	HR	SB
Kenny Williams, St. Louis	1922	153	39	37
Tommy Harper, Milwaukee	1970	154	31	38
Bobby Bonds, New York	1975	145	32	30
Bobby Bonds, California	1977	158	37	41
Bobby Bonds, Chicago-Texas	1978	156	31	43
Joe Carter, Cleveland	1987	149	32	31
Jose Canseco, Oakland	1988	158	42	40
Alex Rodriguez, Seattle	1998	161	42	46
Shawn Green, Toronto	1998	158	35	35

American League

Multiple winners: Rickey Henderson (12); Luis Aparicio (9); Bert Campaneris, George Case and Ty Cobb (6); Kenny Lofton (5); Ben Chapman, Eddie Collins and George Sisler (4); Bob Dillinger, Minnie Minoso and Bill Werber (3); Elmer Flick, Tommy Harper, Clyde Milan, Johnny Mostil, Bill North and Snuffy Stirnweiss (2).

Year		SB
1901	Frank Isbell, Chi	52
1902	Topsy Hartsel, Phi	47
1903	Harry Bay, Cle	45
1904	Elmer Flick, Cle	42
1905	Danny Hoffman, Phi	46
1906	John Anderson, Wash	39
	& Elmer Flick, Cle	39
1907	Ty Cobb, Det	49
1908	Patsy Dougherty, Chi	47
1909	Ty Cobb, Det	76
1910	Eddie Collins, Phi	81
1911	Ty Cobb, Det	83
1912	Clyde Milan, Wash	88
1913	Clyde Milan, Wash	75
1914	Fritz Maisel, NY	74
1915	Ty Cobb, Det	96
1916	Ty Cobb, Det	68
1917	Ty Cobb, Det	55
1918	George Sisler, St.L	45
1919	Eddie Collins, Chi	33
1920	Sam Rice, Wash	63
1921	George Sisler, St.L	35
1922	George Sisler, St.L	51
1923	Eddie Collins, Chi	47
1924	Eddie Collins, Chi	42
1925	Johnny Mostil, Chi	43
1926	Johnny Mostil, Chi	35
1927	George Sisler, St.L	27
1928	Buddy Myer, Bos	30
1929	Charlie Gehringer, Det	28
1930	Marty McManus, Det	23
1931	Ben Chapman, NY	61
1932	Ben Chapman, NY	38
1933	Ben Chapman, NY	27

Year		SB
1934	Bill Werber, Bos	40
1935	Bill Werber, Bos	29
1936	Lyn Lary, St.L	37
1937	Ben Chapman, Wash-Bos	35
	& Bill Werber, Phi	35
1938	Frank Crosetti, NY	27
1939	George Case, Wash	51
1940	George Case, Wash	35
1941	George Case, Wash	33
1942	George Case, Wash	44
1943	George Case, Wash	61
1944	Snuffy Stirnweiss, NY	55
1945	Snuffy Stirnweiss, NY	33
1946	George Case, Cle	28
1947	Bob Dillinger, St.L	34
1948	Bob Dillinger, St.L	28
1949	Bob Dillinger, St.L	20
1950	Dom DiMaggio, Bos	15
1951	Minnie Minoso, Cle-Chi	31
1952	Minnie Minoso, Chi	22
1953	Minnie Minoso, Chi	25
1954	Jackie Jensen, Bos	22
1955	Jim Rivera, Chi	25
1956	Luis Aparicio, Chi	21
1957	Luis Aparicio, Chi	28
1958	Luis Aparicio, Chi	29
1959	Luis Aparicio, Chi	56
1960	Luis Aparicio, Chi	51
1961	Luis Aparicio, Chi	53
1962	Luis Aparicio, Chi	31
1963	Luis Aparicio, Bal	40
1964	Luis Aparicio, Bal	57
1965	Bert Campaneris, KC	51
1966	Bert Campaneris, KC	52

Year		SB
1967	Bert Campaneris, KC	55
1968	Bert Campaneris, Oak	62
1969	Tommy Harper, Sea	73
1970	Bert Campaneris, Oak	42
1971	Amos Otis, KC	52
1972	Bert Campaneris, Oak	52
1973	Tommy Harper, Bos	54
1974	Bill North, Oak	54
1975	Mickey Rivers, CA	70
1976	Bill North, Oak	75
1977	Freddie Patek, KC	53
1978	Ron LeFlore, Det	68
1979	Willie Wilson, KC	83
1980	Rickey Henderson, Oak	100
1981	Rickey Henderson, Oak	56
1982	Rickey Henderson, Oak	130
1983	Rickey Henderson, Oak	108
1984	Rickey Henderson, Oak	66
1985	Rickey Henderson, NY	80
1986	Rickey Henderson, NY	87
1987	Harold Reynolds, Sea	60
1988	Rickey Henderson, NY	93
1989	R. Henderson, NY-Oak	77
1990	Rickey Henderson, Oak	65
1991	Rickey Henderson, Oak	58
1992	Kenny Lofton, Cle	66
1993	Kenny Lofton, Cle	70
1994	Kenny Lofton, Cle	60
1995	Kenny Lofton, Cle	54
1996	Kenny Lofton, Cle	75
1997	Brian Hunter, Det	74
1998	Rickey Henderson, Oak	66

Consecutive Game Streaks

Regular season games through 1998.

Games Played

Gm		Dates of Streak		
2632	Cal Ripken Jr., Bal	5/30/82	to	9/19/98
2130	Lou Gehrig, NY	6/1/25	to	4/30/39
1307	Everett Scott, Bos-NY	6/20/16	to	5/5/25
1207	Steve Garvey, LA-SD	9/3/75	to	7/29/83
1117	Billy Williams, Cubs	9/22/63	to	9/2/70
1103	Joe Sewell, Cle	9/13/22	to	4/30/30
895	Stan Musial, St.L	4/15/52	to	8/23/57
829	Eddie Yost, Wash	4/30/49	to	5/11/55
822	Gus Suhr, Pit	9/11/31	to	6/4/37
798	Nellie Fox, Chisox	8/8/55	to	9/3/60
745	Pete Rose, Cin-Phi	9/2/78	to	8/23/83
740	Dale Murphy, Atl	9/26/81	to	7/8/86
730	Richie Ashburn, Phi	6/7/50	to	4/13/55
717	Ernie Banks, Cubs	8/28/56	to	6/22/61
678	Pete Rose, Cin	9/28/73	to	5/7/78

Others

Gm		Gm	
673	Earl Averill	565	Aaron Ward
652	Frank McCormick	540	Candy LaChance
648	Sandy Alomar Sr.	535	Buck Freeman
618	Eddie Brown	533	Fred Luderus
585	Roy McMillan	511	Clyde Milan
577	George Pinckney	511	Charlie Gehringer
574	Steve Brodie	508	Vada Pinson

Hitting

	Gm	Year
Joe DiMaggio, New York (AL)	56	1941
Willie Keeler, Baltimore (NL)	44	1897
Pete Rose, Cincinnati (NL)	44	1978
Bill Dahlen, Chicago (NL)	42	1894
George Sisler, St. Louis (AL)	41	1922
Ty Cobb, Detroit (AL)	40	1911
Paul Molitor, Milwaukee (AL)	39	1987
Tommy Holmes, Boston (NL)	37	1945
Billy Hamilton, Philadelphia (NL)	36	1894
Fred Clarke, Louisville (NL)	35	1895
Ty Cobb, Detroit (AL)	35	1917
Ty Cobb, Detroit (AL)	34	1912
George Sisler, St. Louis (AL)	34	1925
George McQuinn, St. Louis (AL)	34	1938
Dom DiMaggio, Boston (AL)	34	1949
Benito Santiago, San Diego (NL)	34	1987
George Davis, New York (NL)	33	1893
Hal Chase, New York (AL)	33	1907
Rogers Hornsby, St. Louis (NL)	33	1922
Heinie Manush, Washington (AL)	33	1933
Ed Delahanty, Philadelphia (NL)	31	1899
Nap Lajoie, Cleveland (AL)	31	1906
Sam Rice, Washington, (AL)	31	1924
Willie Davis, Los Angeles (NL)	31	1969
Rico Carty, Atlanta (NL)	31	1970
Ken Landreaux, Minnesota (AL)	31	1980

Annual Pitching Leaders (since 1900)

Winning Percentage

At least 15 wins, except in strike years of 1981 and 1994 (when the minimum was 10).

National League

Multiple winners: Ed Reulbach and Tom Seaver (3); Larry Benton, Harry Brecheen, Jack Chesbro, Paul Derringer, Freddie Fitzsimmons, Don Gullett, Claude Hendrix, Carl Hubbell, Sandy Koufax, Bill Lee, Greg Maddux, Christy Mathewson, Don Newcombe, Preacher Roe and John Smoltz (2).

Year		W-L	Pct
1900	Jesse Tannehill, Pittsburgh	20-6	.769
1901	Jack Chesbro, Pittsburgh	21-10	.677
1902	Jack Chesbro, Pittsburgh	28-6	.824
1903	Sam Leever, Pittsburgh	25-7	.781
1904	Joe McGinnity, New York	35-8	.814
1905	Christy Mathewson, New York	31-8	.795
1906	Ed Reulbach, Chicago	19-4	.826
1907	Ed Reulbach, Chicago	17-4	.810
1908	Ed Reulbach, Chicago	24-7	.774
1909	Howie Camnitz, Pittsburgh	25-6	.806
	& Christy Mathewson, New York	25-6	.806
1910	King Cole, Chicago	20-4	.833
1911	Rube Marquard, New York	24-7	.774
1912	Claude Hendrix, Pittsburgh	24-9	.727
1913	Bert Humphries, Chicago	16-4	.800
1914	Bill James, Boston	26-7	.788
1915	Grover Alexander, Phila.	31-10	.756
1916	Tom Hughes, Boston	16-3	.842
1917	Ferdie Schupp, New York	21-7	.750
1918	Claude Hendrix, Chicago	19-7	.731
1919	Dutch Ruether, Cincinnati	19-6	.760
1920	Burleigh Grimes, Brooklyn	23-11	.676
1921	Bill Doak, St. Louis	15-6	.714
1922	Pete Donohue, Cincinnati	18-9	.667
1923	Dolf Luque, Cincinnati	27-8	.771
1924	Emil Yde, Pittsburgh	16-3	.842
1925	Bill Sherdel, St. Louis	15-6	.714
1926	Ray Kremer, Pittsburgh	20-6	.769
1927	Larry Benton, Boston-NY	17-7	.708
1928	Larry Benton, New York	25-9	.735
1929	Charlie Root, Chicago	19-6	.760
1930	Freddie Fitzsimmons, NY	19-7	.731
1931	Paul Derringer, St. Louis	18-8	.692
1932	Lon Warneke, Chicago	22-6	.786
1933	Ben Cantwell, Boston	20-10	.667
1934	Dizzy Dean, St. Louis	30-7	.811
1935	Bill Lee, Chicago	20-6	.769
1936	Carl Hubbell, New York	26-6	.813
1937	Carl Hubbell, New York	22-8	.733
1938	Bill Lee, Chicago	22-9	.710
1939	Paul Derringer, Cincinnati	25-7	.781
1940	Freddie Fitzsimmons, Bklyn	16-2	.889
1941	Elmer Riddle, Cincinnati	19-4	.826
1942	Larry French, Brooklyn	15-4	.789
1943	Mort Cooper, St. Louis	21-8	.724
1944	Ted Wilks, St. Louis	17-4	.810
1945	Harry Brecheen, St. Louis	14-4	.778
1946.	Murray Dickson, St. Louis	15-6	.714
1947	Larry Jansen, New York	21-5	.808
1948	Harry Brecheen, St. Louis	20-7	.741
1949	Preacher Roe, Brooklyn	15-6	.714
1950	Sal Maglie, New York	18-4	.818
1951	Preacher Roe, Brooklyn	22-3	.880
1952	Hoyt Wilhelm, New York	15-3	.833
1953	Carl Erskine, Brooklyn	20-6	.769
1954	Johnny Antonelli, New York	21-7	.750
1955	Don Newcombe, Brooklyn	20-5	.800
1956	Don Newcombe, Brooklyn	27-7	.794
1957	Bob Buhl, Milwaukee	18-7	.720
1958	Warren Spahn, Milwaukee	22-11	.667
	& Lew Burdette, Milwaukee	20-10	.667
1959	Roy Face, Pittsburgh	18-1	.947
1960	Ernie Broglio, St. Louis	21-9	.700
1961	Johnny Podres, Los Angeles	18-5	.783
1962	Bob Purkey, Cincinnati	23-5	.821
1963	Ron Perranoski, Los Angeles	16-3	.842
1964	Sandy Koufax, Los Angeles	19-5	.792
1965	Sandy Koufax, Los Angeles	26-8	.765
1966	Juan Marichal, San Francisco	25-6	.806
1967	Dick Hughes, St. Louis	16-6	.727
1968	Steve Blass, Pittsburgh	18-6	.750
1969	Tom Seaver, New York	25-7	.781
1970	Bob Gibson, St. Louis	23-7	.767
1971	Don Gullett, Cincinnati	16-6	.727
1972	Gary Nolan, Cincinnati	15-5	.750
1973	Tommy John, Los Angeles	16-7	.696
1974	Andy Messersmith, Los Angeles	20-6	.769
1975	Don Gullett, Cincinnati	15-4	.789
1976	Steve Carlton, Philadelphia	20-7	.741
1977	John Candelaria, Pittsburgh	20-5	.800
1978	Gaylord Perry, San Diego	21-6	.778
1979	Tom Seaver, Cincinnati	16-6	.727
1980	Jim Bibby, Pittsburgh	19-6	.760
1981	Tom Seaver, Cincinnati	14-2	.875
1982	Phil Niekro, Atlanta	17-4	.810
1983	John Denny, Philadelphia	19-6	.760
1984	Rick Sutcliffe, Chicago	16-1	.941
1985	Orel Hershiser, Los Angeles	19-3	.864
1986	Bob Ojeda, New York	18-5	.783
1987	Dwight Gooden, New York	15-7	.682
1988	David Cone, New York	20-3	.870
1989	Mike Bielecki, Chicago	18-7	.720
1990	Doug Drabek, Pittsburgh	22-6	.786
1991	John Smiley, Pittsburgh	20-8	.714
	& Jose Rijo, Cincinnati	15-6	.714
1992	Bob Tewksbury, St. Louis	16-5	.762
1993	Mark Portugal, Houston	18-4	.818
1994	Marvin Freeman, Colorado	10-2	.833
1995	Greg Maddux, Atlanta	19-2	.905
1996	John Smoltz, Atlanta	24-8	.750
1997	Greg Maddux, Atlanta	19-4	.826
1998	John Smoltz, Atlanta	17-3	.850

Note: In 1984, Sutcliffe was also 4-5 with Cleveland for a combined AL-NL record of 20-6 (.769).

American League

Multiple winners: Lefty Grove (5); Chief Bender and Whitey Ford (3); Johnny Allen, Eddie Cicotte, Roger Clemens, Mike Cuellar, Lefty Gomez, Catfish Hunter, Randy Johnson, Walter Johnson, Jim Palmer, Pete Vuckovich and Smokey Joe Wood (2).

Year		W-L	Pct
1901	Clark Griffith, Chicago	24-7	.774
1902	Bill Bernhard, Phila-Cleve	18-5	.783
1903	Cy Young, Boston	28-9	.757
1904	Jack Chesbro, New York	41-12	.774
1905	Andy Coakley, Philadelphia	20-7	.741
1906	Eddie Plank, Philadelphia	19-6	.760
1907	Wild Bill Donovan, Detroit	25-4	.862
1908	Ed Walsh, Chicago	40-15	.727

Year		W-L	Pct
1909	George Mullin, Detroit	29-8	.784
1910	Chief Bender, Philadelphia	23-5	.821
1911	Chief Bender, Philadelphia	17-5	.773
1912	Smokey Joe Wood, Boston	34-5	.872
1913	Walter Johnson, Washington	36-7	.837
1914	Chief Bender, Philadelphia	17-3	.850
1915	Smokey Joe Wood, Boston	15-5	.750
1916	Eddie Cicotte, Chicago	15-7	.682
1917	Reb Russell, Chicago	15-5	.750
1918	Sad Sam Jones, Boston	16-5	.762
1919	Eddie Cicotte, Chicago	29-7	.806
1920	Jim Bagby, Cleveland	31-12	.721
1921	Carl Mays, New York	27-9	.750
1922	Joe Bush, New York	26-7	.788
1923	Herb Pennock, New York	19-6	.760
1924	Walter Johnson, Washington	23-7	.767
1925	Stan Coveleski, Washington	20-5	.800
1926	George Uhle, Cleveland	27-11	.711
1927	Waite Hoyt, New York	22-7	.759
1928	General Crowder, St. Louis	21-5	.808
1929	Lefty Grove, Philadelphia	20-6	.769
1930	Lefty Grove, Philadelphia	28-5	.848
1931	Lefty Grove, Philadelphia	31-4	.886
1932	Johnny Allen, New York	17-4	.810
1933	Lefty Grove, Philadelphia	24-8	.750
1934	Lefty Gomez, New York	26-5	.839
1935	Eldon Auker, Detroit	18-7	.720
1936	Monte Pearson, New York	19-7	.731
1937	Johnny Allen, Cleveland	15-1	.938
1938	Red Ruffing, New York	21-7	.750
1939	Lefty Grove, Boston	15-4	.789
1940	Schoolboy Rowe, Detroit	16-3	.842
1941	Lefty Gomez, New York	15-5	.750
1942	Ernie Bonham, New York	21-5	.808
1943	Spud Chandler, New York	20-4	.833
1944	Tex Hughson, Boston	18-5	.783
1945	Hal Newhouser, Detroit	25-9	.735
1946	Boo Ferriss, Boston	25-6	.806
1947	Allie Reynolds, New York	19-8	.704
1948	Jack Kramer, Boston	18-5	.783
1949	Ellis Kinder, Boston	23-6	.793
1950	Vic Raschi, New York	21-8	.724
1951	Bob Feller, Cleveland	22-8	.733
1952	Bobby Shantz, Philadelphia	24-7	.774
1953	Ed Lopat, New York	16-4	.800
1954	Sandy Consuegra, Chicago	16-3	.842

Year		W-L	Pct
1955	Tommy Byrne, New York	16-5	.762
1956	Whitey Ford, New York	19-6	.760
1957	Dick Donovan, Chicago	16-6	.727
	& Tom Sturdivant, New York	16-6	.727
1958	Bob Turley, New York	21-7	.750
1959	Bob Shaw, Chicago	18-6	.750
1960	Jim Perry, Cleveland	18-10	.643
1961	Whitey Ford, New York	25-4	.862
1962	Ray Herbert, Chicago	20-9	.690
1963	Whitey Ford, New York	24-7	.774
1964	Wally Bunker, Baltimore	19-5	.792
1965	Mudcat Grant, Minnesota	21-7	.750
1966	Sonny Siebert, Cleveland	16-8	.667
1967	Joe Horlen, Chicago	19-7	.731
1968	Denny McLain, Detroit	31-6	.838
1969	Jim Palmer, Baltimore	16-4	.800
1970	Mike Cuellar, Baltimore	24-8	.750
1971	Dave McNally, Baltimore	21-5	.808
1972	Catfish Hunter, Oakland	21-7	.750
1973	Catfish Hunter, Oakland	21-5	.808
1974	Mike Cuellar, Baltimore	22-10	.688
1975	Mike Torrez, Baltimore	20-9	.690
1976	Bill Campbell, Minnesota	17-5	.773
1977	Paul Splittorff, Kansas City	16-6	.727
1978	Ron Guidry, New York	25-3	.893
1979	Mike Caldwell, Milwaukee	16-6	.727
1980	Steve Stone, Baltimore	25-7	.781
1981	Pete Vuckovich, Milwaukee	14-4	.778
1982	Pete Vuckovich, Milwaukee	18-6	.750
	& Jim Palmer, Baltimore	15-5	.750
1983	Rich Dotson, Chicago	22-7	.759
1984	Doyle Alexander, Toronto	17-6	.739
1985	Ron Guidry, New York	22-6	.786
1986	Roger Clemens, Boston	24-4	.857
1987	Roger Clemens, Boston	20-9	.690
1988	Frank Viola, Minnesota	24-7	.774
1989	Bret Saberhagen, Kansas City	23-6	.793
1990	Bob Welch, Oakland	27-6	.818
1991	Scott Erickson, Minnesota	20-8	.714
1992	Mike Mussina, Baltimore	18-5	.783
1993	Jimmy Key, New York	18-6	.750
1994	Jason Bere, Chicago	12-2	.857
1995	Randy Johnson, Seattle	18-2	.900
1996	Charles Nagy, Cleveland	17-5	.773
1997	Randy Johnson, Seattle	20-4	.833
1998	David Wells, NY	18-4	.818

Earned Run Average

Earned Run Averages were based on at least 10 complete games pitched (1900-49), at least 154 innings pitched (1950-60), and at least 162 innings pitched since 1961 in the AL and 1962 in the NL. In the strike years of 1981, '94 and '95, qualifiers had to pitch at least as many innings as the total number of games their team played that season.

National League

Multiple winners: Grover Alexander, Sandy Koufax and Christy Mathewson (5); Greg Maddux (4); Carl Hubbell, Tom Seaver, Warren Spahn and Dazzy Vance (3); Bill Doak, Ray Kremer, Dolf Luque, Howie Pollet, Nolan Ryan, Bill Walker and Bucky Walters (2).

Year		ERA
1900	Rube Waddell, Pit	2.37
1901	Jesse Tannehill, Pit	2.18
1902	Jack Taylor, Chi	1.33
1903	Sam Leever, Pit	2.06
1904	Joe McGinnity, NY	1.61
1905	Christy Mathewson, NY	1.27
1906	Three Finger Brown, Chi	1.04
1907	Jack Pfiester, Chi	1.15
1908	Christy Mathewson, NY	1.43
1909	Christy Mathewson, NY	1.14

Year		ERA
1910	George McQuillan, Phi	1.60
1911	Christy Mathewson, NY	1.99
1912	Jeff Tesreau, NY	1.96
1913	Christy Mathewson, NY	2.06
1914	Bill Doak, St.L	1.72
1915	Grover Alexander, Phi	1.22
1916	Grover Alexander, Phi	1.55
1917	Grover Alexander, Phi	1.86
1918	Hippo Vaughn, Chi	1.74
1919	Grover Alexander, Chi	1.72

Year		ERA
1920	Grover Alexander, Chi	1.91
1921	Bill Doak, St.L	2.59
1922	Rosy Ryan, NY	3.01
1923	Dolf Luque, Cin	1.93
1924	Dazzy Vance, Bklyn	2.16
1925	Dolf Luque, Cin	2.63
1926	Ray Kremer, Pit	2.61
1927	Ray Kremer, Pit	2.47
1928	Dazzy Vance, Bklyn	2.09
1929	Bill Walker, NY	3.09

Year		ERA
1930	Dazzy Vance, Bklyn	2.61
1931	Bill Walker, NY	2.26
1932	Lon Warneke, Chi	2.37
1933	Carl Hubbell, NY	1.66
1934	Carl Hubbell, NY	2.30
1935	Cy Blanton, Pit	2.58
1936	Carl Hubbell, NY	2.31
1937	Jim Turner, Bos	2.38
1938	Bill Lee, Chi	2.66
1939	Bucky Walters, Cin	2.29
1940	Bucky Walters, Cin	2.48
1941	Elmer Riddle, Cin	2.24
1942	Mort Cooper, St.L	1.78
1943	Howie Pollet, St.L	1.75
1944	Ed Heusser, Cin	2.38
1945	Hank Borowy, Chi	2.13
1946	Howie Pollet, St.L	2.10
1947	Warren Spahn, Bos	2.33
1948	Harry Brecheen, St.L	2.24
1949	Dave Koslo, NY	2.50
1950	Jim Hearn, St.L-NY	2.49
1951	Chet Nichols, Bos	2.88
1952	Hoyt Wilhelm, NY	2.43
1953	Warren Spahn, Mil	2.10
1954	Johnny Antonelli, NY	2.30
1955	Bob Friend, Pit	2.83
1956	Lew Burdette, Mil	2.70
1957	Johnny Podres, Bklyn	2.66
1958	Stu Miller, SF	2.47
1959	Sam Jones, SF	2.83
1960	Mike McCormick, SF	2.70
1961	Warren Spahn, Mil	3.02
1962	Sandy Koufax, LA	2.54
1963	Sandy Koufax, LA	1.88
1964	Sandy Koufax, LA	1.74
1965	Sandy Koufax, LA	2.04
1966	Sandy Koufax, LA	1.73
1967	Phil Niekro, Atl	1.87
1968	Bob Gibson, St.L	1.12
1969	Juan Marichal, SF	2.10
1970	Tom Seaver, NY	2.81
1971	Tom Seaver, NY	1.76
1972	Steve Carlton, Phi	1.97
1973	Tom Seaver, NY	2.08
1974	Buzz Capra, Atl	2.28
1975	Randy Jones, SD	2.24
1976	John Denny, St.L	2.52
1977	John Candelaria, Pit	2.34
1978	Craig Swan, NY	2.43
1979	J.R. Richard, Hou	2.71
1980	Don Sutton, LA	2.21
1981	Nolan Ryan, Hou	1.69
1982	Steve Rogers, Mon	2.40
1983	Atlee Hammaker, SF	2.25
1984	Alejandro Peña, LA	2.48
1985	Dwight Gooden, NY	1.53
1986	Mike Scott, Hou	2.22
1987	Nolan Ryan, Hou	2.76
1988	Joe Magrane, St.L	2.18
1989	Scott Garrelts, SF	2.28
1990	Danny Darwin, Hou	2.21
1991	Dennis Martinez, Mon	2.39
1992	Bill Swift, SF	2.08
1993	Greg Maddux, Atl	2.36
1994	Greg Maddux, Atl	1.56
1995	Greg Maddux, Atl	1.63
1996	Kevin Brown, Fla	1.89
1997	Pedro Martinez, Mon	1.90
1998	Greg Maddux, Atl	2.22

Note: In 1945, Borowy had a 3.13 ERA in 18 games with New York (AL) for a combined ERA of 2.65.

American League

Multiple winners: Lefty Grove (9); Roger Clemens (6); Walter Johnson (5); Spud Chandler, Stan Coveleski, Red Faber, Whitey Ford, Lefty Gomez, Ron Guidry, Addie Joss, Hal Newhouser, Jim Palmer, Gary Peters, Luis Tiant and Ed Walsh (2).

Year		ERA
1901	Cy Young, Bos	1.62
1902	Ed Siever, Det	1.91
1903	Earl Moore, Cle	1.77
1904	Addie Joss, Cle	1.59
1905	Rube Waddell, Phi	1.48
1906	Doc White, Chi	1.52
1907	Ed Walsh, Chi	1.60
1908	Addie Joss, Cle	1.16
1909	Harry Krause, Phi	1.39
1910	Ed Walsh, Chi	1.27
1911	Vean Gregg, Cle	1.81
1912	Walter Johnson, Wash	1.39
1913	Walter Johnson, Wash	1.09
1914	Dutch Leonard, Bos	1.01
1915	Smokey Joe Wood, Bos	1.49
1916	Babe Ruth,Bos	1.75
1917	Eddie Cicotte, Chi	1.53
1918	Walter Johnson, Wash	1.27
1919	Walter Johnson, Wash	1.49
1920	Bob Shawkey, NY	2.45
1921	Red Faber, Chi	2.48
1922	Red Faber, Chi	2.80
1923	Stan Coveleski, Cle	2.76
1924	Walter Johnson, Wash	2.72
1925	Stan Coveleski, Wash	2.84
1926	Lefty Grove, Phi	2.51
1927	Wilcy Moore, NY	2.28
1928	Garland Braxton, Wash	2.51
1929	Lefty Grove, Phi	2.81
1930	Lefty Grove, Phi	2.54
1931	Lefty Grove, Phi	2.06
1932	Lefty Grove, Phi	2.84
1933	Monte Pearson, Cle	2.33
1934	Lefty Gomez, NY	2.33
1935	Lefty Grove, Bos	2.70
1936	Lefty Grove, Bos	2.81
1937	Lefty Gomez, NY	2.33
1938	Lefty Grove, Bos	3.08
1939	Lefty Grove, Bos	2.54
1940	Ernie Bonham, NY	1.90
1941	Thornton Lee, Chi	2.37
1942	Ted Lyons, Chi	2.10
1943	Spud Chandler, NY	1.64
1944	Dizzy Trout, Det	2.12
1945	Hal Newhouser, Det	1.81
1946	Hal Newhouser, Det	1.94
1947	Spud Chandler, NY	2.46
1948	Gene Bearden, Cle	2.43
1949	Mel Parnell, Bos	2.77
1950	Early Wynn, Cle	3.20
1951	Saul Rogovin, Det-Chi	2.78
1952	Allie Reynolds, NY	2.06
1953	Ed Lopat, NY	2.42
1954	Mike Garcia, Cle	2.64
1955	Billy Pierce, Chi	1.97
1956	Whitey Ford, NY	2.47
1957	Bobby Shantz, NY	2.45
1958	Whitey Ford, NY	2.01
1959	Hoyt Wilhelm, Bal	2.19
1960	Frank Baumann, Chi	2.67
1961	Dick Donovan, Wash	2.40
1962	Hank Aguirre, Det	2.21
1963	Gary Peters, Chi	2.33
1964	Dean Chance, LA	1.65
1965	Sam McDowell, Cle	2.18
1966	Gary Peters, Chi	1.98
1967	Joe Horlen, Chi	2.06
1968	Luis Tiant, Cle	1.60
1969	Dick Bosman, Wash	2.19
1970	Diego Segui, Oak	2.56
1971	Vida Blue, Oak	1.82
1972	Luis Tiant, Bos	1.91
1973	Jim Palmer, Bal	2.40
1974	Catfish Hunter, Oak	2.49
1975	Jim Palmer, Bal	2.09
1976	Mark Fidrych, Det	2.34
1977	Frank Tanana, Cal	2.54
1978	Ron Guidry, NY	1.74
1979	Ron Guidry, NY	2.78
1980	Rudy May, NY	2.47
1981	Steve McCatty, Oak	2.32
1982	Rick Sutcliffe, Cle	2.96
1983	Rick Honeycutt, Tex	2.42
1984	Mike Boddicker, Bal	2.79
1985	Dave Stieb, Tor	2.48
1986	Roger Clemens, Bos	2.48
1987	Jimmy Key, Tor	2.76
1988	Allan Anderson, Min	2.45
1989	Bret Saberhagen, KC	2.16
1990	Roger Clemens, Bos	1.93
1991	Roger Clemens, Bos	2.62
1992	Roger Clemens, Bos	2.41
1993	Kevin Appier, KC	2.56
1994	Steve Ontiveros, Oak	2.65
1995	Randy Johnson, Sea	2.48
1996	Juan Guzman, Tor	2.93
1997	Roger Clemens, Tor	2.05
1998	Roger Clemens, Tor	2.65

Strikeouts

National League

Multiple winners: Dazzy Vance (7); Grover Alexander (6); Steve Carlton, Christy Mathewson and Tom Seaver (5); Dizzy Dean, Sandy Koufax and Warren Spahn (4); Don Drysdale, Sam Jones and Johnny Vander Meer (3); David Cone, Dwight Gooden, Bill Hallahan, J.R. Richard, Robin Roberts, Nolan Ryan, Curt Schilling, John Smoltz and Hippo Vaughn (2).

Year		SO
1900	Rube Waddell, Pit	130
1901	Noodles Hahn, Cin	239
1902	Vic Willis, Bos	225
1903	Christy Mathewson, NY	267
1904	Christy Mathewson, NY	212
1905	Christy Mathewson, NY	206
1906	Fred Beebe, Chi-St.L	171
1907	Christy Mathewson, NY	178
1908	Christy Mathewson, NY	259
1909	Orval Overall, Chi	205
1910	Earl Moore, Phi	185
1911	Rube Marquard, NY	237
1912	Grover Alexander, Phi	195
1913	Tom Seaton, Phi	168
1914	Grover Alexander, Phi	214
1915	Grover Alexander, Phi	241
1916	Grover Alexander, Phi	167
1917	Grover Alexander, Phi	201
1918	Hippo Vaughn, Chi	148
1919	Hippo Vaughn, Chi	141
1920	Grover Alexander, Chi	173
1921	Burleigh Grimes, Bklyn	136
1922	Dazzy Vance, Bklyn	134
1923	Dazzy Vance, Bklyn	197
1924	Dazzy Vance, Bklyn	262
1925	Dazzy Vance, Bklyn	221
1926	Dazzy Vance, Bklyn	140
1927	Dazzy Vance, Bklyn	184
1928	Dazzy Vance, Bklyn	200
1929	Pat Malone, Chi	166
1930	Bill Hallahan, St.L	177
1931	Bill Hallahan, St.L	159
1932	Dizzy Dean, St.L	191
1933	Dizzy Dean, St.L	199
1934	Dizzy Dean, St.L	195
1935	Dizzy Dean, St.L	190
1936	Van Lingle Mungo, Bklyn	238
1937	Carl Hubbell, NY	159
1938	Clay Bryant, Chi	135
1939	Claude Passeau, Phi-Chi	137
	& Bucky Walters, Cin	137
1940	Kirby Higbe, Phi	137
1941	John Vander Meer, Cin	202
1942	John Vander Meer, Cin	186
1943	John Vander Meer, Cin	174
1944	Bill Voiselle, NY	161
1945	Preacher Roe, Pit	148
1946	Johnny Schmitz, Chi	135
1947	Ewell Blackwell, Cin	193
1948	Harry Brecheen, St.L	149
1949	Warren Spahn, Bos	151
1950	Warren Spahn, Bos	191
1951	Don Newcombe, Bklyn	164
	& Warren Spahn, Bos	164
1952	Warren Spahn, Bos	183
1953	Robin Roberts, Phi	198
1954	Robin Roberts, Phi	185
1955	Sam Jones, Chi	198
1956	Sam Jones, Chi	176
1957	Jack Sanford, Phi	188
1958	Sam Jones, St.L	225
1959	Don Drysdale, LA	242
1960	Don Drysdale, LA	246
1961	Sandy Koufax, LA	269
1962	Don Drysdale, LA	232
1963	Sandy Koufax, LA	306
1964	Bob Veale, Pit	250
1965	Sandy Koufax, LA	382
1966	Sandy Koufax, LA	317
1967	Jim Bunning, Phi	253
1968	Bob Gibson, St.L	268
1969	Ferguson Jenkins, Chi	273
1970	Tom Seaver, NY	283
1971	Tom Seaver, NY	289
1972	Steve Carlton, Phi	310
1973	Tom Seaver, NY	251
1974	Steve Carlton, Phi	240
1975	Tom Seaver, NY	243
1976	Tom Seaver, NY	235
1977	Phil Niekro, Atl	262
1978	J.R. Richard, Hou	303
1979	J.R. Richard, Hou	313
1980	Steve Carlton, Phi	286
1981	F. Valenzuela, LA	180
1982	Steve Carlton, Phi	286
1983	Steve Carlton, Phi	275
1984	Dwight Gooden, NY	276
1985	Dwight Gooden, NY	268
1986	Mike Scott, Hou	306
1987	Nolan Ryan, Hou	270
1988	Nolan Ryan, Hou	228
1989	Jose DeLeon, St.L	201
1990	David Cone, NY	233
1991	David Cone, NY	241
1992	John Smoltz, Atl	215
1993	Jose Rijo, Cin	227
1994	Andy Benes, SD	189
1995	Hideo Nomo, LA	236
1996	John Smoltz, Atl	276
1997	Curt Schilling, Phi	319
1998	Curt Schilling, Phi	300

Pitching Triple Crown Winners

Pitchers who led either league in Earned Run Average, Wins and Strikeouts over a single season.

National League

	Year	ERA	W-L	SO
Tommy Bond, Bos	1877	2.11	40-17	170
Hoss Radbourne, Prov	1884	1.38	60-12	441
Tim Keefe, NY	1888	1.74	35-12	333
John Clarkson, Bos	1889	2.73	49-19	284
Amos Rusie, NY	1894	2.78	36-13	195
Christy Mathewson, NY	1905	1.27	31-8	206
Christy Mathewson, NY	1908	1.43	37-11	259
Grover Alexander, Phi	1915	1.22	31-10	241
Grover Alexander, Phi	1916	1.55	33-12	167
Grover Alexander, Phi	1917	1.86	30-13	201
Hippo Vaughn, Chi	1918	1.74	22-10	148
Grover Alexander, Chi	1920	1.91	27-14	173
Dazzy Vance, Bklyn	1924	2.16	28-6	262
Bucky Walters, Cin	1939	2.29	27-11	137
Sandy Koufax, LA	1963	1.88	25-5	306
Sandy Koufax, LA	1965	2.04	26-8	382
Sandy Koufax, LA	1966	1.73	27-9	317
Steve Carlton, Phi	1972	1.97	27-10	310
Dwight Gooden, NY	1985	1.53	24-4	268

Ties: In 1894, Rusie tied for league lead in wins with Jouett Meekin, NY (36-10); in 1939, Walters tied for league lead in strikeouts with Claude Passeau, Phi-Chi; in 1963, Koufax tied for the league lead in wins with Juan Marichal, SF.

American League

	Year	ERA	W-L	SO
Cy Young, Bos	1901	1.62	33-10	158
Rube Waddell, Phi	1905	1.48	26-11	287
Walter Johnson, Wash	1913	1.09	36-7	243
Walter Johnson, Wash	1918	1.27	23-13	162
Walter Johnson, Wash	1924	2.72	23-7	158
Lefty Grove, Phi	1930	2.54	28-5	209
Lefty Grove, Phi	1931	2.06	31-4	175
Lefty Gomez, NY	1934	2.33	26-5	158
Lefty Gomez, NY	1937	2.33	21-11	194
Hal Newhouser, Det	1945	1.81	25-9	212
Roger Clemens, Tor	1997	2.05	21-7	292
Roger Clemens, Tor	1998	2.65	20-6	271

Ties: In 1998, Clemens tied for league lead in wins with David Cone, NY (20-7) and Rick Helling, Tex (20-7).

American League

Multiple winners: Walter Johnson (12); Nolan Ryan (9); Bob Feller and Lefty Grove (7); Rube Waddell (6); Roger Clemens and Sam McDowell (5); Randy Johnson (4); Lefty Gomez, Mark Langston and Camilo Pascual (3); Len Barker, Tommy Bridges, Jim Bunning, Hal Newhouser, Allie Reynolds, Herb Score, Ed Walsh and Early Wynn (2).

Year		SO
1901	Cy Young, Bos	158
1902	Rube Waddell, Phi	210
1903	Rube Waddell, Phi	302
1904	Rube Waddell, Phi	349
1905	Rube Waddell, Phi	287
1906	Rube Waddell, Phi	196
1907	Rube Waddell, Phi	232
1908	Ed Walsh, Chi	269
1909	Frank Smith, Chi	177
1910	Walter Johnson, Wash.	313
1911	Ed Walsh, Chi	255
1912	Walter Johnson, Wash.	303
1913	Walter Johnson, Wash.	243
1914	Walter Johnson, Wash.	225
1915	Walter Johnson, Wash.	203
1916	Walter Johnson, Wash.	228
1917	Walter Johnson, Wash.	188
1918	Walter Johnson, Wash.	162
1919	Walter Johnson, Wash.	147
1920	Stan Coveleski, Cle	133
1921	Walter Johnson, Wash.	143
1922	Urban Shocker, St.L	149
1923	Walter Johnson, Wash.	130
1924	Walter Johnson, Wash.	158
1925	Lefty Grove, Phi	116
1926	Lefty Grove, Phi	194
1927	Lefty Grove, Phi	174
1928	Lefty Grove, Phi	183
1929	Lefty Grove, Phi	170
1930	Lefty Grove, Phi	209
1931	Lefty Grove, Phi	175
1932	Red Ruffing, NY	190
1933	Lefty Gomez, NY	163
1934	Lefty Gomez, NY	158
1935	Tommy Bridges, Det	163
1936	Tommy Bridges, Det	175
1937	Lefty Gomez, NY	194
1938	Bob Feller, Cle	240
1939	Bob Feller, Cle	246
1940	Bob Feller, Cle	261
1941	Bob Feller, Cle	260
1942	Tex Hughson, Bos	113
	& Bobo Newsom, Wash	113
1943	Allie Reynolds, Cle	151
1944	Hal Newhouser, Det	187
1945	Hal Newhouser, Det	212
1946	Bob Feller, Cle	348
1947	Bob Feller, Cle	196
1948	Bob Feller, Cle	164
1949	Virgil Trucks, Det.	153
1950	Bob Lemon, Cle	170
1951	Vic Raschi, NY	164
1952	Allie Reynolds, NY	160
1953	Billy Pierce, Chi	186
1954	Bob Turley, Bal	185
1955	Herb Score, Cle	245
1956	Herb Score, Cle	263
1957	Early Wynn, Cle	184
1958	Early Wynn, Chi	179
1959	Jim Bunning, Det	201
1960	Jim Bunning, Det	201
1961	Camilo Pascual, Min	221
1962	Camilo Pascual, Min	206
1963	Camilo Pascual, Min	202
1964	Al Downing, NY	217
1965	Sam McDowell, Cle	325
1966	Sam McDowell, Cle	225
1967	Jim Lonborg, Bos	246
1968	Sam McDowell, Cle	283
1969	Sam McDowell, Cle	279
1970	Sam McDowell, Cle	304
1971	Mickey Lolich, Det	308
1972	Nolan Ryan, Cal	329
1973	Nolan Ryan, Cal	383
1974	Nolan Ryan, Cal	367
1975	Frank Tanana, Cal	269
1976	Nolan Ryan, Cal	327
1977	Nolan Ryan, Cal	341
1978	Nolan Ryan, Cal	260
1979	Nolan Ryan, Cal	223
1980	Len Barker, Cle	187
1981	Len Barker, Cle	127
1982	Floyd Bannister, Sea	209
1983	Jack Morris, Det	232
1984	Mark Langston, Sea	204
1985	Bert Blyleven, Cle-Min	206
1986	Mark Langston, Sea	245
1987	Mark Langston, Sea	262
1988	Roger Clemens, Bos	291
1989	Nolan Ryan, Tex	301
1990	Nolan Ryan, Tex	232
1991	Roger Clemens, Bos	241
1992	Randy Johnson, Sea	241
1993	Randy Johnson, Sea	308
1994	Randy Johnson, Sea	204
1995	Randy Johnson, Sea	294
1996	Roger Clemens, Bos	257
1997	Roger Clemens, Tor	292
1998	Roger Clemens, Tor	271

Perfect Games

Seventeen pitchers have thrown perfect games (27 up, 27 down) in major league history. However, the games pitched by Harvey Haddix and Ernie Shore are not considered to be official.

National League

	Game	Date	Score
Lee Richmond	Wor. vs Cle.	6/12/1880	1-0
Monte Ward	Prov. vs Bos.	6/17/1880	5-0
Harvey Haddix	Pit. at Mil.	5/26/1959	0-1*
Jim Bunning	Phi. at NY	6/21/1964	6-0
Sandy Koufax	LA vs Chi.	9/9/1965	1-0
Tom Browning	Cin. vs LA	9/16/1988	1-0
Dennis Martinez	Mon. at LA	7/28/1991	2-0

*Haddix pitched 12 perfect innings before losing in the 13th. Braves' lead-off batter Felix Mantilla reached on a throwing error by Pirates 3B Don Hoak, Eddie Mathews sacrificed Mantilla to 2nd, Hank Aaron was walked intentionally, and Joe Adcock hit a 3-run HR. Adcock, however, passed Aaron on the bases and was only credited with a 1-run double.

American League

	Game	Date	Score
Cy Young	Bos. vs Phi.	5/5/1904	3-0
Addie Joss	Cle. vs Chi.	10/2/1908	1-0
Ernie Shore	Bos. vs Wash.	6/23/1917	4-0*
Charlie Robertson	Chi. at Det.	4/30/1922	2-0
Catfish Hunter	Oak. vs Min.	5/8/1968	4-0
Len Barker	Cle. vs Tor.	5/15/1981	3-0
Mike Witt	Cal. at Tex.	9/30/1984	1-0
Kenny Rogers	Tex. vs Cal.	6/28/1994	4-0
David Wells	NY vs Min.	5/17/1998	4-0

*Babe Ruth started for Boston, walking Senators' lead-off batter Ray Morgan, then was thrown out of game by umpire Brick Owens for arguing the call. Shore came on in relief. Morgan was caught stealing and Shore retired the next 26 batters in a row. While technically not a perfect game—since he didn't start—Shore gets credit anyway.

World Series

Pitcher	Game	Date	Score
Don Larsen	NY vs Bklyn	10/8/1956	2-0

No-Hit Games

Nine innings or more, including perfect games, since 1876. Losing pitchers in **bold** type. **Multiple no-hitters:** Nolan Ryan (7); Sandy Koufax (4); Larry Cocoran, Bob Feller and Cy Young (3); Jim Bunning, Steve Busby, Carl Erskine, Bob Forsch, Pud Galvin, Ken Holtzman, Addie Joss, Hub Leonard, Jim Maloney, Christy Mathewson, Allie Reynolds, Warren Spahn, Bill Stoneham, Virgil Trucks, Johnny Vander Meer and Don Wilson (2).

National League

Year	Date	Pitcher	Result
1876	7/15	George Bradley	St.L vs Har, 2-0
1880	6/12	Lee Richmond	Wor vs Cle,1-0 (perfect game)
	6/17	Monte Ward	Prov vs Buf, 5-0 (perfect game)
	8/19	Larry Corcoran	Chi vs Bos, 6-0
	8/20	Pud Galvin	Buf at Wor, 1-0
1882	9/20	Larry Corcoran	Chi vs Wor, 1-0
1883	7/25	Old Hoss Radbourne	Prov at Cle, 8-0
	9/13	Hugh Daily	Cle at Phi, 1-0
1884	6/27	Larry Cocoran	Chi vs Prov, 6-0
	8/4	Pud Galvin	Buf at Det, 18-0
1885	7/27	John Clarkson	Chi vs Prov, 6-0
	8/29	Charlie Ferguson	Phi vs Prov, 1-0
1891	6/22	Tom Lovett	Bklyn vs NY, 4-0
	7/31	Amos Rusie	NY vs Bklyn, 11-0
1892	8/6	John Stivetts	Bos vs Bklyn, 11-0
	8/22	Ben Sanders	Lou vs Bal, 6-2
	10/22	Bumpus Jones	Cin vs Pit, 7-1 (1st major league game)
1893	8/16	Bill Hawke	Bal vs Wash, 5-0
1897	9/18	Cy Young	Cle vs Cin, 6-0
1898	4/22	Ted Breitenstein	Cin vs Pit, 11-0
	4/22	Jim Hughes	Bal vs Bos, 8-0
	7/8	Frank Donahue	Phi vs Bos, 5-0
	8/21	Walter Thornton	Chi vs Bklyn, 2-0
1899	5/25	Deacon Phillippe	Lou vs NY, 7-0
1900	7/12	Noodles Hahn	Cin vs Phi, 4-0
1901	7/15	Christy Mathewson	NY vs St.L, 5-0
1903	9/18	Chick Fraser	Phi at Chi, 10-0
1905	6/13	Christy Mathewson	NY at Chi, 1-0
1906	5/1	John Lush	Phi at Bklyn, 1-0
	7/20	Mal Eason	Bklyn at St.L, 2-0
1907	5/8	Frank Pfeffer	Bos vs Cin, 6-0
	9/20	Nick Maddox	Pit vs Bkn, 2-1
1908	7/4	Hooks Wiltse	NY vs Phi, 1-0 (10)
	9/5	Nap Rucker	Bklyn vs Bos, 6-0
1912	9/6	Jeff Tesreau	NY at Phi, 3-0
1914	9/9	George Davis	Bos vs Phi, 7-0
1915	4/15	Rube Marquard	NY vs Bklyn, 2-0
	8/31	Jimmy Lavender	Chi at N.Y, 2-0
1916	6/16	Tom Hughes	Bos vs. Pit, 2-0
1917	5/2	Fred Toney	Cin at Chi, 1-0 (10)
1919	5/11	Hod Eller	Cin at St.L, 6-0
1922	5/7	Jesse Barnes	NY vs Phi, 6-0
1924	7/17	Jesse Haines	St.L vs Bos, 5-0
1925	9/17	Dazzy Vance	Bklyn vs Phi, 10-1
1929	5/8	Carl Hubbell	NY vs Pit, 2-0
1934	9/21	Paul Dean	St.L vs Bklyn, 3-0
1938	6/11	Johnny Vander Meer	Cin vs Bos, 3-0
	6/15	Johnny Vander Meer	Cin at Bklyn, 6-0 (consecutive starts)
1940	4/30	Tex Carleton	Bklyn at Cin, 3-0
1941	8/30	Lon Warneke	St.L at Cin, 2-0
1944	4/27	Jim Tobin	Bos vs Bklyn, 2-0
	5/15	Clyde Shoun	Cin vs Bos, 1-0
1946	4/23	Ed Head	Bklyn at NY, 2-0
1947	6/18	Ewell Blackwell	Cin vs Bos, 6-0
1948	9/9	Rex Barney	Bklyn at NY, 2-0
1950	8/11	Vern Bickford	Bos vs Bklyn, 7-0
1951	5/6	Cliff Chambers	Pit at Bos, 3-0
1952	6/19	Carl Erskine	Bklyn vs Chi, 5-0
1954	6/12	Jim Wilson	Mil vs Phi, 2-0
1955	5/12	Sam Jones	Chi vs Pit, 4-0
1956	5/12	Carl Erskine	Bklyn vs NY, 3-0
	9/25	Sal Maglie	Bklyn vs Phi, 5-0
1960	5/15	Don Cardwell	Chi vs St.L, 4-0
	8/18	Lew Burdette	Mil vs Phi, 1-0
	9/16	Warren Spahn	Mil vs Phi, 4-0
1961	4/28	Warren Spahn	Mil vs SF, 1-0
1962	6/30	Sandy Koufax	LA vs NY, 5-0
1963	5/11	Sandy Koufax	LA vs SF, 1-0
	5/17	Don Nottebart	Hou vs Phi, 4-1
	6/15	Juan Marichal	SF vs Hou, 1-0
1964	4/23	**Ken Johnson**	Hou vs Cin, 0-1
	6/4	Sandy Koufax	LA at Phi, 3-0
	6/21	Jim Bunning	Phi at NY, 6-0 (perfect game)
1965	8/19	Jim Maloney	Cin at Chi, 1-0 (10)
	9/9	Sandy Koufax	LA vs Chi, 1-0 (perfect game)
1967	6/18	Don Wilson	Hou vs Atl, 2-0
1968	7/29	George Culver	Cin at Phi, 6-1
	9/17	Gaylord Perry	SF vs St.L, 1-0
	9/18	Ray Washburn	St.L at SF, 2-0 (next day, same park)
1969	4/17	Bill Stoneman	Mon at Phi, 7-0
	4/30	Jim Maloney	Cin vs Hou, 10-0
	5/1	Don Wilson	Hou at Cin, 4-0
	8/19	Ken Holtzman	Chi vs Atl, 3-0
	9/20	Bob Moose	Pit at NY, 4-0
1970	6/12	Dock Ellis	Pit at SD, 2-0
	7/20	Bill Singer	LA vs Phi, 5-0
1971	6/3	Ken Holtzman	Chi at Cin, 1-0
	6/23	Rick Wise	Phi at Cin, 4-0
	8/14	Bob Gibson	St.L at Pit, 11-0
1972	4/16	Burt Hooton	Chi vs Phi, 4-0
	9/2	Milt Pappas	Chi vs SD, 8-0
	10/2	Bill Stoneman	Mon vs NY, 7-0
1973	8/5	Phil Niekro	Atl vs SD, 9-0
1975	8/24	Ed Halicki	SF vs NY, 6-0
1976	7/9	Larry Dierker	Hou vs Mon, 6-0
	8/9	John Candelaria	Pit vs LA, 2-0
	9/29	John Montefusco	SF vs Atl, 9-0
1978	4/16	Bob Forsch	St.L vs Phi, 5-0
	6/16	Tom Seaver	Cin vs St.L, 4-0
1979	4/7	Ken Forsch	Hou vs Atl, 6-0
1980	6/27	Jerry Reuss	LA at SF, 4-0
1981	5/10	Charlie Lea	Mon vs SF, 4-0
	9/26	Nolan Ryan	Hou vs LA, 5-0
1983	9/26	Bob Forsch	St.L vs Mon, 3-0
1986	9/25	Mike Scott	Hou vs SF, 2-0
1988	9/16	Tom Browning	Cin vs LA, 1-0 (perfect game)
1990	6/29	Fernando Valenzuela	LA vs St.L, 6-0
	8/15	Terry Mulholland	Phi vs SF, 6-0
1991	5/23	Tommy Greene	Phi at Mon, 2-0
	7/28	Dennis Martinez	Mon at LA, 2-0 (perfect game)
	9/11	Kent Mercker (6), Mark Wohlers (2) & Alejandro Peña (1)	Atl vs SD, 1-0 (combined no-hitter)
1992	8/17	Kevin Gross	LA vs SF, 2-0
1993	9/8	Darryl Kile	Hou vs NY, 7-1
1994	4/8	Kent Mercker	Atl at LA, 6-0
1995	7/14	Ramon Martinez	LA vs Fla, 7-0
1996	5/11	Al Leiter	Fla vs Col, 11-0

Year	Date	Pitcher	Result
	9/17	Hideo Nomo	LA at Col, 9-0
1997	6/10	Kevin Brown	Fla at SF, 9-0
	7/12	Francisco Cordova (9) Ricardo Rincon (1)	Pit vs. Hou, 3-0 (10 inn.) (combined no-hitter)

American League

Year	Date	Pitcher	Result
1902	9/20	Jimmy Callahan	Chi vs Det, 3-0
1904	5/5	Cy Young	Bos vs Phi, 3-0 (perfect game)
	8/17	Jesse Tannehill	Bos vs Chi, 6-0
1905	7/22	Weldon Henley	Phi at St. L, 6-0
	9/6	Frank Smith	Chi at Det, 15-0
	9/27	Bill Dinneen	Bos vs Chi, 2-0
1908	6/30	Cy Young	Bos at NY, 8-0
	9/18	Dusty Rhoades	Cle vs Bos, 2-0
	9/20	Frank Smith	Chi vs Phi, 1-0
	10/2	Addie Joss	Cle vs Chi, 1-0 (perfect game)
1910	4/20	Addie Joss	Cle at Chi, 1-0
	5/12	Chief Bender	Phi vs Cle, 4-0
1911	7/19	Smokey Joe Wood	Bos vs St. L, 5-0
	8/27	Ed Walsh	Chi vs Bos, 5-0
1912	7/4	George Mullin	Det vs St. L, 7-0
	8/30	Earl Hamilton	St. L at Det, 5-1
1914	5/31	Joe Benz	Chi vs Cle, 6-1
1916	6/16	Rube Foster	Bos vs NY, 2-0
	8/26	Joe Bush	Phi vs Cle, 5-0
	8/30	Hub Leonard	Bos vs St. L, 4-0
1917	4/14	Ed Cicotte	Chi at St. L, 11-0
	4/24	George Mogridge	NY at Bos, 2-1
	5/5	Ernie Koob	St. L vs Chi, 1-0
	5/6	Bob Groom	St. L vs Chi, 3-0
	6/23	Babe Ruth (0) & Ernie Shore (9)	Bos vs Wash, 4-0 (combined no-hitter)
1918	6/3	Hub Leonard	Bos at Det, 5-0
1919	9/10	Ray Caldwell	Cle at NY, 3-0
1920	7/1	Walter Johnson	Wash at Bos, 1-0
1922	4/30	Charlie Robertson	Chi at Det, 2-0 (perfect game)
1923	9/4	Sam Jones	NY at Phi, 2-0
	9/7	Howard Ehmke	Bos at Phi, 4-0
1926	8/21	Ted Lyons	Chi at Bos, 6-0
1931	4/29	Wes Ferrell	Cle vs St. L, 9-0
	8/8	Bob Burke	Wash vs Bos, 5-0
1935	8/31	Vern Kennedy	Chi vs Cle, 5-0
1937	6/1	Bill Dietrich	Chi vs St. L, 8-0
1938	8/27	Monte Pearson	NY vs Cle, 13-0
1940	4/16	Bob Feller	Cle at Chi, 1-0 (Opening Day)
1945	9/9	Dick Fowler	Phi vs St. L, 1-0
1946	4/30	Bob Feller	Cle vs NY, 1-0
1947	7/10	Don Black	Cle vs Phi, 3-0
	9/3	Bill McCahan	Phi vs Wash, 3-0
1948	6/30	Bob Lemon	Cle at Det, 2-0
1951	7/1	Bob Feller	Cle vs Det, 2-1
	7/12	Allie Reynolds	NY vs Cle, 1-0
	9/28	Allie Reynolds	NY vs Bos, 8-0
1952	5/15	Virgil Trucks	Det vs Wash, 1-0
	8/25	Virgil Trucks	Det at NY, 1-0
1953	5/6	Bobo Holloman	St. L vs Phi, 6-0 (first major league start)
1956	7/14	Mel Parnell	Bos vs Chi, 4-0
	10/8	Don Larsen	NY vs Bklyn, 2-0 (perfect W. Series game)
1957	8/20	Bob Keegan	Chi vs Wash, 6-0
1958	7/20	Jim Bunning	Det at Bos, 3-0
	9/2	Hoyt Wilhelm	Bal vs NY, 1-0
1962	5/5	Bo Belinsky	LA vs Bal, 2-0
	6/26	Earl Wilson	Bos vs LA, 2-0
	8/1	Bill Monbouquette	Bos at Chi, 1-0
	8/26	Jack Kralick	Min vs KC, 1-0
1965	9/16	Dave Morehead	Bos vs Cle, 2-0
1966	6/10	Sonny Siebert	Cle vs Wash, 2-0
1967	4/30	**Steve Barber** ($8\frac{2}{3}$) & **Stu Miller** ($\frac{1}{3}$)	Bal vs Det, 1-2 (combined no-hitter)
	8/25	Dean Chance	Min at Cle, 2-1
	9/10	Joel Horlen	Chi vs Det, 6-0
1968	4/27	Tom Phoebus	Bal vs Bos, 6-0
	5/8	Catfish Hunter	Oak vs Min, 4-0 (perfect game)
1969	8/13	Jim Palmer	Bal vs Oak, 8-0
1970	7/3	Clyde Wright	Cal vs Oak, 4-0
	9/21	Vida Blue	Oak vs Min, 6-0
1973	4/27	Steve Busby	KC at Det, 3-0
	5/15	Nolan Ryan	Cal at KC, 3-0
	7/15	Nolan Ryan	Cal at Det, 6-0
	7/30	Jim Bibby	Tex at Oak, 6-0
1974	6/19	Steve Busby	KC at Mil, 2-0
	7/19	Dick Bosman	Cle at Oak, 4-0
	9/28	Nolan Ryan	Cal at Min, 4-0
1975	6/1	Nolan Ryan	Cal vs Bal, 1-0
	9/28	Vida Blue (5), Glenn Abbott (1), Paul Lindblad (1), & Rollie Fingers (2)	Oak vs Cal, 5-0 (combined no-hitter)
1976	7/28	John Odom (5) & Francisco Barrios (4)	Chi at Oak, 2-1 (combined no-hitter)
1977	5/14	Jim Colborn	KC vs Tex, 6-0
	5/30	Dennis Eckersley	Cle vs Cal, 1-0
	9/22	Bert Blyleven	Tex at Cal, 6-0
1981	5/15	Len Barker	Cle vs Tor, 3-0 (perfect game)
1983	7/4	Dave Righetti	NY vs Bos, 4-0
	9/29	Mike Warren	Oak vs Chi, 3-0
1984	4/7	Jack Morris	Det at Chi, 4-0
	9/30	Mike Witt	Cal at Tex, 1-0 (perfect game)
1986	9/19	Joe Cowley	Chi at Cal, 7-1
1987	4/15	Juan Nieves	Mil at Bal, 7-0
1990	6/2	Mark Langston (7) & Mike Witt (2)	Cal vs Sea, 1-0 (combined no-hitter)
	6/2	Randy Johnson	Sea vs Det, 2-0
	6/11	Nolan Ryan	Tex at Oak, 5-0
	6/29	Dave Stewart	Oak at Tor, 5-0
	9/2	Dave Stieb	Tor at Cle, 3-0
1991	5/1	Nolan Ryan	Tex vs Tor, 3-0
	7/13	Bob Milacki (6), Mike Flanagan (1), Mark Williamson (1) & Gregg Olson (1)	Bal at Oak, 2-0 (combined no-hitter)
	8/11	Wilson Alvarez	Chi at Bal, 7-0
	8/26	Bret Saberhagen	KC vs Chi, 7-0
1993	4/22	Chris Bosio	Sea vs Bos, 7-0
	9/4	Jim Abbott	NY vs Cle, 4-0
1994	4/27	Scott Erickson	Min vs Mil, 6-0
	7/28	Kenny Rogers	Tex vs Cal, 4-0 (perfect game)
1996	5/14	Dwight Gooden	NY vs Sea, 2-0
1998	5/17	David Wells	NY vs Min, 4-0 (perfect game)

All-Time Major League Leaders

Based on statistics compiled by *The Baseball Encyclopedia* (9th ed.); through 1998 regular season.

CAREER

Players active in 1998 in **bold** type.

Batting

Note that (*) indicates left-handed hitter and (†) indicates switch-hitter.

Batting Average

		Yrs	AB	H	Avg
1	Ty Cobb*	24	11,429	4191	.367
2	Rogers Hornsby	23	8,137	2930	.358
3	Joe Jackson*	13	4,981	1774	.356
4	Ed Delahanty	16	7,509	2597	.346
5	Tris Speaker*	22	10,197	3514	.345
6	Ted Williams*	19	7,706	2654	.344
7	Billy Hamilton*	14	6,284	2163	.344
8	Willie Keeler*	19	8,585	2947	.343
9	Dan Brouthers*	19	6,711	2296	.342
10	Babe Ruth*	22	8,399	2873	.342
11	Harry Heilmann	17	7,787	2660	.342
12	Pete Browning	13	4,820	1646	.341
13	Bill Terry*	14	6,428	2193	.341
14	George Sisler*	15	8,267	2812	.340
15	Lou Gehrig*	17	8,001	2721	.340
16	Jesse Burkett*	16	8,413	2853	.339
17	**Tony Gwynn***	17	8,648	2928	.339
18	Nap Lajoie	21	9,592	3244	.338
19	Riggs Stephenson	14	4,508	1515	.336
20	Al Simmons	20	8,761	2927	.334
21	Paul Waner*	20	9,459	3152	.333
22	Eddie Collins*	25	9,951	3313	.333
23	**Mike Piazza**	7	3,119	1038	.333
24	Stan Musial*	22	10,972	3630	.331
25	Sam Thompson*	14	6,005	1986	.331

Players Active in 1998

		Yrs	AB	H	Avg
1	Tony Gwynn*	17	8,648	2928	.339
2	Mike Piazza	7	3,119	1038	.333
3	Wade Boggs*	17	8,888	2922	.329
4	Frank Thomas	9	4,406	1416	.321
5	Edgar Martinez	12	4,374	1389	.318
6	Alex Rodriguez	5	2,070	648	.313
7	Kenny Lofton*	8	3,914	1216	.311
8	Mark Grace*	11	6,053	1875	.310
9	Paul Molitor	21	10,835	3319	.306
10	Hal Morris*	11	3,727	1140	.306
11	Larry Walker*	10	4,154	1265	.305
12	Mo Vaughn*	8	3,828	1165	.304
13	Jeff Bagwell	8	4,197	1276	.304

Hits

		Yrs	AB	H	Avg
1	Pete Rose†	24	14,053	**4256**	.303
2	Ty Cobb*	24	11,429	**4191**	.367
3	Hank Aaron	23	12,364	**3771**	.305
4	Stan Musial*	22	10,972	**3630**	.331
5	Tris Speaker*	22	10,197	**3514**	.345
6	Carl Yastrzemski*	23	11,988	**3419**	.285
7	Honus Wagner	21	10,443	**3418**	.327
8	**Paul Molitor**	21	10,835	**3319**	.306
9	Eddie Collins*	25	9,951	**3313**	.333
10	Willie Mays	22	10,881	**3283**	.302
11	Eddie Murray†	21	11,336	**3255**	.287
12	Nap Lajoie	21	9,592	**3244**	.338
13	George Brett*	21	10,349	**3154**	.305
14	Paul Waner*	20	9,459	**3152**	.333
15	Robin Yount	20	11,008	**3142**	.285
16	Dave Winfield	22	11,003	**3110**	.283
17	Rod Carew*	19	9,315	**3053**	.328
18	Lou Brock*	19	10,332	**3023**	.293
19	Al Kaline	22	10,116	**3007**	.297
20	Cap Anson	22	9,108	**3000**	.329
	Roberto Clemente	18	9,454	**3000**	.317
22	Sam Rice*	20	9,269	**2987**	.322
23	Sam Crawford*	19	9,580	**2964**	.309
24	Willie Keeler*	19	8,585	**2947**	.343
25	Frank Robinson	21	10,006	**2943**	.294

Players Active in 1998

		Yrs	AB	H	Avg
1	Paul Molitor	21	10,835	**3319**	.306
2	Tony Gwynn*	17	8,648	**2928**	.339
3	Wade Boggs*	17	8,888	**2922**	.329
4	Cal Ripken Jr.	18	10,433	**2878**	.276
5	Rickey Henderson	20	9,473	**2678**	.283
6	Harold Baines*	19	9,111	**2649**	.291
7	Tim Raines†	20	8,559	**2532**	.296
8	Chili Davis†	18	8,197	**2252**	.275
9	Gary Gaetti	18	8,661	**2223**	.257
10	Willie McGee†	17	7,378	**2186**	.296
11	Joe Carter	16	8,422	**2184**	.259
12	Tony Fernandez†	15	7,303	**2081**	.285
13	Rafael Palmeiro*	13	6,716	**1975**	.294

Games Played

1	Pete Rose	3562
2	Carl Yastrzemski	3308
3	Hank Aaron	3298
4	Ty Cobb	3034
5	Stan Musial	3026
	Eddie Murray	3026
7	Willie Mays	2992
8	Dave Winfield	2973
9	Rusty Staub	2951
10	Brooks Robinson	2896
11	Robin Yount	2856
12	Al Kaline	2834
13	Eddie Collins	2826
14	Reggie Jackson	2820
15	Frank Robinson	2808
16	Tris Speaker	2789
	Honus Wagner	2789
18	Tony Perez	2777
19	Mel Ott	2734
20	George Brett	2707

At Bats

1	Pete Rose	14,053
2	Hank Aaron	12,364
3	Carl Yastrzemski	11,988
4	Ty Cobb	11,429
5	Eddie Murray	11,336
6	Robin Yount	11,008
7	Dave Winfield	11,003
8	Stan Musial	10,972
9	Willie Mays	10,881
10	**Paul Molitor**	10,835
11	Brooks Robinson	10,654
12	Honus Wagner	10,441
13	**Cal Ripken Jr.**	10,433
14	George Brett	10,349
15	Lou Brock	10,332
16	Luis Aparicio	10,230
17	Tris Speaker	10,197
18	Al Kaline	10,116
19	Rabbit Maranville	10,078
20	Frank Robinson	10,006

Total Bases

1	Hank Aaron	6856
2	Stan Musial	6134
3	Willie Mays	6066
4	Ty Cobb	5863
5	Babe Ruth	5793
6	Pete Rose	5752
7	Carl Yastrzemski	5539
8	Eddie Murray	5397
9	Frank Robinson	5373
10	Dave Winfield	5219
11	Tris Speaker	5103
12	Lou Gehrig	5059
13	George Brett	5044
14	Mel Ott	5041
15	Jimmie Foxx	4956
16	Ted Williams	4884
17	Honus Wagner	4868
18	**Paul Molitor**	4854
19	Al Kaline	4852
20	Reggie Jackson	4834

Home Runs

		Yrs	AB	HR	AB/HR
1	Hank Aaron	23	12,364	755	16.4
2	Babe Ruth*	22	8,399	714	11.8
3	Willie Mays	22	10,881	660	16.5
4	Frank Robinson	21	10,006	586	17.1
5	Harmon Killebrew	22	8,147	573	14.2
6	Reggie Jackson*	21	9,864	563	17.5
7	Mike Schmidt	18	8,352	548	15.2
8	Mickey Mantle†	18	8,102	536	15.1
9	Jimmie Foxx	20	8,134	534	15.2
10	Ted Williams*	19	7,706	521	14.8
	Willie McCovey*	22	8,197	521	15.7
12	Eddie Mathews*	17	8,537	512	16.7
	Ernie Banks	19	9,421	512	18.4
14	Mel Ott*	22	9,456	511	18.5
15	Eddie Murray†	21	11,336	504	22.5
16	Lou Gehrig*	17	8,001	493	16.2
17	Willie Stargell*	21	7,927	475	16.7
	Stan Musial*	22	10,972	475	23.1
19	Dave Winfield	22	11,003	465	23.7
20	**Mark McGwire**	13	5,131	457	11.2
21	Carl Yastrzemski*	23	11,988	452	26.5
22	Dave Kingman	16	6,677	442	15.1
23	Andre Dawson	21	9,927	438	22.7
24	Billy Williams*	18	9,350	426	22.0
25	Darrell Evans*	21	8,973	414	21.7

Players Active in 1998

		Yrs	AB	HR	AB/HR
1	Mark McGwire	13	5,131	457	11.2
2	Barry Bonds*	13	6,621	411	16.1
3	Jose Canseco	14	6,042	397	15.2
4	Joe Carter	16	8,422	396	21.3
5	Cal Ripken Jr.	18	10,433	384	27.2
6	Fred McGriff*	13	6,257	358	17.5
7	Gary Gaetti	18	8,661	351	24.7
8	Ken Griffey Jr.*	10	5,226	350	14.9
9	Harold Baines*	19	9,111	348	26.2
10	Darryl Strawberry*	16	5,369	332	16.2
11	Andres Galarraga	14	6,629	332	20.0
12	Chili Davis†	18	8,197	331	24.8
13	Albert Belle	10	4,684	321	14.6
14	Cecil Fielder	13	5,157	319	16.2
15	Rafael Palmeiro*	13	6,716	314	21.4

Runs Batted In

		Yrs	Gm	RBI	P/G
1	Hank Aaron	23	3298	2297	.70
2	Babe Ruth*	22	2503	2211	.88
3	Lou Gehrig*	17	2164	1990	.92
4	Ty Cobb*	24	3034	1961	.65
5	Stan Musial*	22	3026	1951	.64
6	Jimmie Foxx	20	2317	1921	.83
7	Eddie Murray†	21	2980	1917	.64
8	Willie Mays	22	2992	1903	.64
9	Mel Ott*	22	2732	1861	.68
10	Carl Yastrzemski*	23	3308	1844	.56
11	Ted Williams*	19	2292	1839	.80
12	Dave Winfield	22	2973	1833	.62
13	Al Simmons	20	2215	1827	.82
14	Frank Robinson	21	2808	1812	.65
15	Honus Wagner	21	2786	1732	.62
16	Cap Anson	22	2276	1715	.75
17	Reggie Jackson*	21	2820	1702	.60
18	Tony Perez	23	2777	1652	.59
19	Ernie Banks	19	2528	1636	.65
20	Goose Goslin*	18	2287	1609	.70
21	Nap Lajoie	21	2475	1599	.65
22	Mike Schmidt	18	2404	1595	.66
	George Brett*	21	2707	1595	.59
24	Andre Dawson	21	2627	1591	.61
25	Rogers Hornsby	23	2259	1584	.70
	Harmon Killebrew	22	2435	1584	.65

Players Active in 1998

		Yrs	Gm	RBI	P/G
1	Cal Ripken Jr.	18	2704	1514	.56
2	Harold Baines*	19	2567	1480	.58
3	Joe Carter	16	2189	1445	.66
4	Paul Molitor	21	2683	1307	.49
5	Chili Davis†	18	2289	1294	.57
	Gary Gaetti	18	2389	1294	.54
7	Barry Bonds*	13	1898	1216	.64
8	Jose Canseco	14	1600	1214	.76
9	Andres Galarraga	14	1774	1172	.66
10	Mark McGwire	13	1535	1130	.74
11	Bobby Bonilla†	13	1846	1106	.60
	Will Clark*	13	1769	1106	.63
13	Fred McGriff*	13	1753	1088	.62
14	Ruben Sierra†	13	1662	1047	.63
15	Tony Gwynn*	17	2222	1042	.47

Runs

1	Ty Cobb	2245
2	Babe Ruth	2174
	Hank Aaron	2174
4	Pete Rose	2165
5	Willie Mays	2062
6	**Rickey Henderson**	2014
7	Stan Musial	1949
8	Lou Gehrig	1888
9	Tris Speaker	1882
10	Mel Ott	1859
11	Frank Robinson	1829
12	Eddie Collins	1820
13	Carl Yastrzemski	1816
14	Ted Williams	1798
15	**Paul Molitor**	1780
16	Charlie Gehringer	1774
17	Jimmie Foxx	1751
18	Honus Wagner	1735
19	Willie Keeler	1727
20	Cap Anson	1719

Extra Base Hits

1	Hank Aaron	1477
2	Stan Musial	1377
3	Babe Ruth	1356
4	Willie Mays	1323
5	Lou Gehrig	1190
6	Frank Robinson	1186
7	Carl Yastrzemski	1157
8	Ty Cobb	1139
9	Tris Speaker	1132
10	George Brett	1119
11	Ted Williams	1117
	Jimmie Foxx	1117
13	Eddie Murray	1099
14	Dave Winfield	1093
15	Reggie Jackson	1075
16	Mel Ott	1071
17	Pete Rose	1041
18	Andre Dawson	1039
19	Mike Schmidt	1015
20	Rogers Hornsby	1011

Slugging Percentage

1	Babe Ruth	.690
2	Ted Williams	.634
3	Lou Gehrig	.632
4	Jimmie Foxx	.609
5	Hank Greenberg	.605
6	Joe DiMaggio	.579
7	Rogers Hornsby	.577
8	**Albert Belle**	.577
9	**Mark McGwire**	.576
10	**Ken Griffey Jr.**	.568
11	**Juan Gonzalez**	.568
12	Johnny Mize	.562
13	Stan Musial	.559
14	Willie Mays	.557
15	Mickey Mantle	.557
16	**Barry Bonds**	.556
17	Hank Aaron	.555
18	Ralph Kiner	.548
19	Hack Wilson	.545
20	Chuck Klein	.543

Stolen Bases

	Player	SB
1	**Rickey Henderson**	1297
2	Lou Brock	938
3	Billy Hamilton	915
4	Ty Cobb	892
5	**Tim Raines**	803
6	Vince Coleman	752
7	Eddie Collins	743
8	Max Carey	738
9	Honus Wagner	720
10	Joe Morgan	689
11	Arlie Latham	679
12	Willie Wilson	668
13	Bert Campaneris	649
14	Tom Brown	627
15	George Davis	615
16	Dummy Hoy	597
17	**Otis Nixon**	594
18	Maury Wills	586
19	Hugh Duffy	583
	George Van Haltren	583

Walks

	Player	BB
1	Babe Ruth	2056
2	Ted Williams	2019
3	**Rickey Henderson**	1890
4	Joe Morgan	1865
5	Carl Yastrzemski	1845
6	Mickey Mantle	1734
7	Mel Ott	1708
8	Eddie Yost	1614
9	Darrell Evans	1605
10	Stan Musial	1599
11	Pete Rose	1566
12	Harmon Killebrew	1559
13	Lou Gehrig	1508
14	Mike Schmidt	1507
15	Eddie Collins	1503
16	Willie Mays	1463
17	Jimmie Foxx	1452
18	Eddie Mathews	1444
19	Frank Robinson	1420
20	Hank Aaron	1402

Strikeouts

	Player	SO
1	Reggie Jackson	2597
2	Willie Stargell	1936
3	Mike Schmidt	1883
4	Tony Perez	1867
5	Dave Kingman	1816
6	Bobby Bonds	1757
7	Dale Murphy	1748
8	Lou Brock	1730
9	Mickey Mantle	1710
10	Harmon Killebrew	1699
11	Dwight Evans	1697
12	Dave Winfield	1686
13	**Jose Canseco**	1630
14	**Andres Galarraga**	1615
15	**Chili Davis**	1598
16	Lee May	1570
17	Dick Allen	1556
18	Willie McCovey	1550
19	**Gary Gaetti**	1548
20	Dave Parker	1537

Pitching

Note that (*) indicates left-handed pitcher. Active pitching leaders are listed for wins and strikeouts.

Wins

	Player	Yrs	GS	W	L	Pct
1	Cy Young	22	815	**511**	316	.618
2	Walter Johnson	21	666	**416**	279	.599
3	Christy Mathewson	17	551	**373**	188	.665
	Grover Alexander	20	598	**373**	208	.642
5	Warren Spahn*	21	665	**363**	245	.597
6	Kid Nichols	15	561	**361**	208	.634
	Pud Galvin	14	682	**361**	308	.540
8	Tim Keefe	14	594	**342**	225	.603
9	Steve Carlton*	24	709	**329**	244	.574
10	Eddie Plank*	17	527	**327**	193	.629
11	John Clarkson	12	518	**326**	177	.648
12	Don Sutton	23	756	**324**	256	.559
13	Nolan Ryan	27	773	**324**	292	.526
14	Phil Niekro	24	716	**318**	274	.537
15	Gaylord Perry	22	690	**314**	265	.542
16	Old Hoss Radbourn	12	503	**311**	194	.616
	Tom Seaver	20	647	**311**	205	.603
18	Mickey Welch	13	549	**308**	209	.596
19	Lefty Grove*	17	456	**300**	141	.680
	Early Wynn	23	612	**300**	244	.551
21	Tommy John*	26	700	**288**	231	.555
22	Bert Blyleven	22	685	**287**	250	.534
23	Robin Roberts	19	609	**286**	245	.539
24	Tony Mullane	13	505	**285**	220	.564
25	Ferguson Jenkins	19	594	**284**	226	.557
26	Jim Kaat*	25	625	**283**	237	.544
27	Red Ruffing	22	536	**273**	225	.548
28	Burleigh Grimes	19	495	**270**	212	.560
29	Jim Palmer	19	521	**268**	152	.638
30	Bob Feller	18	484	**266**	162	.621

Pitchers Active in 1998

	Player	Yrs	GS	W	L	Pct
1	Dennis Martinez	23	562	**245**	193	.559
2	Roger Clemens	15	449	**233**	124	.653
3	Greg Maddux	13	399	**202**	117	.633
4	Dennis Eckersley	24	361	**197**	171	.535
5	Orel Hershiser	16	428	**190**	133	.588
6	Jimmy Key*	15	389	**186**	117	.614
7	Dwight Gooden	14	374	**185**	103	.642
8	Mark Langston*	15	423	**178**	156	.533
9	Dave Stieb	16	412	**176**	137	.562
10	Tom Glavine*	12	364	**173**	105	.622

Strikeouts

	Player	Yrs	IP	SO	P/9
1	Nolan Ryan	27	5387.0	**5714**	9.54
2	Steve Carlton*	24	5217.1	**4136**	7.13
3	Bert Blyleven	22	4970.1	**3701**	6.70
4	Tom Seaver	20	4782.2	**3640**	6.85
5	Don Sutton	23	5282.1	**3574**	6.09
6	Gaylord Perry	22	5350.1	**3534**	5.94
7	Walter Johnson	21	5923.2	**3508**	5.33
8	Phil Niekro	24	5404.1	**3342**	5.57
9	Ferguson Jenkins	19	4500.2	**3192**	6.38
10	**Roger Clemens**	15	3274.2	**3153**	8.67
11	Bob Gibson	17	3884.1	**3117**	7.22
12	Jim Bunning	17	3760.1	**2855**	6.83
13	Mickey Lolich*	16	3638.1	**2832**	7.01
14	Cy Young	22	7354.2	**2796**	3.42
15	Frank Tanana*	21	4186.2	**2773**	5.96
16	Warren Spahn*	21	5243.2	**2583**	4.43
17	Bob Feller	18	3827.0	**2581**	6.07
18	Jerry Koosman*	19	3839.1	**2556**	5.99
19	Tim Keefe	14	5061.1	**2527**	4.50
20	Christy Mathewson	17	4781.0	**2502**	4.71
21	Don Drysdale	14	3432.0	**2486**	6.52
22	Jack Morris	18	3824.2	**2478**	5.83
23	Jim Kaat*	25	4530.1	**2461**	4.89
24	Sam McDowell*	15	2492.1	**2453**	8.86
25	**Mark Langston***	15	2901.0	**2421**	7.51
26	Luis Tiant	19	3486.1	**2416**	6.24
27	**Dennis Eckersley**	24	3285.2	**2401**	6.58
28	Sandy Koufax*	12	2324.1	**2396**	9.28
29	Charlie Hough	25	3799.1	**2363**	5.60
30	Robin Roberts	19	4688.2	**2357**	4.52

Pitchers Active in 1998

	Player	Yrs	IP	SO	P/9
1	Roger Clemens	15	3274.2	**3153**	8.67
2	Mark Langston*	15	2901.0	**2421**	7.51
3	Dennis Eckersley	24	3285.2	**2401**	6.58
4	Randy Johnson*	11	1978.1	**2329**	10.60
5	David Cone	13	2396.2	**2243**	8.42
6	Dwight Gooden	14	2580.2	**2150**	7.50
7	Dennis Martinez	23	3999.2	**2149**	4.84
8	Greg Maddux	13	2849.1	**2024**	6.39
9	Chuck Finley*	13	2461.2	**1951**	7.13
10	Danny Darwin	21	3016.2	**1942**	5.79

Winning Pct.

		Yrs	W-L	Pct
1	Bob Caruthers	9	218-97	.692
2	Dave Foutz	11	147-66	.690
3	Whitey Ford*	16	236-106	.690
4	Lefty Grove*	17	300-141	.680
5	Vic Raschi	10	132-66	.667
	Mike Mussina	8	118-59	.667
7	Christy Mathewson	17	373-188	.665
8	Larry Corcoran	8	177-90	.663
9	Sam Leever	13	194-101	.658
10	Sal Maglie	10	119-62	.657
11	Sandy Koufax*	12	165-87	.655
12	Johnny Allen	13	142-75	.654
13	**Roger Clemens**	15	233-124	.653
14	Ron Guidry*	14	170-91	.651
15	Lefty Gomez*	14	189-102	.649

Losses

		Yrs	GS	W	L	Pct
1	Cy Young	22	815	511	**316**	.618
2	Pud Galvin	14	682	361	**308**	.540
3	Nolan Ryan	27	773	324	**292**	.526
4	Walter Johnson	21	666	416	**279**	.599
5	Phil Niekro	24	716	318	**274**	.537
6	Gaylord Perry	22	690	314	**265**	.542
7	Jack Powell	16	517	245	**256**	.489
	Don Sutton	23	756	324	**256**	.559
9	Eppa Rixey*	21	552	266	**251**	.515
10	Bert Blyleven	22	685	287	**250**	.534
11	Robin Roberts	19	609	286	**245**	.539
	Warren Spahn*	21	665	363	**245**	.597
13	Early Wynn	23	612	300	**244**	.551
	Steve Carlton*	24	709	329	**244**	.574
15	Jim Kaat*	25	625	283	**237**	.544

Appearances

1 **Dennis Eckersley** 1071
2 Hoyt Wilhelm 1070
3 Kent Tekulve 1050
4 **Jesse Orosco** 1025
5 Lee Smith..................1022
6 Rich Gossage..............1002
7 Lindy McDaniel..............987
8 Rollie Fingers................944
9 Gene Garber 931
10 Cy Young...................906
11 Sparky Lyle 899
12 Jim Kaat....................898
13 Jeff Reardon 880
14 Don McMahon 874
15 Phil Niekro 864

Innings Pitched

1 Cy Young...............7356.0
2 Pud Galvin 5941.1
3 Walter Johnson..........5923.2
4 Phil Niekro 5403.1
5 Nolan Ryan..............5387.0
6 Gaylord Perry............5350.1
7 Don Sutton..............5280.1
8 Warren Spahn 5243.2
9 Steve Carlton 5217.1
10 Grover Alexander 5189.2
11 Kid Nichols..............5084.0
12 Tim Keefe................5061.1
13 Bert Blyleven 4970.1
14 Mickey Welch............4802.0
15 Tom Seaver 4782.2

Earned Run Avg.

1 Ed Walsh 1.82
2 Addie Joss 1.88
3 Three Finger Brown..........2.06
4 Monte Ward 2.10
5 Christy Mathewson 2.13
6 Rube Waddell 2.16
7 Walter Johnson 2.17
8 Orval Overall 2.24
9 Tommy Bond 2.25
10 Will White 2.28
11 Ed Reulbach................2.28
12 Jim Scott 2.32
13 Eddie Plank 2.34
14 Larry Corcoran 2.36
15 Eddie Cicotte...............2.37

Shutouts

1 Walter Johnson..............110
2 Grover Alexander.............90
3 Christy Mathewson............80
4 Cy Young....................76
5 Eddie Plank 69
6 Warren Spahn.................63
7 Nolan Ryan 61
Tom Seaver 61
9 Bert Blyleven 60
10 Don Sutton..................58
11 Three Finger Brown 57
Pud Galvin...................57
Ed Walsh 57
14 Bob Gibson 56
15 Steve Carlton................55

Walks Allowed

1 Nolan Ryan................2795
2 Steve Carlton 1833
3 Phil Niekro 1809
4 Early Wynn................1775
5 Bob Feller 1764
6 Bobo Newsom 1732
7 Amos Rusie 1704
8 Charlie Hough 1665
9 Gus Weyhing 1566
10 Red Ruffing 1541
11 Bump Hadley 1442
12 Warren Spahn 1434
13 Earl Whitehill 1431
14 Tony Mullane 1409
15 Sad Sam Jones............1396

HRs Allowed

1 Robin Roberts 505
2 Ferguson Jenkins.............484
3 Phil Niekro 482
4 Don Sutton..................472
5 Frank Tanana 448
6 Warren Spahn 434
7 Bert Blyleven 430
8 Steve Carlton 414
9 Gaylord Perry...............399
10 Jim Kaat...................395
11 Jack Morris 389
12 Charlie Hough 383
13 Tom Seaver 380
14 Catfish Hunter..............374
15 Jim Bunning................372
Dennis Martinez 372

Saves

1 Lee Smith...................478
2 **John Franco**...............397
3 **Dennis Eckersley**..........390
4 Jeff Reardon 367
5 **Randy Myers** 347
6 Rollie Fingers...............341
7 Tom Henke..................311
8 Rich Gossage 310
9 Bruce Sutter.................300
10 **Jeff Montgomery** 292
11 **Doug Jones** 291
12 **Rick Aguilera** 275
13 Todd Worrell 256
14 **John Wetteland**...........253
15 Dave Righetti...............252
16 **Rod Beck** 250
17 Dan Quisenberry 244
18 Sparky Lyle 238
19 Hoyt Wilhelm 227
20 Gene Garber 218
21 Dave Smith 216
22 **Gregg Olson** 203
23 Bobby Thigpen 201
24 Roy Face 193
Mike Henneman.............193
26 Mitch Williams 192
27 **Trevor Hoffman**...........188
28 Jeff Russell 186
29 Steve Bedrosian 184
Kent Tekulve 184

SINGLE SEASON

Through 1998 regular season.

Batting

Home Runs

		Year	Gm	AB	HR
1	**Mark McGwire**, St.L	1998	155	509	70
2	**Sammy Sosa**, Chi-NL	1998	159	643	66
3	Roger Maris, NY-AL	1961	162	590	61
4	Babe Ruth, NY-AL	1927	151	540	60
5	Babe Ruth, NY-AL	1921	152	540	59
6	Mark McGwire, Oak-St.L	1997	156	540	58
	Hank Greenberg, Det	1938	155	556	58
	Jimmie Foxx, Phi-AL	1932	154	585	58
9	Hack Wilson, Chi-NL	1930	155	585	56
	Ken Griffey Jr., Sea	1997	157	608	56
	Ken Griffey Jr., Sea	1998	161	633	56
12	Babe Ruth, NY-AL	1920	142	458	54
	Mickey Mantle, NY-AL	1961	153	514	54
	Babe Ruth, NY-AL	1928	154	536	54
	Ralph Kiner, Pit	1949	152	549	54
16	Mickey Mantle, NY-AL	1956	150	533	52
	Willie Mays, SF	1965	157	558	52
	George Foster, Cin	1977	158	615	52
	Mark McGwire, Oak	1996	130	423	52
20	Ralph Kiner, Pit	1947	152	565	51
	Cecil Fielder, Det	1990	159	573	51
	Willie Mays, NY-NL	1955	152	580	51
	Johnny Mize, NY-NL	1947	154	586	51

Hits

		Year	AB	H	Avg
1	George Sisler, StL-AL	1920	631	**257**	.407
2	Bill Terry, NY-NL	1930	633	**254**	.401
	Lefty O'Doul, Phi-NL	1929	638	**254**	.398
4	Al Simmons, Phi-AL	1925	658	**253**	.384
5	Rogers Hornsby, StL-NL	1922	623	**250**	.401
6	Chuck Klein, Phi-NL	1930	648	**250**	.386
7	Ty Cobb, Det	1911	591	**248**	.420
8	George Sisler, StL-AL	1922	586	**246**	.420
9	Babe Herman, Bklyn	1930	614	**241**	.393
	Heinie Manush, StL-AL	1928	638	**241**	.378
11	Wade Boggs, Bos	1985	653	**240**	.368
12	Rod Carew, Min	1977	616	**239**	.388
13	Don Mattingly, NY-AL	1986	677	**238**	.352
14	Harry Heilmann, Det	1921	602	**237**	.394
	Paul Waner, Pit	1927	623	**237**	.380
	Joe Medwick, StL-NL	1937	633	**237**	.374
17	Jack Tobin, StL-AL	1921	671	**236**	.352
18	Rogers Hornsby, StL-NL	1921	592	**235**	.397
19	Lloyd Waner, Pit	1929	662	**234**	.353
	Kirby Puckett, Min	1988	657	**234**	.356

Batting Average

From 1900-49

		Year	AB	H	Avg
1	Rogers Hornsby, StL-NL	1924	536	227	.424
2	Nap Lajoie, Phi-AL	1901	543	229	.422
3	George Sisler, StL-AL	1922	586	246	.420
4	Ty Cobb, Det	1911	591	248	.420
5	Ty Cobb, Det	1912	533	227	.410
6	Joe Jackson, Cle	1911	571	233	.408
7	George Sisler, StL-AL	1920	631	257	.407
8	Ted Williams, Bos-AL	1941	456	185	.406
9	Rogers Hornsby, StL-NL	1925	504	203	.403
10	Harry Heilmann, Det	1923	524	211	.403

Since 1950

		Year	AB	H	Avg
1	Tony Gwynn, SD	1994	419	175	.394
2	George Brett, KC	1980	449	175	.390
3	Ted Williams, Bos	1957	420	163	.388
4	Rod Carew, Min	1977	616	239	.388
5	Tony Gwynn, SD	1997	592	220	.372
6	Andres Galarraga, Col	1993	470	174	.370
7	Tony Gwynn, SD	1987	589	218	.370
8	Tony Gwynn, SD	1995	535	197	.368
9	Wade Boggs, Bos	1985	653	240	.368
10	Wade Boggs, Bos	1988	584	214	.366

Total Bases

From 1900-49

		Year	TB
1	Babe Ruth, New York-AL	1921	457
2	Rogers Hornsby, St. Louis-NL	1922	450
3	Lou Gehrig, New York-AL	1927	447
4	Chuck Klein, Philadelphia-NL	1930	445
5	Jimmie Foxx, Philadelphia-AL	1932	438
6	Stan Musial, St. Louis-NL	1948	429
7	Hack Wilson, Chicago-NL	1930	423
8	Chuck Klein, Philadelphia-NL	1932	420
9	Lou Gehrig, New York-AL	1930	419
10	Joe DiMaggio, New York-AL	1937	418

Since 1950

		Year	TB
1	**Sammy Sosa**, Chi-NL	1998	416
2	Larry Walker, Colorado	1997	409
3	Jim Rice, Boston	1978	406
4	Hank Aaron, Milwaukee	1959	400
5	**Albert Belle**, Chi-AL	1998	399
6	Ken Griffey Jr., Seattle	1997	393
7	Ellis Burks, Colorado	1996	392
8	George Foster, Cincinnati	1977	388
	Don Mattingly, New York-AL	1986	388
10	**Ken Griffey Jr.**, Seattle	1998	387

Runs Batted In

From 1900-49

		Year	Avg	HR	RBI
1	Hack Wilson, Chi-NL	1930	.356	56	190
2	Lou Gehrig, NY-AL	1931	.341	46	184
3	Hank Greenberg, Det	1937	.337	40	183
4	Lou Gehrig, NY-AL	1927	.373	47	175
	Jimmie Foxx, Bos-AL	1938	.349	50	175
6	Lou Gehrig, NY-AL	1930	.379	41	174
7	Babe Ruth, NY-AL	1921	.378	59	171
8	Chuck Klein, Phi-NL	1930	.386	40	170
	Hank Greenberg, Det	1935	.328	36	170
10	Jimmie Foxx, Phi-AL	1932	.364	58	169

Since 1950

		Year	Avg	HR	RBI
1	**Sammy Sosa**, Chi-NL	1998	.308	66	158
2	**Juan Gonzalez**, Tex	1998	.318	45	157
3	Tommy Davis, LA-NL	1962	.346	27	153
4	**Albert Belle**, Chi-AL	1998	.328	49	152
5	Andres Galarraga, Col	1996	.304	47	150
6	George Foster, Cin	1977	.320	52	149
7	Johnny Bench, Cin	1970	.293	45	148
	Albert Belle, Cle	1996	.311	48	148
9	Ken Griffey Jr., Sea	1997	.304	56	147
	Mark McGwire, St.L	1998	.299	70	147

Runs

		Year	Runs
1	Babe Ruth, New York-AL	1921	177
2	Lou Gehrig, New York-AL	1936	167
3	Babe Ruth, New York-AL	1928	163
	Lou Gehrig, New York-AL	1931	163
5	Babe Ruth, New York-AL	1920	158
	Babe Ruth, New York-AL	1927	158
	Chuck Klein, Philadelphia-NL	1930	158
8	Rogers Hornsby, Chicago-NL	1929	156
9	Kiki Cuyler, Chicago-NL	1930	155
10	Lefty O'Doul, Philadelphia-NL	1929	152
	Woody English, Chicago-NL	1930	152
	Al Simmons, Philadelphia-AL	1930	152
	Chuck Klein, Philadelphia-NL	1932	152
14	Babe Ruth, New York-AL	1923	151
	Jimmie Foxx, Philadelphia-AL	1932	151
	Joe DiMaggio, New York-AL	1937	151
17	Babe Ruth, New York-AL	1930	150
	Ted Williams, Boston-AL	1940	150
19	Lou Gehrig, New York-AL	1927	149
	Babe Ruth, New York-AL	1931	149

Walks

		Year	BB
1	Babe Ruth, New York-AL	1923	170
2	Ted Williams, Boston-AL	1947	162
	Ted Williams, Boston-AL	1949	162
	Mark McGwire, St. Louis	1998	162
4	Ted Williams, Boston-AL	1946	156
5	Barry Bonds, San Francisco	1996	151
	Eddie Yost, Washington	1956	151
7	Eddie Joost, Philadelphia-AL	1949	149
8	Babe Ruth, New York-AL	1920	148
	Eddie Stanky, Brooklyn	1945	148
	Jimmy Wynn, Houston	1969	148

Extra Base Hits

		Year	EBH
1	Babe Ruth, New York-AL	1921	119
2	Lou Gehrig, New York-AL	1927	117
3	Chuck Klein, Philadelphia-NL	1930	107
4	Chuck Klein, Philadelphia-NL	1932	103
	Hank Greenberg, Detroit	1937	103
	Stan Musial, St. Louis-NL	1948	103
	Albert Belle, Cleveland	1995	103
8	Rogers Hornsby, St. Louis-NL	1922	102
9	Lou Gehrig, New York-AL	1930	100
	Jimmie Foxx, Philadelphia-AL	1933	100

Slugging Percentage

From 1900-49

		Year	Pct
1	Babe Ruth, New York-AL	1920	.847
2	Babe Ruth, New York-AL	1921	.846
3	Babe Ruth, New York-AL	1927	.772
4	Lou Gehrig, New York-AL	1927	.765
5	Babe Ruth, New York-AL	1923	.764
6	Rogers Hornsby, St. Louis-NL	1925	.756
7	Jimmie Foxx, Philadelphia-AL	1932	.749
8	Babe Ruth, New York-AL	1924	.739
9	Babe Ruth, New York-AL	1926	.737
10	Ted Williams, Boston-AL	1941	.735

Since 1950

		Year	Pct
1	**Mark McGwire**, St. Louis	1998	.752
2	Jeff Bagwell, Houston	1994	.750
3	Ted Williams, Boston	1957	.731
4	Mark McGwire, Oakland	1996	.730
5	Frank Thomas, Chicago-AL	1994	.729
6	Larry Walker, Colorado	1997	.720

Stolen Bases

		Year	SB
1	Rickey Henderson, Oakland	1982	130
2	Lou Brock, St. Louis	1974	118
3	Vince Coleman, St. Louis	1985	110
4	Vince Coleman, St. Louis	1987	109
5	Rickey Henderson, Oakland	1983	108
6	Vince Coleman, St. Louis	1986	107
7	Maury Wills, Los Angeles-NL	1962	104
8	Rickey Henderson, Oakland	1980	100
9	Ron LeFlore, Montreal	1980	97
10	Ty Cobb, Detroit	1915	96
11	Omar Moreno, Pittsburgh	1980	96
12	Maury Wills, Los Angeles	1965	94
13	Rickey Henderson, New York-AL	1988	93
14	Tim Raines, Montreal	1983	90
15	Clyde Milan, Washington	1912	88
16	Rickey Henderson, New York-AL	1986	87
17	Ty Cobb, Detroit	1911	83
	Willie Wilson, Kansas City	1979	83
19	Bob Bescher, Cincinnati	1911	81
	Eddie Collins, Philadelphia-AL	1910	81
	Vince Coleman, St. Louis	1988	81

Strikeouts

		Year	SO
1	Bobby Bonds, San Francisco	1970	189
2	Bobby Bonds, San Francisco	1969	187
3	Rob Deer, Milwaukee	1987	186
4	Pete Incaviglia, Texas	1986	185
5	Cecil Fielder, Detroit	1990	182
6	Mike Schmidt, Philadelphia	1975	180
7	Rob Deer, Milwaukee	1986	179
8	Dave Nicholson, Chicago-AL	1963	175
	Gorman Thomas, Milwaukee	1979	175
	Jose Canseco, Oakland	1986	175
	Rob Deer, Detroit	1991	175
	Jay Buhner, Seattle	1997	175

Pinch Hits

Career pinch hits in parentheses.

		Year	PH	
1	John Vander Wal, Colorado	1995	26	(78)
2	Jose Morales, Montreal	1976	25	(123)
3	Dave Philley, Baltimore	1961	24	(93)
	Vic Davalillo, St. Louis	1970	24	(95)
	Rusty Staub, New York-NL	1983	24	(100)

Four tied with 22 each.

Note: The all-time career pinch hit leader is Manny Mota (150).

Four Home Runs in One Game

National League

	Date	H/A	Inn
Bobby Lowe, Boston	5/30/1894	H	9
Ed Delahanty, Philadelphia	7/13/1896	A	9
Chuck Klein, Philadelphia	7/10/1936	A	10
Gil Hodges, Brooklyn	8/31/1950	H	9
Joe Adcock, Milwaukee	7/31/1954	A	9
Willie Mays, San Francisco	4/30/1961	A	9
Mike Schmidt, Philadelphia	4/17/1976	A	10
Bob Horner, Atlanta	7/6/1986	H	9
Mark Whiten, St. Louis	9/7/1993	A	9

American League

	Date	H/A	Inn
Lou Gehrig, New York	6/3/1932	A	9
Pat Seerey, Chicago	7/18/1948	A	11
Rocky Colavito, Cleveland	6/10/1959	A	9

Pitching

Wins

From 1900-49

		Year	W	L	Pct
1	Jack Chesbro, NY-AL	1904	**41**	12	.774
2	Ed Walsh, Chi-AL	1908	**40**	15	.727
3	Christy Mathewson, NY-NL	1908	**37**	11	.771
4	Walter Johnson, Wash	1913	**36**	7	.837
5	Joe McGinnity, NY-NL	1904	**35**	8	.814
6	Smokey Joe Wood, Bos-AL	1912	**34**	5	.872
7	Cy Young, Bos-AL	1901	**33**	10	.767
	Grover Alexander, Phi-NL	1916	**33**	12	.733
	Christy Mathewson, NY-NL	1904	**33**	12	.733
10	Cy Young, Bos-AL	1902	**32**	11	.744

Since 1950

		Year	W	L	Pct
1	Denny McLain, Det.	1968	**31**	6	.838
2	Robin Roberts, Phi-NL	1952	**28**	7	.800
3	Bob Welch, Oak	1990	**27**	6	.818
	Don Newcombe, Bklyn	1956	**27**	7	.794
	Sandy Koufax, LA	1966	**27**	9	.750
	Steve Carlton, Phi.	1972	**27**	10	.730
7	Sandy Koufax, LA	1965	**26**	8	.765
	Juan Marichal, SF	1968	**26**	9	.743

Note: 11 pitchers tied with 25 wins, including Marichal twice.

Earned Run Average

From 1900-49

		Year	ShO	ERA
1	Dutch Leonard, Bos-AL	1914	7	1.01
2	Three Finger Brown, Chi-NL	1906	10	1.04
3	Walter Johnson, Wash	1913	11	1.09
4	Christy Mathewson, NY-NL	1909	8	1.14
5	Jack Pfiester, Chi-NL	1907	3	1.15
6	Addie Joss, Cle	1908	9	1.16
7	Carl Lundgren, Chi-NL	1907	7	1.17
8	Grover Alexander, Phi-NL	1915	12	1.22
9	Cy Young, Bos-AL	1908	3	1.26
10	Three pitchers tied at 1.27			

Since 1950

		Year	ShO	ERA
1	Bob Gibson, St.L	1968	13	1.12
2	Dwight Gooden, NY-NL	1985	8	1.53
3	Greg Maddux, Atl.	1994	3	1.56
4	Luis Tiant, Cle	1968	9	1.60
5	Greg Maddux, Atl	1995	3	1.63
6	Dean Chance, LA-AL	1964	11	1.65
7	Nolan Ryan, Cal	1981	3	1.69
8	Sandy Koufax, LA	1966	5	1.73
9	Sandy Koufax, LA	1964	7	1.74
10	Ron Guidry, NY-AL	1978	9	1.74

Winning Pct.

		Year	W-L	Pct
1	Roy Face, Pit	1959	18-1	.947
2	Rick Sutcliffe, Chi-NL*	1984	16-1	.941
3	Johnny Allen, Cle	1937	15-1	.938
4	Greg Maddux, Atl	1995	19-2	.904
5	Randy Johnson, Sea.	1995	18-2	.900
6	Ron Guidry, NY-AL	1978	25-3	.893
7	Freddie Fitzsimmons, Bklyn	1940	16-2	.889
8	Lefty Grove, Phi-AL	1931	31-4	.886
9	Bob Stanley, Bos.	1978	15-2	.882
10	Preacher Roe, Bklyn	1951	22-3	.880
11	Tom Seaver, Cin	1981	14-2	.875
12	Smokey Joe Wood, Bos-AL	1912	34-5	.872

*Sutcliffe began 1984 with Cleveland and was 4-5 before being traded to the Cubs; his overall winning pct. was .769 (20-6).

Strikeouts

		Year	SO	P/G
1	Nolan Ryan, Cal	1973	**383**	10.57
2	Sandy Koufax, LA	1965	**382**	10.24
3	Nolan Ryan, Cal	1974	**367**	9.92
4	Rube Waddell, Phi-AL	1904	**349**	8.12
5	Bob Feller, Cle	1946	**348**	8.45
6	Nolan Ryan, Cal	1977	**341**	10.26
7	Nolan Ryan, Cal	1972	**329**	10.43
	Randy Johnson, Sea-Hou	1998	**329**	9.68
9	Nolan Ryan, Cal	1976	**327**	10.36
10	Sam McDowell, Cle	1965	**325**	10.71

Appearances

		Year	App	Sv
1	Mike Marshall, LA	1974	**106**	21
2	Kent Tekulve, Pit	1979	**94**	31
3	Mike Marshall, LA	1973	**92**	31
4	Kent Tekulve, Pit	1978	**91**	31
5	Wayne Granger, Cin	1969	**90**	27
	Mike Marshall, Min	1979	**90**	32
	Kent Tekulve, Phi	1987	**90**	3

Saves

		Year	App	Sv
1	Bobby Thigpen, Chi-AL	1990	77	57
2	Randy Myers, Chi-NL	1993	73	53
	Trevor Hoffman, SD	1998	66	53
4	Dennis Eckersley, Oak	1992	69	51
	Rod Beck, Chi-NL	1998	81	51
	Dennis Eckersley, Oak	1990	63	48
6	Rod Beck, SF	1993	76	48
	Jeff Shaw, Cin-LA	1998	73	48
7	Lee Smith, St.L	1991	67	47

Innings Pitched *(since 1920)*

		Year	IP	W-L
1	Wilbur Wood, Chi-AL	1972	**377**	24-17
2	Mickey Lolich, Det	1971	**376**	25-14
3	Bob Feller, Cle	1946	**371**	26-15
4	Grover Alexander, Chi-NL	1920	**363**	27-14
5	Wilbur Wood, Chi-AL	1973	**359**	24-20

Shutouts

		Year	ShO	ERA
1	Grover Alexander, Phi-NL	1916	**16**	1.55
2	Jack Coombs, Phi-AL	1910	**13**	1.30
	Bob Gibson, St.L	1968	**13**	1.12
4	Christy Mathewson, NY-NL	1908	**12**	1.43
	Grover Alexander, Phi-NL	1915	**12**	1.22

Walks Allowed

		Year	BB	SO
1	Bob Feller, Cle	1938	**208**	240
2	Nolan Ryan, Cal	1977	**204**	341
3	Nolan Ryan, Cal	1974	**202**	367
4	Bob Feller, Cle	1941	**194**	260
5	Bobo Newsom, St.L-AL	1938	**192**	226

Home Runs Allowed

		Year	HRs
1	Bert Blyleven, Minnesota	1986	50
2	Robin Roberts, Philadelphia	1956	46
	Bert Blyleven, Minnesota	1987	46
4	Pedro Ramos, Washington	1957	43
5	Denny McLain, Detroit	1966	42

Home Run in First Major League At bat

* on first pitch

A.L.

Luke Stuart, St. Louis, August 8, 1921.
Earl Averill, Cleveland, April 16, 1929.
Ace Parker, Philadelphia, April 30, 1937.
Gene Hasson, Philadelphia, September 9, 1937, first game.
Bill Lefebvre, Boston, June 10, 1938.*
Hack Miller, Detroit, April 23, 1944, second game.
Eddie Pellagrini, Boston, April 22, 1946.
George Vico, Detroit, April 20, 1948.*
Bob Nieman, St. Louis, September 14, 1951.
Bob Tillman, Boston, May 19, 1962.
John Kennedy, Washington, September 5, 1962, first game.
Buster Narum, Baltimore, May 3, 1963.
Gates Brown, Detroit, June 19, 1963.
Bert Campaneris, Kansas City, July 23, 1964.*
Bill Roman, Detroit, September 30, 1964, second game.
Brant Alyea, Washington, September 12, 1965.*
John Miller, New York, September 11, 1966.
Rick Renick, Minnesota, July 11, 1968.
Joe Keough, Oakland, August 7, 1968, second game.
Gene Lamont, Detroit, September 2, 1970, second game.
Don Rose, California, May 24, 1972.*
Reggie Sanders, Detroit, September 1, 1974.
Dave McKay, Minnesota, August 22, 1975.
Al Woods, Toronto, April 7, 1977.
Dave Machemer, California, June 21, 1978.
Gary Gaetti, Minnesota, September 20, 1981.
Andre David, Minnesota, June 29, 1984, first game.
Terry Steinbach, Oakland, September 12, 1986.
Jay Bell, Cleveland, September 29, 1986.*
Junior Felix, Toronto, May 4, 1989.*
Jon Nunnally, Kansas City, April 29, 1995.
Total number of players: 31

N.L.

Joe Harrington, Boston, September 10, 1895.
Bill Duggleby, Philadelphia, April 21, 1898.
Johnny Bates, Boston, April 12, 1906.
Walter Mueller, Pittsburgh, May 7, 1922.
Clise Dudley, Brooklyn, April 27, 1929.*
Gordon Slade, Brooklyn, May 24, 1930.
Eddie Morgan, St. Louis, April 14, 1936.*
Ernie Koy, Brooklyn, April 19, 1938.
Emmett Mueller, Philadelphia, April 19, 1938.
Clyde Vollmer, Cincinnati, May 31, 1942, second game.*
Paul Gillespie, Chicago, September 11, 1942.
Buddy Kerr, New York, September 8, 1943.
Whitey Lockman, New York, July 5, 1945.
Dan Bankhead, Brooklyn, August 26, 1947.
Les Layton, New York, May 21, 1948.
Ed Sanicki, Philadelphia, September 14, 1949.
Ted Tappe, Cincinnati, September 14, 1950, first game.
Hoyt Wilhelm, New York, April 23, 1952.
Wally Moon, St. Louis, April 13, 1954.
Chuck Tanner, Milwaukee, April 12, 1955.*
Bill White, New York, May 7, 1956.
Frank Ernaga, Chicago, May 24, 1957.
Don Leppert, Pittsburgh, June 18, 1961, first game.
Cuno Barragan, Chicago, September 1, 1961.
Benny Ayala, New York, August 27, 1974.
John Montefusco, San Francisco, September 3, 1974.
Jose Sosa, Houston, July 30, 1975.
Johnnie LeMaster, San Francisco, September 2, 1975.
Tim Wallach, Montreal, September 6, 1980.
Carmelo Martinez, Chicago, August 22, 1983.
Mike Fitzgerald, New York, September 13, 1983.
Will Clark, San Francisco, April 8, 1986.
Ricky Jordan, Philadelphia, July 17, 1988.
Jose Offerman, Los Angeles, August 19, 1990.
Dave Eiland, San Diego, April 10, 1992.
Jim Bullinger, Chicago, June 8, 1992, first game.
Jay Gainer, Colorado, May 14, 1993.*
Mitch Lyden, Florida, June 16, 1993.
Garey Ingram, Los Angeles, May 19, 1994.
Jermaine Dye, Atlanta, May 17, 1996.
Dustin Hermanson, Montreal, April 16, 1997.
Brad Fullmer, Montreal, Sept. 2, 1997.
Total number of players: 42

Unassisted Triple Plays

The unassisted triple play is one of the rarest feats in baseball. So much so, in fact, that it has been accomplished only 11 times in major league history. Ironically, in what can only be described as a statistic anomaly, the trick was turned twice in two days in May of 1927.

Player, Position, Team	Date	Opponent
Paul Hines, OF, Providence	May 8, 1878	Boston-NL
Neal Ball, SS, Cleveland	July 19, 1909	Boston-AL
Bill Wambganss, 2B, Cleveland*	Oct. 10, 1920	Brooklyn
George Burns, 1B, Boston-AL	Sept. 14, 1923	Cleveland
Ernie Padgett, SS, Boston-NL	Oct. 6, 1923	Philadelphia
Glenn Wright, SS, Pittsburgh	May 7, 1925	St.Louis-NL
Jimmy Cooney, SS, Chicago-NL	May 30, 1927	Pittsburgh
Johnny Neun, 1B, Detroit	May 31, 1927	Cleveland
Ron Hansen, SS, Washington	July 30, 1968	Cleveland
Mickey Morandini, 2B, Philadelphia	Sept. 20, 1992	Pittsburgh
John Valentin, SS, Boston	July 8, 1994	Seattle

*World Series game

All-Time Winningest Managers

Top 20 Major League career victories through the 1998 season. Career, regular season and postseason (playoffs and World Series) records are noted along with AL and NL pennants and World Series titles won. Managers active during 1998 season in **bold** type.

		Career				Regular Season			Postseason			
		Yrs	W	L	Pct	W	L	Pct	W	L	Pct	Titles
1	Connie Mack	53	**3755**	3967	.486	3731	3948	.486	24	19	.558	9 AL, 5 WS
2	John McGraw	33	**2866**	2012	.588	2840	1984	.589	26	28	.482	10 NL, 3 WS
3	Sparky Anderson	26	**2228**	1855	.547	2194	1834	.545	34	21	.618	4 NL, 1 AL, 3 WS
4	Bucky Harris	29	**2168**	2228	.493	2157	2218	.493	11	10	.524	3 AL, 2 WS
5	Joe McCarthy	24	**2155**	1346	.616	2125	1333	.615	30	13	.698	1 NL, 8 AL, 7 WS
6	Walter Alston	23	**2063**	1634	.558	2040	1613	.558	23	21	.523	7 NL, 4 WS
7	Leo Durocher	24	**2015**	1717	.540	2008	1709	.540	7	8	.467	3 NL, 1 WS
8	Casey Stengel	25	**1942**	1868	.510	1905	1842	.508	37	26	.587	10 AL, 7 WS
9	Gene Mauch	26	**1907**	2044	.483	1902	2037	.483	5	7	.417	—None—
10	Bill McKechnie	25	**1904**	1737	.523	1896	1723	.524	8	14	.364	4 NL, 2 WS
11	Tommy Lasorda	21	**1630**	1469	.526	1599	1439	.526	31	30	.508	4 NL, 2 WS
12	Ralph Houk	20	**1627**	1539	.514	1619	1531	.514	8	8	.500	3 AL, 2 WS
13	Fred Clarke	19	**1609**	1189	.575	1602	1181	.576	7	8	.467	4 NL, 1 WS
14	Dick Williams	21	**1592**	1474	.519	1571	1451	.520	21	23	.477	3 AL, 1 NL, 2 WS
15	**Tony La Russa**	20	**1590**	1445	.524	1564	1425	.523	26	20	.565	3 AL, 1 WS
16	Earl Weaver	17	**1506**	1080	.582	1480	1060	.583	26	20	.565	4 AL, 1 WS
17	Clark Griffith	20	**1491**	1367	.522	1491	1367	.522	0	0	.000	1 AL (1901)
18	**Bobby Cox**	17	**1461**	1181	.553	1418	1145	.553	43	36	.544	4 NL, 1 WS
19	Miller Huggins	17	**1431**	1149	.555	1413	1134	.555	18	15	.545	6 AL, 3 WS
20	Al Lopez	17	**1412**	1012	.583	1410	1004	.584	2	8	.200	2 AL

Notes: John McGraw's postseason record also includes two World Series tie games (1912,'22); Miller Huggins postseason record also includes one World Series tie game (1922).

Where They Managed

Alston—Brooklyn/Los Angeles NL (1954-76); **Anderson**—Cincinnati NL (1970-78), Detroit AL (1979-95); **Clarke**—Louisville NL (1897-99), Pittsburgh NL (1900-15); **Cox**—Atlanta (1978-81, 1990–), Toronto (1982-85); **Durocher**—Brooklyn NL (1939-46,48), New York NL (1948-55), Chicago NL (1966-72), Houston NL (1972-73); **Griffith**—Chicago AL (1901-02), New York AL (1903-08), Cincinnati NL (1909-11), Washington AL (1912-20); **Harris**—Washington AL (1924-28,35-42,50-54), Detroit AL (1929-33,55-56), Boston AL (1934), Philadelphia NL (1943), New York AL (1947-48); **Houk**—New York AL (1961-63,66-73), Detroit AL (1974-78), Boston AL (1981-84); **Huggins**—St. Louis NL (1913-17), New York AL (1918-29); **La Russa**—Chicago AL (1979-86), Oakland (1986-95); St. Louis (1996–) **Lasorda**—Los Angeles NL (1976-96); **Lopez**—Cleveland AL (1951-56), Chicago AL (1957-65,68-69).

Mack—Pittsburgh NL (1894-96), Philadelphia AL (1901-50); **Mauch**—Philadelphia NL (1960-68), Montreal NL (1969-75), Minnesota AL (1976-80), California AL (1981-82,85-87); **McCarthy**—Chicago NL (1926-30), New York AL (1931-46), Boston AL (1948-50); **McGraw**—Baltimore NL (1899), Baltimore AL (1901-02), New York NL (1902-32); **McKechnie**—Newark FL (1915), Pittsburgh NL (1922-26), St. Louis NL (1928-29), Boston NL (1930- 37), Cincinnati NL (1938-46); **Stengel**—Brooklyn NL (1934-36), Boston NL (1938-43), New York AL (1949-60), New York NL (1962-65); **Weaver**—Baltimore AL (1968-82,85-86); **Williams**—Boston AL (1967-69), Oakland AL (1971-73), California AL (1974-76), Montreal NL (1977-81), San Diego NL (1982-85), Seattle AL (1986-88).

Regular Season Winning Pct.

Minimum of 750 victories.

		Yrs	W	L	Pct	Pen
1	Joe McCarthy	24	2125	1333	**.615**	9
2	Charlie Comiskey	12	838	541	**.608**	4
3	Frank Selee	16	1284	862	**.598**	5
4	Billy Southworth	13	1044	704	**.597**	4
5	Frank Chance	11	946	648	**.593**	4
6	John McGraw	33	2784	1959	**.587**	10
7	Al Lopez	17	1410	1004	**.584**	2
8	Earl Weaver	17	1480	1060	**.583**	4
9	Cap Anson	20	1296	947	**.578**	5
10	Fred Clarke	19	1602	1181	**.576**	4
11	Davey Johnson	12	985	727	**.575**	1
12	Steve O'Neill	14	1040	821	**.559**	1
13	Walter Alston	23	2040	1613	**.558**	7
14	Bill Terry	10	823	661	**.555**	3
15	Miller Huggins	17	1413	1134	**.555**	6
16	**Bobby Cox**	17	1418	1145	**.553**	4
17	Billy Martin	16	1253	1013	**.553**	2
18	Harry Wright	18	1000	825	**.548**	3
19	Charlie Grimm	19	1287	1067	**.547**	3
20	Sparky Anderson	26	2194	1834	**.545**	5

World Series Victories

		App	W	L	T	Pct	WS
1	Casey Stengel	10	**37**	26	0	.587	7
2	Joe McCarthy	9	**30**	13	0	.698	7
3	John McGraw	9	**26**	28	2	.482	3
4	Connie Mack	8	**24**	19	0	.558	5
5	Walter Alston	7	**20**	20	0	.500	4
6	Miller Huggins	6	**18**	15	1	.544	3
7	Sparky Anderson	5	**16**	12	0	.571	3
8	Tommy Lasorda	4	**12**	11	0	.522	2
	Dick Williams	4	**12**	14	0	.462	2
10	Frank Chance	4	**11**	9	1	.548	2
	Bucky Harris	3	**11**	10	0	.524	2
	Billy Southworth	4	**11**	11	0	.500	2
	Earl Weaver	4	**11**	13	0	.458	1
	Bobby Cox	4	**11**	14	0	.440	1
15	Whitey Herzog	3	**10**	11	0	.476	1
16	Bill Carrigan	2	**8**	2	0	.800	2
	Danny Murtaugh	2	**8**	6	0	.571	2
	Ralph Houk	3	**8**	8	0	.500	2
	Bill McKechnie	4	**8**	14	0	.364	2
	Tom Kelly	2	**8**	6	0	.571	2
	Joe Torre	2	**8**	2	0	.800	2

Active Managers' Records

Regular season games only; through 1998.

National League

		Yrs	W	L	Pct
1	Tony La Russa, St.L.	20	**1564**	1425	.523
2	Bobby Cox, Atl.	17	**1418**	1145	.553
3	Jim Leyland, Col.	13	**997**	1041	.489
4	Davey Johnson, LA	12	**985**	727	.575
5	Jim Fregosi, Phi	14	**936**	1024	.478
6	Bobby Valentine, NY	11	**769**	772	.499
7	Jack McKeon, Cin.	10	**589**	589	.500
8	Felipe Alou, Mon.	7	**527**	504	.511
9	Phil Garner, Mil.	7	**511**	557	.478
10	Dusty Baker, SF	6	**472**	436	.520
11	Jim Riggleman, Chi.	7	**419**	503	.454
12	Gene Lamont, Pit.	6	**406**	386	.513
13	Buck Showalter, Ari.	5	**378**	365	.509
14	Bruce Bochy, SD	4	**335**	295	.532
15	Larry Dierker, Hou.	2	**186**	138	.574
16	John Boles, Fla	1	**40**	35	.533

American League

		Yrs	W	L	Pct
1	Joe Torre, NY	15	**1176**	1160	.503
2	Lou Piniella, Sea.	12	**940**	866	.520
3	Tom Kelly, Min.	13	**923**	977	.486
4	Mike Hargrove, Cle.	8	**624**	526	.543
5	Johnny Oates, Tex.	7	**620**	571	.521
6	Jimy Williams, Bos	6	**451**	395	.533
7	Art Howe, Oak.	3	**217**	269	.447
8	Ray Miller, Bal.	3	**188**	213	.469
9	Terry Collins, Ana	2	**169**	155	.522
10	Tony Muser, KC	2	**103**	137	.429
11	Tim Johnson, Tor	1	**88**	74	.543
12	Jerry Manuel, Chi.	1	**80**	82	.494
13	Larry Rothschild, TB	1	**63**	99	.389
14	Larry Parrish, Det.	1	**13**	12	.520

Annual Awards

MOST VALUABLE PLAYER

There have been three different Most Valuable Player awards in baseball since 1911—the Chalmers Award (1911-14), presented by the Detroit-based automobile company; the League Award (1922-29), presented by the National and American Leagues; and the Baseball Writers' Award (since 1931), presented by the Baseball Writers' Association of America. Statistics for winning players are provided below. Stats for winning pitchers before advent of Cy Young Award are in MVP Pitchers' Statistics table.

Multiple winners: NL—Barry Bonds, Roy Campanella, Stan Musial and Mike Schmidt (3); Ernie Banks, Johnny Bench, Rogers Hornsby, Carl Hubbell, Willie Mays, Joe Morgan and Dale Murphy (2). **AL**—Yogi Berra, Joe DiMaggio, Jimmie Foxx and Mickey Mantle (3); Mickey Cochrane, Lou Gehrig, Hank Greenberg, Walter Johnson, Roger Maris, Hal Newhouser, Cal Ripken Jr., Frank Thomas, Ted Williams and Robin Yount (2). **NL & AL**—Frank Robinson (2, one in each).

Chalmers Award

National League

Year		Pos	HR	RBI	Avg
1911	Wildfire Schulte, Chi	OF	21	121	.300
1912	Larry Doyle, NY	2B	10	90	.330
1913	Jake Daubert, Bklyn	1B	2	52	.350
1914	Johnny Evers, Bos	2B	1	40	.279

American League

Year		Pos	HR	RBI	Avg
1911	Ty Cobb, Det.	OF	8	144	.420
1912	Tris Speaker, Bos	OF	10	98	.383
1913	Walter Johnson, Wash	P	—	—	—
1914	Eddie Collins, Phi	2B	2	85	.344

League Award

National League

Year		Pos	HR	RBI	Avg
1922	No selection				
1923	No selection				
1924	Dazzy Vance, Bklyn	P	—	—	—
1925	Rogers Hornsby, St.L.	2B-Mgr	39	143	.403
1926	Bob O'Farrell, St.L	C	7	68	.293
1927	Paul Waner, Pit	OF	9	131	.380
1928	Jim Bottomley, St.L.	1B	31	136	.325
1929	Rogers Hornsby, Chi.	2B	39	149	.380

American League

Year		Pos	HR	RBI	Avg
1922	George Sisler, St.L	1B	8	105	.420
1923	Babe Ruth, NY	OF	41	131	.393
1924	Walter Johnson, Wash	P	—	—	—
1925	Roger Peckinpaugh, Wash.	SS	4	64	.294
1926	George Burns, Cle	1B	4	114	.358
1927	Lou Gehrig, NY	1B	47	175	.373
1928	Mickey Cochrane, Phi	C	10	57	.293
1929	No selection				

Most Valuable Player

National League

Year		Pos	HR	RBI	Avg
1931	Frankie Frisch, St.L	2B	4	82	.311
1932	Chuck Klein, Phi	OF	38	137	.348
1933	Carl Hubbell, NY	P	—	—	—
1934	Dizzy Dean, St.L	P	—	—	—
1935	Gabby Hartnett, Chi.	C	13	91	.344
1936	Carl Hubbell, NY	P	—	—	—
1937	Joe Medwick, St.L.	OF	31	154	.374
1938	Ernie Lombardi, Cin	C	19	95	.342
1939	Bucky Walters, Cin	P	—	—	—
1940	Frank McCormick, Cin	1B	19	127	.309
1941	Dolf Camilli, Bklyn	1B	34	120	.285
1942	Mort Cooper, St.L	P	—	—	—
1943	Stan Musial, St.L.	OF	13	81	.357
1944	Marty Marion, St.L	SS	6	63	.267
1945	Phil Cavarretta, Chi	1B	6	97	.355
1946	Stan Musial, St.L.	1B-OF	16	103	.365
1947	Bob Elliott, Bos	3B	22	113	.317
1948	Stan Musial, St.L.	OF	39	131	.376
1949	Jackie Robinson, Bklyn	2B	16	124	.342
1950	Jim Konstanty, Phi	P	—	—	—
1951	Roy Campanella, Bklyn	C	33	108	.325
1952	Hank Sauer, Chi	OF	37	121	.270
1953	Roy Campanella, Bklyn	C	41	142	.312
1954	Willie Mays, NY	OF	41	110	.345

Year		Pos	HR	RBI	Avg
1955	Roy Campanella, Bklyn	C	32	107	.318
1956	Don Newcombe, Bklyn	P	—	—	—
1957	Hank Aaron, Mil	OF	44	132	.322
1958	Ernie Banks, Chi	SS	47	129	.313
1959	Ernie Banks, Chi	SS	45	143	.304
1960	Dick Groat, Pit	SS	2	50	.325
1961	Frank Robinson, Cin	OF	37	124	.323
1962	Maury Wills, LA	SS	6	48	.299
1963	Sandy Koufax, LA	P	—	—	—
1964	Ken Boyer, St.L	3B	24	119	.295
1965	Willie Mays, SF	OF	52	112	.317
1966	Roberto Clemente, Pit	OF	29	119	.317
1967	Orlando Cepeda, St.L	1B	25	111	.325
1968	Bob Gibson, St.L	P	—	—	—
1969	Willie McCovey, SF	1B	45	126	.320
1970	Johnny Bench, Cin	C	45	148	.293
1971	Joe Torre, St.L	3B	24	137	.363
1972	Johnny Bench, Cin	C	40	125	.270
1973	Pete Rose, Cin	OF	5	64	.338
1974	Steve Garvey, LA	1B	21	111	.312
1975	Joe Morgan, Cin	2B	17	94	.327
1976	Joe Morgan, Cin	2B	27	111	.320
1977	George Foster, Cin	OF	52	149	.320
1978	Dave Parker, Pit	OF	30	117	.334
1979	Keith Hernandez, St.L	1B	11	105	.344
	Willie Stargell, Pit	1B	32	82	.281
1980	Mike Schmidt, Phi	3B	48	121	.286
1981	Mike Schmidt, Phi	3B	31	91	.316
1982	Dale Murphy, Atl	OF	36	109	.281
1983	Dale Murphy, Atl	OF	36	121	.302
1984	Ryne Sandberg, Chi	2B	19	84	.314
1985	Willie McGee, St.L	OF	10	82	.353
1986	Mike Schmidt, Phi	3B	37	119	.290
1987	Andre Dawson, Chi	OF	49	137	.287
1988	Kirk Gibson, LA	OF	25	76	.290
1989	Kevin Mitchell, SF	OF	47	125	.291
1990	Barry Bonds, Pit	OF	33	114	.301
1991	Terry Pendleton, Atl	3B	22	86	.319
1992	Barry Bonds, Pit	OF	34	103	.311
1993	Barry Bonds, SF	OF	46	123	.336
1994	Jeff Bagwell, Hou	1B	39	116	.368
1995	Barry Larkin, Cin	SS	15	66	.319
1996	Ken Caminiti, SD	3B	40	130	.326
1997	Larry Walker, Col	OF	49	130	.366

American League

Year		Pos	HR	RBI	Avg
1931	Lefty Grove, Phi	P	—	—	—
1932	Jimmie Foxx, Phi	1B	58	169	.364
1933	Jimmie Foxx, Phi	1B	48	163	.356
1934	Mickey Cochrane, Det	C-Mgr	2	76	.320
1935	Hank Greenberg, Det	1B	36	170	.328
1936	Lou Gehrig, NY	1B	49	152	.354
1937	Charlie Gehringer, Det	2B	14	96	.371
1938	Jimmie Foxx, Bos	1B	50	175	.349
1939	Joe DiMaggio, NY	OF	30	126	.381
1940	Hank Greenberg, Det	OF	41	150	.340
1941	Joe DiMaggio, NY	OF	30	125	.357
1942	Joe Gordon, NY	2B	18	103	.322
1943	Spud Chandler, NY	P	—	—	—
1944	Hal Hewhouser, Det	P	—	—	—
1945	Hal Newhouser, Det	P	—	—	—
1946	Ted Williams, Bos	OF	38	123	.342
1947	Joe DiMaggio, NY	OF	20	97	.315
1948	Lou Boudreau, Cle	SS-Mgr	18	106	.355
1949	Ted Williams, Bos	OF	43	159	.343
1950	Phil Rizzuto, NY	SS	7	66	.324
1951	Yogi Berra, NY	C	27	88	.294
1952	Bobby Shantz, Phi	P	—	—	—
1953	Al Rosen, Cle	3B	43	145	.336
1954	Yogi Berra, NY	C	22	125	.307
1955	Yogi Berra, NY	C	27	108	.272
1956	Mickey Mantle, NY	OF	52	130	.353
1957	Mickey Mantle, NY	OF	34	94	.365
1958	Jackie Jensen, Bos	OF	35	122	.286
1959	Nellie Fox, Chi	2B	2	70	.306
1960	Roger Maris, NY	OF	39	112	.283
1961	Roger Maris, NY	OF	61	142	.269
1962	Mickey Mantle, NY	OF	30	89	.321
1963	Elston Howard, NY	C	28	85	.287
1964	Brooks Robinson, Bal	3B	28	118	.317
1965	Zoilo Versalles, Min	SS	19	77	.273
1966	Frank Robinson, Bal	OF	49	122	.316
1967	Carl Yastrzemski, Bos	OF	44	121	.326
1968	Denny McLain, Det	P	—	—	—
1969	Harmon Killebrew, Min	3B-1B	49	140	.276
1970	Boog Powell, Bal	1B	35	114	.297
1971	Vida Blue, Oak	P	—	—	—
1972	Dick Allen, Chi	1B	37	113	.308
1973	Reggie Jackson, Oak	OF	32	117	.293
1974	Jeff Burroughs, Tex	OF	25	118	.301
1975	Fred Lynn, Bos	OF	21	105	.331
1976	Thurman Munson, NY	C	17	105	.302
1977	Rod Carew, Min	1B	14	100	.388
1978	Jim Rice, Bos	OF-DH	46	139	.315
1979	Don Baylor, Cal	OF-DH	36	139	.296
1980	George Brett, KC	3B	24	118	.390
1981	Rollie Fingers, Mil	P	—	—	—
1982	Robin Yount, Mil	SS	29	114	.331
1983	Cal Ripken Jr., Bal	SS	27	102	.318
1984	Willie Hernandez, Det	P	—	—	—
1985	Don Mattingly, NY	1B	35	145	.324
1986	Roger Clemens, Bos	P	—	—	—
1987	George Bell, Tor	OF	47	134	.308
1988	Jose Canseco, Oak	OF	42	124	.307
1989	Robin Yount, Mil	OF	21	103	.318
1990	Rickey Henderson, Oak	OF	28	61	.325
1991	Cal Ripken Jr., Bal	SS	34	114	.323
1992	Dennis Eckersley, Oak	P	—	—	—
1993	Frank Thomas, Chi	1B	41	128	.317
1994	Frank Thomas, Chi	1B	38	101	.353
1995	Mo Vaughn, Bos	1B	39	126	.300
1996	Juan Gonzalez. Tex	OF-DH	47	144	.314
1997	Ken Griffey Jr., Sea	OF	56	147	.304

MVP Pitchers' Statistics

Pitchers have been named Most Valuable Player on 23 occasions, 10 times in the NL and 13 in the AL. Four have been relief pitchers—Jim Konstanty, Rollie Fingers, Willie Hernandez and Dennis Eckersley.

National League

Year		Gm	W-L	SV	ERA
1924	Dazzy Vance, Bklyn	35	28-6	0	2.16
1933	Carl Hubbell, NY	45	23-12	5	1.66
1934	Dizzy Dean, St.L	50	30-7	7	2.66
1936	Carl Hubbell, NY	42	26-6	3	2.31
1939	Bucky Walters, Cin	39	27-11	0	2.29
1942	Mort Cooper, St.L	37	22-7	0	1.78
1950	Jim Konstanty, Phi	74	16-7	22	2.66

American League

Year		Gm	W-L	SV	ERA
1913	Walter Johnson, Wash	47	36-7	2	1.09
1924	Walter Johnson, Wash	38	23-7	0	2.72
1931	Lefty Grove, Phi	41	31-4	5	2.06
1943	Spud Chandler, NY	30	20-4	0	1.64
1944	Hal Hewhouser, Det	47	29-9	2	2.22
1945	Hal Newhouser, Det	40	25-9	2	1.81
1952	Bobby Shantz, Phi	33	24-7	0	2.48

CY YOUNG AWARD

Voted on by the Baseball Writers Association of America. One award was presented from 1956-66, two since 1967. Pitchers who won the MVP and Cy Young awards in the same season are in **bold** type.

Multiple winners: NL—Steve Carlton and Greg Maddux (4); Sandy Koufax and Tom Seaver (3); Bob Gibson (2). **AL**—Roger Clemens (4); Jim Palmer (3); Denny McLain (2). **NL & AL**—Gaylord Perry (2, one in each).

NL and AL Combined

Year	National League	Gm	W-L	SV	ERA
1956	**Don Newcombe**, Bklyn	38	27-7	0	3.06
1957	Warren Spahn, Mil	39	21-11	3	2.69
1960	Vernon Law, Pit	35	20-9	0	3.08
1962	Don Drysdale, LA	43	25-9	1	2.83
1963	**Sandy Koufax**, LA	40	25-5	0	1.88
1965	Sandy Koufax, LA	43	26-8	2	2.04
1966	Sandy Koufax, LA	41	27-9	0	1.73

Year	American League	Gm	W-L	SV	ERA
1958	Bob Turley, NY	33	21-7	1	2.97
1959	Early Wynn, Chi	37	22-10	0	3.17
1961	Whitey Ford, NY	39	25-4	0	3.21
1964	Dean Chance, LA	46	20-9	4	1.65

Separate League Awards

National League

Year		Gm	W-L	SV	ERA
1967	Mike McCormick, SF	40	22-10	0	2.85
1968	**Bob Gibson**, St.L	34	22-9	0	1.12
1969	Tom Seaver, NY	36	25-7	0	2.21
1970	Bob Gibson, St.L.	34	23-7	0	3.12
1971	Ferguson Jenkins, Chi	39	24-13	0	2.77
1972	Steve Carlton, Phi	41	27-10	0	1.97
1973	Tom Seaver, NY	36	19-10	0	2.08
1974	Mike Marshall, LA	106	15-12	21	2.42
1975	Tom Seaver, NY	36	22-9	0	2.38
1976	Randy Jones, SD	40	22-14	0	2.74
1977	Steve Carlton, Phi	36	23-10	0	2.64
1978	Gaylord Perry, SD	37	21-6	0	2.72
1979	Bruce Sutter, Chi	62	6-6	37	2.23
1980	Steve Carlton, Phi	38	24-9	0	2.34
1981	Fernando Valenzuela, LA	25	13-7	0	2.48
1982	Steve Carlton, Phi	38	23-11	0	3.10
1983	John Denny, Phi	36	19-6	0	2.37
1984	Rick Sutcliffe, Chi	20*	16-1	0	2.69
1985	Dwight Gooden, NY	35	24-4	0	1.53
1986	Mike Scott, Hou	37	18-10	0	2.22
1987	Steve Bedrosian, Phi	65	5-3	40	2.83
1988	Orel Hershiser, LA	35	23-8	1	2.26
1989	Mark Davis, SD	70	4-3	44	1.85
1990	Doug Drabek, Pit	33	22-6	0	2.76
1991	Tom Glavine, Atl	34	20-11	0	2.55
1992	Greg Maddux, Chi	35	20-11	0	2.18
1993	Greg Maddux, Atl	36	20-10	0	2.36
1994	Greg Maddux, Atl	25	16-6	0	1.56
1995	Greg Maddux, Atl	28	19-2	0	1.63
1996	John Smoltz, Atl	35	24-8	0	2.94
1997	Pedro Martinez, Mon.	31	17-8	0	1.90

*NL games only, Sutcliffe pitched 15 games with Cleveland before being traded to the Cubs.

American League

Year		Gm	W-L	SV	ERA
1967	Jim Lonborg, Bos	39	22-9	0	3.16
1968	**Denny McLain**, Det	41	31-6	0	1.96
1969	Denny McLain, Det	42	24-9	0	2.80
	Mike Cuellar, Bal	39	23-11	0	2.38
1970	Jim Perry, Min	40	24-12	0	3.03
1971	**Vida Blue**, Oak	39	24-8	0	1.82
1972	Gaylord Perry, Cle	41	24-16	1	1.92
1973	Jim Palmer, Bal	38	22-9	1	2.40
1974	Catfish Hunter, Oak	41	25-12	0	2.49
1975	Jim Palmer, Bal	39	23-11	1	2.09
1976	Jim Palmer, Bal	40	22-13	0	2.51
1977	Sparky Lyle, NY	72	13-5	26	2.17
1978	Ron Guidry, NY	35	25-3	0	1.74
1979	Mike Flanagan, Bal	39	23-9	0	3.08
1980	Steve Stone, Bal	37	25-7	0	3.23
1981	**Rollie Fingers**, Mil	47	6-3	28	1.04
1982	Pete Vuckovich, Mil	30	18-6	0	3.34
1983	LaMarr Hoyt, Chi	36	24-10	0	3.66
1984	**Willie Hernandez**, Det	80	9-3	32	1.92
1985	Bret Saberhagen, KC	32	20-6	0	2.87
1986	**Roger Clemens**, Bos	33	24-4	0	2.48
1987	Roger Clemens, Bos	36	20-9	0	2.97
1988	Frank Viola, Min	35	24-7	0	2.64
1989	Bret Saberhagen, KC	36	23-6	0	2.16
1990	Bob Welch, Oak	35	27-6	0	2.95
1991	Roger Clemens, Bos	35	18-10	0	2.62
1992	**Dennis Eckersley**, Oak	69	7-1	51	1.91
1993	Jack McDowell, Chi	34	22-10	0	3.37
1994	David Cone, KC	23	16-5	0	2.94
1995	Randy Johnson, Sea	30	18-2	0	2.48
1996	Pat Hentgen, Tor	35	20-10	0	3.22
1997	Roger Clemens, Tor	34	21-7	0	2.05

ROOKIE OF THE YEAR

Voted on by the Baseball Writers Assn. of America. One award was presented from 1947-48. Two awards (one for each league) have been presented since 1949. Winner who was also named MVP is in **bold** type.

NL and AL Combined

Year		Pos
1947	Jackie Robinson, Brooklyn	1B
1948	Alvin Dark, Boston-NL	SS

National League

Year		Pos
1949	Don Newcombe, Bklyn	P
1950	Sam Jethroe, Bos	OF
1951	Willie Mays, NY	OF
1952	Joe Black, Bklyn	P
1953	Jim Gilliam, Bklyn	2B
1954	Wally Moon, St.L	OF
1955	Bill Virdon, St.L.	OF
1956	Frank Robinson, Cin.	OF
1957	Jack Sanford, Phi	P
1958	Orlando Cepeda, SF	1B
1959	Willie McCovey, SF	1B
1960	Frank Howard, LA	OF
1961	Billy Williams, Chi	OF
1962	Ken Hubbs, Chi.	2B
1963	Pete Rose, Cin	2B
1964	Richie Allen, Phi	3B
1965	Jim Lefebvre, LA	2B
1966	Tommy Helms, Cin	3B
1967	Tom Seaver, NY	P
1968	Johnny Bench, Cin	C
1969	Ted Sizemore, LA	2B
1970	Carl Morton, Mon	P
1971	Earl Williams, Atl	C
1972	Jon Matlack, NY	P
1973	Gary Matthews, SF	OF
1974	Bake McBride, St.L.	OF
1975	John Montefusco, SF	P

Year		Pos
1976	Butch Metzger, SD	P
	& Pat Zachry, Cin	P
1977	Andre Dawson, Mon	OF
1978	Bob Horner, Atl	3B
1979	Rick Sutcliffe, LA	P
1980	Steve Howe, LA	P
1981	Fernando Valenzuela, LA	P
1982	Steve Sax, LA	2B
1983	Darryl Strawberry, NY	OF
1984	Dwight Gooden, NY	P
1985	Vince Coleman, St.L	OF
1986	Todd Worrell, St.L	P
1987	Benito Santiago, SD	C
1988	Chris Sabo, Cin	3B
1989	Jerome Walton, Chi	OF
1990	David Justice, Atl	OF
1991	Jeff Bagwell, Hou	1B
1992	Eric Karros, LA	1B
1993	Mike Piazza, LA	C
1994	Raul Mondesi, LA	OF
1995	Hideo Nomo, LA	P
1996	Todd Hollandsworth, LA	OF
1997	Scott Rolen, Phi	3B

American League

Year		Pos
1949	Roy Sievers, St.L	OF
1950	Walt Dropo, Bos	1B
1951	Gil McDougald, NY	3B
1952	Harry Byrd, Phi	P
1953	Harvey Kuenn, Det	SS
1954	Bob Grim, NY	P
1955	Herb Score, Cle	P
1956	Luis Aparicio, Chi	SS
1957	Tony Kubek, NY	INF-OF
1958	Albie Pearson, Wash	OF
1959	Bob Allison, Wash	OF
1960	Ron Hansen, Bal	SS
1961	Don Schwall, Bos	P
1962	Tom Tresh, NY	SS-OF
1963	Gary Peters, Chi	P
1964	Tony Oliva, Min	OF
1965	Curt Blefary, Bal	OF
1966	Tommie Agee, Chi	OF
1967	Rod Carew, Min	2B
1968	Stan Bahnsen, NY	P
1969	Lou Piniella, KC	OF
1970	Thurman Munson, NY	C
1971	Chris Chambliss, Cle	1B
1972	Carlton Fisk, Bos	C
1973	Al Bumbry, Bal	OF
1974	Mike Hargrove, Tex	1B
1975	**Fred Lynn**, Bos	OF
1976	Mark Fidrych, Det	P
1977	Eddie Murray, Bal	DH-1B
1978	Lou Whitaker, Det	2B
1979	John Castino, Min	3B
	& Alfredo Griffin, Tor	SS
1980	Joe Charboneau, Cle	OF-DH
1981	Dave Righetti, NY	P
1982	Cal Ripken Jr., Bal	SS-3B
1983	Ron Kittle, Chi	OF
1984	Alvin Davis, Sea	1B
1985	Ozzie Guillen, Chi	SS
1986	Jose Canseco, Oak	OF
1987	Mark McGwire, Oak	1B
1988	Walt Weiss, Oak	SS
1989	Gregg Olson, Bal	P
1990	Sandy Alomar Jr., Cle	C
1991	Chuck Knoblauch, Min	2B
1992	Pat Listach, Mil	SS
1993	Tim Salmon, Cal	OF
1994	Bob Hamelin, KC	DH
1995	Marty Cordova, Min	OF
1996	Derek Jeter, NY	SS
1997	Nomar Garciaparra, Bos	SS

MANAGER OF THE YEAR

Voted on by the Baseball Writers Association of America. Two awards (one for each league) presented since 1983. Note that (*) indicates manager's team won division championship and (†) indicates unofficial division won in 1994.

Multiple winners: Tony La Russa (3); Sparky Anderson, Dusty Baker, Bobby Cox, Tommy Lasorda and Jim Leyland (2).

National League

Year		Improvement		
1983	Tommy Lasorda, LA	88-74	to	91-71*
1984	Jim Frey, Chi	71-91	to	96-75*
1985	Whitey Herzog, St. L	84-78	to	101-61*
1986	Hal Lanier, Hou	83-79	to	96-66*
1987	Buck Rodgers, Mon	78-83	to	91-71
1988	Tommy Lasorda, LA	73-89	to	94-67*
1989	Don Zimmer, Chi	77-85	to	93-69*
1990	Jim Leyland, Pit	74-88	to	95-67*
1991	Bobby Cox, Atl	65-97	to	94-68*
1992	Jim Leyland, Pit	98-64*	to	96-66*
1993	Dusty Baker, SF	72-90	to	103-59
1994	Felipe Alou, Mon	94-68	to	74-40†
1995	Don Baylor, Col	53-64	to	77-67
1996	Bruce Bochy, SD	70-74	to	91-71
1997	Dusty Baker, SF	68-94	to	90-72

American League

Year		Improvement		
1983	Tony La Russa, Chi	87-75	to	99-63*
1984	Sparky Anderson, Det	92-70	to	104-58*
1985	Bobby Cox, Tor	89-73	to	99-62*
1986	John McNamara, Bos	81-81	to	95-66*
1987	Sparky Anderson, Det	87-75	to	98-64*
1988	Tony La Russa, Oak	81-81	to	104-58*
1989	Frank Robinson, Bal	54-107	to	87-75
1990	Jeff Torborg, Chi	69-92	to	94-68
1991	Tom Kelly, Min	74-88	to	95-67*
1992	Tony La Russa, Oak	84-78	to	96-66*
1993	Gene Lamont, Chi	86-76	to	94-68*
1994	Buck Showalter, NY	88-74	to	70-43†
1995	Lou Piniella, Sea	49-63	to	79-66*
1996	Joe Torre, NY	79-65	to	92-70
	& Johnny Oates, Tex	74-70	to	90-72
1997	Davey Johnson, Bal	88-74	to	98-64

George Steinbrenner's Managerial Merry-Go-Round

As managing general partner of the New York Yankees since 1973, George Steinbrenner has changed managers 21 times in 25 years. In that time, the Yankees have won six AL pennants (1976-78, '81, '96 and '98) and four World Series (1977-78, '96 and '98). Note that (*) indicates interim status. Managers with multiple hitches are Billy Martin (5), and Bob Lemon, Gene Michael and Lou Piniella (2).

	Tenure	W-L
Ralph Houk	1973	80-82
Bill Virdon	1974-75	142-124
Billy Martin	1975-78*	279-192
Dick Howser	1978	0-1
Bob Lemon	1978-79	82-51
Billy Martin	1979	55-40
Dick Howser	1980	103-59
Gene Michael	1981	48-34
Bob Lemon	1981-82	17-22
Gene Michael	1982	44-42
Clyde King	1982	29-33
Billy Martin	1983	91-71
Yogi Berra	1984-85	93-85
Billy Martin	1985	91-54
Lou Piniella	1986-87	179-145
Billy Martin	1988	40-28
Lou Piniella	1988	45-48
Dallas Green	1989	56-65
Bucky Dent	1989-90	36-53
Stump Merrill	1990-91	120-155
Buck Showalter	1992-95	313-268
Joe Torre	1996—	302-184

COLLEGE BASEBALL

College World Series

The NCAA Division I College World Series has been held in Kalamazoo, Mich. (1947-48), Wichita, Kan. (1949) and Omaha, Neb. (since 1950).

Multiple winners: USC (12); Arizona St. (5); LSU and Texas (4); Arizona, CS-Fullerton and Minnesota (3); California, Miami-FL, Michigan, Oklahoma and Stanford (2).

Year	Winner	Coach	Score	Runner-up
1947	California	Clint Evans	8-7	Yale
1948	USC	Sam Barry	9-2	Yale
1949	Texas	Bibb Falk	10-3	W. Forest
1950	Texas	Bibb Falk	3-0	Wash. St.
1951	Oklahoma	Jack Baer	3-2	Tennessee
1952	Holy Cross	Jack Barry	8-4	Missouri
1953	Michigan	Ray Fisher	7-5	Texas
1954	Missouri	Hi Simmons	4-1	Rollins
1955	Wake Forest	Taylor Sanford	7-6	W. Mich.
1956	Minnesota	Dick Siebert	12-1	Arizona
1957	California	Geo. Wolfman	1-0	Penn St.
1958	USC	Rod Dedeaux	8-7	Missouri
1959	Oklahoma St.	Toby Greene	5-3	Arizona
1960	Minnesota	Dick Siebert	2-1	USC
1961	USC	Rod Dedeaux	1-0	Okla. St.
1962	Michigan	Don Lund	5-4	S. Clara
1963	USC	Rod Dedeaux	5-2	Arizona
1964	Minnesota	Dick Siebert	5-1	Missouri
1965	Arizona St.	Bobby Winkles	2-1	Ohio St.
1966	Ohio St.	Marty Karow	8-2	Okla. St.
1967	Arizona St.	Bobby Winkles	11-2	Houston
1968	USC	Rod Dedeaux	4-3	So. Ill.
1969	Arizona St.	Bobby Winkles	10-1	Tulsa
1970	USC	Rod Dedeaux	2-1	Fla. St.
1971	USC	Rod Dedeaux	7-2	So. Ill.
1972	USC	Rod Dedeaux	1-0	Ariz. St.
1973	USC	Rod Dedeaux	4-3	Ariz. St.
1974	USC	Rod Dedeaux	7-3	Miami, FL
1975	Texas	Cliff Gustafson	5-1	S. Carolina
1976	Arizona	Jerry Kindall	7-1	E. Michigan
1977	Arizona St.	Jim Brock	2-1	S. Carolina
1978	USC	Rod Dedeaux	10-3	Ariz. St.
1979	CS-Fullerton	Augie Garrido	2-1	Arkansas
1980	Arizona	Jerry Kindall	5-3	Hawaii
1981	Arizona St.	Jim Brock	7-4	Okla. St.
1982	Miami-FL	Ron Fraser	9-3	Wichita St.
1983	Texas	Cliff Gustafson	4-3	Alabama
1984	CS-Fullerton	Augie Garrido	3-1	Texas
1985	Miami-FL	Ron Fraser	10-6	Texas
1986	Arizona	Jerry Kindall	10-2	Fla. St.
1987	Stanford	M. Marquess	9-5	Okla. St.
1988	Stanford	M. Marquess	9-4	Ariz. St.
1989	Wichita St.	G.Stephenson	5-3	Texas
1990	Georgia	Steve Webber	2-1	Okla. St.
1991	LSU	Skip Bertman	6-3	Wichita St.
1992	Pepperdine	Andy Lopez	3-2	CS-Fullerton
1993	LSU	Skip Bertman	8-0	Wichita St.
1994	Oklahoma	Larry Cochell	13-5	Ga. Tech
1995	CS-Fullerton	Augie Garrido	11-5	USC
1996	LSU	Skip Bertman	9-8	Miami, FL
1997	LSU	Skip Bertman	13-6	Alabama
1998	USC	Mike Gillespie	21-14	Arizona St.

Most Outstanding Player

The Most Outstanding Player has been selected every year of the College World Series since 1949. Winners who did not play for the CWS champion are listed in **bold** type. No player has won the award more than once.

Year
1949 **Charles Teague,** W. Forest, 2B
1950 **Ray VanCleef,** Rutgers, CF
1951 **Sidney Hatfield,** Tenn., P-1B
1952 James O'Neill, Holy Cross, P
1953 **J.L. Smith,** Texas, P
1954 **Tom Yewcic,** Mich. St., C
1955 **Tom Borland,** Okla. St., P
1956 Jerry Thomas, Minn., P
1957 **Cal Emery,** Penn St., P-1B
1958 Bill Thom, USC, P
1959 Jim Dobson, Okla. St., 3B
1960 John Erickson, Minn., 2B
1961 **Littleton Fowler,** Okla. St., P
1962 **Bob Garibaldi,** Santa Clara, P
1963 Bud Hollowell, USC, C
1964 **Joe Ferris,** Maine, P
1965 Sal Bando, Ariz. St., 3B

Year
1966 Steve Arlin, Ohio St., P
1967 Ron Davini, Ariz. St., C
1968 Bill Seinsoth, USC, 1B
1969 John Dolinsek, Ariz. St., LF
1970 **Gene Ammann,** Fla. St., P
1971 **Jerry Tabb,** Tulsa, 1B
1972 Russ McQueen, USC, P
1973 **Dave Winfield,** Minn., P-OF
1974 George Milke, USC, P
1975 Mickey Reichenbach, Texas, 1B
1976 Steve Powers, Arizona, P-DH
1977 Bob Horner, Ariz. St., 3B
1978 Rod Boxberger, USC, P
1979 Tony Hudson, CS-Fullerton, P
1980 Terry Francona, Arizona, LF
1981 Stan Holmes, Ariz. St., LF
1982 Dan Smith, Miami-FL, P

Year
1983 Calvin Schiraldi, Texas, P
1984 John Fishel, CS-Fullerton, LF
1985 Greg Ellena, Miami-FL, LF
1986 Mike Senne, Arizona, DH
1987 Paul Carey, Stanford, RF
1988 Lee Plemel, Stanford, P
1989 Greg Brummett, Wich. St., P
1990 Mike Rebhan, Georgia, P
1991 Gary Hymel, LSU, C
1992 **Phil Nevin,** CS-Fullerton, 3B
1993 Todd Walker, LSU, 2B
1994 Chip Glass, Oklahoma, OF
1995 Mark Kotsay, CS-Fullerton, OF
1996 **Pat Burrell,** Miami-FL, 3B
1997 Brandon Larson, LSU, SS
1998 Wes Rachels, USC, 2B

Annual Awards

Golden Spikes Award

First presented in 1978 by USA Baseball, honoring the nation's best amateur player. Alex Fernandez, the 1990 winner, has been the only junior college player chosen.

Year
1978 Bob Horner, Ariz. St, 2B
1979 Tim Wallach, CS-Fullerton, 1B
1980 Terry Francona, Arizona, OF
1981 Mike Fuentes, Fla. St., OF
1982 Augie Schmidt, N. Orleans, SS
1983 Dave Magadan, Alabama, 1B
1984 Oddibe McDowell, Ariz. St., OF

Year
1985 Will Clark, Miss. St., 1B
1986 Mike Loynd, Fla. St., P
1987 Jim Abbott, Michigan, P
1988 Robin Ventura, Okla. St., 3B
1989 Ben McDonald, LSU, P
1990 Alex Fernandez, Miami-Dade, P
1991 Mike Kelly, Ariz. St., OF

Year
1992 Phil Nevin, CS-Fullerton, 3B
1993 Darren Dreifort, Wichita St., P
1994 Jason Varitek, Ga. Tech, C
1995 Mark Kotsay, CS-Fullerton, OF
1996 Travis Lee, San Diego St., 1B
1997 J.D. Drew, Florida St., OF

Baseball America Player of the Year

Presented to the College Player of the Year since 1981 by *Baseball America.*

Year
1981 Mike Sodders, Ariz. St., 3B
1982 Jeff Ledbetter, Fla. St., OF/P
1983 Dave Magadan, Alabama, 1B
1984 Oddibe McDowell, Ariz. St., OF
1985 Pete Incaviglia, Okla. St., OF
1986 Casey Close, Michigan, OF

Year
1987 Robin Ventura, Okla. St., 3B
1988 John Olerud, Wash. St., 1B/P
1989 Ben McDonald, LSU, P
1990 Mike Kelly, Ariz. St., OF
1991 David McCarty, Stanford, 1B
1992 Phil Nevin, CS-Fullerton, 3B

Year
1993 Brooks Kieschnick, Texas, DH/P
1994 Jason Varitek, Ga. Tech, C
1995 Todd Helton, Tenn., 1B/P
1996 Kris Benson, Clemson, P
1997 J.D. Drew, Florida St., OF
1998 Jeff Austin, Stanford, RHP

Dick Howser Trophy

Presented to the College Player of the Year since 1987 by the American Baseball Coaches Association. Named after the late two-time All-America shortstop and college coach at Florida St., Howser was also a major league manager with Kansas City and the New York Yankees.

Multiple winner: Brooks Kieschnick (2).

Year
1987 Mike Fiore, Miami-FL, OF
1988 Robin Ventura, Okla. St., 3B
1989 Scott Bryant, Texas, DH
1990 Paul Ellis, UCLA, C

Year
1991 Bobby Jones, Fresno St., P
1992 Brooks Kieschnick, Texas, DH/P
1993 Brooks Kieschnick, Texas, DH/P
1994 Jason Varitek, Ga. Tech, C

Year
1995 Todd Helton, Tenn., 1B/P
1996 Kris Benson, Clemson, P
1997 J.D. Drew, Florida St., OF
1998 Eddie Furniss, LSU, 1B

Baseball America Coach of the Year

Presented to the College Coach of the Year since 1981 by *Baseball America.*

Multiple winners: Skip Bertman, Dave Snow and Gene Stephenson (2).

1981 Ron Fraser, Miami-FL
1982 Gene Stephenson, Wichita St.
1983 Barry Shollenberger, Alabama
1984 Augie Garrido, CS-Fullerton
1985 Ron Polk, Mississippi St.
1986 Skip Bertman, LSU
& Dave Snow, Loyola-CA

1987 Mark Marquess, Stanford
1988 Jim Brock, Arizona St.
1989 Dave Snow, Long Beach St.
1990 Steve Webber, Georgia
1991 Jim Hendry, Creighton
1992 Andy Lopez, Pepperdine
1993 Gene Stephenson, Wichita St.

1994 Jim Morris, Miami-FL
1995 Rob Delmonico, Tennessee
1996 Skip Bertman, LSU
1997 Jim Wells, Alabama
1998 Pat Murphy, Arizona St.

All-Time Winningest Coaches

Coaches active in 1998 in **bold** type.

Top 30 Winning Percentage

(Minimum 10 years in Division I)

		Yrs	W	L	T	Pct
1	John Barry	40	619	147	6	.806
2	W.J. Disch	29	465	115	0	.802
3	Cliff Gustafson	29	1427	373	2	.792
4	Harry Carlson	17	143	41	0	.777
5	**Gene Stephenson**	21	1165	346	3	.769
6	Gary Ward	19	953	313	1	.753
7	George Jacobs	11	76	25	0	.752
8	Bobby Winkles	13	524	173	0	.752
9	Frank Sancet	23	831	283	8	.744
10	**Mike Martin**	19	1021	350	3	.744
11	Ron Fraser	30	1271	438	9	.742
12	Bob Wren	23	464	160	4	.742
13	Bibb Falk	25	435	152	0	.741
14	**Skip Bertman**	15	733	267	1	.732
15	Bud Middaugh	22	821	319	1	.720
16	J.F."Pop" McKale	30	302	118	7	.715
17	Jim Brock	28	1100	440	0	.714
18	Toby Green	21	318	132	0	.707
19	Joe Arnold	18	750	313	2	.705
20	**Mark Johnson**	14	616	259	2	.702
21	**Jim Morris**	17	753	319	1	.702
22	Joe Bedenk	32	380	159	3	.701
23	Rod Dedeaux	45	1332	571	11	.699
24	**Bob Hannah**	35	981	419	6	.698
25	Enos Semore	22	851	370	1	.697
26	Dave Keilitz	14	456	208	0	.692
27	Pete Beiden	21	600	268	0	.691
28	Brad Babcock	19	558	251	4	.689
29	Chuck Brayton	33	1162	523	8	.689
30	Chuck Medlar	19	312	141	6	.686

Top 30 Victories

		Yrs	W	L	T	Pct
1	Cliff Gustafson	29	**1427**	373	2	.792
2	Rod Dedeaux	45	**1332**	571	11	.699
3	Ron Fraser	30	**1271**	438	9	.742
4	**Jack Stallings**	38	**1229**	767	5	.614
5	**Augie Garrido**	30	**1228**	563	7	.683
6	Al Ogletree	41	**1217**	713	1	.631
7	Chuck Hartman	38	**1172**	587	3	.666
8	**Gene Stephenson**	21	**1165**	346	3	.769
9	Bobo Brayton	33	**1162**	523	8	.690
10	Bill Wilhelm	36	**1161**	536	10	.683
11	**Bob Bennett**	30	**1157**	655	8	.636
	Larry Hays	28	**1157**	623	2	.649
13	**Larry Cochell**	32	**1115**	627	2	.640
14	Jim Brock	23	**1100**	440	0	.714
15	**Jim Dietz**	27	**1093**	641	18	.624
16	Ron Polk	26	**1043**	486	0	.682
17	**Norm DeBriyn**	29	**1033**	542	6	.653
18	**Richard Jones**	32	**1022**	578	5	.637
19	**Mike Martin**	19	**1021**	350	3	.744
20	**Les Murakami**	28	**1014**	522	4	.658
21	**Bob Hannah**	35	**981**	419	6	.698
22	Gary Adams	28	**960**	680	12	.585
23	Gary Ward	19	**953**	313	1	.753
24	John Winkin	42	**934**	670	11	.582
25	Duane Banks	30	**901**	585	4	.606
26	**Mark Marquess**	22	**895**	467	5	.655
27	**Gary Pullins**	22	**887**	433	6	.669
28	**James Wilson**	39	**873**	624	23	.574
29	Jerry Kindall	24	**861**	578	6	.598
30	Enos Semore	22	**851**	370	1	.697

Other NCAA Champions

Division II

Multiple winners: Florida Southern (8); Cal Poly Pomona and Tampa (3); CS-Northridge, Jacksonville St., Troy St., UC-Irvine and UC-Riverside (2).

Year		Year		Year		Year	
1968	Chapman, CA	1976	Cal Poly Pomona	1984	CS-Northridge	1992	Tampa
1969	Illinois St.	1977	UC-Riverside	1985	Florida Southern	1993	Tampa
1970	CS-Northridge	1978	Florida Southern	1986	Troy St., AL	1994	Central Missouri St.
1971	Florida Southern	1979	Valdosta St., GA	1987	Troy St., AL	1995	Florida Southern
1972	Florida Southern	1980	Cal Poly Pomona	1988	Florida Southern	1996	Kennesaw St., GA
1973	UC-Irvine	1981	Florida Southern	1989	Cal Poly SLO	1997	CS-Chico
1974	UC-Irvine	1982	UC-Riverside	1990	Jacksonville St., AL	1998	Tampa
1975	Florida Southern	1983	Cal Poly Pomona	1991	Jacksonville St., AL		

Division III

Multiple winners: Eastern Conn. St. and Marietta (3); CS-Stanislaus, Glassboro St., Ithaca, Montclair St., Southern Maine and Wm. Paterson, NJ (2).

Year							
		1981	Marietta, OH	1987	Monclair St., NJ	1993	Montclair St., NJ
1976	CS-Stanislaus	1982	Eastern Conn. St.	1988	Ithaca, NY	1994	Wisconsin-Oshkosh
1977	CS-Stanislaus	1983	Marietta, OH	1989	NC-Wesleyan	1995	La Verne, CA
1978	Glassboro St., NJ	1984	Ramapo, NJ	1990	Eastern Conn. St.	1996	Wm. Paterson, NJ
1979	Glassboro St., NJ	1985	Wisconsin-Oshkosh	1991	Southern Maine	1997	Southern Maine
1980	Ithaca, NY	1986	Marietta, OH	1992	Wm. Paterson, NJ	1998	Eastern Conn. St.

Major League Number One Draft Picks

The Major League First-Year Player Draft has been held every year since 1965. Clubs select in reverse order of their won-loss records from the previous regular season with National League and American League teams alternating. AL teams select first in odd-numbered years while NL teams go first in even-numbered years. The pool of draftees consists of graduated high school players, junior or senior college players, Junior college players and anyone over the age of 21. Listed are the top selections from each draft.

Year		Pos	Team	Year		Pos	Team
1965	Rick Monday	OF	Kansas City Athletics	1982	Shawon Dunston	SS	Chicago Cubs
1966	Steve Chilcott	C	New York Mets	1983	Tim Belcher	P	Minnesota Twins
1967	Rom Blomberg	1B	New York Yankees	1984	Shawn Abner	OF	New York Mets
1968	Tim Foli	IF	New York Mets	1985	B.J. Surhoff	C	Milwaukee Brewers
1969	Jeff Burroughs	OF	Washington Senators	1986	Jeff King	IF	Pittsburgh Pirates
1970	Mike Ivie	C	San Diego Padres	1987	Ken Griffey Jr.	OF	Seattle Mariners
1971	Danny Goodwin	C	Chicago White Sox	1988	Andy Benes	P	San Diego Padres
1972	Dave Roberts	IF	San Diego Padres	1989	Ben McDonald	P	Baltimore Orioles
1973	David Clyde	P	Texas Rangers	1990	Chipper Jones	SS	Atlanta Braves
1974	Bill Almon	IF	San Diego Padres	1991	Brien Taylor	P	New York Yankees
1975	Danny Goodwin	C	California Angels	1992	Phil Nevin	3B	Houston Astros
1976	Floyd Bannister	P	Houston Astros	1993	Alex Rodriguez	SS	Seattle Mariners
1977	Harold Baines	OF	Chicago White Sox	1994	Paul Wilson	P	New York Mets
1978	Bob Horner	3B	Atlanta Braves	1995	Darin Erstad	OF/P	California Angels
1979	Al Chambers	OF	Seattle Mariners	1996	Kris Benson	P	Pittsburgh Pirates
1980	Darryl Strawberry	OF	New York Mets	1997	Matt Anderson	P	Detroit Tigers
1981	Mike Moore	P	Seattle Mariners	1998	Pat Burrell	3B	Philadelphia Phillies

Straight to the Majors

Since Major League baseball began its free agent draft in 1965, 17 selections have advanced directly to the major leagues without first playing in the minors

Draft		Pos	Team	Draft		Pos	Team
1967	Mike Adamson, South Carolina	P	Baltimore	1978	Tim Conroy, Gateway HS (Pa.)	P	Oakland
1969	Steve Dunning, Stanford	P	Cleveland		Bob Horner, Arizona St.	IF	Atlanta
1971	Pete Broberg, Dartmouth	P	Washington		Brian Milner, Southwest HS (Tex.)	C	Toronto
	Rob Ellis, Michigan St.	IF	Milwaukee		Mike Morgan, Valley HS (Nev.)	P	Oakland
	Burt Hooton, Texas	P	Chicago	1985	Pete Incaviglia, Oklahoma St.	OF	Montreal
1972	Dave Roberts, Oregon	IF	San Diego	1988	Jim Abbott, Michigan	P	California
1973	Dick Ruthven, Fresno St.	P	Philadelphia	1989	John Olerud, Washington St.	IF	Toronto
1973	David Clyde, Westchester HS (Tex.)	P	Texas				
	Dave Winfield, Minnesota	OF	San Diego				
	Eddie Bane, Arizona St.	P	Minnesota				

College Football

Nebraska coaching mainstay **Tom Osborne** waves good-bye to the game following the Cornhuskers' Orange Bowl win over Tennessee.

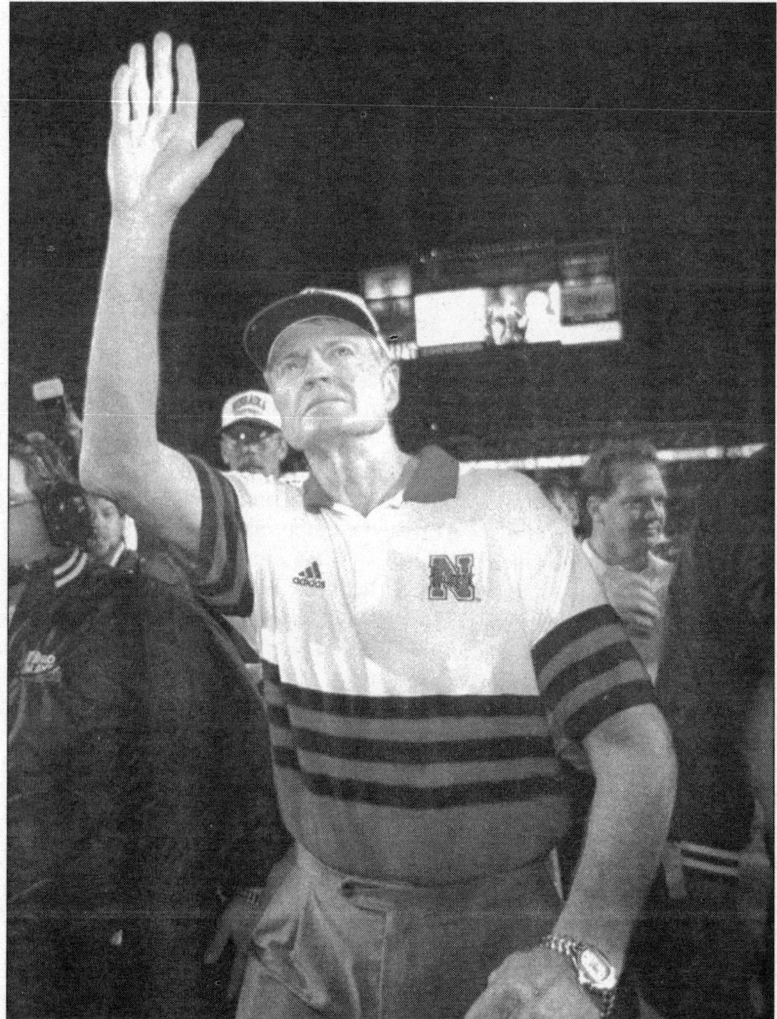

Archive Photos

We are the Co-Champions

Michigan and Nebraska shared the limelight and the national championship in 1997.

by
Chris Fowler

In a deserted parking lot still wet from a tropical shower and strewn with trash, at 2:50 a.m. on January 3, the odyssey of College Football '97 came to a frustrating, controversial, and entirely just end.

Hours earlier, Nebraska had Orange-Bowled-over Tennessee. Pro Player Stadium had long since cleared out, but outside on a temporary set, Lee Corso, Kirk Herbstreit, and I rehashed and dissected and waited for the final Coaches' Poll ballot to be counted. And waited. And waited.

Finally, word came, via my plastic earpiece. Twenty-four coaches had switched their first place vote from unbeaten Michigan, already voted AP champ, to unbeaten Nebraska. There would be two national champions.

First to get the news were two lone Nebraska students in red T-shirts, too stubborn to leave their post next to our set until word arrived. When told during a commercial break that their Huskers had been voted a piece of the title, they hollered, high-fived, and took off running for a victory lap of the empty parking lot.

Then, just to be sure, they came back to hear me announce the poll results on the air, after which they ran off on another loud victory lap. Across town, Nebraska players gathered around TVs as post-game parties erupted. Somebody knocked on Tom Osborne's door, to tell him that his final game had brought Nebraska a co-championship. He managed a smile, as he finished packing for his final flight home as a football coach.

One night earlier, the smiles belonged to Michigan. The Wolverines withstood Washington State in the kind of fairy tale Rose Bowl we

---

Chris Fowler is the host of ESPN's *College GameDay*.

AP/Wide World Photos

Michigan's **Charles Woodson** seemed to hover above the competition this season, picking off this Ryan Leaf pass in the end zone during the first half of the Rose Bowl, and intercepting the Heisman Trophy from Tennessee QB Peyton Manning.

remember watching as kids: Bo or Woody battling the Bruins or Trojans in Pasadena's late afternoon golden glow, as the shadows stretched across that perfectly manicured field at the foot of the San Gabriel Mountains. It seemed a magical setting on those New Years' afternoons, as we watched from our TVs in the frostbelt.

It was no different this day. One hundred thousand people had navigated the winding residential streets that lead down to the world's most famous football stadium to witness the final Rose Bowl under the "old" rules: Big Ten champs versus Pac-10 champs, period. In a few years, when it's Florida State-Nebraska under the lights, it won't feel the same. Trust me, the white shoes, white belt Tournament-of-Roses types who view the football game as a nice little post-parade diversion will be in major denial.

But college football's Brave New World seemed far away that afternoon, as Michigan rallied behind a quarterback who would've been watching the game on TV as a grad student if his brother hadn't talked him into giving college football one more try. Brian Griese won MVP honors and made himself a third-round draft choice that day, and in the closing moments of ABC's broadcast, his dad Bob could finally let his fatherly pride show publicly.

But, typically, the fairy tale ended with a fuss. Was Washington State owed a final second or two? Had a slow-fingered timekeeper denied Ryan Leaf one final heave to the end zone?

It was more ammunition for

AP/Wide World Photos

Peyton Manning, the heavy preseason Heisman Trophy favorite, congratulates winner **Charles Woodson** at the Heisman ceremony in New York. **Randy Moss** chills to their right and **Ryan Leaf** offers his hand to their left.

Nebraska's lobbyists, chiefly quarterback Scott Frost, who begged pollsters to consider that Las Vegas would have favored his Huskers over Michigan in a hypothetical title game.

Frost went further, asking coaches directly: "Which team would you rather play if your job were at stake?"

So, great, now oddsmakers have input in national titles. Two great, undefeated teams. Two sets of championship rings: the only justice possible in an often unjust system. We love this sport, in spite of itself: the only place in sports where pollsters, not players, have the last word. ■

Lee Corso's Ten Most Significant Moments of the Year in College Football

10. The **National Football Foundation honors Jackie Robinson**, UCLA's only four sport letter winner (baseball, basketball, football and track), with its gold medal on the 50th anniversary of Robinson breaking the color barrier in Major League Baseball.

9. For first time in college football history **four #1 teams** (Nebraska, Penn St. twice, Michigan) win their games and drop in the polls. Coaches that run up the score on weaker opponents are vindicated as the margin of victory is proved important to pollsters.

8. Michigan's versatile **Charles Woodson** upsets Tennessee quarterback and heavy preseason favorite Peyton Manning to win the coveted Heisman Trophy. Woodson is the first primarily defensive

AP/Wide World Photos

Eddie Robinson looked in a new direction after the 1997 season, retiring after 55 years at Grambling.

player to win the award in its storied 62-year history.

7. **Colorado forfeits** all five of its wins from the 1997 season after unintentionally allowing an ineligible player to participate. The Buffaloes have had just one other winless season since the football program was established in 1890. The penalty was less severe than it could have been because Colorado reported its infraction to the NCAA.

6. **Notre Dame**, and its 7-5 record, goes to a lesser bowl (Independence) and loses big to LSU, a team it had already beaten.

5. **The Catch.** Nebraska freshman Matt Davison's version of the Immaculate Reception with no time left in regulation against Missouri spoils the stunning upset and forces an overtime. Nebraska goes on to win, 45-38, in OT and the Huskers stay unbeaten and in the hunt for the national title.

4. The **Rose Bowl joins the national title picture** when it becomes part of the Bowl Championship Series, the new name for the old Bowl Alliance. Now a Pac-10 or Big 10 champion can play in another bowl if needed to set-up a national title game.

3. Nebraska head coach **Tom Osborne's retirement**. Osborne, who leaves the game with the highest winning percentage (.836) of any active coach, wins a piece of the national title in his final game.

2. Grambling head coach and living legend **Eddie Robinson retires** as college football's all-time winningest coach. Over his incredible

55-year career Robinson amassed a record of 408-164-15.

1. **Michigan and Nebraska**, the nation's only undefeated teams, split the national title after both teams win their bowl games. Michigan tops the AP Poll, while Nebraska is #1 in the ESPN/*USA Today* coaches' poll. ■

INSIDE THE NUMBERS

by

Chris Fallica, Christian Teja and Team Research

NEBRASK-HUH?

The Cornhuskers were undefeated and won a share of the national championship but exactly who did they beat? A much talked-about game with Ohio St. never materialized and was replaced with Nebraska-Central Florida and Ohio St.-Bowling Green. The mediocrity of the Big XII is not the 'Huskers fault but with non-conference foes Akron and Central Florida, they certainly didn't make it hard on themselves.

Nebraska's Schedule

NCAA Ranking	51st
Opp. Win Pct.	.509
Opp Record	57-55
Non-conference games	Akron, UCF, Washington

Note: Nebraska fans can take heart with the statistical note entitled Who's Number One?.

TOUGH ACTS

Tom Osborne retired with the I-A record for most wins at a single school with his 255 victories at Nebraska. Replacing a 200-game winner has proven a tough task. So while Osborne certainly left the cupboard full for Frank Solich only time will tell how successful the successor will be.

Only seven other men have won more than 200 games at a single school. Note that the three active coaches with 200 wins at one school (Joe Paterno, LaVell Edwards and Bobby Bowden) do not appear on the list below.

	Wins at School	Successor	Wins
T. Osborne, Neb.	255	Frank Solich	?
A. Stagg, Chi.	244	Clark Shaughnessy	17
P. Bryant, Ala.	232	Ray Perkins	32
W. Hayes, Ohio St.	205	Earle Bruce	81
V. Dooley, Ga.	201	Ray Goff	46

Note: Bruce, Perkins and Goff all won well over 50 percent of their games, but the expectations were too much to overcome. Bruce actually won more than 75 percent but was never accepted by OSU alumni and fans.

EDDIE'S EXCELLENCE

Eddie Robinson amassed some staggering numbers in his momentous career at Grambling.

Only coach with 400 wins
Career spanned 11 Presidents
Only eight losing seasons in 57 years
17 conference titles
Career 70.7 winning pct.

WHO'S NUMBER ONE?

Michigan finished the season ranked first in the AP poll while Nebraska took the top spot in the Coaches' poll. But a quick look at the numbers may raise a few eyebrows.

	Team A	Team B
Record	12-0	13-0
Margin of Victory	17.4 ppg	30.2 ppg
vs. Final Reg. Season Top 25	4-0	5-0
Opp. Bowl record	0-6	2-2

Note: Team A is Michigan, Team B is Nebraska. ■

COLLEGE FOOTBALL STATISTICS

THE SEASON IN REVIEW

1997-1998

TOP 25 • BOWLS • STANDINGS

Final AP Top 25 Poll

Voted on by panel of 67 sportswriters & broadcasters and released on Jan. 3, 1998, following the Orange Bowl: winning team receives the Bear Bryant Trophy, given since 1983; first place votes in parentheses, records, total points (based on 25 for 1st, 24 for 2nd, etc.) bowl game result, head coach and career record, preseason rank (released on Aug. 10, 1997) and final regular season rank (released Dec. 7, 1997).

	Team	Final Record	Points	Bowl Game	Head Coach	Aug. 10 Rank	Dec. 7 Rank
1	Michigan (51½)	12-0	1731½	won Rose	Lloyd Carr (3 yrs: 29-8-0)	14	1
2	Nebraska (18½)	13-0	1698½	won Orange	Tom Osborne (25 yrs: 255-49-3)	6	2
3	Florida St.	11-1	1599	won Sugar	Bobby Bowden (32 yrs: 281-83-4)	3	4
4	Florida	10-2	1455	won Citrus	Steve Spurrier (11 yrs: 103-29-2)	2	6
5	UCLA	10-2	1413	won Cotton	Bob Toledo (8 yrs: 44-43-0)	30	5
6	North Carolina	11-1	1397	won Gator	Mack Brown (14 yrs: 87-74-1)	7	7
7	Tennessee	11-2	1320	lost Orange	Phillip Fulmer (6 yrs: 53-11-0)	5	3
8	Kansas St.	11-1	1302	won Fiesta	Bill Snyder (9 yrs: 66-37-1)	23	10
9	Washington St.	10-2	1259	lost Rose	Mike Price (17 yrs: 99-93-0)	44t	8
10	Georgia	10-2	1121	won Outback	Jim Donnan (8 yrs: 79-29-0)	36	12
11	Auburn	10-3	1025	won Peach	Terry Bowden (14 yrs: 111-47-2)	16	13
12	Ohio St.	10-3	975	lost Sugar	John Cooper (21 yrs: 167-73-6)	9	9
13	LSU	9-3	856	won Independence	Gerry DiNardo (7 yrs: 45-34-1)	10	15
14	Arizona St.	8-3	773	won Sun	Bruce Snyder (18 yrs: 108-88-5)	27	16
15	Purdue	9-3	715	won Alamo	Joe Tiller (7 yrs: 48-33-1)	NR	17
16	Penn St.	9-3	706	lost Citrus	Joe Paterno (32 yrs: 298-77-3)	1	11
17	Colorado St.	11-2	673	won Holiday	Sonny Lubick (9 yrs: 62-38-0)	26	18
18	Washington	8-4	617	won Aloha	Jim Lambright (4 yrs: 38-18-1)	4	21
19	So. Mississippi	9-3	490	won Liberty	Jeff Bower (8 yrs: 43-35-1)	37	22
20	Texas A&M	9-4	421	lost Cotton	R.C. Slocum (9 yrs: 83-25-2)	28	20
21	Syracuse	9-4	331	lost Fiesta	Paul Pasqualoni (12 yrs: 104-39-1)	17	14
22	Mississippi	8-4	255	won Motor City	Tommy Tuberville (3 yrs: 19-15-0)	NR	NR
23	Missouri	7-5	175	lost Holiday	Larry Smith (21 yrs: 128-107-7)	NR	19
24	Oklahoma St.	8-4	72	lost Alamo	Bob Simmons (3 yrs: 17-18-0)	NR	24
25	Georgia Tech	7-5	64	won Carquest	George O'Leary (3 yrs: 18-19-0)	41t	NR

Other teams receiving votes: 26. **Arizona** (7-5, 59 points, won Insight.com); 27. **Oregon** (7-5, 50 pts, won Las Vegas); 28. **Air Force** (10-3, 37 pts, lost Las Vegas); 29. **Marshall** (10-3, 33 pts, lost Motor City); 30. **Virginia** (7-4, 31 pts, no bowl); 31. **Clemson** (7-5, 27 pts, lost Peach); 32. **Louisiana Tech** (9-2, 20 pts, no bowl); 33. **Mississippi St.** (7-4, 15 pts, no bowl); 34. **Michigan St.** (7-5, 9 pts, lost Aloha); 35. **Wisconsin** (8-5, 8 pts, no bowl); 36. **New Mexico** (9-4, 6 pts, lost Insight.com); 37. **Cincinnati** (8-4, 5 pts, won Humanitarian); 38. **Notre Dame** (7-6, 3 pts, lost Independence); 39. **Iowa** (7-5, 2 pts, lost Sun); 40. **Virginia Tech** (7-5, 1 pt, lost Gator).

AP Preseason and Final Regular Season Polls

First place votes in parentheses.

Top 25
(Aug. 10, 1997)

	Team	Pts		Team	Pts
1	Penn St. (21)	1566	14	Michigan	797
2	Florida (12)	1548	15	Alabama	673
3	Florida St. (7)	1507	16	Auburn	592
4	Washington (10)	1484	17	Syracuse	585
5	Tennessee (8)	1480	18	Stanford	533
6	Nebraska (4)	1442	19	Brigham Young	375
7	N. Carolina (4)	1333	20	Clemson	352
8	Colorado (3)	1302	21	Iowa	347
9	Ohio St. (1)	1172	22	USC	219
10	LSU	1096	23	Kansas St.	210
11	Notre Dame	1071	24	Wisconsin	198
12	Texas	1042	25	Michigan St.	148
13	Miami	820			

Top 25
(Dec. 7, 1997)

	Team	Pts		Team	Pts
1	Michigan (69)	1749	14	Syracuse	778
2	Nebraska (1)	1681	15	LSU	715
3	Tennessee	1570	16	Arizona St.	610
4	Florida St.	1536	17	Purdue	578
5	UCLA	1386	18	Colorado St.	510
6	Florida	1356	19	Missouri	471
7	N. Carolina	1293	20	Texas A&M	460
8	Washington St.	1292	21	Washington	304
9	Ohio St.	1246	22	So. Mississippi	277
10	Kansas St.	1194	23	Air Force	216
11	Penn St.	994	24	Oklahoma St.	184
12	Georgia	966	25	Michigan St.	140
13	Auburn	952			

1997-98 Bowl Games

Listed by bowls matching highest-ranked teams as of final regular season AP poll (released Dec. 7, 1997). Attendance figures indicate tickets sold.

Bowl		Winner	Regular Season		Loser	Regular Season	Score	Date	Attendance
Rose	#1	Michigan	11-0	#8	Washington St.	10-1	21-16	Jan. 1	101,219
Orange	#2	Nebraska	12-0	#3	Tennessee	11-1	42-17	Jan. 2	72,385
Sugar	#4	Florida St.	10-1	#9	Ohio St.	10-2	31-14	Jan. 1	67,289
Cotton	#5	UCLA	9-2	#20	Texas A&M	9-3	29-23	Jan. 1	59,215
Citrus	#6	Florida	9-2	#11	Penn St.	9-2	21-6	Jan. 1	72,940
Gator	#7	North Carolina	10-1		Va. Tech	7-4	42-3	Jan. 1	54,116
Fiesta	#10	Kansas St.	10-1	#14	Syracuse	9-3	35-18	Dec. 31	69,367
Outback	#12	Georgia	9-2		Wisconsin	8-4	33-6	Jan. 1	56,186
Peach	#13	Auburn	9-3		Clemson	7-4	21-17	Jan. 2	71,212
Independence	#15	LSU	9-2		Notre Dame	7-5	27-9	Dec. 28	50,459
Sun	#16	Arizona St.	8-3		Iowa	7-4	17-7	Dec. 31	49,104
Alamo	#17	Purdue	8-3	#24	Oklahoma St.	8-3	33-20	Dec. 30	55,552
Holiday	#18	Colorado St.	10-2	#20	Missouri	7-4	35-24	Dec. 29	50,761
Aloha	#21	Washington	7-4	#25	Michigan St.	7-4	51-23	Dec. 25	44,598
Liberty	#22	So. Mississippi	8-3		Pittsburgh	6-5	41-7	Dec. 31	50,209
Las Vegas		Oregon	6-5	#23	Air Force	10-2	41-13	Dec. 20	21,514
Carquest		Georgia Tech	6-5		W. Virginia	7-4	35-30	Dec. 29	28,262
Humanitarian		Cincinnati	7-4		Utah St.	6-5	35-19	Dec. 29	16,131
Motor City		Mississippi	8-3		Marshall	10-2	34-31	Dec. 26	43,340
Insight.com		Arizona	6-5		New Mexico	9-3	20-14	Dec. 27	49,385

FAVORITES:

Rose (Michigan by 7½); **Orange** (Nebraska by 13½); **Sugar** (Florida by 6½); **Cotton** (UCLA by 12½); **Citrus** (Florida by 13); **Gator** (North Carolina by 11½); **Fiesta** (Kansas St. by 3½); **Outback** (Georgia by 8½); **Peach** (Auburn by 5); **Independence** (LSU by 6½); **Sun** (Iowa by 6); **Alamo** (Purdue by 4); **Holiday** (Colorado St. by 3½); **Aloha** (Washington by 4½); **Liberty** (Southern Mississippi by 10); **Las Vegas** (Oregon by 3½); **Carquest** (Georgia Tech by 3); **Humanitarian** (Cincinnati by 2½); **Motor City** (Mississippi by 2); **Insight.com** (Arizona by 10).

PER TEAM PAYOUTS:

Rose ($10 million); **FedEx Orange** ($8.5 million); **Nokia Sugar** and **Tostitos Fiesta** ($8.2 million); **CompUSA Florida Citrus** ($3.5 million); **Chick-fil-a Peach** ($3 million); **Southwestern Bell Cotton** ($2.5 million); **Outback** ($1.65 million); **Plymouth Holiday** ($1.35 million); **Toyota Gator** ($1.3 million); **Builders Square Alamo** and **Norwest Sun** ($1 million); **St. Jude's Liberty** ($900,000); **Poulan/Weed Eater Independence** and **Las Vegas** ($800,000); **Carquest**, **Jeep Aloha**, **Insight.com**, **Ford Motor City** and **Sports Humanitarian** ($750,000).

Final Bowl Alliance Poll

Combined point totals of the final regular season AP media and *USA Today*/ESPN coaches' polls to help determine bowl match-ups. Polls were released Dec. 8, 1997.

	AP Poll No.	AP Poll Pts	Coaches No.	Coaches Pts	Total Pts
1 Michigan	1	(1749)	1	(1541½)	3290½
2 Nebraska	2	(1681)	2	(1494½)	3175½
3 Tennessee	3	(1570)	3	(1355)	2925
4 Florida St.	4	(1536)	4	(1354)	2890
5 UCLA	5	(1386)	6	(1192)	2578
6 North Carolina	7	(1293)	5	(1230)	2523
7 Florida	6	(1356)	8	(1134)	2490
8 Washington St.	8	(1292)	7	(1185)	2477
9 Ohio St.	9	(1246)	10	(1067)	2313
10 Kansas St.	10	(1194)	9	(1102)	2296
11 Penn St.	11	(994)	12	(834)	1828
12 Georgia	12	(966)	11	(842)	1808
13 Auburn	13	(952)	13	(772)	1724
14 Syracuse	14	(778)	14	(725)	1503
15 LSU	15	(715)	15	(653)	1368
16 Purdue	17	(578)	16	(533)	1111
17 Arizona St.	16	(610)	18	(457)	1067
18 Colorado St.	18	(510)	17	(532)	1042
19 Texas A&M	20	(460)	19	(391)	851
20 Missouri	19	(471)	20	(335)	806
21 Washington	21	(304)	23	(232)	536
22 So. Mississippi	22	(277)	22	(234)	511
23 Air Force	23	(216)	21	(285)	501
24 Oklahoma St.	24	(184)	24	(185)	369
25 Michigan St.	25	(140)	25	(103)	243

Bowl MVPs

Most Valuable Player, Offensive and Defensive Players of the Game, and Team MVP selections in all 21 bowl games following the 1997 season.

Bowl		Player	Pos
Alamo	Off—	Billy Dicken, Purdue	QB
	Def—	Adrian Beasley, Purdue	SS
Aloha	MVP—	Rashaan Shehee, Washington	RB
Carquest	MVP—	Joe Hamilton, Georgia Tech	QB
Citrus	MVP—	Fred Taylor, Florida	RB
Cotton	Team—	Cade McNown, UCLA	QB
	Team—	Dat Nguyen, Texas A&M	LB
Fiesta	MVP—	Michael Bishop, Kansas St.	QB
Gator	Team—	Chris Keldorf, UNC	QB
	Team—	Al Clark, Virginia Tech	QB
Heritage	MVP—	Steve Wofford, Southern	RB
Holiday	Off—	Darran Hall, Colorado St.	WR
		& Moses Moreno, Colorado St.	QB
Humanitarian	MVP—	Chad Plummer, Cincinnati	QB
Independence	Off—	Rondell Mealey, LSU	RB
	Def—	Arnold Miller, LSU	DE
Insight.com	MVP—	Kelvin Eafon, Arizona	RB
Las Vegas	Team—	Bryce Fisher, Air Force	DT
	Team—	Pat Johnson, Oregon	WR
Liberty	MVP—	Sherrod Gideon, So. Miss.	WR
Motor City	MVP—	Stewart Patridge, Miss.	QB
Orange	Team—	Ahman Green, Nebraska	RB
	Team—	Jamal Lewis, Tennessee	RB
Outback	MVP—	Mike Bobo, Georgia	QB
Peach	Off—	Dameyune Craig, Auburn	QB
	Def—	Takeo Spikes, Auburn	LB
Rose	MVP—	Brian Griese, Michigan	QB
Sun	Team—	Michael Martin, Arizona St.	RB
	Team—	Jason Baker, Iowa	PK
Sugar	MVP—	E.G. Green, Florida St.	WR

Co-National Champions

Michigan and Nebraska each captured a share of the national championship. The Wolverines were ranked first in both the AP and *USA Today*/ESPN coaches' poll entering the bowl season, however, while they retained their top spot in the writers' poll following their 21-16 Rose Bowl win over #8 Washington St., the coaches dropped them a notch to number two in their poll. Nebraska was able to sway enough voters with its 42-17 Orange Bowl win over #3 Tennessee, to earn a share of the national title. Opponents' records and AP rank listed below are day of game.

Michigan Wolverines (12-0)

Date	AP Rank	Opponent	Result
Sept. 13	**#14**	#8 Colorado (1-0)	27-3
Sept. 20	**#8**	Baylor (1-1)	38-3
Sept. 27	**#6**	Notre Dame (1-2)	21-14
Oct. 4	**#6**	at Indiana (1-3)	37-0
Oct. 11	**#6**	Northwestern (2-4)	23-6
Oct. 18	**#5**	#15 Iowa (4-1)	28-24
Oct. 25	**#5**	at #15 Michigan St. (5-1)	23-7
Nov. 1	**#4**	Minnesota (2-6)	24-3
Nov. 8	**#4**	at #2 Penn St. (7-0)	34-8
Nov. 15	**#1**	at #23 Wisconsin (8-2)	26-16
Nov. 22	**#1**	#4 Ohio St. (10-1)	20-14
Jan. 1	**#1**	#8 Washington St. (10-1)†	21-16

†Rose Bowl (at Pasadena)

Final Statistics

Passing (5 Att)	Att	Cmp	Pct.	Yds	TD	Rate
Brian Griese	307	193	62.9	2293	17	140.0
Tom Brady	15	12	80.0	103	0	137.7

Interceptions: Griese 6.

Top Receivers	No	Yds	Avg	Long	TD
Chris Howard	37	276	7.5	26	1
Jerame Tuman	29	437	15.1	53	5
Tai Streets	28	476	17.0	58	6
Russell Shaw	25	284	11.4	39	2
Anthony Thomas	22	219	10.0	28	0
Clarence Williams	22	179	8.1	26	0
Charles Woodson	12	238	19.8	37	2

Top Rushers	Car	Yds	Avg	Long	TD
Chris Howard	199	938	4.7	7	51
Anthony Thomas	137	549	4.0	58	5
Chris Floyd	64	279	4.4	31	2
Clarence Williams	58	266	4.6	16	1
Ray Jackson	11	41	3.7	18	0
Patrick McCall	13	41	3.2	11	1
Tate Schanski	4	25	6.3	11	1
Charles Woodson	5	21	4.2	33	1
Brian Griese	58	20	0.3	40	2

Most Touchdowns	TD	Run	Rec	Ret	Pts
Chris Howard	8	7	1	0	48
Tai Streets	6	0	6	0	36
Anthony Thomas	5	5	0	0	30
Jerame Tuman	5	0	5	0	30
Charles Woodson	4	1	2	1	24
Chris Floyd	2	2	0	0	12
Russell Shaw	2	0	2	0	12

Kicking	FG/Att	Lg	PAT/Att	Pts
Kraig Baker	14/19	42	35/37	77
Jay Feely	3/4	51	2/2	11

Punting	No	Yds	Long	Blk	Avg
Jason Vinson	57	2183	54	0	38.3

Most Interceptions	
Charles Woodson	8
Marcus Ray	5
Tom Hendricks	2
Andre Weathers	2
Six tied with one each.	

Most Sacks	
Glen Steele	7
Josh Williams	7
Dhani Jones	6
James Hall	4
Rob Renes	4
Andre Weathers	4

Nebraska Cornhuskers (13-0)

Date	AP Rank	Opponent	Result
Aug. 30	**#6**	Akron (0-0)	59-14
Sept. 13	**#6**	Central Florida (0-2)	38-24
Sept. 20	**#7**	at #2 Washington (2-0)	27-14
Oct. 4	**#3**	#17 Kansas St. (3-0)	56-26
Oct. 11	**#3**	at Baylor (1-3)	49-21
Oct. 18	**#2**	Texas Tech (3-2)	29-0
Oct. 25	**#1**	at Kansas (4-3)	35-0
Nov. 1	**#1**	Oklahoma (3-5)	69-7
Nov. 8	**#1**	at Missouri (6-3)	45-38 (OT)
Nov. 15	**#3**	Iowa St. (1-8)	77-14
Nov. 28	**#2**	at Colorado (5-5)	27-24
Dec. 6	**#2**	#14 Texas A&M (9-2)*	54-15
Jan. 2	**#2**	#3 Tennessee (11-1)†	42-17

* Big 12 title game (at San Antonio)
† Orange Bowl (at Miami)

Final Statistics

Passing (5 Att)	Att	Cmp	Pct.	Yds	TD	Rate
Scott Frost	171	97	56.7	1362	5	82.5
Frankie London	22	10	45.5	201	0	78.0

Interceptions: Frost 4.

Top Receivers	No	Yds	Avg	Long	TD
Ahman Green	19	182	9.6	39	0
Sheldon Jackson	15	245	16.3	37	2
Kenny Cheatham	14	191	13.6	31	0
Lance Brown	12	226	18.8	35	0
Matt Davison	11	235	21.4	51	1
Bobby Newcombe	8	195	24.4	40	1

Top Rushers	Car	Yds	Avg	Long	TD
Ahman Green	307	2083	6.8	64	24
Scott Frost	193	1155	6.0	34	22
Joel Makovicka	114	746	6.5	43	9
Correll Buckhalter	56	325	5.8	25	6
Frankie London	42	198	4.7	51	3
Bobby Newcombe	19	172	9.1	25	1
Jay Sims	31	148	4.8	16	2
Billy Legate	12	74	6.2	14	0
Dan Alexander	17	69	4.1	18	0
Willie Miller	10	49	4.9	11	1

Most Touchdowns	TD	Run	Rec	Ret	Pts
Ahman Green	24	24	0	0	144
Scott Frost	22	22	0	0	132
Joel Mackovicka	10	9	1	0	60
Correll Buckhalter	6	6	0	0	36
Frankie London	3	3	0	0	18
Bobby Newcombe	3	1	1	1	18
Sheldon Jackson	2	0	2	0	12
Jay Sims	2	2	0	0	12

Kicking	FG/Att	Lg	PAT/Att	Pts
Kris Brown	18/21	46	68/68	122
Ted Retzlaff	0/0	0	7/7	7
Dan Hadefeldt	0/0	0	2/2	2

Punting	No	Yds	Long	Blk	Avg
Jesse Kosch	34	1335	60	2	39.3

Most Interceptions	
Eric Warfield	3

Most Sacks	
Mike Rucker	8½
Grant Wistrom	8½

Rose Bowl

Thursday, Jan. 1, 1998 at Rose Bowl in Pasadena, Calif.

#8 **Washington St.** (Pac-10)	7	0	6	3	**—16**
#1 **Michigan** (Big Ten)	0	7	7	7	**—21**

1st; 03:17; **Washington St.**— Kevin McKenzie 15-yd pass from Ryan Leaf (Rian Lindell kick). 6 plays, 47 yards, 3:09.
2nd; 07:08; **Michigan**— Tai Streets 53-yd pass from Brian Griese (Jay Feely kick). 3 plays, 66 yards, 0:56.
3rd; 08:33; **Washington St.**— Shawn Tims 14-yd run (kick failed). 9 plays, 99 yards, 3:45.
3rd; 05:07; **Michigan**— Streets 58-yd pass from Griese (Kraig Baker kick). 7 plays, 80 yards, 3:26.
4th; 11:21; **Michigan**— Jerame Tuman 23-yd pass from Griese (Baker kick). 14 plays, 77 yards, 5:25.
4th; 07:25; **Washington St.**— Lindell 48-yd Field Goal. 8 plays, 49 yards, 3:56.

Favorite: Michigan by 7½ **Attendance:** 101,219
Field: Grass **Time:** 3:12
Weather: Hazy, 75 degrees, minimal wind

Team Statistics

	WSU	Mich.
Touchdowns	2	3
Rushing	1	0
Passing	1	3
Kick returns	0	0
Interception returns	0	0
Safeties	0	0
Time of possession	27:46	32:14
First downs	18	22
Rushing	4	9
Passing	13	12
Penalties	1	1
3rd down efficiency	7 of 15	10 of 17
4th down efficiency	0 of 0	0 of 0
Total offense (net yards)	398	379
Plays	63	71
Average gain	6.3	5.3
Carries/yards (includ. sacks)	28/67	41/128
Passing yards	331	251
Completions/attempts	17/35	18/30
Times sacked/yards lost	4/28	1/15
Return yardage	2	56
Punt returns/yards	1/2	3/18
Kickoff returns/yards	0/0	2/38
Interceptions/yards	1/0	1/0
Fumbles/lost	0/0	0/0
Penalties/yards	4/43	4/40
Punts/average	6/40.3	6/30.5

INDIVIDUAL STATISTICS

Rushing: WSU–Michael Black 7 carries for 24 yards, DeJuan Gilmore 8 for 20, Shawn Tims 1 for 14, Ryan Leaf 10 for 6, Jason Clayton 2 for 3. MICH–Chris Howard 19 for 70, Anthony Thomas 7 for 20, Chris Floyd 5 for 17, Brian Griese 7 for 13, Charles Woodson 2 for 6, Clarence Williams 1 for 2.

Passing: WSU–Ryan Leaf 17 for 35 for 331 yards and 1 INT. MICH–Brian Griese 18 for 30 for 251 yards and 1 INT.

Receiving: WSU–Chris Jackson 5 catches for 89 yards, Kevin McKenzie 5 for 78, Shawn McWashington 2 for 41, Shawn Tims 2 for 9, Nian Taylor 1 for 46, DeJuan Gilmore 1 for 42, Love Jefferson 1 for 8, Jason Clayton 0 for 18. MICH–Russell Shaw 6 for 49, Tai Streets 4 for 127, Jerame Tuman 2 for 33, Chris Howard 2 for 13, Anthony Thomas 1 for 14, Charles Woodson 1 for 7, Mark Campbell 1 for 7, Clarence Williams 1 for 1.

Orange Bowl

Friday, Jan. 2, 1998 at Pro Player Stadium in Miami, Fla.

#3 **Tennessee** (SEC)	0	3	6	8	**—17**
#2 **Nebraska** (Big 12)	7	7	21	7	**—42**

1st; 13:50; **Nebraska**— Ahman Green 1-yd run (Kris Brown kick). 8 plays, 78 yards, 3:34.
2nd; 03:32; **Nebraska**— Shevin Wiggins 10-yd run (Brown kick). 3 plays, 15 yards, 1:07.
2nd; 06:32; **Tennessee**— Jeff Hall 44-yd Field Goal. 7 plays, 35 yards, 3:00.
3rd; 04:49; **Nebraska**— Scott Frost 1-yd run (Brown kick). 12 plays, 80 yards, 4:49.
3rd; 09:53; **Nebraska**— Frost 11-yd run (Brown kick). 6 plays, 73 yards, 2:53.
3rd; 13:02; **Tennessee**— Peerless Price 5-yd pass from Peyton Manning (pass failed). 9 plays, 72 yards, 3:09.
3rd; 14:31; **Nebraska**— Green 22-yd run (Brown kick). 4 plays, 80 yards, 1:29.
4th; 10:36; **Nebraska**— Frost 9-yd run (Brown kick). 9 plays, 66 yards, 3:53.
4th; 14:02; **Tennessee**— Andy McCullough 3-yd pass from Tee Martin (Travis Stephens pass). 8 plays, 80 yards, 3:26.

Favorite: Nebraska by 13½ **Attendance:** 72,385
Field: Grass **Time:** 3:20
Weather: Partly cloudy, 71 degrees, wind of 15-20 E

Team Statistics

	Tenn.	Neb.
Touchdowns	2	6
Rushing	0	6
Passing	2	0
Kick returns	0	0
Interception returns	0	0
Safeties	0	0
Time of possession	23:57	36:03
First downs	16	30
Rushing	6	22
Passing	9	7
Penalties	1	1
3rd down efficiency	2 of 10	4 of 10
4th down efficiency	1 of 1	1 of 2
Total offense (net yards)	315	534
Plays	56	80
Average gain	5.6	6.7
Carries/yards (includ. sacks)	21/128	68/409
Passing yards	187	125
Completions/attempts	25/35	9/12
Times sacked/yards lost	0/0	1/9
Return yardage	98	88
Punt returns/yards	2/4	3/31
Kickoff returns/yards	5/94	1/29
Interceptions/yards	0/0	1/28
Fumbles/lost	0/0	0/0
Penalties/yards	5/37	8/63
Punts/average	6/52.3	4/39.0

INDIVIDUAL STATISTICS

Rushing: TENN–Jamal Lewis 14 carries for 90 yards, Mark Levine 2 for 30, Tee Martin 1 for 11, Travis Stephens 3 for 6, Peyton Manning 1 for –9. NEB–Ahman Green 29 for 206, Joel Makovicka 9 for 61, Scott Frost 17 for 60, Shevin Wiggins 3 for 28, Jay Sims 4 for 23, Bobby Newcombe 3 for 16, Correll Buckhalter 2 for 14, Dan Alexander 1 for 1.

Passing: TENN–Peyton Manning 21 for 31 for 134 yards and 1 INT, Tee Martin 4 for 4 for 53 yards and 0 INT. NEB–Scott Frost 9 for 12 for 125 yards and 0 INT.

Receiving: TENN–Marcus Nash 5 catches for 53 yards, Jeremaine Copeland 4 for 30, Shawn Bryson 4 for 25, Jamal Lewis 4 for 4, Andy McCullough 3 for 50, Peerless Price 3 for 9, Cedrick Wilson 1 for 13, Derrick Edmonds 1 for 3. NEB–Sheldon Jackson 4 for 56, Ahman Green 3 for 31, Bobby Newcombe 1 for 22, Matt Davison 1 for 16.

Other Final Division I-A Polls

USA Today/ESPN Coaches' Poll

Voted on by panel of 62 Division I-A head coaches; winning team receives the Sears Trophy (originally the McDonald's Trophy, 1991-93); first place votes in parentheses with total points (based on 25 for 1st, 24 for 2nd, etc.).

	Pts		Pts
1 Nebraska (32)	1520	14 Arizona St.	667
2 Michigan (30)	1516	15 Purdue	666
3 Florida St.	1414	16 Colorado St.	646
4 N. Carolina	1292	17 Penn St.	585
5 UCLA	1239	18 Washington	512
6 Florida	1209	19 So. Mississippi	462
7 Kansas St.	1192	20 Syracuse	380
8 Tennessee	1122	21 Texas A&M	359
9 Washington St.	1076	22 Mississippi	188
10 Georgia	1007	23 Missouri	114
11 Auburn	854	24 Oklahoma St.	103
12 Ohio St.	826	25 Air Force	74
13 LSU	786		

Other teams receiving votes: Clemson (58 pts); Georgia Tech (55); Iowa (32); Louisiana Tech (31); Oregon (25); Cincinnati (24); Arizona (23); Mississippi St. (20); Michigan St. (16); New Mexico and Wisconsin (13); Tulane (10); Virginia (9); West Virginia (7); Marshall (4); Notre Dame (1).

NY Times Computer Ratings

Based on an analysis of each team's scores with emphasis on three factors: who won, by what margin, and against what quality of opposition. Computer balances lop-sided scores, notes home field advantage and gives late-season games more weight than those played earlier in the schedule.

The top team is assigned a rating of 1.000, ratings of all other teams reflect their strength relative to strength of No.1 team. Rankings include all regular season games.

	Rating		Rating
1 Nebraska	1.000	14 Air Force	.792
2 Michigan	.996	15 Syracuse	.780
3 Florida St.	.967	16 Washington	.776
4 Tennessee	.957	17 Penn St.	.773
5 Kansas St.	.910	18 Notre Dame	.760
6 UCLA	.901	19 LSU	.752
7 Colorado St.	.897	20 Arizona St.	.735
8 Florida	.881	21 Purdue	.734
9 Ohio St.	.865	22 Marshall	.718
10 Georgia	.846	23 Virginia	.718
11 Washington St.	.840	24 Mississippi	.709
12 N. Carolina	.837	25 Michigan St.	.705
13 Auburn	.823		

FWAA Poll

Voted on by a five-man panel comprised of Tony Barnhart of the *Atlanta Journal-Constitution*, Mark Blaudschun of the *Boston Globe*, Blair Kerkhoff of *The Kansas City Star*, Ivan Maisel of CNN-Sports Illustrated and Dick Weiss of the *New York Daily News*. Each selector voted for one team.

Winning team receives the Grantland Rice Award, given since 1954.

Michigan (5)

NFF's MacArthur Bowl

Voted on by panel of 62 members of the National Football Foundation and College Hall of Fame; winning team receives the NFF's MacArthur Bowl, given since 1959; The McArthur Bowl was the gift of an anonymous donor in the name of General Douglas MacArthur who served for several years as chairman of the Foundation's National Advisory Board. Almost 400 ounces of silver went into the bowl which represents a huge stadium with rows of seats carved in relief.

Michigan

Winningest Teams of the 1990s

Division I-A schools with the best overall winning percentage from 1990-97, through the Jan. 1-2, 1998, bowl games.

National champions: 1990—Colorado (AP, FWAA, NFF) and Georgia Tech (UPI); 1991—Miami-FL (AP) and Washington (FWAA, NFF, *USA Today*/CNN); 1992—Alabama; 1993—Florida St; 1994—Nebraska; 1995—Nebraska; 1996—Florida.; 1997—Michigan (AP, NFF) and Nebraska (*USA Today*/ESPN).

	Overall Record	Bowls W-L-T	Overall Win Pct.
1 Nebraska	87-11-1	4-4-0	.884
2 Florida St.	86-11-1	7-1-0	.883
3 Florida	83-16-1	4-3-0	.835
4 Penn St.	78-20-0	5-3-0	.796
Tennessee	77-19-2	5-3-0	.796
6 Marshall†	89-24-0	0-1-0	.788
7 Miami-FL	74-20-0	3-3-0	.787
8 Texas A&M	75-21-2	2-4-0	.776
9 Colorado	72-20-4	5-2-0	.771
10 Michigan	73-21-3	5-3-0	.768
11 Ohio St.	74-22-3	2-6-0	.763
12 Washington	69-24-1	3-3-0	.739
13 Nevada†	71-26-0	1-2-0	.732
Notre Dame	70-25-2	3-4-0	.732
15 North Carolina	68-26-1	4-2-0	.721
16 Syracuse	67-26-3	5-1-0	.714
17 Kansas St.	65-27-1	3-2-0	.704
Auburn	64-26-3	3-1-0	.704
19 BYU	69-30-2	2-3-1	.693
20 Alabama	66-32-0	5-1-0	.673
21 Toledo	59-28-3	1-0-0	.672
22 Virginia	62-32-1	2-4-0	.658
23 Clemson	60-33-1	2-4-0	.644
24 Iowa	58-35-2	2-3-1	.621
25 Virginia Tech	57-35-1	2-3-0	.618
26 Air Force	60-38-0	6-7-1	.612
27 Texas	56-36-2	1-3-0	.606
28 Colorado St.	58-38-0	2-3-0	.604
29 Georgia	55-36-1	3-1-0	.603
30 UCLA	55-37-0	2-2-0	.598

†Joined I-A as follows: Marshall (1997) and Nevada (1992).

NCAA Division I-A Final Standings

Standings based on conference games only; overall records include postseason games.

Atlantic Coast Conference

	Conference				Overall			
	W	L	PF	PA	W	L	PF	PA
*Florida St.	8	0	347	128	11	1	468	181
*North Carolina	7	1	224	110	11	1	348	146
Virginia	5	3	200	187	7	4	277	242
*Georgia Tech	5	3	200	208	7	5	314	296
*Clemson	4	4	166	158	7	5	292	219
North Carolina St.	3	5	215	199	6	5	325	268
Wake Forest	3	5	166	229	5	6	245	288
Maryland	1	7	109	282	2	9	161	355
Duke	0	8	157	283	2	9	223	341

***Bowls (3-1):** Florida St. (won Sugar); N. Carolina (won Gator); Clemson (lost Peach); Georgia Tech (won Carquest).

Big East Conference

	Conference				Overall			
	W	L	PF	PA	W	L	PF	PA
*Syracuse	6	1	238	104	9	4	441	226
*Virginia Tech	5	2	197	127	7	5	324	227
*West Virginia	4	3	219	167	7	5	360	285
*Pittsburgh	4	3	208	197	6	6	333	354
Miami-FL	3	4	215	191	5	6	314	285
Boston College	3	4	173	176	4	7	237	314
Temple	3	4	150	212	3	8	212	371
Rutgers	0	7	121	347	0	11	191	496

***Bowls (0-4):** Virginia Tech (lost Gator); West Virginia (lost Carquest); Syracuse (lost Fiesta); Pittsburgh (lost Liberty).

Big 12 Conference

North	Conference				Overall			
	W	L	PF	PA	W	L	PF	PA
*Nebraska	9	0	441	145	13	0	607	214
*Kansas St.	7	1	255	132	11	1	418	177
*Missouri	5	3	272	256	7	5	392	367
Colorado	3	5	246	228	5	6	300	295
Kansas	3	5	129	235	5	6	177	279
Iowa St.	1	7	155	321	1	10	214	493

South	Conference				Overall			
	W	L	PF	PA	W	L	PF	PA
*Texas A&M	6	3	261	191	9	4	445	236
*Oklahoma St.	5	3	228	186	8	4	352	233
Texas Tech	5	3	142	121	6	5	245	217
Texas	2	6	294	255	4	7	283	366
Oklahoma	2	6	125	267	4	8	232	379
Baylor	1	7	146	257	2	9	200	375

Big 12 championship game: Nebraska beat Texas A&M, 54-15 (Dec. 6).

***Bowls (2-3):** Nebraska (won Orange); Texas A&M (lost Cotton); Kansas St. (won Fiesta); Missouri (lost Holiday); Oklahoma St. (lost Alamo).

Conference Bowling Results

Postseason records for 1997 season.

	W-L
Conference USA	2-0
Pac-10	5-1
SEC	5-1
ACC	3-1
Big 12	2-3
WAC	1-2
Big Ten	2-5
Mid-Am	0-1
Independents	0-1
Big West	0-1
Big East	0-4

Big Ten Conference

	Conference				Overall			
	W	L	PF	PA	W	L	PF	PA
*Michigan	8	0	215	78	12	0	322	114
*Ohio St.	6	2	253	86	10	3	410	298
*Penn St.	6	2	217	185	9	3	366	254
*Purdue	6	2	285	180	9	3	396	267
*Wisconsin	5	3	165	195	8	5	291	306
*Iowa	4	4	221	106	7	5	411	159
*Michigan St.	4	4	203	148	7	5	342	237
Northwestern	3	5	141	201	5	7	243	288
Minnesota	1	7	119	226	3	9	238	334
Indiana	1	7	74	281	2	9	120	359
Illinois	0	8	76	283	0	11	119	368

***Bowls (2-5):** Michigan (won Rose); Ohio St. (lost Sugar); Penn St. (lost Citrus); Purdue (won Alamo); Wisconsin (lost Outback); Iowa (lost Sun); Michigan St. (lost Aloha).

Big West Conference

	Conference				Overall			
	W	L	PF	PA	W	L	PF	PA
*Utah St.	4	1	211	114	6	6	389	296
Nevada	4	1	227	137	5	6	353	320
Boise St.	3	2	161	127	4	7	285	358
Idaho	2	3	128	170	5	6	302	263
North Texas	2	3	118	175	4	7	232	331
New Mexico St.	0	5	74	196	2	9	236	388

Humanitarian Bowl tiebreaker: Nevada and Utah St. finished the regular season as Big West co-champions. Utah St. earned the right to represent the conference in the Humanitarian Bowl by defeating Nevada 38–19 (Nov. 15).

***Bowls (0-1):** Utah St. (lost Humanitarian).

Conference USA

	Conference				Overall			
	W	L	PF	PA	W	L	PF	PA
*Southern Miss.	6	0	198	85	9	3	337	210
Tulane	5	1	211	124	7	4	375	225
East Carolina	4	2	148	131	5	6	214	298
*Cincinnati	2	4	127	136	8	4	321	252
Memphis	2	4	104	143	4	7	218	243
Houston	2	4	117	189	3	8	216	410
Louisville	0	6	139	236	1	10	245	407

***Bowls (2-0):** Southern Miss. (won Liberty); Cincinnati (won Humanitarian).

Mid-American Conference

Eastern	Conference				Overall			
	W	L	PF	PA	W	L	PF	PA
*Marshall	8	1	339	151	10	3	484	259
Miami-OH	6	2	319	161	8	3	312	226
Ohio	6	2	210	140	8	3	301	177
Bowling Green	3	5	155	209	3	8	191	341
Kent	3	5	242	325	3	8	337	490
Akron	2	7	204	320	2	9	218	435

Western	Conference				Overall			
	W	L	PF	PA	W	L	PF	PA
Toledo	7	2	272	199	9	3	356	268
Western Michigan	6	2	225	190	4	7	329	352
Ball St.	4	4	195	193	5	6	239	260
Eastern Michigan	4	5	295	281	4	7	329	352
Central Michigan	1	7	204	315	2	9	282	479
Northern Illinois	0	8	101	277	0	11	129	382

***Bowls (0-1):** Marshall (lost Motor City).

Pacific 10 Conference

	Conference				Overall			
	W	L	PF	PA	W	L	PF	PA
*Washington St.	7	1	297	246	10	2	483	296
*UCLA	7	1	292	181	10	2	477	247
*Arizona St.	6	2	233	168	9	3	324	210
*Washington	5	3	277	186	8	4	420	259
*Arizona	4	4	222	232	7	5	317	312
USC	4	4	171	181	6	5	233	233
*Oregon	3	5	241	264	7	5	380	350
Stanford	3	5	198	262	5	6	276	317
California	1	7	186	259	3	8	295	339
Oregon St.	0	8	112	250	3	8	195	285

***Bowls (5-1):** Washington St. (lost Rose); UCLA (won Cotton); Arizona St. (won Sun); Washington (won Aloha); Arizona (won Insight.com); Oregon (won Las Vegas).

Southeastern Conference

	Conference				Overall			
Eastern	W	L	PF	PA	W	L	PF	PA
*Tennessee	8	1	285	183	11	2	428	286
*Florida	6	2	274	158	10	2	430	205
*Georgia	6	2	240	155	10	2	380	195
South Carolina	3	5	178	201	5	6	258	279
Kentucky	2	6	212	317	5	6	348	362
Vanderbilt	0	8	52	169	3	8	138	204

	Conference				Overall			
Western	W	L	PF	PA	W	L	PF	PA
*LSU	6	2	229	152	9	3	373	188
*Auburn	6	3	201	189	10	3	340	266
*Mississippi	4	4	145	147	8	4	267	240
Mississippi St.	4	4	154	167	7	4	226	215
Alabama	2	6	157	192	4	7	181	284
Arkansas	2	6	127	224	4	7	246	248

SEC championship game: Tennessee beat Auburn, 30-29 (Dec. 6).

***Bowls (5-1):** Tennessee (lost Orange); Florida (won Citrus); Georgia (won Outback); LSU (won Independence); Mississippi (won Motor City); Auburn (won Peach).

Western Athletic Conference

	Conference				Overall			
Pacific	W	L	PF	PA	W	L	PF	PA
*Colorado St.	8	1	341	111	11	2	477	203
*Air Force	6	2	201	129	10	3	279	190
Fresno St.	5	3	208	166	6	6	318	288
Wyoming	4	4	175	130	7	6	322	227
San Diego St.	4	4	171	199	5	7	257	333
San Jose St.	4	4	191	277	4	7	225	387
UNLV	2	6	205	260	3	8	281	332
Hawaii	1	7	96	238	3	9	189	308

	Conference				Overall			
Mountain	W	L	PF	PA	W	L	PF	PA
*New Mexico	6	3	271	198	9	4	404	274
Rice	5	3	205	189	7	4	306	285
SMU	5	3	185	159	6	5	247	237
Utah	5	3	199	127	6	5	253	200
BYU	4	4	175	167	6	5	250	254
UTEP	3	5	128	201	4	7	162	311
Tulsa	2	6	197	296	2	9	258	426
TCU	1	7	136	237	1	10	172	325

WAC championship game: Colorado St. beat New Mexico, 41-13 (Dec. 6).

***Bowls (1-2):** Colorado St. (won Holiday); New Mexico (lost Insight.com); Air Force (lost Las Vegas).

I-A Independents

	W	L	PF	PA
Louisiana Tech	9	2	364	281
Navy	7	4	398	209
*Notre Dame	7	5	273	238
Ala.-Birmingham	5	6	222	238
Central Florida	5	6	374	303
NE Lousiana	5	7	226	319
Army	4	7	221	311
Arkansas St.	2	9	200	394
SW Louisiana	1	10	176	553

***Bowls (0-1):** Notre Dame (lost Independence).

NCAA Division I-A Individual Leaders

REGULAR SEASON

Total Offense

		Rushing				Passing		Total Offense				
	Cl	Car	Gain	Loss	Net	Att	Yds	Plays	Yds	YdsPP	TDR*	YdsPG
Tim Rattay, La. Tech	So.	64	233	146	87	477	3881	541	3968	7.33	35	360.73
Tim Couch, Kentucky	So.	66	139	264	-125	547	3884	613	3759	6.13	40	341.73
Ryan Leaf, Washington St.	Jr.	72	176	230	-54	375	3637	447	3583	8.02	39	325.73
Daunte Culpepper, C. Florida	Jr.	136	677	239	438	381	3086	517	3524	6.82	30	320.36
John Dutton, Nevada	Sr.	44	134	138	-4	367	3526	411	3522	8.57	21	320.18
Peyton Manning, Tennessee	Sr.	49	103	133	-30	477	3819	526	3789	7.20	39	315.75
Charlie Batch, Eastern Mich.	Sr.	85	327	217	110	434	3280	519	3390	6.53	24	308.18
Thad Busby, Florida St.	Sr.	57	132	148	-16	390	3317	447	3301	7.38	27	300.09
Jose Davis, Kent	So.	50	305	129	176	365	2707	415	2883	6.95	35	288.30
Jon Denton, UNLV	So.	64	204	199	5	374	2586	438	2591	5.92	21	287.89

* Touchdowns responsible for include TD passes and TDs scored.

All-Purpose Yards

	Cl	Gm	Rush	Rec	PR	KOR	Total Yds	YdsPG
Troy Edwards, La. Tech	Jr.	11	190	1707	6	241	2144	194.91
Ricky Williams, Texas	Jr.	11	1893	150	0	0	2043	185.73
Kevin Faulk, LSU	Jr.	9	1144	93	192	217	1646	182.89
Randy Moss, Marshall	So.	12	2	1647	266	263	2178	181.51
Michael Perry, Rice	Jr.	10	1034	44	26	680	1784	178.40
Tutu Atwell, Minnesota	Sr.	12	77	924	296	776	2073	172.75
Jerome Pathon, Washington	Sr.	11	0	1245	209	386	1840	167.27
Tavian Banks, Iowa	Sr.	11	1639	200	0	0	1839	167.18
Ahman Green, Nebraska	Jr.	12	1877	105	0	0	1982	165.17
Sedrick Irvin, Michigan St.	So.	11	1211	339	263	0	1813	164.82

Texas
Ricky Williams
Rushing, Scoring

Wyoming
Brian Lee
Interceptions

Louisiana Tech
Troy Edwards
All-Purpose

UCLA
Cade McNown
Passing Efficiency

Passing Efficiency

(Minimum 15 attempts per game)

	Cl	Gm	Att	Cmp	Cmp Pct	Int	Int Pct	Yds	Yds/ Att	TD	TD Pct	Rating Points
Cade McNown, UCLA	Jr.	11	283	173	61.13	5	1.77	2877	10.17	22	7.77	168.6
Ryan Leaf, Washington St.	Jr.	11	375	210	56.00	10	2.67	3637	9.70	33	8.80	161.2
Joe Germaine, Ohio St.	Sr.	12	184	119	64.67	7	3.80	1674	9.10	15	8.15	160.4
John Dutton, Nevada	Sr.	11	367	225	61.31	6	1.63	3526	9.61	20	5.45	156.7
Brock Huard, Washington	So.	10	244	146	59.84	10	4.10	2140	8.77	23	9.43	156.4
Mike Bobo, Georgia	Sr.	11	306	199	65.03	8	2.61	2751	8.99	19	6.21	155.8
Donovan McNabb, Syracuse	Jr.	12	265	145	54.72	6	2.26	2488	9.39	20	7.78	154.0
Graham Leigh, New Mexico	Jr.	12	276	166	60.14	8	2.90	2318	8.40	24	8.70	153.6
Moses Moreno, Colorado St.	Sr.	12	257	157	61.09	9	3.50	2257	8.78	20	7.78	153.5
Chad Pennington, Marshall	So.	12	428	253	59.11	12	2.80	3480	8.13	39	9.11	151.9
Aaron Brooks, Virginia	Jr.	11	270	164	60.74	7	2.59	2282	8.45	20	7.41	151.0
Tim Rattay, La. Tech	So.	11	477	293	61.43	10	2.10	3881	8.14	34	7.13	149.1
Thad Busby, Florida St.	Sr.	11	390	235	60.26	10	2.56	3317	8.51	25	6.41	147.7

Rushing

	Cl	Car	Yds	TD	YdsPG
Ricky Williams, Texas	Jr.	279	1893	25	172.09
Ahman Green, Nebraska	Jr.	278	1877	22	156.42
Amos Zereoue, West Va.	So.	264	1505	16	150.50
Tavian Banks, Iowa	Sr.	246	1639	17	149.00
Ron Dayne, Wisconsin	So.	249	1421	15	142.10
T. Prentice, Miami-OH	So.	296	1549	25	140.82
Dwayne Harris, Toledo	Jr.	254	1278	10	127.80
Kevin Faulk, LSU	Jr.	205	1144	15	127.11
Demond Parker, Okla.	So.	194	1143	6	127.00
Chris McCoy, Navy	Sr.	246	1370	20	124.55
Curtis Enis, Penn St.	Jr.	228	1363	19	123.91
Fred Taylor, Florida	Sr.	214	1292	13	117.45

Games: All played 11, except Green, Lewis (12); Dayne, Harris, Zereoue (10); Davis, Faulk and Parker (9).

Receptions

	Cl	No	Yds	TD	P/Gm
Eugene Baker, Kent	Jr.	103	1549	18	9.36
Troy Edwards, La. Tech	Jr.	102	1707	13	9.27
Troy Walters, Stanford	Jr.	86	1206	8	7.82
Geoff Noisy, Nevada	Jr.	86	1184	5	7.82
Randy Moss, Marshall	So.	90	1647	25	7.50
Siaha Burley, Cen. Florida	Jr.	77	1106	7	7.00
Antonio Wilson, Idaho	Sr.	77	910	10	7.00
Bobby Shaw, California	Sr.	75	1093	10	6.82
Nakia Jenkins, Utah St.	Sr.	73	1086	6	6.64
Craig Yeast, Kentucky	Jr.	73	873	10	6.64
Desmond Clark, W. Forest	Jr.	72	950	5	6.55
Marcus Nash, Tennessee	Sr.	76	1170	13	6.33

Games: All played 11, except Moss and Nash (12).

Scoring

Non-Kickers

	Cl	TD	Pts	P/Gm
Ricky Williams, Texas	Jr.	25	152*	13.82
Skip Hicks, UCLA	Sr.	25	150	13.64
Travis Prentice, Miami-OH	So.	25	150	13.64
Randy Moss, Marshall	So.	25	152*	12.67
Curtis Enis, Penn St.	Jr.	20	122*	11.09
Ahman Green, Nebraska	Jr.	22	132	11.00
Chris McCoy, Navy	Sr.	20	120	10.91
Tavian Banks, Iowa	Sr.	19	114	10.36
Chris Lemon, Nevada	So.	19	114	10.36
Eugene Baker, Kent	Jr.	18	110*	10.00
Kevin Faulk, LSU	Jr.	15	90	10.00

*Includes one 2-point conversion.

Games: All played 11, except Green, Moss (12); Wood (10); and Faulk (9).

Kickers

	FG/Att	PAT/Att	Pts	P/Gm
Brad Palazzo, Tulane	23/28	40/41	109	9.91
Kris Brown, Nebraska	18/21	62/62	116	9.67
Chris Sailer, UCLA	19/24	49/51	106	9.64
Colby Cason, N. Mexico	21/30	40/45	103	8.58
Martin Gramatica, Kan. St.	19/20	37/38	94	8.55
Kyle Bryant, Texas A&M	18/22	48/48	102	8.50
Shayne Graham, Va. Tech	19/23	35/36	82	8.36
Rian Lindell, Wash. St.	11/16	56/58	89	8.09
Jeff Hall, Tennessee	16/22	47/52	95	7.92
S. Janikowski, Fla. St.	16/21	37/39	84	7.64

Games: All played 11, except Brown, Bryant, Cason (12); Wedel, Dawson and Conway(12).

Field Goals

	Cl	FG/Att	Pct	Lg
Brad Palazzo, Tulane	Jr.	23/28	.821	52
Colby Cason, New Mexico	Sr.	21/30	.700	42
Brian Gowins, Northwestern	Sr.	20/27	.741	52
Martin Gramatica, Kan. St.	Jr.	19/20	.950	55
Shayne Graham, Va. Tech	So.	19/23	.826	48
Chris Sailer, UCLA	Jr.	19/24	.792	56
Kris Brown, Nebraska	Jr.	18/21	.857	46
Kyle Bryant, Texas A&M	Sr.	18/22	.818	51

Games: All played 11, except Brown, Bryant, Cason and Gowins (12).

Longest FG of season: 57 yards by Rian Lindell, Washington St. vs Boise St. (Sept. 27).

Interceptions

	Cl	No	Yds	TD	Lg
Brian Lee, Wyoming	Sr.	8	103	1	56-td
Cedric Donaldson, LSU	Sr.	7	192	2	68
John Noel, La. Tech	Sr.	7	93	0	34
Omarr Smith, San Jose St.	Jr.	7	80	0	41
Tevell Jones, Ohio	Sr.	7	36	0	21
Samari Rolle, Florida St.	Jr.	7	32	0	29
Charles Woodson, Michigan	Jr.	7	7	0	4
Donovin Darius, Syracuse	Sr.	7	56	0	13

Note: Eleven tied with 6 each.

Games: All played 11 except, Darius (12).

Punting

(Minimum of 3.6 per game)

	Cl	No	Yds	Avg
Chad Kessler, LSU	Sr.	39	1961	50.28
John Baker, North Texas	So.	62	2925	47.18
Shane Lechler, Texas A&M	So.	56	2298	46.98
Brad Hill, Tulane	Sr.	42	1940	46.19
Chad Shrout, Hawaii	So.	68	3133	46.07
Rodney Williams, Ga. Tech	So.	47	2145	45.64
Jeff Walker, Miss. St.	So.	45	2049	45.53

Punt Returns

(Minimum of 1.2 per game)

	Cl	No	Yds	TD	Avg
Tim Dwight, Iowa	Sr.	19	367	3	19.32
R.W. McQuarters, Okla. St.	Jr.	32	521	1	16.28
Steve Smith, Utah St.	Sr.	22	344	2	15.64
Nod Washington, Miami-OH	Jr.	12	185	0	15.42
Geoff Turner, Colorado St.	Sr.	20	304	1	15.20
Dee Feaster, Florida St.	So.	14	210	0	15.00
Quinton Spotwood, Syracuse	So.	31	463	4	14.94
Tinker Keck, Cincinnati	Jr.	39	575	4	14.74
Steve Neal, Western Mich.	So.	14	204	1	14.57
Jacquez Green, Florida	Jr.	27	392	2	14.52

Kickoff Returns

(Minimum of 1.2 per game)

	Cl	No	Yds	TD	Avg
Eric Booth, Southern Miss.	Sr.	22	766	2	34.82
Ben Kelly, Colorado	Fr.	25	777	1	31.08
Pat McGrew, Navy	Sr.	15	441	0	29.40
Boo Williams, S. Carolina	So.	18	527	2	29.28
Pat Johnson, Oregon	Sr.	16	462	0	28.88
Allen Rossum, Notre Dame	Sr.	20	570	2	28.50
Ketric Sanford, Houston	So.	19	530	0	27.89
Tony Horne, Clemson	Jr.	18	491	0	27.28
Damon Dunn, Stanford	Sr.	21	566	0	26.95
Tyrone Carter, Minnesota	So.	17	455	0	26.76

NCAA Division I-A Team Leaders

REGULAR SEASON

Scoring Offense

	Gm	Record	Pts	Avg
Nebraska	12	12-0	565	47.1
Washington St.	11	10-1	467	42.5
UCLA	11	9-2	448	40.7
Florida St.	11	10-1	437	39.7
Marshall	12	10-2	453	37.8
Miami-OH	11	8-3	412	37.5
Florida	11	9-2	448	40.7
Colorado St.	12	10-2	442	36.8
Iowa	11	7-4	404	36.7
Navy	11	7-4	398	36.2

Total Offense

	Gm	Plays	Yds	Avg	TD	YdsPG
Nebraska	12	937	6164	6.6	71	513.67
Washington St.	11	808	5524	6.8	60	502.18
Louisiana Tech	11	813	5456	6.7	48	496.00
Tennessee	12	890	5794	6.5	50	482.83
Nevada	11	796	5272	6.6	45	479.27
Kentucky	11	876	5214	6.0	45	474.00
Purdue	11	794	5056	6.4	42	459.64
Florida St.	11	784	4973	6.3	49	452.09
Utah St.	11	835	4933	5.9	45	448.45
Marshall	12	832	5339	6.4	58	444.92

Note: Touchdowns scored by rushing and passing only.

Scoring Defense

	Gm	Record	Pts	Avg
Michigan	11	11-0	98	8.9
Ohio St.	12	10-2	139	11.6
Air Force	12	10-2	149	12.4
Iowa	11	7-4	142	12.9
UNC	11	10-1	143	13.0
Kansas St.	11	10-1	159	14.5
Colorado St.	12	10-2	179	14.9
Florida St.	11	10-1	167	15.2
Syracuse	12	9-3	191	15.9
Ohio	11	8-3	177	16.1

Total Defense

	Gm	Plays	Yds	Avg	TD	YdsPG
Michigan	11	660	2276	3.4	10	206.9
UNC	11	693	2302	3.3	12	209.3
Florida St.	11	717	2655	3.7	22	241.4
Kansas St.	11	702	2825	4.0	18	256.8
Nebraska	12	717	3088	4.3	25	257.3
Navy	11	642	2863	4.5	24	260.3
Iowa	11	733	2927	4.0	18	266.1
Ohio St.	12	820	3215	3.9	13	267.9
Vanderbilt	11	704	3026	4.3	22	275.1
Air Force	12	756	3471	4.6	16	289.3

Note: Opponents' TDs scored by rushing and passing only.

Single Game Highs

INDIVIDUAL

Rushing Yards

Yds	
373	Astron Whatley, Kent vs. Eastern Mich. (Sept. 20)

Rushing & Passing Yards

Yds	
568	John Dutton, Nevada vs. Boise St. (Nov. 8)

Passes Attempted

Att	
66	Tim Couch, Kentucky vs. LSU (Nov. 1)

Receptions

No	
18	Geoffrey Noisy, Nevada vs. Oregon (Sept. 13)

Receiving Yards

Yds	
284	Lennie Johnson, Arkansas St. vs. SW Missouri St. (Nov. 8)

Passing Yards

Yds	
557	John Dutton, Nevada vs. Boise St. (Nov. 8)

Passes Completed

No	
41	Tim Couch, Kentucky vs. Georgia (Oct. 25)
41	Tim Couch, Kentucky vs. LSU (Nov. 1)

TEAM

Points Scored

Pts	
82	Florida vs. Central Mich. (Sept. 6)

Annual Awards

Players of the Year

Charles Woodson, Michigan . . . . .Camp, Heisman
Peyton Manning, Tennessee. .Maxwell

Position Players of the Year

O'Brien Award (Quarterback).Peyton Manning, Tennessee
Unitas Award (Senior QB) . . . .Peyton Manning, Tennessee
Walker Award (Running Back) . . . . .Ricky Williams, Texas
Biletnikoff Award (Receiver) . . . . . . .Randy Moss, Marshall
Groza Award (Kicker) . . . . .Martin Gramatica, Kansas St.
Outland Trophy (Interior Lineman).Aaron Taylor, Nebraska
Lombardi Award (Lineman) . . . .Grant Wistrom, Nebraska
Butkus Award (Linebacker). . .Andy Katzenmoyer, Ohio St.
Thorpe Award (Defensive Back). . . . . . .Charles Woodson, Michigan
Nagurski Award (Defensive Player). . . .Charles Woodson, Michigan
Payton Award (IAA Player of the Year) . . . .Brian Finneran, Villanova
Buchanan Award (IAA Defensive Player) . . .Chris McNeil, North Carolina A&T
Hill Trophy (Div. II Player of the Year) . . . . .Irv Sigler, Bloomsburg University

Coach of the Year

Mike Price, Washington St. . . . . .FWAA, Dodd, *The Sporting News*
Lloyd Carr, Michigan . . . . .AFCA, Camp, Maxwell

Heisman Trophy Vote

Presented since 1935 by the Downtown Athletic Club of New York City and named after former college coach and DAC athletic director John W. Heisman. Voting done by national media and former Heisman winners. Each ballot allows for three names (points based on 3 for 1st, 2 for 2nd and 1 for 3rd).

Top 10 Vote-Getters

	Pos	1st	2nd	3rd	Pts
Charles Woodson, Michigan	DB	433	209	98	1815
Peyton Manning, Tennessee	QB	281	263	174	1543
Ryan Leaf, Washington St.	QB	70	205	241	861
Randy Moss, Marshall	WR	17	205	241	861
Ricky Williams, Texas	RB	4	31	61	135
Curtis Enis, Penn St.	RB	3	18	20	65
Tim Dwight, Iowa	WR	5	3	11	32
Cade McNown, UCLA	QB	0	7	12	26
Tim Couch, Kentucky	QB	0	5	12	22
Amos Zereoue, West Virginia	RB	3	1	10	21

Note: Manning and Dwight were seniors. Enis, Leaf, McNown, Williams and Woodson were juniors. Couch, Moss and Zereoue were sophomores.

Consensus All-America Team

NCAA Division I-A players cited most frequently by the following five selectors: AFCA, AP, FWAA, and Walter Camp Foundation. Holdovers from 1996 All-America team are in **bold** type; (*) indicates unanimous selection.

Offense

	Player	Class	Ht	Wt
WR	Randy Moss*, Marshall	So.	6-5	210
WR	Jacquez Green, Florida	Jr.	5-9	168
TE	Alonzo Mayes*, Oklahoma St.	Sr.	6-6	265
OL	**Aaron Taylor***, Nebraska	Sr.	6-1	305
OL	Benji Olson, Washington	Jr.	6-4	310
OL	Olin Kreutz, Washington	Jr.	6-4	290
OL	Alan Faneca, LSU	Jr.	6-5	310
OL	Chad Overhauser, UCLA	Sr.	6-6	304
QB	Peyton Manning*, Tennessee	Sr.	6-5	222
RB	Ricky Williams*, Texas	Jr.	6-0	220
RB	Curtis Enis, Penn St.	Jr.	6-1	233
K	Chris Sailer, UCLA	Jr.	5-10	190
KR	Tim Dwight, Iowa	Sr.	5-9	185

Defense

	Player	Class	Ht	Wt
DL	Jason Peter, Nebraska	Sr.	6-5	285
DL	Greg Ellis, UNC	Sr.	6-6	265
DL	Andre Wadsworth, Florida St.	Sr.	6-4	282
DL	**Grant Wistrom***, Nebraska	Sr.	6-5	255
LB	Andy Katzenmoyer*, Ohio St.	So.	6-4	260
LB	Brian Simmons, UNC	Sr.	6-4	260
LB	Anthony Simmons, Clemson	Jr.	6-1	225
LB	Sam Cowart, Florida St.	Sr.	6-2	239
DB	Don Darius, Syracuse	Sr.	6-1	205
DB	Brian Lee, Wyoming	Sr.	6-2	200
DB	**Dre' Bly**, UNC	So.	5-10	185
DB	**Charles Woodson***, Michigan	Jr.	6-1	198
P	Chad Kessler, LSU	Sr.	6-1	197

Underclassmen Selected in the 1998 NFL Draft

Forty-one players forfeited the remainder of their college eligibility and declared for the NFL draft in 1998. NFL teams drafted 20 underclassmen. Players listed in alphabetical order; first round selections in **bold** type.

	Pos	Drafted by	Overall pick
Eric Bateman, BYU	OG	N.Y. Jets	149
Mo Collins, Florida	OT	Oakland	23
Curtis Enis, Penn St.	RB	Chicago	5
Alan Faneca, LSU	OG	Pittsburgh	26
Chris Fuamatu-Ma'afala, Utah	RB	Pittsburgh	178
Ahman Green, Nebraska	RB	Seattle	76
Jacquez Green, Florida	WR	Tampa Bay	34
Olin Kreutz, Washington	C	Chicago	64
Ryan Leaf, Washington St.	QB	San Diego	2
R.W. McQuarters, Okla. St.	CB	San Francisco	28
Randy Moss, Marshall	WR	Minnesota	21
Jeremy Newberry, California	C	San Francisco	58
Benji Olson, Washington	OG	Tennessee	139
Anthony Simmons, Clemson	LB	Seattle	15
Takeo Spikes, Auburn	LB	Cincinnati	13
Ryan Thelwell, Minnesota	WR	San Francisco	215
Jeremiah Trotter, Stephen F. Austin	LB	Philadelphia	72
Jason Tucker, Texas Christian	WR	Cincinnati	167
Robert Williams, UNC	CB	Kansas City	128
Charles Woodson, Michigan	CB	Oakland	4

NCAA Division I-AA Final Standings

Standings based on conference games only; overall records include post-season games.

Atlantic 10 Conference

New England	Conf W	L	PF	PA	Overall W	L	PF	PA
New Hampshire	5	3	185	153	5	6	233	226
Connecticut	4	4	280	215	7	4	398	246
Maine	4	4	247	195	5	6	348	275
Rhode Island	2	6	167	226	2	9	216	318
Massachusetts	1	7	101	256	2	9	149	367
Boston U.	1	7	127	270	1	10	162	353

Mid-Atlantic	Conf W	L	PF	PA	Overall W	L	PF	PA
*Villanova	8	0	313	175	12	1	525	288
*Delaware	7	1	263	139	12	2	395	195
Northeastern	5	3	232	197	8	3	320	243
Wm. & Mary	4	4	153	157	7	4	254	203
Richmond	4	4	151	147	6	5	237	183
James Madison	3	5	183	272	5	6	252	337

***Playoffs (3-2):** Delaware (2-1); Villanova (1-1).

Big Sky Conference

	Conf W	L	PF	PA	Overall W	L	PF	PA
*Eastern Wash.	7	1	264	147	12	2	481	245
*Montana	6	2	282	135	8	4	368	206
Montana St.	5	3	158	145	6	5	227	207
Northern Arizona	4	4	219	212	6	5	302	261
Weber St.	4	4	188	182	6	5	257	251
CS-Northridge	4	4	205	210	6	6	370	316
Portland St.	3	5	170	192	4	7	212	294
Idaho St.	2	6	135	241	3	8	188	356
CS-Sacramento	1	7	146	303	1	10	188	408

***Playoffs (2-2):** Eastern Washington (2-1); Montana (0-1).

Conference Playoff Records

Postseason records for 1997 season.

Conference	W-L
Gateway Athletic	5-1
Atlantic 10	3-2
Southland	3-2
Big Sky	2-2
Southern	1-1
Independents	1-2

Gateway Athletic Conference

	Conf W	L	PF	PA	Overall W	L	PF	PA
*Western Ill.	6	0	195	102	11	2	407	229
Northern Iowa	5	1	187	165	7	4	308	339
*Youngstown St.	4	2	176	82	13	2	460	230
SW Missouri St.	3	3	141	154	5	6	266	282
Indiana St.	2	4	66	146	3	8	119	248
Southern Ill.	1	5	143	177	3	8	238	320
Illinois St.	0	6	106	188	2	9	220	333

***Playoffs (5-1):** Youngstown St. (4-0); Western Illinois (1-1).

Ivy League

	Conf W	L	PF	PA	Overall W	L	PF	PA
Harvard	7	0	194	45	9	1	301	123
Dartmouth	6	1	116	103	8	2	208	165
Pennslyvania	5	2	149	117	6	4	198	175
Brown	3	4	171	138	6	4	274	194
Cornell	3	4	145	170	5	5	269	261
Princeton	2	5	87	90	5	5	148	132
Columbia	2	5	106	177	3	7	141	259
Yale	0	7	55	183	1	9	113	250

Playoffs: League does not play postseason games.

Metro-Atlantic Conference

	Conf W	L	PF	PA	Overall W	L	PF	PA
Georgetown	7	0	242	76	8	3	276	178
Duquesne	6	1	206	92	7	3	284	132
Fairfield	4	3	159	147	7	3	244	188
Siena	4	3	194	192	6	3	211	205
Marist	4	3	161	124	6	4	232	141
Canisius	2	5	99	158	4	6	131	205
St. Peters	1	6	108	224	1	9	152	326
†St. John's	0	0	0	0	8	3	206	145
Iona	0	8	54	248	0	10	54	307

†**Note:** The MAAC ruled on Aug. 29, 1997 that St. John's was ineligible to claim the league title because the school violated a league financial aid policy.

Playoffs: No teams invited.

Mid-Eastern Athletic Conference

	Conference				Overall			
	W	L	PF	PA	W	L	PF	PA
*Hampton	7	0	155	72	10	2	258	167
†S. Car. St.	5	2	241	141	9	3	425	264
*Florida A&M	5	2	241	141	9	3	425	264
Howard	4	3	159	168	7	4	308	248
N. Car. A&T	3	4	127	144	7	4	276	230
Morgan St.	2	5	105	145	3	7	149	234
Bethune-Cookman	1	6	107	188	4	7	207	229
Delaware St.	1	6	114	200	3	8	235	312

***Playoffs (0-2):** Florida A&M (0-1); Hampton (0-1).
†**Heritage Bowl:** South Carolina St. lost to SWAC entrant Southern, 34-28 (Dec. 27).

Northeast Conference

	Conference				Overall			
	W	L	PF	PA	W	L	PF	PA
Robert Morris	4	0	140	57	8	3	306	193
Monmouth (NJ)	3	1	129	72	5	4	254	214
Wagner	2	2	92	101	6	4	219	200
Central Conn.	1	3	86	127	5	5	252	214
St. Francis (Pa.)	0	4	38	128	2	9	153	350

Playoffs: No teams invited.

Ohio Valley Conference

	Conference				Overall			
	W	L	PF	PA	W	L	PF	PA
*Eastern Ky.	7	0	257	59	8	4	383	189
Eastern Ill.	5	2	159	124	8	3	267	213
Murray St.	5	2	155	96	7	4	289	172
Tennessee St.	4	2	126	146	4	7	254	331
Tennessee Tech	4	3	131	113	6	5	205	174
Mid. Tenn. St.	2	5	182	185	4	6	292	244
SE Missouri St.	1	6	109	180	4	7	199	244
Tenn.-Martin	0	7	66	275	1	10	123	384

***Playoffs (0-1):** Eastern Kentucky (0-1).

Patriot League

	Conference				Overall			
	W	L	PF	PA	W	L	PF	PA
*Colgate	6	0	256	72	7	5	414	300
Bucknell	5	1	145	99	10	1	282	213
Fordham	4	2	129	117	5	6	215	247
Holy Cross	2	4	75	163	4	7	182	308
Lehigh	2	4	150	189	4	7	307	326
Lafayette	2	4	130	156	3	8	126	233
Towson	0	6	51	140	2	8	126	233

Playoffs (0-1): Colgate (0-1)..

Pioneer League

	Conference				Overall			
	W	L	PF	PA	W	L	PF	PA
Dayton	5	0	188	65	9	1	366	187
San Diego	4	1	195	148	8	3	369	287
Drake	2	3	111	92	8	3	296	158
Butler	2	3	90	133	6	4	196	196
Valparaiso	2	3	86	140	3	7	194	342
Evansville	0	5	90	182	2	8	254	317

Playoffs: No teams invited.

Southern Conference

	Conference				Overall			
	W	L	PF	PA	W	L	PF	PA
*Ga. Southern	7	1	267	98	10	3	423	229
Appalachian St.	6	2	236	144	7	4	294	215
E. Tenn St.	5	3	248	187	7	4	340	242
Furman	5	3	208	176	7	4	281	223
Tenn.-Chatt.	4	4	129	203	7	4	203	244
The Citadel	4	4	119	187	6	5	165	224
W. Carolina	3	5	146	153	3	8	172	206
Wofford	2	6	123	154	3	7	209	212
VMI	0	8	71	245	0	11	93	384

***Playoffs (1-1):** Georgia Southern (1-1).

Southland Conference

	Conference				Overall			
	W	L	PF	PA	W	L	PF	PA
*McNeese St.	6	1	194	88	13	2	395	173
*Northwestern St.	6	1	186	130	8	4	303	231
Stephen F. Austin	5	2	196	141	8	3	296	199
Nicholls St.	3	4	104	175	5	6	168	238
Sam Houston St.	3	4	163	189	5	6	281	279
SW Texas St.	2	5	176	201	5	6	273	276
Troy St.	2	5	132	107	5	6	273	276
Jacksonville St.	1	6	111	231	1	10	199	356

***Playoffs (3-2):** McNeese St. (3-1); Northwestern St. (0-1).

Southwestern Athletic Conference

	Conference				Overall			
	W	L	PF	PA	W	L	PF	PA
†Southern-BR	8	0	287	135	11	1	372	219
*Jackson St.	7	1	283	149	9	3	387	271
Ark.-Pine Bluff	6	2	200	146	8	3	320	188
Texas Southern	4	4	187	176	5	6	249	240
Alcorn St.	4	4	159	162	4	7	192	244
Miss. Valley St.	3	5	173	177	4	6	198	214
Alabama St.	2	6	135	188	3	8	184	242
Grambling	2	6	125	179	3	8	187	258
Prarie View	0	8	66	303	0	9	76	322

***Playoffs (0-1):** Jackson St. (0-1).
†**Heritage Bowl:** Southern-BR beat MEAC entrant South Carolina St., 34-28 (Dec. 27).

NCAA I-AA Independents

	W	L	PF	PA
Cal Poly-SLO	10	1	382	213
*Western Ky.	10	2	429	243
Liberty	9	2	356	195
*Hofstra	9	3	397	295
Morehead St.	7	3	419	317
Elon College	7	4	338	268
Samford	7	4	201	208
South Florida	5	6	307	181
Southern Utah	5	6	312	328
St. Mary's (Ca.)	4	6	253	255
Norfolk St.	3	7	206	200
Buffalo	2	9	229	421
Davidson	2	9	258	271
LaSalle	1	8	104	367
Charleston Southern	1	9	133	326
Austin Peay	0	10	119	440

***Playoffs: (1-2)** Western Kentucky (1-1); Hofstra (0-1).

CS-Northridge
Aaron Flowers
Total Offense

Siena
Reggie Greene
Rushing

Cornell
Eric Krawczyk
Receptions

Western Illinois
Aaron Stecker
Scoring

NCAA Division I-AA Regular Season Leaders

INDIVIDUAL

Passing Efficiency

(Minimum 15 attempts per game)

	Cl	Gm	Att	Cmp	Cmp Pct	Int	Int Pct	Yds	Yds/ Att	TD	TD Pct	Rating Points
Alli Abrew, Cal Poly-SLO	Sr.	11	191	130	68.06	4	2.09	1961	10.27	17	8.90	179.5
Doug Turner, Morehead St.	Sr.	10	290	190	65.52	6	2.07	2869	9.89	29	10.00	177.5
Chris Boden, Villanova	So.	11	345	231	66.96	4	1.16	3079	8.92	36	10.43	174.0
Harry Leons, Eastern Wash.	Sr.	10	257	159	61.87	5	1.95	2588	10.07	21	8.17	169.5
Simon Fuentes, Eastern Ky.	Sr.	11	189	116	61.38	2	1.06	1932	10.22	13	6.88	167.8
Giovanni Carmazzi, Hofstra	Jr.	11	408	288	70.59	8	1.96	3554	8.71	27	6.62	161.7
Mike Stadler, San Diego	So.	11	262	152	58.02	10	3.82	2287	8.73	30	11.45	161.5
Todd Wells, East Tenn. St.	Fr.	11	247	144	58.30	9	3.64	2404	9.73	17	6.88	155.5
Shane Stafford, Connecticut	Sr.	11	296	164	55.41	10	3.38	2814	9.51	23	7.77	154.1
Brian Ginn, Delaware	So.	10	178	97	54.49	3	1.69	1622	9.11	14	7.87	153.6

Total Offense

	Cl	Rush	Pass	Yds	YdsPG
Aaron Flowers, CS-N'ridge	Sr.	-94	3226	3132	348.00
Giovanni Carmazzi, Hofstra	Jr.	153	3554	3707	337.00
O. Sampson, Fla. A&M	Sr.	335	3290	3625	329.55
Travis Brown, N. Arizona	So.	-32	3395	3363	305.73
James Perry, Brown	So.	67	2873	2940	294.00
Mickey Fein, Maine	Jr.	-33	2912	2879	287.90
Chris Boden, Villanova	So.	1	3079	3080	280.00
Chad Salisbury, Buffalo	Jr.	-92	2889	2797	279.70
Doug Turner, Morehead St.	Sr.	-83	2869	2786	278.60
M. Kirby, Jacksonville St.	Jr.	108	2817	2925	265.91

Rushing

	Cl	Car	Yds	TD	YdsPG
Reggie Greene, Siena	Sr.	256	1778	18	197.51
Aaron Stecker, Western Ill.	Jr.	298	1957	24	177.91
Sean Bennett, Evansville	Jr.	235	1668	16	166.80
Rex Prescott, Eastern Wash.	Sr.	212	1494	12	149.40
Claude Mathis, SW Texas	Sr.	311	1595	14	145.00
Jerry Azumah, UNH	Jr.	269	1472	13	142.91
Stan House, Cen. Conn. St.	Sr.	294	1413	12	141.30
Rick Sarille, Wagner	Jr.	243	1274	12	127.40
Steve Wofford, Southern-BR	Jr.	243	1274	12	127.40
Chris Menick, Harvard	So.	247	1267	13	126.70

Games: All played 11, except Bennett, House, Prescott, Sarille and Wagner (10); Green (9).

Receptions

	Cl	No	Yds	TD	P/Gm
Eric Krawczyk, Cornell	Sr.	89	1042	11	8.90
Rameek Wright, Maine	Sr.	88	1176	7	8.00
Mike Furrey, Northern Iowa	Jr.	82	1291	7	7.45
Bryan Kish, Hofstra	Sr.	82	1084	7	7.45
Sean Morey, Brown	Jr.	73	1427	15	7.30
S. Sullivan, St. Mary's (Cal.)	Sr.	72	832	6	7.20
Jerome Henry, CS-N'ridge	Sr.	71	827	8	7.10
Wayne Yearwood, Hofstra	Sr.	76	973	12	6.91
Brian Finneran, Villanova	Sr.	75	1151	17	6.82
Eric Wise, Fairfield	So.	67	698	4	6.70

Games: All played 11, except Henry, Krawczk, Morey, Sullivan and Wise (10).

Interceptions

	Cl	No	Yds	TD	LG
Roderic Parson, Brown	Sr.	8	93	0	35
Tony Booth, JMU	Jr.	8	77	1	37-td
Trevor Bell, Idaho St.	Sr.	8	148	0	50
Derek Carter, Maine	Sr.	8	137	0	50
Paul Serie, Siena	Jr.	7	36	1	72
Chris Tillotson, Columbia	Jr.	7	156	2	73-td
Brian Dunn, Robert Morris	Sr.	7	92	0	37
Reid Ruberti, Georgetown	Sr.	6	150	0	46

Games: All played 11, except Booth, Dunn and Tillotson (10); Ruberti and Serie (9); Parson (8).

Scoring

Non-Kickers

	Cl	TD	XPt	Pts	P/Gm
Aaron Stecker, Western Ill.	Jr.	25	0	150	13.64
Reggie Greene, Siena	Sr.	18	2	110	12.22
Sean Bennett, Evansville	Jr.	20	2	122	12.20
Stan House, Cen. Conn. St.	Sr.	18	2	110	11.80
Rabin Abdullah, Lehigh	Sr.	18	0	108	10.80
Brian Finneran, Villanova	Sr.	17	10	112	10.18

Games: All played 11, except Abdullah, Bennett and House (10); Greene (9).

Kickers

	Cl	FG/Att	PAT/Att	Pts
Dave Ettinger, Hofstra	Sr.	17/22	42/48	93
Juan Toro, Florida A&M	Jr.	17/21	40/45	91
Shonz Lafrenz, McNeese St.	So.	17/26	37/39	88
Scott Shields, Weber St.	Jr.	17/25	24/26	87*
Travis Brawner, SW Mo. St.	So.	21/28	23/25	86

* Includes 2 touchdowns scored.
Games: All played 11.

Field Goals

	Cl	FG/Att	Pct	LG
Travis Brawner, SW Mo. St.	So.	21/28	.750	52
Alex Sierk, Princeton	Jr.	18/21	.857	48
Juan Toro, Florida A&M	Jr.	17/21	.810	37
Dave Ettinger, Hofstra	Sr.	17/25	.773	53
Scott Shields, Weber St.	Jr.	17/25	.680	51
Shonz Lafrenz, McNeese St.	So.	17/26	.654	41
Brian Shallcross, Wm.& Mary	Sr.	15/18	.833	49

Games: All played 11, except Sierk (10).
Longest FG of season: 54 yards by Kris Heppner, Montana vs. Idaho St. (Oct. 11).

Punt/Kickoff Leaders

Punting	Cl	No	Yds	Avg
Barry Cantrell, Fordham	Sr.	65	2980	45.85

Punt Returns	Cl	No	Yds	TD	Avg
Chris Berry, Morehead St.	Sr.	13	273	1	21.00

Kickoff Returns	Cl	No	Yds	TD	Avg
Andy Swafford, Troy St.	Sr.	14	440	1	31.43

TEAM

Scoring Offense

	Gm	Record	Pts	Avg
Morehead St.	10	7-3	419	41.9
Villanova	11	11-0	442	40.2
Dayton	10	9-1	366	36.6
Western Ky.	10	9-1	366	36.6
Connecticut	11	7-4	398	36.2
Eastern Wash.	11	10-1	389	35.4
Florida A&M	11	9-2	388	35.3
Colgate	11	7-4	386	35.1
Hofstra	11	9-2	383	34.8
Cal Poly-SLO	11	10-1	382	34.7
Eastern Ky.	11	8-3	369	33.5
San Diego	11	8-3	369	33.5
Western Ill.	11	10-1	364	33.1
Ga. Southern	11	9-2	364	33.1
Jackson St.	11	9-2	363	33.0
Youngstown St.	11	9-2	360	32.7
Liberty	11	9-2	356	32.4
Delaware	11	10-1	355	32.3

Scoring Defense

	Gm	Record	Pts	Avg
McNeese St.	11	10-1	116	10.5
Harvard	10	9-1	123	12.3
Hampton	11	10-1	139	12.6
Georgetown	11	8-3	143	13.0
St. John's (NY)	11	8-3	145	13.2
Princeton	10	5-5	132	13.2
Duquesne	10	7-3	132	13.2
Eastern Ky.	11	8-3	147	13.4
Marist	10	6-4	141	14.1
Troy St.	11	5-6	157	14.3
Drake	11	8-3	158	14.4
Youngstown St.	11	9-2	160	14.5
Murray St.	11	7-4	172	15.6
Delaware	11	10-1	174	15.8
Tennessee Tech	11	6-5	174	15.8
Ga. Southern	11	9-2	176	16.0
South Fla.	11	5-6	181	16.5
Dartmouth	10	8-2	165	16.5

Total Offense

	Record	Plays	Yds	Avg
Eastern Wash.	10-1	775	5562	505.64
Morehead St.	7-3	743	4955	495.50
Brown	6-4	821	4753	475.30
Florida A&M	9-2	787	5213	473.91
CS-N'ridge	6-6	920	5480	456.67
Western Ky.	9-1	724	4566	456.60
Cal Poly-SLO	10-1	734	5010	455.45
Hofstra	9-2	795	4993	453.91
Northern Ariz.	6-5	876	4927	447.91
Colgate	7-4	786	4857	441.55
Dayton	9-1	671	4394	439.40
Jackson St.	9-2	772	4809	437.18
East Tenn. St.	7-4	764	4755	432.27
Western Ill.	10-1	778	4731	430.09
Villanova	11-0	732	4693	426.64
Southern Utah	5-6	857	4689	426.27
Harvard	9-1	778	4236	423.60
Connecticut	7-4	735	4614	419.45
Monmouth (NJ)	5-4	653	3772	419.11
Montana	8-3	807	4573	415.73

Total Defense

	Record	Plays	Yds	Avg
Marist	6-4	642	2136	213.6
Murray St.	7-4	707	2613	237.5
Hampton	10-1	675	2623	238.5
McNeese St.	10-1	714	2698	245.3
Troy St.	5-6	679	2734	248.5
St. John's (NY)	8-3	742	2739	249.0
Drake	8-3	669	2775	252.3
Grambling	3-8	662	2799	254.5
South Florida	5-6	655	2800	254.5
Princeton	5-5	673	2584	258.4
Northwestern St.	8-3	650	2865	260.5
Richmond	6-5	718	2881	261.9
Harvard	9-1	680	2648	264.8
Georgetown	8-3	646	2660	266.0
Youngstown St.	9-2	693	2947	267.9
Northeastern	8-3	699	3027	275.2
Pennslyvania	6-4	708	2772	277.2
Duquesne	7-3	675	2780	278.0
Eastern Ky.	8-3	725	3068	278.9
Central Conn. St.	5-5	632	2806	280.6

NCAA Playoffs

Division I-AA

First Round (Nov. 29)

at Villanova 49 .... Colgate 28
at Delaware 24 .... Hofstra 14
at Youngstown St. 28 .... Hampton 13
at Ga. Southern 52 .... Florida A&M 37
at Western Kentucky 42 .... Eastern Kentucky 14
at Western Illinois 31 .... Jackson St. 24
at Eastern Wash. 40 .... Northwestern St. 10
at McNeese St. 19 .... Montana 14

Quarterfinals (Dec. 6)

Youngstown St. 37 .... at Villanova 34
at Delaware 16 .... Ga. Southern 7
McNeese St. 14 .... at Western Illinois 12
at Eastern Wash. 38 .... Western Kentucky 21

Semifinals (Dec. 13)

McNeese St. 23 .... at Delaware 21
Youngstown St. 25 .... at Eastern Wash. 14

Championship Game

Dec. 20 at Chattanooga, Tenn. (Att: 14,771)

Youngstown St. 10 .... McNeese St. 9
(13-2) (13-2)

Division II

First Round (Nov. 22)

at New Haven (Conn.) 47 .... Glenville St. (W.Va.) 7
at Slippery Rock (Pa.) 30 .... Ashland (Ohio) 20
at NW Missouri St. 39 .... North Dakota St. 28
at Carson-Newman (Tenn.) 21 .... North Alabama 7
at Albany St. (Ga.) 10 .... Southern Arkansas 0
Northern Colorado 24 .... at Pittsburg St. (Kan.) 16
UC Davis 37 .... at Texas A&M-Kingsville 33
at Angleo St. (Texas) 46 .... Western St. (Colo.) 12

Quarterfinals (Nov. 29)

at New Haven 49 .... Slippery Rock 21
at Carson-Newman 23 .... Albany St. 22
Northern Colorado 35 .... at NW Missouri St. 19
UC Davis 50 .... at Angelo St. 33

Division I-AA, II and III Awards

Players of the Year

Payton Award (Div. I-AA) .... Brian Finneran, WR Villanova (Sr.)
Hill Trophy (Div. II) .... Irv Sigler, RB Bloomsburg University (Sr.)
Gagliardi Trophy (Div. III) .... Billy Borchert, QB Mount Union (Sr.)

Coaches of the Year

AFCA (NCAA Div. I-AA) .... Andy Talley, Villanova
AFCA (College Div. II) .... Joe Glenn, No. Colorado
AFCA (College Div. III) .... Larry Kehres, Mt. Union

Semifinals (Dec. 6)

at New Haven 27 .... UC Davis 25
Northern Colorado 30 .... at Carson-Newman 29

Championship Game

Dec. 13 at Florence, Ala. (Att: 3,352)

Northern Colorado 51 .... New Haven 0
(12-3) (12-2)

Division III

First Round (Nov. 22)

at Mount Union (Ohio) 34 .... Allegheny 30
John Carroll (Ohio) 30 .... at Hanover (Ind.) 20
at Lycoming (Pa.) 27 .... Western Maryland 13
at Rowan (NJ) 43 .... Coast Guard (Conn.) 0
Coll. of New Jersey 34 .... at Cortland St. (N.Y.) 30
Simpson (Iowa) 34 .... at Wis.-Whitewater 31
Augsburg (Minn.) 34 .... at Concordia (Minn.) 22
at Trinity (Texas) 44 .... Catholic (D.C.) 33

Quarterfinals (Nov. 29)

at Mount Union 59 .... John Carroll 7
at Lycoming 46 .... Trinity 26
at Rowan 13 .... College of NJ 7
at Simpson 61 .... Augsburg 21

Semifinals (Dec. 6)

at Mount Union 54 .... Simpson 7
at Lycoming 28 .... Rowan 20

Amos Alonzo Stagg Bowl

Dec. 13 at Salem, Va. (Att: 5,777)

Mount Union 61 .... Lycoming 12
(14-0) (12-1)

NAIA Playoffs

Division I

NAIA returned to a single division playoff for its football championship in 1997.

First round (Nov. 22)

at Geneva College (Pa.) 34 .... Campbellsville Univ. (Ky.) 14
at Jamestown Coll. (ND) 55 .... Benedictine Coll. (Kan.) 30
at Sioux Falls (SD) 57 .... Ottawa Univ. (Kan.) 14
at Evangel Coll. (Mo.) 46 .... McKendree Coll. (Ill.) 6
at Montana Tech 51 .... Minnesota-Crookston 10
at Findlay (Ohio) 40 .... Westminster Coll. (Pa.) 0
at Doane Coll. (Neb.) 53 .... Southwestern Coll. (Kan.) 28
at Willamette Univ. (Ore.) 26 .... Western Ore. Univ. 20, OT

Quarterfinals (Dec. 6)

at Findlay 28 .... Geneva 7
Sioux Falls 29 .... at Jamestown 6
Doane 59 .... at Evangel 20
at Willamette 50 .... Montana Tech 24

Semifinals (Dec. 13)

at Findlay 26 .... Doane 25
at Willamette 17 .... Sioux Falls 7

Championship

Dec. 20 at Savannah, Tenn. (Att: 4,000 est.)

Findlay 14 .... Willamette 7
(14-0) (13-1)

COLLEGE FOOTBALL STATISTICS

THROUGH THE YEARS

1869-1998

BOWLS • ALL-TIME LEADERS

National Champions

Over the last 128 years, there have been 25 major selectors of national champions by way of polls (11), mathematical rating systems (10) and historical research (4). The best-known and most widely circulated of these surveys, the Associated Press poll of sportswriters and broadcasters, first appeared during the 1936 season. Champions prior to 1936 have been determined by retro polls, ratings, and historical research.

The Early Years (1869-1935)

National champions based on the Dickinson mathematical system (DS) and three historical retro polls taken by the College Football Researchers Association (CFRA), the National Championship Foundation (NCF) and the Helms Athletic Foundation (HF). The CFRA and NCF polls start in 1869, college football's inaugural year, while the Helms poll begins in 1883, the first season the game adopted a point system for scoring. Frank Dickinson, an economics professor at Illinois, introduced his system in 1926 and retro-picked winners in 1924 and '25. Bowl game results were counted in the Helms selections, but not in the other three.

Multiple champions: Yale (18); Princeton (17); Harvard (9); Michigan (7); Notre Dame and Penn (4); Alabama, Cornell, Illinois, Pittsburgh and USC (3); California, Georgia Tech, Minnesota and Penn St. (2).

Year		Record
1869	**Princeton**	1-1-0
1870	**Princeton**	1-0-0
1871	No games played	
1872	**Princeton**	1-0-0
1873	**Princeton**	1-0-0
1874	**Yale**	3-0-0
1875	**Princeton** (CFRA)	2-0-0
	& **Harvard** (NCF)	4-0-0
1876	**Yale**	3-0-0
1877	**Yale**	3-0-1
1878	**Princeton**	6-0-0
1879	**Princeton**	4-0-1
1880	**Yale** (CFRA)	4-0-1
	& **Princeton** (NCF)	4-0-1
1881	**Yale**	5-0-1
1882	**Yale**	8-0-0
1883	**Yale**	8-0-0
1884	**Yale**	8-0-1
1885	**Princeton**	9-0-0
1886	**Yale**	9-0-1
1887	**Yale**	9-0-0
1888	**Yale**	13-0-0
1889	**Princeton**	10-0-0
1890	**Harvard**	11-0-0
1891	**Yale**	13-0-0
1892	**Yale**	13-0-0
1893	**Princeton**	11-0-0
1894	**Yale**	16-0-0
1895	**Penn**	14-0-0
1896	**Princeton** (CFRA)	10-0-1
	& **Lafayette** (NCF)	11-0-1
1897	**Penn**	15-0-0
1898	**Harvard**	11-0-0
1899	**Princeton** (CFRA)	12-1-0
	& **Harvard** (NCF, HF)	10-0-1

Year		Record	Bowl Game	Head Coach	Outstanding Player
1900	**Yale**	12-0-0	No bowl	Malcolm McBride	Perry Hale, HB
1901	**Harvard** (CFRA)	12-0-0	No bowl	Bill Reid	Bob Kernan, HB
	& **Michigan** (NCF, HF)	11-0-0	Won Rose	Hurry Up Yost	Neil Snow, E
1902	**Michigan**	11-0-0	No bowl	Hurry Up Yost	Boss Weeks, QB
1903	**Princeton**	11-0-0	No bowl	Art Hillebrand	John DeWitt, G
1904	**Penn** (CFRA, HF)	12-0-0	No bowl	Carl Williams	Andy Smith, FB
	& **Michigan** (NCF)	10-0-0	No bowl	Hurry Up Yost	Willie Heston, HB
1905	**Chicago**	10-0-0	No bowl	Amos Alonzo Stagg	Walter Eckersall, QB
1906	**Princeton**	9-0-1	No bowl	Bill Roper	Cap Wister, E
1907	**Yale**	9-0-1	No bowl	Bill Knox	Tad Jones, HB
1908	**Penn** (CFRA, HF)	11-0-1	No bowl	Sol Metzger	Hunter Scarlett, E
	& **LSU** (NCF)	10-0-0	No bowl	Edgar Wingard	Doc Fenton, QB
1909	**Yale**	12-1-0	No bowl	Howard Jones	Ted Coy, FB
1910	**Harvard** (CFRA, HF)	8-0-1	No bowl	Percy Haughton	Percy Wendell, HB
	& **Pittsburgh** (NCF)	9-0-0	No bowl	Joe Thompson	Ralph Galvin, C
1911	**Princeton** (CFRA, HF)	8-0-2	No bowl	Bill Roper	Sam White, E
	& **Penn St.** (NCF)	8-0-1	No bowl	Bill Hollenback	Dexter Very, E
1912	**Harvard** (CFRA, HF)	9-0-0	No bowl	Percy Haughton	Charley Brickley, HB
	& **Penn St.** (NCF)	8-0-0	No bowl	Bill Hollenback	Dexter Very, E
1913	**Harvard**	9-0-0	No bowl	Percy Haughton	Eddie Mahan, FB
1914	**Army**	9-0-0	No bowl	Charley Daly	John McEwan, C
1915	**Cornell**	9-0-0	No bowl	Al Sharpe	Charley Barrett, QB
1916	**Pittsburgh**	8-0-0	No bowl	Pop Warner	Bob Peck, C
1917	**Georgia Tech**	9-0-0	No bowl	John Heisman	Ev Strupper, HB
1918	**Pittsburgh** (CFRA, HF)	4-1-0	No bowl	Pop Warner	Tom Davies, HB
	& **Michigan** (NCF)	5-0-0	No bowl	Hurry Up Yost	Frank Steketee, FB
1919	**Harvard** (CFRA-tie, HF)	9-0-1	Won Rose	Bob Fisher	Eddie Casey, HB
	Illinois (CFRA-tie)	6-1-0	No bowl	Bob Zuppke	Chuck Carney, E
	& **Notre Dame** (NCF)	9-0-0	No bowl	Knute Rockne	George Gipp, HB
1920	**California**	9-0-0	Won Rose	Andy Smith	Dan McMillan, T

Year		Record	Bowl Game	Head Coach	Outstanding Player
1921	**California** (CFRA)	9-0-1	Tied Rose	Andy Smith	Brick Muller, E
	& **Cornell** (NCF, HF)	8-0-0	No bowl	Gil Dobie	Eddie Kaw, HB
1922	**Princeton** (CFRA)	8-0-0	No bowl	Bill Roper	Herb Treat, T
	California (NCF)	9-0-0	No bowl	Andy Smith	Brick Muller, E
	& **Cornell** (HF)	8-0-0	No bowl	Gil Dobie	Eddie Kaw, HB
1923	**Illinois** (CFRA, HF)	8-0-0	No bowl	Bob Zuppke	Red Grange, HB
	& **Michigan** (NCF)	8-0-0	No bowl	Hurry Up Yost	Jack Blott, C
1924	**Notre Dame**	10-0-0	Won Rose	Knute Rockne	"The Four Horsemen"*
1925	**Alabama** (CFRA, HF)	10-0-0	Won Rose	Wallace Wade	Johnny Mack Brown, HB
	& **Dartmouth** (DS)	8-0-0	No bowl	Jesse Hawley	Swede Oberlander, HB
1926	**Alabama** (CFRA, HF)	9-0-1	Tied Rose	Wallace Wade	Hoyt Winslett, E
	& **Stanford** (DS)	10-0-1	Tied Rose	Pop Warner	Ted Shipkey, E
1927	**Yale** (CFRA)	7-1-0	No bowl	Tad Jones	Bill Webster, G
	& **Illinois** (NCF, HF, DS)	7-0-1	No bowl	Bob Zuppke	Bob Reitsch, C
1928	**Georgia Tech** (CFRA, NCF, HF)	10-0-0	Won Rose	Bill Alexander	Pete Pund, C
	& **USC** (DS)	9-0-1	No bowl	Howard Jones	Jesse Hibbs, T
1929	**Notre Dame**	9-0-0	No bowl	Knute Rockne	Frank Carideo, QB
1930	**Alabama** (CFRA)	10-0-0	Won Rose	Wallace Wade	Fred Sington, T
	& **Notre Dame** (NCF, HF, DS)	10-0-0	No bowl	Knute Rockne	Marchy Schwartz, HB
1931	**USC**	10-1-0	Won Rose	Howard Jones	John Baker, G
1932	**USC** (CFRA, NCF, HF)	10-0-0	Won Rose	Howard Jones	Ernie Smith, T
	& **Michigan** (DS)	8-0-0	No bowl	Harry Kipke	Harry Newman, QB
1933	**Michigan**	8-0-0	No bowl	Harry Kipke	Chuck Bernard, C
1934	**Minnesota**	8-0-0	No bowl	Bernie Bierman	Pug Lund, HB
1935	**Minnesota** (CFRA, NCF, HF)	8-0-0	No bowl	Bernie Bierman	Dick Smith, T
	& **SMU** (DS)	12-1-0	Lost Rose	Matty Bell	Bobby Wilson, HB

*Notre Dame's Four Horsemen were Harry Stuhldreher (QB), Jim Crowley (HB), Don Miller (HB-P) and Elmer Layden (FB).

The Media Poll Years (since 1936)

National champions according to seven media and coaches' polls: Associated Press (since 1936), United Press (1950-57), International News Service (1952-57), United Press International (1958-92), Football Writers Association of America (since 1954), National Football Foundation and Hall of Fame (since 1959) and *USA Today*/CNN (since 1991). In 1991, the American Football Coaches Association switched outlets for its poll from UPI to *USA Today*/CNN and then to *USA Today*/ESPN in 1997.

After 29 years of releasing its final Top 20 poll in early December, AP named its 1965 national champion following that season's bowl games. AP returned to a pre-bowls final vote in 1966 and '67, but has polled its writers and broadcasters after the bowl games since the 1968 season. The FWAA has selected its champion after the bowl games since the 1955 season, the NFF-Hall of Fame since 1971, UPI after 1974, *USA Today*/CNN 1982-96, and *USA Today*/ESPN since 1997.

The Associated Press changed the name of its national championship award from the AP trophy to the Bear Bryant Trophy after the legendary Alabama coach's death in 1983. The Football Writers' trophy is called the Grantland Rice Award (after the celebrated sportswriter) and the NFF-Hall of Fame trophy is called the MacArthur Bowl (in honor of Gen. Douglas MacArthur).

Multiple champions: Notre Dame (9); Alabama (7); Ohio St. and Oklahoma (6); USC and Nebraska (5); Miami-FL and Minnesota (4); Michigan St. and Texas (3); Army, Georgia Tech, Michigan, Penn St. and Pittsburgh (2).

Year		Record	Bowl Game	Head Coach	Outstanding Player
1936	**Minnesota**	7-1-0	No bowl	Bernie Bierman	Ed Widseth, T
1937	**Pittsburgh**	9-0-1	No bowl	Jock Sutherland	Marshall Goldberg, HB
1938	**TCU**	11-0-0	Won Sugar	Dutch Meyer	Davey O'Brien, QB
1939	**Texas A&M**	11-0-0	Won Sugar	Homer Norton	John Kimbrough, FB
1940	**Minnesota**	8-0-0	No Bowl	Bernie Bierman	George Franck, HB
1941	**Minnesota**	8-0-0	No bowl	Bernie Bierman	Bruce Smith, HB
1942	**Ohio St.**	9-1-0	No bowl	Paul Brown	Gene Fekete, FB
1943	**Notre Dame**	9-1-0	No bowl	Frank Leahy	Angelo Bertelli, QB
1944	**Army**	9-0-0	No bowl	Red Blaik	Glenn Davis, HB
1945	**Army**	9-0-0	No bowl	Red Blaik	Doc Blanchard, FB
1946	**Notre Dame**	8-0-1	No bowl	Frank Leahy	Johnny Lujack, QB
1947	**Notre Dame**	9-0-0	No bowl	Frank Leahy	Johnny Lujack, QB
1948	**Michigan**	9-0-0	No bowl	Bennie Oosterbaan	Dick Rifenburg, E
1949	**Notre Dame**	10-0-0	No bowl	Frank Leahy	Leon Hart, E
1950	**Oklahoma**	10-1-0	Lost Sugar	Bud Wilkinson	Leon Heath, FB
1951	**Tennessee**	10-0-0	Lost Sugar	Bob Neyland	Hank Lauricella, TB
1952	**Michigan St.** (AP, UP)	9-0-0	No bowl	Biggie Munn	Don McAuliffe, HB
	& **Georgia Tech** (INS)	12-0-0	Won Sugar	Bobby Dodd	Hal Miller, T
1953	**Maryland**	10-1-0	Lost Orange	Jim Tatum	Bernie Faloney, QB
1954	**Ohio St.** (AP, INS)	10-0-0	Won Rose	Woody Hayes	Howard Cassady, HB
	& **UCLA** (UP, FW)	9-0-0	No bowl	Red Sanders	Jack Ellena, T
1955	**Oklahoma**	11-0-0	Won Orange	Bud Wilkinson	Jerry Tubbs, C
1956	**Oklahoma**	10-0-0	No bowl	Bud Wilkinson	Tommy McDonald, HB
1957	**Auburn** (AP)	10-0-0	No bowl	Shug Jordan	Jimmy Phillips, E
	& **Ohio St.** (UP, FW, INS)	9-1-0	Won Rose	Woody Hayes	Bob White, FB
1958	**LSU** (AP, UPI)	11-0-0	Won Sugar	Paul Dietzel	Billy Cannon, HB
	& **Iowa** (FW)	8-1-1	Won Rose	Forest Evashevski	Randy Duncan, QB

National Champions (Cont.)

Year		Record	Bowl Game	Head Coach	Outstanding Player
1959	**Syracuse**	11-0-0	Won Cotton	Ben Schwartzwalder	Ernie Davis, HB
1960	**Minnesota** (AP, UPI, NFF)	8-2-0	Lost Rose	Murray Warmath	Tom Brown, G
	& **Mississippi** (FW)	10-0-1	Won Sugar	Johnny Vaught	Jake Gibbs, QB
1961	**Alabama** (AP, UPI, NFF)	11-0-0	Won Sugar	Bear Bryant	Billy Neighbors, T
	& **Ohio St.** (FW)	8-0-1	No bowl	Woody Hayes	Bob Ferguson, HB
1962	**USC**	11-0-0	Won Rose	John McKay	Hal Bedsole, E
1963	**Texas**	11-0-0	Won Cotton	Darrell Royal	Scott Appleton, T
1964	**Alabama** (AP, UPI),	10-1-0	Lost Orange	Bear Bryant	Joe Namath, QB
	Arkansas (FW)	11-0-0	Won Cotton	Frank Broyles	Ronnie Caveness, LB
	& **Notre Dame** (NFF)	9-1-0	No bowl	Ara Parseghian	John Huarte, QB
1965	**Alabama** (AP, FW-tie)	9-1-1	Won Orange	Bear Bryant	Paul Crane, C
	& **Michigan St.** (UPI, NFF, FW-tie)	10-1-0	Lost Rose	Duffy Daugherty	George Webster, LB
1966	**Notre Dame** (AP, UPI, FW, NFF-tie)	9-0-1	No bowl	Ara Parseghian	Jim Lynch, LB
	& **Michigan St.** (NFF-tie)	9-0-1	No bowl	Duffy Daugherty	Bubba Smith, DE
1967	**USC**	10-1-0	Won Rose	John McKay	O.J. Simpson, HB
1968	**Ohio St.**	10-0-0	Won Rose	Woody Hayes	Rex Kern, QB
1969	**Texas**	11-0-0	Won Cotton	Darrell Royal	James Street, QB
1970	**Nebraska** (AP, FW)	11-0-1	Won Orange	Bob Devaney	Jerry Tagge, QB
	Texas (UPI, NFF-tie),	10-1-0	Lost Cotton	Darrell Royal	Steve Worster, RB
	& **Ohio St.** (NFF-tie)	9-1-0	Lost Rose	Woody Hayes	Jim Stillwagon, MG
1971	**Nebraska**	13-0-0	Won Orange	Bob Devaney	Johnny Rodgers, WR
1972	**USC**	12-0-0	Won Rose	John McKay	Charles Young, TE
1973	**Notre Dame** (AP, FW, NFF)	11-0-0	Won Sugar	Ara Parseghian	Mike Townsend, DB
	& **Alabama** (UPI)	11-1-0	Lost Sugar	Bear Bryant	Buddy Brown, OT
1974	**Oklahoma** (AP)	11-0-0	No bowl	Barry Switzer	Joe Washington, RB
	& **USC** (UPI, FW, NFF)	10-1-1	Won Rose	John McKay	Anthony Davis, RB
1975	**Oklahoma**	11-1-0	Won Orange	Barry Switzer	Lee Roy Selmon, DT
1976	**Pittsburgh**	12-0-0	Won Sugar	Johnny Majors	Tony Dorsett, RB
1977	**Notre Dame**	11-1-0	Won Cotton	Dan Devine	Ross Browner, DE
1978	**Alabama** (AP, FW, NFF)	11-1-0	Won Sugar	Bear Bryant	Marty Lyons, DT
	& **USC** (UPI)	12-1-0	Won Rose	John Robinson	Charles White, RB
1979	**Alabama**	12-0-0	Won Sugar	Bear Bryant	Jim Bunch, OT
1980	**Georgia**	12-0-0	Won Sugar	Vince Dooley	Herschel Walker, RB
1981	**Clemson**	12-0-0	Won Orange	Danny Ford	Jeff Davis, LB
1982	**Penn St.**	11-1-0	Won Sugar	Joe Paterno	Todd Blackledge, QB
1983	**Miami-FL**	11-1-0	Won Orange	H. Schnellenberger	Bernie Kosar, QB
1984	**BYU**	13-0-0	Won Holiday	LaVell Edwards	Robbie Bosco, QB
1985	**Oklahoma**	11-1-0	Won Orange	Barry Switzer	Brian Bosworth, LB
1986	**Penn St.**	12-0-0	Won Fiesta	Joe Paterno	D.J. Dozier, RB
1987	**Miami-FL**	12-0-0	Won Orange	Jimmy Johnson	Steve Walsh, QB
1988	**Notre Dame**	12-0-0	Won Fiesta	Lou Holtz	Tony Rice, QB
1989	**Miami-FL**	11-1-0	Won Sugar	Dennis Erickson	Craig Erickson, QB
1990	**Colorado** (AP, FW, NFF)	11-1-1	Won Orange	Bill McCartney	Eric Bieniemy, RB
	& **Georgia Tech** (UPI)	11-0-1	Won Citrus	Bobby Ross	Shawn Jones, QB
1991	**Miami-FL** (AP)	12-0-0	Won Orange	Dennis Erickson	Gino Torretta, QB
	& **Washington** (USA, FW, NFF)	12-0-0	Won Rose	Don James	Steve Emtman, DT
1992	**Alabama**	13-0-0	Won Sugar	Gene Stallings	Eric Curry, DE
1993	**Florida St.**	12-1-0	Won Orange	Bobby Bowden	Charlie Ward, QB
1994	**Nebraska**	13-0-0	Won Orange	Tom Osborne	Zach Wiegert, OT
1995	**Nebraska**	12-0-0	Won Fiesta	Tom Osborne	Tommie Frazier, QB
1996	**Florida**	12-1-0	Won Sugar	Steve Spurrier	Danny Wuerffel, QB
1997	**Michigan** (AP)	12-0-0	Won Rose	Lloyd Carr	Charles Woodson, DB
	& **Nebraska** (ESPN/USA)	13-0-0	Won Orange	Tom Osborne	Ahman Green, RB

Number 1 vs. Number 2

Since the Associated Press writers poll started keeping track of such things in 1936, the No. 1 and No. 2 ranked teams in the country have met 31 times; 20 during the regular season and 11 in bowl games. Since the first showdown in 1943, the No. 1 team has beaten the No. 2 team 19 times, lost 10 and there have been two ties. Each showdown is listed below with the date, the match-up, each team's record going into the game, the final score, the stadium and site.

Date	Match-up		Stadium
Oct. 9	**#1** Notre Dame (2-0)	35	Michigan
1943	**#2** Michigan (3-0)	12	(Ann Arbor)
Nov. 20	**#1** Notre Dame (8-0)	14	Notre Dame
1943	**#2** Iowa Pre-Flight (8-0)	13	(South Bend)
Dec. 2	**#1** Army (8-0)	23	Municipal
1944	**#2** Navy (6-2)	7	(Baltimore)
Nov. 10	**#1** Army (6-0)	48	Yankee
1945	**#2** Notre Dame (5-0-1)	0	(New York)
Dec. 1	**#1** Army (8-0)	32	Municipal
1945	**#2** Navy (7-0-1)	13	(Philadelphia)
Nov. 9	**#1** Army (7-0)	0	Yankee
1946	**#2** Notre Dame (5-0)	0	(New York)

Date		Match-up		Stadium
Jan. 1 1963	#1	USC (10-0)	42	ROSE BOWL
	#2	Wisconsin (8-1)	37	(Pasadena)
Oct. 12 1963	#2	Texas (3-0)	28	Cotton Bowl
	#1	Oklahoma (2-0)	7	(Dallas)
Jan. 1 1964	#1	Texas (10-0)	28	COTTON BOWL
	#2	Navy (9-1)	6	(Dallas)
Nov. 19 1966	#1	Notre Dame (8-0)	10	Spartan
	#2	Michigan St. (9-0)	10	(East Lansing)
Sept. 28 1968	#1	Purdue (1-0)	37	Notre Dame
	#2	Notre Dame (1-0)	22	(South Bend)
Jan. 1 1969	#1	Ohio St. (9-0)	27	ROSE BOWL
	#2	USC (9-0-1)	16	(Pasadena)
Dec. 6 1969	#1	Texas (9-0)	15	Razorback
	#2	Arkansas (9-0)	14	(Fayetteville)
Nov. 25 1971	#1	Nebraska (10-0)	35	Owen Field
	#2	Oklahoma (9-0)	31	(Norman)
Jan. 1 1972	#1	Nebraska (12-0)	38	ORANGE BOWL
	#2	Alabama (11-0)	6	(Miami)
Jan. 1 1979	#2	Alabama (10-1)	14	SUGAR BOWL
	#1	Penn St. (11-0)	7	(New Orleans)
Sept. 26 1981	#1	USC (2-0)	28	Coliseum
	#2	Oklahoma (1-0)	24	(Los Angeles)
Jan. 1 1983	#2	Penn St. (10-1)	27	SUGAR BOWL
	#1	Georgia (11-0)	23	(New Orleans)
Oct. 19 1985	#1	Iowa (5-0)	12	Kinnick
	#2	Michigan (5-0)	10	(Iowa City)
Sept. 27 1986	#2	Miami-FL (3-0)	28	Orange Bowl
	#1	Oklahoma (2-0)	16	(Miami)
Jan. 2 1987	#2	Penn St. (11-0)	14	FIESTA BOWL
	#1	Miami-FL (11-0)	10	(Tempe)
Nov. 21 1987	#2	Oklahoma (10-0)	17	Memorial
	#1	Nebraska (10-0)	7	(Lincoln)
Jan. 1 1988	#2	Miami-FL (11-0)	20	ORANGE BOWL
	#1	Oklahoma (11-0)	14	(Miami)
Nov. 26 1988	#1	Notre Dame (10-0)	27	Coliseum
	#2	USC (10-0)	10	(Los Angeles)
Sept. 16 1989	#1	Notre Dame (1-0)	24	Michigan
	#2	Michigan (0-0)	19	(Ann Arbor)
Nov. 16 1991	#2	Miami-FL (8-0)	17	Doak Campbell
	#1	Florida St. (10-0)	16	(Tallahassee)
Jan. 1 1993	#2	Alabama (12-0-0)	34	SUGAR BOWL
	#1	Miama-FL (11-0-0)	13	(New Orleans)
Nov. 13 1993	#2	Notre Dame (9-0)	31	Notre Dame
	#1	Florida St. (9-0)	24	(South Bend)
Jan. 1 1994	#1	Florida St. (11-1)	18	ORANGE BOWL
	#2	Nebraska (11-0)	16	(Miami)
Jan. 2 1996	#1	Nebraska (11-0)	62	FIESTA BOWL
	#2	Florida (12-0)	24	(Tempe)
Nov. 30 1996	#2	Florida St. (10-0)	24	Doak Campbell
	#1	Florida (10-1)	21	(Tallahassee)

Top 50 Rivalries

Top Division I-A and I-AA series records, including games through the 1997 season. All rivalries listed below are renewed annually with the following exceptions. **LSU-Tulane** stopped playing in 1996 but have made plans to renew rivalry no later than 2001.

RECENTLY DISCONTINUED SERIES: **Baylor vs TCU** in 1995 after 102 games (Baylor ahead 48-47-7); **Florida vs Miami-FL** in 1991 after 49 games (Florida ahead, 25-24); **Miami-FL vs Notre Dame** in 1990 after 23 games (ND ahead, 15-7-1).

	Gm	Series Leader
Air Force-Army	32	Air Force (19-12-1)
Air Force-Navy	30	Air Force (20-10-0)
Alabama-Auburn	62	Alabama (35-26-1)
Alabama-Tennessee	80	Alabama (42-31-7)
Arizona-Arizona St.	71	Arizona (41-29-1)
Army-Navy	98	Army (47-44-7)
Auburn-Georgia	101	Auburn (48-45-8)
California-Stanford	100	Stanford (50-39-11)
The Citadel-VMI	57	VMI (28-27-2)
Clemson-S. Carolina	95	Clemson (56-35-4)
Colorado-Nebraska	56	Nebraska (40-14-2)
Colo. St.-Wyoming	87	Colorado St. (45-37-5)
Duke-N. Carolina	83	N. Carolina (44-35-4)
Florida-Florida St.	42	Florida (26-14-2)
Florida-Georgia	76	Georgia (45-29-2)
Florida St.-Miami,FL	41	Miami (23-18-0)
Georgia-Georgia Tech	92	Georgia (52-35-5)
Grambling-Southern	46	Tied (23-23-0)
Harvard-Yale	114	Yale (61-45-8)
Kansas-Kansas St	95	Kansas (61-29-5)
Kentucky-Tennessee	93	Tennessee (61-23-9)
Lafayette-Lehigh	133	Lafayette (71-57-5)
LSU-Tulane	93	LSU (64-22-7)*
Miami,OH-Cincinnati	102	Miami (54-41-7)
Michigan-Michigan St	90	Michigan (59-26-5)
Michigan-Notre Dame	27	Michigan (16-10-1)
Michigan-Ohio St	94	Michigan (54-34-6)
Minnesota-Wisconsin	107	Minnesota (57-42-8)
Mississippi-Miss. St	94	Ole Miss (54-34-6)
Missouri-Kansas	106	Missouri (49-48-9)
Nebraska-Oklahoma	78	Oklahoma (39-36-3)
N. Mexico-N. Mexico St	87	New Mexico (57-25-5)
N. Carolina-N.C. State	87	N. Carolina (57-24-6)
Notre Dame-Purdue	69	Notre Dame (45-22-2)
Notre Dame-USC	69	Notre Dame (39-25-5)
Oklahoma-Okla. St	92	Oklahoma (72-13-7)
Oregon-Oregon St	101	Oregon (51-40-10)
Penn-Cornell	104	Penn (59-40-5)
Penn St.-Pittsburgh	93	Penn St.(48-41-4)
Pittsburgh-West Va	90	Pitt (56-31-3)
Princeton-Yale	120	Yale (64-46-10)
Purdue-Indiana	100	Purdue (60-34-6)
Richmond-Wm.& Mary	107	Wm. & Mary (55-47-5)
Tennessee-Vanderbilt	91	Tennessee (60-26-5)
Texas-Oklahoma	92	Texas (53-34-5)
Texas-Texas A&M	104	Texas (66-33-5)
UCLA-USC	67	USC (34-26-7)
Utah-BYU	73	Utah (44-25-4)
Utah-Utah St	95	Utah (62-29-4)
Washington-Wash. St	90	Washington (58-26-6)

*Disputed series record: Tulane claims LSU leads 61-23-7

Associated Press Final Polls

The Associated Press introduced its weekly college football poll of sportswriters (later, sportswriters and broadcasters) in 1936. The final AP poll was released at the end of the regular season until 1965, when bowl results were included for one year. After a two-year return to regular season games only, the final poll has come out after the bowls since 1968.

1936

Final poll released Nov. 30. Top 20 regular season results after that: **Dec. 5**–#8 Notre Dame tied USC, 13-13; #17 Tennessee tied Ole Miss, 0-0; #18 Arkansas over Texas, 6-0. **Dec. 12**–#16 TCU over #6 Santa Clara, 9-0.

		As of Nov. 30	Head Coach	After Bowls
1	Minnesota	7-1-0	Bernie Bierman	same
2	LSU	9-0-1	Bernie Moore	9-1-1
3	Pittsburgh	7-1-1	Jock Sutherland	8-1-1
4	Alabama	8-0-1	Frank Thomas	same
5	Washington	7-1-1	Jimmy Phelan	7-2-1
6	Santa Clara	7-0-0	Buck Shaw	8-1-0
7	Northwestern	7-1-0	Pappy Waldorf	same
8	Notre Dame	6-2-0	Elmer Layden	6-2-1
9	Nebraska	7-2-0	Dana X. Bible	same
10	Penn	7-1-0	Harvey Harman	same
11	Duke	9-1-0	Wallace Wade	same
12	Yale	7-1-0	Ducky Pond	same
13	Dartmouth	7-1-1	Red Blaik	same
14	Duquesne	7-2-0	John Smith	8-2-0
15	Fordham	5-1-2	Jim Crowley	same
16	TCU	7-2-2	Dutch Meyer	9-2-2
17	Tennessee	6-2-1	Bob Neyland	6-2-2
18	Arkansas	6-3-0	Fred Thomsen	7-3-0
	Navy	6-3-0	Tom Hamilton	same
20	Marquette	7-1-0	Frank Murray	7-2-0

Key Bowl Games

Sugar–#6 Santa Clara over #2 LSU, 21-14; **Rose**– #3 Pitt over #5 Washington, 21-0; **Orange**–#14 Duquesne over Mississippi St., 13-12; **Cotton**–#16 TCU over #20 Marquette, 16-6.

1937

Final poll released Nov. 29. Top 20 regular season results after that: **Dec. 4**–#18 Rice over SMU, 15-7.

		As of Nov. 29	Head Coach	After Bowls
1	Pittsburgh	9-0-1	Jock Sutherland	same
2	California	9-0-1	Stub Allison	10-0-1
3	Fordham	7-0-1	Jim Crowley	same
4	Alabama	9-0-0	Frank Thomas	9-1-0
5	Minnesota	6-2-0	Bernie Bierman	same
6	Villanova	8-0-1	Clipper Smith	same
7	Dartmouth	7-0-2	Red Blaik	same
8	LSU	9-1-0	Bernie Moore	9-2-0
9	Notre Dame	6-2-1	Elmer Layden	same
	Santa Clara	8-0-0	Buck Shaw	9-0-0
11	Nebraska	6-1-2	Biff Jones	same
12	Yale	6-1-1	Ducky Pond	same
13	Ohio St.	6-2-0	Francis Schmidt	same
14	Holy Cross	8-0-2	Eddie Anderson	same
	Arkansas	6-2-2	Fred Thomsen	same
16	TCU	4-2-2	Dutch Meyer	same
17	Colorado	8-0-0	Bunnie Oakes	8-1-0
18	Rice	4-3-2	Jimmy Kitts	6-3-2
19	North Carolina	7-1-1	Ray Wolf	same
20	Duke	7-2-1	Wallace Wade	same

Key Bowl Games

Rose–#2 Cal over #4 Alabama, 13-0; **Sugar**–#9 Santa Clara over #8 LSU, 6-0; **Cotton**–#18 Rice over #17 Colorado, 28-14; **Orange**–Auburn over Michigan St., 6-0.

1938

Final poll released Dec. 5. Top 20 regular season results after that: **Dec. 26**–#14 Cal over Georgia Tech, 13-7.

		As of Dec. 5	Head Coach	After Bowls
1	TCU	10-0-0	Dutch Meyer	11-0-0
2	Tennessee	10-0-0	Bob Neyland	11-0-0
3	Duke	9-0-0	Wallace Wade	9-1-0
4	Oklahoma	10-0-0	Tom Stidham	10-1-0
5	Notre Dame	8-1-0	Elmer Layden	same
6	Carnegie Tech	7-1-0	Bill Kern	7-2-0
7	USC	8-2-0	Howard Jones	9-2-0
8	Pittsburgh	8-2-0	Jock Sutherland	same
9	Holy Cross	8-1-0	Eddie Anderson	same
10	Minnesota	6-2-0	Bernie Bierman	same
11	Texas Tech	10-0-0	Pete Cawthon	10-1-0
12	Cornell	5-1-1	Carl Snavely	same
13	Alabama	7-1-1	Frank Thomas	same
14	California	9-1-0	Stub Allison	10-1-0
15	Fordham	6-1-2	Jim Crowley	same
16	Michigan	6-1-1	Fritz Crisler	same
17	Northwestern	4-2-2	Pappy Waldorf	same
18	Villanova	8-0-1	Clipper Smith	same
19	Tulane	7-2-1	Red Dawson	same
20	Dartmouth	7-2-0	Red Blaik	same

Key Bowl Games

Sugar–#1 TCU over #6 Carnegie Tech, 15-7; **Orange**–#2 Tennessee over #4 Oklahoma, 17-0; **Rose**–#7 USC over #3 Duke, 7-3; **Cotton**–St. Mary's over #11 Texas Tech 20-13.

1939

Final poll released Dec. 11. Top 20 regular season results after that: None.

		As of Dec. 11	Head Coach	After Bowls
1	Texas A&M	10-0-0	Homer Norton	11-0-0
2	Tennessee	10-0-0	Bob Neyland	10-1-0
3	USC	7-0-2	Howard Jones	8-0-2
4	Cornell	8-0-0	Carl Snavely	same
5	Tulane	8-0-1	Red Dawson	8-1-1
6	Missouri	8-1-0	Don Faurot	8-2-0
7	UCLA	6-0-4	Babe Horrell	same
8	Duke	8-1-0	Wallace Wade	same
9	Iowa	6-1-1	Eddie Anderson	same
10	Duquesne	8-0-1	Buff Donelli	same
11	Boston College	9-1-0	Frank Leahy	9-2-0
12	Clemson	8-1-0	Jess Neely	9-1-0
13	Notre Dame	7-2-0	Elmer Layden	same
14	Santa Clara	5-1-3	Buck Shaw	same
15	Ohio St.	6-2-0	Francis Schmidt	same
16	Georgia Tech	7-2-0	Bill Alexander	8-2-0
17	Fordham	6-2-0	Jim Crowley	same
18	Nebraska	7-1-1	Biff Jones	same
19	Oklahoma	6-2-1	Tom Stidham	same
20	Michigan	6-2-0	Fritz Crisler	same

Key Bowl Games

Sugar–#1 Texas A&M over #5 Tulane, 14-13; **Rose** –#3 USC over #2 Tennessee, 14-0; **Orange**–#16 Georgia Tech over #6 Missouri, 21-7; **Cotton**–#12 Clemson over #11 Boston College, 6-3.

1940

Final poll released Dec. 2. Top 20 regular season results after that: **Dec. 7**–#16 SMU over Rice, 7-6.

	As of Dec. 2		Head Coach	After Bowls
1	Minnesota	8-0-0	Bernie Bierman	same
2	Stanford	9-0-0	Clark Shaughnessy	10-0-0
3	Michigan	7-1-0	Fritz Crisler	same
4	Tennessee	10-0-0	Bob Neyland	10-1-0
5	Boston College	10-0-0	Frank Leahy	11-0-0
6	Texas A&M	8-1-0	Homer Norton	9-1-0
7	Nebraska	8-1-0	Biff Jones	8-2-0
8	Northwestern	6-2-0	Pappy Waldorf	same
9	Mississippi St.	9-0-1	Allyn McKeen	10-0-1
10	Washington	7-2-0	Jimmy Phelan	same
11	Santa Clara	6-1-1	Buck Shaw	same
12	Fordham	7-1-0	Jim Crowley	7-2-0
13	Georgetown	8-1-0	Jack Hagerty	8-2-0
14	Penn	6-1-1	George Munger	same
15	Cornell	6-2-0	Carl Snavely	same
16	SMU	7-1-1	Matty Bell	8-1-1
17	Hardin-Simmons	9-0-0	Warren Woodson	same
18	Duke	7-2-0	Wallace Wade	same
19	Lafayette	9-0-0	Hooks Mylin	same
20	–			

Note: Only 19 teams ranked.

Key Bowl Games

Rose–#2 Stanford over #7 Nebraska, 21-13; **Sugar**– #5 Boston College over #4 Tennessee, 19-13; **Cotton**–#6 Texas A&M over #12 Fordham, 13-12; **Orange**–#9 Mississippi St. over #13 Georgetown, 14-7.

1941

Final poll released Dec. 1. Top 20 regular season results after that: **Dec. 6**–#4 Texas over Oregon, 71-7; #9 Texas A&M over #19 Washington St., 7-0; #16 Mississippi St. over San Francisco, 26-13.

	As of Dec. 1		Head Coach	After Bowls
1	Minnesota	8-0-0	Bernie Bierman	same
2	Duke	9-0-0	Wallace Wade	9-1-0
3	Notre Dame	8-0-1	Frank Leahy	same
4	Texas	7-1-1	Dana X. Bible	8-1-1
5	Michigan	6-1-1	Fritz Crisler	same
6	Fordham	7-1-0	Jim Crowley	8-1-0
7	Missouri	8-1-0	Don Faurot	8-2-0
8	Duquesne	8-0-0	Buff Donelli	same
9	Texas A&M	8-1-0	Homer Norton	9-2-0
10	Navy	7-1-1	Swede Larson	same
11	Northwestern	5-3-0	Pappy Waldorf	same
12	Oregon St.	7-2-0	Lon Stiner	8-2-0
13	Ohio St.	6-1-1	Paul Brown	same
14	Georgia	8-1-1	Wally Butts	9-1-1
15	Penn	7-1-1	George Munger	same
16	Mississippi St.	7-1-1	Allyn McKeen	8-1-1
17	Mississippi	6-2-1	Harry Mehre	same
18	Tennessee	8-2-0	John Barnhill	same
19	Washington St.	6-3-0	Babe Hollingbery	6-4-0
20	Alabama	8-2-0	Frank Thomas	9-2-0

Note: 1942 Rose Bowl moved to Durham, N.C., for one year after outbreak of World War II.

Key Bowl Games

Rose–#12 Oregon St. over #2 Duke, 20-16; **Sugar**– #6 Fordham over #7 Missouri, 2-0; **Cotton**–#20 Alabama over #9 Texas A&M, 29-21; **Orange**–#14 Georgia over TCU, 40-26.

1942

Final poll released Nov. 30. Top 20 regular season results after that: **Dec. 5**–#6 Notre Dame tied Great Lakes Naval Station, 13-13; #13 UCLA over Idaho, 40-13; #14 William & Mary over Oklahoma, 14-7; #17 Washington St. lost to Texas A&M, 21-0; #18 Mississippi St. over San Francisco, 19-7. **Dec. 12**–#13 UCLA over USC, 14-7.

	As of Nov. 30		Head Coach	After Bowls
1	Ohio St.	9-1-0	Paul Brown	same
2	Georgia	10-1-0	Wally Butts	11-1-0
3	Wisconsin	8-1-1	Harry Stuhldreher	same
4	Tulsa	10-0-0	Henry Frnka	10-1-0
5	Georgia Tech	9-1-0	Bill Alexander	9-2-0
6	Notre Dame	7-2-1	Frank Leahy	7-2-2
7	Tennessee	8-1-1	John Barnhill	9-1-1
8	Boston College	8-1-0	Denny Myers	8-2-0
9	Michigan	7-3-0	Fritz Crisler	same
10	Alabama	7-3-0	Frank Thomas	8-3-0
11	Texas	8-2-0	Dana X. Bible	9-2-0
12	Stanford	6-4-0	Marchie Schwartz	same
13	UCLA	5-3-0	Babe Horrell	7-4-0
14	William & Mary	8-1-1	Carl Voyles	9-1-1
15	Santa Clara	7-2-0	Buck Shaw	same
16	Auburn	6-4-1	Jack Meagher	same
17	Washington St.	6-1-2	Babe Hollingbery	6-2-2
18	Mississippi St.	7-2-0	Allyn McKeen	8-2-0
19	Minnesota	5-4-0	George Hauser	same
	Holy Cross	5-4-1	Ank Scanlon	same
	Penn St.	6-1-1	Bob Higgins	same

Key Bowl Games

Rose–#2 Georgia over #13 UCLA, 9-0; **Sugar**–#7 Tennessee over #4 Tulsa, 14-7; **Cotton**–#11 Texas over #5 Georgia Tech, 14-7; **Orange**–#10 Alabama over #8 Boston College, 37-21.

1943

Final poll released Nov. 29. Top 20 regular season results after that: **Dec.11**–#10 March Field over #19 Pacific, 19-0.

	As of Nov. 29		Head Coach	After Bowls
1	Notre Dame	9-1-0	Frank Leahy	same
2	Iowa Pre-Flight	9-1-0	Don Faurot	same
3	Michigan	8-1-0	Fritz Crisler	same
4	Navy	8-1-0	Billick Whelchel	same
5	Purdue	9-0-0	Elmer Burnham	same
6	Great Lakes Naval Station	10-2-0	Tony Hinkle	same
7	Duke	8-1-0	Eddie Cameron	same
8	DelMonte Pre-Flight	7-1-0	Bill Kern	same
9	Northwestern	6-2-0	Pappy Waldorf	same
10	March Field	8-1-0	Paul Schissler	9-1-0
11	Army	7-2-1	Red Blaik	same
12	Washington	4-0-0	Ralph Welch	4-1-0
13	Georgia Tech	7-3-0	Bill Alexander	8-3-0
14	Texas	7-1-0	Dana X. Bible	7-1-1
15	Tulsa	6-0-1	Henry Frnka	6-1-1
16	Dartmouth	6-1-0	Earl Brown	same
17	Bainbridge Navy Training School	7-0-0	Joe Maniaci	same
18	Colorado College	7-0-0	Hal White	same
19	Pacific	7-1-0	Amos A. Stagg	7-2-0
20	Penn	6-2-1	George Munger	same

Key Bowl Games

Rose–USC over #12 Washington, 29-0; **Sugar**–#13 Georgia Tech over #15 Tulsa, 20-18; **Cotton**–#14 Texas tied Randolph Field, 7-7; **Orange**–LSU over Texas A&M, 19-14.

Associated Press Final Polls (Cont.)

1944

Final poll released Dec. 4. Top 20 regular season results after that: **Dec. 10**–#3 Randolph Field over #10 March Field, 20-7; #18 Fort Pierce over Kessler Field, 34-7; Morris Field over #20 Second Air Force, 14-7.

		As of Dec. 4	Head Coach	After Bowls
1	Army	9-0-0	Red Blaik	same
2	Ohio St.	9-0-0	Carroll Widdoes	same
3	Randolph Field	10-0-0	Frank Tritico	12-0-0
4	Navy	6-3-0	Oscar Hagberg	same
5	Bainbridge Navy Training School	10-0-0	Joe Maniaci	same
6	Iowa Pre-Flight	10-1-0	Jack Meagher	same
7	USC	7-0-2	Jeff Cravath	8-0-2
8	Michigan	8-2-0	Fritz Crisler	same
9	Notre Dame	8-2-0	Ed McKeever	same
10	March Field	7-0-2	Paul Schissler	7-1-2
11	Duke	5-4-0	Eddie Cameron	6-4-0
12	Tennessee	7-0-1	John Barnhill	7-1-1
13	Georgia Tech	8-2-0	Bill Alexander	8-3-0
14	Norman Pre-Flight	6-0-0	John Gregg	same
15	Illinois	5-4-1	Ray Eliot	same
16	El Toro Marines	8-1-0	Dick Hanley	same
17	Great Lakes Naval Station	9-2-1	Paul Brown	same
18	Fort Pierce	8-0-0	Hamp Pool	9-0-0
19	St. Mary's Pre-Flight	4-4-0	Jules Sikes	same
20	Second Air Force	10-2-1	Bill Reese	10-4-1

Key Bowl Games

Treasury–#3 Randolph Field over #20 Second Air Force, 13-6; **Rose**–#7 USC over #12 Tennessee, 25-0; **Sugar**–#11 Duke over Alabama, 29-26; **Orange**–Tulsa over #13 Georgia Tech, 26-12; **Cotton**–Oklahoma A&M over TCU, 34-0.

1945

Final poll released Dec. 3. Top 20 regular season results after that: None.

		As of Dec. 3	Head Coach	After Bowls
1	Army	9-0-0	Red Blaik	same
2	Alabama	9-0-0	Frank Thomas	10-0-0
3	Navy	7-1-1	Oscar Hagberg	same
4	Indiana	9-0-1	Bo McMillan	same
5	Oklahoma A&M	8-0-0	Jim Lookabaugh	9-0-0
6	Michigan	7-3-0	Fritz Crisler	same
7	St. Mary's-CA	7-1-0	Jimmy Phelan	7-2-0
8	Penn	6-2-0	George Munger	same
9	Notre Dame	7-2-1	Hugh Devore	same
10	Texas	9-1-0	Dana X. Bible	10-1-0
11	USC	7-3-0	Jeff Cravath	7-4-0
12	Ohio St.	7-2-0	Carroll Widdoes	same
13	Duke	6-2-0	Eddie Cameron	same
14	Tennessee	8-1-0	John Barnhill	same
15	LSU	7-2-0	Bernie Moore	same
16	Holy Cross	8-1-0	John DeGrosa	8-2-0
17	Tulsa	8-2-0	Henry Frnka	8-3-0
18	Georgia	8-2-0	Wally Butts	9-2-0
19	Wake Forest	4-3-1	Peahead Walker	5-3-1
20	Columbia	8-1-0	Lou Little	same

Key Bowl Games

Rose–#2 Alabama over #11 USC, 34-14; **Sugar**– #5 Oklahoma A&M over #7 St. Mary's, 33-13; **Cotton**–#10 Texas over Missouri, 40-27; **Orange**–Miami-FL over #16 Holy Cross, 13-6.

1946

Final poll released Dec. 2. Top 20 regular season results after that: None.

		As of Dec. 2	Head Coach	After Bowls
1	Notre Dame	8-0-1	Frank Leahy	same
2	Army	9-0-1	Red Blaik	same
3	Georgia	10-0-0	Wally Butts	11-0-0
4	UCLA	10-0-0	Bert LaBrucherie	10-1-0
5	Illinois	7-2-0	Ray Eliot	8-2-0
6	Michigan	6-2-1	Fritz Crisler	same
7	Tennessee	9-1-0	Bob Neyland	9-2-0
8	LSU	9-1-0	Bernie Moore	9-1-1
9	North Carolina	8-1-1	Carl Snavely	8-2-1
10	Rice	8-2-0	Jess Neely	9-2-0
11	Georgia Tech	8-2-0	Bobby Dodd	9-2-0
12	Yale	7-1-1	Howard Odell	same
13	Penn	6-2-0	George Munger	same
14	Oklahoma	7-3-0	Jim Tatum	8-3-0
15	Texas	8-2-0	Dana X. Bible	same
16	Arkansas	6-3-1	John Barnhill	6-3-2
17	Tulsa	9-1-0	J.O. Brothers	same
18	N.C. State	8-2-0	Beattie Feathers	8-3-0
19	Delaware	9-0-0	Bill Murray	10-0-0
20	Indiana	6-3-0	Bo McMillan	same

Key Bowl Games

Sugar–#3 Georgia over #9 N. Carolina, 20-10; **Rose**– #5 Illinois over #4 UCLA, 45-14; **Orange**–#10 Rice over #7 Tennessee, 8-0; **Cotton**–#8 LSU tied #16 Arkansas, 0-0.

1947

Final poll released Dec. 8. Top 20 regular season results after that: None.

		As of Dec. 8	Head Coach	After Bowls
1	Notre Dame	9-0-0	Frank Leahy	same
2	Michigan	9-0-0	Fritz Crisler	10-0-0
3	SMU	9-0-1	Matty Bell	9-0-2
4	Penn St.	9-0-0	Bob Higgins	9-0-1
5	Texas	9-1-0	Blair Cherry	10-1-0
6	Alabama	8-2-0	Red Drew	8-3-0
7	Penn	7-0-1	George Munger	same
8	USC	7-1-1	Jeff Cravath	7-2-1
9	North Carolina	8-2-0	Carl Snavely	same
10	Georgia Tech	9-1-0	Bobby Dodd	10-1-0
11	Army	5-2-2	Red Blaik	same
12	Kansas	8-0-2	George Sauer	8-1-2
13	Mississippi	8-2-0	Johnny Vaught	9-2-0
14	William & Mary	9-1-0	Rube McCray	9-2-0
15	California	9-1-0	Pappy Waldorf	same
16	Oklahoma	7-2-1	Bud Wilkinson	same
17	N.C. State	5-3-1	Beattie Feathers	same
18	Rice	6-3-1	Jess Neely	same
19	Duke	4-3-2	Wallace Wade	same
20	Columbia	7-2-0	Lou Little	same

Key Bowl Games

Rose–#2 Michigan over #8 USC, 49-0; **Cotton**–#3 SMU tied #4 Penn St., 13-13; **Sugar**–#5 Texas over #6 Alabama, 27-7; **Orange**–#10 Georgia Tech over #12 Kansas, 20-14.

Note: An unprecedented "Who's No. 1?" poll was conducted by AP after the Rose Bowl game, pitting Notre Dame against Michigan. The Wolverines won the vote, 226-119, but AP ruled that the Irish would be the No. 1 team of record.

1948

Final poll released Nov. 29. Top 20 regular season results after that: **Dec. 3**–#12 Vanderbilt over Miami-FL, 33-6. **Dec. 4**–#2 Notre Dame tied USC, 14-14; #11 Clemson over The Citadel, 20-0.

	As of Nov. 29		Head Coach	After Bowls
1	Michigan	9-0-0	Bennie Oosterbaan	same
2	Notre Dame	9-0-0	Frank Leahy	9-0-1
3	North Carolina	9-0-1	Carl Snavely	9-1-1
4	California	10-0-0	Pappy Waldorf	10-1-0
5	Oklahoma	9-1-0	Bud Wilkinson	10-1-0
6	Army	8-0-1	Red Blaik	same
7	Northwestern	7-2-0	Bob Voigts	8-2-0
8	Georgia	9-1-0	Wally Butts	9-2-0
9	Oregon	9-1-0	Jim Aiken	9-2-0
10	SMU	8-1-1	Matty Bell	9-1-1
11	Clemson	9-0-0	Frank Howard	11-0-0
12	Vanderbilt	7-2-1	Red Sanders	8-2-1
13	Tulane	9-1-0	Henry Frnka	same
14	Michigan St.	6-2-2	Biggie Munn	same
15	Mississippi	8-1-0	Johnny Vaught	same
16	Minnesota	7-2-0	Bernie Bierman	same
17	William & Mary	6-2-2	Rube McCray	7-2-2
18	Penn St.	7-1-1	Bob Higgins	same
19	Cornell	8-1-0	Lefty James	same
20	Wake Forest	6-3-0	Peahead Walker	6-4-0

Note: Big Nine "no-repeat" rule kept Michigan from Rose Bowl.

Key Bowl Games

Sugar–#5 Oklahoma over #3 North Carolina, 14-6; **Rose**–#7 Northwestern over #4 Cal, 20-14; **Orange**–Texas over #8 Georgia, 41-28; **Cotton**–#10 SMU over #9 Oregon, 21-13.

1949

Final poll released Nov. 28. Top 20 regular season results after that: **Dec. 2**–#14 Maryland over Miami-FL, 13-0. **Dec. 3**–#1 Notre Dame over SMU, 27-20; #10 Pacific over Hawaii, 75-0.

	As of Nov. 28		Head Coach	After Bowls
1	Notre Dame	9-0-0	Frank Leahy	10-0-0
2	Oklahoma	10-0-0	Bud Wilkinson	11-0-0
3	California	10-0-0	Pappy Waldorf	10-1-0
4	Army	9-0-0	Red Blaik	same
5	Rice	9-1-0	Jess Neely	10-1-0
6	Ohio St.	6-1-2	Wes Fesler	7-1-2
7	Michigan	6-2-1	Bennie Oosterbaan	same
8	Minnesota	7-2-0	Bernie Bierman	same
9	LSU	8-2-0	Gaynell Tinsley	8-3-0
10	Pacific	10-0-0	Larry Siemering	11-0-0
11	Kentucky	9-2-0	Bear Bryant	9-3-0
12	Cornell	8-1-0	Lefty James	same
13	Villanova	8-1-0	Jim Leonard	same
14	Maryland	7-1-0	Jim Tatum	9-1-0
15	Santa Clara	7-2-1	Len Casanova	8-2-1
16	North Carolina	7-3-0	Carl Snavely	7-4-0
17	Tennessee	7-2-1	Bob Neyland	same
18	Princeton	6-3-0	Charlie Caldwell	same
19	Michigan St.	6-3-0	Biggie Munn	same
20	Missouri	7-3-0	Don Faurot	7-4-0
	Baylor	8-2-0	Bob Woodruff	same

Key Bowl Games

Sugar–#2 Oklahoma over #9 LSU, 35-0; **Rose**–#6 Ohio St. over #3 Cal, 17-14; **Cotton**–#5 Rice over #16 North Carolina, 27-13; **Orange**–#15 Santa Clara over #11 Kentucky, 21-13.

1950

Final poll released Nov. 27. Top 20 regular season results after that: **Nov. 30**–#3 Texas over Texas A&M, 17-0. **Dec. 1**–#15 Miami-FL over Missouri, 27–9. **Dec. 2**–#1 Oklahoma over Okla. A&M, 41-14; Navy over #2 Army, 14-2; #4 Tennessee over Vanderbilt, 43-0; #16 Alabama over Auburn, 34-0; #19 Tulsa over Houston, 28-21; #20 Tulane tied LSU, 14-14. **Dec. 9**–#3 Texas over LSU, 21-6.

	As of Nov. 27		Head Coach	After Bowls
1	Oklahoma	9-0-0	Bud Wilkinson	10-1-0
2	Army	8-0-0	Red Blaik	8-1-0
3	Texas	7-1-0	Blair Cherry	9-2-0
4	Tennessee	9-1-0	Bob Neyland	11-1-0
5	California	9-0-1	Pappy Waldorf	9-1-1
6	Princeton	9-0-0	Charlie Caldwell	same
7	Kentucky	10-1-0	Bear Bryant	11-1-0
8	Michigan St.	8-1-0	Biggie Munn	same
9	Michigan	5-3-1	Bennie Oosterbaan	6-3-1
10	Clemson	8-0-1	Frank Howard	9-0-1
11	Washington	8-2-0	Howard Odell	same
12	Wyoming	9-0-0	Bowden Wyatt	10-0-0
13	Illinois	7-2-0	Ray Eliot	same
14	Ohio St.	6-3-0	Wes Fesler	same
15	Miami-FL	8-0-1	Andy Gustafson	9-1-1
16	Alabama	8-2-0	Red Drew	9-2-0
17	Nebraska	6-2-1	Bill Glassford	same
18	Wash. & Lee	8-2-0	George Barclay	8-3-0
19	Tulsa	8-1-1	J.O. Brothers	9-1-1
20	Tulane	6-2-0	Henry Frnka	6-2-1

Key Bowl Games

Sugar–#7 Kentucky over #1 Oklahoma, 13-7; **Cotton**–#4 Tennessee over #3 Texas, 20-14; **Rose**–#9 Michigan over #5 Cal, 14-6; **Orange**–#10 Clemson over #15 Miami-FL, 15-14.

1951

Final poll released Dec. 3. Top 20 regular season results after that: None.

	As of Dec. 3		Head Coach	After Bowls
1	Tennessee	10-0-0	Bob Neyland	10-1-0
2	Michigan St.	9-0-0	Biggie Munn	same
3	Maryland	9-0-0	Jim Tatum	10-0-0
4	Illinois	8-0-1	Ray Eliot	9-0-1
5	Georgia Tech	10-0-1	Bobby Dodd	11-0-1
6	Princeton	9-0-0	Charlie Caldwell	same
7	Stanford	9-1-0	Chuck Taylor	9-2-0
8	Wisconsin	7-1-1	Ivy Williamson	same
9	Baylor	8-1-1	George Sauer	8-2-1
10	Oklahoma	8-2-0	Bud Wilkinson	same
11	TCU	6-4-0	Dutch Meyer	6-5-0
12	California	8-2-0	Pappy Waldorf	same
13	Virginia	8-1-0	Art Guepe	same
14	San Francisco	9-0-0	Joe Kuharich	same
15	Kentucky	7-4-0	Bear Bryant	8-4-0
16	Boston Univ.	6-4-0	Buff Donelli	same
17	UCLA	5-3-1	Red Sanders	same
18	Washington St.	7-3-0	Forest Evashevski	same
19	Holy Cross	8-2-0	Eddie Anderson	same
	Clemson	7-2-0	Frank Howard	7-3-0

Key Bowl Games

Sugar–#3 Maryland over #1 Tennessee, 28-13; **Rose**– #4 Illinois over #7 Stanford, 40-7; **Orange**–#5 Georgia Tech over #9 Baylor, 17-14; **Cotton**–#15 Kentucky over #11 TCU, 20-7.

Associated Press Final Polls (Cont.)

1952

Final poll released Dec. 1. Top 20 regular season results after that: **Dec. 6**–#15 Florida over #20 Kentucky, 27-20.

	As of Dec. 1	Head Coach	After Bowls
1	Michigan St. 9-0-0	Biggie Munn	same
2	Georgia Tech ...11-0-0	Bobby Dodd	12-0-0
3	Notre Dame......7-2-1	Frank Leahy	same
4	Oklahoma 8-1-1	Bud Wilkinson	same
5	USC 9-1-0	Jess Hill	10-1-0
6	UCLA 8-1-0	Red Sanders	same
7	Mississippi 8-0-2	Johnny Vaught	8-1-2
8	Tennessee........8-1-1	Bob Neyland	8-2-1
9	Alabama 9-2-0	Red Drew	10-2-0
10	Texas............8-2-0	Ed Price	9-2-0
11	Wisconsin 6-2-1	Ivy Williamson	6-3-1
12	Tulsa 8-1-1	J.O. Brothers	8-2-1
13	Maryland........7-2-0	Jim Tatum	same
14	Syracuse.........7-2-0	Ben Schwartzwalder	7-3-0
15	Florida 6-3-0	Bob Woodruff	8-3-0
16	Duke 8-2-0	Bill Murray	same
17	Ohio St. 6-3-0	Woody Hayes	same
18	Purdue 4-3-2	Stu Holcomb	same
19	Princeton 8-1-0	Charlie Caldwell	same
20	Kentucky.........5-3-2	Bear Bryant	5-4-2

Note: Michigan St. would officially join Big Ten in 1953.

Key Bowl Games

Sugar–#2 Georgia Tech over #7 Ole Miss, 24-7; **Rose**–#5 USC over #11 Wisconsin, 7-0; **Cotton**–#10 Texas over #8 Tennessee, 16-0; **Orange**–#9 Alabama over #14 Syracuse, 61-6.

1953

Final poll released Nov. 30. Top 20 regular season results after that: **Dec. 5**–#2 Notre Dame over SMU, 40-14.

	As of Nov. 30	Head Coach	After Bowls
1	Maryland.......10-0-0	Jim Tatum	10-1-0
2	Notre Dame......8-0-1	Frank Leahy	9-0-1
3	Michigan St. 8-1-0	Biggie Munn	9-1-0
4	Oklahoma 8-1-1	Bud Wilkinson	9-1-1
5	UCLA 8-1-0	Red Sanders	8-2-0
6	Rice.............8-2-0	Jess Neely	9-2-0
7	Illinois 7-1-1	Ray Eliot	same
8	Georgia Tech.....8-2-1	Bobby Dodd	9-2-1
9	Iowa 5-3-1	Forest Evashevski	same
10	West Virginia.....8-1-0	Art Lewis	8-2-0
11	Texas............7-3-0	Ed Price	same
12	Texas Tech 10-1-0	DeWitt Weaver	11-1-0
13	Alabama 6-2-3	Red Drew	6-3-3
14	Army............7-1-1	Red Blaik	same
15	Wisconsin 6-2-1	Ivy Williamson	same
16	Kentucky.........7-2-1	Bear Bryant	same
17	Auburn 7-2-1	Shug Jordan	7-3-1
18	Duke 7-2-1	Bill Murray	same
19	Stanford 6-3-1	Chuck Taylor	same
20	Michigan 6-3-0	Bennie Oosterbaan	same

Key Bowl Games

Orange–#4 Oklahoma over #1 Maryland, 7-0; **Rose**–#3 Michigan St. over #5 UCLA, 28-20; **Cotton**–#6 Rice over #13 Alabama, 28-6; **Sugar**–#8 Georgia Tech over #10 West Virginia, 42-19.

1954

Final poll released Nov. 29. Top 20 regular season results after that: **Dec. 4**–#4 Notre Dame over SMU, 26-14.

	As of Nov. 29	Head Coach	After Bowls
1	Ohio St. 9-0-0	Woody Hayes	10-0-0
2	UCLA 9-0-0	Red Sanders	same
3	Oklahoma 10-0-0	Bud Wilkinson	same
4	Notre Dame......8-1-0	Terry Brennan	9-1-0
5	Navy............7-2-0	Eddie Erdelatz	8-2-0
6	Mississippi 9-1-0	Johnny Vaught	9-2-0
7	Army............7-2-0	Red Blaik	same
8	Maryland........7-2-1	Jim Tatum	same
9	Wisconsin 7-2-0	Ivy Williamson	same
10	Arkansas 8-2-0	Bowden Wyatt	8-3-0
11	Miami-FL.........8-1-0	Andy Gustafson	same
12	West Virginia.....8-1-0	Art Lewis	same
13	Auburn 7-3-0	Shug Jordan	8-3-0
14	Duke 7-2-1	Bill Murray	8-2-1
15	Michigan 6-3-0	Bennie Oosterbaan	same
16	Virginia Tech 8-0-1	Frank Moseley	same
17	USC 8-3-0	Jess Hill	8-4-0
18	Baylor...........7-3-0	George Sauer	7-4-0
19	Rice.............7-3-0	Jess Neely	same
20	Penn St. 7-2-0	Rip Engle	same

Note: PCC and Big Seven "no-repeat" rules kept UCLA and Oklahoma from Rose and Orange bowls, respectively.

Key Bowl Games

Rose–#1 Ohio St. over #17 USC, 20-7; **Sugar**–#5 Navy over #6 Ole Miss, 21-0; **Cotton**–Georgia Tech over #10 Arkansas, 14-6; **Orange**–#14 Duke over Nebraska, 34-7.

1955

Final poll released Nov. 28. Top 20 regular season results after that: None.

	As of Nov. 28	Head Coach	After Bowls
1	Oklahoma 10-0-0	Bud Wilkinson	11-0-0
2	Michigan St. 8-1-0	Duffy Daugherty	9-1-0
3	Maryland.......10-0-0	Jim Tatum	10-1-0
4	UCLA 9-1-0	Red Sanders	9-2-0
5	Ohio St. 7-2-0	Woody Hayes	same
6	TCU.............9-1-0	Abe Martin	9-2-0
7	Georgia Tech.....8-1-1	Bobby Dodd	9-1-1
8	Auburn 8-1-1	Shug Jordan	8-2-1
9	Notre Dame......8-2-0	Terry Brennan	same
10	Mississippi 9-1-0	Johnny Vaught	10-1-0
11	Pittsburgh 7-3-0	John Michelosen	7-4-0
12	Michigan 7-2-0	Bennie Oosterbaan	same
13	USC 6-4-0	Jess Hill	same
14	Miami-FL.........6-3-0	Andy Gustafson	same
15	Miami-OH 9-0-0	Ara Parseghian	same
16	Stanford 6-3-1	Chuck Taylor	same
17	Texas A&M 7-2-1	Bear Bryant	same
18	Navy............6-2-1	Eddie Erdelatz	same
19	West Virginia.....8-2-0	Art Lewis	same
20	Army............6-3-0	Red Blaik	same

Note: Big Ten "no-repeat" rule kept Ohio St. from Rose Bowl.

Key Bowl Games

Orange–#1 Oklahoma over #3 Maryland, 20-6; **Rose**–#2 Michigan St. over #4 UCLA, 17-14; **Cotton**–#10 Ole Miss over #6 TCU, 14-13; **Sugar**–#7 Georgia Tech over #11 Pitt, 7-0; **Gator**–Vanderbilt over #8 Auburn, 25-13.

1956

Final poll released Dec. 3. Top 20 regular season results after that: **Dec. 8**–#13 Pitt over #6 Miami-FL, 14-7.

		As of Dec. 3	Head Coach	After Bowls
1	Oklahoma	10-0-0	Bud Wilkinson	same
2	Tennessee	10-0-0	Bowden Wyatt	10-1-0
3	Iowa	8-1-0	Forest Evashevski	9-1-0
4	Georgia Tech	9-1-0	Bobby Dodd	10-1-0
5	Texas A&M	9-0-1	Bear Bryant	same
6	Miami-FL	8-0-1	Andy Gustafson	8-1-1
7	Michigan	7-2-0	Bennie Oosterbaan	same
8	Syracuse	7-1-0	Ben Schwartzwalder	7-2-0
9	Michigan St.	7-2-0	Duffy Daugherty	same
10	Oregon St.	7-2-1	Tommy Prothro	7-3-1
11	Baylor	8-2-0	Sam Boyd	9-2-0
12	Minnesota	6-1-2	Murray Warmath	same
13	Pittsburgh	6-2-1	John Michelosen	7-3-1
14	TCU	7-3-0	Abe Martin	8-3-0
15	Ohio St.	6-3-0	Woody Hayes	same
16	Navy	6-1-2	Eddie Erdelatz	same
17	G. Washington	7-1-1	Gene Sherman	8-1-1
18	USC	8-2-0	Jess Hill	same
19	Clemson	7-1-2	Frank Howard	7-2-2
20	Colorado	7-2-1	Dallas Ward	8-2-1

Note: Big Seven "no-repeat" rule kept Oklahoma from Orange Bowl and Texas A&M was on probation.

Key Bowl Games

Sugar–#11 Baylor over #2 Tennessee, 13-7; **Rose**– #3 Iowa over #10 Oregon St., 35-19; **Gator**–#4 Georgia Tech over #13 Pitt, 21-14; **Cotton**–#14 TCU over #8 Syracuse, 28-27; **Orange**–#20 Colorado over #19 Clemson, 27-21.

1957

Final poll released Dec. 2. Top 20 regular season results after that: **Dec. 7**–#10 Notre Dame over SMU, 54-21.

		As of Dec. 2	Head Coach	After Bowls
1	Auburn	10-0-0	Shug Jordan	same
2	Ohio St.	8-1-0	Woody Hayes	9-1-0
3	Michigan St.	8-1-0	Duffy Daugherty	same
4	Oklahoma	9-1-0	Bud Wilkinson	10-1-0
5	Navy	8-1-1	Eddie Erdelatz	9-1-1
6	Iowa	7-1-1	Forest Evashevski	same
7	Mississippi	8-1-1	Johnny Vaught	9-1-1
8	Rice	7-3-0	Jess Neely	7-4-0
9	Texas A&M	8-2-0	Bear Bryant	8-3-0
10	Notre Dame	6-3-0	Terry Brennan	7-3-0
11	Texas	6-3-1	Darrell Royal	6-4-1
12	Arizona St.	10-0-0	Dan Devine	same
13	Tennessee	7-3-0	Bowden Wyatt	8-3-0
14	Mississippi St.	6-2-1	Wade Walker	same
15	N.C. State	7-1-2	Earle Edwards	same
16	Duke	6-2-2	Bill Murray	6-3-2
17	Florida	6-2-1	Bob Woodruff	same
18	Army	7-2-0	Red Blaik	same
19	Wisconsin	6-3-0	Milt Bruhn	same
20	VMI	9-0-1	John McKenna	same

Note: Auburn on probation, ineligible for bowl game.

Key Bowl Games

Rose–#2 Ohio St. over Oregon, 10-7; **Orange**–#4 Oklahoma over #16 Duke, 48-21; **Cotton**–#5 Navy over #8 Rice, 20-7; **Sugar**–#7 Ole Miss over #11 Texas, 39-7; **Gator**–#13 Tennessee over #9 Texas A&M, 3-0.

1958

Final poll released Dec. 1. Top 20 regular season results after that: None.

		As of Dec. 1	Head Coach	After Bowls
1	LSU	10-0-0	Paul Dietzel	11-0-0
2	Iowa	7-1-1	Forest Evashevski	8-1-1
3	Army	8-0-1 •	Red Blaik	same
4	Auburn	9-0-1	Shug Jordan	same
5	Oklahoma	9-1-0	Bud Wilkinson	10-1-0
6	Air Force	9-0-1	Ben Martin	9-0-2
7	Wisconsin	7-1-1	Milt Bruhn	same
8	Ohio St.	6-1-2	Woody Hayes	same
9	Syracuse	8-1-0	Ben Schwartzwalder	8-2-0
10	TCU	8-2-0	Abe Martin	8-2-1
11	Mississippi	8-2-0	Johnny Vaught	9-2-0
12	Clemson	8-2-0	Frank Howard	8-3-0
13	Purdue	6-1-2	Jack Mollenkopf	same
14	Florida	6-3-1	Bob Woodruff	6-4-1
15	South Carolina	7-3-0	Warren Giese	same
16	California	7-3-0	Pete Elliott	7-4-0
17	Notre Dame	6-4-0	Terry Brennan	same
18	SMU	6-4-0	Bill Meek	same
19	Oklahoma St.	7-3-0	Cliff Speegle	8-3-0
20	Rutgers	8-1-0	John Stiegman	same

Key Bowl Games

Sugar–#1 LSU over #12 Clemson, 7-0; **Rose**–#2 Iowa over #16 Cal, 38-12; **Orange**–#5 Oklahoma over #9 Syracuse, 21-6; **Cotton**–#6 Air Force tied #10 TCU, 0-0.

1959

Final poll released Dec. 7. Top 20 regular season results after that: None.

		As of Dec. 7	Head Coach	After Bowls
1	Syracuse	10-0-0	Ben Schwartzwalder	11-0-0
2	Mississippi	9-1-0	Johnny Vaught	10-1-0
3	LSU	9-1-0	Paul Dietzel	9-2-0
4	Texas	9-1-0	Darrell Royal	9-2-0
5	Georgia	9-1-0	Wally Butts	10-1-0
6	Wisconsin	7-2-0	Milt Bruhn	7-3-0
7	TCU	8-2-0	Abe Martin	8-3-0
8	Washington	9-1-0	Jim Owens	10-1-0
9	Arkansas	8-2-0	Frank Broyles	9-2-0
10	Alabama	7-1-2	Bear Bryant	7-2-2
11	Clemson	8-2-0	Frank Howard	9-2-0
12	PennSt.	8-2-0	Rip Engle	9-2-0
13	Illinois	5-3-1	Ray Eliot	same
14	USC	8-2-0	Don Clark	same
15	Oklahoma	7-3-0	Bud Wilkinson	same
16	Wyoming	9-1-0	Bob Devaney	same
17	Notre Dame	5-5-0	Joe Kuharich	same
18	Missouri	6-4-0	Dan Devine	6-5-0
19	Florida	5-4-1	Bob Woodruff	same
20	Pittsburgh	6-4-0	John Michelosen	same

Note: Big Seven "no-repeat" rule kept Oklahoma from Orange Bowl.

Key Bowl Games

Cotton–#1 Syracuse over #4 Texas, 23-14; **Sugar**– #2 Ole Miss over #3 LSU, 21-0; **Orange**–#5 Georgia over #18 Missouri, 14-0; **Rose**–#8 Washington over #6 Wisconsin, 44-8; **Bluebonnet**–#11 Clemson over #7 TCU, 23-7; **Gator**–#9 Arkansas over Georgia Tech, 14-7; **Liberty**–#12 Penn St. over #10 Alabama, 7-0.

The Special Election That Didn't Count

There was one No. 1 vs No. 2 confrontation not noted in the Number 1 vs. Number 2 table on pages 164-5. It came in a special election or re-vote of AP selectors following the 1948 Rose Bowl. Here's what happened: Unbeaten Notre Dame was declared 1947 national champion by AP on Dec. 8, two days after closing out an undefeated season with a 38-7 rout of then third-ranked USC in Los Angeles. Twenty-four days later, however, unbeaten Michigan, AP's final No. 2 team, clobbered now 8th-ranked USC, 49-0, in the Rose Bowl. An immediate cry went up for an unprecedented two-team, "Who's No. 1" ballot and AP gave in. Michigan won the election, 226-119, with 12 voters calling it even. However, AP ruled that the Dec. 8 final poll won by Notre Dame would be the vote of record.

Associated Press Final Polls (Cont.)

1960

Final poll released Nov. 28. Top 20 regular season results after that: **Dec. 3**–UCLA over #10 Duke, 27-6.

		As of Nov. 28	Head Coach	After Bowls
1	Minnesota	8-1-0	Murray Warmath	8-2-0
2	Mississippi	9-0-1	Johnny Vaught	10-0-1
3	Iowa	8-1-0	Forest Evashevski	same
4	Navy	9-1-0	Wayne Hardin	9-2-0
5	Missouri	9-1-0	Dan Devine	10-1-0
6	Washington	9-1-0	Jim Owens	10-1-0
7	Arkansas	8-2-0	Frank Broyles	8-3-0
8	Ohio St.	7-2-0	Woody Hayes	same
9	Alabama	8-1-1	Bear Bryant	8-1-2
10	Duke	7-2-0	Bill Murray	8-3-0
11	Kansas	7-2-1	Jack Mitchell	same
12	Baylor	8-2-0	John Bridgers	8-3-0
13	Auburn	8-2-0	Shug Jordan	same
14	Yale	9-0-0	Jordan Olivar	same
15	Michigan St.	6-2-1	Duffy Daugherty	same
16	Penn St.	6-3-0	Rip Engle	7-3-0
17	New Mexico St.	10-0-0	Warren Woodson	11-0-0
18	Florida	8-2-0	Ray Graves	9-2-0
19	Syracuse	7-2-0	Ben Schwartzwalder	same
	Purdue	4-4-1	Jack Mollenkopf	same

Key Bowl Games

Rose–#6 Washington over #1 Minnesota, 17-7; **Sugar**–#2 Ole Miss over Rice, 14-6; **Orange**–#5 Missouri over #4 Navy, 21-14; **Cotton**–#10 Duke over #7 Arkansas, 7-6; **Bluebonnet**–#9 Alabama tied Texas, 3-3.

1961

Final poll released Dec. 4. Top 20 regular season results after that: None.

		As of Dec. 4	Head Coach	After Bowls
1	Alabama	10-0-0	Bear Bryant	11-0-0
2	Ohio St.	8-0-1	Woody Hayes	same
3	Texas	9-1-0	Darrell Royal	10-1-0
4	LSU	9-1-0	Paul Dietzel	10-1-0
5	Mississippi	9-1-0	Johnny Vaught	9-2-0
6	Minnesota	7-2-0	Murray Warmath	8-2-0
7	Colorado	9-1-0	Sonny Grandelius	9-2-0
8	Michigan St.	7-2-0	Duffy Daugherty	same
9	Arkansas	8-2-0	Frank Broyles	8-3-0
10	Utah St.	9-0-1	John Ralston	9-1-1
11	Missouri	7-2-1	Dan Devine	same
12	Purdue	6-3-0	Jack Mollenkopf	same
13	Georgia Tech	7-3-0	Bobby Dodd	7-4-0
14	Syracuse	7-3-0	Ben Schwartzwalder	8-3-0
15	Rutgers	9-0-0	John Bateman	same
16	UCLA	7-3-0	Bill Barnes	7-4-0
17	Rice	7-3-0	Jess Neely	7-4-0
	Penn St.	7-3-0	Rip Engle	8-3-0
	Arizona	8-1-1	Jim LaRue	same
20	Duke	7-3-0	Bill Murray	same

Note: Ohio St. faculty council turned down Rose Bowl invitation citing concern with OSU's overemphasis on sports.

Key Bowl Games

Sugar–#1 Alabama over #9 Arkansas, 10-3; **Cotton**–#3 Texas over #5 Ole Miss, 12-7; **Orange**–#4 LSU over #7 Colorado, 25-7; **Rose**–#6 Minnesota over #16 UCLA, 21-3; **Gotham**–Baylor over #10 Utah St., 24-9.

1962

Final poll released Dec. 3. Top 10 regular season results after that: None.

		As of Dec. 3	Head Coach	After Bowls
1	USC	10-0-0	John McKay	11-0-0
2	Wisconsin	8-1-0	Milt Bruhn	8-2-0
3	Mississippi	9-0-0	Johnny Vaught	10-0-0
4	Texas	9-0-1	Darrell Royal	9-1-1
5	Alabama	9-1-0	Bear Bryant	10-1-0
6	Arkansas	9-1-0	Frank Broyles	9-2-0
7	LSU	8-1-1	Charlie McClendon	9-1-1
8	Oklahoma	8-2-0	Bud Wilkinson	8-3-0
9	Penn St.	9-1-0	Rip Engle	9-2-0
10	Minnesota	6-2-1	Murray Warmath	same

Key Bowl Games

Rose–#1 USC over #2 Wisconsin, 42-37; **Sugar**–#3 Ole Miss over #6 Arkansas, 17-13; **Cotton**–#7 LSU over #4 Texas, 13-0; **Orange**–#5 Alabama over #8 Oklahoma, 17-0; **Gator**–Florida over #9 Penn St.,17-7.

1963

Final poll released Dec. 9. Top 10 regular season results after that: **Dec.14**–#8 Alabama over Miami-FL, 17-12.

		As of Dec. 9	Head Coach	After Bowls
1	Texas	10-0-0	Darrell Royal	11-0-0
2	Navy	9-1-0	Wayne Hardin	9-2-0
3	Illinois	7-1-1	Pete Elliott	8-1-1
4	Pittsburgh	9-1-0	John Michelosen	same
5	Auburn	9-1-0	Shug Jordan	9-2-0
6	Nebraska	9-1-0	Bob Devaney	10-1-0
7	Mississippi	7-0-2	Johnny Vaught	7-1-2
8	Alabama	7-2-0	Bear Bryant	9-2-0
9	Michigan St.	6-2-1	Duffy Daugherty	same
10	Oklahoma	8-2-0	Bud Wilkinson	same

Key Bowl Games

Cotton–#1 Texas over #2 Navy, 28-6; **Rose**–#3 Illinois over Washington, 17-7; **Orange**–#6 Nebraska over #5 Auburn, 13-7; **Sugar**–#8 Alabama over #7 Ole Miss, 12-7.

1964

Final poll released Nov. 30. Top 10 regular season results after that: **Dec. 5**–Florida over #7 LSU, 20-6.

		As of Nov. 30	Head Coach	After Bowls
1	Alabama	10-0-0	Bear Bryant	10-1-0
2	Arkansas	10-0-0	Frank Broyles	11-0-0
3	Notre Dame	9-1-0	Ara Parseghian	same
4	Michigan	8-1-0	Bump Elliott	9-1-0
5	Texas	9-1-0	Darrell Royal	10-1-0
6	Nebraska	9-1-0	Bob Devaney	9-2-0
7	LSU	7-1-1	Charlie McClendon	8-2-1
8	Oregon St.	8-2-0	Tommy Prothro	8-3-0
9	Ohio St.	7-2-0	Woody Hayes	same
10	USC	7-3-0	John McKay	same

Key Bowl Games

Orange–#5 Texas over #1 Alabama, 21-17; **Cotton**–#2 Arkansas over #6 Nebraska, 10-7; **Rose**– #4 Michigan over #8 Oregon St., 34-7; **Sugar**–#7 LSU over Syracuse, 13-10.

1965

Final poll taken after bowl games for the first time.

	After Bowls	Head Coach	Regular Season
1 Alabama	9-1-1	Bear Bryant	8-1-1
2 Michigan St.	10-1-0	Duffy Daugherty	10-0-0
3 Arkansas	10-1-0	Frank Broyles	10-0-0
4 UCLA	8-2-1	Tommy Prothro	7-1-1
5 Nebraska	10-1-0	Bob Devaney	10-0-0
6 Missouri	8-2-1	Dan Devine	7-2-1
7 Tennessee	8-1-2	Doug Dickey	6-1-2
8 LSU	8-3-0	Charlie McClendon	7-3-0
9 Notre Dame	7-2-1	Ara Parseghian	same
10 USC	7-2-1	John McKay	same

Key Bowl Games

Rankings below reflect final regular season poll, released Nov. 29. No bowls for then #8 USC or #9 Notre Dame. **Rose**–#5 UCLA over #1 Michigan St., 14-12; **Cotton**–LSU over #2 Arkansas, 14-7; **Orange**–#4 Alabama over #3 Nebraska, 39-28; **Sugar**–#6 Missouri over Florida, 20-18; **Bluebonnet**–#7 Tennessee over Tulsa, 27-6; **Gator**–Georgia Tech over #10 Texas Tech, 31-21.

1966

Final poll released Dec. 5, returning to pre-bowl status. Top 10 regular season results after that: None.

	As of Dec. 5	Head Coach	After Bowls
1 Notre Dame	9-0-1	Ara Parseghian	same
2 Michigan St.	9-0-1	Duffy Daugherty	same
3 Alabama	10-0-0	Bear Bryant	11-0-0
4 Georgia	9-1-0	Vince Dooley	10-1-0
5 UCLA	9-1-0	Tommy Prothro	same
6 Nebraska	9-1-0	Bob Devaney	9-2-0
7 Purdue	8-2-0	Jack Mollenkopf	9-2-0
8 Georgia Tech	9-1-0	Bobby Dodd	9-2-0
9 Miami-FL	7-2-1	Charlie Tate	8-2-1
10 SMU	8-2-0	Hayden Fry	8-3-0

Key Bowl Games

Sugar–#3 Alabama over #6 Nebraska, 34-7; **Cotton**–#4 Georgia over #10 SMU, 24-9; **Rose**–#7 Purdue over USC, 14-13; **Orange**–Florida over #8 Georgia Tech, 27-12; **Liberty**–#9 Miami-FL over Virginia Tech, 14-7.

1967

Final poll released Nov. 27. Top 10 regular season results after that: **Dec. 2**–#2 Tennessee over Vanderbilt, 41-14; #3 Oklahoma over Oklahoma St., 38-14; #8 Alabama over Auburn, 7-3.

	As of Nov. 27	Head Coach	After Bowls
1 USC	9-1-0	John McKay	10-1-0
2 Tennessee	8-1-0	Doug Dickey	9-2-0
3 Oklahoma	8-1-0	Chuck Fairbanks	10-1-0
4 Indiana	9-1-0	John Pont	9-2-0
5 Notre Dame	8-2-0	Ara Parseghian	same
6 Wyoming	10-0-0	Lloyd Eaton	10-1-0
7 Oregon St.	7-2-1	Dee Andros	same
8 Alabama	7-1-1	Bear Bryant	8-2-1
9 Purdue	8-2-0	Jack Mollenkopf	same
10 Penn St.	8-2-0	Joe Paterno	8-2-1

Key Bowl Games

Rose–#1 USC over #4 Indiana, 14-3; **Orange**–#3 Oklahoma over #2 Tennessee, 26-24; **Sugar**–LSU over #6 Wyoming, 20-13; **Cotton**–Texas A&M over #8 Alabama, 20-16; **Gator**–#10 Penn St. tied Florida St. 17-17.

1968

Final poll taken after bowl games for first time since close of 1965 season.

	After Bowls	Head Coach	Regular Season
1 Ohio St.	10-0-0	Woody Hayes	9-0-0
2 Penn St.	11-0-0	Joe Paterno	10-0-0
3 Texas	9-1-1	Darrell Royal	8-1-1
4 USC	9-1-1	John McKay	9-0-1
5 Notre Dame	7-2-1	Ara Parseghian	same
6 Arkansas	10-1-0	Frank Broyles	9-1-0
7 Kansas	9-2-0	Pepper Rodgers	9-1-0
8 Georgia	8-1-2	Vince Dooley	8-0-2
9 Missouri	8-3-0	Dan Devine	7-3-0
10 Purdue	8-2-0	Jack Mollenkopf	same
11 Oklahoma	7-4-0	Chuck Fairbanks	7-3-0
12 Michigan	8-2-0	Bump Elliott	same
13 Tennessee	8-2-1	Doug Dickey	8-1-1
14 SMU	8-3-0	Hayden Fry	7-3-0
15 Oregon St.	7-3-0	Dee Andros	same
16 Auburn	7-4-0	Shug Jordan	6-4-0
17 Alabama	8-3-0	Bear Bryant	8-2-0
18 Houston	6-2-2	Bill Yeoman	same
19 LSU	8-3-0	Charlie McClendon	7-3-0
20 Ohio Univ.	10-1-0	Bill Hess	10-0-0

Key Bowl Games

Rankings below reflect final regular season poll, released Dec. 2. No bowls for then #7 Notre Dame and #11 Purdue. **Rose**–#1 Ohio St. over #2 USC, 27-16; **Orange**–#3 Penn St. over #6 Kansas, 15-14; **Sugar**–#9 Arkansas over #4 Georgia, 16-2; **Cotton**–#5 Texas over #8 Tennessee, 36-13; **Bluebonnet**–#20 SMU over #10 Oklahoma, 28-27; **Gator**–#16 Missouri over #12 Alabama, 35-10.

1969

Final poll taken after bowl games.

	After Bowls	Head Coach	Regular Season
1 Texas	11-0-0	Darrell Royal	10-0-0
2 Penn St.	11-0-0	Joe Paterno	10-0-0
3 USC	10-0-1	John McKay	9-0-1
4 Ohio St.	8-1-0	Woody Hayes	same
5 Notre Dame	8-2-1	Ara Parseghian	8-1-1
6 Missouri	9-2-0	Dan Devine	9-1-0
7 Arkansas	9-2-0	Frank Broyles	9-1-0
8 Mississippi	8-3-0	Johnny Vaught	7-3-0
9 Michigan	8-3-0	Bo Schembechler	8-2-0
10 LSU	9-1-0	Charlie McClendon	same
11 Nebraska	9-2-0	Bob Devaney	8-2-0
12 Houston	9-2-0	Bill Yeoman	8-2-0
13 UCLA	8-1-1	Tommy Prothro	same
14 Florida	9-1-1	Ray Graves	8-1-1
15 Tennessee	9-2-0	Doug Dickey	9-1-0
16 Colorado	8-3-0	Eddie Crowder	7-3-0
17 West Virginia	10-1-0	Jim Carlen	9-1-0
18 Purdue	8-2-0	Jack Mollenkopf	same
19 Stanford	7-2-1	John Ralston	same
20 Auburn	8-3-0	Shug Jordan	8-2-0

Key Bowl Games

Rankings below reflect final regular season poll, released Dec. 8. No bowls for then #4 Ohio St., #8 LSU and #10 UCLA.

Cotton–#1 Texas over #9 Notre Dame, 21-17; **Orange**–#2 Penn St. over #6 Missouri, 10-3; **Sugar**–#13 Ole Miss over #3 Arkansas, 27-22; **Rose**–#5 USC over #7 Michigan, 10-3.

Associated Press Final Polls (Cont.)

1970

		After Bowls	Head Coach	Regular Season
1	Nebraska	11-0-1	Bob Devaney	10-0-1
2	Notre Dame	10-1-0	Ara Parseghian	9-0-1
3	Texas	10-1-0	Darrell Royal	10-0-0
4	Tennessee	11-1-0	Bill Battle	10-1-0
5	Ohio St.	9-1-0	Woody Hayes	9-0-0
6	Arizona St.	11-0-0	Frank Kush	10-0-0
7	LSU	9-3-0	Charlie McClendon	9-2-0
8	Stanford	9-3-0	John Ralston	8-3-0
9	Michigan	9-1-0	Bo Schembechler	same
10	Auburn	9-2-0	Shug Jordan	8-2-0
11	Arkansas	9-2-0	Frank Broyles	same
12	Toledo	12-0-0	Frank Lauterbur	11-0-0
13	Georgia Tech	9-3-0	Bud Carson	8-3-0
14	Dartmouth	9-0-0	Bob Blackman	same
15	USC	6-4-1	John McKay	same
16	Air Force	9-3-0	Ben Martin	9-2-0
17	Tulane	8-4-0	Jim Pittman	7-4-0
18	Penn St.	7-3-0	Joe Paterno	same
19	Houston	8-3-0	Bill Yeoman	same
20	Oklahoma	7-4-1	Chuck Fairbanks	7-4-0
	Mississippi	7-4-0	Johnny Vaught	7-3-0

Key Bowl Games

Rankings below reflect final regular season poll, released Dec. 7. No bowls for then #4 Arkansas and #7 Michigan.

Cotton–#6 Notre Dame over #1 Texas, 24-11; **Rose**– #12 Stanford over #2 Ohio St., 27-17; **Orange**–#3 Nebraska over #8 LSU, 17-12; **Sugar**– #5 Tennessee over #11 Air Force, 34-13; **Peach**–#9 Ariz. St. over N. Carolina, 48-26.

1971

		After Bowls	Head Coach	Regular Season
1	Nebraska	13-0-0	Bob Devaney	12-0-0
2	Oklahoma	11-1-0	Chuck Fairbanks	10-1-0
3	Colorado	10-2-0	Eddie Crowder	9-2-0
4	Alabama	11-1-0	Bear Bryant	11-0-0
5	Penn St.	11-1-0	Joe Paterno	10-1-0
6	Michigan	11-1-0	Bo Schembechler	11-0-0
7	Georgia	11-1-0	Vince Dooley	10-1-0
8	Arizona St.	11-1-0	Frank Kush	10-1-0
9	Tennessee	10-2-0	Bill Battle	9-2-0
10	Stanford	9-3-0	John Ralston	8-3-0
11	LSU	9-3-0	Charlie McClendon	8-3-0
12	Auburn	9-2-0	Shug Jordan	9-1-0
13	Notre Dame	8-2-0	Ara Parseghian	same
14	Toledo	12-0-0	John Murphy	11-0-0
15	Mississippi	10-2-0	Billy Kinard	9-2-0
16	Arkansas	8-3-1	Frank Broyles	8-2-1
17	Houston	9-3-0	Bill Yeoman	9-2-0
18	Texas	8-3-0	Darrell Royal	8-2-0
19	Washington	8-3-0	Jim Owens	same
20	USC	6-4-1	John McKay	same

Key Bowl Games

Rankings below reflect final regular season poll, released Dec. 6.

Orange–#1 Nebraska over #2 Alabama, 38-6; **Sugar**–#3 Oklahoma over #5 Auburn, 40-22; **Rose**–#16 Stanford over #4 Michigan, 13-12; **Gator**–#6 Georgia over N. Carolina, 7-3; **Bluebonnet**–#7 Colorado over #15 Houston, 29-17; **Fiesta**–#8 Ariz. St. over Florida St., 45-38; **Cotton**–#10 Penn St. over #12 Texas, 30-6.

1972

		After Bowls	Head Coach	Regular Season
1	USC	12-0-0	John McKay	11-0-0
2	Oklahoma	11-1-0	Chuck Fairbanks	10-1-0
3	Texas	10-1-0	Darrell Royal	9-1-0
4	Nebraska	9-2-1	Bob Devaney	8-2-1
5	Auburn	10-1-0	Shug Jordan	9-1-0
6	Michigan	10-1-0	Bo Schembechler	same
7	Alabama	10-2-0	Bear Bryant	10-1-0
8	Tennessee	10-2-0	Bill Battle	9-2-0
9	Ohio St.	9-2-0	Woody Hayes	9-1-0
10	Penn St.	10-2-0	Joe Paterno	10-1-0
11	LSU	9-2-1	Charlie McClendon	9-1-1
12	North Carolina	11-1-0	Bill Dooley	10-1-0
13	Arizona St.	10-2-0	Frank Kush	9-2-0
14	Notre Dame	8-3-0	Ara Parseghian	8-2-0
15	UCLA	8-3-0	Pepper Rodgers	same
16	Colorado	8-4-0	Eddie Crowder	8-3-0
17	N.C. State	8-3-1	Lou Holtz	7-3-1
18	Louisville	9-1-0	Lee Corso	same
19	Washington St.	7-4-0	Jim Sweeney	same
20	Georgia Tech	7-4-1	Bill Fulcher	6-4-1

Key Bowl Games

Rankings below reflect final regular season poll, released Dec. 4. No bowl for then #8 Michigan.

Rose–#1 USC over #3 Ohio St., 42-17; **Sugar**–#2 Oklahoma over #5 Penn St., 14-0; **Cotton**–#7 Texas over #4 Alabama, 17-13; **Orange**–#9 Nebraska over #12 Notre Dame, 40-6; **Gator**–#6 Auburn over #13 Colorado, 24-3; **Bluebonnet**–#11 Tennessee over #10 LSU, 24-17.

1973

		After Bowls	Head Coach	Regular Season
1	Notre Dame	11-0-0	Ara Parseghian	10-0-0
2	Ohio St.	10-0-1	Woody Hayes	9-0-1
3	Oklahoma	10-0-1	Barry Switzer	same
4	Alabama	11-1-0	Bear Bryant	11-0-0
5	Penn St.	12-0-0	Joe Paterno	11-0-0
6	Michigan	10-0-1	Bo Schembechler	same
7	Nebraska	9-2-1	Tom Osborne	8-2-1
8	USC	9-2-1	John McKay	9-1-1
9	Arizona St.	11-1-0	Frank Kush	10-1-0
	Houston	11-1-0	Bill Yeoman	10-1-0
11	Texas Tech	11-1-0	Jim Carlen	10-1-0
12	UCLA	9-2-0	Pepper Rodgers	same
13	LSU	9-3-0	Charlie McClendon	9-2-0
14	Texas	8-3-0	Darrell Royal	8-2-0
15	Miami-OH	11-0-0	Bill Mallory	10-0-0
16	N.C. State	9-3-0	Lou Holtz	8-3-0
17	Missouri	8-4-0	Al Onofrio	7-4-0
18	Kansas	7-4-1	Don Fambrough	7-3-1
19	Tennessee	8-4-0	Bill Battle	8-3-0
20	Maryland	8-4-0	Jerry Claiborne	8-3-0
	Tulane	9-3-0	Bennie Ellender	9-2-0

Key Bowl Games

Rankings below reflect final regular season poll, released Dec. 3. No bowls for then #2 Oklahoma (probation), #5 Michigan and #9 UCLA.

Sugar–#3 Notre Dame over #1 Alabama, 24-23; **Rose**–#4 Ohio St. over #7 USC, 42-21; **Orange**–#6 Penn St. over #13 LSU, 16-9; **Cotton**–#12 Nebraska over #8 Texas, 19-3; **Fiesta**–#10 Ariz. St. over Pitt, 28-7; **Bluebonnet**–#14 Houston over #17 Tulane, 47-7.

1974

		After Bowls	Head Coach	Regular Season
1	Oklahoma	11-0-0	Barry Switzer	same
2	USC	10-1-1	John McKay	9-1-1
3	Michigan	10-1-0	Bo Schembechler	same
4	Ohio St.	10-2-0	Woody Hayes	10-1-0
5	Alabama	11-1-0	Bear Bryant	11-0-0
6	Notre Dame	10-2-0	Ara Parseghian	9-2-0
7	Penn St.	10-2-0	Joe Paterno	9-2-0
8	Auburn	10-2-0	Shug Jordan	9-2-0
9	Nebraska	9-3-0	Tom Osborne	8-3-0
10	Miami-OH	10-0-1	Dick Crum	9-0-1
11	N.C. State	9-2-1	Lou Holtz	9-2-0
12	Michigan St.	7-3-1	Denny Stolz	same
13	Maryland	8-4-0	Jerry Claiborne	8-3-0
14	Baylor	8-4-0	Grant Teaff	8-3-0
15	Florida	8-4-0	Doug Dickey	8-3-0
16	Texas A&M	8-3-0	Emory Ballard	same
17	Mississippi St.	9-3-0	Bob Tyler	8-3-0
	Texas	8-4-0	Darrell Royal	8-3-0
19	Houston	8-3-1	Bill Yeoman	8-3-0
20	Tennessee	7-3-2	Bill Battle	6-3-2

Key Bowl Games

Rankings below reflect final regular season poll, released Dec. 2. No bowls for #1 Oklahoma (probation) and then #4 Michigan.

Orange–#9 Notre Dame over #2 Alabama, 13-11; **Rose**–#5 USC over #3 Ohio St., 18-17; **Gator**–#6 Auburn over #11 Texas, 27-3; **Cotton**–#7 Penn St. over #12 Baylor, 41-20; **Sugar**–#8 Nebraska over #18 Florida, 13-10; **Liberty**–Tennessee over #10 Maryland, 7-3.

1975

		After Bowls	Head Coach	Regular Season
1	Oklahoma	11-1-0	Barry Switzer	10-1-0
2	Arizona St.	12-0-0	Frank Kush	11-0-0
3	Alabama	11-1-0	Bear Bryant	10-1-0
4	Ohio St.	11-1-0	Woody Hayes	11-0-0
5	UCLA	9-2-1	Dick Vermeil	8-2-1
6	Texas	10-2-0	Darrell Royal	9-2-0
7	Arkansas	10-2-0	Frank Broyles	9-2-0
8	Michigan	8-2-2	Bo Schembechler	8-1-2
9	Nebraska	10-2-0	Tom Osborne	10-1-0
10	Penn St.	9-3-0	Joe Paterno	9-2-0
11	Texas A&M	10-2-0	Emory Bellard	10-1-0
12	Miami-OH	11-1-0	Dick Crum	10-1-0
13	Maryland	9-2-1	Jerry Claiborne	8-2-1
14	California	8-3-0	Mike White	same
15	Pittsburgh	8-4-0	Johnny Majors	7-4-0
16	Colorado	9-3-0	Bill Mallory	9-2-0
17	USC	8-4-0	John McKay	7-4-0
18	Arizona	9-2-0	Jim Young	same
19	Georgia	9-3-0	Vince Dooley	9-2-0
20	West Virginia	9-3-0	Bobby Bowden	8-3-0

Key Bowl Games

Rankings below reflect final regular season poll, released Dec. 1. Texas A&M was unbeaten and ranked 2nd in that poll, but lost to #18 Arkansas, 31-6, in its final regular season game on Dec.6.

Rose–#11 UCLA over #1 Ohio St., 23-10; **Liberty**–#17 USC over #2 Texas A&M, 20-0; **Orange**–#3 Oklahoma over #5 Michigan, 14-6; **Sugar**–#4 Alabama over #8 Penn St., 13-6; **Fiesta**–#7 Ariz. St. over #6 Nebraska, 17-14; **Bluebonnet**–#9 Texas over #10 Colorado, 38-21; **Cotton**–#18 Arkansas over #12 Georgia, 31-10.

1976

		After Bowls	Head Coach	Regular Season
1	Pittsburgh	12-0-0	Johnny Majors	11-0-0
2	USC	11-1-0	John Robinson	10-1-0
3	Michigan	10-2-0	Bo Schembechler	10-1-0
4	Houston	10-2-0	Bill Yeoman	9-2-0
5	Oklahoma	9-2-1	Barry Switzer	8-2-1
6	Ohio St.	9-2-1	Woody Hayes	8-2-1
7	Texas A&M	10-2-0	Emory Bellard	9-2-0
8	Maryland	11-1-0	Jerry Claiborne	11-0-0
9	Nebraska	9-3-1	Tom Osborne	8-3-1
10	Georgia	10-2-0	Vince Dooley	10-1-0
11	Alabama	9-3-0	Bear Bryant	8-3-0
12	Notre Dame	9-3-0	Dan Devine	8-3-0
13	Texas Tech	10-2-0	Steve Sloan	10-1-0
14	Oklahoma St.	9-3-0	Jim Stanley	8-3-0
15	UCLA	9-2-1	Terry Donahue	9-1-1
16	Colorado	8-4-0	Bill Mallory	8-3-0
17	Rutgers	11-0-0	Frank Burns	same
18	Kentucky	8-4-0	Fran Curci	7-4-0
19	Iowa St.	8-3-0	Earle Bruce	same
20	Mississippi St.	9-2-0	Bob Tyler	same

Key Bowl Games

Rankings below reflect final regular season poll, released Nov. 29. No bowl for then #20 Miss. St. (probation).

Sugar–#1 Pitt over #5 Georgia, 27-3; **Rose**–#3 USC over #2 Michigan, 14-6; **Cotton**–#6 Houston over #4 Maryland, 30-21; **Liberty**–#16 Alabama over #7 UCLA, 36-6; **Fiesta**–#8 Oklahoma over Wyoming, 41-7; **Bluebonnet**–#13 Nebraska over #9 Texas Tech, 27-24; **Sun**–#10 Texas A&M over Florida, 37-14; **Orange**–#11 Ohio St. over #12 Colorado, 27-10.

1977

		After Bowls	Head Coach	Regular Season
1	Notre Dame	11-1-0	Dan Devine	10-1-0
2	Alabama	11-1-0	Bear Bryant	10-1-0
3	Arkansas	11-1-0	Lou Holtz	10-1-0
4	Texas	11-1-0	Fred Akers	11-0-0
5	Penn St.	11-1-0	Joe Paterno	10-1-0
6	Kentucky	10-1-0	Fran Curci	same
7	Oklahoma	10-2-0	Barry Switzer	10-1-0
8	Pittsburgh	9-2-1	Jackie Sherrill	8-2-1
9	Michigan	10-2-0	Bo Schembechler	10-1-0
10	Washington	8-4-0	Don James	7-4-0
11	Ohio St.	9-3-0	Woody Hayes	9-2-0
12	Nebraska	9-3-0	Tom Osborne	8-3-0
13	USC	8-4-0	John Robinson	7-4-0
14	Florida St.	10-2-0	Bobby Bowden	9-2-0
15	Stanford	9-3-0	Bill Walsh	8-3-0
16	San Diego St.	10-1-0	Claude Gilbert	same
17	North Carolina	8-3-1	Bill Dooley	8-2-1
18	Arizona St.	9-3-0	Frank Kush	9-2-0
19	Clemson	8-3-1	Charley Pell	8-2-1
20	BYU	9-2-0	LaVell Edwards	same

Key Bowl Games

Rankings below reflect final regular season poll, released Nov. 28. No bowl for then #7 Kentucky (probation).

Cotton–#5 Notre Dame over #1 Texas, 38-10; **Orange**–#6 Arkansas over #2 Oklahoma, 31-6; **Sugar**–#3 Alabama over #9 Ohio St., 35-6; **Rose**–#13 Washington over #4 Michigan, 27-20; **Fiesta**–#8 Penn St. over #15 Ariz. St., 42-30; **Gator**–#10 Pitt over #11 Clemson, 34-3.

Associated Press Final Polls (Cont.)

1978

		After Bowls	Head Coach	Regular Season
1	Alabama	11-1-0	Bear Bryant	10-1-0
2	USC	12-1-0	John Robinson	11-1-0
3	Oklahoma	11-1-0	Barry Switzer	10-1-0
4	Penn St.	11-1-0	Joe Paterno	11-0-0
5	Michigan	10-2-0	Bo Schembechler	10-1-0
6	Clemson	11-1-0	Charley Pell	10-1-0
7	Notre Dame	9-3-0	Dan Devine	8-3-0
8	Nebraska	9-3-0	Tom Osborne	9-2-0
9	Texas	9-3-0	Fred Akers	8-3-0
10	Houston	9-3-0	Bill Yeoman	9-2-0
11	Arkansas	9-2-1	Lou Holtz	9-2-0
12	Michigan St.	8-3-0	Darryl Rogers	same
13	Purdue	9-2-1	Jim Young	8-2-1
14	UCLA	8-3-1	Terry Donahue	8-3-0
15	Missouri	8-4-0	Warren Powers	7-4-0
16	Georgia	9-2-1	Vince Dooley	9-1-1
17	Stanford	8-4-0	Bill Walsh	7-4-0
18	N.C. State	9-3-0	Bo Rein	8-3-0
19	Texas A&M	8-4-0	Emory Bellard (4-2) & Tom Wilson (4-2)	7-4-0
20	Maryland	9-3-0	Jerry Claiborne	9-2-0

Key Bowl Games

Rankings below reflect final regular season poll, released Dec. 4. No bowl for then #12 Michigan St. (probation).

Sugar–#2 Alabama over #1 Penn St., 14-7; **Rose**–#3 USC over #5 Michigan, 17-10; **Orange**–#4 Oklahoma over #6 Nebraska, 31-24; **Gator**–#7 Clemson over #20 Ohio St., 17-15; **Fiesta**–#8 Arkansas tied #15 UCLA, 10-10; **Cotton**–#10 Notre Dame over #9 Houston, 35-34.

1979

		After Bowls	Head Coach	Regular Season
1	Alabama	12-0-0	Bear Bryant	11-0-0
2	USC	11-0-1	John Robinson	10-0-1
3	Oklahoma	11-1-0	Barry Switzer	10-1-0
4	Ohio St.	11-1-0	Earle Bruce	11-0-0
5	Houston	11-1-0	Bill Yeoman	10-1-0
6	Florida St.	11-1-0	Bobby Bowden	11-0-0
7	Pittsburgh	11-1-0	Jackie Sherrill	10-1-0
8	Arkansas	10-2-0	Lou Holtz	10-1-0
9	Nebraska	10-2-0	Tom Osborne	10-1-0
10	Purdue	10-2-0	Jim Young	9-2-0
11	Washington	9-3-0	Don James	8-3-0
12	Texas	9-3-0	Fred Akers	9-2-0
13	BYU	11-1-0	LaVell Edwards	11-0-0
14	Baylor	8-4-0	Grant Teaff	7-4-0
15	North Carolina	8-3-1	Dick Crum	7-3-1
16	Auburn	8-3-0	Doug Barfield	same
17	Temple	10-2-0	Wayne Hardin	9-2-0
18	Michigan	8-4-0	Bo Schembechler	8-3-0
19	Indiana	8-4-0	Lee Corso	7-4-0
20	Penn St.	8-4-0	Joe Paterno	7-4-0

Key Bowl Games

Rankings below reflect final regular season poll, released Dec. 3. No bowl for then #17 Auburn (probation).

Sugar–#2 Alabama over #6 Arkansas, 24-9; **Rose**–#3 USC over #1 Ohio St., 17-16; **Orange**–#5 Oklahoma over #4 Florida St., 24-7; **Sun**–#13 Washington over #11 Texas, 14-7; **Cotton**–#8 Houston over #7 Nebraska, 17-14; **Fiesta**–#10 Pitt over Arizona, 16-10.

1980

		After Bowls	Head Coach	Regular Season
1	Georgia	12-0-0	Vince Dooley	11-0-0
2	Pittsburgh	11-1-0	Jackie Sherrill	10-1-0
3	Oklahoma	10-2-0	Barry Switzer	9-2-0
4	Michigan	10-2-0	Bo Schembechler	9-2-0
5	Florida St.	10-2-0	Bobby Bowden	10-1-0
6	Alabama	10-2-0	Bear Bryant	9-2-0
7	Nebraska	10-2-0	Tom Osborne	9-2-0
8	Penn St.	10-2-0	Joe Paterno	9-2-0
9	Notre Dame	9-2-1	Dan Devine	9-1-1
10	North Carolina	11-1-0	Dick Crum	10-1-0
11	USC	8-2-1	John Robinson	same
12	BYU	12-1-0	LaVell Edwards	11-1-0
13	UCLA	9-2-0	Terry Donahue	same
14	Baylor	10-2-0	Grant Teaff	10-1-0
15	Ohio St.	9-3-0	Earle Bruce	9-2-0
16	Washington	9-3-0	Don James	9-2-0
17	Purdue	9-3-0	Jim Young	8-3-0
18	Miami-FL	9-3-0	H. Schnellenberger	8-3-0
19	Mississippi St.	9-3-0	Emory Bellard	9-2-0
20	SMU	8-4-0	Ron Meyer	8-3-0

Key Bowl Games

Rankings below reflect final regular season poll, released Dec. 8.

Sugar–#1 Georgia over #7 Notre Dame, 17-10; **Orange**–#4 Oklahoma over #2 Florida St., 18-17; **Gator**–#3 Pitt over #18 S. Carolina, 37-9; **Rose**–#5 Michigan over #16 Washington, 23-6; **Cotton**–#9 Alabama over #6 Baylor, 30-2; **Sun**–#8 Nebraska over #17 Miss. St., 31-17; **Fiesta**–#10 Penn St. over #11 Ohio St., 31-19; **Bluebonnet**–#13 N. Carolina over Texas, 16-7.

1981

		After Bowls	Head Coach	Regular Season
1	Clemson	12-0-0	Danny Ford	11-0-0
2	Texas	10-1-1	Fred Akers	9-1-1
3	Penn St.	10-2-0	Joe Paterno	9-2-0
4	Pittsburgh	11-1-0	Jackie Sherrill	10-1-0
5	SMU	10-1-0	Ron Meyer	same
6	Georgia	10-2-0	Vince Dooley	10-1-0
7	Alabama	9-2-1	Bear Bryant	9-1-1
8	Miami-FL	9-2-0	H. Schnellenberger	same
9	North Carolina	10-2-0	Dick Crum	9-2-0
10	Washington	10-2-0	Don James	9-2-0
11	Nebraska	9-3-0	Tom Osborne	9-2-0
12	Michigan	9-3-0	Bo Schembechler	8-3-0
13	BYU	11-2-0	LaVell Edwards	10-2-0
14	USC	9-3-0	John Robinson	9-2-0
15	Ohio St.	9-3-0	Earle Bruce	8-3-0
16	Arizona St.	9-2-0	Darryl Rogers	same
17	West Virginia	9-3-0	Don Nehlen	8-3-0
18	Iowa	8-4-0	Hayden Fry	8-3-0
19	Missouri	8-4-0	Warren Powers	7-4-0
20	Oklahoma	7-4-1	Barry Switzer	6-4-1

Key Bowl Games

Rankings below reflect final regular season poll, released Nov. 30. No bowl for then #5 SMU (probation), #9 Miami-FL (probation), and #17 Ariz. St. (probation).

Orange–#1 Clemson over #4 Nebraska, 22-15; **Sugar**–#10 Pitt over #2 Georgia, 24-20; **Cotton**–#6 Texas over #3 Alabama, 14-12; **Fiesta**–#7 Penn St. over #8 USC, 26-10; **Gator**–#11 N. Carolina over Arkansas, 31-27; **Rose**–#12 Washington over #13 Iowa, 28-0.

1982

		After Bowls	Head Coach	Regular Season
1	Penn St.	11-1-0	Joe Paterno	10-1-0
2	SMU	11-0-1	Bobby Collins	10-0-1
3	Nebraska	12-1-0	Tom Osborne	11-1-0
4	Georgia	11-1-0	Vince Dooley	11-0-0
5	UCLA	10-1-1	Terry Donahue	9-1-1
6	Arizona St.	10-2-0	Darryl Rogers	9-2-0
7	Washington	10-2-0	Don James	9-2-0
8	Clemson	9-1-1	Danny Ford	same
9	Arkansas	9-2-1	Lou Holtz	8-2-1
10	Pittsburgh	9-3-0	Foge Fazio	9-2-0
11	LSU	8-3-1	Jerry Stovall	8-2-1
12	Ohio St.	9-3-0	Earle Bruce	8-3-0
13	Florida St.	9-3-0	Bobby Bowden	8-3-0
14	Auburn	9-3-0	Pat Dye	8-3-0
15	USC	8-3-0	John Robinson	same
16	Oklahoma	8-4-0	Barry Switzer	8-3-0
17	Texas	9-3-0	Fred Akers	9-2-0
18	North Carolina	8-4-0	Dick Crum	7-4-0
19	West Virginia	9-3-0	Don Nehlen	9-2-0
20	Maryland	8-4-0	Bobby Ross	8-3-0

Key Bowl Games

Rankings below reflect final regular season poll, released Dec. 6. No bowl for then #7 Clemson (probation) and #15 USC (probation).

Sugar–#2 Penn St. over #1 Georgia, 27-23; **Orange**–#3 Nebraska over #13 LSU, 21-20; **Cotton**–#4 SMU over #6 Pitt, 7-3; **Rose**–#5 UCLA over #19 Michigan, 24-14; **Aloha**–#9 Washington over #16 Maryland, 21-20; **Fiesta**–#11 Ariz. St. over #12 Oklahoma, 32-21; **Bluebonnet**–#14 Arkansas over Florida, 28-24.

1983

		After Bowls	Head Coach	Regular Season
1	Miami-FL	11-1-0	H. Schnellenberger	10-1-0
2	Nebraska	12-1-0	Tom Osborne	12-0-0
3	Auburn	11-1-0	Pat Dye	10-1-0
4	Georgia	10-1-1	Vince Dooley	9-1-1
5	Texas	11-1-0	Fred Akers	11-0-0
6	Florida	9-2-1	Charley Pell	8-2-1
7	BYU	11-1-0	LaVell Edwards	10-1-0
8	Michigan	9-3-0	Bo Schembechler	9-2-0
9	Ohio St.	9-3-0	Earle Bruce	8-3-0
10	Illinois	10-2-0	Mike White	10-1-0
11	Clemson	9-1-1	Danny Ford	same
12	SMU	10-2-0	Bobby Collins	10-1-0
13	Air Force	10-2-0	Ken Hatfield	9-2-0
14	Iowa	9-3-0	Hayden Fry	9-2-0
15	Alabama	8-4-0	Ray Perkins	7-4-0
16	West Virginia	9-3-0	Don Nehlen	8-3-0
17	UCLA	7-4-1	Terry Donahue	6-4-1
18	Pittsburgh	8-3-1	Foge Fazio	8-2-1
19	Boston College	9-3-0	Jack Bicknell	9-2-0
20	East Carolina	8-3-0	Ed Emory	same

Key Bowl Games

Rankings below reflect final regular season poll, released Dec. 5. No bowl for then #12 Clemson (probation).

Orange–#5 Miami-FL over #1 Nebraska, 31-30; **Cotton**–#7 Georgia over #2 Texas, 10-9; **Sugar**– #3 Auburn over #8 Michigan, 9-7; **Rose**–UCLA over #4 Illinois, 45-9; **Holiday**–#9 BYU over Missouri, 21-17; **Gator**–#11 Florida over #10 Iowa, 14-6; **Fiesta**–#14 Ohio St. over #15 Pitt, 28-23.

1984

		After Bowls	Head Coach	Regular Season
1	BYU	13-0-0	LaVell Edwards	12-0-0
2	Washington	11-1-0	Don James	10-1-0
3	Florida	9-1-1	Charley Pell (0-1-1) & Galen Hall (9-0)	same
4	Nebraska	10-2-0	Tom Osborne	9-2-0
5	Boston College	10-2-0	Jack Bicknell	9-2-0
6	Oklahoma	9-2-1	Barry Switzer	9-1-1
7	Oklahoma St.	10-2-0	Pat Jones	9-2-0
8	SMU	10-2-0	Bobby Collins	9-2-0
9	UCLA	9-3-0	Terry Donahue	8-3-0
10	USC	9-3-0	Ted Tollner	8-3-0
11	South Carolina	10-2-0	Joe Morrison	10-1-0
12	Maryland	9-3-0	Bobby Ross	8-3-0
13	Ohio St.	9-3-0	Earle Bruce	9-2-0
14	Auburn	9-4-0	Pat Dye	8-4-0
15	LSU	8-3-1	Bill Arnsparger	8-2-1
16	Iowa	8-4-1	Hayden Fry	7-4-1
17	Florida St.	7-3-2	Bobby Bowden	7-3-1
18	Miami-FL	8-5-0	Jimmy Johnson	8-4-0
19	Kentucky	9-3-0	Jerry Claiborne	8-3-0
20	Virginia	8-2-2	George Welsh	7-2-2

Key Bowl Games

Rankings below reflect final regular season poll, released Dec. 3. No bowl for then #3 Florida (probation).

Holiday–#1 BYU over Michigan, 24-17; **Orange**–#4 Washington over #2 Oklahoma, 28-17; **Sugar**–#5 Nebraska over #11 LSU, 28-10; **Rose**–#18 USC over #6 Ohio St., 20-17; **Gator**–#9 Okla. St. over #7 S. Carolina, 21-14; **Cotton**–#8 BC over Houston, 45-28; **Aloha**–#10 SMU over #17 Notre Dame, 27-20.

1985

		After Bowls	Head Coach	Regular Season
1	Oklahoma	11-1-0	Barry Switzer	10-1-0
2	Michigan	10-1-1	Bo Schembechler	9-1-1
3	Penn St.	11-1-0	Joe Paterno	11-0-0
4	Tennessee	9-1-2	Johnny Majors	8-1-2
5	Florida	9-1-1	Galen Hall	same
6	Texas A&M	10-2-0	Jackie Sherrill	9-2-0
7	UCLA	9-2-1	Terry Donahue	8-2-1
8	Air Force	12-1-0	Fisher DeBerry	11-1-0
9	Miami-FL	10-2-0	Jimmy Johnson	10-1-0
10	Iowa	10-2-0	Hayden Fry	10-1-0
11	Nebraska	9-3-0	Tom Osborne	9-2-0
12	Arkansas	10-2-0	Ken Hatfield	9-2-0
13	Alabama	9-2-1	Ray Perkins	8-2-1
14	Ohio St.	9-3-0	Earle Bruce	8-3-0
15	Florida St.	9-3-0	Bobby Bowden	8-3-0
16	BYU	11-3-0	LaVell Edwards	11-2-0
17	Baylor	9-3-0	Grant Teaff	8-3-0
18	Maryland	9-3-0	Bobby Ross	8-3-0
19	Georgia Tech	9-2-1	Bill Curry	8-2-1
20	LSU	9-2-1	Bill Arnsparger	9-1-1

Key Bowl Games

Rankings below reflect final regular season poll, released Dec. 9. No bowl for then #6 Florida (probation).

Orange–#3 Oklahoma over #1 Penn St., 25-10; **Sugar**–#8 Tennessee over #2 Miami-FL, 35-7; **Rose**–#13 UCLA over #4 Iowa, 45-28; **Fiesta**–#5 Michigan over #7 Nebraska, 27-23; **Bluebonnet**–#10 Air Force over Texas, 24-16; **Cotton**–#11 Texas A&M over #16 Auburn, 36-16.

Associated Press Final Polls (Cont.)

1986

		After Bowls	Head Coach	Regular Season
1	Penn St.	12-0-0	Joe Paterno	11-0-0
2	Miami-FL	11-1-0	Jimmy Johnson	11-0-0
3	Oklahoma	11-1-0	Barry Switzer	10-1-0
4	Arizona St.	10-1-1	John Cooper	9-1-1
5	Nebraska	10-2-0	Tom Osborne	9-2-0
6	Auburn	10-2-0	Pat Dye	9-2-0
7	Ohio St.	10-3-0	Earle Bruce	9-3-0
8	Michigan	11-2-0	Bo Schembechler	11-1-0
9	Alabama	10-3-0	Ray Perkins	9-3-0
10	LSU	9-3-0	Bill Arnsparger	9-2-0
11	Arizona	9-3-0	Larry Smith	8-3-0
12	Baylor	9-3-0	Grant Teaff	8-3-0
13	Texas A&M	9-3-0	Jackie Sherrill	9-2-0
14	UCLA	8-3-1	Terry Donahue	7-3-1
15	Arkansas	9-3-0	Ken Hatfield	9-2-0
16	Iowa	9-3-0	Hayden Fry	8-3-0
17	Clemson	8-2-2	Danny Ford	7-2-2
18	Washington	8-3-1	Don James	8-2-1
19	Boston College	9-3-0	Jack Bicknell	8-3-0
20	Virginia Tech	9-2-1	Bill Dooley	8-2-1

Key Bowl Games

Rankings below reflect final regular season poll, released Dec. 1.

Fiesta–#2 Penn St. over #1 Miami-FL, 14-10; **Orange**–#3 Oklahoma over #9 Arkansas, 42-8; **Rose**– #7 Ariz. St. over #4 Michigan, 22-15; **Sugar**–#6 Nebraska over #5 LSU, 30-15; **Cotton**–#11 Ohio St. over #8 Texas A&M, 28-12; **Citrus**–#10 Auburn over USC, 16-7; **Sun**–#13 Alabama over #12 Washington, 28-6.

1987

		After Bowls	Head Coach	Regular Season
1	Miami-FL	12-0-0	Jimmy Johnson	11-0-0
2	Florida St.	11-1-0	Bobby Bowden	10-1-0
3	Oklahoma	11-1-0	Barry Switzer	11-0-0
4	Syracuse	11-0-1	Dick MacPherson	11-0-0
5	LSU	10-1-1	Mike Archer	9-1-1
6	Nebraska	10-2-0	Tom Osborne	10-1-0
7	Auburn	9-1-2	Pat Dye	9-1-1
8	Michigan St.	9-2-1	George Perles	8-2-1
9	UCLA	10-2-0	Terry Donahue	9-2-0
10	Texas A&M	10-2-0	Jackie Sherrill	9-2-0
11	Oklahoma St.	10-2-0	Pat Jones	9-2-0
12	Clemson	10-2-0	Danny Ford	9-2-0
13	Georgia	9-3-0	Vince Dooley	8-3-0
14	Tennessee	10-2-1	Johnny Majors	9-2-1
15	South Carolina	8-4-0	Joe Morrison	8-3-0
16	Iowa	10-3-0	Hayden Fry	9-3-0
17	Notre Dame	8-4-0	Lou Holtz	8-3-0
18	USC	8-4-0	Larry Smith	8-3-0
19	Michigan	8-4-0	Bo Schembechler	7-4-0
20	Arizona St.	7-4-1	John Cooper	6-4-1

Key Bowl Games

Rankings below reflect final regular season poll, released Dec. 7.

Orange–#2 Miami-FL over #1 Oklahoma, 20-14; **Fiesta**–#3 Florida St. over #5 Nebraska, 31-28; **Sugar**–#4 Syracuse tied #6 Auburn, 16-16; **Gator**–#7 LSU over #9 S. Carolina, 30-13; **Rose**–#8 Mich. St. over #16 USC, 20-17; **Aloha**–#10 UCLA over Florida, 20-16; **Cotton**–#13 Texas A&M over #12 Notre Dame, 35-10.

1988

		After Bowls	Head Coach	Regular Season
1	Notre Dame	12-0-0	Lou Holtz	11-0-0
2	Miami-FL	11-1-0	Jimmy Johnson	10-1-0
3	Florida St.	11-1-0	Bobby Bowden	10-1-0
4	Michigan	9-2-1	Bo Schembechler	8-2-1
5	West Virginia	11-1-0	Don Nehlen	11-0-0
6	UCLA	10-2-0	Terry Donahue	9-2-0
7	USC	10-2-0	Larry Smith	10-1-0
8	Auburn	10-2-0	Pat Dye	10-1-0
9	Clemson	10-2-0	Danny Ford	9-2-0
10	Nebraska	11-2-0	Tom Osborne	11-1-0
11	Oklahoma St.	10-2-0	Pat Jones	9-2-0
12	Arkansas	10-2-0	Ken Hatfield	10-1-0
13	Syracuse	10-2-0	Dick MacPherson	9-2-0
14	Oklahoma	9-3-0	Barry Switzer	9-2-0
15	Georgia	9-3-0	Vince Dooley	8-3-0
16	Washington St.	9-3-0	Dennis Erickson	8-3-0
17	Alabama	9-3-0	Bill Curry	8-3-0
18	Houston	9-3-0	Jack Pardee	9-2-0
19	LSU	8-4-0	Mike Archer	8-3-0
20	Indiana	8-3-1	Bill Mallory	7-3-1

Key Bowl Games

Rankings below reflect final regular season poll, released Dec. 5.

Fiesta–#1 Notre Dame over #3 West Va., 34-21; **Orange**–#2 Miami-FL over #6 Nebraska, 23-3; **Sugar**–#4 Florida St. over #7 Auburn, 13-7; **Rose**–#11 Michigan over #5 USC, 22-14; **Cotton**–#9 UCLA over #8 Arkansas, 17-3; **Citrus**–#13 Clemson over #10 Oklahoma, 13-6.

1989

		After Bowls	Head Coach	Regular Season
1	Miami-FL	11-1-0	Dennis Erickson	10-1-0
2	Notre Dame	12-1-0	Lou Holtz	11-1-0
3	Florida St.	10-2-0	Bobby Bowden	9-2-0
4	Colorado	11-1-0	Bill McCartney	11-0-0
5	Tennessee	11-1-0	Johnny Majors	10-1-0
6	Auburn	10-2-0	Pat Dye	9-2-0
7	Michigan	10-2-0	Bo Schembechler	10-1-0
8	USC	9-2-1	Larry Smith	8-2-1
9	Alabama	10-2-0	Bill Curry	10-1-0
10	Illinois	10-2-0	John Mackovic	9-2-0
11	Nebraska	10-2-0	Tom Osborne	10-1-0
12	Clemson	10-2-0	Danny Ford	9-2-0
13	Arkansas	10-2-0	Ken Hatfield	10-1-0
14	Houston	9-2-0	Jack Pardee	same
15	Penn St.	8-3-1	Joe Paterno	7-3-1
16	Michigan St.	8-4-0	George Perles	7-4-0
17	Pittsburgh	8-3-1	Mike Gottfried (7-3-1) & Paul Hackett (1-0)	7-3-1
18	Virginia	10-3-0	George Welsh	10-2-0
19	Texas Tech	9-3-0	Spike Dykes	8-3-0
20	Texas A&M	8-4-0	R.C. Slocum	8-3-0

Key Bowl Games

Rankings below reflect final regular season poll, released Dec. 11. No bowl for then #13 Houston (probation).

Orange–#4 Notre Dame over #1 Colorado, 21-6; **Sugar**–#2 Miami-FL over #7 Alabama, 33-25; **Rose**– #12 USC over #3 Michigan, 17-10; **Fiesta**–#5 Florida St. over #6 Nebraska, 41-17; **Cotton**–#8 Tennessee over #10 Arkansas, 31-27; **Hall of Fame**–#9 Auburn over #21 Ohio St., 31-14; **Citrus**–#11 Illinois over #15 Virginia, 31-21.

1990

	After Bowls	Head Coach	Regular Season
1 Colorado	11-1-1	Bill McCartney	10-1-1
2 Georgia Tech	11-0-1	Bobby Ross	10-0-1
3 Miami-FL	10-2-0	Dennis Erickson	9-2-0
4 Florida St.	10-2-0	Bobby Bowden	9-2-0
5 Washington	10-2-0	Don James	9-2-0
6 Notre Dame	9-3-0	Lou Holtz	9-2-0
7 Michigan	9-3-0	Gary Moeller	8-3-0
8 Tennessee	9-2-2	Johnny Majors	8-2-2
9 Clemson	10-2-0	Ken Hatfield	9-2-0
10 Houston	10-1-0	John Jenkins	same
11 Penn St.	9-3-0	Joe Paterno	9-2-0
12 Texas	10-2-0	David McWilliams	10-1-0
13 Florida	9-2-0	Steve Spurrier	same
14 Louisville	10-1-1	H. Schnellenberger	9-1-1
15 Texas A&M	9-3-1	R.C. Slocum	8-3-1
16 Michigan St.	8-3-1	George Perles	7-3-1
17 Oklahoma	8-3-0	Gary Gibbs	same
18 Iowa	8-4-0	Hayden Fry	8-3-0
19 Auburn	8-3-1	Pat Dye	7-3-1
20 USC	8-4-1	Larry Smith	8-3-1

Key Bowl Games

Rankings below reflect final regular season poll, released Dec. 3. No bowl for then #9 Houston (probation), #11 Florida (probation) and #20 Oklahoma (probation).

Orange–#1 Colorado over #5 Notre Dame, 10-9; **Citrus**–#2 Ga. Tech over #19 Nebraska, 45-21; **Cotton**–#4 Miami-FL over #3 Texas, 46-3; **Blockbuster**–#6 Florida St. over #7 Penn St., 24-17; **Rose**–#8 Washington over #17 Iowa, 46-34; **Sugar**–#10 Tennessee over Virginia, 23-22; **Gator**–#12 Michigan over #15 Ole Miss, 35-3.

1991

	After Bowls	Head Coach	Regular Season
1 Miami-FL	12-0-0	Dennis Erickson	11-0-0
2 Washington	12-0-0	Don James	11-0-0
3 Penn St.	11-2-0	Joe Paterno	10-2-0
4 Florida St.	11-2-0	Bobby Bowden	10-2-0
5 Alabama	11-1-0	Gene Stallings	10-1-0
6 Michigan	10-2-0	Gary Moeller	10-1-0
7 Florida	10-2-0	Steve Spurrier	10-1-0
8 California	10-2-0	Bruce Snyder	9-2-0
9 East Carolina	11-1-0	Bill Lewis	10-1-0
10 Iowa	10-1-1	Hayden Fry	10-1-0
11 Syracuse	10-2-0	Paul Pasqualoni	9-2-0
12 Texas A&M	10-2-0	R.C. Slocum	10-1-0
13 Notre Dame	10-3-0	Lou Holtz	9-3-0
14 Tennessee	9-3-0	Johnny Majors	9-2-0
15 Nebraska	9-2-1	Tom Osborne	9-1-1
16 Oklahoma	9-3-0	Gary Gibbs	8-3-0
17 Georgia	9-3-0	Ray Goff	8-3-0
18 Clemson	9-2-1	Ken Hatfield	9-1-1
19 UCLA	9-3-0	Terry Donahue	8-3-0
20 Colorado	8-3-1	Bill McCartney	8-2-1

Key Bowl Games

Rankings below reflect final regular season poll, taken Dec. 2.

Orange–#1 Miami-FL over #11 Nebraska, 22-0; **Rose**–#2 Washington over #4 Michigan, 34-14; **Sugar**–#18 Notre Dame over #3 Florida, 39-28; **Cotton**–#5 Florida St. over #9 Texas A&M, 10-2; **Fiesta**–#6 Penn St. over #10 Tennessee, 42-17; **Holiday**–#7 Iowa tied BYU, 13-13; **Blockbuster**–#8 Alabama over #15 Colorado, 30-25; **Citrus**–#14 California over #13 Clemson, 37-13; **Peach**–#12 East Carolina over #21 N.C. State, 37-34.

1992

	After Bowls	Head Coach	Regular Season
1 Alabama	13-0-0	Gene Stallings	12-0-0
2 Florida St.	11-1-0	Bobby Bowden	10-1-0
3 Miami-FL	11-1-0	Dennis Erickson	11-0-0
4 Notre Dame	10-1-1	Lou Holtz	9-1-1
5 Michigan	9-0-3	Gary Moeller	8-0-3
6 Syracuse	10-2-0	Paul Pasqualoni	9-2-0
7 Texas A&M	12-1-0	R.C. Slocum	12-0-0
8 Georgia	10-2-0	Ray Goff	9-2-0
9 Stanford	10-3-0	Bill Walsh	9-3-0
10 Florida	9-4-0	Steve Spurrier	8-4-0
11 Washington	9-3-0	Don James	9-2-0
12 Tennessee	9-3-0	Johnny Majors (5-3) & Phillip Fulmer (4-0)	8-3-0
13 Colorado	9-2-1	Bill McCartney	9-1-1
14 Nebraska	9-3-0	Tom Osborne	9-2-0
15 Washington St.	9-3-0	Mike Price	8-3-0
16 Mississippi	9-3-0	Billy Brewer	8-3-0
17 N.C. State	9-3-1	Dick Sheridan	9-2-1
18 Ohio St.	8-3-1	John Cooper	8-2-1
19 North Carolina	9-3-0	Mack Brown	8-3-0
20 Hawaii	11-2-0	Bob Wagner	10-2-0

Key Bowl Games

Rankings below reflect final regular season poll, taken Dec. 5.

Sugar–#2 Alabama over #1 Miami-FL, 34-13; **Orange**–#3 Florida St. over #11 Nebraska, 27-14; **Cotton**–#5 Notre Dame over #4 Texas A&M, 28-3; **Fiesta**–#6 Syracuse over #10 Colorado, 26-22; **Rose**–#7 Michigan over #9 Washington, 38-31; **Citrus**–#8 Georgia over #15 Ohio St., 21-14.

1993

	After Bowls	Head Coach	Regular Season
1 Florida St	12-1-0	Bobby Bowden	11-1-0
2 Notre Dame	11-1-0	Lou Holtz	10-1-0
3 Nebraska	11-1-0	Tom Osborne	11-0-0
4 Auburn	11-0-0	Terry Bowden	11-0-0
5 Florida	11-2-0	Steve Spurrier	10-2-0
6 Wisconsin	10-1-1	Barry Alvarez	9-1-1
7 West Virginia	11-1-0	Don Nehlen	11-0-0
8 Penn St.	10-2-0	Joe Paterno	9-2-0
9 Texas A&M	10-2-0	R.C. Slocum	10-1-0
10 Arizona	10-2-0	Dick Tomey	9-2-0
11 Ohio St	10-1-1	John Cooper	9-1-1
12 Tennessee	9-2-1	Phillip Fulmer	9-1-1
13 Boston College	9-3-0	Tom Coughlin	8-3-0
14 Alabama	9-3-1	Gene Stallings	8-3-1
15 Miami-FL	9-3-0	Dennis Erickson	9-2-0
16 Colorado	8-3-1	Bill McCartney	7-3-1
17 Oklahoma	9-3-0	Gary Gibbs	8-3-0
18 UCLA	8-4-0	Terry Donahue	8-3-0
19 North Carolina	10-3-0	Mack Brown	10-2-0
20 Kansas St	9-2-1	Bill Snyder	8-2-1

Key Bowl Games

Rankings below reflect final regular season poll, taken Dec. 5. No bowl for then #5 Auburn (probation).

Orange–#1 Florida St. over #2 Nebraska, 18-16; **Sugar**–#8 Florida over #3 West Virginia, 41-7; **Cotton**–#4 Notre Dame over #7 Texas A&M, 24-21; **Citrus**–#13 Penn St. over #6 Tennessee, 31-13; **Rose**–#9 Wisconsin over #14 UCLA, 21-16; **Fiesta**–#16 Arizona over #10 Miami-FL, 29-0; **Holiday**–#11 Ohio St. over BYU, 28-21; **Gator**–#18 Alabama over #12 North Carolina, 24-10; **Carquest**–#15 Boston College over Virginia, 31-13.

Associated Press Final Polls (Cont.)

1994

		After Bowls	Head Coach	Regular Season
1	Nebraska	13-0-0	Tom Osborne	12-0-0
2	Penn St.	12-0-0	Joe Paterno	11-0-0
3	Colorado	11-1-0	Bill McCartney	10-1-0
4	Florida St	10-1-1	Bobby Bowden	9-1-1
5	Alabama	12-1-0	Gene Stallings	11-1-0
6	Miami-FL	10-2-0	Dennis Erickson	10-1-0
7	Florida	10-2-1	Steve Spurrier	10-1-1
8	Texas A&M	10-0-1	R.C. Slocum	same
9	Auburn	9-1-1	Terry Bowden	same
10	Utah	10-2-0	Ron McBride	9-2-0
11	Oregon	9-4-0	Rich Brooks	9-3-0
12	Michigan	8-4-0	Gary Moeller	7-4-0
13	USC	8-3-1	John Robinson	7-3-1
14	Ohio St.	9-4-0	John Cooper	9-3-0
15	Virginia	9-3-0	George Welsh	8-3-0
16	Colorado St.	10-2-0	Sonny Lubick	10-1-0
17	N.C. State	9-3-0	Mike O'Cain	8-3-0
18	BYU	10-3-0	LaVell Edwards	9-3-0
19	Kansas St	9-3-0	Bill Snyder	9-2-0
20	Arizona	8-4-0	Dick Tomey	8-3-0

Key Bowl Games

Rankings below reflect final regular season poll, taken Dec. 4. No bowls for then #8 Texas A&M (probation) and #9 Auburn (probation).

Orange– #1 Nebraska over #3 Miami-FL, 24-17; **Rose**– #2 Penn St. over #12 Oregon, 38-20; **Fiesta**– #4 Colorado over Notre Dame, 41-24; **Sugar**– #7 Florida St. over #5 Florida, 23-17; **Citrus**– #6 Alabama over #13 Ohio St., 24-17; **Freedom**– #14 Utah over #15 Arizona, 16-13.

1995

		After Bowls	Head Coach	Regular Season
1	Nebraska	12-0-0	Tom Osborne	11-0-0
2	Florida	12-1-0	Steve Spurrier	12-0-0
3	Tennessee	11-1-0	Phillip Fulmer	10-1-0
4	Florida St	10-2-0	Bobby Bowden	9-2-0
5	Colorado	10-2-0	Rick Neuheisel	9-2-0
6	Ohio St.	11-2-0	John Cooper	11-1-0
7	Kansas St.	10-2-0	Bill Snyder	9-2-0
8	Northwestern	10-2-0	Gary Barnett	10-1-0
9	Kansas	10-2-0	Glen Mason	9-2-0
10	Va. Tech	10-2-0	Frank Beamer	9-2-0
11	Notre Dame	9-3-0	Lou Holtz	9-2-0
12	USC	9-2-1	John Robinson	8-2-1
13	Penn St.	9-3-0	Joe Paterno	8-3-0
14	Texas	10-2-1	John Mackovic	10-1-1
15	Texas A&M	9-3-0	R.C. Slocum	8-3-0
16	Virginia	9-4-0	George Welsh	8-4-0
17	Michigan	9-4-0	Lloyd Carr	9-3-0
18	Oregon	9-3-0	Mike Bellotti	9-2-0
19	Syracuse	9-3-0	Paul Pasqualoni	8-3-0
20	Miami-FL	8-3-0	Butch Davis	same

Key Bowl Games

Rankings below reflect final regular season poll, taken Dec. 3. No bowl for then #22 Miami-FL (probation).

Fiesta– #1 Nebraska over #2 Florida, 62-24; **Rose**– #17 USC over #3 Northwestern, 41-32; **Citrus**– #4 (tie) Tennessee over #4 (tie) Ohio St., 20-14; **Orange**– #8 Florida St. over #6 Notre Dame, 31-26; **Cotton**– #7 Colorado over #12 Oregon, 38-6; **Sugar**– #13 Va. Tech over #9 Texas, 28-10; **Holiday**– #10 Kansas St. over Colo. St., 54-21; **Aloha**– #11 Kansas over UCLA, 51-30; **Alamo**– #19 Texas A&M over #14 Michigan, 22-20; **Outback**– #15 Penn St. over #16 Auburn, 43-14; **Peach**– #18 Virginia over Georgia, 34-27; **Gator**– Syracuse over #23 Clemson, 41-0.

1996

		After Bowls	Head Coach	Regular Season
1	Florida	12-1	Steve Spurrier	11-1
2	Ohio St.	11-1	John Cooper	10-1
3	Florida St	11-1	Bobby Bowden	11-0
4	Arizona St.	11-1	Bruce Snyder	11-0
5	BYU	14-1	LaVell Edwards	13-1
6	Nebraska	11-2	Tom Osborne	10-2
7	Penn St.	11-2	Joe Paterno	10-2
8	Colorado	10-2	Rick Neuheisel	9-2
9	Tennessee	10-2	Phillip Fulmer	9-2
10	North Carolina	10-2	Mack Brown	9-2
11	Alabama	10-3	Gene Stallings	9-3
12	LSU	10-2	Gerry DiNardo	9-2
13	Virginia Tech	10-2	Frank Beamer	10-1
14	Miami-FL	9-3	Butch Davis	8-3
15	Northwestern	9-3	Gary Barnett	9-2
16	Washington	9-3	Jim Lambright	9-2
17	Kansas St.	9-3	Bill Snyder	9-2
18	Iowa	9-3	Hayden Fry	8-3
19	Notre Dame	8-3	Lou Holtz	same
20	Michigan	8-4	Lloyd Carr	8-3

Key Bowl Games

Rankings below reflect final regular season poll, taken Dec. 8. No bowl for then #18 Notre Dame and #22 Wyoming.

Sugar– #3 Florida over #1 Florida St., 52-20; **Rose**– #4 Ohio St. over #2 Arizona St., 20-17; **Fiesta**– #7 Penn St. over #20 Texas, 38-15; **Cotton**– #5 BYU over #14 Kansas St., 19-15; **Citrus**– #9 Tennessee over #11 Northwestern, 48-28; **Orange**– #6 Nebraska over #10 Virginia Tech, 41-21; **Gator**– #12 North Carolina over #25 West Virginia, 20-13; **Outback**– #16 Alabama over #15 Michigan, 17-14. **Carquest**– #19 Miami over Virginia, 31-21.

1997

		After Bowls	Head Coach	Regular Season
1	Michigan	12-0	Lloyd Carr	11-0
2	Nebraska	13-0	Tom Osborne	12-0
3	Florida St	11-1	Bobby Bowden	10-1
4	Florida	10-2	Steve Spurrier	9-2
5	UCLA	10-2	Bob Toledo	9-2
6	North Carolina	11-1	Mack Brown (10-1) & Carl Torbush (1-0)	10-1
7	Tennessee	11-2	Phillip Fulmer	11-1
8	Kansas St.	11-1	Bill Snyder	10-1
9	Washington St.	10-2	Mike Price	10-1
10	Georgia	10-2	Jim Donnan	9-2
11	Auburn	10-3	Terry Bowden	9-3
12	Ohio St.	10-3	John Cooper	10-2
13	LSU	9-3	Gerry DiNardo	8-3
14	Arizona St.	8-3	Bruce Snyder	7-3
15	Purdue	9-3	Joe Tiller	8-3
16	Penn St.	9-3	Joe Paterno	9-2
17	Colorado St.	11-2	Sonny Lubick	10-2
18	Washington	8-4	Jim Lambright	7-4
19	So. Mississippi	9-3	Jeff Bower	8-3
20	Texas A&M	9-4	R.C. Slocum	9-3

Key Bowl Games

Rankings below reflect final regular season poll, taken Dec. 7.

Rose– #1 Michigan over #7 Washington St., 21-16; **Orange**– #2 Nebraska over #3 Tennessee, 42-17; **Sugar**– #4 Florida St. over #10 Ohio St., 31-14; **Gator**– #5 North Carolina over Virginia Tech, 42-3; **Cotton**– #6 UCLA over #19 Texas A&M, 29-23; **Citrus**– #8 Florida over #12 Penn St., 21-6; **Fiesta**– #9 Kansas St. over #14 Syracuse, 35-18; **Outback**– #11 Georgia over Wisconsin, 33-6; **Peach**– #13 Auburn over Clemson, 21-17; **Independence**– #15 LSU over Notre Dame, 27-9; **Alamo**– #16 Purdue over #24 Oklahoma St., 33-20; **Holiday**– #17 Colorado St. over #20 Missouri, 35-24.

All-Time AP Top 20

The composite AP Top 20 from the 1936 season through the 1997 season, based on the final rankings of each year. The final AP poll has been taken after the bowl games in 1965 and since 1968. Team point totals are based on 20 points for all 1st place finishes, 19 for each 2nd, etc. Also listed are the number of times each team has been named national champion by AP and times ranked in the final Top 10 and Top 20.

Final AP

		Pts	No.1	Top 10	Top 20
1	Notre Dame	626	8	34	44
2	Michigan	566	2	33	45
3	Oklahoma	558	6	29	41
4	Alabama	551	6	30	41
5	Nebraska	500	4	27	37
6	Ohio St.	499	3	23	40
7	USC	414	3	20	36
8	Tennessee	401	1	20	34
9	Texas	400	2	19	31
10	Penn St	389	2	21	33
11	UCLA	309	0	15	28
12	Auburn	281	1	14	26
13	LSU	277	1	14	25
14	Miami-FL.	264	4	13	21
15	Arkansas	259	0	13	23
16	Florida St	254	1	13	17
17	Georgia	249	1	14	21
18	Michigan St.	238	1	12	19
19	Texas A&M	206	1	11	21
20	Washington	202	0	10	18

Bowl Games

From Jan. 1, 1902 through Jan. 2, 1998. Corporate title sponsors and automatic berths updated through Jan. 1, 1998.

Rose Bowl

City: Pasadena, Calif. **Stadium:** Rose Bowl. **Capacity:** 102,083. **Playing surface:** Grass. **First game:** Jan. 1, 1902. **Playing sites:** Tournament Park (1902, 1916-22), Rose Bowl (1923-41 and since 1943) and Duke Stadium in Durham, N.C. (1942, due to wartime restrictions following Japan's attack at Pearl Harbor on Dec. 7, 1941). **Corporate title sponsors:** AT&T (since 1998).

Automatic berths: Pacific Coast Conference champion vs. opponent selected by PCC (1924-45 seasons); Big Ten champion vs. Pac-10 champion (since 1946 season); #1 vs. #2 on Jan. 3, 2002 (Super Alliance since 1998).

Multiple wins: USC (20); Michigan (8); Ohio St. and Washington (6); Stanford and UCLA (5); Alabama (4); Illinois and Michigan St. (3); California and Iowa (2).

Year	
1902*	Michigan 49, Stanford 0
1916	Washington St. 14, Brown 0
1917	Oregon 14, Penn 0
1918	Mare Island 19, Camp Lewis 7
1919	Great Lakes 17, Mare Island 0
1920	Harvard 7, Oregon 6
1921	California 28, Ohio St. 0
1922	0-0, California vs Wash. & Jeff.
1923	USC 14, Penn St. 0
1924	14-14, Navy vs Washington
1925	Notre Dame 27, Stanford 10
1926	Alabama 20, Washington 19
1927	7-7, Alabama vs Stanford
1928	Stanford 7, Pittsburgh 6
1929	Georgia Tech 8, California 7
1930	USC 47, Pittsburgh 14
1931	Alabama 24, Washington St. 0
1932	USC 21, Tulane 12
1933	USC 35, Pittsburgh 0
1934	Columbia 7, Stanford 0
1935	Alabama 29, Stanford 13
1936	Stanford 7, SMU 0
1937	Pittsburgh 21, Washington 0
1938	California 13, Alabama 0
1939	USC 7, Duke 3
1940	USC 14, Tennessee 0
1941	Stanford 21, Nebraska 13
1942	Oregon St. 20, Duke 16
1943	Georgia 9, UCLA 0
1944	USC 29, Washington 0
1945	USC 25, Tennessee 0
1946	Alabama 34, USC 14
1947	Illinois 45, UCLA 14
1948	Michigan 49, USC 0
1949	Northwestern 20, California 14
1950	Ohio St. 17, California 14
1951	Michigan 14, California 6
1952	Illinois 40, Stanford 7
1953	USC 7, Wisconsin 0
1954	Michigan St. 28, UCLA 20
1955	Ohio St. 20, USC 7
1956	Michigan St. 17, UCLA 14
1957	Iowa 35, Oregon St. 19
1958	Ohio St. 10, Oregon 7
1959	Iowa 38, California 12
1960	Washington 44, Wisconsin 8
1961	Washington 17, Minnesota 7
1962	Minnesota 21, UCLA 3
1963	USC 42, Wisconsin 37
1964	Illinois 17, Washington 7
1965	Michigan 34, Oregon St. 7
1966	UCLA 14, Michigan St. 12
1967	Purdue 14, USC 13
1968	USC 14, Indiana 3
1969	Ohio St. 27, USC 16
1970	USC 10, Michigan 3
1971	Stanford 27, Ohio St. 17
1972	Stanford 13, Michigan 12
1973	USC 42, Ohio St. 17
1974	Ohio St. 42, USC 21
1975	USC 18, Ohio St. 17
1976	UCLA 23, Ohio St. 10
1977	USC 14, Michigan 6
1978	Washington 27, Michigan 20
1979	USC 17, Michigan 10
1980	USC 17, Ohio St. 16
1981	Michigan 23, Washington 6
1982	Washington 28, Iowa 0
1983	UCLA 24, Michigan 14
1984	UCLA 45, Illinois 9
1985	USC 20, Ohio St. 17
1986	UCLA 45, Iowa 28
1987	Arizona St. 22, Michigan 15
1988	Michigan St. 20, USC 17
1989	Michigan 22, USC 14
1990	USC 17, Michigan 10
1991	Washington 46, Iowa 34
1992	Washington 34, Michigan 14
1993	Michigan 38, Washington 31
1994	Wisconsin 21, UCLA 16
1995	Penn St. 38, Oregon 20
1996	USC 41, Northwestern 32
1997	Ohio St. 20, Arizona St. 17
1998	Michigan 21, Washington St. 16

*January game since 1902.

Tiebreakers

The NCAA tiebreaker system was approved for Division I-A bowl games beginning with the 1995 postseason and for regular-season games in 1996. Unlike sudden-death overtime in the NFL, the NCAA tiebreaking procedure gives both teams a chance to score after regulation time has expired. Each team gets an offensive series beginning on the opponent's 25-yard line. A team's possession ends when it scores, turns the ball over or fails to convert a fourth-down play. This untimed procedure is repeated until the score is no longer tied at the end of an overtime period, which consists of one possession per team.

Bowl Games (Cont.)

Fiesta Bowl

City: Tempe, Ariz. **Stadium:** Sun Devil. **Capacity:** 73,656. **Playing surface:** Grass. **First game:** Dec. 27, 1971. **Playing site:** Sun Devil Stadium (since 1971). **Corporate title sponsors:** Sunkist Citrus Growers (1986-91), IBM OS/2 (1993-95) and Frito-Lay Tostitos chips (since 1996) .

Automatic berths: Western Athletic Conference champion vs. at-large opponent (1971-79 seasons); Two of first five picks from 8-team Bowl Coalition pool (1992-94). Bowl Alliance (#1 vs. #2 on Jan. 2, 1996; #3 vs. #5 on Jan. 1, 1997; and #4 vs. #6 on Dec. 31, 1997); Big 12 champion vs. next best team in pool (New Bowl Alliance since 1995); #1 vs. #2 on Jan. 4, 1999 (Super Alliance since 1998).

Multiple wins: Penn St. (6); Arizona St. (5); Florida St. (2).

Year	
1971†	Arizona St. 45, Florida St. 38
1972	Arizona St. 49, Missouri 35
1973	Arizona St. 28, Pittsburgh 7
1974	Oklahoma St. 16, BYU 6
1975	Arizona St. 17, Nebraska 14
1976	Oklahoma 41, Wyoming 7
1977	Penn St. 42, Arizona St. 30
1978	10-10, Arkansas vs UCLA
1979	Pittsburgh 16, Arizona 10
1980	Penn St. 31, Ohio St. 19
1982*	Penn St. 26, USC 10
1983	Arizona St. 32, Oklahoma 21
1984	Ohio St. 28, Pittsburgh 23
1985	UCLA 39, Miami-FL 37
1986	Michigan 27, Nebraska 23
1987	Penn St. 14, Miami-FL 10
1988	Florida St. 31, Nebraska 28
1989	Notre Dame 34, West Va. 21
1990	Florida St. 41, Nebraska 17
1991	Louisville 34, Alabama 7
1992	Penn St. 42, Tennessee 17
1993	Syracuse 26, Colorado 22
1994	Arizona 29, Miami-FL 0
1995	Colorado 41, Notre Dame 24
1996	Nebraska 62, Florida 24
1997	Penn St. 38, Texas 15
1997†	Kansas St. 35, Syracuse 18

†December game from 1971-80 and in '97.

* January game since 1982.

Sugar Bowl

City: New Orleans, La. **Stadium:** Louisiana Superdome. **Capacity:** 77,446. **Playing surface:** AstroTurf. **First game:** Jan. 1, 1935. **Playing sites:** Tulane Stadium (1935-74) and Superdome (since 1975). **Corporate title sponsors:** USF&G Financial Services (1987-95) and Nokia cellular telephones of Finland (starting in 1995).

Automatic berths: SEC champion vs. at-large opponent (1976-91 seasons); SEC champion vs. one of first five picks from 8-team Bowl Coalition pool (1992-94 seasons); #4 vs. #6 on Dec. 31, 1995; #1 vs. #2 on Jan. 2, 1997; and #3 vs. #5 on Jan. 1, 1998; SEC champion vs. next best team in pool (New Bowl Alliance since 1995); #1 vs. #2 on Jan. 3, 2000 (Super Alliance since 1998).

Multiple wins: Alabama (8); Mississippi (5); Georgia Tech, Oklahoma and Tennessee (4); Florida St., LSU and Nebraska (3); Florida, Georgia, Notre Dame, Pittsburgh, Santa Clara and TCU (2).

Year	
1935*	Tulane 20, Temple 14
1936	TCU 3, LSU 2
1937	Santa Clara 21, LSU 14
1938	Santa Clara 6, LSU 0
1939	TCU 15, Carnegie Tech 7
1940	Texas A&M 14, Tulane 13
1941	Boston College 19, Tennessee 13
1942	Fordham 2, Missouri 0
1943	Tennessee 14, Tulsa 7
1944	Georgia Tech 20, Tulsa 18
1945	Duke 29, Alabama 26
1946	Okla. A&M 33, St.Mary's 13
1947	Georgia 20, N. Carolina 10
1948	Texas 27, Alabama 7
1949	Oklahoma 14, N. Carolina 6
1950	Oklahoma 35, LSU 0
1951	Kentucky 13, Oklahoma 7
1952	Maryland 28, Tennessee 13
1953	Georgia Tech 24, Mississippi 7
1954	Georgia Tech 42, West Va. 19
1955	Navy 21, Mississippi 0
1956	Georgia Tech 7, Pittsburgh 0
1957	Baylor 13, Tennessee 7
1958	Mississippi 39, Texas 7
1959	LSU 7, Clemson 0
1960	Mississippi 21, LSU 0
1961	Mississippi 14, Rice 6
1962	Alabama 10, Arkansas 3
1963	Mississippi 17, Arkansas 13
1964	Alabama 12, Mississippi 7
1965	LSU 13, Syracuse 10
1966	Missouri 20, Florida 18
1967	Alabama 34, Nebraska 7
1968	LSU 20, Wyoming 13
1969	Arkansas 16, Georgia 2
1970	Mississippi 27, Arkansas 22
1971	Tennessee 34, Air Force 13
1972	Oklahoma 40, Auburn 22
1972†	Oklahoma 14, Penn St. 0
1973	Notre Dame 24, Alabama 23
1974	Nebraska 13, Florida 10
1975	Alabama 13, Penn St. 6
1977*	Pittsburgh 27, Georgia 3
1978	Alabama 35, Ohio St. 6
1979	Alabama 14, Penn St. 7
1980	Alabama 24, Arkansas 9
1981	Georgia 17, Notre Dame 10
1982	Pittsburgh 24, Georgia 20
1983	Penn St. 27, Georgia 23
1984	Auburn 9, Michigan 7
1985	Nebraska 28, LSU 10
1986	Tennessee 35, Miami-FL 7
1987	Nebraska 30, LSU 15
1988	16-16, Syracuse vs Auburn
1989	Florida St. 13, Auburn 7
1990	Miami-FL 33, Alabama 25
1991	Tennessee 23, Virginia 22
1992	Notre Dame 39, Florida 28
1993	Alabama 34, Miami-FL 13
1994	Florida 41, West Va. 7
1995	Florida St. 23, Florida 17
1995†	Va. Tech 28, Texas 10
1997	Florida 52, Florida St. 20
1998	Florida St. 31, Ohio St. 14

*January game from 1935-72 and since 1977 (except in 1995).

†Game played on Dec. 31 from 1972-75 and in 1995.

Orange Bowl

City: Miami, Fla. **Stadium:** Pro Player Stadium. **Capacity:** 74,916. **Playing surface:** Grass. **First game:** Jan. 1, 1935. **Playing sites:** Orange Bowl (1935 to 1995); Pro Player Stadium (since 1996). **Corporate title sponsor:** Federal Express (since 1989).

Automatic berths: Big 8 champion vs. Atlantic Coast Conference champion (1953-57 seasons); Big 8 champion vs. at-large opponent (1958-63 seasons and 1975-91 seasons); Big 8 champion vs. one of first five picks from 8-team Bowl Coalition pool (1992-94 seasons); #3 vs. #5 on Jan. 1, 1996; #4 vs. #6 on Dec. 31, 1996; and #1 vs. #2 on Jan. 2, 1998 (New Bowl Alliance since 1995); Big East or ACC champion vs. next best team in the pool; #1 vs. #2 Jan. 3, 2001 (Super Alliance since 1998).

Multiple wins: Oklahoma (11); Nebraska (8); Miami-FL (5); Alabama (4); Florida State, Georgia Tech and Penn St. (3); Clemson, Colorado, Georgia, LSU, Notre Dame and Texas (2).

Year
1935* Bucknell 26, Miami-FL 0
1936 Catholic U. 20, Mississippi 19
1937 Duquesne 13, Mississippi St. 12
1938 Auburn 6, Michigan St. 0
1939 Tennessee 17, Oklahoma 0

1940 Georgia Tech 21, Missouri 7
1941 Mississippi St. 14, Georgetown 7
1942 Georgia 40, TCU 26
1943 Alabama 37, Boston College 21
1944 LSU 19, Texas A&M 14
1945 Tulsa 26, Georgia Tech 12
1946 Miami-FL 13, Holy Cross 6
1947 Rice 8, Tennessee 0
1948 Georgia Tech 20, Kansas 14
1949 Texas 41, Georgia 28

1950 Santa Clara 21, Kentucky 13
1951 Clemson 15, Miami-FL 14
1952 Georgia Tech 17, Baylor 14
1953 Alabama 61, Syracuse 6
1954 Oklahoma 7, Maryland 0
1955 Duke 34, Nebraska 7
1956 Oklahoma 20, Maryland 6
1957 Colorado 27, Clemson 21

Year
1958 Oklahoma 48, Duke 21
1959 Oklahoma 21, Syracuse 6

1960 Georgia 14, Missouri 0
1961 Missouri 21, Navy 14
1962 LSU 25, Colorado 7
1963 Alabama 17, Oklahoma 0
1964 Nebraska 13, Auburn 7
1965† Texas 21, Alabama 17
1966 Alabama 39, Nebraska 28
1967 Florida 27, Georgia Tech 12
1968 Oklahoma 26, Tennessee 24
1969 Penn St. 15, Kansas 14

1970 Penn St. 10, Missouri 3
1971 Nebraska 17, LSU 12
1972 Nebraska 38, Alabama 6
1973 Nebraska 40, Notre Dame 6
1974 Penn St. 16, LSU 9
1975 Notre Dame 13, Alabama 11
1976 Oklahoma 14, Michigan 6
1977 Ohio St. 27, Colorado 10
1978 Arkansas 31, Oklahoma 6
1979 Oklahoma 31, Nebraska 24

Year
1980 Oklahoma 24, Florida St. 7
1981 Oklahoma 18, Florida St. 17
1982 Clemson 22, Nebraska 15
1983 Nebraska 21, LSU 20
1984 Miami-FL 31, Nebraska 30
1985 Washington 28, Oklahoma 17
1986 Oklahoma 25, Penn St. 10
1987 Oklahoma 42, Arkansas 8
1988 Miami-FL 20, Oklahoma 14
1989 Miami-FL 23, Nebraska 3

1990 Notre Dame, 21, Colorado 6
1991 Colorado 10, Notre Dame 9
1992 Miami-FL 22, Nebraska 0
1993 Florida St. 27, Nebraska 14
1994 Florida St. 18, Nebraska 16
1995 Nebraska 24, Miami-FL 17
1996 Florida St. 31, Notre Dame 26
1996** Nebraska 41, Virginia Tech 21
1998* Nebraska 42, Tennessee 17

*January game 1935-1996 and '98.
**December game in 1996
†Night game since 1965.

Cotton Bowl

City: Dallas, Tex. **Stadium:** Cotton Bowl. **Capacity:** 68,252. **Playing surface:** Grass. **First game:** Jan 1, 1937. **Playing sites:** Fair Park Stadium (1937) and Cotton Bowl (since 1938). **Corporate title sponsor:** Mobil Corporation (1988-95), Southwestern Bell (since 1997).

Automatic berths: SWC champion vs. at-large opponent (1941-91 seasons); SWC champion vs. one of first five picks from 8-team Bowl Coalition pool (1992-1994 seasons). second pick from Big 12 vs. first choice of WAC champion or second pick from Pac-10 (New Bowl Alliance since 1995).

Multiple wins: Texas (9); Notre Dame (5); Texas A&M (4); Rice (3); Alabama, Arkansas, Georgia, Houston, LSU, Penn St., SMU, Tennessee, TCU and UCLA (2).

Year
1937* TCU 16, Marquette 6
1938 Rice 28, Colorado 14
1939 St. Mary's 20, Texas Tech 13

1940 Clemson 6, Boston College 3
1941 Texas A&M 13, Fordham 12
1942 Alabama 29, Texas A&M 21
1943 Texas 14, Georgia Tech 7
1944 7-7, Texas vs Randolph Field
1945 Oklahoma A&M 34, TCU 0
1946 Texas 40, Missouri 27
1947 0-0, Arkansas vs LSU
1948 13-13, SMU vs Penn St.
1949 SMU 21, Oregon 13

1950 Rice 27, N. Carolina 13
1951 Tennessee 20, Texas 14
1952 Kentucky 20, TCU 7
1953 Texas 16, Tennessee 0
1954 Rice 28, Alabama 6
1955 Georgia Tech 14, Arkansas 6
1956 Mississippi 14, TCU 13
1957 TCU 28, Syracuse 27
1958 Navy 20, Rice 7

Year
1959 0-0, TCU vs Air Force

1960 Syracuse 23, Texas 14
1961 Duke 7, Arkansas 6
1962 Texas 12, Mississippi 7
1963 LSU 13, Texas 0
1964 Texas 28, Navy 6
1965 Arkansas 10, Nebraska 7
1966 LSU 14, Arkansas 7
1966† Georgia 24, SMU 9
1968* Texas A&M 20, Alabama 16
1969 Texas 36, Tennessee 13

1970 Texas 21, Notre Dame 17
1971 Notre Dame 24, Texas 11
1972 Penn St. 30, Texas 6
1973 Texas 17, Alabama 13
1974 Nebraska 19, Texas 3
1975 Penn St. 41, Baylor 20
1976 Arkansas 31, Georgia 10
1977 Houston 30, Maryland 21
1978 Notre Dame 38, Texas 10
1979 Notre Dame 35, Houston 34

Year
1980 Houston 17, Nebraska 14
1981 Alabama 30, Baylor 2
1982 Texas 14, Alabama 12
1983 SMU 7, Pittsburgh 3
1984 Georgia 10, Texas 9
1985 Boston College 45, Houston 28
1986 Texas A&M 36, Auburn 16
1987 Ohio St. 28, Texas A&M 12
1988 Texas A&M 35, Notre Dame 10
1989 UCLA 17, Arkansas 3

1990 Tennessee 31, Arkansas 27
1991 Miami-FL 46, Texas 3
1992 Florida St. 10, Texas A&M 2
1993 Notre Dame 28, Texas A&M 3
1994 Notre Dame 24, Texas A&M 21
1995 USC 55, Texas Tech 14
1996 Colorado 38, Oregon 6
1997 BYU 19, Kansas St. 15
1998 UCLA 29, Texas A&M 23

*January game from 1937-66 and since 1968.
†Game played on Dec. 31, 1966.

Bowl Games (Cont.)

Florida Citrus Bowl

City: Orlando, Fla. **Stadium:** Florida Cirtus Bowl. **Capacity:** 70,188. **Playing surface:** Grass. **First game:** Jan. 1, 1947. **Name change:** Tangerine Bowl (1947-82) and Florida Citrus Bowl (since 1983). **Playing sites:** Tangerine Bowl (1947-72, 1974-82), Florida Field in Gainesville (1973), Orlando Stadium (1983-85) and Florida Citrus Bowl (since 1986). The Tangerine Bowl, Orlando Stadium and Florida Citrus Bowl are all the same stadium. **Corporate title sponsors:** Florida Department of Cirtus (since 1983) and CompUSA (since 1992).

Automatic berths: Championship game of Atlantic Coast Regional Conference (1964-67 seasons); Mid-American Conference champion vs. Southern Conference champion (1968-71 seasons); ACC champion vs. at-large opponent (1988-91 seasons); second pick from SEC vs. second pick from Big 10 (1992-94 seasons); second pick from SEC vs. second pick form Big 10 (New Bowl Alliance since 1995).

Multiple wins: East Texas St., Miami-OH, Tennessee and Toledo (3); Auburn, Catawba, Clemson, East Carolina and Florida (2).

Year	
1947*	Catawba 31, Maryville 6
1948	Catawba 7, Marshall 0
1949	21-21, Murray St. vs Sul Ross St.
1950	St. Vincent 7, Emory & Henry 6
1951	M. Harvey 35, Emory & Henry 14
1952	Stetson 35, Arkansas St. 20
1953	E. Texas St. 33, Tenn. Tech 0
1954	7-7, E. Texas St. vs Arkansas St.
1955	Neb.-Omaha 7, Eastern Ky. 6
1956	6-6, Juniata vs Missouri Valley
1957	W. Texas St. 20, So. Miss. 13
1958	E. Texas St. 10, So. Miss. 9
1958†	E. Texas St. 26, Mo. Valley 7
1960*	Mid. Tenn. 21, Presbyterian 12
1960†	Citadel 27, Tenn. Tech 0
1961	Lamar 21, Middle Tenn. 14
1962	Houston 49, Miami-OH 21
1963	Western Ky. 27, Coast Guard 0
1964	E. Carolina 14, Massachusetts 13
1965	E. Carolina 31, Maine 0
1966	Morgan St. 14, West Chester 6
1967	Tenn-Martin 25, West Chester 8
1968	Richmond 49, Ohio U. 42
1969	Toledo 56, Davidson 33
1970	Toledo 40, Wm. & Mary 12
1971	Toledo 28, Richmond 3
1972	Tampa 21, Kent St. 18
1973	Miami-OH 16, Florida 7
1974	Miami-OH 21, Georgia 10
1975	Miami-OH 20, S. Carolina 7
1976	Oklahoma 49, BYU 21
1977	Florida St. 40, Texas Tech 17
1978	N.C. State 30, Pittsburgh 17
1979	LSU 34, Wake Forest 10
1980	Florida 35, Maryland 20
1981	Missouri 19, Southern Miss. 17
1982	Auburn 33, Boston College 26
1983	Tennessee 30, Maryland 23
1984	17-17, Florida St. vs Georgia
1985	Ohio St. 10, BYU 7
1987*	Auburn 16, USC 7
1988	Clemson 35, Penn St. 10
1989	Clemson 13, Oklahoma 6
1990	Illinois 31, Virginia 21
1991	Georgia Tech 45, Nebraska 21
1992	California 37, Clemson 13
1993	Georgia 21, Ohio St. 14
1994	Penn St. 31, Tennessee 13
1995	Alabama 24, Ohio St. 17
1996	Tennessee 20, Ohio St. 14
1997	Tennessee 48, Northwestern 28
1998	Florida 21, Penn St. 6

*January game from 1947-58, in 1960 and since 1987.

†December game from 1958 and 1960-85.

Gator Bowl

City: Jacksonville, Fla. **Stadium:** ALLTEL Stadium. **Capacity:** 73,000. **Playing surface:** Grass. **First game:** Jan. 1, 1946. **Playing sites:** Gator Bowl (1946-93), Florida Field in Gainesville (1994) and New Gator Bowl (since 1995). Name was changed to ALLTEL Stadium in 1997. **Corporate title sponsors:** Mazda Motors of America, Inc. (1986-91), Outback Steakhouse, Inc. (1992-94) and Toyota Motor Co. (starting in 1995).

Automatic berths: Third pick from SEC vs. sixth pick from 8-team Bowl Coalition pool (1992-94 seasons). second pick from ACC vs. second pick from Big East (New Bowl Alliance since 1995).

Multiple wins: Florida (6); North Carolina (5); Auburn and Clemson (4); Florida St. and Tennessee (3); Georgia, Georgia Tech, Maryland, Oklahoma, Pittsburgh, and Texas Tech (2).

Year	
1946*	Wake Forest 26, S. Carolina 14
1947	Oklahoma 34, N.C. State 13
1948	20-20, Maryland vs Georgia
1949	Clemson 24, Missouri 23
1950	Maryland 20, Missouri 7
1951	Wyoming 20, Wash. & Lee 7
1952	Miami-FL 14, Clemson 0
1953	Florida 14, Tulsa 13
1954	Texas Tech 35, Auburn 13
1954†	Auburn 33, Baylor 13
1955	Vanderbilt 25, Auburn 13
1956	Georgia Tech 21, Pittsburgh 14
1957	Tennessee 3, Texas A&M 0
1958	Mississippi 7, Florida 3
1960*	Arkansas 14, Georgia Tech 7
1960†	Florida 13, Baylor 12
1961	Penn St. 30, Georgia Tech 15
1962	Florida 17, Penn St. 7
1963	N. Carolina 35, Air Force 0
1965*	Florida St. 36, Oklahoma 19
1965†	Georgia Tech 31, Texas Tech 21
1966	Tennessee 18, Syracuse 12
1967	17-17, Florida St. vs Penn St.
1968	Missouri 35, Alabama 10
1969	Florida 14, Tennessee 13
1971*	Auburn 35, Mississippi 28
1971†	Georgia 7, N. Carolina 3
1972	Auburn 24, Colorado 3
1973	Texas Tech 28, Tennessee 19
1974	Auburn 27, Texas 3
1975	Maryland 13, Florida 0
1976	Notre Dame 20, Penn St. 9
1977	Pittsburgh 34, Clemson 3
1978	Clemson 17, Ohio St. 15
1979	N. Carolina 17, Michigan 15
1980	Pittsburgh 37, S. Carolina 9
1981	N. Carolina 31, Arkansas 27
1982	Florida St. 31, West Va. 12
1983	Florida 14, Iowa 6
1984	Oklahoma St. 21, S. Carolina 14
1985	Florida St. 34, Oklahoma St. 23
1986	Clemson 27, Stanford 21
1987	LSU 30, S. Carolina 13
1989*	Georgia 34, Michigan St. 27
1989†	Clemson 27, West Va. 7
1991*	Michigan 35, Mississippi 3
1991†	Oklahoma 48, Virginia 14
1992	Florida 27, N.C. State 10
1993	Alabama 24, N. Carolina 10
1994	Tennessee 45, Va. Tech 23
1996*	Syracuse 41, Clemson 0
1997	N. Carolina 20, West Va. 13
1998	N. Carolina 42, Va. Tech 3

*January game from 1946-54, 1960, 1965, 1971, 1989, 1991 and since 1996.

†December game from 1954-58, 1960-63, 1965-69, 1971-87, 1989 and 1991-94.

Holiday Bowl

City: San Diego, Calif. **Stadium:** Qualcomm. **Capacity:** 71,000. **Playing surface:** Grass. **First game:** Dec. 22, 1978. **Playing sites:** San Diego/Jack Murphy Stadium (since 1978). Name changed to Qualcomm Stadium in 1997. **Corporate title sponsors:** Sea World (1986-90), Thrifty Car Rental (1991-94), Chrysler-Plymouth Division of Chrysler Corp. (1995-97) and U.S. Filter/Culligan Water Tech. (since 1998).

Automatic berths: WAC champion vs. at-large opponent (1978-84, 1986-90 seasons); WAC champ vs. second pick from Big 10 (1991 season); WAC champ vs. third pick from Big 10 (1992-94 seasons). second choice of WAC champion or second pick from Pac-10 vs. third pick from Big 12 (New Bowl Alliance since 1995).

Multiple wins: BYU (4); Iowa and Ohio St. (2).

Year	
1978†	Navy 23, BYU 16
1979	Indiana 38, BYU 37
1980	BYU 46, SMU 45
1981	BYU 38, Washington St. 36
1982	Ohio St. 47, BYU 17
1983	BYU 21, Missouri 17
1984	BYU 24, Michigan 17
1985	Arkansas 18, Arizona St. 17
1986	Iowa 39, San Diego St. 38
1987	Iowa 20, Wyoming 19
1988	Oklahoma St. 62, Wyoming 14
1989	Penn St. 50, BYU 39
1990	Texas A&M 65, BYU 14
1991	13-13, Iowa vs BYU
1992	Hawaii 27, Illinois 17
1993	Ohio St. 28, BYU 21
1994	Michigan 24, Colo. St. 14
1995	Kansas St. 54, Colorado St. 21
1996	Colorado 33, Washington 21
1997	Colorado St. 35, Missouri 24

†December game since 1978.

Outback Bowl

City: Tampa, Fla. **Stadium:** Houlihan's. **Capacity:** 74,300. **Playing surface:** Grass. **First game:** Dec. 23, 1986. **Name change:** Hall of Fame Bowl (1986-95) and Outback Bowl (starting in 1995). **Playing site:** Tampa Stadium (since 1986). Name changed to Houlihan's Stadium in 1996. **Corporate title sponsor:** Outback Steakhouse, Inc. (starting in 1995).

Automatic berths: Fourth pick from ACC vs. fourth pick from Big 10 (1993-94 seasons); third pick from Big 10 vs. third pick from SEC (New Bowl Alliance since 1995).

Multiple wins: Michigan and Syracuse (2).

Year	
1986†	Boston College 27, Georgia 24
1988*	Michigan 28, Alabama 24
1989	Syracuse 23, LSU 10
1990	Auburn 31, Ohio St. 14
1991	Clemson 30, Illinois 0
1992	Syracuse 24, Ohio St. 17
1993	Tennessee 38, Boston Col. 23
1994	Michigan 42, N.C. State 7
1995	Wisconsin 34, Duke 20
1996	Penn St. 43, Auburn 14
1997	Alabama 17, Michigan 14
1998	Georgia 33, Wisconsin 6

†December game in 1986.
*January game since 1988.

Peach Bowl

City: Atlanta, Ga. **Stadium:** Georgia Dome. **Capacity:** 71,228. **Playing surface:** AstroTurf. **First game:** Dec. 30, 1968. **Playing sites:** Grant Field (1968-70), Atlanta-Fulton County Stadium (1971-92) and Georgia Dome (since 1993). **Corporate title sponsor:** Chick-fil-A (since 1998).

Automatic berths: Third pick from ACC vs. at-large opponent (1992 season); third pick from ACC vs. fourth pick from SEC (1993-94 seasons); third pick from ACC vs. fourth pick from SEC (New Bowl Alliance since 1995).

Multiple wins: N.C. State (4); West Virginia (3); Auburn, LSU and Virginia (2).

Year	
1968†	LSU 31, Florida St. 27
1969	West Va. 14, S. Carolina 3
1970	Arizona St. 48, N. Carolina 26
1971	Mississippi 41, Georgia Tech 18
1972	N.C. State 49, West Va. 13
1973	Georgia 17, Maryland 16
1974	6-6, Vanderbilt vs Texas Tech
1975	West Va. 13, N.C. State 10
1976	Kentucky 21, N. Carolina 0
1977	N.C. State 24, Iowa St. 14
1978	Purdue 41, Georgia Tech 21
1979	Baylor 24, Clemson 18
1981*	Miami-FL 20, Va. Tech 10
1981†	West Va. 26, Florida 6
1982	Iowa 28, Tennessee 22
1983	Florida St. 28, N. Carolina 3
1984	Virginia 27, Purdue 24
1985	Army 31, Illinois 29
1986	Va. Tech 25, N.C. State 24
1988*	Tennessee 27, Indiana 22
1988†	N.C. State 28, Iowa 23
1989	Syracuse 19, Georgia 18
1990	Auburn 27, Indiana 23
1992*	E. Carolina 37, N.C. State 34
1993	N. Carolina 21, Miss. St. 17
1993†	Clemson 14, Kentucky 13
1995*	N.C. State 24, Miss. St. 24
1995†	Virginia 34, Georgia 27
1996	LSU 10, Clemson 7
1998*	Auburn 21, Clemson 17

†December game from 1968-79, 1981-86, 1988-90, 1993, 1995 and 1996.
*January game in 1981, 1988, 1992-93, 1995 and 1998.

Alamo Bowl

City: San Antonio, Tex. **Stadium:** Alamodome. **Capacity:** 65,000. **Playing surface:** Turf. **First game:** Dec. 31, 1993. **Playing site:** Alamodome (since 1993). **Corporate title sponsor:** Builders Square (since 1993).

Automatic berths: third pick from SWC vs. fourth pick from Pac-10 (1993-94 seasons); fourth pick from Big 10 vs. fourth pick from Big 12 (New Bowl Alliance 1995).

Multiple wins: None.

Year	
1993†	California 37, Iowa 3
1994	Washington St. 10, Baylor 3
1995	Texas A&M 22, Michigan 20
1996	Iowa 27, Texas Tech 0
1997	Purdue 33, Oklahoma St. 20

†December game since 1993.

Bowl Games (Cont.)

Sun Bowl

City: El Paso, Tex. **Stadium:** Sun Bowl. **Capacity:** 52,000. **Playing surface:** AstroTurf. **First game:** Jan. 1, 1936. **Name changes:** Sun Bowl (1936-85), John Hancock Sun Bowl (1986-88), John Hancock Bowl (1989-93) and Sun Bowl (since 1994). **Playing sites:** Kidd Field (1936-62) and Sun Bowl (since 1963). **Corporate title sponsor:** John Hancock Financial Services (1986-93), Norwest Bank (since 1996).

Automatic berths: Eighth pick from 8-team Bowl Coalition pool vs. at-large opponent (1992); Seventh and eighth picks from 8-team Bowl Coalition pool (1993-94 seasons); third pick from Pac-10 vs. fifth pick from Big 10 (New Bowl Alliance since 1995).

Multiple wins: Texas Western/UTEP (5); Alabama and Wyoming (3); Nebraska, New Mexico St., North Carolina, Oklahoma, Pittsburgh, SW Texas, Stanford, Texas, West Texas St. and West Virginia (2).

Year	
1936*	14-14, Hardin-Simmons vs New Mexico St.
1937	Hardin-Simmons 34, Texas Mines 6
1938	West Va. 7, Texas Tech 6
1939	Utah 26, New Mexico 0
1940	0-0, Catholic U. vs Arizona St.
1941	W. Reserve 26, Arizona St. 13
1942	Tulsa 6, Texas Tech 0
1943	Second Air Force 13, Hardin-Simmons 7
1944	SW Texas 7, New Mexico 0
1945	SW Texas 35, U. of Mexico 0
1946	New Mexico 34, Denver 24
1947	Cincinnati 18, Va. Tech 6
1948	Miami-OH 13, Texas Tech 12
1949	West Va. 21, Texas Mines 12
1950	Tex. Western 33, Georgetown 20
1951	West Texas 14, Cincinnati 13
1952	Texas Tech 25, Pacific 14
1953	Pacific 26, Southern Miss. 7
1954	Tex. Western 37, So. Miss. 14
1955	Tex. Western 47, Florida St. 20
1956	Wyoming 21, Texas Tech 14
1957	Geo. Wash. 13, Tex. Western 0
1958*	Louisville 34, Drake 20
1958†	Wyoming 14, Hardin-Simmons 6
1959	New Mexico St. 28, N. Texas 8
1960	New Mexico St. 20, Utah St. 13
1961	Villanova 17, Wichita 9
1962	West Texas 15, Ohio U. 14
1963	Oregon 21, SMU 14
1964	Georgia 7, Texas Tech 0
1965	Texas Western 13, TCU 12
1966	Wyoming 28, Florida St. 20
1967	UTEP 14, Mississippi 7
1968	Auburn 34, Arizona 10
1969	Nebraska 45, Georgia 6
1970	Georgia Tech 17, Texas Tech 9
1971	LSU 33, Iowa St. 15
1972	N. Carolina 32, Texas Tech 28
1973	Missouri 34, Auburn 17
1974	Miss. St. 26, N. Carolina 24
1975	Pittsburgh 33, Kansas 19
1977*	Texas A&M 37, Florida 14
1977†	Stanford 24, LSU 14
1978	Texas 42, Maryland 0
1979	Washington 14, Texas 7
1980	Nebraska 31, Miss. St. 17
1981	Oklahoma 40, Houston 14
1982	N. Carolina 26, Texas 10
1983	Alabama 28, SMU 7
1984	Maryland 28, Tennessee 27
1985	13-13, Georgia vs Arizona
1986	Alabama 28, Washington 6
1987	Oklahoma St. 35, West Va. 33
1988	Alabama 29, Army 28
1989	Pittsburgh 31, Texas A&M 28
1990	Michigan St. 17, USC 16
1991	UCLA 6, Illinois 3
1992	Baylor 20, Arizona 15
1993	Oklahoma 41, Texas Tech 10
1994	Texas 35, N. Carolina 31
1995	Iowa 38, Washington 18
1996	Stanford 38, Michigan St. 0
1997	Arizona St. 17, Iowa 7

*January game from 1936-58 and in 1977.

†December game from 1958-75 and since 1977.

Insight.com Bowl

City: Tucson, Ariz. **Stadium:** Arizona. **Capacity:** 57,803. **Playing surface:** Grass. **First game:** Dec. 31, 1989. **Name change:** Copper Bowl (1989-1996), Insight.com Bowl (since 1997). **Playing site:** Arizona Stadium (since 1989). **Corporate title sponsors:** Domino's Pizza (1990-91), Weiser Lock (1992-1996) and Insight Enterprises (since 1997).

Automatic berths: Third pick from WAC vs. at-large opponent (1992 season); third pick from WAC vs. fourth pick from Big Eight (1993-94 seasons); second pick from WAC vs. sixth pick from Big 12 (New Bowl Alliance since 1995).

Multiple wins: Arizona (2).

Year	
1989†	Arizona 17, N.C. State 10
1990	California 17, Wyoming 15
1991	Indiana 24, Baylor 0
1992	Washington St. 31, Utah 28
1993	Kansas St. 52, Wyoming 17
1994	BYU 31, Oklahoma 6
1995	Texas Tech 55, Air Force 41
1996	Wisconsin 38, Utah 10
1997	Arizona 20, New Mexico 14

†December game since 1989.

Bowl Matchups of Unbeaten Teams

Date	Bowl	Winner	Head Coach	Score	Loser	Head Coach
1/1/21	Rose	California (8-0)	Andy Smith	28-0	Ohio St. (7-0)	John Wilce
1/2/22	Rose	Wash. & Jeff. (10-0)	Greasy Neale	0-0	California (9-0)	Andy Smith
1/1/27	Rose	Stanford (10-0)	Pop Warner	7-7	Alabama (9-0)	Wallace Wade
1/1/31	Rose	Alabama (9-0)	Wallace Wade	24-0	Washington St. (9-0)	Babe Hollingbery
1/2/39	Orange	Tennessee (10-0)	Bob Neyland	17-0	Oklahoma (10-0)	Tom Stidham
1/1/41	Sugar	Boston College (10-0)	Frank Leahy	19-13	Tennessee (10-0)	Bob Neyland
1/1/52	Sugar	Maryland (9-0)	Jim Tatum	28-13	Tennessee (10-0)	Bob Neyland
1/2/56	Orange	Oklahoma (10-0)	Bud Wilkinson	20-6	Maryland (10-0)	Jim Tatum
1/1/72	Orange	Nebraska (12-0)	Bob Devaney	38-6	Alabama (11-0)	Bear Bryant
12/31/73	Sugar	Notre Dame (10-0)	Ara Parseghian	24-23	Alabama (11-0)	Bear Bryant
1/2/87	Fiesta	Penn St. (11-0)	Joe Paterno	14-10	Miami-FL (11-0)	Jimmy Johnson
1/1/88	Orange	Miami-FL (11-0)	Jimmy Johnson	20-14	Oklahoma (11-0)	Barry Switzer
1/2/89	Fiesta	Notre Dame (11-0)	Lou Holtz	34-21	West Va. (11-0)	Don Nehlen
1/1/93	Sugar	Alabama (12-0)	Gene Stallings	34-13	Miami-FL. (11-0)	Dennis Erickson
1/2/96	Fiesta	Nebraska (11-0)	Tom Osborne	62-24	Florida (12-0)	Steve Spurrier

Liberty Bowl

City: Memphis, Tenn. **Stadium:** Liberty Bowl Memorial. **Capacity:** 62,380. **Playing surface:** Grass. **First game:** Dec. 19, 1959. **Playing sites:** Municipal Stadium in Philadelphia (1959-63), Convention Hall in Atlantic City, N.J. (1964), Memphis Memorial Stadium (1965-75) and Liberty Bowl Memorial Stadium (since 1976). Memphis Memorial Stadium renamed Liberty Bowl Memorial in 1976. **Corporate title sponsor:** St. Jude's Hospital (since 1993), AXA/Equitable (since 1997).

Automatic berths: Commander-in-Chief's Trophy winner (Army, Navy or Air Force) vs. at-large opponent (1989-92 seasons); none (1993 season); first pick from independent group of Cincinnati, East Carolina, Memphis, Southern Miss. and Tulane vs. at-large opponent (for the 1994 and '95 seasons); Conference USA champion vs. fourth pick from the Big East (New Bowl Alliance since 1995).

Multiple wins: Mississippi (4); Penn St. and Tennessee (3); Air Force, Alabama, N.C. State and Syracuse (2).

Year	
1959†	Penn St. 7, Alabama 0
1960	Penn St. 41, Oregon 12
1961	Syracuse 15, Miami-FL 14
1962	Oregon St. 6, Villanova 0
1963	Mississippi St. 16, N.C. State 12
1964	Utah 32, West Virginia 6
1965	Mississippi 13, Auburn 7
1966	Miami-FL 14, Virginia Tech 7
1967	N.C. State 14, Georgia 7
1968	Mississippi 34, Virginia Tech 17
1969	Colorado 47, Alabama 33
1970	Tulane 17, Colorado 3
1971	Tennessee 14, Arkansas 13
1972	Georgia Tech 31, Iowa St. 30
1973	N.C. State 31, Kansas 18
1974	Tennessee 7, Maryland 3
1975	USC 20, Texas A&M 0
1976	Alabama 36, UCLA 6
1977	Nebraska 21, N. Carolina 17
1978	Missouri 20, LSU 15
1979	Penn St. 9, Tulane 6
1980	Purdue 28, Missouri 25
1981	Ohio St. 31, Navy 28
1982	Alabama 21, Illinois 15
1983	Notre Dame 19, Boston Col. 18
1984	Auburn 21, Arkansas 15
1985	Baylor 21, LSU 7
1986	Tennessee 21, Minnesota 14
1987	Georgia 20, Arkansas 17
1988	Indiana 34, S. Carolina 10
1989	Mississippi 42, Air Force 29
1990	Air Force 23, Ohio St. 11
1991	Air Force 38, Mississippi St. 15
1992	Mississippi 13, Air Force 0
1993	Louisville 18, Michigan St. 7
1994	Illinois 30, E. Carolina 0
1995	E. Carolina 19, Stanford 13
1996	Syracuse 30, Houston 17
1997	Southern Miss. 41, Pittsburgh 7

†December game since 1959.

Sunshine Football Classic

City: Miami, Fla. **Stadium:** Pro Player. **Capacity:** 74,915. **Playing surface:** Grass. **First game:** Dec. 28, 1990. **Name change:** Blockbuster Bowl (1990-93), Carquest Bowl (1994-97) and Sunshine Football Classic (since 1998). **Playing site:** Joe Robbie Stadium (since 1990). Name changed to Pro Player Stadium in 1996. **Corporate title sponsors:** Blockbuster Video (1990-93) and Carquest Auto Parts (1993-97).

Automatic berths: Penn St. vs. seventh pick from 8-team Bowl Coalition pool (1992 season); third pick from Big East vs. fifth pick from SEC (1993-94 seasons); third pick from Big East vs. fifth pick from SEC (1995); third pick from Big East vs. fourth pick from ACC (1996-97); fourth pick from Big Ten vs. fourth pick from ACC (since 1998).

Year	
1990†	Florida St. 24, Penn St. 17
1991	Alabama 30, Colorado 25
1993*	Stanford 24, Penn St. 3
1994	Boston College 31, Virginia 13
1995	S. Carolina 24, West Va. 21
1995†	N. Carolina 20, Arkansas 10
1996	Miami-FL 31, Virginia 21
1997	Ga. Tech 35, W. Virginia 30

†December game from 1990-91 and since 1995.
*January game 1993-95.

Aloha Bowl

City: Honolulu, Hawaii. **Stadium:** Aloha. **Capacity:** 50,000. **Playing surface:** AstroTurf. **First game:** Dec. 25, 1982. **Playing site:** Aloha Stadium (since 1982). **Corporate title sponsor:** Jeep Eagle Division of Chrysler (since 1987).

Automatic berths: Second pick from WAC vs. third pick from Big Eight (1992-93 seasons); third pick from Big Eight vs. at-large opponent (1994 season); fifth pick from Big 12 vs. fourth pick from Pac-10 (New Bowl Alliance since 1995).

Multiple wins: Kansas and Washington (2).

Year	
1982†	Washington 21, Maryland 20
1983	Penn St. 13, Washington 10
1984	SMU 27, Notre Dame 20
1985	Alabama 24, USC 3
1986	Arizona 30, N. Carolina 21
1987	UCLA 20, Florida 16
1988	Washington St. 24, Houston 22
1989	Michigan St. 33, Hawaii 13
1990	Syracuse 28, Arizona 0
1991	Georgia Tech 18, Stanford 17
1992	Kansas 23, BYU 20
1993	Colorado 41, Fresno St. 30
1994	Boston Col. 12, Kansas St. 7
1995	Kansas 51, UCLA 30
1996	Navy 42, California 38
1997	Washington 51, Michigan St. 23

†December game since 1982.

Las Vegas Bowl

City: Las Vegas, Nev. **Stadium:** Sam Boyd. **Capacity:** 40,000. **Playing surface:** AstroTurf. **First game:** Dec. 18, 1992. **Playing site:** Sam Boyd Stadium (since 1992).

Automatic berths: Mid-American champion vs. Big West champion (1992-96); none (since 1997).

Note: The MAC and Big West champs have met in a bowl game since 1981, originally in Fresno at the California Bowl (1981-88, 1992) and California Raisin Bowl (1989-91). The results from 1981-91 are included below.

Multiple wins: Fresno St. (4); Bowling Green, San Jose St. and Toledo (2).

Year	
1981†	Toledo 27, San Jose St. 25
1982	Fresno St. 29, Bowling Green 28
1983	Northern Ill. 20, CS-Fullerton 13
1984*	UNLV 30, Toledo 13
1985	Fresno St. 51, Bowling Green 7
1986	San Jose St. 37, Miami-OH 7
1987	E. Michigan 30, San Jose St. 27
1988	Fresno St. 35, W. Michigan 30
1989	Fresno St. 27, Ball St. 6
1990	San Jose St. 48, C. Michigan 24
1991	Bowling Green 28, Fresno St. 21
1992	Bowling Green 35, Nevada 34
1993	Utah St. 42, Ball St. 33
1994	UNLV 52, C. Michigan 24
1995	Toledo 40, Nevada 37 (OT)
1996	Nevada 18, Ball St. 15
1997	Oregon 41, Air Force 13

†December game since 1981.
* Toledo later ruled winner of 1984 game by forfeit because UNLV used ineligible players.

Bowl Games (Cont.)

Independence Bowl

City: Shreveport, La. **Stadium:** Independence. **Capacity:** 50,832. **Playing surface:** Grass. **First game:** Dec. 13, 1976. **Playing site:** Independence Stadium (since 1976). **Corporate title sponsors:** Poulan/Weed Eater (1990-97) and Sanford (since 1998).

Automatic berths: Southland Conference champion vs. at-large opponent (1976-81 seasons); fifth pick from SEC vs. at-large (New Bowl Alliance since 1995).

Multiple wins: Air Force, LSU and Southern Miss (2).

Year	
1976†	McNeese St. 20, Tulsa 16
1977	La. Tech 24, Louisville 14
1978	E. Carolina 35, La. Tech 13
1979	Syracuse 31, McNeese St. 7
1980	Southern Miss 16, McNeese St. 14
1981	Texas A&M 33, Oklahoma St. 16
1982	Wisconsin 14, Kansas St. 3
1983	Air Force 9, Mississippi 3
1984	Air Force 23, Va. Tech 7
1985	Minnesota 20, Clemson 13
1986	Mississippi 20, Texas Tech 17
1987	Washington 24, Tulane 12
1988	Southern Miss 38, UTEP 18
1989	Oregon 27, Tulsa 24
1990	34-34, La. Tech vs Maryland
1991	Georgia 24, Arkansas 15
1992	Wake Forest 39, Oregon 35
1993	Va. Tech 45, Indiana 20
1994	Virginia 20, TCU 10
1995	LSU 45, Michigan St. 26
1996	Auburn 32, Army 29
1997	LSU 27, Notre Dame 9

†December game since 1976.

Humanitarian Bowl

City: Boise, Idaho. **Stadium:** Bronco. **Capacity:** 30,000. **Playing surface:** Turf. **First game:** Dec. 29, 1997. **Playing sites:** Bronco Stadium (since 1997). **Corporate title sponsor:** World Sports Humanitarian Hall of Fame (since 1997).

Automatic berths: Big West champion vs at-large (since 1997 season).

Year	
1997†	Cincinnati 35, Utah St. 19

†December game since 1997.

Motor City Bowl

City: Pontiac, Mich. **Stadium:** Pontiac Silverdome. **Capacity:** 80,368. **Playing surface:** Turf. **First game:** Dec. 26, 1997. **Playing sites:** Pontiac Silverdome (since 1997). **Corporate title sponsor:** Ford Division of Ford Motor Company (since 1997).

Automatic berths: Mid-American champions vs at-large (since 1997 season).

Year	
1997†	Mississippi 34, Marshall 31

†December game since 1997.

Bowl Championship Series

Division I-A football remains the only NCAA sport on any level that does not have a sanctioned national champion. To that end, the Bowl Coalition was formed in 1992 and was updated and renamed the Bowl Alliance in 1995 in an attempt to keep the bowl system intact while forcing an annual championship game between the regular season's two top-ranked teams.

The Bowl Championship Series is the organizers' latest attempt to finally guarantee that the teams ranked No. 1 & No. 2 will play each other in a "national title game" come January. The key difference from the 1992-97 Bowl Coalition/Bowl Alliance is that the Bowl Championship Series will include the Big 10 and Pac-10 champions. These teams, which were originally locked into playing in the Rose Bowl, will be allowed under the new system to move to another bowl game in order to create a match-up featuring the No. 1 & No. 2 teams.

The bowls (the Fiesta, Orange, and Sugar) which made up the old Bowl Alliance kept their spots in this new four-bowl alliance. The Fiesta Bowl will hold the first national championship (No. 1 vs. No. 2) game under the Bowl Championship Series contract on Jan. 4, 1999, followed by the Sugar (Jan. 3, 2000), the Orange (Jan. 3, 2001) and Rose (Jan. 3, 2002). ABC will pay the alliance $525 million over seven years in rights fees for the four "title"games, with the final three years part of an option clause.

The 1992 Coalition, which lasted three seasons, consolidated the resources of four major bowl games (the Cotton, Fiesta, Orange and Sugar), the champions of five major conferences (the ACC, Big East, Big Eight, Southeastern and Southwest) and the national following of independent Notre Dame. It worked two out of three years with No. 1 vs. No. 2 showdowns in the 1993 Sugar Bowl (#2 Alabama over #1 Miami-FL) and 1994 Orange Bowl (#1 Florida St. over #2 Nebraska). The 1995 Orange Bowl had to settle for No. 1 Nebraska beating No. 3 Miami-FL because #2 Penn St., the Big Ten champion, was obligated to play in the Rose Bowl.

The Bowl Alliance, which ended a three-year run after the 1997 season, was an updated version of the Coalition.

Non-Alliance matchups: ALAMO (fourth pick from Big 12 vs. fourth pick from Big 10); ALOHA (fourth pick from Pac-10 vs. fifth pick from Big 12); SUNSHINE FOOTBALL CLASSIC (sixth pick from Big 10 vs. fourth pick from ACC); CITRUS (second pick from Big 10 vs. second pick from SEC); COTTON (first choice of either WAC champ or second pick from Pac-10 vs. second pick from Big 12); OUTBACK (third pick from Big 10 vs. third pick from SEC); HOLIDAY (second choice of either WAC champ or second pick from Pac-10 vs. third pick from Big 12); HUMANITARIAN (Big West champ vs. at-large); INDEPENDENCE (fifth pick from SEC vs. at-large); INSIGHT.COM (second pick from WAC vs. sixth pick from the Big 12); LAS VEGAS (third pick from WAC vs. at-large); LIBERTY (Conference USA champ vs. fourth pick from Big East); MOTOR CITY (MAC champ vs. at-large); and PEACH (third pick from ACC vs. fourth pick from SEC).

All-Time Winningest Division I-A Teams

Schools classified as Division I-A for at least 10 years; through 1997 season (including bowl games).

Top 25 Winning Percentage

								Bowls		1997 Season	
		Yrs	Gm	W	L	T	Pct	App	Record	Bowl	Record
1	Notre Dame	109	1023	753	228	42	.757	22	13-9-0	Lost Indep.	7-6
2	Michigan	118	1066	776	254	36	.745	29	14-15-0	Won Rose	12-0
3	Alabama*	103	1020	717	260	43	.724	48	28-17-3	None	4-7
4	Ohio St.	108	1028	700	275	53	.707	30	13-7-0	Lost Sugar	10-3
5	Oklahoma	103	997	677	267	53	.706	32	20-11-1	None	4-8
6	Texas	105	1041	717	291	33	.705	37	17-18-2	None	4-7
7	Nebraska	108	1054	722	292	40	.704	36	18-18-0	Won Orange	13-0
8	USC	105	983	659	270	54	.698	38	25-13-0	None	6-5
9	Penn St.	111	1055	715	299	41	.697	34	21-11-2	Lost Citrus	9-3
10	Tennessee*	101	1014	677	285	52	.693	38	21-17-0	Lost Orange	11-2
11	Florida St.*	51	556	358	181	17	.659	26	16-8-2	Won Sugar	11-1
12	Washington*	108	968	593	325	50	.638	24	13-10-1	Won Aloha	8-4
13	Central Michigan	97	816	500	280	36	.635	5	3-2-0	None	2-9
14	Miami-OH*	109	940	573	323	44	.633	7	5-2-0	None	8-3
15	LSU*	104	991	603	341	47	.632	31	14-16-1	Won Indep.	9-3
16	Arizona St.	85	769	473	272	24	.631	17	10-6-1	Won Sun	9-3
17	Army	108	1010	611	348	51	.630	4	2-2-0	None	4-7
18	Georgia	104	1021	616	351	54	.630	33	16-14-3	Won Outback	10-2
19	Auburn*	105	987	593	347	74	.625	26	14-10-2	Won Peach	10-3
20	Miami-FL	71	736	443	274	19	.615	22	11-11-0	None	5-6
21	Colorado*	108	988	588	364	36	.613	21	9-12-0	None	0-11
22	Florida	91	913	535	338	40	608	25	12-13-0	Won Citrus	10-2
23	Texas A&M	103	1005	583	34	48	.604	23	12-11-0	Lost Cotton	9-4
24	Syracuse	108	1063	617	397	49	.603	18	10-7-1	Lost Fiesta	9-4
25	UCLA	79	800	464	299	37	.603	21	11-9-1	Won Cotton	10-2

*Includes games forefeited following rulings by the NCAA Executive Council and/or the Committee on Infractions.

Top 50 Victories

		Wins
1	Michigan	776
2	Notre Dame	753
3	Nebraska	722
4	Texas	717
	Alabama	717
6	Penn St.	715
7	Ohio St.	700
8	Tennessee	677
	Oklahoma	677
10	USC	659
11	Syracuse	617
12	Georgia	616
13	Army	611
14	LSU	603
15	Auburn	593
	Washington	593
17	Colorado	588
18	West Virginia	584
	North Carolina	584
20	Texas A&M	583
21	Pittsburgh	582
22	Georgia Tech	574
23	Miami-OH	573
24	Arkansas	571
25	Navy	570
26	Minnesota	568
27	Clemson	553
28	Virginia Tech	548
29	California	546
30	Rutgers	541
31	Michigan St.	540
32	Mississippi	537
33	Florida	535
34	Virginia	533
35	Missouri	525
36	Maryland	522
37	Boston College	517
38	Vanderbilt	515
39	Illinois	510
40	Wisconsin	505
41	Utah	504
42	Kentucky	503
43	Kansas	502
	Stanford	502
45	Central Michigan	500
46	Iowa	494
47	Purdue	491
48	Baylor	488
49	Tulsa	487
50	Arizona	485

Top 30 Bowl Appearances

		App	Record
1	Alabama	48	28-17-3
2	USC	38	25-13-0
	Tennessee	38	21-17-0
4	Texas	37	17-18-2
5	Nebraska	36	18-18-0
6	Penn St	34	21-11-2
7	Georgia	33	16-14-3
8	Oklahoma	32	20-11-1
9	LSU	31	14-16-1
10	Ohio St	30	13-17-0
11	Michigan	29	14-15-0
12	Arkansas	28	9-16-3
13	Georgia Tech	26	18-8-0
	Florida St	26	16-8-2
	Auburn	26	14-10-2
	Mississippi	26	15-11-0
17	Florida	25	12-13-0
18	Washington	24	13-10-1
19	Texas A&M	23	12-11-0
20	Miami-FL	22	11-11-0
	Texas Tech	22	5-16-1
	Notre Dame	22	13-9-0
	Clemson	22	12-10-0
	North Carolina	22	10-12-0
25	Colorado	21	9-12-0
	UCLA	21	11-9-1
27	BYU	20	7-12-1
	Missouri	20	8-12-0
29	Pittsburgh	19	8-11-0
	West Va.	19	8-11-0

Note: Alabama, Georgia, Georgia Tech, Notre Dame and Penn State are the only schools that have won all four of the traditional major bowl games– the Rose, Orange, Sugar and Cotton. Penn State and Notre Dame are the only schools to have won those four and the recently prestigious Fiesta bowl.

Major Conference Champions

Atlantic Coast Conference

Founded in 1953 when charter members all left Southern Conference to form ACC. **Charter members** (7): Clemson, Duke, Maryland, North Carolina, N.C. State, South Carolina and Wake Forest. **Admitted later** (3): Virginia in 1953 (began play in '54), Georgia Tech in 1979 (began play in '83); Florida St. in 1990 (began play in '92). **Withdrew later** (1): South Carolina in 1971 (became an independent after '70 season).

1998 playing membership (9): Clemson, Duke, Florida St., Georgia Tech, Maryland, North Carolina, N.C. State, Virginia and Wake Forest.

Multiple titles: Clemson (13); Maryland (8); Duke and N.C. State (7); Florida St. (6); North Carolina (5); Virginia (2).

Year	
1953	Duke (4-0) & Maryland (3-0)
1954	Duke (4-0)
1955	Maryland (4-0) & Duke (4-0)
1956	Clemson (4-0-1)
1957	N.C. State (5-0-1)
1958	Clemson (5-1)
1959	Clemson (6-1)
1960	Duke (5-1)
1961	Duke (5-1)
1962	Duke (6-0)
1963	North Carolina (6-1) & N.C. State (6-1)
1964	N.C. State (5-2)
1965	Clemson (5-2) & N.C. State (5-2)
1966	Clemson (6-1)
1967	Clemson (6-0)
1968	N.C. State (6-1)
1969	South Carolina (6-0)
1970	Wake Forest (5-1)
1971	North Carolina (6-0)
1972	North Carolina (6-0)
1973	N.C. State (6-0)
1974	Maryland (6-0)
1975	Maryland (5-0)
1976	Maryland (5-0)
1977	North Carolina (5-0-1)
1978	Clemson (6-0)
1979	N.C. State (5-1)
1980	North Carolina (6-0)
1981	Clemson (6-0)
1982	Clemson (6-0)
1983	Clemson (7-0) † & Maryland (5-0)
1984	Maryland (5-0)
1985	Maryland (6-0)
1986	Clemson (5-1-1)
1987	Clemson (6-1)
1988	Clemson (6-1)
1989	Virginia (6-1) & Duke (6-1)
1990	Georgia Tech (6-0-1)
1991	Clemson (6-0-1)
1992	Florida St. (8-0)
1993	Florida St. (8-0)
1994	Florida St. (8-0)
1995	Virginia (7-1) & Florida St. (7-1)
1996	Florida St. (8-0)
1997	Florida St. (8-0)

† On probation, ineligible for championship.

Big East Conference

Founded in 1991 when charter members gave up independent football status to form Big East. **Charter members** (8): Boston College, Miami-FL, Pittsburgh, Rutgers, Syracuse, Temple, Virginia Tech and West Virginia. **Note:** Temple and Virginia Tech are Big East members in football only.

1998 playing membership (8): Boston College, Miami-FL, Pittsburgh, Rutgers, Syracuse, Temple, Virginia Tech and West Virginia.

Conference champion: Member schools needed two years to adjust their regular season schedules in order to begin round-robin conference play in 1993. In the meantime, the 1991 and '92 Big East titles went to the highest-ranked member in the final regular season *USA Today*/CNN coaches' poll.

Multiple titles: Miami-FL (5); Syracuse (3); Virginia Tech (2).

Year	
1991	Miami-FL (2-0, #1) & Syracuse (5-0, #16)
1992	Miami-FL (4-0, #1)
1993	West Virginia (7-0)
1994	Miami-FL (7-0)
1995	Virginia Tech (6-1) & Miami-FL (6-1)
1996	Virginia Tech (6-1), Miami-FL (6-1) & Syracuse (6-1)
1997	Syracuse (6-1)

Big Ten Conference

Originally founded in 1895 as the Intercollegiate Conference of Faculty Representatives, better known as the Western Conference. **Charter members** (7): Chicago, Illinois, Michigan, Minnesota, Northwestern, Purdue and Wisconsin. **Admitted later** (5): Indiana and Iowa in 1899; Ohio St. in 1912; Michigan St. in 1950 (began play in '53); Penn St. in 1990 (began play in '93). **Withdrew later** (2): Michigan in 1907 (rejoined in '17); Chicago in 1940 (dropped football after '39 season). **Note:** Iowa belonged to both the Western and Missouri Valley conferences from 1907-10.

Unofficially called the **Big Ten** from 1912 until Chicago's withdrawal in 1939, then the **Big Nine** from 1940 until Michigan St. began conference play in 1953. Formally named the **Big Ten** in 1984 and has kept the name even after adding Penn St. as its 11th member.

1998 playing membership (11): Illinois, Indiana, Iowa, Michigan, Michigan St., Minnesota, Northwestern, Ohio St., Penn St., Purdue, and Wisconsin.

Multiple titles: Michigan (38); Ohio St. (27); Minnesota (18); Illinois (14); Iowa and Wisconsin (9); Purdue and Northwestern (7); Chicago and Michigan St. (6); Indiana (2).

Year	
1896	Wisconsin (2-0-1)
1897	Wisconsin (3-0)
1898	Michigan (3-0)
1899	Chicago (4-0)
1900	Iowa (3-0-1) & Minnesota (3-0-1)
1901	Michigan (4-0) & Wisconsin (2-0)
1902	Michigan (5-0)
1903	Michigan (3-0-1), Minnesota (3-0-1) & Northwestern (1-0-2)
1904	Minnesota (3-0) & Michigan (2-0)
1905	Chicago (7-0)
1906	Wisconsin (3-0), Minnesota (2-0) & Michigan (1-0)
1907	Chicago (4-0)
1908	Chicago (5-0)
1909	Minnesota (3-0)
1910	Illinois (4-0) & Minnesota (2-0)
1911	Minnesota (3-0-1)
1912	Wisconsin (6-0)
1913	Chicago (7-0)
1914	Illinois (6-0)
1915	Minnesota (3-0-1) & Illinois (3-0-2)
1916	Ohio St. (4-0)
1917	Ohio St. (4-0)
1918	Illinois (4-0), Michigan (2-0) & Purdue (1-0)
1919	Illinois (6-1)
1920	Ohio St. (5-0)
1921	Iowa (5-0)
1922	Iowa (5-0) & Michigan (4-0)
1923	Illinois (5-0) & Michigan (4-0)
1924	Chicago (3-0-3)
1925	Michigan (5-1)
1926	Michigan (5-0) & Northwestern (5-0)
1927	Illinois (5-0) & Minnesota (3-0-1)
1928	Illinois (4-1)
1929	Purdue (5-0)
1930	Michigan (5-0) & Northwestern (5-0)
1931	Purdue (5-1), Michigan (5-1) & Northwestern (5-1)
1932	Michigan (6-0) & Purdue (5-0-1)

Year	
1933	Michigan (5-0-1)
	& Minnesota (2-0-4)
1934	Minnesota (5-0)
1935	Minnesota (5-0)
	& Ohio St. (5-0)
1936	Northwestern (6-0)
1937	Minnesota (5-0)
1938	Minnesota (4-1)
1939	Ohio St. (5-1)
1940	Minnesota (6-0)
1941	Minnesota (5-0)
1942	Ohio St. (5-1)
1943	Purdue (6-0)
	& Michigan (6-0)
1944	Ohio St. (6-0)
1945	Indiana (5-0-1)
1946	Illinois (6-1)
1947	Michigan (6-0)
1948	Michigan (6-0)
1949	Ohio St. (4-1-1)
	& Michigan (4-1-1)
1950	Michigan (4-1-1)
1951	Illinois (5-0-1)
1952	Wisconsin (4-1-1)
	& Purdue (4-1-1)
1953	Michigan St. (5-1)
	& Illinois (5-1)
1954	Ohio St. (7-0)
1955	Ohio St. (6-0)
1956	Iowa (5-1)
1957	Ohio St. (7-0)
1958	Iowa (5-1)
1959	Wisconsin (5-2)
1960	Minnesota (5-1)
	& Iowa (5-1)
1961	Ohio St. (6-0)
1962	Wisconsin (6-1)
1963	Illinois (5-1-1)
1964	Michigan (6-1)
1965	Michigan St. (7-0)
1966	Michigan St. (7-0)
1967	Indiana (6-1),
	Purdue (6-1)
	& Minnesota (6-1)
1968	Ohio St. (7-0)
1969	Ohio St. (6-1)
	& Michigan (6-1)
1970	Ohio St. (7-0)
1971	Michigan (8-0)
1972	Ohio St. (7-1)
	& Michigan (7-1)
1973	Ohio St. (7-0-1)
	& Michigan (7-0-1)
1974	Ohio St. (7-1)
	& Michigan (7-1)
1975	Ohio St. (8-0)
1976	Michigan (7-1)
	& Ohio St. (7-1)
1977	Michigan (7-1)
	& Ohio St. (7-1)
1978	Michigan (7-1)
	& Michigan St. (7-1)
1979	Ohio St. (8-0)
1980	Michigan (8-0)
1981	Iowa (6-2)
	& Ohio St. (6-2)
1982	Michigan (8-1)
1983	Illinois (9-0)
1984	Ohio St. (7-2)
1985	Iowa (7-1)
1986	Michigan (7-1)
	& Ohio St. (7-1)
1987	Michigan St. (7-0-1)
1988	Michigan (7-0-1)
1989	Michigan (8-0)
1990	Iowa (6-2),
	Michigan (6-2),
	Michigan St. (6-2)
	& Illinois (6-2)
1991	Michigan (8-0)
1992	Michigan (6-0-2)
1993	Wisconsin (6-1-1)
	& Ohio St. (6-1-1)
1994	Penn St. (8-0)
1995	Northwestern (8-0)
1996	Ohio St. (7-1)
	& Northwestern (7-1)
1997	Michigan (8-0)

Big 12 Conference

Originally founded in 1907 as the Missouri Valley Intercollegiate Athletic Assn. **Charter members** (5): Iowa, Kansas, Missouri, Nebraska and Washington University of St. Louis. **Admitted later** (11): Drake and Iowa St. (then Ames College) in 1908; Kansas St. (then Kansas College of Applied Science and Agriculture) in 1913; Grinnell (Iowa) College in 1919; Oklahoma in 1920; Oklahoma A&M (now Oklahoma St.) in 1925; Colorado in 1947 (began play in '48); Baylor, Texas, Texas A&M and Texas Tech in 1994 (all four began play in '96).

Withdrew later (1): Iowa in 1911 (left for Big Ten after 1910 season); **Excluded later** (4): Drake, Grinnell, Oklahoma A&M and Washington-MO (left out when MVIAA cut membership to six teams in 1928.

Streamlined MVIAA unofficially called **Big Six** from 1928-47 with surviving members Iowa St., Kansas, Kansas St., Missouri, Nebraska and Oklahoma. Became the **Big Seven** after 1947 season when Colorado came over from the Skyline Conference, and then the **Big Eight** with the return of Oklahoma A&M in 1957. A&M, which resumed conference play in '60, became Oklahoma St. on July 10, 1957. The MVIAA was officially renamed the Big Eight in 1964 and became the **Big 12** after the 1995-96 academic year with the arrival of Baylor, Texas, Texas A&M and Texas Tech from the defunct Southwest Conference.

1998 playing membership (12): Baylor, Colorado, Iowa St., Kansas, Kansas St., Missouri, Nebraska, Oklahoma, Oklahoma St., Texas, Texas A&M and Texas Tech.

Multiple titles: Nebraska (42); Oklahoma (33); Missouri (12); Colorado and Kansas (5); Iowa St. and Oklahoma St. (2).

Year	
1907	Iowa (1-0)
	& Nebraska (1-0)
1908	Kansas (4-0)
1909	Missouri (4-0-1)
1910	Nebraska (2-0)
1911	Iowa St. (2-0-1)
	& Nebraska (2-0-1)
1912	Iowa St. (2-0)
	& Nebraska (2-0)
1913	Missouri (4-0)
	& Nebraska (3-0)
1914	Nebraska (3-0)
1915	Nebraska (4-0)
1916	Nebraska (3-1)
1917	Nebraska (2-0)
1918	Vacant (WW I)
1919	Missouri (4-0-1)
1920	Oklahoma (4-0-1)
1921	Nebraska (3-0)
1922	Nebraska (5-0)
1923	Nebraska (3-0-2)
	& Kansas (3-0-3)
1924	Missouri (5-1)
1925	Missouri (5-1)
1926	Okla. A&M (3-0-1)
1927	Missouri (5-1)
1928	Nebraska (4-0)
1929	Nebraska (3-0-2)
1930	Kansas (4-1)
1931	Nebraska (5-0)
1932	Nebraska (5-0)
1933	Nebraska (5-0)
1934	Kansas St. (5-0)
1935	Nebraska (4-0-1)
1936	Nebraska (5-0)
1937	Nebraska (3-0-2)
1938	Oklahoma (5-0)
1939	Missouri (5-0)
1940	Nebraska (5-0)
1941	Missouri (5-0)
1942	Missouri (4-0-1)
1943	Oklahoma (5-0)
1944	Oklahoma (4-0-1)
1945	Missouri (5-0)
1946	Oklahoma (4-1)
	& Kansas (4-1)
1947	Kansas (4-0-1)
	& Oklahoma (4-0-1)
1948	Oklahoma (5-0)
1949	Oklahoma (5-0)
1950	Oklahoma (6-0)
1951	Oklahoma (6-0)
1952	Oklahoma (5-0-1)
1953	Oklahoma (6-0)
1954	Oklahoma (6-0)
1955	Oklahoma (6-0)
1956	Oklahoma (6-0)
1957	Oklahoma (6-0)
1958	Oklahoma (6-0)
1959	Oklahoma (5-1)
1960	Missouri (7-0)
1961	Colorado (7-0)
1962	Oklahoma (7-0)
1963	Nebraska (7-0)
1964	Nebraska (6-1)
1965	Nebraska (7-0)
1966	Nebraska (6-1)
1967	Oklahoma (7-0)
1968	Kansas (6-1)
	& Oklahoma (6-1)
1969	Missouri (6-1)
	& Nebraska (6-1)
1970	Nebraska (7-0)
1971	Nebraska (7-0)
1972	Nebraska (5-1-1)*
1973	Oklahoma (7-0)
1974	Oklahoma (7-0)
1975	Nebraska (6-1)
	& Oklahoma (6-1)
1976	Colorado (5-2),
	Oklahoma (5-2)
	& Oklahoma St. (5-2)
1977	Oklahoma (7-0)
1978	Nebraska (6-1)
	& Oklahoma (6-1)
1979	Oklahoma (7-0)
1980	Oklahoma (7-0)
1981	Nebraska (7-0)
1982	Nebraska (7-0)
1983	Nebraska (7-0)
1984	Oklahoma (6-1)
	& Nebraska (6-1)
1985	Oklahoma (7-0)
1986	Oklahoma (7-0)
1987	Oklahoma (7-0)
1988	Nebraska (7-0)
1989	Colorado (7-0)
1990	Colorado (7-0)
1991	Nebraska (6-0-1)
	& Colorado (6-0-1)
1992	Nebraska (6-1)
1993	Nebraska (7-0)
1994	Nebraska (7-0)
1995	Nebraska (7-0)

*Oklahoma (6-1) forfeited title in 1972.

Major Conference Champions (Cont.)

Big 12 Championship Game

After expanding to 12 teams and splitting into two divisions in 1996, the Big 12 (formerly the Big Eight) now stages a conference championship game between the two division winners on the first Saturday in December at the Trans World Dome in St. Louis. The divisions: NORTH— Colorado, Iowa St., Kansas, Kansas St., Missouri and Nebraska; SOUTH— Baylor, Oklahoma, Oklahoma St., Texas, Texas A&M and Texas Tech.

Year	Year
1996 Texas 37, Nebraska 27	1997 Nebraska 54, Texas A&M 15

Big West Conference

Originally founded in 1969 as Pacific Coast Athletic Assn. **Charter members** (7): CS-Los Angeles, Fresno St., Long Beach St., Pacific, San Diego St., San Jose St. and UC-Santa Barbara. **Admitted later** (12): CS-Fullerton in 1974; Utah St. in 1977 (began play in '78); UNLV in 1982; New Mexico St. in 1983 (began play in '84); Nevada in 1991 (began play in '92); Arkansas St., Louisiana Tech, Northern Illinois and SW Louisiana in 1992 (all four began play in football only in '93); Boise St., Idaho and North Texas in 1994 (all three began play in '96). **Withdrew later** (13): CS-Los Angeles and UC-Santa Barbara in 1972 (both dropped football after '71 season); San Diego St. in 1975 (became an independent after '75 season); Fresno St. in 1991 (left for WAC after '91 season); Long Beach St. in 1991 (dropped football after '91 season); CS-Fullerton in 1992 (dropped football after '92 season); San Jose St. and UNLV in 1994 (left for WAC after '95 season); Pacific in 1995 (dropped football after '95 season); Arkansas St., Louisiana Tech, Northern Illinois and SW Louisiana in 1995 (all four returned to independent football status after '95 season). **Conference renamed** Big West in 1988.

1998 playing membership (6): Boise St., Idaho, Nevada, New Mexico St., North Texas and Utah St.

Multiple titles: San Jose St. (8); Fresno St. (6); San Diego St. (5); Nevada and Utah St. (4); Long Beach St. (3); CS-Fullerton and SW Louisiana (2).

Year		Year		Year		Year	
1969	San Diego St. (6-0)	1978	San Jose St. (4-1)	1987	San Jose St. (7-0)	1994	UNLV (5-1),
1970	Long Beach St. (5-1)		& Utah St. (4-1)	1988	Fresno St. (7-0)		Nevada (5-1),
	& San Diego St. (5-1)	1979	Utah St. (4-0-1)*	1989	Fresno St. (7-0)		& SW Louisiana (5-1)
1971	Long Beach St. (5-1)	1980	Long Beach St. (5-0)	1990	San Jose St. (7-0)	1995	Nevada (6-0)
1972	San Diego St. (4-0)	1981	San Jose St. (5-0)	1991	Fresno St. (6-1)	1996	Nevada (4-1)
1973	San Diego St. (3-0-1)	1982	Fresno St. (6-0)		& San Jose St. (6-1)		& Utah St. (4-1)
1974	San Diego St. (4-0)	1983	CS-Fullerton (5-1)	1992	Nevada (5-1)	1997	Utah St. (4-1)
1975	San Jose St. (5-0)	1984	CS-Fullerton (6-1)†	1993	Utah St. (5-1)		& Nevada (4-1)
1976	San Jose St. (4-0)	1985	Fresno St. (7-0)		& SW Louisiana (5-1)		
1977	Fresno St. (4-0)	1986	San Jose St. (7-0)				

*San Jose St. (4-0-1) forfeited share of title in 1979.
†UNLV (7-0) forfeited title in 1984.

Conference USA

Founded in 1994 by six independent football schools which began play as a conference in 1996. **Charter members** (6): Cincinnati, Houston, Louisville, Memphis, Southern Mississippi and Tulane. **Admitted later** (2): East Carolina in 1997 and Univ. of Alabama-Birmingham in 1999; **1998 playing members** (7): Cincinnati, East Carolina, Houston, Louisville, Memphis, Southern Mississippi and Tulane.

Multiple titles: Southern Mississippi (2).

Year	Year
1996 Southern Mississippi (4-1)	1997 Southern Mississippi (6-0)
& Houston (4-1)	

Ivy League

First called the "Ivy League" in 1937 by sportswriter Caswell Adams of the *New York Herald Tribune*. Unofficial conference of 10 eastern teams was occasionally referred to as the "Old 10" and included: Army, Brown, Columbia, Cornell, Dartmouth, Harvard, Navy, Pennsylvania, Princeton and Yale. Army and Navy were dropped from the group after 1940. **League formalized** in 1954 for play beginning in 1956. **Charter members** (8): Brown, Columbia, Cornell, Dartmouth, Harvard, Pennsylvania, Princeton, and Yale. League downgraded from Division I to Division I-AA after 1977 season. **1998 playing membership:** the same.

Multiple titles: Dartmouth (17); Yale (12); Harvard and Penn (9); Princeton (8); Cornell (3).

Year		Year		Year		Year	
1956	Yale (7-0)	1968	Harvard (6-0-1)	1978	Dartmouth (6-1)	1989	Princeton (6-1)
1957	Princeton (6-1)		& Yale (6-0-1)	1979	Yale (6-1)		& Yale (6-1)
1958	Dartmouth (6-1)	1969	Dartmouth (6-1),	1980	Yale (6-1)	1990	Cornell (6-1)
1959	Penn (6-1)		Yale (6-1)	1981	Yale (6-1)		& Dartmouth (6-1)
1960	Yale (7-0)		& Princeton (6-1)		& Dartmouth (6-1)	1991	Dartmouth (6-0-1)
1961	Columbia (6-1)	1970	Dartmouth (7-0)	1982	Harvard (5-2),	1992	Dartmouth (6-1)
	& Harvard (6-1)	1971	Cornell (6-1)		Penn (5-2)		& Princeton (6-1)
1962	Dartmouth (7-0)		& Dartmouth (6-1)		& Dartmouth (5-2)	1993	Penn (7-0)
1963	Dartmouth (5-2)	1972	Dartmouth (5-1-1)	1983	Harvard (5-1-1)	1994	Penn (7-0)
	& Princeton (5-2)	1973	Dartmouth (6-1)		& Penn (5-1-1)	1995	Princeton (5-1-1)
1964	Princeton (7-0)	1974	Harvard (6-1)	1984	Penn (7-0)	1996	Dartmouth (7-0)
1965	Dartmouth (7-0)		& Yale (6-1)	1985	Penn (6-1)	1997	Harvard (7-0)
1966	Dartmouth (6-1),	1975	Harvard (6-1)	1986	Penn (7-0)		
	Harvard (6-1)	1976	Brown (6-1)	1987	Harvard (6-1)		
	& Princeton (6-1)		& Yale (6-1)	1988	Penn (6-1)		
1967	Yale (7-0)	1977	Yale (6-1)		& Cornell (6-1)		

Mid-American Conference

Founded in 1946. **Charter members** (6): Butler, Cincinnati, Miami-OH, Ohio University, Western Michigan and Western Reserve (Miami and WMU began play in '48). **Admitted later** (12): Kent St. (now Kent) and Toledo in 1951 (Toledo began play in '52); Bowling Green in 1952; Marshall in 1954; Central Michigan and Eastern Michigan in 1972 (CMU began play in '75 and EMU in '76); Ball St. and Northern Illinois in 1973 (both began play in '75); Akron in 1991 (began play in '92); Marshall and Northern Illinois in 1995 (both resumed play in '97); Buffalo in 1995 (will begin play in '99). **Withdrew later** (5): Butler in 1950 (left for the Indiana Collegiate Conference); Cincinnati in 1953 (went independent); Western Reserve (now Case Western) in 1955 (left for President's Athletic Conference); Marshall in 1969 (went independent); and Northern Illinois in 1986 (went independent).

1998 playing membership (12): Akron, Ball St., Bowling Green, Central Michigan, Eastern Michigan, Kent, Marshall, Miami-OH, Northern Illinois, Ohio University, Toledo and Western Michigan.

Multiple titles: Miami-OH (13); Bowling Green (10); Toledo (8); Ball St. and Ohio University (5); Central Michigan and Cincinnati (4); Western Michigan (2).

Year	
1947	Cincinnati (3-1)
1948	Miami-OH (4-0)
1949	Cincinnati (4-0)
1950	Miami-OH (4-0)
1951	Cincinnati (3-0)
1952	Cincinnati (3-0)
1953	Ohio Univ. (5-0-1) & Miami-OH (3-0-1)
1954	Miami-OH (4-0)
1955	Miami-OH (5-0)
1956	Bowling Green (5-0-1) & Miami-OH (4-0-1)
1957	Miami-OH (5-0)
1958	Miami-OH (5-0)
1959	Bowling Green (6-0)
1960	Ohio Univ. (6-0)
1961	Bowling Green (5-1)
1962	Bowling Green (5-0-1)
1963	Ohio Univ. (5-1)
1964	Bowling Green (5-1)
1965	Bowling Green (5-1) & Miami-OH (5-1)
1966	Miami-OH (5-1) & Western Mich. (5-1)
1967	Toledo (5-1) & Ohio Univ. (5-1)
1968	Ohio Univ. (6-0)
1969	Toledo (5-0)
1970	Toledo (5-0)
1971	Toledo (5-0)
1972	Kent St. (4-1)
1973	Miami-OH (5-0)
1974	Miami-OH (5-0)
1975	Miami-OH (6-0)
1976	Ball St. (4-1)
1977	Miami-OH (5-0)
1978	Ball St. (8-0)
1979	Central Mich. (8-0-1)
1980	Central Mich. (7-2)
1981	Toledo (8-1)
1982	Bowling Green (7-2)
1983	Northern Ill. (8-1)
1984	Toledo (7-1-1)
1985	Bowling Green (9-0)
1986	Miami-OH (6-2)
1987	Eastern Mich. (7-1)
1988	Western Mich. (7-1)
1989	Ball St. (6-1-1)
1990	Central Mich. (7-1) & Toledo (7-1)
1991	Bowling Green (8-0)
1992	Bowling Green (8-0)
1993	Ball St. (7-0-1)
1994	Central Mich. (8-1)
1995	Toledo (7-0-1)
1996	Ball St. (7-1)
1997	Marshall (8-1)

Pacific-10 Conference

Originally founded in 1915 as Pacific Coast Conference. **Charter members** (4): California, Oregon, Oregon St. and Washington. **Admitted later** (6): Washington St. in 1917; Stanford in 1918; Idaho and USC (Southern Cal) in 1922; Montana in 1924; and UCLA in 1928. **Withdrew later** (1): Montana in 1950 (left for the Mountain States Conf.).

The **PCC** dissolved in 1959 and the **AAWU** (Athletic Assn. of Western Universities) was founded. **Charter members** (5): California, Stanford, UCLA, USC and Washington. **Admitted later** (5): Washington St. in 1962; Oregon and Oregon St. in 1964; Arizona and Arizona St. in 1978. **Conference renamed** Pacific-8 in 1968 and Pacific-10 in 1978.

1998 playing membership (10): Arizona, Arizona St., California, Oregon, Oregon St., Stanford, UCLA, USC, Washington and Washington St.

Multiple titles: USC (31); UCLA (16); Washington (14); California (13); Stanford (11); Oregon (5); Oregon St. (4); Washington St. (3); Arizona St. (2).

Year	
1916	Washington (3-0-1)
1917	Washington St. (3-0)
1918	California (3-0)
1919	Oregon (2-1) & Washington (2-1)
1920	California (3-0)
1921	California (5-0)
1922	California (3-0)
1923	California (5-0)
1924	Stanford (3-0-1)
1925	Washington (5-0)
1926	Stanford (4-0)
1927	USC (4-0-1) & Stanford (4-0-1)
1928	USC (4-0-1)
1929	USC (6-1)
1930	Washington St. (6-0)
1931	USC (7-0)
1932	USC (6-0)
1933	Oregon (4-1) & Stanford (4-1)
1934	Stanford (5-0)
1935	California (4-1), Stanford (4-1) & UCLA (4-1)
1936	Washington (6-0-1)
1937	California (6-0-1)
1938	USC (6-1) & California (6-1)
1939	USC (5-0-2) & UCLA (5-0-3)
1940	Stanford (7-0)
1941	Oregon St. (7-2)
1942	UCLA (6-1)
1943	USC (4-0)
1944	USC (3-0-2)
1945	USC (5-1)
1946	UCLA (7-0)
1947	USC (6-0)
1948	California (6-0) & Oregon (6-0)
1949	California (7-0)
1950	California (5-0-1)
1951	Stanford (6-1)
1952	USC (6-0)
1953	UCLA (6-1)
1954	UCLA (6-0)
1955	UCLA (6-0)
1956	Oregon St. (6-1-1)
1957	Oregon (6-2) & Oregon St. (6-2)
1958	California (6-1)
1959	Washington (3-1), USC (3-1) & UCLA (3-1)
1960	Washington (4-0)
1961	UCLA (3-1)
1962	USC (4-0)
1963	Washington (4-1)
1964	Oregon St. (3-1) & USC (3-1)
1965	UCLA (4-0)
1966	USC (4-1)
1967	USC (6-1)
1968	USC (6-0)
1969	USC (6-0)
1970	Stanford (6-1)
1971	Stanford (6-1)
1972	USC (7-0)
1973	USC (7-0)
1974	USC (6-0-1)
1975	UCLA (6-1) & California (6-1)
1976	USC (7-0)
1977	Washington (6-1)
1978	USC (6-1)
1979	USC (6-0-1)
1980	Washington (6-1)
1981	Washington (6-2)
1982	UCLA (5-1-1)
1983	UCLA (6-1-1)
1984	USC (7-1)
1985	UCLA (6-2)
1986	Arizona St. (5-1-1)
1987	USC (7-1) & UCLA (7-1)
1988	USC (8-0)
1989	USC (6-0-1)
1990	Washington (7-1)
1991	Washington (8-0)
1992	Washington (6-2) & Stanford (6-2)
1993	UCLA (6-2), Arizona (6-2) & USC (6-2)
1994	Oregon (7-1)
1995	USC (6-1-1) & Washington (6-1-1)
1996	Arizona St. (8-0)
1997	Washington St. (7-1) & UCLA (7-1)

Major Conference Champions (Cont.)

Southeastern Conference

Founded in 1933 when charter members all left Southern Conference to form SEC. **Charter members** (13): Alabama, Auburn, Florida, Georgia, Georgia Tech, Kentucky, LSU (Louisiana St.), Mississippi, Mississippi St., Sewanee, Tennessee, Tulane and Vanderbilt. **Admitted later** (2): Arkansas and South Carolina in 1990 (both began play in '92). **Withdrew later** (3): Sewanee in 1940; Georgia Tech in 1964; and Tulane in 1966.

1998 playing membership (12): Alabama, Arkansas, Auburn, Florida, Georgia, Kentucky, LSU, Mississippi, Mississippi St., South Carolina, Tennessee and Vanderbilt. **Note:** Conference title decided by championship game between Western and Eastern division winners since 1992.

Multiple titles: Alabama (20); Tennessee (12); Georgia (10); LSU (7); Mississippi (6); Auburn, Florida and Georgia Tech (5); Tulane (3); Kentucky (2).

Year	
1933	Alabama (5-0-1)
1934	Tulane (8-0) & Alabama (7-0)
1935	LSU (5-0)
1936	LSU (6-0)
1937	Alabama (6-0)
1938	Tennessee (7-0)
1939	Tennessee (6-0), Georgia Tech (6-0) & Tulane (5-0)
1940	Tennessee (5-0)
1941	Mississippi St. (4-0-1)
1942	Georgia (6-1)
1943	Georgia Tech (3-0)
1944	Georgia Tech (4-0)
1945	Alabama (6-0)
1946	Georgia (5-0) & Tennessee (5-0)
1947	Mississippi (6-1)
1948	Georgia (6-0)
1949	Tulane (5-1)
1950	Kentucky (5-1)
1951	Georgia Tech (7-0) & Tennessee (5-0)
1952	Georgia Tech (6-0)
1953	Alabama (4-0-3)
1954	Mississippi (5-1)
1955	Mississippi (5-1)
1956	Tennessee (6-0)
1957	Auburn (7-0)
1958	LSU (6-0)
1959	Georgia (7-0)
1960	Mississippi (5-0-1)
1961	Alabama (7-0) & LSU (6-0)
1962	Mississippi (6-0)
1963	Mississippi (5-0-1)
1964	Alabama (8-0)
1965	Alabama (6-1-1)
1966	Alabama (6-0) & Georgia (6-0)
1967	Tennessee (6-0)
1968	Georgia (5-0-1)
1969	Tennessee (5-1)
1970	LSU (5-0)
1971	Alabama (7-0)
1972	Alabama (7-1)
1973	Alabama (8-0)
1974	Alabama (6-0)
1975	Alabama (6-0)
1976	Georgia (5-1) & Kentucky (5-1)
1977	Alabama (7-0) & Kentucky (6-0)
1978	Alabama (6-0)
1979	Alabama (6-0)
1980	Georgia (6-0)
1981	Georgia (6-0) & Alabama (6-0)
1982	Georgia (6-0)
1983	Auburn (6-0)
1984	Florida (5-0-1)*
1985	Florida (5-1)† & Tennessee (5-1)
1986	LSU (5-1)
1987	Auburn (5-0-1)
1988	Auburn (6-1) & LSU (6-1)
1989	Alabama (6-1), Tennessee (6-1) & Auburn (6-1)
1990	Florida (6-1)† & Tennessee (5-1-1)
1991	Florida (7-0)
1992	Alabama (8-0)
1993	Florida (7-1)
1994	Florida (7-1)
1995	Florida (8-0)
1996	Florida (9-0)
1997	Tennessee (8-1)

*Title vacated.

†On probation, ineligible for championship.

Southwest Conference (1914-95)

Founded in 1914 as Southwest Intercollegiate Athletic Conference. **Charter members** (8): Arkansas, Baylor, Oklahoma, Oklahoma A&M (now Oklahoma St.), Rice, Southwestern, Texas and Texas A&M. **Admitted later** (5): SMU (Southern Methodist) in 1918; Phillips University in 1920; TCU (Texas Christian) in 1923; Texas Tech in 1956 (began play in '60); Houston in 1971 (began play in '76). **Withdrew later** (9): Southwestern in 1917 (went independent); Oklahoma in 1920 (left for Missouri Valley after '19 season); Phillips in 1921; Oklahoma A&M (now Oklahoma St.) in 1925 (left for Big Six); Arkansas in 1990 (left for SEC after '91 season); Baylor, Texas, Texas A&M and Texas Tech in 1994 (all four left for Big 12 after '95 season); Rice, SMU and TCU in 1994 (all three left for WAC after '95 season); Houston in 1994 (left for Conference USA after '95 season).

1997 playing membership: Conference folded on June 30, 1996.

Multiple titles: Texas (25); Texas A&M (17); Arkansas (13); SMU (9); TCU (9); Rice (7); Baylor (5); Houston (4); Texas Tech (2).

Year	
1914	No champion
1915	Oklahoma (3-0)
1916	No champion
1917	Texas A&M (2-0)
1918	No champion
1919	Texas A&M (4-0)
1920	Texas (5-0)
1921	Texas A&M (3-0-2)
1922	Baylor (5-0)
1923	SMU (5-0)
1924	Baylor (4-0-1)
1925	Texas A&M (4-1)
1926	SMU (5-0)
1927	Texas A&M (4-0-1)
1928	Texas (5-1)
1929	TCU (4-0-1)
1930	Texas (4-1)
1931	SMU (5-0-1)
1932	TCU (6-0)
1933	Arkansas (4-1)*
1934	Rice (5-1)
1935	SMU (6-0)
1936	Arkansas (5-1)
1937	Rice (4-1-1)
1938	TCU (6-0)
1939	Texas A&M (6-0)
1940	Texas A&M (5-1)
1941	Texas A&M (5-1)
1942	Texas (5-1)
1943	Texas (5-0)
1944	TCU (3-1-1)
1945	Texas (5-1)
1946	Rice (5-1) & Arkansas (5-1)
1947	SMU (5-0-1)
1948	SMU (5-0-1)
1949	Rice (6-0)
1950	Texas (6-0)
1951	TCU (5-1)
1952	Texas (6-0)
1953	Rice (5-1) & Texas (5-1)
1954	Arkansas (5-1)
1955	TCU (5-1)
1956	Texas A&M (6-0)
1957	Rice (5-1)
1958	TCU (5-1)
1959	Texas (5-1), TCU (5-1) & Arkansas (5-1)
1960	Arkansas (6-1)
1961	Texas (6-1) & Arkansas (6-1)
1962	Texas (6-0-1)
1963	Texas (7-0)
1964	Arkansas (7-0)
1965	Arkansas (7-0)
1966	SMU (6-1)
1967	Texas A&M (6-1)
1968	Arkansas (6-1) & Texas (6-1)
1969	Texas (7-0)
1970	Texas (7-0)
1971	Texas (6-1)
1972	Texas (7-0)
1973	Texas (7-0)
1974	Baylor (6-1)
1975	Arkansas (6-1), Texas (6-1) & Texas A&M (6-1)
1976	Houston (7-1) & Texas Tech (7-1)
1977	Texas (8-0)
1978	Houston (7-1)
1979	Houston (7-1) & Arkansas (7-1)
1980	Baylor (8-0)
1981	SMU (7-1)
1982	SMU (7-0-1)
1983	Texas (8-0)
1984	SMU (6-2) & Houston (6-2)
1985	Texas A&M (7-1)
1986	Texas A&M (7-1)
1987	Texas A&M (6-1)
1988	Arkansas (7-0)
1989	Arkansas (7-1)
1990	Texas (8-0)
1991	Texas A&M (8-0)
1992	Texas A&M (7-0)
1993	Texas A&M (7-0)
1994	Baylor, Rice, TCU, Texas and Texas Tech† (4-3)
1995	Texas (7-0)

*Arkansas (4-1) forced to vacate 1933 title for use of ineligible player.

†Texas A&M had the best record (6-0-1) in 1994 but was on probabtion and therefore ineligible for the Southwest championship.

SEC Championship Game

Since expanding to 12 teams and splitting into two divisions in 1992, the SEC has staged a conference championship game between the two division winners on the first Saturday in December. The game has been played at Legion Field in Birmingham, Ala., (1992-93) and the Georgia Dome in Atlanta (since 1994). The divisions: EAST— Florida, Georgia, Kentucky, South Carolina, Tennessee and Vanderbilt; WEST— Alabama, Arkansas, Auburn, LSU, Mississippi and Mississippi St.

Year	Year	Year
1992 Alabama 28, Florida 21	1994 Florida 24, Alabama 23	1996 Florida 45, Alabama 30
1993 Florida 28, Alabama 23	1995 Florida 34, Arkansas 3	1997 Tennessee 30, Auburn 29

Western Athletic Conference

Founded in 1962 when charter members left the Skyline and Border conferences to form the WAC. **Charter members** (6): Arizona and Arizona St. from Border; BYU (Brigham Young), New Mexico, Utah and Wyoming from Skyline. **Admitted later** (12): Colorado St. and UTEP (Texas-El Paso) in 1967 (both began play in '68); San Diego St. in 1978; Hawaii in 1979; Air Force in 1980; Fresno St. in 1991 (began play in '92); Rice, San Jose St., SMU (Southern Methodist), TCU (Texas Christian), Tulsa and UNLV (Nevada-Las Vegas) in 1994 (all began play in '96). **Withdrew later** (2): Arizona and Arizona St. in 1978 (left for Pac-10 after '77 season).

1998 playing membership (16): Air Force, BYU, Colorado St., Fresno St., Hawaii, New Mexico, Rice, San Diego St., San Jose St., SMU, TCU, Tulsa, UNLV, Utah, UTEP and Wyoming.

Multiple titles: BYU (18); Arizona St. and Wyoming (7); New Mexico and Colorado St. (3); Air Force, Arizona, Fresno St. and Utah (2).

Year	
1962	New Mexico (2-1-1)
1963	New Mexico (3-1)
1964	Utah (3-1), New Mexico (3-1) & Arizona (3-1)
1965	BYU (4-1)
1966	Wyoming (5-0)
1967	Wyoming (5-0)
1968	Wyoming (6-1)
1969	Arizona St. (6-1)
1970	Arizona St. (7-0)
1971	Arizona St. (7-0)
1972	Arizona St. (5-1)
1973	Arizona St. (6-1) & Arizona (6-1)
1974	BYU (6-0-1)
1975	Arizona St. (7-0)
1976	BYU (6-1) & Wyoming (6-1)
1977	Arizona St. (6-1) & BYU (6-1)
1978	BYU (5-1)
1979	BYU (7-0)
1980	BYU (6-1)
1981	BYU (7-1)
1982	BYU (7-1)
1983	BYU (7-0)
1984	BYU (8-0)
1985	Air Force (7-1) & BYU (7-1)
1986	San Diego St. (7-1)
1987	Wyoming (8-0)
1988	Wyoming (8-0)
1989	BYU (7-1)
1990	BYU (7-1)
1991	BYU (7-0-1)
1992	Hawaii (6-2), BYU (6-2) & Fresno St. (6-2)
1993	BYU (6-2), Fresno St. (6-2) & Wyoming (6-2)
1994	Colorado St. (7-1)
1995	Colorado St. (6-2), Air Force (6-2), BYU (6-2) & Utah (6-2)
1996	BYU (9-0)
1997	Colorado St. (8-1)

Longest Division I Streaks

Winning Streaks

(Including bowl games)

No		Seasons	Spoiler	Score
47	Oklahoma	1953-57	Notre Dame	7-0
39	Washington	1908-14	Oregon St.	0-0
37	Yale	1890-93	Princeton	6-0
37	Yale	1887-89	Princeton	10-0
35	Toledo	1969-71	Tampa	21-0
34	Penn	1894-96	Lafayette	6-4
31	Oklahoma	1948-50	Kentucky	13-7*
31	Pittsburgh	1914-18	Cleve. Naval	10-9
31	Penn	1896-98	Harvard	10-0
30	Texas	1968-70	Notre Dame	24-11*
29	Miami-FL	1990-93	Alabama	34-13
29	Michigan	1901-03	Minnesota	6-6
28	Alabama†	1991-93	Tennessee	17-17
28	Alabama	1978-80	Mississippi St.	6-3
28	Oklahoma	1973-75	Kansas	23-3
28	Michigan St.	1950-53	Purdue	6-0
27	Nebraska	1901-04	Colorado	6-0
26	Nebraska	1994-96	Arizona St.	19-0
26	Cornell	1921-24	Williams	14-7
26	Michigan	1903-05	Chicago	2-0
25	BYU	1983-85	UCLA	27-24
25	San Diego St.	1965-67	Utah St.	31-25
25	Michigan	1946-49	Army	21-7
25	Army	1944-46	Notre Dame	0-0
25	USC	1931-33	Oregon St.	0-0

***Note:** Kentucky beat Oklahoma in 1951 Sugar Bowl and Notre Dame beat Texas in 1971 Cotton Bowl.

†**Note:** Alabama was forced to forfeit eight victories and one tie in 1993 by the NCAA Committee on Infractions.

Unbeaten Streaks

(Including bowl games)

No	W-T		Seasons	Spoiler	Score
63	59-4	Washington	1907-17	California	27-0
56	55-1	Michigan	1901-05	Chicago	2-0
50	46-4	California	1920-25	Olympic Club	15-0
48	47-1	Oklahoma	1953-57	N. Dame	7-0
48	47-1	Yale	1885-89	Princeton	10-0
47	42-5	Yale	1879-85	Princeton	6-5
44	42-2	Yale	1894-96	Princeton	24-6
42	39-3	Yale	1904-08	Harvard	4-0
39	37-2	N. Dame	1946-50	Purdue	28-14
37	36-1	Oklahoma	1972-75	Kansas	23-3
37	37-0	Yale	1890-93	Princeton	6-0
35	35-0	Toledo	1967-71	Tampa	21-0
35	34-1	Minnesota	1903-05	Wisconsin	16-12

Losing Streaks

No		Seasons	Victim	Score
77	Prairie View	1989–	current streak	
44	Columbia	1983-88	Princeton	16-14
34	Northwestern	1979-82	No. Illinois	31-6
28	Virginia	1958-60	Wm. & Mary	21-6
28	Kansas St.	1944-48	Arkansas St.	37-6
27	Eastern Mich.	1980-82	Kent St.	9-7
27	New Mexico St.	1988-90	CS-Fullerton	43-9

Note: Virginia ended its losing streak in the opening game of the 1961 season.

Major Conference Champions (Cont.)

WAC Championship Game

In addition to expanding to 16 teams and splitting into two divisions in 1996, the WAC now stages a conference championship game between the two division winners on the first Saturday in December at Sam Boyd Stadium in Las Vegas. The divisions: Pacific Division—BYU, Fresno St., Hawaii, New Mexico, San Diego St., San Jose St., UTEP, Utah; Mountain Division—Air Force, Colorado St., Rice, SMU, TCU, Tulsa, UNLV, Wyoming.

Year	
1996	BYU 28, Wyoming 25 (OT)
1997	Colorado St. 41, New Mexico 13

Annual NCAA Division I-A Leaders

Note that Oklahoma A&M is now Oklahoma St. and Texas Mines is now UTEP.

Rushing

Individual championship decided on Rushing Yards (1937-69), and on Yards Per Game (since 1970).

Multiple winners: Troy Davis, Marshall Faulk, Art Luppino, Ed Marinaro, Rudy Mobley, Jim Pilot and O.J. Simpson (2).

Year		Car	Yards
1937	Byron (Whizzer) White, Colorado	181	1121
1938	Len Eshmont, Fordham	132	831
1939	John Polanski, Wake Forest	137	882
1940	Al Ghesquiere, Detroit	146	957
1941	Frank Sinkwich, Georgia	209	1103
1942	Rudy Mobley, Hardin-Simmons	187	1281
1943	Creighton Miller, Notre Dame	151	911
1944	Red Williams, Minnesota	136	911
1945	Bob Fenimore, Oklahoma A&M	142	1048
1946	Rudy Mobley, Hardin-Simmons	227	1262
1947	Wilton Davis, Hardin-Simmons	193	1173
1948	Fred Wendt, Texas Mines	184	1570
1949	John Dottley, Ole Miss	208	1312
1950	Wilford White, Arizona St	199	1502
1951	Ollie Matson, San Francisco	245	1566
1952	Howie Waugh, Tulsa	164	1372
1953	J.C. Caroline, Illinois	194	1256
1954	Art Luppino, Arizona	179	1359
1955	Art Luppino, Arizona	209	1313
1956	Jim Crawford, Wyoming	200	1104
1957	Leon Burton, Arizona St	117	1126
1958	Dick Bass, Pacific	205	1361
1959	Pervis Atkins, New Mexico St	130	971
1960	Bob Gaiters, New Mexico St	197	1338
1961	Jim Pilot, New Mexico St	191	1278
1962	Jim Pilot, New Mexico St	208	1247
1963	Dave Casinelli, Memphis St	219	1016
1964	Brian Piccolo, Wake Forest	252	1044
1965	Mike Garrett, USC	267	1440
1966	Ray McDonald, Idaho	259	1329
1967	O.J. Simpson, USC	266	1415
1968	O.J. Simpson, USC	355	1709
1969	Steve Owens, Oklahoma	358	1523

Year		Car	Yards	P/Gm
1970	Ed Marinaro, Cornell	285	1425	158.3
1971	Ed Marinaro, Cornell	356	1881	209.0
1972	Pete VanValkenburg, BYU	232	1386	138.6
1973	Mark Kellar, Northern Ill	291	1719	156.3
1974	Louie Giammona, Utah St.	329	1534	153.4
1975	Ricky Bell, USC	357	1875	170.5
1976	Tony Dorsett, Pittsburgh	338	1948	177.1
1977	Earl Campbell, Texas	267	1744	158.5
1978	Billy Sims, Oklahoma	231	1762	160.2
1979	Charles White, USC	293	1803	180.3
1980	George Rogers, S. Carolina	297	1781	161.9
1981	Marcus Allen, USC	403	2342	212.9
1982	Ernest Anderson, Okla. St.	353	1877	170.6
1983	Mike Rozier, Nebraska	275	2148	179.0
1984	Keith Byars, Ohio St.	313	1655	150.5
1985	Lorenzo White, Mich. St.	386	1908	173.5
1986	Paul Palmer, Temple	346	1866	169.6
1987	Ickey Woods, UNLV	259	1658	150.7
1988	Barry Sanders, Okla. St.	344	2628	238.9
1989	Anthony Thompson, Ind	358	1793	163.0
1990	Gerald Hudson, Okla. St.	279	1642	149.3
1991	Marshall Faulk, S. Diego St.	201	1429	158.8
1992	Marshall Faulk, S. Diego St.	265	1630	163.0
1993	LeShon Johnson, No. Ill.	327	1976	179.6
1994	Rashaan Salaam, Colorado	298	2055	186.8
1995	Troy Davis, Iowa St.	345	2010	182.7
1996	Troy Davis, Iowa St.	402	2185	198.6
1997	Ricky Williams, Texas	279	1893	172.1

All-Purpose Yardage

Multiple winners: Marcus Allen, Pervis Atkins, Ryan Benjamin, Troy Davis, Louie Giammona, Tom Harmon, Art Luppino, Napolean McCallum, O.J. Simpson, Charles White and Gary Wood (2).

Year		Yards	P/Gm
1937	Byron (Whizzer) White, Colorado	1970	246.3
1938	Parker Hall, Ole Miss	1420	129.1
1939	Tom Harmon, Michigan	1208	151.0
1940	Tom Harmon, Michigan	1312	164.0
1941	Bill Dudley, Virginia	1674	186.0
1942	Complete records not available		
1943	Stan Koslowski, Holy Cross	1411	176.4
1944	Red Williams, Minnesota	1467	163.0
1945	Bob Fenimore, Oklahoma A&M	1577	197.1
1946	Rudy Mobley, Hardin-Simmons	1765	176.5
1947	Wilton Davis, Hardin-Simmons	1798	179.8
1948	Lou Kusserow, Columbia	1737	193.0
1949	Johnny Papit, Virginia	1611	179.0
1950	Wilford White, Arizona St.	2065	206.5
1951	Ollie Matson, San Francisco	2037	226.3
1952	Billy Vessels, Oklahoma	1512	151.2
1953	J.C. Caroline, Illinois	1470	163.3
1954	Art Luppino, Arizona	2193	219.3
1955	Jim Swink, TCU	1702	170.2
	& Art Luppino, Arizona	1702	170.2
1956	Jack Hill, Utah St.	1691	169.1
1957	Overton Curtis, Utah St	1608	160.8
1958	Dick Bass, Pacific	1878	187.8
1959	Pervis Atkins, New Mexico St	1800	180.0
1960	Pervis Atkins, New Mexico St	1613	161.3
1961	Jim Pilot, New Mexico St.	1606	160.6
1962	Gary Wood, Cornell	1395	155.0
1963	Gary Wood, Cornell	1508	167.6
1964	Donny Anderson, Texas Tech	1710	171.0
1965	Floyd Little, Syracuse	1990	199.0
1966	Frank Quayle, Virginia	1616	161.6
1967	O.J. Simpson, USC	1700	188.9
1968	O.J. Simpson, USC	1966	196.6
1969	Lynn Moore, Army	1795	179.5
1970	Don McCauley, North Carolina	2021	183.7
1971	Ed Marinaro, Cornell	1932	214.7

Year		Yards	P/Gm
1972	Howard Stevens, Louisville	2132	213.2
1973	Willard Harrell, Pacific	1777	177.7
1974	Louie Giammona, Utah St	1984	198.4
1975	Louie Giammona, Utah St	2045	185.9
1976	Tony Dorsett, Pittsburgh	2021	183.7
1977	Earl Campbell, Texas	1855	168.6
1978	Charles White, USC	2096	174.7
1979	Charles White, USC	1941	194.1
1980	Marcus Allen, USC	1794	179.4
1981	Marcus Allen, USC	2559	232.6
1982	Carl Monroe, Utah	2036	185.1
1983	Napoleon McCallum, Navy	2385	216.8
1984	Keith Byars, Ohio St	2284	207.6
1985	Napoleon McCallum, Navy	2330	211.8
1986	Paul Palmer, Temple	2633	239.4
1987	Eric Wilkerson, Kent St.	2074	188.6
1988	Barry Sanders, Oklahoma St.	3250	295.5
1989	Mike Pringle, CS-Fullerton	2690	244.6
1990	Glyn Milburn, Stanford	2222	202.0
1991	Ryan Benjamin, Pacific	2995	249.6
1992	Ryan Benjamin, Pacific	2597	236.1
1993	LeShon Johnson, Northern Ill.	2082	189.3
1994	Rashaan Salaam, Colorado	2349	213.5
1995	Troy Davis, Iowa St.	2466	224.2
1996	Troy Davis, Iowa St.	2364	214.9
1997	Troy Edwards, La. Tech	2144	194.9

Total Offense

Individual championship decided on Total Yards (1937-69) and on Yards Per Game (since 1970).

Multiple winners: Johnny Bright, Bob Fenimore, Mike Maxwell and Jim McMahon (2).

Year		Plays	Yards
1937	Byron (Whizzer) White, Colorado	224	1596
1938	Davey O'Brien, TCU	291	1847
1939	Kenny Washington, UCLA	259	1370
1940	Johnny Knolla, Creighton	298	1420
1941	Bud Schwenk, Washington-MO	354	1928
1942	Frank Sinkwich, Georgia	341	2187
1943	Bob Hoernschemeyer, Indiana	355	1648
1944	Bob Fenimore, Oklahoma A&M	241	1758
1945	Bob Fenimore, Oklahoma A&M	203	1641
1946	Travis Bidwell, Auburn	339	1715
1947	Fred Enke, Arizona	329	1941
1948	Stan Heath, Nevada-Reno	233	1992
1949	Johnny Bright, Drake	275	1950
1950	Johnny Bright, Drake	320	2400
1951	Dick Kazmaier, Princeton	272	1827
1952	Ted Marchibroda, Detroit	305	1813
1953	Paul Larson, California	262	1572
1954	George Shaw, Oregon	276	1536
1955	George Welsh, Navy	203	1348
1956	John Brodie, Stanford	295	1642
1957	Bob Newman, Washington St	263	1444
1958	Dick Bass, Pacific	218	1440
1959	Dick Norman, Stanford	319	2018
1960	Billy Kilmer, UCLA	292	1889
1961	Dave Hoppmann, Iowa St	320	1638
1962	Terry Baker, Oregon St	318	2276
1963	George Mira, Miami-FL	394	2318
1964	Jerry Rhome, Tulsa	470	3128
1965	Bill Anderson, Tulsa	580	3343
1966	Virgil Carter, BYU	388	2545
1967	Sal Olivas, New Mexico St.	368	2184
1968	Greg Cook Cincinnati	507	3210
1969	Dennis Shaw, San Diego St	388	3197

Year		Plays	Yards	P/Gm
1970	Pat Sullivan, Auburn	333	2856	285.6
1971	Gary Huff, Florida St	386	2653	241.2
1972	Don Strock, Va. Tech	480	3170	288.2
1973	Jesse Freitas, San Diego St.	410	2901	263.7
1974	Steve Joachim, Temple	331	2227	222.7
1975	Gene Swick, Toledo	490	2706	246.0
1976	Tommy Kramer, Rice	562	3272	297.5
1977	Doug Williams, Gambling	377	3229	293.5
1978	Mike Ford, SMU	459	2957	268.8
1979	Marc Wilson, BYU	488	3580	325.5
1980	Jim McMahon, BYU	540	4627	385.6
1981	Jim McMahon, BYU	487	3458	345.8
1982	Todd Dillon, Long Beach St	585	3587	326.1
1983	Steve Young, BYU	531	4346	395.1
1984	Robbie Bosco, BYU	543	3932	327.7
1985	Jim Everett, Purdue	518	3589	326.3
1986	Mike Perez, San Jose St.	425	2969	329.9
1987	Todd Santos, San Diego St.	562	3688	307.3
1988	Scott Mitchell, Utah	589	4299	390.8
1989	Andre Ware, Houston	628	4661	423.7
1990	David Klingler, Houston	704	5221	474.6
1991	Ty Detmer, BYU	478	4001	333.4
1992	Jimmy Klingler, Houston	544	3768	342.6
1993	Chris Vargas, Nevada	535	4332	393.8
1994	Mike Maxwell, Nevada	477	3498	318.0
1995	Mike Maxwell, Nevada	443	3623	402.6
1996	Josh Wallwork, Wyoming	525	4209	350.8
1997	Tim Rattay, La. Tech	541	3968	360.7

Passing

Individual championship decided on Completions (1937-69), on Completions Per Game (1970-78) and on Passing Efficiency rating points (since 1979).

Multiple winners: Elvis Grbac, Don Heinrich, Jim McMahon, Davey O'Brien and Don Trull (2).

Year		Cmp	Pct	TD	Yds
1937	Davey O'Brien, TCU	94	.402	–	969
1938	Davey O'Brien, TCU	93	.557	–	1457
1939	Kay Eakin, Arkansas	78	.404	–	962
1940	Billy Sewell, Wash. St.	86	.494	–	1023
1941	Bud Schwenk, Wash.-MO	114	.487	–	1457
1942	Ray Evans, Kansas	101	.505	–	1117
1943	Johnny Cook, Georgia	73	.465	–	1007
1944	Paul Rickards, Pittsburgh	84	.472	–	997
1945	Al Dekdebrun, Cornell	90	.464	–	1227
1946	Travis Tidwell, Auburn	79	.500	5	943
1947	Charlie Conerly, Ole Miss	133	.571	18	1367
1948	Stan Heath, Nev-Reno	126	.568	22	2005
1949	Adrian Burk, Baylor	110	.576	14	1428
1950	Don Heinrich, Washington	134	.606	14	1846
1951	Don Klosterman, Loyola-CA	159	.505	9	1843
1952	Don Heinrich, Washington	137	.507	13	1647
1953	Bob Garrett, Stanford	118	.576	17	1637
1954	Paul Larson, California	125	.641	10	1537
1955	George Welsh, Navy	94	.627	8	1319
1956	John Brodie, Stanford	139	.579	12	1633
1957	Ken Ford, H-Simmons	115	.561	14	1254
1958	Buddy Humphrey, Baylor	112	.574	7	1316
1959	Dick Norman, Stanford	152	.578	11	1963
1960	Harold Stephens, H-Simm.	145	.566	3	1254
1961	Chon Gallegos, S. Jose St	117	.594	14	1480
1962	Don Trull, Baylor	125	.546	11	1627

Annual NCAA Division I-A Leaders (Cont.)

Year		Cmp	Pct	TD	Yds
1963	Don Trull, Baylor	174	.565	12	2157
1964	Jerry Rhome, Tulsa	224	.687	32	2870
1965	Bill Anderson, Tulsa	296	.582	30	3464
1966	John Eckman, Wichita St	195	.426	7	2339
1967	Terry Stone, N. Mexico	160	.476	9	1946
1968	Chuck Hixson, SMU	265	.566	21	3103
1969	John Reaves, Florida	222	.561	24	2896

Year		Cmp	P/Gm	TD	Yds
1970	Sonny Sixkiller, Wash	186	18.6	15	2303
1971	Brian Sipe, S. Diego St.	196	17.8	17	2532
1972	Don Strock, Va. Tech	228	20.7	16	3243
1973	Jesse Freitas, S. Diego St.	227	20.6	21	2993
1974	Steve Bartkowski, Cal	182	16.5	12	2580
1975	Craig Penrose, S. Diego St.	198	18.0	15	2660
1976	Tommy Kramer, Rice	269	24.5	21	3317
1977	Guy Benjamin, Stanford	208	20.8	19	2521
1978	Steve Dils, Stanford	247	22.5	22	2943

Year		Cmp	TD	Yds	Rating
1979	Turk Schonert, Stanford	148	19	1922	163.0
1980	Jim McMahon, BYU	284	47	4571	176.9
1981	Jim McMahon, BYU	272	30	3555	155.0
1982	Tom Ramsey, UCLA	191	21	2824	153.5
1983	Steve Young, BYU	306	33	3902	168.5
1984	Doug Flutie, BC	233	27	3454	152.9
1985	Jim Harbaugh, Michigan	139	18	1913	163.7
1986	Vinny Testaverde, Miami-FL	175	26	2557	165.8
1987	Don McPherson, Syracuse	129	22	2341	164.3
1988	Timm Rosenbach, Wash. St.	199	23	2791	162.0
1989	Ty Detmer, BYU	265	32	4560	175.6
1990	Shawn Moore, Virginia	144	21	2262	160.7
1991	Elvis Grbac, Michigan	152	24	1955	169.0
1992	Elvis Grbac, Michigan	112	15	1465	154.2
1993	Trent Dilfer, Fresno St.	217	28	3276	173.1
1994	Kerry Collins, Penn St.	176	21	2679	172.9
1995	Danny Wuerffel, Florida	210	35	3266	178.4
1996	Steve Sarkisian, BYU	278	33	4027	173.6
1997	Cade McNown, UCLA	173	22	2877	168.6

Receptions

Championship decided on Passes Caught (1937-69) and on Catches Per Game (since 1970). Touchdown totals unavailable in 1939 and 1941-45.

Multiple winners: Neil Armstrong, Hugh Campell, Manny Hazard, Reid Moseley, Jason Phillips, Howard Twilley and Alex Van Dyke (2).

Year		No	TD	Yds
1937	Jim Benton, Arkansas	47	7	754
1938	Sam Boyd, Baylor	32	5	537
1939	Ken Kavanaugh, LSU	30	–	467
1940	Eddie Bryant, Virginia	30	2	222
1941	Hank Stanton, Arizona	50	–	820
1942	Bill Rogers, Texas A&M	39	–	432
1943	Neil Armstrong, Okla. A&M	39	–	317
1944	Reid Moseley, Georgia	32	–	506
1945	Reid Moseley, Georgia	31	–	662
1946	Neil Armstrong, Okla. A&M	32	1	479
1947	Barney Poole, Ole Miss	52	8	513
1948	Red O'Quinn, Wake Forest	39	7	605
1949	Art Weiner, N. Carolina	52	7	762
1950	Gordon Cooper, Denver	46	8	569
1951	Dewey McConnell, Wyoming	47	9	725
1952	Ed Brown, Fordham	57	6	774
1953	John Carson, Georgia	45	4	663
1954	Jim Hanifan, California	44	7	569
1955	Hank Burnine, Missouri	44	2	594
1956	Art Powell, San Jose St.	40	5	583
1957	Stuart Vaughan, Utah	53	5	756
1958	Dave Hibbert, Arizona	61	4	606
1959	Chris Burford, Stanford	61	6	756
1960	Hugh Campbell, Wash. St.	66	10	881
1961	Hugh Campbell, Wash. St.	53	5	723
1962	Vern Burke, Oregon St	69	10	1007
1963	Lawrence Elkins, Baylor	70	8	873
1964	Howard Twilley, Tulsa	95	13	1178
1965	Howard Twilley, Tulsa	134	16	1779
1966	Glenn Meltzer, Wichita St	91	4	1115
1967	Bob Goodridge, Vanderbilt	79	6	1114
1968	Ron Sellers, Florida St.	86	12	1496
1969	Jerry Hendren, Idaho	95	12	1452

Year		No	P/Gm	TD	Yds
1970	Mike Mikolayunas, Davidson	87	8.7	8	1128
1971	Tom Reynolds, San Diego St	67	6.7	7	1070
1972	Tom Forzani, Utah St	85	7.7	8	1169
1973	Jay Miller, BYU	100	9.1	8	1181
1974	D. McDonald, San Diego St	86	7.8	7	1157
1975	Bob Farnham, Brown	56	6.2	2	701
1976	Billy Ryckman, La. Tech	77	7.0	10	1382
1977	W. Tolleson, W. Carolina	73	6.6	7	1101
1978	Dave Petzke, Northern Ill	91	8.3	11	1217
1979	Rick Beasley, Appalach. St	74	6.7	12	1205
1980	Dave Young, Purdue	67	6.1	8	917
1981	Pete Harvey, N. Texas St	57	6.3	3	743
1982	Vincent White, Stanford	68	6.8	8	677
1983	Keith Edwards, Vanderbilt	97	8.8	8	909
1984	David Williams, Illinois	101	9.2	8	1278
1985	Rodney Carter, Purdue	98	8.9	4	1099
1986	Mark Templeton, L. Beach St	99	9.0	2	688
1987	Jason Phillips, Houston	99	9.0	3	875
1988	Jason Phillips, Houston	108	9.8	15	1444
1989	Manny Hazard, Houston	142	12.9	22	1689
1990	Manny Hazard, Houston	78	7.8	9	946
1991	Fred Gilbert, Houston	106	9.6	7	957
1992	Sherman Smith, Houston	103	9.4	6	923
1993	Chris Penn, Tulsa	105	9.6	12	1578
1994	Alex Van Dyke, Nevada	98	8.9	10	1246
1995	Alex Van Dyke, Nevada	129	11.7	16	1854
1996	Damond Wilkins, Nevada	114	10.4	4	1121
1997	Eugene Baker, Kent	103	9.4	18	1549

Scoring

Championship decided on Total Points (1937-69) and on Points Per Game (since 1970).

Multiple winners: Tom Harmon and Billy Sims (2).

Year		TD	XP	FG	Pts
1937	Byron (Whizzer) White, Colo	16	23	1	122
1938	Parker Hall, Ole Miss	11	7	0	73
1939	Tom Harmon, Michigan	14	15	1	102
1940	Tom Harmon, Michigan	16	18	1	117
1941	Bill Dudley, Virginia	18	23	1	134
1942	Bob Steuber, Missouri	18	13	0	121
1943	Steve Van Buren, LSU	14	14	0	98
1944	Glenn Davis, Army	20	0	0	120
1945	Doc Blanchard, Army	19	1	0	115
1946	Gene Roberts, Tenn-Chatt	18	9	0	117
1947	Lou Gambino, Maryland	16	0	0	96
1948	Fred Wendt, Texas Mines	20	32	0	152

Year		TD	XP	FG	Pts
1949	George Thomas, Oklahoma	19	3	0	117
1950	Bobby Reynolds, Nebraska	22	25	0	157
1951	Ollie Matson, San Francisco	21	0	0	126
1952	Jackie Parker, Miss. St.	16	24	0	120
1953	Earl Lindley, Utah St.	13	3	0	81
1954	Art Luppino, Arizona	24	22	0	166
1955	Jim Swink, TCU	20	5	0	125
1956	Clendon Thomas, Oklahoma	18	0	0	108
1957	Leon Burton, Ariz. St.	16	0	0	96
1958	Dick Bass, Pacific	18	8	0	116
1959	Pervis Atkins, N. Mexico St.	17	5	0	107
1960	Bob Gaiters, N. Mexico St.	23	7	0	145
1961	Jim Pilot, N. Mexico St.	21	12	0	138
1962	Jerry Logan, W. Texas St.	13	32	0	110
1963	Cosmo Iacavazzi, Princeton	14	0	0	84
	& Dave Casinelli, Memphis St.	14	0	0	84
1964	Brian Piccolo, Wake Forest	17	9	0	111
1965	Howard Twilley, Tulsa	16	31	0	127
1966	Ken Hebert, Houston	11	41	2	113
1967	Leroy Keyes, Purdue	19	0	0	114
1968	Jim O'Brien, Cincinnati	12	31	13	142
1969	Steve Owens, Oklahoma	23	0	0	138

Year		TD	XP	FG	Pts	P/Gm
1970	Brian Bream, Air Force	20	0	0	120	12.0
	& Gary Kosins, Dayton	18	0	0	108	12.0
1971	Ed Marinaro, Cornell	24	4	0	148	16.4
1972	Harold Henson, Ohio St.	20	0	0	120	12.0
1973	Jim Jennings, Rutgers	21	2	0	128	11.6
1974	Bill Marek, Wisconsin	19	0	0	114	12.7
1975	Pete Johnson, Ohio St.	25	0	0	150	13.6
1976	Tony Dorsett, Pitt	22	2	0	134	12.2
1977	Earl Campbell, Texas	19	0	0	114	10.4
1978	Billy Sims, Oklahoma	20	0	0	120	10.9
1979	Billy Sims, Oklahoma	22	0	0	132	12.0
1980	Sammy Winder, So. Miss.	20	0	0	120	10.9
1981	Marcus Allen, USC	23	0	0	138	12.5
1982	Greg Allen, Fla. St	21	0	0	126	11.5
1983	Mike Rozier, Nebraska	29	0	0	174	14.5
1984	Keith Byars, Ohio St	24	0	0	144	13.1
1985	Bernard White, B. Green	19	0	0	114	10.4
1986	Steve Bartalo, Colo. St	19	0	0	114	10.4
1987	Paul Hewitt, S. Diego St.	24	0	0	144	12.0
1988	Barry Sanders, Okla.St.	39	0	0	234	21.3
1989	Anthony Thompson, Ind	25	4	0	154	14.0
1990	Stacey Robinson, No. Ill.	19	6	0	120	10.9
1991	Marshall Faulk, S.D. St.	23	2	0	140	15.6
1992	Garrison Hearst, Georgia	21	0	0	126	11.5
1993	Bam Morris, Texas Tech	22	2	0	134	12.2
1994	Rashaan Salaam, Colo.	24	0	0	144	13.1
1995	Eddie George, Ohio St.	24	0	0	144	12.0
1996	Corey Dillon, Washington	23	0	0	138	12.6
1997	Ricky Williams, Texas	25	2	0	152	13.8

All-Time NCAA Division I-A Leaders

Through the 1997 regular season. The NCAA does not recognize active players among career Per Game leaders.

CAREER

Passing

(Minimum 500 Completions)

	Passing Efficiency	Years	Rating
1	Danny Wuerffel, Florida	1993-96	163.6
2	Ty Detmer, BYU	1988-91	162.7
3	Steve Sarkisian, BYU	1995-96	162.0
4	Billy Blanton, San Diego St.	1993-96	157.1
5	Jim McMahon, BYU	1977-78, 80-81	156.9

	Yards Gained	Years	Yards
1	Ty Detmer, BYU	1988-91	15,031
2	Todd Santos, San Diego St	1984-87	11,425
3	Peyton Manning, Tennessee	1994-97	11,201
4	Eric Zeier, Georgia	1991-94	11,153
5	Alex Van Pelt, Pittsburgh	1989-92	10,913

	Completions	Years	No
1	Ty Detmer, BYU	1988-91	958
2	Todd Santos, San Diego St	1984-87	910
3	Brian McClure, Bowling Green	1982-85	900
4	Erik Wilhelm, Oregon St.	1985-88	870
5	Alex Van Pelt, Pittsburgh	1989-92	845

Rushing

	Yards Gained	Years	Yards
1	Tony Dorsett, Pittsburgh	1973-76	6082
2	Charles White, USC	1976-79	5598
3	Herschel Walker, Georgia	1980-82	5259
4	Archie Griffin, Ohio St	1972-75	5177
5	Darren Lewis, Texas A&M	1987-90	5012

	Yards Per Game	Years	Yards	P/Gm
1	Ed Marinaro, Cornell	1969-71	4715	174.6
2	O.J. Simpson, USC	1967-68	3124	164.4
3	Herschel Walker, Georgia	1980-82	5259	159.4
4	LeShon Johnson, No. Ill.	1992-93	3314	150.6
5	Marshall Faulk, S. Diego St.	1991-93	4589	148.0

Receptions

	Catches	Years	No
1	Aaron Turner, Pacific	1989-92	266
2	Chad Mackey, La. Tech	1993-96	264
3	Terance Mathis, New Mexico	1985-87, 89	263
4	Mark Templeton, Long Beach St	1983-86	262
5	Howard Twilley, Tulsa	1963-65	261

	Catches Per Game	Years	No	P/Gm
1	Manny Hazard, Houston	1989-90	220	10.5
2	Alex Van Dyke, Nevada	1994-95	227	10.3
3	Howard Twilley, Tulsa	1963-65	261	10.0
4	Jason Phillips, Houston	1987-88	207	9.4
5	Bryan Reeves, Nevada	1991-93	234	8.2

	Yards Gained	Years	No	Yards
1	Marcus Harris, Wyoming	1993-96	259	4518
2	Ryan Yarborough, Wyoming	1990-93	229	4357
3	Aaron Turner, Pacific	1989-92	266	4345
4	Terance Mathis, N. Mexico	1985-87, 89	263	4254
5	Chad Mackey, La. Tech	1993-96	264	3789

Total Offense

	Yards Gained	Years	Yards
1	Ty Detmer, BYU	1988-91	14,665
2	Doug Flutie, Boston College	1981-84	11,317
3	Peyton Manning, Tennessee	1994-97	11,020
4	Eric Zeier, Georgia	1991-94	10,841
5	Alex Van Pelt, Pittsburgh	1989-92	10,814

	Yards Per Game	Years	Yards	P/Gm
1	Chris Vargas, Nevada	1992-93	6,417	320.9
2	Ty Detmer, BYU	1988-91	14,665	318.8
3	Mike Perez, San Jose St	1986-87	6,182	309.1
4	Josh Wallwork, Wyoming	1995-96	6,753	307.0
5	Doug Gaynor, L. Beach St.	1984-85	6,710	305.0

All-Time NCAA Division I-A Leaders (Cont.)

All-Purpose Yardage

	Yards Gained	Years	Yards
1	Napoleon McCallum, Navy	1981-85	7172
2	Darrin Nelson, Stanford	1977-78, 80-81	6885
3	Terance Mathis, N. Mexico	1985-87, 89	6691
4	Tony Dorsett, Pittsburgh	1973-76	6615
5	Paul Palmer, Temple	1983-86	6609

	Yards Per Game	Years	Yards	P/Gm
1	Ryan Benjamin, Pacific	1990-92	5706	237.8
2	Sheldon Canley, S. Jose St.	1988-90	5146	205.8
3	Howard Stevens, Louisville	1971-72	3873	193.7
4	O.J. Simpson, USC	1967-68	3666	192.9
5	Alex Van Dyke, Nevada	1994-95	4146	188.5

Miscellaneous

	Interceptions	Years	No
1	Al Brosky, Illinois	1950-52	29
2	John Provost, Holy Cross	1972-74	27
	Martin Bayless, Bowling Green	1980-83	27
4	Tom Curtis, Michigan	1967-69	25
	Tony Thurman, Boston College	1981-84	25
	Tracy Saul, Texas Tech	1989-92	25

	Punting Average*	Years	Avg
1	Todd Sauerbrun, West Va.	1991-94	46.3
2	Reggie Roby, Iowa	1979-82	45.6
3	Greg Montgomery, Mich. St	1985-87	45.4
4	Tom Tupa, Ohio St.	1984-87	45.2
5	Barry Helton, Colorado	1984-87	44.9

*At least 150 punts.

	Punt Return Average*	Years	Avg
1	Jack Mitchell, Oklahoma	1946-48	23.6
2	Gene Gibson, Cincinnati	1949-50	20.5
3	Eddie Macon, Pacific	1949-51	18.9
4	Jackie Robinson, UCLA	1939-40	18.8
	Two tied at 17.7 each.		

*Minimum 1.2 punt returns per game and 30 career returns.

	Kickoff Return Average*	Years	Avg
1	Anthony Davis, USC	1972-74	35.1
2	Eric Booth, So. Miss.	1994-97	32.4
3	Overton Curtis, Utah St	1957-58	31.0
4	Fred Montgomery, New Mexico St.	1991-92	30.5
5	Allie Taylor, Utah St.	1966-68	29.3

*Minimum 1.2 kickoff returns per game and 30 career returns.

Scoring

Non-kickers

	Points	Years	TD	Xpt	FG	Pts
1	Anthony Thompson, Ind.	1986-89	65	4	0	394
2	Marshall Faulk, S.D. St.	1991-93	62	4	0	376
3	Tony Dorsett, Pittsburgh	1973-76	59	2	0	356
4	Glenn Davis, Army	1943-46	59	0	0	354
5	Art Luppino, Arizona	1953-56	48	49	0	337

	Points Per Game	Years	Pts	P/Gm
1	Marshall Faulk, S. Diego St.	1991-93	376	12.1
2	Ed Marinaro, Cornell	1969-71	318	11.8
3	Bill Burnett, Arkansas	1968-70	294	11.3
4	Steve Owens, Oklahoma	1967-69	336	11.2
5	Eddie Talboom, Wyoming	1948-50	303	10.8

	Touchdowns Rushing	Years	No
1	Anthony Thompson, Indiana	1986-89	64
2	Marshall Faulk, S. Diego St.	1991-93	57
3	Steve Owens, Oklahoma	1967-69	56
4	Tony Dorsett, Pittsburgh	1973-76	55
5	Pete Johnson, Ohio St.	1973-76	51

	Touchdowns Passing	Years	No
1	Ty Detmer, BYU	1988-91	121
2	Danny Wuerffel, Florida	1993-96	114
3	David Klingler, Houston	1988-91	91
4	Peyton Manning, Tennessee	1994-97	89
5	Troy Kopp, Pacific	1989-92	87

	Touchdown Catches	Years	No
1	Aaron Turner, Pacific	1989-92	43
2	Ryan Yarborough, Wyoming	1990-93	42
3	Clarkston Hines, Duke	1986-89	38
	Marcus Harris, Wyoming	1993-96	38
5	Terance Mathis, N. Mexico	1985-87, 89	36

Kickers

	Points	Years	FG	XP	Pts
1	Roman Anderson, Hou	1988-91	70	213	423
2	Carlos Huerta, Mia-FL	1988-91	73	178	397
3	Jason Elam, Hawaii	1988-89, 91-92	79	158	395
4	Derek Schmidt, Fla. St	1984-87	73	174	393
5	Luis Zendejas, Ariz. St	1981-84	78	134	368
6	Jeff Jaeger, Wash	1983-86	80	118	358
7	John Lee, UCLA	1982-85	79	116	353
	Max Zendejas, Arizona	1982-85	77	122	353
	Kevin Butler, Georgia	1981-84	77	122	353
10	Derek Mahoney, Fresno St	1990-93	45	216	351

	Field Goals	Years	No
1	Jeff Jaeger, Washington	1983-86	80
2	John Lee, UCLA	1982-85	79
	Jason Elam, Hawaii	1988-89, 91-92	79
4	Philip Doyle, Alabama	1987-90	78
	Luis Zendejas, Arizona St	1981-84	78

SINGLE SEASON

Rushing

Yards Gained	Year	Gm	Car	Yards
Barry Sanders, Okla. St	1988	11	344	2628
Marcus Allen, USC	1981	11	403	2342
Troy Davis, Iowa St.	1996	11	402	2185
Mike Rozier, Nebraska	1983	12	275	2148
Byron Hanspard, Texas Tech	1996	11	339	2084

Yards Per Game	Year	Gm	Yards	P/Gm
Barry Sanders, Okla. St	1988	11	2628	238.9
Marcus Allen, USC	1981	11	2342	212.9
Ed Marinaro, Cornell	1971	9	1881	209.0
Troy Davis, Iowa St.	1996	11	2185	198.6
Byron Hanspard, Texas Tech	1996	11	2084	189.5

Passing

(Minimum 15 Attempts Per Game)

Passing Efficiency	Year	Rating
Danny Wuerffel, Florida	1995	178.4
Jim McMahon, BYU	1980	176.9
Ty Detmer, BYU	1989	175.6
Steve Sarkisian, BYU	1996	173.6
Trent Dilfer, Fresno St.	1993	173.1

Yards Gained	Year	Yards
Ty Detmer, BYU	1990	5188
David Klingler, Houston	1990	5140
Andre Ware, Houston	1989	4699
Jim McMahon, BYU	1980	4571
Ty Detmer, BYU	1989	4560

Completions	Year	Att	No
David Klingler, Houston	1990	643	374
Andre Ware, Houston	1989	578	365
Tim Couch, Kentucky	1997	547	363
Ty Detmer, BYU	1990	562	361
Robbie Bosco, BYU	1985	511	338

Total Offense

Yards Gained	Year	Gm	Plays	Yards
David Klingler, Houston	1990	11	704	5221
Ty Detmer, BYU	1990	12	635	5022
Andre Ware, Houston	1989	11	628	4661
Jim McMahon, BYU	1980	12	540	4627
Ty Detmer, BYU	1989	12	497	4433

Yards Per Game	Year	Gm	Yards	P/Gm
David Klingler, Houston	1990	11	5221	474.6
Andre Ware, Houston	1989	11	4661	423.7
Ty Detmer, BYU	1990	12	5022	418.5
Mike Maxwell, Nevada	1995	9	3623	402.6
Steve Young, BYU	1983	11	4346	395.1

Receptions

Catches	Year	Gm	No
Manny Hazard, Houston	1989	11	142
Howard Twilley, Tulsa	1965	10	134
Alex Van Dyke, Nevada	1995	11	129
Damond Wilkins, Nevada	1996	11	114
Marcus Harris, Wyoming	1996	12	109

Catches Per Game	Year	No	P/Gm
Howard Twilley, Tulsa	1965	134	13.4
Manny Hazard, Houston	1989	142	12.9
Alex Van Dyke, Nevada	1995	129	11.7
Damond Wilkins, Nevada	1996	114	10.4
Jason Phillips, Houston	1988	108	9.8

Yards Gained	Year	No	Yards
Alex Van Dyke, Nevada	1995	129	1854
Howard Twilley, Tulsa	1965	134	1779
Troy Edwards, La. Tech	1997	102	1707
Manny Hazard, Houston	1989	142	1689
Marcus Harris, Wyoming	1996	109	1650

All-Purpose Yardage

Yards Gained	Year	Yards
Barry Sanders, Okla. St	1988	3250
Ryan Benjamin, Pacific	1991	2995
Mike Pringle, CS-Fullerton	1989	2690
Paul Palmer, Temple	1986	2633
Ryan Benjamin, Pacific	1992	2597

Yards Per Game	Year	Yards	P/Gm
Barry Sanders, Okla. St	1988	3250	295.5
Ryan Benjamin, Pacific	1991	2995	249.6
Byron (Whizzer) White, Colo	1937	1970	246.3
Mike Pringle, CS-Fullerton	1989	2690	244.6
Paul Palmer, Temple	1986	2633	239.4

Scoring

Points	Year	TD	Xpt	FG	Pts
Barry Sanders, Okla. St	1988	39	0	0	234
Mike Rozier, Nebraska	1983	29	0	0	174
Lydell Mitchell, Penn St	1971	29	0	0	174
Art Luppino, Arizona	1954	24	22	0	166
Bobby Reynolds, Nebraska	1950	22	25	0	157

Points Per Game	Year	Pts	P/Gm
Barry Sanders, Okla. St	1988	234	21.3
Bobby Reynolds, Nebraska	1950	157	17.4
Art Luppino, Arizona	1954	166	16.6
Ed Marinaro, Cornell	1971	148	16.4
Lydell Mitchell, Penn St	1971	174	15.8

Touchdowns Rushing	Year	No
Barry Sanders, Okla. St	1988	37
Mike Rozier, Nebraska	1983	29
Ricky Williams, Texas	1997	25
Travis Prentice, Miami-OH	1997	25

Several tied with 24 each.

Touchdowns Passing	Year	No
David Klingler, Houston	1990	54
Jim McMahon, BYU	1980	47
Andre Ware, Houston	1989	46
Ty Detmer, BYU	1990	41

Three tied with 39 each.

Touchdown Catches	Year	No
Randy Moss, Marshall	1997	25
Manny Hazard, Houston	1989	22
Desmond Howard, Michigan	1991	19

Five tied with 18 each.

Field Goals	Year	No
John Lee, UCLA	1984	29
Paul Woodside, West Virginia	1982	28
Luis Zendejas, Arizona St	1983	28
Fuad Reveiz, Tennessee	1982	27

Three tied with 25 each.

Miscellaneous

Interceptions	Year	No
Al Worley, Washington	1968	14
George Shaw, Oregon	1951	13

Eight tied with 12 each.

Punting Average*	Year	Avg
Chad Kessler, LSU	1997	50.3
Reggie Roby, Iowa	1981	49.8
Kirk Wilson, UCLA	1956	49.3
Todd Sauerbrun, West Virgina	1994	48.4
Zack Jordan, Colorado	1950	48.2

*Qualifiers for championship.

Punt Return Average*	Year	Avg
Bill Blackstock, Tennessee	1951	25.9
George Sims, Baylor	1948	25.0
Gene Derricotte, Michigan	1947	24.8

*At least 1.2 returns per game.

Kickoff Return Average*	Year	Avg
Paul Allen, BYU	1961	40.1
Tremain Mack, Miami-FL	1996	39.5
Leeland McElroy, Texas A&M	1993	39.3
Forrest Hall, San Francisco	1946	38.2
Tony Ball, Tenn-Chattanooga	1977	36.4

*At least 1.2 kickoff returns per game.

All-Time NCAA Division I-A Leaders (Cont.)

SINGLE GAME

Rushing

Yards Gained	Opponent	Year	Yds
Tony Sands, Kansas	Missouri	1991	396
Marshall Faulk, San Diego St	Pacific	1991	386
Troy Davis, Iowa St.	Missouri	1996	378
Anthony Thompson, Indiana	Wisconsin	1989	377
Astron Whatley, Kent	E. Michigan	1997	373

Passing

Yards Gained	Opponent	Year	Yds
David Klingler, Houston	Arizona St.	1990	716
Matt Vogler, TCU	Houston	1990	690
Scott Mitchell, Utah	Air Force	1988	631
Jeremy Leach, New Mexico	Utah	1989	622
Dave Wilson, Illinois	Ohio St.	1980	621

Completions	Opponent	Year	No
Rusty LaRue, Wake Forest	Duke	1995	55
David Klingler, Houston	SMU	1990	48
Jimmy Klingler, Houston	Rice	1992	46
Sandy Schwab, Northwestern	Michigan	1982	45
Chuck Hartlieb, Iowa	Indiana	1988	44
Jim McMahon, BYU	Colo. St.	1981	44
Matt Vogler, TCU	Houston	1990	44

Total Offense

Yards Gained	Opponent	Year	Yds
David Klingler, Houston	Arizona St.	1990	732
Matt Vogler, TCU	Houston	1990	696
David Klingler, Houston	TCU	1990	625
Scott Mitchell, Utah	Air Force	1988	625
Jimmy Klingler, Houston	Rice	1992	612

Receptions

Catches	Opponent	Year	No
Randy Gatewood, UNLV	Idaho	1994	23
Jay Miller, BYU	New Mexico	1973	22
Rick Eber, Tulsa	Idaho St.	1967	20
Howard Twilley, Tulsa	Colo. St.	1965	19
Ron Fair, Arizona St	Wash. St.	1989	19
Manny Hazard, Houston	TCU	1989	19
Manny Hazard, Houston	Texas	1989	19

Yards Gained	Opponent	Year	Yds
Randy Gatewood, UNLV	Idaho	1994	363
Chuck Hughes, UTEP*	N. Texas St.	1965	349
Rick Eber, Tulsa	Idaho St.	1967	322
Harry Wood, Tulsa	Idaho St.	1967	318
Jeff Evans, N. Mexico St	So. Ill.	1978	316

*UTEP was Texas Western in 1965.

Scoring

Points	Opponent	Year	Pts
Howard Griffith, Illinois	So. Ill.	1990	48
Marshall Faulk, S. Diego St.	Pacific	1991	44
Jim Brown, Syracuse	Colgate	1956	43
Showboat Boykin, Ole Miss	Miss. St.	1951	42
Fred Wendt, UTEP*	N. Mex. St.	1948	42

*UTEP was Texas Mines in 1948.

Touchdowns Rushing	Opponent	Year	No
Howard Griffith, Illinois	So. Ill	1990	8
Showboat Boykin, Ole Miss	Miss. St.	1951	7

Note: Griffith's TD runs (5-51-7-41-5-18-5-3).

Touchdowns Passing	Opponent	Year	No
David Klingler, Houston	E. Wash.	1990	11
Dennis Shaw, San Diego St	N. Mex. St.	1969	9

Note: Klingler's TD passes (5-48-29-7-3-7-40-8-7-8-51).

Touchdown Catches	Opponent	Year	No
Tim Delaney, S. Diego St	N. Mex. St.	1969	6

Note: Delaney's TD catches (2-22-34-31-30-9).

Field Goals	Opponent	Year	No
Dale Klein, Nebraska	Missouri	1985	7
Mike Prindle, W. Mich	Marshall	1984	7

Note: Klein's FGs (32-22-43-44-29-43-43); Prindle's FGs (32-44-42-23-48-41-27).

Extra Points (Kick)	Opponent	Year	No
Terry Leiweke, Houston	Tulsa	1968	13
Derek Mahoney, Fresno St	New Mexico	1991	13

Longest Plays (since 1941)

Rushing	Opponent	Year	Yds
Gale Sayers, Kansas	Nebraska	1963	99
Max Anderson, Ariz. St.	Wyoming	1967	99
Ralph Thompson, W. Texas St	Wich. St.	1970	99
Kelsey Finch, Tennessee	Florida	1977	99
Eric Vann, Kansas	Oklahoma	1997	99

Eleven tied at 98 each.

Passing	Opponent	Year	Yds
Fred Owens to Jack Ford, Portland	St. Mary's	1947	99
Bo Burris to Warren McVea, Houston	Wash. St.	1966	99
Colin Clapton to Eddie Jenkins, Holy Cross	Boston U.	1970	99
Terry Peel to Robert Ford, Houston	Syracuse	1970	99
Terry Peel to Robert Ford, Houston	S. Diego St.	1972	99

Passing	Opponent	Year	Yds
Cris Collinsworth to Derrick Gaffney, Florida	Rice	1977	99
Scott Ankrom to James Maness, TCU	Rice	1984	99
Gino Torretta to Horace Copeland, Miami-FL	Ark.	1991	99
John Paci to Thomas Lewis, Indiana	Penn St.	1993	99

Field Goals	Opponent	Year	Yds
Steve Little, Arkansas	Texas	1977	67
Russell Erxleben, Texas	Rice	1977	67
Joe Williams, Wichita St	So. Ill.	1978	67

Annual Awards

Heisman Trophy

Originally presented in 1935 as the DAC Trophy by the Downtown Athletic Club of New York City to the best college football player east of the Mississippi. In 1936, players across the country were eligible and the award was renamed the Heisman Trophy following the death of former college coach and DAC athletic director John W. Heisman.

Multiple winner: Archie Griffin (2).

Winners in junior year (13): Doc Blanchard (1945), Ty Detmer (1990); Archie Griffin (1974), Desmond Howard (1991), Vic Janowicz (1950), Rashaan Salaam (1994), Barry Sanders (1988), Billy Sims (1978), Roger Staubach (1963), Doak Walker (1948), Herschel Walker (1982), Andre Ware (1989) and Charles Woodson (1997).

Winners on AP national champions (10): Angelo Bertelli (Notre Dame, 1943); Doc Blanchard (Army, 1945); Tony Dorsett (Pittsburgh, 1976); Leon Hart (Notre Dame, 1949); Johnny Lujack (Notre Dame, 1947); Davey O'Brien (TCU, 1938); Bruce Smith (Minnesota, 1941); Charlie Ward (Florida St., 1993); Danny Wuerffel (Florida, 1996); and Charles Woodson (Michigan, 1997).

Year		Points
1935	**Jay Berwanger,** Chicago, HB	84
	2nd–Monk Meyer, Army, HB	29
	3rd–Bill Shakespeare, Notre Dame, HB	23
	4th–Pepper Constable, Princeton, FB	20
1936	**Larry Kelley,** Yale, E	219
	2nd–Sam Francis, Nebraska, FB	47
	3rd–Ray Buivid, Marquette, HB	43
	4th–Sammy Baugh, TCU, HB	39
1937	**Clint Frank,** Yale, HB	524
	2nd–Byron (Whizzer) White, Colo., HB	264
	3rd–Marshall Goldberg, Pitt, HB	211
	4th–Alex Wojciechowicz, Fordham, C	85
1938	**Davey O'Brien,** TCU, QB	519
	2nd–Marshall Goldberg, Pitt, HB	294
	3rd–Sid Luckman, Columbia, QB	154
	4th–Bob MacLeod, Dartmouth, HB	78
1939	**Nile Kinnick,** Iowa, HB	651
	2nd–Tom Harmon, Michigan, HB	405
	3rd–Paul Christman, Missouri, QB	391
	4th–George Cafego, Tennessee, QB	296
1940	**Tom Harmon,** Michigan, HB	1303
	2nd–John Kimbrough, Texas A&M, FB	841
	3rd–George Franck, Minnesota, HB	102
	4th–Frankie Albert, Stanford, QB	90
1941	**Bruce Smith,** Minnesota, HB	554
	2nd–Angelo Bertelli, Notre Dame, QB	345
	3rd–Frankie Albert, Stanford, QB	336
	4th–Frank Sinkwich, Georgia, HB	249
1942	**Frank Sinkwich,** Georgia, TB	1059
	2nd–Paul Governali, Columbia, QB	218
	3rd–Clint Castleberry, Ga. Tech, HB	99
	4th–Mike Holovak, Boston College, FB	95
1943	**Angelo Bertelli,** Notre Dame, QB	648
	2nd–Bob Odell, Penn, HB	177
	3rd–Otto Graham, Northwestern, QB	140
	4th–Creighton Miller, Notre Dame, HB	134
1944	**Les Horvath,** Ohio St., TB-QB	412
	2nd–Glenn Davis, Army, HB	287
	3rd–Doc Blanchard, Army, FB	237
	4th–Don Whitmire, Navy, T	115
1945	**Doc Blanchard,** Army, FB	860
	2nd–Glenn Davis, Army, HB	638
	3rd–Bob Fenimore, Oklahoma A&M, HB	187
	4th–Herman Wedemeyer, St. Mary's, HB	152
1946	**Glenn Davis,** Army, HB	792
	2nd–Charlie Trippi, Georgia, HB	435
	3rd–Johnny Lujack, Notre Dame, QB	379
	4th–Doc Blanchard, Army, FB	267
1947	**Johnny Lujack,** Notre Dame, QB	742
	2nd–Bob Chappuis, Michigan, HB	555
	3rd–Doak Walker, SMU, HB	196
	4th–Charlie Conerly, Mississippi, QB	186
1948	**Doak Walker,** SMU, HB	778
	2nd–Charlie Justice, N. Carolina, HB	443
	3rd–Chuck Bednarik, Penn, C	336
	4th–Jackie Jensen, California, HB	143

Year		Points
1949	**Leon Hart,** Notre Dame, E	995
	2nd–Charlie Justice, N. Carolina, HB	272
	3rd–Doak Walker, SMU, HB	229
	4th–Arnold Galiffa, Army QB	196
1950	**Vic Janowicz,** Ohio St., HB	633
	2nd–Kyle Rote, SMU, HB	280
	3rd–Reds Bagnell, Penn, HB	231
	4th–Babe Parilli, Kentucky, QB	214
1951	**Dick Kazmaier,** Princeton, TB	1777
	2nd–Hank Lauricella, Tennessee, HB	424
	3rd–Babe Parilli, Kentucky, QB	344
	4th–Bill McColl, Stanford, E	313
1952	**Billy Vessels,** Oklahoma, HB	525
	2nd–Jack Scarbath, Maryland, QB	367
	3rd–Paul Giel, Minnesota, HB	329
	4th–Donn Moomaw, UCLA, C	257
1953	**Johnny Lattner,** Notre Dame, HB	1850
	2nd–Paul Giel, Minnesota, HB	1794
	3rd–Paul Cameron, UCLA, HB	444
	4th–Bernie Faloney, Maryland, QB	258
1954	**Alan Ameche,** Wisconsin, FB	1068
	2nd–Kurt Burris, Oklahoma, C	838
	3rd–Howard Cassady, Ohio St., HB	810
	4th–Ralph Guglielmi, Notre Dame, QB	691
1955	**Howard Cassady,** Ohio St., HB	2219
	2nd–Jim Swink, TCU, HB	742
	3rd–George Welsh, Navy, QB	383
	4th–Earl Morrall, Michigan St., QB	323
1956	**Paul Hornung,** Notre Dame, QB	1066
	2nd–Johnny Majors, Tennessee, HB	994
	3rd–Tommy McDonald, Oklahoma, HB	973
	4th–Jerry Tubbs, Oklahoma, C	724
1957	**John David Crow,** Texas A&M, HB	1183
	2nd–Alex Karras, Iowa, T	693
	3rd–Walt Kowalczyk, Mich. St., HB	630
	4th–Lou Michaels, Kentucky, T	330
1958	**Pete Dawkins,** Army, HB	1394
	2nd–Randy Duncan, Iowa, QB	1021
	3rd–Billy Cannon, LSU, HB	975
	4th–Bob White, Ohio St., FB	365
1959	**Billy Cannon,** LSU, HB	1929
	2nd–Richie Lucas, Penn St., QB	613
	3rd–Don Meredith, SMU, QB	286
	4th–Bill Burrell, Illinois, G	196
1960	**Joe Bellino,** Navy, HB	1793
	2nd–Tom Brown, Minnesota, G	731
	3rd–Jake Gibbs, Mississippi, QB	453
	4th–Ed Dyas, Auburn, HB	319
1961	**Ernie Davis,** Syracuse, HB	824
	2nd–Bob Ferguson, Ohio St., HB	771
	3rd–Jimmy Saxton, Texas, HB	551
	4th–Sandy Stephens, Minnesota, QB	543
1962	**Terry Baker,** Oregon St., QB	707
	2nd–Jerry Stovall, LSU, HB	618
	3rd–Bobby Bell, Minnesota, T	429
	4th–Lee Roy Jordan, Alabama, C	321

Annual Awards (Cont.)

Year — Points

- 1963 **Roger Staubach,** Navy, QB 1860
  - 2nd–Billy Lothridge, Ga. Tech, QB 504
  - 3rd–Sherman Lewis, Mich. St., HB 369
  - 4th–Don Trull, Baylor, QB 253
- 1964 **John Huarte,** Notre Dame, QB 1026
  - 2nd–Jerry Rhome, Tulsa, QB 952
  - 3rd–Dick Butkus, Illinois, C 505
  - 4th–Bob Timberlake, Michigan, QB 361
- 1965 **Mike Garrett,** USC, HB 926
  - 2nd–Howard Twilley, Tulsa, E 528
  - 3rd–Jim Grabowski, Illinois, FB 481
  - 4th–Donny Anderson, Texas Tech, HB 408
- 1966 **Steve Spurrier,** Florida, QB 1679
  - 2nd–Bob Griese, Purdue, QB 816
  - 3rd–Nick Eddy, Notre Dame, HB 456
  - 4th–Gary Beban, UCLA, QB 318
- 1967 **Gary Beban,** UCLA, QB 1968
  - 2nd–O.J. Simpson, USC, HB 1722
  - 3rd–Leroy Keyes, Purdue, HB 1366
  - 4th–Larry Csonka, Syracuse, FB 136
- 1968 **O.J. Simpson,** USC, HB 2853
  - 2nd–Leroy Keyes, Purdue, HB 1103
  - 3rd–Terry Hanratty, Notre Dame, QB 387
  - 4th–Ted Kwalick, Penn St., TE 254
- 1969 **Steve Owens,** Oklahoma, HB 1488
  - 2nd–Mike Phipps, Purdue, QB 1344
  - 3rd–Rex Kern, Ohio St., QB 856
  - 4th–Archie Manning, Mississippi, QB 582
- 1970 **Jim Plunkett,** Stanford, QB 2229
  - 2nd–Joe Theismann, Notre Dame, QB 1410
  - 3rd–Archie Manning, Mississippi, QB 849
  - 4th–Steve Worster, Texas, RB 398
- 1971 **Pat Sullivan,** Auburn, QB 1597
  - 2nd–Ed Marinaro, Cornell, RB 1445
  - 3rd–Greg Pruitt, Oklahoma, RB 586
  - 4th–Johnny Musso, Alabama, RB 365
- 1972 **Johnny Rodgers,** Nebraska, FL 1310
  - 2nd–Greg Pruitt, Oklahoma, RB 966
  - 3rd–Rich Glover, Nebraska, MG 652
  - 4th–Bert Jones, LSU, QB 351
- 1973 **John Cappelletti,** Penn St., RB 1057
  - 2nd–John Hicks, Ohio St., OT 524
  - 3rd–Roosevelt Leaks, Texas, RB 482
  - 4th–David Jaynes, Kansas, QB 394
- 1974 **Archie Griffin,** Ohio St., RB 1920
  - 2nd–Anthony Davis, USC, RB 819
  - 3rd–Joe Washington, Oklahoma, RB 661
  - 4th–Tom Clements, Notre Dame, QB 244
- 1975 **Archie Griffin,** Ohio St., RB 1800
  - 2nd–Chuck Muncie, California, RB 730
  - 3rd–Ricky Bell, USC, RB 708
  - 4th–Tony Dorsett, Pitt, RB 616
- 1976 **Tony Dorsett,** Pittsburgh, RB 2357
  - 2nd–Ricky Bell, USC, RB 1346
  - 3rd–Rob Lytle, Michigan, RB 413
  - 4th–Terry Miller, Oklahoma St., RB 197
- 1977 **Earl Campbell,** Texas, RB 1547
  - 2nd–Terry Miller, Oklahoma St., RB 812
  - 3rd–Ken MacAfee, Notre Dame, TE 343
  - 4th–Doug Williams, Grambling, QB 266
- 1978 **Billy Sims,** Oklahoma, RB 827
  - 2nd–Chuck Fusina, Penn St., QB 750
  - 3rd–Rick Leach, Michigan, QB 435
  - 4th–Charles White, USC, RB 354
- 1979 **Charles White,** USC, RB 1695
  - 2nd–Billy Sims, Oklahoma, RB 773
  - 3rd–Marc Wilson, BYU, QB 589
  - 4th–Art Schlichter, Ohio St., QB 251
- 1980 **George Rogers,** South Carolina, RB 1128
  - 2nd–Hugh Green, Pittsburgh, DE 861
  - 3rd–Herschel Walker, Georgia, RB 683
  - 4th–Mark Herrmann, Purdue, QB 405
- 1981 **Marcus Allen,** USC, RB 1797
  - 2nd–Herschel Walker, Georgia, RB 1199
  - 3rd–Jim McMahon, BYU, QB 706
  - 4th–Dan Marino, Pitt, QB 256
- 1982 **Herschel Walker,** Georgia, RB 1926
  - 2nd–John Elway, Stanford, QB 1231
  - 3rd–Eric Dickerson, SMU, RB 465
  - 4th–Anthony Carter, Michigan, WR 142
- 1983 **Mike Rozier,** Nebraska, RB 1801
  - 2nd–Steve Young, BYU, QB 1172
  - 3rd–Doug Flutie, Boston College, QB 253
  - 4th–Turner Gill, Nebraska, QB 190
- 1984 **Doug Flutie,** Boston College, QB 2240
  - 2nd–Keith Byars, Ohio St., RB 1251
  - 3rd–Robbie Bosco, BYU, QB 443
  - 4th–Bernie Kosar, Miami-FL, QB 320
- 1985 **Bo Jackson,** Auburn, RB 1509
  - 2nd–Chuck Long, Iowa, QB 1464
  - 3rd–Robbie Bosco, BYU, QB 459
  - 4th–Lorenzo White, Michigan St., RB 391
- 1986 **Vinny Testaverde,** Miami-FL, QB 2213
  - 2nd–Paul Palmer, Temple, RB 672
  - 3rd–Jim Harbaugh, Michigan, QB 458
  - 4th–Brian Bosworth, Oklahoma, LB 395
- 1987 **Tim Brown**, Notre Dame, WR 1442
  - 2nd–Don McPherson, Syracuse, QB 831
  - 3rd–Gordie Lockbaum, Holy Cross, WR-DB 657
  - 4th–Lorenzo White, Michigan St., RB 632
- 1988 **Barry Sanders,** Oklahoma St., RB 1878
  - 2nd–Rodney Peete, USC, QB 912
  - 3rd–Troy Aikman, UCLA, QB 582
  - 4th–Steve Walsh, Miami-FL, QB 341
- 1989 **Andre Ware,** Houston, QB 1073
  - 2nd–Anthony Thompson, Ind., RB 1003
  - 3rd–Major Harris, West Va., QB 709
  - 4th–Tony Rice, Notre Dame, QB 523
- 1990 **Ty Detmer,** BYU, QB 1482
  - 2nd–Rocket Ismail, Notre Dame, FL 1177
  - 3rd–Eric Bieniemy, Colorado, RB 798
  - 4th–Shawn Moore, Virginia, QB 465
- 1991 **Desmond Howard,** Michigan, WR 2077
  - 2nd–Casey Weldon, Florida St., QB 503
  - 3rd–Ty Detmer, BYU, QB 445
  - 4th–Steve Emtman, Washington, DT 357
- 1992 **Gino Torretta,** Miami-FL, QB 1400
  - 2nd–Marshall Faulk, San Diego St., RB 1080
  - 3rd–Garrison Hearst, Georgia, RB 982
  - 4th–Marvin Jones, Florida St., LB 392
- 1993 **Charlie Ward,** Florida St., QB 2310
  - 2nd–Heath Shuler, Tennessee, QB 688
  - 3rd–David Palmer, Alabama, RB 292
  - 4th–Marshall Faulk, S. Diego St., RB 250
- 1994 **Rashaan Salaam,** Colorado, RB 1743
  - 2nd–Ki-Jana Carter, Penn St., RB 901
  - 3rd–Steve McNair, Alcorn St., QB 655
  - 4th–Kerry Collins, Penn St., QB 639
- 1995 **Eddie George,** Ohio St., RB 1460
  - 2nd–Tommie Frazier, Nebraska, QB 1196
  - 3rd–Danny Wuerffel, Florida, QB 987
  - 4th–Darnell Autry, Northwestern, RB 535
- 1996 **Danny Wuerffel,** Florida, QB 1363
  - 2nd–Troy Davis, Iowa St., RB 1174
  - 3rd–Jake Plummer, Arizona St., QB 685
  - 4th–Orlando Pace, Ohio St., OT 599

Year		Points
1997	**Charles Woodson,** Michigan, DB-WR	1815
	2nd–Peyton Manning, Tennessee, QB	1543
	3rd–Ryan Leaf, Washington St., QB	861
	4th–Randy Moss, Marshall, WR	253

Maxwell Award

First presented in 1937 by the Maxwell Memorial Football Club of Philadelphia, the award is named after Robert (Tiny) Maxwell, a Philadelphia native who was a standout lineman at the University of Chicago at the turn of the century. Like the Heisman, the Maxwell is given to the outstanding college player in the nation. Both awards have gone to the same player in the same season 32 times. Those players are preceded by (#). Glenn Davis of Army and Doak Walker of SMU won both but in different years.

Multiple winner: Johnny Lattner (2).

Year
1937 #Clint Frank, Yale, HB
1938 #Davey O'Brien, TCU, QB
1939 #Nile Kinnick, Iowa, HB
1940 #Tom Harmon, Michigan, HB
1941 Bill Dudley, Virginia, HB
1942 Paul Governali, Columbia, QB
1943 Bob Odell, Penn, HB
1944 Glenn Davis, Army, HB
1945 #Doc Blanchard, Army, FB
1946 Charley Trippi, Georgia, HB
1947 Doak Walker, SMU, HB
1948 Chuck Bednarik, Penn, C
1949 #Leon Hart, Notre Dame, E

1950 Reds Bagnell, Penn, HB
1951 #Dick Kazmaier, Princeton, TB
1952 Johnny Lattner, Notre Dame, HB
1953 #Johnny Lattner, N. Dame, HB
1954 Ron Beagle, Navy, E
1955 #Howard Cassady, Ohio St., HB
1956 Tommy McDonald, Okla., HB
1957 Bob Reifsnyder, Navy, T

Year
1958 #Pete Dawkins, Army, HB
1959 Rich Lucas, Penn St., QB

1960 #Joe Bellino, Navy, HB
1961 Bob Ferguson, Ohio St., HB
1962 #Terry Baker, Oregon St., QB
1963 #Roger Staubach, Navy, QB
1964 Glenn Ressler, Penn St., G
1965 Tommy Nobis, Texas, LB
1966 Jim Lynch, Notre Dame, LB
1967 #Gary Beban, UCLA, QB
1968 #O.J. Simpson, USC, HB
1969 Mike Reid, Penn St., DT

1970 #Jim Plunkett, Stanford, QB
1971 Ed Marinaro, Cornell, RB
1972 Brad Van Pelt, Michigan St., DB
1973 #John Cappelletti, Penn St., RB
1974 Steve Joachim, Temple, QB
1975 #Archie Griffin, Ohio St., RB
1976 #Tony Dorsett, Pitt, RB
1977 Ross Browner, Notre Dame, DE
1978 Chuck Fusina, Penn St., QB

Year
1979 #Charles White, USC, RB

1980 Hugh Green, Pitt, DE
1981 #Marcus Allen, USC, RB
1982 #Herschel Walker, Georgia, RB
1983 #Mike Rozier, Nebraska, RB
1984 #Doug Flutie, Boston Col., QB
1985 Chuck Long, Iowa, QB
1986 #V. Testaverde, Miami-FL, QB
1987 Don McPherson, Syracuse, QB
1988 #Barry Sanders, Okla. St., RB
1989 Anthony Thompson, Indiana, RB

1990 #Ty Detmer, BYU, QB
1991 #Desmond Howard, Mich., WR
1992 #Gino Torretta, Miami-FL, QB
1993 #Charlie Ward, Florida St., QB
1994 Kerry Collins, Penn St., QB
1995 #Eddie George, Ohio St., RB
1996 #Danny Wuerffel, Florida, QB
1997 Peyton Manning, Tennessee, QB

Outland Trophy

First presented in 1946 by the Football Writers Association of America, honoring the nation's outstanding interior lineman. The award is named after its benefactor, Dr. John H. Outland (Kansas, Class of 1898). Players listed in bold type helped lead their team to a national championship (according to AP).

Multiple winner: Dave Rimington (2). **Winners in junior year:** Ross Browner (1976), Steve Emtman (1991), Orlando Pace (1996) and Rimington (1981).

Year
1946 **George Connor**, N. Dame, T
1947 Joe Steffy, Army, G
1948 Bill Fischer, Notre Dame, G
1949 Ed Bagdon, Michigan St., G

1950 Bob Gain, Kentucky, T
1951 Jim Weatherall, Oklahoma, T
1952 Dick Modzelewski, Maryland, T
1953 J.D. Roberts, Oklahoma, G
1954 Bill Brooks, Arkansas, G
1955 Calvin Jones, Iowa, G
1956 Jim Parker, Ohio St., G
1957 Alex Karras, Iowa, T
1958 Zeke Smith, Auburn, G
1959 Mike McGee, Duke, T

1960 **Tom Brown**, Minnesota, G
1961 Merlin Olsen, Utah St., T
1962 Bobby Bell, Minnesota, T
1963 **Scott Appleton**, Texas, T

Year
1964 Steve DeLong, Tennessee, T
1965 Tommy Nobis, Texas, G
1966 Loyd Phillips, Arkansas, T
1967 **Ron Yary**, USC, T
1968 Bill Stanfill, Georgia, T
1969 Mike Reid, Penn St., DT

1970 Jim Stillwagon, Ohio St., MG
1971 **Larry Jacobson**, Neb., DT
1972 Rich Glover, Nebraska, MG
1973 John Hicks, Ohio St., OT
1974 Randy White, Maryland, DT
1975 **Lee Roy Selmon**, Okla., DT
1976 Ross Browner, Notre Dame, DE
1977 Brad Shearer, Texas, DT
1978 Greg Roberts, Oklahoma, G
1979 Jim Richter, N.C. State, C

1980 Mark May, Pittsburgh, OT
1981 Dave Rimington, Nebraska, C

Year
1982 Dave Rimington, Nebraska, C
1983 Dean Steinkuhler, Nebraska, G
1984 Bruce Smith, Virginia Tech, DT
1985 Mike Ruth, Boston College, NG
1986 Jason Buck, BYU, DT
1987 Chad Hennings, Air Force, DT
1988 Tracy Rocker, Auburn, DT
1989 Mohammed Elewonibi, BYU, G

1990 Russell Maryland, Miami-FL, NT
1991 Steve Emtman, Washington, DT
1992 Will Shields, Nebraska, G
1993 Rob Waldrop, Arizona, NG
1994 **Zach Wiegert**, Nebraska, OT
1995 Jonathan Ogden, UCLA, OT
1996 Orlando Pace, Ohio St., OT
1997 Aaron Taylor, Nebraska, G

Butkus Award

First presented in 1985 by the Downtown Athletic Club of Orlando, Fla., to honor the nation's outstanding linebacker. The award is named after Dick Butkus, two-time consensus All-America at Illinois and six-time All-Pro with the Chicago Bears.

Multiple winner: Brian Bosworth (2).

Year
1985 Brian Bosworth, Oklahoma

Year
1986 Brian Bosworth, Oklahoma

Year
1987 Paul McGowan, Florida St.

Annual Awards (Cont.)

Year	Year	Year
1988 Derrick Thomas, Alabama	1991 Erick Anderson, Michigan	1994 Dana Howard, Illinois
1989 Percy Snow, Michigan St.	1992 Marvin Jones, Florida St.	1995 Kevin Hardy, Illinois
1990 Alfred Williams, Colorado	1993 Trev Alberts, Nebraska	1996 Matt Russell, Colorado
		1997 Andy Katzenmoyer, Ohio St.

Lombardi Award

First presented in 1970 by the Rotary Club of Houston, honoring the nation's best lineman. The award is named after pro football coach Vince Lombardi, who, as a guard, was a member of the famous "Seven Blocks of Granite" at Fordham in the 1930s. The Lombardi and Outland awards have gone to the same player in the same year ten times. Those players are preceded by (#). Ross Browner of Notre Dame won both, but in different years.

Multiple winner: Orlando Pace (2).

Year	Year	Year
1970 #Jim Stillwagon, Ohio St., MG	1980 Hugh Green, Pitt, DE	1990 Chris Zorich, Notre Dame, NT
1971 Walt Patulski, Notre Dame, DE	1981 Kenneth Sims, Texas, DT	1991 #Steve Emtman, Wash., DT
1972 #Rich Glover, Nebraska, MG	1982 #Dave Rimington, Neb., C	1992 Marvin Jones, Florida St., LB
1973 #John Hicks, Ohio St., OT	1983 #Dean Steinkuhler, Neb., G	1993 Aaron Taylor, Notre Dame, OT
1974 #Randy White, Maryland, DT	1984 Tony Degrate, Texas, DT	1994 Warren Sapp, Miami-FL, DT
1975 #Lee Roy Selmon, Okla., DT	1985 Tony Casillas, Oklahoma, NG	1995 Orlando Pace, Ohio St., OT
1976 Wilson Whitley, Houston, DT	1986 Cornelius Bennett, Alabama, LB	1996 #Orlando Pace, Ohio St., OT
1977 Ross Browner, Notre Dame, DE	1987 Chris Spielman, Ohio St., LB	1997 Grant Wistrom, Nebraska, DE
1978 Bruce Clark, Penn St., DT	1988 #Tracy Rocker, Auburn, DT	
1979 Brad Budde, USC, G	1989 Percy Snow, Michigan St., LB	

O'Brien Quarterback Award

First presented in 1977 as the O'Brien Memorial Trophy, the award went to the outstanding player in the Southwest. In 1981, however, the Davey O'Brien Educational and Charitable Trust of Ft. Worth renamed the prize the O'Brien National Quarterback Award and now honors the nation's best quarterback. The award is named after 1938 Heisman Trophy-winning QB Davey O'Brien of Texas Christian.

Multiple winners: Ty Detmer, Mike Singletary and Danny Wuerffel (2).

Memorial Trophy

Year	Year
1977 Earl Campbell, Texas, RB	1979 Mike Singletary, Baylor, LB
1978 Billy Sims, Oklahoma, RB	1980 Mike Singletary, Baylor, LB

National QB Award

Year	Year	Year
1981 Jim McMahon, BYU	1987 Don McPherson, Syracuse	1993 Charlie Ward, Florida St.
1982 Todd Blackledge, Penn St.	1988 Troy Aikman, UCLA	1994 Kerry Collins, Penn St.
1983 Steve Young, BYU	1989 Andre Ware, Houston	1995 Danny Wuerffel, Florida
1984 Doug Flutie, Boston College	1990 Ty Detmer, BYU	1996 Danny Wuerffel, Florida
1985 Chuck Long, Iowa	1991 Ty Detmer, BYU	1997 Peyton Manning, Tennessee
1986 Vinny Testaverde, Miami, FL	1992 Gino Torretta, Miami-FL	

Thorpe Award

First presented in 1986 by the Jim Thorpe Athletic Club of Oklahoma City to honor the nation's outstanding defensive back. The award is named after Jim Thorpe–Olympic champion and two-time consensus All-America HB at Carlisle.

Year	Year	Year
1986 Thomas Everett, Baylor	1990 Darryl Lewis, Arizona	1995 Greg Myers, Colorado St.
1987 Bennie Blades, Miami-FL & Rickey Dixon, Oklahoma	1991 Terrell Buckley, Florida St.	1996 Lawrence Wright, Florida
1988 Deion Sanders, Florida St.	1992 Deon Figures, Colorado	1997 Charles Woodson, Michigan
1989 Mike Carrier, USC	1993 Antonio Langham, Alabama	
	1994 Chris Hudson, Colorado	

Payton Award

First presented in 1987 by the Sports Network and Division I-AA sports information directors to honor the nation's outstanding Division I-AA player. The award is named after Walter Payton, the NFL's all-time leading rusher who was an All-America RB at Jackson St.

Year	Year	Year
1987 Kenny Gamble, Colgate, RB	1991 Jamie Martin, Weber St., QB	1995 Dave Dickenson, Montana, QB
1988 Dave Meggett, Towson St., RB	1992 Michael Payton, Marshall, QB	1996 Archie Amerson, N. Arizona, RB
1989 John Friesz, Idaho, QB	1993 Doug Nussmeier, Idaho, QB	1997 Brian Finneran, Villanova, WR
1990 Walter Dean, Grambling, RB	1994 Steve McNair, Alcorn St., QB	

Hill Trophy

First presented in 1986 by the Harlon Hill Awards Committee in Florence, AL, to honor the nation's outstanding Division II player. The award is named after three-time NFL All-Pro Harlon Hill, who played college ball at North Alabama.

Multiple winner: Johnny Bailey (3).

Year	Year	Year
1986 Jeff Bentrim, N. Dakota St., QB	1990 Chris Simdorn, N. Dakota St., QB	1994 Chris Hatcher, Valdosta St., QB
1987 Johnny Bailey, Texas A&I, RB	1991 Ronnie West, Pittsburg St., WR	1995 Ronald McKinnon, N. Alabama, LB
1988 Johnny Bailey, Texas A&I, RB	1992 Ronald Moore, Pittsburg St., RB	1996 Jarrett Anderson, Truman St., RB
1989 Johnny Bailey, Texas A&I, RB	1993 Roger Graham, New Haven, RB	1997 Irv Sigler, Bloomsburg, RB

All-Time Winningest Division I-A Coaches

Minimum of 10 years in Division I-A through 1997 season. Regular season and bowl games included. Coaches active in 1997 in **bold** type.

Top 25 Winning Percentage

		Yrs	W	L	T	Pct
1	Knute Rockne	13	105	12	5	**.881**
2	Frank Leahy	13	107	13	9	**.864**
3	George Woodruff	12	142	25	2	**.846**
4	Barry Switzer	16	157	29	4	**.837**
5	**Tom Osborne**	25	255	49	3	**.836**
6	Percy Haughton	13	96	17	6	**.832**
7	Bob Neyland	21	173	31	12	**.829**
8	Hurry Up Yost	29	196	36	12	**.828**
9	Bud Wilkinson	17	145	29	4	**.826**
10	Jock Sutherland	20	144	28	14	**.812**
11	Bob Devaney	16	136	30	7	**.806**
12	Frank Thomas	19	141	33	9	**.795**
13	**Joe Paterno**	32	298	77	3	**.792**
14	Henry Williams	23	141	34	12	**.786**
15	Gil Dobie	33	180	45	15	**.781**
16	Bear Bryant	38	323	85	17	**.780**
17	Fred Folsom	19	106	28	6	**.779**
18	Bo Schembechler	27	234	65	8	**.775**
19	**Steve Spurrier**	11	103	29	2	**.776**
20	**Bobby Bowden**	32	281	83	4	**.769**
21	Fritz Crisler	18	116	32	9	**.768**
22	Charley Moran	18	122	33	12	**.766**
23	Wallace Wade	24	171	49	10	**.765**
24	Frank Kush	22	176	54	1	**.764**
25	Dan McGugin	30	197	55	19	**.762**

Top 25 Victories

		Yrs	W	L	T	Pct
1	Bear Bryant	38	**323**	85	17	.780
2	Pop Warner	44	**319**	106	32	.733
3	Amos Alonzo Stagg	57	**314**	199	35	.605
4	**Joe Paterno**	32	**298**	77	3	.792
5	**Bobby Bowden**	32	**281**	83	4	.769
6	**Tom Osborne**	25	**255**	49	3	.836
7	Woody Hayes	33	**238**	72	10	.759
8	Bo Schembechler	27	**234**	65	8	.775
	LaVell Edwards	26	**234**	86	3	.729
10	**Hayden Fry**	36	**229**	170	10	.572
11	Lou Holtz	27	**216**	95	7	.690
12	Jess Neely	40	**207**	176	19	.539
13	Warren Woodson	31	**203**	95	14	.673
14	Vince Dooley	25	**201**	77	10	.715
	Eddie Anderson	39	**201**	128	15	.606
16	Jim Sweeney	32	**200**	154	4	.564
17	Dana X. Bible	33	**198**	72	23	.715
18	Dan McGugin	30	**197**	55	19	.762
19	Hurry Up Yost	29	**196**	36	12	.828
20	Howard Jones	29	**194**	64	21	.733
21	Johnny Vaught	25	**190**	61	12	.745
22	John Heisman	36	**185**	70	17	.711
	Johnny Majors	29	**185**	137	10	.572
24	Darrell Royal	23	**184**	60	5	.749
25	**Don Nehlen**	27	**183**	112	8	.617

Note: Eddie Robinson of Division I-AA Grambling St. (1941-42, 1945-97) is the all-time NCAA leader in coaching wins with a 408-165-15 record and .708 winning pct. over 55 seasons.

Where They Coached

Anderson–Loras (1922-24), DePaul (1925-31), Holy Cross (1933-38), Iowa (1939-42), Holy Cross (1950-64); **Bible**–Mississippi College (1913-15), LSU (1916), Texas A&M (1917, 1919-28), Nebraska (1929-36), Texas (1937-46); **Bowden**–Samford (1959-62), West Virginia (1970-75), Florida St. (1976–); **Bryant**–Maryland (1945), Kentucky (1946-53), Texas A&M (1954-57), Alabama (1958-82); **Crisler**–Minnesota (1930-31), Princeton (1932-37), Michigan (1938-47); **Devaney**–Wyoming (1957-61), Nebraska (1962-72); **V. Dooley**–Georgia (1964-88); **Edwards**–BYU (1972–); **Folsom**–Colorado (1895-99, 1901-02), Dartmouth (1903-06), Colorado (1908-15).

Fry–SMU (1962-72), North Texas (1973-78), Iowa (1979–); **Haughton**–Cornell (1899-1900), Harvard (1908-16), Columbia (1923-24); **Hayes**–Denison (1946-48), Miami-OH (1949-50), Ohio St. (1951-78); **Heisman**–Oberlin (1892), Akron (1893), Oberlin (1894), Auburn (1895-99), Clemson (1900-03), Georgia Tech (1904-19), Penn (1920-22), Washington & Jefferson (1923), Rice (1924-27); **Holtz**–William & Mary (1969-71), N.C. State (1972-75), Arkansas (1977-83), Minnesota (1984-85), Notre Dame (1986-96); **Jones**–Syracuse (1908), Yale (1909), Ohio St. (1910), Yale (1913), Iowa (1916-23), Duke (1924), USC (1925-40); **Kush**–Arizona St. (1958-79); **Leahy**–Boston College (1939-40), Notre Dame (1941-43, 1946-53); **Majors**–Iowa St. (1968–72), Pittsburgh (1973–76, 93-96), Tennessee (1977–92); **McGugin**–Vanderbilt (1904-17, 1919-34); **Moran**–Texas A&M (1909-14), Centre (1919-23), Bucknell (1924-26), Catawba (1930-33).

Neely–Rhodes (1924-27), Clemson (1931-39), Rice (1940-66); **Nehlen**–Bowling Green (1968-76), West Virginia (1980–); **Neyland**–Tennessee (1926-34, 1936-40, 1946-52); **Osborne**–Nebraska (1973-97); **Paterno**–Penn St. (1966–); **Rockne**–Notre Dame (1918-30); **Royal**–Mississippi St. (1954-55), Washington (1956), Texas (1957-76); **Schembechler**–Miami-OH (1963-68), Michigan (1969-89); **Spurrier**–Duke (1987-89), Florida (1990–); **Stagg**–Springfield College (1890-91), Chicago (1892-1932), Pacific (1933-46); **Sutherland**–Lafayette (1919-23), Pittsburgh (1924-38); **Sweeney**–Montana St. (1963-67), Washington St. (1968-75), Fresno St. (1976–); **Switzer**–Oklahoma (1973-88).

Thomas–Chattanooga (1925-28), Alabama (1931-42, 1944-46); **Vaught**–Mississippi (1947-70); **Wade**–Alabama (1923-30), Duke (1931-41, 1946-50); **Warner**–Georgia (1895-96), Cornell (1897-98), Carlisle (1899-1903), Cornell (1904-06), Carlisle (1907-13), Pittsburgh (1915-23), Stanford (1924-32), Temple (1933-38); **Wilkinson**–Oklahoma (1947-63); **Williams**–Army (1891), Minnesota (1900-21); **Woodruff**–Penn (1892-1901), Illinois (1903), Carlisle (1905); **Woodson**–Central Arkansas (1935-39), Hardin-Simmons (1941-42, 1946-51), Arizona (1952-56), New Mexico St. (1958-67), Trinity-TX (1972-73); **Yost**–Ohio Wesleyan (1897), Nebraska (1898), Kansas (1899), Stanford (1900), Michigan (1901-23, 1925-26).

All-Time Winningest Division I-A Coaches (Cont.)

All-Time Bowl Appearances

Coaches active in 1997 in **bold** type.

		App	Overall W	L	T
1	Bear Bryant	29	15	12	2
2	**Joe Paterno**	28	18	9	1
3	**Tom Osborne**	25	12	13	0
4	**Bobby Bowden**	21	16	4	1
	Lou Holtz	20	10	8	2
	Vince Dooley	20	8	10	2
	LaVell Edwards	20	7	12	1
8	Johnny Vaught	18	10	8	0
9	**Hayden Fry**	17	7	9	1
	Bo Schembechler	17	5	12	0
11	Johnny Majors	16	9	7	0
	Darrell Royal	16	8	7	1
13	Don James	15	10	5	0
14	Bobby Dodd	13	9	4	0
	Terry Donahue	13	8	4	1
	Barry Switzer	13	8	5	0
	Charlie McClendon	13	7	6	0
18	Earle Bruce	12	7	5	0
	Woody Hayes	12	6	6	0
	Shug Jordan	12	5	7	0
	George Welsh	12	5	7	0

Active Coaches' Victories

(Minimum 5 years in Division I-A.)

		Yrs	W	L	T	Pct
1	Joe Paterno, Penn St	32	**298**	77	3	.792
2	Bobby Bowden, Fla. St.	32	**281**	83	4	.769
3	LaVell Edwards, BYU	26	**234**	86	3	.729
4	Hayden Fry, Iowa	36	**229**	170	10	.572
5	Don Nehlen, West Va.	27	**183**	112	8	.617
6	John Cooper, Ohio St.	21	**167**	73	6	.691
	George Welsh, Virginia	25	**167**	118	4	.583
8	Jackie Sherrill, Miss. St.	20	**146**	82	4	.638
9	Dick Tomey, Arizona	21	**135**	97	7	.579
10	Ken Hatfield, Rice	19	**134**	84	4	.613
11	Larry Smith, Missouri	21	**128**	107	7	.543
12	Dennis Franchione, N. Mexico	15	**113**	55	2	.671
13	Terry Bowden, Auburn	14	**110**	47	2	.698
	Frank Beamer, Va. Tech	17	**110**	79	4	.580
15	Fisher DeBerry, Air Force	14	**108**	63	1	.631
16	Bruce Snyder, Arizona St.	18	**107**	89	6	.545
17	Steve Spurrier, Florida	11	**103**	29	2	.776
18	Mike Price, Wash. St.	17	**99**	93	0	.516
19	Paul Pasqualoni, Syracuse	12	**94**	39	1	.705
20	Mack Brown, Texas	14	**87**	74	1	.540

Note: Only four coaches— **Bill Alexander** of Georgia Tech (1920–44); **Bob Neyland** of Tennessee (1926–34, 36–40, 46–52); **Frank Thomas** of Alabama (1931–42, 44–46) and **Joe Paterno** of Penn State (1966–)— have taken teams to the Rose, Orange, Sugar and Cotton Bowls. Paterno has won all four, while Alexander and Thomas won three and Neyland two.

AFCA Coach of the Year

First presented in 1935 by the American Football Coaches Association. **Multiple winners:** Joe Paterno (4), Bear Bryant (3), John McKay and Darrell Royal (2).

Years
1935 Pappy Waldorf, Northwestern
1936 Dick Harlow, Harvard
1937 Hooks Mylin, Lafayette
1938 Bill Kern, Carnegie Tech
1939 Eddie Anderson, Iowa
1940 Clark Shaughnessy, Stanford
1941 Frank Leahy, Notre Dame
1942 Bill Alexander, Georgia Tech
1943 Amos Alonzo Stagg, Pacific
1944 Carroll Widdoes, Ohio St.
1945 Bo McMillin, Indiana
1946 Red Blaik, Army
1947 Fritz Crisler, Michigan
1948 Bennie Oosterbaan, Michigan
1949 Bud Wilkinson, Oklahoma
1950 Charlie Caldwell, Princeton
1951 Chuck Taylor, Stanford
1952 Biggie Munn, Michigan St.
1953 Jim Tatum, Maryland
1954 Red Sanders, UCLA
1955 Duffy Daugherty, Michigan St.
1956 Bowden Wyatt, Tennessee

Years
1957 Woody Hayes, Ohio St.
1958 Paul Dietzel, LSU
1959 Ben Schwartzwalder, Syracuse
1960 Murray Warmath, Minnesota
1961 Bear Bryant, Alabama
1962 John McKay, USC
1963 Darrell Royal, Texas
1964 Frank Broyles, Arkansas
& Ara Parseghian, Notre Dame
1965 Tommy Prothro, UCLA
1966 Tom Cahill, Army
1967 John Pont, Indiana
1968 Joe Paterno, Penn St.
1969 Bo Schembechler, Michigan
1970 Charlie McClendon, LSU
& Darrell Royal, Texas
1971 Bear Bryant, Alabama
1972 John McKay, USC
1973 Bear Bryant, Alabama
1974 Grant Teaff, Baylor
1975 Frank Kush, Arizona St.
1976 Johnny Majors, Pittsburgh

Years
1977 Don James, Washington
1978 Joe Paterno, Penn St.
1979 Earle Bruce, Ohio St.
1980 Vince Dooley, Georgia
1981 Danny Ford, Clemson
1982 Joe Paterno, Penn St.
1983 Ken Hatfield, Air Force
1984 LaVell Edwards, BYU
1985 Fisher DeBerry, Air Force
1986 Joe Paterno, Penn St.
1987 Dick MacPherson, Syracuse
1988 Don Nehlen, West Virginia
1989 Bill McCartney, Colorado
1990 Bobby Ross, Georgia Tech
1991 Bill Lewis, East Carolina
1992 Gene Stallings, Alabama
1993 Barry Alvarez, Wisconsin
1994 Tom Osborne, Nebraska
1995 Gary Barnett, Northwestern
1996 Bruce Snyder, Arizona St.
1997 Lloyd Carr, Michigan

FWAA Coach of the Year

First presented in 1957 by the Football Writers Association of America. The FWAA and AFCA awards have both gone to the same coach in the same season 27 times. Those double winners are preceded by (#). **Multiple winners:** Woody Hayes and Joe Paterno (3); Lou Holtz, Johnny Majors and John McKay (2).

Year
1957 #Woody Hayes, Ohio St.
1958 #Paul Dietzel, LSU
1959 #Ben Schwartzwalder, Syracuse
1960 #Murray Warmath, Minnesota
1961 Darrell Royal, Texas
1962 #John McKay, USC
1963 #Darrell Royal, Texas
1964 #Ara Parseghian, Notre Dame

Year
1965 Duffy Daugherty, Michigan St.
1966 #Tom Cahill, Army
1967 #John Pont, Indiana
1968 Woody Hayes, Ohio St.
1969 #Bo Schembechler, Michigan
1970 Alex Agase, Northwestern
1971 Bob Devaney, Nebraska
1972 #John McKay, USC

Year
1973 Johnny Majors, Pitt
1974 #Grant Teaff, Baylor
1975 Woody Hayes, Ohio St.
1976 #Johnny Majors, Pitt
1977 Lou Holtz, Arkansas
1978 #Joe Paterno, Penn St.
1979 #Earle Bruce, Ohio St.
1980 #Vince Dooley, Georgia

Year	Year	Year
1981 #Danny Ford, Clemson	1987 #Dick MacPherson, Syracuse	1993 Terry Bowden, Auburn
1982 #Joe Paterno, Penn St.	1988 Lou Holtz, Notre Dame	1994 Rich Brooks, Oregon
1983 Howard Schnellenberger, Miami-FL	1989 #Bill McCartney, Colorado	1995 #Gary Barnett, Northwestern
1984 #LaVell Edwards, BYU	1990 #Bobby Ross, Georgia Tech	1996 #Bruce Snyder, Arizona St.
1985 #Fisher DeBerry, Air Force	1991 Don James, Washington	1997 Mike Price, Washington St.
1986 #Joe Paterno, Penn St.	1992 #Gene Stallings, Alabama	

All-Time NCAA Division I-AA Leaders

CAREER

Total Offense

	Yards Gained	Years	Yards
1	Steve McNair, Alcorn St.	1991-94	16,823
2	Willie Totten, Miss. Valley	1982-85	13,007
3	Jamie Martin, Weber St.	1989-92	12,287
4	Doug Nussmeier, Idaho	1990-93	12,054
5	Neil Lomax, Portland St.	1978-80	11,647

	Yards per Game	Years	Yards	P/Gm
1	Steve McNair, Alcorn St.	1991-94	16,823	400.5
2	Neil Lomax, Portland St.	1978-80	11,647	352.9
3	Dave Dickenson, Montana	1992-95	11,523	329.2
4	Willie Totten, Miss. Valley	1982-85	13,007	325.2
5	Tom Ehrhardt, Rhode Island	1984-85	6,492	309.1

Passing

(Minimum 500 Completions)

	Passing Efficiency	Years	Rating
1	Shawn Knight, William & Mary	1991-94	170.8
2	Dave Dickenson, Montana	1992-95	166.3
3	Doug Nussmeier, Idaho	1990-93	154.4
4	Jay Johnson, Northern Iowa	1989-92	148.9
5	Michael Payton, Marshall	1989-92	148.2

	Yards Gained	Years	Yards
1	Steve McNair, Alcorn St.	1991-94	14,496
2	Willie Totten, Miss. Valley	1982-85	12,711
3	Jamie Martin, Weber St.	1989-92	12,207
4	Neil Lomax, Portland St.	1978-80	11,550
5	Dave Dickenson, Montana	1992-95	11,080

Receiving

	Catches	Years	No
1	Jerry Rice, Miss. Valley	1981-84	301
2	Kasey Dunn, Idaho	1988-91	268
3	Brian Forster, Rhode Island	1983-85,87	245
4	Mark Didio, Connecticut	1988-91	239
5	Rennie Benn, Lehigh	1982-85	237

	Yards Gained	Years	No	Yards
1	Jerry Rice, Miss. Valley	1981-84	301	4693
2	Kasey Dunn, Idaho	1988-91	268	3847
3	Rennie Benn, Lehigh	1982-85	237	3662
4	David Rhodes, Central Fla.	1991-94	213	3618
5	Mark Didio, Connecticut	1988-91	239	3535

Rushing

	Yards Gained	Years	Yards
1	Thomas Haskins, VMI	1993-96	5355
2	Frank Hawkins, Nevada	1977-80	5333
3	Kenny Gamble, Colgate	1984-87	5220
4	Markus Thomas, Eastern Ky.	1989-92	5149
5	Erik Marsh, Lafayette	1991-94	4834

	Yards per Game	Years	Yards	P/Gm
1	Arnold Mickens, Butler	1994-95	3813	190.7
2	Tim Hall, Robert Morris	1994-95	2908	153.1
3	Archie Amerson, N. Ariz.	1995-96	3196	145.3
4	Keith Elias, Princeton	1991-93	4208	140.3
5	Mike Clark, Akron	1984-86	4257	133.0

Miscellaneous

	Interceptions	Years	No
1	Dave Murphy, Holy Cross	1986-89	28
2	Cedric Walker, S.F. Austin	1990-93	25
3	Issiac Holt, Alcorn St.	1981-84	24
	Bill McGovern, Holy Cross	1981-84	24
	Darren Sharper, Wm. & Mary	1993-96	24

	Punting Average	Years	Avg
1	Pumpy Tudors, Tenn.-Chatt.	1989-91	44.4
2	Case de Brujin, Idaho St.	1978-81	43.7
3	Terry Belden, Northern Ariz.	1990-93	43.4
4	George Cimadevilla, East Tenn. St.	1983-86	43.0
5	Harold Alexander, Appalachian St.	1989-92	42.9

	Punt Return Average*	Years	Avg
1	Willie Ware, Miss. Valley	1982-85	16.4
2	Buck Phillips, Western Ill.	1994-95	16.4
3	Tim Egerton, Delaware St.	1986-89	16.1
4	Mark Orlando, Towson St.	1991-94	15.7
5	John Armstrong, Richmond	1984-85	14.4

	Kickoff Return Average*	Years	Avg
1	Troy Brown, Marshall	1991-92	29.7
2	Charles Swann, Indiana St.	1989-91	29.3
3	Craig Richardson, Eastern Wash.	1983-86	28.5
4	Kenyatta Sparks, Southern-BR	1992-95	28.2
5	Kerry Hayes, Western Caro.	1991-94	28.2

*(Minimum 1.2 returns per game)

Scoring

NON-KICKERS

	Points	Years	TD	XP	Pts
1	Sherriden May, Idaho	1991-94	61	0	366
2	Charvez Foger, Nevada	1985-88	60	2	362
3	Kenny Gamble, Colgate	1984-87	57	0	342
4	Rene Ingoglia, U Mass	1992-95	55	2	332
5	Markus Thomas, Eastern Ky.	1989-92	53	4	322

	Touchdowns Passing	Years	No
1	Willie Totten, Miss. Valley	1982-85	139
2	Steve McNair, Alcorn St.	1991-94	119
3	Dave Dickenson, Montana	1992-95	96
4	Doug Nussmeier, Idaho	1990-93	91
5	Neil Lomax, Portland St.	1978-80	88

	Touchdowns Rushing	Years	No
1	Kenny Gamble, Colgate	1984-87	55
2	Rene Ingoglia, UMass	1992-95	54
3	Charvez Foger, Nevada	1985-88	52
4	Markus Thomas, Eastern Ky.	1989-92	51
5	Sherriden May, Idaho	1992-94	50
	Paul Lewis, Boston Univ.	1982-84	50

	Touchdown Catches	Years	No
1	Jerry Rice, Miss. Valley	1981-84	50
2	Rennie Benn, Lehigh	1982-85	44
3	Dedric Ward, N. Iowa	1993-96	41
4	Roy Banks, Eastern Ill.	1983-86	38
	Mike Jones, Tennessee St.	1979-92	38

All-Time NCAA Division I-AA Leaders (Cont.)

KICKERS

	Points	Years	FG	XP	Pts
1	Marty Zendejas, Nevada	1984-87	72	169	385
2	B. Mitchell, Marshall/N. Iowa	1987, 89-91	64	130	322
3	Thayne Doyle, Idaho	1988-91	49	160	307
4	Jose Larios, McNeese St.	1992-95	57	133	304
5	Kirk Roach, W. Carolina	1984-87	71	89	302

	Field Goals	Years	No
1	Marty Zendejas, Nevada	1984-87	72
2	Kirk Roach, Western Carolina	1984-87	71
3	Tony Zendejas, Nevada	1981-83	70
4	B. Mitchell, Marshall/N. Iowa	1987,89-91	64
5	Todd Kurz, Illinois St.	1993-96	59

All-Time Winningest Division I-AA Teams

Includes record at a senior college only, minimum of 20 seasons of competition. Bowl and playoff games are included.

Top 25 Winning Percentage

		Yrs	Gm	W	L	T	Pct.	Playoffs W-L-T
1	Yale	125	1132	784	293	55	.717	0-0-0
2	Florida A&M	65	653	453	182	18	.708	2-4-1
3	Grambling St.	55	588	408	165	15	.707	9-7-0
4	Tennessee St.	70	648	438	180	30	.699	8-2-1
5	Princeton	128	1084	729	305	50	.696	0-0-0
6	Harvard	123	1113	720	343	50	.669	1-0-0
7	Jackson St.	52	532	339	180	13	.649	1-11-1
8	Dartmouth	116	1000	620	334	46	.643	0-0-0
9	Fordham	99	1104	682	369	53	.642	2-3-0
10	Eastern Kentucky	74	734	451	256	27	.633	17-17-0
11	Southern	76	734	449	260	25	.629	6-0-0
12	Pennsylvania	121	1185	722	421	42	.627	0-1-0
13	S. Carolina St.	70	645	389	229	27	.624	6-5-0
14	Dayton	90	850	513	311	26	.619	16-11-0
15	Hofstra	57	542	328	203	11	.615	2-9-0
16	Georgia Southern	29	318	192	119	7	.615	23-5-0
17	McNeese St.	47	506	303	189	14	.613	11-9-0
18	Appalachian St.	68	709	419	261	29	.611	5-11-0
19	Mid. Tennessee St.	81	777	453	296	28	.601	8-9-0
20	Delaware	106	946	545	358	43	.599	22-13-0
21	Youngstown St.	57	575	334	224	17	.596	23-7-0
22	Northern Iowa	99	878	498	333	47	.594	8-10-0
23	Western Kentucky	79	745	427	287	31	.594	8-5-0
24	Alcorn St.	74	646	364	243	39	.594	1-4-0
25	Georgetown	86	726	415	280	31	.593	0-2-0

Top 50 Victories

		Wins
1	Yale	784
2	Princeton	729
3	Pennsylvania	722
4	Harvard	720
5	Fordham	682
6	Dartmouth	620
7	Lafayette	581
8	Cornell	569
9	Delaware	545
10	Holy Cross	532
11	Lehigh	531
12	Dayton	513
13	Bucknell	504
14	Brown	498
	N. Iowa	498
16	Colgate	496
17	Butler	491
18	Drake	475
19	Villanova	470
20	Furman	459
21	William & Mary	456
22	Mid. Tenn. St.	453
	Florida A&M	453
24	E. Kentucky	451
25	Southern-BR	449
26	Massachusetts	447
27	Tennessee St.	438
28	Tenn-Chat	433
29	Hampton	430
30	W. Kentucky	427
31	New Hampshire	426
	VMI	426
33	Northwestern St.	420
34	Appalachian St.	419
35	Howard	416
36	Georgetown	415
37	Maine	412
38	SW Texas St.	411
39	Grambling St.	408
40	Citadel	407
41	Richmond	404
42	Western Ill.	402
43	Idaho St.	396
	Connecticut	396
45	Montana	394
46	S. Carolina St.	389
47	Eastern Ill.	388
48	Murray St.	385
49	SW Missouri St.	381
50	E. Washington	380

Top 30 Playoff Game Appearances

		Games	Record
1	Delaware	36	22-14-0
2	E. Kentucky	34	17-17-0
3	Youngstown St.	30	26-4-0
4	Jacksonville St.	29	19-10-0
5	Georgia Southern	28	23-5-0
6	Dayton	27	16-11-0
7	McNeese St.	20	11-9-0
	Montana	20	11-9-0
9	Troy St.	18	13-5-0
	Furman	18	11-7-0
	N. Iowa	18	8-10-0
12	Boise St.	17	10-7-0
	Mid. Tenn. St.	17	8-9-0
	Idaho	17	6-11-0
15	Grambling St.	16	9-7-0
	Eastern Ill.	16	8-8-0
	Appalachian St.	16	5-11-0
18	W. Kentucky	13	8-5-0

		Games	Record
19	Jackson St.	12	1-11-0
20	Tennessee St.	11	8-2-1
	S.F. Austin St.	11	7-4-0
	S. Carolina St.	11	6-5-0
	Wagner	11	6-5-0
	Villanova	11	3-7-1
	Hofstra	11	2-9-0
26	Montana St.	10	7-1-2
	William & Mary	10	3-7-0
28	Bethune-Cookman	8	6-2-0
	Sam Houston St.	8	4-3-1
	Lehigh	8	4-4-0
	Boston Univ.	8	2-6-0

Active Division I-AA Coaches

Minimum of 5 years as a Division I-A and/or Division I-AA through 1997 season.

Top 5 Winning Percentage

		Yrs	W	L	T	Pct
1	Mike Kelly, Dayton	17	165	28	1	**.853**
2	Al Bagnoli, Pennsylvania	16	130	34	0	**.793**
3	Pete Richardson, Southern	10	87	27	1	**.761**
4	Larry Blakeney, Troy St.	7	63	21	1	**.747**
5	Jim Lyons, Dartmouth	6	44	15	1	**.742**

Top 5 Victories

		Yrs	W	L	T	Pct
1	Roy Kidd, Eastern Ky	34	**280**	103	8	.726
2	Tubby Raymond, Delaware	32	**270**	103	3	.722
3	Ron Randleman, Sam Houston St.	29	**175**	128	6	.576
4	Bill Bowes, New Hampshire	26	**171**	99	5	.631
5	Willie Jeffries, S. Carolina St.	26	**161**	107	6	.599

Note: Eddie Robinson of Grambling St. (1941-42, 1945-97) retired following the 1997 season as the all-time NCAA leader in coaching wins with a 408-165-15 record and a .707 winning pct. over 55 seasons.

Division I-AA Coach of the Year

First presented in 1983 by the American Football Coaches Association.

Multiple winners: Mark Duffner and Erk Russell (2).

Year	
1983	Rey Dempsey, Southern Ill.
1984	Dave Arnold, Montana St.
1985	Dick Sheridan, Furman
1986	Erk Russell, Ga. Southern
1987	Mark Duffner, Holy Cross
1988	Jimmy Satterfield, Furman
1989	Erk Russell, Ga. Southern
1990	Tim Stowers, Ga. Southern
1991	Mark Duffner, Holy Cross
1992	Charlie Taafe, Citadel
1993	Dan Allen, Boston Univ.
1994	Jim Tressel, Youngstown St.
1995	Don Read, Montana
1996	Ray Tellier, Columbia
1997	Andy Talley, Villanova

NCAA Playoffs

Division I-AA

Established in 1978 as a four-team playoff. Tournament field increased to eight teams in 1981, 12 teams in 1982 and 16 teams in 1986. Automatic berths have been awarded to champions of the Big Sky, Gateway, Ohio Valley, Southern, Southland and Atlantic 10 (formerly Yankee) conferences since 1992.

Multiple winners: Georgia Southern and Youngstown St. (4); Eastern Kentucky and Marshall (2).

Year	Winner	Score	Loser
1978	Florida A&M	35-28	Massachusetts
1979	Eastern Kentucky	30-7	Lehigh, PA
1980	Boise St., ID	31-29	Eastern Kentucky
1981	Idaho St.	34-23	Eastern Kentucky
1982	Eastern Kentucky	17-14	Delaware
1983	Southern Illinois	43-7	Western Carolina
1984	Montana St.	19-6	Louisiana Tech
1985	Georgia Southern	44-42	Furman, SC
1986	Georgia Southern	48-21	Arkansas St.
1987	NE Louisiana	43-42	Marshall, WV
1988	Furman, SC	17-12	Georgia Southern
1989	Georgia Southern	37-34	S.F. Austin St.
1990	Georgia Southern	36-13	Nevada-Reno
1991	Youngstown St.	25-17	Marshall
1992	Marshall	31-28	Youngstown St.
1993	Youngstown St.	17-5	Marshall
1994	Youngstown St.	28-14	Boise St.
1995	Montana	22-20	Marshall
1996	Marshall	49-29	Montana
1997	Youngstown St.	10-9	McNeese St.

Division II

Established in 1973 as an eight-team playoff. Tournament field increased to 16 teams in 1988. From 1964-72, eight qualifying NCAA College Division member institutions competed in four regional bowl games, but there was no tournament and no national championship until 1973.

Multiple winners: North Dakota St. (5); North Alabama (3); Northern Colorado, Southwest Texas St. and Troy St. (2).

Year	Winner	Score	Loser
1973	Louisiana Tech	34-0	Western Kentucky
1974	Central Michigan	54-14	Delaware
1975	Northern Michigan	16-14	Western Kentucky
1976	Montana St.	24-13	Akron, OH
1977	Lehigh, PA	33-0	Jacksonville St., AL
1978	Eastern Illinois	10-9	Delaware
1979	Delaware	38-21	Youngstown St., OH
1980	Cal Poly-SLO	21-13	Eastern Illinois
1981	SW Texas St.	42-13	North Dakota St.
1982	SW Texas St.	34-9	UC-Davis
1983	North Dakota St.	41-21	Central St., OH
1984	Troy St., AL	18-17	North Dakota St.
1985	North Dakota St.	35-7	North Alabama
1986	North Dakota St.	27-7	South Dakota
1987	Troy St., AL	31-17	Portland St., OR
1988	North Dakota St.	35-21	Portland St., OR
1989	Mississippi Col.	3-0	Jacksonville St., AL
1990	North Dakota St.	51-11	Indiana, PA
1991	Pittsburg St., KS	23-6	Jacksonville St., AL
1992	Jacksonville St., AL	17-13	Pittsburg St., KS
1993	North Alabama	41-34	Indiana, PA
1994	North Alabama	16-10	Tex. A&M (Kings.)
1995	North Alabama	22-7	Pittsburg St., KS
1996	Northern Colorado	23-14	Carson-Newman
1997	Northern Colorado	51-0	New Haven

Division III

Established in 1973 as a four-team playoff. Tournament field increased to eight teams in 1975 and 16 teams in 1985. From 1969-72, four qualifying NCAA College Division member institutions competed in two regional bowl games, but there was no tournament and no national championship until 1973.

Multiple winners: Augustana (4); Ithaca and Mt. Union (3); Dayton, Widener, WI-La Crosse and Wittenberg (2).

Year	Winner	Score	Loser
1973	Wittenberg, OH	41-0	Juniata, PA
1974	Central, IA	10-8	Ithaca, NY
1975	Wittenberg, OH	28-0	Ithaca, NY
1976	St. John's, MN	31-28	Towson St., MD
1977	Widener, PA	39-36	Wabash, IN
1978	Baldwin-Wallace	24-10	Wittenberg, OH
1979	Ithaca, NY	14-10	Wittenberg, OH
1980	Dayton, OH	63-0	Ithaca, NY
1981	Widener, PA	17-10	Dayton, OH
1982	West Georgia	14-0	Augustana, IL
1983	Augustana, IL	21-17	Union, NY
1984	Augustana, IL	21-12	Central, IA
1985	Augustana, IL	20-7	Ithaca, NY
1986	Augustana, IL	31-3	Salisbury St., MD
1987	Wagner, NY	19-3	Dayton, OH
1988	Ithaca, NY	39-24	Central, IA
1989	Dayton, OH	17-7	Union, NY
1990	Allegheny, PA*	21-14	Lycoming, PA
1991	Ithaca, NY	34-20	Dayton, OH
1992	WI-La Crosse	16-12	Wash. & Jeff., PA
1993	Mt. Union, OH	34-24	Rowan, NJ
1994	Albion, MI	38-15	Wash. & Jeff., PA
1995	WI-La Crosse	36-7	Rowan, NJ
1996	Mt. Union, OH	56-24	Rowan, NJ
1997	Mt. Union, OH	61-12	Lycoming, PA

*Overtime

NAIA Playoffs

Division I

Established in 1956 as two-team playoff. Tournament field increased to four teams in 1958, eight teams in 1978 and 16 teams in 1987 before cutting back to eight teams in 1989. NAIA went back to a single division 16-team playoff in 1997. The title game has ended in a tie four times (1956, '64, '84 and '85).

Multiple winners: Texas A&I (7); Carson-Newman (5); Central Arkansas and Central St., OH (3); Abilene Christian, Central St-OK, Elon, Pittsburg St. and St. John's-MN (2).

Year	Winner	Score	Loser
1956	Montana St.	0-0	St. Joseph's, IN
1957	Pittsburg St., KS	27-26	Hillsdale, MI
1958	NE Oklahoma	19-13	Northern Arizona
1959	Texas A&I	20-7	Lenoir-Rhyne, NC
1960	Lenoir-Rhyne, NC	15-14	Humboldt St., CA
1961	Pittsburg St., KS	12-7	Linfield, OR
1962	Central St., OK	28-13	Lenoir-Rhyne, NC
1963	St. John's, MN	33-27	Prairie View, TX
1964	Concordia, MN	7-7	Sam Houston, TX
1965	St. John's, MN	33-0	Linfield, OR
1966	Waynesburg, PA	42-21	WI-Whitewater
1967	Fairmont St., WV	28-21	Eastern Wash.
1968	Troy St., AL	43-35	Texas A&I
1969	Texas A&I	32-7	Concordia, MN
1970	Texas A&I	48-7	Wofford, SC
1971	Livingston, AL	14-12	Arkansas Tech
1972	East Texas St.	21-18	Car-Newman, TN
1973	Abilene Christian	42-14	Elon, NC
1974	Texas A&I	34-23	Henderson St., AR
1975	Texas A&I	37-0	Salem, WV
1976	Texas A&I	26-0	Central Arkansas
1977	Abilene Christian	24-7	SW Oklahoma
1978	Angelo St., TX	34-14	Elon, NC
1979	Texas A&I	20-14	Central St., OK
1980	Elon, NC	17-10	NE Oklahoma
1981	Elon, NC	3-0	Pittsburg St., KS
1982	Central St., OK	14-11	Mesa, CO
1983	Car-Newman, TN	36-28	Mesa, CO
1984	Car-Newman, TN	19-19	Central Arkansas
1985	Hillsdale, MI	10-10	Central Arkansas
1986	Car-Newman, TN	17-0	Cameron, OK
1987	Cameron, OK	30-2	Car-Newman, TN
1988	Car-Newman, TN	56-21	Adams St., CO
1989	Car-Newman, TN	34-20	Emporia St., KS
1990	Central St., OH	38-16	Mesa, CO
1991	Central Arkansas	19-16	Central St., OH
1992	Central St., OH	19-16	Gardner-Webb, NC
1993	E. Central, OK	49-35	Glenville St., WV
1994	N'eastern St., OK	13-12	Ark-Pine Bluff
1995	Central St., OH	37-7	N'eastern St., OK
1996	SW Oklahoma St.	33-31	Montana Tech
1997	Findlay, OH	14-7	Willamette, ORE

Division II

Established in 1970 as four-team playoff. Tournament field increased to eight teams in 1978 and 16 teams in 1987. NAIA went back to a single division playoff in 1997. The title game has ended in a tie twice (1981 and '87).

Multiple winners: Westminster (6); Findlay, Linfield and Pacific Lutheran (3); Concordia-MN, Northwestern-IA and Texas Lutheran (2).

Year	Winner	Score	Loser
1970	Westminster, PA	21-16	Anderson, IN
1971	Calif. Lutheran	20-14	Westminster, PA
1972	Missouri Southern	21-14	Northwestern, IA
1973	Northwestern, IA	10-3	Glenville St., WV
1974	Texas Lutheran	42-0	Missouri Valley
1975	Texas Lutheran	34-8	Calif. Lutheran
1976	Westminster, PA	20-13	Redlands, CA
1977	Westminster, PA	17-9	Calif. Lutheran
1978	Concordia, MN	7-0	Findlay, OH
1979	Findlay, OH	51-6	Northwestern, IA
1980	Pacific Lutheran	38-10	Wilmington, OH
1981	Austin College, TX	24-24	Concordia, MN
1982	Linfield, OR	33-15	Wm. Jewell, MO
1983	Northwestern, IA	25-21	Pacific Lutheran
1984	Linfield, OR	33-22	Northwestern, IA
1985	WI-La Crosse	24-7	Pacific Lutheran
1986	Linfield, OR	17-0	Baker, KS
1987	Pacific Lutheran	16-16	WI-Stevens Pt.*
1988	Westminster, PA	21-14	WI-La Crosse
1989	Westminster, PA	51-30	WI-La Crosse
1990	Peru St., NE	17-7	Westminster, PA
1991	Georgetown-KY	28-20	Pacific Lutheran
1992	Findlay, OH	26-13	Linfield, OR
1993	Pacific Lutheran	50-20	Westminster, PA
1994	Westminster, PA	27-7	Pacific Lutheran
1995	Findlay, OH	21-21	Central Wash.
1996	Sioux Falls, S.D.	47-25	W. Washington
1997	discontinued		

*Wisconsin-Stevens Point forfeited its entire 1987 schedule due to its use of an ineligible player.

Pro Football

Denver quarterback **John Elway** celebrates with the Vince Lombardi Trophy after leading the Broncos to a 31-24 upset win over the Green Bay Packers in Super Bowl XXXII.

Archive Photos

Bucking the Odds

John Elway and the Denver Broncos broke the AFC's 13-year jinx and upset the Packers in the Super Bowl.

by
Chris Berman

In some ways, it was what many people expected. Kind of. Prior to the start of the '97 season, there were plenty of people who felt the Denver Broncos, often maligned for their failures on Super Sunday, would finally get back to the Big Game. But win it? After all, the AFC was riding a 13-game losing streak in the Super Bowl.

When the smoke finally cleared in San Diego on the final Sunday of January, quarterback John Elway held his head high and the Lombardi Trophy even higher as the Men From Mile High captured their first-ever NFL championship with a 31-24 upset victory over the defending Super Bowl champion Green Bay Packers.

To the odds-makers, it was a huge surprise. After analyzing it afterwards, maybe it shouldn't have been. And the path that Mike Shanahan's club traveled to reach their goal made this title run all the more satisfying.

Of course, much was expected of the Broncos in 1996 as they wrapped up homefield advantage in the AFC by November, only to be stunned by the upstart Jacksonville Jaguars in the Divisional Playoffs.

Six weeks into '97, Shanahan's club again looked primed for a Super Bowl run as they were the league's lone undefeated team (6-0). But by Week 17, they were just playing for the right to host a wild card game as the surprising Kansas City Chiefs had already clinched the AFC West title. With the Jaguars heading to Mile High Stadium for a playoff rematch, even die-hard Broncos' fans were preparing for a bad case of deja vu all over again.

But their team would prove to be very resilient. Primed by the play of a veteran offensive line and the power of AFC rushing leader Terrell Davis, the Broncos eventually ran over the Jaguars (42-17), then gutted out two road

---

Chris Berman is the host of ESPN's *NFL Prime Time*.

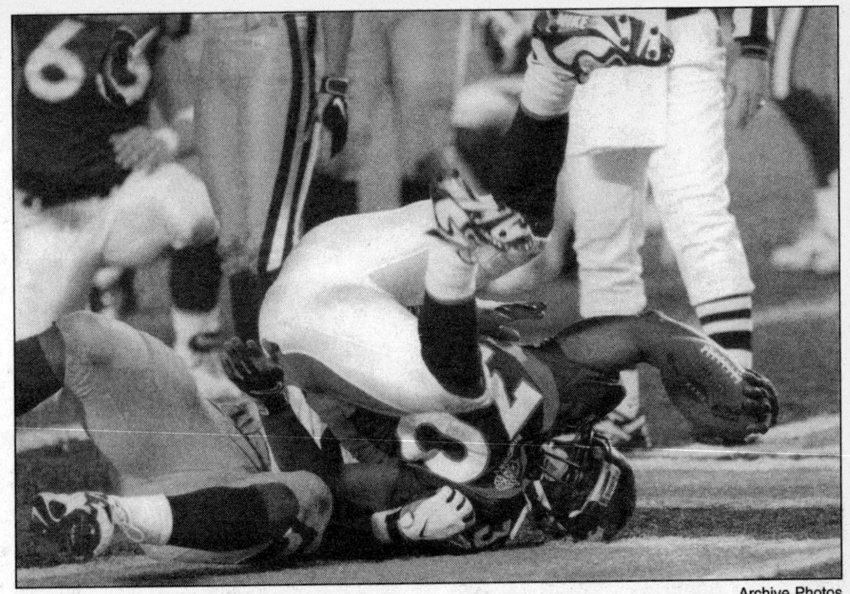

Archive Photos

Super Bowl MVP **Terrell Davis** tumbles into the end zone at San Diego's Qualcomm Stadium for one of his record-breaking three rushing touchdowns.

wins at Kansas City (14-10) and at Pittsburgh (24-21) to reach their fifth Super Bowl.

Their opposition in San Diego would be the defending champion Packers, who had overcome their share of adversity along the way but left little doubt that they would put themselves in position to grab their fourth Lombardi Trophy. Mike Holmgren's team arrived at Super Bowl XXXII riding a seven-game winning streak, and their defense was especially impressive in their playoff conquests of the Tampa Bay Buccaneers (21-7) and San Francisco 49ers (23-10). Quarterback Brett Favre, who became the first player in NFL history to throw 30 or more touchdown passes in four straight seasons, would be named the NFL's Most Valuable Player for an unprecedented third straight year.

In one day, the Broncos not only won a championship, but redemption for the AFC as well. Elway became the first from that fabled Quarterback Class of '83 (Dan Marino, Jim Kelly, Tony Eason, et al.) to win a title. Proud Broncos' owner Pat Bowlen knew what this title meant to his future Hall of Fame signal-caller as he exclaimed, "This one's for John." Meanwhile, Davis firmly established himself as one of the league's premier big-game runners by capturing Super Bowl MVP honors, his 157 yards rushing (along with a Super Bowl record three rushing touchdowns) marking the fourth time in as many playoff games that he had topped the century mark on the ground.

But NFL '97 was also filled with many other memorable moments. We saw only a glimpse of Jerry Rice due to injury, but defenses saw too much

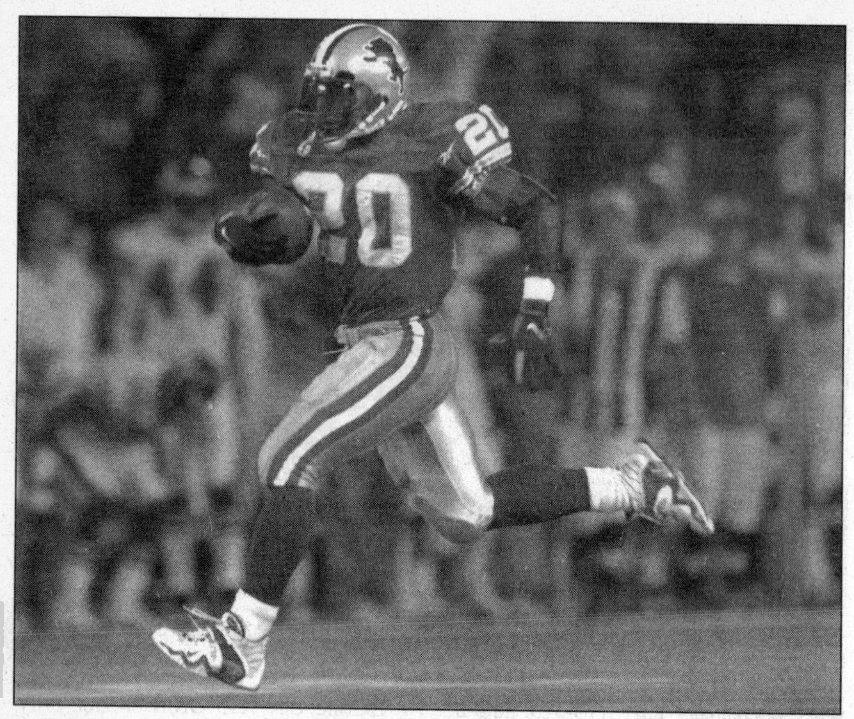

Archive Photos

Barry Sanders scampers across midfield for a 53-yard gain on his last run of the day in the final game of the season against the Jets. The run increases his yardage total to 2,053, the second-highest of all time.

of Barry Sanders, who posted the second-greatest single-season rushing performance in NFL history (2,053 yards) and shared the MVP award with Favre. We saw the resurgence of the Buccaneers, who made the playoffs for the first time since 1982.

Led by a big-time defense (Warren Sapp and Co.) and the 1-2 punch of running backs Warrick Dunn and Mike Alstott, Tony Dungy's team capped their final year at the "Big Sombrero" with a 20-10 victory over the Lions in the wild card round, their first postseason win since 1979. We also witnessed the collapse of the Cowboys, who ended the season with five straight losses and a 6-10 record, culminating with the departure of Barry Switzer. We were shocked by the New York Giants, who despite preseason predictions that they would finish near the bottom of their division, became the first team to ever go undefeated within the NFC East (7-0-1) as Jim Fassel capped his first season at the helm with a division title. And speaking of New York, Bill Parcells brought life back to the Jets and new meaning to their rivalry with the New England Patriots, the Tuna's former employer. The Jets finished the season at a very respectable 9-7, narrowly missing a playoff berth.

While 1997 brought the returns of Mike Ditka and Dick Vermeil back to the sidelines, we also saw the end of several illustrious careers with the retirements of clutch running back Marcus Allen, special teams star Steve Tasker and coaching standout Marv Levy. Most of all, there were the Broncos. No team deserved a championship more. ■

AP/Wide World Photos

Bill Parcells couldn't escape from New York for too long, returning to lead the Jets to a 9-7 mark in his first year at the helm.

John Clayton's Top Ten Highlights of the 1997 NFL season

10. **New Orleans Saints coach Mike Ditka** bets defensive coordinator Zaven Yaralian that his defense can't stop a Tim Brown crossing pattern. It does and Ditka reaches into his pocket for $50 during the game in front of television cameras. Ditka is fined by the league.

9. **The New York Giants**, who enter the season with what is considered the least talented team in the division, win the NFC East. First-year coach Jim Fassel directs his team to a 7-0-1 division record and replaces long-time disappointment Dave Brown with Danny Kanell at quarterback.

8. **The presence of Bill Parcells** along the New York Jets sidelines instantly brings the franchise credibility. He creates plenty of news by benching QB Neil O'Donnell in favor of Glenn Foley and using special teamer Ray Lucas occasionally at QB. He also brings the Jets to within a game of making the playoffs.

7. **Cincinnati halfback Corey Dillon** breaks Jim Brown's 40-year-old rookie rushing record by overpowering the Tennessee Oilers for 246 yards on 39 carries. He averages 116.7 yards over the final eight games of the season.

6. **San Francisco wide receiver Jerry Rice**, trying to make an impossible recovery from knee reconstruction, electrifies 3Com Park on Monday Night Football by catching three passes for 40 yards and a touchdown against Denver. The 49ers clinch home-field advantage with the 34-17 win, but lose Rice again when he reinjures the knee.

5. **The Miami Dolphins**, playing New England for the third time in six weeks, inadvertently allow Patriots defenders to pick up Dan Marino's audible calls in a 17-3 playoff loss. The Pats are so familiar with his hand signals that they start to mimic him in order to make defensive adjustments.

4. **Green Bay coach Mike Holmgren** decides to allow Denver's Terrell Davis to score the game-winning touchdown in Super Bowl XXXII so that Packers QB Brett Favre will have time for one last drive to tie the score. The loss is so devastating to Holmgren that he later admits to being depressed for about a month.

3. **Barry Sanders**, at age 29, becomes the third player in NFL history to rush for 2,000 yards. His 2,053-yard season puts him a mere 2,948 behind all-time leader Walter Payton. Sanders finishes the season with 14 consecutive 100-yard games.

2. **Terrell Davis** replaces Emmitt Smith as the league's championship running back. Like Emmitt, he sets the tone by reminding everyone that a dominating power running game wins championships. His incredible 5.33 yards per carry during the postseason is the best ever.

1. In the final minutes of Super Bowl XXXII, **Denver QB John Elway** breaks a third-down run to his right and courageously lunges into a tackle to complete an eight yard run for a first down at the Packers' four yard line. Two plays later, Terrell Davis scores to give the Broncos a 24-17 lead. It is this sheer determination that keeps the Broncos believing they could end the NFC's domination in the Super Bowl. ■

INSIDE THE NUMBERS

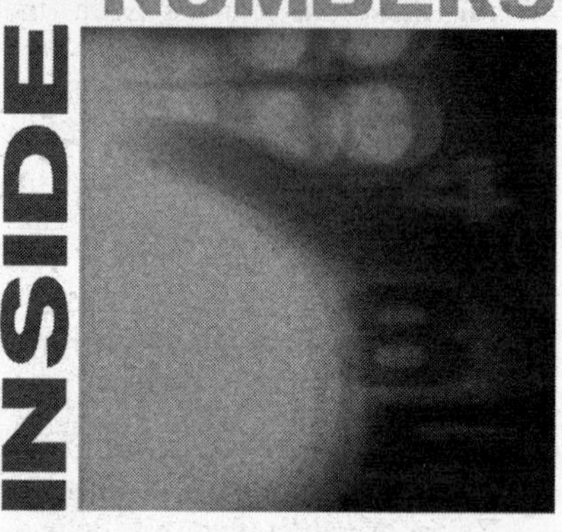

by
Todd Snyder and Craig Wachs

THE 'CELLING POINT

Since the Jets won Super Bowl III following the 1968 season, they have played 28 campaigns, while coach Bill Parcells has coached in 12. But at the point of his arrival, "The Tuna" still dominated his new franchise in almost every statistical category.

	NY Jets (1969-96)	Bill Parcells (1983-96)
Win Pct.	.408	.580
Winning Seasons	6	8
Playoff Appearances	6	7
Super Bowl Appearances	0	3
Division Titles	1	4

CHANGE FOR THE BUCS

There's really no mystery to the Buccaneers' turnaround from 6-10 in 1996 to 10-6 in 1997. Coach Tony Dungy has turned his defense into one of the tops in the NFL, and the rankings confirm it.

	1996	1997
Red Zone Defense	19th	1st
Team Penalties	t-9th	1st
Points Allowed	t-8th	2nd
20-Yard Plays Allowed	7th	1st
Total Defense	11th	3rd

■

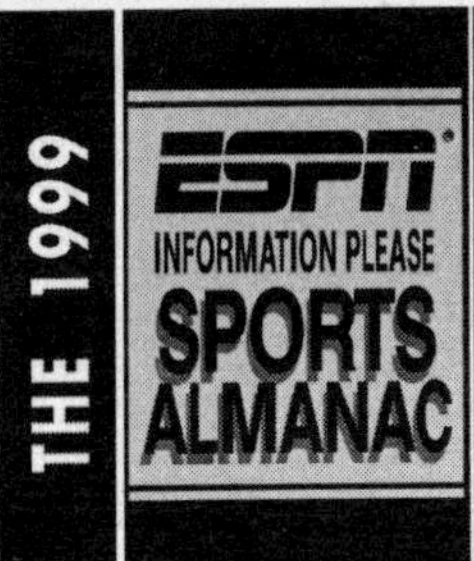

PRO FOOTBALL STATISTICS

THE SEASON IN REVIEW

1997-1998

STANDINGS • PLAYOFFS • DRAFTS

Final NFL Standings

Division champions (*) and Wild Card playoff qualifiers (†) are noted; division champions with two best records received first round byes. Number of seasons listed after each head coach refers to latest tenure with club through 1997 season.

American Football Conference

Eastern Division

	W	L	T	PF	PA	vs Div	vs AFC
*New England	10	6	0	369	289	7-1-0	9-3-0
†Miami	9	7	0	339	327	4-4-0	8-4-0
NY Jets	9	7	0	348	287	2-6-0	6-6-0
Buffalo	6	10	0	255	367	5-3-0	5-7-0
Indianapolis	3	13	0	313	401	2-6-0	2-10-0

1997 Head coaches: NE—Pete Carroll (1st season); **Mia**—Jimmy Johnson (2nd); **NY**—Bill Parcells (1st); **Buf**—Marv Levy (12th); **Ind**—Lindy Infante (2nd).

1996 Standings: 1. New England (11-5); 2. Buffalo (10-6); 3. Indianapolis (9-7); 4. Miami (8-8); 5. NY Jets (1-15).

Central Division

	W	L	T	PF	PA	vs Div	vs AFC
*Pittsburgh	11	5	0	372	307	6-2-0	9-3-0
†Jacksonville	11	5	0	394	318	6-2-0	9-3-0
Tennessee	8	8	0	333	310	2-6-0	4-8-0
Cincinnati	7	9	0	355	405	3-5-0	5-7-0
Baltimore	6	9	1	326	345	3-5-0	4-8-0

1997 Head coaches: Pit—Bill Cowher (6th season); **Jax**—Tom Coughlin (3rd); **Ten**—Jeff Fisher (4th); **Cin**—Bruce Coslet (2nd); **Bal**—Ted Marchibroda (2nd).

1996 Standings: 1. Pittsburgh (10-6); 2. Jacksonville (9-7); 3. Cincinnati (8-8); 4. Houston (8-8); 5. Baltimore (4-12).

Western Division

	W	L	T	PF	PA	vs Div	vs AFC
*Kansas City	13	3	0	375	232	7-1-0	9-3-0
†Denver	12	4	0	472	287	6-2-0	9-3-0
Seattle	8	8	0	365	362	4-4-0	6-6-0
Oakland	4	12	0	324	419	2-6-0	2-10-0
San Diego	4	12	0	266	425	1-7-0	3-9-0

1997 Head coaches: KC—Marty Schottenheimer (9th season); **Den**—Mike Shanahan (3rd); **Sea**—Dennis Erickson (3rd); **Oak**—Joe Bugel (1st); **SD**—Kevin Gilbride (1st).

1996 Standings: 1. Denver (13-3); 2. Kansas City (9-7); 3. San Diego (8-8); 4. Oakland (7-9); 5. Seattle (7-9).

National Football Conference

Eastern Division

	W	L	T	PF	PA	vs Div	vs NFC
*NY Giants	10	5	1	307	265	7-0-1	9-2-1
Washington	8	7	1	327	289	4-3-1	7-4-1
Philadelphia	6	9	1	317	372	3-5-0	4-8-0
Dallas	6	10	0	304	314	3-5-0	4-8-0
Arizona	4	12	0	283	379	2-6-0	3-9-0

1997 Head coaches: NY—Jim Fassel (1st season); **Wash**—Norv Turner (4th); **Phi**—Ray Rhodes (3rd); **Dal**—Barry Switzer (4th); **Ariz**—Vince Tobin (2nd).

1996 Standings: 1. Dallas (10-6); 2. Philadelphia (10-6); 3. Washington (9-7); 4. Arizona (7-9); 5. NY Giants (6-10).

Central Division

	W	L	T	PF	PA	vs Div	vs NFC
*Green Bay	13	3	0	422	282	7-1-0	10-2-0
†Tampa Bay	10	6	0	299	263	3-5-0	7-5-0
†Detroit	9	7	0	379	306	6-2-0	7-5-0
†Minnesota	9	7	0	354	359	3-5-0	6-6-0
Chicago	4	12	0	263	421	1-7-0	2-10-0

1997 Head Coaches: GB—Mike Holmgren (6th season); **TB**—Tony Dungy (2nd); **Det**— Bobby Ross (1st); **Min**—Dennis Green (6th); **Chi**—Dave Wannstedt (5th).

1996 Standings: 1. Green Bay (13-3); 2. Minnesota (9-7); 3. Chicago (7-9); 4. Tampa Bay (6-10); 5. Detroit (5-11).

Western Division

	W	L	T	PF	PA	vs Div	vs NFC
*San Francisco	13	3	0	366	227	8-0-0	11-1-0
Carolina	7	9	0	265	314	4-4-0	5-7-0
Atlanta	7	9	0	320	361	4-4-0	5-7-0
New Orleans	6	10	0	237	327	1-7-0	4-8-0
St. Louis	5	11	0	299	359	3-5-0	5-7-0

1997 Head Coaches: SF—Steve Mariucci (1st season); **Car**—Dom Capers (3rd); **Atl**—Dan Reeves (1st); **NO**—Mike Ditka (1st); **St.L**—Dick Vermeil (1st).

1996 Standings: 1. Carolina (12-4); 2. San Francisco (12-4); 3. St. Louis (6-10); 4. Atlanta (3-13); 5. New Orleans (3-13).

Playoff Tiebreakers

Divisional Championship—AFC: Pittsburgh (11-5) qualified over Jacksonville (11-5) by having more net points in division games. This is the fifth possible tie-breaker. The teams were still tied after the first four tie-breakers were used.

Wild Card berths—AFC: Miami (9-7) qualified over New York Jets (9-7) by winning both regular-season head-to-head matchups.

Home field priority—NFC: San Francisco (13-3) was awarded home field advantage throughout the playoffs over Green Bay (13-3) because of a better won-loss percentage within the conference.

NFL Regular Season Individual Leaders

(* indicates rookies)

Passing Efficiency

(Minimum of 224 attempts)

AFC	Att	Cmp	Cmp Pct	Yds	Avg Gain	TD	Long	Int	Sack/Lost	Rating Points
Mark Brunell, Jax.	435	264	60.7	3281	7.54	18	75	7	33/189	91.2
Jeff George, Oak.	521	290	55.7	3917	7.52	29	76	9	58/430	91.2
Drew Bledsoe, NE	522	314	60.2	3706	7.10	28	76	15	30/258	87.7
John Elway, Den.	502	280	55.8	3635	7.24	27	78	11	34/203	87.5
Jim Harbaugh, Ind.	309	189	61.2	2060	6.67	10	58	4	41/256	86.2
Warren Moon, Sea.	528	313	59.3	3678	6.97	25	60-td	16	30/192	83.7
Dan Marino, Mia.	548	319	58.2	3780	6.90	16	55	11	21/142	80.7
Neil O'Donnell, NYJ	460	259	56.3	2796	6.08	17	70	7	45/289	80.3
Elvis Grbac, KC	314	179	57.0	1943	6.19	11	55-td	6	19/150	79.1
Jeff Blake, Cin.	317	184	58.0	2125	6.70	8	50-td	7	39/244	77.6
Vinny Testaverde, Bal.	470	271	57.7	2971	6.32	18	54-td	15	20/129	75.9
Kordell Stewart, Pit.	440	236	53.6	3020	6.86	21	69-td	17	20/152	75.2
Stan Humphries, SD	225	121	53.8	1488	6.61	5	72-td	6	18/144	70.8
Steve McNair, Ten.	415	216	52.0	2665	6.42	14	55-td	13	31/190	70.4
Todd Collins, Buf.	391	215	55.0	2367	6.05	12	77-td	13	39/278	69.5

NFC	Att	Cmp	Cmp Pct	Yds	Avg Gain	TD	Long	Int	Sack/Lost	Rating Points
Steve Young, SF	356	241	67.7	3029	8.51	19	82	6	35/220	104.7
Chris Chandler, Atl.	342	202	59.1	2692	7.87	20	56	7	39/261	95.1
Brett Favre, GB	513	304	59.3	3867	7.54	35	74	16	25/176	92.6
Brad Johnson, Min.	452	275	60.8	3036	6.72	20	56	12	26/164	84.5
Bobby Hoying, Phi.	225	128	56.9	1573	6.99	11	72-td	6	28/183	83.8
Trent Dilfer, TB	386	217	56.2	2555	6.62	21	59-td	11	32/196	82.8
Scott Mitchell, Det.	509	293	57.6	3484	6.84	19	79	14	41/271	79.6
Troy Aikman, Dal.	518	292	56.4	3283	6.34	19	64-td	12	33/269	78.0
Erik Kramer, Chi.	477	275	57.7	3011	6.31	14	78-td	14	25/149	74.0
Ty Detmer, Phi.	244	134	54.9	1567	6.42	7	57	6	19/94	73.9
Gus Frerotte, Was.	402	204	50.7	2682	6.67	17	52	12	23/146	73.8
Jake Plummer*, Ariz.	296	157	53.0	2203	7.44	15	70-td	15	52/291	73.1
Tony Banks, St.L	487	252	51.7	3254	6.68	14	76	13	43/317	71.5
Danny Kanell, NYG	294	156	53.1	1740	5.92	11	68-td	9	19/171	70.7
Kent Graham, Ariz.	250	130	52.0	1408	5.63	4	47	5	16/115	65.9

Receptions

AFC	No	Yds	Avg	Long	TD
Tim Brown, Oak.	104	1408	13.5	59-td	5
Keenan McCardell, Jax.	85	1164	13.7	60	5
Jimmy Smith, Jax.	82	1324	16.1	75	4
Yancey Thigpen, Pit.	79	1398	17.7	69-td	7
O.J. McDuffie, Mia.	76	943	12.4	55	1
Marvin Harrison, Ind.	73	866	11.9	44	6
Shannon Sharpe, Den.	72	1107	15.4	68-td	3
Andre Rison, KC	72	1092	15.2	45	7
Joey Galloway, Sea.	72	1049	14.6	53-td	12
Rod Smith, Den.	70	1180	16.9	78	12
Keyshawn Johnson, NYJ	70	963	13.8	39	5
Michael Jackson, Bal.	69	918	13.3	54-td	4
Sean Dawkins, Ind.	68	804	11.8	51	2
Ben Coates, NE	66	737	11.2	35	8

NFC	No	Yds	Avg	Long	TD
Herman Moore, Det.	104	1293	12.4	79	8
Rob Moore, Ariz.	97	1584	16.3	47-td	8
Cris Carter, Min.	89	1069	12.0	43	13
Irving Fryar, Phi.	86	1316	15.3	72-td	6
Antonio Freeman, GB	81	1243	15.3	58-td	12
Johnnie Morton, Det.	80	1057	13.2	73-td	6
Michael Irvin, Dal.	75	1180	15.7	55	9
Frank Sanders, Ariz.	75	1017	13.6	70-td	4
Jake Reed, Min.	68	1138	16.7	56	6
Bert Emanuel, Atl.	65	991	15.2	56	9
Terance Mathis, Atl.	62	802	12.9	49	6
Amp Lee, St.L.	61	825	13.5	62	3
Robert Brooks, GB	60	1010	16.8	48	7
Terrell Owens, SF	60	936	15.6	56-td	8

Rushing

AFC	Att	Yards	Avg	Long	TD
Terrell Davis, Den.	369	1750	4.7	50-td	15
Jerome Bettis, Pit.	375	1665	4.4	34	7
Eddie George, Ten.	357	1399	3.9	30	6
Napoleon Kaufman, Oak.	272	1294	4.8	83-td	6
Curtis Martin, NE	274	1160	4.2	70-td	4
Corey Dillon*, Cin.	233	1129	4.8	71-td	10
Adrian Murrell, NYJ	300	1086	3.6	43-td	7
Marshall Faulk, Ind.	264	1054	4.0	45	7
Gary Brown, SD	253	945	3.7	32	4
Karim Abdul-Jabbar, Mia.	283	892	3.2	22	15
Chris Warren, Sea.	200	847	4.2	36-td	4
Antowain Smith*, Buf.	194	840	4.3	56-td	8
Natrone Means, Jax.	244	823	3.4	20	9
Bam Morris, Bal.	204	774	3.8	25	4

NFC	Att	Yards	Avg	Long	TD
Barry Sanders, Det.	335	2053	6.1	82-td	11
Dorsey Levens, GB	329	1435	4.4	52-td	7
Robert Smith, Min.	232	1266	5.5	78-td	6
Ricky Watters, Phi.	285	1110	3.9	28	7
Emmitt Smith, Dal.	261	1074	4.1	44	4
Raymont Harris, Chi.	275	1033	3.8	68-td	10
Garrison Hearst, SF	234	1019	4.4	51	4
Jamal Anderson, Atl.	290	1002	3.5	39	7
Warrick Dunn*, TB	224	978	4.4	76	4
Fred Lane*, Car.	182	809	4.4	50	7
Terry Allen, Was.	210	724	3.4	34	4
Charles Way, NYG	151	698	4.6	42	4
Mike Alstott, TB	176	665	3.8	47-td	7
Tyrone Wheatley, NYG	152	583	3.8	38	4

Detroit Lions
Barry Sanders
Rushing

Miami Dolphins
Karim Abdul-Jabbar
Touchdowns

Minnesota Vikings
John Randle
Sacks

San Francisco 49ers
Steve Young
Passing Efficiency

All-Purpose Yardage

AFC	Rush	Rec	Ret	Total
Terrell Davis, Den.	1750	287	0	2037
Jermaine Lewis, Bal.	35	648	1342	2025
Tamarick Vanover, KC	50	92	1666	1808
Jerome Bettis, Pit.	1665	110	0	1775
Napoleon Kaufman, Oak.	1294	403	0	1697
Steve Broussard, Sea.	418	143	1076	1637
Aaron Bailey, Ind.	20	329	1225	1574
Corey Dillon*, Cin.	1129	259	182	1570
Desmond Howard, Oak.	0	30	1528	1558
Dave Meggett, NE	60	203	1283	1546
Marshall Faulk, Ind.	1054	471	0	1525
Curtis Martin, NE	1160	296	0	1456

NFC	Rush	Rec	Ret	Total
Barry Sanders, Det.	2053	305	0	2358
Kevin Williams, Ariz	-2	273	1920	2191
Brian Mitchell, Wash.	107	438	1536	2081
Eric Guliford, NO	-2	362	1626	1986
Glyn Milburn, Det.	0	77	1748	1825
Dorsey Levens, GB	1435	370	0	1805
Rob Moore, Ariz.	0	1584	0	1584
Ricky Watters, Phi.	1110	440	0	1550
Warrick Dunn*, TB	978	462	48	1488
Robert Smith, Min.	1266	197	0	1463
David Palmer, Min.	36	193	1155	1384
Byron Hanspard*, Atl.	335	53	987	1375

Ret column indicates all kickoff, punt, fumble and interception returns.

Scoring

Touchdowns

AFC	TD	Rush	Rec	Ret	Pts
Karim Abdul-Jabbar, Mia.	16	15	1	0	96
Terrell Davis, Den.	15	15	0	0	96†
Joey Galloway, Sea.	12	0	12	0	72
James Jett, Oak.	12	0	12	0	72
Rod Smith, Den.	12	0	12	0	72
Marcus Allen, KC	11	11	0	0	66
Kordell Stewart, Pit.	11	11	0	0	66
Corey Dillon*, Cin.	10	10	0	0	60
Derrick Alexander, Bal.	9	0	9	0	54
Jerome Bettis, Pit.	9	7	2	0	54
Natrone Means, Jax.	9	9	0	0	54
James Stewart, Jax.	9	8	1	0	54

Eight tied with 8 TDs for 48 Pts.

NFC	TD	Rush	Rec	Ret	Pts
Barry Sanders, Det.	14	11	3	0	84
Cris Carter, Det.	13	0	13	0	84†
Dorsey Levens, GB	12	7	5	0	74*
Antonio Freeman, GB.	12	0	12	0	72
Mike Alstott, TB	10	7	3	0	60
Jamal Anderson, Atl.	10	7	3	0	60
Raymont Harris, Chi.	10	10	0	0	60
Bert Emanuel, Atl.	9	0	9	0	54
Michael Irvin, Dal.	9	0	9	0	54
Terry Kirby, SF	8	6	1	1	52#
Rob Moore, Ariz.	8	0	8	0	50*
Herman Moore, Det.	8	0	8	0	50*
Terrell Owens, SF.	8	0	8	0	48
Chris Calloway, NYG	8	0	8	0	48

* Includes one 2-point conversion.
# Includes two 2-point conversions.
† Includes three 2-point conversions.

Kickers

AFC	PAT	FG	Long	Pts
Mike Hollis, Jax	41/41	31/36	52	134
Jason Elam, Den.	46/46	26/36	53	124
John Hall*, NYJ	36/36	28/41	55	120
Cary Blanchard, Ind.	21/21	32/41	50	117
Olindo Mare*, Mia.	33/33	28/36	50	117
Adam Vinatieri, NE	40/40	25/29	52	115
Al Del Greco, Ten.	32/32	27/35	52	113
Pete Stoyanovich, KC	35/36	26/27	54	113
Matt Stover, Bal.	32/32	26/34	49	110
Greg Davis, Min.-SD	31/32	26/34	45	109
Norm Johnson, Pit.	40/40	22/25	52	106
Todd Peterson, Sea.	37/37	22/28	52	103
Steve Christie, Buf.	21/21	24/30	55	93
Doug Pelfrey, Cin.	41/43	12/16	46	77
Cole Ford, Oak.	33/35	13/22	53	72

NFC	PAT	FG	Long	Pts
Richie Cunningham*, Dal.	24/24	34/37	53	126
Gary Anderson, SF	38/38	29/36	51	125
Ryan Longwell*, GB	48/48	24/30	50	120
Jason Hanson, Det.	39/40	26/29	55	117
Jeff Wilkins, St.L.	32/32	25/37	52	107
Morten Andersen, Atl.	35/35	23/27	55	104
Chris Boniol, Phi.	33/33	22/31	49	99
Brad Daluiso, NYG	27/29	22/32	52	93
Doug Brien, NO	22/22	23/27	53	91
John Kasay, Car.	25/25	22/26	54	91
Jeff Jaeger, Chi.	20/20	21/26	52	83
Scott Blanton, Was.	34/34	16/24	50	82
Michael Husted, TB	32/35	13/17	54	71
Eddie Murray, Min.	23/24	12/17	49	59
Joe Nedney, Mia.-Ariz	19/19	11/17	45	52

Interceptions

AFC	No	Yds	Long	TD
Mark McMillian, KC	8	274	87-td	3
Darryl Williams, Sea.	8	172	44-td	1
Otis Smith, NYJ	6	158	51-td	3
Willie Clay, NE	6	109	53-td	1

Three tied with 5 each.

NFC	No	Yds	Long	TD
Ryan McNeil, St.L	9	127	75-td	1
Keith Lyle, St.L	8	102	39	0
Merton Hanks, SF	6	103	55-td	1
Aeneas Williams, Ariz.	6	95	42-td	2
Jason Sehorn, NYG	6	74	41	1

Punting

AFC	No	Yds	Lg	Avg	In20
Tom Tupa, NE	78	3569	73	45.8	24
Chris Gardocki, Ind.	67	3034	72	45.3	18
Leo Araguz, Oak.	93	4189	63	45.0	28
Bryan Barker, Jax	66	2964	64	44.9	27
Darren Bennett, SD	89	3972	66	44.6	26

NFC	No	Yds	Lg	Avg	In20
Mark Royals, NO	88	4038	66	45.9	21
Matt Turk, Was.	84	3788	62	45.1	32
Craig Hentrich, GB	75	3378	65	45.0	26
Jeff Feagles, Ariz.	91	4028	62	44.3	24
Mitch Berger, Min.	73	3133	65	42.9	22
Mike Horan, St.L	53	2272	60	42.9	10

Sacks

AFC	No
Bruce Smith, Buf.	14.0
Michael Sinclair, Sea.	12.0
Peter Boulware*, Bal.	11.5
Dan Footman, Ind.	10.5
Dan Williams, KC	10.5

NFC	No
John Randle, Min.	15.5
Dana Stubblefield, SF	15.0
Mike Strahan, NYG	14.0
Robert Porcher, Det.	12.5

Punt Returns

(Minimum of 20 returns)

AFC	No	FC	Yards	Avg	Long	TD
Jermaine Lewis, Bal.	28	13	437	15.6	89-td	2
Darrien Gordon, Den.	40	22	543	13.6	94-td	3
Leon Johnson*, NYJ	51	6	619	12.1	66-td	1
Reggie Barlow, Jax.	36	16	412	11.4	52	0
Tamarick Vanover, KC	35	14	383	10.9	82-td	1
Eric Metcalf. SD	45	8	489	10.9	85-td	3

NFC	No	FC	Yds	Avg	Long	TD
David Palmer, Min.	34	19	444	13.1	57	0
Karl Williams, TB	46	12	597	13.0	63	1
Deion Sanders, Dal.	33	12	407	12.3	83-td	1
Brian Mitchell, Was.	38	23	442	11.6	63-td	1
Kevin Williams, Ariz.	40	15	462	11.6	50	0

Kickoff Returns

(Minimum of 20 returns)

AFC	No	Yards	Avg	Long	TD
Aaron Glenn, NYJ	28	741	26.5	96-td	1
Tamarick Vanover, KC	50	1283	25.7	94-td	1
Dave Meggett, NE	33	816	24.7	61	0
Will Blackwell, Pit.	32	791	24.7	97-td	1
Irving Spikes, Mia.	24	565	23.5	48	0
Vaughn Hebron, Den.	43	1009	23.5	46	0

NFC	No	Yards	Avg	Long	TD
Michael Bates, Car.	47	1281	27.3	56	0
Eric Guliford, NO	43	1128	26.2	102-td	1
Kevin Williams, Ariz.	59	1458	24.7	63	0
Byron Hanspard, Atl.	40	987	24.7	99-td	2
Duce Staley*, Phi.	47	1139	24.2	57	0
Glyn Milburn, Det.	55	1315	23.9	69	0

Single Game Highs

(*) indicates overtime game.

Passing

AFC	Att/Cmp	Yds	TD
Warren Moon, Sea. vs. Oak. (10/26)	28/44	409	5
Dan Marino, Mia. vs. NE (11/23)	38/60	389	0
Boomer Esiason, Cin. vs. Phi. (11/30)	27/47	378	4
Jeff George, Oak. vs. NYJ (9/21)	26/38	374	3
Dan Marino, Mia. vs NYJ (10/12)	27/38	372	2

NFC	Att/Cmp	Yds	TD
Tony Banks, St.L vs. Atl. (11/2)*	23/34	401	2
Jake Plummer, Ariz. vs. NYG (11/16)	22/33	388	1
Brett Favre, GB vs. Ind. (11/16)	18/25	363	3
Troy Aikman, Dal. vs. Ten. (11/27)	27/42	356	2
Erik Kramer, Chi. vs. NYJ (11/16)	32/60	354	2

Receiving Yards

AFC	Ct	Yds	TD
Yancey Thigpen, Pit. vs. Jax. (10/26)*	11	196	0
Yancey Thigpen, Pit. vs. Den. (12/7)	6	175	3
Shannon Sharpe, Den. vs Car. (11/9)	8	174	0
Tim Brown, Oak. vs. Jax. (12/21)	14	164	0
Jimmy Smith, Jax. vs. Pit. (9/22)	10	164	1

NFC	Ct	Yds	TD
Isaac Bruce, St.L vs. Atl. (11/2)*	10	233	2
Frank Sanders, Ariz. vs. NYG (11/16)	9	188	1
Rob Moore, Ariz. vs. Pit. (11/30)*	8	188	0
Johnnie Morton, Det. vs. Mia. (12/7)	9	171	1
Antonio Freeman, GB vs. Car. (12/14)	10	166	2

Rushing

AFC	Car	Yds	TD
Corey Dillon, Cin. vs. Ten. (12/4)	39	246	4
Napoleon Kaufman, Oak. vs. Den. (10/19)	28	227	1
Eddie George, Ten. vs. Oak. (8/31)*	35	216	1
Terrell Davis, Den. vs. Cin. (9/21)	27	215	1
Terrell Davis, Den. vs. Buf. (10/26)*	42	207	1

NFC	Car	Yds	TD
Barry Sanders, Det. vs. Ind. (11/23)	24	216	2
Barry Sanders, Det. vs. TB (10/12)	27	215	3†
Dorsey Levens, GB vs. Dal. (11/23)	33	190	2
Barry Sanders, Det. vs. NYJ (12/21)	23	184	1
Robert Smith, Min. vs. Buf. (8/31)	16	169	1

†Sanders had one TD catch and two TD rushes.

NFL Bests

Longest Field Goal
55 yds. ....by 4 players

Longest Run from Scrimmage
83 yds ....Napoleon Kaufman, Oak. vs. Den. (10/19), TD

Longest Pass Play
92 yds.....Eric Zeier to Derrick Alexander, Bal. vs. Sea. (12/7)

Longest Interception Return
100 yds ......Jimmy Hitchcock, NE vs. Mia. (11/23), TD

Longest Punt Return
94 yds..........Darrien Gordon, Den. vs. St.L (9/14), TD

Longest Kickoff Return
102 yds.............Eric Guliford, NO at St.L (8/31), TD
Eric Bieniemy, Cin. at NYG (10/26), TD

NFL Regular Season Team Leaders

Offensive Downs

AFC	First Downs				3rd Downs			4th Downs		
	Tot	Rush	Pass	Pen	Made	Att	Pct	Made	Att	Pct
Denver	340	138	172	30	92	217	42.4	7	16	43.8
Seattle	331	98	207	26	91	224	40.6	8	16	50.0
Pittsburgh	326	154	157	15	98	219	44.7	11	18	61.1
Kansas City	315	129	163	23	93	225	41.3	5	16	31.3
Miami	311	87	199	25	82	217	37.8	13	23	56.5
Cincinnati	310	104	171	35	88	214	41.1	10	20	50.0
Jacksonville	308	103	187	18	82	209	39.2	5	12	41.7
Indianapolis	301	109	171	21	83	219	37.9	10	20	50.0
Baltimore	292	99	176	17	82	227	36.1	12	21	57.1
NY Jets	291	97	173	21	91	238	38.2	12	21	57.1
Tennessee	288	130	136	22	92	219	42.0	9	14	64.3
Buffalo	268	98	144	26	53	212	25.0	11	29	37.9
New England	267	71	173	23	88	218	40.4	3	13	23.1
Oakland	263	74	170	19	65	204	31.9	5	18	27.8
San Diego	251	70	160	21	78	237	32.9	8	21	38.1

NFC	First Downs				3rd Downs			4th Downs		
	Tot	Rush	Pass	Pen	Made	Att	Pct	Made	Att	Pct
Philadelphia	326	105	203	18	90	242	37.2	14	22	63.6
Green Bay	325	103	191	31	80	202	39.6	5	5	100.0
Chicago	305	94	188	23	91	253	36.0	14	27	51.9
Detroit	304	120	166	18	78	221	35.3	8	18	44.4
Washington	300	86	192	22	94	222	42.3	5	13	38.5
Arizona	295	79	186	30	85	242	35.1	11	22	50.0
San Francisco	294	106	167	21	76	209	36.4	4	8	50.0
Minnesota	293	96	177	20	88	223	39.5	5	11	45.5
Carolina	284	91	170	23	99	225	44.0	3	9	33.3
Atlanta	281	88	168	25	74	210	35.2	8	13	61.5
Dallas	279	82	170	27	83	229	36.2	6	13	46.2
NY Giants	273	113	124	36	74	237	31.2	5	9	55.6
St. Louis	271	85	161	25	73	223	32.7	4	11	36.4
Tampa Bay	249	88	134	27	79	204	38.7	5	14	35.7
New Orleans	229	78	127	24	54	207	26.1	14	22	63.6

Overall Club Rankings

Combined AFC and NFC rankings by yards gained on offense and yards given up on defense. Teams listed in alphabetical order with AFC teams in italics.

	Offense			Defense		
	Rush	Pass	Rank	Rush	Pass	Rank
Arizona	30	10	**24**	27	15	**27**
Atlanta	19	22	**23**	8	20	**20**
Baltimore	22	5	**9**	10	28	**25**
Buffalo	14	25	**25**	15	12	**9**
Carolina	15	26	**26**	22	9	**15**
Chicago	16	16	**17**	19	11	**12**
Cincinnati	9	13	**10**	29	21t	**28**
Dallas	20	20	**20**	24	1	**2**
Denver	4	9	**1**	16	5	**5**
Detroit	2	12	**2**	18	13	**14**
Green Bay	12	3	**4**	20	8	**7**
Indianapolis	17	19	**19**	26	4	**10**
Jacksonville	18	4	**7**	13	24	**23**
Kansas City	5	24	**14**	7	16	**11**
Miami	29	2	**11**	17	25	**26**
Minnesota	6	14	**8**	23	29	**29**
New England	26	7	**15**	5	21t	**19**
New Orleans	27	27	**30**	14	6	**4**
NY Giants	7	28	**27**	3	26	**18**
NY Jets	25	15	**22**	21	19	**24**
Oakland	23	8	**13**	30	30	**30**
Philadelphia	10	6	**5**	25	7	**13**
Pittsburgh	1	23	**6**	1	18	**6**
St. Louis	24	17	**21**	9	17	**17**
San Diego	28	21	**28**	11	23	**21**
San Francisco	8	18	**12**	2	2	**1**
Seattle	13	1	**3**	12	14	**8**
Tampa Bay	11	30	**29**	6	10	**3**
Tennessee	3	29	**18**	4	27	**22**
Washington	21	11	**16**	28	3	**16**

Takeaways/Giveaways

AFC	Takeaways			Giveaways			Net
	Int	Fum	Total	Int	Fum	Total	Diff
Kansas City	21	13	34	10	10	20	+14
Denver	18	13	31	11	10	21	+10
New England	19	13	32	15	7	22	+10
Jacksonville	14	15	29	9	11	20	+9
Miami	10	17	27	12	8	20	+7
Tennessee	14	17	31	13	13	26	+5
NY Jets	18	7	25	10	12	22	+3
Cincinnati	13	10	23	9	13	22	+1
Pittsburgh	20	14	34	19	14	33	+1
Oakland	10	12	22	10	14	24	-2
Indianapolis	12	13	25	17	11	28	-3
Seattle	13	16	29	21	11	32	-3
Baltimore	17	11	28	16	16	32	-4
San Diego	15	11	26	21	14	35	-9
Buffalo	15	7	22	25	17	42	-20

NFC	Takeaways			Giveaways			Net
	Int	Fum	Total	Int	Fum	Total	Diff
NY Giants	27	17	44	12	7	19	+25
San Francisco	25	16	41	11	9	20	+21
St. Louis	25	14	39	15	15	30	+9
Minnesota	12	15	27	16	6	22	+5
Atlanta	18	10	28	11	13	24	+4
Tampa Bay	13	13	26	12	11	23	+3
Washington	16	14	30	22	7	29	+1
Green Bay	21	11	32	16	16	32	0
Detroit	17	8	25	17	11	28	-3
Dallas	7	12	19	12	11	23	-4
Philadelphia	14	12	26	16	16	32	-6
Chicago	13	17	30	22	19	41	-11
Carolina	11	11	22	24	15	39	-17
Arizona	15	5	20	22	20	42	-22
New Orleans	16	15	31	33	22	55	-24

AFC Team by Team Statistics

Players with more than one team during the regular season are listed with club they ended season with; (*) indicates rookies.

Baltimore Ravens

Passing (5 Att)	Att	Cmp	Pct	Yds	TD	Rate
Vinny Testaverde	470	271	57.7	2971	18	75.9
Eric Zeier	116	67	57.8	958	7	101.1

Interceptions: Testaverde 15, Zeier 1.

Top Receivers	No	Yds	Avg	Long	TD
Michael Jackson	69	918	13.3	54-td	4
Derrick Alexander	65	1009	15.5	92	9
Eric Green	65	601	9.2	37-td	5
Jermaine Lewis	42	648	15.4	42-td	6
Bam Morris	29	176	6.1	15	0
Earnest Byner	21	128	6.1	17	0

Top Rushers	Car	Yds	Avg	Long	TD
Bam Morris	204	774	3.8	25	4
Earnest Byner	84	313	3.7	19	0
Jay Graham*	81	299	3.7	19	2
Vinny Testaverde	34	138	4.1	16	0

Most Touchdowns	TD	Run	Rec	Ret	Pts
Derrick Alexander	9	0	9	0	54
Jermaine Lewis	8	0	6	2	48
Eric Green	5	0	5	0	30
Michael Jackson	4	0	4	0	26
Bam Morris	4	4	0	0	24
Jay Graham*	2	2	0	0	12

2-Pt. Conversions: Byner, Jackson.

Kicking	PAT/Att	FG/Att	Lg	Pts
Matt Stover	32/32	26/34	49	110

Punts (10 or more)	No	Yds	Long	Avg	In20
Greg Montgomery	83	3540	60	42.7	24

Most Interceptions
Stevon Moore 4

Most Sacks
Peter Boulware* 11½

Buffalo Bills

Passing (5 Att)	Att	Cmp	Pct	Yds	TD	Rate
Todd Collins	391	215	55.0	2367	12	69.5
Alex Van Pelt	124	60	48.4	684	2	37.2

Interceptions: Collins 13, Van Pelt 10.
Waived: Billy Joe Hobert on Oct. 15 (see New Orleans).

Top Receivers	No	Yds	Avg	Long	TD
Andre Reed	60	880	14.7	77-td	5
Quinn Early	60	853	14.2	45	5
Lonnie Johnson	41	340	8.3	62-td	2
Thurman Thomas	30	208	6.9	30	0
Eric Moulds	29	294	10.1	32	0
Antowain Smith*	28	177	6.3	19	0
Jay Riemersma*	26	208	8.0	22	2

Top Rushers	Car	Yds	Avg	Long	TD
Antowain Smith*	194	840	4.3	56-td	8
Thurman Thomas	154	643	4.2	24	1
Darick Holmes	22	106	4.8	19	2
Todd Collins	30	77	2.6	11	0

Most Touchdowns	TD	Run	Rec	Ret	Pts
Antowain Smith*	8	8	0	0	48
Quinn Early	5	0	5	0	30
Andre Reed	5	0	5	0	30
Jay Riemersma*	2	0	2	0	14
Darick Holmes	2	2	0	0	12
Lonnie Johnson	2	0	2	0	12

2-Pt. Conversions: Moulds, Riemersma.

Kicking	PAT/Att	FG/Att	Lg	Pts
Steve Christie	21/21	24/30	55	93

Punts (10 or more)	No	Yds	Long	Avg	In20
Chris Mohr	90	3764	59	41.8	24

Most Interceptions
Five tied with 2 each.

Most Sacks
Bruce Smith 14

Cincinnati Bengals

Passing (5 Att)	Att	Cmp	Pct	Yds	TD	Rate
Jeff Blake	317	184	58.0	2125	8	77.6
Boomer Esiason	186	118	63.4	1478	13	106.9

Interceptions: Blake 7, Esiason 2.

Top Receivers	No	Yds	Avg	Long	TD
Darnay Scott	54	797	14.8	77-td	5
Carl Pickens	52	695	13.4	50-td	5
Tony McGee	34	414	12.2	37	6
Eric Bieniemy	31	249	8.0	21	0
David Dunn	27	414	15.3	39-td	2
Corey Dillon*	27	259	9.6	28	0

Top Rushers	Car	Yds	Avg	Long	TD
Corey Dillon*	233	1129	4.8	71-td	10
Ki-Jana Carter	128	464	3.6	79-td	7
Jeff Blake	45	234	5.2	16	3
Eric Bieniemy	21	97	4.6	20-td	1
Brian Milne	13	32	2.5	5	2

Most Touchdowns	TD	Run	Rec	Ret	Pts
Corey Dillon*	10	10	0	0	60
Ki-Jana Carter	7	7	0	0	42
Tony McGee	6	0	6	0	38
Carl Pickens	5	0	5	0	30
Darnay Scott	5	0	5	0	30

2-Pt. Conversion: McGee.

Kicking	PAT/Att	FG/Att	Lg	Pts
Doug Pelfrey	41/43	12/16	46	77

Punts (10 or more)	No	Yds	Long	Avg	In20
Lee Johnson	81	3471	66	42.9	26

Most Interceptions
Corey Sawyer 4

Most Sacks
Gerald Dixon 8

Denver Broncos

Passing (5 Att)	Att	Cmp	Pct	Yds	TD	Rate
John Elway	502	280	55.8	3635	27	87.5
Bubby Brister	9	6	66.7	48	0	79.9

Interceptions: Elway 11.

Top Receivers	No	Yds	Avg	Long	TD
Shannon Sharpe	72	1107	15.4	68-td	3
Rod Smith	70	1180	16.9	78	12
Ed McCaffrey	45	590	13.1	35	8
Terrell Davis	42	287	6.8	25	0
Willie Green	19	240	12.6	31	2
Dwayne Carswell	12	96	8.0	24-td	1

Top Rushers	Car	Yds	Avg	Long	TD
Terrell Davis	369	1750	4.7	50-td	15
Vaughn Hebron	49	222	4.5	46	1
John Elway	50	218	4.4	23	1
Derek Loville	25	124	5.0	17	1

Most Touchdowns	TD	Run	Rec	Ret	Pts
Terrell Davis	15	15	0	0	96
Rod Smith	12	0	12	0	72
Ed McCaffrey	8	0	8	0	48
Darrien Gordon	4	0	0	4	24
Shannon Sharpe	3	0	3	0	20

2-Pt. Conversions: Davis 3, Sharpe.

Kicking	PAT/Att	FG/Att	Lg	Pts
Jason Elam	46/46	26/36	53	124

Released: Scott Bentley on Oct. 7 (see Atlanta).

Punts (10 or more)	No	Yds	Long	Avg	In20
Tom Rouen	60	2598	57	43.3	22

Most Interceptions
Tyrone Braxton 4
Darrien Gordon 4
Ray Crockett 4

Most Sacks
Alfred Williams 8½
Maa Tanuvasa 8½
Neil Smith 8½

Indianapolis Colts

Passing (5 Att)	Att	Cmp	Pct	Yds	TD	Rate
Jim Harbaugh	309	189	61.2	2060	10	86.2
Paul Justin	140	83	59.3	1046	5	79.6
Kelly Holcomb	73	45	61.6	454	1	44.3

Interceptions: Holcomb 8, Justin 5, Harbaugh 4.

Top Receivers	No	Yds	Avg	Long	TD
Marvin Harrison	73	866	11.9	44	6
Sean Dawkins	68	804	11.8	51	2
Marshall Faulk	47	471	10.0	58	1
Ken Dilger	27	380	14.1	43	3
Aaron Bailey	26	329	12.7	22	3
Brian Stablein	25	253	10.1	30	1

Top Rushers	Car	Yds	Avg	Long	TD
Marshall Faulk	264	1054	4.0	45	7
Zack Crockett	95	300	3.2	20	1
Jim Harbaugh	36	206	5.7	18	0
Lamont Warren	28	80	2.9	11	2

Most Touchdowns	TD	Run	Rec	Ret	Pts
Marshall Faulk	8	7	1	0	48
Marvin Harrison	6	0	6	0	40
Ken Dilger	3	0	3	0	18
Aaron Bailey	3	0	3	0	18
Sean Dawkins	2	0	2	0	12
Lamont Warren	2	2	0	0	12

2-Pt. Conversions: Harrison 2, Stablein, Marcus Pollard.

Kicking	PAT/Att	FG/Att	Lg	Pts
Cary Blanchard	21/21	32/41	50	117

Punts (10 or more)	No	Yds	Long	Avg	In20
Chris Gardocki	67	3034	72	45.3	18

Most Interceptions		Most Sacks	
Jason Belser	2	Dan Footman	10½
Quentin Coryatt	2		
Carlton Gray	2		

Jacksonville Jaguars

Passing (5 Att)	Att	Cmp	Pct	Yds	TD	Rate
Mark Brunell	435	264	60.7	3281	18	91.2
Steve Matthews*	40	26	65.0	275	0	84.9
Rob Johnson	28	22	78.6	344	2	111.9

Interceptions: Brunell 7, Johnson 2.

Top Receivers	No	Yds	Avg	Long	TD
Keenan McCardell	85	1164	13.7	60	5
Jimmy Smith	82	1324	16.1	75	4
James Stewart	41	336	8.2	40	1
Pete Mitchell	35	380	10.9	33	4
Ty Hallock	18	131	7.3	23	1
Willie Jackson	17	206	12.1	45	2

Top Rushers	Car	Yds	Avg	Long	TD
Natrone Means	244	823	3.4	20	9
James Stewart	136	555	4.1	33	8
Mark Brunell	48	257	5.4	15	2
Rob Johnson	10	34	3.4	25-td	1

Most Touchdowns	TD	Run	Rec	Ret	Pts
Natrone Means	9	9	0	0	54
James Stewart	9	8	1	0	54
Keenan McCardell	5	0	5	0	30
Pete Mitchell	4	0	4	0	24
Jimmy Smith	4	0	4	0	24
Willie Jackson	2	0	2	0	14

Three tied with 2 TDs for 12 points.

2-Pt. Conversion: Jackson.

Kicking	PAT/Att	FG/Att	Lg	Pts
Mike Hollis	41/41	31/36	52	134

Punts (10 or more)	No	Yds	Long	Avg	In20
Bryan Barker	66	2964	64	44.9	27

Most Interceptions		Most Sacks	
Deon Figures	5	Clyde Simmons	8½

Kansas City Chiefs

Passing (5 Att)	Att	Cmp	Pct	Yds	TD	Rate
Elvis Grbac	314	179	57.0	1943	11	79.1
Rich Gannon	175	98	56.0	1144	7	79.8
Billy Joe Tolliver	116	64	55.2	677	5	83.2
ATL	115	63	54.8	685	5	83.4
K.C.	1	1	100.0	-8	0	79.2

Interceptions: Grbac 6, Gannon 4, Tolliver 1.
Signed: Tolliver on Nov. 5 (released by Atlanta, Oct. 27).

Top Receivers	No	Yds	Avg	Long	TD
Andre Rison	72	1092	15.2	45	7
Kimble Anders	59	453	7.7	55-td	2
Ted Popson	35	320	9.1	21	2
Tony Gonzalez*	33	368	11.2	30	2

Top Rushers	Car	Yds	Avg	Long	TD
Greg Hill	157	550	3.5	38	0
Marcus Allen	124	505	4.1	30	11
Kimble Anders	79	397	5.0	43	0
Donnell Bennett	94	369	3.9	14	1

Most Touchdowns	TD	Run	Rec	Ret	Pts
Marcus Allen	11	11	0	0	66
Andre Rison	7	0	7	0	42
Danan Hughes	3	0	2	1	18
Mark McMillian	3	0	0	3	18
Tony Richardson	3	0	3	0	18

2-Pt. Conversions: Gonzalez, Tamarick Vanover.

Kicking	PAT/Att	FG/Att	Lg	Pts
Pete Stoyanovich	35/36	26/27	54	113

Punts (10 or more)	No	Yds	Long	Avg	In20
Louie Aguiar	81	3433	65	42.4	28

Most Interceptions		Most Sacks	
Mark McMillian	8	Dan Williams	10½

Miami Dolphins

Passing (5 Att)	Att	Cmp	Pct	Yds	TD	Rate
Dan Marino	548	319	58.2	3780	16	80.7
Craig Erickson	28	13	46.4	165	0	50.4

Interceptions: Marino 11, Erickson 1.

Top Receivers	No	Yds	Avg	Long	TD
O.J. McDuffie	76	943	12.4	55	1
Troy Drayton	39	558	14.3	30-td	4
Jerris McPhail	34	262	7.7	19	1
Karim Abdul-Jabbar	29	261	9.0	36-td	1
Lamar Thomas	28	402	14.4	26	2
Bernie Parmalee	28	301	10.8	29	1

Top Rushers	Car	Yds	Avg	Long	TD
Karim Abdul-Jabbar	283	892	3.2	22	15
Lawrence Phillips	201	677	3.4	28	8
ST.L	183	633	3.5	28	8
MIA	18	44	2.4	8	0
Irving Spikes	63	180	2.9	14	2
Jerris McPhail	17	146	8.6	71-td	1

Signed: Phillips on Dec. 2 (waived by St. Louis, Nov. 20).

Most Touchdowns	TD	Run	Rec	Ret	Pts
Karim Abdul-Jabbar	16	15	1	0	96
Lawrence Phillips	8	8	0	0	48
ST.L	8	8	0	0	48
MIA	0	0	0	0	0
Troy Drayton	4	0	4	0	24

2-Pt. Conversions: None.

Kicking	PAT/Att	FG/Att	Lg	Pts
Olindo Mare*	33/33	28/36	50	117

Punts (10 or more)	No	Yds	Long	Avg	In20
John Kidd	52	2247	58	43.2	13

Waived: Kyle Richardson, Oct. 7 (See Seattle).

Most Interceptions		Most Sacks	
Terrell Buckley	4	Trace Armstrong	5½

New England Patriots

Passing (5 Att)	Att	Cmp	Pct	Yds	TD	Rate
Drew Bledsoe	522	314	60.2	3706	28	87.7
Scott Zolak	9	6	66.7	67	2	128.2

Interceptions: Bledsoe 15.

Top Receivers	No	Yds	Avg	Long	TD
Ben Coates	66	737	11.2	35	8
Shawn Jefferson	54	841	15.6	76	2
Troy Brown	41	607	14.8	67	6
Curtis Martin	41	296	7.2	22	1
Terry Glenn	27	431	16.0	50	2
Vincent Brisby	23	276	12.0	31	2
Sam Gash	22	154	7.0	19	3
Keith Byars	20	189	9.5	51	3

Top Rushers	Car	Yds	Avg	Long	TD
Curtis Martin	274	1160	4.2	70-td	4
Derrick Cullors*	22	101	4.6	24	0
Marrio Grier	33	75	2.3	12	1
Dave Meggett	20	60	3.0	10	1

Most Touchdowns	TD	Run	Rec	Ret	Pts
Ben Coates	8	0	8	0	48
Troy Brown	6	0	6	0	36
Curtis Martin	5	4	1	0	30

Three tied with three each.

2-Pt. Conversions: None.

Kicking	PAT/Att	FG/Att	Lg	Pts
Adam Vinatieri	40/40	25/29	52	115

Punts (10 or more)	No	Yds	Long	Avg	In20
Tom Tupa	78	3569	73	45.8	24

Most Interceptions		Most Sacks	
Willie Clay	6	Chris Slade	9

New York Jets

Passing (5 Att)	Att	Cmp	Pct	Yds	TD	Rate
Neil O'Donnell	460	259	56.3	2796	17	80.3
Glenn Foley	97	56	57.7	705	3	86.5

Interceptions: O'Donnell 7, Foley, Ray Lucas, Leon Johnson 1.

Top Receivers	No	Yds	Avg	Long	TD
Keyshawn Johnson	70	963	13.8	39	5
Wayne Chrebet	58	799	13.8	70	3
Jeff Graham	42	542	12.9	47-td	2
Fred Baxter	27	276	10.2	37	3
Adrian Murrell	27	106	3.9	23	0
Richie Anderson	26	150	5.8	19	1
Kyle Brady	22	238	10.8	24	2

Top Rushers	No	Yds	Avg	Long	TD
Adrian Murrell	300	1086	3.6	43-td	7
Leon Johnson*	48	158	3.3	20	2
Richie Anderson	21	70	3.3	19	0

Most Touchdowns	TD	Run	Rec	Ret	Pts
Adrian Murrell	7	7	0	0	42
Keyshawn Johnson	5	0	5	0	30
Leon Johnson*	4	2	0	2	24
Fred Baxter	3	0	3	0	18
Wayne Chrebet	3	0	3	0	18
Otis Smith	3	0	0	3	18

2-Pt. Conversions: None.

Kicking	PAT/Att	FG/Att	Lg	Pts
John Hall*	36/36	28/41	55	120

Punts (10 or more)	No	Yds	Long	Avg	In20
Brian Hansen	71	3068	58	43.2	20

Most Interceptions		Most Sacks	
Otis Smith	6	Mo Lewis	8

Oakland Raiders

Passing (5 Att)	Att	Cmp	Pct	Yds	TD	Rate
Jeff George	521	290	55.7	3917	29	91.2
David Klingler	7	4	57.1	27	0	26.2

Interceptions: George 9, Klingler.

Top Receivers	No	Yds	Avg	Long	TD
Tim Brown	104	1408	13.5	59-td	5
Rickey Dudley	48	787	16.4	76	7
James Jett	46	804	17.5	56-td	12
Napoleon Kaufman	40	403	10.1	70-td	2
Harvey Williams	16	147	9.2	32-td	2
Derrick Fenner	14	92	6.6	13	0
Kenny Shedd	10	115	11.5	19	0

Top Rushers	Car	Yds	Avg	Long	TD
Napoleon Kaufman	272	1294	4.8	83-td	6
Tim Hall	23	120	5.2	15	0
Harvey Williams	18	70	3.9	13	3
Jeff George	17	44	2.6	12	0
Derrick Fenner	7	24	3.4	7	0

Most Touchdowns	TD	Run	Rec	Ret	Pts
James Jett	12	0	12	0	72
Napoleon Kaufman	8	6	2	0	48
Rickey Dudley	7	0	7	0	42
Tim Brown	5	0	5	0	32
Harvey Williams	5	3	2	0	32

2-Pt. Conversions: Brown, Williams.

Kicking	PAT/Att	FG/Att	Lg	Pts
Cole Ford	33/35	13/22	53	72

Punts (10 or more)	No	Yds	Long	Avg	In20
Leo Araguz	93	4189	63	45.0	28

Most Interceptions	Most Sacks	
Four tied with 2 each.	Anthony Smith	6½

Pittsburgh Steelers

Passing (5 Att)	Att	Cmp	Pct	Yds	TD	Rate
Kordell Stewart	440	236	53.6	3020	21	75.2
Mike Tomczak	24	16	66.7	185	1	68.9

Interceptions: Stewart 17, Tomczak 2.

Top Receivers	No	Yds	Avg	Long	TD
Yancey Thigpen	79	1398	17.7	69-td	7
Charles Johnson	46	568	12.3	49	2
Courtney Hawkins	45	555	12.3	44-td	3
Mark Bruener	18	117	6.5	18-td	6
George Jones*	16	96	6.0	25	1
Jerome Bettis	15	110	7.3	19-td	2
Will Blackwell*	12	168	14.0	46	1

Top Rushers	Car	Yds	Avg	Long	TD
Jerome Bettis	375	1665	4.4	34	7
Kordell Stewart	88	476	5.4	74-td	11
George Jones*	72	235	3.3	32	1
Fred McAfee	13	41	3.2	9	0

Most Touchdowns	TD	Run	Rec	Ret	Pts
Kordell Stewart	11	11	0	0	66
Jerome Bettis	9	7	2	0	54
Yancey Thigpen	7	0	7	0	44
Mark Bruener	6	0	6	0	36
Courtney Hawkins	3	0	3	0	18

2-Pt. Conversions: Thigpen.

Kicking	PAT/Att	FG/Att	Lg	Pts
Norm Johnson	40/40	22/25	52	106

Punts (10 or more)	No	Yds	Long	Avg	In20
Josh Miller	64	2729	72	42.6	17

Most Interceptions		Most Sacks	
Donnell Woolford	4	Carnell Lake	6
Darren Perry	4		

San Diego Chargers

Passing (5 Att)	Att	Cmp	Pct	Yds	TD	Rate
Craig Whelihan*	237	118	49.8	1357	6	58.3
Stan Humphries	225	121	53.8	1488	5	70.8
Jim Everett	75	36	48.0	457	1	49.7
Todd Philcox	28	16	57.1	173	0	60.6

Interceptions: Whelihan 10, Humphries 6, Everett 4, Philcox 1.

Top Receivers	No	Yds	Avg	Long	TD
Tony Martin	63	904	14.3	72-td	6
Freddie Jones*	41	505	12.3	62	2
Eric Metcalf	40	576	14.4	62	2
Terrell Fletcher	39	292	7.5	25	0

Top Rushers	No	Yds	Avg	Long	TD
Gary Brown	253	945	3.7	32	4
Terrell Fletcher	51	161	3.2	13	0
Kenny Bynum*	30	97	3.2	19	0

Most Touchdowns	TD	Run	Rec	Ret	Pts
Tony Martin	6	0	6	0	36
Eric Metcalf	5	0	2	3	30
Gary Brown	4	4	0	0	24
Rodney Harrison	3	0	0	3	18

2-Pt. Conversion: None.

Kicking	PAT/Att	FG/Att	Lg	Pts
Greg Davis	31/32	26/34	45	109
MIN	10/10	7/10	43	31
SD	21/22	19/24	45	78
John Carney	5/5	7/7	41	26

Signed: Davis on Sept. 25 (released by Minn. on Sept. 24.)

Punts (10 or more)	No	Yds	Long	Avg	In20
Darren Bennett	89	3972	66	44.6	26

Most Interceptions
Five tied with 2 each.

Most Sacks
Junior Seau 7

Seattle Seahawks

Passing (5 Att)	Att	Cmp	Pct	Yds	TD	Rate
Warren Moon	528	313	59.3	3678	25	83.7
Jon Kitna*	45	31	68.9	371	1	82.7
John Friesz	36	15	41.7	138	0	18.1

Interceptions: Moon 16, Friesz 3, Kitna 2.

Top Receivers	No	Yds	Avg	Long	TD
Joey Galloway	72	1049	14.6	53-td	12
Mike Pritchard	64	843	13.2	61	2
Chris Warren	45	257	5.7	20	0
James McKnight	34	637	18.7	60-td	6
Carlester Crumpler	31	361	11.6	30	1

Top Rushers	Car	Yds	Avg	Long	TD
Chris Warren	200	847	4.2	36-td	4
Steve Broussard	70	418	6.0	77-td	5
Lamar Smith	91	392	4.3	35	2

Most Touchdowns	TD	Run	Rec	Ret	Pts
Joey Galloway	12	0	12	0	72
Steve Broussard	6	5	1	0	36
James McKnight	6	0	6	0	36
Chris Warren	4	4	0	0	24

2-Pt.Conversions: Smith.

Kicking	PAT/Att	FG/Att	Lg	Pts
Todd Peterson	37/37	22/28	52	103

Punts (10 or more)	No	Yds	Lg	Avg	In20
Rick Tuten	48	2007	65	41.8	15
Rohn Stark	20	813	52	41.7	7
Kyle Richardson	19	804	54	42.3	2
MIA	11	480	54	43.6	0
SEA	8	324	52	40.5	2

Signed: Richardson on Nov. 11 (waived by Miami, Oct. 7); Stark on Nov. 25.

Released: Richardson on Nov. 26.

Most Interceptions
Darryl Williams 8

Most Sacks
Michael Sinclair 12

Tennessee Oilers

Passing (5 Att)	Att	Cmp	Pct	Yds	TD	Rate
Steve McNair	415	216	52.0	2665	14	70.4

Interceptions: McNair 13.

Top Receivers	No	Yds	Avg	Long	TD
Frank Wycheck	63	748	11.9	42	4
Willie Davis	43	564	13.1	46	4
Chris Sanders	31	498	16.1	55-td	3
Derrick Mason*	14	186	13.3	38	0
Rodney Thomas	14	111	7.9	22	0

Top Rushers	Car	Yds	Avg	Long	TD
Eddie George	357	1399	3.9	30	6
Steve McNair	101	674	6.7	47	8
Rodney Thomas	67	310	4.6	25-td	3

Most Touchdowns	TD	Run	Rec	Ret	Pts
Steve McNair	8	8	0	0	48
Eddie George	7	6	1	0	44
Frank Wycheck	4	0	4	0	26
Willie Davis	4	0	4	0	24
Chris Sanders	3	0	3	0	18
Rodney Thomas	3	3	0	0	18

2-Pt. Conversions: George, Wycheck.

Kicking	PAT/Att	FG/Att	Lg	Pts
Al Del Greco	32/32	27/35	52	113

Punts (10 or more)	No	Yds	Long	Avg	In20
Reggie Roby	73	3049	59	41.8	25

Most Interceptions
Darryll Lewis 5
Marcus Robertson 5

Most Sacks
Kenny Holmes* 7
Gary Walker 7

AFC Team Leaders

Offense

	Points		Yardage			
	For	Avg	Rush	Pass	Total	Avg
Denver	472	29.5	2378	3494	5872	367.0
Seattle	365	22.8	1800	3959	5759	359.9
Pittsburgh	372	23.3	2479	3063	5542	346.4
Jacksonville	394	24.6	1720	3704	5424	339.0
Baltimore	326	20.4	1589	3702	5291	330.7
Cincinnati	355	22.2	1966	3316	5282	330.1
Miami	339	21.2	1343	3782	5125	320.3
Oakland	324	20.3	1588	3514	5102	318.9
Kansas City	375	23.4	2171	2893	5064	316.5
New England	369	23.1	1464	3550	5014	313.4
Tennessee	333	20.8	2414	2505	4919	307.4
Indianapolis	313	19.6	1727	3142	4869	304.3
NY Jets	348	21.8	1485	3242	4727	295.4
Buffalo	255	15.9	1782	2875	4657	291.1
San Diego	266	16.6	1416	3089	4505	281.6

Defense

	Points		Yardage			
	Opp	Avg	Rush	Pass	Total	Avg
Denver	17.9	287	1803	2868	4671	291.9
Pittsburgh	19.2	307	1318	3387	4705	294.1
Seattle	22.6	362	1731	3118	4849	303.1
Buffalo	22.9	367	1792	3061	4853	303.3
Indianapolis	25.1	401	2034	2820	4854	303.4
Kansas City	14.5	232	1621	3259	4880	305.0
New England	18.1	289	1616	3459	5075	317.2
San Diego	26.6	425	1698	3468	5166	322.9
Tennessee	19.4	310	1573	3658	5231	326.9
Jacksonville	19.9	318	1734	3504	5238	327.4
NY Jets	17.9	287	1899	3421	5320	332.5
Baltimore	21.6	345	1690	3673	5363	335.2
Miami	20.4	327	1813	3551	5364	335.3
Cincinnati	25.3	405	2223	3459	5682	355.1
Oakland	26.2	419	2246	3870	6116	382.3

NFC Team by Team Statistics

Players with more than one team during the regular season are listed with club they ended season with; (*) indicates rookies.

Arizona Cardinals

Passing (5 Att)	Att	Cmp	Pct	Yds	TD	Rate
Jake Plummer*	296	157	53.0	2203	15	73.1
Kent Graham	250	130	52.0	1408	4	65.9
Stoney Case	55	29	52.7	316	0	54.8

Interceptions: Plummer 15, Graham 5, Case 2.

Top Receivers	No	Yds	Avg	Long	TD
Rob Moore	97	1584	16.3	47-td	8
Frank Sanders	75	1017	13.6	70-td	4
Larry Centers	54	409	7.6	29	1
Chris Gedney	23	261	11.3	37-td	4

Top Rushers	Car	Yds	Avg	Long	TD
Leeland McElroy	135	424	3.1	18	2
Ron Moore	81	278	3.4	27-td	1
ST.L	24	103	4.3	27-td	1
ARIZ	57	175	3.1	16	0
Larry Centers	101	276	2.7	14	1

Signed: Moore on Nov. 3 (released by St. Louis, Oct. 28).

Most Touchdowns	TD	Run	Rec	Ret	Pts
Rob Moore	8	0	8	0	50
Frank Sanders	4	0	4	0	26
Chris Gedney	4	0	4	0	24

2-Pt. Conversion: Moore, Plummer, Sanders.

Kicking	PAT/Att	FG/Att	Lg	Pts
Joe Nedney	19/19	11/17	45	52
Kevin Butler	9/10	8/12	49	33

Signed: Nedney on Oct. 14 (released by Miami, Oct. 6).
Waived: Kevin Butler on Oct. 14.

Punts (10 or more)	No	Yds	Long	Avg	In20
Jeff Feagles	91	4028	62	44.3	24

Most Interceptions Aeneas Williams 6

Most Sacks Eric Swann 7½

Atlanta Falcons

Passing (5 Att)	Att	Cmp	Pct	Yds	TD	Rate
Chris Chandler	342	202	59.1	2692	20	95.1
Tony Graziani*	23	7	30.4	41	0	3.7

Interceptions: Chandler 7, Graziani 2.
Released: Billy Joe Tolliver on Oct. 27 (see Kansas City).

Top Receivers	No	Yds	Avg	Long	TD
Bert Emanuel	65	991	15.2	56	9
Terance Mathis	62	802	12.9	49	6
Harold Green	29	360	12.4	47	0
Jamal Anderson	29	284	9.8	47-td	3

Top Rushers	Car	Yds	Avg	Long	TD
Jamal Anderson	290	1002	3.5	39	7
Byron Hanspard*	53	335	6.3	77	0
Chris Chandler	43	158	3.7	19	0
Harold Green	36	78	2.2	22	1

Most Touchdowns	TD	Run	Rec	Ret	Pts
Jamal Anderson	10	7	3	0	60
Bert Emanuel	9	0	9	0	54
Terance Mathis	6	0	6	0	36
Byron Hanspard*	3	0	1	2	18

2-Pt. Conversions: None.

Kicking	PAT/Att	FG/Att	Lg	Pts
Morten Anderson	35/35	23/27	55	104
Scott Bentley*	4/4	2/3	33	10
DEN	4/4	2/3	33	10
ATL	0/0	0/0	—	0

Signed: Bentley on Dec. 2 (released from Denver, Oct. 7).

Punts (10 or more)	No	Yds	Long	Avg	In20
Dan Stryzinski	89	3498	57	39.3	20

Most Interceptions Ray Buchanan 5

Most Sacks Chuck Smith 12

Carolina Panthers

Passing (5 Att)	Att	Cmp	Pct	Yds	TD	Rate
Kerry Collins	381	200	52.5	2124	11	55.7
Steve Beuerlein	153	89	58.2	1032	6	83.6

Interceptions: Collins 21, Beuerlein 3.

Top Receivers	No	Yds	Avg	Long	TD
Wesley Walls	58	746	12.9	52	6
Rae Carruth*	44	545	12.4	52	4
Scott Greene	40	277	6.9	25	1
Ragib Ismail	36	419	11.6	59-td	2
Mark Carrier	33	436	13.2	36	2
Muhsin Muhammad	27	317	11.7	38	0
Anthony Johnson	21	158	7.5	25	1

Top Rushers	Car	Yds	Avg	Long	TD
Fred Lane*	182	809	4.4	50	7
Anthony Johnson	97	358	3.7	20	0
Tim Biakabutuka	75	299	4.0	26-td	2
Scott Greene	45	157	3.5	10-td	1
Kerry Collins	26	54	2.1	21	1

Most Touchdowns	TD	Run	Rec	Ret	Pts
Fred Lane*	7	7	0	0	42
Wesley Walls	6	0	6	0	36
Rae Carruth*	4	0	4	0	24

2-Pt. Conversions: Johnson, Muhammad.

Kicking	PAT/Att	FG/Att	Lg	Pts
John Kasay	25/25	22/26	54	91

Punts (10 or more)	No	Yds	Long	Avg	In20
Ken Walter*	85	3604	62	42.4	29

Most Interceptions Eric Davis 5

Most Sacks Michael Barrow 8½

Chicago Bears

Passing (5 Att)	Att	Cmp	Pct	Yds	TD	Rate
Erik Kramer	477	275	57.7	3011	14	74.0
Rick Mirer	103	53	51.5	420	0	37.7
Steve Stenstrom	14	8	57.1	70	0	31.0

Interceptions: Kramer 14, Mirer 6, Stenstrom 2.

Top Receivers	No	Yds	Avg	Long	TD
Ricky Proehl	58	753	13.0	78-td	7
Chris Penn	47	576	12.3	33	3
Ryan Wetnight	46	464	10.1	34	1
Bobby Engram	45	399	8.9	23	2
Curtis Conway	30	476	15.9	55-td	1
Raymont Harris	28	115	4.1	16	0

Top Rushers	Car	Yds	Avg	Long	TD
Raymont Harris	275	1033	3.8	68-td	10
Darnell Autry*	112	319	2.8	17	1
Rashaan Salaam	31	112	3.6	17	0

Most Touchdowns	TD	Run	Rec	Ret	Pts
Raymont Harris	10	10	0	0	60
Ricky Proehl	7	0	7	0	44
Chris Penn	3	0	3	0	18
Bobby Engram	2	0	2	0	14
Erik Kramer	2	2	0	0	12

2-Pt. Conversions: Autry, Engram, Jim Flanigan, Mirer, Proehl.

Kicking	PAT/Att	FG/Att	Lg	Pts
Jeff Jaeger	20/20	21/26	52	83

Punts (10 or more)	No	Yds	Lg	Avg	In20
Todd Sauerbrun	95	4059	67	42.7	26

Most Interceptions Walt Harris 5

Most Sacks Jim Flanigan 6
Barry Minter 6

Dallas Cowboys

Passing (5 Att)	Att	Cmp	Pct	Yds	TD	Rate
Troy Aikman	518	292	56.4	3283	19	78.0
Wade Wilson	21	12	57.1	115	0	72.5
Jason Garrett	14	10	71.4	56	0	78.3

Interceptions: Aikman 12.

Top Receivers	No	Yds	Avg	Long	TD
Michael Irvin	75	1180	15.7	55	9
Eric Bjornson	47	442	9.4	32	0
Anthony Miller	46	645	14.0	54	4
Emmitt Smith	40	234	5.9	24	0
Stepfret Williams	30	308	10.3	20	1

Top Rushers	Car	Yds	Avg	Long	TD
Emmitt Smith	261	1074	4.1	44	4
Sherman Williams	121	468	3.9	18	2
Troy Aikman	25	79	3.2	13	0

Most Touchdowns	TD	Run	Rec	Ret	Pts
Michael Irvin	9	0	9	0	54
Emmitt Smith	4	4	0	0	26
Anthony Miller	4	0	4	0	24

Four tied with two each.

2-Pt. Conversion: Bjornson, E. Smith.

Kicking	PAT/Att	FG/Att	Lg	Pts
Richie Cunningham*	24/24	34/37	53	126

Punts (10 or more)	No	Yds	Long	Avg	In20
Toby Gowin*	86	3592	72	41.8	26

Most Interceptions		Most Sacks	
Deion Sanders	2	Shante Carver	6
Omar Stoutmire*	2		

Detroit Lions

Passing (5 Att)	Att	Cmp	Pct	Yds	TD	Rate
Scott Mitchell	509	293	57.6	3484	19	79.6
Frank Reich	30	11	36.7	121	0	21.7

Interceptions: Mitchell 14, Reich 2.

Top Receivers	No	Yds	Avg	Long	TD
Herman Moore	104	1293	12.4	79	8
Johnnie Morton	80	1057	13.2	73-td	6
Barry Sanders	33	305	9.2	66-td	3
David Sloan	29	264	9.1	25	0
Pete Metzelaars	17	144	8.5	22	0
Tommy Vardell	16	218	13.6	37	0

Top Rushers	Car	Yds	Avg	Long	TD
Barry Sanders	335	2053	6.1	82-td	11
Ron Rivers	29	166	5.7	31	1
Tommy Vardell	32	122	3.8	41	6
Scott Mitchell	37	83	2.2	13	1

Most Touchdowns	TD	Run	Rec	Ret	Pts
Barry Sanders	14	11	3	0	84
Herman Moore	8	0	8	0	50
Johnnie Morton	6	0	6	0	36
Tommy Vardell	6	6	0	0	36
Reggie Brown	2	0	0	2	12

Seven tied with one each.

2-Pt. Conversion: Moore.

Kicking	PAT/Att	FG/Att	Lg	Pts
Jason Hanson	39/40	26/29	55	117

Punts (10 or more)	No	Yds	Long	Avg	In20
John Jett	84	3576	60	42.6	24

Most Interceptions		Most Sacks	
Mark Carrier	5	Robert Porcher	12½

Green Bay Packers

Passing (5 Att)	Att	Cmp	Pct	Yds	TD	Rate
Brett Favre	513	304	59.3	3867	35	92.6
Steve Bono	10	5	50.0	29	0	56.3

Interceptions: Favre 16.

Top Receivers	No	Yds	Avg	Long	TD
Antonio Freeman	81	1243	15.3	58-td	12
Robert Brooks	60	1010	16.8	48	7
Dorsey Levens	53	370	7.0	56	5
William Henderson	41	367	9.0	25	1
Mark Chmura	38	417	11.0	32-td	6
Derrick Mayes	18	290	16.1	74	0
Jeff Thomason	9	115	12.8	27	1

Top Rushers	Car	Yds	Avg	Long	TD
Dorsey Levens	329	1435	4.4	52-td	7
Brett Favre	58	187	3.2	16	1
Aaron Hayden	32	148	4.6	21	1
William Henderson	31	113	3.6	15	0

Most Touchdowns	TD	Run	Rec	Ret	Pts
Dorsey Levens	12	7	5	0	74
Antonio Freeman	12	0	12	0	72
Robert Brooks	7	0	7	0	42
Mark Chmura	6	0	6	0	36

2-Pt. Conversion: Levens.

Kicking	PAT/Att	FG/Att	Lg	Pts
Ryan Longwell	48/48	24/30	50	120

Punts (10 or more)	No	Yds	Long	Avg	In20
Craig Hentrich	75	3378	65	45.0	26

Most Interceptions		Most Sacks	
Leroy Butler	5	Reggie White	11

Minnesota Vikings

Passing (5 Att)	Att	Cmp	Pct	Yds	TD	Rate
Brad Johnson	452	275	60.8	3036	20	84.5
Randall Cunningham	88	44	50.0	501	6	71.3

Interceptions: Johnson 12, Cunningham 4.

Top Receivers	No	Yds	Avg	Long	TD
Cris Carter	89	1069	12.0	43	13
Jake Reed	68	1138	16.7	56	6
Robert Smith	37	197	5.3	20	1
Andrew Glover	32	378	11.8	43	3
David Palmer	26	193	7.4	23	1
Charles Evans	21	152	7.2	17	0

Top Rushers	Car	Yds	Avg	Long	TD
Robert Smith	232	1266	5.5	78-td	6
Leroy Hoard	80	235	2.9	20	4
Charles Evans	43	157	3.7	13	2
Brad Johnson	35	139	4.0	28	0
Randall Cunningham	19	127	6.7	28	0

Most Touchdowns	TD	Run	Rec	Ret	Pts
Cris Carter	13	0	13	0	84
Robert Smith	7	6	1	0	42
Jake Reed	6	0	6	0	36
Leroy Hoard	4	4	0	0	24
Andrew Glover	3	0	3	0	18

2-Pt. Conversion: Carter 3, Johnson 2, Evans.

Kicking	PAT/Att	FG/Att	Lg	Pts
Eddie Murray	23/24	12/17	49	59

Signed: Murray on Sept. 24. **Released:** Greg Davis on Sept. 24 (see San Diego).

Punts (10 or more)	No	Yds	Long	Avg	In20
Mitch Berger	73	3133	65	42.9	22

Most Interceptions		Most Sacks	
Dewayne Washington	4	John Randle	15½

New Orleans Saints

Passing (5 Att)	Att	Cmp	Pct	Yds	TD	Rate
Heath Shuler	203	106	52.2	1288	2	46.6
Billy Joe Hobert	161	78	48.4	1024	6	55.5
BUF	30	17	56.7	133	0	40.0
NO	131	61	46.6	891	6	59.0
Danny Wuerffel*	91	42	46.2	518	4	42.3
Doug Nussmeier	32	18	56.3	183	0	33.7

Interceptions: Shuler 14, Hobert 10, Wuerffel 8, Nussmeier 3.
Signed: Hobert on Nov. 19 (waived by Buffalo, Oct. 15).

Top Receivers	No	Yds	Avg	Long	TD
Randal Hill	55	761	13.8	89-td	2
Andre Hastings	48	722	15.0	39	5
Ray Zellars	31	263	8.5	38	0
Eric Guliford	27	362	13.4	47	1
John Farquhar	17	253	14.9	42	1
Irv Smith	17	180	10.6	25	1

Top Rushers	Car	Yds	Avg	Long	TD
Ray Zellars	156	552	3.5	27	4
Mario Bates	119	440	3.7	74-td	4
Troy Davis*	75	271	3.6	20	0

Most Touchdowns	TD	Run	Rec	Ret	Pts
Andre Hastings	5	0	5	0	32
Mario Bates	4	4	0	0	24
Ray Zellars	4	4	0	0	24

2-Pt. Conversions: Hastings.

Kicking	PAT/Att	FG/Att	Lg	Pts
Doug Brien	22/22	23/27	53	91

Punts (10 or more)	No	Yds	Long	Avg	In20
Mark Royals	88	4038	66	45.9	21

Most Interceptions
Sammy Knight* 5

Most Sacks
Wayne Martin 10½

New York Giants

Passing (5 Att)	Att	Cmp	Pct	Yds	TD	Rate
Danny Kanell	294	156	53.1	1740	11	70.7
Dave Brown	180	93	51.7	1023	5	71.1

Interceptions: Kanell 9, Brown 3.

Top Receivers	No	Yds	Avg	Long	TD
Chris Calloway	58	849	14.6	68-td	8
Charles Way	37	304	8.2	62	1
Tiki Barber*	34	299	8.8	29	1
Howard Cross	21	150	7.1	26	2
Erric Pegram	21	90	4.3	14	0
SD	2	7	3.5	4	0
NYG	19	83	4.4	14	0

Signed: Pegram on Oct. 2 (released by San Diego, Sept. 24).

Top Rushers	Car	Yds	Avg	Long	TD
Charles Way	151	698	4.6	42	4
Tyrone Wheatley	152	583	3.8	38	4
Tiki Barber*	136	511	3.8	42	3

Most Touchdowns	TD	Run	Rec	Ret	Pts
Chris Calloway	8	0	8	0	48
Charles Way	5	4	1	0	30
Tiki Barber*	4	3	1	0	26
Tyrone Wheatley	4	4	0	0	24

2-Pt. Conversion: Barber.

Kicking	PAT/Att	FG/Att	Lg	Pts
Brad Daluiso	27/29	22/32	52	93

Punts (10 or more)	No	Yds	Long	Avg	In20
Brad Maynard*	111	4531	57	40.8	33

Most Interceptions
Jason Sehorn 6

Most Sacks
Michael Strahan 14

Philadelphia Eagles

Passing (5 Att)	Att	Cmp	Pct	Yds	TD	Rate
Ty Detmer	244	134	54.9	1567	7	73.9
Bobby Hoying	225	128	56.9	1573	11	83.8
Rodney Peete	118	68	57.6	869	4	78.0

Interceptions: Detmer 6, Hoying 6, Peete 4.

Top Receivers	No	Yds	Avg	Long	TD
Irving Fryar	86	1316	15.3	72-td	6
Kevin Turner	48	443	9.2	36	3
Ricky Watters	48	440	9.2	37	0
Michael Timpson	42	484	11.5	26	2
Freddie Solomon	29	455	15.7	56	3

Top Rushers	Car	Yds	Avg	Long	TD
Ricky Watters	285	1110	3.9	28	7
Charlie Garner	116	547	4.7	26	3
Kevin Turner	18	96	5.3	29	0
Bobby Hoying	16	78	4.9	30	0

Most Touchdowns	TD	Run	Rec	Ret	Pts
Ricky Watters	7	7	0	0	42
Irving Fryar	6	0	6	0	36
Chad Lewis*	4	0	4	0	24
Charlie Garner	3	3	0	0	18
Freddie Solomon	3	0	3	0	18
Kevin Turner	3	0	3	0	18

2-Pt. Conversions: Solomon.

Kicking	PAT/Att	FG/Att	Lg	Pts
Chris Boniol	33/33	22/31	49	99

Punts (10 or more)	No	Yds	Long	Avg	In20
Tom Hutton	87	3660	61	42.1	19

Most Interceptions
Brian Dawkins 3
Troy Vincent 3

Most Sacks
Rhett Hall 8

St. Louis Rams

Passing (5 Att)	Att	Cmp	Pct	Yds	TD	Rate
Tony Banks	487	252	51.7	3254	14	71.5
Mark Rypien	39	19	48.7	270	0	50.2

Interceptions: Banks 13, Rypien 2.

Top Receivers	No	Yds	Avg	Long	TD
Amp Lee	61	825	13.5	62	3
Isaac Bruce	56	815	14.6	59	5
Ernie Conwell	38	404	10.6	46-td	4
Torrance Small	32	488	15.3	46	1
Eddie Kennison	25	404	16.2	76	0

Top Rushers	Car	Yds	Avg	Long	TD
Jerald Moore	104	380	3.7	26	3
Tony Banks	47	186	4.0	23	1
Amp Lee	28	104	3.7	14	0
Craig Heyward	34	84	2.5	8	1

Waived: RB Lawrence Phillips on Nov. 20 (see Miami); RB Ronald Moore on Oct. 28 (see Arizona).

Most Touchdowns	TD	Run	Rec	Ret	PTS
Isaac Bruce	5	0	5	0	30
Ernie Conwell	4	0	4	0	24
Amp Lee	3	0	3	0	18
Jerald Moore	3	3	0	0	18

2-Pt. Conversions: None.

Kicking	PAT/Att	FG/Att	Lg	Pts
Jeff Wilkins	32/32	25/37	52	107

Punts (10 or more)	No	Yds	Long	Avg	In20
Mike Horan	53	2272	60	42.9	10
Will Brice*	41	1713	61	41.8	6

Signed: Horan on Oct. 14. **Released:** Brice on Oct. 13.

Most Interceptions
Ryan McNeil 9

Most Sacks
Leslie O'Neal..........10

San Francisco 49ers

Passing (5 Att)	Att	Cmp	Pct	Yds	TD	Rate
Steve Young	356	241	67.7	3029	19	104.7
Jim Druckenmiller	52	21	40.4	239	1	29.2
Jeff Brohm	24	16	66.7	164	0	68.8

Interceptions: Young, 6, Druckenmiller 4, Brohm 1.

Top Receivers	No	Yds	Avg	Long	TD
Terrell Owens	60	936	15.6	56-td	8
J.J. Stokes	58	733	12.6	36	4
William Floyd	37	321	8.7	44-td	1
Brent Jones	29	383	13.2	33	2
Terry Kirby	23	279	12.1	82	1

Top Rushers	Car	Yds	Avg	Long	TD
Garrison Hearst	234	1019	4.4	51	4
Terry Kirby	125	418	3.3	38	6
William Floyd	78	231	3.0	22	3
Steve Young	50	199	4.0	13	3

Most Touchdowns	TD	Run	Rec	Ret	Pts
Terry Kirby	8	6	1	1	52
Terrell Owens	8	0	8	0	48
Garrison Hearst	6	4	2	0	36
William Floyd	4	3	1	0	24
J.J. Stokes	4	0	4	0	24

2-Pt. Conversions: Kirby 2.

Kicking	PAT/Att	FG/Att	Lg	Pts
Gary Anderson	38/38	29/36	51	125

Punts (10 or more)	No	Yds	Long	Avg	In20
Tommy Thompson	78	3182	55	40.8	22

Most Interceptions Merton Hanks 6

Most Sacks Dana Stubblefield......15

NFC Team Leaders

Offense

	Points		Yardage			
	For	Avg	Rush	Pass	Total	Avg
Detroit	379	23.7	2464	3334	5798	362.4
Green Bay	422	26.4	1909	3705	5614	350.9
Philadelphia	317	19.8	1943	3647	5590	349.4
Minnesota	354	22.1	2041	3313	5354	334.6
San Francisco	375	22.1	1969	3143	5112	319.5
Washington	327	20.4	1615	3383	4998	312.4
Chicago	263	16.4	1746	3241	4987	311.7
Dallas	304	19.0	1637	3141	4778	298.6
St. Louis	299	18.7	1563	3198	4761	297.6
Atlanta	320	20.0	1643	3073	4716	294.8
Arizona	283	17.7	1255	3458	4713	294.6
Carolina	265	16.6	1759	2845	4604	287.8
NY Giants	307	19.2	1988	2525	4513	282.1
Tampa Bay	299	18.7	1934	2442	4376	273.5
New Orleans	237	14.8	1461	2584	4045	252.8

Defense

	Points		Yardage			
	Opp	Avg	Rush	Pass	Total	Avg
San Francisco	265	16.6	1366	2647	4013	250.8
Dallas	314	19.6	1994	2522	4516	282.3
Tampa Bay	263	16.4	1617	3008	4625	289.1
New Orleans	327	20.4	1764	2881	4645	290.3
Green Bay	282	17.6	1876	2951	4827	301.7
Chicago	421	26.3	1858	3030	4888	305.5
Philadelphia	372	23.3	2009	2923	4932	308.3
Detroit	306	19.1	1833	3114	4947	309.2
Carolina	314	19.6	1973	3007	4980	311.3
Washington	289	18.1	2212	2818	5030	314.4
St. Louis	359	22.4	1676	3379	5055	315.9
NY Giants	265	16.6	1451	3616	5067	316.7
Atlanta	361	22.6	1666	3440	5106	319.1
Arizona	379	23.7	2180	3246	5426	339.1
Minnesota	359	22.4	1983	3704	5687	355.4

Tampa Bay Buccaneers

Passing (5 Att)	Att	Cmp	Pct	Yds	TD	Rate
Trent Dilfer	386	217	56.2	2555	21	82.8
Steve Walsh	17	6	35.3	58	0	21.2

Interceptions: Dilfer 11, Walsh 1.

Top Receivers	No	Yds	Avg	Long	TD
Warrick Dunn*	39	462	11.8	59-td	3
Reidel Anthony*	35	448	12.8	38-td	4
Karl Williams	33	486	14.7	55	4
Horace Copeland	33	431	13.1	49	1
Mike Alstott	23	178	7.7	26	3

Top Rushers	Car	Yds	Avg	Long	TD
Warrick Dunn*	224	978	4.4	76	4
Mike Alstott	176	665	3.8	47-td	7
Trent Dilfer	33	99	3.0	17	1
Errict Rhett	31	96	3.1	21	3

Most Touchdowns	TD	Run	Rec	Ret	Pts
Mike Alstott	10	7	3	0	60
Warrick Dunn*	7	4	3	0	42
Karl Williams	5	0	4	1	30
Reidel Anthony*	4	0	4	0	24
Dave Moore	4	0	4	0	24

2-Pt. Conversions: None.

Kicking	PAT/Att	FG/Att	Lg	Pts
Michael Husted	32/35	13/17	54	71

Punts (10 or more)	No	Yds	Long	Avg	In20
Sean Landeta	54	2274	74	42.1	15
Tommy Barnhardt	29	1304	61	39.1	12

Signed: Landeta on Oct. 9.

Most Interceptions Donnie Abraham........5

Most Sacks Warren Sapp........10½

Washington Redskins

Passing (5 Att)	Att	Cmp	Pct	Yds	TD	Rate
Gus Frerotte	402	204	50.7	2682	17	73.8
Jeff Hostetler	144	79	54.9	899	5	56.5

Interceptions: Frerotte 12, Hostetler 10.

Top Receivers	No	Yds	Avg	Long	TD
Jamie Asher	49	474	9.7	24	1
Brian Mitchell	36	438	12.2	69	1
Michael Westbrook	34	559	16.4	40-td	3
Larry Bowie	34	388	11.4	39-td	2
Henry Ellard	32	485	15.2	27	4
Leslie Shephard	29	562	19.4	48	5
Terry Allen	20	172	8.6	38	1
Stephen Davis	18	134	7.4	19	0

Top Rushers	Car	Yds	Avg	Long	TD
Terry Allen	210	724	3.4	34	4
Stephen Davis	141	567	4.0	18	3
Brian Mitchell	23	107	4.7	26	1
Larry Bowie	28	100	3.6	18	2

Most Touchdowns	TD	Run	Rec	Ret	Pts
Terry Allen	5	4	1	0	30
Leslie Shephard	5	0	5	0	30
Larry Bowie	4	2	2	0	24
Henry Ellard	4	0	4	0	24
Brian Mitchell	4	1	1	2	24

Three tied with three each.

2-Pt. Conversions: None.

Kicking	PAT/Att	FG/Att	Lg	Pts
Scott Blanton	34/34	16/24	50	82

Punts (10 or more)	No	Yds	Long	Avg	In20
Matt Turk	84	3788	62	45.1	32

Most Interceptions Chris Dishman..........4; Stanley Richard.........4

Most Sacks Ken Harvey..........9½

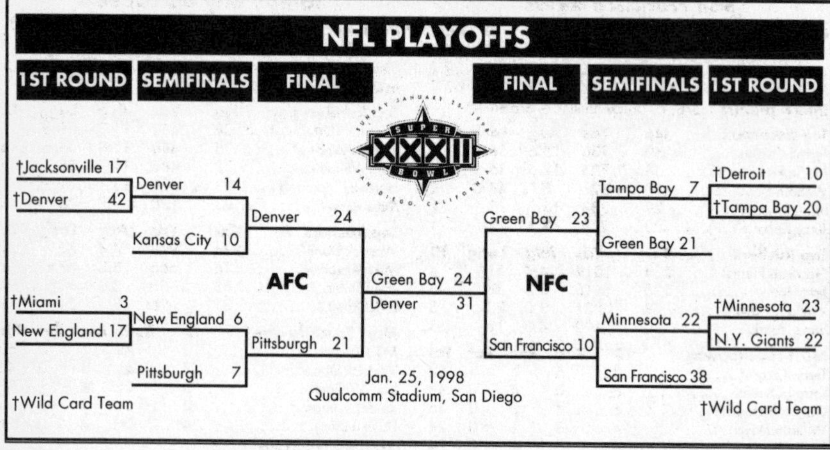

Playoff Game Summaries

Team records listed in parentheses indicate records before game.

WILD CARD ROUND

AFC

Broncos, 42-17

Jacksonville (11-5)	0	7	10	3–	**17**
Denver (12-4)	14	7	0	21–	**42**

Date—Dec. 27. **Att**—74,481. **Time**—3:02.

1st Quarter: DEN—Terrell Davis 2-yd run (Jason Elam kick), 7:39; DEN—Rod Smith 43-yd pass from John Elway (Elam kick), 2:37.

2nd Quarter: DEN—Davis 5-yd run (Elam kick), 10:46; JAX—Natrone Means 1-yd run (Mike Hollis kick), 5:09.

3rd Quarter: JAX—Hollis 38-yd FG, 13:33; JAX—Travis Davis 29-yd blocked punt return (Hollis kick), 9:16.

4th Quarter: DEN—Derek Loville 25-yd run (Elam kick), 13:21; DEN—Loville 8-yd run (Elam kick), 3:43; DEN—Vaughn Hebron 6-yd run (Elam kick), 1:11.

Patriots, 17-3

Miami (9-7)	0	0	0	3–	**3**
New England (10-6)	0	7	10	0–	**17**

Date—Dec. 28. **Att**—60,041. **Time**—3:00.

2nd Quarter: NE—Troy Brown 24-yd pass from Drew Bledsoe (Adam Vinatieri kick), 10:27.

3rd Quarter: NE—Todd Collins 40-yd INT return (Vinatieri kick), 14:05; NE—Vinatieri 22-yd FG, 1:58.

4th Quarter: MIA—Olindo Mare 38-yd FG, 14:51.

NFC

Vikings, 23-22

Minnesota (9-7)	0	3	7	13–	**23**
NY Giants (10-5-1)	0	19	0	3–	**22**

Date—Dec. 27. **Att**—77,497. **Time**—3:08.

1st Quarter: NY—Brad Daluiso 43-yd FG, 6:35; NY—Daluiso 22-yd FG, 2:20.

2nd Quarter: NY—Aaron Pierce 2-yd pass from Danny Kanell (Daluiso kick), 11:33; NY—Daluiso 41-yd FG, 4:54; MIN—Eddie Murray 26-yd FG, 1:47; NY—Daluiso 51-yd FG, :13.

3rd Quarter: MIN—Leroy Hoard 4-yd run (Murray kick), 10:26.

4th Quarter: MIN—Murray 26-yd FG, 14:45; NY—Daluiso 22-yd FG; MIN—Jake Reed 30-yd pass from Randall Cunningham (Murray kick), 1:30; MIN— Murray 24-yd FG, :10.

Buccaneers, 20-10

Detroit (9-7)	0	0	3	7–	**10**
Tampa Bay (10-6)	3	10	7	0–	**20**

Date—Dec. 28. **Att**—73,361. **Time**—3:10.

1st Quarter: TB—Michael Husted 22-yd FG, 5:24.

2nd Quarter: TB—Horace Copeland 9-yd pass from Trent Dilfer (Husted kick), 10:24; TB—Husted 42-yd FG, 6:49.

3rd Quarter: TB—Mike Alstott 31-yd run (Husted kick), 11:06; DET—Jason Hanson 33-yd FG, :28.

4th Quarter: DET— Tommy Vardell 1-yd run (Hanson kick), 7:48.

DIVISIONAL SEMIFINALS

AFC

Steelers, 7-6

New England (11-6)	0	3	0	3—	**6**
Pittsburgh (11-5)	7	0	0	0—	**7**

Date—Jan. 3. **Att**—61,228. **Time**—3:08.

1st Quarter: PIT—Kordell Stewart 40-yd run (Norm Johnson kick), 9:49.

2nd Quarter: NE—Adam Vinatieri 31-yd FG, 7:40.

4th Quarter: NE—Vinatieri 46-yd FG, 12:16.

Broncos, 14-10

Denver (13-4)	0	7	0	7—	**14**
Kansas City (13-3)	0	0	10	0—	**10**

Date—Jan. 4. **Att**—76,965. **Time**—2:59.

2nd Quarter: DEN—Terrell Davis 1-yd run (Jason Elam kick), 1:56.

3rd Quarter: KC—Pete Stoyanovich 20-yd FG, 9:42; KC—Tony Gonzalez 12-yd pass from Elvis Grbac (Stoyanovich kick), :10.

4th Quarter: DEN—Davis 1-yd run (Elam kick), 12:32.

NFC

49ers, 38-22

Minnesota (10-7)	7	0	7	8—	**22**
San Francisco (13-3)	7	14	10	7—	**38**

Date— Jan. 3. **Att**—65,018. **Time**—3:10.

1st Quarter: SF—William Floyd 1-yd run (Gary Anderson kick), 8:03; MIN—Cris Carter 66-yd pass from Randall Cunningham (Eddie Murray kick), 7:26.

2nd Quarter: SF—Terry Kirby 1-yd run (Anderson kick), 6:28; SF—Ken Norton Jr. 23-yd INT return (Anderson kick), 5:41.

3rd Quarter: SF—Anderson 34-yd FG, 8:17; MIN—Carter 3-yd pass from Cunningham (Murray kick), 5:13; SF—Terrell Owens 15-yd pass from Steve Young (Anderson kick), 2:00.

4th Quarter: Kirby 1-yd run (Anderson kick), 7:32; MIN—Matt Hatchette 13-yd pass from Cunningham (Cunningham pass to Chris Walsh for 2-pt. conversion), 3:47.

Packers, 21-7

Tampa Bay (11-6)	0	0	7	0—	**7**
Green Bay (13-3)	7	6	0	8—	**21**

Date—Jan. 4. **Att**—60,327. **Time**—2:57.

1st Quarter: GB—Mark Chmura 3-yd pass from Brett Favre (Ryan Longwell kick), 5:36.

2nd Quarter: GB—Longwell 21-yd FG, 1:52; GB—Longwell 32-yd FG, :02.

3rd Quarter: TB—Mike Alstott 6-yd run (Michael Husted kick), 6:17.

4th Quarter: GB—Dorsey Levens 2-yd run (Favre run for 2-pt. conversion), 13:37.

CONFERENCE CHAMPIONSHIPS

AFC

Broncos, 24-21

Denver (14-4)	7	17	0	0—	**24**
Pittsburgh (12-5)	7	7	0	7—	**21**

Date—Jan. 11. **Att**—61,382. **Time**—2:59.

1st Quarter: DEN—Terrell Davis 8-yd run (Jason Elam kick), 9:18; PIT—Kordell Stewart 33-yd run (Norm Johnson kick), 6:16.

2nd Quarter: PIT—Jerome Bettis 1-yd run (Johnson kick), 12:42; DEN—Elam 43-yd FG, 8:20; DEN—Howard Griffith 15-yd pass from John Elway (Elam kick), 1:47; DEN—Ed McCaffrey 1-yd pass from Elway (Elam kick), :13.

4th Quarter: PIT—Charles Johnson 14-yd pass from Stewart (Johnson kick), 2:46.

NFC

Packers, 23-10

Green Bay (14-3)	3	10	0	10—	**23**
San Francisco (14-3)	0	3	0	7—	**10**

Date—Jan. 11. **Att**—68,987. **Time**—3:00.

1st Quarter: GB—Ryan Longwell 19-yd FG, 2:48.

2nd Quarter: GB—Antonio Freeman 27-yd pass from Brett Favre (Longwell kick), 11:30; SF—Gary Anderson 28-yd FG, :58.

4th Quarter: GB—Longwell 25-yd FG, 5:12; GB—Dorsey Levens 5-yd run (Longwell kick), 3:10; SF—Chuck Levy 95-yd kickoff return (Anderson kick), 2:52.

Super Bowl XXXII

Sunday, Jan. 25 at Qualcomm Stadium, San Diego, Calif.

	1	2	3	4	Total
Green Bay (15-3)	7	7	3	7—	**24**
Denver (15-4)	7	10	7	7—	**31**

1st: GB—Antonio Freeman 22-yd pass from Brett Favre (Ryan Longwell kick), 10:58. Drive: 76 yards in 8 plays. Key play: Favre 13-yd pass to Freeman on 3rd-and-9 to GB 38. DEN—Terrell Davis 1-yd run (Jason Elam kick), 5:39. Drive: 58 yards in 10 plays. Key play: Holding penalty on Doug Evans on 3rd-and-10 to GB 41.

2nd: DEN—John Elway 1-yd run (Elam kick), 14:55. Drive: 45 yards in 8 plays. Key play: Tyrone Braxton interception of Favre pass at GB 45. DEN—Jason Elam 51-yd FG, 12:21. Drive: 0 yards in 4 plays. Key play: Neil Smith recovery of Favre fumble at GB 33. GB—Mark Chmura 6-yd pass from Favre (Longwell kick), :12. Drive: 95 yards in 17 plays. Key play: Favre 21-yd pass to Chmura on 3rd-and-10 to GB 26.

3rd: GB—Longwell 27-yd FG, 11:59. Drive: 17 yards in 7 plays. Key play: Tyrone Williams recovery of Davis fumble at DEN 26. DEN—Davis 1-yd run (Elam kick), 14:26. Drive: 92 yards on 13 plays. Key play: Elway 36-yd pass to Ed McCaffrey to GB 33.

4th: GB—Freeman 13-yd pass from Favre (Longwell kick), 13:32. Drive: 85 yards in 4 plays. Key play: Eugene Robinson 17-yard interception return to GB 15. DEN—Davis 1-yd run (Elam kick), 1:45. Drive: 49 yards in 5 plays. Key play: Davis 2-yd run plus 15-yd face mask penalty on Darius Holland to GB 32.

Favorite: Packers by 11 **Attendance:** 68,912
Field: Grass **Time:** 3:25
Start time: 3:24 PST **TV Rating**: 44.1/66 share (NBC)
MVP—Terrell Davis, Denver (30 carries, 157 yards, 3 TD)

Officials: Ed Hochuli (referee); Jim Quirk (umpire); Ben Montgomery (LJ); Doug Toole (SJ); John Schleyer (HL); Paul Baetz (BJ); Don Dorkowski (FJ).

Team Statistics

	Packers	Broncos
Touchdowns	3	4
Rushing	0	4
Passing	3	0
Returns	0	0
Field Goals made/attempted	1/1	1/1
Time of possession	27:35	32:25
First downs	21	21
Rushing	4	14
Passing	14	5
Penalty	3	2
3rd down efficiency	5/14	5/10
4th down efficiency	0/1	0/0
Total offense (net yards)	351	302
Plays	62	61
Average gain	5.6	5.0
Carries/yards	20/95	39/179
Yards per carry	4.8	4.6
Passing yards	256	123
Completions/attempts	25/42	12/22
Yards per pass	6.1	5.6
Times intercepted	1	1
Times sacked/yards lost	1/1	0/0
Return yardage	121	95
Punt returns/yards	0/0	0/0
Kickoff returns/yards	6/104	5/95
Interceptions/yards	1/17	1/0
Fumbles/lost	2/2	1/1
Penalties/yards	9/59	7/65
Punts/average	4/35.5	4/36.5
Punts blocked	0	0

Individual Statistics

Green Bay Packers

Passing	Att	Cmp	Pct.	Yds	TD	Int
Brett Favre	42	25	59.5	256	3	1

Receiving	No	Yds	Avg	Long	TD
Antonio Freeman	9	126	14.0	27	2
Dorsey Levens	6	56	9.3	22	0
Mark Chmura	4	43	10.8	21	1
Robert Brooks	3	16	5.3	10	0
William Henderson	2	9	4.5	7	0
Terry Mickens	1	6	6.0	6	0
TOTAL	25	256	10.2	27	3

Rushing	Car	Yds	Avg	Long	TD
Dorsey Levens	19	90	4.7	16	0
Robert Brooks	1	5	5.0	5	0
TOTAL	20	95	4.8	16	0

Field Goals	20-29	30-39	40-49	50-59	Total
Ryan Longwell	1-1	0-0	0-0	0-0	1-1

Punting	No	Yds	Long	Avg	In 20	TB
Craig Hentrich	4	142	51	35.5	2	0

Punt Returns	FC	Ret	Yds	Long	Avg	TD
Robert Brooks	1	0	0	0	0.0	0

Kickoff Returns	No	Yds	Long	Avg	TD
Antonio Freeman	6	104	22	17.3	0

Interceptions	No	Yds	Long	Avg	TD
Eugene Robinson	1	17	17	17.0	0

Sacks
none

Most Tackles
Leroy Butler.............7

Denver Broncos

Passing	Att	Cmp	Pct.	Yds	TD	Int
John Elway	22	12	54.5	123	0	1

Receiving	No	Yds	Avg	Long	TD
Shannon Sharpe	5	38	7.6	12	0
Ed McCaffrey	2	45	22.5	36	0
Terrell Davis	2	8	4.0	4	0
Howard Griffith	1	23	23.0	23	0
Vaughn Hebron	1	5	5.0	5	0
Dwayne Carswell	1	4	4.0	4	0
TOTAL	12	123	10.2	36	0

Rushing	Car	Yds	Avg	Long	TD
Terrell Davis	30	157	5.2	27	3
John Elway	5	17	3.4	10	1
Vaughn Hebron	3	3	1.0	27	0
Howard Griffith	1	2	2.0	2	0
TOTAL	39	179	4.6	27	4

Field Goals	20-29	30-39	40-49	50-59	Total
Jason Elam	0-0	0-0	0-0	1-1	1-1

Punting	No	Yds	Long	Avg	In 20	TB
Tom Rouen	4	146	47	36.5	2	0

Punt Returns	FC	Ret	Yds	Long	Avg	TD
Darrien Gordon	2	0	0	0	0	0

Kickoff Returns	No	Yds	Long	Avg	TD
Vaughn Hebron	4	79	32	19.8	0
Keith Burns	1	16	16	16.0	0
TOTAL	5	95	32	19.0	0

Interceptions	No	Yds	Long	Avg	TD
Tyrone Braxton	1	0	0	0.0	0

Sacks
Steve Atwater...........1

Most Tackles
Four tied with 6 each.

Super Bowl Finalists' Playoff Statistics

Green Bay (2-1)

Passing	Att	Cmp	Pct.	Yds	TD	Rating
Brett Favre	97	56	57.7	668	5	83.2

Interceptions: Favre 3.

Receiving	No	Yds	Avg	Long	TD
Antonio Freeman	17	308	18.1	40	3
Dorsey Levens	14	112	8.0	22	0
Mark Chmura	8	81	10.1	21	2
Robert Brooks	7	73	10.4	21	0
William Henderson	5	24	4.8	7	0
Derrick Mayes	3	47	15.7	23	0
Tyrone Davis	1	17	17.0	17	0
Terry Mickens	1	6	6.0	6	0
TOTAL	56	668	11.9	40	5

Rushing	Car	Yds	Avg	Long	TD
Dorsey Levens	71	316	4.5	21	2
William Henderson	5	6	1.2	3	0
Robert Brooks	1	5	5.0	5	0
Brett Favre	7	-8	-1.1	6	0
TOTAL	84	319	3.8	21	2

Touchdowns	TD	Run	Rec	Ret	Pts
Antonio Freeman	3	0	3	0	18
Mark Chmura	2	0	2	0	12
Dorsey Levens	2	2	0	0	12
TOTAL	7	2	5	0	42

Kicking	PAT/Att	FG/Att	Lg	Pts
Ryan Longwell	6/6	6/7	43	24

Punts	No	Yds	Long	Avg	In20
Craig Hentrich	14	538	52	38.4	10

Interceptions		Sacks	
Eugene Robinson	2	Keith McKenzie	3
Mike Prior	1	LeRoy Butler	1
Tyrone Williams	1	Bernardo Harris	1
		Reggie White	1

Denver (4-0)

Passing	Att	Cmp	Pct.	Yds	TD	Rate
John Elway	96	56	58.3	726	3	83.9

Interceptions: Elway 2.

Receiving	No	Yds	Avg	Long	TD
Ed McCaffrey	12	171	14.3	43	1
Shannon Sharpe	12	149	12.4	23	0
Rod Smith	11	205	18.6	43-td	1
Terrell Davis	8	38	4.8	17	0
Howard Griffith	5	58	11.6	23	1
Willie Green	3	51	17.0	22	0
Dwayne Carswell	2	30	15.0	26	0
Vaughn Hebron	2	30	15.0	26	0
Derek Loville	1	10	10.0	10	0
TOTAL	56	726	12.3	43	3

Rushing	Car	Yds	Avg	Long	TD
Terrell Davis	112	581	5.2	59	8
Derek Loville	13	103	7.9	44	2
Vaughn Hebron	11	28	2.5	6-td	1
John Elway	9	25	2.8	10	1
Howard Griffith	5	11	2.2	4	0
TOTAL	150	748	4.1	59	12

Touchdowns	TD	Run	Rec	Ret	Pts
Terrell Davis	8	8	0	0	48
Derek Loville	2	2	0	0	12
John Elway	1	1	0	0	6
Howard Griffith	1	0	1	0	6
Vaughn Hebron	1	1	0	0	6
Ed McCaffrey	1	0	1	0	6
Rod Smith	1	0	1	0	6
TOTAL	15	12	3	0	90

Kicking	PAT/Att	FG/Att	Lg	Pts
Jason Elam	15/15	2/2	51	21

Punts	No	Yds	Long	Avg	In20
Tom Rouen	17	619	53	36.4	6

Most Interceptions		Most Sacks	
Tyrone Braxton	2	Neil Smith	3
		Alfred Williams	2

Packers' 1997 Schedule

Date	Regular Season (13-3)	Result	W-L
Sept. 1*	Chicago (0-0)	W, 38-24	1-0
Sept. 7	at Philadelphia (0-1)	L, 9-10	1-1
Sept. 14	Miami (2-0)	W, 23-18	2-1
Sept. 21	Minnesota (2-1)	W, 38-32	3-1
Sept. 28	at Detroit (2-2)	L, 15-26	3-2
Oct. 5	Tampa Bay (5-0)	W, 21-16	4-2
Oct. 12	at Chicago (0-6)	W, 24-23	5-2
Oct. 19	OPEN DATE	—	—
Oct. 27*	at New England (5-2)	W, 28-10	6-2
Nov. 2	Detroit (4-4)	W, 20-10	7-2
Nov. 9	St. Louis (2-7)	W, 17-7	8-2
Nov. 16	at Indianapolis (0-10)	L, 38-41	8-3
Nov. 23	Dallas (6-5)	W, 45-17	9-3
Dec. 1*	at Minnesota (8-4)	W, 27-11	10-3
Dec. 7	at Tampa Bay (9-4)	W, 17-6	11-3
Dec.14	at Carolina (7-7)	W, 31-10	12-3
Dec. 20†	Buffalo (6-9)	W, 31-21	13-3
Date	**Playoffs (2-1)**	**Result**	**W-L**
Dec. 28	Bye	—	—
Jan. 4	Tampa Bay (11-6)	W, 21-7	14-3
Jan. 11	at San Francisco (14-3)	W, 23-10	15-3
Jan. 25	at Denver (15-4)	L, 24-31	15-4

*Monday; †Saturday.

Broncos' 1997 Schedule

Date	Regular Season (12-4)	Results	W-L
Aug. 31	Kansas City (0-0)	W, 19-3	1-0
Sept. 7	at Seattle (0-1)	W, 35-14	2-0
Sept. 14	St. Louis (1-1)	W, 35-14	3-0
Sept. 21	Cincinnati (1-1)	W, 38-20	4-0
Sept. 28	at Atlanta (0-4)	W, 29-21	5-0
Oct. 6*	New England (4-0)	W, 34-13	6-0
Oct. 12	OPEN DATE	—	—
Oct. 19	at Oakland (2-4)	L, 25-28	6-1
Oct. 26	at Buffalo (4-3)	W, 23-20	7-1
Nov. 2	Seattle (5-3)	W, 30-27	8-1
Nov. 9	Carolina (5-4)	W, 34-0	9-1
Nov. 16	at Kansas City (7-3)	L, 22-24	9-2
Nov. 24*	Oakland (4-7)	W, 31-3	10-2
Nov. 30	at San Diego (4-8)	W, 38-28	11-2
Dec. 7	at Pittsburgh (9-4)	L, 24-35	11-3
Dec. 15*	at San Francisco (12-2)	L, 17-34	11-4
Dec. 21	San Diego (4-11)	W, 38-3	12-4
Date	**Playoffs (4-0)**	**Result**	**W-L**
Dec. 27†	Jacksonville (11-5)	W, 42-17	13-4
Jan. 4	at Kansas City (13-3)	W, 14-10	14-4
Jan. 11	at Pittsburgh (12-5)	W, 24-21	15-4
Jan. 25	Green Bay (15-3)	W, 31-24	16-4

*Monday; †Saturday.

NFL Pro Bowl

48th NFL Pro Bowl Game and 28th AFC-NFC contest (NFC leads series, 15-13). **Date:** Feb. 1 at Aloha Stadium in Honolulu. **Attendance**— 49,995. **Coaches:** Bill Cowher, Pittsburgh (AFC) and Steve Mariucci (NFC). **Player of the Game:** QB Warren Moon of Seattle who was 4 of 8 for 89 yards and rushed for one touchdown.

NFC	7	14	0	3—	**24**
AFC	7	0	7	15—	**29**

1st: NFC—Herman Moore 22-yd pass from Steve Young (Jason Hanson kick), 9:35; AFC—Andre Rison 17-yd pass from Mark Brunell (Mike Hollis kick), :30.

2nd: NFC—Rob Moore 36-yd pass from Young (Hanson kick), 12:10; NFC—Dorsey Levens 12-yd run (Hanson kick), 1:36.

3rd: AFC—Jimmy Smith 14-yd pass from Drew Bledsoe (Hollis kick), 11:31.

4th: NFC—Hanson 35-yd FG, 14:19; AFC—Hollis 48-yd FG, 8:51; AFC—Eddie George 4-yd run (pass failed), 2:31; AFC—Warren Moon 1-yd run, 1:49 (pass failed).

STARTING LINEUPS

As voted on by NFL players and coaches.

American Conference

Pos	Offense	Pos	Defense
WR	Tim Brown, Oak.	E	Bruce Smith, Buf.
WR	Yancey Thigpen, Pit.	E	Neil Smith, Den.
TE	Shannon Sharpe, Den.	T	Ted Washington, Buf.
T	Tony Boselli, Jax.	T	Joel Steed, Pit.
T	Jonathan Ogden, Bal.	LB	Bryce Paup, Buf.
G	Bruce Matthews, Tenn.	LB	Chris Slade, NE
G	Will Shields, KC	LB	Levon Kirkland, Pit.
C	Dermontti Dawson, Pit.	CB	Dale Carter, KC
QB	John Elway, Den.	CB	Aaron Glenn, NYJ
RB	Terrell Davis, Den.	S	Carnell Lake, Pit.
RB	Jerome Bettis, Pit.	S	Darryl Williams, Sea.
K	Mike Hollis, Jax.	P	Bryan Barker, Jax.
KR	Eric Metcalf, SD	ST	Larry Whigham, NE

Note: QB Elway was injured and unable to play.

Reserves

Offense: WR—Andre Rison, KC and Jimmy Smith, Jax.; **TE**—Ben Coates, NE; **T**—Bruce Armstrong, NE; **G**—Ruben Brown, Buf.; **C**—Tom Nalen, Den.; **QB**—Drew Bledsoe, NE and Mark Brunell, Jax.; **RB**—Eddie George, Tenn.; **FB**—Kimble Anders, KC.

Defense: E—Michael Sinclair, Sea.; **T**—Chester McGlockton, Oak.; **LB**—Derrick Thomas, KC and Junior Seau, SD; **CB**—James Hasty, KC; **S**—Blaine Bishop, Tenn.

Replacements: OFFENSE—QB Warren Moon. for Elway. NEED PLAYER—Ray Lewis, Balt., LB.

National Conference

Pos	Offense	Pos	Defense
WR	Herman Moore, Det.	E	Michael Strahan, NYG
WR	Cris Carter, Minn.	E	Reggie White, GB
TE	Wesley Walls, Car.	T	John Randle, Minn.
T	Willie Roaf, NO	T	Dana Stubblefield, SF
T	Todd Steussie, Minn.	LB	Jessie Armstead, NYG
G	R. McDaniel, Minn.	LB	Ken Harvey, Wash.
G	Larry Allen, Dal.	LB	Hardy Nickerson, TB
C	Kevin Glover, Det.	CB	A. Williams, Ariz.
QB	Brett Favre, GB	CB	Deion Sanders, Dal.
RB	Barry Sanders, Det.	S	Merton Hanks, SF
RB	Dorsey Levens, GB	S	Leroy Butler, GB
K	Jason Hanson, Det.	P	Matt Turk, Wash.
KR	Michael Bates, Car.	ST	Travis Jervey, GB

Note: QB Favre, LB Harvey and CB Sanders were injured and unable to play.

Reserves

Offense: WR—Rob Moore, Ariz. and Irving Fryar, Phila.; **TE**—Mark Chmura, GB; **T**— Erik Williams, Dal.; **G**—Kevin Gogan, SF; **C**— Tony Mayberry, TB; **QB**—Steve Young, SF and Trent Dilfer, TB; **RB**—Warrick Dunn, TB; **FB**—Mike Alstott, TB.

Defense: E—Chris Doleman, SF; **T**—Warren Sapp, TB; **LB**—Derrick Brooks, TB and Jessie Tuggle, Atl.; **CB**—Darrell Green, Wash.; **S**—Darren Woodson, Dal.

Replacements: OFFENSE—QB Chris Chandler for Favre. DEFENSE—LB Lee Woodall, SF for Harvey; CB Cris Dishman, Wash. for Sanders; S John Lynch, TB for Woodson. NEED PLAYER—Ken Norton Jr., Dal., LB.

Annual Awards

The NFL does not sanction any of the major postseason awards for players and coaches, but many are given out. Among the presenters for the 1997 regular season were AP, The Maxwell Football Club of Philadelphia, *The Sporting News* and the Pro Football Writers of America. Conference Most Valuable Player awards were also issued by the NFL Players Association.

Most Valuable Player

NFL Barry Sanders, Detroit, RB .....AP*, PFWA, Max, *TSN*
& Brett Favre, Green Bay, QB ....AP*

*For the first time in history, two players tied for the AP award. Sanders and Favre each received 18 of the possible 48 votes.

Offensive Player of the Year

NFL Barry Sanders ....AP, PFWA

Defensive Player of the Year

NFL Dana Stubblefield, San Francisco, DT ....AP, PFWA

Rookies of the Year

NFL	Warrick Dunn, Tampa Bay, RB	PFWA, *TSN*
AFC	Corey Dillon, Cincinnati, RB	NFLPA
NFC	Warrick Dunn	NFLPA
Offense	Warrick Dunn	AP, PFWA
Defense	Peter Boulware, Baltimore, LB	AP, PFWA

Coaches of the Year

NFL Jim Fassel, N.Y. Giants ....AP, *TSN*, PFWA
& Tony Dungee, Tampa Bay ....Max

1997 All-NFL Team

The 1997 All-NFL team combining the All-Pro selections of the Associated Press, *The Sporting News (TSN)* and the Pro Football Writers of America (PFWA). Holdovers from the 1996 All-NFL Team in **bold** type.

Offense

Pos	Player	Selectors
WR—	**Herman Moore**, Detroit	AP, PFWA, *TSN*
WR—	Rob Moore, Arizona	AP, PFWA
WR—	Tim Brown, Oakland	*TSN*
TE—	**Shannon Sharpe**, Denver	AP, PFWA, *TSN*
T—	Tony Boselli, Jacksonville	AP, PFWA, *TSN*
T—	Jonathan Ogden, Baltimore	AP, PFWA, *TSN*
G—	Dave Szott, Kansas City	AP, PFWA
G—	**Larry Allen**, Dallas	AP, PFWA, *TSN*
G—	**Randall McDaniel**, Minnesota	*TSN*
C—	**Dermontti Dawson**, Pittsburgh	AP, *TSN*, PFWA
QB—	**Brett Favre**, Green Bay	AP, PFWA, *TSN*
RB—	**Barry Sanders**, Detroit	AP, PFWA, *TSN*
RB—	**Terrell Davis**, Denver	AP, PFWA, *TSN*
FB—	**Mike Alstott**, Tampa Bay	AP

Defense

Pos	Player	Selectors
DE—	**Bruce Smith**, Buffalo	AP, PFWA, *TSN*
DE—	Michael Strahan, N.Y. Giants	AP, PFWA, *TSN*
DT—	Dana Stubblefield, San Francisco	AP, PFWA, *TSN*
DT—	**John Randle**, Minnesota	AP, PFWA, *TSN*
LB—	Jessie Armstead, N.Y. Giants	AP, PFWA, *TSN*
LB—	John Mobley, Denver	AP, PFWA, *TSN*
LB—	Levon Kirkland, Pittsburgh	AP, PFWA, *TSN*
LB—	Hardy Nickerson, Tampa Bay	AP
CB—	**Aeneas Williams**, Arizona	AP, PFWA, *TSN*
CB—	**Deion Sanders**, Dallas	AP, PFWA, *TSN*
S—	Carnell Lake, Pittsburgh	AP, PFWA, *TSN*
S—	**LeRoy Butler**, Green Bay	AP, PFWA, *TSN*

Specialists

Pos	Player	Selectors
PK—	Pete Stoyanovich, Kansas City	PFWA
PK—	Richie Cunningham, Dallas	AP, *TSN*
P—	Bryan Barker, Jacksonville	AP, PFWA
P—	**Matt Turk**, Washington	*TSN*
KR—	**Michael Bates**, Carolina	PFWA, *TSN*
KR—	**Eric Metcalf**, San Diego	AP
PR—	Darrien Gordon, Denver	PFWA, *TSN*
ST—	Travis Jervey, Green Bay	PFWA

1998 College Draft

First and second round selections at the 63rd annual NFL College Draft held April 18-19, 1998, in New York City. 11 underclassmen were among the first 61 players chosen and are listed in capital LETTERS.

First Round

No	Team	Player	Pos
1	Indianapolis	Peyton Manning, Tennessee	QB
2	**a**-San Diego	RYAN LEAF, Washington St.	QB
3	**b**-Arizona	Andre Wadsworth, Florida St.	DE
4	Oakland	CHARLES WOODSON, Michigan	CB
5	Chicago	CURTIS ENIS, Penn St.	RB
6	St. Louis	Grant Wistrom, Nebraska	DE
7	New Orleans	Kyle Turley, San Diego St.	OT
8	Dallas	Greg Ellis, North Carolina	DE
9	**c**-Jacksonville	Fred Taylor, Florida	RB
10	Baltimore	Duane Starks, Miami-FL	CB
11	Philadelphia	Tra Thomas, Florida St.	OT
12	Atlanta	Keith Brooking, Georgia Tech	LB
13	Cincinnati	TAKEO SPIKES, Auburn	LB
14	Carolina	Jason Peter, Nebraska	DT
15	Seattle	ANTHONY SIMMONS, Clemson	LB
16	Tennessee	Kevin Dyson, Utah	WR
17	**d**-Cincinnati	Brian Simmons, North Carolina	LB
18	**e**-New England	Robert Edwards, Georgia	RB
19	**f**-Green Bay	Vonnie Holliday, North Carolina	DT
20	Detroit	Terry Fair, Tennessee	CB
21	Minnesota	RANDY MOSS, Marshall	WR
22	New England	Tebucky Jones, Syracuse	S
23	**g**-Oakland	MO COLLINS, Florida	OT
24	NY Giants	Shaun Williams, UCLA	S
25	Jacksonville	Donovin Darius, Syracuse	S
26	Pittsburgh	ALAN FANECA, LSU	OG
27	Kansas City	Victor Riley, Auburn	OG
28	San Francisco	R.W. MCQUARTERS, Okla. St.	CB
29	**h**-Miami	John Avery, Mississippi	RB
30	Denver	Marcus Nash, Tennessee	WR

Acquired picks: a—from Arizona; **b**— from San Diego; **c**—from Buffalo; **d**—from Washington; **e**—from NY Jets; **f**—from Miami; **g**—from Tampa Bay; **h**—from Green Bay.

Second Round

No	Team	Player	Pos
31	**i**-Oakland	Leon Bender, Washington St.	DT
32	Indianapolis	Jerome Pathon, Washington	WR
33	**j**-Arizona	Corey Chavous, Vanderbilt	CB
34	**k**-Tampa Bay	JACQUEZ GREEN, Florida	WR
35	Chicago	Tony Parrish, Washington	S
36	Arizona	Anthony Clement, SW Louisiana	OT
37	St. Louis	Robert Holcombe, Illinois	RB
38	Dallas	Flozell Adams, Michigan St.	OT
39	Buffalo	Sam Cowart, Florida St.	LB
40	New Orleans	Cameron Cleeland, Washington	TE
41	**l**-Pittsburgh	Jeremy Staat, Arizona St.	DT
42	Baltimore	Pat Johnson, Oregon	WR
43	Cincinnati	Artell Hawkins, Cincinnati	CB
44	**m**-Miami	Patrick Surtain, Southern Miss.	CB
45	**n**-Tampa Bay	Brian Kelly, USC	CB
46	Tennessee	Samari Rolle, Florida St.	CB
47	Seattle	Todd Weiner, Kansas St.	OT
48	Washington	Stephen Alexander, Oklahoma	TE
49	Miami	Kenny Mixon, LSU	DE
50	Detroit	Germane Crowell, Virginia	WR
51	Minnesota	Kailee Wong, Stanford	DE
52	**o**-New England	Tony Simmons, Wisconsin	WR
53	**p**-Atlanta	Bob Hallen, Kent St.	C
54	New England	Rod Rutledge, Alabama	TE
55	NY Giants	Joe Jurevicius, Penn St.	WR
56	**q**-NY Jets	Dorian Boose, Washington St.	DE
57	Jacksonville	Cordell Taylor, Hampton	CB
58	San Francisco	JEREMY NEWBERRY, California	C
59	**r**-San Diego	Mikhael Ricks, Stephen F. Austin	WR
60	**s**-Detroit	Charlie Batch, E. Michigan	QB
61	Denver	Eric Brown, Mississippi St.	S

Acquired picks: i—compensatory selection; **j**—from San Diego; **k**—from Tampa Bay; **l**— from Philadelphia through NY Jets; **m**—from Carolina; **n**—from Atlanta; **o**—from NY Jets; **p**—from Tampa Bay; **q**—from Pittsburgh; **r**—from Kansas City through Oakland and Tampa Bay; **s**—from Green Bay through Miami.

NFL Head Coaching Changes For 1998

As of March 1, 1998, four new head coaches were in place for the start of the '98 regular season.

AFC	Old Coach	Why Left?	New Coach	Hired	Old Job
Buffalo	Marv Levy	Retired (Dec. 31)	Wade Phillips	Jan. 5	Def. Coord., NFL Bills
Indianapolis	Lindy Infante	Fired (Dec. 22)	Jim Mora	Jan. 12	NBC TV analyst
Oakland	Joe Bugel	Fired (Jan. 6)	Jon Gruden	Jan. 22	Off. Coord., NFL Eagles
NFC	**Old Coach**	**Why Left?**	**New Coach**	**Hired**	**Old Job**
Dallas	Barry Switzer	Resigned (Jan. 9)	Chan Gailey	Feb. 12	Off. Coord., NFL Steelers

Canadian Football League

Final 1997 Standings

Division champions (*) and other playoff qualifiers (†) are noted. Number of seasons listed after each head coach refers to latest tenure with club through 1997 season.

East Division

	W	L	T	Pts	PF	PA	Pct
*Toronto	15	3	0	30	660	327	.833
†Montreal	13	5	0	26	509	532	.722
Winnipeg	4	14	0	8	443	548	.222
Hamilton	2	16	0	4	362	549	.111

1997 Head Coaches: Tor—Don Matthews (2nd year); **Mon**—Dave Ritchie (1st); **Win**—Jeff Reinebold (1st); **Ham**—Don Sutherin (4th, 1-6) replaced on Aug. 11 by Urban Bowman (1-10).

1996 East Div. standings: 1. Toronto (15-3); 2. Montreal (12-6); 3. Hamilton (8-10); 4. Ottawa (3-15).

West Division

	W	L	T	Pts	PF	PA	Pct
*Edmonton	12	6	0	24	479	400	.667
†Calgary	10	8	0	20	519	443	.556
†Saskatchewan	8	10	0	16	413	479	.444
†Brit. Columbia	8	10	0	16	429	536	.444

1997 Head Coaches: Edm—Ron Lancaster (7th season); **Calg**—Wally Buono (8th); **BC**—Adam Rita (1st); **Sask**—Jim Daley (2nd).

1996 West Div. standings: 1. Calgary (13-5); 2. Edmonton (11-7); 3. Winnipeg (9-9); 4. British Columbia (5-13); 5. Saskatchewan (5-13).

CFL Playoffs

Division Semifinals

(Nov. 2)

East: at Montreal 45............British Columbia 35
West: Saskatchewan 33..............at Calgary 30

Division Championships

(Nov. 9)

East: at Toronto 37 ....Montreal 30
West: Saskatchewan 31 ....at Edmonton 30

85th Grey Cup Championship

Sun., Nov. 16, 1997 at Commonwealth Stadium, Edmonton, Alb. (Att: 60,431)

	1	2	3	4	Final
Saskatchewan (10-10)	3	6	0	14	**23**
Toronto (16-3)	7	13	21	6	**47**

Passing: SASK— Reggie Slack 22-37–268, Kevin Mason 0-1–0; TOR— Doug Flutie 30-38–352.

Rushing: SASK— Shawn Daniels 9-35, Mike Saunders 7-26, Slack 1-1; TOR— Robert Drummond 16-128, Mike Clemons 6-45, Flutie 5-35.

Receiving: SASK— Donald Narcisse 7-60, Saunders 6-103, Curtis Mayfield 4-55, Dan Farthing 4-42, Rick Walters 1-8; TOR— Paul Masotti 6-102, Drummond 6-59, Duane Dmytryshyn 6-56, Derrell Mitchell 5-58, Clemons 5-53, Norm Casola 1-13, Andre Kirwan 1-11.

Most Outstanding Player: Doug Flutie, Toronto, QB (Passing— 30 for 38, 352 yds; 3 TD, 1 Int; Rushing—5 carries for 35 yds, 1 TD).

Most Outstanding Canadian: Paul Masotti, Toronto, WR (6 catches for 102 yards).

All-CFL Team

The All-CFL team as selected by a Football Reporters of Canada panel. Holdovers from the 1996 team are in **bold** type.

	Offense		Defense
WR	Milt Stegall, Win.	E	Elfrid Payton, Mon.
WR	Alfred Jackson, B.C.	E	Bobby Jurasin, Sask
T	Neal Fort, Mon.	T	**Rob Waldrop**, Tor.
T	Uzooma Okeke, Mon.	T	Doug Petersen, Mon.
G	Pierre Vercheval, Tor.	LB	**Willie Pless**, Edm.
G	**Fred Childress**, Calg.	LB	Shonte Peoples, Win.
C	**Mike Kiselak**, Tor.	LB	Maurice Kelly, B.C.
QB	**Doug Flutie**, Tor.	CB	Kavis Reed, Edm.
RB	Mike Pringle, Mon.	CB	**Marvin Coleman**, Calg.
RB	**Robert Drummond**, Tor.	DB	**Glenn Rogers**, Edm.
SB	Derrell Mitchell, Tor.	DB	Johnnie Harris, Tor.
SB	**Darren Flutie**, Edm.	S	Lester Smith, Tor.

Specialists
PK—Mike Vanderjagt, Tor.
P—Mike Vanderjagt, Tor.
Special Teams—Mike Clemons, Tor.

Most Outstanding Awards

Player	Doug Flutie, Toronto, QB
Canadian	Sean Millington, Brit. Columbia, FB
Offensive Lineman	Mike Kiselak, Toronto, C
Defensive Player	Willie Pless, Edmonton, LB
Rookie	Darrell Mitchell, Toronto, SB
Tom Pate Award (Sportsmanship)	Mark McLoughlin, Calg., K
Coach	Don Matthews, Toronto

Regular Season Individual Leaders

Passing Efficiency

(Minimum of 200 attempts)

	Att	Cmp	Cmp Pct	Yds	Avg Gain	Tds	TD Pct	Long	Int	Int Pct	Rating
Doug Flutie, Tor.	673	430	63.9	5505	8.2	47	7.0	78	24	3.6	97.8
Jeff Garcia, Calg	566	354	62.5	4573	8.1	33	5.8	52	14	2.5	97.0
Damon Allen, B.C.	583	378	64.8	4653	8.0	21	3.6	73	11	1.9	93.5
Tracy Ham, Mon.	460	261	56.7	3687	8.0	23	5.0	65	12	2.6	88.6
Danny McManus, Edm.	488	293	60.0	4099	8.4	22	4.5	71	19	3.9	85.9
Anthony Calvillo, Ham.	278	160	57.6	2177	7.8	12	4.3	69	11	4.0	80.6
Reggie Slack, Sask.	326	172	52.8	2423	7.4	9	2.8	86	13	4.0	69.8
Chris Vargas, Win.	385	201	52.2	2618	6.8	15	3.9	105	20	5.2	65.3

Rushing

	Car	Yds	Avg	Long	TD
Mike Pringle, Mon.	306	1775	5.8	60	12
Robert Drummond, Tor.	181	1134	6.3	78	12
Ronald Williams, Win.	211	1120	5.3	52	16
Kelvin Anderson, Calg.	246	1088	4.4	34	9
Sean Millington, B.C.	153	865	5.7	54	5
Damon Allen, B.C.	111	837	7.5	28	8
Jeff Garcia, Calg.	135	727	5.4	28	7
Eric Blount, Edm.	177	672	3.8	24	0
Archie Amerson, Ham.	144	630	4.4	64	4
Mike Saunders, Sask.	132	588	4.5	36	5
Tracy Ham, Mon.	82	584	7.1	41	6
Doug Flutie, Tor.	92	542	5.9	34	5
Robert Mimbs, Sask.	113	493	4.4	26	2
Reggie Slack, Sask.	53	406	7.7	36	4
Kevin Mason, Sask.	53	387	7.3	40	3

Receiving

	Rec	Yds	Avg	Long	TD
Milt Stegall, Win.	61	1616	26.5	105	14
Derrell Mitchell, Tor.	77	1457	18.9	71	17
Chris Armstrong, Mon.	80	1411	17.6	65	12
Alfred Jackson, B.C.	79	1322	16.7	73	10
Darren Flutie, Edm.	89	1303	14.6	51	9
Jock Climie, Mon.	89	1214	13.6	43	6
Vince Danielsen, Calg.	91	1174	12.9	52	6
Mike Clemons, Tor.	122	1085	8.9	56	10
Robert Gordon, Edm.	71	1073	15.1	39	7
Terry Vaughn, Calg.	81	1020	12.6	37	9
Paul Masotti, Tor.	77	1011	13.1	51	5
Dan Farthing, Sask.	58	959	16.5	56	4
Donald Narcisse, Sask.	64	950	14.8	47	5
Travis Moore, Calg.	72	931	12.9	41	6
Allen Pitts, Calg.	53	885	16.7	43	8

Touchdowns

	TD	Rush	Rec	Ret	Pts
Robert Drummond, Tor.	18	12	6	0	108
Derrell Mitchell, Tor.	17	0	17	0	102
Ronald Williams, Win	16	16	0	0	96
Mike Clemons, Tor	15	4	10	1	90
Milt Stegall, Win	14	0	14	0	84
Michael Pringle, Mon	13	12	1	0	78
Tony Burse, Edm	13	13	0	0	78
Chris Armstrong, Mon	12	0	12	0	72
Kelvin Anderson, Calg	11	9	2	0	66
Alfred Jackson, B.C.	10	0	10	0	60

Kicking

	PAT	FG	S	Pts
Mike Vanderjagt, Tor.	77/77	33/43	14	190
Sean Fleming, Edm	41/41	41/56	23	187
Mark McLoughlin, Calg	50/50	39/51	7	174
Terry Baker, Mon	50/50	34/52	17	169
Paul McCallum, Sask.	34/34	40/57	11	165
Troy Westwood, Win	40/40	39/54	7	164
Lui Passaglia, B.C.	43/43	35/45	7	155
Paul Osbaldiston, Ham	31/31	24/42	15	118

Punting

	No	Yds	Lg	Avg
Mike Vanderjagt, Tor	118	5303	80	44.9
Anthony Martino, Calg	121	5396	79	44.6
Terry Baker, Mon	111	4932	80	44.4
Paul Osbaldiston, Ham	147	6411	82	43.6
Robert Cameron, Win	143	6192	67	43.3
Lui Passaglia, B.C.	114	4703	76	41.3
Paul McCallum, Sask	135	5568	79	41.2
Sean Fleming, Edm.	115	4667	91	40.6

Sacks

	Sacks
Elfrid Payton, Mon	14
Willie Whitehead, Ham	13
Shonte Peoples, Win	13
Bobby Jurasin. Sask	10
Troy Alexander, Sask.	10
Malvin Hunter, Edm	9
Joe Fleming, B.C.	9
Virgil Robertson, B.C.	9

Interceptions

	No	Yds	Lg	TD
Orlando Steinauer, Ham	7	184	82	1
Kavis Reed, Edm	7	183	59	2
Lester Smith, Tor	6	104	42	1
Glenn Rogers, Edm	6	94	34	0
Brandon Hamilton, Win	5	105	43	1
Tommy Henry, Edm	5	100	45	0
Adrion Smith, Tor.	5	73	37	1
Johnnie Harris, Tor.	5	72	53	0
Rob Hitchcock, Ham	5	43	29	0
Doug Craft, Mon	5	2	2	0

NFL Europe

Final 1998 Standings

	W	L	T	Pct.	PF	PA
*Rhein	7	3	0	.700	198	142
*Frankfurt	7	3	0	.700	167	163
Amsterdam	7	3	0	.700	205	174
Barcelona	4	6	0	.400	185	190
England	3	7	0	.300	161	200
Scotland	2	8	0	.200	153	182

*Clinched World Bowl berth

Note: The teams with the top two records after the regular season advance directly to the World Bowl. Rhein and Frankfurt advanced to the World Bowl over Amsterdam because they had better head-to-head records between the three teams.

World Bowl '98

June 14, 1998 at Waldstadion in Frankfurt
(Att: 47,846)

Rhein (7-3)	10	7	7	10 –	**34**
Frankfurt (7-3)	0	7	3	0 –	**10**

MVP: Jim Arellanes, Rhein, QB (12 for 18, 263 yards and 3 TDs.)

Regular Season Individual Leaders

Passing Efficiency

(Min. 140 pass attempts)

	Att	Cmp	Cmp Pct	Yds	Avg Gain	TD	TD Pct	Long	Int	Int Pct	Rating
Mike Quinn, Rhe	264	133	50.4	1997	7.56	13	4.9	68	3	1.1	87.3
Kurt Warner, Ams	326	165	50.6	2101	6.44	15	4.6	47-td	6	1.8	78.8
Damon Huard, Fran	290	159	54.8	1857	6.40	12	4.1	72	7	2.4	78.2
Josh LaRocca, Eng	257	122	47.5	1641	6.39	14	5.4	74-td	11	4.2	68.6
Jim Ballard, Sco	212	113	53.3	1425	6.72	4	1.8	44	8	3.7	65.1

Scoring

Touchdowns	TD	Rus	Rec	Ret	Pts
Reggie Jones, Eng	7	0	7	0	42
Reggie Brooks, Bar	6	6	0	0	36
Malcolm Thomas, Ams	6	5	1	0	36
Derrick Clark, Rhe	6	6	0	0	36
Mario Bailey, Fran	6	0	6	0	36

Kicking	PAT	FG/FGA	Lg	Pts
M. Burgsmuller, Rhe	21/21	12/13	36	57
Gary Parker, Sco	12/13	13/16	31	51
Silvio Diliberto, Ams	16/18	11/15	44	49
Jess Angoy, Bar	16/18	9/15	46	43
Ralf Kleinmann, Fran	17/20	8/16	46	41

Rushing

	Car	Yards	Avg	Long	TD
Derrick Clark, Rhe	177	739	4.2	44	6
Malcolm Thomas, Ams	150	664	4.4	33	5
Jermaine Chaney, Fran	137	491	3.6	24	2
Carey Bender, Sco	108	441	4.1	44	0
Ralph Dawkins, Ams	104	435	4.2	23	2

Receptions

	No	Yards	Avg	Long	TD
Jason Shelley, Ams	42	559	13.3	46	2
Marcus Robinson, Rhe	39	811	20.8	68	5
Mario Bailey, Fran	38	544	14.3	72	6
Joe Douglass, Ams	38	499	13.1	47-td	5

Two tied with 36 each.

Punting

	No	Yards	Avg	Long	In20
Brian Greenfield, Eng	48	2170	45.2	64	13
Nate Cochran, Rhe	50	2099	42.0	69	17
Jeff Beckley, Bar	67	2745	41.0	61	23
Bill Kushner, Fran	54	2184	40.4	59	12
David Wing, Sco	53	1998	37.7	61	15
Will Brice, Ams	40	1478	37.0	63	14

Sacks

	No
Ed Philion, Rhe	9
Josh Taves, Bar	9
Chick Osborne, Ams	8
Uhuru Hamiter, Eng	7
Mike Croel, Rhe	6
Ben Williams, Eng	5½
Brad Keeney, Sco	5½

Interceptions

	No	Yds	Long	TD
Richard Jones, Rhe	4	114	30	0
Kenyan Branscomb, Fran	4	7	5	0
Dexter Seigler, Ams	3	99	52	0
George McCullough, Bar	3	89	36	1
Chris Hall, Fran	3	67	67-td	1
Kory Blackwell, Sco	3	65	32	1
Greg Evans, Fran	3	52	23	0
Kerry Joseph, Rhe	3	25	25	0

All-NFL Europe League Team

The All-NFL Europe League Team as selected by members of the NFL Europe media.

Pos	Offense	Pos	Defense
QB	Mike Quinn, Rhe	DE	Josh Taves, Bar
RB	Malcolm Thomas, Ams	DT	Chick Osborne, Ams
RB	Derrick Clark, Rhe	DT	Ed Philion, Rhe
WR	Marcus Robinson, Rhe	DE	Uhuru Hamiter, Eng
WR	Mario Bailey, Fran	LB	Hillary Butler, Fran
TE	Vince Marrow, Fran	LB	Juan Long, Bar
G	Joe Andruzzi, Sco	LB	Rich Yurkiewicz, Ams
G	Bob Kronenberg, Rhe	CB	Richard Jones, Rhe
C	Ben Lynch, Fran	CB	Dexter Siegler, Ams
T	Derek West, Rhe	S	Chris Hall, Fran
T	Mike Rockwood, Sco	S	Kerry Joseph, Rhe

Pos	Special Teams
K	Manfred Burgsmuller, Rhe
P	Brian Greenfield, Eng
Spec.	Joe Douglass, Ams

Annual Awards

Offensive MVP	Marcus Robinson, Rhein, WR
Defensive MVP	Josh Taves, Barcelona, DE
Coach of the Year	Dick Curl, Frankfurt

Arena Football

Final 1998 Standings

Division champions (*) and playoff qualifiers (†) are noted; top eight seeds advance to the playoffs.

American Conference

Central Division

	W	L	T	Pct.	PF	PA
*Houston	8	6	0	.571	734	732
Milwaukee	7	7	0	.500	719	718
Iowa	5	9	0	.357	582	716
Grand Rapids	3	11	0	.214	550	710

Western Division

	W	L	T	Pct.	PF	PA
*Arizona	10	4	0	.714	786	650
†San Jose	7	7	0	.500	659	643
Portland	4	10	0	.286	677	762

National Conference

Eastern Division

	W	L	T	Pct.	PF	PA
*Albany	10	4	0	.714	793	692
†New Jersey	8	6	0	.571	679	699
New York	3	11	0	.214	568	717

Southern Division

	W	L	T	Pct.	PF	PA
*Tampa Bay	12	2	0	.857	794	513
†Nashville	9	5	0	.643	711	659
†Orlando	9	5	0	.643	655	623
Florida	3	11	0	.214	637	710

Playoffs

First Round

Arizona 50 .... Houston 36
Orlando 58 .... Nashville 43
New Jersey 66 .... Albany 59
Tampa Bay 65 .... San Jose 46

Semifinals

Tampa Bay 49 .... New Jersey 23
Orlando 38 .... Arizona 33

ArenaBowl XII

August 23, 1998 at the Tampa Bay Ice Palace
(Att: 17,222)

	1	2	3	4	Final
Orlando	10	14	26	12	**62**
Tampa Bay	14	3	8	6	**31**

MVP: Rick Hamilton, Orlando, RB (6 rushes for 82 yards and 3 TDs.)

Regular Season Individual Leaders

Passing Efficiency

	Att	Cmp	Cmp Pct	Yds	Avg Gain	TD	TD Pct	Int	Int Pct	Rating
Mike Pawlawski, Alb	447	293	65.5	3795	8.49	74	16.6	11	2.5	121.4
Sherdrick Bonner, Ari	451	295	65.4	3571	7.92	70	15.5	8	1.8	121.0
Peter Tom Willis, TB	425	255	60.0	3411	8.03	70	16.5	10	2.4	115.3
Rickey Foggie, NJ	358	214	59.8	2812	7.85	56	15.6	9	2.5	113.3
Clint Dolezel, Hou	558	343	61.5	4228	7.58	81	14.5	17	3.0	108.5

Scoring

Touchdowns	TD	Rus	Rec	Ret	PAT	Pts
Eddie Brown, Alb	47	3	43	1	1	284
Calvin Schexnayder, Ari	45	0	44	1	0	270
Oronde Gadsden, Por	38	0	37	1	1	230
George LaFrance, TB	36	0	35	1	0	216
Gary Compton, Mil	35	1	33	1	3	216

Kicking	PAT	2PAT	FG/FGA	Pts
Kenny Stucker, Mil	77/84	0/0	18/36	131
Mike Black, NY	59/67	0/0	23/46	128
Billy Stoyanovich, SJ	74/86	0/0	17/45	125
Bjorn Nittmo, TB	84/93	0/0	13/30	123
Steve Videtich, NJ	71/83	0/1	16/28	119

Rushing

	Car	Yards	Avg	TD
Chad Dukes, Alb	65	364	5.6	10
Rick Hamilton, Orl	66	248	3.8	7
Les Barley, TB	61	232	3.8	15
Travis McDonald, Por	36	189	5.3	0
Mike Maslowski, SJ	33	149	4.5	7

Receptions

	No	Yards	Avg	TD
Calvin Schexnayder, Ari	136	1982	14.6	44
Eddie Brown, Alb	120	1673	13.9	43
Cory Fleming, Nash	112	1376	12.3	29
Alvin Ashley, NJ	102	1194	11.7	30
Gary Compton, Mil	101	1484	14.7	33

Annual Awards

Tinactin Ironman of the Year .... Chad Dukes, Alb
Offensive Player of the Year ..... Calvin Schexnayder, Ari
Defensive Player of the Year .... Johnnie Harris, TB

All-Arena First Team

Pos	
QB	Sherdrick Bonner, Arizona
FB/LB	Chad Dukes, Albany
WR/DB	Alvin Ashley, New Jersey
WR/DB	Rodney Blackshear, Houston
WR/LB	Cory Fleming, Nashville
OS	Calvin Schexnayder, Arizona
OL/DL	Joe Jacobs, Albany
OL/DL	James Baron, Nashville
OL/DL	Willie Wyatt, Tampa Bay
DS	Johnnie Harris, Tampa Bay
DS	Corey Johnson, Nashville
K	Kenny Stucker, Milwaukee

The Super Bowl

The first AFL-NFL World Championship Game, as it was originally called, was played seven months after the two leagues agreed to merge in June of 1966. It became the Super Bowl (complete with roman numerals) by the third game in 1969. The Super Bowl winner has been presented the Vince Lombardi Trophy since 1971. Lombardi, whose Green Bay teams won the first two title games, died in 1970. NFL champions (1966-69) and NFC champions (since 1970) are listed in CAPITAL letters.

Multiple winners: Dallas and San Francisco (5); Pittsburgh (4); Green Bay, Oakland-LA Raiders and Washington (3); Miami and NY Giants (2).

Bowl	Date	Winner	Head Coach	Score	Loser	Head Coach	Site
I	1/15/67	GREEN BAY	Vince Lombardi	35-10	Kansas City	Hank Stram	Los Angeles
II	1/14/68	GREEN BAY	Vince Lombardi	33-14	Oakland	John Rauch	Miami
III	1/12/69	NY Jets	Weeb Ewbank	16-7	BALTIMORE	Don Shula	Miami
IV	1/11/70	Kansas City	Hank Stram	23-7	MINNESOTA	Bud Grant	New Orleans
V	1/17/71	Baltimore	Don McCafferty	16-13	DALLAS	Tom Landry	Miami
VI	1/16/72	DALLAS	Tom Landry	24-3	Miami	Don Shula	New Orleans
VII	1/14/73	Miami	Don Shula	14-7	WASHINGTON	George Allen	Los Angeles
VIII	1/13/74	Miami	Don Shula	24-7	MINNESOTA	Bud Grant	Houston
IX	1/12/75	Pittsburgh	Chuck Noll	16-6	MINNESOTA	Bud Grant	New Orleans
X	1/18/76	Pittsburgh	Chuck Noll	21-17	DALLAS	Tom Landry	Miami
XI	1/9/77	Oakland	John Madden	32-14	MINNESOTA	Bud Grant	Pasadena
XII	1/15/78	DALLAS	Tom Landry	27-10	Denver	Red Miller	New Orleans
XIII	1/21/79	Pittsburgh	Chuck Noll	35-31	DALLAS	Tom Landry	Miami
XIV	1/20/80	Pittsburgh	Chuck Noll	31-19	LA RAMS	Ray Malavasi	Pasadena
XV	1/25/81	Oakland	Tom Flores	27-10	PHILADELPHIA	Dick Vermeil	New Orleans
XVI	1/24/82	SAN FRANCISCO	Bill Walsh	26-21	Cincinnati	Forrest Gregg	Pontiac, MI
XVII	1/30/83	WASHINGTON	Joe Gibbs	27-17	Miami	Don Shula	Pasadena
XVIII	1/22/84	LA Raiders	Tom Flores	38-9	WASHINGTON	Joe Gibbs	Tampa
XIX	1/20/85	SAN FRANCISCO	Bill Walsh	38-16	Miami	Don Shula	Stanford
XX	1/26/86	CHICAGO	Mike Ditka	46-10	New England	Raymond Berry	New Orleans
XXI	1/25/87	NY GIANTS	Bill Parcells	39-20	Denver	Dan Reeves	Pasadena
XXII	1/31/88	WASHINGTON	Joe Gibbs	42-10	Denver	Dan Reeves	San Diego
XXIII	1/22/89	SAN FRANCISCO	Bill Walsh	20-16	Cincinnati	Sam Wyche	Miami
XXIV	1/28/90	SAN FRANCISCO	George Seifert	55-10	Denver	Dan Reeves	New Orleans
XXV	1/27/91	NY GIANTS	Bill Parcells	20-19	Buffalo	Marv Levy	Tampa
XXVI	1/26/92	WASHINGTON	Joe Gibbs	37-24	Buffalo	Marv Levy	Minneapolis
XXVII	1/31/93	DALLAS	Jimmy Johnson	52-17	Buffalo	Marv Levy	Pasadena
XXVIII	1/30/94	DALLAS	Jimmy Johnson	30-13	Buffalo	Marv Levy	Atlanta
XXIX	1/29/95	SAN FRANCISCO	George Seifert	49-26	San Diego	Bobby Ross	Miami
XXX	1/28/96	DALLAS	Barry Switzer	27-17	Pittsburgh	Bill Cowher	Tempe, AZ
XXXI	1/26/97	GREEN BAY	Mike Holmgren	35-21	New England	Bill Parcells	New Orleans
XXXII	1/25/98	Denver	Mike Shanahan	31-24	GREEN BAY	Mike Holmgren	San Diego

Pete Rozelle Award (MVP)

The Most Valuable Player in the Super Bowl. Currently selected by an 11-member panel made up of national pro football writers and broadcasters chosen by the NFL. Presented by *Sport* magazine from 1967-89 and by the NFL since 1990. Named after former NFL commissioner Pete Rozelle in 1990. Winner who did not play for Super Bowl champion is in **bold** type.

Multiple winners: Joe Montana (3); Terry Bradshaw and Bart Starr (2).

Bowl	
I	Bart Starr, Green Bay, QB
II	Bart Starr, Green Bay, QB
III	Joe Namath, NY Jets, QB
IV	Len Dawson, Kansas City, QB
V	**Chuck Howley**, Dallas, LB
VI	Roger Staubach, Dallas, QB
VII	Jake Scott, Miami, S
VIII	Larry Csonka, Miami, RB
IX	Franco Harris, Pittsburgh, RB
X	Lynn Swann, Pittsburgh, WR
XI	Fred Biletnikoff, Oakland, WR
XII	Harvey Martin, Dallas, DE & Randy White, Dallas, DT
XIII	Terry Bradshaw, Pittsburgh, QB
XIV	Terry Bradshaw, Pittsburgh, QB
XV	Jim Plunkett, Oakland, QB
XVI	Joe Montana, San Francisco, QB
XVII	John Riggins, Washington, RB
XVIII	Marcus Allen, LA Raiders, RB
XIX	Joe Montana, San Francisco, QB
XX	Richard Dent, Chicago, DE
XXI	Phil Simms, NY Giants, QB
XXII	Doug Williams, Washington, QB
XXIII	Jerry Rice, San Francisco, WR
XXIV	Joe Montana, San Francisco, QB
XXV	Ottis Anderson, NY Giants, RB
XXVI	Mark Rypien, Washington, QB
XXVII	Troy Aikman, Dallas, QB
XXVIII	Emmitt Smith, Dallas, RB
XXIX	Steve Young, San Francisco, QB
XXX	Larry Brown, Dallas, CB
XXXI	Desmond Howard, Green Bay, KR
XXXII	Terrell Davis, Denver, RB

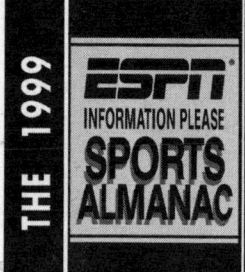

All-Time Super Bowl Leaders

Through Jan. 25, 1998; participants in Super Bowl XXXII in **bold** type.

CAREER

Passing Efficiency

		Gm	Att	Cmp	Cmp%	Yards	Avg Gain	TD	TD%	Int	Int%	Rating
1	Phil Simms, NYG	1	25	22	88.0	268	10.72	3	12.0	0	0.0	150.9
2	Steve Young, SF	2	39	26	66.7	345	8.85	6	15.4	0	0.0	134.1
3	Doug Williams, Wash.	1	29	18	62.1	340	11.72	4	13.8	1	3.4	128.1
4	Joe Montana, SF	4	122	83	68.0	1142	9.36	11	9.0	0	0.0	127.8
5	Jim Plunkett, Raiders	2	46	29	63.0	433	9.41	4	8.7	0	0.0	122.8
6	Terry Bradshaw, Pit	4	84	49	58.3	932	11.10	9	10.7	4	4.8	112.8
7	Troy Aikman, Dal	3	80	56	70.0	689	8.61	5	6.3	1	1.3	111.9
8	Bart Starr, GB	2	47	29	61.7	452	9.62	3	6.4	1	2.1	106.0
9	**Brett Favre**, GB	2	69	39	56.5	502	7.28	5	7.2	1	1.4	97.6
10	Roger Staubach, Dal	4	98	61	62.2	734	7.49	8	8.2	4	4.1	95.4

Ratings based on performance standards established for completion percentage, average gain, touchdown percentage and interception percentage. Quarterbacks are allocated points according to how their statistics measure up to those standards. Minimum 25 passing attempts.

Passing Yards

		Gm	Att	Cmp	Pct	Yds
1	Joe Montana, SF	4	122	83	68.0	1142
2	Terry Bradshaw, Pit	4	84	49	58.3	932
3	Jim Kelly, Buf	4	145	81	55.9	829
4	**John Elway**, Den	4	123	58	47.2	792
5	Roger Staubach, Dal	4	98	61	62.2	734
6	Troy Aikman, Dal	3	80	56	70.0	689
7	**Brett Favre**, GB	2	69	39	56.5	502
8	Fran Tarkenton, Min	3	89	46	51.7	489
9	Bart Starr, GB	2	47	29	61.7	452
10	Jim Plunkett, Raiders	2	46	29	63.0	433
11	Joe Theismann, Wash	2	58	31	53.4	386
12	Len Dawson, KC	2	44	28	63.6	353
13	Steve Young, SF	2	26	39	66.7	345
14	Doug Williams, Wash.	1	29	18	62.1	340
15	Dan Marino, Mia	1	50	29	58.0	318

Super Bowl Appearances

Through Super Bowl XXXII, 11 NFL teams have yet to play for the Vince Lombardi Trophy. In alphabetical order, they are: Arizona, Atlanta, Baltimore Ravens, Carolina, Cleveland, Detroit, Houston, Jacksonville, New Orleans, Seattle and Tampa Bay. Of the 20 teams that have participated, Dallas has the most appearances (8) and, along with San Francisco, has the most titles (5).

App		W	L	Pct	PF	PA
8	Dallas	5	3	.625	221	132
5	San Francisco	5	0	1.000	188	89
5	Pittsburgh	4	1	.800	120	100
5	Washington	3	2	.600	122	103
5	Miami	2	3	.400	74	103
5	Denver	1	4	.200	81	187
4	Green Bay	3	1	.750	127	76
4	Oak/LA Raiders	3	1	.750	111	66
4	Buffalo	0	4	.000	73	139
4	Minnesota	0	4	.000	34	95
2	NY Giants	2	0	1.000	59	39
2	Baltimore Colts	1	1	.500	23	29
2	Kansas City	1	1	.500	33	42
2	Cincinnati	0	2	.000	37	46
2	New England	0	2	.000	31	81
1	Chicago	1	0	1.000	46	10
1	NY Jets	1	0	1.000	16	7
1	LA Rams	0	1	.000	19	31
1	Philadelphia	0	1	.000	10	27
1	San Diego	0	1	.000	26	49

Receptions

		Gm	No	Yds	Avg	TD
1	Jerry Rice, SF	3	28	512	18.3	7
2	Andre Reed, Buf	4	27	323	12.0	0
3	Roger Craig, SF	3	20	212	10.6	3
	Thurman Thomas, Buf	4	20	144	7.2	0
5	Jay Novacek, Dal	3	17	148	8.7	2
6	Lynn Swann, Pit	4	16	364	22.8	3
7	Michael Irvin, Dal	3	16	256	16.0	2
8	Chuck Foreman, Min	3	15	139	9.3	0
9	Cliff Branch, Raiders	3	14	181	12.9	3
10	Don Beebe, Buf	3	12	171	14.3	2
	Preston Pearson, Bal-Pit-Dal	5	12	105	8.8	0
	Kenneth Davis, Buf	4	12	72	6.0	0
	Antonio Freeman, GB	2	12	231	19.3	3
14	John Stallworth, Pit	4	11	268	24.4	3
	Dan Ross, Cin	1	11	104	9.5	2

Rushing

		Gm	Car	Yds	Avg	TD
1	Franco Harris, Pit	4	101	354	3.5	4
2	Larry Csonka, Mia	3	57	297	5.2	2
3	Emmitt Smith, Dal	3	70	289	4.1	5
4	John Riggins, Wash	2	64	230	3.6	2
5	Timmy Smith, Wash	1	22	204	9.3	2
	Thurman Thomas, Buf	4	52	204	3.9	4
7	Roger Craig, SF	3	52	201	3.9	2
8	Marcus Allen, Raiders	1	20	191	9.5	2
9	Tony Dorsett, Dal	2	31	162	5.2	1
10	**Terrell Davis**, Den	1	30	157	5.2	3
11	Mark van Eeghen, Raiders	2	37	153	4.1	0
12	**Dorsey Levens**, GB	2	33	151	4.6	0
13	Kenneth Davis, Buf	4	30	145	4.8	0
14	Rocky Bleier, Pit	4	44	144	3.3	0
15	Walt Garrison, Dal	2	26	139	5.3	0

All-Purpose Yards

		Gm	Rush	Rec	Ret	Total
1	Jerry Rice, SF	3	15	512	0	527
2	Franco Harris, Pit	4	354	114	0	468
3	Roger Craig, SF	3	201	212	0	413
4	Lynn Swann, Pit	4	-7	364	34	391
5	Thurman Thomas, Buf	4	204	144	0	348
6	Emmitt Smith, Dal	3	289	56	0	345
7	**Antonio Freeman**, GB	2	0	231	104	335
8	Andre Reed, Buf	3	0	323	0	323
9	Larry Csonka, Mia	3	297	17	0	314
10	Fulton Walker, Mia	2	0	0	298	298

Scoring

Points

		Gm	TD	FG	PAT	Pts
1	Jerry Rice, SF	3	7	0	0	42
2	Emmitt Smith, Dal.	3	5	0	0	30
3	Roger Craig, SF	3	4	0	0	24
	Franco Harris, Pit	4	4	0	0	24
	Thurman Thomas, Buf	4	4	0	0	24
6	Ray Wersching, SF	2	0	5	7	22
7	Don Chandler, GB	2	0	4	8	20
8	Cliff Branch, Raiders	3	3	0	0	18
	John Stallworth, Pit	4	3	0	0	18
	Lynn Swann, Pit	4	3	0	0	18
	Ricky Watters, SF	1	3	0	0	18
	Terrell Davis, Den	1	3	0	0	18
	Antonio Freeman, GB	2	3	0	0	18
	John Elway, Den	4	3	0	0	18
15	Chris Bahr, Raiders	2	0	3	8	17

Touchdowns

		Gm	Rush	Rec	Ret	TD
1	Jerry Rice, SF	3	0	7	0	7
2	Emmitt Smith, Dal.	3	5	0	0	5
3	Roger Craig, SF	3	2	2	0	4
	Franco Harris, Pit	4	4	0	0	4
	Thurman Thomas, Buf	4	4	0	0	4
6	Cliff Branch, Raiders	3	0	3	0	3
	John Stallworth, Pit	4	0	3	0	3
	Lynn Swann, Pit	4	0	3	0	3
	Ricky Watters, SF	1	1	2	0	3
	Terrell Davis, Den	1	3	0	0	3
	Antonio Freeman, GB	2	0	3	0	3
	John Elway, Den	4	3	0	0	3

13 Twenty-two tied with 2 TDs each:
Marcus Allen, Raiders; Ottis Anderson, NYG; Pete Banaszak, Raiders; Don Beebe, Buf.; Gary Clark, Wash.; Larry Csonka, Mia.; Michael Irvin, Dal.; Butch Johnson, Dal.; Jim Kiick, Mia.; Max McGee, GB; Jim McMahon, Chi.; Bill Miller, Raiders; Joe Montana, SF; Elijah Pitts, GB; Tom Rathman, SF; John Riggins, Wash.; Gerald Riggs, Wash.; Dan Ross, Cin.; Ricky Sanders, Wash.; Timmy Smith, Wash.; John Taylor, SF and Duane Thomas, Dal.

Punting

(Minimum 10 Punts)

		Gm	No	Yds	Avg.
1	Jerrel Wilson, KC	2	11	511	46.5
2	Ray Guy, Raiders	3	14	587	41.9
3	Larry Seiple, Mia	3	15	620	41.3
4	Mike Eischeid, Oak-Min	3	17	698	41.1
5	Danny White, Dal	2	10	406	40.6

Punt Returns

(Minimum 4 returns)

		Gm	No	Yds	Avg.	TD
1	John Taylor, SF	3	6	94	15.7	0
2	Desmond Howard, GB	1	6	90	15.0	0
3	Neal Colzie, Oak	1	4	43	10.8	0
4	Dana McLemore, SF	1	5	51	10.2	0
5	Mike Fuller, Cin	1	4	35	8.8	0

Kickoff Returns

(Minimum 4 returns)

		Gm	No	Yds	Avg.	TD
1	Fulton Walker, Mia	2	8	283	35.4	1
2	Andre Coleman, SD	1	8	242	30.3	1
3	Larry Anderson, Pit	2	8	207	25.9	0
4	Desmond Howard, GB	1	4	154	38.5	1
5	Darren Carrington, Den	1	6	146	24.3	1

Interceptions

		Gm	No	Yds	TD
1	Larry Brown, Dal	2	3	77	0
	Chuck Howley, Dal	2	3	63	0
	Rod Martin, Raiders	2	3	44	0
4	Randy Beverly, NYJ	1	2	0	0
	Mel Blount, Pit	4	2	23	0
	Brad Edwards, Wash	1	2	56	0
	Thomas Everett, Dal.	1	2	22	0
	Jake Scott, Mia	3	2	63	0
	Mike Wagner, Pit.	3	2	45	0
	James Washington, Dal	2	2	25	0
	Barry Wilburn, Wash	1	2	11	0
	Eric Wright, SF	4	2	25	0

Sacks

		Gm	No
1	Charles Haley, SF-Dal	5	4½
2	**Reggie White**, GB	2	3
	Leonard Marshall, NYG	2	3
	Danny Stubbs, SF	2	3
	Jeff Wright, Buf	4	3

Four or More Super Bowl Wins

Dallas Cowboys (5)

Year	Bowl	Head Coach	Quarterback	MVP	Opponent	Score	Site
1972	VI	Tom Landry	Roger Staubach	Staubach	Miami	24-3	New Orleans
1978	XII	Tom Landry	Roger Staubach	Harvey Martin & Randy White	Denver	27-10	New Orleans
1993	XXVII	Jimmy Johnson	Troy Aikman	Aikman	Buffalo	52-17	Pasadena
1994	XXVIII	Jimmy Johnson	Troy Aikman	Emmitt Smith	Buffalo	30-13	Atlanta
1996	XXX	Barry Switzer	Troy Aikman	Larry Brown	Pittsburgh	27-17	Tempe

San Francisco 49ers (5)

Year	Bowl	Head Coach	Quarterback	MVP	Opponent	Score	Site
1982	XVI	Bill Walsh	Joe Montana	Montana	Cincinnati	26-21	Pontiac
1985	XIX	Bill Walsh	Joe Montana	Montana	Miami	38-16	Stanford
1989	XXIII	Bill Walsh	Joe Montana	Jerry Rice	Cincinnati	20-16	Miami
1990	XXIV	George Seifert	Joe Montana	Montana	Denver	55-10	New Orleans
1995	XXIX	George Seifert	Steve Young	Young	San Diego	49-26	Miami

Pittsburgh Steelers (4)

Year	Bowl	Head Coach	Quarterback	MVP	Opponent	Score	Site
1975	IX	Chuck Noll	Terry Bradshaw	Franco Harris	Minnesota	16-6	New Orleans
1976	X	Chuck Noll	Terry Bradshaw	Lynn Swann	Dallas	21-17	Miami
1979	XIII	Chuck Noll	Terry Bradshaw	Bradshaw	Dallas	35-31	Miami
1980	XIV	Chuck Noll	Terry Bradshaw	Bradshaw	LA Rams	31-19	Pasadena

SINGLE GAME

Passing

Yards Gained	Year	Att/Cmp	Yds
Joe Montana, SF vs Cin	1989	36/23	357
Doug Williams, Wash vs Den	1988	29/18	340
Joe Montana, SF vs Mia	1985	35/24	331
Steve Young, SF vs SD	1995	24/36	325
Terry Bradshaw, Pit vs Dal	1979	30/17	318
Dan Marino, Mia vs SF	1985	50/29	318
Terry Bradshaw, Pit vs Rams	1980	21/14	309
John Elway, Den vs NYG	1987	37/22	304
Ken Anderson, Cin vs SF	1982	34/25	300
Joe Montana, SF vs Den	1990	29/22	297

Touchdown Passes	Year	TD	Int
Steve Young, SF vs SD	1995	6	0
Joe Montana, SF vs Den	1990	5	0
Terry Bradshaw, Pit vs Dal	1979	4	1
Doug Williams, Wash vs Den	1988	4	1
Troy Aikman, Dal vs Buf	1993	4	0
Roger Staubach, Dal vs Pit	1979	3	1
Jim Plunkett, Raiders vs Phi	1981	3	0
Joe Montana, SF vs Mia	1985	3	0
Phil Simms, NYG vs Den	1987	3	0
Brett Favre, GB vs Den	1998	3	1

Rushing

Yards Gained	Year	Car	Yds	TD
Timmy Smith, Wash vs Den	1988	22	204	2
Marcus Allen, Raiders vs Wash	1984	20	191	2
John Riggins, Wash vs Mia	1983	38	166	1
Franco Harris, Pit vs Min.	1975	34	158	1
Terrell Davis, Den vs GB	1998	30	157	3
Larry Csonka, Mia vs Min.	1974	33	145	2
Clarence Davis, Raiders vs Min.	1977	16	137	0
Thurman Thomas, Buf vs NYG	1991	15	135	1
Emmitt Smith, Dal vs Buf	1994	30	132	2
Matt Snell, NYJ vs Bal	1969	30	121	1
Tom Matte, Bal vs NYJ	1969	11	116	0
Larry Csonka, Mia vs Wash	1973	15	112	1
Emmitt Smith, Dal vs Buf	1993	22	108	1
Ottis Anderson, NYG vs Buf	1991	21	102	1
Tony Dorsett, Dal vs Pit	1979	16	96	0
Duane Thomas, Dal vs Mia	1972	19	95	1

Scoring

Points	Year	TD	FG	PAT	Pts
Roger Craig, SF vs Mia	1985	3	0	0	18
Jerry Rice, SF vs Den	1990	3	0	0	18
Jerry Rice, SF vs SD	1995	3	0	0	18
Ricky Watters, SF vs SD	1995	3	0	0	18
Terrell Davis, Den vs GB	1998	3	0	0	18
Don Chandler, GB vs Raiders	1968	0	4	3	15

Touchdowns	Year	TD	Rush	Rec
Roger Craig, SF vs Mia	1985	3	1	2
Jerry Rice, SF vs Den	1990	3	0	3
Jerry Rice, SF vs SD	1995	3	0	3
Ricky Watters, SF vs SD	1995	3	1	2
Terrell Davis, Den vs GB	1998	3	3	0

Eighteen tied with 2 TDs each:
(In order of occurrence) Max McGee, GB; Elijah Pitts, GB; Bill Miller, Raiders; Larry Csonka, Mia.; Pete Banaszak, Raiders; John Stallworth, Pit.; Franco Harris, Pit.; Cliff Branch, Oak.; Dan Ross, Cin.; Marcus Allen, Raiders; Jim McMahon, Chi.; Ricky Sanders, Wash.; Timmy Smith, Wash.; Tom Rathman, SF; Gerald Riggs, Wash.; Michael Irvin, Dal.; Emmitt Smith, Dal. (twice); **Antonio Freeman**, GB.

Receiving

Catches	Year	No	Yds	TD
Dan Ross, Cin vs SF	1982	11	104	2
Jerry Rice, SF vs Cin	1989	11	215	1
Tony Nathan, Mia vs SF	1985	10	83	0
Jerry Rice, SF vs SD	1995	10	149	3
Andre Hastings, Pit vs Dal	1996	10	98	0
Ricky Sanders, Wash vs Den	1988	9	193	2
Antonio Freeman, GB vs Den	1998	9	126	2
George Sauer, NYJ vs Bal	1969	8	133	0
Roger Craig, SF vs Cin	1989	8	101	0
Andre Reed, Buf vs NYG	1991	8	62	0
Andre Reed, Buf vs Dal	1993	8	152	0
Ronnie Harmon, SD vs SF	1995	8	68	0
Ernie Mills, Pit vs Dal	1996	8	78	0

Yards Gained	Year	No	Yds	TD
Jerry Rice, SF vs Cin	1989	11	215	1
Ricky Sanders, Wash vs Den	1988	9	193	2
Lynn Swann, Pit vs Dal.	1976	4	161	1
Andre Reed, Buf vs Dal	1993	8	152	0
Jerry Rice, SF vs SD	1995	10	149	3
Jerry Rice, SF vs Den	1990	7	148	3
Max McGee, GB vs KC	1967	7	138	2
George Sauer, NYJ vs Bal	1969	8	133	0
Willie Gault, Chi vs NE.	1986	4	129	0
Antonio Freeman, GB vs Den	1998	9	126	2
Lynn Swann, Pit vs Dal.	1979	7	124	1

All-Purpose Yards

Yards Gained	Year	Run	Rec	Ret	Tot
Desmond Howard, GB vs NE.	1997	0	0	244	244
Andre Coleman, SD vs SF.	1995	0	0	242	242
Ricky Sanders, Wash vs Den	1988	193	-4	46	235
Antonio Freeman, GB vs Den	1998	0	126	104	230
Jerry Rice, SF vs Cin	1989	215	5	0	220
Timmy Smith, Wash vs Den	1988	204	9	0	213
Marcus Allen, Raiders vs Wash	1984	191	18	0	209
Stephen Starring, NE vs Chi.	1986	0	39	153	192
Fulton Walker, Mia vs Wash	1983	0	0	190	190
Thurman Thomas, Buf vs NYG	1991	135	55	0	190
John Riggins, Wash vs Mia	1983	166	15	0	181
Roger Craig, SF vs Cin	1989	74	101	0	175

Interceptions

	Year	No	Yds	TD
Rod Martin, Raiders vs Phi	1981	3	44	0

Six tied with two interceptions each.

Punting

(Minimum 4 punts)

	Year	No	Yds	Avg
Bryan Wagner, SD vs SF.	1995	4	195	48.8
Jerrel Wilson, KC vs Min.	1970	4	194	48.5
Jim Miller, SF vs Cin.	1982	4	185	46.3

Punt Returns

(Minimum 3 returns)

	Year	No	Yds	Avg
John Taylor, SF vs Cin	1989	3	56	18.7
Desmond Howard, GB vs NE.	1997	6	90	15.0
John Taylor, SF vs Den.	1990	3	38	12.7
Kelvin Martin, Dal vs Buf.	1993	3	35	11.7

Kickoff Returns

(Minimum 3 returns)

	Year	No	Yds	Avg
Fulton Walker, Mia vs Wash	1983	4	190	47.5
Desmond Howard, GB vs NE.	1997	4	154	38.5
Larry Anderson, Pit vs Rams	1980	5	162	32.4
Rick Upchurch, Den vs Dal	1978	3	94	31.3

Super Bowl Playoffs

The Super Bowl forced the NFL to set up pro football's first guaranteed multiple-game playoff format. Over the years, the NFL-AFL merger, the creation of two conferences comprised of three divisions each and the proliferation of wild card entries has seen the postseason field grow from four teams (1966), to six (1967-68), to eight (1969-77), to 10 (1978-81, 1983-89), to the present 12 (since 1990).

In 1968, there was a special playoff between Oakland and Kansas City which were both 12–2 and tied for first in the AFL's Western Division. In 1982, when a 57-day players' strike shortened the regular season to just nine games, playoff berths were extended to 16 teams (eight from each conference) and a 15-game tournament was played.

Note that in the following year-by-year summary, records of finalists include all games leading up to the Super Bowl; (*) indicates non-division winners or wild card teams.

1966 Season

AFL Playoffs

Championship...............Kansas City 31, at Buffalo 7

NFL Playoffs

Championship...............Green Bay 34, at Dallas 27

Super Bowl I

Jan. 15, 1967
Memorial Coliseum, Los Angeles
Favorite: Packers by 14 Attendance: 61,946

Kansas City (12-2-1)	0	10	0	0	**—10**
Green Bay (13-2)	7	7	14	7	**—35**

MVP: Green Bay QB Bart Starr (16 for 23, 250 yds, 2 TD, 1 Int)

1967 Season

AFL Playoffs

Championship ....at Oakland 40, Houston 7

NFL Playoffs

Eastern Conference ....at Dallas 52, Cleveland 14
Western Conference ....at Green Bay 28, LA Rams 7
Championship ....at Green Bay 21, Dallas 17

Super Bowl II

Jan. 14, 1968
Orange Bowl, Miami
Favorite: Packers by 13½ Attendance: 75,546

Green Bay (11-4-1)	3	13	10	7	**—33**
Oakland (14-1)	0	7	0	7	**—14**

MVP: Green Bay QB Bart Starr (13 for 24, 202 yds, 1 TD)

1968 Season

AFL Playoffs

Western Div. Playoff ....at Oakland 41, Kansas City 6
AFL Championship ....at NY Jets 27, Oakland 23

NFL Playoffs

Eastern Conference ....at Cleveland 31, Dallas 20
Western Conference ....at Baltimore 24, Minnesota 14
NFL Championship ....Baltimore 34, at Cleveland 0

Super Bowl III

Jan. 12, 1969
Orange Bowl, Miami
Favorite: Colts by 18 Attendance: 75,389

NY Jets (12-3)	0	7	6	3	**—16**
Baltimore (15-1)	0	0	0	7	**—7**

MVP: NY Jets QB Joe Namath (17 for 28, 206 yds)

1969 Season

AFL Playoffs

Inter-Division ....*Kansas City 13, at NY Jets 6
at Oakland 56, *Houston 7
AFL Championship ....Kansas City 17, at Oakland 7

NFL Playoffs

Eastern Conference ....Cleveland 38, at Dallas 14
Western Conference ....at Minnesota 23, LA Rams 20
NFL Championship ....at Minnesota 27, Cleveland 7

Super Bowl IV

Jan. 11, 1970
Tulane Stadium, New Orleans
Favorite: Vikings by 12 Attendance: 80,562

Minnesota (14-2)	0	0	7	0	**—7**
Kansas City (13-3)	3	13	7	0	**—23**

MVP: KC QB Len Dawson (12 for 17, 142 yds, 1 TD, 1 Int)

1970 Season

AFC Playoffs

First Round ....at Baltimore 17, Cincinnati 0
at Oakland 21,*Miami 14
Championship ....at Baltimore 27, Oakland 17

NFC Playoffs

First Round. ....at Dallas 5, *Detroit 0
San Francisco 17, at Minnesota 14
Championship ....Dallas 17, at San Francisco 10

Super Bowl V

Jan. 17, 1971
Orange Bowl, Miami
Favorite: Cowboys by 2½ Attendance: 79,204

Baltimore (13-2-1)	0	6	0	10	**—16**
Dallas (12-4)	3	10	0	0	**—13**

MVP: Dallas LB Chuck Howley (2 interceptions for 22 yds)

1971 Season

AFC Playoffs

First Round............Miami 27, at Kansas City 24 (OT)
*Baltimore 20, at Cleveland 3
Championship ....at Miami 21, Baltimore 0

NFC Playoffs

First Round ....Dallas 20, at Minnesota 12
at San Francisco 24,*Washington 20
Championship ....at Dallas 14, San Francisco 3

Super Bowl VI

Jan. 16, 1972
Tulane Stadium, New Orleans
Favorite: Cowboys by 6 Attendance: 81,023

Dallas (13-3)	3	7	7	7	**—24**
Miami (12-3-1)	0	3	0	0	**—3**

MVP: Dallas QB Roger Staubach (12 for 19, 119 yds, 2 TD)

1972 Season

AFC Playoffs

First Round ....at Pittsburgh 13, Oakland 7
at Miami 20, *Cleveland 14
Championship................Miami 21, at Pittsburgh 17

NFC Playoffs

First Round ....*Dallas 30, at San Francisco 28
at Washington 16, Green Bay 3
Championship ....at Washington 26, Dallas 3

Super Bowl VII

Jan. 14, 1973
Memorial Coliseum, Los Angeles
Favorite: Redskins by 1½ Attendance: 90,182

Miami (16-0)	7	7	0	0	—**14**
Washington (13-3)	0	0	0	7	—**7**

MVP: Miami safety Jake Scott (2 Interceptions for 63 yds)

1973 Season

AFC Playoffs

First Round................at Oakland 33, *Pittsburgh 14
at Miami 34, Cincinnati 16
Championship..................at Miami 27, Oakland 10

NFC Playoffs

First Round ....at Minnesota 27, *Washington 20
at Dallas 27, LA Rams 16
Championship ....Minnesota 27, at Dallas 10

Super Bowl VIII

Jan. 13, 1974
Rice Stadium, Houston
Favorite: Dolphins by 6½ Attendance: 71,882

Minnesota (14-2)	0	0	0	7	—**7**
Miami (12-4)	14	3	7	0	—**24**

MVP: Miami FB Larry Csonka (33 carries, 145 yds, 2 TD)

1974 Season

AFC Playoffs

First Round..................at Oakland 28, Miami 26
at Pittsburgh 32, *Buffalo 14
Championship.............Pittsburgh 24, at Oakland 13

NFC Playoffs

First Round ....at Minnesota 30, St.Louis 14
at LA Rams 19, *Washington 10
Championship ....at Minnesota 14, LA Rams 10

Super Bowl IX

Jan. 12, 1975
Tulane Stadium, New Orleans
Favorite: Steelers by 3 Attendance: 80,997

Pittsburgh (12-3-1)	0	2	7	7	—**16**
Minnesota (12-4)	0	0	0	6	—**6**

MVP: Pittsburgh RB Franco Harris (34 carries, 158 yds, 1 TD)

1975 Season

AFC Playoffs

First Round ....at Pittsburgh 28, Baltimore 10
at Oakland 31, *Cincinnati 28
Championship.............at Pittsburgh 16, Oakland 10

NFC Playoffs

First Round ....at LA Rams 35, St. Louis 23
*Dallas 17, at Minnesota 14
Championship ....Dallas 37, at LA Rams 7

Super Bowl X

Jan. 18, 1976
Orange Bowl, Miami
Favorite: Steelers by 6½ Attendance: 80,187

Dallas (12-4)	7	3	0	7	—**17**
Pittsburgh (14-2)	7	0	0	14	—**21**

MVP: Pittsburgh WR Lynn Swann (4 catches, 161 yds, 1 TD)

1976 Season

AFC Playoffs

First Round ....at Oakland 24, *New England 21
Pittsburgh 40, at Baltimore 14
Championship ....at Oakland 24, Pittsburgh 7

NFC Playoffs

First Round ....at Minnesota 35, *Washington 20
LA Rams 14, at Dallas 12
Championship ....at Minnesota 24, LA Rams 13

Super Bowl XI

Jan. 9, 1977
Rose Bowl, Pasadena
Favorite: Raiders by 4½ Attendance: 103,438

Oakland (15-1)	0	16	3	13	—**32**
Minnesota (13-2-1)	0	0	7	7	—**14**

MVP: Oakland WR Fred Biletnikoff (4 catches, 79 yds)

1977 Season

AFC Playoffs

First Round ....at Denver 34, Pittsburgh 21
*Oakland 37, at Baltimore 31 (OT)
Championship ....at Denver 20, Oakland 17

NFC Playoffs

First Round ....at Dallas 37, *Chicago 7
Minnesota 14, at LA Rams 7
Championship................at Dallas 23, Minnesota 6

Super Bowl XII

Jan. 15, 1978
Louisiana Superdome, New Orleans
Favorite: Cowboys by 6 Attendance: 75,583

Dallas (14-2)	10	3	7	7	—**27**
Denver (14-2)	0	0	10	0	—**10**

MVPs: Dallas DE Harvey Martin and DT Randy White (Cowboys' defense forced 8 turnovers)

A Year Later . . .

Super Bowl champions who did not qualify for the playoffs the following season.

Season		Record	Finish	Season		Record	Finish
1968	Green Bay	6-7-1	3rd in NFL Central	1982	San Francisco	3-6-0*	11th in overall NFC
1970	Kansas City	7-5-2	2nd in AFC West	1987	NY Giants	6-9-0*	5th in NFC East
1980	Pittsburgh	9-7-0	3rd in AFC Central	1988	Washington	7-9-0	3rd in NFC East
1981	Oakland	7-9-0	4th in AFC West	1991	NY Giants	8-8-0	4th in NFC East

* Seasons when player strikes interrupted schedule.

Super Bowl Playoffs (Cont.)

1978 Season

AFC Playoffs

First Round ....*Houston 17, at *Miami 9
Second Round ....Houston 31, at New England 14
at Pittsburgh 33, Denver 10
Championship................at Pittsburgh 34, Houston 5

NFC Playoffs

First Round..............at *Atlanta 14, *Philadelphia 13
Second Round ....at Dallas 27, Atlanta 20
at LA Rams 34, Minnesota 10
Championship ....Dallas 28, at LA Rams 0

Super Bowl XIII

Jan. 21, 1979
Orange Bowl, Miami
Favorite: Steelers by 4 Attendance: 79,484

Pittsburgh (16-2)	7	14	0	14	**—35**
Dallas (14-4)	7	7	3	14	**—31**

MVP: Pittsburgh QB Terry Bradshaw (17 for 30, 318 yds, 4 TD, 1 Int)

1979 Season

AFC Playoffs

First Round...................at *Houston 13, *Denver 7
Second Round.............Houston 17, at San Diego 14
at Pittsburgh 34, Miami 14
Championship ....at Pittsburgh 27, Houston 13

NFC Playoffs

First Round ....at *Philadelphia 27, *Chicago 17
Second Round ....at Tampa Bay 24, Philadelphia 17
LA Rams 21, at Dallas 19
Championship ....LA Rams 9, at Tampa Bay 0

Super Bowl XIV

Jan. 20, 1980
Rose Bowl, Pasadena
Favorite: Steelers by 10½ Attendance: 103,985

LA Rams (11-7)	7	6	6	0	**—19**
Pittsburgh (14-4)	3	7	7	14	**—31**

MVP: Pittsburgh QB Terry Bradshaw (14 for 21, 309 yds, 2 TD, 3 Int)

1980 Season

AFC Playoffs

First Round ....at *Oakland 27, *Houston 7
Second Round...............at San Diego 20, Buffalo 14
Oakland 14, at Cleveland 12
Championship ....Oakland 34, at San Diego 27

NFC Playoffs

First Round..................at *Dallas 34, *LA Rams 13
Second Round ....at Philadelphia 31, Minnesota 16
Dallas 30, at Atlanta 27
Championship...............at Philadelphia 20, Dallas 7

Super Bowl XV

Jan. 25, 1981
Louisiana Superdome, New Orleans
Favorite: Eagles by 3 Attendance: 76,135

Oakland (14-5)	14	0	10	3	**—27**
Philadelphia (14-4)	0	3	0	7	**—10**

MVP: Oakland QB Jim Plunkett (13 for 21, 261 yds, 3 TD)

1981 Season

AFC Playoffs

First Round ....*Buffalo 31, at *NY Jets 27
Second Round...........San Diego 41, at Miami 38 (OT)
at Cincinnati 28, Buffalo 21
Championship ....at Cincinnati 27, San Diego 7

NFC Playoffs

First Round...........*NY Giants 27, at *Philadelphia 21
Second Round ....at Dallas 38, Tampa Bay 0
at San Francisco 38, NY Giants 24
Championship ....at San Francisco 28, Dallas 27

Super Bowl XVI

Jan. 24, 1982
Pontiac Silverdome, Pontiac, Mich.
Favorite: Pick'em Attendance: 81,270

San Francisco (15-3)	7	13	0	6	**—26**
Cincinnati (14-4)	0	0	7	14	**—21**

MVP: San Francisco QB Joe Montana (14 for 22, 157 yds, 1 TD; 6 carries, 18 yds, 1 TD)

1982 Season

A 57-day players' strike shortened the regular season from 16 games to nine. The playoff format was changed to a 16-team tournament open to the top eight teams in each conference.

AFC Playoffs

First Round ....at LA Raiders 27, Cleveland 10
at Miami 28, New England 3
NY Jets 44, at Cincinnati 17
San Diego 31, at Pittsburgh 28
Second Round ....NY Jets 17, at LA Raiders 14
at Miami 34, San Diego 13
Championship ....at Miami 14, NY Jets 0

NFC Playoffs

First Round ....at Washington 31, Detroit 7
at Dallas 30, Tampa Bay 17
at Green Bay 41, St. Louis 16
at Minnesota 30, Atlanta 24
Second Round...........at Washington 21, Minnesota 7
at Dallas 37, Green Bay 26
Championship.............at Washington 31, Dallas 17

Super Bowl XVII

Jan. 30, 1983
Rose Bowl, Pasadena
Favorite: Dolphins by 3 Attendance: 103,667

Miami (10-2)	7	10	0	0	**—17**
Washington (11-1)	0	10	3	14	**—27**

MVP: Washington RB John Riggins (38 carries, 166 yds, 1 TD; 1 catch, 15 yds)

Most Popular Playing Sites

Stadiums hosting more than one Super Bowl.

No		Years
5	Orange Bowl (Miami)	1968-69, 71, 76, 79
5	Rose Bowl (Pasadena)	1977, 80, 83, 87, 93
5	Superdome (N. Orleans)	1978, 81, 86, 90, 97
3	Tulane Stadium (N. Orleans)	1970, 72, 75
2	Joe Robbie Stadium, Miami	1989, 95
2	LA Memorial Coliseum	1967, 73
2	Tampa Stadium	1984, 91
2	Jack Murphy/Qualcomm Stadium (San Diego)	1988, 98

1983 Season

AFC Playoffs

First Round....................at *Seattle 31, *Denver 7
Second Round ....Seattle 27, at Miami 20
at LA Raiders 38, Pittsburgh 10
Championship...............at LA Raiders 30, Seattle 14

NFC Playoffs

First Round..................*LA Rams 24, at *Dallas 17
Second Round ....at San Francisco 24, Detroit 23
at Washington 51, LA Rams 7
Championship ....at Washington 24, San Francisco 21

Super Bowl XVIII

Jan. 22, 1984
Tampa Stadium, Tampa
Favorite: Redskins by 3 Attendance: 72,920

Washington (16-2) ....0 3 6 0 **—9**
LA Raiders (14-4)..............7 14 14 3 **—38**
MVP: LA Raiders RB Marcus Allen (20 carries, 191 yds, 2 TD; 2 catches, 18 yds)

1984 Season

AFC Playoffs

First Round.................at *Seattle 13, *LA Raiders 7
Second Round ....at Miami 31, Seattle 10
Pittsburgh 24, at Denver 17
Championship................at Miami 45, Pittsburgh 28

NFC Playoffs

First Round..............*NY Giants 16, at *LA Rams 13
Second Round.........at San Francisco 21, NY Giants 10
Chicago 23, at Washington 19
Championship ....at San Francisco 23, Chicago 0

Super Bowl XIX

Jan. 20, 1985
Stanford Stadium, Stanford, Calif.
Favorite: 49ers by 3 Attendance: 84,059

Miami (16-2) ....10 6 0 0 **—16**
San Francisco (17-1)............7 21 10 0 **—38**
MVP: San Francisco QB Joe Montana (24 for 35, 331 yds, 2 TD; 5 carries, 59 yards, 1 TD)

1985 Season

AFC Playoffs

First Round ....*New England 26, at *NY Jets 14
Second Round................at Miami 24, Cleveland 21
New England 27, at LA Raiders 20
Championship ....New England 31, at Miami 14

NFC Playoffs

First Round ....at *NY Giants 17, *San Francisco 3
Second Round ....at LA Rams 20, Dallas 0
at Chicago 21, NY Giants 0
Championship ....at Chicago 24, LA Rams 0

Super Bowl XX

Jan. 26, 1986
Louisiana Superdome, New Orleans
Favorite: Bears by 10 Attendance: 73,818

Chicago Bears (17-1).........13 10 21 2 **—46**
New England (14-5)...........3 0 0 7 **—10**
MVP: Chicago DE Richard Dent (Bears defense: 7 sacks, 6 turnovers, 1 safety and gave up just 123 total yards)

1986 Season

AFC Playoffs

First Round.............at *NY Jets 35, *Kansas City 15
Second Round ....at Cleveland 23, NY Jets 20 (OT)
at Denver 22, New England 17
Championship ....Denver 23, at Cleveland 20 (OT)

NFC Playoffs

First Round..............at *Washington 19, *LA Rams 7
Second Round............Washington 27, at Chicago 13
at NY Giants 49, San Francisco 3
Championship ....at NY Giants 17, Washington 0

Super Bowl XXI

Jan. 25, 1987
Rose Bowl, Pasadena
Favorite: Giants by 9½ Attendance: 101,063

Denver (13-5) ....10 0 0 10 **—20**
NY Giants (16-2)...............7 2 17 13 **—39**
MVP: NY Giants QB Phil Simms (22 for 25, 268 yds, 3 TD; 3 carries, 25 yds)

1987 Season

A 24-day players' strike shortened the regular season to 15 games with replacement teams playing for three weeks.

AFC Playoffs

First Round ....at *Houston 23, *Seattle 20 (OT)
Second Round ....at Cleveland 38, Indianapolis 21
at Denver 34, Houston 10
Championship...............at Denver 38, Cleveland 33

NFC Playoffs

First Round..........*Minnesota 44, at *New Orleans 10
Second Round.........Minnesota 36, at San Francisco 24
Washington 21, at Chicago 17
Championship ....at Washington 17, Minnesota 10

Super Bowl XXII

Jan. 31, 1988
San Diego/Jack Murphy Stadium
Favorite: Broncos by 3½ Attendance: 73,302

Washington (13-4) ....0 35 0 7 **—42**
Denver (12-4-1)...............10 0 0 0 **—10**
MVP: Washington QB Doug Williams (18 for 29, 340 yds, 4 TD, 1 Int)

1988 Season

AFC Playoffs

First Round...............*Houston 24, at *Cleveland 23
Second Round.................at Buffalo 17, Houston 10
at Cincinnati 21, Seattle 13
Championship...............at Cincinnati 21, Buffalo 10

NFC Playoffs

First Round ....at *Minnesota 28, *LA Rams 17
Second Round..........at San Francisco 34, Minnesota 9
at Chicago 20, Philadelphia 12
Championship ....San Francisco 28, at Chicago 3

Super Bowl XXIII

Jan. 22, 1989
Joe Robbie Stadium, Miami
Favorite: 49ers by 7 Attendance: 75,129

Cincinnati (14-4)................0 3 10 3 **—16**
San Francisco (12-6)...........3 0 3 14 **—20**
MVP: San Francisco WR Jerry Rice (11 catches, 215 yds, 1 TD; 1 carry, 5 yds)

Super Bowl Playoffs (Cont.)

1989 Season

AFC Playoffs

First Round .... *Pittsburgh 26, at *Houston 23
Second Round .... at Cleveland 34, Buffalo 30
at Denver 24, Pittsburgh 23
Championship .... at Denver 37, Cleveland 21

NFC Playoffs

First Round .... *LA Rams 21, at *Philadelphia 7
Second Round .... LA Rams 19, NY Giants 13 (OT)
at San Francisco 41, Minnesota 13
Championship .... at San Francisco 30, LA Rams 3

Super Bowl XXIV

Jan. 28, 1990
Louisiana Superdome, New Orleans
Favorite: 49ers by 12½ Attendance: 72,919

San Francisco (17-2)	13	14	14	14	**—55**
Denver (13-6)	3	0	7	0	**—10**

MVP: San Francisco QB Joe Montana (22 for 29, 297 yds, 5 TD, 0 Int)

1990 Season

AFC Playoffs

First Round .... at *Miami 17, *Kansas City 16
at Cincinnati 41, *Houston 14
Second Round .... at Buffalo 44, Miami 34
at LA Raiders 20, Cincinnati 10
Championship .... at Buffalo 51, LA Raiders 3

NFC Playoffs

First Round .... *Washington 20, at *Philadelphia 6
at Chicago 16, *New Orleans 6
Second Round .... at San Francisco 28, Washington 10
at NY Giants 31, Chicago 3
Championship .... NY Giants 15, at San Francisco 13

Super Bowl XXV

Jan. 27, 1991
Tampa Stadium, Tampa
Favorite: Bills by 7 Attendance: 73,813

Buffalo (15-4)	3	9	0	7	**—19**
NY Giants (16-3)	3	7	7	3	**—20**

MVP: NY Giants RB Ottis Anderson (21 carries, 102 yds, 1 TD; 1 catch, 7 yds)

1991 Season

AFC Playoffs

First Round .... at *Kansas City 10, *LA Raiders 6
at Houston 17, *NY Jets 10
Second Round .... at Denver 26, Houston 24
at Buffalo 37, Kansas City 14
Championship .... at Buffalo 10, Denver 7

NFC Playoffs

First Round .... *Atlanta 27, at New Orleans 20
*Dallas 17, at *Chicago 13
Second Round .... at Washington 24, Atlanta 7
at Detroit 38, Dallas 6
Championship .... at Washington 41, Detroit 10

Super Bowl XXVI

Jan. 26, 1992
Hubert Humphrey Metrodome, Minneapolis
Favorite: Redskins by 7 Attendance: 63,130

Washington (16-2)	0	17	14	6	**—37**
Buffalo (15-3)	0	0	10	14	**—24**

MVP: Washington QB Mark Rypien (18 for 33, 292 yds, 2 TD, 1 Int)

1992 Season

AFC Playoffs

First Round .... at *Buffalo 41, *Houston 38 (OT)
at San Diego 17, *Kansas City 0
Second Round .... Buffalo 24, at Pittsburgh 3
at Miami 31, San Diego 0
Championship .... Buffalo 29, at Miami 10

NFC Playoffs

First Round .... *Washington 24, at Minnesota 7
*Philadelphia 36, at *New Orleans 20
Second Round .... at San Francisco 20, Washington 13
at Dallas 34, Philadelphia 10
Championship .... Dallas 30, at San Francisco 20

Super Bowl XXVII

Jan. 31, 1993
Rose Bowl, Pasadena
Favorite: Cowboys by 7 Attendance: 98,374

Buffalo (14-5)	7	3	7	0	**—17**
Dallas (15-3)	14	14	3	21	**—52**

MVP: Dallas QB Troy Aikman (22 for 30, 273 yds, 4 TD, 0 Int)

1993 Season

AFC Playoffs

First Round .... at Kansas City 27, *Pittsburgh 24 (OT)
at *LA Raiders 42, *Denver 24
Second Round .... at Buffalo 29, LA Raiders 23
Kansas City 28, at Houston 20
Championship .... at Buffalo 30, Kansas City 13

NFC Playoffs

First Round .... *Green Bay 28, at Detroit 24
at *NY Giants 17, *Minnesota 10
Second Round .... at San Francisco 44, NY Giants 3
at Dallas 27, Green Bay 17
Championship .... at Dallas 38, San Francisco 21

Super Bowl XXVIII

Jan. 30, 1994
Georgia Dome, Atlanta
Favorite: Cowboys by 10½ Attendance: 72,817

Dallas (15-4)	6	0	14	10	**—30**
Buffalo (14-5)	3	10	0	0	**—13**

MVP: Dallas RB Emmitt Smith (30 carries, 132 yds, 2 TDs; 4 catches, 26 yds)

1994 Season

AFC Playoffs

First Round .... at Miami 27, *Kansas City 17
at *Cleveland 20, *New England 13
Second Round .... at Pittsburgh 29, Cleveland 9
at San Diego 22, Miami 21
Championship .... San Diego 17, at Pittsburgh 13

NFC Playoffs

First Round .... at *Green Bay 16, *Detroit 12
*Chicago 25, at Minnesota 18
Second Round .... at San Francisco 44, Chicago 15
at Dallas 35, Green Bay 9
Championship .... at San Francisco 38, Dallas 28

Super Bowl XXIX

Jan. 29, 1995
Joe Robbie Stadium, Miami
Favorite: 49ers by 18 Attendance: 74,107

San Diego (13-5)	7	3	8	8	**—26**
San Francisco (15-3)	14	14	14	7	**—49**

MVP: San Francisco QB Steve Young (24 for 36, 325 yds, 6 TD, 0 Int.)

1995 Season

AFC Playoffs

First Round ....at Buffalo 37, *Miami 22
*Indianapolis 35, at *San Diego 20
Second Round ....at Pittsburgh 40, Buffalo 21
*Indianapolis 10, at Kansas City 7
Championship..........at Pittsburgh 20, *Indianapolis 16

NFC Playoffs

First Round .... at *Philadelphia 58, *Detroit 37
at Green Bay 37, *Atlanta 20
Second Round........ Green Bay 27, at San Francisco 17
at Dallas 30, *Philadelphia 11
Championship .... at Dallas 38, Green Bay 27

Super Bowl XXX

Jan. 28, 1996
Sun Devil Stadium, Tempe, Ariz.
Favorite: Cowboys by 13 ½ Attendance: 76,347

Dallas (14-4)	10	3	7	7	**—27**
Pittsburgh (13-5)	0	7	0	10	**—27**

MVP: Dallas CB Larry Brown (2 Interceptions for 77 yards.)

1996 Season

AFC Playoffs

First Round ....*Jacksonville 30, at *Buffalo 27
at Pittsburgh 42, *Indianapolis 14
Second Round ....*Jacksonville 30, at Denver 27
at New England 28, Pittsburgh 3
Championship........at New England 20, *Jacksonville 6

NFC Playoffs

First Round................. at Dallas 40, *Minnesota 15
at *San Francisco 14, *Philadelphia 0
Second Round ...... at Green Bay 35, *San Francisco 14
at Carolina 26, Dallas 17
Championship .... at Green Bay 30, Carolina 13

Super Bowl XXXI

Jan. 26, 1997
Louisiana Superdome, New Orleans
Favorite: Packers by 14 Attendance: 72,301

New England (13-5)	14	0	7	0	**—21**
Green Bay (15-3)	10	17	8	0	**—35**

MVP: Green Bay KR Desmond Howard (4 kickoff returns for 154 yards and 1 TD, also 6 punt returns for 90 yards)

1997 Season

AFC Playoffs

First Round ....at *Denver 42, *Jacksonville 17
at New England 17, *Miami 3
Second Round............at Pittsburgh 7, New England 6
*Denver 14, at Kansas City 10
Championship .... *Denver 24, at Pittsburgh 21

NFC Playoffs

First Round ....*Minnesota 23, at NY Giants 22
at *Tampa Bay 20, *Detroit 10
Second Round ....at San Francisco 38, *Minnesota 22
at Green Bay 21, *Tampa Bay 7
Championship ....Green Bay 23, at San Francisco 10

Super Bowl XXXII

Jan. 25, 1998
Qualcomm Stadium, San Diego
Favorite: Packers by 11½ Attendance: 68,912

Green Bay (15-3)	7	7	3	7	**—24**
Denver (15-4)	7	10	7	7	**—31**

MVP: Denver RB Terrell Davis (30 carries, 157 yards, 3 TDs; 2 catches, 8 yards)

Before the Super Bowl

The first NFL champion was the Akron Pros in 1920, when the league was called the American Professional Football Association (APFA) and the title went to the team with the best regular season record. The APFA changed its name to the National Football League in 1922.

The first playoff game with the championship at stake came in 1932, when the Chicago Bears (6-1-6) and Portsmouth (Ohio) Spartans (6-1-4) ended the regular season tied for first place. The Bears won the subsequent playoff, 9-0. Due to a snowstorm and cold weather, the game was moved from Wrigley Field to an improvised 80-yard dirt field at Chicago Stadium, making it the first indoor title game as well.

The NFL Championship Game decided the league title until the NFL merged with the AFL and the first Super Bowl was played following the 1966 season.

NFL Champions, 1920-32

Winning player-coaches noted by position.

Multiple winners: Canton-Cleveland Bulldogs and Green Bay (3); Chicago Staleys/Bears (2).

Year	Champion	Head Coach
1920	Akron Pros	Fritz Pollard, HB & Elgie Tobin, QB
1921	Chicago Staleys	George Halas, E
1922	Canton Bulldogs	Guy Chamberlin, E
1923	Canton Bulldogs	Guy Chamberlin, E
1924	Cleveland Bulldogs	Guy Chamberlin, E
1925	Chicago Cardinals	Norm Barry
1926	Frankford Yellow Jackets	Guy Chamberlin, E
1927	New York Giants	Earl Potteiger, QB
1928	Providence Steam Roller	Jimmy Conzelman, HB
1929	Green Bay Packers	Curly Lambeau, QB
1930	Green Bay Packers	Curly Lambeau
1931	Green Bay Packers	Curly Lambeau
1932	Chicago Bears	Ralph Jones

(Bears beat Portsmouth-OH in playoff, 9-0)

Biggest Postseason Blowouts

(since the merger of the NFL and AFL in 1966)

Pts	Winner	Loser	Game	Date
49	at Oakland 56	Houston 7	1969 AFL Inter-Division Champ.	Dec. 21, 1969
48	at Buffalo 51	LA Raiders 3	1990 AFC Champ.	Jan. 20, 1991
46	at NY Giants 49	San Francisco 3	1986 NFC 2nd Rnd.	Jan. 4, 1987
45	San Francisco 55	Denver 10	Super Bowl XXIV	Jan. 28, 1990
44	at Washington 51	LA Rams 7	1983 NFC 2nd Rnd.	Jan. 1, 1984
41	at San Francisco 44	NY Giants 3	1993 NFC 2nd Rnd.	Jan. 15, 1994
38	at Dallas 52	Cleveland 14	1967 NFL East. Conf. Champ.	Dec. 24, 1967
38	at Dallas 38	Tampa Bay 0	1981 NFC 2nd Rnd.	Jan. 2, 1982

NFL-NFC Championship Game

NFL Championship games from 1933-69 and NFC Championship games since the completion of the NFL-AFL merger following the 1969 season.

Multiple winners: Green Bay (10); Dallas (8); Chicago Bears and Washington (7); NY Giants and San Francisco (5); Cleveland Browns, Detroit, Minnesota, and Philadelphia (4); Baltimore (3); Cleveland-LA Rams (2).

Season	Winner	Head Coach	Score	Loser	Head Coach	Site
1933	Chicago Bears	George Halas	23-21	New York	Steve Owen	Chicago
1934	New York	Steve Owen	30-13	Chicago Bears	George Halas	New York
1935	Detroit	Potsy Clark	26- 7	New York	Steve Owen	Detroit
1936	Green Bay	Curly Lambeau	21- 6	Boston Redskins	Ray Flaherty	New York
1937	Washington Redskins	Ray Flaherty	28-21	Chicago Bears	George Halas	Chicago
1938	New York	Steve Owen	23-17	Green Bay	Curly Lambeau	New York
1939	Green Bay	Curly Lambeau	27- 0	New York	Steve Owen	Milwaukee
1940	Chicago Bears	George Halas	73- 0	Washington	Ray Flaherty	Washington
1941	Chicago Bears	George Halas	37- 9	New York	Steve Owen	Chicago
1942	Washington	Ray Flaherty	14- 6	Chicago Bears	Hunk Anderson & Luke Johnsos	Washington
1943	Chicago Bears	Hunk Anderson & Luke Johnsos	41-21	Washington	Arthur Bergman	Chicago
1944	Green Bay	Curly Lambeau	14- 7	New York	Steve Owen	New York
1945	Cleveland Rams	Adam Walsh	15-14	Washington	Dudley DeGroot	Cleveland
1946	Chicago Bears	George Halas	24-14	New York	Steve Owen	New York
1947	Chicago Cardinals	Jimmy Conzelman	28-21	Philadelphia	Greasy Neale	Chicago
1948	Philadelphia	Greasy Neale	7- 0	Chicago Cardinals	Jimmy Conzelman	Philadelphia
1949	Philadelphia	Greasy Neale	14- 0	Los Angeles Rams	Clark Shaughnessy	Los Angeles
1950	Cleveland Browns	Paul Brown	30-28	Los Angeles	Joe Stydahar	Cleveland
1951	Los Angeles	Joe Stydahar	24-17	Cleveland	Paul Brown	Los Angeles
1952	Detroit	Buddy Parker	17- 7	Cleveland	Paul Brown	Cleveland
1953	Detroit	Buddy Parker	17-16	Cleveland	Paul Brown	Detroit
1954	Cleveland	Paul Brown	56-10	Detroit	Buddy Parker	Cleveland
1955	Cleveland	Paul Brown	38-14	Los Angeles	Sid Gillman	Los Angeles
1956	New York	Jim Lee Howell	47- 7	Chicago Bears	Paddy Driscoll	New York
1957	Detroit	George Wilson	59-14	Cleveland	Paul Brown	Detroit
1958	Baltimore	Weeb Ewbank	23-17*	New York	Jim Lee Howell	New York
1959	Baltimore	Weeb Ewbank	31-16	New York	Jim Lee Howell	Baltimore
1960	Philadelphia	Buck Shaw	17-13	Green Bay	Vince Lombardi	Philadelphia
1961	Green Bay	Vince Lombardi	37- 0	New York	Allie Sherman	Green Bay
1962	Green Bay	Vince Lombardi	16- 7	New York	Allie Sherman	New York
1963	Chicago	George Halas	14-10	New York	Allie Sherman	Chicago
1964	Cleveland	Blanton Collier	27- 0	Baltimore	Don Shula	Cleveland
1965	Green Bay	Vince Lombardi	23-12	Cleveland	Blanton Collier	Green Bay
1966	Green Bay	Vince Lombardi	34-27	Dallas	Tom Landry	Dallas
1967	Green Bay	Vince Lombardi	21-17	Dallas	Tom Landry	Green Bay
1968	Baltimore	Don Shula	34- 0	Cleveland	Blanton Collier	Cleveland
1969	Minnesota	Bud Grant	27- 7	Cleveland	Blanton Collier	Minnesota
1970	Dallas	Tom Landry	17-10	San Francisco	Dick Nolan	San Francisco
1971	Dallas	Tom Landry	14- 3	San Francisco	Dick Nolan	Dallas
1972	Washington	George Allen	26- 3	Dallas	Tom Landry	Washington
1973	Minnesota	Bud Grant	27-10	Dallas	Tom Landry	Dallas
1974	Minnesota	Bud Grant	14-10	Los Angeles	Chuck Knox	Minnesota
1975	Dallas	Tom Landry	37- 7	Los Angeles	Chuck Knox	Los Angeles
1976	Minnesota	Bud Grant	24-13	Los Angeles	Chuck Knox	Minnesota
1977	Dallas	Tom Landry	23- 6	Minnesota	Bud Grant	Dallas
1978	Dallas	Tom Landry	28- 0	Los Angeles	Ray Malavasi	Los Angeles
1979	Los Angeles	Ray Malavasi	9- 0	Tampa Bay	John McKay	Tampa Bay
1980	Philadelphia	Dick Vermeil	20- 7	Dallas	Tom Landry	Philadelphia
1981	San Francisco	Bill Walsh	28-27	Dallas	Tom Landry	San Francisco
1982	Washington	Joe Gibbs	31-17	Dallas	Tom Landry	Washington
1983	Washington	Joe Gibbs	24-21	San Francisco	Bill Walsh	Washington
1984	San Francisco	Bill Walsh	23- 0	Chicago	Mike Ditka	San Francisco
1985	Chicago	Mike Ditka	24- 0	Los Angeles	John Robinson	Chicago
1986	New York	Bill Parcells	17- 0	Washington	Joe Gibbs	New York
1987	Washington	Joe Gibbs	17-10	Minnesota	Jerry Burns	Washington
1988	San Francisco	Bill Walsh	28- 3	Chicago	Mike Ditka	Chicago
1989	San Francisco	George Seifert	30- 3	Los Angeles	John Robinson	San Francisco
1990	New York	Bill Parcells	15-13	San Francisco	George Seifert	San Francisco
1991	Washington	Joe Gibbs	41-10	Detroit	Wayne Fontes	Washington
1992	Dallas	Jimmy Johnson	30-20	San Francisco	George Seifert	San Francisco
1993	Dallas	Jimmy Johnson	38-21	San Francisco	George Seifert	Dallas
1994	San Francisco	George Seifert	38-28	Dallas	Barry Switzer	San Francisco
1995	Dallas	Barry Switzer	38-27	Green Bay	Mike Holmgren	Dallas
1996	Green Bay	Mike Holmgren	30-13	Carolina	Dom Capers	Green Bay
1997	Green Bay	Mike Holmgren	23-10	San Francisco	Steve Mariucci	San Francisco

*Sudden death overtime

NFL-NFC Championship Game Appearances

App		W	L	Pct	PF	PA
16	Dallas Cowboys	8	8	.500	361	319
16	NY Giants	5	11	.313	240	322
13	Green Bay Packers	10	3	.769	303	177
13	Chicago Bears	7	6	.538	286	245
12	Boston-Wash.Redskins	7	5	.583	222	255
12	San Francisco	5	7	.417	245	222
12	Cleveland-LA Rams	3	9	.250	123	270
11	Cleveland Browns	4	7	.364	224	253
6	Minnesota	4	2	.667	108	80
6	Detroit	4	2	.667	139	141
5	Philadelphia	4	1	.800	79	48
4	Baltimore Colts	3	1	.750	88	60
2	Chicago Cardinals	1	1	.500	28	28
1	Carolina	0	1	.000	13	30
1	Tampa Bay	0	1	.000	0	9

AFL-AFC Championship Game

AFL Championship games from 1960-69 and AFC Championship games since the completion of the NFL-AFL merger following the 1969 season.

Multiple winners: Buffalo (6); Denver, Miami and Pittsburgh (5); Oakland-LA Raiders (4); Dallas Texans-KC Chiefs (3); Cincinnati, Houston, New England and San Diego (2).

Season	Winner	Head Coach	Score	Loser	Head Coach	Site
1960	Houston	Lou Rymkus	24-16	LA Chargers	Sid Gillman	Houston
1961	Houston	Wally Lemm	10- 3	SD Chargers	Sid Gillman	San Diego
1962	Dallas	Hank Stram	20-17*	Houston	Pop Ivy	Houston
1963	San Diego	Sid Gillman	51-10	Boston Patriots	Mike Holovak	San Diego
1964	Buffalo	Lou Saban	20- 7	San Diego	Sid Gillman	Buffalo
1965	Buffalo	Lou Saban	23- 0	San Diego	Sid Gillman	San Diego
1966	Kansas City	Hank Stram	31- 7	Buffalo	Joel Collier	Buffalo
1967	Oakland	John Rauch	40- 7	Houston	Wally Lemm	Oakland
1968	NY Jets	Webb Ewbank	27-23	Oakland	John Rauch	New York
1969	Kansas City	Hank Stram	17- 7	Oakland	John Madden	Oakland
1970	Baltimore	Don McCafferty	27-17	Oakland	John Madden	Baltimore
1971	Miami	Don Shula	21- 0	Baltimore	Don McCafferty	Miami
1972	Miami	Don Shula	21-17	Pittsburgh	Chuck Noll	Pittsburgh
1973	Miami	Don Shula	27-10	Oakland	John Madden	Miami
1974	Pittsburgh	Chuck Noll	24-13	Oakland	John Madden	Oakland
1975	Pittsburgh	Chuck Noll	16-10	Oakland	John Madden	Pittsburgh
1976	Oakland	John Madden	24- 7	Pittsburgh	Chuck Noll	Oakland
1977	Denver	Red Miller	20-17	Oakland	John Madden	Denver
1978	Pittsburgh	Chuck Noll	34- 5	Houston	Bum Phillips	Pittsburgh
1979	Pittsburgh	Chuck Noll	27-13	Houston	Bum Phillips	Pittsburgh
1980	Oakland	Tom Flores	34-27	San Diego	Don Coryell	San Diego
1981	Cincinnati	Forrest Gregg	27- 7	San Diego	Don Coryell	Cincinnati
1982	Miami	Don Shula	14- 0	NY Jets	Walt Michaels	Miami
1983	LA Raiders	Tom Flores	30-14	Seattle	Chuck Knox	Los Angeles
1984	Miami	Don Shula	45-28	Pittsburgh	Chuck Noll	Miami
1985	New England	Raymond Berry	31-14	Miami	Don Shula	Miami
1986	Denver	Dan Reeves	23-20*	Cleveland	Marty Schottenheimer	Cleveland
1987	Denver	Dan Reeves	38-33	Cleveland	Marty Schottenheimer	Denver
1988	Cincinnati	Sam Wyche	21-10	Buffalo	Marv Levy	Cincinnati
1989	Denver	Dan Reeves	37-21	Cleveland	Bud Carson	Denver
1990	Buffalo	Marv Levy	51-3	LA Raiders	Art Shell	Buffalo
1991	Buffalo	Marv Levy	10- 7	Denver	Dan Reeves	Buffalo
1992	Buffalo	Marv Levy	29-10	Miami	Don Shula	Miami
1993	Buffalo	Marv Levy	30-13	Kansas City	Marty Schottenheimer	Buffalo
1994	San Diego	Bobby Ross	17-13	Pittsburgh	Bill Cowher	Pittsburgh
1995	Pittsburgh	Bill Cowher	20-16	Indianapolis	Ted Marchibroda	Pittsburgh
1996	New England	Bill Parcells	20-6	Jacksonville	Tom Coughlin	New England
1997	Denver	Mike Shanahan	24-21	Pittsburgh	Bill Cowher	Pittsburgh

*Sudden death overtime

AFL-AFC Championship Game Appearances

App		W	L	Pct	PF	PA
12	Oakland-LA Raiders	4	8	.333	228	264
10	Pittsburgh	5	5	.500	207	188
8	Buffalo	6	2	.750	180	92
8	LA-San Diego Chargers	2	6	.250	128	161
7	Miami	5	2	.714	152	115
6	Denver	5	1	.833	149	122
6	Houston	2	4	.333	76	140
4	Dallas Texans/KC Chiefs	3	1	.750	81	61
3	Boston-NE Patriots	2	1	.750	61	71
3	Baltimore-Indy Colts	1	2	.333	43	58
3	Cleveland	0	3	.000	74	98
2	Cincinnati	2	0	1.000	48	17
2	NY Jets	1	1	.500	27	37
1	Seattle	0	1	.000	14	30
1	Jacksonville	0	1	.000	6	20

NFL Divisional Champions

The NFL adopted divisional play for the first time in 1967, splitting both conferences into two four-team divisions—the Capitol and Century divisions in the East and the Central and Coastal divisions in the West. Merger with the AFL in 1970 increased NFL membership to 26 teams and made it necessary for realignment. Two 13-team conferences—the AFC and NFC—were formed by moving established NFL clubs in Baltimore, Cleveland and Pittsburgh to the AFC and rearranging both conferences into Eastern, Central and Western divisions. Expansion has since increased each conference to 15 teams (five per division).

Division champions are listed below; teams that went on to win the Super Bowl are in **bold** type. Note that in the 1980 season, Oakland won the Super Bowl as a wild card team, as did Denver in 1997; and in 1982, the players' strike shortened the regular season to nine games and eliminated divisional play for one season.

Multiple champions (since 1970): **AFC**–Pittsburgh (14); Miami (11); Oakland-LA Raiders (9); Denver (8); Buffalo (7); Cleveland (6); Baltimore-Indianapolis Colts, Cincinnati and San Diego (5); Kansas City and New England (4); Houston (2). **NFC**–San Francisco (16); Dallas (14); Minnesota (12); LA Rams (8); Chicago (6); Washington (5); Green Bay and NY Giants (4); Detroit (3); Philadelphia, St. Louis Cardinals and Tampa Bay (2).

American Football League

Season	East	West
1966	Buffalo	Kansas City
Season	**East**	**West**
1967	Houston	Oakland
1968	**NY Jets**	Oakland
1969	NY Jets	Oakland

National Football League

Season	East		West	
1966	Dallas		**Green Bay**	
Season	**Capitol**	**Century**	**Central**	**Coastal**
1967	Dallas	Cleveland	**Green Bay**	LA Rams
1968	Dallas	Cleveland	Minnesota	Baltimore
1969	Dallas	Cleveland	Minnesota	LA Rams

Note: Kansas City, an AFL second-place team, won the Super Bowl in the 1969 season.

American Football Conference / National Football Conference

Season	East	Central	West	Season	East	Central	West
1970	**Baltimore**	Cincinnati	Oakland	1970	Dallas	Minnesota	San Francisco
1971	Miami	Cleveland	Kansas City	1971	**Dallas**	Minnesota	San Francisco
1972	**Miami**	Pittsburgh	Oakland	1972	Washington	Green Bay	San Francisco
1973	**Miami**	Cincinnati	Oakland	1973	Dallas	Minnesota	LA Rams
1974	Miami	**Pittsburgh**	Oakland	1974	St. Louis	Minnesota	LA Rams
1975	Baltimore	**Pittsburgh**	Oakland	1975	St. Louis	Minnesota	LA Rams
1976	Baltimore	Pittsburgh	**Oakland**	1976	Dallas	Minnesota	LA Rams
1977	Baltimore	Pittsburgh	Denver	1977	**Dallas**	Minnesota	LA Rams
1978	New England	**Pittsburgh**	Denver	1978	Dallas	Minnesota	LA Rams
1979	Miami	**Pittsburgh**	San Diego	1979	Dallas	Tampa Bay	LA Rams
1980	Buffalo	Cleveland	San Diego	1980	Philadelphia	Minnesota	Atlanta
1981	Miami	Cincinnati	San Diego	1981	Dallas	Tampa Bay	**San Francisco**
1982	—	—	—	1982	—	—	—
1983	Miami	Pittsburgh	**LA Raiders**	1983	Washington	Detroit	San Francisco
1984	Miami	Pittsburgh	Denver	1984	Washington	Chicago	**San Francisco**
1985	Miami	Cleveland	LA Raiders	1985	Dallas	**Chicago**	LA Rams
1986	New England	Cleveland	Denver	1986	**NY Giants**	Chicago	San Francisco
1987	Indianapolis	Cleveland	Denver	1987	**Washington**	Chicago	San Francisco
1988	Buffalo	Cincinnati	Seattle	1988	Philadelphia	Chicago	**San Francisco**
1989	Buffalo	Cleveland	Denver	1989	NY Giants	Minnesota	**San Francisco**
1990	Buffalo	Cincinnati	LA Raiders	1990	**NY Giants**	Chicago	San Francisco
1991	Buffalo	Houston	Denver	1991	**Washington**	Detroit	New Orleans
1992	Miami	Pittsburgh	San Diego	1992	**Dallas**	Minnesota	San Francisco
1993	Buffalo	Houston	Kansas City	1993	**Dallas**	Detroit	San Francisco
1994	Miami	Pittsburgh	San Diego	1994	Dallas	Minnesota	**San Francisco**
1995	Buffalo	Pittsburgh	Kansas City	1995	**Dallas**	Green Bay	San Francisco
1996	New England	Pittsburgh	Denver	1996	Dallas	**Green Bay**	Carolina
1997	New England	Pittsburgh	Kansas City	1997	NY Giants	Green Bay	San Francisco

Note: Oakland, an AFC wild card team, won the Super Bowl the 1980 season. Denver, an AFC Wild Card team, won the Super Bowl the 1997 season.

Overall Postseason Games

The postseason records of all NFL teams, ranked by number of playoff games participated in from 1933 through the 1997 season.

Gm		W	L	Pct	PF	PA
51	Dallas Cowboys	32	19	.627	1254	932
37	San Francisco 49ers	23	14	.622	936	712
36	Oakland-LA Raiders	21	15	.583	855	659
36	Pittsburgh Steelers	21	15	.583	801	707
35	Boston-Wash. Redskins	21	14	.600	738	625
34	Minnesota Vikings	14	20	.412	613	746
33	New York Giants	14	19	.424	551	616
33	Cleveland-LA Rams	13	20	.394	501	697
32	Miami Dolphins	17	15	.531	700	650
31	Green Bay Packers	22	9	.710	745	528
30	Cleveland Browns	11	19	.367	596	702
28	Chicago Bears	14	14	.500	579	552
27	Buffalo Bills	14	13	.519	648	612
24	Denver Broncos	13	11	.542	518	604
22	Houston Oilers	9	13	.409	371	533
20	Balt-Indianapolis Colts	10	10	.500	360	389
20	Philadelphia Eagles	9	11	.450	356	369
19	Dallas Texans/KC Chiefs	8	11	.421	301	384
18	LA-San Diego Chargers	7	11	.389	332	428
16	Boston-NE Patriots	7	9	.438	300	332
16	Detroit Lions	7	9	.438	352	377
12	Cincinnati Bengals	5	7	.417	246	257
11	New York Jets	5	6	.455	216	200
7	Seattle Seahawks	3	4	.429	128	139
7	Atlanta Falcons	2	5	.286	139	181
6	Tampa Bay Buccaneers	2	4	.333	68	125
5	Chi-St. L. Cardinals	1	4	.200	81	134
4	Jacksonville Jaguars	2	2	.500	83	116
4	New Orleans Saints	0	4	.000	56	123
2	Carolina Panthers	1	1	.500	39	47

All-Time Postseason Leaders

Through Super Bowl XXXII, Jan. 25, 1998; participants in 1997 season playoffs in **bold** type.

CAREER

Passing Efficiency

Ratings based on performance standards established for completion percentage, average gain, touchdown percentage and interception percentage. Minimum 150 passing attempts.

		Gm	Cmp%	Yds	TD	Int	Rtg
1	Bart Starr	10	61.0	1753	15	3	104.8
2	Troy Aikman	14	66.5	3372	22	13	96.0
3	Joe Montana	23	62.7	5772	45	21	95.6
4	Kenny Anderson	6	66.3	1321	9	6	93.5
5	**Brett Favre**	13	60.4	3098	23	10	92.0
6	Joe Theismann	10	60.7	1782	11	7	91.4
7	**Steve Young**	20	62.4	2855	16	8	88.7
8	Warren Moon	10	64.3	2870	17	14	84.9
9	Ken Stabler	13	57.8	2641	19	13	84.2
10	Bernie Kosar	10	56.3	1953	16	10	83.5

Passing

	Attempts	Gm	Att
1	Joe Montana, S.F.-KC	23	734
2	**John Elway**, Denver	19	565
3	**Dan Marino**, Miami	14	561

	Completions	Gm	Cmp
1	Joe Montana, SF-KC	23	460
2	**Dan Marino**, Miami	14	334
3	Jim Kelly, Buffalo	17	322
4	**John Elway**, Denver	19	310

	Yards Gained	Gm	Yds
1	Joe Montana, SF-KC	23	5772
2	**John Elway**, Denver	19	4273
3	Jim Kelly, Buffalo	17	3863
4	Terry Bradshaw, Pittsburgh	19	3833

Games

	Played	Gm
1	D.D. Lewis, Dallas	27
2	Larry Cole, Dallas	26
3	Charlie Waters, Dallas	25

	Coached	Gm
1	Tom Landry, Dallas	36
	Don Shula, Baltimore-Miami	36
3	Chuck Noll, Pittsburgh	24

Rushing

	Yards Gained	Gm	Car	Yds	Avg
1	Franco Harris	19	400	1556	3.89
2	Emmitt Smith	15	318	1413	4.44
3	Thurman Thomas	19	327	1399	4.28
4	Tony Dorsett	17	302	1383	4.58
5	**Marcus Allen**	16	267	1347	5.04

	Attempts	Gm	Att
1	Franco Harris, Pittsburgh	19	400
2	Thurman Thomas, Buffalo	19	327
3	Emmitt Smith, Dallas	15	318
4	Tony Dorsett, Dallas	17	302

Receiving

	Catches	Gm	No	Yds	Avg
1	Jerry Rice, San Francisco	21	120	1788	14.9
2	Michael Irvin, Dallas	15	83	1283	15.5
3	Andre Reed, Buffalo	19	80	1169	14.6

	Yards Gained	Gm	Yds
1	Jerry Rice, San Francisco	21	1788
2	Cliff Branch, Oakland-LA	22	1289
3	Michael Irvin, Dallas	15	1283
4	Andre Reed, Buffalo	19	1169
5	Fred Biletnikoff, Oakland	19	1167

	Average Gain	Gm	Avg
1	Alvin Harper, Dallas	10	27.3
2	Willie Gault, Chicago-LA	12	23.7
3	Harold Jackson, LA-NE-Minn-Sea	14	22.8

Scoring

	Points	Gm	TD	FG	PAT	Pts
1	Emmitt Smith	15	20	0	0	120
	Thurman Thomas	19	20	0	0	120
3	George Blanda	19	0	22	49	115

	Touchdowns	Gm	Run	Rec	Ret	No
1	Emmitt Smith	15	18	2	0	20
	Thurman Thomas	19	15	5	0	20
3	Jerry Rice	21	0	18	0	18

	Field Goals	Gm	Att	FG	Pct
1	George Blanda	19	39	22	.564
2	Matt Bahr	14	25	21	.840
3	Toni Fritsch	14	28	20	.714

SINGLE GAME

Scoring

	Points Scored	Season	Pts
1	Ricky Watters, SF vs. NYG	1993	30
2	Pat Harder, Det. vs. LA	1952	19
	Paul Hornung, GB vs. NYG	1961	19

	Field Goals	Season	FG
1	Chuck Nelson, Min. vs. SF	1987	5
	Matt Bahr, NYG vs. SF	1990	5
	Steve Christie, Buf. vs. Mia	1992	5
	Brad Daluiso, NYG vs Min	1997	5

Rushing

	Yards Gained	Season	Yds
1	Eric Dickerson, LA Rams vs. Dal	1985	248
2	Keith Lincoln, SD vs. Bos.	1963	206
3	Timmy Smith, Wash. vs. Den	1987	204

	Most Attempts	Season	Att
1	Ricky Bell, T.B. vs. Phi	1979	38
	John Riggins, Wash. vs. Mia	1982	38
3	Lawrence McCutcheon, LA vs. St. L	1975	37
	John Riggins, Wash. vs. Minn	1982	37

Passing

	Attempts	Season	Att
1	Steve Young, SF vs. GB	1995	65
2	Bernie Kosar, Cle. vs. NYJ	1986	64
	Dan Marino, Mia. vs. Buf.	1995	64

	Completions	Season	Cmp
1	Warren Moon, Hou. vs. Buf.	1992	36
2	Dan Fouts, SD vs. Mia.	1981	33
	Bernie Kosar, Cle. vs. NYJ	1986	33
	Dan Marino, Mia. vs. Buf.	1995	33

	Yards Gained	Season	Yds
1	Bernie Kosar, Cle. vs. NYJ	1986	489
2	Dan Fouts, SD vs. Mia.	1981	433
3	Dan Marino, Mia. vs. Buf.	1995	422

Receiving

	Catches	Season	Rec
1	Kellen Winslow, SD vs. Mia	1981	13
	Thurman Thomas, Buf. vs. Cle.	1989	13
	Shannon Sharpe, Den. vs. LA Raiders	1993	13

	Yards Gained	Season	Yds
1	Anthony Carter, Min. vs. SF	1987	227
2	Jerry Rice, SF vs. Cin.	1988	215
3	Tom Fears, LA vs. Chi	1950	198

Champions of Leagues That No Longer Exist

No professional league in American sports has had to contend with more pretenders to the throne than the NFL. Seven times in as many decades a rival league has risen up to challenge the NFL and six of them went under in less than five seasons. Only the fourth American Football League (1960-69) succeeded, forcing the older league to sue for peace and a full partnership in 1966.

Of the six leagues that didn't make it, only the All-America Football Conference (1946-49) lives on—the Cleveland Browns and San Francisco 49ers joined the NFL after the AAFC folded in 1949. The champions of leagues past are listed below.

American Football League I

Year		Head Coach
1926	Philadelphia Quakers (7-2)	Bob Folwell

Note: Philadelphia was challenged to a postseason game by the 7th place New York Giants (8-4-1) of the NFL. The Giants won, 31-0, in a snowstorm.

American Football League II

Year		Head Coach
1936	Boston Shamrocks (8-3)	George Kenneally
1937	Los Angeles Bulldogs (8-0)	Gus Henderson

Note: Boston was scheduled to play 2nd place Cleveland (5-2-2) in the '36 championship game, but the Shamrock players refused to participate because they were owed pay for past games.

American Football League III

Year		Head Coach
1940	Columbus Bullies (8-1-1)	Phil Bucklew
1941	Columbus Bullies (5-1-2)	Phil Bucklew

All-America Football Conference

Year	Winner	Head Coach	Score	Loser	Head Coach	Site
1946	Cleveland Browns	Paul Brown	14-9	NY Yankees	Ray Flaherty	Cleveland
1947	Cleveland Browns	Paul Brown	14-3	NY Yankees	Ray Flaherty	New York
1948	Cleveland Browns	Paul Brown	49-7	Buffalo Bills	Red Dawson	Cleveland
1949	Cleveland Browns	Paul Brown	21-7	S.F. 49ers	Buck Shaw	Cleveland

World Football League

Year	Winner	Head Coach	Score	Loser	Head Coach	Site
1974	Birmingham Americans	Jack Gotta	22-21	Florida Blazers	Jack Pardee	Birmingham
1975	WFL folded Oct. 22.					

United States Football League

Year	Winner	Head Coach	Score	Loser	Head Coach	Site
1983	Michigan Panthers	Jim Stanley	24-22	Philadelphia Stars	Jim Mora	Denver
1984	Philadelphia Stars	Jim Mora	23-3	Arizona Wranglers	George Allen	Tampa
1985	Baltimore Stars	Jim Mora	28-24	Oakland Invaders	Charlie Sumner	E. Rutherford

Defunct Leagues

AFL I (1926): Boston Bulldogs, Brooklyn Horseman, Chicago Bulls, Cleveland Panthers, Los Angeles Wildcats, New York Yankees, Newark Bears, Philadelphia Quakers, Rock Island Independents.

AFL II (1936-37): Boston Shamrocks (1936-37); Brooklyn Tigers (1936); Cincinnati Bengals (1937); Cleveland Rams (1936); Los Angeles Bulldogs (1937); New York Yankees (1936-37); Pittsburgh Americans (1936-37); Rochester Tigers (1936-37).

AFL III (1940-41): Boston Bears (1940); Buffalo Indians (1940-41); Cincinnati Bengals (1940-41); Columbus Bullies (1940-41); Milwaukee Chiefs (1940-41); New York Yankees (1940) renamed Americans (1941).

AAFC (1946-49): Brooklyn Dodgers (1946-48) merged to become Brooklyn-New York Yankees (1949); Buffalo Bisons (1946) renamed Bills (1947-49); Chicago Rockets (1946-48) renamed Hornets (1949); Cleveland Browns (1946-49); Los Angeles Dons (1946-49); Miami Seahawks (1946) became Baltimore Colts (1947-49); New York Yankees (1946-48) merged to become Brooklyn-New York Yankees (1949); San Francisco 49ers (1946-49).

WFL (1974-75): Birmingham Americans (1974) renamed Vulcans (1975); Chicago Fire (1974) renamed Winds (1975); Detroit Wheels (1974); Florida Blazers (1974) became San Antonio Wings (1975); The Hawaiians (1974-75); Houston Texans (1974) became Shreveport (La.) Steamer (1974-75); Jacksonville Sharks (1974) renamed Express (1975); Memphis Southmen (1974) also known as Grizzlies (1975); New York Stars (1974) became Charlotte Hornets (1974-75); Philadelphia Bell (1974-75); Portland Storm (1974) renamed Thunder (1975); Southern California Sun (1974-75).

USFL (1983-85): Arizona Wranglers (1983-84) merged with Oklahoma to become Arizona Outlaws (1985); Birmingham Stallions (1983-85); Boston Breakers (1983) became New Orleans Breakers (1984) and then Portland Breakers (1985); Chicago Blitz (1983-84); Denver Gold (1983-85); Houston Gamblers (1984-85); Jacksonville Bulls (1984-85); Los Angeles Express (1983-85); Memphis Showboats (1984-85).

Michigan Panthers (1983-84) merged with Oakland (1985); New Jersey Generals (1983-85); Oakland Invaders (1983-85); Oklahoma Outlaws (1984) merged with Arizona to become Arizona Outlaws (1985); Philadelphia Stars (1983-84) became Baltimore Stars (1985); Pittsburgh Maulers (1984); San Antonio Gunslingers (1984-85); Tampa Bay Bandits (1983-85); Washington Federals (1983-84) became Orlando Renegades (1985).

NFL Pro Bowl

A postseason All-Star game between the new league champion and a team of professional all-stars was added to the NFL schedule in 1939. In the first game at Wrigley Field in Los Angeles, the NY Giants beat a team made up of players from NFL teams and two independent clubs in Los Angeles (the LA Bulldogs and Hollywood Stars). An all-NFL All-Star team provided the opposition over the next four seasons, but the game was cancelled in 1943.

The Pro Bowl was revived in 1951 as a contest between conference all-star teams: American vs National (1951-53), Eastern vs Western (1954-70), and AFC vs NFC (since 1971). The NFC leads the current series with the AFC, 15-13.

The MVP trophy was named the Dan McGuire Award in 1984 after the late SF 49ers publicist and *Honolulu Advertiser* sports columnist.

Year	Winner	Score	Loser
1939	NY Giants	13-10	All-Stars
1940	Green Bay	16-7	All-Stars
1940	Chicago Bears	28-14	All-Stars
1942	Chicago Bears	35-24	All-Stars
1942	All-Stars	17-14	Washington
1943-50		No game	

Year	Winner	MVP
1951	American, 28-27	Otto Graham, Cle., QB
1952	National, 30-13	Dan Towler, LA, HB
1953	National, 27-7	Don Doll, Det., DB
1954	East, 20-9	Chuck Bednarik, Phi., LB
1955	West, 26-19	Billy Wilson, SF, E
1956	East, 31-30	Ollie Matson, Cards, HB
1957	West, 19-10	Back–Bert Rechichar, Bal.
		Line–Ernie Stautner, Pit.
1958	West, 26-7	Back–Hugh McElhenny, SF
		Line–Gene Brito, Wash.
1959	East, 28-21	Back–Frank Gifford, NY
		Line–Doug Atkins, Chi.
1960	West, 38-21	Back–Johnny Unitas, Bal.
		Line–Big Daddy Lipscomb, Pit.
1961	West, 35-31	Back–Johnny Unitas, Bal.
		Line–Sam Huff, NY
1962	West, 31-30	Back–Jim Brown, Cle.
		Line–Henry Jordan, GB
1963	East, 30-20	Back–Jim Brown, Cle.
		Line–Big Daddy Lipscomb, Pit.
1964	West, 31-17	Back–Johnny Unitas, Bal.
		Line–Gino Marchetti, Bal.
1965	West, 34-14	Back–Fran Tarkenton, Min.
		Line–Terry Barr, Det.
1966	East, 36-7	Back–Jim Brown, Cle.
		Line–Dale Meinhart, St. L.
1967	East, 20-10	Back–Gale Sayers, Chi.
		Line–Floyd Peters, Phi.
1968	West, 38-20	Back–Gale Sayers, Chi.
		Line–Dave Robinson, GB

Year	Winner	MVP
1969	West, 10-7	Back–Roman Gabriel, LA
		Line–Merlin Olsen, LA
1970	West, 16-13	Back–Gale Sayers, Chi.
		Line–George Andrie, Dal.
1971	NFC, 27-6	Back–Mel Renfro, Dal.
		Line–Fred Carr, GB
1972	AFC, 26-13	Off–Jan Stenerud, KC
		Def–Willie Lanier, KC
1973	AFC, 33-28	O.J. Simpson, Buf., RB
1974	AFC, 15-13	Garo Yepremian, Mia., PK
1975	NFC, 17-10	James Harris, LA Rams, QB
1976	NFC, 23-20	Billy Johnson, Hou., KR
1977	AFC, 24-14	Mel Blount, Pit., CB
1978	NFC, 14-13	Walter Payton, Chi., RB
1979	NFC, 13-7	Ahmad Rashad, Min., WR
1980	NFC, 37-27	Chuck Muncie, NO, RB
1981	NFC, 21-7	Eddie Murray, Det., PK
1982	AFC, 16-13	Kellen Winslow, SD, WR
		& Lee Roy Selmon, TB, DE
1983	NFC, 20-19	Dan Fouts, SD, QB
		& John Jefferson, GB, WR
1984	NFC, 45-3	Joe Theismann, Wash., QB
1985	AFC, 22-14	Mark Gastineau, NYJ, DE
1986	NFC, 28-24	Phil Simms, NYG, QB
1987	AFC, 10-6	Reggie White, Phi., DE
1988	AFC, 15-6	Bruce Smith, Buf., DE
1989	NFC, 34-3	Randall Cunningham, Phi., QB
1990	NFC, 27-21	Jerry Gray, LA Rams, CB
1991	AFC, 23-21	Jim Kelly, Buf., QB
1992	NFC, 21-15	Michael Irvin, Dal., WR
1993	AFC, 23-20 (OT)	Steve Tasker, Buf., Sp. Teams
1994	NFC, 17-3	Andre Rison, Atl., WR
1995	AFC, 41-13	Marshall Faulk, Ind., RB
1996	NFC, 20-13	Jerry Rice, SF, WR
1997	AFC, 26-23 (OT)	Mark Brunell, Jax, QB
1998	AFC, 29-24	Warren Moon, Sea., QB

Playing sites: Wrigley Field in Los Angeles (1939); Gilmore Stadium in Los Angeles (both games); Polo Grounds in New York (Jan., 1942); Shibe Park in Philadelphia (Dec., 1942); Memorial Coliseum in Los Angeles (1951-72 and 1979); Texas Stadium in Irving, TX (1973); Arrowhead Stadium in Kansas City (1974); Orange Bowl in Miami (1975); Superdome in New Orleans (1976); Kingdome in Seattle (1977); Tampa Stadium in Tampa (1978) and Aloha Stadium in Honolulu (since 1980).

AFL All-Star Game

The AFL did not play an All-Star game after its first season in 1960 but did stage All-Star games from 1962-70. All-Star teams from the Eastern and Western divisions played each other every year except 1966 with the West winning the series, 6-2. In 1966, the league champion Buffalo Bills met an elite squad made up of the best players from the league's other eight clubs and lost, 30-19.

Year	Winner	MVP
1962	West, 47-27	Cotton Davidson, Oak., QB
1963	West, 21-14	Off–Curtis McClinton, Dal.
		Def–Earl Faison, SD
1964	West, 27-24	Off–Keith Lincoln, SD
		Def–Archie Matsos, Oak.
1965	West, 38-14	Off–Keith Lincoln, SD
		Def–Willie Brown, Den.
1966	All-Stars 30 Buffalo 19	Off–Joe Namath, NY Def–Frank Buncom, SD
1967	East, 30-23	Off–Babe Parilli, Bos.
		Def–Verlon Biggs, NY
1968	East, 25-24	Off–Joe Namath, NY
		& Don Maynard, NY
		Def–Speedy Duncan, SD
1969	West, 38-25	Off–Len Dawson, KC
		Def–George Webster, Hou.
1970	West, 26-3	John Hadl, SD, QB

Playing sites: Balboa Stadium in San Diego (1962-64); Jeppesen Stadium in Houston (1965); Rice Stadium in Houston (1966); Oakland Coliseum (1967); Gator Bowl in Jacksonville (1968-69) and Astrodome in Houston (1970).

NFL Franchise Origins

Here is what the current 30 teams in the National Football League have to show for the years they have put in as members of the American Professional Football Association (APFA), the NFL, the All-America Football Conference (AAFC) and the American Football League (AFL). Years given for league titles indicate seasons championships were won.

American Football Conference

	First Season	League Titles	Franchise Stops
Baltimore Ravens	1996 (NFL)	None	• Baltimore (1996–)
Buffalo Bills	1960 (AFL)	2 AFL (1964-65)	• Buffalo (1960-72) Orchard Park, NY (1973–)
Cincinnati Bengals	1968 (AFL)	None	• Cincinnati (1968–)
Denver Broncos	1960 (AFL)	1 Super Bowl (1997)	• Denver (1960–)
Indianapolis Colts	1953 (NFL)	3 NFL (1958-59,68) 1 Super Bowl (1970)	• Baltimore (1953-83) Indianapolis (1984–)
Jacksonville Jaguars	1995 (NFL)	None	• Jacksonville, FL (1995–)
Kansas City Chiefs	1960 (AFL)	3 AFL (1962,66,69) 1 Super Bowl (1969)	• Dallas (1960-62) Kansas City (1963–)
Miami Dolphins	1966 (AFL)	2 Super Bowls (1972-73)	• Miami (1966–)
New England Patriots	1960 (AFL)	None	• Boston (1960-70) Foxboro, MA (1971–)
New York Jets	1960 (AFL)	1 AFL (1968) 1 Super Bowl (1968)	• New York (1960-83) E. Rutherford, NJ (1984–)
Oakland Raiders	1960 (AFL)	1 AFL (1967) 3 Super Bowls (1976,80,83)	• Oakland (1960-81, 1995–) Los Angeles (1982-94)
Pittsburgh Steelers	1933 (NFL)	4 Super Bowls (1974-75,78-79)	• Pittsburgh (1933–)
San Diego Chargers	1960 (AFL)	1 AFL (1963)	• Los Angeles (1960) San Diego (1961–)
Seattle Seahawks	1976 (NFL)	None	• Seattle (1976–)
Tennessee Oilers	1960 (AFL)	2 AFL (1960-61)	• Houston (1960-96) Memphis (1997) Nashville (1998–)

National Football Conference

	First Season	League Titles	Franchise Stops
Arizona Cardinals	1920 (APFA)	2 NFL (1925,47)	• Chicago (1920-59) St. Louis (1960-87) Tempe, AZ (1988–)
Atlanta Falcons	1966 (NFL)	None	• Atlanta (1966–)
Carolina Panthers	1995 (NFL)	None	• Clemson, SC (1995) Charlotte, NC (1996–)
Chicago Bears	1920 (APFA)	8 NFL (1921, 32-33,40-41,43, 46,63) 1 Super Bowl (1985)	• Decatur, IL (1920) Chicago (1921–)
Dallas Cowboys	1960 (NFL)	5 Super Bowls (1971,77,92-93,95)	• Dallas (1960-70) Irving, TX (1971–)
Detroit Lions	1930 (NFL)	4 NFL (1935,52-53,57)	• Portsmouth, OH (1930-33) Detroit (1934-74) Pontiac, MI (1975–)
Green Bay Packers	1921 (APFA)	11 NFL (1929-31,36,39,44,61-62,65-67) 3 Super Bowls (1966-67,96)	• Green Bay (1921–)
Minnesota Vikings	1961 (NFL)	1 NFL (1969)	• Bloomington, MN (1961-81) Minneapolis, MN (1982–)
New Orleans Saints	1967 (NFL)	None	• New Orleans (1967–)
New York Giants	1925 (NFL)	4 NFL (1927,34,38,56) 2 Super Bowls (1986,90)	• New York (1925-73,75) New Haven, CT (1973-74) E. Rutherford, NJ (1976–)
Philadelphia Eagles	1933 (NFL)	3 NFL (1948-49,60)	• Philadelphia (1933–)
St. Louis Rams	1937 (NFL)	2 NFL (1945,51)	• Cleveland (1937-45) Los Angeles (1946-79) Anaheim (1980-94) St. Louis (1995–)
San Francisco 49ers	1946 (AAFC)	5 Super Bowls (1981,84,88-89,94)	• San Francisco (1946–)
Tampa Bay Buccaneers	1976 (NFL)	None	• Tampa, FL (1976–)
Washington Redskins	1932 (NFL)	2 NFL (1937, 42) 3 Super Bowls (1982, 87, 91)	• Boston (1932-36) Washington, DC (1937-96) Raljon, MD (1997–)

The Growth of the NFL

Of the 14 franchises that comprised the American Professional Football Association in 1920, only two remain—the Arizona Cardinals (then the Chicago Cardinals) and the Chicago Bears (originally the Decatur-IL Staleys). Green Bay joined the APFC in 1921 and the league changed its name to the NFL in 1922. Since then, 54 NFL clubs have come and gone, five rival leagues have expired and two other leagues have been swallowed up.

The NFL merged with the **All-America Football Conference** (1946-49) following the 1949 season and adopted three of its seven clubs—the Baltimore Colts, Cleveland Browns and San Francisco 49ers. The four remaining AAFC teams—the Brooklyn/NY Yankees, Buffalo Bills, Chicago Hornets and Los Angeles Dons—did not survive. After the 1950 season, the financially troubled Colts were sold back to the NFL. The league folded the team and added its players to the 1951 college draft pool. A new Baltimore franchise, also named the Colts, joined the NFL in 1953.

The formation of the **American Football League** (1960-69) was announced in 1959 with ownership lined up in eight cities—Boston, Buffalo, Dallas, Denver, Houston, Los Angeles, Minneapolis and New York. Set to begin play in the autumn of 1960, the AFL was stunned early that year when Minneapolis withdrew to accept an offer to join the NFL as an expansion team in 1961. The new league responded by choosing Oakland to replace Minneapolis and inherit the departed team's draft picks. Since no AFL team actually played in Minneapolis, it is not considered the original home of the Oakland Raiders.

In 1966, the NFL and AFL agreed to a merger that resulted in the first Super Bowl (originally called the AFL-NFL World Championship Game) following the '66 league playoffs. In 1970, the now 10-member AFL officially joined the NFL, forming a 26-team league made up of two conferences of three divisions each.

Expansion/Merger Timetable

For teams currently in NFL.

1921–Green Bay Packers; **1925**–New York Giants; **1930**–Portsmouth-OH Spartans (now Detroit Lions); **1932**–Boston Braves (now Washington Redskins); **1933**–Philadelphia Eagles and Pittsburgh Pirates (now Steelers); **1937**–Cleveland Rams (now St. Louis); **1950**–added AAFC's Cleveland Browns and San Francisco 49ers; **1953**–Baltimore Colts (now Indianapolis).

1960–Dallas Cowboys; **1961**–Minnesota Vikings; **1966**–Atlanta Falcons; **1967**–New Orleans Saints; **1970**–added AFL's Boston Patriots (now New England), Buffalo Bills, Cincinnati Bengals (1968 expansion team), Denver Broncos, Houston Oilers, Kansas City Chiefs, Miami Dolphins (1966 expansion team), New York Jets, Oakland Raiders and San Diego Chargers (the AFL-NFL merger divided the league into two 13-team conferences with old-line NFL clubs Baltimore, Cleveland and Pittsburgh moving to the AFC); **1976**–Seattle Seahawks and Tampa Bay Buccaneers (Seattle was originally in the NFC West and Tampa Bay in the AFC West, but were switched to their current divisions in 1977). **1995**–Carolina Panthers and Jacksonville Jaguars.

City and Nickname Changes

1921—Decatur Staleys move to Chicago; **1922**—Chicago Staleys renamed Bears; **1933**—Boston Braves renamed Redskins; **1937**—Boston Redskins move to Washington; **1934**—Portsmouth (Ohio) Spartans move to Detroit and become Lions; **1941**—Pittsburgh Pirates renamed Steelers; **1943**—Philadelphia and Pittsburgh merge for one season and become Phil-Pitt, or the "Steagles"; **1944**—Chicago Cardinals and Pittsburgh merge for one season and become Card-Pitt; **1946**—Cleveland Rams move to Los Angeles.

1960—Chicago Cardinals move to St. Louis; **1961**—Los Angeles Chargers (AFL) move to San Diego; **1963**—New York Titans (AFL) renamed Jets and Dallas Texans (AFL) move to Kansas City and become Chiefs; **1971**—Boston Patriots become New England Patriots; **1982**—Oakland Raiders move to Los Angeles; **1984**—Baltimore Colts move to Indianapolis; **1988**—St. Louis Cardinals move to Phoenix; **1994**—Phoenix Cardinals become Arizona Cardinals;. **1995**—L.A. Rams move to St. Louis and L.A. Raiders move back to Oakland; **1996**—Cleveland Browns move to Baltimore and become Ravens. City of Cleveland retains rights to team name, colors and all memorabilia; **1997**—Houston Oilers move to Memphis and become Tennessee Oilers; **1998**— Tennessee Oilers move to Vanderbilt Stadium in Nashville.

Defunct NFL Teams

Teams that once played in the APFA and NFL, but no longer exist.

Akron-OH–Pros (1920-25) and Indians (1926); **Baltimore**–Colts (1950); **Boston**–Bulldogs (1926) and Yanks (1944-48); **Brooklyn**–Lions (1926), Dodgers (1930-43) and Tigers (1944); **Buffalo**–All-Americans (1921-23), Bisons (1924-25), Rangers (1926), Bisons (1927,1929); **Canton-OH**–Bulldogs (1920-23,1925-26); **Chicago**–Tigers (1920); **Cincinnati**–Celts (1921) and Reds (1933-34); **Cleveland**–Tigers (1920), Indians (1921), Indians (1923), Bulldogs (1924-25,1927), Indians (1931) and Browns (1950-95); **Columbus-OH**–Panhandles (1920-22) and Tigers (1923-26); **Dallas**–Texans (1952); **Dayton-OH**–Triangles (1920-29).

Detroit–Heralds (1920-21), Panthers (1925-26) and Wolverines (1928); **Duluth-MN**–Kelleys (1923-25) and Eskimos (1926-27); **Evansville-IN**–Crimson Giants (1921-22); **Frankford-PA**–Yellow Jackets (1924-31); **Hammond-IN**–Pros (1920-26); **Hartford**–Blues (1926); **Kansas City**–Blues (1924) and Cowboys (1925-26); **Kenosha-WI**–Maroons (1924); **Los Angeles**–Buccaneers (1926); **Louisville**–Brecks (1921-23) and Colonels (1926); **Marion-OH**–Oorang Indians (1922-23); **Milwaukee**–Badgers (1922-26); **Minneapolis**–Marines (1922-24) and Red Jackets (1929-30); **Muncie-IN**–Flyers (1920-21).

New York–Giants (1921), Yankees (1927-28), Bulldogs (1949) and Yankees (1950-51); **Newark-NJ**–Tornadoes (1930); **Orange-NJ**–Tornadoes (1929); **Pottsville-PA**–Maroons (1925-28); **Providence-RI**–Steam Roller (1925-31); **Racine-WI**–Legion (1922-24) and Tornadoes (1926); **Rochester-NY**–Jeffersons (1920-25); **Rock Island-IL**–Independents (1920-26); **Staten Island-NY**–Stapletons (1929-32); **St. Louis**–All-Stars (1923) and Gunners (1934); **Toledo-OH**–Maroons (1922-23); **Tonawanda-NY**–Kardex (1921), also called Lumbermen; **Washington**–Senators (1921).

Annual NFL Leaders

Individual leaders in NFL (1932-69), NFC (since 1970), AFL (1960-69) and AFC (since 1970).

Passing

Since 1932, the NFL has used several formulas to determine passing leadership, from Total Yards alone (1932-37), to the current rating system—adopted in 1973—that takes Completions, Completion Percentage, Yards Gained, TD Passes, Interceptions, Interception Percentage and other factors into account. The quarterbacks listed below all led the league according to the system in use at the time.

Multiple winners: Sammy Baugh and Steve Young (6); Joe Montana and Roger Staubach (5); Arnie Herber, Sonny Jurgensen, Bart Starr and Norm Van Brocklin (3); Ed Danowski, Otto Graham, Cecil Isbell, Milt Plum and Bob Waterfield (2).

NFL-NFC

Year		Att	Cmp	Yds	TD
1932	Arnie Herber, GB	101	37	639	9
1933	Harry Newman, NY	136	53	973	11
1934	Arnie Herber, GB	115	42	799	8
1935	Ed Danowski, NY	113	57	794	10
1936	Arnie Herber, GB	173	77	1239	11
1937	Sammy Baugh, Wash	171	81	1127	8
1938	Ed Danowski, NY	129	70	848	7
1939	Parker Hall, Cle. Rams	208	106	1227	9
1940	Sammy Baugh, Wash	177	111	1367	12
1941	Cecil Isbell, GB	206	117	1479	15
1942	Cecil Isbell, GB	268	146	2021	24
1943	Sammy Baugh, Wash	239	133	1754	23
1944	Frank Filchock, Wash	147	84	1139	13
1945	Sammy Baugh, Wash	182	128	1669	11
	& Sid Luckman, Chi. Bears	217	117	1725	14
1946	Bob Waterfield, LA	251	127	1747	18
1947	Sammy Baugh, Wash	354	210	2938	25
1948	Tommy Thompson, Phi	246	141	1965	25
1949	Sammy Baugh, Wash	255	145	1903	18
1950	Norm Van Brocklin, LA	233	127	2061	18
1951	Bob Waterfield, LA	176	88	1566	13
1952	Norm Van Brocklin, LA	205	113	1736	14
1953	Otto Graham, Cle	258	167	2722	11
1954	Norm Van Brocklin, LA	260	139	2637	13
1955	Otto Graham, Cle	185	98	1721	15
1956	Ed Brown, Chi. Bears	168	96	1667	11
1957	Tommy O'Connell, Cle	110	63	1229	9
1958	Eddie LeBaron, Wash	145	79	1365	11
1959	Charlie Conerly, NY	194	113	1706	14
1960	Milt Plum, Cle	250	151	2297	21
1961	Milt Plum, Cle	302	177	2416	16
1962	Bart Starr, GB	285	178	2438	12
1963	Y.A. Tittle, NY	367	221	3145	36
1964	Bart Starr, GB	272	163	2144	15
1965	Rudy Bukich, Chi	312	176	2641	20
1966	Bart Starr, GB	251	156	2257	14
1967	Sonny Jurgensen, Wash	508	288	3747	31
1968	Earl Morrall, Bal	317	182	2909	26
1969	Sonny Jurgensen, Wash	442	274	3102	22
1970	John Brodie, SF	378	223	2941	24
1971	Roger Staubach, Dal	211	126	1882	15
1972	Norm Snead, NY	325	196	2307	17
1973	Roger Staubach, Dal	286	179	2428	23
1974	Sonny Jurgensen, Wash	167	107	1185	11
1975	Fran Tarkenton, Min	425	273	2994	25
1976	James Harris, LA	158	91	1460	8
1977	Roger Staubach, Dal	361	210	2620	18
1978	Roger Staubach, Dal	413	231	3190	25
1979	Roger Staubach, Dal	461	267	3586	27
1980	Ron Jaworski, Phi	451	257	3529	27
1981	Joe Montana, SF	488	311	3565	19
1982	Joe Theismann, Wash	252	161	2033	13
1983	Steve Bartkowski, Atl	432	274	3167	22
1984	Joe Montana, SF	432	279	3630	28
1985	Joe Montana, SF	494	303	3653	27
1986	Tommy Kramer, Min	372	208	3000	24
1987	Joe Montana, SF	398	266	3054	31
1988	Wade Wilson, Min	332	204	2746	15
1989	Don Majkowski, GB	599	353	4318	27
1990	Joe Montana, SF	520	321	3944	26
1991	Steve Young, SF	279	180	2517	17
1992	Steve Young, SF	402	268	3465	25
1993	Steve Young, SF	462	314	4023	29
1994	Steve Young, SF	461	324	3969	35
1995	Brett Favre, GB	570	359	4413	38
1996	Steve Young, SF	316	214	2410	14
1997	Steve Young, SF	356	241	3029	19

Note: In 1945, Sammy Baugh and Sid Luckman tied with 8 points on an inverse rating system.

AFL-AFC

Multiple winners: Dan Marino (5); Ken Anderson and Len Dawson (4); Bob Griese, Daryle Lamonica, Warren Moon and Ken Stabler (2).

Year		Att	Cmp	Yds	TD
1960	Jack Kemp, LA	406	211	3018	20
1961	George Blanda, Hou	362	187	3330	36
1962	Len Dawson, Dal	310	189	2759	29
1963	Tobin Rote, SD	286	170	2510	20
1964	Len Dawson, KC	354	199	2879	30
1965	John Hadl, SD	348	174	2798	20
1966	Len Dawson, KC	284	159	2527	26
1967	Daryle Lamonica, Oak	425	220	3228	30
1968	Len Dawson, KC	224	131	2109	17
1969	Greg Cook, Cin	197	106	1854	15
1970	Daryle Lamonica, Oak	356	179	2516	22
1971	Bob Griese, Mia	263	145	2089	19
1972	Earl Morrall, Mia	150	83	1360	11
1973	Ken Stabler, Oak	260	163	1997	14
1974	Ken Anderson, Cin	328	213	2667	18
1975	Ken Anderson, Cin	377	228	3169	21
1976	Ken Stabler, Oak	291	194	2737	27
1977	Bob Griese, Mia	307	180	2252	22
1978	Terry Bradshaw, Pit	368	207	2915	28
1979	Dan Fouts, SD	530	332	4082	24
1980	Brian Sipe, Cle	554	337	4132	30
1981	Ken Anderson, Cin	479	300	3753	29
1982	Ken Anderson, Cin	309	218	2495	12
1983	Dan Marino, Mia	296	173	2210	20
1984	Dan Marino, Mia	564	362	5084	48
1985	Ken O'Brien, NY	488	297	3888	25
1986	Dan Marino, Mia	623	378	4746	44
1987	Bernie Kosar, Cle	389	241	3033	22
1988	Boomer Esiason, Cin	388	223	3572	28
1989	Dan Marino, Mia	550	308	3997	24
1990	Warren Moon, Hou	584	362	4689	33
1991	Jim Kelly, Buf	474	304	3844	33
1992	Warren Moon, Hou	346	224	2521	18
1993	John Elway, Den	551	348	4030	25
1994	Dan Marino, Mia	615	385	4453	30
1995	Jim Harbaugh, Ind	314	200	2575	17
1996	John Elway, Den	466	287	3328	26
1997	Mark Brunell, Jax	435	264	3281	18

Receptions

NFL-NFC

Multiple winners: Don Hutson (8); Raymond Berry, Tom Fears, Pete Pihos, Jerry Rice, Sterling Sharpe and Billy Wilson (3); Dwight Clark, Herman Moore, Ahmad Rashad and Charley Taylor (2).

Year		No	Yds	Avg	TD
1932	Ray Flaherty, NY	21	350	16.7	3
1933	Shipwreck Kelly, Bklyn	22	246	11.2	3
1934	Joe Carter, Phi	16	238	14.9	4
	& Red Badgro, NY	16	206	12.9	1
1935	Tod Goodwin, NY	26	432	16.6	4
1936	Don Hutson, GB	34	536	15.8	8
1937	Don Hutson, GB	41	552	13.5	7
1938	Gaynell Tinsley, Chi. Cards	41	516	12.6	1
1939	Don Hutson, GB	34	846	24.9	6
1940	Don Looney, Phi	58	707	12.2	4
1941	Don Hutson, GB	58	739	12.7	10
1942	Don Hutson, GB	74	1211	16.4	17
1943	Don Hutson, GB	47	776	16.5	11
1944	Don Hutson, GB	58	866	14.9	9
1945	Don Hutson, GB	47	834	17.7	9
1946	Jim Benton, LA	63	981	15.6	6
1947	Jim Keane, Chi. Bears	64	910	14.2	10
1948	Tom Fears, LA	51	698	13.7	4
1949	Tom Fears, LA	77	1013	13.2	9
1950	Tom Fears, LA	84	1116	13.3	7
1951	Elroy Hirsch, LA	66	1495	22.7	17
1952	Mac Speedie, Cle	62	911	14.7	5
1953	Pete Pihos, Phi	63	1049	16.7	10
1954	Pete Pihos, Phi	60	872	14.5	10
	& Billy Wilson, SF	60	830	13.8	5
1955	Pete Pihos, Phi	62	864	13.9	7
1956	Billy Wilson, SF	60	889	14.8	5
1957	Billy Wilson, SF	52	757	14.6	6
1958	Raymond Berry, Bal	56	794	14.2	9
	& Pete Retzlaff, Phi	56	766	13.7	2
1959	Raymond Berry, Bal	66	959	14.5	14
1960	Raymond Berry, Bal	74	1298	17.5	10
1961	Red Phillips, LA	78	1092	14.0	5
1962	Bobby Mitchell, Wash	72	1384	19.2	11
1963	Bobby Joe Conrad, St. L	73	967	13.2	10
1964	Johnny Morris, Chi. Bears	93	1200	12.9	10
1965	Dave Parks, SF	80	1344	16.8	12
1966	Charley Taylor, Wash	72	1119	15.5	12
1967	Charley Taylor, Wash	70	990	14.1	9
1968	Clifton McNeil, SF	71	994	14.0	7
1969	Dan Abramowicz, NO	73	1015	13.9	7
1970	Dick Gordon, Chi	71	1026	14.5	13
1971	Bob Tucker, NY	59	791	13.4	4
1972	Harold Jackson, Phi	62	1048	16.9	4
1973	Harold Carmichael, Phi	67	1116	16.7	9
1974	Charles Young, Phi	63	696	11.0	3
1975	Chuck Foreman, Min	73	691	9.5	9
1976	Drew Pearson, Dal	58	806	13.9	6
1977	Ahmad Rashad, Min	51	681	13.4	2
1978	Rickey Young, Min	88	704	8.0	5
1979	Ahmad Rashad, Min	80	1156	14.5	9
1980	Earl Cooper, SF	83	567	6.8	4
1981	Dwight Clark, SF	85	1105	13.0	4
1982	Dwight Clark, SF	60	913	12.2	5
1983	Roy Green, St. L	78	1227	15.7	14
	Charlie Brown, Wash	78	1225	15.7	8
	& Earnest Gray, NY	78	1139	14.6	5
1984	Art Monk, Wash	106	1372	12.9	7
1985	Roger Craig, SF	92	1016	11.0	6
1986	Jerry Rice, SF	86	1570	18.3	15
1987	J.T. Smith, St. L	91	1117	12.3	8
1988	Henry Ellard, LA	86	1414	16.4	10
1989	Sterling Sharpe, GB	90	1423	15.8	12
1990	Jerry Rice, SF	100	1502	15.0	13
1991	Michael Irvin, Dal	93	1523	16.4	8
1992	Sterling Sharpe, GB	108	1461	13.5	13
1993	Sterling Sharpe, GB	112	1274	11.4	11
1994	Cris Carter, Min	122	1256	10.3	7
1995	Herman Moore, Det	123	1686	13.7	14
1996	Jerry Rice, SF	108	1254	11.6	8
1997	Herman Moore, Det	104	1293	12.4	8

AFL-AFC

Multiple winners: Lionel Taylor (5); Lance Alworth, Haywood Jeffires, Lydell Mitchell and Kellen Winslow (3); Fred Biletnikoff, Todd Christensen, Carl Pickens and Al Toon (2).

Year		No	Yds	Avg	TD
1960	Lionel Taylor, Den	92	1235	13.4	12
1961	Lionel Taylor, Den	100	1176	11.8	4
1962	Lionel Taylor, Den	77	908	11.8	4
1963	Lionel Taylor, Den	78	1101	14.1	10
1964	Charley Hennigan, Hou	101	1546	15.3	8
1965	Lionel Taylor, Den	85	1131	13.3	6
1966	Lance Alworth, SD	73	1383	18.9	13
1967	George Sauer, NY	75	1189	15.9	6
1968	Lance Alworth, SD	68	1312	19.3	10
1969	Lance Alworth, SD	64	1003	15.7	4
1970	Marlin Briscoe, Buf	57	1036	18.2	8
1971	Fred Biletnikoff, Oak	61	929	15.2	9
1972	Fred Biletnikoff, Oak	58	802	13.8	7
1973	Fred Willis, Hou	57	371	6.5	1
1974	Lydell Mitchell, Bal	72	544	7.6	2
1975	Reggie Rucker, Cle	60	770	12.8	3
	& Lydell Mitchell, Bal	60	544	9.1	4
1976	MacArthur Lane, KC	66	686	10.4	1
1977	Lydell Mitchell, Bal	71	620	8.7	4
1978	Steve Largent, Sea	71	1168	16.5	8
1979	Joe Washington, Bal	82	750	9.1	3
1980	Kellen Winslow, SD	89	1290	14.5	9
1981	Kellen Winslow, SD	88	1075	12.2	10
1982	Kellen Winslow, SD	54	721	13.4	6
1983	Todd Christensen, LA	92	1247	13.6	12
1984	Ozzie Newsome, Cle	89	1001	11.2	5
1985	Lionel James, SD	86	1027	11.9	6
1986	Todd Christensen, LA	95	1153	12.1	8
1987	Al Toon, NY	68	976	14.4	5
1988	Al Toon, NY	93	1067	11.5	5
1989	Andre Reed, Buf	88	1312	14.9	9
1990	Haywood Jeffires, Hou	74	1048	14.2	8
	& Drew Hill, Hou	74	1019	13.8	5
1991	Haywood Jeffires, Hou	100	1181	11.8	7
1992	Haywood Jeffires, Hou	90	913	10.1	9
1993	Reggie Langhorne, Ind	85	1038	12.2	3
1994	Ben Coates, NE	96	1174	12.2	7
1995	Carl Pickens, Cin	99	1234	12.5	17
1996	Carl Pickens, Cin	100	1180	11.8	12
1997	Tim Brown, Oak	104	1408	13.5	5

Annual NFL Leaders (Cont.)

Rushing

NFL-NFC

Multiple winners: Jim Brown (8); Walter Payton and Barry Sanders (5); Emmitt Smith and Steve Van Buren (4); Eric Dickerson (3); Cliff Battles, John Brockington, Larry Brown, Bill Dudley, Leroy Kelly, Bill Paschal, Joe Perry, Gale Sayers and Whizzer White (2).

Year		Car	Yds	Avg	TD
1932	Cliff Battles, Bos	148	576	3.9	3
1933	Jim Musick, Bos	173	809	4.7	5
1934	Beattie Feathers, Chi. Bears	119	1004	8.4	8
1935	Doug Russell, Chi. Cards	140	499	3.6	0
1936	Tuffy Leemans, NY	206	830	4.0	2
1937	Cliff Battles, Wash	216	874	4.0	5
1938	Whizzer White, Pit	152	567	3.7	4
1939	Bill Osmanski, Chi. Bears	121	699	5.8	7
1940	Whizzer White, Det	146	514	3.5	5
1941	Pug Manders, Bklyn	111	486	4.4	5
1942	Bill Dudley, Pit	162	696	4.3	5
1943	Bill Paschal, NY	147	572	3.9	10
1944	Bill Paschal, NY	196	737	3.8	9
1945	Steve Van Buren, Phi	143	832	5.8	15
1946	Bill Dudley, Pit	146	604	4.1	3
1947	Steve Van Buren, Phi	217	1008	4.6	13
1948	Steve Van Buren, Phi	201	945	4.7	10
1949	Steve Van Buren, Phi	263	1146	4.4	11
1950	Marion Motley, Cle	140	810	5.8	3
1951	Eddie Price, NY Giants	271	971	3.6	7
1952	Dan Towler, LA	156	894	5.7	10
1953	Joe Perry, SF	192	1018	5.3	10
1954	Joe Perry, SF	173	1049	6.1	8
1955	Alan Ameche, Bal	213	961	4.5	9
1956	Rick Casares, Chi. Bears	234	1126	4.8	12
1957	Jim Brown, Cle	202	942	4.7	9
1958	Jim Brown, Cle	257	1527	5.9	17
1959	Jim Brown, Cle	290	1329	4.6	14
1960	Jim Brown, Cle	215	1257	5.8	9
1961	Jim Brown, Cle	305	1408	4.6	8
1962	Jim Taylor, GB	272	1474	5.4	19
1963	Jim Brown, Cle	291	1863	6.4	12
1964	Jim Brown, Cle	280	1446	5.2	7
1965	Jim Brown, Cle	289	1544	5.3	17
1966	Gale Sayers, Chi	229	1231	5.4	8
1967	Leroy Kelly, Cle	235	1205	5.1	11
1968	Leroy Kelly, Cle	248	1239	5.0	16
1969	Gale Sayers, Chi	236	1032	4.4	8
1970	Larry Brown, Wash	237	1125	4.7	5
1971	John Brockington, GB	216	1105	5.1	4
1972	Larry Brown, Wash	285	1216	4.3	8
1973	John Brockington, GB	265	1144	4.3	3
1974	Lawrence McCutcheon, LA	236	1109	4.7	3
1975	Jim Otis, St. L	269	1076	4.0	5
1976	Walter Payton, Chi	311	1390	4.5	13
1977	Walter Payton, Chi	339	1852	5.5	14
1978	Walter Payton, Chi	333	1395	4.2	11
1979	Walter Payton, Chi	369	1610	4.4	14
1980	Walter Payton, Chi	317	1460	4.6	6
1981	George Rogers, NO	378	1674	4.4	13
1982	Tony Dorsett, Dal	177	745	4.2	5
1983	Eric Dickerson, LA	390	1808	4.6	18
1984	Eric Dickerson, LA	379	2105	5.6	14
1985	Gerald Riggs, Atl	397	1719	4.3	10
1986	Eric Dickerson, LA	404	1821	4.5	11
1987	Charles White, LA	324	1374	4.2	11
1988	Herschel Walker, Dal	361	1514	4.2	5
1989	Barry Sanders, Det	280	1470	5.3	14
1990	Barry Sanders, Det	255	1304	5.1	13
1991	Emmitt Smith, Dal	365	1563	4.3	12
1992	Emmitt Smith, Dal	373	1713	4.6	18
1993	Emmitt Smith, Dal	283	1486	5.3	9
1994	Barry Sanders, Det	331	1883	5.7	7
1995	Emmitt Smith, Dal	377	1773	4.7	25
1996	Barry Sanders, Det	307	1553	5.1	11
1997	Barry Sanders, Det	335	2053	6.1	11

Note: Jim Brown led the NFL in rushing eight of his nine years in the league. The one season he didn't win (1962) he finished fourth (996 yds) behind Jim Taylor, John Henry Johnson of Pittsburgh (1,141 yds) and Dick Bass of the LA Rams (1,033 yds).

AFL-AFC

Multiple winners: Earl Campbell and O.J. Simpson (4); Thurman Thomas (3); Terrell Davis, Eric Dickerson, Cookie Gilchrist, Floyd Little, Jim Nance and Curt Warner (2).

Year		Car	Yds	Avg	TD
1960	Abner Haynes, Dal	157	875	5.6	9
1961	Billy Cannon, Hou	200	948	4.7	6
1962	Cookie Gilchrist, Buf	214	1096	5.1	13
1963	Clem Daniels, Oak	215	1099	5.1	3
1964	Cookie Gilchrist, Buf	230	981	4.3	6
1965	Paul Lowe, SD	222	1121	5.0	7
1966	Jim Nance, Bos	299	1458	4.9	11
1967	Jim Nance, Bos	269	1216	4.5	7
1968	Paul Robinson, Cin	238	1023	4.3	8
1969	Dickie Post, SD	182	873	4.8	6
1970	Floyd Little, Den	209	901	4.3	3
1971	Floyd Little, Den	284	1133	4.0	6
1972	O.J. Simpson, Buf	292	1251	4.3	6
1973	O.J. Simpson, Buf	332	2003	6.0	12
1974	Otis Armstrong, Den	263	1407	5.3	9
1975	O.J. Simpson, Buf	329	1817	5.5	16
1976	O.J. Simpson, Buf	290	1503	5.2	8
1977	Mark van Eeghen, Oak	324	1273	3.9	7
1978	Earl Campbell, Hou	302	1450	4.8	13
1979	Earl Campbell, Hou	368	1697	4.6	19
1980	Earl Campbell, Hou	373	1934	5.2	13
1981	Earl Campbell, Hou	361	1376	3.8	10
1982	Freeman McNeil, NY	151	786	5.2	6
1983	Curt Warner, Sea	335	1449	4.3	13
1984	Earnest Jackson, SD	296	1179	4.0	8
1985	Marcus Allen, LA	380	1759	4.6	11
1986	Curt Warner, Sea	319	1481	4.6	13
1987	Eric Dickerson, Ind	223	1011	4.5	5
1988	Eric Dickerson, Ind	388	1659	4.3	14
1989	Christian Okoye, KC	370	1480	4.0	12
1990	Thurman Thomas, Buf	271	1297	4.8	11
1991	Thurman Thomas, Buf	288	1407	4.9	7
1992	Barry Foster, Pit	390	1690	4.3	11
1993	Thurman Thomas, Buf	355	1315	3.7	6
1994	Chris Warren, Sea	333	1545	4.6	9
1995	Curtis Martin, NE	368	1487	4.0	14
1996	Terrell Davis, Den	345	1538	4.5	13
1997	Terrell Davis, Den	369	1750	4.7	15

Note: Eric Dickerson was traded to Indianapolis from the NFC's LA Rams during the 1987 season. In three games with the Rams, he carried the ball 60 times for 277 yds, a 4.6 avg and 1 TD. His official AFC statistics above came in nine games with the Colts.

Scoring

NFL-NFC

Multiple winners: Don Hutson (5); Dutch Clark, Pat Harder, Paul Hornung, Chip Lohmiller and Mark Moseley (3); Kevin Butler, Mike Cofer, Fred Cox, Jack Manders, Chester Marcol, Eddie Murray, Emmitt Smith, Gordy Soltau and Doak Walker (2).

Year		TD	FG	PAT	Pts
1932	Dutch Clark, Portsmouth	6	3	10	55
1933	Glenn Presnell, Portsmouth	6	6	10	64
	& Ken Strong, NY	6	5	13	64
1934	Jack Manders, Chi. Bears	3	10	31	79
1935	Dutch Clark, Det	6	1	16	55
1936	Dutch Clark, Det	7	4	19	73
1937	Jack Manders, Chi. Bears	5	8	15	69
1938	Clarke Hinkle, GB	7	3	7	58
1939	Andy Farkas, Wash	11	0	2	68
1940	Don Hutson, GB	7	0	15	57
1941	Don Hutson, GB	12	1	20	95
1942	Don Hutson, GB	17	1	33	138
1943	Don Hutson, GB	12	3	26	117
1944	Don Hutson, GB	9	0	31	85
1945	Steve Van Buren, Phi	18	0	2	110
1946	Ted Fritsch, GB	10	9	13	100
1947	Pat Harder, Chi. Cards	7	7	39	102
1948	Pat Harder, Chi. Cards	6	7	53	110
1949	Gene Roberts, NY Giants	17	0	0	102
	& Pat Harder, Chi. Cards	8	3	45	102
1950	Doak Walker, Det	11	8	38	128
1951	Elroy Hirsch, LA	17	0	0	102
1952	Gordy Soltau, SF	7	6	34	94
1953	Gordy Soltau, SF	6	10	48	114
1954	Bobby Walston, Phi	11	4	36	114
1955	Doak Walker, Det	7	9	27	96
1956	Bobby Layne, Det	5	12	33	99
1957	Sam Baker, Wash	1	14	29	77
	& Lou Groza, Cle	0	15	32	77
1958	Jim Brown, Cle	18	0	0	108
1959	Paul Hornung, GB	7	7	31	94
1960	Paul Hornung, GB	15	15	41	176
1961	Paul Hornung, GB	10	15	41	146
1962	Jim Taylor, GB	19	0	0	114
1963	Don Chandler, NY	0	18	52	106
1964	Lenny Moore, Bal	20	0	0	120
1965	Gale Sayers, Chi	22	0	0	132
1966	Bruce Gossett, LA	0	28	29	113
1967	Jim Bakken, St.L	0	27	36	117
1968	Leroy Kelly, Cle	20	0	0	120
1969	Fred Cox, Min	0	26	43	121
1970	Fred Cox, Min	0	30	35	125
1971	Curt Knight, Wash	0	29	27	114
1972	Chester Marcol, GB	0	33	29	128
1973	David Ray, LA	0	30	40	130
1974	Chester Marcol, GB	0	25	19	94
1975	Chuck Foreman, Min	22	0	0	132
1976	Mark Moseley, Wash	0	22	31	97
1977	Walter Payton, Chi	16	0	0	96
1978	Frank Corral, LA	0	29	31	118
1979	Mark Moseley, Wash	0	25	39	114
1980	Eddie Murray, Det	0	27	35	116
1981	Rafael Septien, Dal	0	27	40	121
	& Eddie Murray, Det	0	25	46	121
1982	Wendell Tyler, LA	13	0	0	78
1983	Mark Moseley, Wash	0	33	62	161
1984	Ray Wersching, SF	0	25	56	131
1985	Kevin Butler, Chi	0	31	51	144
1986	Kevin Butler, Chi	0	28	36	120
1987	Jerry Rice, SF	23	0	0	138
1988	Mike Cofer, SF	0	27	40	121
1989	Mike Cofer, SF	0	29	49	136
1990	Chip Lohmiller, Wash	0	30	41	131
1991	Chip Lohmiller, Wash	0	31	56	149
1992	Chip Lohmiller, Wash	0	30	30	120
	& Morten Andersen, NO	0	29	33	120
1993	Jason Hanson, Det	0	34	28	130
1994	Emmitt Smith, Dal	22	0	0	132
	& Fuad Reveiz, Min	0	34	30	132
1995	Emmitt Smith, Dal	25	0	0	150
1996	John Kasay, Car.	0	37	34	145
1997	Richie Cunningham, Dal.	0	34	24	126

AFL-AFC

Multiple winners: Gino Cappelletti (5); Gary Anderson (3); Jim Breech, Roy Gerela, Gene Mingo, Nick Lowery, John Smith, Pete Stoyanovich and Jim Turner (2).

Year		TD	FG	PAT	Pts
1960	Gene Mingo, Den	6	18	33	123
1961	Gino Cappelletti, Bos	8	17	48	147
1962	Gene Mingo, Den	4	27	32	137
1963	Gino Cappelletti, Bos	2	22	35	113
1964	Gino Cappelletti, Bos	7	25	36	155
1965	Gino Cappelletti, Bos	9	17	27	132
1966	Gino Cappelletti, Bos	6	16	35	119
1967	George Blanda, Oak	0	20	56	116
1968	Jim Turner, NY	0	34	43	145
1969	Jim Turner, NY	0	32	33	129
1970	Jan Stenerud, KC	0	30	26	116
1971	Garo Yepremian, Mia	0	28	33	117
1972	Bobby Howfield, NY	0	27	40	121
1973	Roy Gerela, Pit	0	29	36	123
1974	Roy Gerela, Pit	0	20	33	93
1975	O.J. Simpson, Buf	23	0	0	138
1976	Toni Linhart, Bal	0	20	49	109
1977	Errol Mann, Oak	0	20	39	99
1978	Pat Leahy, NY	0	22	41	107
1979	John Smith, NE	0	23	46	115
1980	John Smith, NE	0	26	51	129
1981	Nick Lowery, KC	0	26	37	115
	& Jim Breech, Cin	0	22	49	115
1982	Marcus Allen, LA	14	0	0	84
1983	Gary Anderson, Pit	0	27	38	119
1984	Gary Anderson, Pit	0	24	45	117
1985	Gary Anderson, Pit	0	33	40	139
1986	Tony Franklin, NE	0	32	44	140
1987	Jim Breech, Cin	0	24	25	97
1988	Scott Norwood, Buf	0	32	33	129
1989	David Treadwell, Den	0	27	39	120
1990	Nick Lowery, KC	0	34	37	139
1991	Pete Stoyanovich, Mia	0	31	28	121
1992	Pete Stoyanovich, Mia	0	30	34	124
1993	Jeff Jaeger, LA	0	35	27	132
1994	John Carney, SD	0	34	33	135
1995	Norm Johnson, Pit	0	34	39	141
1996	Cary Blanchard, Ind	0	36	27	135
1997	Mike Hollis, Jax	0	31	41	134

All-Time NFL Leaders

Through 1997 regular season.

CAREER

Players active in 1997 in **bold** type.

Passing Efficiency

Ratings based on performance standards established for completion percentage, average gain, touchdown percentage and interception percentage. Quarterbacks are allocated points according to how their statistics measure up to those standards. Minimum 1500 passing attempts.

		Yrs	Att	Cmp	Cmp%	Yards	Avg Gain	TD	TD%	Int	Int%	Rating
1	**Steve Young**	13	3548	2300	64.8	28,508	8.03	193	5.4	91	2.6	97.0
2	Joe Montana	15	5391	3409	63.2	40,551	7.52	273	5.1	139	2.6	92.3
3	**Brett Favre**	7	3206	1971	61.5	22,591	7.05	182	5.7	95	3.0	89.3
4	**Dan Marino**	15	7452	4453	59.8	55,416	7.44	385	5.2	220	3.0	87.8
5	Jim Kelly	11	4779	2874	60.1	35,467	7.42	237	5.0	175	3.7	84.4
6	Roger Staubach	11	2958	1685	57.0	22,700	7.67	153	5.2	109	3.7	83.4
7	Neil Lomax	8	3153	1817	57.6	22,771	7.22	136	4.3	90	2.9	82.7
8	Sonny Jurgensen	18	4262	2433	57.1	32,224	7.56	255	6.0	189	4.4	82.625
9	Len Dawson	19	3741	2136	57.1	28,711	7.67	239	6.4	183	4.9	82.555
10	**Troy Aikman**	9	3696	2292	62.0	26,016	7.04	129	3.5	110	3.0	82.3
11	Ken Anderson	16	4475	2654	59.3	32,838	7.34	197	4.4	160	3.6	81.9
12	Bernie Kosar	12	3365	1994	59.3	23,301	6.92	124	3.7	87	2.6	81.8
13	Danny White	13	2950	1761	59.7	21,959	7.44	155	5.3	132	4.5	81.7
14	**Dave Krieg**	18	5290	3093	58.5	37,948	7.17	261	4.9	199	3.8	81.5
15	**Warren Moon**	14	6528	3827	58.6	47,465	7.27	279	4.3	224	3.4	81.2
16	**Boomer Esiason**	14	5205	2969	57.0	37,920	7.29	247	4.7	184	3.5	81.1
17	**Jeff Hostetler**	12	2338	1357	58.0	16,430	7.03	94	4.0	71	3.0	80.480
18	**Neil O'Donnell**	8	2519	1438	57.1	16,810	6.67	89	3.5	53	2.1	80.471
19	Bart Starr	16	3149	1808	57.4	24,718	7.85	152	4.8	138	4.4	80.465
20	Ken O'Brien	10	3602	2110	58.6	25,094	6.97	128	3.6	98	2.7	80.436
21	Fran Tarkenton	18	6467	3686	57.0	47,003	7.27	342	5.3	266	4.1	80.354
22	**Scott Mitchell**	7	2016	1146	56.9	14,000	6.94	90	4.5	63	3.1	80.3
23	Dan Fouts	15	5604	3297	58.8	43,040	7.68	254	4.5	242	4.3	80.2
24	**Jeff George**	8	3233	1878	58.1	22,043	6.82	120	3.7	87	2.7	80.1
25	Tony Eason	8	1564	911	58.2	11,142	7.12	61	3.9	51	3.3	79.7

Note: The NFL does not recognize records from the All-American Football Conference (1946-49). If it did, **Otto Graham** would rank 5th (after Marino) with the following stats: 10 Yrs; 2,626 Att; 1,464 Comp; 55.8 Comp Pct; 23,584 Yards; 8.98 Avg Gain; 174 TD; 6.6 TD Pct; 135 Int; 5.1 Int Pct; and 86.6 Rating Pts.

Touchdown Passes

		No
1	**Dan Marino**	385
2	Fran Tarkenton	342
3	Johnny Unitas	290
4	**Warren Moon**	279
5	**John Elway**	278
6	Joe Montana	273
7	**Dave Krieg**	261
8	Sonny Jurgensen	255
9	Dan Fouts	254
10	**Boomer Esiason**	247
11	John Hadl	244
12	Len Dawson	239
13	Jim Kelly	237
14	George Blanda	236
15	John Brodie	214
16	Terry Bradshaw	212
	Y.A. Tittle	212
18	Jim Hart	209
19	**Jim Everett**	203
20	Roman Gabriel	201
21	Phil Simms	199
22	Ken Anderson	197
23	Joe Ferguson	196
	Bobby Layne	196
25	Norm Snead	196
26	Ken Stabler	194
27	**Steve Young**	193
	Steve DeBerg	193
29	Bob Griese	192
30	Sammy Baugh	187
31	Craig Morton	183
32	Steve Grogan	182
	Brett Favre	182
34	Ron Jaworski	179
35	Babe Parilli	178
36	**Vinny Testaverde**	175
37	Charlie Conerly	173
	Joe Namath	173
	Norm Van Brocklin	173
40	Charley Johnson	170
41	Daryle Lamonica	164
	Jim Plunkett	164
43	Earl Morrall	161
44	Joe Theismann	160
45	Tommy Kramer	159

Note: The NFL does not recognize records from the All-American Football Conference (1946-49). If it did, **Y.A. Tittle** would rank 12th (after Hadl) with 242 TDs and **Otto Graham** would rank 37th (after Testaverde) with 174 TDs.

Passes Intercepted

		No
1	George Blanda	277
2	John Hadl	268
3	Fran Tarkenton	266
4	Norm Snead	253
	Johnny Unitas	253
6	Jim Hart	247
7	Bobby Layne	243
8	Dan Fouts	242
9	John Brodie	224
	Warren Moon	224
11	Ken Stabler	222
12	Y.A. Tittle	221
13	**Dan Marino**	220
	Joe Namath	220
	Babe Parilli	220
16	**John Elway**	216
17	Terry Bradshaw	210
18	Joe Ferguson	209
19	Steve Grogan	208
20	Sammy Baugh	203
	Steve DeBerg	203
22	**Dave Krieg**	199
23	Jim Plunkett	198
24	Tobin Rote	191
25	Sonny Jurgensen	189

Passing Yards

		Yrs	Att	Comp	Pct	Yards
1	**Dan Marino**	15	7452	4453	59.8	55,416
2	**John Elway**	15	6894	3913	56.8	48,669
3	**Warren Moon**	14	6528	3827	58.6	47,465
4	Fran Tarkenton	18	6467	3686	57.0	47,003
5	Dan Fouts	15	5604	3297	58.8	43,040
6	Joe Montana	15	5391	3409	63.2	40,551
7	Johnny Unitas	18	5186	2830	54.6	40,239
8	**Dave Krieg**	18	5290	3093	58.5	37,948
9	**Boomer Esiason**	14	5205	2969	57.0	37,920
10	Jim Kelly	11	4779	2874	60.1	35,467
11	**Jim Everett**	12	4923	2841	57.7	34,837
12	Jim Hart	19	5076	2593	51.1	34,665
13	Steve DeBerg	16	4965	2844	57.3	33,872
14	John Hadl	16	4687	2363	50.4	33,503
15	Phil Simms	14	4647	2576	55.4	33,462
16	Ken Anderson	16	4475	2654	59.3	32,838
17	Sonny Jurgensen	18	4262	2433	57.1	32,224
18	John Brodie	17	4491	2469	55.0	31,548
19	Norm Snead	15	4353	2276	52.3	30,797
20	Joe Ferguson	18	4519	2369	52.4	29,817
21	Roman Gabriel	16	4498	2366	52.6	29,444
22	**Vinny Testaverde**	11	4177	2300	55.1	29,223
23	Len Dawson	19	3741	2136	57.1	28,711
24	**Steve Young**	13	3548	2300	64.8	28,508
25	Y.A. Tittle	15	3817	2118	55.5	28,339

Note: The NFL does not recognize records from the All-American Football Conference (1946-49). If it did, **Y.A. Tittle** would rank 16th (after Simms) with the following stats: 17 Yrs; 4,395 Att; 2,427 Comp; 55.2 Pct; and 33,070 Yards.

Rushing

		Yrs	Car	Yards	Avg	TD
1	Walter Payton	13	3838	16,726	4.4	110
2	**Barry Sanders**	9	2719	13,778	5.1	95
3	Eric Dickerson	11	2996	13,259	4.4	90
4	Tony Dorsett	12	2936	12,739	4.3	77
5	Jim Brown	9	2359	12,312	5.2	106
6	**Marcus Allen**	16	3022	12,243	4.1	123
7	Franco Harris	13	2949	12,120	4.1	91
8	**Thurman Thomas**	10	2720	11,405	4.2	63
9	John Riggins	14	2916	11,352	3.9	104
10	O.J. Simpson	11	2404	11,236	4.7	61
11	**Emmitt Smith**	8	2595	11,234	4.3	112
12	Ottis Anderson	14	2562	10,273	4.0	81
13	Earl Campbell	8	2187	9,407	4.3	74
14	Jim Taylor	10	1941	8,597	4.4	83
15	Joe Perry	14	1737	8,378	4.8	53
16	**Ernest Byner**	14	2095	8,261	3.9	56
17	**Herschel Walker**	12	1954	8,225	4.2	61
18	Roger Craig	11	1991	8,189	4.1	56
19	Gerald Riggs	10	1989	8,188	4.1	69
20	Larry Csonka	11	1891	8,081	4.3	64
21	Freeman McNeil	12	1798	8,074	4.5	38
22	James Brooks	12	1685	7,962	4.7	49
23	Mike Pruitt	11	1844	7,378	4.0	51
24	Leroy Kelly	10	1727	7,274	4.2	74
25	George Rogers	7	1692	7,176	4.2	54

Note: The NFL does not recognize records from the All-American Football Conference (1946-49). If it did, **Joe Perry** would rank 13th (after Anderson) with the following stats: 16 Yrs; 1,929 Att; 9,723 Yards; 5.0 Avg; and 71 TD.

Receptions

		Yrs	No	Yards	Avg	TD
1	**Jerry Rice**	13	1057	16,455	15.6	155
2	Art Monk	16	940	12,721	13.5	68
3	**Andre Reed**	13	826	11,764	14.2	80
4	Steve Largent	14	819	13,089	16.0	100
5	**Henry Ellard**	15	807	13,662	16.9	65
6	James Lofton	16	764	14,004	18.3	75
7	**Cris Carter**	11	756	9,436	12.5	89
8	Charlie Joiner	18	750	12,146	16.2	65
9	**Irving Fryar**	14	736	11,427	15.5	75
10	Gary Clark	11	699	10,856	15.5	65
11	**Michael Irvin**	10	666	10,680	16.0	61
12	Ozzie Newsome	13	662	7,980	12.1	47
13	Charley Taylor	13	649	9,110	14.0	79
14	**Andre Rison**	9	641	8,839	13.8	73
15	Drew Hill	15	634	9,831	15.5	60
16	Don Maynard	15	633	11,834	18.7	88
17	Raymond Berry	13	631	9,275	14.7	68
18	**Tim Brown**	10	599	8,588	14.3	60
19	Sterling Sharpe	7	595	8,134	13.7	65
	Anthony Miller	10	595	9,148	15.4	63
21	Harold Carmichael	14	590	8,985	15.2	79
22	Fred Biletnikoff	14	589	8,974	15.2	76
23	**Marcus Allen**	16	587	5,411	9.2	21
24	**Keith Byars**	12	584	5,403	9.3	28
25	Bill Brooks	11	583	8,001	13.7	46

All-Purpose Yards

		Rush	Rec	Ret	Total
1	Walter Payton	16,726	4,538	539	21,803
2	**Herschel Walker**	8,225	4,859	5,084	18,168
3	**Marcus Allen**	12,243	5,411	-6	17,648
4	**Jerry Rice**	614	16,455	6	17,075
5	**Barry Sanders**	13,778	2,632	118	16,528
6	Tony Dorsett	12,739	3,554	33	16,326
7	**Henry Ellard**	50	13,662	1,891	15,603
8	**Thurman Thomas**	11,405	4,084	0	15,489
9	Jim Brown	12,312	2,499	648	15,459
10	Eric Dickerson	13,259	2,137	15	15,411
11	James Brooks	7,962	3,621	3,327	14,910
12	Franco Harris	12,120	2,287	215	14,622
13	**Eric Metcalf**	2,365	5,096	6,982	14,443
14	O.J. Simpson	11,236	2,142	990	14,368
15	James Lofton	246	14,004	27	14,277
16	**Irving Fryar**	180	11,427	2,567	14,174
17	Bobby Mitchell	2,735	7,954	3,389	14,078
18	**Dave Meggett**	1,660	3,023	9,218	13,901
19	**Emmitt Smith**	11,234	2,434	0	13,668
20	**Earnest Byner**	8,261	4,605	631	13,497
21	John Riggins	11,352	2,090	-7	13,435
22	Steve Largent	83	13,089	224	13,396
23	Ottis Anderson	10,273	3,062	29	13,364
24	Drew Hill	19	9,831	3,487	13,337
25	**Mel Gray**	99	164	13,016	13,279

Years played: Allen (16), Anderson (14), Brooks (13), J. Brown (9), Byner (14), Dickerson (11), Dorsett (12), Ellard (15), Fryar (14), Gray (12), Harris (13), Hill (14), Largent (14), Lofton (16), Meggett (9), Metcalf (9), Mitchell (11), Payton (13), Rice (13), Riggins (14), Sanders (9), Simpson (11), Smith (8), Thomas (10) and Walker (12).

All-Time NFL Leaders (Cont.)

Scoring

Points

		Yrs	TD	FG	PAT	Total
1	George Blanda	26	9	335	943	2002
2	Nick Lowery	18	0	383	562	1711
3	Jan Stenerud	19	0	373	580	1699
4	**Gary Anderson**	16	0	385	526	1681
5	**Morten Andersen**	16	0	378	507	1641
6	**Norm Johnson**	16	0	322	592	1558
7	**Eddie Murray**	17	0	337	521	1532
8	Pat Leahy	18	0	304	558	1470
9	Jim Turner	16	1	304	521	1439
10	Matt Bahr	17	0	300	522	1422
11	Mark Moseley	16	0	300	482	1382
12	Jim Bakken	17	0	282	534	1380
13	Fred Cox	15	0	282	519	1365
14	Lou Groza	17	1	234	641	1349
15	Jim Breech	14	0	243	517	1246
16	**Al Del Greco**	16	0	263	435	1224
17	Chris Bahr	14	0	241	490	1213
18	**Kevin Butler**	13	0	265	413	1208
19	Gino Cappelletti	11	42	176	350	1130†
20	Ray Wersching	15	0	222	456	1122
21	Don Cockroft	13	0	216	432	1080
22	Garo Yepremian	14	0	210	444	1074
23	Bruce Gossett	11	0	219	374	1031
24	**Jerry Rice**	13	166	0	0	1000†
25	Sam Baker	15	2	179	428	977

† Cappelletti's total includes four 2-point conversions and Rice's total includes two.

Note: The NFL does not recognize records from the All-American Football Conference (1946-49). If it did, **Lou Groza** would move up to 6th (after Andersen) with the following stats: 21 Yrs; 1 TD; 264 FG, 810 PAT; 1,608 Pts.

Touchdowns

		Yrs	Rush	Rec	Ret	Total
1	**Jerry Rice**	13	10	155	1	166
2	**Marcus Allen**	16	123	21	1	145
3	Jim Brown	9	106	20	0	126
4	Walter Payton	13	110	15	0	125
5	**Emmitt Smith**	8	112	7	0	119
6	John Riggins	14	104	12	0	116
7	Lenny Moore	12	63	48	2	113
8	Don Hutson	11	3	99	3	105
	Barry Sanders	9	95	10	0	105
10	Steve Largent	14	1	100	0	101
11	Franco Harris	13	91	9	0	100
12	Eric Dickerson	11	90	6	0	96
13	Jim Taylor	10	83	10	0	93
14	Tony Dorsett	12	77	13	1	91
	Bobby Mitchell	11	18	65	8	91
16	**Cris Carter**	11	0	89	1	90
	Leroy Kelly	10	74	13	3	90
	Charley Taylor	13	11	79	0	90
19	Don Maynard	15	0	88	0	88
20	Lance Alworth	11	2	85	0	87
21	Ottis Anderson	14	81	5	0	86
	Paul Warfield	13	1	85	0	86
23	Mark Clayton	11	0	84	1	85
	Tommy McDonald	12	0	84	1	85
25	**Herschel Walker**	12	61	21	2	84

Note: The NFL does not recognize records from the All-American Football Conference (1946-49). If it did, **Joe Perry** would tie for 25th (with Walker) with the following stats: 16 Yrs; 71 Rush; 12 Rec; 1 Ret; 84 TDs.

Interceptions

		Yrs	No	Yards	TD
1	Paul Krause	16	81	1185	3
2	Emlen Tunnell	14	79	1282	4
3	Dick (Night Train) Lane	14	68	1207	5
4	Ken Riley	15	65	596	5
5	Ronnie Lott	14	63	730	5

Sacks

		Yrs	No
1	**Reggie White**	13	176½
2	**Bruce Smith**	13	154
3	**Richard Dent**	13	137½
4	**Kevin Greene**	13	133
5	Lawrence Taylor	12	132½

Note: The NFL did not begin officially compiling sacks until 1982. Deacon Jones, who played with the Rams, Chargers and Redskins from 1961-74, is often credited with 173½ sacks. Jack Youngblood (150½) and Alan Page (148) would also make an unofficial top five. Also, Lawrence Taylor has 142 career sacks if you count his rookie year of 1981, the year before sacks became an official stat.

Safeties

		Yrs	No
1	Ted Hendricks	15	4
	Doug English	10	4

Fourteen players tied with three.

Kickoff Returns

Minimum 75 returns.

		Yrs	No	Yards	Avg	TD
1	Gale Sayers	7	91	2781	30.6	6
2	Lynn Chandnois	7	92	2720	29.6	3
3	Abe Woodson	9	193	5538	28.7	5
4	Buddy Young	6	90	2514	27.9	2
5	Travis Williams	5	102	2801	27.5	6

Punting

Minimum 300 punts.

		Yrs	No	Yards	Avg
1	Sammy Baugh	16	338	15,245	45.1
2	Tommy Davis	11	511	22,833	44.7
3	Yale Lary	11	503	22,279	44.3
4	Horace Gillom	7	385	16,872	43.8
	Jerry Norton	11	358	15,671	43.8

Punt Returns

Minimum 75 returns.

		Yrs	No	Yards	Avg	TD
1	**Darrien Gordon**	4	143	1950	13.6	6
2	George McAfee	8	112	1431	12.8	2
3	Jack Christiansen	8	85	1084	12.8	8
4	Claude Gibson	5	110	1381	12.6	3
5	Bill Dudley	9	124	1515	12.2	3

Long-Playing Records

Seasons

		No
1	George Blanda, QB-K	26
2	Earl Morrall, QB	21
3	Jim Marshall, DE	20
	Jackie Slater, OL	20

Games

		No
1	George Blanda, QB-K	340
2	Jim Marshall, DE	282
3	**Clay Matthews**, LB	278

Consecutive Games

		No
1	Jim Marshall, DE	282
2	Mick Tingelhoff, C	240
3	Jim Bakken, K	234

SINGLE SEASON

Passing

Yards Gained	Year	Att	Cmp	Pct	Yds
Dan Marino, Mia	1984	564	362	64.2	5084
Dan Fouts, SD	1981	609	360	59.1	4802
Dan Marino, Mia	1986	623	378	60.7	4746
Dan Fouts, SD	1980	589	348	59.1	4715
Warren Moon, Hou	1991	655	404	61.7	4690
Warren Moon, Hou	1990	584	362	62.0	4689
Neil Lomax, St.L	1984	560	345	61.6	4614
Drew Bledsoe, NE	1994	691	400	57.9	4555
Lynn Dicky, GB	1983	484	286	59.7	4458
Brett Favre, GB	1995	570	359	63.0	4413

Efficiency	Year	Att/Cmp	TD	Rtg
Steve Young, SF	1994	461/324	35	112.8
Joe Montana, SF	1989	386/271	26	112.4
Milt Plum, Cle	1960	250/151	21	110.4
Sammy Baugh, Wash	1945	182/128	11	109.9
Dan Marino, Mia	1984	564/362	48	108.9
Sid Luckman, Bears	1943	202/110	28	107.5
Steve Young, SF	1992	402/268	25	107.0
Bart Starr, GB	1966	251/156	14	105.0
Y.A. Tittle, NYG	1963	367/221	36	104.8
Roger Staubach, Dal	1971	211/126	15	104.8

Receptions

Catches	Year	No	Yds
Herman Moore, Det.	1995	123	1686
Jerry Rice, SF	1995	122	1848
Cris Carter, Min	1995	122	1371
Cris Carter, Min	1994	122	1256
Isaac Bruce, St. L	1995	119	1781
Jerry Rice, SF	1994	112	1499
Sterling Sharpe, GB	1993	112	1274
Michael Irvin, Dal	1995	111	1603
Terance Mathis, Atl	1994	111	1342
Brett Perriman, Det	1995	108	1488
Sterling Sharpe, GB	1992	108	1461
Jerry Rice, SF	1996	108	1254

Rushing

Yards Gained	Year	Car	Yds	Avg
Eric Dickerson, LA Rams	1984	379	2105	5.6
Barry Sanders, Det	1997	335	2053	6.1
O.J. Simpson, Buf.	1973	332	2003	6.0
Earl Campbell, Hou	1980	373	1934	5.2
Barry Sanders, Det.	1994	331	1883	5.7
Jim Brown, Cle	1963	291	1863	6.4
Walter Payton, Chi	1977	339	1852	5.5
Eric Dickerson, LA Rams	1986	404	1821	4.5
O.J. Simpson, Buf.	1975	329	1817	5.5
Eric Dickerson, LA Rams	1983	390	1808	4.6
Emmitt Smith, Dal	1995	377	1773	4.7

Scoring

Points

	Year	TD	PAT	FG	Pts
Paul Hornung, GB	1960	15	41	15	176
Mark Moseley, Wash	1983	0	62	33	161
Gino Cappelletti, Bos	1964	7	38	25	155
Emmitt Smith, Dal	1995	25	0	0	150
Chip Lohmiller, Wash	1991	0	56	31	149
Gino Cappelletti, Bos	1961	8	48	17	147
Paul Hornung, GB	1961	10	41	15	146
Jim Turner, Jets	1968	0	43	34	145
John Kasay, Car.	1996	0	34	37	145
John Riggins, Wash	1983	24	0	0	144
Kevin Butler, Chi.	1985	0	51	31	144
Tony Franklin, NE	1986	0	44	32	140

Touchdowns

	Year	Rush	Rec	Ret	Total
Emmitt Smith, Dal	1995	25	0	0	25
John Riggins, Wash	1983	24	0	0	24
O.J. Simpson, Buf.	1975	16	7	0	23
Jerry Rice, SF	1987	1	22	0	23
Gale Sayers, Chi	1966	14	6	2	22
Chuck Foreman, Min	1975	13	9	0	22
Emmitt Smith, Dal	1994	21	1	0	22
Jim Brown, Cle	1965	17	4	0	21
Joe Morris, NY Giants	1985	21	0	0	21
Terry Allen, Wash	1996	21	0	0	21
Lenny Moore, Bal	1964	16	3	1	20
Leroy Kelly, Cle.	1968	16	4	0	20
Eric Dickerson, LA Rams	1983	18	2	0	20

Note: The NFL regular season schedule grew from 12 games (1947-60) to 14 (1961-77) to 16 (1978-present). The AFL regular season schedule was always 14 games (1960-69).

Touchdowns Passing

	Year	No
Dan Marino, Miami	1984	48
Dan Marino, Miami	1986	44
Brett Favre, Green Bay	1996	39
Brett Favre, Green Bay	1995	38
George Blanda, Houston	1961	36
Y.A. Tittle, NY Giants	1963	36
Brett Favre, Green Bay	1997	35
Steve Young, San Francisco	1994	35
Y.A. Tittle, NY Giants	1962	33
Dan Fouts, San Diego	1981	33
Warren Moon, Houston	1990	33
Jim Kelly, Buffalo	1991	33
Brett Favre, Green Bay	1994	33
Warren Moon, Minnesota	1995	33
Vinny Testaverde, Baltimore	1996	33

Touchdowns Receiving

	Year	No
Jerry Rice, San Francisco	1987	22
Mark Clayton, Miami	1984	18
Sterling Sharpe, Green Bay	1994	18
Don Hutson, Green Bay	1942	17
Elroy (Crazylegs) Hirsch, LA Rams	1951	17
Bill Groman, Houston	1961	17
Jerry Rice, San Francisco	1989	17
Cris Carter, Minnesota	1995	17
Carl Pickens, Cincinnati	1995	17
Art Powell, Oakland	1963	16

Four players tied with 15 each (Rice scored 15 three times).

All-Time NFL Leaders (Cont.)

Touchdowns Rushing

	Year	No
Emmitt Smith, Dallas	1995	25
John Riggins, Washington	1983	24
Joe Morris, NY Giants	1985	21
Emmitt Smith, Dallas	1994	21
Terry Allen, Washington	1996	21
Jim Taylor, Green Bay	1962	19
Earl Campbell, Houston	1979	19
Chuck Muncie, San Diego	1981	19
Eric Dickerson, LA Rams	1983	18
George Rogers, Washington	1986	18
Emmitt Smith, Dallas	1992	18
Jim Brown, Cleveland	1958	17
Jim Brown, Cleveland	1965	17

Field Goals

	Year	Att	No
John Kasay, Carolina	1996	45	37
Cary Blanchard, Indianapolis	1996	40	36
Ali Haji-Sheikh, NY Giants	1983	42	35
Jeff Jaeger, LA Raiders	1993	44	35
Richie Cunningham, Dallas	1997	37	34
Nick Lowery, Kansas City	1990	37	34
Jim Turner, NY Jets	1968	46	34
Jason Hanson, Detroit	1993	43	34
John Carney, San Diego	1994	38	34
Fuad Reveiz, Minnesota	1994	39	34
Norm Johnson, Pittsburgh	1995	41	34
Gary Anderson, Pittsburgh	1985	42	33
Mark Moseley, Washington	1983	47	33
Chester Marcol, Green Bay	1972	48	33

Interceptions

	Year	No
Dick (Night Train) Lane, Detroit	1952	14
Dan Sandifer, Washington	1948	13
Spec Sanders, NY Yanks	1950	13
Lester Hayes, Oakland	1980	13

Kickoff Returns

	Year	Avg
Travis Williams, Green Bay	1967	41.1
Gale Sayers, Chicago Bears	1967	37.7
Ollie Matson, Chicago Cards	1958	35.5

Punting

Qualifiers	Year	Avg
Sammy Baugh, Washington	1940	51.4
Yale Lary, Detroit	1963	48.9
Sammy Baugh, Washington	1941	48.7

Punt Returns

	Year	Avg
Herb Rich, Baltimore	1950	23.0
Jack Christiansen, Detroit	1952	21.5
Dick Christy, NY Titans	1961	21.3
Bob Hayes, Dallas	1968	20.8

Sacks

	Year	No
Mark Gastineau, NY Jets	1984	22
Reggie White, Philadelphia	1987	21
Chris Doleman, Minnesota	1989	21
Lawrence Taylor, NY Giants	1986	20½

Note: The NFL did not begin officially compiling sacks until 1982. Cincinnati's Coy Bacon is widely, although not officially, credited with 26 sacks during the 1976 season.

SINGLE GAME

Passing

Yards Gained	Date	Yds
Norm Van Brocklin, LA vs NY Yanks	9/28/51	554
Warren Moon, Hou at KC	12/16/90	527
Boomer Esiason, Ariz. at Wash.	11/10/96	522
Dan Marino, Mia vs NYJ	10/23/88	521
Phil Simms, NYG vs Cin	10/13/85	513

Completions	Date	No
Drew Bledsoe, NE vs Min	11/13/94	45
Richard Todd, NYJ vs SF	9/21/80	42
Warren Moon, Hou vs Dal	11/10/91	41
Ken Anderson, Cin vs SD	12/20/82	40
Phil Simms, NYG vs Cin	10/13/85	40

Rushing

Yards Gained	Date	Yds
Walter Payton, Chi vs Min	11/20/77	275
O.J. Simpson, Buf vs Det	11/25/76	273
O.J. Simpson, Buf vs NE	9/16/73	250
Willie Ellison, LA Rams vs NO	12/5/71	247
Corey Dillon, Cin vs Ten	12/4/97	246

Receiving

Catches	Date	No
Tom Fears, LA vs GB	12/3/50	18
Clark Gaines, NYJ vs SF	9/21/80	17
Sonny Randle, St.L vs NYG	11/4/62	16
Keenan McCardell, Jax. at St.L.	10/20/96	16
Jerry Rice, S.F. vs LA Rams	11/20/94	16

Yards Gained	Date	Yds
Flipper Anderson, LA Rams vs NO	11/26/89	336
Stephone Paige, KC vs SD	12/22/85	309
Jim Benton, Cle vs Det	11/22/45	303
Cloyce Box, Det vs Bal	12/3/50	302
Jerry Rice, SF at Det	9/25/95	289
John Taylor, SF vs LA Rams	12/11/89	286

All-Purpose Yards

	Date	Yds
Glyn Milburn, Den vs Sea	12/10/95	404
Billy Cannon, Hou vs NY Titans	12/10/61	373
Tyrone Hughes, N.O. vs LA Rams	10/23/94	347
Lionel James, SD vs Raiders	11/10/85	345
Timmy Brown, Phi vs St.L	12/16/62	341
Gale Sayers, Chi vs Min	12/18/66	339
Gale Sayers, Chi vs SF	12/12/65	336
Flipper Anderson, LA Rams vs NO	11/26/89	336

Scoring

Points

	Date	Pts
Ernie Nevers, Chi. Cards vs Chi. Bears	11/28/29	40
Dub Jones, Cle vs Chi. Bears	11/25/51	36
Gale Sayers, Chi vs SF	12/12/65	36
Paul Hornung, GB vs Bal	10/8/61	33
Bob Shaw, Chi. Cards vs Bal	10/2/50	30
Jim Brown, Cle vs Bal	11/1/59	30
Abner Haynes, Dal. Texans vs Oak	11/26/61	30
Billy Cannon, Hou vs NY Titans	12/10/61	30
Cookie Gilchrist, Buf vs NY Jets	12/8/63	30
Kellen Winslow, SD vs Oak	11/22/81	30
Jerry Rice, SF vs Atl	10/14/90	30
James Stewart, Jax vs Phi	10/12/97	30

Note: Nevers celebrated Thanksgiving, 1929, by scoring all the Chicago Cardinals' points on six rushing TDs and four PATs. The Cards beat Red Grange and the Chicago Bears, 40-6.

Touchdowns Passing

	Date	No
Sid Luckman, Chi. Bears vs NYG	11/14/43	7
Adrian Burk, Phi vs Wash	10/17/54	7
George Blanda, Hou vs NY Titans	11/19/61	7
Y.A. Tittle, NYG vs Wash	10/28/62	7
Joe Kapp, Min vs Bal	9/28/69	7

Touchdowns Receiving

	Date	No
Bob Shaw, Chi. Cards vs Bal	10/2/50	5
Kellen Winslow, SD vs Oak	11/22/81	5
Jerry Rice, SF at Atl	10/14/90	5

Touchdowns Rushing

	Date	No
Ernie Nevers, Chi. Cards vs Chi. Bears	11/28/29	6
Jim Brown, Cle vs Bal	11/ 1/59	5
Cookie Gilchrist, Buf vs NY Jets	12/ 8/63	5
James Stewart, Jax vs Phi	10/12/97	5

Field Goals

	Date	No
Jim Bakken, St.L vs Pit	9/24/67	7
Chris Boniol, Dal vs GB	11/18/96	7
Rich Karlis, Min vs LA Rams	11/5/89	7

14 players tied with 6 FGs.

Note: Bakken was 7-for-9, Boniol and Karlis 7-for-7.

Extra Point Kicks

	Date	No
Pat Harder, Cards vs NYG	10/17/48	9
Bob Waterfield, LA Rams vs Bal	10/22/50	9
Charlie Gogolak, Wash vs NYG	11/27/66	9

Interceptions

	No
By 16 players	4

Sacks

	Date	No
Derrick Thomas, KC vs Sea	11/11/90	7
Fred Dean, SF vs NO	11/13/83	6
William Gay, Det vs TB	9/4/83	5½

Longest Plays

Passing (all for TDs)	Date	Yds
Frank Filchock to Andy Farkas, Wash vs Pit	10/15/39	99
George Izo to Bobby Mitchell, Wash vs Cle	9/15/63	99
Karl Sweetan to Pat Studstill, Det vs Bal	10/16/66	99
Sonny Jurgensen to Gerry Allen, Wash vs Chi	9/15/68	99
Jim Plunkett to Cliff Branch, LA Raiders vs Wash	10/2/83	99
Ron Jaworski to Mike Quick, Phi vs Atl	11/10/85	99
Stan Humphries to Tony Martin, SD vs Sea	9/18/94	99
Brett Favre to Robert Brooks, GB vs Chi	9/11/95	99

Runs from Scrimmage (all for TDs)	Date	Yds
Tony Dorsett, Dal vs Min	1/3/83	99
Andy Uram, GB vs Chi. Cards	10/8/39	97
Bob Gage, Pit vs Bears	12/4/49	97
Jim Spavital, Balt. Colts vs GB	11/5/50	96
Bob Hoernschemeyer, Det vs NY Yanks	11/23/50	96

Punts	Date	Yds
Steve O'Neal, NYJ vs Den	9/21/69	98
Joe Lintzenich, Chi. Bears vs NYG	11/15/31	94
Shawn McCarthy, NE vs Buf	11/3/91	93

Field Goals	Date	Yds
Tom Dempsey, NO vs Det	11/8/70	63
Steve Cox, Cle vs Cin	10/21/84	60
Morten Andersen, NO vs Chi	10/27/91	60
Tony Franklin, Phi vs Dal	11/12/79	59
Pete Stoyanovich, Mia vs NYJ	11/12/89	59
Steve Christie, Buf vs Mia	9/26/93	59
Morten Andersen, Atl vs SF	12/24/95	59

Punt Returns (all for TDs)	Date	Yds
Robert Bailey, Rams vs NO	10/23/94	103
Gil LeFebvre, Cin vs Bklyn	12/3/33	98
Charlie West, Min vs Wash	11/3/68	98
Dennis Morgan, Dal vs St.L	10/13/74	98
Terance Mathis, NYJ vs Dal	11/4/90	98
Greg Pruitt, LA Raiders vs Wash.	10/2/83	97

Kickoff Returns (all for TDs)	Date	Yds
Al Carmichael, GB vs Chi. Bears	10/7/56	106
Noland Smith, KC vs Den	12/17/67	106
Roy Green, St.L vs Dal	10/21/79	106

Interception Returns (all for TDs)	Date	Yds
James Willis (14 yds) lateral to Troy Vincent (90 yds), Phi vs Dal	11/3/96	104
Vencie Glenn, SD vs Den	11/29/87	103
Louis Oliver, Mia vs Buf	10/4/92	103

Six players tied with 102-yd returns.

Chicago College All-Star Game

On Aug. 31, 1934, a year after sponsoring Major League Baseball's first All-Star Game, *Chicago Tribune* sports editor Arch Ward presented the first Chicago College All-Star Game at Soldier Field. A crowd of 79,432 turned out to see an all-star team of graduated college seniors battle the 1933 NFL champion Chicago Bears to a scoreless tie. The preseason game was played at Soldier Field and pitted the College All-Stars against the defending NFL champions (1933–1966) or Super Bowl champions (1967–75) every year except 1935 until it was cancelled in 1977. The NFL champs won the series, 31-9-1.

Year
1934 Chi. Bears 0, All-Stars 0
1935 Chi. Bears 5, All-Stars 0
1936 Detroit 7, All-Stars 0
1937 All-Stars 6, Green Bay 0
1938 All-Stars 28, Washington 16
1939 NY Giants 9, All-Stars 0
1940 Green Bay 45, All-Stars 28
1941 Chi. Bears 37, All-Stars 13
1942 Chi. Bears 21, All-Stars 0
1943 All-Stars 27, Washington 7
1944 Chi. Bears 24, All-Stars 21
1945 Green Bay 19, All-Stars 7
1946 All-Stars 16, LA Rams 0
1947 All-Stars 16, Chi. Bears 0
1948 Chi. Cards 28, All-Stars 0

Year
1949 Philadelphia 38, All-Stars 0
1950 All-Stars 17, Philadelphia 7
1951 Cleveland 33, All-Stars 0
1952 LA Rams 10, All-Stars 7
1953 Detroit 24, All-Stars 10
1954 Detroit 31, All-Stars 6
1955 All-Stars 30, Cleveland 27
1956 Cleveland 26, All-Stars 0
1957 NY Giants 22, All-Stars 12
1958 All-Stars 35, Detroit 19
1959 Baltimore 29, All-Stars 0
1960 Baltimore 32, All-Stars 7
1961 Philadelphia 28, All-Stars 14
1962 Green Bay 42, All-Stars 20
1963 All-Stars 20, Green Bay 17

Year
1964 Chi. Bears 28, All-Stars 17
1965 Cleveland 24, All-Stars 16
1966 Green Bay 38, All-Stars 0
1967 Green Bay 27, All-Stars 0
1968 Green Bay 34, All-Stars 17
1969 NY Jets 26, All-Stars 24
1970 Kansas City 24, All-Stars 3
1971 Baltimore 24, All-Stars 17
1972 Dallas 20, All-Stars 7
1973 Miami 14, All-Stars 3
1974 No Game (NFLPA Strike)
1975 Pittsburgh 21, All-Stars 14
1976 Pittsburgh 24, All-Stars 0*

*Downpour flooded field, game called with 1:22 left in 3rd quarter.

Number One Draft Choices

In an effort to blunt the dominance of the Chicago Bears and New York Giants in the 1930s and distribute talent more evenly throughout the league, the NFL established the college draft in 1936. The first player chosen in the first draft was Jay Berwanger, who was college football's first Heisman Trophy winner. In all, 16 Heisman winners have also been the NFL's No.1 draft choice. They are noted in **bold** type. The American Football League (formed in 1960) held its own draft for six years before agreeing to merge with the NFL and select players in a common draft starting in 1967.

Year	Team	
1936	Philadelphia	**Jay Berwanger**, HB, Chicago
1937	Philadelphia	Sam Francis, FB, Nebraska
1938	Cleveland Rams	Corbett Davis, FB, Indiana
1939	Chicago Cards	Ki Aldrich, C, TCU
1940	Chicago Cards	George Cafego, HB, Tennessee
1941	Chicago Bears	**Tom Harmon**, HB, Michigan
1942	Pittsburgh	Bill Dudley, HB, Virginia
1943	Detroit	**Frank Sinkwich**, HB, Georgia
1944	Boston Yanks	**Angelo Bertelli**, QB, N. Dame
1945	Chicago Cards	Charley Trippi, HB, Georgia
1946	Boston Yanks	Frank Dancewicz, QB, N. Dame
1947	Chicago Bears	Bob Fenimore, HB, Okla. A&M
1948	Washington	Harry Gilmer, QB, Alabama
1949	Philadelphia	Chuck Bednarik, C, Penn
1950	Detroit	**Leon Hart**, E, Notre Dame
1951	NY Giants	Kyle Rote, HB, SMU
1952	LA Rams	Bill Wade, QB, Vanderbilt
1953	San Francisco	Harry Babcock, E, Georgia
1954	Cleveland	Bobby Garrett, QB, Stanford
1955	Baltimore	George Shaw, QB, Oregon
1956	Pittsburgh	Gary Glick, DB, Colo. A&M
1957	Green Bay	**Paul Hornung**, QB, N. Dame
1958	Chicago Cards	King Hill, QB, Rice
1959	Green Bay	Randy Duncan, QB, Iowa
1960	NFL–LA Rams	**Billy Cannon**, HB, LSU
	AFL–No choice	
1961	NFL–Minnesota	Tommy Mason, HB, Tulane
	AFL–Buffalo	Ken Rice, G, Auburn
1962	NFL–Washington	**Ernie Davis**, HB, Syracuse
	AFL–Oakland	Roman Gabriel, QB, N.C. State
1963	NFL–LA Rams	**Terry Baker**, QB, Oregon St.
	AFL–Kan.City	Buck Buchanan, DT, Grambling
1964	NFL–San Fran	Dave Parks, E, Texas Tech
	AFL–Boston	Jack Concannon, QB, Boston Col.
1965	NFL–NY Giants	Tucker Frederickson, FB, Auburn
	AFL–Houston	Lawrence Elkins, E, Baylor

Year	Team	
1966	NFL–Atlanta	Tommy Nobis, LB, Texas
	AFL–Miami	Jim Grabowski, FB, Illinois
1967	Baltimore	Bubba Smith, DT, Michigan St.
1968	Minnesota	Ron Yary, T, USC
1969	Buffalo	**O.J. Simpson**, RB, USC
1970	Pittsburgh	Terry Bradshaw, QB, La.Tech
1971	New England	**Jim Plunkett**, QB, Stanford
1972	Buffalo	Walt Patulski, DE, Notre Dame
1973	Houston	John Matuszak, DE, Tampa
1974	Dallas	Ed (Too Tall) Jones, DE, Tenn. St.
1975	Atlanta	Steve Bartkowski, QB, Calif.
1976	Tampa Bay	Lee Roy Selmon, DE, Oklahoma
1977	Tampa Bay	Ricky Bell, RB, USC
1978	Houston	**Earl Campbell**, RB, Texas
1979	Buffalo	Tom Cousineau, LB, Ohio St.
1980	Detroit	**Billy Sims**, RB, Oklahoma
1981	New Orleans	**George Rogers**, RB, S. Carolina
1982	New England	Kenneth Sims, DT, Texas
1983	Baltimore	John Elway, QB, Stanford
1984	New England	Irving Fryar, WR, Nebraska
1985	Buffalo	Bruce Smith, DE, Va. Tech
1986	Tampa Bay	**Bo Jackson**, RB, Auburn
1987	Tampa Bay	**V. Testaverde**, QB, Miami-FL
1988	Atlanta	Aundray Bruce, LB, Auburn
1989	Dallas	Troy Aikman, QB, UCLA
1990	Indianapolis	Jeff George, QB, Illinois
1991	Dallas	Russell Maryland, DT, Miami-FL
1992	Indianapolis	Steve Emtman, DT, Washington
1993	New England	Drew Bledsoe, QB, Washington St.
1994	Cincinnati	Dan Wilkinson, DT, Ohio St.
1995	Cincinnati	Ki-Jana Carter, RB, Penn St.
1996	NY Jets	Keyshawn Johnson, WR, USC
1997	St. Louis	Orlando Pace, OT, Ohio St.
1998	Indianapolis	Peyton Manning, QB, Tennessee

AP/Wide World Photos
Don Shula

Atlanta Falcons
Dan Reeves

New Orleans Saints
Mike Ditka

AP/Wide World Photos
Vince Lombardi

All-Time Winningest NFL Coaches

NFL career victories through the 1997 season. Career, regular season and playoff records are noted along with NFL, AFL and Super Bowl titles won. Coaches active during 1997 season in **bold** type.

		Career					Regular Season				Playoffs			
		Yrs	W	L	T	Pct	W	L	T	Pct	W	L	Pct.	League Titles
1	Don Shula	33	**347**	173	6	.665	328	156	6	.676	19	17	.528	2 Super Bowls and 1 NFL
2	George Halas	40	**324**	151	31	.671	318	148	31	.671	6	3	.667	5 NFL
3	Tom Landry	29	**270**	178	6	.601	250	162	6	.605	20	16	.556	2 Super Bowls
4	Curly Lambeau	33	**229**	134	22	.623	226	132	22	.624	3	2	.600	6 NFL
5	Chuck Noll	23	**209**	156	1	.572	193	148	1	.566	16	8	.667	4 Super Bowls
6	Chuck Knox	22	**193**	158	1	.550	186	147	1	.558	7	11	.389	—None—
7	Paul Brown	21	**170**	108	6	.609	166	100	6	.621	4	8	.333	3 NFL
8	Bud Grant	18	**168**	108	5	.607	158	96	5	.620	10	12	.455	1 NFL
9	**Dan Reeves**	17	**156**	122	1	.561	148	115	1	.563	8	7	.553	—None—
10	**Marv Levy**	17	**154**	120	0	.562	143	112	0	.561	11	8	.579	—None—
11	Steve Owen	23	**153**	108	17	.581	151	100	17	.595	2	8	.200	2 NFL
12	**M. Schottenheimer**	14	**143**	87	1	.621	138	76	1	.644	5	11	.313	—None—
13	Joe Gibbs	12	**140**	65	0	.683	124	60	0	.674	16	5	.762	3 Super Bowls
14	Hank Stram	17	**136**	100	10	.573	131	97	10	.571	5	3	.625	1 Super Bowl and 3 AFL
15	Weeb Ewbank	20	**134**	130	7	.507	130	129	7	.502	4	1	.800	1 Super Bowl, 2 NFL, and 1 AFL
16	**Bill Parcells**	12	**128**	93	1	.579	118	88	1	.572	10	5	.667	2 Super Bowls
17	Sid Gillman	18	**123**	104	7	.541	122	99	7	.550	1	5	.167	1 AFL
18	George Allen	12	**118**	54	5	.681	116	47	5	.705	2	7	.222	—None—
	Mike Ditka	12	**118**	78	0	.602	112	72	0	.609	6	6	.500	1 Super Bowl
20	Don Coryell	14	**114**	89	1	.561	111	83	1	.572	3	6	.333	—None—
21	John Madden	10	**112**	39	7	.731	103	32	7	.750	9	7	.563	1 Super Bowl
22	George Seifert	8	**108**	35	0	.755	98	30	0	.766	10	5	.667	2 Super Bowls
23	Buddy Parker	15	**107**	76	9	.581	104	75	9	.577	3	1	.750	2 NFL
24	Vince Lombardi	10	**105**	35	6	.740	96	34	6	.728	9	1	.900	2 Super Bowls and 5 NFL
	Tom Flores	12	**105**	90	0	.538	97	87	0	.527	8	3	.727	2 Super Bowls

Notes: The NFL does not recognize records from the All-American Football Conference (1946-49). If it did, **Paul Brown** (52-4-3 in four AAFC seasons) would move up to 5th on the all-time list with the following career stats— 25 Yrs; 222 Wins; 112 Losses; 9 Ties; .660 Pct; 9-8 playoff record; and 4 AAFC titles.

The NFL also considers the Playoff Bowl or "Runner-up Bowl" (officially: the Bert Bell Benefit Bowl) as a post-season exhibition game. The Playoff Bowl was contested every year from 1960-69 in Miami between Eastern and Western Conference second place teams. While the games did not count, six of the coaches above went to the Playoff Bowl at least once and came away with the following records— Allen (2-0), Brown (0-1), Grant (0-1), Landry (1-2), Lombardi (1-1) and Shula (2-0).

Where They Coached

Allen—LA Rams (1966-70), Washington (1971-77); **Brown**—Cleveland (1950-62), Cincinnati (1968-75); **Coryell**—St.Louis (1973-77), San Diego (1978-86); **Ditka**— Chicago (1982-92), New Orleans (1997–); **Ewbank**— Baltimore (1954-62), NY Jets (1963-73); **Flores**—Oakland-LA Raiders (1979-87), Seattle (1992-94) **Gibbs**—Washington (1981-92); **Gillman**—LA Rams (1955-59), LA-San Diego Chargers (1960-69), Houston (1973-74).

Grant—Minnesota (1967-83,1985); **Halas**—Chicago Bears (1920-29,33-42,46-55,58-67); **Knox**— LA Rams (1973-77, 1992-94); Buffalo (1978-82), Seattle (1983-91); **Lambeau**— Green Bay (1921-49), Chicago Cards (1950-51), Washington (1952-53); **Landry**—Dallas (1960-88); **Levy**— Kansas City (1978-82), Buffalo (1986-98); **Lombardi**— Green Bay (1959-67), Washington (1969); **Madden**—Oakland (1969-78).

Noll—Pittsburgh (1969-91); **Owen**—NY Giants (1931-53); **Parcells**— NY Giants (1983-90), New England (1993-97), NY Jets (1997—); **Parker**—Chicago Cards (1949), Detroit (1951-56), Pittsburgh (1957-64); **Reeves**— Denver (1981-92), NY Giants (1993-96), Atlanta (1997—); **Schottenheimer**— Cleveland (1984-88), Kansas City (1989—); **Seifert**—San Francisco (1989-96); **Shula**—Baltimore (1963-69), Miami (1970-95); **Stram**—Dallas-Kansas City (1960-74), New Orleans (1976-77).

Top Winning Percentages

Minimum of 85 NFL victories, including playoffs.

		Yrs	W	L	T	Pct
1	George Seifert	8	108	35	0	**.755**
2	Vince Lombardi	10	105	35	6	**.740**
3	John Madden	10	112	39	7	**.731**
4	Joe Gibbs	12	140	65	0	**.683**
5	George Allen	12	118	54	5	**.681**
6	George Halas	40	324	151	31	**.671**
7	Don Shula	33	347	173	6	**.665**
8	Curly Lambeau	33	229	134	22	**.623**
9	**M. Schottenheimer**	14	143	87	1	**.621**
10	Bill Walsh	10	102	63	1	**.617**
11	Paul Brown	21	170	108	6	**.609**
12	Bud Grant	18	168	108	5	**.607**
13	**Mike Ditka**	12	118	78	0	**.602**
14	Tom Landry	29	270	178	6	**.601**
15	Steve Owen	23	153	108	17	**.581**
16	Buddy Parker	15	107	76	9	**.581**
17	**Bill Parcells**	13	128	93	1	**.579**
18	Hank Stram	17	136	100	10	**.573**
19	Chuck Noll	23	209	156	1	**.572**
20	**Marv Levy**	17	154	120	0	**.562**
21	Don Coryell	14	114	89	1	**.561**
22	**Dan Reeves**	17	156	122	1	**.561**
23	Jimmy Conzelman	15	89	68	17	**.560**
24	Chuck Knox	22	193	158	1	**.550**
25	Jim Mora	11	93	78	0	**.544**

Note: If AAFC records are included, **Paul Brown** moves to 8th with a percentage of .660 (25 yrs, 222-112-9) and Buck Shaw would be 11th at .619 (8 yrs, 91-55-5).

Active Coaches' Victories

Through 1997 season, including playoffs.

		Yrs	W	L	T	Pct
1	Dan Reeves, Atlanta	17	**156**	122	1	.561
2	Marty Schottenheimer, KC	14	**143**	87	1	.621
3	Bill Parcells, NY Jets	13	**128**	93	1	.579
4	Mike Ditka, New Orleans	12	**118**	78	0	.602
5	Jim Mora, Indianapolis	11	**93**	78	0	.544
6	Ted Marchibroda, Baltimore	11	**83**	92	1	.474
7	Mike Holmgren, Green Bay	6	**73**	36	0	.670
8	Bill Cowher, Pittsburgh	6	**69**	38	0	.645
9	Jimmy Johnson, Miami	7	**68**	52	0	.567
10	Dick Vermeil, St. Louis	8	**62**	62	0	.500
11	Bobby Ross, Detroit	6	**59**	44	0	.573
12	Dennis Green, Minnesota	5	**57**	45	0	.559
13	Mike Shanahan, Denver	5	**45**	28	0	.616
14	Bruce Coslet, Cincinnati	6	**40**	50	0	.444
15	Dave Wannstedt, Chicago	5	**37**	45	0	.451
16	Ray Rhodes, Philadelphia	3	**27**	23	1	.539
	Dom Capers, Carolina	3	**27**	23	0	.540
18	Tom Coughlin, Jacksonville	3	**26**	26	0	.500
	Norv Turner, Washington	4	**26**	37	1	.414
20	Jeff Fisher, Tennessee	4	**24**	30	0	.444
21	Dennis Erickson, Seattle	3	**23**	25	0	.479
22	Tony Dungee, Tampa Bay	2	**17**	17	0	.500
	Pete Carroll, New England	2	**17**	17	0	.500
	Wade Phillips, Buffalo	3	**17**	20	0	.459
25	Steve Mariucci, San Fran	1	**14**	4	0	.778
26	Vince Tobin, Arizona	2	**11**	21	0	.344
27	Jim Fassel, NY Giants	1	**10**	6	1	.618
28	Kevin Gilbride, San Diego	1	**4**	12	0	.250
29	Jon Gruden, Oakland	0	**0**	0	0	.000
	Chan Gailey, Dallas	0	**0**	0	0	.000

Annual Awards

Most Valuable Player

Unlike other major pro team sports, the NFL does not sanction an MVP award. It gave out the Joe F. Carr Trophy (Carr was NFL president from 1921-39) for nine years but discontinued it in 1947. Since then, four principal MVP awards have been given out: UPI (1953-69), AP (since 1957), the Maxwell Club of Philadelphia's Bert Bell Trophy (since 1959) and the Pro Football Writers Assn. (since 1976). UPI switched to AFC and NFC Player of the Year awards in 1970.

Multiple winners (more than one season): Jim Brown (4); Brett Favre, Johnny Unitas and Y.A. Tittle (3); Earl Campbell, Randall Cunningham, Otto Graham, Don Hutson, Joe Montana, Walter Payton, Barry Sanders, Ken Stabler, Joe Theismann and Steve Young (2).

Year		Awards
1938	Mel Hein, NY Giants, C	Carr
1939	Parker Hall, Cleveland Rams, HB	Carr
1940	Ace Parker, Brooklyn, HB	Carr
1941	Don Hutson, Green Bay, E	Carr
1942	Don Hutson, Green Bay, E	Carr
1943	Sid Luckman, Chicago Bears, QB	Carr
1944	Frank Sinkwich, Detroit, HB	Carr
1945	Bob Waterfield, Cleveland Rams, QB	Carr
1946	Bill Dudley, Pittsburgh, HB	Carr
1947-52	No award	
1953	Otto Graham, Cleveland Browns, QB	UPI
1954	Joe Perry, San Francisco, FB	UPI
1955	Otto Graham, Cleveland, QB	UPI
1956	Frank Gifford, NY Giants, HB	UPI
1957	Y.A. Tittle, San Francisco, QB	UPI
	& Jim Brown, Cleveland, FB	AP
1958	Jim Brown, Cleveland, FB	UPI
	& Gino Marchetti, Baltimore, DE	AP
1959	Johnny Unitas, Baltimore, QB	UPI, Bell
	& Charley Conerly, NY Giants, QB	AP
1960	Norm Van Brocklin, Phi., QB	UPI, AP (tie), Bell
	& Joe Schmidt, Detroit, LB	AP (tie)
1961	Paul Hornung, Green Bay, HB	UPI, AP, Bell
1962	Y.A. Tittle, NY Giants, QB	UPI
	Jim Taylor, Green Bay, FB	AP
	& Andy Robustelli, NY Giants, DE	Bell
1963	Jim Brown, Cleveland, FB	UPI, Bell
	& Y.A. Tittle, NY Giants, QB	AP
1964	Johnny Unitas, Baltimore, QB	UPI, AP, Bell
1965	Jim Brown, Cleveland, FB	UPI, AP
	& Pete Retzlaff, Philadelphia, TE	Bell
1966	Bart Starr, Green Bay, QB	UPI, AP
	& Don Meredith, Dallas, QB	Bell
1967	Johnny Unitas, Baltimore, QB	UPI, AP, Bell
1968	Earl Morrall, Baltimore, QB	UPI, AP
	& Leroy Kelly, Cleveland, RB	Bell
1969	Roman Gabriel, LA Rams, QB	UPI, AP, Bell
1970	John Brodie, San Francisco, QB	AP
	& George Blanda, Oakland, QB-PK	Bell
1971	Alan Page, Minnesota, DT	AP
	& Roger Staubach, Dallas, QB	Bell
1972	Larry Brown, Washington, RB	AP, Bell
1973	O.J. Simpson, Buffalo, RB	AP, Bell
1974	Ken Stabler, Oakland, QB	AP
	& Merlin Olsen, LA Rams, DT	Bell
1975	Fran Tarkenton, Minnesota, QB	AP, Bell
1976	Bert Jones, Baltimore, QB	AP, PFWA
	& Ken Stabler, Oakland, QB	Bell
1977	Walter Payton, Chicago, RB	AP, PFWA
	& Bob Griese, Miami, QB	Bell
1978	Terry Bradshaw, Pittsburgh, QB	AP, Bell
	& Earl Campbell, Houston, RB	PFWA
1979	Earl Campbell, Houston, RB	AP, Bell, PFWA
1980	Brian Sipe, Cleveland, QB	AP, PFWA
	& Ron Jaworski, Philadelphia, QB	Bell
1981	Ken Anderson, Cincinnati, QB	AP, Bell, PFWA

Year		Awards
1982	Mark Moseley, Washington, PK	AP
	Joe Theismann, Washington, QB	Bell
	& Dan Fouts, San Diego, QB	PFWA
1983	Joe Theismann, Washington, QB	AP, PFWA
	& John Riggins, Washington, RB	Bell
1984	Dan Marino, Miami, QB	AP, Bell, PFWA
1985	Marcus Allen, LA Raiders, RB	AP, PFWA
	& Walter Payton, Chicago, RB	Bell
1986	Lawrence Taylor, NY Giants, LB	AP, Bell, PFWA
1987	Jerry Rice, San Francisco, WR	Bell, PFWA
	& John Elway, Denver, QB	AP
1988	Boomer Esiason, Cincinnati, QB	AP, PFWA
	& Randall Cunningham, Phila, QB	Bell
1989	Joe Montana, San Francisco, QB	AP, Bell, PFWA
1990	Randall Cunningham, Phila., QB	Bell, PFWA
	& Joe Montana, San Francisco, QB	AP
1991	Thurman Thomas, Buffalo, RB	AP, PFWA
	& Barry Sanders, Detroit, RB	Bell
1992	Steve Young, San Francisco, QB	AP, Bell, PFWA
1993	Emmitt Smith, Dallas, RB	AP, Bell, PFWA
1994	Steve Young, San Francisco, QB	AP, Bell, PFWA
1995	Brett Favre, Green Bay, QB	AP, Bell, PFWA
1996	Brett Favre, Green Bay, QB	AP, Bell, PFWA
1997*	Barry Sanders, Detroit, RB	AP, Bell, PFWA
	& Brett Favre, Green Bay, QB	AP

*In 1997 for the first time in history, two players tied for the AP MVP award.

NFC Player of the Year

Given out by UPI from 1970-96. Offensive and defensive players honored since 1983. Rookie winners are in **bold** type.

Multiple winners: Eric Dickerson, Reggie White and Mike Singletary (3); Brett Favre, Charles Haley, Walter Payton, Lawrence Taylor and Steve Young (2).

Year		Pos
1970	John Brodie, San Francisco	QB
1971	Alan Page, Minnesota	DT
1972	Larry Brown, Washington	RB
1973	John Hadl, Los Angeles	QB
1974	Jim Hart, St. Louis	QB
1975	Fran Tarkenton, Minnesota	QB
1976	Chuck Foreman, Minnesota	RB
1977	Walter Payton, Chicago	RB
1978	Archie Manning, New Orleans	QB
1979	Ottis Anderson, St. Louis	RB
1980	Ron Jaworski, Philadelphia	QB
1981	Tony Dorsett, Dallas	RB
1982	Mark Moseley, Washington	PK
1983	Off–Eric Dickerson, Los Angeles	RB
	Def–Lawrence Taylor, New York	LB
1984	Off–Eric Dickerson, Los Angeles	RB
	Def–Mike Singletary, Chicago	LB
1985	Off–Walter Payton, Chicago	RB
	Def–Mike Singletary, Chicago	LB
1986	Off–Eric Dickerson, Los Angeles	RB
	Def–Lawrence Taylor, New York	LB
1987	Off–Jerry Rice, San Francisco	WR
	Def–Reggie White, Philadelphia	DE
1988	Off–Roger Craig, San Francisco	RB
	Def–Mike Singletary, Chicago	LB
1989	Off–Joe Montana, San Francisco	QB
	Def–Keith Millard, Minnesota	DT
1990	Off–Randall Cunningham, Philadelphia	QB
	Def–Charles Haley, San Francisco	LB
1991	Off–Mark Rypien, Washington	QB
	Def–Reggie White, Philadelphia	DE
1992	Off–Steve Young, San Francisco	QB
	Def–Chris Doleman, Minnesota	DE
1993	Off–Emmitt Smith, Dallas	RB
	Def–Eric Allen, Philadelphia	CB
1994	Off–Steve Young, San Francisco	QB
	Def–Charles Haley, Dallas	DE
1995	Off–Brett Favre, Green Bay	QB
	Def–Reggie White, Green Bay	DE
1996	Off–Brett Favre, Green Bay	QB
	Def–Kevin Greene, Carolina	LB
1997	UPI awards not given out.	

AFL-AFC Player of the Year

Presented by UPI to the top player in the AFL (1960-69) and AFC (1970-96). Offensive and defensive players have been honored since 1983. Rookie winners are in **bold** type.

Multiple winners: Bruce Smith (4); O.J. Simpson (3); Cornelius Bennett, George Blanda, John Elway, Dan Fouts, Daryle Lamonica, Dan Marino and Curt Warner (2).

Year		Pos
1960	**Abner Haynes**, Dallas Texans	HB
1961	George Blanda, Houston	QB
1962	Cookie Gilchrist, Buffalo	FB
1963	Lance Alworth, San Diego	FL
1964	Gino Cappelletti, Boston	FL-PK
1965	Paul Lowe, San Diego	HB
1966	Jim Nance, Boston	FB
1967	Daryle Lamonica, Oakland	QB
1968	Joe Namath, New York	QB
1969	Daryle Lamonica, Oakland	QB
1970	George Blanda, Oakland	QB-PK
1971	Otis Taylor, Kansas City	WR
1972	O.J. Simpson, Buffalo	RB
1973	O.J. Simpson, Buffalo	RB
1974	Ken Stabler, Oakland	QB
1975	O.J. Simpson, Buffalo	RB
1976	Bert Jones, Baltimore	QB
1977	Craig Morton, Denver	QB
1978	**Earl Campbell**, Houston	RB
1979	Dan Fouts, San Diego	QB
1980	Brian Sipe, Cleveland	QB
1981	Ken Anderson, Cincinnati	QB
1982	Dan Fouts, San Diego	QB
1983	Off–**Curt Warner**, Seattle	RB
	Def–Rod Martin, Los Angeles	LB
1984	Off–Dan Marino, Miami	QB
	Def–Mark Gastineau, New York	DE
1985	Off–Marcus Allen, Los Angeles	RB
	Def–Andre Tippett, New England	LB
1986	Off–Curt Warner, Seattle	RB
	Def–Rulon Jones, Denver	DE
1987	Off–John Elway, Denver	QB
	Def–Bruce Smith, Buffalo	DE
1988	Off–Boomer Esiason, Cincinnati	QB
	Def–Bruce Smith, Buffalo	DE
	& Cornelius Bennett, Buffalo	LB
1989	Off–Christian Okoye, Kansas City	RB
	Def–Michael Dean Perry, Cleveland	NT
1990	Off–Warren Moon, Houston	QB
	Def–Bruce Smith, Buffalo	DE
1991	Off–Thurman Thomas, Buffalo	RB
	Def–Cornelius Bennett, Buffalo	LB

Annual Awards (Cont.)

Year		Pos
1992	Off–Barry Foster, Pittsburgh	RB
	Def–Junior Seau, San Diego	LB
1993	Off–John Elway, Denver	QB
	Def–Rod Woodson, Pittsburgh	CB
1994	Off–Dan Marino, Miami	QB
	Def–Greg Lloyd, Pittsburgh	LB
1995	Off–Jim Harbaugh, Indianapolis	QB
	Def–Bryce Paup, Buffalo	LB
1996	Off–Terrell Davis, Denver	RB
	Def–Bruce Smith, Buffalo	DE
1997	UPI awards not given out.	

NFL-NFC Rookie of the Year

Presented by UPI to the top rookie in the NFL (1955-69) and NFC (1970-96). In 1997, the UPI did not give out awards. The winner designated below was chosen by the NFL Players Association. Players who were the overall first pick in the NFL draft are in **bold** type.

Year		Pos
1955	Alan Ameche, Bal	FB
1956	Lenny Moore, Bal	HB
1957	Jim Brown, Cle	FB
1958	Jimmy Orr, Pit	FL
1959	Boyd Dowler, GB	FL
1960	Gail Cogdill, Det	FL
1961	Mike Ditka, Chi	TE
1962	Ronnie Bull, Chi	FB
1963	Paul Flatley, Min	FL
1964	Charley Taylor, Wash	HB
1965	Gale Sayers, Chi	HB
1966	Johnny Roland, St.L.	HB
1967	Mel Farr, Det	RB
1968	Earl McCullough, Det.	FL
1969	Calvin Hill, Dal	RB
1970	Bruce Taylor, SF	DB
1971	John Brockington, GB	RB
1972	Chester Marcol, GB	PK
1973	Charle Young, Phi	TE
1974	John Hicks, NY	G
1975	Mike Thomas, Wash	RB
1976	Sammy White, Min	WR
1977	Tony Dorsett, Dal	RB
1978	Bubba Baker, Det	DE
1979	Ottis Anderson, St.L.	RB
1980	**Billy Sims**, Det.	RB
1981	**George Rogers**, NO	RB
1982	Jim McMahon, Chi.	QB
1983	Eric Dickerson, LA	RB
1984	Paul McFadden, Phi	PK
1985	Jerry Rice, SF	WR
1986	Reuben Mayes, NO	RB
1987	Robert Awalt, St.L.	TE
1988	Keith Jackson, Phi	TE
1989	Barry Sanders, Det	RB
1990	Mark Carrier, Chi	S
1991	Lawrence Dawsey, TB	WR
1992	Robert Jones, Dal	LB
1993	Jerome Bettis, LA	RB
1994	Bryant Young, SF	DT
1995	Rashaan Salaam, Chi	RB
1996	Simeon Rice, Ari.	DE
1997	Warrick Dunn, TB	RB

AFL-AFC Rookie of the Year

Presented by UPI to the top rookie in the AFL (1960-69) and AFC (1970-96). In 1997, the UPI did not give out awards. The winner designated below was chosen by the NFL Players Association. Players who were the overall first pick in the AFL or NFL draft are in **bold** type.

Year		Pos
1960	Abner Haynes, Dal	HB
1961	Earl Faison, SD	DE
1962	Curtis McClinton, Dal	FB
1963	Billy Joe, Den	FB
1964	Matt Snell, NY	FB
1965	Joe Namath, NY	QB
1966	Bobby Burnett, Buf	HB
1967	George Webster, Hou	LB
1968	Paul Robinson, Cin	RB
1969	Greg Cook, Cin	QB
1970	Dennis Shaw, Buf	QB
1971	**Jim Plunkett**, NE	QB
1972	Franco Harris, Pit.	RB
1973	Bobbie Clark, Cin	RB
1974	Don Woods, SD	RB
1975	Robert Brazile, Hou	LB
1976	Mike Haynes, NE	DB
1977	A.J. Duhe, Mia	DE
1978	**Earl Campbell**, Hou	RB
1979	Jerry Butler, Buf	WR
1980	Joe Cribbs, Buf.	RB
1981	Joe Delaney, KC	RB
1982	Marcus Allen, LA	RB
1983	Curt Warner, Sea	RB
1984	Louis Lipps, Pit	WR
1985	Kevin Mack, Cle	RB
1986	Leslie O'Neal, SD	DE
1987	Shane Conlan, Buf	LB
1988	John Stephens, NE	RB
1989	Derrick Thomas, KC	LB
1990	Richmond Webb, Mia	OT
1991	Mike Croel, Den	LB
1992	Dale Carter, KC	CB
1993	Rick Mirer, Sea	QB
1994	Marshall Faulk, Ind	RB
1995	Curtis Martin, NE	RB
1996	Terry Glenn, NE	WR
1997	Corey Dillon, Cin.	RB

Coach of the Year

Presented by UPI to the top coach in the AFL-NFL (1955-69) and AFC-NFC (1970-96). In 1997, no UPI awards were given out. The 1997 winner indicated is the consensus selection from presenters such as AP, The Maxwell Football Club of Philadelphia, *The Sporting News* and the Pro Football Writers Association. Records indicate how much coach's team improved over one season.

Multiple winners: Don Shula (4); Chuck Knox and Dan Reeves (3); George Allen, Leeman Bennett, Paul Brown, Mike Ditka, George Halas, Tom Landry, Marv Levy, Bill Parcells, Jack Pardee, Sam Rutigliano, Lou Saban, Allie Sherman, Marty Schottenheimer and Bill Walsh (2).

Year		Improvement
1955	NFL–Joe Kuharich, Washington	3-9 to 8-4
1956	NFL–Buddy Parker, Detroit	3-9 to 9-3
1957	NFL–Paul Brown, Cleveland	5-7 to 9-2-1
1958	NFL–Weeb Ewbank, Baltimore	7-5 to 9-3
1959	NFL–Vince Lombardi, Green Bay	1-10-1 to 7-5
1960	NFL–Buck Shaw, Philadelphia	7-5 to 10-2
	AFL–Lou Rymkus, Houston	10-4
1961	NFL–Allie Sherman, New York	6-4-2 to 10-3-1
	AFL–Wally Lemm, Houston	10-4 to 10-3-1
1962	NFL–Allie Sherman, New York	10-3-1 to 12-2
	AFL–Jack Faulkner, Denver	3-11 to 7-7
1963	NFL–George Halas, Chicago	9-5 to 11-1-2
	AFL–Al Davis, Oakland	1-13 to 10-4
1964	NFL–Don Shula, Baltimore	8-6 to 12-2
	AFL–Lou Saban, Buffalo	7-6-1 to 12-2
1965	NFL–George Halas, Chicago	5-9 to 9-5
	AFL–Lou Saban, Buffalo	12-2 to 10-3-1
1966	NFL–Tom Landry, Dallas	7-7 to 10-3-1
	AFL–Mike Holovak, Boston	4-8-2 to 8-4-2
1967	NFL–George Allen, Los Angeles	8-6 to 11-1-2
	AFL–John Rauch, Oakland	8-5-1 to 13-1
1968	NFL–Don Shula, Baltimore	11-1-2 to 13-1
	AFL–Hank Stram, Kansas City	9-5 to 12-2
1969	NFL–Bud Grant, Minnesota	8-6 to 12-2
	AFL–Paul Brown, Cincinnati	3-11 to 4-9-1

Year		Improvement
1970	NFC–Alex Webster, New York	6-8 to 9-5
	AFC–Don Shula, Miami	3-10-1 to 10-4
1971	NFC–George Allen, Washington	6-8 to 9-4-1
	AFC–Don Shula, Miami	10-4 to 10-3-1
1972	NFC–Dan Devine, Green Bay	4-8-2 to 10-4
	AFC–Chuck Noll, Pittsburgh	6-8 to 11-3
1973	NFC–Chuck Knox, Los Angeles	6-7-1 to 12-2
	AFC–John Ralston, Denver	5-9 to 7-5-2
1974	NFC–Don Coryell, St. Louis	4-9-1 to 10-4
	AFC–Sid Gillman, Houston	1-13 to 7-7
1975	NFC–Tom Landry, Dallas	8-6 to 10-4
	AFC–Ted Marchibroda, Baltimore	2-12 to 10-4
1976	NFC–Jack Pardee, Chicago	4-10 to 7-7
	AFC–Chuck Fairbanks, New England	3-11 to 11-3
1977	NFC–Leeman Bennett, Atlanta	4-10 to 7-7
	AFC–Red Miller, Denver	9-5 to 12-2
1978	NFC–Dick Vermeil, Philadelphia	5-9 to 9-7
	AFC–Walt Michaels, New York	3-11 to 8-8
1979	NFC–Jack Pardee, Washington	8-8 to 10-6
	AFC–Sam Rutigliano, Cleveland	8-8 to 9-7
1980	NFC–Leeman Bennett, Atlanta	6-10 to 12-4
	AFC–Sam Rutigliano, Cleveland	9-7 to 11-5
1981	NFC–Bill Walsh, San Francisco	6-10 to 13-3
	AFC–Forrest Gregg, Cincinnati	6-10 to 12-4
1982	NFC–Joe Gibbs, Washington	8-8 to 8-1
	AFC–Tom Flores, Los Angeles	7-9 to 8-1
1983	NFC–John Robinson, Los Angeles	2-7 to 9-7
	AFC–Chuck Knox, Seattle	4-5 to 9-7
1984	NFC–Bill Walsh, San Francisco	10-6 to 15-1
	AFC–Chuck Knox, Seattle	9-7 to 12-4
1985	NFC–Mike Ditka, Chicago	10-6 to 15-1
	AFC–Raymond Berry, New England	9-7 to 11-5
1986	NFC–Bill Parcells, New York	10-6 to 14-2
	AFC–Marty Schottenheimer, Cleveland	8-8 to 12-4
1987	NFC–Jim Mora, New Orleans	7-9 to 12-3
	AFC–Ron Meyer, Indianapolis	3-13 to 9-6
1988	NFC–Mike Ditka, Chicago	11-4 to 12-4
	AFC–Marv Levy, Buffalo	7-8 to 12-4
1989	NFC–Lindy Infante, Green Bay	4-12 to 10-6
	AFC–Dan Reeves, Denver	8-8 to 11-5
1990	NFC–Jimmy Johnson, Dallas	1-15 to 7-9
	AFC–Art Shell, Los Angeles	8-8 to 12-4
1991	NFC–Wayne Fontes, Detroit	6-10 to 12-4
	AFC–Dan Reeves, Denver	5-11 to 12-4
1992	NFC–Dennis Green, Minnesota	8-8 to 11-5
	AFC–Bobby Ross, San Diego	4-12 to 11-5
1993	NFC–Dan Reeves, New York	6-10 to 11-5
	AFC–Marv Levy, Buffalo	11-5 to 12-4
1994	NFC–Dave Wannstedt, Chicago	7-9 to 9-7
	AFC–Bill Parcells, New England	5-11 to 10-6
1995	NFC–Ray Rhodes, Philadelphia	7-9 to 10-6
	AFC–Marty Schottenheimer, Kansas City	9-7 to 13-3
1996	NFC–Dom Capers, Carolina	7-9 to 12-4
	AFC–Tom Coughlin, Jacksonville	4-12 to 9-7
1997	NFL–Jim Fassel, NY Giants	6-10 to 10-5-1

CANADIAN FOOTBALL

The Grey Cup

Earl Grey, the Governor-General of Canada (1904-11), donated a trophy in 1909 for the Rugby Football Championship of Canada. The trophy, which later became known as the Grey Cup, was originally open to competition for teams registered with the Canada Rugby Union. Since 1954, the Cup has gone to the champion of the Canadian Football League (CFL).

Overall multiple winners: Toronto Argonauts (14); Edmonton Eskimos (11); Winnipeg Blue Bombers (9); Hamilton Tiger-Cats and Ottawa Rough Riders (7); Hamilton Tigers (5); Montreal Alouettes and University of Toronto (4); B.C. Lions, Calgary Stampeders and Queen's University (3); Ottawa Senators, Sarnia Imperials, Saskatchewan Roughriders and Toronto Balmy Beach (2).

CFL multiple winners (since 1954): Edmonton (11); Winnipeg (7); Hamilton (6); Ottawa (5); Toronto (4); B.C. Lions and Montreal (3); Calgary and Saskatchewan (2).

Year	Cup Final
1909	Univ. of Toronto 26, Toronto Parkdale 6
1910	Univ. of Toronto 16, Hamilton Tigers 7
1911	Univ. of Toronto 14, Toronto Argonauts 7
1912	Hamilton Alerts 11, Toronto Argonauts 4
1913	Hamilton Tigers 44, Toronto Parkdale 2
1914	Toronto Argonauts 14, Univ. of Toronto 2
1915	Hamilton Tigers 13, Toronto Rowing 7
1916-19	Not held (WWI)
1920	Univ. of Toronto 16, Toronto Argonauts 3
1921	Toronto Argonauts 23, Edmonton Eskimos 0
1922	Queens Univ. 13, Edmonton Elks 1
1923	Queens Univ. 54, Regina Roughriders 0
1924	Queens Univ. 11, Toronto Balmy Beach 3
1925	Ottawa Senators 24, Winnipeg Tigers 1
1926	Ottawa Senators 10, Univ. of Toronto 7
1927	Toronto Balmy Beach 9, Hamilton Tigers 6
1928	Hamilton Tigers 30, Regina Roughriders 0
1929	Hamilton Tigers 14, Regina Roughriders 3
1930	Toronto Balmy Beach 11, Regina Roughriders 6
1931	Montreal AAA 22, Regina Roughriders 0
1932	Hamilton Tigers 25, Regina Roughriders 6
1933	Toronto Argonauts 4, Sarnia Imperials 3
1934	Sarnia Imperials 20, Regina Roughriders 12
1935	Winnipeg 'Pegs 18, Hamilton Tigers 12
1936	Sarnia Imperials 26, Ottawa Rough Riders 20
1937	Toronto Argonauts 4, Winnipeg Blue Bombers 3
1938	Toronto Argonauts 30, Winnipeg Blue Bombers 7
1939	Winnipeg Blue Bombers 8, Ottawa Rough Riders 7
1940	Gm 1: Ottawa Rough Riders 8, Toronto B-Beach 2
	Gm 2: Ottawa Rough Riders 12, Toronto B-Beach 5
1941	Winnipeg Blue Bombers 18, Ottawa Rough Riders 16
1942	Toronto RACF 8, Winnipeg RACF 5
1943	Hamilton Wildcats 23, Winnipeg RACF 14
1944	Montreal HMCS 7, Hamilton Wildcats 6
1945	Toronto Argonauts 35, Winnipeg Blue Bombers 0
1946	Toronto Argonauts 28, Winnipeg Blue Bombers 6
1947	Toronto Argonauts 10, Winnipeg Blue Bombers 9
1948	Calgary Stampeders 12, Ottawa Rough Riders 7
1949	Montreal Alouettes 28, Calgary Stampeders 15
1950	Toronto Argonauts 13, Winnipeg Blue Bombers 0
1951	Ottawa Rough Riders 21, Saskatch. Roughriders 14
1952	Toronto Argonauts 21, Edmonton Eskimos 11
1953	Hamilton Tiger-Cats 12, Winnipeg Blue Bombers 6

Year	Winner	Head Coach	Score	Loser	Head Coach	Site
1954	Edmonton	Frank (Pop) Ivy	26-25	Montreal	Doug Walker	Toronto
1955	Edmonton	Frank (Pop) Ivy	34-19	Montreal	Doug Walker	Vancouver
1956	Edmonton	Frank (Pop) Ivy	50-27	Montreal	Doug Walker	Toronto
1957	Hamilton	Jim Trimble	32-7	Winnipeg	Bud Grant	Toronto
1958	Winnipeg	Bud Grant	35-28	Hamilton	Jim Trimble	Vancouver

The Grey Cup (Cont.)

Year	Winner	Head Coach	Score	Loser	Head Coach	Site
1959	Winnipeg	Bud Grant	21-7	Hamilton	Jim Trimble	Toronto
1960	Ottawa	Frank Clair	16-6	Edmonton	Eagle Keys	Vancouver
1961	Winnipeg	Bud Grant	21-14(OT)	Hamilton	Jim Trimble	Toronto
1962	Winnipeg	Bud Grant	28-27*	Hamilton	Jim Trimble	Toronto
1963	Hamilton	Ralph Sazio	21-10	B.C. Lions	Dave Skrien	Vancouver
1964	B.C. Lions	Dave Skrien	34-24	Hamilton	Ralph Sazio	Toronto
1965	Hamilton	Ralph Sazio	22-16	Winnipeg	Bud Grant	Toronto
1966	Saskatchewan	Eagle Keys	29-14	Ottawa	Frank Clair	Vancouver
1967	Hamilton	Ralph Sazio	24-1	Saskatchewan	Eagle Keys	Ottawa
1968	Ottawa	Frank Clair	24-21	Calgary	Jerry Williams	Toronto
1969	Ottawa	Frank Clair	29-11	Saskatchewan	Eagle Keys	Montreal
1970	Montreal	Sam Etcheverry	23-10	Calgary	Jim Duncan	Toronto
1971	Calgary	Jim Duncan	14-11	Toronto	Leo Cahill	Vancouver
1972	Hamilton	Jerry Williams	13-10	Saskatchewan	Dave Skrien	Hamilton
1973	Ottawa	Jack Gotta	22-18	Edmonton	Ray Jauch	Toronto
1974	Montreal	Marv Levy	20-7	Edmonton	Ray Jauch	Vancouver
1975	Edmonton	Ray Jauch	9-8	Montreal	Marv Levy	Calgary
1976	Ottawa	George Brancato	23-20	Saskatchewan	John Payne	Toronto
1977	Montreal	Marv Levy	41-6	Edmonton	Hugh Campbell	Montreal
1978	Edmonton	Hugh Campbell	20-13	Montreal	Joe Scannella	Toronto
1979	Edmonton	Hugh Campbell	17-9	Montreal	Joe Scannella	Montreal
1980	Edmonton	Hugh Campbell	48-10	Hamilton	John Payne	Toronto
1981	Edmonton	Hugh Campbell	26-23	Ottawa	George Brancato	Montreal
1982	Edmonton	Hugh Campbell	32-16	Toronto	Bob O'Billovich	Toronto
1983	Toronto	Bob O'Billovich	18-17	B.C. Lions	Don Matthews	Vancouver
1984	Winnipeg	Cal Murphy	47-17	Hamilton	Al Bruno	Edmonton
1985	B.C. Lions	Don Matthews	37-24	Hamilton	Al Bruno	Montreal
1986	Hamilton	Al Bruno	39-15	Edmonton	Jack Parker	Vancouver
1987	Edmonton	Joe Faragalli	38-36	Toronto	Bob O'Billovich	Vancouver
1988	Winnipeg	Mike Riley	22-21	B.C. Lions	Larry Donovan	Ottawa
1989	Saskatchewan	John Gregory	43-40	Hamilton	Al Bruno	Toronto
1990	Winnipeg	Mike Riley	50-11	Edmonton	Joe Faragalli	Vancouver
1991	Toronto	Adam Rita	36-21	Calgary	Wally Buono	Winnipeg
1992	Calgary	Wally Buono	24-10	Winnipeg	Urban Bowman	Toronto
1993	Edmonton	Ron Lancaster	33-23	Winnipeg	Cal Murphy	Calgary
1994	B.C. Lions	Dave Ritchie	26-23	Baltimore	Don Matthews	Vancouver
1995	Baltimore	Don Matthews	37-20	Calgary	Wally Buono	Regina
1996	Toronto	Don Matthews	43-37	Edmonton	Ron Lancaster	Hamilton
1997	Toronto	Don Matthews	47-23	Saskatchewan	Jim Daley	Edmonton

*Halted by fog in 4th quarter, final 9:29 played the following day.

CFL Most Outstanding Player

Regular season Player of the Year as selected by The Football Reporters of Canada since 1953.

Multiple winners: Doug Flutie (6); Russ Jackson and Jackie Parker (3); Dieter Brock, Ron Lancaster (2).

Year
1953 Billy Vessels, Edmonton, RB
1954 Sam Etcheverry, Montreal, QB
1955 Pat Abbruzzi, Montreal, RB
1956 Hal Patterson, Montreal, E-DB
1957 Jackie Parker, Edmonton, RB
1958 Jackie Parker, Edmonton, QB
1959 Johnny Bright, Edmonton, RB
1960 Jackie Parker, Edmonton, QB
1961 Bernie Faloney, Hamilton, QB
1962 George Dixon, Montreal, RB
1963 Russ Jackson, Ottawa, QB
1964 Lovell Coleman, Calgary, RB
1965 George Reed, Saskatchewan, RB
1966 Russ Jackson, Ottawa, QB
1967 Peter Liske, Calgary, QB

Year
1968 Bill Symons, Toronto, RB
1969 Russ Jackson, Ottawa, QB
1970 Ron Lancaster, Saskatch., QB
1971 Don Jonas, Winnipeg, QB
1972 Garney Henley, Hamilton, WR
1973 Geo. McGowan, Edmonton, WR
1974 Tom Wilkinson, Edmonton, QB
1975 Willie Burden, Calgary, RB
1976 Ron Lancaster, Saskatch., QB
1977 Jimmy Edwards, Hamilton, RB
1978 Tony Gabriel, Ottawa, TE
1979 David Green, Montreal, RB
1980 Dieter Brock, Winnipeg, QB
1981 Dieter Brock, Winnipeg, QB
1982 Condredge Holloway, Tor., QB

Year
1983 Warren Moon, Edmonton, QB
1984 Willard Reaves, Winnipeg, RB
1985 Merv Fernandez, B.C. Lions, WR
1986 James Murphy, Winnipeg, WR
1987 Tom Clements, Winnipeg, QB
1988 David Williams, B.C. Lions, WR
1989 Tracy Ham, Edmonton, QB
1990 Mike Clemons, Toronto, RB
1991 Doug Flutie, B.C. Lions, QB
1992 Doug Flutie, Calgary, QB
1993 Doug Flutie, Calgary, QB
1994 Doug Flutie, Calgary, QB
1995 Mike Pringle, Baltimore, RB
1996 Doug Flutie, Toronto, QB
1997 Doug Flutie, Toronto, QB

CFL Most Outstanding Rookie

Regular season Rookie of the Year as selected by The Football Reporters of Canada since 1972.

Year
1972 Chuck Ealey, Hamilton, QB
1973 Johnny Rodgers, Montreal, WR
1974 Sam Cvijanovich, Toronto, LB
1975 Tom Clements, Ottawa, QB
1976 John Sciarra, B.C. Lions, QB

Year
1977 Leon Bright, B.C. Lions, WR
1978 Joe Poplawski, Winnipeg, WR
1979 Brian Kelly, Edmonton, WR
1980 William Miller, Winnipeg, RB
1981 Vince Goldsmith, Saskatch., LB

Year
1982 Chris Issac, Ottawa, QB
1983 Johnny Shepherd, Hamilton, RB
1984 Dwaine Wilson, Montreal, RB
1985 Mike Gray, B.C. Lions, DT
1986 Harold Hallman, Calgary, DT

Year	Year	Year
1987 Gill Fenerty, Toronto, RB	1991 Jon Volpe, B.C. Lions, RB	1995 Shalon Baker, Edmonton, WR
1988 Orville Lee, Ottawa, RB	1992 Mike Richardson, Winnipeg, RB	1996 Kelvin Anderson, Calgary, RB
1989 Stephen Jordan, Hamilton, DB	1993 Michael O'Shea, Hamilton, DT	1997 Darrell Mitchell, Toronto, SB
1990 Reggie Barnes, Ottawa, RB	1994 Matt Goodwin, Baltimore, DB	

CFL Most Outstanding Canadian

Regular season Canadian of the Year as selected by The Football Reporters of Canada since 1954.

Multiple Winners: Tony Gabriel and Russ Jackson (4); Ray Elgaard (3); Paul Bennett, Rocky DiPietro, Terry Evanshen, Gerry James, Normie Kwong, Joe Poplawski, David Sapunjis and Jim Young (2).

Year	Year	Year
1953 none selected	1968 Ken Nielsen, Winnipeg, FL	1983 Paul Bennett, Montreal, DB
1954 Gerry James, Winnipeg, RB	1969 Russ Jackson, Ottawa, QB	1984 Nick Arakgi, Montreal, TE
1955 Normie Kwong, Edmonton, RB	1970 Jim Young, B.C. Lions, WR	1985 Paul Bennett, Hamilton, DB
1956 Normie Kwong, Edmonton, RB	1971 Terry Evanshen, Montreal, WR	1986 Joe Poplawski, Winnipeg, SB
1957 Gerry James, Winnipeg, RB	1972 Jim Young, B.C. Lions, WR	1987 Scott Flagel, Winnipeg, S
1958 Ron Howell, Hamilton, FL	1973 Gerry Organ, Ottawa, K	1988 Ray Elgaard, Saskatchewan, SB
1959 Russ Jackson, Ottawa, QB	1974 Tony Gabriel, Hamilton, TE	1989 Rocky DiPietro, Hamilton, SB
1960 Ron Stewart, Ottawa, RB	1975 Jim Foley, Ottawa, WR	1990 Ray Elgaard, Saskatchewan, SB
1961 Tony Pajaczkowski, Calgary, DE	1976 Tony Gabriel, Ottawa, TE	1991 Blake Marshall, Edmonton, FB
1962 Harvey Wylie, Calgary, DB	1977 Tony Gabriel, Ottawa, TE	1992 Ray Elgaard, Saskatchewan, SB
1963 Russ Jackson, Ottawa, QB	1978 Tony Gabriel, Ottawa, TE	1993 David Sapunjis, Calgary, SB
1964 Tommy Grant, Hamilton, FL	1979 Dave Fennell, Edmonton, DT	1994 Gerald Wilcox, Winnipeg, SB
1965 Zeno Karcz, Hamilton, LB	1980 Gerry Dattillio, Montreal, QB	1995 David Sapunjis, Calgary, SB
1966 Russ Jackson, Ottawa, QB	1981 Joe Poplawski, Winnipeg, SB	1996 Leroy Blugh, Edmonton, DE
1967 Terry Evanshen, Calgary, WR	1982 Rocky DiPietro, Hamilton, SB	1997 Sean Millington, B.C. Lions, FB

CFL Coach of the Year

The Annis Stukus Trophy presented by the Edmonton Eskimo Alumni Association to the Coach of the Year as selected by The Football Reporters of Canada.

Multiple Winners: Don Matthews (4); Jack Gotta (3); Wally Buono, Ray Jauch, Cal Murphy, Bob O'Billovich and Mike Riley (2).

Year	Year	Year
1961 Jim Trimble, Hamilton	1974 Marv Levy, Montreal	1987 Bob O'Billovich, Toronto
1962 Steve Owen, Saskatchewan	1975 George Brancato, Ottawa	1988 Mike Riley, Winnipeg
1963 Dave Skrien, B.C. Lions	1976 Bob Shaw, Hamilton	1989 John Gregory, Saskatchewan
1964 Ralph Sazio, Hamilton	1977 Vic Rapp, B.C. Lions	1990 Mike Riley, Winnipeg
1965 Bud Grant, Winnipeg	1978 Jack Gotta, Calgary	1991 Adam Rita, Toronto
1966 Frank Clair, Ottawa	1979 Hugh Campbell, Edmonton	1992 Wally Buono, Calgary
1967 Jerry Williams, Calgary	1980 Ray Jauch, Winnipeg	1993 Wally Buono, Calgary
1968 Eagle Keys, Saskatchewan	1981 Joe Faragalli, Saskatchewan	1994 Don Matthews, Baltimore
1969 Frank Clair, Ottawa	1982 Bob O'Billovich, Toronto	1995 Don Matthews, Baltimore
1970 Ray Jauch, Edmonton	1983 Cal Murphy, Winnipeg	1996 Ron Lancaster, Edmonton
1971 Leo Cahill, Toronto	1984 Cal Murphy, Winnipeg	1997 Don Matthews, Toronto
1972 Jack Gotta, Ottawa	1985 Don Matthews, B.C. Lions	
1973 Jack Gotta, Ottawa	1986 Al Bruno, Hamilton	

All-Time CFL Leaders

Through the 1997 season. Players active in 1997 are in **bold** type.

Passing Yards

	Yrs	Att	Cmp	Yards	Cmp Pct	Avg Gain	TD	Int	Rating
Ron Lancaster	19	6233	3384	50,535	54.3	14.9	333	396	72.4
Matt Dunigan	14	5476	3057	43,857	55.8	14.3	306	211	84.5
Doug Flutie	8	4854	2975	41,355	61.3	13.9	270	155	93.9
Tom Clements	12	4657	2807	39,041	60.3	13.9	252	214	86.1
Damon Allen	13	4955	2667	38,211	53.8	14.3	215	174	78.9
Tracy Ham	10	4405	2364	36,092	53.7	15.3	252	149	85.9
Kent Austin	10	4700	2709	36,030	57.6	13.3	198	191	79.2
Dieter Brock	11	4535	2602	34,830	57.4	13.4	210	158	82.8
Tom Burgess	10	4034	2118	30,308	52.5	14.3	190	191	73.1
Sam Etcheverry	7	2829	1630	25,582	57.6	15.7	183	163	85.3

Rushing Yards

	Yrs	Car	Yards	Avg	TD
George Reed	13	3243	16,116	5.0	134
Johnny Bright	13	1969	10,909	5.5	69
Normie Kwong	13	1745	9,022	5.2	78
Leo Lewis	11	1351	8,861	6.5	48
Dave Thelen	9	1530	8,463	5.5	47

Receiving Yards

	Yrs	Ct	Yards	Avg	TD
Ray Elgaard	14	830	13,198	16.0	78
Brian Kelly	9	575	11,169	19.4	97
Allen Pitts	9	696	11,025	15.8	89
Tom Scott	11	649	10,837	16.7	88
Don Narcisse	11	777	10,551	13.6	67

NFL EUROPE

The World League of American Football was formed in 1991 with hopes of expanding the popularity of the NFL to overseas markets. Funded by the NFL, the inaugural league in 1991 consisted of three European teams (London, Barcelona and Frankfurt), and seven North American teams (New York/New Jersey, Orlando, Montreal, Raleigh-Durham, Birmingham, Sacramento and San Antonio). The second season used the same format with Columbus, Ohio, replacing Raleigh-Durham.

In the fall of 1992, the NFL and WLAF Board of Directors voted to restructure the league to include more European teams. Play was subsequently suspended. In 1993, NFL clubs approved a six-team European-only league to resume play in 1995 with teams in Amsterdam, Barcelona, Frankfurt, London, Rhein and Scotland. In January 1998, the name of the league was changed to NFL Europe.

The World Bowl

The first World Bowl was held in 1991 in front of 61,108 fans at London's Wembley Stadium. In 1991 and 1992, when the league consisted of three divisions, the top team from each division and one wild-card team advanced to the playoffs, with the winners of each game advancing to the World Bowl. Since 1995, the top two regular season teams advance directly to the World Bowl.

Year	Winner	Head Coach	Score	Loser	Head Coach	Site
1991	London	Larry Kennan	21-0	Barcelona	Jack Bicknell	London
1992	Sacramento	Kay Stephenson	21-17	Orlando	Galen Hall	Montreal
1993	No game played.					
1994	No game played.					
1995	Frankfurt	Ernie Stautner	26-22	Amsterdam	Al Luginbill	Amsterdam
1996	Scotland	Jim Criner	32-27	Frankfurt	Ernie Stautner	Edinburgh, Scot.
1997	Barcelona	Jack Bicknell	38-24	Rhein	Galen Hall	Barcelona
1998	Rhein	Galen Hall	34-10	Frankfurt	Dick Curl	Frankfurt

World Bowl MVP

Year
1991 Dan Crossman, London, S
1992 Davis Archer, Sacramento, QB
1993 No game played.

Year
1994 No game played.
1995 Paul Justin, Frankfurt, QB
1996 Yo Murphy, Scotland, WR

Year
1997 Jon Kitna, Barcelona, QB
1998 Jim Arellanes, Rhein, QB

Most Valuable Player

Regular season Offensive and Defensive Most Valuable Players as selected by league head coaches since 1991.

Year
1991 Off–Stan Gelbaugh, London, QB
Def–Anthony Parker, NY/NJ, CB
& Danny Lockett, London, LB
1992 Off–David Archer, Sac., QB
Def–Adrian Jones, Barcelona, CB
1993 No award given out.

Year
1994 No award given out.
1995 Off–Paul Justin, Frankfurt, QB
Def–Malcolm Showell, Ams., DE
1996 Off–Sean LaChapelle, Scot., WR
Def–Ty Parten, Scot., DL

Year
1997 Off–T.J. Rubley, Rhein, QB
Def–Jason Simmons, Scot., DE
1998 Off–Marcus Robinson, Rhe., WR
Def–Josh Taves, Barcelona, DE

Coach of the Year

Year
1991 No award given out.
1992 No award given out.
1993 No award given out.

Year
1994 No award given out.
1995 Ernie Stautner, Frankfurt
1996 Jim Criner, Scotland

Year
1997 Galen Hall, Rhein
1998 Dick Curl, Frankfurt

All-Time Winningest NFL Europe Coaches

Totals include playoff records which are in parentheses. Through the 1998 season. Coaches active in 1998 are in **bold** type.

	Yrs	W	L	T	Pct.	Titles
Jack Bicknell (2-2)	6	34	30	0	.531	1997
Galen Hall (2-2)	5	31	23	0	.574	1998
Al Luginbill (0-1)	4	26	15	0	.634	
Ernie Stautner (1-1)	3	17	15	0	.531	1995
Jim Criner (1-0)	4	17	24	0	.415	1996
Kay Stephenson (2-0)	2	13	9	0	.591	1992
Chan Gailey (0-2)	2	12	9	1	.568	
Larry Kennan (2-0)	1	11	1	0	.917	1991
Mike Riley (0-0)	2	11	9	0	.550	
Mouse Davis (0-1)	2	11	10	0	.524	
Lionel Taylor (0-0)	3	11	17	0	.393	

All-Time NFL Europe Leaders

Through the 1998 season. Players active in 1998 are in **bold** type.

Passing Yards

	Yrs	Yards
Stan Gelbaugh, London	2	4,621
Mike Perez, Frankfurt	2	3,257
Will Furrer, Amsterdam	2	3,231

Rushing Yards

	Yrs	Yards
Siran Stacey, Scotland	3	2,350
Derrick Clark, Rhein	3	1,251
Eric Wilkerson, NY/NJ	2	1,121

Receiving Yards

	Yrs	Yards
Mario Bailey, Frankfurt	4	2,082
Demetrius Davis, Barcelona	4	1,755
Tyree Davis, Barcelona	2	1,593

Receptions

	Yrs	No
Demetrius Davis, Barcelona	4	151
Judd Garrett, London	2	126
Michael Titley, Orl.-Lon.	4	122

College Basketball

Rick who? **Tubby Smith** made everyone forget about his popular predecessor when the Wildcats won it all in 1998.

Archive Photos

Moments of Madness

Bryce Drew's frozen moment epitomized a super NCAA Tournament.

by
Chris Fowler

We watch the NCAA Basketball Tournament because of the "Possibilities."

On a Thursday afternoon in an arena sold out but still far from full, we might see one of the "double-directionals," or some obscure branch campus, take down one of the giants. Or we might see Tyus Edney weaving through Missouri in three seconds flat, or Thomas Hill's facial contortions after Christian Laettner's turnaround drops. In all 63 tournament games, the "Possibility" exists.

March is the month of frozen moments. What precedes it matters little these days.

So we should cherish the NCAA Tournament of 1998. It might have been the best ever. Eighteen games were decided by three points or less. In March, superstars and slickster coaches suddenly fell out of season. Kentucky's championship and the Final Four runs by Utah and Stanford celebrated the collective force of just real solid college basketball players.

And where were you when Bryce Drew's headfirst slide put him at the bottom of a jubilant post-game pile-on? When the world learned about a tiny rural Catholic school called Valpo.

I was in the ESPN hoops "war room." All regions, all the time! A wall of monitors and a table full of catered pasta. And a live (when he's not napping) Dick Vitale in surround sound! OK, so it's not perfect.

But it was a superb place to be on March 13, 1998. On one screen, Western Michigan was validating the selection committee's faith by stunning Clemson. On another: Valparaiso and Ole' Miss.

Chris Fowler is the host of ESPN's *College GameDay*.

AP/Wide World Photos

Homer Drew and his son Bryce embrace moments after the son drained the buzzer-beating game-winner against Mississippi in the first round of the 1998 NCAA Tournament to vault the dad's unheralded Valparaiso team into the next round.

Down one, 2.6 seconds left, Crusader coach Homer Drew calls for "Pacer." It's a play he's hounded his team about for months, they'd groaned and rolled their eyes during endless mock endgame scenarios. Like Latin, or long division, it was something rehearsed endlessly, that you figure you'll never use in the real world.

But here was Jamie Sykes putting his baseball future (and the Arizona Diamondbacks) on hold for one more weekend, to throw a perfect strike. There was the tipped pass - executed better than it had been in practice. And there was Bryce Drew, living the driveway dream or playground fantasy of every kid who's ever shot a basketball: swishing a winning jumper as the clock ticks double zero. Then the Pete Rose slide and the pile-up. And my frozen moment of 1998: a wall full of Homer Drew closeups, the face of your friendly neighborhood pharmacist wearing a "holy-smokes-can-you-believe-it?" grin ear to ear.

He was still wearing that grin a couple weeks later at a Final Four party, and you couldn't blame him. Think about it: under pressure, your team perfectly executes a play you convinced them all along was important that they learn and your kid—who could have played for anybody but decided to pass up the limelight and play for you—hits a buzzer-beater to give your program its biggest win ever. Does it get any better?

In the war room, the collective bedlam of two dozen others almost drowned out Vitale. We weren't rooting for our brackets. We were whooping it up for another one of those moments. One of those "Possibilities" that came to pass before our eyes. ■

Dick Vitale's Highlights of the Year in College Basketball

10. Saint Louis freshman guard **Larry Hughes**, the nation's best diaper dandy, rejuvenates the Billikens and brings basketball excitement back to the Saint Louis campus.

9. **Jim Harrick**, down and out after his departure from UCLA, makes a grand return to the NCAA Tourney, guiding the cinderella Rams of the University of Rhode Island to the tournament's Final Eight.

8. North Carolina forward **Antawn Jamison** sweeps the College Player of the Year awards with his brilliant, unselfish brand of basketball.

7. Father and son **Homer** and **Bryce Drew** shock America as little Valparaiso makes some big noise in the Big Dance against Ole' Miss.

Archive Photos

North Carolina forward **Antawn Jamison** was the consensus Player of the Year thanks in part to explosive plays like the one captured above.

6. The great play of **Duke's brilliant freshmen** keeps them ranked in the Top 5 all year and earns the Blue Devils an ACC regular-season title.

5. **Princeton** proves early on that they can play with the big time programs before eventually losing to Mateen Cleaves and Michigan State in the Tournament.

4. North Carolina's **Bill Guthridge**, a diaper dandy of a head coach, replaces the immortal Dean Smith and the 'Heels don't miss a beat, reaching the Final Four yet again.

3. **Mike Montgomery's Stanford Cardinal** make it to their first Final Four in 56 years, coming from six points down with less than a minute left against Rhode Island in the Midwest Regional final.

2. Rick Majerus's miracle run with Utah. **The Utes** defeat two No. 1-seeds (Arizona and North Carolina) and give Kentucky all they can handle before falling, 78-69, in the national championship game.

1. **Tubby Smith**, less than a year after replacing the wildly-popular Rick Pitino, makes believers out of everyone in Lexington as he guides Kentucky to a national championship in his first season with the Wildcats. ■

THE NUMBERS INSIDE

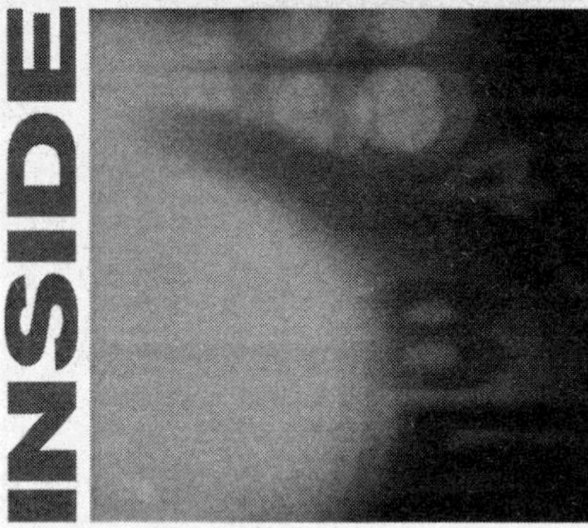

by

Chris Fallica, Steve Rutkowski, Craig Wachs, Jeff Bennett and Team Research

EARLY EXITS

With their loss to Jim Harrick's Rhode Island Rams, Kansas became the latest one-seed to bow out before reaching the Sweet 16. Here's a list of the other teams since the field expanded to 64 in 1985.

Year	No. 1 seed	Lost to
1998	Kansas	Rhode Island
1996	Purdue	Georgia
1994	North Carolina	Boston College
1992	Kansas	UTEP
1990	Oklahoma	North Carolina
1986	St. John's	Auburn
1985	Michigan	Villanova

NO **ONE** ALLOWED

The Kentucky/Utah NCAA final was only the fifth time that a top seed was not involved in the national championship game since seeding began in 1979.

Year	Final
1998	#2 Kentucky def. #3 Utah
1991	#2 Duke def. #3 Kansas
1989	#3 Michigan def. #3 Seton Hall
1981	#3 Indiana def. #2 North Carolina
1980	#2 Louisville def. #8 UCLA

Note: Indiana (1981) is the only lower seed to win an NCAA final not involving a one-seed.

CLAWING BACK

Kentucky's 10-point second half comeback represents the largest deficit overcome in the second half of an NCAA title game. Below is a list of the clutch comebacks.

Year	Champion	Halftime Deficit	Opponent
1998	Kentucky	10	Utah
1963	Loyola-IL	8	Cincinnati
1976	Indiana	6	Michigan
1986	Louisville	3	Duke
1958	Kentucky	3	Seattle
1947	Holy Cross	3	Oklahoma

VOLUNTEERS STREAKING

The Tennessee Lady Vols are owners of the second-longest win streak in NCAA women's basketball history. The Vols, who went 39-0 last year and won the NCAA Tournament, need just win the first 10 games of the 1998-99 season to pass Louisiana Tech as best all-time. Below is a table that shows where Pat Summitt's team currently stacks up.

Years	Team	Games
1980-82	Louisiana Tech	54
1997-98	**Tennessee**	**45**
1985-87	Texas	40
1994-96	UConn	35
1996-97	UConn	33

ELITE 8 BLOWOUTS

A big win in the Elite Eight doesn't necessarily guarantee good things in the Final Four. Utah had the fourth largest Elite Eight blowout and did advance to the championship game but other big winners haven't been so lucky. In fact, besides Utah, only UNLV won their next game.

Year	Winner	Loser	Margin
1992	Cincinnati	Memphis	31
1990	UNLV	Loyola-CA	30
1992	Indiana	UCLA	27
1998	Utah	Arizona	25
1993	Kentucky	FSU	25

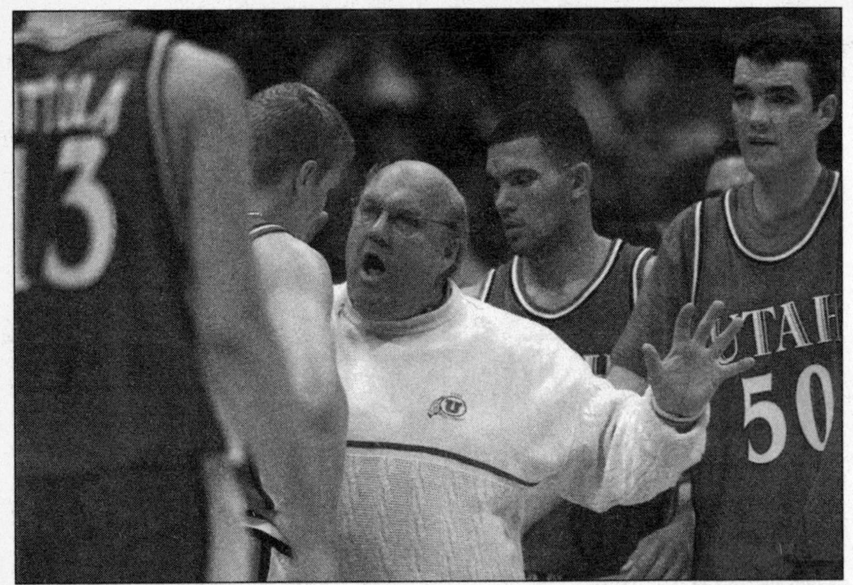

AP/Wide World Photos

Utah head coach **Rick Majerus** talks to his Utes during the Final Four championship game with Kentucky. Apparently his words weren't quite enough because Kentucky prevailed, ending Utah's magnificent tournament run. The convivial Majerus was a media darling during the season, even appearing on *The Tonight Show with Jay Leno.*

FINAL FOURLORN

Stanford Cardinal fans waited a long time for the joys of the 1997-98 season. It was their school's first Final Four appearance in 56 years. In fact, after Stanford won the national championship in 1942 it took them another 47 years before they would even get back into the NCAA Tournament. Here is a list of the longest droughts between Final Four appearances.

Team	Years	Span
Stanford	56	1942-98
Oklahoma St.	44	1951-95
Oklahoma	41	1947-88
Georgetown	39	1943-82
Illinois	37	1952-89

FAMILIAR FACES

The Kentucky Wildcats reached the national title game for the third consecutive season in 1998. The only other team to accomplish this feat since the NCAA Tournament expanded to 64 teams in 1985 is Duke (1990-92). Here is rundown of the teams to make a habit of appearing in the biggest game of the year.

Team	Consecutive Appearances	Titles
UCLA	**7** (1967-73)	7
Cincinnati	**3** (1961-63)	2
Duke	**3** (1990-92)	2
Ohio St.	**3** (1960-62)	1
Kentucky	**3** (1996-98)	2

Final Regular Season AP Men's Top 25 Poll

Taken **before** start of NCAA tournament.

The sportswriters & broadcasters poll: first place votes in parentheses; records through Monday, March 9, 1998; total points (based on 25 for 1st, 24 for 2nd, etc.); record in NCAA tourney and team lost to; head coach (career years and record including 1998 postseason), and preseason ranking. Teams in **bold** type went on to reach NCAA Final Four.

		Mar. 9 Record	Points	NCAA Recap	Head Coach	Preseason Rank
1	**North Carolina** (55)	30-3	1734	4-1 (Utah)	Bill Guthridge (1 yr: 34-4)	4
2	Kansas (13)	34-3	1652	1-1 (Rhode Island)	Roy Williams (10 yrs: 282-62)	2
3	Duke	29-3	1601	3-1 (Kentucky)	Mike Krzyzewski (23 yrs: 505-212)	3
4	Arizona (2)	27-4	1580	3-1 (Utah)	Lute Olson (25 yrs: 565-205)	1
5	**Kentucky**	29-4	1439	6-0	Tubby Smith (7 yrs: 159-66)	8
6	Connecticut	29-4	1429	3-1 (North Carolina)	Jim Calhoun (26 yrs: 520-256)	12
7	**Utah**	25-3	1216	5-1 (Kentucky)	Rick Majerus (14 yrs: 309-111)	16
8	Princeton	26-1	1194	1-1 (Michigan St.)	Bill Carmody (2 yrs: 51-6)	58
9	Cincinnati	26-5	1129	1-1 (West Virginia)	Bob Huggins (17 yrs: 387-149)	28
10	**Stanford**	26-4	1114	4-1 (Kentucky)	Mike Montgomery (20 yrs: 389-209)	14
11	Purdue	26-7	1005	2-1 (Stanford)	Gene Keady (20 yrs: 432-187)	9
12	Michigan	24-8	961	1-1 (UCLA)	Brian Ellerbee (1 yr: 25-9)	25
13	Mississippi	22-6	880	0-1 (Valparaiso)	Rob Evans (6 yrs: 86-81)	23
14	South Carolina	23-7	859	0-1 (Richmond)	Eddie Fogler (11 yrs: 227-144)	7
15	Texas Christian	27-5	784	0-1 (Florida St.)	Billy Tubbs (24 yrs: 519-247)	41t
16	Michigan St.	20-7	717	2-1 (North Carolina)	Tom Izzo (3 yrs: 55-36)	NR
17	Arkansas	23-8	487	1-1 (Utah)	Nolan Richardson (18 yrs: 433-155)	30
18	New Mexico	23-7	474	1-1 (Syracuse)	Dave Bliss (23 yrs: 440-262)	11
19	UCLA	22-8	464	2-1 (Kentucky)	Steve Lavin (2 yrs: 48-17)	6
20	Maryland	19-10	417	2-1 (Arizona)	Gary Williams (20 yrs: 371-240)	27
21	Syracuse	24-8	377	2-1 (Duke)	Jim Boeheim (22 yrs: 528-181)	35
22	Illinois	22-9	366	1-1 (Maryland)	Lon Kruger (16 yrs: 282-205)	40
23	Xavier-OH	22-7	275	0-1 (Washington)	Skip Prosser (5 yrs: 98-47)	10
24	Temple	21-8	124	0-1 (West Virginia)	John Chaney (26 yrs: 581-208)	NR
25	Murray St.	29-3	71	0-1 (Rhode Island)	Mark Gottfried (3 yrs: 68-24)	NR

Others receiving votes: 26. **Clemson** (18-13) 60 pts; 27. **West Virginia** (22-8) 58; 28. **Oklahoma St.** (21-6) 46; 29. **St. John's** (22-9) 45; 30. **Massachusetts** (21-10) 37; 31. **George Washington** (24-8) 32; 32. **UNLV** (20-12) 30; 33. **Rhode Island** (22-8) 24; 34. **Hawaii** (19-8) 16; 35. **UNC-Charlotte** (19-10) 15; 36. **Illinois St.** (24-5) and **Tennessee** (20-8) 10; 38. **Oklahoma** (22-10) 5; 39. **Indiana** (19-11) 4; 40. **Iona** (27-5) 3; 41. **Eastern Michigan** (20-9), **Northern Arizona** (21-7) and **Utah St.** (25-7) 2.

NCAA Men's Division I Tournament Seeds

	WEST		MIDWEST		SOUTH		EAST
1	Arizona (27-4)	1	Kansas (34-3)	1	Duke (29-3)	1	North Carolina (30-3)
2	Cincinnati (26-5)	2	Purdue (26-7)	2	Kentucky (29-4)	2	Connecticut (29-4)
3	Utah (25-3)	3	Stanford (26-4)	3	South Carolina (23-7)	3	Michigan (24-8)
4	Maryland (19-10)	4	Mississippi (22-6)	4	Michigan St. (20-7)	4	New Mexico (23-7)
5	Illinois (22-9)	5	TCU (27-5)	5	Princeton (26-1)	5	Syracuse (24-8)
6	Arkansas (23-8)	6	Clemson (18-13)	6	Xavier (22-7)	6	UCLA (22-8)
7	Temple (21-8)	7	St. John's (22-9)	7	Indiana (19-11)	7	Massachusetts (21-10)
8	Tennessee (20-8)	8	Rhode Island (22-8)	8	UNC-Charlotte (19-10)	8	Oklahoma St. (21-6)
9	Illinois St. (24-5)	9	Murray St. (29-3)	9	Illinois-Chicago (22-5)	9	Geo. Washington (24-8)
10	West Virginia (22-8)	10	Detroit (24-5)	10	Oklahoma (22-10)	10	Saint Louis (21-10)
11	Nebraska (20-11)	11	W. Michigan (20-7)	11	Washington (18-9)	11	Miami (18-9)
12	South Alabama (21-6)	12	Florida St. (17-13)	12	UNLV (20-12)	12	Iona (27-5)
13	Utah St. (25-7)	13	Valparaiso (21-9)	13	E. Michigan (20-9)	13	Butler (22-10)
14	San Francisco (19-10)	14	Coll. of Charleston (24-5)	14	Richmond (22-7)	14	Davidson (20-9)
15	N. Arizona (21-7)	15	Delaware (20-9)	15	F. Dickinson (23-6)	15	S. Carolina St. (22-7)
16	Nicholls St. (19-9)	16	Prairie View A&M (13-16)	16	Navy (19-10)	16	Radford (20-9)

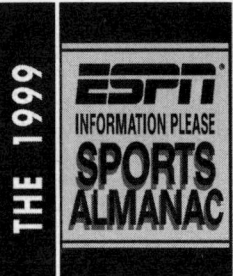

1998 NCAA BASKETBALL MEN'S DIVISION I

EAST

FIRST ROUND March 12-13

1 N. Carolina	88
16 Navy	52
8 NC-Charlotte	77
9 Ill-Chicago	62
5 Princeton	69
12 UNLV	57
4 Michigan St.	83
13 E. Michigan	71
6 Xavier	68
11 Washington	69
3 S. Carolina	61
14 Richmond	62
7 Indiana (OT)	94
10 Oklahoma	87
2 UConn	93
15 F. Dickinson	85

SECOND ROUND March 14-15

N. Carolina	93
(OT) NC-Charlotte	83
Princeton	56
Michigan St.	63
Washington	81
Richmond	66
Indiana	68
UConn	78

REGIONALS March 21-22

N. Carolina	73
Michigan St.	58
Washington	74
UConn	75
N. Carolina	75
UConn	64

East champion: N. Carolina 59

WEST

FIRST ROUND March 12-13

1 Arizona	99
16 Nicholls St.	60
8 Tennessee (OT)	81
9 Illinois St.	82
5 Illinois	64
12 S. Alabama	51
4 Maryland	82
13 Utah St.	68
6 Arkansas	74
11 Nebraska	65
3 Utah	85
14 San. Fran.	68
7 Temple	52
10 W. Virginia	82
2 Cincinnati	65
15 N. Arizona	62

SECOND ROUND March 14-15

Arizona	82
Illinois St.	49
Illinois	61
Maryland	67
Arkansas	69
Utah	75
W. Virginia	75
Cincinnati	74

REGIONALS March 21-22

Arizona	87
Maryland	79
Utah	65
W. Virginia	62
Arizona	51
Utah	76

West champion: Utah 65

SOUTH

FIRST ROUND March 12-13

1 Duke	99
16 Radford	63
8 Okla. St.	74
9 G. Wash.	59
5 Syracuse	63
12 Iona	61
4 N. Mexico	79
13 Butler	62
6 UCLA	65
11 Miami	62
3 Michigan	80
14 Davidson	61
7 U Mass	46
10 St. Louis	51
2 Kentucky	82
15 S. Carolina St.	67

SECOND ROUND March 14-15

Duke	79
Okla. St.	73
Syracuse	56
N. Mexico	46
UCLA	85
Michigan	82
St. Louis	61
Kentucky	88

REGIONALS March 21-22

Duke	80
Syracuse	67
UCLA	68
Kentucky	94
Duke	84
Kentucky	86

South champion: Kentucky 86 (OT)

MIDWEST

FIRST ROUND March 12-13

1 Kansas	110
16 Prairie View	52
8 Rhode Island	97
9 Murray St.	74
5 TCU	87
12 Florida St.	96
4 Mississippi	69
13 Valparaiso	70
6 Clemson	72
11 W. Michigan	75
3 Stanford	67
14 Coll. of Charleston	57
7 St. Johns	64
10 Detroit	66
2 Purdue	95
15 Delaware	56

SECOND ROUND March 14-15

Kansas	75
Rhode Island	80
Florida St.	77
Valparaiso	83
W. Michigan	65
Stanford	83
Detroit	65
Purdue	80

REGIONALS March 21-22

Rhode Island	74
Valparaiso	67
Stanford	67
Purdue	59
Rhode Island	77
Stanford	79

Midwest champion: Stanford 85

NATIONAL CHAMPIONSHIP

Utah 69

Kentucky 78

FINAL FOUR

at The Alamodome
in San Antonio

***

Semifinals: March 28

Finals: March 30

NCAA Men's Championship Game

60th NCAA Division I Championship Game. **Date:** Monday, March 30, at the Alamodome. **Coaches:** Rick Majerus of Utah and Tubby Smith of Kentucky. **Favorite:** Kentucky by 4.

Attendance: 40,509; **Officials:** Jim Burr, Donnee Gray, Mike Sanzere; **TV Rating:** 17.8/28 share (CBS).

Kentucky 78

	Min	FG M-A	FT M-A	Pts	Reb O-T	A	PF
Allen Edwards	24	2-7	0-0	4	0-1	5	0
Scott Padgett	33	6-10	4-4	17	2-5	1	4
Nazr Mohammed	13	5-9	0-0	10	0-2	1	4
Wayne Turner	27	2-5	2-4	6	0-2	4	0
Jeff Sheppard	34	7-14	2-2	16	2-4	3	1
Jamaal Magloire	22	2-3	3-3	7	0-2	1	4
Heshimu Evans	23	3-4	2-2	10	1-6	0	1
Cameron Mills	12	2-4	2-2	8	0-0	1	0
Saul Smith	7	0-0	0-0	0	0-0	0	0
Michael Bradley	5	0-0	0-0	0	0-1	0	1
TOTALS	200	29-57	15-17	78	5-23	15	15

Three-point FG: 5-17 (Evans 2-2, Mills 2-4, Padgett 1-5, Turner 0-1, Sheppard 0-2, Edwards 0-3); **Team Rebounds:** 1; **Blocked Shots:** 6 (Magloire 3, Mohammed 2, Evans); **Turnovers:** 11 (Turner 5, Evans 3, Sheppard 2, Mohammed); **Steals:** 7 (Turner 3, Sheppard 2, Edwards, Evans); **Percentages:** 2-Pt FG (.600), 3-Pt FG (.294), Total FG (.509), Free Throws (.882).

Utah 69

	Min	FG M-A	FT M-A	Pts	Reb O-T	A	PF
Hanno Mottola	28	4-10	6-6	15	4-8	0	4
Alex Jensen	35	5-6	3-3	14	0-2	2	2
Michael Doleac	34	5-12	4-6	15	5-10	1	2
Andre Miller	37	6-15	4-7	16	2-6	5	5
Drew Hansen	32	1-6	0-0	2	1-5	1	2
Britton Johnsen	16	3-4	0-0	7	0-4	0	0
Jordie McTavish	3	0-0	0-0	0	0-0	2	1
David Jackson	10	0-1	0-0	0	0-0	1	2
Trace Caton	5	0-1	0-0	0	0-0	0	0
TOTALS	200	24-55	17-22	69	12-35	12	18

Three-point FG: 4-14 (Jensen 1-1, Doleac 1-1, Johnsen 1-2, Mottola 1-3, Jackson 0-1, Caton 0-1, Hansen 0-2, Miller 0-3); **Team Rebounds:** 4; **Blocked Shots:** 2 (Doleac 2); **Turnovers:** 18 (Miller 8, Mottola 3, Johnsen 3, Hansen 2, Jensen, Doleac); **Steals:** 8 (Hansen 3, Doleac 3, Miller 2). **Percentages:** 2-Pt FG (.488), 3-Pt FG (.286), Total FG (.436), Free Throws (.773).

	1st	2nd	Final
Utah (WAC)	41	28—	**69**
Kentucky (SEC)	31	44—	**78**

THE FINAL FOUR

Alamodome in San Antonio (Mar. 28-30).

Semifinal—Game One

Midwest Regional champ Stanford vs. South Regional champ Kentucky; Saturday, Mar. 28 (5:42 p.m. tipoff). **Coaches:** Mike Montgomery, Stanford and Tubby Smith, Kentucky. **Favorite:** Kentucky by 8½.

	1st	2nd	OT	Final
Stanford (Pac-10)	37	36	12—	**85**
Kentucky (SEC)	32	41	13—	**86**

High scorers— Arthur Lee, Stanford (26) and Jeff Sheppard, Kentucky (27); **Att**— 40,509; **TV rating**— 10.8/25 share (CBS).

Semifinal—Game Two

West Regional champion Utah vs. East Regional champ North Carolina; Saturday, Mar. 28 (8:07 p.m. tipoff). **Coaches:** Rick Majerus, Utah and Bill Guthridge, North Carolina. **Favorite:** North Carolina by 8½.

	1st	2nd	Final
Utah (WAC)	35	30—	**65**
N. Carolina (ACC)	22	37—	**59**

High scorers— Michael Doleac and Andre Miller, Utah (16) and Vince Carter, UNC (21); **Att**— 40,509; **TV rating**— 12.7/24 share (CBS).

Most Outstanding Player

Jeff Sheppard, Senior guard, Kentucky. SEMIFINAL—33 minutes, 27 points, 6 rebounds, 4 assists, 2 steals; FINAL—34 minutes, 16 points, 4 rebounds, 3 assist, 2 steals.

All-Tournament Team

Sheppard and Scott Padgett of Kentucky, center Michael Doleac and guard Andre Miller of Utah and guard Arthur Lee of Stanford.

Final ESPN/*USA Today* Coaches' Poll

Taken **after** NCAA Tournament.

Voted on by a panel of 30 Division I head coaches following the NCAA tournament: first place votes in parentheses with total points (based on 25 for 1st, 24 for 2nd, etc.). Schools on major probation are ineligible to be ranked.

		W-L	Pts	Before NCAAs W-L	Before NCAAs Rank
1	Kentucky (29)	33-4	749	27-4	6
2	Utah	30-4	717	25-3	7
3	North Carolina (1)	34-4	688	30-3	1
4	Stanford	30-5	653	26-4	11
5	Duke	32-4	619	29-3	1
6	Arizona	30-5	599	27-4	2
7	Connecticut	32-5	561	29-4	6
8	Kansas	35-4	510	34-3	3
9	Purdue	28-8	468	26-7	9
10	Michigan St.	22-8	442	20-7	12
11	Rhode Island	25-9	364	22-8	NR
12	UCLA	24-9	347	22-8	17
13	Syracuse	26-9	313	24-8	21
14	Cincinnati	27-6	302	26-5	13
15	Maryland	21-11	298	19-10	24
16	Princeton	27-2	295	26-1	8
17	Michigan	25-9	277	24-8	18
18	West Virginia	24-9	224	22-8	NR
19	South Carolina	23-8	173	23-7	15
20	Mississippi	22-7	170	22-6	10
21	New Mexico	24-8	166	23-7	19
22	Arkansas	24-9	139	23-8	16
23	Valparaiso	23-10	120	21-9	NR
24	Washington	20-10	106	18-9	NR
25	Texas Christian	27-6	90	27-5	16

Others receiving votes: 26. **Illinois** (23-10, 89 pts); 27. **Xavier** (22-8, 58); 28. **NC-Charlotte** (20-11, 47); 29. **Minnesota** (20-15, 28); 30. **Oklahoma St.** (22-7, 26); 31. **Clemson** (18-14, 13); 32. **Illinois St.** (24-6, 11); 33. **St. John's** (21-10, 9); 34. **Detroit** (23-6), **Indiana** (20-12) and **Massachusetts** (21-11, 8); 37. **George Washington** (24-9, 7); 38. **Northern Arizona** (19-8, 6); 39. **Florida St.** (18-14), **Iona** (26-6), **Oklahoma** (21-11) and **Utah St.** (22-8, 5); 43. **Penn St.** (19-13) and **Temple** (21-9, 4), 45. **Georgia** (20-15, 2); 46. **Miami-FL** (18-10) and **Murray St.** (26-4, 1).

NCAA Finalists' Tournament and Season Statistics

At least 10 games played during the overall season.

Kentucky (35-4)

	NCAA Tournament						Overall Season					
				—Per Game—						—Per Game—		
	Gm	FG%	TPts	Pts	Reb	Ast	Gm	FG%	TPts	Pts	Reb	Ast
Jeff Sheppard	6	.522	99	16.5	4.8	2.3	38	.444	521	13.7	4.0	2.7
Nazr Mohammed	6	.533	80	13.3	5.5	0.7	39	.597	468	12.0	7.2	0.7
Scott Padgett	6	.500	82	13.7	5.6	2.2	39	.476	449	11.5	6.5	2.1
Wayne Turner	6	.457	57	9.5	3.2	5.5	39	.481	362	9.3	3.1	4.4
Allen Edwards	6	.522	66	11.0	2.7	3.7	37	.444	341	9.2	3.2	3.3
Jamaal Magloire	6	.714	28	4.7	3.2	0.7	38	.487	192	5.2	4.2	0.3
Cameron Mills	6	.333	17	2.8	1.7	0.3	38	.417	166	4.4	1.5	0.7
Saul Smith	6	.167	3	0.5	0.5	1.2	39	.360	97	2.5	1.0	1.4
Mike Bradley	5	.500	11	2.2	1.6	1.0	32	.667	78	2.4	1.7	0.5
Myron Anthony	3	.571	11	3.7	0.7	0.0	31	.397	10	2.3	1.2	0.2
Ryan Hogan	3	.400	6	2.0	1.0	0.3	19	.269	21	1.1	0.6	0.5
Steve Masiello	3	.000	0	0.0	0.7	0.0	19	.400	11	0.6	0.2	0.3
KENTUCKY	6	.512	514	85.7	36.3	18.8	39	.482	3123	80.1	42.1	17.7
OPPONENTS	6	.372	434	72.3	40.3	12.2	39	.384	2612	67.0	33.9	12.4

Three-pointers: NCAA TOURNAMENT— Sheppard (10-28), Edwards (8-20), Padgett (7-19), Evans (4-8), Anthony (3-4), Mills (3-9), Hogan (2-3), Smith (1-2), Turner (1-5); OVERALL— Sheppard (71-189), Padgett (40-107), Mills (38-87), Edwards (31-106), Turner (21-57), Evans (18-51), Anthony (12-26), Smith (12-42), Hogan (5-12), Masiello (3-4), Team (250-681 for .367 pct.).

Utah (30-4)

	NCAA Tournament						Overall Season					
				—Per Game—						—Per Game—		
	Gm	FG%	TPts	Pts	Reb	Ast	Gm	FG%	TPts	Pts	Reb	Ast
Michael Doleac	6	.523	115	19.2	7.5	1.3	32	.488	516	16.1	7.1	0.5
Andre Miller	6	.500	100	16.7	7.5	6.8	34	.549	483	14.2	5.4	5.2
Hanno Mottola	6	.491	65	10.8	4.8	0.5	34	.489	424	12.5	5.3	0.8
Alex Jensen	6	.563	51	8.5	5.8	1.5	34	.457	232	6.8	5.8	2.3
Britton Johnsen	6	.577	37	6.2	2.2	0.5	21	.456	73	3.5	1.6	0.5
Drew Hansen	6	.458	33	5.5	4.2	1.5	33	.438	182	5.5	3.1	2.1
Trace Caton	6	.357	14	2.3	0.2	0.2	34	.460	137	4.0	1.1	0.7
David Jackson	6	.354	12	2.0	1.2	0.5	32	.415	105	3.3	1.5	1.4
Jordie McTavish	6	.500	8	1.3	0.3	0.8	34	.361	93	2.7	0.7	1.0
Jon Carlisle	2	—	0	0.0	1.0	0.0	30	.565	73	2.4	2.1	0.3
Nate Althoff	1	—	0	0.0	0.0	0.0	17	.667	30	1.8	1.8	0.1
Greg Barratt	0	—	0	0.0	0.0	0.0	15	.306	27	1.8	1.9	0.1
UTAH	6	.502	435	72.5	36.7	13.7	34	.480	2381	70.0	37.0	14.6
OPPONENTS	6	.407	387	64.5	30.5	12.0	34	.386	1959	57.6	27.1	9.4

Three-pointers: NCAA TOURNAMENT— Hansen (6-14), Jensen (4-9), Doleac (2-3), McTavish (2-4), Johnsen (2-6), Caton (2-8), Mottola (2-9), Jackson (1-5), Miller (1-11), Team (22-69 for .319 pct.); OVERALL— Hansen (41-90), Caton (25-60), Jackson (20-50), McTavish (20-56), Miller (20-60), Mottola (16-55), Jensen (14-45), Doleac (13-32), Johnsen (4-13), Barratt (1-5), Team (175-469 for .373 pct.).

Utah's Schedule

Reg. Season
(25-2)

W CS-Fullerton 87-59
W at Weber St.......87-72
W Southern Utah 66-48
W at Loyola Mary....89-50
W UC Irvine 83-45
W Providence 64-58
W at Wake Forest ...62-53
W Utah St...........71-55
W Azusa Pacific.....78-58
W at Oregon St......69-61
W at W.-Milwaukee..65-51
W Rice 73-65
W at BYU...........71-61
W Colorado St. 65-51
W Wyoming 75-58
W at Air Force 57-46
W at UNLV 67-54
L at New Mexico ...74-77
W BYU.............83-68
W at Rice...........60-49
L at Wyoming.......56-62
W at Colorado St. ...60-48
W Air Force.........55-41
W UNLV............79-68
W at UTEP..........71-49
W New Mexico 65-55

WAC Tourney
(0-1)

L at UNLV 51-54

NCAA Tourney
(5-1)

W San Francisco 85-68
W Arkansas.........75-69
W West Virginia 65-62
W Arizona..........76-51
W North Carolina ...65-59
L Kentucky.........69-78

Kentucky's Schedule

Reg. Season
(26-4)

W Morehead St.......88-49
W at G. Washington .70-55
L Arizona..........74-89
W Missouri 77-55
W Clemson 76-61
W at Purdue 89-75
W at Indiana........75-72
W at Canisius 81-54
W Georgia Tech 85-71
W Tulsa 74-53
W American 75-52
L Louisville 76-79
W at Ohio...........95-58
W Vanderbilt........71-62
W at Georgia 90-79
W at Miss. St........77-71
W S. Carolina.......91-70
W Arkansas.........80-77
W Alabama..........70-67
W at Tennessee......85-67
W at Vanderbilt......63-61
L Florida...........78-86
W at LSU 63-61
W at Villanova 79-63
W Tennessee 80-74
L Mississippi 64-73
W at Florida 79-54
W Georgia 85-74
W at Auburn 83-58
W at South Carolina .69-57

SEC Tourney
(3-0)

W Alabama.........82-71
W Arkansas.........99-74
W South Carolina....86-56

NCAA Tourney
(6-0)

W South Carolina St..82-67
W St. Louis 88-61
W UCLA............94-68
W Duke 86-84
W Stanford.....86-85 (OT)
W Utah 78-69

Final NCAA Men's Division I Standings

Conference records include regular season games only. Overall records include all postseason tournament games.

America East Conference

	Conference			Overall		
Team	W	L	Pct	W	L	Pct
*Delaware	13	6	.684	20	10	.667
Boston University	12	7	.632	19	11	.633
Hofstra	11	7	.611	19	12	.613
Vermont	11	7	.611	16	11	.593
Hartford	11	7	.611	15	12	.556
Drexel	10	8	.556	13	15	.464
Northeastern	9	9	.500	14	14	.500
New Hampshire	6	12	.333	10	17	.370
Towson	4	14	.222	8	20	.286
Maine	4	14	.222	7	20	.259

Conf. Tourney Final: Delaware 66, Boston University 58

***NCAA Tourney (0-1):** Delaware (0-1).

Atlantic Coast Conference

	Conference			Overall		
Team	W	L	Pct	W	L	Pct
*Duke	15	1	.895	32	4	.889
*North Carolina	13	3	.842	34	4	.895
*Maryland	10	6	.611	21	11	.656
*Clemson	7	9	.444	18	14	.563
†Wake Forest	7	9	.412	16	14	.533
*Florida St	6	10	.353	18	14	.563
†Georgia Tech	6	10	.353	19	14	.576
†N.C. State	5	11	.333	17	15	.531
Virginia	3	13	.176	11	19	.367

Conf. Tourney Final: North Carolina 83, Duke 68

***NCAA Tourney (10-5):** North Carolina (4-1), Duke (3-1), Maryland (2-1), Florida St. (1-1), Clemson (0-1).

†NIT (4-3): Georgia Tech (2-1), N.C. State (1-1), Wake Forest (1-1).

Atlantic 10 Conference

	Conference			Overall		
East	W	L	Pct	W	L	Pct
*Temple	14	4	.778	21	9	.700
*Rhode Island	13	5	.722	25	9	.735
*Massachusetts	13	5	.722	21	11	.656
†St. Bonaventure	7	11	.389	17	15	.531
St. Joseph's-PA	4	14	.222	11	17	.393
Fordham	2	15	.118	6	21	.222
West	**W**	**L**	**Pct**	**W**	**L**	**Pct**
*Xavier-OH	14	5	.737	22	8	.733
*Geo. Washington	13	6	.684	24	9	.727
†Dayton	12	6	.667	21	12	.636
Virginia Tech	5	12	.294	10	17	.370
Duquesne	5	12	.294	11	19	.367
La Salle	5	12	.294	9	18	.333

Note: There are 12 teams in the Atlantic 10.

Conf. Tourney Final: Xavier 77, George Washington 63

***NCAA Tourney (3-5):** Rhode Island (3-1), George Washington (0-1), Massachusetts (0-1), Temple (0-1), Xavier-OH (0-1).

†NIT Tourney (1-2): Dayton (1-1), St. Bonaventure (0-1).

Big East Conference

	Conference			Overall		
Big East 7	W	L	Pct	W	L	Pct
*Syracuse	14	7	.667	26	9	.743
*Miami-FL	11	8	.579	18	10	.643
†Seton Hall	9	10	.474	15	15	.500
Providence	8	12	.400	13	16	.448
Rutgers	8	13	.381	14	15	.483
†Georgetown	7	13	.350	16	15	.512
Pittsburgh	6	13	.316	11	16	.407
	Conference			**Overall**		
Big East 6	**W**	**L**	**Pct**	**W**	**L**	**Pct**
*Connecticut	18	3	.857	32	5	.865
*St. John's	14	6	.700	22	10	.688
*West Virginia	11	8	.579	24	9	.727
Villanova	9	11	.450	12	17	.414
Notre Dame	7	12	.368	13	14	.481
Boston College	7	13	.350	15	16	.484

Conf. Tourney Final: Connecticut 69, Syracuse 64

***NCAA Tourney (7-5):** Connecticut (3-1), Syracuse (2-1), West Virginia (2-1), Miami (0-1), St. John's (0-1).

†NIT Tourney (1-2): Georgetown (1-1), Seton Hall (0-1).

Big Sky Conference

	Conference			Overall		
Team	W	L	Pct	W	L	Pct
*Northern Arizona	15	3	.833	21	8	.724
Weber St	12	5	.706	14	13	.519
Portland St.	10	6	.625	15	12	.556
Eastern Washington	10	7	.588	16	11	.593
Montana St	11	8	.579	19	11	.633
Montana	9	8	.529	16	14	.533
Cal St.-Northridge	8	10	.444	12	16	.429
Idaho St	2	14	.125	6	20	.231
Cal St.-Sacramento	0	16	.000	1	25	.038

Conf. Tourney Final: Northern Arizona 77, Montana St. 50

***NCAA Tourney (0-1):** Northern Arizona (0-1).

Big South Conference

	Conference			Overall		
Team	W	L	Pct	W	L	Pct
NC-Asheville	11	1	.917	19	9	.679
*Radford	10	2	.833	20	10	.667
MD-Balt. County	6	6	.500	14	14	.500
Liberty	5	7	.417	11	17	.393
Coastal Carolina	4	8	.333	8	19	.296
Winthrop	4	8	.333	7	20	.259
Charleston Southern	2	10	.167	5	22	.185

Conf. Tourney Final: Radford 63, NC-Asheville 61

***NCAA Tourney (0-1):** Radford (0-1).

Final NCAA Men's Division I Standings (Cont.)

Big Ten Conference

Team	Conference W	L	Pct	Overall W	L	Pct
*Illinois	14	4	.778	23	10	.697
*Michigan St	13	4	.765	22	8	.733
*Purdue	14	5	.737	28	8	.778
*Michigan	14	5	.737	25	9	.735
*Indiana	10	8	.556	20	12	.625
†Iowa	9	8	.529	20	11	.645
†Penn St	8	9	.471	19	13	.594
†Minnesota	8	11	.421	20	15	.571
Wisconsin	4	14	.222	12	19	.387
Northwestern	3	14	.176	10	17	.370
Ohio St	1	16	.059	8	22	.267

Note: There are 11 teams in the Big 10.
Conf. Tourney Final: Michigan 76, Purdue 67
***NCAA Tourney (7-5):** Michigan St. (2-1), Purdue (2-1), Illinois (1-1), Indiana (1-1), Michigan (1-1).
†NIT Tourney (9-2): Minnesota (5-0, NIT champions), Penn St. (4-1, NIT runners-up), Iowa (0-1).

Big 12 Conference

Team	Conference W	L	Pct	Overall W	L	Pct
*Kansas	18	1	.947	35	4	.897
*Oklahoma	13	6	.684	22	11	.667
*Oklahoma St.	11	6	.647	22	7	.759
*Nebraska	11	7	.611	20	12	.625
†Missouri	9	9	.500	17	15	.531
Baylor	9	9	.500	14	14	.500
Kansas St	8	10	.444	17	11	.607
Texas	8	11	.421	14	17	.452
Colorado	7	10	.412	13	14	.481
Texas Tech	7	10	.412	13	14	.481
Iowa St.	5	12	.294	12	18	.400
Texas A&M	1	16	.059	7	20	.259

Conf. Tourney Final: Kansas 72, Oklahoma 58
***NCAA Tourney (2-4):** Kansas (1-1), Oklahoma St. (1-1), Oklahoma (0-1), Nebraska (0-1).
†NIT Tourney (0-1): Missouri (0-1).

Big West Conference

Team	Conference W	L	Pct	Overall W	L	Pct
*Utah St	16	3	.842	25	8	.758
Nevada	12	6	.667	15	12	.556
Boise St.	9	8	.529	17	13	.567
Idaho	9	8	.529	15	12	.556
New Mexico St	8	8	.500	18	12	.600
North Texas	4	12	.250	5	21	.192

Team	Conference W	L	Pct	Overall W	L	Pct
†Pacific	16	3	.842	24	10	.706
Cal Poly-SLO	7	9	.438	14	14	.500
Cal St.-Fullerton	7	11	.389	12	16	.429
UC-Irvine	6	11	.353	9	18	.333
Long Beach St	5	12	.294	10	19	.345
UC-Santa Barbara	4	12	.250	7	19	.269

Conf. Tourney Final: Utah St. 78, Pacific 63
***NCAA Tourney (0-1):** Utah St. (0-1).
†NIT Tourney (0-1): Pacific (0-1).

Colonial Athletic Association

Team	Conference W	L	Pct	Overall W	L	Pct
William & Mary	13	3	.813	20	7	.741
†NC-Wilmington	13	3	.813	20	11	.645
*Richmond	12	4	.750	23	8	.742
Old Dominion	8	8	.500	12	16	.429
James Madison	6	10	.375	11	16	.407
George Mason	6	10	.375	9	18	.333
East Carolina	5	11	.313	10	17	.370
American	5	11	.313	9	19	.321
Va. Commonwealth	4	12	.250	9	19	.321

Conf. Tourney Final: Richmond 79, NC-Wilmington 64
***NCAA Tourney (1-1):** Richmond (1-1).
†NIT Tourney (0-1): NC-Wilmington (0-1).

Conference USA

American Division	Conference W	L	Pct	Overall W	L	Pct
*Cincinnati	17	2	.895	27	6	.818
*NC-Charlotte	15	4	.789	20	11	.645
*St. Louis	12	6	.667	22	11	.667
†Marquette	9	9	.500	20	11	.645
Louisville	6	12	.333	12	20	.375
DePaul	3	14	.176	7	23	.233

National Division	Conference W	L	Pct	Overall W	L	Pct
†Memphis	12	5	.706	17	12	.586
†Ala-Birmingham	11	7	.611	21	12	.636
So. Mississippi	11	8	.579	22	10	.688
So. Florida	7	10	.412	17	13	.567
Houston	2	15	.118	9	20	.310
Tulane	2	15	.118	7	22	.241

Conf. Tourney Final: Cincinnati 71, NC-Charlotte 57
***NCAA Tourney (3-3):** Cincinnati (1-1), NC-Charlotte (1-1), Saint Louis (1-1).
†NIT Tourney (4-3): Marquette (2-1), Memphis (1-1), Alabama-Birmingham (1-1).

Ivy League

Team	Conference W	L	Pct	Overall W	L	Pct
*Princeton	14	0	1.000	27	2	.931
Pennsylvania	10	4	.714	17	12	.586
Yale	7	7	.500	12	14	.462
Harvard	6	8	.429	13	13	.500
Columbia	6	8	.429	11	15	.423
Cornell	6	8	.429	9	17	.346
Dartmouth	4	10	.286	7	19	.269
Brown	3	11	.214	6	20	.231

Conf. Tourney Final: Ivy League has no tournament.
***NCAA Tourney (1-1):** Princeton (1-1).

Metro Atlantic Conference

Team	Conference W	L	Pct	Overall W	L	Pct
*Iona	15	3	.833	27	6	.818
†Rider	12	6	.667	18	10	.643
Siena	10	8	.556	17	12	.586
Niagara	10	8	.556	14	13	.519
Canisius	9	9	.500	13	14	.481
Loyola-MD	9	9	.500	12	16	.429
Fairfield	7	11	.389	12	15	.444
Manhattan	7	11	.389	12	17	.414
Marist	7	11	.389	11	17	.393
St. Peter's	4	14	.222	8	19	.296

Conf. Tourney Final: Iona 90, Siena 75
***NCAA Tourney (0-1):** Iona (0-1).
†NIT Tourney (0-1): Rider (0-1).

Mid-American Conference

East	Conference W	L	Pct	Overall W	L	Pct
Akron	13	5	.722	17	10	.630
Miami-OH	10	10	.500	17	12	.586
Kent	9	10	.474	13	17	.433
Marshall	7	11	.389	11	16	.407
Bowling Green	7	11	.389	10	16	.385
Ohio	3	15	.167	5	21	.192

West	Conference W	L	Pct	Overall W	L	Pct
*Western Mich	14	4	.778	21	8	.724
*Eastern Mich	15	5	.750	20	10	.667
†Ball St.	14	5	.737	21	8	.724
Toledo	10	8	.556	15	12	.556
N. Illinois	6	12	.333	10	16	.385
Central Mich	3	15	.167	5	21	.192

Conf. Tourney Final: Eastern Michigan 92, Miami-OH 77
*****NCAA Tourney (1-2):** Western Michigan (1-1), Eastern Michigan (0-1).
†NIT Tourney (0-1): Ball St. (0-1).

Mid-Continent Conference

Team	Conference W	L	Pct	Overall W	L	Pct
*Valparaiso	13	3	.813	23	10	.697
Oral Roberts	12	4	.750	19	12	.613
Youngstown St.	11	5	.688	20	9	.690
Western Illinois	11	5	.688	16	11	.593
Buffalo	9	7	.563	15	13	.536
Missouri-KC	7	9	.437	9	18	.333
Southern Utah	4	12	.250	7	20	.259
Northeastern Illinois	3	13	.188	6	19	.240
Chicago St.	2	14	.125	2	25	.074

Conf. Tourney Final: Valparaiso 67, Youngstown St. 48
*****NCAA Tourney (2-1):** Valparaiso (2-1).

Mid-Eastern Athletic Conference

Team	Conference W	L	Pct	Overall W	L	Pct
*South Carolina St.	21	2	.913	22	8	.733
Coppin St.	19	2	.905	21	8	.724
Hampton	13	7	.650	14	12	.538
Morgan St.	12	8	.600	12	16	.429
Florida A&M	9	11	.450	11	17	.393
MD-Eastern Shore	7	12	.368	9	18	.333
N. Carolina A&T	7	12	.368	8	19	.296
Howard	7	14	.333	8	20	.286
Delaware St.	6	13	.316	8	18	.308
Norfolk St.	1	5	.167	6	21	.222
Bethune-Cookman	1	17	.056	1	25	.038

Note: Norfolk St. did not compete for the conference title in 1997-98, its first year in the conference and NCAA Div. I.
Conf. Tourney Final: South Carolina St. 66, Coppin St. 61
*****NCAA Tourney (0-1):** South Carolina St. (0-1).

Midwestern Collegiate Conference

Team	Conference W	L	Pct	Overall W	L	Pct
*Detroit	12	2	.857	25	6	.806
*Illinois-Chicago	12	2	.857	22	6	.786
*Butler	8	6	.571	22	11	.667
WI-Green Bay	7	7	.500	17	12	.586
Loyola-IL	6	8	.429	15	15	.500
Cleveland St.	6	8	.429	12	15	.444
Wright St	4	10	.286	10	18	.357
WI-Milwaukee	2	12	.167	3	24	.111

Conf. Tourney Final: Butler 70, Wisconsin-Green Bay 51
*****NCAA Tourney (1-3):** Detroit (1-1), Butler (0-1), Illinois-Chicago (0-1).

Missouri Valley Conference

Team	Conference W	L	Pct	Overall W	L	Pct
*Illinois St.	16	2	.889	25	6	.806
†Creighton	12	6	.667	18	10	.643
Wichita St.	11	7	.611	16	15	.516
SW Missouri St.	11	7	.611	16	16	.500
Indiana St.	9	9	.500	16	11	.593
Bradley	9	9	.500	15	14	.517
Evansville	9	9	.500	15	15	.500
Southern Illinois	8	10	.444	14	16	.467
Northern Iowa	4	14	.222	10	17	.370
Drake	0	18	.000	3	24	.111

Conf. Tourney Final: Illinois St. 84, SW Missouri St. 74
*****NCAA Tourney (0-1):** Illinois St. (0-1).
†NIT Tourney (0-1): Creighton (0-1).

Northeast Conference

Team	Conference W	L	Pct	Overall W	L	Pct
†LIU Brooklyn	14	2	.875	21	11	.656
*Fairleigh Dickinson	13	3	.813	23	7	.767
St. Francis-PA	10	6	.625	17	10	.630
St. Francis-NY	10	6	.625	15	12	.556
Mt. St. Mary's	8	8	.500	13	15	.464
Wagner	7	9	.438	13	16	.448
Robert Morris	4	12	.250	8	19	.296
Central Connecticut	3	13	.188	4	22	.154
Monmouth	3	13	.188	4	23	.148

Conf. Tourney Final: Farleigh Dickinson 105, LIU Brooklyn 91
*****NCAA Tourney (0-1):** Farleigh Dickinson (0-1).
†NIT Tourney (0-1): LIU Brooklyn (0-1).

Ohio Valley Conference

Team	Conference W	L	Pct	Overall W	L	Pct
*Murray St.	16	2	.889	29	4	.879
Eastern Illinois	13	5	.722	16	11	.593
Middle Tenn. St.	12	6	.667	19	9	.679
Austin Peay	11	7	.611	17	11	.607
SE Missouri St	10	8	.556	14	13	.519
Tennessee St.	8	10	.444	13	16	.448
Eastern Kentucky	8	10	.444	10	17	.370
Tennessee Tech	5	13	.278	9	21	.300
Tennessee-Martin	5	13	.278	7	20	.259
Morehead St	2	16	.111	3	23	.115

Conf. Tourney Final: Murray St. 92, Tennessee St. 69
*****NCAA Tourney (0-1):** Murray St. (0-1).

Pacific-10 Conference

Team	Conference W	L	Pct	Overall W	L	Pct
*Arizona	17	1	.944	30	5	.857
*Stanford	15	3	.833	30	5	.857
*UCLA	12	6	.667	24	9	.727
*Washington	11	7	.611	20	10	.667
†Arizona St	8	10	.444	18	14	.563
Oregon	8	10	.444	13	14	.481
California	8	10	.444	12	15	.444
USC	5	13	.278	9	19	.321
Oregon St	3	15	.167	13	17	.433
Washington St	3	15	.167	10	19	.345

Conf. Tourney Final: Pac-10 has no tournament.
*****NCAA Tourney (11-4):** Stanford (4-1), Arizona (3-1), UCLA (2-1), Washington (2-1).
†NIT Tourney (0-1): Arizona St. (0-1).

Final NCAA Men's Division I Standings (Cont.)

Patriot League

Team	Conference W	L	Pct	Overall W	L	Pct
*Navy	11	2	.846	19	11	.633
Lafayette	10	3	.769	19	9	.679
Bucknell	8	4	.667	13	15	.464
Colgate	5	7	.417	10	18	.357
Lehigh	4	8	.333	10	17	.370
Holy Cross	3	9	.250	7	20	.259
Army	2	10	.167	8	19	.296

Conf. Tourney Final: Navy 93, Lafayette 85
***NCAA Tourney (0-1):** Navy (0-1).

Southeastern Conference

Eastern Div.	Conference W	L	Pct	Overall W	L	Pct
*Kentucky	17	2	.895	35	4	.897
*South Carolina	13	6	.684	23	8	.742
*Tennessee	10	8	.556	20	9	.690
†Georgia	8	10	.444	20	15	.571
†Vanderbilt	7	10	.412	20	13	.606
†Florida	7	11	.389	14	15	.483

Western Div.	Conference W	L	Pct	Overall W	L	Pct
*Mississippi	13	5	.722	22	7	.759
*Arkansas	12	6	.667	24	9	.727
†Auburn	7	10	.412	16	14	.533
Alabama	7	11	.389	15	16	.484
Mississippi St	4	13	.235	15	15	.500
LSU	2	15	.118	9	18	.333

Conf. Tourney Final: Kentucky 86, South Carolina 56
***NCAA Tourney (7-4):** Kentucky (6-0, NCAA Champions), Arkansas (1-1), Mississippi (0-1), South Carolina (0-1), Tennessee (0-1).
†NIT Tourney (7-4): Georgia (4-1, NIT Third Place), Vanderbilt (2-1), Auburn (1-1), Florida (0-1).

Southern Conference

North Div.	Conference W	L	Pct	Overall W	L	Pct
Appalachian St	13	2	.867	21	8	.724
*Davidson	13	2	.867	20	10	.667
Virginia Military	8	7	.543	14	13	.519
W. Carolina	6	9	.400	12	15	.444
East Tennessee St.	6	9	.400	11	16	.407
NC-Greensboro	6	9	.400	9	19	.321

South Div.	Conference W	L	Pct	Overall W	L	Pct
Tenn-Chattanooga	7	7	.500	13	15	.464
The Citadel	6	8	.429	15	13	.536
Wofford	6	8	.429	9	18	.333
Furman	5	9	.357	9	20	.310
Georgia Southern	4	10	.286	10	18	.357

Conf. Tourney Final: Davidson 66, Appalachian St. 62
***NCAA Tourney (0-1):** Davidson (0-1).

Southland Conference

Team	Conference W	L	Pct	Overall W	L	Pct
*Nicholls St	17	1	.944	19	10	.655
SW Texas St.	11	7	.611	17	11	.607
Texas-San Antonio	10	7	.588	16	11	.593
Northwestern St	10	7	.588	13	14	.481
Texas-Arlington	10	9	.526	13	16	.448
NE Louisiana	8	9	.471	13	16	.448
Sam Houston St	7	9	.438	9	17	.346
Stephen F. Austin	6	10	.375	10	16	.385
McNeese St	4	12	.250	7	19	.269
SE Louisiana	2	14	.125	6	20	.231

Conf. Tourney Final: Nicholls St. 84, Texas-Arlington 81
***NCAA Tourney (0-1):** Nicholls St. (0-1).

Southwestern Athletic Conference

Team	Conference W	L	Pct	Overall W	L	Pct
Texas Southern	14	5	.737	15	16	.484
Jackson St	11	6	.647	14	13	.519
Grambling	11	7	.611	16	12	.571
Southern	10	7	.588	14	13	.519
*Prairie View A&M	9	10	.474	13	17	.433
Alcorn St.	8	9	.471	12	15	.444
Alabama St	7	11	.389	11	17	.393
Miss. Valley St	6	11	.353	6	21	.222
Ark-Pine Bluff	3	13	.188	4	22	.154

Conf. Tourney Final: Prairie View 59, Texas Southern 57
***NCAA Tourney (0-1):** Prairie View (0-1).

Sun Belt Conference

Team	Conference W	L	Pct	Overall W	L	Pct
*South Alabama	14	4	.778	21	7	.750
Arkansas St	14	4	.778	20	9	.690
SW Louisiana	12	6	.667	18	13	.581
Ark-Little Rock	10	8	.556	15	13	.536
New Orleans	9	9	.500	15	12	.556
Louisiana Tech	9	9	.500	12	15	.444
Lamar	7	11	.389	15	14	.517
Western Kentucky	6	12	.333	10	19	.345
Jacksonville	6	12	.333	8	19	.296
Texas-Pan Am	3	15	.167	3	24	.111

Conf. Tourney Final: South Alabama 62, SW Louisiana 59
***NCAA Tourney (0-1):** South Alabama (0-1).

Trans America Athletic Conference

East	Conference W	L	Pct	Overall W	L	Pct
*Col. of Charleston	14	2	.875	24	6	.800
Florida International	13	5	.722	21	8	.724
Central Florida	11	5	.688	17	11	.607
Stetson	8	8	.500	11	15	.423
Florida Atlantic	5	11	.313	5	22	.185
Campbell	4	12	.250	10	17	.370

West	Conference W	L	Pct	Overall W	L	Pct
Georgia St	11	5	.688	16	12	.571
Samford	9	7	.563	14	13	.519
Centenary	8	8	.500	10	20	.333
Jacksonville St	6	10	.375	12	14	.462
Troy St.	5	11	.313	7	19	.269
Mercer	2	14	.125	5	21	.192

Conf. Tourney Final: College of Charleston 72, Florida International 63
***NCAA Tourney (0-1):** College of Charleston (0-1).

West Coast Conference

Team	Conf W	Conf L	Conf Pct	Overall W	Overall L	Overall Pct
†Gonzaga	10	4	.714	24	10	.706
Pepperdine	9	5	.643	17	10	.630
Santa Clara	8	6	.571	18	10	.643
*San Francisco	7	7	.500	19	11	.633
Portland	7	7	.500	14	13	.519
St. Mary's-CA	7	7	.500	12	15	.444
San Diego	5	9	.357	14	14	.500
Loyola Marymount	3	11	.214	7	20	.259

Conf. Tourney Final: San Francisco 80, Gonzaga 76
*__NCAA Tourney (0-1):__ San Francisco (0-1).
†**NIT Tourney (1-1):** Gonzaga (1-1).

Best in Show

Conferences with at least one win in the 1998 NCAA's; number of tournament teams in parentheses.

Conference	W-L	Conference	W-L
Pac-10 (4)	11-4	Conference USA (3)	3-3
ACC (5)	10-5	Atlantic 10 (5)	3-5
Big East (5)	7-5	Big 12 (4)	2-4
Big Ten (5)	7-5	Mid American (2)	1-2
SEC (5)	7-4	Midwestern Col. (3)	1-3
WAC (4)	6-4		

Western Athletic Conference

Pacific	Conf W	Conf L	Conf Pct	Overall W	Overall L	Overall Pct
*TCU	15	1	.938	27	6	.818
†Fresno St	11	5	.688	21	13	.618
Tulsa	9	6	.600	19	12	.613
†Hawaii	8	6	.571	21	9	.700
SMU	6	9	.400	18	10	.643
San Diego St	5	10	.333	13	15	.464
Rice	3	11	.214	6	22	.214
San Jose St.	1	13	.071	3	23	.115

Mountain	Conf W	Conf L	Conf Pct	Overall W	Overall L	Overall Pct
*Utah	12	3	.800	30	4	.882
*New Mexico	13	4	.765	24	8	.750
†Wyoming	9	5	.643	19	9	.679
*UNLV	10	7	.588	20	13	.606
Colorado St	8	6	.571	20	8	.714
BYU	4	10	.286	9	21	.300
UTEP	3	11	.214	12	14	.462
Air Force	2	12	.143	9	16	.360

Conf. Tourney Final: UNLV 56, New Mexico 51
*__NCAA Tourney (6-4):__ Utah (5-1), New Mexico (1-1), Texas Christian (0-1), UNLV (0-1).
†**NIT Tourney (5-4):** Fresno St. (3-2, NIT Fourth Place), Hawaii (2-1), Wyoming (0-1).

Division I Independent

	W	L	Pct
Belmont	9	18	.333

Annual Awards

Player of the Year

Antawn Jamison, North Carolina . . . AP, Naismith, Wooden, NABC, *TSN*, USBWA

Wooden Award Voting

Presented since 1977 by the Los Angeles Athletic Club and named after the former Purdue All-America and UCLA coach John Wooden. Voting done by 984-member panel of national media; candidates must have a cumulative college grade point average of 2.0 (out of 4.0) and be making progress toward graduation.

		Cl	Pos	Pts
1	Antawn Jamison, North Carolina	Jr.	F	5041
2	Raef LaFrentz, Kansas	Sr.	F	3901
3	Mike Bibby, Arizona	So.	G	3629
4	Paul Pierce, Kansas	Jr.	F	2756
5	Miles Simon, Arizona	Sr.	G	2592
6	Vince Carter, North Carolina	Jr.	F	1566
7	Trajan Langdon, Duke	Jr.	G	1539
8	Richard Hamilton, Connecticut	So.	F	1413
9	Michael Doleac, Utah	Sr.	C	1313
10	Ansu Sesay, Mississippi	Jr.	F	1164

Div. II and III Annual Awards

Awarded by the National Association of Basketball Coaches.

Players of the Year

Div. II	Joe Newton, Central Oklahoma
Div. III	Mike Nogelo, Williams (Mass.)

Coaches of the Year

Div. II	Bob Williams, Cal-Davis
Div. III	Bo Ryan, WI-Platteville
NAIA	Bobby Martin, So. Nazarene
JuCo	Terry Carroll, Indian Hills (Ia.) CC

Coaches of the Year

Tom Izzo, Michigan St. . . . AP, USBWA
Bill Guthridge, North Carolina . . . NABC, Naismith

Consensus All-America Team

The NCAA Division I players cited most frequently by the following All-America selectors: AP, U.S. Basketball Writers, National Assn. of Basketball Coaches and Wooden Award Committee. Holdover from the 1996-97 first team is in **bold** type; (*) indicates unanimous first team selection.

First Team

	Class	Hgt	Pos
Antawn Jamison, N. Carolina*	Jr.	6-9	F
Paul Pierce, Kansas*	Jr.	6-7	F
Raef LaFrentz, Kansas*	Sr.	6-11	C
Mike Bibby, Arizona*	So.	6-2	G
Miles Simon, Arizona	Sr.	6-5	G

Second Team

	Class	Hgt	Pos
Pat Garrity, Notre Dame	Sr.	6-9	F
Richard Hamilton, UConn	So.	6-6	F
Ansu Sesay, Mississippi	Sr.	6-9	C
Mateen Cleaves, Michigan St.	So.	6-2	G
Vince Carter, N. Carolina	Jr.	6-6	G

Third Team

	Class	Hgt	Pos
Matt Harpring, Georgia Tech	Sr.	6-8	F
Lee Nailon, TCU	Jr.	6-8	F
Bonzi Wells, Ball St.	Sr.	6-5	F
Trajan Langdon, Duke	Jr.	6-3	G
Andre Miller, Utah	Sr.	6-2	G

NCAA Men's Division I Leaders

Includes games through NCAA and NIT tourneys.

INDIVIDUAL

Scoring

	Cl	Gm	FG%	3FG/Att	FT%	Reb	Ast	Stl	Blk	Pts	Avg	Hi
Charles Jones, LIU-Brooklyn	Sr.	30	45.3	116/337	63.9	156	221	87	8	869	29.0	53
Earl Boykins, Eastern Mich.	Sr.	29	47.2	85/209	81.6	66	160	54	3	746	25.7	45
Lee Nailon, TCU	Jr.	32	55.4	1/2	74.5	285	61	56	33	796	24.9	53
Brett Eppehimer, Lehigh	Jr.	27	39.8	92/231	87.7	60	40	46	0	667	24.7	41
Cory Carr, Texas Tech	Sr.	27	42.3	67/198	86.1	131	69	30	8	628	23.3	39
Pat Garrity, ND	Sr.	27	48.1	40/108	75.0	225	66	17	16	627	23.2	37
Mike Powell, Loyola-Md.	Sr.	28	44.4	46/140	81.2	137	85	55	6	647	23.1	39
Bonzi Wells, Ball St.	Sr.	29	49.0	53/142	68.9	184	95	103	20	662	22.8	39
Xavier Singletary, Howard	So.	23	35.5	71/197	77.0	141	37	24	10	512	22.3	38
Michael Olowokandi, Pacific	Sr.	33	60.8	0/0	48.5	369	26	9	92	734	22.2	35
Antawn Jamison, N. Carolina	Jr.	37	57.9	6/15	66.7	389	30	28	30	822	22.2	36
Michael Redd, Ohio St.	Fr.	30	43.8	46/152	61.9	194	91	61	3	658	21.9	32
Evan Eschmeyer, Northwestern	Sr.	27	61.0	0/0	61.3	290	67	19	24	585	21.7	37
Matt Harpring, Georgia Tech	Sr.	32	45.6	52/168	81.0	302	82	44	7	691	21.6	31
Saddi Washington, W. Michigan	Sr.	29	44.3	57/158	81.0	123	69	56	6	626	21.6	33
De'Teri Mayes, Murray St.	Sr.	33	46.9	103/234	78.4	143	55	44	0	709	21.5	42
Richard Hamilton, Connecticut	So.	37	44.0	99/245	84.3	163	87	54	9	795	21.5	38
Mike Jones, TCU	Sr.	33	48.0	62/164	80.3	188	181	96	1	702	21.3	51
Tyronn Lue, Nebraska	Jr.	32	43.9	78/209	82.8	137	152	63	3	678	21.2	36
Rick Kaye, Eastern Ill.	Sr.	27	43.2	44/148	73.2	123	83	48	3	570	21.1	33

Rebounding

	Cl	Gm	No	Avg
Ryan Perryman, Dayton	Sr.	33	412	12.5
Eric Taylor, St. Francis-Pa.	Sr.	27	321	11.9
Raef LaFrentz, Kansas	Sr.	30	342	11.4
Tremaine Fowlkes, Fresno St.	Jr.	32	359	11.2
Michael Olowokandi, Pacific	Sr.	33	369	11.2
T.J. Lux, Northern Ill.	Jr.	26	289	11.1
Thad Burton, Wright St.	Sr.	28	305	10.9
Allen Ledbetter, Maine	Jr.	27	294	10.9
Rashon Turner, Farleigh Dickenson	Sr.	29	313	10.8
Kenyon Ross, Mississippi Valley St.	Sr.	27	291	10.8
K'Zell Wesson, La Salle	Jr.	27	290	10.7
Evan Eschmeyer, Northwestern	Sr.	27	290	10.7
Antawn Jamison, N. Carolina	Jr.	37	389	10.5
Rocky Walls, Oral Roberts	Sr.	31	325	10.5
Jerome James, Florida A&M	Sr.	27	282	10.4

Assists

	Cl	Gm	No	Avg
Ahlon Lewis, Arizona St.	Sr.	32	294	9.2
Chico Fletcher, Arkansas St.	So.	29	240	8.3
Sean Colson, UNC-Charlotte	Sr.	29	231	8.0
Ed Cota, N. Carolina	So.	37	274	7.4
Charles Jones, LIU-Brooklyn	Sr.	30	221	7.4
Anthony Carter, Hawaii	Sr.	29	212	7.3
Rafer Alston, Fresno St.	Jr.	33	240	7.3
Mateen Cleaves, Michigan St.	So.	30	217	7.2
Craig Claxton, Hofstra	So.	31	224	7.2
Michael Wheeler, Wagner	Jr.	28	197	7.0
Doug Gottlieb, Oklahoma St.	So.	29	201	6.9
Shaheen Holloway, Seton Hall	So.	29	188	6.5
Ali Ton, Davidson	Jr.	30	193	6.4
Robin Kennedy, Nevada	Sr.	28	180	6.4
Jamar Smiley, Illinois St.	Sr.	29	186	6.4
Javier Smith, Robert Morris	Sr.	27	173	6.4
Ryan Robertson, Kansas	Jr.	39	248	6.4

Field Goal Percentage

Minimum 5 Field Goals made per game.

	Cl	Gm	FG	FGA	Pct
Todd MacCulloch, Wash	Jr.	30	225	346	65.0
Ryan Moss, Ark.-Little Rock	Jr.	28	167	257	65.0
Jarrett Stephens, Penn St.	Jr.	31	165	258	64.0
Isaac Spencer, Murray St.	So.	33	171	270	63.3
Brad Miller, Purdue	Sr.	34	191	302	63.2
Zoran Viskovic, Valparasio	Jr.	33	176	280	62.9
Kareem Livingston, Appalachian	Sr.	29	145	231	62.8
David Montgomery, SE Missouri	Jr.	27	141	227	62.1
Travis Lyons, Manhattan	Sr.	29	172	277	62.1
Leon Watson, Texas-San Antonio	So.	27	151	245	61.6

Free Throw Percentage

Minimum 2.5 Free Throws made per game.

	Cl	Gm	FT	FTA	Pct
Matt Sundblad, Lamar	Jr.	27	96	104	92.3
Louis Bullock, Michigan	Jr.	34	123	135	91.1
Shammond Williams, N. Carolina	Sr.	38	133	146	91.1
Kevin Ault, SW Missouri St.	So.	32	99	110	90.0
Clifton Ellis SW Texas	Jr.	28	72	80	90.0
Pete Lisicky, Penn St.	Sr.	32	106	119	89.1
Danny Sprinkle, Montana St.	Jr.	29	73	82	89.0
Mike Wozniak, Cal Poly SLO	So.	27	129	145	89.0
Garrett Davis, Stetson	Jr.	26	87	98	88.8
Arthur Lee, Stanford	Jr.	35	164	185	88.6
Trajan Langdon, Duke	Jr.	36	101	114	88.6

LIU-Brooklyn
Charles Jones
Scoring

Dayton
Ryan Perryman
Rebounding

Ball State
Bonzi Wells
Steals

Arizona State
Ahlon Lewis
Assists

3-Pt Field Goal Percentage

Minimum 1.5 Three-Point FG made per game.

	Cl	Gm	FG	FGA	Pct
Jim Cantamessa, Siena	So.	29	66	117	56.4
Coby Turner, Dayton	Jr.	33	61	118	51.7
Royce Olney, New Mexico	Sr.	25	80	156	51.3
Mike Beam, Harvard	Jr.	25	41	80	51.3
Kenyan Weaks, Florida	So.	26	61	120	50.8
Jaraan Cornell, Purdue	So.	28	61	122	50.0
Matt Langel, Pennslyvania	So.	26	45	90	50.0
Justin Jones, Utah St.	Sr.	33	60	121	49.6
Mike Warhank, Montana	So.	30	52	105	49.5
Rico Hill, Illinois St.	Jr.	30	45	91	49.5

3-Pt Field Goals Per Game

	Cl	Gm	No	Avg
Curtis Staples, Virginia	Sr.	30	130	4.3
Cedric Foster, Mississippi Valley St.	Sr.	22	86	3.9
Charles Jones, LIU-Brooklyn	Sr.	30	116	3.9
Demond Mallet, McNeese St.	So.	26	94	3.6
Cory Johnson, SE Missouri St.	Jr.	27	95	3.5
Denmark Reid, New Mexico St.	Sr.	30	104	3.5
Brett Eppehimer, Lehigh	Jr.	27	92	3.4
Ronnie McCollum, Centenary	Fr.	30	101	3.4

Note: Six tied at 3.3 each.

Blocked Shots

	Cl	Gm	No	Avg
Jerome James, Florida A&M	Sr.	27	125	4.6
Calvin Booth, Penn St.	Jr.	32	140	4.4
Alvin Jones, Georgia Tech	Fr.	33	141	4.3
Etan Thomas, Syracuse	So.	35	138	3.9
Brian Skinner, Baylor	Sr.	28	98	3.5
Tarvis Williams, Hampton	So.	26	83	3.2
Caswell Cyrus, St. Bonaventure	So.	32	99	3.1
Chris Mihm, Texas	Fr.	31	90	2.9
Michael Olowokandi, Pacific	Sr.	33	95	2.9
Erik Nelson, Vermont	Sr.	27	76	2.8
Kenyon Martin, Cincinnati	So.	30	83	2.8

Steals

	CL	Gm	No	Avg
Bonzi Wells, Ball St.	Sr.	29	103	3.6
Pepe Sanchez, Temple	So.	27	93	3.4
Willie Coleman, DePaul	Jr.	30	100	3.3
J.R. Camel, Montana	Jr.	29	90	3.1
Jason Rowe, Loyola-Md.	So.	28	86	3.1
Damian Owens, West Virginia	Sr.	32	97	3.0
Jason Bell, VMI	Jr.	27	79	2.9
Mike Jones, TCU	Sr.	33	96	2.9
Charles Jones, LIU-Brooklyn	Sr.	30	87	2.9
Mike Campbell, LIU-Brooklyn	Sr.	32	89	2.8

Single Game Highs

Individual Points

No		Opponent	Date
53	Charles Jones, LIU-Brooklyn	Medgar Evars	11/26
53	Lee Nailon, TCU	Miss. Valley	12/12
52	Roderic Hall, Texas-San Antonio	Maine	12/6
51	Mike Jones, TCU	Delaware St.	12/3
46	Lee Nailon, TCU	Hawaii	2/12
45	Mike Jones, TCU	Texas-Pan Am	11/29
45	Randy Bolden, Texas Southern	SW Texas St.	12/6
45	Derrick Dial, E. Mich.	Marshall	1/5
45	Earl Boykins, E. Mich.	Western Mich.	2/21
45	Charles Jones, LIU-Brooklyn	Dayton	3/11

Team Points

No		Opponent	Date
179	LIU-Brooklyn	Medgar Evars (NCAA III)	11/26
153	TCU	Texas-Pan Am (NCAA I)	11/29
138	TCU	Delaware St. (NCAA I)	12/3
133	TCU	Morgan St. (NCAA I)	12/6
129	SE Louisiana	Texas College (NAIA I)	11/22
127	Arizona	Arizona St. (NCAA I)	1/15
126	TCU	Hawaii (NCAA I)	2/14

TEAM

Scoring Offense

	Gm	W-L	Pts	Avg
TCU	33	27-6	3209	97.2
LIU-Brooklyn	32	27-5	3102	96.9
Arizona	35	30-5	3177	90.8
Fla. International	29	21-8	2533	87.3
Murray St.	33	29-4	2862	86.7
Southern-La.	27	14-13	2333	86.4
Duke	36	32-4	3082	85.6
Kansas	39	35-4	3300	84.6
Cal Poly SLO	28	14-14	2367	84.5
Arizona St.	32	18-14	2703	84.5
Cal St. Northridge	28	12-16	2356	84.1
Purdue	36	28-8	3014	83.7
Fairleigh Dickenson	30	23-7	2511	83.7
Xavier	30	22-8	2506	83.5
Fresno St.	34	21-13	2835	83.4

Won-Lost Percentage

	W	L	Pct.
Princeton	27	2	.931
Kansas	35	4	.897
Kentucky	35	4	.897
North Carolina	34	4	.895
Duke	32	4	.889
Utah	30	4	.882
Murray St.	29	4	.879
Connecticut	32	5	.865
Arizona	30	5	.857
Stanford	30	5	.857
Cincinnati	27	6	.818
Iona	27	6	.818
TCU	27	6	.818
Detroit	25	6	.806
Illinois St.	25	6	.806

Scoring Defense

	Gm	W-L	Pts	Avg
Princeton	29	27-2	1491	51.4
South Alabama	28	21-7	1526	54.5
Col. of Charleston	30	24-6	1662	55.4
Utah	34	30-4	1959	57.6
Wyoming	28	19-9	1656	59.1
Wisc.-Green Bay	29	17-12	1737	59.9
Marquette	31	20-11	1860	60.0
Temple	30	21-9	1820	60.7
Bradley	29	15-14	1772	61.1
UNC-Wilmington	31	20-11	1905	61.5
William & Mary	27	20-7	1668	61.8
Richmond	31	23-8	1920	61.9
N.C. State	32	17-15	1988	62.1
Colorado St.	29	20-9	1802	62.1

Note: Three tied at 62.2 each.

Field Goal Percentage

	FG	FGA	PCT.
North Carolina	1131	2184	51.8
Northern Arizona	806	1577	51.1
Murray St.	1037	2070	50.1
Princeton	684	1374	49.8
Pacific	841	1692	49.7
TCU	1220	2463	49.5
Kansas	1249	2536	49.3
Indiana	879	1792	49.1
UCLA	985	2011	49.0
Michigan	932	1907	48.9
Arizona	1146	2350	48.8
Washington	843	1729	48.8
South Alabama	665	1371	48.5
Xavier	848	1752	48.4
Purdue	1057	2185	48.4

Scoring Margin

	Off	Def	Mar.
Duke	85.6	64.1	21.5
TCU	97.2	77.9	19.3
Kansas	84.6	67.4	17.2
North Carolina	81.9	65.6	16.3
Arizona	90.8	74.6	16.2
Murray St.	86.7	70.7	16.0
Princeton	66.5	51.4	15.1
Xavier	83.5	68.8	14.7
Col. of Charleston	70.1	55.4	14.7
Kentucky	80.1	67.0	13.1
Cincinnati	76.1	63.2	12.9
Northern Arizona	80.2	67.4	12.8
Connecticut	76.6	63.9	12.7
Iowa	80.2	67.5	12.7
Mississippi	80.5	68.1	12.4
Utah	70.0	57.6	12.4

Field Goal Percentage Defense

	FG	FGA	PCT.
Miami-FL	634	1672	37.9
Bradley	617	1614	38.2
Kentucky	892	2324	38.4
North Carolina	923	2403	38.4
Wyoming	541	1405	38.5
Utah	668	1729	38.6
Col. of Charleston	616	1591	38.7
Temple	620	1599	38.8
Marquette	672	1729	38.9
Colorado St.	612	1570	39.0
Citadel	615	1571	39.1
Tulsa	693	1766	39.2
Pacific	747	1902	39.3
Connecticut	854	2173	39.3
Cincinnati	732	1862	39.3
Florida A&M	707	1798	39.3

Rebound Margin

	Off	Def	Mar
Utah	37.0	27.1	9.9
Stanford	41.3	31.9	9.4
Farleigh Dickenson	45.7	36.5	9.2
Kansas	43.1	34.2	8.9
Michigan St.	39.9	31.0	8.9
Southern Ill.	39.9	31.3	8.6
Cincinnati	40.1	31.8	8.3
Kentucky	42.1	33.9	8.2
South Alabama	34.0	26.4	7.6
North Carolina	39.8	32.3	7.5
St. John's	42.3	35.1	7.2
Michigan	38.6	31.9	6.7
Mississippi	41.5	34.9	6.6
St. Francis	38.5	32.1	6.4
Northwestern	33.4	27.3	6.1

Free Throw Percentage

	FT	FTA	Pct
Siena	574	715	80.3
Montana St.	437	570	76.7
Purdue	657	864	76.0
Montana	472	621	76.0
New Mexico	430	568	75.7
Evansville	454	600	75.7
Wisc-Green Bay	470	625	75.2
Western Mich	477	639	74.6
Arizona St.	493	661	74.6
Hartford	541	730	74.1
Sam Houston St.	382	516	74.0
Penn St.	470	635	74.0
Detroit	472	639	73.9
Xavier	640	867	73.8
Stanford	651	882	73.8

3-point FG Percentage

	3PT	3PTA	Pct
Northern Arizona	254	591	43.0
Utah St.	139	324	42.9
Pennsylvania	223	526	42.4
Harvard	188	448	42.0
Michigan	260	621	41.9
Ill-Chicago	192	460	41.7
Western Mich	209	511	40.9
Stanford	262	642	40.8
Gonzaga	274	678	40.4
New Mexico	301	748	40.2
Oral Roberts	268	667	40.2
Iowa	218	543	40.1
Florida	285	712	40.0
South Carolina St.	174	436	39.9
Richmond	241	605	39.8

3-point FG Made Per Game

	Gm	No	Avg
Florida	29	285	9.8
LIU-Brooklyn	32	310	9.7
North Texas	26	250	9.6
New Mexico	32	301	9.4
Princeton	29	265	9.1
Cal Poly SLO	28	246	8.8
Northern Arizona	29	254	8.8
SE Louisiana	26	227	8.7
Jacksonville St.	26	225	8.7
Oral Roberts	31	268	8.6
CS-Northridge	28	241	8.6
Loyola Marymount	27	231	8.6
Tennessee St.	29	248	8.6
St. Mary's (Cal.)	27	229	8.5
Mississippi Valley	27	227	8.4

Underclassmen in NBA Draft

Twenty Division I players (14 juniors, four sophomores and two freshmen), four high school seniors, three players from overseas, two junior college players, two NAIA players, one Division II junior and one Division II sophomore forfeited the remainder of their college eligibility and declared for the 1998 NBA Draft which took place at GM Place in Vancouver, British Columbia on June 24.

Players are listed in alphabetical order; first round selections in **bold** type, high school players in *italics*.

	Cl	Drafted by	Overall Pick
Rafer Alston, Fresno St.	Jr.	Milwaukee	39
Corey Benjamin, Oregon St.	So.	Chicago	28
Mike Bibby, Arizona	So.	Vancouver	2
Chandar Bingham, Virginia Union	So.	Not drafted	—
Marcus Bullard, Auburn-Montgomery	Jr.	Not drafted	—
Vince Carter, N. Carolina	Jr.	Golden State	5
Wayne Clark, DeKalb (Ga.) JC	Jr.	Not drafted	—
Tim Cole, NE Miss. CC	Jr.	Not drafted	—
Peter Cornell, Loyola-Marymount	Jr.	Not drafted	—
Arthur Davis, St. Joseph's	So.	Not drafted	—
Ricky Davis, Iowa	Fr.	Charlotte	21
Tremaine Fowlkes, Fresno St.	Jr.	Denver	54
Al Harrington, St. Patrick (N.J.) HS	HS	Indiana	25
Larry Hughes, Saint Louis	Fr.	Philadelphia	8
Randell Jackson, Florida St.	Jr.	Not drafted	—
Jerome James, Florida A&M	Jr.	Sacramento	36
Antawn Jamison, N. Carolina	Jr.	Toronto	4
Rashard Lewis, Alief-Elsik (Tex.)	HS	Seattle	32
Tyronn Lue, Nebraska	Jr.	Denver	23
Jelani McCoy, UCLA	Jr.	Seattle	33
Stanislav Medvedenko, Budivelnik (UKR)	—	Not drafted	—
Mark Miller, Ill-Chicago	Jr.	Not drafted	—
Nazr Mohammed, Kentucky	Jr.	Utah	29
Dirk Nowitzki, DJK Wurzburg (GER)	—	Milwaukee	9
Paul Pierce, Kansas	Jr.	Boston	10
Ellis Richardson, Polytechnic (Calif.)	HS	Not drafted	—
Adam Roberts, San Francisco St.	Jr.	Not drafted	—
James Spears, Shaw U.	Jr.	Not drafted	—
Bruno Sudov, Split (CRO)	—	Dallas	35
Robert Traylor, Michigan	Jr.	Dallas	6
Winfred Walton, Fresno St.	So.	Not drafted	—
Jason Williams, Florida	Jr.	Sacramento	7
Korleone Young, Hargrave Mil Acad.	HS	Detroit	40

Note: Lee Nailon of Texas Christian, Lamar Odom of Rhode Island, Bud Eley of Southeast Missouri State, Rico Harris of Los Angeles City College, Marko Jaric of Peristeri (Greece), Sasa Markovic-Theodorakis of Panionios (Greece), and Dimitris Papanikolaou of Olympiakos (Greece) declared for the draft and then withdrew their names before the June 18 deadline.

High School Players to enter NBA

Player	Pro career
Tony Kappen	1946-47
Connie Simmons	1946-56
Joe Graboski	1948-62
Reggie Harding	1963-68
Moses Malone	1974-95
Bill Willoughby	1975-84
Darryl Dawkins	1975-89
Kevin Garnett	1995—
Kobe Bryant	1996—
Jermaine O'Neal	1996—
Tracy McGrady	1997—
Al Harrington	1998—
Rashard Lewis	1998—
Korleone Young	1998—

Note: Kappen started out in the American Basketball League and Malone started out in the American Basketball Association. Because they enrolled in a college, Lloyd Daniels (Mount St. Antonio), Thomas Hamilton (Pittsburgh) and Shawn Kemp (Kentucky/Trinity Valley CC) were not included on this list.

Other Men's 1998 Tournaments

NIT Tournament

The 61st annual National Invitation Tournament had a 32-team field. First three rounds played on home courts of higher seeded teams. Semifinal, Third Place and Championship games played March 24-26 at Madison Square Garden in New York City.

1st Round

at Georgia Tech 88 .... Seton Hall 78
at N.C. State 59 .... Kansas St. 39
at Penn State 82 .... Rider 68
at Auburn 77 .... Southern Miss. 62
at Dayton 95 .... Long Island U. 92
Georgetown 71 .... at Florida 69
at Marquette 80 .... Creighton 68
at Memphis 90 .... Ball State 67
at Minnesota 77 .... Colorado St. 65
Ala-Birmingham 93 .... at Missouri 86
at Vanderbilt 73 .... St. Bonaventure 61
Gonzaga 69 .... at Wyoming 55
Georgia 100 .... at Iowa 93
Fresno St. 73 .... at Pacific 70
at Hawaii 90 .... Arizona St. 73
at Wake Forest 56 .... UNC-Wilmington 52

2nd Round

at Georgia Tech 80 .... Georgetown 79, OT
Penn State 77 .... at Dayton 74
at Minnesota 79 .... Ala-Birmingham 66
at Marquette 75 .... Auburn 60, OT
at Fresno St. 83 .... Memphis 80
at Hawaii 78 .... Gonzaga 70
Vanderbilt 72 .... at Wake Forest 68
Georgia 61 .... N.C. State 55

Quarterfinals

Penn State 75 .... at Georgia Tech 70
at Minnesota 73 .... Marquette 71
at Georgia 79 .... Vanderbilt 65
Fresno St. 85 .... at Hawaii 83

Semifinals

Minnesota 91 .... Fresno St. 89, OT
Penn State 66 .... Georgia 60

Third Place

Georgia 95 .... Fresno St. 79

Championship

Minnesota 79 .... Penn State 72

NCAA Division II

The eight regional winners of the 48-team field: NORTHEAST— St. Rose (27-6); EAST— Fairmont State (27-4); SOUTH ATLANTIC— Virginia Union (27-6); SOUTH— Delta State (27-4); SOUTH CENTRAL— West Texas A&M (26-5); GREAT LAKES— Kentucky Wesleyan (30-3); NORTH CENTRAL— Northern State (27-5); WEST— UC-Davis (31-2).

The Elite Eight was played March 18-21, at the Commonwealth Convention Center in Louisville, Ky. There was no Third Place game.

Quarterfinals

UC-Davis 63 .... West Texas A&M 55
St. Rose 77 .... Fairmont State 73, OT
Virginia Union 67 .... Northern State 63
Kentucky Wesleyan 76 .... Delta State 68

Semifinals

UC-Davis 88 .... St. Rose 76
Kentucky Wesleyan 80 .... Virginia Union 72

Championship

UC-Davis 83 .... Kentucky Wesleyan 77

NCAA Division III

Sixty-four teams played into the 32-team Division III field. The four sectional winners: EAST— Williams College, Mass. (25-4); MID-ATLANTIC— Wilkes, Pa. (26–4); GREAT LAKES— Hope, Mich. (26–5); WEST— Wisconsin-Platteville (30-0).

The Final Four was played March 20-21, at Salem Civic Center in Salem, Va.

Semifinals

Wisc.-Platteville 82 .... Williams 68
Hope 81 .... Wilkes 61

Third Place

Williams 105 .... Wilkes 94

Championship

Wisc-Platteville 69 .... Hope 56

NAIA Division I

The quarterfinalists, in alphabetical order, after two rounds of the 32-team NAIA tournament: Azusa Pacific, Calif. (34-5); Central Washington (19-11); East Central, Okla. (20-9); Georgetown, Ky. (36-3); Incarnate Word, Texas (26-5); Park, Mo. (27-8); St. Vincent, Pa. (28-5); Southern Nazarene, Okla. (29-9).

All tournament games played, March 17-23, at the Mabee Center in Tulsa, Okla. There was no Third Place game.

Quarterfinals: Georgetown def. Central Washington, 92-79; Azusa Pacific def. Incarnate Word, 66-62; Park def. St. Vincent, 73-59; Southern Nazarene def. East Central, 88-86.

Semifinals: Georgetown def. Azusa Pacific, 94-76; Southern Nazarene def. Park, 67–57.

Championship: Georgetown def. Southern Nazarene, 83–69.

NAIA Division II

The semifinalists, in alphabetical order, after three rounds of the 32-team NAIA tournament: Bethel, Ind. (36-3); Mt. Marty College, S.D. (23-9); Northwest Nazarene College, Idaho (27-10); Oregon Tech (26-11).

All tournament games played, March 11-17, at Nampa, Idaho. There was no Third Place game.

Semifinals: Bethel def. Mt. Marty, 88-86; Oregon Tech def. Northwest Nazarene, 82-75.

Championship: Bethel def. Oregon Tech, 89-87.

Legend of the Vols

by Mimi Griffin

For the most part, the 1997-98 season was one of uncertainty. The only constant was the Tennessee Lady Vols, and, oh, were they constant—constantly running, constantly pressuring, constantly dominating.

This team represented a unique blend of talent, experience, youthful enthusiasm and chemistry. The talent and experience made them good, the youthful enthusiasm made them fun to watch and the chemistry made them special. The combination led many to proclaim this the greatest women's collegiate team of all time—and deservedly so. If you watched carefully, you saw a team single handedly elevate the sport to another level.

Their style wasn't necessarily unique. As a matter of fact, it calls to mind another undefeated national championship team, the 1986 University of Texas Lady Longhorns. Both teams played without a true center and tried to hide the fact with their full court pressure on defense and their uptempo style on offense. The Lady Vols, in 1998, however, exhibited a level of intensity, athleticism and cohesiveness beyond anything ever seen in women's basketball.

Their success centers around Chamique Holdsclaw. It is not just Holdsclaw's talent that sets her apart, but also the effect she has on her teammates. Much attention has been paid to Tennessee's fabulous freshmen class this year, but this collection of talent would not have blended as well anywhere but Tennessee because of Holdsclaw. In the media guide, three of the five freshmen listed Chamique as the greatest athlete they knew. She commanded their reverence before they ever set foot on the same court. Consequently, they were willing to subjugate their own self interest for the good of the common goal. Chamique demanded it.

This was not a team with role players and a few superstars. This was a team filled with superstars who willingly opted to play whatever role was necessary to win a national championship. A superior amount of talent and a high level of chemistry are sometimes mutually exclusive. This was not the case with the Lady Vols. This was a big reason why Pat Summitt declared this season and this team one of the most enjoyable that she's had in her 24 years of coaching.

The argument has been made that Holdsclaw is the best player in the history of women's collegiate basketball. After working hard to improve her defense, she finally has a game with no apparent flaws. The manner in which she has handled herself in adversity and triumph has established her as the sport's premier player. Last year she proved she had the maturity, stamina and fortitude to drastically turn around what could have been one of the worst seasons in Lady Vol history. This year she proved she had the focus and mental toughness to maintain the intensity necessary to craft a perfect season. Next year, she can accomplish what no other player has—four consecutive national championships.

Some have proclaimed that Tennessee's dominance is bad for women's basketball. I disagree. Anytime someone raises the bar a little higher, it drives everyone to do better.

In the shadow of Tennessee's perfect season, there were a number of teams that made their mark this year.

An NCAA Tournament bid has always been considered a benchmark accomplishment for any school's program. Through the years, the tournament has also served as a forum for teams to quickly establish or re-establish a national identity.

A list of the teams that took full advantage of this forum in 1998 included Liberty—the "other" undefeated team in the tourney; Rutgers—a collection of brash, young talent that promises big things given time to mature; Iowa State—good coaching and solid teamwork combined for a top 16 seed; UC-Santa Barbara—good talent and coaching but it was their attitude and belief in themselves that left an indelible impression; Harvard—a record setting performance against Stanford proved to one and all that "real" players do attend Ivy League schools; Arkansas—bubble team that turned into the year's Cinderella story with their Final Four appearance; NC State—long on talent and even longer on chemistry which proved to be a key ingredient in their Final Four run; George Washington—a team with lots of heart and gritty determination that put a scare into Connecticut on their home floor in the second round; Notre Dame—a HUGE win over Texas Tech in Lubbock that proved that the previous year's Final Four appearance was no fluke; Purdue—Carolyn Peck's positive coaching style and exceptional consistency by Stephanie White and Ukari Figgs were the keys to their success; Louisiana Tech—they wanted to prove they deserved a higher seed and they did; UCLA—will forever be remembered as the team that was "robbed" of a Sweet 16 appearance. It is unfortunate that the controversy of an official's error marred the memory of a very well played game; North Carolina—came within a breath of spoiling Tennessee's perfect season in a regional final that many considered the championship game.

Despite the dominance of Tennessee, the tournament was anything but predictable. This was a year for many firsts in the NCAA tourney. It was the first time a #16 seed beat a #1 seed and the first time that two #1 seeds did not make the Final Four. It was also the first time a #9 seed (Arkansas) advanced to the Final Four. Expect more of the same in the coming years. This is all part of the unsettled nature of a sport moving to a new plateau. ■

Mimi Griffin is ESPN's Women's NCAA basketball analyst.

Final Regular Season AP Women's Top 25 Poll

Taken **before** start of NCAA tournament.

The sportswriters & broadcasters poll: first place votes in parentheses; records through Sunday, March 10, 1998; total points (based on 25 for 1st, 24 for 2nd, etc.); record in NCAA tourney and team lost to; head coach (career years and record including 1997 postseason), and preseason ranking. Teams in **bold** type went on to reach NCAA Final Four.

		Mar. 10 Record	Points	NCAA Recap	Head Coach	Preseason Rank
1	**Tennessee** (40)	33-0	1000	6-0	Pat Summitt (24 yrs: 664-143)	1
2	Old Dominion	27-2	944	2-1 (N.C. State)	Wendy Larry (14 yrs: 301-122)	3
3	Connecticut	31-2	912	3-1 (N.C. State)	Geno Auriemma (13 yrs: 328-89)	6
4	**Louisiana Tech**	26-3	870	5-1 (Tennessee)	Leon Barmore (16 yrs: 459-71)	2
5	Stanford	21-5	852	0-1 (Harvard)	Tara VanDerveer (19 yrs: 458-121)	4
6	Texas Tech	25-4	817	1-1 (Notre Dame)	Marsha Sharp (16 yrs: 375-125)	8
7	North Carolina	23-6	743	3-1 (Tennessee)	Sylvia Hatchell (23 yrs: 512-205)	5
8	Duke	21-7	681	3-1 (Arkansas)	Gail Goestenkors (6 yrs: 119-61)	19
9	Arizona	21-6	651	2-1 (Connecticut)	Joan Bonvicini (19 yrs: 441-158)	15
10	**North Carolina St.**	21-6	601	4-1 (Louisiana Tech)	Kay Yow (27 yrs: 552-221)	32t
11	Alabama	22-9	574	2-1 (Louisiana Tech)	Rick Moody (9 yrs: 199-81)	11
12	Florida International	28-1	538	1-1 (North Carolina)	Cindy Russo (21 yrs: 440-165)	NR
13	Florida	21-8	536	2-1 (Duke)	Carol Ross (8 yrs: 165-77)	9
14	Clemson	24-7	398	1-1 (Louisiana Tech)	Jim Davis (12 yrs: 252-118)	40
15	Western Kentucky	25-8	382	1-1 (Tennessee)	Steve Small (1 yr: 26-9)	16
16	Illinois	18-9	366	2-1 (North Carolina)	Theresa Grentz (24 yrs: 518-188)	7
17	Virginia	18-9	287	1-1 (Arizona)	Debbie Ryan (21 yrs: 481-165)	NR
18	Vanderbilt	20-8	280	0-1 (Cal-Santa Barbara)	Jim Foster (20 yrs: 416-181)	10
19	Stephen F. Austin	25-3	258	0-1 (Western Ky.)	Royce Chadwick (9 yrs: 201-89)	17
20	Hawaii	24-3	232	0-1 (Arkansas)	Vince Goo (11 yrs: 224-97)	NR
21	Purdue	20-9	148	3-1 (Louisiana Tech)	Carolyn Peck (1 yr: 23-10)	35
22	Drake	25-4	128	0-1 (Colorado St.)	Lisa Bluder (14 yrs: 312-125)	38t
23	Iowa	17-10	115	1-1 (Kansas)	Angie Lee (3 yrs: 63-27)	12
24	Iowa St.	24-7	107	1-1 (Rutgers)	Bill Fennelly (10 yrs: 225-83)	42t
25	UCLA	19-8	88	1-1 (Alabama)	Kathy Olivier (5 yrs: 71-66)	31

Others receiving votes: 26. **Utah** (21-5) 86 pts; 27. **Memphis** (22-7) 70; 28. **Rutgers** (20-9) 61; 29. **Kansas** (21-8) 46; 30. **New Mexico** (26-6) 37; 31. **Wisconsin** (21-9) 32; 32. **Nebraska** (22-9) 26; 33. **SW Missouri St.** (24-5) 22; 34. **Liberty** (28-0) 21; 35. **Arkansas** (18-10) 18; 36. **Georgia** (17-10) and **Washington** (18-9) 14; 38. **Marquette** (22-6) and **Oregon** (17-9) 8; 40. **Virginia Tech** (21-9) 6; 41. **Kent** (23-6) and **UC-Santa Barbara** (26-5) 5; 43. **Colorado St.** (23-5) 4; 44. **Notre Dame** (20-9) 4; 45. **Tulane** (21-6) 2; 46. **Indiana** (19-10), **Rice** (21-8), **Wisconsin-GB** (21-8) and **Youngstown St.** (27-2) 1.

NCAA Women's Division I Tournament Seeds

	WEST	MIDWEST	MIDEAST	EAST
1	Stanford (21-5)	Texas Tech (25-4)	Tennessee (33-0)	Old Dominion (27-2)
2	Duke (21-7)	Alabama (22-9)	North Carolina (24-6)	Connecticut (31-2)
3	Florida (21-8)	Louisiana Tech (26-3)	Illinois (18-9)	Arizona (21-6)
4	Iowa (17-10)	Purdue (20-9)	Iowa St. (24-7)	N.C. State (21-6)
5	Kansas (21-8)	Drake (25-4)	Rutgers (20-9)	Memphis (22-7)
6	Wisconsin (21-9)	Clemson (24-7)	Vanderbilt (20-8)	Virginia (18-9)
7	Utah (21-5)	UCLA (19-8)	Fla. International (28-1)	Georgia (17-10)
8	Hawaii (24-3)	SW Missouri St. (24-5)	Western Ky. (25-8)	New Mexico (26-6)
9	Arkansas (18-10)	Notre Dame (20-9)	Stephen F. Austin (25-3)	Nebraska (22-9)
10	Louisville (19-11)	Michigan (19-9)	Marquette (22-6)	George Washington (19-9)
11	Virginia Tech (21-9)	Miami-FL (19-9)	UC-Santa Barbara (26-5)	SMU (21-7)
12	Tulane (21-6)	Colorado St. (23-5)	Oregon (17-9)	Youngstown St. (27-2)
13	Massachusetts (19-10)	Washington (18-9)	Kent (23-6)	Maine (21-8)
14	Montana (24-5)	Holy Cross (18-9)	Wisconsin-GB (21-8)	Santa Clara (23-7)
15	Mid. Tennessee (18-11)	N.C. Greensboro (21-8)	Howard (23-6)	Fairfield (20-9)
16	Harvard (22-4)	Grambling (23-6)	Liberty (28-0)	St. Francis (22-7)

1998 NCAA BASKETBALL WOMEN'S DIVISION I

1998 NCAA
Goin' to Kansas City
women's FINAL FOUR

EAST

FIRST ROUND March 13-14	SECOND ROUND March 15-16	REGIONALS March 21-23	
1 Old Dominion 92	Old Dominion 75	Old Dominion 54	N.C. State 60
16 St. Francis-PA 39	Nebraska 60		
8 New Mexico 59			
9 Nebraska 76			
5 Memphis 80	Youngstown St. 61	N.C. State 55	
12 Youngstown St. 91	N.C. State 88		
4 N.C. State 89			
13 Maine 64			
6 Virginia 77	Virginia 77	Arizona 57	UConn 52
11 SMU 68	Arizona 94		
3 Arizona 75			
14 Santa Clara 63			
7 Georgia 72	G. Washington 67	UConn 74	
10 G. Washington 74	UConn 75		
2 UConn 93			
15 Fairfield 52			

East champion: N.C. State 65

MIDWEST

FIRST ROUND March 13-14	SECOND ROUND March 15-16	REGIONALS March 21-23	
1 Texas Tech 87	Texas Tech 59	Notre Dame 65	Purdue 65
16 Grambling 75	Notre Dame 74		
8 SW Missouri St. 64			
9 Notre Dame 78			
5 Drake 75	Colorado St. 63	Purdue 70	
12 Colorado St. 81	Purdue 77		
4 Purdue 88			
13 Washington 71			
6 Clemson 60	Clemson 52	La. Tech 71	La. Tech 72
11 Miami (Fla.) 49	La. Tech 74		
3 La. Tech 86			
14 Holy Cross 58			
7 UCLA 65	UCLA 74	Alabama 57	
10 Michigan 58	Alabama 75		
2 Alabama 94			
15 NC-Greensboro 46			

Midwest champion: La. Tech 84

MIDEAST

FIRST ROUND March 13-14	SECOND ROUND March 15-16	REGIONALS March 21-23	
1 Tennessee 102	Tennessee 82	Tennessee 92	Tennessee 76
16 Liberty 58	W. Kentucky 62		
8 W. Kentucky 88			
9 S.F. Austin 76			
5 Rutgers 79	Rutgers 62	Rutgers 60	
12 Oregon 76	Iowa St. 61		
4 Iowa State 79			
13 Kent 76			
6 Vanderbilt (OT) 71	UCSB 65	Illinois 74	N. Carolina 70
11 UC Santa Bar. 76	Illinois 69		
3 Illinois 82			
14 WI-Green Bay 58			
7 Florida Int'l 59	Florida Int'l 72	N. Carolina 80	
10 Marquette 45	N. Carolina 85		
2 N. Carolina 91			
15 Howard 71			

Mideast champion: Tennessee 86

WEST

FIRST ROUND March 13-14	SECOND ROUND March 15-16	REGIONALS March 21-23	
1 Stanford 67	Harvard 64	Arkansas 79	Arkansas 77
16 Harvard 71	Arkansas 82		
8 Hawaii 70			
9 Arkansas 76			
5 Kansas 72	Kansas 62	Kansas 63	
12 Tulane 68	Iowa 58		
4 Iowa 77			
13 U Mass 59			
6 Wisconsin 64	Virginia Tech 57	Florida 58	Duke 72
11 Virginia Tech 75	Florida 89		
3 Florida 85			
14 Montana 64			
7 Utah 61	Louisville 53	Duke 71	
10 Louisville 69	Duke 69		
2 Duke 92			
15 Mid. Tennessee St. 67			

West champion: Arkansas 58

NATIONAL CHAMPIONSHIP

Tennessee 93
La. Tech 75

FINAL FOUR
at Kemper Arena
in Kansas City
***
Semifinals: March 27
Finals: March 29

NCAA Championship Game

Tennessee 93

	Min	FG M-A	FT M-A	Pts	Reb O-T	A	F
Chamique Holdsclaw	36	11-25	3-4	25	4-10	6	0
Tamika Catchings	34	8-16	11-13	27	3-7	2	3
LaShonda Stephens	8	0-2	0-0	0	1-2	0	2
Kellie Jolly	34	7-10	2-2	20	0-4	3	2
Semeka Randall	34	4-9	2-8	10	2-8	2	2
Niya Butts	1	1-1	0-0	2	1-1	0	0
Kyra Elzy	1	0-1	0-0	0	0-0	0	0
Laurie Milligan	1	0-0	0-0	0	0-0	0	0
Misty Greene	1	0-0	0-0	0	0-0	0	0
Brynae Laxton	1	0-0	0-0	0	0-0	0	0
Kristen Clement	15	3-4	0-0	6	0-1	2	1
Teresa Geter	34	1-1	2-7	3	2-7	0	3
TOTALS	200	35-69	19-25	93	13-41	15	13

Three-point FG: 4-9 (Catchings 0-4, Jolly 4-5); **Team Rebounds:** 6; **Blocked Shots:** 5 (Geter 4, Jolly); **Turnovers:** 19 (Catchings 4, Randall 4, Clement 3, Holdsclaw 2, Jolly 2, Elzy, Geter, Laxton, Stephens); **Steals:** 11 (Catchings 4, Jolly 3, Randall 2, Geter, Holdsclaw); **Percentages:** 2-Pt FG (.507); 3-Pt FG (.444); Total FG (.500); Free Throws (.760).

Louisiana Tech 75

	Min	FG M-A	FT M-A	Pts	Reb O-T	A	F
Monica Maxwell	37	7-12	0-0	15	3-8	1	3
Amanda Wilson	31	2-6	0-0	4	1-5	0	4
Alisa Burras	34	9-16	1-5	19	5-10	0	3
LaQuan Stallworth	30	0-6	2-2	2	0-1	9	0
Tamicha Jackson	37	11-25	0-0	26	0-4	5	2
Katie Cochran	1	0-0	0-0	0	0-0	0	0
Jamie Scheppmann	15	1-5	0-0	0	0-0	2	2
Pyria Gilmore	8	0-0	2-2	2	1-1	0	0
Melshika Bowman	7	2-3	0-1	4	0-0	0	2
TOTALS	200	32-73	5-10	75	10-29	17	16

Three-point FG: 6-18 (Maxwell 1-3, Stallworth 0-1, Jackson 4-12, Scheppmann 1-2); **Team Rebounds:** 5; **Blocked Shots:** 7 (Burras 2, Bowman 2, Maxwell, Jackson, Gilmore); **Turnovers:** 20 (Stallworth 5, Jackson 4, Maxwell 3, Wison 3, Burras 2, Scheppmann 2, Bowman); **Steals:** 11 (Wilson 3, Burras 2, Jackson 2, Maxwell 2, Stallworth 2); **Percentages:** 2-Pt FG (.438); 3-Pt FG (.333); Total FG (.418); Free Throws (.500).

Tennessee (SEC)	55	38—	**93**
Louisiana Tech (Sun Belt)	32	43—	**75**

Technical Fouls: None. **Officials:** Sally Bell, Bob Trammell, Wesley Dean. **Attendance:** 17,976. **TV Rating:** 3.7 (ESPN).

Final ESPN/*USA Today* Coaches Poll

Taken **after** NCAA tournament.

Voted on by panel of 60 women's coaches and media following the NCAA tournament: first place votes in parentheses with final overall records.

		W-L
1	Tennessee (60)	39-0
2	Louisiana Tech	31-4
3	North Carolina	27-7
4	N. Carolina St.	27-7
5	Connecticut	34-3
6	Old Dominion	29-3
7	Arkansas	22-11
8	Duke	24-8
9	Arizona	23-7
10	Texas Tech	26-5
11	Purdue	23-10
12	Florida	23-9
13	Alabama	24-10
14	Illinois	20-10
15	Stanford	21-6
16	Rutgers	22-10
17	Notre Dame	22-9
18	Fla. International	29-2
19	Western Kentucky	25-8
20	UCLA	20-9
21	Clemson	25-8
22	Kansas	23-9
23	Virginia	19-10
24	Iowa St.	25-8
25	Vanderbilt	20-9

WOMEN'S FINAL FOUR

at Kemper Arena in Kansas City, Mo. (March 27-29).

Semifinals

Louisiana Tech 84 ....North Carolina St. 65
Tennessee 86 ....Arkansas 58

Championship

Tennessee 93.....................Louisiana Tech 75

Final Records: Tennessee (39-0), Louisiana Tech (31-4), Arkansas (22-11), N.C. State (25-7).

Most Outstanding Player: Chamique Holdsclaw, Tennessee junior forward. SEMIFINAL— 30 minutes, 23 points, 10 rebounds, 1 steal, 2 assists, 2 blocks; FINAL— 36 minutes, 25 points, 10 rebounds, 1 steal, 6 assists.

All-Tournament Team: Holdsclaw, forward Tamika Catchings and guard Kellie Jolly of Tennessee, guard Tamicha Jackson of Louisiana Tech and forward Chasity Melvin of N.C. State.

Annual Awards

Player of the Year

Chamique Holdsclaw, Tennessee....AP, Naismith, USBWA, WBCA

Coach of the Year

Pat Summit, Tennessee .... AP, Naismith, WBCA, Wooden, USBWA

Consensus All-America Team

The NCAA Division I players cited most frequently by the Associated Press, US Basketball Writers Assn., the Women's Basketball Coaches Assn. and the Women's Basketball News Service. Holdover from the 1996-97 All-America first team are in **bold** type; (*) indicates unanimous first team selection.

First Team

	Class	Hgt	Pos
Chamique Holdsclaw, Tenn.*	Jr.	6-2	F
Alicia Thompson, Texas Tech*	Sr.	6-1	F
Murriel Page, Florida	Sr.	6-2	C
Nykesha Sales, UConn	Sr.	6-0	F/G
Ticha Penicheiro, Old Dominion	Sr.	5-11	G

Second Team

	Class	Hgt	Pos
Tracy Reid, N. Carolina	Sr.	5-11	F
Tamika Catchings, Tenn.	Fr.	6-1	F
Kristin Folkl, Stanford	Jr.	6-2	F
Dominique Canty, Alabama	Jr.	5-10	G/F
Adia Barnes, Arizona	Sr.	5-11	F

Other Women's Tournaments

NCAA Division II (Mar. 21 at Pine Bluff, Ark.): Final— North Dakota def. Emporia St. (Kan.), 92–76.

NCAA Division III (Mar. 21 at Gorham, Maine): Final— Washington (Mo.) def. Southern Maine, 77–69.

NAIA Division I (Mar. 24 at Jackson, Tenn.): Final— Union (Tenn.) def. Southern Nazarene (Okla.), 73–70.

NAIA Division II (Mar. 17 at Sioux City, Iowa): Final— Walsh (Ohio) def. Univ. of Mary Hardin-Baylor (Texas), 73-66.

NCAA Women's Division I Leaders

Includes games through NCAA and NIT tourneys.

INDIVIDUAL

Scoring

	Cl	Gm	Pts	Avg
Allison Feaster, Harvard	Sr.	28	797	28.5
Cindy Blodgett, Maine	Sr.	26	704	27.1
Korie Hlede, Duquesne	Sr.	28	758	27.1
Amy O'Brien, Holy Cross	Jr.	30	782	26.1
Tamika Whitmore, Memphis	Jr.	29	754	26.0
Karalyn Church, Vermont	So.	29	712	24.6
Becky Hammon, Colorado St.	Jr.	30	704	23.5
Chamique Holdsclaw, Tennessee	Jr.	39	915	23.5
Alicia Thompson, Texas Tech	Sr.	31	719	23.2
Marlene Stollings, Ohio	Sr.	28	642	22.9
Delores Jones, NE Ill.	Sr.	26	591	22.7
Myndee Larsen, Southern Utah	Sr.	28	618	22.1
Kristina Divjak, Northwestern	Jr.	31	684	22.1
Katrina Prince, Stephen F. Austin	Sr.	28	616	22.0
Kim Knuth, Toledo	Jr.	31	681	22.0
LaTonya Johnson, Memphis	Sr.	30	658	21.9
Adia Barnes, Arizona	Sr.	30	653	21.8
Doninique Canty, Alabama	Jr.	34	732	21.5
Lakeisha Parrish, Troy St.	So.	22	470	21.4
Melanie Halker, Siena	Jr.	26	549	21.1

Assists

	Cl	Gm	No	Avg
Dalma Ivanyi, Fla. International	Jr.	31	294	9.5
Alli Bills, Utah	Sr.	27	212	7.9
Ticha Penicheiro, Old Dominion	Sr.	32	239	7.5
Nicki Taggart, Marquette	Sr.	29	215	7.4
Gina Graziani, Miami-FL	So.	29	210	7.2
Joyce Howard, Texas-San Antonio	Sr.	28	201	7.2
Lisa Witherspoon, Virginia Tech	Jr.	31	219	7.1
Keisha Cox, Drake	Sr.	30	209	7.0
Tori Boudreaux, NE Illinios	Sr.	26	181	7.0
Amber DeWall, Northwestern	Sr.	30	205	6.8
Jennifer O'Brien, Davidson	So.	27	184	6.8
Courtney Kaup, George Mason	So.	28	189	6.8
Ashley Smith, Vanderbilt	Fr.	29	193	6.7
Janel Hollar, Siena	Sr.	28	185	6.6
Brittney Ezell, Alabama	Sr.	34	220	6.5
Amy Vachon, Maine	So.	30	194	6.5
Sabriya Mitchell, Massachusetts	Sr.	30	193	6.4
Laquan Stallworth, La. Tech	Jr.	35	225	6.4
Shanette Lee, Vilanova	Jr.	29	185	6.4
Judy Clark, Northwestern St.	So.	28	177	6.3

Rebounding

	Cl	Gm	No	Avg
Alisha Hill, Howard	Sr.	30	397	13.2
Murriel Page, Florida	Sr.	32	402	12.6
Jessica Zinobile, St. Francis	So.	30	365	12.2
Nyree Roberts, Old Dominion	Sr.	32	384	12.0
Leticia Oseguera, UC-Irvine	Sr.	22	262	11.9
Mfon Udoka, DePaul	Sr.	24	281	11.7
Amy O'Brien, Holy Cross	Jr.	30	344	11.5
Elise James, Robert Morris	So.	26	291	11.2
Amber Hall, Washington	Jr.	28	313	11.2
Kristina Behnfeldt, Marshall	Jr.	29	324	11.2
Felicia Tarver, Prairie View	So.	27	300	11.1
Christie Smith, Stephen F. Austin	Sr.	38	311	11.1
Mercy Aghedo, St. Peter's	So.	28	304	10.9
Allison Feaster, Harvard	Sr.	28	303	10.8
Kym Hope, Miami-FL	Jr.	29	306	10.6

Blocked Shots

	Cl	Gm	No	Avg
Samantha Tomlinson, Troy St.	Sr.	26	107	4.1
Teresa Jenkins, Florida A&M	Jr.	28	98	3.5
DeMya Walker, Virginia	Jr.	29	95	3.3
Myndee Larsen, Southern Utah	Sr.	28	90	3.2
Brooke Wyckoff, Florida St.	Fr.	27	80	3.0

Steals

	Cl	Gm	No	Avg
Ticha Penicheiro, Old Dominion	Sr.	32	161	5.0
Colleen Cook, Youngstown St.	Sr.	31	145	4.7
Shiakiea Carter, Grambling	Sr.	30	123	4.1
Cher Dyson, Stetson	Fr.	26	99	3.8
Jen Ricco, Temple	Sr.	27	96	3.6

TEAM

Scoring Offense

	Gm	W-L	Pts	Avg
Tennessee	39	39-0	3464	88.8
Louisiana Tech	35	31-4	3018	86.2
Stanford	27	21-6	2314	85.7
Western Kentucky	35	26-9	2979	85.1
Stephen F. Austin	29	25-4	2423	83.6
Connecticut	37	34-3	3070	83.0
UC Santa Barbara	33	27-6	2727	82.6
Grambling	30	23-7	2469	82.3
Arkansas St.	30	20-10	2438	81.3

High-Point Games

Individual

No		Opponent	Date
48	Mimi McKinney, Virginia	N. Carolina	1/15
46	Nykesha Sales, UConn	Stanford	12/21
45	Coco Miller, Georgia	Charleston Southern	12/6
43	Cindy Blodgett, Maine	Delaware	2/8
43	Eden Palacio, Pacific	Long Beach St.	2/28

Scoring Defense

	Gm	W-L	Pts	Avg
Princeton	26	16-10	1415	54.4
Old Dominion	32	29-3	1777	55.5
Fla. International	31	29-2	1739	56.1
Villanova	29	19-10	1637	56.4
New Mexico	33	26-7	1869	56.6
St. Joseph's	31	19-12	1757	56.7
Auburn	27	16-11	1531	56.7
Texas-Arlington	27	18-9	1531	56.7
Utah	27	21-6	1531	56.7
Massachusetts	30	19-11	1712	57.1

Scoring Margin

	Off	Def	Mar
Tennessee	88.8	58.7	30.1
Louisiana Tech	86.2	58.5	27.8
Connecticut	83.0	59.4	23.6
Old Dominion	79.1	55.5	23.6
Fla. International	79.6	56.1	23.5
Stephen F. Austin	83.6	65.7	17.9
Western Kentucky	85.1	67.8	17.3
Santa Clara	76.4	59.3	17.0
Hawaii	79.6	62.7	16.9

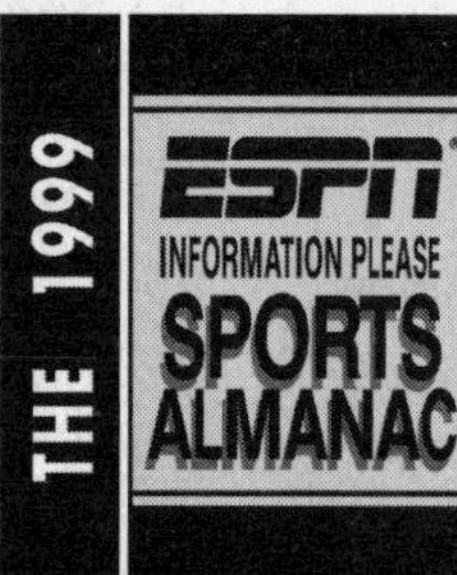

National Champions

The Helms Foundation of Los Angeles, under the direction of founder Bill Schroeder, selected national college basketball champions from 1942-82 and researched retroactive picks from 1901-41. The first NIT tournament and then the NCAA tournament have settled the national championship since 1938, but there are four years (1939, '40, '44 and '54) where the Helms selections differ. Please note that the column titled Outstanding Player is not a list of the official NCAA tournament Most Outstanding Players but rather a subjective list of each team's best player over the course of the season. For a list of official tournament Most Outstanding Players turn to page 307.

Multiple champions (1901-37): Chicago, Columbia and Wisconsin (3); Kansas, Minnesota, Notre Dame, Penn, Pittsburgh, Syracuse and Yale (2). **Multiple champions (since 1938):** UCLA (11); Kentucky (7); Indiana (5); North Carolina (3); Cincinnati, Duke, Kansas, Louisville, N.C. State, Oklahoma A&M (now Oklahoma St.) and San Francisco (2).

Year		Record	Head Coach	Outstanding Player
1901	**Yale**	10-4	No coach	G.M. Clark, F
1902	**Minnesota**	11-0	Louis Cooke	W.C. Deering, F
1903	**Yale**	15-1	W.H. Murphy	R.B. Hyatt, F
1904	**Columbia**	17-1	No coach	Harry Fisher, F
1905	**Columbia**	19-1	No coach	Harry Fisher, F
1906	**Dartmouth**	16-2	No coach	George Grebenstein, F
1907	**Chicago**	22-2	Joseph Raycroft	John Schommer, C
1908	**Chicago**	21-2	Joseph Raycroft	John Schommer, C
1909	**Chicago**	12-0	Joseph Raycroft	John Schommer, C
1910	**Columbia**	11-1	Harry Fisher	Ted Kiendl, F
1911	**St. John's-NY**	14-0	Claude Allen	John Keenan, F/C
1912	**Wisconsin**	15-0	Doc Meanwell	Otto Stangel, F
1913	**Navy**	9-0	Louis Wenzell	Laurence Wild, F
1914	**Wisconsin**	15-0	Doc Meanwell	Gene Van Gent, C
1915	**Illinois**	16-0	Ralph Jones	Ray Woods, G
1916	**Wisconsin**	20-1	Doc Meanwell	George Levis, F
1917	**Washington St**	25-1	Doc Bohler	Roy Bohler, G
1918	**Syracuse**	16-1	Edmund Dollard	Joe Schwarzer, G
1919	**Minnesota**	13-0	Louis Cooke	Arnold Oss, F
1920	**Penn**	22-1	Lon Jourdet	George Sweeney, F
1921	**Penn**	21-2	Edward McNichol	Danny McNichol, G
1922	**Kansas**	16-2	Phog Allen	Paul Endacott, G
1923	**Kansas**	17-1	Phog Allen	Paul Endacott, G
1924	**North Carolina**	25-0	Bo Shepard	Jack Cobb, F
1925	**Princeton**	21-2	Al Wittmer	Art Loeb, G
1926	**Syracuse**	19-1	Lew Andreas	Vic Hanson, F
1927	**Notre Dame**	19-1	George Keogan	John Nyikos, C
1928	**Pittsburgh**	21-0	Doc Carlson	Chuck Hyatt, F
1929	**Montana St.**	36-2	Schubert Dyche	John (Cat) Thompson, F
1930	**Pittsburgh**	23-2	Doc Carlson	Chuck Hyatt, F
1931	**Northwestern**	16-1	Dutch Lonborg	Joe Reiff, C
1932	**Purdue**	17-1	Piggy Lambert	John Wooden, G
1933	**Kentucky**	20-3	Adolph Rupp	Forest Sale, F
1934	**Wyoming**	26-3	Willard Witte	Les Witte, G
1935	**NYU**	19-1	Howard Cann	Sid Gross, F
1936	**Notre Dame**	22-2-1	George Keogan	John Moir, F
1937	**Stanford**	25-2	John Bunn	Hank Luisetti, F

Year		Record	Winner	Head Coach	Outstanding Player
1938	**Temple**	23-2	NIT	James Usilton	Meyer Bloom, G
1939	**Oregon**	29-5	NCAA	Howard Hobson	Slim Wintermute, C
	& **LIU-Brooklyn** (Helms)	24-0	NIT	Clair Bee	Irv Torgoff, F
1940	**Indiana**	20-3	NCAA	Branch McCracken	Marv Huffman, G
	& **USC** (Helms)	20-3	*	Sam Barry	Ralph Vaughn, F
1941	**Wisconsin**	20-3	NCAA	Bud Foster	Gene Englund, F
1942	**Stanford**	27-4	NCAA	Everett Dean	Jim Pollard, F
1943	**Wyoming**	31-2	NCAA	Everett Shelton	Kenny Sailors, G
1944	**Utah**	21-4	NCAA	Vadal Peterson	Arnie Ferrin, F
	& **Army** (Helms)	15-0	**	Ed Kelleher	Dale Hall, F

Year		Record	Winner	Head Coach	Outstanding Player
1945	**Oklahoma A&M**	27-4	NCAA	Hank Iba	Bob Kurland, C
1946	**Oklahoma A&M**	31-2	NCAA	Hank Iba	Bob Kurland, C
1947	**Holy Cross**	27-3	NCAA	Doggie Julian	George Kaftan, F
1948	**Kentucky**	36-3	NCAA	Adolph Rupp	Ralph Beard, G
1949	**Kentucky**	32-2	NCAA	Adolph Rupp	Alex Groza, C
1950	**CCNY**	24-5	NCAA & NIT	Nat Holman	Irwin Dambrot, G
1951	**Kentucky**	32-2	NCAA	Adolph Rupp	Bill Spivey, C
1952	**Kansas**	28-3	NCAA	Phog Allen	Clyde Lovellette, C
1953	**Indiana**	23-3	NCAA	Branch McCracken	Don Schlundt, C
1954	**La Salle**	26-4	NCAA	Ken Loeffler	Tom Gola, F
	& **Kentucky** (Helms)	25-0	***	Adolph Rupp	Cliff Hagan, G
1955	**San Francisco**	28-1	NCAA	Phil Woolpert	Bill Russell, C
1956	**San Francisco**	29-0	NCAA	Phil Woolpert	Bill Russell, C
1957	**North Carolina**	32-0	NCAA	Frank McGuire	Lennie Rosenbluth, F
1958	**Kentucky**	23-6	NCAA	Adolph Rupp	Vern Hatton, G
1959	**California**	25-4	NCAA	Pete Newell	Darrall Imhoff, C
1960	**Ohio St**	25-3	NCAA	Fred Taylor	Jerry Lucas, C
1961	**Cincinnati**	27-3	NCAA	Ed Jucker	Bob Wiesenhahn, F
1962	**Cincinnati**	29-2	NCAA	Ed Jucker	Paul Hogue, C
1963	**Loyola-IL**	29-2	NCAA	George Ireland	Jerry Harkness, F
1964	**UCLA**	30-0	NCAA	John Wooden	Walt Hazzard, G
1965	**UCLA**	28-2	NCAA	John Wooden	Gail Goodrich, G
1966	**Texas Western**	28-1	NCAA	Don Haskins	Bobby Joe Hill, G
1967	**UCLA**	30-0	NCAA	John Wooden	Lew Alcindor, C
1968	**UCLA**	29-1	NCAA	John Wooden	Lew Alcindor, C
1969	**UCLA**	29-1	NCAA	John Wooden	Lew Alcindor, C
1970	**UCLA**	28-2	NCAA	John Wooden	Sidney Wicks, F
1971	**UCLA**	29-1	NCAA	John Wooden	Sidney Wicks, F
1972	**UCLA**	30-0	NCAA	John Wooden	Bill Walton, C
1973	**UCLA**	30-0	NCAA	John Wooden	Bill Walton, C
1974	**N.C. State**	30-1	NCAA	Norm Sloan	David Thompson, F
1975	**UCLA**	28-3	NCAA	John Wooden	Dave Meyers, F
1976	**Indiana**	32-0	NCAA	Bob Knight	Scott May, F
1977	**Marquette**	25-7	NCAA	Al McGuire	Butch Lee, G
1978	**Kentucky**	30-2	NCAA	Joe B. Hall	Jack Givens, F
1979	**Michigan St**	26-6	NCAA	Jud Heathcote	Magic Johnson, G
1980	**Louisville**	33-3	NCAA	Denny Crum	Darrell Griffith, G
1981	**Indiana**	26-9	NCAA	Bob Knight	Isiah Thomas, G
1982	**North Carolina**	32-2	NCAA	Dean Smith	James Worthy, F
1983	**N.C. State**	26-10	NCAA	Jim Valvano	Sidney Lowe, G
1984	**Georgetown**	34-3	NCAA	John Thompson	Patrick Ewing, C
1985	**Villanova**	25-10	NCAA	Rollie Massimino	Ed Pinckney, C
1986	**Louisville**	32-7	NCAA	Denny Crum	Pervis Ellison, C
1987	**Indiana**	30-4	NCAA	Bob Knight	Steve Alford, G
1988	**Kansas**	27-11	NCAA	Larry Brown	Danny Manning, C
1989	**Michigan**	30-7	NCAA	Steve Fisher	Glen Rice, F
1990	**UNLV**	35-5	NCAA	Jerry Tarkanian	Larry Johnson, F
1991	**Duke**	32-7	NCAA	Mike Krzyzewski	Christian Laettner, F/C
1992	**Duke**	34-2	NCAA	Mike Krzyzewski	Christian Laettner, C
1993	**North Carolina**	34-4	NCAA	Dean Smith	Eric Montross, C
1994	**Arkansas**	31-3	NCAA	Nolan Richardson	Corliss Williamson, F
1995	**UCLA**	31-2	NCAA	Jim Harrick	Ed O'Bannon, F
1996	**Kentucky**	34-2	NCAA	Rick Pitino	Tony Delk, G
1997	**Arizona**	25-9	NCAA	Lute Olson	Miles Simon, G
1998	**Kentucky**	35-4	NCAA	Tubby Smith	Jeff Sheppard, G

*USC was beaten by Kansas in the West Regional of the NCAA tournament.
**Army did not lift its policy against postseason play until accepting a bid to the 1961 NIT.
***Unbeaten Kentucky turned down a bid to the 1954 NCAA tournament after the NCAA declared seniors Cliff Hagan, Frank Ramsey and Lou Tsioropoulos ineligible for postseason play.

The Red Cross Benefit Games, 1943-45

For three seasons during World War II, the NCAA and NIT champions met in a benefit game at Madison Square Garden in New York to raise money for the Red Cross. The NCAA champs won all three games.

Year	Winner	Score	Loser
1943	Wyoming (NCAA)	52-47	St. John's (NIT)
1944	Utah (NCAA)	43-36	St. John's (NIT)
1945	Oklahoma A&M (NCAA)	52-44	DePaul (NIT)

NCAA Final Four

The NCAA basketball tournament began in 1939 under the sponsorship of the National Association of Basketball Coaches, but was taken over by the NCAA in 1940. From 1939-51, the winners of the Eastern and Western Regionals played for the national championship, while regional runners-up shared third place. The concept of a Final Four originated in 1952 when four teams qualified for the first national semifinals. Consolation games to determine overall third place were held between regional finalists from 1946-51 and then national semifinalists from 1952-81. Consolation games were discontinued in 1982.

Multiple champions: UCLA (11); Kentucky (7); Indiana (5); North Carolina (3); Cincinnati, Duke, Kansas, Louisville, N.C. State, Oklahoma A&M (now Oklahoma St.) and San Francisco (2).

Year	Champion	Runner-up	Score	Final Two	Third Place	
1939	Oregon	Ohio St.	46-33	@ Evanston, IL	Oklahoma	Villanova
1940	Indiana	Kansas	60-42	@ Kansas City	Duquesne	USC
1941	Wisconsin	Washington St.	39-34	@ Kansas City	Arkansas	Pittsburgh
1942	Stanford	Dartmouth	53-38	@ Kansas City	Colorado	Kentucky
1943	Wyoming	Georgetown	46-34	@ New York	DePaul	Texas
1944	Utah	Dartmouth	42-40 (OT)	@ New York	Iowa St.	Ohio St.
1945	Oklahoma A&M	NYU	49-45	@ New York	Arkansas	Ohio St.

Year	Champion	Runner-up	Score	Final Two	Third Place	Fourth Place
1946	Oklahoma A&M	North Carolina	43-40	@ New York	Ohio St.	California
1947	Holy Cross	Oklahoma	58-47	@ New York	Texas	CCNY
1948	Kentucky	Baylor	58-42	@ New York	Holy Cross	Kansas St.
1949	Kentucky	Oklahoma A&M	46-36	@ Seattle	Illinois	Oregon St.
1950	CCNY	Bradley	71-68	@ New York	N.C. State	Baylor
1951	Kentucky	Kansas St.	68-58	@ Minneapolis	Illinois	Oklahoma A&M

Year	Champion	Runner-up	Score	Third Place	Fourth Place	Final Four
1952	Kansas	St. John's	80-63	Illinois	Santa Clara	@ Seattle
1953	Indiana	Kansas	69-68	Washington	LSU	@ Kansas City
1954	La Salle	Bradley	92-76	Penn St.	USC	@ Kansas City
1955	San Francisco	La Salle	77-63	Colorado	Iowa	@ Kansas City
1956	San Francisco	Iowa	83-71	Temple	SMU	@ Evanston, IL
1957	North Carolina	Kansas	54-53 (3OT)	San Francisco	Michigan St.	@ Kansas City
1958	Kentucky	Seattle	84-72	Temple	Kansas St.	@ Louisville
1959	California	West Virginia	71-70	Cincinnati	Louisville	@ Louisville
1960	Ohio St.	California	75-55	Cincinnati	NYU	@ San Francisco
1961	Cincinnati	Ohio St.	70-65 (OT)	St. Joseph's-PA	Utah	@ Kansas City
1962	Cincinnati	Ohio St.	71-59	Wake Forest	UCLA	@ Louisville
1963	Loyola-IL	Cincinnati	60-58 (OT)	Duke	Oregon St.	@ Louisville
1964	UCLA	Duke	98-83	Michigan	Kansas St.	@ Kansas City
1965	UCLA	Michigan	91-80	Princeton	Wichita St.	@ Portland, OR
1966	Texas Western	Kentucky	72-65	Duke	Utah	@ College Park, MD
1967	UCLA	Dayton	79-64	Houston	North Carolina	@ Louisville
1968	UCLA	North Carolina	78-55	Ohio St.	Houston	@ Los Angeles
1969	UCLA	Purdue	92-72	Drake	North Carolina	@ Louisville
1970	UCLA	Jacksonville	80-69	New Mexico St.	St. Bonaventure	@ College Park, MD
1971	UCLA	Villanova	68-62	Western Ky.	Kansas	@ Houston
1972	UCLA	Florida St.	81-76	North Carolina	Louisville	@ Los Angeles
1973	UCLA	Memphis St.	87-66	Indiana	Providence	@ St. Louis
1974	N.C. State	Marquette	76-64	UCLA	Kansas	@ Greensboro, NC
1975	UCLA	Kentucky	92-85	Louisville	Syracuse	@ San Diego
1976	Indiana	Michigan	86-68	UCLA	Rutgers	@ Philadelphia
1977	Marquette	North Carolina	67-59	UNLV	NC-Charlotte	@ Atlanta
1978	Kentucky	Duke	94-88	Arkansas	Notre Dame	@ St. Louis
1979	Michigan St.	Indiana St.	75-64	DePaul	Penn	@ Salt Lake City
1980	Louisville	UCLA	59-54	Purdue	Iowa	@ Indianapolis
1981	Indiana	North Carolina	63-50	Virginia	LSU	@ Philadelphia

Year	Champion	Runner-up	Score	Third Place		Final Four
1982	North Carolina	Georgetown	63-62	Houston	Louisville	@ New Orleans
1983	N.C. State	Houston	54-52	Georgia	Louisville	@ Albuquerque
1984	Georgetown	Houston	84-75	Kentucky	Virginia	@ Seattle
1985	Villanova	Georgetown	66-64	Memphis St.	St. John's	@ Lexington
1986	Louisville	Duke	72-69	Kansas	LSU	@ Dallas
1987	Indiana	Syracuse	74-73	Providence	UNLV	@ New Orleans
1988	Kansas	Oklahoma	83-79	Arizona	Duke	@ Kansas City
1989	Michigan	Seton Hall	80-79 (OT)	Duke	Illinois	@ Seattle
1990	UNLV	Duke	103-73	Arkansas	Georgia Tech	@ Denver
1991	Duke	Kansas	72-65	North Carolina	UNLV	@ Indianapolis
1992	Duke	Michigan	71-51	Cincinnati	Indiana	@ Minneapolis
1993	North Carolina	Michigan	77-71	Kansas	Kentucky	@ New Orleans
1994	Arkansas	Duke	76-72	Arizona	Florida	@ Charlotte
1995	UCLA	Arkansas	89-78	North Carolina	Oklahoma St.	@ Seattle
1996	Kentucky	Syracuse	76-67	UMass	Mississippi St.	@ E. Rutherford, NJ
1997	Arizona	Kentucky	84-79 (OT)	Minnesota	North Carolina	@ Indianapolis
1998	Kentucky	Utah	78-69	Stanford	North Carolina	@ San Antonio

Note: Six teams have had their standing in the Final Four vacated for using ineligible players: 1961–St. Joseph's-PA (3rd place); 1971–Villanova (Runner-up) and Western Kentucky (3rd place); 1980–UCLA (Runner-up); 1985–Memphis St. (3rd place); 1996–UMass (3rd place).

Most Outstanding Player

A Most Outstanding Player has been selected every year of the NCAA tournament. Winners who did not play for the tournament champion are listed in **bold** type. The 1939 and 1951 winners are unofficial and not recognized by the NCAA. Statistics listed are for Final Four games only.

Multiple winners: Lew Alcindor (3); Alex Groza, Bob Kurland, Jerry Lucas and Bill Walton (2).

Year		Gm	FGM	Pct	3PTM	3PTA	FTM	Pct	Reb	Ast	Blk	Stl	PPG
1939	**Jimmy Hull**, Ohio St.	2	15	—	—	—	10	—	—	—	—	—	20.0
1940	Marv Huffman, Indiana	2	7	—	—	—	4	—	—	—	—	—	9.0
1941	John Kotz, Wisconsin	2	8	—	—	—	6	—	—	—	—	—	11.0
1942	Howie Dallmar, Stanford	2	8	—	—	—	4	.667	—	—	—	—	10.0
1943	Kenny Sailors, Wyoming	2	10	—	—	—	8	.727	—	—	—	—	14.0
1944	Arnie Ferrin, Utah	2	11	—	—	—	6	—	—	—	—	—	14.0
1945	Bob Kurland, Okla. A&M	2	16	—	—	—	5	—	—	—	—	—	18.5
1946	Bob Kurland, Okla. A&M	2	21	—	—	—	10	.667	—	—	—	—	26.0
1947	George Kaftan, Holy Cross	2	18	—	—	—	12	.706	—	—	—	—	24.0
1948	Alex Groza, Kentucky	2	16	—	—	—	5	—	—	—	—	—	18.5
1949	Alex Groza, Kentucky	2	19	—	—	—	14	—	—	—	—	—	26.0
1950	Irwin Dambrot, CCNY	2	12	.429	—	—	4	.500	—	—	—	—	14.0
1951	Bill Spivey, Kentucky	2	20	—	—	—	10	—	—	—	—	—	25.0
1952	Clyde Lovellette, Kansas	2	24	—	—	—	18	—	—	—	—	—	33.0
1953	**B.H. Born**, Kansas	2	17	—	—	—	17	—	—	—	—	—	25.5
1954	Tom Gola, La Salle	2	12	—	—	—	14	—	—	—	—	—	19.0
1955	Bill Russell, San Francisco	2	19	—	—	—	9	—	—	—	—	—	23.5
1956	**Hal Lear**, Temple	2	32	—	—	—	16	—	—	—	—	—	40.0
1957	**Wilt Chamberlain**, Kansas	2	18	.514	—	—	19	.704	—	25	—	—	32.5
1958	**Elgin Baylor**, Seattle	2	18	.340	—	—	12	.750	—	41	—	—	24.0
1959	**Jerry West**, West Virginia	2	22	.667	—	—	22	.688	—	25	—	—	33.0
1960	Jerry Lucas, Ohio St.	2	16	.667	—	—	3	1.000	—	23	—	—	17.5
1961	**Jerry Lucas**, Ohio St.	2	20	.714	—	—	16	.941	—	25	—	—	28.0
1962	Paul Hogue, Cincinnati	2	23	.639	—	—	12	.632	—	38	—	—	29.0
1963	**Art Heyman**, Duke	2	18	.409	—	—	15	.682	—	19	—	—	25.5
1964	Walt Hazzard, UCLA	2	11	.550	—	—	8	.667	10	—	—	—	15.0
1965	**Bill Bradley**, Princeton	2	34	.630	—	—	19	.950	24	—	—	—	43.5
1966	**Jerry Chambers**, Utah	2	25	.532	—	—	20	.833	35	—	—	—	35.0
1967	Lew Alcindor, UCLA	2	14	.609	—	—	11	.458	38	—	—	—	19.5
1968	Lew Alcindor, UCLA	2	22	.629	—	—	9	.900	34	—	—	—	26.5
1969	Lew Alcindor, UCLA	2	23	.676	—	—	16	.640	41	—	—	—	31.0
1970	Sidney Wicks, UCLA	2	15	.714	—	—	9	.600	34	—	—	—	19.5
1971	**Howard Porter**, Villanova	2	20	.488	—	—	7	.778	24	—	—	—	23.5
1972	Bill Walton, UCLA	2	20	.690	—	—	17	.739	41	—	—	—	28.5
1973	Bill Walton, UCLA	2	28	.824	—	—	2	.400	30	—	—	—	29.0
1974	David Thompson, N.C. State	2	19	.514	—	—	11	.786	17	—	—	—	24.5
1975	Richard Washington, UCLA	2	23	.548	—	—	8	.727	20	—	—	—	27.0
1976	Kent Benson, Indiana	2	17	.500	—	—	7	.636	18	—	—	—	20.5
1977	Butch Lee, Marquette	2	11	.344	—	—	8	1.000	6	2	1	1	15.0
1978	Jack Givens, Kentucky	2	28	.651	—	—	8	.667	17	4	1	3	32.0
1979	Magic Johnson, Michigan St.	2	17	.680	—	—	19	.864	17	3	0	2	26.5
1980	Darrell Griffith, Louisville	2	23	.622	—	—	11	.688	7	15	0	2	28.5
1981	Isiah Thomas, Indiana	2	14	.560	—	—	9	.818	4	9	3	4	18.5
1982	James Worthy, N. Carolina	2	20	.741	—	—	2	.286	8	9	0	4	21.0
1983	**Akeem Olajuwon**, Houston	2	16	.552	—	—	9	.643	40	3	2	5	20.5
1984	Patrick Ewing, Georgetown	2	8	.571	—	—	2	1.000	18	1	15	1	9.0
1985	Ed Pinckney, Villanova	2	8	.571	—	—	12	.750	15	6	3	0	14.0
1986	Pervis Ellison, Louisville	2	15	.600	—	—	6	.750	24	2	3	1	18.0
1987	Keith Smart, Indiana	2	14	.636	0	1	7	.778	7	7	0	2	17.5
1988	Danny Manning, Kansas	2	25	.556	0	1	6	.667	17	4	8	9	28.0
1989	Glen Rice, Michigan	2	24	.490	7	16	4	1.000	16	1	0	3	29.5
1990	Anderson Hunt, UNLV	2	19	.613	9	16	2	.500	4	9	1	1	24.5
1991	Christian Laettner, Duke	2	12	.545	1	1	21	.913	17	2	1	2	23.0
1992	Bobby Hurley, Duke	2	10	.417	7	12	8	.800	3	11	0	3	17.5
1993	Donald Williams, N. Carolina	2	15	.652	10	14	10	1.000	4	1	0	2	25.0
1994	Corliss Williamson, Arkansas	2	21	.500	0	0	10	.714	21	8	3	4	26.0
1995	Ed O'Bannon, UCLA	2	16	.457	3	8	10	.769	25	3	1	7	22.5
1996	Tony Delk, Kentucky	2	15	.417	8	16	6	.546	9	2	3	2	22.0
1997	Miles Simon, Arizona	2	17	.459	3	10	17	.773	8	6	0	1	27.0
1998	Jeff Sheppard, Kentucky	2	16	.552	4	10	7	.778	10	7	0	4	21.5

Final Four All-Decade Teams

To celebrate the 50th anniversary of the NCAA tournament in 1989, five All-Decade teams were selected by a blue ribbon panel of coaches and administrators. An All-Time Final Four team was also chosen. Selections were actually made prior to the 1988 tournament.

Selection panel: Vic Bubas, Denny Crum, Wayne Duke, Dave Gavitt, Joe B. Hall, Jud Heathcote, Hank Iba, Pete Newell, Dean Smith, John Thompson and John Wooden.

All-Time Team

	Years
Lew Alcindor, UCLA	1967-69
Larry Bird, Indiana St.	1979
Wilt Chamberlain, Kansas	1957
Magic Johnson, Mich. St	1979
Michael Jordan, N. Carolina	1982

All-1940s

	Years
Ralph Beard, Kentucky	1948-49
Howie Dallmar, Stanford	1942
Dwight Eddleman, Illinois	1949
Arnie Ferrin, Utah	1944
Alex Groza, Kentucky	1948-49
George Kaftan, Holy Cross	1947
Bob Kurland, Okla. A&M	1945-46
Jim Pollard, Stanford	1942
Kenny Sailors, Wyoming	1943
Gerry Tucker, Oklahoma	1947

All-1950s

	Years
Elgin Baylor, Seattle	1958
Wilt Chamberlain, Kansas	1957
Tom Gola, La Salle	1954
K.C. Jones, San Francisco	1955
Clyde Lovellette, Kansas	1952
Oscar Robertson, Cinn.	1959-60
Guy Rodgers, Temple	1958
Lennie Rosenbluth, N. Carolina	1957
Bill Russell, San Francisco	1955-56
Jerry West, West Virginia	1959

All-1960s

	Years
Lew Alcindor, UCLA	1967-69
Bill Bradley, Princeton	1965
Gail Goodrich, UCLA	1964-65
John Havlicek, Ohio St.	1961-62
Elvin Hayes, Houston	1967
Walt Hazzard, UCLA	1964
Jerry Lucas, Ohio St	1960-61
Jeff Mullins, Duke	1964
Cazzie Russell, Michigan	1965
Charlie Scott, N. Carolina	1968-69

All-1970s

	Years
Kent Benson, Indiana	1976
Larry Bird, Indiana St	1979
Jack Givens, Kentucky	1978
Magic Johnson, Mich. St	1979
Marques Johnson, UCLA	1975-76
Scott May, Indiana	1976
David Thompson, N.C. State	1974
Bill Walton, UCLA	1972-74
Sidney Wicks, UCLA	1969-71
Keith Wilkes, UCLA	1972-74

All-1980s

	Years
Steve Alford, Indiana	1987
Johnny Dawkins, Duke	1986
Patrick Ewing, Georgetown	1982-84
Darrell Griffith, Louisville	1980
Michael Jordan, N. Carolina	1982
Rodney McCray, Louisville	1980
Akeem Olajuwon, Houston	1983-84
Ed Pinckney, Villanova	1985
Isiah Thomas, Indiana	1981
James Worthy, N. Carolina	1982

Note: Lew Alcindor later changed his name to Kareem Abdul-Jabbar; Keith Wilkes later changed his first name to Jamaal; and Akeem Olajuwon later changed the spelling of his first name to Hakeem.

Seeds at the Final Four

Year	Seeds (Total)	Teams
1979	1,2,2,9 (14)	Indiana St., **Michigan St.**, DePaul, Pennsylvania
1980	2,5,6,8 (21)	**Louisville**, Iowa, Purdue, UCLA
1981	1,1,2,3 (7)	Virginia, LSU, N. Carolina, **Indiana**
1982	1,1,3,6 (11)	**N. Carolina**, Georgetown, Louisville, Houston
1983	1,1,4,6 (12)	Houston, Louisville, Georgia, **N.C. State**
1984	1,1,2,7 (11)	Kentucky, **Georgetown**, Houston, Virginia
1985	1,1,2,8 (12)	St. John's, Georgetown, Memphis, **Villanova**
1986	1,1,2,11 (15)	Duke, Kansas, **Louisville**, LSU
1987	1,1,2,6 (10)	UNLV, **Indiana**, Syracuse, Providence
1988	1,1,2,6 (10)	Arizona, Oklahoma, Duke, **Kansas**
1989	1,2,3,3 (9)	Illinois, Duke, Seton Hall, **Michigan**
1990	1,3,4,4 (12)	**UNLV**, Duke, Ga. Tech, Arkansas
1991	1,1,2,3 (7)	UNLV, N. Carolina, **Duke**, Kansas
1992	1,2,4,6 (13)	**Duke**, Indiana, Cincinnati, Michigan
1993	1,1,1,2 (5)	**N. Carolina**, Kentucky, Michigan, Kansas
1994	1,2,2,3 (8)	**Arkansas**, Arizona, Duke, Florida
1995	1,2,2,4 (9)	**UCLA**, Arkansas, N. Carolina, Okla. St.
1996	1,1,4,5 (11)	**Kentucky**, UMass, Syracuse, Miss. St.
1997	1,1,1,4 (7)	Kentucky, N. Carolina, Minnesota, **Arizona**
1998	1,2,3,3 (9)	N. Carolina, **Kentucky**, Stanford, Utah

All Time Seeds Records

All-time records of NCAA tournament seeds since tourney expanded to 64 teams in 1985. Records are through the 1998 NCAA Tournament. Note that 1st refers to championships. 2nd refers to runners-up and FF refers to Final Four appearances.

Seed	W	L	Pct.	1st	2nd	FF
1	237	72	.767	9	8	20
2	181	75	.707	5	5	11
3	117	78	.600	2	4	4
4	111	79	.584	1	1	7
5	90	81	.526	0	0	2
6	109	78	.583	2	1	3
7	67	80	.456	0	0	1
8	60	79	.432	1	1	0
9	47	81	.367	0	0	1
10	47	80	.370	0	0	0
11	35	76	.315	0	0	1
12	28	76	.269	0	0	0
13	13	56	.188	0	0	0
14	14	56	.200	0	0	0
15	3	56	.051	0	0	0
16	0	56	.000	0	0	0

Collegiate Commissioners Association Tournament

The Collegiate Commissioners Association staged an eight-team tournament for teams that didn't make the NCAA tournament in 1974 and '75.

Most Valuable Players: 1974–Kent Benson, Indiana: 1975–Bob Elliot, Arizona.

Year	Winner	Score	Loser	Site
1974	Indiana	85-60	USC	St. Louis
1975	Drake	83-76	Arizona	Louisville

NCAA Tournament Appearances

App		W-L	F4	Championships
40	Kentucky	83-35	13	7 (1948-49,51,58,78,96,98)
34	UCLA	75-26	15	11 (1964-65,67-73,75,95)
32	N. Carolina	76-32	14	3 (1957,82,93)
27	Louisville	48-29	7	2 (1980,86)
27	Indiana	51-22	7	5 (1940,53,76,81,87)
27	Kansas	57-27	10	2 (1952,88)
24	Villanova	37-24	3	1 (1985)
24	Notre Dame	25-28	1	None
24	St. John's	23-26	2	None
24	Syracuse	37-25	3	None
23	Arkansas	38-23	6	1 (1994)
22	Duke	60-20	11	2 (1991-92)
22	Kansas St.	27-26	4	None
22	Temple	24-22	2	None
21	Georgetown	36-20	4	1 (1984)
21	Marquette	28-22	2	1 (1977)
21	Princeton	13-25	1	None
20	DePaul	20-23	2	None
20	Michigan	41-19	6	1 (1989)
20	Utah	30-23	4	1 (1944)
20	Connecticut	20-21	0	None
19	Illinois	23-20	4	None
18	Ohio St.	31-17	8	1 (1960)
18	Houston	26-23	5	None
18	BYU	11-21	0	None
18	West Virginia	13-18	1	None
17	Arizona	26-16	3	1 (1997)
17	Cincinnati	33-16	6	2 (1961-62)
17	Iowa	23-19	3	None
17	N.C. State	27-16	3	2 (1974,83)
17	Oklahoma	20-17	3	None
17	Purdue	20-17	2	None
16	Memphis	18-16	2	None
16	Texas	16-19	2	None
16	Missouri	13-16	0	None
16	Oregon St.	12-19	2	None
16	Pennsylvania	13-18	1	None
16	Western Ky.	15-17	1	None

Note: Although all NCAA tournament appearances are included above, the NCAA has officially voided the records of Villanova (4-1) and Western Ky. (4-1) in 1971, UCLA (5-1) in 1980, Oregon St. (2-3) from 1980-82, Memphis (9-5) from 1982-86, DePaul (6-4) from 1986-89, N.C. State (0-2) from 1987-88 and Kentucky (2-1) in 1988.

All-Time NCAA Division I Tournament Leaders

Through 1998; minimum of six games; **Last** column indicates final year played.

CAREER

Scoring

	Points	Yrs	Last	Gm	Pts
1	Christian Laettner, Duke	4	1992	23	407
2	Elvin Hayes, Houston	3	1968	13	358
3	Danny Manning, Kansas	4	1988	16	328
4	Oscar Robertson, Cincinnati	3	1960	10	324
5	Glen Rice, Michigan	4	1989	13	308
6	Lew Alcindor, UCLA	3	1969	12	304
7	Bill Bradley, Princeton	3	1965	9	303
8	Austin Carr, Notre Dame	3	1971	7	289
9	Juwan Howard, Michigan	3	1994	16	280
10	Calbert Cheaney, Indiana	4	1993	13	279

	Average	Yrs	Last	Pts	Avg
1	Austin Carr, Notre Dame	3	1971	289	41.3
2	Bill Bradley, Princeton	3	1965	303	33.7
3	Oscar Robertson, Cincinnati	3	1960	324	32.4
4	Jerry West, West Virginia	3	1960	275	30.6
5	Bob Pettit, LSU	2	1954	183	30.5
6	Dan Issel, Kentucky	3	1970	176	29.3
	Jim McDaniels, Western Ky	2	1971	176	29.3
8	Dwight Lamar, SW Louisiana	2	1973	175	29.2
9	Bo Kimble, Loyola-CA	3	1990	204	29.1
10	David Robinson, Navy	3	1987	200	28.6

Rebounds

	Total	Yrs	Last	Gm	No
1	Elvin Hayes, Houston	3	1968	13	222
2	Lew Alcindor, UCLA	3	1969	12	201
3	Jerry Lucas, Ohio St.	3	1962	12	197
4	Bill Walton, UCLA	3	1974	12	176
5	Christian Laettner, Duke	4	1992	23	169
6	Paul Hogue, Cincinnati	3	1962	12	160
7	Sam Lacey, New Mexico St.	3	1970	11	157
8	Derrick Coleman, Syracuse	4	1990	14	155
9	Akeem Olajuwon, Houston	3	1984	15	153
10	Patrick Ewing, Georgetown	4	1985	18	144

	Average	Yrs	Last	Reb	Avg
1	Johnny Green, Michigan St.	2	1959	118	19.7
2	Artis Gilmore, Jacksonville	2	1971	115	19.2
3	Paul Silas, Creighton	3	1964	111	18.5
4	Len Chappell, Wake Forest	2	1962	137	17.1
5	Elvin Hayes, Houston	3	1968	222	17.1
6	Lew Alcindor, UCLA	3	1969	201	16.8
7	Jerry Lucas, Ohio St.	3	1962	197	16.4
8	Bill Walton, UCLA	3	1974	176	14.7
9	Sam Lacey, New Mexico St.	3	1970	157	14.3
10	Bob Lanier, St. Bonaventure	3	1970	85	14.2

3-Pt Field Goals

	Total	Yrs	Last	Gm	No
1	Bobby Hurley, Duke	4	1993	20	42
2	Jeff Fryer, Loyola-CA	3	1990	7	38
3	Glen Rice, Michigan	4	1989	13	35
4	Anderson Hunt, UNLV	3	1991	15	34
5	Dennis Scott, Georgia Tech	3	1990	8	33

Assists

	Total	Yrs	Last	Gm	No
1	Bobby Hurley, Duke	4	1993	20	145
2	Sherman Douglas, Syracuse	4	1989	14	106
3	Greg Anthony, UNLV	3	1991	15	100
4	Mark Wade, UNLV	2	1987	8	93
	Rumeal Robinson, Michigan	3	1990	11	93

SINGLE TOURNAMENT

Scoring

	Points	Year	Gm	Pts
1	Glen Rice, Michigan	1989	6	184
2	Bill Bradley, Princeton	1965	5	177
3	Elvin Hayes, Houston	1968	5	167
4	Danny Manning, Kansas	1988	6	163
5	Hal Lear, Temple	1956	5	160
	Jerry West, West Virginia	1959	5	160

	Average	Year	Gm	Pts	Avg
1	Austin Carr, Notre Dame	1970	3	158	52.7
2	Austin Carr, Notre Dame	1971	3	125	41.7
3	Jerry Chambers, Utah	1966	4	143	35.8
	Bo Kimble, Loyola-CA	1990	4	143	35.8
5	Bill Bradley, Princeton	1965	5	177	35.4
6	Clyde Lovellette, Kansas	1952	4	141	35.3

Rebounds

	Total	Year	Gm	No	Avg
1	Elvin Hayes, Houston	1968	5	97	19.4
2	Artis Gilmore, Jacksonville	1970	5	93	18.6
3	Elgin Baylor, Seattle	1958	5	91	18.2
4	Sam Lacey, New Mexico St.	1970	5	90	18.0
5	Clarence Glover, Western Ky.	1971	5	89	17.8

Assists

	Total	Year	Gm	No	Avg
1	Mark Wade, UNLV	1987	5	61	12.2
2	Rumeal Robinson, Michigan	1989	6	56	9.3
3	Sherman Douglas, Syracuse	1987	6	49	8.2
4	Bobby Hurley, Duke	1992	6	47	7.8
5	Michael Jackson, Georgetown	1985	6	45	7.5

SINGLE GAME

Scoring

	Points	Year	Pts
1	Austin Carr, Notre Dame vs Ohio Univ	1970	61
2	Bill Bradley, Princeton vs Wichita St.	1965	58
3	Oscar Robertson, Cincinnati vs Arkansas	1958	56
4	Austin Carr, Notre Dame vs Kentucky	1970	52
	Austin Carr, Notre Dame vs TCU	1971	52
6	David Robinson, Navy vs Michigan	1987	50
7	Elvin Hayes, Houston vs Loyola-IL	1968	49
8	Hal Lear, Temple vs SMU	1956	48
9	Austin Carr, Notre Dame vs Houston	1971	47
10	Dave Corzine, DePaul vs Louisville	1978	46
11	Bob Houbregs, Washington vs Seattle	1953	45
	Austin Carr, Notre Dame vs Iowa	1970	45
	Bo Kimble, Loyola-CA vs New Mexico St.	1990	45
14	Seven players tied with 44 each.		

Rebounds

	Total	Year	No
1	Fred Cohen, Temple vs UConn	1956	34
2	Nate Thurmond, Bowl. Green vs Miss. St.	1963	31
3	Jerry Lucas, Ohio St. vs Kentucky	1961	30
4	Toby Kimball, UConn vs St. Joseph's-PA	1965	29
5	Elvin Hayes, Houston vs Pacific	1966	28

Assists

	Total	Year	No
1	Mark Wade, UNLV vs Indiana	1987	18
2	Sam Crawford, N. Mexico St. vs Nebraska	1993	16
3	Kenny Patterson, DePaul vs Syracuse	1985	15
4	Keith Smart, Indiana vs Auburn	1987	15
5	Five players tied with 14 each.		

SINGLE FINAL FOUR GAME

Letters in the **Year** column indicate the following: C for Consolation Game, F for Final and S for Semifinal.

Scoring

	Points	Year	Pts
1	Bill Bradley, Princeton vs Wichita St	1965-C	58
2	Hal Lear, Temple vs SMU	1956-C	48
3	Bill Walton, UCLA vs Memphis St	1973-F	44
4	Bob Houbregs, Washington vs LSU	1953-C	42
	Jack Egan, St. Joseph's-PA vs Utah	1961-C	42*
	Gail Goodrich, UCLA vs Michigan	1965-C	42
7	Jack Givens, Kentucky vs Duke	1978-F	41
8	Oscar Robertson, Cincinnati vs L'ville	1959-C	39
	Al Wood, N. Carolina vs Virginia	1981-S	39
10	Jerry West, West Va. vs Louisville	1959-S	38
	Jerry Chambers, Utah vs Texas Western	1966-S	38
	Freddie Banks, UNLV vs Indiana	1987-S	38

* Four overtimes.

Rebounds

	Total	Year	No
1	Bill Russell, San Francisco vs Iowa	1956-F	27
2	Elvin Hayes, Houston vs UCLA	1967-S	24
3	Bill Russell, San Francisco vs SMU	1956-S	23
4	Four players tied with 22 each.		

Assists

	Total	Year	No
1	Mark Wade, UNLV vs Indiana	1987-S	18
2	Rumeal Robinson, Michigan vs Illinois	1989-S	12
3	Michael Jackson, G'town vs St. John's	1985-S	11
4	Milt Wagner, Louisville vs LSU	1986-S	11
5	Rumeal Robinson, Mich. vs Seton Hall	1989-F	11*

*Overtime.

Teams in Both NCAA and NIT

Fourteen teams played in both the NCAA and NIT tournaments from 1940-52. Colorado (1940), Utah (1944), Kentucky (1949) and BYU (1951) won one of the titles, while CCNY won two in 1950, beating Bradley in both championship games.

Year		NIT	NCAA
1940	Colorado	**Won Final**	Lost 1st Rd
	Duquesne	Lost Final	Lost 2nd Rd
1944	Utah	Lost 1st Rd	**Won Final**
1949	Kentucky	Lost 2nd Rd	**Won Final**
1950	CCNY	**Won Final**	**Won Final**
	Bradley	Lost Final	Lost Final
1951	BYU	**Won Final**	Lost 2nd Rd
	St. John's	Lost 3rd Rd	Lost 2nd Rd
	N.C. State	Lost 2nd Rd	Lost 2nd Rd
	Arizona	Lost 2nd Rd	Lost 1st Rd
1952	St. John's	Lost Final	Lost 2nd Rd
	Dayton	Lost 1st Rd	Lost Final
	Duquesne	Lost 2nd Rd	Lost 2nd Rd
	Saint Louis	Lost 2nd Rd	Lost 2nd Rd

Most Popular Final Four Sites

The NCAA has staged its Men's Division I championship–the Final Two (1939-51) and Final Four (since 1952)–at 29 different arenas and indoor stadiums in 24 different cities. The following facilities have all hosted the event more than once. Note that the RCA Dome is scheduled to host the Final Four again in 2000.

No	Arena	Years
9	Municipal Auditorium (KC)	1940-42, 53-55, 57, 61, 64
7	Madison Sq. Garden (NYC)	1943-48, 50
6	Freedom Hall (Louisville)	1958-59, 62-63, 67, 69
3	Kingdome (Seattle)	1984, 89, 95
	Superdome (New Orleans)	1982, 87, 93
2	Cole Field House (College Park, Md.)	1966, 70
	Edmundson Pavilion (Seattle)	1949, 52
	LA Sports Arena	1968, 72
	RCA Dome (Indianapolis)	1991, 97
	St. Louis Arena	1973, 78
	Spectrum (Philadelphia)	1976, 81

NIT Championship

The National Invitation Tournament began under the sponsorship of the Metropolitan New York Basketball Writers Association in 1938. The NIT is now administered by the Metropolitan Intercollegiate Basketball Association. All championship games have been played at Madison Square Garden.

Multiple winners: St. John's (5); Bradley (4); BYU, Dayton, Kentucky, LIU-Brooklyn, Michigan, Minnesota, Providence, Temple, Virginia and Virginia Tech (2).

Year	Winner	Score	Loser
1938	Temple	60-36	Colorado
1939	LIU-Brooklyn	44-32	Loyola-IL
1940	Colorado	51-40	Duquesne
1941	LIU-Brooklyn	56-42	Ohio Univ.
1942	West Virginia	47-45	Western Ky.
1943	St. John's	48-27	Toledo
1944	St. John's	47-39	DePaul
1945	DePaul	71-54	Bowling Green
1946	Kentucky	46-45	Rhode Island
1947	Utah	49-45	Kentucky
1948	Saint Louis	65-52	NYU
1949	San Francisco	48-47	Loyola-IL
1950	CCNY	69-61	Bradley
1951	BYU	62-43	Dayton
1952	La Salle	75-64	Dayton
1953	Seton Hall	58-46	St. John's
1954	Holy Cross	71-62	Duquesne
1955	Duquesne	70-58	Dayton
1956	Louisville	93-80	Dayton
1957	Bradley	84-83	Memphis St.
1958	Xavier-OH	78-74 (OT)	Dayton
1959	St. John's	76-71 (OT)	Bradley
1960	Bradley	88-72	Providence
1961	Providence	62-59	Saint Louis
1962	Dayton	73-67	St. John's
1963	Providence	81-66	Canisius
1964	Bradley	86-54	New Mexico
1965	St. John's	55-51	Villanova
1966	BYU	97-84	NYU
1967	Southern Illinois	71-56	Marquette
1968	Dayton	61-48	Kansas
1969	Temple	89-76	Boston Coll.
1970	Marquette	65-53	St. John's
1971	North Carolina	84-66	Georgia Tech
1972	Maryland	100-69	Niagara
1973	Virginia Tech	92-91 (OT)	Notre Dame
1974	Purdue	97-81	Utah
1975	Princeton	80-69	Providence
1976	Kentucky	71-67	NC-Charlotte
1977	St. Bonaventure	94-91	Houston
1978	Texas	101-93	N.C. State
1979	Indiana	53-52	Purdue
1980	Virginia	58-55	Minnesota
1981	Tulsa	86-84 (OT)	Syracuse
1982	Bradley	67-58	Purdue
1983	Fresno St.	69-60	DePaul
1984	Michigan	83-63	Notre Dame
1985	UCLA	65-62	Indiana
1986	Ohio St.	73-63	Wyoming
1987	Southern Miss.	84-80	La Salle
1988	Connecticut	72-67	Ohio St.
1989	St. John's	73-65	Saint Louis
1990	Vanderbilt	74-72	Saint Louis
1991	Stanford	78-72	Oklahoma
1992	Virginia	81-76 (OT)	Notre Dame
1993	Minnesota	62-61	Georgetown
1994	Villanova	80-73	Vanderbilt
1995	Virginia Tech	65-64 (OT)	Marquette
1996	Nebraska	60-56	St. Joseph's
1997	Michigan	82-72	Florida St.
1998	Minnesota	79-72	Penn St.

Most Valuable Player

A Most Valuable Player has been selected every year of the NIT tournament. Winners who did not play for the tournament champion are listed in **bold** type.

Multiple winners: None. However, Tom Gola of La Salle is the only player to be named MVP in the NIT (1952) and Most Outstanding Player of the NCAA tournament (1954).

Year	
1938	Don Shields, Temple
1939	**Bill Lloyd**, St. John's
1940	Bob Doll, Colorado
1941	**Frank Baumholtz**, Ohio U.
1942	Rudy Baric, West Virginia
1943	Harry Boykoff, St. John's
1944	Bill Kotsores, St. John's
1945	George Mikan, DePaul
1946	**Ernie Calverley**, Rhode Island
1947	Vern Gardner, Utah
1948	Ed Macauley, Saint Louis
1949	Don Lofgan, San Francisco
1950	Ed Warner, CCNY
1951	Roland Minson, BYU
1952	Tom Gola, La Salle & Norm Grekin, La Salle
1953	Walter Dukes, Seton Hall
1954	Togo Palazzi, Holy Cross
1955	**Maurice Stokes**, St. Francis-PA
1956	Charlie Tyra, Louisville
1957	**Win Wilfong**, Memphis St.
1958	Hank Stein, Xavier-OH
1959	Tony Jackson, St. John's
1960	**Lenny Wilkens**, Providence
1961	Vinny Ernst, Providence
1962	Bill Chmielewski, Dayton
1963	Ray Flynn, Providence
1964	Lavern Tart, Bradley
1965	Ken McIntyre, St. John's
1966	**Bill Melchionni**, Villanova
1967	Walt Frazier, So. Illinois
1968	Don May, Dayton
1969	**Terry Driscoll,** Boston College
1970	Dean Meminger, Marquette
1971	Bill Chamberlain, N. Carolina
1972	Tom McMillen, Maryland
1973	**John Shumate**, Notre Dame
1974	**Mike Sojourner**, Utah
1975	**Ron Lee**, Oregon
1976	**Cedric Maxwell**, NC-Charlotte
1977	Greg Sanders, St. Bonaventure
1978	Ron Baxter, Texas & Jim Krivacs, Texas
1979	Clarence Carter, Indiana & Ray Tolbert, Indiana
1980	Ralph Sampson, Virginia
1981	Greg Stewart, Tulsa
1982	Mitchell Anderson, Bradley
1983	Ron Anderson, Fresno St.
1984	Tim McCormick, Michigan
1985	Reggie Miller, UCLA
1986	Brad Sellers, Ohio St.
1987	Randolph Keys, So. Miss.
1988	Phil Gamble, Connecticut
1989	Jayson Williams, St. John's
1990	Scott Draud, Vanderbilt
1991	Adam Keefe, Stanford
1992	Bryant Stith, Virginia
1993	Voshon Lenard, Minnesota
1994	**Doremus Bennerman**, Siena
1995	Shawn Smith, Va. Tech
1996	Erick Strickland, Nebraska
1997	Robert Traylor, Michigan
1998	Kevin Clark, Minnesota

All-Time NIT Team

As selected by a media panel.

Walt Frazier, S. Illinois
George Mikan, DePaul
Tom Gola, La Salle
Maurice Stokes, St. Francis-PA
Ralph Beard, Kentucky

All-Time Winningest Division I Teams

Top 25 Winning Percentage

Division I schools with best winning percentages through 1997-98 season (including tournament games). Years in Division I only; minimum 20 years. NCAA tournament columns indicate years in tournament, record and number of championships.

		First Year	Yrs	Games	Won	Lost	Tied	Pct	NCAA Tourney Yrs	W-L	Titles
1	Kentucky	1903	95	2250	1720	529	1	**.764**	39	83-35	7
2	North Carolina	1911	88	2308	1709	599	0	**.740**	32	76-32	3
3	UNLV	1959	40	1138	831	307	0	**.730**	13	30-12	1
4	Kansas	1899	100	2379	1665	714	0	**.700**	27	57-27	2
5	UCLA	1920	79	2035	1423	613	0	**.699**	34	79-27	11
6	St. John's	1908	91	2260	1554	706	0	**.688**	24	23-26	0
7	Syracuse	1901	97	2169	1477	692	0	**.681**	24	37-25	0
8	Duke	1906	93	2301	1548	753	0	**.673**	22	60-20	2
9	Western Kentucky	1915	79	2035	1366	669	0	**.671**	16	15-17	0
10	Arkansas	1924	75	1963	1292	671	0	**.658**	23	38-23	1
11	Utah	1909	90	2108	1376	732	0	**.653**	20	30-23	1
12	Louisville	1912	84	2053	1337	716	0	**.651**	27	48-29	2
13	Indiana	1901	98	2197	1430	767	0	**.651**	27	51-22	5
14	Temple	1895	102	2308	1496	812	0	**.648**	22	24-22	0
15	DePaul	1924	75	1833	1187	646	0	**.648**	20	20-23	0
16	Notre Dame	1898	93	2204	1427	776	1	**.647**	24	25-28	0
17	Purdue	1897	100	2141	1383	758	0	**.646**	17	21-17	0
18	Illinois	1906	93	2090	1344	746	0	**.643**	19	23-20	0
19	Weber St.	1963	36	1018	654	364	0	**.642**	11	5-12	0
20	Villanova	1921	78	1990	1268	722	0	**.637**	24	37-24	1
21	Illinois St.	1972	26	788	502	286	0	**.637**	5	3-5	0
22	Penn	1897	98	2288	1454	832	2	**.636**	16	13-18	0
23	Arizona	1906	93	2062	1309	753	0	**.635**	17	26-16	1
24	N.C. State	1913	86	2104	1326	778	0	**.630**	17	27-16	2
25	Murray St.	1926	73	1862	1171	691	0	**.629**	9	1-9	0

Top 35 All-Time Victories

Division I schools with most victories through 1997-98 (including postseason tournaments). Minimum 20 years in Division I.

		Wins			Wins			Wins			Wins
1	Kentucky	1720	10	Indiana	1430	19	Illinois	1344	28	Arkansas	1292
2	North Carolina	1709	11	Notre Dame	1427	20	Bradley	1338	29	Montana St.	1285
3	Kansas	1665	12	UCLA	1423	21	Louisville	1337	30	Villanova	1268
4	St. John's	1554	13	Princeton	1386	22	N.C. State	1326	31	Alabama	1266
5	Duke	1548		Washington	1386	23	Fordham	1319	32	Iowa	1265
6	Temple	1496	15	Purdue	1383	24	Cincinnati	1311	33	Ohio St	1264
7	Syracuse	1477	16	Utah	1376		Washington St.	1311	34	St. Joseph's-PA	1260
8	Oregon St.	1456	17	Western Ky.	1366	26	Arizona	1309	35	USC	1259
9	Penn	1454	18	West Virginia	1349	27	Texas	1296			

Top 25 Single-Season Victories

Division I schools with most victories in a season through 1997-98 (including postseason tournaments). NCAA champions in **bold** type.

		Year	Record
1	UNLV	1987	37-2
	Duke	1986	37-3
3	**Kentucky**	1948	36-3
4	Massachusetts*	1996	35-2
	Georgetown	1985	35-3
	Arizona	1988	35-3
	Kansas	1986	35-4
	Kansas	1998	35-4
	Kentucky	1998	35-4
	Oklahoma	1988	35-4
	UNLV	1990	35-5
	Kentucky	1997	35-5
13	UNLV	1991	34-1
	Duke	1992	34-2
	Kentucky	1996	34-2
	Kansas	1997	34-2
	Kentucky	1947	34-3
	Georgetown	1984	34-3
	Arkansas	1991	34-4
	N. Carolina	1993	34-4
	N. Carolina	1998	34-4
22	Indiana St.	1979	33-1
	Louisville	1980	33-3
	UNLV	1986	33-5
25	**N. Carolina**	1957	32-0
	Indiana	1976	32-0
	Kentucky	1949	32-2
	Kentucky	1951	32-2
	N. Carolina	1982	32-2
	Temple	1988	32-2
	Arkansas	1978	32-3
	Bradley	1986	32-3
	Connecticut*	1996	32-3
	Duke	1998	32-4
	Louisville	1983	32-4
	Kentucky	1986	32-4
	N. Carolina	1987	32-4
	Temple	1987	32-4
	Bradley	1950	32-5
	Connecticut	1998	32-5
	Marshall	1947	32-5
	Houston	1984	32-5
	Bradley	1951	32-6
	Louisville	1986	32-7
	Duke	1991	32-7
	Arkansas	1995	32-7

*NCAA later stripped UMass of its four 1996 tournament victories after learning that center Marcus Camby accepted gifts from an agent. UConn was stripped of its two 1996 tournament victories because two players illegally accepted plane tickets.

Associated Press Final Polls

Taken before NCAA, NIT and Collegiate Commissioner's Association (1974–75) tournaments.

The Associated Press introduced its weekly college basketball poll of sportswriters (later, sportswriters and broadcasters) during the 1948-49 season.

Since the NCAA Division I tournament has determined the national champion since 1939, the final AP poll ranks the nation's best teams through the regular season and conference tournaments.

Except for four seasons (see AP Post-Tournament Final Polls), the final AP poll has been released prior to the NCAA and NIT tournaments and has gone from a Top 10 (1949 and 1963-67) to a Top 20 (1950-62 and 1968-89) to a Top 25 (since 1990).

Tournament champions are in **bold** type.

1949

		Before Tourns	Head Coach	Final Record
1	**Kentucky**	29-1	Adolph Rupp	32-2
2	Oklahoma A&M	21-4	Hank Iba	23-5
3	Saint Louis	22-3	Eddie Hickey	22-4
4	Illinois	19-3	Harry Combes	21-4
5	Western Ky.	25-3	Ed Diddle	25-4
6	Minnesota	18-3	Ozzie Cowles	same
7	Bradley	25-6	Forddy Anderson	27-8
8	**San Francisco**	21-5	Pete Newell	25-5
9	Tulane	24-4	Cliff Wells	same
10	Bowling Green	21-6	Harold Anderson	24-7

NCAA Final Four (at Edmundson Pavilion, Seattle): **Third Place**–Illinois 57, Oregon St. 53. **Championship**–Kentucky 46, Oklahoma A&M 36.

NIT Final Four (at Madison Square Garden): **Semifinals**–San Francisco 49, Bowling Green 39; Loyola-IL 55, Bradley 50. **Third Place**–Bowling Green 82, Bradley 77. **Championship**–San Francisco 48, Loyola-IL 47.

1950

		Before Tourns	Head Coach	Final Record
1	Bradley	28-3	Forddy Anderson	32-5
2	Ohio St.	21-3	Tippy Dye	22-4
3	Kentucky	25-4	Adolph Rupp	25-5
4	Holy Cross	27-2	Buster Sheary	27-4
5	N.C. State	25-5	Everett Case	27-6
6	Duquesne	22-5	Dudey Moore	23-6
7	UCLA	24-5	John Wooden	24-7
8	Western Ky.	24-5	Ed Diddle	25-6
9	St. John's	23-4	Frank McGuire	24-5
10	La Salle	20-3	Ken Loeffler	21-4
11	Villanova	25-4	Al Severance	same
12	San Francisco	19-6	Pete Newell	19-7
13	LIU-Brooklyn	20-4	Clair Bee	20-5
14	Kansas St.	17-7	Jack Gardner	same
15	Arizona	26-4	Fred Enke	26-5
16	Wisconsin	17-5	Bud Foster	same
17	San Jose St.	21-7	Walter McPherson	same
18	Washington St.	19-13	Jack Friel	same
19	Kansas	14-11	Phog Allen	same
20	Indiana	17-5	Branch McCracken	same

Note: Unranked **CCNY**, coached by Nat Holman, won both the NCAAs and NIT. The Beavers entered the postseason at 17-5 and had a final record of 24-5.

NCAA Final Four (at Madison Square Garden): **Third Place**–N. Carolina St. 53, Baylor 41. **Championship**–CCNY 71, Bradley 68.

NIT Final Four (at Madison Square Garden): **Semifinals**–Bradley 83, St. John's 72; CCNY 62, Duquesne 52. **Third Place**–St. John's 69, Duquesne 67 (OT). **Championship**–CCNY 69, Bradley 61.

1951

		Before Tourns	Head Coach	Final Record
1	**Kentucky**	28-2	Adolph Rupp	32-2
2	Oklahoma A&M	27-4	Hank Iba	29-6
3	Columbia	22-0	Lou Rossini	22-1
4	Kansas St.	22-3	Jack Gardner	25-4
5	Illinois	19-4	Harry Combes	22-5
6	Bradley	32-6	Forddy Anderson	same
7	Indiana	19-3	Branch McCracken	same
8	N.C. State	29-4	Everett Case	30-7
9	St. John's	22-3	Frank McGuire	26-5
10	Saint Louis	21-7	Eddie Hickey	22-8
11	**BYU**	22-8	Stan Watts	26-10
12	Arizona	24-4	Fred Enke	24-6
13	Dayton	24-4	Tom Blackburn	27-5
14	Toledo	23-8	Jerry Bush	same
15	Washington	22-5	Tippy Dye	24-6
16	Murray St.	21-6	Harlan Hodges	same
17	Cincinnati	18-3	John Wiethe	18-4
18	Siena	19-8	Dan Cunha	same
19	USC	21-6	Forrest Twogood	same
20	Villanova	25-6	Al Severance	25-7

NCAA Final Four (at Williams Arena, Minneapolis): **Third Place**–Illinois 61, Oklahoma St. 46. **Championship**–Kentucky 68, Kansas St. 58.

NIT Final Four (at Madison Sq. Garden): **Semifinals**–Dayton 69, St. John's 62 (OT); BYU 69, Seton Hall 59. **Third Place**–St. John's 70, Seton Hall 68 (2 OT). **Championship**–BYU 62, Dayton 43.

1952

		Before Tourns	Head Coach	Final Record
1	Kentucky	28-2	Adolph Rupp	29-3
2	Illinois	19-3	Harry Combes	22-4
3	Kansas St.	19-5	Jack Gardner	same
4	Duquesne	21-1	Dudey Moore	23-4
5	Saint Louis	22-6	Eddie Hickey	23-8
6	Washington	25-6	Tippy Dye	same
7	Iowa	19-3	Bucky O'Connor	same
8	**Kansas**	24-3	Phog Allen	28-3
9	West Virginia	23-4	Red Brown	same
10	St. John's	22-3	Frank McGuire	25-5
11	Dayton	24-3	Tom Blackburn	28-5
12	Duke	24-6	Harold Bradley	same
13	Holy Cross	23-3	Buster Sheary	24-4
14	Seton Hall	25-2	Honey Russell	25-3
15	St. Bonaventure	19-5	Ed Melvin	21-6
16	Wyoming	27-6	Everett Shelton	28-7
17	Louisville	20-5	Peck Hickman	20-6
18	Seattle	29-7	Al Brightman	29-8
19	UCLA	19-10	John Wooden	19-12
20	SW Texas St.	30-1	Milton Jowers	same

Note: Unranked La Salle, coached by Ken Loeffler, won the NIT. The Explorers entered the postseason at 21-7 and had a final record of 25-7.

NCAA Final Four (at Edmundson Pavillion, Seattle): **Semifinals**–St. John's 61, Illinois 59; Kansas 74, Santa Clara 59. **Third Place**–Illinois 67, Santa Clara 64. **Championship**–Kansas 80, St. John's 63.

NIT Final Four (at Madison Sq. Garden): **Semifinals**–La Salle 59, Duquesne 46; Dayton 69, St. Bonaventure 62. **Third Place**–St. Bonaventure 48, Duquesne 34. **Championship**–La Salle 75, Dayton 64.

Associated Press Final Polls (Cont.)

1953

		Before Tourns	Head Coach	Final Record
1	**Indiana**	18-3	Branch McCracken	23-3
2	La Salle	25-2	Ken Loeffler	25-3
3	**Seton Hall**	28-2	Honey Russell	31-2
4	Washington	27-2	Tippy Dye	30-3
5	LSU	22-1	Harry Rabenhorst	24-3
6	Kansas	16-5	Phog Allen	19-6
7	Oklahoma A&M	22-6	Hank Iba	23-7
	Kansas St.	17-4	Jack Gardner	same
9	Western Ky.	25-5	Ed Diddle	25-6
10	Illinois	18-4	Harry Combes	same
11	Oklahoma City	18-4	Doyle Parrick	18-6
12	N.C. State	26-6	Everett Case	same
13	Notre Dame	17-4	John Jordan	19-5
14	Louisville	21-5	Peck Hickman	22-6
	Seattle	27-3	Al Brightman	29-4
16	Miami-OH	17-5	Bill Rohr	17-6
17	Eastern Ky.	16-8	Paul McBrayer	16-9
18	Duquesne	18-7	Dudey Moore	21-8
	Navy	16-4	Ben Carnevale	16-5
20	Holy Cross	18-5	Buster Sheary	20-6

NCAA Final Four (at Municipal Auditorium, Kansas City): **Semifinals**–Indiana 80, LSU 67; Kansas 79, Washington 53. **Third Place**–Washington 88, LSU 69. **Championship**–Indiana 69, Kansas 68.

NIT Final Four (at Madison Sq. Garden): **Semifinals**–Seton Hall 74, Manhattan 56; St. John's 64, Duquesne 55. **Third Place**–Duquesne 81, Manhattan 67. **Championship**–Seton Hall 58, St. John's 46.

1954

		Before Tourns	Head Coach	Final Record
1	Kentucky	25-0	Adolph Rupp	same*
2	Indiana	19-3	Branch McCracken	20-4
3	Duquesne	24-2	Dudey Moore	26-3
4	Western Ky.	28-1	Ed Diddle	29-3
5	Oklahoma A&M	23-4	Hank Iba	24-5
6	Notre Dame	20-2	John Jordan	22-3
7	Kansas	16-5	Phog Allen	same
8	**Holy Cross**	23-2	Buster Sheary	26-2
9	LSU	21-3	Harry Rabenhorst	21-5
10	**La Salle**	21-4	Ken Loeffler	26-4
11	Iowa	17-5	Bucky O'Connor	same
12	Duke	22-6	Harold Bradley	same
13	Colorado A&M	22-5	Bill Strannigan	22-7
14	Illinois	17-5	Harry Combes	same
15	Wichita	27-3	Ralph Miller	27-4
16	Seattle	26-1	Al Brightman	26-2
17	N.C. State	26-6	Everett Case	28-7
18	Dayton	24-6	Tom Blackburn	25-7
	Minnesota	17-5	Ozzie Cowles	same
20	Oregon St.	19-10	Slats Gill	same
	UCLA	18-7	John Wooden	same
	USC	17-12	Forrest Twogood	19-14

*Kentucky turned down invitation to NCAA tournament after NCAA declared seniors Cliff Hagan, Frank Ramsey and Lou Tsioropoulos ineligible for postseason play.

NCAA Final Four (at Municipal Auditorium, Kansas City): **Semifinals**–La Salle 69, Penn St. 54; Bradley 74, USC 72. **Third Place**–Penn St. 70, USC 61. **Championship**–La Salle 92, Bradley 76.

NIT Final Four (at Madison Square Garden): **Semifinals**–Duquesne 66, Niagara 51; Holy Cross 75, Western Ky. 69. **Third Place**–Niagara 71, Western Ky. 65. **Championship**–Holy Cross 71, Duquesne 62.

1955

		Before Tourns	Head Coach	Final Record
1	**San Francisco**	23-1	Phil Woolpert	28-1
2	Kentucky	22-2	Adolph Rupp	23-3
3	La Salle	22-4	Ken Loeffler	26-5
4	N.C. State	28-4	Everett Case	same
5	Iowa	17-5	Bucky O'Connor	19-7
6	**Duquesne**	19-4	Dudey Moore	22-4
7	Utah	23-3	Jack Gardner	24-4
8	Marquette	22-2	Jack Nagle	24-3
9	Dayton	23-3	Tom Blackburn	25-4
10	Oregon St.	21-7	Slats Gill	22-8
11	Minnesota	15-7	Ozzie Cowles	same
12	Alabama	19-5	Johnny Dee	same
13	UCLA	21-5	John Wooden	same
14	G. Washington	24-6	Bill Reinhart	same
15	Colorado	16-5	Bebe Lee	19-6
16	Tulsa	20-6	Clarence Iba	21-7
17	Vanderbilt	16-6	Bob Polk	same
18	Illinois	17-5	Harry Combes	same
19	West Virginia	19-10	Fred Schaus	19-11
20	Saint Louis	19-7	Eddie Hickey	20-8

NCAA Final Four (at Municipal Auditorium, Kansas City): **Semifinals**–La Salle 76, Iowa 73; San Francisco 62, Colorado 50. **Third Place**–Colorado 75, Iowa 74. **Championship**–San Francisco 77, La Salle 63.

NIT Final Four (at Madison Square Garden): **Semifinals**–Dayton 79, St. Francis-PA 73 (OT); Duquesne 65, Cincinnati 51. **Third Place**–Cincinnati 96, St. Francis-PA 91 (OT). **Championship**–Duquesne 70, Dayton 58.

1956

		Before Tourns	Head Coach	Final Record
1	**San Francisco**	25-0	Phil Woolpert	29-0
2	N.C. State	24-3	Everett Case	24-4
3	Dayton	23-3	Tom Blackburn	25-4
4	Iowa	17-5	Bucky O'Connor	20-6
5	Alabama	21-3	Johnny Dee	same
6	**Louisville**	23-3	Peck Hickman	26-3
7	SMU	22-2	Doc Hayes	25-4
8	UCLA	21-5	John Wooden	22-6
9	Kentucky	19-5	Adolph Rupp	20-6
10	Illinois	18-4	Harry Combes	same
11	Oklahoma City	18-6	Abe Lemons	20-7
12	Vanderbilt	19-4	Bob Polk	same
13	North Carolina	18-5	Frank McGuire	same
14	Holy Cross	22-4	Roy Leenig	22-5
15	Temple	23-3	Harry Litwack	27-4
16	Wake Forest	19-9	Murray Greason	same
17	Duke	19-7	Harold Bradley	same
18	Utah	21-5	Jack Gardner	22-6
19	Oklahoma A&M	18-8	Hank Iba	18-9
20	West Virginia	21-8	Fred Schaus	21-9

NCAA Final Four (at McGaw Hall, Evanston, IL): **Semifinals**–Iowa 83, Temple 76; San Francisco 76, SMU 68. **Third Place**–Temple 90, SMU 81. **Championship**–San Francisco 83, Iowa 71.

NIT Final Four (at Madison Square Garden): **Semifinals**–Dayton 89, St. Francis-NY 58; Louisville 89, St. Joseph's-PA 79. **Third Place**–St. Joseph's-PA 93, St. Francis-NY 82. **Championship**–Louisville 93, Dayton 80.

1957

		Before Tourns	Head Coach	Final Record
1	**N. Carolina**	27-0	Frank McGuire	32-0
2	Kansas	21-2	Dick Harp	24-3
3	Kentucky	22-4	Adolph Rupp	23-5
4	SMU	21-3	Doc Hayes	22-4
5	Seattle	24-2	John Castellani	24-3
6	Louisville	21-5	Peck Hickman	same
7	West Va.	25-4	Fred Schaus	25-5
8	Vanderbilt	17-5	Bob Polk	same
9	Oklahoma City	17-8	Abe Lemons	19-9
10	Saint Louis	19-7	Eddie Hickey	19-9
11	Michigan St.	14-8	Forddy Anderson	16-10
12	Memphis St.	21-5	Bob Vanatta	24-6
13	California	20-4	Pete Newell	21-5
14	UCLA	22-4	John Wooden	same
15	Mississippi St.	17-8	Babe McCarthy	same
16	Idaho St.	24-2	John Grayson	25-4
17	Notre Dame	18-7	John Jordan	20-8
18	Wake Forest	19-9	Murray Greason	same
19	Canisius	20-5	Joe Curran	22-6
20	Oklahoma A&M	17-9	Hank Iba	same

Note: Unranked **Bradley**, coached by Chuck Orsborn, won the NIT. The Braves entered the tourney at 19-7 and had a final record of 22-7.

NCAA Final Four (at Municipal Auditorium, Kansas City): **Semifinals**–North Carolina 74, Michigan St. 70 (3 OT); Kansas 80, San Francisco 56. **Third Place**–San Francisco 67, Michigan St. 60. **Championship**–North Carolina 54, Kansas 53 (3 OT).

NIT Final Four (at Madison Square Garden): **Semifinals**–Memphis St. 80, St. Bonaventure 78; Bradley 78, Temple 66. **Third Place**–Temple 67, St. Bonaventure 50. **Championship**–Bradley 84, Memphis St. 83.

1958

		Before Tourns	Head Coach	Final Record
1	West Virginia	26-1	Fred Schaus	26-2
2	Cincinnati	24-2	George Smith	25-3
3	Kansas St.	20-3	Tex Winter	22-5
4	San Francisco	24-1	Phil Woolpert	25-2
5	Temple	24-2	Harry Litwack	27-3
6	Maryland	20-6	Bud Millikan	22-7
7	Kansas	18-5	Dick Harp	same
8	Notre Dame	22-4	John Jordan	24-5
9	**Kentucky**	19-6	Adolph Rupp	23-6
10	Duke	18-7	Harold Bradley	same
11	Dayton	23-3	Tom Blackburn	25-4
12	Indiana	12-10	Branch McCracken	13-11
13	North Carolina	19-7	Frank McGuire	same
14	Bradley	20-6	Chuck Orsborn	20-7
15	Mississippi St.	20-5	Babe McCarthy	same
16	Auburn	16-6	Joel Eaves	same
17	Michigan St.	16-6	Forddy Anderson	same
18	Seattle	20-6	John Castellani	24-7
19	Oklahoma St.	19-7	Hank Iba	21-8
20	N.C. State	18-6	Everett Case	same

Note: Unranked **Xavier-OH**, coached by Jim McCafferty, won the NIT. The Musketeers entered the tourney at 15-11 and had a final record of 19-11.

NCAA Final Four (at Freedom Hall, Louisville): **Semifinals**–Kentucky 61, Temple 60; Seattle 73, Kansas St. 51. **Third Place**–Temple 67, Kansas St. 57. **Championship**–Kentucky 84, Seattle 72.

NIT Final Four (at Madison Square Garden): **Semifinals**–Dayton 80, St. John's 56; Xavier-OH 72, St. Bonaventure 53. **Third Place**–St. Bonaventure 84, St. John's 69. **Championship**–Xavier-OH 78, Dayton 74 (OT).

1959

		Before Tourns	Head Coach	Final Record
1	Kansas St.	24-1	Tex Winter	25-2
2	Kentucky	23-2	Adolph Rupp	24-3
3	Mississippi St.	24-1	Babe McCarthy	same*
4	Bradley	23-3	Chuck Orsborn	25-4
5	Cincinnati	23-3	George Smith	26-4
6	N.C. State	22-4	Everett Case	same
7	Michigan St.	18-3	Forddy Anderson	19-4
8	Auburn	20-2	Joel Eaves	same
9	North Carolina	20-4	Frank McGuire	20-5
10	West Virginia	25-4	Fred Schaus	29-5
11	**California**	21-4	Pete Newell	25-4
12	Saint Louis	20-5	John Benington	20-6
13	Seattle	23-6	Vince Cazzetta	same
14	St. Joseph's-PA	22-3	Jack Ramsay	22-5
15	St. Mary's-CA	18-5	Jim Weaver	19-6
16	TCU	19-5	Buster Brannon	20-6
17	Oklahoma City	20-6	Abe Lemons	20-7
18	Utah	21-5	Jack Gardner	21-7
19	St. Bonaventure	20-2	Eddie Donovan	20-3
20	Marquette	22-4	Eddie Hickey	23-6

*Mississippi St. turned down invitation to NCAA tournament because it was an integrated event.

Note: Unranked **St. John's**, coached by Joe Lapchick, won the NIT. The Redmen entered the tourney at 16-6 and had a final record of 20-6.

NCAA Final Four (at Freedom Hall, Louisville): **Semifinals**–West Virginia 94, Louisville 79; California 64, Cincinnati 58. **Third Place**–Cincinnati 98, Louisville 85. **Championship**–California 71, West Virginia 70.

NIT Final Four (at Madison Square Garden): **Semifinals**–Bradley 59, NYU 57; St. John's 76, Providence 55. **Third Place**–NYU 71, Providence 57. **Championship**–St. John's 76, Bradley 71 (OT).

1960

		Before Tourns	Head Coach	Final Record
1	Cincinnati	25-1	George Smith	28-2
2	California	24-1	Pete Newell	28-2
3	**Ohio St.**	21-3	Fred Taylor	25-3
4	**Bradley**	24-2	Chuck Orsborn	27-2
5	West Virginia	24-4	Fred Schaus	26-5
6	Utah	24-2	Jack Gardner	26-3
7	Indiana	20-4	Branch McCracken	same
8	Utah St.	22-4	Cecil Baker	24-5
9	St. Bonaventure	19-3	Eddie Donovan	21-5
10	Miami-FL	23-3	Bruce Hale	23-4
11	Auburn	19-3	Joel Eaves	same
12	NYU	19-4	Lou Rossini	22-5
13	Georgia Tech	21-5	Whack Hyder	22-6
14	Providence	21-4	Joe Mullaney	24-5
15	Saint Louis	19-7	John Benington	19-8
16	Holy Cross	20-5	Roy Leenig	20-6
17	Villanova	19-5	Al Severance	20-6
18	Duke	15-10	Vic Bubas	17-11
19	Wake Forest	21-7	Bones McKinney	same
20	St. John's	17-7	Joe Lapchick	17-8

NCAA Final Four (at the Cow Palace, San Fran.): **Semifinals**–Ohio St. 76, NYU 54; California 77, Cincinnati 69. **Third Place**–Cincinnati 95, NYU 71. **Championship**–Ohio St. 75, California 55.

NIT Final Four (at Madison Square Garden): **Semifinals**–Bradley 82, St. Bonaventure 71; Providence 68, Utah St. 62. **Third Place**–Utah St. 99, St. Bonaventure 93. **Championship**–Bradley 88, Providence 72.

Associated Press Final Polls (Cont.)

1961

		Before Tourns	Head Coach	Final Record
1	Ohio St.	24-0	Fred Taylor	27-1
2	**Cincinnati**	23-3	Ed Jucker	27-3
3	St. Bonaventure	22-3	Eddie Donovan	24-4
4	Kansas St.	22-3	Tex Winter	23-4
5	North Carolina	19-4	Frank McGuire	same
6	Bradley	21-5	Chuck Orsborn	same
7	USC	20-6	Forrest Twogood	21-8
8	Iowa	18-6	S. Scheuerman	same
9	West Virginia	23-4	George King	same
10	Duke	22-6	Vic Bubas	same
11	Utah	21-6	Jack Gardner	23-8
12	Texas Tech	14-9	Polk Robison	15-10
13	Niagara	16-4	Taps Gallagher	16-5
14	Memphis St.	20-2	Bob Vanatta	20-3
15	Wake Forest	17-10	Bones McKinney	19-11
16	St. John's	20-4	Joe Lapchick	20-5
17	St. Joseph's-PA	22-4	Jack Ramsay	25-5
18	Drake	19-7	Maury John	same
19	Holy Cross	19-4	Roy Leenig	22-5
20	Kentucky	18-8	Adolph Rupp	19-9

Note: Unranked **Providence**, coached by Joe Mullaney, won the NIT. The Friars entered the tourney at 20-5 and had a final record of 24-5.

NCAA Final Four (at Municipal Auditorium, Kansas City): **Semifinals**–Ohio St. 95, St. Joseph's-PA 69; Cincinnati 82, Utah 67. **Third Place**–St. Joseph's-PA 127, Utah 120 (4 OT). **Championship**–Cincinnati 70, Ohio St. 65 (OT).

NIT Final Four (at Madison Square Garden) **Semifinals**–St. Louis 67, Dayton 60; Providence 90, Holy Cross 83 (OT). **Third Place**–Holy Cross 85, Dayton 67. **Championship**–Providence 62, St. Louis 59.

1962

		Before Tourns	Head Coach	Final Record
1	Ohio St.	23-1	Fred Taylor	26-2
2	**Cincinnati**	25-2	Ed Jucker	29-2
3	Kentucky	22-2	Adolph Rupp	23-3
4	Mississippi St.	19-6	Babe McCarthy	same
5	Bradley	21-6	Chuck Orsborn	21-7
6	Kansas St.	22-3	Tex Winter	same
7	Utah	23-3	Jack Gardner	same
8	Bowling Green	21-3	Harold Anderson	same
9	Colorado	18-6	Sox Walseth	19-7
10	Duke	20-5	Vic Bubas	same
11	Loyola-IL	21-3	George Ireland	23-4
12	St. John's	19-4	Joe Lapchick	21-5
13	Wake Forest	18-8	Bones McKinney	22-9
14	Oregon St.	22-4	Slats Gill	24-5
15	West Virginia	24-5	George King	24-6
16	Arizona St.	23-3	Ned Wulk	23-4
17	Duquesne	20-5	Red Manning	22-7
18	Utah St.	21-5	Ladell Andersen	22-7
19	UCLA	16-9	John Wooden	18-11
20	Villanova	19-6	Jack Kraft	21-7

Note: Unranked **Dayton**, coached by Tom Blackburn, won the NIT. The Flyers entered the tourney at 20-6 and had a final record of 24-6.

NCAA Final Four (at Freedom Hall, Louisville): **Semifinals**–Ohio St. 84, Wake Forest 68; Cincinnati 72, UCLA 70. **Third Place**–Wake Forest 82, UCLA 80. **Championship**–Cincinnati 71, Ohio St. 59.

NIT Final Four (at Madison Square Garden): **Semifinals**–Dayton 98, Loyola-IL 82; St. John's 76, Duquesne 65. **Third Place**–Loyola-IL 95, Duquesne 84. **Championship**–Dayton 73, St. John's 67.

1963

AP ranked only 10 teams from the 1962-63 season through 1967-68.

		Before Tourns	Head Coach	Final Record
1	Cincinnati	23-1	Ed Jucker	26-2
2	Duke	24-2	Vic Bubas	27-3
3	**Loyola-IL**	24-2	George Ireland	29-2
4	Arizona St.	24-2	Ned Wulk	26-3
5	Wichita	19-7	Ralph Miller	19-8
6	Mississippi St.	21-5	Babe McCarthy	22-6
7	Ohio St.	20-4	Fred Taylor	same
8	Illinois	19-5	Harry Combes	20-6
9	NYU	17-3	Lou Rossini	18-5
10	Colorado	18-6	Sox Walseth	19-7

Note: Unranked **Providence**, coached by Joe Mullaney, won the NIT. The Friars entered the tourney at 21-4 and had a final record of 24-4.

NCAA Final Four (at Freedom Hall, Louisville): **Semifinals**–Loyola-IL 94, Duke 75; Cincinnati 80, Oregon St. 46. **Third Place**–Duke 85, Oregon St. 63. **Championship**–Loyola-IL 60, Cincinnati 58 (OT).

NIT Final Four (at Madison Square Garden): **Semifinals**–Providence 70, Marquette 64; Canisius 61, Villanova 46. **Third Place**–Marquette 66, Villanova 58. **Championship**–Providence 81, Canisius 66.

1964

AP ranked only 10 teams from the 1962-63 season through 1967-68.

		Before Tourns	Head Coach	Final Record
1	**UCLA**	26-0	John Wooden	30-0
2	Michigan	20-4	Dave Strack	23-5
3	Duke	23-4	Vic Bubas	26-5
4	Kentucky	21-4	Adolph Rupp	21-6
5	Wichita St.	22-5	Ralph Miller	23-6
6	Oregon St.	25-3	Slats Gill	25-4
7	Villanova	22-3	Jack Kraft	24-4
8	Loyola-IL	20-5	George Ireland	22-6
9	DePaul	21-3	Ray Meyer	21-4
10	Davidson	22-4	Lefty Driesell	same

Note: Unranked **Bradley**, coached by Chuck Orsborn, won the NIT. The Braves entered the tourney at 20-6 and finished with a record of 23-6.

NCAA Final Four (at Municipal Auditorium, Kansas City): **Semifinals**–Duke 91, Michigan 80; UCLA 90, Kansas St. 84. **Third Place**–Michigan 100, Kansas St. 90. **Championship**–UCLA 98, Duke 83.

NIT Final Four (at Madison Square Garden): **Semifinals**–New Mexico 72, NYU 65; Bradley 67, Army 52. **Third Place**–Army 60, NYU 59. **Championship**–Bradley 86, New Mexico 54.

Undefeated National Champions

Seven NCAA seasons have ended with an undefeated national champion. UCLA has accomplished the feat four times.

Year		W-L
1956	San Francisco	29-0
1957	North Carolina	32-0
1964	UCLA	30-0
1967	UCLA	30-0
1972	UCLA	30-0
1973	UCLA	30-0
1976	Indiana	32-0

1965

AP ranked only 10 teams from the 1962-63 season through 1967-68.

		Before Tourns	Head Coach	Final Record
1	Michigan	21-3	Dave Strack	24-4
2	**UCLA**	24-2	John Wooden	28-2
3	St. Joseph's-PA	25-1	Jack Ramsay	26-3
4	Providence	22-1	Joe Mullaney	24-2
5	Vanderbilt	23-3	Roy Skinner	24-4
6	Davidson	24-2	Lefty Driesell	same
7	Minnesota	19-5	John Kundla	same
8	Villanova	21-4	Jack Kraft	23-5
9	BYU	21-5	Stan Watts	21-7
10	Duke	20-5	Vic Bubas	same

Note: Unranked **St. John's**, coached by Joe Lapchick, won the NIT. The Redmen entered the tourney at 17-8 and finished with a record of 21-8.

NCAA Final Four (at Memorial Coliseum, Portland, OR): **Semifinals**–Michigan 93, Princeton 76; UCLA 108, Wichita St. 89. **Third Place**–Princeton 118, Wichita St. 82. **Championship**–UCLA 91, Michigan 80.

NIT Final Four (at Madison Square Garden): **Semifinals**–Villanova 91, NYU 69; St. John's 67, Army 60. **Third Place**–Army 75, NYU 74. **Championship**– St. John's 55, Villanova 51.

1966

AP ranked only 10 teams from the 1962-63 season through 1967-68.

		Before Tourns	Head Coach	Final Record
1	Kentucky	24-1	Adolph Rupp	27-2
2	Duke	23-3	Vic Bubas	26-4
3	**Texas Western**	23-1	Don Haskins	28-1
4	Kansas	22-3	Ted Owens	23-4
5	St. Joseph's-PA	22-4	Jack Ramsay	24-5
6	Loyola-IL	22-2	George Ireland	22-3
7	Cincinnati	21-5	Tay Baker	21-7
8	Vanderbilt	22-4	Roy Skinner	same
9	Michigan	17-7	Dave Strack	18-8
10	Western Ky.	23-2	Johnny Oldham	25-3

Note: Unranked **BYU**, coached by Stan Watts, won the NIT. The Cougars entered the tourney at 17-5 and had a final record of 20-5.

NCAA Final Four (at Cole Fieldhouse, College Park, MD): **Semifinals**–Kentucky 83, Duke 79; Texas Western 85, Utah 78. **Third Place**–Duke 79, Utah 77. **Championship**–Texas Western 72, Kentucky 65.

NIT Final Four (at Madison Square Garden): **Semifinals**–BYU 66, Army 60; NYU 69, Villanova 63. **Third Place**–Villanova 76, Army 65. **Championship**–BYU 97, NYU 84.

1967

AP ranked only 10 teams from the 1962-63 season through 1967-68.

		Before Tourns	Head Coach	Final Record
1	**UCLA**	26-0	John Wooden	30-0
2	Louisville	23-3	Peck Hickman	23-5
3	Kansas	22-3	Ted Owens	23-4
4	North Carolina	24-4	Dean Smith	26-6
5	Princeton	23-2	B. van Breda Kolff	25-3
6	Western Ky.	23-2	Johnny Oldham	23-3
7	Houston	23-3	Guy Lewis	27-4
8	Tennessee	21-5	Ray Mears	21-7
9	Boston College	19-2	Bob Cousy	21-3
10	Texas Western	20-5	Don Haskins	22-6

Note: Unranked **Southern Illinois**, coached by Jack Hartman, won the NIT. The Salukis entered the tourney at 20-2 and had a final record of 24-2.

NCAA Final Four (at Freedom Hall, Louisville): **Semifinals**–Dayton 76, N. Carolina 62; UCLA 73, Houston 58. **Third Place**–Houston 84, N. Carolina 62. **Championship**–UCLA 79, Dayton 64.

NIT Final Four (at Madison Square Garden): **Semifinals**–Marquette 83, Marshall 78; Southern Ill. 79, Rutgers 70. **Third Place**–Rutgers 93, Marshall 76. **Championship**–Southern Ill. 71, Marquette 56.

1968

AP ranked only 10 teams from the 1962-63 season through 1967-68.

		Before Tourns	Head Coach	Final Record
1	Houston	28-0	Guy Lewis	31-2
2	**UCLA**	25-1	John Wooden	29-1
3	St. Bonaventure	22-0	Larry Weise	23-2
4	North Carolina	25-3	Dean Smith	28-4
5	Kentucky	21-4	Adolph Rupp	22-5
6	New Mexico	23-3	Bob King	23-5
7	Columbia	21-4	Jack Rohan	23-5
8	Davidson	22-4	Lefty Driesell	24-5
9	Louisville	20-6	John Dromo	21-7
10	Duke	21-5	Vic Bubas	22-6

Note: Unranked **Dayton**, coached by Don Donoher, won the NIT. The Flyers entered the tourney at 17-9 and had a final record of 21-9.

NCAA Final Four (at the Sports Arena, Los Angeles): **Semifinals**–N. Carolina 80, Ohio St. 66; UCLA 101, Houston 69. **Third Place**–Ohio St. 89, Houston 85. **Championship**–UCLA 78, N. Carolina 55.

NIT Final Four (at Madison Square Garden): **Semifinals**–Dayton 76, Notre Dame 74 (OT); Kansas 58, St. Peter's 46. **Third Place**–Notre Dame 81, St.Peter's 78. **Championship**–Dayton 61, Kansas 48.

All-Time AP Top 20

The composite AP Top 20 from the 1948-49 season through 1997-98, based on the final regular season rankings of each year. The final AP poll has been taken before the NCAA and NIT tournaments each season since 1949 except in 1953 and '54 and again in 1974 and '75 when the final poll came out after the postseason. Team point totals are based on 20 points for all 1st place finishes, 19 for each 2nd, etc. Also listed are the number of times ranked No.1 by AP going into the tournaments, and times ranked in the pre-tournament Top 10 and Top 20.

		Pts	No.1	Top 10	Top 20
1	Kentucky	568	7	32	37
2	North Carolina	467	4	26	33
3	UCLA	435	7	22	32
4	Duke	317	2	18	27
5	Kansas	293	1	16	23
6	Indiana	290	4	16	22
7	Louisville	233	0	11	22
8	Cincinnati	197	2	9	14
9	Notre Dame	195	0	13	17
10	Michigan	191	2	10	14
11	N.C. State	176	1	9	16
12	UNLV	173	2	8	13
13	Marquette	166	0	11	15
14	Illinois	164	0	8	18
15	Arkansas	158	0	9	13
16	Arizona	157	0	7	14
17	Syracuse	150	0	9	15
18	Ohio St.	149	2	9	10
19	Kansas St	147	1	8	12
20	DePaul	141	2	8	10

Associated Press Final Polls (Cont.)

1969

		Before Tourns	Head Coach	Final Record
1	**UCLA**	25-1	John Wooden	29-1
2	La Salle	23-1	Tom Gola	same*
3	Santa Clara	26-1	Dick Garibaldi	27-2
4	North Carolina	25-3	Dean Smith	27-5
5	Davidson	24-2	Lefty Driesell	26-3
6	Purdue	20-4	George King	23-5
7	Kentucky	22-4	Adolph Rupp	23-5
8	St. John's	22-4	Lou Carnesecca	23-6
9	Duquesne	19-4	Red Manning	21-5
10	Villanova	21-4	Jack Kraft	21-5
11	Drake	23-4	Maury John	26-5
12	New Mexico St.	23-3	Lou Henson	24-5
13	South Carolina	20-6	Frank McGuire	21-7
14	Marquette	22-4	Al McGuire	24-5
15	Louisville	20-5	John Dromo	21-6
16	Boston College	21-3	Bob Cousy	24-4
17	Notre Dame	20-6	Johnny Dee	20-7
18	Colorado	20-6	Sox Walseth	21-7
19	Kansas	20-6	Ted Owens	20-7
20	Illinois	19-5	Harvey Schmidt	same

*On probation

Note: Unranked **Temple**, coached by Harry Litwack, won the NIT. The Owls entered the tourney at 18-8 and finished with a record of 22-8.

NCAA Final Four (at Freedom Hall, Louisville): **Semifinals**–Purdue 92, N. Carolina 65; UCLA 85, Drake 82. **Third Place**–Drake 104, N. Carolina 84. **Championship**–UCLA 92, Purdue 72.

NIT Final Four (at Madison Square Garden): **Semifinals**–Temple 63, Tennessee 58; Boston College 73, Army 61. **Third Place**–Tennessee 64, Army 52. **Championship**–Temple 89, Boston College 76.

1970

		Before Tourns	Head Coach	Final Record
1	Kentucky	25-1	Adolph Rupp	26-2
2	**UCLA**	24-2	John Wooden	28-2
3	St. Bonaventure	22-1	Larry Weise	25-3
4	Jacksonville	23-1	Joe Williams	27-2
5	New Mexico St.	23-2	Lou Henson	27-3
6	South Carolina	25-3	Frank McGuire	25-3
7	Iowa	19-4	Ralph Miller	20-5
8	**Marquette**	22-3	Al McGuire	26-3
9	Notre Dame	20-6	Johnny Dee	21-8
10	N.C. State	22-6	Norm Sloan	23-7
11	Florida St.	23-3	Hugh Durham	23-3
12	Houston	24-3	Guy Lewis	25-5
13	Penn	25-1	Dick Harter	25-2
14	Drake	21-6	Maury John	22-7
15	Davidson	22-4	Terry Holland	22-5
16	Utah St.	20-6	Ladell Andersen	22-7
17	Niagara	21-5	Frank Layden	22-7
18	Western Ky.	22-2	John Oldham	22-3
19	Long Beach St.	23-3	Jerry Tarkanian	24-5
20	USC	18-8	Bob Boyd	18-8

NCAA Final Four (at Cole Fieldhouse, College Park, MD): **Semifinals**–Jacksonville 91, St. Bonaventure 83; UCLA 93, New Mexico St. 77. **Third Place**–N. Mexico St. 79, St. Bonaventure 73. **Championship**–UCLA 80, Jacksonville 69.

NIT Final Four (at Madison Square Garden): **Semifinals**–St. John's 60, Army 59; Marquette 101, LSU 79. **Third Place**–Army 75, LSU 68. **Championship**–Marquette 65, St. John's 53.

1971

		Before Tourns	Head Coach	Final Record
1	**UCLA**	25-1	John Wooden	29-1
2	Marquette	26-0	Al McGuire	28-1
3	Penn	26-0	Dick Harter	28-1
4	Kansas	25-1	Ted Owens	27-3
5	USC	24-2	Bob Boyd	24-2
6	South Carolina	23-4	Frank McGuire	23-6
7	Western Ky.	20-5	John Oldham	24-6
8	Kentucky	22-4	Adolph Rupp	22-6
9	Fordham	25-1	Digger Phelps	26-3
10	Ohio St.	19-5	Fred Taylor	20-6
11	Jacksonville	22-3	Tom Wasdin	22-4
12	Notre Dame	19-7	Johnny Dee	20-9
13	**N. Carolina**	22-6	Dean Smith	26-6
14	Houston	20-6	Guy Lewis	22-7
15	Duquesne	21-3	Red Manning	21-4
16	Long Beach St.	21-4	Jerry Tarkanian	23-5
17	Tennessee	20-6	Ray Mears	21-7
18	Villanova	19-5	Jack Kraft	23-6
19	Drake	20-7	Maury John	21-8
20	BYU	18-9	Stan Watts	18-11

NCAA Final Four (at the Astrodome, Houston): **Semifinals**–Villanova 92, Western Ky. 89 (2 OT); UCLA 68, Kansas 60. **Third Place**–Western Ky. 77, Kansas 75. **Championship**–UCLA 68, Villanova 62.

NIT Final Four (at Madison Square Garden): **Semifinals**–N. Carolina 73, Duke 69; Ga.Tech 76, St. Bonaventure 71 (2 OT). **Third Place**–St. Bonaventure 92, Duke 88 (OT). **Championship**–N. Carolina 84, Ga.Tech 66.

1972

		Before Tourns	Head Coach	Final Record
1	**UCLA**	26-0	John Wooden	30-0
2	North Carolina	23-4	Dean Smith	26-5
3	Penn	23-2	Chuck Daly	25-3
4	Louisville	23-4	Denny Crum	26-5
5	Long Beach St.	23-3	Jerry Tarkanian	25-4
6	South Carolina	22-4	Frank McGuire	24-5
7	Marquette	24-2	Al McGuire	25-4
8	SW Louisiana	23-3	Beryl Shipley	25-4
9	BYU	21-4	Stan Watts	21-5
10	Florida St.	23-5	Hugh Durham	27-6
11	Minnesota	17-6	Bill Musselman	18-7
12	Marshall	23-3	Carl Tacy	23-4
13	Memphis St.	21-6	Gene Bartow	21-7
14	**Maryland**	23-5	Lefty Driesell	27-5
15	Villanova	19-6	Jack Kraft	20-8
16	Oral Roberts	25-1	Ken Trickey	26-2
17	Indiana	17-7	Bob Knight	17-8
18	Kentucky	20-6	Adolph Rupp	21-7
19	Ohio St.	18-6	Fred Taylor	same
20	Virginia	21-6	Bill Gibson	21-7

NCAA Final Four (at the Sports Arena, Los Angeles): **Semifinals**–Florida St. 79, N. Carolina 75; UCLA 96, Louisville 77. **Third Place**–N. Carolina 105, Louisville 91. **Championship**–UCLA 81, Florida St. 76.

NIT Final Four (at Madison Square Garden): **Semifinals**–Maryland 91, Jacksonville 77; Niagara 69, St. John's 67. **Third Place**–Jacksonville 83, St. John's 80. **Championship**–Maryland 100, Niagara 69.

1973

		Before Tourns	Head Coach	Final Record
1	**UCLA**	26-0	John Wooden	30-0
2	N.C. State	27-0	Norm Sloan	same*
3	Long Beach St.	24-2	Jerry Tarkanian	26-3
4	Providence	24-2	Dave Gavitt	27-4
5	Marquette	23-3	Al McGuire	25-4
6	Indiana	19-5	Bob Knight	22-6
7	SW Louisiana	23-2	Beryl Shipley	24-5
8	Maryland	22-6	Lefty Driesell	23-7
9	Kansas St.	22-4	Jack Hartman	23-5
10	Minnesota	20-4	Bill Musselman	21-5
11	North Carolina	22-7	Dean Smith	25-8
12	Memphis St.	21-5	Gene Bartow	24-6
13	Houston	23-3	Guy Lewis	23-4
14	Syracuse	22-4	Roy Danforth	24-5
15	Missouri	21-5	Norm Stewart	21-6
16	Arizona St.	18-7	Ned Wulk	19-9
17	Kentucky	19-7	Joe B. Hall	20-8
18	Penn	20-5	Chuck Daly	21-7
19	Austin Peay	21-5	Lake Kelly	22-7
20	San Francisco	22-4	Bob Gaillard	23-5

*N.C. State was ineligible for NCAA tournament for using improper methods to recruit David Thompson.

Note: Unranked **Virginia Tech**, coached by Don DeVoe, won the NIT. The Hokies entered the tourney at 18-5 and finished with a record of 22-5.

NCAA Final Four (at The Arena, St. Louis): **Semifinals**–Memphis St. 98, Providence 85; UCLA 70, Indiana 59. **Third Place**–Indiana 97, Providence 79. **Championship**–UCLA 87, Memphis St. 66.

NIT Final Four (at Madison Square Garden): **Semifinals**–Va. Tech 74, Alabama 73; Notre Dame 78, N. Carolina 71. **Third Place**–N. Carolina 88, Alabama 69. **Championship**–Va. Tech 92, Notre Dame 91 (OT).

1974

		Before Tourns	Head Coach	Final Record
1	**N.C. State**	26-1	Norm Sloan	30-1
2	UCLA	23-3	John Wooden	26-4
3	Notre Dame	24-2	Digger Phelps	26-3
4	Maryland	23-5	Lefty Driesell	same
5	Providence	26-3	Dave Gavitt	28-4
6	Vanderbilt	23-3	Roy Skinner	23-5
7	Marquette	22-4	Al McGuire	26-5
8	North Carolina	22-5	Dean Smith	22-6
9	Long Beach St.	24-2	Lute Olson	same
10	**Indiana**	20-5	Bob Knight	23-5
11	Alabama	22-4	C.M. Newton	same
12	Michigan	21-4	Johnny Orr	22-5
13	Pittsburgh	23-3	Buzz Ridl	25-4
14	Kansas	21-5	Ted Owens	23-7
15	USC	22-4	Bob Boyd	24-5
16	Louisville	21-6	Denny Crum	21-7
17	New Mexico	21-6	Norm Ellenberger	22-7
18	South Carolina	22-4	Frank McGuire	22-5
19	Creighton	22-6	Eddie Sutton	23-7
20	Dayton	19-7	Don Donoher	20-9

NCAA Final Four (at Greensboro, NC, Coliseum): **Semifinals**–N.C. State 80, UCLA 77 (2 OT); Marquette 64, Kansas 51. **Third Place**–UCLA 78, Kansas 61. **Championship**–N.C. State 76, Marquette 64.

NIT Final Four (at Madison Square Garden): **Semifinals**–Purdue 78, Jacksonville 63; Utah 117, Boston Col. 93. **Third Place**–Boston Col. 87, Jacksonville 77. **Championship**–Purdue 87, Utah 81.

CCA Final Four (at The Arena, St. Louis): Semifinals–Indiana 73, Toledo 72; USC 74, Bradley 73. Championship–Indiana 85, USC 60.

1975

		Before Tourns	Head Coach	Final Record
1	Indiana	29-0	Bob Knight	31-1
2	**UCLA**	23-3	John Wooden	28-3
3	Louisville	24-2	Denny Crum	28-3
4	Maryland	22-4	Lefty Driesell	24-5
5	Kentucky	22-4	Joe B. Hall	26-5
6	North Carolina	21-7	Dean Smith	23-8
7	Arizona St.	23-3	Ned Wulk	25-4
8	N.C.State	22-6	Norm Sloan	22-6
9	Notre Dame	18-8	Digger Phelps	19-10
10	Marquette	23-3	Al McGuire	23-4
11	Alabama	22-4	C.M. Newton	22-5
12	Cincinnati	21-5	Gale Catlett	23-6
13	Oregon St.	18-10	Ralph Miller	19-12
14	**Drake**	16-10	Bob Ortegel	19-10
15	Penn	23-4	Chuck Daly	23-5
16	UNLV	22-4	Jerry Tarkanian	24-5
17	Kansas St.	18-8	Jack Hartman	20-9
18	USC	18-7	Bob Boyd	18-8
19	Centenary	25-4	Larry Little	same
20	Syracuse	20-7	Roy Danforth	23-9

NCAA Final Four (at San Diego Sports Arena): **Semifinals**–Kentucky 95, Syracuse 79; UCLA 75, Louisville 74 (OT). **Third Place**–Louisville 96, Syracuse 88 (OT). **Championship**–UCLA 92, Kentucky 85.

NIT Championship (at Madison Sq. Garden): Princeton 80, Providence 69. No Top 20 teams played in NIT.

CCA Championship (at Freedom Hall, Louisville): Drake 83, Arizona 76. No.14 Drake and No.18 USC were only Top 20 teams in CCA.

1976

		Before Tourns	Head Coach	Final Record
1	**Indiana**	27-0	Bob Knight	32-0
2	Marquette	25-1	Al McGuire	27-2
3	UNLV	28-1	Jerry Tarkanian	29-2
4	Rutgers	28-0	Tom Young	31-2
5	UCLA	24-3	Gene Bartow	28-4
6	Alabama	22-4	C.M. Newton	23-5
7	Notre Dame	22-5	Digger Phelps	23-6
8	North Carolina	25-3	Dean Smith	25-4
9	Michigan	21-6	Johnny Orr	25-7
10	Western Mich.	24-2	Eldon Miller	25-3
11	Maryland	22-6	Lefty Driesell	same
12	Cincinnati	25-5	Gale Catlett	25-6
13	Tennessee	21-5	Ray Mears	21-6
14	Missouri	24-4	Norm Stewart	26-5
15	Arizona	22-8	Fred Snowden	24-9
16	Texas Tech	24-5	Gerald Myers	25-6
17	DePaul	19-8	Ray Meyer	20-9
18	Virginia	18-11	Terry Holland	18-12
19	Centenary	22-5	Larry Little	same
20	Pepperdine	21-5	Gary Colson	22-6

NCAA Final Four (at the Spectrum, Phila.); **Semifinals**–Michigan 86, Rutgers 70; Indiana 65, UCLA 51. **Third Place**–UCLA 106, Rutgers 92. **Championship**–Indiana 86, Michigan 68.

NIT Championship (at Madison Square Garden): Kentucky 71, NC-Charlotte 67. No Top 20 teams played in NIT.

Associated Press Final Polls (Cont.)

1977

		Before Tourns	Head Coach	Final Record
1	**Michigan**	24-3	Johnny Orr	26-4
2	UCLA	24-3	Gene Bartow	25-4
3	Kentucky	24-3	Joe B. Hall	26-4
4	UNLV	25-2	Jerry Tarkanian	29-3
5	North Carolina	24-4	Dean Smith	28-5
6	Syracuse	25-3	Jim Boeheim	26-4
7	**Marquette**	20-7	Al McGuire	25-7
8	San Francisco	29-1	Bob Gaillard	29-2
9	Wake Forest	20-7	Carl Tacy	22-8
10	Notre Dame	21-6	Digger Phelps	22-7
11	Alabama	23-4	C.M. Newton	25-6
12	Detroit	24-3	Dick Vitale	25-4
13	Minnesota	24-3	Jim Dutcher	same*
14	Utah	22-6	Jerry Pimm	23-7
15	Tennessee	22-5	Ray Mears	22-6
16	Kansas St.	23-6	Jack Hartman	24-7
17	NC-Charlotte	25-3	Lee Rose	28-5
18	Arkansas	26-1	Eddie Sutton	26-2
19	Louisville	21-6	Denny Crum	21-7
20	VMI	25-3	Charlie Schmaus	26-4

*On probation

NCAA Final Four (at the Omni, Atlanta): **Semifinals**–Marquette 51, NC-Charlotte, 49; N. Carolina 84, UNLV 83. **Third Place**–UNLV 106, NC-Charlotte 94. **Championship**–Marquette 67, N. Carolina 59.

NIT Championship (at Madison Square Garden): St. Bonaventure 94, Houston 91. No.11 Alabama was only Top 20 team in NIT.

1979

		Before Tourns	Head Coach	Final Record
1	Indiana St.	29-0	Bill Hodges	33-1
2	UCLA	23-4	Gary Cunningham	25-5
3	**Michigan St.**	21-6	Jud Heathcote	26-6
4	Notre Dame	22-5	Digger Phelps	24-6
5	Arkansas	23-4	Eddie Sutton	25-5
6	DePaul	22-5	Ray Meyer	26-6
7	LSU	22-5	Dale Brown	23-6
8	Syracuse	25-3	Jim Boeheim	26-4
9	North Carolina	23-5	Dean Smith	23-6
10	Marquette	21-6	Hank Raymonds	22-7
11	Duke	22-7	Bill Foster	22-8
12	San Francisco	21-6	Dan Belluomini	22-7
13	Louisville	23-7	Denny Crum	24-8
14	Penn	21-5	Bob Weinhauer	25-7
15	Purdue	23-7	Lee Rose	27-8
16	Oklahoma	20-9	Dave Bliss	21-10
17	St. John's	18-10	Lou Carnesecca	21-11
18	Rutgers	21-8	Tom Young	22-9
19	Toledo	21-6	Bob Nichols	22-7
20	Iowa	20-7	Lute Olson	20-8

NCAA Final Four (at Special Events Center, Salt Lake City): **Semifinals**–Michigan St. 101, Penn 67; Indiana St. 76, DePaul 74; **Third Place**–DePaul 96, Penn 93; **Championship**–Michigan St. 75, Indiana St. 64.

NIT Championship (at Madison Square Garden): Indiana 53, Purdue 52. No. 15 Purdue was the only Top 20 team in NIT.

1978

		Before Tourns	Head Coach	Final Record
1	**Kentucky**	25-2	Joe B. Hall	30-2
2	UCLA	24-2	Gary Cunningham	25-3
3	DePaul	25-2	Ray Meyer	27-3
4	Michigan St.	23-4	Jud Heathcote	25-5
5	Arkansas	28-3	Eddie Sutton	32-3
6	Notre Dame	20-6	Digger Phelps	23-8
7	Duke	23-6	Bill Foster	27-7
8	Marquette	24-3	Hank Raymonds	24-4
9	Louisville	22-6	Denny Crum	23-7
10	Kansas	24-4	Ted Owens	24-5
11	San Francisco	22-5	Bob Gaillard	23-6
12	New Mexico	24-3	Norm Ellenberger	24-4
13	Indiana	20-7	Bob Knight	21-8
14	Utah	22-5	Jerry Pimm	23-6
15	Florida St.	23-5	Hugh Durham	23-6
16	North Carolina	23-7	Dean Smith	23-8
17	**Texas**	22-5	Abe Lemons	26-5
18	Detroit	24-3	Dave Gaines	25-4
19	Miami-OH	18-8	Darrell Hedric	19-9
20	Penn	19-7	Bob Weinhauer	20-8

NCAA Final Four (at the Checkerdome, St. Louis): **Semifinals**–Kentucky 64, Arkansas 59; Duke 90, Notre Dame 86. **Third Place**–Arkansas 71, Notre Dame 69. **Championship**–Kentucky 94, Duke 88.

NIT Championship (at Madison Square Garden): Texas 101, N.C. State 93. No. 17 Texas and No. 18 Detroit were only Top 20 teams in NIT.

1980

		Before Tourns	Head Coach	Final Record
1	DePaul	26-1	Ray Meyer	26-2
2	**Louisville**	28-3	Denny Crum	33-3
3	LSU	24-5	Dale Brown	26-6
4	Kentucky	28-5	Joe B. Hall	29-6
5	Oregon St.	26-3	Ralph Miller	26-4
6	Syracuse	25-3	Jim Boeheim	26-4
7	Indiana	20-7	Bob Knight	21-8
8	Maryland	23-6	Lefty Driesell	24-7
9	Notre Dame	20-7	Digger Phelps	20-8
10	Ohio St.	24-5	Eldon Miller	21-8
11	Georgetown	24-5	John Thompson	26-6
12	BYU	24-4	Frank Arnold	24-5
13	St. John's	24-4	Lou Carnesecca	24-5
14	Duke	22-8	Bill Foster	24-9
15	North Carolina	21-7	Dean Smith	21-8
16	Missouri	23-5	Norm Stewart	25-6
17	Weber St.	26-2	Neil McCarthy	26-3
18	Arizona St.	21-6	Ned Wulk	22-7
19	Iona	28-4	Jim Valvano	29-5
20	Purdue	19-9	Lee Rose	23-10

NCAA Final Four (at Market Square Arena, Indianapolis): **Semifinals**–Louisville 80, Iowa 72; UCLA 67, Purdue 62; **Championship**–Louisville 59, UCLA 54.

NIT Championship (at Madison Square Garden): Virginia 58, Minnesota 55. No Top 20 teams played in NIT.

1981

		Before Tourns	Head Coach	Final Record
1	DePaul	27-1	Ray Meyer	27-2
2	Oregon St.	26-1	Ralph Miller	26-2
3	Arizona St.	24-3	Ned Wulk	24-4
4	LSU	28-3	Dale Brown	31-5
5	Virginia	25-3	Terry Holland	29-4
6	North Carolina	25-7	Dean Smith	29-8
7	Notre Dame	22-5	Digger Phelps	23-6
8	Kentucky	22-5	Joe B. Hall	22-6
9	**Indiana**	21-9	Bob Knight	26-9
10	UCLA	20-6	Larry Brown	20-7
11	Wake Forest	22-6	Carl Tacy	22-7
12	Louisville	21-8	Denny Crum	21-9
13	Iowa	21-6	Lute Olson	21-7
14	Utah	24-4	Jerry Pimm	25-5
15	Tennessee	20-7	Don DeVoe	21-8
16	BYU	22-6	Frank Arnold	25-7
17	Wyoming	23-5	Jim Brandenburg	24-6
18	Maryland	20-9	Lefty Driesell	21-10
19	Illinois	20-7	Lou Henson	21-8
20	Arkansas	22-7	Eddie Sutton	24-8

NCAA Final Four (at the Spectrum, Phila.): **Semifinals**–N. Carolina 78, Virginia 65; Indiana 67, LSU 49. **Third Place**–Virginia 78, LSU 74. **Championship**–Indiana 63, N. Carolina 50.

NIT Championship (at Madison Square Garden): Tulsa 86, Syracuse 84. No Top 20 teams played in NIT.

1982

		Before Tourns	Head Coach	Final Record
1	**N. Carolina**	27-2	Dean Smith	32-2
2	DePaul	26-1	Ray Meyer	26-2
3	Virginia	29-3	Terry Holland	30-4
4	Oregon St.	23-4	Ralph Miller	25-5
5	Missouri	26-3	Norm Stewart	27-4
6	Georgetown	26-6	John Thompson	30-7
7	Minnesota	22-5	Jim Dutcher	23-6
8	Idaho	26-2	Don Monson	27-3
9	Memphis St.	23-4	Dana Kirk	24-5
10	Tulsa	24-5	Nolan Richardson	24-6
11	Fresno St.	26-2	Boyd Grant	27-3
12	Arkansas	23-5	Eddie Sutton	23-6
13	Alabama	23-6	Wimp Sanderson	24-7
14	West Virginia	26-3	Gale Catlett	27-4
15	Kentucky	22-7	Joe B. Hall	22-8
16	Iowa	20-7	Lute Olson	21-8
17	Ala-Birmingham	23-5	Gene Bartow	25-6
18	Wake Forest	20-8	Carl Tacy	21-9
19	UCLA	21-6	Larry Farmer	21-6
20	Louisville	20-9	Denny Crum	23-10

NCAA Final Four (at the Superdome, New Orleans): **Semifinals**–N. Carolina 68, Houston 63; Georgetown 50, Louisville 46. **Championship**–N. Carolina 63, Georgetown 62.

NIT Championship (at Madison Square Garden): Bradley 67, Purdue 58. No Top 20 teams played in NIT.

1983

		Before Tourns	Head Coach	Final Record
1	Houston	27-2	Guy Lewis	31-3
2	Louisville	29-3	Denny Crum	32-4
3	St. John's	27-4	Lou Carnesecca	28-5
4	Virginia	27-4	Terry Holland	29-5
5	Indiana	23-5	Bob Knight	24-6
6	UNLV	28-2	Jerry Tarkanian	28-3
7	UCLA	23-5	Larry Farmer	23-6
8	North Carolina	26-7	Dean Smith	28-8
9	Arkansas	25-3	Eddie Sutton	26-4
10	Missouri	26-7	Norm Stewart	26-8
11	Boston College	24-6	Gary Williams	25-7
12	Kentucky	22-7	Joe B. Hall	23-8
13	Villanova	22-7	Rollie Massimino	24-8
14	Wichita St.	25-3	Gene Smithson	same*
15	Tenn-Chatt.	26-3	Murray Arnold	26-4
16	**N.C. State**	20-10	Jim Valvano	26-10
17	Memphis St.	22-7	Dana Kirk	23-8
18	Georgia	21-9	Hugh Durham	24-10
19	Oklahoma St.	24-6	Paul Hansen	24-7
20	Georgetown	21-9	John Thompson	22-10

*On probation

NCAA Final Four (at The Pit, Albuquerque, NM): **Semifinals**–N.C. State 67, Georgia 60; Houston 94, Louisville 81. **Championship**–N.C. State 54, Houston 52.

NIT Championship (at Madison Square Garden): Fresno St. 69, DePaul 60. No Top 20 teams played in NIT.

1984

		Before Tourns	Head Coach	Final Record
1	North Carolina	27-2	Dean Smith	28-3
2	**Georgetown**	29-3	John Thompson	34-3
3	Kentucky	26-4	Joe B. Hall	29-5
4	DePaul	26-2	Ray Meyer	27-3
5	Houston	28-4	Guy Lewis	32-5
6	Illinois	24-4	Lou Henson	26-5
7	Oklahoma	29-4	Billy Tubbs	29-5
8	Arkansas	25-6	Eddie Sutton	25-7
9	UTEP	27-3	Don Haskins	27-4
10	Purdue	22-6	Gene Keady	22-7
11	Maryland	23-7	Lefty Driesell	24-8
12	Tulsa	27-3	Nolan Richardson	27-4
13	UNLV	27-5	Jerry Tarkanian	29-6
14	Duke	24-9	Mike Krzyzewski	24-10
15	Washington	22-6	Marv Harshman	24-7
16	Memphis St.	24-6	Dana Kirk	26-7
17	Oregon St.	22-6	Ralph Miller	22-7
18	Syracuse	22-8	Jim Boeheim	23-9
19	Wake Forest	21-8	Carl Tacy	23-9
20	Temple	25-4	John Chaney	26-5

NCAA Final Four (at the Kingdome, Seattle): **Semifinals**–Houston 49, Virginia 47 (OT); Georgetown 53, Kentucky 40. **Championship**–Georgetown 84, Houston 75.

NIT Championship (at Madison Square Garden): Michigan 83, Notre Dame 63. No Top 20 teams played in NIT.

Highest-Rated College Games on TV

The dozen highest-rated college basketball games seen on U.S. television have been NCAA tournament championship games, led by the 1979 Michigan State-Indiana State final that featured Magic Johnson and Larry Bird.

Listed below are the finalists (winning team first), date of game, TV network, and TV rating and audience share (according to Nielson Media Research).

		Date	Net	Rtg/Sh
1	Michigan St.-Indiana St.	3/26/79	NBC	24.1/38
2	Villanova-Georgetown	4/1/85	CBS	23.3/33
3	Duke-Michigan	4/6/92	CBS	22.7/35
4	N.C. State-Houston	4/4/83	CBS	22.3/32
5	N. Carolina-Michigan	4/5/93	CBS	22.2/34
6	Arkansas-Duke	4/4/94	CBS	21.6/33
7	N. Carolina-Georgetown	3/29/82	CBS	21.6/31
8	UCLA-Kentucky	3/31/75	NBC	21.3/33
9	Michigan-Seton Hall	4/3/89	CBS	21.3/33
10	Louisville-Duke	3/31/86	CBS	20.7/31
11	Indiana-N. Carolina	3/30/81	NBC	20.7/29
12	UCLA-Memphis St.	3/26/73	NBC	20.5/32

Associated Press Final Polls (Cont.)

1985

		Before Tourns	Head Coach	Final Record
1	Georgetown	30-2	John Thompson	35-3
2	Michigan	25-3	Bill Frieder	26-4
3	St. John's	27-3	Lou Carnesecca	31-4
4	Oklahoma	28-5	Billy Tubbs	31-6
5	Memphis St.	27-3	Dana Kirk	31-4
6	Georgia Tech	24-7	Bobby Cremins	27-8
7	North Carolina	24-8	Dean Smith	27-9
8	Louisiana Tech	27-2	Andy Russo	29-3
9	UNLV	27-3	Jerry Tarkanian	28-4
10	Duke	22-7	Mike Krzyzewski	23-8
11	VCU	25-5	J.D. Barnett	26-6
12	Illinois	24-8	Lou Henson	26-9
13	Kansas	25-7	Larry Brown	26-8
14	Loyola-IL	25-5	Gene Sullivan	27-6
15	Syracuse	21-8	Jim Boeheim	22-9
16	N.C. State	20-9	Jim Valvano	23-10
17	Texas Tech	23-7	Gerald Myers	23-8
18	Tulsa	23-7	Nolan Richardson	23-8
19	Georgia	21-8	Hugh Durham	22-9
20	LSU	19-9	Dale Brown	19-10

Note: Unranked **Villanova**, coached by Rollie Massimino, won the NCAAs. The Wildcats entered the tourney at 19-10 and had a final record of 25-10.

NCAA Final Four (at Rupp Arena, Lexington, KY): **Semifinals**– Georgetown 77, St. John's 59; Villanova 52, Memphis St. 45. **Championship**–Villanova 66, Georgetown 64.

NIT Championship (at Madison Square Garden): UCLA 65, Indiana 62. No Top 20 teams played in NIT.

1986

		Before Tourns	Head Coach	Final Record
1	Duke	32-2	Mike Krzyzewski	37-3
2	Kansas	31-3	Larry Brown	35-4
3	Kentucky	29-3	Eddie Sutton	32-4
4	St. John's	30-4	Lou Carnesecca	31-5
5	Michigan	27-4	Bill Frieder	28-5
6	Georgia Tech	25-6	Bobby Cremins	27-7
7	**Louisville**	26-7	Denny Crum	32-7
8	North Carolina	26-5	Dean Smith	28-6
9	Syracuse	25-5	Jim Boeheim	26-6
10	Notre Dame	23-5	Digger Phelps	23-6
11	UNLV	31-4	Jerry Tarkanian	33-5
12	Memphis St.	27-5	Dana Kirk	28-6
13	Georgetown	23-7	John Thompson	24-8
14	Bradley	31-2	Dick Versace	32-3
15	Oklahoma	25-8	Billy Tubbs	26-9
16	Indiana	21-7	Bob Knight	21-8
17	Navy	27-4	Paul Evans	30-5
18	Michigan St.	21-7	Jud Heathcote	23-8
19	Illinois	21-9	Lou Henson	22-10
20	UTEP	27-5	Don Haskins	27-6

NCAA Final Four (at Reunion Arena, Dallas): **Semifinals**–Duke 71, Kansas 67; Louisville 88, LSU 77. **Championship**–Louisville 72, Duke 69.

NIT Championship (at Madison Square Garden): Ohio St. 73, Wyoming 63. No Top 20 teams played in NIT.

1987

		Before Tourns	Head Coach	Final Record
1	UNLV	33-1	Jerry Tarkanian	37-2
2	North Carolina	29-3	Dean Smith	32-4
3	**Indiana**	24-4	Bob Knight	30-4
4	Georgetown	26-4	John Thompson	29-5
5	DePaul	26-2	Joey Meyer	28-3
6	Iowa	27-4	Tom Davis	30-5
7	Purdue	24-4	Gene Keady	25-5
8	Temple	31-3	John Chaney	32-4
9	Alabama	26-4	Wimp Sanderson	28-5
10	Syracuse	26-6	Jim Boeheim	31-7
11	Illinois	23-7	Lou Henson	23-8
12	Pittsburgh	24-7	Paul Evans	25-8
13	Clemson	25-5	Cliff Ellis	25-6
14	Missouri	24-9	Norm Stewart	24-10
15	UCLA	24-6	Walt Hazzard	25-7
16	New Orleans	25-3	Benny Dees	26-4
17	Duke	22-8	Mike Krzyzewski	24-9
18	Notre Dame	22-7	Digger Phelps	24-8
19	TCU	23-6	Jim Killingsworth	24-7
20	Kansas	23-10	Larry Brown	25-11

NCAA Final Four (at the Superdome, New Orleans): **Semifinals**–Syracuse 77, Providence 63; Indiana 97, UNLV 93. **Championship**–Indiana 74, Syracuse 73.

NIT Championship (at Madison Square Garden): Southern Miss. 84, La Salle 80. No Top 20 teams played in NIT.

1988

		Before Tourns	Head Coach	Final Record
1	Temple	29-1	John Chaney	32-2
2	Arizona	31-2	Lute Olson	35-3
3	Purdue	27-3	Gene Keady	29-4
4	Oklahoma	30-3	Billy Tubbs	35-4
5	Duke	24-6	Mike Krzyzewski	28-7
6	Kentucky	25-5	Eddie Sutton	27-6
7	North Carolina	24-6	Dean Smith	27-7
8	Pittsburgh	23-6	Paul Evans	24-7
9	Syracuse	25-8	Jim Boeheim	26-9
10	Michigan	24-7	Bill Frieder	26-8
11	Bradley	26-4	Stan Albeck	26-5
12	UNLV	27-5	Jerry Tarkanian	28-6
13	Wyoming	26-5	Benny Dees	26-6
14	N.C. State	24-7	Jim Valvano	24-8
15	Loyola-CA	27-3	Paul Westhead	28-4
16	Illinois	22-9	Lou Henson	23-10
17	Iowa	22-9	Tom Davis	24-10
18	Xavier-OH	26-3	Pete Gillen	26-4
19	BYU	25-5	Ladell Andersen	26-6
20	Kansas St.	22-8	Lon Kruger	25-9

Note: Unranked **Kansas**, coached by Larry Brown, won the NCAAs. The Jayhawks entered the tourney at 21-11 and had a final record of 27-11.

NCAA Final Four (at Kemper Arena, Kansas City): **Semifinals**–Kansas 66, Duke 59; Oklahoma 86, Arizona 78. **Championship**–Kansas 83, Oklahoma 79.

NIT Championship (at Madison Square Garden): Connecticut 72, Ohio St. 67. No Top 20 teams played in NIT.

1989

		Before Tourns	Head Coach	Final Record
1	Arizona	27-3	Lute Olson	29-4
2	Georgetown	26-4	John Thompson	29-5
3	Illinois	27-4	Lou Henson	31-5
4	Oklahoma	28-5	Billy Tubbs	30-6
5	North Carolina	27-7	Dean Smith	29-8
6	Missouri	27-7	Norm Stewart & Rich Daly	29-8
7	Syracuse	27-7	Jim Boeheim	30-8
8	Indiana	25-7	Bob Knight	27-8
9	Duke	24-7	Mike Krzyzewski	28-8
10	**Michigan**	24-7	Bill Frieder & Steve Fisher	30-7
11	Seton Hall	26-6	P.J. Carlesimo	31-7
12	Louisville	22-8	Denny Crum	24-9
13	Stanford	26-6	Mike Montgomery	26-7
14	Iowa	22-9	Tom Davis	23-10
15	UNLV	26-7	Jerry Tarkanian	29-8
16	Florida St.	22-7	Pat Kennedy	22-8
17	West Virginia	25-4	Gale Catlett	26-5
18	Ball State	28-2	Rick Majerus	29-3
19	N.C. State	20-8	Jim Valvano	22-9
20	Alabama	23-7	Wimp Sanderson	23-8

NCAA Final Four (at The Kingdome, Seattle): **Semifinals**–Seton Hall 95, Duke 78; Michigan 83, Illinois 81. **Championship**–Michigan 80, Seton Hall 79 (OT).

NIT Championship (at Madison Square Garden): St. John's 73, St. Louis 65. No Top 20 teams played in NIT.

1990

		Before Tourns	Head Coach	Final Record
1	Oklahoma	26-4	Billy Tubbs	27-5
2	**UNLV**	29-5	Jerry Tarkanian	35-5
3	Connecticut	28-5	Jim Calhoun	31-6
4	Michigan St.	26-5	Jud Heathcote	28-6
5	Kansas	29-4	Roy Williams	30-5
6	Syracuse	24-6	Jim Boeheim	26-7
7	Arkansas	26-4	Nolan Richardson	30-5
8	Georgetown	23-6	John Thompson	24-7
9	Georgia Tech	24-6	Bobby Cremins	28-7
10	Purdue	21-7	Gene Keady	22-8
11	Missouri	26-5	Norm Stewart	26-6
12	La Salle	29-1	Speedy Morris	30-2
13	Michigan	22-7	Steve Fisher	23-8
14	Arizona	24-6	Lute Olson	25-7
15	Duke	24-8	Mike Krzyzewski	29-9
16	Louisville	26-7	Denny Crum	27-8
17	Clemson	24-8	Cliff Ellis	26-9
18	Illinois	21-7	Lou Henson	21-8
19	LSU	22-8	Dale Brown	23-9
20	Minnesota	20-8	Clem Haskins	23-9
21	Loyola-CA	23-5	Paul Westhead	26-6
22	Oregon St.	22-6	Jim Anderson	22-7
23	Alabama	24-8	Wimp Sanderson	26-9
24	New Mexico St.	26-4	Neil McCarthy	26-5
25	Xavier-OH	26-4	Pete Gillen	28-5

NCAA Final Four (at McNichols Sports Arena, Denver): **Semifinals**–Duke 97, Arkansas 83; UNLV 90, Georgia Tech 81. **Championship**–UNLV 103, Duke 73.

NIT Championship (at Madison Square Garden): Vanderbilt 74, St.Louis 72. No Top 25 teams played in NIT.

1991

		Before Tourns	Head Coach	Final Record
1	UNLV	30-0	Jerry Tarkanian	34-1
2	Arkansas	31-3	Nolan Richardson	34-4
3	Indiana	27-4	Bob Knight	29-5
4	North Carolina	25-5	Dean Smith	29-6
5	Ohio St.	25-3	Randy Ayers	27-4
6	**Duke**	26-7	Mike Krzyzewski	32-7
7	Syracuse	26-5	Jim Boeheim	26-6
8	Arizona	26-6	Lute Olson	28-7
9	Kentucky	22-6	Rick Pitino	same*
10	Utah	28-3	Rick Majerus	30-4
11	Nebraska	26-7	Danny Nee	26-8
12	Kansas	22-7	Roy Williams	27-8
13	Seton Hall	22-8	P.J. Carlesimo	25-9
14	Oklahoma St.	22-7	Eddie Sutton	24-8
15	New Mexico St.	23-5	Neil McCarthy	23-6
16	UCLA	23-8	Jim Harrick	23-9
17	E.Tennessee St.	28-4	Alan LaForce	28-5
18	Princeton	24-2	Pete Carril	24-3
19	Alabama	21-9	Wimp Sanderson	23-10
20	St. John's	20-8	Lou Carnesecca	23-9
21	Mississippi St.	20-8	Richard Williams	20-9
22	LSU	20-9	Dale Brown	20-10
23	Texas	22-8	Tom Penders	23-9
24	DePaul	20-8	Joey Meyer	20-9
25	Southern Miss.	21-7	M.K. Turk	21-8

*On probation

NCAA Final Four (at the Hoosier Dome, Indianapolis): **Semifinals**–Kansas 79, North Carolina 73; Duke 79, UNLV 77. **Championship**–Duke 72, Kansas 65.

NIT Championship (at Madison Square Garden): Stanford 78, Oklahoma 72. No Top 25 teams played in NIT.

1992

		Before Tourns	Head Coach	Final Record
1	**Duke**	28-2	Mike Krzyzewski	34-2
2	Kansas	26-4	Roy Williams	27-5
3	Ohio St.	23-5	Randy Ayers	26-6
4	UCLA	25-4	Jim Harrick	28-5
5	Indiana	23-6	Bob Knight	27-7
6	Kentucky	26-6	Rick Pitino	29-7
7	UNLV	26-2	Jerry Tarkanian	same*
8	USC	23-5	George Raveling	24-6
9	Arkansas	25-7	Nolan Richardson	26-8
10	Arizona	24-6	Lute Olson	24-7
11	Oklahoma St.	26-7	Eddie Sutton	28-8
12	Cincinnati	25-4	Bob Huggins	29-5
13	Alabama	25-8	Wimp Sanderson	26-9
14	Michigan St.	21-7	Jud Heathcote	22-8
15	Michigan	20-8	Steve Fisher	25-9
16	Missouri	20-8	Norm Stewart	21-9
17	Massachusetts	28-4	John Calipari	30-5
18	North Carolina	21-9	Dean Smith	23-10
19	Seton Hall	21-8	P.J. Carlesimo	23-9
20	Florida St.	20-9	Pat Kennedy	22-10
21	Syracuse	21-9	Jim Boeheim	22-10
22	Georgetown	21-9	John Thompson	22-10
23	Oklahoma	21-8	Billy Tubbs	21-9
24	DePaul	20-8	Joey Meyer	20-9
25	LSU	20-9	Dale Brown	21-10

*On probation

NCAA Final Four (at the Metrodome, Minneapolis): **Semifinals**–Michigan 76, Cincinnati 72; Duke 81, Indiana 78. **Championship**–Duke 71, Michigan 51.

NIT Championship (at Madison Square Garden): Virginia 81, Notre Dame 76 (OT). No Top 25 teams played in NIT.

Associated Press Final Polls (Cont.)

1993

		Before Tourns	Head Coach	Final Record
1	Indiana	28-3	Bob Knight	31-4
2	Kentucky	26-3	Rick Pitino	30-4
3	Michigan	26-4	Steve Fisher	31-5
4	**N. Carolina**	28-4	Dean Smith	34-4
5	Arizona	24-3	Lute Olson	24-4
6	Seton Hall	27-6	P.J. Carlesimo	28-7
7	Cincinnati	24-4	Bob Huggins	27-5
8	Vanderbilt	26-5	Eddie Fogler	28-6
9	Kansas	25-6	Roy Williams	29-7
10	Duke	23-7	Mike Krzyzewski	24-8
11	Florida St.	22-9	Pat Kennedy	25-10
12	Arkansas	20-8	Nolan Richardson	22-9
13	Iowa	22-8	Tom Davis	23-9
14	Massachusetts	23-6	John Calipari	24-7
15	Louisville	20-8	Denny Crum	22-9
16	Wake Forest	19-8	Dave Odom	21-9
17	New Orleans	26-3	Tim Floyd	26-4
18	Georgia Tech	19-10	Bobby Cremins	19-11
19	Utah	23-6	Rick Majerus	24-7
20	Western Ky.	24-5	Ralph Willard	26-6
21	New Mexico	24-6	Dave Bliss	24-7
22	Purdue	18-9	Gene Keady	18-10
23	Oklahoma St.	19-8	Eddie Sutton	20-9
24	New Mexico St.	25-7	Neil McCarthy	26-8
25	UNLV	21-7	Rollie Massimino	21-8

NCAA Final Four (at the Superdome, New Orleans): **Semifinals**–North Carolina 78, Kansas 68; Michigan 81, Kentucky 78 (OT). **Championship**–North Carolina 77, Michigan 71.

NIT Championship (at Madison Square Garden): Minnesota 62, Georgetown 61. No. 25 UNLV was the only Top 25 team that played in the NIT.

1994

		Before Tourns	Head Coach	Final Record
1	North Carolina	27-6	Dean Smith	28-7
2	**Arkansas**	25-3	Nolan Richardson	31-3
3	Purdue	26-4	Gene Keady	29-5
4	Connecticut	27-4	Jim Calhoun	29-5
5	Missouri	25-3	Norm Stewart	28-4
6	Duke	23-5	Mike Krzyzewski	28-6
7	Kentucky	26-6	Rick Pitino	27-7
8	Massachusetts	27-6	John Calipari	28-7
9	Arizona	25-5	Lute Olson	29-6
10	Louisville	26-5	Denny Crum	28-6
11	Michigan	21-7	Steve Fisher	24-8
12	Temple	22-7	John Chaney	23-8
13	Kansas	25-7	Roy Williams	27-8
14	Florida	25-7	Lon Kruger	29-8
15	Syracuse	21-6	Jim Boeheim	23-7
16	California	22-7	Todd Bozeman	22-8
17	UCLA	21-6	Jim Harrick	21-7
18	Indiana	19-8	Bob Knight	21-9
19	Oklahoma St.	23-9	Eddie Sutton	24-10
20	Texas	25-7	Tom Penders	26-8
21	Marquette	22-8	Kevin O'Neill	24-9
22	Nebraska	20-9	Danny Nee	20-10
23	Minnesota	20-11	Clem Haskins	21-12
24	Saint Louis	23-5	Charlie Spoonhour	23-6
25	Cincinnati	22-9	Bob Huggins	22-10

NCAA Final Four (at the Charlotte Coliseum): **Semifinals**– Arkansas 91, Arizona 82; Duke 70, Florida 65. **Championship**– Arkansas 76, Duke 72.

NIT Championship (at Madison Square Garden): Villanova 80, Vanderbilt 73. No top 25 teams played in NIT.

1995

		Before Tourns	Head Coach	Final Record
1	**UCLA**	25-2	Jim Harrick	31-2
2	Kentucky	25-4	Rick Pitino	28-5
3	Wake Forest	24-5	Dave Odom	26-6
4	North Carolina	24-5	Dean Smith	28-6
5	Kansas	23-5	Roy Williams	25-6
6	Arkansas	27-6	Nolan Richardson	32-7
7	Massachusetts	26-4	John Calipari	26-5
8	Connecticut	25-4	Jim Calhoun	28-5
9	Villanova	25-7	Steve Lappas	25-8
10	Maryland	24-7	Gary Williams	26-8
11	Michigan St.	22-5	Jud Heathcote	22-6
12	Purdue	24-6	Gene Keady	25-7
13	Virginia	22-8	Jeff Jones	25-9
14	Oklahoma St.	23-9	Eddie Sutton	27-10
15	Arizona	23-7	Lute Olson	23-8
16	Arizona St.	22-8	Bill Frieder	24-9
17	Oklahoma	23-8	Kelvin Sampson	23-9
18	Mississippi St.	20-7	Richard Williams	22-8
19	Utah	27-5	Rick Majerus	28-6
20	Alabama	22-9	David Hobbs	23-10
21	Western Ky.	26-3	Matt Kilcullen	27-4
22	Georgetown	19-9	John Thompson	21-10
23	Missouri	19-8	Norm Stewart	20-9
24	Iowa St.	22-10	Tim Floyd	23-11
25	Syracuse	19-9	Jim Boeheim	20-10

NCAA Final Four (at the Kingdome, Seattle): **Semifinals**– UCLA 74, Oklahoma St. 61; Arkansas 75, North Carolina 68. **Championship**– UCLA 89, Arkansas 78.

NIT Championship (at Madison Square Garden): Virginia Tech 65, Marquette 64 (OT). No top 25 teams played in NIT.

1996

		Before Tourns	Head Coach	Final Record
1	Massachusetts	31-1	John Calipari	35-2
2	**Kentucky**	28-2	Rick Pitino	34-2
3	Connecticut	30-2	Jim Calhoun	32-3
4	Georgetown	26-7	John Thompson	29-8
5	Kansas	26-4	Roy Williams	29-5
6	Purdue	25-5	Gene Keady	26-6
7	Cincinnati	25-4	Bob Huggins	28-5
8	Texas Tech	28-1	James Dickey	30-2
9	Wake Forest	23-5	Dave Odom	26-6
10	Villanova	25-6	Steve Lappas	26-7
11	Arizona	24-6	Lute Olson	26-7
12	Utah	25-6	Rick Majerus	27-7
13	Georgia Tech	22-11	Bobby Cremins	24-12
14	UCLA	23-7	Jim Harrick	23-8
15	Syracuse	24-8	Jim Boeheim	29-9
16	Memphis	22-7	Larry Finch	22-8
17	Iowa St.	23-8	Tim Floyd	24-9
18	Penn St.	21-6	Jerry Dunn	21-7
19	Mississippi St.	22-7	Richard Williams	26-8
20	Marquette	22-7	Mike Deane	23-8
21	Iowa	22-8	Tom Davis	23-9
22	Virginia Tech	22-5	Bill Foster	23-6
23	New Mexico	27-4	Dave Bliss	28-5
24	Louisville	20-11	Denny Crum	22-12
25	North Carolina	20-10	Dean Smith	21-11

NCAA Final Four (at the Meadowlands, E. Rutherford, N.J.): **Semifinals**– Kentucky 81, Massachusetts 74; Syracuse 77, Mississippi St. 69. **Championship**– Kentucky 76, Syracuse 67.

NIT Championship (at Madison Square Garden): Nebraska 60, St. Joseph's 56. No top 25 teams played in NIT.

1997

		Before Tourns	Head Coach	Final Record
1	Kansas	32-1	Roy Williams	34-2
2	Utah	26-3	Rick Majerus	29-4
3	Minnesota	27-3	Clem Haskins	31-4
4	North Carolina	24-6	Dean Smith	28-7
5	Kentucky	30-4	Rick Pitino	35-5
6	South Carolina	24-7	Eddie Fogler	24-8
7	UCLA	21-7	Steve Lavin	24-8
8	Duke	23-8	Mike Krzyzewski	24-9
9	Wake Forest	23-6	Dave Odom	24-7
10	Cincinnati	25-7	Bob Huggins	26-8
11	New Mexico	24-7	Dave Bliss	25-8
12	St. Joseph's	24-6	Phil Martelli	26-7
13	Xavier	22-5	Skip Prosser	23-6
14	Clemson	21-9	Rick Barnes	23-10
15	**Arizona**	19-9	Lute Olsen	25-9
16	Charleston	28-2	John Kresse	29-3
17	Georgia	24-8	Tubby Smith	24-9
18	Iowa St.	20-8	Tim Floyd	22-9
19	Illinois	21-9	Lon Kruger	22-10
20	Villanova	23-9	Steve Lappas	24-10
21	Stanford	20-7	Mike Montgomery	22-8
22	Maryland	21-10	Gary Williams	21-11
23	Boston College	21-8	Jim O'Brien	22-9
24	Colorado	21-9	Ricardo Patton	22-10
25	Louisville	23-8	Denny Crum	26-9

NCAA Final Four (at the RCA Dome, Indianapolis): **Semifinals**– Kentucky 78, Minnesota 69; Arizona 66, North Carolina 58. **Championship**– Arizona 84, Kentucky 79 (OT).

NIT Championship (at Madison Square Garden): Michigan 82, Florida St. 72. No top 25 teams played in NIT.

1998

		Before Tourns	Head Coach	Final Record
1	North Carolina	30-3	Bill Gutheridge	34-4
2	Kansas	34-3	Roy Williams	35-4
3	Duke	29-3	Mike Krzyzewski	32-4
4	Arizona	27-4	Lute Olsen	30-5
5	**Kentucky**	29-4	Tubby Smith	35-4
6	Connecticut	29-4	Jim Calhoun	32-5
7	Utah	25-3	Rick Majerus	30-4
8	Princeton	26-1	Bill Carmody	27-2
9	Cincinnati	26-5	Bob Huggins	27-6
10	Stanford	26-4	Mike Montgomery	30-5
11	Purdue	26-7	Gene Keady	28-8
12	Michigan	24-8	Brian Ellerbe	25-9
13	Mississippi	22-6	Rob Evans	22-7
14	South Carolina	23-7	Eddie Fogler	23-8
15	TCU	27-5	Billy Tubbs	27-6
16	Michigan St.	20-7	Tom Izzo	22-8
17	Arkansas	23-8	Nolan Richardson	24-9
18	New Mexico	23-7	Dave Bliss	24-8
19	UCLA	22-8	Steve Lavin	24-9
20	Maryland	19-10	Gary Williams	21-11
21	Syracuse	24-8	Jim Boeheim	26-9
22	Illinois	22-9	Lon Kruger	23-10
23	Xavier	22-7	Skip Prosser	22-8
24	Temple	21-8	John Chaney	21-9
25	Murray St.	29-3	Mark Gottfried	29-4

NCAA Final Four (at the Alamodome, San Antonio): **Semifinals**– Kentucky 86, Stanford 85 (OT); Utah 65, North Carolina 59. **Championship**– Kentucky 78, Utah 69.

NIT Championship (at Madison Square Garden): Minnesota 79, Penn St. 72. No top 25 teams played in NIT.

AP Post-Tournament Final Polls

The final AP Top 20 poll has been released after the NCAA tournament and NIT four times– in 1953 and '54 and again in 1974 and '75. Those four polls are listed below; teams that were not included in the last regular season polls are in *CAPITAL* italic letters.

1953

		Final Record
1	Indiana	23-3
2	Seton Hall	31-2
3	Kansas	19-6
4	Washington	30-3
5	LSU	24-3
6	La Salle	25-3
7	*ST. JOHN'S*	17-6
8	Okla. A&M	23-7
9	Duquesne	21-8
10	Notre Dame	19-5
11	Illinois	18-4
12	Kansas St.	17-4
13	Holy Cross	20-6
14	Seattle	29-4
15	*WAKE FOREST*	22-7
16	*SANTA CLARA*	20-7
17	Western Ky.	25-6
18	N.C. State	26-6
19	*DEPAUL*	19-9
20	*SW MISSOURI*	24-4

1954

		Final Record
1	Kentucky	25-0
2	La Salle	26-4
3	Holy Cross	26-2
4	Indiana	20-4
5	Duquesne	26-3
6	Notre Dame	22-3
7	*BRADLEY*	19-13
8	Western Ky.	29-3
9	*PENN ST.*	18-6
10	Okla. A&M	24-5
11	USC	19-14
12	*GEO. WASH.*	23-3
13	Iowa	17-5
14	LSU	21-5
15	Duke	22-6
16	*NIAGARA*	24-6
17	Seattle	26-2
18	Kansas	16-5
19	Illinois	17-5
20	*MARYLAND*	23-7

1974

		Final Record
1	N.C. State	30-1
2	UCLA	26-4
3	Marquette	26-5
4	Maryland	23-5
5	Notre Dame	26-3
6	Michigan	22-5
7	Kansas	23-7
8	Providence	28-4
9	Indiana	23-5
10	Long Beach St.	24-2
11	*PURDUE*	22-8
12	North Carolina	22-6
13	Vanderbilt	23-5
14	Alabama	22-4
15	*UTAH*	22-8
16	Pittsburgh	25-4
17	USC	24-5
18	*ORAL ROBERTS*	23-6
19	South Carolina	22-5
20	Dayton	20-9

1975

		Final Record
1	UCLA	28-3
2	Kentucky	26-5
3	Indiana	31-1
4	Louisville	28-3
5	Maryland	24-5
6	Syracuse	23-9
7	N.C. State	22-6
8	Arizona St.	25-4
9	North Carolina	23-8
10	Alabama	22-5
11	Marquette	23-4
12	*PRINCETON*	22-8
13	Cincinnati	23-6
14	Notre Dame	19-10
15	Kansas St.	20-9
16	Drake	19-10
17	UNLV	24-5
18	Oregon St.	19-12
19	*MICHIGAN*	19-8
20	Penn	23-5

Pre-Tournament Records

1953– St. John's (Al DeStefano, 14-5); Wake Forest (Murray Greason, 21-6); Santa Clara (Bob Feerick, 18-6); DePaul (Ray Meyer, 18-7); SW Missouri St. (Bob Vanatta, 19-4 before NAIA tourney). **1954**– Bradley (Forddy Anderson, 15-12); Penn St. (Elmer Gross, 14-5); George Washington (Bill Reinhart, 23-2); Niagara (Taps Gallagher, 22-5); Maryland (Bud Millikan, 23-7). **1974**– Purdue (Fred Schaus, 18-8); Utah (Bill Foster, 19-7); Oral Roberts (Ken Trickey, 21-5). **1975**– Princeton (Pete Carril, 18-8); Michigan (Johnny Orr, 19-7).

Division I Winning Streaks

Full Season

(Including tournaments)

No		Seasons	Broken by	Score
88	UCLA	1971-74	Notre Dame	71-70
60	San Francisco	1955-57	Illinois	62-33
47	UCLA	1966-68	Houston	71-69
45	UNLV	1990-91	Duke	79-77
44	Texas	1913-17	Rice	24-18
43	Seton Hall	1939-41	LIU-Bklyn	49-26
43	LIU-Brooklyn	1935-37	Stanford	45-31
41	UCLA	1968-69	USC	46-44
39	Marquette	1970-71	Ohio St.	60-59
37	Cincinnati	1962-63	Wichita St.	65-64
37	North Carolina	1957-58	West Virginia	75-64
36	N.C. State	1974-75	Wake Forest	83-78
35	Arkansas	1927-29	Texas	26-25

Regular Season

(Not including tournaments)

No		Seasons	Broken by	Score
76	UCLA	1971-74	Notre Dame	71-70
57	Indiana	1975-77	Toledo	59-57
56	Marquette	1970-72	Detroit	70-49
54	Kentucky	1952-55	Georgia Tech	59-58
51	San Francisco	1955-57	Illinois	62-33
48	Penn	1970-72	Temple	57-52
47	Ohio St	1960-62	Wisconsin	86-67
44	Texas	1913-17	Rice	24-18
43	UCLA	1966-68	Houston	71-69
43	LIU-Brooklyn	1935-37	Stanford	45-31
42	Seton Hall	1939-41	LIU-Bklyn	49-26

Home Court

No		Seasons	Broken By	Score
129	Kentucky	1943-55	Georgia Tech	59-58
99	St. Bonaventure	1948-61	Detroit	77-70
98	UCLA	1970-76	Oregon	65-45
86	Cincinnati	1957-64	Kansas	51-47
81	Arizona	1945-51	Kansas St.	76-57
81	Marquette	1967-73	Notre Dame	71-69
80	Lamar	1978-84	Louisiana Tech	68-65
75	Long Beach St.	1968-74	San Francisco	94-84
72	UNLV	1974-78	New Mexico	102-98
71	Arizona	1987-92	UCLA	89-87

Most Improved Teams

Since 1974

Team	Season	W-L	Previous W-L	Games Improved
N.C. A&T	1978	20-8	3-24	16.5
Murray St.	1980	23-8	4-22	16.5
Liberty	1992	22-7	5-23	16.5
North Texas	1976	22-4	6-20	16
Radford	1991	22-7	7-22	15
Tulsa	1981	26-7	8-19	15
Utah St.	1983	20-9	4-23	15
W. Michigan	1992	21-9	5-22	14.5
Tennessee St.	1993	19-10	4-24	14.5
Fresno St.	1978	21-6	7-20	14
James Madison	1987	20-10	5-23	14
Loyola-CA	1988	28-4	12-16	14
Cal Poly-SLO	1996	16-13	1-26	14

All-Time Highest Scoring Teams

SINGLE SEASON

Scoring Offense

Team	Season	Gm	Pts	Avg
Loyola-CA	1990	32	3918	122.4
Loyola-CA	1989	31	3486	112.5
UNLV	1976	31	3426	110.5
Loyola-CA	1988	32	3528	110.3
UNLV	1977	32	3426	107.1
Oral Roberts	1972	28	2943	105.1
Southern-BR	1991	28	2924	104.4
Loyola-CA	1991	31	3211	103.6
Oklahoma	1988	39	4012	102.9
Oklahoma	1989	36	3680	102.2

SINGLE GAME

Highest Scoring

	Score	Opponent	Date
Loyola-CA	186-140	US Int'l	1/5/91
Loyola-CA	181-150	US Int'l	1/31/89
Oklahoma	173-101	US Int'l	11/29/89
Oklahoma	172-112	Loyola-CA	12/15/90
Arkansas	166-101	US Int'l	12/9/89

Scoring Defense

Before 1965

Team	Season	Gm	Pts	Avg
Oklahoma A&M	1948	31	1006	32.5
Oklahoma A&M	1949	28	985	35.2
Oklahoma A&M	1950	27	1059	39.2
Alabama	1948	27	1070	39.6
Creighton	1948	23	925	40.2

Since 1965

Team	Season	Gm	Pts	Avg
Fresno St.	1982	30	1412	47.1
Princeton	1992	28	1349	48.2
Princeton	1991	27	1320	48.9
N.C. State	1982	32	1570	49.1
Princeton	1982	26	1277	49.1

Scoring Margin

Team	Season	Off	Def	Mar
UCLA	1972	94.6	64.3	30.3
N.C. State	1948	75.3	47.2	28.1
Kentucky	1954	87.5	60.3	27.2
Kentucky	1952	82.3	55.4	26.9
UNLV	1991	97.7	71.0	26.7
UCLA	1968	93.4	67.2	26.2
UCLA	1967	89.6	63.7	25.9
Houston	1968	97.8	72.5	25.3
Kentucky	1948	69.0	44.4	24.6
Kentucky	1949	68.2	43.9	24.3

NCAA Champs With Most Losses

11	Kansas (27-11)	1988
10	Villanova (25-10)	1985
10	N.C. State (26-10)	1983
9	Arizona (25-9)	1997
9	Indiana (26-9)	1981

Annual NCAA Division I Leaders

Scoring

The NCAA did not begin keeping individual scoring records until the 1947-48 season. All averages include postseason games where applicable.

Multiple winners: Pete Maravich and Oscar Robertson (3); Darrell Floyd, Charles Jones, Harry Kelly, Frank Selvy and Freeman Williams (2).

Year		Gm	Pts	Avg
1948	Murray Wier, Iowa	19	399	21.0
1949	Tony Lavelli, Yale	30	671	22.4
1950	Paul Arizin, Villanova	29	735	25.3
1951	Bill Mlkvy, Temple	25	731	29.2
1952	Clyde Lovellette, Kansas	28	795	28.4
1953	Frank Selvy, Furman	25	738	29.5
1954	Frank Selvy, Furman	29	1209	41.7
1955	Darrell Floyd, Furman	25	897	35.9
1956	Darrell Floyd, Furman	28	946	33.8
1957	Grady Wallace, S. Carolina	29	906	31.2
1958	Oscar Robertson, Cincinnati	28	984	35.1
1959	Oscar Robertson, Cincinnati	30	978	32.6
1960	Oscar Robertson, Cincinnati	30	1011	33.7
1961	Frank Burgess, Gonzaga	26	842	32.4
1962	Billy McGill, Utah	26	1009	38.8
1963	Nick Werkman, Seton Hall	22	650	29.5
1964	Howie Komives, Bowling Green	23	844	36.7
1965	Rick Barry, Miami-FL	26	973	37.4
1966	Dave Schellhase, Purdue	24	781	32.5
1967	Jimmy Walker, Providence	28	851	30.4
1968	Pete Maravich, LSU	26	1138	43.8
1969	Pete Maravich, LSU	26	1148	44.2
1970	Pete Maravich, LSU	31	1381	44.5
1971	Johnny Neumann, Ole Miss	23	923	40.1
1972	Dwight Lamar, SW La.	29	1054	36.3
1973	Bird Averitt, Pepperdine	25	848	33.9
1974	Larry Fogle, Canisius	25	835	33.4
1975	Bob McCurdy, Richmond	26	855	32.9
1976	Marshall Rodgers, Texas-Pan Am	25	919	36.8
1977	Freeman Williams, Portland St.	26	1010	38.8
1978	Freeman Williams, Portland St.	27	969	35.9
1979	Lawrence Butler, Idaho St	27	812	30.1
1980	Tony Murphy, Southern-BR	29	932	32.1
1981	Zam Fredrick, S. Carolina	27	781	28.9
1982	Harry Kelly, Texas Southern	29	862	29.7
1983	Harry Kelly, Texas Southern	29	835	28.8
1984	Joe Jakubick, Akron	27	814	30.1
1985	Xavier McDaniel, Wichita St	31	844	27.2
1986	Terrance Bailey, Wagner	29	854	29.4
1987	Kevin Houston, Army	29	953	32.9
1988	Hersey Hawkins, Bradley	31	1125	36.3
1989	Hank Gathers, Loyola-CA	31	1015	32.7
1990	Bo Kimble, Loyola-CA	32	1131	35.3
1991	Kevin Bradshaw, US Int'l	28	1054	37.6
1992	Brett Roberts, Morehead St	29	815	28.1
1993	Greg Guy, Texas-Pan Am	19	556	29.3
1994	Glenn Robinson, Purdue	34	1030	30.3
1995	Kurt Thomas, TCU	27	781	28.9
1996	Kevin Granger, Texas Southern	24	648	27.0
1997	Charles Jones, LIU-Brooklyn	30	903	30.1
1998	Charles Jones, LIU-Brooklyn	30	869	29.0

Note: Seventeen underclassmen have won the title. **Sophomores** (4)–Robertson (1958), Maravich (1968), Neumann (1971) and Fogle (1974); **Juniors** (13)–Selvy (1953), Floyd (1955), Robertson (1959), Werkman (1963), Maravich (1969), Lamar (1972), Williams (1977), Kelly (1982), Bailey (1986), Gathers (1989), Guy (1993), Robinson (1994) and Jones (1997).

Rebounds

The NCAA did not begin keeping individual rebounding records until the 1950-51 season. From 1956-62, the championship was decided on highest percentage of recoveries out of all rebounds made by both teams in all games. All averages include postseason games where applicable.

Multiple winners: Artis Gilmore, Jerry Lucas, Xavier McDaniel, Kermit Washington and Leroy Wright (2).

Year		Gm	No	Avg
1951	Ernie Beck, Penn	27	556	20.6
1952	Bill Hannon, Army	17	355	20.9
1953	Ed Conlin, Fordham	26	612	23.5
1954	Art Quimby, Connecticut	26	588	22.6
1955	Charlie Slack, Marshall	21	538	25.6
1956	Joe Holup, G. Washington	26	604	25.6
1957	Elgin Baylor, Seattle	25	508	23.5
1958	Alex Ellis, Niagara	25	536	26.2
1959	Leroy Wright, Pacific	26	652	23.8
1960	Leroy Wright, Pacific	17	380	23.4
1961	Jerry Lucas, Ohio St.	27	470	19.8
1962	Jerry Lucas, Ohio St.	28	499	21.1
1963	Paul Silas, Creighton	27	557	20.6
1964	Bob Pelkington, Xavier-OH	26	567	21.8
1965	Toby Kimball, Connecticut	23	483	21.0
1966	Jim Ware, Oklahoma City	29	607	20.9
1967	Dick Cunningham, Murray St.	22	479	21.8
1968	Neal Walk, Florida	25	494	19.8
1969	Spencer Haywood, Detroit	22	472	21.5
1970	Artis Gilmore, Jacksonville	28	621	22.2
1971	Artis Gilmore, Jacksonville	26	603	23.2
1972	Kermit Washington, American	23	455	19.8
1973	Kermit Washington, American	22	439	20.0
1974	Marvin Barnes, Providence	32	597	18.7
1975	John Irving, Hofstra	21	323	15.4
1976	Sam Pellom, Buffalo	26	420	16.2
1977	Glenn Mosley, Seton Hall	29	473	16.3
1978	Ken Williams, N. Texas	28	411	14.7
1979	Monti Davis, Tennessee St.	26	421	16.2
1980	Larry Smith, Alcorn State	26	392	15.1
1981	Darryl Watson, Miss. Valley St.	27	379	14.0
1982	LaSalle Thompson, Texas	27	365	13.5
1983	Xavier McDaniel, Wichita St.	28	403	14.4
1984	Akeem Olajuwon, Houston	37	500	13.5
1985	Xavier McDaniel, Wichita St.	31	460	14.8
1986	David Robinson, Navy	35	455	13.0
1987	Jerome Lane, Pittsburgh	33	444	13.5
1988	Kenny Miller, Loyola-IL	29	395	13.6
1989	Hank Gathers, Loyola-CA	31	426	13.7
1990	Anthony Bonner, St. Louis	33	456	13.8
1991	Shaquille O'Neal, LSU	28	411	14.7
1992	Popeye Jones, Murray St.	30	431	14.4
1993	Warren Kidd, Mid. Tenn. St.	26	386	14.8
1994	Jerome Lambert, Baylor	24	355	14.8
1995	Kurt Thomas, TCU	27	393	14.6
1996	Marcus Mann, Miss. Valley St.	29	394	13.6
1997	Tim Duncan, Wake Forest	31	457	14.7
1998	Ryan Perryman, Dayton	33	412	12.5

Note: Only three players have ever led the NCAA in scoring and rebounding in the same season: Xavier McDaniel of Wichita St. (1985), Hank Gathers of Loyola-Marymount (1989) and Kurt Thomas of TCU (1995).

Assists

The NCAA did not begin keeping individual assist records until the 1983-84 season. All averages include postseason games where applicable.

Multiple winner: Avery Johnson (2).

Year		Gm	No	Avg
1984	Craig Lathen, IL-Chicago	29	274	9.45
1985	Rob Weingard, Hofstra	24	228	9.50
1986	Mark Jackson, St. John's	36	328	9.11
1987	Avery Johnson, Southern-BR	31	333	10.74
1988	Avery Johnson, Southern-BR	30	399	13.30
1989	Glenn Williams, Holy Cross	28	278	9.93
1990	Todd Lehmann, Drexel	28	260	9.29
1991	Chris Corchiani, N.C. State	31	299	9.65
1992	Van Usher, Tennessee Tech	29	254	8.76
1993	Sam Crawford, N. Mexico St	34	310	9.12
1994	Jason Kidd, California	30	272	9.06
1995	Nelson Haggerty, Baylor	28	284	10.14
1996	Raimonds Miglinieks, UC-Irvine	27	230	8.52
1997	Kenny Mitchell, Dartmouth	26	203	7.81
1998	Ahlon Lewis, Arizona St.	32	294	9.19

Blocked Shots

The NCAA did not begin keeping individual blocked shots records until the 1985-86 season. All averages include postseason games where applicable.

Multiple winner: Keith Closs and David Robinson (2).

Year		Gm	No	Avg
1986	David Robinson, Navy	35	207	5.91
1987	David Robinson, Navy	32	144	4.50
1988	Rodney Blake, St. Joe's-PA	29	116	4.00
1989	Alonzo Mourning, G'town	34	169	4.97
1990	Kenny Green, Rhode Island	26	124	4.77
1991	Shawn Bradley, BYU	34	177	5.21
1992	Shaquille O'Neal, LSU	30	157	5.23
1993	Theo Ratliff, Wyoming	28	124	4.43
1994	Grady Livingston, Howard	26	115	4.42
1995	Keith Closs, Cen. Conn. St.	26	139	5.35
1996	Keith Closs, Cen. Conn. St.	28	178	6.36
1997	Adonal Foyle, Colgate	28	180	6.43
1998	Jerome James, Florida A&M	27	125	4.63

All-Time NCAA Division I Individual Leaders

Through 1997-98; includes regular season and tournament games; **Last** column indicates final year played.

CAREER

Scoring

	Points	Yrs	Last	Gm	Pts
1	Pete Maravich, LSU	3	1970	83	3667
2	Freeman Williams, Port. St.	4	1978	106	3249
3	Lionel Simmons, La Salle	4	1990	131	3217
4	Alphonzo Ford, Miss. Val. St.	4	1993	109	3165
5	Harry Kelly, Texas Southern	4	1983	110	3066
6	Hersey Hawkins, Bradley	4	1988	125	3008
7	Oscar Robertson, Cincinnati	3	1960	88	2973
8	Danny Manning, Kansas	4	1988	147	2951
9	Alfredrick Hughes, Loyola-IL	4	1985	120	2914
10	Elvin Hayes, Houston	3	1968	93	2884
11	Larry Bird, Indiana St.	3	1979	94	2850
12	Otis Birdsong, Houston	4	1977	116	2832
13	Kevin Bradshaw, US Int'l	4	1991	111	2804
14	Allan Houston, Tennessee	4	1993	128	2801
15	Hank Gathers, USC/Loyola-CA	4	1990	117	2723
16	Reggie Lewis, Northeastern	4	1987	122	2708
17	Daren Queenan, Lehigh	4	1988	118	2703
18	Byron Larkin, Xavier-OH	4	1988	121	2696
19	David Robinson, Navy	4	1987	127	2669
20	Wayman Tisdale, Oklahoma	3	1985	104	2661

	Average	Yrs	Last	Pts	Avg
1	Pete Maravich, LSU	3	1970	3667	44.2
2	Austin Carr, Notre Dame	3	1971	2560	34.6
3	Oscar Robertson, Cinn	3	1960	2973	33.8
4	Calvin Murphy, Niagara	3	1970	2548	33.1
5	Dwight Lamar, SW La	2	1973	1862	32.7
6	Frank Selvy, Furman	3	1954	2538	32.5
7	Rick Mount, Purdue	3	1970	2323	32.3
8	Darrell Floyd, Furman	3	1956	2281	32.1
9	Nick Werkman, Seton Hall	3	1964	2273	32.0
10	Willie Humes, Idaho St.	2	1971	1510	31.5
11	William Averitt, Pepperdine	2	1973	1541	31.4
12	Elgin Baylor, Idaho/Seattle	3	1958	2500	31.3
13	Elvin Hayes, Houston	3	1968	2884	31.0
14	Freeman Williams, Port. St.	4	1978	3249	30.7
15	Larry Bird, Indiana St.	3	1979	2850	30.3
16	Bill Bradley, Princeton	3	1965	2503	30.2
17	Rich Fuqua, Oral Roberts	2	1973	1617	29.9
18	Wilt Chamberlain, Kansas	2	1958	1433	29.9
19	Rick Barry, Miami-FL	3	1965	2298	29.8
20	Doug Collins, Illinois St.	3	1973	2240	29.1

	Field Goal Pct.	Yrs	Last	FG	FGA	Pct
1	Ricky Nedd, Appalach. St.	4	1994	412	597	.690
2	Stephen Scheffler, Purdue	4	1990	408	596	.685
3	Steve Johnson, Ore. St.	4	1981	828	1222	.678
4	Murray Brown, Fla. St.	4	1980	566	847	.668
5	Lee Campbell, SW Mo.St.	3	1990	411	618	.665
6	Warren Kidd, M.Tenn.St.	3	1993	496	747	.664
7	Joe Senser, West Chester	4	1979	476	719	.662
8	Kevin McGee, UC-Irvine	2	1982	552	841	.656
9	O. Phillips, Pepperdine	2	1983	404	618	.654
10	Bill Walton, UCLA	3	1974	747	1147	.651

Note: minimum 400 FGs made.

	Free Throw Pct.	Yrs	Last	FT	FTA	Pct
1	Greg Starrick, Ky/So.Ill	4	1972	341	375	.909
2	Jack Moore, Nebraska	4	1982	446	495	.901
3	Steve Henson, Kansas St.	4	1990	361	401	.900
4	Steve Alford, Indiana	4	1987	535	596	.898
5	Bob Lloyd, Rutgers	3	1967	543	605	.898
6	Jim Barton, Dartmouth	4	1989	394	440	.895
7	Tommy Boyer, Arkansas	3	1963	315	353	.892
8	Rob Robbins, N. Mexico	4	1991	309	348	.888
9	Sean Miller, Pitt	4	1992	317	358	.885
10	Ron Perry, Holy Cross	4	1980	680	768	.885
	Joe Dykstra, Western Ill.	4	1983	587	663	.885

Note: minimum 300 FTs made.

	3-Pt Field Goals	Yrs	Last	Gm	3FG
1	Curtis Staples, Virginia	4	1998	122	413
2	Doug Day, Radford	4	1993	117	401
3	Ronnie Schmitz, Missouri-KC	4	1993	112	378
4	Mark Alberts, Akron	4	1993	107	375
5	Bryce Drew, Valparaiso	4	1998	121	364

	3-Pt Field Goal Pct.	Yrs	Last	3FG	Att	Pct
1	Tony Bennett, Wisc-GB	4	1992	290	584	.497
2	Keith Jennings, E.Tenn.St.	4	1991	223	452	.493
3	Kirk Manns, Michigan St.	4	1990	212	446	.475
4	Tim Locum, Wisconsin	4	1991	227	481	.472
5	David Olson, Eastern Ill.	4	1992	262	562	.466

Note: minimum 200 3FGs made.

Rebounds

	Total (before 1973)	Yrs	Last	Gm	No
1	Tom Gola, La Salle	4	1955	118	2201
2	Joe Holup, G. Washington	4	1956	104	2030
3	Charlie Slack, Marshall	4	1956	88	1916
4	Ed Conlin, Fordham	4	1955	102	1884
5	Dickie Hemric, Wake Forest	4	1955	104	1802
6	Paul Silas, Creighton	3	1964	81	1751
7	Art Quimby, Connecticut	4	1955	80	1716
8	Jerry Harper, Alabama	4	1956	93	1688
9	Jeff Cohen, Wm. & Mary	4	1961	103	1679
10	Steve Hamilton, Morehead St.	4	1958	102	1675

	Total (since 1973)	Yrs	Last	Gm	No
1	Tim Duncan, Wake Forest	4	1997	128	1570
2	Derrick Coleman, Syracuse	4	1990	143	1537
3	Ralph Sampson, Virginia	4	1983	132	1511
4	Pete Padgett, Nevada-Reno	4	1976	104	1464
5	Lionel Simmons, La Salle	4	1990	131	1429
6	Anthony Bonner, St. Louis	4	1990	133	1424
7	Tyrone Hill, Xavier-OH	4	1990	126	1380
8	Popeye Jones, Murray St.	4	1992	123	1374
9	Michael Brooks, La Salle	4	1980	114	1372
10	Xavier McDaniel, Wichita St.	4	1985	117	1359

	Average (before 1973)	Yrs	Last	No	Avg
1	Artis Gilmore, Jacksonville	2	1971	1224	22.7
2	Charlie Slack, Marshall	4	1956	1916	21.8
3	Paul Silas, Creighton	3	1964	1751	21.6
4	Leroy Wright, Pacific	3	1960	1442	21.5
5	Art Quimby, Connecticut	4	1955	1716	21.5

Note: minimum 800 rebounds.

	Average (since 1973)	Yrs	Last	No	Avg
1	Glenn Mosley, Seton Hall	4	1977	1263	15.2
2	Bill Campion, Manhattan	3	1975	1070	14.2
3	Pete Padgett, Nevada-Reno	4	1976	1464	14.1
4	Bob Warner, Maine	4	1976	1304	13.6
5	Shaquille O'Neal, LSU	3	1992	1217	13.5

Note: minimum 650 rebounds.

Assists

	Total	Yrs	Last	Gm	No
1	Bobby Hurley, Duke	4	1993	140	1076
2	Chris Corchiani, N.C. State	4	1991	124	1038
3	Keith Jennings, E. Tenn. St.	4	1991	127	983
4	Sherman Douglas, Syracuse	4	1989	138	960
5	Tony Miller, Marquette	4	1995	123	956
6	Greg Anthony, Portland/UNLV	4	1991	138	950
7	Gary Payton, Oregon St.	4	1990	120	938
8	Orlando Smart, San Fran	4	1994	116	902
9	Andre LaFleur, Northeastern	4	1987	128	894
10	Jim Les, Bradley	4	1986	118	884

	Average	Yrs	Last	No	Avg
1	A. Johnson, Cameron/Southern	3	1988	838	8.91
2	Sam Crawford, N. Mexico St.	2	1993	592	8.84
3	Mark Wade, Okla/UNLV	3	1987	693	8.77
4	Chris Corchiani, N.C. State	4	1991	1038	8.37
5	Taurence Chisholm, Delaware	4	1988	877	7.97
6	Van Usher, Tennessee Tech	3	1992	676	7.95
7	Anthony Manuel, Bradley	3	1989	855	7.92
8	Gary Payton, Oregon St.	4	1990	938	7.82
9	Orlando Smart, San Fran	4	1994	902	7.78
10	Tony Miller, Marquette	4	1995	956	7.77

Note: minimum 550 assists.

Blocked Shots

	Average	Yrs	Last	No	Avg
1	Keith Closs, Cen. Conn. St.	2	1996	317	5.87
2	Adonal Foyle, Colgate	3	1997	492	5.66
3	David Robinson, Navy	2	1987	351	5.24
4	Shaquille O'Neal, LSU	3	1992	412	4.58
5	Jerome James, Fla. A&M	3	1998	363	4.48

Note: minimum 200 blocked shots.

Steals

	Average	Yrs	Last	No	Avg
1	Mookie Blaylock, Oklahoma	2	1989	281	3.80
2	Ronn McMahon, Eastern Wash.	3	1990	225	3.52
3	Jason Kidd, California	2	1994	204	3.46
4	Eric Murdock, Providence	4	1991	376	3.21
5	Van Usher, Tennessee Tech	3	1992	270	3.18

Note: minimum 200 steals.

2000 Points/1000 Rebounds

For a combined total of 4000 or more.

		Gm	Pts	Reb	Total
1	Tom Gola, La Salle	118	2462	2201	4663
2	Lionel Simmons, La Salle	131	3217	1429	4646
3	Elvin Hayes, Houston	93	2884	1602	4486
4	Dickie Hemric, W. Forest	104	2587	1802	4389
5	Oscar Robertson, Cinn.	88	2973	1338	4311
6	Joe Holup, G. Wash	104	2226	2030	4256
7	Harry Kelly, TX-Southern	110	3066	1085	4151
8	Danny Manning, Kansas	147	2951	1187	4138
9	Larry Bird, Indiana St.	94	2850	1247	4097
10	Elgin Baylor, Col. Idaho/ Seattle	80	2500	1559	4059
11	Michael Brooks, La Salle	114	2628	1372	4000

Years Played– Baylor (1956-58); **Bird** (1977-79); **Brooks** (1977-80); **Gola** (1952-55); **Hayes** (1966-68); **Hemric** (1952-55); **Holup** (1953-56); **Kelly** (1980-83); **Manning** (1985-88); **Robertson** (1958-60); **Simmons** (1987-90).

SINGLE SEASON

Scoring

	Points	Year	Gm	Pts
1	Pete Maravich, LSU	1970	31	1381
2	Elvin Hayes, Houston	1968	33	1214
3	Frank Selvy, Furman	1954	29	1209
4	Pete Maravich, LSU	1969	26	1148
5	Pete Maravich, LSU	1968	26	1138
6	Bo Kimble, Loyola-CA	1990	32	1131
7	Hersey Hawkins, Bradley	1988	31	1125
8	Austin Carr, Notre Dame	1970	29	1106
9	Austin Carr, Notre Dame	1971	29	1101
10	Otis Birdsong, Houston	1977	36	1090

	Average	Year	Gm	Pts	Avg
1	Pete Maravich, LSU	1970	31	1381	44.5
2	Pete Maravich, LSU	1969	26	1148	44.2
3	Pete Maravich, LSU	1968	26	1138	43.8
4	Frank Selvy, Furman	1954	29	1209	41.7
5	Johnny Neumann, Ole Miss	1971	23	923	40.1
6	Freeman Williams, Port. St.	1977	26	1010	38.8
7	Billy McGill, Utah	1962	26	1009	38.8
8	Calvin Murphy, Niagara	1968	24	916	38.2
9	Austin Carr, Notre Dame	1970	29	1106	38.1
10	Austin Carr, Notre Dame	1971	29	1101	38.0

All-Time NCAA Division I Individual Leaders (Cont.)

	Field Goal Pct.	Year	FG	FGA	Pct
1	Steve Johnson, Oregon St.	1981	235	315	.746
2	Dwayne Davis, Florida	1989	179	248	.722
3	Keith Walker, Utica	1985	154	216	.713
4	Steve Johnson, Oregon St.	1980	211	297	.710
5	Oliver Miller, Arkansas	1991	254	361	.704

	Free Throw Pct.	Year	FT	FTA	Pct
1	Craig Collins, Penn St.	1985	94	98	.959
2	Rod Foster, UCLA	1982	95	100	.950
3	Carlos Gibson, Marshall	1978	84	89	.944
4	Danny Basile, Marist	1994	84	89	.944
5	Jim Barton, Dartmouth	1986	65	69	.942

	3-Pt Field Goal Pct.	Year	3FG	Att	Pct
1	Glenn Tropf, Holy Cross	1988	52	82	.634
2	Sean Wightman, W. Mich	1992	48	76	.632
3	Keith Jennings, E. Tenn. St.	1991	84	142	.592
4	Dave Calloway, Monmouth	1989	48	82	.585
5	Steve Kerr, Arizona	1988	114	199	.573

Assists

	Average	Year	Gm	No	Avg
1	Avery Johnson, Southern-BR	1988	30	399	13.3
2	Anthony Manuel, Bradley	1988	31	373	12.0
3	Avery Johnson, Southern-BR	1987	31	333	10.7
4	Mark Wade, UNLV	1987	38	406	10.7
5	Glenn Williams, Holy Cross	1989	28	278	9.9

Rebounds

	Average (before 1973)	Year	Gm	No	Avg
1	Charlie Slack, Marshall	1955	21	538	25.6
2	Leroy Wright, Pacific	1959	26	652	25.1
3	Art Quimby, Connecticut	1955	25	611	24.4
4	Charlie Slack, Marshall	1956	22	520	23.6
5	Ed Conlin, Fordham	1953	26	612	23.5

	Average (since 1973)	Year	Gm	No	Avg
1	Kermit Washington, American	1973	25	511	20.4
2	Marvin Barnes, Providence	1973	30	571	19.0
3	Marvin Barnes, Providence	1974	32	597	18.7
4	Pete Padgett, Nevada	1973	26	462	17.8
5	Jim Bradley, Northern Ill	1973	24	426	17.8

Blocked Shots

	Average	Year	Gm	No	Avg
1	Adonal Foyle, Colgate	1997	28	180	6.42
2	Keith Closs, Cen. Conn. St.	1996	28	178	6.36
3	David Robinson, Navy	1986	35	207	5.91
4	Keith Closs, Cen. Conn. St.	1995	26	139	5.35
5	Shaquille O'Neal, LSU	1992	30	157	5.23

Steals

	Average	Year	Gm	No	Avg
1	Darron Brittman, Chicago St.	1986	28	139	4.96
2	Aldwin Ware, Florida A&M	1988	29	142	4.90
3	Ronn McMahon, East Wash.	1990	29	130	4.48
4	Pointer Williams, McNeese St.	1996	27	118	4.37
5	Jim Paguaga, St. Francis-NY	1986	28	120	4.29

SINGLE GAME

Scoring

	Points vs Div. I Team	Year	Pts
1	Kevin Bradshaw, US Int'l vs Loyola-CA	1991	72
2	Pete Maravich, LSU vs Alabama	1970	69
3	Calvin Murphy, Niagara vs Syracuse	1969	68
4	Jay Handlan, Wash. & Lee vs Furman	1951	66
	Pete Maravich, LSU vs Tulane	1969	66
	Anthony Roberts, Oral Rbts vs N.C. A&T	1977	66
7	Anthony Roberts, Oral Rbts vs Ore	1977	65
	Scott Haffner, Evansville vs Dayton	1989	65
9	Pete Maravich, LSU vs Kentucky	1970	64
10	Johnny Neumann, Ole Miss vs LSU	1971	63
	Hersey Hawkins, Bradley vs Detroit	1988	63

	Points vs Non-Div. I Team	Year	Pts
1	Frank Selvy, Furman vs Newberry	1954	100
2	Paul Arizin, Villanova vs Phi. NAMC	1949	85
3	Freeman Williams, Port. St. vs Rocky Mt	1978	81
4	Bill Mlkvy, Temple vs Wilkes	1951	73
5	Freeman Williams, Port. St. vs So. Ore	1977	71

Note: Bevo Francis of Division II Rio Grande (Ohio) scored an overall collegiate record 113 points against Hillsdale in 1954. He also scored 84 against Alliance and 82 against Bluffton that same season.

Assists

		Year	No
1	Tony Fairley, Baptist vs Armstrong St.	1987	22
	Avery Johnson, Southern-BR vs TX-South	1988	22
	Sherman Douglas, Syracuse vs Providence	1989	22
4	Mark Wade, UNLV vs Navy	1986	21
	Kelvin Scarborough, N. Mexico vs Hawaii	1987	21
	Anthony Manuel, Bradley vs UC-Irvine	1987	21
	Avery Johnson, Southern-BR vs Ala. St.	1988	21

3-Pt Field Goals

		Year	No
1	Keith Veney, Marshall vs Morehead St.	1996	15
2	Dave Jamerson, Ohio U. vs Charleston	1989	14
	Askia Jones, Kansas St. vs Fresno St.	1994	14
4	Gary Bossert, Niagara vs Siena	1987	12
	Darrin Fitzgerald, Butler vs Detroit	1987	12
	Al Dillard, Arkansas vs Delaware St.	1993	12
	Mitch Taylor, South-BR vs La. Christian	1995	12
	David McMahan, Winthrop vs C. Carolina	1996	12

Rebounds

	Total (before 1973)	Year	No
1	Bill Chambers, Wm. & Mary vs Virginia	1953	51
2	Charlie Slack, Marshall vs M. Harvey	1954	43
3	Tom Heinsohn, Holy Cross vs BC	1955	42
4	Art Quimby, UConn vs BU	1955	40
5	Three players tied with 39 each.		

	Total (since 1973)	Year	No
1	David Vaughn, Oral Roberts vs Brandeis	1973	34
2	Robert Parish, Centenary vs So. Miss	1973	33
3	Durand Macklin, LSU vs Tulane	1976	32
	Jervaughn Scales, South-BR vs Grambling	1994	32
5	Jim Bradley, Northern Ill. vs WI-Milw	1973	31
	Calvin Natt, NE La. vs Ga. Southern	1976	31

Blocked Shots

		Year	No
1	David Robinson, Navy vs NC-Wilmington	1986	14
	Shawn Bradley, BYU vs Eastern Ky	1990	14
	Roy Rogers, Alabama vs Georgia	1996	14
4	Kevin Roberson, Vermont vs UNH	1992	13
	Jim McIlvaine, Marquette vs No. Ill	1993	13
	Keith Closs, C. Conn. St. vs St. Fran-PA.	1994	13

Steals

		Year	No
1	Mookie Blaylock, Oklahoma vs Centenary	1987	13
	Mookie Blaylock, Oklahoma vs Loyola-CA	1988	13
3	Kenny Robertson, Cleve. St. vs Wagner	1988	12
	Terry Evans, Oklahoma vs Florida A&M	1993	12
5	Ten players tied with 11 each.		

Annual Awards

UPI picked the first national Division I Player of the Year in 1955. Since then, the U.S. Basketball Writers Assn. (1959), the Commonwealth Athletic Club of Kentucky's Adolph Rupp Trophy (1961), the Atlanta Tip-Off Club (1969), the National Assn. of Basketball Coaches (1975), and the LA Athletic Club's John Wooden Award (1977) have joined in. UPI discontinued its award in 1997.

Since 1977, the first year all the following awards were given out, the same player has won all of them in the same season 11 times: Marques Johnson in 1977, Larry Bird in 1979, Ralph Sampson in both 1982 and '83, Michael Jordan in 1984, David Robinson in 1987, Lionel Simmons in 1990, Calbert Cheaney in 1993, Glenn Robinson in 1994, Tim Duncan in 1997 and Antawn Jamison in 1998.

United Press International

Voted on by a panel of UPI college basketball writers and first presented in 1955.

Multiple winners: Oscar Robertson, Ralph Sampson and Bill Walton (3); Lew Alcindor and Jerry Lucas (2).

Year
1955 Tom Gola, La Salle
1956 Bill Russell, San Francisco
1957 Chet Forte, Columbia
1958 Oscar Robertson, Cincinnati
1959 Oscar Robertson, Cincinnati
1960 Oscar Robertson, Cincinnati
1961 Jerry Lucas, Ohio St.
1962 Jerry Lucas, Ohio St.
1963 Art Heyman, Duke
1964 Gary Bradds, Ohio St.
1965 Bill Bradley, Princeton
1966 Cazzie Russell, Michigan
1967 Lew Alcindor, UCLA
1968 Elvin Hayes, Houston
1969 Lew Alcindor, UCLA

Year
1970 Pete Maravich, LSU
1971 Austin Carr, Notre Dame
1972 Bill Walton, UCLA
1973 Bill Walton, UCLA
1974 Bill Walton, UCLA
1975 David Thompson, N.C. State
1976 Scott May, Indiana
1977 Marques Johnson, UCLA
1978 Butch Lee, Marquette
1979 Larry Bird, Indiana St.
1980 Mark Aguirre, DePaul
1981 Ralph Sampson, Virginia
1982 Ralph Sampson, Virginia
1983 Ralph Sampson, Virginia
1984 Michael Jordan, N. Carolina

Year
1985 Chris Mullin, St. John's
1986 Walter Berry, St. John's
1987 David Robinson, Navy
1988 Hersey Hawkins, Bradley
1989 Danny Ferry, Duke
1990 Lionel Simmons, La Salle
1991 Shaquille O'Neal, LSU
1992 Jim Jackson, Ohio St.
1993 Calbert Cheaney, Indiana
1994 Glenn Robinson, Purdue
1995 Joe Smith, Maryland
1996 Ray Allen, UConn
1997 award discontinued

U.S. Basketball Writers Association

Voted on by the USBWA and first presented in 1959.

Multiple winners: Ralph Sampson and Bill Walton (3); Lew Alcindor, Jerry Lucas and Oscar Robertson (2).

Year
1959 Oscar Robertson, Cincinnati
1960 Oscar Robertson, Cincinnati
1961 Jerry Lucas, Ohio St.
1962 Jerry Lucas, Ohio St.
1963 Art Heyman, Duke
1964 Walt Hazzard, UCLA
1965 Bill Bradley, Princeton
1966 Cazzie Russell, Michigan
1967 Lew Alcindor, UCLA
1968 Elvin Hayes, Houston
1969 Lew Alcindor, UCLA
1970 Pete Maravich, LSU
1971 Sidney Wicks, UCLA
1972 Bill Walton, UCLA

Year
1973 Bill Walton, UCLA
1974 Bill Walton, UCLA
1975 David Thompson, N.C. State
1976 Adrian Dantley, Notre Dame
1977 Marques Johnson, UCLA
1978 Phil Ford, North Carolina
1979 Larry Bird, Indiana St.
1980 Mark Aguirre, DePaul
1981 Ralph Sampson, Virginia
1982 Ralph Sampson, Virginia
1983 Ralph Sampson, Virginia
1984 Michael Jordan, N. Carolina
1985 Chris Mullin, St. John's
1986 Walter Berry, St. John's

Year
1987 David Robinson, Navy
1988 Hersey Hawkins, Bradley
1989 Danny Ferry, Duke
1990 Lionel Simmons, La Salle
1991 Larry Johnson, UNLV
1992 Christian Laettner, Duke
1993 Calbert Cheaney, Indiana
1994 Glenn Robinson, Purdue
1995 Ed O'Bannon, UCLA
1996 Marcus Camby, UMass
1997 Tim Duncan, Wake Forest
1998 Antawn Jamison, N. Carolina

Rupp Trophy

Voted on by AP sportswriters and broadcasters and first presented in 1961 by the Commonwealth Athletic Club of Kentucky in the name of former University of Kentucky coach Adolph Rupp.

Multiple winners: Ralph Sampson (3); Lew Alcindor, Jerry Lucas, David Thompson and Bill Walton (2).

Year
1961 Jerry Lucas, Ohio St.
1962 Jerry Lucas, Ohio St.
1963 Art Heyman, Duke
1964 Gary Bradds, Ohio St.
1965 Bill Bradley, Princeton
1966 Cazzie Russell, Michigan
1967 Lew Alcindor, UCLA
1968 Elvin Hayes, Houston
1969 Lew Alcindor, UCLA
1970 Pete Maravich, LSU
1971 Austin Carr, Notre Dame
1972 Bill Walton, UCLA
1973 Bill Walton, UCLA

Year
1974 David Thompson, N.C. State
1975 David Thompson, N.C. State
1976 Scott May, Indiana
1977 Marques Johnson, UCLA
1978 Butch Lee, Marquette
1979 Larry Bird, Indiana St.
1980 Mark Aguirre, DePaul
1981 Ralph Sampson, Virginia
1982 Ralph Sampson, Virginia
1983 Ralph Sampson, Virginia
1984 Michael Jordan, N. Carolina
1985 Patrick Ewing, Georgetown
1986 Walter Berry, St. John's

Year
1987 David Robinson, Navy
1988 Hersey Hawkins, Bradley
1989 Sean Elliott, Arizona
1990 Lionel Simmons, La Salle
1991 Shaquille O'Neal, LSU
1992 Christian Laettner, Duke
1993 Calbert Cheaney, Indiana
1994 Glenn Robinson, Purdue
1995 Joe Smith, Maryland
1996 Marcus Camby, UMass
1997 Tim Duncan, Wake Forest
1998 Antawn Jamison, N. Carolina

Naismith Award

Voted on by a panel of coaches, sportswriters and broadcasters and first presented in 1969 by the Atlanta Tip-Off Club in 1969 in the name of the inventor of basketball, Dr. James Naismith.

Multiple winners: Ralph Sampson and Bill Walton (3).

Year	Year	Year
1969 Lew Alcindor, UCLA	1979 Larry Bird, Indiana St.	1989 Danny Ferry, Duke
1970 Pete Maravich, LSU	1980 Mark Aguirre, DePaul	1990 Lionel Simmons, La Salle
1971 Austin Carr, Notre Dame	1981 Ralph Sampson, Virginia	1991 Larry Johnson, UNLV
1972 Bill Walton, UCLA	1982 Ralph Sampson, Virginia	1992 Christian Laettner, Duke
1973 Bill Walton, UCLA	1983 Ralph Sampson, Virginia	1993 Calbert Cheaney, Indiana
1974 Bill Walton, UCLA	1984 Michael Jordan, N. Carolina	1994 Glenn Robinson, Purdue
1975 David Thompson, N.C. State	1985 Patrick Ewing, Georgetown	1995 Joe Smith, Maryland
1976 Scott May, Indiana	1986 Johnny Dawkins, Duke	1996 Marcus Camby, UMass
1977 Marques Johnson, UCLA	1987 David Robinson, Navy	1997 Tim Duncan, Wake Forest
1978 Butch Lee, Marquette	1988 Danny Manning, Kansas	1998 Antawn Jamison, N. Carolina

National Association of Basketball Coaches

Voted on by the National Assn. of Basketball Coaches and presented by the Eastman Kodak Co. from 1975-94.

Multiple winner: Ralph Sampson (2).

Year	Year	Year
1975 David Thompson, N.C. State	1983 Ralph Sampson, Virginia	1991 Larry Johnson, UNLV
1976 Scott May, Indiana	1984 Michael Jordan, N. Carolina	1992 Christian Laettner, Duke
1977 Marques Johnson, UCLA	1985 Patrick Ewing, Georgetown	1993 Calbert Cheaney, Indiana
1978 Phil Ford, North Carolina	1986 Walter Berry, St. John's	1994 Glenn Robinson, Purdue
1979 Larry Bird, Indiana St.	1987 David Robinson, Navy	1995 Shawn Respert, Mich. St.
1980 Michael Brooks, La Salle	1988 Danny Manning, Kansas	1996 Marcus Camby, UMass
1981 Danny Ainge, BYU	1989 Sean Elliott, Arizona	1997 Tim Duncan, Wake Forest
1982 Ralph Sampson, Virginia	1990 Lionel Simmons, La Salle	1998 Antawn Jamison, N. Carolina

Wooden Award

Voted on by a panel of coaches, sportswriters and broadcasters and first presented in 1977 by the Los Angeles Athletic Club in the name of former Purdue All-America and UCLA coach John Wooden. Unlike the other five Player of the Year awards, candidates for the Wooden must have a minimum grade point average of 2.00 (out of 4.00).

Multiple winner: Ralph Sampson (2).

Year	Year	Year
1977 Marques Johnson, UCLA	1985 Chris Mullin, St. John's	1993 Calbert Cheaney, Indiana
1978 Phil Ford, North Carolina	1986 Walter Berry St. John's	1994 Glenn Robinson, Purdue
1979 Larry Bird, Indiana St.	1987 David Robinson, Navy	1995 Ed O'Bannon, UCLA
1980 Darrell Griffith, Louisville	1988 Danny Manning, Kansas	1996 Marcus Camby, UMass
1981 Danny Ainge, BYU	1989 Sean Elliott, Arizona	1997 Tim Duncan, Wake Forest
1982 Ralph Sampson, Virginia	1990 Lionel Simmons, La Salle	1998 Antawn Jamison, N. Carolina
1983 Ralph Sampson, Virginia	1991 Larry Johnson, UNLV	
1984 Michael Jordan, N. Carolina	1992 Christian Laettner, Duke	

Players of the Year and Top Draft Picks

Consensus College Players of the Year and first overall selections in NBA draft since the abolition of the NBA's territorial draft in 1966. Top draft picks who became Rookie of the Year are in **bold** type; (*) indicates top draft pick chosen as junior and (**) indicates top draft pick chosen as sophomore.

Year	Player of the Year	Top Draft Pick
1966	Cazzie Russell, Mich.	Cazzie Russell, NY
1967	Lew Alcindor, UCLA	Jimmy Walker, Det.
1968	Elvin Hayes, Houston	Elvin Hayes, SD
1969	Lew Alcindor, UCLA	**Lew Alcindor**, Milw.
1970	Pete Maravich, LSU	Bob Lanier, Det.
1971	Sidney Wicks, UCLA	Austin Carr, Cle.
1972	Bill Walton, UCLA	LaRue Martin, Port.
1973	Bill Walton, UCLA	Doug Collins, Phi.
1974	Bill Walton, UCLA	Bill Walton, Port.
1975	David Thompson, N.C. St.	David Thompson, Atl.
1976	Scott May, Indiana	John Lucas, Hou.
1977	Marques Johnson, UCLA	Kent Benson, Ind.
1978	Butch Lee, Marquette & Phil Ford, N. Caro.	Mychal Thompson, Port.
1979	Larry Bird, Indiana St.	Magic Johnson, LAL**
1980	Mark Aguirre, DePaul	Joe Barry Carroll, G. St.
1981	Ralph Sampson, Va. & Danny Ainge, BYU	Mark Aguirre, Dal.
1982	Ralph Sampson, Va.	James Worthy, LAL*
1983	Ralph Sampson, Va.	**Ralph Sampson**, Hou.
1984	Michael Jordan, N. Caro.	Akeem Olajuwon, Hou.
1985	Patrick Ewing, G'town & Chris Mullin, St. John's	**Patrick Ewing**, NY
1986	Walter Berry, St. John's	Brad Daugherty, Cle.
1987	David Robinson, Navy	**David Robinson**, SA
1988	Hersey Hawkins, Bradley & Danny Manning, Kan.	Danny Manning, LAC
1989	Sean Elliott, Arizona & Danny Ferry, Duke	Pervis Ellison, Sac.
1990	Lionel Simmons, La Salle	**Derrick Coleman**, NJ
1991	Shaquille O'Neal, LSU	**Larry Johnson**, Char.
1992	Christian Laettner, Duke	**Shaquille O'Neal**, Orl.*
1993	Calbert Cheaney, Ind.	**Chris Webber**, Orl**
1994	Glenn Robinson, Purdue	Glenn Robinson, Mil*
1995	Ed O'Bannon, UCLA & Joe Smith, Maryland	Joe Smith, G. St.**
1996	Marcus Camby, UMass	**Allen Iverson**, Phi.**
1997	Tim Duncan, Wake Forest	**Tim Duncan**, SA
1998	Antawn Jamison, N. Caro.	Michael Olowokandi, LAC

All-Time Winningest Division I Coaches

Minimum of 10 seasons as Division I head coach; regular season and tournament games included; coaches active during 1997-98 in **bold** type.

Top 30 Winning Percentage

		Yrs	W	L	Pct
1	Clair Bee	21	412	87	**.826**
2	Adolph Rupp	41	876	190	**.822**
3	**Jerry Tarkanian**	27	687	157	**.814**
4	John Wooden	29	664	162	**.804**
5	Dean Smith	36	879	254	**.776**
6	Harry Fisher	13	147	44	**.770**
7	Frank Keaney	27	387	117	**.768**
8	George Keogan	24	385	117	**.767**
9	Jack Ramsay	11	231	71	**.765**
10	Vic Bubas	10	213	67	**.761**
11	Chick Davies	21	314	106	**.748**
12	Ray Mears	21	399	135	**.747**
13	**Jim Boeheim**	22	528	181	**.745**
14	Rick Pitino	15	352	124	**.739**
15	Al McGuire	20	405	143	**.739**
16	Everett Case	18	376	133	**.739**
17	Phog Allen	48	746	264	**.739**
18	**John Chaney**	26	581	207	**.737**
19	**Nolan Richardson**	18	433	155	**.736**
20	**Rick Majerus**	14	309	111	**.736**
21	Walter Meanwell	22	280	101	**.735**
22	Bill Musselman	12	232	85	**.732**
23	**Lute Olson**	25	564	208	**.731**
24	**Bob Knight**	33	720	270	**.727**
25	Lew Andreas	25	355	134	**.726**
26	Lou Carnesecca	24	526	200	**.725**
27	Fred Schaus	12	251	96	**.723**
28	Cam Henderson	35	630	243	**.722**
29	**John Thompson**	26	589	233	**.717**
30	**Eddie Sutton**	28	599	241	**.713**

Top 30 Victories

		Yrs	W	L	Pct
1	Dean Smith	36	**879**	254	.776
2	Adolph Rupp	41	**876**	190	.822
3	Hank Iba	41	**767**	338	.694
4	Ed Diddle	42	**759**	302	.715
5	Phog Allen	48	**746**	264	.739
6	Ray Meyer	42	**724**	354	.672
7	**Bob Knight**	33	**720**	270	.727
8	**Norm Stewart**	37	**711**	366	.660
9	**Don Haskins**	37	**703**	341	.673
10	**Lefty Driesell**	36	**699**	347	.668
11	**Jerry Tarkanian**	27	**687**	157	.814
12	**Lou Henson**	35	**681**	343	.665
13	John Wooden	29	**664**	162	.804
14	Ralph Miller	38	**657**	382	.632
15	Marv Harshman	40	**654**	449	.593
16	Gene Bartow	34	**647**	353	.647
17	Cam Henderson	35	**630**	243	.722
18	**Denny Crum**	27	**625**	253	.712
19	Norm Sloan	37	**624**	393	.614
20	**Eddie Sutton**	28	**599**	241	.713
	Slats Gill	36	**599**	392	.604
22	Abe Lemons	34	**597**	344	.634
23	Guy Lewis	30	**592**	279	.680
24	**John Thompson**	26	**589**	233	.717
25	**John Chaney**	26	**581**	207	.737
26	**Eldon Miller**	36	**568**	419	.575
27	**Lute Olson**	25	**564**	208	.730
28	Gary Colson	34	**563**	385	.594
29	Tony Hinkle	41	**557**	393	.586
30	Glenn Wilkes	36	**551**	436	.558

Note: Clarence (Bighouse) Gaines of Division II Winston-Salem St. (1947-93) retired after the 1992-93 season to finish his 47-year career ranked No. 3 on the all-time NCAA list of all coaches regardless of division. His record is 828-446 with a .650 winning percentage.

Where They Coached

Allen–Baker (1906-08), Kansas (1908-09), Haskell (1909), Central Mo. St. (1913-19), Kansas (1920-56); **Andreas**–Syracuse (1925-43; 45-50); **Bartow**–Central Mo. St. (1962-64), Valparaiso (1965-70), Memphis St. (1971-74), Illinois (1975), UCLA (1976-77), UAB (1979-96); **Bee**–Rider (1929-31), LIU-Brooklyn (1932-45, 46-51); **Boeheim**–Syracuse (1977–); **Bubas**–Duke (1960-69); **Carnesecca**–St. John's (1966-70, 74-92); **Case**–N.C. State (1947-64); **Chaney**–Cheyney St. (1973-82), Temple (1983–); **Colson**–Valdosta St. (1959-68), Pepperdine (1969-79), New Mexico (1981-88), Fresno St. (1991-95); **Crum**–Louisville (1972–); **Davies**–Duquesne (1925-43, 47-48); **Diddle**–Western Ky. (1923-64); **Driesell**–Davidson (1961-69), Maryland (1970-86), J. Madison (1989-97), Georgia St. (1997–); **Fisher**–Columbia (1907-16), Army (1922-23, 25).

Gill–Oregon St. (1929-64); **Harshman**–Pacific Lutheran (1946-58), Wash. St. (1959-71), Washington (1972-85); **Haskins**–UTEP (1962–); **Henderson**–Muskingum (1920-22), Davis & Elkins (1923-35), Marshall (1936-55); **Henson**–Hardin-Simmons (1963-66), N. Mexico St. (1967-75), Illinois (1976-96), N. Mexico St. (1997–); **Hinkle**–Butler (1927-42, 46-70); **Iba**–NW Missouri St. (1930-33), Colorado (1934), Oklahoma St. (1935-70); **Keaney**–Rhode Island (1921-48); **Keogan**–St. Louis (1916), Allegheny (1919), Valparaiso (1920-21), Notre Dame (1924-43); **Knight**–Army (1966-71), Indiana (1972–).

Lapchick–St. John's (1937-47, 57-65); **Lemons**–Okla. City (1956-73), Pan American (1974-76), Texas (1977-82), Okla. City (1984-90); **Lewis**– Houston (1957-86); **Majerus**–Marquette (1984-86), Ball St. (1988-89), Utah (1991–); **A. McGuire**–Belmont Abbey (1958-64), Marquette (1965-77); **Meanwell**–Wisconsin (1912-17, 21-34), Missouri (1918-20); **Mears**–Wittenberg (1957-62), Tennessee (1963-77); **Meyer**–DePaul (1943-84); **E. Miller**–Western Mich. (1970–75, Ohio St. (1976–85); Northern Iowa (1986–); **R. Miller**–Wichita St. (1952-64), Iowa (1965-70), Oregon St. (1971-89); **Musselman**–Ashland (1966-71), Minnesota (1972-75), S. Alabama (1996-97); **Olson**–Long Beach St. (1974), Iowa (1975-83), Arizona (1984–), **Pitino**–Boston Univ. (1979-83), Providence (1986-87), Kentucky (1990-97).

Ramsay–St. Joseph's-PA (1956-66); **Richardson**–Tulsa (1981-85), Arkansas (1986–); **Rupp**–Kentucky (1931-72); **Schaus**–West Va. (1955-60), Purdue (1973-78); **Sloan**–Presbyterian (1952-55), Citadel (1957-60), Florida (1961-66), N.C. State (1967-80), Florida (1981-89); **Smith**–North Carolina (1962-97); **Stewart**–No. Iowa (1962-67), Missouri (1968–); **Sutton**–Creighton (1970-74), Arkansas (1975-85), Kentucky (1986-89), Oklahoma St. (1991–); **Tarkanian**–Long Beach St. (1969-73), UNLV (1974-92), Fresno St. (1995–); **Thompson**–Georgetown (1973–); **Wilkes**–Stetson (1958-93); **Wooden**–Indiana St. (1947-48), UCLA (1949-75).

Most NCAA Tournaments

Through 1998; listed are number of appearances, overall tournament record, times reaching Final Four, and number of NCAA championships.

App		W-L	F4	Championships
27	Dean Smith	65-27	11	2 (1982, 93)
22	**Bob Knight**	41-19	5	3 (1976, 81, 87)
21	**Denny Crum**	42-21	6	2 (1980, 86)
20	Adolph Rupp	30-18	6	4 (1948-49, 51, 58)
20	**John Thompson**	34-19	3	1 (1984)
19	**Lute Olson**	31-19	4	1 (1997)
19	**Eddie Sutton**	28-19	2	None
18	**Lou Henson**	19-19	2	None
18	Lou Carnesecca	17-20	1	None
18	**Jim Boeheim**	29-18	2	None
16	John Wooden	47-10	12	10 (1964-65, 67-73, 75)
16	**Jerry Tarkanian**	37-16	4	1 (1990)
15	Digger Phelps	17-17	1	None
15	**Norm Stewart**	12-15	0	None
15	**Gene Keady**	13-15	0	None
14	**Don Haskins**	14-13	1	1 (1966)
14	Guy Lewis	26-18	5	None
14	**Mike Krzyzewski**	43-12	7	2 (1991-92)
14	**John Chaney**	16-14	0	None
13	Dale Brown	15-14	2	None
13	Ray Meyer	14-16	2	None

Active Coaches' Victories

Minimum five seasons in Division I.

		Yrs	W	L	Pct
1	Jim Phelan, Mt. St. Mary's	44	**785**	428	.647
2	Bob Knight, Indiana	33	**720**	270	.727
3	Norm Stewart, Missouri	37	**711**	366	.660
4	Don Haskins, UTEP	37	**703**	341	.673
5	Lefty Driesell, Georgia St.	36	**699**	347	.668
6	Jerry Tarkanian, Fresno St.	27	**687**	157	.814
7	Lou Henson, N. Mexico St.	35	**681**	343	.665
8	Denny Crum, Louisville	27	**625**	253	.712
9	Eddie Sutton, Okla. St.	28	**599**	241	.713
10	John Thompson, Georgetown	26	**589**	233	.717
11	John Chaney, Temple	26	**581**	207	.737
12	Eldon Miller, N. Iowa	36	**568**	419	.575
13	Lute Olson, Arizona	25	**564**	208	.730
14	Hugh Durham, Jacksonville	30	**535**	329	.619
15	Jim Boeheim, Syracuse	22	**528**	181	.745
16	Tom Davis, Iowa	27	**523**	280	.651
17	Jim Calhoun, UConn	26	**520**	256	.670
18	Billy Tubbs, TCU	24	**519**	247	.678
19	Gale Catlett, West Va.	26	**516**	260	.665
20	Mike Krzyzewski, Duke	23	**505**	212	.704

Annual Awards

UPI picked the first national Division I Coach of the Year in 1955. Since then, the U.S. Basketball Writers Assn. (1959), AP (1967), the National Assn. of Basketball Coaches (1969), and the Atlanta Tip-Off Club (1987) have joined in. Since 1987, the first year all five awards were given out, no coach has won all of them in the same season.

United Press International

Voted on by a panel of UPI college basketball writers and first presented in 1955.

Multiple winners: John Wooden (6); Bob Knight, Ray Meyer, Adolph Rupp, Norm Stewart, Fred Taylor and Phil Woolpert (2).

Year
1955 Phil Woolpert, San Francisco
1956 Phil Woolpert, San Francisco
1957 Frank McGuire, North Carolina
1958 Tex Winter, Kansas St.
1959 Adolph Rupp, Kentucky
1960 Pete Newell, California
1961 Fred Taylor, Ohio St.
1962 Fred Taylor, Ohio St.
1963 Ed Jucker, Cincinnati
1964 John Wooden, UCLA
1965 Dave Strack, Michigan
1966 Adolph Rupp, Kentucky
1967 John Wooden, UCLA
1968 Guy Lewis, Houston
1969 John Wooden, UCLA

Year
1970 John Wooden, UCLA
1971 Al McGuire, Marquette
1972 John Wooden, UCLA
1973 John Wooden, UCLA
1974 Digger Phelps, Notre Dame
1975 Bob Knight, Indiana
1976 Tom Young, Rutgers
1977 Bob Gaillard, San Francisco
1978 Eddie Sutton, Arkansas
1979 Bill Hodges, Indiana St.
1980 Ray Meyer, DePaul
1981 Ralph Miller, Oregon St.
1982 Norm Stewart, Missouri
1983 Jerry Tarkanian, UNLV
1984 Ray Meyer, DePaul

Year
1985 Lou Carnesecca, St. John's
1986 Mike Krzyzewski, Duke
1987 John Thompson, Georgetown
1988 John Chaney, Temple
1989 Bob Knight, Indiana
1990 Jim Calhoun, Connecticut
1991 Rick Majerus, Utah
1992 Perry Clark, Tulane
1993 Eddie Fogler, Vanderbilt
1994 Norm Stewart, Missouri
1995 Leonard Hamilton, Miami-FL
1996 Gene Keady, Purdue
1997 award discontinued

U.S. Basketball Writers Association

Voted on by the USBWA and first presented in 1959.

Multiple winners: John Wooden (5); Bob Knight (3); Lou Carnesecca, John Chaney, Ray Meyer and Fred Taylor (2).

Year
1959 Eddie Hickey, Marquette
1960 Pete Newell, California
1961 Fred Taylor, Ohio St.
1962 Fred Taylor, Ohio St.
1963 Ed Jucker, Cincinnati
1964 John Wooden, UCLA
1965 Butch van Breda Kolff, Princeton
1966 Adolph Rupp, Kentucky
1967 John Wooden, UCLA
1968 Guy Lewis, Houston
1969 Maury John, Drake
1970 John Wooden, UCLA
1971 Al McGuire, Marquette
1972 John Wooden, UCLA

Year
1973 John Wooden, UCLA
1974 Norm Sloan, N.C. State
1975 Bob Knight, Indiana
1976 Bob Knight, Indiana
1977 Eddie Sutton, Arkansas
1978 Ray Meyer, DePaul
1979 Dean Smith, North Carolina
1980 Ray Meyer, DePaul
1981 Ralph Miller, Oregon St.
1982 John Thompson, Georgetown
1983 Lou Carnesecca, St. John's
1984 Gene Keady, Purdue
1985 Lou Carnesecca, St. John's
1986 Dick Versace, Bradley

Year
1987 John Chaney, Temple
1988 John Chaney, Temple
1989 Bob Knight, Indiana
1990 Roy Williams, Kansas
1991 Randy Ayers, Ohio St.
1992 Perry Clark, Tulane
1993 Eddie Fogler, Vanderbilt
1994 Charlie Spoonhour, St. Louis
1995 Kelvin Sampson, Oklahoma
1996 Gene Keady, Purdue
1997 Clem Haskins, Minnesota
1998 Tom Izzo, Michigan St.

Associated Press

Voted on by AP sportswriters and broadcasters and first presented in 1967.

Multiple winners: John Wooden (5); Bob Knight (3); Guy Lewis, Ray Meyer, Ralph Miller and Eddie Sutton (2).

Year	Year	Year
1967 John Wooden, UCLA	1978 Eddie Sutton, Arkansas	1989 Bob Knight, Indiana
1968 Guy Lewis, Houston	1979 Bill Hodges, Indiana St.	1990 Jim Calhoun, Connecticut
1969 John Wooden, UCLA	1980 Ray Meyer, DePaul	1991 Randy Ayers, Ohio St.
1970 John Wooden, UCLA	1981 Ralph Miller, Oregon St.	1992 Roy Williams, Kansas
1971 Al McGuire, Marquette	1982 Ralph Miller, Oregon St.	1993 Eddie Fogler, Vanderbilt
1972 John Wooden, UCLA	1983 Guy Lewis, Houston	1994 Norm Stewart, Missouri
1973 John Wooden, UCLA	1984 Ray Meyer, DePaul	1995 Kelvin Sampson, Oklahoma
1974 Norm Sloan, N.C. State	1985 Bill Frieder, Michigan	1996 Gene Keady, Purdue
1975 Bob Knight, Indiana	1986 Eddie Sutton, Kentucky	1997 Clem Haskins, Minnesota
1976 Bob Knight, Indiana	1987 Tom Davis, Iowa	1998 Tom Izzo, Michigan St.
1977 Bob Gaillard, San Francisco	1988 John Chaney, Temple	

National Association of Basketball Coaches

Voted on by NABC membership and first presented in 1969.

Multiple winner: John Wooden (3).

Year	Year	Year
1969 John Wooden, UCLA	1979 Ray Meyer, DePaul	1989 P.J. Carlesimo, Seton Hall
1970 John Wooden, UCLA	1980 Lute Olson, Iowa	1990 Jud Heathcote, Michigan St.
1971 Jack Kraft, Villanova	1981 Ralph Miller, Oregon St. & Jack Hartman, Kansas St.	1991 Mike Krzyzewski, Duke
1972 John Wooden, UCLA	1982 Don Monson, Idaho	1992 George Raveling, USC
1973 Gene Bartow, Memphis St.	1983 Lou Carnesecca, St. John's	1993 Eddie Fogler, Vanderbilt
1974 Al McGuire, Marquette	1984 Marv Harshman, Washington	1994 Nolan Richardson, Arkansas & Gene Keady, Purdue
1975 Bob Knight, Indiana	1985 John Thompson, Georgetown	1995 Jim Harrick, UCLA
1976 Johnny Orr, Michigan	1986 Eddie Sutton, Kentucky	1996 John Calipari, UMass
1977 Dean Smith, North Carolina	1987 Rick Pitino, Providence	1997 Clem Haskins, Minnesota
1978 Bill Foster, Duke & Abe Lemons, Texas	1988 John Chaney, Temple	1998 Bill Guthridge, N. Carolina

Naismith Award

Voted on by a panel of coaches, sportswriters and broadcasters and first presented by the Atlanta Tip-Off Club in 1987 in the name of the inventor of basketball, Dr. James Naismith.

Multiple winner: Mike Krzyzewski (2).

Year	Year	Year
1987 Bob Knight, Indiana	1991 Randy Ayers, Ohio St.	1995 Jim Harrick, UCLA
1988 Larry Brown, Kansas	1992 Mike Krzyzewski, Duke	1996 John Calipari, UMass
1989 Mike Krzyzewski, Duke	1993 Dean Smith, North Carolina	1997 Roy Williams, Kansas
1990 Bobby Cremins, Georgia Tech	1994 Nolan Richardson, Arkansas	1998 Bill Guthridge, N. Carolina

Other Men's Champions

The NCAA has sanctioned national championship tournaments for Divison II since 1957 and Division III since 1975. The NAIA sanctioned a single tournament from 1937-91, then split into two divisions in 1992.

NCAA Div. II Finals

Multiple winners: Kentucky Wesleyan (6); Evansville (5); CS-Bakersfield (3); North Alabama and Virginia Union (2).

Year	Winner	Score	Loser
1957	Wheaton, IL	89-65	Ky. Wesleyan
1958	South Dakota	75-53	St. Michael's, VT
1959	Evansville, IN	83-67	SW Missouri St.
1960	Evansville, IN	90-69	Chapman, CA
1961	Wittenberg, OH	42-38	SE Missouri St.
1962	Mt. St. Mary's, MD	58-57*	CS-Sacramento
1963	South Dakota St.	42-40	Wittenberg, OH
1964	Evansville, IN	72-59	Akron, OH
1965	Evansville, IN	85-82*	Southern Illinois
1966	Ky. Wesleyan	54-51	Southern Illinois
1967	Winston-Salem, NC	77-74	SW Missouri St.
1968	Ky. Wesleyan	63-52	Indiana St.
1969	Ky. Wesleyan	75-71	SW Missouri St.
1970	Phila. Textile	76-65	Tennessee St.
1971	Evansville, IN	97-82	Old Dominion, VA
1972	Roanoke, VA	84-72	Akron, OH
1973	Ky. Wesleyan	78-76*	Tennessee St.
1974	Morgan St., MD	67-52	SW Missouri St.
1975	Old Dominion, VA	76-74	New Orleans
1976	Puget Sound, WA	83-74	Tennessee-Chatt.
1977	Tennessee-Chatt.	71-62	Randolph-Macon
1978	Cheyney, PA	47-40	WI-Green Bay
1979	North Alabama	64-50	WI-Green Bay
1980	Virginia Union	80-74	New York Tech
1981	Florida Southern	73-68	Mt. St. Mary's, MD
1982	Dist. of Columbia	73-63	Florida Southern
1983	Wright St., OH	92-73	Dist. of Columbia
1984	Central Mo.St.	81-77	St. Augustine's,NC
1985	Jacksonville St.	74-73	South Dakota St.
1986	Sacred Heart, CT	93-87	SE Missouri St.
1987	Ky.Wesleyan	92-74	Gannon, PA
1988	Lowell, MA	75-72	AK-Anchorage
1989	N.C. Central	73-46	SE Missouri St.
1990	Ky. Wesleyan	93-79	CS-Bakersfield
1991	North Alabama	79-72	Bridgeport, CT
1992	Virginia Union	100-75	Bridgeport, CT
1993	CS-Bakersfield	85-72	Troy St., AL
1994	CS-Bakersfield	92-86	Southern Ind.
1995	Southern Indiana	71-63	UC-Riverside
1996	Fort Hays St.	70-63	N. Kentucky
1997	CS-Bakersfield	57-56	N. Kentucky
1998	UC-Davis	83-77	Ky. Wesleyan

*Overtime

NCAA Div. III Finals

Multiple winners: North Park (5); WI-Platteville (3); Potsdam St., Scranton and WI-Whitewater (2).

Year	Winner	Score	Loser
1975	LeMoyne-Owen, TN	57-54	Glassboro St., NJ
1976	Scranton, PA	60-57	Wittenberg, OH
1977	Wittenberg, OH	79-66	Oneonta St., NY
1978	North Park, IL	69-57	Widener, PA
1979	North Park, IL	66-62	Potsdam St., NY
1980	North Park, IL	83-76	Upsala, NJ
1981	Potsdam St., NY	67-65*	Augustana, IL
1982	Wabash, IN	83-62	Potsdam St., NY
1983	Scranton, PA	64-63	Wittenberg, OH
1984	WI-Whitewater	103-86	Clark, MA
1985	North Park, IL	72-71	Potsdam St., NY
1986	Potsdam St., NY	76-73	LeMoyne-Owen, TN
1987	North Park, IL	106-100	Clark, MA
1988	Ohio Wesleyan	92-70	Scranton, PA
1989	WI-Whitewater	94-86	Trenton St., NJ
1990	Rochester, NY	43-42	DePauw, IN
1991	WI-Platteville	81-74	Franklin Marshall
1992	Calvin, MI	62-49	Rochester, NY
1993	Ohio Northern	71-68	Augustana, IL
1994	Lebanon Valley, PA	66-59*	NYU
1995	WI-Platteville	69-55	Manchester, IN
1996	Rowan, NJ	100-93	Hope, MI
1997	Illinois Wesleyan	89-86	Neb-Wesleyan
1998	WI-Platteville	69-56	Hope, MI

*Overtime

NAIA Finals, 1937-91

Multiple winners: Grand Canyon, Hamline, Kentucky St. and Tennessee St. (3); Central Missouri, Central St., Fort Hays St. and SW Missouri St. (2).

Year	Winner	Score	Loser
1937	Central Missouri	35-24	Morningside, IA
1938	Central Missouri	45-30	Roanoke, VA
1939	Southwestern, KS	32-31	San Diego St.
1940	Tarkio, MO	52-31	San Diego St.
1941	San Diego St.	36-32	Murray St., KY
1942	Hamline, MN	33-31	SE Oklahoma
1943	SE Missouri St.	34-32	NW Missouri St.
1944	Not held		
1945	Loyola-LA	49-36	Pepperdine, CA
1946	Southern Illinois	49-40	Indiana St.
1947	Marshall, WV	73-59	Mankato St., MN
1948	Louisville, KY	82-70	Indiana St.
1949	Hamline, MN	57-46	Regis, CO
1950	Indiana St.	61-47	East Central, OK
1951	Hamline, MN	69-61	Millikin, IL
1952	SW Missouri St.	73-64	Murray St., KY
1953	SW Missouri St.	79-71	Hamline, MN
1954	St.Benedict's, KS	62-56	Western Illinois
1955	East Texas St.	71-54	SE Oklahoma
1956	McNeese St., LA	60-55	Texas Southern
1957	Tennessee St.	92-73	SE Oklahoma
1958	Tennessee St.	85-73	Western Illinois
1959	Tennessee St.	97-87	Pacific-Luth., WA
1960	SW Texas St.	66-44	Westminster, PA
1961	Grambling, LA	95-75	Georgetown, KY
1962	Prairie View, TX	62-53	Westminster, PA
1963	Pan American, TX	73-62	Western Carolina
1964	Rockhurst, MO	66-56	Pan American, TX
1965	Central St., OH	85-51	Oklahoma Baptist
1966	Oklahoma Baptist	88-59	Georgia Southern
1967	St.Benedict's, KS	71-65	Oklahoma Baptist
1968	Central St., OH	51-48	Fairmont St., WV
1969	Eastern N. Mex	99-76	MD-Eastern Shore
1970	Kentucky St.	79-71	Central Wash.
1971	Kentucky St.	102-82	Eastern Michigan
1972	Kentucky St.	71-62	WI-Eau Claire
1973	Guilford, NC	99-96	MD-Eastern Shore
1974	West Georgia	97-79	Alcorn St., MS
1975	Grand Canyon, AZ	65-54	M'western St., TX
1976	Coppin St., MD	96-91	Henderson St., AR
1977	Texas Southern	71-44	Campbell, NC
1978	Grand Canyon, AZ	79-75	Kearney St., NE
1979	Drury, MO	60-54	Henderson St., AR
1980	Cameron, OK	84-77	Alabama St.
1981	Beth. Nazarene, OK	86-85*	AL-Huntsville
1982	SC-Spartanburg	51-38	Biola, CA
1983	Charleston, SC	57-53	WV-Wesleyan
1984	Fort Hays St., KS	48-46*	WI-Stevens Pt.
1985	Fort Hays St., KS	82-80*	Wayland Bapt., TX
1986	David Lipscomb, TN	67-54	AR-Monticello
1987	Washburn, KS	79-77	West Virginia St.
1988	Grand Canyon, AZ	88-86*	Auburn-Montg, AL
1989	St.Mary's, TX	61-58	East Central, OK
1990	Birm-Southern, AL	88-80	WI-Eau Claire
1991	Oklahoma City	77-74	Central Arkansas

*Overtime

NAIA Div. I Finals

NAIA split tournament into two divisions in 1992.

Multiple winner: Oklahoma City (3).

Year	Winner	Score	Loser
1992	Oklahoma City	82-73*	Central Arkansas
1993	Hawaii Pacific	88-83	Okla. Baptist
1994	Oklahoma City	99-81	Life, GA
1995	Birm-Southern	92-76	Pfeiffer, NC
1996	Oklahoma City	86-80	Georgetown, KY
1997	Life, GA	73-64	Okla. Baptist
1998	Georgetown, KY	83-69	So. Nazarene

*Overtime

NAIA Div. II Finals

NAIA split tournament into two divisions in 1992.

Multiple winner: Bethel, IN (3).

Year	Winner	Score	Loser
1992	Grace, IN	85-79*	Northwestern-IA
1993	Williamette, OR	63-56	Northern St., SD
1994	Eureka, IL	98-95*	Northern St., SD
1995	Bethel, IN	103-95*	NW Nazarene, ID
1996	Albertson, ID	81-72*	Whitworth, WA
1997	Bethel, IN	95-94	Siena Heights, MI
1998	Bethel, IN	89-87	Oregon Tech

*Overtime

Player of the Year and NBA MVP

College Players of the Year who have gone on to win the NBA's Most Valuable Player award:

Bill Russell COLLEGE–San Francisco (1956); PROS–Boston Celtics (1958, 1961, 1962, 1963 and 1965).

Oscar Robertson COLLEGE–Cincinnati (1958, 1959 and 1960); PROS–Cincinnati Royals (1964).

Kareem Abdul-Jabbar COLLEGE–UCLA (1967 and 1969); PROS–Milwaukee Bucks (1971, 1972 and 1974) and LA Lakers (1976, 1977 and 1980).

Bill Walton COLLEGE–UCLA (1972, 1973 and 1974); PROS–Portland Trail Blazers (1978).

Larry Bird COLLEGE–Indiana St. (1979); PROS–Boston Celtics (1984, 1985, and 1986).

Michael Jordan COLLEGE–North Carolina (1984); PROS–Chicago Bulls (1988, 1991, 1992, 1996 and 1998).

David Robinson COLLEGE–Navy (1987); PROS–San Antonio Spurs (1995).

WOMEN

NCAA Final Four

Replaced the Association of Intercollegiate Athletics for Women (AIAW) tournament in 1982 as the official playoff for the national championship.

Multiple winners: Tennessee (6); Louisiana Tech, Stanford and USC (2).

Year	Champion	Head Coach	Score	Runner-up	Third Place	
1982	Louisiana Tech	Sonya Hogg	76-62	Cheyney	Maryland	Tennessee
1983	USC	Linda Sharp	69-67	Louisiana Tech	Georgia	Old Dominion
1984	USC	Linda Sharp	72-61	Tennessee	Cheyney	Louisiana Tech
1985	Old Dominion	Marianne Stanley	70-65	Georgia	NE Louisiana	Western Ky.
1986	Texas	Jody Conradt	97-81	USC	Tennessee	Western Ky.
1987	Tennessee	Pat Summitt	67-44	Louisiana Tech	Long Beach St.	Texas
1988	Louisiana Tech	Leon Barmore	56-54	Auburn	Long Beach St.	Tennessee
1989	Tennessee	Pat Summitt	76-60	Auburn	Louisiana Tech	Maryland
1990	Stanford	Tara VanDerveer	88-81	Auburn	Louisiana Tech	Virginia
1991	Tennessee	Pat Summitt	70-67	Virginia	Connecticut	Stanford
1992	Stanford	Tara VanDerveer	78-62	Western Kentucky	SW Missouri St.	Virginia
1993	Texas Tech	Marsha Sharp	84-82	Ohio St.	Iowa	Vanderbilt
1994	North Carolina	Sylvia Hatchell	60-59	Louisiana Tech	Alabama	Purdue
1995	Connecticut	Geno Auriemma	70-64	Tennessee	Georgia	Stanford
1996	Tennessee	Pat Summitt	83-65	Georgia	Connecticut	Stanford
1997	Tennessee	Pat Summitt	68-59	Old Dominion	Stanford	Notre Dame
1998	Tennessee	Pat Summitt	93-75	Louisiana Tech	Arkansas	N.C. State

Final Four sites: 1982 (Norfolk, Va.), **1983** (Norfolk, Va.), **1984** (Los Angeles), **1985** (Austin), **1986** (Lexington), **1987** (Austin), **1988** (Tacoma), **1989** (Tacoma), **1990** (Knoxville), **1991** (New Orleans), **1992** (Los Angeles), **1993** (Atlanta), **1994** (Richmond), **1995** (Minneapolis), **1996** (Charlotte), **1997** (Cincinnati), **1998** (Kansas City).

Most Outstanding Player

A Most Outstanding Player has been selected every year of the NCAA tournament. Winner who did not play for the tournament champion is listed in **bold,** type.

Multiple winner: Chamique Holdsclaw and Cheryl Miller (2).

Year	Year	Year
1982 Janice Lawrence, La. Tech	1988 Erica Westbrooks, La. Tech	1994 Charlotte Smith, N. Carolina
1983 Cheryl Miller, USC	1989 Bridgette Gordon, Tennessee	1995 Rebecca Lobo, Connecticut
1984 Cheryl Miller, USC	1990 Jennifer Azzi, Stanford	1996 Michelle Marciniak, Tennessee
1985 Tracy Claxton, Old Dominion	1991 **Dawn Staley**, Virginia	1997 Chamique Holdsclaw, Tenn.
1986 Clarissa Davis, Texas	1992 Molly Goodenbour, Stanford	1998 Chamique Holdsclaw, Tenn.
1987 Tonya Edwards, Tennessee	1993 Sheryl Swoopes, Texas Tech	

All-Time NCAA Division I Tournament Leaders

Through 1997-98; minimum of six games; **Last** column indicates final year played.

CAREER

Scoring

	Points	Yrs	Last	Pts	Avg
1	Bridgette Gordon, Tenn	4	1989	388	21.6
2	**Chamique Holdsclaw**, Tenn.	3	1998	382	21.2
3	Cheryl Miller, USC	4	1986	333	20.8
4	Janice Lawrence, La. Tech	3	1984	312	22.3
5	Penny Toler, Long Beach St.	4	1989	291	22.4
6	Dawn Staley, Virginia	4	1992	274	18.3
7	Cindy Brown, Long Beach St	4	1987	263	21.9
8	Venus Lacy, La. Tech	3	1990	263	18.8
9	Clarissa Davis, Texas	3	1989	261	21.8
10	Janet Harris, Georgia	4	1985	254	19.5

Rebounds

	Average	Yrs	Last	No	Avg
1	Cheryl Miller, USC	4	1986	170	10.6
2	Sheila Frost, Tennessee	4	1989	162	9.0
3	Val Whiting, Stanford	4	1993	161	10.1
4	**Chamique Holdsclaw**, Tenn.	3	1998	154	8.6
5	Venus Lacy, La. Tech	3	1990	148	10.6
6	Bridgette Gordon, Tenn	4	1989	142	7.9
7	Kirsten Cummings, Long Beach St.	4	1985	136	10.5
8	Nora Lewis, La. Tech	3	1989	130	9.3
9	Pam McGee, USC	3	1984	127	9.8
10	Daedra Charles, Tenn	3	1991	125	9.6
	Paula McGee, USC	3	1984	125	9.6

SINGLE GAME

Scoring

		Year	Pts
1	Lorri Bauman, Drake vs Maryland	1982	50
2	Sheryl Swoopes, Texas Tech vs Ohio St	1993	47
3	Barbara Kennedy, Clemson vs Penn St	1982	43
4	LaTaunya Pollard, L. Beach St. vs Howard	1982	40
	Cindy Brown, L. Beach St. vs Ohio St.	1987	40
6	Kerry Bascom, UConn vs Toledo	1991	39
	Portia Hill, S.F. Austin St. vs Arkansas	1990	39
	Delmonica DeHorney, Ark. vs Stanford	1990	39
	Sheri Sam, Vanderbilt vs. Harvard	1996	39
10	Connie Swift, Tenn. St. vs. Oregon St.	1995	38

Rebounds

		Year	No
1	Cheryl Taylor, Tenn. Tech vs Georgia	1985	23
	Charlotte Smith, N. Car. vs La. Tech	1994	23
3	Daedra Charles, Tenn. vs SW Missouri	1991	22
4	Cherie Nelson, USC vs Western Ky	1987	21
5	Alison Lang, Oregon vs Missouri	1982	20
	Shelda Arceneaux, S.D. St. vs L. Beach St.	1984	20
	Tracy Claxton, ODU vs Georgia	1985	20
	Brigette Combs, West. Ky. vs West Va	1989	20
	Tandreia Green, West. Ky. vs West Va	1989	20
10	Six tied with 19 each.		

Associated Press Final Top 10 Polls

The Associated Press weekly women's college basketball poll was begun by Mel Greenberg of *The Philadelphia Inquirer* during the 1976-77 season. Although the poll was started as a Top 20 in 1977 and was expanded to a Top 25 in 1990, only the Top 10 from each poll are listed below due to space constraints. The Association of Intercollegiate Athletics for Women (AIAW) Tournament determined the Division I national champion for 1972-81. The NCAA began its women's Division I tournament in 1982. The final AP Polls were taken before the NCAA tournament. Eventual national champions are in **bold** type.

1977
1 **Delta St.**
2 Immaculata
3 St. Joseph's-PA
4 CS-Fullerton
5 Tennessee
6 Tennessee Tech
7 Wayland Baptist
8 Montclair St.
9 S.F. Austin St.
10 N.C. State

1978
1 Tennessee
2 Wayland Baptist
3 N.C. State
4 Montclair St.
5 **UCLA**
6 Maryland
7 Queens-NY
8 Valdosta St.
9 Delta St.
10 LSU

1979
1 **Old Dominion**
2 Louisiana Tech
3 Tennessee
4 Texas
5 S.F. Austin St.
6 UCLA
7 Rutgers
8 Maryland
9 Cheyney
10 Wayland Baptist

1980
1 **Old Dominion**
2 Tennessee
3 Louisiana Tech
4 South Carolina
5 S.F. Austin St.
6 Maryland
7 Texas
8 Rutgers
9 Long Beach St.
10 N.C. State

1981
1 **Louisiana Tech**
2 Tennessee
3 Old Dominion
4 USC
5 Cheyney
6 Long Beach St.
7 UCLA
8 Maryland
9 Rutgers
10 Kansas

1982
1 **Louisiana Tech**
2 Cheyney
3 Maryland
4 Tennessee
5 Texas
6 USC
7 Old Dominion
8 Rutgers
9 Long Beach St.
10 Penn St.

1983
1 **USC**
2 Louisiana Tech
3 Texas
4 Old Dominion
5 Cheyney
6 Long Beach St.
7 Maryland
8 Penn St.
9 Georgia
10 Tennessee

1984
1 Texas
2 Louisiana Tech
3 Georgia
4 Old Dominion
5 **USC**
6 Long Beach St.
7 Kansas St.
8 LSU
9 Cheyney
10 Mississippi

1985
1 Texas
2 NE Louisiana
3 Long Beach St.
4 Louisiana Tech
5 **Old Dominion**
6 Mississippi
7 Ohio St.
8 Georgia
9 Penn St.
10 Auburn

1986
1 **Texas**
2 Georgia
3 USC
4 Louisiana Tech
5 Western Ky.
6 Virginia
7 Auburn
8 Long Beach St.
9 LSU
10 Rutgers

1987
1 Texas
2 Auburn
3 Louisiana Tech
4 Long Beach St.
5 Rutgers
6 Georgia
7 **Tennessee**
8 Mississippi
9 Iowa
10 Ohio St.

1988
1 Tennessee
2 Iowa
3 Auburn
4 Texas
5 **Louisiana Tech**
6 Ohio St.
7 Long Beach St.
8 Rutgers
9 Maryland
10 Virginia

1989
1 **Tennessee**
2 Auburn
3 Louisiana Tech
4 Stanford
5 Maryland
6 Texas
7 Long Beach St.
8 Iowa
9 Colorado
10 Georgia

1990
1 Louisiana Tech
2 **Stanford**
3 Washington
4 Tennessee
5 UNLV
6 S.F. Austin St.
7 Georgia
8 Texas
9 Auburn
10 Iowa

1991
1 Penn St.
2 Virginia
3 Georgia
4 **Tennessee**
5 Purdue
6 Auburn
7 N.C. State
8 LSU
9 Arkansas
10 Western Ky.

1992
1 Virginia
2 Tennessee
3 **Stanford**
4 S.F. Austin St.
5 Mississippi
6 Miami-FL
7 Iowa
8 Maryland
9 Penn St.
10 SW Missouri St.

1993
1 Vanderbilt
2 Tennessee
3 Ohio St.
4 Iowa
5 **Texas Tech**
6 Stanford
7 Auburn
8 Penn St.
9 Virginia
10 Colorado

1994
1 Tennessee
2 Penn St.
3 Connecticut
4 **North Carolina**
5 Colorado
6 Louisiana Tech
7 USC
8 Purdue
9 Texas Tech
10 Virginia

1995
1 **Connecticut**
2 Colorado
3 Tennessee
4 Stanford
5 Texas Tech
6 Vanderbilt
7 Penn St.
8 Louisiana Tech
9 Western Ky.
10 Virginia

1996
1 Louisiana Tech
2 Connecticut
3 Stanford
4 **Tennessee**
5 Georgia
6 Old Dominion
7 Iowa
8 Penn St.
9 Texas Tech
10 Alabama

1997

1 Connecticut
2 Old Dominion
3 Stanford
4 North Carolina
5 Louisiana Tech
6 Georgia
7 Florida
8 Alabama
9 LSU
10 **Tennessee**

1998

1 **Tennessee**
2 Old Dominion
3 Connecticut
4 Louisiana Tech
5 Stanford
6 Texas Tech
7 North Carolina
8 Duke
9 Arizona
10 N.C. State

All-Time AP Top 10

The composite AP Top 10 from the 1976-77 season through 1997-98, based on the final regular season rankings of each year. Team points are based on 10 points for all 1st place finishes, 9 for each 2nd, etc. Also listed are the number of times ranked No. 1 by AP going into the tournaments, and times ranked in the pre-tournament Top 10.

		Pts	No. 1	Top 10
1	Tennessee	142	5	19
2	Louisiana Tech	132	4	17
3	Texas	80	4	17
4	Old Dominion	75	2	10
5	Stanford	58	0	8
6	Georgia	51	0	10
7	Connecticut	45	2	5
8	Long Beach St.	45	0	10
9	Auburn	42	0	8
10	USC	40	1	6

All-Time Winningest Division I Teams

Division I schools with best winning percentages and most victories through 1997-98 (including postseason tournaments). Although official NCAA women's basketball records didn't begin until the 1981-82 season, results from previous seasons are included below.

Top 10 Winning Percentage

		Yrs	W	L	Pct
1	Louisiana Tech	24	676	127	.842
2	Tennessee	30	732	171	.811
3	Montana	20	482	115	.807
4	Texas	24	631	166	.792
5	S. F. Austin St.	26	619	198	.758
6	Old Dominion	29	632	213	.748
7	Mount St. Mary's*	24	477	165	.743
8	Virginia	25	528	197	.728
9	Auburn	27	540	208	.722
10	Mississippi	24	528	212	.714

*Includes records prior to Division I.

Top 10 Victories

		Yrs	W	L	Pct
1	Tennessee	30	732	171	.811
2	Louisiana Tech	24	676	127	.842
3	James Madison	73	633	339	.651
4	Old Dominion	29	632	213	.748
5	Texas	24	631	166	.792
6	S.F. Austin St.	26	619	198	.758
7	Long Beach St.	36	611	250	.710
8	Tennessee Tech	28	606	251	.707
9	Ohio St.	27	540	209	.721
10	Auburn	27	540	208	.722

Annual NCAA Division I Leaders

All averages include postseason games

Scoring

Multiple winner: Cindy Blodgett and Andrea Congreaves (2).

Year		Gm	Pts	Avg
1982	Barbara Kennedy, Clemson	31	908	29.3
1983	LaTaunya Pollard, L. Beach St	31	907	29.3
1984	Deborah Temple, Delta St	28	873	31.2
1985	Anucha Browne, Northwestern	28	855	30.5
1986	Wanda Ford, Drake	30	919	30.6
1987	Tresa Spaulding, BYU	28	810	28.9
1988	LeChandra LeDay, Grambling	28	850	30.4
1989	Patricia Hoskins, Miss. Valley	27	908	33.6
1990	Kim Perrot, SW Louisiana	28	839	30.0
1991	Jan Jensen, Drake	30	888	29.6
1992	Andrea Congreaves, Mercer	28	925	33.0
1993	Andrea Congreaves, Mercer	26	805	31.0
1994	Kristy Ryan, CS-Sacramento	26	727	28.0
1995	Koko Lahanas, CS-Fullerton	29	778	26.8
1996	Cindy Blodgett, Maine	32	889	27.8
1997	Cindy Blodgett, Maine	30	810	27.0
1998	Allison Feaster, Harvard	28	797	28.5

Rebounds

Multiple winner: Patricia Hoskins (2).

Year		Gm	No	Avg
1982	Anne Donovan, Old Dominion	28	412	14.7
1983	Deborah Mitchell, Miss. Col	28	447	16.0
1984	Joy Kellog, Oklahoma City	23	373	16.2
1985	Rosina Pearson, Beth-Cookman	26	480	18.5
1986	Wanda Ford, Drake	30	506	16.9
1987	Patricia Hoskins, Miss. Valley	28	476	17.0
1988	Katie Beck, East Tenn. St.	25	441	17.6
1989	Patricia Hoskins, Miss. Valley	27	440	16.3
1990	Pam Hudson, Northwestern St	29	438	15.1
1991	Tarcha Hollis, Grambling	29	443	15.3
1992	Christy Greis, Evansville	28	383	13.7
1993	Ann Barry, Nevada	25	355	14.2
1994	DeShawne Blocker, E. Tenn. St.	26	450	17.3
1995	Tera Sheriff, Jackson St.	29	401	13.8
1996	Dana Wynne, Seton Hall	29	372	12.8
1997	Etolia Mitchell, Georgia St.	25	330	13.2
1998	Alisha Hill, Howard	30	397	13.2

Note: Wanda Ford (1986) and Patricia Hoskins (1989) each led the country in scoring and rebounds in the same year.

All-Time NCAA Division I Individual Leaders

Through 1997-98; includes regular season and tournament games; Official NCAA women's basketball records began with 1981-82 season. Players who competed earlier than that are not included below; **Last** column indicates final year played.

CAREER

Scoring

	Average	Yrs	Last	Pts	Avg
1	Patricia Hoskins, Miss.Valley St.	4	1989	3122	28.4
2	Sandra Hodge, New Orleans	4	1984	2860	26.7
3	Lorri Bauman, Drake	4	1984	3115	26.0
4	Valorie Whiteside, Aplach St.	4	1988	2944	25.4
5	Joyce Walker, LSU	4	1984	2906	24.8
6	Tarcha Hollis, Grambling	4	1991	2058	24.2
7	Karen Pelphrey, Marshall	4	1986	2746	24.1
8	Erma Jones, Bethune-Cookman	3	1984	2095	24.1
9	Cheryl Miller, USC	4	1986	3018	23.6
10	Chris Starr, Nevada	4	1986	2356	23.3

Rebounds

	Average	Yrs	Last	Reb	Avg
1	Wanda Ford, Drake	4	1986	1887	16.1
2	Patricia Hoskins, Miss.Valley St.	4	1989	1662	15.1
3	Tarcha Hollis, Grambling	4	1991	1185	13.9
4	Katie Beck, East Tenn. St.	4	1988	1404	13.4
5	Marilyn Stephens, Temple	4	1984	1519	13.0
6	Cheryl Taylor, Tenn. Tech	4	1987	1532	12.8
7	Olivia Bradley, West Virginia	4	1985	1484	12.7
8	Judy Mosley, Hawaii	4	1990	1441	12.6
9	Chana Perry,NE La./S. Diego St.	4	1989	1286	12.5
10	Three players tied at 12.2 each.				

SINGLE SEASON

Scoring

	Average	Year	Gm	Pts	Avg
1	Patricia Hoskins, Miss.Valley St.	1989	27	908	33.6
2	Andrea Congreaves, Mercer	1992	28	925	33.0
3	Deborah Temple, Delta St.	1984	28	873	31.2
4	Andrea Congreaves, Mercer	1993	26	805	31.0
5	Wanda Ford, Drake	1986	30	919	30.6
6	Anucha Browne, Northwestern	1985	28	855	30.5
7	LeChandra LeDay, Grambling	1988	28	850	30.4
8	Kim Perrot, SW Louisiana	1990	28	839	30.0
9	Tina Hutchinson, San Diego St.	1984	30	898	29.9
10	Jan Jensen, Drake	1991	30	888	29.6

SINGLE GAME

Scoring

	Average	Year	Pts
1	Cindy Brown, Long Beach St. vs San Jose St.	1987	60
2	Lorri Bauman, Drake vs SW Missouri St.	1984	58
	Kim Perrot, SW La. vs SE La	1990	58
4	Patricia Hoskins, Miss.Valley St. vs South-BR	1989	55
	Patricia Hoskins, Miss.Valley St. vs Ala. St.	1989	55
6	Wanda Ford, Drake vs SW Missouri St.	1986	54
7	Chris Starr, Nevada vs CS-Sacramento	1983	53
	Felisha Edwards, NE La. vs Southern Miss	1991	53
	Sheryl Swoopes, Texas Tech vs Texas	1993	53
10	Three players tied at 52 points each.		

Winningest Active Division I Coaches

Minimum of five seasons as Division I head coach; regular season and tournament games included.

Top 10 Winning Percentage

		Yrs	W	L	Pct
1	Leon Barmore, La. Tech	16	459	71	**.866**
2	Pat Summit, Tennessee	24	664	144	**.822**
3	Robin Selvig, Montana	20	481	115	**.807**
4	Tara VanDerveer, Stanford	19	458	121	**.791**
5	Geno Auriemma, Connecticut	13	328	89	**.787**
6	Bill Sheahan, Mt. St. Mary's	17	371	103	**.783**
7	Jody Conradt, Texas	29	708	212	**.770**
8	Andy Landers, Georgia	19	459	139	**.768**
9	Sonja Hogg, Baylor	15	362	110	**.767**
10	Joe Ciampi, Auburn	21	487	150	**.765**

Top 10 Victories

		Yrs	W	L	Pct
1	Jody Conradt, Texas	29	**708**	212	.770
2	Pat Summitt, Tennessee	24	**664**	144	.822
4	Vivian Stringer, Rutgers	26	**566**	177	.762
3	Sue Gunter, LSU	28	**564**	256	.688
5	Kay Yow, N.C. State	27	**552**	221	.714
6	Theresa Grentz, Illinois	24	**518**	187	.735
8	Sylvia Hatchell, N. Carolina	23	**512**	205	.714
7	Rene Portland, Penn St.	22	**494**	171	.743
9	Joe Ciampi, Auburn	21	**487**	150	.765
	Mike Granelli, St. Peter's	26	**487**	178	.732

Annual Awards

The Broderick Award was first given out to the Women's Division I or Large School Player of the Year in 1977. Since then, the National Assn. for Girls and Women in Sports (1978), the Women's Basketball Coaches Assn. (1983), the Atlanta Tip-Off Club (1983) and the Associated Press (1995) have joined in.

Since 1983, the first year as many as four awards were given out, the same player has won all of them in the same season twice: Cheryl Miller of USC in 1985 and Rebecca Lobo of Connecticut in 1995.

Associated Press

Voted on by AP sportswriters and broadcasters and first presented in 1995.

Year	
1995	Rebecca Lobo, Connecticut
1996	Jennifer Rizzotti, Connecticut
1997	Kara Wolters, Connecticut
1998	Chamique Holdsclaw, Tennessee

Broderick Award

Voted on by a national panel of women's collegiate athletic directors and first presented by the late Thomas Broderick, an athletic outfitter, in 1977. Honda has presented the award since 1987. Basketball Player of the Year is one of 10 nominated for Collegiate Woman Athlete of the Year; (*) indicates player also won Athlete of the Year.

Multiple winners: Chamique Holdsclaw, Nancy Lieberman, Cheryl Miller and Dawn Staley (2).

Year	Year	Year
1977 Lucy Harris, Delta St.*	1985 Cheryl Miller, USC	1993 Sheryl Swoopes, Texas Tech
1978 Anne Meyers, UCLA*	1986 Kamie Ethridge, Texas*	1994 Lisa Leslie, USC
1979 Nancy Lieberman, Old Dominion*	1987 Katrina McClain, Georgia	1995 Rebecca Lobo, Connecticut
1980 Nancy Lieberman, Old Dominion*	1988 Teresa Weatherspoon, La. Tech*	1996 Jennifer Rizzotti, Connecticut
1981 Lynette Woodward, Kansas	1989 Bridgette Gordon, Tennessee	1997 Chamique Holdsclaw, Tennessee
1982 Pam Kelly, La. Tech.	1990 Jennifer Azzi, Stanford	1998 Chamique Holdsclaw, Tennessee*
1983 Anne Donovan, Old Dominion	1991 Dawn Staley, Virginia	
1984 Cheryl Miller, USC*	1992 Dawn Staley, Virginia	

Wade Trophy

Voted on by the National Assn. for Girls and Women in Sports (NAGWS) and awarded for academics and community service as well as player performance. First presented in 1978 in the name of former Delta St. coach Margaret Wade.

Multiple winner: Nancy Lieberman (2).

Year	Year	Year
1978 Carol Blazejowski, Montclair St.	1985 Cheryl Miller, USC	1992 Susan Robinson, Penn St.
1979 Nancy Lieberman, Old Dominion	1986 Kamie Ethridge, Texas	1993 Karen Jennings, Nebraska
1980 Nancy Lieberman, Old Dominion	1987 Shelly Pennefather, Villanova	1994 Carol Ann Shudlick, Minnesota
1981 Lynette Woodward, Kansas	1988 Teresa Weatherspoon, La. Tech	1995 Rebecca Lobo, Connecticut
1982 Pam Kelly, La. Tech	1989 Clarissa Davis, Texas	1996 Jennifer Rizzotti, Connecticut
1983 LaTaunya Pollard, L. Beach St.	1990 Jennifer Azzi, Stanford	1997 DeLisha Milton, Florida
1984 Janice Lawrence, La. Tech	1991 Daedra Charles, Tennessee	1998 Ticha Penicheiro, Old Dominion

Naismith Trophy

Voted on by a panel of coaches, sportwriters and broadcasters and first presented in 1983 by the Atlanta Tip-Off Club in the name of the inventor of basketball, Dr. James Naismith.

Multiple winners: Cheryl Miller (3); Clarissa Davis and Dawn Staley (2).

Year	Year	Year
1983 Anne Donovan, Old Dominion	1989 Clarissa Davis, Texas	1995 Rebecca Lobo, Connecticut
1984 Cheryl Miller, USC	1990 Jennifer Azzi, Stanford	1996 Saudia Roundtree, Georgia
1985 Cheryl Miller, USC	1991 Dawn Staley, Virgina	1997 Kate Starbird, Stanford
1986 Cheryl Miller, USC	1992 Dawn Staley, Virginia	1998 Chamique Holdsclaw, Tennessee
1987 Clarissa Davis, Texas	1993 Sheryl Swoopes, Texas Tech	
1988 Sue Wicks, Rutgers	1994 Lisa Leslie, USC	

Women's Basketball Coaches Association

Voted on by the WBCA and first presented by Champion athletic outfitters in 1983.

Multiple winners: Cheryl Miller and Dawn Staley (2).

Year	Year	Year
1983 Anne Donovan, Old Dominion	1989 Clarissa Davis, Texas	1995 Rebecca Lobo, Connecticut
1984 Janice Lawrence, La. Tech	1990 Venus Lacey, La. Tech	1996 Saudia Roundtree, Georgia
1985 Cheryl Miller, USC	1991 Dawn Staley, Virgina	1997 Kate Starbird, Stanford
1986 Cheryl Miller, USC	1992 Dawn Staley, Virginia	1998 Chamique Holdsclaw, Tennessee
1987 Katrina McClain, Georgia	1993 Sheryl Swoopes, Texas Tech	
1988 Michelle Edwards, Iowa	1994 Lisa Leslie, USC	

Coach of the Year Award

Voted on by the Women's Basketball Coaches Assn. and first presented by Converse athletic outfitters in 1983.

Multiple winners: Jody Conradt, Vivian Stringer and Pat Summitt (2).

Year	Year	Year
1983 Pat Summitt, Tennessee	1989 Tara VanDerveer, Stanford	1995 Gary Blair, Arkansas
1984 Jody Conradt, Texas	1990 Kay Yow, N.C. State	1996 Leon Barmore, La. Tech
1985 Jim Foster, St. Joseph's-PA	1991 Rene Portland, Penn St.	1997 Geno Auriemma, Connecticut
1986 Jody Conradt, Texas	1992 Ferne Labati, Miami-FL	1998 Pat Summitt, Tennessee
1987 Theresa Grentz, Rutgers	1993 Vivian Stringer, Iowa	
1988 Vivian Stringer, Iowa	1994 Marsha Sharp, Texas Tech	

Other Women's Champions

The NCAA has sanctioned national championship tournaments for Division II and Division III since 1982. The NAIA sanctioned a single tournament from 1981-91, then split in to two divisions in 1992.

NCAA Div. II Finals

Multiple winners: North Dakota St. (5); Cal Poly Pomona and Delta St. (3), North Dakota (2).

Year	Winner	Score	Loser
1982	Cal Poly Pomona	93-74	Tuskegee, AL
1983	Virginia Union	73-60	Cal Poly Pomona
1984	Central Mo.St.	80-73	Virginia Union
1985	Cal Poly Pomona	80-69	Central Mo.St.
1986	Cal Poly Pomona	70-63	North Dakota St.
1987	New Haven, CT	77-75	Cal Poly Pomona
1988	Hampton, VA	65-48	West Texas St.
1989	Delta St., MS	88-58	Cal Poly Pomona
1990	Delta St., MS	77-43	Bentley, MA
1991	North Dakota St.	81-74	SE Missouri St.
1992	Delta St., MS	65-63	North Dakota St.
1993	North Dakota St.	95-63	Delta St., MS
1994	North Dakota St.	89-56	CS-San Bernadino
1995	North Dakota St.	98-85	Portland St.
1996	North Dakota St.	105-78	Shippensburg, PA
1997	North Dakota	94-78	S. Indiana
1998	North Dakota	92-76	Emporia St.

NCAA Div. III Finals

Multiple winners: Capital and Elizabethtown (2).

Year	Winner	Score	Loser
1982	Elizabethtown, PA	67-66*	NC-Greensboro
1983	North Central, IL	83-71	Elizabethtown, PA
1984	Rust College, MS	51-49	Elizabethtown, PA
1985	Scranton, PA	68-59	New Rochelle, NY
1986	Salem St., MA	89-85	Bishop, TX
1987	WI-Stevens Pt.	81-74	Concordia, MN
1988	Concordia, MN	65-57	St. John Fisher, NY
1989	Elizabethtown, PA	66-65	CS-Stanislaus
1990	Hope, MI	65-63	St. John Fisher
1991	St. Thomas, MN	73-55	Muskingum, OH
1992	Alma, MI	79-75	Moravian, PA
1993	Central Iowa	71-63	Capital, OH
1994	Capital, OH	82-63	Washington, MO
1995	Capital, OH	59-55	WI-Oshkosh
1996	WI-Oshkosh	66-50	Mt. Union, OH
1997	NYU	72-70	WI-Eau Claire
1998	Washington, MO	77-69	So. Maine

*Overtime

NAIA Finals

Multiple winners: One tournament–SW Oklahoma (4); Div. I tourney–Southern Nazarene (4), Arkansas Tech (2); Div. II tourney–Northern St. and Western Oregon (2).

Year	Winner	Score	Loser
1981	Kentucky St.	73-67	Texas Southern
1982	SW Oklahoma	80-45	Mo. Southern
1983	SW Oklahoma	80-68	AL-Huntsville
1984	NC-Asheville	72-70*	Portland, OR
1985	SW Oklahoma	55-54	Saginaw Val., MI
1986	Francis Marion, SC	75-65	Wayland Baptist, TX
1987	SW Oklahoma	60-58	North Georgia
1988	Oklahoma City	113-95	Claflin, SC
1989	So. Nazarene, OK	98-96	Claflin, SC
1990	SW Oklahoma	82-75	AR-Monticello
1991	Ft. Hays St., KS	57-53	SW Oklahoma
1992	I– Arkansas Tech	84-68	Wayland Baptist, TX
	II– Northern St., SD	73-56	Tarleton St., TX
1993	I– Arkansas Tech	76-75	Union, TN
	II– No. Montana	71-68	Northern St., SD
1994	I– So. Nazarene	97-74	David Lipscomb, TN
	II– Northern St., SD	48-45	Western Oregon
1995	I– So. Nazarene	78-77	SE Oklahoma
	II– Western Oregon	75-67	NW Nazarene, ID
1996	I– So. Nazarene	80-79	SE Oklahoma
	II– Western Oregon	80-77	Huron, SD
1997	I– So. Nazarene	78-73	Union, TN
	II– NW Nazarene	64-46	Black Hills St., SD
1998	I– Union, TN	73-70	So. Nazarene
	II– Walsh, OH	73-66	Mary Hardin-Baylor

*Overtime

AIAW Finals

The Association of Intercollegiate Athletics for Women Large College tournament determined the women's national champion for 10 years until supplanted by the NCAA.

In 1982, most Division I teams entered the first NCAA tournament rather than the last one staged by the AIAW.

Year	Winner	Score	Loser
1972	Immaculata, PA	52-48	West Chester, PA
1973	Immaculata, PA	59-52	Queens College, NY
1974	Immaculata, PA	68-53	Mississippi College
1975	Delta St., MS	90-81	Immaculata, PA
1976	Delta St., MS	69-64	Immaculata, PA
1977	Delta St., MS	68-55	LSU
1978	UCLA	90-74	Maryland
1979	Old Dominion	75-65	Louisiana Tech
1980	Old Dominion	68-53	Tennessee
1981	Louisiana Tech	79-59	Tennessee
1982	Rutgers	83-77	Texas

Pro Basketball

Phil Jackson, **Scottie Pippen** and **Michael Jordan,** the nucleus that brought six NBA titles to Chicago, were apparently broken up following the 1998 season with the hiring of Tim Floyd.

Archive Photos

Last Dance?

Bulls had all the answers for Jazz in the Finals but the real questions began in the offseason.

by

David Aldridge

Here's what the Chicago Bulls do: they come into your town, take your plays, take your heart, take your crowd, take your girl and win it all. The script played out again this past season, as the Bulls again beat the Utah Jazz in six games to capture their sixth NBA championship in eight seasons. Or, more accurately, their sixth straight title when Michael Jordan played a full season.

If it was their last, it provided a perfect symmetry to their dynasty, with two Threepeats to put on the mantle. And if it was their last, it ended as it should, with Jordan hitting the series-clinching basket.

But the Bulls' biggest accomplishment may well have been the continuing cover they provided to a league that was reeling from a number of different problems. Off-court troubles hit the NBA's referees, several of its big star players and a coach or two. More ominously, labor disputes led to the dissolution of the collective bargaining agreement and an owner-led lockout of the players in July.

On the floor, injuries shelved Patrick Ewing, Scottie Pippen, John Stockton and Penny Hardaway for large chunks of the season. But others blossomed. Shaquille O'Neal put up the kinds of numbers and displayed the kind of leadership for the Lakers that's been expected. Gary Payton was an all-pro candidate for the Sonics, who won the Pacific Division. The Hawks, Hornets and Heat all posted 50-win seasons.

But the Sonics were exposed by Los Angeles in the playoffs, and George Karl lost his job. The Lakers still couldn't get past the Jazz in the Western Conference Finals. And the East was its usual fait accompli: no one could beat the Bulls four times in seven games.

There were the usual Great Beginnings. Tim Duncan was as good as

---

David Aldridge is ESPN's NBA analyst.

Archive Photos

The **Bulls** and Chicago mayor **Richard Daley** (second from right), displayed Chicago's championship hardware for over 300,000 fans at a rally in Chicago's Grant Park. Seated left to right are Toni Kukoc, Ron Harper, Dennis Rodman, Scottie Pippen, Michael Jordan, Daley and coach Phil Jackson.

advertised in San Antonio, and kept doing it well into the playoffs. The Nets' Keith Van Horn and Cleveland's Brevin Knight—like Duncan, four-year college players—helped their teams back to the postseason. In Boston, the biggest newcomer wasn't a player, but Coach Rick Pitino. His pressure style and complete control of the franchise put his stamp on a Celtics team that improved dramatically.

In the end though, Chicago's dominance was the story. It has been the story of the decade in the NBA. The only question was whether we've seen the last of the best basketball team–more accurately, the two best basketball players on one team since Russell's Celtics. ■

David Aldridge's Top/Bottom 10 events of the 1997-98 NBA Season

10. **Violet and Dee, come on down.** While many of their male counterparts continue to bite the dust in a tax-evasion scandal, Violet Palmer and Dee Kantner become the first female referees hired by a major sports league. After some amazingly silly questions and stupid statements by players and coaches (and media) during the preseason, Kantner and Palmer have a rather uneventful year.

9. **Let's Make a Deal '97.** In an era where GMs and fans whine about the restrictive nature of the salary

AP/Wide World Photos

Karl Malone and **Dennis Rodman** had their share of run-ins on and off the court. They squared off in the NBA finals and then faced each other in a tag team professional wrestling match. Rodman came out on top in both encounters.

cap, the Sonics, Bucks and Cavaliers put together an old-fashioned blockbuster, primarily involving three superstars. Seattle ships unhappy Shawn Kemp to the Cavaliers. The Cavs move point guard Terrell Brandon to Milwaukee. And the Bucks trade Vin Baker to Seattle. It is that rarest of deals: each team benefits.

8. **Big Coaching Bucks.** Rick Pitino breaks the bank in Boston with a $50 million deal, assuming every basketball-related duty save that of old guys who run the press room. Larry Brown cashes in with a $25 million deal in Philadelphia. Larry Bird ($20 million), P.J. Carlesimo ($15 million) and Phil Jackson ($6 million for one year) also rake in the cake. What in the World of Riles is going on here?

7. **Hell No, I Won't Go.** Players have always had veto power over the years, but have never been as publicly vocal in using them as they were in 1997-98. Kenny Anderson is dealt from Portland to Toronto, but refuses to report until he's shipped to Boston. Doug West displays no interest in playing for Vancouver after being traded from Minnesota—as generally, NBA players treat the two Canadian cities as if they're Beirut and Sarajevo, respectively.

6. **Tonight at the Fights.** The Knicks and Heat ruin a perfectly good playoff game, again, by brawling in the final seconds. This time, Alonzo Mourning and Larry Johnson trade slaps while New York coach Jeff Van Gundy resembles a poodle sliding down

AP/Wide World Photos

NY Knicks coach **Jeff Van Gundy** resorts to his devastating leg hug on Alonzo Mourning in this primetime playoff fight between the Knicks and Heat.

Mourning's leg in a futile attempt to stop the swinging. With Mourning suspended for the deciding fifth game, the Knicks go to Miami and win the series.

5. **Cha-Ching.** After his agent says he's insulted by a $103 million contract offer, 20-year-old Kevin Garnett is signed to a seven-year extension by the Minnesota Timberwolves for $125 million. At the new conference announcing the signing, Garnett says, "it's not about the loot." And "Shaft" wasn't about a butt-kicking detective.

4. **What's the Word about the Bird?** No one, least of all Larry Bird, knows how he'll do as a first-time head coach with the Indiana Pacers. A franchise-record 59 victories later, everyone knows. Bird wins Coach of the Year honors with an amazingly adept handle on dealing with players, delegating authority to his assistants and presenting a stone-faced demeanor that masks his still-fierce competitive instincts. And the Pacers give the Bulls all they want in a hotly-contested seven-game Eastern Conference final.

3. **As the Bulls Turn.** The NBA's best soap opera enjoys record ratings and interest for an eighth season. Will Phil ever speak to Jerry Krause again? Will Scottie Pippen confront Mr. Reinsdorf about his broken promises? Will Tim return from Ames, Iowa, and inherit what's been promised to him? Will Dennis marry himself? And will Michael blow the whole thing up? In the midst of injuries to Pippen, media scrutiny unparalleled in NBA annals—at least three books are on line chronicling Chicago's Last Dance; NBA Entertainment spent a year and shot 1 million feet of film hanging out with the 97-98 team—the Bulls won, again and again.

2. **Labor Pains.** From Day One of the NBA season, owners and players circled each other like the Jets and Sharks, readying for a showdown over the collective bargaining agreement. To what does it come down? It's always about the Benjamins, and it is now: control of $1.7 billion in revenue. And the whole horrible lexicon of labor took center stage: Basketball Related Income, Larry Bird Exceptions, hard and soft caps. And both sides seemed aware of, but not particularly moved by, the threat

of a protracted lockout costing the game fans and support during one of the most vulnerable times in league history.

1. **A Choking Spree.** When the news came down through the transom, no one believed it. He choked his coach? But the details bore it out: Latrell Sprewell attacked his coach, P.J. Carlesimo, during Warriors' practice, starting one of the most bizarre campaigns in memory. The Warriors suspended Sprewell, then terminated his contract. The NBA suspended him for a year. Sprewell retaliated with the help of the players' union, taking the Warriors and the league to arbitration to get his contract reinstated. Somewhat surprisingly, arbitrator John Feerick agrees with much of what Sprewell says and reduces his suspension to seven months, restoring the final three years of his contract. It leaves everyone pondering the question, just what was he thinking? ■

THE NUMBERS

INSIDE

by

Craig Wachs, Todd Snyder and Mike Freer

THREEFEAT

While the Bulls were dominant in the early 1990s, its their three-year run since 1995 that really makes a statement. Not only did the Bulls win three straight titles, pulling the so-called "threepeat repeat," but they also became the first NBA team to win over 200 games in any three year span.

Team	Wins	Star
Bulls 1995-98	205	Jordan
Lakers 1985-88	196	Magic
Celtics 1983-86	193	Bird
76ers 1965-68	192	Chamberlain
Bucks 1969-72	190	Abdul-Jabbar

STRONG FINISHERS

Further illustrating the impressiveness of the Bulls' incredible run, the Finals record of Jordan and Co. is the best in major sports history. Since reaching their first NBA Finals in 1991, the Bulls are undefeated. Here's a look at the best records in the Finals or championships throughout major sports (NBA Finals, Super Bowl, World Series and Stanley Cup Finals).

NBA Bulls	6-0
NFL 49ers	5-0
MLB Blue Jays	2-0
NHL Penguins	2-0
NFL Giants	2-0

SCORE NO MORE

Despite the NBA's efforts to increase scoring, the average points per game has slipped each year during the past six seasons to the lowest level since the 1954-55 season (93.1 ppg). One big reason could be that field goal percentage has steadily slipped as well.

Season	PPG	FG Pct.
1997-98	95.6	45.0
1996-97	96.9	45.5
1995-96	99.5	46.2
1994-95	101.4	46.6
1993-94	101.5	46.6
1992-93	105.3	47.3

■

PRO BASKETBALL STATISTICS

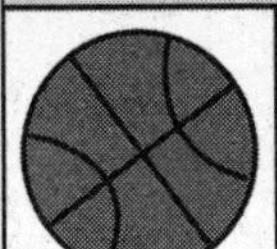

THE SEASON IN REVIEW

1997-1998

STANDINGS • PLAYOFFS

Final NBA Standings

Division champions (*) and playoff qualifiers (†) are noted. Number of seasons listed after each head coach refers to current tenure with club.

Western Conference

Midwest Division

	W	L	Pct	GB	Per Game For	Per Game Opp
*Utah	62	20	.756	—	101.0	94.4
†San Antonio	56	26	.683	6	92.5	88.5
†Minnesota	45	37	.549	17	101.1	100.4
†Houston	41	41	.500	21	98.8	99.5
Dallas	20	62	.244	42	91.4	97.5
Vancouver	19	63	.232	43	96.6	103.9
Denver	11	71	.134	51	89.0	100.8

Head Coaches: Utah— Jerry Sloan (10th season); **Hou**— Rudy Tomjanovich (7th); **Min**— Phil Saunders (3rd); **Dal**— Jim Cleamons (2nd, 4-12) was fired and replaced by GM Don Nelson (16-50) on Dec. 4, 1997; **Den**— Bill Hanzlik (1st); **SA**— Gregg Popovich (2nd); **Van**— Brian Hill (1st).

1996-97 Standings: 1. Utah (64-18); 2. Houston (57-25); 3. Minnesota (40-42); 4. Dallas (24-58); 5. Denver (21-61); 6. San Antonio (20-62); 7. Vancouver (14-68).

Pacific Division

	W	L	Pct	GB	Per Game For	Per Game Opp
*Seattle	61	21	.744	—	100.6	93.4
†LA Lakers	61	21	.744	—	105.5	97.8
†Phoenix	56	26	.683	5	99.6	94.4
†Portland	46	36	.561	15	94.3	92.9
Sacramento	27	55	.329	34	93.1	98.7
Golden St.	19	63	.232	42	88.3	97.4
LA Clippers	17	65	.207	44	95.9	103.3

Head Coaches: Sea— George Karl (7th season); **LAL**— Del Harris (4th); **Port**— Mike Dunleavy (1st); **Pho**— Danny Ainge (2nd); **LAC**— Bill Fitch (4th); **Sac**— Eddie Jordan (2nd); **G.St.**— P.J. Carlesimo (1st).

1996-97 Standings: 1. Seattle (57-25); 2. LA Lakers (56-26); 3. Portland (49-33); 4. Phoenix (40-42); 5. LA Clippers (36-46); 6. Sacramento (34-48); 6. Golden St. (30-52).

Eastern Conference

Atlantic Division

	W	L	Pct	GB	Per Game For	Per Game Opp
*Miami	55	27	.671	—	95.0	90.0
†New Jersey	43	39	.524	12	99.6	98.1
†New York	43	39	.524	12	91.6	89.1
Washington	42	40	.512	13	97.2	96.6
Orlando	41	41	.500	14	90.1	91.2
Boston	36	46	.439	19	95.9	98.5
Philadelphia	31	51	.378	24	93.3	95.7

Head Coaches: Mia— Pat Riley (3rd season); **NJ**— John Calipari (2nd); **NY**— Jeff Van Gundy (3rd); **Wash**— Bernie Bickerstaff (2nd); **Orl**— Chuck Daly (1st); **Bos**— Rick Pitino (1st); **Phi**—Larry Brown (1st).

1996-97 Standings: 1. Miami (61-21); 2. New York (57-25); 3. Orlando (45-37); 4. Washington (44-38) 5. New Jersey (26-56); 6. Philadelphia (22-60); 7. Boston (15-67).

Central Division

	W	L	Pct	GB	Per Game For	Per Game Opp
*Chicago	62	20	.756	—	96.7	89.6
†Indiana	58	24	.707	4	96.0	89.9
†Charlotte	51	31	.622	11	96.6	94.6
†Atlanta	50	32	.610	12	95.8	92.3
†Cleveland	47	35	.573	15	92.5	89.8
Detroit	37	45	.451	25	94.2	92.6
Milwaukee	36	46	.439	26	94.5	96.4
Toronto	16	66	.195	46	94.9	104.2

Head Coaches: Chi— Phil Jackson (9th season); **Ind**— Larry Bird (1st); **Char**— Dave Cowens (2nd); **Atl**— Lenny Wilkens (5th); **Det**— Doug Collins (2nd, 21-24) was fired and replaced by assistant Alvin Gentry (16-21) on Feb. 2 on an interim basis; **Cle**— Mike Fratello (5th); **Mil**— Chris Ford (2nd); **Tor**— Darrell Walker (2nd, 11-38) resigned on Feb. 13 and was replaced by assistant Butch Carter (5-28).

1996-97 Standings: 1. Chicago (69-13); 2. Atlanta (56-26); 3. Charlotte (54-28); 4. Detroit (54-28); 5. Cleveland (42-40); 6. Indiana (39-43); 7. Milwaukee (33-49); 8. Toronto (30-52).

Overall Conference Standings

Sixteen teams—eight from each conference—qualify for the NBA Playoffs; (*) indicates division champions.

Western Conference

		W	L	Home	Away	Div	Conf
1	Utah*	62	20	36-5	26-15	22-2	38-14
2	Seattle*	61	21	35-6	26-15	35-6	26-15
3	LA Lakers	61	21	33-8	28-13	16-8	42-10
4	Phoenix	56	26	30-11	26-15	17-7	37-15
5	San Antonio	56	26	31-10	25-16	18-6	33-19
6	Portland	46	36	26-15	20-21	14-10	33-19
7	Minnesota	45	37	26-15	19-22	14-10	30-22
8	Houston	41	41	24-17	17-24	14-10	29-23
	Sacramento	27	55	21-20	6-35	6-18	18-34
	Dallas	20	62	13-28	7-34	9-15	13-39
	Golden St.	19	63	12-29	7-34	6-18	15-37
	Vancouver	19	63	14-27	5-36	4-20	14-38
	LA Clippers	17	65	11-30	6-35	6-18	14-38
	Denver	11	71	9-32	2-39	3-21	9-43

Eastern Conference

		W	L	Home	Away	Div	Conf
1	Chicago*	62	20	37-4	25-16	21-7	42-12
2	Indiana	58	24	32-9	26-15	19-9	41-13
3	Miami*	55	27	30-11	25-16	18-6	36-18
4	Charlotte	51	31	32-9	19-22	16-12	31-23
5	Atlanta	50	32	29-12	21-20	19-9	34-20
6	Cleveland	47	35	27-14	20-21	14-14	28-26
7	New Jersey	43	39	26-15	17-24	12-12	27-27
8	New York	43	39	28-13	15-26	13-11	27-27
	Washington	42	40	24-17	18-23	12-13	24-30
	Orlando	41	41	24-17	17-24	11-13	24-30
	Detroit	37	45	25-16	12-29	12-16	25-29
	Milwaukee	36	46	21-20	15-26	9-19	20-34
	Boston	36	46	24-17	12-29	12-13	23-31
	Philadelphia	31	51	19-22	12-29	7-17	16-38
	Toronto	16	66	9-32	7-34	2-26	7-47

1998 NBA All-Star Game
East, 135-114

48th NBA All-Star Game. **Date:** Feb. 8, at Madison Square Garden in New York City; **Coaches:** Larry Bird, Indiana (East) and George Karl, Seattle (West); **MVP:** Michael Jordan, Chicago (32 minutes, 23 points).

Starters chosen by fan vote, (for the ninth time in his career, Chicago's Michael Jordan was the leading vote-getter, receiving 1,028,235); bench chosen by conference coaches vote.

Western Conference

Pos	Starters	Min	FG M-A	Pts	Reb	A
F	Kevin Garnett, Minn.	21	6-11	12	4	2
F	Karl Malone, Utah	17	2-4	4	3	2
C	Shaquille O'Neal, LAL	18	5-10	12	4	1
G	Kobe Bryant, LAL	22	7-16	18	6	1
G	Gary Payton, Sea.	24	3-7	7	3	13
	Bench					
F	Vin Baker, Sea.	21	3-12	8	8	0
F	Eddie Jones, LAL	25	7-19	15	11	1
C	David Robinson, SA	22	3-4	15	6	0
G	Mitch Richmond, Sac.	17	4-11	8	1	2
G	Jason Kidd, Pho.	19	0-1	0	1	9
F	Tim Duncan, SA.	14	1-4	2	11	1
G	Nick Van Exel, LAL	20	5-14	13	3	2
	TOTALS	240	46-113	114	61	34

Three-Point FG: 4-23 (Bryant 2-3, Payton 1-3, Van Exel 1-6, Jones 0-7, Richmond 0-2, Garnett 0-1, Duncan 0-1); **Free Throws:** 18-22 (Robinson 9-10, O'Neal 2-4, Bryant 2-2, Baker 2-2, Van Exel 2-2, Jones 1-2); **Percentages:** FG (.407), Three-Pt. FG (.174), Free Throws (.818); **Turnovers:** 18 (Payton 4, Garnett 3, O'Neal 2, Robinson 2, Kidd 2, Duncan 2, Van Exel 2, Bryant); **Steals:** 13 (Garnett 2, Malone 2, Bryant 2, Payton 2, Jones 2, Robinson 2, Baker); **Blocked Shots:** 3 (Robinson 2, Garnett); **Fouls:** 9 (O'Neal 2, Kidd 2, Malone, Bryant, Baker, Jones, Robinson); **Team Rebounds:** 8.

Eastern Conference

Pos	Starters	Min	FG M-A	Pts	Reb	A
F	Shawn Kemp, Cle	25	5-10	12	11	2
F	Grant Hill, Det	28	7-11	15	3	5
C	Dikembe Mutombo, Atl	19	4-5	9	7	0
G	Anfernee Hardaway, Orl	12	3-5	6	0	3
G	Michael Jordan , Chi	32	10-18	23	6	8
	Bench					
G	Tim Hardaway, Mia	17	3-8	8	1	6
C	Jayson Williams, NJ	19	2-3	4	10	1
C	Rik Smits, Ind	21	3-7	10	7	4
F	Reggie Miller, Ind	20	6-8	14	0	0
F	Glen Rice, Cha	16	6-14	16	1	0
G	Steve Smith, Atl	16	6-12	14	3	0
F	Antoine Walker, Bos	15	2-8	4	3	3
	TOTALS	240	57-109	135	52	32

Three-Point FG: 11-25 (Rice 4-6, Smith 2-5, T.Hardaway 2-5, Miller 1-2, Jordan 1-1, Hill 1-1, Kemp 0-1, P.Hardaway 0-1, Walker 0-3); **Free Throws:** 10-13 (Smits 4-4, Jordan 2-3, Kemp 2-2, Mutombo 1-2, Miller 1-2); **Percentages:** FG (.523), Three-Pt. FG (.440), Free Throws (.769); **Turnovers:** 15 (T.Hardaway 6, Kemp 4, Jordan 2, P.Hardaway, Rice, Walker); **Steals:** 10 (Kemp 4, Jordan 3, Hill, Miller, Walker); **Blocked Shots:** 3 (Smits 2, Mutombo); **Fouls:** 13 (Smits 3, Mutombo 3, Kemp 2, Williams 2, Miller 2, Hill); **Team Rebounds:** 5.

	1	2	3	4	F
West	25	33	33	23	—**114**
East	33	34	34	34	—**135**

Halftime— East, 67-58; **Third Quarter—** East, 101-91; **Technical Fouls—** none; **Officials—** Hue Hollins, Bernie Fryer, Bob Delaney; **Attendance—** 18,323; **Time—** 2:04; **TV Rating—** 10.6/17 (NBC).

NBA 3-point Shootout

Eight players are invited to compete in the annual three-point shooting contest held during All-Star weekend, since 1986. Each shooter has 60 seconds to shoot the 25 balls in five racks outside the three-point line. Each ball is worth one point, except the last ball in each rack, which is worth two. Highest scores advance. First prize: $20,000.

First Round	Pts
Dale Ellis, Sea	18
Jeff Hornacek, Utah	17
Charlie Ward, NY	15
Hubert Davis, Dal	15

Failed to advance	
Sam Mack, Van	14
Glen Rice, Cha	13
Reggie Miller, Ind	12
Tracy Murray, Was	12

Semifinals	Pts
Hubert Davis	24
Jeff Hornacek*	15

Failed to advance	
Dale Ellis*	15
Charlie Ward	11

Finals	
Jeff Hornacek	16
Hubert Davis	10

* Hornacek won shootout 11-9 for spot in the final.

NBA/WNBA All-Star 2Ball

The All-Star 2Ball replaced the slam dunk contest in 1998. In it one NBA and one WNBA player, who compete on teams from the same city, are paired up in a competition in which they alternate taking shots from seven designated spots on the half court, accumulating points for every made basket. Each team has one minute to perform, and the point amounts differ according to the distance away from the basket. First prize: $20,000.

Teams: Charlotte— Glen Rice and Andrea Stinson; **Cleveland—** Wesley Person and Michelle Edwards; **Houston—** Clyde Drexler and Cynthia Cooper; **Los Angeles—** Kobe Bryant and Lisa Leslie; **New York—** Allan Houston and Rebecca Lobo; **Phoenix—** Steve Nash and Michele Timms; **Sacramento—** Mitch Richmond and Ruthie Bolton-Holifield; **Salt Lake City—** Karl Malone and Tammi Reiss.

First Round	Pts
Phoenix	49
Cleveland	40
Utah	53
Houston	54
Los Angeles	27
Charlotte	44

First Round	Pts
Sacramento	47
New York	44

Finals	Pts
Utah	61
Houston	73

Washington Wizards
Rod Strickland
Assists

Utah Jazz
Jeff Hornacek
3-pt Shooting Pct.

Toronto Raptors
Marcus Camby
Blocked Shots

Indiana Pacers
Chris Mullin
Free Throw Pct.

NBA Regular Season Individual Leaders

Scoring

	Gm	Min	FG	FG%	3pt/Att	FT	FT%	Reb	Ast	Stl	Blk	Pts	Avg	Hi
Michael Jordan, Chi	82	3181	881	.465	30/126	565	.784	475	283	141	45	2357	28.7	49
Shaquille O'Neal, LAL	60	2175	670	.584	0/0	359	.527	681	142	39	144	1699	28.3	50
Karl Malone, Utah	81	3030	780	.530	2/6	628	.761	834	316	96	70	2190	27.0	56
Mitch Richmond, Sac	70	2569	543	.445	130/334	407	.864	229	279	88	15	1623	23.2	35
Antoine Walker, Bos	82	3268	722	.423	91/292	305	.645	836	273	142	60	1840	22.4	49
Shareef Abdur-Rahim, Van	82	2950	653	.485	21/51	502	.784	581	213	89	76	1829	22.3	32
Glen Rice, Cha	82	3295	634	.457	130/300	428	.849	353	182	77	22	1826	22.3	42
Allen Iverson, Phi	80	3150	649	.461	70/235	390	.729	296	494	176	25	1758	22.0	43
Chris Webber, Was	71	2809	647	.482	65/205	196	.589	674	273	111	124	1555	21.9	36
David Robinson, SA	73	2457	544	.511	1/4	485	.735	775	199	64	192	1574	21.6	39
Michael Finley, Dal	82	3394	675	.449	87/244	326	.784	438	405	132	30	1763	21.5	39
Grant Hill, Det	81	3294	615	.452	3/21	479	.740	623	551	143	53	1712	21.1	37
Tim Duncan, SA	82	3204	706	.549	0/10	319	.662	977	224	55	206	1731	21.1	35
Steve Smith, Atl	73	2857	489	.444	97/276	389	.855	309	292	75	29	1464	20.1	35
Isaiah Rider, Por	74	2786	551	.423	135/420	221	.828	346	231	55	19	1458	19.7	38
Sam Cassell, NJ	75	2606	510	.441	15/80	436	.860	228	603	121	20	1471	19.6	35
Ray Allen, Mil	82	3287	563	.428	134/368	342	.875	405	356	111	12	1602	19.5	40
Reggie Miller, Ind	81	2795	516	.477	164/382	382	.868	232	171	78	11	1578	19.5	35
Vin Baker, Sea	82	2944	631	.542	1/7	311	.591	656	152	91	86	1574	19.2	41
Gary Payton, Sea	82	3145	579	.453	134/397	279	.744	376	679	185	18	1571	19.2	31

Rebounds

	Gm	Off	Def	Tot	Avg
Dennis Rodman, Chi	80	421	780	1201	15.0
Jayson Williams, NJ	65	443	440	883	13.6
Tim Duncan, SA	82	274	703	977	11.9
Dikembe Mutombo, Atl	82	276	656	932	11.4
David Robinson, SA	73	239	536	775	10.6
Karl Malone, Utah	81	189	645	834	10.3
Anthony Mason, Cha	81	177	649	826	10.2
Antoine Walker, Bos	82	270	566	836	10.2
Arvydas Sabonis, Por	73	149	580	729	10.0
Kevin Garnett, Min	82	222	564	786	9.6
Chris Webber, Was	71	176	498	674	9.5
Shawn Kemp, Cle	80	219	526	745	9.3
Charles Oakley, NY	79	218	506	724	9.2
Brian Williams, Det	78	223	472	695	8.9
Zydrunas Ilgauskas, Cle	82	279	444	723	8.8

Assists

	Gm	Ast	Avg
Rod Strickland, Was	76	801	10.5
Jason Kidd, Pho	82	745	9.1
Mark Jackson, Ind	82	713	8.7
Stephon Marbury, Min	82	704	8.6
John Stockton, Utah	64	543	8.5
Tim Hardaway, Mia	81	672	8.3
Gary Payton, Sea	82	679	8.3
Brevin Knight, Cle	80	656	8.2
Damon Stoudamire, Por	71	580	8.2
Sam Cassell, NJ	75	603	8.0
Avery Johnson, SA	75	591	7.9
Nick Van Exel, LAL	64	442	6.9
Grant Hill, Det	81	551	6.8
Mookie Blaylock, Atl	70	469	6.7
David Wesley, Cha	81	529	6.5

Field Goal Pct.

	Gm	FG	Att	Pct
Shaquille O'Neal, LAL	60	670	1147	.584
Bo Outlaw, Orl	82	301	543	.554
Alonzo Mourning, Mia	58	403	732	.551
Tim Duncan, SA	82	706	1287	.549
Vin Baker, Sea	82	631	1164	.542
Dikembe Mutombo, Atl	82	399	743	.537
Antonio McDyess, Pho	81	497	927	.536
Rasheed Wallace, Por	77	466	875	.533
Karl Malone, Utah	81	780	1472	.530
Bryant Reeves, Van	74	492	941	.523

Free Throw Pct.

	Gm	FT	Att	Pct
Chris Mullin, Ind	82	154	164	.939
Jeff Hornacek, Utah	80	285	322	.885
Ray Allen, Mil	82	342	391	.875
Derek Anderson, Cle	66	275	315	.873
Kevin Johnson, Pho	50	162	186	.871
Tracy Murray, Was	82	182	209	.871
Reggie Miller, Ind	81	382	440	.868
Hersey Hawkins, Sea	82	177	204	.868
Christian Laettner, Atl	74	306	354	.864
Mitch Richmond, Sac	70	407	471	.864
Sam Cassell, NJ	75	436	507	.860

3-Point Field Goal Pct.

	Gm	3FG	Att	Pct
Jeff Hornacek, Utah	80	56	127	.441
Chris Mullin, Ind	82	107	243	.440
Hubert Davis, Dal	81	101	230	.439
Steve Kerr, Chi	50	57	130	.438
Glen Rice, Cha	82	130	300	.433
Wesley Person, Cle	82	192	447	.430
Reggie Miller, Ind	81	164	382	.429
Dell Curry, Cha	52	61	145	.421
Eldridge Recasner, Atl	59	62	148	.419

High-Point Games

	Opp	Date	FG-FT–Pts
Karl Malone, Utah	at GS	4/7	18-19–56
Tracy Murray, Wash	at GS	2/10	18-9–50
Shaquille O'Neal, LAL	at NJ	4/2	18-14–50
Michael Jordan, Chi	at LAC	11/21	18-13–49**
Antoine Walker, Bos	at Wash	1/7	21-2–49
Michael Jordan, Chi	vs Atl	12/27	18-11–47
Michael Jordan, Chi	vs. Hou	1/18	16-11–45
Latrell Sprewell, GS	at Min.	10/31	18-5–45

Several tied at 44.

*Overtime.

Blocked Shots

	Gm	Blk	Avg
Marcus Camby, Tor	63	230	3.65
Dikembe Mutombo, Atl	82	277	3.38
Shawn Bradley, Dal	64	214	3.34
Theo Ratliff, Phi	82	258	3.15
David Robinson, SA	73	192	2.63
Tim Duncan, SA	82	206	2.51
Michael Stewart, Sac	81	195	2.41
Shaquille O'Neal, LAL	60	144	2.40
Alonzo Mourning, Mia	58	130	2.24
Bo Outlaw, Orl	82	181	2.21

Steals

	Gm	Stl	Avg
Mookie Blaylock, Atl	70	183	2.61
Brevin Knight, Cle	80	196	2.45
Doug Christie, Tor	78	190	2.44
Gary Payton, Sea	82	185	2.26
Allen Iverson, Phi	80	176	2.20
Eddie Jones, LAL	80	160	2.00
Jason Kidd, Pho	82	162	1.98
Kendall Gill, NJ	81	156	1.93
Hersey Hawkins, Sea	82	148	1.80
Clyde Drexler, Hou	70	126	1.80

Rookie Leaders

Scoring	Gm	FG	FT	Pts	Avg
Tim Duncan, SA	82	706	319	1713	21.1
Keith Van Horn, NJ	62	446	258	1219	19.7
Ron Mercer, Bos	80	515	188	1221	15.3
Zydrunas Ilgauskas, Cle	82	454	230	1139	13.9
Derek Anderson, Cle	66	239	275	770	11.7

Field Goal Pct.	Gm	FG	Att	Pct
Tim Duncan, SA	82	706	1287	.549
Zydrunas Ilgauskas, Cle	82	454	876	.518
Lawrence Funderburke, Sac	52	191	390	.490
Cedric Henderson, Cle	82	348	725	.480
Michael Stewart, Sac	81	155	323	.480

Rebounds	Gm	Off	Def	Tot	Avg
Tim Duncan, SA	82	274	703	977	11.9
Zydrunas Ilgauskas, Cle	82	279	444	723	8.8
Michael Stewart, Sac	81	197	339	536	6.6
Keith Van Horn, NJ	62	142	266	408	6.6
Danny Fortson, Den	80	182	266	448	5.6

Assists	Gm	No	Avg
Brevin Knight, Cle	80	656	8.2
Bobby Jackson, Den	68	317	4.7
Antonio Daniels, Van	74	334	4.5
Anthony Johnson, Sac	77	329	4.3
Chauncey Billups, Tor	80	314	3.9

Personal Fouls

Ervin Johnson, Mil	321
Danny Fortson, Den	314
Shawn Kemp, Cle	310
Rick Fox, LAL	309
Antonio McDyess, Pho	292
Theo Ratliff, Phi	292

Disqualifications

Shawn Kemp, Cle	15
Shawn Bradley, Dal	9
P.J. Brown, Mia	9
Rik Smits, Ind	9
Tyrone Hill, Mil	8
Theo Ratliff, Phi	8

Turnovers

Antoine Walker, Bos	292
Grant Hill, Det	285
Tim Duncan, SA	279
Shawn Kemp, Cle	271
Sam Cassell, NJ	269

Triple Doubles

Grant Hill, Det	4
Jason Kidd, Pho	4
Rod Strickland, Was	3
Mookie Blaylock, Atl	2
Marcus Camby, Tor	2

Minutes Played

Michael Finley, Dal	3394
Glen Rice, Cha	3295
Grant Hill, Det	3294
Ray Allen, Mil	3287
Antoine Walker, Bos	3268

Assist/Turnover Ratio

Nick Van Exel, LAL	4.25
Pooh Richardson, LAC	4.19
Mark Jackson, Ind	4.10
Avery Johnson, SA	3.58
Brevin Knight, Cle	3.38

Team by Team Statistics

At least 16 games played, except where noted. Players who competed for more than one team during the regular season are listed with their final club; (*) indicates rookies.

Atlanta Hawks

	Gm	FG%	Tpts	PPG	RPG	APG
Steve Smith	73	.444	1464	20.1	4.2	4.0
Alan Henderson	69	.485	986	14.3	6.4	1.1
Christian Laettner	74	.485	1020	13.8	6.6	2.6
Dikembe Mutombo	82	.537	1101	13.4	11.4	1.0
Mookie Blaylock	70	.392	921	13.2	4.9	6.7
Tyrone Corbin	79	.439	806	10.2	4.6	2.2
Eldridge Recasner	59	.456	548	9.3	2.4	2.0
Ed Gray*	30	.381	227	7.6	1.5	1.1
Chucky Brown	77	.433	387	5.0	2.4	0.7
Chris Crawford*	40	.418	150	3.8	1.0	0.2
Anthony Miller	37	.558	79	2.1	1.9	0.1
Drew Barry*	27	.474	56	2.1	1.3	1.8
Greg Anderson	50	.444	88	1.8	2.4	0.3

Triple Doubles: Blaylock (2). **3-pt FG leader:** Smith (97).
Steals leader: Blaylock (183). **Blocks leader:** Mutombo (277).
Signed: G Barry (Jan. 20).

Boston Celtics

	Gm	FG%	Tpts	PPG	RPG	APG
Antoine Walker	82	.423	1840	22.4	10.2	3.3
Ron Mercer*	80	.450	1221	15.3	3.5	2.2
Kenny Anderson	61	.398	746	12.2	2.8	5.7
POR	45	.387	567	12.6	3.0	5.4
TOR	0	—	0	0.0	0.0	0.0
BOS	16	.435	179	11.2	2.4	6.3
Dana Barros	80	.461	784	9.8	1.9	3.6
Walter McCarty	82	.404	788	9.6	4.4	2.2
Travis Knight	74	.441	482	6.5	4.9	1.4
Bruce Bowen	61	.409	340	5.6	2.9	1.3
Andrew DeClercq	81	.497	439	5.4	4.8	0.7
Zan Tabak	57	.467	307	5.4	3.7	0.8
TOR	39	.466	248	6.4	3.9	0.9
BOS	18	.473	59	3.3	3.2	0.7
Tyus Edney	52	.431	277	5.3	1.1	2.7
Greg Minor	69	.436	345	5.0	2.2	1.3
Pervis Ellison	33	.571	100	3.0	3.3	0.9

Triple Doubles: Walker (1). **3-pt FG leader:** Barros (100).
Steals leader: Walker (142). **Blocks leader:** Knight (82).
Acquired: G Anderson, C Tabak and F Popeye Jones from Toronto for G Chauncey Billups, G Dee Brown, F John Thomas and F Roy Rogers (Feb. 18).

Charlotte Hornets

	Gm	FG%	Tpts	PPG	RPG	APG
Glen Rice	82	.457	1826	22.3	4.3	2.2
David Wesley	81	.443	1054	13.0	2.6	6.5
Anthony Mason	81	.509	1039	12.8	10.2	4.2
Matt Geiger	78	.505	885	11.3	6.7	1.0
Vlade Divac	64	.498	667	10.4	8.1	2.7
Bobby Phills	62	.446	642	10.4	3.5	3.0
Dell Curry	52	.447	490	9.4	1.9	1.3
Vernon Maxwell	42	.399	291	6.9	1.4	1.6
ORL	11	.333	81	7.4	1.2	1.1
CHA	31	.428	210	3.9	1.1	2.3
J.R. Reid	79	.459	384	4.9	2.7	0.6
B.J. Armstrong	66	.493	261	4.0	1.2	2.3
GS	4	.316	17	4.3	1.8	1.5
CHA	62	.510	244	3.9	1.1	2.3
Travis Williams*	39	.471	136	3.5	2.4	0.5
Cory Beck	59	.459	191	3.2	1.5	1.7
Donald Royal	31	.362	79	2.5	1.3	0.5
ORL	2	.167	5	2.5	2.0	0.5
CHA	29	.381	74	2.6	1.3	0.6
Tony Farmer	27	.321	67	2.5	1.2	0.2

Triple Doubles: none. **3-pt FG leader:** Rice (130).
Steals leader: Wesley (140). **Blocks leader:** Divac (94).
Signed: F Royal (Jan. 14).
Acquired: G Armstrong from Golden State for G Muggsy Bogues and G Tony Delk (Nov. 7).

Chicago Bulls

	Gm	FG%	Tpts	PPG	RPG	APG
Michael Jordan	82	.465	2357	28.7	5.8	3.5
Scottie Pippen	44	.447	841	19.1	5.2	5.8
Toni Kukoc	74	.455	984	13.3	4.4	4.2
Luc Longley	58	.455	663	11.4	5.9	2.8
Ron Harper	82	.441	764	9.3	3.5	2.9
Steve Kerr	50	.454	376	7.5	1.5	1.9
Scott Burrell	80	.424	416	5.3	2.5	0.8
Dennis Rodman	80	.431	375	4.7	15.0	2.9
Randy Brown	71	.384	288	4.1	1.3	2.1
Bill Wennington	48	.436	167	3.5	1.7	0.4
Dickey Simpkins	40	.539	132	3.3	1.9	0.8
GS	19	.458	54	2.8	2.4	0.8
CHI	21	.634	78	3.7	1.5	0.8
Jud Buechler	74	.483	198	2.7	1.0	0.7
Joe Kleine	46	.368	93	2.0	1.7	0.7

Triple Doubles: none. **3-pt FG leader:** Kukoc (63).
Steals leader: Jordan (141). **Blocks leader:** Longley (62).
Signed: F Simpkins (Mar. 2)

Cleveland Cavaliers

	Gm	FG%	Tpts	PPG	RPG	APG
Shawn Kemp	80	.445	1442	18.0	9.3	2.5
Wesley Person	82	.460	1204	14.7	4.4	2.3
Zydrunas Ilgauskas*	82	.518	1139	13.9	8.8	0.9
Derek Anderson*	66	.408	770	11.7	2.8	3.4
Cedric Henderson*	82	.480	832	10.1	4.0	2.0
Brevin Knight*	80	.441	723	9.0	3.2	8.2
Vitaly Potapenko	80	.480	570	7.1	3.9	0.7
Bob Sura	46	.377	267	5.8	2.0	3.7
Danny Ferry	69	.395	291	4.2	1.7	0.9
Carl Thomas	43	.400	148	3.4	1.1	0.4
ORL	4	.800	9	2.3	0.0	0.3
GS	10	.385	62	6.2	1.0	0.9
CLE	29	.386	77	2.7	1.3	0.3
Henry James	28	.407	80	2.9	0.5	0.2
Mitchell Butler	18	.319	37	2.1	1.2	1.0
Scott Brooks	43	.424	79	1.8	0.7	1.1
Shawnelle Scott	41	.444	44	1.1	1.4	0.2

Triple Doubles: none. **3-pt FG leader:** Person (192).
Steals leader: Knight (196). **Blocks leader:** Ilgauskas (135).
Signed: G Brooks (Dec. 12); F Thomas (Feb. 2).

Dallas Mavericks

	Gm	FG%	Tpts	PPG	RPG	APG
Michael Finley	82	.449	1763	21.5	5.3	4.9
Shawn Bradley	64	.422	731	11.4	8.1	0.9
Cedric Ceballos	47	.492	536	11.4	4.7	1.3
PHO	35	.500	333	9.5	4.3	1.0
DAL	12	.478	203	16.9	6.0	2.1
Hubert Davis	81	.456	898	11.1	2.1	1.9
Samaki Walker	41	.486	365	8.9	7.4	0.6
Khalid Reeves	82	.418	717	8.7	2.3	2.8
Erick Strickland	67	.357	511	7.6	2.4	2.5
A.C Green	82	.453	600	7.3	8.1	1.5
Shawn Respert	57	.444	339	5.9	1.8	1.1
TOR	47	.450	257	5.5	1.6	0.9
DAL	10	.429	82	8.2	2.7	1.7
Chris Antsey*	41	.398	240	5.9	3.8	0.9
Martin Muursepp	41	.435	233	5.7	2.8	0.7
Eric Riley	39	.415	139	3.6	3.4	0.6
Bubba Wells*	39	.414	128	3.3	1.7	0.9

Triple Doubles: Bradley and Finley. **3-pt FG leader:** Davis (101).
Steals leader: Finley (132). **Blocks leader:** Bradley (214).
Acquired: F Ceballos from Phoenix for F Dennis Scott (Feb. 18).
Signed: F Riley (Dec.17); G Respert (Mar. 30).

Denver Nuggets

	Gm	FG%	Tpts	PPG	RPG	APG
Johnny Newman	74	.431	1089	14.7	1.9	1.9
LaPhonso Ellis	76	.407	1083	14.3	7.2	2.8
Bobby Jackson*	68	.392	790	11.6	4.4	4.7
Danny Fortson*	80	.452	816	10.2	5.6	1.0
Anthony Goldwire	82	.423	751	9.2	1.8	3.4
Tony Battie*	65	.446	544	8.4	5.4	0.9
Cory Alexander	60	.428	488	8.1	2.4	3.5
SA	37	.414	165	4.5	1.3	1.9
DEN	23	.435	323	14.0	4.3	6.0
Eric Washington*	66	.404	511	7.7	1.9	1.2
Bryant Stith	31	.333	235	7.6	2.1	1.6
Dean Garrett	82	.428	598	7.3	7.9	1.1
Harold Ellis	27	.559	164	6.1	1.9	0.7
Priest Lauderdale	39	.417	144	3.7	2.6	0.5
Kiwane Garris	28	.338	68	2.4	0.7	1.0
Joe Wolf	57	.331	87	1.5	2.2	0.5

Triple Doubles: none. **3-pt FG leader:** Alexander (66). **Steals leader:** Jackson (105). **Blocks leader:** Garrett (133). **Signed:** G Garris (Nov. 24); G H. Ellis (Dec. 15); G Alexander (Mar. 4).

Detroit Pistons

	Gm	FG%	Tpts	PPG	RPG	APG
Grant Hill	81	.452	1712	21.1	7.7	6.8
Brian Williams	78	.511	1261	16.2	8.9	1.2
Jerry Stackhouse	79	.435	1249	15.8	3.4	3.1
PHI	22	.452	353	16.0	3.5	3.0
DET	57	.428	896	15.7	3.3	3.1
Joe Dumars	72	.416	943	13.1	1.4	3.5
Lindsey Hunter	71	.383	862	12.1	3.5	3.2
Malik Sealy	77	.428	591	7.7	2.8	1.3
Theo Ratliff	24	.514	157	6.5	5.0	0.6
Jerome Williams	77	.524	410	5.3	4.9	0.6
Aaron McKie	24	.413	109	4.5	2.8	1.6
Grant Long	40	.427	141	3.5	3.8	0.6
Don Reid	68	.534	238	3.5	2.6	0.4
Eric Montross	48	.424	138	2.9	4.1	0.2
PHI	20	.395	67	3.4	4.6	0.4
DET	28	.456	71	2.5	3.8	0.1
Scot Pollard*	33	.500	89	2.7	2.2	0.3
Rick Mahorn	59	.457	141	2.4	3.3	0.3
Charles O'Bannon*	30	.377	64	2.1	1.1	0.6
Steve Henson	23	.500	36	1.6	0.1	0.2

Triple Doubles: Hill (4). **3-pt FG leader:** Dumars (158). **Steals leader:** Hill (143). **Blocks leader:** Stackhouse (59). **Acquired:** G Jerry Stackhouse and C Eric Montross from Philadelphia for C Theo Ratliff, G Aaron McKie and a conditional first-round draft pick to (Dec. 18).

Individual Single Game Highs

Most Field Goals Made

21 ....Antoine Walker, Bos at Wash (1/7)

Most Field Goals Attempted

39 ....Michael Jordan, Chi vs SA (11/3) 2OT

Most Assists

20 ....Done 4 times

Golden St. Warriors

	Gm	FG%	Tpts	PPG	RPG	APG
Jim Jackson	79	.430	1242	15.7	5.1	4.8
PHI	48	.460	657	13.7	4.7	4.6
GS	31	.402	585	18.9	5.6	5.1
Donyell Marshall	73	.413	1123	15.4	8.6	2.2
Erick Dampier	82	.445	971	11.8	8.7	1.1
Tony Delk	77	.393	781	10.1	2.2	2.2
CHA	3	.750	8	2.7	0.7	1.0
GS	74	.392	773	10.4	2.3	2.3
C. Weatherspoon	79	.441	736	9.3	7.5	1.1
PHI	48	.426	405	8.4	7.0	0.8
GS	31	.458	331	10.7	8.3	1.6
Bimbo Coles	53	.379	423	8.0	2.3	4.7
Jason Caffey	80	.485	583	7.3	4.3	0.8
CHI	51	.503	268	5.3	3.4	0.7
GS	29	.472	315	10.9	5.9	1.1
Brian Shaw	39	.336	251	6.4	3.9	4.4
Mugsy Bogues	61	.437	347	5.7	2.2	5.4
CHA	2	.400	6	3.0	0.5	2.0
GS	59	.437	341	5.8	2.2	5.5
Todd Fuller	57	.420	227	4.0	3.4	0.2
Adonal Foyle*	55	.406	165	3.0	3.3	0.3
Felton Spencer	68	.457	162	2.4	3.3	0.3
Gerald Madkins	19	.382	37	1.9	0.8	2.4
Duane Ferrell	50	.369	94	1.9	0.9	0.5

Triple Doubles: none. **3-pt FG leader:** Marshall (63). **Steals leader:** Marshall (95). **Blocks leader:** Dampier (139). **Signed:** G Madkins (Mar. 5). **Acquired:** G Bogues and G Delk from Charlotte for G B.J. Armstrong (Nov. 7); F Weatherspoon and G Jimmy Jackson from Philadelphia for F Joe Smith and G Brian Shaw (Feb. 17); F Caffey for F David Vaughn and second-round draft picks in 1998 and 2000 (Feb. 19).

Houston Rockets

	Gm	FG%	Tpts	PPG	RPG	APG
Clyde Drexler	70	.427	1287	18.4	4.9	5.5
Hakeem Olajuwon	47	.483	772	16.4	9.8	3.0
Kevin Willis	81	.510	1305	16.1	8.4	1.0
Charles Barkley	68	.485	1036	15.2	11.7	3.2
Matt Maloney	78	.408	669	8.6	1.8	2.8
Eddie Johnson	75	.417	633	8.4	2.0	1.2
Mario Elie	73	.452	612	8.4	2.1	3.0
Matt Bullard	67	.450	466	7.0	2.2	0.9
Othella Harrington	58	.485	350	6.0	3.6	0.4
Rodrick Rhodes*	58	.367	337	5.8	1.2	1.9
Brent Price	72	.413	406	5.6	1.5	2.7
Emanual Davis	45	.444	184	4.1	1.0	1.3
Charles Jones	24	.700	15	0.6	1.0	0.2

Triple Doubles: Barkley (1). **3-pt FG leader:** Maloney (126). **Steals leader:** Drexler (126). **Blocks leader:** Olajuwon (96).

Indiana Pacers

	Gm	FG%	Tpts	PPG	RPG	APG
Reggie Miller	81	.477	1578	19.5	2.9	2.1
Rik Smits	73	.495	1216	16.7	6.9	1.4
Chris Mullin	82	.481	927	11.3	3.0	2.3
Antonio Davis	82	.481	785	9.6	6.8	0.7
Jalen Rose	82	.478	771	9.4	2.4	1.9
Mark Jackson	82	.416	678	8.3	3.9	8.7
Dale Davis	78	.548	626	8.0	7.8	0.9
Travis Best	82	.419	535	6.5	1.5	3.4
Derrick McKey	57	.459	359	6.3	3.7	1.5
Fred Hoiberg	65	.383	261	4.0	1.9	0.7
Austin Croshere*	26	.372	76	2.9	1.7	0.3
Mark Pope*	28	.341	39	1.4	0.9	0.3

Triple Doubles: none. **3-pt FG leader:** Miller (164). **Steals leader:** Mullin (95). **Blocks leader:** Smits (88).

Los Angeles Clippers

	Gm	FG%	Tpts	PPG	RPG	APG
Lamond Murray	79	.481	1220	15.4	6.1	1.8
Rodney Rogers	76	.456	1149	15.1	5.6	2.7
Isaac Austin	78	.466	1055	13.5	7.1	2.2
MIA	52	.474	659	12.7	6.4	1.7
LAC	26	.454	396	15.2	8.7	3.4
Maurice Taylor*	71	.476	815	11.5	4.2	0.7
Eric Piatkowski	67	.452	760	11.3	3.5	1.3
Darrick Martin	82	.377	841	10.3	2.0	4.0
Sharone Wright	69	.445	623	9.0	8.8	0.8
Rumeal Robinson	70	.389	541	7.7	1.6	1.9
Pooh Richardson	69	.372	289	4.2	1.4	3.3
Keith Closs*	58	.449	232	4.0	2.9	0.3
Charles Smith*	34	.392	119	3.5	0.8	0.6
MIA	11	.222	10	0.9	0.7	0.2
LAC	23	.421	109	4.7	0.8	0.8
Stojko Vrankovic	65	.425	195	3.0	4.0	0.6
James Collins	23	.382	59	2.6	0.6	0.1

Triple Doubles: none. **3-pt FG leader:** Martin (107).
Steals leader: Murray (118). **Blocks leader:** Wright (87).
Acquired: F/C Austin, G Smith and a 1998 first-round draft pick from Miami for G Brent Barry (Feb. 19).

Los Angeles Lakers

	Gm	FG%	Tpts	PPG	RPG	APG
Shaquille O'Neal	60	.584	1699	28.3	11.4	2.4
Eddie Jones	80	.484	1349	16.9	3.8	3.1
Kobe Bryant	79	.428	1220	15.4	3.1	2.5
Nick Van Exel	64	.419	881	13.8	3.0	6.9
Rick Fox	82	.471	983	12.0	4.4	3.4
Elden Campbell	81	.463	816	10.1	5.6	1.0
Robert Horry	72	.476	536	7.4	7.5	2.3
Derek Fisher	82	.434	474	5.8	2.4	4.1
Mario Bennett	45	.593	177	3.9	2.8	0.4
Corie Blount	70	.572	253	3.6	4.3	0.5
Sean Rooks	41	.455	139	3.4	2.9	0.6
Jon Barry	49	.365	121	2.5	0.8	1.0

Triple Doubles: none. **3-pt FG leader:** Jones (143).
Steals leader: Jones (160). **Blocks leader:** O'Neal (144).

Miami Heat

	Gm	FG%	Tpts	PPG	RPG	APG
Alonzo Mourning	58	.551	1115	19.2	9.6	0.9
Tim Hardaway	81	.431	1528	18.9	3.7	8.3
Jamal Mashburn	48	.435	723	15.1	4.9	2.8
Voshon Lenard	81	.425	1020	12.6	3.6	2.2
Brent Barry	58	.421	631	10.9	2.9	2.6
LAC	41	.428	561	13.7	3.5	3.2
MIA	17	.371	70	4.1	1.6	1.2
P.J. Brown	74	.471	707	9.6	8.6	1.4
Dan Majerle	72	.419	519	7.2	3.7	2.2
Mark Strickland	51	.539	349	6.8	4.2	0.5
Eric Murdock	82	.422	507	6.2	1.9	2.7
Marty Conlon	18	.452	88	4.9	2.6	0.7
Terry Mills	50	.393	212	4.2	3.0	0.8
Keith Askins	46	.320	111	2.4	2.2	0.6
Duane Causwell	37	.416	89	2.4	2.7	0.1
Rex Walters	38	.453	80	2.1	0.6	0.9
PHI	19	.379	42	2.2	0.5	1.1
MIA	19	.542	38	2.0	0.8	0.7

Triple Doubles: none. **3-pt FG leader:** Hardaway (155).
Steals leader: Hardaway (136). **Blocks leader:** Mourning (130).
Acquired: G Barry from LA Clippers for F/C Isaac Austin, G Charles Smith and a 1998 first-round draft pick (Feb. 19).
Signed: Walters (Jan. 27).

Milwaukee Bucks

	Gm	FG%	Tpts	PPG	RPG	APG
Glenn Robinson	56	.470	1308	23.4	5.5	2.8
Ray Allen	82	.428	1602	19.5	4.9	4.3
Terrell Brandon	50	.464	841	16.8	3.5	7.7
Armon Gilliam	82	.484	921	11.2	5.4	1.3
Tyrone Hill	57	.498	571	10.0	10.7	1.5
Ervin Johnson	81	.537	649	8.0	8.5	0.7
Elliot Perry	81	.430	591	7.3	1.3	2.8
Michael Curry	82	.469	543	6.6	1.2	1.7
Jerald Honeycutt*	38	.407	245	6.4	2.4	0.9
Ricky Pierce	39	.364	151	3.9	1.2	0.9
Andrew Lang	57	.378	152	2.7	2.7	0.3
Jamie Feick	45	.433	102	2.3	2.8	0.4
Litterial Green	21	.217	25	1.2	0.3	0.8

Triple Doubles: none. **3-pt FG leader:** Allen (134).
Steals leader: Allen, Brandon (111). **Blocks leader:** Johnson (158).
Signed: G Pierce (Dec. 4); F Green (Feb. 13).

Minnesota Timberwolves

	Gm	FG%	Tpts	PPG	RPG	APG
Tom Gugliotta	41	.502	823	20.1	8.7	4.1
Kevin Garnett	82	.491	1518	18.5	9.6	4.2
Stephon Marbury	82	.415	1450	17.7	2.8	8.6
Sam Mitchell	81	.464	1000	12.3	4.8	1.3
Anthony Peeler	38	.452	469	12.3	3.2	3.6
VAN	8	.486	79	9.9	2.5	2.9
MIN	30	.445	390	13.0	3.4	3.8
Chris Carr	51	.420	504	9.9	3.0	1.7
Terry Porter	82	.449	777	9.5	2.0	3.3
Cherokee Parks	79	.499	558	7.1	5.5	0.7
Stanley Roberts	74	.495	457	6.2	4.9	0.4
Tom Hammonds	57	.516	346	6.1	4.8	0.6
Reggie Jordan	57	.478	149	2.6	1.7	0.9
Michael Williams	25	.333	64	2.6	0.6	1.3
DeJuan Wheat*	34	.400	57	1.7	0.3	0.7

Triple Doubles: Garnett. **3-pt FG leader:** Marbury (95).
Steals leader: Garnett (139). **Blocks leader:** Garnett (150).
Acquired: G Peeler from Vancouver for G/F Doug West (Feb. 18).

New Jersey Nets

	Gm	FG%	Tpts	PPG	RPG	APG
Keith Van Horn*	62	.426	1219	19.7	6.6	1.7
Sam Cassell	75	.441	1471	19.6	3.0	8.0
Kerry Kittles	77	.440	1328	17.2	4.7	2.3
Kendall Gill	81	.429	1087	13.4	4.8	2.5
Rony Seikaly	56	.432	746	13.3	7.0	1.4
ORL	47	.441	704	15.0	7.6	1.5
NJ	9	.317	42	4.7	4.0	0.9
Jayson Williams	65	.498	837	12.9	13.6	1.0
Chris Gatling	57	.455	656	11.5	5.9	0.9
Sherman Douglas	80	.495	639	8.0	1.7	4.0
Brian Evans	72	.394	321	4.5	1.9	0.8
ORL	44	.374	206	4.7	1.9	0.7
NJ	28	.434	115	4.1	1.9	0.9
David Vaughn	40	.446	162	4.1	3.8	0.5
GS	22	.404	114	5.2	4.6	0.8
CHI	3	1.000	4	1.3	0.3	0.0
NJ	15	.576	44	2.9	3.3	0.1
Lucious Harris	50	.390	191	3.8	1.0	0.8
Jack Haley	16	.278	22	1.4	0.9	0.0
Michael Cage	79	.512	106	1.3	3.9	0.4
Xavier McDaniel	20	.333	25	1.3	1.6	0.5

Triple Doubles: none. **3-pt FG leader:** Kittles (110).
Steals leader: Gill (156). **Blocks leader:** Gill (64).
Acquired: C Seikaly and F Evans from Orlando for G Kevin Edwards, C Yinka Dare, F David Benoit and a conditional 1998 first-round draft pick (Feb. 19).
Signed: G Douglas (Oct. 31); F McDaniel (Nov. 13); F Vaughn (Mar. 7).

New York Knicks

	Gm	FG%	Tpts	PPG	RPG	APG
Patrick Ewing	26	.504	540	20.8	10.2	1.1
Allan Houston	82	.447	1509	18.4	3.3	2.6
Larry Johnson	70	.485	1087	15.5	5.7	2.1
John Starks	82	.393	1059	12.9	2.8	2.7
Chris Mills	80	.433	776	9.7	5.1	1.7
Charles Oakley	79	.440	711	9.0	9.2	2.5
Charlie Ward	82	.455	642	7.8	3.3	5.7
Terry Cummings	74	.467	467	6.3	3.8	0.6
PHI	44	.458	233	5.3	3.4	0.5
NY	30	.477	234	7.8	4.5	0.9
Chris Childs	68	.421	429	6.3	2.4	3.9
Buck Williams	41	.503	202	4.9	4.5	0.5
Chris Dudley	51	.406	157	3.1	5.4	0.4
Anthony Bowie	27	.542	75	2.8	1.0	0.4
Brooks Thompson	30	.411	59	2.0	0.5	0.9
PHO	13	.370	26	2.0	0.4	0.2
NY	17	.448	33	1.9	0.6	1.4
Herb Williams	27	.419	37	1.4	1.1	0.1

Triple Doubles: none. **3-pt FG leader:** Starks (130).
Steals leader: Ward (144). **Blocks leader:** Ewing (58).
Acquired: F Cummings from Philadelphia for C Herb Williams and F Ronnie Grandison (Feb. 19).
Signed: F Bowie (Jan. 6); G Thompson (Jan. 30); C H. Williams (Feb. 25).

Orlando Magic

	Gm	FG%	Tpts	PPG	RPG	APG
Anfernee Hardaway	19	.377	311	16.4	4.0	3.6
Nick Anderson	58	.455	890	15.3	5.1	2.1
Derek Strong	58	.420	736	12.7	7.4	0.9
Horace Grant	76	.459	921	12.1	8.1	2.3
Bo Outlaw	82	.554	783	9.5	7.8	2.6
Mark Price	63	.431	597	9.5	2.0	4.7
Darrell Armstrong	48	.411	442	9.2	3.3	4.9
Derek Harper	66	.417	566	8.6	1.6	3.5
Danny Schayes	74	.418	406	5.5	3.3	0.6
David Benoit	77	.373	420	5.5	2.6	0.3
NJ	53	.379	282	5.3	2.7	0.3
ORL	24	.360	138	5.8	2.6	0.3
Gerald Wilkins	72	.325	380	5.3	1.3	1.1
Kevin Edwards	39	.349	150	3.8	1.4	1.0
NJ	27	.255	91	3.4	1.3	1.0
ORL	12	.339	59	4.9	1.7	1.1
Kevin Ollie*	35	.378	123	3.5	1.1	1.9
DAL	16	.333	46	2.9	1.3	2.0
ORL	19	.411	77	4.1	0.9	1.7
Jason Lawson*	17	.600	26	1.5	1.6	0.3

Triple Doubles: Outlaw. **3-pt FG leader:** Anderson (77).
Steals leader: Outlaw (107). **Blocks leader:** Outlaw (181).
Acquired: G Edwards, C Dare, F Benoit and a conditional first-round draft pick from New Jersey for C Rony Seikaly and F Brian Evans (Feb. 19).
Signed: G Ollie (Mar. 2).

Philadelphia 76ers

	Gm	FG%	Tpts	PPG	RPG	APG
Allen Iverson	80	.461	1758	22.0	3.7	6.2
Derrick Coleman	59	.411	1040	17.6	9.9	2.5
Joe Smith	79	.434	1155	14.6	6.0	1.2
GS	49	.429	846	17.3	6.9	1.4
PHI	30	.448	309	10.3	4.4	0.9
Tim Thomas*	77	.447	845	11.0	3.7	1.2
Theo Ratliff	82	.513	809	9.9	6.7	0.7
DET	24	.514	157	6.5	5.0	0.6
PHI	58	.512	652	11.2	7.3	0.7
Brian Shaw	59	.345	372	6.3	3.6	4.4
GS	39	.336	251	6.4	3.9	4.4
PHI	20	.367	121	6.1	3.2	4.4
Aaron McKie	81	.365	332	4.1	2.9	2.2
DET	24	.413	109	4.5	2.8	1.6
PHI	57	.347	223	3.9	2.9	2.4
Scott Williams	58	.437	237	4.1	3.6	0.5
Mark Davis	71	.447	282	4.0	2.2	1.0
Eric Snow	64	.429	209	3.3	1.3	2.8
SEA	17	.435	25	1.5	0.2	0.8
PHI	47	.429	184	3.9	1.6	3.5
Doug Overton	23	.381	62	2.7	0.6	1.6
Anthony Parker*	37	.397	72	1.9	0.7	0.5

Triple Doubles: none. **3-pt FG leader:** Iverson (70).
Steals leader: Iverson (176). **Blocks leader:** Ratliff (258)
Acquired: F Chambers from Phoenix for G Marko Milic (Nov. 21); F Ratliff, G McKie and a conditional first-round draft pick from Detroit for G Jerry Stackhouse and C Eric Montross (Dec. 18); G Snow from Seattle for a conditional second-round draft pick (Jan 18); F Smith and G Shaw from Golden State for F Clarence Weatherspoon and G Jim Jackson (Feb. 17).

Phoenix Suns

	Gm	FG%	Tpts	PPG	RPG	APG
Rex Chapman	68	.427	1082	15.9	2.5	3.0
Antonio McDyess	81	.536	1225	15.1	7.6	1.3
Cliff Robinson	80	.479	1133	14.2	5.1	2.1
Danny Manning	70	.516	947	13.5	5.6	2.0
Jason Kidd	82	.416	954	11.6	6.2	9.1
Dennis Scott	81	.397	888	11.0	3.0	1.9
DAL	52	.387	707	13.6	3.8	2.5
PHO	29	.438	181	6.2	1.7	0.8
Kevin Johnson	50	.447	476	9.5	3.3	4.9
Steve Nash	76	.459	691	9.1	2.1	3.4
George McCloud	63	.405	456	7.2	3.5	1.3
Mark Bryant	70	.484	291	4.2	3.5	0.7
John Williams	71	.470	255	3.6	4.4	0.7
Marko Milic*	33	.609	92	2.8	0.8	0.4

Triple Doubles: Kidd (4). **3-pt FG leader:** Scott (125).
Steals leader: Kidd (162). **Blocks leader:** McDyess (135).
Acquired: G Milic from Philadelphia for F Tom Chambers (Nov. 21); F Scott from Dallas for F Cedric Ceballos (Feb. 18).

More Individual Single Game Highs

Most 3-point Field Goals Made

9 .... John Starks, NY vs Mil (1/29)*
9 .... Chuck Person, SA at Van (12/30)
9 .... Dennis Scott, Dal. vs. GS (11/20)*

Most 3-point Field Goals Attempted

14 .... Chuck Person, SA at Van (12/30)
14 .... Jaren Jackson, SA at Port. (12/29)
14 .... Isaiah Rider, Port. vs Pho. (11/14)****
14 .... Dennis Scott, Dal. vs. GS (11/20)*

*one overtime
****4-overtimes

Most Free Throws Made

22 .... Michael Jordan, Chi vs NY (4/18)

Most Free Throws Attempted

24 .... Michael Jordan, Chi vs NY (4/18)

Most Blocked Shots

13 .... Shawn Bradley, Dal vs Por (4/7)

Most Steals

10 .... Mookie Blaylock, Atl vs Phi (4/14)

Portland Trailblazers

	Gm	FG%	Tpts	PPG	RPG	APG
Isaiah Rider	74	.423	1458	19.7	4.7	3.1
Damon Stoudamire	71	.411	1225	17.3	4.2	8.2
TOR	49	.425	952	19.4	4.4	8.1
POR	22	.364	273	12.4	3.7	8.2
Arvydis Sabonis	73	.493	1167	16.0	10.0	3.0
Rasheed Wallace	77	.533	1124	14.6	6.2	2.5
Brian Grant	61	.508	737	12.1	9.1	1.4
Walt Williams	59	.386	608	10.3	3.4	2.1
TOR	28	.392	348	12.4	4.2	2.5
POR	31	.378	260	8.4	2.6	1.7
Stacey Augmon	71	.414	403	5.7	3.3	1.2
Carlos Rogers	21	.516	112	5.3	3.2	0.9
TOR	18	.517	108	6.0	3.6	0.9
POR	3	.500	4	1.3	0.7	0.7
Gary Grant	22	.462	105	4.8	2.2	3.8
Jermaine O'Neal	60	.485	269	4.5	3.4	0.3
Rick Brunson*	38	.348	162	4.3	1.5	2.6
Kelvin Cato*	74	.428	282	3.8	3.4	0.3
John Crotty	26	.322	96	3.7	1.2	2.4
Vincent Askew	30	.352	66	2.2	2.3	1.3

Triple Doubles: none. **3-pt FG leader:** Rider (135).
Steals leader: Stoudamire (113). **Blocks leader:** Cato (94).
Acquired: G Stoudamire, F Williams and F Rogers from Toronto for G Kenny Anderson, Alvin Williams, F Gary Trent, two first-round draft picks and cash (Feb. 13).

Sacramento Kings

	Gm	FG%	Tpts	PPG	RPG	APG
Mitch Richmond	70	.445	1623	23.2	3.3	4.0
Corliss Williamson	79	.495	1401	17.7	5.6	2.9
Billy Owens	78	.464	818	10.5	7.5	2.8
Otis Thorpe	74	.471	752	10.2	7.3	3.0
VAN	47	.477	528	11.2	7.9	3.4
SAC	27	.459	224	8.3	6.1	2.5
Olden Polynice	70	.459	550	7.9	6.3	1.5
Anthony Johnson*	77	.371	574	7.5	2.2	4.3
Mahmoud Abdul-Rauf	31	.377	227	7.3	1.2	1.9
Tariq Abdul-Wahad*	59	.403	376	6.4	2.0	0.9
Terry Dehere	77	.399	489	6.4	1.4	2.5
Michael Stewart*	81	.480	375	4.6	6.6	0.8
Chris Robinson	35	.374	162	4.6	1.3	1.1
VAN	16	.365	54	3.4	0.8	0.6
SAC	19	.378	108	5.7	1.7	1.5
Mark Hendrickson	48	.389	163	3.4	3.0	0.9
Kevin Salvadori	16	.077	5	0.3	1.3	0.2

Triple Doubles: none. **3-pt FG leader:** Richmond (130).
Steals leader: Owens (93). **Blocks leader:** Stewart (195).
Acquired: G Robinson and F Otis Thorpe from Vancouver for G Bobby Hurley and F Michael Smith (Feb. 18).
Signed: F Hendrickson (Dec. 23).

San Antonio Spurs

	Gm	FG%	Tpts	PPG	RPG	APG
David Robinson	73	.511	1574	21.6	10.6	2.7
Tim Duncan*	82	.549	1731	21.1	11.9	2.7
Avery Johnson	75	.478	766	10.2	2.0	7.9
Vinny Del Negro	54	.441	513	9.5	2.8	3.4
Sean Elliott	36	.403	334	9.3	3.4	1.7
Jaren Jackson	82	.394	722	8.8	2.6	1.9
Chuck Person	61	.359	409	6.7	3.3	1.4
Monty Williams	72	.448	453	6.3	2.5	1.2
Will Purdue	79	.549	394	5.0	6.8	0.7
Malik Rose	53	.434	158	3.0	1.7	0.4
Carl Herrera	58	.434	170	2.9	1.6	0.4
Reggie Geary	62	.331	152	2.5	1.1	1.2

Triple Doubles: none. **3-pt FG leader:** Jackson (112).
Steals leader: Johnson (84). **Blocks leader:** Duncan (206).

Seattle Supersonics

	Gm	FG%	Tpts	PPG	RPG	APG
Vin Baker	82	.542	1574	19.2	8.0	1.9
Gary Payton	82	.453	1571	19.2	4.6	8.3
Detlef Schrempf	78	.487	1232	15.8	7.1	4.4
Dale Ellis	79	.497	934	11.8	2.3	1.1
Hersey Hawkins	82	.440	862	10.5	4.1	2.7
Sam Perkins	81	.416	580	7.2	3.1	1.4
Jerome Kersey	37	.416	234	6.3	3.6	1.2
Greg Anthony	80	.430	419	5.2	1.4	2.6
Aaron Williams	65	.523	296	4.6	2.3	0.2
Nate McMillan	18	.343	62	3.4	2.2	3.1
Jim McIlvaine	78	.453	247	3.2	3.3	0.2
David Wingate	58	.471	150	2.6	1.4	0.6

Triple Doubles: Payton. **3-pt FG leader:** Payton (134).
Steals leader: Payton (185). **Blocks leader:** McIlvaine (137).

Toronto Raptors

	Gm	FG%	Tpts	PPG	RPG	APG
Doug Christie	78	.428	1287	16.5	5.2	3.6
John Wallace	82	.478	1147	14.0	4.5	1.3
Marcus Camby	63	.412	765	12.1	7.4	1.8
Gary Trent	54	.477	630	11.7	6.3	1.3
POR	41	.493	471	11.5	5.7	1.4
TOR	13	.438	159	12.2	8.0	1.1
Chauncey Billups*	80	.374	893	11.2	2.4	3.9
BOS	51	.390	565	11.1	2.2	4.3
TOR	29	.349	328	11.3	2.7	3.3
Dee Brown	72	.438	658	9.1	2.1	2.1
BOS	41	.427	280	6.8	1.5	1.3
TOR	31	.446	378	12.2	2.9	3.3
Reggie Slater	78	.460	625	8.0	3.9	0.9
Tracy McGrady	64	.450	451	7.0	4.2	1.5
Oliver Miller	64	.461	401	6.3	6.3	3.1
Alvin Williams*	54	.443	324	6.0	1.5	1.9
POR	41	.458	283	6.9	1.5	2.0
TOR	13	.364	41	3.2	1.6	1.5
Shawn Respert	47	.450	257	5.5	1.6	0.9
John Thomas*	54	.487	151	2.8	2.0	0.3
BOS	33	.513	108	3.3	2.1	0.4
TOR	21	.424	43	2.0	1.7	0.2
Chris Garner*	38	.329	53	1.4	0.6	1.2

Triple Doubles: Camby (2). **3-pt FG leader:** Brown (108).
Steals leader: Christie (190). **Blocks leader:** Camby (230).
Acquired: G Kenny Anderson and G Williams from Portland for G Damon Stoudamire, F Walt Williams and F Carlos Rogers (Feb. 13); G Billups, G Brown, F Thomas and F Roy Rogers from Boston for G Kenny Anderson, F Popeye Jones and C Zan Tabak (Feb. 18).

Utah Jazz

	Gm	FG%	Tpts	PPG	RPG	APG
Karl Malone	81	.530	2190	27.0	10.3	3.9
Jeff Hornacek	80	.482	1139	14.2	3.4	4.4
John Stockton	64	.528	770	12.0	2.6	8.5
Bryon Russell	82	.430	738	9.0	4.0	1.2
Shandon Anderson	82	.538	681	8.3	2.8	1.1
Adam Keefe	80	.540	620	7.8	5.5	1.1
Howard Eisley	82	.441	633	7.7	2.0	4.2
Antoine Carr	66	.465	378	5.7	2.0	0.7
Greg Foster	78	.445	441	5.7	3.5	0.7
Greg Ostertag	63	.481	297	4.7	5.9	0.4
Chris Morris	54	.411	233	4.3	2.1	0.4
Jacques Vaughn*	45	.361	139	3.1	0.8	1.9

Triple Doubles: none. **3-pt FG leader:** Russell (73).
Steals leader: Hornacek (109). **Blocks leader:** Ostertag (132).

Vancouver Grizzlies

	Gm	FG%	Tpts	PPG	RPG	APG
Shareef-Abdur-Rahim	82	.485	1829	22.3	7.1	2.6
Bryant Reeves	74	.523	1207	16.3	7.9	2.1
Sam Mack	57	.397	616	10.8	2.3	1.8
Blue Edwards	81	.439	872	10.8	2.7	2.5
Antonio Daniels*	74	.416	579	7.8	1.9	4.5
George Lynch	82	.481	616	7.5	4.4	1.5
Tony Massenburg	61	.479	396	6.5	3.8	0.3
Michael Smith	48	.479	251	5.2	6.4	1.8
SAC	18	.426	69	3.8	5.6	1.6
VAN	30	.504	182	6.1	6.9	2.0
Pete Chilcutt	82	.435	405	4.9	3.7	1.3
Lee Mayberry	79	.375	363	4.6	1.4	4.4
Doug West	38	.374	157	4.1	2.2	1.2
Bobby Hurley	61	.391	250	4.1	1.1	2.9
SAC	34	.409	128	3.8	1.1	2.4
VAN	27	.374	122	4.5	1.1	3.6
Chris Robinson	16	.365	54	3.4	0.8	0.6
Ivano Newbill	28	.351	58	2.1	2.5	0.3

Triple Doubles: none. **3-pt FG leader:** Mack (110). **Steals leader:** Abdur-Rahim (89). **Blocks leader:** Reeves (80). **Acquired:** F West from Minnesota for G Anthony Peeler (Feb. 18); G Hurley and F Smith from Sacramento for F Otis Thorpe and G Chris Robinson (Feb. 18).

Washington Wizards

	Gm	FG%	Tpts	PPG	RPG	APG
Chris Webber	71	.482	1555	21.9	9.5	3.8
Juwan Howard	64	.467	1184	18.5	7.0	3.3
Rod Strickland	76	.434	1349	17.8	5.3	10.5
Tracy Murray	82	.446	1238	15.1	3.4	1.0
Calbert Cheaney	82	.457	1050	12.8	4.0	2.1
Ledell Eackles	42	.429	218	5.2	1.8	0.4
Chris Whitney	82	.355	422	5.1	1.4	2.4
Terry Davis	74	.496	323	4.4	6.5	0.4
Ben Wallace	67	.518	205	3.1	4.8	0.3
God Shammgod*	20	.328	61	3.1	0.4	1.8
Harvey Grant	65	.383	170	2.6	2.6	0.6
Darvin Ham	71	.529	145	2.0	1.8	0.2

Triple Doubles: Strickland (3). **3-pt FG leader:** Murray (158). **Steals leader:** Strickland (126). **Blocks leader:** Webber (124).
Signed: G Eackles (Nov. 28).

More Individual Single Game Highs

Most Rebounds

29 .... Dennis Rodman, Chi vs Atl (12/27)

Most Offensive Rebounds

17 .... Jayson Williams, NJ vs Ind (10/31)

Most Defensive Rebounds

20 .... Dennis Rodman, Chi vs Atl (12/27)

NBA Regular Season Team Leaders

Offense

WEST	PPG	RPG	APG	FG%	3Pt%	FT%
LA Lakers	105.5	43.3	24.5	.481	.350	.680
Minnesota	101.1	42.6	25.2	.461	.347	.739
Utah	101.0	41.1	25.2	.490	.372	.773
Seattle	100.6	38.5	24.2	.473	.395	.721
Phoenix	99.6	42.0	25.9	.468	.356	.749
Houston	98.8	40.7	21.9	.452	.343	.771
Vancouver	96.6	41.4	23.9	.458	.362	.739
LA Clippers	95.9	40.4	18.6	.438	.358	.723
Portland	94.3	44.0	21.5	.451	.309	.737
Sacramento	93.1	41.4	22.4	.442	.351	.687
San Antonio	92.5	44.2	22.4	.468	.350	.688
Dallas	91.4	40.1	18.7	.427	.357	.752
Denver	89.0	39.0	18.9	.417	.323	.772
Golden St.	88.3	45.9	20.8	.413	.272	.710
EAST	**PPG**	**RPG**	**APG**	**FG%**	**3Pt%**	**FT%**
New Jersey	99.6	42.5	20.5	.441	.331	.744
Washington	97.2	42.2	23.2	.452	.339	.691
Chicago	96.7	44.9	23.8	.451	.323	.743
Charlotte	96.6	40.6	23.7	.468	.383	.751
Indiana	96.0	39.3	22.9	.469	.390	.764
Boston	95.9	39.5	22.1	.435	.332	.726
Atlanta	95.8	43.0	19.1	.455	.332	.756
Miami	95.0	42.0	21.5	.450	.354	.739
Toronto	94.9	40.7	21.3	.435	.343	.718
Milwaukee	94.5	39.9	20.1	.456	.353	.767
Detroit	94.2	41.2	19.5	.449	.312	.745
Philadelphia	93.3	41.7	21.1	.443	.300	.737
Cleveland	92.5	40.1	23.1	.454	.372	.756
New York	91.6	41.6	21.8	.447	.335	.772
Orlando	90.1	41.2	20.7	.429	.322	.726

Defense

WEST	PPG	RPG	APG	FG%	3Pt%	FT%
San Antonio	88.5	39.7	19.0	.411	.328	.740
Portland	92.9	39.2	21.5	.431	.343	.722
Seattle	93.4	42.1	22.2	.446	.324	.724
Phoenix	94.4	41.4	22.0	.442	.361	.732
Utah	94.4	36.5	20.6	.439	.357	.757
Golden State	97.4	44.7	24.5	.444	.346	.729
Dallas	97.5	47.2	23.0	.460	.342	.714
LA Lakers	97.8	42.2	22.5	.439	.354	.731
Sacramento	98.7	45.0	22.2	.457	.356	.743
Houston	99.5	41.1	23.3	.469	.365	.744
Minnesota	100.4	43.0	23.3	.448	.358	.742
Denver	100.8	42.6	24.2	.473	.379	.754
LA Clippers	103.3	44.3	22.2	.474	.360	.734
Vancouver	103.9	42.7	25.6	.475	.385	.732
EAST	**PPG**	**RPG**	**APG**	**FG%**	**3Pt%**	**FT%**
New York	89.1	39.0	19.3	.428	.317	.750
Chicago	89.6	39.7	19.5	.431	.322	.729
Cleveland	89.8	38.8	21.9	.433	.344	.755
Indiana	89.9	41.1	19.3	.432	.316	.728
Miami	90.0	40.1	19.9	.429	.331	.744
Orlando	91.2	40.9	21.2	.454	.324	.736
Atlanta	92.3	39.4	21.4	.442	.342	.735
Detroit	92.6	40.5	21.4	.445	.330	.746
Charlotte	94.6	39.3	22.0	.464	.347	.728
Philadelphia	95.7	42.1	23.5	.451	.344	.730
Milwaukee	96.4	39.8	21.3	.461	.327	.743
Washington	96.6	42.6	21.0	.455	.356	.747
New Jersey	98.1	41.4	21.6	.471	.345	.748
Boston	98.5	42.2	22.1	.479	.318	.744
Toronto	104.2	46.0	27.1	.479	.383	.700

Series Summaries

WESTERN CONFERENCE

FIRST ROUND (Best of 5)

	W-L	Avg.	Leading Scorer
San Antonio	3-1	100.5	McDyess (17.8)
Phoenix	1-3	93.0	Johnson (20.5)

Date	Winner	Home Court
Apr. 23	San Antonio, 102-96	at Phoenix
Apr. 25	Phoenix, 108-101	at Phoenix
Apr. 27	San Antonio, 100-88	at San Antonio
Apr. 29	San Antonio, 99-80	at San Antonio

	W-L	Avg.	Leading Scorer
Portland	1-3	99.8	Rider (19.3)
Los Angeles	3-1	104.0	O'Neal (29.0)

Date	Winner	Home Court
Apr. 24	Los Angeles, 104-102	at Los Angeles
Apr. 26	Los Angeles, 108-99	at Los Angeles
Apr. 28	Portland, 99-94	at Portland
Apr. 30	Los Angeles, 110-99	at Portland

	W-L	Avg.	Leading Scorer
Minnesota	2-3	90.2	Peeler (17.6)
Seattle	3-2	96.0	Payton (26.0)

Date	Winner	Home Court
Apr. 24	Seattle, 108-83	at Seattle
Apr. 26	Minnesota, 98-93	at Seattle
Apr. 28	Minnesota, 98-90	at Minnesota
Apr. 30	Seattle, 92-88	at Minnesota
May 2	Seattle, 97-84	at Seattle

	W-L	Avg.	Leading Scorer
Houston	2-3	84.6	Olajuwon (20.4)
Utah	3-2	91.4	Malone (26.6)

Date	Winner	Home Court
Apr. 23	Houston, 103-90	at Utah
Apr. 25	Utah, 105-90	at Utah
Apr. 29	Houston, 89-85	at Houston
May 1	Utah, 93-71	at Houston
May 3	Utah, 84-70	at Utah

SEMIFINALS (Best of 7)

	W-L	Avg.	Leading Scorer
LA Lakers	4-1	105.0	O'Neal (29.0)
Seattle	1-4	94.4	Payton (23.6)

Date	Winner	Home Court
May 4	Seattle, 106-92	at Seattle
May 6	Los Angeles, 92-68	at Seattle
May 8	Los Angeles, 119-103	at Los Angeles
May 10	at Los Angeles, 112-100	at Los Angeles
May 12	Los Angeles, 110-95	at Seattle

	W-L	Avg.	Leading Scorer
San Antonio	1-4	84.8	Duncan (21.0)
Utah	4-1	85.0	Malone (24.6)

Date	Winner	Home Court
May 5	Utah, 83-82	at Utah
May 7	Utah, 109-106 (OT)	at Utah
May 9	San Antonio, 86-64	at San Antonio
May 10	Utah, 82-73	at San Antonio
May 12	Utah, 87-77	at Utah

CHAMPIONSHIP (Best of 7)

	W-L	Avg.	Leading Scorer
LA Lakers	0-4	90.5	O'Neal (31.8)
Utah	4-0	104.0	Malone (30.0)

Date	Winner	Home Court
May 16	Utah, 112-77	at Utah
May 18	Utah, 99-95	at Utah
May 22	Utah, 109-98	at Los Angeles
May 24	Utah, 96-92	at Los Angeles

EASTERN CONFERENCE

FIRST ROUND (Best of 5)

	W-L	Avg.	Leading Scorer
Atlanta	1-3	87.5	Smith (24.8)
Charlotte	3-1	83.8	Rice (22.8)

Date	Winner	Home Court
Apr. 23	Charlotte, 97-87	at Charlotte
Apr. 25	Charlotte, 92-85	at Charlotte
Apr. 28	Atlanta, 96-64	at Atlanta
May 1	Charlotte, 91-82	at Atlanta

	W-L	Avg.	Leading Scorer
Cleveland	1-3	80.8	Kemp (26.0)
Indiana	3-1	88.8	Miller (18.5)

Date	Winner	Home Court
Apr. 23	Indiana, 106-77	at Indiana
Apr. 25	Indiana, 92-86	at Indiana
Apr. 27	Cleveland, 86-77	at Cleveland
Apr. 30	Indiana, 80-74	at Cleveland

	W-L	Avg.	Leading Scorer
New York	3-2	89.6	Houston (23.2)
Miami	2-3	87.4	Hardaway (26.0)

Date	Winner	Home Court
Apr. 24	Miami, 94-79	at Miami
Apr. 26	New York, 96-86	at Miami
Apr. 28	Miami, 91-85	at New York
Apr. 30	New York, 90-85	at New York
May 3	New York, 98-81	at Miami

	W-L	Avg.	Leading Scorer
New Jersey	0-3	95.0	Douglas (18.3)
Chicago	3-0	102.7	Jordan (36.3)

Date	Winner	Home Court
Apr. 24	Chicago, 96-93 (OT)	at Chicago
Apr. 26	Chicago, 96-91	at Chicago
Apr. 29	Chicago, 116-101	at New Jersey

SEMIFINALS (Best of 7)

	W-L	Avg.	Leading Scorer
New York	1-4	87.6	Houston (19.0)
Indiana	4-1	94.2	Miller (24.6)

Date	Winner	Home Court
May 5	Indiana, 93-83	at Indiana
May 7	Indiana, 85-77	at Indiana
May 9	New York, 83-76	at New York
May 10	Indiana, 118-107 (OT)	at New York
May 13	Indiana, 99-88	at Indiana

	W-L	Avg.	Leading Scorer
Charlotte	1-4	80.2	Rice (22.6)
Chicago	4-1	89.8	Jordan (29.6)

Date	Winner	Home Court
May 3	Chicago, 83-70	at Chicago
May 6	Charlotte, 78-76	at Chicago
May 8	Chicago, 103-89	at Charlotte
May 10	Chicago, 94-80	at Charlotte
May 13	Chicago, 93-84	at Chicago

Championship (Best of 7)

	W-L	Avg.	Leading Scorer
Indiana	3-4	91.7	Miller (17.4)
Chicago	4-3	95.9	Jordan (31.7)

Date	Winner	Home Court
May 17	Chicago, 85-79	at Chicago
May 19	Chicago, 104-98	at Chicago
May 23	Indiana, 107-105	at Indiana
May 25	Indiana, 96-94	at Indiana
May 27	Chicago, 106-87	at Chicago
May 29	Indiana, 92-89	at Indiana
May 31	Chicago, 88-83	at Chicago

NBA FINALS (Best of 7)

	W-L	Avg.	Leading Scorer
Chicago	4-2	88.0	Jordan (35.0)
Utah	2-4	80.2	Malone (23.5)

Date	Winner	Home Court
June 3	Utah, 88-85 (OT)	at Utah
June 5	Chicago, 93-88	at Utah
June 7	Chicago, 96-54	at Chicago
June 10	Chicago, 86-82	at Chicago
June 12	Utah, 83-81	at Chicago
June 14	Chicago, 87-86	at Utah

Most Valuable Player
Michael Jordan, Chicago, G
35.0 points, 4.0 rebounds, 2.3 assists

Final Playoff Standings

(Ranked by victories)

	Gm	W	L	Pct	Per Game For	Per Game Opp
Chicago	21	15	6	.714	93.1	86.1
Utah	20	12	7	.650	89.0	86.9
Indiana	16	10	6	.625	91.8	89.5
LA Lakers	13	7	6	.538	100.2	99.0
San Antonio	9	4	5	.444	91.8	88.6
Charlotte	9	4	5	.444	82.8	88.8
Seattle	10	4	6	.400	95.2	97.6
New York	10	4	6	.400	88.6	90.8
Minnesota	5	2	3	.400	90.2	96.0
Houston	5	2	3	.400	84.6	91.4
Miami	5	2	3	.400	87.4	89.6
Portland	4	1	3	.250	99.8	104.0
Phoenix	4	1	3	.250	93.0	100.5
Cleveland	4	1	3	.250	80.8	88.8
Atlanta	4	1	3	.250	87.5	83.8
New Jersey	3	0	3	.000	95.0	102.7

Off-Season Coaching Changes

Team	Old Coach	Why left?	New Coach	Old Job
Chicago	Phil Jackson	Resigned	Tim Floyd	Coach, Iowa St.
Denver	Bill Hanzlik	Fired	Mike D'Antoni	Dir. Player Personnel
LA Clippers	Bill Fitch	Resigned	TBA	
Milwaukee	Chris Ford	Fired	George Karl	Coach, Supersonics
Sacramento	Eddie Jordan	Fired	Rick Adelman	Former Coach, Warriors
Seattle	George Karl	Fired	Paul Westphal	Former Coach, Suns

Note: Due to the off-season NBA lock-out several hirings were delayed.

NBA Playoff Leaders

Scoring

	Gm	FG	FT	Pts	Avg
Michael Jordan, Chicago	21	243	181	680	32.4
Shaquille O'Neal, LA Lakers	13	158	80	396	30.5
Karl Malone, Utah	20	198	130	526	26.3
Tim Hardaway, Miami	5	42	29	130	26.0
Shawn Kemp, Cleveland	4	33	38	104	26.0
Steve Smith, Atlanta	4	39	11	99	24.8
Gary Payton, Seattle	10	87	47	240	24.0
Glen Rice, Charlotte	9	82	30	205	22.8
Allan Houston, New York	10	76	50	211	21.1
Tim Duncan, San Antonio	9	73	40	186	20.7
Hakeem Olajuwon, Houston	5	39	24	102	20.4
Reggie Miller, Indiana	16	98	85	319	19.9
David Robinson, San Antonio	9	57	61	175	19.4
Isaiah Rider, Portland	4	28	20	77	19.3
Sherman Douglas, New Jersey	3	23	7	55	18.3
Antonio McDyess, Phoenix	4	31	9	71	17.8
Damon Stoudamire, Portland	4	25	13	71	17.8
Zydrunas Ilgauskas, Cleveland	4	28	13	69	17.3
Avery Johnson, San Antonio	9	61	34	156	17.3

High Point Games

	Date	FG-FT—Pts
Michael Jordan, Chi vs Utah	6/14	15-12—45
Michael Jordan, Chi vs. Ind	5/19	13-15—41
Michael Jordan, Chi vs NJ	4/24	11-17—39*
Shaquille O'Neal, LAL vs Sea	5/10	17-5—39
Shaquille O'Neal, LAL vs Utah	5/22	15-9—39

Rebounds

	Gm	Off	Def	Tot	Avg
David Robinson, SA	9	41	86	127	14.1
Jayson Williams, NJ	3	20	22	42	14.0
Antonio McDyess, Pho	4	18	35	53	13.3
Dikembe Mutombo, Atl	4	13	38	51	12.8
Dennis Rodman, Chi	21	99	149	248	11.8

Assists

	Gm	No	Avg
Damon Stoudamire, Por	4	38	9.5
Mookie Blaylock, Atl	4	33	8.3
Sherman Douglas, Minn	3	25	8.3
Mark Jackson, Ind	16	133	8.3
Jason Kidd, Pho	4	31	7.8
John Stockton, Utah	20	155	7.8

NBA Finalists' Composite Box Scores

Chicago Bulls (15-6)

	Overall Playoffs						Finals vs. Utah					
				—Per Game—						—Per Game—		
	Gm	FG%	TPts	Pts	Reb	Ast	Gm	FG%	TPts	Pts	Reb	Ast
Michael Jordan	21	.462	680	32.4	5.1	3.5	6	.427	201	33.5	4.0	2.3
Scottie Pippen	21	.415	353	16.8	7.1	5.2	6	.410	94	15.7	6.8	4.8
Toni Kukoc	21	.486	275	13.1	3.9	2.9	6	.500	91	15.2	4.7	2.7
Luc Longley	18	.450	142	7.9	5.0	1.9	6	.444	30	5.0	4.8	1.5
Ron Harper	21	.459	141	6.7	3.7	2.3	6	.364	32	5.3	4.5	2.8
Steve Kerr	21	.434	103	4.9	0.8	1.7	6	.350	23	3.8	0.3	2.5
Dennis Rodman	21	.371	102	4.9	11.8	2.0	6	.462	20	3.3	8.3	1.0
Scott Burrell	21	.438	80	3.8	2.0	0.5	6	.409	21	3.5	2.5	0.0
Bill Wennington	16	.526	44	2.8	0.9	0.2	3	.400	4	1.3	1.0	0.3
Dickey Simpkins	13	.375	16	1.2	1.0	0.2	2	.500	2	1.0	1.5	0.5
Jud Buechler	16	.364	11	0.7	0.7	0.2	6	.600	8	1.3	0.3	0.3
Randy Brown	14	.167	9	0.6	0.6	0.6	2	.333	2	1.0	1.0	0.0
BULLS	21	.445	1956	93.1	41.0	20.5	6	.430	528	88.0	37.7	18.3
OPPONENTS	21	.451	1809	86.1	37.1	19.3	6	.443	481	80.2	38.0	21.3

Three-pointers: PLAYOFFS—Kukoc (23-for-61), Kerr (19-41), Pippen (18-79), Jordan (13-43), Burrell (6-20), Harper (5-19), Buechler (3-5), Rodman (1-4), Team (88-272 for .324 pct.); FINALS—Kukoc (7-for-23), Pippen (6-26), Kerr (5-13), Jordan (4-13), Burrell (1-4), Harper (1-6), Team (26-88 for .295 pct.).

Utah Jazz (13-7)

	Overall Playoffs						Finals vs. Chicago					
				—Per Game—						—Per Game—		
	Gm	FG%	TPts	Pts	Reb	Ast	Gm	FG%	TPts	Pts	Reb	Ast
Karl Malone	20	.471	526	26.3	10.9	3.4	6	.504	150	25.0	10.5	3.8
John Stockton	20	.494	222	11.1	3.0	7.8	6	.490	58	9.7	2.5	8.7
Bryon Russell	20	.469	219	11.0	4.7	1.1	6	.409	53	8.8	5.0	1.3
Jeff Hornacek	20	.416	217	10.9	2.5	3.2	6	.411	64	10.7	2.7	2.7
Shandon Anderson	20	.515	134	6.7	3.2	1.0	6	.500	44	7.3	2.7	0.3
Howard Eisley	20	.368	112	5.6	2.0	4.1	6	.375	28	4.7	2.0	3.8
Chris Morris	17	.406	77	4.5	2.8	0.6	6	.393	26	4.3	2.5	0.5
Antoine Carr	20	.456	88	4.4	2.1	0.6	6	.500	25	4.2	2.0	0.0
Greg Foster	20	.453	82	4.1	3.4	0.3	6	.267	8	1.3	2.3	0.0
Greg Ostertag	19	.565	64	3.4	4.3	0.3	5	.417	11	2.2	3.2	0.0
Adam Keefe	15	.345	31	2.1	2.3	0.1	5	.429	14	2.8	3.4	0.2
Jacque Vaughn	7	.200	7	1.0	0.4	0.6	1	.000	0	0.0	2.0	0.0
JAZZ	20	.455	1779	89.0	39.8	22.3	6	.443	481	80.2	38.0	21.3
OPPONENTS	20	.414	1737	86.9	40.5	16.9	6	.430	528	88.0	37.7	18.3

Three-pointers: PLAYOFFS—Russell (23-for-63), Hornacek (14-30), Stockton (9-26), Eisley (8-27), Morris (7-23), Anderson (3-11), Foster (1-2), Vaughn (1-2), Malone (0-3), Team (66-187 for .353 pct.); FINALS—Russell (6-for-21), Hornacek (3-9), Stockton (2-9), Morris (5-10), Anderson (1-3), Eisley (1-7), Malone (0-1), Morris (0-9), Team (13-60 for .217 pct.).

Annual Awards

Most Valuable Player

The Maurice Podoloff Trophy; voting by 116-member panel of local and national pro basketball writers and broadcasters. Each ballot has five entries; points awarded on 10-7-5-3-1 basis.

	1st	2nd	3rd	4th	5th	Pts
Michael Jordan, Chicago	92	22	2	0	0	1084
Karl Malone, Utah	20	83	11	2	0	842
Gary Payton, Seattle	3	8	50	24	23	431
Shaquille O'Neal, LA Lakers	1	2	33	34	20	311
Tim Duncan, San Antonio	0	1	8	26	23	148
Tim Hardaway, Miami	0	0	2	14	19	71
David Robinson, San Antonio	0	0	2	7	5	36
Vin Baker, Seattle	0	0	3	1	6	24
Grant Hill, Detroit	0	0	1	3	9	23
Scottie Pippen, Chicago	0	0	1	2	3	14
Glen Rice, Charlotte	0	0	0	2	1	7
Antoine Walker, Boston	0	0	1	0	1	6
Jason Kidd, Phoenix	0	0	1	0	0	5
John Stockton, Utah	0	0	1	0	0	5
Mitch Richmond, Sacramento	0	0	0	1	0	3
Reggie Miller, Indiana	0	0	0	0	2	2
Rik Smits, Indiana	0	0	0	0	2	2
Michael Finley, Dallas	0	0	0	0	1	1
Rod Strickland, Washington	0	0	0	0	1	1

All-NBA Teams

Voting by a 116-member panel of local and national pro basketball writers and broadcasters. Each ballot has entries for three teams; points awarded on 5-3-1 basis. First Team repeaters from 1996-97 are in **bold** type.

Pos	First Team	1st	Pts
F	**Karl Malone**, Utah	116	580
F	Tim Duncan, San Antonio	45	370
C	Shaquille O'Neal, LA Lakers	103	544
G	**Michael Jordan**, Chicago	116	580
G	Gary Payton, Seattle	108	561

Pos	Second Team	1st	Pts
F	Grant Hill, Detroit	22	290
F	Vin Baker, Seattle	10	269
C	David Robinson, San Antonio	13	332
G	Tim Hardaway, Miami	2	245
G	Rod Strickland, Washington	4	173

Pos	Third Team	1st	Pts
F	Scottie Pippen, Chicago	23	201
F	Glen Rice, Charlotte	14	179
C	Dikembe Mutombo, Atlanta	0	80
G	Mitch Richmond, Sacramento	0	139
G	Reggie Miller, Indiana	0	124

All-Defensive Teams

Voting by NBA head coaches. Each ballot has entries for two teams; two points given for 1st team, one for 2nd. Coaches cannot vote for own players. First Team repeaters from 1996-97 are in **bold** type.

Pos	First Team	1st	Pts
F	**Scottie Pippen**, Chicago	21	44
F	**Karl Malone**, Utah	10	24
C	**Dikembe Mutombo**, Atlanta	23	48
G	**Gary Payton**, Seattle	24	51
G	**Michael Jordan**, Chicago	25	53

Pos	Second Team	1st	Pts
F	Tim Duncan, San Antonio	7	21
F	Charles Oakley, New York	6	19
C	David Robinson, San Antonio	3	18
G	Mookie Blaylock, Atlanta	3	23
G	Eddie Jones, LA Lakers	0	10

Coach of the Year

The Red Auerbach Trophy; voting by 116-member panel of local and national pro basketball writers and broadcasters. Each ballot has one entry.

	Votes	Improvement
Larry Bird, Indiana	50	39-43 to 53-24
Jerry Sloan, Utah	29	64-18 to 62-20
Mike Fratello, Cleveland	15	42-40 to 47-35
Pat Riley, Miami	5	57-25 to 61-21
Danny Ainge, Phoenix	4	40-42 to 56-26
George Karl, Seattle	4	57-25 to 61-21
Chuck Daly, Orlando	1	45-37 to 41-41
John Calipari, New Jersey	1	26-56 to 43-39
Jeff Van Gundy, New York	1	57-25 to 43-39

Rookie of the Year

The Eddie Gottlieb Trophy; voting by 116-member panel of local and national pro basketball writers and broadcasters. Each ballot has one entry.

	Pos	Votes
Tim Duncan, San Antonio	F	113
Keith Van Horn, New Jersey	F	3

All-Rookie Team

Voting by NBA's 29 head coaches, who cannot vote for players on their team. Each ballot has entries for two five-man teams, regardless of position; two points given for 1st team, one for 2nd. First team votes in parentheses.

First Team	College	Pts
Tim Duncan, San Antonio (28)	Wake Forest	56
Keith Van Horn, New Jersey (28)	Utah	56
Brevin Knight, Cleveland (26)	Stanford	54
Zydrunas Ilgauskas, Cleveland (25)	Atletas-Lithuania	51
Ron Mercer, Boston (23)	Kentucky	50

Second Team	College	Pts
Tim Thomas, Philadelphia (5)	Villanova	30
Cedric Henderson, Cleveland (2)	Memphis	27
Derek Anderson, Cleveland (3)	Kentucky	25
Maurice Taylor, LA Clippers (3)	Michigan	25
Bobby Jackson, Denver (1)	Minnesota	18

IBM Award

Created prior to the 1983-84 season to honor the player who contributes most to his team's overall success and utilizes a computer evalutation of key offensive and defensive statistics to determine an overall leader. The formula is as follows: (Player pts.-FGA+REB+AST+STL+BLK-PF-TO+(team wins x 10) x 250)/(team pts.-FGA+REB+AST+STL+BLK-PF-TO).

	Pos	Pts
Karl Malone, Utah	F	99.69
Tim Duncan, San Antonio	F	98.70
David Robinson, San Antonio	C	96.66
Dennis Rodman, Chicago	F	88.31
Anthony Mason, Charlotte	F	88.29
Michael Jordan, Chicago	G	85.58
Gary Payton, Seattle	G	84.27
Rod Strickland, Washington	G	84.26

Other Awards

Defensive Player of the Year— Dikembe Mutombo, Atlanta; **Most Improved Player**— Alan Henderson, Atlanta; **Sixth Man Award**— Danny Manning, Phoenix; **Kennedy PBWAA Citizenship Award**— Steve Smith, Atlanta; **NBA Sportsmanship Award**— Avery Johnson, San Antonio; ***The Sporting News* Executive of the Year**— Wayne Embry, Cleveland.

1998 College Draft

First and second round picks at the 52nd annual NBA College Draft held June 24, 1998 at General Motors Place in Vancouver. The order of the first 13 positions were determined by a Draft Lottery held May 17, in Secaucus, N.J. Toronto and Vancouver were not eligible to receive the first pick. Positions 14 through 29 reflect regular season records in reverse order. Underclassmen selected are noted in CAPITAL letters.

First Round

	Team	Player	Pos
1	L.A. Clippers	Michael Olowokandi, Pacific	C
2	**a**-Vanvouver	MIKE BIBBY, Arizona	G
3	Denver	Raef LaFrentz, Kansas	F
4	**b**-Toronto	ANTAWN JAMISON, North Carolina	F
5	**b**-Golden State	VINCE CARTER, North Carolina	G
6	**c**-Dallas	ROBERT TRAYLOR, Michigan	F
7	Sacramento	JASON WILLIAMS, Florida	G
8	Philadelphia	LARRY HUGHES, Saint Louis	G
9	**c**-Milwaukee	DIRK NOWITZKI, Germany	C
10	Boston	PAUL PIERCE, Kansas	F
11	Detroit	Bonzi Wells, Ball State	G
12	Orlando	Michael Doleac, Utah	C
13	**d**-Orlando	Keon Clark, UNLV	F
14	Houston	Michael Dickerson, Arizona	G
15	**e**-Orlando	Matt Harpring, Georgia Tech	F
16	**f**-Houston	Bryce Drew, Valparaiso	G
17	Minnesota	Radoslav Nesterovic, Slovenia	C
18	**g**-Houston	Mirsad Turkcan, Turkey	F
19	**h**-Milwaukee	Pat Garrity, Notre Dame	F
20	Atlanta	Roshown McLoed, Duke	F
21	Charlotte	RICKY DAVIS, Iowa	F
22	**i**-L.A. Clippers	Brian Skinner, Baylor	F
23	**j**-Denver	TYRONN LUE, Nebraska	G
24	**k**-San Antonio	Felipe Lopez, St. John's	G
25	Indiana	AL HARRINGTON, St. Patrick's H.S (N.J.)	F
26	L.A. Lakers	Sam Jacobson, Minnesota	G
27	Seattle	Vladimir Stepania, Slovenia	C
28	Chicago	COREY BENJAMIN, Oregon State	G
29	**l**-Utah	NAZR MOHAMMED, Kentucky	C

Second Round

	Team	Player	Pos
30	**m**-Dallas	Ansu Sesay, Mississippi	F
31	**n**-L.A. Lakers	Ruben Patterson, Cincinnati	G
32	**o**-Seattle	RASHARD LEWIS, Alief Elsik H.S. (TX)	F
33	**p**-Seattle	JELANI MCCOY, UCLA	C
34	**q**-Chicago	Shammond Williams, North Carolina	G
35	Dallas	BRUNO SUNDOV, Croatia	C
36	Sacramento	JEROME JAMES, Florida A&M	C
37	Philadelphia	Joe Shaw, Toledo	C
38	**r**-New York	DeMarco Johnson, UNC Charlotte	F
39	Milwaukee	RAFER ALSTON, Fresno State	G
40	Detroit	KORLEONE YOUNG, Hargrave (VA)	F
41	Houston	Cuttino Mobley, Rhode Island	G
42	Orlando	Miles Simon, Arizona	G
43	Washington	Jahidi White, Georgetown	F
44	New York	Sean Marks, California	C
45	**s**-L.A. Lakers	Toby Bailey, UCLA	G
46	Minnesota	Andrae Patterson, Indiana	F
47	**t**-Toronto	Tyson Wheeler, Rhode Island	G
48	Cleveland	Ryan Stack, South Carolina	F
49	**q**-Atlanta	Cory Carr, Texas Tech	G
50	Charlotte	Andrew Betts, Long Beach State	C
51	Miami	Corey Brewer, Oklahoma	G
52	San Antonio	Derrick Dial, Eastern Michigan	G
53	**u**-Dallas	Greg Buckner, Clemson	G
54	**v**-Denver	TREMAINE FOWLKES, Fresno State	F
55	**w**-Denver	Ryan Bowen, Iowa	F
56	**x**-Vancouver	J.R. Henderson, UCLA	F
57	Utah	Torraye Braggs, Xavier	F
58	Chicago	Maceo Baston, Michigan	F

Acquired Picks

FIRST ROUND: **a**-Vancouver won the draft lottery but is not eligible through their expansion agreement with the NBA; **b**-Toronto traded Antawn Jamison to Golden State for Vince Carter and cash; **c**-Dallas traded Robert Traylor to the Bucks for the rights to Dirk Nowitzki and Pat Garrity; **d**-from Washington; **e**-from New Jersey; **f**-from New York via Toronto; **g**-from Portland; **h**-Mavericks traded Garrity, their 1999 first-round pick and players Bubba Wells and Martin Muursepp to the Phoenix Suns for Steve Nash; **i**-from Miami; **j**-from Phoenix, Denver traded Tyronn Lue and forward Tony Battie to the Los Angeles Lakers for guard Nick Van Exel; **k**-San Antonio traded Felipe Lopez and forward Carl Herrera to Vancouver for guard Antonio Daniels; **l**-Utah traded Nazr Mohammed to Philadelphia for a future first-round pick. SECOND ROUND: **m**-from Toronto; **n**-from Vancouver; **o**-from Denver; **p**-from L.A. Clippers; **q**-from Golden State, Chicago traded Shammond Williams to the Atlanta Hawks for Cory Carr and their second round picks in 1999 and 2000; **r**-from Boston; **s**-from New Jersey; **t**-from Portland; **u**-from Phoenix; **v**-from Indiana; **w**-from Seattle; **x**-from L.A. Lakers.

1998 World Championship

Thirteenth World Basketball Championships held July 29-Aug. 9 at Athens, Greece.

Second Round

(*) indicates team advanced to quarterfinals. Other teams relegated to classification games.

Group E	W	L
*Yugoslavia	5	1
*Russia	5	1
*Greece	4	2
*Italy	3	3
Puerto Rico	2	4
Canada	1	5

Group F	W	L
*United States	5	1
*Spain	5	1
*Lithuania	4	2
*Australia	3	3
Argentina	3	3
Brazil	1	5

Most Valuable Player

Dejan Bodiroga, Yugoslavia, 14.7 ppg, 4.9 rpg

Quarterfinals

Aug. 7 at Olympic Stadium.

Russia 82 ... Lithuania 67
United States 80 ... Italy 77
Yugoslavia 70 ... Argentina 62
Greece 69 ... Spain 62

Semifinals

Aug. 8 at Olympic Stadium.

Yugoslavia 78 ... OT ... Greece 73
Russia 66 ... United States 64

Bronze Medal

Aug. 9 at Olympic Stadium.

United States 84 ... Greece 61

Gold Medal

Aug. 9 at Olympic Stadium.

Yugoslavia 64 ... Russia 62

Continental Basketball Association
Final Standings

QW refers to quarters won. Teams get 3 points for a win, 1 point for each quarter won and ½ point for any quarters tied. Avg refers to average points per game played. (*) denotes playoff qualifiers.

American Conference

	W	L	QW	Pts	Home	Road
*Fort Wayne	31	25	116.0	209.0	17-11	14-14
*Rockford	29	27	114.0	201.0	17-11	12-16
*Connecticut	26	30	113.0	191.0	15-13	11-17
Grand Rapids	21	35	101.5	164.5	13-15	8-20

National Conference

	W	L	QW	Pts	Home	Road
*Quad City	38	18	129.5	243.5	22-6	16-12
*Sioux Falls	31	25	114.5	207.5	18-10	13-15
Yakima	26	30	110.0	188.0	17-11	9-19
Idaho	25	31	108.0	183.0	18-10	7-21
La Crosse	25	31	98.0	173.0	17-11	8-20

Playoffs

First two rounds are Best of 5

First Round

Fort Wayne def. Idaho, 3 games to 2
Rockford def. Connecticut, 3 games to 0
Quad City def. La Crosse, 3 games to 0
Sioux Falls def. Yakima, 3 games to 2

Second Round

Quad City def. Rockford, 3 games to 2
Sioux Falls def. Fort Wayne, 3 games to 0

Finals (Best of 7)

Quad City wins series, 4 games to 3

	W-L	Avg	Leading Scorer
Sioux Falls	3-4	81.6	Bob McCann (17.4)
Quad City	4-3	95.6	Jimmy King (21.2)

Date	Winner	Home Court
Apr. 11	Sioux Falls, 95-92	at Quad City
Apr. 13	Quad City, 82-81	at Quad City
Apr. 16	Sioux Falls, 94-93	at Sioux Falls
Apr. 18	Quad City, 108-106	at Sioux Falls
Apr. 19	Sioux Falls, 107-95	at Sioux Falls
Apr. 21	Quad City, 107-85	at Quad City
Apr. 22	Quad City, 92-88	at Quad City

CBA Annual Awards

Most Valuable Player: Jimmy King, Quad City
Newcomer of the Year: Jeff McInnis, Quad City
Rookie of the Year: Alvin Sims, Quad City
Def. Player of the Year: Michael McDonald, Grand Rapids
Coach of the Year: Dan Panaggio, Quad City
Executive of the Year: Tommy Smith, Sioux Falls

CBA Regular Season Individual Leaders

Scoring

	Gm	Pts	Avg
Jason Sasser, Sioux Falls	49	1110	22.7
David Booth, La Crosse	47	873	18.6
Melvin Newbern, Sioux Falls	44	789	17.9
Dan Cross, Connecticut	41	721	17.6
Joe Courtney, Idaho	48	838	17.5

Rebounding

	Gm	Reb	Avg
Devin Davis, Idaho	46	451	9.8
Troy Brown, Connecticut	46	442	9.6
Michael McDonald, Grand Rapids	46	434	9.4
Bob McCann, Sioux Falls	37	338	9.1
Kendrick Warren, Yakima	53	477	9.0

Field Goal Pct.

	FGM	FGA	Pct
Thomas Hamilton, Fort Wayne	206	339	.608
Mikki Moore, Fort Wayne	262	450	.582
Amal McCaskill, Fort Wayne	199	345	.577
Dennis Edwards, Idaho	262	459	.571
Alvin Sims, Quad City	294	517	.569

Assists

	Gm	Ast	Avg
Gerald Madkins, Rockford	31	275	8.9
Ernest Hall, Idaho	48	353	7.4
Damon Bailey, Fort Wayne	52	379	7.3
Randy Livingston, Sioux Falls	28	187	6.7
Keith Johnson, Yakima	56	346	6.2

Blocks

	Gm	Blk	Avg
Jimmy Carruth, Fort Wayne	24	82	3.4
Kendrick Warren, Yakima	53	134	2.5
Nate Huffman, Idaho	56	100	1.8
Michael McDonald, Grand Rapids	46	79	1.7
Mikki Moore, Fort Wayne	55	94	1.7

Steals

	Gm	Stl	Avg
Melvin Newbern, Sioux Falls	44	108	2.5
Adrian Griffin, Connecticut	56	132	2.4
Randy Livingston, Sioux Falls	28	60	2.1
Gerald Madkins, Rockford	31	56	1.8
Keith Johnson, Yakima	56	101	1.8

Women's Professional Basketball

American Basketball League

Final ABL Standings

Conference champions (*) and playoff qualifiers (†) are noted. GB refers to Games Behind leader.

Eastern Conference

	W	L	Pct	GB	Home	Road
*Columbus	36	8	.818	–	21-1	15-7
†New England	24	20	.545	12	17-5	7-15
Atlanta	15	29	.341	21	11-11	4-18
Philadelphia	13	31	.295	23	8-14	5-17

Western Conference

	W	L	Pct	GB	Home	Road
*Portland	27	17	.614	–	16-6	11-11
†Long Beach	26	18	.591	1	15-7	11-11
†Colorado	21	23	.477	6	14-8	7-15
†San Jose	21	23	.477	6	14-8	7-15
Seattle	15	29	.341	12	10-12	5-17

ABL Playoffs

Semifinals (Best of 3)

Date	Result
Feb. 27	Long Beach 72, at Portland 62
Mar. 1	at Long Beach 70, Portland 69
	Long Beach wins series, 2-0

Date	Result
Feb. 28	at Columbus 94, San Jose 88
Mar. 1	Columbus 74, at San Jose 62
	Columbus wins series, 2-0

Finals (Best of 5)

Columbus wins series, 3 games to 2

	W-L	Avg	Leading Scorer
Columbus	3-2	69.4	T. Edwards (16.4)
Long Beach	2-3	66.2	Y. Griffith (16.1)

Date	Winner	Home Court
Mar. 8	Long Beach, 65-62	at Long Beach
Mar. 9	Long Beach, 71-61	at Long Beach
Mar. 11	Columbus, 70-61	at Columbus
Mar. 13	Columbus, 68-53	at Columbus
Mar. 15	Columbus, 86-81	at Columbus

ABL Annual Awards

MVP: Natalie Williams, Portland
Rookie of the Year: Shalonda Enis, Seattle
Def. Player of the Year: Y. Griffith, L. Beach
Coach of the Year: Lin Dunn, Portland

ABL Regular Season Individual Leaders

Scoring

	Gm	Pts	Avg
Natalie Williams, Portland	42	913	21.7
Carolyn Jones, New England	43	934	21.7
Teresa Edwards, Atlanta	42	859	20.5
Yolanda Griffith, Long Beach	41	774	18.9
Shalonda Enis, Seattle	40	728	18.2

Rebounding

	Gm	Reb	Avg
Yolanda Griffith, Long Beach	41	474	11.6
Natalie Williams, Portland	42	477	11.4
Adrienne Goodson, Philadelphia	41	363	8.9
Tari Phillips, Colorado	42	348	8.3
Taj McWilliams, Philadelphia	42	343	8.2

Field Goal Pct.

	Gm	FGM	FGA	Pct
Natalie Williams, Portland	42	336	604	.556
Yolanda Griffith, Long Beach	41	290	540	.537
Tracy Henderson, Atlanta	35	154	288	.535
Crystal Robinson, Colorado	41	221	423	.522
Tari Phillips, Colorado	42	237	472	.502

Assists

	Gm	Ast	Avg
Teresa Edwards, Atlanta	42	283	6.7
Dawn Staley, Philadelphia	42	273	6.5
Andrea Nagy, Long Beach	41	262	6.4
Debbie Black, Colorado	42	253	6.0
Jennifer Azzi, San Jose	42	211	5.0

Blocks

	Gm	Blk	Avg
Kara Wolters, New England	43	63	1.5
Yolanda Griffith, Long Beach	41	57	1.4
Katrina McClain, Atlanta	31	37	1.2
Natalie Williams, Portland	42	47	1.1
Tracy Henderson, Atlanta	35	34	1.0

Steals

	Gm	Stl	Avg
Yolanda Griffith, Long Beach	41	133	3.2
Teresa Edwards, Atlanta	42	115	2.7
Debbie Black, Colorado	42	103	2.5
Dawn Staley, Philadelphia	42	96	2.3
Val Whiting, Seattle	40	91	2.3

Women's National Basketball Association

Final WNBA Standings

Conference champions (*) and playoff qualifiers (†) are noted. GB refers to Games Behind leader.

Eastern Conference

	W	L	Pct	GB	Home	Road
*Cleveland	20	10	.667	–	11-4	9-6
†Charlotte	18	12	.600	2	9-6	9-6
†New York	18	12	.600	2	12-3	6-9
Detroit	17	13	.567	3	11-4	6-9
Washington	3	27	.100	17	3-12	0-15

Western Conference

	W	L	Pct	GB	Home	Road
*Houston	27	3	.900	–	14-1	13-2
†Phoenix	19	11	.633	8	12-3	7-8
Los Angeles	12	18	.400	15	8-7	4-11
Sacramento	8	22	.267	19	5-10	3-12
Utah	8	22	.267	19	5-10	3-12

WNBA Playoffs

Semifinals (Best of 3)

Date	Result
Aug. 22	Houston 85, at Charlotte 71
Aug. 24	at Houston 77, Charlotte 61
	Houston wins series, 2-0

Date	Result
Aug. 22	at Phoenix 78, Cleveland 68
Aug. 24	at Cleveland 67, Phoenix 66
Aug. 25	Phoenix 71, at Cleveland 60
	Phoenix wins series, 2-1

Finals (Best of 3)

Houston wins series, 2 games to 1

	W-L	Avg	Leading Scorer
Houston	2-1	68.3	Cooper (26.3 ppg)
Phoenix	1-2	64.7	Gillom (14.3 pg)

Date	Winner	Home Court
Aug. 27	Phoenix, 54-51	at Phoenix
Aug. 29	Houston, 74-69 OT	at Houston
Sept. 1	Houston 80-71	at Houston

WNBA Regular Season Individual Leaders

Scoring

	Gm	Pts	Avg
Cynthia Cooper, Houston	30	680	22.7
Jennifer Gillom, Phoenix	30	624	20.8
Lisa Leslie, Los Angeles	28	549	19.6
Nikki McCray, Washington	29	512	17.7
Tamecka Dixon, Los Angeles	22	357	16.2

Assists

	Gm	Ast	Avg
Ticha Penicheiro, Sacramento	30	224	7.5
Suzie McConnell Serio, Cleveland	28	178	6.4
Teresa Weatherspoon, New York	30	191	6.4
Michele Timms, Phoenix	30	158	5.3
Penny Toler, Los Angeles	30	143	4.8

Rebounding

	Gm	Reb	Avg
Lisa Leslie, Los Angeles	28	285	10.2
Cindy Brown, Detroit	30	301	10.0
Malgorzata Dydek, Utah	30	227	7.6
Jennifer Gillom, Phoenix	30	219	7.3
Tina Thompson, Houston	27	192	7.1

Blocks

	Gm	Blk	Avg
Malgorzata Dydek, Utah	30	114	3.80
Lisa Leslie, Los Angeles	28	60	2.14
Tangela Smith, Sacramento	28	46	1.64
Vicky Bullett, Charlotte	30	46	1.53
Elena Baranova, Utah	20	30	1.10

Field Goal Pct.

	Gm	FGM	FGA	Pct
Isabelle Fijalkowski, Cleveland	28	146	267	.547
Razija Mujanovic, Detroit	30	106	204	.520
Michelle Griffiths, Phoenix	30	93	184	.505
Janice Braxton, Cleveland	30	108	218	.495
Tracy Reid, Charlotte	30	151	310	.487

Steals

	Gm	Stl	Avg
Teresa Weatherspoon, New York	30	100	3.33
Kim Perrot, Houston	30	84	2.80
Sheryl Swoopes, Houston	29	72	2.48
Ticha Penicheiro, Sacramento	30	67	2.23
Vickey Bullett, Charlotte	30	66	2.20

WNBA Annual Awards

Most Valuable Player: Cynthia Cooper, Houston
Rookie of the Year: Tracy Reid, Charlotte
Newcomer of the Year: Suzie McConnell Serio, Cle.
Def. Player of the Year: Teresa Weatherspoon, N.Y.
Coach of the Year: Van Chancellor, Houston

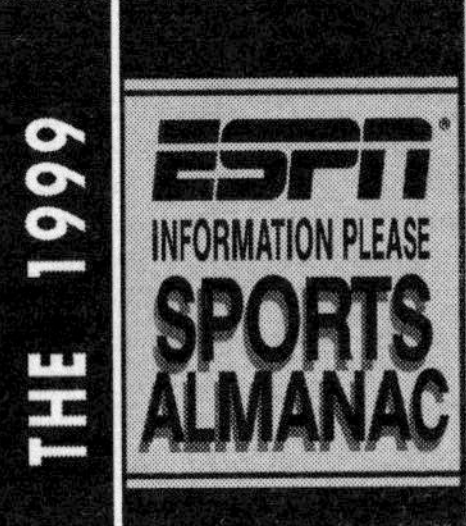

PRO BASKETBALL STATISTICS

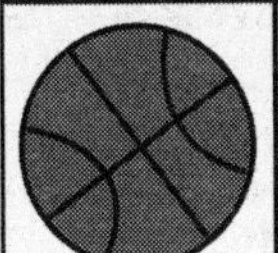

THROUGH THE YEARS

1947-1998

CHAMPIONS• NBA LEADERS

The NBA Finals

Although the National Basketball Association traces its first championship back to the 1946-47 season, the league was then called the Basketball Association of America (BAA). It did not become the NBA until after the 1948-49 season when the BAA and the National Basketball League (NBL) agreed to merge.

In the chart below, the Eastern finalists (representing the NBA Eastern Division from 1947-70, and the NBA Eastern Conference since 1971) are listed in CAPITAL letters. Also, each NBA champion's wins and losses are noted in parentheses after the series score.

Multiple winners: Boston (16); Minneapolis-LA Lakers (11); Chicago Bulls (6); Phi-SF-Golden St. Warriors and Syracuse Nationals-Phi. 76ers (3); Detroit, Houston and New York (2).

Year	Winner	Head Coach	Series	Loser	Head Coach
1947	PHILADELPHIA WARRIORS	Eddie Gottlieb	4-1 (WWWLW)	Chicago Stags	Harold Olsen
1948	Baltimore Bullets	Buddy Jeannette	4-2 (LWWWLW)	PHILA. WARRIORS	Eddie Gottlieb
1949	Minneapolis Lakers	John Kundla	4-2 (WWWLLW)	WASH. CAPITOLS	Red Auerbach
1950	Minneapolis Lakers	John Kundla	4-2 (WLWWLW)	SYRACUSE	Al Cervi
1951	Rochester	Les Harrison	4-3 (WWWLLLW)	NEW YORK	Joe Lapchick
1952	Minneapolis Lakers	John Kundla	4-3 (WLWLWLW)	NEW YORK	Joe Lapchick
1953	Minneapolis Lakers	John Kundla	4-1 (LWWWW)	NEW YORK	Joe Lapchick
1954	Minneapolis Lakers	John Kundla	4-3 (WLWLWLW)	SYRACUSE	Al Cervi
1955	SYRACUSE	Al Cervi	4-3 (WWLLLWW)	Ft. Wayne Pistons	Charley Eckman
1956	PHILADELPHIA WARRIORS	George Senesky	4-1 (WLWWW)	Ft. Wayne Pistons	Charley Eckman
1957	BOSTON	Red Auerbach	4-3 (LWLWWLW)	St. Louis Hawks	Alex Hannum
1958	St. Louis Hawks	Alex Hannum	4-2 (WLWLWW)	BOSTON	Red Auerbach
1959	BOSTON	Red Auerbach	4-0	Mpls. Lakers	John Kundla
1960	BOSTON	Red Auerbach	4-3 (WLWLWLW)	St. Louis Hawks	Ed Macauley
1961	BOSTON	Red Auerbach	4-1 (WWLWW)	St. Louis Hawks	Paul Seymour
1962	BOSTON	Red Auerbach	4-3 (WLLWLWW)	LA Lakers	Fred Schaus
1963	BOSTON	Red Auerbach	4-2 (WWLWLW)	LA Lakers	Fred Schaus
1964	BOSTON	Red Auerbach	4-1 (WWLWW)	SF Warriors	Alex Hannum
1965	BOSTON	Red Auerbach	4-1 (WWLWW)	LA Lakers	Fred Schaus
1966	BOSTON	Red Auerbach	4-3 (LWWWLLW)	LA Lakers	Fred Schaus
1967	PHILADELPHIA 76ERS	Alex Hannum	4-2 (WWLWLW)	SF Warriors	Bill Sharman
1968	BOSTON	Bill Russell	4-2 (WLWLWW)	LA Lakers	B.van Breda Kolff
1969	BOSTON	Bill Russell	4-3 (LLWWLWW)	LA Lakers	B.van Breda Kolff
1970	NEW YORK	Red Holzman	4-3 (WLWLWLW)	LA Lakers	Joe Mullaney
1971	Milwaukee	Larry Costello	4-0	BALT. BULLETS	Gene Shue
1972	LA Lakers	Bill Sharman	4-1 (LWWWW)	NEW YORK	Red Holzman
1973	NEW YORK	Red Holzman	4-1 (LWWWW)	LA Lakers	Bill Sharman
1974	BOSTON	Tommy Heinsohn	4-3 (WLWLWLW)	Milwaukee	Larry Costello
1975	Golden St. Warriors	Al Attles	4-0	WASH. BULLETS	K.C. Jones
1976	BOSTON	Tommy Heinsohn	4-2 (WWLLWW)	Phoenix	John MacLeod
1977	Portland	Jack Ramsay	4-2 (LLWWWW)	PHILA. 76ERS	Gene Shue
1978	WASHINGTON BULLETS	Dick Motta	4-3 (LWLWLWW)	Seattle	Lenny Wilkens
1979	Seattle	Lenny Wilkens	4-1 (LWWWW)	WASH. BULLETS	Dick Motta
1980	LA Lakers	Paul Westhead	4-2 (WLWLWW)	PHILA. 76ERS	Billy Cunningham
1981	BOSTON	Bill Fitch	4-2 (WLWLWW)	Houston	Del Harris
1982	LA Lakers	Pat Riley	4-2 (WLWWLW)	PHILA. 76ERS	Billy Cunningham
1983	PHILADELPHIA 76ERS	Billy Cunningham	4-0	LA Lakers	Pat Riley
1984	BOSTON	K.C. Jones	4-3 (LWLWWLW)	LA Lakers	Pat Riley
1985	LA Lakers	Pat Riley	4-2 (LWWLWW)	BOSTON	K.C. Jones
1986	BOSTON	K.C. Jones	4-2 (WWLWLW)	Houston	Bill Fitch
1987	LA Lakers	Pat Riley	4-2 (WWLWLW)	BOSTON	K.C. Jones
1988	LA Lakers	Pat Riley	4-3 (LWWLLWW)	DETROIT PISTONS	Chuck Daly
1989	DETROIT PISTONS	Chuck Daly	4-0	LA Lakers	Pat Riley
1990	DETROIT	Chuck Daly	4-1 (WLWWW)	Portland	Rick Adelman
1991	CHICAGO	Phil Jackson	4-1 (LWWWW)	LA Lakers	Mike Dunleavy
1992	CHICAGO	Phil Jackson	4-2 (WLWLWW)	Portland	Rick Adelman
1993	CHICAGO	Phil Jackson	4-2 (WWLWLW)	Phoenix	Paul Westphal

Year	Winner	Head Coach	Series	Loser	Head Coach
1994	Houston	Rudy Tomjanovich	4-3 (WLWLLWW)	NEW YORK	Pat Riley
1995	Houston	Rudy Tomjanovich	4-0	ORLANDO	Brian Hill
1996	CHICAGO	Phil Jackson	4-2 (WWWLLW)	Seattle	George Karl
1997	CHICAGO	Phil Jackson	4-2 (WWLLWW)	Utah	Jerry Sloan
1998	CHICAGO	Phil Jackson	4-2 (LWWWLW)	Utah	Jerry Sloan

Note: Four finalists were led by player-coaches: **1948**—Buddy Jeannette (guard) of Baltimore; **1950**—Al Cervi (guard) of Syracuse; **1968**—Bill Russell (center) of Boston; **1969**—Bill Russell (center) of Boston.

Most Valuable Player

Selected by an 11-member media panel. Winner who did not play for the NBA champion is in **bold** type.

Multiple winners: Michael Jordan (6); Magic Johnson (3); Kareem Abdul-Jabbar, Larry Bird, Hakeem Olajuwon and Willis Reed (2).

Year	Year	Year
1969 **Jerry West**, LA Lakers, G	1979 Dennis Johnson, Seattle, G	1989 Joe Dumars, Detroit, G
1970 Willis Reed, New York, C	1980 Magic Johnson, LA Lakers, G/C	1990 Isiah Thomas, Detroit, G
1971 Lew Alcindor, Milwaukee, C	1981 Cedric Maxwell, Boston, F	1991 Michael Jordan, Chicago, G
1972 Wilt Chamberlain, LA Lakers, C	1982 Magic Johnson, LA Lakers, G	1992 Michael Jordan, Chicago, G
1973 Willis Reed, New York, C	1983 Moses Malone, Philadelphia, C	1993 Michael Jordan, Chicago, G
1974 John Havlicek, Boston, F	1984 Larry Bird, Boston, F	1994 Hakeem Olajuwon, Houston, C
1975 Rick Barry, Golden State, F	1985 K. Abdul-Jabbar, LA Lakers, C	1995 Hakeem Olajuwon, Houston, C
1976 Jo Jo White, Boston, G	1986 Larry Bird, Boston, F	1996 Michael Jordan, Chicago, G
1977 Bill Walton, Portland, C	1987 Magic Johnson, LA Lakers, G	1997 Michael Jordan, Chicago, G
1978 Wes Unseld, Washington, C	1988 James Worthy, LA Lakers, F	1998 Michael Jordan, Chicago, G

Note: Lew Alcindor changed his name to Kareem Abdul-Jabbar after the 1970-71 season.

All-Time NBA Playoff Leaders

Through the 1998 playoffs.

CAREER

Years listed indicate number of playoff appearances. Players active in 1998 playoffs in **bold** type.

Points

		Yrs	Gm	Pts	Avg
1	**Michael Jordan**	13	179	5987	33.4
2	Kareem Abdul-Jabbar	18	237	5762	24.3
3	Jerry West	13	153	4457	29.1
4	Larry Bird	12	164	3897	23.8
5	John Havlicek	13	172	3776	22.0
6	Magic Johnson	13	190	3701	19.5
7	**Karl Malone**	13	137	3691	26.9
8	**Hakeem Olajuwon**	13	136	3674	27.0
9	Elgin Baylor	12	134	3623	27.0
10	Wilt Chamberlain	13	160	3607	22.5
11	**Scottie Pippen**	11	178	3217	18.1
12	Kevin McHale	13	169	3182	18.8
13	Dennis Johnson	13	180	3116	17.3
14	Julius Erving	11	141	3088	21.9
15	James Worthy	9	143	3022	21.1
16	**Clyde Drexler**	15	145	2963	20.4
17	Sam Jones	12	154	2909	18.9
18	Robert Parish	16	184	2820	15.3
19	**Charles Barkley**	12	119	2739	23.0
20	Bill Russell	13	165	2673	16.2

Scoring Average

Minimum of 25 games or 700 points.

		Yrs	Gm	Pts	Avg
1	**Michael Jordan**	13	179	5987	33.4
2	Jerry West	13	153	4457	29.1
3	**Hakeem Olajuwon**	13	136	3677	27.0
4	Elgin Baylor	12	134	3623	27.0
5	George Gervin	9	59	1592	27.0
6	**Karl Malone**	13	137	3691	26.9
7	**Shaquille O'Neal**	5	58	1549	26.7
8	Dominique Wilkins	9	55	1421	25.8
9	Bob Pettit	9	88	2240	25.5
10	Rick Barry	7	74	1833	24.8
11	Bernard King	5	28	687	24.5
12	Alex English	10	68	1661	24.4
13	Kareem Abdul-Jabbar	18	237	5762	24.3
14	Paul Arizin	8	49	1186	24.2
15	Larry Bird	12	164	3897	23.8
16	George Mikan	9	91	2141	23.5
17	**Reggie Miller**	8	65	1530	23.5
18	**David Robinson**	7	62	1448	23.4
19	**Charles Barkley**	12	119	2739	23.0
20	Bob Love	6	47	1076	22.9

Field Goals

		Yrs	FG	Att	Pct
1	Kareem Abdul-Jabbar	18	2356	4422	.533
2	**Michael Jordan**	13	2188	4497	.487
3	Jerry West	13	1622	3460	.469
4	Larry Bird	12	1458	3090	.472
5	John Havlicek	13	1451	3329	.436
6	**Hakeem Olajuwon**	12	1469	2771	.530
7	Wilt Chamberlain	13	1425	2728	.522
8	Elgin Baylor	12	1388	3161	.439
9	**Karl Malone**	13	1343	2868	.468
10	Magic Johnson	13	1291	2552	.506

Free Throws

		Yrs	FT	Att	Pct
1	**Michael Jordan**	13	1463	1766	.828
2	Jerry West	13	1213	1507	.805
3	Kareem Abdul-Jabbar	18	1050	1419	.740
4	Magic Johnson	12	1040	1241	.838
5	**Karl Malone**	13	1002	1369	.732
6	Larry Bird	12	901	1012	.891
7	John Havlicek	13	874	1046	.836
8	Elgin Baylor	12	847	1101	.769
9	Kevin McHale	13	766	972	.788
10	Wilt Chamberlain	13	757	1627	.465

Assists

		Yrs	Gm	No	Avg
1	Magic Johnson	13	190	2346	12.3
2	**John Stockton**	14	147	1521	10.3
3	Larry Bird	12	164	1062	6.5
4	**Michael Jordan**	13	179	1022	5.7
5	Dennis Johnson	13	180	1006	5.6

Rebounds

		Yrs	Gm	No	Avg
1	Bill Russell	13	165	4104	24.9
2	Wilt Chamberlain	13	160	3913	24.5
3	Kareem Abdul-Jabbar	18	237	2481	10.5
4	Wes Unseld	12	119	1777	14.9
5	Robert Parish	16	184	1765	9.6

Appearances

	No		No
Kareem Abdul-Jabbar	18	Kevin McHale	13
Robert Parish	16	Dennis Johnson	13
Dolph Schayes	15	Magic Johnson	13
Paul Silas	14	**Michael Jordan**	13
John Stockton	14	**Karl Malone**	13
Wilt Chamberlain	13	**Hakeem Olajuwon**	13
Maurice Cheeks	13	Bill Russell	13
Bob Cousy	13	Chet Walker	13
Hal Greer	13	Jerry West	13
John Havlicek	13		

Games Played

	No		No
K. Abdul-Jabbar	237	John Havlicek	170
Danny Ainge	193	Kevin McHale	169
Magic Johnson	190	Michael Cooper	168
Robert Parish	184	Bill Russell	165
Byron Scott	183	Larry Bird	164
Dennis Johnson	180	Paul Silas	163
Michael Jordan	179	Wilt Chamberlain	160
Scottie Pippen	178		

SINGLE GAME

Points

	Date	FG-FT–Pts
Michael Jordan, Chi at Bos*	4/20/86	22-19–63
Elgin Baylor, LA at Bos	4/14/62	22-17–61
Wilt Chamberlain, Phi vs Syr	3/22/62	22-12–56
Michael Jordan, Chi at Mia	4/29/92	20-16–56
Charles Barkley, Pho vs G.St.	5/4/94	23- 7–56
Rick Barry, SF vs Phi	4/18/67	22-11–55
Michael Jordan, Chi vs Cle	5/1/88	24- 7–55
Michael Jordan, Chi vs Pho	4/16/93	21-13–55
Michael Jordan, Chi vs. Wash	4/27/97	22-10–55

*Double overtime.

Field Goals

	Date	FG	Att
Wilt Chamberlain, Phi vs Syr	3/14/60	24	42
John Havlicek, Bos vs Atl	4/1/73	24	36
Michael Jordan, Chi vs Cle	5/1/88	24	45

Eight tied with 22 each.

Appearances in NBA Finals

Standings of all NBA teams that have reached the NBA Finals since 1947.

App		Titles	Last Won
24	Minneapolis-LA Lakers	11	1988
19	Boston Celtics	16	1986
8	Syracuse Nats-Phila. 76ers	3	1983
7	New York Knicks	2	1973
6	Chicago Bulls	6	1998
6	Phila-SF-Golden St. Warriors	3	1975
5	Ft. Wayne-Detroit Pistons	2	1990
4	Houston Rockets	2	1995
4	St. Louis Hawks	1	1958
4	Baltimore-Washington Bullets	1	1978
3	Portland Trail Blazers	1	1977
3	Seattle SuperSonics	1	1979
2	Milwaukee Bucks	1	1971
2	Phoenix Suns	0	—
2	Utah Jazz	0	—
1	Baltimore Bullets	1	1948
1	Chicago Stags	0	—
1	Orlando Magic	0	—
1	Rochester Royals	0	—
1	Washington Capitols	0	—

Change of address: The St. Louis Hawks now play in Atlanta and the Rochester Royals are now the Sacramento Kings.
Teams now defunct: Baltimore Bullets (1947-55), Chicago Stags (1946-50) and Washington Capitols (1946-51).

Miscellaneous

3-Pt Field Goals	Date	No
Rex Chapman, Pho at Sea	4/25/97	9
Dan Majerle, Pho vs Sea	6/1/93	8

Eight tied with 7 each.

Assists	Date	No
Magic Johnson, LA vs Pho	5/15/84	24
John Stockton, Utah at LA Lakers	5/17/88	24
Magic Johnson, LA Lakers at Port	5/3/85	23
John Stockton, Utah vs Port	4/25/96	23
Doc Rivers, Atl vs Bos	5/16/88	22

Four tied with 21 each.

Rebounds	Date	No
Wilt Chamberlain, Phi vs Bos	4/5/67	41
Bill Russell, Bos vs Phi	3/23/58	40
Bill Russell, Bos vs St.L	3/29/60	40
Bill Russell, Bos vs LA*	4/18/62	40

Three tied with 39 each.
*Overtime.

NBA FINALS

Points

Series		Year	Pts
4-Gm	Hakeem Olajuwon, Hou vs Orl	1995	131
5-Gm	Jerry West, LA vs Bos	1965	169
6-Gm	Michael Jordan, Chi vs Pho	1993	246
7-Gm	Elgin Baylor, LA vs Bos	1962	284

Field Goals

Series		Year	No
4-Gm	Hakeem Olajuwon, Hou vs Orl	1995	56
5-Gm	Michael Jordan, Chi vs LAL	1991	63
6-Gm	Michael Jordan, Chi vs Pho	1993	101
7-Gm	Elgin Baylor, LA vs Bos	1962	101

Assists

Series		Year	No
4-Gm	Bob Cousy, Bos vs Mpls	1959	51
5-Gm	Magic Johnson, LAL vs Chi	1991	62
6-Gm	Magic Johnson, LAL vs Bos	1985	84
7-Gm	Magic Johnson, LA vs Bos	1984	95

Rebounds

Series		Year	No
4-Gm	Bill Russell, Bos vs Mpls	1959	118
5-Gm	Bill Russell, Bos vs St.L	1961	144
6-Gm	Wilt Chamberlain, Phi vs SF	1967	171
7-Gm	Bill Russell, Bos vs LA	1962	189

The National Basketball League

Formed in 1937 by three corporations– General Electric and the Firestone and Goodyear rubber companies of Akron, Ohio– which were interested in moving up from their midwestern industrial league origins and backing a fully professional league. The NBL started with 13 previously independent teams in 1937-38 and although GE, Firestone and Goodyear were gone by late 1942, ran 12 years before merging with the three-year-old Basketball Association of America in 1949 to form the NBA.

Multiple champions: Akron Firestone Non-Skids, Fort Wayne Zollner Pistons, Oshkosh All-Stars (2).

Year	Winner	Series	Loser
1938	Goodyear Wingfoots	2-1	Oshkosh All-Stars
1939	Firestone Non-Skids	3-2	Oshkosh All-Stars
1940	Firestone Non-Skids	3-2	Oshkosh All-Stars
1941	Oshkosh All-Stars	3-0	Sheboygan Redskins
1942	Oshkosh All-Stars	2-1	Ft. Wayne Pistons
1943	Sheboygan Redskins	2-1	Ft. Wayne Pistons
1944	Ft. Wayne Pistons	3-0	Sheboygan Redskins
1945	Ft. Wayne Pistons	3-2	Sheboygan Redskins
1946	Rochester Royals	3-0	Sheboygan Redskins
1947	Chicago Gears	3-2	Rochester Royals
1948	Minneapolis Lakers	3-1	Rochester Royals
1949	Anderson Packers	3-0	Oshkosh All-Stars

NBA All-Star Game

The NBA staged its first All-Star Game before 10,094 at Boston Garden on March 2, 1951. From that year on, the game has matched the best players in the East against the best in the West. Winning coaches are listed first. East leads series, 31-17.

Multiple MVP winners: Bob Pettit (4); Michael Jordan and Oscar Robertson (3); Bob Cousy, Julius Erving, Magic Johnson, Karl Malone and Isiah Thomas (2).

Year		Host	Coaches	Most Valuable Player
1951	East 111, West 94	Boston	Joe Lapchick, John Kundla	Ed Macauley, Boston
1952	East 108, West 91	Boston	Al Cervi, John Kundla	Paul Arizin, Philadelphia
1953	West 79, East 75	Ft. Wayne	John Kundla, Joe Lapchick	George Mikan, Minneapolis
1954	East 98, West 93 (OT)	New York	Joe Lapchick, John Kundla	Bob Cousy, Boston
1955	East 100, West 91	New York	Al Cervi, Charley Eckman	Bill Sharman, Boston
1956	West 108, East 94	Rochester	Charley Eckman, George Senesky	Bob Pettit, St. Louis
1957	East 109, West 97	Boston	Red Auerbach, Bobby Wanzer	Bob Cousy, Boston
1958	East 130, West 118	St. Louis	Red Auerbach, Alex Hannum	Bob Pettit, St. Louis
1959	West 124, East 108	Detroit	Ed Macauley, Red Auerbach	Bob Pettit, St. Louis & Elgin Baylor, Minneapolis
1960	East 125, West 115	Philadelphia	Red Auerbach, Ed Macauley	Wilt Chamberlain, Philadelphia
1961	West 153, East 131	Syracuse	Paul Seymour, Red Auerbach	Oscar Robertson, Cincinnati
1962	West 150, East 130	St. Louis	Fred Schaus, Red Auerbach	Bob Pettit, St. Louis
1963	East 115, West 108	Los Angeles	Red Auerbach, Fred Schaus	Bill Russell, Boston
1964	East 111, West 107	Boston	Red Auerbach, Fred Schaus	Oscar Robertson, Cincinnati
1965	East 124, West 123	St. Louis	Red Auerbach, Alex Hannum	Jerry Lucas, Cincinnati
1966	East 137, West 94	Cincinnati	Red Auerbach, Fred Schaus	Adrian Smith, Cincinnati
1967	West 135, East 120	San Francisco	Fred Schaus, Red Auerbach	Rick Barry, San Francisco
1968	East 144, West 124	New York	Alex Hannum, Bill Sharman	Hal Greer, Philadelphia
1969	East 123, West 112	Baltimore	Gene Shue, Richie Guerin	Oscar Robertson, Cincinnati
1970	East 142, West 135	Philadelphia	Red Holzman, Richie Guerin	Willis Reed, New York
1971	West 108, East 107	San Diego	Larry Costello, Red Holzman	Lenny Wilkens, Seattle
1972	West 112, East 110	Los Angeles	Bill Sharman, Tom Heinsohn	Jerry West, Los Angeles
1973	East 104, West 84	Chicago	Tom Heinsohn, Bill Sharman	Dave Cowens, Boston
1974	West 134, East 123	Seattle	Larry Costello, Tom Heinsohn	Bob Lanier, Detroit
1975	East 108, West 102	Phoenix	K.C. Jones, Al Attles	Walt Frazier, New York
1976	East 123, West 109	Philadelphia	Tom Heinsohn, Al Attles	Dave Bing, Washington
1977	West 125, East 124	Milwaukee	Larry Brown, Gene Shue	Julius Erving, Philadelphia
1978	East 133, West 125	Atlanta	Billy Cunningham, Jack Ramsay	Randy Smith, Buffalo
1979	West 134, East 129	Detroit	Lenny Wilkens, Dick Motta	David Thompson, Denver
1980	East 144, West 136 (OT)	Washington	Billy Cunningham, Lenny Wilkens	George Gervin, San Antonio
1981	East 123, West 120	Cleveland	Billy Cunningham, John MacLeod	Nate Archibald, Boston
1982	East 120, West 118	New Jersey	Bill Fitch, Pat Riley	Larry Bird, Boston
1983	East 132, West 123	Los Angeles	Billy Cunningham, Pat Riley	Julius Erving, Philadelphia
1984	East 154, West 145 (OT)	Denver	K.C. Jones, Frank Layden	Isiah Thomas, Detroit
1985	West 140, East 129	Indiana	Pat Riley, K.C. Jones	Ralph Sampson, Houston
1986	East 139, West 132	Dallas	K.C. Jones, Pat Riley	Isiah Thomas, Detroit
1987	West 154, East 149 (OT)	Seattle	Pat Riley, K.C. Jones	Tom Chambers, Seattle
1988	East 138, West 133	Chicago	Mike Fratello, Pat Riley	Michael Jordan, Chicago
1989	West 143, East 134	Houston	Pat Riley, Lenny Wilkens	Karl Malone, Utah
1990	East 130, West 113	Miami	Chuck Daly, Pat Riley	Magic Johnson, LA Lakers
1991	East 116, West 114	Charlotte	Chris Ford, Rick Adelman	Charles Barkley, Philadelphia
1992	West 153, East 113	Orlando	Don Nelson, Phil Jackson	Magic Johnson, LA Lakers
1993	West 135, East 132 (OT)	Salt Lake City	Paul Westphal, Pat Riley	Karl Malone, Utah & John Stockton, Utah
1994	East 127, West 118	Minneapolis	Lenny Wilkens, George Karl	Scottie Pippen, Chicago
1995	West 139, East 112	Phoenix	Paul Westphal, Brian Hill	Mitch Richmond, Sacramento
1996	East 129, West 118	San Antonio	Phil Jackson, George Karl	Michael Jordan, Chicago
1997	East 132, West 120	Cleveland	Doug Collins, Rudy Tomjanovich	Glen Rice, Charlotte
1998	East 135, West 114	New York	Larry Bird, George Karl	Michael Jordan, Chicago

NBA Franchise Origins

Here is what the current 29 teams in the National Basketball Association have to show for the years they have put in as members of the National Basketball League (NBL), Basketball Association of America (BAA), the NBA, and the American Basketball Association (ABA). League titles are noted by year won.

Western Conference

	First Season		League Titles	Franchise Stops
Dallas Mavericks	1980-81	(NBA)	None	•Dallas (1980–)
Denver Nuggets	1967-68	(ABA)	None	•Denver (1967–)
Golden St. Warriors	1946-47	(BAA)	1 BAA (1947) 2 NBA (1956,75)	•Philadelphia (1946-62) San Francisco (1962-71) Oakland (1971–)
Houston Rockets	1967-68	(NBA)	2 NBA (1994-95)	•San Diego (1967-71) Houston (1971–)
Los Angeles Clippers	1970-71	(NBA)	None	•Buffalo (1970-78) San Diego (1978-84) Los Angeles (1984–)
Los Angeles Lakers	1947-48	(NBL)	1 NBL (1947) 1 BAA (1949) 10 NBA (1950,52-54,72, 80,82,85,87-88)	•Minneapolis (1947-60) Los Angeles (1960-67) Inglewood, CA (1967–)
Minnesota Timberwolves	1989-90	(NBA)	None	•Minneapolis (1989–)
Phoenix Suns	1968-69	(NBA)	None	•Phoenix (1968–)
Portland Trail Blazers	1970-71	(NBA)	1 NBA (1977)	•Portland (1970–)
Sacramento Kings	1945-46	(NBL)	1 NBL (1946) 1 NBA (1951)	•Rochester, NY (1945-58) Cincinnati (1958-72) KC-Omaha (1972-75) Kansas City (1975-85) Sacramento (1985–)
San Antonio Spurs	1967-68	(ABA)	None	•Dallas (1967-73) San Antonio (1973–)
Seattle SuperSonics	1967-68	(NBA)	1 NBA (1979)	•Seattle (1967–)
Utah Jazz	1974-75	(NBA)	None	•New Orleans (1974-79) Salt Lake City (1979–)
Vancouver Grizzlies	1995-96	(NBA)	None	•Vancouver (1995–)

Eastern Conference

	First Season		League Titles	Franchise Stops
Atlanta Hawks	1946-47	(NBL)	1 NBA (1958)	•Tri-Cities (1946-51) Milwaukee (1951-55) St. Louis (1955-68) Atlanta (1968–)
Boston Celtics	1946-47	(BAA)	16 NBA (1957,59-66,68-69 74,76,81,84,86)	•Boston (1946–)
Charlotte Hornets	1988-89	(NBA)	None	•Charlotte (1988–)
Chicago Bulls	1966-67	(NBA)	6 NBA (1991-93,96-98)	•Chicago (1966–)
Cleveland Cavaliers	1970-71	(NBA)	None	•Cleveland (1970-74) Richfield, OH (1974-94) Cleveland (1994–)
Detroit Pistons	1941-42	(NBL)	2 NBL (1944-45) 2 NBA (1989-90)	•Ft. Wayne, IN (1941-57) Detroit (1957-78) Pontiac, MI (1978-88) Auburn Hills, MI (1988–)
Indiana Pacers	1967-68	(ABA)	3 ABA (1970,72-73)	•Indianapolis (1967–)
Miami Heat	1988-89	(NBA)	None	•Miami (1988–)
Milwaukee Bucks	1968-69	(NBA)	1 NBA (1971)	•Milwaukee (1968–)
New Jersey Nets	1967-68	(ABA)	2 ABA (1974,76)	•Teaneck, NJ (1967-68) Commack, NY (1968-69) W. Hempstead, NY (1969-71) Uniondale, NY (1971-77) Piscataway, NJ (1977-81) E. Rutherford, NJ (1981–)
New York Knicks	1946-47	(BAA)	2 NBA (1970,73)	•New York (1946–)
Orlando Magic	1989-90	(NBA)	None	•Orlando, FL (1989–)
Philadelphia 76ers	1949-50	(NBA)	3 NBA (1955,67,83)	•Syracuse, NY (1949-63) Philadelphia (1963–)
Toronto Raptors	1995-96	(NBA)	None	•Toronto (1995–)
Washington Wizards	1961-62	(NBA)	1 NBA (1978)	•Chicago (1961-63) Baltimore (1963-73) Landover, MD (1973–)

Note: The Tri-Cities Blackhawks represented Moline and Rock Island, Ill., and Davenport, Iowa.

The Growth of the NBA

Of the 11 franchises that comprised the Basketball Association of America (BAA) at the start of the 1946-47 season, only three remain—the Boston Celtics, New York Knickerbockers and Golden State Warriors (originally Philadelphia Warriors).

Just before the start of the 1948-49 season, four teams from the more established **National Basketball League** (NBL)—the Ft. Wayne Pistons (now Detroit), Indianapolis Jets, Minneapolis Lakers (now Los Angeles) and Rochester Royals (now Sacramento Kings)—joined the BAA.

A year later, the six remaining NBL franchises—Anderson (Ind.), Denver, Sheboygan (Wisc.), the Syracuse Nationals (now Philadelphia 76ers), Tri-Cities Blackhawks (now Atlanta Hawks) and Waterloo (Iowa)—joined along with the new Indianapolis Olympians and the BAA became the 17-team **National Basketball Association**.

The NBA was down to 10 teams by the 1950-51 season and slipped to eight by 1954-55 with Boston, New York, Philadelphia and Syracuse in the Eastern Division, and Ft. Wayne, Milwaukee (formerly Tri-Cities), Minneapolis and Rochester in the West.

By 1960, five of those surviving eight teams had moved to other cities but by the end of the decade the NBA was a 14-team league. It also had a rival, the **American Basketball Association**, which began play in 1967 with a red, white and blue ball, a three-point line and 11 teams. After a nine-year run, the ABA merged four clubs—the Denver Nuggets, Indiana Pacers, New York Nets and San Antonio Spurs—with the NBA following the 1975-76 season. The NBA adopted the three-point play in 1979-80.

Expansion/Merger Timetable

For teams currently in NBA.

1948—Added NBL's Ft. Wayne Pistons (now Detroit), Minneapolis Lakers (now Los Angeles) and Rochester Royals (now Sacramento Kings); **1949**—Syracuse Nationals (now Philadelphia 76ers) and Tri-Cities Blackhawks (now Atlanta Hawks).

1961—Chicago Packers (now Washington Bullets); **1966**—Chicago Bulls; **1967**—San Diego Rockets (now Houston) and Seattle SuperSonics; **1968**—Milwaukee Bucks and Phoenix Suns.

1970—Buffalo Braves (now Los Angeles Clippers), Cleveland Cavaliers and Portland Trail Blazers; **1974**—New Orleans Jazz (now Utah); **1976**—added ABA's Denver Nuggets, Indiana Pacers, New York Nets (now New Jersey) and San Antonio Spurs.

1980—Dallas Mavericks; **1988**—Charlotte Hornets and Miami Heat; **1989**—Minnesota Timberwolves and Orlando Magic.

1995—Toronto Raptors and Vancouver Grizzlies.

City and Nickname Changes

1951—Tri-Cities Blackhawks, who divided home games between Moline and Rock Island, Ill., and Davenport, Iowa, move to Milwaukee and become the Hawks; **1955**—Milwaukee Hawks move to St. Louis; **1957**—Ft. Wayne Pistons move to Detroit, while Rochester Royals move to Cincinnati.

1960—Minneapolis Lakers move to Los Angeles; **1962**—Chicago Packers renamed Zephyrs, while Philadelphia Warriors move to San Francisco; **1963**—Chicago Zephyrs move to Baltimore and become Bullets, while Syracuse Nationals move to Philadelphia and become 76ers; **1968**—St. Louis Hawks move to Atlanta.

1971—San Diego Rockets move to Houston, while San Francisco Warriors move to Oakland and become Golden State Warriors; **1972**—Cincinnati Royals move to Midwest, divide home games between Kansas City, Mo., and Omaha, Neb., and become Kings; **1973**—Baltimore Bullets move to Landover, Md., outside Washington and become Capital Bullets; **1974**—Capital Bullets renamed Washington Bullets; **1975**—KC-Omaha Kings settle in Kansas City; **1977**—New York Nets move from Uniondale, N.Y., to Piscataway, N.J. (later East Rutherford) and become New Jersey Nets; **1978**—Buffalo Braves move to San Diego and become Clippers; **1979**—New Orleans Jazz move to Salt Lake City and become Utah Jazz.

1984—San Diego Clippers move to Los Angeles; **1985**—Kansas City Kings move to Sacramento; **1997**—Washington Bullets become Washington Wizards.

Defunct NBA Teams

Teams that once played in the BAA and NBA, but no longer exist.

Anderson (Ind.)—Packers (1949-50); **Baltimore**—Bullets (1947-55); **Chicago**—Stags (1946-50); **Cleveland**—Rebels (1946-47); **Denver**—Nuggets (1949-50); **Detroit**—Falcons (1946-47); **Indianapolis**—Jets (1948-49) and Olympians (1949-53). **Pittsburgh**—Ironmen (1946-47); **Providence**—Steamrollers (1946-49); **St. Louis**—Bombers (1946-50); **Sheboygan (Wisc.)**—Redskins (1949-50); **Toronto**—Huskies (1946-47); **Washington**—Capitols (1946-51); **Waterloo (Iowa)**—Hawks (1949-50).

ABA Teams (1967-76)

Anaheim—Amigos (1967-68, moved to LA); **Baltimore**—Claws (1975, never played); **Carolina**—Cougars (1969-74, moved to St. Louis); **Dallas**—Chaparrals (1967-73, called Texas Chaparrals in 1970-71, moved to San Antonio); **Denver**—Rockets (1967-76, renamed Nuggets in 1974-76); **Miami**—Floridians (1968-72, called simply Floridians from 1970-72).

Houston—Mavericks (1967-69, moved to North Carolina); **Indiana**—Pacers (1967-76); **Kentucky**—Colonels (1967-76); **Los Angeles**—Stars (1968-70, moved to Utah); **Memphis**—Pros (1970-75, renamed Tams in 1972 and Sounds in 1974, moved to Baltimore); **Minnesota**—Muskies (1967-68, moved to Miami) and Pipers (1968-69, moved back to Pittsburgh); **New Jersey**—Americans (1967-68, moved to New York).

New Orleans—Buccaneers (1967-70, moved to Memphis); **New York**—Nets (1968-76); **Oakland**—Oaks (1967-69, moved to Washington); **Pittsburgh**—Pipers (1967-68, moved to Minnesota), Pipers (1969-72, renamed Condors in 1970); **St. Louis**—Spirits of St. Louis (1974-76); **San Antonio**—Spurs (1973-76); **San Diego**—Conquistadors (1972-75, renamed Sails in 1975); **Utah**—Stars (1970-75); **Virginia**—Squires (1970-76); **Washington**—Caps (1969-70, moved to Virginia).

Annual NBA Leaders

Scoring

Decided by total points from 1947-69, and per game average since 1970.

Multiple winners: Michael Jordan (10); Wilt Chamberlain (7); George Gervin (4); Neil Johnston, Bob McAdoo and George Mikan (3); Kareem Abdul-Jabbar, Paul Arizin, Adrian Dantley and Bob Pettit (2).

Year		Gm	Pts	Avg
1947	Joe Fulks, Phi	60	1389	23.2
1948	Max Zaslofsky, Chi	48	1007	21.0
1949	George Mikan, Mpls	60	1698	28.3
1950	George Mikan, Mpls	68	1865	27.4
1951	George Mikan, Mpls	68	1932	28.4
1952	Paul Arizin, Phi	66	1674	25.4
1953	Neil Johnston, Phi	70	1564	22.3
1954	Neil Johnston, Phi	72	1759	24.4
1955	Neil Johnston, Phi	72	1631	22.7
1956	Bob Pettit, St.L	72	1849	25.7
1957	Paul Arizin, Phi	71	1817	25.6
1958	George Yardley, Det	72	2001	27.8
1959	Bob Pettit, St.L	72	2105	29.2
1960	Wilt Chamberlain, Phi	72	2707	37.6
1961	Wilt Chamberlain, Phi	79	3033	38.4
1962	Wilt Chamberlain, Phi	80	4029	50.4
1963	Wilt Chamberlain, SF	80	3586	44.8
1964	Wilt Chamberlain, SF	80	2948	36.9
1965	Wilt Chamberlain, SF-Phi	73	2534	34.7
1966	Wilt Chamberlain, Phi	79	2649	33.5
1967	Rick Barry, SF	78	2775	35.6
1968	Dave Bing, Det	79	2142	27.1
1969	Elvin Hayes, SD	82	2327	28.4
1970	Jerry West, LA	74	2309	31.2
1971	Lew Alcindor, Mil	82	2596	31.7
1972	Kareem Abdul-Jabbar, Mil	81	2822	34.8
1973	Nate Archibald, KC-Omaha	80	2719	34.0
1974	Bob McAdoo, Buf	74	2261	30.6
1975	Bob McAdoo, Buf	82	2831	34.5
1976	Bob McAdoo, Buf	78	2427	31.1
1977	Pete Maravich, NO	73	2273	31.1
1978	George Gervin, SA	82	2232	27.2
1979	George Gervin, SA	80	2365	29.6
1980	George Gervin, SA	78	2585	33.1
1981	Adrian Dantley, Utah	80	2452	30.7
1982	George Gervin, SA	79	2551	32.3
1983	Alex English, Den	82	2326	28.4
1984	Adrian Dantley, Utah	79	2418	30.6
1985	Bernard King, NY	55	1809	32.9
1986	Dominique Wilkins, Atl	78	2366	30.3
1987	Michael Jordan, Chi	82	3041	37.1
1988	Michael Jordan, Chi	82	2868	35.0
1989	Michael Jordan, Chi	81	2633	32.5
1990	Michael Jordan, Chi	82	2753	33.6
1991	Michael Jordan, Chi	82	2580	31.5
1992	Michael Jordan, Chi	80	2404	30.1
1993	Michael Jordan, Chi	78	2541	32.6
1994	David Robinson, SA	80	2383	29.8
1995	Shaquille O'Neal, Orl	79	2315	29.3
1996	Michael Jordan, Chi	82	2491	30.4
1997	Michael Jordan, Chi	82	2431	29.7
1998	Michael Jordan, Chi	82	2357	28.7

Note: Lew Alcindor changed his name to Kareem Abdul-Jabbar after the 1970-71 season.

Rebounds

Decided by total rebounds from 1951-69 and per game average since 1970.

Multiple winners: Wilt Chamberlain (11); Dennis Rodman (7); Moses Malone (6); Bill Russell (4); Elvin Hayes and Hakeem Olajuwon (2).

Year		Gm	No	Avg
1951	Dolph Schayes, Syr	66	1080	16.4
1952	Larry Foust, Ft. Wayne	66	880	13.3
	& Mel Hutchins, Mil	66	880	13.3
1953	George Mikan, Mpls	70	1007	14.4
1954	Harry Gallatin, NY	72	1098	15.3
1955	Neil Johnston, Phi	72	1085	15.1
1956	Bob Pettit, St.L	72	1164	16.2
1957	Maurice Stokes, Roch	72	1256	17.4
1958	Bill Russell, Bos	69	1564	22.7
1959	Bill Russell, Bos	70	1612	23.0
1960	Wilt Chamberlain, Phi	72	1941	27.0
1961	Wilt Chamberlain, Phi	79	2149	27.2
1962	Wilt Chamberlain, Phi	80	2052	25.7
1963	Wilt Chamberlain, SF	80	1946	24.3
1964	Bill Russell, Bos	78	1930	24.7
1965	Bill Russell, Bos	78	1878	24.1
1966	Wilt Chamberlain, Phi	79	1943	24.6
1967	Wilt Chamberlain, Phi	81	1957	24.2
1968	Wilt Chamberlain, Phi	82	1952	23.8
1969	Wilt Chamberlain, LA	81	1712	21.1
1970	Elvin Hayes, SD	82	1386	16.9
1971	Wilt Chamberlain, LA	82	1493	18.2
1972	Wilt Chamberlain, LA	82	1572	19.2
1973	Wilt Chamberlain, LA	82	1526	18.6
1974	Elvin Hayes, Cap*	81	1463	18.1
1975	Wes Unseld, Wash	73	1077	14.8
1976	Kareem Abdul-Jabbar, LA	82	1383	16.9
1977	Bill Walton, Port	65	934	14.4
1978	Len Robinson, NO	82	1288	15.7
1979	Moses Malone, Hou	82	1444	17.6
1980	Swen Nater, SD	81	1216	15.0
1981	Moses Malone, Hou	80	1180	14.8
1982	Moses Malone, Hou	81	1188	14.7
1983	Moses Malone, Phi	78	1194	15.3
1984	Moses Malone, Phi	71	950	13.4
1985	Moses Malone, Phi	79	1031	13.1
1986	Bill Laimbeer, Det	82	1075	13.1
1987	Charles Barkley, Phi	68	994	14.6
1988	Michael Cage, LA Clippers	72	938	13.0
1989	Hakeem Olajuwon, Hou	82	1105	13.5
1990	Hakeem Olajuwon, Hou	82	1149	14.0
1991	David Robinson, SA	82	1063	13.0
1992	Dennis Rodman, Det	82	1530	18.7
1993	Dennis Rodman, Det	62	1232	18.3
1994	Dennis Rodman, SA	79	1132	17.3
1995	Dennis Rodman, SA	49	823	16.8
1996	Dennis Rodman, Chi	64	952	14.9
1997	Dennis Rodman, Chi	55	883	16.1
1998	Dennis Rodman, Chi	80	1201	15.0

*The Baltimore Bullets moved to Landover, MD in 1973-74 and became first the Capital Bullets, then the Washington Bullets in 1974-75.

Assists

Decided by total assists from 1952-69 and per game average since 1970.

Multiple winners: John Stockton (9); Bob Cousy (8); Oscar Robertson (6); Magic Johnson and Kevin Porter (4); Andy Phillip and Guy Rodgers (2).

Year		No
1947	Ernie Calverley, Prov	.202
1948	Howie Dallmar, Phi	.120
1949	Bob Davies, Roch	.321
1950	Dick McGuire, NY	.386
1951	Andy Phillip, Phi	.414
1952	Andy Phillip, Phi	.539
1953	Bob Cousy, Bos	.547
1954	Bob Cousy, Bos	.518
1955	Bob Cousy, Bos	.557
1956	Bob Cousy, Bos	.642
1957	Bob Cousy, Bos	.478
1958	Bob Cousy, Bos	.463
1959	Bob Cousy, Bos	.557
1960	Bob Cousy, Bos	.715
1961	Oscar Robertson, Cin	.690
1962	Oscar Robertson, Cin	.899
1963	Guy Rodgers, SF	.825
1964	Oscar Robertson, Cin	.868
1965	Oscar Robertson, Cin	.861
1966	Oscar Robertson, Cin	.847
1967	Guy Rodgers, Chi	.908
1968	Wilt Chamberlain, Phi	.702
1969	Oscar Robertson, Cin	.772
1970	Lenny Wilkens, Sea	9.1
1971	Norm Van Lier, Chi	10.1
1972	Jerry West, LA	9.7
1973	Nate Archibald, KC-O	11.4
1974	Ernie DiGregorio, Buf	8.2
1975	Kevin Porter, Wash	8.0
1976	Slick Watts, Sea	8.1
1977	Don Buse, Ind	8.5
1978	Kevin Porter, Det-NJ	10.2
1979	Kevin Porter, Det	13.4
1980	M.R. Richardson, NY	10.1
1981	Kevin Porter, Wash	9.1
1982	Johnny Moore, SA	9.6
1983	Magic Johnson, LA	10.5
1984	Magic Johnson, LA	13.1
1985	Isiah Thomas, Det	13.9
1986	Magic Johnson, Lakers	12.6
1987	Magic Johnson, Lakers	12.2
1988	John Stockton, Utah	13.8
1989	John Stockton, Utah	13.6
1990	John Stockton, Utah	14.5
1991	John Stockton, Utah	14.2
1992	John Stockton, Utah	13.7
1993	John Stockton, Utah	12.0
1994	John Stockton, Utah	12.6
1995	John Stockton, Utah	12.3
1996	John Stockton, Utah	11.2
1997	Mark Jackson, Den-Ind	11.4
1998	Rod Strickland, Wash	10.5

Field Goal Percentage

Multiple winners: Wilt Chamberlain (9); Artis Gilmore (4); Neil Johnston (3); Bob Feerick, Johnny Green, Alex Groza, Cedric Maxwell, Kevin McHale, Gheorghe Muresan, Shaquille O'Neal, Kenny Sears and Buck Williams (2).

Year		Pct
1947	Bob Feerick, Wash	.401
1948	Bob Feerick, Wash	.340
1949	Arnie Risen, Roch	.423
1950	Alex Groza, Indpls	.478
1951	Alex Groza, Indpls	.470
1952	Paul Arizin, Phi	.448
1953	Neil Johnston, Phi	.452
1954	Ed Macauley, Bos	.486
1955	Larry Foust, Ft.W	.487
1956	Neil Johnston, Phi	.457
1957	Neil Johnston, Phi	.447
1958	Jack Twyman, Cin	.452
1959	Kenny Sears, NY	.490
1960	Kenny Sears, NY	.477
1961	Wilt Chamberlain, Phi	.509
1962	Walt Bellamy, Chi	.519
1963	Wilt Chamberlain, SF	.528
1964	Jerry Lucas, Cin	.527
1965	W. Chamberlain, SF-Phi	.510
1966	Wilt Chamberlain, Phi	.540
1967	Wilt Chamberlain, Phi	.683
1968	Wilt Chamberlain, Phi	.595
1969	Wilt Chamberlain, LA	.583
1970	Johnny Green, Cin	.559
1971	Johnny Green, Cin	.587
1972	Wilt Chamberlain, LA	.649
1973	Wilt Chamberlain, LA	.727
1974	Bob McAdoo, Buf	.547
1975	Don Nelson, Bos	.539
1976	Wes Unseld, Wash	.561
1977	K. Abdul-Jabbar, LA	.579
1978	Bobby Jones, Den	.578
1979	Cedric Maxwell, Bos	.584
1980	Cedric Maxwell, Bos	.609
1981	Artis Gilmore, Chi	.670
1982	Artis Gilmore, Chi	.652
1983	Artis Gilmore, SA	.626
1984	Artis Gilmore, SA	.631
1985	James Donaldson, LAC	.637
1986	Steve Johnson, SA	.632
1987	Kevin McHale, Bos	.604
1988	Kevin McHale, Bos	.604
1989	Dennis Rodman, Det.	.595
1990	Mark West, Pho.	.625
1991	Buck Williams, Port.	.602
1992	Buck Williams, Port.	.604
1993	Cedric Ceballos, Pho	.576
1994	Shaquille O'Neal, Orl	.599
1995	Chris Gatling, G.St.	.633
1996	Gheorghe Muresan, Wash.	.584
1997	Gheorghe Muresan, Wash.	.604
1998	Shaquille O'Neal, LAL	.584

Free Throw Percentage

Multiple winners: Bill Sharman (7); Rick Barry (6); Larry Bird (4); Mark Price and Dolph Schayes (3); Mahmoud Abdul-Rauf, Larry Costello, Ernie DiGregorio, Bob Feerick, Kyle Macy, Calvin Murphy, Oscar Robertson and Larry Siegfried (2).

Year		Pct
1947	Fred Scolari, Wash	.811
1948	Bob Feerick, Wash	.788
1949	Bob Feerick, Wash	.859
1950	Max Zaslofsky, Chi	.843
1951	Joe Fulks, Phi	.855
1952	Bob Wanzer, Roch	.904
1953	Bill Sharman, Bos	.850
1954	Bill Sharman, Bos	.844
1955	Bill Sharman, Bos	.897
1956	Bill Sharman, Bos	.867
1957	Bill Sharman, Bos	.905
1958	Dolph Schayes, Syr	.904
1959	Bill Sharman, Bos	.932
1960	Dolph Schayes, Syr	.892
1961	Bill Sharman, Bos	.921
1962	Dolph Schayes, Syr	.896
1963	Larry Costello, Syr	.881
1964	Oscar Robertson, Cin	.853
1965	Larry Costello, Phi	.877
1966	Larry Siegfried, Bos	.881
1967	Adrian Smith, Cin	.903
1968	Oscar Robertson, Cin	.873
1969	Larry Siegfried, NY	.864
1970	Flynn Robinson, Mil	.898
1971	Chet Walker, Chi	.859
1972	Jack Marin, Bal	.894
1973	Rick Barry, G.St.	.902
1974	Ernie DiGregorio, Buf.	.902
1975	Rick Barry, G.St.	.904
1976	Rick Barry, G.St.	.923
1977	Ernie DiGregorio, Buf.	.945
1978	Rick Barry, G.St.	.924
1979	Rick Barry, Hou	.947
1980	Rick Barry, Hou	.935
1981	Calvin Murphy, Hou	.958
1982	Kyle Macy, Pho	.899
1983	Calvin Murphy, Hou	.920
1984	Larry Bird, Bos	.888
1985	Kyle Macy, Pho	.907
1986	Larry Bird, Bos	.896
1987	Larry Bird, Bos	.910
1988	Jack Sikma, Mil	.922
1989	Magic Johnson, LAL	.911
1990	Larry Bird, Bos	.930
1991	Reggie Miller, Ind	.918
1992	Mark Price, Cle	.947
1993	Mark Price, Cle	.948
1994	M. Abdul-Rauf, Den	.956
1995	Spud Webb, Sac.	.934
1996	M. Abdul-Rauf, Den	.930
1997	Mark Price, G.St.	.906
1998	Chris Mullin, Ind.	.939

Blocked Shots

Decided by per game average since 1973-74 season.

Multiple winners: Kareem Abdul-Jabbar and Mark Eaton (4); George Johnson, Dikembe Mutombo and Hakeem Olajuwon (3); Manute Bol (2).

Year		Gm	No	Avg
1974	Elmore Smith, LA	81	393	4.85
1975	Kareem Abdul-Jabbar, Mil	65	212	3.26
1976	Kareem Abdul-Jabbar, LA	82	338	4.12
1977	Bill Walton, Port	65	211	3.25
1978	George Johnson, NJ	81	274	3.38
1979	Kareem Abdul-Jabbar, LA	80	316	3.95
1980	Kareem Abdul-Jabbar, LA	82	280	3.41
1981	George Johnson, SA	82	278	3.39
1982	George Johnson, SA	75	234	3.12
1983	Tree Rollins, Atl	80	343	4.29
1984	Mark Eaton, Utah	82	351	4.28
1985	Mark Eaton, Utah	82	456	5.56
1986	Manute Bol, Wash	80	397	4.96
1987	Mark Eaton, Utah	79	321	4.06
1988	Mark Eaton, Utah	82	304	3.71
1989	Manute Bol, G.St.	80	345	4.31
1990	Akeem Olajuwon, Hou	82	376	4.59
1991	Hakeem Olajuwon, Hou	56	221	3.95
1992	David Robinson, SA	68	305	4.49
1993	Hakeem Olajuwon, Hou	82	342	4.17
1994	Dikembe Mutombo, Den	82	336	4.10
1995	Dikembe Mutombo, Den	82	321	3.91
1996	Dikembe Mutombo, Den	74	332	4.49
1997	Shawn Bradley, Dal-NJ	73	248	3.40
1998	Marcus Camby, Tor.	63	230	3.65

Steals

Decided by per game average since 1973-74 season.

Multiple winners: Michael Jordan, Micheal Ray Richardson and Alvin Robertson (3); Mookie Blaylock, Magic Johnson and John Stockton (2).

Year		Gm	No	Avg
1974	Larry Steele, Port	81	217	2.68
1975	Rick Barry, G.St.	80	228	2.85
1976	Slick Watts, Sea	82	261	3.18
1977	Don Buse, Ind	81	281	3.47
1978	Ron Lee, Pho	82	225	2.74
1979	M.L. Carr, Det	80	197	2.46
1980	Micheal Ray Richardson, NY	82	265	3.23
1981	Magic Johnson, LA	37	127	3.43
1982	Magic Johnson, LA	78	208	2.67
1983	Micheal Ray Richardson, G. ST-NJ	64	182	2.84
1984	Rickey Green, Utah	81	215	2.65
1985	Micheal Ray Richardson, NJ	82	243	2.96
1986	Alvin Robertson, SA	82	301	3.67
1987	Alvin Robertson, SA	81	260	3.21
1988	Michael Jordan, Chi	82	259	3.16
1989	John Stockton, Utah	82	263	3.21
1990	Michael Jordan, Chi	82	227	2.77
1991	Alvin Robertson, SA	81	246	3.04
1992	John Stockton, Utah	82	244	2.98
1993	Michael Jordan, Chi	78	221	2.83
1994	Nate McMillan, Sea	73	216	2.96
1995	Scottie Pippen, Chi	79	232	2.94
1996	Gary Payton, Sea	81	231	2.85
1997	Mookie Blaylock, Atl.	78	212	2.72
1998	Mookie Blaylock, Atl.	70	183	2.61

Note: Akeem Olajuwon changed the spelling of his first name to Hakeem during the 1990-91 season.

All-Time NBA Regular Season Leaders

Through the 1997-98 regular season.

CAREER

Players active in 1997-98 in **bold** type.

Points

		Yrs	Gm	Pts	Avg
1	Kareem Abdul-Jabbar	20	1560	38,387	24.6
2	Wilt Chamberlain	14	1045	31,419	30.1
3	**Michael Jordan**	13	930	29,277	31.5
4	**Karl Malone**	13	1061	27,782	26.2
5	Moses Malone	19	1329	27,409	20.6
6	Elvin Hayes	16	1303	27,313	21.0
7	Oscar Robertson	14	1040	26,710	25.7
8	Dominique Wilkins	14	1047	26,534	25.3
9	John Havlicek	16	1270	26,395	20.8
10	Alex English	15	1193	25,613	21.5
11	Jerry West	14	932	25,192	27.0
12	**Hakeem Olajuwon**	14	1025	24,422	23.8
13	Robert Parish	21	1611	23,334	14.5
14	Adrian Dantley	15	955	23,177	24.3
15	Elgin Baylor	14	846	23,149	27.4
16	**Charles Barkley**	14	1011	22,852	22.6
17	**Clyde Drexler**	15	1086	22,195	20.4
18	**Patrick Ewing**	13	939	22,079	23.5
19	Larry Bird	13	897	21,791	24.3
20	Hal Greer	15	1122	21,586	19.2
21	Walt Bellamy	14	1043	20,941	20.1
22	Bob Pettit	11	792	20,880	26.4
23	George Gervin	10	791	20,708	26.2
24	**Tom Chambers**	15	1095	20,030	18.3
25	Bernard King	14	874	19,655	22.5
26	Walter Davis	15	1033	19,521	18.9
27	Dolph Schayes	16	1059	19,249	18.2
28	Bob Lanier	14	959	19,248	20.1
29	**Eddie Johnson**	16	1196	19,190	16.0
30	Gail Goodrich	14	1031	19,181	18.6

Scoring Average

Minimum of 400 games or 10,000 points.

		Yrs	Gm	Pts	Avg
1	**Michael Jordan**	13	930	29,277	31.5
2	Wilt Chamberlain	14	1045	31,419	30.1
3	Elgin Baylor	14	846	23,149	27.4
4	**Shaquille O'Neal**	6	406	11,054	27.2
5	Jerry West	14	932	25,192	27.0
6	Bob Pettit	11	792	20,880	26.4
7	**Karl Malone**	13	1061	27,782	26.2
8	George Gervin	10	791	20,708	26.2
9	Oscar Robertson	14	1040	26,710	25.7
10	Dominique Wilkins	14	1047	26,454	25.3
11	**David Robinson**	9	636	15,940	25.1
12	Kareem Abdul-Jabbar	20	1560	38,387	24.6
13	Larry Bird	13	897	21,791	24.3
14	Adrian Dantley	15	955	23,177	24.3
15	Pete Maravich	10	658	15,948	24.2
16	**Hakeem Olajuwon**	14	1025	24,422	23.8
17	**Patrick Ewing**	13	939	22,079	23.5
18	Rick Barry	10	794	18,395	23.2
19	**Mitch Richmond**	10	751	17,371	23.1
20	Paul Arizin	10	713	16,266	22.8
21	George Mikan	9	520	11,764	22.6
22	**Charles Barkley**	14	1011	22,852	22.6
23	Bernard King	14	874	19,655	22.5
24	David Thompson	8	509	11,264	22.1
25	Bob McAdoo	14	852	18,787	22.1
26	Julius Erving	11	836	18,364	22.0
27	Alex English	15	1193	25,613	21.5
28	Elvin Hayes	16	1303	27,313	21.0
29	Billy Cunningham	9	654	13,626	20.8
30	John Havlicek	16	1270	26,395	20.8

NBA-ABA Top 20

Points

All-Time combined regular season scoring leaders, including ABA service (1968-76). NBA players with ABA experience are listed in CAPITAL letters. Players active during 1996-97 are in **bold** type.

		Yrs	Pts	Avg
1	Kareem Abdul-Jabbar	20	38,387	24.6
2	Wilt Chamberlain	14	31,419	30.1
3	JULIUS ERVING	16	30,026	24.2
4	MOSES MALONE	21	29,580	20.3
5	**Michael Jordan**	13	29,277	31.5
6	**Karl Malone**	13	27,782	26.2
7	DAN ISSEL	15	27,482	22.6
8	Elvin Hayes	16	27,313	21.0
9	Oscar Robertson	14	26,710	25.7
10	GEORGE GERVIN	14	26,595	25.1
11	Dominique Wilkins	14	26,534	25.3
12	John Havlicek	16	26,395	20.8
13	Alex English	15	25,613	21.5
14	RICK BARRY	14	25,279	24.8
15	Jerry West	14	25,192	27.0
16	ARTIS GILMORE	17	24,941	18.8
17	**Hakeem Olajuwon**	14	24,422	23.8
18	Robert Parish	21	23,334	14.5
19	Adrian Dantley	15	23,177	24.3
20	Elgin Baylor	14	23,149	27.4

ABA Totals: BARRY (4 yrs, 226 gm, 6884 pts, 30.5 avg); ERVING (5 yrs, 407 gm, 11,662 pts, 28.7 avg); GERVIN (4 yrs, 269 gm, 5887 pts, 21.9 avg); GILMORE (5 yrs, 420 gm, 9362 pts, 22.3 avg); ISSEL (6 yrs, 500 gm, 12,823 pts, 25.6 avg); MALONE (2 yrs, 126 gm, 2171 pts, 17.2 avg).

Field Goals

		Yrs	FG	Att	Pct
1	Kareem Abdul-Jabbar	20	15,837	28,307	.559
2	Wilt Chamberlain	14	12,681	23,497	.540
3	Elvin Hayes	16	10,976	24,272	.452
4	**Michael Jordan**	13	10,958	21,686	.505
5	Alex English	15	10,659	21,036	.507
6	John Havlicek	16	10,513	23,930	.439
7	**Karl Malone**	13	10,290	19,504	.528
8	Dominique Wilkins	14	9,913	21,457	.462
9	**Hakeem Olajuwon**	14	9,706	18,859	.515
10	Robert Parish	21	9,614	17,914	.537

Note: If field goals made in the ABA are included, consider these NBA-ABA totals: Julius Erving (11,818), Dan Issel (10,431), George Gervin (10,368), Moses Malone (10,277) and Rick Barry (9,695).

Free Throws

		Yrs	FT	Att	Pct
1	Moses Malone	19	8531	11,090	.769
2	Oscar Robertson	14	7694	9,185	.838
3	Jerry West	14	7160	8,801	.814
4	**Karl Malone**	13	7133	9,808	.727
5	Dolph Schayes	16	6979	8,273	.844
6	Adrian Dantley	15	6832	8,351	.818
7	**Michael Jordan**	13	6798	8,115	.838
8	Kareem Abdul-Jabbar	20	6712	9,304	.721
9	Bob Pettit	11	6182	8,119	.761
10	**Charles Barkley**	14	6086	8,266	.736

Note: If free throws made in the ABA are included, consider these totals: Moses Malone (9,018), Dan Issel (6,591), Julius Erving (6,256) and Artis Gilmore (6,132).

Assists

		Yrs	Gm	No	Avg
1	**John Stockton**	14	1126	12,713	11.3
2	Magic Johnson	13	906	10,141	11.2
3	Oscar Robertson	14	1040	9,887	9.5
4	Isiah Thomas	13	979	9,061	9.3
5	**Mark Jackson**	11	877	7,538	8.6
6	Maurice Cheeks	15	1101	7,392	6.7
7	Lenny Wilkens	15	1077	7,211	6.7
8	Bob Cousy	14	924	6,955	7.5
9	Guy Rodgers	12	892	6,917	7.8
10	**Kevin Johnson**	11	729	6,687	9.2

Rebounds

		Yrs	Gm	No	Avg
1	Wilt Chamberlain	14	1045	23,924	22.9
2	Bill Russell	13	963	21,620	22.5
3	Kareem Abdul-Jabbar	20	1560	17,440	11.2
4	Elvin Hayes	16	1303	16,279	12.5
5	Moses Malone	19	1329	16,212	12.2
6	Robert Parish	21	1611	14,715	9.1
7	Nate Thurmond	14	964	14,464	15.0
8	Walt Bellamy	14	1043	14,241	13.7
9	Wes Unseld	13	984	13,769	14.0
10	**Buck Williams**	17	1307	13,017	10.0

Note: If rebounds accumulated in the ABA are included, consider the following totals: Moses Malone (17,834) and Artis Gilmore (16,330).

Steals

		Yrs	Gm	No
1	**John Stockton**	14	1126	2620
2	Maurice Cheeks	15	1101	2310
3	**Michael Jordan**	13	930	2306
4	**Clyde Drexler**	15	1086	2207
5	Alvin Robertson	10	779	2112

Note: Steals have only been an official stat since the 1973-74 season.

Blocked Shots

		Yrs	Gm	No
1	**Hakeem Olajuwon**	14	1025	3459
2	Kareem Abdul-Jabbar	20	1560	3189
3	Mark Eaton	11	875	3064
4	**Patrick Ewing**	13	939	2574
5	Tree Rollins	18	1156	2542

Note: Blocked shots have only been an official stat since the 1973-74 season.

Games Played

		Yrs	Career	Gm
1	Robert Parish	21	1976-97	1611
2	Kareem Abdul-Jabbar	20	1970-89	1560
3	Moses Malone	19	1976-95	1329
4	**Buck Williams**	17	1982–	1307
5	Elvin Hayes	16	1969-84	1303

Note: If ABA records are included, consider the following game totals: Moses Malone (1,455) and Artis Gilmore (1,329).

Personal Fouls

		Yrs	Gm	Fouls	DQ
1	Kareem Abdul-Jabbar	20	1560	4657	48
2	Robert Parish	21	1611	4443	86
3	**Buck Williams**	17	1307	4267	58
4	Elvin Hayes	16	1303	4193	53
5	James Edwards	19	1168	4042	96

Note: If ABA records are included, consider the following personal foul totals: Artis Gilmore (4,529) and Caldwell Jones (4,436).

SINGLE SEASON

Scoring Average

		Season	Avg
1	Wilt Chamberlain, Phi	1961-62	50.4
2	Wilt Chamberlain, SF	1962-63	44.8
3	Wilt Chamberlain, Phi	1960-61	38.4
4	Elgin Baylor, LA	1961-62	38.3
5	Wilt Chamberlain, Phi	1959-60	37.6
6	Michael Jordan, Chi	1986-87	37.1
7	Wilt Chamberlain, SF	1963-64	36.9
8	Rick Barry, SF	1966-67	35.6
9	Michael Jordan, Chi	1987-88	35.0
10	Elgin Baylor, LA	1960-61	34.8
	Kareem Abdul-Jabbar, Mil	1971-72	34.8

Field Goal Pct.

		Season	Pct
1	Wilt Chamberlain, LA	1972-73	.727
2	Wilt Chamberlain, SF	1966-67	.683
3	Artis Gilmore, Chi	1980-81	.670
4	Artis Gilmore, Chi	1981-82	.652
5	Wilt Chamberlain, LA	1971-72	.649

Free Throw Pct.

		Season	Pct
1	Calvin Murphy, Hou	1980-81	.958
2	Mahmoud Abdul-Rauf, Den	1993-94	.956
3	Mark Price, Cle	1992-93	.948
4	Mark Price, Cle	1991-92	.947
	Rick Barry, Hou	1978-79	.947

3-Pt Field Goal Pct.

		Season	Pct
1	Steve Kerr, Chi	1994-95	.524
2	Jon Sundvold, Mia	1988-89	.522
3	Tim Legler, Wash	1995-96	.522
4	Steve Kerr, Chi	1995-96	.515
5	Detlef Schrempf, Sea	1994-95	.514

Assists

		Season	Avg
1	John Stockton, Utah	1989-90	14.5
2	John Stockton, Utah	1990-91	14.2
3	Isiah Thomas, Det	1984-85	13.9
4	John Stockton, Utah	1987-88	13.8
5	John Stockton, Utah	1991-92	13.7
6	John Stockton, Utah	1988-89	13.6
7	Kevin Porter, Det	1978-79	13.4
8	Magic Johnson, LA Lakers	1983-84	13.1
9	Magic Johnson, LA Lakers	1988-89	12.8
10	Magic Johnson, LA Lakers	1984-85	12.6
	John Stockton, Utah	1993-94	12.6

Rebounds

		Season	Avg
1	Wilt Chamberlain, Phi	1960-61	27.2
2	Wilt Chamberlain, Phi	1959-60	27.0
3	Wilt Chamberlain, Phi	1961-62	25.7
4	Bill Russell, Bos	1963-64	24.7
5	Wilt Chamberlain, Phi	1965-66	24.6

Blocked Shots

		Season	Avg
1	Mark Eaton, Utah	1984-85	5.56
2	Manute Bol, Wash	1985-86	4.96
3	Elmore Smith, LA	1973-74	4.85
4	Mark Eaton, Utah	1985-86	4.61
5	Hakeem Olajuwon, Hou	1989-90	4.59

Steals

		Season	Avg
1	Alvin Robertson, SA	1985-86	3.67
2	Don Buse, Ind	1976-77	3.47
3	Magic Johnson, LA Lakers	1980-81	3.43
4	Micheal Ray Richardson, NY	1979-80	3.23
5	Alvin Robertson, SA	1986-87	3.21

SINGLE GAME

Points

	Date	FG-FT	Pts
Wilt Chamberlain, Phi vs NY	3/2/62	36-28–	100
Wilt Chamberlain, Phi vs LA***	12/8/61	31-16–	78
Wilt Chamberlain, Phi vs Chi	1/13/62	29-15–	73
Wilt Chamberlain, SF at NY	11/16/62	29-15–	73
David Thompson, Den at Det	4/9/78	28-17–	73
Wilt Chamberlain, SF at LA	11/3/62	29-14–	72
Elgin Baylor, LA at NY	11/15/60	28-15–	71
David Robinson, SA at LAC	4/24/94	26-18–	71
Wilt Chamberlain, SF at Syr	3/10/63	27-16–	70
Michael Jordan, Chi at Cle*	3/28/90	23-21–	69
Wilt Chamberlain, Phi at Chi	12/16/67	30- 8–	68
Pete Maravich, NO vs NYK	2/25/77	26-16–	68
Wilt Chamberlain, Phi vs NY	3/9/61	27-13–	67
Wilt Chamberlain, Phi at St. L	2/17/62	26-15–	67
Wilt Chamberlain, Phi vs NY	2/25/62	25-17–	67
Wilt Chamberlain, SF vs LA	1/11/63	28-11–	67
Wilt Chamberlain, LA vs Pho	2/9/69	29- 8–	66
Wilt Chamberlain, Phi at Cin	2/13/62	24-17–	65
Wilt Chamberlain, Phi at St. L	2/27/62	25-15–	65
Wilt Chamberlain, Phi vs LA	2/7/66	28- 9–	65
Elgin Baylor, Mpls vs Bos	11/8/59	25-14–	64
Rick Barry, G.St. vs Port	3/26/74	30- 4–	64
Michael Jordan, Chi vs Orl	1/16/93	27- 9–	64

*Overtime

***Triple overtime.

Note: Wilt Chamberlain's 100-point game vs New York was played at Hershey, Pa.

Field Goals

	Date	FG	Att
Wilt Chamberlain, Phi vs NY	3/2/62	36	63
Wilt Chamberlain, Phi vs LA***	12/8/61	31	62
Wilt Chamberlain, Phi at Chi	12/16/67	30	40
Rick Barry, G.St. vs Port	2/26/74	30	45

Wilt Chamberlain made 29 four times.

***Triple overtime.

Free Throws

	Date	FT	Att
Wilt Chamberlain, Phi vs NY	3/2/62	28	32
Adrian Dantley, Utah vs Hou	1/4/84	28	29
Adrian Dantley, Utah vs Den	11/25/83	27	31
Adrian Dantley, Utah vs Dal	10/31/80	26	29
Michael Jordan, Chi vs NJ	2/26/87	26	27

3-Pt Field Goals

	Date	No
Dennis Scott, Orl vs Atl	4/18/96	11
Brian Shaw, Mia at Mil	4/8/93	10
Joe Dumars, Det vs Min	11/8/94	10
George McCloud, Dal vs Pho	12/16/95	10*

Many tied with 9 each

* Overtime

Assists

	Date	No
Scott Skiles, Orl vs Den	12/30/90	30
Kevin Porter, NJ vs Hou	2/24/78	29
Bob Cousy, Bos vs Mpls	2/27/59	28
Guy Rodgers, SF vs St.L	3/14/63	28
John Stockton, Utah vs SA	1/15/91	28

Blocked Shots

	Date	No
Elmore Smith, LA vs Port	10/28/73	17
Manute Bol, Wash vs Atl	1/25/86	15
Manute Bol, Wash vs Ind	2/26/87	15
Shaquille O'Neal, Orl at NJ	11/20/93	15

Rebounds

	Date	No
Wilt Chamberlain, Phi vs Bos	11/24/60	55
Bill Russell, Bos vs Syr	2/5/60	51
Bill Russell, Bos vs Phi	11/16/57	49
Bill Russell, Bos vs Det.	3/11/65	49
Wilt Chamberlain, Phi vs Syr	2/6/60	45
Wilt Chamberlain, Phi vs LA	1/21/61	45

Steals

	Date	No
Larry Kenon, San Antonio at KC	12/26/76	11

13 different players tied with 10 each, including Alvin Robertson, who had 10 steals in a game four times.

All-Time Winningest NBA Coaches

Top 25 NBA career victories through the 1997-98 season. Career, regular season and playoff records are noted along with NBA titles won. Coaches active during 1997-98 season in **bold** type.

			Career			Regular Season			Playoffs			
		Yrs	W	L	Pct	W	L	Pct	W	L	Pct	NBA Titles
1	**Lenny Wilkens**	25	**1189**	987	.547	1120	908	.552	69	79	.466	1 (1979)
2	**Pat Riley**	16	**1059**	472	.692	914	387	.703	145	85	.630	4 (1982,85,87-88)
3	Red Auerbach	20	**1037**	548	.654	938	479	.662	99	69	.589	9 (1957, 59-66)
4	**Bill Fitch**	25	**999**	1157	.463	944	1106	.460	55	54	.505	1 (1981)
5	Dick Motta	25	**991**	1087	.477	935	1017	.479	56	70	.444	1 (1978)
6	**Don Nelson**	20	**922**	752	.551	871	691	.558	51	61	.455	None
7	Jack Ramsay	21	**908**	841	.519	864	783	.525	44	58	.431	1 (1977)
8	Cotton Fitzsimmons	21	**867**	824	.513	832	775	.518	35	49	.417	None
9	Gene Shue	22	**814**	908	.473	784	861	.477	30	47	.390	None
10	Red Holzman	18	**754**	652	.536	696	604	.535	58	48	.547	2 (1970, 73)
	John MacLeod	18	**754**	711	.515	707	657	.518	47	54	.465	None
12	**Jerry Sloan**	13	**704**	437	.617	639	379	.628	65	58	.528	None
13	**Larry Brown**	15	**696**	573	.548	655	531	.552	41	42	.494	None
14	**Chuck Daly**	13	**679**	468	.592	605	420	.590	74	48	.607	2 (1989-90)
15	Doug Moe	15	**661**	579	.533	628	529	.543	33	50	.398	None
16	**Phil Jackson**	9	**656**	234	.737	545	193	.738	111	41	.730	6 (1991-93,96-98)
17	K.C. Jones	10	**603**	309	.661	522	252	.674	81	57	.587	2 (1984,86)
18	**Del Harris**	13	**588**	501	.540	550	451	.549	38	50	.432	None
	Al Attles	14	**588**	548	.518	557	518	.518	31	30	.508	1 (1975)
20	**Mike Fratello**	13	**570**	471	.548	550	437	.557	20	34	.370	None
21	**George Karl**	11	**548**	375	.594	503	326	.607	45	49	.479	None
22	Billy Cunningham	8	**520**	235	.689	454	196	.698	66	39	.629	1 (1983)
23	Alex Hannum	12	**518**	446	.536	471	412	.533	47	34	.580	2 (1958, 67)
24	John Kundla	11	**485**	338	.589	423	302	.583	62	36	.633	5 (1949-50, 52-54)
25	Kevin Loughery	17	**480**	683	.413	474	662	.417	6	21	.222	None

Note: The NBA does not recognize records from the National Basketball League (1937-49), the American Basketball League (1961-62) or the American Basketball Assn. (1968-76), so the following NBL, ABL and ABA overall coaching records are not included above: NBL–**John Kundla** (51-19 and a title in 1 year). ABA– **Larry Brown** (249-129 in 4 yrs), **Alex Hannum** (194-164 and one title in 4 yrs), **K.C. Jones** (30-58 in 1 yr); **Kevin Loughery** (189-95 and one title in 3 yrs).

Where They Coached

Attles—Golden St. (1970-80,80-83); **Auerbach**—Washington (1946-49), Tri-Cities (1949-50), Boston (1950-66); **Brown**—Denver (1976-79), New Jersey (1981-83), San Antonio (1988-92), LA Clippers (1992-93), Indiana (1993-97), Philadelphia (1997–); **Cunningham**—Philadelphia (1977-85); **Daly**—Cleveland (1981-82), Detroit (1983-92), New Jersey (1992-94), Orlando (1997–); **Fitch**—Cleveland (1970-79), Boston (1979-83), Houston (1983-88), New Jersey (1989-92), LA Clippers (1994-98); **Fitzsimmons**—Phoenix (1970-72), Atlanta (1972-76), Buffalo (1977-78), Kansas City (1978-84), San Antonio (1984-86), Phoenix (1988-92, 95-96); **Fratello**—Atlanta (1980-90), Cleveland (1993–).

Hannum—St. Louis (1957-58), Syracuse (1960-63), San Francisco (1963-66), Phila. 76ers (1966-68), Houston (1970-71); **Harris**—Houston (1979-83), Milwaukee (1987-92), LA Lakers (1994–); **Holzman**—Milwaukee-St. Louis Hawks (1954-57), NY Knicks (1968-77,78-82); **Jackson**—Chicago (1989-98); **Jones**—Washington (1973-76), Boston (1983-88), Seattle (1990-92); **Karl**—Cleveland (1984-86); Golden St. (1986-88), Seattle (1991-98); **Kundla**—Minneapolis (1948-57,58-59); **Loughery**—Philadelphia (1972-73), NY-NJ Nets (1976-81), Atlanta (1981-83), Chicago (1983-85), Washington (1985-88), Miami (1991-95); **MacLeod**—Phoenix (1973-87), Dallas (1987-89), NY Knicks (1990-91); **Moe**—San Antonio (1976-80), Denver (1981-90), Philadelphia (1992-93).

Motta—Chicago (1968-76), Washington (1976-80), Dallas (1980-87), Sacramento (1990-91), Dallas (1994-96), Denver (1997); **Nelson**—Milwaukee (1976-87), Golden St. (1988-95), New York (1995-96), Dallas (1997–); **Ramsay**—Philadelphia (1968-72), Buffalo (1972-76), Portland (1976-86), Indiana (1986-89); **Riley**—LA Lakers (1981-90), New York (1991-95), Miami (1995–); **Shue**—Baltimore (1967-73), Philadelphia (1973-77), San Diego Clippers (1978-80), Washington (1980-86), LA Clippers (1987-89); **Sloan**—Chicago (1979-82), Utah (1988–); **Wilkens**—Seattle (1969-72), Portland (1974-76), Seattle (1977-85), Cleveland (1986-93), Atlanta (1993–).

Top Winning Percentages

Minimum of 350 victories, including playoffs; coaches active during 1997-98 season in **bold** type.

		Yrs	W	L	Pct
1	**Phil Jackson**	9	656	234	**.737**
2	**Pat Riley**	16	1059	472	**.692**
3	Billy Cunningham	8	520	235	**.689**
4	K.C. Jones	10	603	309	**.661**
5	Red Auerbach	20	1037	548	**.654**
6	**Jerry Sloan**	13	704	437	**.617**
7	Tommy Heinsohn	9	474	296	**.616**
8	**Rudy Tomjanovich**	7	370	233	**.614**
9	**Chris Ford**	7	365	238	**.605**
10	**George Karl**	11	548	375	**.594**
11	**Chuck Daly**	13	679	468	**.592**
12	Larry Costello	10	467	323	**.591**
13	John Kundla	11	485	338	**.589**
14	Rick Adelman	8	393	285	**.580**
15	Bill Sharman	7	368	267	**.580**
16	Al Cervi	9	359	267	**.573**
17	Joe Lapchick	9	356	277	**.562**
18	**Don Nelson**	20	922	752	**.551**
19	**Larry Brown**	15	696	573	**.548**
20	**Mike Fratello**	13	570	471	**.548**
21	**Lenny Wilkens**	25	1189	987	**.547**
22	Bill Russell	8	375	317	**.542**
23	**Del Harris**	13	588	501	**.540**
24	Alex Hannum	12	518	446	**.537**
25	Red Holzman	18	754	651	**.536**

Active Coaches' Victories

Through 1997-98 season, including playoffs.

		Yrs	W	L	Pct
1	Lenny Wilkens, Atlanta	25	**1189**	987	.547
2	Pat Riley, Miami	16	**1059**	472	.692
3	Don Nelson, Dallas	20	**922**	752	.551
4	Jerry Sloan, Utah	13	**704**	437	.617
5	Larry Brown, Philadelphia	15	**696**	573	.548
6	Chuck Daly, Orlando	13	**679**	468	.592
7	Del Harris, LA Lakers	13	**588**	501	.540
8	Mike Fratello, Cleveland	13	**570**	471	.548
9	George Karl, Milwaukee	11	**548**	375	.594
10	Rudy Tomjanovich, Houston	7	**370**	233	.614
11	Rick Adelman, Sacramento	8	**357**	252	.586
12	Bernie Bickerstaff, Wash.	9	**314**	326	.491
13	Mike Dunleavy, Portland	7	**267**	330	.447
14	Brian Hill, Vancouver	5	**227**	185	.551
15	Paul Westphal, Seattle	4	**191**	88	.685
16	P.J. Carlesimo, Golden St.	4	**159**	181	.468
17	Rick Pitino, Boston	3	**132**	127	.510
	Dave Cowens, Charlotte	3	**132**	113	.539
19	Jeff Van Gundy, New York	3	**124**	82	.602
20	Phil Saunders, Minnesota	3	**105**	121	.465
21	Danny Ainge, Phoenix	2	**98**	62	.613
22	Gregg Popovich, San Antonio	2	**73**	73	.500
23	John Calipari, New Jersey	2	**69**	95	.421
24	Larry Bird, Indiana	1	**58**	24	.707
25	Butch Carter, Toronto	1	**5**	28	.152
26	Tim Floyd, Chicago	0	**0**	0	—
27	Mike D'Antoni, Denver	0	**0**	0	—
	TBA, LA Clippers				

Annual Awards

Most Valuable Player

The Maurice Podoloff Trophy for regular season MVP. Named after the first commissioner (then president) of the NBA. Winners first selected by the NBA players (1956-80) then a national panel of pro basketball writers and broadcasters (since 1981). Winners' scoring averages are provided; (*) indicates led league.

Multiple winners: Kareem Abdul-Jabbar (6); Michael Jordan and Bill Russell (5); Wilt Chamberlain (4); Larry Bird, Magic Johnson and Moses Malone (3); Bob Pettit (2).

Year		Avg
1956	Bob Pettit, St. Louis, F	25.7*
1957	Bob Cousy, Boston, G	20.6
1958	Bill Russell, Boston, C	16.6
1959	Bob Pettit, St. Louis, F	29.2*
1960	Wilt Chamberlain, Philadelphia, C	37.6*
1961	Bill Russell, Boston, C	16.9
1962	Bill Russell, Boston, C	18.9
1963	Bill Russell, Boston, C	16.8
1964	Oscar Robertson, Cincinnati, G	31.4
1965	Bill Russell, Boston, C	14.1
1966	Wilt Chamberlain, Philadelphia, C	33.5*
1967	Wilt Chamberlain, Philadelphia, C	24.1
1968	Wilt Chamberlain, Philadelphia, C	24.3
1969	Wes Unseld, Baltimore, C	13.8
1970	Willis Reed, New York, C	21.7
1971	Lew Alcindor, Milwaukee, C	31.7*
1972	Kareem Abdul-Jabbar, Milwaukee, C	34.8*
1973	Dave Cowens, Boston, C	20.5
1974	Kareem Abdul-Jabbar, LA, C	27.0
1975	Bob McAdoo, Buffalo, F	34.5*
1976	Kareem Abdul-Jabbar, LA, C	27.7
1977	Kareem Abdul-Jabbar, LA, C	26.2

Year		Avg
1978	Bill Walton, Portland, C	18.9
1979	Moses Malone, Houston, C	24.8
1980	Kareem Abdul-Jabbar, LA, C	24.8
1981	Julius Erving, Philadelphia, F	24.6
1982	Moses Malone, Houston, C	31.1
1983	Moses Malone, Philadelphia, C	24.5
1984	Larry Bird, Boston, F	24.2
1985	Larry Bird, Boston, F	28.7
1986	Larry Bird, Boston, F	25.8
1987	Magic Johnson, LA Lakers, G	23.9
1988	Michael Jordan, Chicago, G	35.0*
1989	Magic Johnson, LA Lakers, G	22.5
1990	Magic Johnson, LA Lakers, G	22.3
1991	Michael Jordan, Chicago, G	31.5*
1992	Michael Jordan, Chicago, G	30.1*
1993	Charles Barkley, Phoenix, F	25.6
1994	Hakeem Olajuwon, Houston, C	27.3
1995	David Robinson, San Antonio, C	27.6
1996	Michael Jordan, Chicago, G	30.4*
1997	Karl Malone, Utah, F	27.4
1998	Michael Jordan, Chicago, G	28.7*

Note: Lew Alcindor changed his name to Kareem Abdul-Jabbar after the 1970-71 season.

Rookie of the Year

The Eddie Gottlieb Trophy for outstanding rookie of the regular season. Named after the pro basketball pioneer and owner-coach of the first NBA champion Philadelphia Warriors. Winners selected by a national panel of pro basketball writers and broadcasters. Winners' scoring averages provided; (*) indicated led league; winners who were also named MVP are in **bold** type.

Year		Avg
1953	Don Meineke, Ft. Wayne, F	10.8
1954	Ray Felix, Baltimore, C	17.6
1955	Bob Pettit, Milwaukee Hawks, F	20.4
1956	Maurice Stokes, Rochester, F/C	16.8
1957	Tommy Heinsohn, Boston, F	16.2
1958	Woody Sauldsberry, Philadelphia, F/C	12.8
1959	Elgin Baylor, Minneapolis, F	24.9
1960	**Wilt Chamberlain**, Philadelphia, C	37.6*
1961	Oscar Robertson, Cincinnati, G	30.5
1962	Walt Bellamy, Chicago Packers, C	31.6
1963	Terry Dischinger, Chicago Zephyrs, F	25.5
1964	Jerry Lucas, Cincinnati, F/C	17.7
1965	Willis Reed, New York, C	19.5
1966	Rick Barry, San Francisco, F	25.7
1967	Dave Bing, Detroit, G	20.0
1968	Earl Monroe, Baltimore, G	24.3
1969	**Wes Unseld**, Baltimore, C	13.8
1970	Lew Alcindor, Milwaukee Bucks, C	28.8
1971	Dave Cowens, Boston, C	17.0
	& Geoff Petrie, Portland, G	24.8
1972	Sidney Wicks, Portland, F	24.5
1973	Bob McAdoo, Buffalo, C/F	18.0
1974	Ernie DiGregorio, Buffalo, G	15.2
1975	Keith Wilkes, Golden St., F	14.2
1976	Alvan Adams, Phoenix, C	19.0
1977	Adrian Dantley, Buffalo, F	20.3
1978	Walter Davis, Phoenix, G	24.2
1979	Phil Ford, Kansas City, G	15.9
1980	Larry Bird, Boston, F	21.3
1981	Darrell Griffith, Utah, G	20.6
1982	Buck Williams, New Jersey, F	15.5
1983	Terry Cummings, San Diego, F	23.7
1984	Ralph Sampson, Houston, C	21.0
1985	Michael Jordan, Chicago, G	28.2
1986	Patrick Ewing, New York, C	20.0
1987	Chuck Person, Indiana, F	18.8
1988	Mark Jackson, New York, G	13.6
1989	Mitch Richmond, Golden St., G	22.0
1990	David Robinson, San Antonio, C	24.3
1991	Derrick Coleman, New Jersey, F	18.4
1992	Larry Johnson, Charlotte, F	19.2
1993	Shaquille O'Neal, Orlando,C	23.4
1994	Chris Webber, Golden St., F	17.5
1995	Grant Hill, Detroit, F	19.9
	& Jason Kidd, Dallas, G	11.7
1996	Damon Stoudamire, Toronto, G	19.0
1997	Allen Iverson, Philadelphia, G	23.5
1998	Tim Duncan, San Antonio, F/C	21.6

Note: The Chicago Packers changed their name to the Zephyrs after 1961-62 season. Also, Lew Alcindor changed his name to Kareem Abdul-Jabbar after the 1970-71 season.

Sixth Man Award

Awarded to the Best Player Off the Bench for the regular season. Winners selected by a national panel of pro basketball writers and broadcasters.

Multiple winners: Kevin McHale, Ricky Pierce and Detlef Schrempf (2).

Year	
1983	Bobby Jones, Phi., F
1984	Kevin McHale, Bos., F
1985	Kevin McHale, Bos., F
1986	Bill Walton, Bos., F/C
1987	Ricky Pierce, Mil., G/F
1988	Roy Tarpley, Dal., F
1989	Eddie Johnson, Pho., F
1990	Ricky Pierce, Mil., G/F
1991	Detlef Schrempf, Ind., F
1992	Detlef Schrempf, Ind., F
1993	Cliff Robinson, Port., F
1994	Dell Curry, Char., G
1995	Anthony Mason, NY, F
1996	Toni Kukoc, Chi., F
1997	John Starks, NY, G
1998	Danny Manning, Pho., F

Number One Draft Choices

Overall first choices in the NBA draft since the abolition of the territorial draft in 1966. Players who became Rookie of the Year are in **bold** type. The draft lottery began in 1985.

Year		Overall 1st Pick
1966	New York	Cazzie Russell, Michigan
1967	Detroit	Jimmy Walker, Providence
1968	San Diego	Elvin Hayes, Houston
1969	Milwaukee	**Lew Alcindor**, UCLA
1970	Detroit	Bob Lanier, St. Bonaventure
1971	Cleveland	Austin Carr, Notre Dame
1972	Portland	LaRue Martin, Loyola-Chicago
1973	Philadelphia	Doug Collins, Illinois St.
1974	Portland	Bill Walton, UCLA
1975	Atlanta	David Thompson, N.C. State
1976	Houston	John Lucas, Maryland
1977	Milwaukee	Kent Benson, Indiana
1978	Portland	Mychal Thompson, Minnesota
1979	LA Lakers	Magic Johnson, Michigan St.
1980	Golden St	Joe Barry Carroll, Purdue
1981	Dallas	Mark Aguirre, DePaul
1982	LA Lakers	James Worthy, N. Carolina
1983	Houston	**Ralph Sampson**, Virginia
1984	Houston	Akeem Olajuwon, Houston
1985	New York	**Patrick Ewing**, Georgetown
1986	Cleveland	Brad Daugherty, N. Carolina
1987	San Antonio	**David Robinson**, Navy
1988	LA Clippers	Danny Manning, Kansas
1989	Sacramento	Pervis Ellison, Louisville
1990	New Jersey	**Derrick Coleman**, Syracuse
1991	Charlotte	**Larry Johnson**, UNLV
1992	Orlando	**Shaquille O'Neal**, LSU
1993	Orlando	**Chris Webber**, Michigan
1994	Milwaukee	Glenn Robinson, Purdue
1995	Golden St.	Joe Smith, Maryland
1996	Philadelphia	**Allen Iverson**, Georgetown
1997	San Antonio	**Tim Duncan**, Wake Forest
1998	LA Clippers	Michael Olowokandi, Pacific

Note: Lew Alcindor changed his name to Kareem Abdul-Jabbar after the 1970-71 season; Akeem Olajuwon changed his first name to Hakeem in 1991; in 1975 David Thompson signed with Denver of the ABA and did not play for Atlanta; David Robinson joined NBA for 1989-90 season after fulfilling military obligation.

Defensive Player of the Year

Awarded to the Best Defensive Player for the regular season. Winners selected by a national panel of pro basketball writers and broadcasters.

Multiple winners: Dikembe Mutombo (3); Mark Eaton, Sidney Moncrief, Hakeem Olajuwon and Dennis Rodman (2).

Year	Year	Year
1983 Sidney Moncrief, Mil., G	1989 Mark Eaton, Utah, C	1995 Dikembe Mutombo, Den., C
1984 Sidney Moncrief, Mil., G	1990 Dennis Rodman, Det., F	1996 Gary Payton, Sea., G
1985 Mark Eaton, Utah, C	1991 Dennis Rodman, Det., F	1997 Dikembe Mutombo, Atl., C
1986 Alvin Robertson, SA, G	1992 David Robinson, SA, C	1998 Dikembe Mutombo, Atl., C
1987 Michael Cooper, LAL, F	1993 Hakeem Olajuwon, Hou., C	
1988 Michael Jordan, Chi., G	1994 Hakeem Olajuwon, Hou., C	

Most Improved Player

Awarded to the Most Improved Player for the regular season. Winners selected by a national panel of pro basketball writers and broadcasters.

Year	Year	Year
1986 Alvin Robertson, SA, G	1991 Scott Skiles, Orl., G	1996 Gheorghe Muresan, Wash., C
1987 Dale Ellis, Sea., G	1992 Pervis Ellison, Wash., C	1997 Isaac Austin, Miami, C
1988 Kevin Duckworth, Port., C	1993 Mahmoud Abdul-Rauf, Den., G	1998 Alan Henderson, Atl., F
1989 Kevin Johnson, Pho., G	1994 Don MacLean, Wash., F	
1990 Rony Seikaly, Mia., C	1995 Dana Barros, Phi., G	

Coach of the Year

The Red Auerbach Trophy for outstanding coach of the year. Renamed in 1967 for the former Boston coach who led the Celtics to nine NBA titles. Winners selected by a national panel of pro basketball writers and broadcasters. Previous season and winning season records are provided; (*) indicates division title.

Multiple winners: Don Nelson and Pat Riley (3); Bill Fitch, Cotton Fitzsimmons and Gene Shue (2).

Year		Improvement		
1963	Harry Gallatin, St. L	29-51	to	48-32
1964	Alex Hannum, SF	31-49	to	48-32*
1965	Red Auerbach, Bos	59-21*	to	61-18*
1966	Dolph Schayes, Phi	40-40	to	55-25*
1967	Johnny Kerr, Chi	Expan.	to	33-48
1968	Richie Guerin, St. L	39-42	to	56-26*
1969	Gene Shue, Balt	36-46	to	57-25*
1970	Red Holzman, NY	54-28	to	60-22*
1971	Dick Motta, Chi	39-43	to	51-31
1972	Bill Sharman, LA	48-34*	to	69-13*
1973	Tommy Heinsohn, Bos	56-26*	to	68-14*
1974	Ray Scott, Det	40-42	to	52-30
1975	Phil Johnson, KC-Omaha	33-49	to	44-38
1976	Bill Fitch, Cle	40-42	to	49-33*
1977	Tom Nissalke, Hou	40-42	to	49-33*
1978	Hubie Brown, Atl	31-51	to	41-41
1979	Cotton Fitzsimmons, KC	31-51	to	48-34*
1980	Bill Fitch, Bos	29-53	to	61-21*

Year		Improvement		
1981	Jack McKinney, Ind	37-45	to	44-38
1982	Gene Shue, Wash	39-43	to	43-39
1983	Don Nelson, Mil	55-27*	to	51-31*
1984	Frank Layden, Utah	30-52	to	45-37*
1985	Don Nelson, Mil	50-32*	to	59-23*
1986	Mike Fratello, Atl	34-48	to	50-32
1987	Mike Schuler, Port	40-42	to	49-33
1988	Doug Moe, Den	37-45	to	54-28*
1989	Cotton Fitzsimmons, Pho	28-54	to	55-27
1990	Pat Riley, LA Lakers	57-25*	to	63-19*
1991	Don Chaney, Hou	41-41	to	52-30
1992	Don Nelson, GS	44-38	to	55-27
1993	Pat Riley, NY	51-31	to	60-22
1994	Lenny Wilkens, Atl	43-39	to	57-25*
1995	Del Harris, LA Lakers	33-49	to	48-34
1996	Phil Jackson, Chi	47-35	to	72-10*
1997	Pat Riley, Mia	42-40	to	61-21
1998	Larry Bird, Ind	39-43	to	58-24

World Championships

The World Basketball Championships for men and women have been played regularly at four-year intervals (give or take a year) since 1970. The men's tournament began in 1950 and the women's in 1953. The Federation Internationale de Basketball Amateur (FIBA), which governs the World and Olympic tournaments, was founded in 1932. FIBA first allowed professional players from the NBA to participate in 1994.

Men

Multiple wins: Yugoslavia (4); Soviet Union and USA (3); Brazil (2).

Year	
1950	**Argentina**, United States, Chile
1954	**United States**, Brazil, Philippines
1959	**Brazil**, United States, Chile
1963	**Brazil**, Yugoslavia, Soviet Union
1967	**Soviet Union**, Yugoslavia, Brazil
1970	**Yugoslavia**, Brazil, Soviet Union
1974	**Soviet Union**, Yugoslavia, United States
1978	**Yugoslavia**, Soviet Union, Brazil
1982	**Soviet Union**, United States, Yugoslavia
1986	**United States**, Soviet Union, Yugoslavia
1990	**Yugoslavia**, Soviet Union, United States
1994	**United States**, Russia, Croatia
1998	**Yugoslavia**, Russia, United States
2002	at Indianapolis (August)

Women

Multiple wins: Soviet Union and USA (6).

Year	
1953	**United States**, Chile, France
1957	**United States**, Soviet Union, Czechoslovakia
1959	**Soviet Union**, Bulgaria, Czechoslovakia
1964	**Soviet Union**, Czechoslovakia, Bulgaria
1967	**Soviet Union**, South Korea, Czechoslovakia
1971	**Soviet Union**, Czechoslovakia, Brazil
1975	**Soviet Union**, Japan, Czechoslovakia
1979	**United States**, South Korea, Canada
1983	**Soviet Union**, United States, China
1986	**United States**, Soviet Union, Canada
1990	**United States**, Yugoslavia, Cuba
1994	**Brazil**, China, United States
1998	**United States**, Russia, Australia
2002	at China (May)

NBA Photos

50 Greatest Players

In October 1996, as part of its 50th anniversary celebration, the NBA named the 50 greatest players in league history. The voting was done by a league-approved panel of media, former players and coaches, current and former general managers and team executives. The players are listed alphabetically along with the dates of their professional careers and positions. Active players are in **bold** type.

Player	Pos	Player	Pos	Player	Pos
Kareem Abdul-Jabbar, 1969-89	C	George Gervin, 1972-86	G	Bob Pettit, 1954-65	F/C
Nate Archibald, 1970-84	G	Hal Greer, 1958-73	G	**Scottie Pippen**, 1987–	F
Paul Arizin, 1950-61	F/G	John Havlicek, 1962-78	F/G	Willis Reed, 1964-74	C
Charles Barkley, 1984–	F	Elvin Hayes, 1968-84	F/C	Oscar Robertson, 1960-74	G
Rick Barry, 1965-80	F	Magic Johnson, 1979-91, 96	G	**David Robinson**, 1989–	C
Elgin Baylor, 1958-72	F	Sam Jones, 1957-69	G	Bill Russell, 1956-69	C
Dave Bing, 1966-78	G	**Michael Jordan**, 1984-93, 95–	G	Dolph Schayes, 1948-64	F/C
Larry Bird, 1979-92	F	Jerry Lucas, 1963-74	F/C	Bill Sharman, 1950-61	G
Wilt Chamberlain, 1959-73	C	**Karl Malone**, 1985–	F	**John Stockton**, 1984–	G
Bob Cousy, 1950-63, 69-70	G	Moses Malone, 1974-95	C	Isiah Thomas, 1981-94	G
Dave Cowens, 1970-80, 1982-83	C	Pete Maravich, 1970-80	G	Nate Thurmond, 1963-77	C/F
Billy Cunningham, 1965-76	G	Kevin McHale, 1980-93	F	Wes Unseld, 1968-81	C/F
Dave DeBusschere, 1962-74	F	George Mikan, 1946-54, 55-56	C	Bill Walton, 1974-88	C
Clyde Drexler, 1983-98	G	Earl Monroe, 1967-80	G	Jerry West, 1960-74	G
Julius Erving, 1971-87	F	**Hakeem Olajuwon**, 1984–	C	Lenny Wilkens, 1960-75	G
Patrick Ewing, 1985–	C	**Shaquille O'Neal**, 1992–	C	James Worthy, 1982-94	F
Walt Frazier, 1967-80	G	Robert Parish, 1976-97	C		

Note: Rick Barry, Billy Cunningham, Julius Erving, George Gervin and Moses Malone all played part of their pro careers in the ABA.

10 Greatest Coaches

In December 1996, as part of its 50th anniversary celebration, the NBA named the 10 greatest coaches in league history. The voting was done by a league-approved panel of media. The coaches are listed alphabetically along with the dates of their professional coaching careers and overall records, including playoff games, and number of NBA titles won. Active coaches are in **bold** type.

Coach	W	L	Pct.	Titles
Red Auerbach, 1946-66	1037	548	.654	9
Chuck Daly, 1981-94, 97–	679	468	.592	2
Bill Fitch, 1970-98	999	1157	.463	1
Red Holzman, 1953-82	754	652	.536	2
Phil Jackson, 1989-98	656	234	.737	6
John Kundla, 1947-59	485	338	.589	5
Don Nelson, 1976-96, 97–	922	752	.551	0
Jack Ramsay, 1968-89	908	841	.519	1
Pat Riley, 1981–	1059	472	.692	4
Lenny Wilkens, 1969–	1189	987	.547	1
Totals	8688	6449	.574	31

American Basketball Association

ABA Finals

The American Basketball Assn. began play in 1967-68 as a 10-team rival of the 21-year-old NBA. The ABA, which introduced the three-point basket, a multi-colored ball and the All-Star Game Slam Dunk Contest, lasted nine seasons before folding following the 1975-76 season. Four ABA teams–Denver, Indiana, New York and San Antonio–survived to enter the NBA in 1976-77. The NBA also adopted the three-point basket (in 1979-80) and the All-Star Game Slam Dunk Contest. The older league, however, refused to take in the ABA ball.

Multiple winners: Indiana (3); New York (2).

Year	Winner	Head Coach	Series	Loser	Head Coach
1968	Pittsburgh Pipers	Vince Cazzetta	4-3 (WLLWLWW)	New Orleans Bucs	Babe McCarthy
1969	Oakland Oaks	Alex Hannum	4-1 (WLWWW)	Indiana Pacers	Bob Leonard
1970	Indiana Pacers	Bob Leonard	4-2 (WWLWLW)	Los Angeles Stars	Bill Sharman
1971	Utah Stars	Bill Sharman	4-3 (WWLLWLW)	Kentucky Colonels	Frank Ramsey
1972	Indiana Pacers	Bob Leonard	4-2 (WLWLWW)	New York Nets	Lou Carnesecca
1973	Indiana Pacers	Bob Leonard	4-3 (WLLWWLW)	Kentucky Colonels	Joe Mullaney
1974	New York Nets	Kevin Loughery	4-1 (WWWLW)	Utah Stars	Joe Mullaney
1975	Kentucky Colonels	Hubie Brown	4-1 (WWWLW)	Indiana Pacers	Bob Leonard
1976	New York Nets	Kevin Loughery	4-2 (WLWWLW)	Denver Nuggets	Larry Brown

Most Valuable Player

Winners' scoring averages provided; (*) indicates led league.

Multiple winners: Julius Erving (3); Mel Daniels (2).

Year		Avg
1968	Connie Hawkins, Pittsburgh, C	26.8*
1969	Mel Daniels, Indiana, C	24.0
1970	Spencer Haywood, Denver, C	30.0*
1971	Mel Daniels, Indiana, C	21.0
1972	Artis Gilmore, Kentucky, C	23.8
1973	Billy Cunningham, Carolina, F	24.1
1974	Julius Erving, New York, F	27.4*
1975	George McGinnis, Indiana, F	29.8*
	& Julius Erving, New York, F	27.9
1976	Julius Erving, New York, F	29.3*

Rookie of the Year

Winners' scoring averages provided; (*) indicates led league. Rookies who were also named Most Valuable Player are in **bold** type.

Year		Avg
1968	Mel Daniels, Minnesota, C	22.2
1969	Warren Armstrong, Oakland, G	21.5
1970	**Spencer Haywood**, Denver, C	30.0*
1971	Dan Issel, Kentucky, C	29.8*
	& Charlie Scott, Virginia, G	27.1
1972	**Artis Gilmore**, Kentucky, C	23.8
1973	Brian Taylor, New York, G	15.3
1974	Swen Nater, Virginia-SA, C	14.1
1975	Marvin Barnes, St. Louis, C	24.0
1976	David Thompson, Denver, F	26.0

Note: Warren Armstrong changed his name to Warren Jabali after the 1970-71 season.

Coach of the Year

Previous season and winning season records are provided; (*) indicates division title.

Multiple winner: Larry Brown (3).

Year		Improvement		
1968	Vince Cazetta, Pittsburgh			54-24*
1969	Alex Hannum, Oakland	22-56	to	60-18*
1970	Joe Belmont, Denver	44-34	to	51-33*
	& Bill Sharman, LA Stars	33-45	to	43-41
1971	Al Bianchi, Virginia	44-40	to	55-29*
1972	Tom Nissalke, Dallas	30-54	to	42-42
1973	Larry Brown, Carolina	35-49	to	57-27*
1974	Babe McCarthy, Kentucky	56-28	to	53-31
	& Joe Mullaney, Utah	55-29*	to	51-33*
1975	Larry Brown, Denver	37-47	to	65-19*
1976	Larry Brown, Denver	65-19*	to	60-24*

Scoring Leaders

Scoring championship decided by per game point average every season.

Multiple winner: Julius Erving (3).

Year		Gm	Avg	Pts
1968	Connie Hawkins, Pittsburgh	70	1875	26.8
1969	Rick Barry, Oakland	35	1190	34.0
1970	Spencer Haywood, Denver	84	2519	30.0
1971	Dan Issel, Kentucky	83	2480	29.8
1972	Charlie Scott, Virginia	73	2524	34.6
1973	Julius Erving, Virginia	71	2268	31.9
1974	Julius Erving, New York	84	2299	27.4
1975	George McGinnis, Indiana	79	2353	29.8
1976	Julius Erving, New York	84	2462	29.3

ABA All-Star Game

The ABA All-Star Game was an Eastern Division vs Western Division contest from 1968-75. League membership had dropped to seven teams by 1976, the ABA's last season, so the team in first place at the break (Denver) played an All-Star team made up from the other six clubs.

Series: East won 5, West 3 and Denver 1.

Year	Result	Host	Coaches	Most Valuable Player
1968	East 126, West 120	Indiana	Jim Pollard, Babe McCarthy	Larry Brown, New Orleans
1969	West 133, East 127	Louisville	Alex Hannum, Gene Rhodes	John Beasley, Dallas
1970	West 128, East 98	Indiana	Babe McCarthy, Bob Leonard	Spencer Haywood, Denver
1971	East 126, West 122	Carolina	Al Bianchi, Bill Sharman	Mel Daniels, Indiana
1972	East 142, West 115	Louisville	Joe Mullaney, Ladell Andersen	Dan Issel, Kentucky
1973	West 123, East 111	Utah	Ladell Andersen, Larry Brown	Warren Jabali, Denver
1974	East 128, West 112	Virginia	Babe McCarthy, Joe Mullaney	Artis Gilmore, Kentucky
1975	East 151, West 124	San Antonio	Kevin Loughery, Larry Brown	Freddie Lewis, St. Louis
1976	Denver 144, ABA 138	Denver	Larry Brown, Kevin Loughery	David Thompson, Denver

Continental Basketball Association

Formed on April 23, 1946, the CBA is the oldest professional basketball league in the world. Originally named the Eastern Pennsylvania Basketball League, the league changed names several times before becoming known as the Eastern Basketball Association. In 1978, the EBA was redubbed the CBA.

Multiple champions: Allentown and Wilkes-Barre (8); Scranton, Tampa Bay and Williamsport (3); Albany, La Crosse, Pottsville, Rochester and Wilmington (2).

Year
1947 Wilkes-Barre Barons
1948 Reading Keys
1949 Pottsville Packers
1950 Williamsport Billies
1951 Sunbury Mercuries
1952 Potsville Packers
1953 Williamsport Billies
1954 Williamsport Billies
1955 Wilkes-Barre Barons
1956 Wilkes-Barre Barons
1957 Scranton Miners
1958 Wilkes-Barre Barons
1959 Wilkes-Barre Barons
1960 Easton Madisons
1961 Baltimore Bullets
1962 Allentown Jets
1963 Allentown Jets
1964 Camden Bullets
1965 Allentown Jets
1966 Wilmington Blue Bombers
1967 Wilmington Blue Bombers
1968 Allentown Jets
1969 Wilkes-Barre Barons
1970 Allentown Jets
1971 Scranton Apollos
1972 Allentown Jets
1973 Wilkes-Barre Barons
1974 Hartford Capitols
1975 Allentown Jets
1976 Allentown Jets
1977 Scranton Apollos
1978 Wilkes-Barre Barons
1979 Rochester Zeniths
1980 Anchorage Northern Knights
1981 Rochester Zeniths
1982 Lancaster Lightning
1983 Detroit Spirits
1984 Albany Patroons
1985 Tampa Bay Thrillers
1986 Tampa Bay Thrillers
1987 Rapid City Thrillers*
1988 Albany Patroons
1989 Tulsa Fast Breakers
1990 La Crosse Catbirds
1991 Wichita Falls Texans
1992 La Crosse Catbirds
1993 Omaha Racers
1994 Quad City Thunder
1995 Yakima Sun Kings
1996 Sioux Falls Skyforce
1997 Oklahoma City Calvary
1998 Quad City Thunder

*The Tampa Bay Thrillers moved to Rapid City, S.D. at the end of the 1987 regular season.

WOMEN

American Basketball League

League Champions

The American Basketball League began play in 1996 as an eight-team league. Before the 1997-98 season the league added an expansion franchise in Long Beach, Calif. while the Richmond Rage was relocated to Philadelphia. In the spring of 1998, the league announced plans to dissolve an original franchise, the Atlanta Glory, and expand to Chicago and Nashville before the 1998-99 season increasing the league's size to 10 teams. The ABL finals is a best of five series. Each ABL champion's wins and losses are noted in parentheses after the series score.

Multiple winner: Columbus (2).

Year	Champions	Head Coach	Series	Runners-up	Head Coach
1997	Columbus Quest	Brian Agler	3-2 (WLLWW)	Richmond Rage	Lisa Boyer
1998	Columbus Quest	Brian Agler	3-2 (LLWWW)	Long Beach StingRays	Maura McHugh

Most Valuable Player

Winner's scoring averages provided; (*) indicates led league.

Year		Avg.
1997	Nikki McCray, Columbus	19.9
1998	Natalie Williams, Portland	21.9*

Coach of the Year

Previous season and winning season's record are provided; (*) indicates division title.

Year		Improvement
1997	Brian Agler, Columbus	31-9*
1998	Lin Dunn, Portland	14-26 to 27-17

Women's National Basketball Association

League Champions

The WNBA, owned and operated by the NBA, began play in 1997 as an eight-team summer league. The WNBA champion was determined by a single-game playoff between the winners of the semifinals in the league's 1997 inaugural season, before going to a best-of-three championship series in 1998.

Multiple winner: Houston (2).

Year	Champions	Head Coach	Score	Runners-up	Head Coach
1997	Houston Comets	Van Chancellor	65-51	New York Liberty	Nancy Darsch
1998	Houston Comets	Van Chancellor	2-1 (LWW)	Phoenix Mercury	Cheryl Miller

Most Valuable Player

Winner's scoring averages provided; (*) indicates led league.

Year		Avg.
1997	Cynthia Cooper, Houston	22.2*
1998	Cynthia Cooper, Houston	22.7*

Coach of the Year

Previous season and winning season's record are provided; (*) indicates division title.

Year		Improvement
1997	Van Chancellor, Houston	18-10*
1998	Van Chancellor, Houston	18-10 to 27-3*

Hockey

In one of the most moving events of the year, injured Detroit defenseman **Vladimir Konstantinov** is wheeled around the MCI Center ice with the Stanley Cup.

Archive Photos

Championship Wings

Coach Scotty Bowman led the dominant Red Wings to their second consecutive sweep in the Stanley Cup Finals.

by
Steve Levy

Keeping in mind I'm traditionally a "glass is half-full" kind of guy, the 1997-98 NHL season was most definitely less than "half-empty." It was a campaign that had far too many concussions (most notably Anaheim's Paul Kariya and the Rangers' Pat LaFontaine), far too many discussions about contracts and crease violations, and not nearly enough goals. An average of only 5.3 goals were scored per game this season, the lowest total in 42 years.

Nagano only made matters worse. Having NHL stars play in the Olympics seemed like a brilliant idea going in, but turned out to be a disaster for the American and Canadian men, both on and off the ice.

When the season finally did resume, big market teams such as the New York Rangers and the Chicago Blackhawks failed to make the playoffs, the Blackhawks missing out on the postseason for the first time in 29 seasons. And most of those that did qualify didn't perform even close to the way they did in the regular season. The top three seeds in the Eastern Conference, New Jersey, Pittsburgh and Philadelphia, and the No. 2 seed in the West, Colorado, all were eliminated in the first round. And then to top it all off, for an unprecedented fourth consecutive season, the Stanley Cup Finals ended in a four-game sweep.

But as I mentioned earlier, I'm a "glass is half-full" kind of guy, which means we can expect a bounce-back, banner NHL season in 1998-99. And I don't mean to imply that last season

---

Steve Levy is a *SportsCenter* anchor and host of ESPN's *National Hockey Night.*

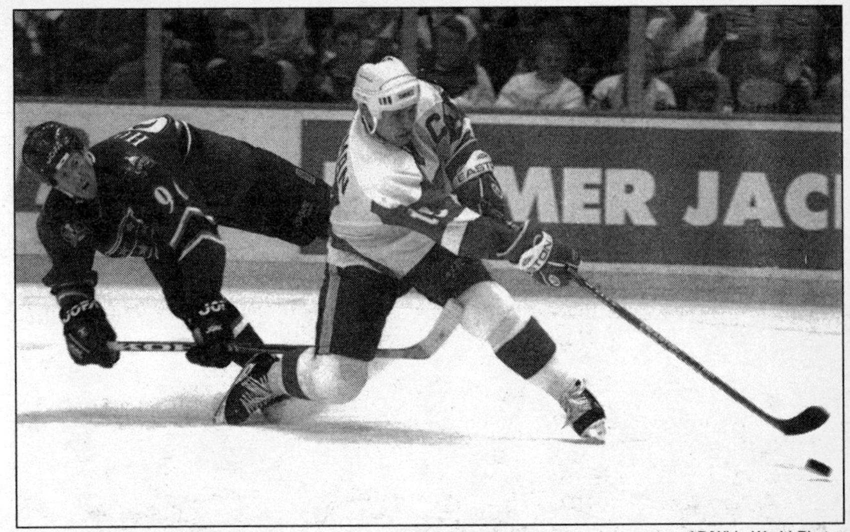

AP/Wide World Photos

Fan favorite **Steve Yzerman** captained the Red Wings to their second consecutive Stanley Cup Finals sweep and finally got the individual recognition he deserved as well, taking home the Conn Smythe Trophy as playoff MVP.

was without any redeeming qualities. After all, I certainly don't hear anyone from Detroit complaining. The Red Wings showed their flat-out dominance over the rest of the league by recording consecutive Stanley Cup Finals sweeps for the first time since the Islanders accomplished the feat in 1981-82 and 82-83. And they did so without dominant goaltending.

And while the Washington Capitals weren't happy at the time with their four and out performance in the Finals, they have to look back with tremendous pride after what was by far the finest season in franchise history. The Capitals, once known for their bad luck and their bad building, moved downtown, turning D.C. "Cap Crazy" with a few breaks and a breakout season by Olie the Goalie (goaltender Olaf Kolzig). They ought to be a lock to win their division this coming season, not that it's much of a division. The NHL will add another team next season (Nashville Predators) with three more being added over the next three seasons. The league has been re-formatted into six divisions with the Caps being joined in the newly-formed Southeast Division by Carolina, Florida and Tampa Bay. Enough said.

Other thoughts from the season that was...Tom Barrasso "penned" quite the comeback season for Pittsburgh. The 33-year-old goaltender finished third in the league in goals-against average (2.07) and second in save percentage (.922), leading Pittsburgh to a 98-point season...The turnaround of the Boston Bruins was the major surprise of the regular season. New head coach Pat Burns worked his magic, getting the most out of Jason Allison and rookie phenom Sergei Samsonov as the Bruins, the league's worst team in 1996-97, reached the playoffs with

AP/Wide World Photos

Dominik Hasek, a.k.a. "The Dominator" was at it again in 1998, leading the Buffalo Sabres to the Eastern Conference Finals and becoming the first goalie in NHL history to win back-to-back Hart and Vezina Trophies. Oh, and he won an Olympic gold medal to boot.

91 points...And while the Bruins were the biggest surprise of the regular season, the biggest shocker in the playoffs had to be the Ottawa Senators' stunning upset of top-seed New Jersey in the first round.

So as I raise my "half-full" glass in the air, here's hoping for a few more hat tricks in the 98-99 season, or a few more goals at the very least. Might we see a third straight Hart Trophy (MVP) for Buffalo goalie Dominik Hasek, or maybe a third straight Cup for the Red Wings? ■

Steve Levy's Top Ten Highlights of the 1997-98 Hockey Season.

10. **Meaningless TV ratings,** as proven by 600 million Disney dollars. So much for the raise I was hoping for.

9. **Gary Suter's brutal cross-check** to the face of Mighty Ducks star Paul Kariya vaults the now San Jose defenseman to Anaheim's public enemy No. 1 status.

8. **The NHL All-Star Game** generates more interest and excitement with a new "North America vs. The World" format, as opposed to the usual "East vs. West."

7. **Rob Blake wins the Norris Trophy.** Barry Melrose was right again. I hate when that happens. But he said that when Blake is healthy, he can be the best defenseman in the game. He proved that, and more, by putting the juice back into L.A. hockey.

AP/Wide World Photos

After seeing the lowest goals per game total in 42 years, the NHL will look to young superstars like Anaheim left wing **Paul Kariya** to find the net more often in 1998-99. Kariya missed most of the season with a concussion after a vicious cross check by Chicago's Gary Suter.

6. **The U.S. women win the gold** at the Olympics, sparking further development of girl's and women's hockey in the states.
5. **Tough to question Dominik Hasek's heart now.** He stars for the Czech Republic to win the gold at the Olympic games, and then becomes the first goaltender in history to win consecutive Hart Trophies.
4. In a time when it's so difficult to repeat, especially in hockey, **the Red Wings do it**. And better yet, they have a full offseason to enjoy it.
3. **Carolina offers Sergei Fedorov** a contract that includes a $12 million bonus for making the conference finals. The Red Wings would have to admit now they made the right move by matching it.
2. **Detroit captain Steve Yzerman** re-emphasizes that he's much more than just a superstar. As a reward, he skates with the Cup for a second consecutive year and wins the Conn Smythe Trophy as playoff MVP, his first major individual NHL trophy.
1. **Detroit's Vladimir Konstantinov**, in uniform, in his wheelchair, is pushed along the MCI Center ice with the Stanley Cup in his lap. It's not just the best minute of the NHL season, but one of the greatest single scenes in sports history. ■

THE NUMBERS

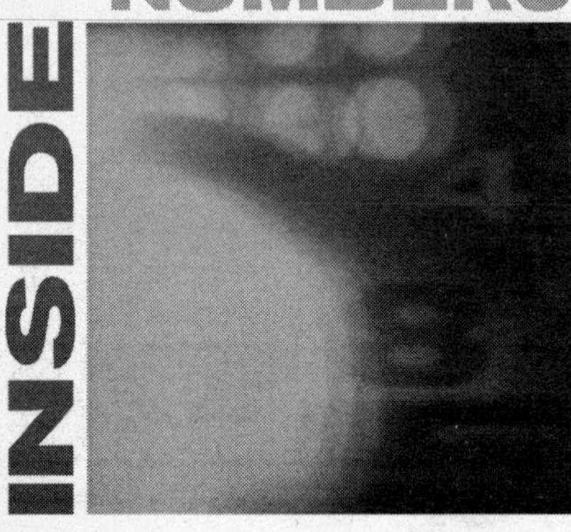

by

Jim Samia

LIGHT ON THE GOALS

The Tampa Bay Lightning scored a woeful 151 goals in the 1997-98 season, including just nine in their last ten games. They became the first team since expansion in 1967-68 to finish the year averaging under two goals per game.

	Games/Goals	Avg
'97-98 Lightning	**82/151**	**1.84**
'67-68 Oak. Seals	74/153	2.07*
'72-73 Islanders	78/170	2.18*
'69-70 Kings	76/168	2.21
'69-70 Oak. Seals	76/169	2.22

* Expansion Team

Note: The 1953-54 Chicago Blackhawks were the last team before Tampa to average less than two goals per game (1.90).

STILL THE (GREAT) ONE

Wayne Gretzky was tops among all Rangers in 1997-98 with 90 points, becoming the 6th player in NHL history to lead his team in scoring at the age of 37 or older. Phil Esposito did it twice for the Rangers in '78-79 and '79-80. The venerable Gordie Howe led the Red Wings in scoring four times after the age of 37, the last time in '69-70 at the age of 42.

'97-98	**Wayne Gretzky, NYR**
'78-80	Phil Esposito, NYR
'74-75	Bob Nevin, LA
'70-71	Jean Beliveau, Mon.
'69-70	Dean Prentice, Pit.
'65-66 & '67-70	Gordie Howe, Det.

MOST OF HIS TEEM'S GOALS

Since the center ice red line was introduced in the 1943-44 season, only five times has a player ended the season with at least 25 percent of his team's goals. Mighty Ducks star Teemu Selanne had the second-highest percentage in 1997-98.

	Goals/Team's	Pct
Brett Hull, St.L, '90-91	86/310	27.7
Teemu Selanne, Ana., '97-98	**52/205**	**25.4**
Brett Hull, St.L, '91-92	70/279	25.1
Peter Bondra, Wash., '94-95	34/136	25.0
Maurice Richard, Mon., '49-50	43/172	25.0

Note: The all-time record is held by Quebec's Joe Malone who scored 39 of his team's 91 goals (42.9 percent) in the 1919-20 season.

PREYING FOR THE PLAYOFFS

The Nashville Predators join the NHL in 1998-99 but could have a bumpy road ahead of them in their inaugural season. Since the 1970-71 season, no team has made the playoffs in their first year of existence. The Atlanta (now Calgary) Flames were the quickest, making it to the postseason in their second year. The Washington Capitals, '97-98 Stanley Cup finalists, waited nine years for postseason play.

	Season
Flames	2nd, '73-74
Panthers	3rd, '95-96
Sharks	3rd, '93-94
Islanders	3rd, '74-75
Sabres	3rd, '72-73

■

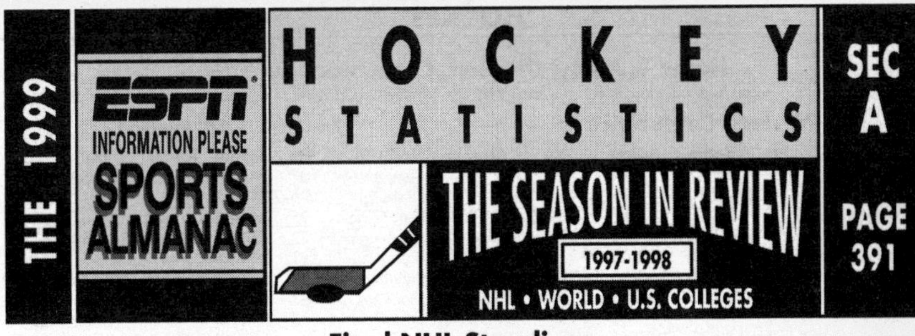

THE 1999
ESPN
INFORMATION PLEASE
SPORTS ALMANAC
HOCKEY
STATISTICS
THE SEASON IN REVIEW
1997-1998
NHL • WORLD • U.S. COLLEGES
SEC
A
PAGE
391

Final NHL Standings

Division champions (*) and playoff qualifiers (†) are noted. Number of seasons listed after each head coach refers to current tenure with club through 1997-98 season.

Western Conference

Central Division

	W	L	T	Pts	GF	GA	Dif
*Dallas	49	22	11	109	242	167	+75
†Detroit	44	23	15	103	250	196	+54
†St. Louis	45	29	8	98	256	204	+52
†Phoenix	35	35	12	82	224	227	-3
Chicago	30	39	13	73	192	199	-7
Toronto	30	43	9	69	194	237	-43

Head Coaches: Dal— Ken Hitchcock (3rd season); **Det**— Scotty Bowman (5th); **St.L**— Joel Quenneville (2nd); **Pho**— Jim Schoenfeld (1st); **Chi**— Craig Hartsburg (3rd); **Tor**— Mike Murphy (2nd).

1996-97 Standings: 1. Dallas (48-26-8, 104 points); 2. Detroit (38-26-18, 94 pts); 3. Phoenix (38-37-7, 83 pts); 4. St. Louis (36-35-11, 83 pts); 5. Chicago (34-35-13, 81 pts); 5. Toronto (30-44-8, 68 pts).

Pacific Division

	W	L	T	Pts	GF	GA	Dif
*Colorado	39	26	17	95	231	205	+26
†Los Angeles	38	33	11	87	227	225	+2
†Edmonton	35	37	10	80	215	224	-9
†San Jose	34	38	10	78	210	216	-6
Calgary	26	41	15	67	217	252	-35
Anaheim	26	43	13	65	205	261	-56
Vancouver	25	43	14	64	224	273	-49

Head Coaches: Col— Marc Crawford (4th season); **LA**— Larry Robinson (3rd); **Edm**— Ron Low (4th); **SJ**— Darryl Sutter (1st); **Cal**— Brian Sutter (1st); **Ana**— Pierre Page (1st); **Van**— fired Tom Renney (2nd, 4-13-2) on Nov. 13 and replaced him with Mike Keenan (21-30-12).

1996-97 Standings: 1. Colorado (49-24-9, 107 points); 2. Anaheim (36-33-13, 85 pts); 3. Edmonton (36-37-9, 81 pts); 4. Vancouver (35-40-7, 77 pts); 5. Calgary (32-41-9, 73 pts); 6. Los Angeles (28-43-11, 67 pts); 7. San Jose (27-47-8, 62 pts).

Eastern Conference

Northeast Division

	W	L	T	Pts	GF	GA	Dif
*Pittsburgh	40	24	18	98	228	188	+40
†Boston	39	30	13	91	221	194	+27
†Buffalo	36	29	17	89	211	187	+24
†Montreal	37	32	13	87	235	208	+27
†Ottawa	34	33	15	83	193	200	-7
Carolina	33	41	8	74	200	219	-19

Head Coaches: Pit— Kevin Constantine (1st season); **Bos**— Pat Burns (1st); **Buf**— Lindy Ruff (1st); **Mon**— Alain Vigneault (1st); **Ott**— Jacques Martin (3rd); **Car**— Paul Maurice (3rd).

1996-97 Standings: 1. Buffalo (40-30-12, 92 points); 2. Pittsburgh (38-36-8, 84 pts); 3. Ottawa (31-36-15, 77 pts); 4. Montreal (31-36-15, 77 pts); 5. Hartford (32-39-11, 75 pts); 6. Boston (26-47-9, 61).

Atlantic Division

	W	L	T	Pts	GF	GA	Dif
*New Jersey	48	23	11	107	225	166	+59
†Philadelphia	42	29	11	95	242	193	+49
†Washington	40	30	12	92	219	202	+17
NY Islanders	30	41	11	71	212	225	-13
NY Rangers	25	39	18	68	197	231	-34
Florida	24	43	15	63	203	256	-53
Tampa Bay	17	55	10	44	151	269	-118

Head Coaches: NJ— Jacques Lemaire (5th); **Phi**— moved Wayne Cashman (1st, 32-20-9) to asst. on March 9 and replaced him with Roger Neilson (10-9-2); **Wash**— Ron Wilson (1st); **NYI**— fired Rick Bowness (2nd, 22-32-9) on March 11 and replaced him with GM Mike Milbury (8-9-2); **NYR**— fired Colin Campbell (4th, 17-24-16) on Feb. 18 and replaced him with John Muckler (8-15-2); **Fla**— fired Doug MacLean (4th, 7-12-4) on Nov. 24 and replaced him with GM Bryan Murray (17-31-11); **TB**— fired Terry Crisp (6th, 2-7-2) on Oct. 26 and replaced him with interim coach Rick Paterson (0-4) and then Jacques Demers (15-44-8) on Nov. 12.

1996-97 Standings: 1. New Jersey (45-23-14, 104 points); 2. Philadelphia (45-24-13, 103 pts); 3. Florida (35-28-19, 89 pts); 4. NY Rangers (38-34-10, 86 pts); 5. Washington (33-40-9, 75 pts); 6. Tampa Bay (32-40-10, 74); 7. NY Islanders (29-41-12, 70 pts).

NHL Realignment for 1998-99

With the Nashville Predators joining the NHL in 1998-99 and three more teams joining in the following two years, the league voted to expand from four divisions to six. Nashville will join the Western Conference's Central Division. Note the Toronto Maple Leafs move from the Western Conference to the Eastern Conference.

Eight teams from each conference will still make the playoffs, with the three division winners being the top three seeds and the five next-best teams filling out the bracket according to record.

Western Conference

Central	Northwest	Pacific
Chicago	Calgary	Anaheim
Detroit	Colorado	Dallas
Nashville	Edmonton	Los Angeles
St. Louis	San Jose	Phoenix
	Vancouver	

Eastern Conference

Atlantic	Northeast	Southeast
New Jersey	Boston	Carolina
NY Islanders	Buffalo	Florida
NY Rangers	Montreal	Tampa Bay
Philadelphia	Ottawa	Washington
Pittsburgh	Toronto	

Home & Away, Division, Conference Records

Sixteen teams— eight from each conference— qualify for the Stanley Cup Playoffs; (*) indicates division champions.

Western Conference

	Pts	Home	Away	Div	Conf
1 Dallas*	109	26-8-7	23-14-4	14-10-4	32-17-7
2 Colorado*	95	21-10-10	18-16-7	16-11-5	28-18-10
3 Detroit	103	25-8-8	19-15-7	13-8-7	27-17-12
4 St. Louis	98	26-10-5	19-19-3	16-11-1	32-20-4
5 Los Angeles	87	22-16-3	16-17-8	19-11-2	29-22-5
6 Phoenix	82	19-16-6	16-19-6	14-10-4	28-22-6
7 Edmonton	80	20-16-5	15-21-5	14-17-1	27-25-4
8 San Jose	78	17-19-5	17-19-5	15-13-4	25-26-5
Chicago	73	14-19-8	16-20-5	6-17-5	16-29-11
Toronto	69	16-20-5	14-23-4	10-17-1	22-27-7
Calgary	67	18-17-6	8-24-9	12-15-5	16-30-10
Anaheim	65	12-23-6	14-20-7	11-17-4	16-32-8
Vancouver	64	15-22-4	10-21-10	11-14-7	16-29-11

Eastern Conference

	Pts	Home	Away	Div	Conf
1 New Jersey*	107	29-10-2	19-13-9	21-6-5	36-13-7
2 Pittsburgh*	98	21-10-10	19-14-8	15-6-7	28-16-12
3 Philadelphia	95	24-11-6	18-18-5	17-11-4	29-19-8
4 Washington	92	23-12-6	17-18-6	17-11-4	28-20-8
5 Boston	91	19-16-6	20-14-7	13-10-5	26-19-11
6 Buffalo	89	20-13-8	16-16-9	12-9-7	25-20-11
7 Montreal	87	15-17-9	22-15-4	9-15-4	22-26-8
8 Ottawa	83	18-16-7	16-17-8	8-13-7	24-22-10
Carolina	74	16-18-7	17-23-1	11-15-2	20-32-4
NY Islanders	71	17-20-4	13-21-7	13-15-4	22-26-8
NY Rangers	68	14-18-9	11-21-9	8-17-7	15-30-11
Florida	63	11-24-6	13-19-9	12-14-6	22-26-8
Tampa Bay	44	11-23-7	6-32-3	7-21-4	10-38-8

1998 NHL All-Star Game

North America, 8-7

48th NHL All-Star Game. **Date:** Jan. 18 at General Motors Place in Vancouver; **Coaches:** Jacques Lemaire, New Jersey (North America) and Ken Hitchcock, Dallas (World); **MVP:** Teemu Selanne, Anaheim right wing (World) — three goals.

In 1998 with the winter Olympics looming, the NHL voted to abandon its usual all-star game format of Eastern Conference vs. Western Conference in favor of a game pitting the North American all-stars vs. the rest of the world's all stars.

Starters were chosen by fan vote while reserves were selected by the NHL's Hockey Operations Department, after consultation from various NHL general managers. Head coaches whose teams were leading the Eastern Conference and Western Conference on Dec. 15 were named all-star head coaches. A coin toss determined which team each would coach.

Mark Messier and Al MacInnis were added to the North American lineup and Jari Kurri and Igor Larionov to the World lineup as special selections by NHL commissioner Gary Bettman.

North America

	Starters	G	A	Pts	PM
W	John LeClair, Philadelphia	1	0	1	0
C	Eric Lindros, Philadelphia	1	0	1	0
D	Ray Bourque, Boston	0	1	1	0
D	Brian Leetch, NY Rangers	0	0	0	0
W	Brendan Shanahan, Detroit	0	0	0	0
	Reserves				
W	Keith Tkachuk, Phoenix	2	1	3	0
D	Chris Chelios, Chicago	0	3	3	0
C	Mike Modano, Dallas	0	3	3	0
W	Theo Fleury, Calgary	1	1	2	2
C	Mark Messier, Vancouver	1	1	2	0
C	Joe Sakic, Colorado	0	2	2	0
C	Wayne Gretzky, NY Rangers	0	2	2	0
W	Tony Amonte, Chicago	1	0	1	0
D	Scott Niedermayer, New Jersey	1	0	1	0
W	Mark Recchi, Montreal	0	1	1	0
W	Shayne Corson, Montreal	0	0	0	0
D	Al MacInnis, St. Louis	0	0	0	0
D	Scott Stevens, New Jersey	0	0	0	0
D	Darryl Sydor, Dallas	0	0	0	0
C	Doug Weight, Edmonton	0	0	0	2
	TOTALS	8	15	23	4

Goaltenders	Mins	Shots	Saves	GA
Patrick Roy, Col.	20:00	7	4	3
Ed Belfour, Dal.	20:00	11	9	2
Martin Brodeur, NJ (W)	20:00	11	9	2
TOTALS	60:00	29	22	7

The World

	Starters	G	A	Pts	PM
W	Teemu Selanne, Anaheim	3	0	3	0
W	Jaromir Jagr, Pittsburgh	1	0	1	0
C	Peter Forsberg, Colorado	0	1	1	0
D	Viacheslav Fetisov, Detroit	0	1	1	2
D	Sandis Ozolinsh, Colorado	0	0	0	0
	Reserves				
C	Saku Koivu, Montreal	0	3	3	0
W	Jere Lehtinen, Dallas	0	3	3	0
D	Igor Kravchuk, Ottawa	1	0	1	0
W	Jari Kurri, Colorado	1	0	1	0
C	Igor Larionov, Detroit	1	0	1	0
W	Peter Bondra, Washington	0	1	1	0
W	Pavel Bure, Vancouver	0	1	1	0
D	Dmitri Mironov, Anaheim	0	1	1	0
C	Mats Sundin, Toronto	0	1	1	0
W	Daniel Alfredsson, Ottawa	0	0	0	0
C	Bobby Holik, New Jersey	0	0	0	0
W	Valeri Kamensky, Colorado	0	0	0	0
D	Nicklas Lidstrom, Detroit	0	0	0	0
W	Zigmund Palffy, NY Islanders	0	0	0	0
D	Sergei Zubov, Dallas	0	0	0	0
	TOTALS	7	12	19	2

Goaltenders	Mins	Shots	Saves	GA
Dominik Hasek, Buf.	20:00	13	10	3
Olaf Kolzig, Wash.	20:00	17	14	3
Nikolai Khabibulin, Pho (L)	20:00	13	11	2
TOTALS	60:00	43	35	8

Score by Periods

	1	2	3	Final
World	3	2	2	— 7
North America	3	3	2	— 8

Power plays: World — 0/2; North America — 1/2. **Officials:** Paul Stewart (referee), Michael Cvik and Shane Heyer (linesmen). **Attendance:** 18,422.

Hat Tricks

Players scored three or more goals in one game a total of 64 times during the 1997-98 regular season. Pavel Bure of Vancouver, Teemu Selanne of Anaheim and Keith Tkachuk of Phoenix led the way with three hat tricks each. (*) indicates rookie.

Four Goals	Date	Score
Eric Daze, Chi at Fla	Mar. 15	Chi, 8-4
Joe Nieuwendyk, Dal vs Ana	Mar. 13	Dal, 6-3
Brian Savage, Mon at NYI	Jan. 8	Mon, 8-2

Three Goals	Date	Score
Jason Allison, Bos vs NYR	Mar. 14	Bos, 5-1
Jason Allison, Bos vs Pho	Jan. 8	Bos, 5-2
Stu Barnes, Pit vs NJ	Jan. 10	Pit, 4-1
Peter Bondra, Wash at NYR	Jan. 8	Wash, 5-3
Doug Brown, Det vs NJ	Dec. 19	Det, 5-4
Pavel Bure, Van vs LA	Dec. 15	Van, 7-0
Pavel Bure, Van at Dal	Oct. 21	Van, 5-1
Pavel Bure, Van at Col	Dec. 6	Col, 6-4
Valeri Bure, Calg vs Edm	Feb. 7	Calg, 4-2
Geoff Courtnall, St.L at Calg	Mar. 22	Calg, 5-3
Alexandre Daigle, Phi vs Det	Mar. 14	Phi, 6-1
Vincent Damphousse, Mon at LA	Nov. 8	Mon, 4-1
Vincent Damphousse, Mon at TB	Mar. 28	Mon, 8-2
Jason Dawe, Buf vs Edm	Nov. 10	Buf, 4-2
Ron Francis, Pit vs NYI	Dec. 29	Pit, 5-1
Dave Gagner, Fla at Pit	Oct. 4	Fla, 5-3
Wayne Gretzky, NYR at Van	Oct. 11	NYR, 6-3
Steve Heinze, Bos at Ott	Apr. 7	Bos, 4-2
Steve Heinze, Bos vs Car	Dec. 6	Bos, 4-1
Brett Hull, St.L vs LA	Oct. 9	St.L, 3-2
Valeri Kamensky, Col at Pit	Jan. 3	Col, 5-4
Sami Kapanen, Car vs Edm	Mar. 15	Car, 4-1
Sami Kapanen, Car at Edm	Nov. 12	Car, 6-4
Paul Kariya, Ana vs Fla	Jan. 21	Ana, 8-3
Derek King, Tor at St.L	Dec. 4	St.L, 4-3
John LeClair, Phi at Mon	Oct. 11	Phi, 6-2
Claude Lemieux, Col at Wash	Nov. 18	Tied, 6-6
Eric Lindros, Phi vs NYI	Dec. 11	Phi, 4-3
Vladimir Malakhov, Mon at Car	Feb. 1	Mon, 6-3
Kirk Maltby, Det at Tor	Dec. 27	Det, 8-1
Shawn McEachern, Ott at Tor	Oct. 22	Ott, 6-2
Marty McInnis, Calg vs Van	Jan. 24	Calg, 5-2
Randy McKay, NJ vs Phi	Mar. 24	NJ, 3-2
Mike Modano, Dal vs Chi	Oct. 10	Dal, 7-0
Glen Murray, LA vs Calg	Apr. 13	LA, 4-2
Joe Nieuwendyk, Dal at Pit	Nov. 5	Dal, 5-2
Adam Oates, Wash at NYI	Oct. 8	Wash, 6-3
Zigmund Palffy, NYI at SJ	Oct. 16	NYI, 5-2
Zigmund Palffy, NYI vs Phi	Jan. 28	NYI, 6-1
Yanic Perreault, LA at Det	Oct. 31	LA, 5-1
Yanic Perreault, LA vs Van	Nov. 11	LA, 8-2
Mark Recchi, Mon at Bos	Oct. 4	Mon, 4-1
Robert Reichel, NYI vs NYR	Nov. 26	NYI, 4-1
Mikael Renberg, TB vs Fla	Mar. 21	TB, 5-1
Gary Roberts, Car vs Tor	Apr. 9	Car, 5-2
Sergei Samsonov*, Bos vs NYI	Apr. 9	Bos, 4-1
Miroslav Satan, Buf at Wash	Mar. 1	Buf, 3-0
Teemu Selanne, Ana vs SJ	Nov. 10	SJ, 6-4
Teemu Selanne, Ana at Ott	Mar. 22	Ana, 5-2
Teemu Selanne, Ana at NYR	Oct. 26	Tied, 3-3
Ray Sheppard, Fla vs Bos	Nov. 26	Fla, 10-5
Cory Stillman, Calg at Det	Oct. 12	Tied, 4-4
Martin Straka, Pit vs Bos	Apr. 18	Pit, 5-2
Jozef Stumpel, LA at Calg	Feb. 3	LA, 6-3
Darryl Sydor, Dal at Car	Jan. 3	Dal, 6-1
Keith Tkachuk, Pho at SJ	Dec. 26	Pho, 4-0
Keith Tkachuk, Pho at Fla	Dec. 1	Pho, 3-2
Keith Tkachuk, Pho vs Ana	Apr. 3	Pho, 6-3
Pat Verbeek, Dal vs Car	Mar. 20	Dal, 6-1
Alexei Yashin, Ott at Col	Jan. 10	Tied, 3-3
Rob Zamuner, TB vs NYR	Nov. 19	TB, 6-3

Game-Winning Goals in Overtime

A total of 219 games were tied after regulation during the 1997-98 regular season, with 54 being resolved in overtime. Teams play one five-minute overtime period during the regular season. (*) indicates rookie.

	Date	Time	Score
Ted Donato, Bos at Pho	Oct. 8	2:09	Bos, 3-2
Brett Hull, St.L vs LA	Oct. 9	3:16	St.L. 3-2
Eric Lindros, Phi at SJ	Oct. 13	1:49	Phi, 3-2
Dave Reid, Dal vs Calg	Oct. 14	1:17	Dal, 5-4
Michael Nylander, Calg vs Col	Oct. 17	4:40	Calg, 6-5
Todd Marchant, Edm at LA	Oct. 19	3:05	Edm, 3-2
Petr Sykora, NJ vs Mon	Oct. 23	4:43	NJ, 2-1
Kevin Hatcher, Pit at Van	Oct. 25	0:41	Pit, 3-2
Jason Dawe, Buf at Car	Oct. 31	3:21	Buf, 3-2
Rob Brown, Pit vs Van	Nov. 1	3:52	Pit, 7-6
Dixon Ward, Buf vs Fla	Nov. 1	1:14	Buf, 4-3
Scott Young, Ana at Calg	Nov. 7	3:34	Ana, 4-3
Valeri Bure, Mon at Ana	Nov. 12	4:07	Mon, 4-3
Jaromir Jagr, Pit vs NYR	Nov. 22	0:25	Pit, 4-3
Ed Jovanovski, Fla at NJ	Nov. 22	4:08	Fla, 2-1
Greg Johnson, Chi at Van	Nov. 22	1:22	Chi, 5-4
Luc Robitaille, LA at Col	Nov. 23	2:43	LA, 2-1
Sandy McCarthy, Calg vs Ana	Nov. 29	1:36	Calg, 3-2
German Titov, Calg vs SJ	Dec. 1	1:22	Calg, 3-2
Joe Juneau, Wash at NYR	Dec. 2	3:45	Wash, 3-2
Jeff Toms, Wash vs Fla	Dec. 5	3:32	Wash, 3-2
Geoff Courtnall, St.L vs Calg	Dec. 6	4:38	St.L, 4-3
Vincent Damphousse, Mon vs St.L	Dec. 10	0:55	Mon, 4-3
Matthew Barnaby, Buf vs Car	Dec. 12	4:45	Buf, 3-2
Michael Nylander, Calg vs Chi	Dec. 16	3:42	Calg, 4-3
Sergei Zubov, Dal at Edm	Dec. 20	1:07	Dal, 2-1
Chris Phillips*, Ott vs Mon	Dec. 23	3:51	Ott, 4-3
Rob Niedermayer, Fla vs NJ	Jan. 1	1:53	Fla, 2-1
Valeri Kamensky, Col at Pit	Jan. 3	3:04	Col, 5-4
Jere Lehtinen, Dal at NJ	Jan. 5	0:34	Dal, 4-3
Steve Heinze, Bos at Mon	Jan. 7	3:13	Bos, 2-1
Jon Battaglia*, Car at NYI	Jan. 10	1:59	Car, 2-1
Joe Sacco, Ana vs Dal	Jan. 11	3:38	Ana, 2-1
Ray Ferraro, LA vs Ana	Jan. 12	2:04	LA, 3-2
Grant Marshall, Dal at St.L	Jan. 14	0:57	Dal, 2-1
Kelly Miller, Wash at TB	Jan. 21	3:32	Wash, 3-2
Eric Lacroix, Col vs Edm	Jan. 26	1:49	Col, 2-1
Michal Pivonka, Wash at Phi	Jan. 31	2:23	Wash, 3-2
Teemu Selanne, Ana vs Chi	Feb. 1	2:51	Ana, 4-3
Scott Fraser*, Edm at Col	Mar. 2	0:11	Edm, 5-4
Jeff O'Neill, Car at Pho	Mar. 6	2:34	Car, 5-4
Alexandre Daigle, Phi vs Pit	Mar. 8	4:03	Phi, 4-3
Dean McAmmond, Edm at Chi	Mar. 9	4:17	Edm, 4-3
Yanic Perreault, LA vs Ana	Mar. 9	4:19	LA, 4-3
Steve Heinze, Bos vs TB	Mar. 16	1:24	Bos, 4-3
Kevin Stevens, NYR vs Mon	Mar. 18	4:41	NYR, 2-1
Shjon Podein, Phi vs NYR	Mar. 22	4:39	Phi, 5-4
Alexei Yashin, Ott at NYR	Mar. 25	3:11	Ott, 3-2
Patrice Brisebois, Mon at TB	Mar. 25	2:34	Mon, 2-1
Bill Lindsay, Fla at Bos	Mar. 28	3:14	Fla, 3-2
Sylvain Cote, Tor vs NYI	Mar. 28	4:56	Tor, 4-3
Daniel Goneau, NYR at Chi	Apr. 5	1:24	NYR, 2-1
Jamie Langenbrunner, Dal vs Wash	Apr. 8	3:28	Dal, 2-1
Scott Stevens, NJ vs Buf	Apr. 15	4:38	NJ, 5-4

Pittsburgh Penguins
Jaromir Jagr
Scoring

Detroit Red Wings
Nicklas Lidstrom
Defensemen Scoring

Dallas Stars
Ed Belfour
Goals Against Avg.

Buffalo Sabres
Dominik Hasek
Save Pct., ShO

NHL Regular Season Individual Leaders

(*) indicates rookie eligible for Calder Trophy.

Scoring

	Pos	Gm	G	A	Pts	+/-	PM	PP	SH	GW	GT	Shots	Pct
Jaromir Jagr, Pittsburgh	R	77	35	67	**102**	17	64	7	0	8	2	262	13.4
Peter Forsberg, Colorado	C	72	25	66	**91**	6	94	7	3	7	1	202	12.4
Pavel Bure, Vancouver	R	82	51	39	**90**	5	48	13	6	4	1	329	15.5
Wayne Gretzky, NY Rangers	C	82	23	67	**90**	-11	28	6	0	4	2	201	11.4
John LeClair, Philadelphia	L	82	51	36	**87**	30	32	16	0	9	1	303	16.8
Zigmund Palffy, NY Islanders	R	82	45	42	**87**	-2	34	17	2	5	1	277	16.2
Ron Francis, Pittsburgh	C	81	25	62	**87**	12	20	7	0	5	2	189	13.2
Teemu Selanne, Anaheim	R	73	52	34	**86**	12	30	10	1	10	3	268	19.4
Jason Allison, Boston	C	81	33	50	**83**	33	60	5	0	8	2	158	20.9
Jozef Stumpel, Los Angeles	C	77	21	58	**79**	17	53	4	0	2	1	162	13.0
Peter Bondra, Washington	R	76	52	26	**78**	14	44	11	5	13	2	284	18.3
Theoren Fleury, Calgary	R	82	27	51	**78**	0	197	3	2	4	1	282	9.6
Adam Oates, Washington	C	82	18	58	**76**	6	36	3	2	3	0	121	14.9
Rod Brind'Amour, Philadelphia	L	82	36	38	**74**	-2	54	10	2	8	0	205	17.6
Mats Sundin, Toronto	C	82	33	41	**74**	-3	49	9	1	5	1	219	15.1
Mark Recchi, Montreal	R	82	32	42	**74**	11	51	9	1	6	0	216	14.8
Tony Amonte, Chicago	R	82	31	42	**73**	21	66	7	3	5	0	296	10.5
Alexei Yashin, Ottawa	C	82	33	39	**72**	6	24	5	0	6	0	291	11.3
Brett Hull, St. Louis	R	66	27	45	**72**	-1	26	10	0	6	0	211	12.8
Eric Lindros, Philadelphia	C	63	30	41	**71**	14	134	10	1	4	0	202	14.9

Goals

Selanne, Ana	52
Bondra, Wash	52
LeClair, Phi	51
Bure, Van	51
Palffy, NYI	45
Tkachuk, Pho	40
Nieuwendyk, Dal	39
Brind'Amour, Phi	36
Jagr, Pit	35
Whitney, Edm-Fla	33
Allison, Bos	33
Sundin, Tor	33
Yashin, Ott	33

Assists

Jagr, Pit	67
Gretzky, NYR	67
Forsberg, Col	66
Francis, Pit	62
Stumpel, LA	58
Oates, Wash	58
Fleury, Calg	51
Allison, Bos	50
Zubov, Dal	47
Turgeon, St.L	46
Hull, St.L	45
Yzerman, Det	45
Weight, Edm	44
Ronning, Pho	44

Defensemen Points

Lidstrom, Det	59
Niedermayer, NJ	57
Zubov, Dal	57
Duchesne, St.L	56
Murphy, Det	52
Ozolinsh, Col	51
Numminen, Pho	51
Blake, LA	50
Leetch, NYR	50
MacInnis, St.L	49
Hatcher, Pit	48
Bourque, Bos	48

Three tied with 46.

Rookie Points

Samsonov, Bos	47
Johnson, Tor	47
Elias, NJ	37
Marleau, SJ	32
Sturm, SJ	30
Ohlund, Van	30
Morris, Calg	29
Axelsson, Bos	27
Cullen, Ana	27
Zednik, Wash	26
Morozov, Pit	26
Arvedson, Ott	26

Plus/Minus

Pronger, St.L	+47
Murphy, Det	+35
Allison, Bos	+33
McKay, NJ	+30
LeClair, Phi	+30
Zubrus, Phi	+29
Shannon, Buf	+26
Modano, Dal	+25
Kristich, Bos	+25
Numminen, Pho	+25
Holik, NJ	+23

Penalty Minutes

Brashear, Van	372
Domi, Tor	365
Oliwa*, NJ	295
Laus, Fla	293
Pilon, NYI	291
Barnaby, Buf	289
Lambert, Ott	250
M. Johnson, LA	249
McCarthy, Calg-TB	241
Ray, Buf	234
Chase, St.L	231

Power Play Goals

Palffy, NYI	17
LeClair, Phi	16
Shanahan, Det	15
Barnes, Pit	15
Corson, Mon	14
Nieuwendyk, Dal	14
Hatcher, Pit	13
Khristich, Bos	13
Bure, Van	13
Sakic, Col	12
Whitney, Edm-Fla	12

Short-Handed Goals

Friesen, SJ	6
Bure, Van	6
Modano, Dal	5
Peca, Buf	5
Bondra, Wash	5
Corkum, Pho	5

Seven tied with four each.

Goaltending

(Minimum 26 games)

	Gm	Min	GAA	GA	Shots	Sv%	EN	ShO	Record	—Offense— G	A	Pts	PM
Ed Belfour, Dallas	61	3581	**1.88**	112	1335	.916	1	9	37-12-10	0	0	0	18
Martin Brodeur, New Jersey	70	4128	**1.89**	130	1569	.917	4	10	43-17-8	0	3	3	10
Tom Barrasso, Pittsburgh	63	3542	**2.07**	122	1556	.922	8	7	31-14-13	0	2	2	14
Dominik Hasek, Buffalo	72	4220	**2.09**	147	2149	.932	3	13	33-23-13	0	2	2	12
Ron Hextall, Philadelphia	46	2688	**2.17**	97	1089	.911	2	4	21-17-7	0	0	0	10
Trevor Kidd, Carolina	47	2685	**2.17**	97	1237	.922	7	3	21-21-3	0	0	0	2
Jamie McLennan, St.Louis	30	1658	**2.17**	60	618	.903	1	2	16-8-2	0	0	0	4
Olaf Kolzig, Washington	64	3788	**2.20**	139	1729	.920	5	5	33-18-10	0	1	1	12
Jeff Hackett, Chicago	58	3441	**2.20**	126	1520	.917	3	8	21-25-11	0	0	0	8
Chris Osgood, Detroit	64	3807	**2.21**	140	1605	.913	5	6	33-20-11	0	0	0	31
Byron Dafoe, Boston	65	3693	**2.24**	138	1602	.914	8	6	30-25-9	0	3	3	2
Ron Tugnutt, Ottawa	42	2236	**2.25**	84	882	.905	6	3	15-14-8	0	0	0	0
Damian Rhodes, Ottawa	50	2743	**2.34**	107	1148	.907	3	5	19-19-7	0	1	1	0
Patrick Roy, Colorado	65	3835	**2.39**	153	1825	.916	5	4	31-19-13	0	3	3	39
Mike Vernon, San Jose	62	3564	**2.46**	146	1401	.896	2	5	30-22-8	0	2	2	24

Wins

Brodeur, NJ	43
Belfour, Dal	37
Kolzig, Wash	33
Osgood, Det	33
Hasek, Buf	33
Barrasso, Pit	31
Roy, Col	31
Vernon, SJ	30
Dafoe, Bos	30
Khabibulin, Pho	30

Shutouts

Hasek, Buf	13
Brodeur, NJ	10
Belfour, Dal	9
Hackett, Chi	8
Joseph, Edm	8
Barrasso, Pit	7
Dafoe, Bos	6
Osgood, Det	6
Four tied with 5 each.	

Save Pct.

Hasek, Buf	.932
Barrasso, Pit	.922
Kidd, Car	.922
Kolzig, Wash	.920
Brodeur, NJ	.917
Hackett, Chi	.917
Roy, Col	.916
Belfour, Dal	.916
Dafoe, Bos	.914
Osgood, Det	.913

Losses

Potvin, Tor	33
Richter, NYR	31
Joseph, Edm	31
Fitzpatrick, TB-Fla	31
Vanbiesbrouck, Fla	29
Salo, NYI	29
Khabibulin, Pho	28
Dafoe, Bos	25
Hackett, Chi	25
Fiset, LA	25

Team Goaltending

WESTERN	GAA	Mins	GA	Shots	Sv%	EN	SO
Dallas	**2.01**	4986	167	1870	.911	4	10
Detroit	**2.35**	4995	196	2118	.907	6	9
Chicago	**2.39**	4999	199	2191	.909	7	10
Colorado	**2.45**	5017	205	2420	.915	7	5
St. Louis	**2.46**	4970	204	1979	.897	6	5
San Jose	**2.61**	4973	216	2020	.893	6	7
Edmonton	**2.70**	4980	224	2313	.903	8	8
Los Angeles	**2.71**	4990	225	2481	.909	4	4
Phoenix	**2.73**	4985	227	2222	.898	5	5
Toronto	**2.86**	4970	237	2352	.899	8	6
Calgary	**3.01**	5016	252	2276	.889	6	0
Anaheim	**3.13**	5007	261	2492	.895	9	4
Vancouver	**3.28**	4996	273	2479	.890	5	3

EASTERN	GAA	Mins	GA	Shots	Sv%	EN	SO
New Jersey	**2.00**	4991	166	1943	.915	4	11
Buffalo	**2.24**	5019	187	2560	.927	3	13
Pittsburgh	**2.25**	5022	188	2202	.915	12	7
Philadelphia	**2.32**	4988	193	2084	.907	2	6
Boston	**2.33**	4995	194	2161	.910	8	9
Ottawa	**2.40**	5002	200	2039	.902	9	8
Washington	**2.43**	4997	202	2292	.912	8	5
Montreal	**2.49**	5009	208	2135	.903	2	5
Carolina	**2.64**	4973	219	2266	.903	10	4
NY Islanders	**2.71**	4982	225	2358	.905	10	8
NY Rangers	**2.76**	5028	231	2299	.900	7	0
Florida	**3.07**	5009	256	2362	.892	5	5
Tampa Bay	**3.24**	4978	269	2377	.887	14	3

Power Play/Penalty Killing

Power play and penalty killing conversions. Power play: No— number of opportunities; GF— goals for; Pct— percentage. Penalty killing: No— number of times shorthanded; GA— goals against; Pct— percentage of penalties killed; SH— shorthanded goals for.

	—Power Play—			—Penalty Killing—			
WESTERN	No	GF	Pct	No	GA	Pct	SH
Dallas	385	77	**20.0**	351	42	88.0	11
Detroit	381	67	**17.6**	376	51	86.4	8
Colorado	425	74	**17.4**	409	53	87.0	8
St. Louis	368	62	**16.8**	367	49	86.6	12
Edmonton	483	77	**15.9**	406	66	83.7	10
Phoenix	384	57	**14.8**	408	66	83.8	10
Los Angeles	366	52	**14.2**	399	63	84.2	10
San Jose	400	54	**13.5**	398	59	85.2	10
Chicago	364	47	**12.9**	382	58	84.8	13
Vancouver	373	48	**12.9**	432	77	82.2	19
Calgary	356	43	**12.1**	430	69	84.0	18
Anaheim	392	46	**11.7**	396	72	81.8	9
Toronto	359	41	**11.4**	372	50	86.6	5

	—Power Play—			—Penalty Killing—			
EASTERN	No	GF	Pct	No	GA	Pct	SH
New Jersey	333	63	**18.9**	309	41	86.7	4
Montreal	372	68	**18.3**	401	62	84.5	13
Philadelphia	399	71	**17.8**	382	51	86.6	7
NY Rangers	351	62	**17.7**	377	55	85.4	0
Boston	359	62	**17.3**	285	44	84.6	5
NY Islanders	364	61	**16.8**	384	54	85.9	11
Pittsburgh	407	67	**16.5**	338	46	86.4	11
Washington	350	55	**15.7**	362	39	89.2	14
Florida	409	55	**13.4**	403	82	79.7	12
Carolina	378	50	**13.2**	391	58	85.2	8
Buffalo	396	51	**12.9**	413	65	84.3	15
Ottawa	375	48	**12.8**	303	47	84.5	6
Tampa Bay	353	33	**9.3**	410	72	82.4	11

Team by Team Statistics

High scorers and goaltenders with at least ten games played. Players who competed for more than one team during the regular season are listed with their final club; (*) indicates rookies eligible for Calder Trophy.

Mighty Ducks of Anaheim

Top Scorers	Gm	G	A	Pts	+/-	PM	PP
Teemu Selanne	73	52	34	86	12	30	10
Steve Rucchin	72	17	36	53	8	13	8
Travis Green	76	19	23	42	-29	82	9
NYI	54	14	12	26	-19	66	8
ANA	22	5	11	16	-10	16	1
Scott Young	73	13	20	33	-13	22	4
Paul Kariya	22	17	14	31	12	23	3
Matt Cullen*	61	6	21	27	-4	23	2
Josef Marha*	23	9	9	18	4	4	3
COL	11	2	5	7	0	4	0
ANA	12	7	4	11	4	0	3
Tomas Sandstrom	77	9	8	17	-25	64	2
Ted Drury	73	6	10	16	-10	82	0
Ruslan Salei	66	5	10	15	7	70	1
David Karpa	78	1	11	12	-3	217	0
Frank Banham*	20	9	2	11	-6	12	1
Kevin Todd	27	4	7	11	-5	12	3
Jamie Pushor	64	2	7	9	3	81	0
DET	54	2	5	7	2	71	0
ANA	10	0	2	2	1	10	0
Jeff Nielsen*	32	4	5	9	-1	16	0
Jason Marshall	72	3	6	9	-8	189	1

Acquired: C Green, D Doug Houda and RW Tony Tuzzolino from NYI for D J.J. Daigneault, RW Joe Sacco and C Mark Janssens (Feb. 6); C Marha from Col. for LW Warren Rychel and a conditional '99 pick (Mar. 24); D Pushor and '98 fourth-round pick from Det. for D Dmitri Mironov (Mar. 24).

Goalies (10 Gm)	Gm	Min	GAA	Record	SV%
Guy Hebert	46	2660	2.93	13-24-6	.903
Mikhail Shtalenkov	40	2049	3.22	13-18-5	.893
ANAHEIM	82	5007	3.13	26-43-13	.895

Shutouts: Hebert (3), Shtalenkov (1). **Assists:** Hebert and Shtalenkov (1). **PM:** Hebert (4).

Boston Bruins

Top Scorers	Gm	G	A	Pts	+/-	PM	PP
Jason Allison	81	33	50	83	33	60	5
Dmitri Khristich	82	29	37	66	25	42	13
Ray Bourque	82	13	35	48	2	80	9
Sergei Samsonov*	81	22	25	47	9	8	7
Steve Heinze	61	26	20	46	8	54	9
Anson Carter	78	16	27	43	7	31	6
Ted Donato	79	16	23	39	6	54	3
Tim Taylor	79	20	11	31	-16	57	1
Rob Dimaio	79	10	17	27	-13	82	0
P.J. Axelsson*	82	8	19	27	-14	38	2
Kyle McLaren	66	5	20	25	13	56	2
Grant Ledyard	71	4	20	24	-4	20	2
VAN	49	2	13	15	-2	14	1
BOS	22	2	7	9	-2	6	1
Dave Ellett	82	3	20	23	3	67	2
Mike Sullivan	77	5	13	18	-1	34	0
Don Sweeney	59	1	15	16	12	24	0
Darren Van Impe	69	3	11	14	-6	40	2
ANA	19	1	3	4	-10	4	0
BOS	50	2	8	10	4	36	2
Joe Thornton*	55	3	4	7	-6	19	0
Hal Gill*	68	2	4	6	4	47	0
Landon Wilson	28	1	5	6	3	7	0

Claimed: D Van Impe off waivers from Ana (Nov. 26); D Ledyard from Van. for '98 eighth-round pick (Mar. 3).

Goalies (10 Gm)	Gm	Min	GAA	Record	SV%
Rob Tallas	14	788	1.83	6-3-3	.926
Byron Dafoe	65	3693	2.24	30-25-9	.914
Jim Carey	10	496	2.90	3-2-1	.893
BOSTON	82	4995	2.33	39-30-13	.910

Shutouts: Dafoe (6), Carey (2) and Tallas (1). **Assists:** Dafoe (3). **PM:** Dafoe (2).

Buffalo Sabres

Top Scorers	Gm	G	A	Pts	+/-	PM	PP
Miroslav Satan	79	22	24	46	2	34	9
Alexei Zhitnik	78	15	30	45	19	102	2
Donald Audette	75	24	20	44	10	59	10
Michael Peca	61	18	22	40	12	57	6
Brian Holzinger	69	14	21	35	-2	36	4
Jason Woolley	71	9	26	35	8	35	3
Derek Plante	72	13	21	34	8	26	5
Michal Grosek	67	10	20	30	9	60	2
Geoff Sanderson	75	11	18	29	1	38	2
CAR	40	7	10	17	-4	14	2
VAN	9	0	3	3	-1	4	0
BUF	26	4	5	9	6	20	0
Matthew Barnaby	72	5	20	25	8	289	0
Curtis Brown	63	12	12	24	11	34	1
Dixon Ward	71	10	13	23	9	42	0
Darryl Shannon	76	3	19	22	26	56	1
Richard Smehlik	72	3	17	20	11	62	0
Jay McKee	56	1	13	14	-1	42	0
Wayne Primeau	69	6	6	12	9	87	2
Vaclav Varada*	27	5	6	11	0	15	0
Randy Burridge	30	4	6	10	0	0	1
Paul Kruse	74	7	2	9	-11	187	0
NYI	62	6	1	7	-12	138	0
BUF	12	1	1	2	1	49	0

Acquired: LW Sanderson from Van. for LW Brad May and '97 third-round pick (Feb. 4); LW Kruse and D Jason Holland from NYI for RW Jason Dawe (Mar. 24).

Goalies (10 Gms)	Gm	Min	GAA	Record	Sv%
Dominik Hasek	72	4220	2.09	33-23-13	.932
Steve Shields	16	785	2.83	3-6-4	.909
BUFFALO	82	5019	2.24	36-29-17	.927

Shutouts: Hasek (13). **Assists:** Hasek (2). **PM:** Hasek (12), Shields (17).

Calgary Flames

Top Scorers	Gm	G	A	Pts	+/-	PM	PP
Theoren Fleury	82	27	51	78	0	197	3
Cory Stillman	72	27	22	49	-9	40	9
Marty McInnis	75	19	25	44	1	34	5
Andrew Cassels	81	17	27	44	-7	32	6
German Titov	68	18	22	40	-1	38	6
Valeri Bure	66	12	26	38	-5	35	2
MON	50	7	22	29	-5	33	2
CALG	16	5	4	9	0	2	0
Michael Nylander	65	13	23	36	10	24	0
Jarome Iginla	70	13	19	32	-10	29	0
Derek Morris*	82	9	20	29	1	88	5
Cale Hulse	79	5	22	27	1	169	1
Jason Wiemer	79	12	10	22	-10	160	3
TB	67	8	9	17	-9	132	2
CALG	12	4	1	5	-1	28	1
Tommy Albelin	69	2	17	19	9	32	1
James Patrick	60	6	11	17	-2	26	1
Hnat Domenichelli*	31	9	7	16	4	6	1
Jim Dowd	48	6	8	14	10	12	0
Joel Bouchard	44	5	7	12	0	57	0
Jamie Allison*	43	3	8	11	3	104	0
Ed Ward	64	4	5	9	-1	122	0

Acquired: RW Bure and future considerations from Mon. for D Zarley Zalapski and LW Jonas Hoglund (Feb. 1); LW Wiemer from TB for RW Sandy McCarthy and '98 third round pick and fifth-round picks (Mar. 24).

Goalies (10 Gm)	Gm	Min	GAA	Record	SV%
Rick Tabaracci	42	2419	2.88	13-22-6	.893
Dwayne Roloson	39	2205	2.99	11-16-8	.890
TOTAL	82	5016	3.01	26-41-15	.889

Shutouts: none. **Assists:** Roloson (4), Tabaracci (1). **PM:** Tabaracci (14), Roloson (10).

Carolina Hurricanes

Top Scorers	Gm	G	A	Pts	+/-	PM	PP
Sami Kapanen	81	26	37	63	9	16	4
Keith Primeau	81	26	37	63	19	110	7
Gary Roberts	61	20	29	49	3	103	4
Nelson Emerson	81	21	24	45	-17	50	6
Jeff O'Neill	74	19	20	39	-8	67	7
Ray Sheppard	71	18	19	37	-11	23	7
FLA	61	14	17	31	-13	21	5
CAR	10	4	2	6	2	2	2
Robert Kron	81	16	20	36	-8	12	4
Martin Gelinas	64	16	18	34	-5	40	3
VAN	24	4	4	8	-6	10	1
CAR	40	12	14	26	1	30	2
Steve Chiasson	66	7	27	34	-2	65	6
Glen Wesley	82	6	19	25	7	36	1
Kevin Dineen	54	7	16	23	-7	105	0
Paul Ranheim	73	5	9	14	-11	28	0
Curtis Leschyshyn	73	2	10	12	-2	45	1
Adam Burt	76	1	11	12	-6	106	0
Steve Leach	45	4	5	9	-19	42	1
Kent Manderville	77	4	4	8	-6	31	0
Kevin Haller	65	3	5	8	-5	94	0
Stu Grimson	82	3	4	7	0	204	0
Sean Hill	55	1	6	7	-5	54	0
OTT	13	1	1	2	-3	6	0
CAR	42	0	5	5	-2	48	0

Acquired: D Hill from Ott. for RW Chris Murray (Nov. 18); LW Gelinas and G Kirk McLean from Van. for G Sean Burke, D Enrico Ciccone and LW Geoff Sanderson (Jan. 2); RW Sheppard from Fla. for G McLean (Mar. 24).

Goalies (10 Gm)	Gm	Min	GAA	Record	Sv%
Trevor Kidd	47	2685	2.17	21-21-3	.922
CAROLINA	82	4973	2.64	33-41-8	.903

Shutouts: Kidd (3). **Assists:** none. **PM:** Kidd (2).

Chicago Blackhawks

Top Scorers	Gm	G	A	Pts	+/-	PM	PP
Tony Amonte	82	31	42	73	21	66	7
Alexei Zhamnov	70	21	28	49	16	61	6
Eric Daze	80	31	11	42	4	22	10
Chris Chelios	81	3	39	42	-7	151	1
Gary Suter	73	14	28	42	1	74	5
Greg Johnson	74	12	22	34	-2	40	4
PIT	5	1	0	1	0	2	0
CHI	69	11	22	33	-2	38	4
Jeff Shantz	61	11	20	31	0	36	1
Sergei Krivokrasov	58	10	13	23	-1	33	1
Eric Weinrich	82	2	21	23	10	106	0
Ethan Moreau	54	9	9	18	0	73	2
Steve Dubinsky	82	5	13	18	-6	57	0
James Black	52	10	5	15	-8	8	2
Jean-Yves Leroux*	66	6	7	13	-2	55	0
Chad Kilger	32	3	9	12	0	10	2
PHO	10	0	1	1	-2	4	0
CHI	22	3	8	11	2	6	2
Jayson More	58	5	7	12	7	61	0
PHO	41	5	5	10	0	53	0
CHI	17	0	2	2	7	8	0
Dimitri Nabokov*	25	7	4	11	-1	10	3
Kevin Miller	37	4	7	11	-4	8	0
Christian LaFlamme*	72	0	11	11	14	59	0

Acquired: C Johnson from Pit. for D Tuomas Gronman (Oct. 22); C Kilger and D More from Pho. for D Keith Carney and RW Jim Cummins (Mar. 4).

Goalies (10 Gm)	Gm	Min	GAA	Record	SV%
Jeff Hackett	58	3441	2.20	21-25-11	.917
Chris Terreri	21	1222	2.41	8-10-2	.906
CHICAGO	82	4999	2.39	30-39-13	.909

Shutouts: Hackett (8), Terreri (2). **Assists:** Terreri (1). **PM:** Hackett (8), Terreri (2).

Colorado Avalanche

Top Scorers	Gm	G	A	Pts	+/-	PM	PP
Peter Forsberg	72	25	66	91	6	94	7
Valeri Kamensky	75	26	40	66	-2	60	8
Joe Sakic	64	27	36	63	0	50	12
Claude Lemieux	78	26	27	53	-7	115	11
Sandis Ozolinsh	66	13	38	51	-12	65	9
Adam Deadmarsh	73	22	21	43	0	125	10
Eric Lacroix	82	16	15	31	0	84	5
Uwe Krupp	78	9	22	31	21	38	5
Rene Corbet	68	16	12	28	8	133	4
Stephane Yelle	81	7	15	22	-10	48	0
Jari Kurri	70	5	17	22	6	12	2
Tom Fitzgerald	80	12	6	18	-4	79	0
FLA	69	10	5	15	-4	57	0
COL	11	2	1	3	0	22	0
Shean Donovan	67	8	10	18	6	70	0
SJ	20	3	3	6	3	22	0
COL	47	5	7	12	3	48	0
Adam Foote	77	3	14	17	-3	124	0
Eric Messier*	62	4	12	16	4	20	0
Jon Klemm	67	6	8	14	-3	30	0
Alexei Gusarov	72	4	10	14	9	42	0
Jeff Odgers	68	5	8	13	5	213	0
Warren Rychel	71	5	6	11	-11	221	1
ANA	63	5	6	11	-10	198	1
COL	8	0	0	0	-1	23	0

Acquired: RW Donovan and '98 first-round pick from SJ for C Mike Ricci and '98 second-round pick (Nov. 20); RW Fitzgerald from Fla. for LW Mark Parrish and '98 third-round pick (Mar. 24); LW Rychel and a conditional '99 pick from Ana. for C Josef Marha (Mar. 24). **Signed:** RW Odgers (Oct. 24).

Goalies (10 Gm)	Gm	Min	GAA	Record	SV%
Craig Billington	23	1162	2.32	8-7-4	.923
Patrick Roy	65	3835	2.39	31-19-13	.916
COLORADO	82	5017	2.45	39-26-17	.915

Shutouts: Roy (4), Billington (1). **Assists:** Roy (3). **PM:** Roy (39), Billington (2).

Dallas Stars

Top Scorers	Gm	G	A	Pts	+/-	PM	PP
Joe Nieuwendyk	73	39	30	69	16	30	14
Mike Modano	52	21	38	59	25	32	7
Sergei Zubov	73	10	47	57	16	16	5
Pat Verbeek	82	31	26	57	15	170	9
Jamie Langenbrunner	81	23	29	52	9	61	8
Darryl Sydor	79	11	35	46	17	51	4
Jere Lehtinen	72	23	19	42	19	20	7
Greg Adams	49	14	18	32	11	20	7
Derian Hatcher	70	6	25	31	9	132	3
Guy Carbonneau	77	7	17	24	3	40	0
Shawn Chambers	57	2	22	24	11	26	1
Mike Keane	83	10	13	23	-12	52	2
NYR	70	8	10	18	-12	47	2
DAL	13	2	3	5	0	5	0
Benoit Hogue	53	6	16	22	7	35	3
Grant Marshall	72	9	10	19	-2	96	3
Dave Reid	65	6	12	18	-15	14	3
Richard Matvichuk	74	3	15	18	7	63	0
Brian Skrudland	72	7	6	13	-6	49	0
NYR	59	5	6	11	-4	39	0
DAL	13	2	0	2	-2	10	0
Bob Bassen	58	3	4	7	-4	57	0
Craig Ludwig	80	0	7	7	21	131	0

Acquired: RW Keane, C Skrudland and '98 or '99 pick from NYR for LW Bob Errey, RW Todd Harvey and '98 fourth-round pick (Mar. 24).

Goalies (10 Gm)	Gm	Min	GAA	Record	SV%
Ed Belfour	61	3581	1.88	37-12-10	.916
Roman Turek	23	1324	2.22	11-10-1	.901
DALLAS	82	4986	2.01	49-22-11	.911

Shutouts: Belfour (9), Turek (1). **Assists:** none. **PM:** Belfour (18), Turek (2).

Detroit Red Wings

Top Scorers	Gm	G	A	Pts	+/-	PM	PP
Steve Yzerman	75	24	45	69	3	46	6
Nicklas Lidstrom	80	17	42	59	22	18	7
Brendan Shanahan	75	28	29	57	6	154	15
Vyacheslav Kozlov	80	25	27	52	14	46	6
Larry Murphy	82	11	41	52	35	37	2
Igor Larionov	69	8	39	47	14	40	3
Dmitri Mironov	77	8	35	43	-7	119	3
ANA	66	6	30	36	-7	115	2
DET	11	2	5	7	0	4	1
Doug Brown	80	19	23	42	17	12	6
Darren McCarty	71	15	22	37	0	157	5
Martin Lapointe	79	15	19	34	0	106	4
Brent Gilchrist	61	13	14	27	4	40	5
Kirk Maltby	65	14	9	23	11	89	2
Kris Draper	64	13	10	23	5	45	1
Tomas Holmstrom	57	5	17	22	6	44	1
Anders Eriksson*	66	7	14	21	21	32	1
Sergei Fedorov	21	6	11	17	10	25	2
Mathieu Dandenault	68	5	12	17	5	43	0
Viacheslav Fetisov	58	2	12	14	4	72	0
Mike Knuble*	53	7	6	13	2	16	0
Bob Rouse	71	1	11	12	-9	57	0
Joe Kocur	63	6	5	11	7	92	0
Aaron Ward	52	5	5	10	-1	47	0

Acquired: D Mironov from Ana for D Jamie Pushor and '98 fourth-round pick (Mar. 24).

Goalies (10 Gm)	Gm	Min	GAA	Record	Sv%
Chris Osgood	64	3807	2.21	33-20-11	.913
Kevin Hodson*	21	988	2.67	9-3-3	.901
DETROIT	82	4995	2.35	44-23-15	.907

Shutouts: Osgood (6), Hodson (2). Osgood and Hodson also shared a shutout. **Assists:** none. **PM:** Osgood (31), Hodson (2).

Edmonton Oilers

Top Scorers	Gm	G	A	Pts	+/-	PM	PP
Doug Weight	79	26	44	70	1	69	9
Dean McAmmond	77	19	31	50	9	46	8
Boris Mironov	81	16	30	46	-8	100	10
Janne Niinimaa	77	4	39	43	13	62	3
PHI	66	3	31	34	6	56	2
EDM	11	1	8	9	7	6	1
Roman Hamrlik	78	9	32	41	-15	70	5
TB	37	3	12	15	-18	22	1
EDM	41	6	20	26	3	48	4
Bill Guerin	59	18	21	39	1	93	9
NJ	19	5	5	10	0	13	1
EDM	40	13	16	29	1	80	8
Todd Marchant	76	14	21	35	9	71	2
Ryan Smyth	65	20	13	33	-24	44	10
Tony Hrkac	49	13	14	27	3	10	7
DAL	13	5	3	8	0	0	3
EDM	36	8	11	19	3	10	4
Mats Lindgren	82	13	13	26	0	42	1
Scott Fraser*	29	12	11	23	6	6	6
Andrei Kovalenko	59	6	17	23	-14	28	1
Kelly Buchberger	81	6	17	23	-10	122	1
Valeri Zelepukin	68	4	18	22	-2	89	0
NJ	35	2	8	10	0	32	0
EDM	33	2	10	12	-2	57	0
Rem Murray	61	9	9	18	-9	39	2
Mike Grier	66	9	6	15	-3	73	1

Acquired: D Hamrlik and C Paul Comrie from TB for D Bryan Marchment, C Jason Bonsignore and C Steve Kelly (Dec. 30); RW Guerin and LW Zelepukin from NJ for C Jason Arnott and D Bryan Muir (Jan. 4); D Niinimaa from Phi. for D Dan McGillis and '98 second-round pick (Mar. 24). **Claimed:** C Hrkac off waivers from Dal. (Jan. 6).

Goalies (10 Gm)	Gm	Min	GAA	Record	Sv%
Bob Essensa	16	825	2.55	6-6-1	.913
Curtis Joseph	71	4132	2.63	29-31-9	.905
EDMONTON	82	4980	2.70	35-37-10	.903

Shutouts: Joseph (8). **Assists:** Joseph (2). **PM:** Joseph (4).

Florida Panthers

Top Scorers	Gm	G	A	Pts	+/-	PM	PP
Ray Whitney	77	33	32	65	9	28	12
EDM	9	1	3	4	-1	0	0
FLA	68	32	29	61	10	28	12
Dave Gagner	78	20	28	48	-21	55	5
Robert Svehla	79	9	34	43	-3	113	3
Scott Mellanby	79	15	24	39	-14	127	6
Radek Dvorak	64	12	24	36	-1	33	2
Dino Ciccarelli	62	16	17	33	-16	70	5
TB	34	11	6	17	-14	42	3
FLA	28	5	11	16	-2	28	2
Viktor Kozlov	64	17	13	30	-3	16	5
SJ	18	5	2	7	-2	2	2
FLA	46	12	11	23	1	14	3
Kirk Muller	70	8	21	29	-14	54	1
Bill Lindsay	82	12	16	28	-2	80	0
Ed Jovanovski	81	9	14	23	-12	158	2
David Nemirovsky	41	9	12	21	-3	8	2
Steve Washburn	58	11	8	19	-6	32	4
Gord Murphy	79	6	11	17	-3	46	3
Jeff Norton	56	4	13	17	-32	44	4
TB	37	4	6	10	-25	26	4
FLA	19	0	7	7	-7	18	0
Rob Niedermayer	33	8	7	15	-9	41	5
Chris Wells	61	5	10	15	4	47	0
Paul Laus	77	0	11	11	-5	293	0

Acquired: LW Kozlov from SJ for '98 first-round pick (Nov. 14); RW Ciccarelli and D Norton from TB for G Mark Fitzpatrick and RW Jody Hull (Jan. 16); G McLean from Car. for RW Ray Sheppard (Mar. 24). **Claimed:** LW Whitney off waivers from Edm. (Nov. 6).

Goalies (10 Gm)	Gm	Min	GAA	Record	Sv%
John Vanbiesbrouck	60	3451	2.87	18-29-11	.899
Kirk McLean	44	2390	3.54	14-21-5	.881
VAN	29	1583	3.68	6-17-4	.879
CAR	8	401	3.29	4-2-0	.878
FLA	7	406	3.25	4-2-1	.894
Kevin Weekes*	11	485	3.96	0-5-1	.870
FLORIDA	82	5009	3.07	24-43-15	.892

Shutouts: Vanbiesbrouck (4), McLean (1 w/Van). **Assists:** Vanbiesbrouck (3), McLean (1 w/Car). **PM:** Vanbiesbrouck (6).

Los Angeles Kings

Top Scorers	Gm	G	A	Pts	+/-	PM	PP
Jozef Stumpel	77	21	58	79	17	53	4
Glen Murray	81	29	31	60	6	54	7
Vladimir Tsyplakov	73	18	34	52	15	18	2
Rob Blake	81	23	27	50	-3	94	11
Yanic Perreault	79	28	20	48	6	32	3
Luc Robitaille	57	16	24	40	5	66	5
Craig Johnson	74	17	21	38	9	42	6
Garry Galley	74	9	28	37	-5	63	7
Sandy Moger	62	11	13	24	4	70	1
Ian Laperriere	77	6	15	21	0	131	0
Russ Courtnall	58	12	6	18	-2	27	1
Sean O'Donnell	80	2	15	17	7	179	0
Philippe Boucher	45	6	10	16	6	49	1
Ray Ferraro	40	6	9	15	-10	42	0
Mattias Norstrom	73	1	12	13	14	90	0
Dan Bylsma	65	3	9	12	9	33	0
Nathan Lafayette	34	5	3	8	2	32	1
Steve McKenna	62	4	4	8	-9	150	1
Doug Zmolek	46	0	8	8	0	111	0
Aki Berg	72	0	8	8	3	61	0
Donald MacLean*	22	5	2	7	-1	4	2

Signed: Free agent RW Courtnall (Nov. 7).

Goalies (10 Gm)	Gm	Min	GAA	Record	Sv%
Jamie Storr*	17	920	2.22	9-5-1	.929
Stephane Fiset	60	3497	2.71	26-25-8	.909
Frederic Chabot	12	554	3.14	3-3-2	.891
LOS ANGELES	82	4990	2.71	38-33-11	.909

Shutouts: Fiset and Storr (2). **Assists:** Fiset (1). **PM:** Fiset (8).

Montreal Canadiens

Top Scorers	Gm	G	A	Pts	+/-	PM	PP
Mark Recchi	82	32	42	74	11	51	9
Vincent Damphousse	76	18	41	59	14	58	2
Saku Koivu	69	14	43	57	8	48	2
Shayne Corson	62	21	34	55	2	108	14
Martin Rucinsky	78	21	32	53	13	84	5
Vladimir Malakhov	74	13	31	44	16	70	8
Brian Savage	64	26	17	43	11	36	8
Patrice Brisebois	79	10	27	37	16	67	5
Dave Manson	81	4	30	34	22	122	2
Benoit Brunet	68	12	20	32	11	61	1
Jonas Hoglund	78	12	13	25	-7	22	4
CALG	50	6	8	14	-9	16	0
MON	28	6	5	11	2	6	4
Marc Bureau	74	13	6	19	0	12	0
Patrick Poulin	78	6	13	19	-4	27	0
TB	44	2	7	9	-3	19	0
MON	34	4	6	10	-1	8	0
Stephane Quintal	71	6	10	16	13	97	0
Scott Thornton	67	6	9	15	0	158	1
Zarley Zalapski	63	3	12	15	-13	63	2
CALG	35	2	7	9	-12	41	2
MON	28	1	5	6	-1	22	0
Sebastien Bordeleau	53	6	8	14	5	36	2

Acquired: LW Poulin, RW Mick Vukota and D Igor Ulanov from TB for RW Stephane Richer, C Darcy Tucker and D David Wilkie (Jan. 15); LW Hoglund and D Zalapski from Calg. for RW Valeri Bure and future cons. (Feb. 1).

Goalies (10 Gm)	Gm	Min	GAA	Record	Sv%
Jocelyn Thibault	47	2652	2.47	19-15-8	.902
Andy Moog	42	2337	2.49	18-17-5	.905
MONTREAL	82	5009	2.49	37-32-13	.903

Shutouts: Moog (3), Thibault (2). **Assists:** Thibault (2). **PM:** Moog (4).

New Jersey Devils

Top Scorers	Gm	G	A	Pts	+/-	PM	PP
Bobby Holik	82	29	36	65	23	100	8
Scott Niedermayer	81	14	43	57	5	27	11
Doug Gilmour	63	13	40	53	10	68	3
Randy McKay	74	24	24	48	30	86	8
Dave Andreychuk	75	14	34	48	19	26	4
Patrik Elias*	74	18	19	37	18	28	5
Petr Sykora	58	16	20	36	0	22	3
Jason Arnott	70	10	23	33	-24	99	4
EDM	35	5	13	18	-16	78	1
NJ	35	5	10	15	-8	21	3
Brian Rolston	76	16	14	30	7	16	0
Denis Pederson	80	15	13	28	-6	97	7
Scott Stevens	80	4	22	26	19	80	1
Steve Thomas	55	14	10	24	4	32	3
Lyle Odelein	79	4	19	23	11	171	1
Doug Bodger	77	9	11	20	-1	57	3
SJ	28	4	6	10	0	32	0
NJ	49	5	5	10	-1	25	3
Bob Carpenter	66	9	9	18	-4	22	0
Sheldon Souray*	60	3	7	10	18	85	0
Brendan Morrison*	11	5	4	9	3	0	0
Kevin Dean	50	1	8	9	12	12	1
Brad Bombardir*	43	1	5	6	11	8	0
Sergei Brylin	18	2	3	5	4	0	0
Krzysztof Oliwa*	73	2	3	5	3	295	0

Acquired: D Bodger and LW Dody Wood from SJ for RW John MacLean and D Ken Sutton (Dec. 7); C Arnott and D Bryan Muir from Edm. for RW Bill Guerin and LW Valeri Zelepukin (Jan. 4).

Goalies (10 Gm)	Gm	Min	GAA	Record	Sv%
Martin Brodeur	70	4128	1.89	43-17-8	.917
Mike Dunham	15	773	2.25	5-5-3	.913
NEW JERSEY	82	4991	2.00	48-23-11	.915

Shutouts: Brodeur (10), Dunham (1). **Assists:** Brodeur (3), Dunham (1). **PM:** Brodeur (10).

New York Islanders

Top Scorers	Gm	G	A	Pts	+/-	PM	PP
Zigmund Palffy	82	45	42	87	-2	34	17
Robert Reichel	82	25	40	65	-11	32	8
Bryan Berard	75	14	32	46	-32	59	8
Bryan Smolinski	81	13	30	43	-16	34	3
Kenny Jonsson	81	14	26	40	-2	58	6
Jason Dawe	81	20	19	39	8	42	4
BUF	68	19	17	36	10	36	4
NYI	13	1	2	3	-2	6	0
Trevor Linden	67	17	21	38	-14	82	5
VAN	42	7	14	21	-13	49	2
NYI	25	10	7	17	-1	33	3
Tom Chorske	82	12	23	35	7	39	1
Sergei Nemchinov	74	10	19	29	3	24	2
Mariusz Czerkawski	68	12	13	25	11	23	2
Joe Sacco	80	11	14	25	0	34	0
ANA	55	8	11	19	-1	24	0
NYI	25	3	3	6	1	10	0
J.J. Daigneault	71	2	21	23	-9	49	1
ANA	53	2	15	17	-10	28	1
NYI	18	0	6	6	1	21	0
Claude Lapointe	78	10	10	20	-9	47	0
Scott Lachance	63	2	11	13	-11	45	1
Mike Hough	74	5	7	12	-4	27	0
Richard Pilon	76	0	7	7	1	291	0

Acquired: C Linden from Van. for D Bryan McCabe, RW Todd Bertuzzi and '98 third-round pick (Feb. 6); C Sacco, D Daigneault and C Mark Janssens from Ana. for C Travis Green, D Doug Houda and RW Tony Tuzzolino (Feb. 6); RW Dawe from Buf. for LW Paul Kruse and D Jason Holland (Mar. 24).

Goalies (10 Gm)	Gm	Min	GAA	Record	Sv%
Wade Flaherty	16	694	1.99	4-4-3	.926
Tommy Salo	62	3461	2.64	23-29-5	.906
Eric Fichaud	17	807	2.97	3-8-3	.905
NY ISLANDERS	82	4982	2.71	30-41-11	.905

Shutouts: Salo (4), Flaherty (3). Flaherty and Salo also shared a shutout. **Assists:** Flaherty and Salo (1). **PM:** Salo (31).

New York Rangers

Top Scorers	Gm	G	A	Pts	+/-	PM	PP
Wayne Gretzky	82	23	67	90	-11	28	6
Pat LaFontaine	67	23	39	62	-16	36	11
Alexei Kovalev	73	23	30	53	-22	44	8
Brian Leetch	76	17	33	50	-36	32	11
Niklas Sundstrom	70	19	28	47	0	24	4
Kevin Stevens	80	14	27	41	-7	130	5
Adam Graves	72	23	12	35	-30	41	10
Tim Sweeney	56	11	18	29	7	26	2
Bruce Driver	75	5	15	20	-3	46	1
Todd Harvey	59	9	10	19	5	104	0
DAL	59	9	10	19	5	104	0
NYR	0	0	0	0	0	0	0
Ulf Samuelsson	73	3	9	12	1	122	0
Bob Errey	71	2	9	11	2	53	0
DAL	59	2	9	11	7	46	0
NYR	12	0	0	0	-5	7	0
Harry York	60	4	6	10	-1	31	0
ST.L	58	4	6	10	0	31	0
NYR	2	0	0	0	-1	0	0
Alexander Karpovtsev	47	3	7	10	-1	38	1
Bill Berg	67	1	9	10	-15	55	0
Jeff Finley	63	1	6	7	-3	55	0

Acquired: RW Harvey, LW Errey and '98 fourth-round pick from Dal. for RW Mike Keane, C Brian Skrudland and '98 or '99 pick (Mar. 24); C York from St.L for C Mike Eastwood (Mar. 24).

Goalies (10 Gm)	Gm	Min	GAA	Record	Sv%
Dan Cloutier*	12	551	2.50	4-5-1	.907
Mike Richter	72	4143	2.66	21-31-15	.903
NY RANGERS	82	5028	2.76	25-39-18	.900

Shutouts: none. **Assists:** Richter (1). **PM:** Cloutier (19), Richter (2).

Ottawa Senators

Top Scorers	Gm	G	A	Pts	+/-	PM	PP
Alexei Yashin	82	33	39	72	6	24	5
Shawn McEachern	81	24	24	48	1	42	8
Daniel Alfredsson	55	17	28	45	7	18	7
Igor Kravchuk	81	8	27	35	-19	8	3
Andreas Dackell	82	15	18	33	-11	24	3
Magnus Arvedson*	61	11	15	26	2	36	0
Vaclav Prospal*	56	6	19	25	-11	21	4
PHI	41	5	13	18	-10	17	4
OTT	15	1	6	7	-1	4	0
Sergei Zholtok	78	10	13	23	-7	16	7
Wade Redden	80	8	14	22	17	27	3
Janne Laukkanen	60	4	17	21	-15	64	2
Denny Lambert	72	9	10	19	4	250	0
Shaun Van Allen	80	4	15	19	4	48	0
Pat Falloon	58	8	10	18	-8	16	3
PHI	30	5	7	12	3	8	1
OTT	28	3	3	6	-11	8	2
Bruce Gardiner	55	7	11	18	2	50	0
Radek Bonk	65	7	9	16	-13	16	1
Chris Phillips*	72	5	11	16	2	38	2
Jason York	73	3	13	16	8	62	0
Randy Cunneyworth	71	2	11	13	-14	63	1

Acquired: C Prospal, RW Falloon and '98 second-round pick from Phi. for RW Alexandre Daigle (Jan. 17).

Goalies (10 Gm)	Gm	Min	GAA	Record	Sv%
Ron Tugnutt	42	2236	2.25	15-14-8	.905
Damian Rhodes	50	2743	2.34	19-19-7	.907
OTTAWA	82	5002	2.40	34-33-15	.902

Shutouts: Rhodes (5), Tugnutt (3). **Assists:** Rhodes (1). **PM:** none.

Philadelphia Flyers

Top Scorers	Gm	G	A	Pts	+/-	PM	PP
John LeClair	82	51	36	87	30	32	16
Rod Brind'Amour	82	36	38	74	-2	54	10
Eric Lindros	63	30	41	71	14	134	10
Chris Gratton	82	22	40	62	11	159	5
Alexandre Daigle	75	16	26	42	-8	14	8
OTT	38	7	9	16	-7	8	4
PHI	37	9	17	26	-1	6	4
Trent Klatt	82	14	28	42	2	16	5
Mike Sillinger	75	21	20	41	-11	50	2
VAN	48	10	9	19	-14	34	1
PHI	27	11	11	22	3	16	1
Dainius Zubrus	69	8	25	33	29	42	1
Eric Desjardins	77	6	27	33	11	36	2
Dan McGillis	80	11	20	31	-21	109	6
EDM	67	10	15	25	-17	74	5
PHI	13	1	5	6	-4	35	1
Paul Coffey	57	2	27	29	3	30	1
Shjon Podein	82	11	13	24	8	53	1
Colin Forbes*	63	12	7	19	2	59	2
Chris Therien	78	3	16	19	5	80	1
Petr Svoboda	56	3	15	18	19	83	2
Dave Babych	53	0	9	9	-9	49	0
VAN	47	0	9	9	-11	37	0
PHI	6	0	0	0	2	12	0

Acquired: RW Daigle from Ott. for C Vaclav Prospal, RW Pat Falloon and '98 second-round pick (Jan. 17); RW Sillinger from Van. for '98 sixth-round pick (Feb. 5); G Burke from Van. for G Garth Snow (Mar. 4); D McGillis and '98 second-round pick from Edm. for D Janne Niinimaa (Mar. 24); D Babych and '98 sixth-round pick from Van. for '98 third-round pick (Mar. 24).

Goalies (10 Gm)	Gm	Min	GAA	Record	Sv%
Ron Hextall	46	2688	2.17	21-17-7	.911
Sean Burke	52	2885	2.95	16-23-9	.896
CAR	25	1415	2.80	7-11-5	.899
VAN	16	838	3.51	2-9-4	.876
PHI	11	632	2.56	7-3-0	.913
PHILADELPHIA	82	4988	2.32	42-29-11	.907

Shutouts: Hextall (4), Burke (2, incl. 1 w/Car.). **Assists:** Burke (2). **PM:** Burke (20), Hextall (10).

Phoenix Coyotes

Top Scorers	Gm	G	A	Pts	+/-	PM	PP
Keith Tkachuk	69	40	26	66	9	147	11
Jeremy Roenick	79	24	32	56	5	103	6
Cliff Ronning	80	11	44	55	5	36	3
Craig Janney	68	10	43	53	5	12	4
Teppo Numminen	82	11	40	51	25	30	6
Rick Tocchet	68	26	19	45	1	157	8
Dallas Drake	60	11	29	40	17	71	3
Mike Gartner	60	12	15	27	-4	24	4
Keith Carney	80	3	19	22	-2	91	1
CHI	60	2	13	15	-7	73	0
PHO	20	1	6	7	5	18	1
Bob Corkum	76	12	9	21	-7	28	0
Oleg Tverdovsky	46	7	12	19	1	12	4
Gerald Diduck	78	8	10	18	14	118	1
Brad Isbister*	66	9	8	17	4	102	1
John Slaney	55	3	14	17	-3	24	1
Darrin Shannon	58	2	12	14	4	26	0
Mark Janssens	74	5	7	12	-21	154	0
ANA	55	4	5	9	-22	116	0
NYI	12	0	0	0	-3	34	0
PHO	7	1	2	3	4	4	0
Juha Ylonen*	55	1	11	12	-3	10	0
Shane Doan	33	5	6	11	-3	35	0
Deron Quint	32	4	7	11	-6	16	1
Mike Stapleton	64	5	5	10	-4	36	1

Acquired: D Carney and RW Jim Cummins from Chi. for D Jay More and C Chad Kilger (Mar. 4); C Janssens from NYI for '98 ninth-round pick (Mar. 24).

Goalies (10 Gm)	Gm	Min	GAA	Record	Sv%
Jim Waite	17	793	2.12	5-6-1	.913
Nikolai Khabibulin	70	4026	2.74	30-28-10	.900
PHOENIX	82	4985	2.73	35-35-12	.898

Shutouts: Khabibulin (4), Waite (1). **Assists:** Khabibulin (2). **PM:** Khabibulin (22), Waite (2).

Pittsburgh Penguins

Top Scorers	Gm	G	A	Pts	+/-	PM	PP
Jaromir Jagr	77	35	67	102	17	64	7
Ron Francis	81	25	62	87	12	20	7
Stu Barnes	78	30	35	65	15	30	15
Kevin Hatcher	74	19	29	48	-3	66	13
Martin Straka	75	19	23	42	-1	28	4
Rob Brown	82	15	25	40	-1	59	4
Fredrik Olausson	76	6	27	33	13	42	2
Alexei Morozov*	76	13	13	26	-4	8	2
Ed Olczyk	56	11	11	22	-9	35	5
Robert Lang	54	9	13	22	7	16	1
BOS	3	0	0	0	1	2	0
PIT	51	9	13	22	6	14	1
Sean Pronger	67	6	15	21	-10	32	1
ANA	62	5	15	20	-9	30	1
PIT	5	1	0	1	-1	2	0
Alex Hicks	58	7	13	20	4	54	0
Brad Werenka	71	3	15	18	15	46	2
Jiri Slegr	73	5	12	17	10	109	1
Andreas Johansson	50	5	10	15	4	20	0
Darius Kasparaitis	81	4	8	12	3	127	0
Robert Dome*	30	5	2	7	-1	12	1
Chris Ferraro*	46	3	4	7	-2	43	0
Tyler Wright	82	3	4	7	-3	112	1
Ian Moran	37	1	6	7	0	19	0
Chris Tamer	79	0	7	7	4	181	0

Acquired: C Pronger from Ana. for G Patrick Lalime (Mar. 24). **Claimed:** C Lang off waivers from Bos. (Oct. 25).

Goalies (10 Gm)	Gm	Min	GAA	Record	Sv%
Peter Skudra*	17	851	1.83	6-4-3	.924
Tom Barrasso	63	3542	2.07	31-14-13	.922
Ken Wregget	15	611	2.75	3-6-2	.904
PITTSBURGH	82	5022	2.25	40-24-18	.915

Shutouts: Barrasso (7). **Assists:** Barrasso (2), Skudra (1). **PM:** Barrasso (14), Wregget (6), Skudra (2).

St. Louis Blues

Top Scorers	Gm	G	A	Pts	+/-	PM	PP
Brett Hull	66	27	45	72	-1	26	10
Pierre Turgeon	60	22	46	68	13	24	6
Geoff Courtnall	79	31	31	62	12	94	6
Steve Duchesne	80	14	42	56	9	32	5
Pavol Demitra	61	22	30	52	11	22	4
Al MacInnis	71	19	30	49	6	80	9
Craig Conroy	81	14	29	43	20	46	0
Jim Campbell	76	22	19	41	0	55	7
Chris Pronger	81	9	27	36	47	180	1
Todd Gill	75	13	17	30	-11	41	7
SJ	64	8	13	21	-13	31	4
ST.L	11	5	4	9	2	10	3
Scott Pellerin	80	8	21	29	14	62	1
Blair Atcheynum	61	11	15	26	5	10	0
Terry Yake	65	10	15	25	1	38	3
Darren Turcotte	62	12	6	18	6	26	3
Pascal Rheaume*	48	6	9	15	4	35	1
Mike Eastwood	58	6	5	11	-2	22	0
NYR	48	5	5	10	-2	16	0
ST.L	10	1	0	1	0	6	0
Chris McAlpine	54	3	7	10	14	36	0
Marc Bergevin	81	3	7	10	-2	90	0
Michel Picard	16	1	8	9	3	29	0
Rudy Poeschek	50	1	7	8	-5	64	0

Acquired: D Gill from SJ for RW Joe Murphy (Mar. 24); C Eastwood from NYR for C Harry York (Mar. 24).

Goalies (10 Gm)	Gm	Min	GAA	Record	Sv%
Jamie McLennan	30	1658	2.17	16-8-2	.903
Grant Fuhr	58	3274	2.53	29-21-6	.898
ST. LOUIS	82	4970	2.46	45-29-8	.897

Shutouts: Fuhr (3), McLennan (2). **Assists:** Fuhr (2). **PM:** Fuhr (6), McLennan (4).

San Jose Sharks

Top Scorers	Gm	G	A	Pts	+/-	PM	PP
Jeff Friesen	79	31	32	63	8	40	7
John MacLean	77	16	27	43	-6	42	6
NJ	26	3	8	11	-6	14	1
SJ	51	13	19	32	0	28	5
Owen Nolan	75	14	27	41	-2	144	3
Patrick Marleau*	74	13	19	32	5	14	1
Bill Houlder	82	7	25	32	13	48	4
Marco Sturm*	74	10	20	30	-2	40	2
Stephane Matteau	73	15	14	29	4	60	1
Murray Craven	67	12	17	29	4	25	2
Bernie Nicholls	60	6	22	28	-4	26	3
Mike Ricci	65	9	18	27	-4	32	5
COL	6	0	4	4	0	2	0
SJ	59	9	14	23	-4	30	5
Tony Granato	59	16	9	25	3	70	3
Marcus Ragnarsson	79	5	20	25	-11	65	3
Joe Murphy	37	9	13	22	9	36	4
ST.L	27	4	9	13	8	22	2
SJ	10	5	4	9	1	14	2
Mike Rathje	81	3	12	15	-4	59	1
Andrei Zyuzin*	56	6	7	13	8	66	2
Bryan Marchment	61	2	11	13	-3	144	0
EDM	27	0	4	4	-2	58	0
TB	22	2	4	6	-3	43	0
SJ	12	0	3	3	2	43	0

Acquired: C Ricci and '98 second-round pick from Col. for RW Shean Donovan and '98 first-round pick (Nov. 20); RW MacLean and D Ken Sutton from NJ for D Doug Bodger and LW Dody Wood (Dec. 7); RW Murphy from St.L for D Todd Gill (Mar. 24); D Marchment and D David Shaw from TB for RW Andrei Nazarov and exch. of '98 picks (Mar. 24).

Goalies (10 Gm)	Gm	Min	GAA	Record	Sv%
Mike Vernon	62	3564	2.46	30-22-8	.896
Kelly Hrudey	28	1360	2.74	4-16-2	.897
SAN JOSE	82	4973	2.61	34-38-10	.893

Shutouts: Vernon (5), Hrudey (1) .**Assists:** Vernon (2). **PM:** Vernon (24), Hrudey (2).

Tampa Bay Lightning

Top Scorers	Gm	G	A	Pts	+/-	PM	PP
Paul Ysebaert	82	13	27	40	-43	32	2
Mikael Renberg	68	16	22	38	-37	34	6
Alexander Selivanov	70	16	19	35	-38	85	4
Stephane Richer	40	14	15	29	-6	41	5
MON	14	5	4	9	1	5	2
TB	26	9	11	20	-7	36	3
Rob Zamuner	77	14	12	26	-31	41	0
Daymond Langkow	68	8	14	22	-9	62	2
Darcy Tucker	74	7	13	20	-14	146	1
MON	39	1	5	6	-6	57	0
TB	35	6	8	14	-8	89	1
Sandy McCarthy	66	8	10	18	-19	241	1
CALG	52	8	5	13	-18	170	1
TB	14	0	5	5	-1	71	0
Mikael Andersson	72	6	11	17	-4	29	0
Karl Dykhuis	78	5	9	14	-8	110	0
Jason Bonsignore*	35	2	8	10	-11	22	0
Cory Cross	74	3	6	9	-24	77	0

Acquired: C Bonsignore, D Bryan Marchment and C Steve Kelly from Edm. for D Roman Hamrlik and C Paul Comrie (Dec. 30); RW Richer, C Tucker and D David Wilkie from Mon. for LW Patrick Poulin, RW Mick Vukota and D Igor Ulanov (Jan. 15); RW Jody Hull and G Fitzpatrick from Fla. for RW Dino Ciccarelli and D Jeff Norton (Jan. 16); RW McCarthy and '98 third and fifth-round picks from Calg. for LW Jason Wiemer (Mar. 24).

Goalies (10 Gm)	Gm	Min	GAA	Record	Sv%
Daren Puppa	26	1456	2.72	5-14-6	.900
Corey Schwab	16	821	2.92	2-9-1	.892
Mark Fitzpatrick	46	2578	3.12	9-31-3	.892
FLA	12	640	3.00	2-7-2	.879
TB	34	1938	3.16	7-24-1	.895
Zac Bierk*	13	433	4.16	1-4-1	.857
TAMPA BAY	82	4978	3.24	17-55-10	.887

Shutouts: Fitzpatrick (2, 1 w/Fla.), Schwab (1). Schwab also shared a shutout with Derek Wilkinson. **Assists:** Fitzpatrick (1). **PM:** Fitzpatrick (16), Puppa (6), Schwab (2).

Toronto Maple Leafs

Top Scorers	Gm	G	A	Pts	+/-	PM	PP
Mats Sundin	82	33	41	74	-3	49	9
Mike Johnson*	82	15	32	47	-4	24	5
Derek King	77	21	25	46	-7	43	4
Igor Korolev	78	17	22	39	-18	22	6
Mathieu Schneider	76	11	26	37	-12	44	4
Fredrik Modin	74	16	16	32	-5	32	1
Sergei Berezin	68	16	15	31	-3	10	3
Steve Sullivan	63	10	18	28	-8	40	1
Sylvain Cote	71	4	21	25	-3	42	1
WASH	59	1	15	16	-5	36	0
TOR	12	3	6	9	2	6	1
Wendel Clark	47	12	7	19	-21	80	4
Alyn McCauley*	60	6	10	16	-7	6	0
Jason Smith	81	3	13	16	-5	100	0
Tie Domi	80	4	10	14	-5	365	0
Todd Warriner	45	5	8	13	5	20	0
Darby Hendrickson	80	8	4	12	-20	67	0
Dimitri Yushkevich	72	0	12	12	-13	78	0
Lonny Bohonos	37	5	4	9	-8	8	0
VAN	31	2	1	3	-9	4	0
TOR	6	3	3	6	1	4	0
Danil Markov*	25	2	5	7	0	28	1
Rob Zettler	59	0	7	7	-8	108	0
Kris King	82	3	3	6	-13	199	0
Martin Prochazka*	29	2	4	6	-1	8	0
Yannick Tremblay*	38	2	4	6	-6	6	1

Acquired: RW Bohonos from Van. for C Brandon Convery (Mar. 7); D Cote from Wash. for D Jeff Brown (Mar. 24).

Goalies (10 Gm)	Gm	Min	GAA	Record	Sv%
Felix Potvin	67	3864	2.73	26-33-7	.906
Glenn Healy	21	1068	2.98	4-10-2	.883
TORONTO	82	4970	2.86	30-43-9	.899

Shutouts: Potvin (5). Healy shared a shutout with Marcel Cousineau. **Assists:** none. **PM:** Potvin (8).

Vancouver Canucks

Top Scorers	Gm	G	A	Pts	+/-	PM	PP
Pavel Bure	82	51	39	90	5	48	13
Mark Messier	82	22	38	60	-10	58	8
Alexander Mogilny	51	18	27	45	-6	36	5
Markus Naslund	76	14	20	34	5	56	2
Todd Bertuzzi	74	13	20	33	-17	121	2
NYI	52	7	11	18	-19	58	1
VAN	22	6	9	15	2	63	1
Jyrki Lumme	74	9	21	30	-25	34	4
Mattias Ohlund*	77	7	23	30	3	76	1
Bret Hedican	71	3	24	27	3	79	1
Brian Noonan	82	10	15	25	-19	62	1
Dave Scatchard*	76	13	11	24	-4	165	0
Bryan McCabe	82	4	20	24	19	209	1
NYI	56	3	9	12	9	145	1
VAN	26	1	11	12	10	64	0
Brad May	63	13	10	23	2	154	4
BUF	36	4	7	11	2	113	0
VAN	27	9	3	12	0	41	4
Peter Zezel	30	5	15	20	15	2	2
NJ	5	0	3	3	2	0	0
VAN	25	5	12	17	13	2	2
Donald Brashear	77	9	9	18	-9	372	0

Acquired: LW May and '97 third-round pick from Buf. for LW Geoff Sanderson (Feb. 4); C Zezel from NJ for '98 fifth-round pick (Feb. 5); D McCabe, RW Bertuzzi and '98 third-round pick from NYI for C Trevor Linden (Feb. 6); G Snow from Phi. for G Sean Burke (Mar. 4);

Goalies (10 Gm)	Gm	Min	GAA	Record	Sv%
Arturs Irbe	41	1999	2.73	14-11-6	.907
Garth Snow	41	2155	2.59	17-15-4	.901
PHI	29	1651	2.43	14-9-4	.902
VAN	12	504	3.10	3-6-0	.901
VANCOUVER	82	4996	3.28	25-43-14	.890

Shutouts: Irbe (2), Snow (1 w/Phi.). **Assists:** none. **PM:** Snow (22), Irbe (2).

Washington Capitals

Top Scorers	Gm	G	A	Pts	+/-	PM	PP
Peter Bondra	76	52	26	78	14	44	11
Adam Oates	82	18	58	76	6	36	3
Calle Johansson	73	15	20	35	-11	30	10
Steve Konowalchuk	80	10	24	34	9	80	2
Joe Juneau	56	9	22	31	-8	26	4
Phil Housley	64	6	25	31	-10	24	4
Jeff Brown	60	4	24	28	5	32	4
CAR	32	3	10	13	-1	16	3
TOR	19	1	8	9	2	10	1
WASH	9	0	6	6	4	6	0
Richard Zednik*	65	17	9	26	-2	28	2
Dale Hunter	82	8	18	26	1	103	0
Andrew Brunette	28	11	12	23	2	12	4
Sergei Gonchar	72	5	16	21	2	66	2
Esa Tikkanen	48	3	18	21	-11	18	1
FLA	28	1	8	9	-7	16	0
WASH	20	2	10	12	-4	2	1
Mark Tinordi	47	8	9	17	9	39	0
Chris Simon	28	7	10	17	-1	38	4
Andrei Nikolishin	38	6	10	16	1	14	1
Jan Bulis*	48	5	11	16	-5	18	0
Craig Berube	74	6	9	15	-3	189	0
Kelly Miller	76	7	7	14	-2	41	0
Todd Krygier	45	2	12	14	-3	30	0

Acquired: LW Tikkanen from Fla. for LW Dwayne Hay and '99 pick (Mar. 8); D Brown from Tor. for D Sylvain Cote (Mar. 24).

Goalies (10 Gm)	Gm	Min	GAA	Record	Sv%
Olaf Kolzig	64	3788	2.20	33-18-10	.920
Bill Ranford	22	1183	2.79	7-12-2	.901
WASHINGTON	82	4997	2.43	40-30-12	.912

Shutouts: Kolzig (5). **Assists:** Kolzig and Ranford (1). **PM:** Kolzig (12).

1998 NHL Draft

First and second round selections at the 36th annual NHL Entry Draft held June 27, 1998, in Buffalo. The order of the first 11 positions were determined by a draft lottery held May 10 in New York. Positions 12 through 27 reflect regular season records in reverse order.

First Round

	Team	Player	Pos
1	**a**-Tampa Bay	Vincent Lecavalier, Rimouski	C
2	**b**-Nashville	David Legwand, Plymouth	C
3	San Jose	Brad Stuart, Regina	D
4	Vancouver	Bryan Allen, Oshawa	D
5	Anaheim	Vitali Vishnevsky, Yaroslavl	D
6	Calgary	Rico Fata, London	C
7	NY Rangers	Manny Malhotra, Guelph	C
8	**c**-Chicago	Mark Bell, Ottawa	C
9	NY Islanders	Michael Rupp, Erie	L
10	**d**-Toronto	Nikolai Antropov, Ust-Kamenogorsk	C
11	Carolina	Jeff Heerema, Sarnia	R
12	**e**-Colorado	Alex Tanguay, Halifax	C
13	Edmonton	Michael Henrich, Barrie	R
14	Phoenix	Patrick DesRochers, Sarnia	G
15	Ottawa	Mathieu Chouinard, Shawinigan	G
16	Montreal	Eric Chouinard, Quebec	C
17	**f**-Colorado	Martin Skoula, Barrie	D
18	Buffalo	Dmitri Kalinin, Chelyabinsk	D
19	**g**-Colorado	Robyn Regehr, Kamloops	D
20	**h**-Colorado	Scott Parker, Kelowna	R
21	**i**-Los Angeles	Mathieu Biron, Shawinigan	D
22	**j**-Philadelphia	Simon Gagne, Quebec	C
23	Pittsburgh	Milan Kraft, Plzen Jr.	C
24	St. Louis	Christian Backman, Frolunda Jr.	D
25	Detroit	Jiri Fischer, Hull	D
26	New Jersey	Mike Van Ryn, Michigan	D
27	**k**-New Jersey	Scott Gomez, Tri-City	C

Second Round

	Team	Player	Pos
28	**l**-Colorado	Ramzi Abid, Chicoutimi	L
29	**m**-San Jose	Jonathan Cheechoo, Belleville	R
30	Florida	Kyle Rossiter, Spokane	D
31	Vancouver	Artem Chubarov, Dynamo	C
32	Anaheim	Stephen Peat, Red Deer	D
33	Calgary	Blair Betts, Prince George	C
34	**n**-Buffalo	Andrew Peters, Oshawa	L
35	Toronto	Petr Svoboda, Havl Brod	D
36	NY Islanders	Chris Nielsen, Calgary	C
37	New Jersey	Christian Berglund, Farjestad Jr.	L
38	**o**-Colorado	Philippe Sauve, Rimouski	G
39	**p**-Dallas	John Erskine, London	D
40	NY Rangers	Randy Copley, Cape Breton	R
41	**q**-St. Louis	Maxim Linnik, St. Thomas	D
42	**r**-Philadelphia	Jason Beckett, Seattle	D
43	Phoenix	Ossi Vaananen, Jokerit Jr.	D
44	Ottawa	Mike Fisher, Sudbury	C
45	Montreal	Mike Ribeiro, Rouyn-Noranda	C
46	Los Angeles	Justin Papineau, Belleville	C
47	Buffalo	Norman Milley, Sudbury	R
48	Boston	Jonathan Girard, Laval	D
49	Washington	Jomar Cruz, Brandon	G
50	**s**-Buffalo	Jaroslav Kristek, Zlin	R
51	Philadelphia	Ian Forbes, Guelph	D
52	Boston	Bobby Allen, Boston Coll.	D
53	Colorado	Steve Moore, Harvard	C
54	Pittsburgh	Alexander Zevakhin, CSKA 2	C
55	**t**-Detroit	Ryan Barnes, Sudbury	L
56	Detroit	Tomek Valtonen, Ilves	L
57	**u**-Dallas	Tyler Bouck, Prince George	R
58	**v**-Ottawa	Chris Bala, Harvard	L

Acquired picks: FIRST ROUND: **a**— from Florida via San Jose; **b**— from Tampa Bay via San Jose; **c**— from Nashville; **d**— from Toronto; **e**— from Chicago; **f**— from San Jose; **g**— from Los Angeles; **h**— from Boston; **i**— from Washington; **j**— from Colorado; **k**— from Dallas; SECOND ROUND: **l**— from Tampa Bay; **m**— from Nashville; **n**— from NY Rangers; **o**— from Chicago; **p**— from Carolina via New Jersey; **q**— from San Jose via Detroit; **r**— from Edmonton; **s**— from Colorado via San Jose; **t**— from St. Louis; **u**— from New Jersey; **v**— from Dallas via Philadelphia.

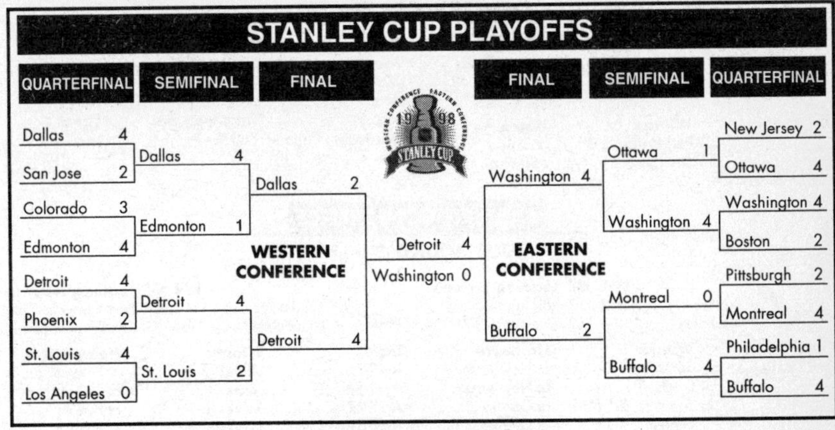

Stanley Cup Playoffs

Series Summaries

WESTERN CONFERENCE

FIRST ROUND (Best of 7)

	W-L	GF	Leading Scorers
Dallas	4-2	16	Modano (3-3-6)
San Jose	2-4	12	Nicholls (0-5-5) & MacLean (2-3-5)

Date	Winner	Home Ice
April 22	Stars, 4-1	at Dallas
April 24	Stars, 5-2	at Dallas
April 26	Sharks, 4-1	at San Jose
April 28	Sharks, 1-0 (OT)	at San Jose
April 30	Stars, 3-2	at Dallas
May 2	Stars, 3-2 (OT)	at San Jose

Shutout: Vernon, San Jose.

	W-L	GF	Leading Scorers
Detroit	4-2	24	Fedorov (6-3-9) & Lidstrom (2-7-9)
Phoenix	2-4	18	Tocchet (6-2-8) & Roenick (5-3-8)

Date	Winner	Home Ice
April 22	Red Wings, 6-3	at Detroit
April 24	Coyotes, 7-4	at Detroit
April 26	Coyotes, 3-2	at Phoenix
April 28	Red Wings, 4-2	at Phoenix
April 30	Red Wings, 3-1	at Detroit
May 3	Red Wings, 5-2	at Phoenix

	W-L	GF	Leading Scorers
Edmonton	4-3	19	Weight (1-7-8)
Colorado	3-4	16	Forsberg (6-5-11)

Date	Winner	Home Ice
April 22	Oilers, 3-2	at Colorado
April 24	Avalanche, 5-2	at Colorado
April 26	Avalanche, 5-4 (OT)	at Edmonton
April 28	Avalanche, 3-1	at Edmonton
April 30	Oilers, 3-1	at Colorado
May 2	Oilers, 2-0	at Edmonton
May 4	Oilers, 4-0	at Colorado

Shutouts: Joseph, Edmonton (2).

	W-L	GF	Leading Scorers
St. Louis	4-0	16	Courtnall (1-6-7)
Los Angeles	0-4	8	Four tied with 3 pts.

Date	Winner	Home Ice
April 23	Blues, 8-3	at St. Louis
April 25	Blues, 2-1	at St. Louis
April 27	Blues, 4-3	at Los Angeles
April 29	Blues, 2-1	at Los Angeles

SEMIFINALS (Best of 7)

	W-L	GF	Leading Scorers
Dallas	4-1	9	Modano (0-4-4)
Edmonton	1-4	5	Four tied with 2 pts.

Date	Winner	Home Ice
May 7	Stars, 3-1	at Dallas
May 9	Oilers, 2-0	at Dallas
May 11	Stars, 1-0 (OT)	at Edmonton
May 13	Stars, 3-1	at Edmonton
May 16	Stars, 2-1	at Dallas

Shutouts: Joseph, Edmonton; Belfour, Dallas

	W-L	GF	Leading Scorers
Detroit	4-2	23	Yzerman (2-8-10)
St. Louis	2-4	13	Campbell (4-1-5)

Date	Winner	Home Ice
May 8	Blues, 4-2	at Detroit
May 10	Red Wings, 6-1	at Detroit
May 12	Red Wings, 3-2	at St. Louis
May 14	Red Wings, 5-2	at St. Louis
May 17	Blues, 3-1	at Detroit
May 19	Red Wings, 6-1	at St. Louis

CHAMPIONSHIP (Best of 7)

	W-L	GF	Leading Scorers
Detroit	4-2	15	Lidstrom (2-4-6) & Murphy (1-5-6)
Dallas	2-4	11	Lehtinen (2-3-5)

Date	Winner	Home Ice
May 24	Red Wings, 2-0	at Dallas
May 26	Stars, 3-1	at Dallas
May 29	Red Wings, 5-3	at Detroit
May 31	Red Wings, 3-2	at Detroit
June 3	Stars, 3-2 (OT)	at Dallas
June 5	Red Wings, 2-0	at Detroit

Shutouts: Osgood, Detroit (2).

EASTERN CONFERENCE

FIRST ROUND (Best of 7)

	W-L	GF	Leading Scorers
Ottawa	4-2	13	Yashin (3-2-5)
New Jersey	2-4	12	Gilmour (5-2-7)

Date	Winner	Home Ice
April 22	Senators, 2-1 (OT)	at New Jersey
April 24	Devils, 3-1	at New Jersey
April 26	Senators, 2-1 (OT)	at Ottawa
April 28	Senators, 4-3	at Ottawa
April 30	Devils, 3-1	at New Jersey
May 2	Senators, 3-1	at Ottawa

	W-L	GF	Leading Scorers
Montreal	4-2	18	Damphousse (2-6-8) & Recchi (3-5-8)
Pittsburgh	2-4	15	Jagr (4-5-9)

Date	Winner	Home Ice
April 23	Canadiens, 3-2 (OT)	at Pittsburgh
April 25	Penguins, 4-1	at Pittsburgh
April 27	Canadiens, 3-1	at Montreal
April 29	Penguins, 6-3	at Montreal
May 1	Canadiens, 5-2	at Pittsburgh
May 3	Canadiens, 3-0	at Montreal

Shutout: Moog, Montreal.

	W-L	GF	Leading Scorers
Buffalo	4-1	18	Four tied with 5 pts.
Philadelphia	1-4	9	Brind'Amour (2-2-4)

Date	Winner	Home Ice
April 22	Sabres, 3-2	at Philadelphia
April 24	Flyers, 3-2	at Philadelphia
April 27	Sabres, 6-1	at Buffalo
April 29	Sabres, 4-1	at Buffalo
May 1	Sabres, 3-2 (OT)	at Philadelphia

	W-L	GF	Leading Scorers
Washington	4-2	15	Oates (3-4-7)
Boston	2-4	13	Allison (2-6-8)

Date	Winner	Home Ice
April 22	Capitals, 3-1	at Washington
April 24	Bruins, 4-3 (2OT)	at Washington
April 26	Capitals, 3-2 (2OT)	at Boston
April 28	Capitals, 3-0	at Boston
May 1	Bruins, 4-0	at Washington
May 3	Capitals, 3-2 (OT)	at Boston

Shutouts: Kolzig, Washington; Dafoe, Boston.

SEMIFINALS (Best of 7)

	W-L	GF	Leading Scorers
Washington	4-1	18	Juneau (2-4-6)
Ottawa	1-4	7	Alfredsson (4-1-5)

Date	Winner	Home Ice
May 7	Capitals, 4-2	at Washington
May 9	Capitals, 6-1	at Washington
May 11	Senators, 4-3	at Ottawa
May 13	Capitals, 2-0	at Ottawa
May 15	Capitals, 3-0	at Washington

Shutouts: Kolzig, Washington (2).

	W-L	GF	Leading Scorers
Buffalo	4-0	17	Audette (2-4-6)
Montreal	0-4	10	Recchi (1-3-4) & Stevenson (3-1-4)

Date	Winner	Home Ice
May 8	Sabres, 3-2 (OT)	at Buffalo
May 10	Sabres, 6-3	at Buffalo
May 12	Sabres, 5-4 (2OT)	at Montreal
May 14	Sabres, 3-1	at Montreal

CHAMPIONSHIP (Best of 7)

	W-L	GF	Leading Scorers
Washington	4-2	13	Nikolishin (1-5-6)
Buffalo	2-4	11	Three tied with 3 each.

	Winner	Home Ice
May 23	Sabres, 2-0	at Washington
May 25	Capitals, 3-2 (OT)	at Washington
May 28	Capitals, 4-3 (OT)	at Buffalo
May 30	Capitals, 2-0	at Buffalo
June 2	Sabres, 2-1	at Washington
June 4	Capitals, 3-2 (OT)	at Buffalo

Shutouts: Hasek, Buffalo; Kolzig, Washington.

STANLEY CUP FINAL (Best of 7)

	W-L	GF	Leading Scorers
Detroit	4-0	13	Brown (3-2-5) & Holmstrom (1-4-5)
Washington	0-4	7	Juneau (1-3-4)

	Winner	Home Ice
June 9	Red Wings, 2-1	at Detroit
June 11	Red Wings, 5-4 (OT)	at Detroit
June 13	Red Wings, 2-1	at Washington
June 16	Red Wings, 4-1	at Washington

Conn Smythe Trophy (MVP)
Steve Yzerman, Detroit, C
22 games, 6 goals, 18 assists, 24 points

Stanley Cup Final Box Scores

Game 1

Tuesday, June 9, at Detroit

Washington .... 0 1 0 — **1**
Detroit .... 2 0 0 — **2**

1st Period: DET— Kocur 4 (Brown, Holmstrom) 14:04; DET— Lidstrom 6 (Yzerman, Holmstrom) 16:18.
2nd Period: WAS— Zednik 7 (Nikolishin, Bondra) 15:57.
Shots on Goal: Washington— 6-4-7–17; Detroit— 10-9-12–31. **Power plays:** Washington 0-4; Detroit 0-3. **Goalies:** Washington, Kolzig (31 shots, 29 saves); Detroit, Osgood (17 shots, 16 saves). **Attendance:** 19,983.

Game 2

Thursday, June 11, at Detroit

Washington .... 0 3 1 0 — **4**
Detroit .... 1 0 3 1 — **5**

1st Period: DET— Yzerman 5 (Holmstrom, Lidstrom) 7:49.
2nd Period: WAS— Bondra 7 (Nikolishin, Brown) 1:51; WAS— Simon 1 (Brown, Hunter) 6:11; WAS— Oates 6 (Juneau, Johansson) 11:03.
3rd Period: DET— Yzerman 6 (Fetisov, McCarty) 6:37 (sh); WAS— Juneau 7 (Gonchar, Bellows) 7:05 (pp); DET— Lapointe 8 (Larionov, Fetisov) 8:08; DET— Brown 2 (unassisted) 15:46.
Overtime: DET— Draper 1 (Lapointe, Shanahan) 15:24.
Shots on Goal: Washington— 8-15-7-3–33; Detroit— 14-14-20-12–60. **Power plays:** Washington 1-4; Detroit 0-4. **Goalies:** Washington, Kolzig (60 shots, 55 saves); Detroit, Osgood (33 shots, 29 saves). **Attendance:** 19,983.

Game 3

Saturday, June 13, at Washington

Detroit .... 1 0 1 — **2**
Washington .... 0 0 1 — **1**

1st Period: DET— Holmstrom 7 (Yzerman, McCarty) 0:35.
3rd Period: WAS— Bellows 5 (Oates, Juneau) 10:35 (pp); DET— Fedorov 10 (Brown, Fetisov) 15:09.
Shots on Goal: Detroit— 13-11-10–34; Washington— 1-12-5–18. **Power plays:** Detroit 0-5; Washington 1-5. **Goalies:** Detroit, Osgood (18 shots, 17 saves); Washington, Kolzig (34 shots, 32 saves). **Attendance:** 19,740.

Game 4

Tuesday, June 16, at Washington

Detroit .... 1 2 1 — **4**
Washington .... 0 1 0 — **1**

1st Period: DET— Brown 3 (Fedorov, Murphy) 10:30 (pp).
2nd Period: DET— Lapointe 9 (Larionov, Rouse) 2:26; WAS— Bellows 6 (Oates, Juneau) 7:49; DET— Murphy 3 (Holmstrom, Fedorov) 11:46 (pp).
3rd Period: DET— Brown 4 (Kozlov, Eriksson) 1:32.
Shots on Goal: Detroit— 14-12-12–38; Washington— 6-14-11–31. **Power plays:** Detroit 3-4; Washington 0-4. **Goalies:** Detroit, Osgood (31 shots, 30 saves); Washington, Kolzig (38 shots, 34 saves). **Attendance:** 19,740.

Stanley Cup Leaders

Scoring

	Gm	G	A	Pts	+/-	PM	PP
Steve Yzerman, Det	22	6	18	**24**	10	22	3
Sergei Fedorov, Det	22	10	10	**20**	0	12	2
Tomas Holmstrom, Det	22	7	12	**19**	9	16	2
Nicklas Lidstrom, Det	22	6	13	**19**	12	8	2
Joe Juneau, Wash	21	7	10	**17**	6	8	1
Adam Oates, Wash	21	6	11	**17**	8	8	1
Martin Lapointe, Det	21	9	6	**15**	6	20	2
Larry Murphy, Det	22	3	12	**15**	12	2	1
Vyacheslav Kozlov, Det	22	6	8	**14**	4	10	1
Mike Modano, Dal	17	4	10	**14**	4	12	1
Andrei Nikolishin, Wash	21	1	13	**14**	4	12	1

Four tied with 13 pts.

Goaltending

(Minimum 420 minutes)

	Gm	Min	W-L	ShO	GAA
Ed Belfour, Dal	17	1039	10-7	1	**1.79**
Curtis Joseph, Edm	12	716	5-7	3	**1.93**
Olaf Kolzig, Wash	21	1351	12-9	4	**1.95**
Byron Dafoe, Bos	6	422	2-4	1	**1.99**
Dominik Hasek, Buf	15	948	10-5	1	**2.03**
Chris Osgood, Det	22	1361	16-6	2	**2.12**
Damian Rhodes, Ott	10	590	5-5	0	**2.14**

Goals

Fedorov, Det	10
Lapointe, Det	9
Campbell, St.L	7
Alfredsson, Ott	7
Guerin, Edm	7
Barnaby, Buf	7
Bondra, Wash	7
Zednik, Wash	7
Juneau, Wash	7
Gonchar, Wash	7
Holmstrom, Det	7

Power Play Goals

Campbell, St.L	4
Guerin, Edm	4
Satan, Buf	4

Ten tied with 3 each.

Plus/Minus

Murphy, Det	+12
Lidstrom, Det	+12
Yzerman, Det	+10

Four tied at +9.

Assists

Yzerman, Det	18
Nikolishin, Wash	13
Lidstrom, Det	13
Murphy, Det	12
Holmstrom, Det	12
Oates, Wash	11

Four tied with 10 each.

Overtime Goals

Juneau, Wash	2

Seventeen tied with 1 each.

Penalty Minutes

Marshall, Dal	47
Tinordi, Wash	42
Hatcher, Dal	39
Zhitnik, Buf	36
O'Donnell, LA	36
McCarty, Det	34
Kocur, Det	30
Gonchar, Wash	30
Maltby, Det	30
Hunter, Wash	30

Wins

Osgood, Det	16-6
Kolzig, Wash	12-9
Hasek, Buf	10-5
Belfour, Dal	10-7
Fuhr, St.L	6-4
Rhodes, Ott	5-5
Joseph, Edm	5-7

Save Pct.

Kolzig, Wash	.941
Hasek, Buf	.938
Joseph, Edm	.928
Belfour, Dal	.922
Osgood, Det	.918
Dafoe, Bos	.912

Final Stanley Cup Standings

				—Goals—		
	Gm	W	L	For	Opp	Dif
Detroit	22	16	6	75	49	+26
Washington	21	12	9	53	44	+9
Buffalo	15	10	5	46	32	+14
Dallas	17	10	7	36	32	+4
St. Louis	10	6	4	29	31	-2
Ottawa	11	5	6	20	30	-10
Edmonton	12	5	7	24	25	-1
Montreal	10	4	6	28	32	-4
Colorado	7	3	4	16	19	-3
New Jersey	6	2	4	12	13	-1
Boston	6	2	4	13	15	-2
Pittsburgh	6	2	4	15	18	-3
San Jose	6	2	4	12	16	-4
Phoenix	6	2	4	18	24	-6
Philadelphia	5	1	4	9	18	-9
Los Angeles	4	0	4	8	16	-8

Finalists' Composite Box Scores

Detroit Red Wings (16–6)

		Overall Playoffs								Finals vs Washington							
Top Scorers	**Pos**	**Gm**	**G**	**A**	**Pts**	**+/-**	**PM**	**PP**	**S**	**GM**	**G**	**A**	**Pts**	**+/-**	**PM**	**PP**	**S**
Steve Yzerman	C	22	6	18	**24**	10	22	3	65	4	2	2	**4**	5	2	0	15
Sergei Fedorov	C	22	10	10	**20**	0	12	2	86	4	1	2	**3**	-1	0	0	21
Tomas Holmstrom	L	22	7	12	**19**	9	16	2	27	4	1	4	**5**	3	2	0	5
Nicklas Lidstrom	D	22	6	13	**19**	12	8	2	59	4	1	1	**2**	3	2	0	16
Martin Lapointe	R	21	9	6	**15**	6	20	2	55	4	2	1	**3**	2	6	0	10
Larry Murphy	D	22	3	12	**15**	12	2	1	36	4	1	1	**2**	3	0	1	13
Vyacheslav Kozlov	L	22	6	8	**14**	4	10	1	47	4	0	1	**1**	-1	0	0	9
Igor Larionov	C	22	3	10	**13**	5	12	0	27	4	0	2	**2**	1	4	0	7
Darren McCarty	R	22	3	8	**11**	9	34	0	46	4	0	2	**2**	4	2	0	7
Brendan Shanahan	L	20	5	4	**9**	5	22	3	60	4	0	1	**1**	2	0	0	11
Doug Brown	R	9	4	2	**6**	-1	0	3	19	4	3	2	**5**	0	0	2	14
Anders Eriksson*	D	18	0	5	**5**	7	16	0	17	4	0	1	**1**	2	4	0	5
Joey Kocur	R	18	4	0	**4**	-3	30	0	13	4	1	0	**1**	-1	4	0	5
Kirk Maltby	L	22	3	1	**4**	2	30	0	31	4	0	0	**0**	-1	6	0	6
Jamie Macoun	D	22	2	2	**4**	3	18	0	21	4	0	0	**0**	-1	0	0	5
Kris Draper	C	19	1	3	**4**	4	12	0	20	4	1	0	**1**	1	2	0	5
Brent Gilchrist	C	15	2	1	**3**	2	12	0	17	0	0	0	**0**	0	0	0	0
Dmitri Mironov	D	7	0	3	**3**	1	14	0	15	0	0	0	**0**	0	0	0	0
Viacheslav Fetisov	D	21	0	3	**3**	4	10	0	14	4	0	3	**3**	2	2	0	5
Bob Rouse	D	22	0	3	**3**	2	16	0	22	4	0	1	**1**	1	2	0	4

Overtime goals— OVERALL (Draper, Shanahan); FINALS (Draper). **Shorthanded goals**— OVERALL (Murphy 2, Yzerman, Fedorov, Lapointe, Maltby); FINALS (Yzerman). **Power Play conversions**—OVERALL (20 for 129, 15.5%); FINALS (3 for 16, 18.8%).

Goaltending	**Gm**	**Min**	**GAA**	**GA**	**SA**	**Sv%**	**W-L**	**Gm**	**Min**	**GAA**	**GA**	**SA**	**Sv %**	**W-L**
Chris Osgood	22	1361	**2.12**	48	588	.918	16-6	4	255	**1.65**	7	99	.929	4-0
TOTAL	22	1367	**2.15**	49	589	.917	16-6	4	255	**1.65**	7	99	.929	4-0

Empty Net Goals— OVERALL (one), FINALS (none). **Shutouts**— OVERALL (Osgood 2), FINALS (none). **Assists**— OVERALL (Osgood), FINALS (none). **Penalty Minutes**— OVERALL (Osgood 12), FINALS (Osgood 2).

Washington Capitals (12–9)

		Overall Playoffs								Finals vs Detroit							
Top Scorers	**Pos**	**Gm**	**G**	**A**	**Pts**	**+/-**	**PM**	**PP**	**S**	**Gm**	**G**	**A**	**Pts**	**+/-**	**PM**	**PP**	**S**
Joe Juneau	C	21	7	10	**17**	6	8	1	54	4	1	3	**4**	-1	0	1	10
Adam Oates	C	21	6	11	**17**	8	8	1	31	4	1	2	**3**	-1	0	0	11
Andrei Nikolishin	C	21	1	13	**14**	4	12	1	29	4	0	2	**2**	-1	2	0	4
Brian Bellows	L	21	6	7	**13**	6	6	2	62	4	2	1	**3**	0	0	1	12
Peter Bondra	R	17	7	5	**12**	4	12	3	48	4	1	1	**2**	-1	4	0	7
Sergei Gonchar	D	21	7	4	**11**	2	30	3	37	4	0	1	**1**	-4	4	0	7
Richard Zednik*	L	17	7	3	**10**	0	16	2	40	4	1	0	**1**	-1	4	0	6
Calle Johansson	D	21	2	8	**10**	9	16	0	42	4	0	1	**1**	-3	2	0	8
Esa Tikkanen	L	21	3	3	**6**	-2	20	1	23	4	0	0	**0**	-5	4	0	3
Phil Housley	D	18	0	4	**4**	-2	4	0	27	4	0	0	**0**	0	2	0	4
Dale Hunter	C	21	0	4	**4**	-1	30	0	14	4	0	1	**1**	-1	2	0	2
Todd Krygier	L	13	1	2	**3**	-2	6	0	12	3	0	0	**0**	-3	2	0	1
Joe Reekie	D	21	1	2	**3**	4	20	0	16	4	0	0	**0**	0	2	0	4
Mark Tinordi	D	21	1	2	**3**	6	42	0	14	4	0	0	**0**	-4	6	0	4
Michal Pivonka	C	13	0	3	**3**	5	0	0	16	0	0	0	**0**	0	0	0	0
Jeff Brown	D	2	0	2	**2**	1	0	0	2	2	0	2	**2**	+1	0	0	2
Mike Eagles	L	12	0	2	**2**	1	2	0	7	2	0	0	**0**	-1	0	0	0
Ken Klee	D	9	1	0	**1**	2	10	0	6	2	0	0	**0**	0	0	0	2
Brendan Witt	D	16	1	0	**1**	-1	14	0	9	0	0	0	**0**	0	0	0	0
Chris Simon	L	18	1	0	**1**	-3	26	0	17	4	1	0	**1**	0	6	0	5
Craig Berube	L	21	1	0	**1**	0	21	0	15	4	0	0	**0**	+1	0	0	5
Kelly Miller	L	10	0	1	**1**	2	4	0	8	2	0	0	**0**	0	0	0	1

Overtime goals— OVERALL (Juneau 2, Bellows, Bondra, Krygier); FINALS (none). **Shorthanded goals**— OVERALL (Juneau, Oates, Gonchar); FINALS (none). **Power Play conversions**— OVERALL (14 for 84, 16.7%); FINALS (2 for 17, 11.8%).

Goaltending	**Gm**	**Min**	**GAA**	**GA**	**SA**	**Sv%**	**W-L**	**Gm**	**Min**	**GAA**	**GA**	**SA**	**Sv%**	**W-L**
Olaf Kolzig	21	1351	**1.95**	44	740	.941	12-9	4	253	**3.08**	13	163	.920	0-4
TOTAL	21	1357	**1.95**	44	740	.941	12-9	4	255	**3.06**	13	163	.920	0-4

Empty Net Goals— OVERALL (none). **Shutouts**— OVERALL (Kolzig 4); FINALS (none). **Assists**— OVERALL (none). **Penalty Minutes**— OVERALL (Kolzig 4), FINALS (none).

Annual Awards

Except for the Vezina Trophy and Adams Award, voting is done by a 54-member panel of the Pro Hockey Writers Association, while full PHWA membership voted for Masterton Trophy. Vezina Trophy voted on by NHL general managers and Adams Award by NHL broadcasters. Points awarded on 10–7–5–3–1 basis except for the Vezina Trophy and the Adams Award which are awarded 5–3–1.

Hart Trophy

For Most Valuable Player

	Pos	1st	2nd	3rd	4th	5th	Pts
Dominik Hasek, Buf	G	43	7	4	0	0–	499
Jaromir Jagr, Pit	R	4	25	16	4	1–	308
Teemu Selanne, Ana	R	5	14	16	4	7–	247
Martin Brodeur, NJ	G	1	5	7	8	11–	115
Wayne Gretzky, NYR	C	1	0	1	9	4–	46
Petr Bondra, Wash	R	0	1	3	5	3–	40

Calder Trophy

For Rookie of the Year

	Pos	1st	2nd	3rd	4th	5th	Pts
Sergei Samsonov, Bos	L	43	9	2	0	0–	503
Mattias Ohlund, Van	D	11	18	10	7	1–	308
Patrik Elias, NJ	R	0	13	15	12	4–	206
Mike Johnson, Tor	R	0	6	14	16	12–	172
Derek Morris, Calg	D	0	4	7	9	9–	99

Norris Trophy

For Best Defenseman

	1st	2nd	3rd	4th	5th	Pts
Rob Blake, LA	27	12	8	2	1–	401
Nicklas Lidstrom, Det	15	22	10	5	0–	369
Chris Pronger, St.L	8	15	23	5	1–	316
Scott Stevens, NJ	3	2	2	9	3–	84
Scott Niedermayer, NJ	0	0	3	10	13–	58

Vezina Trophy

For Outstanding Goaltender

	1st	2nd	3rd	Pts
Dominik Hasek, Buf	24	2	0–	126
Martin Brodeur, NJ	2	14	5–	57
Tom Barrasso, Pit	0	7	5–	26
Ed Belfour, Dal	0	1	7–	10

Lady Byng Trophy

For Sportsmanship and Gentlemanly Play

	Pos	1st	2nd	3rd	4th	5th	Pts
Ron Francis, Pit	C	20	12	11	4	1–	352
Teemu Selanne, Ana	R	10	19	7	6	2–	288
Wayne Gretzky, NYR	C	9	9	14	5	8–	246
Nicklas Lidstrom, Det	D	6	3	5	2	7–	119
Alexei Yashin, Ott	C	2	5	4	5	4–	94
Adam Oates, Wash	C	1	0	2	5	4–	39

Selke Trophy

For Best Defensive Forward

	Pos	1st	2nd	3rd	4th	5th	Pts
Jere Lehtinen, Dal	R	18	13	9	3	3–	328
Michael Peca, Buf	C	9	13	18	8	2–	297
Craig Conroy, St.L	C	12	6	5	3	4–	200
Ron Francis, Pit	C	2	4	6	6	0–	96
Bobby Holik, NJ	C	6	2	1	1	3–	85
Peter Forsberg, Col	C	1	3	2	5	5–	61
Bobby Carpenter, NJ	C	2	1	1	1	1–	36

Adams Award

For Coach of the Year

	1st	2nd	3rd	Pts
Pat Burns, Bos	48	20	6–	306
Larry Robinson, LA	10	27	18–	149
Ken Hitchcock, Dal	17	10	8–	123
Joel Quenneville, St.L	4	13	21–	80
Kevin Constantine, Pit	3	10	16–	61
Jacques Lemaire, NJ	2	3	7–	26

AP/Wide World Photos

Boston's **Pat Burns** became the only coach to win three Adams Awards as the NHL Coach of the Year.

Other Awards

Lester B. Pearson Award (NHL Players Assn. MVP)— Dominik Hasek, Buffalo; **Jennings Trophy** (Goaltenders with a minimum of 25 games played for team with fewest goals against)— Martin Brodeur, New Jersey; **Masterton Trophy** (perseverance, sportsmanship,and dedication to hockey)— Jamie McLennan, St. Louis; **King Clancy Trophy** (leadership and humanitarian contributions to community)— Kelly Chase, St. Louis; **Lester Patrick Trophy** (outstanding service to hockey in the U.S.)— Max McNab, Peter Karmanos, Neal Broten and John Mayasich.

All-NHL Team

Voting by Pro Hockey Writers' Association (PHWA). Holdover from 1996-97 All-NHL first team in **bold** type.

	First Team		Second Team
G	**Dominik Hasek**, Buf	G	Martin Brodeur, NJ
D	Rob Blake, LA	D	Chris Pronger, St.L
D	Nicklas Lidstrom, Det	D	Scott Niedermayer, NJ
C	Peter Forsberg, Col	C	Wayne Gretzky, NYR
R	Jaromir Jagr, Pit	R	**Teemu Selanne**, Ana
L	John LeClair, Phi	L	Keith Tkachuk, Pho

All-Rookie Team

Voting by PHWA. Vote totals not released.

Pos		Pos	
G	Jamie Storr, LA	F	Sergei Samsonov, Bos.
D	Derek Morris, Calg.	F	Mike Johnson, Tor.
D	Mattias Ohlund, Van.	F	Patrik Elias, NJ

Rocket Richard Award

The NHL Board of Governors created the Maurice "Rocket" Richard Award to be given to the league's leading goal scorer beginning with the 1998-99 season. Richard was the first player to score 50 goals in one season and 500 in a career.

U.S. Division I College Hockey

Final regular season standings; overall records, including all postseason tournament games, in parentheses.

Central Collegiate Hockey Assn.

	W	L	T	Pts	GF	GA
*Michigan St. (31-6-4)	21	5	4	46	110	54
*Michigan (32-11-1)	22	7	1	45	109	69
*Ohio St. (27-13-2)	19	10	1	39	106	76
N. Michigan (19-5-4)	15	12	3	33	96	90
Miami-OH (18-14-4)	14	12	4	32	100	87
Lake Superior St. (15-18-4)	12	14	4	28	82	100
Notre Dame (18-19-4)	12	14	4	28	91	89
Ferris St. (15-21-3)	12	15	3	27	88	106
W. Michigan (10-25-3)	9	19	2	20	80	91
Alaska-Fairbanks (10-21-4)	7	20	3	17	87	138
Bowling Green (8-27-3)	6	21	3	15	77	126

Conf. Tourney Final: Michigan St. 3, Ohio St. 2 (2OT).
*__NCAA Tourney (6-2):__ Michigan (4-0), Ohio St. (2-1), Michigan St. (0-1).

Eastern Collegiate Athletic Conf.

	W	L	T	Pts	GF	GA
*Yale (23-9-3)	17	4	1	35	82	44
*Clarkson (23-9-3)	16	4	2	34	86	49
Rennselaer (18-13-4)	11	7	4	26	87	75
Brown (13-16-2)	11	9	2	24	73	64
Harvard (14-17-2)	10	11	1	21	72	78
Colgate (15-15-4)	9	10	3	21	69	75
*Princeton (18-11-7)	7	9	6	20	71	75
Cornell (15-16-2)	9	12	1	19	55	68
Vermont (10-20-4)	7	11	4	18	62	77
St. Lawrence (9-20-4)	8	12	2	18	56	69
Dartmouth (11-13-5)	7	12	3	17	72	77
Union (6-22-4)	4	15	3	11	42	76

Conf. Tourney Final: Princeton 5, Clarkson 4 (OT).
*__NCAA Tourney (0-3):__ Yale (0-1), Clarkson (0-1), Princeton (0-1).

Hockey East Association

	W	L	T	Pts	GF	GA
*Boston University (28-8-2)	18	4	2	38	95	52
*Boston College (28-9-5)	15	5	4	34	107	78
*New Hampshire (25-12-1)	15	8	1	31	104	62
Northeastern (21-15-3)	13	8	3	29	77	78
UMass-Lowell (16-16-3)	11	10	3	25	88	89
Maine (17-15-4)	10	11	3	23	98	89
Providence (15-18-3)	9	13	2	20	65	83
Merrimack (11-26-1)	4	20	0	8	78	128
UMass-Amherst (6-24-3)	3	19	2	8	62	116

Conf. Tourney Final: Boston College 3, Maine 2.
*__NCAA Tourney (4-3):__ Boston College (2-1), New Hampshire (2-1), Boston University (0-1).

Western Collegiate Hockey Assn.

	W	L	T	Pts	GF	GA
*North Dakota (30-8-1)	21	6	1	43	127	80
*Wisconsin (26-14-1)	17	10	1	35	102	88
*Colorado College (26-13-3)	16	10	2	34	111	93
St. Cloud St. (22-16-2)	16	11	1	33	101	90
Minnesota-Duluth (21-17-2)	14	12	2	30	94	90
Minnesota (17-22-0)	12	16	0	24	101	94
Michigan Tech (17-20-3)	10	17	1	21	79	116
Denver (11-25-2)	8	18	2	18	91	119
Alaska-Anchorage (6-26-5)	5	19	4	14	45	81

Conf. Tourney Final: Wisconsin 3, North Dakota 2.
*__NCAA Tourney (1-3):__ Colorado College (1-1), North Dakota (0-1), Wisconsin (0-1).

Independents

(Listed alphabetically)	Gm	W	L	T	Pts	GF	GA
Air Force	34	15	19	0	30	114	128
Army	34	18	15	1	37	156	106
Canisius	26	12	11	3	27	117	114
Connecticut	27	13	13	1	27	89	96
Fairfield	23	11	12	0	22	110	93
Holy Cross	26	16	8	2	34	98	58
Iona	25	4	20	1	9	49	162
Mankato St.	39	16	17	6	38	145	139
Nebraska-Omaha	34	12	19	3	27	101	121
Niagara	27	14	10	3	31	106	80
Villanova	22	2	20	0	4	35	117

USA Today/American Hockey Magazine Coaches Poll

Taken March 23, 1998 before NCAA Tournament. First place votes are in parentheses. Final Four teams are in **bold**.

		League	W	L	T	Pts
1	Michigan St. (10)	CCHA	31	5	4	100
2	North Dakota	WCHA	30	7	1	89
3	**Boston College**	HE	25	8	5	80
4	Boston University	HE	28	7	2	69
5	**Michigan**	CCHA	28	11	1	54
6	Wisconsin	WCHA	26	13	1	49
7	**Ohio St.**	CCHA	24	12	2	44
8	Clarkson	ECAC	23	8	3	29
9	Colorado College	WCHA	25	12	3	20
10	**New Hampshire**	HE	23	11	1	10

Also receiving votes: Yale (4 pts), Princeton (2).

Scoring Leaders

Including postseason games.

	Cl	Gm	G	A	Pts	PPG
Rob Curtis, Fairfield	Jr.	22	27	17	44	**2.00**
Ryan Murray, Fairfield	Sr.	21	12	27	39	**1.86**
Josh Oort, Canisius	Sr.	25	17	28	45	**1.80**
Jason Krog, UNH	Jr.	38	33	33	66	**1.74**
Derek Bekar, UNH	Jr.	35	32	28	60	**1.71**
Marty Reasoner, BC	Jr.	41	31	38	69	**1.68**
Mark Mowers, UNH	Sr.	35	25	31	56	**1.60**
Tom Nolan, UNH	Sr.	37	18	41	59	**1.59**
Mike York, Michigan St.	Jr.	37	25	31	56	**1.51**
Chris Drury, BU	Sr.	38	28	29	57	**1.50**
Rejean Stringer, Merrimack	Jr.	38	11	46	57	**1.50**
Justin Kieffer, Air Force	Jr.	34	24	27	51	**1.50**
Jeff Halpern, Princeton	Jr.	36	28	25	53	**1.47**
Brian Gionta, BC	Fr.	39	29	28	57	**1.46**
Andy Lundbohm, Army	Jr.	30	18	25	43	**1.43**

Goaltending Leaders

Including postseason games; minimum 15 games.

	Cl	Record	Sv%	GAA
Chad Alban, Michigan St.	Sr.	29-4-4	.926	**1.57**
Tom Noble, BU	Sr.	11-4-1	.907	**2.13**
Marty Turco, Michigan	Sr.	31-10-1	.906	**2.18**
Michel Laroque, BU	Jr.	17-4-1	.912	**2.19**
Karl Goehring, N. Dakota	Fr.	23-3-1	.913	**2.27**
Dan Murphy, Clarkson	Sr.	10-9-2	.907	**2.27**
Alex Westlund, Yale	Jr.	20-9-3	.919	**2.32**
Jeff Maund, Ohio St.	Fr.	22-8-0	.922	**2.36**
Chris Bernard, Clarkson	Sr.	13-0-1	.899	**2.43**
Sean Matile, UNH	Jr.	25-12-1	.908	**2.52**

Turco Saves the Day

by Jack Edwards

The Wolverines weren't worried.

Oh, maybe they should have been. Michigan had lost five of its last ten games heading into the NCAA tournament and to some teams it usually pounds with great regularity. On February 27, Ferris State snapped its eight-game losing streak against coach Red Berenson's maize and blue squad. On March 13, Notre Dame snapped its nine-game losing streak against UM. And on March 20 in the semifinals of the CCHA Tournament in Detroit, Ohio State, 0-29-5 against Michigan dating back to November 1989, beat the Wolverines 4-2.

But they weren't worried. They had Marty Turco. All they had to do was keep it close.

This is the goalie who had set the overall NCAA record for career wins, topping Michigan alum Steve Shields' mark of 111. Turco would finish with 127 victories, more than future NHL standouts Ken Dryden, Tony Esposito, Curtis Joseph, Mike Richter and Ed Belfour. When Turco shut out the University of New Hampshire 4-0 in the national semifinals, it was his 15th career shutout. Only Clarkson's Wally Easton (who recorded 16 from 1927-31) had more.

Boston College would provide a greater challenge in the national championship game. After all, the game was at the FleetCenter, a mere trolley ride from the BC campus. The place was sold out, and Eagles fans were shaking the building. Fortunately for Michigan, Turco isn't the kind of guy who can be shaken.

During the 1997-98 season, in the 19 games Michigan had led after one period, it won 18 and tied one. Since February 1995, Turco was 85-0-0 when Michigan had led after two.

But this senior season, which would result in Turco's fourth trip to the Final Four, was perhaps his greatest test. Sixty-three percent of the Wolverines' games were either one-goal games or ties heading into the third period. Fifty-four percent of the Wolverines' games were in that one-goal or tied situation going into the final MINUTE of regulation.

Turco wasn't too shabby. Michigan set a school record with 17 one-goal wins. The previous record had been ten. Seven of the Wolverines' last eight wins were one-goal games. UM played 21 one-goal games overall and that doesn't include four two-goal wins in which it scored empty-netters.

Boston College would send Michigan to OT, tied at two. The Eagles were looking for their first national title in about half a century. Michigan was looking for its second in three years.

The Wolverines could have been worried. But they weren't. Going into overtime at the FleetCenter, Turco was working on an 11-game overtime unbeaten streak. He hadn't allowed an OT goal since Lake Superior State slipped one past him in February 1996. Michigan had gone to OT six times in the '98 season. Turco was 5-0-1.

And what about the 1996 National Championship Game, Michigan's 3-2 win over Colorado College to win its first title in 32 years? You guessed it, that one had come in overtime too.

The two teams went deep into overtime in front of the NCAA-record crowd of 18,276. While Turco had been the constant, the overtime hero probably was going to come from a random draw since eleven different players had scored Michigan's game-winning goals in the one-goal wins.

At 17:51 of the overtime stanza, senior defenseman Chris Fox made the drop pass to Josh Langfeld, who slammed it home past BC goalie Scott Clemmensen. Three-two, Wolverines. In OT.

From 180 feet away at ice level, Turco didn't have a very good view of the goal. But he knew it was coming. He had made sure of it. ■

Jack Edwards is the co-anchor of ESPN's *Sunday SportsDay*.

NCAA Division I Tournament

Regional Seeds

	West		East
1	Michigan St. (31-5-4)	1	Boston U. (28-7-2)
2	North Dakota (30-7-1)	2	**Boston College** (25-8-5)
3	**Michigan** (28-11-1)	3	Clarkson (23-8-3)
4	**Ohio St.** (24-12-2)	4	Wisconsin (26-13-1)
5	Yale (23-8-3)	5	**New Hampshire** (23-11-1)
6	Princeton (18-10-7)	6	Colorado Col. (25-12-3)

West Regional

Held at Yost Arena in Ann Arbor, Mich., March 27-28. Single elimination, two second round winners advance to Final Four.

First Round

Michigan 2 .... Princeton 1
Ohio St. 4 .... Yale 0
(Byes: Michigan St. and North Dakota)

Second Round

Michigan 4 .... North Dakota 3
Ohio St. 4 .... OT .... Michigan St. 3

East Regional

Held at The Pepsi Arena in Albany, NY, March 28-29. Single elimination, two second round winners advance to Final Four.

First Round

New Hampshire 7 .... Wisconsin 4
Colorado College 3 .... Clarkson 1
(Byes: Boston College and Boston University)

Second Round

New Hampshire 4 .... OT .... Boston University 3
Boston College 6 .... Colorado College 1

THE FINAL FOUR

At the FleetCenter in Boston, Mass., April 2 and April 4. Single elimination; no consolation game.

Semifinals

Michigan 4 .... New Hampshire 0
Boston College 5 .... Ohio St. 2

Championship

Michigan 3 .... OT .... Boston College 2

Final records: Michigan (32-11-1); Boston College (27-9-5); New Hampshire (25-12-1); Ohio St. (27-13-2).

Outstanding Player: Marty Turco, Michigan senior goalie; SEMIFINAL— shutout, 19 saves; FINAL— 28 saves.

All-Tournament Team: Turco, forwards Mark Kosick and Josh Langfeld and defenseman Bubba Berenzweig of Michigan; forward Marty Reasoner and defenseman Mike Mottau of Boston College.

Hobey Baker Award

For College Player of the Year. Presented by Koho and USA Hockey, Inc. Voting done by 18-member panel of national media, coaches, pro scouts and a member of USA Hockey. Vote totals not released.

	Cl	Pos
Winner: Chris Drury, BU	Sr.	F
Runner-up: Chad Alban, Michigan St.	Sr.	G

Championship Game

Michigan, 3-2 (OT)

Saturday, April 4, 1998, at the FleetCenter in Boston, Mass.; Attendance: 18,276; TV Rating: 0.7/2 share (ESPN).

Michigan (CCHA)	0	1	1	1	— **3**
Boston College (HE)	1	1	0	0	— **2**

Scoring

1st Period: BC— Kevin Caufield (Mike Mottau), 4:19.

2nd Period: UM— Mark Kosick (Bubba Berenzweig), 7:42; BC— Mike Lephart (Jeff Farkas, Bobby Allen), 18:38 (pp).

3rd Period: UM— Kosick (Bill Muckalt, Chris Fox), 13:48.

Overtime: UM— Josh Langfeld (Fox, Scott Matzka), 17:51.

Goaltenders

Saves: UM— Marty Turco (30 shots/28 saves); BC— Scott Clemmensen (35 shots/32 saves).

Division I All-America

First team Titan Division I All-Americans as chosen by the American Hockey Coaches Association. Holdover from 1996-97 All-America first teams is in **bold** type.

West Team

Pos		Yr	Hgt	Wgt
G	Chad Alban, Michigan St.	Sr.	5-9	166
D	**Dan Boyle**, Miami-OH	Sr.	5-10	170
D	Curtis Murphy, North Dakota	Sr.	5-8	185
F	Hugo Boisvert, Ohio St.	So.	6-0	190
F	Bill Muckalt, Michigan	Sr.	6-0	195
F	Mike York, Michigan St.	Jr.	5-10	190

East Team

Pos		Yr	Hgt	Wgt
G	Marc Robitaille, Northeastern	So.	5-11	175
D	Ray Giroux, Yale	Sr.	6-1	191
D	Tom Poti, Boston University	So.	6-3	205
F	Chris Drury, Boston University	Sr.	5-10	200
F	Mark Mowers, New Hampshire	Sr.	5-10	175
F	Marty Reasoner, Boston College	Jr.	6-1	200

Other NCAA Tournaments

Division II

Two teams selected from limited national field. Championship decided in two games with mini-game (one 15-minute period), if necessary.

Final Two

March 13-14 in Huntsville, Ala.

Championship: GAME ONE— Alabama-Huntsville 6, Bemidji St. (Minn.) 2; GAME TWO— Alabama-Huntsville 5, Bemidji St. 2.

Final records: Alabama-Huntsville (24-3-3), Bemidji St. (22-10-2).

Division III

Final Four

March 20-21 in Plattsburgh, NY.

Semifinals— Wis-Stevens Point 8, Plattsburgh St. 2; Middlebury (Vt.) 5, Augsburg (Minn.) 2. **Third Place**— Plattsburgh St. 9, Augsburg 5. **Championship**— Middlebury 2, Wis-Stevens Point 1.

Final records: Middlebury (24-2-2); Wis-Stevens Point (23-11-0); Plattsburgh St. (26-8-1); Augsburg (21-8-4).

MINOR LEAGUE HOCKEY

American Hockey League

Division champions (*)and playoff qualifiers (†)are noted. GF and GA refer to goals for and against. Losses in overtime are designated in parentheses and worth one point in the standings.

Eastern Conference

Atlantic Division

Team (Affiliate)	W	L	T	Pts	GF	GA
*Saint John (Calg.)	43	24	13	99	231	201
†Fredericton (Mon. & LA)	33	37(5)	10	81	245	244
†Portland (Wash.)	33	35(2)	12	80	241	247
†St. John's (Tor.)	25	37(5)	18	73	233	254

New England Division

Team (Affiliate)	W	L	T	Pts	GF	GA
*Springfield (Pho.)	45	28(2)	7	99	278	248
†Hartford (NYR)	43	25(1)	12	99	272	227
†New Haven (Car. & Fla.)	38	35(2)	7	85	256	239
†Worcester (St.L & Ott.)	34	37(6)	9	83	267	268
Providence (Bos.)	19	54(5)	7	50	211	301

Western Conference

Empire State Division

Team (Affiliate)	W	L	T	Pts	GF	GA
*Albany (NJ)	43	26(6)	11	103	290	223
†Hamilton (Edm)	36	27(5)	17	94	264	242
†Syracuse (Van. & Pit.)	35	34(2)	11	83	272	285
†Adirondack (Det. & TB)	31	40(3)	9	74	245	275
†Rochester (Buf.)	30	38	12	72	238	260

Mid-Atlantic Division

Team (Affiliate)	W	L	T	Pts	GF	GA
*Philadelphia (Phi.)	47	23(2)	10	106	314	249
†Hershey (Col.)	36	37(6)	7	85	238	235
†Kentucky (SJ & NYI)	29	42(3)	9	70	241	278
Cincinnati (Ana.)	23	44(7)	13	66	243	303

Scoring Leaders

	G	A	Pts	PM
Peter White, Phi	27	78	105	28
Steve Guolla, Kent	37	63	100	45
Bob Wren, Cin	42	56	98	149
Daniel Briere, Spr.	36	56	92	42
Stacy Roest, Adi	34	57	91	30

Goaltending Leaders

	GP	GAA	Sv%	Record
Richard Shulmistra, Alb	35	2.32	.918	20-8-4
Robb Stauber, Har	39	2.41	.920	20-10-6
J-Sebastien Giguere, SJ	31	2.46	.926	16-10-3

Calder Cup Finals

	W-L	GF	Leading Scorers
Philadelphia	4-2	22	Maneluk (5-6-11)
Saint John	2-4	19	O'Sullivan (0-8-8)

Date	Winner	Home Ice
May 30	Philadelphia, 3-2 (2OT)	at Philadelphia
May 31	Saint John, 3-2 (OT)	at Philadelphia
June 3	Philadelphia, 4-3 (OT)	at Saint John
June 5	Philadelphia, 6-4	at Saint John
June 7	Saint John, 6-1	at Saint John
June 10	Philadelphia, 6-1	at Philadelphia

International Hockey League

Division champions (*)and playoff qualifiers (†)are noted. GF and GA refer to goals for and against. SOL refers to shootout losses and are worth one point in the standings.

Eastern Conference

Northeast Division

Team (Affiliate)	W	L	SOL	Pts	GF	GA
*Detroit (Indep.)	47	20	15	109	267	242
†Orlando (Indep.)	42	30	10	94	258	251
†Grand Rapids (Indep.)	38	31	13	89	225	243
Quebec (Indep.)	27	48	7	61	211	292

Central Division

Team (Affiliate)	W	L	SOL	Pts	GF	GA
*Fort Wayne (Indep.)	47	29	6	100	270	243
†Cincinnati (Indep.)	40	30	12	92	275	254
†Indianapolis (Chi.)	40	36	6	86	245	261
†Cleveland (Ind.)	35	37	10	80	228	262
†Michigan (Dal.)	36	39	7	79	223	261

Western Conference

Midwest Division

Team (Affiliate)	W	L	SOL	Pts	GF	GA
*Chicago (Indep.)	55	24	3	113	301	258
†Kansas City (Indep.)	41	29	12	94	269	258
†Milwaukee (Indep.)	43	34	5	91	267	262
†Manitoba (Indep.)	39	36	7	85	269	254

Southwest Division

Team (Affiliate)	W	L	SOL	Pts	GF	GA
*Long Beach (Ana.)	53	20	9	115	282	210
†Houston (Indep.)	50	22	10	110	268	214
†Utah (NYI)	47	27	8	102	276	234
†Las Vegas (Pho.)	33	39	10	76	260	305
San Antonio (Indep.)	25	49	8	58	233	334

Scoring Leaders

	G	A	Pts	PM
Patrice Lefebvre, LV	27	88	115	113
Todd Simon, Cin	33	71	104	103
Gilbert Dionne, Cin	41	56	97	52
Steve Maltais, Chi.	43	53	96	118
Brian Wiseman, Hou	26	70	96	86

Goaltending Leaders

	GP	GAA	Sv%	Record
Wade Flaherty, Utah	24	1.80	.936	16-5-3
Mike Buzak, LB	31	1.97	.934	18-6-5
Jeff Reese, Det	46	2.22	.917	27-9-8

Turner Cup Finals

	W-L	GF	Leading Scorers
Chicago	4-3	21	Semak (5-3-8)
Detroit	3-4	17	Carson (3-3-6) & Kesa (3-3-6)

Date	Winner	Home Ice
May 30	Chicago, 4-2	at Chicago
June 2	Detroit, 5-4	at Chicago
June 4	Chicago, 4-3	at Detroit
June 7	Detroit, 3-2	at Detroit
June 9	Detroit, 3-1	at Detroit
June 12	Chicago, 3-1	at Chicago
June 15	Chicago, 3-0	at Chicago

World Hockey Championship

MEN

The World Hockey Championship, held in Zurich and Basel, Switzerland May 1-17, 1998. Top two teams (*) in each pool after preliminary round-robin advance to the qualifying round. Third place teams play in a consolation round. Top two teams from each pool of the qualifying round advance to the semifinals. The semifinals are a best-of-two series with a 10-minute mini-game if necessary. If teams are still tied, a shootout will decide the advancers. Winners meet in the best-of-two final series.

Final Round Robin Standings

POOL A	W-L-T	Pts	GF	GA
*Czech Republic	3-0-0	**6**	20	5
*Belarus	2-1-0	**4**	12	10
Germany	1-2-0	**2**	8	13
Japan	0-3-0	**0**	7	19

POOL B	W-L-T	Pts	GF	GA
*Canada	2-0-1	**5**	12	5
*Slovakia	2-0-1	**5**	9	4
Italy	1-2-0	**2**	8	8
Austria	0-3-0	**0**	3	15

POOL C	W-L-T	Pts	GF	GA
*Sweden	3-0-0	**6**	16	4
*Switzerland	1-2-0	**2**	9	10
United States	1-2-0	**2**	7	11
France	1-2-0	**2**	5	12

Note: Switzerland advances to the qualifying round due to a better goal differential then the United States and France.

POOL D	W-L-T	Pts	GF	GA
*Russia	3-0-0	**6**	19	11
*Finland	2-1-0	**4**	12	4
Latvia	1-2-0	**2**	12	15
Kazakhstan	0-3-0	**0**	6	19

Qualifying Round

POOL E	W-L-T	Pts	GF	GA
*Sweden	3-0-0	**6**	10	2
*Finland	1-1-1	**3**	8	6
Canada	1-1-1	**3**	10	12
Belarus	0-3-0	**0**	5	13

POOL F	W-L-T	Pts	GF	GA
*Czech Republic	2-0-1	**5**	6	3
*Switzerland	1-1-1	**3**	6	6
Russia	1-1-1	**3**	10	7
Slovakia	0-2-1	**1**	2	8

Consolation Round

	W-L-T	Pts	GF	GA
Italy	1-0-1	3	5	1
Latvia	1-0-1	3	6	1
Germany	0-1-1	1	1	6
United States	0-1-1	1	1	5

Note: Only the top two finishers in the consolation round retain their spots in the 1999 World Championship. The United States must now play through a qualifying tournament in November of 1998 in order to be given entry into the 1999 elite group.

Semifinals (best of two)

Sweden 7 .... Switzerland 2
Sweden 4 .... Switzerland 1

Czech Republic 2 .... Finland 2
Finland 4 .... Czech Republic 1

Bronze Medal Game

Czech Republic 4 .... Switzerland 0

Championship (best of two)

Sweden 1 .... Finland 0
Sweden 0 .... Finland 0

Scoring Leaders

	Gm	G	A	Pts	PM
Peter Forsberg, Sweden	7	6	5	**11**	0
Raimo Helminen, Finland	10	2	9	**11**	0
Mats Sundin, Sweden	10	5	6	**11**	6
Ville Peltonen, Finland	10	4	6	**10**	8
Victor Kozlov, Russia	6	4	5	**9**	0
Radek Belohlav, Czech Rep.	9	6	3	**9**	2
Pavel Patera, Czech Rep.	9	6	3	**9**	12
Sergei Berezin, Russia	6	6	2	**8**	2
Olegs Znaroks, Latvia	6	5	3	**8**	2
Alexei Kovalev, Russia	6	5	3	**8**	14
Martin Prochazka, Czech Rep.	8	3	5	**8**	14
Marcel Jenni, Switzerland	9	3	5	**8**	14
Gian-Marco Crameri, Switzerland	9	2	6	**8**	8
Mikael Renberg, Sweden	10	5	3	**8**	6
Kimmo Timonen, Finland	10	2	6	**8**	4

Goaltending Leaders

(At least 180 minutes)	Gm	Min	W-L-T	GAA
Tommy Salo, Sweden	9	540	8-0-0	**0.78**
Ari Sulander, Finland	8	477	3-2-2	**1.26**
Milan Hnilicka, Czech Rep.	8	430	4-1-2	**1.39**
Michael Rosati, Italy	5	298	2-1-2	**1.61**
Miroslav Simonovic, Slovakia	6	359	2-2-2	**2.00**
Felix Potvin, Canada	4	240	3-0-1	**2.00**
Oleg Chevtsov, Russia	4	240	2-1-1	**2.25**
Garth Snow, United States	5	259	1-2-1	**2.77**
Arturs Irbe, Latvia	6	359	3-2-1	**2.84**
David Aebischer, Switzerland	7	375	2-4-1	**2.87**

World All-Star Teams

(Selected by media)

First Team: G— Tommy Salo, Sweden; **D**— Frantisek Kucera, Czech Republic and Jere Karalahti, Finland; **F**— Peter Forsberg, Sweden; Mats Sundin, Sweden; Ville Peltonen, Finland.

Second Team: G— Ari Sulander, Finland; **D**— Marko Kiprusoff, Finland and Mattias Ohlund, Sweden; **F**— Marcel Jenni, Switzerland; Sergei Berezin, Russia; Pavel Patera, Czech Republic.

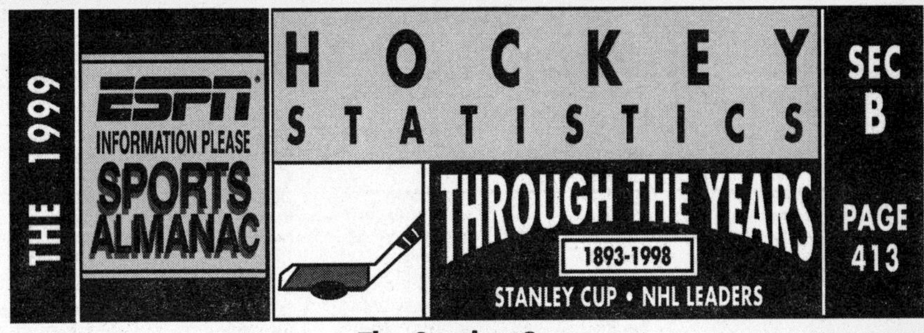

THE 1999
ESPN
INFORMATION PLEASE
SPORTS ALMANAC
HOCKEY
STATISTICS
THROUGH THE YEARS
1893-1998
STANLEY CUP • NHL LEADERS
SEC B
PAGE 413

The Stanley Cup

The Stanley Cup was originally donated to the Canadian Amateur Hockey Association by Sir Frederick Arthur Stanley, Lord Stanley of Preston and 16th Earl of Derby, who had become interested in the sport while Governor General of Canada from 1888 to 1893. Stanley wanted the trophy to be a challenge cup, contested for each year by the best amateur hockey teams in Canada.

In 1893, the Cup was presented without a challenge to the AHA champion Montreal Amateur Athletic Association team. Every year since, however, there has been a playoff. In 1914, Cup trustees limited the field challenging for the trophy to the champion of the eastern professional National Hockey Association (NHA, organized in 1910) and the western professional Pacific Coast Hockey Association (PCHA, organized in 1912).

The NHA disbanded in 1917 and the National Hockey League (NHL) was formed. From 1918 to 1926, the NHL and PCHA champions played for the Cup with the Western Canada Hockey League (WCHL) champion joining in a three-way challenge in 1923 and '24. The PCHA disbanded in 1924, while the WCHL became the Western Hockey League (WHL) for the 1925-26 season and folded the following year. The NHL playoffs have decided the winner of the Stanley Cup ever since.

Champions, 1893-1917

Multiple winners: Montreal Victorias and Montreal Wanderers (4); Montreal Amateur Athletic Association and Ottawa Silver Seven (3); Montreal Shamrocks, Ottawa Senators, Quebec Bulldogs and Winnipeg Victorias (2).

Year	
1893	Montreal AAA
1894	Montreal AAA
1895	Montreal Victorias
1896	(Feb.) Winnipeg Victorias
	(Dec.) Montreal Victorias
1897	Montreal Victorias
1898	Montreal Victorias
1899	Montreal Shamrocks
1900	Montreal Shamrocks

Year	
1901	Winnipeg Victorias
1902	Montreal AAA
1903	Ottawa Silver Seven
1904	Ottawa Silver Seven
1905	Ottawa Silver Seven
1906	Montreal Wanderers
1907	(Jan.) Kenora Thistles
	(Mar.) Montreal Wanderers
1908	Montreal Wanderers

Year	
1909	Ottawa Senators
1910	Montreal Wanderers
1911	Ottawa Senators
1912	Quebec Bulldogs
1913	Quebec Bulldogs
1914	Toronto Blueshirts (NHA)
1915	Vancouver Millionaires (PCHA)
1916	Montreal Canadiens (NHA)
1917	Seattle Metropolitans (PCHA)

Champions Since 1918

Multiple winners: Montreal Canadiens (23); Toronto Arenas-St. Pats-Maple Leafs (13); Detroit Red Wings (9); Boston Bruins and Edmonton Oilers (5); NY Islanders, NY Rangers and Ottawa Senators (4); Chicago Blackhawks (3); Philadelphia Flyers, Pittsburgh Penguins and Montreal Maroons (2).

Year	Winner	Head Coach	Series	Loser	Head Coach
1918	Toronto Arenas	Dick Carroll	3-2 (WLWLW)	Vancouver (PCHA)	Frank Patrick
1919	No Decision*				
1920	Ottawa	Pete Green	3-2 (WWLLW)	Seattle (PCHA)	Pete Muldoon
1921	Ottawa	Pete Green	3-2 (LWWLW)	Vancouver (PCHA)	Frank Patrick
1922	Toronto St. Pats	Eddie Powers	3-2 (LWLWW)	Vancouver (PCHA)	Frank Patrick
1923	Ottawa	Pete Green	3-1 (WLWW)	Vancouver (PCHA)	Frank Patrick
			2-0	Edmonton (WCHL)	K.C. McKenzie
1924	Montreal	Leo Dandurand	2-0	Vancouver (PCHA)	Frank Patrick
			2-0	Calgary (WCHL)	Eddie Oatman
1925	Victoria (WCHL)	Lester Patrick	3-1 (WWLW)	Montreal	Leo Dandurand
1926	Montreal Maroons	Eddie Gerard	3-1 (WWLW)	Victoria (WHL)	Lester Patrick
1927	Ottawa	Dave Gill	2-0 (TWTW)	Boston	Art Ross
1928	NY Rangers	Lester Patrick	3-2 (LWLWW)	Montreal Maroons	Eddie Gerard
1929	Boston	Cy Denneny	2-0	NY Rangers	Lester Patrick
1930	Montreal	Cecil Hart	2-0	Boston	Art Ross
1931	Montreal	Cecil Hart	3-2 (WLLWW)	Chicago	Art Duncan
1932	Toronto	Dick Irvin	3-0	NY Rangers	Lester Patrick
1933	NY Rangers	Lester Patrick	3-1 (WWLW)	Toronto	Dick Irvin
1934	Chicago	Tommy Gorman	3-1 (WWLW)	Detroit	Jack Adams
1935	Montreal Maroons	Tommy Gorman	3-0	Toronto	Dick Irvin
1936	Detroit	Jack Adams	3-1 (WWLW)	Toronto	Dick Irvin
1937	Detroit	Jack Adams	3-2 (LWLWW)	NY Rangers	Lester Patrick
1938	Chicago	Bill Stewart	3-1 (WLWW)	Toronto	Dick Irvin
1939	Boston	Art Ross	4-1 (WLWWW)	Toronto	Dick Irvin

Year	Winner	Head Coach	Series	Loser	Head Coach
1940	NY Rangers	Frank Boucher	4-2 (WWLLWW)	Toronto	Dick Irvin
1941	Boston	Cooney Weiland	4-0	Detroit	Jack Adams
1942	Toronto	Hap Day	4-3 (LLLWWWW)	Detroit	Jack Adams
1943	Detroit	Ebbie Goodfellow	4-0	Boston	Art Ross
1944	Montreal	Dick Irvin	4-0	Chicago	Paul Thompson
1945	Toronto	Hap Day	4-3 (WWWLLLW)	Detroit	Jack Adams
1946	Montreal	Dick Irvin	4-1 (WWWLW)	Boston	Dit Clapper
1947	Toronto	Hap Day	4-2 (LWWWLW)	Montreal	Dick Irvin
1948	Toronto	Hap Day	4-0	Detroit	Tommy Ivan
1949	Toronto	Hap Day	4-0	Detroit	Tommy Ivan
1950	Detroit	Tommy Ivan	4-3 (WLWLLWW)	NY Rangers	Lynn Patrick
1951	Toronto	Joe Primeau	4-1 (WLWWW)	Montreal	Dick Irvin
1952	Detroit	Tommy Ivan	4-0	Montreal	Dick Irvin
1953	Montreal	Dick Irvin	4-1 (WLWWW)	Boston	Lynn Patrick
1954	Detroit	Tommy Ivan	4-3 (WLWWLLW)	Montreal	Dick Irvin
1955	Detroit	Jimmy Skinner	4-3 (WWLLWLW)	Montreal	Dick Irvin
1956	Montreal	Toe Blake	4-1 (WWLWW)	Detroit	Jimmy Skinner
1957	Montreal	Toe Blake	4-1 (WWWLW)	Boston	Milt Schmidt
1958	Montreal	Toe Blake	4-2 (WLWLWW)	Boston	Milt Schmidt
1959	Montreal	Toe Blake	4-1 (WWLWW)	Toronto	Punch Imlach
1960	Montreal	Toe Blake	4-0	Toronto	Punch Imlach
1961	Chicago	Rudy Pilous	4-2 (WLWLWW)	Detroit	Sid Abel
1962	Toronto	Punch Imlach	4-2 (WWLLWW)	Chicago	Rudy Pilous
1963	Toronto	Punch Imlach	4-1 (WWLWW)	Detroit	Sid Abel
1964	Toronto	Punch Imlach	4-3 (WLLWLWW)	Detroit	Sid Abel
1965	Montreal	Toe Blake	4-3 (WWLLWLW)	Chicago	Billy Reay
1966	Montreal	Toe Blake	4-2 (LLWWWW)	Detroit	Sid Abel
1967	Toronto	Punch Imlach	4-2 (LWWLWW)	Montreal	Toe Blake
1968	Montreal	Toe Blake	4-0	St. Louis	Scotty Bowman
1969	Montreal	Claude Ruel	4-0	St. Louis	Scotty Bowman
1970	Boston	Harry Sinden	4-0	St. Louis	Scotty Bowman
1971	Montreal	Al MacNeil	4-3 (LLWWLWW)	Chicago	Billy Reay
1972	Boston	Tom Johnson	4-2 (WWLWLW)	NY Rangers	Emile Francis
1973	Montreal	Scotty Bowman	4-2 (WWLWLW)	Chicago	Billy Reay
1974	Philadelphia	Fred Shero	4-2 (LWWWLW)	Boston	Bep Guidolin
1975	Philadelphia	Fred Shero	4-2 (WWLLWW)	Buffalo	Floyd Smith
1976	Montreal	Scotty Bowman	4-0	Philadelphia	Fred Shero
1977	Montreal	Scotty Bowman	4-0	Boston	Don Cherry
1978	Montreal	Scotty Bowman	4-2 (WWLLWW)	Boston	Don Cherry
1979	Montreal	Scotty Bowman	4-1 (LWWWW)	NY Rangers	Fred Shero
1980	NY Islanders	Al Arbour	4-2 (WLWWLW)	Philadelphia	Pat Quinn
1981	NY Islanders	Al Arbour	4-1 (WWWLW)	Minnesota	Glen Sonmor
1982	NY Islanders	Al Arbour	4-0	Vancouver	Roger Neilson
1983	NY Islanders	Al Arbour	4-0	Edmonton	Glen Sather
1984	Edmonton	Glen Sather	4-1 (WLWWW)	NY Islanders	Al Arbour
1985	Edmonton	Glen Sather	4-1 (LWWWW)	Philadelphia	Mike Keenan
1986	Montreal	Jean Perron	4-1 (LWWWW)	Calgary	Bob Johnson
1987	Edmonton	Glen Sather	4-3 (WWLWLLW)	Philadelphia	Mike Keenan
1988	Edmonton	Glen Sather	4-0	Boston	Terry O'Reilly
1989	Calgary	Terry Crisp	4-2 (WLLWWW)	Montreal	Pat Burns
1990	Edmonton	John Muckler	4-1 (WWLWW)	Boston	Mike Milbury
1991	Pittsburgh	Bob Johnson	4-2 (LWLWWW)	Minnesota	Bob Gainey
1992	Pittsburgh	Scotty Bowman	4-0	Chicago	Mike Keenan
1993	Montreal	Jacques Demers	4-1 (LWWWW)	Los Angeles	Barry Melrose
1994	NY Rangers	Mike Keenan	4-3 (LWWWLLW)	Vancouver	Pat Quinn
1995	New Jersey	Jacques Lemaire	4-0	Detroit	Scotty Bowman
1996	Colorado	Marc Crawford	4-0	Florida	Doug MacLean
1997	Detroit	Scotty Bowman	4-0	Philadelphia	Terry Murray
1998	Detroit	Scotty Bowman	4-0	Washington	Ron Wilson

* The 1919 finals were cancelled after five games due to an influenza epidemic with Montreal and Seattle (PCHA) tied at 2-2-1.

M.J. O'Brien Trophy

Donated by Canadian mining magnate M.J. O'Brien, whose son Ambrose founded the National Hockey Association in 1910. Originally presented to the NHA champion until the league's demise in 1917, the trophy then passed to the NHL champion through 1927. It was awarded to the NHL's Canadian Division winner from 1927-38 and the Stanley Cup runner-up from 1939-50 before being retired in 1950.

NHA winners included the Montreal Wanderers (1910), original Ottawa Senators (1911 and '15), Quebec Bulldogs (1912 and '13), Toronto Blueshirts (1914) and Montreal Canadiens (1916 and '17).

Conn Smythe Trophy

The Most Valuable Player of the Stanley Cup Playoffs, as selected by the Pro Hockey Writers Association. Presented since 1965 by Maple Leaf Gardens Limited in the name of the former Toronto coach, GM and owner, Conn Smythe. Winners who did not play for the Cup champion are in **bold** type.

Multiple winners: Wayne Gretzky, Mario Lemieux, Bobby Orr, Bernie Parent and Patrick Roy (2).

Year	
1965	Jean Beliveau, Mon., C
1966	**Roger Crozier**, Det., G
1967	Dave Keon, Tor., C
1968	**Glenn Hall**, St.L., G
1969	Serge Savard, Mon., D
1970	Bobby Orr, Bos., D
1971	Ken Dryden, Mon., G
1972	Bobby Orr, Bos., D
1973	Yvan Cournoyer, Mon., RW
1974	Bernie Parent, Phi., G
1975	Bernie Parent, Phi., G
1976	**Reggie Leach**, Phi., RW
1977	Guy Lafleur, Mon., RW
1978	Larry Robinson, Mon., D
1979	Bob Gainey, Mon., LW
1980	Bryan Trottier, NYI, C
1981	Butch Goring, NYI, C
1982	Mike Bossy, NYI, RW
1983	Billy Smith, NYI, G
1984	Mark Messier, Edm., LW
1985	Wayne Gretzky, Edm., C
1986	Patrick Roy, Mon., G
1987	**Ron Hextall**, Phi., G
1988	Wayne Gretzky, Edm., C
1989	Al MacInnis, Calg., D
1990	Bill Ranford, Edm., G
1991	Mario Lemieux, Pit., C
1992	Mario Lemieux, Pit., C
1993	Patrick Roy, Mon., G
1994	Brian Leetch, NYR, D
1995	Claude Lemieux, NJ, RW
1996	Joe Sakic, Col., C
1997	Mike Vernon, Det., G
1998	Steve Yzerman, Det., C

Note: Ken Dryden (1971) and Patrick Roy (1986) are the only players to win as rookies.

All-Time Stanley Cup Playoff Leaders

CAREER

Stanley Cup Playoff leaders through 1998. Years listed indicate number of playoff appearances. Players active in 1998 in **bold** type; (DNP) indicates active player did not participate in 1998 playoffs.

Scoring

Points

		Yrs	Gm	G	A	Pts
1	**Wayne Gretzky** (DNP)	16	208	122	260	382
2	**Mark Messier** (DNP)	17	236	109	186	295
3	**Jari Kurri**	14	196	106	127	233
4	Glenn Anderson	15	225	93	121	214
5	**Paul Coffey** (DNP)	15	189	59	136	195
6	Bryan Trottier	17	221	71	113	184
7	Jean Beliveau	17	162	79	97	176
8	Denis Savard	16	169	66	109	175
9	**Doug Gilmour**	14	152	54	117	171
10	Denis Potvin	14	185	56	108	164
11	Mike Bossy	10	129	85	75	160
	Gordie Howe	20	157	68	92	160
	Bobby Smith	13	184	64	96	160
14	Mario Lemieux	7	89	70	85	155
15	**Ray Bourque**	18	168	35	116	151
16	Stan Mikita	18	155	59	91	150
17	Brian Propp	13	160	64	84	148
18	**Larry Murphy**	17	190	35	109	144
	Larry Robinson	20	227	28	116	144
20	Jacques Lemaire	11	145	61	78	139
21	**Adam Oates**	11	126	38	100	138
22	Phil Esposito	15	130	61	76	137
23	**Steve Yzerman**	13	135	52	83	135
24	Guy Lafleur	14	128	58	76	134
25	**Claude Lemieux**	13	179	73	60	133

Goals

		Yrs	Gm	G
1	**Wayne Gretzky** (DNP)	16	208	122
2	**Mark Messier** (DNP)	17	236	109
3	**Jari Kurri**	15	200	106
4	Glenn Anderson	15	225	93
5	Mike Bossy	10	129	85
6	Maurice Richard	15	133	82
7	Jean Beliveau	17	162	79
8	**Dino Ciccarelli** (DNP)	14	141	73
	Claude Lemieux	13	179	73
10	**Esa Tikkanen**	13	186	72
11	Bryan Trottier	17	221	71
12	Mario Lemieux	7	89	70
13	**Brett Hull**	13	108	69
14	Gordie Howe	20	157	68
15	Denis Savard	16	169	66

Assists

		Yrs	Gm	A
1	**Wayne Gretzky** (DNP)	16	208	260
2	**Mark Messier** (DNP)	17	236	186
3	**Paul Coffey** (DNP)	15	189	136
4	**Jari Kurri**	15	200	127
5	Glenn Anderson	15	225	121
6	**Doug Gilmour**	14	152	117
7	Larry Robinson	20	227	116
8	Bryan Trottier	17	221	113
9	**Ray Bourque**	18	168	116
10	Denis Savard	16	169	109
	Larry Murphy	17	190	109
12	Denis Potvin	14	185	108
13	**Adam Oates**	11	126	100
14	Jean Beliveau	17	162	97
15	Bobby Smith	13	184	96

Goaltending

Wins

		Gm	W-L	Pct	GAA
1	**Patrick Roy**	160	99-59	.627	2.38
2	Billy Smith	132	88-36	.710	2.73
3	**Grant Fuhr**	137	86-44	.662	2.98
4	Ken Dryden	112	80-32	.714	2.40
5	**Mike Vernon**	129	75-49	.605	2.68
6	Jacques Plante	112	71-37	.657	2.17
7	**Andy Moog**	132	68-57	.544	3.04
8	Turk Broda	102	58-42	.580	1.98
9	Terry Sawchuk	106	54-48	.529	2.54
10	**Tom Barrasso**	100	53-43	.552	3.09
11	Glenn Hall	115	49-65	.430	2.79
12	Gerry Cheevers	88	47-35	.573	2.69
	Ron Hextall	93	47-43	.522	3.04
14	**Ed Belfour**	85	45-35	.563	2.35
	Tony Esposito	99	45-53	.459	3.07

Shutouts

		Gm	GAA	No
1	Clint Benedict	48	1.80	15
	Jacques Plante	112	2.17	15
3	Turk Broda	102	1.98	13
4	Terry Sawchuk	106	2.54	12
5	**Patrick Roy**	160	2.38	11

Goals Against Average

Minimum of 50 games played

		Gm	Min	GA	GAA
1	**Martin Brodeur**	54	3450	106	1.84
2	George Hainsworth	52	3486	112	1.93
3	Turk Broda	101	6348	211	1.98
4	Jacques Plante	112	6651	241	2.17
5	**Ed Belfour**	85	4981	195	2.35
6	**Patrick Roy**	160	9882	392	2.38
7	Ken Dryden	112	6846	274	2.40
8	Bernie Parent	71	4302	174	2.43
9	Harry Lumley	76	4759	199	2.51
10	Johnny Bower	74	4350	184	2.54

Note: Clint Benedict had an average of 1.80 but played in only 48 games.

Games Played

		Yrs	Gm
1	**Patrick Roy**, Mon-Col	12	160
2	**Grant Fuhr,** Edm-Buf-St.L.	13	137
3	Billy Smith, NY Islanders	13	132
	Andy Moog, Edm-Bos-Dal-Mon	16	132
5	**Mike Vernon**, Calg-Det-SJ	12	129

Appearances in Cup Finals

Standings of all teams that have reached the Stanley Cup championship round, since 1918.

App		Cups	Last Won
32	Montreal Canadiens	23*	1993
21	Toronto Maple Leafs	13†	1967
21	Detroit Red Wings	9	1998
17	Boston Bruins	5	1972
10	New York Rangers	4	1994
10	Chicago Blackhawks	3	1961
7	Philadelphia Flyers	2	1975
6	Edmonton Oilers	5	1990
5	New York Islanders	4	1983
5	Vancouver Millionaires (PCHA)	0	—
4	(original) Ottawa Senators	4	1927
3	Montreal Maroons	2	1935
3	St. Louis Blues	0	—
2	Pittsburgh Penguins	2	1992
2	Calgary Flames	1	1989
2	Victoria Cougars (WCHL-WHL)	1	1925
2	Minnesota North Stars	0	—
2	Seattle Metropolitans (PCHA)	0	—
2	Vancouver Canucks	0	—
1	Colorado Avalanche	1	1996
1	New Jersey Devils	1	1995
1	Buffalo Sabres	0	—
1	Calgary Tigers (WCHL)	0	—
1	Edmonton Eskimos (WCHL)	0	—
1	Florida Panthers	0	—
1	Los Angeles Kings	0	—
1	Washington Capitals	0	—

*Les Canadiens also won the Cup in 1916 for a total of 24. Also, their final with Seattle in 1919 was cancelled due to an influenza epidemic that claimed the life of the Habs' Joe Hall.

†Toronto has won the Cup under three nicknames—Arenas (1918), St. Pats (1922) and Maple Leafs (1932,42,45,47-49,51,62-64,67).

Teams now defunct (7): Calgary Tigers, Edmonton Eskimos, Montreal Maroons, (original) Ottawa Senators, Seattle, Vancouver Millionaires and Victoria. Edmonton (1923) and Calgary (1924) represented the WCHL and later the WHL, while Vancouver (1918,1921-24) and Seattle (1919-20) played out of the PCHA.

Miscellaneous

Championships

		Yrs	Cups
1	Henri Richard, Montreal	18	11
2	Yvan Cournoyer, Montreal	15	10
	Jean Beliveau, Montreal	17	10
4	Claude Provost, Montreal	14	9
5	Jacques Lemaire, Montreal	11	8
	Maurice Richard, Montreal	15	8
	Red Kelly, Detroit-Toronto	19	8

Years in Playoffs

		Yrs	Gm
1	Gordie Howe, Detroit-Hartford	20	157
	Larry Robinson, Montreal-Los Angeles	20	227
3	Red Kelly, Detroit-Toronto	19	164
4	**Kevin Lowe**, Edm-NYR-Edm	18	214
	Henri Richard, Montreal	18	180
	Ray Bourque, Boston	18	168
	Stan Mikita, Chicago	18	155

Games Played

		Yrs	Gm
1	**Mark Messier**, Edm-NYR-Van (DNP)	17	236
2	Larry Robinson, Montreal-Los Angeles	20	227
3	Glenn Anderson, Edm-Tor-NYR-St.L.	15	225
4	Bryan Trottier. NY Isles-Pittsburgh	17	221
5	**Kevin Lowe,** Edm-NYR-Edm	18	214

Penalty Minutes

		Yrs	Gm	Min
1	**Dale Hunter**, Que-Wash	17	167	691
2	Chris Nilan, Mon-NYR-Bos-Mon	12	111	541
3	Willi Plett, Atl-Calg-Min-Bos	10	83	466
4	**Claude Lemieux**, Mon-NJ-Col	13	179	463
5	Dave Williams, Tor-Van-LA	12	83	455

SINGLE SEASON

Scoring

Points

		Year	Gm	G	A	Pts
1	Wayne Gretzky, Edm	1985	18	17	30	47
2	Mario Lemieux, Pit	1991	23	16	28	44
3	Wayne Gretzky, Edm	1988	19	12	31	43
4	Wayne Gretzky, LA	1993	24	15	25	40
5	Wayne Gretzky, Edm	1983	16	12	26	38
6	Paul Coffey, Edm	1985	18	12	25	37
7	Mike Bossy, NYI	1981	18	17	18	35
	Wayne Gretzky, Edm	1984	19	13	22	35
	Doug Gilmour, Tor	1993	21	10	25	35
10	Mario Lemieux, Pit	1992	15	16	18	34
	Mark Messier, Edm	1988	19	11	23	34
	Mark Recchi, Pit	1991	24	10	24	34
	Wayne Gretzky, Edm	1987	21	5	29	34
	Brian Leetch, NYR	1994	23	11	23	34
	Joe Sakic, Col	1996	22	18	16	34

Goals

		Year	Gm	No
1	Reggie Leach, Philadelphia	1976	16	19
	Jari Kurri, Edmonton	1985	18	19
3	Joe Sakic, Colorado	1996	22	18
4	Newsy Lalonde, Montreal	1919	10	17
	Mike Bossy, NY Islanders	1981	18	17
	Wayne Gretzky, Edmonton	1985	18	17
	Steve Payne, Minnesota	1981	19	17
	Mike Bossy, NY Islanders	1982	19	17
	Mike Bossy, NY Islanders	1983	19	17
	Kevin Stevens, Pittsburgh	1991	24	17

Assists

		Year	Gm	No
1	Wayne Gretzky, Edmonton	1988	19	31
2	Wayne Gretzky, Edmonton	1985	18	30
3	Wayne Gretzky, Edmonton	1987	21	29
4	Mario Lemieux, Pittsburgh	1991	23	28
5	Wayne Gretzky, Edmonton	1983	16	26
6	Paul Coffey, Edmonton	1985	18	25
	Doug Gilmour, Toronto	1993	21	25
	Wayne Gretzky, Los Angeles	1993	24	25
9	Al MacInnis, Calgary	1989	22	24
	Mark Recchi, Pittsburgh	1991	24	24

Goaltending

Wins

		Year	Gm	Min	W-L
1	Grant Fuhr, Edm	1988	19	1136	16-2
	Mike Vernon, Det	1997	20	1229	16-4
	Patrick Roy, Mon	1993	20	1293	16-4
	Martin Brodeur, NJ	1995	20	1222	16-4
	Mike Vernon, Calg	1989	22	1381	16-5
	Tom Barrasso, Pit	1992	21	1233	16-5
	Chris Osgood, Det	1998	22	1361	16-6
	Bill Ranford, Edm	1990	22	1401	16-6
	Patrick Roy, Col	1996	22	1454	16-6
	Mike Richter, NYR	1994	23	1417	16-7

Shutouts

		Year	Gm	No
1	Clint Benedict, Mon. Maroons	1926	8	4
	Terry Sawchuk, Detroit	1952	8	4
	Clint Benedict, Mon. Maroons	1928	9	4
	Dave Kerr, NY Rangers	1937	9	4
	Frank McCool, Toronto	1945	13	4
	Ken Dryden, Montreal	1977	14	4
	Bernie Parent, Philadelphia	1975	17	4
	Olaf Kolzig, Washington	1998	21	4
	Mike Richter, NY Rangers	1994	23	4
	Kirk McLean, Vancouver	1994	24	4

Goals Against Average

(Minimum of eight games played.)

		Year	Gm	Min	GA	GAA
1	Terry Sawchuk, Det	1952	8	480	5	0.63
2	Clint Benedict, Mon-M	1928	9	555	8	0.89
3	Turk Broda, Tor	1951	9	509	9	1.06
4	Dave Kerr, NYR	1937	9	553	10	1.11
5	Jacques Plante, Mon	1960	8	489	11	1.35
6	Rogie Vachon, Mon	1969	8	507	12	1.42
7	Jacques Plante, St.L	1969	10	589	14	1.43
8	Frankie Brimsek, Bos	1939	12	863	18	1.50
9	Chuck Gardiner, Chi	1934	8	602	12	1.50
10	Ken Dryden, Mon	1977	14	849	22	1.55

Note: Average determined by games played through 1942-43 season and by minutes played since then.

SINGLE SERIES

Scoring

Points

	Year	Rd	G-A—Pts
Rick Middleton, Bos vs Buf	1983	DF	5-14—19
Wayne Gretzky, Edm vs Chi	1985	CF	4-14—18
Mario Lemieux, Pit vs Wash	1992	DSF	7-10—17
Barry Pedersen, Bos vs Buf	1983	DF	7-9—16
Doug Gilmour, Tor vs SJ	1994	CSF	3-13—16
Jari Kurri, Edm vs Chi	1985	CF	12-3—15
Tim Kerr, Phi vs Pit	1989	DF	10-5—15
Mario Lemieux, Pit vs Bos	1991	CF	6-9—15
Wayne Gretzky, Edm vs LA	1987	DSF	2-13—15

Goals

	Year	Rd	No
Jari Kurri, Edm vs Chi	1985	CF	12
Newsy Lalonde, Mon vs Ott	1919	SF*	11
Tim Kerr, Phi vs Pit	1989	DF	10

Five tied with nine each.

*NHL final prior to Stanley Cup series with Seattle.

Assists

	Year	Rd	No
Rick Middleton, Bos vs Buf	1983	DF	14
Wayne Gretzky, Edm vs Chi	1985	CF	14
Wayne Gretzky, Edm vs LA	1987	DSF	13
Doug Gilmour, Tor vs SJ	1994	CSF	13

Four tied with 11 each.

SINGLE GAME

Scoring

Points

	Date	G	A	Pts
Patrik Sundstrom, NJ vs Wash	4/22/88	3	5	8
Mario Lemieux, Pit vs Phi	4/25/89	5	3	8
Wayne Gretzky, Edm at Calg	4/17/83	4	3	7
Wayne Gretzky, Edm at Win	4/25/85	3	4	7
Wayne Gretzky, Edm vs LA	4/9/87	1	6	7

Goals

	Date	No
Newsy Lalonde, Mon vs Ott	3/1/19	5
Maurice Richard, Mon vs Tor	3/23/44	5
Darryl Sittler, Tor vs Phi	4/22/76	5
Reggie Leach, Phi vs Bos	5/6/76	5
Mario Lemieux, Pit vs Phi	4/25/89	5

Assists

	Date	No
Mikko Leinonen, NYR vs Phi	4/8/82	6
Wayne Gretzky, Edm vs LA	4/9/87	6

Ten tied with five each.

Ten Longest Playoff Overtime Games

The 10 longest overtime games in Stanley Cup history. Note the following Series initials: SF (semifinals), CQF (conference quarterfinal), DSF (division semifinal). QF (quarterfinal) and Final (Cup final). Series winners are in **bold** type; (*) indicates deciding game of series.

		OTs	Elapsed Time	Goal Scorer	Date	Series	Location
1	**Detroit** 1, Montreal Maroons 0	6	176:30	Mud Bruneteau	3/24/36	SF, Gm 1	Montreal
2	**Toronto** 1, Boston 0	6	164:46	Ken Doraty	4/3/33	SF, Gm 5	Toronto
3	**Pittsburgh** 3 Washington 2	4	139:15	Petr Nedved	4/24/96	CQF, Gm 4	Washington
4	Toronto 3, **Detroit** 2	4	130:18	Jack McLean	3/23/43	SF, Gm 2	Detroit
5	**Montreal** 2, NY Rangers 1	4	128:52	Gus Rivers	3/28/30	SF, Gm 1	Montreal
6	**NY Islanders** 3, Washington 2	4	128:47	Pat LaFontaine	4/18/87	DSF, Gm 7*	Washington
7	Buffalo 1, **New Jersey** 0	4	125:43	Dave Hannan	4/27/94	QF, Gm 6	Buffalo
8	**Montreal** 3, Detroit 2	4	121:09	Maurice Richard	3/27/51	SF, Gm 1	Detroit
9	**NY Americans** 3, NY Rangers 2	4	120:40	Lorne Carr	3/27/38	QF, Gm 3*	New York
10	**NY Rangers** 4, Montreal 3	3	119:32	Fred Cook	3/26/32	SF, Gm 2	Montreal

NHL All-Star Game

Three benefit NHL All-Star games were staged in the 1930s for forward Ace Bailey and the families of Howie Morenz and Babe Siebert. Bailey, of Toronto, suffered a fractured skull on a career-ending check by Boston's Eddie Shore. Morenz, the Montreal Canadiens' legend, died of a heart attack at 35 after a severely broken leg ended his career. Siebert, who played with both Montreal teams, drowned at age 35.

The All-Star Game was revived at the start of the 1947-48 season as an annual exhibition match between the defending Stanley Cup champion and All-Stars from the league's other five teams. The format has changed several times since then. The game was moved to midseason in 1966-67 and became an East vs. West contest in 1968-69. The Eastern (East, 1968-1974; Wales, 1975-93) Conference leads the series 18-7-1. In 1998, as a preview for the upcoming Winter Olympics, the East-West format was abandoned for one pitting North American all-stars against all-stars from the rest of the world.

Benefit Games

Date	Occasion		Host	Coaches
2/14/34	Ace Bailey Benefit	Toronto 7, All-Stars 3	Toronto	Dick Irvin, Lester Patrick
11/3/37	Howie Morenz Memorial	All-Stars 6, Montreals* 5	Montreal	Jack Adams, Ceil Hart
10/29/39	Babe Seibert Memorial	All-Stars 5, Canadiens 3	Montreal	Art Ross, Pit Lepine

*Combined squad of Montreal Canadiens and Montreal Maroons.

All-Star Games

Multiple MVP winners: Mario Lemieux (3); Wayne Gretzky, Bobby Hull and Frank Mahovolich (2).

Year		Host	Coaches	Most Valuable Player
1947	All-Stars 4, Toronto 3	Toronto	Dick Irvin, Hap Day	No award
1948	All-Stars 3, Toronto 1	Chicago	Tommy Ivan, Hap Day	No award
1949	All-Stars 3, Toronto 1	Toronto	Tommy Ivan, Hap Day	No award
1950	Detroit 7, All-Stars 1	Detroit	Tommy Ivan, Lynn Patrick	No award
1951	1st Team 2, 2nd Team 2	Toronto	Joe Primeau, Hap Day	No award
1952	1st Team 1, 2nd Team 1	Detroit	Tommy Ivan, Dick Irvin	No award
1953	All-Stars 3, Montreal 1	Montreal	Lynn Patrick, Dick Irvin	No award
1954	All-Stars 2, Detroit 2	Detroit	King Clancy, Jim Skinner	No award
1955	Detroit 3, All-Stars 1	Detroit	Jim Skinner, Dick Irvin	No award
1956	All-Stars 1, Montreal 1	Montreal	Jim Skinner, Toe Blake	No award
1957	All-Stars 5, Montreal 3	Montreal	Milt Schmidt, Toe Blake	No award
1958	Montreal 6, All-Stars 3	Montreal	Toe Blake, Milt Schmidt	No award
1959	Montreal 6, All-Stars 1	Montreal	Toe Blake, Punch Imlach	No award
1960	All-Stars 2, Montreal 1	Montreal	Punch Imlach, Toe Blake	No award
1961	All-Stars 3, Chicago 1	Chicago	Sid Abel, Rudy Pilous	No award
1962	Toronto 4, All-Stars 1	Toronto	Punch Imlach, Rudy Pilous	Eddie Shack, Tor., RW
1963	All-Stars 3, Toronto 3	Toronto	Sid Abel, Punch Imlach	Frank Mahovlich, Tor., LW
1964	All-Stars 3, Toronto 2	Toronto	Sid Abel, Punch Imlach	Jean Beliveau, Mon., C
1965	All-Stars 5, Montreal 2	Montreal	Billy Reay, Toe Blake	Gordie Howe, Det., RW
1966	No game (see below)			
1967	Montreal 3, All-Stars 0	Montreal	Toe Blake, Sid Abel	Henri Richard, Mon., C
1968	Toronto 4, All-Stars 3	Toronto	Punch Imlach, Toe Blake	Bruce Gamble, Tor., G
1969	West 3, East 3	Montreal	Scotty Bowman, Toe Blake	Frank Mahovlich, Det., LW
1970	East 4, West 1	St. Louis	Claude Ruel, Scotty Bowman	Bobby Hull, Chi., LW
1971	West 2, East 1	Boston	Scotty Bowman, Harry Sinden	Bobby Hull, Chi., LW
1972	East 3, West 2	Minnesota	Al MacNeil, Billy Reay	Bobby Orr, Bos., D
1973	East 5, West 4	NY Rangers	Tom Johnson, Billy Reay	Greg Polis, Pit., LW
1974	West 6, East 4	Chicago	Billy Reay, Scotty Bowman	Garry Unger, St.L., C
1975	Wales 7, Campbell 1	Montreal	Bep Guidolin, Fred Shero	Syl Apps Jr., Pit., C
1976	Wales 7, Campbell 5	Philadelphia	Floyd Smith, Fred Shero	Peter Mahovlich, Mon., C
1977	Wales 4, Campbell 3	Vancouver	Scotty Bowman, Fred Shero	Rick Martin, Buf., LW
1978	Wales 3, Campbell 2 (OT)	Buffalo	Scotty Bowman, Fred Shero	Billy Smith, NYI, G
1979	No game (see below)			
1980	Wales 6, Campbell 3	Detroit	Scotty Bowman, Al Arbour	Reggie Leach, Phi., RW
1981	Campbell 4, Wales 1	Los Angeles	Pat Quinn, Scotty Bowman	Mike Liut, St.L., G
1982	Wales 4, Campbell 2	Washington	Al Arbour, Glen Sonmor	Mike Bossy, NYI, RW
1983	Campbell 9, Wales 3	NY Islanders	Roger Neilson, Al Arbour	Wayne Gretzky, Edm., C
1984	Wales 7, Campbell 6	New Jersey	Al Arbour, Glen Sather	Don Maloney, NYR, LW
1985	Wales 6, Campbell 4	Calgary	Al Arbour, Glen Sather	Mario Lemieux, Pit., C
1986	Wales 4, Campbell 3 (OT)	Hartford	Mike Keenan, Glen Sather	Grant Fuhr, Edm., G
1987	No game (see below)			
1988	Wales 6, Campbell 5 (OT)	St. Louis	Mike Keenan, Glen Sather	Mario Lemieux, Pit., C
1989	Campbell 9, Wales 5	Edmonton	Glen Sather, Terry O'Reilly	Wayne Gretzky, LA, C
1990	Wales 12, Campbell 7	Pittsburgh	Pat Burns, Terry Crisp	Mario Lemieux, Pit., C
1991	Campbell 11, Wales 5	Chicago	John Muckler, Mike Milbury	Vincent Damphousse, Tor., LW
1992	Campbell 10, Wales 6	Philadelphia	Bob Gainey, Scotty Bowman	Brett Hull, St.L., RW
1993	Wales 16, Campbell 6	Montreal	Scotty Bowman, Mike Keenan	Mike Gartner, NYR, RW
1994	East 9, West 8	NY Rangers	Jacques Demers, Barry Melrose	Mike Richter, NYR, G
1995	No game (see below)			
1996	East 5, West 4	Boston	Doug MacLean, Scotty Bowman	Ray Bourque, Bos., D
1997	East 11, West 7	San Jose	Doug MacLean, Ken Hitchcock	Mark Recchi, Mon., RW
1998	North America 8, World 7	Vancouver	Jacques Lemaire, Ken Hitchcock	Teemu Selanne, World, RW

No All-Star Game: in 1966 (moved from start of season to mid-season); in 1979 (replaced by Challenge Cup series with USSR); in 1987 (replaced by Rendez-Vous '87 series with USSR); and in 1995 (cancelled when NHL lockout shortened season to 48 games).

NHL Franchise Origins

Here is what the current 27 teams in the National Hockey League have to show for the years they have put in as members of the NHL, the early National Hockey Association (NHA) and the more recent World Hockey Association (WHA). League titles and Stanley Cup championships are noted by year won. The Stanley Cup has automatically gone to the NHL champion since the 1926-27 season. Following the 1992-93 season, the NHL renamed the Clarence Campbell Conference the Western Conference, while the Prince of Wales Conference became the Eastern Conference.

Western Conference

	First Season	League Titles	Franchise Stops
Anaheim, Mighty Ducks of	1993-94 (NHL)	None	•Anaheim, CA (1993–)
Calgary Flames	1972-73 (NHL)	1 Cup (1989)	•Atlanta (1972-80) Calgary (1980–)
Chicago Blackhawks	1926-27 (NHL)	3 Cups (1934,38,61)	•Chicago (1926–)
Colorado Avalanche	1972-73 (WHA)	1 WHA (1977) 1 Cup (1996)	•Quebec City (1972-95) Denver (1995–)
Dallas Stars	1967-68 (NHL)	None	•Bloomington, MN (1967-93) Dallas (1993–)
Detroit Red Wings	1926-27 (NHL)	9 Cups (1936-37,43,50,52,54-55,97,98)	•Detroit (1926–)
Edmonton Oilers	1973-74 (WHA)	5 Cups (1984-85,87-88,90)	•Edmonton (1972–)
Los Angeles Kings	1967-68 (NHL)	None	•Inglewood, CA (1967–)
Nashville Predators	1998-99 (NHL)	None	•Nashville, TN (1998–)
Phoenix Coyotes	1972-73 (WHA)	3 WHA (1976, 78-79)	•Winnipeg (1972-96) Phoenix (1996–)
St. Louis Blues	1967-68 (NHL)	None	•St. Louis (1967–)
San Jose Sharks	1991-92 (NHL)	None	•San Francisco (1991-93) San Jose (1993–)
Vancouver Canucks	1970-71 (NHL)	None	•Vancouver (1970–)

Eastern Conference

	First Season	League Titles	Franchise Stops
Boston Bruins	1924-25 (NHL)	5 Cups (1929,39,41,70,72)	•Boston (1924–)
Buffalo Sabres	1970-71 (NHL)	None	•Buffalo (1970–)
Carolina Hurricanes	1972-73 (WHA)	1 WHA (1973)	•Boston (1972-74) W. Springfield, MA (1974-75) Hartford, CT (1975-78) Springfield, MA (1978-80) Hartford (1980-97) Raleigh (1997–)
Florida Panthers	1993-94 (NHL)	None	•Miami (1993-98) Sunrise, FL (1998–)
Montreal Canadiens	1909-10 (NHA)	2 NHA (1916-17) 2 NHL (1924-25) 24 Cups (1916,24,30-31,44,46,53,56-60,65-66,68-69,71,73,76-79,86,93)	•Montreal (1909–)
New Jersey Devils	1974-75 (NHL)	1 Cup (1995)	•Kansas City (1974-76) Denver (1976-82) E. Rutherford, NJ (1982–)
New York Islanders	1972-73 (NHL)	4 Cups (1980-83)	•Uniondale, NY (1972–)
New York Rangers	1926-27 (NHL)	4 Cups (1928,33,40,94)	•New York (1926–)
Ottawa Senators	1992-93 (NHL)	None	•Ottawa (1992-1996) Kanata, Ont. (1996–)
Philadelphia Flyers	1967-68 (NHL)	2 Cups (1974-75)	•Philadelphia (1967–)
Pittsburgh Penguins	1967-68 (NHL)	2 Cups (1991-92)	•Pittsburgh (1967–)
Tampa Bay Lightning	1992-93 (NHL)	None	•Tampa, FL (1992-93) St. Petersburg, FL (1993-96) Tampa, FL (1996–)
Toronto Maple Leafs	1916-17 (NHA)	2 NHL (1918,22) 13 Cups (1918,22,32,42,45,47-49,51,62-64,67)	•Toronto (1916–)
Washington Capitals	1974-75 (NHL)	None	•Landover, MD (1974-97) Washington, D.C. (1997–)

Note: The Hartford Civic Center roof collapsed after a snowstorm in January 1978, forcing the Whalers to move their home games to Springfield, Mass., for two years.

The Growth of the NHL

Of the four franchises that comprised the National Hockey League (NHL) at the start of the 1917-18 season, only two remain—the Montreal Canadiens and the Toronto Maple Leafs (originally the Toronto Arenas). From 1919-26, eight new teams joined the league, but only four—the Boston Bruins, Chicago Blackhawks (originally Black Hawks), Detroit Red Wings (originally Cougars) and New York Rangers—survived.

It was 41 years before the NHL expanded again, doubling in size for the 1967-68 season with new teams in Los Angeles, Minnesota, Oakland, Philadelphia, Pittsburgh and St. Louis. The league had 16 clubs by the start of the 1972-73 season, but it also had a rival in the **World Hockey Association,** which debuted that year with 12 teams.

The NHL added two more teams in 1974 and merged the struggling Cleveland Barons (originally the Oakland Seals) and Minnesota North Stars in 1978, before absorbing four WHA clubs—the Edmonton Oilers, Hartford Whalers, Quebec Nordiques and Winnipeg Jets—in time for the 1979-80 season. Six expansion teams have joined the league so far in the 1990s, giving the NHL its current 27-team roster. One more will be added in 1999 and two more in 2000 to make it an even 30.

Expansion/Merger Timetable

For teams currently in NHL.

1919—Quebec Bulldogs finally take the ice after sitting out NHL's first two seasons; **1924**—Boston Bruins and Montreal Maroons; **1925**–New York Americans and Pittsburgh Pirates; **1926**—Chicago Black Hawks (now Blackhawks), Detroit Cougars (now Red Wings) and New York Rangers; **1932**—Ottawa Senators return after sitting out 1931-32 season.

1967—California Seals (later Cleveland Barons), Los Angeles Kings, Minnesota North Stars, Philadelphia Flyers, Pittsburgh Penguins and St. Louis Blues.

1970—Buffalo Sabres and Vancouver Canucks; **1972**—Atlanta Flames (now Calgary) and New York Islanders; **1974**—Kansas City Scouts (now New Jersey Devils) and Washington Capitals; **1978**—Cleveland Barons merge with Minnesota North Stars (now Dallas Stars) and team remains in Minnesota; **1979**—added WHA's Edmonton Oilers, Hartford Whalers, Quebec Nordiques (now Colorado Avalanche) and Winnipeg Jets (now Phoenix Coyotes).

1991—San Jose Sharks; **1992**—Ottawa Senators and Tampa Bay Lightning; **1993**—Mighty Ducks of Anaheim and Florida Panthers; **1998**—Nashville Predators.

Looking forward: 1999—Atlanta Thrashers; **2000**—Columbus Blue Jackets and Minnesota Wild.

City and Nickname Changes

1919—Toronto Arenas renamed St. Pats; **1920**—Quebec moves to Hamilton and becomes Tigers (will fold in 1925); **1926**—Toronto St. Pats renamed Maple Leafs; **1929**—Detroit Cougars renamed Falcons.

1930—Pittsburgh Pirates move to Philadelphia and become Quakers (will fold in 1931); **1932**—Detroit Falcons renamed Red Wings; **1934**—Ottawa Senators move to St. Louis and become Eagles (will fold in 1935); **1941**—New York Americans renamed Brooklyn Americans (will fold in 1942).

1967—California Seals renamed Oakland Seals three months into first season; **1970**—Oakland Seals renamed California Golden Seals; **1975**—California Golden Seals renamed Seals; **1976**—California Seals move to Cleveland and become Barons, while Kansas City Scouts move to Denver and become Colorado Rockies; **1978**—Cleveland Barons merge with Minnesota North Stars and become Minnesota North Stars.

1980—Atlanta Flames move to Calgary; **1982**—Colorado Rockies move to East Rutherford, N.J., and become New Jersey Devils; **1986**—Chicago Black Hawks renamed Blackhawks; **1993**—Minnesota North Stars move to Dallas and become Stars. **1995**—Quebec Nordiques move to Denver and become Colorado Avalanche; **1996**—Winnipeg Jets move to Phoenix and become Coyotes; **1997**—Hartford Whalers move to Raleigh and become Carolina Hurricanes.

Defunct NHL Teams

Teams that once played in the NHL, but no longer exist.

Brooklyn—Americans (1941-42, formerly NY Americans from 1925-41); **Cleveland**—Barons (1976-78, originally California-Oakland Seals from 1967-76); **Hamilton (Ont.)**—Tigers (1920-25, originally Quebec Bulldogs from 1919-20); **Montreal**—Maroons (1924-38) and Wanderers (1917-18); **New York**—Americans (1925-41, later Brooklyn Americans for 1941-42); **Oakland**—Seals (1967-76, also known as California Seals and Golden Seals and later Cleveland Barons from 1976-78); **Ottawa**—Senators (1917-31 and 1932-34, later St. Louis Eagles for 1934-35); **Philadelphia**—Quakers (1930-31, originally Pittsburgh Pirates from 1925-30); **Pittsburgh**—Pirates (1925-30, later Philadelphia Quakers for 1930-31); **Quebec**—Bulldogs (1919-20, later Hamilton Tigers from 1920-25); **St. Louis**—Eagles (1934-35), originally Ottawa Senators (1917-31 and 1932-34).

WHA Teams (1972-79)

Baltimore—Blades (1975); **Birmingham**—Bulls (1976-78); **Calgary**—Cowboys (1975-77); **Chicago**—Cougars (1972-75); **Cincinnati**—Stingers (1975-79); **Cleveland**—Crusaders (1972-76, moved to Minnesota); **Denver**—Spurs (1975-76, moved to Ottawa); **Edmonton**—Oilers (1972-79, originally called Alberta Oilers in 1972-73); **Houston**—Aeros (1972-78); **Indianapolis**—Racers (1974-78).

Los Angeles—Sharks (1972-74, moved to Michigan); **Michigan**—Stags (1974-75, moved to Baltimore); **Minnesota**—Fighting Saints (1972-76) and New Fighting Saints (1976-77); **New England**—Whalers (1972-79, played in Boston from 1972-74, West Springfield, MA from 1974-75, Hartford from 1975-78 and Springfield, MA in 1979); **New Jersey**—Knights (1973-74, moved to San Diego); **New York**—Raiders (1972-73, renamed Golden Blades in 1973, moved to New Jersey).

Ottawa—Nationals (1972-73, moved to Toronto) and Civics (1976); **Philadelphia**—Blazers (1972-73, moved to Vancouver); **Phoenix**—Roadrunners (1974-77); **Quebec**—Nordiques (1972-79); **San Diego**—Mariners (1974-77); **Toronto**—Toros (1973-76, moved to Birmingham, AL); **Vancouver**—Blazers (1973-75, moved to Calgary); **Winnipeg**—Jets (1972-79).

Annual NHL Leaders

Art Ross Trophy (Scoring)

Given to the player who leads the league in points scored and named after the former Boston Bruins general manager-coach. First presented in 1948, names of prior leading scorers have been added retroactively. A tie for the scoring championship is broken three ways: 1. total goals; 2. fewest games played; 3. first goal scored.

Multiple Winners: Wayne Gretzky (10); Gordie Howe and Mario Lemieux (6); Phil Esposito (5); Stan Mikita (4); Guy Lafleur (3); Max Bentley, Charlie Conacher, Bill Cook, Babe Dye, Bernie Geoffrion, Bobby Hull, Jaromir Jagr, Elmer Lach, Newsy Lalonde, Joe Malone, Dickie Moore, Howie Morenz, Bobby Orr and Sweeney Schriner (2).

Year		Gm	G	A	Pts
1918	Joe Malone, Mon	20	44	0	44
1919	Newsy Lalonde, Mon	17	23	9	32
1920	Joe Malone, Que	24	39	6	45
1921	Newsy Lalonde, Mon	24	33	8	41
1922	Punch Broadbent, Ott	24	32	14	46
1923	Babe Dye, Tor	22	26	11	37
1924	Cy Denneny, Ott	21	22	1	23
1925	Babe Dye, Tor	29	38	6	44
1926	Nels Stewart, Maroons	36	34	8	42
1927	Bill Cook, NYR	44	33	4	37
1928	Howie Morenz, Mon	43	33	18	51
1929	Ace Bailey, Tor	44	22	10	32
1930	Cooney Weiland, Bos	44	43	30	73
1931	Howie Morenz, Mon	39	28	23	51
1932	Busher Jackson, Tor	48	28	25	53
1933	Bill Cook, NYR	48	28	22	50
1934	Charlie Conacher, Tor	42	32	20	52
1935	Charlie Conacher, Tor	47	36	21	57
1936	Sweeney Schriner, NYA	48	19	26	45
1937	Sweeney Schriner, NYA	48	21	25	46
1938	Gordie Drillon, Tor	48	26	26	52
1939	Toe Blake, Mon	48	24	23	47
1940	Milt Schmidt, Bos	48	22	30	52
1941	Bill Cowley, Bos	46	17	45	62
1942	Bryan Hextall, NYR	48	24	32	56
1943	Doug Bentley, Chi	50	33	40	73
1944	Herbie Cain, Bos	48	36	46	82
1945	Elmer Lach, Mon	50	26	54	80
1946	Max Bentley, Chi	47	31	30	61
1947	Max Bentley, Chi	60	29	43	72
1948	Elmer Lach, Mon	60	30	31	61
1949	Roy Conacher, Chi	60	26	42	68
1950	Ted Lindsay, Det	69	23	55	78
1951	Gordie Howe, Det	70	43	43	86
1952	Gordie Howe, Det	70	47	39	86
1953	Gordie Howe, Det	70	49	46	95
1954	Gordie Howe, Det	70	33	48	81
1955	Bernie Geoffrion, Mon	70	38	37	75
1956	Jean Beliveau, Mon	70	47	41	88
1957	Gordie Howe, Det	70	44	45	89
1958	Dickie Moore, Mon	70	36	48	84
1959	Dickie Moore, Mon	70	41	55	96
1960	Bobby Hull, Chi	70	39	42	81
1961	Bernie Geoffrion, Mon	64	50	45	95
1962	Bobby Hull, Chi	70	50	34	84
1963	Gordie Howe, Det	70	38	48	86
1964	Stan Mikita, Chi	70	39	50	89
1965	Stan Mikita, Chi	70	28	59	87
1966	Bobby Hull, Chi	65	54	43	97
1967	Stan Mikita, Chi	70	35	62	97
1968	Stan Mikita, Chi	72	40	47	87
1969	Phil Esposito, Bos	74	49	77	126
1970	Bobby Orr, Bos	76	33	87	120
1971	Phil Esposito, Bos	78	76	76	152
1972	Phil Esposito, Bos	76	66	67	133
1973	Phil Esposito, Bos	78	55	75	130
1974	Phil Esposito, Bos	78	68	77	145
1975	Bobby Orr, Bos	80	46	89	135
1976	Guy Lafleur, Mon	80	56	69	125
1977	Guy Lafleur, Mon	80	56	80	136
1978	Guy Lafleur, Mon	79	60	72	132
1979	Bryan Trottier, NYI	76	47	87	134
1980	Marcel Dionne, LA	80	53	84	137
1981	Wayne Gretzky, Edm	80	55	109	164
1982	Wayne Gretzky, Edm	80	92	120	212
1983	Wayne Gretzky, Edm	80	71	125	196
1984	Wayne Gretzky, Edm	74	87	118	205
1985	Wayne Gretzky, Edm	80	73	135	208
1986	Wayne Gretzky, Edm	80	52	163	215
1987	Wayne Gretzky, Edm	79	62	121	183
1988	Mario Lemieux, Pit	77	70	98	168
1989	Mario Lemieux, Pit	76	85	114	199
1990	Wayne Gretzky, LA	73	40	102	142
1991	Wayne Gretzky, LA	78	41	122	163
1992	Mario Lemieux, Pit.	64	44	87	131
1993	Mario Lemieux, Pit.	60	69	91	160
1994	Wayne Gretzky, LA	81	38	92	130
1995	Jaromir Jagr, Pit	48	32	38	70
1996	Mario Lemieux, Pit	70	69	92	161
1997	Mario Lemieux, Pit	76	50	72	122
1998	Jaromir Jagr, Pit	77	35	67	102

Note: The three times players have tied for total points in one season the player with more goals has won the trophy. In 1961-62, Hull outscored Andy Bathgate of NY Rangers, 50 goals to 28. In 1979-80, Dionne outscored Wayne Gretzky of Edmonton, 53-51. In 1995, Jagr outscored Eric Lindros of Philadelphia, 32-29.

NHL 500-Goal Scorers

Of the 26 500-goal scorers listed below, four (Ciccarelli, Bobby Hull, Kurri and Lemieux) went on to score over 600, three (Dionne, Esposito and Gartner) scored over 700, and two (Gretzky and Howe) have scored over 800. Players active in 1998 are in **bold** type.

	Date	Game #
Maurice Richard, Mon vs Chi	10/19/57	863
Gordie Howe, Det at NYR	3/14/62	1045
Bobby Hull, Chi vs NYR	2/21/70	861
Jean Beliveau, Mon vs Min	2/11/71	1101
Frank Mahovlich, Mon vs Van	3/21/73	1105
Phil Esposito, Bos vs Det	12/22/74	803
John Bucyk, Bos vs St.L	10/30/75	1370
Stan Mikita, Chi vs Van	2/27/77	1221
Marcel Dionne, LA at Wash	12/14/82	887
Guy Lafleur, Mon at NJ	12/20/83	918
Mike Bossy, NYI vs Bos	1/2/86	647
Gilbert Perreault, Buf vs NJ	3/9/86	1159
Wayne Gretzky, Edm vs Van	11/22/86	575
Lanny McDonald, Calg vs NYI	3/21/89	1107
Bryan Trottier, NYI vs Calg	2/13/90	1104
Mike Gartner, NYR vs Wash	10/14/91	936
Michel Goulet, Chi vs Calg	2/16/92	951
Jari Kurri, LA vs Bos	10/17/92	833
Dino Ciccarelli, Det at LA	1/8/94	946
Mario Lemieux, Pit at NYI	10/26/95	605
Mark Messier, NYR vs Calg	11/6/95	1141
Steve Yzerman, Det vs Col	1/17/96	906
Dale Hawerchuk, St.L at Tor	1/31/96	1103
Brett Hull, St.L vs LA	12/22/96	693
Joe Mullen, Pit at Col	3/14/97	1052
Dave Andreychuk, NJ vs Wash	3/15/97	1070

Goals

Multiple Winners: Bobby Hull (7); Phil Esposito (6); Charlie Conacher, Wayne Gretzky, Gordie Howe and Maurice Richard (5); Bill Cooke, Babe Dye, Brett Hull and Mario Lemieux (3); Jean Beliveau, Doug Bentley, Peter Bondra, Mike Bossy, Bernie Geoffrion, Bryan Hextall, Joe Malone, Teemu Selanne and Nels Stewart (2).

Year		No
1918	Joe Malone, Mon	44
1919	Odie Cleghorn, Mon	23
	& Newsy Lalonde, Mon	23
1920	Joe Malone, Que	39
1921	Babe Dye, Ham-Tor	35
1922	Punch Broadbent, Ott	32
1923	Babe Dye, Tor	26
1924	Cy Denneny, Ott	22
1925	Babe Dye, Tor	38
1926	Nels Stewart, Maroons	34
1927	Bill Cook, NYR	33
1928	Howie Morenz, Mon	33
1929	Ace Bailey, Tor	22
1930	Cooney Weiland, Bos	43
1931	Charlie Conacher, Tor	31
1932	Charlie Conacher, Tor	34
	& Bill Cook, NYR	34
1933	Bill Cook, NYR	28
1934	Charlie Conacher, Tor	32
1935	Charlie Conacher, Tor	36
1936	Charlie Conacher, Tor	23
	& Bill Thoms, Tor	23
1937	Larry Aurie, Det	23
	& Nels Stewart, Bos-NYA	23
1938	Gordie Drillon, Tor	26
1939	Roy Conacher, Bos	26
1940	Bryan Hextall, NYR	24
1941	Bryan Hextall, NYR	26
1942	Lynn Patrick, NYR	32
1943	Doug Bentley, Chi	33
1944	Doug Bentley, Chi	38
1945	Maurice Richard, Mon	50
1946	Gaye Stewart, Tor	37
1947	Maurice Richard, Mon	45
1948	Ted Lindsay, Det	33
1949	Sid Abel, Det	28
1950	Maurice Richard, Mon	43
1951	Gordie Howe, Det	43
1952	Gordie Howe, Det	47
1953	Gordie Howe, Det	49
1954	Maurice Richard, Mon	37
1955	Bernie Geoffrion, Mon	38
	& Maurice Richard, Mon	38
1956	Jean Beliveau, Mon	47
1957	Gordie Howe, Det	44
1958	Dickie Moore, Mon	36
1959	Jean Beliveau, Mon	45
1960	Bronco Horvath, Bos	39
	& Bobby Hull, Chi	39
1961	Bernie Geoffrion, Mon	50
1962	Bobby Hull, Chi	50
1963	Gordie Howe, Det	38
1964	Bobby Hull, Chi	43
1965	Norm Ullman, Tor	42
1966	Bobby Hull, Chi	54
1967	Bobby Hull, Chi	52
1968	Bobby Hull, Chi	44
1969	Bobby Hull, Chi	58
1970	Phil Esposito, Bos	43
1971	Phil Esposito, Bos	76
1972	Phil Esposito, Bos	66
1973	Phil Esposito, Bos	55
1974	Phil Esposito, Bos	68
1975	Phil Esposito, Bos	61
1976	Reggie Leach, Phi	61
1977	Steve Shutt, Mon	60
1978	Guy Lafleur, Mon	60
1979	Mike Bossy, NYI	69
1980	Danny Gare, Buf	56
	Charlie Simmer, LA	56
	& Blaine Stoughton, Hart	56
1981	Mike Bossy, NYI	68
1982	Wayne Gretzky, Edm	92
1983	Wayne Gretzky, Edm	71
1984	Wayne Gretzky, Edm	87
1985	Wayne Gretzky, Edm	73
1986	Jari Kurri, Edm	68
1987	Wayne Gretzky, Edm	62
1988	Mario Lemieux, Pit	70
1989	Mario Lemieux, Pit	85
1990	Brett Hull, St.L	72
1991	Brett Hull, St.L	86
1992	Brett Hull, St.L	70
1993	Alexander Mogilny, Buf	76
	& Teemu Selanne, Win	76
1994	Pavel Bure, Van	60
1995	Peter Bondra, Wash	34
1996	Mario Lemieux, Pit	69
1997	Keith Tkachuk, Pho	52
1998	Teemu Selanne, Ana	52
	& Peter Bondra, Wash	52

Assists

Multiple Winners: Wayne Gretzky (16); Bobby Orr (5); Frank Boucher, Bill Cowley, Phil Esposito, Gordie Howe, Elmer Lach, Mario Lemieux, Stan Mikita and Joe Primeau (3); Syl Apps, Andy Bathgate, Jean Beliveau, Doug Bentley, Art Chapman, Bobby Clarke, Ron Francis, Ted Lindsay, Bert Olmstead, Henri Richard and Bryan Trottier (2).

Year		No
1918	No official records kept.	
1919	Newsy Lalonde, Mon	9
1920	Corbett Denneny, Tor	12
1921	Louis Berlinquette, Mon	9
	Harry Cameron, Tor	9
	& Joe Matte, Ham	9
1922	Punch Broadbent, Ott	14
	& Leo Reise, Ham	14
1923	Ed Bouchard, Ham	12
1924	King Clancy, Ott	8
1925	Cy Denneny, Ott	15
1926	Frank Nighbor, Ott	13
1927	Dick Irvin, Chi	18
1928	Howie Morenz, Mon	18
1929	Frank Boucher, NYR	16
1930	Frank Boucher, NYR	36
1931	Joe Primeau, Tor	32
1932	Joe Primeau, Tor	37
1933	Frank Boucher, NYR	28
1934	Joe Primeau, Tor	32
1935	Art Chapman, NYA	34
1936	Art Chapman, NYA	28
1937	Syl Apps, Tor	29
1938	Syl Apps, Tor	29
1939	Bill Cowley, Bos	34
1940	Milt Schmidt, Bos	30
1941	Bill Cowley, Bos	45
1942	Phil Watson, NYR	37
1943	Bill Cowley, Bos	45
1944	Clint Smith, Chi	49
1945	Elmer Lach, Mon	54
1946	Elmer Lach, Mon	34
1947	Billy Taylor, Det	46
1948	Doug Bentley, Chi	37
1949	Doug Bentley, Chi	43
1950	Ted Lindsay, Det	55
1951	Gordie Howe, Det	43
	& Teeder Kennedy, Tor	43
1952	Elmer Lach, Mon	50
1953	Gordie Howe, Det	46
1954	Gordie Howe, Det	48
1955	Bert Olmstead, Mon	48
1956	Bert Olmstead, Mon	56
1957	Ted Lindsay, Det	55
1958	Henri Richard, Mon	52
1959	Dickie Moore, Mon	55
1960	Don McKenney, Bos	49
1961	Jean Beliveau, Mon	58
1962	Andy Bathgate, NYR	56
1963	Henri Richard, Mon	50
1964	Andy Bathgate, NYR-Tor	58
1965	Stan Mikita, Chi	59
1966	Jean Beliveau, Mon	48
	Stan Mikita, Chi	48
	& Bobby Rousseau, Mon	48
1967	Stan Mikita, Chi	62
1968	Phil Esposito, Bos	49
1969	Phil Esposito, Bos	77
1970	Bobby Orr, Bos	87
1971	Bobby Orr, Bos	102
1972	Bobby Orr, Bos	80
1973	Phil Esposito, Bos	75
1974	Bobby Orr, Bos	90
1975	Bobby Clarke, Phi	89
	& Bobby Orr, Bos	89
1976	Bobby Clarke, Phi	89
1977	Guy Lafleur, Mon	80
1978	Bryan Trottier, NYI	77
1979	Bryan Trottier, NYI	87
1980	Wayne Gretzky, Edm	86
1981	Wayne Gretzky, Edm	109
1982	Wayne Gretzky, Edm	120
1983	Wayne Gretzky, Edm	125
1984	Wayne Gretzky, Edm	118
1985	Wayne Gretzky, Edm	135
1986	Wayne Gretzky, Edm	163
1987	Wayne Gretzky, Edm	121
1988	Wayne Gretzky, Edm	109
1989	Wayne Gretzky, LA	114
	& Mario Lemieux, Pit	114
1990	Wayne Gretzky, LA	102
1991	Wayne Gretzky, LA	122
1992	Wayne Gretzky, LA	90
1993	Adam Oates, Bos	97
1994	Wayne Gretzky, LA	92
1995	Ron Francis, Pit	48
1996	Ron Francis, Pit	92
	& Mario Lemieux, Pit	92
1997	Mario Lemieux, Pit	72
	& Wayne Gretzky, NYR	72
1998	Jaromir Jagr, Pit	67
	& Wayne Gretzky, NYR	67

Goals Against Average

Average determined by games played through 1942-43 season and by minutes played since then. Minimum of 15 games from 1917-18 season through 1925-26; minimum of 25 games since 1926-27 season. Not to be confused with the Vezina Trophy. Goaltenders who posted the season's lowest goals against average, but did not win the Vezina are in **bold** type.

Multiple Winners: Jacques Plante (9); Clint Benedict and Bill Durnan (6); Johnny Bower, Ken Dryden and Tiny Thompson (4); Patrick Roy and Georges Vezina (3); Ed Belfour, Frankie Brimsek, Turk Broda, George Hainsworth, Dominik Hasek, Harry Lumley, Bernie Parent, Pete Peeters and Terry Sawchuk (2).

Year		GAA
1918	Georges Vezina, Mon	3.82
1919	Clint Benedict, Ott	2.94
1920	Clint Benedict, Ott	2.67
1921	Clint Benedict, Ott	3.13
1922	Clint Benedict, Ott	3.50
1923	Clint Benedict, Ott	2.25
1924	Georges Vezina, Mon	2.00
1925	Georges Vezina, Mon	1.87
1926	Alex Connell, Ott	1.17
1927	**Clint Benedict,** Mon-M	1.51
1928	Geo. Hainsworth, Mon	1.09
1929	Geo. Hainsworth, Mon	0.98
1930	Tiny Thompson, Bos	2.23
1931	Roy Worters, NYA	1.68
1932	Chuck Gardiner, Chi	1.92
1933	Tiny Thompson, Bos	1.83
1934	**Wilf Cude,** Det-Mon	1.57
1935	Lorne Chabot, Chi	1.83
1936	Tiny Thompson, Bos	1.71
1937	Norm Smith, Det	2.13
1938	Tiny Thompson, Bos	1.85
1939	Frankie Brimsek, Bos	1.58
1940	Dave Kerr, NYR	1.60
1941	Turk Broda, Tor	2.06
1942	Frankie Brimsek, Bos	2.45
1943	John Mowers, Det	2.47
1944	Bill Durnan, Mon	2.18
1945	Bill Durnan, Mon	2.42
1946	Bill Durnan, Mon	2.60
1947	Bill Durnan, Mon	2.30
1948	Turk Broda, Tor	2.38
1949	Bill Durnan, Mon	2.10
1950	Bill Durnan, Mon	2.20
1951	Al Rollins, Tor	1.77
1952	Terry Sawchuk, Det	1.90
1953	Terry Sawchuk, Det	1.90
1954	Harry Lumley, Tor	1.86
1955	**Harry Lumley,** Tor	1.94
1956	Jacques Plante, Mon	1.86
1957	Jacques Plante, Mon	2.02
1958	Jacques Plante, Mon	2.11
1959	Jacques Plante, Mon	2.16
1960	Jacques Plante, Mon	2.54
1961	Johnny Bower, Tor	2.50
1962	Jacques Plante, Mon	2.37
1963	**Jacques Plante,** Mon	2.49
1964	**Johnny Bower,** Tor	2.11
1965	Johnny Bower, Tor	2.38
1966	**Johnny Bower,** Tor	2.25
1967	Glenn Hall, Chi	2.38
1968	Gump Worsley, Mon	1.98
1969	**Jacques Plante,** St.L	1.96
1970	**Ernie Wakely,** St.L	2.11
1971	**Jacques Plante,** Tor	1.88
1972	Tony Esposito, Chi	1.77
1973	Ken Dryden, Mon	2.26
1974	Bernie Parent, Phi	1.89
1975	Bernie Parent, Phi	2.03
1976	Ken Dryden, Mon	2.03
1977	Bunny Larocque, Mon	2.09
1978	Ken Dryden, Mon	2.05
1979	Ken Dryden, Mon	2.30
1980	Bob Sauve, Buf	2.36
1981	Richard Sevigny, Mon	2.40
1982	**Denis Herron,** Mon	2.64
1983	Pete Peeters, Bos	2.36
1984	**Pat Riggin,** Wash	2.66
1985	**Tom Barrasso,** Buf	2.66
1986	**Bob Froese,** Phi	2.55
1987	**Brian Hayward,** Mon	2.81
1988	**Pete Peeters**, Wash	2.78
1989	Patrick Roy, Mon	2.47
1990	**Mike Liut,** Hart-Wash	2.53
1991	Ed Belfour, Chi	2.47
1992	Patrick Roy, Mon	2.36
1993	**Felix Potvin,** Tor	2.50
1994	Dominik Hasek, Buf	1.95
1995	Dominik Hasek, Buf	2.11
1996	**Ron Hextall**, Phi	2.17
1997	**Martin Brodeur**, NJ	1.88
1998	**Ed Belfour**, Dal	1.88

Penalty Minutes

Multiple Winners: Red Horner (8); Gus Mortson and Dave Schultz (4); Bert Corbeau, Lou Fontinato and Tiger Williams (3); Billy Boucher, Carl Brewer, Red Dutton, Pat Egan, Bill Ezinicki, Joe Hall, Tim Hunter, Keith Magnuson, Chris Nilan and Jimmy Orlando (2).

Year		Min
1918	Joe Hall, Mon	60
1919	Joe Hall, Mon	85
1920	Cully Wilson, Tor	79
1921	Bert Corbeau, Mon	86
1922	Sprague Cleghorn, Mon	63
1923	Billy Boucher, Mon	52
1924	Bert Corbeau, Tor	55
1925	Billy Boucher, Mon	92
1926	Bert Corbeau, Tor	121
1927	Nels Stewart, Mon-M	133
1928	Eddie Shore, Bos	165
1929	Red Dutton, Mon-M	139
1930	Joe Lamb, Ott	119
1931	Harvey Rockburn, Det	118
1932	Red Dutton, NYA	107
1933	Red Horner, Tor	144
1934	Red Horner, Tor	146
1935	Red Horner, Tor	125
1936	Red Horner, Tor	167
1937	Red Horner, Tor	124
1938	Red Horner, Tor	82
1939	Red Horner, Tor	85
1940	Red Horner, Tor	87
1941	Jimmy Orlando, Det	99
1942	Pat Egan, NYA	124
1943	Jimmy Orlando, Det	99
1944	Mike McMahon, Mon	98
1945	Pat Egan, Bos	86
1946	Jack Stewart, Det	73
1947	Gus Mortson, Tor	133
1948	Bill Barilko, Tor	147
1949	Bill Ezinicki, Tor	145
1950	Bill Ezinicki, Tor	144
1951	Gus Mortson, Tor	142
1952	Gus Kyle, Bos	127
1953	Maurice Richard, Mon	112
1954	Gus Mortson, Chi	132
1955	Fern Flaman, Bos	150
1956	Lou Fontinato, NYR	202
1957	Gus Mortson, Chi	147
1958	Lou Fontinato, NYR	152
1959	Ted Lindsay, Chi	184
1960	Carl Brewer, Tor	150
1961	Pierre Pilote, Chi	165
1962	Lou Fontinato, Mon	167
1963	Howie Young, Det	273
1964	Vic Hadfield, NYR	151
1965	Carl Brewer, Tor	177
1966	Reg Fleming, Bos-NYR	166
1967	John Ferguson, Mon	177
1968	Barclay Plager, St.L	153
1969	Forbes Kennedy, Phi-Tor	219
1970	Keith Magnuson, Chi	213
1971	Keith Magnuson, Chi	291
1972	Bryan Watson, Pit	212
1973	Dave Schultz, Phi	259
1974	Dave Schultz, Phi	348
1975	Dave Schultz, Phi	472
1976	Steve Durbano, Pit-KC	370
1977	Tiger Williams, Tor	338
1978	Dave Schultz, LA-Pit	405
1979	Tiger Williams, Tor	298
1980	Jimmy Mann, Win	287
1981	Tiger Williams, Van	343
1982	Paul Baxter, Pit	409
1983	Randy Holt, Wash	275
1984	Chris Nilan, Mon	338
1985	Chris Nilan, Mon	358
1986	Joey Kocur, Det	377
1987	Tim Hunter, Calg	361
1988	Bob Probert, Det	398
1989	Tim Hunter, Calg	375
1990	Basil McRae, Min	351
1991	Rob Ray, Buf	350
1992	Mike Peluso, Chi	408
1993	Marty McSorley, LA	399
1994	Tie Domi, Win	347
1995	Enrico Ciccone, TB	225
1996	Matthew Barnaby, Buf	335
1997	Gino Odjick, Van	371
1998	Donald Brashear, Van	372

All-Time NHL Regular Season Leaders

Through 1998 regular season.

CAREER

Players active during 1998 season in **bold** type.

Points

		Yrs	Gm	G	A	Pts
1	**Wayne Gretzky**	19	1417	885	1910	2795
2	Gordie Howe	26	1767	801	1049	1850
3	Marcel Dionne	18	1348	731	1040	1771
4	**Mark Messier**	19	1354	597	1015	1612
5	Phil Esposito	18	1282	717	873	1590
6	Mario Lemieux	12	745	613	881	1494
7	**Paul Coffey**	18	1268	383	1090	1473
8	Stan Mikita	22	1394	541	926	1467
9	**Ron Francis**	17	1247	428	1006	1434
10	Bryan Trottier	18	1279	524	901	1425
11	**Ray Bourque**	19	1372	375	1036	1411
12	**Steve Yzerman**	15	1098	563	846	1409
	Dale Hawerchuk	16	1188	518	891	1409
14	**Jari Kurri**	17	1251	601	797	1398
15	John Bucyk	23	1540	556	813	1369
16	Guy Lafleur	17	1126	560	793	1353
17	Denis Savard	17	1196	473	865	1338
18	**Mike Gartner**	19	1432	708	627	1335
19	Gilbert Perreault	17	1191	512	814	1326
20	Alex Delvecchio	24	1549	456	825	1281
21	Jean Ratelle	21	1281	491	776	1267
22	Peter Stastny	15	977	450	789	1239
23	Norm Ullman	20	1410	490	739	1229
24	Jean Beliveau	20	1125	507	712	1219
25	Bobby Clarke	15	1144	358	852	1210
26	**Bernie Nicholls**	17	1117	475	732	1207
27	**Dino Ciccarelli**	18	1218	602	591	1193
28	**Doug Gilmour**	15	1125	381	795	1176
29	Bobby Hull	16	1063	610	560	1170
30	Michel Goulet	15	1089	548	604	1152

Goals

		Yrs	Gm	No
1	**Wayne Gretzky**	19	1417	885
2	Gordie Howe	26	1767	801
3	Marcel Dionne	18	1348	731
4	Phil Esposito	18	1282	717
5	**Mike Gartner**	19	1432	708
6	Mario Lemieux	12	745	613
7	Bobby Hull	16	1063	610
8	**Dino Ciccarelli**	18	1218	602
9	**Jari Kurri**	17	1251	601
10	**Mark Messier**	19	1354	597
11	Mike Bossy	10	752	573
12	**Steve Yzerman**	15	1098	563
13	Guy Lafleur	17	1126	560
14	John Bucyk	23	1540	556
15	**Brett Hull**	13	801	554
16	Michel Goulet	15	1089	548
17	Maurice Richard	18	978	544
18	Stan Mikita	22	1394	541
19	Frank Mahovlich	18	1181	533
20	Bryan Trottier	18	1279	524
21	Dale Hawerchuk	16	1188	518
22	**Dave Andreychuk**	16	1158	517
23	Gilbert Perreault	17	1191	512
24	Jean Beliveau	20	1125	507
25	Joe Mullen	17	1062	502
26	Lanny McDonald	16	1111	500
27	Glenn Anderson	16	1128	498
28	Jean Ratelle	21	1281	491
29	Norm Ullman	20	1410	490
30	Darryl Sittler	15	1096	484

Assists

		Yrs	Gm	No
1	**Wayne Gretzky**	19	1417	1910
2	**Paul Coffey**	18	1268	1090
3	Gordie Howe	26	1767	1049
4	Marcel Dionne	18	1348	1040
5	**Ray Bourque**	19	1372	1036
6	**Mark Messier**	19	1354	1015
7	**Ron Francis**	17	1247	1006
8	Stan Mikita	22	1394	926
9	Bryan Trottier	18	1279	901
10	Dale Hawerchuk	16	1188	891
11	Mario Lemieux	12	745	881
12	Phil Esposito	18	1281	873
13	Denis Savard	17	1196	865
14	Bobby Clarke	15	1144	852
15	**Steve Yzerman**	15	1098	846
16	**Larry Murphy**	18	1397	838
17	Alex Delvecchio	24	1549	825
18	Gilbert Perreault	17	1191	814
19	John Bucyk	23	1540	813
20	**Jari Kurri**	17	1251	797

Penalty Minutes

		Yrs	Gm	Min
1	Tiger Williams	14	962	3966
2	**Dale Hunter**	18	1345	3446
3	**Marty McSorley**	15	888	3218
4	Tim Hunter	16	815	3146
5	Chris Nilan	13	688	3043
6	**Bob Probert**	12	648	2701
7	**Rick Tocchet**	14	909	2626
8	Willi Plett	12	834	2572
9	**Pat Verbeek**	16	1147	2532
10	Basil McRae	16	576	2457
	Craig Berube	12	719	2457
13	**Scott Stevens**	16	1200	2440
14	**Joey Kocur**	14	781	2432
15	Jay Wells	18	1098	2359

NHL-WHA Top 15

All-time regular season scoring leaders, including games played in World Hockey Association (1972-79). NHL players with WHA experience are listed in CAPITAL letters. Players active during 1998 are in **bold** type.

Points

		Yrs	G	A	Pts
1	**WAYNE GRETZKY**	20	931	1974	2905
2	GORDIE HOWE	32	975	1383	2358
3	BOBBY HULL	23	913	895	1808
4	Marcel Dionne	18	731	1040	1771
5	**MARK MESSIER**	20	598	1025	1623
6	Phil Esposito	18	717	873	1590
7	Mario Lemieux	12	613	881	1494
8	**Paul Coffey**	18	383	1090	1473
9	Stan Mikita	22	541	926	1467
10	**Ron Francis**	17	428	1006	1434
11	Bryan Trottier	18	524	901	1425
12	**Ray Bourque**	19	375	1036	1411
13	**Steve Yzerman**	15	563	846	1409
	Dale Hawerchuk	16	512	891	1409
15	**Jari Kurri**	17	601	797	1398

WHA Totals: GRETZKY (1 yr, 80 gm, 46-64—110); HOWE (6 yrs, 419 gm, 174-334—508); HULL (7 yrs, 411 gm, 303-335—638); MESSIER (1 yr, 52 gm, 1-10—11).

Years Played

		Yrs	Career	Gm
1	Gordie Howe	26	1946-71, 79-80	1767
2	Alex Delvecchio	24	1950-74	1549
	Tim Horton	24	1949-50, 51-74	1446
4	John Bucyk	23	1955-78	1540
5	Stan Mikita	22	1958-80	1394
	Doug Mohns	22	1953-75	1390
	Dean Prentice	22	1952-74	1378
8	Harry Howell	21	1952-73	1411
	Ron Stewart	21	1952-73	1353
	Jean Ratelle	21	1960-81	1281
	Allan Stanley	21	1948-69	1244
	Eric Nesterenko	21	1951-72	1219
	Marcel Pronovost	21	1950-70	1206
	George Armstrong	21	1949-50, 51-71	1187
	Terry Sawchuk	21	1949-70	971
	Gump Worsley	21	1952-53, 54-74	862

Note: Combined NHL-WHA years played: Howe (32); Howell (24); Bobby Hull (23); Norm Ullman, Nesterenko, Frank Mahovlich and Dave Keon (22).

Games Played

		Yrs	Career	Gm
1	Gordie Howe	26	1946-71, 79-80	1767
2	Alex Delvecchio	24	1950-74	1549
3	John Bucyk	23	1955-78	1540
4	Tim Horton	24	1949-50, 51-74	1446
5	**Mike Gartner**	19	1979—	1432
6	**Wayne Gretzky**	19	1979—	1417
7	Harry Howell	21	1952-73	1411
8	Norm Ullman	20	1955-75	1410
9	**Larry Murphy**	18	1980—	1397
10	Stan Mikita	22	1958-80	1394
11	Doug Mohns	22	1953-75	1390
12	Larry Robinson	20	1972-92	1384
13	Dean Prentice	22	1952-74	1378
14	**Ray Bourque**	19	1979—	1372
15	**Mark Messier**	19	1979—	1354

Note: Combined NHL-WHA games played: Howe (2,186), Dave Keon (1,597), Howell (1,581), Ullman (1,554), Gartner (1,510), Gretzky (1,497), Bobby Hull (1,474), Frank Mahovlich (1,418) and Messier (1406).

Goaltending

Wins

		Yrs	Gm	W	L	T	Pct
1	Terry Sawchuk	21	971	**447**	330	173	.562
2	Jacques Plante	18	837	**434**	246	137	.615
3	Tony Esposito	16	886	**423**	307	151	.566
4	Glenn Hall	18	906	**407**	327	165	.544
5	**Grant Fuhr**	17	806	**382**	271	104	.573
6	**Patrick Roy**	13	717	**380**	224	87	.613
7	**Andy Moog**	18	713	**372**	209	88	.622
8	Rogie Vachon	16	795	**355**	291	115	.542
9	Gump Worsley	21	861	**334**	349	148	.491
10	Harry Lumley	16	804	**333**	326	143	.504
11	**Mike Vernon**	15	624	**331**	201	73	.607
12	**Tom Barrasso**	15	665	**326**	232	76	.574
13	**J. Vanbiesbrouck**	16	717	**306**	285	90	.515
14	Billy Smith	18	680	**305**	233	105	.556
15	Turk Broda	12	629	**302**	224	101	.562
16	Mike Liut	13	663	**294**	271	74	.518
17	Ed Giacomin	13	610	**289**	206	97	.570
18	**Ron Hextall**	12	585	**286**	207	65	.571
	Dan Bouchard	14	655	**286**	232	113	.543
20	Tiny Thompson	12	553	**284**	194	75	.581

Losses

		Yrs	Gm	W	L	T	Pct
1	Gilles Meloche	18	788	270	**351**	131	.446
2	Gump Worsley	21	862	334	**349**	148	.491
3	Terry Sawchuk	21	971	447	**330**	173	.562
4	Glenn Hall	18	906	407	**327**	163	.545
5	Harry Lumley	16	804	333	**326**	143	.504

Goals Against Average

Minimum of 300 games played.

Before 1950

		Gm	Min	GA	GAA
1	George Hainsworth	465	29,415	937	1.91
2	Alex Connell	416	26,030	837	2.01
3	Chuck Gardiner	316	19,687	664	2.02
4	Lorne Chabot	412	25,309	861	2.04
5	Tiny Thompson	552	34,174	1183	2.08

Since 1950

		Gm	Min	GA	GAA
1	**Martin Brodeur**	305	17,387	627	2.16
2	Ken Dryden	397	23,352	870	2.24
3	**Dominik Hasek**	350	20,086	782	2.34
4	Jacques Plante	837	49,633	1965	2.38
5	Glenn Hall	906	53,484	2239	2.51

Shutouts

		Yrs	Games	No
1	Terry Sawchuk	21	971	103
2	George Hainsworth	11	464	94
3	Glenn Hall	18	906	84
4	Jacques Plante	18	837	82
5	Alex Connell	12	417	81
	Tiny Thompson	12	553	81
7	Tony Esposito	16	886	76
8	Lorne Chabot	11	411	73
9	Harry Lumley	16	804	71
10	Roy Worters	12	484	66
11	Turk Broda	14	629	62
12	John Roach	14	492	58
13	Clint Benedict	13	362	57
14	Bernie Parent	13	608	54
	Ed Giacomin	13	610	54

NHL-WHA Top 15

All-Time regular season wins leaders, including games played in World Hockey Association (1972-79). NHL goaltenders with WHA experience are listed in CAPITAL letters. Players active during 1998 are in **bold** type.

Wins

		Yrs	W	L	T	Pct
1	JACQUES PLANTE	19	449	260	138	.612
2	Terry Sawchuk	21	447	330	173	.562
3	Tony Esposito	16	423	307	151	.566
4	Glenn Hall	18	407	327	165	.544
5	**Grant Fuhr**	17	382	271	104	.573
6	**Patrick Roy**	13	380	224	87	.613
7	**Andy Moog**	18	372	209	88	.622
8	Rogie Vachon	16	355	291	115	.542
9	Gump Worsley	21	334	349	148	.491
10	Harry Lumley	16	333	326	143	.504
11	**Mike Vernon**	15	331	201	73	.607
12	GERRY CHEEVERS	16	329	172	83	.634
13	**Tom Barrasso**	15	326	232	76	.574
14	MIKE LIUT	15	324	310	78	.510
15	Billy Smith	18	305	233	105	.556

WHA Totals: CHEEVERS (4 yrs, 191 gm, 99-78-9); LIUT (2 yrs, 81 gm, 31-39-4); PLANTE (1 yr, 31 gm, 15-14-1).

All-Time NHL Regular Season Leaders (Cont.)

SINGLE SEASON

Scoring

Points

		Season	G	A	Pts
1	Wayne Gretzky, Edm	1985-86	52	163	215
2	Wayne Gretzky, Edm	1981-82	92	120	212
3	Wayne Gretzky, Edm	1984-85	73	135	208
4	Wayne Gretzky, Edm	1983-84	87	118	205
5	Mario Lemieux, Pit	1988-89	85	114	199
6	Wayne Gretzky, Edm	1982-83	71	125	196
7	Wayne Gretzky, Edm	1986-87	62	121	183
8	Mario Lemieux, Pit	1987-88	70	98	168
9	Wayne Gretzky, LA	1988-89	54	114	168
10	Wayne Gretzky, Edm	1980-81	55	109	164
11	Wayne Gretzky, LA	1990-91	41	122	163
12	Mario Lemieux, Pit	1995-96	69	92	161
13	Mario Lemieux, Pit	1992-93	69	91	160
14	Steve Yzerman, Det	1988-89	65	90	155
15	Phil Esposito, Bos	1970-71	76	76	152
16	Bernie Nicholls, LA	1988-89	70	80	150
17	Jaromir Jagr, Pit	1995-96	62	87	149
	Wayne Gretzky, Edm	1987-88	40	109	149
19	Pat LaFontaine, Buf	1992-93	53	95	148
20	Mike Bossy, NYI	1981-82	64	83	147

WHA 150 points or more: 154—Marc Tardif, Que. (1977-78).

Goals

		Season	Gm	No
1	Wayne Gretzky, Edm	1981-82	80	92
2	Wayne Gretzky, Edm	1983-84	74	87
3	Brett Hull, St.L	1990-91	78	86
4	Mario Lemieux, Pit	1988-89	76	85
5	Alexander Mogilny, Buf	1992-93	77	76
	Phil Esposito, Bos	1970-71	78	76
	Teemu Selanne, Win	1992-93	84	76
8	Wayne Gretzky, Edm	1984-85	80	73
9	Brett Hull, St.L	1989-90	80	72
10	Jari Kurri, Edm	1984-85	73	71
	Wayne Gretzky, Edm	1982-83	80	71
12	Brett Hull, St.L	1991-92	73	70
	Mario Lemieux, Pit	1987-88	77	70
	Bernie Nicholls, LA	1988-89	79	70
15	Mario Lemieux, Pit	1992-93	60	69
	Mario Lemieux, Pit	1995-96	70	69
	Mike Bossy, NYI	1978-79	80	69
18	Phil Esposito, Bos	1973-74	78	68
	Jari Kurri, Edm	1985-86	78	68
	Mike Bossy, NYI	1980-81	79	68

WHA 70 goals or more: 77—Bobby Hull, Win. (1974-75); 75—Real Cloutier, Que. (1978-79); 71—Marc Tardif, Que. (1975-76); 70—Anders Hedberg, Win. (1976-77).

Assists

		Season	Gm	No
1	Wayne Gretzky, Edm	1985-86	80	163
2	Wayne Gretzky, Edm	1984-85	80	135
3	Wayne Gretzky, Edm	1982-83	80	125
4	Wayne Gretzky, LA	1990-91	78	122
5	Wayne Gretzky, Edm	1986-87	79	121
6	Wayne Gretzky, Edm	1981-82	80	120
7	Wayne Gretzky, Edm	1983-84	74	118
8	Mario Lemieux, Pit	1988-89	76	114
	Wayne Gretzky, LA	1988-89	78	114
10	Wayne Gretzky, Edm	1987-88	64	109
	Wayne Gretzky, Edm	1980-81	80	109
12	Wayne Gretzky, LA	1989-90	73	102
	Bobby Orr, Bos	1970-71	78	102
14	Mario Lemieux, Pit	1987-88	77	98
15	Adam Oates, Bos	1992-93	84	97

WHA 95 assists or more: 106—Andre Lacroix, S.Diego (1974-75).

Goaltending

Wins

		Season	Record
1	Bernie Parent, Phi	1973-74	47-13-12
2	Bernie Parent, Phi	1974-75	44-14- 9
	Terry Sawchuk, Det	1950-51	44-13-13
	Terry Sawchuk, Det	1951-52	44-14-12
5	**Martin Brodeur**, NJ	1997-98	43-17- 8
	Tom Barrasso, Pit	1992-93	43-14- 5
	Ed Belfour, Chi	1990-91	43-19- 7
8	Jacques Plante, Mon	1955-56	42-12-10
	Jacques Plante, Mon	1961-62	42-14-14
	Ken Dryden, Mon	1975-76	42-10- 8
	Mike Richter, NYR	1993-94	42-12- 6

Most WHA wins in one season: 44—Richard Brodeur, Que. (1975-76).

Losses

		Season	Record
1	Gary Smith, Cal	1970-71	19-48- 4
2	Al Rollins, Chi	1953-54	12-47- 7
3	Peter Sidorkiewicz, Ott	1992-93	8-46- 3
4	Harry Lumley, Chi	1951-52	17-44- 9
5	Harry Lumley, Chi	1950-51	12-41-10
	Craig Billington, Ott	1993-94	11-41- 4

Most WHA losses in one season: 36—Don McLeod, Van. (1974-75) and Andy Brown, Ind. (1974-75).

Shutouts

		Season	Gm	No
1	George Hainsworth, Mon	1928-29	44	22
2	Alex Connell, Ottawa	1925-26	36	15
	Alex Connell, Ottawa	1927-28	44	15
	Hal Winkler, Bos	1927-28	44	15
	Tony Esposito, Chi	1969-70	63	15

Most WHA shutouts in one season: 5—Gerry Cheevers, Cle. (1972-73) and Joe Daly, Win. (1975-76).

Goals Against Average

Before 1950

		Season	Gm	GAA
1	George Hainsworth, Mon	1928-29	44	0.98
2	George Hainsworth, Mon	1927-28	44	1.09
3	Alex Connell, Ottawa	1925-26	36	1.17
4	Tiny Thompson, Bos	1928-29	44	1.18
5	Roy Worters, NY Americans	1928-29	38	1.21

Since 1950

		Season	Gm	GAA
1	Tony Esposito, Chi	1971-72	48	1.77
2	Al Rollins, Tor	1950-51	40	1.77
3	Harry Lumley, Tor	1953-54	69	1.86
4	Jacques Plante, Mon	1955-56	64	1.86
5	Martin Brodeur, NJ	1996-97	67	1.88

Penalty Minutes

		Season	PM
1	Dave Schultz, Phi	1974-75	472
2	Paul Baxter, Pit	1981-82	409
3	Mike Peluso, Chi	1991-92	408
4	Dave Schultz, LA-Pit	1977-78	405
5	Marty McSorley, LA	1992-93	399
6	Bob Probert, Det	1987-88	398
7	Basil McRae, Min	1987-88	382
8	Joey Kocur, Det	1985-86	377
9	Tim Hunter, Calg	1988-89	375
10	**Donald Brashear**, Van	1997-98	372

WHA 355 minutes or more: 365—Curt Brackenbury, Min-Que. (1975-76).

SINGLE GAME

Scoring

Points

	Date	G-A—Pts
Darryl Sittler, Tor vs Bos	2/7/76	6-4—10
Maurice Richard, Mon vs Det	12/28/44	5-3— 8
Bert Olmstead, Mon vs Chi	1/9/54	4-4— 8
Tom Bladon, Phi vs Cle	12/11/77	4-4— 8
Bryan Trottier, NYI vs NYR	12/23/78	5-3— 8
Peter Stastny, Que at Wash	2/22/81	4-4— 8
Anton Stastny, Que at Wash	2/22/81	3-5— 8
Wayne Gretzky, Edm vs NJ	11/19/83	3-5— 8
Wayne Gretzky, Edm vs Min	1/4/84	4-4— 8
Paul Coffey, Edm vs Det	3/14/86	2-6— 8
Mario Lemieux, Pit vs St.L	10/15/88	2-6— 8
Bernie Nicholls, LA vs Tor	12/1/88	2-6— 8
Mario Lemieux, Pit vs NJ	12/31/88	5-3— 8

Goals

	Date	No
Joe Malone, Que vs Tor	1/31/20	7
Newsy Lalonde, Mon vs Tor	1/10/20	6
Joe Malone, Que vs Ott	3/10/20	6
Corb Denneny, Tor vs Ham	1/26/21	6
Cy Denneny, Ott vs Ham	3/7/21	6
Syd Howe, Det vs NYR	2/3/44	6
Red Berenson, St.L at Phi	11/7/68	6
Darryl Sittler, Tor vs Bos	2/7/76	6

Assists

	Date	No
Billy Taylor, Det at Chi	3/16/47	7
Wayne Gretzky, Edm vs Wash	2/15/80	7
Wayne Gretzky, Edm at Chi	12/11/85	7
Wayne Gretzky, Edm vs Que	2/14/86	7

24 players tied with 6 each.

Penalty Minutes

	Date	Min
Randy Holt, LA at Phi	3/11/79	67
Frank Bathe, Phi vs LA	3/11/79	55
Russ Anderson, Pit vs Edm	1/19/80	51

Penalties

	Date	No
Chris Nilan, Bos vs Har	3/31/91	10*

Eight tied with 9 each.

* Nilan accumulated six minors, two majors, one 10-minute misconduct and one game misconduct.

The NHL Top 50

To celebrate its fiftieth anniversary, *The Hockey News* presented its list of the "Top 50 NHL Players of All-Time" on January 9, 1998. The list was determined by a panel of 50 hockey experts representing past and present NHL players, coaches, executives and journalists. Voting was conducted before the 1997 Stanley Cup playoffs. Players active during the 1997-98 season are in **bold** type.

No.	Player	Pos
1	**Wayne Gretzky**, 1979—	C
2	Bobby Orr, 1966-1979	D
3	Gordie Howe, 1946-71, 79-80	RW
4	Mario Lemieux, 1984-1997	C
5	Maurice Richard, 1942-1960	RW
6	Doug Harvey, 1947-69	D
7	Jean Beliveau, 1950-71	C
8	Bobby Hull, 1957-72, 79-80	LW
9	Terry Sawchuk, 1949-70	G
10	Eddie Shore, 1926-40	D
11	Guy Lafleur, 1971-85, 88-91	RW
12	**Mark Messier**, 1979—	C
13	Jacques Plante, 1952-65, 67-73	G
14	**Ray Bourque**, 1979—	D
15	Howie Morenz, 1923-37	C
16	Glenn Hall, 1952-71	G
17	Stan Mikita, 1958-80	C
18	Phil Esposito, 1963-81	C
19	Denis Potvin, 1973-88	D
20	Mike Bossy, 1977-87	RW
21	Ted Lindsay, 1944-60, 64-65	LW
22	Red Kelly, 1947-67	D
23	Bobby Clarke, 1969-84	C
24	Larry Robinson, 1972-92	D
25	Ken Dryden, 1970-79	G
26	Frank Mahovlich, 1956-74	LW
27	Milt Schmidt, 1936-42, 45-55	C
28	**Paul Coffey**, 1980—	D
29	Henri Richard, 1955-75	C
30	Bryan Trottier, 1975-92, 93-94	C
31	Dickie Moore, 1951-65, 67-68	LW
32	Newsy Lalonde, 1917-21, 25-27	C
33	Syl Apps, 1936-48	C
34	Bill Durnan, 1943-50	G
35	**Patrick Roy**, 1984—	G
36	Charlie Conacher, 1929-41	RW
37	**Jaromir Jagr**, 1990—	RW
38	Marcel Dionne, 1971-89	C
39	Joe Malone, 1917-24	C
40	**Chris Chelios**, 1983—	D
41	Dit Clapper, 1927-47	D
42	Bernie Geoffrion, 1950-64, 66-68	RW
43	Tim Horton, 1949-50, 51-74	D
44	Bill Cook, 1926-37	RW
45	Johnny Bucyk, 1955-78	LW
46	George Hainsworth, 1926-37	G
47	Gilbert Perreault, 1970-87	C
48	Max Bentley, 1940-43, 45-54	C
49	Brad Park, 1968-85	D
50	**Jari Kurri**, 1980—	RW

All-Time Winningest NHL Coaches

Top 20 NHL career victories through the 1998 season. Career, regular season and playoff records are noted along with NHL titles won. Coaches active during 1998 season in **bold** type.

		Career					Regular Season				Playoffs				
	Yrs	W	L	T	Pct	W	L	T	Pct	W	L	T	Pct	Stanley Cups
1 **Scotty Bowman**	26	1251	594	278	.655	1057	483	278	.658	194	111	0	.636	8 (1973, 76-79, 92, 97-98)
2 Al Arbour	22	904	663	248	.566	781	577	248	.564	123	86	0	.589	4 (1980-83)
3 Dick Irvin	26	790	609	228	.556	690	521	226	.559	100	88	2	.532	4 (1932,44,46,53)
4 Billy Reay	16	599	445	175	.563	542	385	175	.571	57	60	0	.487	None
5 Toe Blake	13	582	292	159	.640	500	255	159	.634	82	37	0	.689	8 (1956-60,65-66,68)
Mike Keenan	13	582	417	111	.574	491	348	111	.575	91	69	0	.569	1 (1994)
7 Glen Sather	11	553	305	110	.628	464	268	110	.616	89	37	0	.706	4 (1984-85,87-88)
8 **Bryan Murray**	13	518	412	126	.550	484	368	126	.559	34	44	0	.436	None
9 Jack Adams	21	475	449	163	.512	423	397	162	.513	52	52	1	.500	3 (1936-37, 43)
10 Fred Shero	10	451	272	119	.606	390	225	119	.612	61	47	0	.565	2 (1974-75)
11 **Jacques Demers**	13	445	459	121	.495	390	416	121	.486	55	43	0	.561	1 (1993)
12 Punch Imlach	15	439	384	148	.528	395	336	148	.534	44	48	0	.478	4 (1962-64,67)
13 Emile Francis	13	433	326	112	.561	393	273	112	.577	40	53	0	.430	None
14 Sid Abel	16	414	470	155	.473	382	426	155	.477	32	44	0	.421	None
15 **Roger Neilson**	14	410	368	128	.523	377	329	128	.529	33	39	0	.458	None
Pat Quinn	12	410	335	102	.544	357	285	102	.548	53	50	0	.515	None
17 **Pat Burns**	9	401	294	96	.568	346	241	96	.577	55	53	0	.509	None
18 Bob Berry	11	395	377	121	.510	384	355	121	.517	11	22	0	.333	None
19 Art Ross	18	393	310	95	.552	361	277	90	.558	32	33	5	.493	1 (1939)
20 Michel Bergeron	10	369	387	104	.490	338	350	104	.492	31	37	0	.456	None

Note: The NHL does not recognize records from the World Hockey Association (1972-79), so the following WHA overall coaching records are not included above: **Demers** (155-164-44 in 4 yrs); **Sather** (103-97-1 in 3 yrs).

Where They Coached

Abel—Chicago (1952-54), Detroit (1957-68,69-70), St. Louis (1971-72), Kansas City (1975-76); **Adams**—Toronto (1922-23), Detroit (1927-47); **Arbour**—St. Louis (1970-73), NY Islanders (1973-86,88-94); **Bergeron**—Quebec (1980-87), NY Rangers (1987-89), Quebec (1989-90); **Berry**—Los Angeles (1978-81), Montreal (1981-84), Pittsburgh (1984-87), St. Louis (1992-94); **Blake**—Montreal (1955-68); **Bowman**—St. Louis (1967-71), Montreal (1971-79), Buffalo (1979-87), Pittsburgh (1991-93), Detroit (1993—); **Burns**—Montreal (1988-92), Toronto (1992-96), Boston (1997—).

Demers—Quebec (1979-80), St. Louis (1983-86), Detroit (1986-90), Montreal (1992-95), Tampa Bay (1997—); **Francis**—NY Rangers (1965-75), St. Louis (1976-77,81-83); **Imlach**—Toronto (1958-69), Buffalo (1970-72), Toronto (1979-81); **Irvin**—Chicago (1930-31,55-56), Toronto (1931-40), Montreal (1940-55); **Keenan**—Philadelphia (1984-88), Chicago (1988-92), NY Rangers (1993-94), St. Louis (1994-96), Vancouver (1997—); **Murray**—Washington (1982-90), Detroit (1990-93), Florida (1997—).

Neilson—Toronto (1977-79), Buffalo (1979-81), Vancouver (1982-83), Los Angeles (1984), NY Rangers (1989-93), Florida (1993-95), Philadelphia (1998—); **Quinn**—Philadelphia (1978-82), Los Angeles (1984-87), Vancouver (1990-94, 96); **Reay**—Toronto (1957-59), Chicago (1963-77); **Ross**—Montreal Wanderers (1917-18), Hamilton (1922-23), Boston (1924-28,29-34,36-39,41-45); **Sather**—Edmonton (1979-89, 93-94); **Shero**—Philadelphia (1971-78), NY Rangers (1978-81).

Top Winning Percentages

Minimum of 275 victories, including playoffs.

	Yrs	W	L	T	Pct.
1 **Scotty Bowman**	26	1251	594	278	**.655**
2 Toe Blake	13	582	292	159	**.640**
3 Glen Sather	11	553	305	110	**.628**
4 Fred Shero	10	451	272	119	**.606**
5 Don Cherry	6	281	177	77	**.597**
6 Tommy Ivan	9	324	205	111	**.593**
7 **Jacques Lemaire**	7	296	193	69	**.592**
8 **Mike Keenan**	13	582	417	111	**.574**
9 Terry Murray	8	327	237	58	**.572**
10 **Pat Burns**	8	401	294	96	**.568**
11 Al Arbour	22	904	663	248	**.566**
12 Billy Reay	16	599	445	175	**.563**
13 Emile Francis	13	433	326	112	**.561**
14 Hap Day	10	308	237	81	**.557**
15 Dick Irvin	26	790	609	228	**.556**
16 Lester Patrick	13	312	242	115	**.552**
17 Art Ross	18	393	310	95	**.552**
18 **Bryan Murray**	13	518	412	126	**.550**
19 Bob Johnson	6	275	223	58	**.547**
20 Pat Quinn	12	410	335	102	**.544**
21 **Brian Sutter**	8	326	274	81	**.538**
22 Punch Imlach	15	439	384	148	**.528**
23 **Roger Neilson**	14	410	368	128	**.523**
24 **Terry Crisp**	9	310	286	78	**.518**
25 Jack Adams	21	475	449	163	**.512**

Active Coaches' Victories

Through 1998 season, including playoffs.

	Yrs	W	L	T	Pct.
1 Scotty Bowman, Det.	26	**1251**	594	278	.655
2 Mike Keenan, Van	13	**582**	417	111	.574
3 Jacques Demers, TB	13	**445**	459	121	.493
4 Roger Neilson, Phi	14	**410**	368	128	.523
Pat Quinn, Tor.	12	**410**	335	102	.544
6 Pat Burns, Bos.	9	**401**	294	96	.568
7 Terry Murray, Fla	8	**327**	237	58	.572
8 Brian Sutter, Calg.	8	**326**	274	81	.538
9 John Muckler, NYR	8	**250**	244	62	.505
10 Jim Schoenfeld, Pho	9	**240**	242	66	.498
11 Ron Wilson, Wash.	5	**176**	191	43	.482
12 Darryl Sutter, SJ	4	**157**	137	36	.530
13 Mike Milbury, NYI.	5	**156**	148	42	.512
Jacques Martin, Ott.	5	**156**	183	57	.466
15 Ken Hitchcock, Dal.	3	**125**	82	24	.593
16 Ron Low, Edm.	4	**116**	139	28	.459
17 Craig Hartsburg, Ana.	3	**112**	110	40	.504
18 Kevin Constantine, Pit.	4	**108**	120	42	.478
19 Paul Maurice, Car.	3	**94**	113	27	.459
20 Larry Robinson, LA	3	**90**	120	40	.440
21 Joel Quenneville, St.L.	2	**71**	52	15	.569
22 Robbie Ftorek, NJ	2	**70**	67	11	.510
23 Lindy Ruff, Buf	1	**46**	34	17	.562
24 Alain Vigneault, Mon.	1	**41**	38	13	.516
25 Dirk Graham, Chi.	0	**0**	0	0	.000
Bob Hartley, Col.	0	**0**	0	0	.000
Barry Trotz, Nash.	0	**0**	0	0	.000

Annual Awards

Hart Memorial Trophy

Awarded to the player "adjudged to be the most valuable to his team" and named after Cecil Hart, the former manager-coach of the Montreal Canadiens. Winners selected by Pro Hockey Writers Assn. (PHWA). Winners' scoring statistics or goaltender W-L records and goals against average are provided; (*) indicates led or tied for league lead.

Multiple Winners: Wayne Gretzky (9); Gordie Howe (6); Eddie Shore (4); Bobby Clarke, Mario Lemieux, Howie Morenz and Bobby Orr (3); Jean Beliveau, Bill Cowley, Phil Esposito, Dominik Hasek, Bobby Hull, Guy Lafleur, Mark Messier, Stan Mikita and Nels Stewart (2).

Year		G	A	Pts
1924	Frank Nighbor, Ottawa, C	10	3	13
1925	Billy Burch, Hamilton, C	20	4	24
1926	Nels Stewart, Maroons, C	34	8	42*
1927	Herb Gardiner, Mon., D	6	6	12
1928	Howie Morenz, Mon., C	33	18	51
1929	Roy Worters, NYA, G	16-13-9,		1.21
1930	Nels Stewart, Maroons, C	39	16	55
1931	Howie Morenz, Mon., C	28	23	51*
1932	Howie Morenz, Mon., C	24	25	49
1933	Eddie Shore, Bos., D	8	27	35
1934	Aurel Joliat, Mon., LW	22	15	37
1935	Eddie Shore, Bos., D	7	26	33
1936	Eddie Shore, Bos., D	3	16	19
1937	Babe Siebert, Mon., D	8	20	28
1938	Eddie Shore, Bos., D	3	14	17
1939	Toe Blake, Mon., LW	24	23	47*
1940	Ebbie Goodfellow, Det., D	11	17	28
1941	Bill Cowley, Bos., C	17	45	62*
1942	Tommy Anderson, NYA, D	12	29	41
1943	Bill Cowley, Bos., C	27	45	72
1944	Babe Pratt, Tor., D	17	40	57
1945	Elmer Lach, Mon., C	26	54	80*
1946	Max Bentley, Chi., C	31	30	61*
1947	Maurice Richard, Mon., RW	45	26	71
1948	Buddy O'Connor, NYR, C	24	36	60
1949	Sid Abel, Det., C	28	26	54
1950	Chuck Rayner, NYR, G	28-30-11;		2.62
1951	Milt Schmidt, Bos., C	22	39	61
1952	Gordie Howe, Det., RW	47	39	86*
1953	Gordie Howe, Det., RW	49	46	95*
1954	Al Rollins, Chi., G	12-47-7;		3.23
1955	Ted Kennedy, Tor., C	10	42	52
1956	Jean Beliveau, Mon., C	47	41	88
1957	Gordie Howe, Det., RW	44	45	89*
1958	Gordie Howe, Det., RW	33	44	77
1959	Andy Bathgate, NYR, RW	40	48	88
1960	Gordie Howe, Det., RW	28	45	73
1961	Bernie Geoffrion, Mon., RW	50	45	95*
1962	Jacques Plante, Mon., G	42-14-14;		2.37*
1963	Gordie Howe, Det., RW	38	48	86*
1964	Jean Beliveau, Mon., C	28	50	78
1965	Bobby Hull, Chi., LW	39	32	71
1966	Bobby Hull, Chi., LW	54	43	97*
1967	Stan Mikita, Chi., C	35	62	97*
1968	Stan Mikita, Chi., C	40	47	87*
1969	Phil Esposito, Bos., C	49	77	126*
1970	Bobby Orr, Bos., D	33	87	120*
1971	Bobby Orr, Bos., D	37	102	139
1972	Bobby Orr, Bos., D	37	80	117
1973	Bobby Clarke, Phi., C	37	67	104
1974	Phil Esposito, Bos., C	68	77	145*
1975	Bobby Clarke, Phi., C	27	89	116
1976	Bobby Clarke, Phi., C	30	89	119
1977	Guy Lafleur, Mon., RW	56	80	136*
1978	Guy Lafleur, Mon., RW	60	72	132*
1979	Bryan Trottier, NYI., C	47	87	134*
1980	Wayne Gretzky, Edm., C	51	86	137*
1981	Wayne Gretzky, Edm., C	55	109	164*
1982	Wayne Gretzky, Edm., C	92	120	212*
1983	Wayne Gretzky, Edm., C	71	125	196*
1984	Wayne Gretzky, Edm., C	87	118	205*
1985	Wayne Gretzky, Edm., C	73	135	208*
1986	Wayne Gretzky, Edm., C	52	163	215*
1987	Wayne Gretzky, Edm., C	62	121	183*
1988	Mario Lemieux, Pit., C	70	98	168*
1989	Wayne Gretzky, LA, C	54	114	168
1990	Mark Messier, Edm., C	45	84	129
1991	Brett Hull, St. L., RW	86	45	131
1992	Mark Messier, NYR, C	35	72	107
1993	Mario Lemieux, Pit., C	69	91	160*
1994	Sergei Fedorov, Det., C	56	64	120
1995	Eric Lindros, Phi., C	29	41	70*
1996	Mario Lemieux, Pit., C	69	92	161*
1997	Dominik Hasek, Buf., G	37-20-10;		2.27
1998	Dominik Hasek, Buf., G	33-23-13,		2.09

Calder Memorial Trophy

Awarded to the most outstanding rookie of the year and named after Frank Calder, the late NHL president (1917-43). Since the 1990-91 season, all eligible candidates must not have attained their 26th birthday by Sept. 15 of their rookie year. Winners selected by PHWA. Winners' scoring statistics or goaltender W-L record & goals against average are provided.

Year		G	A	Pts
1933	Carl Voss, NYR-Det., C	8	15	23
1934	Russ Blinco, Maroons, C	14	9	23
1935	Sweeney Schriner, NYA, LW	18	22	40
1936	Mike Karakas, Chi., G	21-19-8;		1.92
1937	Syl Apps, Tor., C	16	29	45
1938	Cully Dahlstrom, Chi., C	10	9	19
1939	Frankie Brimsek, Bos., G	33-9-1;		1.58
1940	Kilby MacDonald, NYR, LW	15	13	28
1941	John Quilty, Mon., C	18	16	34
1942	Knobby Warwick, NYR, RW	16	17	33
1943	Gaye Stewart, Tor., LW	24	23	47
1944	Gus Bodnar, Tor., C	22	40	62
1945	Frank McCool, Tor., G	24-22-4;		3.22
1946	Edgar Laprade, NYR, C	15	19	34
1947	Howie Meeker, Tor., RW	27	18	45
1948	Jim McFadden, Det., C	24	24	48
1949	Penny Lund, NYR, RW	14	16	30
1950	Jack Gelineau, Bos., G	22-30-15;		3.28
1951	Terry Sawchuk, Det., G	44-13-13;		1.99
1952	Bernie Geoffrion, Mon., RW	30	24	54
1953	Gump Worsley, NYR, G	13-29-8;		3.06
1954	Camille Henry, NYR, LW	24	15	39
1955	Ed Litzenberger, Mon-Chi., RW	23	28	51
1956	Glenn Hall, Det., G	30-24-16;		2.11
1957	Larry Regan, Bos., RW	14	19	33
1958	Frank Mahovlich, Tor., LW	20	16	36
1959	Ralph Backstrom, Mon., C	18	22	40
1960	Billy Hay, Chi., C	18	37	55
1961	Dave Keon, Tor., C	20	25	45
1962	Bobby Rousseau, Mon., RW	21	24	45
1963	Kent Douglas, Tor., D	7	15	22
1964	Jacques Laperriere, Mon., D	2	28	30
1965	Roger Crozier, Det., G	40-23-7;		2.42
1966	Brit Selby, Tor., LW	14	13	27
1967	Bobby Orr, Bos., D	13	28	41
1968	Derek Sanderson, Bos., C	24	25	49
1969	Danny Grant, Min., LW	34	31	65
1970	Tony Esposito, Chi., G	38-17-8;		2.17

Annual Awards (Cont.)

Year		G	A	Pts
1971	Gilbert Perreault, Buf., C	38	34	72
1972	Ken Dryden, Mon., G	39-8-15;		2.24
1973	Steve Vickers, NYR, LW	30	23	53
1974	Denis Potvin, NYI, D	17	37	54
1975	Eric Vail, Atl., LW	39	21	60
1976	Bryan Trottier, NYI, C	32	63	95
1977	Willi Plett, Atl., RW	33	23	56
1978	Mike Bossy, NYI, RW	53	38	91
1979	Bobby Smith, Min., C	30	44	74
1980	Ray Bourque, Bos., D	17	48	65
1981	Peter Stastny, Que., C	39	70	109
1982	Dale Hawerchuk, Win., C	45	58	103
1983	Steve Larmer, Chi., RW	43	47	90
1984	Tom Barrasso, Buf., G	26-12-3;		2.84
1985	Mario Lemieux, Pit., C	43	57	100
1986	Gary Suter, Calg., D	18	50	68
1987	Luc Robitaille, LA, LW	45	39	84
1988	Joe Nieuwendyk, Calg., C	51	41	92
1989	Brian Leetch, NYR, D	23	48	71
1990	Sergei Makarov, Calg., RW	24	62	86
1991	Ed Belfour, Chi., G	43-19-7;		2.47
1992	Pavel Bure, Van., RW	34	26	60
1993	Teemu Selanne, Win., RW	76	56	132
1994	Martin Brodeur, NJ, G	27-11-8;		2.40
1995	Peter Forsberg, Que., C	15	35	50
1996	Daniel Alfredsson, Ott., RW	26	35	61
1997	Bryan Berard, NYI, D	8	40	48
1998	Sergei Samsonov, Bos., LW	22	25	47

Vezina Trophy

From 1927-80, given to the principal goaltender(s) on the team allowing the fewest goals during the regular season. Trophy named after 1920's goalie Georges Vezina of the Montreal Canadiens, who died of tuberculosis in 1926. Since the 1980-81 season, the trophy has been awarded to the most outstanding goaltender of the year as selected by the league's general managers.

Multiple Winners: Jacques Plante (7, one of them shared); Bill Durnan (6); Ken Dryden (5, three shared); Bunny Larocque (4, all shared); Terry Sawchuk (4, one shared); Dominik Hasek (4); Tiny Thompson (4); Tony Esposito (3, one shared); George Hainsworth (3); Glenn Hall (3, two shared); Patrick Roy (3); Ed Belfour (2); Johnny Bower (2, one shared); Frankie Brimsek (2); Turk Broda (2); Chuck Gardiner (2); Charlie Hodge (2, one shared); Bernie Parent (2, one shared); Gump Worsley (2, both shared).

Year		Record	GAA
1927	George Hainsworth, Mon.	28-14-2	1.52
1928	George Hainsworth, Mon.	26-11-7	1.09
1929	George Hainsworth, Mon.	22-7-15	0.98
1930	Tiny Thompson, Bos	38-5-1	2.23
1931	Roy Worters, NYA	18-16-10	1.68
1932	Chuck Gardiner, Chi.	18-19-11	1.92
1933	Tiny Thompson, Bos	25-15-8	1.83
1934	Chuck Gardiner, Chi.	20-17-11	1.73
1935	Lorne Chabot, Chi	26-17-5	1.83
1936	Tiny Thompson, Bos	22-20-6	1.71
1937	Norm Smith, Det	25-14-9	2.13
1938	Tiny Thompson, Bos	30-11-7	1.85
1939	Frankie Brimsek, Bos	33-9-1	1.58
1940	Dave Kerr, NYR	27-11-10	1.60
1941	Turk Broda, Tor	28-14-6	2.06
1942	Frankie Brimsek, Bos	24-17-6	2.45
1943	John Mowers, Det	25-14-11	2.47
1944	Bill Durnan, Mon	38-5-7	2.18
1945	Bill Durnan, Mon	38-8-4	2.42
1946	Bill Durnan, Mon	24-11-5	2.60
1947	Bill Durnan, Mon	34-16-10	2.30
1948	Turk Broda, Tor	32-15-13	2.38
1949	Bill Durnan, Mon	28-23-9	2.10
1950	Bill Durnan, Mon	26-21-17	2.20
1951	Al Rollins, Tor	27-5-8	1.77
1952	Terry Sawchuk, Det	44-14-12	1.90
1953	Terry Sawchuk, Det	32-15-16	1.90
1954	Harry Lumley, Tor	32-24-13	1.86
1955	Terry Sawchuk, Det	40-17-11	1.96
1956	Jacques Plante, Mon	42-12-10	1.86
1957	Jacques Plante, Mon	31-18-12	2.02
1958	Jacques Plante, Mon	34-14-8	2.11
1959	Jacques Plante, Mon	38-16-13	2.16
1960	Jacques Plante, Mon	40-17-12	2.54
1961	Johnny Bower, Tor	33-15-10	2.50
1962	Jacques Plante, Mon	42-14-14	2.37
1963	Glenn Hall, Chi	30-20-16	2.55
1964	Charlie Hodge, Mon.	33-18-11	2.26
1965	Johnny Bower, Tor	13-13-8	2.38
	& Terry Sawchuk, Tor.	17-13-6	2.56
1966	Gump Worsley, Mon	29-14-6	2.36
	& Charlie Hodge, Mon	12-7-2	2.58
1967	Glenn Hall, Chi.	19-5-5	2.38
	& Denis Dejordy, Chi.	22-12-7	2.46
1968	Gump Worsley, Mon	19-9-8	1.98
	& Rogie Vachon, Mon	23-13-2	2.48
1969	Jacques Plante, St.L	18-12-6	1.96
	& Glenn Hall, St.L.	19-12-8	2.17
1970	Tony Esposito, Chi	38-17-8	2.17
1971	Ed Giacomin, NYR	27-10-7	2.16
	& Gilles Villemure, NYR	22-8-4	2.30
1972	Tony Esposito, Chi	31-10-6	1.77
	& Gary Smith, Chi	14-5-6	2.42
1973	Ken Dryden, Mon.	33-7-13	2.26
1974	(Tie) Bernie Parent, Phi	47-13-12	1.89
	Tony Esposito, Chi	34-14-21	2.04
1975	Bernie Parent, Phi.	44-14-10	2.03
1976	Ken Dryden, Mon.	42-10-8	2.03
1977	Ken Dryden, Mon	41-6-8	2.14
	& Bunny Larocque, Mon	19-2-4	2.09
1978	Ken Dryden, Mon	37-7-7	2.05
	& Bunny Larocque, Mon.	22-3-4	2.67
1979	Ken Dryden, Mon.	30-10-7	2.30
	& Bunny Larocque, Mon.	22-7-4	2.84
1980	Bob Sauve, Buf	20-8-4	2.36
	& Don Edwards, Buf.	27-9-12	2.57
1981	Richard Sevigny, Mon	20-4-3	2.40
	Denis Herron, Mon	6-9-6	3.50
	& Bunny Larocque, Mon.	16-9-3	3.03
1982	Billy Smith, NYI	32-9-4	2.97
1983	Pete Peeters, Bos.	40-11-9	2.36
1984	Tom Barrasso, Buf.	26-12-3	2.84
1985	Pelle Lindbergh, Phi	40-17-7	3.02
1986	John Vanbiesbrouck, NYR	31-21-5	3.32
1987	Ron Hextall, Phi	37-21-6	3.00
1988	Grant Fuhr, Edm	40-24-9	3.43
1989	Patrick Roy, Mon	33-5-6	2.47
1990	Patrick Roy, Mon	31-16-5	2.53
1991	Ed Belfour, Chi	43-19-7	2.47
1992	Patrick Roy, Mon.	36-22-8	2.36
1993	Ed Belfour, Chi	41-18-11	2.59
1994	Dominik Hasek, Buf	30-20-6	1.95
1995	Dominik Hasek, Buf	19-14-7	2.11
1996	Jim Carey, Wash	35-24-9	2.26
1997	Dominik Hasek, Buf	37-20-10	2.27
1998	Dominik Hasek, Buf	33-23-13	2.09

Lady Byng Memorial Trophy

Awarded to the player "adjudged to have exhibited the best type of sportsmanship and gentlemanly conduct combined with a high standard of playing ability" and named after Lady Evelyn Byng, the wife of former Canadian Governor General (1921-26) Baron Byng of Vimy. Winners selected by PHWA.

Multiple winners: Frank Boucher (7); Wayne Gretzky and Red Kelly (4); Bobby Bauer, Mike Bossy and Alex Delvecchio (3); Johnny Bucyk, Marcel Dionne, Ron Francis, Paul Kariya, Dave Keon, Stan Mikita, Joey Mullen, Frank Nighbor, Jean Ratelle, Clint Smith and Sid Smith (2).

Year
1925 Frank Nighbor, Ott., C
1926 Frank Nighbor, Ott., C
1927 Billy Burch, NYA, C
1928 Frank Boucher, NYR, C
1929 Frank Boucher, NYR, C
1930 Frank Boucher, NYR, C
1931 Frank Boucher, NYR, C
1932 Joe Primeau, Tor., C
1933 Frank Boucher, NYR, C
1934 Frank Boucher, NYR, C
1935 Frank Boucher, NYR, C
1936 Doc Romnes, Chi., F
1937 Marty Barry, Det., C
1938 Gordie Drillon, Tor., RW
1939 Clint Smith, NYR, C
1940 Bobby Bauer, Bos., RW
1941 Bobby Bauer, Bos., RW
1942 Syl Apps, Tor., C
1943 Max Bentley, Chi., C
1944 Clint Smith, Chi., C
1945 Bill Mosienko, Chi., RW
1946 Toe Blake, Mon., LW
1947 Bobby Bauer, Bos., RW
1948 Buddy O'Connor, NYR, C
1949 Bill Quackenbush, Det., D

Year
1950 Edgar Laprade, NYR, C
1951 Red Kelly, Det., D
1952 Sid Smith, Tor., LW
1953 Red Kelly, Det., D
1954 Red Kelly, Det., D
1955 Sid Smith, Tor., LW
1956 Earl Reibel, Det., C
1957 Andy Hebenton, NYR, RW
1958 Camille Henry, NYR, LW
1959 Alex Delvecchio, Det., LW
1960 Don McKenney, Bos., C
1961 Red Kelly, Tor., D
1962 Dave Keon, Tor., C
1963 Dave Keon, Tor., C
1964 Ken Wharram, Chi., RW
1965 Bobby Hull, Chi., LW
1966 Alex Delvecchio, Det., LW
1967 Stan Mikita, Chi., C
1968 Stan Mikita, Chi., C
1969 Alex Delvecchio, Det., LW
1970 Phil Goyette, St.L., C
1971 Johnny Bucyk, Bos., LW
1972 Jean Ratelle, NYR, C
1973 Gilbert Perreault, Buf., C
1974 Johnny Bucyk, Bos., LW

Year
1975 Marcel Dionne, Det., C
1976 Jean Ratelle, NY-Bos., C
1977 Marcel Dionne, LA, C
1978 Butch Goring, LA, C
1979 Bob MacMillan, Atl., RW
1980 Wayne Gretzky, Edm., C
1981 Rick Kehoe, Pit., RW
1982 Rick Middleton, Bos., RW
1983 Mike Bossy, NYI, RW
1984 Mike Bossy, NYI, RW
1985 Jari Kurri, Edm., RW
1986 Mike Bossy, NYI, RW
1987 Joey Mullen, Calg., RW
1988 Mats Naslund, Mon., LW
1989 Joey Mullen, Calg., RW
1990 Brett Hull, St.L., RW
1991 Wayne Gretzky, LA, C
1992 Wayne Gretzky, LA, C
1993 Pierre Turgeon, NYI, C
1994 Wayne Gretzky, LA, C
1995 Ron Francis, Pit., C
1996 Paul Kariya, Ana., LW
1997 Paul Kariya, Ana., LW
1998 Ron Francis, Pit., C

Note: Bill Quackenbush and Red Kelly are the only defensemen to win the Lady Byng.

James Norris Memorial Trophy

Awarded to the most outstanding defenseman of the year and named after James Norris, the late Detroit Red Wings owner-president. Winners selected by PHWA.

Multiple winners: Bobby Orr (8); Doug Harvey (7); Ray Bourque (5); Chris Chelios, Paul Coffey, Pierre Pilote and Denis Potvin (3); Rod Langway, Brian Leetch and Larry Robinson (2).

Year
1954 Red Kelly, Detroit
1955 Doug Harvey, Montreal
1956 Doug Harvey, Montreal
1957 Doug Harvey, Montreal
1958 Doug Harvey, Montreal
1959 Tom Johnson, Montreal
1960 Doug Harvey, Montreal
1961 Doug Harvey, Montreal
1962 Doug Harvey, NY Rangers
1963 Pierre Pilote, Chicago
1964 Pierre Pilote, Chicago
1965 Pierre Pilote, Chicago
1966 Jacques Laperriere, Montreal
1967 Harry Howell, NY Rangers
1968 Bobby Orr, Boston

Year
1969 Bobby Orr, Boston
1970 Bobby Orr, Boston
1971 Bobby Orr, Boston
1972 Bobby Orr, Boston
1973 Bobby Orr, Boston
1974 Bobby Orr, Boston
1975 Bobby Orr, Boston
1976 Denis Potvin, NY Islanders
1977 Larry Robinson, Montreal
1978 Denis Potvin, NY Islanders
1979 Denis Potvin, NY Islanders
1980 Larry Robinson, Montreal
1981 Randy Carlyle, Pittsburgh
1982 Doug Wilson, Chicago
1983 Rod Langway, Washington

Year
1984 Rod Langway, Washington
1985 Paul Coffey, Edmonton
1986 Paul Coffey, Edmonton
1987 Ray Bourque, Boston
1988 Ray Bourque, Boston
1989 Chris Chelios, Montreal
1990 Ray Bourque, Boston
1991 Ray Bourque, Boston
1992 Brian Leetch, NY Rangers
1993 Chris Chelios, Chicago
1994 Ray Bourque, Boston
1995 Paul Coffey, Detroit
1996 Chris Chelios, Chicago
1997 Brian Leetch, NY Rangers
1998 Rob Blake, Los Angeles

Frank Selke Trophy

Awarded to the outstanding defensive forward of the year and named after the late Montreal Canadiens general manager. Winners selected by the PHWA.

Multiple winners: Bob Gainey (4); Guy Carbonneau (3); Sergei Fedorov (2).

Year
1978 Bob Gainey, Mon., LW
1979 Bob Gainey, Mon., LW
1980 Bob Gainey, Mon., LW
1981 Bob Gainey, Mon., LW
1982 Steve Kasper, Bos., C
1983 Bobby Clarke, Phi., C
1984 Doug Jarvis, Wash., C

Year
1985 Craig Ramsay, Buf., LW
1986 Troy Murray, Chi., C
1987 Dave Poulin, Phi., C
1988 Guy Carbonneau, Mon., C
1989 Guy Carbonneau, Mon., C
1990 Rick Meagher, St.L., C
1991 Dirk Graham, Chi., RW

Year
1992 Guy Carbonneau, Mon., C
1993 Doug Gilmour, Tor., C
1994 Sergei Fedorov, Det., C
1995 Ron Francis, Pit., C
1996 Sergei Fedorov, Det., C
1997 Michael Peca, Buf., C
1998 Jere Lehtinen, Dal., RW

Annual Awards (Cont.)

Jack Adams Award

Awarded to the coach "adjudged to have contributed the most to his team's success" and named after the late Detroit Red Wings coach and general manager. Winners selected by NHL Broadcasters' Assn.; (*) indicates division champion.

Multiple winners: Pat Burns (3); Scotty Bowman, Jacques Demers and Pat Quinn (2).

Year		Improvement		
1974	Fred Shero, Phi	37-30-11	to	50-16-12*
1975	Bob Pulford, LA	41-14-23	to	37-35-8
1976	Don Cherry, Bos	40-26-14	to	48-15-17*
1977	Scotty Bowman, Mon	58-11-11*	to	60- 8-12*
1978	Bobby Kromm, Det.	6-55-9	to	32-34-14
1979	Al Arbour, NYI	48-17-15*	to	51-15-14*
1980	Pat Quinn, Phi	40-25-15	to	48-12-20*
1981	Red Berenson, St.L	34-34-12	to	45-18-17*
1982	Tom Watt, Win	9-57-14	to	33-33-14
1983	Orval Tessier, Chi	30-38-12	to	47-23-10
1984	Bryan Murray, Wash	39-25-16	to	48-27-5
1985	Mike Keenan, Phi	44-26-10	to	53-20-7*
1986	Glen Sather, Edm	49-20-11*	to	56-17-7*
1987	Jacques Demers, Det	17-57-6	to	34-36-10
1988	Jacques Demers, Det	34-36-10	to	41-28-11*
1989	Pat Burns, Mon	45-22-13	to	53-18- 9*
1990	Bob Murdoch, Win	26-42-12	to	37-32-11
1991	Brian Sutter, St.L	37-34-9	to	47-22-11
1992	Pat Quinn, Van	28-43-9	to	42-26-12*
1993	Pat Burns, Tor	30-43-7	to	44-29-11
1994	Jacques Lemaire, NJ	40-37-7	to	47-25-12
1995	Marc Crawford, Que	34-42-8	to	30-13-5*
1996	Scotty Bowman, Det.	33-11-4*	to	62-13-7*
1997	Ted Nolan, Buf	33-42-7	to	40-30-12*
1998	Pat Burns, Bos	26-47-9	to	39-30-13

Lester B. Pearson Award

Awarded to the season's most outstanding player and named after the former diplomat, Nobel Peace Prize winner and Canadian prime minister. Winners selected by the NHL Players Assn.

Multiple winners: Wayne Gretzky (5); Mario Lemieux (4); Guy Lafleur (3); Marcel Dionne, Phil Esposito, Dominik Hasek and Mark Messier (2).

Year
1971 Phil Esposito, Bos., C
1972 Jean Ratelle, NYR, C
1973 Bobby Clarke, Phi., C
1974 Phil Esposito, Bos., C
1975 Bobby Orr, Bos., D
1976 Guy Lafleur, Mon., RW
1977 Guy Lafleur, Mon., RW
1978 Guy Lafleur, Mon., RW
1979 Marcel Dionne, LA, C
1980 Marcel Dionne, LA, C
1981 Mike Liut, St.L., G
1982 Wayne Gretzky, Edm., C
1983 Wayne Gretzky, Edm., C
1984 Wayne Gretzky, Edm., C
1985 Wayne Gretzky, Edm., C
1986 Mario Lemiuex, Pit., C
1987 Wayne Gretzky, Edm., C
1988 Mario Lemieux, Pit., C
1989 Steve Yzerman, Det., C
1990 Mark Messier, Edm., C
1991 Brett Hull, St.L., RW
1992 Mark Messier, NYR, C
1993 Mario Lemieux, Pit., C
1994 Sergei Fedorov, Det., C
1995 Eric Lindros, Phi., C
1996 Mario Lemieux, Pit., C
1997 Dominik Hasek, Buf., G
1998 Dominik Hasek, Buf., G

Bill Masterton Trophy

Awarded to the player who "best exemplifies the qualities of perseverance, sportsmanship and dedication to hockey" and named after the 29-year-old rookie center of the Minnesota North Stars who died of a head injury sustained in a 1968 NHL game. Presented by the PHWA.

Year
1968 Claude Provost, Mon., RW
1969 Ted Hampson, Oak., C
1970 Pit Martin, Chi., C
1971 Jean Ratelle, NYR, C
1972 Bobby Clarke, Phi., C
1973 Lowell MacDonald, Pit., RW
1974 Henri Richard, Mon., C
1975 Don Luce, Buf., C
1976 Rod Gilbert, NYR, RW
1977 Ed Westfall, NYI, RW
1978 Butch Goring, LA, C
1979 Serge Savard, Mon., D
1980 Al MacAdam, Min., RW
1981 Blake Dunlop, St.L., C
1982 Chico Resch, Colo., G
1983 Lanny McDonald, Calg., RW
1984 Brad Park, Det., D
1985 Anders Hedberg, NYR, RW
1986 Charlie Simmer, Bos., LW
1987 Doug Jarvis, Hart., C
1988 Bob Bourne, LA, C
1989 Tim Kerr, Phi., C
1990 Gord Kluzak, Bos., D
1991 Dave Taylor, LA, RW
1992 Mark Fitzpatrick, NYI, G
1993 Mario Lemieux, Pit., C
1994 Cam Neely, Bos., RW
1995 Pat LaFontaine, Buf., C
1996 Gary Roberts, Calg., LW
1997 Tony Granato, SJ, LW
1998 Jamie McLennan, St.L, G

Number One Draft Choices

Overall first choices in the NHL draft since the league staged its first universal amateur draft in 1969. Players are listed with team that selected them; those who became Rookie of the Year are in **bold** type.

Year
1969 Rejean Houle, Mon., LW
1970 **Gilbert Perreault,** Buf., C
1971 Guy Lafleur, Mon., RW
1972 Billy Harris, NYI, RW
1973 **Denis Potvin,** NYI, D
1974 Greg Joly, Wash., D
1975 Mel Bridgman, Phi., C
1976 Rick Green, Wash., D
1977 Dale McCourt, Det., C
1978 **Bobby Smith,** Min., C
1979 Rob Ramage, Colo., D
1980 Doug Wickenheiser, Mon., C
1981 **Dale Hawerchuk,** Win., C
1982 Gord Kluzak, Bos., D
1983 Brian Lawton, Min., C
1984 **Mario Lemieux,** Pit., C
1985 Wendel Clark, Tor., LW/D
1986 Joe Murphy, Det., C
1987 Pierre Turgeon, Buf., C
1988 Mike Modano, Min., C
1989 Mats Sundin, Que., RW
1990 Owen Nolan, Que., RW
1991 Eric Lindros, Que., C
1992 Roman Hamrlik, TB, D
1993 Alexandre Daigle, Ott., C
1994 Ed Jovanovski, Fla., D
1995 **Bryan Berard,** Ott., D
1996 Chris Phillips, Ott., D
1997 Joe Thornton, Bos., C
1998 Vincent Lecavalier, TB, C

World Hockey Association

WHA Finals

The World Hockey Association began play in 1972-73 as a 12-team rival of the 56-year-old NHL. The WHA played for the AVCO World Trophy in its seven playoff finals (Avco Financial Services underwrote the playoffs).

Multiple winners: Winnipeg (3); Houston (2).

Year	Winner	Head Coach	Series	Loser	Head Coach
1973	New England Whalers	Jack Kelley	4-1 (WWLWW)	Winnipeg Jets	Bobby Hull
1974	Houston Aeros	Bill Dineen	4-0	Chicago Cougars	Pat Stapleton
1975	Houston Aeros	Bill Dineen	4-0	Quebec Nordiques	Jean-Guy Gendron
1976	Winnipeg Jets	Bobby Kromm	4-0	Houston Aeros	Bill Dineen
1977	Quebec Nordiques	Marc Boileau	4-3 (LWLWWLW)	Winnipeg Jets	Bobby Kromm
1978	Winnipeg Jets	Larry Hillman	4-0	NE Whalers	Harry Neale
1979	Winnipeg Jets	Larry Hillman	4-2 (WWLWLW)	Edmonton Oilers	Glen Sather

Playoff MVPs—1973—No award; **1974**—No award; **1975**—Ron Grahame, Houston, G; **1976**—Ulf Nilsson, Winnipeg, C; **1977**—Serg Bernier, Quebec, C; **1978**—Bobby Guindon, Winnipeg, C; **1979**—Rich Preston, Winnipeg, RW.

Most Valuable Player

(Gordie Howe Trophy, 1976-79)

Year		G	A	Pts
1973	Bobby Hull, Win., LW	51	52	103
1974	Gordie Howe, Hou., RW	31	69	100
1975	Bobby Hull, Win., LW	77	65	142
1976	Marc Tardif, Que., LW	71	77	148
1977	Robbie Ftorek, Pho., C	46	71	117
1978	Marc Tardif, Que., LW	65	89	154
1979	Dave Dryden, Edm., G	41-17-2; 2.89		

Scoring Leaders

Year		Gm	G	A	Pts
1973	Andre Lacroix, Phi	78	50	74	124
1974	Mike Walton, Min	78	57	60	117
1975	Andre Lacroix, S. Diego	78	41	106	147
1976	Marc Tardif, Que	81	71	77	148
1977	Real Cloutier, Que	76	66	75	141
1978	Marc Tardif, Que	78	65	89	154
1979	Real Cloutier, Que	77	75	54	129

Note: In 1979, 18 year-old Rookie of the Year Wayne Gretzky finished third in scoring (46-64—110).

Rookie of the Year

Year		G	A	Pts
1973	Terry Caffery, N. Eng., C	39	61	100
1974	Mark Howe, Hou., LW	38	41	79
1975	Anders Hedberg, Win., RW	53	47	100
1976	Mark Napier, Tor., RW	43	50	93
1977	George Lyle, N. Eng., LW	39	33	72
1978	Kent Nilsson, Win., C	42	65	107
1979	Wayne Gretzky, Ind.-Edm., C	46	64	110

Best Goaltender

Year		Record	GAA
1973	Gerry Cheevers, Cleveland	32-20-0	2.84
1974	Don McLeod, Houston	33-13-3	2.56
1975	Ron Grahame, Houston	33-10-0	3.03
1976	Michel Dion, Indianapolis	14-15-1	2.74
1977	Ron Grahame, Houston	27-10-2	2.74
1978	Al Smith, New England	30-20-3	3.22
1979	Dave Dryden, Edmonton	41-17-2	2.89

Best Defenseman

Year	
1973	J.C. Tremblay, Quebec
1974	Pat Stapleton, Chicago
1975	J.C. Tremblay, Quebec
1976	Paul Shmyr, Cleveland
1977	Ron Plumb, Cincinnati
1978	Lars-Erik Sjoberg, Winnipeg
1979	Rick Ley, New England

Coach of the Year

Year		Improvement		
1973	Jack Kelley, N. Eng			46-30-2*
1974	Billy Harris, Tor	35-39-4	to	41-33-4
1975	Sandy Hucul, Pho	Expan.	to	39-31-8
1976	Bobby Kromm, Win	38-35-5	to	52-27-2*
1977	Bill Dineen, Hou	53-27-0*	to	50-24-6*
1978	Bill Dineen, Hou	50-24-6*	to	42-34-4
1979	John Brophy, Birm	36-41-3	to	32-42-6

*Won Division.

WHA All-Star Game

The WHA All-Star Game was an Eastern Division vs Western Division contest from 1973-75. In 1976, the league's five Canadian-based teams played the nine teams in the US. Over the final three seasons–East played West in 1977; AVCO Cup champion Quebec played a WHA All-Star team in 1978; and in 1979, a full WHA All-Star team played a three-game series with Moscow Dynamo of the Soviet Union.

Year	Result	Host	Coaches	Most Valuable Player
1973	East 6, West 2	Quebec	Jack Kelley, Bobby Hull	Wayne Carleton, Ottawa
1974	East 8, West 4	St. Paul, MN	Jack Kelley, Bobby Hull	Mike Walton, Minnesota
1975	West 6, East 4	Edmonton	Bill Dineen, Ron Ryan	Rejean Houle, Quebec
1976	Canada 6, USA 1	Cleveland	Jean-Guy Gendron, Bill Dineen	Can—Real Cloutier, Que. USA—Paul Shmyr, Cleve.
1977	East 4, West 2	Hartford	Jacques Demers, Bobby Kromm	East—L. Levasseur, Min. West—W. Lindstrom, Win.
1978	Quebec 5, WHA 4	Quebec	Marc Boileau, Bill Dineen	Quebec—Marc Tardif WHA—Mark Howe, NE
1979	WHA def. Moscow Dynamo 3 games to none (4-2, 4-2, 4-3)	Edmonton	Larry Hillman, P. Iburtovich	No awards

World Championship

Men

The World Hockey Championship tournament has been played regularly since 1930. The International Ice Hockey Federation (IIHF), which governs both the World and Winter Olympic tournaments, considers the Olympic champions from 1920-68 to also be the World champions. However the IIHF has not recognized an Olympic champion as World champion since 1968. The IIHF has sanctioned separate World Championships in Olympic years three times–in 1972, 1976 and again in 1992. The world championship is officially vacant for the three Olympic years from 1980-88.

Multiple winners: Soviet Union/Russia (23); Canada (21); Sweden (7); Czechoslovakia (6); USA (2).

Year		Year		Year		Year	
1920	Canada	1950	Canada	1967	Soviet Union	1984	Not held
1924	Canada	1951	Canada	1968	Soviet Union	1985	Czechoslovakia
1928	Canada	1952	Canada	1969	Soviet Union	1986	Soviet Union
1930	Canada	1953	Sweden	1970	Soviet Union	1987	Sweden
1931	Canada	1954	Soviet Union	1971	Soviet Union	1988	Not held
1932	Canada	1955	Canada	1972	Czechoslovakia	1989	Soviet Union
1933	United States	1956	Soviet Union	1973	Soviet Union	1990	Soviet Union
1934	Canada	1957	Sweden	1974	Soviet Union	1991	Sweden
1935	Canada	1958	Canada	1975	Soviet Union	1992	Sweden
1936	Great Britain	1959	Canada	1976	Czechoslovakia	1993	Russia
1937	Canada	1960	United States	1977	Czechoslovakia	1994	Canada
1938	Canada	1961	Canada	1978	Soviet Union	1995	Finland
1939	Canada	1962	Sweden	1979	Soviet Union	1996	Czech Republic
1940-46	Not held	1963	Soviet Union	1980	Not held	1997	Canada
1947	Czechoslovakia	1964	Soviet Union	1981	Soviet Union	1998	Sweden
1948	Canada	1965	Soviet Union	1982	Soviet Union		
1949	Czechoslovakia	1966	Soviet Union	1983	Soviet Union		

Women

The women's World Hockey Championship tournament is governed by the International Ice Hockey Federation (IIHF). With women's hockey being accepted as a full-medal sport at the 1998 Winter Olympics in Nagano, the 1997 World Championship served as a qualifier. **Multiple winners:** Canada (4).

Year		Year		Year		Year	
1990	Canada	1992	Canada	1994	Canada	1997	Canada

Canada vs. USSR Summits

The first competition between the Soviet National Team and the NHL took place Sept. 2-28, 1972. A team of NHL All-Stars emerged as the winner of the heralded 8-game series, but just barely—winning with a record of 4-3-1 after trailing 1-3-1.

Two years later a WHA All-Star team played the Soviet Nationals and could win only one game and tie three others in eight contests. Two other Canada vs USSR series took place during NHL All-Star breaks: the three-game Challenge Cup at New York in 1979, and the two-game Rendez-Vous '87 in Quebec City in 1987.

The NHL All-Stars played the USSR in a three-game Challenge Cup series in 1979.

1972 Team Canada vs. USSR

NHL All-Stars vs Soviet National Team.

Date	City	Result	Goaltenders
9/2	Montreal	USSR, 7-3	Tretiak/Dryden
9/4	Toronto	Canada, 4-1	Esposito/Tretiak
9/6	Winnipeg	Tie, 4-4	Tretiak/Esposito
9/8	Vancouver	USSR, 5-3	Tretiak/Dryden
9/22	Moscow	USSR, 5-4	Tretiak/Esposito
9/24	Moscow	Canada, 3-2	Dryden/Tretiak
9/26	Moscow	Canada, 4-3	Esposito/Tretiak
9/28	Moscow	Canada, 6-5	Dryden/Tretiak

Standings

	W	L	T	Pts	GF	GA
Team Canada (NHL)	4	3	1	9	32	32
Soviet Union	3	4	1	7	32	32

Leading Scorers

1. Phil Esposito, Canada, (7-6—13); **2.** Aleksandr Yakushev, USSR (7-4—11); **3.** Paul Henderson, Canada (7-2—9); **4.** Boris Shadrin, USSR (3-5—8); **5.** Valeri Kharlamov, USSR (3-4—7) and Vladimir Petrov, USSR (3-4—7); **7.** Bobby Clarke, Canada (2-4—6) and Yuri Liapkin, USSR (1-5—6).

1974 Team Canada vs. USSR

WHA All-Stars vs Soviet National Team.

Date	City	Result	Goaltenders
9/17	Quebec City	Tie, 3-3	Tretiak/Cheevers
9/19	Toronto	Canada, 4-1	Cheevers/Tretiak
9/21	Winnipeg	USSR, 8-5	Tretiak/McLeod
9/23	Vancouver	Tie, 5-5	Tretiak/Cheevers
10/1	Moscow	USSR, 3-2	Tretiak/Cheevers
10/3	Moscow	USSR, 5-2	Tretiak/Cheevers
10/5	Moscow	Tie, 4-4	Cheevers/Tretiak
10/6	Moscow	USSR, 3-2	Sidelinkov/Cheevers

Standings

	W	L	T	Pts	GF	GA
Soviet Union	4	1	3	11	32	27
Team Canada (WHA)	1	4	3	5	27	32

Leading Scorers

1. Bobby Hull, Canada (7-2—9); **2.** Aleksandr Yakushev, USSR (6-2—8), Ralph Backstrom, Canada (4-4—8) and Valeri Kharlamov, USSR (2-6—8); **5.** Gordie Howe, Canada (3-4—7), Andre Lacroix, Canada (1-6—7) and Vladimir Petrov, USSR (1-6—7).

1979 Challenge Cup Series

NHL All-Stars vs Soviet National Team

Date	City	Result	Goaltenders
2/8	New York	NHL, 4-2	K. Dryden/Tretiak
2/10	New York	USSR, 5-4	Tretiak/K. Dryden
2/11	New York	USSR, 6-0	Myshkin/Cheevers

Rendez-Vous '87

NHL All-Stars vs Soviet National Team

Date	City	Result	Goaltenders
2/11	Quebec	NHL, 4-3	Fuhr/Belosheykhin
2/13	Quebec	USSR, 5-3	Belosheykhin/Fuhr

The Canada Cup

After organizing the historic 8-game Team Canada-Soviet Union series of 1972, NHL Players Association executive director Alan Eagleson and the NHL created the Canada Cup in 1976. For the first time, the best players from the world's six major hockey powers—Canada, Czechoslovakia, Finland, Russia, Sweden and the USA—competed together in one tournament.

1976

Round Robin Standings

	W	L	T	Pts	GF	GA
Canada	4	1	0	8	22	6
Czechoslovakia	3	1	1	7	19	9
Soviet Union	2	2	1	5	23	14
Sweden	2	2	1	5	16	18
United States	1	3	1	3	14	21
Finland	1	4	0	2	16	42

Finals (Best of 3)

Date	City	Score
9/13	Toronto	Canada 6, Czechoslovakia 0
9/15	Montreal	Canada 5, Czechoslovakia 4 (OT)

Note: Darryl Sittler scored the winning goal for Canada at 11:33 in overtime to clinch the Cup, 2 games to none.

Leading Scorers

1. Victor Hluktov, USSR (5-4—9), Bobby Orr, Canada (2-7—9) and Denis Potvin, Canada (1-8—9); **4.** Bobby Hull, Canada (5-3—8) and Milan Novy, Czechoslovakia (5-3—8).

Team MVPs

Canada—Rogie Vachon
Czech.—Milan Novy
USSR—Alexandr Maltsev
Sweden—Borje Salming
USA—Robbie Ftorek
Finland—Matti Hagman

Tournament MVP—Bobby Orr, Canada

1981

Round Robin Standings

	W	L	T	Pts	GF	GA
Canada	4	0	1	9	32	13
Soviet Union	3	1	1	7	20	13
Czechoslovakia	2	1	2	6	21	13
United States	2	2	1	5	17	19
Sweden	1	4	0	2	13	20
Finland	0	4	1	1	6	31

Semifinals

Date	City	Score
9/11	Ottawa	USSR 4, Czechoslovakia 1
9/11	Montreal	Canada 4, United States 1

Finals

Date	City	Score
9/13	Montreal	USSR 8, Canada 1

Leading Scorers

1. Wayne Gretzky, Canada (5-7—12); **2.** Mike Bossy, Canada (8-3—11), Bryan Trottier, Canada (3-8—11), Guy Lafleur, Canada (2-9—11), Alexei Kasatonov, USSR (1-10—11).

All-Star Team

Goal—Vladislav Tretiak, USSR; **Defense**—Arnold Kadlec, Czech. and Alexei Kasatonov, USSR; **Forwards**—Mike Bossy, Canada, Gil Perreault, Canada, and Sergei Shepelev, USSR. **Tournament MVP**—Tretiak.

1984

Round Robin Standings

	W	L	T	Pts	GF	GA
Soviet Union	5	0	0	10	22	7
United States	3	1	1	7	21	13
Sweden	3	2	0	6	15	16
Canada	2	2	1	5	23	18
West Germany	0	4	1	1	13	29
Czechoslovakia	0	4	1	1	10	21

Semifinals

Date	City	Score
9/12	Edmonton	Sweden 9, United States 2
9/15	Montreal	Canada 3, USSR 2 (OT)

Note: Mike Bossy scored the winning goal for Canada at 12:29 in overtime.

Finals (Best of 3)

Date	City	Score
9/16	Calgary	Canada 5, Sweden 2
9/18	Edmonton	Canada 6, Sweden 5

Leading Scorers

1. Wayne Gretzky, Canada (5-7—12); **2.** Michel Goulet, Canada (5-6—11), Kent Nilsson, Sweden (3-8—11), Paul Coffey, Canada (3-8—11); **5.** Hakan Loob, Sweden (6-4—10).

All-Star Team

Goal—Vladimir Myshkin, USSR; **Defense**—Paul Coffey, Canada and Rod Langway, USA; **Forwards**—Wayne Gretzky, Canada, John Tonelli, Canada, and Sergei Makarov, USSR. **Tournament MVP**—Tonelli.

1987

Round Robin Standings

	W	L	T	Pts	GF	GA
Canada	3	0	2	8	19	13
Soviet Union	3	1	1	7	22	13
Sweden	3	2	0	6	17	14
Czechoslovakia	2	2	1	5	12	15
United States	2	3	0	4	13	14
Finland	0	5	0	0	9	23

Semifinals

Date	City	Score
9/8	Hamilton	USSR 4, Sweden 2
9/9	Montreal	Canada 5, Czechoslovakia 3

Finals (Best of 3)

Date	City	Score
9/11	Montreal	USSR 6, Canada 5 (OT)
9/13	Hamilton	Canada 6, USSR 5 (2 OT)
9/15	Hamilton	Canada 6, USSR 5

Note: In Game 1, Alexander Semak of USSR scored at 5:33 in overtime. In Game 2, Mario Lemieux of Canada scored at 10:01 in the second overtime period. Lemieux also won Game 3 on a goal with 1:26 left in regulation time.

Leading Scorers

1. Wayne Gretzky, Canada (3-18—21); **2.** Mario Lemieux, Canada (11-7—18); **3.** Sergei Makarov, USSR (7-8—15); **4.** Vladimir Krutov, USSR (7-7—14); **5.** Viacheslav Bykov, USSR (2-7—9); **6.** Ray Bourque, Canada (2-6—8).

All-Star Team

Goal—Grant Fuhr, Canada; **Defense**—Ray Bourque, Canada and Viacheslav Fetisov, USSR; **Forwards**—Wayne Gretzky, Canada, Mario Lemieux, Canada, and Vladimir Krutov, USSR. **Tournament MVP**—Gretzky.

1991

Round Robin Standings

	W	L	T	Pts	GF	GA
Canada	3	0	2	8	21	11
United States	4	1	0	8	19	15
Finland	2	2	1	5	10	13
Sweden	2	3	0	4	13	17
Soviet Union	1	3	1	3	14	14
Czechoslovakia	1	4	0	2	11	18

Semifinals

Date	City	Score
9/11	Hamilton	United States 7, Finland 3
9/12	Toronto	Canada 4, Sweden 0

Finals (Best of 3)

Date	City	Score
9/14	Montreal	Canada 4, United States 1
9/16	Hamilton	Canada 4, United States 2

Leading Scorers

1. Wayne Gretzky, Canada (4-8—12); **2.** Steve Larmer, Canada (6-5—11); **3.** Brett Hull, USA (2-7—9); **4.** Mike Modano, USA (2-7—9); **5.** Mark Messier, Canada (2-6—8).

All-Star Team

Goal—Bill Ranford, Canada; **Defense**—Al MacInnis, Canada and Chris Chelios, USA; **Forwards**—Wayne Gretzky, Canada, Jeremy Roenick, USA and Mats Sundin, Sweden. **Tournament MVP**—Bill Ranford.

The World Cup

Formed jointly by the NHL and the NHL Players Association in cooperation with the International Ice Hockey Federation. The inaugural World Cup held games in nine different cities throughout North America and Europe, the most ever by a single international hockey tournament.

1996

Round Robin Standings

European Pool	W	L	T	Pts	GF	GA
Sweden	3	0	0	6	14	3
Finland	2	1	0	4	17	11
Germany	1	2	0	2	11	15
Czech Republic	0	3	0	0	4	17

North American Pool	W	L	T	Pts	GF	GA
United States	3	0	0	6	19	8
Canada	2	1	0	4	11	10
Russia	1	2	0	2	12	14
Slovakia	0	3	0	0	10	18

Semifinals

Date	City	Score
9/7	Philadelphia	Canada 3, Sweden 2 (OT)
9/8	Ottawa	United States 5, Russia 2

Finals (Best of 3)

Date	City	Score
9/10	Philadelphia	Canada 4, United States 3 (OT)
9/12	Montreal	United States 5, Canada 2
9/14	Montreal	United States 5, Canada 2

Leading Scorers

1. Brett Hull, USA (7-4—11); **2.** John LeClair, USA (6-4—10); **3.** Mats Sundin, Sweden (4-3—7); Wayne Gretzky, Canada (3-4—7); Doug Weight, USA (3-4—7); Paul Coffey, Canada (0-7—7); Brian Leetch, USA (0-7—7).

All-Tournament Team

Goal—Mike Richter, USA; **Defense**—Calle Johansson, Sweden and Chris Chelios, USA; **Forwards**—Brett Hull, USA; John LeClair, USA and Mats Sundin, Sweden. **Tournament MVP**—Mike Richter, USA.

U.S. DIVISION I COLLEGE HOCKEY

NCAA Final Four

The NCAA Division I hockey tournament began in 1948 and was played at the Broadmoor Ice Palace in Colorado Springs from 1948-57. Since 1958, the tournament has moved around the country, stopping for consecutive years only at Boston Garden from 1972-74. Consolation games to determine third place were played from 1949-89 and discontinued in 1990.

Multiple Winners: Michigan (9); North Dakota (6); Denver and Wisconsin (5); Boston University (4); Lake Superior St., Michigan Tech and Minnesota (3); Colorado College, Cornell, Michigan St. and RPI (2).

Year	Champion	Head Coach	Score	Runner-up	Third Place
1948	Michigan	Vic Heyliger	8-4	Dartmouth	Colorado College and Boston College

Year	Champion	Head Coach	Score	Runner-up	Third Place	Score	Fourth Place
1949	Boston College	Snooks Kelley	4-3	Dartmouth	Michigan	10-4	Colorado Col.
1950	Colorado College	Cheddy Thompson	13-4	Boston Univ.	Michigan	10-6	Boston College
1951	Michigan	Vic Heyliger	7-1	Brown	Boston Univ.	7-4	Colorado College
1952	Michigan	Vic Heyliger	4-1	Colorado Col.	Yale	4-1	St. Lawrence
1953	Michigan	Vic Heyliger	7-3	Minnesota	RPI	6-3	Boston Univ.
1954	RPI	Ned Harkness	5-4*	Minnesota	Michigan	7-2	Boston College
1955	Michigan	Vic Heyliger	5-3	Colorado Col.	Harvard	6-3	St. Lawrence
1956	Michigan	Vic Heyliger	7-5	Michigan Tech	St. Lawrence	6-2	Boston College
1957	Colorado College	Tom Bedecki	13-6	Michigan	Clarkson	2-1†	Harvard
1958	Denver	Murray Armstrong	6-2	North Dakota	Clarkson	5-1	Harvard
1959	North Dakota	Bob May	4-3*	Michigan St.	Boston College	7-6†	St. Lawrence
1960	Denver	Murray Armstrong	5-3	Michigan Tech	Boston Univ.	7-6	St. Lawrence
1961	Denver	Murray Armstrong	12-2	St. Lawrence	Minnesota	4-3	RPI
1962	Michigan Tech	John MacInnes	7-1	Clarkson	Michigan	5-1	St. Lawrence
1963	North Dakota	Barry Thorndycraft	6-5	Denver	Clarkson	5-3	Boston College
1964	Michigan	Allen Renfrew	6-3	Denver	RPI	2-1	Providence
1965	Michigan Tech	John MacInnes	8-2	Boston College	North Dakota	9-5	Brown
1966	Michigan St.	Amo Bessone	6-1	Clarkson	Denver	4-3	Boston Univ.
1967	Cornell	Ned Harkness	4-1	Boston Univ.	Michigan St.	6-1	North Dakota
1968	Denver	Murray Armstrong	4-0	North Dakota	Cornell	6-1	Boston College
1969	Denver	Murray Armstrong	4-3	Cornell	Harvard	6-5†	Michigan Tech

Year	Champion	Head Coach	Score	Runner-up	Third Place	Score	Fourth Place
1970	Cornell	Ned Harkness	6-4	Clarkson	Wisconsin	6-5	Michigan Tech
1971	Boston Univ.	Jack Kelley	4-2	Minnesota	Denver	1-0	Harvard
1972	Boston Univ.	Jack Kelley	4-0	Cornell	Wisconsin	5-2	Denver
1973	Wisconsin	Bob Johnson	4-2	Denver	Boston College	3-1	Cornell
1974	Minnesota	Herb Brooks	4-2	Michigan Tech	Boston Univ.	7-5	Harvard
1975	Michigan Tech	John MacInnes	6-1	Minnesota	Boston Univ.	10-5	Harvard
1976	Minnesota	Herb Brooks	6-4	Michigan Tech	Brown	8-7	Boston Univ.
1977	Wisconsin	Bob Johnson	6-5*	Michigan	Boston Univ.	6-5	N. Hampshire
1978	Boston Univ.	Jack Parker	5-3	Boston College	Bowl. Green	4-3	Wisconsin
1979	Minnesota	Herb Brooks	4-3	North Dakota	Dartmouth	7-3	N. Hampshire
1980	North Dakota	Gino Gasparini	5-2	N. Michigan	Dartmouth	8-4	Cornell
1981	Wisconsin	Bob Johnson	6-3	Minnesota	Mich. Tech	5-2	N. Michigan
1982	North Dakota	Gino Gasparini	5-2	Wisconsin	Northeastern	10-4	N. Hampshire
1983	Wisconsin	Jeff Sauer	6-2	Harvard	Providence	4-3	Minnesota
1984	Bowling Green	Jerry York	5-4*	Minn-Duluth	North Dakota	6-5†	Michigan St.
1985	RPI	Mike Addesa	2-1	Providence	Minn-Duluth	7-6†	Boston College
1986	Michigan St.	Ron Mason	6-5	Harvard	Minnesota	6-4	Denver
1987	North Dakota	Gino Gasparini	5-3	Michigan St.	Minnesota	6-3	Harvard
1988	Lake Superior St.	Frank Anzalone	4-3*	St. Lawrence	Maine	5-2	Minnesota
1989	Harvard	Billy Cleary	4-3*	Minnesota	Michigan St.	7-4	Maine

Year	Champion	Head Coach	Score	Runner-up	Third Place
1990	Wisconsin	Jeff Sauer	7-3	Colgate	Boston College and Boston Univ.
1991	Northern Michigan	Rick Comley	8-7*	Boston Univ.	Maine and Clarkson
1992	Lake Superior St.	Jeff Jackson	5-3	Wisconsin	Michigan and Michigan St.
1993	Maine	Shawn Walsh	5-4	Lake Superior St.	Boston Univ. and Michigan
1994	Lake Superior St.	Jeff Jackson	9-1	Boston Univ.	Harvard and Minnesota
1995	Boston Univ.	Jack Parker	6-2	Maine	Michigan and Minnesota
1996	Michigan	Red Berenson	3-2*	Colorado Col.	Vermont and Boston Univ.
1997	North Dakota	Dean Blais	6-4	Boston Univ.	Colorado College and Michigan
1998	Michigan	Red Berenson	3-2*	Boston College	New Hampshire and Ohio St.

***Championship game overtime goals:** **1954**—1:54; **1959**—4:22; **1977**—0: 23; **1984**—7:11 in 4th OT; **1988**—4:46; **1989**—4:16; **1991**—1:57 in 3rd OT; **1996**—3:35; **1998**—17:51.

†Consolation game overtimes ended in 1st OT except in 1957, '59, and '69, which all ended in 2nd OT.

Note: Runners-up Denver (1973) and Wisconsin (1992) had participation voided by the NCAA for using ineligible players.

Most Outstanding Player

The Most Outstanding Players of each NCAA Div. I tournament since 1948. Winners of the award who did not play for the tournament champion are in **bold** type. In 1960, three players, none on the winning team, shared the award.

Multiple Winners: Lou Angotti and Marc Behrend (2).

Year

1948 **Joe Riley,** Dartmouth, F
1949 **Dick Desmond,** Dart., G
1950 **Ralph Bevins,** Boston U., G
1951 **Ed Whiston,** Brown, G
1952 **Ken Kinsley,** Colo. Col., G
1953 John Matchefts, Mich., F
1954 Abbie Moore, RPI, F
1955 **Phil Hilton,** Colo. Col., D
1956 Lorne Howes, Mich., G
1957 Bob McCusker, Colo. Col., F
1958 Murray Massier, Denver, F
1959 Reg Morelli, N. Dakota, F
1960 **Lou Angotti,** Mich. Tech, F; **Bob Marquis,** Boston U., F; & **Barry Urbanski,** BU, G
1961 Bill Masterton, Denver, F
1962 Lou Angotti, Mich. Tech, F
1963 Al McLean, N. Dakota, F

Year

1964 Bob Gray, Michigan, G
1965 Gary Milroy, Mich. Tech, F
1966 Gaye Cooley, Mich. St., G
1967 Walt Stanowski, Cornell, D
1968 Gerry Powers, Denver, G
1969 Keith Magnuson, Denver, D
1970 Dan Lodboa, Cornell, D
1971 Dan Brady, Boston U., G
1972 Tim Regan, Boston, U., G
1973 Dean Talafous, Wisc., F
1974 Brad Shelstad, Minn., G
1975 Jim Warden, Mich. Tech, G
1976 Tom Vanelli, Minn., F
1977 Julian Baretta, Wisc., G
1978 Jack O'Callahan, Boston U., D
1979 Steve Janaszak, Minn., G
1980 Doug Smail, N. Dakota, F
1981 Marc Behrend, Wisc., G

Year

1982 Phil Sykes, N. Dakota, F
1983 Marc Behrend, Wisc., G
1984 Gary Kruzich, Bowl. Green, G
1985 **Chris Terreri**, Prov., G
1986 Mike Donnelly, Mich. St., F
1987 Tony Hrkac, N. Dakota, F
1988 Bruce Hoffort, Lk. Superior, G
1989 Ted Donato, Harvard, F
1990 Chris Tancill, Wisconsin, F
1991 Scott Beattie, No. Mich., F
1992 Paul Constantin, Lk. Superior, F
1993 Jim Montgomery, Maine, F
1994 Sean Tallaire, Lk. Superior, F
1995 Chris O'Sullivan, Boston U., F
1996 Brendan Morrison, Michigan, F
1997 Matt Henderson, N. Dakota, F
1998 Marty Turco, Michigan, G

Hobey Baker Award

College hockey's Player of the Year award; voted on by a national panel of sportswriters, broadcasters, college coaches and pro scouts. First presented in 1981 by the Decathlon Athletic Club of Bloomington, Minn., in the name of the Princeton collegiate hockey and football star who was killed in a plane crash.

Year

1981 Neal Broten, Minnesota, F
1982 George McPhee, Bowl. Green, F
1983 Mark Fusco, Harvard, D
1984 Tom Kurvers, Minn-Duluth, D
1985 Bill Watson, Minn-Duluth, F
1986 Scott Fusco, Harvard, F

Year

1987 Tony Hrkac, North Dakota, F
1988 Robb Stauber, Minnesota, G
1989 Lane MacDonald, Harvard, F
1990 Kip Miller, Michigan St., F
1991 Dave Emma, Boston College, F
1992 Scott Pellerin, Maine, F

Year

1993 Paul Kariya, Maine, F
1994 Chris Marinucci, Minn-Duluth, F
1995 Brian Holzinger, Bowl. Green, F
1996 Brian Bonin, Minnesota, F
1997 Brendan Morrison, Michigan, F
1998 Chris Drury, Boston U., F

Coach of the Year

The Penrose Memorial Trophy, voted on by the American Hockey Coaches Association and first presented in 1951 in the name of Colorado gold and copper magnate Spencer T. Penrose. Penrose built the Broadmoor hotel and athletic complex in Colorado Springs that originally hosted the NCAA hockey championship from 1948-57.

Multiple winners: Len Ceglarski and Charlie Holt (3); Rick Comley, Eddie Jeremiah, Snooks Kelly, John MacInnes, Jack Parker, Jack Riley and Cooney Weiland (2).

Year
1951 Eddie Jeremiah, Dartmouth
1952 Cheedy Thompson, Colo. Col.
1953 John Mariucci, Minnesota
1954 Vic Heyliger, Michigan
1955 Cooney Weiland, Harvard
1956 Bill Harrison, Clarkson
1957 Jack Riley, Army
1958 Harry Cleverly, BU
1959 Snooks Kelly, BC

1960 Jack Riley, Army
1961 Murray Armstrong, Denver
1962 Jack Kelley, Colby
1963 Tony Frasca, Colorado Col.
1964 Tom Eccleston, Providence
1965 Jim Fullerton, Brown
1966 Amo Bessone, Michigan St. & Len Ceglarski, Clarkson
1967 Eddie Jeremiah, Dartmouth

Year
1968 Ned Harkness, Cornell
1969 Charlie Holt, New Hampshire

1970 John MacInnes, Michigan Tech
1971 Cooney Weiland, Harvard
1972 Snooks Kelly, BC
1973 Len Ceglarski, BC
1974 Charlie Holt, New Hampshire
1975 Jack Parker, BU
1976 John MacInnes, Michigan Tech
1977 Jerry York, Clarkson
1978 Jack Parker, BU
1979 Charlie Holt, New Hampshire

1980 Rick Comley, No. Michigan
1981 Bill O'Flarety, Clarkson
1982 Fern Flaman, Northeastern
1983 Bill Cleary, Harvard
1984 Mike Sertich, Minn-Duluth
1985 Len Ceglarski, BC

Year
1986 Ralph Backstrom, Denver
1987 Gino Gasparini, N. Dakota
1988 Frank Anzalone, Lk. Superior
1989 Joe March, St. Lawrence

1990 Terry Slater, Colgate
1991 Rick Comley, No. Michigan
1992 Ron Mason, Michigan St.
1993 George Gwozdecky, Miami-OH
1994 Don Lucia, Colorado Col.
1995 Shawn Walsh, Maine
1996 Bruce Crowder, UMass-Lowell
1997 Dean Blais, N. Dakota
1998 Tim Taylor, Yale

Note: 1960 winner Jack Riley won the award for coaching the USA to its first hockey gold medal in the Winter Olympics at Squaw Valley.

All-Time Tournament Appearances

	App	Record
Boston Univ.	24	32-28-0
Minnesota	22	28-24-0
Michigan	21	34-14-0
Boston College	19	15-28-0
Michigan St.	18	22-21-1
Wisconsin	17	29-15-1
Harvard	16	14-24-1
Clarkson	16	12-19-0
North Dakota	15	25-12-0
Denver	13	19-11-0
Colorado Coll.	13	11-14-0
St. Lawrence	12	5-21-0
Cornell	11	10-12-0
Lake Superior St.	10	20-11-1
Michigan Tech	10	13-9-0
Bowling Green	9	8-12-1
New Hampshire	9	5-13-0
RPI	8	8-8-1

	App	Record
Maine	7	14-10-0
Providence	7	9-12-0
N. Michigan	6	8-7-0
Dartmouth	5	4-5-0
Minn.-Duluth	4	5-6-0
Brown	4	2-5-0
Northeastern	3	3-3-1
UMass-Lowell	3	2-3-1
Ala-Anchorage	3	2-5-0
Vermont	3	1-4-0
W. Michigan	3	0-4-0
Yale	2	1-2-0
Miami-OH	2	0-2-0
Colgate	1	3-1-0
Ohio St.	1	2-1-0
Merrimack	1	2-2-0
Princeton	1	0-1-0
St. Cloud St.	1	0-2-0

Note: The NCAA voided tournament participation of Denver in 1973 and Wisconsin in 1992 for using ineligible players.

NCAA All-Time Team

To celebrate the 50th anniversary of the NCAA tournament in 1997, the NCAA announced its 50th Anniversary Team and introduced it during the 1997 championship game in Milwaukee. The team was chosen by current Division I coaches, coaches of teams that have participated in the NCAA tournament, and members of the Division I Hockey Committee. Players named to the team had to have played in at least one NCAA tournament game. Tournament years are listed below.

Forwards

Tony Amonte, Boston Univ., 1981, '83
Lou Angotti, Michigan Tech, 1960, '62
Red Berenson, Michigan, 1962
Bill Cleary, Harvard, 1955
Tony Hrkac, North Dakota, 1987
Paul Kariya, Maine, 1993
Bill Masterton, Denver, 1960, '61
John Matchetts, Michigan, 1951, '53
John Mayasich, Minnesota, 1953, '54
Jim Montgomery, Maine, 1990, '91, '92, '93
Tom Rendall, Michigan, 1955, '56, '57
Phil Sykes, North Dakota, 1979, '80, '82

Defensemen

Chris Chelios, Wisconsin, 1982, '83
Bruce Driver, Wisconsin, 1981, '82, '83
George Konik, Denver, 1960, '61
Dan Lodboa, Cornell, 1970
Keith Magnuson, Denver, 1968, '69
Jack O'Callahan, Boston Univ., 1976, '77, '78

Goaltenders

Marc Behrend, Wisconsin, 1981, '83
Ken Dryden, Cornell, 1967, '68, '69
Chris Terreri, Providence, 1983, '85

College Sports

Do you think she's getting bored? **Chamique Holdslaw** led Tennessee to an undefeated season and its third consecutive national championship.

AP/Wide World Photos

The Last Game

Nebraska football coach Tom Osborne called it a career after the 1997 season, and he went out on top.

by
Steve Cyphers

I was in Duluth, Minnesota when I heard the news that December afternoon, and I was in Lincoln before midnight.

Tom Osborne was retiring. After 25 years as Nebraska's head football coach, after 13 conference championships, after back-to-back national titles in 1994-95 and the Lawrence Phillips controversy, Doctor Tom was calling it quits.

He didn't want to. He still loved it all, the players, the strategy, and of course, the "brain tests" every Saturday. But unfortunately he had to. His heart told him so. There was the bypass surgery in 1985, and then the electric shock treatments to stop his atrial fibrillation on the night of the Iowa State game in November of last season. At the age of 60, Osborne simply couldn't continue coaching the only way he ever knew how – fourteen hours a day, six, sometimes seven days a week.

But there was one more game, the final game, in the 1998 FedEx Orange Bowl against third-ranked Tennessee. And for three weeks, it was "the" story line. The Nebraska players all talked about how they would not let him go out with a loss. Not now. The Huskers were undefeated going in with a slim chance at their third national championship in four years. Osborne played it cool and talked as he always had. This was just another game, game number 307 in a career that spanned a quarter-century. He didn't waver at all, not in private and not at the numerous pregame press conferences. He would prepare this team the way he prepared every team – to win.

With Michigan having wrapped up the Rose Bowl (and a No. 1 ranking in at least one of the polls) the day before, the Husker mentality was more that of a golfer than a football team

---

Steve Cyphers is a reporter for ESPN's *SportsCenter* and *College GameDay.*

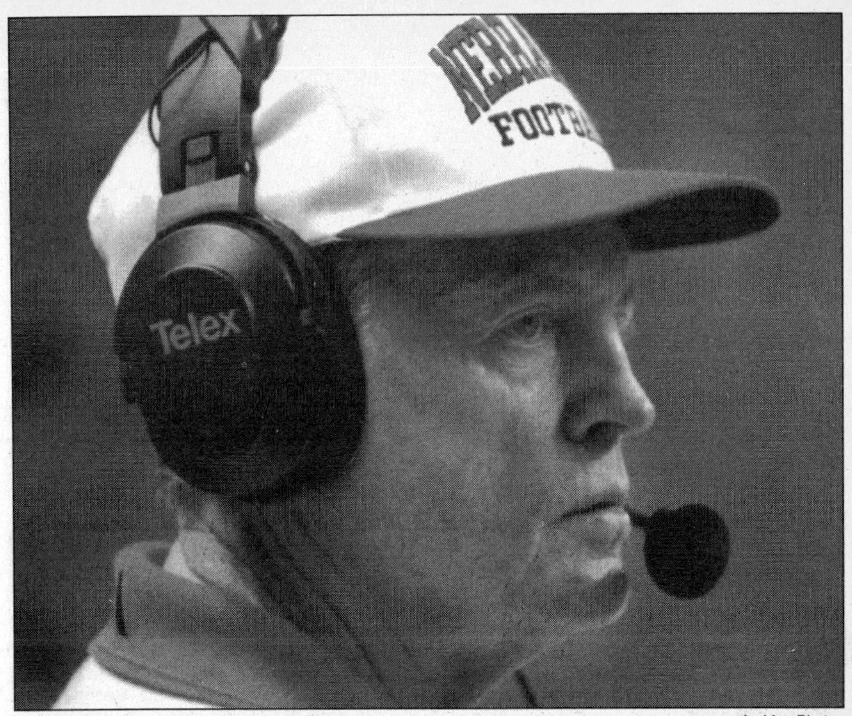

Archive Photos

Tom Osborne retired from Nebraska after the 1997-98 season but not before winning 255 games (.836 pct.) and three national championships during his magnificent 25-year career.

when they took the field. This team had a number in mind, a margin of victory that would be convincing to the pollsters.

Nebraska had control at the half, 14-3. And then, according to some of his players, Osborne broke character. In his final halftime speech, he actually alluded to the national championship, suggesting to his team that if they wanted to win it, their play must improve.

They listened. Control converted to dominance in the third quarter with vintage Osborne-like power football. They started with 80 yards and a touchdown in 12 plays to open the second half. The next series went for 73 yards in six plays for another score. At the end of the third quarter, Nebraska owned Tennessee. And the Vols knew it. One of them approached the Husker sideline saying, "Call 'em off, coach. Call off the dogs."

Running back Ahman Green finished with an Orange Bowl record 206 rushing yards and three touchdowns. Quarterback Scott Frost ran for two more and passed for 125 yards. The final was 42-17.

But Osborne never changed expression. That night could have been any night over the last two decades. The piercing eyes, the gum chewing, the calm demeanor – it never changed. Except in the tunnel on the way to the locker room, when someone offered their congratulations. From 30 feet

AP/Wide World Photos

While most college sophomores were spring-breaking in Cancun or Florida in early April, Georgia Tech's **Matt Kuchar** opted for the Augusta (Ga.) National Golf Club. Here, the 19-year-old U.S. Amateur winner blasts out of the sand at the second hole during the first round of the Masters.

away, I saw what appeared to be a smile, not a gloating smile, or a smug one, but one that suggested that after 25 years and 307 games, Tom Osborne was happy. ■

Steve Cyphers' Top Ten Highlights of the 1998 College Sports Season

10. **Eight teams agree to bolt the WAC** amidst financial concerns and form their own conference after the 1998-99 season. The conference, who had just expanded to 16 teams in 1996, vows to live on.
9. **Syracuse lacrosse coach Roy Simmons Jr. retires.** One of the more fascinating head coaches in all of college sports leaves the Orangemen after 28 years, a 290-96 record (.751 pct.) and six NCAA championships.
8. **Kuchar wows 'em at the Masters.** Sure, 41-year-old Mark O'Meara takes home the green jacket, but Kuchar, the 19-year-old sophomore from Georgia Tech, finishes just nine strokes back and wins the crowd over with his infectious smile.
7. **Mark McGwire's alma mater USC** wins the College World Series in a 21-14 slugfest over Arizona State. It is the Trojan's record 12th world series title. The ridiculously high score finally persuades the NCAA to place restrictions on aluminum bats.

AP/Wide World Photos

Stanford's **Tom Wilkens** was a three-time winner at the 1998 NCAA Swimming and Diving Championship at Auburn, one of the Cardinal's five national titles, as they continued to shine in the world of college athletics.

6. **Three college wrestlers die** within 33 days of each other while trying to cut weight. The deaths of these athletes, all of whom were starving and dehydrating themselves, prompted new policies by the NCAA that include a ban on rubber suits, saunas and diuretics.

5. **Guard Bryce Drew beats Mississippi** with a last-second three-point bomb that sends tiny Valparaiso to the Sweet 16 for the first time in school history.

4. **The NCAA gets a big bill.** A federal jury rules in May that the NCAA must pay $67 million in damages to 1,900 assistant coaches whose salaries had been restricted to $16,000 per year.

3. **What does Stanford know** that the rest of the NCAA doesn't? The Cardinal win championships in five separate sports and take the Sears Directors' Cup for the fourth consecutive year.

2. **Arizona finds defending its Division I basketball title** too difficult against Rick Majerus and his gutty (no pun intended) Utah team, who in turn find winning it all equally difficult against first-year head coach Tubby Smith and the Kentucky Wildcats.

1. **Chamique Holdsclaw is not as good** as we were led to believe. She's better. Pat Summitt's Tennessee Lady Vols win their third consecutive Division I women's basketball title. ■

INSIDE THE NUMBERS

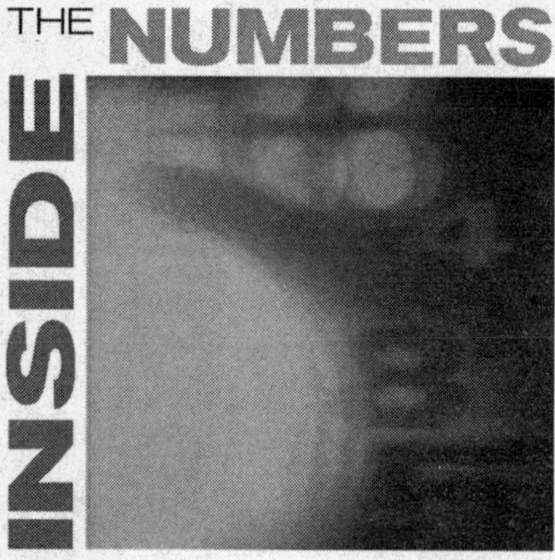

by

Chris Fallica and Team Research

ACTIVE COACHING LEGENDS

Tom Osborne retired after the 1997-98 season after 25 years and three titles with Nebraska. The following list highlights the active Division I football and basketball coaches that have the longest tenure and have at least one title with their current team.

	Years	Titles
Don Haskins, UTEP	37	1
Joe Paterno, Penn St.	32	2
Bob Knight, Indiana	27	3
Denny Crum, Louisville	27	2
LaVell Edwards, BYU	26	1
John Thompson, G'Town	26	1

Note: The longest tenure for any pro coach belongs to Tom Kelly of the Minnesota Twins with 13 years.

CLOSE TO THE **SUMMITT**

Tennessee women's basketball coach Pat Summitt is matching legendary UCLA coach John Wooden title for title. The Vols' win in 1998 gave her six wins in her 24-year career. Wooden had six in his first 24 years and ended his career with ten. Only Wooden has won more than three titles in a row (7) and Summitt has won the last three.

	Titles	Final 4s
John Wooden	10	12
Pat Summitt	**6**	**10**
Adolph Rupp	4	6
Bobby Knight	3	5

CARDINAL SUPREMACY

Stanford has won at least one NCAA national championship every year since 1976-77. They've never been more dominant than in the '90s, winning a total of 35 titles through 1997-98. Last year, they won their fourth consecutive Sears Directors' Cup with five overall titles and a remarkable eleven top-three finishes. The following table indicates the amount of championships won in each of the last five seasons. Note the "slip-ups" in 1990-91 and '95-96.

	Titles		Titles
'97-98	5	'92-93	4
'96-97	6	'91-92	5
'95-96	2	'90-91	1
'94-95	5	'89-90	3
'93-94	4		

THREE STRAIGHT FOURS

Kentucky reached the Final Four round for the third consecutive year in 1998, making them only the ninth men's basketball team in history to accomplish that feat. Only seven more years to tie UCLA's record of ten.

	Final 4s
UCLA, '67-76	10
Cincinnati, '59-63	5
Duke, '88-92	5
Houston, '82-84	3
Kentucky, '96–	**3**
North Carolina, '67-69	3
Ohio St., '44-46	3
Ohio St., '60-62	3
San Francisco, '55-57	3

Note: Only Duke and Kentucky have been to three straight since the tournament field went to 64 teams in 1985. ■

NCAA Division I Basketball Schools

1998-99 Season

Conferences and coaches as of Sept. 21, 1998.

Joining Mid-American in 1998-99: BUFFALO from Mid-Continent.

Joining Mid-Continent in 1998-99: OAKLAND and INDIANA UNIVERSITY-PURDUE UNIVERSITY INDIANAPOLIS from Division II.

Joining Northeast in 1998-99: MD-BALTIMORE COUNTY from Big South and QUINNIPIAC from Division II.

Joining Southern in 1998-99: COLLEGE OF CHARLESTON from Trans America.

Joining Southland in 1998-99: LAMAR from Sun Belt.

Joining Sun Belt in 1998-99: FLORIDA INTERNATIONAL from Trans America.

Joining Trans America in 1998-99: JACKSONVILLE from Sun Belt.

Joining Big South in 1999-2000: HIGH POINT from Division II.

Joining Big South in 1999-2000: ELON from Division II.

Joining Sun Belt in 1999-2000: DENVER from Division II.

	Nickname	Conference	Head Coach	Location	Colors
Air Force	Falcons	WAC	Reggie Minton	Colo. Springs, CO	Blue/Silver
Akron	Zips	Mid-American	Dan Hipsher	Akron, OH	Blue/Gold
Alabama	Crimson Tide	SEC-West	Mark Gottfried	Tuscaloosa, AL	Crimson/White
Alabama St.	Hornets	SWAC	Rob Spivery	Montgomery, AL	Black/Gold
Ala-Birmingham	Blazers	USA	Murry Bartow	Birmingham, AL	Green/Gold
Alcorn St.	Braves	SWAC	Davey Whitney	Lorman, MS	Purple/Gold
American	Eagles	Colonial	Art Perry	Washington, DC	Red/Blue
Appalachian St.	Mountaineers	Southern	Buzz Peterson	Boone,NC	Black/Gold
Arizona	Wildcats	Pac-10	Lute Olson	Tucson, AZ	Cardinal/Navy
Arizona St.	Sun Devils	Pac-10	Rob Evans	Tempe, AZ	Maroon/Gold
Arkansas	Razorbacks	SEC-West	Nolan Richardson	Fayetteville, AR	Cardinal/White
Ark.-Little Rock	Trojans	Sun Belt	Wimp Sanderson	Little Rock, AR	Maroon/White
Ark.-Pine Bluff	Golden Lions	SWAC	Harold Blevins	Pine Bluff, AR	Black/Gold
Arkansas St.	Indians	Sun Belt	Dickey Nutt	State Univ., AR	Scarlet/Black
Army	Cadets, Black Knights	Patriot	Pat Harris	West Point, NY	Black/Gold/Gray
Auburn	Tigers	SEC-West	Cliff Ellis	Auburn, AL	Orange/Blue
Austin Peay St.	Governors	Ohio Valley	Dave Loos	Clarksville, TN	Red/White
Ball St.	Cardinals	Mid-American	Ray McCallum	Muncie, IN	Cardinal/White
Baylor	Bears	Big 12	Harry Miller	Waco, TX	Green/Gold
Bethune-Cookman	Wildcats	Mid-Eastern	Horace Broadnax	Daytona Beach, FL	Maroon/Gold
Boise St.	Broncos	Big West	Rod Jensen	Boise, ID	Orange/Blue
Boston College	Eagles	Big East	Al Skinner	Chestnut Hill, MA	Maroon/Gold
Boston University	Terriers	America East	Dennis Wolff	Boston, MA	Scarlet/White
Bowling Green	Falcons	Mid-American	Dan Dakich	Bowling Green, OH	Orange/Brown
Bradley	Braves	Mo. Valley	Jim Molinari	Peoria, IL	Red/White
BYU	Cougars	WAC	Steve Cleveland	Provo, UT	Royal Blue/White
Brown	Bears	Ivy	Frank Dobbs	Providence, RI	Brown/Cardinal/White
Bucknell	Bison	Patriot	Pat Flannery	Lewisburg, PA	Orange/Blue
Buffalo	Bulls	Mid-American	Tim Cohane	Buffalo, NY	Royal Blue/White
Butler	Bulldogs	Midwestern	Barry Collier	Indianapolis, IN	Blue/White
California	Golden Bears	Pac-10	Ben Braun	Berkeley, CA	Blue/Gold
Cal Poly SLO	Mustangs	Big West	Jeff Schneider	San Luis Obispo, CA	Green/Gold
CS-Fullerton	Titans	Big West	Bob Hawking	Fullerton, CA	Blue/Orange/White
CS-Northridge	Matadors	Big Sky	Bobby Braswell	Northridge, CA	Red/White/Black
CS-Sacramento	Hornets	Big Sky	Tom Abatemarco	Sacramento, CA	Green/Gold
Campbell	Fighting Camels	Trans Am	Billy Lee	Buies Creek, NC	Orange/Black
Canisius	Golden Griffins	Metro Atlantic	Mike MacDonald	Buffalo, NY	Blue/Gold
Centenary	Gentlemen	Trans Am	Billy Kennedy	Shreveport, LA	Maroon/White
Central Conn. St.	Blue Devils	Northeast	Howie Dickenman	New Britain, CT	Blue/White
Central Florida	Golden Knights	Trans Am	Kirk Speraw	Orlando, FL	Black/Gold
Central Michigan	Chippewas	Mid-American	Jay Smith	Mt. Pleasant, MI	Maroon/Gold

NCAA Division I Basketball Schools (Cont.)

	Nickname	Conference	Head Coach	Location	Colors
Charleston So.	Buccaneers	Big South	Tom Conrad	Charleston, SC	Blue/Gold
Chicago St.	Cougars	Mid-Continent	Bo Ellis	Chicago, IL	Green/White
Cincinnati	Bearcats	USA	Bob Huggins	Cincinnati, OH	Red/Black
The Citadel	Bulldogs	Southern	Pat Dennis	Charleston, SC	Blue/White
Clemson	Tigers	ACC	Larry Shyatt	Clemson, SC	Purple/Orange
Cleveland St.	Vikings	Midwestern	Rollie Massimino	Cleveland, OH	Forest Green/White
Coastal Carolina	Chanticleers	Big South	Pete Strickland	Conway, SC	Green/Bronze/Black
Colgate	Red Raiders	Patriot	Emmett Davis	Hamilton, NY	Maroon/Gray/White
College of Charleston	Cougars	Southern	John Kresse	Charleston, SC	Maroon/White
Colorado	Buffaloes	Big 12	Ricardo Patton	Boulder, CO	Silver/Gold/Black
Colorado St.	Rams	WAC	Ritchie McKay	Ft. Collins, CO	Green/Gold
Columbia	Lions	Ivy	Armond Hill	New York, NY	Lt. Blue/White
Connecticut	Huskies	Big East	Jim Calhoun	Storrs, CT	Blue/White
Coppin St.	Eagles	Mid-Eastern	Ron Mitchell	Baltimore, MD	Royal Blue/Gold
Cornell	Big Red	Ivy	Scott Thompson	Ithaca, NY	Carnelian/White
Creighton	Bluejays	Mo. Valley	Dana Altman	Omaha, NE	Blue/White
Dartmouth	Big Green	Ivy	Dave Faucher	Hanover, NH	Green/White
Davidson	Wildcats	Southern	Bob McKillop	Davidson, NC	Red/Black
Dayton	Flyers	Atlantic 10	Oliver Purnell	Dayton, OH	Red/Blue
DePaul	Blue Demons	USA	Pat Kennedy	Chicago, IL	Scarlet/Blue
Delaware	Fightin' Blue Hens	America East	Mike Brey	Newark, DE	Blue/Gold
Delaware St.	Hornets	Mid-Eastern	James Dubose	Dover, DE	Red/Columbia Blue
Detroit Mercy	Titans	Midwestern	Perry Watson	Detroit, MI	Red/White/Blue
Drake	Bulldogs	Mo. Valley	Kurt Kanaskie	Des Moines, IA	Blue/White
Drexel	Dragons	America East	Bill Herrion	Philadelphia, PA	Navy Blue/Gold
Duke	Blue Devils	ACC	Mike Krzyzewski	Durham, NC	Royal Blue/White
Duquesne	Dukes	Atlantic 10	Darelle Porter	Pittsburgh, PA	Red/Blue
East Carolina	Pirates	Colonial	Joe Dooley	Greenville, NC	Purple/Gold
East Tenn. St.	Buccaneers	Southern	Ed DeChellis	Johnson City, TN	Blue/Gold
Eastern Illinois	Panthers	Ohio Valley	Rick Samuels	Charleston, IL	Blue/Gray
Eastern Kentucky	Colonels	Ohio Valley	Scott Perry	Richmond, KY	Maroon/White
Eastern Michigan	Eagles	Mid-American	Milton Barnes	Ypsilanti, MI	Green/White
Eastern Washington	Eagles	Big Sky	Steve Aggers	Cheney, WA	Red/White
Evansville	Aces	Mo. Valley	Jim Crews	Evansville, IN	Purple/White
Fairfield	Stags	Metro Atlantic	Tim O'Toole	Fairfield, CT	Cardinal Red
Fairleigh Dickinson	Knights	Northeast	Tom Green	Teaneck, NJ	Blue/Black
Florida	Gators	SEC-East	Billy Donovan	Gainesville, FL	Orange/Blue
Florida A&M	Rattlers	Mid-Eastern	Mickey Clayton	Tallahassee, FL	Orange/Green
Florida Atlantic	Owls	Trans Am	Kevin Billerman	Boca Raton, FL	Blue/Red
Florida Int'l	Golden Panthers	Sun Belt	Shakey Rodriguez	Miami, FL	Blue/Gold
Florida St.	Seminoles	ACC	Steve Robinson	Tallahassee, FL	Garnet/Gold
Fordham	Rams	Atlantic 10	Nick Macarchuk	Bronx, NY	Maroon/White
Fresno St.	Bulldogs	WAC	Jerry Tarkanian	Fresno, CA	Cardinal/Blue
Furman	Paladins	Southern	Larry Davis	Greenville, SC	Purple/White
George Mason	Patriots	Colonial	Jim Larranaga	Fairfax, VA	Green/Gold
George Washington	Colonials	Atlantic 10	Tom Penders	Washington, DC	Buff/Blue
Georgetown	Hoyas	Big East	John Thompson	Washington, DC	Blue/Gray
Georgia	Bulldogs, 'Dawgs	SEC-East	Ron Jirsa	Athens, GA	Red/Black
Georgia Southern	Eagles	Southern	Gregg Polinsky	Statesboro, GA	Blue/White
Georgia St.	Panthers	Trans Am	Lefty Driesell	Atlanta, GA	Roy. Blue/White
Georgia Tech	Yellow Jackets	ACC	Bobby Cremins	Atlanta, GA	Old Gold/White
Gonzaga	Bulldogs, Zags	West Coast	Dan Monson	Spokane, WA	Blue/White/Red
Grambling St.	Tigers	SWAC	Lacey Reynolds	Grambling, LA	Black/Gold
Hampton	Pirates	Mid-Eastern	Steve Merfeld	Hampton, VA	Royal Blue/White
Hartford	Hawks	America East	Paul Brazeau	W. Hartford, CT	Scarlet/White
Harvard	Crimson	Ivy	Frank Sullivan	Cambridge, MA	Crimson/Black/White
Hawaii	Rainbows	WAC	Riley Wallace	Honolulu, HI	Green/White
Hofstra	Flying Dutchmen	America East	Jay Wright	Hempstead, NY	Blue/White/Gold
Holy Cross	Crusaders	Patriot	Bill Raynor	Worcester, MA	Royal Purple
Houston	Cougars	USA	Clyde Drexler	Houston, TX	Scarlet/White
Howard	Bison	Mid-Eastern	Kirk Saulny	Washington, DC	Blue/White/Red
Idaho	Vandals	Big West	David Farrar	Moscow, ID	Silver/Gold
Idaho St.	Bengals	Big Sky	Doug Oliver	Pocatello, ID	Orange/Black
Illinois	Fighting Illini	Big Ten	Lon Kruger	Champaign, IL	Orange/Blue
Illinois St.	Redbirds	Mo. Valley	Kevin Stallings	Normal, IL	Red/White
Indiana	Hoosiers	Big Ten	Bob Knight	Bloomington, IN	Cream/Crimson
IU/PU-Indianapolis	Metros	Mid-Continent	Ron Hunter	Indianapolis, IN	Red/Gold

	Nickname	Conference	Head Coach	Location	Colors
Indiana St.	Sycamores	Mo. Valley	Royce Waltman	Terre Haute, IN	Blue/White
Iona	Gaels	Metro Atlantic	Jeff Ruland	New Rochelle, NY	Maroon/Gold
Iowa	Hawkeyes	Big Ten	Tom Davis	Iowa City, IA	Old Gold/Black
Iowa St.	Cyclones	Big 12	Larry Eustachy	Ames, IA	Cardinal/Gold
Jackson St.	Tigers	SWAC	Andy Stoglin	Jackson, MS	Blue/White
Jacksonville	Dolphins	Trans Am	Hugh Durham	Jacksonville, FL	Green/White
Jacksonville St.	Gamecocks	Trans Am	Mark Turgeon	Jacksonville, AL	Red/White
James Madison	Dukes	Colonial	Sherman Dillard	Harrisonburg, VA	Purple/Gold
Kansas	Jayhawks	Big 12	Roy Williams	Lawrence, KS	Crimson/Blue
Kansas St.	Wildcats	Big 12	Tom Asbury	Manhattan, KS	Purple/White
Kent	Golden Flashes	Mid-American	Gary Waters	Kent, OH	Navy Blue/Gold
Kentucky	Wildcats	SEC-East	Tubby Smith	Lexington, KY	Blue/White
La Salle	Explorers	Atlantic 10	Speedy Morris	Philadelphia, PA	Blue/Gold
Lafayette	Leopards	Patriot	Fran O'Hanlon	Easton, PA	Maroon/White
Lamar	Cardinals	Southland	Grey Giovanine	Beaumont, TX	Red/White
Lehigh	Mountain Hawks, Engineers	Patriot	Sal Mentesana	Bethlehem, PA	Brown/White
Liberty	Flames	Big South	Mel Hankinson	Lynchburg, VA	Red/White/Blue
Long Beach St.	49ers	Big West	Wayne Morgan	Long Beach, CA	Black/Gold
LIU-Brooklyn	Blackbirds	Northeast	Ray Martin	Brooklyn, NY	Blue/White
LSU	Fighting Tigers	SEC-West	John Brady	Baton Rouge, LA	Purple/Gold
Louisiana Tech	Bulldogs	Sun Belt	Keith Richard	Ruston, LA	Red/Blue
Louisville	Cardinals	USA	Denny Crum	Louisville, KY	Red/Black/White
Loyola Marymount	Lions	West Coast	Charles Bradley	Los Angeles, CA	Crimson/Blue
Loyola-IL	Ramblers	Midwestern	Larry Farmer	Chicago, IL	Maroon/Gold
Loyola-MD	Greyhounds	Metro Atlantic	Dino Gaudio	Baltimore, MD	Green/Gray
Maine	Black Bears	America East	John Giannini	Orono, ME	Blue/White
Manhattan	Jaspers	Metro Atlantic	John Leonard	Riverdale, NY	Kelly Green/White
Marist	Red Foxes	Metro Atlantic	Dave Magarity	Poughkeepsie, NY	Red/White
Marquette	Golden Eagles	USA	Mike Deane	Milwaukee, WI	Blue/Gold
Marshall	Thundering Herd	Mid-American	Greg White	Huntington, WV	Green/White
Maryland	Terrapins, Terps	ACC	Gary Williams	College Park, MD	Red/Wt./Black/Gold
MD-Balt. County	Retrievers	Northeast	Tom Sullivan	Baltimore, MD	Black/Gold/Red
MD-Eastern Shore	Hawks	Mid-Eastern	Lonnie Williams	Princess Anne, MD	Maroon/Gray
Massachusetts	Minutemen	Atlantic 10	James Bruiser Flint	Amherst, MA	Maroon/White
McNeese St.	Cowboys	Southland	Ron Everhart	Lake Charles, LA	Blue/Gold
Memphis	Tigers	USA	Tic Price	Memphis, TN	Blue/Gray
Mercer	Bears	Trans Am	Mark Slonaker	Macon, GA	Orange/Black
Miami-FL	Hurricanes	Big East	Leonard Hamilton	Coral Gables, FL	Orange/Green/White
Miami-OH	RedHawks	Mid-American	Charlie Coles	Oxford, OH	Red/White
Michigan	Wolverines	Big Ten	Brian Ellerbe	Ann Arbor, MI	Maize/Blue
Michigan St.	Spartans	Big Ten	Tom Izzo	East Lansing, MI	Green/White
Middle Tenn. St.	Blue Raiders	Ohio Valley	Randy Wiel	Murfreesboro, TN	Blue/White
Minnesota	Golden Gophers	Big Ten	Clem Haskins	Minneapolis, MN	Maroon/Gold
Mississippi	Ole Miss, Rebels	SEC-West	Rod Barnes	Oxford, MS	Red/Blue
Mississippi St.	Bulldogs	SEC-West	Rick Stansbury	Starkville, MS	Maroon/White
Miss. Valley St.	Delta Devils	SWAC	Lafayette Stribling	Itta Bena, MS	Green/White
Missouri	Tigers	Big 12	Norm Stewart	Columbia, MO	Old Gold/Black
Missouri-KC	Kangaroos	Mid-Continent	Bob Sundvold	Kansas City, MO	Blue/Gold
Monmouth	Hawks	Northeast	Dave Calloway	W. Long Branch, NJ	Royal Blue/White
Montana	Grizzlies	Big Sky	Don Holst	Missoula, MT	Copper/Silver/Gold
Montana St.	Bobcats	Big Sky	Mick Durham	Bozeman, MT	Blue/Gold
Morehead St.	Eagles	Ohio Valley	Kyle Macy	Morehead, KY	Blue/Gold
Morgan St.	Bears	Mid-Eastern	Chris Fuller	Baltimore, MD	Blue/Orange
Mt. St. Mary's	Mountaineers	Northeast	Jim Phelan	Emmitsburg, MD	Blue/White
Murray St.	Racers	Ohio Valley	Tevester Anderson	Murray, KY	Blue/Gold
Navy	Midshipmen	Patriot	Don DeVoe	Annapolis, MD	Navy Blue/Gold
Nebraska	Cornhuskers	Big 12	Danny Nee	Lincoln, NE	Scarlet/Cream
Nevada	Wolf Pack	Big West	Pat Foster	Reno, NV	Silver/Blue
New Hampshire	Wildcats	America East	Jeff Jackson	Durham, NH	Blue/White
New Mexico	Lobos	WAC	Dave Bliss	Albuquerque, NM	Cherry/Silver
New Mexico St.	Aggies	Big West	Lou Henson	Las Cruces, NM	Crimson/White
New Orleans	Privateers	Sun Belt	Joey Stiebing	New Orleans, LA	Royal Blue/Silver
Niagara	Purple Eagles	Metro Atlantic	Joe Mihalich	Lewiston, NY	Purple/White/Gold
Nicholls St.	Colonels	Southland	Rickey Broussard	Thibodaux, LA	Red/Gray
Norfolk State	Spartans	Mid-Eastern	Mel Coleman	Norfolk, VA	Green/Gold
North Carolina	Tar Heels	ACC	Bill Guthridge	Chapel Hill, NC	Carolina Blue/White
North Carolina A&T	Aggies	Mid-Eastern	Roy Thomas	Greensboro, NC	Blue/Gold
North Carolina St.	Wolfpack	ACC	Herb Sendek	Raleigh, NC	Red/White
NC-Asheville	Bulldogs	Big South	Eddie Biedenbach	Asheville, NC	Royal Blue/White

NCAA Division I Basketball Schools (Cont.)

	Nickname	Conference	Head Coach	Location	Colors
NC-Charlotte	49ers	USA	Bobby Lutz	Charlotte, NC	Green/White
NC-Greensboro	Spartans	Southern	Randy Peele	Greensboro, NC	Gold/White/Navy
NC-Wilmington	Seahawks	Colonial	Jerry Wainwright	Wilmington, NC	Green/Gold/Navy
North Texas	Mean Green	Big West	Vic Trilli	Denton, TX	Green/White
NE Louisiana	Indians	Southland	Mike Vining	Monroe, LA	Maroon/Gold
Northeastern	Huskies	America East	Rudy Keeling	Boston, MA	Red/Black
Northern Arizona	Lumberjacks	Big Sky	Ben Howland	Flagstaff, AZ	Blue/Gold
Northern Illinois	Huskies	Mid-American	Brian Hammel	De Kalb, IL	Cardinal/Black
Northern Iowa	Panthers	Mo. Valley	Sam Weaver	Cedar Falls, IA	Purple/Old Gold
Northwestern	Wildcats	Big Ten	Kevin O'Neill	Evanston, IL	Purple/White
Northwestern St.	Demons	Southland	J.D. Barnett	Natchitoches, LA	Purple/Orange/Wt.
Notre Dame	Fighting Irish	Big East	John MacLeod	Notre Dame, IN	Gold/Blue
Oakland University	Pioneers	Mid-Continent	Greg Kampe	Rochester, MI	Black/Gold
Ohio University	Bobcats	Mid-American	Larry Hunter	Athens, OH	Hunter Green/White
Ohio St.	Buckeyes	Big Ten	Jim O'Brien	Columbus, OH	Scarlet/Gray
Oklahoma	Sooners	Big 12	Kelvin Sampson	Norman, OK	Crimson/Cream
Oklahoma St.	Cowboys	Big 12	Eddie Sutton	Stillwater, OK	Orange/Black
Old Dominion	Monarchs	Colonial	Jeff Capel	Norfolk, VA	Slate Blue/Silver
Oral Roberts	Golden Eagles	Mid-Continent	Barry Hinson	Tulsa, OK	Navy Blue/White
Oregon	Ducks	Pac-10	Ernie Kent	Eugene, OR	Green/Yellow
Oregon St.	Beavers	Pac-10	Eddie Payne	Corvallis, OR	Orange/Black
Pacific	Tigers	Big West	Bob Thomason	Stockton, CA	Orange/Black
Pennsylvania	Quakers	Ivy	Fran Dunphy	Philadelphia, PA	Red/Blue
Penn St.	Nittany Lions	Big Ten	Jerry Dunn	University Park, PA	Blue/White
Pepperdine	Waves	West Coast	Lorenzo Romar	Malibu, CA	Blue/Orange
Pittsburgh	Panthers	Big East	Ralph Willard	Pittsburgh, PA	Gold/Blue
Portland	Pilots	West Coast	Rob Chavez	Portland, OR	Purple/White
Portland St.	Vikings	Big Sky	Joel Sobotka	Portland, OR	Green/White
Prairie View A&M	Panthers	SWAC	Elwood Plummer	Prairie View, TX	Purple/Gold
Princeton	Tigers	Ivy	Bill Carmody	Princeton, NJ	Orange/Black
Providence	Friars	Big East	Tim Welsh	Providence, RI	Black/White
Purdue	Boilermakers	Big Ten	Gene Keady	W. Lafayette, IN	Old Gold/Black
Quinnipiac	Braves	Northeast	Joe DeSantis	Hamden, CT	Blue/Gold
Radford	Highlanders	Big South	Ron Bradley	Radford, VA	Blue/Red/Green/Wt.
Rhode Island	Rams	Atlantic 10	Jim Harrick	Kingston, RI	Lt. Blue/White/Navy
Rice	Owls	WAC	Willis Wilson	Houston, TX	Blue/Gray
Richmond	Spiders	Colonial	John Beilein	Richmond, VA	Red/Blue
Rider	Broncs	Metro Atlantic	Don Harnum	Lawrenceville, NJ	Cranberry/White
Robert Morris	Colonials	Northeast	Jim Boone	Moon Township, PA	Blue/White
Rutgers	Scarlet Knights	Big East	Kevin Bannon	New Brunswick, NJ	Scarlet
St. Bonaventure	Bonnies	Atlantic 10	Jim Baron	St. Bonaventure, NY	Brown/White
St. Francis-NY	Terriers	Northeast	Ron Ganulin	Brooklyn, NY	Red/Blue
St. Francis-PA	Red Flash	Northeast	Tom McConnell	Loretto, PA	Red/White
St. John's	Red Storm	Big East	Mike Jarvis	Jamaica, NY	Red/White
St. Joseph's-PA	Hawks	Atlantic 10	Phil Martelli	Philadelphia, PA	Crimson/Gray
Saint Louis	Billikens	USA	Charlie Spoonhour	St. Louis, MO	Blue/White
St. Mary's-CA	Gaels	West Coast	Dave Bollwinkel	Moraga, CA	Red/Blue
St. Peter's	Peacocks	Metro Atlantic	Rodger Blind	Jersey City, NJ	Blue/White
Sam Houston St.	Bearkats	Southland	Bob Marlin	Huntsville, TX	Orange/White
Samford	Bulldogs	Trans Am	Jimmy Tillette	Birmingham, AL	Red/Blue
San Diego	Toreros	West Coast	Brad Holland	San Diego, CA	Lt. Blue/Navy
San Diego St.	Aztecs	WAC	Fred Trenkle	San Diego, CA	Scarlet/Black
San Francisco	Dons	West Coast	Phil Mathews	San Francisco, CA	Green/Gold
San Jose St.	Spartans	WAC	Phil Johnson	San Jose, CA	Gold/White/Blue
Santa Clara	Broncos	West Coast	Dick Davey	Santa Clara, CA	Bronco Red/White
Seton Hall	Pirates	Big East	Tommy Amaker	South Orange, NJ	Blue/White
Siena	Saints	Metro Atlantic	Paul Hewitt	Loudonville, NY	Green/Gold
South Alabama	Jaguars	Sun Belt	Bob Weltlich	Mobile, AL	Red/White/Blue
South Carolina	Gamecocks	SEC-East	Eddie Fogler	Columbia, SC	Garnet/Black
South Carolina St.	Bulldogs	Mid-Eastern	Cy Alexander	Orangeburg, SC	Garnet/Blue
South Florida	Bulls	USA	Seth Greenberg	Tampa, FL	Green/Gold
SE Missouri St.	Indians	Ohio Valley	Gary Garner	Cape Girardeau, MO	Red/Black
SE Louisiana	Lions	Southland	John Lyles	Hammond, LA	Green/Gold
Southern Illinois	Salukis	Mo. Valley	Bruce Weber	Carbondale, IL	Maroon/White
SMU	Mustangs	WAC	Mike Dement	Dallas, TX	Red/Blue
Southern Miss.	Golden Eagles	USA	James Green	Hattiesburg, MS	Black/Gold
Southern Utah	Thunderbirds	Mid-Continent	Bill Evans	Cedar City, UT	Scarlet/White

	Nickname	Conference	Head Coach	Location	Colors
Southern-BR	Jaguars	SWAC	Tommy Green	Baton Rouge, LA	Blue/Gold
SW Missouri St.	Bears	Mo. Valley	Steve Alford	Springfield, MO	Maroon/White
SW Texas St.	Bobcats	Southland	Mike Miller	San Marcos, TX	Maroon/Gold
SW Louisiana	Ragin' Cajuns	Sun Belt	Jessie Evans	Lafayette, LA	Vermilion/White
Stanford	Cardinal	Pac-10	Mike Montgomery	Stanford, CA	Cardinal/White
S.F. Austin St.	Lumberjacks	Southland	Derek Allister	Nacogdoches, TX	Purple/White
Stetson	Hatters	Trans Am	Murray Arnold	DeLand, FL	Green/White
Syracuse	Orangemen	Big East	Jim Boeheim	Syracuse, NY	Orange
Temple	Owls	Atlantic 10	John Chaney	Philadelphia, PA	Cherry/White
Tennessee	Volunteers	SEC-East	Jerry Green	Knoxville, TN	Orange/White
Tenn-Chattanooga	Mocs	Southern	Henry Dickerson	Chattanooga, TN	Navy Blue/Old Gold
Tenn-Martin	Skyhawks	Ohio Valley	Cal Luther	Martin, TN	Orange/Wt./Royal Blue
Tennessee St.	Tigers	Ohio Valley	Frankie Allen	Nashville, TN	Blue/White
Tennessee Tech	Golden Eagles	Ohio Valley	Jeff Lebo	Cookeville, TN	Purple/Gold
Texas	Longhorns	Big 12	Rick Barnes	Austin, TX	Burnt Orange/White
Texas A&M	Aggies	Big 12	Melvin Watkins	College Station, TX	Maroon/White
TCU	Horned Frogs	WAC	Billy Tubbs	Ft. Worth, TX	Purple/White
Texas Southern	Tigers	SWAC	Robert Moreland	Houston, TX	Maroon/Gray
Texas Tech	Red Raiders	Big 12	James Dickey	Lubbock, TX	Scarlet/Black
TX-Arlington	Mavericks	Southland	Eddie McCarter	Arlington, TX	Royal Blue/White
TX-Pan American	Broncs	Independent	Delray Brooks	Edinburg, TX	Green/White
TX-San Antonio	Roadrunners	Southland	Tim Carter	San Antonio, TX	Orange/Navy/White
Toledo	Rockets	Mid-American	Stan Joplin	Toledo, OH	Blue/Gold
Towson	Tigers	America East	Mike Jaskulski	Towson, MD	Gold/White/Black
Troy St.	Trojans	Trans Am	Don Maestri	Troy, AL	Cardinal/Silver/Black
Tulane	Green Wave	USA	Perry Clark	New Orleans, LA	Olive Green/Sky Blue
Tulsa	Golden Hurricane	WAC	Bill Self	Tulsa, OK	Blue/Red/Gold
UC-Irvine	Anteaters	Big West	Pat Douglass	Irvine, CA	Blue/Gold
UCLA	Bruins	Pac-10	Steve Lavin	Los Angeles, CA	Blue/Gold
UC-Santa Barbara	Gauchos	Big West	Bob Williams	Santa Barbara, CA	Blue/Gold
UIC	Flames	Midwestern	Jim Collins	Chicago, IL	Navy Blue/Red
UNLV	Runnin' Rebels	WAC	Billy Bayno	Las Vegas, NV	Scarlet/Gray
USC	Trojans	Pac-10	Henry Bibby	Los Angeles, CA	Cardinal/Gold
Utah	Utes	WAC	Rick Majerus	Salt Lake City, UT	Crimson/White
Utah St.	Aggies	Big West	Stew Morrill	Logan, UT	Navy Blue/White
UTEP	Miners	WAC	Don Haskins	El Paso, TX	Orange/Blue/Wt.
Valparaiso	Crusaders	Mid-Continent	Homer Drew	Valparaiso, IN	Brown/Gold
Vanderbilt	Commodores	SEC-East	Jan van Breda Kolff	Nashville, TN	Black/Gold
Vermont	Catamounts	America East	Tom Brennan	Burlington, VT	Green/Gold
Villanova	Wildcats	Big East	Steve Lappas	Villanova, PA	Blue/White
Virginia	Cavaliers	ACC	Pete Gillen	Charlottesville, VA	Orange/Blue
VCU	Rams	Colonial	Mack McCarthy	Richmond, VA	Black/Gold
VMI	Keydets	Southern	Bart Bellairs	Lexington, VA	Red/White/Yellow
Virginia Tech	Hokies, Gobblers	Atlantic 10	Bob Hussey	Blacksburg, VA	Orange/Maroon
Wagner	Seahawks	Northeast	Tim Capstraw	Staten Island, NY	Green/White
Wake Forest	Demon Deacons	ACC	Dave Odom	Winston-Salem, NC	Old Gold/Black
Washington	Huskies	Pac-10	Bob Bender	Seattle, WA	Purple/Gold
Washington St.	Cougars	Pac-10	Kevin Eastman	Pullman, WA	Crimson/Gray
Weber St.	Wildcats	Big Sky	Ron Abegglen	Ogden, UT	Purple/White
West Virginia	Mountaineers	Big East	Gale Catlett	Morgantown, WV	Old Gold/Blue
Western Carolina	Catamounts	Southern	Phil Hopkins	Cullowhee, NC	Purple/Gold
Western Illinois	Leathernecks	Mid-Continent	Jim Kerwin	Macomb, IL	Purple/Gold
Western Kentucky	Hilltoppers	Sun Belt	Dennis Felton	Bowling Green, KY	Red/White
Western Michigan	Broncos	Mid-American	Bob Donewald	Kalamazoo, MI	Brown/Gold
Wichita St.	Shockers	Mo. Valley	Randy Smithson	Wichita, KS	Yellow/Black
William & Mary	Tribe	Colonial	Charlie Woollum	Williamsburg, VA	Green/Gold/Silver
Winthrop	Eagles	Big South	Gregg Marshall	Rock Hill, SC	Garnet/Gold
Wisconsin	Badgers	Big Ten	Dick Bennett	Madison, WI	Cardinal/White
WI-Green Bay	Phoenix	Midwestern	Mike Heideman	Green Bay, WI	Green/White/Red
WI-Milwaukee	Panthers	Midwestern	Ric Cobb	Milwaukee, WI	Black/Gold
Wofford	Terriers	Southern	Richard Johnson	Spartanburg, SC	Old Gold/Black
Wright St.	Raiders	Midwestern	Ed Schilling	Dayton, OH	Green/Gold
Wyoming	Cowboys	WAC	Steve McClain	Laramie, WY	Brown/Yellow
Xavier	Musketeers	Atlantic 10	Skip Prosser	Cincinnati, OH	Blue/White
Yale	Bulldogs, Elis	Ivy	Dick Kuchen	New Haven, CT	Yale Blue/White
Youngstown St.	Penguins	Mid-Continent	Dan Peters	Youngstown, OH	Red/White

NCAA Division I-A Football Schools

1998 Season

Conferences and coaches as of Sept. 1, 1998.

Joining Conference USA in 1998: ARMY from Independent.
Joining Mid-American in 1999: BUFFALO from Div. I-AA Independent.
Joining Conference USA in 1999: ALABAMA–BIRMINGHAM from Independent.

	Nickname	Conference	Head Coach	Location	Colors
Air Force	Falcons	WAC-Pacific	Fisher DeBerry	Colo. Springs, CO	Blue/Silver
Akron	Zips	Mid-American	Lee Owens	Akron, OH	Blue/Gold
Alabama	Crimson Tide	SEC-West	Mike DuBose	Tuscaloosa, AL	Crimson/White
Alabama-Birm.	Blazers	Independent	Watson Brown	Birmingham, AL	Green/Gold/White
Arizona	Wildcats	Pac-10	Dick Tomey	Tucson, AZ	Cardinal/Navy
Arizona St.	Sun Devils	Pac-10	Bruce Snyder	Tempe, AZ	Maroon/Gold
Arkansas	Razorbacks	SEC-West	Houston Nutt	Fayetteville, AR	Cardinal/White
Arkansas St.	Indians	Independent	Joe Hollis	State Univ., AR	Scarlet/Black
Army	Cadets, Black Knights	USA	Bob Sutton	West Point, NY	Black/Gold/Gray
Auburn	Tigers	SEC-West	Terry Bowden	Auburn, AL	Orange/Blue
Ball St.	Cardinals	Mid-American	Bill Lynch	Muncie, IN	Cardinal/White
Baylor	Bears	Big 12	Dave Roberts	Waco, TX	Green/Gold
Boise St.	Broncos	Big West	Dirk Koetter	Boise, ID	Orange/Blue
Boston College	Eagles	Big East	Tom O'Brien	Chestnut Hill, MA	Maroon/Gold
Bowling Green	Falcons	Mid-American	Gary Blackney	Bowling Green, OH	Orange/Brown
BYU	Cougars	WAC-Mountain	LaVell Edwards	Provo, UT	Royal Blue/White
California	Golden Bears	Pac-10	Tom Holmoe	Berkeley, CA	Blue/Gold
Central Florida	Golden Knights	Independent	Mike Kruczek	Orlando, FL	Black/Gold
Central Michigan	Chippewas	Mid-American	Dick Flynn	Mt. Pleasant, MI	Maroon/Gold
Cincinnati	Bearcats	USA	Rick Minter	Cincinnati, OH	Red/Black
Clemson	Tigers	ACC	Tommy West	Clemson, SC	Purple/Orange
Colorado	Buffaloes	Big 12	Rick Neuheisel	Boulder, CO	Silver/Gold/Black
Colorado St.	Rams	WAC-Pacific	Sonny Lubick	Ft. Collins, CO	Green/Gold
Duke	Blue Devils	ACC	Fred Goldsmith	Durham, NC	Royal Blue/White
East Carolina	Pirates	USA	Steve Logan	Greenville, NC	Purple/Gold
Eastern Michigan	Eagles	Mid-American	Rick Rasnick	Ypsilanti, MI	Green/White
Florida	Gators	SEC-East	Steve Spurrier	Gainesville, FL	Orange/Blue
Florida St.	Seminoles	ACC	Bobby Bowden	Tallahassee, FL	Garnet/Gold
Fresno St.	Bulldogs	WAC-Pacific	Pat Hill	Fresno, CA	Cardinal/Blue
Georgia	Bulldogs	SEC-East	Jim Donnan	Athens, GA	Red/Black
Georgia Tech	Yellow Jackets	ACC	George O'Leary	Atlanta, GA	Old Gold/White
Hawaii	Rainbow Warriors	WAC-Pacific	Fred vonAppen	Honolulu, HI	Green/White
Houston	Cougars	USA	Kim Helton	Houston, TX	Scarlet/White
Idaho	Vandals	Big West	Chris Tormey	Moscow, ID	Silver/Gold
Illinois	Fighting Illini	Big Ten	Ron Turner	Champaign, IL	Orange/Blue
Indiana	Hoosiers	Big Ten	Cam Cameron	Bloomington, IN	Cream/Crimson
Iowa	Hawkeyes	Big Ten	Hayden Fry	Iowa City, IA	Old Gold/Black
Iowa St.	Cyclones	Big 12	Dan McCarney	Ames, IA	Cardinal/Gold
Kansas	Jayhawks	Big 12	Terry Allen	Lawrence, KS	Crimson/Blue
Kansas St.	Wildcats	Big 12	Bill Snyder	Manhattan, KS	Purple/White
Kent	Golden Flashes	Mid-American	Dean Pees	Kent, OH	Navy Blue/Gold
Kentucky	Wildcats	SEC-East	Hal Mumme	Lexington, KY	Blue/White
LSU	Fighting Tigers	SEC-West	Gerry DiNardo	Baton Rouge, LA	Purple/Gold
Louisiana Tech	Bulldogs	Independent	Gary Crowton	Ruston, LA	Red/Blue
Louisville	Cardinals	USA	John L. Smith	Louisville, KY	Red/Black/White
Marshall	Thundering Herd	Mid-American	Bob Pruett	Huntington, WV	Green/White
Maryland	Terrapins, Terps	ACC	Ron Vanderlinden	College Park, MD	Red/White/Black/Gold
Memphis	Tigers	USA	Rip Scherer	Memphis, TN	Blue/Gray
Miami-FL	Hurricanes	Big East	Butch Davis	Coral Gables, FL	Orange/Green/White
Miami-OH	RedHawks	Mid-American	Randy Walker	Oxford, OH	Red/White
Michigan	Wolverines	Big Ten	Lloyd Carr	Ann Arbor, MI	Maize/Blue
Michigan St.	Spartans	Big Ten	Nick Saban	E. Lansing, MI	Green/White
Minnesota	Golden Gophers	Big Ten	Glen Mason	Minneapolis, MN	Maroon/Gold
Mississippi	Ole Miss, Rebels	SEC-West	Tommy Tuberville	Oxford, MS	Cardinal/Navy Blue
Mississippi St.	Bulldogs	SEC-West	Jackie Sherrill	Starkville, MS	Maroon/White
Missouri	Tigers	Big 12	Larry Smith	Columbia, MO	Old Gold/Black
Navy	Midshipmen	Independent	Charlie Weatherbie	Annapolis, MD	Navy Blue/Gold
Nebraska	Cornhuskers	Big 12	Frank Solich	Lincoln, NE	Scarlet/Cream
Nevada	Wolf Pack	Big West	Jeff Tisdel	Reno, NV	Silver/Blue

	Nickname	Conference	Head Coach	Location	Colors
New Mexico	Lobos	WAC-Mountain	Rocky Long	Albuquerque, NM	Cherry/Silver
New Mexico St.	Aggies	Big West	Tony Samuel	Las Cruces, NM	Crimson/White
North Carolina	Tar Heels	ACC	Carl Torbush	Chapel Hill, NC	Carolina Blue/White
North Carolina St.	Wolfpack	ACC	Mike O'Cain	Raleigh, NC	Red/White
North Texas	Eagles	Big West	Darrell Dickey	Denton, TX	Green/White
NE Louisiana	Indians	Independent	Ed Zaunbrecher	Monroe, LA	Maroon/Gold
Northern Illinois	Huskies	Mid-American	Joe Novak	De Kalb, IL	Cardinal/Black
Northwestern	Wildcats	Big Ten	Gary Barnett	Evanston, IL	Purple/White
Notre Dame	Fighting Irish	Independent	Bob Davie	Notre Dame, IN	Gold/Blue
Ohio University	Bobcats	Mid-American	Jim Grobe	Athens, OH	Ohio Green/White
Ohio St.	Buckeyes	Big Ten	John Cooper	Columbus, OH	Scarlet/Gray
Oklahoma	Sooners	Big 12	John Blake	Norman, OK	Crimson/Cream
Oklahoma St.	Cowboys	Big 12	Bob Simmons	Stillwater, OK	Orange/Black
Oregon	Ducks	Pac-10	Mike Bellotti	Eugene, OR	Green/Yellow
Oregon St.	Beavers	Pac-10	Mike Riley	Corvallis, OR	Orange/Black
Penn St.	Nittany Lions	Big Ten	Joe Paterno	University Park, PA	Blue/White
Pittsburgh	Panthers	Big East	Walt Harris	Pittsburgh, PA	Blue/Gold
Purdue	Boilermakers	Big Ten	Joe Tiller	W. Lafayette, IN	Old Gold/Black
Rice	Owls	WAC-Mountain	Ken Hatfield	Houston, TX	Blue/Gray
Rutgers	Scarlet Knights	Big East	Terry Shea	New Brunswick, NJ	Scarlet
San Diego St.	Aztecs	WAC-Pacific	Ted Tollner	San Diego, CA	Scarlet/Black
San Jose St.	Spartans	WAC-Pacific	Dave Baldwin	San Jose, CA	Gold/White/Blue
South Carolina	Gamecocks	SEC-East	Brad Scott	Columbia, SC	Garnet/Black
SMU	Mustangs	WAC-Mountain	Mike Cavan	Dallas, TX	Red/Blue
Southern Miss.	Golden Eagles	USA	Jeff Bower	Hattiesburg, MS	Black/Gold
SW Louisiana	Ragin' Cajuns	Independent	Nelson Stokley	Lafayette, LA	Vermilion/White
Stanford	Cardinal	Pac-10	Tyrone Willingham	Stanford, CA	Cardinal/White
Syracuse	Orangemen	Big East	Paul Pasqualoni	Syracuse, NY	Orange
Temple	Owls	Big East	Bobby Wallace	Philadelphia, PA	Cherry/White
Tennessee	Volunteers	SEC-East	Phillip Fulmer	Knoxville, TN	Orange/White
Texas	Longhorns	Big 12	Mack Brown	Austin,TX	Burnt Orange/White
Texas A&M	Aggies	Big 12	R.C. Slocum	College Station, TX	Maroon/White
TCU	Horned Frogs	WAC-Mountain	Dennis Franchione	Ft. Worth, TX	Purple/White
Texas Tech	Red Raiders	Big 12	Spike Dykes	Lubbock, TX	Scarlet/Black
Toledo	Rockets	Mid-American	Gary Pinkel	Toledo, OH	Blue/Gold
Tulane	Green Wave	USA	Tommy Bowden	New Orleans, LA	Olive Green/Sky Blue
Tulsa	Golden Hurricane	WAC-Mountain	Dave Rader	Tulsa, OK	Blue/Gold
UCLA	Bruins	Pac-10	Bob Toledo	Los Angeles, CA	Blue/Gold
UNLV	Rebels	WAC-Pacific	Jeff Horton	Las Vegas, NV	Scarlet/Gray
USC	Trojans	Pac-10	Paul Hackett	Los Angeles, CA	Cardinal/Gold
Utah	Utes	WAC-Mountain	Ron McBride	Salt Lake City, UT	Crimson/White
Utah St.	Aggies	Big West	Dave Arslanian	Logan, UT	Navy Blue/White
UTEP	Miners	WAC-Mountain	Charlie Bailey	El Paso, TX	Orange/Blue/Wt.
Vanderbilt	Commodores	SEC-East	Woody Widenhofer	Nashville, TN	Black/Gold
Virginia	Cavaliers	ACC	George Welsh	Charlottesville, VA	Orange/Blue
Virginia Tech	Hokies, Gobblers	Big East	Frank Beamer	Blacksburg, VA	Orange/Maroon
Wake Forest	Demon Deacons	ACC	Jim Caldwell	Winston-Salem, NC	Old Gold/Black
Washington	Huskies	Pac-10	Jim Lambright	Seattle, WA	Purple/Gold
Washington St.	Cougars	Pac-10	Mike Price	Pullman, WA	Crimson/Gray
West Virginia	Mountaineers	Big East	Don Nehlen	Morgantown, WV	Old Gold/Blue
Western Michigan	Broncos	Mid-American	Gary Darnell	Kalamazoo, MI	Brown/Gold
Wisconsin	Badgers	Big Ten	Barry Alvarez	Madison, WI	Cardinal/White
Wyoming	Cowboys	WAC-Pacific	Dana Dimel	Laramie, WY	Brown/Yellow

Out of WAC

In May 1998, presidents of eight Western Athletic Conference schools voted to leave the 16-team league and form a new conference, effective July 31, 1999. The WAC, however, vows to live on with the eight remaining teams.

Remaining WAC

Fresno St., SMU, Hawaii, TCU, Rice, UTEP, San Jose St., Tulsa

New Conference

Air Force, New Mexico, Brigham Young, San Diego St., Colorado St., Utah, UNLV, Wyoming

NCAA Division I-AA Football Schools

1998 Season

Coaches as of Sept. 1, 1998.

Joining Northeast in 1998: SACRED HEART from Division II.
Joining Metro Atlantic in 1999: LA SALLE from independent.
Joining Northeast in 1999: STONYBROOK from Division II.

	Nickname	Conference	Head Coach	Location	Colors
Alabama St.	Hornets	SWAC	Ron Dickerson	Montgomery, AL	Black/Gold
Alcorn St.	Braves	SWAC	Johnny Thomas	Lorman, MS	Purple/Gold
Appalachian St.	Mountaineers	Southern	Jerry Moore	Boone, NC	Black/Gold
Ark.-Pine Bluff	Golden Lions	SWAC	Lee Hardman	Pine Bluff, AR	Black/Gold
Austin Peay St.	Governors	Independent	Bill Schmitz	Clarksville, TN	Red/White
Bethune-Cookman	Wildcats	Mid-Eastern	Alvin Wyatt	Daytona Beach, FL	Maroon/Gold
Brown	Bears	Ivy	Phil Estes	Providence, RI	Brown/Red/White
Bucknell	Bison	Patriot	Tom Gadd	Lewisburg, PA	Orange/Blue
Buffalo	Bulls	Independent	Craig Cirbus	Buffalo, NY	Blue/White
Butler	Bulldogs	Pioneer	Ken LaRose	Indianapolis, IN	Blue/White
Cal Poly SLO	Mustangs	Independent	Larry Welsh	San Luis Obispo, CA	Green/Gold
CS-Northridge	Matadors	Big Sky	Ron Ponciano	Northridge, CA	Red/White/Black
CS-Sacramento	Hornets	Big Sky	John Volek	Sacramento, CA	Green/Gold
Canisius	Golden Griffins	Metro Atlantic	Chuck Williams	Buffalo, NY	Blue/Gold
Central Conn. St.	Blue Devils	Northeast	Sal Cintorino	New Britain, CT	Blue/White
Charleston So.	Buccaneers	Independent	David Dowd	Charleston, SC	Blue/Gold
The Citadel	Bulldogs	Southern	Don Powers	Charleston, SC	Blue/White
Colgate	Red Raiders	Patriot	Dick Biddle	Hamilton, NY	Maroon/White/Gray
Columbia	Lions	Ivy	Ray Tellier	New York, NY	Lt. Blue/White
Connecticut	Huskies	Atlantic 10	Skip Holtz	Storrs, CT	Blue/White
Cornell	Big Red	Ivy	Pete Mangurian	Ithaca, NY	Carnelian/White
Dartmouth	Big Green	Ivy	John Lyons	Hanover, NH	Green/White
Davidson	Wildcats	Independent	Tim Landis	Davidson, NC	Red/Black
Dayton	Flyers	Pioneer	Mike Kelly	Dayton, OH	Red/Blue
Delaware	Blue Hens	Atlantic 10	Tubby Raymond	Newark, DE	Blue/Gold
Delaware St.	Hornets	Mid-Eastern	John McKenzie	Dover, DE	Red/Blue
Drake	Bulldogs	Pioneer	Rob Ash	Des Moines, IA	Blue/White
Duquesne	Dukes	Metro Atlantic	Greg Gattuso	Pittsburgh, PA	Red/Blue
East Tenn. St.	Buccaneers	Southern	Paul Hamilton	Johnson City, TN	Blue/Gold
Eastern Illinois	Panthers	Gateway	Bob Spoo	Charleston, IL	Blue/Gray
Eastern Kentucky	Colonels	Ohio Valley	Roy Kidd	Richmond, KY	Maroon/White
Eastern Wash.	Eagles	Big Sky	Mike Kramer	Cheney, WA	Red/White
Fairfield	Stags	Metro Atlantic	Kevin Kiesel	Fairfield, CT	Cardinal Red
Florida A&M	Rattlers	Mid-Eastern	Billy Joe	Tallahassee, FL	Orange/Green
Fordham	Rams	Patriot	Ken O'Keefe	Bronx, NY	Maroon/White
Furman	Paladins	Southern	Bobby Johnson	Greenville, SC	Purple/White
Georgetown	Hoyas	Metro Atlantic	Bob Benson	Washington, DC	Blue/Gray
Georgia Southern	Eagles	Southern	Paul Johnson	Statesboro, GA	Blue/White
Grambling St.	Tigers	SWAC	Doug Williams	Grambling, LA	Black/Gold
Hampton	Pirates	Mid-Eastern	Joe Taylor	Hampton, VA	Royal Blue/White
Harvard	Crimson	Ivy	Tim Murphy	Cambridge, MA	Crimson/Black/White
Hofstra	Flying Dutchmen	Independent	Joe Gardi	Hempstead, NY	Gray/White/Gold
Holy Cross	Crusaders	Patriot	Dan Allen	Worcester, MA	Royal Purple
Howard	Bison	Mid-Eastern	Steve Wilson	Washington, DC	Blue/Wt./Red
Idaho St.	Bengals	Big Sky	Tom Walsh	Pocatello, ID	Orange/Black
Illinois St.	Redbirds	Gateway	Todd Berry	Normal, IL	Red/White
Indiana St.	Sycamores	Gateway	Tim McGuire	Terre Haute, IN	Royal Blue/White
Iona	Gaels	Metro Atlantic	Fred Mariani	New Rochelle, NY	Maroon/Gold
Jackson St.	Tigers	SWAC	James Carson	Jackson, MS	Blue/White
Jacksonville St.	Gamecocks	Southland	Mike Williams	Jacksonville, AL	Red/White
James Madison	Dukes	Atlantic 10	Alex Wood	Harrisonburg, VA	Purple/Gold
Lafayette	Leopards	Patriot	Bill Russo	Easton, PA	Maroon/White
La Salle	Explorers	Metro Atlantic	Bill Manlove	Philadelphia, PA	Blue/Gold
Lehigh	Engineers	Patriot	Kevin Higgins	Bethlehem, PA	Brown/White
Liberty	Flames	Independent	Sam Rutigliano	Lynchburg, VA	Red/White/Blue
Maine	Black Bears	Atlantic 10	Jack Cosgrove	Orono, ME	Blue/White
Marist	Red Foxes	Metro Atlantic	Jim Parady	Poughkeepsie, NY	Red/White
Massachusetts	Minutemen	Atlantic 10	Mark Whipple	Amherst, MA	Maroon/White
McNeese St.	Cowboys	Southland	Bobby Keasler	Lake Charles, LA	Blue/Gold

	Nickname	Conference	Head Coach	Location	Colors
Middle Tenn. St.	Blue Raiders	Ohio Valley	Boots Donnelly	Murfreesboro, TN	Blue/White
Miss. Valley St.	Delta Devils	SWAC	Larry Dorsey	Itta Bena, MS	Green/White
Monmouth	Hawks	Northeast	Kevin Callahan	W. Long Branch, NJ	Royal Blue/White
Montana	Grizzlies	Big Sky	Mick Dennehy	Missoula, MT	Maroon/Gray
Montana St.	Bobcats	Big Sky	Cliff Hysell	Bozeman, MT	Blue/Gold
Morehead St.	Eagles	Independent	Matt Ballard	Morehead, KY	Blue/Gold
Morgan St.	Bears	Mid-Eastern	Stump Mitchell	Baltimore, MD	Blue/Orange
Murray St.	Racers	Ohio Valley	Denver Johnson	Murray, KY	Blue/Gold
New Hampshire	Wildcats	Atlantic 10	Bill Bowes	Durham, NH	Blue/White
Nicholls St.	Colonels	Southland	Darren Barbier	Thibodaux, LA	Red/Gray
Norfolk State	Spartans	Mid-Eastern	Darnell Moore	Norfolk, VA	Green/Gold
North Carolina A&T	Aggies	Mid-Eastern	Bill Hayes	Greensboro, NC	Blue/Gold
Northeastern	Huskies	Atlantic 10	Barry Gallup	Boston, MA	Red/Black
Northern Ariz.	Lumberjacks	Big Sky	Jerome Souers	Flagstaff, AZ	Blue/Gold
Northern Iowa	Panthers	Gateway	Mike Dunbar	Cedar Falls, IA	Purple/Old Gold
Northwestern St.	Demons	Southland	Sam Goodwin	Natchitoches, LA	Purple/White
Pennsylvania	Quakers	Ivy	Al Bagnoli	Philadelphia, PA	Red/Blue
Portland St.	Vikings	Big Sky	Tim Walsh	Portland, OR	Green/Gray
Prairie View A&M	Panthers	SWAC	Gregory Johnson	Prairie View, TX	Purple/Gold
Princeton	Tigers	Ivy	Steve Tosches	Princeton, NJ	Orange/Black
Rhode Island	Rams	Atlantic 10	Floyd Keith	Kingston, RI	Light Blue/Navy/Wt.
Richmond	Spiders	Atlantic 10	Jim Reid	Richmond, VA	Red/Blue
Robert Morris	Colonials	Independent	Joe Walton	Moon Township, PA	Blue/White
Sacred Heart	Pioneers	Northeast	Tom Radulski	Fairfield, CT	Scarlet/White
St. Francis-PA	Red Flash	Northeast	Kevin Doherty	Loretto, PA	Red/White
St. John's-NY	Red Storm	Metro Atlantic	Bob Ricca	Jamaica, NY	Red/White
St. Mary's-CA	Gaels	Independent	Mike Rasmussen	Moraga, CA	Red/Blue
St. Peter's	Peacocks	Metro Atlantic	Mark Collins	Jersey City, NJ	Blue/White
Sam Houston St.	Bearkats	Southland	Ron Randleman	Huntsville, TX	Orange/White
Samford	Bulldogs	Independent	Pete Hurt	Birmingham, AL	Crimson/Blue
San Diego	Toreros	Pioneer	Kevin McGarry	San Diego, CA	Lt. Blue/Navy
Siena	Saints	Metro Atlantic	Ed Zaloom	Loudonville, NY	Green/Gold
South Carolina St.	Bulldogs	Mid-Eastern	Willie Jeffries	Orangeburg, SC	Garnet/Blue
South Florida	Bulls	Indepedent	Jim Leavitte	Tampa, FL	Green/Gold
SE Missouri St.	Indians	Ohio Valley	John Mumford	Cape Girardeau, MO	Red/Black
Southern-BR	Jaguars	SWAC	Pete Richardson	Baton Rouge, LA	Blue/Gold
Southern Illinois	Salukis	Gateway	Jan Quarless	Cardondale, IL	Maroon/White
Southern Utah	Thunderbirds	Independent	C. Ray Gregory	Cedar City, UT	Scarlet/White
SW Missouri St.	Bears	Gateway	Del Miller	Springfield, MO	Maroon/White
SW Texas St.	Bobcats	Southland	Bob DeBesse	San Marcos, TX	Maroon/Gold
S.F. Austin St.	Lumberjacks	Southland	John Pearce	Nacogdoches, TX	Purple/White
Tenn-Chattanooga	Mocs	Southern	Buddy Green	Chattanooga, TN	Navy Blue/Old Gold
Tenn-Martin	Skyhawks	Ohio Valley	Jim Marshall	Martin, TN	Orange/White/Blue
Tennessee St.	Tigers	Ohio Valley	L.C. Cole	Nashville, TN	Blue/White
Tennessee Tech	Golden Eagles	Ohio Valley	Mike Hennigan	Cookeville, TN	Purple/Gold
Texas Southern	Tigers	SWAC	Bill Thomas	Houston, TX	Maroon/Gray
Towson	Tigers	Patriot	Gordy Combs	Towson, MD	Gold/White
Troy St.	Trojans	Southland	Larry Blakeney	Troy, AL	Cardinal/Gray/Black
Valparaiso	Crusaders	Pioneer	Tom Horne	Valparaiso, IN	Brown/Gold
Villanova	Wildcats	Atlantic 10	Andy Talley	Villanova, PA	Blue/White
VMI	Keydets	Southern	Ted Cain	Lexington, VA	Red/White/Yellow
Wagner	Seahawks	Northeast	Walt Hameline	Staten Island, NY	Green/White
Weber St.	Wildcats	Big Sky	Jerry Graybeal	Ogden, UT	Royal Purple/White
Western Carolina	Catamounts	Southern	Bill Bleil	Cullowhee, NC	Purple/Gold
Western Illinois	Leathernecks	Gateway	Randy Ball	Macomb, IL	Purple/Gold
Western Kentucky	Hilltoppers	Independent	Jack Harbaugh	Bowling Green, KY	Red/White
William & Mary	Tribe	Atlantic 10	Jimmye Laycock	Williamsburg, VA	Green/Gold/Silver
Wofford	Terriers	Southern	Mike Ayers	Spartanburg, SC	Old Gold/Black
Yale	Bulldogs, Elis	Ivy	Jack Siedlecki	New Haven, CT	Yale Blue/White
Youngstown St.	Penguins	Gateway	Jim Tressel	Youngstown, OH	Red/White

Native American Nicknames Down to 9

At the start of the 1998-99 academic year the number of Native American nickname variations stood at 9 in Division I basketball and football: INDIANS (3)– Arkansas St., Northeast Louisiana and Southeast Missouri St.; BRAVES (2)– Alcorn St. and Bradley; CHIPPEWAS– Central Michigan; FIGHTING ILLINI– Illinois; SEMINOLES– Florida St.; and TRIBE– William & Mary.

Texas
Mack Brown
North Carolina to Texas

USC
Paul Hackett
NFL's Chiefs to USC

Providence
Pete Gillen
Providence to Virginia

St. John's
Mike Jarvis
G. Washington to St. John's

Coaching Changes

New head coaches were named at 14 Division 1-A and 13 Division 1-AA football schools while 46 Division 1 basketball schools changed head coaches after the 1997-98 season. Coaching changes listed below are as of September 21, 1998.

Division I-A Football

	Old Coach	Record	Why Left?	New Coach	Old Job
Arkansas	Danny Ford	4-7	Resigned	Houston Nutt	Coach, Boise St.
Boise St.	Houston Nutt	4-7	to Arkansas*	Dirk Koetter	Off. coord., Oregon
Central Florida	Gene McDowell	5-6	Resigned	Mike Kruczek†	Off. coord., Central Florida
Kent	Jim Corrigall	3-8	Fired	Dean Pees	Def. coord., Michigan St.
Louisville	Ron Cooper	1-10	Fired	John L. Smith	Coach, Utah St.
Nebraska	Tom Osborne	12-0	Retired	Frank Solich	Asst., Nebraska
New Mexico	Dennis Franchione	9-3	to TCU*	Rocky Long	Def. coord., UCLA
North Carolina	Mack Brown	10-1	to Texas*	Carl Torbush	Def. coord., North Carolina
North Texas	Matt Simon	4-7	Reassigned	Darrell Dickey	Off. coord., SMU
Temple	Ron Dickerson	3-8	Resigned	Bobby Wallace	Coach, North Alabama
Texas	John Mackovic	4-7	Reassigned	Mack Brown	Coach, North Carolina
TCU	Pat Sullivan	1-10	Resigned	Dennis Franchione	Coach, New Mexico
USC	John Robinson	6-5	Fired	Paul Hackett	Off coord., NFL's Chiefs
Utah St.	John L. Smith	6-5	to Louisville*	Dave Arslanian	Coach, Weber St.

* as head coach
† on an interim basis

Division I-AA Football

	Old Coach	Record	Why Left?	New Coach	Old Job
Alabama St.	Houston Markham	3-8	Fired	Ron Dickerson	Coach, Temple
Alcorn St.	Cardell Jones	4-7	Fired	Johnny Thomas	Fmr. Asst., Ark-Pine Bluff
Brown	Mark Whipple	6-4	to Massachusetts*	Phil Estes	Asst., Brown
CS-Northridge	Jim Fenwick	5-7	to New Mexico**	Ron Ponciano	Def. coord., CS-Northridge
Cornell	Jim Hofher	5-5	to North Carolina**	Pete Mangurian	Asst., NFL's Falcons
Fordham	Nick Quartaro	5-6	to Iowa St.**	Ken O'Keefe	Coach, Allegheny (Div. III)
Grambling St.	Eddie Robinson	3-8	Retired	Doug Williams	Coach, Morehouse
Indiana St.	Dennis Raetz	3-8	Reassigned	Tim McGuire	Def. coord., Indiana St.
Iona	Harold Crocker	0-10	Resigned	Fred Mariani	Asst., Fordham
Massachusetts	Mike Hodges	2-9	Resigned	Mark Whipple	Coach, Brown
Northern Arizona	Steve Axman	6-5	Resigned	Jerome Souers	Def. coord., Montana
St. Francis-PA	Pete Maycock	2-9	Fired	Kevin Doherty	Def. coord., Marist
Weber St.	Dave Arslanian	6-4	to Utah St.*	Jerry Graybeal	Def. coord., E. Washington

* as head coach
** as assistant coach

Division I Basketball

	Old Coach	Record	Why Left?	New Coach	Old Job
Alabama	David Hobbs	15-16	Fired	Mark Gottfried	Coach, Murray St.
Arizona St.	Don Newman	18-13	Interim#	Rob Evans	Coach, Mississippi
Chicago St.	Phil Gary	2-25	Fired	Bo Ellis	Asst., Marquette
Clemson	Rick Barnes	18-13	to Texas*	Larry Shyatt	Coach, Wyoming
Coastal Carolina	Michael Hopkins	8-19	Resigned	Pete Strickland	Asst., Dayton
Colgate	Jack Bruen	3-3	Deceased$	Emmett Davis	Asst., Navy

	Old Coach	Record	Why Left?	New Coach	Old Job
Colorado St.	Stew Morrill	20-8	to Utah St.*	Ritchie McKay	Coach, Portland St.
Duquesne	Scott Edgar	11-19	Fired	Darelle Porter	Asst., Duquesne
Fairfield	Paul Cormier	12-15	Resigned	Tim O'Toole	Asst., Seton Hall
Geo. Washington	Mike Jarvis	24-8	to St. Johns*	Tom Penders	Coach, Texas
Houston	Alvin Brooks	9-20	Fired	Clyde Drexler	Player, NBA's Rockets
Howard	Mike McLeese	8-20	Fired	Kirk Saulny	Asst., NC-Wilmington
Idaho St.	Herb Williams	6-20	Resigned	Doug Oliver	Asst., Stanford
Iona	Tim Welsh	27-5	to Providence*	Jeff Ruland	Asst., Iona
Iowa St.	Tim Floyd	12-18	to NBA's Bulls*	Larry Eustachy	Coach, Utah St.
Jacksonville St.	Bill Jones	12-14	Retired	Mark Turgeon	Asst., NBA's 76ers
Liberty	Randy Dunton	11-17	Interim	Mel Hankinson	Asst., West Virginia
LIU-Brooklyn	Ray Haskins	21-10	Resigned	Ray Martin	Asst., Miami (OH)
Louisiana Tech	Jim Woolridge	12-15	to NBA's Bulls**	Keith Richard	Asst., La. Tech
Loyola-Chicago	Ken Burmeister	15-15	Fired	Larry Farmer	Asst., Rhode Island
Mississippi	Rob Evans	22-6	to Arizona State*	Roderick Barnes	Asst., Mississippi
Mississippi St.	Richard Williams	15-15	Retired	Rick Stansbury	Asst., Mississippi St.
Monmouth	Wayne Szoke	1-13	Resigned&	Dave Calloway	Asst., Monmouth
Montana	Blaine Taylor	16-14	to Stanford**	Don Holst†	Asst., Montana
Murray St.	Mark Gottfried	29-3	to Alabama*	Tevester Anderson	Asst., Murray State
New Mexico St.	Neil McCarthy	18-12	Reassigned@	Lou Henson	Fmr. Coach, Illinois
Niagara	Jack Armstrong	14-13	Fired	Joe Mihalich	Asst., LaSalle
Norfolk St.	Michael Bernard	6-21	Fired	Mel Coleman	Asst., Norfolk St.
NC-Charlotte	Melvins Watkins	19-10	to Texas A&M*	Bobby Lutz	Asst., NC-Charlotte
Northern Iowa	Eldon Miler	10-17	Resigned	Sam Weaver	Asst., Iowa St.
Portland St.	Ritchie McKay	15-12	to Colorado St.*	Joel Sobotka	Asst., Portland St.
Providence	Pete Gillen	13-16	to Virginia*	Tim Welsh	Coach, Iona
St. John's	Fran Fraschilla	22-9	Resigned	Mike Jarvis	Coach, G. Washington
Sam Houston St.	Jerry Hopkins	9-17	Reassigned	Bob Marlin	Asst., Alabama
San Jose St.	Stan Morrison	3-23	Resigned	Phil Johnson	Asst., Arizona
Southern Illinois	Rich Herrin	14-16	Resigned	Bruce Weber	Asst., Purdue
Tennessee Tech	Frank Harrell	9-21	Resigned	Jeff Lebo	Fmr. Asst., So. Carolina
Texas	Tom Penders	14-17	Resigned	Rick Barnes	Coach, Clemson
Texas A&M	Tony Barone	7-20	Reassigned	Melvin Watkins	Coach, NC-Charlotte
Utah St.	Larry Eustachy	25-8	to Iowa St.*	Stew Morrill	Coach, Colorado St.
UC-Santa Barbara	Jerry Pimm	7-19	Reassigned	Bob Williams	Coach, UC-Davis
Virginia	Jeff Jones	11-19	Resigned	Pete Gillen	Coach, Providence
VCU	Sonny Smith	9-19	Retired	Mack McCarthy	Fmr. Coach, Tenn-Chatt.
Western Kentucky	Matt Kilcullen	10-19	Fired+	Dennis Felton	Asst., Clemson
Winthrop	Dan Kenney	7-20	Fired	Gregg Marshall	Asst., Marshall
Wyoming	Larry Shyatt	19-8	to Clemson*	Steve McClain	Asst., TCU

* as head coach
** as assistant coach
# Newman took over for Bill Frieder, who resigned under pressure on September 10, 1997.
$ Bruen died of pancreatic cancer on December 19, 1997 at the age of 48. Asst. Paul Aiello coached for the remainder of the season.
† on an interim basis
& Szoke resigned on January 17, 1998 and Asst. Dave Calloway was named interim head coach.
@ McCarthy was reassigned to become assistant athletic director on October 16, 1997. Lou Henson was chosen as an interim and named permanent head coach on February 19, 1998.
+ Kilcullen was fired on February 14, 1998 with only four games remaining. Assistant coaches finished the season.

Housecleaning

There are three Division I member institutions with new football and men's basketball head coaches for the 1998-99 season.

	Football		Basketball	
School	Old Coach	New Coach	Old Coach	New Coach
Iona	Harold Crocker	Fred Mariani	Tim Welsh	Jeff Ruland
Texas	John Mackovic	Mack Brown	Tom Penders	Rick Barnes
Utah St.	John L. Smith	Dave Arslanian	Larry Eustachy	Stew Morrill

1997-98 Directors' Cup

Officially, the Sears Directors' Cup and sponsored by the National Association of Collegiate Directors of Athletics. Introduced in 1993-94 to honor the nation's best overall NCAA Division I athletic department (combining men's and women's sports), winners in NCAA Division II and III and NAIA were named for the first time following the 1995-96 season.

Standings computed by NACDA with points awarded for each Div. I school's finish in 20 sports (top 10 scoring sports for both men and women). Div. II schools are awarded points in 14 sports (top 7 scoring sports for both men and women). Div III schools are awarded points in 18 sports (top 9 scoring sports for both men and women). NAIA schools are awarded points in 12 sports (top 6 scoring sports for both men and women). National champions in each sport earn 100 points, while 2nd through 64th-place finishers earn decreasing points depending on the size of the tournament field. Division I-A football points based on final *USA Today*/ESPN Coaches Top 25 poll. Listed below are team conferences (for Div. I only), combined Final Four finishes (1st thru 4th place) for men's and women's programs, overall points in **bold** type, and the previous year's ranking (for Div. I only).

Division I

		Conf	1-2-3-4	Pts	96-97 Rank
1	Stanford	Pac-10	5-3-3-0	**1010**	1
2	Florida	SEC	1-2-1-0	**660**	5
	N. Carolina	ACC	2-0-2-1	**660**	2
4	UCLA	Pac-10	2-1-0-0	**630**	3
5	Michigan	Big Ten	1-1-0-1	**620**	11
6	Arizona	Pac-10	0-2-1-1	**510**	6
7	Georgia	SEC	1-1-2-0	**500**	NR
8	Washington	Pac-10	1-0-1-0	**460**	11
9	Nebraska	Big 12	1-0-0-0	**450**	4
10	LSU	SEC	0-1-2-1	**440**	10
	USC	Pac-10	1-1-0-0	**440**	8
12	Arizona St.	Pac-10	1-1-0-0	**430**	13
13	Virginia	ACC	0-2-2-0	**420**	22
14	Arkansas	SEC	2-1-1-0	**400**	NR
15	Penn St.	Big Ten	1-1-0-1	**380**	20
	Texas	Big 12	2-0-1-0	**380**	7
17	Minnesota	Big Ten	0-1-0-0	**370**	15
18	BYU	WAC	1-0-1-0	**360**	16
19	California	Pac-10	1-0-0-0	**330**	25
	Colorado	Big 12	1-0-2-0	**330**	21
	Maryland	ACC	1-1-0-0	**330**	NR
	Tennessee	SEC	1-0-0-1	**330**	17
23	Ohio St.	Big Ten	0-0-1-0	**320**	8
24	Oklahoma St.	Big 12	0-0-1-2	**310**	NR
25	Auburn	SEC	0-1-0-0	**300**	19
	Clemson	ACC	0-1-1-0	**300**	NR
	Princeton	Ivy	1-0-0-2	**300**	NR

Division II

		1-2-3-4	Pts
1	CS-Bakersfield	2-1-1-0	**530**
2	UC-Davis	1-0-1-1	**420**
3	Abilene Christian	3-1-0-0	**330**
	Barry, FL	0-3-1-0	**330**
5	Florida Southern	1-1-1-0	**320**
6	Northern Colorado	1-0-0-0	**310**
7	Lynn, FL	1-1-1-0	**290**
8	Adams St., CO	1-0-2-0	**270**
9	South Dakota	1-1-0-0	**260**
10	North Dakota St.	1-0-0-0	**250**
11	Bloomsburg, PA	1-0-0-0	**240**
	Western St., CO	0-0-1-1	**240**
13	Cent. Missouri St.	0-1-2-0	**230**
	North Dakota	1-0-0-0	**230**
	South Dakota St.	0-1-0-0	**230**
16	Edinboro, PA	0-0-0-1	**210**
	Lewis, IL	0-1-1-2	**210**
	Truman St., MO	0-0-1-1	**210**
19	Drury, MO	1-1-0-0	**200**
20	Columbus St., GA	0-1-0-0	**180**
	St. Augustine's, NC	1-1-0-0	**180**
22	Ashland, OH	0-0-0-0	**170**
	Central Oklahoma	0-0-0-1	**170**
	Northern Michigan	0-0-1-1	**170**
	Tampa, FL	1-0-0-0	**170**
	West Texas A&M	1-0-0-0	**170**
	W. Virginia Wesleyan	0-1-0-0	**170**

Division III

		1-2-3-4	Pts
1	UC-San Diego	2-1-1-0	**490**
2	Cortland St., NY	1-1-1-0	**460**
	College of New Jersey	1-1-0-0	**460**
4	Middlebury, VT	1-2-2-0	**430**
	Williams, MA	0-2-1-1	**430**
6	Mt. Union, OH	1-2-2-0	**390**
7	Wisconsin-Stevens Pt.	1-1-0-0	**355**
8	Wisconsin-La Crosse	0-0-2-2	**350**
9	Amherst, MA	0-0-1-1	**340**
10	Washington, MO	1-0-1-1	**320**
11	Wisconsin-Oshkosh	0-0-1-1	**310**
12	Kenyon, OH	2-1-0-0	**300**
13	North Central, IL	2-0-1-0	**290**
14	Emory, GA	0-0-1-0	**280**
	Rowan, NJ	0-0-1-1	**280**
16	Simpson, IA	0-0-2-1	**250**
	Wisconsin-Eau Claire	0-1-0-0	**250**
18	Gustavus Adolphus, MN	0-0-1-0	**240**
	Hobart/William Smith (NY)	1-1-0-0	**240**
	Ithaca, NY	0-0-0-0	**240**
21	Christopher Newport, VA	2-0-1-0	**230**
	Methodist, NC	2-0-0-0	**230**
23	Hope, MI	0-1-0-0	**220**
24	Johns Hopkins, MD	0-0-0-0	**210**
25	Augsburg, MN	1-0-0-0	**200**
	Calvin, MI	0-0-0-0	**200**
	Gettysburg, PA	0-0-0-0	**200**
	St. Thomas, MN	0-0-0-0	**200**

NAIA

		1-2-3-4	Pts
1	Simon Fraser, BC	4-3-1-1	**740**
2	Mobile, AL	2-1-1-1	**530**
3	Findlay, OH	1-0-2-1	**420**
4	Oklahoma City	1-0-2-0	**390**
5	Puget Sound, WA	1-2-0-0	**380**
6	Southern Nazarene, OK	0-3-0-0	**350**
7	Life, GA	1-1-0-1	**300**
8	Azusa Pacific, CA	0-1-1-0	**290**
	Berry, GA	1-0-1-0	**290**
	Pacific Lutheran, WA	0-0-0-1	**290**
11	BYU - Hawaii	2-0-1-0	**270**
12	Rockhurst, MO	0-1-0-0	**260**
	Western Washington	1-0-0-0	**260**
14	Doane, NE	0-0-2-0	**250**
	Mary, ND	0-2-0-0	**250**
	Westmont, CA	0-0-2-0	**250**
17	Lindewood, MO	1-0-0-0	**240**
18	Auburn-Montgomery, AL	0-1-1-0	**230**
	Union, TN	1-0-0-0	**230**
20	Cumberland, KY	0-0-0-0	**210**
	Nebraska Wesleyan	0-0-0-0	**210**
	Willamette, OR	0-1-0-0	**210**
23	Phillips, OK	0-0-0-0	**200**
24	McKendree, IL	0-0-0-0	**190**
	Walsh, OH	1-0-0-0	**190**
	Western Oregon	0-0-0-0	**190**

NCAA Division I Schools on Probation

As of Sept. 1, 1998, there were 21 Division I member institutions serving NCAA probations.

School	Sport	Yrs	Penalty To End
Louisville	M Basketball	2	9/21/98
Montana St.	M Basketball	2	9/22/98
Mississippi	Football	4	9/30/98
Alabama St.	W Volleyball	3	9/30/98
	W Track	3	9/30/98
	& M Basketball	3	9/30/98
Miami-FL	Football	3	11/10/98
	Baseball	3	11/10/98
	W Golf	3	11/10/98
	& M Tennis	3	11/10/98
Texas A&M	Football	5	1/6/99
Georgia	Football	2	1/31/99
Kansas St.	W Basketball	2	5/31/99
Grambling St.	Football	2	6/2/99
	& M & W Basketball	2	6/2/99
Bethune-Cookman	Football	4	6/2/99
	M/W Basketball	4	6/2/99
	M Tennis	4	6/2/99
	& W Track	4	6/2/99
Michigan St.	Football	4	12/1/99
UCLA	Softball	3	2/1/00
	& M Basketball	3	4/30/01
Cal-Berkeley	M Basketball	3	6/1/00
Maine	M Ice Hockey	4	6/3/00
	Baseball	4	6/3/00
	Football	4	6/3/00
	M/W Track and XC	4	6/3/00
	W Soccer	4	6/3/00
	Field Hockey	4	6/3/00
	M Basketball	4	6/3/00
	& M Golf	4	6/3/00
Texas-Pan American	M Basketball	8	7/25/00
Weber St.	M Basketball	4	8/7/00
SE Missouri St.	M Basketball	3	1/31/01
Texas Southern	M/W Track and XC	5	8/11/01
	Football	5	8/11/01
	Baseball	5	8/11/01
	M Tennis	5	8/11/01
	& M Golf	5	8/11/01
Texas Tech	M & W Basketball	4	4/24/02
	Football	4	4/24/02
	Baseball	4	4/24/02
Texas-El Paso	M & W Basketball	5	5/1/02
	Football	5	5/1/02
	& W Rifle	5	5/1/02
Gonzaga	Entire Program	4	6/5/02

Remaining postseason and TV sanctions
1998-99 postseason ban: None.
1998-99 television ban: None.

NCAA Graduation Rates

The following table compares graduation rates of NCAA Division I student athletes with the entire student body in those schools. Years given denote the year in which students entered college. Rates are based on students who received an athletics scholarship and who graduated in six years or less. All figures are percentages.

Source: NCAA Graduation-Rate Disclosure, 1992-1997.

	1985	1986	1987	1988	1989	1990
All Student Athletes	52	57	57	58	58	58
Entire Student Body	54	55	56	57	57	56
Male Student Athletes	48	52	53	53	53	53
Male Student Body	52	54	54	55	55	54
Female Student Athletes	61	68	67	69	67	68
Female Student Body	55	57	58	58	59	58
Div I-A Football Players	48	53	55	56	56	52
Male Basketball Players	43	44	46	42	44	45
Female Basketball Players	57	57	62	65	65	67

1997-98 NCAA Team Champions

Thirteen schools won two or more national championships during the 1997-98 academic year, led by Division I Stanford with five and Division II Abilene Christian with three.

Multiple winners: FIVE— Stanford (Div. I men's cross country, women's volleyball, men's swimming & diving, women's swimming & diving and men's tennis). **THREE**— Abilene Christian (Div. II men's indoor track, women's indoor track and women's outdoor track). **TWO**— Arkansas (Div. I men's indoor track and men's outdoor track); Cal State-Bakersfield (Div. II men's soccer and men's swimming); Christopher Newport (Div. III women's indoor track and women's outdoor track); Kenyon, OH (Div. III men's swimming & diving and women's swimming & diving); Methodist, NC (Div. III men's golf and Div. II/III women's golf); Michigan (Div. I-A football and Div. I ice hockey); North Carolina (Div. I field hockey and women's soccer); North Central, IL (Div. III men's cross country and men's outdoor track); Texas (Div. I women's indoor track and women's outdoor track); UCLA (Div. I men's soccer and National division of men's volleyball); UC-San Diego (Div. III women's soccer and women's volleyball).

Overall titles in parentheses; (*) indicates defending champions.

FALL

Cross Country

Men

Div.	Winner		Runner-Up	Score
I	Stanford*	(2)	Arkansas	53-56
II	South Dakota	(1)	Cent. Missouri St.	78-83
III	North Central, IL	(10)	Mt. Union, OH	94-96

Women

Div.	Winner		Runner-Up	Score
I	Brigham Young	(1)	Stanford*	100-102
II	Adams St., CO*	(6)	Lewis, IL	37-103
III	Cortland St.	(7)	Wisc.-Eau Claire	148-167

Field Hockey

Div.	Winner		Runner-Up	Score
I	North Carolina*	(4)	Old Dominion	3-2
II	Bloomsburg, PA*	(4)	Kutztown, PA	2-0
III	William Smith	(2)	Cortland St.	3-0

Football

Div.	Winner		Runner-Up	Score
I-A	Michigan	(9)	Nebraska	AP poll
	Nebraska	(5)	Michigan	ESPN/USA
I-AA	Youngstown St.	(4)	McNeese St.	10-9
II	Northern Colo.*	(2)	New Haven, CT	51-0
III	Mt. Union, OH*	(3)	Lycoming, PA	61-12

Note: There is no official Div. I-A playoff.

Soccer

Men

Div.	Winner		Runner-Up	Score
I	UCLA	(3)	Virginia	2-0
II	CS-Bakersfield	(1)	Lynn, FL	1-0
III	Wheaton, IL	(2)	Coll. of New Jersey*	3-0

Women

Div.	Winner		Runner-Up	Score
I	North Carolina*	(14)	Connecticut	2-0
II	Franklin Pierce, NH*	(4)	W. Virg. Wesleyan	3-0
III	UC-San Diego*	(4)	William Smith	1-0

Volleyball

Women

Div.	Winner		Runner-Up	Score
I	Stanford*	(4)	Penn St.	5 games
II	W. Texas A&M	(3)	Barry, FL	5 games
III	UC-San Diego	(7)	Juniata, PA	5 games

Water Polo

Div.	Winner		Runner-Up	Score
National	Pepperdine	(1)	USC	8-7 (2OT)

WINTER

Basketball

Men

Div.	Winner		Runner-Up	Score
I	Kentucky	(7)	Utah	78-69
II	UC-Davis	(1)	Kentucky Wesleyan	83-77
III	Wisc.-Platteville	(3)	Hope, MI	69-56

Women

Div.	Winner		Runner-Up	Score
I	Tennessee*	(6)	Louisiana Tech	93-75
II	North Dakota*	(2)	Emporia St.	92-76
III	Washington, MO	(1)	Southern Maine	77-69

Fencing

Div.	Winner		Runner-Up	Score
Combined	Penn St.*	(6)	Notre Dame	149-147

Gymnastics

Div.	Winner		Runner-Up	Margin
Men	California*	(4)	Iowa	by 1.525
Women	Georgia	(4)	Florida	by 1.375

Ice Hockey

Div.	Winner		Runner-Up	Score
I	Michigan	(9)	Boston College	3-2 (OT)
II	Alabama-Huntsville	(2)	Bemidji St., MN*	6-2, 5-2†
III	Middlebury, VT*	(4)	Wisc-Stevens Point	2-1

†Div. II championship is decided by a two-game series.

Real Gender Equity

Schools whose men's and women's teams won NCAA championships in the same sport, or its equivalent during the 1997-98 season.

School	Div.	Sports
Stanford	I	Men's swimming Women's swimming
Abilene Christian	II	Men's indoor track Women's indoor track
Kenyon, OH	III	Men's swimming Women's swimming
Methodist, NC	III II/III	Men's golf Women's golf

Rifle

Div.	Winner		Runner-Up	Score
Combined	West Va.*	(13)	Ala.-Fairbanks	6214-6211

Skiing

Div.	Winner		Runner-Up	Score
Combined	Colorado	(14)	Utah*	654-651½

Swimming & Diving

Men

Div.	Winner		Runner-Up	Score
I	Stanford	(8)	Auburn*	599-394½
II	CS-Bakersfield	(9)	Drury, MO	730-637
III	Kenyon, OH*	(19)	UC-San Diego	726-395

Women

Div.	Winner		Runner-Up	Score
I	Stanford	(8)	Arizona	422-378
II	Drury, MO*	(2)	CS-Bakersfield	578½-386
III	Kenyon, OH*	(15)	Denison, OH	693½-522

Indoor Track

Men

Div.	Winner		Runner-Up	Score
I	Arkansas*	(14)	Stanford	56-36½
II	Abilene Christian*	(6)	St. Augustine's	97-59
III	Lincoln, PA	(4)	Mt. Union, OH	53-48

Women

Div.	Winner		Runner-Up	Score
I	Texas	(4)	LSU*	60-30
II	Abilene Christian*	(10)	South Dakota	66-43
III	Chris. Newport*	(6)	Wheaton, MA	31-28

Wrestling

Div.	Winner		Runner-Up	Score
I	Iowa*	(18)	Minnesota	115-102
II	N. Dakota St.	(2)	S. Dakota St.	112-78
III	Augsburg, MN*	(5)	Wartburg, IA	132-90

SPRING

Baseball

Div.	Winner		Runner-Up	Score
I	USC	(12)	Arizona St.	21-14
II	Tampa	(3)	Kennesaw St., GA	6-1
III	Eastern Conn. St.	(3)	Montclair St., NJ	16-1

Golf

Men

Div.	Winner		Runner-Up	Score
I	UNLV	(1)	Clemson	1118-1121
II	Florida Southern	(9)	Columbus St.*	1168-1175
III	Methodist, NC*	(8)	Otterbein, OH	1143-1179

Women

Div.	Winner		Runner-Up	Score
I	Arizona St.*	(6)	Florida	1155-1173
II and III	Methodist	(2)	Florida Southern	1254-1259

Lacrosse

Men

Div.	Winner		Runner-Up	Score
I	Princeton*	(5)	Maryland	15-5
II	Adelphi, NY	(5)	C.W. Post, NY	18-6
III	Washington, MD	(1)	Nazareth, NY*	16-10

Women

Div.	Winner		Runner-Up	Score
National	Maryland*	(6)	Virginia	11-5
III	Coll. of New Jersey	(9)	Williams, MA	12-11 (OT)

Rowing

Women

Div.	Winner		Runner-Up	Score
National	Washington*	(2)†	Brown	91-85

† The 1997 National Collegiate Women's Rowing Championships were the first to be sponsored by the NCAA. National championships had been held without NCAA sponsorship since 1979 with Washington winning seven titles.

Softball

Div.	Winner		Runner-Up	Score
I	Fresno St.	(1)	Arizona*	1-0
II	California, PA*	(2)	Barry	2-1
III	Wisc.-Stevens Point	(1)	Chapman, CA	3-1

Tennis

Note that both Div. II tournaments were team-only.

Men

Div.	Winner		Runner-Up	Score
I	Stanford*	(16)	Georgia	4-0
II	Lander, SC*	(6)	Barry	5-1
III	UC Santa Cruz	(4)	Williams, MA	4-2

Women

Div.	Winner		Runner-Up	Score
I	Florida	(3)	Duke	5-1
II	Lynn, FL*	(2)	Armstrong Atlantic	5-2
III	Skidmore	(1)	Kenyon, OH*	5-1

Outdoor Track

Men

Div.	Winner		Runner-Up	Score
I	Arkansas*	(8)	Stanford	58½-51
II	St. Augustine's	(8)	Abilene Christian*	97-80
III	North Central, IL	(3)	Lincoln, PA	91-73

Women

Div.	Winner		Runner-Up	Score
I	Texas	(2)	UCLA	60-55
II	Abilene Christian	(8)	St. Augustine's*	120-78
III	Chris. Newport	(6)	Wheaton, MA	69-50

Volleyball

Men

Div.	Winner		Runner-Up	Score
National	UCLA	(17)	Pepperdine	3 games

Georgia
Kim Arnold
Gymnastics

Vermont
Thorodd Bakken
Skiing

Arkansas
Robert Howard
Track & Field

SMU
Lars Frolander
Swimming

1997-98 Division I Individual Champions

Repeat champions in **bold** type.

FALL

Cross-country

	Men (10,000 meters)	Time
1	Mebrahtom Keflezighi, UCLA	28:54
2	Kevin Sullivan, Michigan	29:01
3	Bernard Lagat, Washington St.	29:05

	Women (5,000 meters)	Time
1	Carrie Tollefson, Villanova	16:29
2	Amy Skieresz, Arizona	16:39
3	Angela Graham, Boston College	16:47

WINTER

Fencing

Men

Event		Record
Foil	Ayo Griffin, Yale	21-4
Epee	George Hentea, St. John's	18-7
Sabre	Luke LaValle, Notre Dame	19-6

Women

Event		Record
Foil	Felicia Zimmermann, Stanford	23-2
Epee	Charlotte Walker, Penn St.	22-3

Gymnastics

Men

Event		Points
All-Around	Travis Romagnoli, Illinois	58.225
Floor Exercise	Darin Gerlach, Temple	9.8125
Pommel Horse	Josh Birckelbaw, California	9.8250
Rings	Dan Fink, Oklahoma	9.8875
Vault	Travis Romagnoli, Illinois	9.7125
Horizontal Bar	Todd Bishop, Oklahoma	9.9375
Parallel Bars	**Marshall Nelson**, Nebraska	9.7875

Women

Event		Points
All-Around	**Kim Arnold**, Georgia	39.625
Vault (tie)	**Susan Hines**, Florida	9.8625
	& Larissa Fontaine, Stanford	9.8625
Uneven Bars	Heidi Moneymaker, UCLA	9.9500
Balance Beam (tie)	Betsy Hamm, Florida,	9.8750
	Kim Arnold, Georgia,	9.8750
	& Jenni Beathard, Georgia	9.8750
Floor Exercise (tie)	Karin Lichey, Georgia	9.9500
	& Stella Umeh, UCLA	9.9500

Rifle

Combined Smallbore

		Points
1	Karyn Juziuk, Xavier	1169
2	Jeff Odor, Wyoming	1167
3	Ron Nelson, West Virginia	1167

Air Rifle

		Points
1	Emily Caruso, Norwich	393
2	Dan Jordan, Ala.-Fairbanks	393
3	Kelly Mansfield, Ala-Fairbanks	392

Skiing

Men

Event		Time
Slalom	Christian Hutter, Denver	1:41.86
Giant Slalom	David Viele, Dartmouth	1:48.45
10-k Classical	Thorodd Bakken, Vermont	27:52.6
20-k Freestyle	**Thorodd Bakken**, Vermont	52:40.6

Women

Event		Time
Slalom	Brooke Laundon, Middlebury	1:29.77
Giant Slalom	Caroline Gedde-Dahl, Colorado	1:52.50
5-k Classical	Line Selnes, Colorado	15:49.3
15-k Freestyle	Line Selnes, Colorado	41:19.4

Wrestling

Wgt	Champion	Runner-Up
118	Teague Moore, Okla. St.	David Morgan, Mich. St.
126	**Eric Guerrero**, Okla. St.	Eric Jetton, Wisc.
134	**Mark Ironside**, Iowa	Shawn Enright, Ohio
142	Jeff McGinness, Iowa	Casey Cunningham, C. Mich.
150	Eric Siebert, Illinois	Chad Kraft, Minnesota
158	Dwight Gardner, Ohio	Hardell Moore, Okla. St.
167	Joe Williams, Iowa	Brandon Slay, Penn.
177	Mitch Clark, Ohio St.	Vertus Jones, W. Va.
190	Tim Hartung, Minn.	Jason Robison, Edinboro
Hvy	Stephen Neal, CS-Bakers.	Trent Hynek, Iowa St.

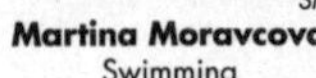

SMU
Martina Moravcova
Swimming

Georgia
Debbie Ferguson
Track & Field

Minnesota
James McLean
Golf

Stanford
Bob Bryan
Tennis

Swimming & Diving

(*) indicates meet record

Men

Event (yards)		**Time**
50 free	Brendon Dedekind, Florida St.	19.22
100 free	**Lars Frolander**, SMU	42.12
200 free	Ryk Neethling, Arizona	1:34.19
500 free	Ryk Neethling, Arizona	4:13.42
1650 free	**Ryk Neethling**, Arizona	14:32.50
100 back	**Neil Walker**, Texas	46.66
200 back	Tate Blahnik, Stanford	1:41.21
100 breast	**Jeremy Linn**, Tennessee	53:01
200 breast	Tom Wilkens, Stanford	1:55.02
100 butterfly	**Lars Frolander**, SMU	45.99
200 butterfly	Matthew Pierce, Stanford	1:43.68
200 IM	Tom Wilkens, Stanford	1:45.16
400 IM	**Tom Wilkens**, Stanford	3:43.96
200 free relay	Stanford	1:16.76
400 free relay	Stanford	2:51.37
800 free relay	Texas	6:23.78
200 medley relay	**Auburn**	1:25.24
400 medley relay	Stanford	3:07.73

Diving		**Points**
1-meter	**Rio Ramirez**, Miami-FL	630.70
3-meter	Bryan Gillooly, Miami-FL	631.40
Platform	Brent Robert, Alabama	834.45

Women

Event (yards)		**Time**
50 free	**Catherine Fox**, Stanford	22.21
100 free	**Martina Moravcova**, SMU	48.81
200 free	**Martina Moravcova**, SMU	1:45.11
500 free	Cristina Teuscher, Colum.-Barn.	4:35.45
1650 free	**Trina Jackson**, Arizona	15:49.25
100 back	**Catherine Fox**, Stanford	52.71
200 back	Misty Hyman, Stanford	1:53.12
100 breast	Kristy Kowal, Georgia	59.05
200 breast	Kristy Kowal, Georgia	2:09.14
100 butterfly	Misty Hyman, Stanford	51.34
200 butterfly	Misty Hyman, Stanford	1:55.70
200 IM	**Martina Moravcova**, SMU	1:57.37
400 IM	Cristina Teuscher, Colum.-Barn.	4:05.62
200 free relay	**Arizona**	1:29.16
400 free relay	Arizona	3:15.77
800 free relay	Arizona	7:10.79
200 medley relay	Stanford	1:37.80
400 medley relay	Stanford	3:33.61

Diving		**Points**
1-meter	**Vera Ilyina**, Texas	495.70
3-meter	**Vera Ilyina**, Texas	612.60
Platform	Kathy Pesek, Tennessee	659.65

Indoor Track

(*) indicates meet record

Men

Event		**Time**
55 meters	Ja Warren Hooker, Washington	6.13
200 meters	Shawn Crawford, Clemson	20.69
400 meters	Davian Clarke, Miami-FL	45.86
800 meters	**David Krummenacker**, Ga. Tech	1:47.52
Mile	Kevin Sullivan, Michigan	4:03.54
3000 meters	**Adam Goucher**, Coloradp	7:46.03*
5000 meters	Brad Hauser, Stanford	13:58.50
55-m hurdles	Larry Wade, Texas A&M	7.11
4x400-m relay	Baylor	3:06.38
Distance medley relay	Washington St.	9:29.54*

Event		**Hgt/Dist**
High Jump	Kenny Evans, Arkansas	7-6
Pole Vault	Vesa Rantanen, Minnesota	18-2½
Long Jump	Bashir Yamini, Iowa	26-0¼
Triple Jump	**Robert Howard**, Arkansas	54-1¼
Shot Put	Brad Snyder, So. Carolina	66-4¼
35-lb Throw	Libor Charfreitag, SMU	69-8

Women

Event		**Time**
55 meters	Kwajalein Butler, LSU	6.78
200 meters	Lakeisha Backus, Texas	23.18
400 meters	Suziann Reid, Texas	52.57
800 meters	Hazel Clark, Florida	2:02.53
Mile	Carmen Douma, Villanova	4:37.74
3000 meters	Katie McGregor, Michigan	9:24.68
5000 meters	**Amy Skieresz**, Arizona	15:54.58
55-m hurdles	Angie Vaughn, Texas	7.41*
4x400-m relay	Baylor	3:33.93
Distance medley relay	Michigan	11:03.28*

Event		**Hgt/Dist**
High Jump	Erin Aldrich, Texas	6-4¼
Pole Vault	Melissa Price, Fresno St.	13-10
Long Jump	Trecia Smith, Pittsburgh	21-6¼
Triple Jump	Trecia Smith, Pittsburgh	46-1¼
Shot Put	Teri Tunks, SMU	60-5¼*
20-lb Throw	Lisa Misipeka, So.Carolina	70-5¼

Spring

Golf

Men

		Total
1	James McLean, Minnesota	71-66-65-69—271
2	Chris Berry, UNLV	70-68-67-67—272
	Joel Kribel, Stanford	69-67-68-68—272
	J.J. Henry, TCU	67-67-70-68—272
	Charles Warren, Clemson	69-66-67-70—272

Women

		Total
1	Jennifer Rosales, USC	68-66-73-72—279
2	Christina Kuld, Tulsa	70-72-68-72—282
3	Grace Park, Arizona St.	65-65-77-76—283

Tennis

Men

Singles— Bob Bryan (Stanford) def. Paul Goldstein (Stanford), 6-3, 6-2.

Doubles— Bob Byran & Mike Bryan (Stanford) def. Kelly Gullett & Robert Lindstedt (Pepperdine), 6-7 (6), 6-2, 6-4.

Women

Singles— Vanessa Webb (Duke) def. Ania Bleszynski (Stanford), 6-3, 6-4.

Doubles— Amanda Augustus & Amy Jensen (California) def. Dawn Buth & Stephanie Nickitas (Florida), 7-5, 6-3.

Outdoor Track

(*) indicates meet record

Men

Event		Time
100 meters	Leonard Myles-Mills, BYU	10.20
200 meters	Curtis Perry, LSU	20.40
400 meters	Jerome Davis, USC	45.18
800 meters	Khadevis Robinson, TCU	1:46.04
1500 meters	**Seneca Lassiter**, Arkansas	3:42.34
5000 meters	Adam Goucher, Colorado	13:31.64
10,000 meters	Brad Hauser, Stanford	28:31.30
110-m hurdles	Larry Wade, Texas A&M	13.37
400-m hurdles	Angelo Taylor, Ga. Tech	48.14
3000-m steeple	Matt Kerr, Arkansas	8:36.95
4x100-m relay	TCU	38.04*
4x400-m relay	Georgia Tech	3:01.89

Event		Hgt/Dist
High Jump	Nathan Leeper, Kansas St.	7-5¾
Pole Vault	Toby Stevenson, Stanford	18-2½
Long Jump	**Robert Howard**, Arkansas	27-5½
Triple Jump	**Robert Howard**, Arkansas	55-8¼
Shot Put	Brad Snyder, So. Carolina	64-7¾
Discus	Casey Malone, Colorado St.	200-2
Javelin	Esko Mikkola, Arizona	268-7*
Hammer	Libor Charfreitag, SMU	237-2
Decathlon	Klaus Ambrosch, Arizona	7825 pts

Women

Event		Time
100 meters	Debbie Ferguson, Georgia	10.94
200 meters	Debbie Ferguson, Georgia	22.66
400 meters	Suziann Reid, Texas	51.22
800 meters	Hazel Clark, Florida	2:02.16
1500 meters	Carmen Douma, Villanova	4:16.04
3000 meters	Monal Chokshi, Stanford	9:20.18
5000 meters	**Amy Skieresz**, Arizona	15:37.77*
10,000 meters	**Amy Skieresz**, Arizona	33:04.12
100-m hurdles	Angie Vaughn, Texas	12.82
400-m hurdles	Rosa Jolivet, Texas A&M	55.24
4x100-m relay	Texas	42.76
4x400-m relay	**Texas**	3:28.65

Event		Hgt/Dist
High Jump	Erin Aldrich, Texas	6-4
Pole Vault	Bianca Maran, Cal Poly	12-5½
Long Jump	Angie Brown, George Mason	21-7½
Triple Jump	Trecia Smith, Pittsburgh	45-10½
Shot Put	**Tressa Thompson**, Nebraska	61-2¼*
Discus	**Seilala Sua**, UCLA	210-8*
Javelin	**Windy Dean**, SMU	184-8
Hammer	Lisa Misipeka, So. Carolina	209-4*
Heptathlon	**Tiffany Lott**, BYU	5982 pts

Most Outstanding Players

Men

Baseball	Wes Rachels, USC
Basketball	Jeff Sheppard, Kentucky
Cross-country	Mebrahtom Keflezighi, UCLA*
Golf	James McLean, Minnesota*
Gymnastics	Travis Romagnoli, Illinois*
Ice Hockey	Marty Turco, Michigan
Lacrosse	Corey Popham, Princeton
Soccer: Offense	Seth George, UCLA
Soccer: Defense	Matt Reis, UCLA
Swimming & Diving	Lars Frolander, SMU
Tennis	Bob Bryan, Stanford*
Track: Indoor	Robert Howard, Arkansas*
Track: Outdoor	Robert Howard, Arkansas*
Volleyball	Adam Naeve, UCLA
Water Polo	Jeremy Pope, Alan Herrmann & Merrill Moses, Pepperdine
Wrestling	Joe Williams, Iowa

Women

Basketball	Chamique Holdsclaw, Tennessee
Cross-country	Carrie Tollefson, Villanova*
Golf	Jennifer Rosales*
Gymnastics	Kim Arnold, Georgia*
Lacrosse	Cathy Nelson, Maryland
Soccer: Offense	Robin Confer, UNC
Soccer: Defense	Siri Mullinix, UNC
Softball	Amanda Scott, Fresno St.
Swimming & Diving	Martina Moravcova, SMU
Tennis	Vanessa Webb, Duke*
Track: Indoor	Trecia Smith, Pittsburgh*
Track: Outdoor	Amy Skieresz, Arizona* & Debbie Ferguson, Georgia*
Volleyball	Terri Zemaitis, Penn St.

(*) indicates won individual or all-around NCAA championship; There were no official Outstanding Players in field hockey or the men's and women's combined sports of fencing, riflery and skiing. Outstanding players in indoor and outdoor track are the individuals earning the most points in the NCAA Championships.

1997-98 NAIA Team Champions

Total NAIA titles in parentheses.

FALL

Cross Country: MEN'S–Lubbock Christian, TX (8); WOMEN'S– Simon Fraser, BC (4). **Football:** MEN'S– Findlay, OH (4). **Soccer:** MEN'S– Seattle, WA (1); WOMEN'S– Mobile, AL (1). **Volleyball:** WOMEN'S– BYU-Hawaii (8).

WINTER

Basketball: MEN'S– Division I: Georgetown, KY (1) and Division II: Bethel, IN (3); WOMEN'S– Division I: Union, TX (1) and Division II: Walsh, OH (1). **Swimming & Diving:** MEN'S– Simon Fraser, BC (1); WOMEN'S– Puget Sound, WA (4). **Indoor Track:** MEN'S– Lindenwood, MO (1); WOMEN'S– Simon Fraser, BC (3). **Wrestling:** MEN'S– Montana St.-Northern (3).

SPRING

Baseball: MEN'S– Albertson, ID (1); **Golf:** MEN'S– Berry, GA (1); WOMEN'S– Mobile, AL (1); **Softball:** WOMEN'S– Western Washington (1); **Tennis:** MEN'S– Oklahoma City (1); WOMEN'S– BYU-Hawaii (2); **Outdoor Track:** MEN'S– Life, GA (2); WOMEN'S– Simon Fraser, BC (2).

Annual NCAA Division I Team Champions

Men's and Women's NCAA Division I team champions from Cross-country to Wrestling. Rowing is included, although the NCAA does not sanction championships on the men's side. The 1997 season was the first for NCAA sanctioned women's rowing championships. Also see Team champions for baseball, basketball, football, golf, ice hockey, soccer and tennis in the appropriate chapters throughout the almanac. See pages 460-462 for list of 1997-98 individual champions.

CROSS-COUNTRY

Men

Stanford placed five runners in the top 25 to outdistance Arkansas for the second straight year to win the Division I Men's Cross Country Championships. The Cardinal finished with 53 points, compared to the Razorbacks' 56 over the 10,000-meter course. Leading the way for the champions were Nathan Nutter and Brad Hauser, who finished 8th and 10th, respectively. Mebrahtom Keflezighi won UCLA's first-ever individual title with a time of 28:54. (*Greenville, S.C.; Nov. 24, 1997.*)

Multiple winners: Michigan St. and Arkansas (8); UTEP (7); Oregon and Villanova (4); Drake, Indiana, Penn St. and Wisconsin (3); Iowa St., San Jose St., Stanford and Western Michigan (2).

Year	Year	Year	Year	Year
1938 Indiana	1950 Penn St.	1963 San Jose St.	1976 UTEP	1989 Iowa St.
1939 Michigan St.	1951 Syracuse	1964 Western Mich.	1977 Oregon	1990 Arkansas
1940 Indiana	1952 Michigan St.	1965 Western Mich.	1978 UTEP	1991 Arkansas
1941 Rhode Island	1953 Kansas	1966 Villanova	1979 UTEP	1992 Arkansas
1942 Indiana	1954 Oklahoma St.	1967 Villanova	1980 UTEP	1993 Arkansas
& Penn St.	1955 Michigan St.	1968 Villanova	1981 UTEP	1994 Iowa St.
1943 Not held	1956 Michigan St.	1969 UTEP	1982 Wisconsin	1995 Arkansas
1944 Drake	1957 Notre Dame	1970 Villanova	1983 Vacated	1996 Stanford
1945 Drake	1958 Michigan St.	1971 Oregon	1984 Arkansas	1997 Stanford
1946 Drake	1959 Michigan St.	1972 Tennessee	1985 Wisconsin	
1947 Penn St.	1960 Houston	1973 Oregon	1986 Arkansas	
1948 Michigan St.	1961 Oregon St.	1974 Oregon	1987 Arkansas	
1949 Michigan St.	1962 San Jose St.	1975 UTEP	1988 Wisconsin	

Women

Brigham Young won its first women's cross-country team title by taking five of the top 46 individual spots. The Cougars registered 100 points to edge defending champion Stanford by only two points. Carrie Tollefson of Villanova won the individual crown in 16:29, holding off defending champion Amy Skieresz of Arizona to give the Wildcats a championships-high seventh individual title. (*Greenville, S.C.; Nov. 24, 1997.*)

Multiple winners: Villanova (6); Oregon, Virginia and Wisconsin (2).

Year	Year	Year	Year	Year
1981 Virginia	1985 Wisconsin	1989 Villanova	1993 Villanova	1997 Brigham Young
1982 Virginia	1986 Texas	1990 Villanova	1994 Villanova	
1983 Oregon	1987 Oregon	1991 Villanova	1995 Providence	
1984 Wisconsin	1988 Kentucky	1992 Villanova	1996 Stanford	

FENCING

Men & Women

Penn St. took home its fourth consecutive fencing title with a two-point victory over host Notre Dame. Charlotte Walker defeated Nicole Dygert of St. John's (NY) in women's epee for the Lions' only individual title. Going into the last day, Penn St. trailed the Irish by three points but rallied to win with 149 points. Individually, Notre Dame's Luke LaValle beat Michael Golia of Penn in men's sabre, George Hentea of St. John's knocked off Stanford's Eric Tribbett in men's epee and Yale's Ayo Griffin won the school's first individual title with a 15-13 victory over Penn's Yaron Roth in the men's foil. In the finals of the women's foil, Felicia Zimmermann of Stanford defeated her teammate Erinn Smart. (*Notre Dame, Ind.; Mar. 19-22, 1998.*)

Multiple winners: Penn St. (6); Columbia/Barnard (2). **Note:** Prior to 1990, men and women held separate championships. Men's multiple winners included: NYU (12); Columbia (11); Wayne St. (7); Navy, Notre Dame and Penn (3); Illinois (2). Women's multiple winners included: Wayne St. (3); Yale (2).

Year	Year	Year	Year	Year
1990 Penn St.	1992 Columbia/	1993 Columbia/	1994 Notre Dame	1996 Penn St.
1991 Penn St.	Barnard	Barnard	1995 Penn St.	1997 Penn St.
				1998 Penn St.

FIELD HOCKEY

Women

North Carolina won its third consecutive field hockey title and fourth overall with a 3-2 win over Old Dominion. ODU got on the scoreboard first after a Marina DiGiacomo score, but the Tar Heels answered with three goals of their own form Cindy Werley, Nancy Pelligreen and Joy Driscoll. The UNC defense was also strong as they allowed just four shots on goaltender Jana Withrow. The Tar Heels concluded the year at 20-3 and improved their record to 67-4 during their three-year reign. (*Storrs, Ct.; Nov. 23, 1997.*)

Multiple winners: Old Dominion (7); North Carolina (4); Connecticut and Maryland (2).

Year	Year	Year	Year	Year
1981 Connecticut	1985 Connecticut	1989 N. Carolina	1993 Maryland	1997 N. Carolina
1982 Old Dominion	1986 Iowa	1990 Old Dominion	1994 J. Madison	
1983 Old Dominion	1987 Maryland	1991 Old Dominion	1995 N. Carolina	
1984 Old Dominion	1988 Old Dominion	1992 Old Dominion	1996 N. Carolina	

Annual NCAA Division I Team Champions (Cont.)

GYMNASTICS

Men

California defended its national title at the NCAA Men's Gymnastics Championships, scoring a well-balanced 231.2 points in the process. Iowa and Illinois finished second and third, respectively. The Golden Bears completed a perfect season that included an undefeated dual record and first-place finishes in their conference, region and preliminaries. Josh Birckelbaw was the only individual winner for California, taking the pommel horse. Illinois' Travis Romagnoli took first place in the vault on his way to the all-around title. Nebraska's Marshall Nelson was the only repeat champion, winning the parallel bars for the second year in a row. *(University Park, Pa.; Apr. 16-18, 1998.)*

Multiple winners: Illinois and Penn St. (9); Nebraska (8); California and So. Illinois (4); Iowa St., Oklahoma and Stanford (3); Florida St., Michigan, Ohio St. and UCLA (2).

Year	Year	Year	Year	Year
1938 Chicago	1955 Illinois	1967 So.Illinois	& Oklahoma	1990 Nebraska
1939 Illinois	1956 Illinois	1968 California	1978 Oklahoma	1991 Oklahoma
1940 Illinois	1957 Penn St.	1969 Iowa	1979 Nebraska	1992 Stanford
1941 Illinois	1958 Michigan St.	& Michigan (T)	1980 Nebraska	1993 Stanford
1942 Illinois	& Illinois	1970 Michigan &	1981 Nebraska	1994 Nebraska
1943-47 Not held	1959 Penn St.	Michigan (T)	1982 Nebraska	1995 Stanford
1948 Penn St.	1960 Penn St.	1971 Iowa St.	1983 Nebraska	1996 Ohio St.
1949 Temple	1961 Penn St.	1972 So. Illinois	1984 UCLA	1997 California
1950 Illinois	1962 USC	1973 Iowa St.	1985 Ohio St.	1998 California
1951 Florida St.	1963 Michigan	1974 Iowa St.	1986 Arizona St.	(T) indicates won
1952 Florida St.	1964 So. Illinois	1975 California	1987 UCLA	trampoline competi-
1953 Penn St.	1965 Penn St.	1976 Penn St.	1988 Nebraska	tion (1969-70).
1954 Penn St.	1966 So.Illinois	1977 Indiana St.	1989 Illinois	

Women

Georgia claimed its fourth women's gymnastics title, their first in five years, with an all-around effort that accumulated a point total of 197.725. Karin Lichey finished first in three different events during the team competition to lead the Bulldogs over fellow Southeastern Conference members Florida (196.350) and Alabama (196.300). Georgia's Kim Arnold won the individual all-around crown for the second year in a row, just edging out Lichey for the title. As well as the all-around title, Arnold also tied for the top spot in the balance beam with teammate Jenni Beathard and Florida's Betsy Hamm. Lichey and UCLA's Stella Umeh tied for the floor exercise title. (*Los Angeles, Calif.; Apr. 16-18, 1998.*)

Multiple Winners: Utah (9); Georgia (4); Alabama (3).

Year	Year	Year	Year	Year
1982 Utah	1986 Utah	1990 Utah	1994 Utah	1998 Georgia
1983 Utah	1987 Georgia	1991 Alabama	1995 Utah	
1984 Utah	1988 Alabama	1992 Utah	1996 Alabama	
1985 Utah	1989 Georgia	1993 Georgia	1997 UCLA	

LACROSSE

Men

Princeton defeated Maryland 15-5 to win its third consecutive lacrosse championship behind 17 saves from goalie Corey Popham, the most outstanding player of the tournament. The Tigers finished the season at 14-1, while the Terps were 14-3. The game opened up in the second half as Princeton finished the game on a 12-2 run. Jesse Hubbard led the attack with four goals, while Chris Massey netted three and Jon Hess had two goals and four assists. (*New Brunswick, N.J.; May 23-25, 1998.*)

Multiple winners: Johns Hopkins (7); Syracuse (6); Princeton (5); North Carolina (4); Cornell (3); Maryland (2).

Year	Year	Year	Year	Year
1971 Cornell	1977 Cornell	1983 Syracuse	1989 Syracuse	1995 Syracuse
1972 Virginia	1978 Johns Hopkins	1984 Johns Hopkins	1990 Syracuse	1996 Princeton
1973 Maryland	1979 Johns Hopkins	1985 Johns Hopkins	1991 North Carolina	1997 Princeton
1974 Johns Hopkins	1980 Johns Hopkins	1986 North Carolina	1992 Princeton	1998 Princeton
1975 Maryland	1981 North Carolina	1987 Johns Hopkins	1993 Syracuse	
1976 Cornell	1982 North Carolina	1988 Syracuse	1994 Princeton	

Women

Goalie Alex Kahoe made 21 saves to lead Maryland to an 11-5 win against Virginia, giving the Terrapins a record fourth-straight women's lacrosse national championship and their sixth overall. Cathy Nelson scored four goals for Maryland, Christie Jenkins scored twice and Quinn Carney added three assists. Maryland finished off the season with seven straight wins and the final game was its 10th consecutive NCAA tournament win. (*Baltimore, Md.; May 15-17, 1998.*)

Multiple winners: Maryland (6); Penn St., Temple and Virginia (2).

Year	Year	Year	Year	Year
1982 Massachusetts	1986 Maryland	1990 Harvard	1994 Princeton	1998 Maryland
1983 Delaware	1987 Penn St.	1991 Virginia	1995 Maryland	
1984 Temple	1988 Temple	1992 Maryland	1996 Maryland	
1985 New Hampshire	1989 Penn St.	1993 Virginia	1997 Maryland	

RIFLE

Men & Women

West Virginia won its fourth consecutive team title and its 10th in the last 11 years with a close 6,214-6,211 victory over Alaska-Fairbanks. West Virginia, led by a record 396 points from Marcos Scrivner, posted a 1,556 in air rifle and a 1,177 in smallbore in the team competitions. This year's individual champs were the first for their respective schools. In air rifle, Norwich's Emily Caruso shot 393 for the win. Karyn Juziuk of Xavier won the smallbore title with a prone score of 396, a standing score of 385 and a kneeling count of 388 for an aggregate 1,169. (*Murray, Ky.; Mar. 5-7, 1998.*)

Multiple winners: West Virginia (13); Tennessee Tech (3); Murray St. (2).

Year	Year	Year	Year	Year
1980 Tenn. Tech	1984 West Virginia	1988 West Virginia	1992 West Virginia	1996 West Virginia
1981 Tenn. Tech	1985 Murray St.	1989 West Virginia	1993 West Virginia	1997 West Virginia
1982 Tenn. Tech	1986 West Virginia	1990 West Virginia	1994 AK-Fairbanks	1998 West Virginia
1983 West Virginia	1987 Murray St.	1991 West Virginia	1995 West Virginia	

ROWING

NCAA Championships

Women

Washington continued its rowing mastery, winning the NCAA Women's Rowing Championship for the second consecutive year. The Huskies were all locked up with Brown and Virginia going into the varsity eights, the championships' final race, but as in the inaugural race in 1997, they emerged victorious. Washington took the eights in 6:52.0, pushing past runner-up UMass (6:55.3) and Brown (6:57.0). Washington finished with 91 points overall, followed by Brown (85) and Virginia (76). (*Gainesville, Ga.; May 29-31, 1998*).

Multiple winners: Washington (2).

Year	Overall winner	Varsity Eights	Year	Overall winner	Varsity Eights
1997	Washington	Washington	1998	Washington	Washington

Intercollegiate Rowing Association Regatta

VARSITY EIGHTS

Men

Princeton made a valiant charge down the stretch to win the 96th rowing of the IRA championships. It was the Tigers' third IRA win overall and their second in the past three years. Princeton crossed the line in 5:31.1, outracing western super powers Washington (5:32.2) and California (5:38.6), who finished second and third, respectively. Princeton caught Washington with 800 meters to go and then took charge with a push in the final 300 to earn the victory. Penn, Northeastern and Georgetown rounded out the top six. *(Cooper River, Camden, N.J.; May 30, 1998.)*

The IRA was formed in 1895 by several Northeastern colleges after Harvard and Yale quit the Rowing Association (established in 1871) to stage an annual race of their own. Since then the IRA Regatta has been contested over courses of varing lengths in Poughkeepsie, N.Y., Marietta, Ohio, Syracuse, N.Y. and Camden, N.J.

Distances: 4 miles (1895-97,1899-1916,1925-41); 3 miles (1898,1921-24,1947-49,1952-63,1965-67); 2 miles (1920,1950-51); 2000 meters (1964, since 1968).

Multiple winners: Cornell (24); Navy (13); Washington (11); California (10); Penn (9); Brown and Wisconsin (7); Syracuse (6); Columbia (4); Princeton (3); Northeastern (2).

Year	Year	Year	Year	Year
1895 Columbia	1916 Syracuse	1939 California	1963 Cornell	1984 Navy
1896 Cornell	1917-19 Not held	1940 Washington	1964 California	1985 Princeton
1897 Cornell	1920 Syracuse	1941 Washington	1965 Navy	1986 Brown
1898 Penn	1921 Navy	1942-46 Not held	1966 Wisconsin	1987 Brown
1899 Penn	1922 Navy	1947 Navy	1967 Penn	1988 Northeastern
1900 Penn	1923 Washington	1948 Washington	1968 Penn	1989 Penn
1901 Cornell	1924 Washington	1949 California	1969 Penn	1990 Wisconsin
1902 Cornell	1925 Navy	1950 Washington	1970 Washington	1991 Northeastern
1903 Cornell	1926 Washington	1951 Wisconsin	1971 Cornell	1992 Dartmouth, Navy & Penn†
1904 Syracuse	1927 Columbia	1952 Navy	1972 Penn	1993 Brown
1905 Cornell	1928 California	1953 Navy	1973 Wisconsin	1994 Brown
1906 Cornell	1929 Columbia	1954 Navy*	1974 Wisconsin	1995 Brown
1907 Cornell	1930 Cornell	1955 Cornell	1975 Wisconsin	1996 Princeton
1908 Syracuse	1931 Navy	1956 Cornell	1976 California	1997 Washington
1909 Cornell	1932 California	1957 Cornell	1977 Cornell	1998 Princeton
1910 Cornell	1933 Not held	1958 Cornell	1978 Syracuse	
1911 Cornell	1934 California	1959 Wisconsin	1979 Brown	
1912 Cornell	1935 California	1960 California	1980 Navy	
1913 Syracuse	1936 Washington	1961 California	1981 Cornell	
1914 Columbia	1937 Washington	1962 Cornell	1982 Cornell	
1915 Cornell	1938 Navy		1983 Brown	

*In 1954, Navy was disqualified because of an ineligible coxwain; no trophies were given.
†First dead heat in history of IRA Regatta.

Annual NCAA Division I Team Champions (Cont.)

The Harvard-Yale Regatta

Harvard made it two in a row and 13 of the last 14 as it outpaced Yale in the 133rd Harvard/Yale Regatta for varsity eights on June 6, 1998. Harvard sprinted out to an early lead in choppy water and simply continued to expand its lead through the calmer two and three-mile marks. Harvard completed the four-mile course on the Thames River in New London, Conn. in 20:32.3, six lengths ahead of the Elis, the largest margin of victory since 1992. The Harvard/Yale Regatta is the nation's oldest intercollegiate sporting event. Harvard holds an 81-52 series edge.

National Rowing Championship
VARSITY EIGHTS

Men

National championship raced annually from 1982-96 in Bantam, Ohio over a 2,000-meter course on Lake Harsha. Winner received the Herschede Cup. Regatta discontinued in 1997.

Multiple winners: Harvard (6); Brown (3); Wisconsin (2).

Year	Champion	Time	Runner-up	Time
1982	Yale	5:50.8	Cornell	5:54.15
1983	Harvard	5:59.6	Washington	6:00.0
1984	Washington	5:51.1	Yale	5:55.6
1985	Harvard	5:44.4	Princeton	5:44.87
1986	Wisconsin	5:57.8	Brown	5:59.9
1987	Harvard	5:35.17	Brown	5:35.63
1988	Harvard	5:35.98	Northeastern	5:37.07
1989	Harvard	5:36.6	Washington	5:38.93
1990	Wisconsin	5:52.5	Harvard	5:56.84
1991	Penn	5:58.21	Northeastern	5:58.48
1992	Harvard	5:33.97	Dartmouth	5:34.28
1993	Brown	5:54.15	Penn	5:56.98
1994	Brown	5:24.52	Harvard	5:25.83
1995	Brown	5:23.40	Princeton	5:25.83
1996	Princeton	5:57.47	Penn	6:03.28
1997	discontinued			

Women

National championship held over various distances at 10 different venues from 1979-96. Distances– 1000 meters (1979-81); 1500 meters (1982-83); 1000 meters (1984); 1750 meters (1985); 2000 meters (1986-88, since 1991); 1852 meters (1989-90). Winner received the Ferguson Bowl. Regatta discontinued in 1997.

Multiple winners: Washington (7); Princeton (4); Boston University (2).

Year	Champion	Time	Runner-up	Time
1979	Yale	3:06	California	3:08.6
1980	California	3:05.4	Oregon St.	3:05.8
1981	Washington	3:20.6	Yale	3:22.9
1982	Washington	4:56.4	Wisconsin	4:59.83
1983	Washington	4:57.5	Dartmouth	5:03.02
1984	Washington	3:29.48	Radcliffe	3:31.08
1985	Washington	5:28.4	Wisconsin	5:32.0
1986	Wisconsin	6:53.28	Radcliffe	6:53.34
1987	Washington	6:33.8	Yale	6:37.4
1988	Washington	6:41.0	Yale	6:42.37
1989	Cornell	5:34.9	Wisconsin	5:37.5
1991	Boston Univ.	7:03.2	Cornell	7:06.21
1992	Boston Univ.	6:28.79	Cornell	6:32.79
1993	Princeton	6:40.75	Washington	6:43.86
1994	Princeton	6:11.38	Yale	6:14.46
1995	Princeton	6:11.98	Washington	6:12.69
1996	Brown	6:45.7	Princeton	6:49.3
1997	discontinued			

SKIING

Men & Women

In the closest competition since 1964, Colorado squeaked by defending champion Utah by 2½ points to win the National Collegiate Men's and Women's Skiing Championships. The Buffaloes were led by Line Selnes, who swept both women's Nordic races, taking the 5-K classical in 15:49.3 and the 15-K freestyle in 41:19.4. Colorado also got a victory from Caroline Gedde-Dahl in the women's giant slalom. They finished with 654 points overall, edging runner-up Utah (651½) and third-place finisher Denver (638). Vermont's Thorodd Bakken joined Selnes as a double winner, defending his title in the 20-K freestyle and adding the 10-K classical. (*Bozeman, Mont.; Mar. 11-14, 1998.*)

Multiple winners: Colorado and Denver (14); Utah (9); Vermont (5); Dartmouth and Wyoming (2).

Year	
1954	Denver
1955	Denver
1956	Denver
1957	Denver
1958	Dartmouth
1959	Colorado
1960	Colorado
1961	Denver
1962	Denver
1963	Denver
1964	Denver
1965	Denver
1966	Denver
1967	Denver
1968	Wyoming
1969	Denver
1970	Denver
1971	Denver
1972	Colorado
1973	Colorado
1974	Colorado
1975	Colorado
1976	Colorado & Dartmouth
1977	Colorado
1978	Colorado
1979	Colorado
1980	Vermont
1981	Utah
1982	Colorado
1983	Utah
1984	Utah
1985	Wyoming
1986	Utah
1987	Utah
1988	Utah
1989	Vermont
1990	Vermont
1991	Colorado
1992	Vermont
1993	Utah
1994	Vermont
1995	Colorado
1996	Utah
1997	Utah
1998	Colorado

SOFTBALL

Women

Nina Lindenberg's leadoff home run in the bottom of the sixth, her 13th of the season, gave Fresno State a 1-0 victory over Arizona and its first NCAA Division I softball championship. The Wildcats, ranked No. 1 all season, finished with a 67-4 record while Fresno State finished 52-11. Amanda Scott got the win for the Bulldogs with a stunning three-hitter as she struck out six and walked none for her 25th win of the year. Arizona's 67 victories established an NCAA record for a single season. (*Oklahoma City, Okla.; May 21-25, 1998.*)

Multiple winners: UCLA (8); Arizona (5); Texas A&M (2).

Year	Year	Year	Year	Year
1982 UCLA	1986 CS-Fullerton	1990 UCLA	1994 Arizona	1998 Fresno St.
1983 Texas A&M	1987 Texas A&M	1991 Colorado	1995 UCLA*	
1984 UCLA	1988 UCLA	1992 UCLA	1996 Arizona	
1985 UCLA	1989 UCLA	1993 Arizona	1997 Arizona	

*Title was later vacated due to action by the NCAA Committee on Infractions.

SWIMMING & DIVING

Men

Stanford scored 599 points to defeat host Auburn (394½) and Texas (362½) for their eighth NCAA swimming and diving championship. Stanford's Tom Wilkens and Arizona's Ryk Neethling each won three events, but the Cardinal got much-needed help from Matthew Pierce (200 butterfly) and Tate Blahnik, who defeated world champion Lenny Krayzelburg of USC in the 200-yard backstroke. Stanford also claimed the 400-yard freestyle relay. SMU senior Lars Frolander won the 100-yard freestyle and the 100-yard butterfly and was named the tournament's most outstanding swimmer. Alabama's Brent Robert won the platform diving event while Rio Ramirez and Bryan Gillooly of Miami-FL took the 1-meter and 3-meter dives, respectively. (*Auburn, Ala.; Mar. 26-28, 1998.*)

Multiple winners: Michigan and Ohio St. (11); USC (9); Stanford (8); Indiana and Texas (6); Yale (4); California and Florida (2).

1937 Michigan	1950 Ohio St.	1963 USC	1976 USC	1989 Texas
1938 Michigan	1951 Yale	1964 USC	1977 USC	1990 Texas
1939 Michigan	1952 Ohio St.	1965 USC	1978 Tennessee	1991 Texas
1940 Michigan	1953 Yale	1966 USC	1979 California	1992 Stanford
1941 Michigan	1954 Ohio St.	1967 Stanford	1980 California	1993 Stanford
1942 Yale	1955 Ohio St.	1968 Indiana	1981 Texas	1994 Stanford
1943 Ohio St.	1956 Ohio St.	1969 Indiana	1982 UCLA	1995 Michigan
1944 Yale	1957 Michigan	1970 Indiana	1983 Florida	1996 Texas
1945 Ohio St.	1958 Michigan	1971 Indiana	1984 Florida	1997 Auburn
1946 Ohio St.	1959 Michigan	1972 Indiana	1985 Stanford	1998 Stanford
1947 Ohio St.	1960 USC	1973 Indiana	1986 Stanford	
1948 Michigan	1961 Michigan	1974 USC	1987 Stanford	
1949 Ohio St.	1962 Ohio St.	1975 USC	1988 Texas	

Women

Stanford won its sixth NCAA women's swimming title and its eighth overall. The Cardinal were led by Catherine Fox, who won two individual events and and swam on the winning legs of two NCAA-record setting relay teams. Misty Hyman swept both butterfly events, setting an NCAA record in the 100, and also took the 200-yard backstroke. Runner-up Arizona won all three freestyle relays and overtook Georgia on the final day of competition. Kristy Kowal swept both breaststoke events to pace the Bulldogs.

Cristina Teuscher of Columbia-Barnard became the school's first female national champion, winning two events including the 500-yard freestyle (4:35.45) where she narrowly missed the American record set by Janet Evans. Martina Moravcova of SMU repeated as NCAA champ in three of her events (100 and 200-yard freestyles and the 200-yard individual medley) to increase her total to nine overall championship titles. Texas' Vera Ilyina claimed the 1 and 3-meter diving crowns. (*Minneapolis, Minn.; Mar. 19-21, 1998.*)

Multiple winners: Stanford (8); Texas (7).

Year	Year	Year	Year	Year
1982 Florida	1986 Texas	1990 Texas	1994 Stanford	1998 Stanford
1983 Stanford	1987 Texas	1991 Texas	1995 Stanford	
1984 Texas	1988 Texas	1992 Stanford	1996 Stanford	
1985 Texas	1989 Stanford	1993 Stanford	1997 USC	

Annual NCAA Division I Team Champions (Cont.)

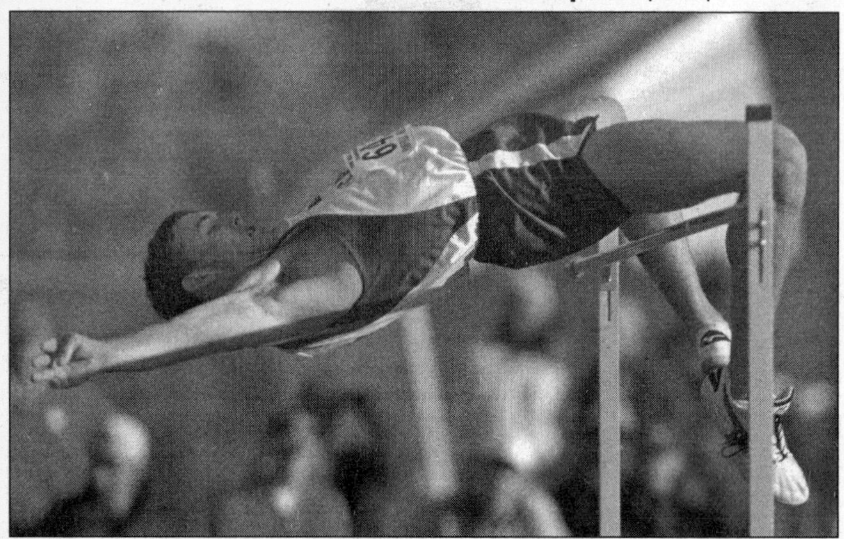

AP/Wide World Photos

Kansas State's **Nathan Leeper** (yes, Leeper) clears the bar at 7'5¾ to win the high jump at the NCAA Outdoor Track and Field Championships in Buffalo.

INDOOR TRACK

Men

Arkansas compiled 56 points to cruise to its 14th indoor track championship in the last 15 years and its second consecutive. Stanford was the runner-up with 36½ points and Clemson and Washington St. tied for third with 26. Razorback star Robert Howard won the triple jump title for the third straight year with a leap of 54-1¼ and teammate Kenny Evans jumped 7-6 for an unexpected victory in the high jump. Georgia Tech's David Krummenacker and Colorado's Adam Goucher were also repeat champions, Krummenacker taking the 800-m and Goucher setting a meet record (7:46.03) in the 3000-m. The distance medley relay team from Washington St. also took first in record fashion, clocking in at 9:29.54. (*Indianapolis, Ind.; March 13-14, 1998.*)

Multiple winners: Arkansas (14); UTEP (7); Kansas and Villanova (3); USC (2).

Year	Year	Year	Year	Year
1965 Missouri	1972 USC	1979 Villanova	1986 Arkansas	1993 Arkansas
1966 Kansas	1973 Manhattan	1980 UTEP	1987 Arkansas	1994 Arkansas
1967 USC	1974 UTEP	1981 UTEP	1988 Arkansas	1995 Arkansas
1968 Villanova	1975 UTEP	1982 UTEP	1989 Arkansas	1996 George Mason
1969 Kansas	1976 UTEP	1983 SMU	1990 Arkansas	1997 Arkansas
1970 Kansas	1977 Washington St.	1984 Arkansas	1991 Arkansas	1998 Arkansas
1971 Villanova	1978 UTEP	1985 Arkansas	1992 Arkansas	

Women

Texas amassed a championships record 60 points to win its fourth Division I women's indoor track championship, it's first since 1990. LSU placed second with 30 points and saw its streak of five consecutive crowns come to an end. The Longhorns really took control of the meet when Suziann Reid captured the 400-m race and teammate Toya Brown took third. Lakeisha Backus (200-m), Angie Vaughn (55-m hurdles) and high jumper Erin Aldrich also claimed victories to pace Texas. Pittsburgh's Trecia Smith was the meet's only double champion with wins in both the long jump and the triple jump. SMU's Teri Tunks was the first shot-putter in championships history to break the 60-foot barrier with a toss of 60-5¼. Arizona's Amy Skieresz was the only repeat champion with her win in the 5000-m race. (*Indianapolis, Ind.; March 13-14, 1998.*)

Multiple winners: LSU (8); Texas (4); Nebraska (2).

Year	Year	Year	Year	Year
1983 Nebraska	1987 LSU	1990 Texas	1993 LSU	1996 LSU
1984 Nebraska	1988 Texas	1991 LSU	1994 LSU	1997 LSU
1985 Florida St.	1989 LSU	1992 Florida	1995 LSU	1998 Texas
1986 Texas				

OUTDOOR TRACK

Men

Robert Howard swept the long jump and the triple jump for the second straight year to lead Arkansas to its seventh consecutive NCAA Division I Outdoor Track and Field Championships. The Razorbacks finished with 58½ points, coming from behind to top runner-up Stanford (51) and TCU (43). Arkansas was also paced by Seneca Lassiter, who repeated as 1500-m champ and steeplechase winner Matt Kerr. Meet records were set by TCU's 4x100-m relay team and Arizona's Esko Mikkola, who shattered the previous mark in the javelin throw. Howard joined former Razorback Mike Conley as the only two men to ever sweep both jumps in consecutive years. (*Buffalo, N.Y.; June 3-6, 1998.*)

Multiple winners: USC (26); Arkansas and UCLA (8); UTEP (6); Illinois and Oregon (5); Kansas, LSU and Stanford (3); SMU and Tennessee (2).

Year	Year	Year	Year	Year
1921 Illinois	1938 USC	1954 USC	1970 BYU, Kansas & Oregon	1985 Arkansas
1922 California	1939 USC	1955 USC	1971 UCLA	1986 SMU
1923 Michigan	1940 USC	1956 UCLA	1972 UCLA	1987 UCLA
1924 Not held	1941 USC	1957 Villanova	1973 UCLA	1988 UCLA
1925 Stanford*	1942 USC	1958 USC	1974 Tennessee	1989 LSU
1926 USC*	1943 USC	1959 Kansas	1975 UTEP	1990 LSU
1927 Illinois*	1944 Illinois	1960 Kansas	1976 USC	1991 Tennessee
1928 Stanford	1945 Navy	1961 USC	1977 Arizona St.	1992 Arkansas
1929 Ohio St.	1946 Illinois	1962 Oregon	1978 UCLA & UTEP	1993 Arkansas
1930 USC	1947 Illinois	1963 USC	1979 UTEP	1994 Arkansas
1931 USC	1948 Minnesota	1964 Oregon	1980 UTEP	1995 Arkansas
1932 Indiana	1949 USC	1965 Oregon & USC	1981 UTEP	1996 Arkansas
1933 LSU	1950 USC	1966 UCLA	1982 UTEP	1997 Arkansas
1934 Stanford	1951 USC	1967 USC	1983 SMU	1998 Arkansas
1935 USC	1952 USC	1968 USC	1984 Oregon	
1936 USC	1953 USC	1969 San Jose St.		
1937 USC				

(*) indicates unofficial championship.

Women

It had to end sometime. LSU's run of 11 consecutive Division I women's outdoor track championships finally came to an end in 1998 as Texas vaulted to the top. It was the second outdoor title for the Longhorns, who finished runner-up in three of the last four championships, last year by just one point. Texas amassed 60 points for the title, behind victories from Suziann Reid in the 400-m, Angie Vaughn in the 100-m hurdles and Erin Aldrich in the high jump. They also won both the 4x100-m relay and the 4x400-m relay.

UCLA finished in second with 55 points while BYU and SMU tied for third with 45. Georgia's Debbie Ferguson was a double winner in the 100 and 200-m and Arizona's Amy Skieresz continued to dominate the distance events, claiming titles in the 5,000-m and 10,000-m for the second consecutive year. (*Buffalo, N.Y.; June 3-6, 1998.*)

Multiple winners: LSU (11); Texas and UCLA (2).

Year	Year	Year	Year	Year
1982 UCLA	1986 Texas	1990 LSU	1994 LSU	1998 Texas
1983 UCLA	1987 LSU	1991 LSU	1995 LSU	
1984 Florida St.	1988 LSU	1992 LSU	1996 LSU	
1985 Oregon	1989 LSU	1993 LSU	1997 LSU	

VOLLEYBALL

Men

UCLA rebounded from last year's defeat to Stanford in the championship match to reclaim their spot atop the Division I men's volleyball world. The Bruins upended top-seeded Pepperdine in three straight games 15-11, 15-11, 15-7 to win the title. It was their third win in the past four years and 17th overall under head coach Al Scates. The tournament's outstanding player, Adam Naeve, led UCLA with 23 kills in the match, while Evan Thatcher and Tom Stillwell had 21 and 18, respectively. It was the sixth consecutive year in which UCLA made it to the championship final. (*Honolulu, Hawaii; May 2, 1998.*)

Multiple winners: UCLA (17); Pepperdine and USC (4).

Year	Year	Year	Year	Year
1970 UCLA	1976 UCLA	1982 UCLA	1988 USC	1994 Penn St.
1971 UCLA	1977 USC	1983 UCLA	1989 UCLA	1995 UCLA
1972 UCLA	1978 Pepperdine	1984 UCLA	1990 USC	1996 UCLA
1973 San Diego St.	1979 UCLA	1985 Pepperdine	1991 Long Beach St.	1997 Stanford
1974 UCLA	1980 USC	1986 Pepperdine	1992 Pepperdine	1998 UCLA
1975 UCLA	1981 UCLA	1987 UCLA	1993 UCLA	

Annual NCAA Division I Team Champions (Cont.)

Women

Stanford won its fourth women's volleyball title in the last six years and its second in a row by beating Penn State in the five-game championship match. The Cardinal jumped out to an early lead, grabbing the first two games 15-6 and 15-10, but Penn State wouldn't go down quietly, making a stirring comeback in games three and four (15-2 and 17-15). Kristin Folkl took over for the Cardinal in the decisive game five, planting five kills in a 15-9 victory. Penn State's Terri Zemaitis, the tournament's most outstanding player, was immense for the Nittany Lions, recording 25 kills and 25 digs in the match. (*Spokane, Wash.; Dec. 20, 1997.*)

Multiple winners: Stanford (4); Hawaii and UCLA (3); Long Beach St. and Pacific (2).

Year	Year	Year	Year	Year
1981 USC	1985 Pacific	1989 Long Beach St.	1993 Long Beach St.	1997 Stanford
1982 Hawaii	1986 Pacific	1990 UCLA	1994 Stanford	
1983 Hawaii	1987 Hawaii	1991 UCLA	1995 Nebraska	
1984 UCLA	1988 Texas	1992 Stanford	1996 Stanford	

WATER POLO

Men

In the 28 years of organized NCAA Division I Water Polo, only five teams had won the national championship. This year, Pepperdine made it six. The Waves' Andy Bruininga scored the winning tally with 44 seconds left in the second overtime of the championship game to give his team an 8-7 victory over USC. Jeremy Pope netted two goals for Pepperdine and was named most outstanding player along with teammates Alan Herrmann and Merrill Moses. (*Ft. Lauderdale, Fla.; Dec. 7, 1997.*)

Multiple winners: California (11); Stanford (8); UCLA (5); UC-Irvine (3).

Year	Year	Year	Year	Year
1969 UCLA	1975 California	1981 Stanford	1987 California	1993 Stanford
1970 UC-Irvine	1976 Stanford	1982 UC-Irvine	1988 California	1994 Stanford
1971 UCLA	1977 California	1983 California	1989 UC-Irvine	1995 UCLA
1972 UCLA	1978 Stanford	1984 California	1990 California	1996 UCLA
1973 California	1979 UC-S. Barbara	1985 Stanford	1991 California	1997 Pepperdine
1974 California	1980 Stanford	1986 Stanford	1992 California	

WRESTLING

Men

Joe Williams, Mark Ironside and Jeff McGinness each claimed championships in their respective weight classes to lead Iowa to the NCAA team wrestling title. It was the fourth consecutive title for the Hawkeyes, their seventh in the last eight years, and their 18th overall. Iowa accumulated 115 points, 13 more than runner-up Minnesota. Williams, who took the title at 167-pounds after winning the 158-pound division the previous two years, was named Most Outstanding Wrestler. It was the first championship under interim coach Jim Zalesky, currently at the helm while coaching legend Dan Gable is on leave. A sellout crowd of 12,007 watched the finals. (*Cleveland, Ohio; Mar. 19-21, 1998.*)

Multiple winners: Oklahoma St. (30); Iowa (18); Iowa St. (8); Oklahoma (7).

Year	Year	Year	Year	Year
1928 Okla. A&M*	1941 Okla. A&M	1957 Oklahoma	1971 Okla. St.	1985 Iowa
1929 Okla. A&M	1942 Okla. A&M	1958 Okla. St.	1972 Iowa St.	1986 Iowa
1930 Okla. A&M	1943-45 Not held	1959 Okla. St.	1973 Iowa St.	1987 Iowa St.
1931 Okla. A&M*	1946 Okla. A&M	1960 Oklahoma	1974 Oklahoma	1988 Arizona St.
1932 Indiana*	1947 Cornell Col.	1961 Okla. St.	1975 Iowa	1989 Okla. St.
1933 Okla. A&M*	1948 Okla. A&M	1962 Okla. St.	1976 Iowa	1990 Okla. St.
& Iowa St.*	1949 Okla. A&M	1963 Oklahoma	1977 Iowa St.	1991 Iowa
1934 Okla. A&M	1950 Northern Iowa	1964 Okla. St.	1978 Iowa	1992 Iowa
1935 Okla. A&M	1951 Oklahoma	1965 Iowa St.	1979 Iowa	1993 Iowa
1936 Oklahoma	1952 Oklahoma	1966 Okla. St.	1980 Iowa	1994 Okla. St.
1937 Okla. A&M	1953 Penn St.	1967 Michigan St.	1981 Iowa	1995 Iowa
1938 Okla. A&M	1954 Okla. A&M	1968 Okla. St.	1982 Iowa	1996 Iowa
1939 Okla. A&M	1955 Okla. A&M	1969 Iowa St.	1983 Iowa	1997 Iowa
1940 Okla. A&M	1956 Okla. A&M	1970 Iowa St.	1984 Iowa	1998 Iowa

(*) indicates unofficial champions. Note: Oklahoma A&M became Oklahoma St. in 1958.

Halls of Fame & Awards

American tennis great **Jimmy Connors** was inducted into the International Tennis Hall of Fame in 1998. Connors won a men's record 109 singles titles, including eight Grand Slams, in his storied career.

Archive Photos

BASEBALL

National Baseball Hall of Fame & Museum

Established in 1935 by Major League Baseball to celebrate the game's 100th anniversary. **Address:** P.O. Box 590, Cooperstown, NY 13326. **Telephone:** (607) 547-7200.

Eligibility: Nominated players must have played at least part of 10 seasons in the major leagues and be retired for at least five but no more than 20 years. Voting done by Baseball Writers' Association of America. Certain nominated players not elected by the writers can become eligible via the Veterans' Committee 23 years after retirement. The Hall of Fame board of directors voted unanimously on Feb. 4, 1991, to exclude players on baseball's ineligible list from consideration. Pete Rose is the only living ex-player on that list.

Class of 1998 (4): BBWAA vote— pitcher **Don Sutton**, Los Angeles (1966-80), Houston (1981-82), Milwaukee (1982-84), Oakland (1985), California (1985-87), Los Angleles (1988). VETERAN'S COMMITTEE vote—shortstop **George Davis**, Cleveland-NL (1890-92), New York-NL (1893-1901, 1903), Chicago-AL (1902, 1904-09); centerfielder **Larry Doby**, Cleveland (1947-55, 58), Chicago-AL (1956-57, 59), Detroit (1959); former AL President **Lee McPhail, Jr.** (1974-83); Negro Leagues pitcher **Wilber Rogan**, KC Monarchs (1920-38).

1998 Top 10 vote-getters (473 BBWAA ballots cast, 355 needed to elect): 1. **Don Sutton** (386); 2. **Tony Perez** (321); 3. **Ron Santo** (204); 4. **Jim Rice** (203); 5. **Gary Carter** (200); 6. **Steve Garvey** (195); 7. **Bruce Sutter** (147); 8. **Tommy John** (129), 9. **Jim Kaat** (129), 10. **Dave Parker** (116).

Elected first year on ballot (31): Hank Aaron, Ernie Banks, Johnny Bench, Lou Brock, Rod Carew, Steve Carlton, Ty Cobb, Bob Feller, Bob Gibson, Reggie Jackson, Walter Johnson, Al Kaline, Sandy Koufax, Mickey Mantle, Christy Mathewson, Willie Mays, Willie McCovey, Joe Morgan, Stan Musial, Jim Palmer, Brooks Robinson, Frank Robinson, Jackie Robinson, Babe Ruth, Mike Schmidt, Tom Seaver, Warren Spahn, Willie Stargell, Honus Wagner, Ted Williams and Carl Yastrzemski.

Members are listed with years of induction; (+) indicates deceased members.

Catchers

Bench, Johnny 1989
Berra, Yogi 1972
\+ Bresnahan, Roger 1945
\+ Campanella, Roy..........1969
\+ Cochrane, Mickey.........1947
\+ Dickey, Bill 1954
\+ Ewing, Buck 1939
\+ Ferrell, Rick.............1984
\+ Hartnett, Gabby 1955
\+ Lombardi, Ernie...........1986
\+ Schalk, Ray 1955

1st Basemen

\+ Anson, Cap 1939
\+ Beckley, Jake 1971
\+ Bottomley, Jim............1974
\+ Brouthers, Dan............1945
\+ Chance, Frank.............1946
\+ Connor, Roger.............1976
\+ Foxx, Jimmie..............1951
\+ Gehrig, Lou 1939
\+ Greenberg, Hank 1956
\+ Kelly, George.............1973
Killebrew, Harmon 1984
McCovey, Willie 1986
\+ Mize, Johnny 1981
\+ Sisler, George 1939
\+ Terry, Bill...............1954

2nd Basemen

Carew, Rod 1991
\+ Collins, Eddie............1939
Doerr, Bobby 1986
\+ Evers, Johnny 1946
Fox, Nellie 1997
\+ Frisch, Frankie 1947
\+ Gehringer, Charlie 1949
\+ Herman, Billy 1975
\+ Hornsby, Rogers 1942
\+ Lajoie, Nap 1937
\+ Lazzeri, Tony 1991
Morgan, Joe...............1990
\+ Robinson, Jackie 1962
Schoendienst, Red.........1989

Shortstops

Aparicio, Luis............1984
\+ Appling, Luke............1964
\+ Bancroft, Dave...........1971
Banks, Ernie..............1977
Boudreau, Lou 1970
\+ Cronin, Joe..............1956
Davis, George 1998
\+ Jackson, Travis..........1982
\+ Jennings, Hugh 1945
\+ Maranville, Rabbit.......1954
Reese, Pee Wee............1984
Rizzuto, Phil 1994
\+ Sewell, Joe 1977
\+ Tinker, Joe..............1946
\+ Vaughan, Arky............1985
\+ Wagner, Honus 1936
\+ Wallace, Bobby...........1953
\+ Ward, Monte 1964

3rd Basemen

\+ Baker, Frank.............1955
\+ Collins, Jimmy 1945
Kell, George..............1983
\+ Lindstrom, Fred 1976
Mathews, Eddie............1978
Robinson, Brooks..........1983
Schmidt, Mike 1995
\+ Traynor, Pie 1948

Left Fielders

Brock, Lou................1985
\+ Burkett, Jesse 1946
\+ Clarke, Fred.............1945
\+ Delahanty, Ed............1945
\+ Goslin, Goose 1968
\+ Hafey, Chick 1971
\+ Kelley, Joe..............1971
Kiner, Ralph 1975
\+ Manush, Heinie 1964
\+ Medwick, Joe.............1968
Musial, Stan 1969
\+ O'Rourke, Jim............1945
\+ Simmons, Al..............1953
Stargell, Willie..........1988
\+ Wheat, Zack 1959
Williams, Billy 1987
Williams, Ted 1966
Yastrzemski, Carl.........1989

Center Fielders

\+ Ashburn, Richie 1995
\+ Averill, Earl............1975
\+ Carey, Max 1961
\+ Cobb, Ty.................1936
\+ Combs, Earle.............1970
DiMaggio, Joe.............1955
Doby, Larry...............1998
\+ Duffy, Hugh 1945
\+ Hamilton, Billy 1961
\+ Mantle, Mickey 1974
Mays, Willie..............1979
\+ Roush, Edd 1962
Snider, Duke..............1980
\+ Speaker, Tris............1937
\+ Waner, Lloyd 1967
\+ Wilson, Hack.............1979

Right Fielders

Aaron, Hank 1982
+ Clemente, Roberto..........1973
+ Crawford, Sam 1957
+ Cuyler, Kiki................1968
+ Flick, Elmer.................1963
+ Heilmann, Harry 1952
+ Hooper, Harry 1971

Jackson, Reggie............1993
Kaline, Al 1980
+ Keeler, Willie..............1939
+ Kelly, King 1945
+ Klein, Chuck...............1980
+ McCarthy, Tommy 1946
+ Ott, Mel 1951

+ Rice, Sam 1963
Robinson, Frank............1982
+ Ruth, Babe 1936
Slaughter, Enos 1985
+ Thompson, Sam............1974
+ Waner, Paul 1952
+ Youngs, Ross 1972

Pitchers

+ Alexander, Grover 1938
+ Bender, Chief..............1953
+ Brown, Mordecai 1949
Bunning, Jim...............1996
Carlton, Steve 1994
+ Chesbro, Jack 1946
+ Clarkson, John.............1963
+ Coveleski, Stan 1969
+ Dean, Dizzy...............1953
+ Drysdale, Don 1984
+ Faber, Red 1964
Feller, Bob 1962
Fingers, Rollie..............1992
Ford, Whitey 1974
+ Galvin, Pud 1965
Gibson, Bob................1981
+ Gomez, Lefty 1972
+ Grimes, Burleigh 1964
+ Grove, Lefty 1947

+ Haines, Jess 1970
+ Hoyt, Waite 1969
+ Hubbell, Carl 1947
Hunter, Catfish.............1987
Jenkins, Ferguson...........1991
+ Johnson, Walter............1936
+ Joss, Addie................1978
+ Keefe, Tim.................1964
Koufax, Sandy.............1972
Lemon, Bob 1976
+ Lyons, Ted.................1955
Marichal, Juan.............1983
+ Marquard, Rube 1971
+ Mathewson, Christy 1936
+ McGinnity, Joe.............1946
Niekro, Phil 1997
Newhouser, Hal............1992
+ Nichols, Kid 1949
Palmer, Jim 1990

+ Pennock, Herb 1948
Perry, Gaylord 1991
+ Plank, Eddie...............1946
+ Radbourne, Old Hoss........1939
+ Rixey, Eppa 1963
Roberts, Robin 1976
+ Ruffing, Red 1967
+ Rusie, Amos 1977
Seaver, Tom 1992
Spahn, Warren 1973
Sutton, Don................1998
+ Vance, Dazzy..............1955
+ Waddell, Rube.............1946
+ Walsh, Ed.................1946
+ Welch, Mickey.............1973
Wilhelm, Hoyt 1985
+ Willis, Vic.................1995
Wynn, Early...............1972
+ Young, Cy.................1937

Managers

+ Alston, Walter 1983
+ Durocher, Leo..............1994
+ Hanlon, Ned 1996
+ Harris, Bucky 1975
+ Huggins, Miller 1964
Lasorda, Tommy............1997

Lopez, Al 1977
+ Mack, Connie 1937
+ McCarthy, Joe 1957
+ McGraw, John 1937
+ McKechnie, Bill 1962

+ Robinson, Wilbert 1945
+ Stengel, Casey.............1966
Weaver, Earl 1996

Umpires

+ Barlick, Al.................1989
+ Conlan, Jocko 1974
+ Connolly, Tom 1953

+ Evans, Billy...............1973
+ Hubbard, Cal..............1976

+ Klem, Bill.................1953
+ McGowan, Bill.............1992

From Negro Leagues

+ Bell, Cool Papa (OF)........1974
+ Charleston, Oscar (1B-OF)...1976
+ Dandridge, Ray (3B)........1987
+ Day, Leon (P-OF-2B) 1995
+ Dihigo, Martin (P-OF) 1977

+ Foster, Rube (P-Mgr) 1981
+ Foster, Willie (P)...........1996
+ Gibson, Josh (C) 1972
Irvin, Monte (OF)...........1973
+ Johnson, Judy (3B)..........1975

+ Leonard, Buck (1B) 1972
+ Lloyd, Pop (SS)............1977
+ Paige, Satchel (P) 1971
+ Rogan, Wilber (P) 1998
+ Wells, Willie (SS)...........1997

Pioneers and Executives

+ Barrow, Ed 1953
+ Bulkeley, Morgan...........1937
+ Cartwright, Alexander 1938
+ Chadwick, Henry 1938
+ Chandler, Happy...........1982
+ Comiskey, Charles..........1939
+ Cummings, Candy..........1939
+ Frick, Ford 1970

+ Giles, Warren 1979
+ Griffith, Clark.............1946
+ Harridge, Will 1972
+ Hulbert, William 1995
+ Johnson, Ban 1937
+ Landis, Kenesaw 1944
+ MacPhail, Larry 1978
MacPhail, Lee 1998

+ Rickey, Branch 1967
+ Spalding, Al...............1939
+ Veeck, Bill.................1991
+ Weiss, George.............1971
+ Wright, George............1937
+ Wright, Harry 1953
+ Yawkey, Tom...............1980

Ford Frick Award

First presented in 1978 by the Hall of Fame for meritorious contributions by baseball broadcasters. Named in honor of the late newspaper reporter, broadcaster, National League president and commissioner, the Frick Award does not constitute induction into the Hall of Fame.

Year	
1978	Mel Allen & Red Barber
1979	Bob Elson
1980	Russ Hodges
1981	Ernie Harwell
1982	Vin Scully
1983	Jack Brickhouse
1984	Curt Gowdy

Year	
1985	Buck Canel
1986	Bob Prince
1987	Jack Buck
1988	Lindsey Nelson
1989	Harry Caray
1990	Byrum Saam
1991	Joe Garagiola

Year	
1992	Milo Hamilton
1993	Chuck Thompson
1994	Bob Murphy
1995	Bob Wolff
1996	Herb Carneal
1997	Jimmy Dudley
1998	Jaime Jarrin

Baseball (Cont.)

J.G. Taylor Spink Award

First presented in 1962 by the Baseball Writers' Association of America for meritorious contributions by members of the BBWAA. Named in honor of the late publisher of *The Sporting News*, the Spink Award does not constitute induction into the Hall of Fame. Winners are honored in the year following their selection.

Year	
1962	J.G. Taylor Spink
1963	Ring Lardner
1964	Hugh Fullerton
1965	Charley Dryden
1966	Grantland Rice
1967	Damon Runyon
1968	H.G. Salsinger
1969	Sid Mercer
1970	Heywood C. Broun
1971	Frank Graham
1972	Dan Daniel, Fred Lieb & J. Roy Stockton
1973	Warren Brown, John Drebinger & John F. Kieran
1974	John Carmichael & James Isaminger
1975	Tom Meany & Shirley Povich
1976	Harold Kaese & Red Smith
1977	Gordon Cobbledick & Edgar Munzel
1978	Tim Murnane & Dick Young
1979	Bob Broeg & Tommy Holmes
1980	Joe Reichler & Milt Richman
1981	Bob Addie & Allen Lewis
1982	Si Burick
1983	Ken Smith
1984	Joe McGuff
1985	Earl Lawson
1986	Jack Lang
1987	Jim Murray
1988	Bob Hunter & Ray Kelly
1989	Jerome Holtzman
1990	Phil Collier
1991	Ritter Collett
1992	Leonard Koppett & Buzz Saidt
1993	John Wendell Smith
1994	No award
1995	Joseph Durso
1996	Charley Feeney
1997	Sam Lacy

Major League Baseball's All-Time Team—Then and Now

The Baseball Writers' Association of America originally selected an all-time team as part of major league baseball's 100th anniversary, announcing the outcome of its vote on July 21, 1969. Vote totals were not released. Recently, another vote was released when a panel of 36 BWAA members picked an all-time team for the Classic Sports Network just before the 1997 All-Star Game. This time around vote totals were given, the single outfield category was divided into three (left, center and right) and two recently popularized positions—the designated hitter and relief pitcher—were added. In the most recent vote two points were awarded for first-place votes and one point for second place. Point totals follow the names with the number of first-place votes in parentheses. All-time team members are listed in **bold** type

1969 Vote

C **Mickey Cochrane**, Bill Dickey, Roy Campanella

1B **Lou Gehrig**, George Sisler, Stan Musial

2B **Rogers Hornsby**, Charlie Gehringer, Eddie Collins

SS **Honus Wagner**, Joe Cronin, Ernie Banks

3B **Pie Traynor**, Brooks Robinson, Jackie Robinson

OF **Babe Ruth**, **Ty Cobb**, **Joe DiMaggio**, Ted Williams, Tris Speaker, Willie Mays

RHP **Walter Johnson**, Christy Mathewson, Cy Young

LHP **Lefty Grove**, Sandy Koufax, Carl Hubbell

Mgr. **John McGraw**, Casey Stengel, Joe McCarthy

1969 Vote All-Time Outstanding Player: **Ruth**, Cobb, Wagner, DiMaggio

1997 Vote

C **Johnny Bench** (24) 52; Yogi Berra (4) 22; Roy Campanella (4) 17; Mickey Cochrane (1) 5; Bill Dickey (1) 4; Gabby Hartnett (1) 3; Carlton Fisk 2.

1B **Lou Gehrig** (31) 66½; Jimmie Foxx (3) 19; George Sisler (2) 8; Willie McCovey 6; Hank Greenberg 2½; Stan Musial, Eddie Murray, Mark McGwire and Frank Thomas 1.

2B **Rogers Hornsby** (17) 44; Joe Morgan (6) 23; Jackie Robinson (6) 15; Charley Gehringer (4) and Napolean Lajoie (3) 11; Eddie Collins (1) 3; Rod Carew 2; Ryne Sandberg 1.

SS **Honus Wagner** (23) 55; Cal Ripken Jr. (6) 24; Ozzie Smith (5) 16; Ernie Banks (1) 8; Lou Boudreau and Luke Appling 1.

3B **Mike Schmidt** (21) 50; Brooks Robinson (13) 37; Eddie Mathews 5; George Brett (1) 8; Pie Traynor 3; Pete Rose (1) 2; Frank Baker, Al Rosen and Wade Boggs 1.

LF **Ted Williams** (32) 68; Stan Musial (4) 36; Pete Rose, Ralph Kiner, Rickey Henderson and Barry Bonds 1.

CF **Willie Mays** (25) 57; Ty Cobb (7) 22; Joe DiMaggio (3) 17; Mickey Mantle (1) 10; Tris Speaker 2.

RF **Babe Ruth** (31) 67; Hank Aaron (5) 36; Frank Robinson 2; Al Kaline, Roberto Clemente and Tony Gwynn 1.

DH **Paul Molitor** (22) 48; Harold Baines (3) 12; Don Baylor (1) 10; Edgar Martinez (2) 9; Ty Cobb (2) 6; Hal McRae (1) 5; Mickey Mantle (1) and Dave Parker (1) 3; Joe DiMaggio (1) 2; Lee May, Frank Robinson and Tony Oliva 1.

RHP **Walter Johnson** (9) 30, Cy Young (12) 25; Christy Mathewson (5) 18; Bob Feller (4) 10; Bob Gibson (2) 9; Nolan Ryan (2) 7; Tom Seaver (1) 3; Greg Maddux (1), Grover Cleveland Alexander and Juan Marichal 2.

LHP **Sandy Koufax** (11) 32; Warren Spahn (11) 28; Lefty Grove (8) 25; Steve Carlton (4) 12; Carl Hubbell 6; Whitey Ford (1) 3; Eddie Plank (1) 2.

RP **Dennis Eckersley** (16) 40; Rollie Fingers (9) 29; Lee Smith (4) 13; Hoyt Wilhelm (3) 10; Rich Gossage (3) 9; Bruce Sutter (1) 6, Dan Quisenberry 1.

Mgr. **Casey Stengel** (6) 22, Joe McCarthy (6) 18; Connie Mack (7) 17; John McGraw (6) 14; Sparky Anderson (3) 11; Leo Durocher (2) 6; Dick Williams (1) 4; Billy Martin (1) 3; Al Lopez (1), Ned Hanlon (1), Whitey Herzog (1), Earl Weaver and Bobby Cox 2; Tony La Russa 1.

BASKETBALL

Naismith Memorial Basketball Hall of Fame

Established in 1949 by the National Association of Basketball Coaches in memory of the sport's inventor, Dr. James Naismith. Original Hall opened in 1968 and current Hall in 1985. **Address:** 1150 West Columbus Avenue, Springfield, MA 01105. **Telephone:** (413) 781-6500.

Eligibility: Nominated players and referees must be retired for five years, coaches must have coached 25 years or be retired for five, and contributors must have already completed their noteworthy service to the game. Voting done by 24-member honors committee made up of media representatives, Hall of Fame members and trustees. Any nominee not elected after five years becomes eligible for consideration by the Veterans' Committee after a five-year wait.

Class of 1998 (7): PLAYERS—forward **Larry Bird** NBA (Boston, 1979-92); guard **Marques Haynes**, Harlem Globetrotters (1947-53, 1972-79), Magicians (1953-72, 1981-83); center **Arnie Risen** NBA (Indianapolis, 1945-47; Rochester 1948-55; Boston, 1955-58). COACHES—**Judy Conradt**, college (Sam Houston St., 1969-73; Texas-Arlington, 1973-76; Texas, 1976-present); **Alex Hannum**, NBA (St. Louis, 1956-58; Syracuse, 1960-63; San Francisco, 1963-66; Philadelphia, 1966-68; San Diego, 1969-71); **Aleksandar Nikolic**, Yugoslavian National Team (1953-78); **Lenny Wilkens**, NBA (Seattle, 1969-72; Portland, 1974-76; Seattle, 1977-85; Cleveland, 1986-93; Atlanta, 1993-present).

1998 finalists (nominated but not elected): PLAYERS—Larry Costello, Adrian Dantley, Gus Johnson, Sidney Moncrief and Chet Walker. COACHES— Harley Redin, John Thompson, Tex Winter and Ubiratan Pereira Maciel. CONTRIBUTOR—Grady Lewis.

Note: John Wooden and **Lenny Wilkens**, who was rehonored by the Hall in 1998, are the only members to be inducted as both a player and a coach.

Members are listed with years of induction; (+) indicates deceased members.

Men

Abdul-Jabbar, Kareem 1995
Archibald, Nate............1991
Arizin, Paul...............1977
+ Barlow, Thomas (Babe)......1980
Barry, Rick 1987
Baylor, Elgin..............1976
+ Beckman, John.............1972
Bellamy, Walt..............1993
Belov, Sergei 1992
Bing, Dave 1990
Bird, Larry................1998
+ Borgmann, Benny 1961
Bradley, Bill 1982
+ Brennan, Joe 1974
Cervi, Al 1984
Chamberlain, Wilt..........1978
+ Cooper, Charles (Tarzan)....1976
+ Cosic, Kresimir...........1996
Cousy, Bob.................1970
Cowens, Dave 1991
Cunningham, Billy..........1986
+ Davies, Bob 1969
+ DeBernardi, Forrest.......1961
DeBusschere, Dave 1982
+ Dehnert, Dutch............1968
+ Endacott, Paul 1971
English, Alex 1997
Erving, Julius (Dr. J).........1993
Foster, Bud 1964
Frazier, Walt 1987
+ Friedman, Marty 1971
+ Fulks, Joe 1977
Gale, Laddie 1976
Gallatin, Harry 1991
Gates, William (Pop) 1989
Gervin, George.............1996
Gola, Tom..................1975
Goodrich, Gail 1996
Greer, Hal 1981
+ Gruenig, Robert...........1963
Hagan, Cliff...............1977
+ Hanson, Victor............1960
Havlicek, John 1983
Hawkins, Connie............1992
Hayes, Elvin...............1990
Haynes, Marques 1998
Heinsohn, Tom..............1986
+ Holman, Nat 1964
Houbregs, Bob..............1987
Howell, Bailey 1997
+ Hyatt, Chuck 1959
Issel, Dan 1993
+ Jeannette, Buddy..........1994
+ Johnson, Bill (Skinny)........1976
+ Johnston, Neil 1990
Jones, K. C................1989
Jones, Sam 1983
+ Krause, Edward (Moose) 1975
Kurland, Bob 1961
Lanier, Bob................1992
+ Lapchick, Joe 1966
Lovellette, Clyde..........1988
Lucas, Jerry...............1979
Luisetti, Hank 1959
Macauley, Ed...............1960
+ Maravich, Pete............1987
Martin, Slater.............1981
+ McCracken, Branch 1960
+ McCracken, Jack..........1962
+ McDermott, Bobby 1988
McGuire, Dick 1993
Mikan, George 1959
Mikkelsen, Vern 1995
Monroe, Earl 1990
Murphy, Calvin 1993
+ Murphy, Charles (Stretch)....1960
+ Page, Harlan (Pat)........1962
Pettit, Bob 1970
Phillip, Andy..............1961
+ Pollard, Jim..............1977
Ramsey, Frank 1981
Reed, Willis 1981
Risen, Arnie 1998
Robertson, Oscar...........1979
+ Roosma, John..............1961
Russell, Bill 1974
+ Russell, John (Honey) 1964
Schayes, Dolph 1972
+ Schmidt, Ernest J 1973
+ Schommer, John............1959
+ Sedran, Barney 1962
Sharman, Bill 1975
+ Steinmetz, Christian 1961
Thompson, David............1996
+ Thompson, John (Cat) 1962
Thurmond, Nate 1984
Twyman, Jack...............1982
Unseld, Wes................1988
+ Vandivier, Robert (Fuzzy) 1974
+ Wachter, Ed..............1961
Walton, Bill...............1993
Wanzer, Bobby 1987
West, Jerry 1979
Wilkens, Lenny.............1989
Wooden, John 1960
Yardley, George 1996

Women

Blazejowski, Carol 1994
Crawford, Joan 1997
Curry, Denise..............1997
Donovan, Anne 1995
Harris, Lucy 1992
Lieberman-Cline, Nancy.....1996
Meyers, Ann................1993
Miller, Cheryl.............1995
Semenova, Juliana 1993
White, Nera................1992

Teams

Buffalo Germans 1961
First Team 1959
New York Renaissance......1963
Original Celtics 1959

Basketball (Cont.)

Referees

+ Enright, Jim 1978
+ Hepbron, George 1960
+ Hoyt, George 1961
+ Kennedy, Pat 1959
+ Leith, Lloyd 1982
+ Mihalik, Red 1986
Nucatola, John 1977
+ Quigley, Ernest (Quig) 1961
+ Shirley, J. Dallas 1979
+ Strom, Earl 1995
Tobey, Dave 1961
+ Walsh, David 1961

Coaches

+ Allen, Forrest (Phog) 1959
+ Anderson, Harold (Andy) 1984
Auerbach, Red 1968
+ Barry, Sam 1978
+ Blood, Ernest (Prof) 1960
+ Cann, Howard 1967
+ Carlson, Henry (Doc) 1959
Carnesecca, Lou 1992
Carnevale, Ben 1969
Carril, Pete 1997
+ Case, Everett 1981
Conradt, Judy 1998
Crum, Denny 1994
Daly, Chuck 1994
+ Dean, Everett 1966
Diaz-Miguel, Antonio 1997
+ Diddle, Ed 1971
+ Drake, Bruce 1972
Gaines, Clarence (Bighouse) 1981
Gardner, Jack 1983
+ Gill, Amory (Slats) 1967
Gomelsky, Aleksandr 1995
Hannum, Alex 1998
Harshman, Marv 1984
Haskins, Don 1997
+ Hickey, Eddie 1978
+ Hobson, Howard (Hobby) 1965
Holzman, Red 1986
+ Iba, Hank 1968
+ Julian, Alvin (Doggie) 1967
+ Keaney, Frank 1960
+ Keogan, George 1961
Knight, Bob 1991
Kundla, John 1995
+ Lambert, Ward (Piggy) 1960
Litwack, Harry 1975
+ Loeffler, Ken 1964
+ Lonborg, Dutch 1972
+ McCutchan, Arad 1980
McGuire, Al 1992
+ McGuire, Frank 1976
+ Meanwell, Walter (Doc) 1959
Meyer, Ray 1978
Miller, Ralph 1988
Nikolic, Aleksandar 1998
Ramsay, Jack 1992
Rubini, Cesare 1994
+ Rupp, Adolph 1968
+ Sachs, Leonard 1961
+ Shelton, Everett 1979
Smith, Dean 1982
Taylor, Fred 1985
+ Wade, Margaret 1984
Watts, Stan 1985
Wilkens, Lenny 1998
Wooden, John 1972
+ Woolpert, Phil 1992

Contributors

+ Abbott, Senda Berenson 1984
+ Bee, Clair 1967
+ Brown, Walter A 1965
+ Bunn, John 1964
+ Douglas, Bob 1971
+ Duer, Al 1981
Fagen, Clifford B 1983
+ Fisher, Harry 1973
+ Fleisher, Larry 1991
+ Gottlieb, Eddie 1971
+ Gulick, Luther 1959
+ Harrison, Les 1979
+ Hepp, Ferenc 1980
+ Hickox, Ed 1959
+ Hinkle, Tony 1965
+ Irish, Ned 1964
+ Jones, R. William 1964
+ Kennedy, Walter 1980
+ Liston, Emil (Liz) 1974
McLendon, John 1978
+ Mokray, Bill 1965
+ Morgan, Ralph 1959
+ Morgenweck, Frank (Pop) 1962
+ Naismith, James 1959
Newell, Pete 1978
+ O'Brien, John J. (Jack) 1961
+ O'Brien, Larry 1991
+ Olsen, Harold G 1959
+ Podoloff, Maurice 1973
+ Porter, Henry (H.V.) 1960
+ Reid, William A 1963
+ Ripley, Elmer 1972
+ St. John, Lynn W 1962
+ Saperstein, Abe 1970
+ Schabinger, Arthur 1961
+ Stagg, Amos Alonzo 1959
Stankovic, Boris 1991
+ Steitz, Ed 1983
+ Taylor, Chuck 1968
+ Teague, Bertha 1984
+ Tower, Oswald 1959
+ Trester, Arthur (A.L.) 1961
+ Wells, Cliff 1971
+ Wilke, Lou 1982

Curt Gowdy Award

First presented in 1990 by the Hall of Fame Board of Trustees for meritorious contributions by the media. Named in honor of the former NBC sportscaster, the Gowdy Award does not constitute induction into the Hall of Fame.

Year	
1990	Curt Gowdy & Dick Herbert
1991	Dave Dorr & Marty Glickman
1992	Sam Goldaper & Chick Hearn
1993	Leonard Lewin & Johnny Most
1994	Leonard Koppett & Cawood Ledford
1995	Dick Enberg & Bob Hammel
1996	Billy Packer & Bob Hentzen
1997	Marv Albert & Bob Ryan
1998	Dick Vitale

BOWLING

National Bowling Hall of Fame & Museum

The National Bowling Hall is one museum with separate wings for honorees of the American Bowling Congress (ABC), Professional Bowlers' Association (PBA) and Women's International Bowling Congress (WIBC). The museum does not include the new Ladies Pro Bowlers Tour Hall of Fame, which is located in Las Vegas. **Address:** 111 Stadium Plaza, St. Louis, MO 63102. **Telephone:** (314) 231-6340.

Professional Bowlers Association

Established in 1975. **Eligibility:** Nominees must be PBA members and at least 35 years old. Voting done by 50-member panel that includes writers who have covered bowling for at least 12 years.

Class of 1998 (2): PERFORMANCE—**Serniz Teata** and **Pete Weber**.

Members are listed with years of induction; (+) indicates deceased members.

Performance

+ Allen, Bill 1983
Anthony, Earl 1986
Aulby, Mike 1996
Berardi, Joe 1990
Bluth, Ray 1975
Buckley, Roy 1992

Burton, Nelson Jr 1979
Carter, Don 1975
Colwell, Paul 1991
Cook, Steve 1993
Davis, Dave 1978
Dickinson, Gary............ 1988
Durbin, Mike 1984
+ Fazio, Buzz 1976
Ferraro, Dave.............. 1997
Godman, Jim 1987
Hardwick, Billy 1977
Holman, Marshall 1990
Hudson, Tommy 1989
Husted, Dave 1996
Johnson, Don 1977
Laub, Larry 1985
Monacelli, Amleto 1997
Ozio, David 1995
Pappas, George 1986
Petraglia, John 1982
Ritger, Dick 1978
Roth, Mark 1987
Salvino, Carmen 1975
Smith, Harry............... 1975
Soutar, Dave 1979
Stefanich, Jim.............. 1980
Teata, Serniz 1998
Voss, Brian 1994
Webb, Wayne.............. 1993
Weber, Dick............... 1975
Weber, Pete 1998
+ Welu, Billy 1975
Williams, Walter Ray Jr...... 1995
Zahn, Wayne............... 1981

Veterans

Allison, Glenn 1984
Asher, Barry............... 1988
Foremsky, Skee 1992
Guenther, Johnny........... 1986
+ Joseph, Joe................ 1985
Limongello, Mike 1994
Marzich, Andy.............. 1990
McCune, Don............... 1991
McGrath, Mike 1988
Schlegel, Ernie............. 1997
+ St. John, Jim 1989
Strampe, Bob 1987

Meritorious Service

+ Antenora, Joe.............. 1993
Archibald, John 1989
Clemens, Chuck............ 1994
Elias, Eddie 1976
Esposito, Frank............. 1975
Evans, Dick................ 1986
Firestone, Raymond......... 1987
Fisher, E.A. (Bud)........... 1984
+ Frantz, Lou 1978
Golden, Harry 1983
Hoffman, Ted Jr 1985
Jowdy, John 1988
Kelley, Joe................. 1989
Lichstein, Larry 1996
+ Nagy, Steve 1977
Pezzano, Chuck............ 1975
Reichert, Jack.............. 1992
+ Richards, Joe 1976
Schenkel, Chris 1976
Stitzlein, Lorraine........... 1980
Thompson, Al.............. 1991
Zeller, Roger............... 1995

American Bowling Congress

Established in 1941 and open to professional and amateur bowlers. **Eligibility:** Nominated bowlers must have competed in at least 20 years of ABC tournaments. Voting done by 170-member panel made up of ABC officials, Hall of Fame members and media representatives.

Class of 1998 (3): PERFORMANCE— **Barry Asher** and **Draold Meisel**. MERITORIOUS SERVICE— **Jack Reichert**.

Members are listed with years of induction; (+) indicates deceased members.

Performance

Allison, Glenn 1979
Anthony, Earl 1986
Asher, Barry............... 1998
+ Asplund, Harold 1978
Baer, Gordy 1987
Beach, Bill 1991
+ Benkovic, Frank............ 1958
Berlin, Mike 1994
+ Billick, George............. 1982
+ Blouin, Jimmy 1953
Bluth, Ray 1973
+ Bodis, Joe................. 1941
+ Bomar, Buddy 1966
+ Brandt, Allie............... 1960
+ Brosius, Eddie 1976
+ Bujack, Fred............... 1967
Bunetta, Bill 1968
Burton, Nelson Jr........... 1981
+ Burton, Nelson Sr 1964
+ Campi, Lou................ 1968
+ Carlson, Adolph 1941
Carter, Don 1970
+ Caruana, Frank 1977
+ Cassio, Marty 1972
+ Castellano, Graz........... 1976
+ Clause, Frank............. 1980
Cohn, Alfred 1985
+ Crimmins, Johnny 1962
Davis, Dave 1990
+ Daw, Charlie 1941
+ Day, Ned 1952
Dickinson, Gary............ 1992
+ Easter, Sarge 1963
Ellis, Don.................. 1981
+ Falcaro, Joe 1968
+ Faragalli, Lindy 1968
+ Fazio, Buzz 1963
Fehr, Steve 1993
+ Gersonde, Russ 1968
+ Gibson, Therm 1965
Godman, Jim 1987
Goike, Robert.............. 1996
Golembiewski, Billy......... 1979
Griffo, Greg 1995
Guenther, Johnny........... 1988
Hardwick, Billy 1985
Hart, Bob 1994
Hennessey, Tom 1976
Hoover, Dick 1974
Horn, Bud 1992
Howard, George............ 1986
Jackson, Eddie............. 1988
Johnson, Don 1982
Johnson, Earl 1987
+ Joseph, Joe................ 1969
+ Jouglard, Lee 1979
+ Kartheiser, Frank 1967
+ Kawolics, Ed 1968
+ Kissoff, Joe 1976
+ Klares, John 1982
+ Knox, Billy 1954
+ Koster, John 1941
+ Krems, Eddie 1973
Kristof, Joe 1968
+ Krumske, Paul............. 1968
+ Lange, Herb 1941
+ Lauman, Hank 1976
Lillard, Bill................. 1972
Lindemann, Tony 1979
+ Lindsey, Mort 1941
+ Lippe, Harry............... 1989
Lubanski, Ed............... 1971
Lucci, Vince Sr 1978
+ Marino, Hank.............. 1941
+ Martino, John.............. 1969
Marzich, Andy............. 1993
McGrath, Mike 1993
+ McMahon, Junie 1967
+ Meisel, Draold 1998
+ Mercurio, Skang 1967
+ Meyers, Norm 1984
+ Nagy, Steve 1963
Norris, Joe 1954
O'Donnell, Chuck 1968
Pappas, George 1989
+ Patterson, Pat 1974
Ritger, Dick 1984
+ Rogoznica, Andy.......... 1993
Salvino, Carmen 1979
Schissler, Les.............. 1991
Schlegel, Ernie............. 1997
Schroeder, Jim 1990
+ Schwoegler, Connie 1968
Semiz, Teata.............. 1991
+ Sielaff, Lou 1968
+ Sinke, Joe 1977
+ Sixty, Billy 1961
Smith, Harry............... 1978
+ Smith, Jimmy 1941
Soutar, Dave 1985
+ Sparando, Tony 1968
+ Spinella, Barney 1968
+ Steers, Harry 1941
Stefanich, Jim.............. 1983
+ Stein, Otto Jr 1971

Bowling (Cont.)

Stoudt, Bud ... 1991
Strampe, Bob ... 1977
+ Thoma, Sykes ... 1971
Toft, Rod ... 1991
Tountas, Pete ... 1989
+ Totsky, Mike ... 1996
Tucker, Bill ... 1988
Tuttle, Tommy ... 1995
+ Varipapa, Andy ... 1957
+ Ward, Walter ... 1959
Weber, Dick ... 1970
+ Welu, Billy ... 1975
+ Wilman, Joe ... 1951
+ Wolf, Phil ... 1961
Wonders, Rich ... 1990
+ Young, George ... 1959
Zahn, Wayne ... 1980
Zikes, Les ... 1983
+ Zunker, Gil ... 1941

Pioneers

+ Allen, Lafayette Jr. ... 1994
+ Briell, Frank ... 1996
+ Carow, Rev. Charles ... 1995
+ Celestine, Sydney ... 1993
+ Curtis, Thomas ... 1993
de Freitas, Eric ... 1994
Hall, William Sr. ... 1994
Hirashima, Hirohito ... 1995
+ Karpf, Samuel ... 1993
+ Moore, Henry ... 1996
+ Pasdeloup, Frank ... 1993
+ Rhodman, Bill ... 1997
+ Satow, Masao ... 1994
+ Schutte, Louis ... 1993
Shimada, Fuzzy ... 1997
Stein, Louis ... 1997
+ Thompson, William V. ... 1993
+ Timm, Dr. Henry ... 1993

Meritorious Service

+ Allen, Harold ... 1966
Archibald, John ... 1996
+ Baker, Frank ... 1975
+ Baumgarten, Elmer ... 1963
+ Bellisimo, Lou ... 1986
+ Bensinger, Bob ... 1969
+ Chase, LeRoy ... 1972
+ Coker, John ... 1980
+ Collier, Chuck ... 1963
+ Cruchon, Steve ... 1983
+ Ditzen, Walt ... 1973
+ Doehrman, Bill ... 1968
Elias, Eddie ... 1985
Esposito, Frank ... 1997
Evans, Dick ... 1992
Franklin, Bill ... 1992
+ Hagerty, Jack ... 1963
+ Hattstrom, H.A. (Doc) ... 1980
+ Hermann, Cornelius ... 1968
+ Howley, Pete ... 1941
+ Kennedy, Bob ... 1981
+ Langtry, Abe ... 1963
+ Levine, Sam ... 1971
+ Luby, David ... 1969
Luby, Mort Jr. ... 1988
+ Luby, Mort Sr. ... 1974
Matzelle, Al ... 1995
+ McCullough, Howard ... 1971
+ Patterson, Morehead ... 1985
+ Petersen, Louie ... 1963
Pezzano, Chuck ... 1982
Picchietti, Remo ... 1993
Pluckhahn, Bruce ... 1989
+ Raymer, Milt ... 1972
+ Reed, Elmer ... 1978
Reichert, Jack ... 1998
Rudo, Milt ... 1984
Schenkel, Chris ... 1988
+ Sweeney, Dennis ... 1974
Tessman, Roger ... 1994
+ Thum, Joe ... 1980
Weinstein, Sam ... 1970
+ Whitney, Eli ... 1975
Wolf, Fred ... 1976

Women's International Bowling Congress

Established in 1953. **Eligibility:** Performance nominees must have won at least one WIBC Championship Tournament title, a WIBC Queens tournament title or an international competition title and have bowled in at least 15 national WIBC Championship Tournaments (unless injury or illness cut career short).

Class of 1998 (3): PERFORMANCE—**Cindy C. Coburn** and **Ashie Gonzalez**; MERITORIOUS SERVICE—**Mitzi Herold**.

Members are listed with years of induction; (+) indicates deceased members.

Performance

Abel, Joy ... 1984
Adamek, Donna ... 1996
Ann, Patty ... 1995
Bolt, Mae ... 1978
Bouvia, Gloria ... 1987
Boxberger, Loa ... 1984
Buckner, Pam ... 1990
+ Burling, Catherine ... 1958
+ Burns, Nina ... 1977
Cantaline, Anita ... 1979
Carter, LaVerne ... 1977
Carter, Paula ... 1994
Coburn, Cindy C. ... 1998
Coburn, Doris ... 1976
Costello, Pat ... 1986
Costello, Patty ... 1989
Dryer, Pat ... 1978
Duval, Helen ... 1970
Fellmeth, Catherine ... 1970
Fothergill, Dotty ... 1980
+ Fritz, Deane ... 1966
Garms, Shirley ... 1971
Gianulias, Nikki ... 1997
Gloor, Olga ... 1976
Gonzalez, Ashie ... 1998
Graham, Linda ... 1992
Graham, Mary Lou ... 1989
+ Greenwald, Goldie ... 1953
Grinfelds, Vesma ... 1991
+ Harman, Janet ... 1985
+ Hartrick, Stella ... 1972
+ Hatch, Grayce ... 1953
Havlish, Jean ... 1987
+ Hoffman, Martha ... 1979
Holm, Joan ... 1974
+ Humphreys, Birdie ... 1979
Ignizio, Mildred ... 1975
Jacobson, D.D ... 1981
+ Jaeger, Emma ... 1953
Kelly, Annese ... 1985
+ Knechtges, Doris ... 1983
Kuczynski, Betty ... 1981
Ladewig, Marion ... 1964
Martin, Sylvia Wene ... 1966
Martorella, Millie ... 1975
+ Matthews, Merle ... 1974
+ McCutcheon, Floretta ... 1956
Merrick, Marge ... 1980
+ Mikiel, Val ... 1979
Miller, Carol ... 1997
+ Miller, Dorothy ... 1954
Mivelaz, Betty ... 1991
Mohacsi, Mary ... 1994
Morris, Betty ... 1983
Nichols, Lorrie ... 1989
Norman, Edie Jo ... 1993
Norton, Virginia ... 1988
Notaro, Phyllis ... 1979
Ortner, Bev ... 1972
+ Powers, Connie ... 1973
Rickard, Robbie ... 1994
+ Robinson, Leona ... 1969
Romeo, Robin ... 1995
+ Rump, Anita ... 1962
+ Ruschmeyer, Addie ... 1961
+ Ryan, Esther ... 1963
+ Sablatnik, Ethel ... 1979
+ Schulte, Myrtle ... 1965
+ Shablis, Helen ... 1977
Sill, Aleta ... 1996
+ Simon, Violet (Billy) ... 1960
+ Small, Tess ... 1971
+ Smith, Grace ... 1968
Soutar, Judy ... 1976
+ Stockdale, Louise ... 1953
Toepfer, Elvira ... 1976
+ Twyford, Sally ... 1964
+ Warmbier, Marie ... 1953
Wilkinson, Dorothy ... 1990
+ Winandy, Cecelia ... 1975
Zimmerman, Donna ... 1982

Meritorious Service

Baetz, Helen 1977
+ Baker, Helen 1989
+ Banker, Gladys 1994
+ Bayley, Clover 1992
+ Berger, Winifred 1976
+ Bohlen, Philena 1955
Borschuk, Lo 1988
+ Botkin, Freda 1986
+ Chapman, Emily 1957
+ Crowe, Alberta 1982
+ Dornblaser, Gertrude 1979
Duffy, Agnes 1987
Finke, Gertrude 1990
+ Fisk, Rae 1983
+ Haas, Dorothy 1977
Herold, Mitzi 1998
+ Higley, Margaret 1969
+ Hochstadter, Bee 1967
+ Kay, Nora 1964
+ Kelly, Ellen 1979
Kelone, Theresa 1978
+ Knepprath, Jeannette 1963
+ Lasher, Iolia 1967
Marrs, Mabel 1979
+ McBride, Bertha 1968
+ Menne, Catherine 1979
Mitchell, Flora 1996
+ Mraz, Jo 1959
O'Connor, Billie 1992
+ Phaler, Emma 1965
+ Porter, Cora 1986
+ Quin, Zoe 1979
+ Rishling, Gertrude 1972
Simone, Anne 1991
Sloan, Catherine 1985
+ Speck, Berdie 1966
Spitalnick, Mildred 1994
+ Spring, Alma 1979
+ Switzer, Pearl 1973
Todd, Trudy 1993
+ Veatch, Georgia 1974
+ White, Mildred 1975
+ Wood, Ann 1970

Ladies Pro Bowlers Hall of Fame

Established in 1995 by the Ladies Pro Bowlers Tour. The LPBT has since been renamed the Professional Women Bowlers Association. **Address:** Sam's Town Hotel, Gambling Hall and Bowling Center, 5111 Boulder Highway, Las Vegas, NV 89122. **Telephone:** (815) 332-5756.

Eligibility: Nominees in performance category must have at least five titles from organizations including All-Star, World Invitational, LPBT, WPBA, PWBA, TPA and LPBA. Voting done by 10-member committee of bowling writers appointed by LPBT president John Falzone.

Class of 1998 (4): PERFORMANCE—**Tish Johnson** and **Aleta Sill**. PIONEERS—**Joy Able** and **Bev Ortner**.

Members are listed with year of induction; (+) indicates deceased member.

Performance

Adamek, Donna 1995
Colburn-Carroll, Cindy 1997
Costello, Pat 1997
Costello, Patty 1995
Fothergill, Dotty 1995
Gianulias, Nikki 1996
Grinfelds, Vesma 1997
Johnson, Tish 1998
Ladewig, Marion 1995
Martorella, Millie 1995
Morris, Betty 1995
Nichols, Lorrie 1996
Romeo, Robin 1996
Sill, Aleta 1998
Wagner, Lisa 1996

Pioneers

Able, Joy 1998
Boxberger, Loa 1997
Carter, LaVerne 1995
Coburn, Doris 1996
Duval, Helen 1995
Garms, Shirley 1995
Ortner, Bev 1998
Soutar, Judy 1997
Zimmerman, Donna 1996

Builders

Buhler, Janet 1996
Keller, Pearl 1997
Robinson, Jeanette 1996
Sommer Jr., John 1997
+ Veatch, Georgia 1995

BOXING

International Boxing Hall of Fame

Established in 1989 and opened in 1990. **Address:** 1 Hall of Fame Drive, Canastota, NY 13032. **Telephone:** (315) 697-7095.

Eligibility: All nominees must be retired for five years. Voting done by 142-member panel made up of Boxing Writers' Association members and world-wide boxing historians.

Class of 1998 (13): MODERN ERA—**Sammy Angott** (featherweight), **Miguel Canto** (flyweight), **Antonio Cervantes** (welterweight), **Matthew Saad Muhammad** (light heavyweight). OLD TIMERS—**Joe Choynski** (heavyweight), **Frankie Genaro** (flyweight), **George "Kid" Lavigne** (lightweight), **Benny Lynch** (flyweight), **Sammy Mandell** (lightweight). PIONEERS—**Prof. Mike Donovan** (middleweight). NON-PARTICIPANTS— **William A. Brady** (manager), **Lou Duva** (manager/promoter) and **Herman Taylor** (promoter).

Members are listed with year of induction; (+) indicates deceased member.

Modern Era

Ali, Muhammad 1990
+ Angott, Sammy 1998
Arguello, Alexis 1992
+ Armstrong, Henry 1990
Basilio, Carmen 1990
Benitez, Wilfredo 1996
Benvenuti, Nino 1992
+ Berg, Jackie (Kid) 1994
+ Brown, Joe 1996
+ Burley, Charley 1992
Canto, Miguel 1998
+ Cerdan, Marcel 1991
Cervantes, Antonio 1998
+ Charles, Ezzard 1990
+ Conn, Billy 1990
+ Elorde, Gabriel (Flash) 1993
Foster, Bob 1990
Frazier, Joe 1990
Fullmer, Gene 1991
Gavilan, Kid 1990
Giardello, Joey 1993
Gomez, Wilfredo 1995
+ Graham, Billy 1992
+ Graziano, Rocky 1991
Griffith, Emile 1990
Hagler, Marvelous Marvin . . . 1993
Harado, Masahiko (Fighting) . 1995
Jack, Beau 1991
Jofre, Eder 1992
Johnson, Harold 1993
LaMotta, Jake 1990
Leonard, Sugar Ray 1997
+ Liston, Sonny 1991
+ Louis, Joe 1990
+ Marciano, Rocky 1990
Maxim, Joey 1994
Montgomery, Bob 1995
+ Monzon, Carlos 1990
Moore, Archie 1990

Boxing (Cont.)

Muhammad, Matthew Saad .1998
Napoles, Jose 1990
Norton, Ken 1992
Olivares, Ruben............1991
Ortiz, Carlos 1991
Ortiz, Manuel 1996
Patterson, Floyd............1991
Pep, Willie 1990
+ Perez, Pasqual.............1995
Pryor, Aaron...............1996
+ Robinson, Sugar Ray........1990
+ Rodriguez, Luis 1997
Saddler, Sandy 1990
+ Sanchez, Salvadore 1991
Schmeling, Max.............1992
Spinks, Michael............1994
+ Tiger, Dick 1991
Torres, Jose................1997
+ Walcott, Jersey Joe 1990
+ Williams, Ike 1990
+ Wright, Chalky 1997
+ Zale, Tony.................1991
Zarate, Carlos 1994
+ Zivic, Fritzie 1993

Old-Timers

Ambers, Lou 1992
+ Attell, Abe.................1990
+ Baer, Max..................1995
+ Britton, Jack 1990
+ Brown, Panama Al 1992
+ Burns, Tommy..............1996
+ Canzoneri, Tony 1990
+ Carpentier, Georges........1991
+ Chocolate, Kid.............1991
+ Choynski, Joe..............1998
+ Corbett, James J............1990
+ Darcy, Les.................1993
+ Delaney, Jack..............1996
+ Dempsey, Jack 1990
+ Dempsey, Jack (Nonpareil) ..1992
+ Dillon, Jack................1995
+ Dixon, George.............1990
+ Driscoll, Jem...............1990
+ Dundee, Johnny............1991
+ Fitzsimmons, Bob...........1990
+ Flowers, Theodore (Tiger)....1993
+ Gans, Joe 1990
+ Genaro, Frankie 1998
+ Gibbons, Mike.............1992
+ Gibbons, Tommy 1993
+ Greb, Harry 1990
+ Griffo, Young 1991
+ Herman, Pete 1997
+ Jackson, Peter..............1990
+ Jeanette, Joe...............1997
+ Jeffries, James J 1990
+ Johnson, Jack..............1990
+ Ketchel, Stanley............1990
+ Kilbane, Johnny 1995
+ LaBarba, Fidel 1996
+ Langford, Sam 1990
+ Leonard, Benny 1990
+ Lavigne, George (Kid) 1998
+ Lewis, John Henry 1994
+ Lewis, Ted (Kid) 1992
+ Loughran, Tommy 1991
+ Lynch, Benny 1998
+ Mandell, Sammy 1998
+ McAuliffe, Jack 1995
+ McCoy, Charles (Kid) 1991
+ McFarland, Packey 1992
+ McGovern, Terry 1990
McLarnin, Jimmy 1991
+ Miller, Freddie 1997
+ Nelson, Battling............1992
+ O'Brien, Philadelphia Jack...1994
+ Rosenbloom, Maxie 1993
+ Ross, Barney...............1990
+ Ryan, Tommy 1991
+ Sharkey, Jack 1994
+ Stribling, Young 1996
+ Tunney, Gene..............1990
+ Villa, Pancho 1994
+ Walcott, Jersey Joe 1991
+ Walker, Mickey 1990
+ Welsh, Freddie.............1997
+ Wilde, Jimmy..............1990
+ Williams, Kid..............1996
+ Wills, Harry 1992

Pioneers

+ Belcher, Jem 1992
+ Brain, Ben.................1994
+ Broughton, Jack 1990
+ Burke, James (Deaf).........1992
+ Cribb, Tom 1991
+ Donovan, Prof. Mike........1998
+ Duffy, Paddy...............1994
+ Figg, James 1992
+ Jackson, Gentleman John....1992
+ Johnson, Tom 1995
+ King, Tom 1992
+ Langham, Nat 1992
+ Mace, Jem 1990
+ Mendoza, Daniel 1990
+ Molineaux, Tom............1997
+ Morrisey, John 1996
+ Pearce, Henry 1993
+ Sam, Dutch................1997
+ Sayers, Tom 1990
Spring, Tom 1992
+ Sullivan, John L 1990
+ Thompson, William.........1991
+ Ward, Jem 1995

Non-Participants

+ Andrews, Thomas S 1992
+ Arcel, Ray.................1991
+ Blackburn, Jack 1992
+ Brady, William A...........1998
Brenner, Teddy.............1993
+ Chambers, John Graham 1990
Clancy, Gil................1993
+ Coffroth, James W..........1991
+ D'Amato, Cus..............1995
+ Donovan, Arthur 1993
Dundee, Angelo............1992
Dundee, Chris 1994
+ Dunphy, Don 1993
Duva, Lou 1998
+ Egan, Pierce...............1991
+ Fleischer, Nat..............1990
+ Fox, Richard K. 1997
Futch, Eddie 1994
+ Goldman, Charley 1992
+ Goldstein, Ruby............1994
+ Humphreys, Joe 1997
+ Jacobs, Jimmy 1993
+ Jacobs, Mike 1990
+ Kearns, Jack (Doc)..........1990
King, Don 1997
+ Liebling, A.J 1992
+ Lonsdale, Lord 1990
Markson, Harry.............1992
Mercante, Arthur...........1995
+ Muldoon, William..........1996
Odd, Gilbert 1995
+ Parker, Dan 1996
+ Parnassus, George 1991
+ Queensberry, Marquis of....1990
+ Rickard, Tex 1990
+ Siler, George 1995
+ Solomons, Jack 1995
Steward, Emanuel..........1996
+ Taub, Sam.................1994
+ Taylor, Herman 1998
+ Walker, James J. (Jimmy) 1992

Old *Ring* Hall Members Not in Int'l. Boxing Hall

Nat Fleischer, the late founder and editor-in-chief of *The Ring*, established his magazine's Boxing Hall of Fame in 1954, but it was abandoned after the 1987 inductions. One hundred and ten members of the old *Ring* Hall have been elected to the International Hall since 1989. The 49 boxers and one sportswriter who have yet to be elected to the International Hall are listed below with their year of induction into the *Ring* Hall.

Modern Group

+ Apostoli, Fred.............1978
+ Braddock, James J..........1964
+ Escobar, Sixto 1975
+ Garcia, Ceferino 1977
+ Jenkins, Lew 1976
+ Lesnevich, Gus.............1973
+ Petrolle, Billy...............1962
+ Shirai, Yoshio..............1977
+ Tendler, Lew 1961

Old-Timers

+ Berlenbach, Paul 1971
+ Britt, Jimmy 1976
+ Chaney, George (K.O.) 1974
+ Corbett, Young II 1965
+ Coulon, Johnny 1965
+ Fields, Jackie 1977
+ Houck, Leo 1969
+ Jeffra, Harry 1982
+ Kid, The Dixie 1975
+ Klaus, Frank 1974
+ Levinsky, Battling 1966
+ Maher, Peter. 1978
+ McVey, Sam 1986
+ Mitchell, Charley 1957
+ Ortiz, Manuel 1985
+ Papke, Billy. 1972
+ Ritchie, Willie. 1962
+ Root, Jack 1961
+ Sharkey, Tom 1959
+ Smith, Jeff 1969
+ Taylor, Bud 1986
+ Willard, Jess. 1977
+ Wolgast, Ad. 1958

Pioneers

+ Aaron, Barney (Young) 1967
+ Chambers, Arthur 1954
+ Chandler, Tom 1972
+ Clark, Nobby 1971
+ Collyer, Sam 1964
+ Donnelly, Dan 1960
+ Goss, Joe 1969
+ Gully, John 1959
+ Heenan, John C. 1954
+ Hyer, Jacob 1968
+ Hyer, Tom 1954
+ Jackling, Thomas 1985
+ Kilrain, Jack 1965
+ Molineaux, Tom 1958
+ Price, Ned. 1962
+ Richmond, Bill 1956
+ Ryan, Paddy. 1973

Non-Participant

+ Daniel, Dan (sportswriter). . . .1977

FOOTBALL

College Football Hall of Fame

Established in 1955 by the National Football Foundation. **Address:** 111 South St. Joseph St., South Bend, IN 46601. **Telephone:** (219) 235-9999.

Eligibility: Nominated players must be out of college 10 years and a first team All-America pick by a major selector during their careers; coaches must be retired three years. Voting done by 12-member panel of athletic directors, conference and bowl officials and media representatives. 1996 was the first year representatives from NCAA Div. I-AA, II, and III, and the NAIA are eligible for induction.

Class of 1998 (9): LARGE COLLEGE—OT/DT **Kenneth Dement**, SE Missouri St. (1951-54); QB **Richard Ritchie**, Texas A&M (1973-77); DB **Donnie Shell**, South Carolina St. (1970-73). SMALL COLLEGE— QB **Jeff Bentrim**, North Dakota St. (1983-86); DB **Tom Deery**, Widener (1979-81), OG/DT **Larry Pugh**, Westminster, Pa. (1961-64). COACHES—**Bob Keade**, Augustana, Ill. (1979-94); **Chuck Klausing**, Indiana, Pa. (1964-69), Carnegie Mellon (1976-94); **Ad Rutschman**, Linfield (1968-91).

Note: Bobby Dodd and **Amos Alonzo Stagg** are the only members to be honored as both players and coaches.

Players are listed with final year they played in college and coaches are listed with year of induction; (+) indicates deceased members.

Players

+ Abell, Earl-Colgate 1915
Agase, Alex-Purdue/Ill 1946
+ Agganis, Harry-Boston U 1952
Albert, Frank-Stanford. 1941
+ Aldrich, Ki-TCU 1938
+ Aldrich, Malcolm-Yale. 1921
+ Alexander, Joe-Syracuse. 1920
Alworth, Lance-Arkansas 1961
+ Ameche, Alan-Wisconsin 1954
+ Ames, Knowlton-Princeton . . .1889
Amling, Warren-Ohio St. 1946
Anderson, Dick-Colorado. . . .1967
Anderson, Donny-Tex.Tech . . .1966
+ Anderson, Hunk-N.Dame 1921
Atkins, Doug-Tennessee. 1952
Babich, Bob-Miami-OH 1968
+ Bacon, Everett-Wesleyan 1912
+ Bagnell, Reds-Penn 1950
+ Baker, Hobey-Princeton. 1913
+ Baker, John-USC 1931
+ Baker, Moon-N'western 1926
Baker, Terry-Oregon St 1962
+ Ballin, Harold-Princeton 1914
+ Banker, Bill-Tulane 1929
Banonis, Vince-Detroit. 1941
+ Barnes, Stan-California. 1921
+ Barrett, Charles-Cornell. 1915
+ Baston, Bert-Minnesota 1916
+ Battles, Cliff-WV Wesleyan . .1931
Baugh, Sammy-TCU 1936
Baughan, Maxie-Ga.Tech. . . .1959
+ Bausch, James-Kansas. 1930
Beagle, Ron-Navy 1955
Beban, Gary-UCLA 1967
Bechtol, Hub-Texas 1946
Beck, Ray-Ga. Tech 1951
+ Beckett, John-Oregon 1916
Bednarik, Chuck-Penn 1948
Behm, Forrest-Nebraska 1940
Bell, Bobby-Minnesota 1962
Bellino, Joe-Navy. 1960
Below, Marty-Wisconsin. 1923
+ Benbrook, Al-Michigan. 1910
+ Berry, Charlie-Lafayette. 1924
Bertelli, Angelo-N.Dame. 1943
Berwanger, Jay-Chicago 1935
+ Bettencourt, L.-St.Mary's 1927
Biletnikoff, Fred-Fla.St. 1964
Blanchard, Doc-Army 1946
+ Blozis, Al-Georgetown 1942
Bock, Ed-Iowa St 1938
Bomar, Lynn-Vanderbilt 1924
+ Bomeisler, Bo-Yale 1913
+ Booth, Albie-Yale 1931
+ Borries, Fred-Navy 1934
+ Bosley, Bruce-West Va. 1955
Bosseler, Don-Miami,FL. 1956
Bottari, Vic-California 1938
+ Boynton, Ben-Williams 1920
+ Brewer, Charles-Harvard 1895
+ Bright, Johnny-Drake 1951
Brodie, John-Stanford 1956
+ Brooke, George-Penn 1895
Brown, Bob-Nebraska 1963
Brown, Geo-Navy/S.Diego St.1947
+ Brown, Gordon-Yale 1900
Brown, Jim-Syracuse 1956
+ Brown, John, Jr.-Navy 1913
+ Brown, Johnny Mack-Ala 1925
+ Brown, Tay-USC. 1932
+ Bunker, Paul-Army 1902
Burford, Chris-Stanford 1959
Burton, Ron-N'western 1959
Butkus, Dick-Illinois 1964
+ Butler, Robert-Wisconsin 1912
+ Cafego, George-Tenn 1939
+ Cagle, Red-SWLa/Army. 1929
+ Cain, John-Alabama 1932
Cameron, Ed-Wash.& Lee . . .1924
+ Campbell, David-Harvard . . .1901
Campbell, Earl-Texas. 1977
+ Cannon, Jack-N.Dame 1929
Cappelletti, John-Penn St 1973
+ Carideo, Frank-N.Dame 1930
+ Carney, Charles-Illinois 1921
Caroline, J.C.-Illinois 1954
Carpenter, Bill-Army 1959
+ Carpenter, Hunter-Va.Tech . . .1905
Carroll, Chas.-Washington. . .1928
Casanova, Tommy-LSU 1971
+ Casey, Edward-Harvard 1919
Cassady, Howard-Ohio St . . .1955
+ Chamberlin, Guy-Neb. 1915
Chapman, Sam-California . . .1938
Chappuis, Bob-Michigan 1947
+ Christman, Paul-Missouri 1940
+ Clark, Dutch-Colo. Col. 1929
Cleary, Paul-USC 1947
+ Clevenger, Zora-Indiana. 1903

Football (Cont.)

Cloud, Jack-Wm. & Mary ...1948
+ Cochran, Gary-Princeton 1897
+ Cody, Josh-Vanderbilt 1919
Coleman, Don-Mich.St 1951
+ Conerly, Charlie-Miss 1947
Connor, George-HC/ND 1947
+ Corbin, William-Yale........1888
Corbus, William-Stanford....1933
+ Cowan, Hector-Princeton 1889
+ Coy, Edward (Tad)-Yale 1909
+ Crawford, Fred-Duke........1933
Crow, John David-Tex.A&M..1957
+ Crowley, Jim-Notre Dame....1924
Csonka, Larry-Syracuse 1967
Cutter, Slade-Navy 1934
+ Czarobski, Ziggie-N.Dame ..1947
Dale, Carroll-Va.Tech 1959
+ Dalrymple, Gerald-Tulane ...1931
+ Dalton, John-Navy..........1911
+ Daly, Chas.-Harvard/Army ..1902
Daniell, Averell-Pitt..........1936
+ Daniell, James-Ohio St 1941
+ Davies, Tom-Pittsburgh 1921
+ Davis, Ernie-Syracuse 1961
Davis, Glenn-Army 1946
Davis, Robert-Ga.Tech 1947
Dawkins, Pete-Army 1958
Dement, Kenneth, SE Mo. St..1998
DeLong, Steve-Tennessee 1964
+ DeRogatis, Al-Duke 1948
+ DesJardien, Paul-Chicago....1914
+ Devine, Aubrey-Iowa 1921
+ DeWitt, John-Princeton 1903
Dial, Buddy-Rice 1958
Ditka, Mike-Pittsburgh 1960
Dobbs, Glenn-Tulsa.........1942
+ Dodd, Bobby-Tennessee 1930
Donan, Holland-Princeton....1950
+ Donchess, Joseph-Pitt........1929
Dorsett, Tony-Pitt............1976
+ Dougherty, Nathan-Tenn.....1909
Drahos, Nick-Cornell........1940
+ Driscoll, Paddy-N'western ...1917
+ Drury, Morley-USC 1927
Dudley, Bill-Virginia.........1941
Duncan, Randy-Iowa.........1958
Easley, Kenny-UCLA 1980
+ Eckersall, Walter-Chicago ...1906
+ Edwards, Turk-Wash.St......1931
+ Edwards, Wm.-Princeton 1899
+ Eichenlaub, Ray-N.Dame....1914
Eisenhauer, Steve-Navy 1953
Elkins, Larry-Baylor 1964
Elliott, Bump-Mich/Purdue ...1947
Elliott, Pete-Michigan........1948
Elmendorf, Dave-Tex. A&M ..1970
Evans, Ray-Kansas..........1947
+ Exendine, Albert-Carlisle 1907
Falaschi, Nello-S.Clara......1936
Fears, Tom-S.Clara/UCLA ...1947
+ Feathers, Beattie-Tenn 1933
Fenimore, Bob-Okla.St 1946
+ Fenton, Doc-LSU............1909
Ferguson, Bob-Ohio St. 1961
Ferraro, John-USC 1944
Fesler, Wes-Ohio St.........1930
+ Fincher, Bill-Ga.Tech 1920
Fischer, Bill-Notre Dame.....1948
+ Fish, Hamilton-Harvard......1909
+ Fisher, Robert-Harvard 1911
+ Flowers, Allen-Ga.Tech......1920

Flowers, Charlie-Ole Miss....1959
+ Fortmann Danny-Colgate 1935
Francis, Sam-Nebraska 1936
Franco, Ed-Fordham 1937
+ Frank, Clint-Yale............1937
Franz, Rodney-California 1949
Frederickson, Tucker-Auburn .1964
+ Friedman, Benny-Michigan ..1926
Gabriel, Roman-N.C. State ..1961
Gain, Bob-Kentucky 1950
+ Galiffa, Arnold-Army 1949
Gallarneau, Hugh-Stanford ..1940
+ Garbisch, Edgar-W.& J./Army.1924
Garrett, Mike-USC..........1965
+ Gelbert, Charles-Penn.......1896
+ Geyer, Forest-Oklahoma.....1915
Gibbs, Jake-Miss 1960
Giel, Paul-Minnesota........1953
Gifford, Frank-USC 1951
+ Gilbert, Walter-Auburn 1936
Gilmer, Harry-Alabama 1947
+ Gipp, George-N.Dame 1920
+ Gladchuk, Chet-Boston Col ..1940
Glass, Bill-Baylor 1956
Glover, Rich-Nebraska 1972
Goldberg, Marshall-Pitt......1938
Goodreault, Gene-BC 1940
+ Gordon, Walter-Calif 1918
+ Governali, Paul-Columbia ...1942
Grabowski, Jim-Illinois 1965
Graham, Otto-N'western 1943
+ Grange, Red-Illinois.........1925
+ Grayson, Bobby-Stanford....1935
Green, Hugh-Pitt 1980
+ Green, Jack-Tulane/Army....1945
Greene, Joe-N.Texas St 1968
Griese, Bob-Purdue 1966
Griffin, Archie-Ohio St 1975
Groom, Jerry-Notre Dame ...1950
+ Gulick, Merle-Toledo/Hobart.1929
+ Guyon, Joe-Ga.Tech 1918
Hadl, John-Kansas..........1961
+ Hale, Edwin-Miss.College ...1921
Hall, Parker-Miss 1938
Ham, Jack-Penn St..........1970
+ Hamilton, Bob-Stanford......1935
+ Hamilton, Tom-Navy 1926
+ Hanson, Vic-Syracuse 1926
+ Harder, Pat-Wisconsin 1942
+ Hardwick, Tack-Harvard.....1914
+ Hare, T.Truxton-Penn 1900
+ Harley, Chick-Ohio St........1919
+ Harmon, Tom-Michigan 1940
+ Harpster, Howard-Carnegie..1928
+ Hart, Edward-Princeton......1911
Hart, Leon-Notre Dame......1949
Hartman, Bill-Georgia.......1937
+ Hazel, Homer-Rutgers 1924
+ Hazeltine, Matt-Calif........1954
+ Healey, Ed.-Dartmouth 1916
+ Heffelfinger, Pudge-Yale 1891
+ Hein, Mel-Washington St....1930
+ Heinrich, Don-Washington 1952
Hendricks, Ted-Miami,FL.....1968
+ Henry, Pete-Wash&Jeff 1919
+ Herschberger, C.-Chicago ...1898
+ Herwig, Robert-Calif........1937
+ Heston, Willie-Michigan.....1904
+ Hickman, Herman-Tenn......1931
+ Hickok, William-Yale........1894
Hill, Dan-Duke 1938

+ Hillebrand, Art-Princeton 1899
+ Hinkey, Frank-Yale..........1894
Hinkle, Carl-Vanderbilt 1937
Hinkle, Clarke-Bucknell......1931
Hirsch, Elroy-Wisc./Mich....1943
+ Hitchcock, James-Auburn 1932
Hoffmann, Frank-N.Dame ...1931
+ Hogan, James J.-Yale 1904
+ Holland, Brud-Cornell.......1938
+ Holleder, Don-Army.........1955
+ Hollenback, Bill-Penn........1908
Holovak, Mike-Boston Col ...1942
Holub, E.J.-Texas Tech.......1960
Hornung, Paul-N.Dame 1956
+ Horrell, Edwin-California 1924
+ Horvath, Les-Ohio St........1944
+ Howe, Arthur-Yale..........1911
+ Howell, Dixie-Alabama......1934
+ Hubbard, Cal-Centenary 1926
+ Hubbard, John-Amherst 1906
+ Hubert, Pooley-Ala..........1925
Huff, Sam-West Virginia.....1955
Humble, Weldon-Rice 1946
Hunley, Ricky-Arizona.......1983
+ Hunt, Joe-Texas A&M 1927
Huntington, Ellery-Colgate ...1914
+ Hutson, Don-Alabama.......1934
+ Ingram, Jonas-Navy 1906
+ Isbell, Cecil-Purdue 1937
+ Jablonsky, J.-Army/Wash....1933
+ Janowicz, Vic-Ohio St.......1951
+ Jenkins, Darold-Missouri.....1941
+ Jensen, Jackie-California 1948
+ Joesting, Herbert-Minn 1927
Johnson, Bob-Tennessee 1967
+ Johnson, Jimmie-Carlisle/
Northwestern 1903
Johnson, Ron-Michigan......1968
+ Jones, Calvin-Iowa..........1955
+ Jones, Gomer-Ohio St.......1935
Jordan, Lee Roy-Alabama....1962
+ Juhan, Frank-U.of South 1910
Justice, Charlie-N.Car.......1949
+ Kaer, Mort-USC 1926
Karras, Alex-Iowa 1957
Kavanaugh, Ken-LSU........1939
+ Kaw, Edgar-Cornell.........1922
Kazmaier, Dick-Princeton 1951
+ Keck, James-Princeton.......1921
Kelley, Larry-Yale 1936
+ Kelly, Wild Bill-Montana.....1926
Kenna, Doug-Army 1944
+ Kerr, George-Boston Col 1941
+ Ketcham, Henry-Yale........1913
Keyes, Leroy-Purdue 1968
+ Killinger, Glenn-Penn St 1921
+ Kilpatrick, John-Yale 1910
Kimbrough, John-Tex A&M...1940
+ Kinard, Frank-Mississippi 1937
+ King, Phillip-Princeton 1893
+ Kinnick, Nile-Iowa..........1939
+ Kipke, Harry-Michigan 1923
+ Kitzmiller, John-Oregon......1930
+ Koch, Barton-Baylor 1931
+ Koppisch, Walt-Columbia ...1924
Kramer, Ron-Michigan 1956
Kroll, Alex-Rutgers 1961
Krueger, Charlie-Tex. A&M ..1957
Kutner, Malcolm-Texas 1941
Kwalick, Ted-Penn St........1968
+ Lach, Steve-Duke 1941

+ Lane, Myles-Dartmouth 1927
Lattner, Johnny-N.Dame 1953
Lauricella, Hank-Tenn 1952
+ Lautenschlaeger, Les-Tulane .. 1925
+ Layden, Elmer-N.Dame 1924
+ Layne, Bobby-Texas 1947
+ Lea, Langdon-Princeton 1895
LeBaron, Eddie-Pacific 1949
+ Leech, James-VMI 1920
+ Lester, Darrell-TCU 1935
Lilly, Bob-TCU 1960
Little, Floyd-Syracuse 1966
+ Lio, Augie-Georgetown 1940
+ Locke, Gordon-Iowa 1922
+ Lourie, Don-Princeton 1921
Lucas, Richie-Penn St 1959
+ Luckman, Sid-Columbia 1938
Lujack, Johnny-N.Dame 1947
+ Lund, Pug-Minnesota 1934
Lynch, Jim-Notre Dame 1966
+ Macomber, Bart-Illinois 1915
MacLeod, Robert-Dart. 1938
Maegle, Dick-Rice 1954
+ Mahan, Eddie-Harvard 1915
Majors, John-Tennessee 1956
+ Mallory, William-Yale 1923
Mancha, Vaughn-Ala 1947
+ Mann, Gerald-SMU 1927
Manning, Archie-Miss. 1970
Manske, Edgar-N'western ... 1933
Marinaro, Ed-Cornell 1971
Markov, Vic-Washington 1937
+ Marshall, Bobby-Minn 1906
Martin, Jim-Notre Dame 1949
Matson, Ollie-San Fran 1952
Matthews, Ray-TCU 1927
+ Maulbetsch, John-Mich 1914
+ Mauthe, Pete-Penn St. 1912
+ Maxwell, Robert-Chicago/ Swarthmore 1906
McAfee, George-Duke 1939
McAfee, Ken-Notre Dame ... 1977
+ McClung, Thomas-Yale 1891
McColl, Bill-Stanford 1951
+ McCormick, Jim-Princeton ... 1907
McDonald, Tommy-Okla 1956
+ McDowall, Jack-N.C.State ... 1927
McElhenny, Hugh-Wash 1951
+ McEver, Gene-Tennessee 1931
+ McEwan, John-Army 1916
McFadden, Banks-Clemson .. 1939
McFadin, Bud-Texas 1950
McGee, Mike-Duke 1959
+ McGinley, Edward-Penn 1924
+ McGovern, John-Minn 1910
McGraw, Thurman-Colo.St. .. 1949
+ McKeever, Mike-USC 1960
+ McLaren, George-Pitt 1918
+ McMillan, Dan-USC/Calif ... 1922
+ McMillin, Bo-Centre 1921
+ McWhorter, Bob-Georgia ... 1913
+ Mercer, LeRoy-Penn 1912
Meredith, Don-SMU 1959
Merritt, Frank-Army 1943
+ Metzger, Bert-N.Dame 1930
+ Meylan, Wayne-Nebraska ... 1967
Michaels, Lou-Kentucky 1957
Michels, John-Tennessee 1952
Mickal, Abe-LSU 1935
Miller, Creighton-N.Dame ... 1943
+ Miller, Don-Notre Dame 1924
+ Miller, Eugene-Penn St 1913
+ Miller, Fred-Notre Dame 1928

Miller, Rip-Notre Dame 1924
Millner, Wayne-N.Dame 1935
+ Milstead, C.A.-Wabash/Yale .. 1923
+ Minds, John-Penn 1897
Minisi, Skip-Penn/Navy 1947
Modzelewski, Dick-Md. 1952
+ Moffat, Alex-Princeton 1883
+ Molinski, Ed-Tenn 1940
Montgomery, Cliff-Columbia . 1933
Moomaw, Donn-UCLA 1952
+ Morley, William-Columbia ... 1902
Morris, George-Ga.Tech. 1952
Morris, Larry-Ga.Tech 1954
+ Morton, Bill-Dartmouth 1931
Morton, Craig-California 1964
+ Moscrip, Monk-Stanford 1935
+ Muller, Brick-California 1922
+ Nagurski, Bronko-Minn 1929
+ Nevers, Ernie-Stanford 1925
+ Newell, Marshall-Harvard ... 1893
Newman, Harry-Michigan ... 1932
Newsome, Ozzie-Alabama .. 1977
Nielson, Gifford-BYU 1977
Nobis, Tommy-Texas 1965
Nomellini, Leo-Minnesota 1949
+ Oberlander, Andrew-Dart ... 1925
+ O'Brien, Davey-TCU 1938
+ O'Dea, Pat-Wisconsin 1899
Odell, Bob-Penn 1943
+ O'Hearn, Jack-Cornell 1915
Olds, Robin-Army 1942
+ Oliphant, Elmer-Army/Pur ... 1917
Olsen, Merlin-Utah St 1961
Onkotz, Dennis-Penn St. 1969
+ Oosterbaan, Bennie-Mich ... 1927
O'Rourke, Charles-BC 1940
+ Orsi, John-Colgate 1931
+ Osgood, Win-Cornell/Penn .. 1892
Osmanski, Bill-Holy Cross ... 1938
+ Owen, George-Harvard 1922
Owens, Jim-Oklahoma 1949
Owens, Steve-Oklahoma 1969
Page, Alan-Notre Dame 1966
Pardee, Jack-Texas A&M 1956
Parilli, Babe-Kentucky 1951
Parker, Ace-Duke 1936
Parker, Jackie-Miss.St 1953
Parker, Jim-Ohio St 1956
+ Pazzetti, Vince-Lehigh 1912
+ Peabody, Chub-Harvard 1941
+ Peck, Robert-Pittsburgh 1916
Pellegrini, Bob-Maryland 1955
+ Pennock, Stan-Harvard 1914
Pfann, George-Cornell 1923
+ Phillips, H.D.-Sewanee 1904
Phillips, Loyd-Arkansas 1966
Pihos, Pete-Indiana 1946
Pingel, John-Michigan St 1938
+ Pinckert, Erny-USC 1931
Plunkett, Jim-Stanford 1970
+ Poe, Arthur-Princeton 1899
+ Pollard, Fritz-Brown 1916
Poole, B.-Miss/NC/Army 1947
Powell, Marvin-USC 1976
Pregulman, Merv-Michigan .. 1943
+ Price, Eddie-Tulane 1949
+ Pund, Peter-Georgia Tech 1928
Ramsey, G.-Wm&Mary 1942
Redman, Rick-Wash 1964
+ Reeds, Claude-Oklahoma ... 1913
Reid, Mike-Penn St. 1969
Reid, Steve-Northwestern 1936
+ Reid, William-Harvard 1899

Reifsnyder, Bob-Navy 1958
Renfro, Mel-Oregon 1963
+ Rentner, Pug-N'western 1932
+ Reynolds, Bob-Stanford 1935
+ Reynolds, Bobby-Nebraska .. 1952
Richter, Les-California 1951
Richter, Pat-Wisconsin 1962
+ Riley, Jack-Northwestern 1931
Rimington, Dave-Nebraska .. 1982
+ Rinehart, Chas.-Lafayette 1897
Ritchie, Richard-Tex.A&M 1998
Roberts, J. D.-Oklahoma 1953
+ Robeson, Paul-Rutgers 1918
Robinson, Dave-Penn St. 1962
Robinson, Jerry-UCLA 1978
+ Rodgers, Ira-West Va. 1919
+ Rogers, Ed-Carlisle/Minn 1903
Rogers, George-S. Carolina .. 1980
Romig, Joe-Colorado 1961
+ Rosenberg, Aaron-USC 1933
Rote, Kyle-SMU 1950
+ Routt, Joe-Texas A&M 1937
+ Salmon, Red-Notre Dame 1903
+ Sauer, George-Nebraska 1933
Savitsky, George-Penn 1947
Saxton, Jimmy-Texas 1961
Sayers, Gale-Kansas 1964
Scarbath, Jack-Maryland 1952
+ Scarlett, Hunter-Penn 1908
Schloredt, Bob-Wash 1960
+ Schoonover, Wear-Ark. 1929
+ Schreiner, Dave-Wisconsin ... 1942
+ Schultz, Germany-Mich 1908
+ Schwab, Dutch-Lafayette 1922
+ Schwartz, Marchy-N.Dame .. 1931
+ Schwegler, Paul-Wash 1931
Scott, Clyde-Navy/Arkansas . 1948
Scott, Richard-Navy 1947
Scott, Tom-Virginia 1953
+ Seibels, Henry-Sewanee 1899
Sellers, Ron-Florida St 1968
Selmon, Lee Roy-Okla 1975
+ Shakespeare, Bill-N.Dame ... 1935
Shell, Donnie-S.Carolina St... 1998
+ Shelton, Murray-Cornell 1915
+ Shevlin, Tom-Yale 1905
+ Shively, Bernie-Illinois 1926
+ Simons, Monk-Tulane 1934
Simpson, O.J.-USC 1968
Sims, Billy-Oklahoma 1979
Singletary, Mike-Baylor 1980
Sington, Fred-Alabama 1930
+ Sinkwich, Frank-Georgia 1942
+ Sitko, Emil-Notre Dame 1949
+ Skladany, Joe-Pittsburgh 1933
+ Slater, Duke-Iowa 1921
+ Smith, Bruce-Minnesota 1941
Smith, Bubba-Michigan St ... 1966
+ Smith, Clipper-N.Dame 1927
+ Smith, Ernie-USC 1932
Smith, Harry-USC 1939
Smith, Jim Ray-Baylor 1954
Smith, Riley-Alabama 1935
+ Smith, Vernon-Georgia 1931
+ Snow, Neil-Michigan 1901
Sparlis, Al-UCLA 1945
+ Spears, Clarence-Dart. 1915
Spears, W.D.-Vanderbilt 1927
+ Sprackling, Wm.-Brown 1911
+ Sprague, Bud-Army/Texas ... 1928
Spurrier, Steve-Florida 1966
Stafford, Harrison-Texas 1932
+ Stagg, Amos Alonzo-Yale 1889

Football (Cont.)

+ Starcevich, Max-Wash 1936
Staubach, Roger-Navy 1964
+ Steffen, Walter-Chicago 1908
Steffy, Joe-Tenn/Army 1947
+ Stein, Herbert-Pitt 1921
Steuber, Bob-Missouri 1943
+ Stevens, Mal-Yale 1923
Stillwagon, Jim-Ohio St. 1970
+ Stinchcomb, Pete-Ohio St 1920
+ Stevenson, Vincent-Penn 1905
Strom, Brock-Air Force 1959
+ Strong, Ken-NYU 1928
+ Strupper, Ev-Ga.Tech 1917
+ Stuhldreher, Harry-N.Dame 1924
+ Sturhan, Herb-Yale 1926
+ Stydahar, Joe-West Va 1935
+ Suffridge, Bob-Tennessee 1940
+ Suhey, Steve-Penn St 1947
Sullivan, Pat-Auburn 1971
+ Sundstrom, Frank-Cornell 1923
Swann, Lynn-USC 1973
+ Swanson, Clarence-Neb. 1921
+ Swiacki, Bill-Columbia/HC 1947
Swink, Jim-TCU 1956
Taliafarro, Geo.-Indiana 1948
Tarkenton, Fran-Georgia 1960
+ Tavener, John-Indiana 1944
+ Taylor, Chuck-Stanford 1942
Thomas, Aurelius-Ohio St 1957
+ Thompson, Joe-Pittsburgh 1907
+ Thorne, Samuel-Yale 1895
+ Thorpe, Jim-Carlisle 1912
+ Ticknor, Ben-Harvard 1930
+ Tigert, John-Vanderbilt 1904
Tinsley, Gaynell-LSU 1936
Tipton, Eric-Duke 1938
+ Tonnemaker, Clayton-Minn 1949
+ Torrey, Bob-Pennsylvania 1905
+ Travis, Brick-Missouri 1920
Trippi, Charley-Georgia 1946
+ Tryon, Edward-Colgate 1925
Tubbs, Jerry-Oklahoma 1956
Turner, Bulldog-H.Simmons 1939
Twilley, Howard-Tulsa 1965
+ Utay, Joe-Texas A&M 1907
+ Van Brocklin, Norm-Ore 1948
+ Van Sickel, Dale-Florida 1929
+ Van Surdam, H.-Wesleyan 1905
+ Very, Dexter-Penn St 1912
Vessels, Billy-Oklahoma 1952
+ Vick, Ernie-Michigan 1921
+ Wagner, Hube-Pittsburgh 1913
Walker, Doak-SMU 1949
+ Wallace, Bill-Rice 1935
+ Walsh, Adam-N.Dame 1924
+ Warburton, Cotton, USC 1934
Ward, Bob-Maryland 1951
+ Warner, William-Cornell 1904
+ Washington, Kenny-UCLA 1939
+ Weatherall, Jim-Okla. 1951
Webster, George-Mich. St 1966
Wedemeyer, H.-St. Mary's 1947
+ Weekes, Harold-Columbia 1902
Weiner, Art-N. Carolina 1949
+ Weir, Ed-Nebraska 1925
+ Welch, Gus-Carlisle 1914
+ Weller, John-Princeton 1935
+ Wendell, Percy-Harvard 1912
+ West, Belford-Colgate 1919
+ Westfall, Bob-Michigan 1941
+ Weyand, Babe-Army 1915
+ Wharton, Buck-Penn 1896
+ Wheeler, Arthur-Princeton 1894
White, Byron-Colorado 1938
White, Charles-USC 1979
White, Danny-Ariz. St. 1973
White, Randy-Maryland 1974
Whitmire, Don-Navy/Ala. 1944
+ Wickhorst, Frank-Navy 1926
Widseth, Ed-Minnesota 1936
+ Wildung, Dick-Minnesota 1942
Williams, Bob-N. Dame 1950
Williams, Froggie-Rice 1949
Willis, Bill-Ohio St 1944
Wilson, Bobby-SMU 1935
+ Wilson, George-Wash 1925
+ Wilson, Harry-Army/Penn St 1926
Wilson, Marc-BYU 1979
Wilson, Mike-Lafayette 1928
Wistert, Albert-Michigan 1942
Wistert, Alvin-Michigan 1949
+ Wistert, Whitey-Michigan 1933
+ Wojciechowicz, Alex-Fordham 1937
+ Wood, Barry-Harvard 1931
+ Wyant, Andy-Chicago 1894
+ Wyatt, Bowden-Tenn 1938
+ Wyckoff, Clint-Cornell 1895
+ Yarr, Tommy-N.Dame 1931
Yary, Ron-USC 1967
+ Yoder, Lloyd-Carnegie 1926
+ Young, Claude-Illinois 1946
+ Young, Harry-Wash.& Lee 1916
+ Young, Waddy-Okla 1938
Youngblood, Jack-Florida 1970
Zarnas, Gustave-Ohio St. 1937

Coaches

+ Aillet, Joe 1989
+ Alexander, Bill 1951
+ Anderson, Ed 1971
+ Armstrong, Ike 1957
+ Bachman, Charlie 1978
+ Banks, Earl 1992
+ Baujan, Harry 1990
+ Bell, Matty 1955
+ Bezdek, Hugo 1954
+ Bible, Dana X. 1951
+ Bierman, Bernie 1955
Blackman, Bob 1987
+ Blaik, Earl (Red) 1965
Broyles, Frank 1983
+ Bryant, Paul (Bear) 1986
+ Butts, Wally 1997
+ Caldwell, Charlie 1961
+ Camp, Walter 1951
Casanova, Len 1977
+ Cavanaugh, Frank 1954
+ Colman, Dick 1990
+ Crisler, Fritz 1954
+ Daugherty, Duffy 1984
+ Devaney, Bob 1981
Devine, Dan 1985
+ Dobie, Gil 1951
+ Dodd, Bobby 1993
+ Donohue, Michael 1951
Dooley, Vince 1994
+ Dorais, Gus 1954
+ Edwards, Bill 1986
+ Engle, Rip 1973
Faurot, Don 1961
+ Gaither, Jake 1973
Gillman, Sid 1989
+ Godfrey, Ernest 1972
Graves, Ray 1990
+ Gustafson, Andy 1985
+ Hall, Edward 1951
+ Harding, Jack 1980
+ Harlow, Richard 1954
+ Harman, Harvey 1981
+ Harper, Jesse 1971
+ Haughton, Percy 1951
+ Hayes, Woody 1983
+ Heisman, John W 1954
+ Higgins, Robert 1954
+ Hollingberry, Babe 1979
+ Howard, Frank 1989
+ Ingram, Bill 1973
James, Don 1997
+ Jennings, Morley 1973
+ Jones, Biff 1954
+ Jones, Howard 1951
+ Jones, Tad 1958
+ Jordan, Lloyd 1978
+ Jordan, Ralph (Shug) 1982
+ Kerr, Andy 1951
Kush, Frank 1995
+ Leahy, Frank 1970
+ Little, George 1955
+ Little, Lou 1960
+ Madigan, Slip 1974
Maurer, Dave 1991
McClendon, Charley 1986
+ McCracken, Herb 1973
+ McGugin, Dan 1951
McKay, John 1988
+ McKeen, Allyn 1991
+ McLaughry, Tuss 1962
+ Merritt, John 1994
+ Meyer, Dutch 1956
+ Mollenkopf, Jack 1988
+ Moore, Bernie 1954
+ Moore, Scrappy 1980
+ Morrison, Ray 1954
+ Munger, George 1976
+ Munn, Clarence (Biggie) 1959
+ Murray, Bill 1974
+ Murray, Frank 1983
+ Mylin, Ed (Hooks) 1974
+ Neale, Earle (Greasy) 1967
+ Neely, Jess 1971
+ Nelson, David 1987
+ Neyland, Robert 1956
+ Norton, Homer 1971
+ O'Neill, Frank (Buck) 1951
+ Owen, Bennie 1951
Parseghian, Ara 1980
+ Perry, Doyt 1988
+ Phelan, Jimmy 1973
+ Prothro, Tommy 1991
Ralston, John 1992
+ Robinson, E.N. 1955
+ Rockne, Knute 1951
+ Romney, Dick 1954
+ Roper, Bill 1951
Royal, Darrell 1983
+ Sanders, Henry (Red) 1996
+ Sanford, George 1971
Schembechler, Bo 1993
+ Schmidt, Francis 1971

+ Schwartzwalder, Ben 1982
+ Shaughnessy, Clark. 1968
+ Shaw, Buck. 1972
+ Smith, Andy 1951
+ Snavely, Carl 1965
+ Stagg, Amos Alonzo. 1951
+ Sutherland, Jock. 1951
+ Tatum, Jim. 1984
+ Thomas, Frank 1951
+ Vann, Thad. 1987
Vaught, Johnny. 1979
+ Wade, Wallace. 1955
+ Waldorf, Lynn (Pappy) 1966
+ Warner, Glenn (Pop). 1951
+ Wieman, E.E. (Tad). 1956
+ Wilce, John 1954
+ Wilkinson, Bud 1969
+ Williams, Henry. 1951
+ Woodruff, George. 1963
+ Woodson, Warren 1989
+ Wyatt, Bowden 1997
+ Yost, Fielding (Hurry Up) 1951
+ Zuppke, Bob. 1951

Small College

Players

Bentrim, Jeff-N.Dakota St. . . .1998
Brasdshaw, Terry-La. Tech. . . .1969
+ Buchanan, Buck-Grambling . .1962
Cichy, Joe-N.Dakota St. 1970
Deery, Tom-Widener, PA. 1998
+ Delaney, Joe-N'western St.. . .1980
Dement, Kenneth-SE Mo. St. .1998
Den Herder, Vern-Central IA..1970
Dryer, Fred-San Diego St.. . . .1968
Dudek, Joe-Plymouth St. 1985
Grinnell, William-Tufts. 1934
Hawkins, Frank-Nevada. 1980
Holt, Pierce-Angelo St. 1987
Johnson, Billy-Widener, PA . . .1973
Johnson, Gary-Grambling St.. .1974
Lomax, Neil-Portland St.. 1980
McGriff, Tyrone-Jackson St. . .1974
Montgomery, Wilbert-Ab. Christ. . .1976
O'Brien, Ken-UC–Davis 1982
Payton, Walter-Jackson St. . . .1974
Pugh, Larry-Westminster 1998
Reasons, Gary-N'western St. .1983
Taylor, Bruce-Boston U. 1969
Thomsen, Lynn-Augustana . . .1986
Youngblood, Jim-Tenn. Tech . .1972

Coaches

+ Burry, Harold 1996
Butterfield, Jim 1997
+ Hoernemann, Paul. 1997
Keade, Bob 1998
Klausing, Chuck. 1998
Rutschman, Ad. 1998
Sherman, Edgar. 1996
+ Steinke, Gilbert 1996
+ Tressel, Lee 1996

Pro Football Hall of Fame

Established in 1963 by National Football League to commemorate the sport's professional origins. **Address:** 2121 George Halas Drive NW, Canton, OH 44708. **Telephone:** (330) 456-8207.

Eligibility: Nominated players must be retired five years, coaches must be retired, and contributors can still be active. Voting done by 36-member panel made up of media representatives from all 30 NFL cities, one PFWA representative and five selectors-at-large.

Class of 1998 (5): PLAYERS—DB **Paul Krause**, Washington (1964-67) and Minnesota (1968-79); WR **Tommy McDonald**, Philadelphia (1957-63), Dallas (1964), L.A. Rams (1965-66), Atlanta (1967) and Cleveland (1968); OT **Anthony Munoz**, Cincinnati (1980-92); LB **Mike Singletary**, Chicago (1981-92); C **Dwight Stephenson**, Miami (1980-87)

Quarterbacks

Baugh, Sammy. 1963
Blanda, George (also PK) . . .1981
Bradshaw, Terry. 1989
+ Clark, Dutch 1963
+ Conzelman, Jimmy 1964
Dawson, Len. 1987
+ Driscoll, Paddy. 1965
Fouts, Dan 1993
Graham, Otto 1965
Griese, Bob 1990
+ Herber, Arnie. 1966
Jurgensen, Sonny. 1983
+ Layne, Bobby. 1967
+ Luckman, Sid 1965
Namath, Joe. 1985
Parker, Clarence (Ace) 1972
Starr, Bart 1977
Staubach, Roger 1985
Tarkenton, Fran 1986
Tittle, Y.A. 1971
Unitas, Johnny 1979
+ Van Brocklin, Norm. 1971
+ Waterfield, Bob. 1965

Running Backs

+ Battles, Cliff 1968
Brown, Jim 1971
Campbell, Earl. 1991
Canadeo, Tony 1974
Csonka, Larry. 1987
Dorsett, Tony. 1994
Dudley, Bill 1966
Gifford, Frank 1977
+ Grange, Red 1963
+ Guyon, Joe. 1966
Harris, Franco 1990
+ Hinkle, Clarke 1964
Hornung, Paul 1986
Johnson, John Henry. 1987
Kelly, Leroy. 1994
+ Leemans, Tuffy 1978
Matson, Ollie. 1972
McAfee, George 1966
McElhenny, Hugh 1970
+ McNally, Johnny (Blood) 1963
Moore, Lenny. 1975
Motley, Marion 1968
+ Nagurski, Bronko 1963
+ Nevers, Ernie. 1963
Payton, Walter. 1993
Perry, Joe 1969
Riggins, John 1992
Sayers, Gale 1977
Simpson, O.J 1985
+ Strong, Ken 1967
Taylor, Jim. 1976
+ Thorpe, Jim. 1963
Trippi, Charley. 1968
Van Buren, Steve 1965
Walker, Doak. 1986

Ends & Wide Receivers

Alworth, Lance. 1978
+ Badgro, Red. 1981
Berry, Raymond 1973
Biletnikoff, Fred 1988
+ Chamberlin, Guy. 1965
Ditka, Mike. 1988
Fears, Tom 1970
+ Hewitt, Bill 1971
Hirsch, Elroy (Crazylegs) 1968
+ Hutson, Don 1963
Joiner, Charlie 1996
Largent, Steve 1995
Lavelli, Dante 1975
Mackey, John 1992
Maynard, Don 1987
McDonald, Tommy 1998
+ Millner, Wayne 1968
Mitchell, Bobby 1983
Pihos, Pete 1970
Smith, Jackie 1994
Taylor, Charley. 1984
Warfield, Paul 1983
Winslow, Kellen. 1995

Linemen (pre-World War II)

+ Edwards, Turk (T)...........1969
+ Fortmann, Dan (G)...........1985
+ Healey, Ed (T)...........1964
+ Hein, Mel (C)...........1963
+ Henry, Pete (T)...........1963
+ Hubbard, Cal (T)...........1963
+ Kiesling, Walt (G)...........1966
+ Kinard, Bruiser (T)...........1971
+ Lyman, Link (T)...........1964
+ Michalske, Mike (G)...........1964

Musso, George (T-G)...........1982
+ Stydahar, Joe (T)...........1967
+ Trafton, George (C)...........1964

Turner, Bulldog (C)...........1966
+ Wojciechowicz, Alex (C)...........1968

Offensive Linemen

Bednarik, Chuck (C-LB)...........1967
Brown, Roosevelt (T)...........1975
Dierdorf, Dan (T)...........1996
Gatski, Frank (C)...........1985
Gregg, Forrest (T-G)...........1977
Groza, Lou (T-PK)...........1974
Hannah, John (G)...........1991
Jones, Stan (T-G-DT)...........1991
Langer, Jim (C)...........1987
Little, Larry (G)...........1993
McCormack, Mike (T)...........1984
Mix, Ron (T-G)...........1979
Munoz, Anthony (T)...........1998
Otto, Jim (C)...........1980
Parker, Jim (G)...........1973
Ringo, Jim (C)...........1981
St. Clair, Bob (T)...........1990
Stephenson, Dwight (C)...........1998
Shell, Art (T)...........1989
Upshaw, Gene (G)...........1987
Webster, Mike (C)...........1997

Defensive Linemen

Atkins, Doug...........1982
+ Buchanan, Buck...........1990

Creekmur, Lou...........1996
Davis, Willie...........1981
Donovan, Art...........1968
+ Ford, Len...........1976

Greene, Joe...........1987
Jones, Deacon...........1980
+ Jordan, Henry...........1995

Lilly, Bob...........1980
Marchetti, Gino...........1972
Nomellini, Leo...........1969
Olsen, Merlin...........1982
Page, Alan...........1988
Robustelli, Andy...........1971
Selmon, Lee Roy...........1995
Stautner, Ernie...........1969
Weinmeister, Arnie...........1984
White, Randy...........1994
Willis, Bill...........1977

Linebackers

Bell, Bobby...........1983
Butkus, Dick...........1979
Connor, George (DT-OT)...........1975
+ George, Bill...........1974

Ham, Jack...........1988
Hendricks, Ted...........1990
Huff, Sam...........1982
Lambert, Jack...........1990
Lanier, Willie...........1986
+ Nitschke, Ray...........1978

Schmidt, Joe...........1973
Singletary, Mike...........1998

Defensive Backs

Adderley, Herb...........1980
Barney, Lem...........1992
Blount, Mel...........1989
Brown, Willie...........1984
+ Christiansen, Jack...........1970

Haynes, Mike...........1997
Houston, Ken...........1986
Johnson, Jimmy...........1994
Krause, Paul...........1998
Lane, Dick (Night Train)...........1974
Lary, Yale...........1979
Renfro, Mel...........1996
+ Tunnell, Emlen...........1967

Wilson, Larry...........1978
Wood, Willie...........1989

Placekicker

Stenerud, Jan...........1991

Coaches

+ Brown, Paul...........1967

Ewbank, Weeb...........1978
+ Flaherty, Ray...........1976

Gibbs, Joe...........1996
Gillman, Sid...........1983
Grant, Bud...........1994
+ Halas, George...........1963
+ Lambeau, Curly...........1963

Landry, Tom...........1990
+ Lombardi, Vince...........1971
+ Neale, Earle (Greasy)...........1969

Noll, Chuck...........1993
+ Owen, Steve...........1966

Shula, Don...........1997
Walsh, Bill...........1993

Contributors

+ Bell, Bert...........1963
+ Bidwill, Charles...........1967
+ Carr, Joe...........1963

Davis, Al...........1992
+ Finks, Jim...........1995
+ Halas, George...........1963

Hunt, Lamar...........1972
+ Mara, Tim...........1963

Mara, Wellington...........1997
+ Marshall, George...........1963
+ Ray, Hugh (Shorty)...........1966
+ Reeves, Dan...........1967
+ Rooney, Art...........1964
+ Rozelle, Pete...........1985

Schramm, Tex...........1991

Dick McCann Award

First presented in 1969 by the Pro Football Writers of America for long and distinguished reporting on pro football. Named in honor of the first director of the Hall, the McCann Award does not constitute induction into the Hall of Fame.

Year	
1969	George Strickler
1970	Arthur Daley
1971	Joe King
1972	Lewis Atchison
1973	Dave Brady
1974	Bob Oates
1975	John Steadman
1976	Jack Hand
1977	Art Daley
1978	Murray Olderman
1979	Pat Livingston
1980	Chuck Heaton
1981	Norm Miller
1982	Cameron Snyder
1983	Hugh Brown
1984	Larry Felser
1985	Cooper Rollow
1986	Bill Wallace
1987	Jerry Magee
1988	Gordon Forbes
1989	Vito Stellino
1990	Will McDonough
1991	Dick Connor
1992	Frank Luska
1993	Ira Miller
1994	Don Pierson
1995	Ray Didinger
1996	Paul Zimmerman
1997	Bob Roesler
1998	Dave Anderson

NFL's 75th Anniversary All-Time Team

Selected by a 15-member panel of former players, NFL and Pro Football Hall of Fame officials and media representatives and released Sept. 1, 1994.

Offense

Wide Receivers (4): Lance Alworth, Raymond Berry, Don Hutson and Jerry Rice
Tight Ends (2): Mike Ditka and Kellen Winslow
Tackles (3): Roosevelt Brown, Forrest Gregg and Anthony Munoz
Guards (3): John Hannah, Jim Parker and Gene Upshaw
Centers (2): Mel Hein and Mike Webster
Quarterbacks (4): Sammy Baugh, Otto Graham, Joe Montana and Johnny Unitas
Running Backs (6): Jim Brown, Marion Motley, Bronko Nagurski, Walter Payton, O.J. Simpson and Steve Van Buren

Defense

Ends (3): Deacon Jones, Gino Marchetti and Reggie White
Tackles (3): Joe Greene, Bob Lilly and Merlin Olsen
Linebackers (7): Dick Butkus, Jack Ham, Ted Hendricks, Jack Lambert, Willie Lanier, Ray Nitschke and Lawrence Taylor
Cornerbacks (4): Mel Blount, Mike Haynes, Dick (Night Train) Lane and Rod Woodson
Safties (3): Ken Houston, Ronnie Lott and Larry Wilson

Specialists

Placekicker: Jan Stenerud
Punter: Ray Guy
Kick Returner: Gale Sayers
Punt Returner: Billy (White Shoes) Johnson

Pete Rozelle Award

First presented in 1989 by the Hall of Fame for exceptional longtime contributions to radio and TV in pro football. Named in honor of the former NFL commissioner, who was also a publicist and GM for the LA Rams, the Rozelle Award does not constitute induction into the Hall of Fame.

Year
1989 Bill McPhail
1990 Lindsey Nelson
1991 Ed Sabol
1992 Chris Schenkel

Year
1993 Curt Gowdy
1994 Pat Summerall
1995 Frank Gifford
1996 Jack Buck

Year
1997 Charlie Jones
1998 Val Pinchbeck Jr.

Canadian Football Hall of Fame

Established in 1963. Current Hall opened in 1972. **Address:** 58 Jackson Street West, Hamilton, Ontario, L8P 1L4. **Telephone:** (905) 528-7566.

Eligibility: Nominated players must be retired three years, but coaches and builders can still be active. Voting done by 15-member panel of Canadian pro and amateur football officials.

Class of 1998 (5): PLAYERS—PK **Dave Cutler**, Edmonton (1969-84); WR **Joe Poplawski**, Winnipeg (1978-86); WR/S/PK **Larry Robinson**, Calgary (1961-74); SB **Tom Scott**, Winnipeg (1974-78), Edmonton (1978-85). BUILDER—**Bernard Custis**.

Members are listed with year of induction; (+) indicates deceased members.

Players

Ah You, Junior 1997
Atchison, Ron 1978
Bailey, Byron 1975
Baker, Bill 1994
Barrow, John 1976
+ Batstone, Harry 1963
+ Beach, Ormond 1963
Benecick, Al 1996
Box, Ab 1965
+ Breen, Joe 1963
+ Bright, Johnny 1970
Brown, Tom 1984
Brock, Dieter 1995
Campbell, Jerry (Soupy) 1996
Casey, Tom 1964
Charlton, Ken 1992
Clarke, Bill 1996
Clements, Tom 1994
Coffey, Tommy Joe 1977
+ Conacher, Lionel 1963
Copeland, Royal 1988
Corrigall, Jim 1990
+ Cox, Ernest 1963
+ Craig, Ross 1964
+ Cronin, Carl 1967
Cutler, Dave 1998
+ Cutler, Wes 1968
Dalla Riva, Peter 1993
DiPietro, Rocky 1997
+ Dixon, George 1974
+ Eliowitz, Abe 1969
+ Emerson, Eddie 1963
Etcheverry, Sam 1969
Evanshen, Terry 1984
Faloney, Bernie 1974
+ Fear, A.H. (Cap) 1967
Fennell, Dave 1990
+ Ferraro, John 1966
Fieldgate, Norm 1979
Fleming, Willie 1982
Gabriel, Tony 1985
Gaines, Gene 1994
+ Gall, Hugh 1963
Golab, Tony 1964
Grant, Tom 1995
Gray, Herbert 1983
+ Griffing, Dean 1965
+ Hanson, Fritz 1963
Harris, Wayne 1976
Harrison, Herm 1993
Helton, John 1986
Henley, Garney 1979
Hinton, Tom 1991
+ Huffman, Dick 1987
+ Isbister, Bob Sr. 1965
Jackson, Russ 1973
+ Jacobs, Jack 1963
+ James, Eddie (Dynamite) 1963
James, Gerry 1981
+ Kabat, Greg 1966
Kapp, Joe 1984
Keeling, Jerry 1989
Kelly, Brian 1991
Kelly, Ellison 1992
Kepley, Dan 1996
Krol, Joe 1963
Kwong, Normie 1969
Lancaster, Ron 1982
+ Lawson, Smirle 1963
+ Leadlay, Frank (Pep) 1963
+ Lear, Les 1974
Lewis, Leo 1973

Lunsford, Earl 1983
Luster, Marv 1990
Luzzi, Don 1986
+ McCance, Ches 1976
+ McGill, Frank 1965
McQuarters, Ed 1988
Miles, Rollie 1980
+ Molson, Percy 1963
Morris, Frank 1983
+ Morris, Ted 1964
Mosca, Angelo 1987
+ Nelson, Roger 1986
Neumann, Peter 1979
O'Quinn, John (Red) 1981
Pajaczkowski, Tony 1988
Parker, Jackie 1971
Patterson, Hal 1971
Poplawski, Joe 1998
Perry, Gordon 1970
+ Perry, Norm 1963
Ploen, Ken 1975
+ Quilty, S.P. (Silver) 1966
+ Rebholz, Russ 1963
Reed, George 1979
+ Reeve, Ted 1963
Rigney, Frank 1985
Robinson, Larry 1998
+ Rodden, Mike 1964
+ Rowe, Paul 1964
Ruby, Martin 1974
+ Russel, Jeff 1963
Scott, Tom 1998
+ Scott, Vince 1982
Shatto, Dick 1975
+ Simpson, Ben 1963
Simpson, Bob 1976
+ Sprague, David 1963
Stevenson, Art 1969
Stewart, Ron 1977
+ Stirling, Hugh (Bummer) 1966
Sutherin, Don 1992
Symons, Bill 1997
Thelen, Dave 1989
+ Timmis, Brian 1963
Tinsley, Bud 1982
+ Tommy, Andy 1989
+ Trawick, Herb 1975
+ Tubman, Joe 1968
Tucker, Whit 1993
Urness, Ted 1989
Vaughan, Kaye 1978
Wagner, Virgil 1980
+ Welch, Hawley (Huck) 1964
Wilkinson, Tom 1987
Wilson, Al 1997
Wylie, Harvey 1980
Young, Jim 1991
+ Zock, Bill 1985

Builders

+ Back, Leonard 1971
+ Bailey, Harold 1965
+ Ballard, Harold 1987
+ Berger, Sam 1993
+ Brook, Tom 1975
+ Brown, D. Wes 1963
+ Chipman, Arthur 1969
Clair, Frank 1981
+ Cooper, Ralph 1992
Coulter, Bruce 1997
+ Crighton, Hec 1986
+ Currie, Andrew 1974
Custis, Bernard 1998
+ Davies, Dr. Andrew 1969
+ DeGruchy, John 1963
Dojack, Paul 1978
+ Duggan, Eck 1981
+ DuMoulin, Seppi 1963
+ Foulds, Willliam 1963
Fulton, Greg 1995
Gaudaur, J.G. (Jake) 1984
Gibson, Frank 1996
Grant, Bud 1983
+ Grey, Lord Earl 1963
+ Griffith, Dr. Harry 1963
+ Halter, Sydney 1966
+ Hannibal, Frank 1963
+ Hayman, Lew 1975
+ Hughes, W.P. (Billy) 1974
Keys, Eagle 1990
Kimball, Norman 1991
+ Kramer, R.A. (Bob) 1987
+ Lieberman, M.I. (Moe) 1973
+ McBrien, Harry 1978
+ McCaffrey, Jimmy 1967
+ McCann, Dave 1966
McNaughton, Don 1994
+ McPherson, Don 1983
+ Metras, Johnny 1980
+ Montgomery, Ken 1970
+ Newton, Jack 1964
+ Preston, Ken 1990
+ Ritchie, Alvin 1963
+ Ryan, Joe B. 1968
Sazio, Ralph 1988
+ Shaughnessy, Frank (Shag) ..1963
+ Shouldice, W.T. (Hap) 1977
+ Simpson, Jimmie 1986
+ Slocomb, Karl 1989
+ Spring, Harry 1976
Stukus, Annis 1974
+ Taylor, N.J. (Piffles) 1963
+ Tindall, Frank 1985
+ Warner, Clair 1965
+ Warwick, Bert 1964
+ Wilson, Seymour 1984

GOLF

World Golf Hall of Fame

A new World Golf Hall of Fame opened its doors in 1998 at the World Golf Village outside of Jacksonville, Fla. The 71 members of the former Hall of Fame (established in 1974 but inactive since 1993) in Pinehurst, N.C. and LPGA Hall of Fame were "grandfathered" into the new Hall.

Eligibility: Professionals have three avenues into the WGHF. A PGA Tour player qualifies for the ballot if he has at least 10 victories in approved tournaments, or at least two victories among The Players Championship, Masters, U.S. Open, British Open and PGA Championship, is at least 40 years old and has been a member of the Tour for 10 years. A senior PGA Tour player qualifies if he has been a Senior Tour member for five years and has 20 wins between the PGA Tour and Senior Tour or five wins among the PGA majors, the Players Championship and the senior majors (US Senior Open, Tradition, PGA Seniors' Championship and Senior Players Championship). Any player qualifying for the LPGA Hall automatically qualifies for the WGHF. Nominees must have played 10 years on the LPGA tour and won 30 official events, including two major championships; 35 official events and one major; or 40 official events and no majors. For players not eligible for either the PGA Tour or the LPGA Hall of Fame, a body of over 300 international golf writers and historians will vote each year.

Members are listed with year of induction; (+) indicates deceased members.

Class of 1998 (2): MEN—**Nick Faldo** and **Johnny Miller**.

Note: Seve Ballesteros has already been voted in but will not be inducted until 1999.

Men

+ Anderson, Willie 1975
+ Armour, Tommy 1976
+ Ball, John, Jr 1977
+ Barnes, Jim 1989
+ Boros, Julius 1982
+ Braid, James 1976
Casper, Billy 1978
Cooper, Lighthorse Harry 1992
+ Cotton, Thomas 1980
+ Demaret, Jimmy 1983
DeVicenzo, Roberto 1989
+ Evans, Chick 1975
Faldo, Nick 1998
Floyd, Ray 1989
+ Guldahl, Ralph 1981
+ Hagen, Walter 1974
+ Hilton, Harold 1978
+ Hogan, Ben 1974
Irwin, Hale 1992
+ Jones, Bobby 1974
+ Little, Lawson 1980
Littler, Gene 1990
+ Locke, Bobby 1977
+ Middlecoff, Cary 1986
Miller, Johnny 1998
+ Morris, Tom Jr. 1975
+ Morris, Tom Sr 1976
Nelson, Byron 1974
Nicklaus, Jack 1974
+ Ouimet, Francis 1974

Palmer, Arnold 1974
Player, Gary...............1974
Runyan, Paul 1990
Sarazen, Gene 1974
+ Smith, Horton.............1990
Snead, Sam 1974
+ Taylor, John H 1975
Thomson, Peter............1988
+ Travers, Jerry 1976
+ Travis, Walter.............1979
Trevino, Lee 1981
+ Vardon, Harry 1974
Watson, Tom 1988

Women

Berg, Patty 1974
Bradley, Pat 1991
Carner, JoAnne 1985
Haynie, Sandra............1977
+ Howe, Dorothy C.H 1978
Jameson, Betty 1951
King, Betsy................1995
Lopez, Nancy 1989
Mann, Carol...............1977
Rawls, Betsy...............1987
Sheehan, Patty............1993
Suggs, Louise 1979
+ Vare, Glenna Collett 1975
+ Wethered, Joyce 1975
Whitworth, Kathy 1982
Wright, Mickey 1976
+ Zaharias, Babe Didrikson ...1974

Contributors

Campbell, William 1990
+ Corcoran, Fred 1975
+ Crosby, Bing...............1978
+ Dey, Joe 1975
+ Graffis, Herb 1977
+ Harlow, Robert.............1988
Hope, Bob 1983
Jones, Robert Trent 1987
+ Roberts, Clifford...........1978
Rodriguez, Chi Chi 1992
+ Ross, Donald 1977
+ Shore, Dinah 1994
+ Tufts, Richard 1992

Old PGA Hall Members Not in PGA/World Hall

The original PGA Hall of Fame was established in 1940 by the PGA of America, but abandoned after the 1982 inductions in favor of the PGA/World Hall of Fame. Twenty-seven members of the old PGA Hall have been elected to the PGA/World Hall since then. Players yet to make the cut are listed below with year of induction into old PGA Hall.

+ Brady, Mike 1960
+ Burke, Billy 1966
Burke, Jack Jr 1975
+ Cruickshank, Bobby 1967
+ Diegel, Leo................1955
+ Dudley, Ed 1964
+ Dutra, Olin 1962
+ Farroll, Johnny 1961
Ford, Doug................1975
+ Ghezzi, Vic 1965
+ Harbert, Chick 1968
Harper, Chandler 1969
+ Harrison, Dutch 1962
+ Hutchison, Jock Sr 1959
+ McDermott, John 1940
+ Mangrum, Lloyd............1964
+ McLeod, Fred..............1960
+ Picard, Henry..............1961
+ Revolta, Johnny 1963
+ Shute, Denny 1957
+ Smith, Alex................1940
+ Smith, Macdonald..........1954
+ Wood, Craig 1956

HOCKEY

Hockey Hall of Fame

Established in 1945 by the National Hockey League and opened in 1961. **Address:** BCE Place, 30 Yonge Street, Toronto, Ontario, M5E 1X8. **Telephone:** (416) 360-7735.

Eligibility: Nominated players and referees must be retired three years. Voting done by 15-member panel made up of pro and amateur hockey personalities and media representatives. A 15-member Veterans Committee selects older players.

Class of 1998 (4): PLAYERS— forward **Michel Goulet**, Quebec (1979-90), Chicago (1990-94); forward **Peter Stastny**, Quebec (1980-90), New Jersey (1989-93), St. Louis (1993-95); VETERAN— forward **Roy Conacher**, Boston (1939-46), Detroit (1946-47), Chicago (1947-52); BUILDER— **Athol "Pere" Murray** (Notre Dame college founder).

Members are listed with year of induction; (+) indicates deceased members.

Forwards

Abel, Sid..................1969
+ Adams, Jack..............1959
Apps, Syl 1961
Armstrong, George 1975
+ Bailey, Ace................1975
+ Bain, Dan 1945
+ Baker, Hobey..............1945
Barber, Bill 1990
+ Barry, Marty...............1965
Bathgate, Andy 1978
+ Bauer, Bobby 1996
Beliveau, Jean 1972
+ Bentley, Doug.............1964
+ Bentley, Max 1966
+ Blake, Toe.................1966
Bossy, Mike 1991
+ Boucher, Frank.............1958
+ Bowie, Dubbie 1945
+ Broadbent, Punch 1962
Bucyk, John (Chief) 1981
+ Burch, Billy 1974
Clarke, Bobby 1987
+ Colville, Neil 1967
+ Conacher, Charlie..........1961
Conacher, Roy.............1998
+ Cook, Bill 1952
+ Cook, Bun.................1995
Cournoyer, Yvan 1982
+ Cowley, Bill 1968
+ Crawford, Rusty............1962
+ Darragh, Jack.............1962
+ Davidson, Scotty 1950
+ Day, Hap 1961
Delvecchio, Alex 1977
+ Denneny, Cy...............1959
Dionne, Marcel 1992
+ Drillon, Gordie.............1975
+ Drinkwater, Graham 1950
Dumart, Woody............1992
+ Dunderdale, Tommy 1974
+ Dye, Babe.................1970
Esposito, Phil 1984
+ Farrell, Arthur.............1965
+ Foyston, Frank 1958
+ Frederickson, Frank.........1958
Gainey, Bob...............1992
+ Gardner, Jimmy 1962
Geoffrion, Bernie...........1972
+ Gerard, Eddie 1945
Gilbert, Rod 1982
+ Gilmour, Billy 1962
Goulet, Michel.............1998
+ Griffis, Si..................1950
+ Hay, George 1958
+ Hextall, Bryan 1969
+ Hooper, Tom..............1962
Howe, Gordie 1972
+ Howe, Syd 1965
Hull, Bobby 1983
+ Hyland, Harry 1962
+ Irvin, Dick.................1958
+ Jackson, Busher 1971
+ Joliat, Aurel 1947
+ Keats, Duke 1958
Kennedy, Ted (Teeder).......1966
Keon, Dave 1986
Lach, Elmer................1966
Lafleur, Guy 1988
+ Lalonde, Newsy............1950
Laprade, Edgar 1993
Lemaire, Jacques 1984
Lemieux, Mario 1997

Hockey (Cont.)

+ Lewis, Herbie 1989
Lindsay, Ted 1966
+ MacKay, Mickey 1952
Mahovlich, Frank 1981
+ Malone, Joe 1950
+ Marshall, Jack 1965
+ Maxwell, Fred 1962
McDonald, Lanny 1992
+ McGee, Frank 1945
+ McGimsie, Billy 1962
Mikita, Stan 1983
Moore, Dickie 1974
+ Morenz, Howie 1945
+ Mosienko, Bill 1965
+ Nighbor, Frank 1947
+ Noble, Reg 1962
+ O'Connor, Buddy 1988
+ Oliver, Harry 1967
Olmstead, Bert 1985
+ Patrick, Lynn 1980
Perreault, Gilbert 1990
+ Phillips, Tom 1945
+ Primeau, Joe 1963
Pulford, Bob 1991
+ Rankin, Frank 1961
Ratelle, Jean 1985
Richard, Henri 1979
Richard, Maurice (Rocket) 1961
+ Richardson, George 1950
+ Roberts, Gordie 1971
+ Russel, Blair 1965
+ Russell, Ernie 1965
+ Ruttan, Jack 1962
+ Scanlan, Fred 1965
Schmidt, Milt 1961
+ Schriner, Sweeney 1962
+ Seibert, Oliver 1961
Shutt, Steve 1993
+ Siebert, Babe 1964
Sittler, Darryl 1989
+ Smith, Alf 1962
Smith, Clint 1991
+ Smith, Hooley 1972
+ Smith, Tommy 1973
+ Stanley, Barney 1962
Stastny, Peter 1998
+ Stewart, Nels 1962
+ Stuart, Bruce 1961
+ Taylor, Fred (Cyclone) 1947
+ Trihey, Harry 1950
Trottier, Bryan 1997
Ullman, Norm 1982
+ Walker, Jack 1960
+ Walsh, Marty 1962
Watson, Harry 1994
+ Watson, Harry (Moose) 1962
+ Weiland, Cooney 1971
+ Westwick, Harry (Rat) 1962
+ Whitcroft, Fred 1962

Goaltenders

+ Benedict, Clint 1965
Bower, Johnny 1976
Brimsek, Frankie 1966
+ Broda, Turk 1967
Cheevers, Gerry 1985
+ Connell, Alex 1958
Dryden, Ken 1983
+ Durnan, Bill 1964
Esposito, Tony 1988
+ Gardiner, Chuck 1945
Giacomin, Eddie 1987
+ Hainsworth, George 1961
Hall, Glenn 1975
+ Hern, Riley 1962
+ Holmes, Hap 1972
+ Hutton, J.B. (Bouse) 1962
+ Lehman, Hughie 1958
+ LeSueur, Percy 1961
+ Lumley, Harry 1980
+ Moran, Paddy 1958
Parent, Bernie 1984
+ Plante, Jacques 1978
Rayner, Chuck 1973
+ Sawchuk, Terry 1971
Smith, Billy 1993
+ Thompson, Tiny 1959
Tretiak, Vladislav 1989
+ Vezina, Georges 1945
Worsley, Gump 1980
+ Worters, Roy 1969

Defensemen

Boivin, Leo 1986
+ Boon, Dickie 1952
Bouchard, Butch 1966
+ Boucher, George 1960
+ Cameron, Harry 1962
+ Clancy, King 1958
+ Clapper, Dit 1947
+ Cleghorn, Sprague 1958
+ Conacher, Lionel 1994
Coulter, Art 1974
+ Dutton, Red 1958
Flaman, Fernie 1990
Gadsby, Bill 1970
+ Gardiner, Herb 1958
+ Goheen, F.X. (Moose) 1952
+ Goodfellow, Ebbie 1963
+ Grant, Mike 1950
+ Green, Wilf (Shorty) 1962
+ Hall, Joe 1961
+ Harvey, Doug 1973
Horner, Red 1965
+ Horton, Tim 1977
Howell, Harry 1979
+ Johnson, Ching 1958
+ Johnson, Ernie 1952
Johnson, Tom 1970
Kelly, Red 1969
Laperriere, Jacques 1987
Lapointe, Guy 1993
+ Laviolette, Jack 1962
+ Mantha, Sylvio 1960
+ McNamara, George 1958
Orr, Bobby 1979
Park, Brad 1988
+ Patrick, Lester 1947
Pilote, Pierre 1975
+ Pitre, Didier 1962
Potvin, Denis 1991
+ Pratt, Babe 1966
Pronovost, Marcel 1978
+ Pulford, Harvey 1945
Quackenbush, Bill 1976
Reardon, Kenny 1966
Robinson, Larry 1995
+ Ross, Art 1945
Salming, Borje 1996
Savard, Serge 1986
Seibert, Earl 1963
+ Shore, Eddie 1947
+ Simpson, Joe 1962
Stanley, Allan 1981
+ Stewart, Jack 1964
+ Stuart, Hod 1945
+ Wilson, Gordon (Phat) 1962

Referees & Linesmen

Armstrong, Neil 1991
Ashley, John 1981
Chadwick, Bill 1964
D'Amico, John 1993
+ Elliott, Chaucer 1961
+ Hayes, George 1988
+ Hewitson, Bobby 1963
+ Ion, Mickey 1961
Pavelich, Matt 1987
+ Rodden, Mike 1962
+ Smeaton, J. Cooper 1961
Storey, Red 1967
Udvari, Frank 1973

Builders

+ Adams, Charles 1960
+ Adams, Weston W. Sr 1972
+ Ahearn, Frank 1962
+ Ahearne, J.F. (Bunny) 1977
+ Allan, Sir Montagu 1945
Allen, Keith 1992
Arbour, Al 1996
+ Ballard, Harold 1977
+ Bauer, Fr. David 1989
+ Bickell, J.P. 1978
Bowman, Scotty 1991
+ Brown, George 1961
+ Brown, Walter 1962
+ Buckland, Frank 1975
Butterfield, Jack 1980
+ Calder, Frank 1945
+ Campbell, Angus 1964
+ Campbell, Clarence 1966
+ Cattarinich, Joseph 1977
+ Dandurand, Leo 1963
Dilio, Frank 1964
+ Dudley, George 1958
+ Dunn, James 1968
Francis, Emile 1982

+ Gibson, Jack 1976
+ Gorman, Tommy 1963
+ Griffiths, Frank A. 1993
+ Hanley, Bill.................1986
+ Hay, Charles 1984
+ Hendy, Jim 1968
+ Hewitt, Foster..............1965
+ Hewitt, W.A 1945
+ Hume, Fred.................1962
+ Imlach, Punch..............1984
Ivan, Tommy...............1964
+ Jennings, Bill...............1975
+ Johnson, Bob 1992
+ Juckes, Gordon 1979
+ Kilpatrick, John 1960
+ Knox, Seymour III 1993
+ Leader, Al..................1969
LeBel, Bob..................1970
+ Lockhart, Tom 1965
+ Loicq, Paul 1961
+ Mariucci, John 1985
Mathers, Frank.............1992
+ McLaughlin, Frederic 1963
+ Milford, Jake 1984
Molson, Hartland 1973
+ Murray, Athol (Pere) 1998
+ Nelson, Francis 1945
+ Norris, Bruce 1969
+ Norris, James D 1962
+ Norris, James Sr 1958
+ Northey, William...........1945
+ O'Brien, J.A 1962
O'Neill, Brian 1994
Page, Fred 1993
+ Patrick, Frank..............1958
+ Pickard, Allan 1958
+ Pilous, Rudy 1985
Poile, Bud 1990
Pollock, Sam...............1978
+ Raymond, Donat 1958
+ Robertson, John Ross........1945
+ Robinson, Claude 1945
+ Ross, Philip................1976
Sather, Glen...............1997
Sebetzki, Gunther 1995
+ Selke, Frank 1960
Sinden, Harry 1983
+ Smith, Frank...............1962
+ Smythe, Conn..............1958
Snider, Ed..................1988
+ Stanley, Lord of Preston 1945
+ Sutherland, James 1945
+ Tarasov, Anatoli............1974
Torrey, Bill.................1995
+ Turner, Lloyd..............1958
+ Tutt, William Thayer 1978
Voss, Carl 1974
+ Waghorne, Fred 1961
+ Wirtz, Arthur 1971
Wirtz, Bill..................1976
Ziegler, John...............1987

Note: Alan Eagleson was inducted into the Hockey Hall of Fame in 1989 but resigned in 1998 after being found guilty of fraud.

Elmer Ferguson Award

First presented in 1984 by the Professional Hockey Writers' Association for meritorious contributions by members of the PHWA. Named in honor of the late Montreal newspaper reporter, the Ferguson Award does not constitute induction into the Hall of Fame and is not necessarily an annual presentation.

1984 Jacques Beauchamp, Jim Burchard, Red Burnett, Dink Carroll, Jim Coleman, Ted Damata, Marcel Desjardins, Jack Dulmage, Milt Dunnell, Elmer Ferguson, Tom Fitzgerald, Trent Frayne, Al Laney, Joe Nichols, Basil O'Meara, Jim Vipond & Lewis Walter
1985 Charlie Barton, Red Fisher, George Gross, Zotique L'Esperance, Charles Mayer & Andy O'Brien
1986 Dick Johnston, Leo Monahan & Tim Moriarty
1987 Bill Brennan, Rex MacLeod, Ben Olan & Fran Rosa
1988 Jim Proudfoot & Scott Young
1989 Claude Larochelle & Frank Orr
1990 Bertrand Raymond
1991 Hugh Delano
1992 No award
1993 Al Strachan
1994 No award
1995 Jake Gatecliff
1996 No award
1997 Ken McKenzie
1998 Yvon Pedneault

Foster Hewitt Award

First presented in 1984 by the NHL Broadcasters' Association for meritorious contributions by members of the NHLBA. Named in honor of Canada's legendary "Voice of Hockey," the Hewitt Award does not constitute induction into the Hall of Fame and is not necessarily an annual presentation.

1985 Budd Lynch & Doug Smith
1986 Wes McKnight & Lloyd Pettit
1987 Bob Wilson
1988 Dick Irvin
1989 Dan Kelly
1990 Jiggs McDonald
1991 Bruce Martyn
1992 Jim Robson
1993 Al Shaver
1994 Ted Darling
1995 Brian McFarlane
1996 Bob Cole
1997 Gene Hart
1998 Howie Meeker

U.S. Hockey Hall of Fame

Established in 1968 by the Eveleth (Minn.) Civic Association Project H Committee and opened in 1973. **Address:** 801 Hat Trick Ave., P.O. Box 657, Eveleth, MN 55734. **Telephone:** (218) 744-5167.

Eligibility: Nominated players and referees must be American-born and retired five years; coaches must be American-born and must have coached predominantly American teams. Voting done by 12-member panel made up of Hall of Fame members and U.S. hockey officials.

Class of 1997 (3): PLAYERS—**William D. Nyrop**, **Timothy Sheehy**. COACH—**Charles E. Holt Jr.**

Members are listed with year of induction; (+) indicates deceased members.

Players

+ Abel, Clarence (Taffy).......1973
+ Baker, Hobey..............1973
Bartholome, Earl 1977
+ Bessone, Peter 1978
Blake, Bob 1985
Boucha, Henry.............1995
Brimsek, Frankie 1973
Cavanaugh, Joe 1994
+ Chaisson, Ray 1974
Chase, John 1973
Christian, Bill 1984
Christian, Roger............1989
Cleary, Bill 1976
Cleary, Bob 1981
+ Conroy, Tony 1975
Dahlstrom, Carl (Cully)......1973
+ DesJardins, Vic.............1974
+ Desmond, Richard..........1988
+ Dill, Bob 1979
Everett, Doug 1974
Ftorek, Robbie 1991
+ Garrison, John 1974
Garrity, Jack...............1986
+ Goheen, Frank (Moose) 1973
Grant, Wally 1994
+ Harding, Austie 1975
Iglehart, Stewart 1975
Ikola, Willard..............1990
Johnson, Virgil 1974
+ Karakas, Mike 1973

+ Palmer, Winthrop ... 1973

Kirrane, Jack ... 1987
+ Lane, Myles ... 1973
Langevin, Dave ... 1993
Larson, Reed ... 1996
+ Linder, Joe ... 1975
+ LoPresti, Sam ... 1973
+ Mariucci, John ... 1973
Matchefts, John ... 1991
Mayasich, John ... 1976
McCartan, Jack ... 1983
Moe, Bill ... 1974
Morrow, Ken ... 1995
+ Moseley, Fred ... 1975
+ Murray, Hugh (Muzz) Sr. ... 1987
+ Nelson, Hub ... 1978
+ Nyrop, William D. ... 1997
Olson, Eddie ... 1977
+ Owen, George ... 1973
+ Palmer, Winthrop ... 1973
Paradise, Bob ... 1989
Purpur, Clifford (Fido) ... 1974
Riley, Bill ... 1977
+ Romnes, Elwin (Doc) ... 1973
Rondeau, Dick ... 1985
Sheehey, Timothy ... 1997
+ Williams, Tom ... 1981
+ Winters, Frank (Coddy) ... 1973
+ Yackel, Ken ... 1986

Coaches

+ Almquist, Oscar ... 1983
Bessone, Amo ... 1992
Brooks, Herb ... 1990
Ceglarski, Len ... 1992
+ Fullerton, James ... 1992
Gambucci, Sergio ... 1996
+ Gordon, Malcolm ... 1973
Harkness, Ned ... 1994
Heyliger, Vic ... 1974
Holt Jr., Charles E. ... 1997
Ikola, Willard ... 1990
+ Jeremiah, Eddie ... 1973
+ Johnson, Bob ... 1991
Kelley, Jack ... 1993
+ Kelly, John (Snooks) ... 1974
Pleban, Connie ... 1990
Riley, Jack ... 1979
+ Ross, Larry ... 1988
+ Thompson, Cliff ... 1973
+ Stewart, Bill ... 1982
+ Winsor, Ralph ... 1973

Referee

Chadwick, Bill ... 1974

Contributor

Schulz, Charles M. ... 1993

Administrators

+ Brown, George ... 1973
+ Brown, Walter ... 1973
Bush, Walter ... 1980
Clark, Don ... 1978
Claypool, Jim ... 1995
+ Gibson, J.L. (Doc) ... 1973
+ Jennings, Bill ... 1981
+ Kahler, Nick ... 1980
+ Lockhart, Tom ... 1973
Marvin, Cal ... 1982
Patrick, Craig ... 1996
Ridder, Bob ... 1976
Trumble, Hal ... 1970
+ Tutt, Thayer ... 1973
Wirtz, Bill ... 1967
+ Wright, Lyle ... 1973

Members of Both Hockey and U.S. Hockey Halls of Fame

Players
Hobey Baker
Frankie Brimsek
Frank (Moose) Goheen
John Mariucci

Coach
Bob Johnson

Referee
Bill Chadwick

Builders
George Brown
Walter Brown
Doc Gibson
Bill Jennings
Tom Lockhart
Thayer Tutt
Bill Wirtz

HORSE RACING

National Horse Racing Hall of Fame

Established in 1950 by the Saratoga Springs Racing Association and opened in 1955. **Address:** National Museum of Racing and Hall of Fame, 191 Union Ave., Saratoga Springs, NY 12866. **Telephone:** (518) 584-0400.

Eligibility: Nominated horses must be retired five years; jockeys must be active at least 15 years; trainers must be active at least 25 years. Voting done by 100-member panel of horse racing media.

Class of 1998 (6): JOCKEY—**Jacinto Vasquez**. TRAINERS—**Bill Mott** and **Ansel Williamson**. HORSES—**Bayakoa**, **Fort Marcy** and **Riva Ridge**.

Members are listed with year of induction; (+) indicates deceased members.

Jockeys

+ Adams, Frank (Dooley)* ... 1970
+ Adams, John ... 1965
+ Aitcheson, Joe Jr.* ... 1978
+ Arcaro, Eddie ... 1958
Atkinson, Ted ... 1957
Baeza, Braulio ... 1976
Bailey, Jerry ... 1995
+ Barbee, George ... 1996
+ Bassett, Carroll* ... 1972
+ Blum, Walter ... 1987
+ Bostwick, George H.* ... 1968
+ Boulmetis, Sam ... 1973
+ Brooks, Steve ... 1963
Brumfield, Don ... 1996
+ Burns, Tommy ... 1983
+ Butwell, Jimmy ... 1984
Cauthen, Steve ... 1994
+ Coltiletti, Frank ... 1970
Cordero, Angel Jr. ... 1988
+ Crawford, Robert (Specs)* ... 1973
Day, Pat ... 1991
Delahoussaye, Eddie ... 1993
+ Ensor, Lavelle (Buddy) ... 1962
+ Fator, Laverne ... 1955
Fishback, Jerry* ... 1992
+ Garner, Andrew (Mack) ... 1969
+ Garrison, Snapper ... 1955
+ Griffin, Henry ... 1956
+ Guerin, Eric ... 1972
Hartack, Bill ... 1959
Hawley, Sandy ... 1992
+ Johnson, Albert ... 1971
+ Knapp, Willie ... 1969
+ Kummer, Clarence ... 1972
+ Kurtsinger, Charley ... 1967
+ Loftus, Johnny ... 1959
Longden, Johnny ... 1958
Maher, Danny ... 1955
+ McAtee, Linus ... 1956
McCarron, Chris ... 1989
+ McCreary, Conn ... 1974
+ McKinney, Rigan ... 1968
+ McLaughlin, James ... 1955
+ Miller, Walter ... 1955
+ Murphy, Isaac ... 1955
+ Neves, Ralph ... 1960
+ Notter, Joe ... 1963
+ O'Connor, Winnie ... 1956

+ Odom, George 1955
+ O'Neill, Frank 1956
+ Parke, Ivan 1978
+ Patrick, Gil 1970
Pincay, Laffit Jr. 1975
+ Purdy, Sam 1970
+ Reiff, John 1956
+ Robertson, Alfred 1971
Rotz, John L. 1983
+ Sande, Earl 1955
+ Schilling, Carroll 1970
Shoemaker, Bill 1958
+ Simms, Willie 1977
+ Sloan, Todhunter 1955
+ Smithwick, A. Patrick* 1973
Stevens, Gary 1997
+ Stout, James 1968
+ Taral, Fred 1955
+ Tuckman, Bayard Jr.* 1973
Turcotte, Ron 1979
+ Turner, Nash 1955
Ussery, Robert 1980
Vasquez, Jacinto 1998
Velasquez, Jorge 1990
+ Woolfe, George 1955
+ Workman, Raymond 1956
Ycaza, Manuel 1977

*Steeplechase jockey

Trainers

+ Barrera, Laz 1979
+ Bedwell, H. Guy 1971
+ Brown, Edward D. 1984
Burch, Elliot 1980
+ Burch, Preston M. 1963
+ Burch, W.P. 1955
+ Burlew, Fred 1973
+ Byers, J.D. (Dilly) 1967
+ Childs, Frank E. 1968
+ Cocks, W. Burling 1985
Conway, James P. 1996
Croll, Jimmy 1994
+ Duke, William 1956
+ Feustel, Louis 1964
+ Fitzsimmons, J. (Sunny Jim) . . 1958
Frankel, Bobby 1995
+ Gaver, John M. 1966
+ Healey, Thomas 1955
+ Hildreth, Samuel 1955
+ Hirsch, Max 1959
+ Hirsch, W.J. (Buddy) 1982
+ Hitchcock, Thomas Sr. 1973
+ Hughes, Hollie 1973
+ Hyland, John 1956
+ Jacobs, Hirsch 1958
Jerkens, H. Allen 1975
Johnson, Philip 1997
+ Johnson, William R. 1986
+ Jolley, LeRoy 1987
+ Jones, Ben A. 1958
Jones, H.A. (Jimmy) 1959
+ Joyner, Andrew 1955
Kelly, Tom 1993
Laurin, Lucien 1977
+ Lewis, J. Howard 1969
+ Luro, Horatio 1980
+ Madden, John 1983
+ Maloney, Jim 1989
Martin, Frank (Pancho) 1981
McAnally, Ron 1990
+ McDaniel, Henry 1956
+ Miller, MacKenzie 1987
+ Molter, William, Jr. 1960
Mott, Bill 1998
+ Mulholland, Winbert 1967
+ Neloy, Eddie 1983
Nerud, John 1972
+ Parke, Burley 1986
+ Penna, Angel Sr. 1988
+ Pincus, Jacob 1988
+ Rogers, John 1955
+ Rowe, James Sr. 1955
Schulhofer, Scotty 1992
Sheppard, Jonathan 1990
+ Smith, Robert A. 1976
+ Smithwick, Mike 1976
+ Stephens, Woody 1976
+ Thompson, H.J. 1969
+ Trotsek, Harry 1984
Van Berg, Jack 1985
+ Van Berg, Marion 1970
+ Veitch, Sylvester 1977
+ Walden, Robert 1970
Walsh, Michael 1997
+ Ward, Sherrill 1978
Whiteley, Frank Jr. 1978
Whittingham, Charlie 1974
+ Williamson, Ansel 1998
Winfrey, W.C. (Bill) 1971

Horses

Year foaled in parentheses.

+ Ack Ack (1966) 1986
Affectionately (1960) 1989
Affirmed (1975) 1980
All-Along (1979) 1990
+ Alsab (1939) 1976
+ Alydar (1975) 1989
Alysheba (1984) 1993
+ American Eclipse (1814) 1970
+ Armed (1941) 1963
+ Artful (1902) 1956
+ Arts and Letters (1966) 1994
+ Assault (1943) 1964
+ Battleship (1927) 1969
+ Bayakoa (1984) 1998
+ Bed O'Roses (1947) 1976
+ Beldame (1901) 1956
+ Ben Brush (1893) 1955
+ Bewitch (1945) 1977
+ Bimelech (1937) 1990
+ Black Gold (1919) 1989
+ Black Helen (1932) 1991
+ Blue Larkspur (1926) 1957
+ Bold 'n Determined (1977) . . 1997
+ Bold Ruler (1954) 1973
+ Bon Nouvel (1960) 1976
+ Boston (1833) 1955
+ Broomstick (1901) 1956
+ Buckpasser (1963) 1970
+ Busher (1942) 1964
+ Bushranger (1930) 1967
+ Cafe Prince (1970) 1985
+ Carry Back (1958) 1975
+ Cavalcade (1931) 1993
+ Challendon (1936) 1977
+ Chris Evert (1971) 1988
+ Cicada (1959) 1967
+ Citation (1945) 1959
+ Coaltown (1945) 1983
+ Colin (1905) 1956
+ Commando (1898) 1956
+ Count Fleet (1940) 1961
+ Crusader (1923) 1995
+ Dahlia (1971) 1981
+ Damascus (1964) 1974
+ Dark Mirage (1965) 1974
+ Davona Dale (1976) 1985
+ Desert Vixen (1970) 1979
+ Devil Diver (1939) 1980
+ Discovery (1931) 1969
+ Domino (1891) 1955
+ Dr. Fager (1964) 1971
Easy Goer (1986) 1997
+ Eight 30 (1936) 1994
+ Elkridge (1938) 1966
+ Emperor of Norfolk (1885) . . 1988
+ Equipoise (1928) 1957
+ Exterminator (1915) 1957
+ Fairmount (1921) 1985
+ Fair Play (1905) 1956
+ Firenze (1885) 1981
Flatterer (1979) 1994
Foolish Pleasure (1972) 1995
+ Forego (1971) 1979
+ Fort Marcy (1964) 1998
+ Gallant Bloom (1966) 1977
+ Gallant Fox (1927) 1957
+ Gallant Man (1954) 1987
+ Gallorette (1942) 1962
+ Gamely (1964) 1980
Genuine Risk (1977) 1986
+ Good and Plenty (1900) 1956
+ Go For Wand (1987) 1996
+ Granville (1933) 1997
+ Grey Lag (1918) 1957
+ Hamburg (1895) 1986
+ Hanover (1884) 1955
+ Henry of Navarre (1891) . . . 1985
+ Hill Prince (1947) 1991
+ Hindoo (1878) 1955
+ Imp (1894) 1965
+ Jay Trump (1957) 1971
John Henry (1975) 1990
+ Johnstown (1936) 1992
+ Jolly Roger (1922) 1965
+ Kingston (1884) 1955
+ Kelso (1957) 1967
+ Kentucky (1861) 1983
Lady's Secret (1982) 1992
La Prevoyante (1970) 1995
+ L'Escargot (1963) 1977
+ Lexington (1850) 1955
+ Longfellow (1867) 1971
+ Luke Blackburn (1877) 1956
+ Majestic Prince (1966) 1988
+ Man o' War (1917) 1957
+ Miss Woodford (1880) 1967
+ Myrtlewood (1933) 1979
+ Nashua (1952) 1965
+ Native Dancer (1950) 1963
+ Native Diver (1959) 1978
+ Northern Dancer (1961) 1976
+ Neji (1950) 1966

+ Oedipus (1941)............1978
+ Old Rosebud (1911)........1968
+ Omaha (1932)............1965
+ Pan Zareta (1910).........1972
+ Parole (1873)............1984
Personal Ensign (1984).....1993
+ Peter Pan (1904)..........1956
Princess Rooney (1980).....1991
+ Real Delight (1949).........1987
+ Regret (1912)............1957
+ Reigh Count (1925)........1978
Riva Ridge (1969)..........1998
+ Roamer (1911)............1981
+ Roseben (1901)............1956
+ Round Table (1954)........1972
+ Ruffian (1972)............1976
+ Ruthless (1864)............1975
+ Salvator (1886)............1955
+ Sarazen (1921)............1957
+ Seabiscuit (1933)..........1958
+ Searching (1952)..........1978
Seattle Slew (1974)........1981
+ Secretariat (1970)..........1974
+ Shuvee (1966)............1975
+ Silver Spoon (1956)........1978
+ Sir Archy (1805)...........1955
+ Sir Barton (1916)..........1957
Slew o'Gold (1980)........1992
+ Sun Beau (1925)...........1996
Sunday Silence (1986)......1996
+ Stymie (1941)............1975
+ Susan's Girl (1969).........1976
+ Swaps (1952)............1966
+ Sword Dancer (1956).......1977
+ Sysonby (1902)............1956
+ Ta Wee (1966)............1994
+ Tim Tam (1955)............1985
+ Tom Fool (1949)...........1960
+ Top Flight (1929)...........1966
+ Tosmah (1961).............1984
+ Twenty Grand (1928).......1957
+ Twilight Tear (1941)........1963
+ War Admiral (1934)........1958
+ Whirlaway (1938).........1959
+ Whisk Broom II (1907)......1979
Zaccio (1976).............1990
+ Zev (1920)................1983

Exemplars of Racing

+ Hanes, John W............1982
+ Jeffords, Walter M..........1973
Mellon, Paul...............1989
Widener, George D........1971

Harness Racing Living Hall of Fame

Established by the U.S. Harness Writers Association (USHWA) in 1958. **Address:** Trotting Horse Museum, 240 Main Street, P.O. Box 590, Goshen, NY 10924; **Telephone:** (914) 294-6330.

Eligibility: Open to all harness racing drivers, trainers and executives. Voting done by USHWA membership. There are 73 members of the Living Hall of Fame, but only the 37 drivers and trainer-drivers are listed below.

Class of 1998 (5): TRAINER-DRIVER—**Ray Remmen** and **Charles Sylvester**. EXECUTIVE—**William Brown**. HORSES— **Cam Fella** and **Mack Lobell**.

Members are listed with years of induction; (+) indicates deceased members.

Trainer-Drivers

Abbatiello, Carmine........1986
Abbatiello, Tony............1995
Ackerman, Doug...........1995
+ Avery, Earle...............1975
+ Baldwin, Ralph.............1972
Beissinger, Howard.........1975
Bostwick, Dunbar...........1989
+ Cameron, Del..............1975
Campbell, John............1991
+ Chapman, John............1980
Cruise, Jimmy..............1987
Dancer, Stanley............1970
+ Ervin, Frank...............1969
Farrington, Bob............1980
Filion, Herve...............1976
+ Garnsey, Glen.............1983
Galbraith, Clint............1990
Gilmour, Buddy............1990
Harner, Levi...............1986
+ Haughton, Billy............1969
+ Hodgins, Clint.............1973
Insko, Del.................1981
Kopas, Jack...............1996
Lachance, Michel..........1996
Miller, Del..................1969
+ O'Brien, Joe...............1971
O'Donnell, Bill.............1991
Patterson, John Sir..........1994
+ Pownall, Harry.............1971
Remmen, Ray..............1998
Riegle, Gene..............1992
+ Russell, Sanders............1971
+ Shively, Bion..............1968
Sholty, George.............1985
Simpson, John Sr...........1972
+ Smart, Curly..............1970
Sylvester, Charles..........1998
Waples, Keith.............1987
Waples, Ron...............1994

MEDIA

National Sportscasters and Sportswriters Hall of Fame

Established in 1959 by the National Sportscasters and Sportswriters Association. **Mailing Address:** P.O. Box 559, Salisbury, NC 28144. A permanent museum is scheduled to open in early 1998. **Telephone:** (704) 633-4275.

Eligibility: Nominees must be active for at least 25 years. Voting done by NSSA membership and other media representatives.

Members are listed with year of induction; (+) indicates deceased members.

Sportscasters

+ Allen, Mel.................1972
+ Barber, Walter (Red)........1973
+ Brickhouse, Jack...........1983
Buck, Jack.................1990
+ Caray, Harry..............1989
+ Cosell, Howard............1993
+ Dean, Dizzy...............1976
+ Dunphy, Don..............1986
+ Elson, Bob................1995
Enberg, Dick..............1996
Glickman, Marty...........1992
Gowdy, Curt..............1981
Harwell, Ernie.............1989
Hearn, Chick..............1997
+ Hodges, Russ.............1975
+ Hoyt, Waite..............1987
+ Husing, Ted..............1963
Jackson, Keith.............1995
+ McCarthy, Clem...........1970
McKay, Jim...............1987
+ McNamee, Graham........1964
+ Nelson, Lindsey............1979
+ Prince, Bob................1986
Schenkel, Chris............1981
+ Scott, Ray.................1982
Scully, Vin.................1991
+ Stern, Bill................1974
Summerall, Pat.............1994

Sportswriters

Anderson, Dave............1990
Bisher, Furman............1989
Broeg, Bob................1997
Burick, Si................1985
+ Cannon, Jimmy...........1986
+ Carmichael, John P......1994
+ Connor, Dick............1992
+ Considine, Bob..........1980
+ Daley, Arthur...........1976
Durslag, Mel..............1995
+ Gould, Alan.............1990
+ Graham, Frank Sr........1995
+ Grimsley, Will..........1987
Heinz, W.C................1987
Jenkins, Dan..............1996
+ Kieran, John............1971
+ Lardner, Ring...........1967
+ Murphy, Jack............1988
+ Murray, Jim.............1978
Olderman, Murray..........1993
+ Parker, Dan.............1975
Pope, Edwin...............1994
+ Povich, Shirley.........1984
+ Rice, Grantland.........1962
+ Runyon, Damon...........1964
Russell, Fred.............1988
Sherrod, Blackie..........1991
+ Smith, Walter (Red).....1977
+ Spink, J.G. Taylor......1969
+ Ward, Arch..............1973
+ Woodward, Stanley.......1974

American Sportscasters Hall of Fame

Established in 1984 by the American Sportscasters Association. **Address:** 5 Beekman Street, Suite 814, New York, NY 10038. A permanent museum site is in the planning stages. **Telephone:** (212) 227-8080.

Eligibility: nominations made by selection committee of previous winners, voting by ASA membership.

Class of 1998 (1): **Jack Whitaker**.

Members are listed with year of induction; (+) indicates deceased members.

+ Allen, Mel..............1985
+ Barber, Walter (Red)....1984
+ Brickhouse, Jack........1985
Buck, Jack................1990
+ Caray, Harry............1989
+ Cosell, Howard..........1993
+ Dunphy, Don.............1984
Glickman, Marty...........1993
Gowdy, Curt...............1985
Harwell, Ernie............1991
Hearn, Chick..............1995
+ Husing, Ted.............1984
Jackson, Keith............1994
+ McCarthy, Clem..........1987
McKay, Jim................1987
+ McNamee, Graham.........1984
+ Nelson, Lindsey.........1986
Schenkel, Chris...........1997
Scully, Vin...............1992
+ Stern, Bill.............1984
Whitaker, Jack............1998

MOTORSPORTS

Motorsports Hall of Fame of America

Established in 1989. **Mailing Address:** P.O. Box 194, Novi, MI 48376. **Telephone:** (810) 349-7223.

Eligibility: Nominees must be retired at least three years or engaged in their area of motor sports for at least 20 years. Areas include: open wheel, stock car, dragster, sports car, motorcycle, off road, power boat, air racing and land speed records.

Class of 1998 (3): DRIVERS—**Jack Brabham** (open wheel) and **Rick Mears** (open wheel). CONTRIBUTORS—**Takeo Hirashima**.

Members are listed with year of induction; (+) indicates deceased members.

Drivers

Allison, Bobby............1992
Andretti, Mario...........1990
Arfons, Art...............1991
+ Baker, Cannonball.......1989
Bettenhausen, Tony........1997
Brabham, Jack.............1998
Breedlove, Craig..........1993
+ Campbell, Sir Malcolm...1994
Cantrell, Bill............1992
+ Chenoweth, Dean.........1991
Chrisman, Art.............1997
+ Clark, Jim..............1990
+ Cook, Betty.............1996
Cunningham, Briggs........1997
Davis, Jim................1997
DeCoster, Roger...........1994
+ DePalma, Ralph..........1992
+ DePaolo, Peter..........1995
+ Donahue, Mark...........1990
Foyt, A.J.................1989
Garlits, Don..............1989
Glidden, Bob..............1994
Gurney, Dan...............1991
Hanauer, Chip.............1995
Hill, Phil................1989
+ Holbert, Al.............1993
+ Horn, Ted...............1993
Jarrett, Ned..............1997
Jenkins, Bill (Grumpy)....1996
Johnson, Junior...........1991
Jones, Parnelli...........1992
Kalitta, Connie...........1992
Leonard, Joe..............1991
+ McLaren, Bruce..........1995
Mann, Dick................1993
+ Mays, Rex...............1995
Mears, Rick...............1998
+ Meyer, Louis............1993
Muldowney, Shirley........1990
+ Muncy, Bill.............1989
+ Musson, Ron.............1993
Nordskog, Bob.............1997
+ Oldfield, Barney........1989
Parks, Wally..............1993
Pearson, David............1993
+ Petrali, Joe............1992
Petty, Lee................1996
Petty, Richard............1989
Prudhomme, Don............1991
+ Revson, Peter...........1996
+ Roberts, Fireball.......1995
Roberts, Kenny............1990
Rutherford, Johnny........1996
+ Shaw, Wilbur............1991
Smith, Malcolm............1996
+ Thompson, Mickey........1990
Unser, Al.................1991
Unser, Bobby..............1994
+ Vukovich, Bill Sr.......1992
Ward, Rodger..............1995
+ Wood, Gar...............1990
Yarborough, Cale..........1994

Pilots

+ Cochran, Jacqueline.....1993
+ Curtiss, Glenn..........1990
+ Doolittle, Jimmy........1989
+ Earhart, Amelia.........1992
+ Falck, Bill.............1994
Greenmayer, Darryl........1997
+ Turner, Roscoe..........1991

Contributors

+ Agajanian, J.C..........1992
Bignotti, George..........1993
+ Black, Keith............1995
Chapman, Colin............1997
+ Chevrolet, Louis........1995
Duesenberg, Fred..........1997
Economacki, Chris.........1994
+ Ford, Henry.............1996
+ France, Bill Sr.........1990
Hall, Jim.................1994
+ Hulman, Tony............1991
Little, Bernie............1994
Penske, Roger.............1995
+ Rickenbacker, Eddie.....1994
+ Rose, Mauri.............1996
Shelby, Carroll...........1992
Watson, A.J...............1996

Motorsports (Cont.)

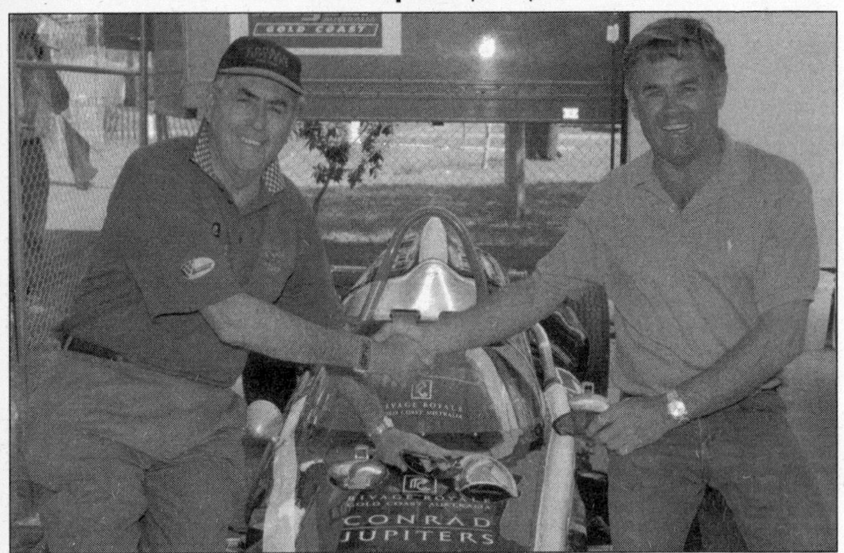

AP/Wide World Photos

Racing legends **Jack Brabham** of Australia (left) and American **Al Unser Sr.** pictured above in a meeting in 1996, were both honored in 1998. Brabham was inducted into the Motorsports Hall of Fame of America while Unser was enshrined at the International Motorsports Hall of Fame. Now both men are members of both organizations.

International Motorsports Hall of Fame

Established in 1990 by the International Motorsports Hall of Fame Commission. **Mailing Address:** P.O. Box 1018, Talladega, AL 35160. **Telephone:** (205) 362-5002.

Eligibility: Nominees must be retired from their specialty in motorsports for five years. Voting done by 150-member panel made up of the world-wide auto racing media.

Class of 1998 (6): DRIVERS—**Davey Allison**, **Rudolph Caracciola**, **Tazio Nuvolari**, and **Al Unser Sr.** CONTRIBUTERS—**Banjo Matthews** and **Roger Penske**.

Members are listed with year of induction; (+) indicates deceased members.

Drivers

Allison, Bobby 1993
+ Allison, Davey 1998
+ Ascari, Alberto............1992
Baker, Buck................1990
+ Bettenhausen, Tony 1991
Brabham, Jack 1990
+ Campbell, Sir Malcolm......1990
+ Caracciola, Rudolph........1998
+ Clark, Jim 1990
+ DePalma, Ralph............1991
+ Donahue, Mark 1990
+ Evans, Richie 1996
+ Fangio, Juan Manuel 1990
+ Flock, Tim 1991
+ Gregg, Peter 1992
Gurney, Dan................1990
+ Haley, Donald 1996
+ Hill, Graham 1990
Hill, Phil 1991
+ Holbert, Al 1993
+ Isaac, Bobby 1996
Jarrett, Ned 1991
Johnson, Junior............1990
Jones, Parnelli 1990
Lauda, Niki................1993
Lorenzen, Fred 1991
+ Lund, Tiny.................1994
+ Mays, Rex.................1993
+ McLaren, Bruce 1991
+ Meyer, Louis..............1992
Moss, Stirling 1990
+ Nuvolari, Tazio 1998
+ Oldfield, Barney 1990
Parsons, Benny............1994
Pearson, David 1993
Petty, Lee..................1990
+ Roberts, Fireball...........1990
Roberts, Kenny............1992
Rose, Mauri 1994
Rutherford, Johnny.........1996
+ Shaw, Wilbur.............1991
Stewart, Jackie............1990
Surtees, John 1996
Thomas, Herb.............1994
+ Turner, Curtis 1992
Unser, Al Sr...............1998
Unser, Bobby 1990
+ Vukovich, Bill 1991
Ward Rodger..............1992
+ Weatherly, Joe............1994
Yarborough, Cale 1993

Contributors

Bignotti, George 1993
+ Chapman, Colin 1994
+ Chevrolet, Louis 1992
+ Ferrari, Enzo 1994
+ Ford, Henry 1993
+ France, Bill Sr.............1990
Granatelli, Andy 1992
+ Hulman, Tony.............1990
Marcum, John 1994
+ Matthews, Banjo 1998
Moody, Ralph 1994
Parks, Wally..............1992
Penske, Roger 1998
+ Porsche, Ferdinand........1996
+ Rickenbacker, Eddie 1992
Shelby, Carroll............1991
+ Thompson, Mickey 1990
Yunick, Smokey 1990

OLYMPICS

U.S. Olympic Hall of Fame

Established in 1983 by the United States Olympic Committee. **Mailing Address:** U.S. Olympic Committee, 1750 East Boulder Street, Colorado Springs, CO 80909. Plans for a permanent museum site have been suspended due to lack of funding. **Telephone:** (719) 578-4529.

Eligibility: Nominated athletes must be five years removed from active competition. Voting done by National Sportscasters and Sportswriters Association, Hall of Fame members and the USOC board members of directors.

Voting for membership in the Hall was suspended in 1993.

Members are listed with year of induction; (+) indicates deceased members.

Teams

1956 Basketball Dick Boushka, Carl Cain, Chuck Darling, Bill Evans, Gib Ford, Burdy Haldorson, Bill Hougland, Bob Jeangerard, K.C. Jones, Bill Russell, Ron Tomsic, +Jim Walsh and coach +Gerald Tucker.

1960 Basketball Jay Arnette, Walt Bellamy, Bob Boozer, Terry Dischinger, Burdy Haldorson, Darrall Imhoff, Allen Kelley, +Lester Lane, Jerry Lucas, Oscar Robertson, Adrian Smith, Jerry West and coach Pete Newell.

1964 Basketball Jim Barnes, Bill Bradley, Larry Brown, Joe Caldwell, Mel Counts, Richard Davies, Walt Hazzard, Luke Jackson, John McCaffrey, Jeff Mullins, Jerry Shipp, George Wilson and coach +Hank Iba.

1960 Ice Hockey Billy Christian, Roger Christian, Billy Cleary, Bob Cleary, Gene Grazia, Paul Johnson, Jack Kirrane, John Mayasich, Jack McCartan, Bob McKay, Dick Meredith, Weldon Olson, Ed Owen, Rod Paavola, Larry Palmer, Dick Rodenheiser, +Tom Williams and coach Jack Riley.

1980 Ice Hockey Bill Baker, Neal Broten, Dave Christian, Steve Christoff, Jim Craig, Mike Eruzione, John Harrington, Steve Janaszak, Mark Johnson, Ken Morrow, Rob McClanahan, Jack O'Callahan, Mark Pavelich, Mike Ramsey, Buzz Schneider, Dave Silk, Eric Strobel, Bob Suter, Phil Verchota, Mark Wells and coach Herb Brooks.

The Olympic Order

Established in 1974 by the International Olympic Committee (IOC) to honor athletes, officials and media members who have made remarkable contributions to the Olympic movement. The IOC's Council of the Olympic Order is presided over by the IOC president and active IOC members are not eligible for consideration. Through 1998, only three American officials have received the Order's highest commendation—the gold medal:

Avery Brundage, president of USOC (1928-53) and IOC (1952-72), was given the award posthumously in 1975.

Peter Ueberroth, president of Los Angeles Olympic Organizing Committee, was given the award in 1984.

Billy Payne, president of the Atlanta Committee for the Olympic Games, was given the award in 1996.

Alpine Skiing

Mahre, Phil................1992

Bobsled

\+ Eagan, Eddie (see Boxing)...1983

Boxing

Clay, Cassius*.............1983
\+ Eagan, Eddie (see Bobsled)..1983
Foreman, George..........1990
Frazier, Joe................1989
Leonard, Sugar Ray........1985
Patterson, Floyd............1987

*Clay changed name to Muhammad Ali in 1964.

Cycling

Carpenter-Phinney, Connie...1992

Diving

King, Miki.................1992
Lee, Sammy...............1990
Louganis, Greg...........1985
McCormick, Pat............1985

Figure Skating

Albright, Tenley............1988
Button, Dick...............1983
Fleming, Peggy............1983
Hamill, Dorothy............1991
Hamilton, Scott............1990

Gymnastics

Conner, Bart...............1991
Retton, Mary Lou...........1985
Vidmar, Peter..............1991

Rowing

\+ Kelly, Jack Sr...............1990

Speed Skating

Heiden, Eric..............1983

Swimming

Babashoff, Shirley..........1987
Caulkins, Tracy............1990
\+ Daniels, Charles..........1988
de Varona, Donna..........1987
\+ Kahanamoku, Duke.........1984
\+ Madison, Helene...........1992
Meyer, Debbie.............1986
Naber, John...............1984
Schollander, Don..........1983
Spitz, Mark...............1983
\+ Weissmuller, Johnny........1983

Track & Field

Beamon, Bob..............1983
Boston, Ralph.............1985
\+ Calhoun, Lee.............1991
Campbell, Milt............1992
Davenport, Willie..........1991
Davis, Glenn..............1986
\+ Didrikson, Babe...........1983
Dillard, Harrison..........1983
Evans, Lee................1989
\+ Ewry, Ray................1983
Fosbury, Dick.............1992
Jenner, Bruce.............1986
Johnson, Rafer............1983
\+ Kraenzlein, Alvin..........1985
Lewis, Carl...............1985
Mathias, Bob..............1983
Mills, Billy.................1984
Morrow, Bobby............1989
Moses, Edwin..............1985
O'Brien, Parry............1984
Oerter, Al.................1983
\+ Owens, Jesse.............1983
\+ Paddock, Charley..........1991
Richards, Bob.............1983
\+ Rudolph, Wilma............1983
\+ Sheppard, Mel.............1989
Shorter, Frank.............1984
\+ Thorpe, Jim...............1983
Toomey, Bill...............1984
Tyus, Wyomia.............1985
Whitfield, Mal.............1988
\+ Wykoff, Frank.............1984

Weight Lifting

\+ Davis, John................1989
Kono, Tommy..............1990

Wrestling

Gable, Dan...............1985

Contributors

Arledge, Roone............1989
\+ Brundage, Avery...........1983
\+ Bushnell, Asa.............1990
Hull, Col. Don.............1992
\+ Iba, Hank................1985
\+ Kane, Robert..............1986
\+ Kelly, Jack Jr..............1992
McKay, Jim................1988
Miller, Don...............1984
Simon, William............1991
Walker, LeRoy.............1987

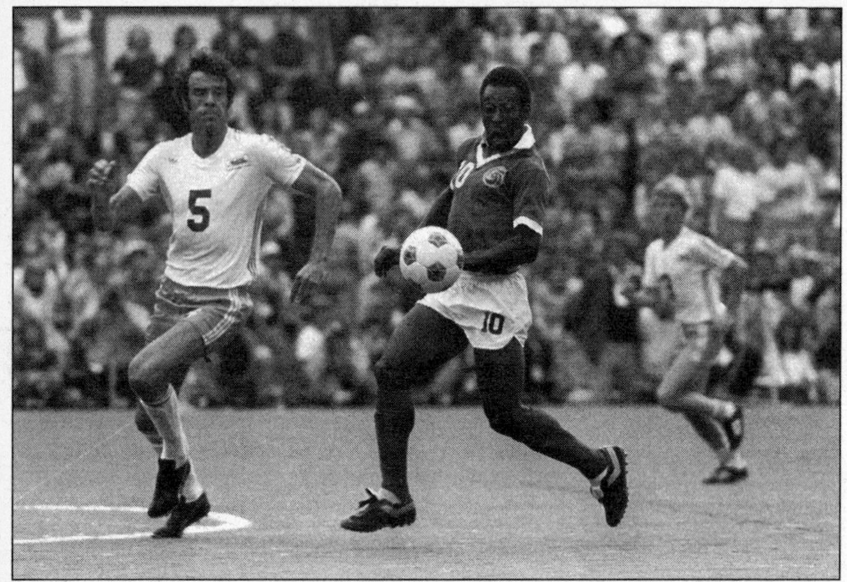

AP/Wide World Photos

Pele, pictured above in the 1977 North American Soccer League title game, was among ten players in the inaugural class inducted into the International Soccer Hall of Champions in 1998.

SOCCER

International Soccer Hall of Champions

Established in 1998 by FIFA, soccer's international governing body. Located at Disneyland Paris.

Eligibility: Nominated players and coaches must be retired at least five years. Nominations made by a committee composed of FIFA members, the Hall of Champions management and three ad hoc members then submit a list to a panel of 32 soccer journalists from around the world who also have the chance to add nominees of their own as well as voting for a specific number of candidates in each category.

Inaugural Class of 1998 (18): PLAYERS—**Pelé**, **Franz Beckenbauer**, **Johan Cruyff**, **Alfredo di Stefano**, **Michel Plantini**, **Sir Bobby Charlton**, **Sir Stanley Matthews**, **Ferenc Puskas**, **Eusebio** and **Lev Yashin**. COACHES—**Rinus Michels** and **Sir Matt Busby**. REFEREES—**Michel Vautrot**. CLUB TEAMS—**Real Madrid**. NATIONAL TEAMS—**Brazil**. PIONEERS—**Jules Rimet**. MEDIA—**Jacques Goddett**. FOR THE GOOD OF THE GAME—**Horst Dassler**.

National Soccer Hall of Fame

Established in 1950 by the Philadelphia Oldtimers Association. First exhibit unveiled in Oneonta, NY in 1982. Moved into present building in 1987. New Hall of Fame planned at Wright National Soccer Campus in Oneonta. **Address:** 5-11 Ford Avenue, Oneonta, NY 13820. **Telephone:** (607) 432-3351.

Eligibility: Nominated players must have represented the U.S. in international competition and be retired five years; other categories include Meritorious Service and Special Commendation.

Nominations made by state organizations and a veterans' committee. Voting done by nine-member committee made up of Hall of Famers, U.S. Soccer officials and members of the national media.

Class of 1998 (4): PLAYERS—**Franz Beckenbauer** and **April Heinrichs**. CONTRIBUTORS—**Peter Collins** and **Patrick Smith**.

Members are listed with home state and year of induction; (+) indicates deceased members.

Members

Abronzino, Umberto (CA) ...1971
Aimi, Milton (TX) 1991
+ Alonso, Julie (NY) 1972
+ Andersen, William (NY).....1956
+ Ardizzone, John (CA).......1971
+ Armstrong, James (NY)......1952
+ Auld, Andrew (RI) 1986
Bahr, Walter (PA)...........1976
Barr, George (NY)..........1983
+ Barriskill, Joe (NY)..........1953
+ Beardsworth, Fred (MA).....1965
Beckenbauer, Franz (Ger) ...1998
Berling, Clay (CA)..........1995
Bernabei, Ray (PA) 1978
Best, John O. (CA)..........1982
+ Bookie, Michael (PA)........1986
+ Booth, Joseph (CT)..........1952
Borghi, Frank (MO).........1976
Boulos, Frenchy (NY) 1980
+ Boxer, Matt (CA) 1961
Bradley, Gordon (Eng) 1996
+ Briggs, Lawrence E. (MA)....1978
+ Brittan, Harold (PA).........1951
+ Brock, John (MA)...........1950
+ Brown, Andrew M. (OH) 1950
+ Brown, David (NJ)..........1951
Brown, George (NJ) 1995

Brown, James (NY) 1986
+ Cahill, Thomas W (NY) 1950
+ Carenza, Joe (MO).........1982
+ Caraffi, Ralph (OH).........1959
Chacurian, Chico (CT) 1992
+ Chesney, Stan (NY).........1966
Chyzowych, Walter (PA) 1997
+ Coll, John (NY) 1986
+ Collins, George M. (MA) 1951
Collins, Peter (NY)..........1998
+ Colombo, Charlie (MO).....1976
+ Commander, Colin (OH) 1967
+ Cordery, Ted (CA)..........1975
+ Craddock, Robert (PA) 1959
+ Craggs, Edmund (WA)......1969
Craggs, George (WA) 1981
+ Cummings, Wilfred R. (IL) ...1953
+ Delach, Joseph (PA).........1973
DeLuca, Enzo (NY) 1979
+ Dick, Walter (CA) 1989
Diorio, Nick (PA) 1974
+ Donaghy, Edward J. (NY) ...1951
+ Donelli, Buff (PA) 1954
+ Donnelly, George (NY)......1989
+ Douglas, Jimmy (NJ) 1954
+ Dresmich, John W. (PA) 1968
+ Duff, Duncan (CA)..........1972
+ Dugan, Thomas (NJ) 1951
+ Dunn, James (MO) 1974
Edwards, Gene (WI)........1985
Ely, Alexander (PA) 1997
+ Epperleim, Rudy (NJ) 1951
+ Fairfield, Harry (PA) 1951
Feibusch, Ernst (CA) 1984
+ Ferguson, John (PA).........1950
+ Fernley, John A. (MA).......1951
+ Ferro, Charles (NY).........1958
+ Fishwick, George E. (IL) 1974
+ Flamhaft, Jack (NY).........1964
+ Fleming, Harry G. (PA)......1967
+ Florie, Thomas (NJ) 1986
+ Foulds, Pal (MA) 1953
+ Foulds, Sam (MA) 1969
+ Fowler, Dan (NY)...........1970
+ Fowler, Peg (NY) 1979
Fricker, Werner (PA) 1992
+ Fryer, William J. (NJ) 1951
+ Gaetjens, Joe (NY) 1976
+ Gallagher, James (NY)......1986
+ Garcia, Pete (MO) 1964
+ Gentle, James (PA)..........1986
Getzinger, Rudy (IL).........1991
+ Giesler, Walter (MO) 1962
Glover, Teddy (NY) 1965
+ Gonsalves, Billy (MA).......1950
Gormley, Bob (PA)..........1989
+ Gould, David L. (PA) 1953
+ Govier, Sheldon (IL).........1950
Greer, Don (CA) 1985
Gryzik, Joe (IL).............1973
+ Guelker, Bob (MO) 1980
Guennel, Joe (CO) 1980
Harker, Al (PA).............1979
+ Healy, George (MI).........1951

Heilpern, Herb (NY) 1988
Heinrichs, April (CO) 1998
+ Hemmings, William (IL)......1961
+ Hudson, Maurice (CA) 1966
Hunt, Lamar (TX) 1982
Hynes, John (NY)...........1977
+ Iglehart, Alfredda (MD) 1951
+ Japp, John (PA) 1953
+ Jeffrey, William (PA) 1951
Jewell, Frank (FA)...........1996
+ Johnson, Jack (IL) 1952
Kabanica, Mike (WI) 1987
Kehoe, Bob (MO) 1990
Kelly, Frank (NJ)............1994
+ Kempton, George (WA) 1950
Keough, Harry (MO)........1976
+ Klein, Paul (NJ) 1953
Kleinaitis, Al (IN)...........1995
+ Koszma, Oscar (CA)........1964
Kracher, Frank (IL) 1983
Kraft, Granny (MD).........1984
+ Kraus, Harry (NY)..........1963
Kropfelder, Nicholas........1996
+ Kunter, Rudy (NY) 1963
+ Lamm, Kurt (NY) 1979
Lang, Millard (MD) 1950
Larson, Bert (CT) 1988
Leonard, Abbot (Eng) 1996
+ Lewis, H. Edgar (PA) 1950
Lombardo, Joe (NY) 1984
Long, Denny (MO)...........1993
+ MacEwan, John J. (MI) 1953
+ Maca, Joe (NY) 1976
+ Magnozzi, Enzo (NY).......1978
+ Maher, Jack (IL) 1970
+ Manning, Dr. Randolf (NY) ..1950
+ Marre, John (MO) 1953
McBride, Pat (MO) 1994
+ McClay, Allan (MA) 1971
+ McGhee, Bart (NY).........1986
+ McGrath, Frank (MA).......1978
+ McGuire, Jimmy (NY).......1951
+ McGuire, John (NY) 1951
+ McIlveney, Eddie (PA).......1976
McLaughlin, Bennie (PA).....1977
+ McSkimming, Dent (MO) 1951
Merovich, Pete (PA).........1971
+ Mieth, Werner (NJ) 1974
+ Millar, Robert (NY) 1950
Miller, Al (OH) 1995
+ Miller, Milton (NY)..........1971
+ Mills, Jimmy (PA) 1954
Monson, Lloyd (NY) 1994
Moore, James F. (MO) 1971
Moore, Johnny (CA) 1997
+ Moorehouse, George (NY) ..1986
+ Morrison, Robert (PA) 1951
+ Morrissette, Bill (MA) 1967
Nanoski, Jukey (PA).........1993
+ Netto, Fred (IL) 1958
Newman, Ron (CA).........1992
+ Niotis, D.J. (IL) 1963
+ O'Brien, Shamus (NY) 1990
Olaff, Gene (NJ) 1971

+ Oliver, Arnie (MA)..........1968
Oliver, Len (PA) 1996
+ Palmer, William (PA) 1952
Pariani, Gino (MO).........1976
+ Patenaude, Bert (MA).......1971
+ Pearson, Eddie (GA)........1990
+ Peel, Peter (IL).............1951
Pelé (Brazil) 1993
Peters, Wally (NJ) 1967
Phillipson, Don (CO)........1987
+ Piscopo, Giorgio (NY) 1978
+ Pomeroy, Edgar (CA) 1955
+ Ramsden, Arnold (TX).......1957
+ Ratican, Harry (MO)........1950
Reese, Doc (MD) 1957
+ Renzulli, Pete (NY)..........1951
Ringsdorf, Gene (MD).......1979
Roe, James (MO)...........1997
Roth, Werner (NY)..........1989
+ Rottenberg, Jack (NJ) 1971
Roy, Willy (IL)..............1989
+ Ryan, Hun (PA).............1958
+ Sager, Tom (PA) 1968
Saunders, Harry (NY).......1981
Schaller, Willy (IL) 1995
Schellscheidt, Mannie (NJ)...1990
Schillinger, Emil (PA) 1960
+ Schroeder, Elmer (PA) 1951
+ Scwarcz, Erno (NY) 1951
+ Shields, Fred (PA) 1968
+ Single, Erwin (NY)..........1981
+ Slone, Philip (NY) 1986
+ Smith, Alfred (PA) 1951
Smith, Patrick (OH) 1998
+ Souza, Ed (MA)............1976
Souza, Clarkie (MA)........1976
+ Spalding, Dick (PA).........1951
+ Stark, Archie (NJ) 1950
+ Steelink, Nicolaas (CA) 1971
+ Steur, August (NY)..........1969
+ Stewart, Douglas (PA).......1950
+ Stone, Robert T. (CO) 1971
+ Swords, Thomas (MA) 1976
+ Tintle, Joseph (NJ) 1952
+ Tracey, Ralph (MO).........1986
+ Triner, Joseph (IL) 1951
+ Vaughan, Frank (MO).......1986
+ Walder, Jimmy (PA).........1971
+ Wallace, Frank (MO) 1976
+ Washauer, Adolph (CA).....1977
+ Webb, Tom (WA)...........1987
+ Weir, Alex (NY)............1975
+ Weston, Victor (WA)........1956
+ Wilson, Peter (NJ) 1950
+ Wood, Alex (MI) 1986
+ Woods, John W. (IL) 1952
Woosnam, Phil (GA)........1997
Yeagley, Jerry (IN)..........1989
+ Young, John (CA)...........1958
+ Zampini, Dan (PA)..........1963
Zerhusen, Al (CA) 1978

SWIMMING

International Swimming Hall of Fame

Established in 1965 by the U.S. College Coaches' Swim Forum. **Address:** One Hall of Fame Drive, Ft. Lauderdale, FL 33316. **Telephone:** (954) 462-6536.

Categories for induction are: swimming, diving, water polo, synchronized swimming, coaching, pioneers and contributors. Of the 481 members, 266 are from the United States. Contributors are not included in the following list. Only U.S. men, women and coaches listed below.

Members are listed with year of induction; (+) indicates deceased members.

U.S. Men

+ Anderson, Miller 1967
Barrowman, Mike 1997
Biondi, Matt 1997
+ Boggs, Phil 1985
Brack, Walter 1997
Breen, George 1975
+ Browning, Skippy 1975
Bruner, Mike 1988
Burton, Mike 1977
+ Cann, Tedford 1967
Carey, Rick 1993
Clark, Earl 1972
Clark, Steve 1966
Cleveland, Dick 1991
Clotworthy, Robert 1980
+ Crabbe, Buster 1965
+ Daniels, Charlie 1965
Degener, Dick 1971
DeMont, Rick 1990
Dempsey, Frank 1996
+ Desjardins, Pete 1966
Edgar, David 1996
+ Faricy, John 1990
+ Farrell, Jeff 1968
+ Fick, Peter 1978
+ Flanagan, Ralph 1978
Ford, Alan 1966
Furniss, Bruce 1987
Gaines, Rowdy 1995
Garton, Tim 1997
Glancy, Harrison 1990
+ Goodwin, Budd 1971
Graef, Jed 1988
Haines, George 1977
Hall, Gary 1981
+ Harlan, Bruce 1973
+ Hebner, Harry 1968
Hencken, John 1988
Hickcox, Charles 1976
Higgins, John 1971
Holiday, Harry 1991
Irwin, Juno Stover 1980
Jastremski, Chet 1977
+ Kahanamoku, Duke 1965
+ Kealoha, Warren 1968
Kiefer, Adolph 1965
Kinsella, John 1986
+ Kojac, George 1968
Konno, Ford 1972
+ Kruger, Stubby 1986
+ Kuehn, Louis 1988
+ Langer, Ludy 1988
Larson, Lance 1980
Lee, Dr. Sammy 1968
+ LeMoyne, Harry 1988
Louganis, Greg 1993
Lundquist, Steve 1990
Mann, Thompson 1984
McCormick, Pat 1965
+ McDermott, Turk 1969
+ McGillivray, Perry 1981
McKenzie, Don 1989
McKinney, Frank 1975
McLane, Jimmy 1970
+ Medica, Jack 1966
Montgomery, Jim 1986
Mullikan, Bill 1984
Naber, John 1982
Nakama, Keo 1975
+ O'Connor, Wally 1966
Oyakawa, Yoshi 1979
+ Patnik, Al 1969
Phillips, William Berge 1997
+ Riley, Mickey 1977
+ Ris, Wally 1966
Robie, Carl 1976
Roper, Gail 1997
Ross, Clarence 1988
+ Ross, Norman 1967
Roth, Dick 1987
+ Ruddy, Joe 1986
Russell, Doug 1985
Saari, Roy 1976
+ Schaeffer, E. Carroll 1968
Scholes, Clarke 1980
Schollander, Don 1965
Shaw, Tim 1989
+ Sheldon, George 1989
+ Skelton, Robert 1988
Smith, Bill 1966
+ Smith, Dutch 1979
+ Smith, Jimmy 1992
Smith, R. Jackson 1983
Spitz, Mark 1977
Stack, Allen 1979
Stickles, Ted 1995
Stock, Tom 1989
+ Swendsen, Clyde 1991
Tobian, Gary 1978
Troy, Mike 1971
Vande Weghe, Albert 1990
Vassallo, Jesse 1997
+ Verdeur, Joe 1966
Vogel, Matt 1996
+ Vollmer, Hal 1990
Wayne, Marshall 1981
Webster, Bob 1970
+ Weissmuller, Johnny 1965
+ White, Al 1965
Wrightson, Bernie 1984
Yorzyk, Bill 1971

U.S. Women

Anderson, Terry 1986
Atwood, Sue 1992
Babashoff, Shirley 1982
Ball, Catie 1976
+ Bauer, Sybil 1967
Bean, Dawn Pawson 1996
Belote, Melissa 1983
Bleibtrey, Ethelda 1967
+ Boyle, Charlotte 1988
Burke, Lynne 1978
Bush, Lesley 1986
Callen, Gloria 1984
Caretto, Patty 1987
Carr, Cathy 1988
Caulkins, Tracy 1990
+ Chadwick, Florence 1970
Chandler, Jennifer 1987
Cohen, Tiffany 1996
+ Coleman, Georgia 1966
Cone, Carin 1984
Costie, Candy 1995
Crlenkovich, Helen 1981
Curtis, Ann 1966
Daniel, Ellie 1997
de Varona, Donna 1969
Dean, Penny 1996
+ Dorfner, Olga 1970
Draves, Vickie 1969
Duenkel, Ginny 1985
Ederle, Gertrude 1965
Ellis, Kathy 1991
Ferguson, Cathy 1978
Finneran, Sharon 1985
+ Galligan, Claire 1970
+ Garatti-Seville, Eleanor 1992
Gestring, Marjorie 1976
Gossick, Sue 1988
+ Guest, Irene 1990
Hall, Kaye 1979
Henne, Jan 1979
Holm, Eleanor 1966
Hunt-Newman, Virginia 1993
Johnson, Gail 1983
Josephson, Karen 1997
Josephson, Sarah 1997
Kane, Marion 1981
+ Kaufman, Beth 1967
Kight, Lenore 1981
King, Micki 1978
Kolb, Claudia 1975
+ Lackie, Ethel 1969
Linehan, Kim 1997
Lord-Landon, Alice 1993
+ Madison, Helene 1966
Mann, Shelly 1966
McGrath, Margo 1989
McKim, Josephine 1991
Meagher, Mary T. 1993
+ Meany, Helen 1971
Meyer, Debbie 1977
Mitchell, Michele 1995
Moe, Karen 1992
Morris, Pam 1965
Neilson, Sandra 1986
Neyer, Megan 1997
+ Norelius, Martha 1967
Olsen, Zoe-Ann 1989
O'Rourke, Heidi 1980
+ Osipowich, Albina 1986

Pedersen, Susan 1995
Pinkston, Betty Becker 1967
Pope, Paula Jean Meyers 1979
Potter, Cynthia 1987
+ Poynton, Dorothy 1968
+ Rawls, Katherine 1965
Redmond, Carol 1989
Riggin, Aileen 1967
Ross, Anne 1984
Rothammer, Keena 1991
Ruiz-Conforto, Tracie 1993
Ruuska, Sylvia 1976
Schuler, Carolyn 1989
Seller, Peg 1988
+ Smith, Caroline 1988
Stouder, Sharon 1972
+ Toner, Vee 1995
+ Vilen, Kay 1978
Von Saltza, Chris 1966
Oho Wahle 1996
+ Wainwright, Helen 1972
+ Watson, Lillian (Pokey) 1984
Wehselau, Mariechen 1989
Welshons, Kim 1988
Wichman, Sharon 1991
Williams, Esther 1966
+ Woodbridge, Margaret 1989

U.S. Coaches

+ Armbruster, Dave 1966
+ Bachrach, Bill 1966
Billingsley, Hobie 1983
+ Brandsten, Ernst 1966
+ Brauninger, Stan 1972
+ Cady, Fred 1969
+ Center, George (Dad) 1991
Chavoor, Sherman 1977
+ Cody, Jack 1970
Counsilman, Dr. James 1976
+ Curtis, Katherine 1979
Daland, Peter 1977
+ Daughters, Ray 1971
Draves, Lyle 1989
Gambril, Don 1983
Haines, George 1977
Handley, L. de B. 1967
Hannula, Dick 1987
Kimball, Dick 1985
+ Kiphuth, Bob 1965
Mann, Matt II 1965
+ McCormick, Glen 1995
Moriarty, Phil 1980
Mowerson, Robert 1986
Muir, Bob 1989
+ Neuschaufer, Al 1967
Nitzkowski, Monte 1991
O'Brien, Ron 1988
+ Papenguth, Richard 1986
+ Peppe, Mike 1966
+ Pinkston, Clarence 1966
+ Robinson, Tom 1965
Sakamoto, Soichi 1966
+ Sava, Charlie 1970
+ Schlueter, Walt 1978
Schubert, Mark 1997
Smith, Dick 1979
Stager, Gus 1982
Thornton, Nort 1995
Tinkham, Stan 1989

TENNIS

International Tennis Hall of Fame

Originally the National Tennis Hall of Fame. Established in 1953 by James Van Alen and sanctioned by the U.S. Tennis Association in 1954. Renamed the International Tennis Hall of Fame in 1976. **Address:** 194 Bellevue Ave., Newport, RI 02840. **Telephone:** (401) 849-3990.

Eligibility: Nominated players must be five years removed from being a "significant factor" in competitive tennis. Voting done by members of the international tennis media.

Class of 1998 (2): PLAYERS— **Jimmy Connors** and **Herman David**.

Members are listed with year of induction; (+) indicates deceased members.

Men

+ Adee, George 1964
+ Alexander, Fred 1961
+ Allison, Wilmer 1963
+ Alonso, Manuel 1977
+ Ashe, Arthur 1985
+ Behr, Karl 1969
Borg, Bjorn 1987
+ Borotra, Jean 1976
Bromwich, John 1984
+ Brookes, Norman 1977
+ Brugnon, Jacques 1976
Budge, Don 1964
+ Campbell, Oliver 1955
+ Chace, Malcolm 1961
+ Clark, Clarence 1983
+ Clark, Joseph 1955
+ Clothier, William 1956
+ Cochet, Henri 1976
Connors, Jimmy 1998
Cooper, Ashley 1991
+ Crawford, Jack 1979
David, Herman 1998
+ Doeg, John 1962
+ Doherty, Lawrence 1980
+ Doherty, Reginald 1980
Drobny, Jaroslav 1983
+ Dwight, James 1955
Emerson, Roy 1982
+ Etchebaster, Pierre 1978
Falkenburg, Bob 1974
Fraser, Neale 1984
+ Garland, Chuck 1969
+ Gonzales, Pancho 1968
+ Grant, Bryan (Bitsy) 1972
+ Griffin, Clarence 1970
+ Hackett, Harold 1961
Hewitt, Bob 1992
+ Hoad, Lew 1980
+ Hovey, Fred 1974
+ Hunt, Joe 1966
+ Hunter, Frank 1961
+ Johnston, Bill 1958
+ Jones, Perry 1970
Kodes, Jan 1990
Kramer, Jack 1968
+ Lacoste, Rene 1976
+ Larned, William 1956
Larsen, Art 1969
Laver, Rod 1981
+ Lott, George 1964
Mako, Gene 1973
+ McKinley, Chuck 1986
+ McLoughlin, Maurice 1957
McMillan, Frew 1992
+ McNeill, Don 1965
Mulloy, Gardnar 1972
+ Murray, Lindley 1958
+ Myrick, Julian 1963
Nastase, Ilie 1991
Newcombe, John 1986
+ Nielsen, Arthur 1971
Olmedo, Alex 1987
+ Osuna, Rafael 1979
Parker, Frank 1966
+ Patterson, Gerald 1989
Patty, Budge 1977
+ Perry, Fred 1975
+ Pettitt, Tom 1982
Pietrangeli, Nicola 1986
+ Quist, Adrian 1984
Ralston, Dennis 1987
+ Renshaw, Ernest 1983
+ Renshaw, William 1983
+ Richards, Vincent 1961
+ Riggs, Bobby 1967
Roche, Tony 1986
Rosewall, Ken 1980
Santana, Manuel 1984
Savitt, Dick 1976
Schroeder, Ted 1966
+ Sears, Richard 1955
Sedgman, Frank 1979
Segura, Pancho 1984
Seixas, Vic 1971
+ Shields, Frank 1964
+ Slocum, Henry 1955
Smith, Stan 1987
Stolle, Fred 1985
Talbert, Bill 1967
+ Tilden, Bill 1959
Trabert, Tony 1970
Van Ryn, John 1963
Vilas, Guillermo 1991
+ Vines, Ellsworth 1962
+ von Cramm, Gottfried 1977
+ Ward, Holcombe 1956
+ Washburn, Watson 1965
+ Whitman, Malcolm 1955
+ Wilding, Anthony 1978
+ Williams, Richard 2nd 1957
Wood, Sidney 1964
+ Wrenn, Robert 1955
+ Wright, Beals 1956

Tennis (Cont.)

Women

+ Atkinson, Juliette 1974
Austin, Bunny 1997
Austin, Tracy 1992
+ Barger-Wallach, Maud 1958
Betz Addie, Pauline.......... 1965
+ Bjurstedt Mallory, Molla 1958
Bowrey, Lesley Turner 1997
Brough Clapp, Louise 1967
+ Browne, Mary 1957
Bueno, Maria 1978
+ Cahill, Mabel 1976
Casals, Rosie 1996
+ Connolly Brinker, Maureen .. 1968
+ Dod, Charlotte (Lottie) 1983
+ Douglass Chambers, Dorothy .. 1981
Evert, Chris 1995
Fry Irvin, Shirley 1970
Gibson, Althea 1971
Goolagong Cawley, Evonne .. 1988
+ Hansell, Ellen 1965
Hard, Darlene 1973
Hart, Doris 1969
Haydon Jones, Ann 1985
Heldman, Gladys 1979
+ Hotchkiss Wightman, Hazel ... 1957
+ Jacobs, Helen Hull 1962
King, Billie Jean 1987
+ Lenglen, Suzanne 1978
Mandlikova, Hana 1994
+ Marble, Alice 1964
+ McKane Godfree, Kitty 1978
+ Moore, Elisabeth 1971
Mortimer Barrett, Angela 1993
+ Nuthall Shoemaker, Betty 1977
Osborne duPont, Margaret 1967
+ Palfrey Danzig, Sarah 1963
+ Roosevelt, Ellen 1975
+ Round Little, Dorothy 1986
+ Ryan, Elizabeth 1972
+ Sears, Eleanora 1968
Smith Court, Margaret 1979
+ Sutton Bundy, May 1956
+ Townsend Toulmin, Bertha 1974
Wade, Virginia 1989
+ Wagner, Marie 1969
+ Wills Moody Roark, Helen 1959

Contributors

+ Baker, Lawrence Sr 1975
Chatrier, Philippe 1992
Collins, Bud 1994
Cullman, Joseph F. 3rd 1990
+ Danzig, Allison 1968
+ Davis, Dwight 1956
+ Gray, David 1985
+ Gustaf, V (King of Sweden) .. 1980
+ Hester, W.E. (Slew) 1981
+ Hopman, Harry 1978
Hunt, Lamar 1993
+ Laney, Al 1979
Martin, Alastair 1973
Martin, William M. 1982
Maskell, Dan 1996
+ Outerbridge, Mary 1981
+ Pell, Theodore 1966
+ Tingay, Lance 1982
+ Tinling, Ted 1986
+ Van Alen, James 1965
+ Wingfield, Walter Clopton ... 1997

TRACK & FIELD

National Track & Field Hall of Fame

Established in 1974 by the The Athletics Congress (now USA Track & Field). Originally located in Charleston, WV, the Hall moved to Indianapolis in 1983 and reopened at the Hoosier Dome in 1986. **Address:** One RCA Dome, Indianapolis, IN 46225. **Telephone:** (317) 261-0500.

Eligibility: Nominated athletes must be retired three years and coaches must have coached at least 20 years if retired or 35 years if still coaching. Voting done by 800-member panel made up of Hall of Fame and USA Track & Field officials, Hall of Fame members, current U.S. champions and members of the Track & Field Writers of America.

Class of 1997 (4): MEN—**Henry Carr**, **Herny Laskau** and **Renaldo Nehemiah**; WOMEN—**Evelyn Ashford**.

Members are listed with year of induction; (+) indicates deceased members.

Men

+ Albritton, Dave 1980
Ashenfelter, Horace 1975
+ Bausch, James 1979
Beamon, Bob 1977
Beatty, Jim 1990
Bell, Greg 1988
+ Boeckmann, Dee 1976
Boston, Ralph 1974
Bragg, Don 1996
+ Calhoun, Lee 1974
Campbell, Milt 1989
Carr, Henry 1997
+ Clark, Ellery 1991
Connolly, Harold 1984
Courtney, Tom 1978
+ Cunningham, Glenn 1974
+ Curtis, William 1979
Davenport, Willie 1982
Davis, Glenn 1974
Davis, Harold 1974
Dillard, Harrison 1974
Dumas, Charley 1990
Evans, Lee 1983
+ Ewell, Barney 1986
+ Ewry, Ray 1974
+ Flanagan, John 1975
Fosbury, Dick 1981
+ Gordien, Fortune 1979
Greene, Charlie 1992
+ Hahn, Archie 1983
+ Hardin, Glenn 1978
Hayes, Bob 1976
Held, Bud 1987
Hines, Jim 1979
+ Houser, Bud 1979
+ Hubbard, DeHart 1979
Jenkins, Charlie 1992
Jenner, Bruce 1980
+ Johnson, Cornelius 1994
Johnson, Rafer 1974
Jones, Hayes 1976
Kelley, John 1980
Kiviat, Abel 1985
+ Kraenzlein, Alvin 1974
Laird, Ron 1986
+ Lash, Don 1995
Laskau, Henry 1997
Liquori, Marty 1995
Long, Dr. Dallas 1996
Mathias, Bob 1974
Matson, Randy 1984
McCluskey, Joe 1996
+ Meadows, Earle 1996
+ Meredith, Ted 1982
+ Metcalfe, Ralph 1975
+ Milburn, Rod 1993
Mills, Billy 1976
Moore, Tom 1988
Morrow, Bobby 1975
+ Mortensen, Jess 1992
Moses, Edwin 1994
+ Myers, Lawrence 1974
Nehemiah, Renaldo 1997
O'Brien, Parry 1974
Oerter, Al 1974
+ Osborn, Harold 1974
+ Owens, Jesse 1974
+ Paddock, Charley 1976
Patton, Mel 1985
+ Peacock, Eulace 1987
+ Prefontaine, Steve 1976
+ Ray, Joie 1976
+ Rice, Greg 1977
Richards, Bob 1975
+ Rose, Ralph 1976
Ryun, Jim 1980
+ Scholz, Jackson 1977
Schul, Bob 1991
Seagren, Bob 1986
+ Sheppard, Mel 1976
+ Sheridan, Martin 1988
Shorter, Frank 1989
Sime, Dave 1981
+ Simpson, Robert 1974
Smith, Tommie 1978
+ Stanfield, Andy 1977
Steers, Les 1974
+ Tewksbury, Dr. Walter 1996
Thomas, John 1985
+ Thomson, Earl 1977

+ Thorpe, Jim ... 1975
+ Tolan, Eddie ... 1982
Toomey, Bill ... 1975
+ Towns, Forrest (Spec) ... 1976
Warmerdam, Cornelius ... 1974
Whitfield, Mal ... 1974
Wilkins, Mac ... 1993
+ Williams, Archie ... 1992
Wohlhuter, Rick ... 1990
Woodruff, John ... 1978
Wottle, Dave ... 1982
+ Wykoff, Frank ... 1977
Young, George ... 1981

Women

Ashford, Evelyn ... 1997
Brisco, Valerie ... 1995
Coachman, Alice ... 1975
+ Copeland, Lillian ... 1994
+ Didrikson, Babe ... 1974
Faggs, Mae ... 1976
Ferrell, Barbara ... 1988
+ Griffith Joyner, Florence ... 1995
+ Hall Adams, Evelyne ... 1988
Heritage, Doris Brown ... 1990
+ Jackson, Nell ... 1989
Manning, Madeline ... 1984
McDaniel, Mildred ... 1983
McGuire, Edith ... 1979
Ritter, Louise ... 1995
Robinson, Betty ... 1977
+ Rudolph, Wilma ... 1974
+ Schmidt, Kate ... 1994
+ Shiley Newhouse, Jean ... 1993
+ Stephens, Helen ... 1975
Tyus, Wyomia ... 1980
+ Walsh, Stella ... 1975
Watson, Martha ... 1987
White, Willye ... 1981

Coaches

+ Abbott, Cleve ... 1996
+ Baskin, Weems ... 1982
+ Beard, Percy ... 1981
Bell, Sam ... 1992
Botts, Tom ... 1983
Bowerman, Bill ... 1981
Bush, Jim ... 1987
+ Cromwell, Dean ... 1974
+ Doherty, Ken ... 1976
+ Easton, Bill ... 1975
+ Elliott, Jumbo ... 1981
+ Giegengack, Bob ... 1978
+ Hamilton, Brutus ... 1974
+ Haydon, Ted ... 1975
+ Hayes, Billy ... 1976
+ Haylett, Ward ... 1979
+ Higgins, Ralph ... 1982
+ Hillman, Harry ... 1976
+ Hurt, Edward ... 1975
+ Hutsell, Wilbur ... 1977
+ Jones, Thomas ... 1977
Jordan, Payton ... 1982
+ Littlefield, Clyde ... 1981
+ Moakley, Jack ... 1988
+ Murphy, Michael ... 1974
Rosen, Mel ... 1995
+ Snyder, Larry ... 1978
Temple, Ed ... 1989
+ Templeton, Dink ... 1976
Walker, LeRoy ... 1983
+ Wilt, Fred ... 1981
+ Winter, Bud ... 1985
Wolfe, Vern ... 1996
Wright, Stan ... 1993
+ Yancy, Joseph ... 1984

Contributors

+ Abramson, Jesse ... 1981
Andersen, Roxanne ... 1991
+ Bakjian, Andy ... 1986
+ Brundage, Avery ... 1974
+ Ferris, Dan ... 1974
+ Griffith, John ... 1979
+ Lebow, Fred ... 1994
+ Nelson, Bert ... 1991
Nelson, Cordner ... 1988
+ Sullivan, James ... 1977

VOLLEYBALL

Volleyball Hall of Fame

Established in 1985. **Address:** P.O. Box 1895, 444 Dwight St., Holyoke, MA 01041 **Telephone:** (413) 536-0926.

Eligibility: Nominees must have contributed at least seven years of outstanding service to volleyball within his/her respective category. Nominees in the player or official category must be retired for five years. A nominee may appear on the ballot a maximum of seven times at which point he/she can be nominated in the Veterans category an unlimited number of times. Voting is done by a panel of no more than 30 individuals from the greater volleyball community.

Class of 1998 (3): MEN— **Steve Timmons, Craig Buck** and **Dusty Dvorak**; WOMEN— **Paula Weishoff**; LEADER— **Bill Baird**; COACH— **Yasutaka Matsudaira**

Members are listed with year of induction; (+) indicates deceased members.

Men

Bright, Mike ... 1993
Buck, Craig ... 1998
Dvorak, Dusty ... 1998
Engen, Rolf ... 1991
+ Haine, Thomas ... 1991
O'Hara, Michael ... 1989
Rundle, Larry ... 1994
Selznick, Eugene ... 1988
Stanley, Jon ... 1992
Timmons, Steve ... 1998
Velasco, Pedro "Pete" ... 1997
Von Hagen, Ron ... 1992

Women

Bright, Patti ... 1996
Dowdell, Patty ... 1994
Gregory, Kathy ... 1989
Green, Debbie ... 1995
+ Hyman, Flo ... 1988
Peppler, Mary Jo ... 1990
Ward, Jane ... 1988
Weishoff, Paula ... 1998

Coaches

Banachowski, Andy ... 1997
Beal, Douglas ... 1989
Coleman, Dr. James ... 1992
DeGroot, Col. Edward ... 1990
Dunphy, Marv ... 1994
Matsudaira, Yasutaka ... 1998
Scates, Al ... 1993
Selinger, Arie ... 1995
Shondell, Donald ... 1996
+ Wilson, Harry ... 1988

Leaders

Baird, Bill ... 1998
+ Fisher, Dr. George J. ... 1991
Friermood, Dr. Harold T. ... 1986
+ Gibson, Leonard ... 1988
+ Koch, John ... 1994
+ Lindsey, Robert L. ... 1995
Monaco, Jr., Albert ... 1997
+ Morgan, Dr. William G. ... 1985

Officials

Davies, Glen ... 1989
+ Fish, Alton ... 1990
Ignacio, Catalino ... 1991
Kennedy, Merton H. ... 1992
Miller, C.L. (Bobb) ... 1995

WOMEN

International Women's Sports Hall of Fame

Established in 1980 by the Women's Sports Foundation. **Address:** Women's Sports Foundation, Eisenhower Park, East Meadow, NY 11554. **Telephone:** (516) 542-4700.

Eligibility: Nominees' achievements and commitment to the development of women's sports must be internationally recognized. Athletes are elected in two categories—Pioneer (before 1960) and Contemporary (since 1960). Members are divided below by sport for the sake of easy reference; (*) indicates member inducted in Pioneer category. Coaching nominees must have coached at least 10 years.

Class of 1997 (4): CONTEMPORARY—**Evelyn Ashford** (track and field) and **Diana Golden Brosnihan** (skiing). PIONEER—**Barbara Ann Scott-King** (figure skating). COACHES—**Gail Emery** (synchorinized swimming).

Members are listed with year of induction; (+) indicates deceased members.

Alpine Skiing
Cranz, Christl* 1991
Golden Brosnihan, Diana....1997
Lawrence, Andrea Mead*...1983
Moser-Pröll, Annemarie 1982

Auto Racing
Guthrie, Janet..............1980

Aviation
+ Coleman, Bessie*..........1992
+ Earhart, Amelia*...........1980
+ Marvingt, Marie*..........1987

Badminton
Hashman, Judy Devlin* 1995

Baseball
Stone, Toni*...............1993

Basketball
Meyers, Ann...............1985
Miller, Cheryl..............1991

Bowling
Ladewig, Marion*..........1984

Cycling
Carpenter Phinney, Connie ..1990

Diving
King, Micki................1983
McCormick, Pat*...........1984
Riggin, Aileen*............1988

Equestrian
Hartel, Lis.................1994

Fencing
Schacherer-Elek, Ilona* 1989

Figure Skating
Albright, Tenley*...........1983
+ Blanchard, Theresa Weld* ..1989
Fleming, Peggy 1981
Heiss Jenkins, Carol*.......1992
+ Henie, Sonja*.............1982
Protopopov, Ludmila 1992
Rodnina, Irena.............1988
Scott-King, Barbara Ann* ...1997

Golf
Berg, Patty*...............1980
Carner, JoAnne............1987
Hicks, Betty*..............1995
Mann, Carol...............1982
Rawls, Betsy*..............1986
Suggs, Louise*.............1987
+ Vare, Glenna Collett*.......1981
Whitworth, Kathy 1984
Wright, Mickey 1981

Golf/Track & Field
+ Zaharias, Babe Didrikson* ..1980

Gymnastics
Caslavska, Vera............1991
Comaneci, Nadia 1990
Korbut, Olga 1982
Latynina, Larysa* 1985
Retton, Mary Lou...........1993
Tourischeva, Lyudmila.......1987

Shooting
Murdock, Margaret.........1988

Softball
Joyce, Joan................1989

Speed Skating
+ Klein Outland, Kit* 1993
Young, Sheila..............1981

Swimming
Caulkins, Tracy 1986
+ Chadwick, Florence* 1996
Curtis Cuneo, Ann* 1985
de Varona, Donna..........1983
Ederle, Gertrude* 1980
Fraser, Dawn 1985
Holm, Eleanor* 1980
Meagher, Mary T...........1993
Meyer-Reyes, Debbie 1987

Tennis
+ Connolly, Maureen*........1987
+ Dod, Charlotte (Lottie)*......1986
Evert, Chris................1981
Gibson, Althea* 1980
Goolagong Cawley, Evonne .1989
+ Hotchkiss Wightman, Hazel*...1986
King, Billie Jean............1980
+ Lenglen, Suzanne* 1984
Navratilova, Martina 1984
+ Sears, Eleanora*...........1984
Smith Court, Margaret 1986

Track & Field
Ashford, Evelyn 1997
Blankers-Koen, Fanny*......1982
Cheng, Chi.................1994
Coachman Davis, Alice* 1991
Faggs Star, Aeriwentha Mae* ..1996
Manning Mims, Madeline ...1987
+ Rudolph, Wilma............1980
+ Stephens, Helen* 1983
Szewinska, Irena...........1992
Tyus, Wyomia 1981
Waitz, Grete 1995
White, Willye..............1988

Volleyball
+ Hyman, Flo...............1986

Water Skiing
McGuire, Willa Worthington*...1990

Orienteering
Kringstad, Annichen 1995

Coaches
Applebee, Constance.......1991
Backus, Sharron............1993
Conradt, Judy..............1995
Emery, Gail 1997
Grossfeld, Muriel...........1991
Holum, Diana..............1996
Jacket, Barbara 1995
+ Jackson, Nell 1990
Kanakogi, Rusty............1994
Summitt, Pat Head..........1990
+ Wade, Margaret...........1992

Women's Global Challenge

The Women's Sports Foundation has announced the creation of the "Women's Global Challenge" to feature the best amateur and professional female athletes and to be held every two years beginning in 1999. The inaugural event will be held over a five-day period from April 28 through May 2, 1999 in Washington D.C. and will consist of eight sports — basketball, beach volleyball, diving, figure skating, gymnastics, soccer, swimming and track & field. The top ten athletes in each individual sport and the top four to eight teams in each team sport will be invited to compete. The inaugural "Challenge" will be broadcast by CBS, Lifetime Television and Trans World International and will be syndicated to an estimated 100 countries.

RETIRED NUMBERS

Major League Baseball

The New York Yankees have retired the most uniform numbers (14) in the major leagues; followed the Brooklyn/Los Angeles Dodgers (9), the Pittsburgh Pirates and St. Louis Cardinals (8), the Chicago White Sox (7) and the New York/San Francisco Giants (6). **Nolan Ryan** has had his number retired by three teams—#34 by Texas and Houston and #30 by California. Four players and a manager have had their numbers retired by two teams: **Hank Aaron**—#44 by the Boston/Milwaukee/Atlanta Braves and the Milwaukee Brewers; **Rod Carew**—#29 by Minnesota and California; **Rollie Fingers**—#34 by Milwaukee and Oakland; **Frank Robinson**—#20 by Cincinnati and Baltimore; and **Casey Stengel**—#37 by the New York Yankees and New York Mets.

Numbers retired in 1998 (4): CLEVELAND—#21 worn by pitcher **Bob Lemon** (1946-58 with Indians); CINCINNATI—#8 second baseman **Joe Morgan** (1972-1979 with Reds), #18 worn by first baseman **Ted Kluszewski** (1947-57 with Reds), #20 worn by right fielder **Frank Robinson**.

American League

Three AL teams—the Seattle Mariners, Tampa Bay Devil Rays and the Toronto Blue Jays—have not retired any numbers. The Blue Jays have a "level of excellence" which includes Dave Steib (#11) and George Bell (#37). Both numbers are currently being used, however.

Anaheim Angels

26 Gene Autry
29 Rod Carew
30 Nolan Ryan
50 Jimmie Reese

Baltimore Orioles

4 Earl Weaver
5 Brooks Robinson
20 Frank Robinson
22 Jim Palmer
33 Eddie Murray

Boston Red Sox

1 Bobby Doerr
4 Joe Cronin
8 Carl Yastrzemski
9 Ted Williams

Chicago White Sox

2 Nellie Fox
3 Harold Baines
4 Luke Appling
9 Minnie Minoso
11 Luis Aparicio
16 Ted Lyons
19 Billy Pierce
72 Carlton Fisk

Cleveland Indians

3 Earl Averill
5 Lou Boudreau
14 Larry Doby
18 Mel Harder
19 Bob Feller
21 Bob Lemon

Detroit Tigers

2 Charlie Gehringer
5 Hank Greenberg
6 Al Kaline
16 Hal Newhouser

Kansas City Royals

5 George Brett
10 Dick Howser
20 Frank White

Minnesota Twins

3 Harmon Killebrew
6 Tony Oliva
14 Kent Hrbek
29 Rod Carew
34 Kirby Puckett

New York Yankees

1 Billy Martin
3 Babe Ruth
4 Lou Gehrig
5 Joe DiMaggio
7 Mickey Mantle
8 Yogi Berra & Bill Dickey
9 Roger Maris
10 Phil Rizzuto
15 Thurman Munson
16 Whitey Ford
23 Don Mattingly
32 Elston Howard
37 Casey Stengel
44 Reggie Jackson

Oakland Athletics

27 Catfish Hunter
34 Rollie Fingers

Texas Rangers

34 Nolan Ryan

National League

Three NL teams—the Arizona Diamondbacks, Colorado Rockies and the Florida Marlins—have not retired any numbers. San Francisco has honored former NY Giants Christy Mathewson and John McGraw even though they played before numbers were worn.

Atlanta Braves

3 Dale Murphy
21 Warren Spahn
35 Phil Niekro
41 Eddie Mathews
44 Hank Aaron

Chicago Cubs

14 Ernie Banks
26 Billy Williams

Cincinnati Reds

1 Fred Hutchinson
5 Johnny Bench
8 Joe Morgan
18 Ted Kluszewski
20 Frank Robinson

Houston Astros

25 Jose Cruz
32 Jim Umbricht
33 Mike Scott
34 Nolan Ryan
40 Don Wilson

Los Angeles Dodgers

1 Pee Wee Reese
2 Tommy Lasorda
4 Duke Snider
19 Jim Gilliam
24 Walter Alston
32 Sandy Koufax
39 Roy Campanella
42 Jackie Robinson
53 Don Drysdale

Milwaukee Brewers

19 Robin Yount
34 Rollie Fingers
44 Hank Aaron

Montreal Expos

8 Gary Carter
10 Rusty Staub & Andre Dawson

New York Mets

14 Gil Hodges
37 Casey Stengel
41 Tom Seaver

Philadelphia Phillies

1 Richie Ashburn
20 Mike Schmidt
32 Steve Carlton
36 Robin Roberts

Pittsburgh Pirates

1 Billy Meyer
4 Ralph Kiner
8 Willie Stargell
9 Bill Mazeroski
20 Pie Traynor
21 Roberto Clemente
33 Honus Wagner
40 Danny Murtaugh

St. Louis Cardinals

1 Ozzie Smith
2 Red Schoendienst
6 Stan Musial
14 Ken Boyer
17 Dizzy Dean
20 Lou Brock
45 Bob Gibson
85 August (Gussie) Busch

San Diego Padres

6 Steve Garvey
35 Randy Jones

San Francisco Giants

3 Bill Terry
4 Mel Ott
11 Carl Hubbell
24 Willie Mays
27 Juan Marichal
44 Willie McCovey

Retired Numbers (Cont.)

National Basketball Association

Boston has retired the most numbers (20) in the NBA; followed by Portland (8); the Los Angeles Lakers, New York Knicks and the KC/Sacramento Kings have (7); Detroit, Milwaukee and the Rochester/Cincinnati Royals have (6); Cleveland and the Syracuse Nats/Philadelphia 76ers (5). Six players have had their numbers retired by two teams: **Kareem Abdul-Jabbar**—#33 by LA Lakers and Milwaukee; **Wilt Chamberlain**—#13 by the Los Angeles Lakers and Philadelphia; **Julius Erving**—#6 by Philadelphia and #32 by New Jersey; **Bob Lanier**—#16 by Detroit and Milwaukee; **Oscar Robertson**—#1 by Milwaukee and #14 by Sacramento; and **Nate Thurmond**—#42 by Cleveland and Golden State.

Numbers retired in 1998 (4): BOSTON—#00 worn by center **Robert Parish** (1980-94 with Celtics); DETROIT—#2 for coach Chuck Daly (1983-92 with Pistons); HOUSTON—#24 worn by center **Moses Malone** (1977-82 with Rockets); SAN ANTONIO—#00 worn by guard **Johnny Moore** (1980-88,89-90 with Spurs).

Eastern Conference

Three Eastern teams—the Miami Heat, Orlando Magic, and Toronto Raptors—have not retired any numbers.

Boston Celtics

1 Walter A. Brown
2 Red Auerbach
3 Dennis Johnson
6 Bill Russell
10 Jo Jo White
14 Bob Cousy
15 Tom Heinsohn
16 Tom (Satch) Sanders
17 John Havlicek
18 Dave Cowens
19 Don Nelson
21 Bill Sharman
22 Ed Macauley
23 Frank Ramsey
24 Sam Jones
25 K.C. Jones
32 Kevin McHale
33 Larry Bird
35 Reggie Lewis
00 Robert Parish
Loscy Jim Loscutoff
Radio mic Johnny Most

Atlanta Hawks

9 Bob Pettit
23 Lou Hudson

Charlotte Hornets

6 Fans ("Sixth Man")

Chicago Bulls

4 Jerry Sloan
10 Bob Love
23 Michael Jordan

Cleveland Cavaliers

7 Bingo Smith
22 Larry Nance
34 Austin Carr
42 Nate Thurmond
43 Brad Daugherty

Detroit Pistons

2 Chuck Daly
11 Isiah Thomas
15 Vinnie Johnson
16 Bob Lanier
21 Dave Bing
40 Bill Laimbeer

Indiana Pacers

30 George McGinnis
34 Mel Daniels
35 Roger Brown

Milwaukee Bucks

1 Oscar Robertson
2 Junior Bridgeman
4 Sidney Moncrief
14 Jon McGlocklin
16 Bob Lanier
32 Brian Winters
33 Kareem Abdul-Jabbar

New York Knicks

10 Walt Frazier
12 Dick Barnett
15 Dick McGuire & Earl Monroe
19 Willis Reed
22 Dave DeBusschere
24 Bill Bradley
613 Red Holzman

New Jersey Nets

3 Drazen Petrovic
4 Wendell Ladner
23 John Williamson
25 Bill Melchionni
32 Julius Erving

Philadelphia 76ers

6 Julius Erving
10 Maurice Cheeks
13 Wilt Chamberlain
15 Hal Greer
24 Bobby Jones
32 Billy Cunningham
P.A. mic Dave Zinkoff

Washington Wizards

11 Elvin Hayes
25 Gus Johnson
41 Wes Unseld

Western Conference

Three Western teams—the Los Angeles Clippers, Minnesota Timberwolves and Vancouver Grizzlies—have not retired any numbers.

Dallas Mavericks

15 Brad Davis

Denver Nuggets

2 Alex English
33 David Thompson
40 Byron Beck
44 Dan Issel

Golden St. Warriors

14 Tom Meschery
16 Al Attles
24 Rick Barry
42 Nate Thurmond

Houston Rockets

23 Calvin Murphy
24 Moses Malone
45 Rudy Tomjanovich

Los Angeles Lakers

13 Wilt Chamberlain
22 Elgin Baylor
25 Gail Goodrich
32 Magic Johnson
33 Kareem Abdul-Jabbar
42 James Worthy
44 Jerry West

Phoenix Suns

5 Dick Van Arsdale
6 Walter Davis
33 Alvan Adams
42 Connie Hawkins
44 Paul Westphal

Portland Trail Blazers

1 Larry Weinberg
13 Dave Twardzik
15 Larry Steele
20 Maurice Lucas
32 Bill Walton
36 Lloyd Neal
45 Geoff Petrie
77 Jack Ramsay

Sacramento Kings

1 Nate Archibald
6 Fans ("Sixth Man")
11 Bob Davies
12 Maurice Stokes
14 Oscar Robertson
27 Jack Twyman
44 Sam Lacey

San Antonio Spurs

13 James Silas
44 George Gervin
00 Johnny Moore

Seattle SuperSonics

19 Lenny Wilkens
32 Fred Brown
43 Jack Sikma
Radio Mic Bob Blackburn

Utah Jazz

1 Frank Layden
7 Pete Maravich
35 Darrell Griffith
53 Mark Eaton

National Football League

The Chicago Bears have retired the most uniform numbers (13) in the NFL; followed by the New York Giants (9); the Dallas Texans/Kansas City Chiefs (8); the Baltimore-Indianapolis Colts, the Boston-New England Patriots and San Francisco (7); Detroit (6); Cleveland and Philadelphia (5). No player has ever had his number retired by more than one NFL team.

Numbers retired in 1998 (2): NEW YORK GIANTS—#4 worn by fullback, defensive back, quarterback **Tuffy Leemans** (1936-43 with Giants); SAN FRANCISCO—#16 quarterback **Joe Montana** (1979-92 with 49ers)

AFC

Five AFC teams—the Baltimore Ravens, Buffalo Bills, Oakland Raiders, Pittsburgh Steelers and Jacksonville Jaguars—have not retired any numbers. The Cleveland Browns have retired five numbers— #14 Otto Graham, #32 Jim Brown, #45 Ernie Davis, #46 Don Fleming and #76 Lou Groza.

Cincinnati Bengals

54 Bob Johnson

Denver Broncos

18 Frank Tripucka
44 Floyd Little

Tennessee Oilers

34 Earl Campbell
43 Jim Norton
63 Mike Munchak
65 Elvin Bethea

Indianapolis Colts

19 Johnny Unitas
22 Buddy Young
24 Lenny Moore
70 Art Donovan
77 Jim Parker
82 Raymond Berry
89 Gino Marchetti

Kansas City Chiefs

3 Jan Stenerud
16 Len Dawson
28 Abner Haynes
33 Stone Johnson
36 Mack Lee Hill
63 Willie Lanier
78 Bobby Bell
86 Buck Buchanan

Miami Dolphins

12 Bob Griese

New England Patriots

14 Steve Grogan
20 Gino Cappelletti
40 Mike Haynes
57 Steve Nelson
73 John Hannah
79 Jim Hunt
89 Bob Dee

New York Jets

12 Joe Namath
13 Don Maynard

San Diego Chargers

14 Dan Fouts

Seattle Seahawks

12 Fans ("12th Man")
80 Steve Largent

NFC

Atlanta, Dallas and the Carolina Panthers are the only NFC teams that haven't officially retired any numbers. The Falcons haven't issued uniforms #10 (Steve Bartowski), #23 (Bobby Butler), #31 (William Andrews), #57 (Jeff Van Note and Clay Mathews), #60 (Tommy Nobis) and #78 (Mike Kenn) since those players retired. The Cowboys have a "Ring of Honor" at Texas Stadium that includes nine players and one coach—Tony Dorsett, Chuck Howley, Lee Roy Jordan, Tom Landry, Bob Lilly, Don Meredith, Don Perkins, Mel Renfro, Roger Staubach and Randy White.

Arizona Cardinals

8 Larry Wilson
77 Stan Mauldin
88 J.V. Cain
99 Marshall Goldberg

Chicago Bears

3 Bronko Nagurski
5 George McAfee
7 George Halas
28 Willie Galimore
34 Walter Payton
40 Gale Sayers
41 Brian Piccolo
42 Sid Luckman
51 Dick Butkus
56 Bill Hewitt
61 Bill George
66 Bulldog Turner
77 Red Grange

Detroit Lions

7 Dutch Clark
22 Bobby Layne
37 Doak Walker
56 Joe Schmidt
85 Chuck Hughes
88 Charlie Sanders

Green Bay Packers

3 Tony Canadeo
14 Don Hutson
15 Bart Starr
66 Ray Nitschke

Minnesota Vikings

10 Fran Tarkenton
88 Alan Page

New Orleans Saints

31 Jim Taylor
81 Doug Atkins

New York Giants

1 Ray Flaherty
4 Tuffy Leemans
7 Mel Hein
11 Phil Simms
14 Y.A. Tittle
32 Al Blozis
40 Joe Morrison
42 Charlie Conerly
50 Ken Strong
56 Lawrence Taylor

Philadelphia Eagles

15 Steve Van Buren
40 Tom Brookshier
44 Pete Retzlaff
60 Chuck Bednarik
70 Al Wistert
99 Jerome Brown

St. Louis Rams

7 Bob Waterfield
74 Merlin Olsen
78 Jackie Slater

San Francisco 49ers

12 John Brodie
16 Joe Montana
34 Joe Perry
37 Jimmy Johnson
39 Hugh McElhenny
70 Charlie Krueger
73 Leo Nomellini
87 Dwight Clark

Tampa Bay Bucs

63 Lee Roy Selmon

Wash. Redskins

33 Sammy Baugh

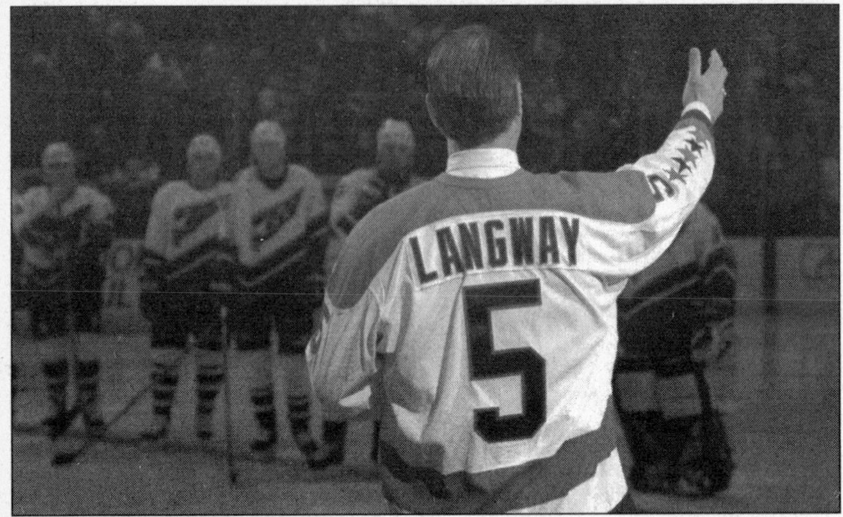

AP/Wide World Photos

Washington Capitals great **Rod Langway**, one of the greatest American-born defensemen in history, had his number 5 retired by the Caps in 1998.

National Hockey League

The Boston Bruins and Montreal Canadiens have retired the most uniform numbers (7) in the NHL; followed by Detroit (6); the N.Y. Islanders (5); Buffalo, Chicago, St. Louis and Philadelphia (4); and the Boston-New England-Hartford Whalers, Los Angeles Kings and Quebec Nordiques-Colorado Avalanche (3). Two players have had their numbers retired by two teams: Gordie Howe—#9 by Detroit and Hartford; and Bobby Hull—#9 by Chicago and Winnipeg.

Numbers retired in 1998 (2): BLACKHAWKS—#18 worn by center **Denis Savard** (1980-90 with Blackhawks). CAPITALS—#5 worn by defenseman **Rod Langway** (1982-93 with Capitals).

Eastern Conference

Four Eastern teams—the Carolina Hurricanes, New Jersey Devils, Tampa Bay Lightning and Florida Panthers—have not retired any numbers. The Hartford Whalers had retired three numbers: #2 Rick Ley, #9 Gordie Howe and #19 John McKenzie.

Boston Bruins

2 Eddie Shore
3 Lionel Hitchman
4 Bobby Orr
5 Dit Clapper
7 Phil Esposito
9 John Bucyk
15 Milt Schmidt

Buffalo Sabres

2 Tim Horton
7 Rick Martin
11 Gilbert Perreault
14 Rene Robert

Montreal Canadiens

1 Jacques Plante
2 Doug Harvey
4 Jean Beliveau
7 Howie Morenz
9 Maurice Richard
10 Guy Lafleur
16 Henri Richard

New York Islanders

5 Denis Potvin
9 Clark Gilles
22 Mike Bossy
23 Bob Nystrom
31 Billy Smith

New York Rangers

1 Eddie Giacomin
7 Rod Gilbert

Ottawa Senators

8 Frank Finnigan

Philadelphia Flyers

1 Bernie Parent
4 Barry Ashbee
7 Bill Barber
16 Bobby Clarke

Pittsburgh Penguins

21 Michel Briere

Washington Capitals

5 Rod Langway
7 Yvon Labre

Western Conference

Three Western teams—the Colorado Avalanche, San Jose Sharks and Mighty Ducks of Anaheim—have not retired any numbers. Note, the Quebec Nordiques retired the numbers of J.C. Tremblay (3), Marc Tardiff (8) and Michel Goulet (16) but these numbers have been worn since the team moved to Colorado.

Calgary Flames

9 Lanny McDonald

Chicago Blackhawks

1 Glenn Hall
9 Bobby Hull
18 Denis Savard
21 Stan Mikita
35 Tony Esposito

Dallas Stars

8 Bill Goldsworthy
19 Bill Masterton

Detroit Red Wings

1 Terry Sawchuk
6 Larry Aurie
7 Ted Lindsay
9 Gordie Howe
10 Alex Delvecchio
12 Sid Abel

Edmonton Oilers

3 Al Hamilton

Los Angeles Kings

16 Marcel Dionne
18 Dave Taylor
30 Rogie Vachon

Phoenix Coyotes

9 Bobby Hull
25 Thomas Steen

St. Louis Blues

3 Bob Gassoff
8 Barclay Plager
11 Brian Sutter
24 Bernie Federko

Toronto Maple Leafs

5 Bill Barilko
6 Ace Bailey

Vancouver Canucks

12 Stan Smyl

AWARDS

Associated Press Athletes of the Year

Selected annually by AP newspaper sports editors since 1931.

Male

Golfer Tiger Woods, who shocked the world with his record-breaking Masters victory and led the PGA Tour in money won with over $2 million in his first full season, won the AP Athlete of the Year award for 1997. Woods, who also won his third straight U.S. Amateur title before turning pro, became the first minority to win a major golf championship.

The Top 10 vote-getters (first place votes in parentheses): 1. **Tiger Woods**, golf (53), 231 pts; 2. **Barry Sanders**, football (17), 100 pts; 3. **Evander Holyfield**, boxing (19), 98 pts; 4. **Michael Jordan**, basketball (15), 87 pts; 5. **Brett Favre**, football (13), 84 pts; 6. **Ken Griffey Jr.**, baseball (7), 79 pts; 7. **Jeff Gordon**, auto racing (8), 69 pts; 8. **Roger Clemens**, baseball (11), 68 pts; 9. **Mark McGwire**, baseball (9), 61 pts; 10. **Mario Lemieux**, hockey (5), 31 pts.

Multiple winners: Michael Jordan (3); Don Budge, Sandy Koufax, Carl Lewis, Joe Montana and Byron Nelson (2).

Year	
1931	**Pepper Martin**, baseball
1932	**Gene Sarazen**, golf
1933	**Carl Hubbell**, baseball
1934	**Dizzy Dean**, baseball
1935	**Joe Louis**, boxing
1936	**Jesse Owens**, track
1937	**Don Budge**, tennis
1938	**Don Budge**, tennis
1939	**Nile Kinnick**, college football
1940	**Tom Harmon**, college football
1941	**Joe DiMaggio**, baseball
1942	**Frank Sinkwich**, college football
1943	**Gunder Haegg**, track
1944	**Byron Nelson**, golf
1945	**Byron Nelson**, golf
1946	**Glenn Davis**, college football
1947	**Johnny Lujack**, college football
1948	**Lou Boudreau**, baseball
1949	**Leon Hart**, college football
1950	**Jim Konstanty**, baseball
1951	**Dick Kazmaier**, college football
1952	**Bob Mathias**, track
1953	**Ben Hogan**, golf
1954	**Willie Mays**, baseball
1955	**Hopalong Cassady**, col. football
1956	**Mickey Mantle**, baseball
1957	**Ted Williams**, baseball
1958	**Herb Elliott**, track
1959	**Ingemar Johansson**, boxing
1960	**Rafer Johnson**, track
1961	**Roger Maris**, baseball
1962	**Maury Wills**, baseball
1963	**Sandy Koufax**, baseball
1964	**Don Schollander**, swimming
1965	**Sandy Koufax**, baseball
1966	**Frank Robinson**, baseball
1967	**Carl Yastrzemski**, baseball
1968	**Denny McLain**, baseball
1969	**Tom Seaver**, baseball
1970	**George Blanda**, pro football
1971	**Lee Trevino**, golf
1972	**Mark Spitz**, swimming
1973	**O.J. Simpson**, pro football
1974	**Muhammad Ali**, boxing
1975	**Fred Lynn**, baseball
1976	**Bruce Jenner**, track
1977	**Steve Cauthen**, horse racing
1978	**Ron Guidry**, baseball
1979	**Willie Stargell,** baseball
1980	**U.S. Olympic hockey team**
1981	**John McEnroe**, tennis
1982	**Wayne Gretzky**, hockey
1983	**Carl Lewis**, track
1984	**Carl Lewis**, track
1985	**Dwight Gooden**, baseball
1986	**Larry Bird**, pro basketball
1987	**Ben Johnson**, track
1988	**Orel Hershiser**, baseball
1989	**Joe Montana**, pro football
1990	**Joe Montana**, pro football
1991	**Michael Jordan**, pro basketball
1992	**Michael Jordan**, pro basketball
1993	**Michael Jordan**, pro basketball
1994	**George Foreman,** boxing
1995	**Cal Ripken Jr.**, baseball
1996	**Michael Johnson**, track
1997	**Tiger Woods**, golf

Female

Seventeen-year-old tennis phenom Martina Hingis, winner of three Grand Slam titles in 1997, won the AP Female Athlete of the Year Award. Hingis made it to the finals of the French Open, the only Grand Slam she didn't win, just weeks after suffering a knee injury when she was thrown from a horse. She finished the year with a 75-5 record and 12 titles.

The Top 10 vote-getters (first place votes in parentheses): 1. **Martina Hingis**, tennis (92), 363 points; 2. **Annika Sorenstam**, golf (20), 178 pts; 3. **Mia Hamm**, socccer (9), 95 pts; 4. **Chamique Holdsclaw**, basketball (8), 69 pts; 5. **Cynthia Cooper**, basketball (11), 67 pts; 6. **Tara Lipinski**, figure skating (13), 66 pts; 7. **Marion Jones**, track (4), 35 pts; 8. **Christy Martin**, boxing (5), 34 pts; 9. **Venus Williams**, tennis (2), 25 pts; 10. **Michelle Kwan**, figure skating (2), 22 pts.

Multiple winners: Babe Didrikson Zaharias (6); Chris Evert (4); Patty Berg and Maureen Connolly (3); Tracy Austin, Althea Gibson, Billie Jean King, Nancy Lopez, Alice Marble, Martina Navratilova, Wilma Rudolph, Monica Seles, Kathy Whitworth and Mickey Wright (2).

Year	
1931	**Helene Madison**, swimming
1932	**Babe Didrikson**, track
1933	**Helen Jacobs**, tennis
1934	**Virginia Van Wie**, golf
1935	**Helen Wills Moody**, tennis
1936	**Helen Stephens**, track
1937	**Katherine Rawls**, swimming
1938	**Patty Berg**, golf
1939	**Alice Marble**, tennis
1940	**Alice Marble**, tennis
1941	**Betty Hicks Newell**, golf
1942	**Gloria Callen**, swimming
1943	**Patty Berg**, golf
1944	**Ann Curtis**, swimming
1945	**Babe Didrikson Zaharias**, golf
1946	**Babe Didrikson Zaharias**, golf
1947	**Babe Didrikson Zaharias**, golf
1948	**Fanny Blankers-Koen**, track
1949	**Marlene Bauer**, golf
1950	**Babe Didrikson Zaharias**, golf
1951	**Maureen Connolly**, tennis
1952	**Maureen Connolly**, tennis
1953	**Maureen Connolly**, tennis
1954	**Babe Didrikson Zaharias**, golf
1955	**Patty Berg**, golf
1956	**Pat McCormick**, diving
1957	**Althea Gibson**, tennis
1958	**Althea Gibson**, tennis
1959	**Maria Bueno**, tennis
1960	**Wilma Rudolph**, track
1961	**Wilma Rudolph**, track
1962	**Dawn Fraser**, swimming
1963	**Mickey Wright**, golf
1964	**Mickey Wright**, golf
1965	**Kathy Whitworth**, golf
1966	**Kathy Whitworth**, golf
1967	**Billie Jean King**, tennis
1968	**Peggy Fleming**, skating
1969	**Debbie Meyer**, swimming
1970	**Chi Cheng**, track
1971	**Evonne Goolagong,** tennis
1972	**Olga Korbut**, gymnastics
1973	**Billie Jean King**, tennis
1974	**Chris Evert**, tennis
1975	**Chris Evert**, tennis
1976	**Nadia Comaneci**, gymnastics
1977	**Chris Evert**, tennis
1978	**Nancy Lopez**, golf
1979	**Tracy Austin**, tennis
1980	**Chris Evert Lloyd**, tennis
1981	**Tracy Austin**, tennis

Awards (Cont.)

Year	Year	Year
1982 **Mary Decker Tabb**, track	1988 **Florence Griffith Joyner**, track	1994 **Bonnie Blair**, speed skating
1983 **Martina Navratilova**, tennis	1989 **Steffi Graf**, tennis	1995 **Rebecca Lobo**, col. basketball
1984 **Mary Lou Retton**, gymnastics	1990 **Beth Daniel**, golf	1996 **Amy Van Dyken**, swimming
1985 **Nancy Lopez**, golf	1991 **Monica Seles**, tennis	1997 **Martina Hingis**, tennis
1986 **Martina Navratilova**, tennis	1992 **Monica Seles**, tennis	
1987 **Jackie Joyner-Kersee**, track	1993 **Sheryl Swoopes**, basketball	

UPI International Athletes of the Year

Selected annually by United Press International's European newspaper sports editors from 1974-95.

Male

Multiple winners: Sebastian Coe, Alberto Juantorena and Carl Lewis (2).

Year	Year	Year
1974 **Muhammad Ali**, boxing	1982 **Daley Thompson**, track	1990 **Stefan Edberg**, tennis
1975 **Joao Oliveira**, track	1983 **Carl Lewis**, track	1991 **Sergei Bubka**, track
1976 **Alberto Juantorena**, track	1984 **Carl Lewis**, track	1992 **Kevin Young**, track
1977 **Alberto Juantorena**, track	1985 **Steve Cram**, track	1993 **Miguel Indurain**, cycling
1978 **Henry Rono**, track	1986 **Diego Maradona**, soccer	1994 **Johan Olav Koss**, speed skating
1979 **Sebastian Coe**, track	1987 **Ben Johnson**, track	1995 **Jonathan Edwards**, track
1980 **Eric Heiden**, speed skating	1988 **Matt Biondi**, swimming	1996 discontinued
1981 **Sebastian Coe**, track	1989 **Boris Becker**, tennis	

Female

Multiple winners: Nadia Comaneci, Steffi Graf, Marita Koch and Monica Seles (2).

Year	Year	Year
1974 **Irena Szewinska**, track	1982 **Marita Koch**, track	1990 **Merlene Ottey**, track
1975 **Nadia Comaneci**, gymnastics	1983 **Jarmila Kratochvilova**, track	1991 **Monica Seles**, tennis
1976 **Nadia Comaneci**, gymnastics	1984 **Martina Navratilova**, tennis	1992 **Monica Seles**, tennis
1977 **Rosie Ackermann**, track	1985 **Mary Decker Slaney**, track	1993 **Wang Junxia**, track
1978 **Tracy Caulkins**, swimming	1986 **Heike Drechsler**, track	1994 **Le Jingyi**, swimming
1979 **Marita Koch**, track	1987 **Steffi Graf**, tennis	1995 **Gwen Torrence**, track
1980 **Hanni Wenzel**, alpine skiing	1988 **Florence Griffith Joyner**, track	1996 discontinued
1981 **Chris Evert Lloyd**, tennis	1989 **Steffi Graf**, tennis	

Jesse Owens International Trophy

Presented annually by the International Amateur Athletic Association since 1981 and selected by a worldwide panel of electors. The Jesse Owens International Trophy is named after the late American Olympic champion, who won four gold medals at the 1936 Summer Games in Berlin.

Year	Year	Year
1981 **Eric Heiden**, speed skating	1987 **Greg Louganis**, diving	1994 **Wang Junxia**, track
1982 **Sebastian Coe**, track	1988 **Ben Johnson**, track	1995 **Johan Olva Koss**, speed skating
1983 **Mary Decker**, track	1990 **Roger Kingdom**, track	1996 **Michael Johnson**, track
1984 **Edwin Moses**, track	1991 **Greg LeMond**, cycling	1997 **Michael Johnson**, track
1985 **Carl Lewis**, track	1992 **Mike Powell**, track	1998 **Haile Gebrselassie**, track
1986 **Said Aouita**, track	1993 **Vitaly Scherbo**, gymnastics	

James E. Sullivan Memorial Award

Presented annually by the Amateur Athletic Union since 1930. The Sullivan Award is named after the former AAU president and given to the athlete who, "by his or her performance, example and influence as an amateur, has done the most during the year to advance the cause of sportsmanship." An athlete cannot win the award more than once.

The 1997 winner was college football quarterback **Peyton Manning**. Manning, although finishing second behind Charles Woodson in the Heisman Trophy voting, led the Tennessee Volunteers to an 11-2 record and the SEC championship. The other nine finalists are listed alphabetically: **Char Carvin**, swimming; **J.D. Drew**, baseball; **Tim Duncan**, basketball; **Les Gutches**, wrestling; **Chamique Holdsclaw**, basketball; **Trinity Johnson**, softball; **Linda Mastandrea**, disabled sports; **Jenny Thompson**, swimming; **Blaine Wilson**, gymnastics. Vote totals were not released.

Year	Year	Year
1930 **Bobby Jones**, golf	1941 **Leslie MacMitchell**, track	1952 **Horace Ashenfelter**, track
1931 **Barney Berlinger**, track	1942 **Cornelius Warmerdam**, track	1953 **Sammy Lee**, diving
1932 **Jim Bausch**, track	1943 **Gilbert Dodds**, track	1954 **Mal Whitfield**, track
1933 **Glenn Cunningham**, track	1944 **Ann Curtis**, swimming	1955 **Harrison Dillard**, track
1934 **Bill Bonthron**, track	1945 **Doc Blanchard**, football	1956 **Pat McCormick**, diving
1935 **Lawson Little**, golf	1946 **Arnold Tucker**, football	1957 **Bobby Morrow**, track
1936 **Glenn Morris**, track	1947 **John B. Kelly, Jr.**, rowing	1958 **Glenn Davis**, track
1937 **Don Budge**, tennis	1948 **Bob Mathias**, track	1959 **Parry O'Brien**, track
1938 **Don Lash**, track	1949 **Dick Button**, skating	1960 **Rafer Johnson**, track
1939 **Joe Burk**, rowing	1950 **Fred Wilt**, track	1961 **Wilma Rudolph**, track
1940 **Greg Rice**, track	1951 **Bob Richards**, track	1963 **John Pennel**, track

Year
1964 **Don Schollander**, swimming
1965 **Bill Bradley**, basketball
1966 **Jim Ryun**, track
1967 **Randy Matson**, track
1968 **Debbie Meyer**, swimming
1969 **Bill Toomey**, track
1970 **John Kinsella**, swimming
1971 **Mark Spitz**, swimming
1972 **Frank Shorter**, track
1973 **Bill Walton**, basketball
1974 **Rich Wohlhuter**, track
1975 **Tim Shaw**, swimming

Year
1976 **Bruce Jenner**, track
1977 **John Naber**, swimming
1978 **Tracy Caulkins**, swimming
1979 **Kurt Thomas**, gymnastics
1980 **Eric Heiden**, speed skating
1981 **Carl Lewis**, track
1982 **Mary Decker**, track
1983 **Edwin Moses**, track
1984 **Greg Louganis**, diving
1985 **Joan B. Samuelson**, track
1986 **Jackie Joyner-Kersee**, track
1987 **Jim Abbott**, baseball

Year
1988 **Florence Griffith Joyner**, track
1989 **Janet Evans**, swimming
1990 **John Smith**, wrestling
1991 **Mike Powell**, track
1992 **Bonnie Blair**, speed skating
1993 **Charlie Ward**, football
1994 **Dan Jansen**, speed skating
1995 **Bruce Baumgartner**, wrestling
1996 **Michael Johnson**, track
1997 **Peyton Manning**, football

USOC Sportsman & Sportswoman of the Year

To the outstanding overall male and female athletes from within the U.S. Olympic Committee member organizations. Winners are chosen from nominees of the national governing bodies for Olympic and Pan American Games and affiliated organizations. Voting is done by members of the national media, USOC board of directors and Athletes' Advisory Council.

Sportsman

Multiple winners: Eric Heiden and Michael Johnson (3); Matt Biondi and Greg Louganis (2).

Year
1974 **Jim Bolding**, track
1975 **Clint Jackson**, boxing
1976 **John Naber**, swimming
1977 **Eric Heiden**, speed skating
1978 **Bruce Davidson**, equestrian
1979 **Eric Heiden**, speed skating
1980 **Eric Heiden**, speed skating
1981 **Scott Hamilton**, fig. skating

Year
1982 **Greg Louganis**, diving
1983 **Rick McKinney**, archery
1984 **Edwin Moses**, track
1985 **Willie Banks**, track
1986 **Matt Biondi**, swimming
1987 **Greg Louganis**, diving
1988 **Matt Biondi**, swimming
1989 **Roger Kingdom**, track

Year
1990 **John Smith**, wrestling
1991 **Carl Lewis**, track
1992 **Pablo Morales**, swimming
1993 **Michael Johnson**, track
1994 **Dan Jansen**, speed skating
1995 **Michael Johnson**, track
1996 **Michael Johnson**, track
1997 **Pete Sampras**, tennis

Sportswoman

Multiple winners: Bonnie Blair, Tracy Caulkins, Jackie Joyner-Kersee and Sheila Young Ochowicz (2).

Year
1974 **Shirley Babashoff**, swimming
1975 **Kathy Heddy**, swimming
1976 **Sheila Young**, speedskating
1977 **Linda Fratianne**, fig. skating
1978 **Tracy Caulkins**, swimming
1979 **Sippy Woodhead**, swimming
1980 **Beth Heiden**, speed skating
1981 **Sheila Ochowicz**, speed skating & cycling

Year
1982 **Melanie Smith**, equestrian
1983 **Tamara McKinney**, skiing
1984 **Tracy Caulkins**, swimming
1985 **Mary Decker Slaney**, track
1986 **Jackie Joyner-Kersee**, track
1987 **Jackie Joyner-Kersee**, track
1988 **Florence Griffith Joyner**, track
1989 **Janet Evans**, swimming
1990 **Lynn Jennings**, track

Year
1991 **Kim Zmeskal**, gymnastics
1992 **Bonnie Blair**, speed skating
1993 **Gail Devers**, track
1994 **Bonnie Blair**, speed skating
1995 **Picabo Street**, skiing
1996 **Amy Van Dyken**, swimming
1997 **Tara Lipinski,** figure skating

Honda Broderick Cup

To the outstanding collegiate woman athlete of the year in NCAA competition. Winner is chosen from nominees in each of the NCAA's 10 competitive sports. Final voting is done by member athletic directors. Award is named after founder and sportswear manufacturer Thomas Broderick.

Multiple winner: Tracy Caulkins (2).

Year		
1977	**Lucy Harris**, Delta St	basketball
1978	**Ann Meyers**, UCLA	basketball
1979	**Nancy Lieberman**, Old Dominion	basketball
1980	**Julie Shea**, N.C. State	track & field
1981	**Jill Sterkel**, Texas	swimming
1982	**Tracy Caulkins**, Florida	swimming
1983	**Deitre Collins**, Hawaii	volleyball
1984	**Tracy Caulkins**, Florida	swimming
	& **Cheryl Miller**, USC	basketball
1985	**Jackie Joyner**, UCLA	track & field
1986	**Kamie Ethridge**, Texas	basketball
1987	**Mary T. Meagher**, California	swimming

Year		
1988	**Teresa Weatherspoon**, La. Tech	basketball
1989	**Vicki Huber**, Villanova	track
1990	**Suzy Favor**, Wisconsin	track
1991	**Dawn Staley**, Virginia	basketball
1992	**Missy Marlowe**, Utah	gymnastics
1993	**Lisa Fernandez**, UCLA	softball
1994	**Mia Hamm**, North Carolina	soccer
1995	**Rebecca Lobo**, UConn	basketball
1996	**Jennifer Rizzotti**, UConn	basketball
1997	**Cindy Daws**, Notre Dame	soccer
1998	**Chamique Holdsclaw**, Tennessee	basketball

Flo Hyman Award

Presented annually since 1987 by the Women's Sports Foundation for "exemplifying dignity, spirit and commitment to excellence" and named in honor of the late captain of the 1984 U.S. Women's Volleyball team. Voting by WSF members.

Year
1987 **Martina Navratilova**, tennis
1988 **Jackie Joyner-Kersee**, track
1989 **Evelyn Ashford**, track
1990 **Chris Evert**, tennis

Year
1991 **Diana Golden**, skiing
1992 **Nancy Lopez**, golf
1993 **Lynette Woodward**, basketball
1994 **Patty Sheehan**, golf

Year
1995 **Mary Lou Retton**, gymnastics
1996 **Donna de Varona**, swimming
1997 **Billie Jean King**, tennis

Awards (Cont.)

ESPY Awards

The ESPY Awards, which represent the convergence of the sports and entertainment communities, were created by ESPN in 1993 and are given for Excellence in Sports Performance in more than 30 categories. ESPYs are awarded by a panel of sports executives, journalists and retired athletes whose decisions are based on the performances of the nominees during the year preceding the awards ceremony. Note that not all categories are listed below.

Breakthrough Athlete of the Year

1993 Gary Sheffield, San Diego Padres
1994 Mike Piazza, Los Angeles Dodgers
1995 Jeff Bagwell, Houston Astros
1996 Hideo Nomo, Los Angeles Dodgers
1997 Tiger Woods, golf
1998 Nomar Garciaparra, Boston Red Sox

Coach/Manager of the Year

1993 Jimmy Johnson, Dallas Cowboys
1994 Jimmy Johnson, Dallas Cowboys
1995 George Siefert, San Francisco 49ers
1996 Gary Barnett, Northwestern
1997 Joe Torre, New York Yankees
1998 Jim Leyland, Florida Marlins

Comeback Athlete of the Year

1993 Dave Winfield, Toronto Blue Jays
1994 Mario Lemieux, Pittsburgh Penguins
1995 Dan Marino, Miami Dolphins
1996 Michael Jordan, Chicago Bulls
1997 Evander Holyfield, boxer
1998 Roger Clemens, Toronto Blue Jays

Outstanding Female Athlete of the Year

1993 Monica Seles, tennis
1994 Julie Krone, jockey
1995 Bonnie Blair, speed skater
1996 Rebecca Lobo, basketball
1997 Amy Van Dyken, swimming
1998 Mia Hamm, soccer

Outstanding Male Athlete of the Year

1993 Michael Jordan, Chicago Bulls
1994 Barry Bonds, San Francisco Giants
1995 Steve Young, San Francisco 49ers
1996 Cal Ripken, Baltimore Orioles
1997 Michael Johnson, Olympic sprinter
1998 Tiger Woods, golf

Outstanding Performance Under Pressure

1993 Christian Laettner, Duke
1994 Joe Carter, Toronto Blue Jays
1995 Mark Messier, New York Rangers
1996 Martin Broduer, New Jersey Devils
1997 Kerri Strug, Olympic gymnast
1998 Terrell Davis, Denver Broncos

Outstanding Team

1993 Dallas Cowboys
1994 Toronto Blue Jays
1995 New York Rangers
1996 UConn women's hoops
1997 New York Yankees
1998 Denver Broncos

Outstanding Baseball Performer of the Year

1993 Dennis Eckersley, Oakland A's
1994 Barry Bonds, San Francisco Giants
1995 Jeff Bagwell, Houston Astros
1996 Greg Maddux, Atlanta Braves
1997 Ken Caminiti, San Diego Padres
1998 Larry Walker, Colorado Rockies

Outstanding Pro Football Performer of the Year

1993 Emmitt Smith, Dallas Cowboys
1994 Emmitt Smith, Dallas Cowboys
1995 Barry Sanders, Detroit Lions
1996 Brett Favre, Green Bay Packers
1997 Brett Favre, Green Bay Packers
1998 Barry Sanders, Detroit Lions

Outstanding Pro Basketball Performer of the Year

1993 Michael Jordan, Chicago Bulls
1994 Charles Barkley, Phoenix Suns
1995 Hakeem Olajuwon, Houston Rockets
1996 Hakeem Olajuwon, Houston Rockets
1997 Michael Jordan, Chicago Bulls
1998 Michael Jordan, Chicago Bulls

Outstanding Pro Hockey Performer of the Year

1993 Mario Lemieux, Pittsburgh Penguins
1994 Mario Lemieux, Pittsburgh Penguins
1995 Mark Messier, New York Rangers
1996 Eric Lindros, Philadelphia Flyers
1997 Joe Sakic, Colorado Avalanche
1998 Mario Lemieux, Pittsburgh Penguins

Outstanding College Football Performer of the Year

1993 Garrison Hearst, Georgia
1994 Charlie Ward, Florida State
1995 Rashaan Salaam, Colorado
1996 Eddie George, Ohio State
1997 Danny Wuerffel, Florida
1998 Peyton Manning, Tennessee

Time Man of the Year

Since Charles Lindbergh was named *Time* magazine's first Man of the Year for 1927, two individuals with significant sports credentials have won the honor.

Year
1984 **Peter Ueberroth**, president of the Los Angeles Olympic Organizing Committee.
1991 **Ted Turner**, owner-president of Turner Broadcasting System, founder of CNN cable news network, owner of the Atlanta Braves (NL) and Atlanta Hawks (NBA), and former winning America's Cup skipper.

Outstanding College Basketball Performer of the Year

1993 Christian Laettner, Duke
1994 Bobby Hurley, Duke
1995 Grant Hill, Duke
1996 Ed O'Bannon, UCLA
1997 Tim Duncan, Wake Forest
1998 Keith Van Horn, Utah

Outstanding Women's College Hoops Performer of the Year

1993 Dawn Staley, Virginia
1994 Sheryl Swoopes, Texas Tech
1995 Charlotte Smith, North Carolina
1996 Rebecca Lobo, Connecticut
1997 Saudia Roundtree, Georgia
1998 Chamique Holdsclaw, Tennessee

Outstanding Men's Tennis Performer of the Year

1993 Jim Courier
1994 Pete Sampras
1995 Pete Sampras
1996 Pete Sampras
1997 Pete Sampras
1998 Pete Sampras

Outstanding Women's Tennis Performer of the Year

1993 Monica Seles
1994 Steffi Graf
1995 Aranxta Sanchez Vicario
1996 Steffi Graf
1997 Steffi Graf
1998 Martina Hingis

Outstanding Men's Golf Performer of the Year

1993 Fred Couples
1994 Nick Price
1995 Nick Price
1996 Corey Pavin
1997 Tom Lehman
1998 Tiger Woods

Outstanding Women's Golf Performer of the Year

1993 Dottie Monroe
1994 Betsy King
1995 Laura Davies
1996 Annika Sorenstam
1997 Karrie Webb
1998 Annika Sorenstam

Outstanding Jockey of the Year

1994 Mike Smith
1995 Chris McCarron
1996 Jerry Bailey
1997 Jerry Bailey
1998 Gary Stevens

Outstanding Bowling Performer of the Year

1995 Norm Duke
1996 Mike Aulby
1997 Bob Learn Jr.
1998 Walter Ray Williams Jr.

Outstanding Auto Racing Performer of the Year

1993 Nigel Mansell
1994 Nigel Mansell
1995 Al Unser Jr.
1996 Jeff Gordon
1997 Jimmy Vasser
1998 Jeff Gordon

Outstanding Men's Track Performer of the Year

1993 Kevin Young
1994 Michael Johnson
1995 Dennis Mitchell
1996 Michael Johnson
1997 Michael Johnson
1998 Wilson Kipketer

Outstanding Women's Track Performer of the Year

1993 Evelyn Ashford
1994 Gail Devers
1995 Gwen Torrence
1996 Kim Batten
1997 Marie-Jose Perec
1998 Marion Jones

Outstanding Boxing Performer of the Year

1993 Riddick Bowe
1994 Evander Holyfield
1995 George Foreman
1996 Roy Jones Jr.
1997 Evander Holyfield
1998 Evander Holyfield

Game of the Year

1996 AFC championship between Colts and Steelers
1997 Ohio State edges Arizona State in the Rose Bowl
1998 Super Bowl XXXII, Broncos over Packers

Arthur Ashe Award for Courage

Presented since 1993 on the annual ESPN "ESPYs" telecast. Given to a member of the sports community who has exemplified the same courage, spirit and determination to help others despite personal hardship that characterized Arthur Ashe, the late tennis champion and humanitarian. Voting done by select 26-member committee of media and sports personalities.

Year
1993 **Jim Valvano**, basketball
1994 **Steve Palermo**, baseball
1995 **Howard Cosell**, TV & radio
1996 **Loretta Clairborne**, special olympics
1997 **Muhammad Ali**, boxing
1998 **Dean Smith**, college basketball

Awards (Cont.)

The Hickok Belt

Officially known as the S. Rae Hickok Professional Athlete of the Year Award and presented by the Kickik Manufacturing Co. of Arlington, Texas, from 1950-76. The trophy was a large belt of gold, diamonds and other jewels, reportedly worth $30,000 in 1976, the last year it was handed out. Voting was done by 270 newspaper sports editors from around the country.

Multiple winner: Sandy Koufax (2).

Year	
1950	**Phil Rizzuto**, baseball
1951	**Allie Reynolds**, baseball
1952	**Rocky Marciano**, boxing
1953	**Ben Hogan**, golf
1954	**Willie Mays**, baseball
1955	**Otto Graham**, football
1956	**Mickey Mantle**, baseball
1957	**Carmen Basilio**, boxing
1958	**Bob Turley**, baseball
1959	**Ingemar Johansson**, boxing
1960	**Arnold Palmer**, golf
1961	**Roger Maris**, baseball
1962	**Maury Wills**, baseball
1963	**Sandy Koufax**, baseball
1964	**Jim Brown**, football
1965	**Sandy Koufax**, baseball
1966	**Frank Robinson**, baseball
1967	**Carl Yastrzemski**, baseball
1968	**Joe Namath**, football
1969	**Tom Seaver**, baseball
1970	**Brooks Robinson**, baseball
1971	**Lee Trevino**, golf
1972	**Steve Carlton**, baseball
1973	**O.J. Simpson**, football
1974	**Muhammad Ali**, boxing
1975	**Pete Rose**, baseball
1976	**Ken Stabler**, football
1977	Discontinued

ABC's "Wide World of Sports" Athlete of the Year

Selected annually by the producers of ABC Sports since 1962.

Multiple winner: Greg LeMond (2).

Year	
1962	**Jim Beatty**, track
1963	**Valery Brumel**, track
1964	**Don Schollander**, swimming
1965	**Jim Clark**, auto racing
1966	**Jim Ryun**, track
1967	**Peggy Fleming**, figure skating
1968	**Bill Toomey**, track
1969	**Mario Andretti**, auto racing
1970	**Willis Reed**, basketball
1971	**Lee Trevino**, golf
1972	**Olga Korbut**, gymnastics
1973	**O.J. Simpson**, football & **Jackie Stewart**, auto racing
1974	**Muhammad Ali**, boxing
1975	**Jack Nicklaus**, golf
1976	**Nadia Comaneci**, gymnastics
1977	**Steve Cauthen**, horse racing
1978	**Ron Guidry**, baseball
1979	**Willie Stargell**, baseball
1980	**U.S. Olympic hockey team**
1981	**Sugar Ray Leonard**, boxing
1982	**Wayne Gretzky**, hockey
1983	**Australia II**, yachting
1984	**Edwin Moses**, track
1985	**Pete Rose**, baseball
1986	**Debi Thomas**, figure skating
1987	**Dennis Conner**, yachting
1988	**Greg Louganis**, diving
1989	**Greg LeMond**, cycling
1990	**Greg LeMond**, cycling
1991	**Carl Lewis**, track & **Kim Zmeskal**, gymnastics
1992	**Bonnie Blair**, speed skating
1993	**Evander Holyfield**, boxing
1994	**Al Unser Jr.**, auto racing
1995	**Miguel Induráin**, cycling
1996	**Michael Johnson**, track
1997	**Tiger Woods**, golf

The Sporting News Sportsman of the Year

Selected annually by the editors of *The Sporting News* since 1968. 'Man of the Year' changed to 'Sportsman' of the Year in 1993.

Year	
1968	**Denny McLain**, baseball
1969	**Tom Seaver**, baseball
1970	**John Wooden**, basketball
1971	**Lee Trevino**, golf
1972	**Charles O. Finley**, baseball
1973	**O.J. Simpson**, pro football
1974	**Lou Brock**, baseball
1975	**Archie Griffin**, football
1976	**Larry O'Brien**, basketball
1977	**Steve Cauthen**, horse racing
1978	**Ron Guidry**, baseball
1979	**Willie Stargell**, baseball
1980	**George Brett**, baseball
1981	**Wayne Gretzky**, hockey
1982	**Whitey Herzog**, baseball
1983	**Bowie Kuhn**, baseball
1984	**Peter Ueberroth**, LA Olympics
1985	**Pete Rose**, baseball
1986	**Larry Bird**, pro basketball
1987	No award
1988	**Jackie Joyner-Kersee**, track
1989	**Joe Montana**, football
1990	**Nolan Ryan**, baseball
1991	**Michael Jordan**, basketball
1992	**Mike Krzyzewski**, col. bask.
1993	**Cito Gaston** & **Pat Gillick**, baseball
1994	**Emmitt Smith**, pro football
1995	**Cal Ripken Jr.**, baseball
1996	**Joe Torre**, baseball
1997	**Mark McGwire**, baseball

Presidential Medal of Freedom

Since President John F. Kennedy established the Medal of Freedom as America's highest civilian honor in 1963, only nine sports figures have won the award. Note that (*) indicates the presentation was made posthumously.

Year		President
1963	**Bob Kiphuth**, swimming	Kennedy
1976	**Jesse Owens**, track & field	Ford
1977	**Joe DiMaggio**, baseball	Ford
1983	**Paul (Bear) Bryant***, football	Reagan
1984	**Jackie Robinson***, baseball	Reagan
1986	**Earl (Red) Blaik**, football	Reagan
1991	**Ted Williams**, baseball	Bush
1992	**Richard Petty**, auto racing	Bush
1993	**Arthur Ashe***, tennis	Clinton

TROPHY CASE

From the first organized track meet at Olympia in 776 B.C., to the Atlanta Summer Olympics over 2,700 years later, championships have been officially recognized with prizes that are symbolically rich and eagerly pursued. Here are 15 of the most coveted trophies in America.

(Illustrations by Lynn Mercer Michaud)

America's Cup

First presented by England's Royal Yacht Squadron to the winner of an invitational race around the Isle of Wight on Aug. 22, 1851. . . originally called the Hundred Guinea Cup. . . renamed after the U.S. boat America, winner of the first race. . . made of sterling silver and designed by London jewelers R. & G. Garrard. . . measures 2 feet, 3 inches high and weighs 16 lbs. . . originally cost 100 guineas ($500), now valued at $250,000 . . . bell-shaped base added in 1958. . . challenged for every three to four years. . . trophy held by yacht club sponsoring winning boat...Cup was badly damaged when a Maori protester repeatedly smashed it with a sledgehammer on March 14, 1997. It was sent back to the original maker and fully restored.

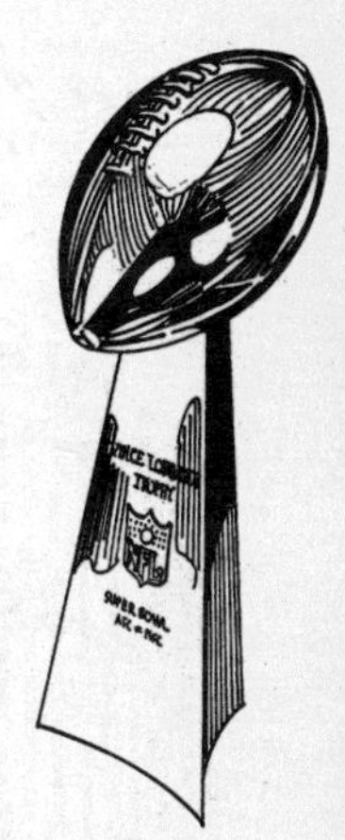

Vince Lombardi Trophy

First presented at the AFL-NFL World Championship Game (now Super Bowl) on Jan. 15, 1967. . . originally called the World Championship Game Trophy . . . renamed in 1971 in honor of former Green Bay Packers GM-coach and two-time Super Bowl winner Vince Lombardi, who died in 1970 as coach of Washington . . . made of sterling silver and designed by Tiffany & Co. of New York . . . measures 21 inches high and weighs 7 lbs (football depicted is regulation size). . . valued at $12,500. . . competed for annually- . . . winning team keeps trophy.

Olympic Gold Medal

First presented by International Olympic Committee in 1908 (until then winners received silver medals). . . second and third place finishers also got medals of silver and bronze for first time in 1908. . . each medal must be at least 2.4 inches in diameter and 0.12 inches thick. . . the gold medal is actually made of silver, but must be gilded with at least 6 grams (0.21 ounces) of pure gold. . . the medals for the 1996 Atlanta Games were designed by Malcolm Grear Designers and produced by Reed & Barton of Taunton, Mass...604 gold, 604 silver and 630 bronze medals were made. . . competed for every two years as Winter and Summer Games alternate. . . winners keep medals.

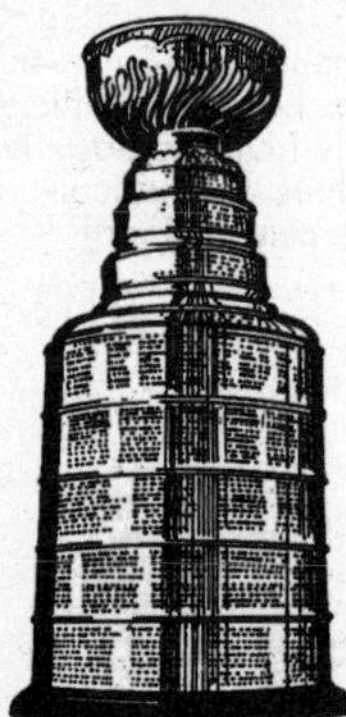

Stanley Cup

Donated by Lord Stanley of Preston, the Governor General of Canada and first presented in 1893. . . original cup was made of sterling silver by an unknown London silversmith and measured 7 inches high with an 11½-inch diameter. . . in order to accommodate all the rosters of winning teams, the cup now measures 35½ inches high with a base 54 inches around and weighs 32 lbs-. . . originally bought for 10 guineas ($48.67), it is now insured for $75,000. . . actual cup retired to Hall of Fame and replaced in 1970. . . presented to NHL playoff champion since 1918. . . trophy loaned to winning team for one year.

World Cup

First presented by the Federation Internationale de Football Association (FIFA). . . originally called the World Cup Trophy. . . renamed the Jules Rimet Cup (after the then FIFA president) in 1946, but retired by Brazil after that country's third title in 1970. . . new World Cup trophy created in 1974. . . designed by Italian sculptor Silvio Gazzaniga and made of solid 18 carat gold with two malachite rings inlaid at the base. . . measures 14.2 inches high and weighs 11 lbs. . . insured for $200,000 (U.S.). . . competed for every four years. . . winning team gets gold-plated replica.

Commissioner's Trophy

First presented by the Commissioner of baseball to the winner of the 1967 World Series. . . also known as the World Championship Trophy. . . made of brass and gold plate with an ebony base and a baseball in the center made of pewter with a silver finish. . . designed by Balfour & Co. of Attleboro, Mass. . . 30 pennants represent 15 AL and 15 NL teams . . . measures 30 inches high and 36 inches around at the base and weighs 30 lbs. . . valued at $15,000. . . competed for annually. . . winning team keeps trophy.

Larry O'Brien Trophy

First presented in 1978 to winner of NBA Finals. . . originally called the Walter A. Brown Trophy after the league pioneer and Boston Celtics owner (an earlier NBA championship bowl was also named after Brown). . . renamed in 1984 in honor of outgoing commissioner O'Brien, who served from 1975-84 . . . made of sterling silver with 24 carat gold overlay and designed by Tiffany & Co. of New York. . . measures 2 feet high and weighs 14½ lbs (basketball depicted is regulation size). . . valued at $13,500. . . competed for annually. . . winning team keeps trophy.

Heisman Trophy

First presented in 1935 to the best college football player east of the Mississippi by the Downtown Athletic Club of New York. . . players across the entire country eligible since 1936. . . originally called the DAC Trophy. . . renamed in 1936 following the death of DAC athletic director and former college coach John W. Heisman. . . made of bronze and designed by New York sculptor Frank Eliscu, it measures 13½ in. high, 6½ in. wide and 14 in. long at the base and weighs 25 lbs. . . valued at $2,000 . . . voting done by national media and former Heisman winners. . . awarded annually. . . winner keeps trophy.

James E. Sullivan Memorial Award

First presented by the Amateur Athletic Union (AAU) in 1930 as a gold medal and given to the nation's outstanding amateur athlete. . . trophy given since 1933. . . named after the amateur sports movement pioneer, who was a founder and past president of AAU and the director of the 1904 Olympic Games in St. Louis. . . made of bronze with a marble base, it measures 17½ in. high and 11 in. wide at the base and weighs 13½ lbs. . . valued at $2,500. . . voting done by AAU and USOC officials, former winners and selected media. . . awarded annually. . . winner keeps trophy.

Ryder Cup

Donated in 1927 by English seed merchant Samuel Ryder, who offered the gold cup for a biennial match between teams of golfing pros from Great Britain and the United States. . . the format changed in 1977 to include the best players on the European PGA Tour . . . made of 14 carat gold on a wood base and designed by Mappin and Webb of London. . . the golfer depicted on the top of the trophy is Ryder's friend and teaching pro Abe Mitchell. . . . the cup measures 16 in. high and weighs 4 lbs. . . insured for $50,000 . . . competed for every two years at alternating British and U.S. sites . . . the cup is held by the PGA headquarters of the winning side.

Davis Cup

Donated by American college student and U.S. doubles champion Dwight F. Davis in 1900 and presented by the International Tennis Federation (ITF) to the winner of the annual 16-team men's competition. . . officially called the International Lawn Tennis Challenge Trophy. . . made of sterling silver and designed by Shreve, Crump and Low of Boston, the cup has a matching tray (added in 1921) and a very heavy two-tiered base containing rosters of past winning teams. . . it stands 34½ in. high and 108 in. around at the base and weighs 400 lbs. . . insured for $150,000. . . competed for annually. . . trophy loaned to winning country for one year.

Borg-Warner Trophy

First presented by the Borg-Warner Automotive Co. of Chicago in 1936 to the winner of the Indianapolis 500. . . replaced the Wheeler-Schebler Trophy which went to the 400-mile leader from 1911-32. . . made of sterling silver with bas-relief sculptured heads of each winning driver and a gold bas-relief head of Tony Hulman, the owner of the Indy Speedway from 1945-77 . . . designed by Robert J. Hill and made by Gorham, Inc. of Rhode Island . . . measures 51½ in. high and weighs over 80 lbs. . . new base added in 1988 and the entire trophy restored in 1991. . . competed for annually. . . insured for $1 million. . . trophy stays at Speedway Hall of Fame. . . winner gets a 14-in. high replica valued at $30,000.

NCAA Championship Trophy

First presented in 1952 by the NCAA to all 1st, 2nd and 3rd place teams in sports with sanctioned tournaments. . . 1st place teams receive gold-plated awards, 2nd place award is silver-plated and 3rd is bronze. . . replaced silver cup given to championship teams from 1939-1951. . . made of walnut, the trophy stands 24¾ in. high, 14⅛ in. wide and 4½ in. deep at the base and weighs 15 lbs . . . designed by Medallic Art Co. of Danbury, Conn. and made by House of Usher of Kansas City since 1990. . . valued at $500. . . competed for annually. . . winning teams keep trophies.

World Championship Belt

First presented in 1921 by the World Boxing Association, one of the three organizations (the World Boxing Council and International Boxing Federation are the others) generally accepted as sanctioning legitimate world championship fights. . . belt weighs 8 lbs. and is made of hand tanned leather. . . the outsized buckle measures 10½ in. high and 8 in. wide, is made of pewter with 24 carat gold plate and contains crystal and semi-precious stones . . . side panels of polished brass are for engraving title bout results . . . currently made by Phil Valentino Originals of Jersey City, N.J.. . . champions keep belts even if they lose their title.

World Championship Ring

Rings decorated with gems and engraving date back to ancient Egypt where the wealthy wore heavy gold and silver rings to indicate social status. . . championship rings in sports serve much the same purpose, indicating the wearer is a champion. . . As an example, the Dallas Cowboys' ring for winning Superbowl XXX on Jan. 28, 1996 was designed by Diamond Cutters International of Houston. . . each ring is made of 14–carat yellow gold, weighs 48–51 penny weights and features five trimmed marquis diamonds interlocking in the shape of the Cowboys' star logo as well as five more marquis diamonds (for the team's five Super Bowl wins) on a bed of 51 smaller diamonds. . . rings were appraised at over $30,000 each.

Who's Who

Muhammad Ali, owner of one of the world's most recognizable faces, stings like a bee in this photo from 1975.

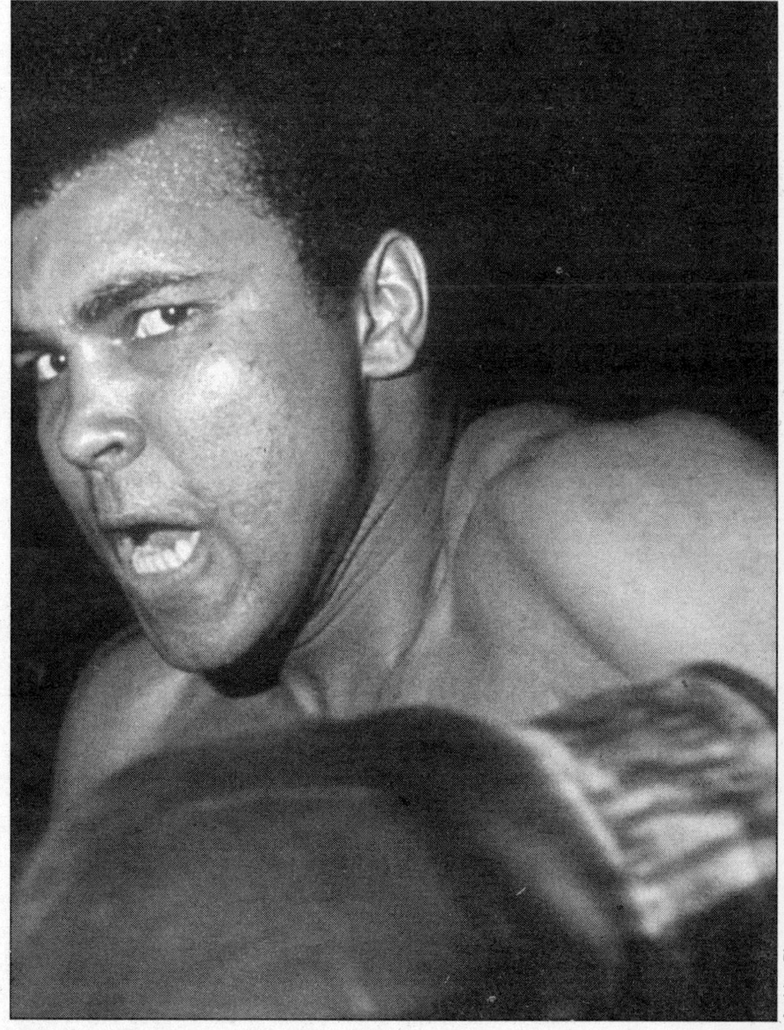

Archive Photos

Sports Personalities

Eight hundred forty-nine entries dating back to the turn of the century. Entries updated through September 21, 1998.

Hank Aaron (b. Feb. 5, 1934): Baseball OF; led NL in HRs and RBI 4 times each and batting twice with Milwaukee and Atlanta Braves; MVP in 1957; played in 24 All-Star Games, all-time leader in HRs (755) and RBI (2,297), 3rd in hits (3,771); executive with Braves and TBS, Inc.

Kareem Abdul-Jabbar (b. Lew Alcindor, Apr. 16, 1947): Basketball C; led UCLA to 3 NCAA titles (1967-69); Final 4 MOP 3 times; Player of Year twice; led Milwaukee (1) and LA Lakers (5) to 6 NBA titles; playoff MVP twice (1971,85), regular season MVP 6 times (1971-72,74,76-77,80); retired in 1989 after 20 seasons as all-time leader in over 20 categories.

Andre Agassi (b. Apr. 29, 1970): Tennis; former No. 1 men's player in the world with 38 career tournament wins and 3 grand slam titles; won Wimbledon in 1992, U.S. Open as unseeded entry in '94 and Australian Open in 1996; helped U.S. win 2 Davis Cup finals (1990,92).

Troy Aikman (b. Nov. 21, 1966): Football QB; consensus All-America at UCLA (1988); 1st overall pick in 1989 NFL Draft (by Dallas); led Cowboys to 3 Super Bowl titles (1992,93,95 seasons); MVP in Super Bowl XXVII.

Marv Albert (b. June 12, 1941): Radio-TV; Former NBC announcer and radio broadcaster for the New York Knicks, Rangers and Giants who pled guilty to a misdemeanor assault charge amid embarrassing allegations of his sex life. One of NBC's top play-by- play announcers who worked five NBA Finals, one NBA All-Star Game, the 1992 Summer Olympics in Barcelona and the 1994 Basketball World Championships. Rehired to MSG network in 1998.

Tenley Albright (b. July 18, 1935): Figure skater; 2-time world champion (1953,55); won Olympic silver (1952) and gold (1956) medals; became a surgeon.

Grover Cleveland (Pete) Alexander (b. Feb. 26, 1887, d. Nov. 4, 1950): Baseball RHP; won 20 or more games 9 times; 373 career wins and 90 shutouts.

Muhammad Ali (b. Cassius Clay, Jan. 17, 1942): Boxer; 1960 Olympic light heavyweight champion; only 3-time world heavyweight champ (1964-67, 1974-78,1978-79); defeated Sonny Liston (1964), George Foreman (1974) and Leon Spinks (1978) for title; fought Joe Frazier in 3 memorable bouts (1971-75), winning twice; adopted Black Muslim faith in 1964 and changed name; stripped of title in 1967 after conviction for refusing induction into U.S. Army; verdict reversed by Supreme Court in 1971; career record of 56-5 with 37 KOs and 19 successful title defenses; lit the flaming cauldron to signal the beginning of the 1996 Summer Olympics in Atlanta.

Forrest (Phog) Allen (b. Nov. 18, 1885, d. Sept. 16, 1974): Basketball; college coach 48 years; directed Kansas to NCAA title (1952); 5th on all-time Div. I list with 746 career wins.

Bobby Allison (b. Dec. 3, 1937): Auto racer; 3-time winner of Daytona 500 (1978,82,88); NASCAR national champ in 1983; father of Davey.

Davey Allison (b. Feb. 25, 1961, d. July 13, 1993): Auto racer; stock car Rookie of Year (1987); winner of 19 NASCAR races, including 1992 Daytona 500; killed at age 32 in helicopter accident at Talladega Superspeedway; son of Bobby.

Roberto Alomar (b. Feb. 5, 1968): Baseball; member of two World Series champions as a Toronto Blue Jay; six-time Gold Glove second baseman; seven-time All-Star; MVP of 1992 ALCS; became known well beyond baseball for spitting in the face of umpire John Hirschbeck during final weekend of 1996 season; named MVP of 1998 All-Star Game.

Walter Alston (b. Dec. 1, 1911, d. Oct. 1, 1984): Baseball; managed Brooklyn-LA Dodgers 23 years, won 7 pennants and 4 World Series (1955,59,63,65); retired after 1976 season with 2,063 wins (2,040 regular season and 23 postseason).

Sparky Anderson (b. Feb. 22, 1934): Baseball; only manager to win World Series in each league—Cincinnati in NL (1975-76) and Detroit in AL (1984); 3rd-ranked skipper on all-time career list with 2,228 wins (2,194 regular season and 34 postseason).

Willie Anderson (b. May 1878, d. Oct. 25, 1910): Scottish golfer; became a US citizen and won 4 U.S. Opens, including 3 straight (1901,03-05).

Mario Andretti (b. Feb. 28, 1940): Auto racer; 4-time USAC-CART national champion (1965-66,69,84); only driver to win Daytona 500 (1967), Indy 500 (1969) and Formula One world title (1978); Indy 500 Rookie of Year (1965); retired following 1994 racing season ranked 1st in poles (67) and starts (407) and 2nd in wins (52) on all-time IndyCar list; father of Michael and Jeff, uncle of John.

Michael Andretti (b. Oct. 5, 1962): Auto racer; 1991 CART national champion with single-season record 8 wins; Indy 500 Rookie of Year (1984); left IndyCar circuit for ill-fated Formula One try in 1993; returned to IndyCar in '94; son of Mario.

Earl Anthony (b. Apr. 27, 1938): Bowler; 6-time PBA Bowler of Year; 41 career titles; first to earn $100,000 in 1 season (1975); first to earn $1 million in career. Came out of retirement in '96.

Said Aouita (b. Nov. 2, 1959): Moroccan runner; won gold (5000m) and bronze (800m) in 1984 Olympics; won 5000m at 1987 World Championships; formerly held 2 world records recognized by IAAF—2000m and 5000m.

Luis Aparicio (b. Apr. 29, 1934): Baseball SS; retired as all-time leader in most games, assists and double plays by shortstop; led AL in stolen bases 9 times (1956-64); 506 career steals.

Al Arbour (b. Nov. 1, 1932): Hockey; coached NY Islanders to 4 straight Stanley Cup titles (1980-83); retired after 1993-94 season 2nd on all-time career list with 902 wins (779 regular season and 123 postseason); elected to Hockey Hall of Fame in 1996.

Eddie Arcaro (b. Feb. 19, 1916, d. Nov. 14, 1997): Jockey; 2-time Triple Crown winner (Whirlaway in 1941, Citation in '48); from 1938-55, he won Kentucky Derby 5 times, Preakness and Belmont 6 times each.

Roone Arledge (b. July 8, 1931): Sports TV innovator of live events, anthology shows, Olympic coverage and "Monday Night Football"; ran ABC Sports from 1968-86; has run ABC News since 1977.

Henry Armstrong (b. Dec. 12, 1912, d. Oct. 22, 1988): Boxer; held feather-, light- and welterweight titles simultaneously in 1938; pro record 152-21-8 with 100 KOs.

Arthur Ashe (b. July 10, 1943, d. Feb. 6, 1993): Tennis; first black man to win U.S. Championship (1968) and Wimbledon (1975); 1st U.S. player to earn $100,000 in 1 year (1970); won Davis Cup as player (1968-70) and captain (1981-82); wrote black sports history, *Hard Road to Glory*; announced in 1992 that he was infected with AIDS virus from a blood transfusion during 1983 heart surgery; in 1997, the new home for the U.S. Open was named Arthur Ashe Stadium.

Evelyn Ashford (b. Apr. 15, 1957): Track & Field; winner of 4 Olympic gold medals—100m in 1984, and 4x100m in 1984, '88 and '92; also won silver medal in 100m in '88; member of 5 U.S. Olympic teams (1976-92); Inducted into Track and Field and Women's Sports Halls of Fame in 1998.

Red Auerbach (b. Sept. 20, 1917): Basketball; 2nd winningest coach (regular season and playoffs) in NBA history; won 1,037 times in 20 years; as coach-GM, led Boston to 9 NBA titles, including 8 in a row (1959-66); also coached defunct Washington Capitols (1946-49); NBA Coach of the Year award named after him; retired as Celtics coach in 1966 and as GM in '84; club president from 1970 to 1997.

Tracy Austin (b. Dec. 12, 1962): Tennis; youngest player to win U.S. Open (age 16 in 1979); won 2nd U.S. Open in '81; named AP Female Athlete of Year twice before she was 20; recurring neck and back injuries shortened career after 1983; youngest player ever inducted into Tennis Hall of Fame (age 29 in 1992).

Paul Azinger (b. Jan. 6, 1960): Golf; PGA Player of Year (1987); 11 career wins, including '93 PGA Championship; missed most of '94 season overcoming lymphoma (a form of cancer) in right shoulder blade.

Donovan Bailey (b. Dec. 16, 1967): Track; Jamaican-born Canadian sprinter who is currently the world's fastest human; world record holder for the 100m (9.84) set in gold medal-winning performance at 1996 Olympics; set indoor record in 50m (5.56) in 1996; member of Canadian 4x100 relay that won gold in 1996 Olympics.

Oksana Baiul (b. Feb. 26, 1977): Ukrainian figure skater; 1993 world champion at age 15; edged Nancy Kerrigan by a 5-4 judges' vote for 1994 Olympic gold medal.

Hobey Baker (b. Jan. 15, 1892, d. Dec. 21, 1918): Football and hockey star at Princeton (1911-14); member of college football and pro hockey Halls of Fame; college hockey Player of Year award named after him; killed in plane crash.

Seve Ballesteros (b. Apr. 9, 1957): Spanish golfer; has won British Open 3 times (1979,84,88) and Masters twice (1980,83); 3-time European Golfer of Year (1986,88,91); has led Europe to 5 Ryder Cup titles (1985,87,89,95,97); 72 world-wide victories.

Ernie Banks (b. Jan. 31, 1931): Baseball SS-1B; led NL in home runs and RBI twice each; 2-time MVP (1958-59) with Chicago Cubs; 512 career HRs.

Roger Bannister (b. Mar. 23, 1929): British runner; first to run mile in less than 4 minutes (3:59.4 on May 6, 1954).

Walter (Red) Barber (b. Feb. 17, 1908, d. Oct. 22, 1992): Radio-TV; renowned baseball play-by-play broadcaster for Cincinnati, Brooklyn and N.Y. Yankees from 1934-66; won Peabody Award for radio commentary in 1991.

Charles Barkley (b. Feb. 20, 1963): Basketball F; 5-time All-NBA 1st team with Philadelphia and Phoenix; traded to Suns for 3 players (June 17, 1992); U.S. Olympic Dream Team member in '92; NBA regular season MVP in 1993. Traded to Houston Rockets in 1996.

Leon Barmore (b. June 3, 1944): college basketball coach; respected coach of Louisiana Tech Lady Techsters; career win pct. of .866 (459-71, 16 yrs) entering 1998-99 season is best all-time.

Rick Barry (b. Mar. 28, 1944): Basketball F; only player to lead both NBA and ABA in scoring; 5-time All-NBA 1st team; Finals MVP with Golden St. in 1975.

Sammy Baugh (b. Mar. 17, 1914): Football QB-DB-P; led Washington to NFL titles in 1937 (his rookie year) and '42; led league in passing 6 times, punting 4 times and interceptions once.

Elgin Baylor (b. Sept. 16, 1934): Basketball F; MOP of Final 4 in 1958; led Minneapolis-LA Lakers to 8 NBA Finals; 10-time All-NBA 1st team (1959-65,67-69); LA Clippers' vice president of basketball operations.

Bob Beamon (b. Aug. 29, 1946): Track & Field; won 1968 Olympic gold medal in long jump with world record (29-ft, 2½in.) that shattered old mark by nearly 2 feet; record finally broken by 2 inches in 1991 by Mike Powell.

Franz Beckenbauer (b. Sept. 11, 1945): Soccer; captain of West German World Cup champions in 1974 then coached West Germany to World Cup title in 1990; invented sweeper position; played in U.S. for NY Cosmos (1977-80,83); Member of International Soccer Hall of Champions.

Boris Becker (b. Nov. 22, 1967): German tennis player; 3-time Wimbledon champ (1985-86,89); youngest male (17) to win Wimbledon; led country to 1st Davis Cup win in 1988; has also won U.S. (1989) and Australian (1991,96) Opens.

Chuck Bednarik (b. May 1, 1925): Football C-LB; 2-time All-America at Penn and 7-time All-Pro with NFL Eagles as both center (1950) and linebacker (1951-56); missed only 3 games in 14 seasons; led Eagles to 1960 NFL title as a 35-year-old two-way player.

Clair Bee (b. Mar. 2, 1896, d. May 20, 1983): Basketball coach who led LIU to 2 undefeated seasons (1936,39) and 2 NIT titles (1939,41); his teams won 95 percent of their games between 1931-51, including 43 in a row from 1935-37; coached NBA Baltimore Bullets from 1952-54, but was only 34-116; contributions to game include 1-3-1 zone defense, 3-second rule and NBA 24-second clock; also authored sports manuals and fictional Chip Hilton sports books for kids.

Jean Beliveau (b. Aug. 31, 1931): Hockey C; led Montreal to 10 Stanley Cups in 17 playoffs; playoff MVP (1965); 2-time regular season MVP (1956,64).

Bert Bell (b. Feb. 25, 1895, d. Oct. 11, 1959): Football; team owner and 2nd NFL commissioner (1946-59); proposed college draft in 1935 and instituted TV blackout rule.

Albert Belle (b. August 25, 1966): Baseball OF; tremendous hitter and stupendous troublemaker; in strike-shortened 1995 season, became first player in major league history to hit 50 homers and 50 doubles in a season; five-time All-Star; three-time AL RBI leader; was fined $50,000 for a profanity-laced tirade aimed at NBC's Hannah Storm during 1995 World Series; in 1996, was suspended for a brutal hit on Brewers' Fernando Vina; suspended in 1994 for ten games for using a corked bat.

Deane Beman (b. Apr. 22, 1938): Golf; 1st commissioner of PGA Tour (1974-94); introduced "stadium golf"; as player, won U.S. Amateur twice and British Amateur once.

Johnny Bench (b. Dec. 7, 1947): Baseball C; led NL in HRs twice and RBI 3 times; 2-time regular season MVP (1970,72) with Cincinnati, World Series MVP in 1976; 389 career HRs.

Patty Berg (b. Feb. 13, 1918): Golfer; 57 career pro wins, including 15 majors; 3-time AP Female Athlete of Year (1938,43,55).

Chris Berman (b. May 10, 1955): Radio-TV; 5-time Sportscaster of Year known for his nicknames and jovial studio anchoring on ESPN; play-by-play man only year Brown University football team won Ivy League (1976); began doing weekly highlights on "Monday Night Football"in 1996.

Yogi Berra (b. May 12, 1925): Baseball C; played on 10 World Series winners with NY Yankees; holds WS records for games played (75), at bats (259) and hits (71); 3-time AL MVP (1951,54-55); managed both Yankees (1964) and NY Mets (1973) to pennants.

Jay Berwanger (b. Mar. 19, 1914): Football HB; Univ. of Chicago star; won 1st Heisman Trophy in 1935.

Gary Bettman (b. June 2, 1952): Hockey; former NBA executive, who was named first commissioner of NHL on Dec. 11, 1992; took office on Feb. 1, 1993.

Matt Biondi (b. Oct. 8, 1965): Swimmer; won 7 medals in 1988 Olympics, including 5 gold (2 individual, 3 relay); has won a total of 11 medals (8 gold, 2 silver and a bronze) in 3 Olympics (1984,88,92).

Larry Bird (b. Dec. 7, 1956): Basketball F; college Player of Year (1979) at Indiana St.; 1980 NBA Rookie of Year; 9-time All-NBA 1st team; 3-time regular season MVP (1984-86); led Boston to 3 NBA titles (1981,84, 86); 2-time Finals MVP (1984,86); U.S. Olympic Dream Team member in '92; in 1997, named coach of Indiana Pacers and won Coach of the Year honors in first season; inducted into Hall of Fame in 1998.

The Black Sox: Eight Chicago White Sox players who were banned from baseball for life in 1921 for allegedly throwing the 1919 World Series— RHP Eddie Cicotte (1884-1969), OF Happy Felsch (1891-1964), 1B Chick Gandil (1887-1970), OF Shoeless Joe Jackson (1889-1951), INF Fred McMullin (1891-1952), SS Swede Risberg (1894-1975), 3B-SS Buck Weaver (1890-1956), and LHP Lefty Williams (1893-1959).

Earl (Red) Blaik (b. Feb. 15, 1897, d. May 6, 1989): Football; coached Army to consecutive national titles in 1944-45; 166 career wins and 3 Heisman winners (Blanchard, Davis, Dawkins).

Bonnie Blair (b. Mar. 18, 1964): Speedskater; only American woman to win 5 Olympic gold medals in Winter or Summer Games; won 500-meters in 1988, then 500m and 1,000m in both 1992 and '94; added 1,000m bronze in 1988; Sullivan Award winner (1992); retired on 31st birthday as reigning world sprint champ.

Hector (Toe) Blake (b. Aug. 21, 1912, d. May 17, 1995): Hockey LW; led Montreal to 2 Stanley Cups as a player and 8 more as coach; regular season MVP in 1939.

Felix (Doc) Blanchard (b. Dec. 11, 1924): Football FB; 3-time All-America; led Army to national titles in 1944-45; Glenn Davis' running mate; won Heisman Trophy and Sullivan Award in 1945.

George Blanda (b. Sept. 17, 1927): Football QB-PK; pro football's all-time leading scorer (2,002 points); led Houston to 2 AFL titles (1960-61); played 26 pro seasons; retired at 48.

Fanny Blankers-Koen (b. Apr. 26, 1918): Dutch sprinter; 30-year-old mother of two, who won 4 gold medals (100m, 200m, 800m hurdles and 4x100m relay) at 1948 Olympics.

Drew Bledsoe (b. Feb. 14, 1972): Football QB; 1st overall pick in 1993 NFL draft (by New England); holds NFL season record for most passes attempted (691) and game records for most passes completed (45) and attempted (70).

Wade Boggs (b. June 15, 1958): Baseball 3B; 5 AL batting titles (1983,85-88) with Boston Red Sox; 11-time All-Star; two Gold Gloves.

Barry Bonds (b. July 24, 1964): Baseball OF; 3-time NL MVP, twice with Pittsburgh (1990,92) and once with San Francisco (1993); NL's HR and RBI leader in 1993; became only second player to hit 40 homers and steal 40 bases in same season in 1996; son of Bobby.

Bjorn Borg (b. June 6, 1956): Swedish tennis player; 2-time Player of Year (1979-80); won 6 French Opens and 5 straight Wimbledons (1976-80); led Sweden to 1st Davis Cup win in 1975; retired in 1983 at age 26; attempted unsuccessful comeback in 1991.

Mike Bossy (b. Jan. 22, 1957): Hockey RW; led NY Isles to 4 Stanley Cups; playoff MVP in 1982; 50 goals or more 9 straight years; 573 career goals.

Ralph Boston (b. May 9, 1939): Track & Field; medaled in 3 consecutive Olympic long jumps— gold (1960), silver (1964), bronze (1968).

Ray Bourque (b. Dec. 28, 1960): Hockey D; 12-time All-NHL 1st team, has won Norris Trophy 5 times (1987-88,1990-91,94) with Boston. '96 All-Star Game MVP.

Bobby Bowden (b. Nov. 8, 1929): Football; coached Florida St. to a national title in 1993; over 270 career wins, including a 16-4-1 bowl record in 32 years as coach at Samford, West Va. and FSU; father of Terry.

Terry Bowden (b. Feb. 24, 1956): Football; led Auburn to 11-0 record in his first season as Division I-A head coach in 1993; NCAA probation earned under previous staff prevented bowl appearance; son of Bobby.

Riddick Bowe (b. Aug. 10, 1967): Boxing; won world heavyweight title with unanimous decision over champion Evander Holyfield on Nov. 13, 1992; lost title to Holyfield on majority decision Nov. 6, 1993; in 1996, was fined $250,000 because members of his entourage caused a riot at Madison Square Garden after opponent Andrew Golota was disqualified for repeated low blows.

Scotty Bowman (b. Sept. 18, 1933): Hockey coach; all-time winningest NHL coach in both regular season and playoffs over 25 seasons; Coached a record-tying eight Stanley Cup winners with Montreal (1973,76-79), Pittsburgh (1992) and Detroit (1997,98).

Jack Brabham (b. Apr. 2, 1926): Australian auto racer; 3-time Formula One champion (1959-60,66); 14 career wins. Member of the Hall of Fame.

Bill Bradley (b. July 28, 1943): Basketball F; 2-time All-America at Princeton; Player of the Year and Final 4 MOP in 1965; captain of gold medal-winning 1964 U.S. Olympic team; Sullivan Award winner (1965); led NY Knicks to 2 NBA titles (1970,73); U.S. Senator (D, N.J.) 1979-95.

Pat Bradley (b. Mar. 24, 1951): Golfer; 2-time LPGA Player of Year (1986,91); has won all four majors on LPGA tour, including 3 du Maurier Classics; inducted into the LPGA Hall of Fame on Jan. 18, 1992; entered 1999 among all-time LPGA money leaders and tournament winners (31).

Terry Bradshaw (b. Sept. 2, 1948): Football QB; led Pittsburgh to 4 Super Bowl titles (1975-76,79-80); 2-time Super Bowl MVP (1979-80) and regular season MVP in 1978.

George Brett (b. May 15, 1953): Baseball 3B-1B; AL batting champion in 3 different decades (1976,80,90); MVP in 1980; led KC to World Series title in 1985; retired after 1993 season with 3,154 hits and .305 career average.

Valerie Brisco-Hooks (b. July 6, 1960): Track & Field; won three gold medals at the 1984 Olympics (200 meters, 400 meters and 4x100 relay); first athlete to ever win the 200 and 400 in the same Olympics.

Lou Brock (b. June 18, 1939): Baseball OF; former all-time stolen base leader (938); led NL in steals 8 times; led St. Louis to 2 World Series titles (1964,67); had 3,023 career hits.

Herb Brooks (b. Aug. 5, 1937): Hockey; former U.S. Olympic player (1964,68) who coached 1980 team to gold medal; coached Minnesota to 3 NCAA titles (1974,76,78); also coached NY Rangers, Minnesota and New Jersey in NHL.

Jim Brown (b. Feb. 17, 1936): Football FB; All-America at Syracuse (1956) and NFL Rookie of Year (1957); led NFL in rushing 8 times; 8-time All-Pro (1957-61,63-65); 3-time MVP (1958,63,65) with Cleveland; ran for 12,312 yards and scored 126 touchdowns in just 9 seasons.

Larry Brown (b. Sept. 14, 1940): Basketball; played in ACC, AAU, 1964 Olympics and ABA; 3-time assist leader (1968-70) and 3-time Coach of Year (1973,75-76) in ABA; coached ABA's Carolina and Denver and NBA's Denver, N. J., San Antonio, LA Clippers, Indiana and Phila.; also coached UCLA to NCAA Final (1980) and Kansas to NCAA title (1988).

Mordecai (Three-Finger) Brown (b. Oct. 18, 1876, d. Feb. 14, 1948): Baseball; nickname derived from loss of three fingers in a childhood accident; injury gave him a particularly nasty curve ball; won the decisive game of the the 1907 World Series as a Chicago Cub; in 1908, first pitcher to record 4 consecutive shutouts and finished at 29-9; career record of 239-130 with lifetime ERA of 2.06; member of Hall of Fame.

Paul Brown (b. Sept. 7, 1908, d. Aug. 5, 1991): Football innovator; coached Ohio St. to national title in 1942; in pros, directed Cleveland Browns to 4 straight AAFC titles (1946-49) and 3 NFL titles (1950,54-55); formed Cincinnati Bengals as head coach and part-owner in 1968 (reached playoffs in '70).

Valery Brumel (b. Apr. 14, 1942): Soviet high jumper; dominated event from 1961-64; broke world record 5 times; won silver medal in 1960 Olympics and gold in 1964; highest jump was 7-5.

Avery Brundage (b. Sept. 28, 1887, d. May 5, 1975): Amateur sports czar for over 40 years as president of AAU (1928-35), U.S. Olympic Committee (1929-53) and Int'l Olympic Committee (1952-72).

Paul (Bear) Bryant (b. Sept. 11, 1913, d. Jan. 26, 1983): Football; coached at 4 colleges over 38 years; directed Alabama to 5 national titles (1961,64-65,78-79); 323-85-17 record; 15 bowl wins, including 8 Sugar Bowls.

Sergey Bubka (b. Dec. 4, 1963): Ukrainian pole vaulter; 1st man to clear 20 feet both indoors and out (1991); holder of indoor (20-2) and outdoor (20-1¾) world records as of Sept. 1, 1998; 6-time world champion (1983,87,91,93,95,97); won Olympic gold medal in 1988, but failed to clear any height in 1992 Games.

Buck Buchanan (b. Sept. 10, 1940, d. July 16, 1992): Football; played both ways in college at Grambling; first player chosen in the first AFL draft by the Dallas Texans who later became the KC Chiefs; missed one game in a 13-year pro career; played in six AFL All-Star games and two Pro Bowls at def. tackle; defensive star of the Chiefs team that won Super Bowl IV; later coached for the New Orleans Saints and Cleveland Browns; member of Pro Football Hall of Fame.

Don Budge (b. June 13, 1915): Tennis; in 1938 became 1st player to win the Grand Slam— the French, Wimbledon, U.S. and Australian titles in 1 year; led U.S. to 2 Davis Cups (1937-38); turned pro in late '38.

Maria Bueno (b. Oct. 11, 1939): Brazilian tennis player; won 4 U.S. Championships (1959,63-64,66) and 3 Wimbledons (1959-60,64).

Leroy Burrell (b. Feb. 21, 1967): Track & Field; set former world record of 9.85 in 100 meters, July 6, 1994; previously held record (9.90) in 1991; member of 4 world record-breaking 4 x 100m relay teams.

George Bush (b. June 12, 1924): 41st President of U.S. (1989-93) and avid sportsman; played 1B on 1947 and '48 Yale baseball teams that placed 2nd in College World Series; captain of 1948 team.

Susan Butcher (b. Dec. 26, 1956): Sled Dog racer; 4-time winner of Iditarod Trail race (1986-88,90).

Dick Butkus (b. Dec. 9, 1942): Football LB; 2-time All-America at Illinois (1963-64); All-Pro 7 of 9 NFL seasons with Chicago Bears.

Dick Button (b. July 18, 1929): Figure skater; 5-time world champion (1948-52); 2-time Olympic champ (1948,52); Sullivan Award winner (1949); won Emmy Award as Best Analyst for 1980-81 TV season.

Walter Byers (b. Mar. 13, 1922): College athletics; 1st exec. director of NCAA, serving from 1951-88.

Frank Calder (b. Nov. 17, 1877, d. Feb. 4, 1943): Hockey; 1st NHL president (1917-43); guided league through its formative years; NHL's Rookie of the Year award named after him.

Lee Calhoun (b. Feb. 23, 1933, d. June 22, 1989): Track & Field; won consecutive Olympic gold medals in the 110m hurdles (1956,60).

Walter Camp (b. Apr. 7, 1859, d. Mar. 14, 1925): Football coach and innovator; established scrimmage line, center snap, downs, 11 players per side; elected 1st All-America team (1889).

Roy Campanella (b. Nov. 19, 1921, d. June 26, 1993): Baseball C; 3-time NL MVP (1951,53,55); led Brooklyn to 5 pennants and 1st World Series title (1955); career cut short when 1958 car accident left him paralyzed.

Clarence Campbell (b. July 9, 1905, d. June 24, 1984): Hockey; 3rd NHL president (1946-77), league tripled in size from 6 to 18 teams during his tenure.

Earl Campbell (b. Mar. 29, 1955): Football RB; won Heisman Trophy in 1977; led NFL in rushing 3 times; 3-time All-Pro; 2-time MVP (1978-79) at Houston.

John Campbell (b. Apr. 8, 1955): Harness racing; 4-time winner of Hambletonian (1987,88,90,95); 3-time Driver of Year; first driver to go over $100 million in career winnings.

Milt Campbell (b. Dec. 9, 1933): Track & Field; won silver medal in 1952 Olympic decathlon and gold medal in '56.

Jimmy Cannon (b. 1910, d. Dec. 5, 1973): Tough, opinionated New York sportswriter and essayist who viewed sports as an extension of show business; protégé of Damon Runyon; covered World War II for *Stars & Stripes*.

Jose Canseco (b. July 2, 1964): Baseball OF/DH; A.L. Rookie of the Year in 1986 and Most Valuable Player in 1988 with the Oakland A's; in 1988 he became the first player in history to hit 40 HRs and steal 40 bases in one season; led A.L. in HRs in 1988 and tied for lead in 1991.

Jennifer Capriati (b. Mar. 29, 1976): Tennis; youngest Grand Slam semifinalist ever (age 14 in 1990 French Open); also youngest to win a match at Wimbledon (1990); upset Steffi Graf to win gold medal at 1992 Olympics; left tour in '94 due to personal problems including an arrest for marijuana possession.

Harry Caray (b. Mar. 1, 1917, d. Feb. 18, 1998): Radio-TV; baseball play-by-play broadcaster for St. Louis Cardinals, Oakland, Chicago White Sox and Cubs since 1945; father of sportscaster Skip and grandfather of sportscaster Chip.

Rod Carew (b. Oct. 1, 1945): Baseball 2B-1B; led AL in batting 7 times (1969,72-75,77-78) with Minnesota; MVP in 1977; had 3,053 career hits.

Steve Carlton (b. Dec. 22, 1944): Baseball LHP; won 20 or more games 6 times; 4-time Cy Young winner (1972,77,80,82) with Philadelphia; 329-244 career record.

JoAnne Carner (b. Apr. 4, 1939): Golfer; 5-time U.S. Amateur champion; 2-time U.S. Open champ; 3-time LPGA Player of Year (1974,81-82); 7th in career wins (42).

Cris Carter (b. Nov. 25, 1965): Football; wide receiver for the Minnesota Vikings; twice caught 122 passes in a season (1994, '95), the first time establishing an NFL record for catches in a season that was beaten by Detroit's Herman Moore a year later.

Don Carter (b. July 29, 1926): Bowler; 6-time Bowler of Year (1953-54,57-58,60-61); voted Greatest of All-Time in 1970.

Alexander Cartwright (b. Apr. 17, 1820, d. July 12, 1892): Baseball; engineer and draftsman who spread gospel of baseball from New York City to California gold fields; widely regarded as the father of modern game; his guidelines included setting 3 strikes for an out and 3 outs for each half inning.

Billy Casper (b. June 4, 1931): Golfer; 2-time PGA Player of Year (1966,70); has won U.S. Open (1959,66), Masters (1970), U.S. Senior Open (1983); compiled 51 PGA Tour wins and 9 on Senior Tour.

Tracy Caulkins (b. Jan. 11, 1963): Swimmer; won 3 gold medals (2 individual) at 1984 Olympics; set 5 world records and won 48 U.S. national titles from 1978-84; Sullivan Award winner (1978); 2-time Honda Broderick Cup winner (1982,84).

Steve Cauthen (b. May 1, 1960): Jockey; became youngest jockey (18) to win the Triple Crown with Affirmed in 1978; won a record $6.1 million in 1977, winning the Eclipse Award as the nation's top rider and the award for AP male athlete of the year.

Evonne Goolagong Cawley (b. July 31, 1951): Australian tennis player; won Australian Open 4 times, Wimbledon twice (1971,80), French once (1971).

Florence Chadwick (b. Nov. 9, 1917, d. Mar. 15, 1995): Dominant distance swimmer of 1950s; set English Channel records from France to England (1950) and England to France (1951 and '55).

Wilt Chamberlain (b. Aug. 21, 1936): Basketball C; consensus All-America in 1957 and '58 at Kansas; Final Four MOP in 1957; led NBA in scoring 7 times and rebounding 11 times; 7-time All-NBA first team; 4-time MVP (1960,66-68) in Philadelphia; scored 100 points vs. NY Knicks in Hershey, Pa., Mar. 2, 1962; led 76ers (1967) and LA Lakers (1972) to NBA titles; Finals MVP in 1972.

A.B. (Happy) Chandler (b. July 14, 1898, d. June 15, 1991): Baseball; former Kentucky governor and U.S. Senator who succeeded Judge Landis as commissioner in 1945; backed Branch Rickey's move in 1947 to make Jackie Robinson 1st black player in major leagues; deemed too pro-player and ousted by owners in 1951.

Julio Cesar Chavez (b. July 12, 1962): Mexican boxer; world jr. welterweight champ (1989-94); also held titles as jr. lightweight (1984-87) and lightweight (1987-89); fought Pernell Whitaker to controversial draw for welterweight title on Sept. 10, 1993; career record of 101-2-2 record with 84 KOs; 90-bout unbeaten streak ended Jan. 29, 1994 when Frankie Randall won title on split decision; Chavez won title back four months later.

Linford Christie (b. Apr. 2, 1960): British sprinter; won 100-meter gold medals at both 1992 Olympics (9.96) and '93 World Championships (9.87); set indoor world record in 200-meters (20.25) on Feb. 19, 1995 in Lievin, France.

Jim Clark (b. Mar. 14, 1936, d. Apr. 7, 1968): Scottish auto racer; 2-time Formula One world champion (1963,65); won Indy 500 in 1965; killed in car crash.

Bobby Clarke (b. Aug. 13, 1949): Hockey C; led Philadelphia Flyers to consecutive Stanley Cups in 1974-75; 3-time regular season MVP (1973,75-76); currently Flyers general manager.

Ron Clarke (b. Feb. 21, 1937): Australian runner; from 1963-70 set 17 world records in races from 2 miles to 20,000 meters; never won Olympic gold medal.

Roger Clemens (b. Aug. 4, 1962): Baseball RHP; twice fanned MLB record 20 batters in 9-inning game (April 29, 1986 and Sept. 18, 1996); 4 Cy Young Awards with Boston (1986-87,91) and Toronto (1997); AL MVP in 1986.

Roberto Clemente (b. Aug. 18, 1934, d. Dec. 31, 1972): Baseball OF; hit over .300 13 times with Pittsburgh; led NL in batting 4 times; World Series MVP in 1971; regular season MVP in 1966; had 3,000 career hits; killed in plane crash.

Ty Cobb (b. Dec. 18, 1886, d. July 17, 1961): Baseball OF; all-time highest career batting average (.367); hit over .400 3 times; led AL in batting 12 times and stolen bases 6 times with Detroit; MVP in 1911; had 4,191 career hits and 892 steals.

Mickey Cochrane (b. Apr. 6, 1903, d. June 28, 1962): Baseball C; led Philadelphia A's (1929-30) and Detroit (1935) to 3 World Series titles; 2-time AL MVP (1928,34).

Sebastian Coe (b. Sept. 29, 1956): British runner; won gold medal in 1500m and silver medal in 800m at both 1980 and '84 Olympics; long time world record holder in 800m and 1000m; elected to Parliament as Conservative in 1992.

Paul Coffey (b. June 1, 1961): Hockey D; holds NHL record for goals, assists and points by a defenseman; member of four Stanley Cup championship teams at Edmonton (1984-85,87) and Pittsburgh (1991).

Rocky Colavito (b. August 10, 1933): Baseball OF; six-time all-star who hit 374 HRs over his 14-year career; hugely popular in Cleveland where he played from 1955-59 and then 1965-67; led the league in HRs in 1959 with 42 and RBI in 1965 with 108; hit four consecutive HRs in one game.

Eddie Collins (b. May 2, 1887, d. Mar. 25, 1951): Baseball 2B; led Phila. A's (1910-11) and Chicago White Sox (1917) to 3 World Series titles; AL MVP in 1914; had 3,311 career hits and 743 stolen bases.

Nadia Comaneci (b. Nov. 12, 1961): Romanian gymnast; 1st to record perfect 10 in Olympics; won 3 individual golds at 1976 Olympics and 2 more in '80.

Lionel Conacher (b. May 24, 1901, d. May 26, 1954): Canada's greatest all-around athlete; NHL hockey (2 Stanley Cups), CFL football (1 Grey Cup), minor league baseball, soccer, lacrosse, track, amateur boxing champion; member of Parliament (1949-54).

Tony Conigliaro (b. Jan. 7, 1945, d. Feb. 24, 1990): Baseball OF; hit 24 HRs as a 19-year-old rookie (1964) with the Red Sox; became youngest in history to lead the AL in HRs (32) the following year; won the pennant with the 1967 "Impossible Dream" Red Sox; hit in the face with a fastball earlier in the season; came back to hit 36 HRs in 1970 but was never the same.

Gene Conley (b. Nov. 10, 1930): Baseball and Basketball; played for World Series and NBA champions with Milwaukee Braves (1957) and Boston Celtics (1959-61); winning pitcher in 1954 All-Star Game; 91-96 record in 11 seasons.

Dennis Conner (b. Sept. 16, 1942): Sailing; 3-time America's Cup-winning skipper aboard *Freedom* (1980), *Stars & Stripes* (1987) and the *Stars & Stripes* catamaran (1988); only American skipper to lose Cup, first in 1983 when *Australia II* beat *Liberty* and again in '95 when New Zealand's *Black* Magic swept Conner and his *Stars & Stripes* crew aboard the borrowed *Young America*.

Maureen Connolly (b. Sept. 17, 1934, d. June 21, 1969): Tennis; in 1953 1st woman to win Grand Slam (at age 18); riding accident ended her career in '54; won both Wimbledon and U.S. titles 3 times (1951-53); 3-time AP Female Athlete of Year (1951-53).

Jimmy Connors (b. Sept. 2, 1952): Tennis; No.1 player in world 5 times (1974-78); won 5 U.S. Opens, 2 Wimbledons and 1 Australian; rose from No. 936 at the close of 1990 to U.S. Open semifinals in 1991 at age 39; NCAA singles champ (1971); all-time leader in pro singles titles (109) and matches won at U.S. Open (98) and Wimbledon (84); inducted into Hall of Fame in 1998.

Jack Kent Cooke (b. Oct. 25, 1912, d. April 6, 1997): Football; sole owner of NFL Washington Redskins from 1985-97; teams have won 2 Super Bowls (1988,92); also owned NBA Lakers and NHL Kings in LA; built LA Forum for $12 million in 1967.

Angel Cordero Jr. (b. Nov. 8, 1942): Jockey; retired third on all-time list with 7,057 wins in 38,646 starts; won Kentucky Derby 3 times (1974,76,85), Preakness twice and Belmont once; 2-time Eclipse Award winner (1982-83).

Howard Cosell (b. Mar. 25, 1920, d. Apr. 23, 1995): Radio-TV; former ABC commentator on *Monday Night Football* and *Wide World of Sports*, who energized TV sports journalism with abrasive "tell it like it is" style.

Bob Costas (b. Mar. 22, 1952): Radio-TV; NBC anchor for NBA, NFL and Summer Olympics as well as baseball play-by-play man; 8-time Emmy winner and 6-time Sportscaster of Year.

James (Doc) Counsilman (b. Dec. 28, 1920): Swimming; coached Indiana men's swim team to 6 NCAA championships (1968-73); coached the 1964 and '76 U.S. men's Olympic teams that won a combined 21 of 24 gold medals; in 1979 became oldest person (59) to swim English Channel; retired in 1990 with dual meet record of 287-36-1.

Fred Couples (b. Oct. 3, 1959): Golfer; 2-time PGA Tour Player of the Year (1991,92); 14 Tour victories, including 1992 Masters.

Jim Courier (b. Aug. 17, 1970): Tennis; No. 1 player in world in 1992, has won two Australian Opens (1992-93) and two French (1991-92); played on 1992 Davis Cup winner; Nick Bollettieri Academy classmate of Andre Agassi.

Margaret Smith Court (b. July 16, 1942): Australian tennis player; won Grand Slam in both singles (1970) and mixed doubles (1963 with Ken Fletcher); record 24 Grand Slam singles titles— 11 Australian, 5 U.S., 5 French and 3 Wimbledon.

Bob Cousy (b. Aug. 9, 1928): Basketball G; led NBA in assists 8 times; 10-time All-NBA 1st team; 1957 MVP; led Boston to 6 NBA titles (1957,59-63).

Buster Crabbe (b. Feb. 7, 1910, d. Apr. 23, 1983): Swimmer; 2-time Olympic freestyle medalist with bronze in 1928 (1500m) and gold in '32 (400m); became movie star and King of Serials as Flash Gordon and Buck Rogers.

Ben Crenshaw (b. Jan. 11, 1952): Golfer; co-NCAA champion with Tom Kite in 1972; battled Graves' disease in mid-1980s; 19 career Tour victories; won Masters for second time on April 9, 1995 and dedicated it to 90-year-old mentor Harvey Penick, who had died on April 2; captain of 1999 Ryder Cup team.

Joe Cronin (b. Oct. 12, 1906, d. Sept. 7, 1984): Baseball SS; hit over .300 and drove in over 100 runs 8 times each; player-manager in Washington and Boston (1933-47); AL president (1959-73).

Larry Csonka (b. Dec. 25, 1946): Football RB; powerful runner and blocker who gained 8,081 yards in 11 seasons in the AFL and NFL; won two consecutive Super Bowls with the Miami Dolphins (1973-74) and was named MVP in the latter, rushing for 145 yards and two TDs; member of the College and Pro Football Halls of Fame.

Ann Curtis (b. Mar. 6, 1926): Swimming; won 2 gold medals and 1 silver in 1948 Olympics; set 4 world and 18 U.S. records during career; 1st woman and swimmer to win Sullivan Award (1944).

Chuck Daly (b. July 20, 1930): Basketball; coached Detroit to two NBA titles (1989-90) before leaving in 1992 to coach New Jersey; retired after 1993-94 season; coached NBA "Dream Team" to gold medal in 1992 Olympics; unretired in 1997 to coach Orlando Magic.

John Daly (b. Apr. 28, 1966): Golfer; surprise winner of 1991 PGA Championship as unknown 25-year-old; battled through personal troubles in 1994 to return in '95 and win 2nd major at British Open, beating Italy's Costantino Rocca in 4-hole playoff.

Stanley Dancer (b. July 25, 1927): Harness racing; winner of 4 Hambletonians; trainer-driver of Triple Crown winners in trotting (Nevele Pride in 1968 and Super Bowl in '72) and pacing (Most Happy Fella in 1970).

Tamas Darnyi (b. June 3, 1967): Hungarian swimmer; 2-time double gold medal winner in 200m and 400m individual medley at 1988 and '92 Olympics; also won both events in 1986 and '91 world championships; set world records in both at '91 worlds; 1st swimmer to break 2 minutes in 200m IM (1:59:36).

Al Davis (b. July 4, 1929): Football; GM-coach of Oakland 1963-66; helped force AFL-NFL merger as AFL commissioner in 1966; returned to Oakland as managing general partner and directed club to 3 Super Bowl wins (1977,81,84); defied fellow NFL owners and moved Raiders to LA in 1982; turned down owners' 1995 offer to build him a new stadium in LA and moved back to Oakland instead.

Dwight Davis (b. July 5, 1879, d. Nov. 28, 1945): Tennis; donor of Davis Cup; played for winning U.S. team in 1st two Cup finals (1900,02); won U.S. and Wimbledon doubles titles in 1901; Secretary of War (1925-29) under President Coolidge.

Glenn Davis (b. Dec. 26, 1924): Football HB; 3-time All-America; led Army to national titles in 1944-45; Doc Blanchard's running mate; won Heisman Trophy in 1946.

John Davis (b. Jan. 12, 1921, d. July 13, 1984): Weightlifting; 6-time world champion; 2-time Olympic super-heavyweight champ (1948,52); undefeated from 1938-53.

Dizzy Dean (b. Jan. 16 1911, d. July 17, 1974): Baseball RHP; led NL in strikeouts and complete games 4 times; last NL pitcher to win 30 games (30-7 in 1934); MVP in 1934 with St. Louis; 150-83 record.

Dave DeBusschere (b. Oct. 16, 1940): Basketball F; youngest coach in NBA history (24 in 1964); player-coach of Detroit Pistons (1964-67); played in 8 All-Star games; won 2 NBA titles as player with NY Knicks; ABA commissioner (1975-76); also pitched 2 seasons for Chicago White Sox (1962-63) with 3-4 record.

Pierre de Coubertin (b. Jan. 1, 1863, d. Sept. 2, 1937): French educator; father of the Modern Olympic Games; IOC president from 1896-1925.

Anita DeFrantz (b. Oct. 4, 1952): Olympics; attorney who is one of 2 American delegates to the International Olympic Committee (James Easton is the other); first woman to represent U.S. on IOC; member of USOC Executive Committee; member of bronze medal U.S. women's eight-oared shell at Montreal in 1976.

Jack Dempsey (b. June 24, 1895, d. May 31, 1983): Boxer; world heavyweight champion from 1919-26; lost title to Gene Tunney, then lost "Long Count" rematch in 1927 when he floored Tunney in 7th round but failed to retreat to neutral corner; pro record 64-6-9 with 49 KOs.

Donna de Varona (b. Apr. 26, 1947): Swimming; won gold medals in 400 IM and 400 freestyle relay at 1964 Olympics; set 18 world records during career; co-founder of Women's Sports Foundation in 1974.

Gail Devers (b. Nov. 19, 1966): Track & Field; fastest-ever woman sprinter-hurdler; overcame thyroid disorder (Graves' disease) that sidelined her in 1989-90 and nearly resulted in having both feet amputated; won Olympic gold medal in 100 meters in 1992 and '96; world champion in 100 meters (1993) and 100-meter hurdles (1993,95).

Klaus Dibiasi (b. Oct. 6, 1947): Italian diver; won 3 consecutive Olympic gold medals in platform event (1968,72,76).

Eric Dickerson (b. Sept. 2, 1960): Football RB; led NFL in rushing 4 times (1983-84,86,88); ran for single-season record 2,105 yards in 1984; NFC Rookie of Year in 1983; All-Pro 5 times; traded from LA Rams to Indianapolis (Oct. 31, 1987) in 3-team, 10-player deal (including draft picks) that also involved Buffalo; 3rd on all-time career rushing list with 13,259 yards in 11 seasons.

Joe DiMaggio (b. Nov. 25, 1914): Baseball OF; hit safely in 56 straight games (1941); led AL in batting, HRs and RBI twice each; 3-time MVP (1939,41,47); hit .325 with 361 HRs over 13 seasons; led NY Yankees to 10 World Series titles.

Marcel Dionne (b. Aug. 3, 1951): Hockey C; third on NHL's all-time points list (1,771) and goals list (731); tied Wayne Gretzky for the league lead in points (137) in 1980; scored 50 goals in a season 6 times; won the Lady Byng Award for gentlemanly play in 1975 with Detroit and in 1977 with the L.A. Kings; member of the Hockey Hall of Fame.

Mike Ditka (b. Oct. 18, 1939): Football; All-America at Pitt (1960); NFL Rookie of Year (1961); 5-time Pro Bowl tight end for Chicago Bears; also played for Philadelphia and Dallas in 12-year career; returned to Chicago as head coach in 1982; won Super Bowl XX; compiled 112-68-0 record in 11 seasons with Bears; left Bears in 1992 and worked as a broadcaster at NBC for four years; named head coach of New Orleans Saints in 1997.

Charlotte (Lottie) Dod (b. Sept. 24, 1871, d. June 27, 1960): British athlete; was 5-time Wimbledon singles champion (1887-88,91-93); youngest player ever to win Wimbledon (15 in 1887); archery silver medalist at 1908 Olympics; member of national field hockey team in 1899; British Amateur golf champ in 1904.

Tony Dorsett (b. Apr. 7, 1954): Football RB; won Heisman Trophy leading Pitt to national title in 1976; all-time NCAA Div. I-A rushing leader with 6,082 yards entering 1998; led Dallas to Super Bowl title as NFC Rookie of Year (1977); NFC Player of Year (1981); ranks 4th on all-time NFL list with 12,739 yards gained in 12 years; holds NFL record for longest run from scrimmage (99 yards vs. Minn. in 1983).

James (Buster) Douglas (b. Apr. 7, 1960): Boxing; 42-1 shot who knocked out undefeated Mike Tyson in 10th round on Feb. 10, 1990 to win heavyweight title in Tokyo; 8½ months later, lost only title defense to Evander Holyfield by KO in 3rd round.

The Dream Team Head coach Chuck Daly's "Best Ever" 12-man NBA All-Star squad that headlined the 1992 Summer Olympics in Barcelona and easily won the basketball gold medal; co-captained by Larry Bird and Magic Johnson, with veterans Charles Barkley, Clyde Drexler, Patrick Ewing, Michael Jordan, Karl Malone, Chris Mullin, Scottie Pippen, David Robinson, John Stockton and Duke's Christian Laettner.

Dream Team II Head coach Don Nelson's 12-man NBA All-Star squad that cruised to gold medal at 1994 World Basketball Championships in Toronto— Derrick Coleman, Joe Dumars, Kevin Johnson, Larry Johnson, Shawn Kemp, Dan Majerle, Reggie Miller, Alonzo Mourning, Shaquille O'Neal, Mark Price, Steve Smith and Dominique Wilkins.

Dream Team III Head coach Lenny Wilkens' 12-man NBA All-Star squad that represented the U.S. at the 1996 Summer Olympics in Atlanta— Anfernee Hardaway, Grant Hill, Karl Malone, Reggie Miller, Hakeem Olajuwon, Shaquille O'Neal, Gary Payton, Scottie Pippen, Mitch Richmond, David Robinson, Glenn Robinson and John Stockton.

Heike Drechsler (b. Dec. 16, 1964): German long jumper and sprinter; East German before reunification in 1991; set world long jump record (24-2¼) in 1988; won long jump gold medals at 1992 Olympics and 1983 and '93 World Championships; won silver medal in long jump and bronze medals in both 100- and 200-meter sprints at 1988 Olympics.

Ken Dryden (b. Aug. 8, 1947): Hockey G; led Montreal to 6 Stanley Cup titles; playoff MVP as rookie in 1971; won or shared 5 Vezina Trophies; 2.24 career GAA; currently Pres. and G.M. of Toronto Maple Leafs.

Don Drysdale (b. July 23, 1936, d. July 3, 1993): Baseball RHP; led NL in strikeouts 3 times and games started 4 straight years; pitched record 6 shutouts in a row in 1968; won Cy Young (1962); had 209-166 record and hit 29 HRs in 14 years.

Charley Dumas (b. Feb. 12, 1937): U.S. high jumper; first man to clear 7 feet (7-0½) on June 29, 1956; won gold medal at 1956 Olympics.

Margaret Osborne du Pont (b. Mar. 4, 1918): Tennis; won 5 French, 7 Wimbledon and an unprecedented 25 U.S. national titles in singles, doubles and mixed doubles from 1941-62.

Roberto Duran (b. June 16, 1951): Panamanian boxer; one of only 4 fighters to hold 4 different world titles— lightweight (1972-79), welterweight (1980), junior middleweight (1983) and middleweight (1989-90); lost famous "No Mas" welterweight title bout when he quit in 8th round against Sugar Ray Leonard (1980); pro record of 101-13 (69 KOs) as of Aug. 1998.

Leo Durocher (b. July 27, 1905, d. Oct. 7, 1991): Baseball; managed in NL 24 years; won 2,015 games, including postseason; 3 pennants with Brooklyn (1941) and NY Giants (1951,54); won World Series in 1954.

Eddie Eagan (b. Apr. 26, 1898, d. June 14, 1967): Only athlete to win gold medals in both Summer and Winter Olympics (Boxing–1920, Bobsled–1932).

Alan Eagleson (b. Apr. 24, 1933): Hockey; Toronto lawyer, agent and 1st executive director of NHL Players Assn. (1967-90); midwived Team Canada vs. Soviet series (1972) and Canada Cup; charged with racketeering and defrauding NHLPA in indictment handed down by U.S. grand jury in 1994; was sentenced to 18 months in jail in Jan. 1998 after pleading guilty; removed from Hall of Fame in 1998.

Dale Earnhardt (b. Apr. 29, 1952): Auto racer; 7-time NASCAR national champion (1980,86-87,90-91,93-94); Rookie of Year in 1979; all-time NASCAR money leader with over $32 million won and 3rd on career wins list with 71; finally won Daytona 500 in 1998 on 20th attempt.

Dick Ebersol (b. July 28, 1947): Radio-TV; protégé of ABC Sports czar Roone Arledge; key NBC exec in launching of *Saturday Night Live* in 1975; became president of NBC Sports in 1989, won U.S. TV rights to both 2000 Summer and 2002 Winter Olympics with combined bid of $1.27 billion in August 1995.

Dennis Eckersley (b. Oct. 3, 1954): Baseball P; began his career as a starter in 1975 with the Cleveland Indians; pitched a no-hitter against California in 1977; won 20 games in 1978 with Boston; moved to the bullpen after 12 seasons as a starter and became one of the best closers of all time with Oakland; won the AL Cy Young Award and MVP (1992).

Stefan Edberg (b. Jan. 19, 1966): Swedish tennis player; 2-time No.1 player (1990-91); 2-time winner of Australian Open (1985,87), Wimbledon (1988,90) and U.S. Open (1991-92).

Gertrude Ederle (b. Oct. 23, 1906): Swimmer; 1st woman to swim English Channel, breaking men's record by 2 hours in 1926; won 3 medals in 1924 Olympics.

Krisztina Egerszegi (b. Aug. 16, 1974): Hungarian swimmer; 3-time gold medal winner (100m and 200m backstroke and 400m IM) in 1992 Olympics; also won a gold (200m back) and silver (100m back) in 1988 Games; youngest (age 14) ever to win swimming gold. Won fifth gold medal (200m back) at '96 Games.

Todd Eldredge (b. Aug. 28, 1971): Figure Skater; five-time U.S. champion (1990,91,95,97,98); 1996 World Champion; has won U.S. titles at all three levels (novice, junior and senior); most decorated American figure skater without an Olympic medal.

Bill Elliott (b. Oct. 8, 1955): Auto racer; 2-time winner of Daytona 500 (1985,87); NASCAR national champ in 1988; entered 1998 with 40 NASCAR wins.

Herb Elliott (b. Feb. 25, 1938): Australian runner; undefeated from 1958-60; ran 17 sub-4:00 miles; 3 world records; won gold medal in 1500 meters at 1960 Olympics; retired at age 22.

John Elway (b. June 28, 1960): Football QB; All-American at Stanford; first overall pick in the fabled quarterback draft of 1983; famous for his last-minute, game-winning scoring drives; led Broncos to three Super Bowl losses before a win over Green Bay in Super Bowl XXXII; 1987 NFL MVP; four-time Pro Bowl selection; first QB to receive a pass in the Super Bowl (1987); one of only two QBs in league history (Marino) to throw for over 3,000 yards in 12 seasons; dangerous runner, with over 30 rushing TDs in his career and more than 3,000 rushing yards.

Roy Emerson (b. Nov. 3, 1936): Australian tennis player; won 12 majors in singles— 6 Australian, 2 French, 2 Wimbledon and 2 U.S. from 1961-67.

Kornelia Ender (b. Oct. 25, 1958): East German swimmer; 1st woman to win 4 gold medals at one Olympics (1976), all in world-record time.

Julius Erving (b. Feb. 22, 1950): Basketball F; in ABA (1971-76)— 3-time MVP, 2-time playoff MVP, led NY Nets to 2 titles (1974,76); in NBA (1976-87)— 5-time All-NBA 1st team, MVP in 1981, led Philadelphia 76ers to title in 1983.

Phil Esposito (b. Feb. 20, 1942): Hockey C; 1st NHL player to score 100 points in a season (126 in 1969); 6-time All-NHL 1st team with Boston (1969-74); 2-time MVP (1969,74); 5-time scoring champ; star of 1972 Canada-Soviet series; president-GM of Tampa Bay Lightning.

Janet Evans (b. Aug. 28, 1971): Swimmer; won 3 individual gold medals (400m & 800m freestyle, 400m IM) at 1988 Olympics; 1989 Sullivan Award winner; entered 1998 as world record-holder in 400m, 800m and 1500m freestyles; won 1 gold (800m) and 1 silver (400m) at 1992 Olympics.

Lee Evans (b. Feb. 25, 1947): Track & Field; dominant quarter-miler in world from 1966-72; world record in 400m set at 1968 Olympics stood 20 years.

Chris Evert (b. Dec. 21, 1954): Tennis; No.1 player in world 5 times (1975-77,80-81); won at least 1 Grand Slam singles title every year from 1974-86; 18 majors in all— 7 French, 6 U.S., 3 Wimbledon and 2 Australian; retired after 1989 season.

Weeb Ewbank (b. May 6, 1907): Football; only coach to win NFL and AFL titles; led Baltimore to 2 NFL titles (1958-59) and NY Jets to Super Bowl III win.

Patrick Ewing (b. Aug. 5, 1962): Basketball C; 3-time All-America; led Georgetown to 3 NCAA Finals and 1984 title; Final 4 MOP in '84; NBA Rookie of Year with New York in '86; All-NBA in 1990; on U.S. Olympic gold medal-winning teams in 1984 and '92; named one of the NBA's 50 greatest players of all-time.

Ray Ewry (b. Oct. 14, 1873, d. Sept. 29, 1937): Track & Field; won 10 gold medals over 4 consecutive Olympics (1900,04,06,08); all events he won (Standing HJ, LJ and TJ) were discontinued in 1912.

Nick Faldo (b. July 18, 1957): British golfer; 3-time winner of British Open (1987,90,92) and Masters (1989, 90, 96); 3-time European Golfer of Year (1989-90,92); PGA Player of Year in 1990.

Juan Manuel Fangio (b. June 24, 1911, d. July 17, 1995): Argentine auto racer; 5-time Formula One world champion (1951,54-57); 24 career wins, retired in 1958.

Brett Favre (b. Oct. 10, 1969): Football QB; Selected in the second round (33rd overall) by the Atlanta Falcons in the 1991 NFL draft; traded to Green Bay Packers in 1992; league MVP in 1995, '96 and '97; five-time Pro Bowl QB; 100th TD pass came in his 62nd game, third-fastest in league history; 39 TD passes in 1996 season broke his own NFC record of 38 set in 1995; led Packers to Super Bowl victory in 1997.

Sergei Fedorov (b. Dec. 13, 1969): Hockey C; first Russian to win NHL Hart Trophy as 1993-94 regular season MVP; 3-time All-Star with Detroit.

Bob Feller (b. Nov. 3, 1918): Baseball RHP; led AL in strikeouts 7 times and wins 6 times with Cleveland; threw 3 no-hitters and 12 one-hitters; 266-162 record.

Tom Ferguson (b. Dec. 20, 1950): Rodeo; 6-time All-Around champion (1974-79); 1st cowboy to win $100,000 in one season (1978); 1st to win $1 million in career (1986).

Cecil Fielder (b. Sept. 21, 1963): Baseball 1B; returned from one season with Hanshin Tigers in Japan to hit 51 HRs for Detroit Tigers in 1990; led MLB in RBI 3 straight years (1990-92); AL MVP runner-up in 1990 and '91.

Herve Filion (b. Feb. 1, 1940): Harness racing; 10-time Driver of Year; all-time leader in races won with 14,783 in 35 years.

Rollie Fingers (b. Aug. 25, 1946): Baseball RHP; relief ace with 341 career saves; won AL MVP and Cy Young awards in 1981 with Milwaukee; World Series MVP in 1974 with Oakland.

Charles O. Finley (b. Feb. 22, 1918, d. Feb, 19, 1997): Baseball owner; moved KC A's to Oakland in 1968; won 3 straight World Series from 1972-74; also owned teams in NHL and ABA.

Bobby Fischer (b. Mar. 9, 1943): Chess; at 15, became youngest international grandmaster in chess history; only American to hold world championship (1972-75); was stripped of title in 1975 after refusing to defend against Anatoly Karpov and became recluse; re-emerged to defeat old foe and former world champion Boris Spassky in 1992.

Carlton Fisk (b. Dec. 26, 1947): Baseball C; holds all-time major league record for games caught (2,229); also all-time HR leader for catchers (376); AL Rookie of Year (1972) and 10-time All-Star; hit epic, 12th-inning Game 6 homer for Boston Red Sox in 1975 World Series.

Emerson Fittipaldi (b. Dec. 12, 1946): Brazilian auto racer; 2-time Formula One world champion (1972,74); 2-time winner of Indy 500 (1989,93); won overall IndyCar title in 1989.

Bob Fitzsimmons (b. May 26, 1863, d. Oct. 22, 1917): British boxer; held three world titles— middleweight (1881-97), heavyweight (1897-99) and light heavyweight (1903-05); pro record 40-11 with 32 KOs.

James (Sunny Jim) Fitzsimmons (b. July 23, 1874, d. Mar. 11, 1966): Horse racing; trained horses that won over 2,275 races, including 2 Triple Crown winners— Gallant Fox in 1930 and Omaha in '35.

Jim Fixx (b. Apr. 23, 1932, d. July 20, 1984): Running; author who popularized the sport of running; his 1977 bestseller *The Complete Book of Running*, is credited with helping start America's fitness revolution; died of a heart attack while running.

Larry Fleisher (b. Sept. 26, 1930, d. May 4, 1989): Basketball; led NBA players union from 1961-89; increased average yearly salary from $9,400 in 1967 to $600,000 without a strike.

Peggy Fleming (b. July 27, 1948): Figure skating; 3-time world champion (1966-68); won Olympic gold medal in 1968.

Curt Flood (b. Jan. 18, 1938, d. Jan. 20, 1997): Baseball OF; played 15 years (1956-69,71) mainly with St. Louis; hit over .300 6 times with 7 Gold Gloves; refused trade to Phillies in 1969; lost challenge to baseball's reserve clause in Supreme Court in 1972 (see Peter Seitz).

Ray Floyd (b. Sept. 14, 1942): Golfer; has 22 PGA victories in 4 decades; joined Senior PGA Tour in 1992; has won Masters (1976), U.S. Open (1986), PGA twice (1969,82) and PGA Seniors Championship (1995); only player to ever win on PGA and Senior tours in same year (1992); member of 8 Ryder Cup teams and captain in 1989.

Doug Flutie (b. Oct. 23, 1962): Football QB; won Heisman Trophy with Boston College (1984); has played in USFL, NFL and CFL; 6-time CFL MVP with B.C. Lions (1991), Calgary (1992-94) and Toronto (1996-97); led Calgary to Grey Cup title in '92 and Toronto in 1996-97; returned to NFL with Buffalo in 1998.

Gerald Ford (b. July 14, 1913): 38th President of the U.S.; lettered as center on undefeated Michigan football teams in 1932 and '33; MVP on 1934 squad.

Whitey Ford (b. Oct. 21, 1928): Baseball LHP; all-time leader in World Series wins (10); led AL in wins 3 times; won Cy Young and World Series MVP in 1961 with NY Yankees; 236-106 record

George Foreman (b. Jan. 10, 1949): Boxer; Olympic heavyweight champ (1968); world heavyweight champ (1973-74 and 94-95); lost title to Muhammad Ali (KO-8th) in '74; recaptured it on Nov. 5, 1994 at age 45 with a 10-round KO of WBA/IBF champ Michael Moorer, becoming the oldest man to win heavyweight crown; named AP Male Athlete of Year 20 years after losing title to Ali; stripped of WBA title on Mar. 4, 1995 after declining to fight No. 1 contender; successfully defended title at age 46 against 26-year-old Axel Schultz of Germany in controversial majority decision on Apr. 22; gave up IBF title in June after refusing rematch with Schultz.

Dick Fosbury (b. Mar. 6, 1947): Track & Field; revolutionized high jump with back-first "Fosbury Flop"; won gold medal at 1968 Olympics.

The Four Horsemen Senior backfield that led Notre Dame to national collegiate football championship in 1924; put together as sophomores by Irish coach Knute Rockne; immortalized by sportswriter Grantland Rice, whose report of the Oct. 19, 1924, Notre Dame-Army game began: "Outlined against a blue, gray October sky the Four Horsemen rode again . . ."; HB Jim Crowley (b. Sept. 10, 1902, d. Jan. 15, 1986), FB Elmer Layden (b. May 4, 1903, d. June 30, 1973), HB Don Miller (b. May 30, 1902, d. July 28, 1979) and QB Harry Stuhldreher (b. Oct. 14, 1901, d. Jan. 26, 1965).

The Four Musketeers French quartet that dominated men's tennis in 1920s and '30s, winning 8 straight French singles titles (1925-32), 6 Wimbledons in a row (1924-29) and 6 consecutive Davis Cups (1927-32)— Jean Borotra (b. Aug. 13, 1898, d. July 17, 1994), Jacques Brugnon (b. May 11, 1895, d. Mar. 20, 1978), Henri Cochet (b. Dec. 14, 1901, d. Apr. 1, 1987), Rene Lacoste (b. July 2, 1905, d. Oct. 13, 1996).

Nellie Fox (b. Dec. 25, 1927, d. Dec. 1, 1975): Baseball 2B; batted .306 in 1959 to win the AL MVP award with the pennant-winning Chicago White Sox; led the league in fielding percentage six times, hits four times and triples once; ended his 19-year career with 2,663 hits, 1,279 runs and .288 average.

Jimmie Foxx (b. Oct. 22, 1907, d. July 21, 1967): Baseball 1B; led AL in HRs 4 times and batting twice; won Triple Crown in 1933; 3-time MVP (1932-33,38) with Philadelphia and Boston; hit 30 HRs or more 12 years in a row; 534 career HRs.

A.J. Foyt (b. Jan. 16, 1935): Auto racer; 7-time USAC-CART national champion (1960-61,63-64,67,75,79); 4-time Indy 500 winner (1961,64,67,77); only driver in history to win Indy 500, Daytona 500 (1972) and 24 Hours of LeMans (1967 with Dan Gurney); retired in 1993 as all-time IndyCar wins leader with 67.

Bill France Sr. (b. Sept. 26, 1909, d. June 7, 1992): Stock car pioneer and promoter; founded NASCAR in 1948; guided race circuit through formative years; built both Daytona (Fla.) Int'l Speedway and Talladega (Ala.) Superspeedway.

Dawn Fraser (b. Sept. 4, 1937): Australian swimmer; won gold medals in 100m freestyle at 3 consecutive Olympics (1956,60,64).

Joe Frazier (b. Jan. 12, 1944): Boxer; 1964 Olympic heavyweight champion; world heavyweight champ (1970-73); fought Muhammad Ali 3 times and won once; pro record 32-4-1 with 27 KOs.

Walt Frazier (b. March 29, 1945): Basketball G; won the NBA championship two times (1970 and 73) with the New York Knicks; 35 points and 19 assists in the 1970 championship game vs. the Lakers; averaged 18.9 PPG and 6.1 APG over his career; four-time all-NBA and a member of the Hall of Fame; nick-named "Clyde the Glide."

Ford Frick (b. Dec. 19, 1894, d. Apr. 8, 1978): Baseball; sportswriter and radio announcer who served as NL president (1934-51) and commissioner (1951-65); convinced record-keepers to list Roger Maris' and Babe Ruth's season records separately; major leagues moved to West Coast and expanded from 16 to 20 teams during his tenure.

Frankie Frisch (b. Sept. 9, 1898, d. Mar. 12, 1973): Baseball 2B; played on 8 NL pennant winners in 19 years with NY and St. Louis; hit .300 or better 11 years in a row (1921-31); MVP in 1931; player-manager from 1933-37.

Dan Gable (b. Oct. 25, 1948): Wrestling; career wrestling record of 118-1 at Iowa St., where he was a 2-time NCAA champ (1968,69) and tourney MVP in 1969 (137 lbs); won gold medal (149 lbs) at 1972 Olympics; coached U.S. freestyle team in 1988; coached Iowa to 9 straight NCAA titles (1978-86) and has added six more since 1991.

Eddie Gaedel (b. June 8, 1925, d. June 18, 1961): Baseball PH; St. Louis Browns' midget whose career lasted one at bat (he walked) on Aug 19, 1951.

Clarence (Big House) Gaines (b. May 21, 1924): Basketball; retired as coach of Div. II Winston-Salem after 1992-93 season with 828-447 record in 47 years; ranks 3rd on all-time NCAA list behind Dean Smith (879) and Adolph Rupp (876).

Alonzo (Jake) Gaither (b. Apr. 11, 1903, d. Feb. 18, 1994): Football; head coach at Florida A&M for 25 years; led Rattlers to 6 national black college titles; retired after 1969 season with record of 203-36-4 and a winning percentage of .844; coined phrase, "I like my boys agile, mobile and hostile."

Cito Gaston (b. Mar. 17, 1944): Baseball; managed Toronto to consecutive World Series titles (1992-93); first black manager to win Series; shared *The Sporting News* 1993 Man of Year award with Blue Jays GM Pat Gillick.

Lou Gehrig (b. June 19, 1903, d. June 2, 1941): Baseball 1B; played in 2,130 consecutive games from 1925-39 a major league record until Cal Ripken Jr. surpassed it in 1995; led AL in RBI 5 times and HRs 3 times; drove in 100 runs or more 13 years in a row; 2-time MVP (1927,36); hit .340 with 493 HRs over 17 seasons; led NY Yankees to 6 World Series titles; died at age 37 of Amyotrophic Lateral Sclerosis (ALS), a rare and incurable disease of the nervous system now better known as Lou Gehrig's disease.

Bernie Geoffrion (b. Feb. 14, 1931): Hockey RW; credited with popularizing the slap shot, earning his nickname "Boom Boom"; scored 30 goals in 1952 to win the NHL's Calder Trophy (Rookie of the Year Award); won the MVP award (Hart) in 1955; became the second player in history to score 50 goals in one season; led the league in points in 1955 and 61; won 6 Stanley Cups with Montreal; member of the Hockey Hall of Fame.

George Gervin (b. April 27, 1952): Basketball G/F; joined the ABA in 1972 and came to the NBA with San Antonio in 1976; a five-time NBA all-star; led the league in scoring four times; scored 26,595 points with an average of 25.1 per game; known as the "Iceman" because of his cool style; elected to the Basketball Hall of Fame in 1996.

A. Bartlett Giamatti (b. Apr. 14, 1938, d. Sept. 1, 1989): Scholar and 7th commissioner of baseball; banned Pete Rose for life for betting on Major League games and associating with known gamblers; also served as president of Yale (1978-86) and National League (1986-89).

Joe Gibbs (b. Nov. 25, 1940): Football; coached Washington to 140 victories and 3 Super Bowl titles in 12 seasons before retiring in 1993; owner of NASCAR racing team that won 1993 Daytona 500.

Althea Gibson (b. Aug. 25, 1927): Tennis; won both Wimbledon and U.S. championships in 1957 and '58; 1st black to play in either tourney and 1st to win each title.

Bob Gibson (b. Nov. 9, 1935): Baseball RHP; won 20 or more games 5 times; won 2 NL Cy Youngs (1968,70); MVP in 1968; led St. Louis to 2 World Series titles (1964,67); 251-174 record.

Josh Gibson (b. Dec. 21, 1911, d. Jan. 20, 1947): Baseball C; the "Babe Ruth of the Negro Leagues"; Satchel Paige's battery mate with Pittsburgh Crawfords. The Negro Leagues did not keep accurate records but Gibson hit 84 home runs in one season and his Baseball Hall of Fame plaque says he hit "almost 800" home runs in his seventeen-year career.

Kirk Gibson (b. May 28, 1957): Baseball OF; All-America flanker at Mich. St. in 1978; chose baseball career and was AL playoff MVP with Detroit in 1984 and NL regular season MVP with Los Angeles in 1988.

Frank Gifford (b. Aug. 16, 1930): Football HB; 4-time All-Pro (1955-57,59); NFL MVP in 1956; led NY Giants to 3 NFL title games; TV sportscaster since 1958, beginning career while still a player; scandal struck the married Gifford after he was videotaped in a compromising position with a former stewardess in 1997.

Sid Gillman (b. Oct. 26, 1911): Football innovator; only coach in both College and Pro Football Halls of Fame; led college teams at Miami-OH and Cincinnati to combined 81-19-2 record from 1944-54; coached LA Rams (1955-59) in NFL, then led LA-San Diego Chargers to 5 Western titles and 1 league championship in first six years of AFL.

George Gipp (b. Feb. 18, 1895, d. Dec. 14, 1920): Football FB; died of throat infection 2 weeks before he made All-America; rushed for 2,341 yards, scored 156 points and averaged 38 yards a punt in 4 years (1917-20).

Marc Girardelli (b. July 18, 1963): Luxembourg Alpine skier; Austrian native who refused to join Austrian Ski Federation because he wanted to be coached by his father; won unprecedented 5th overall World Cup title in 1993; winless at Olympics, although he won 2 silver medals in 1992.

Tom Glavine (b. Mar. 26, 1996): Baseball LHP; Atlanta Braves' pitcher led the majors in wins from 1991-95 with 91; won NL Cy Young award in 1991 with 20 wins and a 2.55 ERA; six-time All-Star and was the NL starter twice; World Series MVP (1995).

Tom Gola (b. Jan. 13, 1933): Basketball F; 4-time All-America and 1955 Player of Year at La Salle; MOP in 1952 NIT and '54 NCAA Final 4, leading Pioneers to both titles; won NBA title as rookie with Philadelphia Warriors in 1956; 4-time NBA All-Star.

Marshall Goldberg (b. Oct. 24, 1917): Football HB; 2-time consensus All-America at Pittsburgh (1937-38); led Pitt to national championship in 1937; played with NFL champion Chicago Cardinals 10 years later.

Lefty Gomez (b. Nov. 26, 1908, d. Feb. 17, 1989): Baseball LHP; 4-time 20-game winner with NY Yankees; holds World Series record for most wins (6) without a defeat; pitched on 5 world championship clubs in 1930s.

Pancho Gonzales (b. May 9, 1928, d. July 3, 1995): Tennis; won consecutive U.S. Championships in 1947-48 before turning pro at 21; dominated pro tour from 1950-61; in 1969 at age 41, played longest Wimbledon match ever (5:12), beating Charlie Pasarell 22-24,1-6,16-14,6-3,11-9.

Bob Goodenow (b. Oct. 29, 1952): Hockey; succeeded Alan Eagleson as executive director of NHL Players Assn. in 1990; led players out on 10-day strike (Apr. 1-10) in 1992 and during 103-day owners' lockout in 1994-95.

Gail Goodrich (b. April 23, 1943): Basketball G; starred at UCLA and won two national championships in 1964 and 1965 under legendary coach John Wooden's tutelage; won the NBA championship with the L.A. Lakers in 1972 and led the team in scoring (25.9 ppg); averaged 18.6 ppg over his 14-year career.

Jeff Gordon (b. Aug. 4, 1971): Auto racer; NASCAR Rookie of Year (1993); two-time Winston Cup champion (1995,97); won inaugural Brickyard 400 in 1994; in 1997, at 25 became youngest winner of the Daytona 500 and became the second (and final) winner of the Winston Million, a $1 million bonus prize, for winning the Daytona 500, the Coca Cola 600 and the Southern 500.

Dr. Harold Gores (b. Sept. 20, 1909, d. May 28, 1993): Educator and first president of Education Facilities Laboratories in New York; in 1964 hired Monsanto Co. to produce a synthetic turf that kids could play on in city schoolyards; resulting ChemGrass proved too expensive for playground use, but it was just what the Houston Astros were looking for in 1966 to cover the floor of the Astrodome, where grass refused to grow. Thus, AstroTurf was born.

Goose Gossage (b. July 5, 1951): Baseball RHP; Nine-time All Star (1975-78, 80-82, 84-85); intimidating relief pitcher; Fireman of the Year in 1975 with White Sox and 1978 with Yankees; led A.L. in saves with 26 (1975), 27 (1978); 1,002 career appearances; 310 saves.

Shane Gould (b. Nov. 23, 1956): Australian swimmer; set world records in 5 different freestyle events between July 1971 and Jan. 1972; won 3 gold medals, a silver and bronze in 1972 Olympics then retired at age 16.

Alf Goullet (b. Apr. 5, 1891, d. Mar. 11, 1995): Cycling; Australian who gained fame and fortune early in century as premier performer on U.S. 6-day bike race circuit; won 8 annual races at Madison Square Garden with 6 different partners from 1913-23.

Curt Gowdy (b. July 31, 1919): Radio-TV; former radio voice of NY Yankees and then Boston Red Sox from 1949-66; TV play-by-play man for AFL, NFL and major league baseball; has broadcast World Series, All-Star Games, Rose Bowls, Super Bowls, Olympics and NCAA Final Fours for all 3 networks; hosted "The American Sportsman."

Steffi Graf (b. June 14, 1969): German tennis player; won Grand Slam and Olympic gold medal in 1988 at age 19; won three of four majors in 1993, '95 and '96; has won 21 Grand Slam titles— 7 at Wimbledon, 5 French, 5 U.S. and 4 Australian Opens.

Otto Graham (b. Dec. 6, 1921): Football QB and basketball All-America at Northwestern; in pro ball, led Cleveland Browns to 7 league titles in 10 years, winning 4 AAFC championships (1946-49) and 3 NFL (1950,54-55); 5-time All-Pro; 2-time NFL MVP (1953,55).

Red Grange (b. June 13, 1903, d. Jan. 28, 1991): Football HB; 3-time All-America at Illinois who brought 1st huge crowds to pro football when he signed with Chicago Bears in 1925; formed 1st AFL with manager-promoter C.C. Pyle in 1926, but league folded and he returned to Bears.

Bud Grant (b. May 20, 1927): Football and Basketball; only coach to win 100 games in both CFL and NFL and only member of both CFL and U.S. Pro Football Halls of Fame; led Winnipeg to 4 Grey Cup titles (1958-59,61-62) in 6 appearances, but his Minnesota Vikings lost all 4 Super Bowl attempts in 1970s; all-time rank of 3rd in CFL wins (122) and 8th in NFL wins (168); also All-Big Ten at Minnesota in both football and basketball in late 1940s; a 3-time CFL All-Star offensive end; also member of 1950 NBA champion Minneapolis Lakers.

Rocky Graziano (b. June 7, 1922, d. May 22, 1990): Boxer; world middleweight champion (1946-47); fought Tony Zale for title 3 times in 21 months, losing twice; pro record 67-10-6 with 52 KOs; movie "Somebody Up There Likes Me" based on his life.

Hank Greenberg (b. Jan. 1, 1911, d. Sept. 4, 1986): Baseball 1B; led AL in HRs and RBI 4 times each; 2-time MVP (1935,40) with Detroit; 331 career HRs, including 58 in 1938.

Joe Greene (b. Sept. 24, 1946): Football DT; 5-time All-Pro (1972-74,77,79); led Pittsburgh to 4 Super Bowl titles in 1970s; nicknamed "Mean Joe".

Bud Greenspan (b. Sept. 18, 1926): Filmmaker specializing in the Olympic Games; has won Emmy awards for 22-part "The Olympiad" (1976-77) and historical vignettes for ABC-TV's coverage of 1980 Winter Games; won 1994 Emmy award for edited special on Lillehammer Winter Olympics.

Wayne Gretzky (b. Jan. 26, 1961): Hockey C; 10-time NHL scoring champion; 9-time regular season MVP (1979-87,89) and 9-time All-NHL first team; has scored 200 points or more in a season 4 times; led Edmonton to 4 Stanley Cups (1984-85,87-88); 2-time playoff MVP (1985,88); traded to LA Kings (Aug. 9, 1988); broke Gordie Howe's all-time NHL goal scoring record of 801 on Mar. 23, 1994; all-time NHL leader in points, goals and assists; also all-time Stanley Cup leader in points, goals and assists; spent the end of the 1996 season with the St. Louis Blues and then signed a free agent contract with the New York Rangers.

Bob Griese (b. Feb. 3, 1945): Football QB; 2-time All-Pro (1971,77); led Miami to undefeated season (17-0) in 1972 and consecutive Super Bowl titles (1973-74).

Ken Griffey Jr. (b. Nov. 21, 1969): Baseball OF; overall 1st pick of 1987 draft by Seattle; 8-time Gold Glove winner; 8-time All-Star; in 1997, set major league record for home runs in April with 13; in many categories, is among the youngest ever to reach certain plateaus, like 200 homers, 300 homers and 1,000 hits; Mariners all-time leader in home runs and RBIs; MVP of 1992 All-Star game at age 23; hit home runs in 8 consecutive games in 1993; son of Ken Sr. and in 1990 they became the first father-son combination to appear in the same major league lineup.

Archie Griffin (b. Aug. 21, 1954): Football RB; only college player to win two Heisman Trophies (1974-75); rushed for 5,177 yards in career at Ohio St.

Emile Griffith (b. Feb. 3, 1938): Boxer; world welterweight champion (1961,62-63,63-65); world middleweight champ (1966-67,67-68); pro record 85-24-2 with 23 KOs.

Dick Groat (b. Nov. 4, 1930): Basketball and Baseball SS; 2-time basketball All-America at Duke and college Player of Year in 1951; won NL MVP award as shortstop with Pittsburgh in 1960; won World Series with Pirates (1960) and St. Louis (1964).

Lefty Grove (b. Mar. 6, 1900, d. May 23, 1975): Baseball LHP; won 20 or more games 8 times; led AL in ERA 9 times and strikeouts 7 times; 31-4 record and MVP in 1931 with Philadelphia; 300-141 record.

Lou Groza (b. Jan. 25, 1924): Football T-PK; 6-time All-Pro; played in 13 championship games for Cleveland from 1946-67; kicked winning field goal in 1950 NFL title game; 1,608 career points (1,349 in NFL).

Janet Guthrie (b. Mar. 7, 1938): Auto racer; in 1977, became 1st woman to race in Indianapolis 500; placed 9th at Indy in 1978.

Tony Gwynn (b. May 9, 1960): Baseball OF; 8-time NL batting champion (1984,87-89,94-97) at San Diego, 12-time All-Star; played basketball at San Diego St. leaving as school's all-time assist leader; drafted in 10th round of 1981 NBA draft by San Diego Clippers.

Harvey Haddix (b. Sept. 18, 1925, d. Jan. 9, 1994): Baseball LHP; pitched 12 perfect innings for Pittsburgh, but lost to Milwaukee in the 13th, 1-0 (May 26, 1959); won Game 7 of 1960 World Series.

Walter Hagen (b. Dec. 21, 1892, d. Oct. 5, 1969): Pro golf pioneer; won 2 U.S. Opens (1914,19), 4 British Opens (1922,24,28-29), 5 PGA Championships (1921,24-27) and 5 Western Opens; retired with 40 PGA wins; 6-time U.S. Ryder Cup captain.

Marvin Hagler (b. May 23, 1954): Boxer; world middleweight champion 1980-87; enjoyed his nickname "Marvelous Marvin" so much he had his name legally changed; pro record of 62-3-2 with 52 KOs.

George Halas (b. Feb. 2, 1895, d. Oct. 31, 1983): Football pioneer; MVP in 1919 Rose Bowl; player-coach-owner of Chicago Bears from 1920-83; signed Red Grange in 1925; coached Bears for 40 seasons and won 8 NFL titles (1921,32-33,40-41,43,46,63); 2nd on all-time career list with 324 wins; elected to NFL Hall of Fame in 1963.

Dorothy Hamill (b. July 26, 1956): Figure skater; won Olympic gold medal and world championship in 1976; Ice Capades headliner from 1977-84; bought financially-strapped Ice Capades in 1993 and sold it several years later.

Scott Hamilton (b. Aug. 28, 1958): Figure skater; 4-time world champion (1981-84); won gold medal at 1984 Olympics.

Mia Hamm (b. Mar. 17, 1972): Soccer; Member of the U.S. gold medal team at the 1996 Olympics in Atlanta; named U.S. Soccer's female Athlete of the Year for four consecutive years (1994-97); MVP of both U.S. Women's Cup '97, after scoring six goals in three games, and U.S. Women's Cup '95; made the U.S. National Team at 15; a three-time collegiate All-American; ACC's all-time leading scorer in goals (103), assists (72) and points (278); led the Univ. of North Carolina to four consecutive national championships

Tonya Harding (b. Nov. 12, 1970): Figure skater; 1991 U.S. women's champion; involved in bizarre plot hatched by ex-husband Jeff Gillooly to injure rival Nancy Kerrigan on Jan. 6, 1994 and keep her off Olympic team; won '94 U.S. women's title in Kerrigan's absence; denied any role in assault and sued USOC when her berth on Olympic team was threatened; finished 8th at Lillehammer (Kerrigan recovered and won silver medal); pleaded guilty on Mar. 16 to conspiracy to hinder investigation; stripped of 1994 title by U.S. Figure Skating Assn.

Tom Harmon (b. Sept. 28, 1919, d. Mar. 17, 1990): Football HB; 2-time All-America at Michigan; won Heisman Trophy in 1940; played with AFL NY Americans in 1941 and NFL LA Rams (1946-47); World War II fighter pilot who won Silver Star and Purple Heart; became radio-TV commentator.

Franco Harris (b. Mar. 7, 1950): Football RB; ran for over 1,000 yards a season 8 times; rushed for 12,120 yards in 13 years; led Pittsburgh to 4 Super Bowl titles.

Leon Hart (b. Nov. 2, 1928): Football E; only player to win 3 national championships in college and 3 more in the NFL; won his titles at Notre Dame (1946-47,49) and with Detroit Lions (1952-53,57); 3-time All-America and last lineman to win Heisman Trophy (1949); All-Pro on both offense and defense in 1951.

Bill Hartack (b. Dec. 9, 1932): Jockey; won Kentucky Derby 5 times (1957,60,62,64,69), Preakness 3 times (1956,64,69), but the Belmont only once (1960).

Doug Harvey (b. Dec. 19, 1924, d. Dec. 26, 1989): Hockey D; 10-time All-NHL 1st team; won Norris Trophy 7 times (1955-58,60-62); led Montreal to 6 Stanley Cups.

Dominik Hasek (b. Jan. 29, 1965): Czech hockey G; 2-time NHL MVP (1997,98) with Buffalo; 4-time Vezina Trophy winner (1994,95,97,98); led NHL with a 1.95 GAA in 1993-94— the first sub-2.00 GAA since Bernie Parent in 1974; led Czech Republic to Olympic gold medal in 1998 at Nagano.

Billy Haughton (b. Nov. 2, 1923, d. July 15, 1986): Harness racing; 4-time winner of Hambletonian; trainer-driver of one Pacing Triple Crown winner (1968); 4,910 career wins.

João Havelange (b. May 8, 1916): Soccer; Brazilian-born president of Federation Internationale de Football Assoc. (FIFA) 1974-98; also member of International Olympic Committee.

John Havlicek (b. Apr. 8, 1940): Basketball; played in 3 NCAA Finals at Ohio St. (1960-62); led Boston to 8 NBA titles (1963-66,68-69,74,76); Finals MVP in 1974; 4-time All-NBA 1st team.

Bob Hayes (b. Dec. 20, 1942): Track & Field and Football; won gold medal in 100m at 1964 Olympics; All-Pro SE for Dallas in 1966; convicted of drug trafficking in 1979 and served 18 months of a 5-year sentence.

Elvin Hayes (b. Nov. 17, 1945): Basketball C; Known as "the Big E"; Overall number one pick of the 1968 NBA draft; Three-time All-NBA first team (1975,77,79); 1978 Finals MVP; Twelve-time NBA all-star (1969-80); named to NBA's 50 Greatest Players; 6th leading scorer in NBA history with 27,313 points; member of NBA Hall of Fame.

Woody Hayes (b. Feb. 14, 1913, d. Mar. 12, 1987): Football; coached Ohio St. to 3 national titles (1954,57,68) and 4 Rose Bowl victories; 238 career wins in 28 seasons at Denison, Miami-OH and OSU.

Thomas Hearns (b. Oct. 18, 1958): Boxer; has held world titles as welterweight, light middleweight, middleweight and light heavyweight; four career losses have come against Sugar Ray Leonard, Marvin Hagler and twice to Iran Barkley; entered 1998 with pro record of 57-4-1 and 45 KOs.

Eric Heiden (b. June 14, 1958): Speedskater; 3-time overall world champion (1977-79); won all 5 men's gold medals at 1980 Olympics, setting records in each; Sullivan Award winner (1980).

Mel Hein (b. Aug. 22, 1909, d. Jan. 31, 1992): Football C; NFL All-Pro 8 straight years (1933-40); MVP in 1938 with NY Giants; didn't miss a game in 15 seasons.

John W. Heisman (b. Oct. 23, 1869, d. Oct. 3, 1936): Football; coached at 9 colleges from 1892-1927; won 185 games; Director of Athletics at Downtown Athletic Club in NYC (1928-36); DAC named Heisman Trophy after him.

Carol Heiss (b. Jan. 20, 1940): Figure skater; 5-time world champion (1956-60); won Olympic silver medal in 1956 and gold in '60; married 1956 men's gold medalist Hayes Jenkins.

Rickey Henderson (b. Dec. 25, 1958): Baseball OF; AL playoff MVP (1989) and AL regular season MVP (1990); set single-season base stealing record of 130 in 1982; has led AL in steals a record 11 times; broke Lou Brock's all-time record of 938 on May 1, 1991; all-time leader in steals and HRs as leadoff batter.

Sonja Henie (b. Apr. 8, 1912, d. Oct. 12, 1969): Norwegian figure skater; 10-time world champion (1927-36); won 3 consecutive Olympic gold medals (1928,32,36); became movie star.

Foster Hewitt (b. Nov. 21, 1902, d. Apr. 21, 1985): Radio-TV; Canada's premier hockey play-by-play broadcaster from 1923-81; coined phrase, "He shoots, he scores!"

Graham Hill (b. Feb. 15, 1929, d. Nov. 29, 1975): British auto racer; 2-time Formula One world champion (1962,68); won Indy 500 in 1966; killed in plane crash; father of fellow driver Damon.

Phil Hill (b. Apr. 20, 1927): Auto racer; first U.S. driver to win Formula One championship (1961); 3 career wins (1958-64).

Martina Hingis (b. Sept. 30, 1980): Tennis player; in March 1997 at 16 years, 6 months, she became the youngest No. 1 ranked player since the ranking system began in 1975; won the 1997 Wimbledon, U.S. Open and Australian Open, one of only three teenagers to win three Grand Slam events in one year; led tour in wins (75) in 1997; first woman to surpass the $3 million mark in earnings for one season (1997).

Max Hirsch (b. July 30, 1880, d. Apr. 3, 1969): Horse racing; trained 1,933 winners from 1908-68; won Triple Crown with Assault in 1946.

Tommy Hitchcock (b. Feb. 11, 1900, d. Apr. 19, 1944): Polo; world class player at 20; achieved 10-goal rating 18 times from 1922-40.

Lew Hoad (b. Nov. 23, 1934, d. July 3, 1994): Australian tennis player; 2-time Wimbledon winner (1956-57); won Australian, French and Wimbledon titles in 1956, but missed capturing Grand Slam at Forest Hills when beaten by Ken Rosewall in 4-set final.

Gil Hodges (b. Apr. 4, 1924, d. Apr. 2, 1972): Baseball 1B-Manager; won three consecutive Gold Gloves (1957-59); Tied Major League record with four Home Runs in one game on Aug 31, 1950; drove in 100 runs in seven consecutive seasons (1949-55); hit 370 home runs and 1,274 RBIs lifetime; won 660 games as a manager (Senators and Mets).

Ben Hogan (b. Aug. 13, 1912, d. July 25, 1997): Golfer; 4-time PGA Player of Year; one of only four players to win all four Grand Slam titles (others are Nicklaus, Player and Sarazen); won 4 U.S. Opens, 2 Masters, 2 PGAs and 1 British Open between 1946-53; only player to win three of the four current majors in one year when he won Masters, U.S. Open and British Open in 1953; nearly killed in Feb. 2, 1949 car accident, but came back to win U.S. Open in '50; third on all-time list with 63 career wins.

Eleanor Holm (b. Dec. 6, 1913): Swimmer; won gold medal in 100m backstroke at 1932 Olympics; thrown off '36 U.S. team for drinking champagne in public and shooting craps on boat to Germany.

Nat Holman (b. Oct. 18, 1896, d. Feb. 12, 1995): Basketball pioneer; played with Original Celtics (1920-28); coached CCNY to both NCAA and NIT titles in 1950 (a year later, several of his players were caught up in a point-shaving scandal); 423 career wins.

Larry Holmes (b. Nov. 3, 1949): Boxer; heavyweight champion (WBC or IBF) from 1978-85; successfully defended title 20 times before losing to Michael Spinks; returned from first retirement in 1988 and was KO'd in 4th by champ Mike Tyson; launched second comeback in 1991; fought and lost title bids against Evander Holyfield in '92 and Oliver McCall in '95; entered 1998 with record of 66-6 and 42 KOs.

Lou Holtz (b. Jan. 6, 1937): Football; coached Notre Dame to national title in 1988; 2-time Coach of Year (1977,88) retired after 1996 season with 216-95-7 record in 27 seasons with 5 schools— Wm. & Mary (3 years), N.C. State (4), Arkansas (7), Minnesota (2) and ND (11); also coached NFL NY Jets for 13 games (3-10) in 1976.

Evander Holyfield (b. Oct. 19, 1962): Boxer; KO'd Buster Douglas in 3rd round to become world hvywt. champion in 1990; 2 of first 4 title defenses included wins over 42-year-old ex-champs George Foreman and Larry Holmes; lost title to Riddick Bowe by unanimous dec. in 1992; beat Bowe by majority dec. to reclaim title in 1993; lost title again to Michael Moorer by majority dec. in 1994; after retiring in '94 due to an apparent heart defect, he returned to the ring in 1995 with a clean bill of health; defeated Mike Tyson in 1996 to win WBA belt; in 1997 rematch, Tyson was disqualified for twice biting Holyfield's ear.

Red Holzman (b. Aug. 10, 1920): Basketball; played for NBL and NBA champions at Rochester (1946,51); coached NY Knicks to 2 NBA titles (1970,73); Coach of Year (1970); ranks 10th on all-time NBA list with 754 wins (including playoffs).

Rogers Hornsby (b. Apr. 27, 1896, d. Jan. 5, 1963): Baseball 2B; hit .400 three times, including .424 in 1924; led NL in batting 7 times; 2-time MVP (1925,29); career average of .358 over 23 years is all-time highest in NL.

Paul Hornung (b. Dec. 23, 1935): Football HB-PK; only Heisman Trophy winner to play for losing team (2-8 Notre Dame in 1956); 3-time NFL scoring leader (1959-61) at Green Bay; 176 points in 1960, an all-time record; MVP in 1961; suspended by NFL for 1963 season for betting on his own team.

Gordie Howe (b. Mar. 31, 1928): Hockey RW; played 32 seasons in NHL and WHA from 1946-80; led NHL in scoring 6 times; All-NHL 1st team 12 times; MVP 6 times in NHL (1952-53,57-58,60,63) with Detroit and once in WHA (1974) with Houston; ranks 2nd on all-time NHL list in goals (801) and points (1,850) to Wayne Gretzky; played with sons Mark and Marty at Houston (1973-77) and New England-Hartford (1977-80).

Cal Hubbard (b. Oct. 31, 1900, d. Oct. 19, 1977): Member of college football, pro football and baseball halls of fame; 9 years in NFL; 4-time All-Pro at end and tackle; AL umpire (1936-51).

Carl Hubbell (b. June 22, 1903, d. Nov. 21, 1988): Baseball LHP; led NL in wins and ERA 3 times each; 2-time MVP (1933,36) with NY Giants; fanned Ruth, Gehrig, Foxx, Simmons and Cronin in succession in 1934 All-Star Game; 253-154 career record.

Sam Huff (b. Oct. 4, 1934): Football LB; glamorized NFL's middle linebacker position with NY Giants from 1956-63; subject of "The Violent World of Sam Huff" TV special in 1961; helped club win 6 division titles and a world championship (1956).

Miller Huggins (b. Mar. 27, 1879, d. Sept. 25, 1929): Baseball; managed NY Yankees from 1918 until his death late in '29 season; led Yanks to 6 pennants and 3 World Series titles from 1921-28.

H. Wayne Huizenga (b. Dec. 29, 1937): Owner; formerly vice chairman of Viacom Inc. and chairman/CEO of Blockbuster Entertainment; majority owner of MLB's Florida Marlins and 100-percent owner of NFL Miami Dolphins, NHL Florida Panthers and Pro Player Stadium; criticized for dismantling 1997 World Champion Marlins in off-season to cut payroll.

Bobby Hull (b. Jan. 3, 1939): Hockey LW; led NHL in scoring 3 times; 2-time MVP (1965-66) with Chicago; All-NHL first team 10 times; jumped to WHA in 1972, 2-time MVP there (1973,75) with Winnipeg; scored 913 goals in both leagues; father of Brett.

Brett Hull (b. Aug. 9, 1964): Hockey RW; NHL MVP in 1991 with St. Louis; holds single season RW scoring record with 86 goals; he and father Bobby have both won Hart (MVP), Lady Byng (sportsmanship) and All-Star Game MVP trophies.

Jim (Catfish) Hunter (b. Apr. 8, 1946): Baseball RHP; won 20 games or more 5 times (1971-75); played on 5 World Series winners with Oakland and NY Yankees; threw perfect game in 1968; won AL Cy Young Award in 1974; 224-166 career record.

Ibrahim Hussein (b. June 3, 1958): Kenyan distance runner; 3-time winner of Boston Marathon (1988,91-92) and 1st African runner to win in Boston; won New York Marathon in 1987.

Don Hutson (b. Jan. 31, 1913, d. June 24, 1997): Football E-PK; led NFL in receptions 8 times and interceptions once; 9-time All-Pro (1936,38-45) for Green Bay; 99 career TD catches.

Flo Hyman (b. July 31, 1954, d. Jan. 24, 1986): Volleyball; 3-time All-America spiker at Houston and captain of 1984 U.S. Women's Olympic team; died of heart attack caused by Marfan Syndrome during a match in Japan in 1986.

Hank Iba (b. Aug. 6, 1904, d. Jan. 15, 1993): Basketball; coached Oklahoma A&M to 2 straight NCAA titles (1945-46); 767 career wins in 41 years; coached U.S. Olympic team to 2 gold medals (1964,68), but lost to Soviets in controversial '72 final.

Mike Ilitch (b. July 20, 1929): Baseball and Hockey owner; owns Little Caesar's, the international pizza chain; bought Detroit Red Wings of NHL for $8 million in 1982 and AL Detroit Tigers for $85 million in 1992.

Punch Imlach (b. Mar. 15, 1918, d. Dec. 1, 1987): Hockey; directed Toronto to 4 Stanley Cups (1962-64,67) in 11 seasons as GM-coach.

Miguel Induráin (b. July 16, 1964): Spanish cyclist; won a record 5th straight Tour de France in 1995, joining legends Jacques Anquetil and Bernard Hinault of France and Eddy Merckx of Belgium as the only 5-time winners; won gold in time trial at '96 Olympics; retired in 1997.

Hale Irwin (b. June 3, 1945): Golfer; oldest player ever to win U.S. Open (45 in 1990); NCAA champion in 1967; 20 PGA victories, including 3 U.S. Opens (1974,79,90); 5-time Ryder Cup team member; joined senior PGA tour in 1995 and had already won 17 titles through Aug. 1998.

Bo Jackson (b. Nov. 30, 1962): Baseball OF and Football RB; won Heisman Trophy in 1985 and MVP of baseball All-Star Game in 1989; starter for both baseball's KC Royals and NFL's LA Raiders in 1988 and '89; severely injured left hip Jan. 13, 1991, in NFL playoffs; waived by Royals but signed by Chicago White Sox in 1991; missed entire 1992 season recovering from hip surgery; played for White Sox in 1993 and California in '94 before retiring.

Joe Jackson (b. July 16, 1889, d. Dec. 5, 1951): Baseball OF; hit .300 or better 11 times; nicknamed "Shoeless Joe"; career average of .356 (see Black Sox).

Phil Jackson (b. Sept. 17, 1945): Basketball; NBA champion as reserve forward with New York in 1973 (injured when Knicks won in '70); coached Chicago to six NBA titles in eight years (1991-93, 96-98); coach of the year in 1996 and 97; all-time leader in winning percentage for NBA coaches with 500 or more wins.

Reggie Jackson (b. May 18, 1946): Baseball OF; led AL in HRs 4 times; MVP in 1973; played on 5 World Series winners with Oakland, NY Yankees; 1977 Series MVP with 5 HRs; 563 career HRs; all-time strikeout leader (2,597); member of the Hall of Fame.

Dr. Robert Jackson (b. Aug. 6, 1932): Surgeon; revolutionized sports medicine by popularizing the use of othroscopic surgery to treat injuries; learned technique from Japanese physician that allowed athletes to return quickly from potentially career-ending injuries.

Helen Jacobs (b. Aug. 6, 1908): Tennis; 4-time winner of U.S. Championship (1932-35); Wimbledon winner in 1936; lost 4 Wimbledon finals to arch-rival Helen Wills Moody.

Jaromir Jagr (b. Feb. 15, 1972): Hockey RW; Fifth overall pick by Pittsburgh (1990); NHL All-Rookie team (1991); NHL All-Star (1992-93,96-98); Won Art Ross Trophy (1995); NHL All-Star First Team (1995,96); NHL single season record for most points by a right winger (149); NHL single season record for most assists by a right winger (87); led NHL in game-winning goals with 12 (1996).

Dan Jansen (b. June 17, 1965): Speedskater; 1993 world record-holder in 500m; fell in 500m and 1,000m in 1988 Olympics at Calgary after learning of death of sister Jane; placed 4th in 500m and didn't attempt 1,000m 4 years later in Albertville; fell in 500m at '94 Games in Lillehammer, but finally won an Olympic medal with world record (1:12.43) effort in 1,000m, then took victory lap with baby daughter Jane in his arms; won 1994 Sullivan Award.

James J. Jeffries (b. Apr. 15, 1875, d. Mar. 3, 1953): Boxer; world heavyweight champion (1899-1905); retired undefeated but came back to fight Jack Johnson in 1910 and lost (KO,15th).

David Jenkins (b. June 29, 1936): Figure skater; brother of Hayes; 3-time world champion (1957-59); won gold medal at 1960 Olympics.

Hayes Jenkins (b. Mar. 23, 1933): Figure skater; 4-time world champion (1953-56); won gold medal at 1956 Olympics; married 1960 women's gold medalist Carol Heiss.

Bruce Jenner (b. Oct. 28, 1949): Track & Field; won gold medal in 1976 Olympic decathlon.

Jackie Jensen (b. Mar. 9, 1927, d. July 14, 1982): Football RB and Baseball OF; All-America at California in 1948; American League MVP with Boston Red Sox in 1958.

Ben Johnson (b. Dec. 30, 1961): Canadian sprinter; set 100m world record (9.83) at 1987 World Championships; won 100m at 1988 Olympics, but flunked drug test and forfeited gold medal; 1987 world record revoked in '89 for admitted steroid use; returned drug-free in 1991, but performed poorly; banned for life by IAAF in 1993 for testing positive after a meet in Montreal.

Bob Johnson (b. Mar. 4, 1931, d. Nov. 26, 1991): Hockey; coached Pittsburgh Penguins to 1st Stanley Cup title in 1991; led Wisconsin to 3 NCAA titles (1973,77,81) in 15 years; also coached 1976 U.S. Olympic team and NHL Calgary (1982-87).

Earvin (Magic) Johnson (b. Aug. 14, 1959): Basketball G; led Michigan St. to NCAA title in 1979 and was Final 4 MOP; All-NBA 1st team 9 times; 3-time MVP (1987,89-90); led LA Lakers to 5 NBA titles; 3-time Finals MVP (1980, 82, 87); 2nd all-time in NBA assists with 10,141; retired on Nov. 7, 1991 after announcing he was HIV-positive; returned to score 25 points in 1992 NBA All-Star Game; U.S. Olympic Dream Team member in '92; announced NBA comeback then retired again before start of 1992-93 season; named head coach of Lakers on Mar. 23, 1994, but finished season at 5-11 and quit; later became minority owner of team; came back a final time and played 32 games during 1995-96 season before retiring for good.

Jack Johnson (b. Mar. 31, 1878, d. June 10, 1946): Boxer; controversial heavyweight champion (1908-15) and 1st black to hold title; defeated Tommy Burns for crown at age 30; fled to Europe in 1913 after Mann Act conviction; lost title to Jess Willard in Havana, but claimed to have taken a dive; pro record 78-8-12 with 45 KOs.

Jimmy Johnson (b. July 16, 1943): Football; All-SWC defensive lineman on Arkansas' 1964 national championship team; coached Miami-FL to national title in 1987; college record of 81-34-3 in 10 years; hired by old friend and new Dallas owner Jerry Jones to succeed Tom Landry in 1989; went 1-15 in '89, then led Cowboys to consecutive Super Bowl victories in 1992 and '93 seasons; quit in 1994 after feuding with Jones; became TV analyst; replaced Don Shula as Miami Dolphins head coach in 1996.

Judy Johnson (b. Oct. 26, 1899, d. June 13, 1989): Baseball IF; one of the great stars of the Negro Leagues; a great fielding third baseman who regularly batted over .300; when baseball integrated Johnson's playing days were over but he coached and scouted for the Philadelphia Athletics, Boston Braves and Philadelphia Phillies; member of Hall of Fame.

Junior Johnson (b. 1930): Auto Racing; won the second Daytona 500 in 1960; also won 13 NASCAR races in 1965, including the Rebel 300 at Darlington; retired from racing to become a highly successful car owner; his first driver was Bobby Allison.

Michael Johnson (b. Sep 13, 1967): Track & Field; Shattered world record in 200m (19.32) and set Olympic record in 400m (43.49) to become first man to win the gold in both races in the same Olympic Games at Atlanta in 1996; two-time world champion in 200 (1991,95) and three-time world champ in 400 (1993,95,97).

Rafer Johnson (b. Aug. 18, 1934): Track & Field; won silver medal in 1956 Olympic decathlon and gold medal in 1960.

Walter Johnson (b. Nov. 6, 1887, d. Dec. 10, 1946): Baseball RHP; won 20 games or more 10 straight years; led AL in ERA 5 times, wins 6 times and strikeouts 12 times; twice MVP (1913, 24) with Washington; all-time leader in shutouts (110) and 2nd in wins (416); nicknamed "Big Train."

Ben A. Jones (b. Dec. 31, 1882, d. June 13, 1961): Horse racing; Calumet Farm trainer (1939-47); saddled 6 Kentucky Derby champions, including 2 Triple Crown winners—Whirlaway in 1941 and Citation in '48.

Bobby Jones (b. Mar. 17, 1902, d. Dec. 18, 1971): Won U.S. and British Opens plus U.S. and British Amateurs in 1930 to become golf's only Grand Slam winner ever; from 1922-30, won 4 U.S. Opens, 5 U.S. Amateurs, 3 British Opens, and played in 6 Walker Cups; founded Masters tournament in 1934.

Deacon Jones (b. Dec. 9, 1938): Football DE; 5-time All-Pro (1965-69) with LA Rams; unofficial all-time NFL sack leader with 173½ in 14 years.

Jerry Jones (b. Oct. 13, 1942): Football; owner-GM of Dallas Cowboys; maverick who bought declining team (3-13) and Texas Stadium for $140 million in 1989; hired old pal Jimmy Johnson to replace legendary Tom Landry as coach; their partnership led Cowboys to 2 Super Bowl titles (1993-94); when feud developed in 1994, he fired Johnson and hired Barry Switzer, who won Super Bowl in 1996; defied NFL Properties by signing separate sponsorship deals with Pepsi and Nike in 1995, causing NFL to file a $300 million lawsuit against him.

Roy Jones Jr. (b. Jan. 16, 1969): Boxing; robbed of gold medal at 1988 Summer Olympics due to an error in scoring; still voted Outstanding Boxer of the Games; won IBF middleweight crown by beating Bernard Hopkins in 1993; moved up to super middleweight and won IBF title from James Toney in 1994; moved up to light heavyweight division winning WBC title in 1997 and WBA title in '98.

Michael Jordan (b. Feb. 17, 1963): Basketball G; College Player of Year with North Carolina in 1984; led NBA in scoring 7 years in a row (1987-93) and also 1996-98; 10-time All-NBA 1st team; 5-time regular season MVP (1988,91-92,96,98) and 6-time MVP of NBA Finals (1991-93,96-98); 3-time AP Male Athlete of Year; led U.S. Olympic team to gold medals in 1984 and '92; stunned sports world when he retired at age 30 on Oct. 6, 1993; signed as OF with Chicago White Sox and spent summer of '94 in Double A with Birmingham; struggled with .204 average; made one of the most anticipated comebacks in sports history when he returned to the Bulls lineup on Mar. 19, 1995 and shot 7-for-28; lost first playoff series since 1990 when Bulls were eliminated by Orlando in second round; led Bulls to 6 NBA titles (1991-93,96-98); in 1997, as part of the league's 50th anniversary celebration, named as one of the NBA's 50 Greatest Players. Duh.

Florence Griffith Joyner (b. Dec. 21, 1959, d. Sept. 21, 1998): Track & Field; set world records in 100 and 200 meters in 1988; won 3 gold medals at '88 Olympics (100m, 200m, 4x100m relay); Sullivan Award winner (1988); retired in 1989; named as co-chairperson of President's Council on Physical Fitness and Sports in 1993.

Jackie Joyner-Kersee (b. Mar. 3, 1962): Track & Field; 2-time world champion in both long jump (1987,91) and heptathlon (1987,93); won heptathlon gold medals at 1988 and '92 Olympics and LJ gold at '88 Games; also won Olympic silver (1984) in heptathlon and bronze (1992,96) in LJ; Sullivan Award winner (1986); only woman to receive *The Sporting News* Man of Year award.

Sonny Jurgensen (b. Aug. 23, 1934): Football QB; played 18 seasons with Philadelphia and Washington; led NFL in passing twice (1967,69); All-Pro in 1961; 255 career TD passes.

Duke Kahanamoku (b. Aug. 24, 1890, d. Jan. 22, 1968): Swimmer; won 3 gold medals and 2 silver over 3 Olympics (1912,20,24); also surfing pioneer.

Al Kaline (b. Dec. 19, 1934): Baseball; youngest player (at age 20) to win batting title (led AL with .340 in 1955); had 3,007 hits, 399 HRs in 22 years with Detroit.

Anatoly Karpov (b. May 23, 1951): Chess; Soviet world champion from 1975-85; regained International Chess Federation (FIDE) version of championship in 1993 when countryman Garry Kasparov was stripped of title after forming new Professional Chess Association.

Garry Kasparov (b. Apr. 13, 1963): Chess; Azerbaijani who became youngest player (22 years, 210 days) ever to win world championship as Soviet in 1985; defeated countryman Anatoly Karpov for title; split with International Chess Federation (FIDE) to form Professional Chess Association (PCA) in 1993; stripped of FIDE title in '93 but successfully defended PCA title against Briton Nigel Short; beat IBM supercomputer "Deep Blue" 4 games to 2 in 1996 much-publicized match in New York; lost rematch to computer in 1997.

Ewing Kauffman (b. Sept. 21, 1916, d. Aug. 1, 1993): Baseball; pharmaceutical billionaire and long-time owner of Kansas City Royals; Royals Stadium renamed for Kauffman on July 2, 1993, one month before his death.

Mike Keenan (b. Oct. 21, 1949): Hockey; coach who finally led NY Rangers to Stanley Cup title in 1994 after 53 unsuccessful years; quit a month later in pay dispute and signed with St. Louis as coach-GM; since moved on to Vancouver; entered 1998-99 season tied for fifth all-time with 582 wins (including playoffs).

Kipchoge (Kip) Keino (b. Jan. 17, 1940): Kenyan runner; policeman who beat USA's Jim Ryun to win 1,500m gold medal at 1968 Olympics; won again in steeplechase at 1972 Summer Games; his success spawned long line of international distance champions from Kenya.

Johnny Kelley (b. Sept. 6, 1907): Distance runner; ran in his 61st and final Boston Marathon at age 84 in 1992, finishing in 5:58:36; won Boston twice (1935,45) and was 2nd 7 times.

Jim Kelly (b. Feb. 14, 1960): Football QB; led Buffalo to four consecutive Super Bowl appearances, and is only QB to lose four times; named to AFC Pro Bowl team 5 times.

Walter Kennedy (b. June 8, 1912, d. June 26, 1977): Basketball; 2nd NBA commissioner (1963-75); league doubled in size to 18 teams during his term of office.

Nancy Kerrigan (b. Oct. 13, 1969): Figure skating; 1993 U.S. women's champion and Olympic medalist in 1992 (bronze) and '94 (silver); victim of Jan. 6, 1994 assault at U.S. nationals in Detroit when Shane Stant clubbed her in right knee with metal baton after a practice session; conspiracy hatched by Jeff Gillooly, ex-husband of rival Tonya Harding; although unable to compete in nationals, she quickly recovered and was granted berth on Olympic team; finished 2nd in Lillehammer to Oksana Baiul of Ukraine by a 5-4 judges' vote.

Billy Kidd (b. Apr. 13, 1943): Skiing; the first great American male Alpine skier; first American male to win an Olympic medal when he won a silver in the slalom and a bronze in the Alpine combined in 1964; competed respectably with the great Jean-Claude Killy; won the world Alpine combined event in 1970, which was the first world championship for an American male.

Harmon Killebrew (b. June 29, 1936): Baseball 3B-1B; led AL in HRs 6 times and RBI 3 times; MVP in 1969 with Minnesota; 573 career homers ranks him fifth all-time.

Jean-Claude Killy (b. Aug. 30, 1943): French alpine skier; 2-time World Cup champion (1967-68); won 3 gold medals at 1968 Olympics in Grenoble; co-president of 1992 Winter Games in Albertville.

Ralph Kiner (b. Oct. 27, 1922): Baseball OF; led NL in home runs 7 straight years (1946-52) with Pittsburgh; 369 career HRs and 1,015 RBI in 10 seasons; long-time NY Mets announcer.

Betsy King (b. Aug. 13, 1955): Golfer; 2-time LPGA Player of Year (1984,89), who entered 1998 as Tour's all-time money winner with $5,980,113; 3-time winner of Dinah Shore (1987,90,97) and 2-time winner of U.S. Open (1989,90); 31 overall Tour wins; member of LPGA Hall of Fame.

Billie Jean King (b. Nov. 22, 1943): Tennis; women's rights pioneer; Wimbledon singles champ 6 times; U.S. champ 4 times; first woman athlete to earn $100,000 in one year (1971); beat 55-year-old Bobby Riggs 6-4,6-3,6-3, in "Battle of the Sexes" to win $100,000 at Astrodome in 1973.

Don King (b. Aug. 20, 1931): Boxing promoter; first major black promoter who controlled heavyweight title from 1978-90 while Larry Holmes and Mike Tyson were champions; 1st big promotion was Muhammad Ali's fight against George Foreman in 1974; former numbers operator who served 4 years for manslaughter (1967-70); acquitted of tax evasion and fraud in 1985; regained control of heavyweight title in 1994 with wins by Oliver McCall (WBC) and Bruce Seldon (WBA); other fighters he promoted include Roberto Duran and Julio Cesar Chavez; also famous for his gravity-defying hairstyle and his catchphrase "Only in America!".

Karch Kiraly (b. Nov. 3, 1960): Volleyball; USA's preeminent volleyball player; led UCLA to three NCAA championships (1979,81,82); played on US national teams that won Olympic gold medals in 1984 and '88, world championships in '82 and '86; won the inaugural gold medal for Olympic beach volleyball with Kent Steffes in 1996.

Tom Kite (b. Dec. 9, 1949): Golfer; entered 1998 as 2nd on all-time PGA Tour money list with over $10 million; finally won 1st major with victory in 1992 U.S. Open at Pebble Beach; co-NCAA champion with Ben Crenshaw (1972); PGA Rookie of Year (1973); PGA Player of Year (1989); captain of losing 1997 US Ryder Cup team

Gene Klein (b. Jan. 29, 1921, d. Mar. 12, 1990): Horseman; won 3 Eclipse awards as top owner (1985-87); his filly Winning Colors won 1988 Kentucky Derby; also owned San Diego Chargers football team (1966-84).

Bob Knight (b. Oct. 25, 1940): Basketball; has coached Indiana to 3 NCAA titles (1976,81,87); 3-time Coach of Year (1975-76,89); coached 1984 U.S. Olympic team to gold medal; 7th on all-time NCAA list with 720 wins in 33 years as of 1998.

Phil Knight (b. Feb. 24, 1938): Founder and chairman of Nike, Inc., the multi-billion dollar shoe and fitness company founded in 1972 and based in Beaverton, Ore.; stable of endorsees includes Michael Jordan, Tiger Woods and Brazilian soccer phenom Ronaldo; named "The Most Powerful Man in Sports" by *The Sporting News* in 1992.

Bill Koch (b. June 7, 1955): Cross-country skiing; first highly accomplished American male in his sport; first American male to win a cross-country Olympic medal when he took home a silver in the 30-kilometer race in 1976; in 1982, he was the first American male to win the Nordic World Cup.

Olga Korbut (b. May 16, 1955): Soviet gymnast; 3 gold medals at 1972 Olympics; first to perform back somersault on balance beam.

Johann Olav Koss (b. Oct. 29, 1968): Norwegian speedskater; won three gold medals at 1994 Olympics in Lillehammer with world records in the 1,500m, 5,000m and 10,000m; also won 1,500m gold and 10,000m silver in 1992 Games; retired shortly after '94 Olympics.

Sandy Koufax (b. Dec. 30, 1935): Baseball LHP; led NL in strikeouts 4 times and ERA 5 straight years; won 3 Cy Young Awards (1963,65,66) with LA Dodgers; MVP in 1963; 2-time World Series MVP (1963, 65); threw perfect game against Chicago Cubs (1-0, Sept. 9, 1965) and had 3 other no-hitters in 1962, '63 and '64.

Alvin Kraenzlein (b. Dec. 12, 1876, d. Jan. 6, 1928): Track & Field; won 4 individual gold medals in 1900 Olympics (60m, long jump and the 110m and 200m hurdles).

Ingrid Kristiansen (b. Mar. 21, 1956): Norwegian runner; 2-time Boston Marathon winner (1986,89); won New York City Marathon in 1989; entered 1998 as world record holder in the marathon.

Julie Krone (b. July 24, 1963): Jockey; only woman to ride winning horse in a Triple Crown race when she captured Belmont Stakes aboard Colonial Affair in 1993; entered 1998 as all-time winningest female jockey with over 3,000 wins.

Mike Krzyzewski (b. Feb. 13, 1947): Basketball; has coached Duke to 7 Final Four appearances; won consecutive NCAA titles in 1991 and '92; missed most of 1994-95 season with a back injury and stress-related exhaustion; 23-year record of 505-212.

Bowie Kuhn (b. Oct. 28, 1926): Baseball Commissioner; Elected commissioner on Feb. 4, 1969 and served until Sept. 30, 1984; kept Willie Mays and Mickey Mantle out of baseball for their employment with casinos; handed down one-year suspensions of several players for drug involvement; nixed Charlie Finley's sale of three players for $3.5 million; baseball enjoyed unprecedented attendance and television contracts during his reign.

Alan Kulwicki (b. Dec. 14, 1954, d. Apr. 1, 1993): Auto racer; 1992 NASCAR national champion; 1st college grad and Northerner to win title; NASCAR Rookie of Year in 1986; famous for driving car backwards on victory lap; killed at age 38 in plane crash near Bristol, Tenn.

Michelle Kwan (b. July 7, 1980): Figure Skater; 1998 Olympic silver medalist at Nagano; U.S. and World Champion in 1996 and 1998; was U.S. alternate to the Olympics in 1994 as a 13-year-old.

Marion Ladewig (b. Oct. 30, 1914): Bowler; named Woman Bowler of the Year 9 times (1950-54,57-59,63).

Guy Lafleur (b. Sept. 20, 1951): Hockey RW; led NHL in scoring 3 times (1976-78); 2-time MVP (1977-78), played for 5 Stanley Cup winners in Montreal; playoff MVP in 1977; returned to NHL as player in 1988 after election to Hall of Fame; retired again in 1991 with 560 goals and 1,353 points.

Napoleon (Nap) Lajoie (b. Sept. 5, 1874, d. Feb. 7, 1959): Baseball 2B; led AL in batting 3 times (1901,03-04); batted .422 in 1901; hit .339 for career with 3,251 hits.

Jack Lambert (b. July 8, 1952): Football LB; 6-time All-Pro (1975-76,79-82); led Pittsburgh to 4 Super Bowl titles.

Kenesaw Mountain Landis (b. Nov. 20, 1866, d. Nov. 25, 1944): U.S. District Court judge who became first baseball commissioner (1920-44); banned eight Chicago Black Sox from baseball for life.

Tom Landry (b. Sept. 11, 1924): Football; All-Pro DB for NY Giants (1954); coached Dallas for 29 years (1960-88); won 2 Super Bowls (1972,78); 3rd on NFL all-time list with 270 wins.

Steve Largent (b. Sept. 28, 1954): Football WR; retired in 1989 after 14 years in Seattle with then NFL records in passes caught (819) and TD passes caught (100); elected to U.S. House of Representatives (R, Okla.) in 1994 and Pro Football Hall of Fame in '95.

Don Larsen (b. Aug. 7, 1929): Baseball RHP; NY Yankees hurler who pitched the only perfect game in World Series history— a 2-0 victory over Brooklyn in Game 5 of the 1956 Series (Oct. 8); Series MVP that year; had career record of 81-91 in 14 seasons with 6 clubs.

Tommy Lasorda (b. Sept. 22, 1927): Baseball; managed LA Dodgers to 2 World Series titles (1981,88) in 4 appearances; retired as manager during 1996 season with 1,599 regular-season wins in 21 years; named interim GM of Dodgers in 1998; member of Baseball Hall of Fame.

Larissa Latynina (b. Dec. 27, 1934): Soviet gymnast; won total of 18 medals, (9 gold) in 3 Olympics (1956,60,64).

Nikki Lauda (b. Feb. 22, 1949): Austrian auto racer; 3-time world Formula One champion (1975,77,84); 25 career wins from 1971-85.

Rod Laver (b. Aug. 9, 1938): Australian tennis player; only player to win Grand Slam twice (1962,69); Wimbledon champion 4 times; 1st to earn $1 million in prize money.

Andrea Mead Lawrence (b. Apr. 19, 1932): Alpine skier; won 2 gold medals at 1952 Olympics.

Bobby Layne (b. Dec. 19, 1926, d. Dec. 1, 1986): Football QB; college star at Texas; master of 2-minute offense; led Detroit to 4 divisional titles and 3 NFL championships in 1950s.

Frank Leahy (b. Aug. 27, 1908, d. June 21, 1973): Football; coached Notre Dame to four national titles (1943,46-47,49); career record of 107-13-9 for a winning pct. of .864.

Brian Leetch (b. Mar. 3, 1968): Hockey D; NHL Rookie of Year in 1989; won Norris Trophy as top defenseman in 1992; Conn Smythe Trophy winner as playoffs' MVP in 1994 when he helped lead NY Rangers to 1st Stanley Cup title in 54 years.

Jacques Lemaire (b. Sept. 7, 1945): Hockey C; member of 8 Stanley Cup champions in Montreal; scored 366 goals in 12 seasons; coached Canadiens from 1983-85; directed New Jersey Devils to surprising 4-game sweep of Detroit to win 1995 Stanley Cup.

Claude Lemieux (b. July 16, 1965): Hockey RW; member of Stanley Cup championship teams in Montreal (1986), New Jersey (1995) and Colorado (1996); playoff MVP with Devils in '95 and Colorado in 96; no relation to Mario.

Mario Lemieux (b. Oct. 5, 1965): Hockey C; 6-time NHL scoring leader (1988-89,92-93,96,97); Rookie of Year (1985); 4-time All-NHL 1st team (1988-89,93,96); 3-time regular season MVP (1988,93,96); 3-time All-Star Game MVP; led Pittsburgh to consecutive Stanley Cup titles (1991 and '92) and was playoff MVP both years; won 1993 scoring title despite missing 24 games to undergo radiation treatments for Hodgkin's disease; missed 62 games during 1993-94 season and entire 94-95 season due to back injuries and fatigue; returned in 1995-96 to lead NHL in scoring and win the MVP trophy; retired after 1996-97 season and inducted into the Hall of Fame.

Greg LeMond (b. June 26, 1961): Cyclist; 3-time Tour de France winner (1986,89-90); only non-European to win the event; retired in Dec. 1994 after being diagnosed with a rare muscular disease known as mitochondrial myopathy.

Ivan Lendl (b. Mar. 7, 1960): Czech tennis player; No.1 player in world 4 times (1985-87,89); has won both French and U.S. Opens 3 times and Australian twice; owns 94 career tournament wins.

Suzanne Lenglen (b. May 24, 1899, d. July 4, 1938): French tennis player; dominated women's tennis from 1919-26; won both Wimbledon and French singles titles 6 times.

Sugar Ray Leonard (b. May 17, 1956): Boxer; light welterweight Olympic champ (1976); won world welterweight title 1979 and four more titles; retired after losing to Terry Norris on Feb. 9, 1991, with record of 36-2-1 and 25 KOs; misguided comeback in 1997 resulted in resounding defeat by Hector Camacho.

Marv Levy (b. Aug. 3, 1928): Football; coached Buffalo to four consecutive Super Bowls, but is one of two coaches who are 0-4 (Bud Grant is the other); won 50 games and two CFL Grey Cups with Montreal (1974,77).

Carl Lewis (b. July 1, 1961): Track & Field; won 9 Olympic gold medals; 4 in 1984 (100m, 200m, 4x100m, LJ), 2 in '88 (100m, LJ), 2 in '92 (4x100m, LJ) and 1 in '96 (LJ); has record 8 World Championship titles and 9 medals in all; Sullivan Award winner (1981); two-time AP Male Athlete of the Year (1983-84).

Nancy Lieberman-Cline (b. July 1, 1958): Basketball; 3-time All-America and 2-time Player of Year (1979-80); led Old Dominion to consecutive AIAW titles in 1979 and '80; played in defunct WPBL and WABA and became 1st woman to play in men's pro league (USBL) in 1986; played in the inaugural season of the WNBA for the Phoenix Mercury and named coach/GM of Detroit Shock in '98.

Eric Lindros (b. Feb. 28, 1973): Hockey C; No. 1 pick in 1991 NHL draft by the Nordiques; sat out 1991-92 season rather than play in Quebec; traded to Philadelphia in 1992 for 6 players, 2 No. 1 picks and $15 million; elected Flyers captain at age 22; won Hart Trophy as league MVP in 1995.

Tara Lipinski (b. June 10, 1982): Figure Skater; won the 1998 women's figure skating gold medal at the Olympics in Nagano, becoming the youngest in history (15 yrs., 7 mos.) to do so; she and Michelle Kwan gave the U.S. its first 1-2 finish in that event since 1956; 1997 U.S. and World champion; turned pro in April 1998.

Sonny Liston (b. May 8, 1932, d. Dec. 30, 1970): Boxer; heavyweight champion (1962-64), who knocked out Floyd Patterson twice in the first round, then lost title to Muhammad Ali (then Cassius Clay) in 1964; pro record of 50-4 with 39 KOs.

Rebecca Lobo (b. Oct. 6, 1973): Basketball F; women's college basketball Player of the Year in 1995; led Connecticut to undefeated season (35-0) and national title; member of 1996 U.S. Olympic team; helped lead NY Liberty to WNBA's first championship game in 1997 but lost to Houston Comets.

Vince Lombardi (b. June 11, 1913, d. Sept. 3, 1970): Football; coached Green Bay to 5 NFL titles; won first 2 Super Bowls (1967-68); died as NFL's all-time winningest coach with percentage of .740 (105-35-6); Super Bowl trophy named in his honor.

Johnny Longden (b. Feb. 14, 1907): Jockey; first to win 6,000 races; rode Count Fleet to Triple Crown in 1943.

Nancy Lopez (b. Jan. 6, 1957): Golfer; 4-time LPGA Player of the Year (1978-79,85,88); Rookie of Year (1977); 3-time winner of LPGA Championship; reached Hall of Fame by age 30 with 35 victories; entered 1998 with 48 career wins.

Donna Lopiano (b. Sept. 11, 1946): Former basketball and softball star who was women's athletic director at Texas for 18 years before leaving to become executive director of Women's Sports Foundation in 1992.

Greg Louganis (b. Jan. 29, 1960): U.S. diver; won platform and springboard gold medals at both 1984 and '88 Olympics; revealed on Feb. 22, 1995 that he has AIDS.

Joe Louis (b. May 13, 1914, d. Apr. 12, 1981): Boxer; world heavyweight champion from June 22, 1937 to Mar. 1, 1949; his reign of 11 years, 8 months longest in division history; successfully defended title 25 times; retired in 1949, but returned to lose title shot against successor Ezzard Charles in 1950 and then to Rocky Marciano in '51; pro record of 63-3 with 49 KOs.

Sid Luckman (b. Nov. 21, 1916, d. July 5, 1998): Football QB; 6-time All-Pro; led Chicago Bears to 4 NFL titles (1940-41,43,46); MVP in 1943.

Hank Luisetti (b. June 16, 1916): Basketball F; 3-time All-America at Stanford (1935-38); revolutionized game with one-handed shot.

Johnny Lujack (b. Jan. 4, 1925): Football QB; led Notre Dame to three national titles (1943,46-47); won Heisman Trophy in 1947.

Darrell Wayne Lukas (b. Sept. 2, 1935): Horse racing; 4-time Eclipse-winning trainer who saddled Horses of Year Lady's Secret in 1988 and Criminal Type in 1990; first trainer to earn over $100 million in purses; led nation in earnings 11 times from 1983-94; Grindstone's Kentucky Derby win in 1996 gave him six Triple Crown wins in a row; has won Preakness four times and Kentucky Derby and Belmont three times.

Gen. Douglas MacArthur (b. Jan. 26, 1880, d. Apr. 5, 1964): Controversial U.S. general of World War II and Korea; president of U.S. Olympic Committee (1927-28); college football devotee, National Football Foundation MacArthur Bowl (for No.1 team) named after him.

Connie Mack (b. Dec. 22, 1862, d. Feb. 8, 1956): Baseball owner; managed Philadelphia A's until he was 87 (1901-50); all-time major league wins leader with 3,755, including World Series; won 9 AL pennants and 5 World Series (1910-11,13,29-30); also finished last 17 times.

Andy MacPhail (b. Apr. 5, 1953): Baseball; Chicago Cubs president, who was GM of 2 World Series champions in Minnesota (1987,91); won first title at age 34; son of Lee, grandson of Larry.

Larry MacPhail (b. Feb. 3, 1890, d. Oct. 1, 1975): Baseball executive and innovator; introduced major leagues to night games at Cincinnati (May 24, 1935); won pennant in Brooklyn (1941) and World Series with NY Yankees (1947); father of Lee.

Lee MacPhail (b. Oct. 25, 1917): Baseball; AL president (1974-83); president of owners' Player Relations Committee (1984-85); also GM of Baltimore (1959-65) and NY Yankees (1967-74); son of Larry and father of Andy.

John Madden (b. Apr. 10, 1936): Football and Radio-TV; won 112 games and a Super Bowl (1976 season) as coach of Oakland Raiders; has won 10 Emmy Awards since 1982 as NFL analyst with CBS and Fox; signed 4-year, $32 million deal with Fox in 1994— a richer contract than any NFL player at the time.

Greg Maddux (b. Apr. 14, 1966): Baseball RHP; won unprecedented 4 straight NL Cy Young Awards with Cubs (1992) and Atlanta (1993-95); led NL in ERA three times (1993-95) entering 1998.

Larry Mahan (b. Nov. 21, 1943): Rodeo; 6-time All-Around world champion (1966-70,73).

Phil Mahre (b. May 10, 1957): Alpine skier; 3-time World Cup overall champ (1981-83); finished 1-2 with twin brother Steve in 1984 Olympic slalom.

Karl Malone (b. July 24, 1963): Basketball F; 10-time All-NBA 1st team (1989-98) with Utah; member of the 1992 and '96 Olympic Dream Teams; league MVP in 1997; named one of the NBA's 50 greatest players.

Moses Malone (b. Mar. 23, 1955): Basketball C; signed with Utah of ABA at age 19; led NBA in rebounding 6 times; 4-time All-NBA 1st team; 3-time NBA MVP (1979,82-83); Finals MVP with Philadelphia in 1983; played in 21st pro season in 1994-95.

Nigel Mansell (b. Aug. 8, 1953): British auto racer; won 1992 Formula One driving championship with record 9 victories and 14 poles; quit Grand Prix circuit to race Indy cars in 1993; 1st rookie to win IndyCar title; 3rd driver to win IndyCar and F1 titles; returned to F1 after 1994 IndyCar season and won '94 Australian Grand Prix; left F1 again on May 23, 1995 with 31 wins and 32 poles in 15 years.

Mickey Mantle (b. Oct. 20, 1931, d. Aug. 13, 1995): Baseball OF; named after Hall of Fame catcher Mickey Cochrane; led AL in home runs 4 times; won Triple Crown in 1956; hit 52 HRs in 1956 and 54 in '61; 3-time MVP (1956-57,62); hit 536 career HRs; played in 12 World Series with NY Yankees and won 7 times; all-time Series leader in HRs (18), RBI (40), runs (42) and strikeouts (54).

Diego Maradona (b. Oct. 30, 1960): Soccer F; captain and MVP of 1986 World Cup champion Argentina; also led national team to 1990 World Cup final; consensus Player of Decade in 1980s; led Napoli to 2 Italian League titles (1987,90) and UEFA Cup (1989); tested positive for cocaine and suspended 15 months by FIFA in 1991; returned to World Cup as Argentine captain in 1994, but was kicked out of tournament after two games when doping test found 5 banned substances in his urine.

Pete Maravich (b. June 27, 1947, d. Jan. 5, 1988): Basketball; NCAA scoring leader 3 times at LSU (1968-70); averaged NCAA-record 44.2 points a game over career; Player of Year in 1970; NBA scoring champ in '77 with New Orleans.

Alice Marble (b. Sept. 28, 1913, d. Dec. 13, 1990): Tennis; 4-time U.S. champion (1936,38-40); won Wimbledon in 1939; swept U.S. singles, doubles and mixed doubles from 1938-40.

Rocky Marciano (b. Sept. 1, 1923, d. Aug. 31, 1969): Boxer; heavyweight champion (1952-56); retired undefeated; pro record of 49-0 with 43 KOs; killed in plane crash in Iowa.

Juan Marichal (b. Oct. 20, 1938): Baseball RHP; won 21 or more games 6 times for S.F. Giants from 1963-69; ended 16-year career at 243-142.

Dan Marino (b. Sept. 15, 1961): Football QB; 4-time leading passer in AFC (1983-84,86,89); set NFL single-season records for TD passes (48) and passing yards (5,084) with Miami in 1984; all-time leader in career TD passes, passing yards, attempts and completions.

Roger Maris (b. Sept. 10, 1934, d. Dec. 14, 1985): Baseball OF; broke Babe Ruth's season HR record with 61 in 1961; 2-time AL MVP (1960-61) with NY Yankees; 275 HRs in 12 years.

Billy Martin (b. May 16, 1928, d. Dec. 25, 1989): Baseball; 5-time manager of NY Yankees; won 2 pennants and 1 World Series (1977); also managed Minnesota, Detroit, Texas and Oakland; played on 5 Yankee world champions in 1950s.

Casey Martin (b. June 2, 1972): Golfer; Rookie on the Nike Tour in 1998; suffers from a birth defect in his right leg known as Klippel-Trenauney-Webber Syndrome; won lawsuit against the PGA Tour for the right to use a golf cart during competition under the Americans with Disabilities Act; took first place at his first Nike Tour event, the Lakeland Classic, with a final round 69.

Christy Martin (b. June 12, 1968): Boxing; Lightweight women's champion; known as "the Coal Miner's Daughter"; captured title Jan. 13, 1996.

Eddie Mathews (b. Oct. 13, 1931): Baseball 3B; led NL in HRs twice (1953,59); hit 30 or more home runs 9 straight years; 512 career HRs.

Christy Mathewson (b. Aug. 12, 1880, d. Oct. 7, 1925): Baseball RHP; won 22 or more games 12 straight years (1903-14); 373 career wins; pitched 3 shutouts in 1905 World Series.

Bob Mathias (b. Nov. 17, 1930): Track & Field; youngest winner of decathlon with gold medal in 1948 Olympics at age 17; first to repeat as decathlon champ in 1952; Sullivan Award winner (1948); 4-term member of U.S. Congress (R, Calif.) from 1967-74.

Ollie Matson (b. May 1, 1930): Football HB; All-America at San Francisco (1951); bronze medal winner in 400m at 1952 Olympics; 4-time All-Pro for NFL Chicago Cardinals (1954-57); traded to LA Rams for 9 players in 1959; accounted for 12,884 all-purpose yards and scored 73 TDs in 14 seasons.

Don Mattingly (b. Apr. 20, 1961): Baseball 1B; American League MVP (1985); won AL batting title in 1984 (.343) and led AL with 207 hits and 44 doubles; led majors with 145 RBI in 1985; led AL with 238 hits (Yankee record), 53 doubles and a .573 slugging percentage in 1986; won 9 Gold Glove Awards (1985-89, 91-94); Back injury shortened career.

Willie Mays (b. May 6, 1931): Baseball OF; nicknamed the "Say Hey Kid"; led NL in HRs and stolen bases 4 times each; 2-time MVP (1954,65) with NY-SF Giants; Hall of Famer who played in 24 All-Star Games; 660 HRs and 3,283 hits in career.

Bill Mazeroski (b. Sept. 5, 1936): Baseball 2B; career .260 hitter who won the 1960 World Series for Pittsburgh with a lead-off HR in the bottom of the 9th inning of Game 7; the pitcher was Ralph Terry of the NY Yankees, the count was 1-0 and the score was tied 9-9; also a sure-fielder, Maz won 8 Gold Gloves in 17 seasons.

Bob McAdoo (b. Sept. 25, 1951): Basketball F/C; 1972 *Sporting News* First Team All-American; NBA Rookie of the Year (1973); NBA MVP (1975); All-NBA First Team (1975); Led NBA in scoring three consecutive years (1974-76); Played in five NBA All-Star games (1974-78); two championships with Los Angeles Lakers (1982,85).

Joe McCarthy (b. Apr. 21, 1887, d. Jan. 13, 1978): Baseball; first manager to win pennants in both leagues (Chicago Cubs in 1929 and NY Yankees in 1932); greatest success came with Yankees when he won seven pennants and six World Series championships from 1936 to 1943; first manager to win four World Series in a row (1936-39); finished his career with the Boston Red Sox (1948-'50); lifetime record of 2125-1333; member of Baseball Hall of Fame.

Mark McCormack (b. Nov. 6, 1930): Founder and CEO of International Management Group (IMG), the sports management conglomerate which represents, among others, Joe Montana, Wayne Gretzky, Arnold Palmer, Andre Agassi and Pete Sampras.

Pat McCormick (b. May 12, 1930): U.S. diver; won women's platform and springboard gold medals in both 1952 and '56 Olympics.

Willie McCovey (b. Jan. 10, 1938): Baseball 1B; led NL in HRs 3 times and RBI twice; MVP in 1969 with SF; 521 career HRs; indicted for tax evasion in July 1995, pled guilty.

John McEnroe (b. Feb. 16, 1959): Tennis; No.1 player in the world 4 times (1981-84); 4-time U.S. Open singles champ (1979-81,84); 3-time Wimbledon champ (1981,83-84); has played on 5 Davis Cup winners (1978-79,81-82,92); won NCAA singles title (1978); finished career with 77 championships in singles, 77 more in men's doubles (including 9 Grand Slam titles), and U.S. Davis Cup records for years played (13) and singles matches won (41).

John McGraw (b. Apr. 7, 1873, d. Feb. 25, 1934): Baseball; managed NY Giants to 9 NL pennants between 1905-24; won 3 World Series (1905,21-22); 2nd on all-time career list with 2,810 wins in 33 seasons (2,784 regular season and 26 World Series).

Frank McGuire (b. Nov. 8, 1916, d. Oct. 11, 1994): Basketball; winner of 731 games as high school, college and pro coach; only coach to win 100 games at 3 colleges— St. John's (103), North Carolina (164) and South Carolina (283); won 550 games in 30 college seasons; 1957 UNC team went 32-0 and beat Kansas 54-53 in triple OT to win NCAA title; coached NBA Philadelphia Warriors to 49-31 record in 1961-62 season, but refused to move with team to San Francisco.

Mark McGwire (b. Oct. 1, 1963): Baseball 1B; *Sporting News* college player of the year (1984); Member of 1984 U.S. Olympic baseball team; won AL Rookie of the Year and hit rookie-record 49 HRs in 1987; broke Roger Maris' season home run record (61) 1998 with St. Louis; only player with at least 50 HRs in 3 straight seasons.

Jim McKay (b. Sept. 24, 1921): Radio-TV; host and commentator of ABC's Olympic coverage and "Wide World of Sports" show since 1961; 12-time Emmy winner; also given Peabody Award in 1988 and Life Achievement Emmy in 1990; became part owner of Baltimore Orioles in 1993.

John McKay (b. July 5, 1923): Football; coached USC to 3 national titles (1962,67,72); won Rose Bowl 5 times; reached NFL playoffs 3 times with Tampa Bay.

Tamara McKinney (b. Oct. 16, 1962): Skiing; only American woman to win overall Alpine World Cup championship (1983); won World Cup slalom (1984) and giant slalom titles twice (1981,83).

Denny McLain (b. Mar. 29, 1944): Baseball RHP; last pitcher to win 30 games (1968); 2-time Cy Young winner (1968-69) with Detroit; convicted of racketeering, extortion and drug possession in 1985, served 29 months of 25-year jail term, sentence overturned when court ruled he had not received a fair trial; he has faced subsequent legal troubles.

Rick Mears (b. Dec. 3, 1951): Auto racer; 3-time CART national champ (1979,81-82); 4-time winner of Indianapolis 500 (1979,84,88,91) and only driver to win 6 Indy 500 poles; Indy 500 Rookie of Year (1978); retired after 1992 season with 29 IndyCar wins and 40 poles.

Mark Messier (b. Jan. 18, 1961): Hockey C; 2-time Hart Trophy winner as MVP with Edmonton (1990) and NY Rangers (1992); captain of 1994 Rangers team that won 1st Stanley Cup since 1940; ranks 2nd (behind Gretzky) in all-time playoff points and assists; signed free agent contract with Vancouver Canucks in 1997.

Anne Meyers (b. Mar. 26, 1955): Basketball G; In 1974, became first high school student to play for U.S. national team; 4-time All-American at UCLA (1976-79); member of 1976 U.S. Olympic team; Broderick Award and Cup winner (1978); Signed $50,000 no cut contract with NBA's Indiana Pacers (1980); married Dodger all-time great Don Drysdale.

George Mikan (b. June 18, 1924): Basketball C; 3-time All-America (1944-46); led DePaul to NIT title (1945); led Minneapolis Lakers to 5 NBA titles in 6 years (1949-54); first commissioner of ABA (1967-69).

Stan Mikita (b. May 20, 1940): Hockey C; led NHL in scoring 4 times; won both MVP and Lady Byng awards in 1967 and '68 with Chicago.

Cheryl Miller (b. Jan. 3, 1964): Basketball; 3-time College Player of Year (1984-86); led USC to NCAA title and U.S. to Olympic gold medal in 1984; coached USC to 44-14 record in 2 seasons before quitting to join Turner Sports as NBA reporter; coach/GM of WNBA's Phoenix Mercury.

Del Miller (b. July 5, 1913): Harness racing; driver, trainer, owner, breeder, seller and track owner; drove to 2,441 wins from 1939-90.

Marvin Miller (b. Apr. 14, 1917): Baseball labor leader; executive director of Players' Assn. from 1966-82; increased average salary from $19,000 to over $240,000; led 13-day strike in 1972 and 50-day walkout in '81.

Tommy Moe (b. Feb. 17, 1970): Alpine skier; won Downhill and placed 2nd in Super-G at 1994 Winter Olympics; 1st U.S. man to win 2 Olympic alpine medals in one year.

Paul Molitor (b. Aug. 22, 1956): Baseball DH-1B; All-America SS at Minnesota in 1976; signed as free agent by Toronto in 1992, after 15 years with Milwaukee; led Blue Jays to 2nd straight World Series title as MVP (1993); hit .418 in 2 Series appearances (1982,93); holds World Series record with five hits in one game; got career hit 3,000 with a triple on Sept. 16, 1996.

Joe Montana (b. June 11, 1956): Football QB; led Notre Dame to national title in 1977; led San Francisco to 4 Super Bowl titles in 1980s; only 3-time Super Bowl MVP; 2-time NFL MVP (1989-90); led NFL in passing 5 times; missed all of 1991 season and nearly all of '92 after elbow surgery; traded to Kansas City in 1993; ranks 2nd in all-time passing efficiency (92.3), 6th in TD passes (273) and yards passing (40,551).

Helen Wills Moody (b. Oct. 6, 1905, d. Jan. 1, 1998): Tennis; won 8 Wimbledon singles titles, 7 U.S. and 4 French from 1923-38.

Warren Moon (b. Nov. 18, 1956): Football QB; MVP of 1978 Rose Bowl with Washington; MVP of CFL with Edmonton in 1983; led Eskimos to 5 consecutive Grey Cup titles (1978-82) and was playoff MVP twice (1980,82); joined Houston of NFL in 1984; led NFL in attempts, completions and yards in 1990 and '91; picked for 8 Pro Bowls.

Archie Moore (b. Dec. 13, 1913): Boxer; world light-heavyweight champion (1952-60); pro record 199-26-8 with 145 KOs.

Michael Moorer (b. Nov. 12, 1967): Boxer; became 1st left-hander to win heavyweight title when he scored majority decision over Evander Holyfield on Apr. 22, 1994; lost title to George Foreman on 10th round KO Nov. 5, 1994; pro record of 37-1 with 30 KOs.

Noureddine Morceli (b. Feb. 28, 1970): Algerian runner; 3-time world champion at 1,500 meters (1991,93, 95); holder of world records in several middle distance events.

Howie Morenz (b. June 21, 1902, d. Mar. 8, 1937): Hockey C; 3-time NHL MVP (1928,31-32); led Montreal Canadiens to 3 Stanley Cups; voted Outstanding Player of the Half-Century in 1950.

Joe Morgan (b. Sept. 19, 1943): Baseball 2B; led NL in walks 4 times; regular-season MVP both years he led Cincinnati to World Series titles (1975-76); 3rd behind Babe Ruth and Ted Williams in career walks with 1,865.

Bobby Morrow (b. Oct. 15, 1935): Track & Field; won 3 gold medals at 1956 Olympics (100m, 200m and 4x400m relay).

Willie Mosconi (b. June 27, 1913, d. Sept. 12, 1993): Pocket Billiards; 14-time world champion from 1941-57.

Annemarie Moser-Pröll (b. Mar. 27, 1953): Austrian alpine skier; won World Cup overall title 6 times (1971-75,79); all-time women's World Cup leader in career wins with 61; won Downhill in 1980 Olympics.

Edwin Moses (b. Aug. 31, 1955): Track & Field; won 400m hurdles at 1976 and '84 Olympics, bronze medal in '88; also winner of 122 consecutive races from 1977-87.

Marion Motley (b. June 5, 1920): Football FB; all-time leading AAFC rusher; rushed for over 4,700 yards and 31 TDs for Cleveland Browns (1946-53).

Calvin Murphy (b. May 9, 1948): Basketball G; NBA All-Rookie team (1971); holds NBA single season free throw percentage (.958); third all-time career free throw pct. (.892); elected to Basketball Hall of Fame in 1992; though only 5'9" and 165 pounds, he is regarded as one of the best guards ever.

Dale Murphy (b. Mar. 12, 1956): Baseball OF; led NL in RBI 3 times and HRs twice; 2-time MVP (1982-83) with Atlanta; also played with Philadelphia and Colorado; retired in 1993 with 398 HRs.

Jack Murphy (b. Feb. 5, 1923, d. Sept. 24, 1980): Sports editor and columnist of *The San Diego Union* from 1951-80; instrumental in bringing AFL Chargers south from LA in 1961, landing Padres as NL expansion team in '69; and lobbying for 54,000-seat San Diego stadium that would later bear his name.

Eddie Murray (b. Feb. 24, 1956): Baseball 1B-DH; AL Rookie of Year in 1977; became 20th player in history, but only 2nd switch hitter (after Pete Rose) to get 3,000 hits; belted 500th homer off Detroit's Felipe Lira on Sept. 6, 1996.

Jim Murray (b. Dec. 29, 1919, d. Aug. 16, 1998): Sports columnist for *LA Times* 1961-98; 14-time Sportswriter of the Year; won Pulitzer Prize for commentary in 1990.

Ty Murray (b. Oct. 11, 1969): Rodeo cowboy; 6-time All-Around world champion (1989-94); Rookie of Year in 1988; youngest (age 20) to win All-Around title; set single season earnings mark with $297,896 in 1993; career shortened by injury.

Stan Musial (b. Nov. 21, 1920): Baseball OF-1B; led NL in batting 7 times; 3-time MVP (1943,46,48) with St. Louis; played in 24 All-Star Games; had 3,630 career hits and .331 average.

John Naber (b. Jan. 20, 1956): Swimmer; won 4 gold medals and a silver in 1976 Olympics.

Bronko Nagurski (b. Nov. 3, 1908, d. Jan. 7, 1990): Football FB-T; All-America at Minnesota (1929); All-Pro with Chicago Bears (1932-34); charter member of college and pro Halls of Fame.

James Naismith (b. Nov. 6, 1861, d. Nov. 28, 1939): Canadian physical education instructor who invented basketball in 1891 at the YMCA Training School (now Springfield College) in Springfield, Mass.

Joe Namath (b. May 31, 1943): Football QB; signed for unheard-of $400,000 as rookie with AFL's NY Jets in 1965; 2-time All-AFL (1968-69) and All-NFL (1972); led Jets to Super Bowl upset as MVP in '69.

Ilie Nastase (b. July 19, 1946): Romanian tennis player; No.1 in the world twice (1972-73); won U.S. (1972) and French (1973) Opens; has since entered Romanian politics.

Martina Navratilova (b. Oct. 18, 1956): Tennis player; No.1 player in the world 7 times (1978-79,82-86); won her record 9th Wimbledon singles title in 1990; also won 4 U.S. Opens, 3 Australian and 2 French; in all, won 18 Grand Slam singles titles and 37 Grand Slam doubles titles; retired as all-time leader among men and women in singles titles (167) and money won ($20.3 million) over 21 years.

Cosmas Ndeti (b. Nov. 24, 1971): Kenyan distance runner; winner of three consecutive Boston Marathons (1993-95), set course record of 2:07:15 in 1994.

Earle (Greasy) Neale (b. Nov. 5, 1891, d. Nov. 2, 1973): Baseball and Football; hit .357 for Cincinnati in 1919 World Series; also played with pre-NFL Canton Bulldogs; later coached Philadelphia Eagles to 2 NFL titles (1948-49).

Primo Nebiolo (b. July 14, 1923): Italian president of International Amateur Athletic Federation (IAAF) since 1981; also an at-large member of International Olympic Committee; regarded as dictatorial, but credited with elevating track & field to world class financial status.

Byron Nelson (b. Feb. 4, 1912): Golfer; 2-time winner of both Masters (1937,42) and PGA (1940,45); also U.S. Open champion in 1939; won 19 tournaments in 1945, including 11 in a row; also set all-time PGA stroke average with 68.33 strokes per round over 120 rounds in '45.

Lindsey Nelson (b. May 25, 1919, d. June 10, 1995): Radio-TV; all-purpose play-by-play broadcaster for CBS, NBC and others; 4-time Sportscaster of the Year (1959-62); voice of Cotton Bowl for 25 years and NY Mets from 1962-78; given Life Achievement Emmy Award in 1991.

Ernie Nevers (b. July 11, 1903, d. May 3, 1976): Football FB; earned 11 letters in four sports at Stanford; played pro football, baseball and basketball; scored 40 points for Chicago Cardinals in one NFL game (1929).

Paula Newby-Fraser (b. June 2, 1962): Zimbabwean triathlete; 8-time winner of Ironman Triathlon in Hawaii; established women's record of 8:55:28 in 1992.

John Newcombe (b. May 23, 1944): Australian tennis player; No.1 player in world 3 times (1967,70-71); won Wimbledon 3 times and U.S. and Australian championships twice each.

Pete Newell (b. Aug. 31, 1915): Basketball; coached at Univ. of San Francisco, Michigan St. and the Univ. of California; first coach to win NIT (San Francisco-1949), NCAA (California-1959) and Olympic gold medal (1960); later served as the general manager of the San Diego Rockets and LA Lakers in the NBA; member of Basketball Hall of Fame.

Bob Neyland (b. Feb. 17, 1892, d. Mar. 28, 1962): Football; 3-time coach at Tennessee; had 173-31-12 record in 21 years; won national title in 1951; Vols' stadium named for him; also Army general who won Distinguished Service Cross as supply officer in World War II.

Jack Nicklaus (b. Jan. 21, 1940): Golfer; all-time leader in major tournament wins with 20— including 6 Masters, 5 PGAs, 4 U.S. Opens and 3 British Opens; oldest player to win Masters (46 in 1986); PGA Player of Year 5 times (1967,72-73,75-76); named Golfer of the Century by PGA in 1988; 6-time Ryder Cup player and 2-time captain (1983,87); won NCAA title (1961) and 2 U.S. Amateurs (1959,61); 70 PGA Tour wins (2nd to Sam Snead's 81); third win in Tradition in 1995 gave him 7 majors in 6 years on Senior PGA Tour; nicknamed "the Golden Bear".

Chuck Noll (b. Jan. 5, 1932): Football; coached Pittsburgh to 4 Super Bowl titles (1975-76,79-80); retired after 1991 season ranked 5th on all-time list with 209 wins (including playoffs) in 23 years.

Greg Norman (b. Feb. 10, 1955): Australian golfer; PGA Tour's all-time money winner ($11.9 million), passing Tom Kite on Aug. 27, 1995; 73 tournament wins worldwide; 2-time British Open winner (1986,93); lost Masters by a stroke in both 1986 (to Jack Nicklaus) and '87 (to Larry Mize in sudden death).

James D. Norris (b. Nov. 6, 1906, d. Feb. 25, 1966): Boxing promoter and NHL owner; president of International Boxing Club from 1949 until U.S. Supreme Court ordered its break-up (for anti-trust violations) in 1958; only NHL owner to win Stanley Cups in two cities: Detroit (1936-37,43) and Chicago (1961).

Paavo Nurmi (b. June 13, 1897, d. Oct. 2, 1973): Finnish runner; won 9 gold medals (6 individual) in 1920, '24 and '28 Olympics; from 1921-31 broke 23 world outdoor records in events ranging from 1,500 to 20,000 meters.

Dan O'Brien (b. July 18, 1966): Track & Field; Olympic decathlon gold medalist (1996); set world record in decathlon (8,891 pts) on Sept. 4-5, 1992, after shockingly failing to qualify for event at U.S. Olympic Trials; three-time gold medalist at World Championships (1991,93,95).

Larry O'Brien (b. July 7, 1917, d. Sept. 27, 1990): Basketball; former U.S. Postmaster General and 3rd NBA commissioner (1975-84), league absorbed 4 ABA teams and created salary cap during his term in office.

Al Oerter (b. Sept. 19, 1936): Track & Field; his 4 discus gold medals in consecutive Olympics from 1956-68 is an unmatched Olympic record.

Sadaharu Oh (b. May 20, 1940): Baseball 1B; led Japan League in HRs 15 times; 9-time MVP for Tokyo Giants; hit 868 HRs in 22 years.

Hakeem Olajuwon (b. Jan. 21, 1963): Basketball C; Nigerian native who was consensus All-America in 1984 and Final Four MOP in 1983 for Houston; overall 1st pick by Houston Rockets in 1984 NBA draft; led Rockets to back-to-back NBA titles (1994-95); regular season MVP ('94) and Finals MVP (1994-95); 6-time All-NBA 1st team (1987-89,93-95). Member of Dream Team III.

José Maria Olazábal (b. Feb. 5, 1966): Spanish golfer; Has 14 worldwide victories; won only major at '94 Masters.

Barney Oldfield (b. Jan. 29, 1878, d. Oct. 4, 1946): Auto racing pioneer; drove cars built by Henry Ford; first man to drive car a mile per minute (1903).

Walter O'Malley (b. Oct. 9, 1903, d. Aug. 9, 1979): Baseball owner; moved Brooklyn Dodgers to Los Angeles after 1957 season; won 4 World Series (1955,59,63,65).

Shaquille O'Neal (b. Mar. 6, 1972): Basketball C; 2-time All-America at LSU (1991-92); overall 1st pick (as a junior) by Orlando in 1992 NBA draft; Rookie of Year in 1993; led NBA in scoring in 1995; member of Dream Teams II and III. Signed with LA Lakers in 1996.

Bobby Orr (b. Mar. 20, 1948): Hockey D; 8-time Norris Trophy winner as best defenseman; led NHL in scoring twice and assists 5 times; All-NHL 1st team 8 times; regular season MVP 3 times (1970-72); playoff MVP twice (1970,72) with Boston.

Tom Osborne (b. Feb. 23, 1937): Football; Nebraska head coach from 1973-97; career record of 255-49-3; his win pct. of .835 is fifth all-time; finally won national championship in 1994; followed it with 2nd national title in '95 and shared national title with Michigan in '97.

Mel Ott (b. Mar. 2, 1909, d. Nov. 21, 1958): Baseball OF; joined NY Giants at age 16; led NL in HRs 6 times; had 511 HRs and 1,860 RBI in 22 years.

Kristin Otto (b. Feb. 7, 1966): East German swimmer; 1st woman to win 6 gold medals (4 individual) at one Olympics (1988).

Francis Ouimet (b. May 8, 1893, d. Sept. 3, 1967): Golfer; won 1913 U.S. Open as 20-year-old amateur playing on Brookline, Mass. course where he used to caddie; won U.S. Amateur twice; 8-time Walker Cup player.

Steve Owen (b. Apr. 21, 1898, d. May 17, 1964): Football; All-Pro guard (1927); coached NY Giants for 23 years (1931-53); won 153 career games and 2 NFL titles (1934,38).

Jesse Owens (b. Sept. 12, 1913, d. Mar. 31, 1980): Track & Field; broke 5 world records in one afternoon at Big Ten Championships (May 25, 1935); a year later, he upstaged Hitler by winning 4 golds (100m, 200m, 4x100m relay and long jump) at 1936 Olympics in Berlin.

Alan Page (b. Aug. 7, 1945): Football DE; All-America at Notre Dame in 1966 and member of two national championship teams; 6-time NFL All-Pro and 1971 Player of Year with Minnesota Vikings; later a lawyer who was elected to Minnesota Supreme Court in 1992.

Satchel Paige (b. July 7, 1906, d. June 6, 1982): Baseball RHP; pitched 55 career no-hitters over 20 seasons in Negro Leagues, entered major leagues with Cleveland in 1948 at age 42; had 28-31 record in 5 years; returned to AL at age 59 to start 1 game for Kansas City in 1965 (went 3 innings, gave up a hit and got a strikeout).

Arnold Palmer (b. Sept. 10, 1929): Golfer; winner of 4 Masters, 2 British Opens and a U.S. Open; 2-time PGA Player of Year (1960,62); 1st player to earn over $1 million in career (1968); annual PGA Tour money leader award named after him; 60 wins on PGA Tour and 10 more on Senior Tour.

Jim Palmer (b. Oct. 15, 1945): Baseball RHP; 3-time Cy Young Award winner (1973,75-76); won 20 or more games 8 times with Baltimore; 1991 comeback attempt at age 45 scrubbed in spring training.

Bill Parcells (b. Aug. 22, 1941): Football; coached NY Giants to 2 Super Bowl titles (1987,91); retired after 1990 season then returned in '93 as coach of New England; led Patriots to Super Bowl loss in 1997; left Patriots in 1997 and signed to coach the New York Jets.

Jack Pardee (b. Apr. 19, 1936): Football; All-America linebacker at Texas A&M; 2-time All-Pro with LA Rams (1963) and Washington (1971); 2-time NFL Coach of Year (1976,79) and winner of 87 games in 11 seasons; only man hired as head coach in NFL, WFL, USFL and CFL; also coached at Univ. of Houston.

Bernie Parent (b. Apr. 3, 1945): Hockey G; led Philadelphia Flyers to 2 Stanley Cups as playoff MVP (1974,75); 2-time Vezina Trophy winner; posted 55 career shutouts and 2.55 GAA in 13 seasons.

Joe Paterno (b. Dec. 21, 1926): Football; has coached Penn St. to 2 national titles (1982,86) and 18-9-1 bowl record in 31 years; also had three unbeaten teams that didn't finish No. 1; 4-time Coach of Year (1968,78,82,86); leads all active Div. I-A coaches with over 300 wins (including bowls).

Craig Patrick (b. May 20, 1946): Hockey; 3rd generation Patrick to have name inscribed on Stanley Cup; GM of 2-time Cup champion Pittsburgh Penguins (1991-92); also captain of 1969 NCAA champion at Denver; assistant coach-GM of 1980 gold medal-winning U.S. Olympic team; scored 72 goals in 8 NHL seasons and won 69 games in 3 years as coach; grandson of Lester.

Lester Patrick (b. Dec. 30, 1883, d. June 1, 1960): Hockey; pro hockey pioneer as player, coach and general manager for 43 years; led NY Rangers to Stanley Cups as coach (1928,33) and GM (1940); grandfather of Craig.

Floyd Patterson (b. Jan. 4, 1935): Boxer; Olympic middleweight champ in 1952; world heavyweight champion (1956-59,60-62); 1st to regain heavyweight crown; fought Ingemar Johansson 3 times in 22 months from 1959-61 and won last two; pro record 55-8-1 with 40 KOs.

Walter Payton (b. July 25, 1954): Football RB; NFL's all-time leading rusher with 16,726 yards; scored 125 career TDs; All-Pro 7 times with Chicago; MVP in 1977; led Bears to Super Bowl title in Jan. 1986.

Pelé (b. Oct. 23, 1940): Brazilian soccer F; given name— Edson Arantes do Nascimento; led Brazil to 3 World Cup titles (1958,62,70); came to U.S. in 1975 to play for NY Cosmos in NASL; scored 1,281 goals in 22 years; currently Brazil's minister of sport.

Roger Penske (b. Feb. 20, 1937): Auto racing; national sports car driving champion (1964); established racing team in 1961; co-founder of Championship Auto Racing Teams (CART); Penske Racing entered 1995 with a record 91 IndyCar victories, including 10 Indianapolis 500s and 9 IndyCar points titles; shocked racing world by failing to qualify car for 1995 Indy 500.

Willie Pep (b. Sept. 19, 1922): Boxer; 2-time world featherweight champion (1942-48,49-50); pro record 230-11-1 with 65 KOs.

Marie-Jose Perec (b. 1968): Track & Field; French sprinter who became 2nd woman to win the 200m and 400m events in the same Olympics (1996); her time in the 400 (48.25) set an Olympic record; Valerie Brisco-Hooks did it in the boycotted 1984 games; also won the 400M in 1992 Games.

Fred Perry (b. May 18, 1909, d. Feb. 2, 1995): British tennis player; 3-time Wimbledon champ (1934-36); first player to win all four Grand Slam singles titles, though not in same year; last native to win All-England men's title.

Gaylord Perry (b. Sept. 15, 1938): Baseball RHP; only pitcher to win a Cy Young Award in both leagues; retired in 1983 with 314-265 record and 3,534 strikeouts over 22 years and with 8 teams; brother Jim won 215 games for family total of 529.

Bob Pettit (b. Dec. 12, 1932): Basketball F; All-NBA 1st team 10 times (1955-64); 2-time MVP (1956,59) with St. Louis Hawks; first player to score 20,000 points.

Richard Petty (b. July 2, 1937): Auto racer; 7-time winner of Daytona 500; 7-time NASCAR national champ (1964,67,71-72,74-75,79); first stock car driver to win $1 million in career; all-time NASCAR leader in races won (200), poles (127) and wins in a single season (27 in 1967); retired after 1992 season; son of Lee (54 career wins) and father of Kyle (7 career wins).

Laffit Pincay Jr. (b. Dec. 29, 1946): Jockey; 5-time Eclipse Award winner (1971,73-74,79,85); winner of 3 Belmonts and 1 Kentucky Derby (aboard Swale in 1984); entered 1998 with more than 8,500 career wins, trailing only Bill Shoemaker's 8,833.

Scottie Pippen (b. Sept. 25, 1965): Basketball; Chicago Bulls forward has started on six NBA champions (1991-93, 96-98); 3-time all-NBA first team (1994-96). Voted one of NBA's 50 Greatest Players.

Nelson Piquet (b. Aug. 17, 1952): Brazilian auto racer; 3-time Formula One world champion (1981,83, 87); left circuit in 1991 with 23 career wins.

Rick Pitino (b. Sept. 18, 1952): Basketball; won 1996 NCAA title in his 7th year at Kentucky; previously coached the New York Knicks in the NBA (96-81 overall), Providence College (42-23) and Boston University (46-24); in 1997, became coach and president of Boston Celtics.

Jacques Plante (b. Jan. 17, 1929, d. Feb. 27, 1986): Hockey G; led Montreal to 6 Stanley Cups (1953,56-60); won 7 Vezina Trophies; MVP in 1962; first goalie to regularly wear a mask; posted 82 shutouts with 2.38 GAA.

Gary Player (b. Nov. 1, 1936): South African golfer; 3-time winner of Masters and British Open; only player in 20th century to win British Open in three different decades (1959,68,74); one of only four players to win all four Grand Slam titles (others are Hogan, Nicklaus and Sarazen); has also won 2 PGAs, a U.S. Open and 2 U.S. Senior Opens; owner of 21 wins on PGA Tour and 17 more on Senior Tour.

Jim Plunkett (b. Dec. 5, 1947): Football QB; Heisman Trophy winner (Stanford) in 1970; AFL Rookie of the Year in 1971; led Oakland-LA Raiders to Super Bowl wins in 1981 and '84; MVP in '81.

Maurice Podoloff (b. Aug. 18, 1890, d. Nov. 24, 1985): Basketball; engineered merger of Basketball Assn. of America and National Basketball League into NBA in 1949; NBA commissioner (1949-63); league MVP trophy named after him.

Fritz Pollard (b. Jan. 27, 1894, d. May 11, 1986): Football; 1st black All-America RB (1916 at Brown); 1st black to play in Rose Bowl; 7-year NFL pro (1920-26); 1st black NFL coach, at Milwaukee and Hammond, Ind.

Sam Pollock (b. Dec. 15, 1925): Hockey GM; managed NHL Montreal Canadiens to 9 Stanley Cups in 14 years (1965-78).

Denis Potvin (b. Oct. 29, 1953): Hockey D; won Norris Trophy 3 times (1976,78-79); 5-time All-NHL 1st-team; led NY Islanders to 4 Stanley Cups.

Mike Powell (b. Nov. 10, 1963): Track & Field; broke Bob Beamon's 23-year-old long jump world record by 2 inches with leap of 29-ft., 4½ in. at the 1991 World Championships; Sullivan Award winner (1991); won long jump silver medals in 1988 and '92 Olympics; repeated as world champ in 1993.

Steve Prefontaine (b. Jan. 25, 1951, d. June 1, 1975): Track & Field; All-America distance runner at Oregon; first athlete to win same event at NCAA championships 4 straight years (5,000 meters from 1970-73); finished 4th in 5,000 at 1972 Munich Olympics; first athlete to endorse Nike running shoes; killed in a one-car accident.

Nick Price (b. Jan. 28, 1957): Zimbabwean golfer; PGA Tour Player of Year in 1993 and '94; became 1st since Nick Faldo in 1990 to win 2 Grand Slam titles in same year when he took British Open and PGA Championship in 1994; also won PGA in '92.

Alain Prost (b. Feb. 24, 1955): French auto racer; 4-time Formula One world champion (1985-86,89,93); sat out 1992 then returned to win title in 1993; retired after '93 season as all-time F1 wins leader with 51.

Kirby Puckett (b. Mar. 14, 1961): Baseball OF; led Minnesota Twins to World Series titles in 1987 and '91; retired in 1996 due to an eye ailment with a batting title (1989), 2,304 hits and a .318 career average in 12 seasons.

C.C. Pyle (b. 1882, d. Feb. 3, 1939): Promoter; known as "Cash and Carry"; hyped Red Grange's pro football debut by arranging 1925 barnstorming tour with Chicago Bears; had Grange bolt NFL for new AFL in 1926 (AFL folded in '27); also staged 2 Transcontinental Races (1928-29), known as "Bunion Derbies."

Bobby Rahal (b. Jan. 10, 1953): Auto racer; 3-time PPG Cup champ (1986,87,92); 24 career Indy-Car wins, including 1986 Indy 500.

Jack Ramsay (b. Feb. 21, 1925): Basketball; coach who won 239 college games with St. Joseph's-PA in 11 seasons and 906 NBA games (including playoffs) with 4 teams over 21 years; placed 3rd in 1961 Final Four; led Portland to NBA title in 1977.

Bill Rassmussen (b. Oct. 15, 1932): Radio-TV; unemployed radio broadcaster who founded ESPN, the nation's first 24-hour all-sports cable-TV network, in 1978; bought out by Getty Oil in 1981.

Willis Reed (b. June 25, 1942): Basketball C; led NY Knicks to NBA titles in 1970 and '73, Finals MVP both years; regular season MVP 1970. Voted one of NBA's 50 Greatest Players.

Pee Wee Reese (b. July 23, 1919): Baseball SS; member of Brooklyn/Los Angeles Dodgers from 1940-58; led NL in runs scored (132) in 1949 and stolen bases (30) in 1952; hit over .300 in a season once (.309 in 1954); led the NL in putouts four times; real name is Harold H. Reese.

Mary Lou Retton (b. Jan. 24, 1968): Gymnast; won gold medal in women's All-Around at the 1984 Olympics; also won 2 silvers and 2 bronzes.

Butch Reynolds (b. June 8, 1964): Track & Field; set current world record in 400 meters (43.29) in 1988; banned for 2½ years for allegedly failing drug test in 1990; sued IAAF and won $27.4 million judgment in 1992, but award was voided in '94.

Grantland Rice (b. Nov. 1, 1880, d. July 13, 1954): First celebrated American sportswriter; chronicled the Golden Age of Sport in 1920s; immortalized Notre Dame's "Four Horsemen."

Jerry Rice (b. Oct. 13, 1962): Football WR; 2-time Div. I-AA All-America at Mississippi Valley St. (1983-84); 10-time All-Pro; regular season MVP in 1987 and Super Bowl MVP in 1989 with San Francisco; NFL all-time leader in touchdowns and receptions.

Henri Richard (b. Feb. 29, 1936): Hockey C; leap year baby who played on more Stanley Cup championship teams (11) than anybody else; at 5-foot-7, known as the "Pocket Rocket"; brother of Maurice.

Maurice Richard (b. Aug. 4, 1921): Hockey RW; the "Rocket"; 8-time NHL 1st team All-Star; MVP in 1947; 1st to score 50 goals in one season (1944-45); 544 career goals; played on 8 Stanley Cup winners in Montreal.

Bob Richards (b. Feb. 2, 1926): Track & Field; pole vaulter, ordained minister and original *Wheaties* pitchman, who won gold medals at 1952 and '56 Olympics; remains only 2-time Olympic pole vault champ.

Tex Rickard (b. Jan. 2, 1870, d. Jan. 6, 1929): Promoter who handled boxing's first $1 million gate (Dempsey vs. Carpentier in 1921); built Madison Square Garden in 1925; founded NY Rangers as Garden tenant in 1926 and named NHL team after himself (Tex's Rangers); also built Boston Garden in 1928.

Eddie Rickenbacker (b. Oct. 8, 1890, d. July 23, 1973): Mechanic and auto racer; became America's top flying ace (22 kills) in World War I; owned Indianapolis Speedway (1927-45) and ran Eastern Air Lines (1938-59).

Branch Rickey (b. Dec. 20, 1881, d. Dec. 9, 1965): Baseball innovator; revolutionized game with creation of modern farm system while general manager of St. Louis Cardinals (1917-42); integrated major leagues in 1947 as president-GM of Brooklyn Dodgers when he brought up Jackie Robinson (whom he had signed on Oct. 23, 1945); later GM of Pittsburgh Pirates.

Leni Riefenstahl (b. Aug. 22, 1902): German filmmaker of 1930s; directed classic sports documentary "Olympia" on 1936 Berlin Summer Olympics; infamous, however, for also making 1934 Hitler propaganda film "Triumph of the Will."

Roy Riegels (b. Apr. 4, 1908, d. Mar. 26, 1993): Football; California center who picked up fumble in 2nd quarter of 1929 Rose Bowl and raced 70 yards in the wrong direction to set up a 2-point safety in 8-7 loss to Georgia Tech.

Bobby Riggs (b. Feb. 25, 1918, d. Oct. 25, 1995): Tennis; won Wimbledon once (1939) and U.S. title twice (1939,41); legendary hustler who made his biggest score in 1973 as 55-year-old male chauvinist challenging the best women players; beat No. 1 Margaret Smith Court 6-2,6-1, but was thrashed by No. 2 Billie Jean King, 6-4,6-3,6-3 in nationally televised "Battle of the Sexes" on Sept. 20, before 30,492 at the Astrodome.

Pat Riley (b. Mar. 20, 1945): Basketball; coached LA Lakers to 4 of their 5 NBA titles in 1980s (1982,85,87-88); coached New York from 1991-95; 2-time Coach of Year (1990,93) and all-time NBA leader in playoff wins (137); quit Knicks after 1994-95 season with year left on contract; signed with Miami Heat on Sept. 2 as coach, team president and part-owner after Knicks agreed to drop tampering charges in exchange for $1 million and a conditional first round draft pick.

Cal Ripken Jr. (b. Aug. 24, 1960): Baseball SS; broke Lou Gehrig's major league Iron Man record of 2,130 consecutive games played on Sept. 6, 1995; record streak began on May 30, 1982; 2-time AL MVP (1983,91) for Baltimore; AL Rookie of Year (1982); AL starter in All-Star Game since 1984; holds record for career home runs by a shortstop.

Phil Rizzuto (b. Sept. 25, 1918): Baseball SS; nicknamed "the Scooter"; AL MVP with the Yankees in 1950; five-time All-Star; retired in 1956 and became Yankees radio and television announcer; elected to the Hall of Fame in 1994.

Joe Robbie (b. July 7, 1916, d. Jan. 7, 1990): Football; original owner of Miami Dolphins (1966-90); won 2 Super Bowls (1973-74); built $115-million Robbie Stadium (now named Pro Player Stadium) with private funds in 1987.

Oscar Robertson (b. Nov. 24, 1938): Basketball G; 3-time College Player of Year (1958-60) at Cincinnati; led 1960 U.S. Olympic team to gold medal; NBA Rookie of Year (1961); 9-time All-NBA 1st team; MVP in 1964 with Cincinnati Royals; NBA champion in 1971 with Milwaukee Bucks; 3rd in career assists with 9,887.

Paul Robeson (b. Apr. 8, 1898, d. Jan. 23, 1976): Black 4-sport star and 2-time football All-America (1917-18) at Rutgers; 3-year NFL pro; also scholar, lawyer, singer, actor and political activist; long-tainted by Communist sympathies, he was finally inducted into College Football Hall of Fame in 1995.

Brooks Robinson (b. May 18, 1937): Baseball 3B; led AL in fielding 12 times from 1960-72 with Baltimore; AL MVP in 1964; World Series MVP in 1970; 16 Gold Gloves; entered Hall of Fame in 1983.

David Robinson (b. Aug. 6, 1965): Basketball C; College Player of Year at Navy in 1987; overall 1st pick by San Antonio in 1987 NBA draft; served in military from 1987-89; NBA Rookie of Year in 1990 and MVP in '95; 2-time All-NBA 1st team (1991,92); led NBA in scoring in 1994; member of 1988, '92 and '96 U.S. Olympic teams.

Eddie Robinson (b. Feb. 13, 1919): Football; head coach at Div. I-AA Grambling from 1941-97; winningest coach in college history (408-165-15); led Tigers to 8 national black college titles.

Frank Robinson (b. Aug. 31, 1935): Baseball OF; won MVP in NL (1961) and AL (1966); Triple Crown winner and World Series MVP in 1966 with Baltimore; 1st black manager in major leagues with Cleveland in 1975; also managed in SF and Baltimore.

Jackie Robinson (b. Jan. 31, 1919, d. Oct. 24, 1972): Baseball 1B-2B-3B; 4-sport athlete at UCLA (baseball, basketball, football and track); hit .387 with K.C. Monarchs of Negro Leagues in 1945; signed by Brooklyn Dodgers on Oct. 23, 1945 and broke major league baseball's color line in 1947; Rookie of Year in 1947 and NL's MVP in '49; hit .311 over 10 seasons. His #42 was retired by MLB in 1997.

Sugar Ray Robinson (b. May 3, 1921, d. Apr. 12, 1989): Boxer; world welterweight champion (1946-51); 5-time middleweight champ; retired at age 45 after 25 years in the ring; pro record 174-19-6 with 109 KOs.

Knute Rockne (b. Mar. 4, 1888, d. Mar. 31, 1931): Football; coached Notre Dame to 3 consensus national titles (1924,29,30), highest winning pecentage in college history (.881) with record of 105-12-5 over 13 seasons; killed in plane crash.

Bill Rodgers (b. Dec. 23, 1947): Distance runner; won Boston and New York City marathons 4 times each from 1975-80.

Dennis Rodman (b. May 13, 1961): Basketball F; ferocious rebounder and tenacious defender; also known for dyeing his hair various colors and for getting suspended regularly; in 1997, he was suspended for 11 games for kicking a courtside cameraman in the groin; led the NBA in rebounding 7 years in a row, 1992-98; member of 5 NBA champion teams, Detroit Pistons (1989,90) and Chicago Bulls (1996-98); 2-time All Star (1990,92), 2-time defensive player of the year (1990-91) and 6-time member of the NBA All-Defensive team (1989-93,96).

Irina Rodnina (b. Sept. 12, 1949): Soviet figure skater; won 10 world championships and 3 Olympic gold medals in pairs competition from 1971-80.

Alex Rodriguez (b. July 27, 1975): Baseball SS; highly-touted prospect exploded on the scene in 1996 with a .358 batting average (led AL), 36 home runs, 123 RBIs and league-leading 141 runs.

Diann Roffe-Steinrotter (b. Mar. 24, 1967): Alpine skier; 2-time Olympic medalist in Super-G; won silver at Albertville in 1992, then gold at Lillehammer in '94.

Ronaldo (b. Sept. 22, 1976): Soccer; Brazilian forward who has been compared to the great Pele; signed with a first division club in Brazil, Cruzeiro Belo Horizonte, before he was 18 and scored 58 goals in 60 games; named to the Brazilian National Team when he was 17; named FIFA Player of the Year in 1996 and '97; European Player of the Year in '97; named to 1998 World Cup MVP.

Art Rooney (b. Jan. 27, 1901, d. Aug. 25, 1988): Race track legend and pro football pioneer; bought Pittsburgh Steelers franchise in 1933 for $2,500; finally won NFL title with 1st of 4 Super Bowls in 1974 season.

Theodore Roosevelt (b. Oct. 27, 1858, d. Jan. 6, 1919): 26th President of the U.S.; physical fitness buff who boxed as undergraduate at Harvard; credited with presidential assist in forming of Intercollegiate Athletic Assn. (now NCAA) in 1905-06.

Mauri Rose (b. May 26, 1906, d. Jan. 1, 1981): Auto racer; 3-time winner of Indy 500 (1941,47-48).

Murray Rose (b. Jan. 6, 1939): Australian swimmer; won 3 gold medals at 1956 Olympics; added a gold, silver and bronze in 1960.

Pete Rose (b. Apr. 14, 1941): Baseball OF-IF; all-time hits leader with 4,256; led NL in batting 3 times; regular-season MVP in 1973; World Series MVP in 1975; had 44-game hitting streak in '78; managed Cincinnati (1984-89); banned for life in 1989 for conduct detrimental to baseball; convicted of tax evasion in 1990 and sentenced to 5 months in prison; released Jan. 7, 1991.

Ken Rosewall (b. Nov. 2, 1934): Tennis; won French and Australian singles titles at age 18; U.S. champ twice, but never won Wimbledon.

Mark Roth (b. Apr. 10, 1951): Bowler; 4-time PBA Player of Year (1977-79,84); entered 1998 with 34 tournament wins; victory in Apr. 15, 1995 Foresters Open was first in 7 years; U.S. Open champ in 1984.

Alan Rothenberg (b. Apr. 10, 1939): Soccer; president of U.S. Soccer 1990-98; surprised European skeptics by directing hugely successful 1994 World Cup tournament; successfully got oft-delayed outdoor Major League Soccer off ground in 1996.

Patrick Roy (b. Oct. 5, 1965): Hockey G; led Montreal to 2 Stanley Cup titles; playoff MVP as rookie in 1986 and again in '93; has won Vezina Trophy 3 times (1989-90,92). Won 3rd Stanley Cup with Colorado ('96).

Pete Rozelle (b. Mar. 1, 1926, d. December 6, 1996): Football; NFL Commissioner from 1960-89; presided over growth of league from 12 to 28 teams, merger with AFL, creation of Super Bowl and advent of huge TV rights fees.

Wilma Rudolph (b. June 23, 1940, d. Nov. 12, 1994): Track & Field; won 3 gold medals (100m, 200m and 4x100m relay) at 1960 Olympics; also won relay silver in '56 Games; 2-time AP Athlete of Year (1960-61) and Sullivan Award winner in 1961.

Damon Runyon (b. Oct. 4, 1884, d. Dec. 10, 1946): Kansas native who gained fame as New York journalist, sports columnist and short-story writer; best known for 1932 story collection, "Guys and Dolls."

Adolph Rupp (b. Sept. 2, 1901, d. Dec. 10, 1977): Basketball; 2nd in all-time college coacing wins with 876; led Kentucky to 4 NCAA championships (1948-49,51,58) and 1 NIT title (1946).

Bill Russell (b. Feb. 12, 1934): Basketball C; won titles in college, Olympics and pros; 5-time NBA MVP; led Boston to 11 titles from 1957-69; also became first black NBA head coach in 1966.

Babe Ruth (b. Feb. 6, 1895, d. Aug. 16, 1948): Baseball LHP-OF; two-time 20-game winner with Boston Red Sox (1916-17); had a 94-46 record with a 2.28 ERA, while he was 3-0 in the World Series with an ERA of 0.87; sold to New York Yankees for $100,000 in 1920; AL MVP in 1923; led AL in slugging average 13 times, HRs 12 times, RBI 6 times and batting once (.378 in 1924); hit 60 HRs in 1927 and at least 54 3 other times; ended career with Boston Braves in 1935 with 714 HRs, 2,211 RBI and a batting average of .342; remains all-time leader in walks (2,056) and slugging average (.690); member of the Hall of Fame's inaugural class of 1936.

Johnny Rutherford (b. Mar. 12, 1938): Auto racer; 3-time winner of Indy 500 (1974,76,80); CART national champion in 1980.

Nolan Ryan (b. Jan. 31, 1947): Baseball RHP; author of record 7 no-hitters against Kansas City and Detroit (1973), Minnesota (1974), Baltimore (1975), LA Dodgers (1981), Oakland A's (1990) and Toronto (1991 at age 44); 2-time 20-game winner (1973-74); 2-time NL leader in ERA (1981,87); led AL in strikeouts 9 times and NL twice in 27 years; retired after 1993 season with 324 wins, 292 losses and all-time records for strikeouts (5,714) and walks (2,795); never won Cy Young Award.

Samuel Ryder (b. Mar. 24, 1858, d. Jan. 2, 1936): Golf; English seed merchant who donated the Ryder Cup in 1927 for competition between pro golfers from Great Britain and the U.S.; made his fortune by coming up with idea of selling seeds in small packages.

Toni Sailer (b. Nov. 17, 1935): Austrian skier; 1st to win 3 alpine gold medals in Winter Olympics— taking downhill, slalom and giant slalom events in 1956.

Alberto Salazar (b. Aug. 7, 1958): Track and Field; set one world and six U.S. records during his career; broke 12-year-old record at New York Marathon in 1981 and broke Boston Marathon record in 1982; won three straight NY Marathons (1980-82); qualified for the 1980 and 1984 U.S. Olympic teams

Juan Antonio Samaranch (b. July 17, 1920): Native of Barcelona, Spain; president of International Olympic Committee since 1980; reelected in 1996 after IOC's move in '95 to bump membership age limit to 80.

Pete Sampras (b. Aug. 12, 1971): Tennis; No.1 player in world in 1993,94,95,96,97; overtaken briefly as No. 1 in 1995 by Andre Agassi but later regained the top ranking that year; youngest ever U.S. Open men's champion (19 years, 28 days) in 1990; has won 11 majors: 2 Australian Opens (1994,97), 5 Wimbledons (1993,94,95,97,98) and 4 U.S. Opens (1990,93,95,96).

Joan Benoit Samuelson (b. May 16, 1957): Distance runner; has won Boston Marathon twice (1979,83); won first women's Olympic marathon in 1984 Games at Los Angeles; Sullivan Award recipient in 1985.

Arantxa Sanchez Vicario (b. Dec. 18, 1971): Spanish tennis player; entered 1998 season with 26 tour victories, winner of French Open (1989,94,98) and U.S. Open (1994) and was finalist in three of four Grand Slam finals in '95; teamed with Conchita Martinez to win 3 of 4 Federation Cups from 1991-94.

Earl Sande (b. Nov. 13, 1898, d. Aug. 19, 1968): Jockey; rode Gallant Fox to Triple Crown in 1930; won 5 Belmonts and 3 Kentucky Derbies.

Barry Sanders (b. July 16, 1968): Football RB; won 1988 Heisman Trophy as junior at Oklahoma St.; all-time NCAA single season leader in rushing (2,628 yards), scoring (234 points) and TDs (39); 4-time NFL rushing leader with Detroit Lions (1990,94,96,97); NFC Rookie of Year (1988); 2-time NFL Player of Year (1991,97); NFC MVP (1994); rushed for 2,053 yards in 1997, second-best season total ever; No. 2 all-time rusher with more than 14,000 yards.

Deion Sanders (b. Aug. 9, 1967): Baseball OF and Football DB-KR-WR; 2-time All-America at Florida St. in football (1987-88); 4-time NFL All-Pro with Atlanta and San Francisco (1991-94); led majors in triples (14) with Atlanta in 1992 and hit .533 in World Series the same year; signed with San Francisco 49ers as free agent in 1994 and helped Niners win Super Bowl XXIX; only athlete to play in both World Series and Super Bowl.

Abe Saperstein (b. July 4, 1901, d. Mar. 15, 1966): Basketball; founded all-black, Harlem Globetrotters barnstorming team in 1927; coached sharpshooting comedians to 1940 world pro title in Chicago and established troupe as game's foremost goodwill ambassadors; also served as 1st commissioner of American Basketball League (1961-62).

Gene Sarazen (b. Feb. 27, 1902): Golfer; one of only four players to win all four Grand Slam titles (others are Hogan, Nicklaus and Player); won Masters, British Open, 2 U.S. Opens and 3 PGA titles between 1922-35; invented sand wedge in 1930.

Glen Sather (b. Sept. 2, 1943): Hockey; GM-coach of 4 Stanley Cup winners in Edmonton (1984-85,87-88) and GM-only for another in 1990; ranks 7th on all-time NHL list with 553 wins (including playoffs); entered Hockey Hall of Fame in 1997.

Terry Sawchuk (b. Dec. 28, 1929, d. May 31, 1970): Hockey G; recorded 103 shutouts in 21 NHL seasons; 4-time Vezina Trophy winner; played on 4 Stanley Cup winners at Detroit and Toronto; posted career 2.52 GAA.

Gale Sayers (b. May 30, 1943): Football HB; 2-time All-America at Kansas; NFL Rookie of Year (1965) and 5-time All-Pro with Chicago; scored then-record 22 TDs in rookie year.

Chris Schenkel (b. Aug. 21, 1923): Radio-TV; 4-time Sportscaster of Year; easy-going baritone who covered basketball, bowling, football, golf and the Olympics for ABC and CBS; host of ABC's Pro Bowlers Tour for 33 years; received lifetime achievement Emmy Award in 1993.

Vitaly Scherbo (b. Jan. 13, 1972): Russian gymnast; winner of unprecedented 6 gold medals in gymnastics, including men's All-Around, for Unified Team in 1992 Olympics; won 3 bronze in '96 Games.

Mike Schmidt (b. Sept. 27, 1949): Baseball 3B; led NL in HRs 8 times; 3-time MVP (1980,81,86) with Philadelphia; 548 career HRs and 10 Gold Gloves; inducted into Hall of Fame in 1995.

Don Schollander (b. Apr. 30, 1946): Swimming; won 4 gold medals at 1964 Olympics, plus one gold and one silver in 1968; won Sullivan Award in 1964.

Dick Schultz (b. Sept. 5, 1929): Reform-minded executive director of NCAA from 1988-93; announced resignation on May 11, 1993 in wake of special investigator's report citing Univ. of Virginia with improper student-athlete loan program during Schultz's tenure as athletic director (1981-87); named executive director of the USOC on June 23, 1995.

Michael Schumacher (b. Jan. 3, 1969): Auto racer; entered 1998 Formula One's active win leader with 22 career victories; world champion in 1994 and '95.

Bob Seagren (b. Oct. 17, 1946): Track & Field; won gold medal in pole vault at 1968 Olympics; broke world outdoor record 5 times.

Tom Seaver (b. Nov. 17, 1944): Baseball RHP; won 3 Cy Young Awards (1969,73,75); had 311 wins, 3,640 strikeouts and 2.86 ERA over 20 years.

George Seifert (b. Jan. 22, 1940): Football; coached San Francisco to a record 17 wins in his 1st season as head coach in 1989; guided 49ers to Super Bowl-winning seasons in 1989 and '94.

Peter Seitz (b. May 17, 1905, d. Oct. 17, 1983): Baseball arbitrator; ruled on Dec. 23, 1975 that players who perform for one season without a signed contract can become free agents; decision ushered in big money era for players.

Monica Seles (b. Dec. 2, 1973): Yugoslav tennis player; No.1 in the world in 1991 and '92 after winning Australian, French and U.S. Opens both years; 4-time winner of Australian and 3-time winner of French; winner of 30 singles titles in just 5 years before she was stabbed in the back by Steffi Graf fan Gunter Parche on Apr. 30, 1993 during match in Hamburg, Germany; spent remainder of 1993, all of '94 and most of '95 recovering; returned to WTA Tour with win at the Canadian Open on Aug. 20, 1995; comeback complete with 1996 Australian Open win.

Bud Selig (b. July 30, 1934): Baseball; Milwaukee car dealer who bought AL Seattle Pilots for $10.8 million in 1970 and moved team to Midwest; as de facto comissioner, he presided over 232-day players' strike that resulted in cancellation of World Series for first time since 1904 and delayed opening of 1995 season until Apr. 25; officially named baseball's ninth commissioner on July 2, 1998.

Frank Selke (b. May 7, 1893, d. July 3, 1985): Hockey; GM of 6 Stanley Cup champions in Montreal (1953,56-60); the annual NHL trophy for best defensive forward bears his name.

Ayrton Senna (b. Mar. 21, 1960, d. May 1, 1994): Brazilian auto racer; 3-time Formula One champion (1988,90-91); died as all-time F1 leader in poles (65) and 2nd in wins (41); killed in crash at Imola, Italy during '94 San Marino Grand Prix.

Wilbur Shaw (b. Oct. 13, 1902, d. Oct. 30, 1954): Auto racer; 3-time winner and 3-time runner-up of Indy 500 from 1933-1940.

Patty Sheehan (b. Oct. 27, 1956): Golfer; LPGA Player of Year in 1983; clinched entry into LPGA Hall of Fame with her 30th career win in 1993; 3 LPGA titles (1983-84,93) and 2 U.S. Opens (1992,94).

Bill Shoemaker (b. Aug. 19, 1931): Jockey; all-time career wins leader with 8,833; 3-time Eclipse Award winner as jockey (1981) and special award recipient (1976,81); won Belmont 5 times, Kentucky Derby 4 times and Preakness twice; oldest jockey to win Kentucky Derby (age 54, aboard Ferdinand in 1986); retired in 1990 to become trainer; paralyzed in 1991 auto accident but continued to train horses.

Eddie Shore (b. Nov. 25, 1902, d. Mar. 16, 1985): Hockey D; only NHL defenseman to win Hart Trophy as MVP 4 times (1933,35-36,38); led Boston Bruins to Stanley Cup titles in 1929 and '39; had 105 goals and 1,047 penalty minutes in 14 seasons.

Frank Shorter (b. Oct. 31, 1947): Track & Field; won gold medal in marathon at 1972 Olympics, 1st American to win in 64 years.

Don Shula (b. Jan. 4, 1930): Football; retired after 1995 season with an NFL-record 347 career wins (including playoffs) and a winning percentage of .670; one of only two NFL coaches with 300 wins (George Halas); took six teams to Super Bowl and won twice with Miami (1973-74); 4-time Coach of Year, twice with Baltimore (1964,68) and twice with Miami (1970-71); coached 1972 Dolphins to 17-0 record, the only undefeated team in NFL history.

Al Simmons (b. May 22, 1902, d. May 26, 1956): Baseball OF; led AL in batting twice (1930-31) with Philadelphia A's and knocked in 100 runs or more 11 straight years (1924-34).

O.J. Simpson (b. July 9, 1947): Football RB; won Heisman Trophy in 1968 at USC; ran for 2,003 yards in NFL in 1973; All-Pro 5 times; MVP in 1973; rushed for 11,236 career yards; TV analyst and actor after career ended; arrested June 17, 1994 as suspect in double murder of ex-wife Nicole Brown Simpson and her friend Ronald Goldman; acquitted on Oct. 3, 1995 by a Los Angeles jury in criminal trial but forced to make financial reparations after losing wrongful death civil suit.

George Sisler (b. Mar. 24, 1893, d. Mar. 26, 1973): Baseball 1B; hit over .400 twice (1920,22); 257 hits in 1920 still a major league record.

Mary Decker Slaney (b. Aug. 4, 1958): U.S. middle distance runner; has held 7 separate American track & field records from the 800 to 10,000 meters; won both 1,500 and 3,000 meters at 1983 World Championships in Helsinki, but no Olympic medals.

Raisa Smetanina (b. Feb. 29, 1952): Russian Nordic skier; all-time Winter Olympics medalist with 10 cross-country medals (4 gold, 5 silver and a bronze) in 5 appearances (1976,80,84,88,92) for USSR and Unified Team.

Billy Smith (b. Dec. 12, 1950): Hockey G; led NY Islanders to 4 consecutive Stanley Cups (1980-83); won Vezina Trophy in 1982; Stanley Cup MVP in 1983.

Dean Smith (b. Feb. 28, 1931): Basketball; No. 1 on all-time NCAA coaches victory list (879); led North Carolina to 25 NCAA tournaments in 34 years, reaching Final Four 10 times and winning championship twice (1982,93); coached U.S. Olympic team to gold medal in 1976.

Emmitt Smith (b. May 15, 1969): Football RB; consensus All-America (1989) at Florida; 4-time NFL rushing leader (1991-93,95); 4-time All-Pro (1992-95); regular season and Super Bowl MVP in 1993; played on three Super Bowl champions (1992, '93 and '95 seasons).

John Smith (b. Aug. 9, 1965): Wrestler; 2-time NCAA champion for Oklahoma St. at 134 lbs (1987-88) and Most Outstanding Wrestler of '88 championships; 3-time world champion; gold medal winner at 1988 and '92 Olympics at 137 lbs; won Sullivan Award (1990); coached Oklahoma St. to 1994 NCAA title and brother Pat was Most Outstanding Wrestler.

Lee Smith (b. Dec. 4, 1957): Baseball RHP; 3-time NL saves leader (1983,91-92); retired as all-time saves leader with 478 and an ERA of 3.03; 10 seasons with 30 or more saves and 3 times saved over 40.

Michelle Smith (b. Apr. 7, 1969): Swimmer; Irish woman who won three gold medals at the 1996 Olympics; accused of using performance-enhancing drugs but passed all tests until she was suspended for 4 years by FINA in 1998 for tampering with a urine sample.

Ozzie Smith (b. Dec. 26, 1954): Baseball SS; won 13 straight Gold Gloves (1980-92); played in 12 straight All-Star Games (1981-92); MVP of 1985 NL playoffs; holds all-time assist record for shortstops with 8,375.

Walter (Red) Smith (b. Sept. 25, 1905, d. Jan. 15, 1982): Sportswriter for newspapers in Philadelphia and New York from 1936-82; won Pulitzer Prize for commentary in 1976.

Conn Smythe (b. Feb. 1, 1895, d. Nov. 18, 1980): Hockey pioneer; built Maple Leaf Gardens in 1931; managed Toronto to 7 Stanley Cups before retiring in 1961.

Sam Snead (b. May 27, 1912): Golfer; won both Masters and PGA 3 times and British Open once; runner-up in U.S. Open 4 times; PGA Player of Year in 1949; oldest player (52 years, 10 months) to win PGA event with Greater Greensboro Open title in 1965; all-time PGA Tour career victory leader with 81.

Duke Snider (b. Sept. 26, 1926): Baseball OF; hit 40 or more home runs five straight seasons (1953-57); played in six World Series with the Dodgers and batted .286 with 11 home runs; nicknamed "Duke of Flatbush"; in 18 seasons hit 407 home runs, scored 1,259 runs and had 1,333 RBI.

Annika Sorenstam (b. Oct. 9, 1970): Swedish golfer; won the 1995 U.S. Women's Open as her first LPGA victory; won the event again in 1996; College Player of the Year and NCAA champion in 1991.

Sammy Sosa (b. Nov. 12, 1968): Baseball OF; slugging Chicago Cub who surpassed Roger Maris' season home run record (61), just after Cardinal Mark McGwire did, in 1998.

Javier Sotomayor (b. Oct. 13, 1967): Cuban high jumper; first man to clear 8 feet (8-0) on July 29, 1989; won gold medal at 1992 Olympics with jump of only 7-ft, 8-in.; broke world record with leap of 8-0½ in 1993.

Warren Spahn (b. Apr. 23, 1921): Baseball LHP; led NL in wins 8 times; won 20 or more games 13 times; Cy Young winner in 1957; most career wins (363) by a left-hander.

Tris Speaker (b. Apr. 4, 1888, d. Dec. 8, 1958): Baseball OF; all-time leader in outfield assists (449) and doubles (793); had .344 career batting average and 3,515 hits.

J.G. Taylor Spink (b. Nov. 6, 1888, d. Dec. 7, 1962): Publisher of *The Sporting News* from 1914-62; Baseball Writers' Assn. annual meritorious service award named after him.

Leon Spinks (b. July 11, 1953): Boxing; won heavyweight crown in split decision over Muhammad Ali in Feb.1978; Ali regained title seven months later; won gold medal in light heavyweight division at 1976 Olympics; brother Michael won the heavyweight title in 1983; were the only brothers to hold world titles; known more for frequent traffic violations and lavish lifestyle than bouts late in career; filed for bankruptcy in 1986.

Mark Spitz (b. Feb. 10, 1950): Swimmer; set 23 world and 35 U.S. records; won all-time record 7 gold medals (4 individual, 3 relay) in 1972 Olympics; also won 4 medals (2 gold, a silver and a bronze) in 1968 Games for a total of 11; comeback attempt at age 41 foundered in 1991.

Latrell Sprewell (b. Sept. 8, 1970): Basketball G; became an NBA All-Star in just his second pro season out of Alabama; led Golden State in scoring four years in a row; made headlines in 1997 after being suspended by the NBA for attacking Warriors head coach P.J. Carlesimo during a practice.

Amos Alonzo Stagg (b. Aug. 16, 1862, d. Mar. 17, 1965): Football innovator; coached at U. of Chicago for 41 seasons and College of the Pacific for 14 more; 314-199-35 record; elected to both college football and basketball Halls of Fame.

Willie Stargell (b. Mar. 6, 1940): Baseball OF-1B; led NL in home runs twice (1971,73); 475 career HRs; NL co-MVP and World Series MVP in 1979.

Bart Starr (b. Jan. 9, 1934): Football QB; led Green Bay to 5 NFL titles and 2 Super Bowl wins from 1961-67; regular season MVP in 1966; MVP of Super Bowls I and II.

Roger Staubach (b. Feb. 5, 1942): Football QB; Heisman Trophy winner as Navy junior in 1963; led Dallas to 2 Super Bowl titles (1972,78) and was Super Bowl MVP in 1972; 5-time leading passer in NFC (1971,73,77-79).

George Steinbrenner (b. July 4, 1930): Baseball; principal owner of NY Yankees since 1973; teams have won 5 pennants and 3 World Series (1977-78,96); has changed managers 21 times and GMs 11 times in 25 years; ordered by baseball commissioner Fay Vincent in 1990 to surrender control of club for dealings with small-time gambler; reinstated on Mar. 1, 1993.

Casey Stengel (b. July 30, 1890, d. Sept. 29, 1975): Baseball; player for 14 years and manager for 25; outfielder and lifetime .284 hitter with 5 clubs (1912-25); guided NY Yankees to 10 AL pennants and 7 World Series titles from 1949-60; 1st NY Mets skipper from 1962-65.

Ingemar Stenmark (b. Mar. 18, 1956): Swedish alpine skier; 3-time World Cup overall champ (1976-78); posted 86 World Cup wins in 16 years; won 2 gold medals at 1980 Olympics.

Helen Stephens (b. Feb. 3, 1918, d. Jan. 17, 1994): Track & Field; set 3 world records in 100-yard dash and 4 more in 100 meters in 1935-36; won gold medals in 100 meters and 4x100-meter relay in 1936 Olympics; retired in 1937.

Woody Stephens (b. Sept. 1, 1913, d. Aug. 22, 1998): Horse racing; trainer who saddled an unprecedented 5 straight winners in Belmont Stakes (1982-86); also had two Kentucky Derby winners (1974,84); trained 1982 Horse of Year Conquistador Cielo; won Eclipse award as nation's top trainer in 1983.

David Stern (b. Sept. 22, 1942): Basketball; marketing expert and NBA commissioner since 1984; took office the year Michael Jordan turned pro; has presided over stunning artistic and financial success of NBA both nationally and internationally; league has grown from 23 teams to 29 during his watch and opened offices worldwide; oversaw launch of WNBA in 1997.

Teófilo Stevenson (b. Mar. 29, 1952): Cuban boxer; won 3 consecutive gold medals as Olympic heavyweight (1972,76,80); did not turn pro.

Jackie Stewart (b. June 11, 1939): Auto racer; won 27 Formula One races and 3 world driving titles from 1965-73.

John Stockton (b. Mar 26, 1962): Basketball G; all-time NBA leader in every major assist category, including most in a season (1,164), highest average in a season (14.4 per game) and most overall (12,713); also holds the NBA record for career steals (2,620); All-NBA team in '94 and '95; member of 1992 and '96 US Olympic basketball Dream Teams; 8-time All-Star.

Dwight Stones (b. Dec. 6, 1953): Track & Field; set three world records in the high jump, the last in 1976 (7-7¼); won bronze medal at 1972 Summer Games and silver in 1976; won NCAA indoor and outdoor titles in 1976; competed until 1979 when he was suspended for taking money for a television appearance; attempted comeback in 1983 but failed to make 1984 Olympic squad.

Curtis Strange (b. Jan. 30, 1955): Golfer; won consecutive U.S. Open titles (1988-89); 3-time leading money winner on PGA Tour (1985,87-88); first PGA player to win $1 million in one year (1988).

Picabo Street (b. Apr. 3, 1971): Skiing; 2-time Olympic medalist, gold (Super G in 1998) and silver (downhill in 1994); her '95 World Cup downhill series title first-ever by U.S. women.

Kerri Strug (b. Nov. 19, 1977): Gymnastics; delivered the most dramatic moment of the 1996 Summer Olympics when she completed a vault (9.712) after spraining her ankle; the second vault assured the first all-around gold medal for a US Women's gymnastics team after poor vaulting by her teammates had put the medal in doubt; a poor performance by the Russian team on the beam had clinched the gold medal for the US but Strug was unaware when she made the second vault; the injury prevented her from participating in any individual events.

Louise Suggs (b. Sept. 7, 1923): Golfer; won 11 majors and 50 LPGA events overall from 1949-62.

James E. Sullivan (b. Nov. 18, 1862, d. Sept. 16, 1914): Track & Field; pioneer who founded Amateur Athletic Union (AAU) in 1888; director of St. Louis Olympic Games in 1904; AAU's annual Sullivan Award for performance and sportsmanship named after him.

John L. Sullivan (b. Oct. 15, 1858, d. Feb. 2, 1918): Boxer; world heavyweight champion (1882-92); last of bare-knuckle champions.

Pat Summitt (b. June 14, 1952): Basketball; women's basketball coach at Tennessee (1974–); 2nd all-time in career victories to Jody Conradt of Texas; coached 1984 US women's basketball team to its first Olympic gold medal; has coached Lady Vols to 6 national championships (1987,89,91,96,97,98).

Don Sutton (b. April 2, 1945): Baseball RHP; won 324 games and tossed 58 shutouts in his 23-year career; recorded NL record five career one-hitters; lost 13 straight games to the Cubs–a major league record for consecutive losses to one team; played with Dodgers, Astros, Brewers, Athletics, Angels and was a four-time All-Star; elected to Hall of Fame in 1998.

Lynn Swann (b. Mar. 7, 1952): Football WR; played nine seasons with Pittsburgh (1974-82); appeared in four Super Bowls and had 16 catches for 364 yards and three TDs; named MVP of Super Bowl X for 4-161, 1 TD performance; member of ABC Sports television broadcasting crew.

Barry Switzer (b. Oct. 5, 1937): Football; coached Oklahoma to 3 national titles (1974-75,85); 4th on all-time winningest pct list at .837 (157-29-4); resigned in 1989 after OU was slapped with 3-year NCAA probation and 5 players were brought up on criminal charges; hired as Dallas Cowboys head coach in 1994 and led team to victory in Super Bowl XXX in 1996.

Paul Tagliabue (b. Nov. 24, 1940): Football; NFL attorney who was elected league's 4th commissioner in 1989; ushered in salary cap in 1994; league expanded by 2 teams in 1995 for 1st time since '76; brought $300 million suit against Dallas owner Jerry Jones on Sept. 18, 1995 for Jones' rogue sponsorship deals with Pepsi and Nike.

Anatoli Tarasov (b. 1918, d. June 23, 1995): Hockey; coached Soviet Union to 9 straight world championships and 3 Olympic gold medals (1964,68,72).

Jerry Tarkanian (b. Aug. 30, 1930): Basketball; 3rd all-time winningest college coach with .814 win pct.; record of 687-157 in 27 years at Long Beach St., UNLV and Fresno St.; led UNLV to 4 Final Fours and 1 national title (1990); fought 16-year battle with NCAA over purity of UNLV program; quit as coach after going 26-2 in 1991-92; fired after 20 games (9-11) as coach of NBA San Antonio Spurs in 1992; unretired in 1995 to coach his alma mater, Fresno St.

Fran Tarkenton (b. Feb. 3, 1940): Football QB; 2-time NFL All-Pro (1973,75); Player of Year (1975); threw for 47,003 yards and 342 TDs (both former NFL records) in 18 seasons with Minnesota Vikings and NY Giants.

Chuck Taylor (b. June 24, 1901, d. June 23, 1969): Converse traveling salesman whose name came to grace the classic, high-top canvas basketball sneakers known as "Chucks"; over 500 million pairs have been sold since 1917; he also ran clinics worldwide and edited Converse Basketball Yearbook from 1922-68.

Lawrence Taylor (b. Feb. 4, 1959): Football LB; All-America at North Carolina (1980); only defensive player in NFL history to be consensus Player of Year (1986); led NY Giants to Super Bowl titles in 1986 and '90 seasons; played in a record 10 Pro Bowls (1981-90); retired after 1993 season with 132½ sacks.

Gustavo Thoeni (b. Feb. 28, 1951): Italian alpine skier; 4-time World Cup overall champion (1971-73,75); won giant slalom at 1972 Olympics.

Frank Thomas (b. May 27, 1968): Baseball 1B; All-America at Auburn in 1989; 2-time AL MVP with Chicago (1993,94); five-time All Star; first player in major league history to hit .300, hit at least 20 home runs and have over 100 walks, RBIs and runs scored in seven straight seasons; has hit 40 home runs 3 times (1993,95,96); nicknamed "the Big Hurt."

Isiah Thomas (b. Apr. 30, 1961): Basketball; led Indiana to NCAA title as sophomore and Final 4 MOP in 1981; consensus All-America guard in '81; led Detroit to 2 NBA titles in 1989 and '90; NBA Finals MVP in 1990; 3-time All-NBA 1st team (1984-86); retired in 1994 at age 33 after tearing right Achilles tendon.

Thurman Thomas (b. May 16, 1966): Football RB; 3-time AFC rushing leader (1990-91,93); 2-time All-Pro (1990-91); NFL Player of Year (1991); led Buffalo to 4 straight Super Bowls (1991-94).

Daley Thompson (b. July 30, 1958): British Track & Field; won consecutive gold medals in decathlon at 1980 and '84 Olympics.

John Thompson (b. Sept. 2, 1941): Basketball; has coached centers Patrick Ewing, Alonzo Mourning and Dikembe Mutombo at Georgetown; reached NCAA tourney final 3 out of 4 years with Ewing, winning title in 1984; also led Hoyas to 6 Big East tourney titles; coached 1988 U.S. Olympic team to bronze medal.

Bobby Thomson (b. Oct. 25, 1923): Baseball OF; career .270 hitter who won the 1951 NL pennant for the NY Giants with a 1-out, 3-run HR in the bottom of the 9th inning of Game 3 of a best-of-3 playoff with Brooklyn; the pitcher was Ralph Branca, the count was 0-1 and the Dodgers were ahead 4-2; the Giants had trailed Brooklyn by 13½ games on Aug. 11.

Jim Thorpe (b. May 28, 1888, d. May 28, 1953): 2-time All-America in football; won both pentathlon and decathlon at 1912 Olympics; stripped of medals a month later for playing semi-pro baseball prior to Games; medals restored in 1982; played major league baseball (1913-19) and pro football (1920-26,28); chosen "Athlete of the Half Century" by AP in 1950.

Bill Tilden (b. Feb. 10, 1893, d. June 5, 1953): Tennis; won 7 U.S. and 3 Wimbledon titles in 1920s; led U.S. to 7 straight Davis Cup victories (1920-26).

Tinker to Evers to Chance Chicago Cubs double play combination from 1903-10; immortalized in poem by New York sportswriter Franklin P. Adams— SS Joe Tinker (1880-1948), 2B Johnny Evers (1883-1947) and 1B Frank Chance (1877-1924); all 3 managed the Cubs and made the Hall of Fame.

Y.A. Tittle (b. Oct. 24, 1926): Football QB; played 17 years in AAFC and NFL; All-Pro 4 times; league MVP with San Francisco (1957) and NY Giants (1962); passed for 28,339 career yards.

Alberto Tomba (b. Dec. 19, 1966): Italian alpine skier; all-time Olympic alpine medalist with 5 (3 gold, 2 silver); became 1st alpine skier to win gold medals in 2 consecutive Winter Games when he won the slalom and giant slalom in 1988 then repeated in the GS in '92; also won silvers in slalom in 1992 and '94; won 1st overall World Cup championship along with slalom and giant slalom titles in 1995.

Vladislav Tretiak (b. Apr. 25, 1952): Hockey G; led USSR to Olympic gold medals in 1972 and '76; starred for Soviets against Team Canada in 1972, and again in 2 Canada Cups (1976,81).

Lee Trevino (b. Dec. 1, 1939): Golfer; 2-time winner of 3 majors—U.S. Open (1968,71), British Open (1971-72) and PGA (1974,84); Player of Year once on PGA Tour (1971) and 3 times with Seniors (1990,92,94); 27 PGA Tour wins and 27 more on Senior Tour.

Bryan Trottier (b. July 17, 1956): Hockey C; led NY Islanders to 4 straight Stanley Cups (1980-83); Rookie of Year (1976); scoring champion (134 points) and regular season MVP in 1979; playoff MVP (1980); added 5th and 6th Cups with Pittsburgh in 1991 and '92; entered Hockey Hall of Fame in 1997.

Gene Tunney (b. May 25, 1897, d. Nov. 7, 1978): Boxer; world heavyweight champion from 1926-28; beat 31-year-old champ Jack Dempsey in unanimous 10 round decision in 1926; beat him again in famous "long count" rematch in '27; quit while still champion in 1928 with 65-1-1 record and 47 KOs.

Ted Turner (b. Nov. 19, 1938): Sportsman and TV mogul; skippered *Courageous* to America's Cup win in 1977; owner of both Atlanta Braves and Hawks; owner of superstation WTBS, and cable stations CNN and TNT; founder of Goodwill Games; 1991 *Time* Man of Year.

Mike Tyson (b. June 30, 1966): Boxer; youngest (age 19) to win heavyweight title (WBC in 1986); undisputed champ from 1987 until upset loss to 42-1 shot Buster Douglas on Feb. 10, 1990, in Tokyo; found guilty on Feb. 10, 1992, of raping 18-year-old Miss Black America contestant Desiree Washington in Indianapolis on July 19, 1991; sentenced to 6-year prison term; released May 9, 1995 after serving 3 years; reclaimed WBC and WBA belts with wins over Frank Bruno and Bruce Seldon in 1996; lost WBA title to Evander Holyfield in 1996; brought his career to a halt when he bit Holyfield twice in the ear during their WBA championship fight in 1997; see career fight record in Boxing chapter.

Wyomia Tyus (b. Aug. 29, 1945): Track & Field; 1st woman to win consecutive Olympic gold medals in 100m (1964-68).

Peter Ueberroth (b. Sept. 2, 1937): Organizer of 1984 Summer Olympics in LA; 1984 *Time* Man of Year; baseball commissioner from 1984-89; headed Rebuild Los Angeles for one year after 1992 riots.

Johnny Unitas (b. May 7, 1933): Football QB; led Baltimore Colts to 2 NFL titles (1958-59) and a Super Bowl win (1971); All-Pro 5 times; 3-time MVP (1959,64,67); passed for 40,239 career yards and 290 TDs.

Al Unser Jr. (b. Apr. 19, 1962): Auto racer; 2-time CART-IndyCar national champion (1990,94); captured Indy 500 for 2nd time in 3 years in '94, giving Unser family 9 overall titles at the Brickyard; 31 IndyCar wins in 16 years; son of Al and nephew of Bobby.

Al Unser Sr. (b. May 29, 1939): Auto racer; 3-time USAC-CART national champion (1970,83,85); 4-time winner of Indy 500 (1970-71,78,87); retired in 1994 ranked 3rd on all-time IndyCar list with 39 wins; younger brother of Bobby and father of Little Al.

Bobby Unser (b. Feb. 20, 1934): Auto racer; 2-time USAC-CART national champion (1968,74); 3-time winner of Indy 500 (1968,75,81); retired after 1981 season; ranks 4th on all-time IndyCar list with 35 wins.

Gene Upshaw (b. Aug. 15, 1945): Football G; 2-time All-AFL and 3-time All-NFL selection with Oakland; helped lead Raiders to 2 Super Bowl titles in 1976 and '80 seasons; executive director of NFL Players Assn. since 1987; agreed to application of salary cap in 1994.

Jim Valvano (b. Mar. 10, 1946, d. Apr. 28, 1993): Basketball; coach at North Carolina St. whose team upset Houston to win national title in 1983; in 19 seasons as a coach appeared in eight NCAA tournaments; twice voted ACC Coach of the Year; career record 346-212; athletic director at N.C. State 1986-89 when a recruiting and admissions scandal forced him out of the position; worked as a television broadcaster for ESPN and ABC; died of a year long battle with cancer; The V Foundation for cancer research is named for him.

Norm Van Brocklin (b. Mar. 15, 1926, d. May 2, 1983): Football QB-P; led NFL in passing 3 times and punting twice; led LA Rams (1951) and Philadelphia (1960) to NFL titles; MVP in 1960.

Amy Van Dyken (b. Feb. 17, 1973): Swimming; first American woman to win four gold medals in one Olympics (1996); won the individual 50M freestyle, 100M butterfly, and was on the US team for the 4x100 freestyle and 4x50 medley.

Johnny Vander Meer (b. Nov. 2, 1914, d. Oct. 6, 1997): Baseball LHP; only major leaguer to pitch consecutive no-hitters (June 11 & 15, 1938).

Harold S. Vanderbilt (b. July 6, 1884, d. July 4, 1970): Sportsman; successfully defended America's Cup 3 times (1930, 34,37); also invented contract bridge in 1926.

Glenna Collett Vare (b. June 20, 1903, d. Feb. 10, 1989): Golfer; won record 6 U.S. Women's Amateur titles from 1922-35; "the female Bobby Jones."

Andy Varipapa (b. Mar. 31, 1891, d. Aug. 25, 1984): Bowler; trick-shot artist; won consecutive All-Star match game titles (1947-48) at age 55 and 56.

Mo Vaughn (b. Dec. 15, 1967): Baseball 1B; slugger for Boston Red Sox; led team to 1995 Eastern Div. title and named AL MVP with 39 homers, 126 RBI, .300 batting average and 11 stolen bases; 3-time All-Star.

Bill Veeck (b. Feb. 9, 1914, d. Jan. 2, 1986): Maverick baseball executive; owned AL teams in Cleveland, St. Louis and Chicago from 1946-80; introduced ballpark giveaways, exploding scoreboards, Wrigley Field's ivy-covered walls and midget Eddie Gaedel; won World Series with Indians (1948) and pennant with White Sox (1959).

Jacques Villeneuve (b. Apr. 9, 1971): Canadian auto racer; Indianapolis 500 runner-up and IndyCar Rookie of Year in 1994; won 500 and IndyCar driving championship in 1995; jumped to Formula One racing in 1996 and won the F1 title in 1997.

Fay Vincent (b. May 29, 1938): Baseball; became 8th commissioner after death of A. Bartlett Giamatti in 1989; presided over World Series earthquake, owners' lockout and banishment of NY Yankees owner George Steinbrenner in his first year on the job; contentious relationship with owners resulted in his resignation on Sept. 7, 1992, four days after 18-9 "no confidence" vote.

Lasse Viren (b. July 22, 1949): Finnish runner; won gold medals at 5,000 and 10,00 meters in 1972 Munich Olympics; repeated 5,000/10,000 double in 1976 Games and added a 5th place in the marathon.

Dick Vitale (b. June 9, 1939): Broadcaster; Radio and television commentator for ESPN and ABC Sports known for his enthusiastic, almost spastic style; had successful college and pro basketball coaching career with the University of Detroit (1973-77) and the Detroit Pistons (1978-79); he's been nominated for a Cable ACE award eight times and won once in 1995.

Lanny Wadkins (b. Dec. 5, 1949): Golfer; member of 8 Ryder Cup teams and captain of 1995 team; 21 PGA Tour wins.

Honus Wagner (b. Feb. 24, 1874, d. Dec. 6, 1955): Baseball SS; hit .300 for 17 consecutive seasons (1897-1913) with Louisville and Pittsburgh; led NL in batting 8 times; ended career with 3,430 career hits, a .329 average and 722 stolen bases.

Lisa Wagner (b. May 19, 1961): Bowler; 3-time LPBT Player of Year (1983,88,93); 1980's Bowler of Decade; first woman to earn $100,000 in a season; entered 1998 season with a record 30 pro titles.

Grete Waitz (b. Oct. 1, 1953): Norwegian runner; 9-time winner of New York City Marathon from 1978-88; won silver medal at 1984 Olympics.

Jersey Joe Walcott (b. Jan. 31, 1914, d. Feb. 27, 1994): Boxer; oldest heavyweight (37) to ever win the championship; lost four championship bouts before knocking out Ezzard Charles in the seventh round in 1951; lost the title the following year, losing to Rocky Marciano; won 50 bouts, 30 by knockout, lost 17 and fought one draw as a professional; later became sheriff of Camden County, NJ.

Doak Walker (b. Jan. 1, 1927): Football HB; won Heisman Trophy as SMU junior in 1948; led Detroit to 2 NFL titles (1952-53); All-Pro 4 times in 6 years.

Herschel Walker (b. Mar. 3, 1962): Football RB; led Georgia to national title as freshman in 1980; won Heisman in 1982 then jumped to USFL in '83; signed by Dallas after USFL folded; led NFL in rushing in 1988; traded to Minnesota in 1989 for 5 players and 6 draft picks; has since played for Philadelphia and NY Giants and again with Dallas.

Rusty Wallace (b. Aug. 14, 1956): Auto racing; NASCAR Winston Cup Champion in 1989 and runner up in 1980, 1988 and 1993; recorded 18 victories and $3,616,226 in 1993-94; has earned $1 million in earnings seven different seasons.

Bill Walsh (b. Nov. 30, 1931): Football; coached San Francisco to 3 Super Bowl titles (1982,85,89); retired after 1989 Super Bowl with 102 wins in 10 seasons; returned to college coaching in 1992 for his second stint at Stanford; retired again after 1994 season.

Bill Walton (b. Nov. 5, 1952): Basketball C; 3-time College Player of Year (1972-74); led UCLA to 2 national titles (1972-73); led Portland to NBA title as MVP in 1977; regular season MVP in 1978.

Arch Ward (b. Dec. 27, 1896, d. July 9, 1955): Promoter and sports editor of *Chicago Tribune* from 1930-55; founder of baseball All-Star Game (1933), Chicago College All-Star Football Game (1934) and the All-America Football Conference (1946-49).

Charlie Ward (b. Oct. 12, 1970): Football QB and Basketball G; led Florida St. to national football championship in 1993; 1st Heisman Trophy winner to play for national champs since Tony Dorsett in 1976, won Sullivan Award same year; 3-year starter for FSU basketball team; not taken in NFL Draft; 1st round pick of NY Knicks in 1994 NBA draft.

Glenn (Pop) Warner (b. Apr. 5, 1871, d. Sept. 7, 1954): Football innovator; coached at 7 colleges over 49 years; 319 career wins 2nd only to Bear Bryant's 323 in Div. I-A; produced 47 All-Americas, including Jim Thorpe and Ernie Nevers.

Tom Watson (b. Sept. 4, 1949): Golfer; 6-time PGA Player of the Year (1977-80,82,84); has won 5 British Opens, 2 Masters and a U.S. Open; 4-time Ryder Cup member and captain of 1993 team; 33 PGA tour wins.

Earl Weaver (b. Aug. 14, 1930): Baseball; managed the Baltimore Orioles to six Eastern Division titles, four AL pennants and a World Series victory in 1970; was ejected 91 times and suspended four times for outbursts against umpires; record of 1,480 wins and 1,060 losses from 1968-82 and 85-86.

Dick Weber (b. Dec. 23, 1929): Bowler; 3-time PBA Bowler of the Year (1961,63,65); won 30 PBA titles in 4 decades.

Johnny Weissmuller (b. June 2, 1904, d. Jan. 20 1984): Swimmer; won 3 gold medals at 1924 Olympics and 2 more at 1928 Games; became Hollywood's most famous Tarzan.

Jerry West (b. May 28, 1938): Basketball G; 2-time All-America and NCAA Final 4 MOP (1959) at West Virginia; led 1960 U.S. Olympic team to gold medal; 10-time All-NBA 1st-team; NBA finals MVP (1969); led LA Lakers to NBA title once as player (1972) and 5 times as GM in 1980s; his silhouette serves as the NBA's logo.

Pernell Whitaker (b. Jan. 2, 1964): Boxer; won Olympic gold medal as lightweight in 1984; has won 4 world championships as lightweight, jr. welterweight, welterweight and jr. middleweight; outfought but failed to beat Julio Cesar Chavez when Sept. 10, 1993 welterweight title defense ended in controversial draw.

Bill White (b. Jan. 28, 1934): Baseball; NL president and highest ranking black executive in sports from 1989-94; as 1st baseman, won 7 Gold Gloves and hit .286 with 202 HRs in 13 seasons.

Byron (Whizzer) White (b. June 8, 1917): Football; All-America HB at Colorado (1937); signed with Pittsburgh in 1938 for the then largest contract in pro history ($15,800); took Rhodes Scholarship in 1939; returned to NFL in 1940 to lead league in rushing and retired in 1941; named to U.S. Supreme Court by President Kennedy in 1962 and stepped down in 1993.

Reggie White (b. Dec. 19, 1961): Football DE; consensus All-America in 1983 at Tennessee; 7-time All-NFL (1986-92) with Philadelphia; signed as free agent with Green Bay in 1993 for $17 million over 4 years; all-time NFL leader in sacks; played key role in Packers 1997 Super Bowl victory; made headlines in 1998 after making controversial public comments about gays and minorities.

Kathy Whitworth (b. Sept. 27, 1939): Golf; 7-time LPGA Player of the Year (1966-69,71-73); won 6 majors; 88 tour wins, most on LPGA or PGA tour.

Hazel Hotchkiss Wightman (b. Dec. 20, 1886, d. Dec. 5, 1974): Tennis; won 16 U.S. national titles; 4-time U.S. Women's champion (1909-11,19); donor of Wightman Cup.

Hoyt Wilhelm (b. July 26, 1923): Baseball RHP; Knuckleballer who is all-time leader in games pitched (1,070), games finished (651) and games won in relief (123); had career ERA of 2.52 and 227 saves; 1st relief pitcher inducted into Hall of Fame (1985); threw no-hitter vs. NY Yankees (1958); also hit lone HR of career in first major league at bat (1952).

Lenny Wilkens (b. Oct. 28, 1937): Basketball; NBA's all-time winningest coach (1189-987); MVP of 1960 NIT as Providence guard; played 15 years in NBA, including 4 as player-coach; MVP of 1971 All-Star Game; coached Seattle to NBA title in 1979; Coach of Year in 1994 with Atlanta; one of only two men (John Wooden) to be honored by the Hall of Fame as player and coach.

Dominique Wilkins (b. Jan. 12, 1960): Basketball F; last player to lead NBA in scoring (1986) before Michael Jordan's reign; All-NBA 1st team in 1986; elder statesman of Dream Team II.

Bud Wilkinson (b. Apr. 23, 1916, d. Feb. 9, 1994): Football; played on 1936 national championship team at Minnesota; coached Oklahoma to 3 national titles (1950,55,56); won 4 Orange and 2 Sugar Bowls; teams had winning streaks of 47 (1953-57) and 31 (1948-50); retired after 1963 season with 145-29-4 record in 17 years; also coached St. Louis of NFL to 9-20 record in 1978-79.

Ted Williams (b. Aug. 30, 1918): Baseball OF; led AL in batting 6 times, and HRs and RBI 4 times each; won Triple Crown twice (1942,47); 2-time MVP (1946,49); last player to bat .400 when he hit .406 in 1941; Marine Corps combat pilot who missed three full seasons during World War II (1943-45) and most of two others (1952-53) during Korean War; hit .344 lifetime with 521 HRs in 19 years with Boston Red Sox.

Walter Ray Williams Jr. (b. Oct. 6, 1959): Bowling and Horseshoes; 3-time PBA Bowler of Year (1986,93,96); won 6 World Horseshoe Pitching titles.

Hack Wilson (b. Apr. 26, 1900, d. Nov. 23, 1948): Baseball; as a Chicago Cub, he produced one of baseball's most outstanding seasons in 1930 with 56 homeruns, .356 batting average, 105 walks and, most amazingly, a major league record 190 RBIs that still stands; finished with 1,461 hits, 244 homers, 1,062 RBIs; member of Baseball Hall of Fame.

Dave Winfield (b. Oct. 3, 1951): Baseball OF-DH; selected in 4 major sports league drafts in 1973— NFL, NBA, ABA, and MLB; chose baseball and has played in 12 All-Star Games over 22-year career; at age 41, helped lead Toronto to World Series title in 1992; 3,110 hits and 465 HRs.

Katarina Witt (b. Dec. 3, 1965): East German figure skater; 4-time world champion (1984-85,87-88); won consecutive Olympic gold medals (1984,88).

John Wooden (b. Oct. 14, 1910): Basketball; College Player of Year at Purdue in 1932; coached UCLA to 10 national titles (1964-65,67-73,75); one of only two men (Lenny Wilkens) to be honored by the Hall of Fame as player and coach.

Tiger Woods (b. Dec. 30, 1975): Golfer; became youngest player (age 18) and first minority to win U.S. Amateur in 1994, won it again in '95 and '96; turned pro in Sept. of '96 and won the fifth event he entered, the Las Vegas Invitational; in his first full year on the tour, he won six of the 25 events he entered and broke the single season money record; won 1997 Masters by a record 18 under par and 13 stroke margin of victory, the latter being a record for all majors.

Mickey Wright (b. Feb. 14, 1935): Golfer; won 3 of 4 majors (LPGA, U.S. Open, Titleholders) in 1961; 4-time winner of both U.S. Open and LPGA titles; 82 career wins including 13 majors.

Early Wynn (b. Jan. 6, 1920): Baseball RHP; won 20 games 5 times; Cy Young winner in 1959; 300-244 record in 23 years.

Kristi Yamaguchi (b. July 12, 1971): Figure Skating; finished second in the 1991 American nationals but won the world title that year; dominated the sport in 1992 by winning the national, world and Olympic titles and then turned professional.

Cale Yarborough (b. Mar. 27, 1940): Auto racer; 3-time NASCAR national champion (1976-78); 4-time winner of Daytona 500 (1968,77,83-84); ranks 5th on NASCAR all-time list with 83 wins.

Carl Yastrzemski (b. Aug. 22, 1939): Baseball OF; led AL in batting 3 times; won Triple Crown and MVP in 1967; had 3,419 hits and 452 HRs in 23 years with Boston; member of Hall of Fame.

Cy Young (b. Mar. 29, 1867, d. Nov. 4, 1955): Baseball RHP; all-time leader in wins (511), losses (313), complete games (751) and innings pitched (7,356); had career 2.63 ERA in 22 years (1890-1911); 30-game winner 5 times and 20-game winner 11 other times; threw 3 no-hitters and perfect game (1904); AL and NL pitching awards named after him.

Sheila Young (b. Oct. 14, 1950): Speed skater and cyclist; 1st U.S. athlete to win 3 medals at Winter Olympics (1976); won speed skating overall and sprint cycling world titles in 1976.

Steve Young (b. Oct. 11, 1961): Football QB; All-America at BYU (1983); NFL Player of Year (1992) with S.F. 49ers; only QB to lead NFL in passer rating 4 straight years (1991-94); rating of 112.8 in 1994 was highest ever; threw record 6 TD passes in MVP performance in Super Bowl XXIX; holds NFL career records for highest passer rating (97.0) and completion percentage (64.8), entering 1998.

Robin Yount (b. Sept. 16, 1955): Baseball SS-OF; AL MVP at 2 positions— as SS in 1982 and OF in '89; retired after 1993 season with 3,142 hits, 251 HRs and a major-league-record 123 sacrifice flies after 20 seasons with Milwaukee Brewers.

Steve Yzerman (b. May 9, 1965): Hockey C; Captained the Detroit Red Wings to back-to-back Stanley Cup sweeps in '96-97 and '97-98; took home the Conn Smythe Trophy as the playoff MVP in 1998.

Mario Zagalo (b. Aug. 9, 1931): Soccer; Brazilian forward who is one of only two men (Franz Beckenbauer is the other) to serve as both captain (1962) and coach (1970,94) of World Cup champion.

Babe Didrikson Zaharias (b. June 26, 1911, d. Sept. 27, 1956): All-around athlete who was chosen AP Female Athlete of Year 6 times from 1932-54; won 2 gold medals (javelin and 80-meter hurdles) and a silver (high jump) at 1932 Olympics; took up golf in 1935 and went on to win 55 pro and amateur events; won 10 majors, including 3 U.S. Opens (1948,50,54); helped found LPGA in 1949; chosen female "Athlete of the Half Century" by AP in 1950.

Tony Zale (b. May 29, 1913, d. March 20, 1997): Boxer; 2-time world middleweight champion (1941-47,48); fought Rocky Graziano for title 3 times in 21 months in 1947-48, winning twice; pro record 67-18-2 with 44 KOs.

Frank Zamboni (b. Jan. 16, 1901, d. July 27, 1988): Mechanic, ice salesman and skating rink owner in Paramount, Calif.; invented 1st ice-resurfacing machine in 1949; over 4,000 sold in more than 33 countries since.

Emil Zatopek (b. Sept. 19, 1922): Czech distance runner; winner of 1948 Olympic gold medal at 10,000 meters; 4 years later, won unprecedented Olympic triple crown (5,000 meters, 10,000 meters and marathon) at 1952 Games in Helsinki.

John Ziegler (b. Feb. 9, 1934): Hockey; NHL president from 1977-92; negotiated settlement with rival WHA in 1979 that led to inviting four WHA teams (Edmonton, Hartford, Quebec and Winnipeg) to join NHL; stepped down June 12, 1992, 2 months after settling 10-day players' strike.

Kim Zmeskal (b. Feb 6, 1976): Gymnastics; Won three U.S. all-around championships in a row (1990-'92); first American gymnast to win the all-around competition in the world championships (1991); only athlete to win two golds in the 1992 world championships (balance beam and floor exercise).

Pirmin Zurbriggen (b. Feb. 4, 1963): Swiss alpine skier; 4-time World Cup overall champ (1984,87-88,90) and 3-time runner-up; 40 World Cup wins in 10 years; won gold and bronze medals at 1988 Olympics.

Ballparks & Arenas

The pool behind the right-center field fence at Arizona's Bank One Ballpark is the ultimate symbol of the changing nature of big league stadium design.

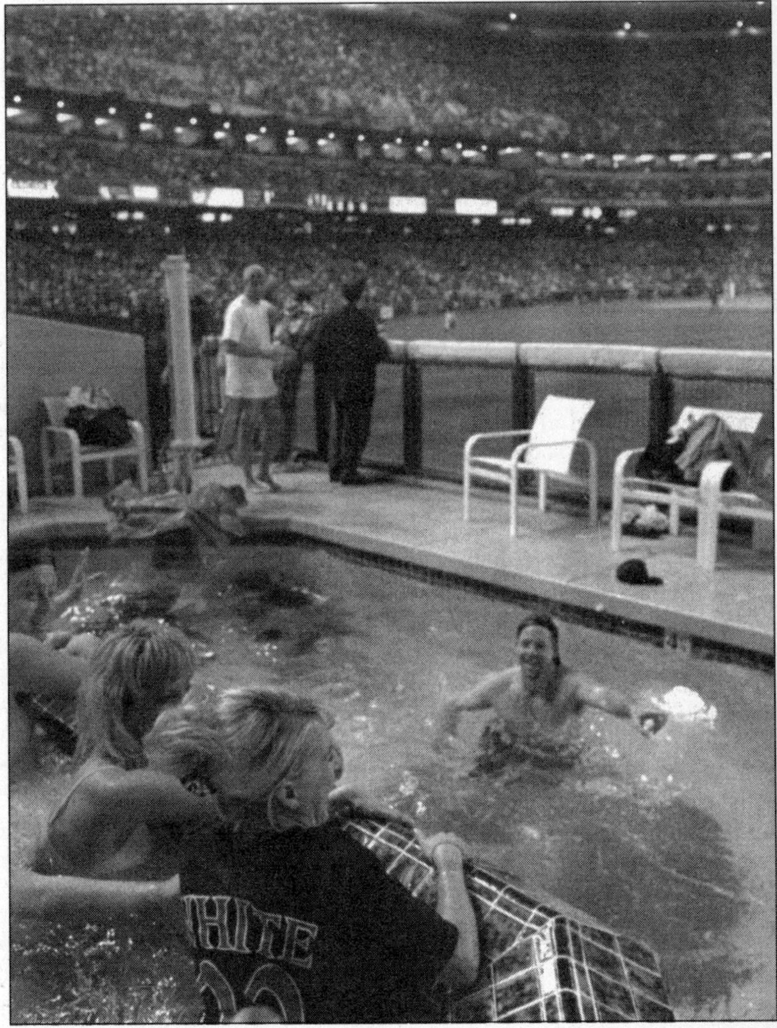

AP/Wide World Photos

Padres know best

The San Diego Padres' ownership had a novel idea: build a good team before asking for a publicly-funded park.

by
Karl Ravech

The plan in San Diego is, and always has been, different. Unlike Baltimore, where the baseball fans have been as faithful as man's best friend, and unlike Cleveland, where an owner had deep pockets and reasoned that if he built a beautiful new ballpark, success on and off the field would result (he was right), the approach in San Diego was unique.

The game plan for team owner John Moores and President and CEO Larry Lucchino was as follows: build a better baseball team, build a stronger fan base and as a result, build a new stadium. Oh yeah, the catch, have the public fund two-thirds of the $411 million facility.

Let's remember folks this was an organization that in 1994, the year before Moores and Lucchino bought it, had the worst record in Major League Baseball. This is the same organization that with some perverse sense of pride also wore those incredibly hideous mustard-yellow and brown uniforms. Suffice it to say that in the world of public relations the Padres were not tearing the cover off the ball. Yet the foundation that was laid with a blockbuster 12-player deal in 1995, three years later had grown into a baseball machine. In 1998, the San Diego Padres were a first-place team with a mission, win the World Series, build a new ballpark.

The concept was not lost on players. In fact, since the opening of spring training they were as aware of the fact they were playing for a new park as they were playing for a pennant. For better or worse, the modern-day player knows as much about the business side of the game as he does the rotation on a curveball. Wally Joyner, Ken Caminiti and Tony Gwynn all say they have seen the effects new ballparks have on communities. What's amazing is that if and when a new stadium does

---

Karl Ravech has been an ESPN anchor and reporter since 1993.

AP/Wide World Photos

San Diego Mayor **Susan Golding** and Padres President and CEO **Larry Lucchino** share a good laugh during a public hearing announcing plans to build a largely publicly-funded downtown ballpark. Depending on how the voters feel, the two of them might not be in such high spirits come election day.

get built, it's very likely none of the key players from this make-or-break season will still be playing.

In Denver, Cleveland, Baltimore and Arlington, Texas attendance is up across the board. While a new stadium does not guarantee success, it is hard to argue with these numbers. This decade seven new Major League Baseball facilities have been built and, within two years, six of the teams made it to the postseason. The seventh (the Orioles) did it four years after Camden Yards opened its gates.

On paper it was perfect. Finish the season with the best record in the division. Win a World Series in October, have a parade in the city and then on November 3 have the voters go to the polls in such a state of baseball euphoria that there would be no decision on which lever to pull. Still baseball executives know better than most, game plans that look perfect on paper don't always play out the way they should on the field. ■

Karl Ravech's Top Ten List of Ballparks and Arenas in the News

10. **Long Island, NY**— The sky is falling on Long Island. The Islanders' owners fear that the scoreboard and speaker system are in danger of collapse. They've threatened to play their home games elsewhere. Some advice: tighten the screws on the scoreboard and loosen the wallets a little.

9. **Milwaukee**— It's not exactly the Bud Bowl since Mr. Selig is (as we suggested in last year's edition) the Commish, but the fact is Miller Park is well on its way to becoming one of the best beer

AP/Wide World Photos

The **Boston Garden**, opened in 1928, was painstakingly demolished in 1998. The modern and massive FleetCenter, built just a foot away from the Garden, dwarves its distinguished neighbor and proves a classic example of how time marches on.

spots in baseball. Growing slowly, but on schedule to open in 2001. Fans will be able to get a decent beer, but how about a decent team?

8. **Pittsburgh**— One of the most exciting stories in Pennsylvania. PNC Park is set to be ready for play in 2001. It will seat 38,000 fans, about twice as many people as the Pirates get for a game now. Iron City Brew just won't cut it, how about bringing Jim Leyland and Barry Bonds together for a final run.

7. **New York City**— I hope you're sitting down. There is a slim chance that George Steinbrenner will be running the Yankees, New York Knicks and New York Rangers. Cablevision wants to buy the Yankees for $500 million and, in turn, has offered Steinbrenner control of the three teams (Cablevision already owns the other two). This for a guy who dropped $73 million to buy the Yankees. If it happens there won't be enough newspaper to go around.

6. **Boston**— It is very possible that the bats of both Mark McGwire and Sammy Sosa end up in Fenway Park or a reasonable facsimile. Rumors are circulating that the Hall of Fame would relocate to Boston. Why not, with all the history? The best news of all for Red Sox fans, right next door would be a brand new Fenway Park. Let it happen people, don't let the FleetCenter be a hindrance to progress.

5. **San Diego**— Padres team owners John Moores and Larry Lucchino have done more for the people of San Diego than the mayor, now they need votes. On November 3 polls open for a vote on a new stadium. Will a winning team be

AP/Wide World Photos

The grand opening of **Raymond James Stadium**, the new home of the Tampa Bay Buccaneers, on Sept. 20, 1998 was a spectacular affair. A B-52 bomber appears to be investigating reports of pirate activity in the area as it flies over the field, which is equipped with a life-sized replica of a 19th-century pirate ship.

enough to convince the people to open their pocketbooks?

4. **Phoenix**— In a season in which attendance has passed their wildest imaginations, the true test of the power of the BOB will come in the offseason. With revenue streams flowing like water into the outfield pool, can the Diamondbacks bring the game's best talent to play in the desert? If Bernie Williams or Randy Johnson end up playing for Buck Showalter will every team then say, "our stadium is outdated, if we don't get a place to swim, we'll sink?"

3. **Miami**— Wayne Huizenga will sell his team to stock-market maven John Henry. He's a guy who is used to taking risks but also knows a good investment. He locked up GM Dave Dombrowski for five years at $1 million per and word is former U.S. Senate Majority Leader George Mitchell may be on board as well. He'll need him. Mitchell can work a room, but can he work and entire city into helping finance a new building?

2. **Detroit**— One of the great baseball towns in America has suffered long enough. What a nightmare of a season in 1998. A team with so much promise fell flat on its face. A manager whose popularity with his players was very high got canned and with regards to a new place to play...well they broke ground. It's a big hole. Forget about 1999, they're thinking 2000.

It's a franchise that's literally rebuilding, it's just taking longer than expected.

1. **Houston**— Five minutes before the trading deadline, Astros GM Gerry Hunsicker called Seattle just to check on the status of Randy Johnson. He got a call back and was told, "produce two minor leaguers and he's yours." Done deal and the Big Unit brought big dreams to Houston. They get a new stadium in the year 2000. How about naming it "Randy's Ranch?" He stays, the fans stay and everyone is happy. ■

THE NUMBERS INSIDE

by
Team Research

STRUCTURAL DEFECTS

In 1998, Yankee Stadium became the third baseball park to need significant repair in the 1990s. Ironically, it doesn't seem that the tenants of the crumbling edifices have fared all that badly when suddenly forced out of their home fields by emergency repairs.

Year	Stadium/Problem	Result
1998	Yankee Stadium/ support beam damage	Anaheim series cancelled. Yankees win nine of next ten games.
1994	Kingdome/ceiling tiles fall from roof	20 game road trip. Mariners go 11-9
1991	Olympic Stadium/ 35 ton block collapses	26 game road trip. Expos go 13-13.

COSTLY CONVERTIBLES

Retractable-roof stadiums are the latest rage in Major League Baseball. There are six teams that either already do or will play in parks with retractable lids when they open in the next few years. The stadium cost or estimated costs (in millions) are listed with each.

Team	Opening	Cost
Blue Jays	1989	$570
Diamondbacks	1998	$354
Mariners	1999	$500
Brewers	2000	$394
Astros	2000	$260
Mets	2002	$500

STADIA MANIA

Construction costs of new big league stadiums have skyrocketed recently. The desire to build venues with more and more bells and whistles has helped make the average cost go through the retractable roof. Below is the average cost of stadiums and arenas used by current teams, broken down by the era in which it was built: recent (1990-present), previous (1960-89) and early (pre-1960). All figures are in millions of dollars.

League	Recent	Previous	Early
MLB	$223	$160	$27
NFL	$224	$101	$55
NBA	$162	$103	$8
NHL	$165	$73	$30

■

1998

BASEBALL

Arizona (NL): Bank One Ballpark (Bank One is the title sponsor) opened on March 31, 1998. It is located one block from America West Arena and features a retractable roof; seats 48,500; grass field; includes 69 luxury suites and six larger party suites; estimated cost: $350 million.

Tampa Bay (AL): Tropicana Field, formerly known as the ThunderDome and the Florida Suncoast Dome when it opened in 1990, was renovated to accommodate the expansion Devil Rays. Located in St. Petersburg at the corner of 16th St. and 1st Ave. South; seats 48,000 for baseball; indoor, artificial turf field; includes 66 luxury suites; estimated cost: $50 million.

NFL FOOTBALL

Baltimore (AFC): Ravens' stadium (title sponsor pending) opened on August 8, 1998 with a 19-14 exhibition win for the Ravens over the Chicago Bears. The open-air, grass-field stadium is located in Camden Yards next to Oriole Park and cost an estimated $200 million. It seats 68,400 and includes 108 luxury suites.

Tampa Bay (NFC): Construction of Raymond James Stadium (Raymond James Financial is title sponsor) is nearing completion. The open-air, grass-field stadium will house the Buccaneers (as well as the University of South Florida and the MLS Mutiny) and will be located across from Legend's Field in West Tampa. Stadium will have a 103 x 78-foot replica of pirate ship in the north end zone complete with a fog machine, six smoke cannons, four confetti cannons and two concussion cannons; stadium will seat 65,000 and include 120 luxury suites; to be part of larger complex and include the team's training facility as well; estimated cost: $165 million. Opening date set for September 20, 1998 for the Buccaneers game with the Chicago Bears.

NHL HOCKEY

Florida (East): Construction of National Car Rental Center (National Car Rental is title sponsor) started in November 1996. To be located in Sunrise, Fla., west of Ft. Lauderdale; will seat 19,088 for hockey and 20,184 for basketball including 70 luxury suites and four larger party suites; estimated cost: $184 million. Panthers' home opener slated for the fall of 1998.

1999

BASEBALL

Seattle (AL): Groundbreaking for SAFECO Field (SAFECO Corp. is the title sponsor) occurred on March 8, 1998. To be located on the site of the old Kingdome parking lot; seating capacity of 45,611 for baseball only; retractable-roof, grass field; would include 66 luxury suites and 12 larger party suites; estimated cost: $498 million. Earliest Mariners' home opener would be July 1999.

NBA BASKETBALL

Atlanta (East) The New Atlanta Arena (title sponsor pending) for the NBA Hawks and NHL-expansion Thrashers is under construction. Stadium will have a capacity of 20,000 for basketball and 18,750 for hockey including 96 luxury suites; located on the old site of the Omni which was demolished on July 27, 1997. The Hawks home opener is scheduled for the 1999 season in the $213 million facility. In the meantime, the Hawks will split home games between the Georgia Dome and Georgia Tech's Alexander Memorial Stadium.

Denver (West): Groundbreaking for Pepsi Center (Pepsi-Cola is the title sponsor) took place on November 20, 1997. To be built by team owner Ascent Entertainment, along with a television studio on downtown site adjacent to the new Elitch Gardens theme park; will seat 19,309 for NBA Nuggets and 18,129 for NHL Avalanche; will include 95 luxury suites; estimated cost: $160 million. Nuggets' home opener planned for October 1999.

Indiana (East): Construction for 18,500-seat Conseco Fieldhouse (Conseco Inc. is the title sponsor) is underway. The building will be located in downtown Indianapolis between Pennsylvania and Delaware streets. Estimated cost: $175 million. The arena will contain at least 65 luxury suites and serve as home to the Pacers and IHL's Indianapolis Ice. Earliest Pacers' home opener would be October 1999.

Los Angeles (West): Groundbreaking for the Staples Center (Staples Inc. is the title sponsor), which will house the NBA Lakers and Clippers and NHL Kings, occurred this past winter. It will be the first facility to host three major professional teams during the same season. The complex, which is located near the downtown L.A. Convention Center, will have 20,000 seats for basketball, 19,000 seats for hockey, 160 prime-level suites and 2,500 club seats. The $240 million project is targeted for completion for the 1999-2000 season.

Miami (East): Groundbreaking for American Airlines Arena (American Airlines is the title sponsor) took place in the fall of 1997; arena will be located on the FEC tract next to Bayside on the Miami waterfront. Estimated cost: $228 million. Arena will seat approximately 20,000 for the NBA Heat and house 156 luxury suites. Heat home opener set for some time during 1999-2000 NBA season.

Toronto (East): Construction of Air Canada Centre (Air Canada is the title sponsor) is underway. The new home to the NBA Raptors and NHL Maple Leafs will be located on site of Old Canada Post Building at corner of Bay Street and Lake Shore Road; will seat 19,800 for basketball and 18,800 for hockey; will include 65 suites on the 200 level; estimated cost: $172 million (US). Raptors' home opener scheduled for February 1999.

NFL FOOTBALL

Cleveland (expansion team): Construction of new stadium for resurrected Browns is underway. The 70,300-seat open-air stadium will be located on the old site of Cleveland Stadium and include 116 luxury suites. Grand opening for the $280 million facility is scheduled for the Browns' debut in 1999.

Nashville (AFC): Construction for Tennessee Stadium to house the relocated and eventually renamed Tennessee Oilers is underway. The natural grass, open-air stadium will seat 67,000 and have 144 luxury suites. To be located in the East Bank area of downtown Nashville. Estimated cost: $290 million. Earliest opening would be June 1999.

NHL HOCKEY

Atlanta (expansion team): The New Atlanta Arena (title sponsor pending) for the NHL-expansion Thrashers and NBA Hawks is under construction. Will have a capacity of 18,750 for hockey and 20,000 for basketball including 96 luxury suites; located on the old site of the Omni which was demolished on July 27, 1997. The Thrashers' home opener is scheduled for the 1999 season in the $213 million facility.

Carolina (East): Groundbreaking for The Raleigh Entertainment and Sports Arena (title sponsor pending) took place on July 22, 1997. The building, located next to Carter Finley Stadium and the North Carolina State Fairgrounds, will have a capacity of 19,000 for the NHL Hurricanes and 20,000 for basketball and include 75 luxury suites; estimated cost: $152 million. The arena was scheduled to be completed in the fall of 1998 but the Hurricanes will not start playing there until the 1999-2000 season. The arena will also be home to N.C. State basketball.

Colorado (West): Groundbreaking for Pepsi Center (Pepsi-Cola is the title sponsor) took place on November 20, 1997. To be built by team owner Ascent Entertainment, along with a television studio on downtown site adjacent to the new Elitch Gardens theme park; will seat 18,129 for NHL Avalanche and 19,309 for NBA Nuggets; will include 95 luxury suites; estimated cost: $160 million. Avalanche's home opener planned for October 1999.

Los Angeles (West): Groundbreaking for the new Staples Center (Staples Inc. is the title sponsor), which will house the NBA Lakers and Clippers and NHL Kings, occurred this past winter. The complex, which is located near the downtown L.A. Covention Center, will have 20,000 seats for basketball, 19,000 seats for hockey, 160 prime-level suites and 2,500 club seats. The $240 million project is targeted for completion for the 1999-2000 season.

Toronto (East): Construction of Air Canada Centre (Air Canada is the title sponsor) is underway. The new home to the NHL Maple Leafs and NBA Raptors will be located on site of Old Canada Post Building at corner of Bay Street and Lake Shore Road; will seat 18,800 for hockey and 19,800 for basketball; will include 65 suites on the 200 level; estimated cost: $172 million (US). Leafs' home opener scheduled for February 1999.

2000

BASEBALL

Detroit (AL): Ground was broken for Tiger Ballpark on October 29, 1997. Located near a new stadium for the Detroit Lions in downtown Detroit's Foxtown Theater district about one mile from existing Tiger Stadium; baseball-only park would seat approximately 40,000 and have 80 luxury suites; estimated cost: $260 million. Grand opening slated for opening day 2000.

Houston (NL): Groundbreaking for the Ballpark at Union Station on the east side of downtown Houston occurred on October 30, 1997. The natural grass ballpark will feature a retractable roof which can open and close in 20 minutes; will seat 42,000 and have over 60 luxury suites; left field will be connected to Union train station, which will also house the Astros administrative offices, retail stores and a cafe; estimated cost between $260 million. Grand opening slated for opening day 2000.

Milwaukee (AL): Groundbreaking for Miller Park (Miller Brewing Co. is the title sponsor) on a site adjacent to the existing County Stadium took place Nov. 9, 1996. The retractable-roof stadium will have natural grass, an asymmetrical outfield and seat approximately 43,000; estimated cost: $250 million. Brewers' home opener scheduled for April 2000.

San Francisco (NL): Construction of Pacific Bell Park (Pacific Bell is the title sponsor) in underway; to be located on the waterfront at China Basin; the open-air baseball-only park will seat 42,000, including 5,300 club seats and 65 luxury suites; estimated cost: $262 million. Giants' home opener scheduled for April 2000.

NFL FOOTBALL

Cincinnati (AFC): Groundbreaking for Paul Brown Stadium took place on April 25, 1998. The project will cost approximately $400 million. The open-air, grass-field stadium will have a futuristic design and seat 66,965 for football; will include approximately 104 luxury suites; Bengals' home opener scheduled for August 2000.

NHL HOCKEY

Columbus (expansion): Groundbreaking for Nationwide Arena (Nationwide Insurance is the title sponsor) took place on May 26, 1998. The privately-funded arena for the NHL expansion Columbus Blue Jackets will seat 18,500 for hockey and cost an estimated $150 million. The building will have 76 luxury suites and is scheduled to open in October 2000.

Minnesota (expansion): Groundbreaking for New Saint Paul Arena took place on June 23, 1998. The multi-purpose arena will seat 18,600 for the NHL expansion Minnesota Wild, including 74 luxury suites, and have a transparent glass exterior. The building, located in downtown St. Paul, will cost an estimated $130 million and is scheduled to open in September 2000.

2001

BASEBALL

Pittsburgh (NL): PNC Park (PNC Bank is the title sponsor) is in planning stages. To be located on a site on the Allegheny River between Three Rivers Stadium and the Sixth Street Bridge. The baseball-only park would seat approximately 38,000, have 64 luxury suites and cost an estimated $228 million; Stadium would be part of city's larger construction project, including enlarged convention center and new ballpark for NFL's Steelers; earliest Pirates' home opener would be April 2001.

NFL FOOTBALL

Pittsburgh (AFC): New open-air, grass-field stadium would seat 65,000 and contain 120 luxury suites. To be located 300 yards west of Three Rivers Stadium as part of city's larger construction project, including enlarged convention center and new ballpark for MLB's Pirates. Estimated cost for new football stadium: $233 million. Earliest opening would be September 2001.

San Francisco (NFC): Groundbreaking for as-yet-unnamed stadium set for fall of 1998. To be part of larger complex including shopping mall and parking garage located at Candlestick Point. Estimated cost of entire complex: $525 million. The open-air, grass stadium would seat 75,000 and include 200 luxury suites. To be located in same area as 3Com Park. Earliest opening would be September 2001.

2002

BASEBALL

New York (NL): New ballpark is in planning stages. To be located adjacent to Shea Stadium in Queens. The retractable-roof stadium would seat 45,000, including 78 luxury suites and 5,000 club seats. The stadium will have a grass field on a platform that can be rolled out into the parking lot to receive enough sunshine and moisture. With the field out the stadium could seat 60,000 for hockey, basketball or other events. Estimated cost: $500 million. Earliest opening would be April 2002.

San Diego (NL): New ballpark is in planning stages. To be located on a one-square-block downtown lot and be part of a larger redevelopment project that would include a new hotel, office space and retail space. The as-yet-unnamed baseball-only park would seat approximately 42,000. Earliest Padres' home opener would be April 2002.

NFL FOOTBALL

Seattle (AFC): Construction for the as-yet-unnamed stadium is set to begin in April 2000. Stadium and exhibition center are to be located on old site of Kingdome; would seat 72,000 and include 112 luxury suites and 10,000 club seats; open-air, grass-field would cost an estimated $400 million. The Seahawks would compete at Husky Stadium for two years during construction. Earliest Seahawks home opener would be August 2002.

2003

BASEBALL

Cincinnati (NL): New ballpark is in planning stages. Many details, including the site, are still to be determined. Estimated cost of project: $235 million. Earliest opening would be spring 2003. Stay tuned.

Home, Sweet Home

The home fields, home courts and home ice of the AL, NL, NBA, NFL, CFL, NHL, NCAA Division I-A college football and Division I basketball. Also included are Formula One, IndyCar, Indy Racing League and NASCAR auto racing tracks.

Attendance figures for the 1997 NFL regular season and the 1997-98 NBA and NHL regular seasons are provided. See Baseball chapter for 1998 AL and NL attendance figures.

MAJOR LEAGUE BASEBALL

American League

Team	Ballpark	Built	Capacity	LF	LCF	CF	RCF	RF	Field
				—Outfield Fences—					
Anaheim Angels	**Edison International Field of Anaheim**	1966	**46,000**	333	386	404	386	370	Grass
Baltimore Orioles	**Oriole Park at Camden Yards**	1992	**48,188**	333	410	400	373	318	Grass
Boston Red Sox	**Fenway Park**	1912	**33,871**	315	379	390	380	302	Grass
Chicago White Sox	**Comiskey Park**	1991	**44,321**	347	375	400	375	347	Grass
Cleveland Indians	**Jacobs Field**	1994	**43,368**	325	370	405	375	325	Grass
Detroit Tigers	**Tiger Stadium**	1912	**46,945**	340	365	440	375	325	Grass
Kansas City Royals	**Kauffman Stadium**	1973	**40,625**	330	375	400	375	330	Grass
Minnesota Twins	**Hubert H. Humphrey Metrodome**	1982	**48,678**	343	385	408	367	327	Turf
New York Yankees	**Yankee Stadium**	1923	**57,746**	318	399	408	385	314	Grass
Oakland Athletics	**Oakland-Alameda County Coliseum**	1966	**43,662**	330	367	400	367	330	Grass
Seattle Mariners	**The Kingdome**	1976	**59,166**	331	389	405	380	312	Turf
	& SAFECO Field	1999	**45,611**	TBA	TBA	TBA	TBA	TBA	Grass
Tampa Bay Devil Rays	**Tropicana Field**	1990	**45,200**	315	415	407	409	322	Turf
Texas Rangers	**The Ballpark in Arlington**	1994	**49,166**	332	390	400	381	325	Grass
Toronto Blue Jays	**SkyDome**	1989	**50,516**	328	375	400	375	328	Turf

National League

Team	Ballpark	Built	Capacity	LF	LCF	CF	RCF	RF	Field
				—Outfield Fences—					
Arizona Diamondbacks	**Bank One Ballpark**	1998	**48,500**	330	374	407	374	334	Grass
Atlanta Braves	**Turner Field**	1996	**50,062**	335	380	401	385	330	Grass
Chicago Cubs	**Wrigley Field**	1914	**38,902**	355	368	400	368	353	Grass
Cincinnati Reds	**Cinergy Field**	1970	**52,952**	330	375	404	375	330	Turf
Colorado Rockies	**Coors Field**	1995	**50,200**	347	390	415	375	350	Grass
Florida Marlins	**Pro Player Stadium**	1987	**42,631**	330	385	434	385	345	Grass
Houston Astros	**The Astrodome**	1965	**54,370**	325	375	400	375	325	Turf
Los Angeles Dodgers	**Dodger Stadium**	1962	**56,000**	330	385	395	385	330	Grass
Milwaukee Brewers	**County Stadium**	1953	**53,192**	315	392	402	392	315	Grass
Montreal Expos	**Olympic Stadium**	1976	**46,500**	325	375	404	375	325	Turf
New York Mets	**Shea Stadium**	1964	**55,775**	338	371	410	371	338	Grass
Philadelphia Phillies	**Veterans Stadium**	1971	**62,409**	330	371	408	371	330	Turf
Pittsburgh Pirates	**Three Rivers Stadium**	1970	**47,972**	335	375	400	375	335	Turf
St. Louis Cardinals	**Busch Stadium**	1966	**49,625**	330	372	402	372	330	Grass
San Diego Padres	**Qualcomm Stadium**	1967	**53,166**	327	370	405	370	327	Grass
San Francisco Giants	**3Com Park**	1960	**63,000**	335	365	400	365	328	Grass

Rank by Capacity

AL		NL	
Seattle	59,166	San Francisco	63,000
New York	57,746	Philadelphia	62,409
Toronto	50,516	Los Angeles	56,000
Texas	49,166	New York	55,775
Minnesota	48,678	Houston	54,370
Baltimore	48,188	Milwaukee	53,192
Detroit	46,945	San Diego	53,166
Anaheim	46,000	Cincinnati	52,952
Tampa Bay	45,200	Colorado	50,200
Chicago	44,321	Atlanta	50,062
Oakland	43,662	St. Louis	49,625
Cleveland	43,368	Arizona	48,500
Kansas City	40,625	Pittsburgh	47,972
Boston	33,871	Montreal	46,500
		Florida	42,631
		Chicago	38,902

Rank by Age

AL		NL	
Boston	1912	Chicago	1914
Detroit	1912	Milwaukee	1953
New York	1923	San Francisco	1960
Anaheim	1966	Los Angeles	1962
Oakland	1966	New York	1964
Kansas City	1973	Houston	1965
Seattle	1976	St. Louis	1966
Minnesota	1982	San Diego	1967
Toronto	1989	Cincinnati	1970
Tampa Bay	1990	Pittsburgh	1970
Chicago	1991	Philadelphia	1971
Baltimore	1992	Montreal	1976
Cleveland	1994	Florida	1987
Texas	1994	Colorado	1995
		Atlanta	1996
		Arizona	1998

Note: New York's Yankee Stadium (AL) was rebuilt in 1976.

Major League Baseball (Cont.)
Home Fields

Listed below are the principal home fields used through the years by current American and National League teams. The NL became a major league in 1876, the AL in 1901.

The capacity figures in the right-hand column indicate the largest seating capacity of the ballpark while the club played there. Capacity figures before 1915 (and the introduction of concrete grandstands) are sketchy at best and have been left blank.

American League

Anaheim Angels

1961	Wrigley Field (Los Angeles)	20,457
1962-65	Dodger Stadium	56,000
1966–	Edison International Field of Anaheim (1966 capacity-43,250)	46,000

Baltimore Orioles

1901	Lloyd Street Grounds (Milwaukee)	–
1902-53	Sportsman's Park II (St. Louis)	30,500
1954-91	Memorial Stadium (Baltimore)	53,371
1992–	Camden Yards	48,188

Boston Red Sox

1901-11	Huntington Ave. Grounds	–
1912–	Fenway Park (1934 capacity-27,000)	33,871

Chicago White Sox

1901-10	Southside Park	–
1910-90	Comiskey Park I	43,931
1991–	Comiskey Park II	44,321

Cleveland Indians

1901-09	League Park I	–
1910-46	League Park II	21,414
1932-93	Cleveland Stadium	74,483
1994–	Jacobs Field	43,368

Detroit Tigers

1901-11	Bennett Park	–
1912–	Tiger Stadium (1912 capacity-23,000)	46,945

Kansas City Royals

1969-72	Municipal Stadium	35,020
1973–	Kauffman Stadium (1973 capacity-40,762)	40,625

Minnesota Twins

1901-02	American League Park (Washington, DC)	–
1903-60	Griffith Stadium	27,410
1960-81	Metropolitan Stadium (Bloomington, MN)	45,919
1982–	HHH Metrodome (Minneapolis) (1982 capacity-54,000)	48,678

New York Yankees

1901-02	Oriole Park (Baltimore)	–
1903-12	Hilltop Park (New York)	–
1913-22	Polo Grounds II	38,000
1923-73	Yankee Stadium I	67,224
1974-75	Shea Stadium	55,101
1976–	Yankee Stadium II (1976 capacity-57,145)	57,746

Oakland Athletics

1901-08	Columbia Park (Philadelphia)	–
1909-54	Shibe Park	33,608
1955-67	Municipal Stadium (Kansas City)	35,020
1968–	Oakland Alameda County Coliseum (1968 capacity-48,621)	43,662

Seattle Mariners

1977-99	The Kingdome	59,166
1999–	SAFECO Field	45,611

Tampa Bay Devil Rays

1990–	Tropicana Field	45,200

Texas Rangers

1961	Griffith Stadium (Washington, DC)	27,410
1962-71	RFK Stadium	45,016
1972-93	Arlington Stadium (Texas)	43,521
1994–	The Ballpark in Arlington	49,166

Toronto Blue Jays

1977-89	Exhibition Stadium	43,737
1989–	SkyDome (1989 capacity-49,500)	50,516

Ballpark Name Changes: ANAHEIM—**Edison International Field of Anaheim** originally Anaheim Stadium (1966-98); CHICAGO—**Comiskey Park I** originally White Sox Park (1910-12), then Comiskey Park in 1913, then White Sox Park again in 1962, then Comiskey Park again in 1976; CLEVELAND—**League Park** renamed Dunn Field in 1920, then League Park again in 1928; Cleveland Stadium originally Municipal Stadium (1932-74); DETROIT—**Tiger Stadium** originally Navin Field (1912-37), then Briggs Stadium (1938-60); KANSAS CITY—**Kauffman Stadium** originally Royals Stadium (1973-93); LOS ANGELES—**Dodger Stadium** referred to as Chavez Revine by AL while Angels played there (1962-65); PHILADELPHIA—**Shibe Park** renamed Connie Mack Stadium in 1953; ST. LOUIS—**Sportsman's Park** renamed Busch Stadium in 1953; WASHINGTON—**Griffith Stadium** originally National Park (1892-1920), **RFK Stadium** originally D.C. Stadium (1961-68).

National League

Arizona Diamondbacks

1998–	Bank One Ballpark	48,500

Atlanta Braves

1876-94	South End Grounds I (Boston)	–
1894-1914	South End Grounds II	–
1915-52	Braves Field	40,000
1953-65	County Stadium (Milwaukee)	43,394
1966-96	Atlanta-Fulton County Stadium (1966 capacity-50,000)	52,769
1997–	Turner Field	50,062

Chicago Cubs

1876-77	State Street Grounds	–
1878-84	Lakefront Park	–
1885-91	West Side Park	–
1891-93	Brotherhood Park	–
1893-1915	West Side Grounds	–
1916–	Wrigley Field (1916 capacity-16,000)	38,902

Cincinnati Reds

1876-79	Avenue Grounds	–
1880	Bank Street Grounds	–
1890-1901	Redland Field I	–
1902-11	Palace of the Fans	–
1912-70	Crosley Field	29,603
1970–	Cinergy Field	52,952
	(1970 capacity-52,000)	

Colorado Rockies

1993-94	Mile High Stadium (Denver)	76,100
1995–	Coors Field	50,200

Florida Marlins

1993–	Pro Player Stadium (Miami)	42,631

Houston Astros

1962-64	Colt Stadium	32,601
1965–	The Astrodome	54,370
	(1965 capacity-45,011)	

Los Angeles Dodgers

1890	Washington Park I (Brooklyn)	–
1891-97	Eastern Park	–
1898-1912	Washington Park II	–
1913-56	Ebbets Field	31,497
1957	Ebbets Field	31,497
	& Roosevelt Stadium (Jersey City)	24,167
1958-61	Memorial Coliseum (Los Angeles)	93,600
1962–	Dodger Stadium	56,000

Milwaukee Brewers

1969	Sick's Stadium (Seattle)	59,166
1970–	County Stadium (Milwaukee)	53,192
	(1970 capacity-46,620)	

Montreal Expos

1969-76	Jarry Park	28,000
1977–	Olympic Stadium	46,500
	(1977 capacity-58,500)	

New York Mets

1962-63	Polo Grounds	55,987
1964–	Shea Stadium	55,775
	(1964 capacity-55,101)	

Philadelphia Phillies

1883-86	Recreation Park	–
1887-94	Huntingdon Ave. Grounds	–
1895-1938	Baker Bowl	18,800
1938-70	Shibe Park	33,608
1971–	Veterans Stadium	62,409
	(1971 capacity-56,371)	

Pittsburgh Pirates

1887-90	Recreation Park	–
1891-1909	Exposition Park	–
1909-70	Forbes Field	35,000
1970–	Three Rivers Stadium	47,972
	(1970 capacity-50,235)	

St. Louis Cardinals

1876-77	Sportsman's Park I	–
1885-86	Vandeventer Lot	–
1892-1920	Robison Field	18,000
1920-66	Sportsman's Park II	30,500
1966–	Busch Stadium	49,625
	(1966 capacity-50,126)	

San Diego Padres

1969–	Qualcomm Stadium	53,166
	(1969 capacity-47,634)	

San Francisco Giants

1876	Union Grounds (Brooklyn)	–
1883-88	Polo Grounds I (New York)	–
1889-90	Manhattan Field	–
1891-1957	Polo Grounds II	55,987
1958-59	Seals Stadium (San Francisco)	22,900
1960–	3Com Park	63,000
	(1960 capacity-42,553)	

Ballpark Name Changes: ATLANTA—**Atlanta-Fulton County Stadium** originally Atlanta Stadium (1966-74), **Turner Field** originally Centennial Olympic Stadium (1996); CHICAGO—**Wrigley Field** originally Weeghman Park (1914-17), then Cubs Park (1918-25); CINCINNATI—**Redland Field** originally League Park (1890-93), **Crosley Field** originally Redland Field II (1912-33) and **Cinergy Field** originally Riverfront Stadium (1970-96); FLORIDA—**Pro Player Stadium** originally Joe Robbie Stadium (1987-96); HOUSTON—**Astrodome** originally Harris County Domed Stadium before it opened in 1965; PHILADELPHIA—**Shibe Park** renamed Connie Mack Stadium in 1953; ST. LOUIS—**Robison Field** originally Vandeventer Lot, then League Park, then Cardinal Park all before becoming Robison Field in 1901, **Sportsman's Park** renamed Busch Stadium in 1953, and **Busch Stadium** originally Busch Memorial Stadium (1966-82); SAN DIEGO—**Qualcomm Stadium** originally San Diego Stadium (1967-81) and San Diego/Jack Murphy Stadium (1982-96); SAN FRANCISCO—**3Com Park** originally Candlestick Park (1960-95).

NATIONAL BASKETBALL ASSOCIATION

Western Conference

Team	Arena	Location	Built	Capacity
Dallas Mavericks	**Reunion Arena**	Dallas, Texas	1980	**18,042**
Denver Nuggets	**McNichols Arena**	Denver, Colo.	1975	**17,171**
Golden State Warriors	**New Oakland Coliseum**	Oakland, Calif.	1997	**19,200**
Houston Rockets	**Compaq Center**	Houston, Texas	1975	**16,285**
Los Angeles Clippers	**Los Angeles Sports Arena**	Los Angeles, Calif.	1959	**16,021**
	& **Arrowhead Pond**	Anaheim, Calif.	1993	**18,211**
Los Angeles Lakers	**Great Western Forum**	Inglewood, Calif.	1967	**17,505**
Minnesota Timberwolves	**Target Center**	Minneapolis, Minn.	1990	**19,006**
Phoenix Suns	**America West Arena**	Phoenix, Ariz.	1992	**19,023**
Portland Trail Blazers	**Rose Garden**	Portland, Ore.	1995	**19,980**
Sacramento Kings	**ARCO Arena**	Sacramento, Calif.	1988	**17,317**
San Antonio Spurs	**Alamodome**	San Antonio, Texas	1993	**20,557**
Seattle SuperSonics	**Key Arena at Seattle Center**	Seattle, Wash.	1962	**17,100**
Utah Jazz	**Delta Center**	Salt Lake City, Utah	1991	**19,911**
Vancouver Grizzlies	**General Motors Place**	Vancouver, B.C.	1995	**19,193**

Notes: Seattle's Key Arena was originally the Seattle Coliseum before being rebuilt in 1995; San Antonio's Alamodome seating is expandable to hold 32,500 while Portland's Rose Garden was "downsized" from a capacity of 21,538 to 19,980 prior to the 1998-99 season; the Los Angeles Clippers are scheduled to play eight of 41 regular season home games at the Arrowhead Pond in Anaheim in 1998-99.

National Basketball Association (Cont.)

Eastern Conference

Team	Arena	Location	Built	Capacity
Atlanta Hawks	**Georgia Dome**	Atlanta, Ga.	1992	**21,570**
	& **Alexander Memorial Coliseum**	Atlanta, Ga.	1956	**9,300**
Boston Celtics	**FleetCenter**	Boston, Mass.	1995	**18,624**
Charlotte Hornets	**Charlotte Coliseum**	Charlotte, N.C.	1988	**24,042**
Chicago Bulls	**United Center**	Chicago, Ill.	1994	**21,711**
Cleveland Cavaliers	**Gund Arena**	Cleveland, Ohio	1994	**20,562**
Detroit Pistons	**The Palace of Auburn Hills**	Auburn Hills, Mich.	1988	**21,454**
Indiana Pacers	**Market Square Arena**	Indianapolis, Ind.	1974	**16,530**
Miami Heat	**Miami Arena**	Miami, Fla.	1988	**15,200**
Milwaukee Bucks	**Bradley Center**	Milwaukee, Wisc.	1988	**18,717**
New Jersey Nets	**Continental Airlines Arena**	E. Rutherford, N.J.	1981	**20,029**
New York Knicks	**Madison Square Garden**	New York, N.Y.	1968	**19,763**
Orlando Magic	**Orlando Arena**	Orlando, Fla.	1989	**17,248**
Philadelphia 76ers	**First Union Center**	Philadelphia, Pa.	1996	**20,444**
Toronto Raptors	**SkyDome**	Toronto, Ont.	1989	**20,125**
	& **Air Canada Centre**	Toronto, Ont.	1999	**19,800**
Washington Wizards	**MCI Center**	Washington, DC	1997	**20,500**

Notes: Atlanta is scheduled to play 12 regular season games at Georgia Tech's Alexander Memorial Coliseum in 1998-99; Toronto will play their home games at SkyDome before moving into the new Air Canada Centre in February of 1999.

Rank by Capacity

West		East	
San Antonio	20,557	Charlotte	24,042
Portland	19,980	Chicago	21,711
Utah	19,911	Atlanta	21,570
Golden St.	19,200	Detroit	21,454
Vancouver	19,193	Cleveland	20,562
Phoenix	19,023	Washington	20,500
Minnesota	19,006	Philadelphia	20,444
Dallas	18,042	Toronto	20,125
LA Lakers	17,505	New Jersey	20,029
Sacramento	17,317	New York	19,763
Denver	17,171	Milwaukee	18,717
Seattle	17,100	Boston	18,624
Houston	16,285	Orlando	17,248
LA Clippers	16,021	Indiana	16,530
		Miami	15,200

Note: Alamodome seating is expandable to 32,500 and Georgia Dome seating is expandable to 34,821.

Rank by Age

West		East	
LA Clippers	1959	New York	1968
Seattle	1962	Atlanta	1972
LA Lakers	1967	Indiana	1974
Denver	1975	New Jersey	1981
Houston	1975	Charlotte	1988
Dallas	1980	Detroit	1988
Sacramento	1988	Miami	1988
Minnesota	1990	Milwaukee	1988
Utah	1991	Orlando	1989
Phoenix	1992	Toronto	1989
San Antonio	1993	Chicago	1994
Portland	1995	Cleveland	1994
Vancouver	1995	Boston	1995
Golden St.	1997	Philadelphia	1996
		Washington	1997

Note: The Seattle Coliseum was rebuilt and renamed Key Arena in 1995.

1997-98 NBA Attendance

Official overall attendance in the NBA for the 1997-98 season was 20,352,157 for an average per game crowd of 17,117 over 1,189 games. Teams in each conference are ranked by attendance over 41 home games based on total tickets distributed; sellouts are listed in S/O column. Numbers in parentheses indicate rank in 1996-97.

Western Conference

	Team	Attendance	S/O	Average
1	Portland (1)	823,070	9	20,075
2	Utah (2)	815,969	38	19,902
3	San Antonio (5)	783,455	11	19,109
4	Phoenix (3)	779,943	41	19,023
5	Minnesota (7)	738,572	12	18,014
6	Seattle (6)	699,952	41	17,072
7	LA Lakers (8)	691,994	26	16,878
8	Houston (10)	666,685	41	16,285
9	Vancouver (9)	660,457	2	16,109
10	Sacramento (4)	605,434	5	14,767
11	Dallas (12)	541,541	5	13,208
12	Golden St. (11)	500,286	3	12,202
13	Denver (13)	483,791	2	11,800
14	LA Clippers (14)	408,699	3	9,968
	TOTAL	9,199,848	239	16,029

Note: LA Clippers played 33 games at LA Sports Arena (2 sellouts and 9,128 avg.) and eight at The Arrowhead Pond in Anaheim (1 sellout and 13,435 avg.)

Eastern Conference

	Team	Attendance	S/O	Average
1	Chicago (2)	983,444	41	23,986
2	Charlotte (1)	959,616	23	23,405
3	New York (4)	810,283	41	19,763
4	Washington (7)	801,240	23	19,542
5	Detroit (3)	794,567	17	19,380
6	Boston (10)	743,422	28	18,132
7	New Jersey (9)	719,020	15	17,537
8	Atlanta (15)	715,502	11	17,451
9	Orlando (6)	701,647	28	17,113
10	Cleveland (8)	694,629	6	16,942
11	Toronto (5)	675,325	2	16,471
12	Philadelphia (13)	655,417	7	15,986
13	Indiana (11)	645,302	12	15,739
14	Milwaukee (12)	638,034	6	15,562
15	Miami (14)	614,861	24	14,997
	TOTAL	11,152,309	284	18,134

Note: Washington played 5 games at USAir Arena (4 sellouts and 18,661 avg.) and 36 at their new MCI Center (19 sellouts, 19,665 avg.).

Home Courts

Listed below are the principal home courts used through the years by current NBA teams. The largest capacity of each arena is noted in the right-hand column. ABA arenas (1972-76) are included for Denver, Indiana, New Jersey and San Antonio.

Western Conference

Dallas Mavericks

1980– Reunion Arena 18,042

Denver Nuggets

1967-75 Auditorium Arena 6,841
1975– McNichols Sports Arena 17,171
(1975 capacity-16,700)

Golden State Warriors

1946-52 Philadelphia Arena 7,777
1952-62 Convention Hall (Philadelphia) 9,200
& Philadelphia Arena 7,777
1962-64 Cow Palace (San Francisco) 13,862
1964-66 Civic Auditorium 7,500
& (USF Memorial Gym) 6,000
1966-67 Cow Palace, Civic Auditorium
& Oakland Coliseum Arena 15,000
1967-71 Cow Palace 14,500
1971-96 Oakland Coliseum Arena 15,025
(1971 capacity-12,905)
1996-97 San Jose Arena 18,500
1997– New Oakland Coliseum 19,200

Houston Rockets

1967-71 San Diego Sports Arena 14,000
1971-72 Hofheinz Pavilion (Houston) 10,218
1972-73 Hofheinz Pavilion 10,218
& HemisFair Arena (San Antonio) 10,446
1973-75 Hofheinz Pavilion 10,218
1975– Compaq Center 16,285
(1975 capacity-15,600)

Los Angeles Clippers

1970-78 Memorial Auditorium (Buffalo) 17,300
1978-84 San Diego Sports Arena 12,167
1985-94 Los Angeles Sports Arena 16,005
1994– Los Angeles Sports Arena 16,021
& Arrowhead Pond 18,211

Los Angeles Lakers

1948-60 Minneapolis Auditorium 10,000
1960-67 Los Angeles Sports Arena 14,781
1967– Great Western Forum (Inglewood, CA) .. 17,505
(1967 capacity-17,086)

Minnesota Timberwolves

1989-90 Hubert H. Humphrey Metrodome 23,000
1990– Target Center 19,006

Phoenix Suns

1968-92 Arizona Veterans' Memorial Coliseum .. 14,487
1992– America West Arena 19,023

Portland Trail Blazers

1970-95 Memorial Coliseum 12,888
1995– Rose Garden 19,980
(1995 capacity-21,538)

Sacramento Kings

1948-55 Edgarton Park Arena (Rochester, NY) 5,000
1955-58 Rochester War Memorial 10,000
1958-72 Cincinnati Gardens 11,438
1972-74 Municipal Auditorium (Kansas City) 9,929
& Omaha (NE) Civic Auditorium 9,136
1974-78 Kemper Arena (Kansas City) 16,785
& Omaha Civic Auditorium 9,136
1978-85 Kemper Arena 16,785
1985-88 ARCO Arena I 10,333
1988– ARCO Arena II 17,317
(1988 capacity-16,517)

San Antonio Spurs

1967-70 Memorial Auditorium (Dallas) 8,088
& Moody Coliseum (Dallas) 8,500
1970-71 Moody Coliseum 8,500
Tarrant Convention Center (Ft. Worth) ... 13,500
& Municipal Coliseum (Lubbock) 10,400
1971-73 Moody Coliseum 9,500
& Memorial Auditorium 8,088
1973-93 HemisFair Arena (San Antonio) 16,057
1993– The Alamodome 20,557

Seattle SuperSonics

1967-78 Seattle Center Coliseum 14,098
1978-85 Kingdome 40,192
1985-94 Seattle Center Coliseum 14,252
1994-95 Tacoma Dome 19,000
1995– Key Arena at Seattle Center 17,100

Utah Jazz

1974-75 Municipal Auditorium 7,853
& Louisiana Superdome 47,284
1975-79 Superdome 47,284
1979-83 Salt Palace (Salt Lake City) 12,519
1983-84 Salt Palace 12,519
& Thomas & Mack Center (Las Vegas) .. 18,500
1985-91 Salt Palace 12,616
1991– Delta Center 19,911

Vancouver Grizzlies

1995– General Motors Place 19,193

Eastern Conference

Atlanta Hawks

1949-51 Wharton Field House (Moline, IL) 6,000
1951-55 Milwaukee Arena 11,000
1955-68 Kiel Auditorium (St. Louis) 10,000
1968-72 Alexander Mem. Coliseum (Atlanta) 7,166
1972-96 The Omni 16,378
1997– Georgia Dome 21,570
& Alexander Mem. Coliseum 9,300

Boston Celtics

1946-95 Boston Garden 14,890
1995– FleetCenter 18,624

Note: From 1975-95 the Celtics played some regular season games at the Hartford Civic Center (15,418).

Charlotte Hornets

1988– Charlotte Coliseum 24,042
(1988 capacity-23,500)

Chicago Bulls

1966-67 Chicago Amphitheater 11,002
1967-94 Chicago Stadium 18,676
1994– United Center 21,711

Cleveland Cavaliers

1970-74 Cleveland Arena 11,000
1974-94 The Coliseum (Richfield, OH) 20,273
1994– Gund Arena 20,562

National Basketball Association (Cont.)

Detroit Pistons

1948-52	North Side H.S. Gym (Ft. Wayne, IN)	3,800
1952-57	Memorial Coliseum (Ft. Wayne)	9,306
1957-61	Olympia Stadium (Detroit)	14,000
1961-78	Cobo Arena	11,147
1978-88	Silverdome (Pontiac, MI)	22,366
1988–	The Palace of Auburn Hills	21,454

Indiana Pacers

1967-74	State Fairgrounds (Indianapolis)	9,479
1974–	Market Square Arena (1974 capacity-17,287)	16,530

Miami Heat

1988–	Miami Arena	15,200

Milwaukee Bucks

1968-88	Milwaukee Arena (The Mecca)	11,052
1988–	Bradley Center	18,717

New Jersey Nets

1967-68	Teaneck (NJ) Armory	3,500
1968-69	Long Island Arena (Commack, NY)	6,500
1969-71	Island Garden (W. Hempstead, NY)	5,200
1971-77	Nassau Coliseum (Uniondale, NY)	15,500
1977-81	Rutgers Ath. Center (Piscataway, NJ)	9,050
1981–	Continental Airlines Arena (E. Rutherford, NJ)	20,029

New York Knicks

1946-68	Madison Sq. Garden III (50th St.)	18,496
1968–	Madison Sq. Garden IV (33rd St.) (1968 capacity-19,694)	19,763

Orlando Magic

1989–	Orlando Arena	17,248

Philadelphia 76ers

1949-51	State Fair Coliseum (Syracuse, NY)	7,500
1951-63	Onondaga County (NY) War Memorial	8,000
1963-67	Convention Hall (Philadelphia)	12,000
	& Philadelphia Arena	7,777
1967-96	CoreStates Spectrum	18,136
1996–	First Union Center	20,444

Toronto Raptors

1995-99	SkyDome	20,125
1999–	Air Canada Centre	19,800

Washington Wizards

1961-62	Chicago Amphitheater	11,000
1962-63	Chicago Coliseum	7,100
1963-73	Baltimore Civic Center	12,289
1973-97	USAir Arena (Landover, MD)	18,756
1997–	MCI Center	20,500

Note: From 1988-96 the Wizards (then Bullets) played four regular season games at Baltimore Arena (12,756).

Building Name Changes: HOUSTON– **Compaq Center** originally The Summit (1975-97); NEW JERSEY– **Continental Airlines Arena** originally Byrne Meadowlands Arena (1981-96); PHILADELPHIA– **First Union Center** originally the CoreStates Center (1996-98) and **CoreStates Spectrum** originally The Spectrum (1967-94); WASHINGTON– **USAir Arena** originally Capital Centre (1973-93).

NATIONAL FOOTBALL LEAGUE

American Football Conference

		Location	Built	Capacity	Field
Baltimore Ravens	**Ravens' Stadium**	Baltimore, Md.	1998	**68,400**	Grass
Buffalo Bills	**Rich Stadium**	Orchard Park, N.Y.	1973	**80,024**	Turf
Cincinnati Bengals	**Cinergy Field**	Cincinnati, Ohio	1970	**60,389**	Turf
Denver Broncos	**Mile High Stadium**	Denver, Colo.	1948	**76,208**	Grass
Indianapolis Colts	**RCA Dome**	Indianapolis, Ind.	1984	**60,599**	Turf
Jacksonville Jaguars	**ALLTEL Stadium**	Jacksonville, Fla.	1995	**73,000**	Grass
Kansas City Chiefs	**Arrowhead Stadium**	Kansas City, Mo.	1972	**79,409**	Grass
Miami Dolphins	**Pro Player Stadium**	Miami, Fla.	1987	**75,192**	Grass
New England Patriots	**Foxboro Stadium**	Foxboro, Mass.	1971	**60,292**	Grass
New York Jets	**Giants Stadium**	E. Rutherford, N.J.	1976	**77,803**	Turf
Oakland Raiders	**Oakland-Alameda County Coliseum**	Oakland, Calif.	1966	**63,026**	Grass
Pittsburgh Steelers	**Three Rivers Stadium**	Pittsburgh, Pa.	1970	**59,600**	Turf
San Diego Chargers	**Qualcomm Stadium**	San Diego, Calif.	1967	**71,000**	Grass
Seattle Seahawks	**Kingdome**	Seattle, Wash.	1976	**66,400**	Turf
Tennessee Oilers	**Vanderbilt Stadium**	Nashville, Tenn.	1981	**41,600**	Turf

National Football Conference

		Location	Built	Capacity	Field
Arizona Cardinals	**Sun Devil Stadium**	Tempe, Ariz.	1958	**73,273**	Grass
Atlanta Falcons	**Georgia Dome**	Atlanta, Ga.	1992	**71,228**	Turf
Carolina Panthers	**Ericsson Stadium**	Charlotte, N.C.	1996	**75,248**	Grass
Chicago Bears	**Soldier Field**	Chicago, Ill.	1924	**66,944**	Grass
Dallas Cowboys	**Texas Stadium**	Irving, Texas	1971	**65,675**	Turf
Detroit Lions	**Pontiac Silverdome**	Pontiac, Mich.	1975	**80,368**	Turf
Green Bay Packers	**Lambeau Field**	Green Bay, Wisc.	1957	**60,790**	Grass
Minnesota Vikings	**Hubert H. Humphrey Metrodome**	Minneapolis, Minn.	1982	**64,182**	Turf
New Orleans Saints	**Louisiana Superdome**	New Orleans, La.	1975	**69,420**	Turf
New York Giants	**Giants Stadium**	E. Rutherford, N.J.	1976	**78,148**	Turf
Philadelphia Eagles	**Veterans Stadium**	Philadelphia, Pa.	1971	**65,352**	Turf
St. Louis Rams	**Trans World Dome**	St. Louis, Mo.	1995	**66,000**	Turf
San Francisco 49ers	**3Com Park**	San Francisco, Calif.	1960	**70,140**	Grass
Tampa Bay Buccaneers	**Raymond James Stadium**	Tampa, Fla.	1998	**65,000**	Grass
Washington Redskins	**Jack Kent Cooke Stadium**	Raljon, MD	1997	**78,600**	Grass

Rank by Capacity

AFC		NFC	
Buffalo	80,024	Detroit	80,368
Kansas City	79,409	Washington	78,600
NY Jets	77,803	NY Giants	78,148
Denver	76,208	Carolina	75,248
Miami	75,192	Arizona	73,273
Jacksonville	73,000	Atlanta	71,228
San Diego	71,000	San Francisco	70,140
Baltimore	68,400	New Orleans	69,420
Seattle	66,400	Chicago	66,944
Oakland	63,026	St. Louis	66,000
Indianapolis	60,599	Dallas	65,675
Cincinnati	60,389	Philadelphia	65,352
New England	60,292	Tampa Bay	65,000
Pittsburgh	59,600	Minnesota	64,182
Tennessee	41,600	Green Bay	60,790

Rank by Age

AFC		NFC	
Denver	1948	Chicago	1924
Oakland	1966	Green Bay	1957
San Diego	1967	Arizona	1958
Cincinnati	1970	San Francisco	1960
Pittsburgh	1970	Dallas	1971
New England	1971	Philadelphia	1971
Kansas City	1972	New Orleans	1975
Buffalo	1973	Detroit	1975
NY Jets	1976	NY Giants	1976
Seattle	1976	Minnesota	1982
Tennessee	1981	Atlanta	1992
Indianapolis	1984	St. Louis	1995
Miami	1987	Carolina	1996
Jacksonville	1995	Washington	1997
Baltimore	1998	Tampa Bay	1998

1997 NFL Attendance

Official overall paid attendance in the NFL for the 1997 season was 14,715,299 for an average per game crowd of 61,314 over 240 games. Teams in each conference are ranked by attendance over eight home games. Rank column indicates rank in entire league. Numbers in parentheses indicate conference rank in 1996.

AFC

		Attendance	Rank	Average
1	Kansas City (1)	610,192	1	76,274
2	Denver (3)	590,189	3	73,774
3	Miami (4)	574,811	5	71,851
4	Jacksonville (5)	558,147	6	69,768
5	NY Jets (12)	549,836	8	68,730
6	Buffalo (2)	523,763	11	65,470
7	New England (7)	477,431	18	59,679
8	Baltimore (6)	475,236	19	59,405
9	San Diego (9)	465,906	20	58,238
10	Pittsburgh (8)	462,533	21	57,817
11	Seattle (14)	462,124	22	57,766
12	Indianapolis (10)	451,455	23	56,432
13	Cincinnati (13)	446,287	24	55,786
14	Oakland (11)	375,499	28	46,937
15	Tennessee (15)	224,401	30	28,050
	TOTAL	7,247,810	—	60,398

NFC

		Attendance	Rank	Average
1	Washington (11)	605,592	2	75,699
2	NY Giants (2)	582,422	4	72,803
3	Detroit (6)	554,898	7	69,362
4	Tampa Bay (13)	543,514	9	67,939
5	Philadelphia (3)	535,783	10	66,973
6	Carolina (1)	523,691	12	65,461
7	St. Louis (7)	518,468	13	64,809
8	Dallas (4)	511,767	14	63,971
9	San Francisco (5)	502,351	15	62,794
10	Minnesota (10)	486,921	16	60,865
11	Green Bay (8)	481,494	17	60,187
12	New Orleans (15)	443,714	25	55,464
13	Chicago (9)	421,900	26	52,738
14	Arizona (14)	379,547	27	47,443
15	Atlanta (12)	375,427	29	46,928
	TOTAL	7,467,489	—	62,229

Home Fields

Listed below are the principal home fields used through the years by current NFL teams. The largest capacity of each stadium is noted in the right-hand column. All-America Football Conference stadiums (1946-49) are included for Cleveland and San Francisco.

AFC

Baltimore Ravens

1946-95	Cleveland Stadium (1946 capacity-85,703)	78,512
1996-97	Memorial Stadium (Baltimore)	65,000
1998–	Ravens' Stadium	68,400

Buffalo Bills

1960-72	War Memorial Stadium	45,748
1973–	Rich Stadium (Orchard Park, NY) (1973 capacity-80,020)	80,024

Cincinnati Bengals

1968-69	Nippert Stadium (Univ. of Cincinnati)	26,500
1970–	Cinergy Field (1970 capacity-56,200)	60,389

Denver Broncos

1960–	Mile High Stadium (1960 capacity-34,000)	76,208

Indianapolis Colts

1953-83	Memorial Stadium (Baltimore)	60,020
1984–	RCA Dome (Indianapolis) (1984 capacity-60,127)	60,599

Jacksonville Jaguars

1995–	ALLTEL Stadium	73,000

Kansas City Chiefs

1960-62	Cotton Bowl (Dallas)	72,000
1963-71	Municipal Stadium (Kansas City)	47,000
1972–	Arrowhead Stadium (1972 capacity-78,097)	79,409

Miami Dolphins

1966-86	Orange Bowl	75,206
1987–	Pro Player Stadium (1987 capacity-75,500)	75,192

National Football League (Cont.)

New England Patriots

1960-62 Nickerson Field (Boston Univ.) 17,369
1963-68 Fenway Park 33,379
1969 Alumni Stadium (Boston College).......26,000
1970 Harvard Stadium 37,300
1971– Foxboro Stadium 60,292
(1971 capacity-61,114)

New York Jets

1960-63 Polo Grounds 55,987
1964-83 Shea Stadium 60,372
1984– Giants Stadium (E. Rutherford, NJ) 77,803

Oakland Raiders

1960 Kesar Stadium (San Francisco).........59,636
1961 Candlestick Park......................42,500
1962-65 Frank Youell Field (Oakland)............20,000
1966-81 Oakland-Alameda County Coliseum 54,587
1982-94 Memorial Coliseum (Los Angeles) 67,800
1995– Oakland-Alameda County Coliseum 63,026

Pittsburgh Steelers

1933-57 Forbes Field..........................35,000
1958-63 Forbes Field..........................35,000
& Pitt Stadium 54,500
1964-69 Pitt Stadium 54,500
1970– Three Rivers Stadium 59,600
(1970 capacity-49,000)

San Diego Chargers

1960 Memorial Coliseum (Los Angeles) 92,604
1961-66 Balboa Stadium (San Diego) 34,000
1967– Qualcomm Stadium 71,000
(1967 capacity-54,000)

Seattle Seahawks

1976-94 Kingdome 66,000
1994 Kingdome 66,400
& Husky Stadium 72,500
1995– Kingdome 66,400

Tennessee Oilers

1960-64 Jeppesen Stadium (Houston)...........23,500
1965-67 Rice Stadium (Rice Univ.)..............70,000
1968-96 Astrodome...........................59,969
1997 Liberty Bowl (Memphis) 62,380
1998 Vanderbilt Stadium (Nashville) 41,600

Ballpark Name Changes: Baltimore—**Cleveland Stadium** originally Municipal Stadium (1932-74); CINCINNATI—**Cinergy Field** originally Riverfront Stadium (1970–96); DENVER—**Mile High Stadium** originally Bears Stadium (1948-66); INDIANAPOLIS—**RCA Dome** originally Hoosier Dome (1984-94); Jacksonville—**ALLTEL Stadium** originally Jacksonville Municipal Stadium (1995-97); MIAMI—**Pro Player Stadium** originally Joe Robbie Stadium (1987-96); NEW ENGLAND—**Foxboro Stadium** originally Schaefer Stadium (1971-82), then Sullivan Stadium (1983-89); SAN DIEGO—**Qualcomm Stadium** originally San Diego Stadium (1967-81) then San Diego/Jack Murphy Stadium (1981-96).

NFC

Arizona Cardinals

1920-21 Normal Field (Chicago)................7,500
1922-25 Comiskey Park 28,000
1926-28 Normal Field 7,500
1929-59 Comiskey Park 52,000
1960-65 Busch Stadium (St. Louis)..............34,000
1966-87 Busch Memorial Stadium..............54,392
1988– Sun Devil Stadium (Tempe, AZ) 73,273

Atlanta Falcons

1966-91 Atlanta-Fulton County Stadium 59,643
1992– Georgia Dome 71,228

Carolina Panthers

1995 Memorial Stadium (Clemson, SC)........81,473
1996– Ericsson Stadium 75,248

Chicago Bears

1920 Staley Field (Decatur, IL) ....–
1921-70 Wrigley Field (Chicago) 37,741
1971– Soldier Field 66,944
(1971 capacity-55,049)

Dallas Cowboys

1960-70 Cotton Bowl..........................72,132
1971– Texas Stadium (Irving, TX).............65,675
(1971 capacity-65,101)

Detroit Lions

1930-33 Spartan Stadium (Portsmouth, OH) 8,200
1934-37 Univ. of Detroit Stadium..............25,000
1938-74 Tiger Stadium 54,468
1975– Pontiac Silverdome...................80,368
(1975 capacity-80,638)

Green Bay Packers

1921-22 Hagemeister Brewery Park..................–
1923-24 Bellevue Park ....–
1925-56 City Stadium I.......................24,800
1957– Lambeau Field.......................60,790
(1957 capacity-32,150)

Note: The Packers played games in Milwaukee from 1933-94: at Borchert Field, State Fair Park and Marquette Stadium (1933-52), and County Stadium (1953-94).

Minnesota Vikings

1961-81 Metropolitan Stadium (Bloomington) 48,446
1982– HHH Metrodome (Minneapolis)........64,182
(1982 capacity-62,220)

New Orleans Saints

1967-74 Tulane Stadium 80,997
1975– Louisiana Superdome.................69,420
(1975 capacity-74,472)

New York Giants

1925-55 Polo Grounds II.......................55,200
1956-73 Yankee Stadium I 63,800
1973-74 Yale Bowl (New Haven, CT)...........70,896
1975 Shea Stadium 60,372
1976– Giants Stadium (E. Rutherford, NJ) 78,148
(1976 capacity-76,800)

Philadelphia Eagles

1933-35 Baker Bowl 18,800
1936-39 Municipal Stadium 73,702
1940 Shibe Park...........................33,608
1941 Municipal Stadium 73,702
1942 Shibe Park...........................33,608
1943 Forbes Field (Pittsburgh)...............34,528
1944-57 Shibe Park 33,608
1958-70 Franklin Field (Univ. of Penn.) 60,546
1971– Veterans Stadium 65,352
(1971 capacity-65,000)

San Francisco 49ers

1946-70	Kezar Stadium	59,636
1971–	3Com Park (1971 capacity-61,246)	70,140

St. Louis Rams

1937-42	Municipal Stadium (Cleveland)	85,703
1945	Suspended operations for one year.	
1944-45	Municipal Stadium	85,703
1946-79	Memorial Coliseum (Los Angeles)	92,604
1980-94	Anaheim Stadium	69,008
1995–	Trans World Dome	66,000

Tampa Bay Buccaneers

1976-97	Houlihan's Stadium	74,300
1998–	Raymond James Stadium	65,000

Washington Redskins

1932	Braves Field (Boston)	40,000
1933-36	Fenway Park	27,000
1937-60	Griffith Stadium (Washington, DC)	35,000
1961-97	RFK Stadium	56,454
1997–	Jack Kent Cooke Stadium (Raljon, MD)	78,600

Ballpark Name Changes: ATLANTA—**Atlanta-Fulton County Stadium** originally Atlanta Stadium (1966-74); CHICAGO— **Wrigley Field** originally Cubs Park (1916-25), also, Comiskey Park originally White Sox Park (1910-12); DETROIT— **Tiger Stadium** originally Navin Field (1912-37), then Briggs Stadium (1938-60), also, **Pontiac Silverdome** originally Pontiac Metropolitan Stadium (1975); GREEN BAY—**Lambeau Field** originally City Stadium II (1957-64); PHILADELPHIA—**Shibe Park** renamed Connie Mack Stadium in 1953; ST. LOUIS—**Busch Memorial Stadium** renamed Busch Stadium in 1983; SAN FRANCISCO—**3Com Park** originally Candlestick Park (1960-94); TAMPA BAY—**Houlihan's Stadium** originally Tampa Stadium (1976-96); WASHINGTON—**RFK Stadium** originally D.C. Stadium (1961-68).

NATIONAL HOCKEY LEAGUE

Western Conference

Team	Arena	Location	Built	Capacity
Anaheim, Mighty Ducks of	**Arrowhead Pond**	Anaheim, Calif.	1993	**17,174**
Calgary Flames	**Canadian Airlines Saddledome**	Calgary, Alb.	1983	**18,810**
Chicago Blackhawks	**United Center**	Chicago, Ill.	1994	**20,500**
Colorado Avalanche	**McNichols Arena**	Denver, Colo.	1975	**16,061**
Dallas Stars	**Reunion Arena**	Dallas, Texas	1980	**16,924**
Detroit Red Wings	**Joe Louis Arena**	Detroit, Mich.	1979	**19,783**
Edmonton Oilers	**Edmonton Coliseum**	Edmonton, Alb.	1974	**16,437**
Los Angeles Kings	**Great Western Forum**	Inglewood, Calif.	1967	**16,005**
Nashville Predators	**Nashville Arena**	Nashville, Tenn.	1994	**18,000**
Phoenix Coyotes	**America West**	Phoenix, Ariz.	1992	**16,210**
St. Louis Blues	**Kiel Center**	St. Louis, Mo.	1994	**19,260**
San Jose Sharks	**San Jose Arena**	San Jose, Calif.	1993	**17,190**
Vancouver Canucks	**General Motors Place**	Vancouver, B.C.	1995	**18,422**

Eastern Conference

Team	Arena	Location	Built	Capacity
Boston Bruins	**FleetCenter**	Boston, Mass.	1995	**17,565**
Buffalo Sabres	**Marine Midland Arena**	Buffalo, N.Y.	1996	**18,595**
Carolina Hurricanes	**Greensboro Coliseum**	Greensboro, N.C.	1959	**21,500**
Florida Panthers	**National Car Rental Center**	Sunrise, Fla.	1998	**19,088**
Montreal Canadiens	**Molson Centre**	Montreal, Que.	1996	**21,273**
New Jersey Devils	**Continental Airlines Arena**	E. Rutherford, N.J.	1981	**19,040**
New York Islanders	**Nassau Veterans' Mem. Coliseum**	Uniondale, N.Y.	1972	**16,297**
New York Rangers	**Madison Square Garden**	New York, N.Y.	1968	**18,200**
Ottawa Senators	**Corel Centre**	Kanata, Ont.	1996	**18,500**
Philadelphia Flyers	**First Union Center**	Philadelphia, Pa.	1996	**19,463**
Pittsburgh Penguins	**Civic Arena**	Pittsburgh, Pa.	1961	**17,181**
Tampa Bay Lightning	**Ice Palace**	Tampa Bay, Fla.	1996	**19,500**
Toronto Maple Leafs	**Maple Leaf Gardens**	Toronto, Ont.	1931	**15,746**
	& **Air Canada Centre**	Toronto, Ont.	1999	**18,800**
Washington Capitals	**MCI Center**	Washington, D.C.	1997	**20,000**

Note: Toronto will play their home games at Maple Leaf Gardens before moving to the Air Canada Centre on Feb. 20, 1999.

Rank by Capacity

Western		Eastern	
Chicago	20,500	Carolina	21,500
Detroit	19,783	Montreal	21,273
St. Louis	19,260	Washington	20,000
Calgary	18,810	Tampa Bay	19,500
Vancouver	18,422	Philadelphia	19,463
Nashville	18,000	Florida	19,088
San Jose	17,190	New Jersey	19,040
Anaheim	17,174	Buffalo	18,595
Dallas	16,924	Ottawa	18,500
Edmonton	16,437	NY Rangers	18,200
Phoenix	16,210	Boston	17,565
Colorado	16,061	Pittsburgh	17,181
Los Angeles	16,005	NY Islanders	16,297
		Toronto	15,746

Rank by Age

Western		Eastern	
Los Angeles	1967	Toronto	1931
Edmonton	1974	Carolina	1959
Colorado	1975	Pittsburgh	1961
Detroit	1979	NY Rangers	1968
Dallas	1980	NY Islanders	1972
Calgary	1983	New Jersey	1981
Phoenix	1992	Boston	1995
Anaheim	1993	Montreal	1996
San Jose	1993	Ottawa	1996
Chicago	1994	Buffalo	1996
St. Louis	1994	Philadelphia	1996
Nashville	1994	Tampa Bay	1996
Vancouver	1995	Washington	1997
		Florida	1998

National Hockey League (Cont.)

1997-98 NHL Attendance

Official overall paid attendance for the 1997-98 season according to the NHL accounting office was 17,253,206 (paid tickets) for an average per game crowd of 16,185 over 1,066 games. This amounts to a one percent decrease over 1996-97 totals. Teams in each conference are ranked by attendance over 41 home games. There were no neutral site games. Number of sellouts are listed in S/O column. Numbers in parentheses indicate rank in 1996-97. Note that before the 1997-98 season, Carolina moved from Hartford to the Greensboro (N.C.) Coliseum until their new arena in Raleigh is completed.

Western Conference

		Attendance	S/O	Average
1	Detroit (1)	819,303	41	19,983
2	Chicago (2)	752,611	11	18,356
3	San Jose (3)	701,494	19	17,110
4	Vancouver (4)	696,437	13	16,986
5	Anaheim (6)	693,235	25	16,908
6	Calgary (5)	690,745	3	16,847
7	St. Louis (7)	755,014	23	18,415
8	Dallas (10)	674,423	22	16,449
9	Edmonton (9)	666,033	22	16,245
10	Colorado (8)	658,471	41	16,060
11	Toronto (11)	644,098	34	15,710
12	Phoenix (12)	631,591	16	15,405
13	Los Angeles (13)	533,792	11	13,019
	TOTAL	8,917,247	281	16,730

Eastern Conference

		Attendance	S/O	Average
1	Montreal (1)	851,645	19	20,772
2	Philadelphia (2)	800,285	23	19,519
3	NY Rangers (3)	746,200	41	18,200
4	Tampa Bay (4)	568,579	0	13,868
5	Buffalo (5)	641,034	10	15,635
6	Pittsburgh (6)	617,900	3	15,071
7	New Jersey (7)	710,160	18	17,321
8	Washington (8)	626,285	7	15,275
9	Boston (9)	619,006	4	15,098
10	Ottawa (10)	686,787	13	16,751
11	Florida (11)	602,536	40	14,696
12	Carolina (12)	372,519	0	9,086
13	NY Islanders (13)	493,023	7	12,025
	TOTAL	8,335,959	185	15,640

Home Ice

Listed below are the principal home buildings used through the years by current NHL teams. The largest capacity of each arena is noted in the right hand column. World Hockey Association arenas (1972-76) are included for Edmonton, Hartford (now Carolina), Quebec (now Colorado) and Winnipeg (now Phoenix).

Western Conference

Anaheim, Mighty Ducks of

1993– Arrowhead Pond 17,174

Calgary Flames

1972-80 The Omin (Atlanta) 15,278
1980-83 Calgary Corral 7,424
1983– Canadian Airlines Saddledome (1983 capacity-16,674) 18,810

Chicago Blackhawks

1926-29 Chicago Coliseum 5,000
1929-94 Chicago Stadium 17,317
1994– United Center 20,500

Colorado Avalanche

1972-95 Le Colisee de Quebec 15,399
1995– McNichols Arena (Denver) 16,061

Dallas Stars

1967-93 Met Center (Bloomington, MN) 15,174
1993– Reunion Arena (Dallas) 16,924

Detroit Red Wings

1926-27 Border Cities Arena (Windsor, Ont.) 3,200
1927-79 Olympia Stadium (Detroit) 16,700
1979– Joe Louis Arena 19,783

Edmonton Oilers

1972-74 Edmonton Gardens 7,200
1974– Edmonton Coliseum 16,437
(1974 capacity-15,513)

Los Angeles Kings

1967– Great Western Forum (Inglewood) 16,005
(1967 capacity-15,651)

Note: The Kings played 17 games at Long Beach Sports Arena and LA Sports Arena at the start of the 1967-68 season.

Nashville Predators

1998– Nashville Arena 18,000

Phoenix Coyotes

1972–96 Winnipeg Arena 15,393
(1972 capacity-10,177)
1996– America West (Phoenix) 16,210

St. Louis Blues

1967-94 St. Louis Arena 17,188
1994– Kiel Center 19,260

San Jose Sharks

1991-93 Cow Palace (Daly City, CA) 11,100
1993– San Jose Arena 17,190

Vancouver Canucks

1970-95 Pacific Coliseum 16,150
1995– General Motors Place 18,422

Building Name Changes: CALGARY—**Canadian Airlines Saddledome** originally Olympic Saddledome (1983-1995); DALLAS—**Met Center** in Minneapolis originally Metropolitan Sports Center (1967-82); EDMONTON—**Edmonton Coliseum** originally Northlands Coliseum (1974-94); LOS ANGELES—**Great Western Forum** originally The Forum (1967-88); ST. LOUIS—**St. Louis Arena** renamed The Checkerdome in 1977, then St. Louis Arena again in 1982.

Eastern Conference

Boston Bruins

1924-28 Boston Arena....6,200
1928-95 Boston Garden....14,448
1995– FleetCenter....17,565

Buffalo Sabres

1970-96 Memorial Auditorium (The Aud)....16,284
(1970 capacity-10,429)
1996– Marine Midland Arena....18,595

Carolina Hurricanes

1972-73 Boston Garden....14,442
1973-74 Boston Garden (regular season)....14,442
West Springfield (MA) Big E (playoffs)....5,513
1974-75 West Springfield Big E....5,513
& Hartford (CT) Civic Center....10,507
1975-77 Hartford Civic Center....10,507
1977-78 Hartford Civic Center....10,507
& Springfield (MA) Civic Center....7,725
1978-79 Springfield Civic Center....7,725
1979-80 Springfield Civic Center....7,725
& Hartford Civic Center II....14,250
1980-97 Hartford Civic Center II....15,635
1997– Greensboro Coliseum....21,500

Note: The Hartford Civic Center roof caved in January 1978, forcing the Whalers to move their home games to Springfield, MA for two years.

Florida Panthers

1993-98 Miami Arena....14,703
1998– National Car Rental Center....19,088

Montreal Canadiens

1910-20 Jubilee Arena....3,200
1913-18 Montreal Arena (Westmount)....6,000
1918-26 Mount Royal Arena....6,750
1926-68 Montreal Forum I....15,500
1968-96 Montreal Forum II....17,959
1996– Molson Centre....21,273

New Jersey Devils

1974-76 Kemper Arena (Kansas City)....16,300
1976-82 McNichols Arena (Denver)....15,900
1982– Continental Airlines Arena....19,040
(1982 capacity-19,023)

New York Islanders

1972– Nassau Veterans' Mem. Coliseum....16,297
(1972 capacity-14,500)

New York Rangers

1925-68 Madison Square Garden III....15,925
1968– Madison Square Garden IV....18,200
(1968 capacity-17,250)

Ottawa Senators

1992-95 Ottawa Civic Center....10,755
1996– Corel Centre (Kanata)....18,500

Philadelphia Flyers

1967-96 CoreStates Spectrum....17,380
(1967 capacity-14,558)
1996– First Union Center....19,463

Pittsburgh Penguins

1967– Civic Arena....17,181
(1967 capacity-12,508)

Tampa Bay Lightning

1992-93 Expo Hall (Tampa)....10,500
1993-96 ThunderDome (St. Petersburg)....26,000
1996– Ice Palace....19,500

Toronto Maple Leafs

1917-31 Mutual Street Arena....8,000
1931– Maple Leaf Gardens....15,746
(1931 capacity-13,542)

Washington Capitals

1974-97 USAir Arena (Landover, MD)....18,130
1997– MCI Center....20,000

Building Name Changes: NEW JERSEY—**Continental Airlines Arena** originally Meadowlands Arena (1982-96); PHILADELPHIA—**First Union Center** originally the CoreStates Center (1996-98) and **CorEStates Spectrum** originally The Spectrum (1967-94); WASHINGTON—**USAir Arena** originally Capital Centre (1974-93).

AUTO RACING

Formula One, NASCAR Winston Cup, CART and Indy Racing League (IRL) racing circuits. Qualifying records accurate as of Aug. 1, 1998. Capacity figures for NASCAR, CART and IRL tracks are approximate and pertain to grandstand seating only. Standing room and hillside terrain seating featured at most road courses are not included.

CART

	Location	Miles	Qual.mph record	Set by	Seats
Belle Isle Park	Detroit, Mich.	2.1**	108.649	Nigel Mansell (1994)	18,000
Burke Lakefront Airport	Cleveland, Ohio	2.37**	147.512	Gil de Ferran (1995)	36,000
California Speedway	Fontana, Calif.	2.0	—	First race in 1997	69,000
Exhibition Place	Toronto, Ont.	1.78**	110.396	Jacques Villeneuve (1995)	60,000
Laguna Seca Raceway	Monterey, Calif.	2.24*	118.666	Bryan Herta (1997)	8,000
Long Beach	Long Beach, Calif.	1.85**	109.639	Gil de Ferran (1996)	45,000
Homestead Motorsports Complex	Homestead, Fla.	1.5	198.590	Paul Tracy (1996)	50,000
Houston Grand Prix	Houston, Tex.	1.68**	—	First race in late 1998	TBA
Michigan International Speedway	Brooklyn, Mich.	2.0	234.275	Mario Andretti (1993)	70,000
Mid-Ohio Sports Car Course	Lexington, Ohio	2.25*	123.766	Dario Franchitti (1998)	6,000
The Milwaukee Mile	West Allis, Wisc.	1.0	185.500	Patrick Charpentier (1998)	36,800
Nazareth Speedway	Nazareth, Pa.	1.0	190.737	Paul Tracy (1996)	35,000
Pacific Place	Vancouver, B.C.	1.65**	110.293	Scott Goodyear (1993)	65,000
Portland International Raceway	Portland, Ore.	1.95	121.341	Bryan Herta (1998)	27,000
Piquet International Raceway	Rio de Janeiro, Brazil	1.6	167.084	Alex Zanardi (1996)	80,000
Road America	Elkhart Lake, Wisc.	4.0*	142.206	Jacques Villeneuve (1995)	10,000
Surfers Paradise	Gold Coast, Australia	2.804	106.053	Nigel Mansell (1994)	55,000
Twin Ring Motegi	Motegi, Japan	1.549	217.964	Jimmy Vasser (1998)	50,000

*Road courses (not ovals). **Temporary street circuits.

Auto Racing (Cont.)

Indy Racing League

Founded by Indianapolis Motor Speedway president Tony George, the Indy Racing League competes with CART and fielded eight races, anchored by the Indianapolis 500, in 1997.

	Location	Miles	Qual.mph Record	Set by	Seats
Atlanta Motor Speedway	Hampton, Ga.	1.54	—	First race was late 1998	78,000
Charlotte Motor Speedway	Concord, N.C.	1.5	217.164	Tony Stewart (1997)	140,000
Dover Downs Int'l. Speedway	Dover, Del.	1.0	185.204	Tony Stewart (1998)	55,000
Indianapolis Motor Speedway	Indianapolis, Ind.	2.5	232.618	Arie Luyendyk (1996)	265,000
Las Vegas Motor Speedway	Las Vegas, Nev.	1.5	226.491	Arie Luyendyk (1996)	107,000
New Hampshire Int'l. Speedway	Loudon, N.H.	1.01	177.436	Andre Ribeiro (1995)	75,000
Phoenix International Raceway	Phoenix, Ariz.	1.0	181.952	Bryan Herta (1995)	50,000
Pikes Peak Int'l. Raceway	Fountain, Colo.	1.0	176.117	Scott Sharp (1997)	42,787
Texas Motor Speedway	Fort Worth, Tex.	1.5	224.448	Tony Stewart (1998)	150,061
Walt Disney World Speedway	Orlando, Fla.	1.1	181.388	Buddy Lazier (1996)	55,000

Note: The IRL announced it currently has no future plans to hold races at New Hampshire International Speedway.

NASCAR

	Location	Miles	Qual.mph Record	Set By	Seats
Atlanta Motor Speedway	Hampton, Ga.	1.54	197.478	Geoff Bodine (1997)	78,000
Bristol International Raceway	Bristol, Tenn.	0.533	125.093	Mark Martin (1995)	65,000
California Speedway	Fontana, Calif.	2.0	183.753	Greg Sacks (1997)	80,000
Charlotte Motor Speedway	Concord, N.C.	1.5	185.759	Ward Burton (1994)	140,000
Darlington International Raceway	Darlington, N.C.	1.37	173.797	Ward Burton (1996)	55,000
Daytona International Speedway	Daytona Beach, Fla.	2.5	210.364	Bill Elliott (1987)	97,900
Dover Downs International Speedway	Dover, Del.	1.0	155.898	Rusty Wallace (1998)	55,000
Indianapolis Motor Speedway	Indianapolis, Ind.	2.5	177.736	Ernie Irvan (1997)	265,000
Las Vegas Motor Speedway	Las Vegas, Nev.	1.5	168.224	Dale Jarrett (1998)	107,000
Martinsville Speedway	Martinsville, Va.	0.526	94.129	Ted Musgrave (1994)	56,000
Michigan International Speedway	Brooklyn, Mich.	2.0	186.611	Jeff Gordon (1995)	70,000
New Hampshire Int'l Speedway	Loudon, N.H.	1.058	129.423	Ken Schrader (1997)	60,000
North Carolina Motor Speedway	Rockingham, N.C.	1.017	157.885	Mark Martin (1997)	55,000
Phoenix International Raceway	Phoenix, Ariz.	1.0	131.579	Bobby Hamilton (1996)	50,000
Pocono International Raceway	Long Pond, Pa.	2.5	169.725	Jeff Gordon (1996)	77,000
Richmond International Raceway	Richmond, Va.	0.75	124.757	Jeff Gordon (1995)	71,350
Sears Point International Raceway	Sonoma, Calif.	2.52*	92.807	Mark Martin (1997)	42,500
Talladega Superspeedway	Talladega, Ala.	2.66	212.809	Bill Elliott (1987)	85,000
Texas Motor Speedway	Ft. Worth, Tex.	1.5	175.105	Jeff Gordon (1997)	150,061
Watkins Glen	Watkins Glen, N.Y.	2.45*	120.733	Dale Earnhardt (1996)	35,000

*Road courses (not ovals).

Notes: Richmond sells reserved seats only (no infield) for Winston Cup races.

Formula One

Race track capacity figures unavailable.

Grand Prix		Miles	Qual.mph Record	Set by
Argentine	**Oscar A. Galvez** (Buenos Aires)	2.645	112.722	Jacques Villeneuve (1997)
Austrian	**A1-Ring** (Zeltwig, Austria)	2.683	134.657	Jacques Villeneuve (1997)
Australian	**Albert Park** (Melbourne)	3.274	132.731	Jacques Villeneuve (1997)
Belgian	**Spa-Francorchamps**	4.333	141.123	Nigel Mansell (1992)
Brazilian	**Interlagos** (Sao Paulo)	2.687	127.799	Nigel Mansell (1992)
British	**Silverstone** (Towcester)	3.247	148.043	Nigel Mansell (1992)
Canadian	**Circuit Gilles Villeneuve** (Montreal)	2.747	127.181	David Coulthard (1998)
European	**Nürburgring** (Nürburg/Eifel, Germany)	2.822	131.219	Teo Fabi (1985)
French	**Magny Cours** (Nevers)	2.641	128.709	Nigel Mansell (1992)
German	**Hockenheimring** (Hockenheim)	4.235	156.722	Nigel Mansell (1991)
Hungarian	**Hungaroring** (Budapest)	2.465	117.602	Riccardo Patrese (1992)
Italian	**Autodromo di Nazionale, Monza** (Milan)	3.604	159.951	Ayrton Senna (1991)
Japanese	**Suzuka** (Nagoya)	3.641	138.515	Gerhard Berger (1991)
Monaco	**Monte Carlo**	2.068	96.286	Heinz-Harald Frentzen (1997)
Pacific	**T1 Circuit Aida** (Japan)	2.301	117.970	Ayrton Senna (1994)
Portuguese	**Autodromo do Estoril**	2.703	133.224	Nigel Mansell (1992)
San Marino	**Ferrari Circuit** (Imola, Italy)	3.040	138.265	Ayrton Senna (1994)
Spanish	**Catalunya** (Barcelona)	2.937	138.205	Jacques Villeneuve (1997)

SOCCER

World's Premier Soccer Stadiums

(Listed by city)

Stadium	Location	Seats
Olimpiako	Athens, Greece	74,160
Eden Park	Auckland, New Zealand	48,000
Nou Camp	Barcelona, Spain	115,000
Olympiastadion	Berlin, Germany	76,234
Népstadion	Budapest, Hungary	72,000
Monumental	Buenos Aires, Argentina	77,000
D.A. Nasser	Cairo, Egypt	100,000
Westfalenstadion	Dortmund, Germany	42,800
Lansdowne Road	Dublin, Ireland	51,000
Hampden Park	Glasgow, Scotland	50,000
Ellis Park	Johannesburg, S. Africa	62,000
Republikansky	Kiev, Ukraine	100,000
Estadio da Luz	Lisbon, Portugal	130,000
Wembley	London, England	80,000
Santiago Bernabeu	Madrid, Spain	110,000
Azteca	Mexico City, Mexico	114,000
Guiseppe Meazza	Milan, Italy	83,107
Centenario	Montevideo, Uruguay	76,609
Luzhniki Stadion	Moscow, Russia	100,000
Olympiastadion	Munich, Germany	74,000
San Paolo	Naples, Italy	72,810
Parc des Princes	Paris, France	49,700
Rose Bowl	Pasadena, Calif.	102,083
Spartakiadni Stadion	Prague, Czech Republic	250,000
Rungnado	Pyongyang, N. Korea	150,000
Maracana	Rio de Janeiro, Brazil	165,000
King Fahd II	Riyadh, Saudi Arabia	75,000
Olimpico	Rome, Italy	82,922
Stade de France	Saint-Denis, France	80,000
Nacional	Santiago, Chile	75,000
Morumbi	Sao Paulo, Brazil	120,000
Olympic Stadium	Seoul, S. Korea	100,000
Olympic Stadium	Sydney, Australia	120,000
Olympic Stadium	Tokyo, Japan	62,000
Delle Alpi	Turin, Italy	71,012
Prater	Vienna, Austria	62,958
Dziesieiolecia	Warsaw, Poland	100,000

1999 FIFA Women's World Cup Stadiums

The 2nd FIFA Women's World Cup of Soccer will be held across the United States from June 19 to July 10, 1999. Listed below are the stadiums which will host the 32 World Cup matches. Note that many of the stadiums have been transformed to soccer accommodations and their seating capacities are reflected below. The Cup final will be held July 10 at the Rose Bowl in Pasadena, California.

Stadium	Location	Built	Seats
Foxboro Stadium	Foxboro, Mass.	1971	22,385
Soldier Field	Chicago, Ill.	1924	24,000
Rose Bowl	Los Angeles, Calif.	1922	28,000
Giants Stadium	East Rutherford, N.J.	1976	25,576
Civic Stadium	Portland, Ore.	1923	27,396
Spartan Stadium	San Jose, Calif.	1933	26,000
Stanford Stadium	Palo Alto, Calif.	1921	20,000
J. K. Cooke Stadium	Raljon, Md.	1997	28,167

Major League Soccer

The 12-team MLS is the only U.S. Division I professional outdoor league sanctioned by FIFA and U.S. Soccer. Note that all capacity figures are approximate given the adjustments of football stadium seating to soccer.

Western Conference

	Stadium	Built	Seats	Field
Chicago Fire	Soldier Field	1924	24,995	Grass
Colorado Rapids	Mile High	1948	17,500	Grass
Dallas Burn	Cotton Bowl	1935	25,704	Grass
Kansas City Wizards	Arrowhead	1972	20,269	Grass
L.A. Galaxy	Rose Bowl	1922	26,000	Grass
San Jose Clash	Spartan	1933	26,000	Grass

Eastern Conference

	Stadium	Built	Seats	Field
Columbus Crew	Ohio Stadium	1922	25,134	Grass
D.C. United	RFK	1961	26,169	Grass
Metro Stars (N.Y./N.J.)	Giants	1976	25,576	Both
Miami Fusion	Lockhart	1998	20,450	Grass
N.E. Revolution	Foxboro	1971	24,481	Grass
Tampa Bay Mutiny	Houlihan's	1967	24,776	Grass

MISCELLANEOUS

Minor League Baseball

AAA Ballparks
International League

East		Built	Seats	Field
Buffalo (Indians)	**Northamericare Park**	1988	20,900	Grass
Ottawa (Expos)	**JetForm Park**	1993	10,332	Grass
Pawtucket (Red Sox)	**McCoy Stadium**	1942	7,002	Grass
Rochester (Orioles)	**Frontier Field**	1997	10,600	Grass
Scranton/Wilkes-Barre (Phillies)	**Lackawanna County Stadium**	1989	10,832	Turf
Syracuse (Blue Jays)	**P&C Stadium**	1997	11,100	Turf

Miscellaneous (Cont.)

West		Built	Seats	Field
Columbus (Yankees)	**Cooper Stadium**	1932	15,000	Turf
Indianapolis (Reds)	**Victory Field**	1996	15,500	Grass
Louisville (Cardinals)	**Cardinal Stadium**	1957	33,500	Turf
Toledo (Tigers)	**Ned Skeldon Stadium**	1965	10,197	Grass
South		**Built**	**Seats**	**Turf**
Charlotte (Marlins)	**Knights Castle**	1990	10,002	Grass
Durham (Braves)	**Durham Bulls Athletic Park**	1994	10,000	Grass
Norfolk (Mets)	**Harbor Park**	1993	12,059	Grass
Richmond (Braves)	**The Diamond**	1985	12,134	Grass

Pacific Coast League

East Division		Built	Seats	Field
Oklahoma	**Southwestern Bell Stadium**	1961	15,000	Grass
Memphis	**Tim McCarver Stadium**	1963	8,800	Grass
Nashville (White Sox)	**Herschel Greer Stadium**	1978	15,500	Grass
New Orleans (Astros)	**Zephyr Field**	1997	10,000	Grass
Central Division		**Built**	**Seats**	**Field**
Albuquerque (Dodgers)	**Albuquerque Sports Stadium**	1969	10,510	Grass
Colorado Springs (Rockies)	**Sky Sox Stadium**	1988	9,000	Grass
Iowa (Cubs)	**Sec Taylor Stadium**	1992	10,800	Grass
Omaha (Royals)	**Rosenblatt Stadium**	1948	22,000	Turf
North Division		**Built**	**Seats**	**Field**
Calgary (Pirates)	**Burns Stadium**	1966	8,000	Grass
Edmonton (Athletics)	**TELUS Field**	1995	9,200	Grass
Tacoma (Mariners)	**Cheney Stadium**	1960	9,600	Grass
Vancouver (Angels)	**Nat Bailey Stadium**	1951	6,500	Grass
South Division		**Built**	**Seats**	**Field**
Las Vegas (Padres)	**Cashman Field**	1982	9,334	Grass
Fresno (Giants)	**Beiden Field**	1987	7,500	Grass
Salt Lake (Twins)	**Franklin Quest Field**	1993	15,500	Grass
Tucson (Brewers)	**Tucson Electric**	1998	11,000	Grass

Japanese Baseball League

Central League

		Location	Seats
Chunichi Dragons	**Nagoya Stadium**	Nagoya	35,000
	& **Nagoya Dome**	Nagoya	40,500
Hanshin Tigers	**Koshien Stadium**	Nisinomiya	55,000
Hiroshima Carp	**Hiroshima Shimin Stadium**	Hiroshima	32,000
Yakult Swallows	**Jingu Stadium**	Tokyo	48,785
Yokohama BayStars	**Yokohama Stadium**	Yokohama	30,000
Yomiuri Giants	**Tokyo Dome**	Tokyo	48,000

Pacific League

		Location	Seats
Chiba Lotte Marines	**Chiba Marine Stadium**	Chiba	30,000
Fukuoka Daiei Hawks	**Fukuoka Dome**	Fukuoka	49,000
Kintetsu Buffaloes	**Fujidera Stadium**	Osaka	32,000
Nippon Ham Fighters	**Tokyo Dome**	Tokyo	48,000
Orix Blue Wave	**Kobe Green**	Kobe	35,000
Seibu Lions	**Seibu Stadium**	Tokorozawa	37,000

Women's Professional Basketball

American Basketball League

		Location	Built	Seats
Chicago Condors	**UIC Pavilion**	Chicago, Ill.	1982	7,800
Colorado Xplosion	**Denver Coliseum**	Denver, Colo.	1953	9,300
	& **McNichols Arena**	Denver, Colo.	1975	14,500
Columbus Quest	**Batelle Hall**	Columbus, Ohio	1980	6,313
	St. John Arena	Ohio St. Univ.	1956	13,276
Nashville Noise	**Municipal Auditorium**	Nashville, Tenn.	1962	8,700
New England Blizzard	**Hartford Civic Center**	Hartford, Conn.	1975	15,340
Philadelphia Rage	**The Apollo**	Philadelphia, Pa.	1997	10,000
Portland Power	**Memorial Coliseum**	Portland, Ore.	1960	10,934
San Jose Lasers	**San Jose Event Center**	San Jose, Calif.	1989	4,550
	& **San Jose Arena**	San Jose, Calif.	1993	18,500
Seattle Reign	**Mercer Arena**	Seattle, Wash.	1929	4,623

Women's National Basketball Association

The WNBA teams play in the same arenas as the NBA teams in their respective cities. However, the capacities of the venues are "down-sized" for most games. The new, smaller capacity for WNBA games is listed below.

Team	Arena	Location	Built	Seats
Charlotte Sting	**Charlotte Coliseum**	Charlotte, N.C.	1988	24,042
Cleveland Rockers	**Gund Arena**	Cleveland, Ohio	1994	20,562
Detroit Shock	**The Palace of Auburn Hills**	Auburn Hills, Mich.	1988	21,454
Houston Comets	**Compaq Center**	Houston, Tex.	1975	16,285
Los Angeles Sparks	**Great Western Forum**	Inglewood, Calif.	1967	17,505
New York Liberty	**Madison Square Garden**	New York, N.Y.	1968	19,763
Phoenix Mercury	**America West Arena**	Phoenix, Ariz.	1992	19,023
Sacramento Monarchs	**ARCO Arena**	Sacramento, Calif.	1988	17,317
Utah Starzz	**Delta Center**	Salt Lake City, Utah	1991	19,911
Washington Mystics	**MCI Center**	Washington, D.C.	1997	20,500

Canadian Football League

East Division

Team	Stadium	Location	Built	Seats	Field
Hamilton Tiger-Cats	**Ivor Wynne Stadium**	Hamilton, Ont.	1932	29,183	Turf
Montreal Alouettes	**Molson Stadium (McGill)**	Montreal, Que.	1976	18,025	Turf
Toronto Argonauts	**SkyDome**	Toronto, Ont.	1989	52,595	Turf
Winnipeg Blue Bombers	**Winnipeg Stadium**	Winnipeg, Man.	1953	33,675	Turf

West Division

Team	Stadium	Location	Built	Seats	Field
British Columbia Lions	**B.C. Place**	Vancouver, B.C.	1983	59,478	Turf
Calgary Stampeders	**McMahon Stadium**	Calgary, Alb.	1960	37,317	Turf
Edmonton Eskimos	**Commonwealth Stadium**	Edmonton, Alb.	1978	60,051	Grass
Saskatchewan Roughriders	**Taylor Field**	Regina, Sask.	1948	27,732	Turf

NFL Europe

Team	Stadium	Location	Seats
Amsterdam Admirals	**Amsterdam Arena**	Amsterdam, Netherlands	51,328
Barcelona Dragons	**Estadi Olimpic de Monthuic**	Barcelona, Spain	54,000
Berlin (expansion)	**Jahn-Sportspark**	Berlin, Germany	20,000
Frankfurt Galaxy	**Waldstadion**	Frankfurt, Germany	54,000
Rhein Fire	**Rheinstadion**	Dusseldorf, Germany	57,000
Scottish Claymores	**Murrayfield Stadium**	Edinburgh, Scotland	67,000

Arena Football League

American Conference

Western Division		Location	Built	Seats
Arizona Rattlers	**America West Arena**	Phoenix, Ariz.	1992	16,923
Portland Forest Dragons	**Rose Garden**	Portland, Ore.	1995	18,800
San Jose SaberCats	**San Jose Arena**	San Jose, Calif.	1990	16,929
Central Division				
Iowa Barnstormers	**Veterans Auditorium**	Des Moines, Iowa	1955	11,250
Grand Rapids Rampage	**Van Andel Arena**	Grand Rapids, Mich.	1996	10,040
Milwaukee Mustangs	**Bradley Center**	Milwaukee, Wisc.	1988	17,819
Houston Terror	**Compaq Center**	Houston, Texas	1975	15,050

National Conference

Southern Division		Location	Built	Seats
Florida Bobcats	**W. Palm Beach Auditorium**	W. Palm Beach, Fla.	1966	4,700
Nashville Kats	**Nashville Arena**	Nashville, Tenn.	1996	16,200
N.Y. CityHawks	**Madison Square Garden**	New York, N.Y.	1968	18,900
Orlando Predators	**Orlando Arena**	Orlando, Fla.	1989	16,613
Eastern Division		**Location**	**Built**	**Seats**
Albany Firebirds	**Pepsi Arena**	Albany, N.Y.	1990	13,652
Buffalo Destroyers	**Marine Midland Arena**	Buffalo, N.Y.	1996	18,250
New Jersey Red Dogs	**Continental Airlines Arena**	E. Rutherford, N.J.	1981	17,500
Tampa Bay Storm	**Ice Palace**	Tampa Bay, Fla.	1996	20,282

Horse Racing

Triple Crown race tracks

Race	Racetrack	Seats	Infield
Kentucky Derby	Churchill Downs	48,500	100,000
Preakness	Pimlico Race Course	40,000	60,000
Belmont Stakes	Belmont Park	32,491	50,000

Record crowds: Kentucky Derby– 163,628 (1974); Preakness– 98,896 (1989); Belmont– 82,694 (1971).

Tennis

Grand Slam center courts

Event	Main Stadium	Seats
Australian Open	Melbourne Park	16,000
French Open	Stade Roland Garros	16,500
Wimbledon	Centre Court	13,118
U.S. Open	Arthur Ashe Stadium	23,000

COLLEGE BASKETBALL

The 50 Largest Arenas

The 50 largest arenas in Division I for the 1998-99 NCAA regular season. Note that (*) indicates part-time home court.

	Arena	Seats	Home Team
1	Carrier Dome	**33,000**	Syracuse
2	Thompson-Boling Arena	**24,535**	Tennessee
3	Rupp Arena	**23,000**	Kentucky
4	Marriott Center	**22,700**	BYU
5	Dean Smith Center	**21,572**	N. Carolina
6	The Rose Garden	**21,401**	Portland St.
7	First Union Center	**21,000**	Villanova*
8	MCI Center	**20,600**	Georgetown*
9	The Pyramid	**20,142**	Memphis
10	Continental Airlines Arena	**20,029**	Seton Hall*
11	Kiel Center	**20,000**	Saint Louis
12	Marine Midland Arena	**19,500**	Canisius* & Niagara*
13	Bud Walton Arena	**19,200**	Arkansas
14	Bradley Center	**19,150**	Marquette
15	Freedom Hall	**18,865**	Louisville
16	Thomas & Mack Center	**18,500**	UNLV
17	Madison Square Garden	**18,470**	St. John's*
18	First Union Spectrum	**18,060**	Villanova* & LaSalle*
19	University Arena (The Pit)	**18,018**	New Mexico
20	Rosemont Horizon	**17,500**	DePaul*
	Value City Arena	**17,500**	Ohio St.
22	Assembly Hall	**17,357**	Indiana
23	Pittsburgh Civic Arena	**16,725**	Pittsburgh*
24	Assembly Hall	**16,450**	Illinois
25	Allen Field House	**16,300**	Kansas
26	Hartford Civic Center	**16,294**	UConn*
27	Erwin Center	**16,175**	Texas
28	LA Sports Arena	**15,509**	USC
29	Carver-Hawkeye Arena	**15,500**	Iowa
	Pepsi Arena	**15,500**	Siena*
31	Memorial Gymnasium	**15,311**	Vanderbilt
32	Bryce Jordan Center	**15,261**	Penn St.
33	Miami Arena	**15,200**	Miami
34	Breslin Events Center	**15,138**	Michigan St.
35	Coleman Coliseum	**15,043**	Alabama
36	Arena-Auditorium	**15,028**	Wyoming
37	Huntsman Center	**15,000**	Utah
38	Cole Fieldhouse	**14,500**	Maryland
39	McKale Center	**14,489**	Arizona
40	Joel Memorial Coliseum	**14,407**	Wake Forest
41	Williams Arena	**14,321**	Minnesota
42	Devaney Sports Center	**14,200**	Nebraska
43	University Activity Center	**14,198**	Arizona St.
44	Maravich Assembly Ctr.	**14,164**	LSU
45	Mackey Arena	**14,123**	Purdue
46	Hilton Coliseum	**14,020**	Iowa St.
47	WVU Coliseum	**14,000**	West Va.
48	Henry Goodman Arena	**13,610**	Cleveland St.
49	Crisler Arena	**13,562**	Michigan
50	U. of Dayton Arena	**13,511**	Dayton

Division I Conference Home Courts

NCAA Division I conferences for the 1998-99 season. Teams with home games in more than one arena are noted.

America East

	Home Floor	Seats
Boston University	Case Gym	2,500
Delaware	Bob Carpenter Center	5,000
Drexel	Phys. Education Center	2,300
Hartford	The Sports Center	4,475
Hofstra	Physical Fitness Center	2,500
Maine	Alfond Arena	5,712
New Hampshire	Whittemore Center	7,200
Northeastern	Cabot Gym	2,500
Towson St.	Towson Center	5,000
Vermont	Patrick Gym	3,228

Atlantic Coast

	Home Floor	Seats
Clemson	Littlejohn Coliseum	11,020
Duke	Cameron Indoor Stadium	9,314
Florida St.	Leon County Civic Center	12,500
Georgia Tech	Alexander Mem. Stadium	10,020
Maryland	Cole Field House	14,500
North Carolina	Dean Smith Center	21,572
N.C. State	Reynolds Coliseum	12,500
Virginia	University Hall	8,864
Wake Forest	Joel Mem. Coliseum	14,407

Biggest Not Fullest

While Syracuse continues to have the largest basketball arena in the nation, it finished behind Kentucky for the third straight year in attendance rankings. After 11 consecutive years at the top, Syracuse lost the attendance title to Kentucky in 1996, the same year the Orangemen lost to the Wildcats in the Final Four championship game. Kentucky averaged 23,946 fans over 12 home games during the 1997-98 season. Syracuse finished second with 21,124 over 16. For the 22nd straight season the Big Ten had the highest average attendance for conferences with 12,450 fans per game.

Atlantic 10

	Home Floor	Seats
Dayton	U. of Dayton Arena	13,511
Duquesne	Palumbo Center	6,200
Fordham	Rose Hill Gym	3,470
G. Washington	Smith Center	5,000
La Salle	First Union Spectrum	18,060
	& Hayman Center	4,000
Massachusetts	Mullins Center	9,493
Rhode Island	Keaney Gymnasium	3,385
	& Providence Civic Center	12,993
St. Bonaventure	Reilly Center	6,000
St. Joseph's-PA	Alumni Mem. Fieldhouse	3,200
Temple	Apollo Center	10,224
Virginia Tech	Cassell Coliseum	10,052
Xavier-OH	Cincinnati Gardens	10,100

Note: There are 12 schools in the Atlantic 10.

Big East

	Home Floor	Seats
Boston College	Conte Forum	8,606
Connecticut	Gampel Pavilion	10,027
	& Hartford Civic Center	16,294
Georgetown	MCI Center	20,600
Miami-FL	Miami Arena	15,200
Notre Dame	Joyce Center	11,418
Pittsburgh	Fitzgerald Field House	6,798
	& Pittsburgh Civic Arena	16,725
Providence	Providence Civic Center	12,993
Rutgers	Brown Athletic Center	9,000
St. John's	Alumni Hall	6,008
	& Madison Square Garden	18,470
Seton Hall	Continental Airlines Arena	20,029
Syracuse	Carrier Dome	33,000
Villanova	The Pavilion	6,500
	First Union Center	21,000
	& First Union Spectrum	18,060
West Virginia	WVU Coliseum	14,000

Big Sky

	Home Floor	Seats
CS-Northridge	The Matadome	3,000
CS-Sacramento	Memorial Auditorium	2,603
Eastern Wash.	Reese Court	5,000
Idaho St	Holt Arena	8,721
Montana	Dahlberg Arena	8,950
Montana St	Alterowitz Gym	3,500
Northern Ariz.	Walkup Skydome	7,000
Portland St.	Rose Garden	21,401
Weber St	Dee Events Center	12,000

Big South

	Home Floor	Seats
Charleston So	CSU Fieldhouse	1,500
	& N. Charleston Coliseum	13,000
Coastal Carolina	Kimbel Gymnasium	1,800
	& Myrtle Beach Con. Center	5,000
Liberty	Vines Center	9,000
NC-Asheville	Justice Center	1,570
	& Asheville Civic Center	6,800
Radford	Dedmon Center	5,000
Winthrop	Winthrop Coliseum	6,100

Big Ten

	Home Floor	Seats
Illinois	Assembly Hall	16,450
Indiana	Assembly Hall	17,357
Iowa	Carver-Hawkeye Arena	15,500
Michigan	Crisler Arena	13,562
Michigan St	Breslin Events Center	15,138
Minnesota	Williams Arena	14,321
Northwestern	Welsh-Ryan Arena	8,117
Ohio St.	Value City Arena	17,500
Penn St	Bryce Jordan Center	15,261
Purdue	Mackey Arena	14,123
Wisconsin	Wisconsin Field House	11,500

Note: There are 11 schools in the Big Ten.

Big 12

North	Home Floor	Seats
Colorado	Coors Events Conference Ctr.	11,198
Iowa St.	Hilton Coliseum	14,020
Kansas	Allen Fieldhouse	16,300
Kansas St.	Bramlage Coliseum	13,500
Missouri	Hearnes Center	13,300
Nebraska	Devaney Sports Center	14,200
South	**Home Floor**	**Seats**
Baylor	Ferrell Center	10,084
Oklahoma	Lloyd Noble Center	11,100
Oklahoma St.	Gallagher-Iba Arena	6,381
Texas	Erwin Center	16,175
Texas A&M	Reed Arena	12,700
Texas Tech	Lubbock Muni. Coliseum	8,174

Note: The Big Eight became the Big 12 in 1996-97 with the addition of Baylor, Texas, Texas A&M and Texas Tech from the SWC, which folded after the 1995-96 school year.

Big West

	Home Floor	Seats
Boise St.	BSU Pavilion	12,380
Cal Poly SLO	Mott Gym	3,500
CS-Fullerton	Titan Gym	3,500
Idaho	Kibbie Dome	10,000
Long Beach St	The Pyramid	5,000
Nevada	Lawlor Events Center	11,200
New Mexico St	Pan American Center	13,071
North Texas	The Super Pit	10,000
Pacific	Spanos Center	6,150
UC-Irvine	Bren Events Center	5,000
UC-Santa Barbara	The Thunderdome	6,000
Utah St.	The Smith Spectrum	10,270

Colonial

	Home Floor	Seats
American	Bender Arena	5,000
East Carolina	Minges Coliseum	7,500
George Mason	Patriot Center	10,000
James Madison	JMU Convocation Center	7,612
NC-Wilmington	Trask Coliseum	6,100
Old Dominion	Norfolk Scope	10,253
Richmond	Robins Center	9,171
VCU	Siegel Center	7,500
Wm. & Mary	William & Mary Hall	10,000

Conference USA

	Home Floor	Seats
Ala-Birmingham	Bartow Arena	8,500
Cincinnati	Shoemaker Center	13,176
DePaul	Rosemont Horizon	17,500
Houston	Hofheinz Pavilion	10,245
Louisville	Freedom Hall	18,865
Marquette	Bradley Center	19,150
Memphis	The Pyramid	20,142
NC-Charlotte	Halton Arena	9,105
Saint Louis	Kiel Center	20,000
South Florida	Sun Dome	10,411
Southern Miss	Green Coliseum	8,095
Tulane	Fogelman Arena	3,600

Ivy League

	Home Floor	Seats
Brown	Pizzitola Sports Center	2,800
Columbia	Levien Gymnasium	3,408
Cornell	Newman Arena	4,750
Dartmouth	Leede Arena	2,200
Harvard	Briggs Athletic Center	2,195
Penn	The Palestra	8,700
Princeton	Jadwin Gymnasium	7,500
Yale	Lee Amphitheater	3,100

Metro Atlantic

	Home Floor	Seats
Canisius	Marine Midland Arena	19,500
	& Koessler Athletic Center	1,800
Fairfield	Alumni Hall	2,479
Iona	Mulcahy Center	3,200
Loyola-MD	Reitz Arena	3,000
Manhattan	Draddy Gymnasium	3,000
Marist	McCann Center	3,944
Niagara	Marine Midland Arena	19,500
	& Gallagher Center	3,200
Rider	Alumni Gymnasium	1,650
St. Peter's	Yanitelli Center	3,200
Siena	Pepsi Arena	15,500

College Basketball (Cont.)

Mid American

	Home Floor	Seats
Akron	JAR Arena	5,942
Ball St	University Arena	11,500
Bowling Green	Anderson Arena	5,200
Central Mich	Rose Arena	6,000
Eastern Mich	Convocation Center	4,800
Kent	MAC Center	6,327
Marshall	Henderson Center	10,291
Miami-OH	Millett Hall	9,200
Northern Illinois	Chick Evans Field House	6,044
Ohio Univ	The Convo	13,000
Toledo	Savage Hall	9,000
Western Mich	University Arena	5,800

Mid-Continent

	Home Floor	Seats
Buffalo	Alumni Arena	8,500
Chicago St	Dickens Athletic Center	2,500
Missouri-K.C	Municipal Auditorium	11,126
NE Illinois	Phys. Ed. Complex	2,000
Oral Roberts	Mabee Center	10,575
Southern Utah	Centrum	5,300
Valparaiso	Athletics-Recreation Center	4,500
Western Ill	Western Hall	5,139
Youngstown St	Beeghly Center	8,000

Mid-Eastern Athletic

	Home Floor	Seats
Bethune-Cookman	Moore Gym	3,000
Coppin St	Coppin Center	3,000
Delaware St	Memorial Hall	3,000
Florida A&M	Gaither Gym	3,350
Hampton	Hampton Convocation Center	7,200
Howard	Burr Gym	3,000
MD-East.Shore	Tawes Gym	1,200
Morgan St	Baltimore City CC	2,000
N. Carolina A&T	Corbett Sports Center	7,500
S. Carolina St	SHM Center	3,200

Midwestern

	Home Floor	Seats
Butler	Hinkle Fieldhouse	11,043
Cleveland St	CSU Convocation Center	13,610
Detroit Mercy	Calihan Hall	8,837
IL-Chicago	UIC Pavilion	8,000
Loyola-IL	Gentile Center	5,200
WI-Green Bay	Brown County Arena	5,600
WI-Milwaukee	Wisconsin Center	10,938
Wright St	Nutter Center	10,632

Missouri Valley

	Home Floor	Seats
Bradley	Carver Arena	10,825
Butler	Hinkle Fieldhouse	11,043
Creighton	Omaha Civic Auditorium	9,000
Drake	Knapp Center	7,002
Evansville	Roberts Stadium	12,300
Illinois St.	Redbird Arena	10,200
Indiana St	Hulman Center	10,200
Northern Iowa	UNI-Dome	10,000
Southern Ill	SIU Arena	10,014
SW Missouri St.	Hammons Student Center	8,846
Wichita St.	Levitt Arena	10,545

Northeast

	Home Floor	Seats
Central Conn. St.	Detrick Gym	4,500
Farleigh Dickinson	Rothman Center	5,000
LIU-Brooklyn	Schwartz Athletic Center	1,200
MD-Balt. County	UMBC Fieldhouse	9,024
Monmouth	Boylan Gym	2,500
Mt. St. Mary's	Knott Arena	3,196
Quinnipiac	Burt Kahn Court	1,500
Robert Morris	Sewall Center	3,056
St. Francis-NY	Phys. Ed. Center	1,400
St. Francis-PA	DeGol Arena	3,500
Wagner	Spiro Sports Center	2,000

Ohio Valley

	Home Floor	Seats
Austin Peay	Dunn Center	9,000
Eastern Illinois	Lantz Gym	6,000
Eastern Ky	McBrayer Arena	6,500
Middle Tenn. St	Murphy Center	11,520
Morehead St	Johnson Arena	6,500
Murray St	Regional Special Events Ctr.	8,000
SE Missouri St	Show Me Center	7,000
Tennessee-Martin	Skyhawk Arena	6,700
Tennessee St	Gentry Complex	10,500
Tennessee Tech	Eblen Center	10,152

Pacific-10

	Home Floor	Seats
Arizona	McKale Center	14,489
Arizona St	Univ. Activity Center	14,198
California	Oakland Coliseum	19,200
Oregon	McArthur Court	9,087
Oregon St	Gill Coliseum	10,400
Stanford	Maples Pavilion	7,500
UCLA	Pauley Pavilion	12,819
USC	LA Sports Arena	15,509
Washington	Hec Edmundson Pavilion	7,800
Washington. St.	Friel Court	12,058

Patriot League

	Home Floor	Seats
Army	Christl Arena	5,043
Bucknell	Davis Gym	2,380
Colgate	Cotterell Court	3,000
Holy Cross	Hart Recreation Center	3,600
Lafayette	Kirby Field House	3,500
Lehigh	Stabler Arena	5,600
Navy	Alumni Hall	5,710

Southeastern

Eastern	Home Floor	Seats
Florida	O'Connell Center	12,000
Georgia	Stegeman Coliseum	10,523
Kentucky	Rupp Arena	23,000
South Carolina	McGuire Arena	12,401
Tennessee	Thompson-Boling Arena	24,535
Vanderbilt	Memorial Gymnasium	15,311

Western	Home Floor	Seats
Alabama	Coleman Coliseum	15,043
Arkansas	Bud Walton Arena	19,200
Auburn	Eaves-Memorial Coliseum	10,108
LSU	Maravich Assembly Center	14,164
Mississippi	Tad Smith Coliseum	8,135
Mississippi St	Humphrey Coliseum	10,000

Southern

	Home Floor	Seats
Appalachian St	Varsity Gymnasium	8,000
The Citadel	McAlister Field House	6,200
Coll. of Charleston	Kresse Arena	3,500
Davidson	Belk Arena	5,700
E. Tenn. St	Memorial Center	12,000
Furman	Timmons Arena	5,000
Ga. Southern	Hanner Fieldhouse	5,500
NC-Greensboro	Fleming Gymnasium	2,320
Tenn-Chatt	UTC Arena	11,218
VMI	Cameron Hall	5,029
W. Carolina	Ramsey Center	7,286
Wofford	Johnson Arena	3,500

Southland

	Home Floor	Seats
McNeese St	Burton Coliseum	8,000
Nicholls St	Stopher Gym	3,800
NE Louisiana	Ewing Coliseum	8,000
Northwestern St	Prather Coliseum	3,900
Sam Houston St	Johnson Coliseum	6,172
SE Louisiana	University Center	7,500
SW Texas St	Strahan Coliseum	7,200
S.F. Austin St.	W.R. Johnson Coliseum	7,200
TX-Arlington	Texas Hall	4,200
TX-San Antonio	Convocation Center	5,100

Southwestern

	Home Floor	Seats
Alabama St	Joe Reed Acadome	7,000
Alcorn St	Whitney Complex	7,000
Grambling St.	Memorial Gym	4,500
Jackson St	Williams Center	8,000
Miss.Valley	Harrison Athletic Complex	6,000
Prairie View	The Baby Dome	6,600
Southern-BR	Clark Activity Center	7,500
TX Southern	Health & P.E. Building	8,100

Sun Belt

	Home Floor	Seats
Ark-Little Rock	Barton Coliseum	8,303
Ark-Pine Bluff	Health & Phy. Ed. Complex	4,500
Arkansas St	Convocation Center	10,563
Florida International	Golden Panther Arena	5,000
Louisiana Tech	Thomas Assembly Center	8,000
New Orleans	Lakefront Arena	10,000
South Alabama	Mitchell Center	10,000
SW Louisiana	The Cajundome	12,800
Western Ky	E.A. Diddle Arena	11,300

Trans America

	Home Floor	Seats
Campbell	Carter Gym	945
Centenary	Gold Dome	3,000
Central Fla	UCF Arena	5,100
Fla. Atlantic	FAU Gym	5,000
Florida Int'l	Golden Panther Arena	5,000
Georgia St	GSU Sports Arena	4,200
Jacksonville St.	Mathews Coliseum	5,500
Mercer	Macon Coliseum	8,500
Samford	Seibert Hall	4,000
Stetson	Edmunds Center	5,000
Troy St	Sartain Hall	3,500

West Coast

	Home Floor	Seats
Gonzaga	Martin Centre	4,000
Loyola-CA	Gersten Pavilion	4,156
Pepperdine	Firestone Fieldhouse	3,104
Portland	Chiles Center	5,000
St. Mary's-CA	McKeon Pavilion	3,500
San Diego	USD Sports Center	2,500
San Francisco	War Memorial Gym	5,300
Santa Clara	Toso Pavilion	5,000

Western Athletic

Mountain	Home Floor	Seats
BYU	Marriott Center	22,700
New Mexico	University Arena (The Pit)	18,018
Rice	Autry Court	5,000
SMU	Moody Coliseum	8,998
TCU	Daniel-Meyer Coliseum	7,166
Tulsa	Tulsa Conv. Center	8,659
Utah	Huntsman Center	15,000
UTEP	Haskins Center	12,222

Pacific	Home Floor	Seats
Air Force	Clune Arena	6,003
Colorado St	Moby Arena	9,000
Fresno St.	Selland Arena	10,132
Hawaii	Special Events Arena	10,225
San Diego St	Aztec Bowl Arena	12,000
San Jose St.	The Events Center	5,000
UNLV	Thomas & Mack Center	18,500
Wyoming	Arena-Auditorium	15,028

Future NCAA Final Four Sites

Men

Year	Arena	Seats	Location
1999	ThunderDome	32,351	St. Petersburg
2000	RCA Dome	47,100	Indianapolis
2001	Metrodome	50,000	Minneapolis
2002	Georgia Dome	40,000	Atlanta
2003	Louisiana Superdome	53,500	New Orleans

Women

Year	Arena	Seats	Location
1999	San Jose Arena	17,500	San Jose
2000	First Union Spectrum	16,975	Philadelphia
2001	Kiel Center	20,000	St. Louis
2002	Alamodome	26,000	San Antonio

COLLEGE FOOTBALL

The 40 Largest I-A Stadiums

The 40 largest stadiums in NCAA Division I-A college football heading into the 1998 season. Note that (*) indicates stadium not on campus.

	Stadium	Location	Seats	Home Team	Conference	Built	Field
1	Michigan Stadium	Ann Arbor, Mich.	**107,501**	Michigan	Big Ten	1927	Grass
2	Neyland Stadium	Knoxville, Tenn.	**102,854**	Tennessee	SEC-East	1921	Grass
3	Rose Bowl*	Pasadena, Calif.	**98,636**	UCLA	Pac-10	1922	Grass
4	Beaver Stadium	University Park, Pa.	**93,967**	Penn St.	Big Ten	1960	Grass
5	LA Memorial Coliseum*	Los Angeles, Calif.	**92,000**	USC	Pac-10	1923	Grass
6	Ohio Stadium	Columbus, Ohio	**89,841**	Ohio St.	Big Ten	1922	Grass
7	Sanford Stadium	Athens, Ga.	**86,117**	Georgia	SEC-East	1929	Grass
8	Stanford Stadium	Stanford, Calif.	**85,500**	Stanford	Pac-10	1921	Grass
9	Jordan-Hare Stadium	Auburn, Ala.	**85,214**	Auburn	SEC-West	1939	Grass
10	Bryant-Denny Stadium	Tuscaloosa, Ala.	**83,453**	Alabama	SEC-West	1929	Grass
11	Legion Field*	Birmingham, Ala.	**83,091**	Alabama/UAB	SEC/Indy	1927	Grass
12	Florida Field	Gainesville, Fla.	**83,000**	Florida	SEC-East	1929	Grass
13	Memorial Stadium	Clemson, S.C.	**81,474**	Clemson	ACC	1942	Grass
14	Williams-Brice Stadium	Columbia, S.C.	**80,250**	South Carolina	SEC-East	1934	Grass
15	Notre Dame Stadium	Notre Dame, Ind.	**80,225**	Notre Dame	Independent	1930	Grass
16	Doak Campbell Stadium	Tallahasse, Fla.	**80,000**	Florida St.	ACC	1950	Grass
17	Tiger Stadium	Baton Rouge, La.	**79,940**	LSU	SEC-West	1924	Grass
18	Royal-Memorial Stadium	Austin, Tex.	**77,809**	Texas	Big 12-South	1924	Grass
19	Camp Randall Stadium	Madison, Wisc.	**76,129**	Wisconsin	Big Ten	1917	Turf
20	Oklahoma Memorial Field	Norman, Okla.	**75,004**	Oklahoma	Big 12-South	1924	Grass
21	Memorial Stadium	Berkeley, Calif.	**74,909**	California	Pac-10	1923	Grass
22	Memorial Stadium	Lincoln, Neb.	**73,650**	Nebraska	Big 12-North	1923	Turf
23	Qualcomm Stadium*	San Diego, Calif.	**73,400**	San Diego St.	WAC-Pac.	1967	Grass
24	Sun Devil Stadium	Tempe, Ariz.	**73,379**	Arizona St.	Pac-10	1959	Grass
25	Husky Stadium	Seattle, Wash.	**72,500**	Washington	Pac-10	1920	Turf
26	Orange Bowl*	Miami, Fla.	**72,314**	Miami-FL	Big East	1935	Grass
27	Spartan Stadium	East Lansing, Mich.	**72,027**	Michigan St.	Big Ten	1957	Turf
28	Memorial Stadium	Champaign, Ill.	**70,904**	Illinois	Big Ten	1923	Turf
29	Kinnick Stadium	Iowa City, Iowa	**70,397**	Iowa	Big Ten	1929	Grass
30	Kyle Field	College Station, Tex.	**70,210**	Texas A&M	Big 12-South	1925	Grass
31	Citrus Bowl*	Orlando, Fla.	**70,188**	Central Florida	Independent	1936	Grass
32	Rice Stadium	Houston, Tex.	**70,000**	Rice	WAC-Mtn.	1950	Turf
33	Cotton Bowl*	Dallas, Tex.	**68,252**	SMU	WAC-Mtn.	1932	Grass
34	Ross-Ade Stadium	W. Lafayette, Ind.	**67,861**	Purdue	Big Ten	1924	Grass
35	Veterans Stadium*	Philadelphia, Pa.	**66,592**	Temple	Big East	1971	Turf
36	Cougar Stadium	Provo, Utah	**65,000**	BYU	WAC-Mtn.	1964	Grass
37	Superdome*	New Orleans, La.	**64,767**	Tulane	USA	1975	Turf
38	HHH Metrodome*	Minneapolis, Minn.	**63,699**	Minnesota	Big Ten	1982	Turf
39	Mountaineer Field	Morgantown, W. Va.	**63,500**	West Virginia	Big East	1980	Turf
40	Liberty Bowl*	Memphis, Tenn.	**62,380**	Memphis	Conf. USA	1965	Grass

Note: Kentucky is undertaking a $24 million expansion and renovation of Commonwealth Stadium (which currently seats 57,800) that will increase capacity to approximately 68,000 prior to the 1999 season.

1998 Conference Home Fields

NCAA Division I-A conference by conference listing includes member teams heading into the 1998 season. Note that (*) indicates stadium is not on campus.

Atlantic Coast

	Stadium	Built	Seats	Field
Clemson	Memorial	1942	81,474	Grass
Duke	Wallace Wade	1929	33,941	Grass
Florida St	Doak Campbell	1950	80,000	Grass
Ga. Tech	Dodd	1913	46,000	Grass
Maryland	Byrd	1950	48,055	Grass
N. Carolina	Kenan Memorial	1927	60,000	Grass
N.C. State	Carter-Finley	1966	53,500†	Grass
Virginia	Harrison Field	1931	40,000	Grass
Wake Forest	Groves	1968	31,500	Grass

† Grass bank holds additional 10,000.

Big East

	Stadium	Built	Seats	Field
Boston Col	Alumni	1957	44,500	Turf
Miami-FL	Orange Bowl*	1935	72,314	Grass
Pittsburgh	Pitt	1925	56,150	Turf
Rutgers	Rutgers	1994	41,500	Grass
Syracuse	Carrier Dome	1980	59,550	Turf
Temple	Veterans*	1971	66,592	Turf
Va. Tech	Lane	1965	50,000	Grass
West Va	Mountaineer Fld.	1980	63,500	Turf

University of Michigan

Michigan Stadium added more than 5,000 seats in 1998. The Wolverines can once again lay claim to playing their home games at the nation's largest college football venue.

Big Ten

	Stadium	Built	Seats	Field
Illinois	Memorial	1923	70,904	Turf
Indiana	Memorial	1960	52,354	Turf
Iowa	Kinnick	1929	70,397	Grass
Michigan	Michigan	1927	107,501	Grass
Michigan St	Spartan	1957	72,027	Turf
Minnesota	Metrodome*	1982	63,699	Turf
Northwestern	Ryan Field	1926	49,256	Grass
Ohio St.	Ohio	1922	89,841	Grass
Penn St	Beaver	1960	93,967	Grass
Purdue	Ross-Ade	1924	67,861	Grass
Wisconsin	Camp Randall	1917	76,129	Turf

Big 12

NORTH	Stadium	Built	Seats	Field
Colorado	Folsom Field	1924	51,808	Turf
Iowa St.	Trice Field	1975	43,000	Grass
Kansas	Memorial	1921	50,250	Turf
Kansas St.	Wagner Field	1968	42,000	Turf
Missouri	Faurot Field	1926	62,000	Grass
Nebraska	Memorial	1923	72,700	Turf
SOUTH	**Stadium**	**Built**	**Seats**	**Field**
Baylor	Floyd Casey	1950	50,000	Turf
Oklahoma	Memorial	1924	75,004	Grass
Oklahoma St	Lewis Field	1920	50,614	Turf
Texas	Royal-Mem.	1924	77,809	Grass
Texas A&M	Kyle Field	1925	70,210	Grass
Texas Tech	Jones	1947	47,000	Turf

With the breakup of the Southwest Conference on June 30, 1996, the Big Eight became the Big 12 with the addition of Baylor, Texas, Texas A&M and Texas Tech from the SWC.

Note: The annual Oklahoma-Texas game has been played at the Cotton Bowl (capacity 68,252) in Dallas since 1937.

Big West

	Stadium	Built	Seats	Field
Boise St	Bronco	1970	30,000	Turf
Idaho	Kibbie Dome	1975	16,000	Turf
Nevada	Mackay	1967	31,545	Grass
New Mexico St	Aggie Memorial	1978	30,343	Grass
North Texas	Fouts Field	1952	30,500	Turf
Utah St.	Romney	1968	30,257	Grass

Note: Pacific dropped its football program after the 1995 season. Also, Arkansas St., Louisiana Tech, Northern Illinois and SW Louisiana all became independent while Boise St. and Idaho moved up from I-AA.

Conference USA

	Stadium	Built	Seats	Field
Army	Michie	1924	39,929	Turf
Houston	Robertson	1942	20,500	Grass
Cincinnati	Nippert	1924	35,000	Turf
E. Carolina	Dowdy-Ficklen	1963	43,000	Grass
Louisville	Papa John's Cardinal	1998	45,000	Grass
Memphis	Liberty Bowl*	1965	62,380	Grass
Southern Miss	Roberts	1976	33,000	Grass
Tulane	Superdome*	1975	64,767	Turf

I-A Independents

	Stadium	Built	Seats	Field
Alabama-Birm.	Legion	1927	83,091	Grass
Arkansas St	Indian	1974	33,410	Grass
C. Florida	Citrus Bowl	1936	70,188	Grass
Louisiana Tech	Joe Aillet	1968	30,600	Grass
Navy	Navy-Marine Corps Memorial	1959	30,000	Grass
NE Louisiana	Malone	1978	30,427	Grass
Notre Dame	Notre Dame	1930	80,225	Grass
SW Louisiana	Cajun Field	1971	31,000	Grass

College Football (Cont.)

Mid-American

	Stadium	Built	Seats	Field
Akron	Rubber Bowl*	1940	35,202	Turf
Ball St	Ball State	1967	21,581	Grass
Bowling Green	Doyt Perry	1966	30,599	Grass
Central Mich	Kelly/Shorts	1972	20,086	Turf
Eastern Mich.	Rynearson	1969	30,200	Turf
Kent	Dix	1969	30,520	Turf
Marshall	Marshall	1991	30,000	Turf
Miami-OH	Fred Yager	1983	30,012	Grass
Northern Ill	Huskie	1965	31,000	Turf
Ohio Univ	Peden	1929	20,000	Grass
Toledo	Glass Bowl	1937	26,248	Turf
Western Mich	Waldo	1939	30,200	Grass

Pacific-10

	Stadium	Built	Seats	Field
Arizona	Arizona	1928	57,803	Grass
Arizona St	Sun Devil	1959	73,379	Grass
California	Memorial	1923	74,909	Grass
Oregon	Autzen	1967	41,698	Turf
Oregon St	Parker	1953	35,362	Turf
Stanford	Stanford	1921	85,500	Grass
UCLA	Rose Bowl*	1922	98,636	Grass
USC	LA Coliseum*	1923	92,000	Grass
Washington	Husky	1920	72,500	Turf
Washington St	Martin	1972	37,600	Turf

Southeastern

EASTERN	Stadium	Built	Seats	Field
Florida	Florida Field	1929	83,000	Grass
Georgia	Sanford	1929	86,117	Grass
Kentucky	Commonwealth	1973	55,453	Grass
S. Carolina	Williams-Brice	1934	80,250	Grass
Tennessee	Neyland	1921	102,854	Grass
Vanderbilt	Vanderbilt	1981	41,600	Turf

WESTERN	Stadium	Built	Seats	Field
Alabama	Bryant-Denny	1929	83,453	Grass
	& Legion	1927	83,091	Grass
Arkansas	Razorback	1938	50,019	Grass
	& War Memorial*	1948	53,727	Grass
Auburn	Jordan-Hare	1939	85,214	Grass
LSU	Tiger	1924	79,940	Grass
Mississippi	Vaught-Hem'way	1941	42,577	Grass
Miss. St	Scott Field	1915	40,656	Grass

Notes: EAST– Kentucky is expanding Commonwealth Stadium to increase capacity to approximately 68,000 prior to the 1999 season; Vanderbilt Stadium was rebuilt in 1981.

SEC Championship Game

The first two SEC Championship Games were played at Legion Field in Birmingham, Ala., in 1992 and 1993. The game was moved to Atlanta's 71,228-seat Georgia Dome in 1994.

Western Athletic

Mountain	Stadium	Built	Seats	Field
BYU	Cougar	1964	65,000	Grass
New Mexico	University	1960	31,218	Grass
Rice	Rice	1950	70,000	Turf
SMU	Cotton Bowl*	1932	68,252	Grass
TCU	Amon Carter	1929	44,830	Grass
Tulsa	Skelly	1930	40,385	Turf
Utah	Rice	1927	32,500	Grass
UTEP	Sun Bowl*	1963	52,000	Turf

Pacific	Stadium	Built	Seats	Field
Air Force	Falcon	1962	52,480	Grass
Colorado St.	Hughes	1968	30,000	Grass
Fresno St	Bulldog	1980	41,031	Grass
Hawaii	Aloha*	1975	50,000	Turf
San Diego St	Qualcomm*	1967	73,400	Grass
San Jose St	Spartan	1933	30,478	Grass
UNLV	Sam Boyd*	1971	35,000	Turf
Wyoming	War Memorial	1950	33,500	Grass

WAC Championship Game

The WAC championship game between division winners is played at Sam Boyd Stadium in Las Vegas.

Bowl Games

Listed alphabetically and updated as of Sept. 1, 1998. The Bowl Championship Series calls for the national championship game (No. 1 vs. No. 2) to rotate between the Fiesta Bowl (1999), Sugar Bowl (2000), Orange Bowl (2001) and Rose Bowl (2002). See The Bowl Championship Series.

	Stadium	Built	Seats	Field
Alamo	Alamodome	1993	65,000	Turf
Aloha	Aloha	1975	50,000	Turf
Copper	Arizona	1928	57,803	Grass
Cotton	Cotton	1930	68,252	Grass
Fiesta	Sun Devil	1959	73,471	Grass
Fla. Citrus	Fla. Citrus Bowl	1936	65,000	Grass
Gator	Alltel	1995	72,223	Grass
Holiday	Qualcomm	1967	71,000	Grass
Independence	Independence	1936	50,459	Grass
Las Vegas	Sam Boyd	1971	40,000	Turf

	Stadium	Built	Seats	Field
Liberty	Liberty Bowl	1965	62,800	Grass
Motor City	Pontiac Silverdome	1975	80,368	Turf
Orange	Pro Player	1987	75,192	Grass
Outback	Houlihan's	1967	65,000	Grass
Peach	Georgia Dome	1992	71,228	Turf
Rose	Rose Bowl	1922	102,083	Grass
Sugar	Superdome	1975	76,000	Turf
Sun	Sun Bowl	1963	57,127	Turf
Sunshine Classic	Pro Player	1987	74,916	Grass

Playing Sites

Alamo— San Antonio; **Aloha**— Honolulu; **Carquest**— Miami; **Copper**— Tucson; **Cotton**— Dallas; **Fiesta**— Tempe; **Florida Citrus**— Orlando; **Gator**— Jacksonville; **Holiday**— San Diego; **Independence**— Shreveport; **Las Vegas**— Las Vegas; **Liberty**— Memphis; **Motor City**— Pontiac; **Orange**— Miami; **Outback**— Tampa; **Peach**— Atlanta; **Rose**— Pasadena; **Sugar**— New Orleans; **Sun**— El Paso.

Business

Beanie Baby giveaways took the sports nation by storm in 1998, as kids flocked to the ballparks whenever the famous collectors toys were handed out.

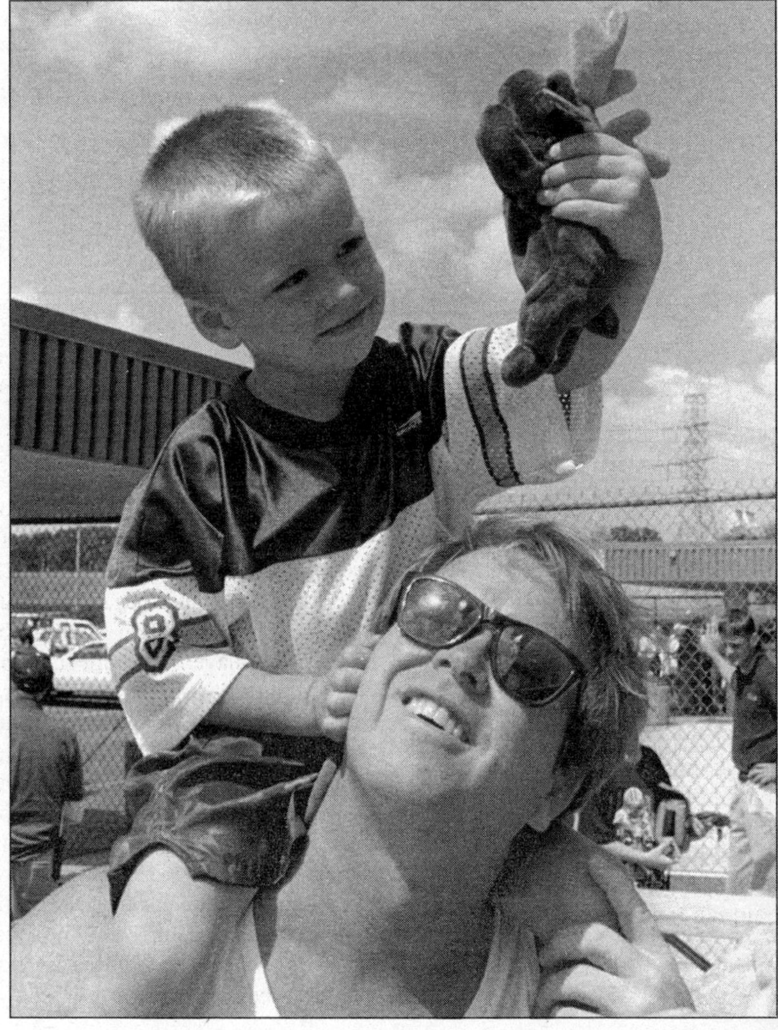

AP/Wide World Photos

The Browns are Back in Town

With a new owner and a new stadium under construction, the pieces are coming together for Cleveland's return to the NFL.

by
Bob Stevens

In a story that could only be fiction, or modern-day sports, the man who admitted he had a "front row seat" for the move of one of football's most storied franchises, the Cleveland Browns, now owns the "new" Browns. Yes, this is a story about money, mountains of it, but also about all the other things that make sports such great theater–lust, deceit, greed and blackmail. Everything but murder–so far.

Al Lerner is a billionaire. Chances are you have one of his MBNA credit cards. A minority owner and close friend of Art Modell, he didn't just introduce Modell to Maryland, he provided the plane where the papers were signed. The almost universal (except in Baltimore) negative fallout from the franchise shift led to a split between the pair. Lerner, however, continued his contact with a lawyer he'd hired to help with a case a quarter-century ago (NFL commissioner Paul Tagliabue) and a Cleveland politician he'd backed when he was a long-shot candidate for mayor (current mayor Michael White).

While Cleveland began construction on the $280 million stadium that never would have been built for Modell, and selling over 41,000 personal seat licenses that Modell never could have dreamed of peddling, Lerner continued to stay in the background, as was his style. Despite calls from Mayor White, Lerner's soul was still seared by the "Browns to Baltimore" circus, and he didn't want to be in the limelight again. Until he got a call from a Youngstown, Ohio native who was looking for a new job.

Bob Stevens is an anchor for ESPN's *Sports-Center*.

The brawn, the brains and the bucks. Former Browns quarterback **Bernie Kosar** (l) stands with **Carmen Policy** (c) and **Al Lerner** (r) on Sept. 8 after their $530 million proposal to own the new Cleveland Browns was unanimously accepted by the NFL.

Carmen Policy was president of the San Francisco 49ers during a decade of excellence that included three Super Bowls. He was considered one of the NFL's shrewdest manipulators of the complex salary cap rules. But he'd had a personal and professional falling out with his long-time friend, Edward DeBartolo, Jr., whose involvement in a gaming project in Louisiana prompted a federal probe, forcing him to transfer the team to his sister.

Policy wanted a football team to run, Lerner had the money, mutual friend Tagliabue played matchmaker, and the "Dream Team" was born. It was complemented by two critical endorsements. Former Browns quarterback Bernie Kosar, arguably the most popular player in Cleveland sports history, wanted to be on the winning team. Mayor White eschewed his earlier expectations of some minority ownership of the team and along with Kosar, sold Clevelanders that Lerner was "only helping a friend" when he aided Modell's move.

While Minnesota nearly had to run a national want-ad to find San Antonio's Red McCombs to buy the playoff-caliber Vikings for $250 million, seven different groups announced their intention of spending at least $350 million for the Browns sans players or coaches. After listening to current owners ponder a "billion dollar bid," Lerner's bid of $530 million proved the highest after four votes of the other owners in September and after Modell himself, who had lobbied against his old friend Lerner, finally caved in and backed the Lerner/Policy group. However, Modell and his Baltimore Ravens (and another mobile

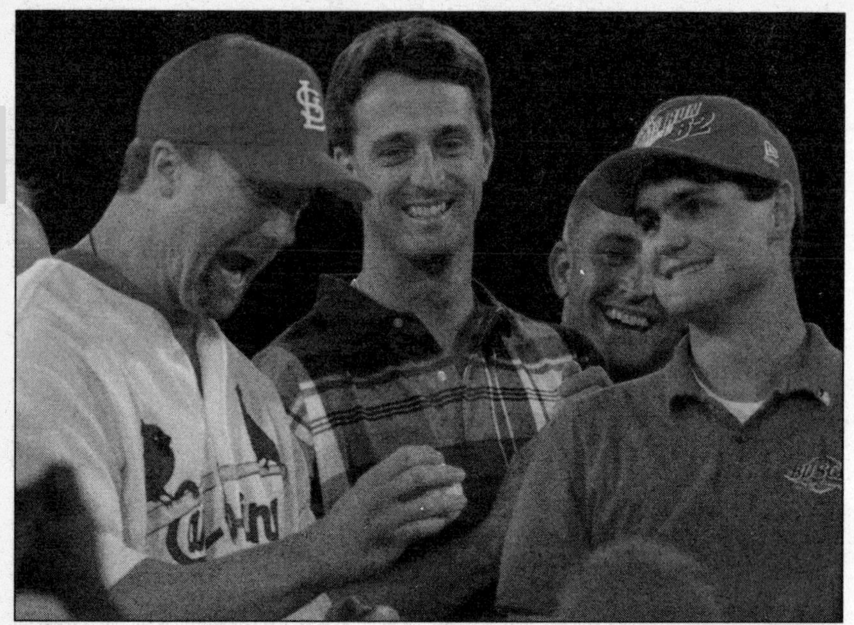

AP/Wide World Photos

St. Louis slugger **Mark McGwire** (l) reacts to receiving his 62nd home run ball from grounds crew worker **Tim Forneris** (r) as Roger Maris Jr. and Kevin Maris look on. The ball could have possibly fetched up to $1 million.

team of the '90s, the St. Louis Rams) won't get one of the $17 million shares that the other owners pocketed.

What did Lerner get for more than twice the Vikings' price and nearly three times more than the cost of the 1993 expansion teams? Well for starters, he gets the first pick in the '99 NFL draft. Plus he gets a number of cast-offs from the other NFL teams and he hasn't spent a dime of his salary cap on free agents–yet. He's expected to haul in at least $30 million a year in new stadium revenues and will get a $70 million share of the new TV deal. And he might just get to take the bullet-proof glass off his car in Cleveland.

Was it worth it? Ask the guy who buys the next item up for bids, the Washington Redskins, or the eventual expansion team in Los Angeles. It might take more than a good credit card to pay for them. ■

Bob Stevens' Top Ten 1998 Sports Business Highlights

10. **Marketing job of the year.** WNBA's Washington Mystics finish 3-27 on the court, but still lead the league in attendance, averaging 15,910 fans per game and breaking the 20,000-fan barrier twice.

9. **Beanie Baby days.** Even if you didn't have Mark McGwire coming to your park, just give away Beanie Babies and draw better than 10,000 fans per game over your usual average. Beanie Babies

given out at baseball's All-Star Game sold for $500 on the spot.

8. **Senior Tour golfer Hale Irwin** became the first to break the $2 million mark in tour earnings in 1997. He does it again in '98, becoming the PGA Tour's all-time leading money winner–at age 54.

7. **Peyton Manning signs** a six-year, $48 million deal with the Indianapolis Colts. Five years ago, top pick Drew Bledsoe signed a six-year, $14.4 million deal. Fifteen years ago, rookie quarterback John Elway signed a five-year deal for $5 million...total.

6. **The NBA television deal.** Without even accepting any outside bids, and with Michael Jordan's future cloudy, the NBA still more than doubles its take for the next four years. NBC and Turner Broadcasting pony up $2.64 billion. Cost of lockout: as yet undetermined.

5. **Mark McGwire cleans up.** The 62nd home run ball ends up costing him nothing, and he makes a dollar for every Cardinal ticket sold over 2.8 million.

4. **Murdoch goes shopping.** The media tycoon purchases the Los Angeles Dodgers and Dodger Stadium ($350 million), continues football for Fox ($4.4 billion), and acquires soccer's Manchester United (reported to be worth $1 billion). Not a bad year.

3. **Disney on ice.** The NHL signs a five-year $600 million broadcasting deal with Disney to begin in 1999, just a tad higher than Fox's five-year, $216 million deal ending in 1998.

AP/Wide World Photos

Media mogul **Rupert Murdoch** (c) seemed to grab whatever he could get his hands on in 1998, spending a total of close to $6 billion for the Los Angeles Dodgers, soccer's Manchester United and NFL football for Fox.

2. **The Florida Marlins.** After buying the 1997 World Series, owner H. Wayne Huizenga auctions off most of his talent, slashes payroll down to $10 million, and puts the team up for sale for $150 million, World Series Trophy included. Fans still pay the price as World Series tickets double, now costing $150 and $100. Go figure.

1. **The NFL television deal.** Disney (ABC/ESPN), CBS and Fox pay $17.6 billion from 1998-2005 to televise NFL games, over $70 million per team, per year. The $2.2 billion deal is double the cost of the previous four-year deal. NBC, who was outbid by CBS for the rights to the AFC, will be without pro football for the first time since 1965. ■

THE NUMBERS INSIDE

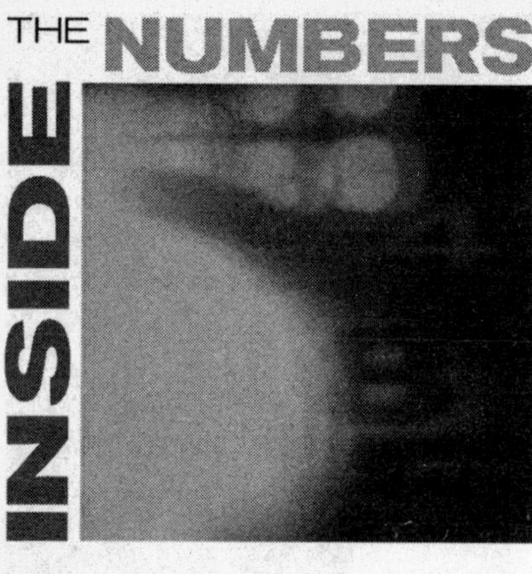

by
Steve Rutkowski, Craig Wachs and Paul Kinney

EXPENSIVE **EXPANSION**

The most recent expansion teams in each of the four major sports have cost owners some serious cash, none more than the recent Cleveland Browns sale to Al Lerner that carried a whopping $530 million price tag. The NHL's new Nashville Predators were a relative "bargain" at just $80 million.

NFL	Cleveland, '99	$530M
MLB	Arizona/Tampa Bay, '98	130M
NBA	Toronto/Vancouver, '95	125M
NHL	Nashville, '98	80M

FULL **ENDORSEMENT**

Like he's done with the competition in the NBA, Michael Jordan has dominated endorsement money in the '90s. He has been one of the top three highest paid athletes in the world every year since 1991, and in 1997 earned a whopping $78.3 million ($31 million in salary, $47 million in endorsements).

	Endorsement Earnings, '90s
Michael Jordan	$240.2M
Arnold Palmer	97.5
Jack Nicklaus	80.8
Andre Agassi	77.5
Shaquille O'Neal	70.9

Source: Forbes Magazine

THE NEED FOR **SPEED**

Last year, Dolphins quarterback Dan Marino joined the growing list of prominent athletes now involved in auto racing ownership. It's just another way that Marino is linked to future Hall of Fame quarterback Joe Montana. Montana is a partner with Target/Chip Ganassi Racing, which has won the last two CART championships. Championships just seem to follow that guy around, huh?

Dan Marino (NFL)	NASCAR
Walter Payton (NFL)	CART
Joe Montana (NFL)	CART
Brad Daugherty (NBA)	NASCAR
Julius Erving (NBA)	NASCAR
Joe Washington (NFL)	NASCAR

ACTING UP

OK, back to Jordan. Is there anything (besides Major League Baseball) that this guy doesn't do well? Check out where his movie, "Space Jam," ranked in its opening weekend, as compared to movies starring other athletes. Keep in mind that Jordan had Bugs Bunny as a co-star, and the other movies didn't.

	Movie	**Opening Weekend** (Gross)
Michael Jordan	Space Jam	$27.5M
Ray Allen	He Got Game	7.6M
Dennis Rodman	Double Team	5.2M
Shaquille O'Neal	Kazaam	5.0M
Gheorghe Muresan	My Giant	3.1M
Shaquille O'Neal	Steel	0.9M

■

1997-98 Top Rated TV Sports Events

Final 1997-98 network television ratings for nationally-telecast sports events, according to Nielsen Media Research. Covers period from Oct. 1, 1997 through Aug. 23, 1998. Events are listed with ratings points and audience share; each ratings point represents 980,000 households and shares indicate percentage of TV sets in use.

Multiple entries: SPORTS—NFL Football (40); Winter Olympics (14); Major League Baseball (8); NBA Basketball (9); NCAA Basketball and College Football bowl games (2). NETWORKS—NBC (29); CBS (17); ABC (16); FOX (13).

		Date	Net	Rtg/Sh
1	**Super Bowl XXXII** (Broncos vs Packers)	1/25/98	NBC	44.5/67
2	**NFC Championship Game** (Packers at 49ers)	1/11/98	FOX	26.2/47
3	**AFC Championship Game** (Broncos at Steelers)	1/11/98	NBC	25.0/54
4	**MLB World Series-Game 7** (Indians at Marlins)	10/26/97	NBC	24.5/39
5	**Winter Olympics** (Women's figure skating finals, women's GS)	2/20/98	CBS	23.2/38
6	**AFC Playoff Game** (Broncos at Chiefs)	1/4/98	NBC	22.9/42
7	**NBA Finals-Game 6** (Bulls at Jazz)	6/14/98	NBC	22.3/38
8	**Winter Olympics** (Women's figure skating short program, men's GS)	2/18/98	CBS	20.7/32
9	**NFL Playoff Game** (Buccaneers at Packers)	1/4/98	FOX	20.2/46
	Winter Olympics (Pairs figure skating, men's combined downhill)	2/8/98	CBS	20.2/30
11	**NBA Finals-Game 5** (Jazz at Bulls)	6/12/98	NBC	19.8/37
12	**Winter Olympics** (Men's figure skating short program, men's Super G)	2/12/98	CBS	19.3/30
13	**NBA Finals-Game 4** (Jazz at Bulls)	6/10/98	NBC	19.1/33
	NBA Eastern Conference Finals-Game 7 (Pacers at Bulls)	5/31/98	NBC	19.1/33
15	**Winter Olympics** (Pairs figure skating, ski jumping, speedskating)	2/10/98	CBS	18.2/30
16	**NFC Wildcard Playoff Game** (Lions at Buccaneers)	12/28/97	FOX	18.1/37
17	**Monday Night Football** (Broncos at 49ers)	12/15/97	ABC	18.0/31
	Winter Olympics (Ice dancing, bobsled, speedskating)	2/15/98	CBS	18.0/28
	NBA Finals-Game 1 (Bulls at Jazz)	6/3/98	NBC	18.0/32
20	**NCAA Men's Basketball Championship Game** (Kentucky vs Utah)	3/30/98	CBS	17.8/28
	AFC Wildcard Game (Dolphins at Patriots)	12/28/97	NBC	17.8/43
22	**Rose Bowl** (Wash. St. vs Michigan)	1/1/98	ABC	17.6/32
23	**NFL Regular Season Late Game** (Various teams)	12/21/97	NBC	17.4/36
24	**MLB World Series-Game 5** (Marlins at Indians)	10/23/97	NBC	17.2/30
25	**Winter Olympics** (Opening Ceremonies)	2/6/98	CBS	17.1/29
	AFC Playoff Game (Jaguars at Broncos)	12/27/97	ABC	17.1/37
27	**Monday Night Football** (Packers at Patriots)	10/27/97	ABC	16.8/32
	Monday Night Football (Packers at Vikings)	12/1/97	ABC	16.8/28
29	**NBA Finals-Game 2** (Bulls at Jazz)	6/5/98	NBC	16.6/31

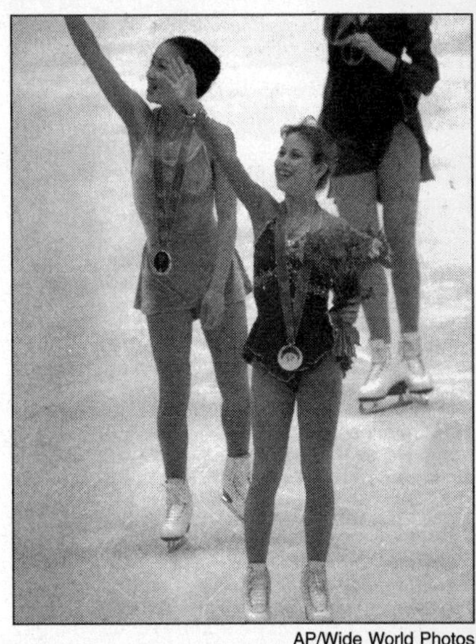

AP/Wide World Photos

Nancy and Tonya it wasn't, but **Tara Lipinski** (c) and **Michelle Kwan** (l) made the Olympic women's figure skating finals the fifth-highest watched sports event of the year.

		Date	Net	Rtg/Sh
30	**NFL Regular Season Late Game** (Various teams)	11/2/97	FOX	16.5/31
31	**NFL Regular Season Late Game** (Various teams)	12/7/97	FOX	16.3/32
32	**NBA Finals-Game 3** (Jazz at Bulls)	6/7/98	NBC	16.2/28
33	**NFL Regular Season Late Game** (Various teams)	11/16/97	FOX	15.8/30
34	**Monday Night Football** (Steelers at Chiefs)	11/3/97	ABC	15.7/26
35	**AFC Playoff Game** (Patriots at Steelers)	1/3/98	NBC	15.6/40
	MLB World Series-Game 3 (Marlins at Indians)	10/21/97	NBC	15.6/27
37	**MLB World Series-Game 4** (Marlins at Indians)	10/22/97	NBC	15.5/26
	MLB World Series-Game 6 (Indians at Marlins)	10/25/97	NBC	15.5/28
39	**Winter Olympics** (Men's figure skating long program, women's combined downhill, speedskating)	2/14/98	CBS	15.4/28
40	**Monday Night Football** (Panthers at Cowboys)	12/8/97	ABC	15.3/25
	Winter Olympics (Freestyle skiing, men's combined slalom, luge)	2/11/98	CBS	15.3/24
	Monday Night Football (Patriots at Dolphins)	12/22/97	ABC	15.3/27

		Date	Net	Rtg/Sh
43	**NFC Playoff Game** (Vikings at 49ers)	1/3/98	FOX	15.1/32
44	**MLB World Series-Game 2** (Indians at Marlins)	10/19/97	NBC	15.0/24
45	**NFL Regular Season Early Game** (Various teams)	11/23/97	FOX	14.9/35
	NFL Regular Season Late Game (Various teams)	10/26/97	NBC	14.9/28
	Winter Olympics (Ice dancing, freestyle skiing, ski jumping)	2/16/98	CBS	14.9/23
48	**Winter Olympics** (Women's Super G, speedskating, luge)	2/9/98	CBS	14.8/23
	Winter Olympics (Women's downhill, ice dancing)	2/13/98	CBS	14.8/26
50	**NFL Thanksgiving Day Late Game** (Oilers at Cowboys)	11/27/97	NBC	14.7/40
51	**Monday Night Football** (Cowboys at Redskins)	10/13/97	ABC	14.4/24
52	**Monday Night Football** (49ers at Eagles)	11/10/97	ABC	14.3/24
53	**NFC Playoff Game** (Vikings at Giants)	12/27/97	ABC	14.2/37
	Monday Night Football (49ers at Panthers)	9/29/97	ABC	14.2/24
55	**Monday Night Football** (Patriots at Broncos)	10/6/97	ABC	13.9/23
	NFL Regular Season Late Game (Various teams)	11/23/97	NBC	13.9/28
	Winter Olympics (Women's figure skating preview, women's slalom, speedskating)	2/19/98	CBS	13.9/22
58	**NBA Eastern Conference Finals-Game 6** (Bulls at Pacers)	5/29/98	NBC	13.8/26
59	**Winter Olympics** (Freestyle skiing, women's combined slalom)	2/17/98	CBS	13.5/21
60	**Monday Night Football** (Bills at Dolphins)	11/17/97	ABC	13.4/22
61	**FedEx Orange Bowl** (Nebraska vs Tennessee)	1/2/98	CBS	13.3/23
	MLB 1998 All-Star Game (Denver, Colorado)	7/7/98	NBC	13.3/25
	NFL Regular Season Late Game (Various teams)	10/19/97	NBC	13.3/30
64	**NFL Regular Season Early Game** (Various teams)	12/7/97	NBC	13.0/30
	MLB NLCS-Game 6 (Marlins at Braves)	10/14/97	NBC	13.0/22
	NFL Regular Season Early Game (Various teams)	11/9/97	FOX	13.0/31
	Monday Night Football (Raiders at Broncos)	11/24/97	ABC	13.0/22
68	**NFL Regular Season Early Game** (Various teams)	11/30/97	FOX	12.9/29
	NFL Regular Season Late Game (Various teams)	11/30/97	NBC	12.9/25
70	**Monday Night Football** (Bills at Colts)	10/20/97	ABC	12.8/22
	NFL Regular Season Late Game (Various teams)	12/14/97	FOX	12.8/27
72	**NCAA Men's Basketball National Semifinal** (Utah vs North Carolina)	3/28/98	CBS	12.7/24
73	**NFL Thanksgiving Day Game** (Bears at Lions)	11/27/97	FOX	12.6/35
74	**NBA Eastern Conference Finals-Game 5** (Pacers at Bulls)	5/27/98	NBC	12.5/23
	NFL Regular Season Early Game (Various teams)	10/5/97	FOX	12.5/32

AP/Wide World Photos

Rabid Green Bay Packers fans, often known as "Cheeseheads," helped make Super Bowls XXXI and XXXII two of the most-watched TV programs of all time.

All-Time Top-Rated TV Programs

NFL Football dominates television's All-Time Top-Rated 50 Programs with 21 Super Bowls and the 1981 NFC Championship Game making the list. Rankings based on surveys taken from January 1961 through May 17, 1998; include only sponsored programs seen on individual networks; and programs under 30 minutes scheduled duration are excluded. Programs are listed with ratings points, audience share and number of households watching, according to Nielsen Media Research.

Multiple entries: The Super Bowl (21); "Roots" (7); "The Beverly Hillbillies" and "The Thorn Birds" (3); "The Bob Hope Christmas Show," "The Ed Sullivan Show," "Gone With The Wind" and 1994 Winter Olympics (2).

	Program	Episode/Game	Net	Date	Rating	Share	Households
1	M*A*S*H (series)	Final episode	CBS	2/28/83	**60.2**	77	50,150,000
2	Dallas (series)	"Who Shot J.R.?"	CBS	11/21/80	**53.3**	76	41,470,000
3	Roots (mini-series)	Part 8	ABC	1/30/77	**51.1**	71	36,380,000
4	**Super Bowl XVI**	49ers 26, Bengals 21	CBS	1/24/82	**49.1**	73	40,020,000
5	**Super Bowl XVII**	Redskins 27, Dolphins 17	NBC	1/30/83	**48.6**	69	40,480,000
6	**XVII Winter Olympics**	Women's Figure Skating	CBS	2/23/94	**48.5**	64	45,690,000
7	**Super Bowl XX**	Bears 46, Patriots 10	NBC	1/26/86	**48.3**	70	41,490,000
8	Gone With the Wind (movie)	Part 1	NBC	11/7/76	**47.7**	65	33,960,000
9	Gone with the Wind (movie)	Part 2	NBC	11/8/76	**47.4**	64	33,750,000
10	**Super Bowl XII**	Cowboys 27, Broncos 10	CBS	1/15/78	**47.2**	67	34,410,000
11	**Super Bowl XIII**	Steelers 35, Cowboys 31	NBC	1/21/79	**47.1**	74	35,090,000
12	Bob Hope Special	Christmas Show	NBC	1/15/70	**46.6**	64	27,260,000
13	**Super Bowl XVIII**	Raiders 38, Redskins 9	CBS	1/22/84	**46.4**	71	38,800,000
	Super Bowl XIX	49ers 38, Dolphins 16	ABC	1/20/85	**46.4**	63	39,390,000
15	**Super Bowl XIV**	Steelers 31, Rams 19	CBS	1/20/80	**46.3**	67	35,330,000
16	**Super Bowl XXX**	Cowboys 27, Steelers 17	NBC	1/28/96	**46.0**	68	44,114,400
	ABC Theater (special)	"The Day After"	ABC	11/20/83	**46.0**	62	38,550,000
18	Roots (mini-series)	Part 6	ABC	1/28/77	**45.9**	66	32,680,000
	The Fugitive (series)	Final episode	ABC	8/29/67	**45.9**	72	25,700,000
20	**Super Bowl XXI**	Giants 39, Broncos 20	CBS	1/25/87	**45.8**	66	40,030,000
21	Roots (mini-series)	Part 5	ABC	1/27/77	**45.7**	71	32,540,000
22	**Super Bowl XXVIII**	Cowboys 30, Bills 13	NBC	1/29/94	**45.5**	66	42,860,000
	Cheers	Final episode	NBC	5/20/93	**45.5**	64	42,360,500
24	The Ed Sullivan Show	Beatles' 1st appearance	CBS	2/9/64	**45.3**	60	23,240,000
25	**Super Bowl XXVII**	Cowboys 52, Bills 17	NBC	1/31/93	**45.1**	66	41,988,100
26	Bob Hope Special	Christmas Show	NBC	1/14/71	**45.0**	61	27,050,000
27	Roots (mini-series)	Part 3	ABC	1/25/77	**44.8**	68	31,900,000
28	**Super Bowl XXXII**	Denver 31, Green Bay 24	NBC	1/25/98	**44.5**	67	43,630,000
29	**Super Bowl XI**	Raiders 32, Vikings 14	NBC	1/9/77	**44.4**	73	31,610,000
	Super Bowl XV	Raiders 27, Eagles 10	NBC	1/25/81	**44.4**	63	34,540,000
31	**Super Bowl VI**	Cowboys 24, Dolphins 3	CBS	1/16/72	**44.2**	74	27,450,000
32	**XVII Winter Olympics**	Women's Figure Skating	CBS	2/25/94	**44.1**	64	41,540,000
	Roots (mini-series)	Part 2	ABC	1/24/77	**44.1**	62	31,400,000
34	The Beverly Hillbillies	Regular episode	CBS	1/8/64	**44.0**	65	22,570,000
35	Roots (mini-series)	Part 4	ABC	1/26/77	**43.8**	66	31,190,000
	The Ed Sullivan Show	Beatles' 2nd appearance	CBS	2/16/64	**43.8**	60	22,445,000
37	**Super Bowl XXIII**	49ers 20, Bengals 16	NBC	1/22/89	**43.5**	68	39,320,000
38	The Academy Awards	John Wayne wins Oscar	ABC	4/7/70	**43.4**	78	25,390,000
39	**Super Bowl XXXI**	Packers 35, Patriots 21	FOX	1/26/97	**43.3**	65	42,000,000
40	The Thorn Birds (mini-series)	Part 3	ABC	3/29/83	**43.2**	62	35,990,000
41	The Thorn Birds (mini-series)	Part 4	ABC	3/30/83	**43.1**	62	35,900,000
42	**NFC Championship Game**	49ers 28, Cowboys 27	CBS	1/10/82	**42.9**	62	34,940,000
43	The Beverly Hillbillies	Regular episode	CBS	1/15/64	**42.8**	62	21,960,000
44	**Super Bowl VII**	Dolphins 14, Redskins 7	NBC	1/14/73	**42.7**	72	27,670,000
45	The Thorn Birds (mini-series)	Part 2	ABC	3/28/83	**42.5**	59	35,400,000
46	**Super Bowl IX**	Steelers 16, Vikings 6	NBC	1/12/75	**42.4**	72	29,040,000
	The Beverly Hillbillies	Regular episode	CBS	2/26/64	**42.4**	60	21,750,000
48	**Super Bowl X**	Steelers 21, Cowboys 17	CBS	1/18/76	**42.3**	78	29,440,000
	ABC Sunday Night Movie	"Airport"	ABC	11/11/73	**42.3**	63	28,000,000
	ABC Sunday Night Movie	"Love Story"	ABC	10/1/72	**42.3**	62	27,410,000
	Cinderella	Musical special	CBS	2/22/65	**42.3**	59	22,250,000
	Roots (mini-series)	Part 7	ABC	1/29/77	**42.3**	65	30,120,000

Note: The final Seinfeld episode on May 14, 1998 became the 64th highest-watched program of all time (41.3/58).

All-Time Top-Rated Cable TV Sports Events

All-time cable television for sports events, according to ESPN and Turner Sports research. Covers period from Sept. 1, 1980 through Sept. 1, 1998.

NFL Telecasts

		Date	Net	Rtg
1	Chicago at Minnesota	12/6/87	ESPN	17.6
2	Detroit at Miami	12/25/94	ESPN	15.1
3	Chicago at Minnesota	12/3/89	ESPN	14.7
4	Cleveland at San Fran	11/29/87	ESPN	14.2
5	Pittsburgh at Houston	12/30/90	ESPN	13.8

Non-NFL Telecasts

		Date	Net	Rtg
1	NBA: Detroit-Boston	6/1/88	TBS	8.8
2	NBA: Chicago-Detroit	5/31/89	TBS	8.2
3	NBA: Detroit-Boston	5/26/88	TBS	8.1
4	NCAA: G'town-St. John's	2/27/85	ESPN	8.0
5	NBA: Chicago-Orlando	5/10/95	TNT	7.9

Teams Bought in 1998

Seven major league clubs acquired new majority owners or significant minority owners from Nov. 1, 1997 through Sept. 1, 1998. See Business essay and updates chapter for Cleveland Browns sale.

Major League Baseball

Los Angeles Dodgers: After remaining under the same family ownership since 1950, the Dodgers were sold by Peter O'Malley to Rupert Murdoch's Fox Group on March 19, 1998 for $350 million. The deal also includes Dodger Stadium, 300 surrounding acres and training complexes in Florida and the Dominican Republic. The sale of the team to Fox was a controversial one because the media powerhouse has contracts with 22 of the 30 major league teams and it was feared that they would be monopolizing the game. The deal, however, was approved by a vote of 14-1 with Ted Turner, Vice Chairman of Time Warner and owner of the Braves, the only "no" vote.

Texas Rangers: Tom Hicks, CEO of Hicks, Muse, Tate and Furst, Inc. and owner of over 400 radio stations worldwide, purchased the Rangers on June 16, 1998. The $250 million deal, which also includes the lease to The Ballpark in Arlington and 270 acres of land, was bought from the original ownership of 28 partners that included Texas Governor George W. Bush. Hicks is also the owner of the NHL's Dallas Stars.

NFL Football

Minnesota Vikings: After months of speculation, Red McCombs purchased the Vikings for $250 million on July 28, 1998 after a group led by author Tom Clancy fell through with their financial plan to purchase the franchise. McCombs has owned the San Antonio Spurs and the Denver Nuggets, but never an NFL team.

NBA Basketball

New Jersey Nets: A group of businessmen led by Finn Wentworth and Stanley Gale of Wentworth and Gale LLC, a real estate investment firm, acquired a majority stake in the Nets on June 30, 1998. The current Nets' ownership consists of seven partners including David Gerstein, who owns approximately 25 percent, and will remain as the minority owner. The group reportedly paid $150 million for a 65 percent share of the NBA franchise. According to numerous reports, the new owners intend to keep the team in New Jersey, but they discussed moving from East Rutherford to Newark.

NHL Hockey

New York Islanders: New York Sports Ventures, a group headed by former Phoenix Coyotes owner Steven Gluckstern and partner Howard Milstein, purchased the Islanders from John O. Pickett Jr. on February 26, 1998 for $195 million. Pickett had originally sold the team to John Spano in January 1997 for $165 million, but Spano failed to meet his deadline for a $17 million payment and was later indicted on fraud charges in an unrelated case.

Edmonton Oilers: Edmonton Investors Group Ltd., a local partnership consisting of 17 Edmonton businesses, purchased the Oilers from Peter Pocklington on March 13, 1998 for $70 million. The group bid for the franchise after the NBA's Houston Rockets owner Les Alexander bought the franchise for $82 million and announced that he planned to move the team to Houston. Under the Location Agreement, Alexander was forced to wait 30 days before completing the deal, at which point local offers were given preference if they intended to keep the franchise in Edmonton until 2004.

Tampa Bay Lightning: Arthur L. Williams and ALW Sports Management, Inc. purchased the Lightning and the rights to their arena, the Ice Palace, on May 18, 1998 from Kokusai Green, a Japanese company that received criticism for its lack of involvement in the organization. The bid by Williams was lower than the reported $130 million offer from NBA's Detroit Pistons owner William Davidson, but Williams' deal allowed for concessions and vendor contracts to remain as it was with the original ownership.

Major TV Deals in 1997-98

NFL Football

The NFL hit the television jackpot in January 1998, signing brand new eight-year contracts with ABC, CBS, ESPN and FOX worth a total of $17.6 billion. The $2.2 million average per year more than doubles the price per year of the previous contracts. After four years without professional football, **CBS** outbid NBC, agreeing to pay $4 billion over the eight years for the exclusive rights to televise AFC games. **ABC** upped their ante to $4 billion, as well, in order to keep the rights to all Monday Night Football games, a part of ABC for 27 years. **ESPN**, who had previously split all Sunday night games with TNT, now gets all Sunday night games for a total of $4.8 billion or a yearly average of $600 million, the highest package of anyone. **Fox**, who had outbid CBS in 1993 for the rights to NFC games, held onto the NFC for eight more years with a bid of $4.4 billion.

NBA Basketball

In November 1997, Turner Broadcasting and NBC inked new television deals with the NBA worth over $2.6 billion for four years, beginning with the 1998-99 season and ending in 2001-2002. **Turner** (which includes both TBS and TNT) will pay $890 million for the right to show 80 regular-season games and approximately 40 playoff contests. **NBC** will shell out $1.75 billion for a lineup that now includes 32 regular-season games and 31 in the playoffs.

NHL Hockey

The NHL signed a new five-year contract in August 1998 with the Walt Disney Co. worth $600 million. Under the agreement, which begins with the 1999-2000 season and runs through 2003-04, **ESPN** will pay $350 million for all cable rights and $250 million for broadcast rights, which it will show on **ABC** Sports. Both ESPN and ABC are owned by Disney. ABC will televise anywhere from four to seven regular-season games, six early-round playoff games and up to five Stanley Cup Finals games. ESPN (and espn2) will increase their telecasts to close to 200 games per year, including comprehensive coverage of the Stanley Cup playoffs.

Top 10 Salaries In Each Sport

The top 10 highest paid athletes over the 1997-98 season for the NFL, NBA, Major League Baseball and NHL. Note that the salaries are for the most recent season only, and are not based on yearly averages. Figures are in millions of dollars.

Source: Street & Smith's SportsBusiness Journal.

NFL

		Position	Team	Salary
1	Troy Aikman	Quarterback	Dallas	$5.871
2	Drew Bledsoe	Quarterback	N. England	5.193
3	Trent Dilfer	Quarterback	Tampa Bay	4.523
4	Dan Marino	Quarterback	Miami	4.34
5	Brett Favre	Quarterback	Green Bay	4.124
6	Ray Buchanan	Cornerback	Atlanta	4.0
	Scott Mitchell	Quarterback	Detroit	4.0
8	Jerry Rice	Wide receiver	San Fran.	3.954
9	Junior Seau	Linebacker	San Diego	3.78
10	Neil O'Donnell	Quarterback	NY Jets	3.65

MLB

		Position	Team	Salary
1	Gary Sheffield	Right field	Los Angeles	$10.0
	Albert Belle	Left field	Chicago-AL	10.0
3	Greg Maddux	Pitcher	Atlanta	9.6
4	Barry Bonds	Left field	San Fran.	8.9
5	Mark McGwire	First base	St. Louis	8.33
6	Bernie Williams	Center field	NY Yankees	8.25
7	Ken Griffey Jr.	Center field	Seattle	8.01
8	Mike Piazza	Catcher	NY Mets	8.0
	Sammy Sosa	Right field	Chicago-NL	8.0
	Andres Galarraga	First base	Atlanta	8.0

NBA

		Position	Team	Salary
1	Michael Jordan	Guard	Chicago	$33.14
2	Patrick Ewing	Center	New York	20.5
3	Horace Grant	Forward	Orlando	14.285
4	Shaquille O'Neal	Center	LA Lakers	12.85
5	David Robinson	Center	San Antonio	12.397
6	Alonzo Mourning	Center	Miami	11.255
7	Juwan Howard	Center	Washington	11.25
8	Gary Payton	Guard	Seattle	10.514
9	Dikembe Mutombo	Center	Atlanta	9.61
10	Chris Webber	Forward	Washington	9.0

NHL

		Position	Team	Salary
1	Joe Sakic	Center	Colorado	$17.0
2	Sergei Fedorov	Center	Detroit	16.0
3	Chris Gratton	Center	Philadelphia	10.0
4	Eric Lindros	Center	Philadelphia	7.5
5	Wayne Gretzky	Center	NY Rangers	6.5
6	Mark Messier	Center	Vancouver	6.0
7	Pavel Bure	Right wing	Vancouver	5.5
	Paul Kariya	Left wing	Anaheim	5.5
9	Jaromir Jagr	Right wing	Pittsburgh	5.35
10	Steve Yzerman	Center	Detroit	5.079

Highest and Lowest Ticket Prices

The most expensive and least expensive average ticket prices for NFL, NBA, Major League Baseball and NHL franchises over the 1997-98 season.

Source: Team Marketing Report, Street & Smith's SportsBusiness Journal

NFL

	Highest	Venue	Avg. Price
1	Washington	Jack Kent Cooke	$52.92
2	Oakland	Oakland-Alameda	51.41
3	San Francisco	3Com Park	45.00
4	Dallas	Texas Stadium	43.48
5	Philadelphia	Veterans Stadium	42.83

	Lowest	Venue	Avg. Price
1	NY Jets	Giants Stadium	$30.16
2	Atlanta	Georgia Dome	31.49
3	Seattle	Kingdome	32.65
4	St. Louis	Trans World Dome	33.57
5	Cincinnati	Cinergy Field	34.09

MLB

	Highest	Venue	Avg. Price
1	Boston	Fenway Park	$20.63
2	NY Yankees	Yankee Stadium	20.51
3	Baltimore	Camden Yards	19.77
4	Cleveland	Jacobs Field	17.35
5	Atlanta	Turner Field	17.18

	Lowest	Venue	Avg. Price
1	Minnesota	HHH Metrodome	$8.22
2	Cincinnati	Cinergy Field	8.37
3	Pittsburgh	Three Rivers Stadium	9.33
4	Montreal	Olympic Stadium	9.98
5	Milwaukee	County Stadium	10.28

NBA

	Highest	Venue	Avg. Price
1	Portland	The Rose Garden	$47.49
2	Chicago	United Center	42.97
3	NY Knicks	Madison Sq. Garden	42.14
4	Houston	Compaq Center	41.92
5	Orlando	Orlando Arena	40.07

	Lowest	Venue	Avg. Price
1	LA Clippers	L.A. Mem. Sports Arena & Arrowhead Pond	$24.81
2	Charlotte	Charlotte Coliseum	25.57
3	Milwaukee	Bradley Center	26.67
4	Minnesota	Target Center	27.38
5	Atlanta	Georgia Dome & Georgia Tech	27.61

NHL

	Highest	Venue	Avg. Price
1	Pittsburgh	Civic Center	$56.28
2	Boston	FleetCenter	53.56
3	Philadelphia	First Union Center	52.75
4	New Jersey	Continental Airlines	50.60
5	Washington	US Airways Arena & MCI Center	50.36

	Lowest	Venue	Avg. Price
1	Dallas	Reunion Arena	$28.74
2	Calgary	Canadian Airlines Saddledome	29.04
3	Buffalo	Marine Midland	31.46
4	Phoenix	America West Arena	33.34
5	San Jose	San Jose Arena	33.90

1998 MLB Team Payrolls

Major League Baseball continues to be under fire because with no salary cap in place, teams in small markets can't possibly match the talent of those in larger markets. Listed are the 1998 opening day payrolls of all 30 MLB teams, along with the team's average salary.

Source: The Associated Press.

	Team	Payroll (000s)	Average (000s)
1	Baltimore	$68,988	$2,555
2	NY Yankees	63,461	2,441
3	Cleveland	59,584	2,128
4	Atlanta	59,536	2,126
5	Texas	55,305	1,975
6	St. Louis	52,575	1,753
7	Seattle	52,027	1,678
8	Boston	51,647	1,781
9	NY Mets	49,518	1,651
10	Chicago-NL	49,433	1,831
11	Toronto	48,666	1,738
12	Los Angeles	47,970	1,654
13	Colorado	47,435	1,694
14	San Diego	45,368	1,745
15	Houston	40,629	1,451
16	San Francisco	40,571	1,560
17	Anaheim	38,702	1,290
18	Chicago-AL	36,840	1,474
19	Philadelphia	34,370	1,228
20	Florida	33,434	1,238
21	Kansas City	32,963	1,177
22	Milwaukee	32,393	1,117
23	Arizona	30,572	1,054
24	Minnesota	26,183	1,091
25	Tampa Bay	25,318	873
26	Detroit	22,725	784
27	Cincinnati	21,995	758
28	Oakland	20,063	669
29	Pittsburgh	13,352	477
30	Montreal	9,162	352

The 1997 *Forbes* Top 40

The 40 highest-paid athletes of 1997 (including salary, winnings, endorsements, etc.), according to the Dec. 15, 1997 issue of *Forbes* magazine. Nationality, birth date, and each athlete's rank on the 1996 list are also given. Age refers to athlete's age as of Dec. 31, 1997.

	Athlete	Sport	Salary/ Winnings	Other Income	Total	Nat	Birthdate	Age	1996 Rank
1	Michael Jordan	Basketball	$31.3	$47.0	$78.3	USA	Feb. 17, 1963	34	2
2	Evander Holyfield	Boxing	53.0	1.3	54.3	USA	Oct. 19, 1962	35	6
3	Oscar De La Hoya	Boxing	37.0	1.0	38.0	USA	Feb. 4, 1973	24	17
4	Michael Schumacher	Auto Racing	25.0	10.0	35.0	GBR	Jan. 3, 1969	28	3
5	Mike Tyson	Boxing	27.0	0.0	27.0	USA	June 30, 1966	31	1
6	Tiger Woods	Golf	2.1	24.0	26.1	USA	Dec. 30, 1975	21	26
7	Shaquille O'Neal	Basketball	12.9	12.5	25.4	USA	Mar. 6, 1972	25	4
8	Dale Earnhardt	Auto Racing	3.6	15.5	19.1	USA	Apr. 29, 1952	45	20
9	Joe Sakic	Hockey	17.8	0.1	17.9	CAN	July 7, 1969	28	NR
10	Grant Hill	Basketball	5.0	12.0	17.0	USA	Oct. 5, 1972	25	18
11	Greg Norman	Golf	3.2	13.0	16.2	AUS	Feb. 10, 1955	42	38
12	Arnold Palmer	Golf	0.1	16.0	16.1	USA	Sept. 10, 1929	68	8
13	Horace Grant	Basketball	14.5	0.4	14.9	USA	July 4, 1965	32	NR
14	George Foreman	Boxing	10.2	4.5	14.7	USA	Jan 10, 1949	48	36
15	Pete Sampras	Tennis	6.5	8.0	14.5	USA	Aug. 12, 1971	26	16
16	Andre Agassi	Tennis	0.1	14.0	14.1	USA	Apr. 29, 1970	27	7
17	Cal Ripken Jr.	Baseball	6.7	6.5	13.2	USA	Aug. 24, 1960	37	11
18	David Robinson	Basketball	11.2	2.0	13.2	USA	Aug. 6, 1965	32	21
19	Ken Griffey Jr.	Baseball	8.8	4.2	13.0	USA	Nov. 21, 1969	28	19
20	Alonzo Mourning	Basketball	9.5	3.5	13.0	USA	Feb. 8, 1970	27	NR
21	Michael Chang	Tennis	2.5	9.5	12.0	USA	Feb. 22, 1972	25	24
22	Naseem Hamed	Boxing	9.5	2.5	12.0	GBR	Feb. 12, 1974	23	NR
23	Juwan Howard	Basketball	10.0	1.2	11.2	USA	Feb. 7, 1973	24	NR
24	Gary Payton	Basketball	9.0	2.2	11.2	USA	July 23, 1968	29	NR
25	Greg Maddux	Baseball	10.2	0.8	11.0	USA	April 14, 1966	31	NR
26	Hakeem Olajuwon	Basketball	9.5	1.5	11.0	NGR	Jan. 21, 1963	34	22
27	Dennis Rodman	Basketball	5.0	6.0	11.0	USA	May 13, 1961	34	9
28	Wayne Gretzky	Hockey	5.9	5.0	10.9	CAN	Jan. 26, 1961	36	14
29	Mike Piazza	Baseball	7.0	3.6	10.6	USA	Sept. 4, 1968	29	NR
30	Reggie Miller	Basketball	9.2	1.2	10.4	USA	Aug. 24, 1965	32	NR
31	Albert Belle	Baseball	10.0	0.4	10.4	USA	Aug. 25, 1966	31	NR
32	Jeff Gordon	Auto Racing	3.8	6.5	10.3	USA	Aug. 4, 1971	26	NR
33	Barry Sanders	Football	8.4	1.8	10.2	USA	July 16, 1968	29	NR
34	Chris Gratton	Hockey	10.0	0.1	10.1	CAN	July 5, 1975	22	NR
35	Lennox Lewis	Boxing	9.5	0.2	9.7	GBR	Sept. 2, 1965	32	NR
36	Michael Moorer	Boxing	9.6	0.0	9.6	USA	Nov. 12, 1967	30	NR
37	Sammy Sosa	Baseball	9.3	0.2	9.5	DOM	Nov. 12, 1968	29	NR
38	Jack Nicklaus	Golf	0.3	9.0	9.3	USA	Jan. 20, 1940	57	33
39	Frank Thomas	Baseball	7.2	2.1	9.3	USA	Mar. 27, 1968	29	30
40	Brett Favre	Football	5.6	3.6	9.2	USA	Oct. 10, 1969	28	NR

AWARDS

The Peabody Award

Presented annually since 1940 for outstanding achievement in radio and television broadcasting. Only 13 Peabodys have been given for sports programming. Named after Georgia banker and philanthropist George Foster Peabody, the awards are administered by the Henry W. Grady College of Journalism and Mass Communication at the University of Georgia. Documentary filmmaker Bud Greenspan won a Personal Peabody award in 1996 for his series of Olympic films.

Television

Year

1960 **CBS** for coverage of 1960 Winter and Summer Olympic Games

1966 ABC's **"Wide World of Sports"** (for Outstanding Achievement in Promotion of International Understanding).

1968 **ABC Sports** coverage of both the 1968 Winter and Summer Olympic Games.

1972 **ABC Sports** coverage of the 1972 Summer Olympics in Munich.

1973 **Joe Garagiola** of NBC Sports (for "The Baseball World of Joe Garagiola").

1976 **ABC Sports** coverage of both the 1976 Winter and Summer Olympic Games.

1984 **Roone Arledge**, president of ABC News & Sports (for significant contributions to news and sports programming).

1986 **WFAA-TV**, Dallas for its investigation of the Southern Methodist University football program.

1988 **Jim McKay** of ABC Sports (for pioneering efforts and career accomplishments in the world of TV sports).

1991 **CBS Sports** coverage of the 1991 Masters golf tournament & **HBO Sports** and Black Canyon Productions for the baseball special "When It Was A Game."

1995 **Kartemquin Educational Films** and **KTCA-TV** in St. Paul, MN, presented on PBS for "Hoop Dreams" & Turner Original Productions for the baseball special "Hank Aaron: Chasing the Dream."

Radio

Year

1974 **WSB** radio in Atlanta for "Henry Aaron: A Man with a Mission."

1991 **Red Barber** of National Public Radio (for his six decades as a broadcaster and his 10 years as a commentator on NPR's "Morning Edition").

National Emmy Awards
Sports Programming

Presented by the Academy of Television Arts and Sciences since 1948. Eligibility period covered the calendar year from 1948-57 and since 1988.

Multiple major award winners: ABC "Wide World of Sports" (19), NFL Films Football coverage (10); ABC Olympics coverage (9); ABC "Monday Night Football" (8); CBS NFL Football coverage, ESPN "Outside the Lines" series (6); CBS NCAA Basketball coverage and CBS "NFL Today" (5); ESPN "SportsCenter" and NBC Olympics coverage (4); ABC "The American Sportsman," ABC Indianapolis 500 coverage, ESPN "GameDay" and HBO "Real Sports with Bryant Gumbel" (3); ABC Kentucky Derby coverage, ABC "Sportsbeat," Bud Greenspan Olympic specials, CBS Olympics coverage, CBS Golf coverage, ESPN "Speedworld," Fox "NFL Sunday", MTV Sports series and NBC World Series coverage (2).

1949

Coverage—"Wrestling" (KTLA, Los Angeles)

1950

Program—"Rams Football" (KNBH-TV, Los Angeles)

1954

Program—"Gillette Cavalcade of Sports" (NBC)

1965-66

Programs—"Wide World of Sports" (ABC), "Shell's Wonderful World of Golf" (NBC) and "CBS Golf Classic" (CBS)

1966-67

Program—"Wide World of Sports" (ABC)

1967-68

Program—"Wide World of Sports" (ABC)

1968-69

Program—"1968 Summer Olympics" (ABC)

1969-70

Programs—"NFL Football" (CBS) and "Wide World of Sports" (ABC)

1970-71

Program—"Wide World of Sports" (ABC)

1971-72

Program—"Wide World of Sports" (ABC)

1972-73

News Special—"Coverage of Munich Olympic Tragedy" (ABC)

Sports Programs—"1972 Summer Olympics" (ABC) and "Wide World of Sports" (ABC)

1973-74

Program—"Wide World of Sports" (ABC)

1974-75

Non-Edited Program—"Jimmy Connors vs. Rod Laver Tennis Challenge" (CBS)

Edited Program—"Wide World of Sports" (ABC)

1975-76

Live Special—"1975 World Series: Cincinnati vs. Boston" (NBC)

Live Series—"NFL Monday Night Football" (ABC)

Edited Specials—"1976 Winter Olympics" (ABC)and "Triumph and Tragedy: The Olympic Experience" (ABC)

Edited Series—"Wide World of Sports" (ABC)

1976-77

Live Special—"1976 Summer Olympics" (ABC)

Live Series—"The NFL Today/NFL Football" (CBS)

Edited Special—"1976 Summer Olympics Preview" (ABC)

Edited Series—"The Olympiad" (PBS)

1977-78

Live Special—"Muhammad Ali vs. Leon Spinks Heavyweight Championship Fight" (CBS)

Live Series—"The NFL Today/NFL Football" (CBS)

Edited Special—"The Impossible Dream: Ballooning Across the Atlantic" (CBS)

Edited Series—"The Way It Was" (PBS)

National Emmy Awards (Cont.)

1978-79

Live Special—"Super Bowl XIII: Pittsburgh vs Dallas" (NBC)
Live Series—"NFL Monday Night Football" (ABC)
Edited Special—"Spirit of '78: The Flight of Double Eagle II" (ABC)
Edited Series—"The American Sportsman" (ABC)

1979-80

Live Special—"1980 Winter Olympics" (ABC)
Live Series—"NCAA College Football" (ABC)
Edited Special—"Gossamer Albatross: Flight of Imagination" (CBS)
Edited Series—"NFL Game of the Week" (NFL Films)

1980-81

Live Special—"1981 Kentucky Derby" (ABC)
Live Series—"PGA Golf Tour" (CBS)
Edited Special—"Wide World of Sports 20th Anniversary Show" (ABC)
Edited Series—"The American Sportsman" (ABC)

1981-82

Live Special—"1982 NCAA Basketball Final: North Carolina vs Georgetown" (CBS)
Live Series—"NFL Football" (CBS)
Edited Special—"1982 Indianapolis 500" (ABC)
Edited Seris—"Wide World of Sports" (ABC)

1982-83

Live Special—"1982 World Series: St. Louis vs Milwaukee" (NBC)
Live Series—"NFL Football" (CBS)
Edited Special—"Wimbledon '83" (NBC)
Edited Series—"Wide World of Sports" (ABC)
Journalism—"ABC Sportsbeat" (ABC)

1983-84

No awards given.

1984-85

Live Special—"1984 Summer Olympics" (ABC)
Live Series—No award given
Edited Special—"Road to the Super Bowl '85" (NFL Films)
Edited Series—"The American Sportsman" (ABC)
Journalism—"ABC Sportsbeat" (ABC), "CBS Sports Sunday" (CBS), Dick Schaap features (ABC) and 1984 Summer Olympic features (ABC)

1985-86

No awards given.

1986-87

Live Special—"1987 Daytona 500" (CBS)
Live Series—"NFL Football" (CBS)
Edited Special—"Wide World of Sports 25th Anniversary Special" (ABC)
Edited Series—"Wide World of Sports" (ABC)

1987-88

Live Special—"1987 Kentucky Derby" (ABC)
Live Series—"NFL Monday Night Football" (ABC)
Edited Special—"Paris-Roubaix Bike Race" (CBS)
Edited Series—"Wide World of Sports" (ABC)

1988

Live Special —"1988 Summer Olympics" (NBC)
Live Series—"1988 NCAA Basketball" (CBS)
Edited Special—"Road to the Super Bowl '88" (NFL Films)
Edited Series—"Wide World of Sports" (ABC)
Studio Show—"NFL GameDay" (ESPN)
Journalism—1988 Summer Olympic reporting (NBC)

1989

Live Special—"1989 Indianapolis 500" (ABC)
Live Series—"NFL Monday Night Football" (ABC)
Edited Special—"Trans-Antarctica! The International Expedition" (ABC)
Edited Series—"This is the NFL" (NFL Films)
Studio Show—"NFL Today" (CBS)
Journalism—1989 World Series Game 3 earthquake coverage (ABC)

1990

Live Special—"1990 Indianapolis 500" (ABC)
Live Series—"1990 NCAA Basketball Tournament" (CBS)
Edited Special—"Road to Super Bowl XXIV" (NFL Films)
Edited Series—"Wide World of Sports" (ABC)
Studio Show—"SportsCenter" (ESPN)
Journalism—"Outside the Lines: The Autograph Game" (ESPN)

1991

Live Special—"1991 NBA Finals: Chicago vs LA Lakers" (NBC)
Live Series—"1991 NCAA Basketball Tournament" (CBS)
Edited Special—"Wide World of Sports 30th Anniversary Special" (ABC)
Edited Series—"This is the NFL" (NFL Films)
Studio Show—"NFL GameDay" (ESPN) and "NFL Live" (NBC)
Journalism—"Outside the Lines: Steroids–Whatever It Takes" (ESPN)

1992

Live Special—"1992 Breeders' Cup" (NBC)
Live Series—"1992 NCAA Basketball Tournament" (CBS)
Edited Special—"1992 Summer Olympics" (NBC)
Edited Series—"MTV Sports" (MTV)
Studio Show—"The NFL Today" (CBS)
Journalism—"Outside the Lines: Portraits in Black and White" (ESPN)

1993

Live Special—"1993 World Series" (CBS)
Live Series—"Monday Night Football" (ABC)
Edited Special—"Road to the Super Bowl" (NFL Films)
Edited Series—"This is the NFL" (NFL Films)
Studio Show—"The NFL Today" (CBS)
Journalism (TIE)—"Outside the Lines: Mitch Ivey Feature" (ESPN) and "SportsCenter: University of Houston Football" (ESPN).
Feature—"Arthur Ashe: His Life, His Legacy" (NBC).

1994

Live Special —"NHL Stanley Cup Finals" (ESPN)
Live Series —"Monday Night Football" (ABC)
Edited Special —"Lillehammer '94: 16 Days of Glory" (Disney/Cappy Productions)
Edited Series —"MTV Sports" (MTV)
Studio Show —"NFL GameDay" (ESPN)
Journalism —"1994 Winter Olympic Games: Mossad feature" (CBS)
Feature (TIE) —"Heroes of Telemark" on Winter Olympic Games (CBS); and "SportsCenter: Vanderbilt running back Brad Gaines" (ESPN).

"Baseball" Wins Prime Time Emmy

Ken Burns's miniseries "Baseball" won the 1994 Emmy Award for Outstanding Informational Series. The nine-part documentary aired from Sept. 18-28, 1994 and ran more than 18 hours, drawing the largest audience in PBS history.

1995

Live Special —"Cal Ripken 2131" (ESPN)
Live Series —"ESPN Speedworld" (ESPN)
Edited Special (quick turn-around) —"Outside the Lines: Playball– Opening Day in America" (ESPN)
Edited Special (long turn-around) —"Lillehammer, an Olympic Diary" (CBS)
Edited Series —"NFL Films Presents" (NFL Films)
Studio Show (TIE) —"NFL GameDay" (ESPN) and "Fox NFL Sunday"(Fox)
Journalism —"Real Sports with Bryant Gumbel: Broken Promises" (HBO)
Feature (TIE) —"SportsCenter: Jerry Quarry" (ESPN) and "Real Sports with Bryant Gumbel: Coach" (HBO).

1996

Live Special —"1996 World Series" (Fox)
Live Series —"ESPN Speedworld" (ESPN)
Edited Special —"Football America" (TNT/NFL Films)
Edited Series —"NFL Films Presents" (NFL Films)
Live Event Turnaround —"The Centennial Olympic Games" (NBC)
Studio Show —"SportsCenter" (ESPN)
Journalism —"Outside the Lines: AIDS in Sports" (ESPN)
Feature —"Real Sports with Bryant Gumbel: 1966 Texas Western NCAA Champs" (HBO).

1997

Live Special —"The NBA Finals" (NBC)
Live Series —"NFL Monday Night Football" (ABC)
Edited Special —"Ironman Triathlon World Championship" (NBC/World Triathlon Corporation)
Edited Series —"NFL Films Presents" (NFL Films)
Live Event Turnaround —"Outside The Lines: Inside The Kentucky Derby" (ESPN)
Studio Show —"Fox NFL Sunday" (FOX)
Journalism —"Real Sports With Bryant Gumbel: Pros and Cons" (HBO)
Feature —"NFL Films Presents: Eddie George" (NFL Films).

Sportscasters of the Year National Emmy Awards

An Emmy Award for Sportscasters was first introduced in 1968 and given for Outstanding Host/Commentator for the 1967-68 TV season. Two awards, one for Outstanding Host or Play-by-Play and the other for Outstanding Analyst, were first presented in 1981 for the 1980-81 season. Three awards, for Outstanding Studio Host, Play-by-Play and Analyst, have been given since the 1993 season

Multiple winners: John Madden (11); Bob Costas and Jim McKay (9); Dick Enberg (4); Al Michaels (3); Keith Jackson (2). Note that Jim McKay has won a total of 12 Emmy awards: eight for Host/Commentator, one for Host/Play-by-Play, two for Sports Writing, and one for News Commentary.

Season	Host/Commentator
1967-68	Jim McKay, ABC
1968-69	No award
1969-70	No award
1970-71	Jim McKay, ABC & Don Meredith, ABC
1971-72	No award
1972-73	Jim McKay, ABC
1973-74	Jim McKay, ABC
1974-75	Jim McKay, ABC
1975-76	Jim McKay, ABC
1976-77	Frank Gifford, ABC
1977-78	Jack Whitaker, CBS
1978-79	Jim McKay, ABC
1979-80	Jim McKay, ABC

Season	Host/Play-by-Play
1980-81	Dick Enberg, NBC
1981-82	Jim McKay, ABC
1982-83	Dick Enberg, NBC
1983-84	No award
1984-85	George Michael, NBC
1985-86	No award
1986-87	Al Michaels, ABC
1987-88	Bob Costas, NBC
1988	Bob Costas, NBC
1989	Al Michaels, ABC
1990	Dick Enberg, NBC
1991	Bob Costas, NBC
1992	Bob Costas, NBC

Season	Analyst
1980-81	Dick Button, ABC
1981-82	John Madden, CBS
1982-83	John Madden, CBS
1983-84	No award
1984-85	No award
1985-86	No award
1986-87	John Madden, CBS
1987-88	John Madden, CBS
1988	John Madden, CBS
1989	John Madden, CBS
1990	John Madden, CBS
1991	John Madden, CBS
1992	John Madden, CBS

Year	Studio Host
1993	Bob Costas, NBC
1994	Bob Costas, NBC
1995	Bob Costas, NBC
1996	Bob Costas, NBC
1997	Dan Patrick, ESPN

Year	Play-by-Play
1993	Dick Enberg, NBC
1994	Keith Jackson, ABC
1995	Al Michaels, ABC
1996	Keith Jackson, ABC
1997	Bob Costas, NBC

Year	Analyst
1993	Billy Packer, CBS
1994	John Madden, Fox
1995	John Madden, Fox
1996	Howie Long, Fox
1997	Cris Collinsworth, HBO/NBC

Life Achievement Emmy Award

For outstanding work as an exemplary television sportscaster over many years.

Year	
1989	Jim McKay
1990	Lindsey Nelson
1991	Curt Gowdy
1992	Chris Schenkel
1993	Pat Summerall
1994	Howard Cosell
1995	Vin Scully
1996	Frank Gifford
1997	Jim Simpson

National Sportscasters and Sportswriters Assn. Award

Sportscaster of the Year presented annually since 1959 by the National Sportcasters and Sportswriters Association, based in Salisbury, N.C. Voting is done by NSSA members and selected national media.

Multiple winners: Bob Costas (7); Chris Berman and Keith Jackson (5); Lindsey Nelson and Chris Schenkel (4); Dick Enberg, Al Michaels and Vin Scully (3); Curt Gowdy and Ray Scott (2).

Year		Year		Year		Year	
1959	Lindsey Nelson	1969	Curt Gowdy	1979	Dick Enberg	1988	Bob Costas
1960	Lindsey Nelson	1970	Chris Schenkel	1980	Dick Enberg & Al Michaels	1989	Chris Berman
1961	Lindsey Nelson	1971	Ray Scott	1981	Dick Enberg	1990	Chris Berman
1962	Lindsey Nelson	1972	Keith Jackson	1982	Vin Scully	1991	Bob Costas
1963	Chris Schenkel	1973	Keith Jackson	1983	Al Michaels	1992	Bob Costas
1964	Chris Schenkel	1974	Keith Jackson	1984	John Madden	1993	Chris Berman
1965	Vin Scully	1975	Keith Jackson	1985	Bob Costas	1994	Chris Berman
1966	Curt Gowdy	1976	Keith Jackson	1986	Al Michaels	1995	Bob Costas
1967	Chris Schenkel	1977	Pat Summerall	1987	Bob Costas	1996	Chris Berman
1968	Ray Scott	1978	Vin Scully			1997	Bob Costas

American Sportscasters Association Award

Sportscaster of the Year presented annually from 1984-94, with the exception of 1988, by the New York-based American Sportscasters Association. Two awards presented starting in 1995 to honor top play-by-play personality and studio host. Voting done by ASA members and officials.

Multiple winners: Dick Enberg (5); Bob Costas (4); Chris Berman (3).

Sportscaster of the Year

Year		Year	
1984	Dick Enberg	1990	Dick Enberg
1985	Vin Scully	1991	Bob Costas
1986	Dick Enberg	1992	Bob Costas
1987	Dick Enberg	1993	Bob Costas
1988	No award	1994	Pat Summerall
1989	Bob Costas		

Play-by-Play

Year	
1995	Al Michaels
1996	Marv Albert
1997	Dick Enberg

Studio Host

Year	
1995	Chris Berman
1996	Chris Berman
1997	Chris Berman

The Pulitzer Prize

The Pulitzer Prizes for journalism, letters and music have been presented annually since 1917 in the name of Joseph Pulitzer (1847-1911), the publisher of the *New York World*. Prizes are awarded by the president of Columbia University on the recommendation of a board of review. Fourteen Pulitzers have been awarded for newspaper sports reporting, sports commentary and sports photography.

News Coverage

1935 **Bill Taylor,** *NY Herald Tribune*, for his reporting on the 1934 America's Cup yacht races.

Special Citation

1952 **Max Kase**, *NY Journal-American*, for his reporting on the 1951 college basketball point-shaving scandal.

Meritorious Public Service

1954 *Newsday* (Garden City, N.Y.) for its expose of New York State's race track scandals and labor racketeering.

General Reporting

1956 **Arthur Daley,** *NY Times*, for his 1955 columns.

Investigative Reporting

1981 **Clark Hallas** & **Robert Lowe,** *(Tucson) Arizona Daily Star*, for their 1980 investigation of the University of Arizona athletic department.

Specialized Reporting

1985 **Randall Savage** & **Jackie Crosby,** Macon (Ga.) *Telegraph and News, for their 1984 investigation of athletics and academics at the University of Georgia and Georgia Tech.*

Feature Writing

1996 **Lisa Pollak**, *Baltimore Sun*, for her story "The Umpire's Son" about baseball umpire John Hirschbeck and his son.

Commentary

1976 **Red Smith**, *NY Times*, for his 1975 columns.

1981 **Dave Anderson,** *NY Times*, for his 1980 columns.

1990 **Jim Murray**, *LA Times*, for his 1989 columns.

Photography

1949 **Nat Fein,** *NY Herald Tribune*, for his photo, "Babe Ruth Bows Out."

1952 **John Robinson** & **Don Ultang,** *Des Moines* (Iowa) *Register and Tribune, for their sequence of six pictures of the 1951 Drake-Oklahoma A&M football game, in which Drake's Johnny Bright had his jaw broken.*

1985 **The Photography Staff** of the *Orange County* (Calif.) *Register, for their coverage of the 1984 Summer Olympics in Los Angeles.*

1993 **William Snyder** & **Ken Geiger,** *The Dallas Morning News*, for their coverage of the 1992 Summer Olympics in Barcelona, Spain.

Sportswriter of the Year

NSSA Award

Presented annually since 1959 by the National Sportscasters and Sportswriters Association, based in Salisbury, N.C. Voting is done by NSSA members and selected national media.

Multiple winners: Jim Murray (14); Frank Deford (6); Rick Reilly and Red Smith (5); Will Grimsley (4); Peter Gammons (3).

Year
1959 Red Smith, *NY Herald-Tribune*
1960 Red Smith, *NY Herald-Tribune*
1961 Red Smith, *NY Herald-Tribune*
1962 Red Smith, *NY Herald-Tribune*
1963 Arthur Daley, *NY Times*
1964 Jim Murray, *LA Times*
1965 Red Smith, *NY Herald-Tribune*
1966 Jim Murray, *LA Times*
1967 Jim Murray, *LA Times*
1968 Jim Murray, *LA Times*
1969 Jim Murray, *LA Times*
1970 Jim Murray, *LA Times*
1971 Jim Murray, *LA Times*
1972 Jim Murray, *LA Times*

Year
1973 Jim Murray, *LA Times*
1974 Jim Murray, *LA Times*
1975 Jim Murray, *LA Times*
1976 Jim Murray, *LA Times*
1977 Jim Murray, *LA Times*
1978 Will Grimsley, AP
1979 Jim Murray, *LA Times*
1980 Will Grimsley, AP
1981 Will Grimsley, AP
1982 Frank Deford, *Sports Ill.*
1983 Will Grimsley, AP
1984 Frank Deford, *Sports Ill.*
1985 Frank Deford, *Sports Ill.*
1986 Frank Deford, *Sports Ill.*

Year
1987 Frank Deford, *Sports Ill.*
1988 Frank Deford, *Sports Ill.*
1989 Peter Gammons, *Sports Ill.*
1990 Peter Gammons, *Boston Globe*
1991 Rick Reilly, *Sports Ill.*
1992 Rick Reilly, *Sports Ill.*
1993 Peter Gammons, *Boston Globe*
1994 Rick Reilly, *Sports Ill.*
1995 Rick Reilly, *Sports Ill.*
1996 Rick Reilly, *Sports Ill.*
1997 Dave Kindred, *The Sporting News*

Best Newspaper Sports Sections of 1997

Winners of the Annual Associated Press Sports Editors contest for best daily and Sunday sports sections. Awards are divided into different categories, based on circulation figures. Selections are made by a committee of APSE members.

Circulation Over 175,000

Top 10 Daily

Boston Globe
Chicago Tribune
Dallas Morning News
Sun Sentinal (Ft. Lauderdale)
Los Angeles Times
Miami Herald
New York Times
Philadelphia Daily News
USA Today
Washington Post

Top 10 Sunday

Atlanta Journal and Constitution
Boston Globe
Chicago Tribune
Dallas Morning News
Sun Sentinal (Ft. Lauderdale)
Los Angeles Times
Miami Herald
New York Daily News
Orange County Register
Washington Post

Circulation 50,000-175,000

Top 10 Daily

Akron Beacon Journal
Asbury Park Press
Gannett Suburban (White Plains, NY)
Lexington (Ky.) *Herald-Leader*
Munster (Ind.) *Times*
Raleigh News and Observer
The Hackensack Record
San Francisco Examiner
The News Tribune (Tacoma, Wash.)
Wichita Eagle

Top 10 Sunday

Akron Beacon Journal
Asbury Park Press
Contra Costa Times (Walnut Creek, Cal.)
Lexington (Ky.) *Herald-Leader*
Munster (Ind.) *Times*
Quad-City Times (Davenport, Iowa)
Raleigh News and Observer
The Record (Hackensack, N.J.)
San Francisco Examiner
The News Tribune (Tacoma, Wash.)

Best Sportswriting of 1997

Winners of the Annual Associated Press Sports Editors Contest for best sportswriting in 1997. Eventual winners were chosen from five finalists in each writing division. Selections are made by a committee of APSE members. Note the investigative writing division included all circulation categories.

Circulation over 175,000

Column: Mitch Albom, *Detroit Free Press*
Enterprise: Mike Fish, Jeff Schultz, Mike Tierney and Matt Winkeljohn, *Atlanta Journal and Constitution*
Feature: Mitch Albom, *Detroit Free Press*
Game Story: Michael Madden, *Boston Globe*
News story: Sallie Hoffmeister and Ross Newhan, *Los Angeles Times*

Circulation 50,000-175,000

Column: Adrian Wojnarowski, *Fresno Bee*
Enterprise: Chris Poore and Mark Story, *Lexington* (Ky.) *Herald-Leader*
Feature: Chuck Culpepper, *Lexington* (Ky.) *Herald-Leader*
Game Story: Tom Spousta, *Sarasota Herald-Tribune*
News story: Matt Steinmetz, *Contra Costa Times* (Walnut Creek, Cal.)

All Categories

Investigative: John Valenti, *Newsday*

Directory of Organizations

Listing of the major sports organizations, teams and media addresses and officials as Sept. 1, 1998.

AUTO RACING

CART
(Championship Auto Racing Teams, Inc.)
755 W. Big Beaver Rd., Suite 800, Troy, MI 48084
(248) 362-8800
President-CEO .... Andrew Craig
Director of Publicity .... Mike Zizzo

IRL
(Indy Racing League)
4565 West 16th St., Indianapolis, IN 46222
(317) 484-6526
Chairman .... Mari George
President .... Tony George
V.P./Exec. Director .... Leo Mehl
Director of Public Relations .... Fred Nation

FIA— Formula One
(Federation Internationale de L'Automobile)
8 Bis Rue Boissy D'anglas 75008 Paris, France
TEL: 011-33-1-4312-4455
President .... Max Mosley
Secretary General .... Pierre de Coninck
Director of Public Relations .... Francesco Longanesi

NASCAR
(National Assn. for Stock Car Auto Racing)
P.O. Box 2875, Daytona Beach, FL 32120
(904) 253-0611
President .... William C. France
Director of Communications-Worldwide .... John Griffin

NHRA
(National Hot Rod Association)
2035 Financial Way, Glendora, CA 91741
(626) 914-4761
President .... Dallas Gardner
Executive V.P./General Manager .... Tom Compton
Director of Communications .... Denny Darnell

MAJOR LEAGUE BASEBALL

Office of the Commissioner
350 Park Ave., 17th Floor, New York, NY 10022
(212) 339-7800
Commissioner .... Bud Selig
President-COO .... Paul Beeston
General Counsel .... Thomas Ostertag
Executive Dir. of Public Relatons .... Richard Levin

Player Relations Committee
350 Park Ave., New York, NY 10022
(212) 339-7400
Chief Labor Negotiator .... Randy Levine
Associate Counsels .... John Westhoff & Louis Melendez

Major League Baseball Players Association
12 East 49th St., 24th Floor, New York, NY 10017
(212) 826-0808
Exec. Director & General Counsel .... Donald Fehr
Special Assistant .... Mark Belanger

AL

American League Office
350 Park Ave., 18th Floor, New York, NY 10022
(212) 339-7600
President .... Gene Budig
V.P., Admin. & Media Affairs .... Phyllis Merhige

Anaheim Angels
P. O. Box 2000, Anaheim, CA 92803
(714) 940-2000
Chairman .... Gene Autry
Minority Owner .... Walt Disney Co.
President & CEO .... Tony Tavares
V.P. & General Manager .... Bill Bavasi
Director of Communications .... Tim Mead

Baltimore Orioles
333 West Camden St., Baltimore, MD 21201
(410) 685-9800
CEO .... Peter Angelos
Vice Chairman, Business & Finance .... Joseph Foss
General Manager .... Pat Gillick
Director of Public Relations .... John Maroon

Boston Red Sox
Fenway Park, 4 Yawkey Way, Boston, MA 02215
(617) 267-9440
General Partner .... Jean R. Yawkey Trust
CEO .... John Harrington
Exec. V.P. & General Manager .... Dan Duquette
Director of Communications .... Kevin Shea

Chicago White Sox
Comiskey Park, 333 W. 35th St., Chicago, IL 60616
(312) 674-1000
Chairman .... Jerry Reinsdorf
Vice Chairman .... Eddie Einhorn
Senior V.P. & General Manager .... Ron Schueler
Director of Public Relations .... Scott Reifert

Cleveland Indians
Jacobs Field, 2401 Ontario St., Cleveland, OH 44115
(216) 420-4200
Owner-Chairman-CEO .... Richard Jacobs
Exec. V.P. & General Manager .... John Hart
V.P., Public Relations .... Bob DiBiasio

Detroit Tigers
Tiger Stadium, 2121 Trumbull Ave., Detroit, MI 48216
(313) 962-4000
Owner-Chairman .... Mike Ilitch
Owner-Secretary-Treasurer .... Marian Ilitch
President-CEO .... John McHale Jr.
General Manager-VP .... Randy Smith
Director of Public Relations .... Tyler Barnes

Kansas City Royals
P.O. Box 419969, Kansas City, MO 64141
(816) 921-8000
Owner .... Greater K.C. Community Foundation
Chairman-CEO .... David Glass
Exec. V.P. & General Manager .... Herk Robinson
Director of Media Relations .... Steve Fink

Minnesota Twins
Hubert H. Humphrey Metrodome
34 Kirby Puckett Place, Minneapolis, MN 55415
(612) 375-1366
Owner .... Carl Pohlad
President .... Jerry Bell
V.P. & General Manager .... Terry Ryan
Manager of Media Relations .... Sean Harlin

New York Yankees
Yankee Stadium, Bronx, NY 10451
(718) 293-4300
Principal Owner .... George Steinbrenner
General Partners .... Hal Steinbrenner & Joe Molloy
V.P. & General Manager .... Brian Cashman
Dir. of Media Relations/Publicity .... Rick Cerrone

Oakland Athletics
Oakland-Alameda County Coliseum
Oakland, CA 94621
(510) 638-4900
Co-Owners ....Steve Schott and Ken Hofmann
President ....Sandy Alderson
General Manager ....Billy Beane
Baseball Information Manager ....Mike Selleck

Seattle Mariners
P.O. Box 4100, Seattle, WA 98104
(206) 346-4000
Chairman-CEO ....John Ellis
President-COO ....Chuck Armstrong
V.P., Baseball Operations ....Woody Woodward
Director of Public Relations ....Dave Aust

Tampa Bay Devil Rays
Tropicana Field, One Tropicana Dr., St. Petersburg, FL 33705
(813) 825-3137
Managing General Partner/CEO ....Vincent J. Naimoli
Senior V.P. Baseball Ops./GM ....Chuck Lamar
VP Public Relations ....Rick Vaughn

Texas Rangers
1000 Ballpark Way, Arlington, TX 76011
(817) 273-5222
Owner ....Thomas Hicks
President ....Tom Schieffer
V.P., General Manager ....Doug Melvin
V.P., Public Relations ....John Blake

Toronto Blue Jays
SkyDome, One Blue Jays Way, Suite 3200
Toronto, Ontario M5V 1J1
(416) 341-1000
Chairman/CEO ....Sam Pollock
Exec. V.P. & General Manager ....Gord Ash
Vice President of Media ....Howie Starkman

NL

National League Office
350 Park Ave., New York, NY 10022
(212) 339-7700
President ....Leonard Coleman
Exec. Dir. of Public Relations ....Ricky Clemons

Arizona Diamondbacks
P.O. Box 2095, Phoenix, AZ 85001
(602) 462-6500
Chief Executive Officer ....Jerry Colangelo
President ....Rich H. Dozer
V.P. & General Manager ....Joe Garagiola Jr.
Media Relations Mgr. ....Bob Crawford

Atlanta Braves
P.O. Box 4064, Atlanta, GA 30302
(404) 522-7630
Owner ....Ted Turner
President ....Stan Kasten
Exec. V.P. & General Manager ....John Schuerholz
Director of Public Relations ....Jim Schultz

Chicago Cubs
1060 West Addison St., Chicago, IL 60613
(773) 404-2827
Owner ....The Tribune Company
President-CEO ....Andy MacPhail
General Manager ....Ed Lynch
Director of Media Relations ....Sharon Pannozzo

Cincinnati Reds
100 Cinergy Field, Cincinnati, OH 45202
(513) 421-4510
General Partner-President-CEO ....Marge Schott
General Manager ....Jim Bowden
Director of Media Relations ....Rob Butcher

Colorado Rockies
Coors Field, 2001 Blake St., Denver, CO 80205
(303) 292-0200
Chairman-President-CEO ....Jerry McMorris
Executive V.P. & General Manager ....Bob Gebhard
Senior V.P. of Business Ops. ....Keli McGregor
Director of Public Relations ....Jay Alves

Florida Marlins
2267 N.W. 199th St., Miami, FL 33056
(305) 626-7400
Owner ....Wayne Huizenga
Exec. V.P. & General Manager ....Dave Dombrowski
Director of Media Relations ....Ron Colangelo

Houston Astros
The Astrodome, P.O. Box 288, Houston, TX 77001
(713) 799-9500
Chairman-CEO ....Drayton McLane Jr.
President ....Tal Smith
General Manager ....Gerry Hunsicker
Director of Media Relations ....Rob Matwick

Los Angeles Dodgers
1000 Elysian Park Ave., Los Angeles, CA 90012
(213) 224-1500
Owner ....Fox Group
President ....Bob Graziano
General Manager ....Kevin Malone
Director of Publicity ....Derrick Hall

Milwaukee Brewers
County Stadium, P.O. Box 3099, Milwaukee, WI 53201
(414) 933-4114
President-CEO ....Wendy Selig-Prieb
Senior V.P., Baseball Operations ....Sal Bando
Director of Media Relations ....Jon Greenberg

Montreal Expos
P.O. Box 500, Station M, Montreal, Quebec H1V 3P2
(514) 253-3434
General Partner-President ....Claude Brochu
V.P./General Manager ....Jim Beattie
V.P., Baseball Operations ....Bill Stoneman
Director of Media Relations ....Peter Loyello

New York Mets
123-01 Roosevelt Ave., Flushing, NY 11368
(718) 507-6387
Chairman ....Nelson Doubleday
President-CEO ....Fred Wilpon
General Manager ....Steve Phillips
Director of Media Relations ....Jay Horwitz

Philadelphia Phillies
P.O. Box 7575, Philadelphia, PA 19101
(215) 463-6000
Managing Gen. Partner/Pres./CEO ...David Montgomery
General Partner/Chairman ....Bill Giles
General Manager ....Ed Wade
V.P. of Public Relations ....Larry Shenk

Pittsburgh Pirates
P.O. Box 7000, Pittsburgh, PA 15212
(412) 323-5000
Managing General Partner ....Kevin McClatchy
COO ....Richard Freeman
Senior V.P. & General Manager ....Cam Bonifay
Director of Media Relations ....Jim Trdinich

St. Louis Cardinals
250 Stadium Plaza, St. Louis, MO 63102
(314) 421-3060
Owner ....Frederick O. Hanser
President ....Mark Lamping
V.P. & General Manager ....Walt Jocketty
Director of Public Relations ....Brian Bartow

San Diego Padres
P.O. Box 122000, San Diego, CA 92112
(619) 881-6500
Chairman .... John Moores
President-CEO .... Larry Lucchino
V.P., Baseball Operations & G.M .... Kevin Towers
Director of Media Relations .... Glenn Geffner

San Francisco Giants
3Com Park at Candlestick Point, San Francisco, CA 94124
(415) 468-3700
Managing General Partner .... Peter Magowan
Executive V.P./COO .... Laurence Baer
Senior V.P. & General Manager .... Brian Sabean
V.P. of Communications .... Bob Rose

PRO BASKETBALL

NBA

League Office
Olympic Tower, 645 Fifth Ave., New York, NY 10022
(212) 407-8000
Commissioner .... David Stern
Senior V.P. of Basketball Ops. .... Rod Thorn
Deputy Commissioner .... Russell Granik
V.P., Public Relations .... Brian McIntyre
Director of Media Relations .... Chris Rienza

NBA Players Association
1700 Broadway, Suite 1400, New York, NY 10019
(212) 655-0880
Exec. Director .... William Hunter
General Counsel .... Robert Lanza
President .... Patrick Ewing

Atlanta Hawks
One CNN Center, South Tower, Suite 405
Atlanta, GA 30303
(404) 827-3800
Owner .... Ted Turner
President .... Stan Kasten
General Manager .... Pete Babcock
Director of Media Relations .... Arthur Triche

Boston Celtics
151 Merrimac St., 4th Floor, Boston, MA 02114
(617) 523-6050
Chairman .... Paul Gaston
President & Head Coach .... Rick Pitino
General Manager .... Chris Wallace
V.P. of Media Relations .... Jeff Twiss

Charlotte Hornets
100 Hive Drive, Charlotte, NC 28217
(704) 357-0252
Owner .... George Shinn
Executive V.P., Basketball Operations .... Bob Bass
V.P. of Public Relations .... Harold Kaufman

Chicago Bulls
United Center, 1901 West Madison St.
Chicago, IL 60612
(312) 455-4000
Chairman .... Jerry Reinsdorf
V.P., Basketball Operations .... Jerry Krause
Director of Media Services .... Tim Hallam

Cleveland Cavaliers
One Centre Court, Cleveland, OH 44115
(216) 420-2000
Owner-Chairman .... Gordon Gund
Owner-Vice Chairman .... George Gund III
President & COO .... Wayne Embry
Director of Media Relations .... Bob Zink

Dallas Mavericks
Reunion Arena, 777 Sports St., Dallas, TX 75207
(972) 988-0117
Owners .. Ross Perot Jr., David McDavid & Frank Zaccanelli
General Manager .... Don Nelson
VP Communications .... Kevin Sullivan

Denver Nuggets
1635 Clay St., Denver, CO 80204
(303) 893-6700
Owner .... Ascent Ent. Group
General Manager .... Dan Issel
Director of Media Services .... Tommy Sheppard

Detroit Pistons
The Palace of Auburn Hills
Two Championship Dr., Auburn Hills, MI 48326
(248) 377-0100
Managing Partner .... William Davidson
President .... Tom Wilson
V.P. of Player Personnel .... Rick Sund
V.P. of Public Relations .... Matt Dobek

Golden State Warriors
1011 Broadway, Oakland, CA 94607
(510) 986–2200
Owner-CEO .... Chris Cohan
General Manager .... Garry St. Jean
Director of Public Relations .... Raymond Ridder

Houston Rockets
2 Greenway Plaza, Suite 400, Houston, TX 77046
(713) 627-3865
Owner .... Leslie L. Alexander
COO .... Ken Harmon
Sr. Exec. V.P. of Basketball Affairs .... Robert Barr
Manager of Team Communications .... Tim Frank

Indiana Pacers
300 East Market St., Indianapolis, IN 46204
(317) 263-2100
Owners .... Melvin Simon & Herb Simon
President .... Donnie Walsh
General Manager .... David Kahn
Executive V.P./Head Coach .... Larry Bird
Director of Media Relations .... David Benner

Los Angeles Clippers
L.A. Sports Arena
3939 S. Figueroa St., Los Angeles, CA 90037
(213) 745-0400
Owner-Chairman .... Donald T. Sterling
Executive V.P. .... Andy Roeser
V.P., Basketball Operations .... Elgin Baylor
Director of Communications .... Jill Wiggins

Los Angeles Lakers
Great Western Forum
3900 W. Manchester Blvd., Inglewood, CA 90305
(310) 419-3100
Owner .... Jerry Buss
Exec. V.P., Basketball Operations .... Jerry West
General Manager .... Mitch Kupchak
Director of Public Relations .... John Black

Miami Heat
Suntrust International Bldg, 1 SE 3rd Ave., Suite 2300, Miami, FL 33131
(305) 577-4328
Managing General Partner .... Micky Arison
President & Head Coach .... Pat Riley
General Manager .... Randy Pfund
Director of Media Relations .... Tim Donovan

Milwaukee Bucks
Bradley Center, 1001 N. Fourth St., Milwaukee, WI 53203
(414) 227-0500
President .... Sen. Herb Kohl (D., Wisc.)
General Manager .... Bob Weinhauer
Director of Publicity .... Bill King II

Minnesota Timberwolves
Target Center
600 First Ave. North, Minneapolis, MN 55403
(612) 673-1600
Owner .... Glen Taylor
President .... Rob Moor
V.P., Basketball Operations .... Kevin McHale
Dir. of Public Relations/Communications .... Kent Wipf

New Jersey Nets
390 Murray Hill Pkwy., East Rutherford, NJ 07073
(201) 935-8888
Chairman/CEO .... Henry Taub
President/COO .... Michael Rowe
Exec. V.P. of Basketball Ops. .... John Calipari
Director of Public Relations .... John Mertz

New York Knickerbockers
Madison Square Garden
2 Penn Plaza, 14th Floor, New York, NY 10121
(212) 465-6000
Owner .... ITT Corp./Cablevision Systems Inc.
President (MSG) .... Dave Checketts
Pres. (Knicks) & General Manager .... Ernie Grunfeld
Director of Public Relations .... Chris Weiller

Orlando Magic
Orlando Arena
One Magic Place, Orlando, FL 32801
(407) 916-2400
Owner .... Rich DeVos
President .... Bob Vander Weide
V.P., Basketball Ops. & GM .... John Gabriel
Dir. of Publicity/Media Relations .... Alex Martins

Philadelphia 76ers
CoreStates Center
One CoreStates Complex, Philadelphia, PA 19148
(215) 339-7600
Owner-President .... Pat Croce
General Manager .... Billy King
Player Personnel Director .... Kevin O'Connor
Director of Public Relations .... Jody Silverman

Phoenix Suns
P.O. Box 1369, Phoenix, AZ 85001
(602) 379-7900
President-CEO .... Jerry Colangelo
V.P., Administration-G.M. .... Bryan Colangelo
V.P., Dir. of Player Personnel .... Dick Van Arsdale
Media Relations Director .... Julie Fie

Portland Trail Blazers
One Center Court, Suite 200
Portland, OR 97227
(503) 234-9291
Owner-Chairman .... Paul Allen
President & General Manager .... Bob Whitsitt
Assistant General Manager .... Jim Paxson
Director of Communications .... John Christensen

Sacramento Kings
One Sports Parkway, Sacramento, CA 95834
(916) 928-0000
Managing General Partner .... Jim Thomas
President .... Rick Benner
V.P., Basketball Operations .... Geoff Petrie
Director of Media Relations .... Troy Hanson

San Antonio Spurs
Alamodome
100 Montana St., San Antonio, TX 78203
(210) 554-7700
Chairman .... Peter Holt
GM & Head Coach .... Gregg Popovich
Director of Player Personnel .... Sam Schuler
Director of Media Services .... Tom James

Seattle SuperSonics
190 Queen Anne Ave. N., Suite 200, Seattle, WA 98109
(206) 281-5800
Owner-Chairman .... Barry Ackerley
President & General Manager .... Wally Walker
V.P. of Basketball Ops. .... Billy McKinney
Director of Media Relations .... Cheri Hanson

Toronto Raptors
20 Bay St., Suite 1702, Toronto, Ontario M5J 2N8
(416) 214-2255
President .... Richard Peddie
V.P./General Manager .... Glen Grunwald
V.P of Comms./Community Dev. .... John Lashway

Utah Jazz
Delta Center, 301 West South Temple
Salt Lake City, UT 84101
(801) 325-2500
Owner .... Larry Miller
General Manager .... Tim Howells
President .... Frank Layden
Director of Media Relations .... Kim Turner

Vancouver Grizzlies
General Motors Place, 800 Griffiths Way
Vancouver, B.C. V6B 6G1
(604) 899-4666
Owner .... Orca Bay Sports & Ent.
Chairman .... John E. McCaw Jr.
CEO .... Stephen T. Bellringer
President & GM .... Stu Jackson
Director of Media Relations .... Steve Frost

Washington Wizards
MCI Center, 601 F Street NW, Washington, D.C., 20004
(202) 661-5000
Chairman .... Abe Pollin
President .... Susan O'Malley
Executive V.P. & GM .... Wes Unseld
Director of Public Relations .... Maureen Lewis

Other Men's Pro Leagues

Continental Basketball Association
400 North 5th St., Suite 1425, Phoenix, AZ 85004
(602) 254-6677
Interim Commissioner .... Gary Hunter
Dir. of Media Relations .... Troy Furr

Member teams (9): Connecticut Pride, Ft. Wayne (IN) Fury, Grand Rapids Hoops, Idaho Stampede, LaCrosse Bobcats, Quad City (IL) Thunder, Rockford (IL) Lightning, Sioux Falls (SD) Skyforce, and Yakima (WA) Sun Kings.

United States Basketball League
46 Quirk Road, Milford, CT 06460
(203) 877-9508
Commissioner .... Daniel T. Meisenheimer III
Dir. of Public Relations .... Sean Fisher

Member teams (12): Atlanta Trojans, Atlantic City Seagulls, Camden (NJ) Power, Columbus Cagerz, Connecticut Skyhawks, Jacksonville Barracudas, Long Island Surf, New Jersey Shorecats, New Hampshire Thunder Loons, Raleigh Cougars, Tampa Bay Windjammers, Washington D.C. Congressionals.

Women's Pro Leagues

American Basketball League
1900 Embarcadero Road, Suite 110
Palo Alto, CA 94303
(650) 856-3225
Co-Founders .... Steve Hams, Anne Cribbs & Gary Cavalli
Chief Operating Officer .... Jim Weyermann
V.P. of Basketball Operations .... Tracey Williams
Director of Media Relations .... Dean Jutilla

Chicago Condors
322 South Green St., Ste. 208
Chicago, IL 60661
(312) 409-4143
General Manager ....Allison Hodges
Head Coach ....Jim Cleamons
Director of Media Relations ....Mark Himmelstein

Colorado Xplosion
800 Grant St., Suite 410
Denver, CO 80203
(303) 832-2225
General Manager ....Lark Birdsong
Head Coach ....Linda Hargrove
Director of Media Relations ....Tim Simmons

Columbus Quest
Columbus Conv. Center, 400 N. High St.
Columbus, OH 43215
(614) 464-2378
General Manager ....Bill McGillis
Head Coach ....Brian Agler

Nashville Noise
231 Third Avenue North
Nashville, TN 37201
(615) 843-8430
General Manager ....Mike Kopp
Head Coach ....Candi Harvey
Director of Media Relations ....Chris Jewell

New England Blizzard
179 Allyn St., Suite 403
Hartford, CT 06103
(860) 522-4667
Interim GM ....Christopher Sienko
Head Coach ................................K.C. Jones
Director of Media Relations ....Steve Raczynski

Philadelphia Rage
123 Chestnut St., 4th Floor
Philadelphia, PA 19106
(215) 629-1976
General Manager ....Jonathan Matthews
Head Coach ....Anne Donovan
Director of Media Relations ....Kirk Sampson

Portland Power
439 North Broadway
Portland, OR 97227
(503) 249-1130
General Manager ....Linda Weston
Head Coach ....Lin Dunn
Director of Media Relations ....Nelson Holmberg

San Jose Lasers
1530 Parkmoor Ave., Suite A
San Jose, CA 95128
(408) 271-1500
General Manager ....Christine Forter
Head Coach/Asst. GM ....Angela Beck
Director of Media Relations ....Shana Daum

Seattle Reign
400 Mercer St., Suite 408
Seattle, WA 98109
(206) 285-5225
General Manager ....Karen Bryant
Head Coach ....Tammy Holder
Director of Media Relations ....Cindy Fester

❧ ❧ ❧

Women's National Basketball Association
645 5th Ave., New York, NY 10022
(212) 688-9622
President ....Val Ackerman
Director of Communications ....Alice McGillian
Director of Media Relations ....Mark Pray

Charlotte Sting
3308 Oaklace Blvd., Ste. B
Charlotte, NC 28208
(704) 357-0252
Executive V.P. ....Sam Russo
GM/Head Coach ....Marynell Meadors
Director of Media Relations ....Cheryl Harden

Cleveland Rockers
Gund Arena, One Center Court
Cleveland, OH 44115
(216) 420-2000
President/COO ....Wayne Embry
Head Coach ....Linda Hill-MacDonald
Director of Media Relations ....Lori Montgomery

Detroit Shock
The Palace at Auburn Hills, Two Championship Dr.
Auburn Hills, MI 48326
(248) 377-0100
GM/Head Coach ....Nancy Lieberman-Cline
Asst. GM/Dir. of PR ....Patrick E. Auerbach

Houston Comets
Two Greenway Plaza, Suite 400
Houston, TX 77046-3865
(713) 627-9622
Owner/President ....Leslie L. Alexander
GM/Head Coach ....Van Chancellor
Director of Media Relations ....Tom Savage

Los Angeles Sparks
Great Western Forum, 3900 W. Manchester Blvd.
Inglewood, CA 90306
(310) 330-2434
General Manager ....Rhonda Windham
Head Coach ....Orlando Woolridge
Director of Media Relations ....Stacey Stewart

New York Liberty
Two Penn Plaza
New York, NY 10121
(212) 564-9622
General Manager ....Carol Blazejowski
Head Coach ....Nancy Darsch
Director of Public Relations ....Maureen Coyle

Phoenix Mercury
America West Arena, 201 E. Jefferson St.
Phoenix, AZ 85004
(602) 514-8333
Chairman/CEO ....Jerry Colangelo
GM/Head Coach ....Cheryl Miller
Director of Communications ....Nedia Kia

Sacramento Monarchs
ARCO Arena, One Sports Pkwy.
Sacramento, CA 95834
(916) 928-0000
General Manager ....Jerry Reynolds
Head Coach ....Heidi VanDerveer
Director of Communications ....Andrea Lepore

Utah Starzz
Delta Center, 301 West South Temple
Salt Lake City, UT 84101
(801) 355-7827
General Manager ....Tim R. Howells
Head Coach ....Frank Layden
Director of Public/Comm. Relations ....Scott Miller

Washington Mystics
MCI Center, 601 F St. NW
Washington D.C. 20004
(202) 661-5000
Executive V.P./GM ....Wes Unseld
Interim Head Coach ....Cathy Parson
Director of Public Relations ....Julie Demeo

BOWLING

ABC
(American Bowling Congress)
5301 South 76th St., Greendale, WI 53129
(414) 421-6400
Executive Director .... Roger Dalken
Director of PR/Marketing .... Bryan LeMonds

BPAA
(Bowling Proprietors' Assn. of America)
P.O. Box 5802, Arlington, TX 76005
(817) 649-5105
CEO .... Don A. Harris
President .... Charlie Brehob
Director of Public Relations .... Cary Richmond

PWBA
(Professional Women's Bowling Association)
7171 Cherryvale Blvd., Rockford, IL 61112
(815) 332-5756
President .... John Falzone
Media Director .... Dan Leary

PBA
(Professional Bowlers Association)
1720 Merriman Road, P.O. Box 5118, Akron, OH 44334
(330) 836-5568
Commissioner .... Mark Gerberich
Public Relations Director .... Dave Schroeder

WIBC
(Women's International Bowling Congress, Inc.)
5301 South 76th St., Greendale, WI 53129
(414) 421-9000
President .... Joyce Deitch
Public Relations Manager .... Bryan LeMonds

BOXING

IBF
(International Boxing Federation)
134 Evergreen Place, 9th Floor,
East Orange, NJ 07018
(973) 414-0300
President .... Robert W. Lee
Executive Secretary .... Marian Muhammad
Champs. & Ratings Chairman .... Doug Beavers
P.O. Box 7577, Portsmouth, VA 23707
(757) 399-6608

WBA
(World Boxing Association)
P.O. Box 377, Maracay 2110–A
Venezuela
TEL: 011-58-44-63-1584
President .... Gilberto Mendoza
General Counsel/U.S. Spokesman .... Jimmy Binns
1735 Market St., 39th Floor, Phila., PA 19103
(215) 557-8000
Ratings Chairman .... Bolivar Icaza
P.O. Box 1833, Panama 1, Rep. de Panama
TEL: 011-507-63-5167

WBC
(World Boxing Council)
Genova 33-503, Col. Juarez,
MEXICO, 06600, D.F., Mexico
TEL: 011-525-533-3787
President .... Jose Sulaiman
Ratings Chairman .... Frank Quill
Press Information/U.S. Spokesman .... John Brister
411 Ballentine St., Bay St. Louis, MS 39520
(601) 467-3304

WBO
(World Boxing Organization)
1st Federal Bldg., 1056 Ave Munoz Revera, Suite 714, San Juan, P.R. 00927
(787) 765-4444
President .... Francisco Paco Valcarcel
Past Pres./Attorney .... Louis Batista Salas
Ratings Chairman .... Louis Perez
Public Relations Dir. .... Mario Rivera-Martino

Don King Productions, Inc.
501 Fairway Dr., Deerfield Beach, FL 33441
(954) 418-5800
President .... Don King
Dir. of Boxing Ops. .... Bob Goodman
Director of Public Relations .... Greg Fritz

Top Rank
3980 Howard Hughes Pkwy. Ste. 580, Las Vegas, NV 89109
(702) 732-2717
Chairman .... Bob Arum
Director of Marketing .... Michael Malitz

COLLEGE SPORTS

CCA
(Collegiate Commissioners Association)
800 South Broadway, Suite 400, Walnut Creek, CA 94596
(925) 932-4411
President .... Michael Tranghese (Big East)
Exec. V.P. .... Linda Bruno (Atlantic-10)
Secretary-Treasurer .... David Price (Pac-10)

NAIA
(National Assn. of Intercollegiate Athletics)
6120 South Yale, Suite 1450, Tulsa, OK 74136
(918) 494-8828
President-CEO .... Steve Baker
Public Relations Director .... Kevin Henry

NCAA
(National Collegiate Athletic Association)
6201 College Blvd., Overland Park, KS 66211
(913) 339-1906
Chief Operating Officer .... Daniel Boggan Jr.
President .... Cedric Dempsey
Group Exec. Dir. for Enforcement .... David Berst
Director of Public Relations .... Wallace I. Renfro

WSF
(Women's Sports Foundation)
Eisenhower Park, East Meadow, NY 11554
(516) 542-4700
Executive Director .... Donna Lopiano
President .... Benita Fitzgerald-Mosley
Public Relations Director .... Paula Hunt

Major NCAA Conferences

See pages 445-453 for basketball coaches, football coaches, nicknames and colors of all Division I basketball schools and Division I-A and I-AA football schools.

ATLANTIC COAST CONFERENCE
P.O. Drawer ACC
Greensboro, NC 27417-6724
(336) 854-8787 Founded: 1953
Commissioner .... John Swofford
Asst. Commis. of Media Relations .... Brian Morrison

1998-99 members: BASKETBALL & FOOTBALL (9)—Clemson, Duke, Florida St., Georgia Tech, Maryland, North Carolina, North Carolina St., Virginia and Wake Forest.

Clemson University
Clemson, SC 29633 Founded: 1889
SID: (864) 656-2114 Enrollment: 16,403
President .... Deno Curris
Athletic Director .... Bobby Robinson
Sports Information Director .... Tim Baurret

Duke University
Durham, NC 27708 Founded: 1838
SID: (919) 684-2633 Enrollment: 6,272
President .... Nannerl Keohane
Athletic Director .... Joe Alleva
Sports Information Director .... Mike Cragg

Florida State University
Tallahassee, FL 32316 Founded: 1857
SID: (850) 644-1403 Enrollment: 30,519
President .... Talbot (Sandy) D'Alemberte
Athletic Director .... Dave Hart Jr.
Sports Information Director .... Rob Wilson

Georgia Tech
Atlanta, GA 30332 Founded: 1885
SID: (404) 894-5445 Enrollment: 13,000
President .... Wayne Clough
Athletic Director .... Dave Braine
Sports Information Director .... Mike Finn

University of Maryland
College Park, MD 20741 Founded: 1807
SID: (301) 314-7064 Enrollment: 33,600
President .... Dr. Clayton D. Mote Jr.
Athletic Director .... Deborah Yow
Sports Information Director .... Dave Haglund

University of North Carolina
Chapel Hill, NC 27514 Founded: 1789
SID: (919) 962-2123 Enrollment: 24,439
Chancellor .... Michael K. Hooker
Athletic Director .... Dick Baddour
Sports Information Director .... Steve Kirschner

North Carolina State University
Raleigh, NC 27695 Founded: 1887
SID: (919) 515-2102 Enrollment: 28,281
Chancellor .... Mary Anne E. Fox
Athletic Director .... Les Robinson
Sports Information Director .... TBA

University of Virginia
Charlottesville, VA 22903 Founded: 1819
SID: (804) 982-5500 Enrollment: 18,417
President .... John T. Casteen III
Athletic Director .... Terry Holland
Sports Information Director .... Rich Murray

Wake Forest University
Winston-Salem, NC 27109 Founded: 1834
SID: (336) 758-5640 Enrollment: 3,841
President .... Thomas K. Hearn Jr.
Athletic Director .... Ron Wellman
Sports Information Director .... John Justus

❧ ❧ ❧

BIG EAST CONFERENCE
56 Exchange Terrace
Providence, RI 02903
(401) 272-9108 Founded: 1979
Commissioner .... Mike Tranghese
Assoc. Commissioner/P.R .... John Paquette

1998-99 members: BASKETBALL (13)— Boston College, Connecticut, Georgetown, Miami-FL, Notre Dame, Pittsburgh, Providence, Rutgers, St. John's, Seton Hall, Syracuse, Villanova and West Virginia; FOOTBALL (8)— Boston College, Miami-FL, Pittsburgh, Rutgers, Syracuse, Temple, Virginia Tech and West Virginia.

Boston College
Chestnut Hill, MA 02167 Founded: 1863
SID: (617) 552-3004 Enrollment: 8,958
President .... Rev. William P. Leahy, S.J.
Athletic Director .... Gene DeFillippo
Sports Information Director .... Chris Cameron

University of Connecticut
Storrs, CT 06269 Founded: 1881
SID: (860) 486-3531 Enrollment: 22,316
President .... Harry J. Hartley
Athletic Director .... Lew Perkins
Sports Information Director .... Tim Tolokan

Georgetown University
Washington, DC 20057 Founded: 1789
SID: (202) 687-2492 Enrollment: 6,394
President .... Rev. Leo J. O'Donovan, S.J.
Athletic Director .... Joseph C. Lang
Sports Information Director .... Bill Shapland

University of Miami
Coral Gables, FL 33124 Founded: 1926
SID: (305) 284-3244 Enrollment: 13,842
President .... Edward T. Foote II
Athletic Director .... Paul Dee
Sports Information Director .... Bob Burda

University of Notre Dame
Notre Dame, IN 46556 Founded: 1842
SID: (219) 631-7516 Enrollment: 10,359
President .... Rev. Edward (Monk) Malloy
Athletic Director .... Michael Wadsworth
Sports Information Director .... John Heisler

University of Pittsburgh
Pittsburgh, PA 15213 Founded: 1787
SID: (412) 648-8240 Enrollment: 32,187
Chancellor .... Mark A. Nordenberg
Athletic Director .... Steve Pederson
Sports Information Director .... E.J. Borghetti

Providence College
Providence, RI 02918 Founded: 1917
SID: (401) 865-2272 Enrollment: 3,596
President .... Philip A. Smith, OP
Athletic Director .... John Marinatto
Sports Information Director .... Tim Connor

Rutgers University
New Brunswick, NJ 08903 Founded: 1766
SID: (732) 445-4200 Enrollment: 33,500
President .... Francis L. Lawrence
Athletic Director .... Robert E. Mulcahy III
Sports Information Director .... TBA

St. John's University
Jamaica, NY 11439 Founded: 1870
SID: (718) 990-6367 Enrollment: 17,250
President .... Rev. Donald J. Harrington, CM
Athletic Director .... Edward J. Manetta Jr.
Sports Information Director .... Dominic Scianna

Seton Hall University
South Orange, NJ 07079 Founded: 1856
SID: (201) 761-9493 Enrollment: 10,538
Chancellor .... Rev. Thomas R. Peterson, OP
Athletic Director .... Jeff Fogelson
Sports Information Director .... John Wooding

Syracuse University
Syracuse, NY 13244 Founded: 1870
SID: (315) 443-2608 Enrollment: 10,200
Chancellor .... Kenneth Shaw
Athletic Director .... Jake Crouthamel
Sports Information Director .... Sue Edson

Temple University
Philadelphia, PA 19122 Founded: 1884
SID: (215) 204-7445 Enrollment: 31,000
President ....Peter J. Liacouras
Athletic Director ....David O'Brien
Sports Information Director ....Brian Kirschner

Villanova University
Villanova, PA 19085 Founded: 1842
SID: (610) 519-4120 Enrollment: 5,995
President ....Rev. Edmund J. Dobbin, OSA
Athletic Director ....Tim Hofferth
Sports Information Director ....Karen Frascona

Virginia Tech
Blacksburg, VA 24061 Founded: 1872
SID: (540) 231-6796 Enrollment: 23,674
President ....Paul Torgersen
Athletic Director ....Jim Weaver
Sports Information Director ....Dave Smith

West Virginia University
Morgantown, WV 26507 Founded: 1867
SID: (304) 293-2821 Enrollment: 23,000
President ....David Hardesty
Athletic Director ....Ed Pastilong
Sports Information Director ....Shelly Poe

❧ ❧ ❧

BIG 12 CONFERENCE
2201 Stemmons Fwy., 28th Floor, Dallas, TX 75207
(214) 742-1212 Founded: 1996
Interim Commissioner ....Dave Martin
Media Relations Director ....Bo Carter

1998-99 members: BASKETBALL & FOOTBALL (12)—Baylor, Colorado, Iowa St., Kansas, Kansas St., Missouri, Nebraska, Oklahoma, Oklahoma St., Texas, Texas A&M and Texas Tech.

Baylor University
Waco, TX 76711 Founded: 1845
SID: (254) 710-2743 Enrollment: 12,000
President ....Robert B. Sloan
Athletic Director ....Tom Stanton
Sports Information Director ....Brian McCallum

University of Colorado
Boulder, CO 80309 Founded: 1876
SID: (303) 492-5626 Enrollment: 24,622
President ....Dr. John Buechner
Athletic Director ....Dick Tharp
Sports Information Director ....Dave Plati

Iowa State University
Ames, IA 50011 Founded: 1858
SID: (515) 294-3372 Enrollment: 25,000
President ....Martin Jischke
Athletic Director ....Eugene Smith
Sports Information Director ....Tom Kroeschell

University of Kansas
Lawrence, KS 66045 Founded: 1866
SID: (785) 864-3417 Enrollment: 25,200
Chancellor ....Robert Hemenway
Athletic Director ....Bob Frederick
Sports Information Director ....Dean Buchan

Kansas State University
Manhattan, KS 66502 Founded: 1863
SID: (785) 532-6735 Enrollment: 20,400
President ....Jon Wefald
Athletic Director ....Max Urick
Sports Information Director ....Kent Brown

University of Missouri
Columbia, MO 65205 Founded: 1839
SID: (573) 882-3241 Enrollment: 22,500
Chancellor ....Richard Wallace
Athletic Director ....Michael Alden
Sports Information Director ....Bob Brendel

University of Nebraska
Lincoln, NE 68588 Founded: 1869
SID: (402) 472-2263 Enrollment: 25,000
Chancellor ....Dr. James Moeser
Athletic Director ....Bill Byrne
Sports Information Director ....Chris Anderson

University of Oklahoma
Norman, OK 73019 Founded: 1890
SID: (405) 325-8231 Enrollment: 25,000
President ....David Boren
Athletic Director ....Joe Castiglione
Sports Information Director ....Mike Prusinski

Oklahoma State University
Stillwater, OK 74078 Founded: 1890
SID: (405) 744-5749 Enrollment: 18,500
President ....James Halligan
Athletic Director ....Terry Don Phillips
Sports Information Director ....Steve Buzzard

University of Texas
Austin, TX 78713 Founded: 1883
SID: (512) 471-7437 Enrollment: 47,719
President ....Dr. Larry Faulkner
Athletic Director ....De Loss Dodds
Sports Information Director ....Dave Saba

Texas A&M University
College Station, TX 77843 Founded: 1876
SID: (409) 845-5725 Enrollment: 43,031
President ....Ray Bowen
Athletic Director ....Wally Groff
Sports Information Director ....Alan Cannon

Texas Tech University
Lubbock, TX 79409 Founded: 1923
SID: (806) 742-2770 Enrollment: 25,000
Chancellor ....John Montford
Athletic Director ....Gerald Myers
Sports Information Director ....Richard Kilwien

❧ ❧ ❧

BIG TEN CONFERENCE
1500 West Higgins Road
Park Ridge, IL 60068-6300
(847) 696-1010 Founded: 1895
Commissioner ....Jim Delany
Dir. of Information Services ....Sue Ryan

1998-99 members: BASKETBALL & FOOTBALL (11)—Illinois, Indiana, Iowa, Michigan, Michigan St., Minnesota, Northwestern, Ohio St., Penn St., Purdue and Wisconsin.

University of Illinois
Champaign, IL 61820 Founded: 1867
SID: (217) 333-1390 Enrollment: 36,000
President ....James J. Stukel
Athletic Director ....Ron Guenther
Dir. of Communications ....Dave Johnson

Indiana University
Bloomington, IN 47405 Founded: 1820
SID: (812) 855-9399 Enrollment: 35,551
President ....Myles Brand
Athletic Director ....Clarence Doninger
Sports Information Director ....Kit Klingelhoffer

University of Iowa
Iowa City, IA 52242 Founded: 1847
SID: (319) 335-9411 Enrollment: 27,871
President ....Mary Sue Coleman
Athletic Director ....Bob Bowlsby
Sports Information Director ....Phil Haddy

University of Michigan
Ann Arbor, MI 48109 Founded: 1817
SID: (313) 763-1381 Enrollment: 36,450
President ....Lee Bollinger
Athletic Director ....Tom Goss
Sports Information Director ....Bruce Madej

Michigan State University
East Lansing, MI 48824 Founded: 1855
SID: (517) 355-2271 Enrollment: 42,603
President ....Peter McPherson
Athletic Director ....Merritt J. Norvell Jr.
Sports Information Director ....John Lewandowski

University of Minnesota
Minneapolis, MN 55455 Founded: 1851
SID: (612) 625-4090 Enrollment: 38,000
President ....Mark Yudof
Athletic Director ....Dr. Mark Dienhart
Sports Information Director ....Marc Ryan

Northwestern University
Evanston, IL 60208 Founded: 1851
SID: (847) 491-7503 Enrollment: 7,400
President ....Henry S. Bienen
Athletic Director ....Rick Taylor
Sports Information Director ....Brad Hurlbut

Ohio State University
Columbus, OH 43210 Founded: 1870
SID: (614) 292-6861 Enrollment: 48,300
President ....William E. Kirwan
Athletic Director ....Andy Geiger
Sports Information Director ....Gerry Erring

Penn State University
University Park, PA 16802 Founded: 1855
SID: (814) 865-1757 Enrollment: 38,200
President ....Graham Spanier
Athletic Director ....Tim Curley
Sports Information Director ....Jeff Nelson

Purdue University
West Lafayette, IN 47907 Founded: 1869
SID: (765) 494-3202 Enrollment: 35,156
President ....Steven C. Beering
Athletic Director ....Morgan Burke
Sports Information Director ....Mark Adams

University of Wisconsin
Madison, WI 53711 Founded: 1848
SID: (608) 262-1811 Enrollment: 39,826
Chancellor ....David Ward
Athletic Director ....Pat Richter
Sports Information Director ....Steve Malchow

❧ ❧ ❧

BIG WEST CONFERENCE
Two Corporate Park, Suite 206
Irvine, CA 92606
(949) 261-2525 Founded: 1969
Commissioner ....Dennis Farrell
Director of Information ....TBA

1998-99 members: BASKETBALL (12)— Boise St., CS-Fullerton, Cal Poly-SLO, Idaho, Long Beach St., Nevada, New Mexico St., North Texas, Pacific, UC-Irvine, UC-Santa Barbara, Utah St.; FOOTBALL (6)— Boise St., Idaho, Nevada, New Mexico St., North Texas, Utah St.

Boise State
Boise, ID 83725 Founded: 1932
SID: (208) 385-1515 Enrollment: 15,422
President ....Charles P. Ruch
Athletic Director ....Gene Bleymaier
Sports Information Director ....Max Corbet

Cal State-Fullerton
Fullerton, CA 92834 Founded: 1957
SID: (714) 278-3970 Enrollment: 24,000
President ....Milton A. Gordon
Athletic Director ....John Easterbrook
Sports Information Director ....Mel Franks

Cal Poly SLO
San Luis Obispo, CA 93407 Founded: 1901
SID: (805) 756-6531 Enrollment: 17,000
President ....Dr. Warren J. Baker
Athletic Director ....John McCutcheon
Sports Information Director ....Jason Sullivan

University of Idaho
Moscow, ID 83844 Founded: 1889
SID: (208) 885-0211 Enrollment: 11,027
President ....Bob Hoover
Athletic Director ....Mike Bohn
Sports Information Director ....Becky Pavll

Long Beach State
Long Beach, CA 90840 Founded: 1949
SID: (562) 985-8569 Enrollment: 27,431
President ....Robert Maxson
Athletic Director ....Bill Shumard
Sports Information Director ....Steve Janisch

University of Nevada
Reno, NV 89557 Founded: 1874
SID: (702) 784-4600 Enrollment: 12,500
President ....Joe Crowley
Athletic Director ....Chris Ault
Sports Information Director ....Paul Stuart

New Mexico State University
Las Cruces, NM 88003 Founded: 1888
SID: (505) 646-3929 Enrollment: 15,008
President ....Dr. William Conroy
Athletic Director ....Jim Paul
Sports Information Director ....Steve Shutt

University of North Texas
Denton, TX 76203 Founded: 1890
SID: (940) 565-2476 Enrollment: 26,400
Chancellor ....Dr. Alfred F. Hurley
Athletic Director ....Craig Helwig
Sports Information Director ....Sean Johnson

University of the Pacific
Stockton, CA 95211 Founded: 1851
SID: (209) 946-2479 Enrollment: 6,000
President ....Donald DeRosa
Athletic Director ....Michael McNeely
Sports Information Director ....Mike Millerick

University of California, Irvine
Irvine, CA 92697 Founded: 1962
SID: (949) 824-5814 Enrollment: 17,395
Chancellor ....Ralph Cicerone
Athletic Director ....Dan Guerrero
Sports Information Director ....Bob Olson

University of California, Santa Barbara
Santa Barbara, CA 93106 Founded: 1944
SID: (805) 893-3428 Enrollment: 18,200
Chancellor ....Henry Yang
Athletic Director ....Gary Cunningham
Sports Information Director ....Bill Mahoney

Utah State University
Logan, UT 84322 Founded: 1888
SID: (435) 797-1361 Enrollment: 20,808
President ....George Emert
Interim Athletic Director ....Ken Peterson
Sports Information Director ....Mike Strauss

❧ ❧ ❧

CONFERENCE USA
35 East Wacker Drive, Suite 650, Chicago, IL 60601
(312) 553-0483 Founded: 1995
Commissioner ....Mike Slive
Asst. Commissioner ....Brian Teter

1998-99 members: BASKETBALL (12)— UAB, Cincinnati, DePaul, Houston, Louisville, Marquette, Memphis, UNC-Charlotte, Saint Louis, South Florida, Southern Miss and Tulane; FOOTBALL (8)— Army, Cincinnati, East Carolina, Houston, Louisville, Memphis, Southern Miss and Tulane.

University of Alabama at Birmingham
Birmingham, AL 35294 Founded: 1969
SID: (205) 934-0722 Enrollment: 15,850
President ....Dr. W. Ann Reynolds
Athletic Director ....Gene Bartow
Sports Information Director ....Grant Shingleton

Army— U.S. Military Academy
West Point, NY 10996 Founded: 1802
SID: (914) 938-3303 Enrollment: 4,000
Superintendent ....Lt. Gen. Daniel W. Christman
Athletic Director ....Al Vanderbush
Sports Information Director ....Bob Beretta

University of Cincinnati
Cincinnati, OH 45221 Founded: 1819
SID: (513) 556-5191 Enrollment: 35,000
President ....Dr. Joseph A. Steger
Athletic Director ....Bob Goin
Sports Information Director ....Tom Hathaway

DePaul University
Chicago, IL 60614 Founded: 1898
SID: (773) 325-7525 Enrollment: 17,133
President ....Rev. John P. Minogue
Athletic Director ....Bill Bradshaw
Sports Information Director ....John Lanctot

East Carolina University
Greenville, NC 27858 Founded: 1907
SID: (919) 328-4522 Enrollment: 17,851
Chancellor ....Richard Eakin
Athletic Director ....Mike Hamrick
Sports Information Director ....Norm Reilly

University of Houston
Houston, TX 77204 Founded: 1927
SID: (713) 743-9404 Enrollment: 30,757
President ....Arthur Smith
Athletic Director ....Chet Gladchuk
Sports Information Director ....Donna Turner

University of Louisville
Louisville, KY 40292 Founded: 1798
SID: (502) 852-6581 Enrollment: 22,000
President ....Dr. John W. Shumaker
Athletic Director ....Tom Jurich
Sports Information Director ....Kenny Klein

Marquette University
Milwaukee, WI 53233 Founded: 1881
SID: (414) 288-7447 Enrollment: 10,600
President ....Rev. Robert A. Wild S.J.
Athletic Director ....Bill Cords
Sports Information Director ....Kathleen Hohl

University of Memphis
Memphis, TN 38152 Founded: 1912
SID: (901) 678-2337 Enrollment: 19,851
President ....V. Lane Rawlins
Athletic Director ....R.C. Johnson
Sports Information Director ....Bob Winn

University of North Carolina at Charlotte
Charlotte, NC 28223 Founded: 1946
SID: (704) 547-4937 Enrollment: 15,895
Chancellor ....J. H. Woodward
Athletic Director ....Judy Rose
Sports Information Director ....Tom Whitestone

Saint Louis University
St. Louis, MO 63103 Founded: 1818
SID: (314) 977-2524 Enrollment: 11,000
President ....Rev. Lawrence Biondi
Athletic Director ....Doug Woolard
Sport Information Director ....Doug McIlhagga

University of South Florida
Tampa, FL 33620 Founded: 1956
SID: (813) 974-4086 Enrollment: 37,000
President ....Betty Castor
Atheltic Director ....Paul Griffin
Sports Information Director ....John Gerdes

University of Southern Mississippi
Hattiesburg, MS 39406 Founded: 1910
SID: (601) 266-4503 Enrollment: 14,000
President ....Dr. Horace W. Fleming Jr.
Athletic Director ....Bill McLellan
Sports Information Director ....Regiel Napier

Tulane University
New Orleans, LA 70118 Founded: 1834
SID: (504) 865-5506 Enrollment: 11,000
President ....Dr. Scott S. Cowen
Athletic Director ....Sandy Barbour
Sports Information Director ....Scott Stricklin

❧ ❧ ❧

MID-AMERICAN CONFERENCE
Four SeaGate, Suite 102, Toledo, OH 43609
(419) 249-7177 Founded: 1946
Commissioner ....Jerry Ippoliti
Asst. Director of Communications ....Shawn Robinson

1998-99 members: BASKETBALL (13)— Akron, Ball St., Bowling Green, Buffalo, Central Michigan, Eastern Michigan, Kent, Marshall, Miami-OH, Northern Illinois, Ohio University, Toledo and Western Michigan; FOOTBALL (12)— all but Buffalo.

New in 1999: FOOTBALL (1)— Buffalo.

University of Akron
Akron, OH 44325 Founded: 1870
SID: (330) 972-7468 Enrollment: 24,252
President ....Marion Ruebel
Athletic Director ....TBA
Sports Information Director ....Jeff Brewer

Ball State University
Muncie, IN 47306 Founded: 1918
SID: (317) 285-8242 Enrollment: 19,115
President ....John Worthen
Athletic Director ....Andrea Seger
Sports Information Director ....Joe Hernandez

Bowling Green State University
Bowling Green, OH 43403 Founded: 1910
SID: (419) 372-7075 Enrollment: 16,900
President ....Sidney Ribeau
Athletic Director ....Ron Zwierlein
Sports Information Director ....Steve Barr

University of Buffalo
Buffalo, NY 14260 Founded: 1846
SID: (716) 645-6311 Enrollment: 23,000
President ....William P. Greiner
Athletic Director ....Nelson Townsend
Sports Information Director ....Paul Vecchio

Central Michigan University
Mt. Pleasant, MI 48859 Founded: 1892
SID: (517) 774-3277 Enrollment: 16,957
President ....Leonard Plachta
Athletic Director ....Herb Deromedi
Sports Information Director ....Fred Stabley Jr.

Eastern Michigan University
Ypsilanti, MI 48197 Founded: 1849
SID: (313) 487-0317 Enrollment: 24,000
President ....William Shelton
Interim Athletic Director ....Carole Houston
Sports Information Director ....Jim Streeter

Kent State University
Kent, OH 44242 Founded: 1910
SID: (330) 672-2110 Enrollment: 29,862
President ....Carol Cartwright
Athletic Director ....Laing Kennedy
Sports Information Director ....Dale Gallagher

Marshall University
Huntington, WV 25715 Founded: 1837
SID: (304) 696-4660 Enrollment: 17,000
President ....J. Wade Gilley
Athletic Director ....Lance West
Sports Information Director ....Clark Haptonstall

Miami University
Oxford, OH 45056 Founded: 1809
SID: (513) 529-4327 Enrollment: 15,000
President ....James C. Garland
Athletic Director ....Joel Maturi
Sports Information Director ....Mike Wolf

Northern Illinois University
DeKalb, IL 60115 Founded: 1895
SID: (815) 753-1706 Enrollment: 22,092
President ....John LaTourette
Athletic Director ....Cary Groth
Sports Information Director ....Michael Korcek

Ohio University
Athens, OH 45701 Founded: 1804
SID: (614) 593-1298 Enrollment: 27,605
President ....Robert Glidden
Athletic Director ....Tom Boeh
Sports Information Director ....George Mauzy

University of Toledo
Toledo, OH 43606 Founded: 1872
SID: (419) 530-3790 Enrollment: 21,692
President ....Frank E. Horton
Athletic Director ....Pete Liske
Sports Information Director ....Paul Helgren

Western Michigan University
Kalamazoo, MI 49008 Founded: 1903
SID: (616) 387-4138 Enrollment: 25,689
President ....Diether Haenicke
Athletic Director ....Kathy Beauregard
Sports Information Director ....John Beatty

PACIFIC-10 CONFERENCE
800 South Broadway, Suite 400, Walnut Creek, CA 94596
(925) 932-4411 Founded: 1915
Commissioner ....Thomas Hansen
Asst. Commissioner, Public Relations ....Jim Muldoon

1998-99 members: BASKETBALL & FOOTBALL (10)—Arizona, Arizona St., California, Oregon, Oregon St., Stanford, UCLA, USC, Washington and Washington St.

University of Arizona
Tucson, AZ 85721 Founded: 1885
SID: (520) 621-4163 Enrollment: 33,504
President ....Peter Likins
Athletic Director ....Jim Livengood
Sports Information Director ....Tom Duddleston

Arizona State University
Tempe, AZ 85287 Founded: 1885
SID: (602) 965-6592 Enrollment: 42,626
President ....Lattie F. Coor
Athletic Director ....Kevin White
Sports Information Director ....Mark Brand

University of California
Berkeley, CA 94720 Founded: 1868
SID: (510) 642-5363 Enrollment: 30,000
Chancellor ....Robert Berdahl
Athletic Director ....John Kasser
Sports Information Director ....Kevin Reneau

University of Oregon
Eugene, OR 97401 Founded: 1876
SID: (541) 346-5488 Enrollment: 17,500
President ....David Frohnmeyer
Athletic Director ....Bill Moos
Sports Information Director ....Dave Williford

Oregon State University
Corvallis, OR 97331 Founded: 1868
SID: (541) 737-3720 Enrollment: 14,500
President ....Paul G. Risser
Athletic Director ....Mitch Barnhart
Sports Information Director ....Hal Cowan

Stanford University
Stanford, CA 94305 Founded: 1891
SID: (650) 723-4418 Enrollment: 13,075
President ....Gerhard Casper
Athletic Director ....Ted Leland
Sports Information Director ....Gary Migdol

UCLA— Univ. of California, Los Angeles
Los Angeles, CA 90024 Founded: 1919
SID: (310) 206-6831 Enrollment: 34,000
Chancellor ....Albert Carnesale
Athletic Director ....Pete Dalis
Sports Information Director ....Marc Dellins

USC— Univ. of Southern California
Los Angeles, CA 90089 Founded: 1880
SID: (213) 740-8480 Enrollment: 28,190
President ....Steven Sample
Athletic Director ....Mike Garrett
Sports Information Director ....Tim Tessalone

University of Washington
Seattle, WA 98195 Founded: 1861
SID: (206) 543-2230 Enrollment: 25,000
President ....Richard McCormick
Athletic Director ....Barbara Hedges
Sports Information Director ....Jim Daves

Female Athletic Directors

As of Sept. 1, 1998, there were 17 female athletic directors at the nation's 308 NCAA Div. I schools. Here they are (in alphabetical order): Eve Atkinson, Lafayette; Sandy Barbour, Tulane; Kathy Beauregard, Western Mich.; Judith Davidson, CS-Sacramento; Vivian L. Fuller, Tennessee St.; Cary Groth, N. Illinois; Barbara Hedges, Washington; Judy Macleod, Tulsa; Marilyn McNeil, Monmouth; Patricia Meiser-McKnett, Hartford; Andrea Myers, Indiana St.; Judith Ray, New Hampshire; Judy Rose, NC-Charlotte; Andrea Seger, Ball St.; Helen Smiley, W. Illinois; Suzanne Tyler, Maine; Deborah Yow, Maryland.

Washington State University
Pullman, WA 99164 — Founded: 1890
SID: (509) 335-0270 — Enrollment: 20,020
President ....Samuel Smith
Athletic Director ....Rick Dickson
Sports Information Director ....Rod Commons

❧ ❧ ❧

SOUTHEASTERN CONFERENCE
2201 Civic Center Blvd.
Birmingham, AL 35203
(205) 458-3000 — Founded: 1933
Commissioner ....Roy Kramer
Asst. Commis. of Media Relations ....Charles Bloom

1998-99 members: BASKETBALL & FOOTBALL (12)—Alabama, Arkansas, Auburn, Florida, Georgia, Kentucky, LSU, Mississippi St., Ole Miss, South Carolina, Tennessee and Vanderbilt.

University of Alabama
Tuscaloosa, AL 35487 — Founded: 1831
SID: (205) 348-6084 — Enrollment: 18,500
President ....Dr. Andrew Sorensen
Athletic Director ....Robert Bockrath
Sports Information Director ....Larry White

University of Arkansas
Fayetteville, AR 72701 — Founded: 1871
SID: (501) 575-2751 — Enrollment: 14,600
Chancellor ....John White
Athletic Director ....Frank Broyles
Women's Athletic Director ....Bev Lewis
Sports Information Director ....Rick Schaeffer

Auburn University
Auburn, AL 36831 — Founded: 1856
SID: (334) 844-9800 — Enrollment: 22,122
President ....William V. Muse
Athletic Director ....David Housel
Sports Information Director ....Kent Partridge

University of Florida
Gainesville, FL 32604 — Founded: 1853
SID: (352) 375-4683 ext. 6100 — Enrollment: 40,000
President ....John Lombardi
Athletic Director ....Jeremy Foley
Sports Information Director ....John Humenik

University of Georgia
Athens, GA 30603 — Founded: 1785
SID: (706) 542-1621 — Enrollment: 30,000
President ....Michael F. Adams
Athletic Director ....Vince Dooley
Sports Information Director ....Claude Felton

University of Kentucky
Lexington, KY 40506 — Founded: 1865
SID: (606) 257-3838 — Enrollment: 24,200
President ....Charles T. Wethington Jr.
Athletic Director ..........................C.M. Newton
Sports Information Director ....Rena Vicini

LSU— Louisiana State University
Baton Rouge, LA 70894 — Founded: 1860
SID: (504) 388-8226 — Enrollment: 28,077
Chancellor ....William L. Jenkins
Athletic Director ....Joe Dean
Sports Information Director ....Herb Vincent

Mississippi State University
Starkville, MS 39762 — Founded: 1878
SID: (601) 325-2703 — Enrollment: 15,645
President ....Dr. Malcolm Portera
Athletic Director ....Larry Templeton
Sports Information Director ....Mike Nemeth

Ole Miss
U. of M., MS 38677 — Founded: 1848
SID: (601) 232-7522 — Enrollment: 13,168
Chancellor ....Dr. Robert C. Khayat
Athletic Director ....John Shafer
Sports Information Director ....Langston Rogers

University of South Carolina
Columbia, SC 29208 — Founded: 1801
SID: (803) 777-5204 — Enrollment: 25,435
President ....John Palms
Athletic Director ....Mike McGee
Sports Information Director ....Kerry Tharp

University of Tennessee
Knoxville, TN 37916 — Founded: 1794
SID: (423) 974-1212 — Enrollment: 25,039
President ....Joe Johnson
Athletic Director ....Doug Dickey
Women's Athletic Director ....Joan Cronan
Sports Information Director ....Bud Ford

Vanderbilt University
Nashville, TN 37212 — Founded: 1873
SID: (615) 322-4121 — Enrollment: 5,927
Chancellor ....Joe B. Wyatt
Athletic Director ....Todd Turner
Sports Information Director ....Rod Williamson

❧ ❧ ❧

WESTERN ATHLETIC CONFERENCE
9250 East Costilla Ave., Suite 300
Englewood, CO 80112
(303) 799-9221 — Founded: 1962
Commissioner ....Karl Benson
Directors of Communications .....Dave Chaffin & Lisa Vad

1998-99 members: BASKETBALL & FOOTBALL (16)—Air Force, BYU, Colorado St., Fresno St., Hawaii, New Mexico, Rice, San Diego St., San Jose St., SMU, TCU, Tulsa, UNLV, Utah, UTEP and Wyoming.

U.S. Air Force Academy
US Academy, CO 80840 — Founded: 1959
SID: (719) 333-2313 — Enrollment: 4,100
Superintendent ....Lt. Gen. Tad Oelstrom
Athletic Director ....Col. Randall W. Spetman
Sports Information Director ....Dave Kellogg

Brigham Young University
Provo, UT 84602 — Founded: 1875
SID: (801) 378-4911 — Enrollment: 27,000
President ....Merril J. Bateman
Athletic Director ....Rondo Fehlberg
Sports Information Director ....Ralph Zobell

Colorado State University
Fort Collins, CO 80523 — Founded: 1870
SID: (970) 491-5067 — Enrollment: 22,344
President ....Dr. Albert Yates
Athletic Director ....Tim Wieser
Sports Information Director ....Gary Ozzello

Fresno State University
Fresno, CA 93740 — Founded: 1911
SID: (209) 278-2509 — Enrollment: 18,902
President ....Dr. John D. Welty
Athletic Director ....Dr. Al Bohl
Sports Information Director ....Rose Pietrzak

University of Hawaii
Honolulu, HI 96822 — Founded: 1907
SID: (808) 956-7523 — Enrollment: 19,062
President ....Dr. Kenneth Mortimer
Athletic Director ....Hugh Yoshida
Sports Information Director ....Lois Manin

University of New Mexico
Albuquerque, NM 87131 — Founded: 1889
SID: (505) 277-2026 — Enrollment: 22,890
Interim President ....Dr. William Gordon
Athletic Director ....Rudy Davalos
Sports Information Director ....Greg Remington

Rice University
Houston, TX 77005 — Founded: 1912
SID: (713) 737-5775 — Enrollment: 2,600
President ....Dr. Malcolm Gillis
Athletic Director ....Bobby May
Sports Information Director ....Bill Cousins

San Diego State University
San Diego, CA 92182 — Founded: 1897
SID: (619) 594-5547 — Enrollment: 29,000
President ....Dr. Stephen L. Weber
Athletic Director ....Rick Bay
Sports Information Director ....John Rosenthal

San Jose State University
San Jose, CA 95192 — Founded: 1857
SID: (408) 924-1217 — Enrollment: 27,000
President ....Dr. Robert Caret
Athletic Director ....Chuck Bell
Sports Information Director ....Lawrence Fan

SMU— Southern Methodist University
Dallas, TX 75275 — Founded: 1911
SID: (214) 768-2883 — Enrollment: 9,172
President ....Dr. R. Gerald Turner
Athletic Director ....Jim Copeland
Sports Information Director ....Jon Jackson

TCU— Texas Christian University
Fort Worth, TX 76129 — Founded: 1873
SID: (817) 257-7969 — Enrollment: 7,240
Chancellor ....Dr. Michael Ferrari
Athletic Director ....Eric Hyman
Sports Information Director ....Rick Covington

University of Tulsa
Tulsa, OK 74104 — Founded: 1894
SID: (918) 631-2395 — Enrollment: 4,300
President ....Dr. Bob Lawless
Athletic Director ....Judy MacLeod
Sports Information Director ....Don Tomkalski

University of Utah
Salt Lake City, UT 84112 — Founded: 1850
SID: (801) 581-3510 — Enrollment: 26,359
President ....Dr. Bernard Machen
Athletic Director ....Dr. Chris Hill
Sports Information Director ....Liz Abel

UNLV— University of Nevada, Las Vegas
Las Vegas, NV 89154 — Founded: 1957
SID: (702) 895-3207 — Enrollment: 20,200
President ....Dr. Carol Harter
Athletic Director ....Charles Cavognaro
Sports Information Director ....Jim Gemma

UTEP— University of Texas at El Paso
El Paso, TX 79902 — Founded: 1914
SID: (915) 747-6653 — Enrollment: 15,393
President ....Dr. Diana Natalicio
Athletic Director ....Bob Stull
Sports Information Director ....Derek Smolik

University of Wyoming
Laramie, WY 82071 — Founded: 1886
SID: (307) 766-2256 — Enrollment: 10,600
President ....Dr. Philip Dubois
Athletic Director ....Lee Moon
Sports Information Director ....Kevin McKinney

MAJOR INDEPENDENTS

Division I-A football independents in 1998.

Arkansas State University
State University, AR 72467 — Founded: 1909
SID: (870) 972-2541 — Enrollment: 10,050
President ....Les Wyatt
Athletic Director ....Barry Dowd
Sports Information Director ....Gina Bowman

University of Central Florida
Orlando, FL 32816 — Founded: 1963
SID: (407) 823-2729 — Enrollment: 28,500
President ....Dr. John C. Hitt
Athletic Director ....Steve Sloan
Sports Information Director ....John Marini

Louisiana Tech University
Ruston, LA 71272 — Founded: 1894
SID: (318) 257-3144 — Enrollment: 9,664
President ....Dan Reneau
Athletic Director ....Jim Oakes
Sports Information Director ....Byron Avery

Navy— U.S. Naval Academy
Annapolis, MD 21402 — Founded: 1845
SID: (410) 268-6226 — Enrollment: 4,000
Superintendent ....Adm. John Ryan
Athletic Director ....Jack Lengyel
Sports Information Director ....Scott Strasemeier

Northeast Louisiana University
Monroe, LA 71209 — Founded: 1931
SID: (318) 342-5460 — Enrollment: 10,942
President ....Lawson Swearingen, Jr.
Athletic Director ....Richard Giannini
Sports Information Director ....Robby Edwards

University of Notre Dame
Notre Dame, IN 46556 — Founded: 1842
SID: (219) 631-7516 — Enrollment: 10,359
President ....Rev. Edward (Monk) Malloy
Athletic Director ....Michael Wadsworth
Sports Information Director ....John Heisler

University of Southwestern Louisiana
Lafayette, LA 70506 — Founded: 1898
SID: (318) 482-6331 — Enrollment: 17,000
President ....Ray Authement
Athletic Director ....Nelson Schexnayder
Sports Information Director ....Dan McDonald

❧ ❧ ❧

OTHER MAJOR DIVISION I CONFERENCES

Conferences that play either Division I basketball or Division I-AA football, or both.

America East
10 High St., Suite 860
Boston, MA 02110
(617) 695-6369 — Founded: 1979
Commissioner ....Chris Monasch
Director of Communications ....Matt Bourque

1998-99 members: BASKETBALL (10)— Boston University, Delaware, Drexel, Hartford, Hofstra, Maine, New Hampshire, Northeastern, Towson and Vermont.

Division I Hockey Conferences

The four Division I hockey conferences are the Eastern Collegiate Athletic Conference (ECAC) in Centerville, Mass., (508) 771-5060; the Central Collegiate Hockey Assn. (CCHA) in Ann Arbor, Mich. (248) 888-0600; Hockey East in Lawrence, Mass., (978) 687-8535 and the Western Collegiate Hockey Assn. in Madison, Wisc. (608) 829-0100.

Atlantic 10 Conference
2 Penn Center Plaza
Philadelphia, PA 19102 Founded: 1976
(215) 751-0500 A-10 Football founded: 1997
Commissioner ....Linda Bruno
Director of Communications ....Ray Cella

1998-99 members: BASKETBALL (12)— Dayton, Duquesne, Fordham, George Washington, La Salle, Massachusetts, Rhode Island, St. Bonaventure, St. Joseph's-PA, Temple, Virginia Tech and Xavier-OH. FOOTBALL (11)— Connecticut, Delaware, James Madison, Maine, Massachusetts, New Hampshire, Northeastern, Rhode Island, Richmond, Villanova and William & Mary.

Big Sky Conference
P.O. Box 1459
Ogden, UT 84402
(801) 392-1978, ext. 2 Founded: 1963
Commissioner ....Douglas Fullerton
Director of Information ....Ron Loghry

1998-99 members: BASKETBALL & FOOTBALL (9)— Cal St. Northridge, Cal. St. Sacramento, Eastern Washington, Idaho St., Montana, Montana St., Northern Arizona, Portland St. and Weber St.

Big South Conference
6428 Bannington Dr., Ste A
Charlotte, NC 28226
(704) 341-7990 Founded: 1983
Commissioner ....Kyle Kallander
Director of Media Relations ....Shannon Fritts

1998-99 members: BASKETBALL (6)— Charleston Southern, Coastal Carolina, Liberty, NC-Asheville, Radford, and Winthrop.

Colonial Athletic Association
8625 Patterson Ave.
Richmond, VA 23229
(804) 754-1616 Founded: 1985
Commissioner ....Thomas E. Yeager
Sports Information Director ....Steve Vehorn

1998-99 members: BASKETBALL (9)— American, East Carolina, George Mason, James Madison, NC-Wilmington, Old Dominion, Richmond, Virginia Commonwealth and William & Mary.

Gateway Football Conference
1000 Union Station, Suite 105
St. Louis, MO 63103
(314) 421-2268 Founded: 1985
Commissioner ....Patty Viverito
Asst. Commissioner, Information ....Mike Kern

1998 members: FOOTBALL (7)— Illinois St., Indiana St., Northern Iowa, Southern Illinois, SW Missouri St., Western Illinois and Youngstown St..

Ivy League
330 Alexander Street
Princeton, NJ 08544
(609) 258-6426 Founded: 1954
Executive Director ....Jeffrey Orleans
Director of Information ....Chuck Yrigoyen

1998-99 members: BASKETBALL & FOOTBALL (8)— Brown, Columbia, Cornell, Dartmouth, Harvard, Pennsylvania, Princeton and Yale.

Metro Atlantic Athletic Conference
1090 Amboy Avenue
Edison, NJ 08837
(732) 225-0202 Founded: 1980
Commissioner ....Richard Ensor
Director of Media Relations ....TBA

1998-99 members: BASKETBALL (10)— Canisius, Fairfield, Iona, Loyola-MD, Manhattan, Marist, Niagara, Rider, St. Peter's and Siena. FOOTBALL (9)— Canisius, Duquesne, Fairfield, Georgetown, Iona, Marist, St. John's, St. Peter's and Siena.

Mid-Continent Conference
340 West Butterfield Rd., Ste 3D
Elmhurst, IL 60126
(630) 516-0661 Founded: 1982
Commissioner ....Jon Steinbrecher
Asst. Commiss. for Media Relations ....Jeff Reynolds

1998-99 members: BASKETBALL (9)— Chicago St., Indiana U-Purdue U Indianapolis, Missouri/K.C., Oakland, Oral Roberts, Southern Utah, Valparaiso, Western Illinois, Youngstown St.

Mid-Eastern Athletic Conference
102 North Elm St. SE Building, Suite 401
Greensboro, NC 27401
(336) 275-9961 Founded: 1970
Commissioner ....Charles S. Harris
Director of Media Relations ....Larry Barber

1998-99 members: BASKETBALL (11)— Bethune-Cookman, Coppin St., Delaware St., Florida A&M, Hampton, Howard, MD-Eastern Shore, Morgan St., Norfolk St., North Carolina A&T and South Carolina St.; FOOTBALL (9)— all but Coppin St. and MD-Eastern Shore.

Midwestern Collegiate Conference
201 South Capitol Ave., Suite 500
Indianapolis, IN 46225
(317) 237-5622 Founded: 1979
Commissioner ....John LeCrone
Director of Communications ....Terry Powers

1998-99 members: BASKETBALL (8)— Butler, Cleveland St., Detroit Mercy, Illinois-Chicago, Loyola-IL, Wisconsin-Green Bay, Wisconsin-Milwaukee and Wright St.

Missouri Valley Conference
1000 St. Louis Union Station, Suite 105
St. Louis, MO 63103
(314) 421-0339 Founded: 1907
Commissioner ....Doug Elgin
Asst. Commissioner ....Jack Watkins

1998-99 members: BASKETBALL (10)— Bradley, Creighton, Drake, Evansville, Illinois St., Indiana St., Northern Iowa, Southern Illinois, SW Missouri St., and Wichita St.

Northeast Conference
220 Old New Brunswick Rd.
Piscataway, NJ 08854
(732) 562-0877 Founded: 1981
Commissioner ....John Iamarino
Asst. Commissioner, Media Relations .....Denise Gormley

1998-99 members: BASKETBALL (11)— Cent. Conn. St., Fairleigh Dickinson, LIU-Brooklyn, Maryland-Baltimore County, Monmouth, Mount St. Mary's, Quinnipiac, Robert Morris, St. Francis-NY, St. Francis-PA and Wagner. FOOTBALL (6)—Cent. Conn. St., Monnouth, Robert Morris, Sacred Heart, St. Francis (PA) and Wagner.

Ohio Valley Conference
278 Franklin Road, Suite 103
Brentwood, TN 37027
(615) 371-1698 Founded: 1948
Commissioner ....Dan Beebe
Asst. Commis., Info. and Champs. ....Rob Washburn

1998-99 members: BASKETBALL (10)— Austin Peay St., Eastern Illinois, Eastern Kentucky, Middle Tennessee St., Morehead St., Murray St., SE Missouri St., Tennessee-Martin, Tennessee St. and Tennessee Tech; FOOTBALL (8)— all but Austin Peay and Morehead St.

Patriot League
3897 Adler Place, Building C, Suite 310
Bethlehem, PA 18017
(610) 691-2414 Founded: 1984
Executive Director ....Constance Hurlbut
Director of Information ....Todd Newcomb

1998-99 members: BASKETBALL (7)— Army, Bucknell, Colgate, Holy Cross, Lafayette, Lehigh and Navy; FOOTBALL (7)— Bucknell, Colgate, Fordham, Holy Cross, Lafayette, Lehigh and Towson.

Pioneer Football League
1000 St. Louis Union Station, Suite 105
St. Louis, MO 63103
(314) 421-2268 Founded: 1993
Commissioner ....Patty Viverito
Media Relations ....Cindy Kern

1998 members: FOOTBALL (5): Butler, Dayton, Drake, San Diego and Valparaiso.

Southern Conference
1 West Pack Square, Suite 1508
Asheville, NC 28801
(828) 255-7872 Founded: 1921
Commissioner ....Alfred B. White
Asst. Commissioner, Public Affairs ....Heather Czeczok

1998-99 members: BASKETBALL (12)— Appalachian St., The Citadel, College of Charleston, Davidson, East Tennessee St., Furman, Georgia Southern, UNC-Greensboro, Tennessee-Chattanooga, VMI, Western Carolina and Wofford; FOOTBALL (9)—all except College of Charleston, Davidson and UNC-Greensboro.

Southland Conference
8150 North Central Expressway, Suite 930
Dallas, TX 75206
(214) 750-7522 Founded: 1963
Commissioner ....Greg Sankey
Director of Media Relations ....Bruce Ludlow

1998-99 members: BASKETBALL (12)— Lamar, McNeese St., Nicholls St., North Texas, NE Louisiana, Northwestern St., Sam Houston St., SE Louisiana, Southwest Texas St., Stephen F. Austin St., Texas-Arlington and Texas-San Antonio; FOOTBALL (8)— Jacksonville St., McNeese St., Nicholls St., Northwestern St., Sam Houston St., Southwest Texas St., Stephen F. Austin St. and Troy St.

Southwestern Athletic Conference
1500 Sugar Bowl Drive, Superdome
New Orleans, LA 70112
(504) 523-7574 Founded: 1920
Commissioner ....Rudy Washington
Director of Publicity ....Lonza Hardy Jr.

1998-99 members: BASKETBALL & FOOTBALL (9)— Alabama St., Alcorn St., Arkansas-Pine Bluff, Grambling St., Jackson St., Mississippi Valley St., Prairie View A&M, Southern-Baton Rouge and Texas Southern.

Sun Belt Conference
One Galleria Boulevard, Suite 2115
Metairie, LA 70001
(504) 834-6600 Founded: 1976
Commissioner ....Craig Thompson
Director of Media Services ....Dayna Wells

1998-99 members: BASKETBALL (8)— Arkansas-Little Rock, Arkansas St., Florida International, Louisiana Tech, New Orleans, South Alabama, SW Louisiana and Western Kentucky.

Trans America Athletic Conference
The Commons, 3370 Vineville Ave., Suite 108-B,
Macon, GA 31204
(912) 474-3394 Founded: 1978
Commissioner ....Bill Bibb
Director of Information ....Tom Snyder

1998-99 members: BASKETBALL (11)— Campbell, Centenary, Central Florida, Florida Atlantic, Georgia St., Jacksonville, Jacksonville St., Mercer, Samford, Stetson and Troy St.

West Coast Conference
1200 Bayhill Dr.
San Bruno, CA 94066
(650) 873-8622 Founded: 1952
Commissioner ....Michael Gilleran
Director of Information ....Don Ott

1998-99 members: BASKETBALL (8)— Gonzaga, Loyola Marymount, Pepperdine, Portland, St. Mary's, San Diego, San Francisco and Santa Clara.

PRO FOOTBALL

National Football League

League Office
280 Park Ave., New York, NY 10017
(212) 450-2000
Commissioner ....Paul Tagliabue
President ....Neil Austrian
Exec. V.P. & League Counsel ....Jeff Pash
AFC Info. Coordinator ....Dan Masonson
NFC Info. Coordinator ....Chris McCloskey

NFL Management Council
280 Park Ave., New York, NY 10017
(212) 450-2000
Chairman ....Harold Henderson
V.P. & General Counsel ....Dennis Curran

NFL Players Association
2021 L Street NW, Suite 600
Washington, DC 20036
(202) 463-2200
Executive Director ....Gene Upshaw
Asst. Exec. Director ....Doug Allen
General Counsel ....Richard Berthelsen
Director of Public Relations ....Frank Woschitz

AFC

Baltimore Ravens
11001 Owings Mills Blvd.
Owings Mills, MD 21117
(410) 654-6200
Owner-President ....Arthur B. Modell
Exec. V.P., Legal & Administration ....Jim Bailey
Executive V.P. to President ....David Modell
V.P., Public Relations ....Kevin Byrne

Buffalo Bills
One Bills Drive, Orchard Park, NY 14127
(716) 648-1800
Owner-President ....Ralph C. Wilson Jr.
Exec. V.P. & General Manager ....John Butler
Director of Media Relations ....Scott Berchtold

Cincinnati Bengals
One Bengals Drive, Cincinnati, OH 45204
(513) 621-3550
Chairman ....Austin Knowlton
President & General Manager ....Mike Brown
Public Relations Director ....Jack Brennan

Denver Broncos
13655 Broncos Parkway, Englewood, CO 80112
(303) 649-9000
Owner-President-CEO ....Pat Bowlen
General Manager ....John Beake
Director of Media Relations ....Jim Saccomano

Indianapolis Colts
7001 W 56th St., Indianapolis, IN 46254
(317) 297-2658
Owner-CEO ....Jim Irsay
President ....Bill Polian
Dir. of Football Operations ....Dom Anice
Director of Public Relations ....Craig Kelley

Jacksonville Jaguars
One ALLTEL Stadium Place
Jacksonville, FL 32202
(904) 633-6000
Chairman-CEO-President ....Wayne Weaver
Sr. V.P., Football Operations ....Michael Huyghue
Exec. Director of Communications ....Dan Edwards

Kansas City Chiefs
One Arrowhead Drive, Kansas City, MO 64129
(816) 924-9300
Owner-Founder .... Lamar Hunt
Chairman .... Jack Steadman
President-CEO-General Manager .... Carl Peterson
Director of Public Relations .... Bob Moore

Miami Dolphins
7500 SW 30th St., Davie, FL 33314
(954) 452-7000
Owner-Chairman .... Wayne Huizenga
President & COO .... Eddie Jones
GM & Head Coach .... Jimmy Johnson
V.P., Media Relations .... Harvey Greene

New England Patriots
Foxboro Stadium, Route 1, Foxboro, MA 02035
(508) 543-8200
Owner-President-CEO & General Manager ...... Bob Kraft
Dir. of Player Personnel .... Bobby Grier
Director of Public Relations .... Don Lowery

New York Jets
1000 Fulton Ave., Hempstead, NY 11550
(516) 560-8100
Owner-Chairman .... Leon Hess
President .... Steve Gutman
Chief Football Ops. Officer & Head Coach .... Bill Parcells
Director of Public Relations .... Frank Ramos

Oakland Raiders
1220 Harborbay Parkway, Alameda, CA 94502
(510) 864-5000
Managing General Partner .... Al Davis
Executive Assistant .... Al LoCasale
Director of Public Relations .... Mike Taylor

Pittsburgh Steelers
300 Stadium Circle, Pittsburgh, PA 15212
(412) 323-0300
Owner-President .... Dan Rooney
VPs .... John McGinley, Art Rooney Jr. & Art Rooney II
Communications Coordinator .... Ron Whal

San Diego Chargers
4020 Murphy Canyon Rd., San Diego, CA 92123
(619) 874-4500
Owner-Chairman .... Alex Spanos
President -Vice Chairman .... Dean Spanos
General Manager .... Bobby Beathard
Director of Public Relations .... Bill Johnston

Seattle Seahawks
11220 NE 53rd Street, Kirkland, WA 98033
(425) 827-9777
Owner .... Paul Allen
President .... Bob Whitsitt
V.P., Football Operations .... Randy Mueller
Public Relations Director .... Dave Pearson

Tennessee Oilers
P.O. Box 198497, Nashville, TN 37219
(615) 733-3000
Owner-President .... K.S. (Bud) Adams Jr.
Exec. V.P. & General Manager .... Floyd Reese
Director of Media Services .... Tony Wyllie

NFC

Arizona Cardinals
P.O. Box 888, Phoenix, AZ 85001
(602) 379-0101
Owner-President .... Bill Bidwill
Vice President .... Bill Bidwill, Jr.
Dir. of Player Personnel .... Bob Ferguson
Public Relations Director .... Paul Jensen

Atlanta Falcons
One Falcon Place
Suwanee, GA 30024
(770) 945-1111
Owner-President .... Taylor Smith
Exec. V.P. Football Ops./Head Coach .... Dan Reeves
V.P., Football Ops. .... Ron Hill
Director of Public Relations .... Charlie Taylor

Carolina Panthers
800 South Mint St.
Charlotte, NC 28202-1502
(704) 358-7000
Founder-Owner .... Jerry Richardson
President .... Mark Richardson
Dir. of Player Personnel .... Jack Bushofsky
Director of Communications .... Charlie Dayton

Chicago Bears
1000 Football Drive
Lake Forest, IL 60045
(847) 295-6600
Owner-Chairman .... Edward McCaskey
President-CEO .... Mike McCaskey
V.P., Football Operations .... Ted Phillips
Director of Public Relations .... Bryan Harlan

Dallas Cowboys
Cowboys Center
One Cowboys Parkway, Irving, TX 75063
(972) 556-9900
Owner-President-GM .... Jerry Jones
V.P./Dir. of Player Personnel .... Stephen Jones
Public Relations Director .... Rich Dalrymple

Detroit Lions
Pontiac Silverdome
1200 Featherstone Rd., Pontiac, MI 48342
(248) 335-4131
Owner-President .... William Clay Ford
Executive V.P. & COO .... Chuck Schmidt
Director of Media Relations .... Mike Murray

Green Bay Packers
1265 Lombardi Ave., P.O. Box 10628
Green Bay, WI 54307
(920) 496-5700
President-CEO .... Bob Harlan
Exec. V.P. & General Manager .... Ron Wolf
Exec. Dir. of Public Relations .... Lee Remmel

Minnesota Vikings
9520 Viking Drive
Eden Prairie, MN 55344
(612) 828-6500
Owner .... Red McCombs
President-CEO .... TBA
V.P., Team Operations .... Jeff Diamond
Public Relations Asst. .... Bob Hagen

New Orleans Saints
5800 Airline Drive
Metairie, LA 70003
(504) 733-0255
Owner .... Tom Benson
President & General Manager .... Bill Kuharich
V.P. of Football Ops./Asst. GM .... Chet Franklin
Director of Media/Public Relations .... Greg Bensel

New York Giants
Giants Stadium
East Rutherford, NJ 07073
(201) 935-8111
President/co-CEO .... Wellington Mara
Chairman/co-CEO .... Preston Robert Tisch
V.P. & General Manager .... Ernie Accorsi
V.P. of Communications .... Pat Hanlon

Philadelphia Eagles
Veterans Stadium
3501 S. Broad St.
Philadelphia, PA 19148-5298
(215) 463-2500
Owner ....Jeff Lurie
Executive V.P. ....Joe Banner
Director of Football Operations ....Tom Modrak
Director of Public Relations ....Ron Howard

St. Louis Rams
One Rams Way, St. Louis, MO 63045
(314) 982-7267
Owner-Chairman ....Georgia Frontiere
President ....John Shaw
V.P., Football Operations ....Lynn Stiles
Director of Public Relations ....Rick Smith

San Francisco 49ers
4949 Centennial Blvd.
Santa Clara, CA 95054
(408) 562-4949
Owners ..Edward DeBartolo Jr., Denise DeBartolo-York and Edward J. DeBartolo Corp.
Interim President ....Larry Thrailkill
V.P., Football Operations ....Dwight Clark
Director of Public Relations ....Rodney Knox

Tampa Bay Buccaneers
One Buccaneer Place, Tampa, FL 33607
(813) 870-2700
Owner-President ....Malcolm Glazer
General Manager ....Rich McKay
Director of Communications ....Reggie Roberts

Washington Redskins
Redskin Park
P.O. Box 17247, Washington D.C. 20041
(703) 478-8900
President ....John Kent Cooke Sr.
General Manager ....Charley Casserly
Director of Public Relations ....Mike McCall

Canadian Football League

League Office
CFL Building, 110 Eglinton Avenue West, 5th Floor
Toronto, Ontario M4R 1A3
(416) 322-9650
Chairman/Acting Commissioner ....John Tory
President/COO ....Jeff Giles
V.P., Football Operations ....Ed Chalupka
Manager of Communications ....Jim Neish

CFL Players Association
467 Speers Rd., Unit 5, Oakville, Ontario L6K 3S4
(905) 844-7852
President ....Dan Ferrone
Legal Counsel ....Ed Molstad

British Columbia Lions
10605 135th St., Surrey, B.C. V3T 4C8
(604) 930-5466
Owner ....David Braylay
President & CEO ....Glen Ringdal
Dir. of Media/Public Relations ....Colin Metcalfe

Calgary Stampeders
McMahon Stadium, 1817 Crowchild Trail, NW
Calgary, Alberta T2M 4R6
(403) 289-0205
Owner ....Sig Gutsche
President ....Stan Schwartz
General Manager & Head Coach ....Wally Buono
V.P., Marketing & Communications ....Ron Rooke

Edmonton Eskimos
9023 111th Ave.
Edmonton, Alberta T5B 0C3
(403) 448-1525
Owner ....Community-owned
President ....Hugh Campbell
General Manager ....Tom Higgins
Asst. General Manager of Adm. ....Mike Thome

Hamilton Tiger-Cats
75 Balsam Ave. N, Hamilton, Ontario L8L 8C1
(905) 547-2418
Chairman/Owner ....David M. Macdonald
Vice Chairman/Owner ....George Grant
GM/Dir. of Business Ops. ....Neil Lumsden
Communications Director ....Norm Miller

Montreal Alouettes
4545 Avenue Pierre-De Coubertin
P.O. Box 65, Station M
Montreal, Quebec H1V 3L6
(514) 254-2400
Owner ....Robert Wetenhall
President & CEO ....Larry Smith
Dir. of Football Ops/GM ....Jim Popp
Dir. of Communications ....Louis-Phillippe Doraif

Saskatchewan Roughriders
2940 — 10th Avenue, P.O. Box 1277
Regina, Saskatchewan S4P 3B8
(306) 569-2323
Owner ....Community-owned
President ....Bob Ellard
CEO & General Manager ....Alan Ford
Media Coordinator ....Tony Playter

Toronto Argonauts
SkyDome Gate 3
Suite 1300, P.O. Box 2005, Station B
Toronto, Ontario M5T 3H8
(416) 341-5151
Owners ....Labatt Breweries
President ....Bob Nicholson
General Manager & Head Coach ....Don Matthews
Director of Public Relations ....Greg Mandziuk

Winnipeg Blue Bombers
1465 Maroons Road, Winnipeg, Manitoba R3G 0L6
(204) 784-2583
Owner ....Community-owned
President ....Don Bryk
Dir. Football Operations & Head Coach .....Jeff Reinebold
Manager of Media Relations ..................J.D. Boyd

NFL Europe

President ....Oliver Luck
Public Relations Director ....David Tossell
U.S. Public Relations Assistant ....Michael Signora

League Offices

London
26A Albemarle St.
London, England W1X 3FA
011-44-171-355-1955

New York
280 Park Avenue
New York, NY 10017
(212) 450-2000

Member teams (6): Amsterdam Admirals, Barcelona Dragons, Berlin (as yet unnamed), Frankfurt Galaxy, Rhein Fire (Dusseldorf), Scottish Claymores (Edinburgh).

Arena Football League
75 E Wacker, Suite 400
Chicago, IL 60601
(312) 332-5510
Commissioner ....C. David Baker
President/General Counsel ....Ronald J. Kurpiers II
V.P., Football Operations ....Jerry Trice
Media Services ....David Cooper

Member teams (15): American Conference— Arizona Rattlers, Grand Rapids Rampage, Houston Thunderbears, Iowa Barnstormers, Milwaukee Mustangs, Portland (OR) Forest Dragons and San Jose Sabrecats. National Conference— Albany (NY) Firebirds, Florida Bob Cats, Nashville Kats, New Jersey Red Dogs, New York Cityhawks, Orlando Predators and Tampa Bay Storm. Expansion Team in 1999— Buffalo Destroyers.

GOLF

LPGA Tour
(Ladies' Professional Golf Association)
100 International Golf Drive
Daytona Beach, FL 32124
(904) 274-6200
Commissioner ....Jim Ritts
Deputy Commissioner ....Jim Webb
Director of Communications ....Leslie King

PGA of America
100 Avenue of the Champions
Palm Beach Gardens, FL 33410
(561) 624-8400
President ....Ken Lindsay
CEO ....Jim Awtrey
Director of Communications ....Terry McSweeney

PGA European Tour
Wentworth Drive, Virginia Water
Surrey, England GU25 4LX
TEL: 011-44-1344-842881
Executive Director ....Ken Schofield
Director of Communications ....Mitchell Platts

PGA Tour
112 PGA Tour Blvd., Ponte Vedra, FL 32082
(904) 285-3700
Commissioner ....Tim Finchem
Director of Information ....Dave Lancer

Royal & Ancient Golf Club of St. Andrews
St. Andrews, Fife, Scotland KY16 9JD
TEL: 011-44-1334-472112
Secretary ....Michael Bonallack
Deputy Secretary ....George Wilson

USGA
(United States Golf Association)
P.O. Box 708, Liberty Corner Road, Far Hills, NJ 07931
(908) 234-2300
President ....Buzz Taylor
Executive Director ....David Fay
Sr. Director of Communications ....Marty Parkes

PRO HOCKEY

NHL

National Hockey League

Commissioner ....Gary Bettman
Senior V.P., COO ....Stephen Solomon
Senior V.P., Dir. of Hockey Ops. ....Colin Campbell
V.P., Public Relations ....Arthur Pincus

League Offices

Montreal
1800 McGill College Ave., Suite 2600
Montreal, Quebec H3A 3J6
(514) 288-9220

New York
251 Sixth Ave., 47th Floor
New York, NY 10020
(212) 789-2000

Toronto
75 International Blvd., Suite 300
Rexdale, Ontario M9W 6L9
(416) 798-0809

NHL Players' Association
777 Bay St., Suite 2400, P.O. Box 121
Toronto, Ontario M5G 2C8
(416) 408-4040
Executive Director ....Bob Goodenow
Associate Counsel ....Ian Pulver,
J.P. Barry and Jeff Citron
Media Relations Mgr. ....Devin Smith

Anaheim, Mighty Ducks of
Arrowhead Pond of Anaheim
Anaheim, CA 92806
(714) 940-2900
Owner ....Walt Disney Co.
Anaheim Sports, Inc. Pres. ....Tony Tavares
President/GM ....Pierre Gauthier
Mgr. Communications and Team Services .....Rob Scichili

Boston Bruins
1 FleetCenter, Suite 250, Boston, MA 02114
(617) 624-1900
Owner ....Jeremy Jacobs
President & General Manager ....Harry Sinden
Director of Media Relations ....Heidi Holland

Buffalo Sabres
Marine Midland Arena, One Seymour H. Knox III Plaza,
Buffalo, NY 14203-3096
(716) 855-4100
COO ....Timothy Rigas
General Manager ....Darcy Regier
Director of Public Relations ....Michael Gilbert

Calgary Flames
Canadian Airlines Saddledome, P.O. Box 1540 Station M
Calgary, Alberta T2P 3B9
(403) 777-2177
Owners ....Harley Hotchkiss, Grant A. Bartlett, Murray Edwards, Ronald V. Joyce, Alvin G. Libin, Allan P. Markin, J.R. McCaig, Byron and Daryl Seamen
President & CEO ....Ron Bremner
V.P. & General Manager ....Al Coates
Director of Communications ....Peter Hanlon

Carolina Hurricanes
5000 Aerial Center Pkwy., Suite 100
Morrisville, NC 27560
(919) 467-7825
Owner-CEO ....Peter Karmanos Jr.
General Partner ....Thomas Thewes
President & General Manager ....Jim Rutherford
Dir., Media Relations/Team Services ....Chris Brown

Chicago Blackhawks
United Center, 1901 West Madison St.
Chicago, IL 60612
(312) 455-7000
Owner-President ....William Wirtz
General Manager ....Bob Murray
Executive Director of P.R. ....Jim DeMaria

Colorado Avalanche
1635 Clay St., Denver, CO 80204
(303) 893-6700
Owner .... Ascent Entertainment Corp.
Governor/Chairman .... Charlie Lyons
President/GM/Alt. Governor .... Pierre Lacroix
Dir., Media Relations/Team Services .... Jean Martineau

Dallas Stars
211 Cowboys Parkway, Irving, TX 75063
(972) 868-2890
Owner .... Thomas O. Hicks
President .... Jim Lites
General Manager .... Bob Gainey
Director of Public Relations .... Larry Kelly

Detroit Red Wings
Joe Louis Arena, 600 Civic Center Drive
Detroit, MI 48226
(313) 396-7544
Owner/President .... Mike Ilitch
Owner/Secretary-Treasurer .... Marian Ilitch
General Manager .... Ken Holland
Director of Media Relations .... John Hahn

Edmonton Oilers
11230 110th St., 2nd Flr.
Edmonton, Alberta, T5G 3G8
(403) 414-4000
Owners .... Many (34)
President & General Manager .... Glen Sather
Exec. V.P. & Assistant GM .... Bruce MacGregor
Director of Public Relations .... Bill Tuele

Florida Panthers
Broward County Arena, 2555 NW 137th Way
Sunrise, FL 33323
(954) 835-7000
Owner .... Wayne Huizenga
President .... Bill Torrey
General Manager .... Bryan Murray
Dir. of Public & Media Relations .... Mike Hanson

Los Angeles Kings
Great Western Forum, 3900 West Manchester Blvd.
Inglewood, CA 90305
(310) 419-3160
Majority Owners .... Philip Anschutz and Ed Roski
President .... Tim Leiweke
General Manager .... Dave Taylor
Director of Media Relations .... Mike Altieri

Montreal Canadiens
Molson Centre, 1260 Gauchetière St. West
Montreal, Quebec H3B 5E8
(514) 932-2582
Owner .... Molson Companies, Ltd.
Chairman-President .... Ronald Corey
General Manager .... Rejean Houle
Director of Communications .... Don Beauchamp

Nashville Predators
501 Broadway
Nashville, TN 57203
(615) 770-2300
Chairman and Maj. Owner .... Craig Leipold
President .... Jack Diller
General Manager .... David Poile
Manager of Public Relations .... Frank Buonomo

New Jesey Devils
Continental Airlines Arena, P.O. Box 504
East Rutherford, NJ 07073
(201) 935-6050
Chairman .... John McMullen
President & GM .... Lou Lamoriello
Director of Public Relations .... Mike Levine

New York Islanders
Nassau Veterans' Memorial Coliseum, Uniondale, NY 11553
(516) 794-4100
Owner .... Stephen Gluckstern
V.P. & General Manager .... Mike Milbury
Director of Media Relations .... Chris Botta

New York Rangers
2 Penn Plaza, 14th Floor, New York, NY 10121
(212) 465-6486
Owner .... Cablevision Systems Inc.
President (MSG) .... Dave Checketts
President & General Manager .... Neil Smith
Director of Public Relations .... John Rosasco

Ottawa Senators
1000 Palladium Dr., Kanata, Ontario, K2V 1A5
(613) 599-0250
Chairman & Gov. .... Rod Bryden
President & CEO .... Roy Mlakar
General Manager .... Rick Dudley
Director of Media Relations .... Phil Legault

Philadelphia Flyers
One CoreStates Complex, Philadelphia, PA 19148
(215) 465-4500
Chairman .... Ed Snider
President & General Manager .... Bob Clarke
Director of Media Relations .... Joe Klueg

Phoenix Coyotes
Cellular One Ice Den, 9375 E. Bell Rd.
Scottsdale, AZ 85260
(602) 473-5600
Owner .... Richard Burke
President .... Shawn Hunter
General Manager .... Bobby Smith
Director of Media Relations .... Richard Nairn

Pittsburgh Penguins
Civic Arena, Pittsburgh, PA 15219
(412) 642-1800
Owners .... Roger Marino & Howard Baldwin
Exec. V.P. & General Manager .... Craig Patrick
V.P., Communications .... Thomas McMillan

St. Louis Blues
Kiel Center, 1401 Clark Ave., St. Louis, MO 63103
(314) 622-2500
President-CEO .... Mark Sauer
General Manager .... Larry Pleau
Director of Public Relations .... Jeff Trammel

San Jose Sharks
525 West Santa Clara St., San Jose, CA 95113
(408) 287-7070
Owner-Chairman .... George Gund III
Co-Owner .... Gordon Gund
President-CEO .... Greg Jamison
Exec. V.P.& GM .... Dean Lombardi
Director of Media Relations .... Ken Arnold

Tampa Bay Lightning
401 Channelside Drive, Tampa, FL 33602
(813) 229-2658
Owner .... Art Williams
General Manager .... Phil Esposito
Asst. General Manager .... Tony Esposito
Director of Public Relations .... Jay Preble

Toronto Maple Leafs
Maple Leaf Gardens
60 Carlton Street, Toronto, Ontario M5B 1L1
(416) 977-1641
Chairman-CEO .... Steve Stavro
President-GM .... Ken Dryden
Assoc. GM .... Mike Smith
Media Relations .... Pat Park

Vancouver Canucks
General Motors Place, 800 Griffiths Way
Vancouver, B.C. V6B 6G1
(604) 899-4600
Owner .... Orca Bay Sports and Ent.
Chairman .... John McCaw Jr.
CEO .... Stephen Bellringer
President & General Manager .... Brian Burke
Dir. of Public & Media Relations .... TBA

Washington Capitals
MCI Center, 601 F St. NW
Washington, D.C. 20004
(202) 628-3200
Chairman .... Abe Pollin
President .... Dick Patrick
V.P. & General Manager .... George McPhee
V.P. of Communications .... Matt Williams

AHL

American Hockey League
425 Union St., W. Springfield, MA 01089
(413) 781-2030
President .... David Andrews
Sr. VP of Hockey Operations .... Gordon Anziano
Manager, Communications/PR .... Brent Maurer

IHL

International Hockey League
1577 N. Woodward Ave., Suite 212, Bloomfield Hills, MI 48304
(248) 258-0580
President/CEO .... Doug Moss
VP, Communications .... Bill Jameson

IIHF

International Ice Hockey Federation
Parkring 11
CH-8002 Zurich, Switzerland
TEL: 011-411-289-8600
President .... Rene Fasel
General Secretary .... Jan-Ake Edvinsson
PR/Marketing Mgr. .... Kimmo Leinonen

HORSE RACING

Breeders' Cup Limited
2525 Harrodsburg Road, Suite 500
Lexington, KY 40504
(606) 223-5444
President .... D.G. Van Clief, Jr.
Communications Manager .... John Garry

National Museum of Racing and Hall of Fame
191 Union Ave., Saratoga Springs, NY 12866
(518) 584-0400
Executive Director .... Peter Hammell
Assistant Director .... Catherine Maguire
Communications Officer .... Richard Hamilton

The Jockeys' Guild
P.O. Box 250, Lexington, KY 40588-0250
(606) 259-3211
President .... Gary Stevens
National Manager .... John Giovanni
Communications .... John Ball

NTRA
(National Thoroughbred Racing Association)
2343 Alexandria Drive, Ste. 210, Lexington, KY 40504
(606) 223-0658
CEO-Commissioner .... Tim Smith
Executive Dir. .... Nick Nicholson
Sr. V.P., Marketing .... Rick Baedeker

TRA
(Thoroughbred Racing Associations of N. America, Inc.)
420 Fair Hill Drive, Suite 1, Elkton, MD 21921
(410) 392-9200
President .... Harold G. Handel
Executive V.P .... Chris Scherf

TRC
(Thoroughbred Racing Communications)
40 East 52nd Street
New York, NY 10022
(212) 371-5910
Executive Director .... Tom Merritt
Director of Media Relations .... Bob Curran

USTA
(United States Trotting Association)
750 Michigan Ave., Columbus, OH 43215
(614) 224-2291
President .... Corwin Nixon
Executive V.P .... Fred Noe
Director of Public Relations .... John Pawlak

MEDIA

PERIODICALS

ESPN, The Magazine
19 E 34th St., 7th Floor
New York, NY 10016
(212) 515-1000
Editor in Chief .... John Papanek
Executive Editors .... Gary Hoenig, Steve Wulf
V.P., Publisher .... Michael Rooney
Public Relations Manager .... Kim Shapiro

Sports Illustrated
Time & Life Bldg., Rockefeller Center
New York, NY 10020
(212) 522-1212
President .... Michael J. Klingensmith
Managing Editor .... William Colson
Executive Editors . . B. Peter Carry, Rob Fleder, David Bauer

The Sporting News
10176 Corporate Square Dr., Suite 200
St. Louis, MO 63132
(314) 997-7111
Senior V.P./Editorial Director .... John D. Rawlings
President .... James H. Nuckols

The Sports Business Daily
120 West Morehead St., Ste. 250
Charlotte, NC 28202
(704) 973-1500
President .... Sal Schiliro
Editor .... Abe Madkour
Media Relations Mgr. .... Bill Magrath

USA Today
1000 Wilson Blvd., Arlington, VA 22229
(703) 276-3400
Owner .... Gannett Co.
President-Publisher .... Tom Curley
Managing Editor/Sports .... Monte Lorell

WIRE SERVICES

Associated Press
50 Rockefeller Plaza, New York, NY 10020
(212) 621-1630
Sports Editor .... Terry Taylor
Deputy Sports Editor .... Brian Friedman

United Press International
1510 H Street, Washington, DC 20005
(202) 898-8000
Sports Editor .... Ron Colbert

The Sports Network
95 James Way, Suite 107 & 109
Southampton, PA 18966
(215) 942-7890
President .... Mickey Charles
Director of Operations .... Phil Sokol
Managing Editor .... Jim Gillis

Sportsticker
600 Plaza Two, Harborside Financial Ctr., Jersey City, NJ 07311
(201) 309-1200
Vice President & General Manager .... Rick Alessandri
Exec. Director, News .... Jim Morganthaler

TV NETWORKS

ABC Sports
47 West 66th St., 13th Floor, New York, NY 10023
(212) 456-4867
President .... Steve Bornstein
Senior V.P., Production .... Steve Anderson
Exec. V.P./GM .... Brian McAndrews
Director of Information .... Mark Mandel

CBC Sports
P.O. Box 500, Station A 5H 100
Toronto, Ontario M5W 1E6
(416) 205-6523
Head of Sports .... Alan Clark
Sr. Executive Producer .... Joel Darling
Publicist .... Susan Procter

Classic Sports Network
300 Park Ave. South, 6th & 7th Floor, New York, NY 10010
(212) 529-8000
President .... Steve Greenberg
Senior V.P., Program Productions .... Douglas Warshaw
Director of Public Relations .... Gil Larsen

CBS Sports
51 West 52nd St., 25th Floor, New York, NY 10019
(212) 975-5230
President .... Sean McManus
Executive Producer .... Terry Ewert
Sr. V.P., Programming/Bus. Affairs .... Tony Petitti
V.P.,Public Relations .... Leslie Ann Wade

ESPN
ESPN Plaza, Bristol, CT 06010
(860) 585-2000
President-CEO .... Steve Bornstein
Sr. V.P., Programming .... John Wildhack
Sr. V.P. & Executive Editor .... John Walsh
Asst. Managing Editor/News Dir. .... Vince Doria
Director of Communications .... Mike Soltys

FOX Sports
10201 W. Pico Blvd., Los Angeles, CA 90035
(310) 369-1000
President .... David Hill
Exec. Producer .... Ed Goren
V.P., Media Relations (NYC) .... Vince Wladika

The Golf Channel
7580 Commerce Center Drive, Orlando, FL 32819
(407) 345-4653
President-CEO .... Joe Gibbs
V.P., Production .... Mike Whelan
Director of Public Relations .... Debra Sweeney

HBO Sports
1100 Ave. of the Americas, New York, NY 10036
(212) 512-1987
President-CEO .... Seth Abraham
V.P., Executive Producer .... Ross Greenburg
Sr. V.P., Programming .... Lou DiBella
Director of Publicity .... Ray Stallone

MTV Sports
1633 Broadway, 32nd Floor, New York, NY 10019
(212) 654-6177
Coordinating Producer .... Gregory Choa
Publicity Contact .... Sheryl Jones

NBC Sports
30 Rockefeller Plaza, New York, NY 10112
(212) 664-2160
Chairman .... Dick Ebersol
President .... Ken Schanzer
Executive Producer .... Tommy Roy
Director of Public Relations .... Ed Markey

Rainbow Sports
150 Crossways Park West
Woodbury, NY 11797
(516) 396-3000
President/CEO .... Josh Sapan
Sr. V.P., Programming & Ops. .... Mark Shuken
Vice President of Marketing .... Dan Ronayne

TSN-The Sports Network
2225 Shepherd Ave. East, Suite 100
Willowdale, Ontario, M2J-5C2
(416) 494-1212
Chairman & CEO .... Gordon Craig
President .... Rick Brace
Public Relations Manager .... David Rosenbloom

Turner Sports
One CNN Center
13th Floor, Atlanta, GA 30303
(404) 827-1735
President .... Dr. Harvey Schiller
Vice President, Production .... Mike Pearl
Sr. V.P., Programming .... Kevin O'Malley
V.P. of Public Relations .... Greg Hughes

Univision (Spanish)
9405 NW 41st St., Miami, FL 33178
(305) 471-3900
Sports Director .... Jorge Hidalgo
Publicity Coordinator .... Rosalyn Sariol

USA Network
1230 Ave. of the Americas, New York, NY 10020
(212) 408-9100
V.P., Production in Sports .... Gordon Beck
V.P., Sports Programming .... Kevin Landry
Dir. of Media Relations .... Jane Wallace

OLYMPICS

IOC
(International Olympic Committee)
Chateau de Vidy
CH-1007 Lausanne, Switzerland
TEL: 011-41-21-621-6111
President .... Juan Antonio Samaranch
Director General .... Francois Carrard
Secretary General .... Francoise Zweifel
Dir. of International Cooperation .... Fekrou Kidane
Director of Information .... Michele Verdier

2000 SUMMER GAMES

Sydney Olympic Organizing Committee
GPO Box 2000, Sydney, Australia NSW 2001
TEL: 011-61-29-297-2000
Time difference: 14 hours ahead of New York (EDT)
CEO ..... Sandy Hollway
M.P., President ..... Hon. Michael Knight
GM, Media ..... Milton Cockburn
(Games of XXVIIth Olympiad, Sept. 15-Oct. 1)

2002 WINTER GAMES

Salt Lake Olympic Organizing Committee
257 East, 200 South, Suite 600, Salt Lake City, UT 84111
(801) 322-2002
Chairman ..... Robert H. Garff
President & CEO ..... Frank Joklik
Sr. Vice Presidents ..... Dave Johnson, Gordon Crabtree
Senior V.P., Communications ..... Shelly Thomas
(XIXth Olympic Winter Games, Feb. 8-24)

2004 SUMMER GAMES

Athens Olympic Organizing Committee
Zappio, Megaro, Athens, Greece
TEL: 011-30-1-12004
Time difference: 7 hours ahead of New York (EDT)
Chairman ..... Stratis Stratigis
Managing Director ..... Kostas Bakouris
(XXVIIIth Olympic Summer Games, Aug. 13-29)

COA
(Canadian Olympic Association)
2380 Avenue Pierre Dupuy, Montreal, Quebec H3C-3R4
(514) 861-3371
CEO ..... Carol Anne Letheren
President ..... Bill Warren
IOC members ..... Carol Anne Letheren & Richard Pound
Media Relations ..... Lisa Beatty (Tor.) ..... Dina Bell (Ott.)

USOC
(United States Olympic Committee)
One Olympic Plaza, Colorado Springs, CO 80909
(719) 632-5551
President ..... Bill Hybl
Director ..... Dick Schultz
IOC members .Anita DeFrantz, James Easton & George Killian
Director of Public/Media Relations ..... Mike Moran

1999 PAN AMERICAN GAMES

Pan American Games Society
(Winnipeg 1999, Inc.)
500 Shaftesbury Blvd., Winninpeg, Manitoba R3P 0M1
(204) 985-1999
President-CEO ..... Don MacKenzie
Executive V.P. ..... Tim Ryan
Communications Manager ..... Dave Ulrich
(XIIIth Pan American Games, July 23-Aug. 8)

U.S. OLYMPICS TRAINING CENTERS

Colorado Springs Training Center
One Olympic Plaza, Colorado Springs, CO 80909
(719) 578-4500 ext. 5500
Sr. Dir. of Sport Services ..... Benita Fitzgerald-Mosley
Director ..... John Smyth

Lake Placid Training Center
421 Old Military Road, Lake Placid, NY 12946
(518) 523-2600
Director ..... Jack Favro
Operations Manager ..... Tracy Lamb

San Diego Training Center
2800 Olympic Parkway, Chula Vista, CA 91915
(619) 656-1500
Director ..... Patrice Milkovich

U.S. OLYMPIC ORGANIZATIONS

National Archery Association
One Olympic Plaza, Colorado Springs, CO 80909
(719) 578-4576
President ..... Jane Johnson
Executive Director ..... George Greenway
Media Contact ..... Bill Kellick

U.S. Badminton Association
One Olympic Plaza, Colorado Springs, CO 80909
(719) 578-4808
President ..... Steve Kearney
Executive Director ..... Holly Martin

USA Baseball
3400 E Camino Camtestre, Tucson, AZ 85716
(520) 327-9700
President ..... Mark Marquess
Executive Director & CEO ..... Daniel F. O'Brien
Dir. of Media Relations ..... George Doig

USA Basketball
5465 Mark Dabling Blvd., Colorado Springs, CO 80918
(719) 590-4800
President ..... Russell Granik
Executive Director ..... Warren S. Brown
Director of Public Relations ..... Craig Miller

U.S. Biathlon Association
29 Ethan Allen Ave.
Colchester, VT 05446
(802) 654-7833
President ..... Lyle Nelson
Exec. Director ..... Stephen Sands
Director of Summer Biathlon ..... Jerry Kokesh
Public Relations Contact ..... Mary Grace

U.S. Bobsled and Skeleton Federation
421 Old Military Road
Lake Placid, NY 12946
(518) 523-1842
President ..... Jim Morris
Executive Director ..... Matt Roy
Media/P.R. Director ..... Becky Matanic

USA Boxing
One Olympic Plaza, Colorado Springs, CO 80909
(719) 578-4506
President ..... Gary Tony
Executive Director ..... Chris Campbell
Dir. of Media/Public Relations ..... Shilpa Bakre

U.S. Canoe and Kayak Team
421 Old Military Rd., P.O. Box 789
Lake Placid, NY 12946
(518) 523-1855
Chairman ..... Helen Collins
Executive Director ..... Terry Kent
Public Relations Director ..... Lisa Fish

USA Curling
1100 Center Point Drive, Box 866
Stevens Point, WI 54481
(715) 344-1199
President ..... Clark Higgins
Executive Director ..... David Garber
Media Contact ..... Rick Patzke

USA Cycling
One Olympic Plaza
Colorado Springs, CO 80909
(719) 578-4581
President ..... Mike Plant
Executive Director & CEO ..... Lisa Voight
Managing Director ..... Evan Call
Managing Editors ..... Kip Kipmickler, Frank Stanley

United States Diving, Inc.
Pan American Plaza, Suite 430,
201 South Capitol Avenue, Indianapolis, IN 46225
(317) 237-5252
President .... Steve McFarland
Executive Director .... Todd Smith
Director of Communications .... Seth Pederson

U.S. Equestrian Team
Pottersville Road, Gladstone, NJ 07934
(908) 234-1251
President .... D.D. Matz
Executive Director .... Bob Standish
Director of Public Relations .... Marty Bauman
(508) 698-6810

U.S. Fencing Association
One Olympic Plaza, Colorado Springs, CO 80909
(719) 578-4511
President .... Donald Alperstien
Executive Director .... Michael Massik
Media Relations Coord. .... Coleen Walker-Mar

U.S. Field Hockey Assocation
One Olympic Plaza, Colorado Springs, CO 80909
(719) 578-4567
President .... Jenepher Shillingford
Executive Director .... Jane Betts
Director of Media/Public Relations .... TBA

U.S. Figure Skating Association
20 First Street, Colorado Springs, CO 80906
(719) 635-5200
President .... James W. Disbrow
Executive Director .... John Filefevre
Director of Events .... Heather Linhart

USA Gymnastics (Artistic & Rythmic)
Pan American Plaza, Suite 300
201 South Capitol Avenue, Indianapolis, IN 46225
(317) 237-5050
President-Exec. Director .... Robert V. Colarossi
Director of Public Relations .... Craig Bohnert

USA Hockey, Inc.
1775 Bob Johnson Dr., Colorado Springs, CO 80906
(719) 576-8724
President .... Walter Bush Jr.
Executive Director .... Dave Ogrean
Dir. of Public Relations & Media .... Darryl Seibel

United States Judo, Inc.
One Olympic Plaza, Suite 202
Colorado Springs, CO 80909
(719) 578-4730
President .... Yosh Uchida
Media Contact .... Clay Morgan

U.S. Luge Association
P.O. Box 651, Lake Placid, NY 12946
(518) 523-2071
President .... Doug Bateman
Executive Director .... Ron Rossi
Public Relations Manager .... Sandy Caligiore
Communications Manager .... Dmitry Feld

U.S. Modern Pentathlon Association
7330 San Pedro, Box 10 San Antonio, TX 78216
(210) 528-2999
President .... Dr. Risto Hurme
Executive Director .... Dean Billick

U.S. Rowing
Pan American Plaza, Suite 400
201 South Capitol Avenue, Indianapolis, IN 46225
(317) 237-5656
President .... Dave Vogel
Executive Director .... Frank Coyle
Media Contact .... Maureen Merhoff

U.S. Sailing Association
P.O. Box 1260, 15 Maritime Drive, Portsmouth, RI 02871
(401) 683-0800
President .... James P. Muldoon
Executive Director .... Terry D. Harper
Media Liaison .... Barby MacGowan
(401) 849-0220

U.S. Shooting Team
One Olympic Plaza, Colorado Springs, CO 80909
(719) 578-4670
Executive Director .... Robert Jursnick
Public Relations Director .... Michelle Petty

U.S. Ski & Snowboard Assoc.
P.O. Box 100, 1500 Kearns Blvd., Park City, UT 84060
(801) 649-9090
Chairman .... Jim McCarthy
CEO/President .... Bill Marolt
V.P. of Public Relations .... Tom Kelly
Public Information Manager .... Deborah Engen

U.S. Soccer Federation
U.S. Soccer House
1801-1811 South Prairie Ave., Chicago, IL 60616
(312) 808-1300
President .... Dr. S. Robert Contiguglia
Exec. Director/Sec. General .... Hank Steinbrecher
Director of Communications .... Jim Trecker

Amateur Softball Association
2801 N.E. 50th Street, Oklahoma City, OK 73111
(405) 424-5266
President .... Bill Humphrey
Executive Director .... Ron Radigonda
Director of Communications .... Ron Babb

U.S. Speedskating
P.O. Box 16157, Rocky River, OH 44116
(440) 899-0128
President .... Bill Cushman
Executive Director .... Katie Marquard
Public Relations Director .... TBA

U.S.A. Swimming
One Olympic Plaza, Colorado Springs, CO 80909
(719) 578-4578
President .... Carol Zaleski
Executive Director .... Chuck Weilgus
Director of Communications .... Charlie Snyder

U.S. Synchronized Swimming, Inc.
Pan American Plaza, Suite 901
201 South Capitol Avenue, Indianapolis, IN 46225
(317) 237-5700
President .... Laurette Longmire
Executive Director .... Debbie Hesse
Media Relations Director .... Brian Eaton

USA Table Tennis
One Olympic Plaza, Colorado Springs, CO 80909
(719) 578-4583
President .... James McQueen
Executive Director .... Kevin T. Carlon
Communications Director .... TBA

USA Team Handball
1903 Towers Ferry Rd., Ste. 230, Atlanta, GA 30339
(770) 956-7660
President .... Dennis Berkholtz
Executive Director .... TBA
Program Coordinator .... Danette Leininger

U.S. Tennis Association
70 West Red Oak Lane, White Plains, NY 10604
(914) 696-7000
President .... Harry Marmion
Executive Director .... Richard D. Fermin
Dir. of Communications .... Page Dahl Crosland

USA Track and Field
P.O. Box 120, Indianapolis, IN 46206
(317) 261-0500
President .... Patricia Rico
CEO .... Craig Masback
Press Information Director .... Pete Cava

USA Triathlon
3595 East Fountain Blvd., Ste. F-1, Colorado Springs, CO 80910
(719) 597-9090
President .... Johnathon Grinder
Executive Director .... Steven M. Locke
Deputy Director/Media Contact .... Tim Yount

USA Volleyball
3595 East Fountain Blvd., Suite I2
Colorado Springs, CO 80910
(719) 637-8300
President .... Rebecca Howard
Director of Communications .... Lorene Graves

United States Water Polo
1685 W. Uintah St., Colorado Springs, CO 80904
(719) 634-0699
President .... Brett Bernard
Executive Director .... Bruce Wigo
Dir. of Media/Public Relations .... Kyle Utsumi

USA Weightlifting
One Olympic Plaza, Colorado Springs, CO 80909
(719) 578-4508
President .... Brian Derwin
Exec. Dir./Comm. Dir. .... James J. Fox

USA Wrestling
6155 Lehman Drive, Colorado Springs, CO 80918
(719) 598-8181
President .... Bruce Baumgartner
Executive Director .... Jim Scherr
Dir. of Communications .... Gary Abbott

PAN AMERICAN SPORT ORGANIZATIONS

USA Bowling
5301 South 76th St., Greendale, WI 53129
(414) 421-9008
President .... Elaine Hagin
Executive Director .... Gerald Koenig

USA National Karate-Do Federation, Inc.
P.O. Box 77083, 8351 15th Ave. NW, Seattle, WA 98177-7083
(206) 440-8386
President .... Julius Thiry
Executive Director .... TBA
Public/Media Information .... Howard High

United States Raquetball Association
1685 West Uintah, Colorado Springs, CO 80904
(719) 635-5396
President .... Otto Dietrich
Executive Director .... Luke Saint Onge
Assoc. Exec. Dir/Comm. .... Linda Mojer

USA Roller Skating
P.O. Box 6579, Lincoln, NE 68506
(402) 483-7551
President .... Betty Ann Danna
Executive Director .... George Pickard
Information Director .... Jean Stanek

U.S. Squash Racquets Association
P.O. Box 1216 (23 Cynwyd Rd.)
Bala Cynwyd, PA 19004
(610) 667-4006
President .... E. Taylor Quick
Executive Director .... Craig W. Brand

U.S. Taekwondo Union
One Olympic Plaza, Colorado Springs, CO 80909
(719) 578-4632
President .... Dr. Sang Chul Lee
Executive Director .... R. Jay Warwick

American Water Ski Association
799 Overlook Drive, S.E., Winter Haven, FL 33884
(941) 324-4341
President .... Andrea Plough
Executive Director .... Steve McDermett
Director of Communications .... Greg Nixon

AFFILIATED ORGANIZATIONS

U.S. Orienteering Federation
P.O. Box 1444, Forest Park, GA 30298
(404) 363-2110
President .... Gary Kraght
Executive Director .... Robin Shannonhouse
Media Contact .... Jon Nash

USA Rugby
3595 East Fountain Blvd., Ste. M2
Colorado Springs, CO 80910
(719) 637-1022
President .... Anne Barry
Executive VP .... Neal Brendel
Communications Director .... Mia Shapiro

U.S. Sports Acrobatics Federation
P.O. Box 41356, Sacramento, CA 95841-0356
(916) 488-9499
President .... Tonya Case-Patterson

USA Trampoline & Tumbling
P.O. Box 306, Brownfield, TX 79316-0306
(806) 637-8670
President .... Paul H. Parilla
Executive Director .... Ann Sims

Underwater Society of America
164 N Bascom Ave., San Jose, CA 95128
(408) 286-8840
President/Exec. Dir. .... Michael Gower
Director of Public Relations .... Carol Rose

SOCCER

FIFA

(Federation Internationale de Football Assn.)
P.O. Box 85, 8030 Zurich, Switzerland
TEL: 011-41-1-384-9595
President .... Joao Havelange
General Secretary .... Joseph Blatter
Director of Communications .... Keith Cooper

MLS

Major League Soccer
110 E. 42nd Street, 10th Floor
New York, NY 10017
(212) 450-1200
Founder .... Alan I. Rothenberg
Commissioner .... Douglas G. Logan
Director of Communications .... Dan Courtemanche

Chicago Fire
311 W Superior St., #444
Chicago, IL 60610
(312) 705-7200
Investor/Operator .... Philip F. Anschutz
General Manager .... Peter Wilt
Media Relations .... Adam Low

Colorado Rapids
555 17th Street, Suite 3350, Denver, CO 80202
(303) 299-1570
Investor/Operator ....Philip F. Anschutz
General Manager ....Dan Counce
Media Relations ....Ben Grossman

Columbus Crew
77 E. Nationwide Blvd., Columbus, OH 43215
(614) 221-2739
Investor/Operator ....Lamar Hunt and Family
President/GM ....Jamey Rootes
Director of Media Relations ....Jeff Wuerth

Dallas Burn
2602 McKinney, Suite 200
Dallas, TX 75204
(214) 979-0303
Investor/Operator ....League-owned
President/GM ....Billy Hicks
Director of Media Relations ....Chris Ward

Kansas City Wizards
706 Broadway St., Suite 108
Kansas City, MO 64105
(816) 472-4625
Investor/Operator ....Lamar Hunt and Family
General Manager ....Doug Newman
Director of Media Relations ....Chris Taylor

Los Angeles Galaxy
1640 So. Sepulveda Blvd., Suite 114
Los Angeles, CA 90025
(310) 445-1260
Investor/Operator ....LA Soccer Partners
Chairman ....Mark Rapaport
General Manager ....Danny Villanueva Jr.
Director of Media Relations ....Luis Gonzalez

Miami Fusion
2200 Commercial Blvd., Ste. 104
Ft. Lauderdale, FL 33309
(954) 717-2200
Investor/Operator ....Kenneth Horowitz
V.P./General Manager ....Leandro Stillitano
Director of Media Relations ....Gabe Gabor

New England Revolution
Foxboro Stadium, Route 1
Foxboro, MA 02035
(508) 543-0350
Investor/Operator ....Robert Kraft and Family
General Manager ....Brian O'Donovan
Director of Media Relations ....Derek Aframe

New York/New Jersey MetroStars
One Harmon Plaza, 3rd Floor
Seacausus, NJ 07094
(201) 583-7000
Investor/Operator ....John Kluge and Stuart Subotnick
Vice President/GM ....Charlie Stillitano
Media Relations ....Richard Schneider

San Jose Clash
1265 El Camino Real, 2nd Floor
Santa Clara, CA 95050
(408) 241-9922
Investor/Operator ....League-owned
President/GM ....Peter Bridgwater
Director of Media Relations ....Rick La Plante

Tampa Bay Mutiny
1408 N. Westshore Blvd., Suite 1004
Tampa, FL 33607
(813) 288-0096
Investor/Operator ....League-owned
General Manager ....Nick Sakiewicz
Director of Media Relations ....Jim Henderson

Washington D.C. United
13832 Redskin Drive
Herndon, VA 20171
(703) 478-6600
Owner ....Washington Soccer, L.P.
President/GM ....Kevin Payne
Director of Media Relations ....Rick Lawes

Other Soccer

CONCACAF
(Confederation of North, Central American & Caribbean Association Football)
725 Fifth Ave., 17th Floor, New York, NY 10022
(212) 308-0044
President ....Jack Austin Warner
General Secretary ....Chuck Blazer
Press Officer ....Carlos Giron

U.S. Soccer
(United States Soccer Federation)
Soccer House, 1801-1811 South Prairie Ave.
Chicago, IL 60616
(312) 808-1300
President ....Dr. S. Robert Contiguglia
Exec. Director/Sec. General ....Hank Steinbrecher
Director of Communications ....Jim Trecker

CISL
(Continental Indoor Soccer League)
16027 Ventura Blvd., Suite 605, Encino, CA 91436
(818) 906-7627
Commissioner ....Ron Weinstein
League Counsel ....Dan Grigsby
Director of Media Relations ....Tim Sullivan

Member teams (11): Eastern Division— Dallas Sidekicks, Detroit Safari, Houston Hotshots, Indiana Twisters, Monterrey La Raza, Washington Warthogs. Western Division— Anaheim Splash, Arizona Sandsharks, Portland Pride, Sacramento Knights, Seattle SeaDogs.

NPSL
(National Professional Soccer League)
115 Dewalt Avenue NW, 5th Fl.
Canton, OH 44702
(330) 455-4625
Commissioner ....Steve M. Paxos
Director of Operations ....Paul Luchowski
Communications Coordinator ....Keri Alexander

Member teams (14): American Conference— Baltimore Spirit, Cincinnati Silverbacks, Cleveland Crunch, Harrisburg Heat and Philadelphia Kixx . National Conference—Buffalo Blizzard, Detroit Rockers, Edmonton Drillers, Kansas City Attack, Milwaukee Wave, St. Louis Ambush and Wichita Wings. Expansion Teams— Florida Thundercats and Montreal Impact.

USISL
(United Systems of Independent Soccer Leagues)
14497 N. Dale Mabry Hwy., Ste. 201
Tampa, FL 33618
(813) 963-3909
Commissioner ....Francisco Marcos
Administrative Manager ....Beverly Wright
Director of Public Relations ....Bryan Chenault

SWIMMING

FINA
(Federation Internationale de Natation Amateur)
9 ave de Beaumont, 1012 Lausanne, Switzerland
TEL: 011-4121-312-6602
President ....Mustapha Larfaoui
General Secretary ....Gunnar Werner

TENNIS

ATP Tour
(Association of Tennis Professionals)
201 ATP Tour Blvd., Ponte Vedra Beach, FL 32082
(904) 285-8000
Chief Executive Officer ....Mark Miles
V.P., Communications ....Pete Alfano
Dir. of Media Services ....Joe Lynch

ITF
(International Tennis Federation)
Palliser Rd., Barons Court
London, England W14 9EN
TEL: 011-44-171-381-8060
President ....Brian Tobin
Media Administrator ....Ian Barnes

World TeamTennis
445 North Wells, Suite 404, Chicago, IL 60610
(312) 245-5300
Chief Executive Officer ....Billie Jean King
Executive Director ....Ilana Kloss
Communications Director ....Tracey Donnelly

USTA
(United States Tennis Association)
70 West Red Oak Lane, White Plains, NY 10604
(914) 696-7000
President ....Harry Marmian
Executive Director ....Richard D. Fermin
Dir. of Communications ....Page Dahl Crosland

WTA Tour
(Women's Tennis Association)
1266 East Main St. 4th Floor, Stamford, CT 06902
(203) 978-1740
CEO ....Bartlett H. McGuire
COO ....Elizabeth Garger
Communications Director ....Joe Favorito

TRACK & FIELD

IAAF
(International Ameteur Athletics Federation)
17 Rue Princesse Florestine
BP 359, MC-98007, Monaco Cedex
TEL: 011-377-10-88-88
President ....Primo Nebiolo
General Secretary ....Istvan Gyulai
Director of Information ....Giorgio Reinei

AAU
(Amateur Athletic Union)
c/o Walt Disney World Resorts, P.O. Box 10000, Lake Buena Vista, FL 32830-1000
(407) 934-7200
President ....Bobby Dodd
P.R./Communications ....Deanne Hoover

USA Track & Field
P.O. Box 120
Indianapolis, IN 46206
(317) 261-0500
President ....Patricia Rico
CEO ....Craig Masbak
Director of Information ....Pete Cava

YACHTING

1999-2000 America's Cup

New Zealand Defense Committee
(Royal New Zealand Yacht Squadron)
P.O. Box 1927, Auckland, New Zealand
TEL: 011-64-9-357-6712
Time difference: 16 hours ahead of New York (EDT)
Exec. Director & Contact ....Alan Sefton
(Next America's Cup defense scheduled to begin in Oct. 1999 and run through Feb. 2000, off the coast of Auckland.)

MISCELLANEOUS

All-American Soap Box Derby
P.O. Box 7225, Akron, OH 44306
(330) 733-8723
President .......................F.A. Wahl
Chairman of the Board ....John Piscitelli
Executive Director ....Anthony DeLuca
Public Relations Director ....Bob Troyer

American Powerboating Association
P.O. Box 377, Eastpointe, MI 48021
(810) 773-9700
President ....Steven David
Executive Director ....Gloria Urbin

Association of Surfing Professionals
P.O. Box 309, Huntingon Beach, CA 92648
(949) 851-2774
President ....Gary Linden
Executive Director ....Graham Stapelberg

BASS, Inc.
(Bass Anglers Sportsmen Society)
5845 Carmichael Road, Mongomery, AL 36117
(334) 272-9530
CEO ....Helen Sevier
Publicity Director ....Ann Lewis

Iditarod Trail Committee
P.O. Box 870800, Wasilla, AK 99687
(907) 376-5155
Executive Director ....Stan Hooley
Race Director ....Joanne Potts

International Game Fish Association
1301 East Atlantic Blvd., Pompano Beach, FL 33060
(954) 941-3474
Chairman ....George Matthews
President ....Mike Leach
Editor ....Ray Crawford

Little League Baseball Incorporated
P.O. Box 3485, Williamsport, PA 17701
(717) 326-1921
CEO-President ....Steven Keener
Director of Communications ....Dennis Sullivan
Dir., Publications/Media Relations ....Lance Van Auken

National Association for Girls and Women in Sport
1900 Association Drive, Reston, VA 20191
(703) 476-3452
Executive Director ....Diana Everett
President ....Donna Pastore

National Lacrosse League
237 Main St., Ste 1500, Buffalo, NY 14203
(716) 855-1NLL
Commissioner .... John Livsey Jr.
V.P. of Public Relations .... Bruce Wawrzyniak
Member teams (7): Baltimore, Buffalo, Ontario, Philadelphia, Rochester (N.Y.), Syracuse (N.Y.) and Long Island (N.Y.).

National Rifle Assocation
11250 Waples Mill Road, Fairfax, VA 22030
(703) 267-1000
Executive VP .... Wayne LaPierre
Public Affairs Director .... Bill Powers

National Sports Foundation
P.O. Box 888886, Atlanta, GA 30356
(770) 698-8600
Executive Director .... Ed Harris

NORBA
(National Off-Road Bicycle Association)
One Olympic Plaza, Colorado Springs, CO 80909
(719) 578-4717
Sr. Managing Director .... Philip M. Milburn
Director of Competition .... Eric Moore

Professional Billiards Tour, Inc.
4412 Commercial Way, Spring Hill, FL 34606
(352) 596-7808
CEO .... Don Mackey

Professional Rodeo Cowboys Association
101 Pro Rodeo Drive, Colorado Springs, CO 80919
(719) 593-8840
Commissioner .... Steve Hatchell
Director of Public Relations .... Steve Fleming

Roller Hockey International
3773 Cherry Creek N Drive, Ste. 575, Denver, CO 80209
(303) 331-7960
Commissioner .... Ralph Backstrom
CEO .... Bernie Mullin
Media Relations .... Mark Ehrhart

Special Olympics
1325 G St. NW Suite 500, Washington, DC 20005
(202) 628-3630
Founder .... Eunice Kennedy Shriver
COB .... Sargent Shriver
COO .... Kim Elliott
Sr. Media Relations Manager .... Mike Janes

U.S. Polo Association
4059 Iron Works Pkwy., Ste. 1, Lexington, KY 40511
(606) 255-0593
Executive Director .... George Alexander Jr.

U.S. Pro Beach Volleyball
P.O. Box 57, Huntington Beach, CA 92648
(714) 536-4900
President .... Gary Pope

U.S. Windsurfing
P.O. Box 978, Hood River, OR 97031
(541) 386-8708
President .... Bill Collins
Executive Director .... Holly Macpherson

Wheelchair Sports USA
3595 East Fountain Blvd., Suite L-1
Colorado Springs, CO 80910
(719) 574-1150
Chairman .... Paul DePace
Executive Director .... Patricia Shepherd

Commissioners and Presidents

Chief Executives of Established Major Sports Organizations since 1876

Major League Baseball

Commissioner	Tenure
Kenesaw Mountain Landis*	1920-44
Albert (Happy) Chandler	1945-51
Ford Frick	1951-65
William Eckert	1965-68
Bowie Kuhn	1969-84
Peter Ueberroth	1984-89
A. Bartlett Giamatti*	1989
Fay Vincent	1989-92
Bud Selig†	1998—

*Died in office.
†Served as interim commissioner from 1992-98.

National League

President	Tenure
Morgan G. Bulkeley	1876
William A. Hulbert*	1877-82
A.G. Mills	1883-84
Nicholas Young	1885-1902
Henry Pulliam*	1903-09
Thomas J. Lynch	1910-13
John K. Tener	1914-18
John A. Heydler	1918-34
Ford Frick	1935-51
Warren Giles	1951-69
Charles (Chub) Feeney	1970-86
A. Bartlett Giamatti	1987-89
Bill White	1989-94
Leonard Coleman	1994—

*Died in office.

American League

President	Tenure
Bancroft (Ban) Johnson	1901-27
Ernest Barnard*	1927-31
William Harridge	1931-59
Joe Cronin	1959-73
Lee McPhail	1974-83
Bobby Brown	1984-94
Gene Budig	1994—

*Died in office.

NBA

Commissioner	Tenure
Maurice Podoloff	1949-63
Walter Kennedy	1963-75
Larry O'Brien	1975-84
David Stern	1984—

NFL

President	Tenure
Jim Thorpe	1920
Joe Carr	1921-39
Carl Storck	1939-41
Commissioner	
Elmer Layden	1941-46
Bert Bell*	1946-59
Austin Gunsel	1959-60
Pete Rozelle	1960-89
Paul Tagliabue	1989—

*Died in office.

NHL

President	Tenure
Frank Calder*	1917-43
Red Dutton	1943-46
Clarence Campbell	1946-77
John Ziegler	1977-92
Gil Stein	1992-93
Commissioner	
Gary Bettman	1993—

*Died in office.

NCAA

Executive Director	Tenure
Walter Byers	1951-88
Dick Schultz	1988-93
Cedric Dempsey	1993—

IOC

President	Tenure
Demetrius Vikelas, Greece	1894-96
Baron Pierre de Coubertin, France	1896-1925
Count Henri de Baillet-Latour, Belgium	1925-42
Vacant	1942-46
J. Sigfried Edstrom, Sweden	1946-52
Avery Brundage, USA	1952-72
Lord Michael Killanin, Ireland	1972-80
Juan Antonio Samaranch, Spain	1980—

Olympics

Fifteen-year-old **Tara Lipinski**, who would score an upset win over teammate Michelle Kwan in the ladies figure skating finals, reacts after finishing her free skate program.

AP/Wide World Photos

Street of Gold

Picabo Street showed what she's made of in Nagano, winning gold on her rebuilt knee.

by
Jack Edwards

The season shouldn't be remembered for the crash which could have taken her life. It should be remembered for the legendary comeback.

Fourteen months before she was in the starting gate in Japan, Picabo Street was on the operating table at the Steadman Hawkins Clinic in Vail, having her left knee reconstructed. She had blown-out two ligaments, torn some cartilage, and damaged a bone in a training slam in December of '97.

Eleven days before she was in the starting gate in Japan, Street was unconscious, rag-dolling as she slid to a stop on a Swedish slope. She had been the victim of a freak binding release at 75 miles per hour. After all that, she did what Jerry Rice wanted to do: she made the comeback which few thought could be done, and stood to savor her triumph. (Rice had attempted to come back very quickly from a blown ACL, and–on a knee which needed a brace–fractured his kneecap).

Street's victory came in the closest race in Olympic history. She won the women's super G by one one-hundredth of a second, the smallest increment of time used in the sport. The top 11 racers finished within six-tenths of a second of one another.

What Street did probably never will be done again–at least not until the next breakthrough in sports medicine. No one comes back one year and two months after a career-threatening wreck to win on the World Cup, much less in that super-heated crucible of the Olympics–where the briefest hesitation twists psyches and the smallest mistakes shatter poise–these races come just once or twice in a career.

Street has The Gift. It is likely that many people have it, but only an infinitesimally small group of them realize it, act on it, and dare to visualize a reality that is on the far side of reason. In the Olympic super G, she took that gift way wide of the "quad" turn, a series of four gates which drew

---

Jack Edwards was in Nagano for ESPN

AP/Wide World Photos

The surprise winner of the women's super G at Nagano, America's **Picabo Street** rips around a gate in her gold medal run. It was the first time that Street, who wore longer downhill skis in the race, had ever really skied the course at Hakuba. Her only other time on the mountain was when she skied down riding on the back of a coach while her knee was still healing.

the racers around a near-hairpin turn. She could have panicked when she got out of her desired line, losing impetus. Instead, she channeled her anger into positive energy and tore off for the bottom of the hill, not caring what was behind her. Her time looked good - but she had to wait, as the big guns all took their shots.

Michaela Dorfmeister of Austria gave Street the biggest scare. Her splits were good enough to win. Where that hundredth got away from Dorfmeister–or where Street found it...is the stuff of which legend is made.

And Street is a legend. She won in Nagano, neither by luck nor by fate but by the strength of her character.

* * * * *

Just 30 days later, in Switzerland, Street got a little bit back coming off a jump in the final downhill of the season. She had a choice - to hit the net face-first at 60 miles per hour, or to put her feet in there. She went-in feet first. She snapped her left femur and tore the ACL in her right knee.

There will be no 1999 season for Street. At this writing, she is training at least to give herself the option of coming back for 2000–and the Salt Lake games of 2002. If she does race again, it'll be for herself. Street–two times a World Cup season downhill champion, a world champion, an Olympic silver–and gold-medalist, the winningest speed-event racer (male or female) in North American history–has nothing left to prove. ■

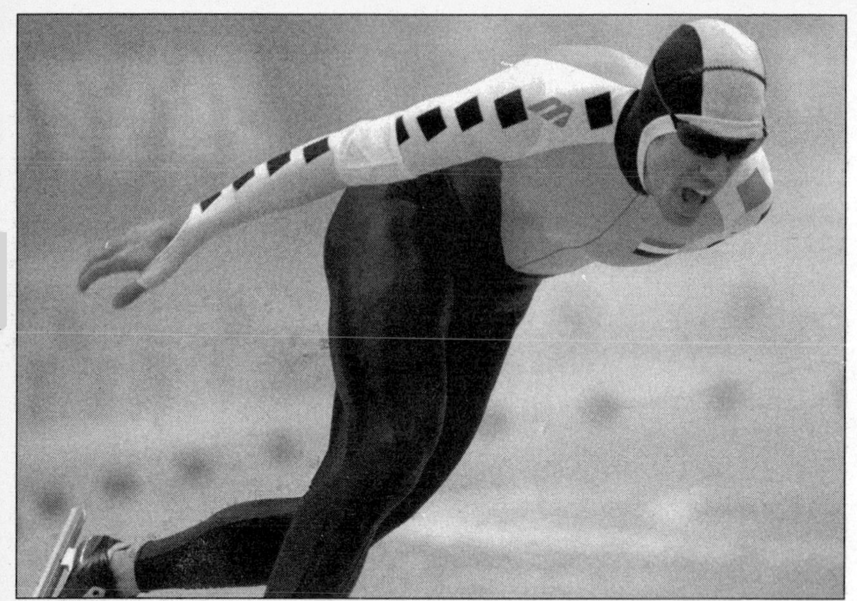

AP/Wide World Photos

Dutch speedskater **Gianni Romme** set world records in two events in Nagano. Technological advances have caused controversy and changed speedskating forever. The tiny rubber racing stripes on the skaters' skin-tight suits, as seen on Romme's hood, seem insignificant at first glance. But, along with the new clap skates, these racing "stripes", which cut down on air resistance, are believed to have contributed to record times at Nagano.

Jack Edwards' Top Ten Olympic Moments of the Year

10. Norway's **Bjorn Dählie adds to his legend** with his winter games-record eighth career Olympic gold medal and 12th medal overall in a come-from-behind victory in the 50km. Dählie, solidifying his place as the greatest cross-country skier of his time, won a gold in the 10km and the 40km relay and a silver in the 15km race earlier in Nagano.

9. Americans **Eric Bergoust and Nikki Stone win** Freestyle Aerials gold medals. Bergoust scores a world record 255.64 points with two quadruple twisting triple flips while Stone, the only woman in the competition to do a triple somersault, edges out China's Xu Nannan.

8. **Netherlands dominates** speed skating competition winning five out of 10 gold medals and 11 medals overall. Dutch star Gianni Romme sets world records in the 5km and 10km events with the controversial new striped racing suits and clap skates.

7. Canadian snowboarder **Ross Rebagliati wins** his sport's first gold medal in the Giant Slalom, then tests positive for marijuana. Rebagliati claims he is a victim of second-hand smoke and after several days of legal wrangling Rebagliati retains his medal and gains a guest spot on Jay Leno.

6. Tiny **Tara Lipinski** out jumps fellow American **Michelle Kwan** in women's figure skating. Lipinski,

AP/Wide World Photos

U.S. Olympic women's hockey teammates **Cammi Granato**, left, and **Karyn Bye** show off the gold medals they won after the U.S. defeated Canada, 3-1, in the tournament's gold medal game.

15, becomes the youngest Olympic figure skating champion in history topping Kwan, the favorite. It is the first 1-2 finish for the United States in women's figure skating since 1956.

5. The **U.S. women's hockey team wins** the sport's inaugural gold medal with a 3-1 victory over archrival Canada. The Americans get 22 saves and superb play from goaltender Sarah Tueting in the gold medal game.

4. **Hermann Maier** comes back from an epic crash in downhill to win super G gold. Austria's "Herminator", the downhill favorite, submitted his entry for a new "agony of defeat" video with his spectacular wipe out on a sharp left turn early in the course. A battered and bruised Maier would bounce back to win the super G three days later and the giant slalom four days after that for his second gold medal.

3. Banzai! **Japanese ski jumpers win** the team gold in the large hill competition. Masahiko Harada, who caved in to pressure at Lillehammer to cost Japan the gold, comes up big along with his teammates as host nation Japan captured the gold in front of 50,000 delirious fans.

2. **Czech Republic beats the NHL** star-laden teams from the U.S., Canada and Russia for the gold medal. Czech goaltender Dominik Hasek dominates opposing goalscorers and Petr Svoboda nets the game-winner against the Russians for the gold.

1. **Picabo Street wins** the women's super G by 0.01 seconds, the closest Alpine race in Olympic history. Street, wearing longer downhill skis no less, completes her long comeback attacking the course to take gold in an event that is not among her best. ■

INSIDE THE NUMBERS

by

Andrew Villa, Jim Samia and Craig Wachs

SEEING DOUBLE

Tara Lipinski and Michelle Kwan gave the U.S. two spots on the women's figure skating medal platform for the fourth time in Winter Olympic history. The only other countries to have double medal winners in women's figure skating were Great Britain in 1906 and Sweden in 1920. Below is a list of the U.S. doubles.

Year	Skaters
1998	T. Lipinski (gold)
	M. Kwan (silver)
1992	K. Yamaguchi (gold)
	N. Kerrigan (bronze)
1960	C. Heiss (gold)
	B. Roles (bronze)
1956	T. Albright (gold)
	C. Heiss (silver)

MEDAL HAUL

The U.S. Olympic team matched its best Winter Olympics performance ever, set at Lillehammer, at the Games in Nagano. Here is a list of the best medal performances for the U.S. in the Winter Games.

Year	Host	Totals	Golds
1998	Nagano	13	6
1994	Lillehammer	13	6
1980	Lake Placid	12	6
1932	Lake Placid	12	6
1992	Albertville	11	5
1952	Oslo	11	4

NAGANOPE!

Heading into the Nagano Olympics, offense was considered the biggest strength of the U.S. men's hockey team. In the end, it turned out to be their biggest weakness. The U.S. forwards, many of whom were among the NHL's leading scorers at the time, couldn't score at all in the Olympics.

Forward	NHL goals	Olympic goals
John LeClair	38	0
Keith Tkachuk	35	0
Tony Amonte	20	0
Doug Weight	18	0
J. Langenbrunner	17	0
Jeremy Roenick	16	0
Bill Guerin	12	0

GOLD TO DUST

Since winning Olympic gold in 1980 the best showing in the next five Olympics for the U.S. hockey team was in 1992 when they finished fourth, just missing a medal. It's been downright discouraging the rest of the time.

Year	Record	Finish
1998	1-3-0	6th
1994	1-1-3	8th
1992	5-2-1	4th
1988	2-3-0	7th
1984	1-2-2	7th

Note: The 1992 team was 4-0-1 prior to the medal round. ■

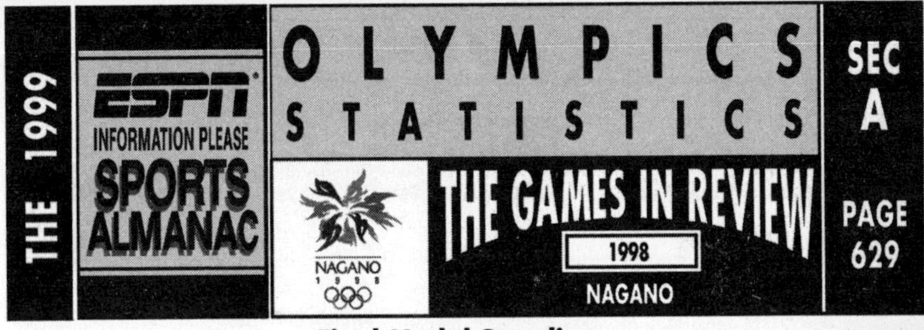

THE 1999
ESPN
INFORMATION PLEASE
SPORTS
ALMANAC
OLYMPICS
STATISTICS
NAGANO
1998
THE GAMES IN REVIEW
1998
NAGANO
SEC
A
PAGE
629

Final Medal Standings

National Medal Standings are not recognized by the IOC. The unofficial point totals are based on three points for every gold medal, two for each silver and one for each bronze.

		G	S	B	Medals	Points
1	Germany	12	9	8	29	62
2	Norway	10	10	5	25	55
3	Russia	9	6	3	18	42
4	Canada	6	5	4	15	32
5	Austria	3	5	9	17	28
	United States	6	3	4	13	28
7	Netherlands	5	4	2	11	25
8	Japan	5	1	4	10	21
9	Finland	2	4	6	12	20
	Italy	2	6	2	10	20
11	China	0	6	2	8	14
12	France	2	1	5	8	13
	Switzerland	2	2	3	7	13
	South Korea	3	1	2	6	13
15	Czech Republic	1	1	1	3	6
16	Sweden	0	2	1	3	5
17	Bulgaria	1	0	0	1	3
18	Denmark	0	1	0	1	2
	Ukraine	0	1	0	1	2
	Belarus	0	0	2	2	2
	Kazakhstan	0	0	2	2	2
22	Australia	0	0	1	1	1
	Belgium	0	0	1	1	1
	Great Britain	0	0	1	1	1

1994 Lillehammer Top 10: 1. **Norway** (26 medals, 57 points); 2. **Russia** (23 medals, 53 pts.); 3. **Germany** (24 medals, 49 pts.); 4. **Italy** (20 medals, 39 pts.); 5. **United States** (13 medals, 30 pts.); 6. **Canada** (13 medals, 25 pts.); 7. **Switzerland** (9 medals, 19 pts.); 8. **Austria** (9 medals, 16 pts.); 9. **South Korea** (6 medals, 15 pts.); 10. **Japan** (5 medals, 9 pts.).

Leading Medal Winners

Number of medals won on the left; gold, silver and bronze breakdown on right. USA medalists in **bold** type.

MEN

No		Sport	G-S-B
4	Bjorn Dählie, NOR	Cross-country	3-1-0
3	Kazuyoshi Funaki, JPN	Ski Jumping	2-1-0
3	Rintje Ritsma, NET	Sp. Skating	0-1-2
3	Mika Myllylae, FIN	Cross-country	1-0-2
2	Gianni Romme, NET	Sp. Skating	2-0-0
2	Thomas Alsgaard, NOR	Cross-country	2-0-0
2	Hermann Maier, AUT	Alpine	2-0-0
2	Bjarte Engen Vik, NOR	Nordic Comb.	2-0-0
2	Ids Postma, NET	Sp. Skating	1-1-0
2	Jani Soininen, FIN	Ski Jumping	1-1-0
2	Erling Jevne, NOR	Cross-country	1-1-0
2	Ole Bjoerndalen, NOR	Biathlon	1-1-0
2	Halvard Hanevold, NOR	Biathlon	1-1-0
2	Kim Dong Sung, KOR	ST Sp. Skating	1-1-0
2	Christoph Langen, GER	Bobsled	1-0-1
2	Markus Zimmerman, GER	Bobsled	1-0-1
2	Eric Bedard, CAN	ST Sp. Skating	1-0-1
2	Masahiko Harada, JPN	Ski Jumping	1-0-1
2	Hiroyasu Shimizu, JPN	Sp. Skating	1-0-1
2	Lasse Kjus, NOR	Alpine	0-2-0
2	Samppa Lajunen, FIN	Nordic Comb.	0-2-0
2	Silvio Fauner, ITA	Cross-country	0-1-1
2	Li Jiajun, CHN	ST Sp. Skating	0-1-1
2	An Yulong, CHN	ST Sp. Skating	0-1-1
2	Andreas Widhoelzl, AUT	Ski Jumping	0-0-2

WOMEN

No		Sport	G-S-B
5	Larissa Lazutina, RUS	Cross-country	3-1-1
3	Olga Danilova, RUS	Cross-country	2-1-0
3	Katja Seizinger, GER	Alpine	2-0-1
3	Lee-Kyung Chun, KOR	ST Sp. Skating	2-0-1
3	G. Niemann-Stirnemann, GER	Sp. Skating	1-2-0
3	Ursula Disl, GER	Biathlon	1-1-1
3	Yang S. Yang, CHN	ST Sp. Skating	0-3-0
2	Marianne Timmer, NET	Sp. Skating	2-0-0
2	Galina Kukleva, GER	Biathlon	1-1-0
2	Deborah Compagnoni, ITA	Alpine	1-1-0
2	Claudia Pechstein, GER	Sp. Skating	1-1-0
2	Hilde Gerg, GER	Alpine	1-0-1
2	Catriona LeMay Doan, CAN	Sp. Skating	1-0-1
2	Katrin Apel, GER	Biathlon	1-0-1
2	Annie Perreault, CAN	ST Sp. Skating	1-0-1
2	Katerina Neumannova, CZR	Cross-country	0-1-1
2	Bente Martinsen, NOR	Cross-country	0-1-1
2	Anita Moen-Guidon, NOR	Cross-country	0-1-1
2	**Chris Witty, USA**	Sp. Skating	0-1-1
2	Stefania Belmondo, ITA	Cross-country	0-1-1
2	Alexandra Meissnitzer, AUT	Alpine	0-1-1

Medal Sports

Medal winners in individual sports contested at Nagano, Japan from Feb. 7-22, 1998.

ALPINE SKIING

Medal breakdown (10 events): **11 medals**— Austria (3-4-4); **Six**— Germany (3-1-2); **Four**— Norway (1-3-0); **Two**— Italy (1-1-0), France (1-0-1) and Switzerland (0-1-1); **One**— United States (1-0-0), Sweden (0-1-0) and Australia (0-0-1).

MEN

Downhill

		Time
1	Jean-Luc Cretier, FRA	1:50.11
2	Lasse Kjus, NOR	1:50.51
3	Hannes Trinkl, AUT	1:50.63

Top 10 USA: 9th, Kyle Rasmussen (1:51.09).

Slalom

		Time
1	Hans-Petter Buraas, NOR	1:49.31
2	Ole Christian Furuseth, NOR	1:50.64
3	Thomas Sykora, AUT	1:50.68

Best USA: 15th, Matthew Grosjean (1:52.56).

Giant Slalom

		Time
1	Hermann Maier, AUT	2:38.51
2	Stefan Eberharter, AUT	2:39.36
3	Michael Von Gruenigen, SWI	2:39.69

Best USA: 20th, Daron Rahlves (2:43.59).

Super G

		Time
1	Hermann Maier, AUT	1:34.82
2	Didier Cuche, SWI	1:35.43
2	Hans Knauss, AUT	1:35.43

Top 10 USA: 7th, Daron Rahlves (1:35.96); 8th, Tommy Moe (1:35.97).

Combined

		DH	SL	Time
1	Mario Reiter, AUT	5th	1st	3:08.06
2	Lasse Kjus, NOR	2nd	2nd	3:08.65
3	Christian Mayer, AUT	3rd	4th	3:10.11

Best USA: No American finished in the top 15.

WOMEN

Downhill

		Time
1	Katja Seizinger, GER	1:28.89
2	Pernilla Wiberg, SWE	1:29.18
3	Florence Masnada, FRA	1:29.37

Top 10 USA: 6th, Picabo Street (1:29.54).

Slalom

		Time
1	Hilde Gerg, GER	1:32.40
2	Deborah Compagnoni, ITA	1:32.46
3	Zali Steggall, AUS	1:32.67

Best USA: 13th, Julie M.J. Parisien (1:36.35).

Giant Slalom

		Time
1	Deborah Compagnoni, ITA	2:50.59
2	Alexandra Meissnitzer, AUT	2:52.39
3	Katja Seizinger, GER	2:52.61

Best USA: 28th, Julie M.J. Parisien (3:02.78).

Super G

		Time
1	Picabo Street, USA	1:18.02
2	Michaela Dorfmeister, AUT	1:18.03
3	Alexandra Meissnitzer, AUT	1:18.09

Next best USA: 29th, Kathleen Monahan (1:20.25).

Combined

		DH	SL	Time
1	Katja Seizinger, GER	1st	5th	2:40.74
2	Martina Ertl, GER	2nd	1st	2:40.92
3	Hilde Gerg, GER	5th	2nd	2:41.50

Top 10 USA: 7th, Caroline Lalive (9th, 10th; 2:44.76); 9th, Alexandra Shaffer (14th, 7th; 2:45.24).

FIGURE SKATING

All four events consist of a short program (two minutes and 40 seconds) and a long program (4:30 for men and 4:00 for women). Skaters are ranked on technical merit and artistic impression in a consensus vote by nine judges. Factored placements (FP) are determined by multiplying the final short program rank by 0.5 and then adding that number to the final long program.

Medal breakdown (4 events): **Five medals**— Russia (3-2-0); **Two**— United States (1-1-0) and France (0-0-2); **One**— Canada (0-1-0), China (0-0-1) and Germany (0-0-1).

MEN

		FP
1	Ilia Kulik, RUS	1.5
2	Elvis Stojko, CAN	4.0
3	Philippe Candeloro, FRA	4.5

Top 10 USA: 4th, Todd Eldredge (5.5); 7th, Michael Weiss (11.5).

PAIRS

		FP
1	Oksana Kazakova & Artur Dmitriev, RUS	1.5
2	Elena Berezhnaya & Anton Sikharulidze, RUS	3.5
3	Mandy Wotzel & Ingo Steuer, GER	4.0

Top 10 USA: 4th, Kyoko Ina & Jason Dungjen (6.0); 8th, Jenni Meno & Todd Sand (12.0).

WOMEN

		FP
1	Tara Lipinski, USA	2.0
2	Michelle Kwan, USA	2.5
3	Lu Chen, CHN	5.0

Next best USA: 17th, Nicole Bobek (25.5).

ICE DANCING

		FP
1	Pasha Grishuk & Yevgeny Platov, RUS	2.0
2	Anjelika Krylova & Oleg Ovsyannikov, RUS	4.0
3	Marina Anissina & Gwendal Peizerat, FRA	7.0

Top 10 USA: 7th, Elizabeth Punsalan & Jerod Swallow (14.0).

BIATHLON

Cross-country (any style) and rifle shooting (.22 caliber, small-bore, standing and prone). MT indicates missed targets

Medal breakdown (6 events): **Five medals**— Norway (2-2-1) and Germany (2-1-2); **Three**— Russia (1-1-1); **One**— Bulgaria (1-0-0), Italy (0-1-0), Ukraine (0-1-0), Belarus (0-0-1) and Finland (0-0-1).

MEN

10 kilometers

		MT	Time
1	Ole Einar Bjoerndalen, NOR	0	27:16.2
2	Frode Andresen, NOR	2	28:17.8
3	Ville Raikkonen, FIN	1	28:21.7

Best USA: 49th, Dan Westover (1 MT; 30:39.5).

20 kilometers

		MT	Time
1	Halvard Hanevold, NOR	1	56:16.4
2	Pier Alberto Carrara, ITA	0	56:21.9
3	Aleksei Aidarov, BLR	1	56:46.5

Best USA: 42nd, Jay Hakkinen (4 MTs; 1:02:10.3).

4 x 7.5-km Relay

		MT	Time
1	Germany	6	1:21:36.2
2	Norway	7	1:21:56.3
3	Russia	7	1:22:19.3

GER— Ricco Gross, Peter Sendel, Sven Fischer, Frank Luck; **NOR**— Egil Gjelland, Halvard Hanevold, Dag Bjoerndalen, Ole Einar Bjoerndalen; **RUS**— Pavel Mouslimov, Vladimir Dratschev, Serguei Tarassov, Victor Maigourov.

USA entry: 17th; Jay Hakkinen, Dan Westover, Andrew Erickson, Robert Rosser (15 MTs; 1:28:13.9).

WOMEN

7.5 kilometers

		MT	Time
1	Galina Koukleva, RUS	1	23:08.0
2	Ursula Disl, GER	1	23:08.7
3	Katrin Apel, GER	1	23:32.4

Best USA: 33rd, Kristina Sabasteanski (1 MT; 25:12.2).

15 kilometers

		MT	Time
1	Ekaterina Dafovska, BUL	1	54:52.0
2	Elena Petrova, UKR	1	55:09.8
3	Ursula Disl, GER	1	55:17.9

Best USA: 55th, Stacey Ann Wooley (2 MTs; 1:03:57.3); 56th, Kara Salmela (5 MTs; 1:04:43.7).

4 x 7.5-km Relay

		MT	Time
1	Germany	11	1:40:13.6
2	Russia	9	1:40:25.2
3	Norway	10	1:40:37.3

GER— Ursula Disl, Martina Zellner, Katrin Apel, Petra Behle; **RUS**— Olga Melnik, Galina Koukleva, Albina Akhatova, Olga Romasko; **NOR**— Ann-Elen Skjelbreid, Annette Sikveland, Margit Gunn Andreassen, Liv Grete Skjelbreid.

USA entry: 15th, Ntala Skinner, Stacey Ann Wooley, Kara Salmela, Kristina Sabasteanski (12 MTs; 1:48:30.2).

CROSS-COUNTRY SKIING

There are two techniques in cross-country: classical (diagonal stride) and freestyle (skating style). The Freestyle Pursuit consists of a classical race (10 km for men, 5 km for women) followed the next day by a freestyle race (15 km for men, 10 km for women). The starting order in the Freestyle Pursuit is determined by the finish of the classical leg. Relays consist of two classical and two freestyle legs.

Medal breakdown (10 events): **Nine medals**— Norway (4-3-2); **Eight**— Russia (5-2-1); **Four**— Italy (0-2-2); **Three**— Finland (1-0-2); **Two**— Austria (0-1-1) and Czech Republic (0-1-1); **One**— Sweden (0-1-0) and Kazakhstan (0-0-1).

MEN

10-km Classical

		Time
1	Bjorn Dählie, NOR	27:24.5
2	Markus Gandler, AUT	27:32.5
3	Mika Myllylae, FIN	27:40.1

Best USA: 41st, John Bauer (29:58.4); 43rd, Patrick Weaver (30:04.4).

15-km Freestyle Pursuit

		Time
1	Thomas Alsgaard, NOR	1:07:01.7
2	Bjorn Dählie, NOR	1:07:02.8
3	Vladimir Smirnov, KAZ	1:07:31.5

Best USA: 40th, Patrick Weaver (1:12:31.1).

30-km Classical

		Time
1	Mika Myllylae, FIN	1:33:55.8
2	Erling Jevne, NOR	1:35:27.1
3	Silvio Fauner, ITA	1:36:08.5

Best USA: 37th, Justin Wadsworth (1:42:21.1).

50-km Freestyle

		Time
1	Bjorn Dählie, NOR	2:05:08.2
2	Niklas Jonsson, SWE	2:05:16.3
3	Christian Hoffmann, AUT	2:06:01.8

Best USA: 35th, Marcus Nash (2:17:37.8).

4 x 10-km Mixed Relay

		Time
1	Norway	1:40:55.7
2	Italy	1:40:55.9
3	Finland	1:42:15.5

NOR— Sture Sivertsen, Erling Jevne, Bjorn Dählie, Thomas Alsgaard; **ITA**— Marco Albarello, Fulvio Valbusa, Fabio Maj, Silvio Fauner; **FIN**— Harri Kirvesniemi, Mika Myllylae, Sami Repo, Jari Isometsae.

USA entry: 17th; Marcus Nash, John Bauer, Patrick Weaver, Justin Wadsworth (1:48:16.4).

WOMEN

5-km Classical

		Time
1	Larissa Lazutina, RUS	17:37.9
2	Katerina Neumannova, CZE	17:42.7
3	Bente Martinsen, NOR	17:49.4

Best USA: 51st, Kerrin Petty (1:58.7).

10-km Freestyle Pursuit

		Time
1	Larissa Lazutina, RUS	46:06.9
2	Olga Danilova, RUS	46:13.4
3	Katerina Neumannova, CZE	46:14.2

Best USA: 52nd, Kerrin Petty (51:49.2).

15-km Classical

		Time
1	Olga Danilova, RUS	46:55.4
2	Larissa Lazutina, RUS	47:01.0
3	Anita Moen-Guidon, NOR	47:52.6

Best USA: 47th, Kerrin Petty (52:45.3); 48th, Suzanne King (52:58.9).

30-km Freestyle

		Time
1	Julija Tchepalova, RUS	1:22:01.5
2	Stefania Belmondo, ITA	1:22:11.7
3	Larissa Lazutina, RUS	1:23:15.7

Best USA: 36th, Laura Wilson (1:33:10.6).

4 x 5 Mixed Relay

		Time
1	Russia	55:13.5
2	Norway	55:38.0
3	Italy	56:53.3

RUS— Nina Gavryliouk, Olga Danilova, Elena Valbe, Larissa Lazutina; **NOR—** Bente Martinsen, Marit Mikkelsplass, Elin Nilsen, Anita Moen-Guidon; **ITA—** Karin Moroder, Gabriella Paruzzi, Manuela Di Centa, Stefania Belmondo.

USA entry: 15th; Kerrin Petty, Suzanne King, Laura McCabe, Laura Wilson (1:00:51.2).

ICE HOCKEY

Medal breakdown (2 events): **Two medals**— Finland (0-0-2); **One medal**— Czech Republic (1-0-0), United States (1-0-0), Canada (0-1-0) and Russia (0-1-0)

MEN

Preliminary Round Standings

Group A	G	W-L-T	Pts	GF	GA
*Kazakhstan	3	2-1-0	**4**	14	11
Slovakia	3	1-1-1	**3**	9	9
Italy	3	1-2-0	**2**	11	11
Austria	3	0-1-2	**2**	9	12

Group B	G	W-L-T	Pts	GF	GA
*Belarus	3	2-0-1	**5**	14	4
Germany	3	2-1-0	**4**	7	9
France	3	1-2-0	**2**	5	8
Japan	3	0-2-1	**1**	5	10

* Advanced to final round competition.

Placement round: 9th place— Germany 4, Slovakia 2; **11th place**— France 5, Italy 1; **13th place**— Japan 4, Australia 3 (shootout).

Final Round Standings

Group C	G	W-L-T	Pts	GF	GA
Russia	3	3-0-0	**6**	15	6
Czech Republic	3	2-1-0	**4**	12	4
Finland	3	1-2-0	**2**	11	9
Kazakhstan	3	0-3-0	**0**	6	25

Group D	G	W-L-T	Pts	GF	GA
Canada	3	3-0-0	**6**	12	3
Sweden	3	2-1-0	**4**	11	7
United States	3	1-2-0	**2**	8	10
Belarus	3	0-3-0	**0**	4	15

Quarterfinals

Czech Republic 4 .... United States 1
Russia 4 .... Belarus 1
Canada 4 .... Kazakhstan 1
Finland 2 .... Sweden 1

Semifinals

Czech Republic 2 .... Canada 1, SH
Russia 7 .... Finland 4

Bronze Medal

Finland 3 .... Canada 2

Gold Medal

Czech Republic 1 .... Russia 0

Gold Medal Game

	1	2	3	F
Czech Republic	0	0	1	1
Russia	0	0	0	0

Scoring: 3RD PERIOD— Petr Svoboda, CZE (Pavel Patera, Martin Prochazka), 48:08.

Goaltenders: CZECH REPUBLIC— Dominik Hasek (20 shots, 20 saves); RUSSIA— Mikhail Shtalenkov (21 shots, 20 saves).

Leading Scorers

	Gm	G	A	Pts	PM
Teemu Selanne, FIN	5	4	6	**10**	8
Saku Koivu, FIN	6	2	8	**10**	4
Pavel Bure, RUS	6	9	0	**9**	2
Alexandr Koreshkov, KAZ	7	3	6	**9**	2
Philippe Bozon, FRA	4	5	2	**7**	4
Konstantin Shafranov, KAZ	7	4	3	**7**	6
Dominik Lavoie, AUT	4	5	1	**6**	8
Jere Lehtinen, FIN	6	4	2	**6**	2
Alexei Yashin, RUS	6	3	3	**6**	0
Serge Poudrier, FRA	4	2	4	**6**	4
Sergei Fedorov, RUS	6	1	5	**6**	8

Leading Goaltenders

(Minimum 180 min.)

	Gm	Min	SV%	GAA
Dominik Hasek, CZE	6	370	.961	**0.97**
Patrick Roy, CAN	6	369	.935	**1.46**
Mikhail Shtalenkov, RUS	5	290	.931	**1.65**
Tommy Salo, SWE	4	238	.913	**2.27**
Dusty Imoo, JPN	3	189	.925	**2.54**
Igor Murin, SVK	4	240	.845	**3.25**
Mike Anthony Rosati, ITA	4	215	.848	**3.35**

WOMEN

Final Standings

	Gm	W-L-T	Pts	GF	GA
United States	6	6-0-0	**12**	36	8
Canada	6	4-2-0	**8**	29	15
Finland	6	4-2-0	**8**	31	11
China	6	2-4-0	**4**	11	19
Sweden	5	1-4-0	**2**	10	21
Japan	5	0-5-0	**0**	2	45

Bronze Medal

Finland 4 .... China 1

Gold Medal

United States 3 .... Canada 1

Gold Medal Game

	1	2	3	F
Canada	0	0	1	1
United States	0	1	2	3

Scoring: 2ND PERIOD— Gretchen Ulion, USA (Sandra Whyte, Suzanne Merz), 22:38 (pp). 3RD PERIOD— Shelley Looney, USA (Sandra Whyte, Ulion Gretchen), 50:57 (pp); Danielle Goyette, CAN (Haley Wickenheiser, Geraldine Heaney), 55:59 (pp); Sandra Whyte, USA (unassisted), 59:52.

Goaltenders: CANADA— Manon Rheaume (23 shots, 21 saves); UNITED STATES— Sarah Tueting (22 shots, 21 saves).

Leading Scorers

	Gm	G	A	Pts	PM
Hanna-Riikka Nieminen, FIN	6	7	5	**12**	4
Danielle Goyette, CAN	6	8	1	**9**	10
Karyn Bye, USA	6	5	3	**8**	4
Kathryn King, USA	6	4	4	**8**	2
Catherine Granato, USA	6	4	4	**8**	0
Gretchen Ulion, USA	6	3	5	**8**	4
Hayley Wickenheiser, CAN	6	2	6	**8**	4
Therese Brisson, CAN	6	5	2	**7**	6
Kirsi Maaria Haenninen, FIN	6	4	3	**7**	6
Laurie Baker, USA	6	4	3	**7**	6

Leading Goaltenders

(Minimum 150 min.)

	Gm	Min	SV%	GAA
Sarah Tueting, USA	4	209	.938	**1.15**
Manon Rheaume, CAN	4	208	.926	**1.15**
Tuula Katriina Puputti, FIN	5	270	.896	**1.55**
Sara DeCosta, USA	3	150	.875	**1.59**
Hong Guo, CHN	6	349	.893	**2.75**
Lesley Reddon, CAN	3	150	.781	**3.58**

LUGE

Medal breakdown (3 events): **Five medals**— Germany (3-1-1); **Two**— United States (0-1-1); **One**— Italy (0-1-0) and Austria (0-0-1).

MEN

Singles

		Time
1	Georg Hackl, GER	3:18.436
2	Armin Zoeggeler, ITA	3:18.939
3	Jens Mueller, GER	3:19.093

Top 10 USA: 6th, Wendel Suckow (3:19.728); 9th, Adam Heidt (3:20.098).

Doubles

		Time
1	Stefan Krausse & Jan Behrendt, GER	1:41.105
2	Christopher Thorpe & Gordy Sheer, USA	1:41.127
3	Mark Grimmette & Brian Martin, USA	1:41.217

WOMEN

Singles

		Time
1	Silke Kraushaar, GER	3:23.779
2	Barbara Niedernhuber, GER	3:23.781
3	Angelika Neuner, AUT	3:24.253

Top 10 USA: 6th, Erin Warren (3:25.328); 8th, Bethany Calcaterra-McMahon (3:25.558).

SHORT TRACK SPEED SKATING

The short track oval is 111 meters (364 feet).

Medal breakdown (6 events): **Six medals**— Korea (3-1-2) and China (0-5-1); **Four**— Canada (2-0-2); **Two**— Japan (1-0-1).

MEN

500 meters

		Time
1	Takafumi Nishitani, JPN	42.862
2	Yulong An, CHN	43.022
3	Hitoshi Uematsu, JPN	43.713

Best USA: No Americans qualified for final.

1000 meters

		Time
1	Dong-Sung Kim, KOR	1:32.375
2	Jiajun Li, CHN	1:32.428
3	Eric Bedard, CAN	1:32.661

Best USA: 4th, Andrew Gabel (1:33.518).

5000M Relay

		Time
1	Canada	7:06.075
2	Korea	7:06.776
3	China	7:11.559

Best USA: No Americans qualified for the final.

WOMEN

500 meters

		Time
1	Annie Perreault, CAN	46.568
2	Yang S.Yang, CHN	46.627

Finalist #3 was disqualified and finalist #4 did not finish the race.

Best USA: No Americans qualified for the final.

1000 meters

		Time
1	Lee-Kyung Chun, KOR	1:42.776
2	Yang S.Yang, CHN	1:43.343
3	Hye-Kyung Won, KOR	1:43.361

Best USA: No Americans qualified for the final.

3000M Relay

		Time	
1	Korea	4:16.260	**WR**
2	China	4:16.383	
3	Canada	4:21.205	

Best USA: The United States did not qualify for the final.

SPEED SKATING

The long track oval measures 400 meters (1,312 feet). Distance laps: 500m (1¼ laps); 1,000m (2½ laps); 1,500m (3¾ laps); 3,000m (7½ laps); 5,000 (12½ laps); 10,000m (25 laps).

Medal breakdown (10 events): **11 medals**— Netherlands (5-4-2); **Six**— Germany (2-3-1); **Five**— Canada (1-2-2); **Three**— Japan (1-0-2); **Two**— United States (0-1-1); **One**— Norway (1-0-0), Belgium (0-0-1) and Kazakhstan (0-0-1).

MEN

500 meters

		Time
1	Hiroyasu Shimizu, JPN	71.35
2	Jeremy Wotherspoon, CAN	71.84
3	Kevin Overland, CAN	71.86

Best USA: 23rd, Marc Pelchat (73.35); 25th, David Cruikshank (73.53).

Note: Times reflected are a combination of two heats with each skater racing once on the inside lane and once in the outside lane.

1000 meters

		Time	
1	Ids Postma, NET	1:10.64	OR
2	Jan Bos, NET	1:10.71	
3	Hiroyasu Shimizu, JPN	1:11.00	

Top 10 USA: 7th, Casey Fitzrandolph (1:11.64); 8th, KC Boutiette (1:11.75).

1500 meters

		Time	
1	Aadne Sondral, NOR	1:47.87	WR
2	Ids Postma, NET	1:48.13	
3	Rintje Ritsma, NET	1:48.52	

Top 10 USA: 5th, KC Boutiette (1:50.04).

5000 meters

		Time	
1	Gianni Romme, NET	6:22.20	WR
2	Rintje Ritsma, NET	6:28.24	
3	Bart Veldkamp, BEL	6:28.31	

Best USA: 14th, KC Boutiette (6:39.67), 16th, David Tamburrino (6:41.19).

10,000 meters

		Time	
1	Gianni Romme, NET	13:15.33	WR
2	Bob De Jong, NET	13:25.76	
3	Rintje Ritsma, NET	13:28.19	

Top 10 USA: 8th, KC Boutiette (13:44.03).

WOMEN

500 meters

		Time
1	Catriona Lemay-Doan, CAN	76.60
2	Susan Auch, CAN	76.93
3	Tomomi Okazaki, JPN	77.10

Top 10 USA: 10th, Christine Witty (78.53).

Note: Times reflected are a combination of two heats with each skater racing once on the inside lane and once in the outside lane.

1000 meters

		Time	
1	Marianne Timmer, NET	1:16.51	OR
2	Christine Witty, USA	1:16.79	
3	Catriona Lemay-Doan, CAN	1:17.37	

Top 10 USA: 6th, Becky Sundstrom (1:18.23); 9th, Moira D'Andrea (1:18.38).

1500 meters

		Time	
1	Marianne Timmer, NET	1:57.58	WR
2	Gunda Niemann-Stirnemann, GER	1:58.66	
3	Christine Witty, USA	1:58.97	

Top 10 USA: 8th, Jennifer Rodriguez (2:00.97).

3000 meters

		Time	
1	Gunda Niemann-Stirnemann, GER	4:07.29	OR
2	Claudia Pechstein, GER	4:08.47	
3	Anna Friesinger, GER	4:09.44	

Top 10 USA: 4th, Jennifer Rodriguez (4:11.64); 6th, Kirstin Holum (4:12.24).

5000 meters

		Time	
1	Claudia Pechstein, GER	6:59.61	WR
2	Gunda Niemann-Stirnemann, GER	6:59.65	
3	Lyudmila Prokasheva, KAZ	7:11.14	

Top 10 USA: 7th, Kirstin Holum (7:14.20); 10th, Jennifer Rodriguez (7:16.78).

FREESTYLE SKIING

Aerials consist of two jumps with points awarded for execution and precision (50%), height and distance (20%) and landing (30%). Moguls consist of turns executed on a bumpy course (50%), two aerials (25%) and elapsed time (25%).

Medal breakdown (4 events): **Three medals**— United States (3-0-0); **Two**— Finland (0-1-1); **One**— Japan (1-0-0), China (0-1-0), France (0-1-0), Germany (0-1-0), Belarus (0-0-1), Norway (0-0-1) and Switzerland (0-0-1).

MEN

Aerials

		Points
1	Eric Bergoust, USA	255.64
2	Sebastien Foucras, FRA	248.79
3	Dmitri Dashchinsky, BLR	240.79

Top 10 USA: 5th, Britt Swartley (231.6).

Moguls

		Points
1	Jonny Moseley, USA	26.93
2	Janne Lahtela, FIN	26.00
3	Sami Mustonen, FIN	25.76

Top 10 USA: 10th, Alexander Wilson (24.68).

WOMEN

Aerials

		Points
1	Nikki Stone, USA	193.00
2	Nannan Xu, CHN	186.97
3	Colette Brand, SWI	171.83

Best USA: No other Americans qualified for the final.

Moguls

		Points
1	Tae Satoya, JPN	25.06
2	Tatjana Mittermayer, GER	24.62
3	Kari Traa, NOR	24.09

Top 10 USA: 4th, Donna Weinbrecht (24.02); 8th, Elizabeth McIntyre (23.72); 10th, Ann Battelle (23.65).

NORDIC COMBINED

Three jumps off normal hill (best two count) followed the next day by a 15-km cross-country race. The cross-country starting order determined by finish in ski jump. The times shown are adjusted to include the competitors' staggered start time.

Medal breakdown (2 events): **Two medals**— Norway (2-0-0) and Finland (0-2-0); **One**— France (0-0-1) and Russia (0-0-1).

Individual

		Time
1	Bjarte Engen Vik, NOR	41:21.1
2	Samppa Lajunen, FIN	41:48.6
3	Balerij Stoljarov, RUS	41:49.3

Best USA: 20th, Todd Lodwick (44.57.4)

Team

		Time
1	Norway	54:11.5
2	Finland	55:30.4
3	France	55:53.4

USA entry: 10th, John Jarrett, Tim Tetreault, Bill Demong, Todd Lodwick (55:53.6).

BOBSLED

Medal breakdown (2 events): **Two medals**— Germany (1-0-1); **One**— Canada (1-0-0), Italy (0-1-0), Switzerland (0-1-0), France (0-0-1) and Great Britain (0-0-1).

Two-Man

		Time
1	Italy I	3:37.24
1	Canada I	3:37.24
3	Germany I	3:37.89

ITA I— Guenther Huber & Antonio Tartaglia; **CAN I—** Pierre Fritz Lueders & David G. MacEachern; **GER I—** Christoph Langen & Markus Zimmermann.

Top 10 USA: 7th, USA II— James Herberich & Robert Olesen (3:38.53).

Four-Man

		Time
1	Germany II	2:39.41
2	Switzerland I	2:40.01
3	Great Britain I	2:40.06
3	France I	2:40.06

GER II— Christoph Langen, Markus Zimmermann, Marco Jakobs, Olaf Hampel; **SWI I—** Marcel Rohner, Markus Nuessli, Markus Wasser, Beat Seitz; **GBR—** Sean Olsson Dean Martin Ward, Courtney Orville Rumbolt, Paul Jason Attwood; **FRA I—** Bruno Mingeon, Emmanuel Hostache, Eric Le Chanony, Max Robert.

Top 10 USA: 5th, USA I— Brian Shimer, Nathan Minton, Randy Jones, Garreth Hines (2:40.08).

CURLING

Teams attempt to slide a 20kg (42lbs) stone into a three-circle target six feet in diameter called "the house". The team with the stone closest to the center gets a point. All stones of the winning team which are closer to the center than is the nearest stone of the opponent are also given one point each. After 10 rounds or "ends" the team with the most points wins.

Medal breakdown (2 events): **Two medals**— Canada (1-1-0); **One**— Switzerland (1-0-0), Denmark (0-1-0), Norway (0-0-1), Sweden (0-0-1).

MEN
Round Robin Standings

	G	W-L-T	PF	PA
*Canada	7	6-1-0	57	32
*Switzerland	7	5-2-0	44	28
*Norway	7	5-2-0	42	35
*United States	7	3-4-0	34	46
Japan	7	3-4-0	36	42
Sweden	7	3-4-0	32	40
Britain	7	2-5-0	32	47
Germany	7	1-6-0	38	50

* Qualified for next round.

Tiebreakers (loser out): United States 5, Sweden 2; United States 5, Japan 4.

Semifinals

Canada 7 ... United States 1
Switzerland 8 ... Norway 7

Bronze Medal

Norway 9 ... United States 4

Gold Medal

Switzerland 9 ... Canada 3

WOMEN
Round Robin Standings

	G	W-L-T	PF	PA
*Canada	7	6-1-0	51	34
*Sweden	7	6-1-0	54	32
*Denmark	7	5-2-0	46	34
*Britain	7	4-3-0	38	44
Japan	7	2-5-0	34	41
Norway	7	2-5-0	41	45
United States	7	2-5-0	47	47
Germany	7	1-6-0	32	51

* Qualified for next round.

Semifinals

Canada 6 ... Britain 5
Denmark 7 ... Sweden 5

Bronze Medal

Sweden 10 ... Britain 6

Gold Medal

Canada 7 ... Denmark 5

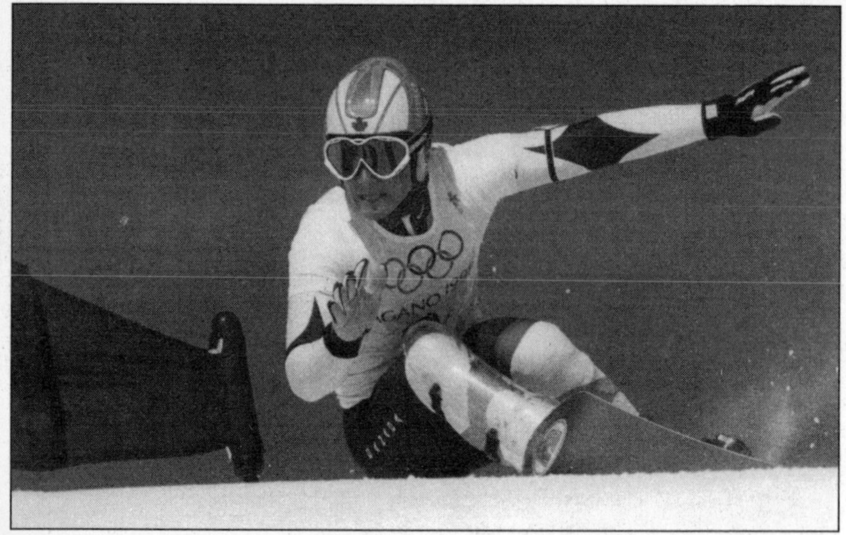

Archive Photos

Canadian snowboarder **Ross Rebagliati** became the first ever Olympic medalist in snowboarding with his gold medal run in the slalom on Mt.Yakebitai (north of Nagano). Rebagliati would nearly lose the medal days later when he tested positive for marijuana. Second-hand smoke strikes again.

SKI JUMPING

Each contestant gets two jumps with points awarded for distance and style. The normal hill is 90 meters (295 feet) and the large hill is 120 meters (394 feet).

Medal breakdown (3 events): **Four medals**— Japan (2-1-1); **Two**— Finland (1-1-0) and Austria (0-0-2); **One**— Germany (0-1-0).

Normal Hill

		1st (ft)	2nd (ft)	Pts
1	Jani Soininen, FIN	295	292	234.5
2	Kazuyoshi Funaki, JPN	287	297	233.5
3	Andreas Widhoelzl, AUT	289	270	232.5

Best USA: No Americans qualified for final.

Large Hill

		1st (ft)	2nd (ft)	Pts
1	Kazuyoshi Funaki, JPN	413	435	272.3
2	Jani Soininen, FIN	425	415	260.8
3	Masahiko Harada, JPN	394	446	258.3

Best USA: 30th, Casey Colby (298, 298; 165.8 pts)

Team (Large Hill)

		Pts
1	Japan	933.0
2	Germany	897.4
3	Austria	881.5

JPN— Takanobu Okabe, Hiroya Saito, Masahiko Harada, Kazuyoshi Funaki; **GER**— Sven Hannawald, Martin Schmitt, Hansjoerg Jaekle, Dieter Thoma; **AUT**— Reinhard Schwarzenberger, Martin Hoellwarth, Stefan Horngacher, Andreas Widhoelzl.

USA entry: 12th; Michael Keuler, Alan Alborn, Randy Weber, Casey Colby (490.7 pts).

SNOWBOARDING

Medal breakdown (4 events): **Two medals**— Germany (1-1-0), Switzerland (1-0-1), Norway (0-2-0) and United States (0-0-2); **One**— Canada (1-0-0), France (1-0-0), Italy (0-1-0) and Austria (0-0-1).

MEN

Halfpipe

		Pts
1	Gian Simmen, SWI	85.2
2	Daniel Franck, NOR	82.4
3	Ross Powers, USA	82.1

Next best USA: 16th, Todd Richards (69.6).

Giant Slalom

		Time
1	Ross Rebagliati, CAN	2:03.96
2	Thomas Prugger, ITA	2:03.98
3	Ueli Kestenholz, SWI	2:04.08

Top 10 USA: 6th, Christopher Klug (2:05.25).

WOMEN

Halfpipe

		Pts
1	Nicola Thost, GER	74.6
2	Stine Brun Kjeldaas, NOR	74.2
3	Shannon Dunn, USA	72.8

Other Top 10 USA: 4th, Cara-Beth Burnside (72.6).

Giant Slalom

		Time
1	Karine Ruby, FRA	2:17.34
2	Heidi Renoth, GER	2:19.17
3	Brigitte Koeck, AUT	2:19.42

Best USA: 12th, Sondra Van Ert, 2:26.56.

The Winter Olympics

The move toward a winter version of the Olympics began in 1908 when figure skating made an appearance at the Summer Games in London. Ten-time world champion Ulrich Salchow of Sweden, who originated the backwards, one revolution jump that bears his name, and Madge Syers of Britain were the first singles champions. Germans Anna Hubler and Heinrich Berger won the pairs competition.

Organizers of the 1916 Summer Games in Berlin planned to introduce a "Skiing Olympia," featuring nordic events in the Black Forest, but the Games were cancelled after the outbreak of World War I in 1914.

The Games resumed in 1920 at Antwerp, Belgium, where figure skating returned and ice hockey was added as a medal event. Sweden's Gillis Grafstrom and Magda Julin took individual honors, while Ludovika and Walter Jakobsson were the top pair. In hockey, Canada won the gold medal with the United States second and Czechoslovakia third.

Despite the objections of Modern Olympics' founder Baron Pierre de Coubertin and the resistance of the Scandinavian countries, which had staged their own Nordic championships every four or five years from 1901-26 in Sweden, the International Olympic Committee sanctioned an "International Winter Sports Week" at Chamonix, France, in 1924. The 11-day event, which included nordic skiing, speed skating, figure skating, ice hockey and bobsledding, was a huge success and was retroactively called the First Olympic Winter Games.

Seventy years after those first cold weather Games, the 17th edition of the Winter Olympics took place in Lillehammer, Norway, in 1994. The event ended the four-year Olympic cycle of staging both Winter and Summer Games in the same year and began a new schedule that calls for the two Games to alternate every two years.

Year	No	Location	Dates	Nations	Most medals	USA Medals
1924	I	Chamonix, FRA	Jan. 25-Feb. 4	16	Norway (4-7-6–17)	1-2-1– 4 (3rd)
1928	II	St. Moritz, SWI	Feb. 11-19	25	Norway (6-4-5–15)	2-2-2– 6 (2nd)
1932	III	Lake Placid, USA	Feb. 4-15	17	USA (6-4-2–12)	6-4-2–12 (1st)
1936	IV	Garmisch-Partenkirchen, GER	Feb. 6-16	28	Norway (7-5-3–15)	1-0-3– 4 (T-5th)
1940-**a**	–	Sapporo, JPN	Cancelled (WWII)			
1944	–	Cortina d'Ampezzo, ITA	Cancelled (WWII)			
1948	V	St. Moritz, SWI	Jan. 30-Feb. 8	28	Norway (4-3-3–10), Sweden (4-3-3–10) & Switzerland (3-4-3–10)	3-4-2– 9 (4th)
1952-**b**	VI	Oslo, NOR	Feb. 14-25	30	Norway (7-3-6–16)	4-6-1–11 (2nd)
1956-**c**	VII	Cortina d'Ampezzo, ITA	Jan. 26-Feb. 5	32	USSR (7-3-6–16)	2-3-2– 7 (T-4th)
1960	VIII	Squaw Valley, USA	Feb. 18-28	30	USSR (7-5-9–21)	3-4-3–10 (2nd)
1964	IX	Innsbruck, AUT	Jan. 29-Feb. 9	36	USSR (11-8-6–25)	1-2-3– 6 (7th)
1968-**d**	X	Grenoble, FRA	Feb. 6-18	37	Norway (6-6-2–14)	1-5-1– 7 (T-7th)
1972	XI	Sapporo, JPN	Feb. 3-13	35	USSR (8-5-3–16)	3-2-3– 8 (6th)
1976-**e**	XII	Innsbruck, AUT	Feb. 4-15	37	USSR (13-6-8–27)	3-3-4–10 (T-3rd)
1980	XIII	Lake Placid, USA	Feb. 14-23	37	E. Germany (9-7-7–23)	6-4-2–12 (3rd)
1984	XIV	Sarajevo, YUG	Feb. 7-19	49	USSR (6-10-9–25)	4-4-0– 8 (T-5th)
1988	XV	Calgary, CAN	Feb. 13-28	57	USSR (11-9-9–29)	2-1-3– 6 (T-8th)
1992-**f**	XVI	Albertville, FRA	Feb. 8-23	63	Germany (10-10-6–26)	5-4-2–11 (6th)
1994-**g**	XVII	Lillehammer, NOR	Feb. 12-27	67	Norway (10-11-5–26)	6-5-2–13 (T-5th)
1998	XVIII	Nagano, JPN	Feb. 7-22	72	Germany (12-9-8–29)	6-3-4–13 (5th)
2002	XIX	Salt Lake City, USA	Feb. 8-24			

a–The 1940 Winter Games are originally scheduled for Sapporo, but Japan resigns as host in 1937 when the Sino-Japanese war breaks out. St. Moritz is the next choice, but the Swiss feel that ski instructors should not be considered professionals and the IOC withdraws its offer. Finally, Garmisch-Partenkirchen is asked to serve again as host, but the Germans invade Poland in 1939 and the Games are eventually cancelled.

b–Germany and Japan are allowed to rejoin the Olympic community for the first time since World War II. Though a divided country, the Germans send a joint East-West team.

c–The Soviet Union (USSR) participates in its first Winter Olympics and takes home the most medals, including the gold medal in ice hockey.

d–East Germany and West Germany officially send separate teams for the first time and will continue to do so through 1988.

e–The IOC grants the 1976 Winter Games to Denver in May 1970, but in 1972 Colorado voters reject a $5 million bond issue to finance the undertaking. Denver immediately withdraws as host and the IOC selects Innsbruck, the site of the 1964 Games, to take over.

f–Germany sends a single team after East and West German reunification in 1990 and the USSR competes as the Unified Team after the breakup of the Soviet Union in 1991.

g–The IOC moves the Winter Games' four-year cycle ahead two years in order to separate them from the Summer Games and alternate Olympics every two years.

1924

Chamonix

The first Winter Olympic Games were actually called "The International Winter Sports Week" and went on for 11 days in the French Alps, 60 miles northeast of Grenoble.

As expected, the Scandinavians dominated the 16–nation field. Norway and Finland won 27 of the 43 medals available, including all four Nordic events and four of the five speed skating races. Speed skater Clas Thunberg of Finland and Norwegian Nordic skier and jumper Thorleif Haug each won three gold medals.

American speed skater Charles Jewtraw won the first event of the Games with an upset in the 500 meters. But the most remarkable U.S. medal was the bronze won by Anders Haugen in the ski jump. Due to a scoring error at the time he didn't receive it until 1974 – when he was 83 years old.

In its first four hockey games, Canada beat Switzerland 33–0, Czechoslovakia 30–0, Sweden 22–0 and Great Britain 19–2, before winning the tournament with a 6–1 victory over the U.S. in the final.

Top 5 Standings

National medal standings are not recognized by the IOC. The unofficial point totals are based on 3 points for a gold medal, 2 for a silver and 1 for a bronze. Total medals are in parentheses.

		Gold	Silver	Bronze	Points
1	Norway (17)	4	7	6	32
2	Finland (10)	4	3	3	21
3	Austria (3)	2	1	0	8
	USA (4)	1	2	1	8
5	Switzerland (2)	1	0	1	4
	Great Britain (3)	0	1	2	4

Leading Medal Winners

Number of individual medals won on the left; gold, silver and bronze breakdown to the right.

No		Sport	G-S-B
5	Clas Thunberg, FIN	Sp. Skate	3-1-1
5	Roald Larsen, NOR	Sp. Skate	0-2-3
3	Thorleif Haug, NOR	X-country & Nordic Combined	3-0-0
3	Julius Skutnabb, FIN	Sp. Skate	1-1-1
3	Johan Gröttumsbråten, NOR	X-country & Nordic Combined	0-1-2
2	Thoralf Strömstad, NOR	X-country & Nordic Combined	0-2-0

Bobsled

Event		Time
4-Man	SWI (Eduard Scherrer, Alfred Neveu, Alfred Schläppi, Heinrich Schläppi)	5:45.54

Figure Skating

Event		Points
Men	Gillis Grafström, SWE	367.89
Women	Herma Planck-Szabó, AUT	299.17
Pairs	Helene Engelmann & Albert Berger, AUT	10.64

Ice Hockey

Championship Round

Records include games played in two 4-team preliminary pools. Canada and Sweden qualified from one pool, the U.S. and Britain from the other.

		Gm	W-L-T	GF	GA
1	Canada	5	5-0-0	110	3
2	USA	5	4-1-0	73	6
3	Great Britain	5	3-2-0	40	38
4	Sweden	5	2-3-0	21	49

Semifinals: Canada over Britain, 19–2; USA over Sweden, 20–0. **Third place:** Britain over Sweden, 4–3 (also decided European title). **Final:** Canada over USA, 6–1.

Nordic Skiing

Cross Country

Event		Time
18km	Thorleif Haug, NOR	1:14:31
50km	Thorleif Haug, NOR	3:44:32

Ski Jumping

Event		Points
90m	Jacob Thams, NOR	18.906

Nordic Combined

Event		Points
18km/Jump	Thorleif Haug, NOR	18.906

Speed Skating

Event		Time
500m	Charles Jewtraw, USA	44.0
1500m	Clas Thunberg, FIN	2:20.8
5000m	Clas Thunberg, FIN	8:39.0
10,000m	Julius Skutnabb, FIN	18:04.8
Combined	Clas Thunberg, FIN	5.5 pts

1928

St. Moritz

Sonja Henie of Norway was only 11 years old in 1924 when she participated in her first Olympics and finished last in women's figure skating. Three years later, she won the world championship at age 14 and the year after that was Olympic champion at 15.

Henie would go on to win two more gold medals, a record that her coach, men's champion Gillis Grafstrom of Sweden, set in 1928 with his third straight victory in the Winter Games.

Otherwise, St. Moritz was plagued with warm weather that slowed bobsled and cross-country runs and cancelled the 10,000–meter speed skating race. Speed skater Bernt Evensen of Norway led the Games with three medals, sharing the 500–meter title with Finland's Clas Thunberg. Norway also got two gold medals from Johan Gröttumsbråten in cross-country and the Nordic Combined and led the 25 nations competing with six gold and 15 overall medals. The U.S. edged Sweden for second place.

Top 5 Standings

National medal standings are not recognized by the IOC. The unofficial point totals are based on 3 points for a gold medal, 2 for a silver and 1 for a bronze. Total medals are in parentheses.

	Gold	Silver	Bronze	Points
1 Norway (15)	6	4	5	31
2 USA (6)	2	2	2	12
3 Sweden (5)	2	2	1	11
4 Finland (4)	2	1	1	9
5 Austria (4)	0	3	1	7

Leading Medal Winners

Number of individual medals won on the left; gold, silver and bronze breakdown to the right.

No		Sport	G-S-B
3	Bernt Evensen, NOR	Sp. Skate	1-1-1
2	Johan Gröttumsbråten, NOR	X-country	2-0-0
2	Clas Thunberg, FIN	Sp. Skate	2-0-0
2	Jennison Heaton, USA	Bobsled & Cresta	1-1-0
2	Ivar Ballangrud, NOR	Sp. Skate	1-0-1

Note: Evensen also placed second in the 10,000–meter Speed Skating race that was later disallowed due to thawing ice conditions.

Bobsled

Event		Time
5-Man	USA (Billy Fiske, Nion Tucker, Geoff Mason, Clifford Gray, Richard Parke)	3:20.5

Cresta (Toboggan)

Event		Time
1-Man	Jennison Heaton, USA	3:01.8

Figure Skating

Event		Points
Men	Gillis Grafström, SWE	1630.75
Women	Sonja Henie, NOR	2452.25
Pairs	Andrée Joly & Pierre Brunet, FRA	100.50

Ice Hockey

Championship Round

(Overall record in parentheses)

	Gm	W-L-T	Pts	GF	GA
1 Canada (3-0-0)	3	3-0-0	6	38	0
2 Sweden (3-1-1)	3	2-1-0	4	7	12
3 Switzerland (2-2-1)	3	1-2-0	2	4	17
4 Britain (2-4-0)	3	0-3-0	0	1	21

Note: Canada received a bye to the 4–team championship round robin. The 10 other competing countries—not including the USA which did not send a team—were divided into three pools with the winners advancing to the final round. The Canadians routed Sweden, 11–0; Britain 14–0 and the Swiss, 13–0.

Nordic Skiing

Cross Country

Event		Time
18km	Johan Gröttumsbråten, NOR	1:37:01
50km	Per Erik Hedlund, SWE	4:52:03

Ski Jumping

Event		Points
90m	Alf Andersen, NOR	19.208

Nordic Combined

Event		Points
18km/Jump	Johan Gröttumsbråten, NOR	17.833

Speed Skating

Event		Time	
500m	Bernt Evensen, NOR & Clas Thunberg, FIN	43.4	OR
1500m	Clas Thunberg, FIN	2:21.1	
5000m	Ivar Ballangrud, NOR	8:50.5	
10,000m	No decision (thawing of ice)		

Note: Irving Jaffee of USA had the fastest time in the 10,000 meters (18:36.5) before the race was cancelled.

1932

Lake Placid

Back in 1928, American Irving Jaffee had the fastest time in the 10,000–meter speed skating race at St. Moritz only to lose his gold medal when thawing ice made it necessary to call the event off with no official winner.

Four years later, Jaffee won the 10,000 and the 5,000–meter races and local hero Jack Shea won at 500 and 1,500 meters as the U.S. swept all four speed skating events—which were run as actual races (not timed heats) for the first time in Olympic history.

Billy Fiske, who had driven the 5–man U.S. bobsled to a gold medal at St. Moritz when he was only 16, steered the 4–man sled to victory in 1932. On board was Eddie Eagan, the 1920 Olympic light heavyweight champion, who remains the only athlete ever to win gold medals in both the Winter and Summer Games.

Canada won its fourth consecutive hockey gold medal, but 38–year-old Gillis Grafstrom of Sweden missed in his bid for a fourth straight men's figure skating title, placing second to 22–year-old Austrian Karl Schafer.

Top 5 Standings

National medal standings are not recognized by the IOC. The unofficial point totals are based on 3 points for a gold medal, 2 for a silver and 1 for a bronze. Total medals are in parentheses.

	Gold	Silver	Bronze	Points
1 USA (12)	6	4	2	28
2 Norway (10)	3	4	3	20
3 Canada (7)	1	1	5	10
4 Sweden (3)	1	2	0	7
5 Finland (3)	1	1	1	6

Leading Medal Winners

Number of individual medals won on the left; gold, silver and bronze breakdown to the right.

No		Sport	G-S-B
2	Irving Jaffee, USA	Sp. Skate	2-0-0
2	Jack Shea, USA	Sp. Skate	2-0-0
2	Veli Saarinen, FIN	X-country	1-0-1
2	Alex Hurd, CAN	Sp. Skate	0-1-1
2	William Logan, CAN	Sp. Skate	0-0-2

Bobsled

Event		Time
2-Man	USA (J.Hubert Stevens & Curtis Stevens)	8:14.74
4-Man	USA (Billy Fiske, Eddie Eagan, Clifford Gray, Jay O'Brien)	7:53.68

Figure Skating

Event		Points
Men	Karl Schäfer, AUT	2602.0
Women	Sonja Henie, NOR	2302.5
Pairs	Andrée Joly Brunet & Pierre Brunet, FRA	76.7

Ice Hockey

	Gm	W-L-T	Pts	GF	GA
1 Canada	6	5-0-1	11	32	4
2 USA	6	4-1-1	9	27	5
3 Germany	6	2-4-0	4	7	26
4 Poland	6	0-6-0	0	3	34

Note: Due to the worldwide Depression, only four teams competed. Each side played the other teams twice. Canada beat the U.S., 2–1, in their first game and tied the Americans, 2–2, in triple overtime in the second. A win by the U.S. in Game 2 would have resulted in a third contest to decide the gold medal.

Nordic Skiing

Cross Country

Event		Time
18km	Sven Utterström, SWE	1:23.07
50km	Veli Saarinen, FIN	4:28.00

Ski Jumping

Event		Points
90m	Birger Rudd, NOR	228.1

Nordic Combined

Event		Points
18km/Jump	Johan Gröttumsbråten, NOR	446.00

Speed Skating

Event		Time	
500m	Jack Shea, USA	43.4	OR
1500m	Jack Shea, USA	2:57.5	
5000m	Irving Jaffee, USA	9:40.8	
10,000m	Irving Jaffee, USA	19:13.6	

Note: For the only time in the history of the Winter Games, all events were staged as races rather than two-man heats against the clock.

1936

Garmisch-Partenkirchen

The fourth Winter Olympic Games were held in the neighboring villages of Garmisch and Partenkirchen in Germany's Bavarian Alps and included Alpine skiing for the first time.

Also featured in these Games were Norwegians Ivar Ballangrud and Sonja Henie, and Rudi Ball—the Jewish star of the German hockey team.

Ballangrud won three individual gold medals and narrowly missed a fourth in speed skating, but his heroics paled compared to the attention lavished on Henie, who won her third straight gold medal. A week later, she won the world championship for the 10th year in a row, then turned pro. Moving to the U.S., she toured in her own skating show, starred in nine Hollywood movies and was worth more than $45 million when she died in 1969 at age 57.

Ball, who had been the best player on Germany's bronze medal-winning hockey team in 1932, was invited back from voluntary exile in France to lead the 1936 German squad. He was the only Jew on the German Winter Olympic team and his presence was a token gesture by the government of Adolf Hitler to mollify anxious IOC officials who objected to the Nazis' fervent anti-Semitism.

The story of the hockey tournament, however, wasn't one German Jew, but 11 British Canadians, who led Britain to the gold medal and stopped Canada's undefeated Olympic winning streak at 20. The best of the imported Brits was goaltender Jimmy Foster, who allowed just three goals in eight games.

After winning six gold medals in 1932, the U.S. had to settle for one this time, in the two-man bobsled driven by Ivan Brown.

Top 10 Standings

National medal standings are not recognized by the IOC. The unofficial point totals are based on 3 points for a gold medal, 2 for a silver and 1 for a bronze. Total medals are in parentheses.

		Gold	Silver	Bronze	Pts
1	Norway (15)	7	5	3	34
2	Germany (6)	3	3	0	15
3	Sweden (7)	2	2	3	13
4	Finland (6)	1	2	3	10
5	Switzerland (3)	1	2	0	7
6	Austria (4)	1	1	2	7
7	Great Britain (3)	1	1	1	6
8	USA (4)	1	0	3	6
9	Canada (1)	0	1	0	2
10	France (1)	0	0	1	1
	Hungary (1)	0	0	1	1

Leading Medal Winners

Number of individual medals won on the left; gold, silver and bronze breakdown to the right.

No		Sport	G-S-B
4	Ivar Ballangrud, NOR	Sp. Skate	3-1-0
3	Oddbjörn Hagen, NOR	X-country & Nordic Combined	1-2-0
3	Birger Vasenius, FIN	Sp. Skate	0-2-1
2	Ernst Baier, GER	Fig. Skate	1-1-0
2	Joseph Beerli, SWI	Bobsled	1-1-0
2	Erik Larsson, SWE	X-country	1-0-1
2	Fritz Feierabend, SWI	Bobsled	0-2-0
2	Olaf Hoffsbakken, NOR	X-country	0-2-0
2	Sverre Brodahl, NOR	X-country	0-1-1

Alpine Skiing

MEN

Event		Pts
Combined	Franz Pfnür, GER	99.25

WOMEN

Event		Pts
Combined	Christl Cranz, GER	97.06

Bobsled

Event		Time
2-Man	USA (Ivan Brown & Alan Washbond)	5:29.29
4-Man	SWI (Pierre Musy, Arnold Gartmann, Charles Bouvier, Joseph Beerli)	5:19.85

Figure Skating

Event		Points
Men	Karl Schäfer, AUT	2959.0
Women	Sonja Henie, NOR	425.5
Pairs	Maxi Herber & Ernst Baier, GER	11.5

Ice Hockey

Championship Round

(Overall records in parentheses)

		Gm	W-L-T	Pts	GF	GA
1	Great Britain (5-0-2)	3	2-0-1	5	7	1
2	Canada (7-1-0)	3	2-1-0	4	9	2
3	USA (5-2-1)	3	1-1-1	3	2	1
4	Czechoslovakia (5-3-0)	3	0-3-0	0	0	14

Scores: Britain beat Canada, 2–1; Czech., 5–0; and tied the U.S., 0–0 (OT). Canada beat Czech., 7–0, and the U.S., 1–0. The U.S. beat Czech., 2–0.

Nordic Skiing

Cross Country

Event		Time
18km	Erik-August Larsson, SWE	1:14:38
50km	Elis Wiklund, SWE	3:30:11
4x10km	FIN (Sulo Nurmela, Klaes Karppinen, Matti Lähde, Kalle Jalkanen)	2:41:33

Ski Jumping

Event		Points
90m	Birger Rudd, NOR	232.0

Nordic Combined

Event		Points
18km/Jump	Oddbjörn Hagen, NOR	430.3

Speed Skating

Event		Time	
500m	Ivar Ballangrud, NOR	43.4	=OR
1500m	Charles Mathisen, NOR	2:19.2	OR
5000m	Ivar Ballangrud, NOR	8:19.6	OR
10,000m	Ivar Ballangrud, NOR	17:24.3	OR

1948

St. Moritz

The Winter Games originally scheduled for Sapporo, Japan (1940) and Cortina d'Ampezzo, Italy (1944) were cancelled because of World War II. Untouched by the war, the Swiss resort town of St. Moritz was picked to host the 1948 Games and 28 countries sent 706 athletes to compete.

The United States sent two hockey teams, one sanctioned by the American Olympic Committee and one by the American Hockey Association. The IOC ruled that the AOC team could march in the opening parade and the AHA team could play in the tournament, but neither would be eligible for a medal. Canada and Czechoslovakia each finished with 7–0–1 records, but the Canadians won the gold medal by goal differential, 64–62. Czech team member Jaroslav Drobny later distinguished himself as a tennis player, winning the men's singles title at Wimbledon in 1954.

Dick Button of Englewood, N.J., became the first American to win a figure skating gold medal, an achievement that also earned him the Sullivan Award as U.S. amateur athlete of the year.

Alpine skier Gretchen Fraser won a gold medal in the slalom and a silver in the combined for the Americans. French Alpine skier Henri Oreiller was the men's top individual performer with two golds and a bronze.

Top 10 Standings

National medal standings are not recognized by the IOC. The unofficial point totals are based on 3 points for a gold medal, 2 for a silver and 1 for a bronze. Total medals are in parentheses.

		Gold	Silver	Bronze	Pts
1	Norway (10)	4	3	3	21
	Sweden (10)	4	3	3	21
3	Switzerland (10)	3	4	3	20
4	USA (9)	3	4	2	19
5	Austria (8)	1	3	4	13
6	Finland (6)	1	3	2	11
7	France (5)	2	1	2	10
8	Canada (3)	2	0	1	7
9	Belgium (2)	1	1	0	5
10	Italy (1)	1	0	0	3

Leading Medal Winners

Number of individual medals won on the left; gold, silver and bronze breakdown to the right.

MEN

No		Sport	G-S-B
3	Henri Oreiller, FRA	Alpine	2-0-1
2	Martin Lundström, SWE	X-country	2-0-0
2	Nils Östensson, SWE	X-country	1-1-0
2	Åke Seyffarth, SWE	Sp. Skate	1-1-0
2	Gunnar Eriksson, SWE	X-country	1-0-1
2	Karl Molitor, SWI	Alpine	1-0-1
2	James Couttet, FRA	Alpine	0-1-1
2	Odd Lundberg, NOR	Sp. Skate	0-1-1

WOMEN

No		Sport	G-S-B
2	Trude Beiser, AUT	Alpine	1-1-0
2	Gretchen Fraser, USA	Alpine	1-1-0
2	Erika Mahringer, AUT	Alpine	0-0-2

Alpine Skiing

MEN

Event		Pts
Downhill	Henri Oreiller, FRA	2:55.0
Slalom	Edi Reinalter, SWI	2:10.3
Combined	Henri Oreiller, FRA	3.27 pts

WOMEN

Event		Pts
Downhill	Hedy Schlunegger, SWI	2:28.3
Slalom	Gretchen Fraser, USA	1:57.2
Combined	Trude Beiser, AUT	6.58 pts

Bobsled

Event		Time
2-Man	SWI (Felix Endrich & Friedrich Waller)	5:29.2
4-Man	USA (Francis Tyler, Patrick Martin, Edward Rimkus, William D'Amico	5:20.1

Cresta (Toboggan)

Event		Time
1-Man	Nino Bibbia, ITA	5:23.2

Figure Skating

Event		Points
Men	Dick Button, USA	191.177
Women	Barbara Ann Scott, CAN	163.077
Pairs	Micheline Lannoy & Pierre Baugniet, BEL	11.227

Ice Hockey

		Gm	W-L-T	Pts	GF	GA
1	Canada	8	7-0-1	15	69	5
2	Czechoslovakia	8	7-0-1	15	80	18
3	Switzerland	8	6-2-0	12	67	21
4	USA (AHA)	8	5-3-0	10	86	33
5	Sweden	8	4-4-0	8	55	28
6	Great Britain	8	3-5-0	6	39	47
7	Poland	8	2-6-0	4	20	97
8	Austria	8	1-7-0	2	33	77
9	Italy	8	0-8-0	0	24	156

Note: Canada won championship on goal differential, 64–62.

Nordic Skiing

Cross Country

Event		Time
18km	Martin Lundstrom, SWE	1:13:50.0
50km	Nils Karlsson, SWE	3:47:48.0
4x10km	SWE (Nils Östensson, Nils Täpp, Gunnar Eriksson, Martin Lundström)	2:32:08.0

Ski Jumping

Event		Points
90m	Peter Hugsted, NOR	228.1

Nordic Combined

Event		Points
18km/Jump	Heikki Hasu, FIN	448.80

Speed Skating

Event		Time	
500m	Finn Helgesen, NOR	43.1	OR
1500m	Sverre Farstad, NOR	2:17.6	OR
5000m	Reidar Liaklev, NOR	8:29.4	
10,000m	Åke Seyffarth, SWE	17:26.3	

1952

Oslo

Dick Button, who had revolutionized figure skating with his athletic jumps and spins at St. Moritz in 1948, repeated his gold medal performance in '52. The 22–year-old Harvard senior also won the world championship for the fifth straight year, then turned pro.

Andrea Mead Lawrence, a 19–year-old whose parents built the Pico Peak ski resort in Vermont became the first U.S. skier to win two Olympic gold medals, taking both the slalom and giant slalom.

The star of the Games, however, was 28–year-old Norwegian truck driver Hjalmar Andersen who, urged on by his cheering countrymen, won three speed skating gold medals in three days and set Olympic records in two of the races.

The U.S. finished second to Norway in the overall medal count and was runner-up to Canada in hockey. The gold medal was the Canadians' seventh in eight Olympics and, as it turned out, their last.

Top 10 Standings

National medal standings are not recognized by the IOC. The unofficial point totals are based on 3 points for a gold medal, 2 for a silver and 1 for a bronze. Total medals are in parentheses.

		Gold	Silver	Bronze	Pts
1	Norway (16)	7	3	6	33
2	USA (11)	4	6	1	25
3	Finland (9)	3	4	2	19
4	Austria (8)	2	4	2	16
5	Germany (7)	3	2	2	15
6	Holland (3)	0	3	0	6
7	Canada (2)	1	0	1	4
	Italy (2)	1	0	1	4
	Sweden (4)	0	0	4	4
10	Great Britain (1)	1	0	0	3

Leading Medal Winners

Number of individual medals won on the left; gold, silver and bronze breakdown to the right.

MEN

No		Sport	G-S-B
3	Hjalmar Andersen, NOR	Sp. Skate	3-0-0
2	Andreas Ostler, GER	Bobsled	2-0-0
2	Lorenz Nieberl, GER	Bobsled	2-0-0
2	Hallgeir Brenden, NOR	X-country	1-1-0
2	Stein Eriksen, NOR	Alpine	1-1-0
2	Heikki Hasu, FIN	X-country & Nordic Combined	1-1-0
2	Tapio Mäkelä, FIN	X-country	1-1-0
2	Othmar Schneider, AUT	Alpine	1-1-0
2	Paavo Lonkila, FIN	X-country	1-0-1
2	Stan Benham, USA	Bobsled	0-2-0
2	Kees Broekman, NED	Sp. Skate	0-2-0
2	Patrick Martin, USA	Bobsled	0-2-0
2	Magnar Estenstad, NOR	X-country	0-1-1
2	Christian Pravda, AUT	Alpine	0-1-1
2	Fritz Feierabend, SWI	Bobsled	0-0-2
2	Stephan Waser, SWI	Bobsled	0-0-2

WOMEN

No		Sport	G-S-B
3	Annemarie Buchner, GER	Alpine	0-1-2
2	Andrea Mead Lawrence, USA	Alpine	2-0-0

Alpine Skiing

MEN

Event		Time
Downhill	Zeno Colò, ITA	2:30.8
Slalom	Othmar Schneider, AUT	2:00.0
G.Slalom	Stein Eriksen, NOR	2:25.0

WOMEN

Event		Time
Downhill	Trude Jochum-Beiser, AUT	1:47.1
Slalom	Andrea Mead Lawrence, USA	2:10.6
G.Slalom	Andrea Mead Lawrence, USA	2:06.8

Bobsled

Event		Time
2-Man	GER (Andreas Ostler & Lorenz Nieberl)	5:24.54
4-Man	GER (Andreas Ostler, Friedrich Kuhn, Lorenz Nieberl, Franz Kemser)	5:07.84

Ice Hockey

		Gm	W-L-T	Pts	GF	GA
1	Canada	8	7-0-1	15	71	14
2	USA	8	6-1-1	13	43	21
3	Sweden	8	6-2-0	12	48	19
4	Czechoslovakia	8	6-2-0	12	47	18
5	Switzerland	8	4-4-0	8	40	40
6	Poland	8	2-5-1	5	21	56
7	Finland	8	2-6-0	4	21	60
8	Germany	8	1-6-1	3	21	53
9	Norway	8	0-8-0	0	15	46

Note: Sweden defeated Czechoslovakia 5–3, in a playoff game to decide third place and the 1952 European championship.

Nordic Skiing

MEN

Cross Country

Event		Time
18km	Hallgeir Brenden, NOR	1:01:34.0
50km	Veikko Hakulinen, FIN	3:33:33.0
4x10km	FIN (Heikki, Hasu, Paavo Lonkila, Urpo Korhonen, Tapio Mäkelä)	2:20:16.0

Ski Jumping

Event		Points
90m	Arnfinn Bergman, NOR	226.0

Nordic Combined

Event		Points
18km/Jump	Simon Slåttvik, NOR	51.621

WOMEN

Cross-Country

Event		Time
10km	Lydia Widerman, FIN	41:40.0

Speed Skating

MEN

Event		Time	
500m	Ken Henry, USA	43.2	
1500m	Hjalmar Andersen, NOR	2:20.4	
5000m	Hjalmar Andersen, NOR	8:10.6	OR
10,000m	Hjalmar Andersen, NOR	16:45.8	OR

1956

Cortina d'Ampezzo

The Soviet Union emerged from the shadows of the Cold War in 1952 to make its Olympic debut at the Summer Games in Helsinki. Finishing a close second to the United States in overall medal count (74–71), the Russians served notice that they were an athletic superpower to be reckoned with.

In 1956, the USSR made its first appearance in the Winter Games and not only outmedaled the 32–nation field, but dethroned Canada as hockey champion. Four of the USSR's seven gold medals came in speed skating, where Yevgeny Grishin led the way with gold medals in the 500 and 1,500 meters.

Despite a shortage of snow in northern Italy, the outstanding performance of the VIIth Winter Games belonged to a skier named Sailer. By winning the downhill, slalom and giant slalom, Toni Sailer of Austria became the first skier to sweep all three Alpine events and only the fifth winter athlete to win three gold medals at one Olympics.

Swedish cross-country skier Sixten Jernberg, who would eventually participate in three Winter Games and win a total of nine medals, led all contestants in Cortina with four, including a gold at 50 kilometers.

The women's and men's figure skating titles were won by Americans Tenley Albright and Hayes Jenkins, who were both reigning world champions. Albright had won a silver medal in 1952, while Jenkins had finished fourth.

Top 10 Standings

National medal standings are not recognized by the IOC. The unofficial point totals are based on 3 points for a gold medal, 2 for a silver and 1 for a bronze. Total medals are in parentheses.

		Gold	Silver	Bronze	Pts
1	USSR (16)	7	3	6	33
2	Austria (11)	4	3	4	22
3	Sweden (10)	2	4	4	18
4	Finland (7)	3	3	1	16
5	Switzerland (6)	3	2	1	14
	USA (7)	2	3	2	14
7	Norway (4)	2	1	1	9
8	Italy (3)	1	2	0	7
9	Germany (2)	1	0	1	4
	Canada (3)	0	1	2	4

Leading Medal Winners

Number of individual medals won on the left; gold, silver and bronze breakdown to the right.

MEN

No		Sport	G-S-B
4	Sixten Jernberg, SWE	X-country	1-2-1
3	Toni Sailer, AUT	Alpine	3-0-0
3	Veikko Hakulinen, FIN	X-country	1-2-0
3	Pavel Kolchin, USSR	X-country	1-0-2
2	Yevgeny Grishin, USSR	Sp. Skate	2-0-0
2	Sigvard Ericsson, SWE	Sp. Skate	1-1-0
2	Fedor Terentyev, USSR	X-country	1-0-1
2	Renzo Alvera, ITA	Bobsled	0-2-0
2	Eugenio Monti, ITA	Bobsled	0-2-0
2	Andreas Molterer, AUT	Alpine	0-1-1
2	Oleg Goncharenko, USSR	Sp. Skate	0-0-2

WOMEN

No		Sport	G-S-B
2	Lyubov Kozyreva, USSR	X-country	1-1-0
2	Radya Eroshina, USSR	X-country	0-2-0
2	Sonja Edstrom, SWE	X-country	0-0-2

Alpine Skiing

MEN

Event		Time
Downhill	Toni Sailer, AUT	2:52.2
Slalom	Toni Sailer, AUT	3:14.7
G.Slalom	Toni Sailer, AUT	3:00.1

WOMEN

Event		Time
Downhill	Madeleine Berthod, SWI	1:40.7
Slalom	Renée Colliard, SWI	1:52.3
G.Slalom	Ossi Reichert, GER	1:56.5

Bobsled

Event		Time
2-Man	ITA (Lamberto Dalla Costa & Giacomo Conti)	5:30.14
4-Man	SWI (Franz Kapus, Gottfried Diener, Robert Alt, Heinrich Angst)	5:10.44

Figure Skating

Event		Time
Men	Hayes Jenkins, USA	166.43
Women	Tenley Albright, USA	169.67
Pairs	Elisabeth Schwartz & Kurt Oppelt, AUT	11.31

Ice Hockey

(Overall records in parentheses)

		Gm	W-L-T	Pts	GF	GA
1	USSR (7-0-0)	5	5-0-0	10	25	5
2	USA (5-2-0)	5	4-1-0	8	26	12
3	Canada (6-2-0)	5	3-2-0	6	23	11
4	Sweden (2-4-1)	5	1-3-1	3	10	22
5	Czechoslovakia (3-4-0)	5	1-4-0	2	20	30
6	Germany (1-5-2)	5	0-4-1	1	6	35

Note: The USSR beat the U.S., 4–0, and Canada, 2–0. The U.S. beat Canada, 4–1.

Nordic Skiing

MEN

Cross Country

Event		Time
15km	Hallgeir Brenden, NOR	49:39.0
30km	Veikko Hakulinen, FIN	1:44:06.0
50km	Sixten Jernberg, SWE	2:50:27.0
4x10km	USSR (Fedor Terentyev, Pavel Kolchin, Nikolai Anikin, Vladimir Kuzin)	2:15:30.0

Ski Jumping

Event		Points
90m	Antti Hyvärinen, FIN	227.0

Nordic Combined

Event		Points
15km/Jump	Sverre Stenersen, NOR	455.000

WOMEN

Cross Country

Event		Time
10km	Lyubov Kosyreva, USSR	38:11.0
3x5km	FIN (Sirkka Polkunen, Mirja Hietamies, Siira Rantanen)	1:09:01.0

Speed Skating

MEN

Event		Time	
500m	Yevgeny Grishin, USSR	40.2	WR
1500m	Yevgeny Grishin, USSR & Yuri Mikhailov, USSR	2:08.6	WR
5000m	Boris Shilkov, USSR	7:48.7	OR
10,000m	Sigvard Ericsson, SWE	16:35.9	OR

1960

Squaw Valley

The first Winter Olympics in the U.S. since 1932 was held at an obscure California ski resort near Lake Tahoe that had no bobsled run and in the days leading up to the opening ceremony, no snow. Luckily, an 11th hour drop in temperature changed a drenching rain into a much-needed blizzard and the Games got off to a wintry start.

The most exciting venue, however, was indoors at Blyth Arena where the underdog U.S. hockey team upset the Russians and Canadians to win the gold medal for the first time ever. Led by forwards Billy Cleary and Roger Christian and goaltender Jack McCarten, the Americans beat Canada 2–1, Russia 3–2, and the Czechs 9–4, in their last three games to clinch the title.

Blyth was also where Carol Heiss and David Jenkins won the women's and men's figure skating gold medals. Heiss had won a silver and Jenkins a bronze in 1956. Shortly after the Games, Heiss married Jenkins' older brother Hayes, the men's gold medalist in '56.

Outside, speed skater Yevgeny Grishin of the USSR won at 500 and 1,500 meters for the second Olympics in a row. In fact, Grishin's victory in the 1,500 was his second straight tie at that distance—sharing gold medals with teammate Yuri Mikhailov in 1956 and Norway's Roald Aas in '60. This was also the first year women could compete in speed skating and the Soviets' Lydia Skoblikova won twice, at 1,500 and 3,000 meters. She would go on to win four gold medals at Innsbruck in 1964.

At 35, three-time Olympic cross-country skier Veikko Hakulinen of Finland was the only athlete at Squaw Valley to claim three medals (for a career total of seven). He came from 20 seconds back on the anchor leg to win gold in the 40-kilometer relay.

Nineteen-year-old Alpine skier Penny Pitou was America's top medalist, placing second in both the downhill and slalom events. She was later married for a few years to 1964 men's downhill champion Egon Zimmermann of Austria.

Top 10 Standings

National medal standings are not recognized by the IOC. The unofficial point totals are based on 3 points for a gold medal, 2 for a silver and 1 for a bronze. Total medals are in parentheses.

		Gold	Silver	Bronze	Pts
1	USSR (21)	7	5	9	40
2	USA (10)	3	4	3	20
3	Germany (8)	4	3	1	19
4	Norway (6)	3	3	0	15
	Sweden (7)	3	2	2	15
	Finland (8)	2	3	3	15
7	Austria (6)	1	2	3	10
8	Canada (4)	2	1	1	9
9	Switzerland (2)	2	0	0	6
10	France (3)	1	0	2	5

Leading Medal Winners

Number of individual medals won on the left; gold, silver and bronze breakdown to the right.

MEN

No		Sport	G-S-B
3	Veikko Hakulinen, FIN	X-country	1-1-1
2	Yevgeny Grishin, USSR	Sp. Skate	2-0-0
2	Håkon Brusveen, NOR	X-country	1-1-0
2	Knut Johannesen, NOR	Sp. Skate	1-1-0
2	Sixten Jernberg, SWE	X-country	1-1-0
2	Viktor Kosichkin, USSR	Sp. Skate	1-1-0
2	Ernst Hinterseer, AUT	Alpine	1-0-1
2	Rolf Rämgård, SWE	X-country	0-1-1
2	Nikolai Anikin, USSR	X-country	0-0-2

WOMEN

No		Sport	G-S-B
2	Lydia Skoblikova, USSR	Sp. Skate	2-0-0
2	Maria Gusakova, USSR	X-country	1-1-0
2	Helga Haase, GER	Sp. Skate	1-1-0
2	Penny Pitou, USA	Alpine	0-2-0
2	Lyubov Baranova, USSR	X-country	0-2-0
2	Radya Eroshina, USSR	X-country	0-1-1

Alpine Skiing

MEN

Event		Time
Downhill	Jean Vuarnet, FRA	2:06.0
Slalom	Ernst Hinterseer, AUT	2:08.9
G.Slalom	Roger Staub, SWI	1:48.3

WOMEN

Event		Time
Downhill	Heidi Biebl, GER	1:37.6
Slalom	Anne Heggtveit, CAN	1:49.6
G.Slalom	Avonne Rüegg, SWI	1:39.9

Biathlon

Event		MT	Adj.Time
20 km	Klas Lestander, SWE	0	1:33:21.6

Figure Skating

Event		Time
Men	David Jenkins, USA	1440.2
Women	Carol Heiss, USA	1490.1
Pairs	Barbara Wagner & Robert Paul, CAN	80.4

Ice Hockey

Championship Round

(Overall records in parentheses)

		Gm	W-L-T	Pts	GF	GA
1	USA (7-0-0)	5	5-0-0	10	29	11
2	Canada (6-1-0)	5	4-1-0	8	31	12
3	USSR (4-2-1)	5	2-2-1	5	24	19
4	Czechoslovakia (3-4-0)	5	2-3-0	4	21	23
5	Sweden (2-4-1)	5	1-3-1	3	19	19
6	Germany (1-6-0)	5	0-5-0	0	5	45

Note: The U.S. beat Canada, 2–1, the USSR, 3–2, and Czech., 9–4, in its last three games. Canada beat the USSR, 8–5, and Sweden tied the Russians, 2–2.

Nordic Skiing

MEN

Cross Country

Event		Time
15km	Håkon Brusveen, NOR	51:55.5
30km	Sixten Jernberg, SWE	1:51:03.9
50km	Kalevi Hämäläinen, FIN	2:59:06.3
4x10km	FIN (Toimi Alatalo, Eero Mäntyranta, Väinö Huhtala, Veikko Hakulinen)	2:18:45.6

Ski Jumping

Event		Points
80m	Helmut Recknagel, GER	227.2

Nordic Combined

Event		Points
15km/Jump	Georg Thoma, GER	457.952

WOMEN

Cross Country

Event		Time
10km	Marija Gusakova, USSR	39:46.6
3x5km	SWE (Irma Johansson, Britt Strandberg, Sonja Ruthström)	1:04:21.4

Speed Skating

MEN

Event		Time	
500m	Yevgeny Grishin, USSR	40.2	=WR
1500m	Roald Aas, NOR	2:10.4	WR
	& Yevgeny Grishin, USSR	2:10.4	WR
5000m	Viktor Kosichkin, USSR	7:51.3	
10,000m	Knut Johannesen, NOR	15:46.6	

WOMEN

Event		Time	
500m	Helga Haase, GER	45.9	
1000m	Klara Guseva, USSR	1:34.1	
1500m	Lydia Skoblikova, USSR	2:25.2	WR
3000m	Lydia Skoblikova, USSR	5:14.3	

1964

Innsbruck

Death and unseasonably mild weather hung over the ninth Winter Games in the Tyrolean Alps.

Two athletes, 50–year-old British luger Kazimierz Kay-Skyszpeski and 19–year-old Australian downhill skier Ross Milne, were killed taking practice runs less than a week before the Games began. And three years before, on Feb. 15, 1961, a plane crash in Belgium had killed 18 members of the U.S. figure skating team—including America's top female skater, 16-year-old Laurence Owen.

Springlike temperatures plagued Innsbruck both before and during the Games, forcing the Austrian military to carry in over 50,000 cubic meters of snow from higher elevations.

The USSR won 11 gold medals—a combined seven by speed skater Lydia Skoblikova (4) and cross-country skier Claudia Boyarskikh (3). Other stars included the skiing Goitschel sisters, Christine and Marielle, of France; and cross-country skiers Eero Mäntyranta of Finland and 34-year-old Sixten Jernberg of Sweden.

The lone U.S. gold medal was won by 23-year-old barber Terry McDermott in speed skating.

Top 10 Standings

National medal standings are not recognized by the IOC. The unofficial point totals are based on 3 points for a gold medal, 2 for a silver and 1 for a bronze. Total medals are in parentheses.

		Gold	Silver	Bronze	Pts
1	USSR (25)	11	8	6	55
2	Norway (15)	3	6	6	27
3	Austria (12)	4	5	3	25
4	Finland (10)	3	4	3	20
5	France (7)	3	4	0	17
6	Sweden (7)	3	3	1	16
	Germany (8)	3	2	3	16
8	USA (6)	1	2	3	10
9	Holland (2)	1	1	0	5
	Canada (3)	1	0	2	5
	Italy (4)	0	1	3	5

Leading Medal Winners

Number of individual medals won on the left; gold, silver and bronze breakdown to the right.

MEN

No		Sport	G-S-B
3	Eero Mäntyranta, FIN	X-country	2-1-0
3	Sixten Jernberg, SWE	X-country	2-0-1
2	Toralf Engan, NOR	Ski Jump	1-1-0
2	Veikko Kankkonen, FIN	Ski Jump	1-1-0
2	Assar Rönnlund, SWE	X-country	1-1-0
2	Knut Johannesen, NOR	Sp. Skate	1-0-1
2	Pepi Stiegler, AUT	Alpine	1-0-1
2	Harald Grönningen, NOR	X-country	0-2-0
2	Fred Maier, NOR	Sp. Skate	0-1-1
2	Arto Tiainen, FIN	X-country	0-1-1
2	Torgeir Brandtzaeg, NOR	Ski jump	0-0-2
2	Eugenio Monti, ITA	Bobsled	0-0-2
2	Sergio Siorpaes, ITA	Bobsled	0-0-2
2	Igor Voronchikin, USSR	X-country	0-0-2

WOMEN

No		Sport	G-S-B
4	Lydia Skoblikova, USSR	Sp. Skate	4-0-0
3	Claudia Boyarskikh, USSR	X-country	3-0-0
2	Christine Goitschel, FRA	Alpine	1-1-0
2	Marielle Goitschel, FRA	Alpine	1-1-0
2	Eudokia Mekshilo, USSR	X-country	1-1-0
2	Alevtina Kolchina, USSR	X-country	1-0-1
2	Mirja Lehtonen, FIN	X-country	0-1-1
2	Kaija Mustonen, FIN	Sp. Skate	0-1-1
2	Jean Saubert, USA	Alpine	0-1-1
2	Irina Yegorova, USSR	Sp. Skate	0-2-0

Alpine Skiing

MEN

Event		Time
Downhill	Egon Zimmermann, AUT	2:18.16
Slalom	Pepi Stiegler, AUT	2:11.13
G.Slalom	Francois Bonlieu, FRA	1:46.71

Note: In the Slalom, Billy Kidd (2nd) and Jimmy Heuga (3rd) won first U.S. men's Alpine medals ever.

WOMEN

Event		Time
Downhill	Christl Haas, AUT	1:55.39
Slalom	Christine Goitschel, FRA	1:29.86
G.Slalom	Marielle Goitschel, FRA	1:52.24

Biathlon

Event		MT	Adj.Time
20 km	Vladimir Melanin, USSR	0	1:20:26.8

Bobsled

Event		Time
2-Man	GBR (Tony Nash & Robin Dixon)	4:21.90
4-Man	CAN (Victor Emery, Peter Kirby, Doug Anakin, John Emery)	4:14.46

Figure Skating

Event		Points
Men	Manfred Schnelldorfer, GER	1916.9
Women	Sjoukje Dijkstra, NED	2018.5
Pairs	Lyudmila Belousova & Oleg Protopopov, USSR	104.4

Ice Hockey

Championship Round

(Overall records in parentheses)

		Gm	W-L-T	Pts	GF	GA
1	USSR (8-0-0)	7	7-0-0	14	54	10
2	Sweden (6-2-0)	7	5-2-0	10	47	16
3	Czechoslovakia (6-2-0)	7	5-2-0	10	38	19
4	Canada (6-2-0)	7	5-2-0	10	32	17
5	USA (3-5-0)	7	2-5-0	4	29	33
6	Finland (3-5-0)	7	2-5-0	4	10	31
7	Germany (3-5-0)	7	2-5-0	4	13	49
8	Switzerland (1-7-0)	7	0-7-0	0	9	57

Luge

MEN

Event		Time
1-Seat	Thomas Köhler, GER	3:26.77
2-Seat	Josef Feistmantl & Manfred Stengl, AUT	1:41.62

WOMEN

Event		Time
1-Seat	Ortrun Enderlein, GER	3:24.67

Nordic Skiing

MEN

Cross Country

Event		Time
15km	Eero Mäntyranta, FIN	50:54.1
30km	Eero Mäntyranta, FIN	1:30:50.7
50km	Sixten Jernberg, SWE	2:43:52.6
4x10km	SWE (Karl-Åke Asph, Sixten Jernberg Janne Stefansson, Assar Rönnlund)	2:18:34.6

Ski Jumping

Event		Points
70m	Veikko Kankkonen, FIN	229.9
80m	Toralf Engan, NOR	230.7

Nordic Combined

Event		Points
15km/Jump	Tormod Knutsen, NOR	469.28

WOMEN

Cross-country

Event		Time
5km	Claudia Boyarskikh, USSR	17:50.5
10km	Claudia Boyarskikh, USSR	40:24.3
3x5km	USSR (Alevtina Kolchina, Eudokia Mekshilo, Claudia Boyarskikh)	59:20.2

Speed Skating

MEN

Event		Time	
500m	Terry McDermott, USA	40.1	OR
1500m	Ants Antson, USSR	2:10.3	
5000m	Knut Johannesen, NOR	7:38.4	OR
10,000m	Jonny Nilsson, SWE	15:50.1	

WOMEN

Event		Time	
500m	Lydia Skoblikova, USSR	45.0	OR
1000m	Lydia Skoblikova, USSR	1:33.2	OR
1500m	Lydia Skoblikova, USSR	2:22.6	OR
3000m	Lydia Skoblikova, USSR	5:14.9	

1968

Grenoble

For the first time since they began attending the Winter Games in 1956, the Russians did not win the most medals—Norway did.

This was also the first year that the IOC permitted East and West Germany to participate as separate countries.

The host French team finished fourth in the overall standings—their best showing ever—thanks mainly to 24-year-old Jean-Claude Killy, who became the first skier to sweep all three Alpine events since Tony Sailer in 1956.

Killy was awarded his third gold medal in the slalom only after original winner Karl Schranz of Austria was disqualified for missing two gates on his second run in the two-heat race. Schranz had been allowed to retake his second heat run when a spectator interrupted his initial attempt, but officials ruled the missed gates came before the interruption.

Once again, the U.S. won only one gold medal—19-year-old Peggy Fleming in women's figure skaiting. Three of the five silver medals won by the U.S. came in one event—the women's 500-meter speed skating race, where Jenny Fish, Dianne Holum and Mary Myers tied for second place with a time of 46.3 seconds.

Top 10 Standings

National medal standings are not recognized by the IOC. The unofficial point totals are based on 3 points for a gold medal, 2 for a silver and 1 for a bronze. Total medals are in parentheses.

		Gold	Silver	Bronze	Pts
1	Norway (14)	6	6	2	32
2	USSR (13)	5	5	3	28
3	Austria (11)	3	4	4	21
4	France (9)	4	3	2	20
5	Holland (9)	3	3	3	18
6	Sweden (8)	3	2	3	16
7	USA (7)	1	5	1	14
8	West Germany (7)	2	2	3	13
9	Italy (4)	4	0	0	12
10	East Germany (5)	1	2	2	9
	Finland (5)	1	2	2	9

Leading Medal Winners

Number of individual medals won on the left; gold, silver and bronze breakdown to the right.

MEN

No		Sport	G-S-B
3	Jean-Claude Killy, FRA	Alpine	3-0-0
3	Eero Mäntyranta, FIN	X-country	0-1-2
2	Eugenio Monti, ITA	Bobsled	2-0-0
2	Luciano De Paolis, ITA	Bobsled	2-0-0
2	Ole Ellefsaeter, NOR	X-country	2-0-0
2	Harald Grönningen, NOR	X-country	2-0-0
2	Thomas Köhler, E.Ger.	Luge	1-1-0
2	Fred Maier, NOR	Sp. Skate	1-1-0
2	Odd Martinsen, NOR	X-country	1-1-0
2	Jiri Raska, CZE	Ski Jump	1-1-0
2	Manfred Schmid, AUT	Luge	1-1-0
2	Magnar Solberg, NOR	Biathlon	1-1-0
2	Aleksandr Tikhonov, USSR	Biathlon	1-1-0
2	Kees Verkerk, NED	Sp. Skate	1-1-0
2	Klaus Bonsack, E. Ger.	Luge	1-0-1
2	Vladimir Goundartsev, USSR	Biathlon	1-0-1
2	Gunnar Larsson, SWE	X-country	0-1-1

WOMEN

No		Sport	G-S-B
3	Toini Gustafsson, SWE	X-country	2-1-0
2	Carolina Geijssen, NED	Sp. Skate	1-1-0
2	Nancy Greene, CAN	Alpine	1-1-0
2	Berit Mördre, NOR	X-country	1-1-0
2	Kaija Mustonen, FIN	Sp. Skate	1-1-0
2	Lyudmila Titova, USSR	Sp. Skate	1-1-0
2	Inger Aufles, NOR	X-country	1-0-1
2	Annie Famose, FRA	Alpine	0-1-1
2	Dianne Holum, USA	Sp. Skate	0-1-1
2	Galina Kulakova, USSR	X-country	0-1-1
2	Christina Kaiser, NED	Sp. Skate	0-0-2
2	Alevtina Kolchina, USSR	X-country	0-0-2

Alpine Skiing

MEN

Event		Time
Downhill	Jean-Claude Killy, FRA	1:59.85
Slalom	Jean-Claude Killy, FRA	1:39.73
G.Slalom	Jean-Claude Killy, FRA	3:29.28

WOMEN

Event		Time
Downhill	Olga Pall, AUT	1:40.87
Slalom	Marielle Goitschel, FRA	1:25.86
G.Slalom	Nancy Greene, CAN	1:51.97

Biathlon

Event		MT	Adj.Time
20 km	Magnar Solberg, NOR	0	1:13:45.9
4x7.5km	USSR (Tikonov, Pousanov, Mamatov, Goundartsev)	2	2:13:02.4

Bobsled

Event		Time
2-Man	ITA (Eugenio Monti & Luciano De Paolis)	4:41.54
4-Man	ITA (Monti, De Paolis, Zandonella, Armano)	2:17.39

Figure Skating

Event		Points
Men	Wolfgang Schwarz, AUT	1904.1
Women	Peggy Fleming, USA	1970.5
Pairs	Lyudmila Belousova & Oleg Protopopov, USSR	315.2

Ice Hockey

Group A

(Overall records in parentheses)

		Gm	W-L-T	Pts	GF	GA
1	USSR	7	6-1-0	12	48	10
2	Czecholslovakia	7	5-1-1	11	33	17
3	Canada	7	5-2-0	10	28	15
4	Sweden	7	4-2-1	9	23	18
5	Finland (4-3-1)	7	3-3-1	9	17	23
6	USA	7	2-4-1	5	23	28
7	West Germany (2-6-0)	7	1-6-0	2	13	39
8	East Germany (1-7-0)	7	0-7-0	0	13	48

Note: Finland and the two Germanys had to win an elimination round game to qualify for Group A. Their overall records are in parentheses.

Luge

MEN

Event		Time
1-Seat	Manfred Schmid, AUT	2:52.48
2-Seat	Klaus Bonsack & Thomas Köhler, E. Ger	1:35.85

WOMEN

Event		Time
1-Seat	Erica Lechner, ITA	2:28.66

Note: Defending champion Ortrun Enderlein and teammate Anna Maria Müller of East Germany finished 1–2, but were disqualified for heating the blades of their toboggans.

Nordic Skiing

MEN

Cross Country

Event		Time
15km	Harold Grönningen, NOR	47:54.2
30km	Franco Nones, ITA	1:35:39.2
50km	Ole Ellefsaeter, NOR	2:28:45.8
4x10km	NOR (Martinsen, Tyldum, Grönningen, Ellefsaeter)	2:08:33.5

Ski Jumping

Event		Points
70m	Jiri Raska, CZE	216.5
90m	Vladimir Beloussov, USSR	231.3

Nordic Combined

Event		Points
15km/Jump	Franz Keller, W. Ger.	449.04

WOMEN

Cross-country

Event		Time
5km	Toini Gustafsson, SWE	16:45.2
10km	Toini Gustafsson, SWE	36:46.5
3x5km	NOR (Aufles, Damon-Enger, Mördre)	57:30.0

Speed Skating

MEN

Event		Time	
500m	Erhard Keller, W. Ger.	40.3	
1500m	Kees Verkerk, NED	2:03.4	OR
5000m	Fred Maier, NOR	7:22.4	WR
10,000m	Johnny Höglin, SWE	15:23.6	OR

WOMEN

Event		Time	
500m	Lyudmila Titova, USSR	46.1	
1000m	Carolina Geijssen, NED	1:32.6	OR
1500m	Kaija Mustonen, FIN	2:22.4	OR
3000m	Johanna Schut, NED	4:56.2	OR

1972

Sapporo

The biggest controversy in the 48–year history of the Winter Games erupted just three days before the opening ceremonies were scheduled to get underway in northern Japan. That's when retiring IOC president Avery Brundage threatened to disqualify 40 Alpine skiers for professionalism.

At Grenoble in 1968, Brundage had demanded that all trademarks be removed from competitors' skis, but settled for having the offensive skis taken away from medal winners before they could be photographed. Now, the 84–year-old guardian of the Olympic flame wanted all the pros thrown out.

A compromise was reached when the IOC executive committee voted 28–14 to make an example of skiing's most commercialized star, 33–year-old Austrian World Cup champion Karl Schranz, who reportedly earned over $50,000 a year "testing" ski equipment.

All other offenders were allowed to participate.

Said Schranz after being banished: "This thing of amateur purity is something that dates back to the 19th century when amateur sportsmen were regarded as gentlemen and everyone else was an outcast. The Olympics should be a competition of skill and strength and speed—and no more."

Schranz retired after the Games, having never won an Olympic gold medal.

Top 10 Standings

National medal standings are not recognized by the IOC. The unofficial point totals are based on 3 points for a gold medal, 2 for a silver and 1 for a bronze. Total medals are in parentheses.

		Gold	Silver	Bronze	Pts
1	USSR (16)	8	5	3	37
2	East Germany (14)	4	3	7	25
3	Switzerland (10)	4	3	3	21
	Norway (12)	2	5	5	21
5	Holland (9)	4	3	2	20
6	USA (8)	3	2	3	16
7	West Germany (5)	3	1	1	12
8	Italy (5)	2	2	1	11
9	Austria (5)	1	2	2	9
	Finland (5)	0	4	1	9

Leading Medal Winners

Number of individual medals won on the left; gold, silver and bronze breakdown to the right.

MEN

No		Sport	G-S-B
3	Ard Schenk, NED	Sp. Skate	3-0-0
3	Vyacheslav Vedenine, USSR	X-country	2-0-1
3	Pål Tyldum, NOR	X-country	1-2-0
2	Fedor Simashov, USSR	X-country	1-1-0
2	Gustav Thöni, ITA	Alpine	1-1-0
2	Wolfgang Zimmerer, W. Ger.	Bobsled	1-0-1
2	Peter Utzschneider, W. Ger.	Bobsled	1-0-1
2	Jean Wicki, SWI	Bobsled	1-0-1
2	Edy Hubacher, SWI	Bobsled	1-0-1
2	Roar Grönvold, NOR	Sp. Skate	0-2-0
2	Ivar Formo, NOR	X-country	0-1-1
2	Johs Harviken, NOR	X-country	0-1-1
2	Hansjorg Knauthe, E. Ger.	Biathlon	0-1-1
2	Wolfram Fiedler, E. Ger.	Luge	0-0-2
2	Sten Stensen, NOR	Sp. Skate	0-0-2

WOMEN

No		Sport	G-S-B
3	Galina Kulakova, USSR	X-country	3-0-0
3	Marjatta Kajosmaa, FIN	X-country	0-2-1
2	Marie-Theres Nadig, SWI	Alpine	2-0-0
2	Dianne Holum, USA	Sp. Skate	1-1-0
2	Christina Baas-Kaiser, NED	Sp. Skate	1-1-0
2	Alevtina Olunina, USSR	X-country	1-1-0
2	Anne Henning, USA	Sp. Skate	1-0-1
2	Annemarie Pröll, FRA	Alpine	0-2-0
2	Atje Keulen-Deelstra, NED	Sp. Skate	0-1-1

Alpine Skiing

MEN

Event		Time
Downhill	Bernhard Russi, SWI	1:51.43
Slalom	Francisco Ochoa, SPA	1:49.27
G.Slalom	Gustav Thöni, ITA	3:09.62

WOMEN

Event		Time
Downhill	Marie-Theres Nadig, SWI	1:36.68
Slalom	Barbara Cochran, USA	1:31.24
G.Slalom	Marie-Theres Nadig, SWI	1:29.90

Biathlon

Event		MT	Adj.Time
20 km	Magnar Solberg, NOR	2	1:15:55.50
4x7.5km	USSR (Tikonov, Safine, Biakov Mamatov)	3	1:51:44.92

Bobsled

Event		Time
2-Man	W. Ger. (Wolfgang Zimmerer & Peter Utzschneider)	4:57.07
4-Man	SWI (Wicki, Hubacher Leutenegger, Carmichel)	4:43.07

Figure Skating

Event		Points
Men	Ondrej Nepela, CZE	2739.1
Women	Trixi Schuba, AUT	2751.5
Pairs	Irina Rodnina & Aleksei Ulanov, USSR	420.4

Ice Hockey

Group A

(Overall records in parentheses)

		Gm	W-L-T	Pts	GF	GA
1	USSR (4-0-1)	5	4-0-1	9	33	13
2	USA (4-2-0)	5	3-2-0	6	18	15
3	Czechoslovakia (4-2-0)	5	3-2-0	6	26	13
4	Sweden (3-2-1)	5	2-2-1	5	17	13
5	Finland (3-3-0)	5	2-3-0	4	14	24
6	Poland (1-5-0)	5	0-5-0	0	9	39

Note: Pivotal game—USSR over Czech., 5–2, in final contest for both teams. The 5–1 U.S. victory over the Czechs gave the Americans second place. Canada did not send a team, having withdrawn from international amateur competition in 1969 to protest use of "professional amateurs" by Russia and other eastern bloc countries. Also, the USSR received a bye to Group A while the other seven teams had to win a one-game elimination round to qualify.

Luge

MEN

Event		Time
1-Seat	Wolfgang Scheidel, E. Ger.	3:27.58
2-Seat	TIE—Horst Hörnlein & Reinhard Bredow, E. Ger.	1:28.35
	—Paul Hildgartner & Walter Plaikner, ITA	1:28.35

WOMEN

Event		Time
1-Seat	Anna-Maria Müller, E. Ger.	2:59.18

Nordic Skiing

MEN

Cross Country

Event		Time
15km	Sven-Ake Lundbäck, SWE	45:28.24
30km	Vyachelav Vedenine, USSR	1:36:31.15
50km	Pål Tyldum, NOR	2:43:14.75
4x10km	USSR (Voronkov, Skobov, Simachev Vedenine)	2:04:47.94

Ski Jumping

Event		Points
70m	Yukio Kasaya, JPN	244.2
90m	Wojciech Fortuna, POL	219.9

Nordic Combined

Event		Points
15km/Jump	Ulrich Wehling, E. Ger.	413.340

WOMEN

Cross-country

Event		Time
5km	Galina Kulakova, USSR	17:00.50
10km	Galina Kulakova, USSR	34:17.82
3x5km	USSR (Moukhatcheva, Olunina, Kulakova)	48:46.15

Speed Skating

MEN

Event		Time	
500m	Erhard Keller, W. Ger.	39.44	OR
1500m	Ard Schenk, NED	2:02.96	OR
5000m	Ard Schenk, NED	7:23.61	
10,000m	Ard Schenk, NED	15:01.35	OR

WOMEN

Event		Time	
500m	Anne Henning, USA	43.33	OR
1000m	Monika Pflug, W. Ger.	1:31.40	OR
1500m	Dianne Holum, USA	2:20.85	OR
3000m	Christina Baas-Kaiser, NED	4:52.14	OR

1976

Innsbruck

The IOC originally gave the 1976 Winter Games to Denver, but in 1972 Colorado voters rejected a $5 million bond issue to finance the undertaking. Denver immediately withdrew as host and the IOC called on Innsbruck, site of the 1964 Games.

For the second straight Winter Carnival the USSR and East Germany finished 1–2 in overall medals. In 1972, Dutch speed skater Ard Schenk and Soviet cross-country skier Galina Kulakova each won three gold medals. In '76, nobody won three, but 25–year-old West German skier Rosi Mittermaier almost did—winning two golds and a silver in the women's Alpine events.

The Russian hockey team, which had won the gold medal in 1972 and then battled the NHL's Team Canada to a virtual standoff six months later, returned with most of the same players and won its fourth straight Olympic title.

In figure skating, 19–year-old Dorothy Hamill of the U.S. and John Curry of Britain won gold medals. Both were coached by Carlo Fassi, who also coached Peggy Fleming in 1968.

Also, Bill Koch became the first U.S. skier to ever win an Olympic cross-country medal when he placed second in the 30–kilometer race.

Top 10 Standings

National medal standings are not recognized by the IOC. The unofficial point totals are based on 3 points for a gold medal, 2 for a silver and 1 for a bronze. Total medals are in parentheses.

		Gold	Silver	Bronze	Pts
1	USSR (27)	13	6	8	59
2	East Germany (19)	7	5	7	38
3	USA (10)	3	3	4	19
	West Germany (10)	2	5	3	19
5	Norway (7)	3	3	1	16
6	Finland (7)	2	4	1	15
7	Austria (6)	2	2	2	12
8	Switzerland (5)	1	3	1	10
	Holland (6)	1	2	3	10
10	Italy (4)	1	2	1	8

Leading Medal Winners

Number of individual medals won on the left; gold, silver and bronze breakdown to the right.

MEN

No		Sport	G-S-B
3	Hans van Helden, NED	Sp. Skate	0-0-3
2	Bernhard Germeshausen, E. Ger.	Bobsled	2-0-0
2	Nikolai Kruglov, USSR	Biathlon	2-0-0
2	Meinhard Nehmer, E. Ger.	Bobsled	2-0-0
2	Ivar Formo, NOR	X-country	1-1-0
2	Piet Kleine, NED	Sp. Skate	1-1-0
2	Nikolai Bazhuko, USSR	X-country	1-0-1
2	Aleksandr Elizarov, USSR	Biathlon	1-0-1
2	Arto Koivisto, FIN	X-country	1-0-1
2	Hans Rinn, E. Ger.	Luge	1-0-1
2	Sergei Saveliev, USSR	X-country	1-0-1
2	Karl Schnabl, AUT	Ski Jump	1-0-1
2	Sten Stensen, NOR	Sp. Skate	1-1-0
2	Neikki Ikola, FIN	Biathlon	0-2-0
2	Yevgeny Beliaev, USSR	X-country	0-1-1
2	Josef Benz, SWI	Bobsled	0-1-1
2	Valery Muratov, USSR	Sp. Skate	0-1-1
2	Erich Scharer, SWI	Bobsled	0-1-1
2	Manfred Schumann, W. Ger.	Bobsled	0-1-1
2	Wolfgang Zimmerer, W. Ger.	Bobsled	0-1-1
2	Ivan Garanin, USSR	X-country	0-0-2

WOMEN

No		Sport	G-S-B
4	Tatiana Averina, USSR	Sp. Skate	2-0-2
3	Rosi Mittermaier, W. Ger.	Alpine	2-1-0
3	Raisa Smetanina, USSR	X-country	2-1-0
3	Helena Takalo, FIN	X-country	1-2-0
3	Sheila Young, USA	Sp. Skate	1-1-1
2	Galina Kulakova, USSR	X-country	1-0-1

Alpine Skiing

MEN

Event		Time
Downhill	Franz Klammer, AUT	1:45.73
Slalom	Piero Gros, ITA	2:03.29
G.Slalom	Heini Hemmi, SWI	3:26.97

WOMEN

Event		Time
Downhill	Rosi Mittermaier, W. Ger.	1:46.16
Slalom	Rosi Mittermaier, W. Ger.	1:30.54
G.Slalom	Kathy Kreiner, CAN	1:29.13

Note: Mittermaier finished second in the GS, missing the first women's alpine sweep by an eighth of a second.

Biathlon

Event		MT	Adj.Time
20 km	Nikolai Kruglov, USSR	2	1:14:12.26
4x7.5km	USSR (Elizarov, Biakov, Kruglov Tikonov)	0	1:57:55.64

Bobsled

Event		Time
2-Man	E. Ger. (Meinhard Nehmer & Bernhard Germeshausen)	3:44.42
4-Man	E. Ger (Nehmer, Babock, Germeshausen, Lehmann)	3:40.43

Figure Skating

Event		Points
Men	John Curry, GBR	192.74
Women	Dorothy Hamill, USA	193.80
Pairs	Irina Rodnina & Aleksandr Zaitsev, USSR	140.54
Dance	Lyudmila Pakhomova & Aleksandr Gorshkov, USSR	209.92

Ice Hockey

Group A

(Overall records in parentheses)

		Gm	W-L-T	Pts	GF	GA
1	USSR (6-0-0)	5	5-0-0	10	40	11
2	Czechoslovakia (3-2-0)	4	2-2-0	6	17	10
3	West Germany (3-3-0)	5	2-3-0	4	21	24
4	Finland (3-3-0)	5	2-3-0	4	19	18
5	USA (3-3-0)	5	2-3-0	4	15	21
6	Poland (1-4-0)	5	0-4-0	0	9	37

Note: Czechoslovakia's 7–1 win over Poland was disallowed when a Czech player flunked a random post-game drug test. The Czechs were given a loss and their goals vs. Poland were deleted from the records. The U.S. missed a bronze medal in its final game with a 4–1 loss to West Germany.

Luge

MEN

Event		Time
1-Seat	Dettlef Günther, E. Ger.	3:27.688
2-Seat	Hans Rinn & Norbert Hahn, E. Ger.	1:25.604

WOMEN

Event		Time
1-Seat	Margit Schumann, E. Ger.	2:50.621

Nordic Skiing

MEN

CROSS COUNTRY

Event		Time
15km	Nikolai Bazhukov, USSR	43:58.47
30km	Sergei Saveliev, USSR	1:30:29.38
50km	Ivar Formo, NOR	2:37:30.05
4x10km	FIN (Pitkänen, Mieto Teurajärvi, Koivisto)	2:07:59.72

Ski Jumping

Event		Points
70m	Hans-Goerg Aschenbach, E. Ger.	252.0
90m	Karl Schnabl, AUT	234.8

Nordic Combined

Event		Points
15km/Jump	Ulrich Wehling, E. Ger.	423.39

WOMEN

Cross-country

Event		Time
5km	Helena Takalo, FIN	15:48.69
10km	Raisa Smetanina, USSR	30:13.41
4x5km	USSR (Baldycheva, Amosova Smetanina, Kulakova)	1:07:49.75

Speed Skating

MEN

Event		Time	
500m	Yevgeny Kulikov, USSR	39.17	OR
1000m	Peter Mueller, USA	1:19.32	
1500m	Jan Egil Storholt, NOR	1:59.38	OR
5000m	Sten Stensen, NOR	7:24.48	
10,000m	Piet Kleine, NED	14:50.59	OR

WOMEN

Event		Time	
500m	Sheila Young, USA	42.76	OR
1000m	Tatiana Averina, USSR	1:28.43	OR
1500m	Galina Stepanskaya, USSR	2:16.58	OR
3000m	Tatiana Averina, USSR	4:45.19	OR

1980

Lake Placid

Eric and the Miracles.

Over 1,100 athletes from 37 countries participated in the 1980 Winter Games, but the only ones most people will ever remember are 21-year-old American speed skater Eric Heiden, who won five individual gold medals, and the U.S. hockey team—a bunch of college kids (average age 22) who beat the unbeatable Russians.

No one before or since Heiden has won five individual gold medals in a single Olympic Games (three of swimmer Mark Spitz's seven gold medals were for relay races). And Heiden's sweep of the men's speed skating events has never been duplicated.

The hockey team, on the other hand, was a decided underdog. Seeded seventh out of 12 teams in the first round, they had also been routed, 10–3, by the Soviet Union in an exhibition game only a week before the Olympics.

Nevertheless, the Americans reached the final round with a 4–0–1 record. Playing in front of a boisterous, flag-waving home crowd, the U.S. upset the Soviets, 4–3 (captain Mike Eruzione scored the winning goal midway through the third period and goalie Jim Craig made 39 saves), then beat Finland, 4–2, to win the gold medal. "Do you believe in miracles?" asked ABC-TV announcer Al Michaels as the final seconds ticked off against the Russians. "Ye-s-s-s!"

That game was played on Feb. 22—five days short of exactly 20 years after the 1960 U.S. team beat the USSR, 3–2, on their way to the gold medal at Squaw Valley. Other links to the past included right wing Dave Christian, whose father Billy and uncle Roger were linemates on the 1960 team, and coach Herb Brooks, who had been the last player cut from the 1960 squad.

Swedish Alpine skier Ingemar Stenmark, who would retire in 1989 with 86 World Cup victories, won the slalom and GS for his only two Olympic wins.

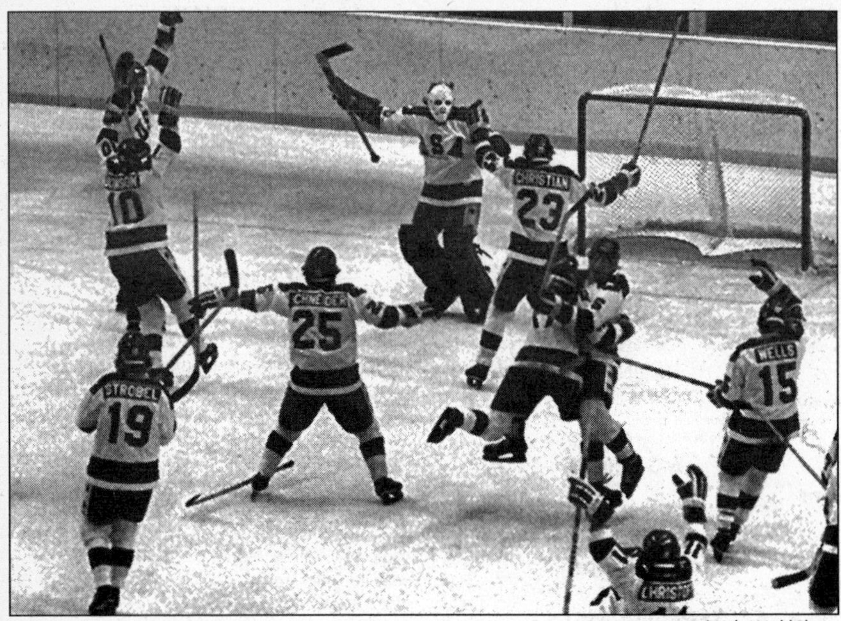

AP/Wide World Photos

The **U.S. Hockey team** celebrates one of the greatest moments in American sports history, a 4-3 win over the heavily-favored Soviet team.

Top 10 Standings

National medal standings are not recognized by the IOC. The unofficial point totals are based on 3 points for a gold medal, 2 for a silver and 1 for a bronze. Total medals are in parentheses.

		Gold	Silver	Bronze	Pts
1	USSR (22)	10	6	6	48
	East Germany (23)	9	7	7	48
3	USA (12)	6	4	2	28
4	Finland (9)	1	5	3	16
5	Austria (7)	3	2	2	15
	Norway (10)	1	3	6	15
7	Sweden (4)	3	0	1	10
	Liechtenstein (4)	2	2	0	10
9	Holland (4)	1	2	1	8
	Switzerland (5)	1	1	3	8

Leading Medal Winners

Number of individual medals won on the left; gold, silver and bronze breakdown to the right.

MEN

No		Sport	G-S-B
5	Eric Heiden, USA	Sp. Skating	5-0-0
3	Nikolai Zimatov, USSR	X-country	3-0-0
3	Anatoly Alyabiev, USSR	Biathlon	2-0-1
3	Frank Ullrich, E. Ger.	Biathlon	1-2-0
3	Juha Mieto, FIN	X-country	0-2-1
2	Ingemar Stenmark, SWE	Alpine	2-0-0
2	Vladimir Alikin,USSR	Biathlon	1-1-0
2	Josef Benz, SWI	Bobsled	1-1-0
2	Hans Jurgen Gerhardt, E. Ger.	Bobsled	1-1-0
2	Bernhard Germeshausen, E. Ger.	Bobsled	1-1-0
2	Vasili Rochev, USSR	X-country	1-1-0
2	Erich Schärer, SWI	Bobsled	1-1-0
2	Bogdan Musiol, E. Ger.	Bobsled	1-0-1
2	Meinhard Nehmer, E. Ger.	Bobsled	1-0-1
2	Kai Arne Stenshjemmet, NOR	Sp. Skate	0-2-0
2	Ove Aunli, NOR	X-country	0-1-1
2	Eberhard Rosch, E. Ger.	Biathlon	0-1-1
2	Tom Erik Oxholm, NOR	Sp. Skate	0-0-2

WOMEN

No		Sport	G-S-B
3	Hanni Wenzel, LIE	Alpine	2-1-0
2	Barbara Petzold, E. Ger.	X-country	2-0-0
2	Raisa Smetanina, USSR	X-country	1-1-0
2	Natalia Petruseva, USSR	Sp. Skate	1-0-1
2	Leah Mueller, USA	Sp. Skate	0-2-0
2	Hilkka Riihivuori, FIN	X-country	0-2-0
2	Sabine Becker, E. Ger.	Sp. Skate	0-1-1

Alpine Skiing

MEN

Event		Time
Downhill	Leonhard Stock, AUT	1:45.50
Slalom	Ingemar Stenmark, SWE	1:44.26
G.Slalom	Ingemar Stenmark, SWE	2:40.74

WOMEN

Event		Time
Downhill	Annemarie Moser-Pröll, AUT	1:37.52
Slalom	Hanni Wenzel, LIE	1:25.09
G.Slalom	Hanni Wenzel, LIE	2:41.66

Biathlon

Event		MT	Adj.Time
10km	Frank Ullrich, E. Ger.	2	32:10.69
20 km	Anatoly Alyabiev, USSR	0	1:08:16.31
4x7.5km	USSR (Alikin, Tikonov, Barnashov, Alyabiev)	0	1:34:03.27

Bobsled

Event		Time
2-Man	SWI (Erich Schärer & Josef Benz)	4:09.36
4-Man	E. Ger (Nehmer, Musiol, Germeshausen, Gerhardt)	3:59.92

Figure Skating

Event		Points
Men	Robin Cousins, GBR	189.48
Women	Anett Pötzsch, E. Ger.	189.00
Pairs	Irina Rodnina & Aleksandr Zaitsev, USSR	147.26
Dance	Natalia Linichuk & Gennady Karponosov, USSR	205.48

Ice Hockey

Medal Round

(Overall records in parentheses)

		Gm	W-L-T	Pts	GF	GA
1	USA (6-0-1)	3	2-0-1	5	10	7
2	USSR (6-1-0)	3	2-1-0	4	16	8
3	Sweden (4-1-2)	3	0-1-2	2	7	14
4	Finland (3-3-1)	3	0-2-1	1	7	11

Note: Games against common oppenents carried over from the preliminary round. FIRST ROUND—USA tied Sweden, 2–2, and USSR over Finland, 4–2. MEDAL ROUND—USA over USSR, 4–3, and Finland, 4–2; USSR over Sweden, 9–2; and Sweden tied Finland, 3–3.

Luge

MEN

Event		Time
1-Seat	Bernhard Glass, E. Ger.	2:54.796
2-Seat	Hans Rinn & Norbert Hahn, E. Ger.	1:19.331

WOMEN

Event		Time
1-Seat	Vera Zozulia, USSR	2:36.537

Nordic Skiing

MEN

Cross Country

Event		Time
15km	Thomas Wassberg, SWE	41:57.63
30km	Nikolai Zimyatov, USSR	1:27:02.80
50km	Nikolai Zimyatov, USSR	2:27:24.60
4x10km	USSR (Rochev, Bazhukov, Beliaev, Zimyatov)	1:57:03.46

Ski Jumping

Event		Points
70m	Anton Innauer, AUT	266.3
90m	Jouko Törmänen, FIN	271.0

Nordic Combined

Event		Points
15km/Jump	Ulrich Wehling, E. Ger.	432.200

WOMEN

Cross-country

Event		Time
5km	Raisa Smetanina, USSR	15:06.92
10km	Barbara Petzold, E. Ger.	30:31.54
4x5km	E. Ger. (Rostock, Anding, Hesse, Petzold)	1:02:11.10

Speed Skating

MEN

Event		Time	
500m	Eric Heiden, USA	38.03	OR
1000m	Eric Heiden, USA	1:15.18	OR
1500m	Eric Heiden, USA	1:55.44	OR
5000m	Eric Heiden, USA	7:02.29	OR
10,000m	Eric Heiden, USA	14:28.13	WR

WOMEN

Event		Time	
500m	Karin Enke, E. Ger.	41.78	OR
1000m	Natalia Petruseva, USSR	1:24.10	OR
1500m	Annie Borckink, NED	2:10.95	OR
3000m	Bjoerg Eva Jensen, NOR	4:32.13	OR

1984

Sarajevo

In 1980, the Soviet Union and East Germany finished the Winter Games in a virtual tie for the unofficial team championship. The USSR won more gold medals (10–9), but the GDR won more overall medals (23–22).

In 1984, the East Germans edged into the lead in the battle of state-controlled athletic programs, winning three more golds (9–6), while the Soviets won one more overall medal (25–24).

Karin Enke was the top East German performer, taking two gold medals and two silvers in the four women's speed skating events. Teammate Andrea Schöne won a gold and two silvers. Cross-country skier Marja-Liisa Hämäläinen of Finland was the only athlete to win three events and one of only three—Enke and Swedish cross-country skier Gunde Svan were the others—to win four overall medals.

The U.S. hockey team failed to qualify for the medal round, but the men's Alpine ski team, which had never won an event before, won twice. Bill Johnson took the downhill and the Mahre brothers, Phil and Steve, finished 1–2 in the slalom.

Top 10 Standings

National medal standings are not recognized by the IOC. The unofficial point totals are based on 3 points for a gold medal, 2 for a silver and 1 for a bronze. Total medals are in parentheses.

		Gold	Silver	Bronze	Pts
1	East Germany (24)	9	9	6	51
2	USSR (25)	6	10	9	47
3	Finland (13)	4	3	6	24
4	USA (8)	4	4	0	20
5	Sweden (8)	4	2	2	18
6	Norway (9)	3	2	4	17
7	Switzerland (5)	2	2	1	11
8	Canada (4)	2	1	1	9
	West Germany (4)	2	1	1	9
10	Czechoslovakia (6)	0	2	4	8

Leading Medal Winners

Number of individual medals won on the left; gold, silver and bronze breakdown to the right.

MEN

No		Sport	G-S-B
4	Gunde Svan, SWE	X-country	2-1-1
3	Gaétan Boucher, CAN	Sp. Skating	2-0-1
3	Peter Angerer, W. Ger.	Biathlon	1-1-1
3	Eirik Kvalfoss, NOR	Biathlon	1-1-1
3	Aki Karvonen, FIN	X-country	0-1-2
2	Wolfgang Hoppe, E. Ger.	Bobsled	2-0-0
2	Dietmar Schauerhammer, E. Ger.	Bobsled	2-0-0
2	Thomas Wassberg, SWE	X-country	2-0-0
2	Tomas Gustafson, SWE	Sp. Skate	1-1-0
2	Igor Malkov, USSR	Sp. Skate	1-1-0
2	Matti Nykänen, FIN	Ski Jump	1-1-0
2	Jens Weissflog, E. Ger.	Ski Jump	1-1-0
2	Nikolai Zimyatov, USSR	X-country	1-1-0
2	Sergei Khlebnikov, USSR	Sp. Skate	0-2-0
2	Bernhard Lehmann, E. Ger.	Bobsled	0-2-0
2	Bogdan Musiol, E. Ger.	Bobsled	0-2-0
2	Aleksandr Zavialov, USSR	X-country	0-2-0
2	Harri Kirvesniemi, FIN	X-country	0-0-2
2	Rene Schofisch, E. Ger.	Sp. Skate	0-0-2

WOMEN

No		Sport	G-S-B
4	Marja-Liisa Hämäläinen, FIN	X-country	3-0-1
4	Karin Enke, E. Ger.	Sp. Skating	2-2-0
3	Andrea Schöne, E. Ger.	Sp. Skating	1-2-0
2	Berit Aunli, NOR	X-country	1-1-0
2	Anne Jahren, NOR	X-country	1-0-1
2	Brit Pettersen, NOR	X-country	1-0-1
2	Kvetoslava Jeriova, CZE	X-country	0-1-1
2	Perrine Pelen, FRA	Alpine	0-1-1
2	Natalia Petruseva, USSR	Sp. Skate	0-0-2

Alpine Skiing

MEN

Event		Time
Downhill	Bill Johnson, USA	1:45.59
Slalom	Phil Mahre, USA	1:39.41
G.Slalom	Max Julen, SWI	2:41.18

WOMEN

Event		Time
Downhill	Michela Figini, SWI	1:13.36
Slalom	Paoletta Magoni, ITA	1:36.47
G.Slalom	Debbie Armstrong, USA	2:20.98

Biathlon

Event		MT	Adj.Time
10km	Erik Kvalfoss, NOR	2	30:53.8
20 km	Peter Angerer, W. Ger	2	1:11:52.7
4x7.5km	USSR (Vasiliev, Kachkarov, Algimantas, Buligin)	2	1:38:51.7

Bobsled

Event		Time
2-Man	E. Ger. (Wolfgang Hoppe & Dietmar Schauerhammer)	3:25.56
4-Man	E. Ger. (Hoppe, Wetzig, Schauerhammer, Kirchner)	3:20.22

Figure Skating

Event		Points
Men	Scott Hamilton, USA	3.4
Women	Katarina Witt, E. Ger.	3.2
Pairs	Elena Valova & Oleg Vasiliev, USSR	1.4
Dance	Jayne Torvill & Christopher Dean, GBR	2.0

Ice Hockey

Medal Round

(Overall records in parentheses)

	Gm	W-L-T	Pts	GF	GA
1 USSR (7-0-0)	3	3-0-0	6	16	1
2 Czechoslovakia (6-1-0)	3	2-1-0	4	6	3
3 Sweden (4-2-1)	3	1-2-0	2	3	12
4 Canada (4-3-0)	3	0-3-0	0	0	10

Note: Games against common opponents carried over from the preliminary round. MEDAL ROUND—the USSR beat Sweden, 10–1, Canada, 4–0, and the Czechs, 2–0, the Czechs beat Canada, 4–0, and Sweden, 2–0; and Sweden beat Canada, 2–0.

Also: The U.S., featuring future NHL stars Chris Chelios and Pat LaFontaine, failed to qualify for the Medal Round, finishing 7th overall with a record of 2–2–2.

Luge

MEN

Event		Time
1-Seat	Paul Hildgartner, ITA	3:04.258
2-Seat	Hans Stanggassinger & Franz Wembacher, W. Ger.	1:23.620

WOMEN

Event		Time
1-Seat	Steffi Martin, E. Ger.	2:46.570

Nordic Skiing

MEN

Cross Country

Event		Time
15km	Gunde Svan, SWE	41:25.6
30km	Nikolai Zimyatov, USSR	1:28:56.3
50km	Thomas Wassberg, SWE	2:15:55.8
4x10km	SWE (Wassberg, Kohlberg, Ottoson, Svan)	1:55:06.3

Ski Jumping

Event		Points
70m	Jens Weissflog, E. Ger.	215.2
90m	Matti Nykänen, FIN	231.2

Nordic Combined

Event		Points
15km/Jump	Tom Sandberg, NOR	422.595

WOMEN

Cross-country

Event		Time
5km	Marja-Liisa Hämäläinen, FIN	17:04.0
10km	Marja-Liisa Hämäläinen, FIN	31:44.2
20km	Marja-Liisa Hämäläinen, FIN	1:01:45.0
4x5km	NOR (Nybråten, Jahren, Pettersen Aunli)	1:06:49.7

Speed Skating

MEN

Event		Time
500m	Sergei Fokichev, USSR	38.19
1000m	Gaétan Boucher, CAN	1:15.80
1500m	Gaétan Boucher, CAN	1:58.36
5000m	Tomas Gustafson, SWE	7:12.28
10,000m	Igor Malkov, USSR	14:39.90

WOMEN

Event		Time	
500m	Christa Rothenburger, E. Ger.	41.02	OR
1000m	Karin Enke, E. Ger.	1:21.61	OR
1500m	Karin Enke, E. Ger.	2:03.42	WR
3000m	Andrea Schöne, E. Ger.	4:24.79	OR

1988

Calgary

A record 1,750 athletes from 57 nations came to western Canada for the first Olympics north of the U.S. border. The Games featured an indoor speed skating oval and sporadic chinook winds that sent temperatures into the unwintry 70s.

Matti Nykänen of Finland became the first pure ski jumper to capture three titles, winning gold medals at 70 and 90 meters and adding a third in the new team jumping competition.

Nykänen may have been the most decorated jumper in Calgary, but he wasn't the most celebrated. That honor belonged to Michael (Eddie the Eagle) Edwards, the accident-prone flying plasterer from Britain. Edwards finished 58th and last in the 70–meter jump and 55th and last in the 90–meter and was welcomed home after the Games by hundreds of fans at London's Heathrow Airport.

Back on the serious side, Dutch speed skater Yvonne van Gennip won three gold medals; East German figure skater Katarina Witt won her second straight women's title; and the USSR beat East Germany in both gold and overall medals in the last winterized confrontation of Communist superpowers.

Top 10 Standings

National medal standings are not recognized by the IOC. The unofficial point totals are based on 3 points for a gold medal, 2 for a silver and 1 for a bronze. Total medals are in parentheses.

		Gold	Silver	Bronze	Pts
1	USSR (29)	11	9	9	60
2	East Germany (25)	9	10	6	53
3	Switzerland (15)	5	5	5	30
4	Austria (10)	3	5	2	21
5	Finland (7)	4	1	2	16
	West Germany (8)	2	4	2	16
7	Netherlands (7)	3	2	2	15
8	Sweden (6)	4	0	2	14
9	USA (6)	2	1	3	11
10	Italy (5)	2	1	2	10

Leading Medal Winners

Number of individual medals won on the left; gold, silver and bronze breakdown to the right.

MEN

No		Sport	G-S-B
3	Matti Nykänen, FIN	Ski Jump	3-0-0
3	Valery Medvedtsev, USSR	Biathlon	1-2-0
3	Vladimir Smirnov, USSR	X-country	0-2-1
2	Alberto Tomba, ITA	Alpine	2-0-0
2	Frank-Peter Rötsch, E. Ger.	Biathlon	2-0-0
2	Gunde Svan, SWE	X-country	2-0-0
2	Tomas Gustafson, SWE	Sp. Skate	2-0-0
2	Hubert Strolz, AUT	Alpine	1-1-0
2	Mikhail Deviatiarov, USSR	X-country	1-1-0
2	Hippolyt Kempf, SWI	Nordic Comb.	1-1-0
2	Jens-Uwe Mey, E. Ger.	Sp. Skate	1-1-0
2	Alexei Prokurorov, USSR	X-country	1-1-0
2	Sergei Chepikov, USSR	Biathlon	1-0-1
2	Ianis Kipours, USSR	Bobsled	1-0-1
2	Vladimir Kozlov, USSR	Bobsled	1-0-1
2	Franck Piccard, FRA	Alpine	1-0-1
2	Pirmin Zurbriggen, SWI	Alpine	1-0-1
2	Wolfgang Hoppe, E. Ger.	Bobsled	0-2-0
2	Bogdan Musiol, E. Ger.	Bobsled	0-2-0
2	Matjaz Debelak, YUG	Ski Jump	0-1-1
2	Michael Hadschieff, AUT	Sp. Skate	0-1-1
2	Erik Johnsen, NOR	Ski Jump	0-1-1
2	Klaus Sulzenbacher, AUT	Nordic Comb.	0-1-1
2	Leo Visser, NED	Sp. Skate	0-1-1
2	Johann Passler, ITA	Biathlon	0-0-2

WOMEN

No		Sport	G-S-B
3	Yvonne van Gennip, NED	Sp. Skating	3-0-0
3	Tamara Tikhonova, USSR	X-country	2-1-0
3	Marjo Matikänen, FIN	X-country	1-0-2
3	Andrea Ehrig, E. Ger.	Sp. Skating	0-2-1
3	Karin Kania, E. Ger.	Sp. Skating	0-2-1
2	Vreni Schneider, SWI	Alpine	2-0-0
2	Anfissa Reztsova, USSR	X-country	1-1-0
2	Christa Rothenburger, E. Ger.	Sp. Skate	1-1-0
2	Bonnie Blair, USA	Sp. Skate	1-0-1
2	Vida Ventsene, USSR	X-country	1-0-1
2	Brigitte Oertli, SWI	Alpine	0-2-0
2	Christa Kinshofer, W. Ger.	Alpine	0-1-1
2	Raisa Smetanina, USSR	X-country	0-1-1
2	Karen Percy, CAN	Alpine	0-0-2
2	Maria Walliser, SWI	Alpine	0-0-2
2	Gabi Zange, E. Ger.	Sp. Skate	0-0-2

Alpine Skiing

MEN

Event		Time
Downhill	Pirmin Zurbriggen, SWI	1:59.63
Slalom	Alberto Tomba, ITA	1:39.47
G.Slalom	Alberto Tomba, ITA	2:06.37
Super GS	Franck Piccard, FRA	1:39.66
Combined	Hubert Strolz, AUT	36.55 pts

WOMEN

Event		Time
Downhill	Marina Kiehl, W. Ger.	1:25.86
Slalom	Vreni Schneider, SWI	1:36.69
G.Slalom	Vreni Schneider, SWI	2:06.49
Super GS	Sigrid Wolf, AUT	1:19.03
Combined	Anita Wachter, AUT	29.25 pts

Biathlon

Event		MT	Adj.Time
10km	Frank-Peter Rötsch, E. Ger.	1	25:08.1
20 km	Frank-Peter Rötsch, E. Ger.	3	56:33.3
4x7.5km	USSR (Vasiliev, Chepikov Popov, Medvedtsev)	0	1:22:30.0

Bobsled

Event		Time
2-Man	USSR (Ianis Kipours & Vladimir Kozlov)	3:53.48
4-Man	SWI (Fasser, Meier, Fässler, Stocker)	3:47.51

Figure Skating

Event		Points
Men	Brian Boitano, USA	3.0
Women	Katarina Witt, E. Ger.	4.2
Pairs	Ekaterina Gordeeva & Sergei Grinkov, USSR	1.4
Dance	Natalya Bestemianova & Andrei Bukin, USSR	2.0

Ice Hockey

Medal Round

(Overall records in parentheses)

		Gm	W-L-T	Pts	GF	GA
1	USSR (7-1-0)	5	4-1-0	8	25	7
2	Finland (5-2-1)	5	3-1-1	7	18	10
3	Sweden (4-1-3)	5	2-1-2	6	15	16
4	Canada (5-2-1)	5	5-2-1	5	17	14
5	West Germany (4-4-0)	5	1-4-0	2	8	26
6	Czecholsovakia (4-4-0)	5	1-4-0	2	12	22

Note: Games against common opponents carried over from the preliminary round. The USSR lost its final game to Finland, 2–1, after clinching the gold medal.

Also: The U.S. finished 4th in its preliminary pool with a 2–3 record. The top three teams in each of two 6–team pools qualified for the medal round.

Luge

MEN

Event		Time
1-Seat	Jens Müller, E. Ger.	3:05.548
2-Seat	Joerg Hoffmann & Jochen Pietzsch, E. Ger.	1:31.940

WOMEN

Event		Time
1-Seat	Steffi Martin Walter, E. Ger.	3:03.973

Nordic Skiing

MEN

Cross Country

Event		Time
15 km	Mikhail Deviatiarov, USSR	41:18.9
30 km	Alexei Prokurorov, USSR	1:24:26.3
50 km	Gunde Svan, SWE	2:04:30.9
4x10 km	SWE (Ottosson, Wassberg, Svan, Mogren)	1:43:58.6

Ski Jumping

Event		Points
70m	Matti Nykänen, FIN	229.1
90m	Matti Nykänen, FIN	224.0
Team	FIN (Nikkola, Nykänen, Ylipulli, Puikkonen)	634.4

Nordic Combined

Event		Points
Individ.	Hippolyt Kempf, SWI	432.23
Team	W. Ger. (Pohl, Schwarz, Müller)	792.08

WOMEN

Cross-country

Event		Time
5km	Marjo Matikänen, FIN	15:04.0
10km	Vida Ventsene, USSR	30:08.3
20km	Tamara Tikhonova, USSR	55:53.6
4x5km	USSR (Nagueikina, Gavriliuk, Tikhonova, Reztsova)	59:51.1

Speed Skating

MEN

Event		Time	
500m	Jens-Uwe Mey, E. Ger.	36.45	WR
1000m	Nikolai Gouliaev, USSR	1:13.03	OR
1500m	André Hoffmann, E. Ger.	1:52.06	WR
5000m	Tomas Gustafson, SWE	6:44.63	WR
10,000m	Tomas Gustafson, SWE	13:48.20	WR

WOMEN

Event		Time	
500m	Bonnie Blair, USA	39.10	WR
1000m	Christa Rothenburger, E. Ger.	1:17.65	WR
1500m	Yvonne van Gennip, NED	2:00.68	OR
3000m	Yvonne van Gennip, NED	4:11.94	WR
5000m	Yvonne van Gennip, NED	7:14.13	WR

1992

Albertville

The first Olympics since the reunification of Germany in 1990 and the breakup of the Soviet Union in 1991 resulted in a record 2,174 athletes from 65 countries as the Winter Games were staged in the French Alps for the third time. Despite all the political turmoil at home, Germany's combined East-West squad and the Unified Team of ex-Soviet athletes were again the biggest winners with the Germans edging the Unifieds in total medals, 26-23.

The female stars of the UT cross-country contingent made the most medal news as Lyubov Egorova (3 gold and 2 silver) and Elena Valbe (1 gold and 4 bronze), each won five and 39–year-old Raisa Smetanina set a Winter Games record with her 10th career medal as a member of the victorious 20–kilometer relay team.

Norway won as many gold medals (9) as the Unified Team, thanks mainly to cross-country skiers Bjorn Dahlie and Vegard Ulvang, who each carried off three golds and a silver. Norwegians also won gold in alpine skiing for the first time in 40 years as Finn Christian Jagge (slalom) and Kjetil Andre Aamodt (Super G) made like Stein Eriksen in 1952.

Led by Bonnie Blair's victories at 500 and 1,000 meters in speed skating, women won all five gold medals collected by the U.S. Blair was joined by figure skater Kristi Yamaguchi, freestyle skier Donna Weinbrecht and short track speed skater Cathy Turner.

Top 10 Standings

National medal standings are not recognized by the IOC. The unofficial point totals are based on 3 points for a gold medal, 2 for a silver and 1 for a bronze. Total medals are in parentheses.

		Gold	Silver	Bronze	Points
1	Germany (26)	10	10	6	56
2	Unified Team (23)	9	6	8	47
3	Norway (20)	9	6	5	44
4	Austria (21)	6	7	8	40
5	Italy (14)	4	6	4	28
6	United States (11)	5	4	2	25
7	France (9)	3	5	1	20
8	Finland (7)	3	1	3	14
	Canada (7)	2	3	2	14
10	Japan (7)	1	2	4	11

Leading Medal Winners

Number of individual medals won on the left; gold, silver and bronze breakdown to the right.

MEN

No		Sport	G-S-B
4	Bjorn Dählie, NOR	X-country	3-1-0
4	Vegard Ulvang, NOR	X-country	3-1-0
3	Mark Kirchner, GER	Biahtlon	2-1-0
3	Toni Nieminen, FIN	Ski Jump	2-0-1
3	Martin Hollwarth, AUT	Ski Jump	0-3-0
3	Giorgio Vanzetta, ITA	X-country	0-1-2
2	Kim Ki Hoon, S.Kor	ST Sp. Skate	2-0-0
2	Ricco Gross, GER	Biathlon	1-1-0
2	Johann Koss, NOR	Sp. Skate	1-1-0
2	Alberto Tomba, ITA	Alpine	1-1-0
2	Ernst Vettori, AUT	Ski Jump	1-1-0
2	Kjetil Andre Aamodt, NOR	Alpine	1-0-1
2	Donat Acklin, SWI	Bobsled	1-0-1
2	Geir Karlstad, NOR	Sp. Skate	1-0-1
2	Terje Langli, NOR	X-country	1-0-1
2	Gustav Weder, SWI	Bobsled	1-0-1
2	Lee Joon Ho, S.Kor	ST Sp. Skate	1-0-1
2	Marco Albarello, ITA	X-country	0-2-0
2	Frederic Blackburn, CAN	ST Sp. Skate	0-2-0
2	Marc Girardelli, LUX	Alpine	0-2-0
2	Heinz Kuttin, AUT	Ski Jump	0-1-1
2	Mikael Lofren, SWE	Biathlon	0-0-2
2	Klaus Sulzenbacher, AUT	Nordic Comb.	0-0-2
2	Leo Visser, NED	Sp. Skate	0-0-2

WOMEN

No		Sport	G-S-B
5	Lyubov Egorova, UT	X-country	3-2-0
5	Elena Valbe, UT	X-country	1-0-4
3	Gunda Niemann, GER	Sp. Skate	2-1-0
3	Antje Misersky, GER	Biathlon	1-2-0
3	Stefania Belmondo, ITA	X-country	1-1-1
2	Bonnie Blair, USA	Sp.Skate	2-0-0
2	Petra Kronberger, AUT	Alpine	2-0-0
2	Marjut Lukkarinen, FIN	X-country	1-1-0
2	Cathy Turner, USA	ST Sp. Skate	1-1-0
2	Anfisa Reztsova, UT	Biathlon	1-0-1
2	Ye Qiaobo, CHN	Sp. Skate	0-2-0
2	Anita Wachter, AUT	Alpine	0-2-0
2	Heike Warnicke, GER	Sp. Skate	0-2-0
2	Elena Belova, UT	Biathlon	0-0-2

Alpine Skiing

MEN

Event		Time
Downhill	Patrick Ortlieb, AUT	1:50.37
Slalom	Finn Christian Jagge, NOR	1:44.39
Giant Slalom	Alberto Tomba, ITA	2:06.98
Super G	Kjetil Andre Aamodt, NOR	1:13.04
Combined	Josef Polig, ITA	14.58 pts

WOMEN

Event		Time
Downhill	Kerrin Lee-Gartner, CAN	1:52.55
Slalom	Petra Krenberger, AUT	1:32.68
Giant Slalom	Pernilla Wiberg, SWE	2:12.74
Super G	Deborah Compagnoni, ITA	1:21.22
Combined	Petra Kronberger, AUT	2.55 pts

Biathlon

MEN

Event		MT	Time
10 km	Mark Kircher, GER	0	26:02.3
20 km	Yevgeny Redkine, UT	0	57:34.4
4x7.5 km relay	Germany (Gross, Steinigen, Kirchner, Fischer)	0	1:24:43.5

WOMEN

Event		MT	Time
7.5 km	Anfisa Reztsova, UT	3	24:29.2
15 km	Antje Misersky, GER	1	51:47.2
3x7.5 km relay	France (Niogret, Claudel, Briand)	0	1:15:55.6

Bobsled

Event		Time
2-Man	SWI (Weder & Acklin)	4:03.26
4-Man	AUT (Appelt, Winkler, Haidacher, Schroll)	3:53.90

Figure Skating

Event		FP
Men	Viktor Petrenko, UT	1.5
Women	Kristi Yamaguchi, USA	1.5
Pairs	Natalya Mishkutienok & Artur Dmitriev	1.5
Dance	Marina Klimova & Sergei Ponomarenko, UT	2.0

Freestyle Skiing

Event		Pts
Men's Moguls	Edgar Grospiron, FRA	25.81
Women's Moguls	Donna Weinbrecht, USA	23.69

Ice Hockey

Round Robin Standings

First four teams in each group advanced to medal round.

Group A	Gm	W-L-T	Pts	GF	GA
United States	5	4-0-1	9	18	7
Sweden	5	3-0-2	8	22	11
Finland	5	3-1-1	7	22	11
Germany	5	2-3-0	4	11	12
Italy	5	1-4-0	2	18	24
Poland	5	0-5-0	0	4	30

Group B	Gm	W-L-T	Pts	GF	GA
Canada	5	4-1-0	8	28	9
Unified Team	5	4-1-0	8	32	10
Czechoslovakia	5	4-1-0	8	25	15
France	5	2-3-0	4	14	22
Switzerland	5	1-4-0	2	13	25
Norway	5	0-5-0	0	7	38

Note: First place tie broken by goal differential in common games.

Quarterfinals

Canada 3 .... Germany 3
(Canada wins shootout, 3-2)

Czechoslovakia 3 .... Sweden 1

USA 4 .... France 1

Unified Team 6 .... Finland 1

Semifinals

Canada 4 .... Czechoslovakia 2

Unified Team 5 .... USA 2

Bronze Medal

Czechoslovakia 6 .... USA 1

Gold Medal

Unified Team 3 .... Canada 1

Luge

MEN

Event		Time
Singles	Georg Hackl,. GER	3:02.363
Doubles	Stefan Krausse & Jan Behrendt, GER	1:32.053

WOMEN

Event		Time
Singles	Doris Neuner, AUT	3:06.696

Nordic Skiing

MEN

Cross-Country

Event		Time
10 km	Vegard Ulvang, NOR	27:36.0
15 km	Bjorn Dählie, NOR	38:01.9
30 km	Vegard Ulvang, NOR	1:22:27.8
50 km	Bjorn Dählie, NOR	2:03:41.5
4x10 km	NOR (Langli, Ulvang, Skjedal, Dahlie)	1:39:26.0

Ski Jumping

Event		Pts
90 m	Ernst Vettori, AUT	222.8
120 m	Toni Nieminen, FIN	239.5
Team (120 m)	FIN (Nikkola, Laitinen, Laakkonen, Nieminen)	644.4

Nodic Combined

Event		Pts
Indiv.	Fabrice Guy, FRA	426.47
Team	JPN (Mikata, Kono, Ogiwara)	1247.18

WOMEN

Cross-Country

Event		Time
5 km	Marjut Lukkarinen, FIN	14:13.8
10 km	Lyubov Egorova, RUS	25:53.7
15 km	Lyubov Egorova, RUS	42:20.8
30 km	Stefania Belmondo, ITA	1:22:30.1
4x5 km	UT (Valbe, Smetanina, Lasutina, Egorova)	59:34.8

Speed Skating

MEN

Long Track

Event		Time
500m	Uwe-Jens Mey, GER	37.14
1000m	Olaf Zinke, GER	1:14.85
1500m	Johann Olav Koss, NOR	1:54.81
5000m	Geir Karlstad, NOR	6:59.97
10,000m	Bart Veldkamp,. NED	14:12.12

Short Track

Event		Time	
1000m	Ki-Hoon Kim, S. Kor	1:30.76	WR
4x1250m	S.Kor (Kim, Lee, Jmo, Song)	7:14.02	WR

WOMEN

Long Track

Event		Time
500m	Bonnie Blair, USA	40.33
1000m	Bonnie Blair, USA	1:21.90
1500m	Jacqueline Borner, GER	2:05.87
3000m	Gunda Niemann, GER	4:19.90
5000m	Gunda Niemann, GER	7:31.57

Short Track

Event		Time
500m	Cathy Turner, USA	47.04
4x750m	CAN (Cutrone, Daigle, Lambert, Perreault)	4:36.62

1994

Lillehammer

For better or worse, the Lillehammer games may be best evoked in most people's memories by two names. Tonya and Nancy. It was an ugly attack before the U.S. Figure Skating Championships on skater Nancy Kerrigan by cohorts of teammate and rival Tonya Harding that set up the most anticipated moment of the Games. Harding's goons were arrested following the Kerrigan clubbing and charged in a plot to improve Harding's chances of medaling by removing Kerrigan from competition. The plan failed and Kerrigan did compete, finishing with the silver medal. She actually tied 16-year-old Ukrainian orphan Oksana Baiul but missed the gold on the artistic merit tie-breaker. Harding, who had to threaten a lawsuit to avoid being barred from the Games by the USOC, ended up in eighth. The broadcast of the women's skating final was the sixth highest-rated program of any sort in U.S. television history.

There are so many more names symbolic of these games, however. Norway's Johann Olav Koss set three world records and won three golds in the men's 1500-, 5000- and 10,000-meter speed skating events. American speed skaters had success as well. Dan Jansen finally caught that elusive medal, winning the 1000-meter gold with a world record in his final event. Bonnie Blair won two golds in the women's 500 and 1000-meter races. And those were just the speedskaters.

The games were the most environmentally-friendly Olympics in history as well. Norway's recycling and energy-saving techniques were so successful that the IOC revised its procedure for choosing host cities as a result.

Top 10 Standings

National medal standings are not recognized by the IOC. The unofficial point totals are based on 3 points for a gold medal, 2 for a silver and 1 for a bronze. Total medals are in parentheses.

		Gold	Silver	Bronze	Points
1	Norway (26)	10	11	5	57
2	Russia (23)	11	8	4	53
3	Germany (24)	9	7	8	49
4	Italy (20)	7	5	8	39
5	United States (13)	6	5	2	30
6	Canada (13)	3	6	4	25
7	Switzerland (9)	3	4	2	19
8	Austria (9)	2	3	4	16
9	South Korea (6)	4	1	1	15
10	Japan (5)	1	2	2	9

Leading Medal Winners

Number of individual medals won on the left; gold, silver and bronze breakdown to the right.

MEN

No		Sport	G-S-B
4	Bjorn Dählie, NOR	X-country	2-2-0
3	Johann Olav Koss, NOR	Sp. Skating	3-0-0
3	Vladimir Smirnov, KAZ	X-country	1-2-0
3	Sergei Tarasov, RUS	Biathlon	1-1-1
3	Kjetil Andre Aamodt, NOR	Alpine	0-2-1
3	Mika Myllyla, FIN	X-country	0-1-2
2	Markus Wasmeier, GER	Alpine	2-0-0
2	Jens Weissflog, GER	Ski Jumping	2-0-0
2	Donat Acklin, SWI	Bobsled	1-1-0
2	Thomas Alsgaard, NOR	X-country	1-1-0

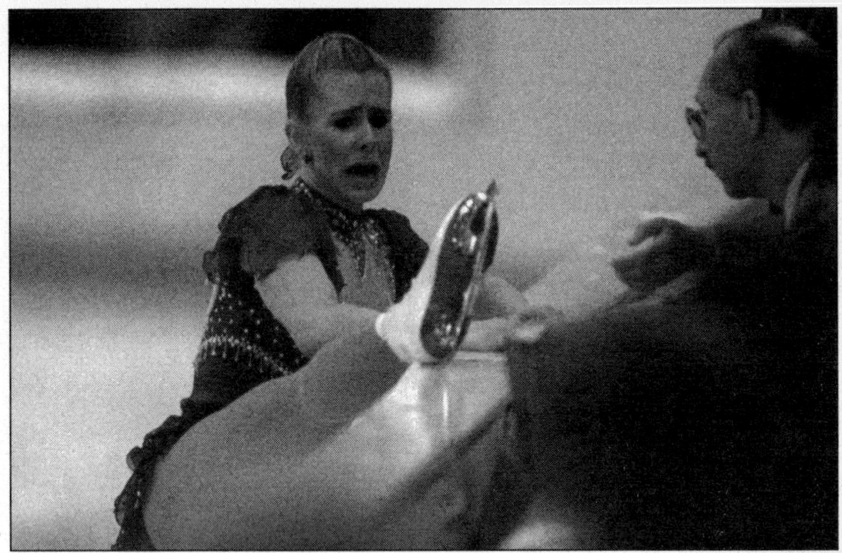

AP/Wide World Photos

In 1994, **Tonya Harding** desperately pleaded with the judges to allow her a restart because of a bum skate. Unfortunately for Harding, it would not be the last time she'd have to plead her case in front of a judge.

No		Sport	G-S-B
2	Espen Bredesen, NOR	Ski Jumping	1-1-0
2	Ji-Hoon Chae, S.Kor	ST Sp. Skating	1-1-0
2	Ricco Gross, GER	Biathlon	1-1-0
2	Takanori Kono, JPN	Nordic Comb.	1-1-0
2	Frank Luck,. GER	Biathlon	1-1-0
2	Fred Borre Lundberg, NOR	Nordic Comb.	1-1-0
2	Tommy Moe, USA	Alpine	1-1-0
2	Sergei Chepikov, RUS	Biathlon	1-1-0
2	Mirko Vuillermin, ITA	ST. Sp. Skating	1-1-0
2	Gustav Weder, SWI	Bobsled	1-1-0
2	Marco Albarello, ITA	X-Country	1-0-1
2	Silvio Fauner, ITA	X-Country	1-0-1
2	Sven Fischer, GER	Biathlon	1-0-1
2	Dieter Thoma, GER	Ski Jumping	1-0-1
2	Kjell Storelid, NOR	Sp. Skating	0-2-0
2	Sergei Klevchenya, RUS	Sp. Skating	0-1-1
2	Rintje Ritsma, NED	Sp. Skating	0-1-1
2	Sture Sivertsen, NOR	X-Country	0-1-1
2	Bjarte Engen Vik, NOR	Nordic Comb.	0-1-1
2	Andreas Goldberger, AUT	Ski Jumping	0-0-2

WOMEN

No		Sport	G-S-B
5	Manuela Di Centa, ITA	X-Country	2-2-1
4	Lyubov Egorova, RUS	X-Country	3-1-0
3	Vreni Schneider, SWI	Alpine	1-1-1
2	Myriam Bedard, CAN	Biathlon	2-0-0
2	Bonnie Blair, USA	Sp. Skating	2-0-0
2	Lee-Kyung Chun, S. Kor	ST Sp. Skating	2-0-0
2	Emese Hunyady, AUT	Sp. Skating	1-1-0
2	Nina Gavriluk, RUS	X-Country	1-0-1
2	So-Hee Kim, S. Kor	ST Sp. Skating	1-0-1
2	Claudia Pechstein, GER	Sp. Skating	1-0-1
2	Cathy Turner, USA	ST Sp. Skating	1-0-1
2	Ann Briand, FRA	Biathlon	0-1-1
2	Ursula Disl, GER	Biathlon	0-1-1
2	Gunda Niemann, GER	Sp. Skating	0-1-1
2	Stefina Belmondo, ITA	X-Country	0-0-2
2	M.L. Kirvesniemi, FIN	X-Country	0-0-2
2	Isolde Kostner, ITA	Alpine	0-0-2
2	Amy Peterson, USA	ST Sp. Skating	0-0-2

Alpine Skiing

MEN

Event		Time
Downhill	Tommy Moe, USA	1:45.75
Slalom	Thomas Stangassinger, AUT	2:02.02
Giant Slalom	Markus Wasmeier, GER	2:52.46
Super G	Markus Wasmeier, GER	1:32.53
Combined	Lasse Kjus, NOR	3:17.53

WOMEN

Event		Time
Downhill	Katja Seizinger, GER	1:35.93
Slalom	Vreni Schneider, SWI	1:56.01
Giant Slalom	Deborah Compagnoni, ITA	2:30.97
Super G	Diann Roffe-Steinrotter, USA	1:22.15
Combined	Pernilla Wiberg, SWE	3:05.16

Biathlon

MEN

Event		MT	Time
10-k	Sergei Chepikov, RUS	0	28:07.0
20-k	Sergei Tarasov, RUS	3	57:25.3
4x7.5-k relay	Germany	0	1:30:22.1

WOMEN

Event		MT	Time
7.5-k	Myriam Bedard, CAN	2	26:08.8
15-k	Myriam Bedard, CAN	2	52:06.6
4x7.5-k relay	Russia	0	1:47:19.5

Bobsled

Event		Time
2-Man	SWI (Weder & Acklin)	3:30.81
4-Man	GER (Czudaj, Brannasch, Hampel, Szelig)	3:27.78

Freestyle Skiing

MEN

Event		Pts
Aerials	Andreas Schoenbaechler, SWI	234.67
Moguls	Jean-Luc Brassard, CAN	27.24

WOMEN

Event		Pts
Aerials	Lina Cherjazova, UZB	166.84
Moguls	Stine Lise Hattestad, NOR	25.97

Figure Skating

Event		FP
Men	Alexei Urmanov, RUS	1.5
Women	Oksana Baiul, UKR	2.0
Pairs	Ekaterina Gordeeva & Sergei Grinkov, RUS	1.5
Dance	Oksana Gritschuk & Yevgeny Platov, RUS	3.0

Ice Hockey

Round Robin Standings

First four teams in each group advanced to medal round.

Group A	Gm	W-L-T	Pts	GF	GA
Finland	5	5-0-0	10	25	4
Germany	5	3-2-0	6	11	14
Czech Republic	5	3-2-0	6	16	11
Russia	5	3-2-0	6	20	14
Austria	5	1-4-0	2	13	28
Norway	5	0-5-0	0	5	19

Note: Second place tie broken by goal differential in common games.

Group B	Gm	W-L-T	Pts	GF	GA
Slovakia	5	3-0-2	8	26	14
Canada	5	3-1-1	7	17	11
Sweden	5	3-1-1	7	23	13
United States	5	1-1-3	5	21	17
Italy	5	1-4-0	2	15	31
France	5	0-4-1	1	11	27

Note: Second place tie broken by goal differential in common games.

Quarterfinals

Sweden 3 .... Germany 0
Canada 3 .... OT .... Czech Republic 2
Finland 6 .... United States 1
Russia 3 .... OT .... Slovakia 2

Semifinals

Sweden 4 .... Russia 3
Canada 5 .... Finland 3

Bronze Medal

Finland 4 .... Russia 0

Gold Medal

Sweden 2 .... OT .... Canada 2
(Sweden wins shootout, 3-2)

Luge

MEN

Event		Time
Singles	Georg Hackl,. GER	3:21.571
Doubles	Kurt Brugger & Wilfried Huber, ITA	1:36.720

WOMEN

Event		Time
Singles	Gerda Weissensteiner, ITA	3:15.517

Nordic Skiing

MEN

Cross-Country

Event		Time
10 km	Bjorn Dählie, NOR	24:20.1
15 km	Bjorn Dählie, NOR	1:00:08.8
30 km	Thomas Alsgaard, NOR	1:12:26.4
50 km	Vladimir Smirnov, KAZ	2:07:20.3
4x10 km	ITA (De Zolt, Albarello, Vanzetta, Fauner)	1:41:15.0

Ski Jumping

Event		Pts
90 m	Espen Bredesen, NOR	282.0
120 m	Jens Weissflog, GER	274.5
Team (120 m)	GER (Jaekle, Duffner, Thoma, Weissflog)	970.1

Nodic Combined

Event		Pts
Indiv.	Fred Borre Lundberg, NOR	457.970
Team	JPN (Kono, Abe, Ogiwara)	1368.860

WOMEN

Cross-Country

Event		Time
5 km	Lyubov Egorova, RUS	14:08.8
10 km	Lyubov Egorova, RUS	41:38.1
15 km	Manuela Di Centa, ITA	39:44.5
30 km	Manuela Di Centa, ITA	1:25:41.6
4x5 km	RUS (Valbe, Lazutina, Gavriluk, Egorova)	57:12.5

Speed Skating

MEN

Long Track

Event		Time	
500m	Aleksandr Golubev, RUS	36.33	OR
1000m	Dan Jansen, USA	1:12.43	WR
1500m	Johann Olav Koss, NOR	1:51.29	WR
5000m	Johann Olav Koss, NOR	6:34.96	WR
10,000m	Johann Olav Koss, NOR	13:30.55	WR

Short Track

Event		Time	
500m	Ji-Hoon Chae, S. Kor	43.45	
1000m	Ki-Hoon Kim, S. Kor	1:34.57	
5000m relay	Italy	7:11.74	OR

WOMEN

Long Track

Event		Time
500m	Bonnie Blair, USA	39.25
1000m	Bonnie Blair, USA	1:18.74
1500m	Emese Hunyady, AUT	2:02.19
3000m	Svetlana Bazhanova, RUS	4:17.43
5000m	Claudia Pechstein, GER	7:14.37

Short Track

Event		Time	
500m	Cathy Turner, USA	45.98	OR
1000m	Lee-Kyung Chun, S. Kor	1:36.87	
3000m Relay	South Korea	4:26.64	WR

Event-by-Event

Gold medal winners from 1924-98 in the following events: Alpine Skiing, Biathlon, Bobsled, Cross-country Skiing, Curling, Figure Skating, Ice Hockey, Luge, Nordic Combined, Ski Jumping, Snowboarding and Speed Skating.

ALPINE SKIING

MEN

Multiple gold medals: Jean-Claude Killy, Toni Sailer and Alberto Tomba (3); Hermann Maier, Henri Oreiller, Ingemar Stenmark and Markus Wasmeier (2).

Downhill

Year		Time	Year		Time
1948	Henri Oreiller, FRA	2:55.0	1976	Franz Klammer AUT	1:45.73
1952	Zeno Colò, ITA	2:30.8	1980	Leonhard Stock, AUS	1:45.50
1956	Toni Sailer, AUT	2:52.2	1984	Bill Johnson, USA	1:45.59
1960	Jean Vuarnet, FRA	2:06.0	1988	Pirmin Zurbriggen, SWI	1:59.63
1964	Egon Zimmermann, AUT	2:18.16	1992	Patrick Ortlieb, AUT	1:50.37
1968	Jean-Claude Killy, FRA	1:59.85	1994	Tommy Moe, USA	1:45.75
1972	Bernhard Russi, SWI	1:51.43	1998	Jean-Luc Cretier, FRA	1:50.11

Slalom

Year		Time	Year		Time
1948	Edi Reinalter, SWI	2:10.3	1976	Piero Gros, ITA	2:03.29
1952	Othmar Schneider, AUT	2:00.0	1980	Ingemar Stenmark, SWE	1:44.26
1956	Toni Sailer, AUT	3:14.7	1984	Phil Mahre, USA	1:39.41
1960	Ernst Hinterseer, AUT	2:08.9	1988	Alberto Tomba, ITA	1:39.47
1964	Pepi Stiegler, AUT	2:11.13	1992	Finn Christian Jagge, NOR	1:44.39
1968	Jean-Claude Killy, FRA	1:39.73	1994	Thomas Stangassinger, AUT	2:02.02
1972	Francisco Ochoa, SPA	1:49.27	1998	Hans-Petter Buraas, NOR	1:49.31

Giant Slalom

Year		Time	Year		Time
1952	Stein Eriksen, NOR	2:25.0	1980	Ingemar Stenmark, SWE	2:40.74
1956	Toni Sailer, AUS	3:00.1	1984	Max Julen, SWI	2:41.18
1960	Roger Staub, SWI	1:48.3	1988	Alberto Tomba, ITA	2:06.37
1964	Francois Bonlieu, FRA	1:46.71	1992	Alberto Tomba, ITA	2:06.98
1968	Jean-Claude Killy, FRA	3:29.28	1994	Markus Wasmeier, GER	2:52.46
1972	Gustav Thöni, ITA	3:09.62	1998	Hermann Maier, AUT	2:38.51
1976	Heini Hemmi, SWI	3:26.97			

Super Giant Slalom

Year		Time	Year		Time
1988	Frank Piccard, FRA	1:39.66	1994	Markus Wasmeier, GER	1:32.53
1992	Kjetil Andre Aamadt, NOR	1:13.04	1998	Hermann Maier, AUT	1:34.82

Alpine Combined

Year		Points	Year		Points
1936	Franz Pfnür, GER	99.25	1992	Josef Polig, ITA	14.58
1948	Henri Oreiller, FRA	3.27	**Year**		**Time**
1952-84	Not held		1994	Lasse Kjus, NOR	3:17.53
1988	Hubert Strolz, AUT	36.55	1998	Mario Reiter, AUT	3:08.06

WOMEN

Multiple gold medals: Deborah Compagnoni, Vreni Schneider and Katja Seizinger (3); Marielle Goitschel, Trude Jochum-Beiser, Petra Kronberger, Andrea Mead Lawrence, Rosi Mittermaier, Marie-Theres Nadig, Hanni Wenzel and Pernilla Wiberg (2).

Downhill

Year		Time	Year		Time
1948	Hedy Schlunegger, SWI	2:28.3	1976	Rosi Mittermaier, W. Ger	1:46.16
1952	Trude Jochum-Beiser, AUT	1:47.1	1980	Annemarie Moser-Pröll, AUT	1:37.52
1956	Madeleine Berthod, SWI	1:40.7	1984	Michela Figini, SWI	1:13.36
1960	Heidi Biebl, GER	1:37.6	1988	Marina Kiehl, W. Ger	1:25.86
1964	Christl Haas, AUT	1:55.39	1992	Kerrin Lee-Gartner, CAN	1:52.55
1968	Olga Pall, AUT	1:40.87	1994	Katja Seizinger, GER	1:35.93
1972	Marie-Theres Nadig, SWI	1:36.68	1998	Katja Seizinger, GER	1:28.89

Slalom

Year		Time	Year		Time
1948	Gretchen Fraser, USA	1:57.2	1976	Rosi Mittermaier, W. Ger	1:30.54
1952	Andrea Mead Lawrence, USA	2:10.6	1980	Hanni Wenzel, LIE	1:25.09
1956	Renée Colliard, SWI	1:52.3	1984	Paoletta Magoni, ITA	1:36.47
1960	Anne Heggtveit, CAN	1:49.6	1988	Vreni Schneider, SWI	1:36.69
1964	Christine Goitschel, FRA	1:29.86	1992	Petra Kronberger, AUT	1:32.68
1968	Marielle Goitschel, FRA	1:25.86	1994	Vreni Schneider, SWI	1:56.01
1972	Barbara Cochran, USA	1:31.24	1998	Hilde Gerg, GER	1:32.40

Giant Slalom

Year		Time	Year		Time
1952	Andrea Mead Lawrence, USA	2:06.8	1980	Hanni Wenzel, LIE	2:41.66
1956	Ossi Reichert, GER	1:56.5	1984	Debbie Armstrong, USA	2:20.98
1960	Yvonne Rügg, SWI	1:39.9	1988	Vreni Schneider, SWI	2:06.49
1964	Marielle Goitschel, FRA	1:52.24	1992	Pernilla Wiberg, SWE	2:12.74
1968	Nancy Greene, CAN	1:51.97	1994	Deborah Compagnoni, ITA	2:30.97
1972	Marie-Theres Nadig, SWI	1:29.90	1998	Deborah Compagnoni, ITA	2:50.59
1976	Kathy Kreiner, CAN	1:29.13			

Super Giant Slalom

Year		Time	Year		Time
1988	Sigrid Wolf, AUT	1:19.03	1998	Picabo Street, USA	1:18.02
1992	Deborah Compagnoni, ITA	1:21.22			
1994	Diann Roffe-Steinrotter, USA	1:22.15			

Alpine Combined

Year		Points	Year		Points
1936	Christl Cranz, GER	97.06	1992	Petra Kronberger, AUT	2.55
1948	Trude Beiser, AUT	6.58	**Year**		**Time**
1952-84	Not held		1994	Pernilla Wiberg, SWE	3:05.16
1988	Anita Wachter, AUT	29.25	1998	Katja Seizinger, GER	2:40.74

BIATHLON

MEN

Multiple gold medals (including relays): Aleksandr Tikhonov (4); Mark Kirchner and Ricco Gross (3); Anatoly Alyabyev, Ivan Biakov, Sergei Chepikov, Sven Fischer, Frank Luck, Viktor Mamatov, Frank-Peter Roetsch, Magnar Solberg and Dmitri Vasilyev (2).

10 kilometers

Year		Time	Year		Time
1980	Frank Ullrich, E. Ger	32:10.69	1992	Mark Kirchner, GER	26:02.3
1984	Erik Kvalfoss, NOR	30:53.8	1994	Sergei Chepikov, RUS	28:07.0
1988	Frank-Peter Roetsch, E. Ger	25:08.1	1998	Ole Einar Bjoerndalen, NOR	27:16.2

20 kilometers

Year		Time	Year		Time
1960	Klas Lestander, SWE	1:33:21.6	1984	Peter Angerer, W. Ger	1:11:52.7
1964	Vladimir Melanin, USSR	1:20:26.8	1988	Frank-Peter Roetsch, E. Ger	56:33.3
1968	Magnar Solberg, NOR	1:13:45.9	1992	Yevgeny Redkine, UT	57:34.4
1972	Magnar Solberg, NOR	1:15:55.50	1994	Sergei Tarasov, RUS	57:25.3
1976	Nikolai Kruglov, USSR	1:14:12.26	1998	Halvard Hanevold, NOR	56:16.4
1980	Anatoly Alyabyev, USSR	1:08:16.31			

4x7.5-kilometer Relay

Year		Time	Year		Time	Year		Time
1968	Soviet Union	2:13:02.4	1980	Soviet Union	1:34:03.27	1992	Germany	1:24:43.5
1972	Soviet Union	1:51:44.92	1984	Soviet Union	1:38:51.7	1994	Germany	1:30:22.1
1976	Soviet Union	1:57:55.64	1988	Soviet Union	1:22:30.0	1998	Germany	1:21.36.2

WOMEN

Multiple gold medals (including relays): Myriam Bedard and Anfisa Reztsova (2). Note that Reztsova won a third gold medal in 1988 in the Cross-country 4x5-kilometer Relay.

7.5 kilometers

Year		Time	Year		Time
1992	Anfisa Reztsova, UT	24:29.2	1998	Galina Koukleva, RUS	23:08.0
1994	Myriam Bedard, CAN	26:08.8			

15 kilometers

Year		Time	Year		Time
1992	Antje Misersky, GER	51:47.2	1998	Ekaterina Dafovska, BUL	54:52.0
1994	Myriam Bedard, CAN	52:06.6			

4x7.5 kilometer Relay

Year		Time	Year		Time	Year		Time
1992	France	1:15:55.6	1994	Russia	1:47:19.5	1998	Germany	1:40:13.6

Note: Event featured three skiers per team in 1992.

BOBSLED

Multiple gold medals: DRIVERS–Meinhard Nehmer (3); Billy Fiske, Wolfgang Hoppe, Eugenio Monti, Andreas Ostler and Gustav Weder (2). CREW–Bernard Germeshausen (3); Donat Acklin, Luciano De Paolis, Cliff Gray, Lorenz Nieberl and Dietmar Schauerhammer (2).

Two-Man

Year		Time
1932	United States (Hubert Stevens)	8:14.74
1936	United States (Ivan Brown)	5:29.29
1948	Switzerland (Felix Endrich)	5:29.2
1952	Germany (Andreas Ostler)	5:24.54
1956	Italy (Lamberto Dalla Costa)	5:30.14
1960	Not held	
1964	Great Britain (Anthony Nash)	4:21.90
1968	Italy (Eugenio Monti)	4:41.54
1972	West Germany (Wolfgang Zimmerer)	4:57.07
1976	East Germany (Meinhard Nehmer)	3:44.42
1980	Switzerland (Erich Schärer)	4:09.36
1984	East Germany (Wolfgang Hoppe)	3:25.56
1988	Soviet Union (Janis Kipurs)	3:54.19
1992	Switzerland I (Gustav Weder)	4:03.26
1994	Switzerland I (Gustav Weder)	3:30.81
1998	Italy I (Guenther Huber)	3:37.24

Four-Man

Year		Time
1924	Switzerland (Eduard Scherrer)	5:45.54
1928	United States (Billy Fiske)	3:20.5
1932	United States (Billy Fiske)	7:53.68
1936	Switzerland (Pierre Musy)	5:19.85
1948	United States (Francis Tyler)	5:20.1
1952	Germany (Andreas Ostler)	5:07.84
1956	Switzerland (Franz Kapus)	5:10.44
1960	Not held	
1964	Canada (Vic Emery)	4:14.46
1968	Italy (Eugenio Monti)	2:17.39
1972	Switzerland (Jean Wicki)	4:43.07
1976	East Germany (Meinhard Nehmer)	3:40.43
1980	East Germany (Meinhard Nehmer)	3:59.92
1984	East Germany (Wolfgang Hoppe)	3:20.22
1988	Switzerland (Ekkehard Fasser)	3:47.51
1992	Austria I (Ingo Appelt)	3:53.90
1994	Germany II (Harald Czudaj)	3:27.78
1998	Germany II (Christoph Langen)	2:39.41

Note: Five-man sleds were used in 1928.

CROSS-COUNTRY SKIING

There have been two significant changes in men's and women's Cross-country racing since the end of the 1984 Winter Games in Sarajevo. First, the classical and freestyle (i.e., skating) techniques were designated for specific events beginning in 1988, and the Pursuit race was introduced in 1992.

MEN

Multiple gold medals (including relays): Bjorn Dählie (8); Sixten Jernberg, Gunde Svan, Thomas Wassberg and Nikolai Zimyatov (4); Veikko Hakulinen, Eero Mäntyranta and Vegard Ulvang (3); Hallgeir Brenden, Harald Grönningen, Thorlief Haug, Jan Ottoson, Pål Tyldum and Vyacheslav Vedenine (2).

Multiple gold medals (including Nordic Combined): Johan Gröttumsbråten and Thorlief Haug (3).

10-kilometer Classical

Year		Time
1924-88	Not held	
1992	Vegard Ulvang, NOR	27:36.0
1994	Bjorn Dählie, NOR	24:20.1
1998	Bjorn Dählie, NOR	27:24.5

15-kilometer Freestyle Pursuit

A 15-km Freestyle race in which the starting order is determined by order of finish in the 10-km Classical race. Time given is combined time of both events.

Year		Time
1924-88	Not held	
1992	Bjorn Dählie, NOR	1:05:37.9
1994	Bjorn Dählie, NOR	1:00.08.8
1998	Thomas Alsgaard, NOR	1:07:01.7

15-kilometer Classical (Discont.)

Discontinued in 1992 and replaced by 15-km Freestyle Pursuit. Event was held over 18 kilometers from 1924-52.

Year		Time
1924	Thorleif Haug, NOR	1:14:31.0
1928	Johan Gröttumsbråten, NOR	1:37:01.0
1932	Sven Utterström, SWE	1:23:07.0
1936	Erik-August Larsson, SWE	1:14:38.0
1948	Martin Lundström, SWE	1:13:50.0
1952	Hallgeir Brenden, NOR	1:01:34.0
1956	Hallgeir Brenden, NOR	49:39.0
1960	Hakon Brusveen NOR	51:55.5
1964	Eero Mäntyranta, FIN	50:54.1
1968	Harald Grönningen, NOR	47:54.2
1972	Sven-Ake Lundback, SWE	45:28.24
1976	Nikolai Bazhukov, USSR	43:58.47
1980	Thomas Wassberg, SWE	41:57.63
1984	Gunde Svan, SWE	41:25.6
1988	Mikhail Devyatyarov, USSR	41:18.9

Youngest and Oldest Gold Medalists in an Individual Event

Youngest: MEN– Toni Nieminen, Finland, Large Hill Ski Jumping, 1992 (16 years, 261 days); WOMEN–Tara Lipinski, United States, Figure Skating, 1998 (15 years, 256 days).

Oldest: MEN– Magnar Solberg, NOR, 20-km Biathlon, 1972 (35 years, 4 days); WOMEN– Christina Baas-Kaiser, Holland, 3,000m Speed Skating, 1972 (33 years, 268 days).

30-kilometer Freestyle

Year	Time	Year	Time
1924-52 Not held		1980 Nikolai Zimyatov, USSR	1:27:02.80
1956 Veikko Hakulinen, FIN	1:44:06.0	1984 Nikolai Zimyatov, USSR	1:28:56.3
1960 Sixten Jernberg, SWE	1:51:03.9	1988 Alexi Prokurorov, USSR	1:24:26.3
1964 Eero Mäntyranta, FIN	1:30:50.7	1992 Vegard Ulvang, NOR	1:22:27.8
1968 Franco Nones, ITA	1:35:39.2	1994 Thomas Alsgaard, NOR	1:12:26.4
1972 Vyacheslav Vedenine, USSR	1:36:31.15	1998 not held	
1976 Sergei Saveliev, USSR	1:30:29.38		

30-kilometer Classical

Year	Time
1998 Mila Myllylae, FIN	1:33:55.8

50-kilometer Classical

Year	Time	Year	Time
1924 Thorleif Haug, NOR	3:44:32.0	1968 Ole Ellefsaeter, NOR	2:28:45.8
1928 Per Erik Hedlund, SWE	4:52:03.0	1972 Päl Tyldum, NOR	2:43:14.75
1932 Veli Saarinen, FIN	4:28:00.0	1976 Ivar Formo, NOR	2:37:30.05
1936 Elis Wiklund, SWE	3:30:11.0	1980 Nikolai Zimyatov, USSR	2:27:24.60
1948 Nils Karlsson, SWE	3:47:48.0	1984 Thomas Wassberg, SWE	2:15:55.8
1952 Veikko Hakulinen, FIN	3:33:33.0	1988 Gunde Svan, SWE	2:04:30.9
1956 Sixten Jernberg, SWE	2:50:27.0	1992 Bjorn Dählie, NOR	2:03:41.5
1960 Kalevi Hämäläinen, FIN	2:59:06.3	1994 Vladimir Smirnov, KAZ	2:07:20.3
1964 Sixten Jernberg, SWE	2:43:52.6	1998 not held	

50-kilometer Freestyle

Year	Time
1998 Bjorn Dälie, NOR	2:05:08.2

4x10-kilometer Mixed Relay

Two Classical and two Freestyle legs.

Year		Time	Year		Time	Year		Time
1936	Finland	2:41:33.0	1964	Sweden	2:18:34.6	1984	Sweden	1:55:06.3
1948	Sweden	2:32:08.0	1968	Norway	2:08:33.5	1988	Sweden	1:43:58.6
1952	Finland	2:20:16.0	1972	Soviet Union	2:04:47.94	1992	Norway	1:39:26.0
1956	Soviet Union	2:15:30.0	1976	Finland	2:07:59.72	1994	Italy	1:41:15.0
1960	Finland	2:18:45.6	1980	Soviet Union	1:57:03.46	1998	Norway	1:40:55.7

WOMEN

Multiple gold medals (including relays): Lyubov Egorova (6); Galina Kulakova and Raisa Smetanina (4); Claudia Boyarskikh and Marja-Liisa Hämäläinen (3); Manuela Di Centa, Toini Gustafsson, Larisa Lazutina, Barbara Petzold and Elena Valbe (2).

Multiple gold medals (including relays and Biathlon): Anfisa Reztsova (2).

5-kilometer Classical

Year	Time	Year	Time
1952-60 Not held		1984 Marja-Liisa Hämäläinen, FIN	17:04.0
1964 Claudia Boyarskikh, USSR	17:50.5	1988 Marjo Matikainen, FIN	15:04.0
1968 Toini Gustafsson, SWE	16:45.2	1992 Marjut Lukkarinen, FIN	14:13.8
1972 Galina Kulakova, USSR	17:00.50	1994 Lyubov Egorova, RUS	14:08.8
1976 Helena Takalo, FIN	15:48.69	1998 Larissa Lazutina, RUS	17:37.9
1980 Raisa Smetanina, USSR	15:06.92		

10-kilometer Freestyle Pursuit

A 10-km Freestyle race in which the starting order is determined by order of finish in the 5-km Classical race. Time given is combined time of both events.

Year	Time	Year	Time
1952-88 Not held		1994 Lyubov Egorova, RUS	41:38.1
1992 Lyubov Egorova, UT	40:07.7	1998 Larissa Lazutina, RUS	17:37.9

10-kilometer Classical (Discont.)

Discontinued in 1992 and replaced by 10-km Freestyle Pursuit. Event was held over 18 kilometers from 1924-52.

Year	Time	Year	Time
1952 Lydia Wideman, FIN	41:40.0	1972 Galina Kulakova, USSR	34:17.82
1956 Lyubov Kosyreva, USSR	38:11.0	1976 Raisa Smetanina, USSR	30:13.41
1960 Maria Gusakova, USSR	39:46.6	1980 Barbara Petzold, E. Ger.	30:31.54
1964 Claudia Boyarskikh, USSR	40:24.3	1984 Marja-Liisa Hämäläinen, FIN	31:44.2
1968 Toini Gustafsson, SWE	36:46.5	1988 Vida Venciene, USSR	30:08.3

15-kilometer Freestyle

Year	Time	Year	Time
1952-88 Not held		1994 Manuela Di Centa, ITA	39:44.5
1992 Lyubov Egorova, UT	42:20.8	1998 not held	

15-kilometer Classical

Year	Time
1998 Olga Danilova, RUS	46:55.4

30-kilometer Classical

Event was held over 20 kilometers from 1984-88.

Year	Time	Year	Time
1984 Marja-Liisa Hämäläinen, FIN	1:01:45.0	1994 Manuela Di Centa, ITA	1:25:41.6
1988 Tamara Tikhonova, USSR	55:53.6	1998 not held	
1992 Stefania Belmondo, ITA	1:22:30.1		

30-kilometer Freestyle

Year	Time
1998 Julija Tchepalova, RUS	1:22:01.5

4x5-kilometer Mixed Relay

Two Classical and two Freestyle legs. Event featured three skiers per team from 1956-72.

Year		Time	Year		Time	Year		Time
1956	Finland	1:09:01.0	1972	Soviet Union	48:46.15	1988	Soviet Union	59:51.1
1960	Sweden	1:04:21.4	1976	Soviet Union	1:07:49.75	1992	Unified Team	59:34.8
1964	Soviet Union	59:20.2	1980	East Germany	1:02:11.10	1994	Russia	57:12.5
1968	Norway	57:30.0	1984	Norway	1:06:49.7	1998	Russia	55:13.5

CURLING

MEN

Year	
1998	**Switzerland**, Canada, Norway

WOMEN

Year	
1998	**Canada**, Denmark, Sweeden

FIGURE SKATING

MEN

Multiple gold medals: Gillis Grafström (3); Dick Button and Karl Schäfer (2).

Year			Year			Year		
1908	Ulrich Salchow	SWE	1948	Dick Button	USA	1976	John Curry	GBR
1912	Not held		1952	Dick Button	USA	1980	Robin Cousins	GBR
1920	Gillis Grafström	SWE	1956	Hayes Alan Jenkins	USA	1984	Scott Hamilton	USA
1924	Gillis Grafström	SWE	1960	David Jenkins	USA	1988	Brian Boitano	USA
1928	Gillis Grafström	SWE	1964	Manfred Schnelldorfer	GER	1992	Victor Petrenko	UT
1932	Karl Schäfer	AUT	1968	Wolfgang Schwarz	AUT	1994	Alexei Urmanov	RUS
1936	Karl Schäfer	AUT	1972	Ondrej Nepela	CZE	1998	Ilia Kulik	RUS

WOMEN

Multiple gold medals: Sonja Henie (3); Katarina Witt (2).

Year			Year			Year		
1908	Madge Syers	GBR	1952	Jeanette Altwegg	GBR	1984	Katarina Witt	E. Ger
1912	Not held		1956	Tenley Albright	USA	1988	Katarina Witt	E. Ger
1920	Magda Julin-Mauroy	SWE	1960	Carol Heiss	USA	1992	Kristi Yamaguchi	USA
1924	Herma Planck-Szabö	AUT	1964	Sjoukje Dijkstra	HOL	1994	Oksana Baiul	UKR
1928	Sonja Henie	NOR	1968	Peggy Fleming	USA	1998	Tara Lipinski	USA
1932	Sonja Henie	NOR	1972	Beatrix Schuba	AUT			
1936	Sonja Henie	NOR	1976	Dorothy Hamill	USA			
1948	Barbara Ann Scott	CAN	1980	Anett Pötzsch	E. Ger			

PAIRS

Multiple gold medals: MEN–Pierre Brunet, Artur Dmitriev, Sergei Grinkov, Oleg Protopopov and Aleksandr Zaitsev (2). WOMEN–Irina Rodnina (3); Ludmila Belousova, Ekaterina Gordeeva and Andree Joly Brunet (2).

Year		
1908	Anna Hübler & Heinrich Burger	Germany
1912	Not held	
1920	Ludovika & Walter Jakobsson	Finland
1924	Helene Engelmann & Alfred Berger	Austria
1928	Andrée Joly & Pierre Brunet	France
1932	Andrée & Pierre Brunet	France
1936	Maxi Herber & Ernst Baier	Germany
1948	Micheline Lannoy & Pierre Baugniet	Belgium
1952	Ria & Paul Falk	Germany
1956	Elisabeth Schwartz & Kurt Oppelt	Austria
1960	Barbara Wagner & Robert Paul	Canada
1964	Ludmila Belousova & Oleg Protopopov	USSR
1968	Ludmila Belousova & Oleg Protopopov	USSR
1972	Irina Rodnina & Aleksei Ulanov	USSR
1976	Irina Rodnina & Aleksandr Zaitsev	USSR
1980	Irina Rodnina & Aleksandr Zaitsev	USSR
1984	Elena Valova & Oleg Vasiliev	USSR
1988	Ekaterina Gordeeva & Sergei Grinkov	USSR
1992	Natalya Mishkutienok & Arthur Dmitriev	UT
1994	Ekaterina Gordeeva & Sergei Grinkov	RUS
1998	Oksana Kazakova & Artur Dmitriev	RUS

Ice Dancing

Multiple gold medals: Yevegny Platov (2).

Year		
1976	Lyudmila Pakhomova & Aleksandr Gorshkov	USSR
1980	Natalia Linichuk & Gennady Karponosov	USSR
1984	Jayne Torvill & Christopher Dean	Great Britain
1988	Natalia Bestemianova & Andrei Bukin	USSR
1992	Marina Klimova & Sergei Ponomarenko	UT
1994	Oksana Gritschuk & Yevgeny Platov	RUS
1998	Pasha Grishuk & Yevgeny Platov	RUS

FREESTYLE SKIING

MEN

Aerials

Year		Points
1994	Andreas Schoebaechler, SWI	234.67
1998	Eric Bergoust, USA	255.6

Moguls

Year		Points
1994	Jean-Luc Brassard, CAN	27.24
1998	Jonny Moseley, USA	26.93

WOMEN

Aerials

Year		Points
1994	Lina Cherjazova, UZB	166.84
1998	Nikki Stone, USA	193.00

Moguls

Year		Points
1994	Stine Lise Hattestad, NOR	25.97
1998	Tae Satoya, JPN	25.06

ICE HOCKEY

MEN

Multiple gold medals: Soviet Union/Unified Team (8); Canada (6); United States (2).

Year	
1920	**Canada**, United States Czechoslovakia
1924	**Canada**, United States, Great Britain
1928	**Canada**, Sweden, Switzerland
1932	**Canada**, United States, Germany
1936	**Great Britain**, Canada, United States
1948	**Canada**, Czechoslovakia, Switzerland
1952	**Canada**, United States, Sweden
1956	**Soviet Union**, United States, Canada
1960	**United States**, Canada, Soviet Union
1964	**Soviet Union**, Sweden, Czechoslovakia
1968	**Soviet Union**, Czechoslovakia, Canada
1972	**Soviet Union**, United States, Czechoslovakia
1976	**Soviet Union**, Czechoslovakia, West Germany
1980	**United States**, Soviet Union, Sweden
1984	**Soviet Union**, Czechoslovakia, Sweden
1988	**Soviet Union**, Finland, Sweden
1992	**Unified Team**, Canada, Czechoslovakia
1994	**Sweden**, Canada, Finland
1998	**Czech Repbulic**, Russia, Finland

WOMEN

Year	
1998	**United States**, Canada, Finland

U.S. Gold Medal Hockey Teams

1960

Forwards: Billy Christian, Roger Christian, Billy Cleary, Gene Grazia, Paul Johnson, Bob McVey, Dick Meredith, Weldy Olson, Dick Rodenheiser and Tom Williams. **Defensemen:** Bob Cleary, Jack Kirrane (captain), John Mayasich, Bob Owen and Rod Paavola. **Goaltenders:** Jack McCartan and Larry Palmer. **Coach:** Jack Riley.

1980

Forwards: Neal Broten, Steve Christoff, Mike Eruzione (captain), John Harrington, Mark Johnson, Rob McClanahan, Mark Pavelich, Buzz Schneider, Dave Silk, Eric Strobel, Phil Verchota and Mark Wells. **Defensemen:** Bill Baker, Dave Christian, Ken Morrow, Jack O'Callahan, Mike Ramsey and Bob Suter. **Goaltenders:** Jim Craig and Steve Janaszak. **Coach:** Herb Brooks.

1998

Forwards: Laurie Baker, Alana Blahoski, Lisa Brown-Miller, Karen Bye, Tricia Dunn, Cammi Granato, Katie King, Shelley Looney, A.J. Mleczko, Jenny Schmidgall, Gretchen Ulion, Sandra Whyte. **Defensemen:** Chris Bailey, Colleen Coyne, Sue Mertz, Tara Mounsey, Vicki Movessian, Angela Ruggiero. **Goaltenders:** Sarah DeCosta and Sarah Tueting. **Coach:** Ben Smith.

LUGE

MEN

Multiple gold medals: (including doubles): Georg Hackl (3); Norbert Hahn, Paul Hildgartner, Thomas Kohler and Hans Rinn (2).

Singles

Year		Time
1964	Thomas Köhler, GER	3:26.77
1968	Manfred Schmid, AUT	2:52.48
1972	Wolfgang Scheidel, E. Ger	3:27.58
1976	Dettlef Günther, E. Ger	3:27.688
1980	Bernhard Glass, E. Ger	2:54.796
1984	Paul Hildgartner, ITA	3:04.258
1988	Jens Müller, E. Ger	3:05.548
1992	Georg Hackl, GER	3:02.363
1994	Georg Hackl, GER	3:21.571
1998	Georg Hackl, GER	3:18.436

Doubles

Year		Time
1964	Austria	1:41.62
1968	East Germany	1:35.85
1972	(TIE) East Germany	1:28.35
	& Italy	1:28.35
1976	East Germany	1:25.604
1980	East Germany	1:19.331
1984	West Germany	1:23.620
1988	East Germany	1:31.940
1992	Germany	1:32.053
1994	Italy	1:36.720
1998	Germany	1:41.105

WOMEN

Multiple gold medals: Steffi Martin Walter (2).

Singles

Year		Time
1964	Ortrun Enderlein, GER	3:24.67
1968	Erica Lechner, ITA	2:28.66
1972	Anna-Maria Müller, E. Ger	2:59.18
1976	Margit Schumann, E. Ger	2:50.621
1980	Vera Zozulya, USSR	2:36.537
1984	Steffi Martin, E. Ger	2:46.570
1988	Steffi Martin Walter, E. Ger	3:03.973
1992	Doris Neuner, AUT	3:06.696
1994	Gerda Weissensteiner, ITA	3:15.517
1998	Silke Kraushaar, GER	3:23.779

NORDIC COMBINED

Multiple gold medals: Ulrich Wehling (3); Johan Gröttumsbråten (2).

Individual

Year		Points
1924	Thorleif Haug, NOR	18.906
1928	Johan Gröttumsbråten, NOR	17.833
1932	Johan Gröttumsbråten, NOR	446.00
1936	Oddbjörn Hagen, NOR	430.3
1948	Heikki Hasu, FIN	448.80
1952	Simon Slattvik, NOR	451.621
1956	Sverre Stenersen, NOR	455.000
1960	Georg Thoma, GER	457.952
1964	Tormod Knutsen, NOR	469.28
1968	Franz Keller, W. Ger	449.04
1972	Ulrich Wehling, E. Ger	413.340
1976	Ulrich Wehling, E. Ger	423.39
1980	Ulrich Wehling, E. Ger	432.200
1984	Tom Sandberg, NOR	422.595
1988	Hippolyt Kempf, SWI	432.230
1992	Fabrice Guy, FRA	426.470
1994	Fred Borre Lundberg, NOR	457.970
		Time
1998	Bjarte Engen Vik, NOR	41:21.1

Team

Year		Points
1924-84	Not held	
1988	West Germany	792.08
1992	Japan	1247.180
1994	Japan	1368.860
		Time
1998	Norway	54:11.5

SKI JUMPING

Multiple gold medals (including team jumping): Matti Nykänen (4); Jens Weissflog (3); Birger Ruud and Toni Nieminen (2).

Normal Hill–90 Meters

Year		Points
1924-60	Not held	
1964	Veikko Kankkonen, FIN	229.9
1968	Jiri Raska, CZE	216.5
1972	Yukio Kasaya, JPN	244.2
1976	Hans-Georg Aschenbach, E. Ger	252.0
1980	Anton Innauer, AUT	266.3
1984	Jens Weissflog, E. Ger	215.2
1988	Matti Nykänen, FIN	229.1
1992	Ernst Vettori, AUT	222.8
1994	Espen Bredesen, NOR	282.0
1998	Jani Soininen, FIN	234.5

Note: Jump held at 70 meters from 1964-92.

Large Hill-120 Meters

Year		Points	Year		Points
1924	Jacob Tullin Thams, NOR	18.960	1968	Vladimir Beloussov, USSR	231.3
1928	Alf Andersen, NOR	19.208	1972	Wojciech Fortuna, POL	219.9
1932	Birger Ruud, NOR	228.1	1976	Karl Schäabl, AUT	234.8
1936	Birger Ruud, NOR	232.0	1980	Jouko Törmänen, FIN	271.0
1948	Petter Hugsted, NOR	228.1	1984	Matti Nykänen, FIN	231.2
1952	Arnfinn Bergmann, NOR	226.0	1988	Matti Nykänen, FIN	224.0
1956	Antti Hyvärinen, FIN	227.0	1992	Toni Nieminen, FIN	239.5
1960	Helmut Recknagel, GER	227.2	1994	Jens Weissflog, GER	274.5
1964	Toralf Engan, NOR	230.7	1998	Kazuyoshi Funaki, JPN	272.3

Note: Jump held at various lengths from 1924-56; at 80 meters from 1960-64; and at 90 meters from 1968-88.

Team Large Hill

Year		Points	Year		Points
1924-84	Not held		1994	Germany	970.1
1988	Finland	634.4	1998	Japan	933.0
1992	Finland	644.4			

SNOWBOARDING

MEN

Halfpipe

Year		Points
1998	Gian Simmen, SWI	85.2

Giant Slalom

Year		Points
1998	Ross Rebagliati, CAN	2:03.96

WOMEN

Halfpipe

Year		Points
1998	Nicola Thost, GER	74.6

Giant Slalom

Year		Points
1998	Karine Ruby, FRA	2:17.34

SPEED SKATING

MEN

Multiple gold medals: Eric Heiden and Clas Thunberg (5); Ivar Ballangrud, Yevgeny Grishin and Johann Olav Koss (4); Hjalmar Andersen, Tomas Gustafson, Irving Jaffee and Ard Schenk (3); Gaétan Boucher, Knut Johannesen, Erhard Keller, Uwe-Jens Mey, Gianni Romme and Jack Shea (2). Note that Thunberg's total includes the All-Around, which was contested for the only time in 1924.

500 meters

Year		Time		Year		Time	
1924	Charles Jewtraw, USA	44.0		1968	Erhard Keller, W. Ger	40.3	
1928	(TIE) Bernt Evensen, NOR	43.4	OR	1972	Erhard Keller, W. Ger.	39.44	OR
	& Clas Thunberg, FIN	43.4	OR	1976	Yevgeny Kulikov, USSR	39.17	OR
1932	Jack Shea, USA	43.4	=OR	1980	Eric Heiden, USA	38.03	OR
1936	Ivar Ballangrud, NOR	43.4	=OR	1984	Sergei Fokichev, USSR	38.19	
1948	Finn Helgesen, NOR	43.1	OR	1988	Uwe-Jens Mey, E. Ger	36.45	WR
1952	Ken Henry, USA	43.2		1992	Uwe-Jens Mey, GER	37.14	
1956	Yevgeny Grishin, USSR	40.2	=WR	1994	Aleksandr Golubev, RUS	36.33	OR
1960	Yevgeny Grishin, USSR	40.2	=WR	1998	Hiroyashu Shimizu, JPN	71.35	OR
1964	Terry McDermott, USA	40.1	OR				

1000 meters

Year		Time		Year		Time	
1924-72	Not held			1988	Nikolai Gulyaev, USSR	1:13.03	OR
1976	Peter Mueller, USA	1:19.32		1992	Olaf Zinke, GER	1:14.85	
1980	Eric Heiden, USA	1:15.18	OR	1994	Dan Jansen, USA	1:12.43	WR
1984	Gaétan Boucher, CAN	1:15.80		1998	Ids Postma, NET	1:10.64	OR

1500 meters

Year		Time		Year		Time	
1924	Clas Thunberg, FIN	2:20.8		1964	Ants Antson, USSR	2:10.3	
1928	Clas Thunberg, FIN	2:21.1		1968	Kees Verkerk, NET	2:03.4	OR
1932	Jack Shea, USA	2:57.5		1972	Ard Schenk, NET	2:02.96	OR
1936	Charles Mathisen, NOR	2:19.2	OR	1976	Jan Egil Storholt, NOR	1:59.38	OR
1948	Sverre Farstad, NOR	2:17.6	OR	1980	Eric Heiden, USA	1:55.44	OR
1952	Hjalmar Andersen, NOR	2:20.4		1984	Gaétan Boucher, CAN	1:58.36	
1956	(TIE)Yevgeny Grishin, USSR	2:08.6	WR	1988	Andre Hoffman, E. Ger	1:52.06	WR
	& Yuri Mikhailov, USSR	2:08.6	WR	1992	Johann Olav Koss, NOR	1:54.81	
1960	(TIE) Roald Aas, NOR	2:10.4		1994	Johann Olav Koss, NOR	1:51.29	WR
	& Yevgeny Grishin, USSR	2:10.4		1998	Aadne Sondral, NOR	1:47.87	WR

5000 meters

Year		Time	
1924	Clas Thunberg, FIN	8:39.0	
1928	Ivar Ballangrud, NOR	8:50.5	
1932	Irving Jaffee, USA	9:40.8	
1936	Ivar Ballangrud, NOR	8:19.6	OR
1948	Reidar Liaklev, NOR	8:29.4	
1952	Hjalmar Andersen, NOR	8:10.6	OR
1956	Boris Shilkov, USSR	7:48.7	OR
1960	Viktor Kosichkin, USSR	7:51.3	
1964	Knut Johannesen, NOR	7:38.4	OR
1968	Fred Anton Maier, NOR	7:22.4	WR
1972	Ard Schenk, NET	7:23.61	
1976	Sten Stensen, NOR	7:24.48	
1980	Eric Heiden, USA	7:02.29	OR
1984	Tomas Gustafson, SWE	7:12.28	
1988	Tomas Gustafson, SWE	6:44.63	WR
1992	Geir Karlstad, NOR	6:59.97	
1994	Johann Olav Koss, NOR	6:34.96	WR
1998	Gianni Romme, NET	6:22.20	WR

10,000 meters

Year		Time	
1924	Julius Skutnabb, FIN	18:04.8	
1928	Irving Jaffee, USA*	18:36.5	
1932	Irving Jaffee, USA	19:13.6	
1936	Ivar Ballangrud, NOR	17:24.3	OR
1948	Ake Seyffarth, SWE	17:26.3	
1952	Hjalmar Andersen, NOR	16:45.8	OR
1956	Sigvard Ericsson, SWE	16:35.9	OR
1960	Knut Johannesen, NOR	15:46.6	WR
1964	Jonny Nilsson, SWE	15:50.1	
1968	Johnny Höglin, SWE	15:23.6	OR
1972	Ard Schenk, NET	15:01.35	OR
1976	Piet Kleine, NET	14:50.59	OR
1980	Eric Heiden, USA	14:28.13	WR
1984	Igor Malkov, USSR	14:39.90	
1988	Tomas Gustafson, SWE	13:48.20	WR
1992	Bart Veldkamp, NET	14:12.12	
1994	Johann Olav Koss, NOR	13:30.55	WR
1998	Gianni Romme, NET	13:15.33	WR

*Unofficial, according to the IOC. Jaffee recorded the fastest time, but the event was called off in progress due to thawing ice.

WOMEN

Multiple gold medals: Lydia Skoblikova (6); Bonnie Blair (5); Karin Enke, Gunda Niemann-Stirnemann and Yvonne van Gennip (3); Tatiana Averina, Claudia Pechstein and Christa Rothenburger (2).

500 meters

Year		Time	
1960	Helga Haase, GER	45.9	
1964	Lydia Skoblikova, USSR	45.0	OR
1968	Lyudmila Titova, USSR	46.1	
1972	Anne Henning, USA	43.33	OR
1976	Sheila Young, USA	42.76	OR
1980	Karin Enke, E. Ger	41.78	OR
1984	Christa Rothenburger, E. Ger	41.02	OR
1988	Bonnie Blair, USA	39.10	WR
1992	Bonnie Blair, USA	40.33	
1994	Bonnie Blair, USA	39.25	
1998	Catriona Lemay-Doan, CAN	76.60	OR

1000 meters

Year		Time	
1960	Klara Guseva, USSR	1:34.1	
1964	Lydia Skoblikova, USSR	1:33.2	OR
1968	Carolina Geijssen, NET	1:32.6	OR
1972	Monika Pflug, W. Ger	1:31.40	OR
1976	Tatiana Averina, USSR	1:28.43	OR
1980	Natalia Petruseva, USSR	1:24.10	OR
1984	Karin Enke, E. Ger	1:21.61	OR
1988	Christa Rothenburger, E. Ger	1:17.65	WR
1992	Bonnie Blair, USA	1:21.90	
1994	Bonnie Blair, USA	1:18.74	
1998	Marianne Timmer, NET	1:16.51	OR

1500 meters

Year		Time	
1960	Lydia Skoblikova, USSR	2:25.2	WR
1964	Lydia Skoblikova, USSR	2:22.6	OR
1968	Kaija Mustonen, FIN	2:22.4	OR
1972	Dianne Holum, USA	2:20.85	OR
1976	Galina Stepanskaya, USSR	2:16.58	OR
1980	Annie Borckink, NET	2:10.95	OR
1984	Karin Enke, E. Ger	2:03.42	WR
1988	Yvonne van Gennip, NET	2:00.68	OR
1992	Jacqueline Börner, GER	2:05.87	
1994	Emese Hunyady, AUT	2:02.19	
1998	Marianne Timmer, NET	1:57.58	WR

3000 meters

Year		Time	
1960	Lydia Skoblikova, USSR	5:14.3	
1964	Lydia Skoblikova, USSR	5:14.9	
1968	Johanna Schut, NET	4:56.2	OR
1972	Christina Baas-Kaiser, NET	4:52.14	OR
1976	Tatiana Averina, USSR	4:45.19	OR
1980	Bjorg Eva Jensen, NOR	4:32.13	OR
1984	Andrea Schöne, E. Ger	4:24.79	OR
1988	Yvonne van Gennip, NET	4:11.94	WR
1992	Gunda Niemann, GER	4:19.90	
1994	Svetlana Bazhanova, RUS	4:17.43	
1998	Gunda Niemann-Stirnemann, GER	4:07.29	OR

5000 meters

Year		Time	
1960-84	Not held		
1988	Yvonne van Gennip, NET	7:14.13	WR
1992	Gunda Niemann, GER	7:31.57	
1994	Claudia Pechstein, GER	7:14.37	
1998	Claudia Pechstein, GER	6:59.61	WR

AP/Wide World Photos

Norway's **Bjorn Dählie** collapses after crossing the finish line first in the 50km freestyle cross country event at Nagano. Perhaps it was all the gold around his neck. Norway has won more Winter Olympic medals than any other nation. Having guys like Dählie, who has more medals than any other Winter Olympic athlete, doesn't hurt.

All-Time Leading Medal Winners

MEN

No		Sport	G-S-B
12	Bjorn Dählie, NOR	Cross-country	8-4-0
9	Sixten Jernberg, SWE	Cross-country	4-3-2
7	Clas Thunberg, FIN	Speed Skating	5-1-1
7	Ivar Ballangrud, NOR	Speed Skating	4-2-1
7	Veikko Hakulinen, FIN	Cross-country	3-3-1
7	Eero Mäntyranta, FIN	Cross-country	3-2-2
7	Bogdan Musiol, E. Ger/GER	Bobsled	1-5-1
6	Gunde Svan, SWE	Cross-country	4-1-1
6	Vegard Ulvang, NOR	Cross-country	3-2-1
6	Johan Gröttumsbråten, NOR	Nordic	3-1-2
6	Wolfgang Hoppe, E. Ger/GER	Bobsled	2-3-1
6	Eugenio Monti, ITA	Bobsled	2-2-2
6	Vladimir Smirnov, USSR/UT/KAZ	X-country	1-4-1
6	Mika Myllylae, FIN	Cross-country	1-1-4
6	Roald Larsen, NOR	Speed Skating	0-2-4
5	**Eric Heiden, USA**	Speed Skating	5-0-0
5	Yevgeny Grishin, USSR	Speed Skating	4-1-0
5	Johann Olav Koss, NOR	Speed Skating	4-1-0
5	Matti Nykänen, FIN	Ski Jumping	4-1-0
5	Aleksandr Tikhonov, USSR	Biathlon	4-1-0
5	Nikolai Zimyatov, USSR	Cross-country	4-1-0
5	Alberto Tomba, ITA	Alpine	3-2-0
5	Harald Grönningen, NOR	Cross-country	2-3-0
5	Päl Tyldum, NOR	Cross-country	2-3-0
5	Knut Johannesen, NOR	Speed Skating	2-2-1
5	Kjetil André Aamodt, NOR	Alpine	1-2-2
5	Peter Angerer, W. Ger/GER	Biathlon	1-2-2
5	Juha Mieto, FIN	Cross-country	1-2-2
5	Fritz Feierabend, SWI	Bobsled	0-3-2
5	Rintje Ritsma, NET	Speed Skating	0-2-3

WOMEN

No		Sport	G-S-B
10	Raisa Smetanina, USSR/UT	Cross-country	4-5-1
9	Lyubov Egorova, UT/RUS	Cross-country	6-3-0
8	Galina Kulakova, USSR	Cross-country	4-2-2
8	Karin (Enke) Kania, E. Ger	Speed Skating	3-4-1
8	Gunda Neimann-Stirnemann, GER	Speed Skating	3-4-1
7	Larisa Lazutina, UT/RUS	Cross-country	5-1-1
7	Marja-Liisa (Hämäläinen) Kirvesniemi, FIN	Cross-country	3-0-4
7	Elena Valbe, UT/RUS	Cross-country	3-0-4
7	Andrea (Mitscherlich, Schöne) Ehrig, E. Ger	Speed Skating	1-5-1
7	Stefania Belmondo, ITA	Cross-country	1-2-4
6	Lydia Skoblikova, USSR	Speed Skating	6-0-0
6	**Bonnie Blair, USA**	Speed Skating	5-0-1
6	Manuela Di Centa, ITA	Cross-country	2-2-2
5	Lee-Kyung Chun, KOR	ST Sp. Skating	4-0-1
5	Anfisa Reztsova, USSR/UT	CC/Biathlon	3-1-1
5	Vreni Schneider, SWI	Alpine	3-1-1
5	Katja Seizinger, GER	Alpine	3-0-2
5	Claudia Pechstien, GER	Speed Skating	2-1-2
5	Helena Takalo, FIN	Cross-country	1-3-1
5	Ursula Disl, GER	Biathlon	1-2-2
5	Alevtina Kolchina, USSR	Cross-country	1-1-3

Athletes with Winter and Summer Medals

Only three athletes have won medals in both the Winter and Summer Olympics:

Eddie Eagan, USA– Light Heavyweight Boxing gold (1920) and Four-man Bobsled gold (1932).

Jacob Tullin Thams, Norway– Ski Jumping gold (1924) and 8-meter Yachting silver (1936).

Christa Luding-Rothenburger, East Germany– Speed Skating gold at 500 meters (1984) and 1,000m (1988), silver at 500m (1988) and bronze at 500m (1992) and Match Sprint Cycling silver (1988). Luding- Rothenburger is the only athlete to ever win medals in both Winter and Summer Games in the same year.

Games Medaled In

MEN– **Aamodt** (1992,94); **Angerer** (1980,84,88); **Ballangrud**(1928,32,36); **Dählie** (1992,94,98); **Feierabend** (1936,48,52); **Grishin** (1956,60,64); **Gröttumsbråten** (1924,28,32); **Grönningen** (1960,64,68); **Hakulinen** (1952,56,60); **Heiden** (1980); **Hoppe** (1984,88,92,94); **Jernberg** (1956,60,64); **Johannesen** (1956,60,64); **Koss** (1992,94). **Larsen** (1924,28); **Mäntyranta** (1960,64,68); **Mieto** (1976,80,84); **Monti** (1956,60,64,68); **Musiol** (1980,84,88,92); **Myllylae** (1994,98); **Nykänen** (1984,88); **Ritsma** (1994,98); **Smirnov** (1988,92,94,98); **Svan** (1984,88); **Thunberg** (1924,28); **Tikhonov** (1968,72,76,80); **Tomba** (1988,92,94); **Tyldum** (1968,72,76); **Ulvang** (1988,92,94); **Zimyatov** (1980,84).

WOMEN– **Belmondo** (1992,94,98); **Blair** (1988,92,94); **Chun** (1994,98); **Di Centa** (1992,94); **Disl** (1994,98); **Egorova** (1992,94); **Ehrig** (1976,80,84,88); **Kania** (1980,84,88); **Kirvesniemi** (1984,88,94); **Kolchina** (1956,64,68); **Kulakova** (1968,72,76,80); **Lazutina** (1992,94,98); **Niemann-Stirnemann** (1992,94,98); **Pechstein** (1992,94,98); **Reztsova** (1988,92,94); **Schneider** (1988,92,94); **Seizinger** (1992,94,98); **Skoblikova** (1960,64); **Smetanina** (1976,80,84,88,92); **Takalo** (1972,76,80); **Valbe** (1992,94,98).

Most Gold Medals

MEN

No		Sport	G-S-B
5	Bjorn Dählie, NOR	Cross-country	5-3-0
5	Clas Thunberg, FIN	Speed Skating	5-1-1
5	**Eric Heiden, USA**	Speed Skating	5-0-0
4	Sixten Jernberg, SWE	Cross-country	4-3-2
4	Ivar Ballangrud, NOR	Speed Skating	4-2-1
4	Gunde Svan, SWE	Cross-country	4-1-1
4	Yevgeny Grishin, USSR	Speed Skating	4-1-0
4	Johann Olav Koss, NOR	Speed Skating	4-1-0
4	Matti Nykänen, FIN	Ski Jumping	4-1-0
4	Aleksandr Tikhonov, USSR	Biathlon	4-1-0
4	Nikolai Zimyatov, USSR	Cross-country	4-1-0
4	Thomas Wassberg, SWE	Cross-country	4-0-0
3	Veikko Hakulinen, FIN	Cross-country	3-3-1
3	Eero Mäntyranta, FIN	Cross-country	3-2-2
3	Vegard Ulvang, NOR	Cross-country	3-2-1
3	Alberto Tomba, ITA	Alpine	3-2-0
3	Johan Gröttumsbråten, NOR	Nordic	3-1-2
3	Bernhard Germeshausen, E. Ger	Bobsled	3-1-0
3	Gillis Grafström, SWE	Figure Skating	3-1-0
3	Tomas Gustafson, SWE	Speed Skating	3-1-0
3	Vladislav Tretiak, USSR	Ice Hockey	3-1-0
3	Jens Weissflog, E. Ger/GER	Ski Jumping	3-1-0
3	Meinhard Nehmer, E. Ger	Bobsled	3-0-1
3	Hjalmar Andersen, NOR	Speed Skating	3-0-0
3	Vitaly Davydov, USSR	Ice Hockey	3-0-0
3	Anatoly Firsov, USSR	Ice Hockey	3-0-0
3	Thorleif Haug, NOR	Cross-country	3-0-0
3	**Irving Jaffee, USA**	Speed Skating	3-0-0
3	Andrei Khomoutov, USSR/UT	Ice Hockey	3-0-0
3	Jean-Claude Killy, FRA	Alpine	3-0-0
3	Viktor Kuzkin, USSR	Ice Hockey	3-0-0
3	Aleksandr Ragulin, USSR	Ice Hockey	3-0-0
3	Toni Sailer, AUT	Alpine	3-0-0
3	Ard Schenk, NET	Speed Skating	3-0-0
3	Ulrich Wehling, E. Ger	Ski Jumping	3-0-0

WOMEN

No		Sport	G-S-B
6	Lyubov Egorova, UT/RUS	Cross-country	6-3-0
6	Lydia Skoblikova, USSR	Speed Skating	6-0-0
5	Larissa Lazutina, UT/RUS	Cross-country	5-1-1
5	**Bonnie Blair, USA**	Speed Skating	5-0-1
4	Raisa Smetanina, USSR/UT	Cross-country	4-5-1
4	Galina Kulakova, USSR	Cross-country	4-2-2
4	Lee-Kyung Chun, KOR	ST Sp. Skating	4-0-1
3	Karin (Enke) Kania, E. GER	Speed Skating	3-4-1
3	Gunda Neimann-Stirnemann, GER	Speed Skating	3-4-1
3	Anfisa Reztsova, USSR/UT	CC/Biathlon	3-1-1
3	Vreni Schneider, SWI	Alpine	3-1-1
3	Marja-Liisa (Hämäläinen) Kirvesniemi, FIN	Cross-country	3-0-4
3	Elena Valbe, UT/RUS	Cross-country	3-0-4
3	Katja Seizinger, GER	Alpine	3-0-2
3	Claudia Boyarskikh, USSR	Cross-country	3-0-0
3	Sonja Henie, NOR	Figure Skating	3-0-0
3	Irina Rodnina, USSR	Figure Skating	3-0-0
3	Yvonne van Gennip, NET	Speed Skating	3-0-0

All-Time Leading USA Medalists

MEN

No		Sport	G-S-B
5	Eric Heiden	Speed Skating	5-0-0
3*	Irving Jaffee	Speed Skating	3-0-0
3	Pat Martin	Bobsled	1-2-0
3	John Heaton	Bobsled/Cresta	0-2-1
2	Dick Button	Figure Skating	2-0-0
2†	Eddie Eagan	Boxing/Bobsled	2-0-0
2	Billy Fiske	Bobsled	2-0-0
2	Cliff Gray	Bobsled	2-0-0
2	Jack Shea	Speed Skating	2-0-0
2	Billy Cleary	Ice Hockey	1-1-0
2	Jennison Heaton	Bobsled/Cresta	1-1-0
2	John Mayasich	Ice Hockey	1-1-0

No		Sport	G-S-B
2	Terry McDermott	Speed Skating	1-1-0
2	Dick Meredith	Ice Hockey	1-1-0
2	Tommy Moe	Alpine	1-1-0
2	Weldy Olson	Ice Hockey	1-1-0
2	Dick Rodenheiser	Ice Hockey	1-1-0
2	David Jenkins	Figure Skating	1-1-0
2	Stan Benham	Bobsled	0-2-0
2	Herb Drury	Ice Hockey	0-2-0
2	Eric Flaim	Sp. Skate/ST Sp. Skate	0-2-0
2	Frank Synott	Ice Hockey	0-2-0
2	John Garrison	Ice Hockey	0-1-1

*Jaffee is generally given credit for a third gold medal in the 10,000-meter Speed Skating race of 1928. He had the fastest time before the race was cancelled due to thawing ice. The IOC considers the race unofficial.

†Eagan won the Light Heavyweight boxing title at the 1920 Summer Games in Antwerp and the four-man Bobsled at the 1932 Winter Games in Lake Placid. He is the only athlete ever to win gold medals in both the Winter and Summer Olympics.

WOMEN

No		Sport	G-S-B
6	Bonnie Blair	Speed Skating	5-0-1
4	Cathy Turner	ST Sp. Skating	2-1-1
4	Dianne Holum	Speed Skating	1-2-1
3	Sheila Young	Speed Skating	1-1-1
3	Leah Poulos Mueller	Speed Skating	0-3-0
3	Beatrix Loughran	Figure Skating	0-2-1
3	Amy Peterson	ST Sp. Skating	0-2-1
2	Andrea Mead Lawrence	Alpine	2-0-0
2	Tenley Albright	Figure Skating	1-1-0
2	Gretchen Fraser	Alpine	1-1-0
2	Carol Heiss	Figure Skating	1-1-0
2	Picabo Street	Alpine	1-1-0
2	Diann Roffe-Steinrotter	Alpine	1-1-0
2	Anne Henning	Speed Skating	1-0-1
2	Penny Pitou	Alpine	0-2-0
2	Nancy Kerrigan	Figure Skating	0-1-1
2	Jean Saubert	Alpine	0-1-1
2	Chris Witty	Sp. Skating	0-1-1
2	Nikki Ziegelmeyer	ST Sp. Skating	0-1-1

Notes: The Cresta run is undertaken on a heavy sled ridden head first in the prone position and has only been held at St. Moritz in 1928 and '48. Also, the term ST Sp. Skating refers to Short Track (or pack) Speed Skating.

All-Time Medal Standings, 1924-98

All-time Winter Games medal standings, according to *The Golden Book of the Olympic Games* and updated through 1998. Medal counts include figure skating medals (1908 and '20) and hockey medals (1920) awarded at the Summer Games. National medal standings for the Winter and Summer Games are not recognized by the IOC.

		G	S	B	Total
1	Norway	83	87	69	239
2	Soviet Union (1956-88)	78	57	59	194
3	**United States**	59	59	41	159
4	Austria	39	53	53	145
5	Finland	38	49	48	135
6	East Germany (1956-88)	43	39	36	118
7	Sweden	39	28	35	102
8	Switzerland	29	31	32	92
9	Germany (1928-36,92–)	35	30	25	90
10	Canada	25	25	29	79
11	Italy	27	27	23	77
12	Netherlands	19	23	19	61
	France	18	17	26	61
14	West Germany (1952-88)	18	20	19	57
15	Russia (1994–)	21	14	7	42
16	Japan	8	9	12	29
17	Czechoslovakia (1924-92)	2	8	16	26
18	Great Britain	7	4	13	24
19	Unified Team (1992)	9	6	8	23
20	South Korea	9	3	4	16
21	China	0	10	4	14
22	Liechtenstein	2	2	5	9
23	Hungary	0	2	4	6
24	Kazakhstan (1994–)	1	2	2	5
	Belgium	1	1	3	5
26	Poland	1	1	2	4
	Yugoslavia (1924-88)	0	3	1	4
	Belarus (1994–)	0	2	2	4
29	Czech Republic (1998—)	1	1	1	3
	Ukraine (1994–)	1	1	1	3
	Slovenia (1992–)	0	0	3	3
32	Bulgaria	1	0	1	2
	Spain	1	0	1	2
	Luxembourg	0	2	0	2
	North Korea	0	1	1	2
	Australia	0	0	2	2
37	Uzbekistan (1994–)	1	0	0	1
	Denmark	0	1	0	1
	New Zealand	0	1	0	1
	Romania	0	0	1	1

Combined totals	G	S	B	Total
Germany/E. Ger/W. Ger	96	89	80	265
USSR/UT/Russia	108	77	74	259

Notes: Athletes from the USSR participated in the Winter Games from 1956-88, returned as the Unified Team in 1992 after the breakup of the Soviet Union (in 1991) and then competed for the independent republics of Belarus, Kazakhstan, Russia, Ukraine, Uzbekistan and three others in 1994. Yugoslavia divided into Croatia and Bosnia-Herzegovina in 1991, while Czechoslovakia split into Slovenia and the Czech Republic the same year.

Germany was barred from the Olympics in 1924 and 1948 as an aggressor nation in both World Wars I and II. Divided into East and West Germany after WWII, both countries competed under one flag from 1952-64, then as separate teams from 1968-88. Germany was reunified in 1990.

Modern Olympic Games

The original Olympic Games were celebrated as a religious festival from 776 B.C. until 393 A.D., when Roman emperor Theodosius I banned all pagan festivals (the Olympics celebrated the Greek god Zeus). On June 23, 1894, French educator Baron Pierre de Coubertin, speaking at the Sorbonne in Paris to a gathering of international sports leaders, proposed that the ancient games be revived on an international scale. The idea was enthusiastically received and the Modern Olympics were born. The first Olympics were held two years later in Athens, where 311 athletes from 14 nations competed in the ancient Panathenaic stadium to large and enthusiastic crowds. Americans captured nine out of 12 track and field events, but Greece won the most medals with 47.

The Summer Olympics

Year	No	Location	Dates	Nations	Most medals	USA Medals	
1896	I	Athens, GRE	Apr. 6-15	14	Greece (10-19-18—47)	11- 6- 2— 19	(2nd)
1900	II	Paris, FRA	May 20-Oct. 28	26	France (26-37-32—95)	18-14-15— 47	(2nd)
1904	III	St. Louis, USA.	July 1-Nov. 23	13	USA (78-84-82—244)	78-84-82—244	(1st)
1906-**a**	—	Athens, GRE	Apr. 22-May 2	20	France (15-9-16—40)	12- 6- 6— 24	(3rd)
1908	IV	London, GBR	Apr. 27-Oct. 31	22	Britain (54-46-38—138)	23-12-12— 47	(2nd)
1912	V	Stockholm, SWE	May 5-July 22	28	Sweden (23-24-17—64)	25-18-20— 63	(2nd)
1916	VI	Berlin, GER	Cancelled (WWI)				
1920	VII	Antwerp, BEL	Apr. 20-Sept. 12	29	USA (41-27-27—95)	41-27-27— 95	(1st)
1924	VIII	Paris, FRA	May 4-July 27	44	USA (45-27-27—99)	45-27-27— 99	(1st)
1928	IX	Amsterdam, NET	May 17-Aug. 12	46	USA (22-18-16—56)	22-18-16— 56	(1st)
1932	X	Los Angeles, USA.	July 30-Aug. 14	37	USA (41-32-30—103)	41-32-30—103	(1st)
1936	XI	Berlin, GER	Aug. 1-16	49	Germany (33-26-30-89)	24-20-12— 56	(2nd)
1940-**b**	XII	Tokyo, JPN	Cancelled (WWII)				
1944	XIII	London, GBR	Cancelled (WWII)				
1948	XIV	London, GBR	July 29-Aug. 14	59	USA (38-27-19—84)	38-27-19— 84	(1st)
1952-**cd**	XV	Helsinki, FIN	July 19-Aug. 3	69	USA (40-19-17—76)	40-19-17— 76	(1st)
1956-**e**	XVI	Melbourne, AUS	Nov. 22-Dec .8	72	USSR (37-29-32—98)	32-25-17— 74	(2nd)
1960	XVII	Rome, ITA	Aug. 25-Sept. 11	83	USSR (43-29-31—103)	34-21-16— 71	(2nd)
1964	XVIII	Tokyo, JPN	Oct. 10-24	93	USSR (30-31-35—96)	36-26-28— 90	(2nd)
1968-**f**	XIX	Mexico City, MEX	Oct. 12-27	113	USA (45-28-34—107)	45-28-34—107	(1st)
1972	XX	Munich, W. GER	Aug. 26-Sept. 10	122	USSR (50-27-22—99)	33-31-30— 94	(2nd)
1976-**g**	XXI	Montreal, CAN	July 17-Aug. 1	88	USSR (49-41-35—125)	34-35-25— 94	(3rd)
1980-**h**	XXII	Moscow, USSR	July 19-Aug. 3	81	USSR (80-69-46—195)	Boycotted Games	
1984-**i**	XXIII	Los Angeles, USA.	July 28-Aug. 12	140	USA (83-61-30—174)	83-61-30—174	(1st)
1988	XXIV	Seoul, S. KOR	Sept. 17-Oct. 2	160	USSR (55-31-46—132)	36-31-27— 94	(3rd)
1992-**j**	XXV	Barcelona, SPA	July 25-Aug. 9	172	UT (45-38-29—112)	37-34-37—108	(2nd)
1996	XXVI	Atlanta, USA	July 20-Aug. 4	197	USA (44-32-25—101)	44-32-25—101	(1st)
2000	XXVII	Sydney, AUS	Sept. 15-Oct. 1				
2004	XXVIII	Athens, GRE	Aug. 13-29				

a—The 1906 Intercalated Games in Athens are considered unofficial by the IOC because they did not take place in the four-year cycle established in 1896. However, most record books include these interim games with the others.

b—The 1940 Summer Games are originally scheduled for Tokyo, but Japan resigns as host after the outbreak of the Sino-Japanese war in 1937. Helsinki is the next choice, but the IOC cancels the Games after Russian troops invade Finland in 1939.

c—Germany and Japan are allowed to rejoin Olympic community for first Summer Games since 1936. Though a divided country, the Germans send a joint East-West team.

d—The Soviet Union (USSR) participates in its first Olympics, Winter or Summer, since the Russian revolution in 1917 and takes home the second most medals (22-30-19—71).

e—Due to Australian quarantine laws, the equestrian events for the 1956 Games are held in Stockholm, June 10-17.

f—East Germany and West Germany send separate teams for the first time and will continue to do so through 1988.

g—The 1976 Games are boycotted by 32 nations, most of them from black Africa, because the IOC will not ban New Zealand. Earlier that year, a rugby team from New Zealand had toured racially-segregated South Africa.

h—The 1980 Games are boycotted by 64 nations, led by the USA, to protest the Russian invasion of Afghanistan on Dec. 27, 1979.

i—The 1984 Games are boycotted by 14 Eastern Bloc nations, led by the USSR, to protest America's overcommercialization of the Games, inadequate security and an anti-Soviet attitude by the U.S. government. Most believe, however, the communist walkout is simply revenge for 1980.

j—Germany sends a single team after East and West German reunification in 1990 and the USSR competes as the Unified Team after the breakup of the Soviet Union in 1991.

Event-by-Event

Gold medal winners from 1896-1996 in the following events: Baseball, Basketball, Boxing, Diving, Field Hockey, Gymnastics, Soccer, Swimming, Tennis, and Track & Field.

BASEBALL

Multiple gold medals: Cuba (2).

Year		Year	
1992	**Cuba**, Taiwan, Japan	1996	**Cuba**, Japan, United States

BASKETBALL

MEN

Multiple gold medals: USA (11); USSR (2).

Year		Year	
1936	**United States**, Canada, Mexico	1972	**Soviet Union**, United States, Cuba
1948	**United States**, France, Brazil	1976	**United States**, Yugoslavia, Soviet Union
1952	**United States**, Soviet Union, Uruguay	1980	**Yugoslavia**, Italy, Soviet Union
1956	**United States**, Soviet Union, Uruguay	1984	**United States**, Spain, Yugoslavia
1960	**United States**, Soviet Union, Brazil	1988	**Soviet Union**, Yugoslavia, United States
1964	**United States**, Soviet Union, Brazil	1992	**United States**, Croatia, Lithuania
1968	**United States**, Yugoslavia, Soviet Union	1996	**United States**, Yugoslavia, Lithuania

U.S. Medal-Winning Men's Basketball Teams

1936 (gold medal): Sam Balter, Ralph Bishop, Joe Fortenberry, Tex Gibbons, Francis Johnson, Carl Knowles, Frank Lubin, Art Mollner, Don Piper, Jack Ragland, Carl Shy, Willard Schmidt, Duane Swanson and William Wheatley. Coach–Jim Needles; Assistant–Gene Johnson. Final: USA over Canada, 19-8.

1948 (gold medal): Cliff Barker, Don Barksdale, Ralph Beard, Louis Beck, Vince Boryla, Gordon Carpenter, Alex Groza, Wallace Jones, Bob Kurland, Ray Lumpp, R.C. Pitts, Jesse Renick, Robert (Jackie) Robinson and Ken Rollins. Coach–Omar Browning; Assistant–Adolph Rupp. Final: USA over France, 65-21.

1952 (gold medal): Ron Bontemps, Mark Freiberger, Wayne Glasgow, Charlie Hoag, Bill Hougland, John Keller, Dean Kelley, Bob Kenney, Bob Kurland, Bill Lienhard, Clyde Lovellette, Frank McCabe, Dan Pippin and Howie Williams. Coach–Warren Womble; Assistant–Forrest (Phog) Allen. Final: USA over USSR, 36-25.

1956 (gold medal): Dick Boushka, Carl Cain, Chuck Darling, Bill Evans, Gib Ford, Burdy Haldorson, Bill Hougland, Bob Jeangerard, K.C. Jones, Bill Russell, Ron Tomsic, Jim Walsh. Coach–Gerald Tucker; Assistant–Bruce Drake. Final: USA over USSR, 89-55.

1960 (gold medal): Jay Arnette, Walt Bellamy, Bob Boozer, Terry Dischinger, Jerry Lucas, Oscar Robertson, Adrian Smith, Burdy Haldorson, Darrall Imhoff, Allen Kelley, Lester Lane and Jerry West. Coach–Pete Newell; Assistant–Warren Womble. Final round: USA defeated USSR (81-57), Italy (112-81) and Brazil (90-63) in round robin.

1964 (gold medal): Jim (Bad News) Barnes, Bill Bradley, Larry Brown, Joe Caldwell, Mel Counts, Dick Davies, Walt Hazzard, Lucious Jackson, Pete McCaffrey, Jeff Mullins, Jerry Shipp and George Wilson. Coach–Hank Iba; Assistant–Henry Vaughn. Final: USA over USSR, 73-59.

1968 (gold medal): Mike Barrett, John Clawson, Don Dee, Cal Fowler, Spencer Haywood, Bill Hosket, Jim King, Glynn Saulters, Charlie Scott, Mike Silliman, Ken Spain, and JoJo White. Coach–Hank Iba; Assistant–Henry Vaughn. USA over Yugoslavia, 65-50.

1972 (silver medal refused): Mike Bantom, Jim Brewer, Tom Burleson, Doug Collins, Kenny Davis, Jim Forbes, Tom Henderson, Bobby Jones, Dwight Jones, Kevin Joyce, Tom McMillen and Ed Ratleff. Coach–Hank Iba; Assistants– John Bach and Don Haskins. Final: USSR over USA, 51-50.

1976 (gold medal): Tate Armstrong, Quinn Buckner, Kenny Carr, Adrian Dantley, Walter Davis, Phil Ford, Ernie Grunfeld, Phil Hubbard, Mitch Kupchak, Tommy LaGarde, Scott May and Steve Sheppard. Coach–Dean Smith; Assistants–Bill Guthridge and John Thompson. Final: USA over Yugoslavia, 95-74.

1980 (no medal): USA boycotted Moscow Games. Final: Yugoslavia over Italy, 86-77.

1984 (gold medal): Steve Alford, Patrick Ewing, Vern Fleming, Michael Jordan; Joe Kleine, Jon Koncak, Chris Mullin, Sam Perkins, Alvin Robertson, Wayman Tisdale, Jeff Turner and Leon Wood. Coach–Bobby Knight; Assistants– Don Donoher and George Raveling. Final: USA over Spain, 96-65.

1988 (bronze medal): Stacey Augmon, Willie Anderson, Bimbo Coles, Jeff Grayer, Hersey Hawkins, Dan Majerle, Danny Manning, Mitch Richmond, J.R. Reid, David Robinson, Charles D. Smith and Charles E. Smith. Coach–John Thompson; Assistants–George Raveling and Mary Fenlon. Final: USSR over Yugoslavia, 76-63.

1992 (gold medal): Charles Barkley, Larry Bird, Clyde Drexler, Patrick Ewing, Magic Johnson, Michael Jordan, Christian Laettner, Karl Malone, Chris Mullin, Scottie Pippen, David Robinson and John Stockton. Coach–Chuck Daly; Assistants–Lenny Wilkens, Mike Krzyzewski and P.J. Carlesimo. Final: USA over Croatia, 117-85.

1996 (gold medal): Charles Barkley, Anfernee Hardaway, Grant Hill, Karl Malone, Reggie Miller, Hakeem Olajuwon, Shaquille O'Neal, Gary Payton, Scottie Pippen, David Robinson and John Stockton. Coach–Lenny Wilkens; Assistants–Bobby Cremins, Clem Haskins and Jerry Sloan. Final: USA over Yugoslavia, 95-69.

WOMEN

Multiple gold medals: USA and USSR/UT (3).

Year		Year	
1976	**Soviet Union**, United States, Bulgaria	1988	**United States**, Yugoslavia, Soviet Union
1980	**Soviet Union**, Bulgaria, Yugoslavia	1992	**Unified Team**, China, United States
1984	**United States**, South Korea, China	1996	**United States**, Brazil, Australia

U.S. Gold Medal-Winning Women's Basketball Teams

1984: Cathy Boswell, Denise Curry, Anne Donovan, Teresa Edwards, Lea Henry, Janice Lawrence, Pamela McGee, Carol Menken-Schaudt, Cheryl Miller, Kim Mulkey, Cindy Noble, Lynette Woodard. Coach–Pat Summitt; Assistant–Kay Yow. Final: USA over South Korea, 85-55.

1988: Cindy Brown, Vicky Bullett, Cynthia Cooper, Anne Donovan, Teresa Edwards, Kamie Ethridge, Jennifer Gillom, Bridgette Gordon, Andrea Lloyd, Katrina McClain, Suzie McConnell, Teresa Weatherspoon. Coach–Kay Yow; Assistants–Sylvia Hatchell and Susan Yow. Final: USA over Yugoslavia, 77-70.

1996: Jennifer Azzi, Ruthie Bolton, Teresa Edwards, Venus Lacy, Lisa Leslie, Rebecca Lobo, Katrina McClain, Nikki McCray, Carla McGee, Dawn Staley, Katy Steding and Sheryl Swoopes. Coach—Tara VanDerveer; Assistants–Ceal Barry, Nancy Darsch and Marian Washington. Final: USA over Brazil, 111-87.

BOXING

Multiple gold medals: László Papp and Teófilo Stevenson (3); Ariel Hernandez, Angel Herrera, Oliver Kirk, Jerzy Kulej, Boris Lagutin, Harry Mallin, Felix Savon and Hector Vinent (2). All fighters won titles in consecutive Olympics, except Kirk, who won both the bantamweight and featherweight titles in 1904 (he only had to fight once in each division).

Light Flyweight (106 lbs)

Year		Final Match	Year		Final Match
1968	Francisco Rodriguez, VEN	Decision, 3-2	1984	Paul Gonzales, USA	Default
1972	György Gedó, HUN	Decision, 5-0	1988	Ivailo Hristov, BUL	Decision, 5-0
1976	Jorge Hernandez, CUB	Decision, 4-1	1992	Rogelio Marcelo, CUB	Decision, 24-10
1980	Shamil Sabyrov, USSR	Decision, 3-2	1996	Daniel Petrov Bojilov, BUL	Decision, 19-6

Flyweight (112 lbs)

Year		Final Match	Year		Final Match
1904	George Finnegan, USA	Stopped, 1st	1964	Fernando Atzori, ITA	Decision, 4-1
1920	Frank Di Gennara, USA	Decision	1968	Ricardo Delgado, MEX	Decision, 5-0
1924	Fidel LaBarba, USA	Decision	1972	Georgi Kostadinov, BUL	Decision, 5-0
1928	Antal Kocsis, HUN	Decision	1976	Leo Randolph, USA	Decision, 3-2
1932	István Énekes, HUN	Decision	1980	Peter Lessov, BUL	Stopped, 2nd
1936	Willi Kaiser, GER	Decision	1984	Steve McCrory, USA	Decision, 4-1
1948	Pascual Perez, ARG	Decision	1988	Kim Kwang-Sun, S. Kor	Decision, 4-1
1952	Nate Brooks, USA	Decision, 3-0	1992	Su Choi-Chol, N. Kor	Decision, 12-2
1956	Terence Spinks, GBR	Decision	1996	Maikro Romero, CUB	Decision, 12-11
1960	Gyula Török, HUN	Decision, 3-2			

Bantamweight (119 lbs)

Year		Final Match	Year		Final Match
1904	Oliver Kirk, USA	Stopped, 3rd	1960	Oleg Grigoryev, USSR	Decision
1908	Henry Thomas, GBR	Decision	1964	Takao Sakurai, JPN	Stopped, 2nd
1920	Clarence Walker, SAF	Decision	1968	Valery Sokolov, USSR	Stopped, 2nd
1924	William Smith, SAF	Decision	1972	Orlando Martinez, CUB	Decision, 5-0
1928	Vittorio Tamagnini, ITA	Decision	1976	Gu Yong-Ju, N. Kor	Decision, 5-0
1932	Horace Gwynne, CAN	Decision	1980	Juan Hernandez, CUB	Decision, 5-0
1936	Ulderico Sergo, ITA	Decision	1984	Maurizio Stecca, ITA	Decision, 4-1
1948	Tibor Csik, HUN	Decision	1988	Kennedy McKinney, USA	Decision, 5-0
1952	Pentti Hämäläinen, FIN	Decision, 2-1	1992	Joel Casamayor, CUB	Decision, 14-8
1956	Wolfgang Behrendt, GER	Decision	1996	Istvan Kovacs, HUN	Decision, 14-7

Featherweight (125 lbs)

Year		Final Match	Year		Final Match
1904	Oliver Kirk, USA	Decision	1960	Francesco Musso, ITA	Decision, 4-1
1908	Richard Gunn, GBR	Decision	1964	Stanislav Stepashkin, USSR	Decision, 3-2
1920	Paul Fritsch, FRA	Decision	1968	Antonio Roldan, MEX	Won on Disq.
1924	John Fields, USA	Decision	1972	Boris Kousnetsov, USSR	Decision, 3-2
1928	Lambertus van Klaveren, HOL	Decision	1976	Angel Herrera, CUB	KO, 2nd
1932	Carmelo Robledo, ARG	Decision	1980	Rudi Fink, E. Ger	Decision, 4-1
1936	Oscar Casanovas, ARG	Decision	1984	Meldrick Taylor, USA	Decision, 5-0
1948	Ernesto Formenti, ITA	Decision	1988	Giovanni Parisi, ITA	Stopped, 1st
1952	Jan Zachara, CZE	Decision, 2-1	1992	Andreas Tews, GER	Decision, 16-7
1956	Vladimir Safronov, USSR	Decision	1996	Somluck Kamsing, THA	Decision, 8-5

Lightweight (132 lbs)

Year		Final Match	Year		Final Match
1904	Harry Spanger, USA	Decision	1960	Kazimierz Pazdzior, POL	Decision, 4-1
1908	Frederick Grace, GBR	Decision	1964	Józef Grudzien, POL	Decision
1920	Samuel Mosberg, USA	Decision	1968	Ronnie Harris, USA	Decision, 5-0
1924	Hans Nielsen, DEN	Decision	1972	Jan Szczepanski, POL	Decision, 5-0
1928	Carlo Orlandi, ITA	Decision	1976	Howard Davis, USA	Decision, 5-0
1932	Lawrence Stevens, SAF	Decision	1980	Angel Herrera, CUB	Stopped, 3rd
1936	Imre Harangi, HUN	Decision	1984	Pernell Whitaker, USA	Foe quit, 2nd
1948	Gerald Dreyer, SAF	Decision	1988	Andreas Zuelow, E. Ger	Decision, 5-0
1952	Aureliano Bolognesi, ITA	Decision, 2-1	1992	Oscar De La Hoya, USA	Decision, 7-2
1956	Richard McTaggart, GBR	Decision	1996	Hocine Soltani, ALG	Tiebreak, 3-3

Light Welterweight (139 lbs)

Year		Final Match	Year		Final Match
1952	Charles Adkins, USA	Decision, 2-1	1964	Jerzy Kulej, POL	Decision, 5-0
1956	Vladimir Yengibaryan, USSR	Decision	1968	Jerzy Kulej, POL	Decision, 3-2
1960	Bohumil Nemecek, CZE	Decision, 5-0	1972	Ray Seales, USA	Decision, 3-2

Boxing (Cont.)

Year		Final Match	Year		Final Match
1976	Ray Leonard, USA	Decision, 5-0	1988	Vyacheslav Yanovsky, USSR	Decision, 5-0
1980	Patrizio Oliva, ITA	Decision, 4-1	1992	Hector Vinent, CUB	Decision, 11-1
1984	Jerry Page, USA	Decision, 5-0	1996	Hector Vinent, CUB	Decision, 20-13

Welterweight (147 lbs)

Year		Final Match	Year		Final Match
1904	Albert Young, USA	Decision	1964	Marian Kasprzyk, POL	Decision, 4-1
1920	Bert Schneider, CAN	Decision	1968	Manfred Wolke, E. Ger	Decision, 4-1
1924	Jean Delarge, BEL	Decision	1972	Emilio Correa, CUB	Decision, 5-0
1928	Edward Morgan, NZE	Decision	1976	Jochen Bachfeld, E. Ger	Decision, 3-2
1932	Edward Flynn, USA	Decision	1980	Andrés Aldama, CUB	Decision, 4-1
1936	Sten Suvio, FIN	Decision	1984	Mark Breland, USA	Decision, 5-0
1948	Julius Torma, CZE	Decision	1988	Robert Wangila, KEN	KO, 2nd
1952	Zygmunt Chychla, POL	Decision, 3-0	1992	Michael Carruth, IRE	Decision, 13-10
1956	Nicolae Linca, ROM	Decision, 3-2	1996	Oleg Saitov, RUS	Decision, 14-9
1960	Nino Benvenuti, ITA	Decision, 4-1			

Light Middleweight (156 lbs)

Year		Final Match	Year		Final Match
1952	László Papp, HUN	Decision, 3-0	1976	Jerzy Rybicki, POL	Decision, 5-0
1956	László Papp, HUN	Decision	1980	Armando Martinez, CUB	Decision, 4-1
1960	Skeeter McClure, USA	Decision, 4-1	1984	Frank Tate, USA	Decision, 5-0
1964	Boris Lagutin, USSR	Decision, 4-1	1988	Park Si-Hun, S. Kor	Decision, 3-2
1968	Boris Lagutin, USSR	Decision, 5-0	1992	Juan Lemus, CUB	Decision, 6-1
1972	Dieter Kottysch, W.Ger	Decision, 3-2	1996	David Reid, USA	KO, 3rd

Middleweight (165 lbs)

Year		Final Match	Year		Final Match
1904	Charles Mayer, USA	Stopped, 3rd	1960	Eddie Crook, USA	Decision, 3-2
1908	John Douglas, GBR	Decision	1964	Valery Popenchenko, USSR	Stopped, 1st
1920	Harry Mallin, GBR	Decision	1968	Christopher Finnegan, GBR	Decision, 3-2
1924	Harry Mallin, GBR	Decision	1972	Vyacheslav Lemechev, USSR	KO, 1st
1928	Piero Toscani, ITA	Decision	1976	Michael Spinks, USA	Stopped, 3rd
1932	Carmen Barth, USA	Decision	1980	José Gomez, CUB	Decision, 4-1
1936	Jean Despeaux, FRA	Decision	1984	Shin Joon-Sup, S. Kor	Decision, 3-2
1948	László Papp, HUN	Decision	1988	Henry Maske, E. Ger	Decision, 5-0
1952	Floyd Patterson, USA	KO, 1st	1992	Ariel Hernandez, CUB	Decision, 12-7
1956	Gennady Schatkov, USSR	KO, 1st	1996	Ariel Hernandez, CUB	Decision, 11-3

Light Heavyweight (178 lbs)

Year		Final Match	Year		Final Match
1920	Eddie Eagan, USA	Decision	1964	Cosimo Pinto, ITA	Decision, 3-2
1924	Harry Mitchell, GBR	Decision	1968	Dan Poznjak, USSR	Default
1928	Victor Avendaño, ARG	Decision	1972	Mate Parlov, YUG	Stopped, 2nd
1932	David Carstens, SAF	Decision	1976	Leon Spinks, USA	Stopped, 3rd
1936	Roger Michelot, FRA	Decision	1980	Slobodan Kacar, YUG	Decision, 4-1
1948	George Hunter, SAF	Decision	1984	Anton Josipovic, YUG	Default
1952	Norvel Lee, USA	Decision, 3-0	1988	Andrew Maynard, USA	Decision, 5-0
1956	Jim Boyd, USA	Decision	1992	Torsten May, GER	Decision, 8-3
1960	Cassius Clay, USA	Decision, 5-0	1996	Vasilii Jirov, KAZ	Decision, 17-4

Note: Cassius Clay changed his name to Muhammad Ali after winning the world heavyweight championship in 1964.

Heavyweight (201 lbs)

Year		Final Match	Year		Final Match
1984	Henry Tillman, USA	Decision, 5-0	1992	Felix Savon, CUB	Decision, 14-1
1988	Ray Mercer, USA	KO, 1st	1996	Felix Savon, CUB	Decision, 20-2

Super Heavyweight (Unlimited)

Year		Final Match	Year		Final Match
1904	Samuel Berger, USA	Decision	1960	Franco De Piccoli, ITA	KO, 1st
1908	Albert Oldham, GBR	KO, 1st	1964	Joe Frazier, USA	Decision, 3-2
1920	Ronald Rawson, GBR	Decision	1968	George Foreman, USA	Stopped, 2nd
1924	Otto von Porat, NOR	Decision	1972	Teófilo Stevenson, CUB	Default
1928	Arturo Rodriguez Jurado, ARG	Stopped, 1st	1976	Teófilo Stevenson, CUB	KO, 3rd
1932	Santiago Lovell, ARG	Decision	1980	Teófilo Stevenson, CUB	Decision, 4-1
1936	Herbert Runge, GER	Decision	1984	Tyrell Biggs, USA	Decision, 4-1
1948	Rafael Iglesias, ARG	KO, 2nd	1988	Lennox Lewis, CAN	Stopped, 2nd
1952	Ed Sanders, USA	Won on Disq.*	1992	Roberto Balado, CUB	Decision, 13-2
1956	Pete Rademacher, USA	Stopped, 1st	1996	Vladimir Klichko, UKR	Decision, 7-3

* Sanders' opponent, Ingemar Johansson was disqualified in 2nd round for not trying.

DIVING

MEN

Multiple gold medals: Greg Louganis (4); Klaus Dibiasi (3); Pete Desjardins, Sammy Lee, Bob Webster and Albert White (2).

Springboard

Year		Points	Year		Points
1908	Albert Zürner, GER	85.5	1960	Gary Tobian, USA	170.00
1912	Paul Günther, GER	79.23	1964	Ken Sitzberger, USA	159.90
1920	Louis Kuehn, USA	675.4	1968	Bernie Wrightson, USA	170.15
1924	Albert White, USA	696.4	1972	Vladimir Vasin, USSR	594.09
1928	Pete Desjardins, USA	185.04	1976	Phil Boggs, USA	619.05
1932	Michael Galitzen, USA	161.38	1980	Aleksandr Portnov, USSR	905.03
1936	Richard Degener, USA	163.57	1984	Greg Louganis, USA	754.41
1948	Bruce Harlan, USA	163.64	1988	Greg Louganis, USA	730.80
1952	David Browning, USA	205.29	1992	Mark Lenzi, USA	676.53
1956	Bob Clotworthy, USA	159.56	1996	Ni Xiong, CHN	701.46

Platform

Year		Points	Year		Points
1904	George Sheldon, USA	12.66	1956	Joaquin Capilla, MEX	152.44
1906	Gottlob Walz, GER	156.0	1960	Bob Webster, USA	165.56
1908	Hjalmar Johansson, SWE	83.75	1964	Bob Webster, USA	148.58
1912	Erik Adlerz, SWE	73.94	1968	Klaus Dibiasi, ITA	164.18
1920	Clarence Pinkston, USA	100.67	1972	Klaus Dibiasi, ITA	504.12
1924	Albert White, USA	97.46	1976	Klaus Dibiasi, ITA	600.51
1928	Pete Desjardins, USA	98.74	1980	Falk Hoffmann, E. Ger	835.65
1932	Harold Smith, USA	124.80	1984	Greg Louganis, USA	710.91
1936	Marshall Wayne, USA	113.58	1988	Greg Louganis, USA	638.61
1948	Sammy Lee, USA	130.05	1992	Sun Shuwei, CHN	677.31
1952	Sammy Lee, USA	156.28	1996	Dmitri Saoutine, RUS	692.34

WOMEN

Multiple gold medals: Pat McCormick (4); Ingrid Engel-Krämer and Fu Mingxia (3); Vicki Draves, Dorothy Poynton Hill, Gao Min (2).

Springboard

Year		Points	Year		Points
1920	Aileen Riggin, USA	539.9	1964	Ingrid Engel-Kräamer, GER	145.00
1924	Elizabeth Becker, USA	474.5	1968	Sue Gossick, USA	150.77
1928	Helen Meany, USA	78.62	1972	Micki King, USA	450.03
1932	Georgia Coleman, USA	87.52	1976	Jennifer Chandler, USA	506.19
1936	Marjorie Gestring, USA	89.27	1980	Irina Kalinina, USSR	725.91
1948	Vicki Draves, USA	108.74	1984	Sylvie Bernier, CAN	530.70
1952	Pat McCormick, USA	147.30	1988	Gao Min, CHN	580.23
1956	Pat McCormick, USA	142.36	1992	Gao Min, CHN	572.40
1960	Ingrid Krämer, GER	155.81	1996	Fu Mingxia, CHN	547.68

Platform

Year		Points	Year		Points
1912	Greta Johansson, SWE	39.9	1964	Lesley Bush, USA	99.80
1920	Stefani Fryland-Clausen, DEN	34.6	1968	Milena Duchková, CZE	109.59
1924	Caroline Smith, USA	33.2	1972	Ulrika Knape, SWE	390.00
1928	Elizabeth Becker Pinkston, USA	31.6	1976	Elena Vaytsekhovskaya, USSR	406.59
1932	Dorothy Poynton, USA	40.26	1980	Martina Jäschke, E. Ger	596.25
1936	Dorothy Poynton Hill, USA	33.93	1984	Zhou Jihong, CHN	435.51
1948	Vicki Draves, USA	68.87	1988	Xu Yanmei, CHN	445.20
1952	Pat McCormick, USA	79.37	1992	Fu Mingxia, CHN	461.43
1956	Pat McCormick, USA	84.85	1996	Fu Mingxia, CHN	521.58
1960	Ingrid Krämer, GER	91.28			

FIELD HOCKEY

MEN

Multiple gold medals: India (8); Great Britain and Pakistan (3); West Germany/Germany (2).

Year		Year	
1908	**Great Britain**, Ireland, Scotland	1964	**India**, Pakistan, Australia
1920	**Great Britain**, Denmark, Belgium	1968	**Pakistan**, Australia, India
1928	**India**, Netherlands, Germany	1972	**West Germany**, Pakistan, India
1932	**India**, Japan, United States	1976	**New Zealand**, Australia, Pakistan
1936	**India**, Germany, Netherlands	1980	**India**, Spain, Soviet Union
1948	**India**, Great Britain, Netherlands	1984	**Pakistan**, West Germany, Great Britain
1952	**India**, Netherlands, Great Britain	1988	**Great Britain**, West Germany, Netherlands
1956	**India**, Pakistan, Germany	1992	**Germany**, Australia, Pakistan
1960	**Pakistan**, India, Spain	1996	**Netherlands**, Spain, Australia

Field Hockey (Cont.)

WOMEN

Multiple gold medals: Australia (2).

Year	
1980	**Zimbabwe**, Czechoslovakia, Soviet Union
1984	**Netherlands**, West Germany, United States
1988	**Australia**, South Korea, Netherlands
1992	**Spain**, Germany, Great Britain
1996	**Australia**, South Korea, Netherlands

GYMNASTICS

MEN

At least 4 gold medals (including team events): Sawao Kato (8); Nikolai Andrianov, Viktor Chukarin and Boris Shakhlin (7); Akinori Nakayama and Vitaly Scherbo (6); Yukio Endo, Anton Heida, Mitsuo Tsukahara and Takashi Ono (5); Vladimir Artemov, Georges Miez and Valentin Muratov (4).

All-Around

Year		Points
1900	Gustave Sandras, FRA	302
1904	Julius Lenhart, AUT	69.80
1906	Pierre Payssé, FRA	97.0
1908	Alberto Braglia, ITA	317.0
1912	Alberto Braglia, ITA	135.0
1920	Giorgio Zampori, ITA	88.35
1924	Leon Stukelj, YUG	110.340
1928	Georges Miez, SWI	247.500
1932	Romeo Neri, ITA	140.625
1936	Alfred Schwarzmann, GER	113.100
1948	Veikko Huhtanen, FIN	229.7
1952	Viktor Chukarin, USSR	115.7
1956	Viktor Chukarin, USSR	114.25
1960	Boris Shakhlin, USSR	115.95
1964	Yukio Endo, JPN	115.95
1968	Sawao Kato, JPN	115.9
1972	Sawao Kato, JPN	114.650
1976	Nikolai Andrianov, USSR	116.65
1980	Aleksandr Dityatin, USSR	118.65
1984	Koji Gushiken, JPN	118.7
1988	Vladimir Artemov, USSR	119.125
1992	Vitaly Scherbo, UT	59.025
1996	Li Xiaoshuang, CHN	58.423

Horizontal Bar

Year		Points
1896	Hermann Weingärtner, GER	–
1904	(TIE) Anton Heida, USA	40
	& Edward Hennig, USA	40
1924	Leon Stukelj, YUG	19.73
1928	Georges Miez, SWI	19.17
1932	Dallas Bixler, USA	18.33
1936	Aleksanteri Saarvala, FIN	19.367
1948	Josef Stalder, SWI	19.85
1952	Jack Günthard, SWI	19.55
1956	Takashi Ono, JPN	19.60
1960	Takashi Ono, JPN	19.60
1964	Boris Shakhlin, USSR	19.625
1968	(TIE) Akinori Nakayama, JPN	19.55
	& Mikhail Voronin, USSR	19.55
1972	Mitsuo Tsukahara, JPN	19.725
1976	Mitsuo Tsukahara, JPN	19.675
1980	Stoyan Deltchev, BUL	19.825
1984	Shinji Morisue, JPN	20.00
1988	(TIE) Vladimir Artemov, USSR	19.900
	& Valeri Lyukin, USSR	19.900
1992	Trent Dimas, USA	9.875
1996	Andreas Wecker, GER	9.850

Parallel Bars

Year		Points
1896	Alfred Flatow, GER	–
1904	George Eyser, USA	44
1924	August Güttinger, SWI	21.63
1928	Ladislav Vácha, CZE	18.83
1932	Romeo Neri, ITA	18.97
1936	Konrad Frey, GER	19.067
1948	Michael Reusch, SWI	19.75
1952	Hans Eugster, SWI	19.65
1956	Viktor Chukarin, USSR	19.20
1960	Boris Shakhlin, USSR	19.40
1964	Yukio Endo, JPN	19.675
1968	Akinori Nakayama, JPN	19.475
1972	Sawao Kato, JPN	19.475
1976	Sawao Kato, JPN	19.675
1980	Aleksandr Tkachyov, USSR	19.775
1984	Bart Conner, USA	19.95
1988	Vladimir Artemov, USSR	19.925
1992	Vitaly Scherbo, UT	9.900
1996	Rustam Sharipov, UKR	9.837

Vault

Year		Points
1896	Karl Schumann, GER	–
1904	(TIE) George Eyser, USA	36
	& Anton Heida, USA	36
1924	Frank Kriz, USA	9.98
1928	Eugen Mack, SWI	9.58
1932	Savino Guglielmetti, ITA	18.03
1936	Alfred Schwarzmann, GER	19.20
1948	Paavo Aaltonen, FIN	19.55
1952	Viktor Chukarin, USSR	19.20
1956	(TIE) Helmut Bantz, GER	18.85
	& Valentin Muratov, USSR	18.85
1960	(TIE) Takashi Ono, JPN	19.35
	& Boris Shakhlin, USSR	19.35
1964	Haruhiro Yamashita, JPN	19.60
1968	Mikhail Voronin, USSR	19.00
1972	Klaus Köste, E. Ger	18.85
1976	Nikolai Andrianov, USSR	19.45
1980	Nikolai Andrianov, USSR	19.825
1984	Lou Yun, CHN	19.95
1988	Lou Yun, CHN	19.875
1992	Vitaly Scherbo, UT	9.856
1996	Alexei Nemov, RUS	9.787

Pommel Horse

Year		Points	Year		Points
1896	Louis Zutter, SWI	–	1964	Miroslav Cerar, YUG	19.525
1904	Anton Heida, USA	42	1968	Miroslav Cerar, YUG	19.325
1924	Josef Wilhelm, SWI	21.23	1972	Viktor Klimenko, SOV	19.125
1928	Hermann Hänggi, SWI	19.75	1976	Zoltán Magyar, HUN	19.70
1932	Istvän Pelle, HUN	19.07	1980	Zoltán Magyar, HUN	19.925
1936	Konrad Frey, GER	19.333	1984	(TIE) Li Ning, CHN	19.95
1948	(TIE) Paavo Aaltonen, FIN	19.35		& Peter Vidmar, USA	19.95
	Veikko Huhtanen, FIN	19.35	1988	(TIE) Dmitri Bilozerchev, USSR	19.95
	& Heikki Savolainen, FIN	19.35		& Zsolt Borkai, HUN	19.95
1952	Viktor Chukarin, USSR	19.50		Lyubomir Geraskov, BUL	19.95
1956	Boris Shakhlin, USSR	19.25	1992	(TIE) Pae Gil-Su, N. Kor	9.925
1960	(TIE) Eugen Ekman, FIN	19.375		& Vitaly Scherbo, UT	9.925
	& Boris Shakhlin, USSR	19.375	1996	Li Donghua, SWI	9.875

Rings

Year		Points	Year		Points
1896	Ioannis Mitropoulos, GRE	–	1968	Akinori Nakayama, JPN	19.45
1904	Hermann Glass, USA	45	1972	Akinori Nakayama, JPN	19.35
1924	Francesco Martino, ITA	21.553	1976	Nikolai Andrianov, USSR	19.65
1928	Leon Stukelj, YUG	19.25	1980	Aleksandr Dityatin, USSR	19.875
1932	George Gulack, USA	18.97	1984	(TIE) Koji Gushiken, JPN	19.85
1936	Alois Hudec, CZE	19.433		& Li Ning, CHN	19.85
1948	Karl Frei, SWI	19.80	1988	(TIE) Holger Behrendt, E. Ger	19.925
1952	Grant Shaginyan, USSR	19.75		& Dmitri Bilozerchev, USSR	19.925
1956	Albert Azaryan, USSR	19.35	1992	Vitaly Scherbo, UT	9.937
1960	Albert Azaryan, USSR	19.725	1996	Yuri Chechi, ITA	9.887
1964	Takuji Haytta, JPN	19.475			

Floor Exercise

Year		Points	Year		Points
1932	Istvan Pelle, HUN	9.60	1972	Nikolai Andrianov, USSR	19.175
1936	Georges Miez, SWI	18.666	1976	Nikolai Andrianov, USSR	19.45
1948	Ferenc Pataki, HUN	19.35	1980	Roland Brückner, E. Ger	19.75
1952	William Thoresson, SWE	19.25	1984	Li Ning, CHN	19.925
1956	Valentin Muratov, USSR	19.20	1988	Sergei Kharkov, USSR	19.925
1960	Nobuyuki Aihara, JPN	19.45	1992	Li Xiaosahuang, CHN	9.925
1964	Franco Menichelli, ITA	19.45	1996	Ioannis Melissanidis, GRE	9.850
1968	Sawao Kato, JPN	19.475			

Team Combined Exercises

Year		Points	Year		Points
1904	United States	374.43	1956	Soviet Union	568.25
1906	Norway	19.00	1960	Japan	575.20
1908	Sweden	438	1964	Japan	577.95
1912	Italy	265.75	1968	Japan	575.90
1920	Italy	359.855	1972	Japan	571.25
1924	Italy	839.058	1976	Japan	576.85
1928	Switzerland	1718.625	1980	Soviet Union	598.60
1932	Italy	541.850	1984	United States	591.40
1936	Germany	657.430	1988	Soviet Union	593.35
1948	Finland	1358.30	1992	Unified Team	585.45
1952	Soviet Union	574.40	1996	Russia	576.778

WOMEN

At least 4 gold medals (including team events): Larissa Latynina (9); Vera Cáslavská (7); Polina Astakhova, Nadia Comaneci, Agnes Keleti and Nelli Kim (5); Olga Korbut, Ecaterina Szabó and Lyudmila Tourischeva (4).

All-Around

Year		Points	Year		Points
1952	Maria Gorokhovskaya, USSR	76.78	1976	Nadia Comaneci, ROM	79.275
1956	Larissa Latynina, USSR	74.933	1980	Yelena Davydova, USSR	79.15
1960	Larissa Latynina, USSR	77.031	1984	Mary Lou Retton, USA	79.175
1964	Vera Cáslavská, CZE	77.564	1988	Yelena Shushunova, USSR	79.662
1968	Vera Cáslavská, CZE	78.25	1992	Tatiana Gutsu, UT	39.737
1972	Lyudmila Tourischeva, USSR	77.025	1996	Lilia Podkopayeva, UKR	39.255

Vault

Year		Points	Year		Points
1952	Yekaterina Kalinchuk, USSR	19.20	1960	Margarita Nikolayeva, USSR	19.316
1956	Larissa Latynina, USSR	18.833	1964	Vera Cáslavská, CZE	19.483

Gymnastics (Cont.)

Year		Points
1968	Vera Cáslavská, CZE	19.775
1972	Karin Janz, E. Ger	19.525
1976	Nelli Kim, USSR	19.80
1980	Natalia Shaposhnikova, USSR	19.725
1984	Ecaterina Szabó, ROM	19.875
1988	Svetlana Boginskaya, USSR	19.905
1992	(TIE) Henrietta Onodi, HUN	9.925
	& Lavinia Milosovici, ROM	9.925
1996	Simona Amanar, ROM	9.775

Uneven Bars

Year		Points
1952	Margit Korondi, HUN	19.40
1956	Agnes Keleti, HUN	18.966
1960	Polina Astakhova, USSR	19.616
1964	Polina Astakhova, USSR	19.332
1968	Vera Cáslavská, CZE	19.65
1972	Karin Janz, E. Ger	19.675
1976	Nadia Comaneci, ROM	20.00
1980	Maxi Gnauck, E. Ger	19.875
1984	(TIE) Julianne McNamora, USA	19.95
	& Ma Yanhong, CHN	19.95
1988	Daniela Silivas, ROM	20.00
1992	Lu Li, CHN	10.00
1996	Svetlana Chorkina, RUS	9.850

Balance Beam

Year		Points
1952	Nina Bocharova, USSR	19.22
1956	Agnes Keleti, HUN	18.80
1960	Eva Bosakova, CZE	19.283
1964	Vera Cáslavská, CZE	19.449
1968	Natalya Kuchinskaya, USSR	19.65
1972	Olga Korbut, USSR	19.40
1976	Nadia Comaneci, ROM	19.95
1980	Nadia Comaneci, ROM	19.80
1984	(TIE) Simona Pauca, ROM	19.80
	& Ecaterina Szabó, ROM	19.80
1988	Daniela Silivas, ROM	19.924
1992	Tatiana Lyssenko, UT	9.975
1996	Shannon Miller, USA	9.862

Floor Exercise

Year		Points
1952	Agnes Keleti, HUN	19.36
1956	(TIE) Agnes Keleti, HUN	18.733
	& Larissa Latynina, USSR	18.733
1960	Larissa Latynina, USSR	19.583
1964	Larissa Latynina, USSR	19.599
1968	(TIE) Vera Cáslavská, CZE	19.675
	& Larissa Petrik, USSR	19.675
1972	Olga Korbut, USSR	19.575
1976	Nelli Kim, USSR	19.85
1980	(TIE) Nadia Comaneci, ROM	19.875
	& Nelli Kim, USSR	19.875
1984	Ecaterina Szabó, ROM	19.975
1988	Daniela Silivas, ROM	19.937
1992	Lavinia Milosovici, ROM	10.000
1996	Lilia Podkopayeva, UKR	9.887

Team Combined Exercises

Year		Points
1928	Holland	316.75
1936	Germany	506.50
1948	Czechoslovakia	445.45
1952	Soviet Union	527.03
1956	Soviet Union	444.800
1960	Soviet Union	382.320
1964	Soviet Union	280.890
1968	Soviet Union	382.85
1972	Soviet Union	380.50
1976	Soviet Union	466.00
1980	Soviet Union	394.90
1984	Romania	392.02
1988	Soviet Union	395.475
1992	Unified Team	395.666
1996	United States	389.225

SOCCER

MEN

Multiple gold medals: Great Britain and Hungary (3); Uruguay and USSR (2).

Year	
1900	**Great Britain**, France, Belgium
1904	**Canada**, USA I, USA II
1906	**Denmark**, Smyrna (Int'l entry), Greece
1908	**Great Britain**, Denmark, Netherlands
1912	**Great Britain**, Denmark, Netherlands
1920	**Belgium**, Spain, Netherlands
1924	**Uruguay**, Switzerland, Sweden
1928	**Uruguay**, Argentina, Italy
1936	**Italy**, Austria, Norway
1948	**Sweden**, Yugoslavia, Denmark
1952	**Hungary**, Yugoslavia, Sweden
1956	**Soviet Union**, Yugoslavia, Bulgaria
1960	**Yugoslavia**, Denmark, Hungary
1964	**Hungary**, Czechoslovakia, Germany
1968	**Hungary**, Bulgaria, Japan
1972	**Poland**, Hungary, East Germany & Soviet Union
1976	**East Germany**, Poland, Soviet Union
1980	**Czechoslovakia**, East Germany, Soviet Union
1984	**France**, Brazil, Yugoslavia
1988	**Soviet Union**, Brazil, West Germany
1992	**Spain**, Poland, Ghana
1996	**Nigeria**, Argentina, Brazil

WOMEN

Year	
1996	**United States**, China, Norway

SWIMMING

World and Olympic records below that appear to be broken or equaled by winning times in subsequent years, but are not so indicated, were all broken in preliminary heats leading up to the finals. Some events were not held at every Olympics.

MEN

At least 4 gold medals (including relays): Mark Spitz (9); Matt Biondi (8); Charles Daniels, Tom Jager, Don Schollander, and Johnny Weissmuller (5); Tamás Darnyi, Roland Matthes, John Naber, Aleksandr Popov, Murray Rose, Vladimir Salnikov and Henry Taylor (4).

50-meter Freestyle

Year		Time	
1904	Zoltán Halmay, HUN (50 yds)	28.0	
1906-84	Not held		
1988	Matt Biondi, USA	22.14	WR
1992	Aleksandr Popov, UT	21.91	OR
1996	Aleksandr Popov, RUS	22.13	

100-meter Freestyle

Year		Time	
1896	Alfréd Hajós, HUN	1:22.2	OR
1904	Zoltán Halmay, HUN (100 yds)	1:02.8	
1906	Charles Daniels, USA	1:13.4	
1908	Charles Daniels, USA	1:05.6	WR
1912	Duke Kahanamoku, USA	1:03.4	
1920	Duke Kahanamoku, USA	1:00.4	WR
1924	Johnny Weissmuller, USA	59.0	OR
1928	Johnny Weissmuller, USA	58.6	OR
1932	Yasuji Miyazaki, JPN	58.2	
1936	Ferenc Csik, HUN	57.6	
1948	Wally Ris, USA	57.3	OR
1952	Clarke Scholes, USA	57.4	
1956	Jon Henricks, AUS	55.4	OR
1960	John Devitt, AUS	55.2	OR
1964	Don Schollander, USA	53.4	OR
1968	Michael Wenden, AUS	52.2	WR
1972	Mark Spitz, USA	51.22	WR
1976	Jim Montgomery, USA	49.99	WR
1980	Jorg Woithe, E. Ger	50.40	
1984	Rowdy Gaines, USA	49.80	OR
1988	Matt Biondi, USA	48.63	OR
1992	Aleksandr Popov, UT	49.02	
1996	Aleksandr Popov, RUS	48.74	

200-meter Freestyle

Year		Time	
1900	Frederick Lane, AUS (220 yds)	2:25.2	OR
1904	Charles Daniels, USA (220 yds)	2:44.2	
1968	Michael Wenden, AUS	1:55.2	OR
1972	Mark Spitz, USA	1:52.78	WR
1976	Bruce Furniss, USA	1:50.29	WR
1980	Sergei Kopliakov, USSR	1:49.81	OR
1984	Michael Gross, W. Ger	1:47.44	WR
1988	Duncan Armstrong, AUS	1:47.25	WR
1992	Yevgeny Sadovyi, UT	1:46.70	OR
1996	Danyon Loader, NZE	1:47.63	

400-meter Freestyle

Year		Time	
1896	Paul Neumann, AUT (550m)	8:12.6	
1904	Charles Daniels, USA (440 yds)	6:16.2	
1906	Otto Scheff, AUT	6:23.8	
1908	Henry Taylor, GBR	5:36.8	
1912	George Hodgson, CAN	5:24.4	
1920	Norman Ross, USA	5:26.8	
1924	Johnny Weissmuller, USA	5:04.2	OR
1928	Alberto Zorilla, ARG	5:01.6	OR
1932	Buster Crabbe, USA	4:48.4	OR
1936	Jack Medica, USA	4:44.5	OR
1948	Bill Smith, USA	4:41.0	OR
1952	Jean Boiteux, FRA	4:30.7	OR
1956	Murray Rose, AUS	4:27.3	OR
1960	Murray Rose, AUS	4:18.3	OR
1964	Don Schollander, USA	4:12.2	WR
1968	Mike Burton, USA	4:09.0	OR
1972	Bradford Cooper, AUS*	4:00.27	OR
1976	Brian Goodell, USA	3:51.93	WR
1980	Vladimir Salnikov, USSR	3:51.31	OR
1984	George DiCarlo, USA	3:51.23	OR
1988	Uwe Dassler, E. Ger	3:46.95	WR
1992	Yevgeny Sadovyi, UT	3:45.00	WR
1996	Danyon Loader, NZE	3:47.97	

*Australian Cooper finished second to Rick DeMont of the U.S., who was disqualified when he flunked the post-race drug test (his asthma medication was on the IOC's banned list).

1500-meter Freestyle

Year		Time	
1896	Alfréd Hajós, HUN (1200m)	18:22.2	OR
1900	John Arthur Jarvis, GBR (1000m)	13:40.2	
1904	Emil Rausch, GER (1 mile)	27:18.2	
1906	Henry Taylor, GBR (1 mile)	28:28.0	
1908	Henry Taylor, GBR	22:48.4	WR
1912	George Hodgson, CAN	22:00.0	WR
1920	Norman Ross, USA	22:23.2	
1924	Andrew (Boy) Charlton, AUS	20:06.6	WR
1928	Arne Borge, SWE	19:51.8	OR
1932	Kusuo Kitamura, JPN	19:12.4	OR
1936	Noboru Terada, JPN	19:13.7	
1948	James McLane, USA	19:18.5	
1952	Ford Konno, USA	18:30.3	OR
1956	Murray Rose, AUS	17:58.9	
1960	Jon Konrads, AUS	17:19.6	OR
1964	Robert Windle, AUS	17:01.7	OR
1968	Mike Burton, USA	16:38.9	OR
1972	Mike Burton, USA	15:52.58	WR
1976	Brian Goodell, USA	15:02.40	WR
1980	Vladimir Salnikov, USSR	14:58.27	WR
1984	Mike O'Brien, USA	15:05.20	
1988	Vladimir Salnikov, USSR	15:00.40	
1992	Kieren Perkins, AUS	14:43.48	WR
1996	Kieren Perkins, AUS	14:56.40	

Swimming (Cont.)

100-meter Backstroke

Year		Time		Year		Time	
1904	Walter Brack, GER (100 yds)	1:16.8		1956	David Theile, AUS	1:02.2	OR
1908	Arno Bieberstein, GER	1:24.6	WR	1960	David Theile, AUS	1:01.9	OR
1912	Harry Hebner, USA	1:21.2		1968	Roland Matthes, E. Ger	58.7	OR
1920	Warren Kealoha, USA	1:15.2		1972	Roland Matthes, E. Ger	56.58	OR
1924	Warren Kealoha, USA	1:13.2	OR	1976	John Naber, USA	55.49	WR
1928	George Kojac, USA	1:08.2	WR	1980	Bengt Baron, SWE	56.33	
1932	Masaji Kiyokawa, JPN	1:08.6		1984	Rick Carey, USA	55.79	
1936	Adolf Kiefer, USA	1:05.9	OR	1988	Daichi Suzuki, JPN	55.05	
1948	Allen Stack, USA	1:06.4		1992	Mark Tewksbury, CAN	53.98	OR
1952	Yoshinobu Oyakawa, USA	1:05.4	OR	1996	Jeff Rouse, USA	54.10	

200-meter Backstroke

Year		Time		Year		Time	
1900	Ernst Hoppenberg, GER	2:47.0		1980	Sándor Wládar, HUN	2:01.93	
1964	Jed Graef, USA	2:10.3	WR	1984	Rick Carey, USA	2:00.23	
1968	Roland Matthes, E. Ger	2:09.6	OR	1988	Igor Poliansky, USSR	1:59.37	
1972	Roland Matthes, E. Ger	2:02.82	=WR	1992	Martin Lopez-Zubero, SPA	1:58.47	OR
1976	John Naber, USA	1:59.19	WR	1996	Brad Bridgewater, USA	1:58.54	

100-meter Breaststroke

Year		Time		Year		Time	
1968	Don McKenzie, USA	1:07.7	OR	1984	Steve Lundquist, USA	1:01.65	WR
1972	Nobutaka Taguchi, JPN	1:04.94	WR	1988	Adrian Moorhouse, GBR	1:02.04	
1976	John Hencken, USA	1:03.11	WR	1992	Nelson Diebel, USA	1:01.50	OR
1980	Duncan Goodhew, GBR	1:03.44		1996	Fred deBurghgraeve, BEL	1:00.60	

200-meter Breaststroke

Year		Time		Year		Time	
1908	Frederick Holman, GBR	3:09.2	WR	1960	Bill Mulliken, USA	2:37.4	
1912	Walter Bathe, GER	3:01.8	OR	1964	Ian O'Brien, AUS	2:27.8	WR
1920	Hakan Malmroth, SWE	3:04.4		1968	Felipe Muñoz, MEX	2:28.7	
1924	Robert Skelton, USA	2:56.6		1972	John Hencken, USA	2:21.55	WR
1928	Yoshiyuki Tsuruta, JPN	2:48.8	OR	1976	David Wilkie, GBR	2:15.11	WR
1932	Yoshiyuki Tsuruta, JPN	2:45.4		1980	Robertas Zhulpa, USSR	2:15.85	
1936	Tetsuo Hamuro, JPN	2:41.5	OR	1984	Victor Davis, CAN	2:13.34	WR
1948	Joseph Verdeur, USA	2:39.3	OR	1988	József Szabó, HUN	2:13.52	
1952	John Davies, AUS	2:34.4	OR	1992	Mike Barrowman, USA	2:10.16	WR
1956	Masaru Furukawa, JPN	2:34.7*	OR	1996	Norbert Rozsa, HUN	2:12.57	

*In 1956, the butterfly stroke and breaststroke were separated into two different events.

100-meter Butterfly

Year		Time		Year		Time	
1968	Doug Russell, USA	55.9	OR	1984	Michael Gross, W. Ger	53.08	WR
1972	Mark Spitz, USA	54.27	WR	1988	Anthony Nesty, SUR	53.0	OR
1976	Matt Vogel, USA	54.35		1992	Pablo Morales, USA	53.32	
1980	Pär Arvidsson, SWE	54.92		1996	Dennis Pankratov, RUS	52.27	

200-meter Butterfly

Year		Time		Year		Time	
1956	Bill Yorzyk, USA	2:19.3	OR	1980	Sergei Fesenko, USSR	1:59.76	
1960	Mike Troy, U	2:12.8	WR	1984	Jon Sieben, AUS	1:57.04	WR
1964	Kevin Berry, AUS	2:06.6	WR	1988	Michael Gross, W. Ger	1:56.94	OR
1968	Carl Robie, USA	2:08.7		1992	Melvin Stewart, USA	1:56.26	OR
1972	Mark Spitz, USA	2:00.70	WR	1996	Dennis Pankratov, RUS	1:56.51	
1976	Mike Bruner, USA	1:59.23	WR				

200-meter Individual Medley

Year		Time		Year		Time	
1968	Charles Hickcox, USA	2:12.0	OR	1988	Tamás Darnyi, HUN	2:00.17	WR
1972	Gunnar Larsson, SWE	2:07.17	WR	1992	Tamás Darnyi, HUN	2:00.76	
1984	Alex Baumann, CAN	2:01.42	WR	1996	Attila Czene, HUN	1:59.91	

400-meter Individual Medley

Year		Time		Year		Time	
1964	Richard Roth, USA	4:45.4	WR	1984	Alex Baumann, CAN	4:17.41	WR
1968	Charles Hickcox, USA	4:48.4		1988	Tamás Darnyi, HUN	4:14.75	WR
1972	Gunnar Larsson, SWE	4:31.98	OR	1992	Tamás Darnyi, HUN	4:14.23	OR
1976	Rod Strachan, USA	4:23.68	WR	1996	Tom Dolan, USA	4:14.90	
1980	Aleksandr Sidorenko, USSR	4:22.89	OR				

4x100-meter Freestyle Relay

Year		Time		Year		Time	
1964	United States	3:32.2	WR	1984	United States	3:19.03	WR
1968	United States	3:31.7	WR	1988	United States	3:16.53	WR
1972	United States	3:26.42	WR	1992	United States	3:16.74	
1976-80	Not held			1996	United States	3:15.41	

4x200-meter Freestyle Relay

Year		Time		Year		Time	
1906	Hungary (x250m)	16:52.4		1960	United States	8:10.2	WR
1908	Great Britain	10:55.6	WR	1964	United States	7:52.1	WR
1912	Australia/New Zealand	10:11.6	WR	1968	United States	7:52.33	
1920	United States	10:04.4	WR	1972	United States	7:35.78	WR
1924	United States	9:53.4	WR	1976	United States	7:23.22	WR
1928	United States	9:36.2	WR	1980	Soviet Union	7:23.50	
1932	Japan	8:58.4	WR	1984	United States	7:15.69	WR
1936	Japan	8:51.5	WR	1988	United States	7:12.51	WR
1948	United States	8:46.0	WR	1992	Unified Team	7:11.95	WR
1952	United States	8:31.1	OR	1996	United States	7:14.84	
1956	Australia	8:23.6	WR				

4x100-meter Medley Relay

Year		Time		Year		Time	
1960	United States	4:05.4	WR	1980	Australia	3:45.70	
1964	United States	3:58.4	WR	1984	United States	3:39.30	WR
1968	United States	3:54.9	WR	1988	United States	3:36.93	WR
1972	United States	3:48.16	WR	1992	United States	3:36.93	=WR
1976	United States	3:42.22	WR	1996	United States	3:34.84	

WOMEN

At least 4 gold medals (including relays): Kristin Otto (6); Krisztina Egerszegi and Jenny Thompson (5), Kornelia Ender, Janet Evans, Dawn Fraser and Amy Van Dyken (4).

50-meter Freestyle

Year		Time		Year		Time	
1988	Kristin Otto, E. Ger	25.49	OR	1996	Amy Van Dyken, USA	24.87	
1992	Yang Wenyi, CHN	24.79	WR				

100-meter Freestyle

Year		Time		Year		Time	
1912	Fanny Durack, AUS	1:22.2		1964	Dawn Fraser, AUS	59.5	OR
1920	Ethelda Bleibtrey, USA	1:13.6	WR	1968	Jan Henne, USA	1:00.0	
1924	Ethel Lackie, USA	1:12.4		1972	Sandra Neilson, USA	58.59	OR
1928	Albina Osipowich, USA	1:11.0	OR	1976	Kornelia Ender, E. Ger	55.65	WR
1932	Helene Madison, USA	1:06.8	OR	1980	Barbara Krause, E. Ger	54.79	WR
1936	Rie Mastenbroek, HOL	1:05.9	OR	1984	(TIE) Nancy Hogshead, USA	55.92	
1948	Greta Andersen, DEN	1:06.3			Carrie Steinseifer, USA	55.92	
1952	Katalin Szöke, HUN	1:06.8		1988	Kristin Otto, E. Ger	54.93	
1956	Dawn Fraser, AUS	1:02.0	WR	1992	Zhuang Yong, CHN	54.65	OR
1960	Dawn Fraser, AUS	1:01.2	OR	1996	Le Jingyi, CHN	54.50	

200-meter Freestyle

Year		Time		Year		Time	
1968	Debbie Meyer, USA	2:10.5	OR	1984	Mary Wayte, USA	1:59.23	
1972	Shane Gould, AUS	2:03.56	WR	1988	Heike Friedrich, E. Ger	1:57.65	OR
1976	Kornelia Ender, E. Ger	1:59.26	WR	1992	Nicole Haislett, USA	1:57.90	
1980	Barbara Krause, E. Ger	1:58.33	OR	1996	Claudia Poll, COS	1:58.16	

400-meter Freestyle

Year		Time		Year		Time	
1920	Ethelda Bleibtrey, USA (300m)	4:34.0	WR	1964	Ginny Duenkel, USA	4:43.3	OR
1924	Martha Norelius, USA	6:02.2	OR	1968	Debbie Meyer, USA	4:31.8	OR
1928	Martha Norelius, USA	5:42.8	WR	1972	Shane Gould, AUS	4:19.44	WR
1932	Helene Madison, USA	5:28.5	WR	1976	Petra Thümer, E. Ger	4:09.89	WR
1936	Rie Mastenbroek, HOL	5:26.4	OR	1980	Ines Diers, E. Ger	4:08.76	OR
1948	Ann Curtis, USA	5:17.8	OR	1984	Tiffany Cohen, USA	4:07.10	OR
1952	Valéria Gyenge, HUN	5:12.1	OR	1988	Janet Evans, USA	4:03.85	WR
1956	Lorraine Crapp, AUS	4:54.6	OR	1992	Dagmar Hase, GER	4:07.18	
1960	Chris von Saltza, USA	4:50.6	OR	1996	Michelle Smith, IRE	4:07.25	

800-meter Freestyle

Year		Time		Year		Time	
1968	Debbie Meyer, USA	9:24.0	OR	1984	Tiffany Cohen, USA	8:24.95	OR
1972	Keena Rothhammer, USA	8:53.68	WR	1988	Janet Evans, USA	8:20.20	OR
1976	Petra Thümer, E. Ger	8:37.14	WR	1992	Janet Evans, USA	8:25.52	
1980	Michelle Ford, AUS	8:28.90	OR	1996	Brooke Bennett, USA	8:27.89	

Swimming (Cont.)

100-meter Backstroke

Year		Time		Year		Time	
1924	Sybil Bauer, USA	1:23.2	**OR**	1968	Kaye Hall, USA	1:06.2	**WR**
1928	Maria Braun, HOL	1:22.0		1972	Melissa Belote, USA	1:05.78	**OR**
1932	Eleanor Holm, USA	1:19.4		1976	Ulrike Richter, E. Ger	1:01.83	**OR**
1936	Dina Senff, HOL	1:18.9		1980	Rica Reinisch, E. Ger	1:00.86	**WR**
1948	Karen-Margrete Harup, DEN	1:14.4	**OR**	1984	Theresa Andrews, USA	1:02.55	
1952	Joan Harrison, SAF	1:14.3		1988	Kristin Otto, E. Ger	1:00.89	
1956	Judy Grinham, GBR	1:12.9	**OR**	1992	Krisztina Egerszegi, HUN	1:00.68	**OR**
1960	Lynn Burke, USA	1:09.3	**OR**	1996	Beth Botsford, USA	1:01.19	
1964	Cathy Ferguson, USA	1:07.7	**WR**				

200-meter Backstroke

Year		Time		Year		Time	
1968	Pokey Watson, USA	2:24.8	**OR**	1984	Jolanda de Rover, NET	2:12.38	
1972	Melissa Belote, USA	2:19.19	**WR**	1988	Krisztina Egerszegi, HUN	2:09.29	**OR**
1976	Ulrike Richter, E. Ger	2:13.43	**OR**	1992	Krisztina Egerszegi, HUN	2:07.06	**OR**
1980	Rica Reinisch, E. Ger	2:11.77	**WR**	1996	Krisztina Egerszegi, HUN	2:07.83	

100-meter Breaststroke

Year		Time		Year		Time	
1968	Djurdjica Bjedov, YUG	1:15.8	**OR**	1984	Petra van Staveren, NET	1:09.88	**OR**
1972	Cathy Carr, USA	1:13.58	**WR**	1988	Tania Dangalakova, BUL	1:07.95	**OR**
1976	Hannelore Anke, E. Ger	1:11.16		1992	Yelena Rudkovskaya, UT	1:08.00	
1980	Ute Geweniger, E. Ger	1:10.22		1996	Penny Heyns, S. Afr.	1:07.73	

200-meter Breaststroke

Year		Time		Year		Time	
1924	Lucy Morton, GBR	3:33.2	**OR**	1968	Sharon Wichman, USA	2:44.4	**OR**
1928	Hilde Schrader, GER	3:12.6		1972	Beverley Whitfield, AUS	2:41.71	**OR**
1932	Clare Dennis, AUS	3:06.3	**OR**	1976	Marina Koshevaya, USSR	2:33.35	**WR**
1936	Hideko Maehata, JPN	3:03.6		1980	Lina Kaciusyte, USSR	2:29.54	**OR**
1948	Petronella van Vliet, NET	2:57.2		1984	Anne Ottenbrite, CAN	2:30.38	
1952	Éva Székely, HUN	2:51.7	**OR**	1988	Silke Hörner, E. Ger	2:26.71	**WR**
1956	Ursula Happe, GER	2:53.1	**OR**	1992	Kyoko Iwasaki, JPN	2:26.65	**OR**
1960	Anita Lonsbrough, GBR	2:49.5	**WR**	1996	Penny Heyns, S. Afr.	2:25.41	
1964	Galina Prozumenshikova, USSR	2:46.4	**OR**				

100-meter Butterfly

Year		Time		Year		Time	
1956	Shelly Mann, USA	1:11.0	**OR**	1980	Caren Metschuck, E. Ger	1:00.42	
1960	Carolyn Schuler, USA	1:09.5	**OR**	1984	Mary T. Meagher, USA	59.26	
1964	Sharon Stouder, USA	1:04.7	**WR**	1988	Kristin Otto, E. Ger	59.00	**OR**
1968	Lynn McClements, AUS	1:05.5		1992	Qian Hong, CHN	58.62	**OR**
1972	Mayumi Aoki, JPN	1:03.34	**WR**	1996	Amy Van Dyken, USA	59.13	
1976	Kornelia Ender, E. Ger	1:00.13	**=WR**				

200-meter Butterfly

Year		Time		Year		Time	
1968	Ada Kok, NET	2:24.7	**OR**	1984	Mary T. Meagher, USA	2:06.90	**OR**
1972	Karen Moe, USA	2:15.57	**WR**	1988	Kathleen Nord, E. Ger	2:09.51	
1976	Andrea Pollack, E. Ger	2:11.41	**OR**	1992	Summer Sanders, USA	2:08.67	
1980	Ines Geissler, E. Ger	2:10.44	**OR**	1996	Susan O'Neill, AUS	2:07.76	

200-meter Individual Medley

Year		Time		Year		Time	
1968	Claudia Kolb, USA	2:24.7	**OR**	1988	Daniela Hunger, E. Ger	2:12.59	**OR**
1972	Shane Gould, AUS	2:23.07	**WR**	1992	Lin Li, CHN	2:11.65	**WR**
1984	Tracy Caulkins, USA	2:12.64	**OR**	1996	Michelle Smith, IRE	2:13.93	

400-meter Individual Medley

Year		Time		Year		Time	
1964	Donna de Varona, USA	5:18.7	**OR**	1984	Tracy Caulkins, USA	4:39.24	
1968	Claudia Kolb, USA	5:08.5	**OR**	1988	Janet Evans, USA	4:37.76	
1972	Gail Neall, AUS	5:02.97	**WR**	1992	Krisztina Egerszegi, HUN	4:36.54	
1976	Ulrike Tauber, E. Ger	4:42.77	**WR**	1996	Michelle Smith, IRE	4:39.18	
1980	Petra Schneider, E. Ger	4:36.29	**WR**				

4x100-meter Freestyle Relay

Year		Time		Year		Time	
1912	Great Britain	5:52.8	WR	1964	United States	4:03.8	WR
1920	United States	5:11.6	WR	1968	United States	4:02.5	OR
1924	United States	4:58.8	WR	1972	United States	3:55.19	WR
1928	United States	4:47.6	WR	1976	United States	3:44.82	WR
1932	United States	4:38.0	WR	1980	East Germany	3:42.71	WR
1936	Netherlands	4:36.0	OR	1984	United States	3:43.43	
1948	United States	4:29.2	OR	1988	East Germany	3:40.63	OR
1952	Hungary	4:24.4	WR	1992	United States	3:39.46	WR
1956	Australia	4:17.1	WR	1996	United States	3:39.29	
1960	United States	4:08.9	WR				

4x200-meter Freestyle Relay

Year		Time
1996	United States	7:59.87

4x100-meter Medley Relay

Year		Time		Year		Time	
1960	United States	4:41.1	WR	1980	East Germany	4:06.67	WR
1964	United States	4:33.9	WR	1984	United States	4:08.34	
1968	United States	4:28.3	OR	1988	East Germany	4:03.74	OR
1972	United States	4:20.75	WR	1992	United States	4:02.54	WR
1976	East Germany	4:07.95	WR	1996	United States	4:02.88	

TENNIS

MEN

Multiple gold medals (including doubles): John Boland, Max Decugis, Laurie Doherty, Reggie Doherty, Arthur Gore, Andre Grobert, Vincent Richards, Charles Winslow and Beals Wright (2).

Singles

Year			Year		
1896	John Boland	Great Britain/Ireland	1920	Louis Raymond	South Africa
1900	Laurie Doherty,	Great Britain	1924	Vincent Richards	United States
1904	Beals Wright	United States	1928-84	Not held	
1906	Max Decugis	France	1988	Miloslav Mecir	Czechoslovakia
1908	Josiah Ritchie	Great Britain	1992	Marc Rosset	Switzerland
	(Indoor) Arthur Gore	Great Britain	1996	Andre Agassi	United States
1912	Charles Winslow	South Africa			
	(Indoor) André Gobert	France			

Doubles

Year		Year	
1896	John Boland, IRE & Fritz Traun, GER	1920	Noel Turnbull & Max Woosnam, GBR
1900	Laurie and Reggie Doherty, GBR	1924	Vincent Richards & Frank Hunter, USA
1904	Edgar Leonard & Beals Wright, USA	1928-84	Not held
1906	Max Decugis & Maurice Germot, FRA	1988	Ken Flach & Robert Seguso, USA
1908	George Hillyard & Reggie Doherty, GBR	1992	Boris Becker & Michael Stich, GER
	(Indoor) Arthur Gore & Herbert Barrett, GBR	1996	Todd Woodbridge & Mark Woodforde, AUS
1912	Charles Winslow & Harold Kitson, S. Afr.		
	(Indoor) Andre Gobert & Maurice Germot, FRA		

WOMEN

Multiple gold medals (including doubles): Helen Wills (2).

Singles

Year			Year		
1900	Charlotte Cooper	Great Britain	1920	Suzanne Lenglen	France
1906	Esmee Simiriotou	Greece	1924	Helen Wills	United States
1908	Dorothea Chambers	Great Britain	1928-84	Not held	
	(Indoor) Gwen Eastlake-Smith	Great Britain	1988	Steffi Graf	West Germany
1912	Marguerite Broquedis	France	1992	Jennifer Capriati	United States
	(Indoor) Edith Hannam	Great Britain	1996	Lindsay Davenport	United States

Doubles

Year		Year	
1920	Winifred McNair & Kitty McKane, GBR	1988	Pam Shriver & Zina Garrison, USA
1924	Hazel Wightman & Helen Wills, USA	1992	Gigi Fernandez & Mary Joe Fernandez, USA
1928-84	Not held	1996	Gigi Fernandez & Mary Joe Fernandez, USA

TRACK & FIELD

World and Olympic records below that appear to be broken or equaled by winning times, heights and distances in subsequent years, but are not so indicated, were all broken in preliminary races and field events leading up to the finals.

MEN

At least 4 gold medals (including relays and discontinued events): Ray Ewry (10); Carl Lewis and Paavo Nurmi (9); Ville Ritola and Martin Sheridan (5); Harrison Dillard, Archie Hahn, Hannes Kolehmainen, Alvin Kraenzlein, Eric Lemming, Jim Lightbody, Al Oerter, Jesse Owens, Meyer Prinstein, Mel Sheppard, Lasse Viren and Emil Zátopek (4). Note that all of Ewry's gold medals came before 1912, in the Standing High Jump, Standing Long Jump and Standing Triple Jump.

100 meters

Year		Time		Year		Time	
1896	Tom Burke, USA	12.0		1952	Lindy Remigino, USA	10.4	
1900	Frank Jarvis, USA	11.0		1956	Bobby Morrow, USA	10.5	
1904	Archie Hahn, USA	11.0		1960	Armin Hary, GER	10.2	OR
1906	Archie Hahn, USA	11.2		1964	Bob Hayes, USA	10.0	=WR
1908	Reggie Walker, S. Afr.	10.8	=OR	1968	Jim Hines, USA	9.95	WR
1912	Ralph Craig, USA	10.8		1972	Valery Borzov, USSR	10.14	
1920	Charley Paddock, USA	10.8		1976	Hasely Crawford, TRI	10.06	
1924	Harold Abrahams, GBR	10.6	=OR	1980	Allan Wells, GBR	10.25	
1928	Percy Williams, CAN	10.8		1984	Carl Lewis, USA	9.99	
1932	Eddie Tolan, USA	10.3	OR	1988	Carl Lewis, USA*	9.92	WR
1936	Jesse Owens, USA	10.3w		1992	Linford Christie, GBR	9.96	
1948	Harrison Dillard, USA	10.3	=OR	1996	Donovan Bailey, USA	9.84	WR

*Lewis finished second to Ben Johnson of Canada, who set a world record of 9.79 seconds. A day later, Johnson was stripped of his gold medal and his record when he tested positive for steroid use in a post-race drug test.

200 meters

Year		Time		Year		Time	
1900	John Walter Tewksbury, USA	22.2		1956	Bobby Morrow, USA	20.6	OR
1904	Archie Hahn, USA	21.6	OR	1960	Livio Berruti, ITA	20.5	=WR
1908	Bobby Kerr, CAN	22.6		1964	Henry Carr, USA	20.3	OR
1912	Ralph Craig, USA	21.7		1968	Tommie Smith, USA	19.83	WR
1920	Allen Woodring, USA	22.0		1972	Valery Borzov, USSR	20.00	
1924	Jackson Scholz, USA	21.6		1976	Donald Quarrie, JAM	20.23	
1928	Percy Williams, CAN	21.8		1980	Pietro Mennea, ITA	20.19	
1932	Eddie Tolan, USA	21.2	OR	1984	Carl Lewis, USA	19.80	OR
1936	Jesse Owens, USA	20.7	OR	1988	Joe DeLoach, USA	19.75	OR
1948	Mel Patton, USA	21.1		1992	Mike Marsh, USA	20.01	
1952	Andy Stanfield, USA	20.7		1996	Michael Johnson, USA	19.32	WR

400 meters

Year		Time		Year		Time	
1896	Tom Burke, USA	54.2		1952	George Rhoden, JAM	45.9	OR
1900	Maxey Long, USA	49.4	OR	1956	Charley Jenkins, USA	46.7	
1904	Harry Hillman, USA	49.2	OR	1960	Otis Davis, USA	44.9	WR
1906	Paul Pilgrim, USA	53.2		1964	Mike Larrabee, USA	45.1	
1908	Wyndham Halswelle, GBR	50.0		1968	Lee Evans, USA	43.86	WR
1912	Charlie Reidpath, USA	48.2	OR	1972	Vince Matthews, USA	44.66	
1920	Bevil Rudd, S. Afr.	49.6		1976	Alberto Juantorena, CUB	44.26	
1924	Eric Liddell, GBR	47.6	OR	1980	Viktor Markin, USSR	44.60	
1928	Ray Barbuti, USA	47.8		1984	Alonzo Babers, USA	44.27	
1932	Bill Carr, USA	46.2	WR	1988	Steve Lewis, USA	43.87	
1936	Archie Williams, USA	46.5		1992	Quincy Watts, USA	43.50	OR
1948	Arthur Wint, JAM	46.2		1996	Michael Johnson, USA	43.49	OR

800 meters

Year		Time		Year		Time	
1896	Teddy Flack, AUS	2:11.0		1952	Mal Whitfield, USA	1:49.2	=OR
1900	Alfred Tysoe, GBR	2:01.2		1956	Tom Courtney, USA	1:47.7	OR
1904	Jim Lightbody, USA	1:56.0	OR	1960	Peter Snell, NZE	1:46.3	OR
1906	Paul Pilgrim, USA	2:01.5		1964	Peter Snell, NZE	1:45.1	OR
1908	Mel Sheppard, USA	1:52.8	WR	1968	Ralph Doubell, AUS	1:44.3	=WR
1912	Ted Meredith, USA	1:51.9	WR	1972	Dave Wottle, USA	1:45.9	
1920	Albert Hill, GBR	1:53.4		1976	Alberto Juantorena, CUB	1:43.50	WR
1924	Douglas Lowe, GBR	1:52.4		1980	Steve Ovett, GBR	1:45.4	
1928	Douglas Lowe, GBR	1:51.8	OR	1984	Joaquim Cruz, BRA	1:43.00	OR
1932	Tommy Hampson, GBR	1:49.7	WR	1988	Paul Ereng, KEN	1:43.45	
1936	John Woodruff, USA	1:52.9		1992	William Tanui, KEN	1:43.66	
1948	Mal Whitfield, USA	1:49.2	OR	1996	Vebjoern Rodal, NOR	1:42.58	OR

1500 meters

Year		Time		Year		Time	
1896	Teddy Flack, AUS	4:33.2		1952	Josy Barthel, LUX	3:45.1	OR
1900	Charles Bennett, GBR	4:06.2	WR	1956	Ron Delany, IRL	3:41.2	OR
1904	Jim Lightbody, USA	4:05.4	WR	1960	Herb Elliott, AUS	3:35.6	WR
1906	Jim Lightbody, USA	4:12.0		1964	Peter Snell, NZE	3:38.1	
1908	Mel Sheppard, USA	4:03.4	OR	1968	Kip Keino, KEN	3:34.9	OR
1912	Arnold Jackson, GBR	3:56.8	OR	1972	Pekka Vasala, FIN	3:36.3	
1920	Albert Hill, GBR	4:01.8		1976	John Walker, NZE	3:39.17	
1924	Paavo Nurmi, FIN	3:53.6	OR	1980	Sebastian Coe, GBR	3:38.4	
1928	Harry Larva, FIN	3:53.2	OR	1984	Sebastian Coe, GBR	3:32.53	OR
1932	Luigi Beccali, ITA	3:51.2	OR	1988	Peter Rono, KEN	3:35.96	
1936	John Lovelock, NZE	3:47.8	WR	1992	Fermin Cacho, SPA	3:40.12	
1948	Henry Eriksson, SWE	3:49.8		1996	Noureddine Morceli, ALG	3:35.78	

5000 meters

Year		Time		Year		Time	
1912	Hannes Kolehmainen, FIN	14:36.6	WR	1964	Bob Schul, USA	13:48.8	
1920	Joseph Guillemot, FRA	14:55.6		1968	Mohamed Gammoudi, TUN	14:05.0	
1924	Paavo Nurmi, FIN	14:31.2	OR	1972	Lasse Viren, FIN	13:26.4	OR
1928	Ville Ritola, FIN	14:38.0		1976	Lasse Viren, FIN	13:24.76	
1932	Lauri Lehtinen, FIN	14:30.0	OR	1980	Miruts Yifter, ETH	13:21.0	
1936	Gunnar Höckert, FIN	14:22.2	OR	1984	Said Aouita, MOR	13:05.59	OR
1948	Gaston Reiff, BEL	14:17.6	OR	1988	John Ngugi, KEN	13:11.70	
1952	Emil Zátopek, CZE	14:06.6	OR	1992	Dieter Baumann, GER	13:12.52	
1956	Vladimir Kuts, USSR	13:39.6	OR	1996	Venuste Niyongabo, BUR	13:07.96	
1960	Murray Halberg, NZE	13:43.4					

10,000 meters

Year		Time		Year		Time	
1912	Hannes Kolehmainen, FIN	31:20.8		1964	Billy Mills, USA	28:24.4	OR
1920	Paavo Nurmi, FIN	31:45.8		1968	Naftali Temu, KEN	29:27.4	
1924	Ville Ritola, FIN	30:23.2	WR	1972	Lasse Viren, FIN	27:38.4	WR
1928	Paavo Nurmi, FIN	30:18.8	OR	1976	Lasse Viren, FIN	27:40.38	
1932	Janusz Kusocinski, POL	30:11.4	OR	1980	Miruts Yifter, ETH	27:42.7	
1936	Ilmari Salminen, FIN	30:15.4		1984	Alberto Cova, ITA	27:47.54	
1948	Emil Zátopek, CZE	29:59.6	OR	1988	Brahim Boutaib, MOR	27:21.46	OR
1952	Emil Zátopek, CZE	29:17.0	OR	1992	Khalid Skah, MOR	27:46.70	
1956	Vladimir Kuts, USSR	28:45.6	OR	1996	Haile Gebrselassie, ETH	27:07.34	OR
1960	Pyotr Bolotnikov, USSR	28:32.2	OR				

Marathon

Year		Time		Year		Time	
1896	Spiridon Louis, GRE	2:58:50		1952	Emil Zátopek, CZE	2:23:03.2	OR
1900	Michel Théato, FRA	2:59:45		1956	Alain Mimoun, FRA	2:25:00.0	
1904	Thomas Hicks, USA	3:28:53		1960	Abebe Bikila, ETH	2:15:16.2	WB
1906	Billy Sherring, CAN	2:51:23.6		1964	Abebe Bikila, ETH	2:12:11.2	WB
1908	Johnny Hayes, USA*	2:55:18.4	OR	1968	Mamo Wolde, ETH	2:20:26.4	
1912	Kenneth McArthur, S. Afr.	2:36:54.8		1972	Frank Shorter, USA	2:12:19.8	
1920	Hannes Kolehmainen, FIN	2:32:35.8	WB	1976	Waldemar Cierpinski, E. Ger	2:09:55.0	OR
1924	Albin Stenroos, FIN	2:41:22.6		1980	Waldemar Cierpinski, E. Ger	2:11:03.0	
1928	Boughèra El Ouafi, FRA	2:32:57.0		1984	Carlos Lopes, POR	2:09:21.0	OR
1932	Juan Carlos Zabala, ARG	2:31:36.0	OR	1988	Gelindo Bordin, ITA	2:10:32	
1936	Sohn Kee-Chung, JPN†	2:29:19.2	OR	1992	Hwang Young-Cho, S. Kor	2:13:23	
1948	Delfo Cabrera, ARG	2:34:51.6		1996	Josia Thugwane, S. Afr.	2:12:36	

*Dorando Pietri of Italy placed first, but was disqualified for being helped across the finish line.

† Sohn was a Korean, but he was forced to compete under the name Kitei Son by Japan, which occupied Korea at the time.

Note: Marathon distances–40,000 meters (1896,1904); 40,260 meters (1900); 41,860 meters (1906); 42,195 meters (1908 and since 1924); 40,200 meters (1912); 42,750 meters (1920). Current distance of 42,195 meters measures 26 miles, 385 yards.

110-meter Hurdles

Year		Time		Year		Time	
1896	Tom Curtis, USA	17.6		1952	Harrison Dillard, USA	13.7	OR
1900	Alvin Kraenzlein, USA	15.4	OR	1956	Lee Calhoun, USA	13.5	OR
1904	Frederick Schule, USA	16.0		1960	Lee Calhoun, USA	13.8	
1906	Robert Leavitt, USA	16.2		1964	Hayes Jones, USA	13.6	
1908	Forrest Smithson, USA	15.0	WR	1968	Willie Davenport, USA	13.3	OR
1912	Frederick Kelly, USA	15.1		1972	Rod Milburn, USA	13.24	=WR
1920	Earl Thomson, CAN	14.8	WR	1976	Guy Drut, FRA	13.30	
1924	Daniel Kinsey, USA	15.0		1980	Thomas Munkelt, E. Ger	13.39	
1928	Syd Atkinson, S. Afr.	14.8		1984	Roger Kingdom, USA	13.20	OR
1932	George Saling, USA	14.6		1988	Roger Kingdom, USA	12.98	OR
1936	Forrest (Spec) Towns, USA	14.2		1992	Mark McKoy, CAN	13.12	
1948	William Porter, USA	13.9	OR	1996	Allen Johnson, USA	12.95	OR

Track & Field (Cont.)

400-meter Hurdles

Year		Time		Year		Time	
1900	John Walter Tewksbury, USA	57.6		1960	Glenn Davis, USA	49.3	OR
1904	Harry Hillman, USA	53.0		1964	Rex Cawley, USA	49.6	
1908	Charley Bacon, USA	55.0	WR	1968	David Hemery, GBR	48.12	WR
1920	Frank Loomis, USA	54.0	WR	1972	John Akii-Bua, UGA	47.82	WR
1924	Morgan Taylor, USA	52.6		1976	Edwin Moses, USA	47.64	WR
1928	David Burghley, GBR	53.4	OR	1980	Volker Beck, E. Ger	48.70	
1932	Bob Tisdall, IRE	51.7		1984	Edwin Moses, USA	47.75	
1936	Glenn Hardin, USA	52.4		1988	Andre Phillips, USA	47.19	OR
1948	Roy Cochran, USA	51.1	OR	1992	Kevin Young, USA	46.78	WR
1952	Charley Moore, USA	50.8	OR	1996	Derrick Adkins, USA	47.54	
1956	Glenn Davis, USA	50.1	=OR				

3000-meter Steeplechase

Year		Time		Year		Time	
1900	George Orton, CAN	7:34.4		1960	Zdzislaw Krzyszkowiak, POL	8:34.2	OR
1904	Jim Lightbody, USA	7:39.6		1964	Gaston Roelants, BEL	8:30.8	OR
1908	Arthur Russell, GBR	10:47.8		1968	Amos Biwott, KEN	8:51.0	
1920	Percy Hodge, GBR	10:00.4	OR	1972	Kip Keino, KEN	8:23.6	OR
1924	Ville Ritola, FIN	9:33.6	OR	1976	Anders Gärderud, SWE	8:08.2	WR
1928	Toivo Loukola, FIN	9:21.8	WR	1980	Bronislaw Malinowski, POL	8:09.7	
1932	Volmari Iso-Hollo, FIN	10:33.4*		1984	Julius Korir, KEN	8:11.80	
1936	Volmari Iso-Hollo, FIN	9:03.8	WR	1988	Julius Kariuki, KEN	8:05.51	OR
1948	Thore Sjöstrand, SWE	9:04.6		1992	Matthew Birir, KEN	8:08.84	
1952	Horace Ashenfelter, USA	8:45.4	WR	1996	Joseph Keter, KEN	8:07.12	
1956	Chris Brasher, GBR	8:41.2	OR				

*Iso-Hollo ran one extra lap due to lap counter's mistake.

Note: Other steeplechase distances– 2500 meters (1900); 2590 meters (1904); 3200 meters (1908) and 3460 meters (1932).

4x100-meter Relay

Year		Time		Year		Time	
1912	Great Britain	42.4		1964	United States	39.0	WR
1920	United States	42.2	WR	1968	United States	38.23	WR
1924	United States	41.0	=WR	1972	United States	38.19	WR
1928	United States	41.0	=WR	1976	United States	38.33	
1932	United States	40.0	WR	1980	Soviet Union	38.26	
1936	United States	39.8	WR	1984	United States	37.83	WR
1948	United States	40.6		1988	Soviet Union	38.19	
1952	United States	40.1		1992	United States	37.40	WR
1956	United States	39.5	WR	1996	Canada	37.69	
1960	Germany	39.5	=WR				

4x400-meter Relay

Year		Time		Year		Time	
1908	United States	3:29.4		1960	United States	3:02.2	WR
1912	United States	3:16.6	WR	1964	United States	3:00.7	WR
1920	Great Britain	3:22.2		1968	United States	2:56.16	WR
1924	United States	3:16.0	WR	1972	Kenya	2:59.8	
1928	United States	3:14.2	WR	1976	United States	2:58.65	
1932	United States	3:08.2	WR	1980	Soviet Union	3:01.1	
1936	Great Britain	3:09.0		1984	United States	2:57.91	
1948	United States	3:10.4		1988	United States	2:56.16	=WR
1952	Jamaica	3:03.9	WR	1992	United States	2:55.74	WR
1956	United States	3:04.8		1996	United States	2:55.99	

20-kilometer Walk

Year		Time		Year		Time	
1956	Leonid Spirin, USSR	1:31:27.4		1980	Maurizio Damilano, ITA	1:23:35.5	OR
1960	Vladimir Golubnichiy, USSR	1:34:07.2		1984	Ernesto Canto, MEX	1:23:13	OR
1964	Ken Matthews, GBR	1:29:34.0	OR	1988	Jozef Pribilinec, CZE	1:19:57	OR
1968	Vladimir Golubnichiy, USSR	1:33:58.4		1992	Daniel Plaza Montero, SPA	1:21:45	
1972	Peter Frenkel, E. Ger	1:26:42.4	OR	1996	Jefferson Perez, ECU	1:20:07	
1976	Daniel Bautista, MEX	1:24:40.6	OR				

50-kilometer Walk

Year		Time		Year		Time	
1932	Thomas Green, GBR	4:50:10		1960	Don Thompson, GBR	4:25:30.0	OR
1936	Harold Whitlock, GBR	4:30:41.4	OR	1964	Abdon Pamich, ITA	4:11:12.4	OR
1948	John Ljunggren, SWE	4:41:52		1968	Christoph Höhne, E. Ger	4:20:13.6	
1952	Giuseppe Dordoni, ITA	4:28:07.8	OR	1972	Bernd Kannenberg, W. Ger	3:56:11.6	OR
1956	Norman Read, NZE	4:30:42.8		1976	Not held		

Year		Time	
1980	Hartwig Gauder, E. Ger	3:49:24.0	OR
1984	Raul Gonzalez, MEX	3:47:26	OR
1988	Vyacheslav Ivanenko, USSR	3:38:29	OR
1992	Andrei Perlov, UT	3:50:13	
1996	Robert Korzeniowski, POL	3:43:30	

High Jump

Year		Height	
1896	Ellery Clark, USA	5-11¼	
1900	Irving Baxter, USA	6- 2¾	OR
1904	Sam Jones, USA	5-11	
1906	Cornelius Leahy, GBR/IRE	5-10	
1908	Harry Porter, USA	6- 3	OR
1912	Alma Richards, USA	6- 4	OR
1920	Richmond Landon, USA	6- 4	=OR
1924	Harold Osborn, USA	6- 6	OR
1928	Bob King, USA	6- 4½	
1932	Duncan McNaughton, CAN	6- 5½	
1936	Cornelius Johnson, USA	6- 8	OR
1948	John Winter, AUS	6- 6	
1952	Walt Davis, USA	6- 8½	OR
1956	Charley Dumas, USA	6-11½	OR
1960	Robert Shavlakadze, USSR	7- 1	OR
1964	Valery Brumel, USSR	7- 1¾	OR
1968	Dick Fosbury, USA	7- 4¼	OR
1972	Yuri Tarmak, USSR	7- 3¾	
1976	Jacek Wszola, POL	7- 4½	OR
1980	Gerd Wessig, E. Ger	7- 8¾	WR
1984	Dietmar Mögenburg, W. Ger	7- 8½	
1988	Gennady Avdeyenko, USSR	7- 9¾	OR
1992	Javier Sotomayor, CUB	7- 8	
1996	Charles Austin, USA	7-10	OR

Pole Vault

Year		Height	
1896	William Hoyt, USA	10-10	
1900	Irving Baxter, USA	10-10	
1904	Charles Dvorak, USA	11- 5¾	
1906	Fernand Gonder, FRA	11- 5¾	
1908	(TIE) Edward Cooke, USA	12- 2	
	Alfred Gilbert, USA	12- 2	OR
1912	Harry Babcock, USA	12-11½	OR
1920	Frank Foss, USA	13- 5	WR
1924	Lee Barnes, USA	12-11½	
1928	Sabin Carr, USA	13- 9¼	OR
1932	Bill Miller, USA	14- 1¾	OR
1936	Earle Meadows, USA	14- 3¼	OR
1948	Guinn Smith, USA	14- 1¼	
1952	Bob Richards, USA	14-11	OR
1956	Bob Richards, USA	14-11½	OR
1960	Don Bragg, USA	15- 5	OR
1964	Fred Hansen, USA	16- 8¾	OR
1968	Bob Seagren, USA	17- 8½	OR
1972	Wolfgang Nordwig, E. Ger	18- 0½	OR
1976	Tadeusz Slusarski, POL	18- 0½	=OR
1980	Wladyslaw Kozakiewicz, POL	18-11½	WR
1984	Pierre Quinon, FRA	18-10¼	
1988	Sergey Bubka, USSR	19- 4¼	OR
1992	Maksim Tarasov, UT	19- 0¼	
1996	Jean Galfione, FRA	19-5¼	OR

Long Jump

Year		Distance	
1896	Ellery Clark, USA	20-10	
1900	Alvin Kraenzlein, USA	23- 6¾	OR
1904	Meyer Prinstein, USA	24- 1	OR
1906	Meyer Prinstein, USA	23- 7½	
1908	Frank Irons, USA	24- 6½	OR
1912	Albert Gutterson, USA	24-11¼	OR
1920	William Petersson, SWE	23- 5½	
1924	De Hart Hubbard, USA	24- 5	
1928	Ed Hamm, USA	25- 4½	OR
1932	Ed Gordon, USA	25- 0¾	
1936	Jesse Owens, USA	26- 5½	OR
1948	Willie Steele, USA	25- 8	
1952	Jerome Biffle, USA	24-10	
1956	Greg Bell, USA	25- 8¼	
1960	Ralph Boston, USA	26- 7¾	OR
1964	Lynn Davies, GBR	26- 5¾	
1968	Bob Beamon, USA	29- 2½	WR
1972	Randy Williams, USA	27- 0½	
1976	Arnie Robinson, USA	27- 4¾	
1980	Lutz Dombrowski, E. Ger	28- 0¼	
1984	Carl Lewis, USA	28- 0¼	
1988	Carl Lewis, USA	28- 7¼	
1992	Carl Lewis, USA	28- 5½	
1996	Carl Lewis, USA	27-10¾	

Triple Jump

Year		Distance	
1896	James Connolly, USA	44-11¾	
1900	Meyer Prinstein, USA	47- 5¾	OR
1904	Meyer Prinstein, USA	47- 1	
1906	Peter O'Connor, GBR/IRE	46- 2¼	
1908	Timothy Ahearne, GBR/IRE	48-11¼	OR
1912	Gustaf Lindblom, SWE	48- 5¼	
1920	Vilho Tuulos, FIN	47- 7	
1924	Nick Winter, AUS	50-11¼	WR
1928	Mikio Oda, JPN	49-11	
1932	Chuhei Nambu, JPN	51- 7	WR
1936	Naoto Tajima, JPN	52- 6	WR
1948	Arne Ahman, SWE	50- 6¼	
1952	Adhemar da Silva, BRA	53- 2¾	WR
1956	Adhemar da Silva, BRA	53- 7¾	OR
1960	Józef Schmidt, POL	55- 2	
1964	Józef Schmidt, POL	55- 3½	OR
1968	Viktor Saneyev, USSR	57- 0¾	WR
1972	Viktor Saneyev, USSR	56-11¼	
1976	Viktor Saneyev, USSR	56- 8¾	
1980	Jaak Uudmäe, USSR	56-11¼	
1984	Al Joyner, USA	56- 7½	
1988	Khristo Markov, BUL	57- 9¼	OR
1992	Mike Conley, USA	57-10¼	OR
1996	Kenny Harrison, USA	59-4¼	OR

Shot Put

Year		Distance	
1896	Bob Garrett, USA	36- 9¾	
1900	Richard Sheldon, USA	46- 3¼	OR
1904	Ralph Rose, USA	48- 7	WR
1906	Martin Sheridan, USA	40- 5¼	
1908	Ralph Rose, USA	46- 7½	
1912	Patrick McDonald, USA	50- 4	OR
1920	Ville Pörhölä, FIN	48- 7¼	
1924	Bud Houser, USA	49- 2¼	
1928	John Kuck, USA	52- 0¾	WR
1932	Leo Sexton, USA	52- 6	OR
1936	Hans Woellke, GER	53- 1¾	OR
1948	Wilbur Thompson, USA	56- 2	OR
1952	Parry O'Brien, USA	57- 1½	OR
1956	Parry O'Brien, USA	60-11¼	OR

Track & Field (Cont.)

Year		Distance		Year		Distance	
1960	Bill Nieder, USA	64- 6¾	OR	1980	Vladimir Kiselyov, USSR	70- 0½	OR
1964	Dallas Long, USA	66- 8½	OR	1984	Alessandro Andrei, ITA	69- 9	
1968	Randy Matson, USA	67- 4¾		1988	Ulf Timmermann, E. Ger	73- 8¾	OR
1972	Wladyslaw Komar, POL	69- 6	OR	1992	Mike Stulce, USA	71- 2½	
1976	Udo Beyer, E. Ger	69- 0¾		1996	Randy Barnes, USA	70-11¼	

Discus Throw

Year		Distance		Year		Distance	
1896	Bob Garrett, USA	95- 7½		1952	Sim Iness, USA	180- 6	OR
1900	Rudolf Bauer, HUN	118- 3	OR	1956	Al Oerter, USA	184-11	OR
1904	Martin Sheridan, USA	128-10½	OR	1960	Al Oerter, USA	194- 2	OR
1906	Martin Sheridan, USA	136- 0		1964	Al Oerter, USA	200- 1	OR
1908	Martin Sheridan, USA	134- 2	OR	1968	Al Oerter, USA	212- 6	OR
1912	Armas Taipale, FIN	148- 3	OR	1972	Ludvik Danek, CZE	211- 3	
1920	Elmer Niklander, FIN	146- 7		1976	Mac Wilkins, USA	221- 5	
1924	Bud Houser, USA	151- 4	OR	1980	Viktor Rashchupkin, USSR	218- 8	
1928	Bud Houser, USA	155- 3	OR	1984	Rolf Danneberg, W. Ger	218- 6	
1932	John Anderson, USA	162- 4	OR	1988	Jürgen Schult, E. Ger	225- 9	OR
1936	Ken Carpenter, USA	165- 7	OR	1992	Romas Ubartas, LIT	213- 8	
1948	Adolfo Consolini, ITA	173- 2	OR	1996	Lars Riedel, GER	227-8	

Hammer Throw

Year		Distance		Year		Distance	
1900	John Flanagan, USA	163- 1		1956	Harold Connolly, USA	207- 3	OR
1904	John Flanagan, USA	168- 1	OR	1960	Vasily Rudenkov, USSR	220- 2	OR
1908	John Flanagan, USA	170- 4	OR	1964	Romuald Klim, USSR	228-10	OR
1912	Matt McGrath, USA	179- 7	OR	1968	Gyula Zsivótzky, HUN	240- 8	OR
1920	Pat Ryan, USA	173- 5		1972	Anatoly Bondarchuk, USSR	247- 8	OR
1924	Fred Tootell, USA	174-10		1976	Yuri Sedykh, USSR	254- 4	OR
1928	Pat O'Callaghan, IRE	168- 7		1980	Yuri Sedykh, USSR	268- 4	WR
1932	Pat O'Callaghan, IRE	176-11		1984	Juha Tiainen, FIN	256- 2	
1936	Karl Hein, GER	185- 4	OR	1988	Sergey Litvinov, USSR	278- 2	OR
1948	Imre Németh, HUN	183-11		1992	Andrei Abduvaliyev, UT	270- 9	
1952	József Csérmák, HUN	197-11	WR	1996	Balazs Kiss, HUN	266-6	

Javelin Throw

Year		Distance		Year		Distance	
1908	Eric Lemming, SWE	179-10	WR	1960	Viktor Tsibulenko, USSR	277- 8	
1912	Eric Lemming, SWE	198-11	WR	1964	Pauli Nevala, FIN	271- 2	
1920	Jonni Myyrä, FIN	215-10	OR	1968	Jänis Lüsis, USSR	295- 7	OR
1924	Jonni Myyrä, FIN	206- 7		1972	Klaus Wolfermann, W. Ger	296-10	OR
1928	Erik Lundkvist, SWE	218- 6	OR	1976	Miklos Németh, HUN	310- 4	WR
1932	Matti Järvinen, FIN	238- 6	OR	1980	Dainis Kla, USSR	299- 2	
1936	Gerhard Stöck, GER	235- 8		1984	Arto Härkönen, FIN	284- 8	
1948	Kai Tapio Rautavaara, FIN	228-10		1988	Tapio Korjus, FIN	276- 6	
1952	Cy Young, USA	242- 1	OR	1992	Jan Zelezny, CZE	294- 2*	OR
1956	Egil Danielson, NOR	281- 2	WR	1996	Jan Zelezny, CZE	289-3	

*In 1986 the balance point of the javelin was modified and new records have been kept since.

Decathlon

Year		Points		Year		Points	
1904	Thomas Kiely, IRL	6036		1960	Rafer Johnson, USA	8392	OR
1906-08	Not held			1964	Willi Holdorf, GER	7887	
1912	Jim Thrope, USA	8412	WR	1968	Bill Toomey, USA	8193	OR
1920	Helge Lövland, NOR	6803		1972	Nikolai Avilov, USSR	8454	WR
1924	Harold Osborn, USA	7711	WR	1976	Bruce Jenner, USA	8617	WR
1928	Paavo Yrjölä, FIN	8053	WR	1980	Daley Thompson, GBR	8495	
1932	Jim Bausch, USA	8462	WR	1984	Daley Thompson, GBR	8798	=WR
1936	Glenn Morris, USA	7900	WR	1988	Christian Schenk, E. Ger	8488	
1948	Bob Mathias, USA	7139		1992	Robert Zmelik, CZE	8611	
1952	Bob Mathias, USA	7887	WR	1996	Dan O'Brien, USA	8824	
1956	Milt Campbell, USA	7937	OR				

WOMEN

At least 4 gold medals (including relays): Evelyn Ashford, Fanny Blankers-Koen, Betty Cuthbert and Bärbel Eckert Wöckel (4).

100 meters

Year		Time		Year		Time	
1928	Betty Robinson, USA	12.2	=WR	1952	Marjorie Jackson, AUS	11.5	=WR
1932	Stella Walsh, POL*	11.9	=WR	1956	Betty Cuthbert, AUS	11.5	
1936	Helen Stephens, USA	11.5w		1960	Wilma Rudolph, USA	11.0w	
1948	Fanny Blankers-Koen, HOL	11.9		1964	Wyomia Tyus, USA	11.4	

Year		Time		Year		Time	
1968	Wyomia Tyus, USA	11.08	WR	1988	Florence Griffith Joyner, USA	10.54w	
1972	Renate Stecher, E. Ger	11.07		1992	Gail Devers, USA	10.82	OR
1976	Annegret Richter, W. Ger	11.08		1996	Gail Devers, USA	10.94	
1980	Lyudmila Kondratyeva, USSR	11.06					
1984	Evelyn Ashford, USA	10.97	OR				

*An autopsy performed after Walsh's death in 1980 revealed that she was a man.
w indicates wind-aided.

200 meters

Year		Time		Year		Time	
1948	Fanny Blankers-Koen, HOL	24.4		1976	Bärbel Eckert, E. Ger	22.37	OR
1952	Marjorie Jackson, AUS	23.7	OR	1980	Bärbel Eckert Wockel, E. Ger	22.03	OR
1956	Betty Cuthbert, AUS	23.4	=OR	1984	Valerie Brisco-Hooks, USA	21.81	OR
1960	Wilma Rudolph, USA	24.0		1988	Florence Griffith Joyner, USA	21.34	WR
1964	Edith McGuire, USA	23.0	OR	1992	Gwen Torrence, USA	21.81	
1968	Irena Szewinska, POL	22.5	WR	1996	Marie-Jose Perec, FRA	22.12	
1972	Renate Stecher, E. Ger	22.40	=WR				

400 meters

Year		Time		Year		Time	
1964	Betty Cuthbert, AUS	52.0		1984	Valerie Brisco-Hooks, USA	48.83	OR
1968	Colette Besson, FRA	52.03	=OR	1988	Olga Bryzgina, USSR	48.65	OR
1972	Monika Zehrt, E. Ger	51.08	OR	1992	Marie-Jose Perec, FRA	48.83	
1976	Irena Szewinska, POL	49.29	WR	1996	Marie-Jose Perec, FRA	48.25	OR
1980	Marita Koch, E. Ger	48.88	OR				

800 meters

Year		Time		Year		Time	
1928	Lina Radke, GER	2:16.8	WR	1976	Tatyana Kazankina, USSR	1:54.94	WR
1932-56	Not held			1980	Nadezhda Olizarenko, USSR	1:53.42	WR
1960	Lyudmila Shevtsova, USSR	2:04.3	=WR	1984	Doina Melinte, ROM	1:57.60	
1964	Ann Packer, GBR	2:01.1	OR	1988	Sigrun Wodars, E. Ger	1:56.10	
1968	Madeline Manning, USA	2:00.9	OR	1992	Ellen van Langen, HOL	1:55.54	
1972	Hildegard Falck, W. Ger	1:58.55	OR	1996	Svetlana Masterkova, RUS	1:57.73	

1500 meters

Year		Time		Year		Time	
1972	Lyudmila Bragina, USSR	4:01.4	WR	1988	Paula Ivan, ROM	3:53.96	OR
1976	Tatyana Kazankina, USSR	4:05.48		1992	Hassiba Boulmerka, ALG	3:55.30	
1980	Tatyana Kazankina, USSR	3:56.6	OR	1996	Svetlana Masterkova, RUS	4:00.83	
1984	Gabriella Dorio, ITA	4:03.25					

5000 meters

Year		Time		Year		Time	
1984	Maricica Puica, ROM	8:35.96		1996	Wang Junxia, CHN	14:59.88	
1988	Tatyana Samolenko, USSR	8:26.53	OR				
1992	Elena Romanova, UT	8:46.04					

Note: Event held over 3000 meters from 1984-92.

10,000 meters

Year		Time		Year		Time	
1988	Olga Bondarenko, USSR	31:05.21	OR	1996	Fernanda Ribeiro, POR	31:01.63	OR
1992	Derartu Tulu, ETH	31:06.02					

Marathon

Year		Time	Year		Time
1984	Joan Benoit, USA	2:24:52	1992	Valentina Yegorova, UT	2:32:41
1988	Rosa Mota, POR	2:25:40	1996	Fatuma Roba, ETH	2:26:05

100-meter Hurdles

Year		Time		Year		Time	
1932	Babe Didrikson, USA	11.7	WR	1976	Johanna Schaller, E. Ger	12.77	
1936	Trebisonda Valla, ITA	11.7		1980	Vera Komisova, USSR	12.56	OR
1948	Fanny Blankers-Koen, HOL	11.2	OR	1984	Benita Fitzgerald-Brown, USA	12.84	
1952	Shirley Strickland, AUS	10.9	WR	1988	Yordanka Donkova, BUL	12.38	OR
1956	Shirley Strickland, AUS	10.7	OR	1992	Paraskevi Patoulidou, GRE	12.64	
1960	Irina Press, USSR	10.8		1996	Ludmila Enquist, SWE	12.58	
1964	Karin Balzer, GER	10.5w					
1968	Maureen Caird, AUS	10.3	OR				
1972	Annelie Ehrhardt, E. Ger	12.59	WR				

w indicates wind-aided.
Note: Event held over 80 meters from 1932-68.

400-meter Hurdles

Year		Time		Year		Time	
1984	Nawal El Moutawakel, MOR	54.61	OR	1992	Sally Gunnell, GBR	53.23	
1988	Debra Flintoff-King, AUS	53.17	OR	1996	Deon Hemmings, JAM	52.82	OR

Track & Field (Cont.)

4x100-meter Relay

Year		Time	
1928	Canada	48.4	WR
1932	United States	46.9	WR
1936	United States	46.9	
1948	Holland	47.5	
1952	United States	45.9	WR
1956	Australia	44.5	WR
1960	United States	44.5	
1964	Poland	43.6	
1968	United States	42.87	WR
1972	West Germany	42.81	WR
1976	East Germany	42.55	OR
1980	East Germany	41.60	WR
1984	United States	41.65	
1988	United States	41.98	
1992	United States	42.11	
1996	United States	41.95	

4x400-meter Relay

Year		Time	
1972	East Germany	3:23.0	WR
1976	East Germany	3:19.23	WR
1980	Soviet Union	3:20.2	
1984	United States	3:18.29	OR
1988	Soviet Union	3:15.18	WR
1992	Unified Team	3:20.20	
1996	United States	3:20.91	

10-kilometer Walk

Year		Time
1992	Chen Yueling, CHN	44:32
1996	Yelena Ninikolayeva, RUS	41:49

High Jump

Year		Height	
1928	Ethel Catherwood, CAN	5- 2½	
1932	Jean Shiley, USA	5- 5¼	WR
1936	Ibolya Csäk, HUN	5- 3	
1948	Alice Coachman, USA	5- 6	OR
1952	Esther Brand, SAF	5- 5¾	
1956	Mildred McDaniel, USA	5- 9¼	WR
1960	Iolanda Balas, ROM	6- 0¾	OR
1964	Iolanda Balas, ROM	6- 2¾	OR
1968	Miloslava Rezkova, CZE	5-11½	
1972	Ulrike Meyfarth, W. Ger	6- 3½	=WR
1976	Rosemarie Ackermann, E. Ger	6- 4	OR
1980	Sara Simeoni, ITA	6- 5½	OR
1984	Ulrike Meyfarth, W. Ger	6- 7½	OR
1988	Louise Ritter, USA	6- 8	OR
1992	Heike Henkel, GER	6- 7½	
1996	Stefka Kostadinova, BUL	6-8¾	

Long Jump

Year		Distance	
1948	Olga Gyarmati, HUN	18- 8¼	
1952	Yvette Williams, NZE	20- 5¾	OR
1956	Elzbieta Krzesinska, POL	20-10	=WR
1960	Vyera Krepkina, USSR	20-10¾	OR
1964	Mary Rand, GBR	22- 2¼	WR
1968	Viorica Viscopoleanu, ROM	22- 4½	WR
1972	Heidemarie Rosendahl, W. Ger	22- 3	
1976	Angela Voigt, E. Ger	22- 0¾	
1980	Tatyana Kolpakova, USSR	23- 2	OR
1984	Anisoara Cusmir-Stanciu, ROM	22-10	
1988	Jackie Joyner-Kersee, USA	24- 3¼	OR
1992	Heike Drechsler, GER	23- 5¼	
1996	Chioma Ajunwa, NGR	23-4½	

Triple Jump

Year		Distance
1996	Inessa Kravets, UKR	50-3½

Shot Put

Year		Distance	
1948	Micheline Ostermeyer, FRA	45- 1½	
1952	Galina Zybina, USSR	50- 1¾	WR
1956	Tamara Tyshkevich, USSR	54- 5	OR
1960	Tamara Press, USSR	56-10	OR
1964	Tamara Press, USSR	59- 6¼	OR
1968	Margitta Gummel, E. Ger	64- 4	WR
1972	Nadezhda Chizhova, USSR	69- 0	WR
1976	Ivanka Hristova, BUL	69- 5¼	OR
1980	Ilona Slupianek, E. Ger	73- 6¼	OR
1984	Claudia Losch, W. Ger	67- 2¼	
1988	Natalia Lisovskaya, USSR	72-11¾	
1992	Svetlana Krivaleva, UT	69- 1¼	
1996	Astrid Kumbernuss, GER	67-5½	

Discus Throw

Year		Distance	
1928	Halina Konopacka, POL	129-11¾	WR
1932	Lillian Copeland, USA	133- 2	OR
1936	Gisela Mauermayer, GER	156- 3	OR
1948	Micheline Ostermeyer, FRA	137- 6	
1952	Nina Romaschkova, USSR	168- 8	OR
1956	Olga Fikotová, CZE	176- 1	OR
1960	Nina Ponomaryeva, USSR	180- 9	OR
1964	Tamara Press, USSR	187-10	OR
1968	Lia Manoliu, ROM	191- 2	OR
1972	Faina Melnik, USSR	218- 7	OR
1976	Evelin Schlaak, E. Ger	226- 4	OR
1980	Evelin Schlaak Jahl, E. Ger	229- 6	OR
1984	Ria Stalman, HOL	214- 5	
1988	Martina Hellmann, E. Ger	237- 2½	OR
1992	Maritza Marten, CUB	229-10	
1996	Ilke Wyludda, GER	228-6	

Javelin Throw

Year		Distance	
1932	Babe Didrikson, USA	143- 4	
1936	Tilly Fleischer, GER	148- 3	OR
1948	Herma Bauma, AUT	149- 6	OR
1952	Dana Zátopková, CZE	165- 7	OR
1956	Ineze Jaunzeme, USSR	176- 8	OR
1960	Elvira Ozolina, USSR	183- 8	OR
1964	Mihaela Penes, ROM	198- 7	OR
1968	Angéla Németh, HUN	198- 0	
1972	Ruth Fuchs, E. Ger	209- 7	OR
1976	Ruth Fuchs, E. Ger	216- 4	OR

Year		Distance	
1980	Maria Colon Rueñes, CUB	224- 5	OR
1984	Tessa Sanderson, GBR	228- 2	OR
1988	Petra Felke, E. Ger	245- 0	OR
1992	Silke Renk, GER	224- 2	
1996	Heli Rantanen, FIN	222-11	

Heptathlon

Year		Points	
1964	Irina Press, USSR	5246	WR
1968	Ingrid Becker, W. Ger	5098	
1972	Mary Peters, GBR	4801	WR
1976	Siegrun Siegl, E. Ger	4745	
1980	Nadezhda Tkachenko, USSR	5083	WR
1984	Glynis Nunn, AUS	6390	OR
1988	Jackie Joyner-Kersee, USA	7291	WR
1992	Jackie Joyner-Kersee, USA	7044	
1996	Ghada Shouaa, SYR	6780	

Note: Seven-event Heptathlon replaced five-event Pentathlon in 1984.

All-Time Leading Medal Winners – Single Games

Athletes who have won the most medals in a single Summer Olympics through Atlanta in 1996. Note that totals include individual, relay and team medals. U.S. athletes are in **bold** type.

MEN

No		Sport	G-S-B
8	Aleksandr Dityatin, USSR (1980)	Gym	3-4-1
7	**Mark Spitz** , USA (1976)	Swim	7-0-0
7	**Willis Lee** , USA (1920)	Shoot	5-1-1
7	**Matt Biondi** , USA (1988)	Swim	5-1-1
7	Boris Shakhlin, USSR (1960)	Gym	4-2-1
7	**Lloyd Spooner** , USA (1920)	Shoot	4-1-2
7	Mikhail Voronin, USSR (1968)	Gym	2-4-1
7	Nikolai Andrianov, USSR (1976)	Gym	2-4-1
6	Vitaly Scherbo, UT (1992)	Gym	6-0-0
6	Li Ning, CHN (1984)	Gym	3-2-1
6	Akinori Nakayama, JPN (1968)	Gym	4-1-1
6	Takashi Ono, JPN (1960)	Gym	3-1-2
6	Viktor Chukarin, USSR (1956)	Gym	4-2-0
6	Konrad Frey, GER (1936)	Gym	3-1-2
6	Ville Ritola, FIN (1924)	Track	4-2-0
6	Hubert Van Innis, BEL (1920)	Arch	4-2-0
6	**Carl Osburn** , USA (1920)	Shoot	4-1-1
6	Louis Richardet, SWI (1906)	Shoot	3-3-0
6	**Anton Heida** , USA (1904)	Gym	5-1-0
6	**George Eyser** , USA (1904)	Gym	3-2-1
6	**Burton Downing** , USA (1904)	Cycle	2-3-1
6	Alexei Nemov, RUS (1996)	Gym	2-1-3

WOMEN

No		Sport	G-S-B
7	Maria Gorokhovskaya, USSR (1952)	Gym	2-5-0
6	Kristin Otto, E. Ger (1988)	Swim	6-0-0
6	Agnes Keleti, HUN (1956)	Gym	4-2-0
6	Vera Cáslavská, CZE (1968)	Gym	4-2-0
6	Larisa Latynina, USSR (1956)	Gym	4-1-1
6	Larisa Latynina, USSR (1960)	Gym	3-2-1
6	Daniela Silivas, ROM (1988)	Gym	3-2-1
6	Larisa Latynina, USSR (1964)	Gym	2-2-2
6	Margit Korondi, HUN, (1956)	Gym	1-1-4
5	Kornelia Ender, E. Ger (1976)	Swim	4-1-0
5	Ecaterina Szabó, ROM (1984)	Gym	4-1-0
5	Shane Gould, AUS (1972)	Swim	3-1-1
5	Nadia Comaneci, ROM (1976)	Gym	3-1-1
5	Karin Janz, E. Ger (1972)	Gym	2-2-1
5	Ines Diers, E. Ger (1980)	Swim	2-2-1
5	**Shirley Babashoff**, USA (1976)	Swim	1-4-0
5	**Mary Lou Retton**, USA (1984)	Gym	1-2-2
5	**Shannon Miller**, USA (1992)	Gym	0-2-3

All-Time Leading Medal Winners – Career

All Nations

Most Overall Medals

MEN

No		Sport	G-S-B
15	Nikolai Andrianov, USSR	Gymnastics	7-5-3
13	Boris Shakhlin, USSR	Gymnastics	7-4-2
13	Edoardo Mangiarotti, ITA	Fencing	6-5-2
13	Takashi Ono, JPN	Gymnastics	5-4-4
12	Paavo Nurmi, FIN	Track/Field	9-3-0
12	Sawao Kato, JPN	Gymnastics	8-3-1
11	**Mark Spitz**, USA	Swimming	9-1-1
11*	**Matt Biondi**, USA	Swimming	8-2-1
11	Viktor Chukarin, USSR	Gymnastics	7-3-1
11	**Carl Osburn**, USA	Shooting	5-4-2
10	**Ray Ewry**, USA	Track/Field	10-0-0
10	**Carl Lewis**, USA	Track/Field	9-1-0
10	Aladár Gerevich, HUN	Fencing	7-1-2
10	Akinori Nakayama, JPN	Gymnastics	6-2-2
10	Aleksandr Dityatin, USSR	Gymnastics	3-6-1
9	Vitaly Scherbo, BLR	Gymnastics	6-0-3
9	**Martin Sheridan**, USA	Track/Field	5-3-1
9	Zoltán Halmay, HUN	Swimming	3-5-1
9	Giulio Gaudini, ITA	Fencing	3-4-2
9	Mikhail Voronin, USSR	Gymnastics	2-6-1
9	Heikki Savolainen, FIN	Gymnastics	2-1-6
9	Yuri Titov, USSR	Gymnastics	1-5-3

* Includes gold medal as preliminary member of 1st-place relay team.

Note: Medals won by Ewry (2-0-0), Sheridan (2-3-0) and Halmay (1-1-0) at the 1906 Intercalated games are not officially recognized by the IOC.

Games Participated In

Andrianov (1972,76,80); **Biondi** (1984,88,92); **Chukarin** (1952,56); **Dityatin** (1976,80); **Ewry** (1900,04,06,08); **Gerevich** (1932,36,48,52,56,60); **Gaudini** (1928,32,36); **Halmay** (1900,04,06,08); **Kato** (1968,72,76); **Lewis** (1984,88,92,96); **Mangiarotti** (1936,48,52,56,60); **Nakayama** (1968,72); **Nurmi** (1920,24,28); **Ono** (1952,56,60,64); **Osburn** (1912,20, 24); **Savolainen** (1928,32,36,48,52); **Scherbo**(1992,96): **Shakhlin** (1956,60,64); **Sheridan** (1904,06,08); **Spitz** (1968,72); **Titov** (1956,60,64); **Voronin** (1968,72).

All-Time Leading Medal Winners – Career (Cont.)

WOMEN

No		Sport	G-S-B
18	Larissa Latynina, USSR	Gymnastics	9-5-4
11	Vera Cáslavská, CZE	Gymnastics	7-4-0
10	Agnes Keleti, HUN	Gymnastics	5-3-2
10	Polina Astaknova, USSR	Gymnastics	5-2-3
9	Nadia Comaneci, ROM	Gymnastics	5-3-1
9	Lyudmila Tourischeva, USSR	Gymnastics	4-3-2
8	Kornelia Ender, E. Ger	Swimming	4-4-0
8	Dawn Fraser, AUS	Swimming	4-4-0
8	**Shirley Babashoff**, USA	Swimming	2-6-0
8	Sofia Muratova, USSR	Gymnastics	2-2-4
7	Krisztina Egerszegi, HUN	Swimming	5-1-1
7	Irena Kirszenstein Szewinska, POL	Track/Field	3-2-2
7	Shirley Strickland, AUS	Track/Field	3-1-3
7	Maria Gorokhovskaya, USSR	Gymnastics	2-5-0
7	Ildikó Ságiné-Ujlaki-Rejtö, HUN	Fencing	2-3-2
7	**Shannon Miller**, USA	Gymnastics	2-2-3
7	Merlene Ottey, JAM	Track/Field	0-2-5

Games Participated In

Astaknova (1956,60,64); **Babashoff** (1972,76); **Cáslavská** (1960,64,68); **Comaneci** (1976,80); **Egerszegi** (1988,92,96) **Ender** (1972,76); **Fraser** (1956,60,64); **Gorokhovskaya** (1952); **Keleti** (1952,56); **Latynina** (1956,60,64); **Miller** (1992,96); **Muratova** (1956,60); **Ottey** (1980,84,88,92,96) **Sdágine-Ujlaki-Rejtä** (1960,64,68,72,76); **Strickland** (1948,52,56); **Szewinska** (1964,68,72,76,80); **Tourischeva** (1968, 72,76).

Most Individual Medals

Not including team competition.

	Sport	G-S-B
Men: 12-Nikolai Andrianov, USSR	Gym	6-3-3
Women: 14-Larissa Latynina, USSR	Gym	7-4-3

Most Gold Medals

MEN

No		Sport	G-S-B
10	**Ray Ewry**, USA	Track/Field	10-0-0
9	Paavo Nurmi, FIN	Track/Field	9-3-0
9	**Mark Spitz**, USA	Swimming	9-1-1
9	**Carl Lewis**, USA	Track/Field	9-1-0
8	Sawao Kato, JPN	Gymnastics	8-3-1
8*	**Matt Biondi**, USA	Swimming	8-2-1
7	Nikolai Andrianov, USSR	Gymnastics	7-5-3
7	Boris Shakhlin, USSR	Gymnastics	7-4-2
7	Viktor Chukarin, USSR	Gymnastics	7-3-1
7	Aladar Gerevich, HUN	Fencing	7-1-2

* Includes gold medal as preliminary member of 1st-place relay team.

WOMEN

No		Sport	G-S-B
9	Larissa Latynina, USSR	Gymnastics	9-5-4
7	Vera Cáslavská, CZE	Gymnastics	7-4-0
6	Kristin Otto, E. Ger	Swimming	6-0-0
5	Agnes Keleti, HUN	Gymnastics	5-3-2
5	Nadia Comaneci, ROM	Gymnastics	5-3-1
5	Polina Astaknova, USSR	Gymnastics	5-2-3
5	Krisztina Egerszegi, HUN	Swimming	5-1-1
5	**Jenny Thompson**, USA	Swimming	5-1-0
4	Kornelia Ender, E. Ger	Swimming	4-4-0
4	Dawn Fraser, AUS	Swimming	4-4-0
4	Lyudmila Tourischeva, USSR	Gymnastics	4-3-2
4	**Evelyn Ashford**, USA	Track/Field	4-1-0
4	**Janet Evans**, USA	Swimming	4-1-0
4	Fanny Blankers-Koen, NET	Track/Field	4-0-0
4	Betty Cuthbert, AUS	Track/Field	4-0-0
4	**Pat McCormick**, USA	Diving	4-0-0
4	**Amy Van Dyken**, USA	Swimming	4-0-0
4	Bärbel Eckert Wäckel, E. Ger	Track/Field	4-0-0

Most Silver Medals

MEN

No		Sport	G-S-B
6	Alexandr Dityatin, USSR	Gymnastics	3-6-1
6	Mikhail Voronin, USSR	Gymnastics	2-6-1
5	Nikolai Andrianov, USSR	Gymnastics	7-5-3
5	Edoardo Mangiarotti, ITA	Fencing	6-5-2
5	Zoltán Halmay, HUN	Swimming	3-5-1
5	Gustavo Marzi, ITA	Fencing	2-5-0
5	Yuri Titov, USSR	Gymnastics	1-5-3
5	Viktor Lisitsky, USSR	Gymnastics	0-5-0

WOMEN

No		Sport	G-S-B
6	**Shirley Babashoff**, USA	Swimming	2-6-0
5	Larissa Latynina, USSR	Gymnastics	9-5-4
5	Maria Gorokhovskaya, USSR	Gymnastics	2-5-0
4	Vera Cáslavská, CZE	Gymnastics	7-4-0
4	Kornelia Ender, E. Ger	Swimming	4-4-0
4	Dawn Fraser, AUS	Swimming	4-4-0
4	Erica Zuchold, E. Ger	Gymnastics	0-4-1

Most Bronze Medals

MEN

No		Sport	G-S-B
6	Heikki Savolainen, FIN	Gymnastics	2-1-6
5	Daniel Revenu, FRA	Fencing	1-0-5
5	Philip Edwards, CAN	Track/Field	0-0-5
5	Adrianus Jong, NET	Fencing	0-0-5

WOMEN

No		Sport	G-S-B
5	Merlene Ottey, JAM	Track/Field	0-2-5
4	Larissa Latynina, USSR	Gymnastics	9-5-4
4	Sofia Muratova, USSR	Gymnastics	2-2-4

All-Time Leading USA Medal Winners

Most Overall Medals

MEN

No		Sport	G-S-B
11	Mark Spitz	Swimming	9-1-1
11*	Matt Biondi	Swimming	8-2-1
11	Carl Osburn	Shooting	5-4-2
10	Ray Ewry	Track/Field	10-0-0
10	Carl Lewis	Track/Field	9-1-0
9	Martin Sheridan	Track/Field	5-3-1
8	Charles Daniels	Swimming	5-1-2
7†	Tom Jager	Swimming	5-1-1
7	Willis Lee	Shooting	5-1-1
7	Lloyd Spooner	Shooting	4-1-2
6	Anton Heida	Gymnastics	5-1-0
6	Don Schollander	Swimming	5-1-0
6	Johnny Weissmuller	Swim/Water Polo	5-0-1
6	Alfred Lane	Shooting	5-0-1
6	Jim Lightbody	Track/Field	4-2-0
6	George Eyser	Gymnastics	3-2-1
6	Michael Plumb	Equestrian	2-4-0
6	Burton Downing	Cycling	2-3-1
6	Bob Garrett	Track/Field	2-2-2

*Includes gold medal as prelim. member of 1st-place relay team.

† Includes 3 gold medals as prelim. member of 1st-place relay teams.

Note: Medals won by Ewry (2-0-0) and Sheridan (2-3-0) at the 1906 Intercalated games are not officially recognized by the IOC.

Games Participated In

Biondi (1984,88,92); **Daniels** (1904,06,08); **Downing** (1904); **Ewry** (1900,04,06,08); **Eyser** (1904); **Garrett** (1896,1900); **Heida** (1904); **Jager** (1984,88,92); **Lane** (1912,20); **Lee** (1920); **Lewis** (1984,88,92,96); **Lightbody** (1904,06); **Osburn** (1912,20,24); **Plumb** (1960, 64,68,72,76,84); **Schollander** (1964, 68); **Sheridan** (1904,06,08); **Spitz** (1968,72); **Spooner** (1920); **Weissmuller** (1924,28).

WOMEN

No		Sport	G-S-B
8	Shirley Babashoff	Swimming	2-6-0
7	Shannon Miller	Gymnastics	2-2-3
6	Jenny Thompson	Swimming	5-1-0
6	Jackie Joyner-Kersee	Track/Field	3-1-2
5	Evelyn Ashford	Track/Field	4-1-0
5	Janet Evans	Swimming	4-1-0
5*	Mary T. Meagher	Swimming	3-1-1
5	Florence Griffith Joyner	Track/Field	3-2-0
5	Mary Lou Retton	Gymnastics	1-2-2
4	Pat McCormick	Diving	4-0-0
4	Amy Van Dyken	Swimming	4-0-0
4	Valerie Brisco-Hooks	Track/Field	3-1-0
4	Nancy Hogshead	Swimming	3-1-0
4	Sharon Stouder	Swimming	3-1-0
4	Wyomia Tyus	Track/Field	3-1-0
4	Wilma Rudolph	Track/Field	3-0-1
4	Chris von Saltza	Swimming	3-1-0
4	Sue Pederson	Swimming	2-2-0
4	Jan Henne	Swimming	2-1-1
4	Dorothy Poynton Hill	Diving	2-1-1
4*	Summer Sanders	Swimming	2-1-1
4*	Dara Torres	Swimming	2-1-1
4	Kathy Ellis	Swimming	2-0-2
4	Georgia Coleman	Diving	1-2-1

*Includes silver medal as prelim. member of 2nd-place relay team.

Games Participated In

Ashford (1976,84,88,92); **Babashoff** (1972,76); **Brisco-Hooks** (1984,88); **Coleman** (1928,32); **Ellis** (1964); **Evans** (1988,92); **Griffith Joyner** (1984,88); **Henne** (1968); **Hogshead** (1984); **Joyner-Kersee** (1984,88,92,96); **McCormick** (1952,56); **Meagher** (1984,88); **Miller** (1992, 96); **Pederson** (1968); **Poynton Hill** (1928,32,36); **Retton** (1984); **Rudolph** (1956,60); **Sanders** (1992); **Stouder** (1964); **Thompson** (1988,92,96);**Torres** (1984,88,92); **Tyus** (1964,68); **Van Dyken** (1996); **von Saltza** (1960).

Most Gold Medals

MEN

No		Sport	G-S-B
10	Raymond Ewry	Track/Field	10-0-0
9	Mark Spitz	Swimming	9-1-1
9	Carl Lewis	Track/Field	9-1-0
8*	Matt Biondi	Swimming	8-2-1
5	Carl Osburn	Shooting	5-4-2
5	Martin Sheridan	Track/Field	5-3-1
5	Charles Daniels	Swimming	5-1-2
5†	Tom Jager	Swimming	5-1-1
5	Willis Lee	Shooting	5-1-1
5	Anton Heida	Gymnastics	5-1-0
5	Don Schollander	Swimming	5-1-0
5	Johnny Weissmuller	Swim/Water Polo	5-0-1
5	Alfred Lane	Shooting	5-0-1
5	Morris Fisher	Shooting	5-0-0
4	Jim Lightbody	Track/Field	4-2-0
4	Lloyd Spooner	Shooting	4-1-2
4	Greg Louganis	Diving	4-1-0
4	John Naber	Swimming	4-1-0
4	Meyer Prinstein	Track/Field	4-1-0
4	Mel Sheppard	Track/Field	4-1-0
4	Marcus Hurley	Cycling	4-0-1
4	Harrison Dillard	Track/Field	4-0-0
4	Archie Hahn	Track/Field	4-0-0
4	Alvin Kraenzlein	Track/Field	4-0-0
4	Al Oerter	Track/Field	4-0-0
4	Jesse Owens	Track/Field	4-0-0

*Includes gold medal as prelim. member of 1st-place relay team.
† Includes 3 gold medals as prelim. member of 1st-place relay teams.

WOMEN

No		Sport	G-S-B
5	Jenny Thompson	Swimming	5-1-0
4	Evelyn Ashford	Track/Field	4-1-0
4	Janet Evans	Swimming	4-1-0
4	Pat McCormick	Diving	4-0-0
4	Amy Van Dyken	Swimming	4-0-0
3	Florence Griffith Joyner	Track/Field	3-2-0
3	Jackie Joyner-Kersee	Track/Field	3-1-2
3*	Mary T. Meagher	Swimming	3-1-1
3	Valerie Brisco-Hooks	Track/Field	3-1-0
3	Nancy Hogshead	Swimming	3-1-0
3	Sharon Stouder	Swimming	3-1-0
3	Wyomia Tyus	Track/Field	3-1-0
3	Chris von Saltza	Swimming	3-1-0
3	Wilma Rudolph	Track/Field	3-0-1
3	Melissa Belote	Swimming	3-0-0
3	Ethelda Bleibtrey	Swimming	3-0-0
3	Tracy Caulkins	Swimming	3-0-0
3*	Nicole Haislett	Swimming	3-0-0
3	Helen Madison	Swimming	3-0-0
3	Debbie Meyer	Swimming	3-0-0
3	Sandra Neilson	Swimming	3-0-0
3	Martha Norelius	Swimming	3-0-0
3*	Carrie Steinseifer	Swimming	3-0-0

*Includes gold medal as prelim. member of 1st-place relay team.

Most Silver Medals

MEN

No		Sport	G-S-B
4	Carl Osburn	Shooting	5-4-2
4	Michael Plumb	Equestrian	2-4-0
3	Martin Sheridan	Track/Field	5-3-1
3	Burton Downing	Cycling	2-3-1
3	Irving Baxter	Track/Field	2-3-0
3	Earl Thomson	Equestrian	2-3-0

WOMEN

No		Sport	G-S-B
6	Shirley Babashoff	Swimming	2-6-0

All-Time Medal Standings, 1896-1996

All-time Summer Games medal standings, according to *The Golden Book of the Olympic Games*. Medal counts include the 1906 Intercalated Games which are not recognized by the IOC.

		G	S	B	Total
1	**United States**	832	634	553	2019
2	USSR (1952-88)	395	319	296	1010
3	Great Britain	169	223	218	610
4	France	175	179	206	560
5	Sweden	132	151	174	457
6	Italy	166	135	144	445
	East Germany (1956-88)	159	150	136	445
8	Hungary	142	129	155	426
9	Germany (1896-36,92–)	124	121	134	379
10	West Germany (1952-88)	77	104	120	301
11	Finland	99	80	113	292
	Australia	86	85	121	292
13	Japan	92	8p	97	278
14	Romania	63	77	99	239
15	Poland	50	67	110	227
16	Canada	48	78	90	216
17	Netherlands	49	58	81	188
18	Bulgaria	43	76	63	182
19	Switzerland	46	69	59	174
20	China	52	63	49	164
21	Denmark	38	60	57	155
22	Czechoslovakia (1924-92)	49	49	44	142
23	Belgium	37	49	49	135
24	South Korea	38	42	46	126
25	Norway	45	41	38	124
26	Greece	28	42	43	113
27	Unified Team (1992)	45	38	29	112
28	Cuba	44	33	31	108
29	Yugoslavia (1924-88, 96–)	27	31	32	90
30	Austria	18	31	34	83
31	New Zealand	29	12	29	70
32	Russia	26	24	18	68
33	Spain	22	25	17	64
34	Turkey	30	16	13	59
35	South Africa	19	18	21	58
36	Brazil	12	13	29	54
37	Argentina	13	21	16	50
38	Kenya	14	17	16	47
39	Mexico	9	13	19	41
40	Iran	5	13	18	36
41	Jamaica	5	16	9	30
42	North Korea	8	6	12	26
43	Estonia	7	6	10	23
44	Great Britain/Ireland	6	11	3	20
45	Ireland	8	5	6	19
46	Ethiopia	8	1	7	16
	Egypt	6	5	5	16
48	India	8	3	4	15
	Portugal	3	4	8	15
50	Nigeria	2	5	7	14
	Mongolia	0	5	9	14
52	Czech Republic	4	3	4	11
	Morocco	4	2	5	11
54	Indonesia	3	4	3	10
	Pakistan	3	3	4	10
56	Uruguay	2	1	6	9
	Trinidad & Tobago	1	2	6	9
	Philippines	0	2	7	9
59	Venezuela	1	2	5	8
	Chile	0	6	2	8
61	Algeria	3	0	4	7
	Latvia	0	5	2	7
63	Uganda	1	3	2	6
	Tunisia	1	2	3	6
	Thailand	1	1	4	6
	Colombia	0	2	4	6
	Bohemia	0	1	5	6
	Puerto Rico	0	1	5	6
69	Croatia	1	2	2	5
	Chinese Taipei	0	3	2	5
71	Peru	1	3	0	4
	Bahamas	1	1	2	4
	Lithuania	1	0	3	4
	Namibia	0	4	0	4
	Lebanon	0	2	2	4
	Slovenia	0	2	2	4
	Ghana	0	1	3	4
	Luxenbourg	2	1	0	3
	Slovakia	1	1	1	3
	Israel	0	1	2	3
	Malaysia	0	1	2	3
82	Armenia	1	1	0	2
	Costa Rica	1	1	0	2
	Syria	1	1	0	2
	Japan/Korea	1	0	1	2
	Surinam	1	0	1	2
	Tanzania	0	2	0	2
	Cameroon	0	1	1	2
	Great Britain/USA	0	1	1	2
	Haiti	0	1	1	2
	Iceland	0	1	1	2
	Moldova	0	1	1	2
	Russia/Estonia	0	1	1	2
	United Arab Republic	0	1	1	2
	Uzbekistan	0	1	1	2
	Zambia	0	1	1	2
	The Antilles	0	0	2	2
	Georgia	0	0	2	2
	Panama	0	0	2	2
100	Australia/New Zealand	1	0	0	1
	Burundi	1	0	0	1
	Cuba/USA	1	0	0	1
	Denmark/Sweden	1	0	0	1
	Ecuador	1	0	0	1
	Gr. Britain/Ireland/Germany	1	0	0	1
	Gr. Britain/Ireland/USA	1	0	0	1
	Hong Kong	1	0	0	1
	Ireland/USA	1	0	0	1
	Zimbabwe	1	0	0	1
	Azerbaijan	0	1	0	1
	Belgium/Greece	0	1	0	1
	Ceylon	0	1	0	1
	France/USA	0	1	0	1
	France/Gr. Britain/Ireland	0	1	0	1
	Ivory Coast	0	1	0	1
	Netherlands Antilles	0	1	0	1
	Senegal	0	1	0	1
	Singapore	0	1	0	1
	Smyrna	0	1	0	1
	Tonga	0	1	0	1
	Virgin Islands	0	1	0	1
	Australia/Great Britain	0	0	1	1
	Bermuda	0	0	1	1
	Bohemia/Great Britain	0	0	1	1
	Djibouti	0	0	1	1
	Dominican Republic	0	0	1	1
	France/Great Britain	0	0	1	1
	Guyana	0	0	1	1
	Iraq	0	0	1	1
	Mexico/Spain	0	0	1	1
	Mozambique	0	0	1	1
	Niger	0	0	1	1
	Qatar	0	0	1	1
	Scotland	0	0	1	1
	Thessalonika	0	0	1	1
	Wales	0	0	1	1

Combined totals:	**G**	**S**	**B**	**Total**
USSR/UT/Russia	466	381	343	1190
Germany/E. Ger/W. Ger	360	375	390	1125

International Sports

Italian climbing ace **Marco Pantani** joins the protest with the rest of his fellow bikers on the French concrete before the start of the 12th stage of the Tour de France.

Archive Photos

Drug Pedalers

"The Pirate" took the gold in France, but his victory was overshadowed by drug scandals and protests.

by
Jack Edwards

Cycling's dirty little secret exploded into public view at a border crossing, the day before the 1998 Tour de France began. In his official car, a Team Festina trainer–in violation of French law–had large quantities of masking agents and performance-enhancing drugs, including the banned synthetic blood-doping hormone EPO.

EPO boosts oxygen delivery to muscles but dangerously thickens blood. It has been anecdotally connected to deaths of cyclists who had heart attacks in their sleep. However, because tests can't detect EPO, it is the substance of choice for rule-breakers.

Festina was the best team in the world. It had French rider Richard Virenque, an unprecedented four-time defending King of the Mountains [KOM] as Tour climbing champion. Although Virenque said he never had used banned performance-enhancing substances, the Tour expelled him and his eight teammates. The remaining racers staged a two-hour sit-down strike in sympathy.

Five teams withdrew. Police held the '98 KOM leader Rodolfo Massi for so long that he missed the start of a stage and was disqualified. Journalists digging for stories found medical waste in one team's rubbish. French police pounced on even shaky leads, raiding team hotels. They took one TVM rider out of the shower and led him and his teammates off for questioning.

American Bobby Julich bemoaned France's lack of protection against search and seizure, sympathizing with the detained riders. Julich had been having the ride of his life, in second place for most of the Tour. The last stage in the Alps was supposed to have been his chance to overtake Italy's Marco Pantani, who had climbed from

Jack Edwards is the co-anchor of ESPN's Sunday *SportsDay* and rides up to 110 miles per week in warm-weather months.

AP/Wide World Photos

Amidst all of the scandals, there was actually a race, and a pretty decent one at that. Eventual winner **Marco Pantani** is shown here, flanked by American **Bobby Julich** during the 16th stage.

an eight-minute deficit to lead. But another rider protest stifled Julich's chances, annulling a stage for the first time in Tour history.

Clashes with the law overwhelmed battles for the yellow jersey. Five riders eventually confessed to using EPO, but the majority of European riders suggested they would abandon the Tour if police conducted any more night raids.

That sentiment was not unanimous.

"I believe that the Tour has to continue," Pantani said, "because sport has to win this battle as well. If we don't continue, the sport will lose."

Pantani was raising the bar for cycling. He was trying to become just the fifth man ever to win both the Tour of Italy and the Tour de France in the same year. To do it, he had to stay within 5:55 of time-trial specialist Jan Ullrich in the penultimate stage. Ullrich won the stage, moving past Julich and into second place overall, but he couldn't catch "The Pirate."

The nickname is a sad twist, for robbers who rode dirty and tested clean plundered Pantani's glory. Julich's brilliant third-place finish and Ullrich's second after last year's win cast them as stars who will shine for years to come.

But the drug scandal casts a shadow which blots out that light. Until the sport of cycling–not some police force–punishes the users, innocent athletes will suffer in the darkness of suspicion. ■

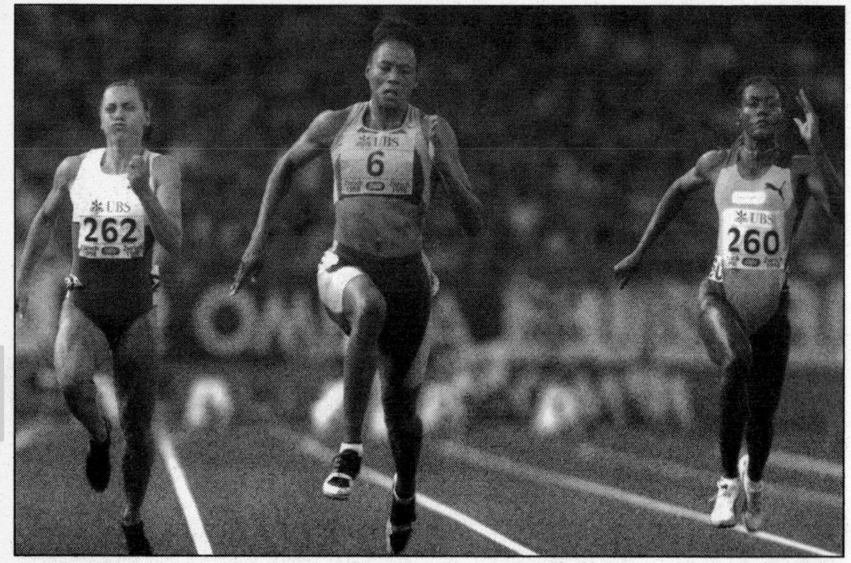

Archive Photos

Former North Carolina basketball star **Marion Jones** (c), the world's top female sprinter and long jumper, was almost perfect in 1997-98, once going undefeated in 37 consecutive events over a 12-month span.

Jack Edwards' Top Ten Newsmakers of the Year in International Sports

10. **Chinese swimmer Yuan Yuan** is caught, just before the world championships in January, carrying enough Human Growth Hormone into Australia to supply 13 patients for a week.
9. **Yuan Yuan claims** she was bringing the HGH "to friends."
8. **A United States swimming coach** says that if Yuan Yuan was bringing it to friends, "I'm Mao Tse-tung."
7. **Maria Mutola** of Mozambique continues to dominate the 800-meter run. She breaks the ten-year-old 800-meter indoor record in February, to go along with the 1000-meter record she already owned.
6. Seventeen-year-old gymnast **Sang Lan** of China falls during warm-ups for the vault at the Goodwill Games and breaks her neck, causing paralysis below the shoulders.
5. At the Goodwill Games, **Jackie Joyner-Kersee** comes from behind to win her final heptathlon, and retires.
4. **Marion Jones emerges** as the successor to Joyner-Kersee as track and field's leading female athlete.
3. **Heather Fuhr** leads a 1-2 Canadian sweep of the women's pro division at the 1997 Hawaii Ironman.
2. **Thomas Hellriegel** leads a 1-2-3 German sweep of the Hawaii Ironman as German men take five of the top eight spots.
1. **Marco Pantani** holds off Jan Ullrich and American Bobby Julich to win the drug-marred Tour de France. ■

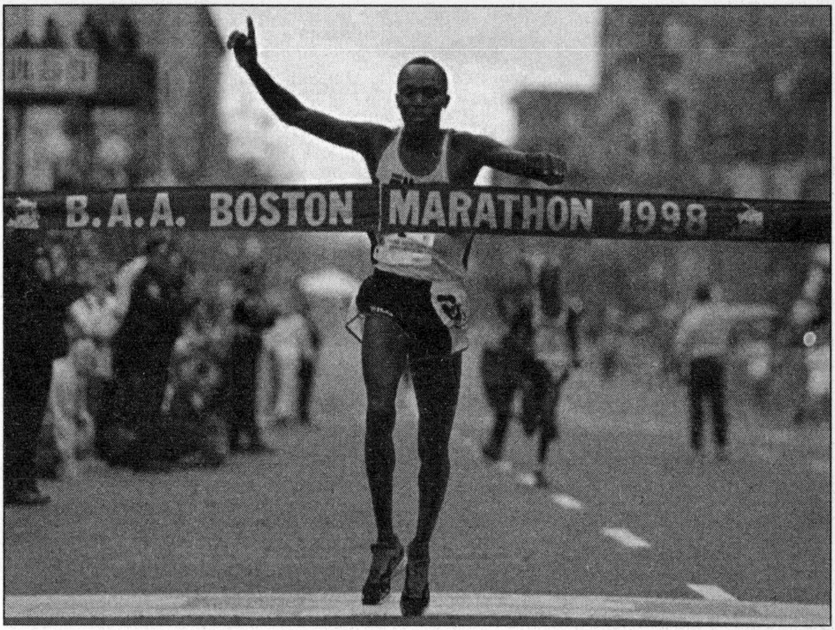

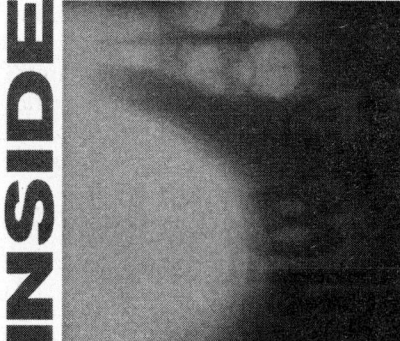

AP/Wide World Photos

Moses Tanui of Kenya breaks the finish line tape on April 20, 1998 for his second Boston Marathon win in the past three years.

by

Team Research

VICTOIRE!

Marco Pantani's 1998 Tour de France win gave Italy nine victories over the Tour's 85-year history. France leads all countries with 36 career wins, although they haven't produced a winner since Bernard Hinault in 1985. The United States has had three victories, all by Greg LeMond ('86, '89 and '90).

	Tour Wins
France	36
Belgium	18
Italy	9
Spain	8
Luxembourg	4
United States	3

Note: The 1946 Tour, the first after World War II, was shortened to a five-day race. It was won by France's Jean Lazarides but is not considered an official Tour win.

JACK(IE) OF ALL TRADES

Jackie Joyner-Kersee, who retired from regular competition in July 1998, was anointed "the world's greatest athlete" by *Track & Field News* and "the greatest multi-event athlete ever,

AP/Wide World Photos

Jackie Joyner-Kersee, quite possibly the greatest female athlete the world has ever seen, makes her final throw in the heptathlon javelin at the Goodwill Games on July 22, 1998. It is her last heptathlon before retirement, and as usual...she won.

man or woman" by former decathlon champ Bruce Jenner. If you disagree, take a look at just a partial list of her accomplishments below. She's also found the time to become a registered NFL agent, a chief executive of a sports marketing firm, and the head of her own community center in St. Louis.

Olympic Medals:	6 (3G, 1S, 2B)
World Record:	Heptathlon (7291 pts)
American Records:	Long Jump-outdoors (24-7)
	Long Jump-indoors (23-4¾)
	Indoor 50-m hurdles (6.67)
	Indoor 60-m hurdles (7.81)

Three-time NCAA heptathlon champion
Broderick Cup winner (1985)
UCLA basketball-four-year starter
ABL's Richmond Rage - played 17 games

BOSTON...BY THE NUMBERS

With close to one million spectators and 1,200 media representatives, the Boston Marathon is the second-largest single-day sporting event in the world, behind only the Super Bowl. Here are some behind the scenes stats from the 1998 edition.

Registered runners	11,425
Volunteers	7,000
Gallons of spring water	34,750
Paper cups used	1 million
Port-o-johns	600
Safety pins	48,000
Aspirin tablets	25,000
Blankets	1,500

Sources: *Boston Globe,* BAA, AP, John Hancock Financial Services ■

TRACK & FIELD

World, Olympic and American Records

As of Sept. 21, 1998

World outdoor records officially recognized by the International Amateur Athletics Federation (IAAF); (p) indicates record is pending ratification by the IAAF.

MEN

Running

Event		Time		Date Set	Location
100 meters:	**World**	9.84	**Donovan Bailey**, Canada	July 27, 1996	Atlanta
	Olympic	9.84	Bailey (same as World)	—	—
	American	9.85	Leroy Burrell	July 6, 1994	Lausanne, SWI
200 meters:	**World**	19.32	**Michael Johnson**, USA	Aug. 1, 1996	Atlanta
	Olympic	19.32	Johnson (same as World)	—	—
	American	19.32	Johnson (same as World)	—	—
400 meters:	**World**	43.29	**Butch Reynolds,** USA	Aug. 17, 1988	Zurich
	Olympic	43.49	Michael Johnson, USA	July 29, 1996	Atlanta
	American	43.29	Reynolds (same as World)	—	—
800 meters:	**World**	1:41.11	**Wilson Kipketer**, Denmark	Aug. 24, 1997	Cologne
	Olympic	1:42.58	Vebjoern Rodal, Norway	July 31, 1996	Atlanta
	American	1:42.60	Johnny Gray	Aug. 28, 1985	Koblenz, W. Ger.
1000 meters:	**World**	2:12.18	**Sebastian Coe,** Great Britain	July 11, 1981	Oslo
	Olympic		Not an event	—	—
	American	2:13.9	Rick Wohlhuter	July 30, 1974	Oslo
1500 meters:	**World**	3:26.00	**Hicham El Guerrouj,** Morocco	July 14, 1998	Rome
	Olympic	3:32.53	Sebastian Coe, Great Britain	Aug. 11, 1984	Los Angeles
	American	3:29.77	Sydney Maree	Aug. 25, 1985	Cologne
Mile:	**World**	3:44.39	**Noureddine Morceli,** Algeria	Sept. 5, 1993	Rieti, ITA
	Olympic		Not an event	—	—
	American	3:47.69	Steve Scott	July 7, 1982	Oslo
2000 meters:	**World**	4:47.88	**Noureddine Morceli,** Algeria	July 3, 1995	Paris
	Olympic		Not an event	—	—
	American	4:52.44	Jim Spivey	Sept. 15, 1987	Lausanne, SWI
3000 meters:	**World**	7:20.67	**Daniel Komen**, Kenya	Sept. 1, 1996	Riete, ITA
	Olympic		Not an event	–	–
	American	7:30.84p	Bob Kennedy	Aug. 8, 1998	Monte Carlo
5000 meters:	**World**	12:39.36	**Haile Gebrselassie**, Ethiopia	June 13, 1998	Helsinki
	Olympic	13:05.59	Said Aouita, Morocco	Aug. 11, 1984	Los Angeles
	American	12:58.21	Bob Kennedy	Aug. 14, 1996	Zurich
10,000 meters:	**World**	26:22.75	**Haile Gebrselassie**, Ethiopia	June 1, 1998	Hengelo, HOL
	Olympic	27:07.34	Haile Gebrselassie, Ethiopia	July 29, 1996	Atlanta
	American	27:20.56	Mark Nenow	Sept. 5, 1986	Brussels
20,000 meters:	**World**	56:55.6	**Arturo Barrios,** Mexico	Mar. 30, 1991	La Fleche, FRA
	Olympic		Not an event	—	–
	American	58:15.0	Bill Rodgers	Aug. 9, 1977	Boston
Marathon:	**World**	2:06:05	**Ronaldo da Costa,** Brazil	Sept. 20, 1998	Berlin
	Olympic	2:09:21	Carlos Lopes, Portugal	Aug. 12, 1984	Los Angeles
	American	2:09:35	Jerry Lawson	Oct. 19, 1997	Chicago
		2:08:52*	Alberto Salazar	Apr. 19, 1982	Boston

Note: The Mile run is 1,609.344 meters and the Marathon is 42,194.988 meters (26 miles, 385 yards).
*Former American record no longer officially recognized.

Walking

Event		Time		Date Set	Location
20 km:	**World**	1:17:25.6	**Bernardo Segura,** Mexico	May 7, 1994	Fana, NOR
	Olympic	1:19:57	Jozef Pribilinec, Czechoslovakia	Sept. 23, 1988	Seoul
	American	1:24:26.9	Allen James	May 7, 1994	Fana, NOR
50 km:	**World**	3:40:57.9	**Thierry Toutain**, France	Sept. 29, 1996	Hericourt, FRA
	Olympic	3:38:29	Vyacheslav Ivanenko, USSR	Sept. 30, 1988	Seoul
	American	3:59:41.2	Herm Nelson	June 9, 1996	Seattle

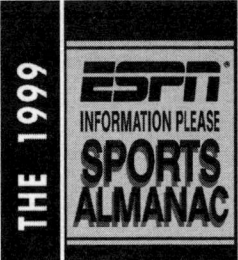

Hurdles

Event		Time		Date Set	Location
110 meters:	**World**	12.91	**Colin Jackson,** Great Britain	Aug. 20, 1993	Stuttgart
	Olympic	12.95	Allen Johnson, USA	July 29, 1996	Atlanta
	American	12.92	Roger Kingdom	Aug. 16, 1989	Zurich
		12.92	Allen Johnson	June 23, 1996	Atlanta
400 meters:	**World**	46.78	**Kevin Young,** USA	Aug. 6, 1992	Barcelona
	Olympic	46.78	Young (same as World)	–	–
	American	46.78	Young (same as World)	–	–

Note: The hurdles at 110 meters are 3 feet, 6 inches high and the hurdles at 400 meters are 3 feet. There are 10 hurdles in both races.

Steeplechase

Event		Time		Date Set	Location
3000 meters:	**World**	7:55.72	**Bernard Barmasai**, Kenya	Aug. 24, 1997	Cologne
	Olympic	8:05.51	Julius Kariuki, Kenya	Sept. 30, 1988	Seoul
	American	8:09.17	Henry Marsh	Aug. 28, 1985	Koblenz

Note: A steeplechase course consists of 28 hurdles (3 feet high) and seven water jumps (12 feet long).

Relays

Event		Time		Date Set	Location
4 x 100m:	**World**	37.40	**USA** (Marsh, Burrell, Mitchell, C. Lewis)	Aug. 8, 1992	Barcelona
		37.40	**USA** (Drummond, Cason, Mitchell, Burrell)	Aug. 21, 1993	Stuttgart
	Olympic	37.40	USA (same as World)	–	–
	American	37.40	USA (same as World)	–	–
4 x 200m:	**World**	1:18.68	**USA** (Marsh, Burrell, Heard, C. Lewis)	Apr. 17, 1994	Walnut, Calif.
	Olympic		Not an event	–	–
	American	1:18.68	USA (same as World)	–	–
4 x 400m:	**World**	2:54.20p	**USA** (Young, Pettigrew, Washington, Johnson)	July 22, 1998	Uniondale, NY
	Olympic	2:55.74	USA (Valmon, Watts, Johnson, S. Lewis)	Aug. 8, 1992	Barcelona
	American	2:54.20p	USA (same as World)	–	–
4 x 800m:	**World**	7:03.89	**Great Britain** (Elliott, Cook, Cram, Coe)	Aug. 30, 1982	London
	Olympic		Not an event	–	–
	American	7:06.5	SMTC (J. Robinson, Mack, E. Jones, Gray)	Apr. 26, 1986	Walnut, Calif.
4 x 1500m:	**World**	14:38.8	**West Germany** (Wessinghage, Hudak, Lederer, Fleschen)	Aug. 17, 1977	Cologne
	Olympic		Not an event	–	–
	American	14:46.3	USA (Aldredge, Clifford, Harbour, Duits)	June 24, 1979	Bourges, FRA

Field Events

Event		Mark		Date Set	Location
High Jump:	**World**	8-0½	**Javier Sotomayor,** Cuba	July 27, 1993	Salamanca, SPA
	Olympic	7-10	Charles Austin, USA	July 28, 1996	Atlanta
	American	7-10½	Charles Austin	Aug. 7, 1991	Zurich
Pole Vault:	**World**	20-1¾	**Sergey Bubka,** Ukraine	July 31, 1994	Sestriere, ITA
	Olympic	19-5¼	Jean Galfione, France	Aug. 2, 1996	Atlanta
		19-5¼	Igor Trandenkov, Russia	Aug. 2, 1996	Atlanta
		19-5¼	Andrei Tiwontschik, Germany	Aug. 2, 1996	Atlanta

World Outdoor Records Set in 1998

World outdoor records set or equaled between Oct. 1, 1997 and Sept. 21, 1998; (p) indicates record is pending ratification by the IAAF.

MEN

Event	Name	Record	Old Mark	Former Holder
1500 meters	**Hicham El Guerrouj**, MOR	3:26.00	3:27.37	Noureddine Morceli, ALB (1995)
5000 meters	**Haile Gebrselassie**, ETH	12:39.36	12:39.74	Daniel Komen, KEN (1997)
10,000 meters	**Haile Gebrselassie**, ETH	26:22.75	26:27.85	Paul Tergat, KEN (1997)
Marathon†	**Ronaldo da Costa**, BRA	2:06:05	2:06:50	Belayneh Densimo, ETH (1988)
4 x 400m relay	**Young, Pettigrew, Washington, Johnson**, USA	2:54.20p	2:54.29	Valmon, Watts, Reynolds, Johnson, USA (1993)

WOMEN

	Name	Record	Old Mark	Former Holder
5000 meters	**Jiang Bo**, CHN	14:28.09p	14:31.27	Dong Yanmei, CHN (1997)
1 Hour	**Tegla Loroupe**, KEN	18,340 meters(p)	18,084 meters	Silvana Cruciata, ITA (1981)
Marathon†	**Tegla Loroupe**, KEN	2:20:47	2:21:06	Ingrid Kristiansen, NOR (1985)
Pole Vault	**Emma George**, AUS	15-0	14-11	Emma George, AUS (1996)
Pole Vault	**Emma George**, AUS	15-0¼	15-0	Emma George, AUS (1996)
Pole Vault	**Emma George**, AUS	15-0¾p	15-0¼	Emma George, AUS (1996)
Hammer Throw	**Mihaela Melinte**, ROM	239-11*	239-10	Olga Kuzenkova, RUS (1997)

†The IAAF does not officially recognize world records for road races.

*Kuzenkova had set the mark at 242-1 earlier in the year but becuase no drug test was performed, the record was not ratified by the IAAF.

Event	Mark		Date Set	Location
	American 19-8½	Jeff Hartwig	July 21, 1998	Uniondale, NY
Long Jump:	**World** 29-4¾*	**Ivan Pedroso,** Cuba	July 29, 1995	Sestriere, ITA
	...............29-4½	**Mike Powell,** USA	Aug. 30, 1991	Tokyo
	Olympic 29-2½	Bob Beamon, USA	Oct. 18, 1968	Mexico City
	American 29-4½	Powell (same as World)	–	–
Triple Jump:	**World** 60- 0¼	**Jonathan Edwards,** GBR	Aug. 7, 1995	Göteborg
	Olympic 59-4¼	Kenny Harrison, USA	July 27, 1996	Atlanta
	American 59-4¼	Kenny Harrison (same as Olympic)	–	–
Shot Put:	**World** 75-10¼	**Randy Barnes,** USA	May 20, 1990	Los Angeles
	Olympic......73- 8¾	Ulf Timmermann, East Germany	Sept. 23, 1988	Seoul
	American 75-10¼	Barnes (same as World)	–	–
Discus:	**World** 243- 0	**Jurgen Schult**, East Germany	June 6, 1986	Neubrandenburg
	Olympic 227- 8	Lare Reidel, Germany	July 31, 1996	Atlanta
	American 237-4	Ben Plucknett	July 7, 1981	Stockholm
Javelin:	**World** 323- 1	**Jan Zelezny**, Czech Republic	May 25, 1996	Jena, GER
	Olympic 294-2	Jan Zelezny, Czechoslovakia	Aug. 8, 1992	Barcelona
	American 285-10	Tom Pukstys	May 25, 1997	Jena, GER
Hammer:	**World** 284- 7	**Yuriy Sedykh**, USSR	Aug. 30, 1986	Stuttgart
	Olympic 278- 2	Sergey Litvinov, USSR	Sept. 26, 1988	Seoul
	American 270- 9	Lance Deal	Sept. 7, 1996	Milan

Note: The international weights for men— **Shot** (16 lbs); **Discus** (4 lbs/6.55 oz); **Javelin** (minimum 1 lb/124¼ oz.); **Hammer** (16 lbs).
*Apparent world record disallowed because of interference with wind gauge at altitude.

Decathlon

	Points		Date Set	Location
Ten Events:	**World** 8891	**Dan O'Brien,** USA	Sept. 4-5, 1992	Talence, FRA
	Olympic 8847	Daley Thompson, Great Britain	Aug. 8-9, 1984	Los Angeles
	American 8891	O'Brien (same as World)	–	–

Note: O'Brien's WR times and distances, in order over two days— **100m** (10.43); **LJ** (26- 6¼); **Shot** (54- 9¼); **HJ** (6- 9½); **400m** (48.51); **110m H** (13.98); **Discus** (159- 4); **PV** (16- 4¾); **Jav** (205-4); **1500m** (4:42.10).

WOMEN
Running

Event	Time		Date Set	Location
100 meters:	**World** 10.49	**Florence Griffith Joyner,** USA	July 16, 1988	Indianapolis
	Olympic.......10.62	Florence Griffith Joyner, USA	Sept. 24, 1988	Seoul
	American......10.49	Griffith Joyner (same as World)	–	–
200 meters:	**World** 21.34	**Florence Griffith Joyner,** USA	Sept. 29, 1988	Seoul
	Olympic.......21.34	Griffith Joyner (same as World)	–	–
	American......21.34	Griffith Joyner (same as World)	–	–
400 meters:	**World** 47.60	**Marita Koch,** East Germany	Oct. 6, 1985	Canberra, AUS
	Olympic 48.65	Olga Bryzgina, USSR	Sept. 26, 1988	Seoul
	American......48.83	Valerie Brisco	Aug. 6, 1984	Los Angeles
800 meters:	**World** 1:53.28	**Jarmila Kratochvilova,** Czech.	July 26, 1983	Munich
	Olympic 1:53.42	Nadezhda Olizarenko, USSR	July 27, 1980	Moscow
	American ...1:56.43p	Jearl Miles-Clark	Aug. 12, 1998	Zurich
1000 meters:	**World** 2:28.98	**Svetlana Masterkova**, Russia	Aug. 23, 1996	Brussels
	Olympic	Not an event	–	–
	American 2:33.93	Suzy Hamilton	June 4, 1995	Eugene, Ore.
1500 meters:	**World** 3:50.46	**Qu Yunxia,** China	Sept. 11, 1993	Beijing
	Olympic 3:53.96	Paula Ivan, Romania	Oct. 1, 1988	Seoul
	American 3:57.12	Mary Slaney	July 26, 1983	Stockholm
Mile:	**World** 4:12.56	**Svetlana Masterkova**, Russia	Aug. 14, 1996	Zurich
	Olympic	Not an event	–	–
	American 4:16.71	Mary Slaney	Aug. 21, 1985	Zurich
2000 meters:	**World** 5:25.36	**Sonia O'Sullivan,** Ireland	July 8, 1994	Edinburgh
	Olympic............	Not an event	–	–
	American 5:32.7	Mary Slaney	Aug. 3, 1984	Eugene
3000 meters:	**World** 8:06.11	**Wang Junxia**, China	Sept. 13, 1993	Beijing
	Olympic 8:26.53	Tatyana Samolenko, USSR	Sept. 25, 1988	Seoul
	American 8:25.83	Mary Slaney	Sept. 7, 1985	Rome
5000 meters:	**World**....14:28.09p	**Jiang Bo,** China	Oct. 23, 1997	Shanghai
	Olympic	Not an event	–	–
	American ...14:52.49	Regina Jacobs	July 4, 1998	Brunswick, ME
10,000 meters:	**World** 29:31.78	**Wang Junxia,** China	Sept. 8, 1993	Beijing
	Olympic....31:05.21	Olga Bondarenko, USSR	Sept. 30, 1988	Seoul
	American...31:19.89	Lynn Jennings	Aug. 7, 1992	Barcelona
Marathon:	**World** 2:20:47	**Tegla Loroupe**, Kenya	Apr. 19, 1998	Rotterdam
	Olympic 2:24:52	Joan Benoit, USA	Aug. 5, 1984	Los Angeles
	American 2:21:21	Joan Benoit Samuelson	Oct. 20, 1985	Chicago

Note: The Mile run is 1,609.344 meters and the Marathon is 42,194.988 meters (26 miles, 385 yards).

Relays

Event	Time		Date Set	Location
4 x 100m:	**World**........41.37	**East Germany** (Gladisch, Rieger, Auerswald, Gohr);	Oct. 6, 1985	Canberra, AUS
	Olympic.......41.60	East Germany (Muller, Wockel, Auerswald, Gohr)	Aug. 1, 1980	Moscow
	American......41.47	USA (Gaines, Jones, Miller, Devers)	Aug. 9, 1997	Athens
4 x 200m:	**World**......1:28.15	**East Germany** (Gohr, Muller, Wockel, Koch)	Aug. 9, 1980	Jena, E. Ger.
	Olympic.............	Not an event	—	—
	American....1:29.64	Nike International (Roberts, Miller, Green, Jones)	Apr. 25, 1998	Philadelphia
4 x 400m:	**World**......3:15.17	**USSR** (Ledovskaya, Nazarova, Pinigina, Bryzgina)	Oct. 1, 1988	Seoul
	Olympic.....3:15.17	USSR (same as World)	—	—
	American....3:15.51	USA (Howard, Dixon, Brisco, Griffith Joyner)	Oct. 1, 1988	Seoul
4 x 800m:	**World**......7:50.17	**USSR** (Olizarenko, Gurina, Borisova, Podyalovskaya)	Aug. 5, 1984	Moscow
	Olympic.............	Not an event	—	—
	American....8:17.09	Athletics West (Addison, Arbogast, Decker Slaney, Mullen)	Apr. 24, 1983	Walnut, CA

Hurdles

Event	Time		Date Set	Location
100 meters:	**World**........12.21	**Yordanka Donkova,** Bulgaria	Aug. 20, 1988	Stara Zagora, BUL
	Olympic.......12.38	Yordanka Donkova, Bulgaria	Sept. 30, 1988	Seoul
	American......12.46	Gail Devers	Aug. 20, 1993	Stuttgart
400 meters:	**World**........52.61	**Kim Batten,** USA	Aug. 11, 1995	Göteborg
	Olympic.......53.17	Debra Flintoff-King, Australia	Sept. 28, 1988	Seoul
	American......52.61	Batten (same as World)	—	—

Note: The hurdles at 110 meters are 3 feet, 6 inches high and the hurdles at 400 meters are 3 feet. There are 10 hurdles in both races.

Walking

Event	Time		Date Set	Location
5 km:	**World**.....20:13.26	**Kerry Saxby-Junna**, Australia	Feb. 25, 1996	Hobart, AUS
	Olympic	Not an event	—	—
	American...21:28.17	Teresa Vaill	Apr. 24, 1993	Philadelphia
10 km:	**World**........41:04	**Yelena Nikolayeva,** Russia	Apr. 20, 1996	Sochi, RUS
	Olympic.......41.49	Yelena Nikolayeva, Russia	July 29, 1996	Atlanta
	American......44:17	Michelle Rohl	Aug. 7, 1995	Göteborg

Field Events

Event	Mark		Date Set	Location
High Jump:	**World** 6-10¼	**Stefka Kostadinova**, Bulgaria	Aug. 30, 1987	Rome
	Olympic.........6- 8	Louise Ritter, USA	Sept. 30, 1988	Seoul
	American........6- 8	Louise Ritter	July 8, 1988	Austin
	................6- 8	Ritter (see Olympic)	—	—
Pole Vault:	**World** 15-0¾p	**Emma George**, Australia	March 21, 1998	Brisbane, AUS
	Olympic	Not an event	—	—
	American 14-7¼	Stacy Dragila	May 10, 1997	Modesto, CA
Long Jump:	**World**.......24- 8¼	**Galina Chistyakova,** USSR	June 11, 1988	Leningrad
	Olympic......24- 3¼	Jackie Joyner-Kersee, USA	Sept. 29, 1988	Seoul
	American.......24- 7	Jackie Joyner-Kersee	May 22, 1994	New York
Triple Jump:	**World**.....50-10¼p	**Inessa Kravets,** Ukraine	Aug. 8, 1995	Göteborg
	Olympic 50-3½	Inessa Kravets, Ukraine	July 31, 1998	Atlanta
	American 47-3½	Sheila Hudson	July 8, 1996	Stockholm
Shot Put:	**World**.........74- 3	**Natalya Lisovskaya,** USSR	June 7, 1987	Moscow
	Olympic......73- 6¼	Ilona Slupianek, E. Germany	July 24, 1980	Moscow
	American.....66- 2½	Ramona Pagel	June 25, 1988	San Diego
Discus:	**World** 252- 0	**Gabriele Reinsch,** E. Germany	July 9, 1988	Neubrandenburg
	Olympic 237- 2½	Martina Hellmann, E. Germany	Sept. 29, 1988	Seoul
	American 216- 10	Carol Cady	May 31, 1986	San Jose
Javelin:	**World** 262- 5	**Petra Felke**, E. Germany	Sept. 9, 1988	Potsdam, E. Ger.
	Olympic 245- 0	Petra Felke, E. Germany	Sept. 26, 1988	Seoul
	American 227- 5	Kate Schmidt	Sept. 10, 1977	Furth, W. Ger.
Hammer:	**World**.......239-11	**Mihaela Melinte**, Romania	July 16, 1998	Poiana Brasov
	Olympic	Not an event	—	—
	American 220-1	Amy Palmer	Apr. 3, 1998	Austin, TX

Note: The international weights for women— **Shot** (8 lbs/13 oz); **Discus** (2 lbs/3.27 oz); **Javelin** (minimum 1 lb/5.16 oz); **Hammer** (16 lbs).

Heptathlon

	Points		Date Set	Location
Seven Events:	**World** 7291	**Jackie Joyner-Kersee,** USA	Sept. 23-24, 1988	Seoul
	Olympic 7291	Joyner-Kersee (same as World)	—	—
	American 7291	Joyner-Kersee (same as World)	—	—

Note: Joyner-Kersee's WR times and distances, in order over two days— **100m H** (12.69); **HJ** (61¼); **Shot** (51-10); **200m** (22.56); **LJ** (2310¼); **Jav** (149-10); **800m** (2:08.51).

World Indoor Records Set in 1998

World indoor records set or equaled between Oct. 1, 1997 and Sept. 1, 1998.

MEN

Event		Record	Old Mark	Former Holder
60 meters	**Maurice Greene**, USA	6.41*	6.41	Andre Cason, USA (1992)
60 meters	**Maurice Greene**, USA	6.39	6.41	Cason/Greene, USA (1992 & 98)
3000 meters	**Haile Gebrselassie**, ETH	7:26.14p	7:30.72	Haile Gebrselassie, ETH (1996)
3000 meters	**Daniel Komen**, KEN	7:24.90p	7:26.14	Haile Gebrselassie, ETH (1998)
5000 meters	**Daniel Komen**, KEN	12:51.48p	12:59.04	Haile Gebrselassie, ETH (1997)

* Greene tied the mark set by Andre Cason in 1992.

WOMEN

Event		Record	Old Mark	Former Holder
800 meters	**Maria Mutola**, MOZ	1:56.36	1:56.40	Christine Wachtel, EG (1988)
Triple Jump	**Ashia Hansen**, GBR	49-9	49-3¾	Yoland Chen, RUS (1995)
Pole Vault	**Daniela Bartova**, CZE	14-5½	14-5¼	Emma George, AUS (1996) & Stacy Dragila, USA (1997)
Pole Vault	**Vala Flosadottir**, ICE	14-6	14-5½	Daniela Bartova, CZE (1998)
Pole Vault	**Daniela Bartova**, CZE	14-6¼	14-6	Vala Flosadottir, ICE (1998)
Pole Vault	**Vala Flosadottir**, ICE	14-6¾	14-6¼	Daniela Bartova, CZE (1998)
Pole Vault	**Anzhela Balakhonova**, UKR	14-7¼	14-6¾	Vala Flosadottir, ICE (1998)
Pole Vault	**Emma George**, AUS	14-8	14-7¼	Anzhela Balakhonova, UKR (1998)
Pole Vault	**Stacy Dragila**, USA	14-8¼	14-8	Emma George, AUS (1998)
Pole Vault	**Daniela Bartova**, CZE	14-8¼	14-8¼	Stacy Dragila, USA (1998)
Pole Vault	**Emma George**, AUS	14-9¼	14-8¼	Dragila/Bartova (1998)
Pole Vault	**Emma George**, AUS	14-11p	14-9¼	Emma George (1998)

World and American Indoor Records

As of Sept. 1, 1998

World indoor records officially recognized by the International Amateur Athletics Federation (IAAF); (p) indicates record is pending ratification by the IAAF; (a) indicates record was set at an altitude over 1000 meters.

MEN

Running

Event	Time		Date Set	Location
50 meters:	**World**........5.56a	**Donovan Bailey,** Canada	Feb. 9, 1996	Reno, NV
	American 5.61	James Sanford, USA	Feb. 20, 1981	San Diego
60 meters:	**World**.........6.39	**Maurice Greene,** USA	Feb. 3, 1998	Madrid
	American 6.39	Greene (same as World)	–	–
200 meters:	**World**........19.92	**Frankie Fredericks,** Namibia	Feb. 18, 1996	Lievin, FRA
	American 20.40	Jeff Williams	Feb. 18, 1996	Lievin, FRA
		& Kevin Little	Mar. 8, 1997	Paris
400 meters:	**World**........44.63	**Michael Johnson,** USA	Mar. 4, 1995	Atlanta
	American 44.63	Johnson (same as World)	—	—
800 meters:	**World**......1:42.67	**Wilson Kipketer,** Kenya	Mar. 9, 1997	Paris
	American 1:45.00	Johnny Gray	Mar. 8, 1992	Sindelfingen, GER
1000 meters:	**World**......2:15.26	**Noureddine Morceli,** Algeria	Feb. 22, 1992	Birmingham, ENG
	American 2:18.19	Ocky Clark	Feb. 12, 1989	Stuttgart
1500 meters:	**World**......3:31.17	**Hicham El Guerrouj**, Morocco	Feb. 2, 1997	Stuttgart
	American 3:38.12	Jeff Atkinson	Mar. 5, 1989	Budapest
Mile:	**World**......3:48.45	**Hicham El Guerrouj**, Morocco	Feb. 12, 1997	Ghent, BEL
	American 3:51.8	Steve Scott	Feb. 20, 1981	San Diego
3000 meters:	World......7:24.90p	**Daniel Komen,** Kenya	Feb. 6, 1998	Budapest
	American 7:39.94	Steve Scott	Feb. 10, 1989	E. Rutherford, N.J.
5000 meters:	**World**....12:51.48p	**Daniel Komen,** Kenya	Feb. 19, 1998	Stockholm
	American...13:20.55	Doug Padilla	Feb. 12, 1982	New York

Note: The Mile run is 1,609.344 meters.

Hurdles

Event		Time		Date Set	Location
50 meters:	**World**	6.25	**Mark McKoy,** Canada	Mar. 5, 1986	Kobe, JPN
	American	6.35	Greg Foster	Jan. 27, 1985	Rosemont, Ill.
		6.35	Greg Foster	Jan. 31, 1987	Ottawa
60 meters:	**World**	7.30	**Colin Jackson**, Britain	Mar. 6, 1994	Sindelfingen, GER
	American	7.36	Greg Foster	Jan. 16, 1987	Los Angeles

Note: The hurdles for both distances are 3 feet, 6 inches high. There are four hurdles in the 50 meters and five in the 60.

Relays

Event		Time		Date Set	Location
4x200 meters:	**World**	1:22.11	**Great Britain**	Mar. 3, 1991	Glasgow
	American	1:22.71	National Team	Mar. 3, 1991	Glasgow
4x400 meters:	**World**	3:03.05	**Germany**	Mar. 10, 1991	Seville
	American	3:03.24	National Team	Mar. 10, 1991	Seville

Field Events

Events		Time		Date Set	Location
High Jump:	**World**	7-11½	**Javier Sotomayor,** Cuba	Mar. 4, 1989	Budapest
	American	7-10½	Hollis Conway	Mar. 10, 1991	Seville
Pole Vault:	**World**	20-2	**Sergey Bubka,** Ukraine	Feb. 21, 1993	Donyetsk, UKR
	American	19- 3¾	Billy Olson	Jan. 25, 1986	Albuquerque
Long Jump:	**World**	28- 10¼	**Carl Lewis,** USA	Jan. 27, 1984	New York
	American	28- 10¼	Lewis (same as World)	—	—
Triple Jump:	**World**	58-6	**Aliecer Urrutia,** Cuba	Mar. 1, 1997	Sindelfingen, GER
	American	58-3¼	Mike Conley	Feb. 27, 1987	New York
Shot Put:	**World**	74-4¼	**Randy Barnes**, USA	Jan. 20, 1989	Los Angeles
	American	74-4¼	Barnes (same as World)	—	—

Note: The international shot put weight for men is 16 lbs.

Heptathlon

		Points		Date Set	Location
Seven Events:	**World**	6476	**Dan O'Brien,** USA	Mar. 13-14, 1993	Toronto
	American	6476	O'Brien (same as World)	—	—

Note: O'Brien's WR times and distances, in order over two days— **60m** (6.67); **LJ** (25-8¾); **SP** (52-6¾); **HJ** (6-11¾); **60m H** (7.85); **PV** (17-0¾); **1000m** (2:57.96).

WOMEN

Running

Event		Time		Date Set	Location
50 meters:	**World**	5.96	**Irina Privalova,** Russia	Feb. 9, 1995	Madrid
	American	6.07a	Gwen Torrence	Feb. 9, 1996	Reno, NV
60 meters:	**World**	6.92	**Irina Privalova,** Russia	Feb. 11, 1993	Madrid
		6.92	**Irina Privalova,** Russia	Feb. 9, 1995	Madrid
	American	6.95	Gail Devers	Mar. 12, 1993	Toronto
		6.95p	Marion Jones	Mar. 7, 1998	Maebashi, JPN
200 meters:	**World**	21.87	**Merlene Ottey,** Jamaica	Feb. 13, 1993	Lievin, FRA
	American	22.33	Gwen Torrence	Mar. 2, 1996	Atlanta
400 meters:	**World**	49.59	**Jarmila Kratochvilova,** Czech.	Mar. 7, 1982	Milan
	American	50.64	Diane Dixon	Mar. 10, 1991	Seville
800 meters:	**World**	1:56.36	**Maria Mutola,** Mozambique	Feb. 22, 1998	Lievin, FRA
	American	1:58.9	Mary Slaney	Feb. 22, 1980	San Diego
1000 meters:	**World**	2:31.23	**Maria Mutola,** Mozambique	Feb. 25, 1996	Stockholm
	American	2:37.6	Mary Slaney	Jan. 21, 1989	Portland
1500 meters:	**World**	4:00.27	**Doina Melinte,** Romania	Feb. 9, 1990	E. Rutherford, N.J.
	American	4:00.8	Mary Slaney	Feb. 8, 1980	New York
Mile:	**World**	4:17.13	**Doina Melinte,** Romania	Feb. 9, 1990	E. Rutherford, N.J.
	American	4:20.5	Mary Slaney	Feb. 19, 1982	San Diego
3000 meters:	**World**	8:33.82	**Elly van Hulst,** Holland	Mar. 4, 1989	Budapest
	American	8:40.45	Lynn Jennings	Feb. 23, 1990	New York
5000 meters:	**World**	15:03.17	**Liz McGolgan,** Great Britain	Feb. 22, 1992	Birmingham, ENG
	American	15:22.64	Lynn Jennings	Jan. 7, 1990	Hanover, N.H.

Note: The Mile run is 1,609.344 meters.

Hurdles

Event		Time		Date Set	Location
50 meters:	**World**	6.58	**Cornelia Oschkenat,** E. Ger.	Feb. 20, 1988	East Berlin
	American	6.67a	Jackie Joyner-Kersee	Feb. 10, 1995	Reno, Nev.
60 meters:	**World**	7.69	**Lyudmila Narozhilenko,** USSR	Feb. 4, 1990	Chelyabinsk, USSR
	American	7.81	Jackie Joyner-Kersee	Feb. 5, 1989	Fairfax, Va.

Note: The hurdles for both distances are 2 feet, 9 inches high. There are four hurdles in the 50 meters and five in the 60.

Walking

Event		Time		Date Set	Location
3000 meters:	**World**	11:44.00	**Alina Ivanova,** Russia	Feb. 7, 1992	Moscow
	American	12:20.79	Debbi Lawrence	Mar. 12, 1993	Toronto

Relays

Event		Time		Date Set	Location
4x200 meters:	**World**	1:32.55	**West Germany**	Feb. 20, 1988	Dortmund, W. Ger.
	American	1:33.24	National Team	Feb. 12, 1994	Glasgow
4x400 meters:	**World**	3:26.84	**Russia**	Mar. 9, 1997	Paris
	American	3:27.66	National Team	Mar. 9, 1997	Paris
4x800 meters:	**World**	8:18.71	**Russia**	Feb. 4, 1994	Moscow
	American	8:25.5p	Villanova	Feb. 7, 1987	Gainesville, Fla.

Field Events

Event		Mark		Date Set	Location
High Jump:	**World**	6- 9½	**Heike Henkel,** Germany	Feb. 9, 1992	Karlsruhe, GER
	American	6-7p	Tisha Waller	Feb. 28, 1998	Atlanta
Pole Vault:	**World**	14-11p	**Emma George,** Australia	Mar. 26, 1998	Adelaide, AUS
	American	14- 8¼p	Stacy Dragila	Mar. 8, 1998	Sindelfingen, GER
Long Jump:	**World**	24- 2¼	**Heike Drechsler,** E. Germany	Feb. 13, 1988	Vienna
	American	23- 4¾	Jackie Joyner-Kersee	Mar. 5, 1992	Atlanta
Triple Jump:	**World**	49-9	**Ashia Hansen,** Great Britain	Feb. 28, 1998	Valencia, Spain
	American	46- 8¼	Sheila Hudson	Mar. 4, 1995	Atlanta
Shot Put:	**World**	73-10	**Helena Fibingerova,** Czech.	Feb. 19, 1977	Jablonec, CZE
	American	65- 0¾	Ramona Pagel	Feb. 20, 1987	Inglewood, Calif.

Note: The international shotput weight for women is 8 lbs. and 13 oz.

Pentathlon

		Points		Date Set	Location
Five Events:	**World**	4991	**Irina Byelova,** Russia	Feb. 14-15, 1992	Berlin
	American	4632	Kym Carter	Mar. 10, 1995	Barcelona

Note: Byelova's WR times and distances, in order over two days– **60m H** (8.22); **HJ** (6-4); **SP** (43- 5¾); **LJ** (21-1¾); **800m** (2:10.26).

SWIMMING

VIIIth FINA World Championships

The 8th FINA World Championships in swimming, diving, synchronized swimming and water polo held in Perth, Australia (Jan. 7-18). Note that (CR) indicates course record.

Final Medal Standings–Top Ten

		G	S	B	Total
1	United States	17	6	9	32
2	Australia	7	8	10	25
3	China	6	8	4	18
4	Russia	11	3	3	17
5	Germany	1	7	6	14
6	Netherlands	1	4	3	8
	Japan	0	4	4	8
8	Italy	2	2	2	6
	France	1	4	1	6
10	Ukraine	3	1	0	4
	Hungary	1	1	2	4
	Canada	0	1	3	4

MEN

Event		Time	
50m free	Bill Pilczuk, USA	22.29	
100m free	Alexander Popov, RUS	48.93	**CR**
200m free	Michael Klim, AUS	1:47.41	
400m free	Ian Thorpe, AUS	3:46.29	
1500m free	Grant Hackett, AUS	14:51.70	
100m back	Lenny Krayzelburg, USA	55.00	
200m back	Lenny Krayzelburg, USA	1:58.84	
100m breast	Frederik Deburghgraeve, BEL	1:01.34	
200m breast	Kurt Grote, USA	2:13.40	
100m fly	Michael Klim, AUS	52.25	**CR**
200m fly	Denys Sylantyev, UKR	1:56.61	
200m I.M.	Marcel Wouda, NET	2:01.18	
400m I.M.	Tom Dolan, USA	4:14.95	
5k open water	Alexei Akatiev, RUS	55:18.6	
25k open water	Alexei Akatiev, RUS	5:05:42.1	

WOMEN

Event		Time	
50m free	Amy Van Dyken, USA	25.15	
100m free	Jenny Thompson, USA	54.95	
200m free	Claudia Poll, CST	1:58.90	
400m free	Yan Chen, CHN	4:06.72	
800m free	Brooke Bennett, USA	8:28.71	
100m back	Lea Maurer, USA	1:01.16	
200m back	Roxanna Maracineanu, FRA	2:11.26	
100m breast	Kristy Kowal, USA	1:08.42	
200m breast	Agnes Kovacs, HUN	2:25.45	**CR**
100m fly	Jenny Thompson, USA	58.46	**CR**
200m fly	Susie O'Neill, AUS	2:07.93	**CR**
200m I.M.	Yanyan Wu, CHN	2:10.88	**CR**
400m I.M.	Yan Chen, CHN	4:36.66	
5k open water	Erica Rose, USA	59:23.5	
25k open water	Tobie Smith, USA	5:31:20.1	

Men's Relays

Event		Time	
400m free	United States (Scott Tucker, Neil Walker, Jon Olsen, Gary Hall Jr.)	3:16.69	**CR**
800m free	Australia (Michael Klim, Grant Hackett, Ian Thorpe, Daniel Kowalski)	7:12.48	
400m med	Australia (Matt Welsh, Phil Rogers, Michael Klim, Chris Fydler)	3:37.98	

Women's Relays

Event		Time
400m free	United States (Lindsey Farella, Amy Van Dyken, B.J. Bedford, Jenny Thompson)	3:42.11
800m free	Germany (Franziska Van Almsick, Dagmar Hase, Silvia Szalai, Kerstin Kielgass)	8:01.46
400m med	United States (Lea Maurer, Kristy Kowal, Jenny Thompson, Amy Van Dyken)	4:01.93

Diving

MEN

Event		Pts
1-meter spring	Yu Zhuocheng, CHN	417.54
3-meter spring	Dmitry Sautin, RUS	746.79
Platform	Dmitry Sautin, RUS	750.99

WOMEN

Event		Pts
1-meter spring	Irina Lashko, RUS	296.07
3-meter spring	Yulia Pakhalina, RUS	544.52
Platform	Olena Zhupyna, UKR	550.41

Synchronized Swimming

Event		Pts
Solo	Olga Sedakova, RUS	99.304
Duet	Olga Brousnikina & Olga Sedakova, RUS	99.400
Team	Russia	99.317

Water Polo

Men's Final: Spain 6 .... Hungary 4
Women's Final: Italy 7 .... Netherlands 6

World, Olympic and American Records

As of Sept. 1, 1998

World long course records officially recognized by the Federation Internationale de Natation Amateur (FINA). Note that (ph) indicates preliminary heat; (r) relay lead-off split; and (s) indicates split time.

MEN

Freestyle

Distance		Time		Date Set	Location
50 meters:	**World**	21.81	**Tom Jager,** USA	Mar. 24, 1990	Nashville
	Olympic	21.91	Aleksandr Popov, Unified Team	July 30, 1992	Barcelona
	American	21.81	Jager (same as World)	—	—
100 meters:	**World**	48.21	**Alexander Popov,** Russia	June 18, 1994	Monte Carlo
	Olympic	48.63	Matt Biondi, USA	Sept.22, 1988	Seoul
	American	48.42	Matt Biondi	Aug. 10, 1988	Austin, Tex.
200 meters:	**World**	1:46.69	**Giorgio Lamberti,** Italy	Aug. 15, 1989	Bonn, W. Ger.
	Olympic	1:46.70	Yevgeny Sadovyi, Unified Team	July 26, 1992	Barcelona
	American	1:47.72ph	Matt Biondi	Aug. 8, 1988	Austin, Tex.
400 meters:	**World**	3:43.80	**Kieren Perkins,** Australia	Sept. 9, 1994	Rome
	Olympic	3:45.00	Yevgeny Sadovyi, Unified Team	July 29, 1992	Barcelona
	American	3:48.06	Matt Cetlinski	Aug. 11, 1988	Austin, Tex.
800 meters:	**World**	7:46.00s	**Kieren Perkins,** Australia	Aug. 24, 1994	Victoria, CAN
	Olympic		Not an event	—	—
	American	7:52.45	Sean Killion	July 27, 1987	Clovis, Calif.
1500 meters:	**World**	14:41.66	**Kieren Perkins,** Australia	Aug. 24, 1994	Victoria, CAN
	Olympic	14:43.48	Kieren Perkins, Australia	July 31, 1992	Barcelona
	American	15:01.51	George DiCarlo	June 30, 1984	Indianapolis

Backstroke

Distance		Time		Date Set	Location
100 meters:	**World**	53.86r	**Jeff Rouse,** USA	July 31, 1992	Barcelona
	Olympic	53.98	Mark Tewksbury, Canada	July 30, 1992	Barcelona
	American	53.86r	Rouse (same as World)	–	–
200 meters:	**World**	1:56.57	**Martin Zubero,** Spain	Nov. 23, 1991	Tuscaloosa, Ala.
	Olympic	1:58.47	Martin Zubero, Spain	July 28, 1992	Barcelona
	American	1:57.38	Lenny Krayzelburg	Aug. 12, 1998	Clovis, Cal.

Breaststroke

Distance		Time		Date Set	Location
100 meters:	**World**	1:00.60p	**Fred deBurghgraeve,** Belgium	July 20, 1996	Atlanta
	Olympic	1:00.60	deBurghgraeve, BEL (same as World)	—	—
	American	1:00.77	Jeremy Linn, USA	July 20, 1996	Atlanta
200 meters:	**World**	2:10.16	**Mike Barrowman,** USA	July 29, 1992	Barcelona
	Olympic	2:10.16	Barrowman (same as World)	—	—
	American	2:10.16	Barrowman (same as World)	—	—

Butterfly

Distance		Time		Date Set	Location
100 meters:	**World**	52.15	**Michael Klim,** Australia	Oct. 9, 1997	Brisbane, AUS
	Olympic	52.27	Denis Pankratov, Russia	July 24, 1996	Atlanta
	American	52.76	Neil Walker	Aug. 12, 1997	Fukuoka, JPN
200 meters:	**World**	1:55.22	**Denis Pankratov,** Russia	June 14, 1995	Canet, FRA
	Olympic	1:56.26	Melvin Stewart, USA	July 30, 1992	Barcelona
	American	1:55.69	Melvin Stewart	Jan. 12, 1991	Perth, AUS

Individual Medley

Distance		Time		Date Set	Location
200 meters:	**World**	1:58.16	**Jani Sievinen,** Finland	Sept. 11, 1994	Rome
	Olympic	1:59.91	Atilla Czene, Hungary	July 25, 1996	Atlanta
	American	2:00.11	David Wharton	Aug. 20, 1989	Tokyo
400 meters:	**World**	4:12.30	**Tom Dolan,** USA	Sept. 6, 1994	Rome
	Olympic	4:14.23	Tamas Darnyi, Hungary	July 27, 1992	Barcelona
	American	4:12.30	Dolan (same as World)	–	–

Relays

Distance	Time		Date Set	Location
4x100m medley:	**World** 3:34.84	**USA** (Rouse, Linn, Henderson, Hall Jr.)	July 26, 1996	Atlanta
	Olympic 3:34.84	USA (same as World)	—	—
	American 3:34.84	USA (same as World)	—	—
4x100m free:	**World** 3:15.11	**USA** (Fox, Hudepohl, Olsen, Hall)	Aug. 12, 1995	Atlanta
	Olympic 3:15.41	USA (Olsen, Davis, Schumacher, Hall Jr.)	July 23, 1996	Atlanta
	American 3:15.11	USA (same as World)	—	—
4x200m free:	**World** 7:11.95	**Unified Team** (Lepikov, Pychnenko, Taianovitch, Sadovyi)	July 27, 1992	Barcelona
	Olympic 7:11.95	Unified Team (same as World)	—	—
	American 7:12.51	USA (Dalbey, Cetlinski, Gjertsen, Biondi)	Sept. 21, 1988	Seoul

WOMEN

Freestyle

Distance	Time		Date Set	Location
50 meters:	**World**........24.51	**Le Jingyi,** China	Sept. 11, 1994	Rome
	Olympic.......24.79	Yang Wenyi, China	July 31, 1992	Barcelona
	American......24.87	Amy Van Dyken	July 26, 1996	Atlanta
100 meters:	**World**........54.01	**Le Jingyi,** China	Sept. 5, 1994	Rome
	Olympic.......54.65	Zhaung Yong, China	July 26, 1992	Barcelona
	American.....54.48p	Jenny Thompson	Mar. 1, 1992	Indianapolis
200 meters:	**World**......1:56.78	**Franziska Van Almsick,** Ger.	Sept. 6, 1994	Rome
	Olympic.....1:57.65	Heike Friedrich, E. Germany	Sept. 21, 1988	Seoul
	American....1:57.90	Nicole Haislett	July 27, 1992	Barcelona
400 meters:	**World**......4:03.85	**Janet Evans,** USA	Sept. 22, 1988	Seoul
	Olympic.....4:03.85	Evans (same as World)	—	—
	American....4:03.85	Evans (same as World)	—	—
800 meters:	**World**......8:16.22	**Janet Evans,** USA	Aug. 20, 1989	Tokyo
	Olympic.....8:20.20	Janet Evans, USA	Sept. 24, 1988	Seoul
	American....8:16.22	Evans (same as World)	—	—
1500 meters:	**World**.....15:52.10	**Janet Evans**, USA	Mar. 26, 1988	Orlando
	Olympic	Not an event	—	—
	American...15:52.10	Evans (same as World)	—	—

Backstroke

Distance	Time		Date Set	Location
100 meters:	**World** 1:00.16r	**He Cihong,** China	Sept. 10, 1994	Rome
	Olympic.....1:00.68	Krisztina Egerszegi, Hungary	July 28, 1992	Barcelona
	American ...1:00.77r	Lea Maurer	Jan. 14, 1998	Perth, AUS
200 meters:	**World**......2:06.62	**Krisztina Egerszegi,** Hungary	Aug. 25, 1991	Athens
	Olympic.....2:07.06	Krisztina Egerszegi, Hungary	July 31, 1992	Barcelona
	American....2:08.60	Betsy Mitchell	June 27, 1986	Orlando

Breaststroke

Distance	Time		Date Set	Location
50 meters:	**World**........30.95	**Penny Heyns**, South Africa	Aug. 1, 1998	East Meadow, NY
100 meters:	**World**......1:07.02	**Penny Heyns**, South Africa	July 21, 1996	Atlanta
	Olympic.....1:07.02	Penny Heyns (same as World)	—	—
	American....1:08.09	Amanda Beard	July 21, 1996	Atlanta
200 meters:	**World**......2:24.76	**Rebecca Brown**, Australia	Mar. 16, 1994	Queensland, AUS
	Olympic.....2:26.65	Kyoko Iwasaki, Japan	July 27, 1992	Barcelona
	American....2:25.35	Anita Nall	Mar. 2, 1992	Indianapolis

Butterfly

Distance	Time		Date Set	Location
100 meters:	**World**........57.93	**Mary T. Meagher,** USA	Aug. 16, 1981	Brown Deer, Wisc.
	Olympic.......58.62	Qian Hong, China	July 29, 1992	Barcelona
	American......57.93	Meagher (same as World)	—	—
200 meters:	**World**......2:05.96	**Mary T. Meagher,** USA	Aug. 13, 1981	Brown Deer, Wisc.
	Olympic.....2:06.90	Mary T. Meagher, USA	Aug. 4, 1984	Los Angeles
	American....2:05.96	Meagher (same as World)	—	—

Individual Medley

Distance	Time		Date Set	Location
200 meters:	**World**......2:09.72	**Yanyan Wu,** China	Oct. 17, 1997	Shanghai
	Olympic.....2:11.65	Lin Li	July 30, 1992	Barcelona
	American....2:11.91	Summer Sanders	July 28, 1992	Barcelona
400 meters:	**World**......4:34.79	**Yan Chen**, China	Oct. 13, 1997	Shanghai
	Olympic.....4:36.29	Petra Schneider, E. Germany	July 26, 1980	Moscow
	American....4:37.58	Summer Sanders	July 30, 1992	Barcelona

Relays

Distance		Time		Date Set	Location
4x100m free:	**World**	3:37.91	**China** (Jingyi, S.Ying, L. Ying, Lu)	Sept. 7, 1994	Rome
	Olympic	3:39.29	USA (Martino, Van Dyken, Fox, Thompson)	July 22, 1996	Atlanta
	American	3:39.29	USA (same as Olympic)	—	—
4x200m free:	**World**	7:55.47	**E. Germany** (Stellmach, Strauss, Mohring, Friedrich)	Aug. 18, 1987	Strasbourg, FRA
	Olympic	7:59.87	USA (Jackson, Teuscher, Taormina, Thompson)	July 25, 1996	Atlanta
	American	7:59.87	USA (same as Olympic)	—	—
4x100m medley:	**World**	4:01.67	**China** (Cihong, Guohong, Limin, Jingyi)	Sept. 10, 1994	Rome
	Olympic	4:02.54	USA (Loveless, Nall, Ahmann-Leighton, Thompson)	July 30, 1992	Barcelona
	American	4:01.93	USA (Maurer, Kowal, Thompson, Van Dyken)	Jan. 16, 1998	Perth, AUS

WINTER SPORTS

Alpine Skiing

1998 U.S. Championships

at Jackson, Wyoming (March 17-25)

MEN

Slalom

1 Sacha Gros 1:36.72
2 Andrezej Bachleda 1:37.93
3 Andy LeRoy 1:38.34

Giant Slalom

1 Bode Miller 2:01.00
2 Dane Spencer 2:01.07
Thomas Grandi 2:01.07

Downhill

1 Ed Podivinsky 1:08.87
2 A.J. Kitt 1:09.13
3 Daron Rahlves 1:09.16

WOMEN

Slalom

1 Kristina Koznick 1:37.22
2 Tasha Nelson 1:38.16
3 Alex Krebs 1:39.49

Giant Slalom

1 Sarah Schleper 2:03.74
2 Julie Parisien 2:03.89
3 Caroline Lalive 2:03.97

Downhill

1 Kirsten Clark 1:13.55
2 Jonna Mendes 1:14.12
3 Julie Parisien 1:14.14

Note: The Men's and Women's Super G competitions were cancelled due to adverse weather conditions.

World Cup Champions

MEN

Overall ... Hermann Maier, AUT
Downhill ... Andreas Schifferer, AUT
Slalom ... Thomas Sykora, AUT
Giant Slalom ... Hermann Maier, AUT
Super G ... Hermann Maier, AUT
Nation's Cup ... Austria

WOMEN

Overall ... Katja Seizinger, GER
Downhill ... Katja Seizinger, GER
Slalom ... Ylva Nowen, SWE
Giant Slalom ... Martina Ertl, GER
Super G ... Katja Seizinger, GER
Nation's Cup ... Germany

Top Five Standings (Men)

Overall 1. Hermann Maier, AUT (1685 pts); 2. Andreas Schifferer, AUT (1114); 3. Stefan Eberharter, AUT (1030); 4. Kjetil Andre Aamodt, NOR (901); 5. Hans Knauss, AUT (888). *Best USA*— Daron Rahlves (t-57th, 130 pts).

Downhill 1. Andreas Schifferer, AUT (655 pts); 2. Hermann Maier, AUT (479); 3. Nicolas Burtin, FRA (469); 4. Didier Cuche, SWI (424); 5. Jean-Luc Cretier, FRA (414). *Best USA*— Tommy Moe (t-35th, 45 pts).

Slalom 1. Thomas Sykora, AUT (521 pts); 2. Thomas Stangassinger, AUT (517); 3. Hans-Peter Buraas, NOR (420); 4. Finn Christian Jagge, NOR (345); 5. Kiminobu Kimura, JPN (316). *Best USA*— Matt Grosjean (32nd, 38 pts).

Giant Slalom 1. Hermann Maier, AUT (620 pts); 2. Michael von Gruenigen, SWI (560); 3. Christian Mayer, AUT (429); 4. Stefan Eberharter, AUT (388); 5. Hans Knauss, AUT (375). *Best USA*— Bode Miller (36th, 27 pts).

Super G 1. Hermann Maier, AUT (400 pts); 2. Hans Krauss, AUT (256); 3. Stefan Eberharter, AUT (220); 4. Patrik Jaerbyn, SWE (195); 5. Andreas Schifferer, AUT (185). *Best USA*— Daron Rhalves (t-11th, 113 pts).

Top Five Standings (Women)

Overall 1. Katja Seizinger, GER (1655 pts); 2. Martina Ertl, GER (1508); 3. Hilde Gerg, GER (1391); 4. Deborah Compagnoni, ITA (912); 5. Alexandra Meissnitzer, AUT (884). *Best USA*— Kristina Koznick (11th, 560 pts).

Downhill 1. Katja Seizinger, GER (520 pts); 2. Renate Goetschl, AUT (392); 3. Isolde Kostner, ITA (292); 4. Melanie Suchet, FRA (237); 5. Hilde Gerg, GER (224). *Best USA*— Picabo Street (17th, 102 pts).

Slalom 1. Ylva Nowen, SWE (620 pts); 2. Kristina Koznick, USA (560); 3. Hilde Gerg, GER (451); 4. Urska Hrovat, SLO (423); 5. Martina Ertl, GER (320).

Giant Slalom 1.Martina Ertl, GER (591 pts); 2. Deborah Compagnoni, ITA (565); 3. Alexandra Meissnitzer, AUT (445); 4. Sonja Nef, SWI (359); 5. Andrine Flemmen, NOR (296). *Best USA*— Sarah Schleper (t-46th, 7 pts).

Super G 1. Katja Seizinger, GER (445 pts); 2. Renate Goetschl, AUT (305); 3. Isolde Kostner, ITA (266); 4. Martina Ertl, GER (259); 5. Melanie Suchet, FRA (228). *Best USA*— Picabo Street (24th, 54 pts).

Combined Nation's Cup 1. Austria (13570 pts); 2. Germany (6085); 3. Italy (6001); 4. Switzerland (5609); 5. France (5025); 6. Norway (4069); 7. Sweden (2284); 8. Slovenia (2171); 9. United States (1243); 10. Canada (905).

Freestyle Skiing

1998 U.S. Championships

at Sugarloaf, Maine (March 26-29)

MEN

Acro		Pts
1	Steve Roxberg	26.00
2	Justin Holland	22.85
3	William T. Boyle	20.85

Moguls		Pts
1	Jonny Moseley	27.11
2	Garth Hager	26.32
3	Alex Wilson	25.52

Aerials		Pts
1	Matt Chojnacki	235.97
2	Eric Bergoust	213.85
3	Britt Swartley	209.39

Dual Moguls

1 Garth Hager
2 Alex Wilson
3 Caleb Martin

WOMEN

Acro		Pts
1	Maria Guarnieri	25.45
2	Lara Rosenbaum	24.30
3	Erin Reinhardt	22.80

Moguls		Pts
1	Liz McIntyre	24.66
2	Ann Battelle	24.63
3	Jillian Vogtli	24.54

Aerials		Pts
1	Nikki Stone	182.13
2	Kelly Hilliman	145.13
3	Emily Cook	133.03

Dual Moguls

1 Ann Battelle
2 Michelle Roark
3 Liz McIntyre

World Cup Champions

MEN

Overall	Fabrice Becker, FRA
Aerials	Eric Bergoust, USA
Moguls	Jonny Moseley, USA
Dual Moguls	Johann Gregoire, FRA
Acroski	Ian Edmondson, USA
Nation's Cup	Canada

WOMEN

Overall	Nikki Stone, USA
Aerials	Kirstie Marshall, AUS
Moguls	Kari Traa, NOR
Dual Moguls	Kari Traa, NOR
Acroski	Oksana Kushenko, RUS
Nation's Cup	United States

Cross Country Skiing

1998 U.S. Championships

at Bend, Oregon (March 28-Apr. 2)

MEN

10-k Classic

1	Marcus Nash	25:18.7
2	John Bauer	25:51.8
3	Justin Wadsworth	25:56.2

15-k Freestyle

1	Marcus Nash	32:18.8
2	Justin Wadsworth	32:46.4
3	Patrick Weaver	32:46.6

30-k Freestyle

1	Patrick Weaver	1:11:57.9
2	Justin Wadsworth	1:12:05.4
3	Carl Swenson	1:13:08.2

WOMEN

5-k Classic

1	Wendy Kay Wagner	15:02.8
2	Lines Selnes	15:11.6
3	Laura Wilson	15:13.1

10-k Freestyle

1	Laura Wilson	24:41.1
2	Lines Selnes	25:03.3
3	Jennifer Douglas	25:05.8

15-k Freestyle

1	Laura Wilson	40:52.6
2	Lines Selnes	40:57.2
3	Jennifer Douglas	41:38.3

World Cup Champions

MEN

1 Thomaas Alsgaard, NOR
2 Bjorn Dählie, NOR
3 Vladimir Smirnov, KAZ
4 Mikhail Bitvinov, AUT
5 Jari Isometsaie, FIN

WOMEN

1 Larissa Lazhutina, RUS
2 Bente Martinsen, NOR
3 Stefania Belmondo, ITA
4 Anita Moen-Guidon, NOR
5 Marit Mikkelsplass, NOR

Nordic Combined
World Cup Champions

1 Bjarte Engen Vik, NOR
2 Mario Stecher, AUT
3 Felix Gottwald, AUT
4 Todd Lodwick, USA
5 Hannu Manninen, FIN

Ski Jumping
World Cup Champions

1 Andreas Widhoelzl, AUT
2 Primoz Peterka, SLO
3 Kazuyoshi Funaki, JPN
4 Masahiko Harada, JPN
5 Dieter Thomas, GER
Sven Hannawald, GER

Snowboarding
World Cup Final Standings

MEN

Overall	Pts
1 Alexander Koller, AUT	990.32
2 Richard Richardsson, SWE	821.33
3 Dieter Moherndl, GER	757.86
Halfpipe	**Pts**
1 Fredrik Sterner, SWE	5480
2 Klas Vangen, NOR	4550
3 Kim Christiansen, NOR	2300
Slalom	**Pts**
1 Richard Richardsson, SWE	3800
2 Dejan Kosir, SLO	3780
3 Dieter Moherndl, GER	3520
Giant Slalom	**Pts**
1 Nicolas Conti, FRA	3600
2 Peter Pechhacker, AUT	3148
3 Harald Walder, AUT	3130
Snowboard Cross	**Pts**
1 Alexander Koller, AUT	2450
2 Daniel Biveson, SWE	1160
3 Drew Neilson, CAN	1000

WOMEN

Overall	Pts
1 Karine Ruby, FRA	1723.33
2 Manuela Riegler, AUT	1449.99
3 Ursula Fingerlos, AUT	1030.33
Halfpipe	**Pts**
1 Doriane Vidal, FRA	4970
2 Sabine Wehr-Hassler, GER	4280
3 Stine Brun Kjeldaas, NOR	3260
Slalom	**Pts**
1 Karine Ruby, FRA	4700
2 Marion Posch, ITA	4500
3 Manuela Riegler, AUT	4420
Giant Slalom	**Pts**
1 Karine Ruby, FRA	9400
2 Isabelle Blanc, FRA	4740
3 Lidia Trettel, ITA	4610
Snowboard Cross	**Pts**
1 Ursula Fingerlos, AUT	2200
2 Manuela Riegler, AUT	2140
3 Maria Tikhvinskja, RUS	1300

Speed Skating
World Cup Champions

MEN

500 meters .... Jeremy Wotherspoon, CAN
1000 meters .... Jeremy Wotherspoon, CAN
1500 meters .... Ids Postma, NET
5000 meters .... Gianni Romme, NET

WOMEN

500 meters .... Catriona LeMay-Doan, CAN
1000 meters .... Catriona LeMay-Doan, CAN
1500 meters .... Gunda Niemann-Stirnemann, GER
3000 meters .... Gunda Niemann-Stirnemann, GER

1998 World Championships

at Heerenveen, Netherlands (March 13-16)

MEN

500 meters .... Ids Postma, NET
1500 meters .... Ids Postma, NET
5000 meters .... Ids Postma, NET
10,000 meters .... Bart Veldkamp, BEL
All-Around .... Ids Postma, NET

WOMEN

500 meters .... Chris Witty, USA
1500 meters .... Gunda Niemann-Stirnemann, GER
3000 meters .... Gunda Niemann-Stirnemann, GER
5000 meters .... Gunda Niemann-Stirnemann, GER
All-Around .... Gunda Niemann-Stirnemann, GER

Figure Skating
World Championships

at Minneapolis, Minn. (March 29-April 5)

Men's — 1. Alexei Yagudin, Russia; 2. Todd Eldredge, USA; 3. Evgeni Plushenko, Russia

Women's — 1. Michelle Kwan, USA; 2. Irina Slutskaya, Russia; 3. Maria Butyrskaya, Russia

Pairs — 1. Elena Berezhnaya & Anton Sikharulidze, Russia; 2. Jenni Meno & Todd Sand, USA; 3. Peggy Schwarz & Mirko Muller, Germany

Ice Dance — 1. Anjelika Krylova & Oleg Ovsiannikov, Russia; 2. Marina Anissina & Gwendal Peizerat, France; 3. Shae-Lynn Bourne & Victor Kraatz, Canada

U.S. Championships

at Philadelphia, Pa. (Jan. 4-11)

Men's .... Todd Eldredge
Women's .... Michelle Kwan
Pairs .... Kyoko Ina & Jason Dungjen
Ice Dance .... Elizabeth Punsalan & Jerod Swallow

European Championships

at Milan, Italy (Jan. 13-18)

Men's .... Alexei Yagudin, Russia
Women's .... Maria Butyrskaya, Russia
Pairs .... Elena Berezhnaya & Anton Sikharulidze, Russia
Ice Dance .... Pasha Grishuk & Yevgeny Platov, Russia

SUMMER SPORTS

Cross-country

IAAF World Championships

The 26th IAAF World Cross Country Championships held at Marrakech, Morroco (Mar. 21-22)

MEN 12 km (7.46 mi) ... 1. Paul Tergat, KEN 34:01
2. Paul Koech, KEN 34:06
3. Assefa Mezegebu, ETH 34:28
Best USA— Bob Kennedy, 16th, 35:18

WOMEN 8 km (4.97 mi) ... 1. Sonia O'Sullivan, IRE 25:39
2. Paula Radcliffe, GBR 25:42
3. Gete Wami, ETH 25:49
Best USA— Deena Drossin, 20th, 27:06

Cycling

Tour de France

The 85th Tour de France (July 12-August 2) ran 21 stages plus a prologue, covering just over 2,400 miles starting in Dublin, Ireland, passing through the Pyrenees and the Alps and finishing on the Avenue des Champs-Elysees in Paris.

Italy's Marco Pantani, a.k.a "The Pirate" became the first Italian Tour champion since 1965. He overtook defending champion Jan Ullrich in the exhausting mountain stages and finished with a time of 92 hours, 49 minutes and 46 seconds. His time was three minutes, 21 seconds ahead of runner-up Ullrich. American Bobby Julich was consistent throughout and wound up in third.

The 1998 Tour will, however, be known for its ever present drug scandals and ensuing biker strikes. Just days before the start of the race, a Festina Team car was busted for having 400 doses of performance-enhancing drugs. The entire team was later ousted from the race. After days of unannounced police raids and intense media scrutiny, bikers fought back by climbing off their bikes and sitting in the road before the 12th stage. In all, only 96 of the 189 riders that began the race, finished.

	Rider	Team	Behind
1	Marco Pantani, ITA	Mercatone Uno	—
2	Jan Ullrich, GER	Telekom	3:21
3	Bobby Julich, USA	Cofidis	8:08
4	Christophe Rinero, FRA	Cofidis	9:16
5	Michael Boogerd, NET	Rabobank	11:26
6	Jean-Cyril Robin, FRA	U.S. Postal	14:57
7	Roland Meier, SWI	Cofidis	15:13
8	Daniele Nardello, ITA	Mapei	16:07
9	Guiseppe di Grande, ITA	Mapei	17:35
10	Axel Merckx, BEL	Polti3	17:39

Other Worldwide Champions

1998 UCI (Union Cycliste Internationale) Elite Results

MEN

Mediterranean Tour (FRA)	Rodolfo Massi, ITA
Tour of Valencia (SPA)	Pascal Chanteur, FRA
Het Volk (BEL)	Peter Van Petegem, BEL
Paris-Nice (FRA)	Frank Vandenbroucke, BEL
Tirreno-Adriatico (ITA)	Rolf Jaermann, SWI
Criterium International (FRA)	Christophe Moreau, FRA
Tour of the Basque Country (SPA)	Inigo Cuesta, SPA
Ghent-Wevelgen (BEL)	Frank Vandenbroucke, BEL
Fleche Wallone (BEL)	Bo Hamburger, DEN
Tour de Romandie (SWI)	Laurent Dufaux, SWI
Giro d'Italia (ITA)	Marco Pantani, ITA
Dauphine Libere (FRA)	Armand De Las Cuevas, FRA
Tour of Switzerland (SWI)	Stephan Garzelli, ITA
Tour of Netherlands (NET)	Rolf Sorensen, DEN
Tour of Spain (SPA)	ends Sept. 27
World Time Trial	ends Oct. 9
World Pro Road Race	ends Oct. 11

WOMEN

First Union USPRO Champ. (USA)	Petra Rossner, GER
Tour de L'Aude (FRA)	Fabiana Luperini, ITA
H-P International (USA)	Linda Jackson, CAN
Giro d'Italia Femminile (ITA)	Fabiana Luperini, ITA
Tour Cycliste Feminin (FRA)	Edita Pucinskaite, LIT

Mountain Biking

1998 Grundig/UCI World Cup Champions

MEN

Cross Country	Cadel Evans, AUS
Downhill	Nicolas Vouilloz, FRA
Dual	Brian Lopes, USA

WOMEN

Cross Country	Alison Sydor, CAN
Downhill	Anne-Caroline Chausson, FRA
Dual	Katrina Miller, AUS

Marathons

Boston Marathon

102nd edition of the Boston Marathon, held Monday, April 20, 1998 and run, as always, from Hopkinton through Ashland, Framingham, Natick, Wellesley, Newton and Brookline to Boston, Mass. Kenya's Moses Tanui outkicked fellow countryman Joseph Chebet to win for the second time in the past three years. He finished in two hours, seven minutes and 34 seconds, the third best time in Boston Marathon history, and just three seconds ahead of Chebet, who recorded the fourth best time.

Ethiopia's Fatuma Roba ran the third fastest women's time (2:23:21) in Boston Marathon history to win her second consecutive race. She finished three minutes and 56 seconds ahead of her nearest competitor.

Franz Nietlispach of Swiitzerland dominated the men's wheelchair division (1:21:52) and Australia's Louise Sauvage (1:41:19) came from behind to nip American Jean Driscoll at the finish line for her second consecutive win in the women's wheelchair division. Winners in the men's and women's divisions earned $80,000. **Distance:** 26.2 miles.

MEN

		Time
1	Moses Tanui, KEN	2:07:34
2	Joseph Chebet, KEN	2:07:37
3	Gert Thys, S.Afr.	2:07:52
4	Andre Ramos, BRA	2:08:26
5	John Kagwe, KEN	2:08:51
6	German Silva, MEX	2:08:56
7	Alejandro Gomez, SPA	2:12:34
8	Turbo Tumo, ETH	2:13:06
9	Rey Jose-Ramon, SPA	2:13:12
10	Takayuki Inubushi, JPN	2:13:15

Best USA: 17th— Joseph McVeigh, New Jersey, 2:16:48

WOMEN

		Time
1	Fatuma Roba, ETH	2:23:21
2	Renata Paradowska, POL	2:27:17
3	Anuta Catuna, ROM	2:27:34
4	Manuela Machado, POR	2:29:13
5	Colleen de Reuck, S. Afr	2:29:43
6	Irina Kazakova, FRA	2:30:44
7	Jane Salumae, EST	2:31:20
8	Hiroko Nomura, JPN	2:31:58
9	Irina Timofeyeva, RUS	2:32:32
10	Aurica Buia, JPN	2:34:17

Best USA: 11th— Mary-Lynn B. Currier, Massachusetts, 2:35:18

WHEELCHAIR (Men)

		Time
1	Franz Nietlispach, SWI	1:21:52
2	Krige Schabort, S. Afr.	1:26:37
3	Saul Mendoza, MEX	1:26:38
4	Philippe Couprie, FRA	1:26:40
5	Scot A. Hollonbeck, USA	1:27:17

WHEELCHAIR (Women)

		Time
1	Louise Sauvage, AUS	1:41:19
2	Jean L. Driscoll, USA	1:41:19
3	Monica S. Wetterstrom, SWE	1:44:17
4	Rose M. Winand, USA	1:48:09
5	Miriam Nibley, USA	1:51:08

Other 1998 Winners

Los Angeles

Date		Winner	Time
Mar. 29	Men	Zebedayo Bayo, TAN	2:11:21
	Women	Lornah Kiplagat, KEN	2:34:03

London

Date		Winner	Time
Apr. 26	Men	Abel Anton, SPA	2:07:56
	Women	Catherina McKiernan, IRE	2:26:25

Rotterdam

Date		Winner	Time
Apr. 19	Men	Fabian Roncero, SPA	2:07:26
	Women	Tegla Loroupe, KEN	2:20:47

Late 1997

New York City

Date		Winner	Time
Nov. 2	Men	John Kagwe, KEN	2:08:12
	Women	Franziska Rochat-Moser, SWI	2:28:43

Fukuoka

Date		Winner	Time
Dec. 7	Men	Josiah Thugwane, S. Afr.	2:07:28

(No women's division)

Rowing

World Rowing Championships

at Cologne, Germany (Sept. 6-13)

MEN

Eights	United States, 5:38.78
Coxed Pairs	Australia, 6:45.01
Coxed Fours	Australia, 6:09.43
Coxless Pairs	Germany, 6:22.32
Coxless Fours	Great Britain, 5:48.06
Single Sculls	Rob Waddell, NZ, 6:39.65
Double Sculls	Germany, 6:13.20
Quad Sculls	Italy, 5:51.19

WOMEN

Eights	Romania, 6:14.62
Coxless Pairs	Canada, 7:05.19
Coxless Fours	Ukraine, 6:30.63
Single Sculls	Irina Fedotova, RUS, 7:25.09
Double Sculls	Great Britain, 6:48.85
Quad Sculls	Germany, 6:24.38

TRACK & FIELD

IAAF World Championships

While the Summer Olympics have served as the unofficial world outdoor championships for track and field throughout the century, a separate World Championship meet was started in 1983 by the International Amateur Athletic Federation (IAAF). The meet was held every four years from 1983-91, but began an every-other-year cycle in 1993. World Championship sites include Helsinki (1983), Rome (1987), Tokyo (1991), Stuttgart (1993), Göteborg, Sweden (1995), Athens (1997) and Seville (1999). Note that (WR) indicates world record and (CR) indicates championship meet record.

MEN

Multiple gold medals (including relays): Carl Lewis (8); Michael Johnson (7); Sergey Bubka (6); Calvin Smith and Lars Riedel (4); Donovan Bailey, Greg Foster, Haile Gebrselassie, Werner Gunthor, Moses Kiptanui, Noureddine Morceli, Dan O'Brien and Butch Reynolds (3); Andrey Abduvaliyev, Leroy Burrell, Andre Cason, Maurizio Damilano, John Godina, Allen Johnson, Wilson Kipketer, Ismael Kirui, Billy Konchellah, Sergey Litvinov, Dennis Mitchell, Edwin Moses, Ivan Pedroso, Mike Powell, Javier Sotmayor and Jan Zelezny (2).

100 Meters

Year		Time	
1983	Carl Lewis, USA	10.07	
1987	Carl Lewis, USA	9.93	
1991	Carl Lewis, USA	9.86	WR
1993	Linford Christie, GBR	9.87	
1995	Donovan Bailey, CAN	9.97	
1997	Maurice Greene, USA	9.86	=CR

Note: Ben Johnson was the original winner in 1987, but was stripped of his title and world record time (9.83) following his 1989 admission of drug taking.

200 Meters

Year		Time	
1983	Calvin Smith, USA	20.14	
1987	Calvin Smith, USA	20.16	
1991	Michael Johnson, USA	20.01	
1993	Frank Fredericks, NAM	19.85	
1995	Michael Johnson, USA	19.79	CR
1997	Ato Boldon, USA	20.04	

400 Meters

Year		Time	
1983	Bert Cameron, JAM	45.05	
1987	Thomas Schonlebe, E.Ger	44.33	
1991	Antonio Pettigrew, USA	44.57	
1993	Michael Johnson, USA	43.65	
1995	Michael Johnson, USA	43.39	CR
1997	Michael Johnson, USA	44.12	

800 Meters

Year		Time	
1983	Willi Wülbeck, W.Ger	1:43.65	
1987	Billy Konchellah, KEN	1:43.06	CR
1991	Billy Konchellah, KEN	1:43.99	
1993	Paul Ruto, KEN	1:44.71	
1995	Wilson Kipketer, DEN	1:45.08	
1997	Wilson Kipketer, DEN	1:43.38	

1500 Meters

Year		Time	
1983	Steve Cram, GBR	3:41.59	
1987	Abdi Bile, SOM	3:36.80	
1991	Noureddine Morceli, ALG	3:32.84	CR
1993	Noureddine Morceli, ALG	3:34.24	
1995	Noureddine Morceli, ALG	3:33.73	
1997	Hicham El Guerrouj, MAR	3:35.83	

5000 Meters

Year		Time	
1983	Eammon Coghlan, IRE	13:28.53	
1987	Said Aouita, MOR	13:26.44	
1991	Yobes Ondieki, KEN	13:14.45	
1993	Ismael Kirui, KEN	13:02.75	CR
1995	Ismael Kirui, KEN	13:16.77	
1997	Daniel Komen, KEN	13:07.38	

10,000 Meters

Year		Time	
1983	Alberto Cova, ITA	28:01.04	
1987	Paul Kipkoech, KEN	27:38.63	
1991	Moses Tanui, KEN	27:38.74	
1993	Haile Gebrselassie, ETH	27:46.02	
1995	Haile Gebrselassie, ETH	27:12.95	CR
1997	Haile Gebrselassie, ETH	27:24.58	

Marathon

Year		Time	
1983	Rob de Castella, AUS	2:10:03	CR
1987	Douglas Wakiihuri, KEN	2:11:48	
1991	Hiromi Taniguchi, JPN	2:14:57	
1993	Mark Plaatjes, USA	2:13:57	
1995	Martin Fíz, SPA	2:11:41	
1997	Abel Anton, SPA	2:13:16	

110-Meter Hurdles

Year		Time	
1983	Greg Foster, USA	13.42	
1987	Greg Foster, USA	13.21	
1991	Greg Foster, USA	13.06	
1993	Colin Jackson, GBR	12.91	WR
1995	Allen Johnson, USA	13.00	
1997	Allen Johnson, USA	12.93	

400-Meter Hurdles

Year		Time	
1983	Edwin Moses, USA	47.50	
1987	Edwin Moses, USA	47.46	
1991	Samuel Matete, ZAM	47.64	
1993	Kevin Young, USA	47.18	CR
1995	Derrick Adkins, USA	47.98	
1997	Stephane Diagana, FRA	47.70	

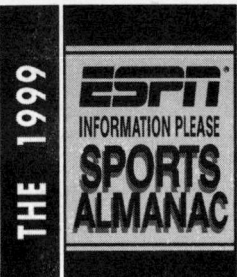

Track & Field (Cont.)

3000-Meter Steeplechase

Year		Time	
1983	Patriz Ilg, W. Ger	8:15.06	
1987	Francesco Panetta, ITA	8:08.57	
1991	Moses Kiptanui, KEN	8:12.59	
1993	Moses Kiptanui, KEN	8:06.36	
1995	Moses Kiptanui, KEN	8:04.16	CR
1997	Wilson B. Kipketer, KEN	8:05.84	

4 x 100-Meter Relay

Year		Time	
1983	United States	37.86	WR
1987	United States	37.90	
1991	United States	37.50	WR
1993	United States	37.48	CR
1995	Canada	38.31	
1997	Canada	37.86	

4 x 400-Meter Relay

Year		Time	
1983	Soviet Union	3:00.79	
1987	United States	2:57.29	
1991	Great Britain	2:57.53	
1993	United States	2:54.29	WR
1995	United States	2:57.32	
1997	United States	2:56.47	

20-Kilometer Walk

Year		Time	
1983	Ernesto Canto, MEX	1:20.49	
1987	Maurizio Damilano, ITA	1:20.45	
1991	Maurizio Damilano, ITA	1:19.37	CR
1993	Valentin Massana, SPA	1:22.31	
1995	Michele Didoni, ITA	1:19.59	
1997	Daniel Garcia, MEX	1:21:43	

50-Kilometer Walk

Year		Time	
1983	Ronald Weigel, E. Ger	3:43:08	
1987	Hartwig Gauder, E. Ger	3:40:53	CR
1991	Aleksandr Potashov, USSR	3:53:09	
1993	Jesus Angel Garcia, SPA	3:41:41	
1995	Valentin Kononen, FIN	3:43.42	
1997	Robert Korzeniowski, POL	3:44:46	

High Jump

Year		Height	
1983	Gennedy Avdeyenko, USSR	7- 7¼	
1987	Patrik Sjoberg, SWE	7- 9¾	
1991	Charles Austin, USA	7- 9¾	
1993	Javier Sotomayor, CUB	7-10½	CR
1995	Troy Kemp, BAH	7- 9¼	
1997	Javier Sotomayor, CUB	7- 9¼	

Pole Vault

Year		Height	
1983	Sergey Bubka, USSR	18- 8¼	
1987	Sergey Bubka, USSR	19- 2¼	
1991	Sergey Bubka, USSR	19- 6¼	CR
1993	Sergey Bubka, UKR	19- 8¼	
1995	Sergey Bubka, UKR	19- 5	
1997	Sergey Bubka, UKR	19- 8½	CR

Long Jump

Year		Distance	
1983	Carl Lewis, USA	28- 0¾	
1987	Carl Lewis, USA	28- 0¼	
1991	Mike Powell, USA	29- 4½	WR
1993	Mike Powell, USA	28- 2¼	
1995	Ivan Pedroso, CUB	28- 6½	
1997	Ivan Pedroso, CUB	27- 7½	

Triple Jump

Year		Distance	
1983	Zdzislaw Hoffmann, POL	57- 2	
1987	Khristo Markov, BUL	58- 9	
1991	Kenny Harrison, USA	58- 4	
1993	Mike Conley, USA	58- 7¼	
1995	Jonathan Edwards, GBR	60- 0¼	WR
1997	Yoelvis Quesada, CUB	58- 6¾	

Shot Put

Year		Distance	
1983	Edward Sarul, POL	70- 2¼	
1987	Werner Günthör, SWI	72-11¼	CR
1991	Werner Günthör, SWI	71- 1¼	
1993	Werner Günthör, SWI	72- 1	
1995	John Godina, USA	70- 5¼	
1997	John Godina, USA	70- 4¼	

Discus

Year		Distance	
1983	Imrich Bugar, CZE	222- 2	
1987	Jurgen Schult, E. Ger	225- 6	
1991	Lars Riedel, GER	217- 2	
1993	Lars Riedel, GER	222- 2	
1995	Lars Riedel, GER	225- 7	CR
1997	Lars Riedel, GER	224- 10	

Hammer Throw

Year		Distance	
1983	Sergey Litvinov, USSR	271- 3	
1987	Sergey Litvinov, USSR	272- 6	CR
1991	Yuri Sedykh, USSR	268- 0	
1993	Andrey Abduvaliyev, TAJ	267-10	
1995	Andrey Abduvaliyev, TAJ	267- 7	
1997	Heinz Weis, GER	268-4	

Javelin

Year		Distance	
1983	Detlef Michel, E. Ger	293- 7	
1987	Seppo Raty, FIN	274- 1	
1991	Kimmo Kinnunen, FIN	297-11	CR
1993	Jan Zelezny, CZE	282- 1	
1995	Jan Zelezny, CZE	293-11	
1997	Marius Corbett, S. Afr.	290-0	

Decathlon

Year		Points	
1983	Daley Thompson, GBR	8714	
1987	Torsten Voss, E. Ger	8680	
1991	Dan O'Brien, USA	8812	
1993	Dan O'Brien, USA	8817	CR
1995	Dan O'Brien, USA	8695	
1997	Tomas Dvorak, CZE	8837	CR

WOMEN

Multiple gold medals (including relays): Gail Devers and Jackie Joyner-Kersee (4); Tatyana Samolenko Dorovskikh, Silke Gladisch, Marita Koch, Jearl Miles, Merlene Ottey and Gwen Torrence (3); Hassiba Boulmerka, Sabine Braun, Olga Bryzgina, Mary Decker, Heike Daute Drechsler, Chryste Gaines, Trine Hattestad, Martina Optiz Hellmann, Marion Jones, Stefka Kostadinova, Katrin Krabbe, Jarmila Kratochvilova, Astrid Kumbernuss, Marie-José Pérec, Ana Quirot and Huang Zhihong (2).

100 Meters

Year		Time	
1983	Marlies Gohr, E. Ger	10.97	
1987	Silke Gladisch, E. Ger	10.90	
1991	Katrin Krabbe, GER	10.99	
1993	Gail Devers, USA	10.81	CR
1995	Gwen Torrence, USA	10.85	
1997	Marion Jones, USA	10.83	

200 Meters

Year		Time	
1983	Marita Koch, E. Ger	22.13	
1987	Silke Gladisch, E. Ger	21.74	CR
1991	Katrin Krabbe, GER	22.09	
1993	Merlene Ottey, JAM	21.98	
1995	Merlene Ottey, JAM	22.12	
1997	Zhanna Pintusevich, UKR	22.32	

400 Meters

Year		Time	
1983	Jarmila Kratochvilova, CZE	47.99	WR
1987	Olga Bryzgina, USSR	49.38	
1991	Marie-José Pérec, FRA	49.13	
1993	Jearl Miles, USA	49.82	
1995	Marie-José Pérec, FRA	49.28	
1997	Cathy Freeman, AUS	49.77	

800 Meters

Year		Time	
1983	Jarmila Kratochvilova, CZE	1:54.68	CR
1987	Sigrun Wodars, E. Ger	1:55.26	
1991	Lilia Nurutdinova, USSR	1:57.50	
1993	Maria Mutola, MOZ	1:55.43	
1995	Ana Quirot, CUB	1:56.11	
1997	Ana Quirot, CUB	1:57.14	

1500 Meters

Year		Time	
1983	Mary Decker, USA	4:00.90	
1987	Tatiana Samolenko, USSR	3:58.56	CR
1991	Hassiba Boulmerka, ALG	4:02.21	
1993	Liu Dong, CHN	4:00.50	
1995	Hassiba Boulmerka, ALG	4:02.42	
1997	Carla Sacramento, POR	4:04.24	

5000 Meters

Held as 3000-meter race from 1983-93

Year		Time	
1983	Mary Decker, USA	8:34.62	
1987	Tatyana Samolenko, USSR	8:38.73	
1991	T. Samolenko Dorovskikh, USSR	8:35.82	
1993	Qu Yunxia, CHN	8:28.71	CR
1995	Sonia O'Sullivan, IRE	14:46.47	CR
1997	Gabriela Szabo, ROM	14:57.68	

10,000 Meters

Year		Time	
1983	Not held		
1987	Ingrid Kristiansen, NOR	31:05.85	
1991	Liz McColgan, GBR	31:14.31	
1993	Wang Junxia, CHN	30:49.30	CR
1995	Fernanda Ribeiro, POR	31:04.99	
1997	Sally Barsosio, KEN	31:32.92	

Marathon

Year		Time	
1983	Grete Waitz, NOR	2:28:09	
1987	Rose Mota, POR	2:25:17	CR
1991	Wanda Panfil, POL	2:29:53	
1993	Junko Asari, JPN	2:30:03	
1995	Manuela Machado, POR	2:25:39	
1997	Hiromi Suzuki, JPN	2:29:48	

100-Meter Hurdles

Year		Time	
1983	Bettine Jahn, E. Ger	12.35w	
1987	Ginka Zagorcheva, BUL	12.34	CR
1991	Lyudmila Narozhilenko, USSR	12.59	
1993	Gail Devers, USA	12.46	
1995	Gail Devers, USA	12.68	
1997	Ludmila Engquist, SWE	12.50	

w indicates wind-aided.

400-Meter Hurdles

Year		Time	
1983	Yekaterina Fesenko, USSR	54.14	
1987	Sabine Busch, E. Ger	53.62	
1991	Tatiana Ledovskaya, USSR	53.11	
1993	Sally Gunnell, GBR	52.74	WR
1995	Kim Batten, USA	52.61	WR
1997	Nezha Bidouane, MOR	52.97	

4 x 100-Meter Relay

Year		Time	
1983	East Germany	41.76	
1987	United States	41.58	
1991	Jamaica	41.94	
1993	Russia	41.49	CR
1995	United States	42.12	
1997	United States	41.47	CR

4 x 400-Meter Relay

Year		Time	
1983	East Germany	3:19.73	
1987	East Germany	3:18.63	
1991	Soviet Union	3:18.43	
1993	United States	3:16.71	CR
1995	United States	3:22.39	
1997	Germany	3:20.92	

10-Kilometer Walk

Year		Time	
1983	Not held		
1987	Irina Strakhova, USSR	44:12	
1991	Alina Ivanova, USSR	42:57	
1993	Sari Essayah, FIN	42:59	
1995	Irina Stankina, RUS	42:13	CR
1997	Anna Sidoti, ITA	42:55	

High Jump

Year		Height	
1983	Tamara Bykova, USSR	6- 7	
1987	Stefka Kostadinova, BUL	6-10¼	WR
1991	Heike Henkel, GER	6- 8¾	
1993	Ioamnet Quintero, CUB	6- 6¼	
1995	Stefka Kostadinova, BUL	6- 7	
1997	Hanne Haugland, NOR	6- 6¼	

Track & Field (Cont.)

Long Jump

Year		Distance	
1983	Heike Daute, E. Ger	23-10¼w	
1987	Jackie Joyner-Kersee, USA	24- 1¾	CR
1991	Jackie Joyner-Kersee, USA	24- 0¼	
1993	Heike Drechsler, GER	23- 4	
1995	Fiona May, ITA	22-10¾w	
1997	Lyudmila Galkina, RUS	23- 1¾	

w indicates wind-aided.

Triple Jump

Year		Distance	
1983	Not held		
1987	Not held		
1991	Not held		
1993	Ana Biryukova, RUS	46- 6¼	WR
1995	Inessa Kravets, UKR	50-10¾	WR
1997	Sarka Kasparkova, CZE	49-10½	

Shot Put

Year		Distance	
1983	Helena Fibingerova, CZE	69- 0	
1987	Natalia Lisovskaya, USSR	69- 8	CR
1991	Huang Zhihong, CHN	68- 4	
1993	Huang Zhihong, CHN	67- 6	
1995	Astrid Kumbernuss, GER	69- 7½	
1997	Astrid Kumbernuss, GER	67- 11½	

Discus

Year		Distance	
1983	Martina Opitz, E. Ger	226- 2	
1987	Martina Opitz Hellmann, E. Ger	235- 0	CR
1991	Tsvetanka Khristova, BUL	233- 0	
1993	Olga Burova, RUS	221- 1	
1995	Ellina Zvereva, BLR	225- 2	
1997	Beatrice Faumuina, NZL	219-3	

Javelin

Year		Distance	
1983	Tiina Lillak, FIN	232- 4	
1987	Fatima Whitbread, GBR	251- 5	CR
1991	Xu Demei, CHN	225- 8	
1993	Trine Hattestad, NOR	227- 0	
1995	Natalya Shikolenko, BLR	221- 8	
1997	Trine Hattestad, NOR	225- 8	

Heptathlon

Year		Points	
1983	Ramona Neubert, E. Ger	6770	
1987	Jackie Joyner-Kersee, USA	7128	CR
1991	Sabine Braun, GER	6672	
1993	Jackie Joyner-Kersee, USA	6837	
1995	Ghada Shouaa, SYR	6651	
1997	Sabine Braun, GER	6739	

Marathons

Boston

America's oldest regularly contested foot race, the Boston Marathon is held on Patriots' Day every April. It has been run at four different distances: 24 miles, 1232 yards (1897-1923); 26 miles, 209 yards (1924-26); 26 miles, 385 yards (1927-52, since 1957); 25 miles, 958 yards (1953-56).

MEN

Multiple winners: Clarence DeMar (7); Gerard Cote and Bill Rodgers (4); Ibrahim Hussein, Cosmas Ndeti and Leslie Pawson (3); Tarzan Brown, Jim Caffrey, John A. Kelley, John Miles, Eino Oksanen, Toshihiko Seko, Geoff Smith, Moses Tanui and Aurele Vandendriessche (2).

Year		Time
1897	John McDermott, New York	2:55:10
1898	Ronald McDonald, Massachusetts	2:42:00
1899	Lawrence Brignolia, Massachusetts	2:54:38
1900	Jim Caffrey, Canada	2:39:44
1901	Jim Caffrey, Canada	2:29:23
1902	Sam Mellor, New York	2:43:12
1903	J.C. Lorden, Massachusetts	2:41:29
1904	Mike Spring, New York	2:38:04
1905	Fred Lorz, New York	2:38:25
1906	Tim Ford, Massachusetts	2:45:45
1907	Tom Longboat, Canada	2:24:24
1908	Tom Morrissey, New York	2:25:43
1909	Henri Renaud, New Hampshire	2:53:36
1910	Fred Cameron, Nova Scotia	2:28:52
1911	Clarence DeMar, Massachusetts	2:21:39
1912	Mike Ryan, Illinois	2:21:18
1913	Fritz Carlson, Minnesota	2:25:14
1914	James Duffy, Canada	2:25:01
1915	Edouard Fabre, Canada	2:31:41
1916	Arthur Roth, Massachusetts	2:27:16
1917	Bill Kennedy, New York	2:28:37
1918	World War relay race	
1919	Carl Linder, Massachusetts	2:29:13
1920	Peter Trivoulidas, New York	2:29:31
1921	Frank Zuna, New Jersey	2:18:57
1922	Clarence DeMar, Massachusetts	2:18:10
1923	Clarence DeMar, Massachusetts	2:23:37
1924	Clarence DeMar, Massachusetts	2:29:40
1925	Charles Mellor, Illinois	2:33:00
1926	John Miles, Nova Scotia	2:25:40
1927	Clarence DeMar, Massachusetts	2:40:22
1928	Clarence DeMar, Massachusetts	2:37:07
1929	John Miles, Nova Scotia	2:33:08
1930	Clarence DeMar, Massachusetts	2:34:48
1931	James Henigan, Massachusetts	2:46:45
1932	Paul deBruyn, Germany	2:33:36
1933	Leslie Pawson, Rhode Island	2:31:01
1934	Dave Komonen, Canada	2:32:53
1935	John A. Kelley, Massachusetts	2:32:07
1936	Ellison (Tarzan) Brown, Rhode Island	2:33:40
1937	Walter Young, Canada	2:33:20
1938	Leslie Pawson, Rhode Island	2:35:34
1939	Ellison (Tarzan) Brown, Rhode Island	2:28:51
1940	Gerard Cote, Canada	2:28:28
1941	Leslie Pawson, Rhode Island	2:30:38
1942	Joe Smith, Massachusetts	2:26:51
1943	Gerard Cote, Canada	2:28:25
1944	Gerard Cote, Canada	2:31:50
1945	John A. Kelley, Massachusetts	2:30:40
1946	Stylianos Kyriakides, Greece	2:29:27
1947	Yun Bok Suh, Korea	2:25:39
1948	Gerard Cote, Canada	2:31:02
1949	Karle Leandersson, Sweden	2:31:50
1950	Kee Yonh Ham, Korea	2:32:39
1951	Shigeki Tanaka, Japan	2:27:45
1952	Doroteo Flores, Guatemala	2:31:53
1953	Keizo Yamada, Japan	2:18:51
1954	Veiko Karvonen, Finland	2:20:39
1955	Hideo Hamamura, Japan	2:18:22
1956	Antti Viskari, Finland	2:14:14
1957	John J. Kelley, Connecticut	2:20:05
1958	Franjo Mihalic, Yugoslavia	2:25:54

Year	Time
1959 Eino Oksanen, Finland	2:22:42
1960 Paavo Kotila, Finland	2:20:54
1961 Eino Oksanen, Finland	2:23:39
1962 Eino Oksanen, Finland	2:23:48
1963 Aurele Vandendriessche, Belgium	2:18:58
1964 Aurele Vandendriessche, Belgium	2:19:59
1965 Morio Shigematsu, Japan	2:16:33
1966 Kenji Kimihara, Japan	2:17:11
1967 David McKenzie, New Zealand	2:15:45
1968 Amby Burfoot, Connecticut	2:22:17
1969 Yoshiaki Unetani, Japan	2:13:49
1970 Ron Hill, England	2:10:30
1971 Alvaro Mejia, Colombia	2:18:45
1972 Olavi Suomalainen, Finland	2:15:39
1973 Jon Anderson, Oregon	2:16:03
1974 Neil Cusack, Ireland	2:13:39
1975 Bill Rodgers, Massachusetts	2:09:55
1976 Jack Fultz, Pennsylvania	2:20:19
1977 Jerome Drayton, Canada	2:14:46
1978 Bill Rodgers, Massachusetts	2:10:13
1979 Bill Rodgers, Massachusetts	2:09:27
1980 Bill Rodgers, Massachusetts	2:12:11
1981 Toshihiko Seko, Japan	2:09:26
1982 Alberto Salazar, Oregon	2:08:52
1983 Greg Meyer, New Jersey	2:09:00
1984 Geoff Smith, England	2:10:34
1985 Geoff Smith, England	2:14:05
1986 Rob de Castella, Australia	2:07:51
1987 Toshihiko Seko, Japan	2:11:50
1988 Ibrahim Hussein, Kenya	2:08:43
1989 Abebe Mekonnen, Ethiopia	2:09:06
1990 Gelindo Bordin, Italy	2:08:19
1991 Ibrahim Hussein, Kenya	2:11:06
1992 Ibrahim Hussein, Kenya	2:08:14
1993 Cosmas Ndeti, Kenya	2:09:33
1994 Cosmas Ndeti, Kenya	2:07:15*
1995 Cosmas Ndeti, Kenya	2:09:22
1996 Moses Tanui, Kenya	2:09:16
1997 Lameck Aguta, Kenya	2:10:34
1998 Moses Tanui, Kenya	2:07:34

*Course record.

WOMEN

Multiple winners: Rosa Mota and Uta Pippig (3); Joan Benoit, Miki Gorman, Ingrid Kristiansen, Olga Markova and Fatuma Roba (2).

Year	Time
1972 Nina Kuscsik, New York	3:08:58
1973 Jacqueline Hansen, California	3:05:59
1974 Miki Gorman, California	2:47:11
1975 Liane Winter, West Germany	2:42:24
1976 Kim Merritt, Wisconsin	2:47:10
1977 Miki Gorman, California	2:48:33
1978 Gayle Barron, Georgia	2:44:52
1979 Joan Benoit, Maine	2:35:15
1980 Jacqueline Gareau, Canada	2:34:28
1981 Allison Roe, New Zealand	2:26:46
1982 Charlotte Teske, West Germany	2:29:33
1983 Joan Benoit, Maine	2:22:43
1984 Lorraine Moller, New Zealand	2:29:28
1985 Lisa Larsen Weidenbach, Mass	2:34:06
1986 Ingrid Kristiansen, Norway	2:24:55
1987 Rosa Mota, Portugal	2:25:21
1988 Rosa Mota, Portugal	2:24:30
1989 Ingrid Kristiansen, Norway	2:24:33
1990 Rosa Mota, Portugal	2:25:23
1991 Wanda Panfil, Poland	2:24:18
1992 Olga Markova, CIS	2:23:43
1993 Olga Markova, Russia	2:25:27
1994 Uta Pippig, Germany	2:21:45*
1995 Uta Pippig, Germany	2:25:11
1996 Uta Pippig, Germany	2:27:12
1997 Fatuma Roba, Ethiopia	2:26:23
1998 Fatuma Roba, Ethiopia	2:23:21

*Course record.

New York City

Started in 1970, the New York City Marathon is run in the fall, usually on the first Sunday in November. The route winds through all of the city's five boroughs and finishes in Central Park.

MEN

Multiple winners: Bill Rodgers (4); Alberto Salazar (3); Tom Fleming, Orlando Pizzolato and German Silva (2).

Year	Time
1970 Gary Muhrcke, USA	2:31:38
1971 Norman Higgins, USA	2:22:54
1972 Sheldon Karlin, USA	2:27:52
1973 Tom Fleming, USA	2:21:54
1974 Norbert Sander, USA	2:26:30
1975 Tom Fleming, USA	2:19:27
1976 Bill Rodgers, USA	2:10:09
1977 Bill Rodgers, USA	2:11:28
1978 Bill Rodgers, USA	2:12:12
1979 Bill Rodgers, USA	2:11:42
1980 Alberto Salazar, USA	2:09:41
1981 Alberto Salazar, USA	2:08:13
1982 Alberto Salazar, USA	2:09:29
1983 Rod Dixon, New Zealand	2:08:59
1984 Orlando Pizzolato, Italy	2:14:53
1985 Orlando Pizzolato, Italy	2:11:34
1986 Gianni Poli, Italy	2:11:06
1987 Ibrahim Hussein, Kenya	2:11:01
1988 Steve Jones, Wales	2:08:20
1989 Juma Ikangaa, Tanzania	2:08:01*
1990 Douglas Wakiihuri, Kenya	2:12:39
1991 Salvador Garcia, Mexico	2:09:28
1992 Willie Mtolo, South Africa	2:09:29
1993 Andres Espinosa, Mexico	2:10:04
1994 German Silva, Mexico	2:11:21
1995 German Silva, Mexico	2:11:00
1996 Giacomo Leone, Italy	2:09:54
1997 John Kagwe, Kenya	2:08:12

*Course record.

Track & Field (Cont.)

WOMEN

Multiple winners: Grete Waitz (9); Miki Gorman, Nina Kuscsik and Tegla Laroupe (2).

Year		Time
1970	No Finisher	
1971	Beth Bonner, USA	2:55:22
1972	Nina Kuscsik, USA	3:08:41
1973	Nina Kuscsik, USA	2:57:07
1974	Katherine Switzer, USA	3:07:29
1975	Kim Merritt, USA	2:46:14
1976	Miki Gorman, USA	2:39:11
1977	Miki Gorman, USA	2:43:10
1978	Grete Waitz, Norway	2:32:30
1979	Grete Waitz, Norway	2:27:33
1980	Grete Waitz, Norway	2:25:41
1981	Allison Roe, New Zealand	2:25:29
1982	Grete Waitz, Norway	2:27:14
1983	Grete Waitz, Norway	2:27:00
1984	Grete Waitz, Norway	2:29:30
1985	Grete Waitz, Norway	2:28:34
1986	Grete Waitz, Norway	2:28:06
1987	Priscilla Welch, Britain	2:30:17
1988	Grete Waitz, Norway	2:28:07
1989	Ingrid Kristiansen, Norway	2:25:30
1990	Wanda Panfil, Poland	2:30:45
1991	Liz McColgan, Scotland	2:27:23
1992	Lisa Ondieki, Australia	2:24:40*
1993	Uta Pippig, Germany	2:26:24
1994	Tegla Laroupe, Kenya	2:27:37
1995	Tegla Laroupe, Kenya	2:28:06
1996	Anuta Catuna, Romania	2:28:18
1997	Franziska Rochat-Moser, Switz.	2:28:43

*Course record.

Annual Awards

Track & Field News Athletes of the Year

Voted on by an international panel of track and field experts and presented since 1959 for men and 1974 for women.

MEN

Multiple winners: Carl Lewis (3); Sergey Bubka, Sebastian Coe, Michael Johnson, Alberto Juantorena, Noureddine Morceli, Jim Ryun and Peter Snell (2).

Year		Event
1959	Martin Lauer, W. Germany	110H/Decathlon
1960	Rafer Johnson, USA	Decathlon
1961	Ralph Boston, USA	Long Jump/110 Hurdles
1962	Peter Snell, New Zealand	800/1500
1963	C.K. Yang, Taiwan	Decathlon/Pole Vault
1964	Peter Snell, New Zealand	800/1500
1965	Ron Clarke, Australia	5000/10,000
1966	Jim Ryun, USA	800/1500
1967	Jim Ryun, USA	1500
1968	Bob Beamon, USA	Long Jump
1969	Bill Toomey, USA	Decathlon
1970	Randy Matson, USA	Shot Put
1971	Rod Milburn, USA	110 Hurdles
1972	Lasse Viren, Finland	5000/10,000
1973	Ben Jipcho, Kenya	1500/5000/Steeplechase
1974	Rick Wohlhuter, USA	800/1500
1975	John Walker, New Zealand	800/1500
1976	Alberto Juantorena, Cuba	400/800
1977	Alberto Juantorena, Cuba	400/800
1978	Henry Rono, Kenya	5000/10,000/Steeplechase
1979	Sebastian Coe, Great Britain	800/1500
1980	Edwin Moses, USA	400 Hurdles
1981	Sebastian Coe, Great Britain	800/1500
1982	Carl Lewis, USA	100/200/Long Jump
1983	Carl Lewis, USA	100/200/Long Jump
1984	Carl Lewis, USA	100/200/Long Jump
1985	Said Aouita, Morocco	1500/5000
1986	Yuri Sedykh, USSR	Hammer Throw
1987	Ben Johnson, Canada	100
1988	Sergey Bubka, USSR	Pole Vault
1989	Roger Kingdom, USA	110 Hurdles
1990	Michael Johnson, USA	200/400
1991	Sergey Bubka, USSR	Pole Vault
1992	Kevin Young, USA	400 Hurdles
1993	Noureddine Morceli, Algeria	Mile/1500/3000
1994	Noureddine Morceli, Algeria	Mile/1500/3000
1995	Haile Gebrselassie, Ethopia	5000/10,000
1996	Michael Johnson, USA	200/400
1997	Wilson Kipketer, Denmark	800

WOMEN

Multiple winners: Marita Koch (4); Jackie Joyner-Kersee (3); Evelyn Ashford (2).

Year		Event
1974	Irena Szewinska, Poland	100/200/400
1975	Faina Melnik, USSR	Shot Put/Discus
1976	Tatiana Kazankina, USSR	800/1500
1977	Rosemarie Ackermann, E. Germany	High Jump
1978	Marita Koch, E. Germany	100/200/400
1979	Marita Koch, E. Germany	100/200/400
1980	Ilona Briesenick, E. Germany	Shot Put
1981	Evelyn Ashford, USA	100/200
1982	Marita Koch, E. Germany	100/200/400
1983	Jarmila Kratochvilova, Czech	200/400/800
1984	Evelyn Ashford, USA	100
1985	Marita Koch, E. Germany	100/200/400
1986	Jackie Joyner-Kersee, USA	Heptathlon/Long Jump
1987	Jackie Joyner-Kersee, USA	100H/Heptathlon/LJ
1988	Florence Griffith Joyner, USA	100/200
1989	Ana Quirot, Cuba	400/800
1990	Merlene Ottey, Jamaica	100/200
1991	Heike Henkel, Germany	High Jump
1992	Heike Drechsler, Germany	Long Jump
1993	Wang Junxia, China	1500/3000/10,000
1994	Jackie Joyner-Kersee, USA	100H/Heptathlon/LJ
1995	Sonia O'Sullivan, Ireland	1500/3000/5000
1996	Svetlana Masterkova, Russia	800/1500
1997	Marion Jones, USA	100/200

SWIMMING & DIVING

FINA World Championships

While the Summer Olympics have served as the unofficial world championships for swimming and diving throughout the century, a separate World Championship meet was started in 1973 by the International Amateur Swimming Federation (FINA). The meet was held three times between 1973-78, then every four years since then. Sites have included Belgrade (1973); Cali, COL (1975); West Berlin (1978); Guayaquil, ECU (1982); Madrid (1986); Perth (1991 & 98) and Rome (1994).

MEN

Most gold medals (including relays): Jim Montgomery (7); Matt Biondi (6); Rowdy Gaines (5); Joe Bottom, Tamas Darnyi, Michael Gross, Tom Jager, Michael Klim, David McCagg, Vladimir Salnikov and Tim Shaw (4); Billy Forrester, Andras Hargitay, Roland Matthes, John Murphy, Alexander Popov, Jeff Rouse, Norbert Rozsa and David Wilkie (3).

50-Meter Freestyle

Year		Time	
1973-82	Not held		
1986	Tom Jager, USA	22.49	
1991	Tom Jager, USA	22.16	CR
1994	Alexander Popov, RUS	22.17	
1998	Bill Pilczuk, USA	22.29	

100-Meter Freestyle

Year		Time	
1973	Jim Montgomery, USA	51.70	
1975	Tim Shaw, USA	51.25	
1978	David McCagg, USA	50.24	
1982	Jorg Woithe, E. Ger	50.18	
1986	Matt Biondi, USA	48.94	
1991	Matt Biondi, USA	49.18	
1994	Alexander Popov, RUS	49.12	
1998	Alexander Popov, RUS	48.93	CR

200-Meter Freestyle

Year		Time	
1973	Jim Montgomery, USA	1:53.02	
1975	Tim Shaw, USA	1:52.04	
1978	Billy Forrester, USA	1:51.02	
1982	Michael Gross, W. Ger	1:49.84	
1986	Michael Gross, W. Ger	1:47.92	
1991	Giorgio Lamberti, ITA	1:47.27	
1994	Antti Kasvio, FIN	1:47.32	CR
1998	Michael Klim, AUS	1:47.41	

400-Meter Freestyle

Year		Time	
1973	Rick DeMont, USA	3:58.18	
1975	Tim Shaw, USA	3:54.88	
1978	Vladimir Salnikov, USSR	3:51.94	
1982	Vladimir Salnikov, USSR	3:51.30	
1986	Rainer Henkel, W. Ger	3:50.05	
1991	Jorg Hoffman, GER	3:48.04	
1994	Kieren Perkins, AUS	3:43.80	WR
1998	Ian Thorpe, AUS	3:46.29	

1500-Meter Freestyle

Year		Time	
1973	Stephen Holland, AUS	15:31.85	
1975	Tim Shaw, USA	15:28.92	
1978	Vladimir Salnikov, USSR	15:03.99	
1982	Vladimir Salnikov, USSR	15:01.77	
1986	Rainer Henkel, W. Ger	15:05.31	
1991	Jorg Hoffman, GER	14:50.36	WR
1994	Kieren Perkins, AUS	14:50.52	
1998	Grant Hackett, AUS	14:51.70	

100-Meter Backstroke

Year		Time	
1973	Roland Matthes, E. Ger	57.47	
1975	Roland Matthes, E. Ger	58.15	
1978	Bob Jackson, USA	56.36	
1982	Dirk Richter, E. Ger	55.95	
1986	Igor Polianski, USSR	55.58	
1991	Jeff Rouse, USA	55.23	
1994	Martin Lopez-Zubero, SPA	55.17	CR
1998	Lenny Krayzelburg, USA	55.00	

200-Meter Backstroke

Year		Time	
1973	Roland Matthes, E. Ger	2:01.87	
1975	Zoltan Varraszto, HUN	2:05.05	
1978	Jesse Vassallo, USA	2:02.16	
1982	Rick Carey, USA	2:00.82	
1986	Igor Polianski, USSR	1:58.78	CR
1991	Martin Zubero, SPA	1:59.52	
1994	Vladimir Selkov, RUS	1:57.42	
1998	Lenny Krayzelburg, USA	1:58.84	

100-Meter Breaststroke

Year		Time	
1973	John Hencken, USA	1:04.02	
1975	David Wilkie, GBR	1:04.26	
1978	Walter Kusch, W. Ger	1:03.56	
1982	Steve Lundquist, USA	1:02.75	
1986	Victor Davis, CAN	1:02.71	
1991	Norbert Rozsa, HUN	1:01.45	WR
1994	Norbert Rozsa, HUN	1:01.24	
1998	Frederik Deburghgraeve, BEL	1:01.34	

200-Meter Breaststroke

Year		Time	
1973	David Wilkie, GBR	2:19.28	
1975	David Wilkie, GBR	2:18.23	
1978	Nick Nevid, USA	2:18.37	
1982	Victor Davis, CAN	2:14.77	WR
1986	Jozsef Szabo, HUN	2:14.27	
1991	Mike Barrowman, USA	2:11.23	WR
1994	Norbert Rozsa, HUN	2:12.81	
1998	Kurt Grote, USA	2:13.40	

100-Meter Butterfly

Year		Time	
1973	Bruce Robertson, CAN	55.69	
1975	Greg Jagenburg, USA	55.63	
1978	Joe Bottom, USA	54.30	
1982	Matt Gribble, USA	53.88	
1986	Pablo Morales, USA	53.54	
1991	Anthony Nesty, SUR	53.29	
1994	Rafal Szukala, POL	53.51	
1998	Michael Klim, AUS	52.25	CR

200-Meter Butterfly

Year		Time	
1973	Robin Backhaus, USA	2:03.32	
1975	Billy Forrester, USA	2:01.95	
1978	Mike Bruner, USA	1:59.38	
1982	Michael Gross, W. Ger	1:58.85	
1986	Michael Gross, W. Ger	1:56.53	
1991	Melvin Stewart, USA	1:55.69	WR
1994	Denis Pankratov, RUS	1:56.54	
1998	Denys Sylantyev, UKR	1:56.61	

200-Meter Individual Medley

Year		Time	
1973	Gunnar Larsson, SWE	2:08.36	
1975	Andras Hargitay, HUN	2:07.72	
1978	Graham Smith, CAN	2:03.65	WR
1982	Alexander Sidorenko, USSR	2:03.30	
1986	Tamás Darnyi, HUN	2:01.57	
1991	Tamás Darnyi, HUN	1:59.36	WR
1994	Janis Sievinen, FIN	1:58.16	WR
1998	Marcel Wouda, NET	2:01.18	

Swimming & Diving (Cont.)

400-Meter Individual Medley

Year		Time	
1973	Andras Hargitay, HUN	4:31.11	
1975	Andras Hargitay, HUN	4:32.57	
1978	Jesse Vassallo, USA	4:20.05	WR
1982	Ricardo Prado, BRA	4:19.78	WR
1986	Tamás Darnyi, HUN	4:18.98	
1991	Tamás Darnyi, HUN	4:12.36	WR
1994	Tom Dolan, USA	4:12.30	WR
1998	Tom Dolan, USA	4:14.95	

4 x 100-Meter Freestyle Relay

Year		Time	
1973	United States	3:27.18	
1975	United States	3:24.85	
1978	United States	3:19.74	
1982	United States	3:19.26	WR
1986	United States	3:19.98	
1991	United States	3:17.15	
1994	United States	3:16.90	
1998	United States	3:16.69	CR

4 x 200-Meter Freestyle Relay

Year		Time	
1973	United States	7:33.22	WR
1975	West Germany	7:39.44	
1978	United States	7:20.82	
1982	United States	7:21.09	
1986	East Germany	7:15.91	
1991	Germany	7:13.50	CR
1994	Sweden	7:17.34	
1998	Australia	7:12.48	

4 x 100-Meter Medley Relay

Year		Time	
1973	United States	3:49.49	
1975	United States	3:49.00	
1978	United States	3:44.63	
1982	United States	3:40.84	WR
1986	United States	3:41.25	
1991	United States	3:39.66	
1994	United States	3:37.74	CR
1998	Australia	3:37.98	

WOMEN

Most gold medals (including relays): Kornelia Ender (8); Kristin Otto (7); Tracy Caulkins, Heike Friedrich, Le Jingyi, Rosemarie Kother, Ulrike Richter and Jenny Thompson (4); Hannalore Anke, Lu Bin, He Cihong, Janet Evans, Nicole Haislett, Lui Limin, Birgit Meineke, Joan Pennington, Manuela Stellmach, Amy Van Dyken, Renate Vogel and Cynthia Woodhead (3).

50-Meter Freestyle

Year		Time	
1973-82	Not held		
1986	Tamara Costache, ROM	25.28	WR
1991	Zhuang Yong, CHN	25.47	
1994	Le Jingyi, CHN	24.51	WR
1998	Amy Van Dyken, USA	25.15	

100-Meter Freestyle

Year		Time	
1973	Kornelia Ender, E. Ger	57.54	
1975	Kornelia Ender, E. Ger	56.50	
1978	Barbara Krause, E. Ger	55.68	
1982	Birgit Meineke, E. Ger	55.79	
1986	Kristin Otto, E. Ger	55.05	
1991	Nicole Haislett, USA	55.17	
1994	Le Jingyi, CHN	54.01	WR
1998	Jenny Thompson, USA	54.95	

200-Meter Freestyle

Year		Time	
1973	Keena Rothhammer, USA	2:04.99	
1975	Shirley Babashoff, USA	2:02.50	
1978	Cynthia Woodhead, USA	1:58.53	WR
1982	Annemarie Verstappen, HOL	1:59.53	
1986	Heike Friedrich, E. Ger	1:58.26	
1991	Hayley Lewis, AUS	2:00.48	
1994	Franziska Van Almsick, GER	1:56.78	WR
1998	Claudia Poll, CST	1:58.90	

400-Meter Freestyle

Year		Time	
1973	Heather Greenwood, USA	4:20.28	
1975	Shirley Babashoff, USA	4:22.70	
1978	Tracey Wickham, AUS	4:06.28	WR
1982	Carmela Schmidt. E. Ger	4:08.98	
1986	Heike Friedrich, E. Ger	4:07.45	
1991	Janet Evans, USA	4:08.63	
1994	Yang Aihua, CHN	4:09.64	
1998	Yan Chen, CHN	4:06.72	

800-Meter Freestyle

Year		Time	
1973	Novella Calligaris, ITA	8:52.97	
1975	Jenny Turrall, AUS	8:44.75	
1978	Tracey Wickham, AUS	8:25.94	
1982	Kim Linehan, USA	8:27.48	
1986	Astrid Strauss, E. Ger	8:28.24	
1991	Janet Evans, USA	8:24.05	CR
1994	Janet Evans, USA	8:29.85	
1998	Brooke Bennett, USA	8:28.71	

100-Meter Backstroke

Year		Time	
1973	Ulrike Richter, E. Ger	1:05.42	
1975	Ulrike Richter, E. Ger	1:03.30	
1978	Linda Jezek, USA	1:02.55	
1982	Kristin Otto, E. Ger	1:01.30	
1986	Betsy Mitchell, USA	1:01.74	
1991	Krisztina Egerszegi, HUN	1:01.78	
1994	He Cihong, CHN	1:00.57	WR
1998	Lea Maurer, USA	1:01.16	

200-Meter Backstroke

Year		Time	
1973	Melissa Belote, USA	2:20.52	
1975	Birgit Treiber, E. Ger	2:15.46	WR
1978	Linda Jezek, USA	2:11.93	WR
1982	Cornelia Sirch, E. Ger	2:09.91	WR
1986	Cornelia Sirch, E. Ger	2:11.37	
1991	Krisztina Egerszegi, HUN	2:09.15	
1994	He Cihong, CHN	2:07.40	CR
1998	Roxanna Maracineanu, FRA	2:11.26	

100-Meter Breaststroke

Year		Time	
1973	Renate Vogel, E. Ger	1:13.74	
1975	Hannalore Anke, E. Ger	1:12.72	
1978	Julia Bogdanova, USSR	1:10.31	WR
1982	Ute Geweniger, E. Ger	1:09.14	
1986	Sylvia Gerasch, E. Ger	1:08.11	WR
1991	Linley Frame, AUS	1:08.81	
1994	Samantha Riley, AUS	1:07.69	WR
1998	Kristy Kowal, USA	1:08.42	

200-Meter Breaststroke

Year		Time	
1973	Renate Vogel, E. Ger	2:40.01	
1975	Hannalore Anke, E. Ger	2:37.25	
1978	Lina Kachushite, USSR	2:31.42	WR
1982	Svetlana Varganova, USSR	2:28.82	
1986	Silke Hoerner, E. Ger	2:27.40	WR

Year		Time	
1991	Elena Volkova, USSR	2:29.53	
1994	Samantha Riley, AUS	2:26.87	
1998	Agnes Kovacs, HUN	2:25.45	CR

100-Meter Butterfly

Year		Time	
1973	Kornelia Ender, E. Ger	1:02.53	
1975	Kornelia Ender, E. Ger	1:01.24	WR
1978	Joan Pennington, USA	1:00.20	
1982	Mary T. Meagher, USA	.59.41	
1986	Kornelai Gressler, E. Ger	.59.51	
1991	Qian Hong, CHN	.59.68	
1994	Liu Limin, CHN	.58.98	
1998	Jenny Thompson, USA	.58.46	CR

200-Meter Butterfly

Year		Time	
1973	Rosemarie Kother, E. Ger	2:13.76	
1975	Rosemarie Kother, E. Ger	2:15.92	
1978	Tracy Caulkins, USA	2:09.78	WR
1982	Ines Geissler, E. Ger	2:08.66	
1986	Mary T. Meagher, USA	2:08.41	
1991	Summer Sanders, USA	2:09.24	
1994	Liu Limin, CHN	2:07.25	CR
1998	Susie O'Neill, AUS	2:07.93	CR

200-Meter Individual Medley

Year		Time	
1973	Andre Huebner, E. Ger	2:20.51	
1975	Kathy Heddy, USA	2:19.80	
1978	Tracy Caulkins, USA	2:19.80	WR
1982	Petra Schneider, E. Ger	2:11.79	CR
1986	Kristin Otto, E. Ger	2:15.56	
1991	Lin Li, CHN	2:13.40	
1994	Lu Bin, CHN	2:12.34	
1998	Yanyan Wu, CHN	2:10.88	CR

400-Meter Individual Medley

Year		Time	
1973	Gudrun Wegner, E. Ger	4:57.71	
1975	Ulrike Tauber, E. Ger	4:52.76	
1978	Tracy Caulkins, USA	4:40.83	WR
1982	Petra Schneider, E. Ger	4:36.10	WR
1986	Kathleen Nord, E. Ger	4:43.75	
1991	Lin Li, CHN	4:41.45	
1994	Dai Guohong, CHN	4:39.14	
1998	Yan Chen, CHN	4:36.66	

4 x 100-Meter Freestyle Relay

Year		Time	
1973	East Germany	3:52.45	
1975	East Germany	3:49.37	
1978	United States	3:43.43	WR
1982	East Germany	3:43.97	
1986	East Germany	3:40.57	
1991	United States	3:43.26	
1994	China	3:37.91	WR
1998	United States	3:42.11	

4 x 200-Meter Freestyle Relay

Year		Time	
1973-82	Not held		
1986	East Germany	7:59.33	WR
1991	Germany	8:02.56	
1994	China	7:57.96	CR
1998	Germany	8:01.46	

4 x 100-Meter Medley Relay

Year		Time	
1973	East Germany	4:16.84	
1975	East Germany	4:14.74	
1978	United States	4:08.21	
1982	East Germany	4:05.8	WR
1986	East Germany	4:04.82	
1991	United States	4:06.51	
1994	China	4:01.67	CR
1998	United States	4:01.93	

Diving

Multiple Gold Medals: MEN– Greg Louganis (5); Phil Boggs and Dmitry Sautin (3); Klaus Dibiasi and Yu Zhuocheng (2). WOMEN– Irina Kalinina and Gao Min (3); Fu Mingxia (2).

MEN

1-Meter Springboard

Year		Pts
1991	Edwin Jongejans, HOL	588.51
1994	Evan Stewart, ZIM	382.14
1998	Yu Zhuocheng, CHN	417.54

3-Meter Springboard

Year		Pts
1973	Phil Boggs, USA	618.57
1975	Phil Boggs, USA	597.12
1978	Phil Boggs, USA	913.95
1982	Greg Louganis, USA	752.67
1986	Greg Louganis, USA	750.06
1991	Kent Ferguson, USA	650.25
1994	Yu Zhuocheng, CHN	655.44
1998	Dmitry Sautin, RUS	746.79

Platform

Year		Pts
1973	Klaus Dibiasi, ITA	559.53
1975	Klaus Dibiasi, ITA	547.98
1978	Greg Louganis, USA	844.11
1982	Greg Louganis, USA	634.26
1986	Greg Louganis, USA	668.58
1991	Sun Shuwei, CHN	626.79
1994	Dmitry Sautin, RUS	634.71
1998	Dmitry Sautin, RUS	750.99

WOMEN

1-Meter Springboard

Year		Pts
1991	Gao Min, CHN	478.26
1994	Chen Lixia, CHN	279.30
1998	Irina Lashko, RUS	296.07

3-Meter Springboard

Year		Pts
1973	Christa Koehler, E. Ger	442.17
1975	Irina Kalinina, USSR	489.81
1978	Irina Kalinina, USSR	691.43
1982	Megan Neyer, USA	501.03
1986	Gao Min, CHN	582.90
1991	Gao Min, CHN	539.01
1994	Tan Shuping, CHN	548.49
1998	Yulia Pakhalina, RUS	544.52

Platform

Year		Pts
1973	Ulrike Knape, SWE	406.77
1975	Janet Ely, USA	403.89
1978	Irina Kalinina, USSR	412.71
1982	Wendy Wyland, USA	438.79
1986	Chen Lin, CHN	449.67
1991	Fu Mingxia, CHN	426.51
1994	Fu Mingxia, CHN	434.04
1998	Olena Zhupyna	550.41

ALPINE SKIING

World Cup Overall Champions

World Cup Overall Champions (downhill and slalom events combined) since the tour was organized in 1967.

MEN

Multiple winners: Marc Girardelli (5), Gustavo Thoeni and Pirmin Zurbriggen (4); Phil Mahre, and Ingemar Stenmark (3); Jean-Claude Killy and Karl Schranz (2).

Year	
1967	Jean-Claude Killy, France
1968	Jean Claude Killy, France
1969	Karl Schranz, Austria
1970	Karl Schranz, Austria
1971	Gustavo Thoeni, Italy
1972	Gustavo Thoeni, Italy
1973	Gustavo Thoeni, Italy
1974	Piero Gros, Italy
1975	Gustavo Thoeni, Italy
1976	Ingemar Stenmark, Sweden
1977	Ingemar Stenmark, Sweden
1978	Ingemar Stenmark, Sweden
1979	Peter Luescher, Switzerland
1980	Andreas Wenzel, Liechtenstein
1981	Phil Mahre, USA
1982	Phil Mahre, USA
1983	Phil Mahre, USA
1984	Pirmin Zurbriggen, Switzerland
1985	Marc Girardelli, Luxembourg
1986	Marc Girardelli, Luxembourg
1987	Pirmin Zurbriggen, Switzerland
1988	Pirmin Zurbriggen, Switzerland
1989	Marc Girardelli, Luxembourg
1990	Pirmin Zurbriggen, Switzerland
1991	Marc Girardelli, Luxembourg
1992	Paul Accola, Switzerland
1993	Marc Girardelli, Luxembourg
1994	Kjetil Andre Aamodt, Norway
1995	Alberto Tomba, Italy
1996	Lasse Kjus, Norway
1997	Luc Alphand, France
1998	Hermann Maier, Austria

WOMEN

Multiple winners: Annemarie Moser-Proell (6); Petra Kronberger and Vreni Schneider (3); Michela Figini, Nancy Greene, Erika Hess, Katja Seizinger, Maria Walliser and Hanni Wenzel (2).

Year	
1967	Nancy Greene, Canada
1968	Nancy Greene, Canada
1969	Gertrud Gabi, Austria
1970	Michele Jacot, France
1971	Annemarie Pröll, Austria
1972	Annemarie Pröll, Austria
1973	Annemarie Pröll, Austria
1974	Annemarie Pröll, Austria
1975	Annemarie Moser-Pröll, Austria
1976	Rosi Mittermaier, W. Germany
1977	Lise-Marie Morerod, Switzerland
1978	Hanni Wenzel, Liechtenstein
1979	Annemarie Moser-Pröll, Austria
1980	Hanni Wenzel, Liechtenstein
1981	Marie-Theres Nadig,Switzerland
1982	Erika Hess, Switzerland
1983	Tamara McKinney, USA
1984	Erika Hess, Switzerland
1985	Michela Figini, Switzerland
1986	Maria Walliser, Switzerland
1987	Maria Walliser, Switzerland
1988	Michela Figini, Switzerland
1989	Vreni Schneider, Switzerland
1990	Petra Kronberger, Austria
1991	Petra Kronberger, Austria
1992	Petra Kronberger, Austria
1993	Anita Wachter, Austria
1994	Vreni Schneider, Switzerland
1995	Vreni Schneider, Switzerland
1996	Katja Seizinger, Germany
1997	Pernilla Wiberg, Sweden
1998	Katja Seizinger, Germany

TOUR DE FRANCE

The world's premier cycling event, the Tour de France is staged throughout the country (sometimes passing through neighboring countries) over four weeks. The 1946 Tour, however, the first after World War II, was only a five-day race.

Multiple winners: Jacques Anquetil, Bernard Hinault, Miguel Induráin and Eddy Merckx (5); Louison Bobet, Greg LeMond and Phillippe Thys (3); Gino Bartali Ottavio Bottecchia, Fausto Coppi, Laurent Fignon, Nicholas Frantz, Firmin Lambot, André Leducq, Sylvere Maes, Antonin Magne, Lucien Petit-Breton and Bernard Thevenet (2).

Year	
1903	Maurice Garin, France
1904	Henri Cornet, France
1905	Louis Trousselier, France
1906	René Pottier, France
1907	Lucien Petit-Breton, France
1908	Lucien Petit-Breton, France
1909	Francois Faber, Luxembourg
1910	Octave Lapize, France
1911	Gustave Garrigou, France
1912	Odile Defraye, Belgium
1913	Philippe Thys, Belgium
1914	Philippe Thys, Belgium
1915-18	Not held
1919	Firmin Lambot, Belgium
1920	Philippe Thys, Belgium
1921	Léon Scieur, Belgium
1922	Firmin Lambot, Belgium
1923	Henri Pelissier, France
1924	Ottavio Bottecchia, Italy
1925	Ottavio Bottecchia, Italy
1926	Lucien Buysse, Belgium
1927	Nicholas Frantz, Luxembourg
1928	Nicholas Frantz, Luxembourg
1929	Maurice Dewaele, Belgium
1930	André Leducq, France
1931	Antonin Magne, France
1932	André Leducq, France
1933	Georges Speicher, France
1934	Antonin Magne, France
1935	Romain Maes, Belgium
1936	Sylvere Maes, Belgium
1937	Roger Lapebie, France
1938	Gino Bartali, Italy
1939	Sylvere Maes, Belgium
1940-45	Not held
1946	Jean Lazarides, France
1947	Jean Robic, France
1948	Gino Bartali, Italy
1949	Fausto Coppi, Italy
1950	Ferdinand Kubler, Switzerland
1951	Hugo Koblet, Switzerland
1952	Fausto Coppi, Italy
1953	Louison Bobet, France
1954	Louison Bobet, France
1955	Louison Bobet, France
1956	Roger Walkowiak, France
1957	Jacques Anquetil, France
1958	Charly Gaul, Luxembourg
1959	Federico Bahamontes, Spain
1960	Gastone Nencini, Italy
1961	Jacques Anquetil, France
1962	Jacques Anquetil, France
1963	Jacques Anquetil, France
1964	Jacques Anquetil, France
1965	Felice Gimondi, Italy
1966	Lucien Aimar, France
1967	Roger Pingeon, France
1968	Jan Janssen, Holland
1969	Eddy Merckx, Belgium
1970	Eddy Merckx, Belgium
1971	Eddy Merckx, Belgium
1972	Eddy Merckx, Belgium
1973	Luis Ocana, Spain
1974	Eddy Merckx, Belgium
1975	Bernard Thevenet, France
1976	Lucien van Impe, Belgium
1977	Bernard Thevenet, France
1978	Bernard Hinault, France
1979	Bernard Hinault, France
1980	Joop Zoetemelk, Holland
1981	Bernard Hinault, France
1982	Bernard Hinault, France
1983	Laurent Fignon, France
1984	Laurent Fignon, France
1985	Bernard Hinault, France
1986	Greg LeMond, USA
1987	Stephen Roche, Ireland
1988	Pedro Delgado, Spain

Year		Year		Year	
1989	Greg LeMond, USA	1993	Miguel Induráin, Spain	1997	Jan Ullrich, Germany
1990	Greg LeMond, USA	1994	Miguel Induráin, Spain	1998	Marco Pantani, Italy
1991	Miguel Induráin, Spain	1995	Miguel Induráin, Spain		
1992	Miguel Induráin, Spain	1996	Bjarne Riis, Denmark		

FIGURE SKATING

World Champions

Skaters who won World and Olympic championships in the same year are listed in **bold** type.

MEN

Multiple winners: Ulrich Salchow (10); Karl Schafer (7); Dick Button (5); Willy Bockl, Kurt Browning, Scott Hamilton and Hayes Jenkins (4); Emmerich Danzer, Gillis Grafstrom, Gustav Hugel, David Jenkins, Fritz Kachler, Ondrej Nepela and Elvis Stojko (3); Brian Boitano, Gilbert Fuchs, Jan Hoffmann, Felix Kaspar, Vladimir Kovalev and Tim Wood (2).

Year	
1896	Gilbert Fuchs, Germany
1897	Gustav Hugel, Austria
1898	Henning Grenander, Sweden
1899	Gustav Hugel, Austria
1900	Gustav Hugel, Austria
1901	Ulrich Salchow, Sweden
1902	Ulrich Salchow, Sweden
1903	Ulrich Salchow, Sweden
1904	Ulrich Salchow, Sweden
1905	Ulrich Salchow, Sweden
1906	Gilbert Fuchs, Germany
1907	Ulrich Salchow, Sweden
1908	**Ulrich Salchow**, Sweden
1909	Ulrich Salchow, Sweden
1910	Ulrich Salchow, Sweden
1911	Ulrich Salchow, Sweden
1912	Fritz Kachler, Austria
1913	Fritz Kachler, Austria
1914	Gosta Sandhal, Sweden
1915-21	Not held
1922	Gillis Grafstrom, Sweden
1923	Fritz Kachler, Austria
1924	**Gillis Grafstrom,** Sweden
1925	Willy Bockl, Austria
1926	Willy Bockl, Austria
1927	Willy Bockl, Austria
1928	Willy Bockl, Austria
1929	Gillis Grafstrom, Sweden
1930	Karl Schafer, Austria
1931	Karl Schafer, Austria
1932	**Karl Schafer**, Austria
1933	Karl Schafer, Austria
1934	Karl Schafer, Austria
1935	Karl Schafer, Austria
1936	**Karl Schafer**, Austria
1937	Felix Kaspar, Austria
1938	Felix Kaspar, Austria
1939	Graham Sharp, Britain
1940-46	Not held
1947	Hans Gerschwiler, Switzerland
1948	**Dick Button**, USA
1949	Dick Button, USA
1950	Dick Button, USA
1951	Dick Button, USA
1952	**Dick Button**, USA
1953	Hayes Jenkins, USA
1954	Hayes Jenkins, USA
1955	Hayes Jenkins, USA
1956	**Hayes Jenkins**, USA
1957	David Jenkins, USA
1958	David Jenkins, USA
1959	David Jenkins, USA
1960	Alan Giletti, France
1961	Not held
1962	Donald Jackson, Canada
1963	Donald McPherson, Canada
1964	**Manfred Schnelldorfer**, W. Ger
1965	Alain Calmat, France
1966	Emmerich Danzer, Austria
1967	Emmerich Danzer, Austria
1968	Emmerich Danzer, Austria
1969	Tim Wood, USA
1970	Tim Wood, USA
1971	Ondrej Nepela, Czechoslovakia
1972	**Ondrej Nepela**, Czechoslovakia
1973	Ondrej Nepela, Czechoslovakia
1974	Jan Hoffmann, E. Germany
1975	Sergie Volkov, USSR
1976	**John Curry**, Britain
1977	Vladimir Kovalev, USSR
1978	Charles Tickner, USA
1979	Vladimir Kovalev, USSR
1980	Jan Hoffmann, E. Germany
1981	Scott Hamilton, USA
1982	Scott Hamilton, USA
1983	Scott Hamilton, USA
1984	**Scott Hamilton**, USA
1985	Alexander Fadeev, USSR
1986	Brian Boitano, USA
1987	Brian Orser, Canada
1988	**Brian Boitano**, USA
1989	Kurt Browning, Canada
1990	Kurt Browning, Canada
1991	Kurt Browning, Canada
1992	**Viktor Petrenko**, CIS
1993	Kurt Browning, Canada
1994	Elvis Stojko, Canada
1995	Elvis Stojko, Canada
1996	Todd Eldredge, USA
1997	Elvis Stojko, Canada
1998	Alexei Yagudin, Russia

WOMEN

Multiple winners: Sonja Henie (10); Carol Heiss and Herma Planck Szabo (5); Lily Kronberger and Katarina Witt (4); Sjoukje Dijkstra, Peggy Fleming, Meray Horvath (3); Tenley Albright, Linda Fratianne, Michelle Kwan, Anett Poetzsch, Beatrix Schuba, Barbara Ann Scott, Gabriele Seyfert, Megan Taylor, Alena Vrzanova, and Kristi Yamaguchi (2).

Year	
1906	Madge Syers, Britain
1907	Madge Syers, Britian
1908	Lily Kronberger, Hungary
1909	Lily Kronberger, Hungary
1910	Lily Kronberger, Hungary
1911	Lily Kronberger, Hungary
1912	Meray Horvath, Hungary
1913	Meray Horvath, Hungary
1914	Meray Horvath, Hungary
1915-21	Not held
1922	Herma Planck-Szabo, Austria
1923	Herma Planck-Szabo, Austria
1924	**Herma Planck-Szabo**, Austria
1925	Herma Planck-Szabo, Austria
1926	Herma Planck-Szabo, Austria
1927	Sonja Henie, Norway
1928	**Sonja Henie**, Norway
1929	Sonja Henie, Norway
1930	Sonja Henie, Norway
1931	Sonja Henie, Norway
1932	**Sonja Henie**, Norway
1933	Sonja Henie, Norway
1934	Sonja Henie, Norway
1935	Sonja Henie, Norway
1936	**Sonja Henie**, Norway
1937	Cecilia Colledge, Britain
1938	Megan Taylor, Britain
1939	Megan Taylor, Britain
1940-46	Not held
1947	Barbara Ann Scott, Canada
1948	**Barbara Ann Scott**, Canada
1949	Alena Vrzanova,Czechoslovakia
1950	Alena Vrzanova,Czechoslovakia
1951	Jeannette Altwegg, Britain
1952	Jacqueline Du Bief, France
1953	Tenley Albright, USA
1954	Gundi Busch, W. Germany
1955	Tenley Albright, USA
1956	Carol Heiss, USA
1957	Carol Heiss, USA
1958	Carol Heiss, USA
1959	Carol Heiss, USA
1960	**Carol Heiss**, USA
1961	Not held
1962	Sjoukje Dijkstra, Holland
1963	Sjoukje Dijkstra, Holland
1964	**Sjoukje Dijkstra**, Holland
1965	Petra Burka, Canada
1966	Peggy Fleming, USA
1967	Peggy Fleming, USA
1968	**Peggy Fleming**, USA
1969	Gabriele Seyfert, E. Germany

Year	
1970	Gabriele Seyfert, E. Germany
1971	Beatrix Schuba, Austria
1972	**Beatrix Schuba**, Austria
1973	Karen Magnussen, Canada
1974	Christine Errath, E. Germany
1975	Dianne DeLeeuw, Holland
1976	**Dorothy Hamill**, USA
1977	Linda Fratianne, USA
1978	Anett Poetzsch, E. Germany
1979	Linda Fratianne, USA
1980	**Anett Poetzsch**, E. Germany
1981	Denise Biellmann, Switzerland
1982	Elaine Zayak, USA
1983	Rosalyn Sumners, USA
1984	**Katarina Witt**, E. Germany
1985	Katarina Witt, E. Germany
1986	Debi Thomas, USA
1987	Katarina Witt, E. Germany
1988	**Katarina Witt**, E. Germany
1989	Midori Ito, Japan
1990	Jill Trenary, USA
1991	Kristi Yamaguchi, USA
1992	**Kristi Yamaguchi**, USA
1993	Oksana Baiul, Ukraine
1994	Yuka Sato, Japan
1995	Lu Chen, China
1996	Michelle Kwan, USA
1997	Tara Lipinski, USA
1998	Michelle Kwan, USA

U.S. Champions

Skaters who won U.S., World and Olympic championships in same year are in **bold** type.

MEN

Multiple winners: Dick Button and Roger Turner (7); Sherwin Badger, Todd Eldredge and Robin Lee (5); Brian Boitano, Scott Hamilton, David Jenkins, Hayes Jenkins and Charles Tickner (4); Gordon McKellen, Nathaniel Niles and Tim Wood (3); Scott Allen, Christopher Bowman, Scott Davis, Eugene Turner and Gary Visconti (2).

Year	
1914	Norman Scott
1915-17	Not held
1918	Nathaniel Niles
1919	Not held
1920	Sherwin Badger
1921	Sherwin Badger
1922	Sherwin Badger
1923	Sherwin Badger
1924	Sherwin Badger
1925	Nathaniel Niles
1926	Chris Christenson
1927	Nathaniel Niles
1928	Roger Turner
1929	Roger Turner
1930	Roger Turner
1931	Roger Turner
1932	Roger Turner
1933	Roger Turner
1934	Roger Turner
1935	Robin Lee
1936	Robin Lee
1937	Robin Lee
1938	Robin Lee
1939	Robin Lee
1940	Eugene Turner
1941	Eugene Turner
1942	Robert Specht
1943	Arthur Vaughn
1944-45	Not held
1946	Dick Button
1947	Dick Button
1948	**Dick Button**
1949	Dick Button
1950	Dick Button
1951	Dick Button
1952	**Dick Button**
1953	Hayes Jenkins
1954	Hayes Jenkins
1955	Hayes Jenkins
1956	**Hayes Jenkins**
1957	David Jenkins
1958	David Jenkins
1959	David Jenkins
1960	David Jenkins
1961	Bradley Lord
1962	Monty Hoyt
1963	Thomas Litz
1964	Scott Allen
1965	Gary Visconti
1966	Scott Allen
1967	Gary Visconti
1968	Tim Wood
1969	Tim Wood
1970	Tim Wood
1971	John (Misha) Petkevich
1972	Ken Shelley
1973	Gordon McKellen
1974	Gordon McKellen
1975	Gordon McKellen
1976	Terry Kubicka
1977	Charles Tickner
1978	Charles Tickner
1979	Charles Tickner
1980	Charles Tickner
1981	Scott Hamilton
1982	Scott Hamilton
1983	Scott Hamilton
1984	**Scott Hamilton**
1985	Brian Boitano
1986	Brian Boitano
1987	Brian Boitano
1988	**Brian Boitano**
1989	Christopher Bowman
1990	Todd Eldredge
1991	Todd Eldredge
1992	Christopher Bowman
1993	Scott Davis
1994	Scott Davis
1995	Todd Eldredge
1996	Rudy Galindo
1997	Todd Eldredge
1998	Todd Eldredge

WOMEN

Multiple winners: Maribel Vinson (9); Theresa Weld Blanchard and Gretchen Merrill (6); Tenley Albright, Peggy Fleming, and Janet Lynn (5); Linda Fratianne and Carol Heiss (4); Dorothy Hamill, Beatrix Loughran, Rosalyn Summers, Joan Tozzer and Jill Trenary (3); Michelle Kwan, Yvonne Sherman and Debi Thomas (2).

Year	
1914	Theresa Weld
1915-17	Not held
1918	Rosemary Beresford
1919	Not held
1920	Theresa Weld
1921	Theresa Blanchard
1922	Theresa Blanchard
1923	Theresa Blanchard
1924	Theresa Blanchard
1925	Beatrix Loughran
1926	Beatrix Loughran
1927	Beatrix Loughran
1928	Maribel Vinson
1929	Maribel Vinson
1930	Maribel Vinson
1931	Maribel Vinson
1932	Maribel Vinson
1933	Maribel Vinson
1934	Suzanne Davis
1935	Maribel Vinson
1936	Maribel Vinson
1937	Maribel Vinson
1938	Joan Tozzer
1939	Joan Tozzer
1940	Joan Tozzer
1941	Jane Vaughn
1942	Jane Sullivan
1943	Gretchen Merrill
1944	Gretchen Merrill
1945	Gretchen Merrill
1946	Gretchen Merrill
1947	Gretchen Merrill
1948	Gretchen Merrill
1949	Yvonne Sherman
1950	Yvonne Sherman
1951	Sonya Klopfer
1952	Tenley Albright
1953	Tenley Albright
1954	Tenley Albright
1955	Tenley Albright
1956	Tenley Albright
1957	Carol Heiss
1958	Carol Heiss
1959	Carol Heiss
1960	**Carol Heiss**
1961	Laurence Owen
1962	Barbara Pursley
1963	Lorraine Hanlon
1964	Peggy Fleming
1965	Peggy Fleming
1966	Peggy Fleming
1967	Peggy Fleming
1968	**Peggy Fleming**
1969	Janet Lynn
1970	Janet Lynn
1971	Janet Lynn
1972	Janet Lynn
1973	Janet Lynn
1974	Dorothy Hamill
1975	Dorothy Hamill
1976	**Dorothy Hamill**
1977	Linda Fratianne
1978	Linda Fratianne
1979	Linda Fratianne
1980	Linda Fratianne
1981	Elaine Zayak
1982	Rosalyn Sumners
1983	Rosalyn Sumners
1984	Rosalyn Sumners
1985	Tiffany Chin
1986	Debi Thomas
1987	Jill Trenary
1988	Debi Thomas
1989	Jill Trenary
1990	Jill Trenary
1991	Tonya Harding
1992	**Kristi Yamaguchi**
1993	Nancy Kerrigan
1994	vacated*
1995	Nicole Bobek
1996	Michelle Kwan
1997	Tara Lipinski
1998	Michelle Kwan

* Tonya Harding was stripped of the 1994 women's title and banned from membership in the U.S. Figure Skating Assn. for life on June 30, 1994 for violating the USFSA Code of Ethics after she pleaded guilty to a charge of conspiracy to hinder the prosecution related to the Jan. 6, 1994 attack on Nancy Kerrigan.

Soccer

Football euphoria hit millions of French fans on the Champs D'Elysees the day after their national team beat Brazil to become world champions.

AP/Wide World Photos

French Toast

Zinedine Zidane and his fellow Frenchmen gave their nation a reason to raise their glasses, blowing out the defending champion Brazilians in the final of a superb World Cup.

by
Bob Ley

Imagine a World Cup team: a lineup in flux, forwards unable to score goals, its population hardly on the edge of their seats, the coach at odds with the media. That's a formula for both disaster and triumph, a profile of both the U.S. and French national teams in World Cup '98.

Over a million Frenchmen celebrated on the Champs D'Elysees in the hours after France's 3-0 pasting of Brazil in the final. The immigrant neighborhoods around Le Stade de France in suburban St. Denis became a sea of Algerian flags in celebration of Zinedine Zidane, whose two headers stunned the defending champs, and ignited a national celebration. It took all month for the celebrated French ennui to erode, for coach Aime Jacquet to reach détente with a critical media, and for his team's offense to catch up with its imperious Gallic defense.

At the other end of soccer's food chain, well recovered from jet lag by the time France exulted, was the U.S. team. Finishing dead last in the field of 32, it left a bitter legacy of disappointment. Two months before the Cup, coach Steve Sampson dropped longtime captain John Harkes from the squad. Against Germany he gambled on a young midfield, and a new alignment. Three shots off goal posts heralded disaster against Iran. Carping and criticism during the tournament from several players injected a real world feeling into American soccer. Following his team's elimination, Sampson resigned.

The Cup's biggest disappointment was Brazil, whose *jogo bonito* and *joie de vivre* was showcased only in short

---

Bob Ley, a *SportsCenter* anchor since 1979, was the lead announcer for ESPN and ABC at the World Cup in France.

AP/Wide World Photos

France's **Zinedine Zidane** puts his head on the ball and the ball in the net, scoring the opening goal for France in the World Cup final against Brazil.

spurts. No one may ever know the truth about the hours before the final, when Ronaldo received hospital treatment, and the official lineup listed the World Player of the Year as a substitute.

Ronaldo did start, but was clearly off his game. But no more so than the Brazilian defense. Their back line was susceptible in the air, and slow to react, a weakness that was nearly fatal against the game Danes, who were the true purveyors of attacking soccer.

Germany fielded a familiar, veteran team, and was unceremoniously dumped in the quarterfinals. The best the Germans could muster against Croatia was a studs-high strategy, and the resulting first half red-card led to a humiliating exit. Italy had to juggle the skills of strikers Christian Vieri, Roberto Baggio, and Alessandro Del Piero. But without any midfield vision, a quarterfinal finish was just reward.

The Dutch were a popular pre-Cup choice to break into the circle of champions, a sentiment validated with their dramatic late victories over Yugoslavia and Argentina. Had Patrick Kluivert played to his clippings, the gold trophy might well have motored north.

But the Croatians best exemplified the new reality in soccer. Newly independent for seven years and fighting accusations that their national flag dated from a Nazi puppet regime, the Croatians grabbed the world spotlight in their first World Cup appearance. They provided both the ultimate high and low. Davor Suker was top scorer. But cynicism hit a new peak, when defender Slaven Bilic's play-acting cost French defender Laurent Blanc an

AP/Wide World Photos

Forward **Robert Pires** and defender **Marcel Desailly**, both French, kiss the **World Cup trophy** immediately following their 3-0 win over Brazil in the championship game of the World Cup at the Stade de France in Saint Denis.

undeserved red card and a chance to play in France's triumphant final. ■

Bob Ley's Top Ten Images on French Post Cards

10. **Michael Owen's goal against Argentina.** England manager Glen Hoddle's indecision on giving the brilliant young striker playing time seems insane in retrospect. In one of many of his World Cup highlights, Owen sped past Argentine defender Jose Chamot and then made Roberto Ayala look bad before easily beating goalkeeper Carlos Roa with a high shot to the far post.

9. **Dennis Bergkamp's goal against Argentina.** The Dutchman showed world-class control and finishing in the 89th minute of Holland's victory on a spectacular play that went the length of the field. Bergkamp brought down the long pass from Frank de Boer, beat defender Roberto Ayala, and won it with his right foot just 32 seconds away from extra time.

8. **Gianluca Pagliuca's save on Tore Andre Flo of Norway.** In the game's 72nd minute, the towering Norwegian headed a cross

AP/Wide World Photos

Goalkeeper **Kasey Keller** and the rest of the U.S. national team were left flailing in France, losing all three of their games. Above, Keller lunges, unsuccessfully, to stop a shot from Iran's Hamid Estili in his team's 2-1 loss to the Iranians.

from Erik Mykland in what appeared to be a sure goal but Pagliuca reacted with lightning quickness to stop the ball on the goal line.

7. **Mexico's resilience.** Three first-round come-from-behind results, and they nearly did in Germany.

6. **Scotland's Tartan Army.** Someday the game's best fans will cheer a second-round match. This could have been the year. The Scots might have scored the upset of the tournament in the World Cup opener against defending champions Brazil until a fluky own goal by Scottish defender Tommy Boyd put the Brazilians up for good.

5. **Diving.** Croatian defender Slaven Bilic got Laurent Blanc red-carded with a dive, forcing Blanc to sit out the final against Brazil—a potentially crushing blow to the French. Bilic wasn't the only player/thespian. Even child prodigy Owen set up a penalty kick this way.

4. **Esse Barhamast's redemption.** A day-old replay stopped the global savaging of the tournament's only American referee for awarding Norway a late-game penalty shot in their surprising win over Brazil.

3. **Denmark vs. Brazil.** Five goals and a 93rd minute crossbar. A lesson for all. Brazilian coach Mario Zagallo had this to say about his

team's victory, "It was a match that showed the way football should be played. Denmark could just as easily have won 3-2 but we gave everything to win. I'm almost as tired as the players."

2. **Marcel Desailly of France.** The French defender, usually a midfielder with his club side, proves to be the most reliable player of the month. When Blanc was lost for the final to a red card, Desailly answered every challenge.

1. **Iranian Fan Warmup.** Before the highly-anticipated game against the U.S.—the country they call "The Great Satan"—where else could they gather and wave flags, but at the one McDonald's in downtown Lyon? ■

INSIDE THE NUMBERS

by

Christian Teja

BYE BYE BRAZIL

Brazil's three-goal loss in the World Cup final against France was the worst defeat in its 80-match World Cup history. They have suffered just five two-goal losses in World Cup play. Here is a list of Brazil biggest World Cup beatings.

Year	Opponent	Score	Round
1998	France	0-3	final
1974	Netherlands	0-2	2nd round
1966	Portugal	1-3	group play
1966	Hungary	1-3	group play
1954	Hungary	2-4	quarterfinals
1934	Spain	1-3	1st round

RED, WHITE, AND BLUE

Despite the United States' dismal performance at the World Cup in France, departed head coach Steve Sampson is the first coach of U.S. Soccer to compile a winning record since Alkis Panagoulias did it from 1983-85. Below is a list of recent national team coaches and their win-loss records.

Coach	Tenure	W-L-T
Steve Sampson	1995-98	26-22-14
Bora Milutinovic	1991-95	30-35-30
Bob Gansler	1982, 1989-91	16-20-6
Lothar Osiander	1986-88	9-13-7
Alkis Panagoulias	1983-85	7-6-8
Walter Chyzowych	1976-81	14-14-12

GREEDY HOSTS

France became the sixth nation to win the World Cup as the host. Uruguay and Italy won the first two World Cups as hosts, but since then only four other host nations have taken the trophy. Also, of the seven nations that have won the World Cup, the nation that has the most titles (Brazil with 4) is the only one to never have won it as the host country. Brazil has only hosted one World Cup, losing to Uruguay in the 1950 Final.

Year	Host winner
1998	France
1978	Argentina
1974	West Germany
1966	England
1934	Italy
1930	Uruguay

■

1998 World Cup Tournament

The 16th World Cup hosted by France from June 10-July 12, 1998.

First Round

Round robin; each team played the other three teams in its group once. Note that three points were awarded for a win and one point for a tie. (*) indicates team advanced to second round.

Group A	Gm	W	L	T	Pts	GF	GA
*Brazil	3	2	1	0	**6**	6	3
*Norway	3	1	0	2	**5**	5	4
Morocco	3	1	1	1	**4**	5	5
Scotland	3	0	2	1	**1**	2	6

Results

6/10	St. Denis (80,000)	Brazil 2, Scotland 1
6/10	Montpellier (29,750)	Morocco 2, Norway 2
6/16	Nantes (33,266)	Brazil 3, Morocco 0
6/16	Bordeaux (30,236)	Scotland 1, Norway 1
6/23	Marseille (60,000)	Norway 2, Brazil 1
6/23	St. Etienne (36,000)	Morocco 3, Scotland 0

Group B	Gm	W	L	T	Pts	GF	GA
*Italy	3	2	0	1	**7**	7	3
*Chile	3	0	0	3	**3**	4	4
Austria	3	0	1	2	**2**	3	4
Cameroon	3	0	1	2	**2**	2	5

Results

6/11	Bordeaux (36,500)	Italy 2, Chile 2
6/11	Toulouse (37,500)	Cameroon 1, Austria 1
6/17	Montpellier (35,500)	Italy 3, Cameroon 0
6/17	St. Etienee (30,392)	Chile 1, Austria 1
6/23	St. Denis (80,000)	Italy 2, Austria 1
6/23	Nantes (40,000)	Chile 1, Cameroon 1

Group C	Gm	W	L	T	Pts	GF	GA
*France	3	3	0	0	**9**	9	1
*Denmark	3	1	1	1	**4**	3	3
South Africa	3	0	1	2	**2**	3	6
Saudi Arabia	3	0	2	1	**1**	2	7

Results

6/12	Marseille (60,000)	France 3, South Africa 0
6/12	Lens (38,140)	Denmark 1, Saudi Arabia 0
6/18	St. Denis (80,000)	France 4, Saudi Arabia 0
6/18	Toulouse (37,500)	South Africa 1, Denmark 1
6/24	Lyon (44,000)	France 2, Denmark 1
6/24	Bordeaux (36,500)	South Africa 2, Saudi Arabia 2

Group D	Gm	W	L	T	Pts	GF	GA
*Nigeria	3	2	1	0	**6**	5	5
*Paraguay	3	1	0	2	**5**	3	1
Spain	3	1	1	1	**4**	8	4
Bulgaria	3	0	2	1	**1**	1	7

Results

6/12	Montpellier (27,650)	Paraguay 0, Bulgaria 0
6/13	Nantes (33,257)	Nigeria 3, Spain 2
6/19	St. Etienne (36,000)	Spain 0, Paraguay 0
6/19	Paris (49,300)	Nigeria 1, Bulgaria 0
6/24	Lens (41,275)	Spain 6, Bulgaria 1
6/24	Toulouse (37,500)	Paraguay 3, Nigeria 1

Group E	Gm	W	L	T	Pts	GF	GA
*Netherlands	3	1	0	2	**5**	7	2
*Mexico	3	1	0	2	**5**	7	5
Belgium	3	0	0	3	**3**	3	3
South Korea	3	0	2	1	**1**	2	9

Results

6/13	St. Denis (75,000)	Netherlands 0, Belgium 0
6/13	Lyon (37,588)	Mexico 3, South Korea 1
6/20	Marseille (60,000)	Netherlands 5, South Korea 0
6/20	Bordeaux (36,500)	Belgium 2, Mexico 2
6/25	St. Etienne (36,000)	Netherlands 2, Mexico 2
6/25	Paris (49,300)	Belgium 1, South Korea 1

Group F	Gm	W	L	T	Pts	GF	GA
*Germany	3	2	0	1	**7**	6	2
*Yugoslavia	3	2	0	1	**7**	4	2
Iran	3	1	2	0	**3**	2	4
United States	3	0	3	0	**0**	1	5

Results

6/14	St. Etienne (30,342)	Yugoslavia 1, Iran 0
6/15	Paris (43,815)	Germany 2, USA 0
6/21	Lens (41,275)	Germany 2, Yugoslavia 2
6/21	Lyon (44,000)	Iran 2, USA 1
6/25	Montepellier (35,500)	Germany 2, Iran 0
6/25	Nantes (40,000)	Yugoslavia 1, USA 0

Group G	Gm	W	L	T	Pts	GF	GA
*Romania	3	2	0	1	**7**	4	2
*England	3	2	1	0	**6**	5	2
Colombia	3	1	2	0	**3**	1	3
Tunisia	3	0	2	1	**1**	1	4

Results

6/15	Lyon (37,572)	Romania 1, Colombia 0
6/15	Marseille (54,587)	England 2, Tunisia 0
6/22	Toulouse (37,5000)	Romania 2, England 1
6/22	Montpellier (35,500)	Colombia 1, Tunisia 0
6/26	Paris (80,000)	Romania 1, Tunisia 1
6/26	Lens (41,275)	England 2, Colombia 0

Group H	Gm	W	L	T	Pts	GF	GA
*Argentina	3	3	0	0	**9**	7	0
*Croatia	3	2	1	0	**6**	4	2
Jamaica	3	1	2	0	**3**	3	9
Japan	3	0	3	0	**0**	1	4

Results

6/14	Toulouse (33,400)	Argentina 1, Japan 0
6/14	Lens (38,058)	Croatia 3, Jamaica 1
6/20	Nantes (40,000)	Croatia 1, Japan 0
6/21	Paris (49,300)	Argentina 5, Jamaica 0
6/26	Bordeaux (36,500)	Argentina 1, Croatia 0
6/26	Lyon (44,000)	Jamaica 2, Japan 1

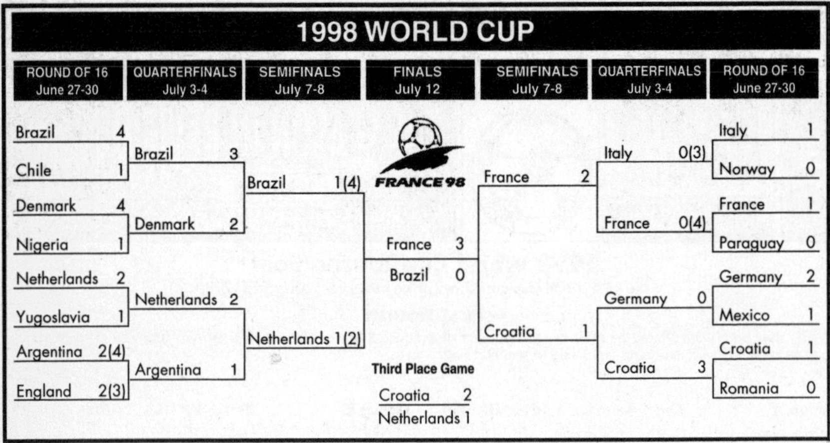

Round of 16

Single elimination with two 15 minute sudden-death "golden goal" overtime periods. If still tied, games are decided by shootout.

6/27 Paris (49,300) ....Brazil 4, Chile 1
6/27 Marseille (60,000)..................Italy 1, Norway 0
6/28 Lens (41,250) ....France 1, Paraguay 0 (2OT)
6/28 St. Denis (80,000) ....Denmark 4, Nigeria 1
6/29 Toulouse (37,500) ...Netherlands 2, Yugoslavia 1
6/29 Montpellier (35,500) ......Germany 2, Mexico 1
6/30 Bordeaux (36,500) ....Croatia 1, Romania 0
6/30 St. Etienne (36,000) .Argentina 2, England 2 (SO)*

*Argentina won shootout, 4-3.

Quarterfinals

7/3 St. Denis (77,000) ....France 0, Italy 0 (SO)*
7/3 Nantes (35,500)............Brazil 3, Denmark 2
7/4 Marseille (55,000).....Netherlands 2, Argentia 1
7/4 Lyon (39,100) ....Croatia 3, Germany 0

*France won shootout, 4-3.

Semifinals

7/7 Marseille (54,000)...Brazil 1, Netherlands 1 (SO)*
7/8 St. Denis (76,000)...........France 2, Croatia 1

*Brazil won shootout, 4-2.

Third Place

7/11 Paris (45,500)...........Croatia 2, Netherlands 1

Final

7/12 St. Denis (75,000) ....France 3, Brazil 0

World Cup All-Star Team

Voting done by FIFA Technical Study Group and announced on July 10 before the July 12 championship game.

GK	Jose Luis Chilavert, PAR	M	Michael Laudrup, DEN
GK	Fabien Barthez, FRA	M	Edgar Davids, NED
D	Lilian Thurman, FRA	M	Rivaldo, BRA
D	Frank de Boer, NED	M	Zinedine Zidane, FRA
D	Marcel Desailly, FRA	F	Brian Laudrup, DEN
D	Carlos Gamarra, PAR	F	Dennis Bergkamp, NED
D	Roberto Carlos, BRA	F	Davor Suker, CRO
M	Dunga, BRA	F	Ronaldo, BRA

France 3, Brazil 0

World Cup final played July 12, 1998 at Stade de France in St. Denis, France. **Attendance:** 75,000; **Referee:** Said Belqola (Morocco); **Assistants:** Achmat Salie (So. Africa), Mark Warren (England); **Time of Possesion:** BRA-33:32, FRA-23:37.

	1	2–	F
Brazil	0	0–	0
France	2	1–	3

Scoring
First Half: FRA—Zinedine Zidane, 27th and 46th minutes
Second Half: FRA—Emmanuel Petit, 92nd.

	Brazil		France
1	Taffarel	16	Barthez, Fabien
2	Cafu	3	Lizarazu, Bixente
3	Aldair	8	Desailly, Marcel
4	Baiano, Junior	15	Thuram, Lilian
6	Carlos, Roberto	18	Leboeuf, Frank
5	Sampaio, Cesar	6	Djorkaeff, Youri
	21 Edmundo (74th)		4 Vieira, Patrick (75th)
8	Dunga	7	Deschamps, Didier
10	Rivaldo	10	Zidane, Zinedine
18	Leonardo	17	Petit, Emmanuel
	19 Denilson (46th)	19	Karembeu, Christian
20	Bebeto		14 Boghossian, Alain (57th)
9	Ronaldo	9	Guivarc'h, Stephane
			21 Dugarry, Christophe (66th)

Brazil	France
Yellow Cards	**Yellow Cards**
Baiano (34th)	Deschamps (38th)
	Desailly (47th)
	Karembeu (55th)
	Desailly (68th)
Red Cards	**Red Cards**
none	Desailly (68th)

Brazil	Match Stats	France
6	Corners	3
5	Offsides	3
12	Shots	14
6	SOG	5
1	Yellow Cards	4
0	Red Cards	1
15	Fouls	13

FIFA Top 50 World Rankings

FIFA announced a new monthly world ranking system on Aug. 13, 1993 designed to "provide a constant international comparison of national team performances." The rankings are based on a mathematical formula that weighs strength of schedule, importance of matches and goals scored for and against. Games considered include World Cup qualifying and final rounds, Continental championship qualifying and final rounds, and friendly matches. At the end of the year, FIFA designates a Team of the Year. Teams of the Year so far have been Germany (1993) and Brazil (1994-97).

1997

		Points	1996 Rank
1	Brazil	73.45	1
2	Germany	65.41	2
3	Czech Republic	64.92	5
4	England	61.26	12
5	Mexico	60.80	11
6	France	60.36	3
7	Romania	60.35	16
8	Denmark	59.95	6
9	Italy	59.59	10
10	Colombia	59.44	4
11	Spain	59.13	8
12	Russia	58.35	7
13	Norway	58.29	14
14	Japan	57.98	21
15	Morocco	57.87	27
16	Chile	57.75	26
17	Argentina	57.74	22
18	Sweden	57.47	17
19	Croatia	56.95	24
20	Yugoslavia	56.90	55
21	Zambia	56.73	20
22	Netherlands	55.89	9
23	Tunisia	55.58	23
24	Bolivia	54.82	39
25	Austria	54.59	34
26	**USA**	54.42	18
27	South Korea	54.35	44
28	Ecuador	54.23	33
29	Paraguay	53.97	38
30	Portugal	53.11	13
31	South Africa	53.08	19
32	Egypt	53.04	28
33	Saudi Arabia	52.94	37
34	Slovakia	52.89	30
35	Australia	52.68	50
36	Bulgaria	52.36	15
37	Scotland	52.27	29
38	Peru	51.70	54
39	Jamaica	51.61	32
40	Uruguay	50.78	43
41	Belgium	50.49	42
42	Greece	49.92	35
43	Turkey	49.30	31
44	Kuwait	48.47	62
45	Lithuania	47.32	48
46	Iran	47.10	83
47	Ireland	47.07	36
48	Poland	46.15	53
49	Ukraine	45.91	59
50	United Arab Emirates	45.86	60

1998 (as of Sept. 16)

		Points	1997 Rank
1	Brazil	73.67	1
2	France	69.21	6
3	Germany	67.75	2
4	Croatia	66.64	19
5	Argentina	65.29	17
6	Czech Republic	64.79	3
7	Italy	64.53	9
8	Yugoslavia	64.16	20
9	Netherlands	62.77	22
10	Mexico	61.89	5
11	England	61.36	4
12	Chile	59.49	16
13	Romania	59.08	7
14	Spain	58.63	11
15	Morocco	58.60	15
16	Norway	58.51	13
17	**USA**	57.04	26
18	Denmark	55.91	8
19	Egypt	55.49	8
	South Korea	55.49	27
21	Japan	54.57	14
22	Paraguay	54.37	29
23	Zambia	54.23	21
24	Colombia	53.92	10
25	Sweden	53.13	18
26	Tunisia	52.96	23
27	Russia	52.87	12
28	Belgium	52.52	41
29	Austria	52.45	25
30	Jamaica	52.32	39
31	South Africa	51.98	31
32	Saudi Arabia	50.67	33
33	Slovakia	50.30	34
34	Poland	50.24	48
35	Uruguay	48.99	40
36	Australia	48.08	35
37	Cameroon	48.01	53
	Iran	48.01	46
39	Scotland	47.88	37
40	Israel	47.52	61
41	Portugal	46.83	30
42	Georgia	45.58	69
43	Thailand	45.45	54
44	Trinidad and Tobago	45.03	55
45	Ivory Coast	44.98	52
46	Angola	44.90	58
47	Bulgaria	44.69	36
48	China	44.40	55
49	Ukraine	44.30	49
50	Costa Rica	43.65	51

CONCACAF Golf Cup

Championship for the Confederation of North, Central American and Carribean Association Football (CONCACAF). Contested for every two years since its revival in 1991. Held Feb. 1-15, 1998 in the United States.

First Round

Round Robin; each team plays the other teams in its group once. Note that three points are awarded for a win and one for a tie. (*) indicates team advanced to semifinals.

Group 1	W	L	T	GA	GA	Pts
*Jamaica	2	0	1	5	2	7
*Brazil	1	0	2	5	1	5
Guatemala	0	1	2	3	4	2
El Salvador	0	2	1	0	6	1

RESULTS: **Feb. 1**—El Salvador 0, Guatemala 0; **Feb. 3**—Brazil 0, Jamaica 0; **Feb. 5**—Brazil 1, Guatemala 1; **Feb. 8**—Jamaica 3, Guatemala 2; Brazil 4, El Salvador 0; **Feb. 9**—Jamaica 2, El Salvador 0.

Group 2	W	L	T	GF	GA	Pts
*Mexico	2	0	0	6	2	6
Trinidad & Tobago	1	1	0	5	5	3
Honduras	0	2	0	1	5	0

RESULTS: **Feb. 1**—Trinidad & Tobago 3, Honduras 1; **Feb. 4**—Mexico 4, Trinidad & Tobago 2; **Feb. 7**—Mexico 2, Honduras 0.

Group 3	W	L	T	GF	GA	Pts
*United States	2	0	0	5	1	6
Costa Rica	1	1	0	8	4	3
Cuba	0	2	0	2	10	0

RESULTS: **Feb. 1**—United States 3, Cuba 0; **Feb. 4**—Costa Rica 7, Cuba 2; **Feb. 7**—United States 2, Costa Rica 1.

Semifinals

Feb. 10 Los Angeles (12,298) ....United States 1, Brazil 0
Feb. 12 Los Angeles (45,507).......Mexico 1, Jamaica 0

Third Place

Feb. 15 Los Angeles (91,255) ....Brazil 1, Jamaica 0

Final

Feb. 15 Los Angeles (91,255) ..Mexico 1, United States 0

African Nations Cup

Contested for the 21st time since its inception in 1957. Held Feb. 7-28, 1998 in Burkina Faso.

First Round

Round Robin; each team plays the other teams in its group once. Note that three points are awarded for a win and one for a tie. (*) indicates team advanced to quarterfinals.

Group A	W	L	T	GF	GA	Pts
*Cameroon	2	0	1	5	3	7
*Burkina Faso	2	1	0	3	2	6
Guinea	1	1	1	3	3	4
Algeria	0	3	0	2	5	0

RESULTS: **Feb. 7**—Cameroon 1, Burkina Faso 0; **Feb. 8**—Guinea 1, Algeria 0; **Feb. 11**—Cameroon 2, Guinea 2; Burkina Faso 2, Algeria 1; **Feb. 15**—Burkina Faso 1, Guinea 0; Cameroon 2, Algeria 1.

Group B	W	L	T	GF	GA	Pts
*Tunisia	2	1	0	5	4	6
*Congo	2	1	0	4	3	6
Ghana	1	2	0	3	3	3
Togo	1	2	0	4	6	3

RESULTS: **Feb. 9**—Congo 2, Togo 1; Ghana 2, Tunisia 0; **Feb. 12**—Tunisia 2, Congo 1; Togo 2, Ghana 1; **Feb. 16**—Congo 1, Ghana 0; Tunisia 3, Togo 1.

Group C	W	L	T	GF	GA	Pts
*Ivory Coast	2	0	1	10	6	7
*South Africa	1	0	2	5	2	5
Angola	0	1	2	5	8	2
Namibia	0	2	1	7	11	1

RESULTS: **Feb. 8**—South Africa 0, Angola 0; Ivory Coast 4, Namibia 3; **Feb. 11**—South Africa 1, Ivory Coast 1; **Feb. 12**—Angola 3, Namibia 3; **Feb. 16**—South Africa 5, Namibia 2; Ivory Coast 4, Angola 1.

Group D	W	L	T	GF	GA	Pts
*Morocco	2	0	1	5	1	7
*Egypt	2	1	0	6	1	6
Zambia	1	1	1	4	6	4
Mozambique	0	3	0	1	8	0

RESULTS: **Feb. 9**—Zambia 1, Morocco 1; **Feb. 10**—Egypt 2, Mozambique 0; **Feb. 13**—Egypt 4, Zambia 0; Morocco 3, Mozambique 0; **Feb. 17**—Zambia 3, Mozambique 1; Morocco 1, Egypt 0.

Quarterfinals

Feb. 20 .... Congo 2, Cameroon 1
Feb. 21 .... Burkina Faso 1, Tunisia 0 (8-7 P.K.)
Feb. 21 .... Egypt 1, Ivory Coast 0 (5-4 P.K.)
Feb. 22 .... South Africa 2, Morocco 1

Semifinals

Feb. 25 .... South Africa 2, Congo 1
Feb. 25 .... Egypt 2, Burkina Faso 0

Third Place

Feb. 27 .... Congo 4, Burkina Faso 4 (4-1 P.K.)

Final

Feb. 28 .... Egypt 2, South Africa 0

Women's World Cup '99 Qualifying

Qualifying records through Oct. 5, 1998 for 16-team FIFA Women's World Cup to be held in the United States June 19-July 10, 1999. The host and defending champion United States received an automatic bid. Note that three points are awarded for a win and one for a tie. (*) indicates team has qualified for United States '99. As of Oct. 5, 1998, 10 of 16 teams were determined. The qualifiers were the United States, Canada, Brazil, Sweden, Denmark, Italy, Norway, North Korea, China and Japan

Africa

Two teams qualify. Final qualification tournament was scheduled to be played in Nigeria Oct. 3-18, 1998. Patricipants were Cameroon, Congo, Egypt, Ghana, Morocco, Mozambique, Nigeria and South Africa.

Asia

Three teams qualify. Note that (†) indicates team advanced to semifinals.

Group A	W	L	T	GF	GA	Pts
†Japan	3	0	0	31	0	9
India	2	1	0	13	1	6
Hong Kong	1	2	0	1	12	3
Guam	0	3	0	0	32	0

Group B	W	L	T	GF	GA	Pts
†China	3	0	0	27	1	9
†North Korea	2	1	0	23	4	6
Uzbekistan	1	2	0	2	17	3
Philippines	0	3	0	2	32	0

Group C	W	L	T	GF	GA	Pts
†Taiwan	2	0	0	7	0	6
South Korea	1	1	0	11	1	3
Kazakstan	0	2	0	0	17	0

Semifinals

*North Korea 1 .... Japan 0
*China 10 .... Taiwan 0

Finals

China 2 .... North Korea 0

Third Place

*Japan 2 .... Taiwan 0

CONCACAF

Two or three teams qualify including the host United States which receives and automatic bid. The tournament runner-up advances to a two-leg playoff against the runner-up from South America.

Group A	W	L	T	GF	GA	Pts
†Canada	3	0	0	39	0	9
†Guatemala	2	1	0	10	4	6
Martinique	1	2	0	9	16	3
Puerto Rico	0	3	0	0	38	0

Group B	W	L	T	GF	GA	Pts
†Mexico	2	0	1	12	4	7
†Costa Rica	2	1	0	6	5	6
Trinidad & Tobago	1	1	1	5	6	4
Haiti	0	3	0	3	12	0

Semifinals

Mexico 8 .... Guatemala 0
Canada 2 .... Costa Rica 0

Finals

*Canada 1 .... Mexico 0

Third Place

Costa Rica 4 .... Guatemala 0

REMAINING GAME: South America runner-up (Argentina) vs. CONCACAF runner up (Mexico) in a two-leg playoff.

Europe

Six teams qualify. Each group winner in round robin play qualifies while the second place teams advance to a two-leg playoff. Winners of the two leg playoffs matching Russia with Finland and Germany with Ukraine also will qualify for the World Cup. Note (†) indicates team advanced to playoff.

Group 1	W	L	T	GF	GA	Pts
*Sweden	6	0	0	18	5	18
†Ukraine	3	3	0	9	13	9
Iceland	1	3	2	5	9	5
Spain	0	4	2	5	10	2

Group 2	W	L	T	GF	GA	Pts
*Italy	5	0	1	11	4	16
†Finland	3	2	1	6	5	10
France	2	2	2	9	7	8
Switzerland	0	6	0	2	12	0

Group 3	W	L	T	GF	GA	Pts
*Norway	4	1	1	13	5	13
†Germany	4	2	0	9	5	12
Netherlands	2	3	1	5	10	7
England	1	5	0	3	10	3

Group 4	W	L	T	GF	GA	Pts
*Denmark	6	0	0	22	3	18
†Russia	4	2	0	15	9	12
Portugal	2	4	0	4	15	6
Belgium	0	6	0	5	19	0

South America

One of two teams will qualify. Tournament runner-up will advance to a two-leg playoff against the runner-up from CONCACAF. Note (†) indicates team advanced to semifinals.

Group A	W	L	T	GF	GA	Pts
†Brazil	4	0	0	42	1	12
†Peru	3	1	0	5	17	9
Colombia	2	2	0	11	16	6
Chile	1	3	0	6	7	3
Venezuela	0	4	0	2	25	0

Group B	W	L	T	GF	GA	Pts
†Argentina	4	0	0	16	1	12
†Ecuador	2	1	1	10	6	7
Paraguay	2	2	0	6	10	6
Uruguay	0	2	2	6	8	2
Bolivia	0	3	15	5	18	1

Semifinals

Brazil 11 .... Ecuador 1
Argentina 1 (4) .... Peru 1 (3)

Final

*Brazil 7 .... Argentina 1

REMAINING GAME: South America runner-up (Argentina) vs. CONCACAF runner up (Mexico) in a two-leg playoff.

Oceania

One team qualifies. Final qualifying tournament was scheduled to played in Auckland, New Zealand Oct. 3-18, 1998. Participants were Australia, Fiji, New Zealand, Papua New Guinea, Tonga and Western Samoa.

U.S. Men's National Team 1998 Schedule and Results

Through Oct. 15, 1998. World Cup matches are in **bold** type.

Date		Result	USA Goals	Site	Crowd
Jan. 24	Sweden	W, 1-0	Wegerle	Orlando, Fla.	12,773
Feb. 1	Cuba*	W, 3-0	Wegerle, Wynalda, Moore	Oakland, Calif.	11,234
Feb. 7	Costa Rica*	W, 2-1	Pope, Radosavljevic	Oakland, Calif.	36,240
Feb. 10	Brazil*	W, 1-0	Radosavljevic	Los Angeles, Calif.	12,298
Feb. 15	Mexico*	L, 0-1	—	Los Angeles, Calif.	91,255
Feb. 21	Netherlands	L, 0-1	—	Miami, Fla.	20,379
Feb. 25	Belgium	L, 0-2	—	Brussels, Belgium	15,894
Mar. 14	Paraguay	T, 2-2	Deering, Balboa	San Diego, Calif.	15,253
Apr. 22	Austria	W, 3-0	Hejduk, McBride, Reyna	Vienna, Austria	17,00
May 16	F.Y.R. Macedonia	T, 0-0	—	San Jose, Calif.	23,861
May 24	Kuwait	W, 2-0	Stewart, Ramos	Portland, Ore.	25,343
May 30	Scotland	T, 0-0	—	Washington, D.C.	46,037
Jun. 15	**Germany**	L, 0-2	—	Paris, France	43,615
Jun. 21	**Iran**	L, 1-2	McBride	Lyon, France	44,000
June 25	**Yugoslavia**	L, 0-1	—	Nantes, France	39,500

*CONCACAF Gold Cup Tournament

Overall record: 6-6-3. **World Cup record:** 0-3-0. **Team scoring:** Goals for– 15; Goals against– 13.

1998 U.S. Men's National Team Statistics

Individual records for season through Oct. 15, 1998. Note that the column labeled "Career C/G" refers to career caps and goals.

Forwards	GP	GS	Mins	G	A	Pts	Career C/G
Jovan Kirovski	1	1	45	0	0	0	25/4
Roy Lassiter	3	1	110	0	0	0	24/4
Brian McBride	8	3	358	2	0	4	23/6
Joe-Max Moore	12	10	895	1	2	4	70/17
Preki Radosavljevic	14	1	425	2	2	6	26/4
Ernie Stewart	8	7	641	1	0	2	50/6
David Wagner	2	2	109	0	0	0	8/0
Roy Wegerle	11	8	558	2	0	4	41/7
Eric Wynalda	12	7	724	1	3	5	102/32

Defenders	GP	GS	Mins	G	A	Pts	Career C/G
Jeff Agoos	11	9	834	0	2	2	87/3
Marcelo Balboa	4	3	257	1	0	2	127/13
Greg Berhalter	2	2	135	0	0	0	4/0
Mike Burns	14	13	1170	0	0	0	75/0
Chad Deering	6	6	519	1	0	2	11/1
Thomas Dooley	8	7	659	0	0	0	80/7
Alexi Lalas	7	6	540	0	1	1	98/9
Eddie Pope	11	11	945	1	0	2	25/3
David Regis	5	5	450	0	0	0	5/0
Greg Vanney	1	1	90	0	0	0	3/0
Martin Vasquez	0	0	0	0	0	0	7/0

Midfielders	GP	GS	Mins	G	A	Pts	Career C/G
John Harkes	7	7	630	0	0	0	90/6
Frankie Hejduk	9	8	695	1	0	2	14/2
Chris Henderson	2	0	44	0	0	0	78/3
Cobi Jones	14	13	1026	0	0	0	110/8
Brian Maisonneuve	7	5	449	0	1	1	10/0
Tab Ramos	5	3	209	1	0	2	82/7
Claudio Reyna	9	8	705	1	2	4	62/6
Mike Sorber	1	1	45	0	0	0	67/2

Goalkeepers	GP	GS	Mins	Record	SO	Career Caps
Brad Friedel	4	4	360	3-1-0	2	57
Kasey Keller	10	10	900	3-5-2	5	35
Juergen Sommer	1	1	90	0-0-1	0	8

Yellow cards: Mike Burns and Alexi Lalas (3), John Harkes, Frankie Hejduk, Joe-Max Moore and Cladio Reyna (2), Greg Berhalter, Chad Deerin, Eddie Pope, Preki Radosavljevic, David Regis and Roy Wegerle. **Red cards:** none.
Head coach: Steve Sampson; **Assistant coach:** Clive Charles; **Goal coach:** Milutin Soskic; **General Manager:** Tom King; **Captain:** Thomas Dooley

U.S. Women's National Team
1998 Schedule and Results

Date	Opponent	Result	USA Goals	Site	Crowd
Jan. 18	Sweden*	W, 3-0	Venturini, Milbrett, Keller	Guangzhou, China	1,500
Jan. 21	China*	T, 0-0	—	Guangzhou, China	3,200
Jan. 24	Norway*	W, 3-0	Venturini, Hamm, Parlow	Guangzhou, China	750
Mar. 15	Finland†	W, 2-0	Akers, Chastain	Olhão, Portugal	250
Mar. 17	China†	W, 4-1	Hamm (3), Lilly	Loulé, Portugal	300
Mar. 19	Norway†	L, 1-4	Chastain	Lagos, Portugal	250
Mar. 21	Sweden†	W, 3-1	Foudy, Chastain, Lilly	Quarteire, Portugal	250
April 24	Argentina	W, 8-1	Milbrett (3), Akers, Hamm (2), Keller (2)	Fullerton, Calif.	10,099
April 26	Argentina	W, 7-0	Lilly, Milbrett (2), Akers, Chastain, Foudy, Own Goal	San Jose, Calif.	14,608
May 8	Iceland	W, 6-0	Milbrett, Hamm (2), Whalen, Venturini, Keller	Indianapolis, Ind.	5,123
May 10	Iceland	W, 1-0	Neaton	Bethlehem, Pa.	5,811
May 17	Japan	W, 2-1	Keller (2)	Tokyo, Japan	23,774
May 21	Japan	W, 2-0	Lilly, Keller	Kobe, Japan	1,039
May 24	Japan	W, 3-0	Chastain, Lilly, Venturini	Yokohama, Japan	34,985
May 30	New Zealand	W, 5-0	Parlow, Keller (2), Fair, Milbrett	Washington, D.C.	46,037
June 25	Germany	T, 1-1	Parlow	St. Louis, Mo.	5,938
June 28	Germany	W, 4-2	Lilly, Hamm (3)	Chicago, Ill.	13,107
July 26	Denmark #	W, 5-0	Milbrett, Akers, Hamm (3)	Long Island, N.Y.	6,970
July 27	China #	W, 2-0	Hamm (2)	Long Island, N.Y.	11,307
Aug. 2	Canada	W, 4-0	Keller (2), Milbrett, Foudy	Orlando, Fla.	34,416
Sept. 12	Mexico @	W, 9-0	Hamm (2), Lilly (2), Milbrett, MacMillan, Fawcett, Venturini, Keller	Foxboro, Mass.	35,462
Sept. 16	Russia @	W, 4-0	Hamm (2), Milbrett (2)	Rochester, N.Y.	13,125
Sept. 20	Brazil @	W, 3-0	Fawcett, Akers, Keller	Richmond, Va.	9,147

*Guangzhou International Women's Tournament
†Algarve Cup Tournament
#1998 Goodwill Games
@NIKE U.S. Women's Cup '98
Overall record: 20-1-2.
Team Scoring: Goals For– 81; Goals against– 11.

1998 U.S. Women's National Team Statistics

Individual records for entire 1998 season. Note that the column labeled "Career C/G" refers to career caps and goals.

Forwards	GP	GS	Mins	G	A	Pts	Career C/G
Robin Confer	2	0	46	0	0	0	7/1
Danielle Fotopolous	1	0	14	0	0	0	9/4
Mia Hamm	20	20	1511	20	20	60	156/101
Debbie Keller	22	7	918	13	2	28	45/17
Tiffeny Milbrett	19	18	1326	13	9	35	101/46
Nathalie Neaton	2	0	56	1	0	2	4/3
Cindy Parlow	13	7	765	3	1	7	42/17

Defenders	GP	GS	Mins	G	A	Pts	Career C/G
Brandi Chastain	23	21	1841	5	5	15	78/16
Amanda Cromwell	2	0	45	0	0	0	51/1
Lorrie Fair	15	6	801	1	1	3	35/1
Joy Fawcett	23	23	1902	2	3	7	125/17
Carla Overbeck	22	22	1793	0	0	0	127/7
Christie Pearce	18	13	1074	0	1	1	36/2
Kate Sobrero	12	8	776	0	0	0	12/0

Midfielders	GP	GS	Mins	G	A	Pts	Career C/G
Michelle Akers	15	15	932	5	3	13	126/98
Justi Baumgardt	4	0	100	0	1	1	14/2
Julie Foudy	23	22	1710	3	7	13	137/24
Kristine Lilly	23	23	1869	8	10	26	162/61
Shannon MacMillan	23	13	1229	1	2	4	62/14
Tiffany Roberts	10	2	362	0	0	0	67/6
Jill Rutten	1	0	20	0	0	0	1/0
Tisha Venturini	22	10	1181	5	2	12	110/37
Sara Whalen	16	0	429	1	1	3	23/1

Goalkeepers	GP	GS	Mins	Record	SO	Career Caps
Tracy Ducar	6	6	450	5-0-0	4	20
Briana Scurry	18	16	1530	14-1-2	4	77
Saskia Webber	1	1	90	1-0-0	1	20

Yellow Cards: Kristine Lilly (3), Brandi Chastain and Shannon MacMillan (2), Joy Fawcett, Julie Foudy, Mia Hamm, Cindy Parlow, Christie Pearce and Kate Sobrero. **Red Cards:** none.
Head coach: Tony DiCiccio; **Assistant coaches:** Lauren Gregg and April Heinrichs; **Co-Captain:** Julie Foudy and Carla Overbeck.

Club Team Competition

1997 Toyota Cup

Also known as the Intercontinental Cup; a year-end match for the World Club Championship between the European Cup and Copa Libertadores winners. Played Dec. 2, 1997, before 55,000 at Tokyo's National Stadium.

Final

Borussia Dortmund (Germany) 2 ....Cruzeiro (Brazil) 0
Scoring: Borussia Dortmund— Zorc, 34th minute; Herrlich 85th.

SOUTH AMERICA

1998 Liberatadores Cup

Contested by the league champions of South America's football union. Two-leg Semifinals and two-leg Final; home teams listed first. Winner Vasco da Gama of Brazil plays European Cup champion Real Madrid of Spain in the 1998 World Club Championship in Tokyo in December.

Final Four: Barcelona (Ecuador), Cerro Porteño (Paraguay), River Plate (Argentina) and Vasco da Gama (Brazil).

Semifinals

Barcelona vs. Cerro Porteño

Barcelona 1 ....Cerro Porteño 0
Cerro Porteño 2 ....Barcelona 1
Aggregate tied 2-2, Barcelona wins 4-3 on penalty kicks

River Plate vs. Vasco da Gama

Vasco da Gama 1 ....River Plate 0
River Plate 1 ....Vasco da Gama 1
Vasco da Gama wins 2-1 on aggregate

Final

Vasco da Gama 2......................... Barcelona 0
Barcelona 1 ....Vasco da Gama 2
Vasco da Gama wins on aggregate, 4-1

EUROPE

There are three European club competitions sanctioned by the Union of European Football Associations (UEFA). The **European Cup** (officially, the Champions' Cup) is a knockout contest between national league champions of UEFA member countries; the **Cup Winners' Cup** is between winners of domestic cup competitions (note that a double winner– league and cup titles– would play for the European Cup and be replaced in the Cup Winners' Cup by the team it defeated in the domestic cup final); and the **UEFA Cup** is between the so-called "best of the rest," usually the national league runners-up. Note that home teams are listed first.

1997-98 European Cup

Champions League: Six-game double round robin in four 4-team groups (Sept. 17-Dec. 10, 1997); top two teams in each group advance to quarterfinal round. Winner Real Madrid plays Libertadores Cup champion Vasco da Gama of Brazil in the 1998 World Club Championship this December in Tokyo.

Round Robin Standings

Group A	W	L	T	GF	GA	Pts
*Borussia Dortmund (GER)	5	1	0	14	3	15
Parma (ITA)	2	1	3	6	5	9
Sparta Prague (CZE)	1	3	2	6	11	5
Galatasaray (TUR)	1	4	1	4	11	4

Group B	W	L	T	GF	GA	Pts
*Manchester Utd. (ENG)	5	1	0	14	5	15
*Juventus (ITA)	4	2	0	12	8	12
Feyenoord (NED)	3	3	0	8	10	9
Kosice (SLO)	0	6	0	2	13	0

Group C	W	L	T	GF	GA	Pts
*Dynamo Kiev (UKR)	3	1	2	13	6	11
PSV Eindhoven (NED)	2	1	3	9	8	9
Newcastle (ENG)	2	3	1	7	8	7
Barcelona (SPA)	1	3	2	7	14	5

Group D	W	L	T	GF	GA	Pts
*Real Madrid (SPA)	4	1	1	15	4	13
Rosenborg (NOR)	3	1	2	13	8	11
Olympiakos (GRE)	1	3	2	6	14	5
FC Porto (POR)	1	4	1	3	11	4

Group E	W	L	T	GF	GA	Pts
*Bayern Munich (GER)	4	2	0	13	6	12
Paris-St. Germain (FRA)	4	2	0	11	10	12
Besiktas (TUR)	2	4	0	6	9	6
IFK Goteborg (SWE)	2	4	0	4	9	6

Group F	W	L	T	GF	GA	Pts
*AS Monaco	4	1	1	15	8	13
*Bayer Leverkusen (GER)	4	1	1	11	7	13
Sporting Lisbon (POR)	2	3	1	9	11	7
Lierse (BEL)	0	5	1	3	12	1

EUROPE (Cont.)

Quarterfinals

Two legs, total goals; home team listed first.

Borussia Dortmund vs. Bayern Munich

Mar. 4 –Bayern Munich 0.........Borussia Dortmund 0
Mar. 18 –Borussia Dortmund 1.........Bayern Munich 0
Borussia Dortmund wins 1-0 on aggregate

AS Monaco vs. Manchester United

Mar. 4 –AS Monaco 0...........Manchester United 0
Mar. 18 –Manchester United 1............AS Monaco 1
1-1 aggregate, AS Monaco advances on away goals

Bayer Leverkusen vs. Real Madrid

Mar. 4 –Bayer Leverkusen 1.............Real Madrid 1
Mar. 18 –Real Madrid 3.............Bayer Leverkusen 0
Real Madrid wins 4-1 on aggregate

Juventus of Turin vs. Dynamo Kiev

Mar. 4 –Juventus 1.....................Dynamo Kiev 1
Mar. 18 –Dynamo Kiev 1...................Juventus 4
Juventus wins 5-2 on aggregate

Semifinals

Two legs, total goals; home team listed first.

Juventus of Turin vs. AS Monaco

Apr. 1 –Juventus 4.....................AS Monaco 1
Apr. 15 –AS Monaco 3....................Juventus 2
Juentus of Turin wins 6-4 on aggregate

Real Madrid vs. Borussia Dortmund

Apr. 1 –Real Madrid 2...........Borussia Dortmund 0
Apr. 15 –Borussia Dortmund 0...........Real Madrid 0
Real Madrid wins 2-0 on aggregate

Final

May 20 at Amsterdam ArenA

Real Madrid 1 ....Juventus 0
Scoring: Real Madrid— Predrag Mijatovic, 71st minute.

1998 Cup Winners' Cup

Two-leg Semifinals one-game Final; home team listed first.
Final Four: Chelsea (England), Lokomotiv Moscow (Russia), VfB Stuttgart (Germany) and Vicneza (Italy).

Semifinals

Chelsea vs. Vicenza

Apr. 2 –Vicenza 1 ....Chelsea 0
Apr. 16 –Chelsea 3 ....Vicenza 1
Barcelona wins 3-2 on aggregate

VfB Stuttgart vs. Lokomotiv Moscow

Apr. 2 –VfB Stuttgart 2 ....Lokomotiv Moscow 1
Apr. 16 –Lokomotiv Moscow 0 ....VfB Stuttgart 1
VfB Stuttgart wins 3-1 on aggregate

Final

May 14 at Stockholm, Sweden

Chelsea 1 .... VfB Stuttgart 0
Goal: Chelsea— Gianfranco Zola, 72nd minute.

1998 UEFA Cup

Two-leg Semifinals, one-game Final; home team listed first.
Final Four: Atletico de Madrid (Spain), Internazionale of Milan (Italy), Lazio of Rome (Italy) and Spartak Moscow (Russia).

Semifinals

Atletico de Madrid vs. Lazio of Rome

Mar. 31 –Atletico Madrid 0 ....Lazio 1
Apr. 14 –Lazio 0 ....Atletico Madrid 0
Lazio wins 1-0 on aggregate

Inter Milan vs. Spartak Moscow

Mar. 31 –Inter Milan 2 ....Spartak Moscow 1
Apr. 14 –Spartak Moscow 1 ....Inter Milan 2
Inter Milan wins 2-1 on aggregate

Final

May 6 at Paris

Inter Milan 3 ....Lazio 0
Goals: Inter Milan— Ivan Zamorano 4th minute; Javier Zanetti 60th; Ronaldo 70th.

Major League Soccer

1998 Final Regular Season Standings

Conference champions (*) and playoff qualifiers (†) are noted. SOW refers to shootout wins. Teams receive three points for a win and one point for a shootout win. SOW are included in W (win) column. The GF and GA columns refer to Goals For and Goals Against in regulation play. Number of seasons listed after each head coach refers to current tenure with club through the 1998 season.

Eastern Conference

	Team	W	L	Pts	GF	GA	SOW
*	D.C. United	24	8	58	74	48	7
†	Columbus	15	17	45	67	56	0
†	NY/NJ	15	17	39	54	63	3
†	Miami	15	17	35	46	68	5
	Tampa Bay	12	20	34	46	57	1
	New England	11	21	29	53	66	2

Head Coaches: DC— Bruce Arena (3rd season); Clb— Tim Hankinson (1st); NY/NJ— replaced Alfonso Mondelo (1st, 14-17) with Bora Multinovic on Sept. 21; TB— John Kowalski (1st); NE— replaced Tom Rongen (2nd, 8-18) with Walter Zenga on Aug. 24.

Western Conference

	Team	W	L	Pts	GF	GA	SOW
*	Los Angeles	24	8	68	85	44	2
†	Chicago	20	12	56	62	45	2
†	Colorado	16	16	44	62	69	2
†	Dallas	15	17	37	43	59	4
	San Jose	13	19	33	48	60	3
	Kansas City	12	20	32	45	50	2

Head Coaches: LA— Octavio Zambrano (2nd season); Chi— Bob Bradley (1st); Colo— Glenn Myernick (2nd); Dal— David Dir (3rd); SJ— Brian Quinn (2nd); KC— Ron Newman (3rd).

Leading Scorers

Points

	Gm	G	A	Pts
Stern John, Clb	27	26	5	57
Cobi Jones, LA	24	19	13	51
Welton, LA	31	17	11	45
Roy Lassiter, DC	31	18	8	44
Raul Diaz Arce, NE	32	18	8	44
Jaime Moreno, D.C.	31	16	11	43
Mauricio Cienfuegos, LA	30	13	16	42
Marco Etcheverry, DC	29	10	19	39
Ronald Cerritos, SJ	31	13	12	38
Eduardo Hurtado, NY/NJ	29	11	15	37

Goals

	Gm	No
Stern John, Clb	27	26
Cobi Jones, LA	24	19
Roy Lassiter, DC	31	18
Raul Diaz Arce, NE	32	18
Welton, LA	31	17
Jaime Moreno, DC	31	16
Giovanni Savarese, NY/NJ	30	14
Wolde Harris, Col	27	13
Mauricio Cienfuegos, LA	30	13
Ronald Cerritos, SJ	31	13

Assists

	Gm	No
Marco Etcheverry, DC	29	19
Mauricio Cienfuegos, LA	30	16
Joe-Max Moore, NE	21	15
Eduardo Hurtado, NY/NJ	29	15
Jerzy Podbrozny, Chi	26	14
Martin Machon, LA	31	14
Cobi Jones, LA	24	13
Preki, KC	25	13
Adrian Paz, Colo	28	13

Six players tied with 12 each.

Shots

	Gm	No
Stern John, Clb	27	116
Eduardo Hurtado, NY/NJ	29	101
Roy Lassiter, DC	31	101
Jason Kreis, Dal	30	97
Paul Bravo, Col	30	90
Raul Diaz Arce, NE	32	90

Shots on Goal

	Gm	No
Roy Lassiter, DC	31	52
Raul Diaz Arce, NE	32	51
Ronald Cerritos, SJ	31	50
Eduardo Hurtado, NY/NJ	29	48
Jaime Moreno, DC	31	48

Game-Winning Goals

	Gm	GWG
Stern John, Clb	27	6
Jason Kreis, Dal	30	6
Diego Serna, Mia	26	5
Mauricio Cienfuegos, LA	30	5
Roy Lassiter, DC	31	5
Ronald Cerritos, SJ	31	5

Shootout Goals

	Gm	No
Marco Etcheverry, DC	29	5
Imad Baba, NE	30	5
Eddie Lewis, SJ	32	5

Five tied with four each.

Fouls Committed

	Gm	No
Richie Williams, DC	31	66
Eduardo Hurtado, NY/NJ	29	64
Leonel Alvarez, Dal	27	63
Raul Diaz Arce, NE	32	57
Diego Serna, Mia	26	56

Fouls Suffered

	Gm	No
Diego Serna, Mia	26	89
Roman Kosecki, Chi	25	87
Adrian Paz, Col	28	82
Brian McBride, Clb	24	68
Stern John, Clb	27	68

Offsides

	Gm	Offs
Raul Diaz Arce, NE	32	44
Roy Lassiter, DC	31	41
Ronald Cerritos, SJ	31	41
Alan Prampin, TB	31	41

Corner Kicks

	Gm	CKs
Marco Etcheverry, DC	29	198
Adrian Paz, Col	28	94
Joe-Max Moore, NE	21	78
Peter Nowak, Chi	24	77
Preki, KC	25	75

Minutes Played

	Mins
Raul Diaz Arce, NE	2878
Eddie Lewis, SJ	2835
Chris Armas, Chi	2790
Lubos Kubik, Chi	2790
Tony Meola, NY/NJ	2790

Leading Goaltenders

Goals Against Avg.

	Gm	Min	Shts	Svs	GAA	W-L
Zach Thornton, Chi	25	2076	118	85	1.17	16-8
Kevin Hartman, LA	29	2544	146	103	1.38	22-7
Scott Garlick, DC	25	2205	129	88	1.43	19-5
Mike Ammann, KC	27	2430	134	85	1.56	11-16
David Kramer, SJ	24	2125	132	82	1.65	10-14
Thomas Ravelli, TB	23	2053	179	131	1.67	7-13
Juergen Sommer, Clb	21	1890	143	106	1.67	11-10
Mark Dodd, Dal	25	2205	182	134	1.71	11-13
Marcus Hahnemann, Col.	28	2520	200	138	1.86	16-12
Jeff Cassar, Mia	21	1890	151	107	1.95	12-9

Saves

	Gm	No
Tony Meola, NY/NJ	31	164
Marcus Hahnemann, Clb	28	138
Mark Dodd, Dal	25	134
Thomas Ravelli, TB	23	131
Ian Feuer, NE	26	113

Shutouts

	Gm	No
Zach Thornton, Chi	25	8
Scott Garlick, DC	25	7
Kevin Hartman, LA	29	7
Mark Dodd, Dal	25	6
David Kramer, SJ	24	5
Mike Ammann, KC	27	5
Ian Feuer, NE	26	5

Save Percentage

	Svs	SOG	SV Pct
Juergen Sommer, Clb	106	143	.741
Mark Dodd, Dal	134	182	.736
Thomas Ravelli, TB	131	179	.732
Zach Thornton, Chi	85	118	.750
Jeff Cassar, Mia	107	151	.709

MLS Attendance

Number in parentheses indicates last year's rank. Note that Chicago and Miami were expansion teams in 1998.

	Gm	Total	Avg
Los Angeles (2)	16	348,549	21,784
New England (1)	16	307,004	19,187
Chicago	16	286,190	17,886
N.Y./N.J.(3)	16	264,316	16,519
Wash. D.C. (4)	16	256,127	16,007
Colorado (7)	16	236,995	14,812
San Jose (6)	16	218,450	13,653
Columbus (5)	16	196,394	12,274
Dallas (9)	16	175,162	10,947
Tampa Bay (8)	16	164,999	10,312
Miami	16	164,548	10,284
Kansas City (10)	16	129,163	8,072
TOTAL	192	2,747,897	14,312

MLS All-Star Game

USA, 6-1

Date: Sunday, Aug. 2, 1998 at Florida Citrus Bowl in Orlando, Fla.; **Attendance:** 34,416; **Coaches:** Octavio Zombrano, LA (MLS World) and Bruce Arena, D.C. (MLS USA); **MVP:** Brian McBride, Columbus Crew forward (USA) — one goal, two assists.

	1	2	Final
MLS World	0	1	— **1**
MLS USA	4	2	— **6**

Scoring

1st Half: USA— Tab Ramos (Brian McBride, Marcelo Balboa) 5; USA— Alexi Lalas (unassisted) 15; USA— Brian McBride (Cobi Jones) 16; USA— Preki (Brian McBride, John Harkes) 40.

2nd Half: USA— Roy Lassiter (Jeff Agoos) 78; USA— Cobi Jones (Paul Bravo) 83; World— Mauricio Ramos (Jorge Campos) 89.

Goaltenders

Saves: USA— Tony Meola 5, Zach Thornton 2; World— Thomas Ravelli 4, Jorge Campos 1.

Playoffs

Quarterfinals (Best of 3)

WESTERN

Chicago Fire vs. Colorado Rapids

Date	Result	Site
Oct. 1	Fire, 2-1 (3-2 SO)	at Chicago
Oct. 5	Fire, 1-0	at Colorado

Fire win series, 2-0

Los Angeles Galaxy vs. Dallas Burn

Date	Result	Site
Oct. 1	Galaxy, 6-1	at Los Angeles
Oct. 4	Galaxy, 3-2	at Dallas

Galaxy win series, 2-0

EASTERN

Columbus Crew vs. N.Y./N.J. Metrostars

Date	Result	Site
Sept. 30	Crew, 5-3	at Columbus
Oct. 3	Crew, 2-1 (3-2 SO)	at New Jersey

Crew win series, 2-0

D.C. United vs. Miami Fusion

Date	Result	Site
Sept. 30	United, 2-1	at Washington, D.C.
Oct. 4	United, 1-0 (3-2 SO)	at Miami

United win series, 2-0

Semifinals (Best of 3)

Chicago Fire vs. Los Angeles Galaxy

D.C. United vs. Columbus Crew

See Updates Chapter for results.

Team-by-Team Statistics

Players who played with more than one club during the season are listed with final team.

Eastern Conference

Columbus Crew

	Pos	Gm	Min	G	A	Pts
Stern John	F	27	2170	26	5	57
Brian McBride	F	24	2117	10	7	27
Jason Farrell	M	28	2002	5	10	20
Jeff Cunningham	F	25	1076	8	1	17
Robert Warzycha	M	25	1752	2	10	14
Andy Williams	F	13	976	1	12	14
Brian Maisonneuve	M	13	902	3	7	13
Billy Thompson	M	29	2191	1	8	10
Rob Smith	M	24	1502	3	2	8
Ansil Elcock	D	28	2409	0	8	8
Todd Yeagley	M	27	1958	2	2	6
Marcelo Carrera	F	16	596	1	3	5
Thomas Dooley	M/D	23	2008	1	2	4
Brian West	F	13	478	1	2	4
Scott Cannon	D	15	750	0	3	3
Michael Clark	D	30	2571	0	2	2
Andrew Gregor	M	10	357	0	2	2
Mike Lapper	D	7	560	1	0	2
Ricardo Iribarren	D	24	1779	0	2	2
Juergen Sommer	GK	21	1890	0	1	1
Jimmy Glenn	F	5	242	0	1	1
Ubusuku Abukusumo	D	7	309	0	0	0

Goalkeepers	Gm	Min	W-L	Shts	Svs	GAA
Juergen Sommer	21	1890	11-10	143	106	1.67
Mark Dougherty	11	989	4-6	78	49	1.91
David Winner	1	1	0-1	0	0	0.00

D.C. United

	Pos	Gm	Min	G	A	Pts
Roy Lassiter	F	31	2691	18	8	44
Jaime Moreno	F	31	2610	16	11	43
Marco Etcheverry	M	29	2590	10	19	39
John Harkes	M	29	2600	6	6	18
Ben Olsen	M	31	2107	4	8	16
Tony Sanneh	M	17	1367	5	6	16
Richie Williams	M	31	2672	3	4	10
Brian Kamler	M	22	1743	1	4	6
A.J. Wood	F	19	417	3	0	6
Jeff Agoos	D	21	1780	1	4	6
Carey Talley	D	29	1757	0	2	2
Eddie Pope	D	20	1754	1	0	2
Geoff Aunger	D	22	1389	0	2	2
Mike Slivinski	M	16	258	0	1	1
Clint Peay	D	6	393	0	1	1
Mario Gori	D	17	842	0	0	0
Carlos Llamosa	D	18	1444	0	0	0
Judah Cooks	M	1	90	0	0	0
Curt Onalfo	D	3	72	0	0	0
Danny Care	D	1	45	0	0	0
Lyle Yorks	M	1	4	0	0	0

Goalkeepers	Gm	Min	W-L	Shts	Svs	GAA
Scott Garlick	25	2205	19-5	129	88	1.43
Tom Presthus	6	495	5-1	28	19	1.45

New York/New Jersey MetroStars

	Pos	Gm	Min	G	A	Pts
Eduardo Hurtado	F	29	2526	11	15	37
Giovanni Savarese	F	30	2163	14	7	35
Jim Rooney	M	28	2040	8	5	21
Brian Kelly	M	29	2160	6	3	15
Diego Sonora	D	30	2572	3	7	13
Marcelo Vega	M	17	1055	1	6	8
Miles Joseph	F	15	479	3	2	8
Tab Ramos	M	17	1455	1	5	7
Mike Sorber	M	28	2158	0	6	6
Alexi Lalas	D	25	2250	2	0	4
Mike Duhaney	D	14	962	1	2	4
Mike Petke	D	12	27	1	1	3
Kerry Zavagnin	D	18	754	0	2	2
Billy Walsh	M	8	337	0	2	2
Arley Palacious	D	24	1986	0	1	1
Rhett Harty	D	7	544	0	1	1
Ramiro Corrales	D	4	301	0	1	1
Tony Meola	GK	31	2790	0	1	1
Mark Semioli	D	10	829	0	0	0
Christian da Silva	D	3	177	0	0	0
Jeff Zaun	D	4	360	0	0	0

Goalkeepers	Gm	Min	W-L	Shts	Svs	GAA
Tony Meola	31	2790	14-17	236	164	2.00
Tim Howard	1	90	1-0	8	5	1.00

Miami Fusion

	Pos	Gm	Min	G	A	Pts
Diego Serna	F	26	1988	11	9	31
Paulinho McLaren	F	16	1176	5	6	16
Carlos Valderrama	M	18	1542	2	12	16
Dan Stebbins	F	24	1263	6	3	15
Marcelo Herrera	M/F	17	1441	5	4	14
Henry Gutierrez	M	26	1784	5	3	13
Nelson Vargas	M	18	719	2	4	8
Jerry Tamashiro	F	12	524	3	0	6
Leo Cullen	D	31	2680	1	4	6
Kris Kelderman	M/D	21	1187	0	5	5
Pablo Mastroeni	M	23	1611	0	4	4
Jason Boyce	F	15	597	0	3	3
Tyrone Marshall	F	9	349	1	0	2
Matt Kmosko	M/D	27	2232	0	2	2
Carlos Parra	M	18	1367	0	2	2
Roger Thomas	M	5	310	1	0	2
John Maessner	M	27	1575	0	1	1
Wade Webber	D	28	2488	0	1	1
Brian Taylor	M/F	6	288	0	1	1
Cle Kooiman	D	14	1260	0	0	0
Joey Martinez	D	6	390	0	0	0
Matt Knowles	D	7	548	0	0	0
Allen Kozic	M	2	57	0	0	0

Goalkeepers	Gm	Min	W-L	Shts	Svs	GAA
Jeff Cassar	21	1890	12-9	151	107	1.95
Matt Napoleon	4	360	1-3	45	32	3.00
David Winner	4	271	2-2	23	16	1.99

New England Revolution

	Pos	Gm	Min	G	A	Pts
Raul Diaz Arce	F	32	2878	18	8	44
Joe-Max Moore	F	21	1864	7	15	29
Edwin Gorter	M	28	2394	7	7	21
Imad Baba	M	30	2484	5	4	14
Damian	F	15	954	4	2	10
Mike Burns	M	23	2025	1	8	10
Ivan McKinley	D	28	2282	4	1	9
Johnny Torres	F	20	1179	2	3	7
Ted Chronopoulos	D	23	1960	2	3	7
Jair	M	11	643	3	1	7
Paul Keegan	F	20	892	1	4	6
Richard Goulooze	D	29	2529	1	2	4
Manny Motajo	D	15	1012	0	2	2
Carlos Rocha	F	16	537	0	1	1
Jamar Beasley	F	3	49	0	1	1
David Nakhid	M	18	1350	0	0	0
Janusz Michallik	D	12	759	0	0	0
Dahir Mohammed	D	7	423	0	0	0
Brian Dunseth	D	18	1416	0	0	0
Jesse Van Saun	F	5	117	0	0	0
Tom McLaughlin	F	1	29	0	0	0

Goalkeepers	Gm	Min	W-L	Shts	Svs	GAA
Ian Feuer	26	2336	8-15	180	113	2.12
Jeff Causey	9	544	3-6	35	24	1.82

Tampa Bay Mutiny

	Pos	Gm	Min	G	A	Pts
Mauricio Ramos	M	22	1932	9	9	27
Alan Prampin	F	31	2450	7	11	25
Paul Dougherty	F	29	2015	6	12	24
Steve Ralston	M	30	2521	5	8	18
Musa Shannon	M/F	18	823	7	2	16
Dominic Kinnear	M	24	868	3	5	11
Jorge Salcedo	M	26	1909	1	7	9
Roy Wegerle	F	17	1265	3	3	9
Gilmar	M/F	12	909	3	2	8
Frankie Hejduk	D	18	1618	3	1	7
Chris Houser	D	24	2005	1	5	7
Paul Young	F	14	768	0	5	5
Jan Eriksson	D	29	2342	2	1	5
Frank Yallop	D	32	2703	1	1	3
Guillermo Jara	F	16	571	0	3	3
Sam George	M	21	1591	0	1	1
Brian Loftin	F	8	219	0	1	1
Evans Wise	M	17	764	0	1	1
Eric Quill	F	4	141	0	0	0
Jacek Ziober	F	3	196	0	0	0
Adam Frye	D	10	710	0	0	0
Chad McCarty	D	6	540	0	0	0
R.T. Moore	D	2	62	0	0	0

Goalkeepers	Gm	Min	W-L	Shts	Svs	GAA
Thomas Ravelli	23	2053	7-13	179	131	1.67
Doug Petras	12	827	5-7	71	49	2.07

Western Conference

Chicago Fire

	Pos	Gm	Min	G	A	Pts
Ante Razov	F	30	2091	10	9	29
Roman Kosecki	F	25	1999	9	9	27
Jerzy Podbrozny	F	26	1979	6	14	26
Peter Nowak	M	24	1921	6	12	24
Lubos Kubik	D	31	2790	7	8	22
Josh Wolff	F	14	651	8	3	19
Frank Klopas	M/F	27	1497	6	4	16
Chris Armas	M	31	2790	1	10	12
Rich Kotschau	M	24	1973	4	3	11
Jesse Marsch	M	29	2199	2	3	7
C.J. Brown	D	28	2470	2	0	4
Diego Gutierrez	D	13	812	0	3	3
Francis Okaroh	D	26	2294	0	3	3
Zak Ibsen	M/D	27	908	0	1	1
Zach Thornton	GK	25	2076	0	1	1
Andre Lewis	D	13	623	0	1	1
Josh Keller	M	15	827	0	0	0
Tony Kuhn	F	5	137	0	0	0
Tom Soehn	D	20	1543	0	0	0
Manny Lagos	M/F	1	11	0	0	0
Michael Richardson	D	1	6	0	0	0

Goalkeepers	Gm	Min	W-L	Shts	Svs	GAA
Zach Thornton	25	2076	16-8	118	85	1.17
Jorge Campos	8	714	4-3	49	33	1.89
Scott Coufal	1	90	0-1	5	2	3.00

Colorado Rapids

	Pos	Gm	Min	G	A	Pts
Paul Bravo	M	30	2579	11	8	30
Wolde Harris	F	27	1133	13	4	30
Ross Paule	M	30	2503	10	6	26
Waldir	F	23	1382	6	6	18
Adrian Paz	M	28	2313	2	13	17
Marcelo Balboa	D	26	2290	5	5	15
Chris Henderson	M	28	1915	2	9	13
David Vaudreuil	M/D	27	2177	3	4	10
Marquinho	M	11	596	3	3	9
Marquis White	F	20	492	4	1	9
Peter Vermes	D	31	2675	2	5	9
Joey DiGiamarino	M	23	1554	3	2	8
Chris Martinez	D	28	2358	0	7	7
Tahj Jakins	D	22	1147	0	4	4
Steve Trittschuh	D	30	2700	1	1	3
Marcus Hahnemann	GK	28	2520	0	2	2
Sean Henderson	M	21	1266	0	0	0
Jason Bent	M	12	890	0	0	0
Andre Nunley	D	1	1	0	0	0

Goalkeepers	Gm	Min	W-L	Shts	Svs	GAA
Marcus Hahnemann	28	2520	16-12	200	138	1.86
Paul Grafer	4	360	0-4	39	20	4.25

Dallas Burn

	Pos	Gm	Min	G	A	Pts
Jason Kreis	M	30	2578	9	8	26
Dante Washington	F	28	1852	7	5	19
Mickey Trotman	F	23	1278	5	3	13
Jorge Rodriguez	D	30	2569	4	2	10
Gerell Elliott	F	17	1100	3	1	7
Brian Haynes	M	31	1414	3	1	7
Chad Deering	M	14	1114	3	1	7
Oscar Pareja	M	19	1486	0	7	7
Ted Eck	M/F	31	2331	2	2	6
Leonel Alvarez	M	27	2338	0	6	6
Temoc Suarez	M	20	831	1	4	6
Mark Santel	M/D	21	1634	0	4	4
Richard Farrer	M/D	28	2119	1	2	4
Jorge Flores	M	14	777	1	0	2
Alain Sutter	M	4	341	0	2	2
Mark Dodd	GK	25	2205	0	1	1
Brandon Pollard	D	29	2373	0	0	0
Eric Dade	D	20	1393	0	0	0
Brian Bates	D	6	286	0	0	0
Juan Sastoque	F	3	49	0	0	0
Chris Brown	D	1	16	0	0	0
Darren Sawatzky	M/F	1	3	0	0	0

Goalkeepers	Gm	Min	W-L	Shts	Svs	GAA
Mark Dodd	25	2205	11-13	182	134	1.71
Garth Lagerwey	8	630	4-3	44	28	2.00
Matt Jordan	1	45	0-1	4	1	6.00

Kansas City Wizards

	Pos	Gm	Min	G	A	Pts
Preki	M	25	2164	10	13	33
Mo Johnston	F	26	2080	11	2	24
Paul Wright	M/F	30	2060	6	6	18
Vitalis Takawira	F	29	1769	7	3	17
Mark Chung	M	30	2551	2	8	12
Paul Rideout	F	27	2114	4	3	11
Ryan Tinsley	M	30	2305	2	5	9
Scott Vermillion	D	22	1955	1	3	5
Pete Marino	F	11	276	1	0	2
Scott Uderitz	D	22	1660	0	2	2
Uche Okafor	D	22	1967	0	2	2
Goran Hunjak	M	12	261	0	2	2
Refik Sabanadzovic	M	21	1644	0	2	2
Sean Bowers	D	29	2565	0	1	1
Chris Snitko	GK	5	450	0	1	1
Chris Klein	M	17	782	0	0	0
Matt McKeon	D	22	1875	0	0	0
Brian Johnson	M	6	140	0	0	0
Jake Dancy	D	2	135	0	0	0
Brian Bliss	D	3	106	0	0	0
Nino Da Silva	M	1	32	0	0	0
Joh DeBrito	F	9	267	0	0	0

Goalkeepers	Gm	Min	W-L	Shts	Svs	GAA
Mike Ammann	27	2430	11-16	134	85	1.56
Chris Snitko	5	450	1-4	27	18	1.60

Los Angeles Galaxy

	Pos	Gm	Min	G	A	Pts
Cobi Jones	M	24	2136	19	13	51
Welton	F	31	2435	17	11	45
Mauricio Cienfuegos	M	30	2640	13	16	42
Marin Machon	D	31	2588	6	14	26
Carlos Hermosillo	F	18	1530	6	12	24
Clint Mathis	M	30	1550	5	10	20
Ezra Hendrickson	D	27	1946	5	8	18
Greg Vanney	M	31	2321	3	3	9
Wellington Sanchez	M	13	698	1	4	6
Steve Jolley	M	28	2093	2	2	6
Jor Franchino	D	16	736	0	4	4
Paul Caligiuri	D	18	1293	1	1	3
Danny Pena	D	25	2049	0	2	2
Jose Vasquez	D	8	291	1	0	2
Daniel Hernandez	M	17	458	0	1	1
Kevin Hartman	GK	29	2544	0	1	1
Robin Fraser	D	29	2456	0	0	0
Jose Botello	F	2	27	0	0	0
David Quesada	F	1	9	0	0	0
Dan Calichman	D	8	682	0	0	0
Lawrence Lozzano	M	1	75	0	0	0

Goalkeepers	Gm	Min	W-L	Shts	Svs	GAA
Kevin Hartman	29	2544	22-7	146	103	1.38
Matt Reis	5	336	2-1	24	18	1.34

San Jose Clash

	Pos	Gm	Min	G	A	Pts
Ronald Cerritos	F	31	2702	13	12	38
Eric Wynalda	F	16	1424	6	5	17
Victor Mella	M	31	2350	4	6	14
Braeden Cloutier	M	30	2078	3	5	11
Jeff Baicher	F	20	1099	4	3	11
Eddie Lewis	M	32	2835	3	4	10
Francisco Uribe	F	12	734	2	5	9
Oscar Draguicevich	D	13	774	4	1	9
Harut Karapetyan	F	20	532	4	0	8
Martin Vasquez	M	28	2076	0	7	7
Wade Barrett	M	26	1921	2	2	6
Richard Gough	D	19	1609	2	1	5
John Doyle	D	28	2431	1	2	4
Shawn Medved	M	19	1059	0	3	3
Brian Sebapole	F	12	238	0	3	3
Troy Dayak	D	11	607	0	1	1
Vicente Figueroa	D	20	1005	0	0	0
Tim Weaver	D	12	1080	0	0	0
Esmundo Rodriguez	M	3	52	0	0	0
Tim Martin	D	23	1847	0	0	0

Goalkeepers	Gm	Min	W-L	Shts	Svs	GAA
David Kramer	24	2125	10-14	132	82	1.65
Andy Kirk	9	755	3-5	56	34	2.50

U.S. Open Cup

Dating back to 1914, the U.S. Open Cup is the oldest soccer competition in the United States and is among the oldest in the world. The U.S. Open Cup is a single-elimination tournament open to all amateur and professional teams in the United States. Thirty-two teams competed for the 85-year-old Dewar Cup trophy in the 1998 U.S. Open Cup.

Quarterfinals

July 22, 1998 at the Cotton Bowl, Dallas and Finley Stadium, Chattanooga

Columbus Crew (MLS) def. Miami Fusion (MLS), 3-0

Tampa Bay Mutiny (MLS) def. NY/NJ Metrostars (MLS), 4-0

Chicago Fire (MLS) def. San Jose Clash (MLS), 1-1 (4-3 PK)

Dallas Burn (MLS) def. Nashville Metros (A-League), 5-1

Semifinals

Aug. 4, 1998 at Zephyr Field, New Orleans

Columbus Crew def. NY/NJ Metrostars, 1-0

Chicago Fire def. Dallas Burn, 3-2

Final

Oct. 30, 1998 at Soldier Field, Chicago

Chicago Fire vs. Columbus Crew

Other U.S. Pro Leagues

A-League Final Standings (Outdoor)

The A-League serves as a type of minor league system for Major League Soccer. The division II outdoor league is part of the United Systems of Independent Soccer Leagues (USISL) and is recognized by U.S. Soccer. MLS and the USISL have an agreement where MLS teams can assign players to the A-League and call-up A-League players when desired. Also, the U.S. Pro-40 Select team is made-up of players from the MLS's Project 40 program. Project 40 is a joint venture between MLS and U.S. Soccer aimed at developing young American players, giving them the chance to train with MLS clubs and play games at various professional levels. The U.S. Pro-40 team played all their games on the road.

Eastern Conference

Northeast Division	W	L	Pts	GF	GA
* Rochester Raging Rhinos	24	4	70	72	15
† Montreal Impact	21	7	47	47	33
Staten Island Vipers	16	12	46	46	37
Long Island Rough Riders	17	11	45	46	35
Worcester Wildfire	12	16	32	37	50
Toronto Lynx	9	19	25	27	42
Connecticut Wolves	7	21	11	32	57

Atlantic Division	W	L	Pts	GF	GA
* Richmond Kickers	21	7	57	48	22
† Hershey Wildcats	19	9	53	51	31
Hampton Roads Mariners	16	12	46	44	39
Charleston Battery	12	16	34	37	40
Jacksonville Cyclones	10	18	30	36	53
Atlanta Ruckus	7	21	21	31	67
Raleigh Flyers	5	23	15	31	66

Western Conference

Central Division	W	L	Pts	GF	GA
* Nashville Metros	20	8	56	70	31
† Minnesota Thunder	19	9	51	52	33
Milwaukee Rampage	17	11	49	61	39
New Orleans Storm	15	13	43	53	50
Cincinnati Riverhawks	11	17	33	48	65
El Paso Patriots	12	16	60	51	54
Albuquerque Geckos	5	23	15	39	100

Pacific Division	W	L	Pts	GF	GA
* San Diego Flash	21	7	61	58	23
† Seattle Sounders	18	10	52	63	28
Orange County Zodiac	16	12	46	49	43
Vancouver 86ers	15	13	41	55	42
U.S. Pro-40 Select	11	17	31	45	55
San Francisco Bay Seals	10	18	28	31	47
California Jaguars	6	22	15	32	95

Note: Three points are awarded for a victory in regulation or overtime. One point is awarded for a shootout win. Shootouts occur if a game is tied after a 15-minute sudden-death overtime.

Playoffs

Semifinals (Best of 3)

Eastern Conference

Rochester vs. Hershey

Sept. 26	Raging Rhinos, 3-1	at Rochester
Sept. 30	Raging Rhinos, 1-0	at Hershey

Rochester wins series, 2-0

Western Conference

Minnesota vs. San Diego

Sept. 26	Thunder, 2-1	at Minnesota
Sept. 30	Thunder, 2-1	at San Diego

Minnesota wins series, 2-0

Final

Oct. 17 at Rochester.
Minnesota vs. Rochester
See Updates Chapter for results.

NPSL Final Standings (Indoor)

Division champions (*) and playoff qualifiers (†) are noted. PF and PA stand for points for and points against. Division champions drew first-round playoff byes.

American Conference

East Division	W	L	Pct.	GB	PF	PA
*Philadelphia Kixx	26	14	.650	—	569	484
†Harrisburg Heat	21	19	.525	5	530	518
Baltimore Spirit	12	28	.300	14	487	569

Central Division	W	L	Pct.	GB	PF	PA
*Milwaukee Wave	28	12	.700	—	593	486
†Cleveland Crunch	21	19	.525	7	627	612
†Cincinnati Silverbacks	15	25	.375	13	563	604

National Conference

North Division	W	L	Pct.	GB	PF	PA
*Buffalo Blizzard	21	19	.525	—	495	504
†Edmonton Drillers	18	22	.450	3	428	418
Montreal Impact	16	24	.400	5	455	518
Detroit Rockers	13	27	.325	8	464	571

Midwest Division	W	L	Pct	GB	PF	PA
*St. Louis Ambush	27	13	.675	—	625	513
†Wichita Wings	22	18	.550	5	575	559
†Kansas City Attack	20	20	.500	7	442	497

Playoffs

American Conference

First Round (Best of 3): Harrisburg def. Cincinnati (2-1)

Semifinals (Best of 3): Philadelphia def. Cleveland (2-0); Milwaukee def. Harrisburg (2-0)

Finals (Best of 5): Milwaukee def. Philadelphia (3-1)

National Conference

First Round (Best of 3): Kansas City def. Edmonton (2-0)

Semifinals (Best of 3): Buffalo def. Wichita (2-0); St. Louis def. Kansas City (2-0).

Finals (Best of 5): St. Louis def. Wichita (3-1)

Championship (Best of 7)

	W-L	GF	GA
Milwaukee	4-1	80	60
St. Louis	1-4	60	80

Date	Result	Site
May 2	Wave, 16-14	at Milwaukee
May 3	Wave, 18-10	at Milwaukee
May 8	Wave, 17-14	at St. Louis
May 10	Ambush, 12-8	at St. Louis
May 12	Wave, 21-10	at Milwaukee

Colleges

MEN

1997 Final *Soccer America* Top 20

Final 1997 regular season poll including games through Nov. 17. Conducted by the national weekly *Soccer America* and released in the Dec. 1st issue. Listing includes records through conference playoffs as well as NCAA tournament record and team lost to. Teams in **bold** type went on to reach NCAA Final Four. All tournament games decided by penalty kicks are considered ties.

		Nov.17 Record	NCAA Recap
1	**Indiana**	20-0-0	3-1 (UCLA)
2	**UCLA**	17-2-0	5-0
3	SMU	17-2-0	2-1 (St. Louis)
4	Washington	14-2-2	1-1 (UCLA)
5	South Carolina	15-2-1	1-1 (Clemson)
6	**Virginia**	15-3-3	4-1 (UCLA)
7	Creighton	15-4-1	1-1 (St. Louis)
8	American	15-3-4	2-1 (Virginia)
9	Maryland	15-5-1	1-1 (American)
10	St. John's	17-3-2	1-1 (South Florida)
11	Duke	15-5-0	did not play
12	**Saint Louis**	14-4-3	3-1 (Virginia)
13	Rutgers	14-6-1	0-1 (Maryland)
14	VA Commonwealth	15-3-4	0-1 (Georgetown)
15	Stanford	13-4-2	0-1 (Washington)
16	Clemson	9-6-3	2-1 (UCLA)
17	Gonzaga	14-4-0	did not play
18	Southwest Missouri	13-4-3	0-1 (St. Louis)
19	Boston University	14-5-2	0-1 (Dartmouth)
20	Florida International	14-5-1	0-1 (South Florida)

NCAA Division I Tournament

First Round (Nov. 21-23)

at Indiana 2 ... 3 OT ... Butler 1
Bowling Green 1 ... at Marquette 0
at St. John's 2 ... Brown 1
South Florida 3 ... at Florida Int'l 1
at UCLA 3 ... Santa Clara 0
at Washington 2 ... 2 OT ... Stanford 1
at Clemson 5 ... UNC-Charlotte 0
at South Carolina 3 ... Charleston Southern 0
at SMU 1 ... Rider 0
at Dartmouth 5 ... Boston University 1
at Saint Louis 2 ... Southwest Missouri 0
Creighton 3 ... 2 OT ... at Air Force 2
at American 2 ... 4 OT ... William & Mary 1
Maryland 1 ... at Rutgers 0
Georgetown 2 ... at VA Commonwealth 0
at Virginia 3 ... Howard 0

Second Round (Nov. 30-Dec. 1)

at Indiana 4 ... Bowling Green 0
South Florida 2 ... at St. John's 1
at UCLA 1 ... Washington 0
Clemson 1 ... 2 OT ... at South Carolina 0
at SMU 2 ... Dartmouth 0
at St. Louis 1 ... Creighton 0
at American 1 ... Maryland 0
at Virginia 5 ... Georgetown 1

Quarterfinals (Dec. 7)

at Indiana 6 ... South Florida 0
at UCLA 2 ... Clemson 1
St. Louis 0 ... 4 OT ... at SMU 0
(St. Louis advances on PK's)
at Virginia 2 ... 2 OT ... American 1

FINAL FOUR

at Richmond, Va. (Dec. 12 and 14)

Semifinals

UCLA 1 ... OT ... Indiana 0
Virginia 3 ... St. Louis 1

Championship

UCLA 2 ... Virginia 0

Scoring: UCLA— Seth George (Martin Bruno, Josh Keller) 79:37; UCLA— George (McKinley Tennyson Jr.) 81:57.

Attendance: 20,143

Final records: UCLA (22-2), Virginia (19-4-3).

WOMEN

1997 Final *Soccer America* Top 20

Final 1997 regular season poll including games through Nov. 10. Conducted by the national weekly *Soccer America* and released in the Nov. 24th issue. Listing includes records through conference playoffs as well as NCAA tournament record and team lost to. Teams in **bold** type went on to reach NCAA Final Four. All tournament games decided by penalty kicks are considered ties.

		Nov.10 Record	NCAA Recap
1	**North Carolina**	22-0-1	5-0
2	**Notre Dame**	20-0-1	3-1 (Connecticut)
3	**Santa Clara**	17-2-1	3-1 (North Carolina)
4	Texas A&M	18-2-0	0-1 (SMU)
5	**Connecticut**	19-3-0	4-1 (North Carolina)
6	Nebraska	17-3-0	1-1 (Notre Dame)
7	Florida	19-2-1	1-1 (North Carolina)
8	Portland	14-4-0	0-1 (UCLA)
9	William & Mary	18-4-0	2-1 (Connecticut)
10	Clemson	13-6-0	2-1 (Santa Clara)
11	Hartford	18-1-1	1-1 (Connecticut)
12	Virginia	13-4-2	1-1 (William & Mary)
13	Maryland	12-8-2	0-1 (George Mason)
14	Duke	14-5-1	0-1 (UNC Greensboro)
15	SMU	16-4-1	1-1 (UCLA)
16	UCLA	17-2-0	2-1 (Notre Dame)
17	Minnesota	17-2-2	1-1 (Santa Clara)
18	Michigan	18-3-1	0-1 (Nebraska)
19	Harvard	11-3-2	2-1 (North Carolina)
20	Georgia	15-5-1	0-1 (Clemson)

NCAA Division I Tournament

First Round (Nov. 15-16)

at North Carolina 6 ... Wake Forest 0
at Florida 3 ... Vanderbilt 2
at Harvard 2 ... Massachusetts 0
George Mason 2 ... at Maryland 1
UNC Greensboro 3 ... 2 OT ... at Duke 2
at Clemson 1 ... Georgia 0
at Minnesota 2 ... WI-Milwaukee 1
at Santa Clara 1 ... BYU 0
at Connecticut 3 ... Fairfield 0
at Hartford 4 ... Colgate 0
William & Mary 3 ... 2 OT ... at Penn St. 2
at Virginia 3 ... James Madison 1
UCLA 1 ... at Portland 0
SMU 1 ... at Texas A&M 0
at Nebraska 5 ... Michigan 1
at Notre Dame 7 ... Cincinnati 1

Second Round (Nov. 23)

at North Carolina 5 .... Florida 0
at Harvard 2 .... 3 OT .... George Mason 1
at Clemson 5 .... UNC Greensboro 0
at Santa Clara 5 .... Minnesota 1
at Connecticut 2 .... 2 OT .... Hartford 1
William & Mary 1 .... at Virginia 0
UCLA 3 .... at SMU 2
at Notre Dame 6 .... Nebraska 0

Quarterfinals (Nov. 29-30)

at Notre Dame 8 .... UCLA 0
at Connecticut 4 .... William & Mary 0
at North Carolina 1 .... Harvard 0
at Santa Clara 3 .... Clemson 0

FINAL FOUR

at Santa Clara, Calif. (Dec. 5 and 7)

Semifinals

Santa Clara 2 .... North Carolina 1
Connecticut 2 .... Notre Dame 1

Championship

North Carolina 2 .... Connecticut 0

Scoring: NC— Cindy Parlow (Raven McDonald, Lindsay Stoecker) 20:03; NC— Robin Confer (Nel Fettig) 87:46.

Attendance: 9,460

Final records: North Carolina (27-0-1), Connecticut (23-4).

1997 Annual Awards

Men's Players of the Year

Hermann Trophy .... Johnny Torres, Creighton, F
MAC Award .... Johnny Torres, Creighton, F
Soccer America .... Ben Olsen, Virginia, MF/F

Women's Player of the Year

Hermann Trophy .... Cindy Parlow, North Carolina, F
MAC Award .... Cindy Parlow, North Carolina, F
Soccer America .... Sara Whalen, Connecticut, F

NSCAA Coaches of the Year

Division I: Women's .... Len Tsantiris, Connecticut
Men's .... Sigi Schmid, UCLA

Division I All-America Teams

MEN

The combined 1997 first team All-America selections of the National Soccer Coaches Association of America (NSCAA) and the 11 *Soccer America* MVPs. Holdovers from the combined 1996 All-America team are in **bold** type.

GOALKEEPERS— Matthew Jordan, Clemson, Sr.; Matt Reis, UCLA, Sr.

DEFENDERS— **Pete Santora**, Furman, Sr.; **Kevin Daly**, St. John's, Sr.; Leo Cullen, Maryland, Sr.

MIDFIELDERS— Daniel Hernandez, Southern Methodist, Sr.; **Alen Kozic**, Florida Int'l, Jr.; Ben Olsen, Virginia, Jr.; Kevin Quigley, St. Louis, Sr.; Lazo Alavanja, Indiana, Jr.

FORWARDS— Wade Barrett, William & Mary, Sr.; **Siggi Eyjolfsson**, UNC Greensboro, Jr.; Dema Kovalenko, Indiana, So.; **Johnny Torres**, Creighton, Sr.; Scott Pearson, American, Sr.; Seth George, UCLA, Jr.

WOMEN

The combined 1997 first team All-America selections of the National Soccer Coaches Association of America (NSCAA) and the 11 *Soccer America* MVPs. Holdovers from the combined 1996 All-America team are in **bold** type.

GOALKEEPER— LaKeysia Beene, Notre Dame, So.

DEFENDERS— Jennifer Grubb, Notre Dame, So.; Kate Sobrero, Notre Dame, Sr.; Stephanie Yarem, Georgia, Jr.; **Staci Wilson**, North Carolina, Sr..

MIDFIELDERS— Erin Baxter, Florida, Jr.; Ann Cook, William & Mary, Sr.; Erica Iverson, UMass, Sr.; Jennifer McElmury, Minnesota, Sr.; Laurie Schwoy, Soph.; **Justi Baumgardt**, Portland, Sr.; Anne Makinen, Notre Dame, Fr.

FORWARDS— Traci Arkenberg, UCLA, Sr.; **Cindy Parlow**, North Carolina, Jr.; **Sara Whalen**, UConn, Sr.; Mandy Clemens, Santa Clara, So.; Robin Confer, North Carolina, Sr.

Small College Final Fours

MEN

NCAA Division II

at Cal St. Bakersfield (Dec. 5-7)

Semifinals: Cal St. Bakersfield def. Truman State (Mo.), 2-0; Lynn (Fla.) def. Southern Conn. St., 1-0.

Championship: Cal St. Bakersfield def. Lynn, 1-0. Final records: Cal St. Bakersfield (20-4), Lynn (19-2).

NCAA Division III

at Mary Washington (Nov. 28-29)

Semifinals: College of New Jersey def. Amherst (Mass.), 2-1; Wheaton (Ill.) def. Mary Washington, 2-1.

Championship: Wheaton def. College of New Jersey, 3-0. Final records: Wheaton (24-0-1), College of New Jersey (17-6).

NAIA

at Birmingham, Ala. (Nov. 28-29)

Semifinals: Rockhurst (Mo.) def. Mobile (Ala.), 4-3; Seattle (Wash.) def. William Carey (Miss.), 3-2 (OT).

Championship: Seattle def. Rockhurst, 2-1 (OT).

WOMEN

NCAA Division II

at Cal St. Dominguez Hills (Dec. 5-7)

Semifinals: West Va. Wesleyan def. Lynn (Fla.), 1-0 (OT); Franklin Pierce (NH) def. Cal St. Dominguez Hills, 4-3.

Championship: Franklin Pierce def. West Va. Wesleyan, 3-0. Final records: Franklin Pierce (21-0), West Va. Wesleyan (21-2-1).

NCAA Division III

at Elizabethtown, N.J. (Nov. 22-23)

Semifinals: Washington (Mo.) def. UC San Diego, 2-0; William Smith (N.Y.) def. Elizabethtown (N.J.), 0-0 (William Smith advanced on PK's)

Championship: UC San Diego def. William Smith, 1-0. Final records: UC San Diego (20-2), William Smith (18-4).

NAIA

at San Antonio (Nov. 28-29)

Semifinals: Mobile (Ala.) def. Berry (Ga.), 3-1; Simon Fraser (B.C.) def. Westmont (Calif.), 1-0.

Championship: Mobile def. Simon Fraser, 2-1 (OT).

SOCCER STATISTICS

THROUGH THE YEARS

1900-1998

WORLD • US • COLLEGE

The World Cup

The Federation Internationale de Football Association (FIFA) began the World Cup championship tournament in 1930 with a 13-team field in Uruguay. Sixty-four years later, 138 countries competed in qualifying rounds to fill 24 berths in the 1994 World Cup finals. FIFA increased the World Cup '98 tournament field from 24 to 32 teams, including automatic berths for defending champion Brazil and host France. The other 30 slots are allotted by region: Europe (14), Africa (5), South America (4), CONCACAF (3), Asia (3), and the one remaining position to the winner of a playoff between the fourth place team in Asia and the champion of Oceania.

The United States hosted the World Cup for the first time in '94 and American crowds shattered tournament attendance records (see Year-by-Year Comparisons). Tournaments have now been played three times in North America (Mexico 2 and U.S.), four times in South America (Argentina, Chile, Brazil and Uruguay) and nine times in Europe (France 2, Italy 2, England, Spain, Sweden, Switzerland and West Germany).

Brazil retired the first World Cup (called the Jules Rimet Trophy after FIFA's first president) in 1970 after winning it for the third time. The new trophy, first presented in 1974, is known as simply the World Cup.

Multiple winners: Brazil (4); Italy and West Germany (3); Argentina and Uruguay (2).

Year	Champion	Manager	Score	Runner-up	Host Country	Third Place
1930	Uruguay	Alberto Suppici	4-2	Argentina	Uruguay	No game
1934	Italy	Vittório Pozzo	2-1*	Czechoslovakia	Italy	Germany 3, Austria 2
1938	Italy	Vittório Pozzo	4-2	Hungary	France	Brazil 4, Sweden 2
1942-46	Not held					
1950	Uruguay	Juan Lopez	2-1	Brazil	Brazil	No game
1954	West Germany	Sepp Herberger	3-2	Hungary	Switzerland	Austria 3, Uruguay 1
1958	Brazil	Vicente Feola	5-2	Sweden	Sweden	France 6, W. Ger. 3
1962	Brazil	Aimoré Moreira	3-1	Czechoslovakia	Chile	Chile 1, Yugoslavia 0
1966	England	Alf Ramsey	4-2*	W. Germany	England	Portugal 2, USSR 1
1970	Brazil	Mario Zagalo	4-1	Italy	Mexico	W. Ger. 1, Uruguay 0
1974	West Germany	Helmut Schoen	2-1	Holland	W. Germany	Poland 1, Brazil 0
1978	Argentina	Cesar Menotti	3-1*	Holland	Argentina	Brazil 2, Italy 1
1982	Italy	Enzo Bearzot	3-1	W. Germany	Spain	Poland 3, France 2
1986	Argentina	Carlos Bilardo	3-2	W. Germany	Mexico	France 4, Belgium 2*
1990	West Germany	Franz Beckenbauer	1-0	Argentina	Italy	Italy 2, England 1
1994	Brazil	Carlos Parreira	0-0†	Italy	USA	Sweden 4, Bulgaria 0
1998	France	Aimé Jacquet	3-0	Brazil	France	Croatia 2, Holland 1
2002	at Japan/South Korea					

*Winning goals scored in overtime (no sudden death); †Brazil defeated Italy in shootout (3-2) after scoreless overtime period (30 minutes).

All-Time World Cup Leaders

Career Goals

World Cup scoring leaders through 1998. Years listed are years played in World Cup.

	No
Gerd Müller, West Germany (1970, 74)	14
Just Fontaine, France (1958)	13
Pelé, Brazil (1958, 62, 66, 70)	12
Sandor Kocsis, Hungary (1954)	11
Juergen Klinsmann, Germany (1990, 94, 98)	11
Helmut Rahn, West Germany (1954, 58)	10
Teofilo Cubillas, Peru (1970, 78)	10
Gregorz Lato, Poland (1974, 78, 82)	10
Gary Lineker, England (1986, 90)	10

Most Valuable Player

Officially, the Golden Ball Award, the Most Valuable Player of the World Cup tournament has been selected since 1982 by a panel of international soccer journalists.

Year		Year	
1982	Paolo Rossi, Italy	1994	Romario, Brazil
1986	Diego Maradona, Arg.	1998	Ronaldo, Brazil
1990	Toto Schillaci, Italy		

Single Tournament Goals

World Cup tournament scoring leaders through 1998.

Year		Gm	No
1930	Guillermo Stabile, Argentina	4	8
1934	Angelo Schiavio, Italy	3	4
	Oldrich Nejedly, Czechoslovakia	4	4
	& Edmund Conen, Germany	4	4
1938	Leônidas, Brazil	3	8
1950	Ademir, Brazil	6	7
1954	Sandor Kocsis, Hungary	5	11
1958	Just Fontaine, France	6	13
1962	Drazen Jerkovic, Yugoslavia	6	5
1966	Eusébio, Portugal	6	9
1970	Gerd Müller, West Germany	6	10
1974	Grzegorz Lato, Poland	7	7
1978	Mario Kempes, Argentina	7	6
1982	Paolo Rossi, Italy	7	6
1986	Gary Lineker, England	5	6
1990	Toto Schillaci, Italy	7	6
1994	Oleg Salenko, Russia	3	6
	Hristo Stoichkov, Bulgaria	7	6
1998	Davor Suker, Croatia	7	6

All-Time World Cup Ranking Table

Since the first World Cup in 1930, Brazil is the only country to play in all 16 final tournaments and win the championship four times. The FIFA All-Time Table below ranks all nations that have ever qualified for a World Cup final tournament by points earned through 1998. Victories, which earned two points from 1930-90, were awarded three points starting in 1994. Note that Germany's appearances include 10 made by West Germany from 1954-90. Participants in the 1998 World Cup final are in **bold** type.

		App	Gm	W	L	T	Pts	GF	GA
1	**Brazil**	16	80	53	13	14	**120**	173	78
2	**Germany**	14	78	45	16	17	**107**	162	103
3	**Italy**	14	66	38	12	16	**92**	105	62
4	**Argentina**	12	57	29	18	10	**68**	100	69
5	**England**	10	45	20	12	13	**53**	62	42
6	**France**	10	41	21	14	6	**48**	86	58
7	**Spain**	10	40	16	14	10	**42**	61	48
8	**Yugoslavia**	9	37	16	13	8	**40**	60	46
9	Uruguay	9	37	15	14	8	**38**	61	52
	Russia	8	34	16	12	6	**38**	60	40
11	Sweden	9	38	14	15	9	**37**	66	60
	Netherlands	7	31	14	9	9	**37**	56	36
13	Hungary	9	32	15	14	3	**33**	87	57
14	Poland	5	25	13	7	5	**31**	39	29
15	**Austria**	7	29	12	13	4	**28**	43	47
16	Czech Rep.	8	30	11	14	5	**27**	44	45
17	**Mexico**	11	37	8	19	10	**26**	39	75
18	**Belgium**	10	32	9	16	7	**25**	40	56
19	**Romania**	7	21	8	8	5	**21**	30	32
20	**Chile**	7	25	7	12	6	**20**	31	40
21	**Scotland**	8	23	4	12	7	**15**	25	41
	Switzerland	7	22	6	13	3	**15**	33	51
23	**Bulgaria**	7	26	3	15	8	**14**	22	53
	Paraguay	5	15	4	6	5	**14**	19	27
25	**Cameroon**	4	14	3	5	6	**12**	13	26
26	Portugal	2	9	6	3	0	**12**	19	12
27	Peru	4	15	4	8	3	**11**	19	31
	No. Ireland	3	13	3	5	5	**11**	13	23
	Denmark	2	9	5	3	1	**11**	19	13
30	**Croatia**	1	7	5	2	0	**10**	11	5
31	**USA**	6	17	4	12	1	**9**	18	38
32	**Morocco**	4	13	2	7	4	**8**	12	18
	Colombia	4	13	3	8	2	**8**	14	23
	Nigeria	2	8	4	4	0	**8**	13	13
35	Ireland	2	9	1	3	5	**7**	4	7
	Norway	2	8	2	3	3	**7**	7	8
37	East Germany	1	6	2	2	2	**6**	5	5
38	**Saudi Arabia**	2	7	2	4	1	**5**	7	13
	Algeria	2	6	2	3	1	**5**	6	10
	Wales	1	5	1	1	3	**5**	4	4
41	**South Korea**	5	14	0	10	4	**4**	11	43
	Tunisia	2	6	1	3	2	**4**	4	6
	Costa Rica	1	4	2	2	0	**4**	4	6
44	**Iran**	2	6	1	4	1	**3**	4	12
	North Korea	1	4	1	2	1	**3**	5	9
	Cuba	1	3	1	1	1	**3**	5	12
47	Egypt	2	4	0	2	2	**2**	3	6
	Honduras	1	3	0	1	2	**2**	2	3
	Israel	1	3	0	1	2	**2**	1	3
	Turkey	1	3	1	2	0	**2**	10	11
51	Bolivia	3	6	0	5	1	**1**	1	20
	Australia	1	3	0	2	1	**1**	0	5
	Kuwait	1	3	0	2	1	**1**	2	6
54	El Salvador	2	6	0	6	0	**0**	1	22
	Canada	1	3	0	3	0	**0**	0	5
	East Indies	1	1	0	1	0	**0**	0	6
	Greece	1	3	0	3	0	**0**	0	10
	Haiti	1	3	0	3	0	**0**	2	14
	Iraq	1	3	0	3	0	**0**	1	4
	New Zealand	1	3	0	3	0	**0**	2	12
	UAE	1	3	0	3	0	**0**	2	11
	Zaire	1	3	0	3	0	**0**	0	14

The United States in the World Cup

While the United States has fielded a national team every year of the World Cup, only five of those teams have been able to make it past the preliminary competition and qualify for the final World Cup tournament. The 1994 national team automatically qualified because the U.S. served as host of the event for the first time. The U.S. has played in three of the first four World Cups (1930, '34 and '50) and each of the last three (1990, '94 and '98). The Americans have a record of 4-12-1 in 17 World Cup matches, with two victories in 1930, a 1-0 upset of England in 1950, and a 2-1 shocker over Colombia in 1994.

1930

1st Round Matches

United States 3 .... Belgium 0
United States 3 .... Paraguay 0

Semifinals

Argentina 6 .... United States 1

U.S. Scoring–Bert Patenaude (3), Bart McGhee (2), James Brown, Thomas Florie.

1934

1st Round Match

Italy 7 .... United States 1

U.S. Scoring–Buff Donelli (who later became a noted college and NFL football coach).

1950

1st Round Matches

Spain 3 .... United States 1
United States 1 .... England 0
Chile 5 .... United States 2

U.S. Scoring–Joe Gaetjens, Joe Maca, John Souza, Frank Wallace.

1990

1st Round Matches

Czechoslovakia 5 .... United States 1
Italy 1 .... United States 0
Austria 2 .... United States 1

U.S. Scoring–Paul Caligiuri, Bruce Murray.

1994

1st Round Matches

United States 1 .... Switzerland 1
United States 2 .... Colombia 1
Romania 1 .... United States 0

Round of 16

Brazil 1 .... United States 0

Overall U.S. Scoring– Eric Wynalda, Ernie Stewart, own goal (Colombia defender Andres Escobar).

1998

1st Round Matches

Germany 2 .... United States 0
Iran 2 .... United States 1
Yugoslavia 1 .... United States 0

Overall U.S. Scoring– Brian McBride.

World Cup Finals

Brazil and West Germany (now Germany) have played in the most Cup finals with six. Note that a four-team round robin determined the 1950 championship–the deciding game turned out to be the last one of the tournament between Uruguay and Brazil.

1930

Uruguay 4, Argentina 2

(at Montevideo, Uruguay)

		1	2–T
July 30	Uruguay (4-0)	1	3–4
	Argentina (4-1)	2	0–2

Goals: Uruguay–Pablo Dorado (12th minute), Pedro Cea (54th), Santos Iriarte (68th), Castro (89th); Argentina–Carlos Peucelle (20th), Guillermo Stabile (37th).

Uruguay–Ballesteros, Nasazzi, Mascheroni, Andrade, Fernandez, Gestido, Dorado, Scarone, Castro, Cea, Iriarte.

Argentina–Botasso, Della Torre, Paternoster, J. Evaristo, Monti, Suarez, Peucelle, Varallo, Stabile, Ferreira, M. Evaristo.

Attendance: 90,000. **Referee:** Langenus (Belgium).

1934

Italy 2, Czechoslovakia 1 (OT)

(at Rome)

		1	2	OT–T
June 10	Italy (4-0-1)	0	1	1–2
	Czechoslovakia (3-1)	0	1	0–1

Goals: Italy–Raimondo Orsi (80th minute), Angelo Schiavio (95th); Czechoslovakia–Puc (70th).

Italy–Combi, Monzeglio, Allemandi, Ferraris IV, Monti, Bertolini, Guaita, Meazza, Schiavio, Ferrari, Orsi.

Czechoslovakia–Planicka, Zenisek, Ctyroky, Kostalek, Cambal, Krcil, Junek, Svoboda, Sobotka, Nejedly, Puc.

Attendance: 55,000. **Referee:** Eklind (Sweden).

1938

Italy 4, Hungary 2

(at Paris)

		1	2–T
June 19	Italy (4-0)	3	1–4
	Hungary (3-1)	1	1–2

Goals: Italy–Gino Colaussi (5th minute), Silvio Piola (16th), Colassi (35th), Piola (82nd); Hungary–Titkos (7th), Georges Sarosi (70th).

Italy–Olivieri, Foni, Rava, Serantoni, Andreolo, Locatelli, Biavati, Meazza, Piola, Ferrari, Colaussi.

Hungary–Szabo, Polgar, Biro, Szalay, Szucs, Lazar, Sas, Vincze, G. Sarosi, Szengeller, Titkos.

Attendance: 65,000. **Referee:** Capdeville (France).

1950

Uruguay 2, Brazil 1

(at Rio de Janeiro)

		1	2–T
July 16	Uruguay (3-0-1)	0	2–2
	Brazil (4-1-1)	0	1–1

Goals: Uruguay–Juan Schiaffino (66th minute), Chico Ghiggia (79th); Brazil–Friaca (47th).

Uruguay–Maspoli, M. Gonzales, Tejera, Gambetta, Varela, Andrade, Ghiggia, Perez, Miguez, Schiaffino, Moran.

Brazil–Barbosa, Augusto, Juvenal, Bauer, Danilo, Bigode, Friaça, Zizinho, Ademir, Jair, Chico.

Attendance: 199,854. **Referee:** Reader (England).

1954

West Germany 3, Hungary 2

(at Berne, Switzerland)

		1	2–T
July 4	West Germany (4-1)	2	1–3
	Hungary (4-1)	2	0–2

Goals: West Germany–Max Morlock (10th minute), Helmut Rahn (18th), Rahn (84th); Hungary–Ferenc Puskas (4th), Zoltan Czibor (9th).

West Germany–Turek, Posipal, Liebrich, Kohlmeyer, Eckel, Mai, Rahn, Morlock, O. Walter, F. Walter, Schaefer.

Hungary–Grosics, Buzansky, Lorant, Lantos, Bozsik, Zakarias, Czibor, Kocsis, Hidegkuti, Puskas, J. Toth.

Attendance: 60,000. **Referee**: Ling (England).

1958

Brazil 5, Sweden 2

(at Stockholm)

		1	2–T
June 29	Brazil (5-0-1)	2	3–5
	Sweden (4-1-1)	1	1–2

Goals: Brazil–Vava (9th minute), Vava (32nd), Pelé (55th), Mario Zagalo (68th), Pelé (90th); Sweden–Nils Liedholm (3rd), Agne Simonsson (80th).

Brazil–Gilmar, D. Santos, N. Santos, Zito, Bellini, Orlando, Garrincha, Didi, Vava, Pelé, Zagalo.

Sweden–Svensson, Bergmark, Axbom, Boerjesson, Gustavsson, Parling, Hamrin, Gren, Simonsson, Liedholm, Skoglund.

Attendance: 49,737. **Referee:** Guigue (France).

1962

Brazil 3, Czechoslovakia 1

(at Santiago, Chile)

		1	2–T
June 17	Brazil (5-0-1)	1	2–3
	Czechoslovakia (3-2-1)	1	0–1

Goals: Brazil–Amarildo (17th minute), Zito (68th), Vava (77th); Czechoslovakia–Josef Masopust (15th).

Brazil–Gilmar, D. Santos, N. Santos, Zito, Mauro, Zozimo, Garrincha, Didi, Vava, Amarildo, Zagalo.

Czechoslovakia–Schroiff, Tichy, Novak, Pluskal, Popluhar, Masopust, Pospichal, Scherer, Kvasniak, Kadraba, Jelinek.

Attendance: 68,679. **Referee:** Latishev (USSR).

1966

England 4, West Germany 2 (OT)

(at London)

		1	2	OT–T
July 30	England (5-0-1)	1	1	2–4
	West Germany (4-1-1)	1	1	0–2

Goals: England–Geoff Hurst (18th minute), Martin Peters (78th), Hurst (101st), Hurst (120th); West Germany–Helmut Haller (12th), Wolfgang Weber (90th).

England–Banks, Cohen, Wilson, Stiles, J. Charlton, Moore, Ball, Hurst, B. Charlton, Hunt, Peters.

West Germany–Tilkowski, Hottges, Schnellinger, Beckenbauer, Schulz, Weber, Haller, Seeler, Held, Overath, Emmerich.

Attendance: 93,802. **Referee:** Dienst (Switzerland).

1970

Brazil 4, Italy 1

(at Mexico City)

		1	2–T
June 21	Brazil (6-0)	1	3–4
	Italy (3-1-2)	1	0–1

Goals: Brazil–Pelé (18th minute), Gerson (65th), Jairzinho (70th), Carlos Alberto (86th); Italy–Roberto Boninsegna (37th).

Brazil–Felix, C. Alberto, Everaldo, Clodoaldo, Brito, Piazza, Jairzinho, Gerson, Tostão, Pelé, Rivelino.

Italy–Albertosi, Burgnich, Facchetti, Bertini (Juliano, 73rd), Rosato, Cera, Domenghini, Mazzola, Boninsegna (Rivera, 84th), De Sisti, Riva.

Attendance: 107,412. **Referee:** Glockner (E. Germany).

1974

West Germany 2, Holland 1

(at Munich)

		1	2–T
July 7	West Germany (6-1)	2	0–2
	Holland (5-1-1)	1	0–1

Goals: West Germany–Paul Breitner (25th minute, penalty kick), Gerd Müller (43rd); Holland–Johan Neeskens (1st, penalty kick).

West Germany–Maier, Beckenbauer, Vogts, Breitner, Schwarzenbeck, Overath, Bonhof, Hoeness, Grabowski, Muller, Holzenbein.

Holland–Jongbloed, Suurbier, Rijsbergen (De Jong, 58th), Krol, Haan, Jansen, Van Hanegem, Neeskens, Rep, Cruyff, Rensenbrink (R. Van de Kerkhof, 46th).

Attendance: 77,833. **Referee:** Taylor (England).

1978

Argentina 3, Holland 1 (OT)

(at Buenos Aires)

		1	2	OT–T
June 25	Argentina (5-1-1)	1	0	2–3
	Holland (3-2-2)	0	1	0–1

Goals: Argentina–Mario Kempes (37th minute), Kempes (104th), Daniel Bertoni (114th); Holland–Dirk Nanninga (81st).

Argentina–Fillol, Olguin, L. Galvan, Passarella, Tarantini, Ardiles (Larrosa, 65th), Gallego, Kempes, Luque, Bertoni, Ortiz (Houseman, 77th).

Holland–Jongbloed, Jansen (Suurbier, 72nd), Brandts, Krol, Poortvliet, Haan, Neeskens, W. Van de Kerkhof, R. Van de Kerkhof, Rep (Nanninga, 58th), Rensenbrink.

Attendance: 77,260. **Referee:** Gonella (Italy).

1982

Italy 3, West Germany 1

(at Madrid)

		1	2–T
July 11	Italy (4-0-3)	0	3–3
	West Germany (4-2-1)	0	1–1

Goals: Italy–Paolo Rossi (57th minute), Marco Tardelli (68th), Alessandro Altobelli (81st); West Germany–Paul Breitner (83rd).

Italy–Zoff, Scirea, Gentile, Cabrini, Collovati, Bergomi, Tardelli, Oriali, Conti, Rossi, Graziani (Altobelli, 8th, and Causio, 89th).

West Germany–Schumacher, Stielike, Kaltz, Briegel, K.H. Forster, B. Forster, Breitner, Dremmler (Hrubesch, 61st), Littbarski, Fischer, Rummenigge (Muller, 69th).

Attendance: 90,080. **Referee:** Coelho (Brazil).

1986

Argentina 3, West Germany 2

(at Mexico City)

		1	2–T
June 29	Argentina (6-0-1)	1	2–3
	West Germany (4-2-1)	0	2–2

Goals: Argentina–Jose Brown (22nd minute), Jorge Valdano (55th), Jorge Burruchaga (83rd); West Germany–Karl-Heinz Rummenigge (73rd), Rudi Voller (81st).

Argentina–Pumpido, Cuciuffo, Olarticoechea, Ruggeri, Brown, Batista, Burruchaga (Trobbiani, 89th), Giusti, Enrique, Maradona, Valdano.

West Germany–Schumacher, Jakobs, B. Forster, Berthold, Briegel, Eder, Brehme, Matthaus, Rummenigge, Magath (Hoeness, 61st), Allofs (Voller, 46th).

Attendance: 114,590. **Referee:** Filho (Brazil).

1990

West Germany 1, Argentina 0

(at Rome)

		1	2–T
July 8	West Germany (6-0-1)	0	1–1
	Argentina (4-2-1)	0	0–0

Goals: West Germany–Andreas Brehme (85th minute, penalty kick).

West Germany–Illgner, Berthold (Reuter, 73th), Kohler, Augenthaler, Buchwald, Brehme, Haessler, Matthaus, Littbarski, Klinsmann, Voller.

Argentina: Goycoechea, Ruggeri (Monzon, 46th), Simon, Serrizuela, Lorenzo, Basualdo, Troglio, Burruchaga (Calderon, 53rd), Sensini, Dezotti, Maradona.

Attendance: 73,603. **Referee:** Codesal (Mexico).

1994

Brazil 0, Italy 0 (SO)

(at Pasadena, Calif.)

		1	2	OT–T
July 17	Brazil (6-0-1)	0	0	0–0*
	Italy (4-2-1)	0	0	0–0

*Brazil wins shootout, 3-2.

Shootout (five shots each, alternating): ITA– Baresi (miss, 0-0); BRA– Santos (blocked, 0-0): ITA– Albertini (goal, 1-0); BRA–Romario (goal, 1-1); ITA– Evani (goal, 2-1); BRA– Branco (goal, 2-2); ITA– Massaro (blocked, 2-2); BRA– Dunga (goal, 2-3); ITA–R. Baggio (miss, 2-3).

Brazil– Taffarel, Jorginho (Cafu, 21st minute), Branco, Aldair, Santos, Mazinho, Silva, Dunga, Zinho (Viola, 106th), Bebeto, Romario.

Italy– Pagliuca, Mussi (Apolloni, 35th minute), Baresi, Benarrivo, Maldini, Albertini, D. Baggio (Evani, 95th), Berti, Donadoni, R. Baggio, Massaro.

Attendance: 94,194. **Referee:** Puhl (Hungary).

1998

France 3, Brazil 0

(at Paris)

		1	2– T
July 12	Brazil (6-1-0)	0	0– 0
	France (6-0-0)	2	1– 3

Goals: France– Zinedine Zidane (27th and 46th minutes), Petit (92).

Brazil– Taffarel, Cafu, Aldair, Baiano, Carlos, Sampaio (Edmundo, 74th minute), Dunga, Rivaldo, Leonardo (Denilson, 46th minute), Bebeto, Ronaldo.

France– Barthez, Lizarazu, Desailly, Thuram, Leboeuf, Djorkaeff (Viera, 75th minute), Deschamps, Zidane, Petit, Karembeu (Boghossian, 57th minute), Guivarc'h, Dugarry.

Attendance: 75,000. **Referee:** Belqola (Morocco).

Year-by-Year Comparisons

How the 15 World Cup tournaments have compared in nations qualifying, matches played, players participating, goals scored, average goals per game, overall attendance and attendance per game.

Year	Host	Continent	Nations	Matches	Players	Goals Scored	Goals Per Game	Attendance Overall	Attendance Per Game
1930	Uruguay	So. America	13	18	189	70	3.8	589,300	32,739
1934	Italy	Europe	16	17	208	70	4.1	361,000	21,235
1938	France	Europe	15	18	210	84	4.7	376,000	20,889
1942-46	Not held								
1950	Brazil	So. America	13	22	192	88	4.0	1,044,763	47,489
1954	Switzerland	Europe	16	26	233	140	5.3	872,000	33,538
1958	Sweden	Europe	16	35	241	126	3.6	819,402	23,411
1962	Chile	So. America	16	32	252	89	2.8	892,812	27,900
1966	England	Europe	16	32	254	89	2.8	1,464,944	45,780
1970	Mexico	No. America	16	32	270	95	3.0	1,690,890	52,840
1974	West Germany	Europe	16	38	264	97	2.6	1,809,953	47,630
1978	Argentina	So. America	16	38	277	102	2.7	1,685,602	44,358
1982	Spain	Europe	24	52	396	146	2.8	2,108,723	40,552
1986	Mexico	No. America	24	52	414	132	2.5	2,393,031	46,020
1990	Italy	Europe	24	52	413	115	2.2	2,516,354	48,391
1994	United States	No. America	24	52	437	140	2.7	3,587,088	68,982
1998	France	Europe	32	64	704	171	2.7	2,775,400	43,366

World Team of the 20th Century

The team, comprised of the century's best players, was voted on by a panel that included 250 international soccer journalists and released on June 10, 1998 in conjunction with the opening of the 1998 World Cup. The panel first selected the European and South American Teams of the Century and then chose the World Team from those two lists.

World Team

Pos	
GK	Lev Yashin, Soviet Union
D	Carlos Alberto, Brazil
D	Franz Beckenbauer, West Germany
D	Bobby Moore, England
D	Nilton Santos, Brazil
MF	Johan Cryuff, Netherlands
MF	Alfredo Di Stefano, Argentina
MF	Michel Platini, France
F	Pele, Brazil
F	Garrincha, Brazil
F	Diego Maradona, Argentina

European Team

Pos	
GK	Lev Yashin, Soviet Union
D	Paolo Maldini, Italy
D	Franz Beckenbauer, West Germany
D	Bobby Moore, England
D	Franco Baresi, Italy
MF	Johan Cryuff, Netherlands
MF	Eusebio, Portugal
MF	Michel Platini, France
F	Ferenc Puskas, Hungary
F	Bobby Charlton, England
F	Marco Van Basten, Netherlands

South American Team

Pos	
GK	Ubaldo Fillol, Argentina
D	Carlos Alberto, Brazil
D	Elias Figueroa, Chile
D	Daniel Passarella, Argentina
D	Nilton Santos, Brazil
MF	Didi, Brazil
MF	Alfredo Di Stefano, Argentina
MF	Rivelino, Brazil
F	Pele, Brazil
F	Garrincha, Brazil
F	Diego Maradona, Argentina

World Cup Shootouts

Introduced in 1982; winning sides in **bold** type.

Year	Round		Final	SO
1982	Semi	**W. Germany** vs. France	3-3	(5-4)
	Semi	**W. Germany** vs. England	1-1	(4-3)
1986	Quarter	**Belgium** vs. Spain	1-1	(5-4)
	Quarter	**France** vs. Brazil	1-1	(4-3)
	Quarter	**W. Germany** vs. Mexico	0-0	(4-1)
1990	Second	**Ireland** vs. Romania	0-0	(5-4)
	Quarter	**Argentina** vs. Yugoslavia	0-0	(3-2)
	Semi	**Argentina** vs. Italy	1-1	(4-3)
1994	Second	**Bulgaria** vs. Mexico	1-1	(3-1)
	Quarter	**Sweden** vs. Romania	2-2	(5-4)
	Final	**Brazil** vs. Italy	0-0	(3-2)
1998	Second	**Argentina** vs. England	2-2	(4-3)
	Quarter	**France** vs. Italy	0-0	(4-3)

OTHER WORLDWIDE COMPETITION

The Olympic Games

Held every four years since 1896, except during World War I (1916) and World War II (1940-44). Soccer was not a medal sport in 1896 at Athens or in 1932 at Los Angeles. By agreement between FIFA and the IOC, Olympic soccer competition is currently limited to players 23 years old and under.

Multiple winners: England and Hungary (3); Soviet Union and Uruguay (2).

MEN

Year	
1900	**England**, France, Belgium
1904	**Canada**, USA I, USA II
1906	**Denmark**, Smyrna (Int'l entry), Greece
1908	**England**, Denmark, Holland
1912	**England**, Denmark, Holland
1920	**Belgium**, Spain, Holland
1924	**Uruguay**, Switzerland, Sweden
1928	**Uruguay**, Argentina, Italy
1936	**Italy**, Austria, Norway
1948	**Sweden**, Yugoslavia, Denmark
1952	**Hungary**, Yugoslavia, Sweden
1956	**Soviet Union**, Yugoslavia, Bulgaria
1960	**Yugoslavia**, Denmark, Hungary
1964	**Hungary**, Czechoslovakia, East Germany
1968	**Hungary**, Bulgaria, Japan
1972	**Poland**, Hungary, East Germany
1976	**East Germany**, Poland, Soviet Union
1980	**Czechoslovakia**, East Germany, Soviet Union
1984	**France**, Brazil, Yugoslavia
1988	**Soviet Union**, Brazil, West Germany
1992	**Spain**, Poland, Ghana
1996	**Nigeria**, Argentina, Brazil

WOMEN

Year	
1996	**USA**, China, Norway

The Under-20 World Cup

Held every two years since 1977. Officially, The World Youth Championship for the FIFA/Coca-Cola Cup.

Multiple winners: Argentina and Brazil (3); Portugal (2).

Year		Year	
1977	Soviet Union	1989	Portugal
1979	Argentina	1991	Portugal
1981	West Germany	1993	Brazil
1983	Brazil	1995	Argentina
1985	Brazil	1997	Argentina
1987	Yugoslavia	1999	(at South America)

The Under-17 World Cup

Held every two years since 1985. Officially, The U-17 World Tournament for the FIFA/JVC Cup.

Multiple winners: Ghana and Nigeria (2).

Year		Year	
1985	Nigeria	1993	Nigeria
1987	Soviet Union	1995	Ghana
1989	Saudi Arabia	1997	Brazil
1991	Ghana	1999	(at New Zealand)

Indoor World Championship

First held in 1989. FIFA's only Five-a-Side tournament.

Multiple winners: Brazil (3).

Year		Year	
1989	Brazil	1996	Brazil
1992	Brazil		

Women's World Cup

First held in 1991. Officially, the FIFA Women's World Championship.

Year		Year	
1991	United States	1999	(at United States)
1995	Norway		

Confederations' Cup

First held in 1992. Contested by the Continental champions of Africa, Asia, Europe, North America and South America and originally called the Intercontinental Championship for the King Fahd Cup until it was redubbed the FIFA/Confederation's Cup for the King Fahd Trophy in 1997.

Year		Year	
1992	Argentina	1997	Brazil
1995	Denmark	1999	(at Mexico)

CONTINENTAL COMPETITION

European Championship

Held every four years since 1960. Officially, the European Football Championship. Winners receive the Henri Delaunay trophy, named for the frenchman who first proposed the idea of a European Soccer Championship in 1927. The first one would not be played until five years after his death in 1955.

Multiple winner: West Germany (2).

Year		Year		Year		Year	
1960	Soviet Union	1972	West Germany	1984	France	1996	Germany
1964	Spain	1976	Czechoslovakia	1988	Holland	2000	(at Belgium/ Netherlands)
1968	Italy	1980	West Germany	1992	Denmark		

Copa America

Held irregularly since 1916. Unofficially, the Championship of South America.

Multiple winners: Argentina and Uruguay (14); Brazil (5); Paraguay and Peru (2).

Year		Year		Year		Year	
1916	Uruguay	1927	Argentina	1949	Brazil	1979	Paraguay
1917	Uruguay	1929	Argentina	1953	Paraguay	1983	Uruguay
1919	Brazil	1935	Uruguay	1955	Argentina	1987	Uruguay
1920	Uruguay	1937	Argentina	1956	Uruguay	1989	Brazil
1921	Argentina	1939	Peru	1957	Argentina	1991	Argentina
1922	Brazil	1941	Argentina	1958	Argentina	1993	Argentina
1923	Uruguay	1942	Uruguay	1959	Uruguay	1995	Uruguay
1924	Uruguay	1945	Argentina	1963	Bolivia	1997	Brazil
1925	Argentina	1946	Argentina	1967	Uruguay	1999	(at Paraguay)
1926	Uruguay	1947	Argentina	1975	Peru		

African Nations' Cup

Contested since 1957 and held every two years since 1968.

Multiple winners: Egypt and Ghana (4); Congo/Zaire (3); Cameroon and Nigeria (2).

Year		Year		Year		Year	
1957	Egypt	1970	Sudan	1982	Ghana	1994	Nigeria
1959	Egypt	1972	Congo	1984	Cameroon	1996	South Africa
1962	Ethiopia	1974	Zaire	1986	Egypt	1998	Egypt
1963	Ghana	1976	Morocco	1988	Cameroon	2000	(at Zimbabwe)
1965	Ghana	1978	Ghana	1990	Algeria		
1968	Zaire	1980	Nigeria	1992	Ivory Coast		

CONCACAF Gold Cup

The Confederation of North, Central American and Caribbean Football Championship. Contested irregularly from 1963-81 and revived as CONCACAF Gold Cup in 1991.

Multiple winners: Mexico (6); Costa Rica (2).

Year		Year		Year		Year	
1963	Costa Rica	1969	Costa Rica	1977	Mexico	1993	Mexico
1965	Mexico	1971	Mexico	1981	Honduras	1996	Mexico
1967	Guatemala	1973	Haiti	1991	United States	1998	Mexico

CLUB COMPETITION

Toyota Cup

Also known as the World Club Championship. Contested annually in December between the winners of the European Cup and South America's Copa Libertadores. Four European Cup winners refused to participate in the championship match in the 1970s and were replaced each time by the European Cup runner-up: Panathinaikos (Greece) for Ajax Amsterdam (Holland) in 1971; Juventus (Italy) for Ajax in 1973; Atlético Madrid (Spain) for Bayern Munich (West Germany) in 1974; and Malmo (Sweden) for Nottingham Forest (England) in 1979. Another European Cup winner, Marseille of France, was prohibited by the Union of European Football Associations (UEFA) from playing for the 1993 Toyota Cup because of its involvement in the match-rigging scandal.

Best-of-three game format from 1960-68, then a two-game/total goals format from 1969-79. Toyota became Cup sponsor in 1980, changed the format to a one-game championship and moved it to Toyko.

Multiple winners: AC Milan, Nacional and Penarol (3); Ajax Amsterdam, Independiente, Inter-Milan, Juventus, Santos and Sao Paulo (2).

Year		Year		Year	
1960	Real Madrid (Spain)	1973	Independiente (Argentina)	1986	River Plate (Argentina)
1961	Peñarol (Uruguay)	1974	Atlético Madrid (Spain)	1987	FC Porto (Portugal)
1962	Santos (Brazil)	1975	Not held	1988	Nacional (Uruguay)
1963	Santos (Brazil)	1976	Bayern MunichW. Germany)	1989	AC Milan (Italy)
1964	Inter Milan (Italy)	1977	Boca Juniors (Argentina)	1990	AC Milan (Italy)
1965	Inter Milan (Italy)	1978	Not held	1991	Red Star (Yugoslavia)
1966	Penarol (Uruguay)	1979	Olimpia (Paraguay)	1992	Sao Paulo (Brazil)
1967	Racing Club (Argentina)	1980	Nacional (Uruguay)	1993	Sao Paulo (Brazil)
1968	Estudiantes (Argentina)	1981	Flamengo (Brazil)	1994	Velez Sarsfield (Argentina)
1969	AC Milan (Italy)	1982	Peñarol (Uruguay)	1995	Ajax Amsterdam (Holland)
1970	Feyenoord (Holland)	1983	Gremio (Brazil)	1996	Juventus (Italy)
1971	Nacional (Uruguay)	1984	Independiente (Argentina)	1997	Borussia Dortmund (Germany)
1972	Ajax Amsterdam (Holland)	1985	Juventus (Italy)		

European Cup

Contested annually since the 1955-56 season by the league champions of the member countries of the Union of European Football Associations (UEFA).

Multiple winners: Real Madrid (7); AC Milan (5); Ajax Amsterdam and Liverpool (4); Bayern Munich (3); Benfica, Inter-Milan, Juventus and Nottingham Forest (2).

Year
1956 Real Madrid (Spain)
1957 Real Madrid (Spain)
1958 Real Madrid (Spain)
1959 Real Madrid (Spain)
1960 Real Madrid (Spain)
1961 Benfica (Portugal)
1962 Benfica (Portugal)
1963 AC Milan (Italy)
1964 Inter Milan (Italy)
1965 Inter Milan (Italy)
1966 Real Madrid (Spain)
1967 Glasgow Celtic (Scotland)
1968 Manchester United (England)
1969 AC Milan (Italy)
1970 Feyenoord (Holland)

Year
1971 Ajax Amsterdam (Holland)
1972 Ajax Amsterdam (Holland)
1973 Ajax Amsterdam (Holland)
1974 Bayern Munich (W. Germany)
1975 Bayern Munich (W. Germany)
1976 Bayern Munich (W. Germany)
1977 Liverpool (England)
1978 Liverpool (England)
1979 Nottingham Forest (England)
1980 Nottingham Forest (England)
1981 Liverpool (England)
1982 Aston Villa (England)
1983 SV Hamburg (W. Germany)
1984 Liverpool (England)
1985 Juventus (Italy)

Year
1986 Steaua Bucharest (Romania)
1987 FC Porto (Portugal)
1988 PSV Eindhoven (Holland)
1989 AC Milan (Italy)
1990 AC Milan (Italy)
1991 Red Star Belgrade (Yugo.)
1992 Barcelona (Spain)
1993 Marseille (France)*
1994 AC Milan (Italy)
1995 Ajax Amsterdam (Holland)
1996 Juventus (Italy)
1997 Borussia Dortmund (Germany)
1998 Real Madrid (Spain)

*title vacated

European Cup Winner's Cup

Contested annually since the 1960-61 season by the cup winners of the member countries of the Union of European Football Associations (UEFA).

Multiple winners: Barcelona (4); AC Milan, RSC Anderlecht, Chelsea and Dinamo Kiev (2).

Year
1961 Fiorentina (Italy)
1962 Atletico Madrid (Spain)
1963 Tottenham Hotspur (England)
1964 Sporting Lisbon (Portugal)
1965 West Ham United (England)
1966 Borussia Dortmund (W.Germany)
1967 Bayern Munich (W. Germany)
1968 AC Milan (Italy)
1969 Slovan Bratislava (Czech.)
1970 Manchester City (England)
1971 Chelsea (England)
1972 Glasgow Rangers (Scotland)
1973 AC Milan (Italy)

Year
1974 FC Magdeburg (E. Germany)
1975 Dinamo Kiev (USSR)
1976 RSC Anderlecht (Belgium)
1977 SV Hamburg (W. Germany)
1978 RSC Anderlecht (Belgium)
1979 Barcelona (Spain)
1980 Valencia (Spain)
1981 Dinamo Tbilisi (USSR)
1982 Barcelona (Spain)
1983 Aberdeen (Scotland)
1984 Juventus (Italy)
1985 Everton (England)
1986 Dinamo Kiev (USSR)

Year
1987 Ajax Amsterdam (Holland)
1988 Mechelen (Belgium)
1989 Barcelona (Spain)
1990 Sampdoria (Italy)
1991 Manchester United (England)
1992 Werder Bremen (Germany)
1993 Parma (Italy)
1994 Arsenal (England)
1995 Real Zaragoza (Spain)
1996 Paris St. Germain (France)
1997 Barcelona (Spain)
1998 Chelsea (England)

UEFA Cup

Contested annually since the 1957-58 season by teams other than league champions and cup winners of the Union of European Football Associations (UEFA). Teams selected by UEFA based on each country's previous performance in the tournament. Teams from England were banned from UEFA Cup play from 1985-90 for the criminal behavior of their supporters.

Multiple winners: Barcelona, Inter Milan and Juventus (3); Borussia Mönchengladbach, IFK Göteborg, Leeds United, Liverpool, Real Madrid, Tottenham Hotspur and Valencia (2).

Year
1958 Barcelona (Spain)
1959 Not held
1960 Barcelona (Spain)
1961 AS Roma (Italy)
1962 Valencia (Spain)
1963 Valencia (Spain)
1964 Real Zaragoza (Spain)
1965 Ferencvaros (Hungary)
1966 Barcelona (Spain)
1967 Dinamo Zagreb (Yugoslavia)
1968 Leeds United (England)
1969 Newcastle United (England)
1970 Arsenal (England)
1971 Leeds United (England)
1972 Tottenham Hotspur (England)

Year
1973 Liverpool (England)
1974 Feyenoord (Holland)
1975 Borussia Mönchengladbach (W. Germany)
1976 Liverpool (England)
1977 Juventus (Italy)
1978 PSV Eindhoven (Holland)
1979 Borussia Mönchengladbach (W. Germany)
1980 Eintracht Frankfurt (W. Germany)
1981 Ipswich Town (England)
1982 IFK Göteborg (Sweden)
1983 RSC Anderlecht (Belgium)
1984 Tottenham Hotspur (England)
1985 Real Madrid (Spain)

Year
1986 Real Madrid (Spain)
1987 IFK Göteborg (Sweden)
1988 Bayer Leverkusen (W. Germany)
1989 Napoli (Italy)
1990 Juventus (Italy)
1991 Inter Milan (Italy)
1992 Ajax Amsterdam (Holland)
1993 Juventus (Italy)
1994 Inter Milan (Italy)
1995 Parma (Italy)
1996 Bayern Munich (Germany)
1997 Schalke 04 (Germany)
1998 Inter Milan (Italy)

Copa Libertadores

Contested annually since the 1955-56 season by the league champions of South America's football union.

Multiple winners: Independiente (7); Peñarol (5); Estudiantes and Nacional-Uruguay (3); Boca Juniors, Cruzeiro, Gremio, Olimpia, River Plate, Santos and São Paulo (2).

Year	Year	Year
1960 Peñarol (Uruguay)	1973 Independiente (Argentina)	1986 River Plate (Argentina)
1961 Peñarol (Uruguay)	1974 Independiente (Argentina)	1987 Peñarol (Uruguay)
1962 Santos (Brazil)	1975 Independiente (Argentina)	1988 Nacional (Uruguay)
1963 Santos (Brazil)	1976 Cruzeiro (Brazil)	1989 Nacional Medellin (Colombia)
1964 Independiente (Argentina)	1977 Boca Juniors (Argentina)	1990 Olimpia (Paraguay)
1965 Independiente (Argentina)	1978 Boca Juniors (Argentina)	1991 Colo Colo (Chile)
1966 Peñarol (Uruguay)	1979 Olimpia (Paraguay)	1992 São Paulo (Brazil)
1967 Racing Club (Argentina)	1980 Nacional (Uruguay)	1993 São Paulo (Brazil)
1968 Estudiantes de la Plata (Argentina)	1981 Flamengo (Brazil)	1994 Velez Sarsfield (Argentina)
1969 Estudiantes de la Plata (Argentina)	1982 Peñarol (Uruguay)	1995 Gremio (Brazil)
1970 Estudiantes de la Plata (Argentina)	1983 Gremio (Brazil)	1996 River Plate (Argentina)
1971 Nacional (Uruguay)	1984 Independiente (Argentina)	1997 Cruzeiro (Brazil)
1972 Independiente (Argentina)	1985 Argentinos Jrs. (Argentina)	1998 Vasco da Gama (Brazil)

Annual Awards

World Player of the Year

Presented by FIFA, the European Sports Magazine Association (ESM) and Adidas, the sports equipment manufacturer, since 1991. Winners are selected by national team coaches from around the world.

Year		Nat'l Team	Year		Nat'l Team
1991	Lothar Matthäus, Inter Milan	Germany	1995	George Weah, AC Milan	Liberia
1992	Marco Van Basten, AC Milan	Holland	1996	Ronaldo, Barcelona	Brazil
1993	Roberto Baggio, Juventus	Italy	1997	Ronaldo, Inter Milan	Brazil
1994	Romario, Barcelona	Brazil			

European Player of the Year

Officially, the "Ballon d'Or" and presented by *France Football* magazine since 1956. Candidates are limited to European players in European leagues and winners are selected by a panel of 49 European soccer journalists.

Multiple winners: Johan Cruyff, Michel Platini and Marco Van Basten (3); Franz Beckenbauer, Alfredo di Stéfano, Kevin Keegan and Karl-Heinz Rummenigge (2).

Year		Nat'l Team	Year		Nat'l Team
1956	Stanley Matthews, Blackpool	England	1977	Allan Simonsen, B. Mönchengladbach	Denmark
1957	Alfredo di Stéfano, Real Madrid	Arg./Spain	1978	Kevin Keegan, SV Hamburg	England
1958	Raymond Kopa, Real Madrid	France	1979	Kevin Keegan, SV Hamburg	England
1959	Alfredo di Stéfano, Real Madrid	Arg./Spain	1980	K.H. Rummenigge, Bayern Munich	W. Ger.
1960	Luis Suarez, Barcelona	Spain	1981	K.H. Rummenigge, Bayern Munich	W. Ger.
1961	Enrique Sivori, Juventus	Arg./Italy	1982	Paolo Rossi, Juventus	Italy
1962	Josef Masopust, Dukla Prague	Czech.	1983	Michel Platini, Juventus	France
1963	Lev Yashin, Dinamo Moscow	Soviet Union	1984	Michel Platini, Juventus	France
1964	Denis Law, Manchester United	Scotland	1985	Michel Platini, Juventus	France
1965	Eusébio, Benfica	Portugal	1986	Igor Belanov, Dinamo Kiev	Soviet Union
1966	Bobby Charlton, Manchester United	England	1987	Ruud Gullit, AC Milan	Holland
1967	Florian Albert, Ferencvaros	Hungary	1988	Marco Van Basten, AC Milan	Holland
1968	George Best, Manchester United	No. Ireland	1989	Marco Van Basten, AC Milan	Holland
1969	Gianni Rivera, AC Milan	Italy	1990	Lothar Matthäus, Inter Milan	W. Ger.
1970	Gerd Müller, Bayern Munich	W. Ger.	1991	Jean-Pierre Papin, Marseille	France
1971	Johan Cruyff, Ajax Amsterdam	Holland	1992	Marco Van Basten, AC Milan	Holland
1972	Franz Beckenbauer, Bayern Munich	W. Ger.	1993	Roberto Baggio, Juventus	Italy
1973	Johan Cruyff, Barcelona	Holland	1994	Hristo Stoitchkov, Barcelona	Bulgaria
1974	Johan Cruyff, Barcelona	Holland	1995	George Weah, AC Milan	Liberia
1975	Oleg Blokhin, Dinamo Kiev	Soviet Union	1996	Matthias Sammer, Bor. Dortmund	Germany
1976	Franz Beckenbauer, Bayern Munich	W. Ger.	1997	Ronaldo, Inter Milan	Brazil

South American Player of the Year

Presented by El Pais of Uruguay since 1971. Candidates are limited to South American players in South American leagues and winners are selected by a panel of 80 Latin American sports editors.

Multiple winners: Elias Figueroa and Zico (3); Enzo Francescoli, Diego Maradona and Carlos Valderrama (2).

Year		Nat'l Team	Year		Nat'l Team
1971	Tostao, Cruzeiro	Brazil	1978	Mario Kempes, Valencia	Argentina
1972	Teofilo Cubillas, Alianza Lima	Peru	1979	Diego Maradona, Argentinos Juniors	Argentina
1973	Pelé, Santos	Brazil	1980	Diego Maradona, Boca Juniors	Argentina
1974	Elias Figueroa, Internacional	Chile	1981	Zico, Flamengo	Brazil
1975	Elias Figueroa, Internacional	Chile	1982	Zico, Flamengo	Brazil
1976	Elias Figueroa, Internacional	Chile	1983	Socrates, Corinthians	Brazil
1977	Zico, Flamengo	Brazil	1984	Enzo Francescoli, River Plate	Uruguay

Year		Nat'l Team
1985	Julio Cesar Romero, Fluminense	Paraguay
1986	Antonio Alzamendi, River Plate	Uruguay
1987	Carlos Valderrama, Deportivo Cali	Colombia
1988	Ruben Paz, Racing Buenos Aires	Uruguay
1989	Bebeto, Vasco da Gama	Brazil
1990	Raul Amarilla, Olimpia	Paraguay
1991	Oscar Ruggeri, Velez Sarsfield	Argentina
1992	Rai, Sao Paulo	Brazil
1993	Carlos Valderrama, Atl. Junior	Colombia
1994	Cafu, Sao Paulo	Brazil
1995	Enzo Francescoli, River Plate	Uruguay
1996	Jose Luis Chilavert, Velez Sarsfield	Paraguay
1997	Marcelo Salas, River Plate	Chile

African Player of the Year

Officially, the African "Ballon d'Or" and presented by *France Football* magazine since 1970. All African players are eligible for the award and winners are selected by a panel of 52 African soccer journalists.

Multiple winners: George Weah (4); Abedi Pelé (3); Roger Milla and Thomas N'Kono (2).

Year	
1970	Salif Keita, Mali
1971	Ibrahim Sunday, Ghana
1972	Cherif Souleymane, Guinea
1973	Tshimimu Bwanga, Zaire
1974	Paul Moukila, Congo
1975	Ahmed Faras, Morocco
1976	Roger Milla, Cameroon
1977	Dhiab Tarak, Tunisia
1978	Abdul Razak, Ghana
1979	Thomas N'Kono, Cameroon
1980	Jean Manga Onguene, Cameroon
1981	Lakhdar Belloumi, Algeria
1982	Thomas N'Kono, Cameroon
1983	Mahmoud Al-Khatib, Egypt
1984	Theophile Abega, Cameroon
1985	Mohamed Timoumi, Morocco
1986	Badou Zaki, Morocco
1987	Rabah Madjer, Algeria
1988	Kalusha Bwalya, Zambia
1989	George Weah, Liberia
1990	Roger Milla, Cameroon
1991	Abedi Pelé, Ghana
1992	Abedi Pelé, Ghana
1993	Abedi Pelé, Ghana
1994	George Weah, Liberia
1995	George Weah, Liberia
1996	George Weah, Liberia
1997	Victor Ikpeba, Nigeria

U.S. Player of the Year

Presented by Honda and the Spanish-speaking radio show "Futbol de Primera" since 1991. Candidates are limited to American players who have played with the U.S. National Team and winners are selected by a panel of U.S. soccer journalists.

Multiple winner: Eric Wynalda (2).

Year	
1991	Hugo Perez
1992	Eric Wynalda
1993	Thomas Dooley
1994	Marcelo Balboa
1995	Alexi Lalas
1996	Eric Wynalda
1997	Eddie Pope

U.S. PRO LEAGUES

OUTDOOR

Major League Soccer

Sanctioned by U.S. Soccer and FIFA, the international soccer federation. MLS was founded on the heels of the successful 1994 World Cup tournament hosted by the United States and it remains the only FIFA-sanctioned division I outdoor league in the United States. The MLS title game is known as the MLS Cup.

Multiple Winner: D.C. United (2).

MLS Cup

Year	Winner	Head Coach	Score	Loser	Head Coach	Site
1996	D.C. United	Bruce Arena	3-2	Los Angeles Galaxy	Lothar Osiander	Foxboro, Mass.
1997	D.C. United	Bruce Arena	2-1	Colorado Rapids	Glen Myernick	Washington, D.C.

MLS Cup '96

D.C. United, 3-2 (OT)

Oct. 20 at Foxboro Stadium, Foxboro, Mass.

Attendance: 34,643

	1	2	OT	
Los Angeles Galaxy	1	1	0	**—2**
D.C. United	0	2	1	**—3**

First Half: LA–Eduardo Hurtado (Mauricio Cienfuegos), 5th minute.

Second Half: LA–Chris Armas (unassisted), 56th; DC–Tony Sanneh (Marco Etcheverry), 73rd; DC–Shawn Medved (unassisted), 82nd.

Overtime: DC-Eddie Pope (Etcheverry), 94th.

MVP: Marco Etcheverry, D.C. United, Midfielder

MLS Cup '97

D.C. United, 2-1

Oct. 26 at RFK Stadium, Washington, D.C..

Attendance: 57,431

	1	2	
Colorado Rapids	0	1	**—1**
D.C. United	1	1	**—2**

First Half: DC–Jaime Moreno (Tony Sanneh, David Vaudreuil), 37th minute.

Second Half: DC–Sanneh (John Harkes, Richie Williams), 68th; COL–Adrian Paz (David Patino, Matt Kmosko), 75th.

MVP: Jaime Moreno, D.C. United, Forward

Regular Season

Most Valuable Player

1996	Carlos Valderrama, Tampa Bay
1997	Preki, Kansas City

Leading Scorer	G	A	Pts
1996 Roy Lassiter, Tampa Bay	27	4	58
1997 Stern John, Columbus	26	5	57

National Professional Soccer League (1967)

Not sanctioned by FIFA, the international soccer federation. The NPSL recruited individual players to fill the rosters of its 10 teams. The league lasted only one season.

	Playoff Final			Regular Season			
Year	**Winner**	**Score(s)**	**Loser**	**Leading Scorer**	**G**	**A**	**Pts**
1967	Oakland Clippers	0-1, 4-1	Baltimore Bays	Yanko Daucik, Toronto	20	8	48

United Soccer Association (1967)

Sanctioned by FIFA. Originally called the North American Soccer League, it became the USA to avoid being confused with the National Professional Soccer League (see above). Instead of recruiting individual players, the USA imported 12 entire teams from Europe to represent its 12 franchises. It, too, only lasted a season. The league champion Los Angeles Wolves were actually Wolverhampton of England and the runner-up Washington Whips were Aberdeen of Scotland.

	Playoff Final			Regular Season			
Year	**Winner**	**Score**	**Loser**	**Leading Scorer**	**G**	**A**	**Pts**
1967	Los Angeles Wolves	6-5 (OT)	Washington Whips	Roberto Boninsegna, Chicago	10	1	21

North American Soccer League (1968-84)

The NPSL and USA merged to form the NASL in 1968 and the new league lasted until 1985. The NASL championship was known as the Soccer Bowl from 1975-84. One game decided the NASL title every year but five. There were no playoffs in 1969; a two-game/aggregate goals format was used in 1968 and '70; and a best-of-three games format was used in 1971 and '84; (*) indicates overtime and (†) indicates game decided by shootout.

Multiple winners: NY Cosmos (5); Chicago (2).

	Playoff Final			Regular Season			
Year	**Winner**	**Score(s)**	**Loser**	**Leading Scorer**	**G**	**A**	**Pts**
1968	Atlanta Chiefs	0-0,3-0	San Diego Toros	John Kowalik, Chicago	30	9	69
1969	Kansas City Spurs	No game	Atlanta Chiefs	Kaiser Motaung, Atlanta	16	4	36
1970	Rochester Lancers	3-0,1-3	Washington Darts	Kirk Apostolidis, Dallas	16	3	35
1971	Dallas Tornado	1-2*,4-1,2-0	Atlanta Chiefs	Carlos Metidieri, Rochester	19	8	46
1972	New York Cosmos	2-1	St. Louis Stars	Randy Horton, New York	9	4	22
1973	Philadelphia Atoms	2-0	Dallas Tornado	Kyle Rote Jr., Dallas	10	10	30
1974	Los Angeles Aztecs	3-3†	Miami Toros	Paul Child, San Jose	15	6	36
1975	Tampa Bay Rowdies	2-0	Portland Timbers	Steve David, Miami	23	6	52
1976	Toronto Metros	3-0	Minnesota Kicks	Giorgio Chinaglia, New York	19	11	49
1977	New York Cosmos	2-1	Seattle Sounders	Steve David, Los Angeles	26	6	58
1978	New York Cosmos	3-1	Tampa Bay Rowdies	Giorgio Chinaglia, New York	34	11	79
1979	Vancouver Whitecaps	2-1	Tampa Bay Rowdies	Oscar Fabbiani, Tampa Bay	25	8	58
1980	New York Cosmos	3-0	Ft. Laud. Strikers	Giorgio Chinaglia, New York	32	13	77
1981	Chicago Sting	0-0†	New York Cosmos	Giorgio Chinaglia, New York	29	16	74
1982	New York Cosmos	1-0	Seattle Sounders	Giorgio Chinaglia, New York	20	15	55
1983	Tulsa Roughnecks	2-0	Toronto Blizzard	Roberto Cabanas, New York	25	16	66
1984	Chicago Sting	2-1,3-2	Toronto Blizzard	Steve Zungul, Golden Bay	20	10	50

Note: In 1969, Kansas City won the NASL regular season championship with 110 points to 109 for Atlanta. There were no playoffs.

Regular Season MVP

Regular season Most Valuable Player as designated by the NASL.

Multiple winner: Carlos Metidieri (2).

Year		Year		Year	
1967	Rueben Navarro, Phila (NPSL)	1973	Warren Archibald, Miami	1979	Johan Cruyff, Los Angeles
1968	John Kowalik, Chicago	1974	Peter Silvester, Baltimore	1980	Roger Davies, Seattle
1969	Cirilio Fernandez, KC	1975	Steve David, Miami	1981	Giorgio Chinaglia, New York
1970	Carlos Metidieri, Rochester	1976	Pelé, New York	1982	Peter Ward, Seattle
1971	Carlos Metidieri, Rochester	1977	Franz Beckenbauer, New York	1983	Roberto Cabanas, New York
1972	Randy Horton, New York	1978	Mike Flanagan, New England	1984	Steve Zungul, Golden Bay

A-League (American Professional Soccer League)

The American Professional Soccer League was formed in 1990 with the merger of the Western Soccer League and the New American Soccer League. The APSL was officially sanctioned as an outdoor pro league in 1992 and changed its name to the A-League in 1995.

Multiple winner: Colorado and Seattle (2).

Year		Year		Year		Year	
1990	Maryland Bays	1992	Colorado Foxes	1994	Montreal Impact	1996	Seattle Sounders
1991	SF Bay Blackhawks	1993	Colorado Foxes	1995	Seattle Sounders	1997	Milwaukee Rampage

INDOOR

Major Soccer League (1978-92)

Originally the Major Indoor Soccer League from 1978-79 season through 1989-90. The MISL championship was decided by one game in 1980 and 1981; a best-of-three games series in 1979, best-of-five games in 1982 and 1983; and best-of-seven games since 1984. The MSL folded after the 1991-92 season.

Multiple winners: San Diego (8); New York (4).

	Playoff Final			Regular Season			
Year	**Winner**	**Series**	**Loser**	**Leading Scorer**	**G**	**A**	**Pts**
1979	New York Arrows	2-0 (WW)	Philadelphia	Fred Grgurev, Philadelphia	46	28	74
1980	New York Arrows	7-4 (1 game)	Houston	Steve Zungul, New York	90	46	136
1981	New York Arrows	6-5 (1 game)	St. Louis	Steve Zungul, New York	108	44	152
1982	New York Arrows	3-2 (LWWLW)	St. Louis	Steve Zungul, New York	103	60	163
1983	San Diego Sockers	3-2 (WWLLW)	Baltimore	Steve Zungul, NY/Golden Bay	75	47	122
1984	Baltimore Blast	4-1 (LWWWW)	St. Louis	Stan Stamenkovic, Baltimore	34	63	97
1985	San Diego Sockers	4-1 (WWLWW)	Baltimore	Steve Zungul, San Diego	68	68	136
1986	San Diego Sockers	4-3 (WLLLWWW)	Minnesota	Steve Zungul, Tacoma	55	60	115
1987	Dallas Sidekicks	4-3 (LLWWLWW)	Tacoma	Tatu, Dallas	73	38	111
1988	San Diego Sockers	4-0	Cleveland	Eric Rasmussen, Wichita	55	57	112
1989	San Diego Sockers	4-3 (LWWWLLW)	Baltimore	Preki, Tacoma	51	53	104
1990	San Diego Sockers	4-2 (LWWWLW)	Baltimore	Tatu, Dallas	64	49	113
1991	San Diego Sockers	4-2 (WLWLWW)	Cleveland	Tatu, Dallas	78	66	144
1992	San Diego Sockers	4-2 (WWWLLW)	Dallas	Zoran Karic, Cleveland	39	63	102

Playoff MVPs

MSL playoff Most Valuable Players, selected by a panel of soccer media covering the playoffs.

Multiple winners: Zungul (4); Quinn (2).

Year		Year	
1979	Shep Messing, NY	1986	Brian Quinn, SD
1980	Steve Zungul, NY	1987	Tatu, Dallas
1981	Steve Zungul, NY	1988	Hugo Perez, SD
1982	Steve Zungul, NY	1989	Victor Nogueira, SD
1983	Juli Veee, SD	1990	Brian Quinn, SD
1984	Scott Manning, Bal.	1991	Ben Collins, SD
1985	Steve Zungul, SD	1992	Thompson Usiyan, SD

Regular Season MVPs

MSL regular season Most Valuable Players, selected by a panel of soccer media from every city in the league.

Multiple winner: Zungul (6); Nogueira and Tatu (2).

Year		Year	
1979	Steve Zungul, NY	1986	Steve Zungul, SD/Tac.
1980	Steve Zungul, NY	1987	Tatu, Dallas
1981	Steve Zungul, NY	1988	Erik Rasmussen, Wich.
1982	Steve Zungul, NY & Stan Terlecki, Pit.	1989	Preki, Tacoma
1983	Alan Mayer, SD	1990	Tatu, Dallas
1984	Stan Stamenkovic, Bal.	1991	Victor Nogueira, SD
1985	Steve Zungul, SD	1992	Victor Nogueira, SD

NASL Indoor Champions (1980-84)

The North American Soccer League started an indoor league in the fall of 1979. The indoor NASL, which featured many of the same teams and players who played in the outdoor NASL, crowned champions from 1980-82 before suspending play. It was revived for the 1983-84 indoor season but folded for good in 1984.

Multiple winners: San Diego (2).

Year		Year		Year		Year	
1980	Memphis Rogues	1982	San Diego Sockers	1983	Play suspended	1984	San Diego Sockers
1981	Edmonton Drillers						

National Professional Soccer League

The winter indoor NPSL began as the American Indoor Soccer Association in 1984-85, then changed its name in 1989-90.

Multiple winner: Canton (5); Cleveland and Kansas City (2).

Year		Year		Year		Year	
1985	Canton (OH) Invaders	1989	Canton Invaders	1993	Kansas City Attack	1997	Kansas City Attack
1986	Canton Invaders	1990	Canton Invaders	1994	Cleveland Crunch	1998	Milwaukee Wave
1987	Louisville Thunder	1991	Chicago Power	1995	St. Louis Ambush		
1988	Canton Invaders	1992	Detroit Rockers	1996	Cleveland Crunch		

Continental Indoor Soccer League (1993-97)

The summer indoor CISL played its first season in 1993 and folded following the 1997 season.

Multiple winners: Monterrey (2).

Year		Year		Year		Year	
1993	Dallas Sidekicks	1995	Monterrey La Raza	1996	Monterrey La Raza	1997	Seattle Seadogs
1994	Las Vegas Dustdevils						

U.S. COLLEGES

NCAA Men's Division I Champions

NCAA Division I champions since the first title was contested in 1959. The championship has been shared three times–in 1967, 1968 and 1989. There was a playoff for third place from 1974-81.

Multiple winners: Saint Louis (10); San Francisco and Virginia (5); Indiana and UCLA (3); Clemson, Howard and Michigan St. (2).

Year	Winner	Head Coach	Score	Runner-up	Host/Site	Semifinalists
1959	Saint Louis	Bob Guelker	5-2	Bridgeport	UConn	West Chester, CCNY
1960	Saint Louis	Bob Guelker	3-2	Maryland	Brooklyn	West Chester, UConn
1961	West Chester	Mel Lorback	2-0	Saint Louis	Saint Louis	Bridgeport, Rutgers
1962	Saint Louis	Bob Guelker	4-3	Maryland	Saint Louis	Mich. St., Springfield
1963	Saint Louis	Bob Guelker	3-0	Navy	Rutgers	Army, Maryland
1964	Navy	F.H. Warner	1-0	Michigan St.	Brown	Army, Saint Louis
1965	Saint Louis	Bob Guelker	1-0	Michigan St.	Saint Louis	Army, Navy
1966	San Francisco	Steve Negoesco	5-2	LIU-Brooklyn	California	Army, Mich. St.
1967-**a**	Michigan St. & Saint Louis	Gene Kenney Harry Keough	0-0	–	Saint Louis	LIU-Bklyn, Navy
1968-**b**	Michigan St. & Maryland	Gene Kenney Doyle Royal	2-2 (2 OT)	–	Ga. Tech	Brown, San Jose St.
1969	Saint Louis	Harry Keough	4-0	San Francisco	San Jose St.	Harvard, Maryland
1970	Saint Louis	Harry Keough	1-0	UCLA	SIU-Ed'sville	Hartwick, Howard
1971-**c**	Howard	Lincoln Phillips	3-2	Saint Louis	Miami	Harvard, San Fran.
1972	Saint Louis	Harry Keough	4-2	UCLA	Miami	Cornell, Howard
1973	Saint Louis	Harry Keough	2-1 (OT)	UCLA	Miami	Brown, Clemson
Year	**Winner**	**Head Coach**	**Score**	**Runner-up**	**Host/Site**	**Third Place**
1974	Howard	Lincoln Phillips	2-1 (4OT)	Saint Louis	Saint Louis	Hartwick 3, UCLA 1
1975	San Francisco	Steve Negoesco	4-0	SIU-Ed'sville	SIU-Ed'sville	Brown 2, Howard 0
1976	San Francisco	Steve Negoesco	1-0	Indiana	Penn	Hartwick 4, Clemson 3
1977	Hartwick	Jim Lennox	2-1	San Francisco	California	SIU-Ed'sville 3, Brown 2
1978-**d**	San Francisco	Steve Negoesco	4-3 (OT)	Indiana	Tampa	Clemson 6, Phi. Textile 2
1979	SIU-Ed'sville	Bob Guelker	3-2	Clemson	Tampa	Penn St. 2, Columbia 1
1980	San Francisco	Steve Negoesco	4-3 (OT)	Indiana	Tampa	Ala. A&M 2, Hartwick 0
1981	Connecticut	Joe Morrone	2-1 (OT)	Alabama A&M	Stanford	East. Ill. 4, Phi. Textile 2
Year	**Winner**	**Head Coach**	**Score**	**Runner-up**	**Host/Site**	**Semifinalists**
1982	Indiana	Jerry Yeagley	2-1 (8 OT)	Duke	Ft. Lauderdale	UConn, SIU-Ed'sville
1983	Indiana	Jerry Yeagley	1-0 (2 OT)	Columbia	Ft. Lauderdale	UConn, Virginia
1984	Clemson	I.M. Ibrahim	2-1	Indiana	Seattle	Hartwick, UCLA
1985	UCLA	Sigi Schmid	1-0 (8 OT)	American	Seattle	Evansville, Hartwick
1986	Duke	John Rennie	1-0	Akron	Tacoma	Fresno St., Harvard
1987	Clemson	I.M. Ibrahim	2-0	San Diego St.	Clemson	Harvard, N. Carolina
1988	Indiana	Jerry Yeagley	1-0	Howard	Indiana	Portland, S. Carolina
1989-**e**	Santa Clara & Virginia	Steve Sampson Bruce Arena	1-1 (2 OT)	– –	Rutgers	Indiana, Rutgers
1990-**f**	UCLA	Sigi Schmid	0-0 (PKs)	Rutgers	South Fla.	Evansville, N.C. State
1991-**g**	Virginia	Bruce Arena	0-0 (PKs)	Santa Clara	Tampa	Indiana, Saint Louis
1992	Virginia	Bruce Arena	2-0	San Diego	Davidson	Davidson, Duke
1993	Virginia	Bruce Arena	2-0	South Carolina	Davidson	CS-Fullerton, Princeton
1994	Virginia	Bruce Arena	1-0	Indiana	Davidson	Rutgers, UCLA
1995	Wisconsin	Jim Launder	2-0	Duke	Richmond	Portland, Virginia
1996	St. John's	Dave Masur	4-1	Fla. International	Richmond	Creighton, NC-Charlotte
1997	UCLA	Sigi Schmid	2-0	Virginia	Richmond	Indiana, Saint Louis

a–game declared a draw due to inclement weather after regulation time; **b**–game declared a draw after two overtimes; **c**–Howard vacated title for using ineligible player; **d**–San Francisco vacated title for using ineligible player; **e**–game declared a draw due to inclement weather after two overtimes. **f**–UCLA wins on penalty kicks (4-3) after four overtimes; **g**–Virginia wins on penalty kicks (3-1) after four overtimes.

Women's NCAA Division I Champions

NCAA Division I women's champions since the first tournament was contested in 1982.

Multiple winner: North Carolina (14).

Year	Winner	Score	Runner-up	Year	Winner	Score	Runner-up
1982	North Carolina	2-0	Central Florida	1990	North Carolina	6-0	Connecticut
1983	North Carolina	4-0	George Mason	1991	North Carolina	3-1	Wisconsin
1984	North Carolina	2-0	Connecticut	1992	North Carolina	9-1	Duke
1985	George Mason	2-0	North Carolina	1993	North Carolina	6-0	George Mason
1986	North Carolina	2-0	Colorado College	1994	North Carolina	5-0	Notre Dame
1987	North Carolina	1-0	Massachusetts	1995	Notre Dame	1-0 (3OT)	Portland
1988	North Carolina	4-1	N.C. State	1996	North Carolina	1-0 (2OT)	Notre Dame
1989	North Carolina	2-0	Colorado College	1997	North Carolina	2-0	Connecticut

Annual Awards

MEN

Hermann Trophy

College Player of the Year. Voted on by Division I college coaches and selected sportswriters and first presented in 1967 in the name of Robert Hermann, one of the founders of the North American Soccer League. **Multiple winners:** Mike Fisher, Mike Seerey, Ken Snow and Al Trost (2).

Year
1967 Dov Markus, LIU
1968 Manuel Hernandez, San Jose St.
1969 Al Trost, Saint Louis
1970 Al Trost, Saint Louis
1971 Mike Seerey, Saint Louis
1972 Mike Seerey, Saint Louis
1973 Dan Counce, Saint Louis
1974 Farrukh Quraishi, Oneonta St.
1975 Steve Ralbovsky, Brown
1976 Glenn Myernick, Hartwick
1977 Billy Gazonas, Hartwick

Year
1978 Angelo DiBernardo, Indiana
1979 Jim Stamatis, Penn St.
1980 Joe Morrone, Jr. UConn
1981 Armando Betancourt, Indiana
1982 Joe Ulrich, Duke
1983 Mike Jeffries, Duke
1984 Amr Aly, Columbia
1985 Tom Kain, Duke
1986 John Kerr, Duke
1987 Bruce Murray, Clemson
1988 Ken Snow, Indiana

Year
1989 Tony Meola, Virginia
1990 Ken Snow, Indiana
1991 Alexi Lalas, Rutgers
1992 Brad Friedel, UCLA
1993 Claudio Reyna, Virginia
1994 Brian Maisonneuve, Indiana
1995 Mike Fisher, Virginia
1996 Mike Fisher, Virginia
1997 Johnny Torres, Creighton

Missouri Athletic Club Award

College Player of the Year. Voted on by men's team coaches around the country from Division I to junior college level and first presented in 1986 by the Missouri Athletic Club of St. Louis. **Multiple winner:** Claudio Reyna and Ken Snow (2).

Year
1986 John Kerr, Duke
1987 John Harkes, Virginia
1988 Ken Snow, Indiana
1989 Tony Meola, Virginia

Year
1990 Ken Snow, Indiana
1991 Alexi Lalas, Rutgers
1992 Claudio Reyna, Virginia
1993 Claudio Reyna, Virginia

Year
1994 Todd Yeagley, Indiana
1995 Matt McKeon, St. Louis
1996 Mike Fisher, Virginia
1997 Johnny Torres, Creighton

WOMEN

Hermann Trophy

Women's College Player of the year. Voted on by Division I college coaches and selected sportswriters and first presented in 1988 in the name of Robert Hermann, one of the founders of the North American Soccer League. **Multiple winner:** Mia Hamm (2).

Year
1988 Michelle Akers, Central Fla.
1989 Shannon Higgins, N. Carolina
1990 April Kater, Massachusetts
1991 Kristine Lilly, N. Carolina

Year
1992 Mia Hamm, N. Carolina
1993 Mia Hamm, N. Carolina
1994 Tisha Venturini, N. Carolina
1995 Shannon McMillan, Portland

Year
1996 Cindy Daws, Notre Dame
1997 Cindy Parlow, N. Carolina

Missouri Athletic Club Award

Women's College Player of the Year. Voted on by women's team coaches around the country from Division I to junior college level and first presented in 1991 by the Missouri Athletic Club of St. Louis. **Multiple winner:** Mia Hamm (2).

Year
1991 Kristine Lilly, N. Carolina
1992 Mia Hamm, N. Carolina
1993 Mia Hamm, N. Carolina

Year
1994 Tisha Venturini, N. Carolina
1995 Shannon McMillan, Portland
1996 Cindy Daws, Notre Dame

Year
1997 Cindy Parlow, N. Carolina

Coach of the Year

MEN

Men's Coach of the Year. Voted on by the National Soccer Coaches Association of America. **Multiple winner:** J. Yeagley (3).

Year
1973 Robert Guelker, SIU-Edwardsville
1974 Jack MacKenzie, Quincy College
1975 Paul Reinhardt, Vermont
1976 Jerry Yeagley, Indiana
1977 Klass Deboer, Cleveland St.
1978 Cliff McCrath, Seattle Pacific
1979 Walter Bahr, Penn St.
1980 Jerry Yeagley, Indiana
1981 Schellas Hyndman, E. Illinois

Year
1982 John Rennie, Duke
1983 Dieter Ficken, Columbia
1984 James Lennox, Hartwick
1985 Peter Mehleft, American
1986 Steve Parker, Akron
1987 Anson Dorrance, N. Carolina
1988 Keith Tucker, Howard
1989 Steve Sampson, Santa Clara
1990 Bob Reasso, Rutgers

Year
1991 Mitch Murray, Santa Clara
1992 Charles Slagle, Davidson
1993 Bob Bradley, Princeton
1994 Jerry Yeagley, Indiana
1995 Jim Launder, Wisconsin
1996 Dave Masur, St. John's
1997 Sigi Schmid, UCLA

WOMEN

Women's Coach of the Year. Voted on by the National Soccer Coaches Association of America. **Multiple winners:** Kalenkeni M. Banda, Anson Dorrance and Chris Petrucelli (2).

Year
1982 Anson Dorrance, N. Carolina
1983 David Lombardo, Keene St.
1984 Phillip Picince, Brown
1985 Kalenkeni M. Banda, UMass
1986 Anson Dorrance, N. Carolina
1987 Kalenkeni M. Banda, UMass

Year
1988 Larry Gross, N.C. State
1989 Austin Daniels, Hartford
1990 Lauren Gregg, Virginia
1991 Greg Ryan, Wisc-Madison
1992 Bell Hempen, Duke
1993 Jac Cicala, George Mason

Year
1994 Chris Petrucelli, Norte Dame
1995 Chris Petrucelli, Norte Dame
1996 John Walker, Nebraska
1997 Len Tsantiris, UConn

Bowling

Career PBA Tour money leader **Walter Ray Williams Jr.** continued to shine in 1998 with another $100,000 year.

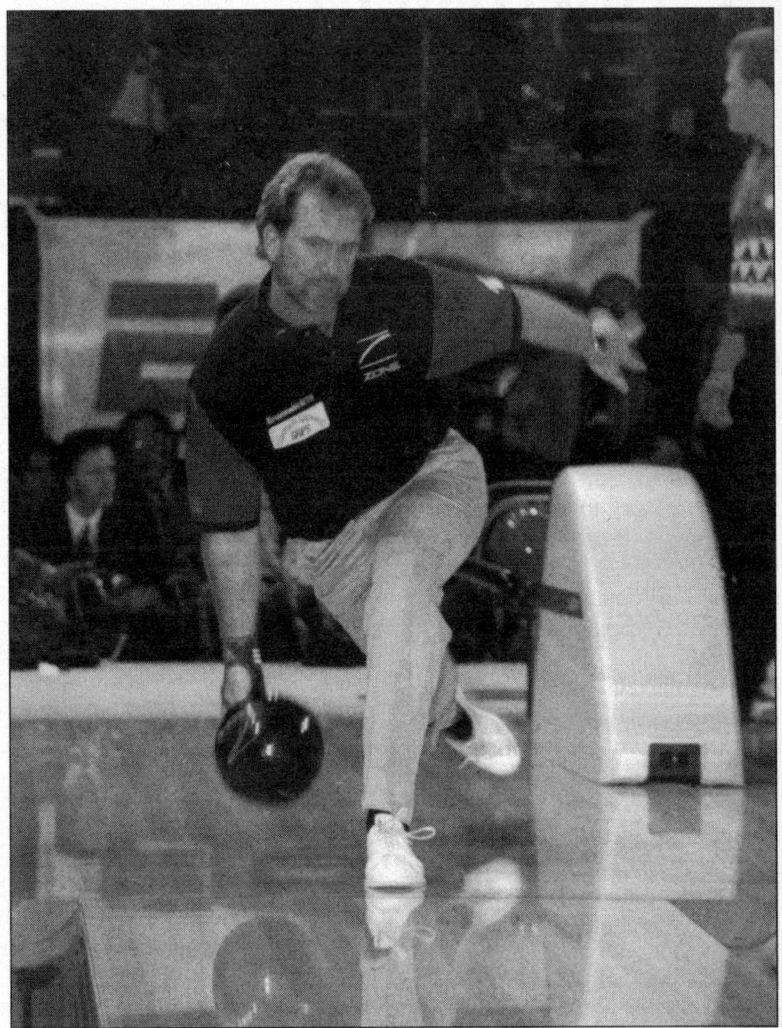

PBA Tour

A Bohnified Champion

Parker Bohn III is in the driver's seat for his first PBA Player of the Year award.

by
Mike Durbin

Although it might seem that Player of the Year honors on all three bowling tours (PBA, PWBA, Senior PBA) is assured, there is still plenty of room at the top. Parker Bohn III, 35, of Jackson, N.J., has been *the* story through September on the men's Professional Bowlers Tour in 1998. He has done it all, winning four titles in six championship round finishes, capping things off with a win in the Japan Cup. He bowled a 300 during the televised championship round of the prestigious ABC Masters, and at the time of this writing, leads the earnings list with more than $165,000.

But it ain't over till it's over, especially when you've got a guy named Walter Ray Williams Jr. on your tail. With eight tournaments including the Brunswick World Tournament of Champions remaining, both Williams, the 1997 Player of the Year and all-time PBA Tour money winner, and Tim Criss are more than capable of derailing Bohn. Williams has two wins to his credit, one in the BPAA U.S. Open, and has a slight lead on both Bohn and Criss on the average list. Both Williams and Criss have accumulated over $100,000 in winnings and have a comparable match play record. A strong finish by either and any stumble by Bohn should make for a very interesting race.

The PBA Hall of Fame had an eventful year in 1998 with the inductions of Pete Weber in the Performance category and Teata Semiz in the Veteran/Senior category. Weber joined his father, the legendary Dick Weber, in becoming the first father-son pair ever elected. Weber, who won 24 titles over his career and was voted

---

Mike Durbin is an analyst for ESPN's bowling coverage and a bowler on the Sr. PBA Tour.

PBA Tour

After finishing second to Walter Ray Williams Jr. in earnings in 1997, **Parker Bohn III** is leading the pack in 1998.

1980 Rookie of the Year, is one of only four bowlers to win bowling's "Triple Crown" (National Championship, U.S. Open and Tournament of Champions). He is also the youngest player to accumulate career earnings in excess of $1 million and currently stands second on the PBA's all-time earnings list. Semiz has three wins to his credit on the National Tour, eight on the Senior Tour, and is the oldest player (63) to win a tournament.

The Senior PBA thus far has been thoroughly dominated by 53-year-old Pete Couture of Titusville, Fla. He became only the second player to win over $100,000 in one year on the Senior Tour (Gary Dickinson accomplished the feat in 1997) and won the coveted ABC Senior Masters tournament in August. Couture won the 1995 Senior Rookie of the Year award and this year appears to be a lock for Senior Player of the Year.

Continuing its history of being the second-longest running live sports series on network television, the Pro Bowlers Tour marked its 38th year with a change to the CBS network. The contract was recently extended through the year 2000 and featured a new announcing team (Gary Seibel and Marshall Holman) and a brand new format. The tour also implemented heavier Brunswick gold pins in championship rounds.

AP/Wide World Photos

Bowling continues its attempt to increase its popularity and reach new markets. Having the guy on the left as a spokesman certainly can't hurt. **Michael Jordan**, shown here with AMF president and CEO **Doug Stanard** (r), signed a five-year deal in late 1997 to endorse AMF bowling products.

With over $100,000 in earnings in 1998, Aleta Sill has the inside track for Player of the Year on the PWBA Tour. She has won two tournaments, including the BPAA U.S. Open, and is set to become the first woman in the history of the tour to surpass the $1 million mark in career earnings. With seven tournaments that include the AMF Gold Cup, the Brunswick World Open and the Sam's Town Invitational, the fall tour will go a long way towards deciding the champion. Average leader Carol Gianotti-Block and the always tough Kim Adler continue to impress and could make a run at Sill. ■

Mike Durbin's Top Ten Highlights from the year in Bowling

10. **John Handegard** retires from the senior tour to take ownership of a bowling center in Texas, comes back, wins the Senior Tournament of Champions, and then retires again.
9. **Pete Couture** wins the first Major of his career, the ABC Senior Masters tournament, and pockets $60,000 in the process. He defeats a tenacious Ron Garr 234-213 in the final game.

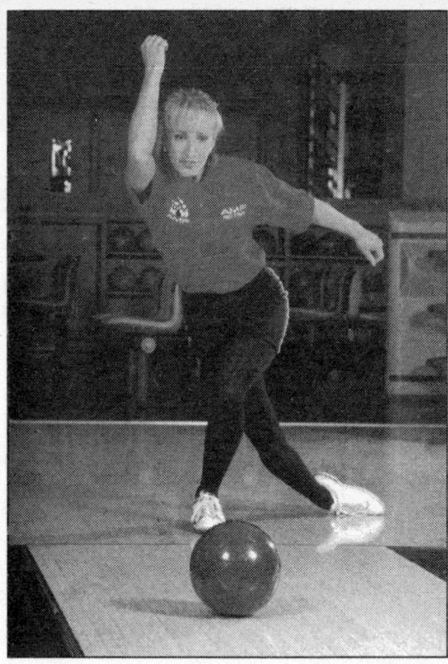

PWBA Tour

With two wins and one second-place finish in the first 16 PWBA tournaments, **Kim Adler** found herself behind only Aleta Sill on the 1998 money list.

8. **Hurricane Georges** rips through southern Florida, cutting the Naples Senior Open down to 27 games. It is the first time in history that a PBA tournament is cut short.

7. **Brian Voss wins** the Johnny Petraglia Open, giving him at least one title in 12 consecutive years. He is two years away from tying Earl Anthony's streak of 14.

6. **PBA signs a broadcasting deal with CBS** to show nine telecasts beginning in April and including the ABC Masters, and adds two broadcasts to its ESPN schedule.

5. **PBA introduces the Brunswick Pro Pin** to championship rounds on the National Tour. The pin is gold with black crowns and is heavier than other tour pins, making it more challenging for the bowlers.

4. **Pete Weber**, the youngest bowler (26) to break the $1 million mark in career earnings, joins his father, Dick, in the PBA Hall of Fame.

3. **Parker Bohn III rolls** a perfect 300 during the televised portion of the ABC Masters, becoming the 12th player in PBA history to throw a televised 300 game.

2. **Mike Aulby defeats Bohn** in the final round, 224-192, to become the first three-time winner of the ABC Masters.

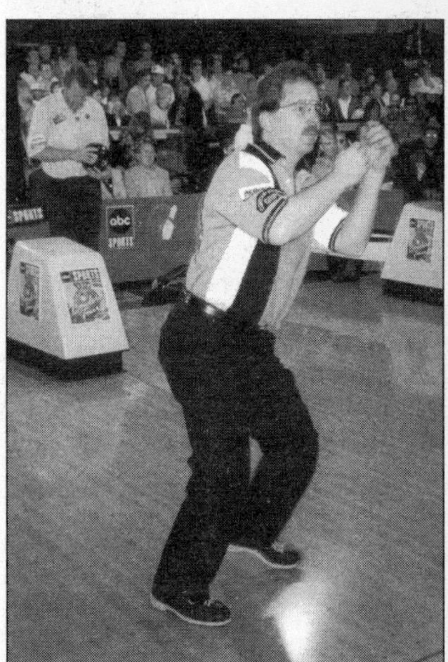

PBA Tour

Mike Aulby needed all the body english he could muster up to defeat Parker Bohn III for his third ABC Masters title.

1. Hall of Famers **Aleta Sill and Walter Ray Williams Jr.** each capture BPAA U.S. Open titles. Sill, the 12th seed heading into the bracket portion of the tournament, leads wire to wire in the final game to crush runner-up Tammy Turner (276-151). No. 1 seeded Williams wins a see-saw battle with Tim Criss. ■

INSIDE THE NUMBERS

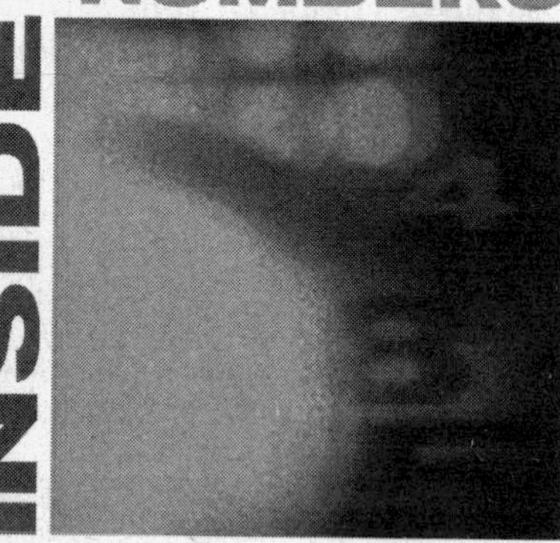

by

Team Research

BAD SEEDS?

In the first ten tournaments of the 1998 Senior PBA Tour (through Sept. 10), the top seed entering the championship round has emerged the victor only three times. On the PBA Tour, however, the top seeds have fared much better, taking nine of 17 tournaments throughout the spring schedule.

Seed	Senior PBA Wins	PBA Wins
1st	3	9
2nd	0	5
3rd	2	2
4th	0*	1
5th	5	0

*Oddly enough, no fourth seed has won a senior title since 1993.

PICTURE PERFECT

Parker Bohn III's perfect 300 at the ABC Masters was the twelfth televised perfect game since the PBA Tour began broadcasting in 1962. Maybe these guys are getting too good. Of the twelve perfectionists listed below, seven accomplished the feat in the last five years.

1967	Jack Biondolillo	Akron, OH
1969	John Guenther	San Jose, CA
1974	Jim Stefanich	Alameda, CA
1987	Pete McCordic	Torrence, CA
1988	Bob Benoit*	Grand Prairie, TX
1993	Mike Aulby	Wichita, KS
1994	Johnny Petraglia	Toledo, OH
	Butch Soper	Reno, NV
1996	C.K. Moore	Austin, TX
	Bob Learn Jr.	Erie, PA
1997	Steve Hoskins	Rochester, NY
1998	Parker Bohn III	Reno, NV

*First 300 game in a title match ■

PWBA Tour

Aleta Sill broke the $100,000 mark once again in 1998 and now aims to become the PWBA's first million dollar woman.

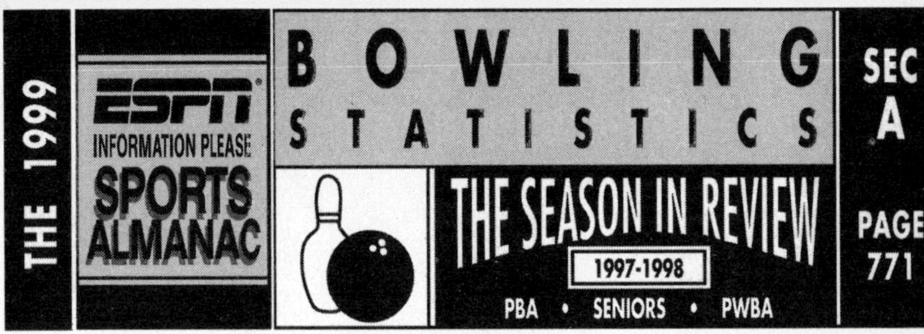

THE 1999
ESPN
INFORMATION PLEASE
SPORTS
ALMANAC
BOWLING
STATISTICS
THE SEASON IN REVIEW
1997-1998
PBA • SENIORS • PWBA
SEC
A
PAGE
771

Tournament Results

Winners of stepladder finals in all PBA, Seniors and PWBA tournaments from Oct. 29, 1997, through Sept. 12, 1998; major tournaments in **bold** type. See Updates Chapter for later results.

PBA

Late 1997 Fall Tour

Final	Event	Winner	Earnings	Score	Runner-up
Oct. 29	Ebonite Challenge (Ind.)	John Mazza	$21,000	220-212	Dave D'Entremont
Nov. 5	Ebonite Challenge (Va.)	Amleto Monacelli	10,000	222-213	Steve Hoskins
Nov. 12	**Bayer/Brunswick TPC**	Steve Hoskins	40,000	233-194	Danny Wiseman
Dec. 11	Merit Showdown	Walter Ray Williams Jr.	30,000	654-570†	Wendy Macpherson
Dec. 14	Merit Mixed Doubles Champ.	Tim Criss/Carol Gianotti-Block	40,000	453-411†	Pete Weber/Carolyn Dorin-Ballard

†Scoring in the Merit Showdown and Mixed Doubles events is based on total pins.

1998 Winter/Spring Tour

Final	Event	Winner	Earnings	Score	Runner-up
Jan. 25	Brentwood Classic	Parker Bohn III	$16,000	239-222	Tom Baker
Jan. 31	Long John Silver's Classic	Ricky Ward	16,000	279-226	Butch Soper
Feb. 7	Columbia 300 Open	Roger Bowker	22,000	279-258	Butch Soper
Feb. 14	Peoria Open	David Traber	16,000	248-229	Walter Ray Williams Jr.
Feb. 21	**PBA National Championship**	Pete Weber	28,000	277-236	David Ozio
Feb. 28	Flagship Open	Walter Ray Williams Jr.	19,000	202-146	Steve Jaros
Apr. 11	**BPAA U.S. Open**	Walter Ray Williams Jr.	40,000	221-189	Tim Criss
Apr. 18	**Bayer/Brunswick TPC**	Dennis Horan Jr.	40,000	245-202	Parker Bohn III
May 2	Tucson Open	Norm Duke	16,000	279-256	Eric Forkel
May 9	**ABC Masters**	Mike Aulby	50,000	224-192	Parker Bohn III
May 16	Greater Detroit Open	Parker Bohn III	16,000	290-248	Doug Kent
May 23	Johnny Petraglia Open	Brian Voss	28,000	238-230	Tim Criss
May 30	Greater Harrisburg Open	Parker Bohn III	16,000	268-181	Steve Hoskins
June 13	Showboat Invitational	Jason Couch	46,000	205-181	Amleto Monacelli
June 20	AC Delco Classic	Steve Hoskins	52,000	230-202	Tim Criss
June 27	Oregon Open	Danny Wiseman	19,000	213-191	Sean Swanson
July 2	Northwest Classic	Tim Criss	16,000	245-207	Butch Soper

Note: The American Bowling Congress Masters tournament is not a PBA Tour event.

1998 Fall Tour Schedules

PBA

Events: Japan Cup – Tokyo (Sept. 17-20); National Finance Championship – Virginia Beach, VA (Oct. 3-7); Long Island Open – Coram, NY (Oct. 10-14); Greater Rochester Open – Rochester, NY (Oct. 17-21); Bay City Classic – Bay City, MI (Oct. 24-28); Indianapolis Open – Indianapolis, IN (Oct. 31-Nov. 4); Wichita Open – Wichita, KS (Nov. 7-11); Kansas City Open – Overland Park, KS (Nov. 11-15); **Brunswick World Tournament of Champions** – Reno, NV (Nov. 17-22).

SENIOR PBA

Events: Greater Sebring Senior Open – Sebring, FL (Sept. 13-17); Naples Senior Open – Naples, FL (Sept. 20-24); Jackson Senior Open – Jackson, TN (Oct. 4-8); Davenport Senior Open – Davenport, IA (Oct. 11-15).

PWBA

Events: Visionary Bowling Products Classic – Lancaster, OH (Sept. 13-17); Track Triton Open – Rossford, OH (Sept. 20-24); Columbia 300 Delaware Open – New Castle, DE (Sept. 27-Oct. 1); Storm Three Rivers Open – Pittsburgh, PA (Oct. 4-8); **AMF Gold Cup** – Richmond, VA (Oct. 11-15); Brunswick World Open – Chicago, IL (Oct. 18-22); **Sam's Town Invitational** – Las Vegas, NV (Nov. 14-21).

SENIOR PBA

1998 Spring/Summer Tour

Final	Event	Winner	Earnings	Score	Runner-up
March 12	Greater Albany Senior Open	Pete Couture	$9,000	242-224	Gary Dickinson
March 19	Vermont Senior Classic	John Hricsina	8,000	215-215*	Pete Couture
July 2	Boise Senior Open	Pete Couture	8,000	223-211	Dale Eagle
July 16	Seattle Senior Open	Gene Stus	8,000	216-188	John Hricsina
July 23	Northwest Senior Classic	Gene Stus	8,000	216-199	Steve Neff
Aug. 1	Showboat Senior Invitational	Don Helling	22,000	248-201	Mike Durbin
Aug. 15	**ABC Senior Masters**	Pete Couture	60,000	234-213	Ron Garr
Aug. 20	Glass City Senior Open	Gary Dickinson	9,000	231-218	Bob Glass
Aug. 28	National Championship	Johnny Petraglia	21,000	214-182	Avery LeBlanc
Sept. 9	The Villages Senior Open	Phil Barnes	7,000	225-213	Roger Tramp
Sept. 10	The Villages Senior Tournament of Champions	John Handegard	10,000	269-245	Pete Couture

*After tying at 215, Hricsina defeated Couture 10-9 in a sudden-death roll-off to decide the championship.

PWBA*

Late 1997 Fall Tour

Final	Event	Winner	Earnings	Score	Runner-up
Nov. 22	**Sam's Town Invitational**	Kim Adler	$17,000	257-206	Carolyn Dorin-Ballard
Dec. 11	Merit Showdown	Walter Ray Williams	30,000	654-570†	Wendy Macpherson
Dec. 14	Merit Mixed Doubles Champ.	Carol Gianotti-Block/ Tim Criss	40,000	453-411†	Carolyn Dorin-Ballard/ Pete Weber

†Scoring in the Merit Showdown and Mixed Doubles is based on total pins.

1998 Winter/Spring Tour

Final	Event	Winner	Earnings	Score	Runner-up
Feb. 5	Lubbock Open	Tish Johnson	$9,000	268-211	Carol Gianotti-Block
Feb. 12	Rocket City Challenge	Ann Marie Duggan	9,000	234-212	Carol Gianotti-Block
Feb. 19	Jacksonville Classic	Dana Miller-Mackie	11,000	279-211	Cathy Dorin
Feb. 26	Greater Sebring (Fla.) Open	Kendra Cameron	9,000	269-184	Kim Canady
Mar. 5	Greater Orlando Classic	Carolyn Dorin-Ballard	9,000	246-234	Dana Miller-Mackie
Mar. 12	Greater Atlanta Open	Leanne Barrette	9,000	223-212	Carol Gianotti-Block

1998 Summer/Fall Tour

Final	Event	Winner	Earnings	Score	Runner-up
Apr. 11	**BPAA U.S. Open**	Aleta Sill	$40,000	276-151	Tammy Turner
May 7	Omaha Open	Marianne DiRupo	9,000	183-157	Carol Gianotti-Block
May 16	**WIBC Queens**	Lynda Norry	20,000	213-157	Karen Stroud
May 21	St. Claire Classic	Dede Davidson	9,000	237-178	Aleta Sill
July 16	Lehigh Valley Classic	Leanne Barrette	9,000	216-152	Carol Dorin-Ballard
July 23	Southern Virginia Open	Aleta Sill	9,000	203-180	Tammy Turner
July 30	Chattanooga Open	Kim Adler	9,000	183-182	Carolyn Dorin-Ballard
Aug. 5	Lady Ebonite Classic	Michelle Feldman	11,000	205-192	Kim Adler
Aug. 13	Clabber Girl Open	Kim Adler	10,000	200-197	Carol Gianotti-Block
Aug. 20	Hammer Players Championship	Yvette Smith	16,000	203-197	Wendy Macpherson

Note: The Women's International Bowling Congress Queens tournament is not an official PWBA Tour event.

* The Ladies Professional Bowling Tour (LPBT) officially changed its name to Professional Women's Bowling Association (PWBA) in 1998.

1997-98 *Bowlers Journal International* All-American Teams

The 60th annual All-American First and Second teams as selected by the editors of *Bowlers Journal International.*

MEN		WOMEN	
First Team	**Second Team**	**First Team**	**Second Team**
Parker Bohn III	Tom Baker	Marianne DiRupo	Kim Adler
Steve Hoskins	Jason Couch	Carolyn Dorin-Ballard	Leanne Barrette
Amleto Monacelli	Tim Criss	Carol Gianotti-Block	Anne Marie Duggan
Pete Weber	Norm Duke	Liz Johnson	Dana Miller-Mackie
Walter Ray Williams Jr.	Doug Kent	Wendy Macpherson	Aleta Sill

Tour Leaders

Official standings for 1997 and unofficial standings for 1998. Note that (TB) indicates Tournaments Bowled; (CR) Championship Rounds as Stepladder Finalist; and (1st) Titles Won.

Final 1997

PBA

Top 10 Money Winners

		TB	CR	1st	Earnings
1	Walter Ray Williams Jr.	25	14	3	$352,044
2	Parker Bohn III	25	8	2	273,185
3	Pete Weber	23	11	2	252,184
4	Brian Voss	25	7	2	199,035
5	Amleto Monacelli	20	4	2	185,155
6	Norm Duke	22	6	2	160,220
7	Doug Kent	26	6	1	149,830
8	Steve Hoskins	22	5	2	166,695
9	Tim Criss	26	7	2	182,675
10	Wayne Webb	25	4	2	139,469

Top 10 Averages

		TB	Games	Avg
1	Walter Ray Williams Jr.	25	947	222.00
2	Pete Weber	23	867	221.23
3	Parker Bohn III	25	830	220.39
4	Amleto Monacelli	20	768	219.44
5	Brian Voss	25	866	219.40
6	Norm Duke	22	821	218.89
7	Ricky Ward	21	577	217.27
8	Steve Jaros	27	929	217.20
9	Bob Learn Jr.	25	794	216.84
10	John Mazza	19	485	216.69

SENIOR PBA

Top 5 Money Winners

		TB	CR	1st	Earnings
1	Gary Dickinson	16	8	3	$109,240
2	Larry Laub	16	5	3	59,255
3	John Hricsina	16	4	1	50,015
4	Gene Stus	16	6	1	49,685
5	Pete Couture	16	7	1	45,425

Top 5 Averages

		TB	Games	Avg
1	Gary Dickinson	16	674	224.45
2	George Pappas	9	337	222.99
3	Earl Anthony	12	410	222.76
4	Pete Couture	16	693	222.37
5	Larry Laub	16	666	221.93

LPBT

Top 10 Money Winners

		TB	CR	1st	Earnings
1	Wendy Macpherson	21	13	4	$165,425
2	Carol Gianotti-Block	19	12	3	142,400
3	Carolyn Dorin-Ballard	21	10	1	104,500
4	Liz Johnson	19	8	3	95,850
5	Marianne DiRupo	19	9	1	92,050
6	Kim Adler	19	4	2	77,500
7	Leanne Barrette	17	6	1	67,875
8	Sandra Jo Odom	16	2	1	62,402
9	Anne Marie Duggan	18	5	1	62,240
10	Nikki Gianulias	19	3	1	62,213

Note: Earnings include WIBC Queens.

Top 5 Averages

		TB	Games	Avg
1	Wendy Macpherson	21	915	214.68
2	Marianne DiRupo	19	859	213.08
3	Carolyn Dorin-Ballard	21	911	212.96
4	Carol Gianotti-Block	19	850	212.94
5	Liz Johnson	19	844	211.44

1998 (through Sept. 12)

PBA

Top 10 Money Winners

		TB	CR	1st	Earnings
1	Parker Bohn III	14	5	3	$116,805
2	Tim Criss	17	4	1	103,545
3	Walter Ray Williams Jr.	17	3	2	101,250
4	Mike Aulby	14	4	1	81,780
5	Steve Hoskins	17	3	1	78,240
6	Jason T. Couch	16	2	1	75,820
7	Pete Weber	13	4	1	57,785
8	Amleto Monacelli	14	3	0	55,242
9	Dennis Horan Jr.	15	1	1	52,855
10	Ricky Ward	12	1	1	49,735

Top 10 Averages

		TB	Games	Avg
1	Walter Ray Williams Jr.	17	600	223.82
2	Parker Bohn III	14	402	223.40
3	Tim Criss	17	607	221.96
4	Pete Weber	13	419	221.84
5	Norm Duke	15	461	220.68
6	Thomas Baker	17	567	220.55
7	Ryan R. Shafer	17	589	220.42
8	Amleto Monacelli	14	495	220.21
9	Jason T. Couch	16	552	220.11
10	Ricky Ward	12	333	219.66

SENIOR PBA

Top 5 Money Winners

		TB	CR	1st	Earnings
1	Pete Couture	9	7	3	$104,500
2	Gary Dickinson	9	4	1	52,150
3	Ron Garr	7	1	0	37,932
4	Gene Stus	9	4	2	36,870
5	Mike Durbin	8	5	0	34,110

Top 5 Averages

		TB	Games	Avg
1	Pete Couture	9	373	226.56
2	Gary Dickinson	9	420	224.04
3	Dale Eagle	9	416	223.98
4	Mike Durbin	8	327	223.88
5	John Hricsina	9	344	223.33

PWBA

Top 10 Money Winners

		TB	CR	1st	Earnings
1	Aleta Sill	16	5	2	$100,285
2	Kim Adler	16	7	2	83,060
3	Carol Gianotti-Block	16	8	0	78,750
4	Marianne DiRupo	16	4	1	64,400
5	Tammy Turner	16	3	0	55,955
6	Dede Davidson	16	5	1	51,225
7	Leanne Barrette	16	3	2	51,150
8	Tish Johnson	16	5	1	47,075
9	Carolyn Dorin-Ballard	16	3	1	45,495
10	Wendy Macpherson	16	3	0	44,840

Note: Earnings include WIBC Queens.

Top 5 Averages

		TB	Games	Avg
1	Carol Gianotti-Block	16	647	216.20
2	Kim Adler	16	597	215.93
3	Dede Davidson	16	488	215.29
4	Marianne DiRupo	16	611	214.44
5	Carolyn Dorin-Ballard	16	612	214.41

Major Championships

MEN

BPAA U.S. Open

Started in 1941 by the Bowling Proprietors' Association of America, 18 years before the founding of the Professional Bowlers Association. Originally the BPAA All-Star Tournament, it became the U.S. Open in 1971. There were two BPAA All-Star tournaments in 1955, in January and December.

Multiple winners: Don Carter and Dick Weber (4); Dave Husted (3); Del Ballard, Jr., Marshall Holman, Junie McMahon, Connie Schwoegler, Andy Varipapa and Pete Weber (2)

Year	
1942	John Crimmons
1943	Connie Schwoegler
1944	Ned Day
1945	Buddy Bomar
1946	Joe Wilman
1947	Andy Varipapa
1948	Andy Varipapa
1949	Connie Schwoegler
1950	Junie McMahon
1951	Dick Hoover
1952	Junie McMahon
1953	Don Carter
1954	Don Carter
1955	Steve Nagy
1956	Bill Lillard
1957	Don Carter
1958	Don Carter
1959	Billy Welu
1960	Harry Smith
1961	Bill Tucker
1962	Dick Weber
1963	Dick Weber
1964	Bob Strampe
1965	Dick Weber
1966	Dick Weber
1967	Les Schissler
1968	Jim Stefanich
1969	Billy Hardwick
1970	Bobby Cooper
1971	Mike Limongello
1972	Don Johnson
1973	Mike McGrath
1974	Larry Laub
1975	Steve Neff
1976	Paul Moser
1977	Johnny Petraglia
1978	Nelson Burton Jr.
1979	Joe Berardi
1980	Steve Martin
1981	Marshall Holman
1982	Dave Husted
1983	Gary Dickinson
1984	Mark Roth
1985	Marshall Holman
1986	Steve Cook
1987	Del Ballard Jr.
1988	Pete Weber
1989	Mike Aulby
1990	Ron Palombi Jr.
1991	Pete Weber
1992	Robert Lawrence
1993	Del Ballard Jr.
1994	Justin Hromek
1995	Dave Husted
1996	Dave Husted
1997	Not held
1998	Walter Ray Williams Jr.

PBA National Championship

The Professional Bowlers Association was formed in 1958 and its first national championship tournament was held in Memphis in 1960. The tournament has been held in Toledo, Ohio, since 1981.

Multiple winners: Earl Anthony (6); Mike Aulby, Dave Davis, Mike McGrath, Pete Weber and Wayne Zahn (2).

Year	
1960	Don Carter
1961	Dave Soutar
1962	Carmen Salvino
1963	Billy Hardwick
1964	Bob Strampe
1965	Dave Davis
1966	Wayne Zahn
1967	Dave Davis
1968	Wayne Zahn
1969	Mike McGrath
1970	Mike McGrath
1971	Mike Limongello
1972	Johnny Guenther
1973	Earl Anthony
1974	Earl Anthony
1975	Earl Anthony
1976	Paul Colwell
1977	Tommy Hudson
1978	Warren Nelson
1979	Mike Aulby
1980	Johnny Petraglia
1981	Earl Anthony
1982	Earl Anthony
1983	Earl Anthony
1984	Bob Chamberlain
1985	Mike Aulby
1986	Tom Crites
1987	Randy Pedersen
1988	Brian Voss
1989	Pete Weber
1990	Jim Pencak
1991	Mike Miller
1992	Eric Forkel
1993	Ron Palombi Jr.
1994	David Traber
1995	Scott Alexander
1996	Butch Soper
1997	Rick Steelsmith
1998	Pete Weber

Brunswick World Tournament of Champions

Originally the Firestone Tournament of Champions (1965-93), the tournament has also been sponsored by General Tire (1994) and Brunswick Corp. (since 1995). Held annually in Akron, Ohio from 1965-94, the T of C was moved to suburban Chicago in 1995.

Multiple winners: Mike Durbin (3); Earl Anthony, Jim Godman, Marshall Holman and Mark Williams (2).

Year	
1965	Billy Hardwick
1966	Wayne Zahn
1967	Jim Stefanich
1968	Dave Davis
1969	Jim Godman
1970	Don Johnson
1971	Johnny Petraglia
1972	Mike Durbin
1973	Jim Godman
1974	Earl Anthony
1975	Dave Davis
1976	Marshall Holman
1977	Mike Berlin
1978	Earl Anthony
1979	George Pappas
1980	Wayne Webb
1981	Steve Cook
1982	Mike Durbin
1983	Joe Berardi
1984	Mike Durbin
1985	Mark Williams
1986	Marshall Holman
1987	Pete Weber
1988	Mark Williams
1989	Del Ballard Jr.
1990	Dave Ferraro
1991	David Ozio
1992	Marc McDowell
1993	George Branham III
1994	Norm Duke
1995	Mike Aulby
1996	Dave D'Entremont
1997	John Gant

ABC Masters Tournament

Sponsored by the American Bowling Congress. The Masters is not a PBA event, but is considered one of the four major tournaments on the men's tour and is open to qualified pros and amateurs.

Multiple winners: Mike Aulby (3); Earl Anthony, Billy Golembiewski, Dick Hoover and Billy Welu (2).

Year	Year	Year	Year
1951 Lee Jouglard	1963 Harry Smith	1975 Eddie Ressler	1987 Rick Steelsmith
1952 Willard Taylor	1964 Billy Welu	1976 Nelson Burton Jr.	1988 Del Ballard Jr.
1953 Rudy Habetler	1965 Billy Welu	1977 Earl Anthony	1989 Mike Aulby
1954 Red Elkins	1966 Bob Strampe	1978 Frank Ellenburg	1990 Chris Warren
1955 Buzz Fazio	1967 Lou Scalia	1979 Doug Myers	1991 Doug Kent
1956 Dick Hoover	1968 Pete Tountas	1980 Neil Burton	1992 Ken Johnson
1957 Dick Hoover	1969 Jim Chestney	1981 Randy Lightfoot	1993 Norm Duke
1958 Tom Hennessey	1970 Don Glover	1982 Joe Berardi	1994 Steve Fehr
1959 Ray Bluth	1971 Jim Godman	1983 Mike Lastowski	1995 Mike Aulby
1960 Billy Golembiewski	1972 Bill Beach	1984 Earl Anthony	1996 Ernie Schlegel
1961 Don Carter	1973 Dave Soutar	1985 Steve Wunderlich	1997 Jason Queen
1962 Billy Golembiewski	1974 Paul Colwell	1986 Mark Fahy	1998 Mike Aulby

WOMEN

BPAA U.S. Open

Started by the Bowling Proprietors' Association of America in 1949, 11 years before the founding of the Professional Women's Bowling Association. Originally the BPAA Women's All-Star Tournament, it became the U.S. Open in 1971. There were two BPAA All-Star tournaments in 1955, in January and December. Note that (a) indicates amateur.

Multiple winners: Marion Ladewig (8); Donna Adamek, Paula Sperber Carter, Pat Costello, Dotty Fothergill, Dana Miller-Mackie, Aleta Sill and Sylvia Wene (2).

Year	Year	Year	Year
1949 Marion Ladewig	1961 Phyllis Notaro	1975 Paula Sperber Carter	1988 Lisa Wagner
1950 Marion Ladewig	1962 Shirley Garms	1976 Patty Costello	1989 Robin Romeo
1951 Marion Ladewig	1963 Marion Ladewig	1977 Betty Morris	1990 Dana Miller-Mackie
1952 Marion Ladewig	1964 LaVerne Carter	1978 Donna Adamek	1991 Anne Marie Duggan
1953 Not held	1965 Ann Slattery	1979 Diana Silva	1992 Tish Johnson
1954 Marion Ladewig	1966 Joy Abel	1980 Pat Costello	1993 Dede Davidson
1955 Sylvia Wene	1967 Gloria Simon	1981 Donna Adamek	1994 Aleta Sill
1955 Anita Cantaline	1968 Dotty Fothergill	1982 Shinobu Saitoh	1995 Cheryl Daniels
1956 Marion Ladewig	1969 Dotty Fothergill	1983 Dana Miller	1996 Liz Johnson
1957 Not held	1970 Mary Baker	1984 Karen Ellingsworth	1997 Not held
1958 Merle Matthews	1971 a-Paula Sperber	1985 Pat Mercatanti	1998 Aleta Sill
1959 Marion Ladewig	1972 a-Lorrie Koch	1986 Wendy Macpherson	
1960 Sylvia Wene	1973 Millie Martorella	1987 Carol Norman	
	1974 Pat Costello		

WIBC Queens

Sponsored by the Women's International Bowling Congress, the Queens is a double elimination, match play tournament. It is not a PWBA event, but is open to qualified pros and amateurs. Note that (a) indicates amateur.

Multiple winners: Millie Martorella (3); Donna Adamek, Dotty Fothergill, Aleta Sill and Katsuko Sugimoto (2).

Year	Year	Year	Year
1961 Janet Harman	1971 Millie Martorella	1981 Katsuko Sugimoto	1991 Dede Davidson
1962 Dorothy Wilkinson	1972 Dotty Fothergill	1982 Katsuko Sugimoto	1992 Cindy Coburn-Carroll
1963 Irene Monterosso	1973 Dotty Fothergill	1983 Aleta Sill	1993 Jan Schmidt
1964 D.D. Jacobson	1974 Judy Soutar	1984 Kazue Inahashi	1994 Anne Marie Duggan
1965 Betty Kuczynski	1975 Cindy Powell	1985 Aleta Sill	1995 Sandra Postma
1966 Judy Lee	1976 Pam Rutherford	1986 Cora Fiebig	1996 Lisa Wagner
1967 Millie Martorella	1977 Dana Stewart	1987 Cathy Almeida	1997 Sandra Jo Odom
1968 Phyllis Massey	1978 Loa Boxberger	1988 Wendy Macpherson	1998 Lynda Norry
1969 Ann Feigel	1979 Donna Adamek	1989 Carol Gianotti	
1970 Millie Martorella	1980 Donna Adamek	1990 a-Patty Ann	

Sam's Town Invitational

Originally held in Milwaukee as the Pabst Tournament of Champions, but discontinued after one year (1981). The event was revived in 1984, moved to Las Vegas and renamed the Sam's Town Tournament of Champions. Since then it has been known as the LPBT Tournament of Champions (1985), the Sam's Town National Pro/Am (1986-88) and the Sam's Town Invitational (since 1989).

Multiple winners: Tish Johnson (3); Aleta Sill (2).

Year		Year		Year		Year	
1981	Cindy Coburn	1986	Aleta Sill	1991	Lorrie Nichols	1995	Michelle Mullen
1982-83	Not held	1987	Debbie Bennett	1992	Tish Johnson	1996	Carol Gianotti-Block
1984	Aleta Sill	1988	Donna Adamek	1993	Robin Romeo	1997	Kim Adler
1985	Patty Costello	1989	Tish Johnson	1994	Tish Johnson		

Major Championships (Cont.)

WPBA National Championship (1960-1980)

The Women's Professional Bowling Association National Championship tournament was discontinued when the WPBA broke up in 1981. The WPBA changed its name from the Professional Women Bowlers Association (PWBA) in 1978.

Multiple winners: Patty Costello (3); Dotty Fothergill (2).

Year	Year	Year	Year	Year
1960 Marion Ladewig	1965 Helen Duval	1970 Bobbe North	1975 Pam Buckner	1980 Donna Adamek
1961 Shirley Garms	1966 Judy Lee	1971 Patty Costello	1976 Patty Costello	
1962 Stephanie Balogh	1967 Betty Mivelaz	1972 Patty Costello	1977 Vesma Grinfelds	
1963 Janet Harman	1968 Dotty Fothergill	1973 Betty Morris	1978 Toni Gillard	
1964 Betty Kuczynski	1969 Dotty Fothergill	1974 Pat Costello	1979 Cindy Coburn	

Annual Leaders

Average

PBA Tour

The George Young Memorial Award, named after the late ABC Hall of Fame bowler. Based on at least 16 national PBA tournaments from 1959-78, and at least 400 games of tour competition since 1979.

Multiple winners: Mark Roth (6); Earl Anthony (5); Marshall Holman and Walter Ray Williams Jr. (3); Norm Duke, Billy Hardwick, Don Johnson and Wayne Zahn (2).

Year	Avg	Year	Avg	Year	Avg
1962 Don Carter	212.84	1974 Earl Anthony	219.34	1986 John Gant	214.38
1963 Bill Hardwick	210.35	1975 Earl Anthony	219.06	1987 Marshall Holman	216.80
1964 Ray Bluth	210.51	1976 Mark Roth	215.97	1988 Mark Roth	218.04
1965 Dick Weber	211.90	1977 Mark Roth	218.17	1989 Pete Weber	215.43
1966 Wayne Zahn	208.63	1978 Mark Roth	219.83	1990 Amleto Monacelli	218.16
1967 Wayne Zahn	212.14	1979 Mark Roth	221.66	1991 Norm Duke	218.21
1968 Jim Stefanich	211.90	1980 Earl Anthony	218.54	1992 Dave Ferraro	219.70
1969 Billy Hardwick	212.96	1981 Mark Roth	216.70	1993 Walter Ray Williams Jr.	222.98
1970 Nelson Burton Jr.	214.91	1982 Marshall Holman	216.15	1994 Norm Duke	222.83
1971 Don Johnson	213.98	1983 Earl Anthony	216.65	1995 Mike Aulby	225.49
1972 Don Johnson	215.29	1984 Marshall Holman	213.91	1996 Walter Ray Williams Jr.	225.37
1973 Earl Anthony	215.80	1985 Mark Baker	213.72	1997 Walter Ray Williams Jr.	222.00

PWBA Tour

Based on at least 282 games of tour competition.

Multiple winners: Leanne Barrette, Nikki Gianulias and Lisa Rathgeber Wagner (3); Anne Marie Duggan, Wendy Macpherson and Aleta Sill (2).

Year	Avg	Year	Avg	Year	Avg
1981 Nikki Gianulias	213.71	1987 Wendy Macpherson	211.11	1993 Tish Johnson	215.39
1982 Nikki Gianulias	210.63	1988 Lisa Wagner	213.02	1994 Anne Marie Duggan	213.47
1983 Lisa Rathgeber	208.50	1989 Lisa Wagner	211.87	1995 Anne Marie Duggan	215.79
1984 Aleta Sill	210.68	1990 Leanne Barrette	211.53	1996 Tammy Turner	215.23
1985 Aleta Sill	211.10	1991 Leanne Barrette	211.48	1997 Wendy Macpherson	214.68
1986 Nikki Gianulias	213.89	1992 Leanne Barrette	211.36		

Money Won

PBA Tour

Multiple winners: Earl Anthony (6); Mark Roth, Dick Weber and Walter Ray Williams Jr. (4); Mike Aulby (3); Don Carter (2).

Year	Earnings	Year	Earnings	Year	Earnings
1959 Dick Weber	$7,672	1972 Don Johnson	$56,648	1985 Mike Aulby	$201,200
1960 Don Carter	22,525	1973 Don McCune	69,000	1986 Walter Ray Williams Jr.	145,550
1961 Dick Weber	26,280	1974 Earl Anthony	99,585	1987 Pete Weber	179,516
1962 Don Carter	49,972	1975 Earl Anthony	107,585	1988 Brian Voss	225,485
1963 Dick Weber	46,333	1976 Earl Anthony	110,833	1989 Mike Aulby	298,237
1964 Bob Strampe	33,592	1977 Mark Roth	105,583	1990 Amleto Monacelli	204,775
1965 Dick Weber	47,675	1978 Mark Roth	134,500	1991 David Ozio	225,585
1966 Wayne Zahn	54,720	1979 Mark Roth	124,517	1992 Marc McDowell	176,215
1967 Dave Davis	54,165	1980 Wayne Webb	116,700	1993 Walter Ray Williams Jr.	296,370
1968 Jim Stefanich	67,375	1981 Earl Anthony	164,735	1994 Norm Duke	273,753
1969 Billy Hardwick	64,160	1982 Earl Anthony	134,760	1995 Mike Aulby	219,792
1970 Mike McGrath	52,049	1983 Earl Anthony	135,605	1996 Walter Ray Williams Jr.	241,330
1971 Johnny Petraglia	85,065	1984 Mark Roth	158,712	1997 Walter Ray Williams Jr.	352,044

WPBA and PWBA Tours

WPBA leaders through 1980; PWBA leaders since 1981.

Multiple winners: Aleta Sill (6); Donna Adamek (4); Patty Costello, Tish Johnson and Betty Morris (3); Dotty Fothergill and Wendy Macpherson.

Year	Earnings	Year	Earnings	Year	Earnings
1965 Betty Kuczynski	$ 3,792	1976 Patty Costello	$39,585	1987 Betty Morris	$63,735
1966 Joy Abel	5,795	1977 Betty Morris	23,802	1988 Lisa Wagner	105,500
1967 Shirley Garms	4,920	1978 Donna Adamek	31,000	1989 Robin Romeo	113,750
1968 Dotty Fothergill	16,170	1979 Donna Adamek	26,280	1990 Tish Johnson	94,420
1969 Dotty Fothergill	9,220	1980 Donna Adamek	31,907	1991 Leanne Barrette	87,618
1970 Patty Costello	9,317	1981 Donna Adamek	41,270	1992 Tish Johnson	96,872
1971 Vesma Grinfelds	4,925	1982 Nikki Gianulias	45,875	1993 Aleta Sill	57,995
1972 Patty Costello	11,350	1983 Aleta Sill	42,525	1994 Aleta Sill	126,325
1973 Judy Cook	11,200	1984 Aleta Sill	81,452	1995 Tish Johnson	123,440
1974 Betty Morris	30,037	1985 Aleta Sill	52,655	1996 Wendy Macpherson	107,230
1975 Judy Soutar	20,395	1986 Aleta Sill	36,962	1997 Wendy Macpherson	165,425

All-Time Leaders

All-time leading money winners on the PBA and PWBA tours, through 1997. PBA figures date back to 1959, while PWBA figures include Women's Pro Bowlers Association (WPBA) earnings through 1980. National tour titles are also listed.

Money Won

PBA Top 20

		Titles	Earnings
1	Walter Ray Williams Jr.	24	$2,076,003
2	Pete Weber	23	2,019,015
3	Mike Aulby	25	1,855,075
4	Marshall Holman	22	1,590,745
5	Brian Voss	18	1,616,760
6	Amleto Monacelli	18	1,597,991
7	Mark Roth	34	1,496,271
8	Dave Husted	13	1,494,578
9	Earl Anthony	41	1,441,060
10	Parker Bohn III	13	1,395,453
11	Wayne Webb	20	1,285,346
12	Norm Duke	13	1,274,251
13	David Ozio	11	1,222,514
14	Gary Dickinson	8	1,169,911
15	Del Ballard Jr.	12	1,097,967
16	Mark Williams	7	1,059,157
17	Dave Ferraro	9	1,044,176
18	Tom Baker	9	1,031,690
19	Dick Weber	26	918,203
20	Johnny Petraglia	14	912,620

WPBA-PWBA Top 12

		Titles	Earnings
1	Aleta Sill	28	$866,937
2	Tish Johnson	21	811,410
3	Lisa Wagner	30	736,743
4	Wendy Macpherson	13	678,779
5	Anne Marie Duggan	14	669,756
6	Robin Mossonite	16	627,094
7	Leanne Barrette	17	625,633
8	Nikki Gianulias	19	586,087
9	Carol Gianotti-Block	12	584,789
10	Cheryl Daniels	10	568,461
11	Jeanne Naccarato	9	482,197
12	Lorrie Nichols	15	481,091

Senior PBA Top 5

		Titles	Earnings
1	John Handegard	13	$368,946
2	Gene Stus	8	332,895
3	Teata Semiz	8	312,115
4	Gary Dickinson	9	309,999
5	John Hricsina	6	303,097

Annual Awards

MEN

BWAA Bowler of the Year

Winners selected by Bowling Writers Association of America.

Multiple winners: Earl Anthony and Don Carter (6); Mark Roth and Walter Ray Williams Jr. (4); Mike Aulby and Dick Weber (3); Buddy Bomar, Ned Day, Billy Hardwick, Don Johnson, and Steve Nagy (2).

Year	Year	Year	Year
1942 Johnny Crimmins	1957 Don Carter	1972 Don Johnson	1987 Marshall Holman
1943 Ned Day	1958 Don Carter	1973 Don McCune	1988 Brian Voss
1944 Ned Day	1959 Ed Lubanski	1974 Earl Anthony	1989 Mike Aulby
1945 Buddy Bomar	1960 Don Carter	1975 Earl Anthony	1990 Amleto Monacelli
1946 Joe Wilman	1961 Dick Weber	1976 Earl Anthony	1991 David Ozio
1947 Buddy Bomar	1962 Don Carter	1977 Mark Roth	1992 Marc McDowell
1948 Andy Varipapa	1963 Dick Weber	1978 Mark Roth	1993 Walter Ray Williams Jr.
1949 Connie Schwoegler	1964 Billy Hardwick	1979 Mark Roth	1994 Norm Duke
1950 Junie McMahon	1965 Dick Weber	1980 Wayne Webb	1995 Mike Aulby
1951 Lee Jouglard	1966 Wayne Zahn	1981 Earl Anthony	1996 Walter Ray Williams Jr.
1952 Steve Nagy	1967 Dave Davis	1982 Earl Anthony	1997 Walter Ray Williams Jr.
1953 Don Carter	1968 Jim Stefanich	1983 Earl Anthony	
1954 Don Carter	1969 Billy Hardwick	1984 Mark Roth	
1955 Steve Nagy	1970 Nelson Burton Jr.	1985 Mike Aulby	
1956 Bill Lillard	1971 Don Johnson	1986 Walter Ray Williams Jr.	

Annual Awards (Cont.)

PBA Player of the Year

Winners selected by members of Professional Bowlers Association. The PBA Player of the Year has differed from the BWAA Bowler of the Year four times–in 1963, '64, '89 and '92.

Multiple winners: Earl Anthony (6); Mark Roth and Walter Ray Williams Jr. (4); Mike Aulby, Billy Hardwick, Don Johnson and Amleto Monacelli (2).

Year		Year		Year		Year	
1963	Billy Hardwick	1972	Don Johnson	1981	Earl Anthony	1990	Amleto Monacelli
1964	Bob Strampe	1973	Don McCune	1982	Earl Anthony	1991	David Ozio
1965	Dick Weber	1974	Earl Anthony	1983	Earl Anthony	1992	Dave Ferraro
1966	Wayne Zahn	1975	Earl Anthony	1984	Mark Roth	1993	Walter Ray Williams Jr.
1967	Dave Davis	1976	Earl Anthony	1985	Mike Aulby	1994	Norm Duke
1968	Jim Stefanich	1977	Mark Roth	1986	Walter Ray Williams Jr.	1995	Mike Aulby
1969	Billy Hardwick	1978	Mark Roth	1987	Marshall Holman	1996	Walter Ray Williams Jr.
1970	Nelson Burton Jr.	1979	Mark Roth	1988	Brian Voss	1997	Walter Ray Williams Jr.
1971	Don Johnson	1980	Wayne Webb	1989	Amleto Monacelli		

PBA Rookie of the Year

Winners selected by members of Professional Bowlers Association.

Year		Year		Year		Year	
1964	Jerry McCoy	1973	Steve Neff	1982	Mike Steinbach	1991	Ricky Ward
1965	Jim Godman	1974	Cliff McNealy	1983	Toby Contreras	1992	Jason Couch
1966	Bobby Cooper	1975	Guy Rowbury	1984	John Gant	1993	Mark Scroggins
1967	Mike Durbin	1976	Mike Berlin	1985	Tom Crites	1994	Tony Ament
1968	Bob McGregor	1977	Steve Martin	1986	Marc McDowell	1995	Billy Myers Jr.
1969	Larry Lichstein	1978	Joseph Groskind	1987	Ryan Shafer	1996	C.K. Moore
1970	Denny Krick	1979	Mike Aulby	1988	Rick Steelsmith	1997	Anthony Lombardo
1971	Tye Critchlow	1980	Pete Weber	1989	Steve Hoskins		
1972	Tommy Hudson	1981	Mark Fahy	1990	Brad Kiszewski		

WOMEN

BWAA Bowler of the Year

Winners selected by Bowling Writers Association of America.

Multiple winners: Marion Ladewig (9); Donna Adamek and Lisa Rathgeber Wagner (4); Tish Johnson and Betty Morris (3); Patty Costello, Dotty Forthergill, Shirley Garms, Wendy Macpherson, Val Mikiel, Aleta Sill, Judy Soutar and Sylvia Wene (2).

Year		Year		Year		Year	
1948	Val Mikiel	1961	Shirley Garms	1974	Betty Morris	1987	Betty Morris
1949	Val Mikiel	1962	Shirley Garms	1975	Judy Soutar	1988	Lisa Wagner
1950	Marion Ladewig	1963	Marion Ladewig	1976	Patty Costello	1989	Robin Romeo
1951	Marion Ladewig	1964	LaVerne Carter	1977	Betty Morris	1990	Tish Johnson
1952	Marion Ladewig	1965	Betty Kuczynski	1978	Donna Adamek	1991	Leanne Barrette
1953	Marion Ladewig	1966	Joy Abel	1979	Donna Adamek	1992	Tish Johnson
1954	Marion Ladewig	1967	Millie Martorella	1980	Donna Adamek	1993	Lisa Wagner
1955	Sylvia Wene	1968	Dotty Fothergill	1981	Donna Adamek	1994	Anne Marie Duggan
1956	Anita Cantaline	1969	Dotty Fothergill	1982	Nikki Gianulias	1995	Tish Johnson
1957	Marion Ladewig	1970	Mary Baker	1983	Lisa Rathgeber	1996	Wendy Macpherson
1958	Marion Ladewig	1971	Paula Sperber	1984	Aleta Sill	1997	Wendy Macpherson
1959	Marion Ladewig	1972	Patty Costello	1985	Aleta Sill		
1960	Sylvia Wene	1973	Judy Soutar	1986	Lisa Wagner		

PWBA Player of the Year

Winners selected by members of Professional Women's Bowling Association. The PWBA Player of the Year has differed from the BWAA Bowler of the Year three times–in 1985, '86 and '90.

Multiple winners: Lisa Rathgeber Wagner (3); Leanne Barrette, Tish Johnson and Wendy Macpherson (2).

Year		Year		Year		Year	
1983	Lisa Rathgeber	1987	Betty Morris	1991	Leanne Barrette	1995	Tish Johnson
1984	Aleta Sill	1988	Lisa Wagner	1992	Tish Johnson	1996	Wendy Macpherson
1985	Patty Costello	1989	Robin Romeo	1993	Lisa Wagner	1997	Wendy Macpherson
1986	Jeanne Maiden	1990	Leanne Barrette	1994	Anne Marie Duggan		

WPBA and PWBA Rookie of the Year

Winners selected by members of Women's Professional Bowlers Association (1978-80) and the Professional Women's Bowling Association (since 1981).

Year		Year		Year		Year	
1978	Toni Gillard	1983	Anne Marie Pike	1988	Mary Martha Cerniglia	1993	Kathy Zielke
1979	Nikki Gianulias	1984	Paula Vidad	1989	Kim Terrell	1994	Tammy Turner
1980	Lisa Rathgeber	1985	Dede Davidson	1990	Debbie McMullen	1995	Krissy Stewart
1981	Cindy Mason	1986	Wendy Macpherson	1991	Kim Kahrman	1996	Liz Johnson
1982	Carol Norman	1987	Paula Drake	1992	Marianne DiRupo	1997	Lisa Bishop

Horse Racing

Hall of Fame jockey **Jerry Bailey** knows when he's got a good thing, and he had one in "Horse of the Year" favorite **Skip Away** in 1998.

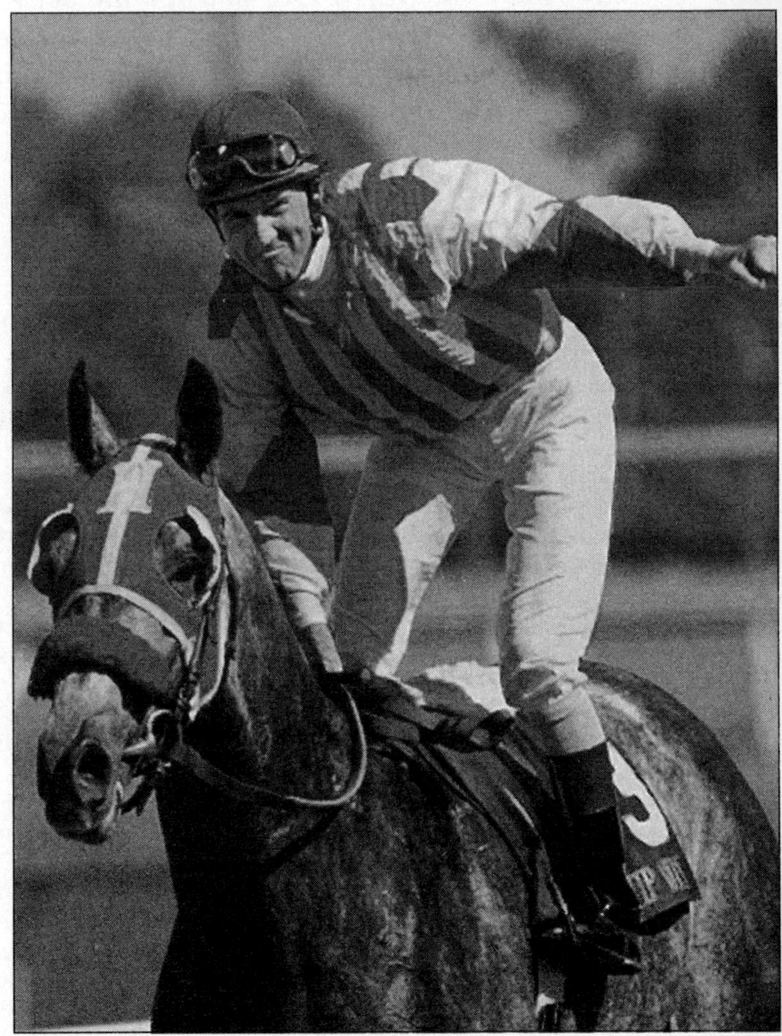

AP/Wide World Photos

Real Close

Skip Away ruled in 1998, and for the second consecutive year, a Bob Baffert-trained horse challenged for the Triple Crown–and came up just short.

by
Hank Goldberg

When Hall of Fame jockey Jerry Bailey was asked to compare Skip Away with Cigar, he said it was like having two children. "You don't love one over the other."

Bailey has certainly been blessed with both mounts. Cigar won a record $9,999,815 in his illustrious career. Skip Away can surpass that all-time earnings mark with a win in the Jockey Club Gold Cup at Belmont, and will then attempt to accomplish what no other horse has, record consecutive wins in the Breeders' Cup Classic. Then, Carolyn and Sonny Hine's superstar will call it a career.

At this writing, Skip Away had crossed the finish line first on nine straight occasions, which makes him a cinch for Horse of the Year. Last year, he finished second to Favorite Trick, who was eight-for-eight in 1997 as a two-year-old. "Skippy" showed his dominance at the Woodward Stakes in September, dusting an all-star field that included Gentlemen, Free House and Coronado's Quest.

The aforementioned Favorite Trick finished a disappointing eighth under jockey Pat Day in the Kentucky Derby and out of the top 10 in overall earnings for the year. Predictably, he never outran his pedigree, which suggested that he could not negotiate the classic distances.

Again, it was the California-based trainer, Bob Baffert, who saddled the Derby and the Preakness winner in Mike Pegram's Real Quiet, another horse who was not bred to go the mile and a quarter. As was the case in 1997, Baffert narrowly missed out on the Triple Crown. Last year, Silver Charm won the first two legs and was thwarted by Touch Gold in the Belmont. This time around, the spoiler

Hank Goldberg is an analyst for ESPN's horse racing coverage.

Archive Photos

Missed it by that much. **Victory Gallop** (l) and jockey Gary Stevens came up on the outside to nip **Real Quiet** (jockey Kent Desormeaux) at the wire to win the 130th Belmont Stakes on June 6. Real Quiet was attempting to become the first horse since Affirmed in 1978 to win the Triple Crown.

was Victory Gallop. Runner-up to Real Quiet in the first two legs, Victory Gallop reversed positions at the Belmont, coming from behind to win by a nose. The inquiry sign went up, but it was a tiring Real Quiet who drifted out and the result stood.

The Triple Crown had its share of controversy off the track as well. At the nationally-televised post-position draw for the Kentucky Derby, two horses (Artax and Rock and Roll) apparently drew the No. 15 spot. Human error was at fault and an embarrassed Churchill Downs ruled that a redraw was in order. It was believed to be the first redraw in the Derby's 124-year history.

The Preakness day in mid-May was marred by an area power failure that interrupted betting at most of Pimlico's windows for several hours. With a crowd of over 91,000 on hand, an estimated $1.5 million on-track handle was lost.

The horse racing industry had a very active year, hiring Tim Smith, a sports marketing veteran, as Commissioner/CEO of the fledgling National Thoroughbred Racing Association (NTRA). A multi-million dollar advertising campaign was launched, incorporating the theme, "Go Baby Go."

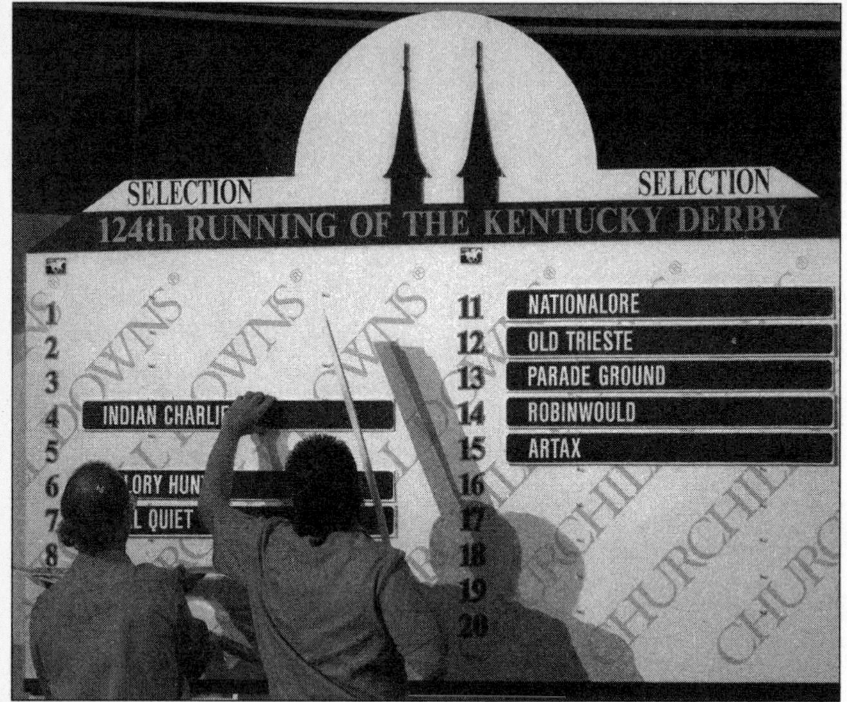

AP/Wide World Photos

Track workers remove horses' name cards from the selection board at the nationally-televised **Kentucky Derby post-position draw** after two horses apparently drew the 15th pick. Amidst a chorus of boos, embarrassed race officials called for a redraw.

Among the organization's promotions was a nationally-televised All-Star Jockey Championship from Lone Star Park in Grand Prairie, Texas. Shane Sellers won the inaugural event, beating out 11 other competitors. The NTRA also made deals with the ABC and Fox television networks for a "Road to the Triple Crown" series and a schedule of premier races for older horses, respectively. ■

Hank Goldberg's Top Stories of the Year in Horse Racing

10. **Elusive Quality** runs the fastest one-mile race in history (1:31⅗) in the Poker Handicap on the turf at Belmont. The previous standard had been held by Atticus, who ran a 1:31⅘ at Santa Anita on March 1, 1997.

9. **Horse racing Hall of Fame inductees** include Bill Mott (trainer), Jacinto Vasquez (jockey), Riva Ridge (contemporary male), Bayakoa (contemporary female) and Fort Marcy (horse of yesteryear).

8. **Breeders Cup purses rise** to $13 million with the 1999 addition of a $1 million turf race at a mile and a quarter for fillies and mares.

7. **Angel Cordero quits** training horses after six years to become a jockey's agent.

AP/Wide World Photos

Trainer **Bob Baffert** strikes a quarterback pose with the Kentucky Derby trophy after Real Quiet won the 124th running of the Kentucky Derby on May 2, 1998.

6. Hall of Fame jockey **Sandy Hawley retires** from riding at the age of 49.
5. Still going strong, **Earlie Fires** becomes the 13th jock to win 6,000 races.
4. On a sad note, **Hall of Fame trainer Woody Stephens** passes away in August at the age of 84. Among his many achievements, he is best remembered for saddling five straight Belmont Stakes winners from 1982-86.
3. **Real Quiet** takes the first two legs of the Triple Crown and seems to be in control of the Belmont until Victory Gallop charges down the backstretch and nips him at the wire to spoil the party.
2. Continuing his torrid 1997 pace, **Skip Away** seems to do whatever he wants in 1998 and puts his claim in as the most dominant horse since Cigar.
1. **The 1997 Eclipse Award Winners:**

Two-Year-Old Colt:
Favorite Trick
Two-Year-Old Filly:
Countess Diana
Three-Year-Old Colt:
Silver Charm
Three-Year-Old Filly:
Ajina
Older Horse, Colt or Gelding:
Skip Away
Older Horse, Filly or Mare:
Hidden Lake
Male Turf Horse:
Chief Bearhart
Female Turf Horse:
Ryafan
Sprinter:
Smoke Glacken
Steeplechase Horse:
Lonesome Glory
Horse of the Year:
Favorite Trick ■

THE NUMBERS INSIDE

by
Christian Teja

SECOND FIDDLE

Victory Gallop is one of 14 horses to have placed second in the first two legs of the Triple Crown and he became one of just five to go on to win the Belmont. Of the five Belmont winners listed below, all but Sword Dancer spoiled Triple Crown attempts.

	Spolier	Spoiled bid for
1998	Victory Gallop	Real Quiet
1989	Easy Goer	Sunday Silence
1987	Bet Twice	Alysheba
1969	Arts and Letters	Majestic Prince
1959	Sword Dancer	–

Note: Alydar is the only horse to have finished second in all three races, finishing second to Affirmed in all three as Affirmed won the Triple Crown in 1978.

GOING THE EXTRA **MILE**

Real Quiet has now raced 15 times in his career. Each of his first six races were under a mile and he never finished better than third in any of them.

In October 1997, he raced more than a mile for the first time and picked up his first win. Since then, he hasn't raced in a distance shorter than 1$\frac{1}{16}$ miles, and he's accumulated three more wins, including the Kentucky Derby and the Preakness. At 1½ miles, the Belmont was the longest race of his career.

	1 Mile or Less	Over 1 Mile
Starts	6	9
Win	0	4
Place	0	3
Show	4	1

WHEN TWO LEGS AREN'T ENOUGH

With Real Quiet's Derby and Preakness wins, 43 horses have now won any two legs of the Triple Crown. Since Affirmed won the Triple Crown in 1978, six horses have won the first two legs only to fall short in the Belmont.

		Belmont Finish
1998	Real Quiet	2nd
1997	Silver Charm	2nd
1989	Sunday Silence	2nd
1987	Alysheba	4th
1981	Pleasant Colony	3rd
1979	Spectacular Bid	3rd

Note: Two horses have won the first two Triple Crown legs, only to be forced out of the Belmont due to injury (Burgoo King in 1932 and Bold Venture in 1936).

DERBY JINX

In 1979, Spectacular Bid won the Kentucky Derby as post-time race favorite and since then, no other favorite has accomplished the feat. In 1998, Indian Charlie kept up the long running tradition of failures by favorites by coming in third. Here is where race-time favorites have finished in the past twenty years and over the entire history of the Derby.

	Since 1979	All-Time
Win	1	48
Place	3	27
Show	3	10
Other	13	39

■

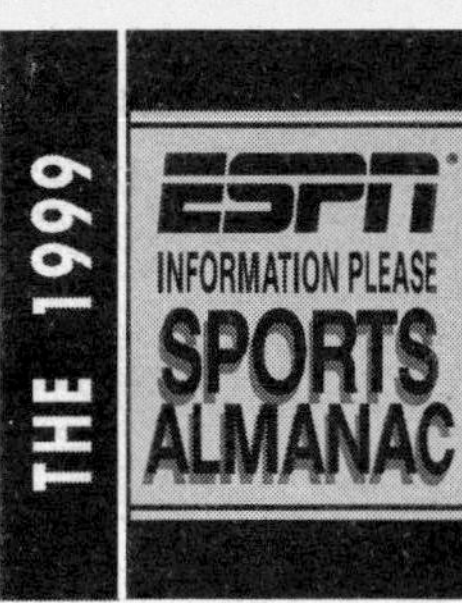

HORSE RACING STATISTICS

THE SEASON IN REVIEW

1997-1998

THOROUGHBRED • HARNESS

Thoroughbred Racing
Major Stakes Races

Winners of major stakes races from Oct. 11, 1997 through Sept. 20, 1998; (T) indicates turf race course; (F) indicates furlongs. See Updates for later results.

LATE 1997

Date	Race	Track	Miles	Winner	Jockey	Purse
Oct. 11	Hawthorne Gold Cup	Hawthorne	1¼	Buck's Boy	Mark Guidry	$300,000
Nov. 2	Yellow Ribbon Stakes	Santa Anita	1¼ (T)	Ryafan	Alex Solis	500,000
Nov. 8	Breeders' Cup Classic	Hollywood	1¼	Skip Away	Mike Smith	4,400,000
Nov. 8	Breeders' Cup Turf	Hollywood	1½ (T)	Chief Bearhart	Jose Santos	2,000,000
Nov. 8	Breeders' Cup Distaff	Hollywood	1⅛	Ajina	Mike Smith	1,000,000
Nov. 8	Breeders' Cup Mile	Hollywood	1	Spinning World	Cash Asmussen	1,100,000
Nov. 8	Breeders' Cup Juvenile	Hollywood	1 1/16	Favorite Trick	Pat Day	1,000,000
Nov. 8	Breeders' Cup Juv. Fil.	Hollywood	1 1/16	Countess Diana	Shane Sellers	1,030,000
Nov. 8	Breeders' Cup Sprint	Hollywood	6 F	Elmhurst	Corey Nakatani	1,180,000
Nov. 23	Japan Cup	Tokyo Racecourse	1½ (T)	Pilsudski	Michael Kinane	2,690,714
Nov. 30	Matriarch Stakes	Hollywood	1¼ (T)	Ryafan	Alex Solis	420,000
Nov. 30	Hollywood Derby	Hollywood	1⅛ (T)	Subordination	Jerry Bailey	300,000
Dec. 14	Hollywood Turf Cup	Hollywood	1½ (T)	River Bay	Alex Solis	500,000
Dec. 14	Hollywood Futurity	Hollywood	1 1/16	Real Quiet	Kent Desormeaux	470,000

Note: The purse for the Japan Cup was 376,700,000 Yen. The amount listed above is an estimate in U.S. dollars, based on an exchange rate of 140.

1998

Date	Race	Track	Miles	Winner	Jockey	Purse
Jan. 4	Spectacular Bid B.C. Stakes*	Gulfstream	6 F	Time Limit	Jerry Bailey	$75,000
Jan. 17	Holy Bull Stakes*	Gulfstream	1 1/16	Cape Town	Jerry Bailey	100,000
Jan. 18	Golden Gate Derby	Golden Gate	1 1/16	Clover Hunter	Russell Baze	200,000
Jan. 31	Hutcheson Stakes*	Gulfstream	7 F	Time Limit	Jerry Bailey	100,000
Feb. 1	Santa Catalina Stakes*	Santa Anita	1 1/16	Artax	Chris McCarron	107,200
Feb. 7	Charles H. Strub Stakes	Santa Anita	1¼	Silver Charm	Gary Stevens	500,000
Feb. 7	Donn Handicap	Gulfstream	1⅛	Skip Away	Jerry Bailey	300,000
Feb. 7	San Vicente Stakes*	Santa Anita	7 F	Sea of Secrets	Kent Desormeaux	100,000
Feb. 21	Fountain of Youth Stakes*	Gulfstream	1 1/16	Lil's Lad	Jerry Bailey	200,000
Feb. 28	Southwest Stakes*	Oaklawn	1	Hot Wells	Calvin Borel	75,000
Feb. 28	Gulfstream Park Handicap	Gulfstream	1¼	Skip Away	Jerry Bailey	500,000
Mar. 1	Rampart Handicap	Gulfstream	1 1/16	Dance for Three	Joe Bravo	200,000
Mar. 1	San Rafael Stakes*	Santa Anita	1	Orville N Wilbur's	Corey Nakatani	200,000
Mar. 7	El Camino Real Derby*	Bay Meadows	1 1/16	Event of the Year	Russell Baze	110,000
Mar. 7	Santa Anita Handicap	Santa Anita	1¼	Malek	Alex Solis	1,000,000
Mar. 8	Santa Margarita Handicap	Santa Anita	1⅛	Toda Una Dama	Goncalino Almeida	300,000
Mar. 14	Swale Stakes*	Gulfstream	7 F	Favorite Trick	Pat Day	100,000
Mar. 14	Florida Derby*	Gulfstream	1⅛	Cape Town	Shane Sellers	750,000
Mar. 14	San Felipe Stakes*	Santa Anita	1 1/16	Artax	Chris McCarron	250,000
Mar. 15	Louisiana Derby*	Fairgrounds	1 1/16	Comic Strip	Shane Sellers	500,000
Mar. 15	Santa Anita Oaks	Santa Anita	1 1/16	Hedonist	Kent Desormeaux	250,000
Mar. 21	Rebel Stakes*	Oaklawn	1 1/16	Victory Gallop	Eibar Coa	125,000
Mar. 21	Gotham Stakes*	Aqueduct	1	Wasatch	Jerry Bailey	150,000
Mar. 22	Tampa Bay Derby*	Tampa Bay	1 1/16	Parade Ground	Pat Day	150,000
Mar. 28	Dubai Classic	Nad al-Sheba	1¼	Silver Charm	Gary Stevens	4,000,000
Mar. 29	Jim Beam Stakes*	Turfway	1⅛	Event of the Year	Russell Baze	600,000
Apr. 4	Santa Anita Derby*	Santa Anita	1⅛	Indian Charlie	Gary Stevens	450,000
Apr. 4	Flamingo Stakes	Hialeah	1⅛	Chilito	Gary Boulanger	200,000
Apr. 4	Ashland Stakes	Keeneland	1 1/16	Well Chosen	Charles Woods Jr.	555,500
Apr. 4	Oaklawn Handicap	Oaklawn	1⅛	Precocity	Carlos Gonzalez	750,000
Apr. 8	Lafayette Stakes*	Keeneland	7 F	Dontletthebigonego	Willie Martinez	108,800
Apr. 10	Apple Blossom Handicap	Oaklawn	1 1/16	Escena	Jerry Bailey	500,000

Date	Race	Track	Miles	Winner	Jockey	Purse
Apr. 11	Blue Grass Stakes*	Keeneland	1⅛	Halory Hunter	Gary Stevens	$700,000
Apr. 11	Arkansas Derby*	Oaklawn	1⅛	Victory Gallop	Alex Solis	500,000
Apr. 11	Wood Memorial*	Aqueduct	1⅛	Coronado's Quest	Robbie Davis	500,000
Apr. 11	Bay Shore Stakes*	Aqueduct	7 F	Limit Out	Jean-Luc Samyn	100,000
Apr. 18	Federico Tesio Stakes*	Pimlico	1⅛	Thomas Jo	Steve Hamilton	150,000
Apr. 18	California Derby	Golden Gate	9 F (T)	Prime Meridian	Rafael Q. Meza	200,000
Apr. 19	San Juan Capistrano Handicap	Santa Anita	1¾ (T)	Amerique	Eddie Delahoussaye	400,000
Apr. 19	Lexington Stakes*	Keeneland	1 1/16	Classic Cat	Robby Albarado	368,225
Apr. 19	Lone Star Derby*	Lone Star	1 1/16	Smolderin Heart	Tim Doocy	250,000
Apr. 25	Derby Trial*	Churchill Downs	1	Souvenir Copy	David Flores	113,300
May 1	Kentucky Oaks	Churchill Downs	1⅛	Keeper Hill	David Flores	500,000
May 2	**Kentucky Derby***	Churchill Downs	1¼	Real Quiet	Kent Desormeaux	1,000,000
May 2	Withers Stakes*	Belmont	1	Dice Dancer	Jorge Chavez	150,000
May 9	Pimlico Special	Pimlico	1 3/16	Skip Away	Jerry Bailey	750,000
May 9	Illinois Derby*	Sportsman's Park	1⅛	Yarrow Brae	Willie Martinez	500,000
May 15	Black-Eyed Susan Stakes	Pimlico	1⅛	Added Gold	John Velazquez	200,000
May 16	**Preakness Stakes***	Pimlico	1 3/16	Real Quiet	Kent Desormeaux	1,000,000
May 24	Peter Pan Stakes*	Belmont	1⅛	Grand Slam	Jerry Bailey	150,000
May 25	Metropolitan Mile	Belmont	1	Wild Rush	Jerry Bailey	500,000
May 25	Hollywood Turf Handicap	Hollywood Park	1¼ (T)	Storm Trooper	Kent Desormeaux	400,000
May 30	Massachusetts Handicap	Suffolk Downs	1⅛	Skip Away	Jerry Bailey	500,000
May 31	The Californian	Hollywood Park	1⅛	Mud Route	Chris McCarron	250,000
June 6	Riva Ridge Stakes*	Belmont	7 F	Coronado's Quest	Mike Smith	125,000
June 6	Vodafone English Derby	Epsom Downs	1½ (T)	High-Rise	Olivier Peslier	1,297,975
June 6	**Belmont Stakes***	Belmont	1½	Victory Gallop	Gary Stevens	1,000,000
June 7	Acorn Stakes	Belmont	1	Jersey Girl	Mike Smith	150,000
June 14	Leonard Richards Stakes*	Delaware	1 1/16	Scatmandu	Richard Migliore	150,000
June 14	Shoemaker BC Mile	Hollywood	1 (T)	Labeeb	Kent Desormeaux	400,000
June 21	Affirmed Handicap*	Hollywood Park	1 1/16	Old Trieste	Chris McCarron	150,000
June 21	Queen's Plate	Woodbine	1¼	Archers Bay	Kent Desormeaux	425,800
June 27	Mother Goose Stakes	Belmont	1⅛	Jersey Girl	Mike Smith	200,000
June 27	Jersey Shore BC*	Monmouth	7 F	Good and Tough	Herb McCauley	75,000
June 28	Irish Derby	Curragh	1½ (T)	Dream Well	Cash Asmussen	700,000
June 28	Hollywood Gold Cup	Hollywood Park	1¼	Skip Away	Jerry Bailey	1,000,000
July 4	Beverly Hills Handicap	Hollywood Park	1¼ (T)	Squeak	Gary Stevens	300,000
July 4	Suburban Handicap	Belmont	1¼	Frisk Me Now	Eddie King	350,000
July 12	Dwyer Stakes*	Belmont	1 1/16	Coronado's Quest	Mike Smith	150,000
July 12	Hollywood Oaks	Hollywood Park	1⅛	Manistique	Gary Stevens	200,000
July 18	Frank J. DeFrancis Memorial	Laurel Park	6 F	Kelly Kip	Jean-Luc Samyn	300,000
July 19	Ohio Derby*	Thistledown	1⅛	Classic Cat	Shane Sellers	300,000
July 19	Swaps Stakes*	Hollywood Park	1⅛	Old Trieste	Chris McCarron	500,000
July 19	Coaching Club Am. Oaks	Belmont	1¼	Banshee Breeze	Jerry Bailey	250,000
July 20	Vanity Handicap	Hollywood	1⅛	Escena	Jerry Bailey	350,000
July 25	K. George VI and Q. Elizabeth Diamond Stakes	Ascot	1½ (T)	Swain	Frankie Dettori	776,300
Aug. 2	Go for Wand Handicap	Saratoga	1⅛	Aldiza	Mike Smith	250,000
Aug. 2	Eddie Read Handicap	Del Mar	1⅛ (T)	Subordination	David Flores	300,000
Aug. 8	Whitney Handicap	Saratoga	1⅛	Awesome Again	Pat Day	400,000
Aug. 9	Haskell Invitational*	Monmouth	1⅛	Coronado's Quest	Mike Smith	1,000,000
Aug. 9	Jim Dandy Stakes*	Saratoga	1⅛	Favorite Trick	Pat Day	250,000
Aug. 15	Pacific Classic	Del Mar	1¼	Free House	Chris McCarron	1,000,000
Aug. 22	Alabama Stakes	Saratoga	1¼	Banshee Breeze	Jerry Bailey	250,000
Aug. 28	Personal Ensign Handicap†	Saratoga	1¼	Tomisue's Delight	Pat Day	400,000
Aug. 29	King's Bishop Stakes*	Saratoga	7 F	Secret Firm	Edgar Prado	200,000
Aug. 29	Travers Stakes*	Saratoga	1¼	Coronado's Quest	Mike Smith	750,000
Aug. 30	Philip H. Iselin Handicap	Monmouth	1 1/16	Skip Away	Jerry Bailey	500,000
Aug. 30	Saratoga Cup Handicap	Saratoga	1¼	Awesome Again	Pat Day	300,000
Aug. 30	Remington Park Derby	Remington	1 1/16	Classic Cat	Shane Sellers	300,000
Sept. 12	Man o' War Stakes	Belmont	1⅜ (T)	Daylami	Jerry Bailey	400,000
Sept. 19	Woodward Stakes	Belmont	1⅛	Skip Away	Jerry Bailey	500,000
Sept. 19	Ruffian Handicap	Belmont	1 1/16	Sharp Cat	Corey Nakatani	250,000
Sept. 20	Woodbine Mile	Woodbine	1	Labeeb	Kent Desormeaux	750,000

* VISA 3-Year-Old Championship Series race (see tables on p. 788).

† formerly known as John A. Morris Handicap.

Note: The Arlington International Racecourse in Arlington Heights, Ill., which hosted the Arlington Million ($1,000,000 purse), Beverly D. Stakes ($500,000), Secretariat Stakes ($400,000) and Round Table Stakes ($100,000), closed after the 1997 season.

The 1998 Triple Crown

Thoroughbred racing's Triple Crown for 3-year-olds consists of the Kentucky Derby, Preakness Stakes and Belmont Stakes run over six weeks on May 2, May 16 and June 6, respectively.

124th KENTUCKY DERBY

Grade I for three-year olds; 8th race at Churchill Downs in Louisville. **Date**— May 2, 1998; **Distance**— 1¼ miles; **Stakes Purse**— $1,000,000 ($700,000 to winner; $170,000 for 2nd; $85,000 for 3rd; $45,000 for 4th); **Track**— Cloudy and Fast; **Off**— 5:29 p.m. EDT; **Favorite**— Indian Charlie (7-2 odds).

Winner— Real Quiet; **Field**— 15 horses; **Time**— 2:02⅕; **Start**— Good for all but Old Trieste (stumbled); **Won**— Driving; **Sire**— Quiet American; **Dam**— Really Blue; **Record** (going into race)— 12 starts, 2 wins, 2 seconds, 5 thirds; **Last start**— 2nd in Santa Anita Derby (Apr. 4); **Breeder**— Little Hill Farm (Ky.).

Order of Finish	Jockey	PP	1/4	1/2	3/4	Mile	Stretch	Finish	To $1
Real Quiet	Kent Desormeaux	3	8-1½	6-1	6-½	1-1	1-1½	1-½	8.40
Victory Gallop	Alex Solis	13	14-½	15	14-1½	7-1	3-hd	2-2¼	14.60
Indian Charlie	Gary Stevens	8	4-1	5-2	4-hd	2-½	2-2	3-hd	2.70
Halory Hunter	Corey Nakatani	4	15	12-½	12-1½	6-1	5-6	4-1	6.60
Cape Town	Jerry Bailey	11	6-hd	8-hd	8-½	4-1½	4½	5-8	4.60
Parade Ground	Shane Sellers	10	13-1½	13½	13½	10-1	6-hd	6-nk	22.30
Hanuman Highway	David Flores	6	9-1	9-½	7-½	9-1	8-5	7-nk	22.50
Favorite Trick	Pat Day	7	5-1½	4-hd	5-1½	5½	7-hd	8-6¾	4.40
Nationalore	Goncalino Almeida	1	12-hd	14-½	15	11-1½	9-3	9-4¾	109.60
Old Trieste	Robbie Albarado	14	2-1½	1-1	1-3½	3-1	10-4	10-3¾	32.10
Chilito	Gary Boulanger	5	3-2	3-3	3-½	8-1½	11-5	11-7¼	34.80
Robinwould	Earlie Fires	15	7-hd	7-1	9-½	13-5	12-2	12-4½	69.80
Artax	Chris McCarron	12	10-2	10-3	10-1	12-2	13-12	13-22¾	11.50
Rock and Roll	Francisco Torres	9	1-½	2-2	2-hd	15	14-15	14-10¾	50.60
Basic Trainee	John Velazquez	2	11-½	11-½	11-½	14-2	15	15	69.80

Times— 22⅗; 45⅗; 1:10⅗; 1:35⅗; 2:02⅕.

$2 Mutual Prices— #2 Real Quiet ($18.80, $8.80, $5.80); #12 Victory Gallop ($13.00, $7.60); #7 Indian Charlie ($4.20). **Exacta**— (2-12) for $291.80; **Trifecta**— (2-12-7) for $1,221.00; **Superfecta**— (2-12-7-3) for $3,007.40; **Pick Six**— (2-2-10-12-8-2) (6-correct) $1,383.00; **Scratched**— none. **Overweights**— none. **Attendance**— 143,215; **TV Rating**— 6.1/18 (ABC).

Trainers & Owners (by finish): **1**— Bob Baffert & Mike Pegram; **2**— Elliott Walden & Prestonwood Farm; **3**— Bob Baffert & Earnhardt/John T. Gaines; **4**— Nick Zito & Celtic Pride Stable; **5**— D. Wayne Lukas & Overbrook Farm; **6**— Neil Howard & W.S. Farish & Stephen Hilbert; **7**— Kathy Walsh & Budget Stable; **8**— Bill Mott & Joseph Lacombe; **9**—Myung Kwon Cho & Myung Kwon Cho; **10**— Mike Puype & Cobra Farm; **11**— Graham Motion & Lazy Lane Farms; **12**— Jerry Calvin & Bill/ Dee Davenport; **13**— Randy Bradshaw & Paraneck Stable; **14**— Bill Mott & Madeline Paulsen/Jenny Craig; **15**— Jorge Romero & Luis Gambotto & Enrique Ocejo.

123rd PREAKNESS STAKES

Grade I for three-year olds; 10th race at Pimlico in Baltimore. **Date**— May 16, 1998; **Distance**— 1³⁄₁₆ miles; **Stakes Purse**— $1,000,000 ($650,000 to winner; $200,000 for 2nd; $100,000 for 3rd; $50,000 for 4th); **Track**— Fast and Clear; **Off**— 5:29 p.m. EDT; **Favorite**— Real Quiet (2-1).

Winner— Real Quiet; **Field**— 10 horses; **Time**— 1:54⅘; **Start**— Good for all; **Won**— Driving; **Sire**— Quiet American; **Dam**— Really Blue; **Record** (going into race)— 13 starts, 3 wins, 2 seconds, 5 thirds; **Last start**— Won the Kentucky Derby (May 2); **Breeder**— Little Hill Farm (Ky.).

Order of Finish	Jockey	PP	1/4	1/2	3/4	Stretch	Finish	To $1
Real Quiet	Kent Desormeaux	10	8-4	6-hd	5-1	1-½	1-2¼	2.50
Victory Gallop	Gary Stevens	9	7-1½	8-5	4-1	2-2	2-¾	2.00
Classic Cat	Robbie Albarado	3	6-hd	5-1	6-½	3-1	3-3¾	12.30
Hot Wells	Edgar Prado	7	9-2	9-3½	8-4	4-1	4-nk	25.20
Black Cash	Shane Sellers	2	2-½	3-1	7-3	5-2	5-hd	7.10
Spartan Cat	Rick Wilson	1	10	10	10	6-½	6-9¾	98.80
Baquero	Pat Day	6	1-1½	1-2½	1-½	7-3½	7-7¼	14.60
Basic Trainee	Cornelio Velasquez	5	3-½	2-½	3-hd	9-6	8-no	63.80
Cape Town	Jerry Bailey	4	4-1	4-4	2-hd	8-1	9-5	2.90
Silver's Prospect	Frank Douglas	8	5-½	7-hd	9-2½	10	10	98.00

Times— 46⅗; 1:11; 1:35⅘; 1:54⅘.

$2 Mutual Prices— #11 Real Quiet ($7.00, $3.60, $3.00); #10 Victory Gallop ($3.20, $2.80); #3 Indian Charlie ($4.80).

Exacta— (11-10) for $14.80; **Trifecta**— (11-10-3) for $97.40; **Pick Six**— none; **Scratched**— Coronado's Quest. **Overweights**— none. **Attendance**— 91,122; **TV Rating**— 3.6/11 (ABC).

Trainers & Owners (by finish): **1**— Bob Baffert & Mike Pegram; **2**— Elliot Walden & Prestonwood Farm; **3**— David Cross & Gary Garber; **4**— Tom Amoss & So What's Nu Stable; **5**— Patrick Byrne & Frank Stronach; **6**— Richard Dutrow & Marathon Farms (Peter Angelos); **7**— D. Wayne Lukas & Robert/Beverly Lewis; **8**— Jorge Romero & Luis Gambotto/Enrique Ocejo; **9**— D. Wayne Lukas & Overbrook Farm; **10**— Jean Rofe & Robert G. Sowder.

130th BELMONT STAKES

Grade I for three-year olds; 9th race at Belmont Park in Elmont, N.Y. **Date**— June 6, 1998; **Distance**— 1½ miles; **Stakes Purse**— $1,000,000 ($600,000 to winner; $200,000 for 2nd; $110,000 for 3rd; $60,000 for 4th; $30,000 for 5th); **Track**— Fast and Clear; **Off**— 5:29 p.m. EDT; **Favorite**— Real Quiet (6-5).

Winner— Victory Gallop; **Field**— 11 horses; **Time**— 2:29; **Start**— Good for all; **Won**— Driving; **Sire**— Cryptoclearance (Fappiano); **Dam**— Victorious Lil (Vice Regent); **Record** (going into race): 9 starts, 5 wins, 3 second; **Last Start**— 2nd in Preakness Stakes (May 16); **Breeder**— Tall Oaks Farm.

Order of Finish	Jockey	PP	1/4	1/2	Mile	1 1/4-M	Stretch	Finish	To $1
Victory Gallop	Gary Stevens	9	10-1	10-1	9-3	5-1½	2-3	1-no	4.50
Real Quiet	Kent Desormeaux	7	6-1½	6-1½	3-½	1-½	1-4	2-6	0.80
Thomas Jo	Chris McCarron	1	7-½	7-1½	7-1½	4-½	3-hd	3-1¼	28.50
Parade Ground	Pat Day	4	9-hd	9-1	8-½	8-1	5-hd	4-2½	20.40
Raffie's Majesty	Jorge Chavez	8	2-hd	5-½	6-1½	6-4	4-½	5-4	13.90
Chilito	Robbie Davis	3	1-1½	1-1	1-½	2-½	6-8	6-4	85.75
Grand Slam	Jerry Bailey	11	3-hd	2-1	2-½	3-6	7-1	7-nk	7.20
Classic Cat	John Velazquez	5	11	11	10-4	10-13	8-6	8-9½	10.40
Limit Out	Jean-Luc Samyn	6	4-1½	3-hd	5-hd	7-½	9-10	9-11	20.90
Yarrow Brae	Mike Smith	10	5-hd	4-1½	4-2	9-½	10-14	10-20	32.25
Basic Trainee	Joe Bravo	2	8-1	8-hd	11	11	11	11	113.25

Times— 23⅗ ; 48⅗; 1:13⅖; 1:37⅖; 2:02⅘; 2:29.
$2 Mutual Prices— #11 Victory Gallop ($11.00, $3.60, $3.20); #8 Real Quiet ($3.00, $2.60); #2 Thomas Jo ($5.30).
Exacta— (11-8) for $17.60; **Trifecta**— (11-8-2) for $275.00; **Pick Three**— (2-1-11) for $27.00; **Scratched**— Hanuman Highway and Hot Wells. **Overweights**— None. **Attendance**— 80,162; **TV Rating**— 5.9/18 share (ABC).
Trainers & Owners (by finish): **1**— Elliott Walden & Prestonwood Farm; **2**— Bob Baffert & Mike Pegram; **3**— Jimmy Jerkens & Earle Mack/Team Valor; **4**— Neil Howard & W.S. Farish/Stephen Hilbert; **5**— H. James Bond & Barrios/Lester/Prieger; **6**— H. Graham Motion & Lazy Lane Farm; **7**— D. Wayne Lukas & Baker/Cornstein/Mack; **8**— David Cross & Gary Garber; **9**— Allen Jerkens & Joseph Shields Jr.; **10**— D. Wayne Lukas & Mrs. John Magnier/Michael Tabor; **11**— Jorge Romero & Luis Gambotto and Enrique Ocejo.

NTRA National Thoroughbred Poll

(Sept. 20, 1998)

The NTRA Thoroughbred Poll conducted by Thoroughbred Racing Communications, Inc. and covering races through Sept. 20, 1998. Rankings are based on the votes of 20 sports and thoroughbred media representatives. First place votes are in parentheses.

		Pts	Age	Sex	'98 Record Sts—1-2-3	Owner	Trainer
1	Skip Away (19)	199	5	Horse	7—7-0-0	Carolyn Hine	Sonny Hine
2	Awesome Again	133	4	Colt	4—4-0-0	Stronach Stable	Patrick Byrne
3	Gentlemen	120	6	Horse	5—1-2-0	R.D. Hubbard	Richard Mandella
4	Real Quiet	106	3	Colt	6—2-3-0	Mike Pegram	Bob Baffert
5	Victory Gallop	99	3	Colt	7—3-4-0	Prestonwood Farms	Elliott Walden
6	Silver Charm (1)	94	4	Colt	5—3-1-0	Bob & Beverly Lewis	Bob Baffert
7	Coronado's Quest	70	3	Colt	9—5-2-0	Stuart Janney III	Shug McGaughey
8	Free House	68	4	Colt	3—2-0-0	J. Toffan & T. McCaffery	Paco Gonzalez
9	Joyeux Danseur	55	5	Horse	4—4-0-0	B. Wayne Hughes	Albert Stall Jr.
10	Sharp Cat	28	4	Filly	3—3-0-0	The Thoroughbred Corp.	D. Wayne Lukas

Others receiving votes: 11. Mossflower (21 points); **12.** Memories of Silver (20); **13.** Labeeb (19); **14.** Fiji (14); **15.** Kelly Kip (14); **16.** Jersey Girl (12); **17.** Banshee Breeze (8); **18.** Escena and Touch Gold (5); **20.** Tap to Music (3); **21.** Ladies Din, Malek, and Maxzene (2); **24.** Precocity (1).

Final VISA 3–year–old Series Standings

The VISA Championship Series consists of 44 stakes races to determine the VISA 3-Year-Old Champion. Points are awarded to the first, second and third-place finishers as follows: Triple Crown races are scored 15-10-7; Grade I races are scored 10-7-5; Grade II races 7-5-3; and Grade III and ungraded 5-3-1. Top 20 horses and jockeys are listed below.

Horses

		Pts
1	Victory Gallop	66
2	Real Quiet	62
3	Coronado's Quest	51
4	Classic Cat	21
5	Grand Slam	20
6	Lil's Lad	19
7	Cape Town	18
8	Artax	17
	Indian Charlie	17
10	Favorite Trick	15
	Halory Hunter	15
	Yarrow Brae	15
13	Dice Dancer	13
	Souvenir Copy	13
15	Event of the Year	12
	Old Trieste	12
	Thomas Jo	12
	Time Limit	12
19	Good and Tough	11
	Hot Wells	11
	Parade Ground	11
	Scatmandu	11

Jockeys

		Pts
1	Kent Desormeaux	72
2	Gary Stevens	71
3	Jerry Bailey	64
4	Mike Smith	47
5	Pat Day	40
6	Shane Sellers	38
7	Chris McCarron	36
8	Alex Solis	27
9	Robbie Albarado	20
10	Willie Martinez	17
11	Jorge Chavez	16
12	Eibar Coa	15
13	Jean-Luc Samyn	14
14	David Flores	13
	Corey Nakatani	13
	Edgar Prado	13
17	Russell Baze	12
	Richard Migliore	12
19	Julie Krone	11
20	Robbie Davis	10

1997–98 Money Leaders

Official Top 10 standings for 1997 and unofficial Top 10 standings for 1998, through Sept. 20.

Final 1997

HORSES	Age	Sts	1-2-3	Earnings
Skip Away	4	11	4-5-2	$4,089,000
Gentlemen	5	6	4-0-1	2,125,300
Siphon	6	6	2-3-0	2,121,000
Chief Bearhart	4	7	5-2-0	2,011,259
Deputy Commander	3	10	4-2-1	1,849,440
Silver Charm	3	7	3-4-0	1,638,750
Touch Gold	3	7	4-0-0	1,522,313
Marlin	4	10	4-0-2	1,521,600
Free House	3	10	3-2-3	1,336,910
Favorite Trick	2	8	8-0-0	1,231,998

JOCKEYS	Mts	1st	Earnings
Jerry Bailey	1145	273	$18,320,743
Gary Stevens	950	197	15,861,224
Mike Smith	1279	241	14,730,546
Pat Day	1217	266	14,060,954
Alex O. Solis	1373	255	13,517,376
Shane Sellers	1385	280	13,042,441
Corey Nakatani	836	169	11,334,806
Chris McCarron	649	129	10,701,231
Kent Desormeaux	1063	186	10,560,690
Jorge Chavez	1440	259	9,093,180

TRAINERS	Sts	1st	Earnings
D. Wayne Lukas	854	175	$10,351,397
Richard Mandella	364	70	9,632,774
Bill Mott	618	128	9,474,680
Bob Baffert	430	113	8,867,128
Jerry Hollendorfer	938	229	5,206,224
Wallace Dollase	182	48	5,027,430
Mark Frostad	235	66	4,863,931
Hubert Hine	132	22	4,805,791
David Hofmans	295	53	4,444,182
John Kimmel	432	97	4,393,272

1998 (through Sept. 20)

HORSES	Age	Sts	1-2-3	Earnings
Silver Charm	4	5	3-1-0	$2,990,430
Skip Away	5	7	7-0-0	2,630,000
Real Quiet	3	6	2-3-0	1,788,800
Victory Gallop	3	7	3-4-0	1,695,000
Coronado's Quest	3	9	5-2-0	1,619,550
Escena	5	8	4-3-0	992,425
Awesome Again	4	4	4-0-0	943,590
Malek	5	3	1-1-0	840,000
Precocity	4	9	2-4-1	838,970
Labeeb	6	3	3-0-0	837,060

JOCKEYS	Mts	1st	Earnings
Jerry Bailey	844	205	$13,181,385
Gary Stevens	702	139	12,804,663
Kent Desormeaux	823	156	11,204,927
Pat Day	947	193	10,436,897
Corey Nakatani	743	164	8,756,895
Shane Sellers	991	196	8,405,959
Chris McCarron	536	122	8,205,722
Alex O. Solis	746	109	7,260,879
Edgar Prado	1404	329	6,667,520
John Velazquez	1046	171	6,363,247

TRAINERS	Sts	1st	Earnings
Bob Baffert	378	98	$10,008,621
Bill Mott	451	111	6,812,105
D. Wayne Lukas	433	78	5,421,209
Jerry Hollendorfer	667	178	5,035,031
Neil Drysdale	196	52	4,602,822
Richard Mandella	242	42	4,432,347
Claude McGaughey III	224	51	4,058,318
W. Elliott Walden	336	55	3,945,572
Ronald McAnally	284	51	3,743,008
Todd Pletcher	394	76	3,736,919

Harness Racing

1997–98 Major Stakes Races

Winners of major stakes races from Nov. 7, 1997 through Sept. 24, 1998; all paces and trots cover one mile; (BC) indicates year-end Breeders' Crown series. See Updates for later results.

LATE 1997

Date	Race	Raceway	Winner	Time	Driver	Purse
Nov. 7	Three Diamonds Pace	Garden St.	Mybrowneyedgirl	1:53⅕	Cat Manzi	$506,700
Nov. 7	Valley Victory	Garden St.	Buzzin Brian	1:57⅗	Jim Morrill Jr.	332,100
Nov. 14	Windy City Pace	Maywood	Arturo	1:54⅖	Dave Palone	270,000
Nov. 14	Governor's Cup	Garden St.	Sealed N Delivered	1:52⅖	Ron Pierce	590,600

1998 (through Sept. 24)

Date	Race	Raceway	Winner	Time	Driver	Purse
May 2	Berry's Creek	Meadowlands	Resurgent Dragon	1:51⅗	Jack Moiseyev	$300,000
May 25	New Jersey Classic	Meadowlands	Shady Character	1:51⅕	Mike Lachance	500,000
June 20	North America Cup	Woodbine	Straight Path	1:51⅖	Mike Lachance	1,000,000
July 10	Del Miller Memorial	Meadowlands	Fern	1:54⅘	Luc Ouellette	340,000
July 11	Meadowlands Pace	Meadowlands	A Day In A Life	1:51⅕	Luc Ouellette	1,000,000
July 18	Maple Leaf Trot	Woodbine	Hanko Angus	1:54	Rick Zeron	315,500
July 25	Budweiser Beacon Course	Meadowlands	Muscles Yankee	1:54⅗	John Campbell	400,000
July 25	Art Rooney Pace	Yonkers	Shady Character	1:53⅗	Jim Morrill Jr.	333,282
Aug. 1	BC Open Pace	Meadowlands	Red Bow Tie	1:50⅕	Luc Ouellette	340,000
Aug. 1	BC Open Trot	Meadowlands	Moni Maker	1:52⅗	Wally Hennessey	500,000
Aug. 1	BC Mare Pace	Meadowlands	Jays Table	1:49⅗	John Campbell	282,500
Aug. 6	Sweetheart Pace	Meadowlands	Mattaroni	1:52⅘	John Campbell	517,600
Aug. 6	Peter Haughton Memorial	Meadowlands	Enjoy Lavec	1:56⅘	Jimmy Takter	458,000
Aug. 6	Merrie Annabelle Final	Meadowlands	Rae	1:58⅖	Wally Hennessey	412,000
Aug. 7	Woodrow Wilson Pace	Meadowlands	Grinfromeartoear	1:52⅗	Luc Ouellette	660,250
Aug. 8	**Hambletonian**	Meadowlands	Muscles Yankee	1:52⅖	John Campbell	1,000,000
Aug. 8	Hambletonian Oaks	Meadowlands	Fern	1:55	Luc Ouellette	500,000
Aug. 8	Nat Ray	Meadowlands	Moni Maker	1:52⅘	Wally Hennessey	300,000
Aug. 15	Adios Final	Ladbroke	Artist Stena	1:52⅕	Mike Lachance	500,000

Date	Race	Raceway	Winner	Time	Driver	Purse
Aug. 23	Confederation Cup XXII	Flamboro	Rustler Hanover	1:53⅘	Paul MacDonell	$459,000
Aug. 29	Metro Stakes	Woodbine	Grinfromeartoear	1:52⅘	Luc Ouellette	600,100
Sept. 5	Cane Pace	Freehold	Shady Character	1:53⅖	Mike Lachance	379,941
Sept. 24	**Little Brown Jug**	Delaware	Shady Character	1:52⅗	Ron Pierce	566,630

1997–98 Money Leaders

Official Top 10 standings for 1997 and unofficial Top 10 standings for 1998 through Sept. 20.

Final 1997

HORSES	Age	Sts	1-2-3	Earnings
Malabar Man	3th	14	11-3-0	$1,485,417
Western Dreamer	3pg	29	14-7-3	1,349,401
Village Jasper	3ph	30	14-6-3	1,057,595
Arturo	3ph	30	9-8-9	991,475
Dream Away	3ph	22	10-5-1	986,399
Steinam's Place	3pf	19	14-2-0	897,033
Gothic Dream	3ph	24	5-6-2	895,199
Lord Stormont	3tg	23	20-1-1	839,553
No Nonsense Woman	3tf	17	14-3-0	838,563
Armbro Plato	3tg	22	12-3-2	663,942

DRIVERS	Mts	1st	Earnings
Mike Lachance	2138	343	$9,119,093
John Campbell	1567	254	8,821,469
Luc Ouellette	2418	449	6,054,722
Jack Moiseyev	2216	301	5,759,150
Tony Morgan	3362	773	5,505,853
Ronald Pierce	1785	226	5,208,705
Cat Manzi	3147	464	4,716,642
Doug Brown	1815	318	4,634,223
George Brennan	2617	415	4,427,075
Steven Condren	1508	226	4,359,226

1998 (through Sept. 20)

HORSES	Age	Sts	1-2-3	Earnings
Muscles Yankee	3tc	7	6-1-0	$943,612
Shady Character	3pc	14	7-3-2	819,407
Day In A Life	3pc	16	5-5-2	743,681
Grinfromeartoear	2pc	6	6-0-0	730,175
David Raymond	3tc	15	7-5-2	665,729
Straight Path	3pc	17	8-6-1	660,830
Pacific Fella	5ph	21	9-3-4	652,365
Red Bow Tie	4pg	25	13-3-2	644,137
Dragon Again	3pc	13	5-2-5	595,503
Fern	3tf	14	9-1-2	520,729

DRIVERS	Mts	1st	Earnings
John Campbell	1432	297	$7,606,436
Luc Ouellette	2026	463	7,381,196
Mike Lachance	1645	236	6,556,550
George Brennan	2184	369	5,426,790
Jack Moiseyev	1951	291	4,384,410
Cat Manzi	2212	296	4,252,038
Anthony Morgan	2163	516	4,159,869
Ronald Pierce	1818	222	4,055,430
James Morrill	1721	210	3,520,154
Stephen Condren	1262	192	3,472,700

Hambletonian Society/Breeders Crown Standardbred Poll

Final Poll conducted by Harness Racing Communications as of Sept. 21, 1998 and based on the votes of 35 harness racing media representatives. Number in parentheses indicates first place votes. (p-pacer, t-trotter, h-horse, f-filly, m-mare, c-colt, g-gelding)

		Pts	Age/Gait/Sex	'98 Sts—1-2-3	Earnings
1	Moni Maker (22)	322	5tm	13—8-3-2	$1,019,918*
2	Muscles Yankee (13)	317	3tc	7—6-1-0	943,612
3	Red Bow Tie	238	4pg	25—13-3-2	644,137
4	Falcon's Icon	186	2pc	9—9-0-0	295,825
5	Grinfromeartoear	179	2pc	6—6-0-0	730,175
6	Pacific Fella	136	5ph	21—9-3-4	652,365
7	Shady Character	123	3pc	14—7-3-2	819,407
8	Artiscape	90	3pc	9—7-1-1	382,613
9	Galleria	83	3pf	10—4-4-2	502,350
10	Kick Tail	50	3tc	12—7-1-3	475,212

Others receiving votes: 11. Fern (48 points); **12.** Armbro Romance (35); **13.** Mattaroni, David Raymond and Hanko Angus (20); **16.** Dragon Again (18); **17.** Jays Table (13); **18.** Day In A Life (9); **19.** Noble Ability and Shania (4); **21.** Extreme Velocity, Browning Blue Chip, Hi Ho Silverheel's, Howard's Sister and Glorys Comet (2).

*includes foreign earnings

Steeplechase Racing
1997–98 Major Stakes Races

Winners of major steeplechase races from Nov. 16, 1997 through Aug. 27, 1998. See Updates for later results.

LATE 1997

Date	Race	Location	Miles	Winner	Jockey	Purse
Nov. 16	Colonial Cup	Camden, S.C.	2 ¾	Lonesome Glory	Blythe Miller	$115,900

1998

Date	Race	Location	Miles	Winner	Jockey	Purse
April 11	Atlanta Cup	Kingston, Ga.	2	Soringoverseattle	Jonathan Kiser	$100,000
April 18	Grand National	Butler, Md.	3	Buck Jakes	Anne Moran	30,000
April 25	Maryland Hunt Cup	Glyndon, Md.	4	Florida Law	J. Gillet	50,000
May 2	Virginia Gold Cup	The Plains, Va.	4	Saluter	Jack Fisher	40,000
May 9	Iroquois	Nashville, Tenn.	3	Rowdy Irishman	Vincent Marzullo	100,000
Aug. 27	N.Y. Turf Writers Cup	Saratoga, N.Y.	2 ⅜	Hokan	Sean Clancy	100,000

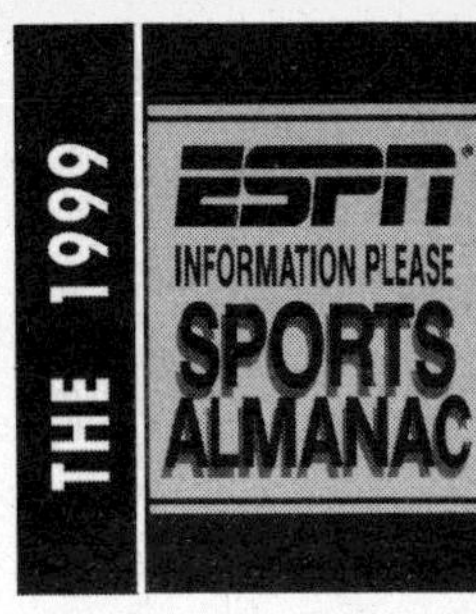

HORSE RACING STATISTICS

THROUGH THE YEARS

1867-1998

THOROUGHBRED • HARNESS

Thoroughbred Racing

The Triple Crown

The term "Triple Crown" was coined by sportswriter Charles Hatton while covering the 1930 victories of Gallant Fox in the Kentucky Derby, Preakness Stakes and Belmont Stakes. Before then, only Sir Barton (1919) had won all three races in the same year. Since then, nine horses have won the Triple Crown. Two trainers, James (Sunny Jim) Fitzsimmons and Ben A. Jones, have saddled two Triple Crown champions, while Eddie Arcaro is the only jockey to ride two champions.

Year		Jockey	Trainer	Owner	Sire/Dam
1919	**Sir Barton**	Johnny Loftus	H. Guy Bedwell	J.K.L. Ross	Star Shoot/Lady Sterling
1930	**Gallant Fox**	Earl Sande	J.E. Fitzsimmons	Belair Stud	Sir Gallahad III/Marguerite
1935	**Omaha**	Willie Saunders	J.E. Fitzsimmons	Belair Stud	Gallant Fox/Flambino
1937	**War Admiral**	Charley Kurtsinger	George Conway	Samuel Riddle	Man o' War/Brushup
1941	**Whirlaway**	Eddie Arcaro	Ben A. Jones	Calumet Farm	Blenheim II/Dustwhirl
1943	**Count Fleet**	Johnny Longden	Don Cameron	Mrs. J.D. Hertz	Reigh Count/Quickly
1946	**Assault**	Warren Mehrtens	Max Hirsch	King Ranch	Bold Venture/Igual
1948	**Citation**	Eddie Arcaro	Ben A. Jones	Calumet Farm	Bull Lea/Hydroplane II
1973	**Secretariat**	Ron Turcotte	Lucien Laurin	Meadow Stable	Bold Ruler/Somethingroyal
1977	**Seattle Slew**	Jean Cruguet	Billy Turner	Karen Taylor	Bold Reasoning/My Charmer
1978	**Affirmed**	Steve Cauthen	Laz Barrera	Harbor View Farm	Exclusive Native/Won't Tell You

Note: Gallant Fox (1930) is the only Triple Crown winner to sire another Triple Crown winner, Omaha (1935). Wm. Woodward Sr., owner of Belair Stud, was breeder-owner of both horses and both were trained by Sunny Jim Fitzsimmons.

Triple Crown Near Misses

Forty-three horses have won two legs of the Triple Crown. Of those, fourteen won the Kentucky Derby (KD) and Preakness Stakes (PS) only to be beaten in the Belmont Stakes (BS). Two others, Burgoo King (1932) and Bold Venture (1936), each won the Derby and Preakness but were forced out of the Belmont with the same injury–a bowed tendon–that effectively ended their racing careers. In 1978, Alydar finished second to Affirmed in all three races, the only time that has happened. Note that the Preakness preceded the Kentucky Derby in 1922, '23 and '31; (*) indicates won on disqualification.

Year		KD	PS	BS
1877	**Cloverbrook**	DNS	won	won
1878	**Duke of Magenta**	DNS	won	won
1880	**Grenada**	DNS	won	won
1881	**Saunterer**	DNS	won	won
1895	**Belmar**	DNS	won	won
1920	**Man o' War**	DNS	won	won
1922	**Pillory**	DNS	won	won
1923	**Zev**	won	12th	won
1931	**Twenty Grand**	won	2nd	won
1932	**Burgoo King**	won	won	DNS
1936	**Bold Venture**	won	won	DNS
1939	**Johnstown**	won	5th	won
1940	**Bimelech**	2nd	won	won
1942	**Shut Out**	won	5th	won
1944	**Pensive**	won	won	2nd
1949	**Capot**	2nd	won	won
1950	**Middleground**	won	2nd	won
1953	**Native Dancer**	2nd	won	won
1955	**Nashua**	2nd	won	won
1956	**Needles**	won	2nd	won
1958	**Tim Tam**	won	won	2nd

Year		KD	PS	BS
1961	**Carry Back**	won	won	7th
1963	**Chateaugay**	won	2nd	won
1964	**Northern Dancer**	won	won	3rd
1966	**Kauai King**	won	won	4th
1967	**Damascus**	3rd	won	won
1968	**Forward Pass**	won*	won	2nd
1969	**Majestic Prince**	won	won	2nd
1971	**Canonero II**	won	won	4th
1972	**Riva Ridge**	won	4th	won
1974	**Little Current**	5th	won	won
1976	**Bold Forbes**	won	3rd	won
1979	**Spectacular Bid**	won	won	3rd
1981	**Pleasant Colony**	won	won	3rd
1984	**Swale**	won	7th	won
1987	**Alysheba**	won	won	4th
1988	**Risen Star**	3rd	won	won
1989	**Sunday Silence**	won	won	2nd
1991	**Hansel**	10th	won	won
1994	**Tabasco Cat**	6th	won	won
1995	**Thunder Gulch**	won	3rd	won
1997	**Silver Charm**	won	won	2nd
1998	**Real Quiet**	won	won	2nd

The Triple Crown Challenge (1987-93)

Seeking to make the Triple Crown more than just a media event and to insure that owners would not be attracted to more lucrative races, officials at Churchill Downs, the Maryland Jockey Club and the New York Racing Association created Triple Crown Productions in 1985 and announced that a $1 million bonus would be given to the horse that performs best in the Kentucky Derby, Preakness Stakes and Belmont Stakes. Furthermore, a bonus of $5 million would be presented to any horse winning all three races.

Revised in 1991, the rules stated that the winning horse must: 1. finish all three races; 2. earn points by finishing first, second, third or fourth in at least one of the three races; and 3. earn the highest number of points based on the following system–10 points to win, five to place, three to show and one to finish fourth. In the event of a tie, the $1 million is distributed equally among the top point-getters. From 1987-90, the system was five points to win, three to place and one to show. The Triple Crown Challenge was discontinued in 1994.

Year		KD	PS	BS	Pts
1987	1 **Bet Twice**	2nd	2nd	1st –	11
	2 Alysheba	1st	1st	4th –	10
	3 Cryptoclearance	4th	3rd	2nd –	4
1988	1 **Risen Star**	3rd	1st	1st –	11
	2 Winning Colors	1st	3rd	6th –	6
	3 Brian's Time	6th	2nd	3rd –	4
1989	1 **Sunday Silence**	1st	1st	2nd –	13
	2 Easy Goer	2nd	2nd	1st –	11
	3 Hawkster	5th	5th	5th –	0
1990	1 **Unbridled**	1st	2nd	4th –	8
	2 Summer Squall	2nd	1st	DNR –	8
	3 Go and Go	DNR	DNR	1st –	5
	(Unbridled was only horse to run all three races.)				

Year		KD	PS	BS	Pts
1991	1 **Hansel**	10th	1st	1st –	20
	2 Strike the Gold	1st	6th	2nd –	15
	3 Mane Minister	3rd	3rd	3rd –	9
1992	1 **Pine Bluff**	5th	1st	3rd –	13
	2 Casual Lies	2nd	3rd	5th –	8
	(No other horses ran all three races.)				
1993	1 **Sea Hero**	1st	5th	7th –	10
	2 Wild Gale	3rd	8th	3rd –	6
	(No other horses ran all three races.)				

Kentucky Derby

For three-year-olds. Held the first Saturday in May at Churchill Downs in Louisville, Ky. Inaugurated in 1875. Originally run at 1½ miles (1875-95), shortened to present 1¼ miles in 1896.

Trainers with most wins: Ben Jones (6); Dick Thompson (4); Sunny Jim Fitzsimmons, Max Hirsch and D. Wayne Lukas (3).

Jockeys with most wins: Eddie Arcaro and Bill Hartack (5); Bill Shoemaker (4); Angel Cordero Jr., Issac Murphy, Earl Sande and Gary Stevens (3).

Winning fillies: Regret (1915), Genuine Risk (1980) and Winning Colors (1988).

Year		Time	Jockey	Trainer	2nd place	3rd place
1875	**Aristides**	2:37¾	Oliver Lewis	Ansel Anderson	Volcano	Verdigris
1876	**Vagrant**	2:38¼	Bobby Swim	James Williams	Creedmore	Harry Hill
1877	**Baden-Baden**	2:38	Billy Walker	Ed Brown	Leonard	King William
1878	**Day Star**	2:37¼	Jimmy Carter	Lee Paul	Himyar	Leveler
1879	**Lord Murphy**	2:37	Charlie Shauer	George Rice	Falsetto	Strathmore
1880	**Fonso**	2:37½	George Lewis	Tice Hutsell	Kimball	Bancroft
1881	**Hindoo**	2:40	Jim McLaughlin	James Rowe Sr.	Lelex	Alfambra
1882	**Apollo**	2:40¼	Babe Hurd	Green Morris	Runnymede	Bengal
1883	**Leonatus**	2:43	Billy Donohue	John McGinty	Drake Carter	Lord Raglan
1884	**Buchanan**	2:40¼	Isaac Murphy	William Bird	Loftin	Audrain
1885	**Joe Cotton**	2:37¼	Babe Henderson	Alex Perry	Bersan	Ten Booker
1886	**Ben Ali**	2:36½	Paul Duffy	Jim Murphy	Blue Wing	Free Knight
1887	**Montrose**	2:39¼	Isaac Lewis	John McGinty	Jim Gore	Jacobin
1888	**MacBeth II**	2:38¼	George Covington	John Campbell	Gallifet	White
1889	**Spokane**	2:34½	Thomas Kiley	John Rodegap	Proctor Knott	Once Again
1890	**Riley**	2:45	Isaac Murphy	Edward Corrigan	Bill Letcher	Robespierre
1891	**Kingman**	2:52¼	Isaac Murphy	Dud Allen	Balgowan	High Tariff
1892	**Azra**	2:41½	Lonnie Clayton	John Morris	Huron	Phil Dwyer
1893	**Lookout**	2:39¼	Eddie Kunze	Wm. McDaniel	Plutus	Boundless
1894	**Chant**	2:41	Frank Goodale	Eugene Leigh	Pearl Song	Sigurd
1895	**Halma**	2:37½	Soup Perkins	Byron McClelland	Basso	Laureate
1896	**Ben Brush**	2:07¾	Willie Simms	Hardy Campbell	Ben Eder	Semper Ego
1897	**Typhoon II**	2:12½	Buttons Garner	J.C. Cahn	Ornament	Dr. Catlett
1898	**Plaudit**	2:09	Willie Simms	John E. Madden	Lieber Karl	Isabey
1899	**Manuel**	2:12	Fred Taral	Robert Walden	Corsini	Mazo
1900	**Lieut. Gibson**	2:06¼	Jimmy Boland	Charles Hughes	Florizar	Thrive
1901	**His Eminence**	2:07¾	Jimmy Winkfield	F.B. Van Meter	Sannazarro	Driscoll
1902	**Alan-a-Dale**	2:08¾	Jimmy Winkfield	T.C. McDowell	Inventor	The Rival
1903	**Judge Himes**	2:09	Hal Booker	J.P. Mayberry	Early	Bourbon
1904	**Elwood**	2:08½	Shorty Prior	C.E. Durnell	Ed Tierney	Brancas
1905	**Agile**	2:10¾	Jack Martin	Robert Tucker	Ram's Horn	Layson
1906	**Sir Huon**	2:08⅘	Roscoe Troxler	Pete Coyne	Lady Navarre	James Reddick
1907	**Pink Star**	2:12⅗	Andy Minder	W.H. Fizer	Zal	Ovelando
1908	**Stone Street**	2:15⅕	Arthur Pickens	J.W. Hall	Sir Cleges	Dunvegan
1909	**Wintergreen**	2:08⅕	Vincent Powers	Charles Mack	Miami	Dr. Barkley

Year	Time	Jockey	Trainer	2nd place	3rd place
1910 **Donau**	2:06⅖	Fred Herbert	George Ham	Joe Morris	Fighting Bob
1911 **Meridian**	2:05	George Archibald	Albert Ewing	Governor Gray	Colston
1912 **Worth**	2:09⅖	C.H. Shilling	Frank Taylor	Duval	Flamma
1913 **Donerail**	2:04⅘	Roscoe Goose	Thomas Hayes	Ten Point	Gowell
1914 **Old Rosebud**	2:03⅖	John McCabe	F.D. Weir	Hodge	Bronzewing
1915 **Regret**	2:05⅖	Joe Notter	James Rowe Sr.	Pebbles	Sharpshooter
1916 **George Smith**	2:04	Johnny Loftus	Hollie Hughes	Star Hawk	Franklin
1917 **Omar Khayyam**	2:04⅗	Charles Borel	C.T. Patterson	Ticket	Midway
1918 **Exterminator**	2:10⅘	William Knapp	Henry McDaniel	Escoba	Viva America
1919 **SIR BARTON**	2:09⅘	Johnny Loftus	H. Guy Bedwell	Billy Kelly	Under Fire
1920 **Paul Jones**	2:09	Ted Rice	Billy Garth	Upset	On Watch
1921 **Behave Yourself**	2:04⅕	Charles Thompson	Dick Thompson	Black Servant	Prudery
1922 **Morvich**	2:04⅗	Albert Johnson	Fred Burlew	Bet Mosie	John Finn
1923 **Zev**	2:05⅖	Earl Sande	David Leary	Martingale	Vigil
1924 **Black Gold**	2:05⅕	John Mooney	Hanly Webb	Chilhowee	Beau Butler
1925 **Flying Ebony**	2:07⅗	Earl Sande	William Duke	Captain Hal	Son of John
1926 **Bubbling Over**	2:03⅘	Albert Johnson	Dick Thompson	Bagenbaggage	Rock Man
1927 **Whiskery**	2:06	Linus McAtee	Fred Hopkins	Osmand	Jock
1928 **Reigh Count**	2:10⅖	Chick Lang	Bert Michell	Misstep	Toro
1929 **Clyde Van Dusen**	2:10⅘	Linus McAtee	Clyde Van Dusen	Naishapur	Panchio
1930 **GALLANT FOX**	2:07⅗	Earl Sande	Jim Fitzsimmons	Gallant Knight	Ned O.
1931 **Twenty Grand**	2:01⅘	Charley Kurtsinger	James Rowe Jr.	Sweep All	Mate
1932 **Burgoo King**	2:05⅕	Eugene James	Dick Thompson	Economic	Stepenfetchit
1933 **Brokers Tip**	2:06⅘	Don Meade	Dick Thompson	Head Play	Charley O.
1934 **Cavalcade**	2:04	Mack Garner	Bob Smith	Discovery	Agrarian
1935 **OMAHA**	2:05	Willie Saunders	Jim Fitzsimmons	Roman Soldier	Whiskolo
1936 **Bold Venture**	2:03⅗	Ira Hanford	Max Hirsch	Brevity	Indian Broom
1937 **WAR ADMIRAL**	2:03⅕	Charley Kurtsinger	George Conway	Pompoon	Reaping Reward
1938 **Lawrin**	2:04⅘	Eddie Arcaro	Ben Jones	Dauber	Can't Wait
1939 **Johnstown**	2:03⅖	James Stout	Jim Fitzsimmons	Challedon	Heather Broom
1940 **Gallahadion**	2:05	Carroll Bierman	Roy Waldron	Bimelech	Dit
1941 **WHIRLAWAY**	2:01⅖	Eddie Arcaro	Ben Jones	Staretor	Market Wise
1942 **Shut Out**	2:04⅖	Wayne Wright	John Gaver	Alsab	Valdina Orphan
1943 **COUNT FLEET**	2:04	Johnny Longden	Don Cameron	Blue Swords	Slide Rule
1944 **Pensive**	2:04⅕	Conn McCreary	Ben Jones	Broadcloth	Stir Up
1945 **Hoop Jr**	2:07	Eddie Arcaro	Ivan Parke	Pot O'Luck	Darby Dieppe
1946 **ASSAULT**	2:06⅗	Warren Mehrtens	Max Hirsch	Spy Song	Hampden
1947 **Jet Pilot**	2:06⅘	Eric Guerin	Tom Smith	Phalanx	Faultless
1948 **CITATION**	2:05⅖	Eddie Arcaro	Ben Jones	Coaltown	My Request
1949 **Ponder**	2:04⅕	Steve Brooks	Ben Jones	Capot	Palestinian
1950 **Middleground**	2:01⅗	William Boland	Max Hirsch	Hill Prince	Mr. Trouble
1951 **Count Turf**	2:02⅗	Conn McCreary	Sol Rutchick	Royal Mustang	Ruhe
1952 **Hill Gail**	2:01⅗	Eddie Arcaro	Ben Jones	Sub Fleet	Blue Man
1953 **Dark Star**	2:02	Hank Moreno	Eddie Hayward	Native Dancer	Invigorator
1954 **Determine**	2:03	Raymond York	Willie Molter	Hasty Road	Hasseyampa
1955 **Swaps**	2:01⅘	Bill Shoemaker	Mesh Tenney	Nashua	Summer Tan
1956 **Needles**	2:03⅖	David Erb	Hugh Fontaine	Fabius	Come On Red
1957 **Iron Liege**	2:02⅕	Bill Hartack	Jimmy Jones	Gallant Man	Round Table
1958 **Tim Tam**	2:05	Ismael Valenzuela	Jimmy Jones	Lincoln Road	Noureddin
1959 **Tomy Lee**	2:02⅕	Bill Shoemaker	Frank Childs	Sword Dancer	First Landing
1960 **Venetian Way**	2:02⅖	Bill Hartack	Victor Sovinski	Bally Ache	Victoria Park
1961 **Carry Back**	2:04	John Sellers	Jack Price	Crozier	Bass Clef
1962 **Decidedly**	2:00⅖	Bill Hartack	Horatio Luro	Roman Line	Ridan
1963 **Chateaugay**	2:01⅘	Braulio Baeza	James Conway	Never Bend	Candy Spots
1964 **Northern Dancer**	2:00	Bill Hartack	Horatio Luro	Hill Rise	The Scoundrel
1965 **Lucky Debonair**	2:01⅕	Bill Shoemaker	Frank Catrone	Dapper Dan	Tom Rolfe
1966 **Kauai King**	2:02	Don Brumfield	Henry Forrest	Advocator	Blue Skyer
1967 **Proud Clarion**	2:00⅗	Bobby Ussery	Loyd Gentry	Barbs Delight	Damascus
1968 **Forward Pass***	—	Ismael Valenzuela	Henry Forrest	Francie's Hat	T.V. Commercial
1969 **Majestic Prince**	2:01⅘	Bill Hartack	Johnny Longden	Arts and Letters	Dike
1970 **Dust Commander**	2:03⅖	Mike Manganello	Don Combs	My Dad George	High Echelon
1971 **Canonero II**	2:03⅕	Gustavo Avila	Juan Arias	Jim French	Bold Reason
1972 **Riva Ridge**	2:01⅘	Ron Turcotte	Lucien Laurin	No Le Hace	Hold Your Peace
1973 **SECRETARIAT**	1:59⅖	Ron Turcotte	Lucien Laurin	Sham	Our Native
1974 **Cannonade**	2:04	Angel Cordero Jr.	Woody Stephens	Hudson County	Agitate
1975 **Foolish Pleasure**	2:02	Jacinto Vasquez	LeRoy Jolley	Avatar	Diabolo
1976 **Bold Forbes**	2:01⅗	Angel Cordero Jr.	Laz Barrera	Honest Pleasure	Elocutionist
1977 **SEATTLE SLEW**	2:02⅕	Jean Cruguet	Billy Turner	Run Dusty Run	Sanhedrin

Kentucky Derby (Cont.)

Year	Time	Jockey	Trainer	2nd place	3rd place
1978 **AFFIRMED**	2:01⅕	Steve Cauthen	Laz Barrera	Alydar	Believe It
1979 **Spectacular Bid**	2:02⅖	Ron Franklin	Bud Delp	General Assembly	Golden Act
1980 **Genuine Risk**	2:02	Jacinto Vasquez	LeRoy Jolley	Rumbo	Jaklin Klugman
1981 **Pleasant Colony**	2:02	Jorge Velasquez	John Campo	Woodchopper	Partez
1982 **Gato Del Sol**	2:02⅖	E. Delahoussaye	Eddie Gregson	Laser Light	Reinvested
1983 **Sunny's Halo**	2:02⅕	E. Delahoussaye	David Cross Jr.	Desert Wine	Caveat
1984 **Swale**	2:02⅖	Laffit Pincay Jr.	Woody Stephens	Coax Me Chad	At The Threshold
1985 **Spend A Buck**	2:00⅕	Angel Cordero Jr.	Cam Gambolati	Stephan's Odyssey	Chief's Crown
1986 **Ferdinand**	2:02⅘	Bill Shoemaker	Chas. Whittingham	Bold Arrangement	Broad Brush
1987 **Alysheba**	2:03⅖	Chris McCarron	Jack Van Berg	Bet Twice	Avies Copy
1988 **Winning Colors**	2:02⅕	Gary Stevens	D. Wayne Lukas	Forty Niner	Risen Star
1989 **Sunday Silence**	2:05	Pat Valenzuela	Chas. Whittingham	Easy Goer	Awe Inspiring
1990 **Unbridled**	2:02	Craig Perret	Carl Nafzger	Summer Squall	Pleasant Tap
1991 **Strike the Gold**	2:03	Chris Antley	Nick Zito	Best Pal	Mane Minister
1992 **Lil E. Tee**	2:03	Pat Day	Lynn Whiting	Casual Lies	Dance Floor
1993 **Sea Hero**	2:02⅖	Jerry Bailey	Mack Miller	Prairie Bayou	Wild Gale
1994 **Go For Gin**	2:03⅗	Chris McCarron	Nick Zito	Strodes Creek	Blumin Affair
1995 **Thunder Gulch**	2:01⅕	Gary Stevens	D. Wayne Lukas	Tejano Run	Timber Country
1996 **Grindstone**	2:01	Jerry Bailey	D. Wayne Lukas	Cavonnier	Prince of Thieves
1997 **Silver Charm**	2:02⅖	Gary Stevens	Bob Baffert	Captain Bodgit	Free House
1998 **Real Quiet**	2:02⅕	Kent Desormeaux	Bob Baffert	Victory Gallop	Indian Charlie

*Dancer's Image finished first (in 2:02½), but was disqualified after traces of prohibited medication were found in his system.

Preakness Stakes

For three-year-olds. Held two weeks after the Kentucky Derby at Pimlico Race Course in Baltimore, Md. Inaugurated 1873. Originally run at 1½ miles (1873-88), then at 1¼ miles (1889), 1½ miles (1890), 1¹⁄₁₆ miles (1894-1900), 1 mile & 70 yards (1901-07), 1¹⁄₁₆ miles (1908), 1 mile (1909-1910), 1⅛ miles (1911-24), and the present 1³⁄₁₆ miles since 1925

Trainers with most wins: Robert W. Walden (7); T.J. Healey (5); Sunny Jim Fitzsimmons, Jimmy Jones and D. Wayne Lukas (4); and J. Whalen (3).

Jockeys with most wins: Eddie Arcaro (6); Pat Day (5); G. Barbee, Bill Hartack and Lloyd Hughes (3).

Winning fillies: Flocarline (1903), Whimsical (1906), Rhine Maiden (1915) and Nellie Morse (1924).

Year	Time	Jockey	Trainer	2nd place	3rd place
1873 **Survivor**	2:43	G. Barbee	A.D. Pryor	John Boulger	Artist
1874 **Culpepper**	2:56½	W. Donohue	H. Gaffney	King Amadeus	Scratch
1875 **Tom Ochiltree**	2:43½	L. Hughes	R.W. Walden	Viator	Bay Final
1876 **Shirley**	2:44¾	G. Barbee	W. Brown	Rappahannock	Compliment
1877 **Cloverbrook**	2:45½	C. Holloway	J. Walden	Bombast	Lucifer
1878 **Duke of Magenta**	2:41¾	C. Holloway	R.W. Walden	Bayard	Albert
1879 **Harold**	2:40½	L. Hughes	R.W. Walden	Jericho	Rochester
1880 **Grenada**	2:40½	L. Hughes	R.W. Walden	Oden	Emily F.
1881 **Saunterer**	2:40½	T. Costello	R.W. Walden	Compensation	Baltic
1882 **Vanguard**	2:44½	T. Costello	R.W. Walden	Heck	Col. Watson
1883 **Jacobus**	2:42½	G. Barbee	R. Dwyer	Parnell	(2-horse race)
1884 **Knight of Ellerslie**	2:39½	S. Fisher	T.B. Doswell	Welcher	(2-horse race)
1885 **Tecumseh**	2:49	Jim McLaughlin	C. Littlefield	Wickham	John C.
1886 **The Bard**	2:45	S. Fisher	J. Huggins	Eurus	Elkwood
1887 **Dunboyne**	2:39½	W. Donohue	W. Jennings	Mahoney	Raymond
1888 **Refund**	2:49	F. Littlefield	R.W. Walden	Bertha B.*	Glendale
1889 **Buddhist**	2:17½	W. Anderson	J. Rogers	Japhet	(2-horse race)
1890 **Montague**	2:36¾	W. Martin	E. Feakes	Philosophy	Barrister
1891-93 Not held					
1894 **Assignee**	1:49¼	F. Taral	W. Lakeland	Potentate	Ed Kearney
1895 **Belmar**	1:50½	F. Taral	E. Feakes	April Fool	Sue Kittie
1896 **Margrave**	1:51	H. Griffin	Byron McClelland	Hamilton II	Intermission
1897 **Paul Kauvar**	1:51¼	T. Thorpe	T.P. Hayes	Elkins	On Deck
1898 **Sly Fox**	1:49¾	W. Simms	H. Campbell	The Huguenot	Nuto
1899 **Half Time**	1:47	R. Clawson	F. McCabe	Filigrane	Lackland
1900 **Hindus**	1:48⅖	H. Spencer	J.H. Morris	Sarmatian	Ten Candles
1901 **The Parader**	1:47⅕	F. Landry	T.J. Healey	Sadie S.	Dr. Barlow
1902 **Old England**	1:45⅘	L. Jackson	G.B. Morris	Maj. Daingerfield	Namtor
1903 **Flocarline**	1:44⅘	W. Gannon	H.C. Riddle	Mackey Dwyer	Rightful
1904 **Bryn Mawr**	1:44⅕	E. Hildebrand	W.F. Presgrave	Wotan	Dolly Spanker
1905 **Cairngorm**	1:45⅘	W. Davis	A.J. Joyner	Kiamesha	Coy Maid
1906 **Whimsical**	1:45	Walter Miller	T.J. Gaynor	Content	Larabie
1907 **Don Enrique**	1:45⅖	G. Mountain	J. Whalen	Ethon	Zambesi
1908 **Royal Tourist**	1:46⅖	Eddie Dugan	A.J. Joyner	Live Wire	Robert Cooper
1909 **Effendi**	1:39⅘	Willie Doyle	F.C. Frisbie	Fashion Plate	Hill Top

Year		Time	Jockey	Trainer	2nd place	3rd place
1910	**Layminster**	1:40⅗	R. Estep	J.S. Healy	Dalhousie	Sager
1911	**Watervale**	1:51	Eddie Dugan	J. Whalen	Zeus	The Nigger
1912	**Colonel Holloway**	1:56⅗	C. Turner	D. Woodford	Bwana Tumbo	Tipsand
1913	**Buskin**	1:53⅖	James Butwell	J. Whalen	Kleburne	Barnegat
1914	**Holiday**	1:53⅘	A. Schuttinger	J.S. Healy	Brave Cunarder	Defendum
1915	**Rhine Maiden**	1:58	Douglas Hoffman	F. Devers	Half Rock	Runes
1916	**Damrosch**	1:54⅘	Linus McAtee	A.G. Weston	Greenwood	Achievement
1917	**Kalitan**	1:54⅖	E. Haynes	Bill Hurley	Al M. Dick	Kentucky Boy
1918	**War Cloud**	1:53⅗	Johnny Loftus	W.B. Jennings	Sunny Slope	Lanius
1918	**Jack Hare Jr**	1:53⅖	Charles Peak	F.D. Weir	The Porter	Kate Bright
1919	**SIR BARTON**	1:53	Johnny Loftus	H. Guy Bedwell	Eternal	Sweep On
1920	**Man o' War**	1:51⅗	Clarence Kummer	L. Feustel	Upset	Wildair
1921	**Broomspun**	1:54⅕	F. Coltiletti	James Rowe Sr.	Polly Ann	Jeg
1922	**Pillory**	1:51⅗	L. Morris	Thomas Healey	Hea	June Grass
1923	**Vigil**	1:53⅗	B. Marinelli	Thomas Healey	General Thatcher	Rialto
1924	**Nellie Morse**	1:57⅕	John Merimee	A.B. Gordon	Transmute	Mad Play
1925	**Coventry**	1:59	Clarence Kummer	William Duke	Backbone	Almadel
1926	**Display**	1:59⅘	John Maiben	Thomas Healey	Blondin	Mars
1927	**Bostonian**	2:01⅗	Whitey Abel	Fred Hopkins	Sir Harry	Whiskery
1928	**Victorian**	2:00⅕	Sonny Workman	James Rowe Jr.	Toro	Solace
1929	**Dr. Freeland**	2:01⅗	Louis Schaefer	Thomas Healey	Minotaur	African
1930	**GALLANT FOX**	2:00⅗	Earl Sande	Jim Fitzsimmons	Crack Brigade	Snowflake
1931	**Mate**	1:59	George Ellis	J.W. Healy	Twenty Grand	Ladder
1932	**Burgoo King**	1:59⅘	Eugene James	Dick Thompson	Tick On	Boatswain
1933	**Head Play**	2:02	Charley Kurtsinger	Thomas Hayes	Ladysman	Utopian
1934	**High Quest**	1:58⅕	Robert Jones	Bob Smith	Cavalcade	Discovery
1935	**OMAHA**	1:58⅖	Willie Saunders	Jim Fitzsimmons	Firethorn	Psychic Bid
1936	**Bold Venture**	1:59	George Woolf	Max Hirsch	Granville	Jean Bart
1937	**WAR ADMIRAL**	1:58⅖	Charley Kurtsinger	George Conway	Pompoon	Flying Scot
1938	**Dauber**	1:59⅘	Maurice Peters	Dick Handlen	Cravat	Menow
1939	**Challedon**	1:59⅘	George Seabo	Louis Schaefer	Gilded Knight	Volitant
1940	**Bimelech**	1:58⅗	F.A. Smith	Bill Hurley	Mioland	Gallahadion
1941	**WHIRLAWAY**	1:58⅘	Eddie Arcaro	Ben Jones	King Cole	Our Boots
1942	**Alsab**	1:57	Basil James	Sarge Swenke	Requested & Sun Again (dead heat)	
1943	**COUNT FLEET**	1:57⅖	Johnny Longden	Don Cameron	Blue Swords	Vincentive
1944	**Pensive**	1:59⅕	Conn McCreary	Ben Jones	Platter	Stir Up
1945	**Polynesian**	1:58⅘	W.D. Wright	Morris Dixon	Hoop Jr.	Darby Dieppe
1946	**ASSAULT**	2:01⅖	Warren Mehrtens	Max Hirsch	Lord Boswell	Hampden
1947	**Faultless**	1:59	Doug Dodson	Jimmy Jones	On Trust	Phalanx
1948	**CITATION**	2:02⅖	Eddie Arcaro	Jimmy Jones	Vulcan's Forge	Bovard
1949	**Capot**	1:56	Ted Atkinson	J.M. Gaver	Palestinian	Noble Impulse
1950	**Hill Prince**	1:59⅕	Eddie Arcaro	Casey Hayes	Middleground	Dooly
1951	**Bold**	1:56⅖	Eddie Arcaro	Preston Burch	Counterpoint	Alerted
1952	**Blue Man**	1:57⅖	Conn McCreary	Woody Stephens	Jampol	One Count
1953	**Native Dancer**	1:57⅘	Eric Guerin	Bill Winfrey	Jamie K.	Royal Bay Gem
1954	**Hasty Road**	1:57⅖	Johnny Adams	Harry Trotsek	Correlation	Hasseyampa
1955	**Nashua**	1:54⅗	Eddie Arcaro	Jim Fitzsimmons	Saratoga	Traffic Judge
1956	**Fabius**	1:58⅖	Bill Hartack	Jimmy Jones	Needles	No Regrets
1957	**Bold Ruler**	1:56⅕	Eddie Arcaro	Jim Fitzsimmons	Iron Liege	Inside Tract
1958	**Tim Tam**	1:57⅕	Ismael Valenzuela	Jimmy Jones	Lincoln Road	Gone Fishin'
1959	**Royal Orbit**	1:57	William Harmatz	R. Cornell	Sword Dancer	Dunce
1960	**Bally Ache**	1:57⅗	Bobby Ussery	Jimmy Pitt	Victoria Park	Celtic Ash
1961	**Carry Back**	1:57⅗	Johnny Sellers	Jack Price	Globemaster	Crozier
1962	**Greek Money**	1:56⅕	John Rotz	V.W. Raines	Ridan	Roman Line
1963	**Candy Spots**	1:56⅕	Bill Shoemaker	Mesh Tenney	Chateaugay	Never Bend
1964	**Northern Dancer**	1:56⅘	Bill Hartack	Horatio Luro	The Scoundrel	Hill Rise
1965	**Tom Rolfe**	1:56⅕	Ron Turcotte	Frank Whiteley	Dapper Dan	Hail To All
1966	**Kauai King**	1:55⅖	Don Brumfield	Henry Forrest	Stupendous	Amberoid
1967	**Damascus**	1:55⅕	Bill Shoemaker	Frank Whiteley	In Reality	Proud Clarion
1968	**Forward Pass**	1:56⅘	Ismael Valenzuela	Henry Forrest	Out Of the Way	Nodouble
1969	**Majestic Prince**	1:55⅗	Bill Hartack	Johnny Longden	Arts and Letters	Jay Ray
1970	**Personality**	1:56⅕	Eddie Belmonte	John Jacobs	My Dad George	Silent Screen
1971	**Canonero II**	1:54	Gustavo Avila	Juan Arias	Eastern Fleet	Jim French
1972	**Bee Bee Bee**	1:55⅗	Eldon Nelson	Red Carroll	No Le Hace	Key To The Mint
1973	**SECRETARIAT**	1:54⅖	Ron Turcotte	Lucien Laurin	Sham	Our Native
1974	**Little Current**	1:54⅗	Miguel Rivera	Lou Rondinello	Neapolitan Way	Cannonade
1975	**Master Derby**	1:56⅖	Darrel McHargue	Smiley Adams	Foolish Pleasure	Diabolo
1976	**Elocutionist**	1:55	John Lively	Paul Adwell	Play The Red	Bold Forbes

Preakness Stakes (Cont.)

Year	Time	Jockey	Trainer	2nd place	3rd place
1977 **SEATTLE SLEW**	1:54 2/5	Jean Cruguet	Billy Turner	Iron Constitution	Run Dusty Run
1978 **AFFIRMED**	1:54 2/5	Steve Cauthen	Laz Barrera	Alydar	Believe It
1979 **Spectacular Bid**	1:54 1/5	Ron Franklin	Bud Delp	Golden Act	Screen King
1980 **Codex**	1:54 1/5	Angel Cordero Jr.	D. Wayne Lukas	Genuine Risk	Colonel Moran
1981 **Pleasant Colony**	1:54 3/5	Jorge Velasquez	John Campo	Bold Ego	Paristo
1982 **Aloma's Ruler**	1:55 2/5	Jack Kaenel	John Lenzini Jr.	Linkage	Cut Away
1983 **Deputed Testamony**	1:55 2/5	Donald Miller Jr.	Bill Boniface	Desert Wine	High Honors
1984 **Gate Dancer**	1:53 3/5	Angel Cordero Jr.	Jack Van Berg	Play On	Fight Over
1985 **Tank's Prospect**	1:53 2/5	Pat Day	D. Wayne Lukas	Chief's Crown	Eternal Prince
1986 **Snow Chief**	1:54 4/5	Alex Solis	Melvin Stute	Ferdinand	Broad Brush
1987 **Alysheba**	1:55 4/5	Chris McCarron	Jack Van Berg	Bet Twice	Cryptoclearance
1988 **Risen Star**	1:56 1/5	E. Delahoussaye	Louie Roussel III	Brian's Time	Winning Colors
1989 **Sunday Silence**	1:53 4/5	Pat Valenzuela	Chas. Whittingham	Easy Goer	Rock Point
1990 **Summer Squall**	1:53 3/5	Pat Day	Neil Howard	Unbridled	Mister Frisky
1991 **Hansel**	1:54	Jerry Bailey	Frank Brothers	Corporate Report	Mane Minister
1992 **Pine Bluff**	1:55 3/5	Chris McCarron	Tom Bohannan	Alydeed	Casual Lies
1993 **Prairie Bayou**	1:56 3/5	Mike Smith	Tom Bohannan	Cherokee Run	El Bakan
1994 **Tabasco Cat**	1:56 2/5	Pat Day	D. Wayne Lukas	Go For Gin	Concern
1995 **Timber Country**	1:54 2/5	Pat Day	D. Wayne Lukas	Oliver's Twist	Thunder Gulch
1996 **Louis Quatorze**	1:53 2/5	Pat Day	Nick Zito	Skip Away	Editor's Note
1997 **Silver Charm**	1:54 2/5	Gary Stevens	Bob Baffert	Free House	Captain Bodgit
1998 **Real Quiet**	1:54 4/5	Kent Desormeaux	Bob Baffert	Victory Gallop	Classic Cat

* Later named Judge Murray.

Belmont Stakes

For three-year-olds. Held three weeks after Preakness Stakes at Belmont Park in Elmont, N.Y. Inaugurated in 1867 at Jerome Park, moved to Morris Park in 1890 and Belmont Park in 1905.

Originally run at 1 mile and 5 furlongs (1867-89), then 1 1/4 miles (1890-1905), 1 3/8 miles (1906-25), and the present 1 1/2 miles since 1926.

Trainers with most wins: James Rowe, Sr. (8); Sam Hildreth (7); Sunny Jim Fitzsimmons (6); Woody Stephens (5); Max Hirsch and Robert W. Walden (4); Elliott Burch, Lucien Laurin, D. Wayne Lukas, F. McCabe and D. McDaniel (3).

Jockeys with most wins: Eddie Arcaro and Jim McLaughlin (6); Earl Sande and Bill Shoemaker (5); Braulio Baeza, Laffit Pincay, Jr and James Stout (3).

Winning fillies: Ruthless (1867) and Tanya (1905).

Year	Time	Jockey	Trainer	2nd place	3rd place
1867 **Ruthless**	3:05	J. Gilpatrick	A.J. Minor	DeCourcey	Rivoli
1868 **General Duke**	3:02	Bobby Swim	A. Thompson	Northumberland	Fanny Ludlow
1869 **Fenian**	3:04 1/4	C. Miller	J. Pincus	Glenelg	Invercauld
1870 **Kingfisher**	2:59 1/2	W. Dick	R. Colston	Foster	Midday
1871 **Harry Bassett**	2:56	W. Miller	D. McDaniel	Stockwood	By the Sea
1872 **Joe Daniels**	2:58 1/4	James Roe	D. McDaniel	Meteor	Shylock
1873 **Springbok**	3:01 3/4	James Roe	D. McDaniel	Count d'Orsay	Strachino
1874 **Saxon**	2:39 1/2	G. Barbee	W. Prior	Grinstead	Aaron Pennington
1875 **Calvin**	2:42 1/4	Bobby Swim	A. Williams	Aristides	Milner
1876 **Algerine**	2:40 1/2	Billy Donohue	Major Doswell	Fiddlesticks	Barricade
1877 **Cloverbrook**	2:46	C. Holloway	J. Walden	Loiterer	Baden-Baden
1878 **Duke of Magenta**	2:43 1/2	L. Hughes	R.W. Walden	Bramble	Sparta
1879 **Spendthrift**	2:42 3/4	George Evans	T. Puryear	Monitor	Jericho
1880 **Grenada**	2:47	L. Hughes	R.W. Walden	Ferncliffe	Turenne
1881 **Saunterer**	2:47	T. Costello	R.W. Walden	Eole	Baltic
1882 **Forester**	2:43	Jim McLaughlin	L. Stuart	Babcock	Wyoming
1883 **George Kinney**	2:42 1/2	Jim McLaughlin	James Rowe Sr.	Trombone	Renegade
1884 **Panique**	2:42	Jim McLaughlin	James Rowe Sr.	Knight of Ellerslie	Himalaya
1885 **Tyrant**	2:43	Paul Duffy	W. Claypool	St. Augustine	Tecumseh
1886 **Inspector B**	2:41	Jim McLaughlin	F. McCabe	The Bard	Linden
1887 **Hanover**	2:43 1/2	Jim McLaughlin	F. McCabe	Oneko	(2-horse race)
1888 **Sir Dixon**	2:40 1/4	Jim McLaughlin	F. McCabe	Prince Royal	(2-horse race)
1889 **Eric**	2:47 1/4	W. Hayward	J. Huggins	Diablo	Zephyrus
1890 **Burlington**	2:07 3/4	Pike Barnes	A. Cooper	Devotee	Padishah
1891 **Foxford**	2:08 3/4	Ed Garrison	M. Donavan	Montana	Laurestan
1892 **Patron**	2:12	W. Hayward	L. Stuart	Shellbark	(2-horse race)
1893 **Commanche**	1:53 1/4	Willie Simms	G. Hannon	Dr. Rice	Rainbow
1894 **Henry of Navarre**	1:56 1/2	Willie Simms	B. McClelland	Prig	Assignee
1895 **Belmar**	2:11 1/2	Fred Taral	E. Feakes	Counter Tenor	Nanki Poo
1896 **Hastings**	2:24 1/2	H. Griffin	J.J. Hyland	Handspring	Hamilton II
1897 **Scottish Chieftain**	2:23 1/4	J. Scherrer	M. Byrnes	On Deck	Octagon

Year	Time	Jockey	Trainer	2nd place	3rd place
1898 **Bowling Brook**	2:32	F. Littlefield	R.W. Walden	Previous	Hamburg
1899 **Jean Beraud**	2:23	R. Clawson	Sam Hildreth	Half Time	Glengar
1900 **Ildrim**	2:21¼	Nash Turner	H.E. Leigh	Petruchio	Missionary
1901 **Commando**	2:21	H. Spencer	James Rowe Sr.	The Parader	All Green
1902 **Masterman**	2:22⅗	John Bullman	J.J. Hyland	Renald	King Hanover
1903 **Africander**	2:21¾	John Bullman	R. Miller	Whorler	Red Knight
1904 **Delhi**	2:06⅗	George Odom	James Rowe Sr.	Graziallo	Rapid Water
1905 **Tanya**	2:08	E. Hildebrand	J.W. Rogers	Blandy	Hot Shot
1906 **Burgomaster**	2:20	Lucien Lyne	J.W. Rogers	The Quail	Accountant
1907 **Peter Pan**	N/A	G. Mountain	James Rowe Sr.	Superman	Frank Gill
1908 **Colin**	N/A	Joe Notter	James Rowe Sr.	Fair Play	King James
1909 **Joe Madden**	2:21⅗	E. Dugan	Sam Hildreth	Wise Mason	Donald MacDonald
1910 **Sweep**	2:22	James Butwell	James Rowe Sr.	Duke of Ormonde	(2-horse race)
1911-12 Not held					
1913 **Prince Eugene**	2:18	Roscoe Troxler	James Rowe Sr.	Rock View	Flying Fairy
1914 **Luke McLuke**	2:20	Merritt Buxton	J.F. Schorr	Gainer	Charlestonian
1915 **The Finn**	2:18⅖	George Byrne	E.W. Heffner	Half Rock	Pebbles
1916 **Friar Rock**	2:22	E. Haynes	Sam Hildreth	Spur	Churchill
1917 **Hourless**	2:17⅘	James Butwell	Sam Hildreth	Skeptic	Wonderful
1918 **Johren**	2:20⅖	Frank Robinson	A. Simons	War Cloud	Cum Sah
1919 **SIR BARTON**	2:17⅖	John Loftus	H. Guy Bedwell	Sweep On	Natural Bridge
1920 **Man o' War**	2:14⅕	Clarence Kummer	L. Feustel	Donnacona	(2-horse race)
1921 **Grey Lag**	2:16⅘	Earl Sande	Sam Hildreth	Sporting Blood	Leonardo II
1922 **Pillory**	2:18⅘	C.H. Miller	T.J. Healey	Snob II	Hea
1923 **Zev**	2:19	Earl Sande	Sam Hildreth	Chickvale	Rialto
1924 **Mad Play**	2:18⅘	Earl Sande	Sam Hildreth	Mr. Mutt	Modest
1925 **American Flag**	2:16⅘	Albert Johnson	G.R. Tompkins	Dangerous	Swope
1926 **Crusader**	2:32⅕	Albert Johnson	George Conway	Espino	Haste
1927 **Chance Shot**	2:32⅖	Earl Sande	Pete Coyne	Bois de Rose	Flambino
1928 **Vito**	2:33⅕	Clarence Kummer	Max Hirsch	Genie	Diavolo
1929 **Blue Larkspur**	2:32⅘	Mack Garner	C. Hastings	African	Jack High
1930 **GALLANT FOX**	2:31⅗	Earl Sande	Jim Fitzsimmons	Whichone	Questionnaire
1931 **Twenty Grand**	2:29⅗	Charley Kurtsinger	James Rowe Jr.	Sun Meadow	Jamestown
1932 **Faireno**	2:32⅘	Tom Malley	Jim Fitzsimmons	Osculator	Flag Pole
1933 **Hurryoff**	2:32⅗	Mack Garner	H. McDaniel	Nimbus	Union
1934 **Peace Chance**	2:29⅕	W.D. Wright	Pete Coyne	High Quest	Good Goods
1935 **OMAHA**	2:30⅗	Willie Saunders	Jim Fitzsimmons	Firethorn	Rosemont
1936 **Granville**	2:30	James Stout	Jim Fitzsimmons	Mr. Bones	Hollyrood
1937 **WAR ADMIRAL**	2:28⅗	Charley Kurtsinger	George Conway	Sceneshifter	Vamoose
1938 **Pasteurized**	2:29⅖	James Stout	George Odom	Dauber	Cravat
1939 **Johnstown**	2:29⅗	James Stout	Jim Fitzsimmons	Belay	Gilded Knight
1940 **Bimelech**	2:29⅗	Fred Smith	Bill Hurley	Your Chance	Andy K.
1941 **WHIRLAWAY**	2:31	Eddie Arcaro	Ben Jones	Robert Morris	Yankee Chance
1942 **Shut Out**	2:29⅕	Eddie Arcaro	John Gaver	Alsab	Lochinvar
1943 **COUNT FLEET**	2:28⅕	Johnny Longden	Don Cameron	Fairy Manhurst	Deseronto
1944 **Bounding Home**	2:32⅕	G.L. Smith	Matt Brady	Pensive	Bull Dandy
1945 **Pavot**	2:30⅕	Eddie Arcaro	Oscar White	Wildlife	Jeep
1946 **ASSAULT**	2:30⅘	Warren Mehrtens	Max Hirsch	Natchez	Cable
1947 **Phalanx**	2:29⅖	R. Donoso	Syl Veitch	Tide Rips	Tailspin
1948 **CITATION**	2:28⅕	Eddie Arcaro	Jimmy Jones	Better Self	Escadru
1949 **Capot**	2:30⅕	Ted Atkinson	John Gaver	Ponder	Palestinian
1950 **Middleground**	2:28⅗	William Boland	Max Hirsch	Lights Up	Mr. Trouble
1951 **Counterpoint**	2:29	David Gorman	Syl Veitch	Battlefield	Battle Morn
1952 **One Count**	2:30⅕	Eddie Arcaro	Oscar White	Blue Man	Armageddon
1953 **Native Dancer**	2:28⅗	Eric Guerin	Bill Winfrey	Jamie K.	Royal Bay Gem
1954 **High Gun**	2:30⅘	Eric Guerin	Max Hirsch	Fisherman	Limelight
1955 **Nashua**	2:29	Eddie Arcaro	Jim Fitzsimmons	Blazing Count	Portersville
1956 **Needles**	2:29⅘	David Erb	Hugh Fontaine	Career Boy	Fabius
1957 **Gallant Man**	2:26⅗	Bill Shoemaker	John Nerud	Inside Tract	Bold Ruler
1958 **Cavan**	2:30⅕	Pete Anderson	Tom Barry	Tim Tam	Flamingo
1959 **Sword Dancer**	2:28⅖	Bill Shoemaker	Elliott Burch	Bagdad	Royal Orbit
1960 **Celtic Ash**	2:29⅕	Bill Hartack	Tom Barry	Venetian Way	Disperse
1961 **Sherluck**	2:29⅕	Braulio Baeza	Harold Young	Globemaster	Guadalcanal
1962 **Jaipur**	2:28⅘	Bill Shoemaker	B. Mulholland	Admiral's Voyage	Crimson Satan
1963 **Chateaugay**	2:30⅕	Braulio Baeza	James Conway	Candy Spots	Choker
1964 **Quadrangle**	2:28⅖	Manuel Ycaza	Elliott Burch	Roman Brother	Northern Dancer
1965 **Hail to All**	2:28⅖	John Sellers	Eddie Yowell	Tom Rolfe	First Family
1966 **Amberoid**	2:29⅗	William Boland	Lucien Laurin	Buffle	Advocator

Belmont Stakes (Cont.)

Year	Time	Jockey	Trainer	2nd place	3rd place
1967 **Damascus**	2:28⅘	Bill Shoemaker	F.Y. Whiteley Jr.	Cool Reception	Gentleman James
1968 **Stage Door Johnny**	2:27⅕	Gus Gustines	John Gaver	Forward Pass	Call Me Prince
1969 **Arts and Letters**	2:28⅘	Braulio Baeza	Elliott Burch	Majestic Prince	Dike
1970 **High Echelon**	2:34	John Rotz	John Jacobs	Needles N Pens	Naskra
1971 **Pass Catcher**	2:30⅖	Walter Blum	Eddie Yowell	Jim French	Bold Reason
1972 **Riva Ridge**	2:28	Ron Turcotte	Lucien Laurin	Ruritania	Cloudy Dawn
1973 **SECRETARIAT**	2:24	Ron Turcotte	Lucien Laurin	Twice A Prince	My Gallant
1974 **Little Current**	2:29⅕	Miguel Rivera	Lou Rondinello	Jolly Johu	Cannonade
1975 **Avatar**	2:28⅕	Bill Shoemaker	Tommy Doyle	Foolish Pleasure	Master Derby
1976 **Bold Forbes**	2:29	Angel Cordero Jr.	Laz Barrera	McKenzie Bridge	Great Contractor
1977 **SEATTLE SLEW**	2:29⅗	Jean Cruguet	Billy Turner	Run Dusty Run	Sanhedrin
1978 **AFFIRMED**	2:26⅘	Steve Cauthen	Laz Barrera	Alydar	Darby Creek Road
1979 **Coastal**	2:28⅗	Ruben Hernandez	David Whiteley	Golden Act	Spectacular Bid
1980 **Temperence Hill**	2:29⅘	Eddie Maple	Joseph Cantey	Genuine Risk	Rockhill Native
1981 **Summing**	2:29	George Martens	Luis Barerra	Highland Blade	Pleasant Colony
1982 **Conquistador Cielo**	2:28⅕	Laffit Pincay Jr.	Woody Stephens	Gato Del Sol	Illuminate
1983 **Caveat**	2:27⅘	Laffit Pincay Jr.	Woody Stephens	Slew o' Gold	Barberstown
1984 **Swale**	2:27⅕	Laffit Pincay Jr.	Woody Stephens	Pine Circle	Morning Bob
1985 **Creme Fraiche**	2:27	Eddie Maple	Woody Stephens	Stephan's Odyssey	Chief's Crown
1986 **Danzig Connection**	2:29⅘	Chris McCarron	Woody Stephens	Johns Treasure	Ferdinand
1987 **Bet Twice**	2:28⅕	Craig Perret	Jimmy Croll	Cryptoclearance	Gulch
1988 **Risen Star**	2:26⅖	E. Delahoussaye	Louie Roussel III	Kingpost	Brian's Time
1989 **Easy Goer**	2:26	Pat Day	Shug McGaughey	Sunday Silence	Le Voyageur
1990 **Go And Go**	2:27⅕	Michael Kinane	Dermot Weld	Thirty Six Red	Baron de Vaux
1991 **Hansel**	2:28	Jerry Bailey	Frank Brothers	Strike the Gold	Mane Minister
1992 **A.P. Indy**	2:26	E. Delahoussaye	Neil Drysdale	My Memoirs	Pine Bluff
1993 **Colonial Affair**	2:29⅘	Julie Krone	Scotty Schulhofer	Kissin Kris	Wild Gale
1994 **Tabasco Cat**	2:26⅘	Pat Day	D. Wayne Lukas	Go For Gin	Strodes Creek
1995 **Thunder Gulch**	2:32	Gary Stevens	D. Wayne Lukas	Star Standard	Citadeed
1996 **Editor's Note**	2:28⅘	Rene Douglas	D. Wayne Lukas	Skip Away	My Flag
1997 **Touch Gold**	2:28⅘	Chris McCarron	David Hofmans	Silver Charm	Free House
1998 **Victory Gallop**	2:29	Gary Stevens	Elliott Walden	Real Quiet	Thomas Jo

Breeders' Cup Championship

Inaugurated on Nov. 10, 1984, the Breeders' Cup Championship consists of seven races on one track on one day late in the year to determine thoroughbred racing's principle champions.

The Breeders' Cup has been held at the following tracks (in alphabetical order): Aqueduct Racetrack (N.Y.) in 1985; Belmont Park (N.Y.) in 1990 and '95; Churchill Downs (Ky.) in 1988, '91 and '94; Gulfstream Park (Fla.) in 1989 and '92; Hollywood Park (Calif.) in 1984, '87 and '97; Santa Anita Park (Calif.) in 1986 and '93 and Woodbine (Toronto) in 1996.

Trainers with most wins: D. Wayne Lukas (13); Shug McGaughey (7); Neil Drysdale (5); Ron McAnally and Bill Mott (4); Francois Boutin (3).

Jockeys with most wins: Pat Day (9); Mike Smith (8); Eddie Delahoussaye and Laffit Pincay Jr.(7); Jerry Bailey, Chris McCarron, Jose Santos and Pat Valenzuela (6); Angel Cordero, Craig Perret and Gary Stevens (4); Corey Nakatani and Randy Romero (3).

Juvenile

Distances: one mile (1984-85, 87); 1$\frac{1}{16}$ miles (1986 and since 1988).

Year	Time	Jockey	Trainer	2nd place	3rd place
1984 **Chief's Crown**	1:36⅕	Don MacBeth	Roger Laurin	Tank's Prospect	Spend A Buck
1985 **Tasso**	1:36⅕	Laffit Pincay Jr.	Neil Drysdale	Storm Cat	Scat Dancer
1986 **Capote**	1:43⅘	Laffit Pincay Jr.	D. Wayne Lukas	Qualify	Alysheba
1987 **Success Express**	1:35⅕	Jose Santos	D. Wayne Lukas	Regal Classic	Tejano
1988 **Is It True**	1:46⅗	Laffit Pincay Jr.	D. Wayne Lukas	Easy Goer	Tagel
1989 **Rhythm**	1:43⅗	Craig Perret	Shug McGaughey	Grand Canyon	Slavic
1990 **Fly So Free**	1:43⅖	Jose Santos	Scotty Schulhofer	Take Me Out	Lost Mountain
1991 **Arazi**	1:44⅗	Pat Valenzuela	Francois Boutin	Bertrando	Snappy Landing
1992 **Gilded Time**	1:43⅖	Chris McCarron	Darrell Vienna	It'sali'lknownfact	River Special
1993 **Brocco**	1:42⅘	Gary Stevens	Randy Winick	Blumin Affair	Tabasco Cat
1994 **Timber Country**	1:44⅖	Pat Day	D. Wayne Lukas	Eltish	Tejano Run
1995 **Unbridled's Song**	1:41⅗	Mike Smith	James Ryerson	Hennessy	Editor's Note
1996 **Boston Harbor**	1:43⅖	Jerry Bailey	D. Wayne Lukas	Acceptable	Ordway
1997 **Favorite Trick**	1:41⅖	Pat Day	Patrick Byrne	Dawson's Legacy	Nationalore

Juvenile Fillies

Distances: one mile (1984-85, 87); 1 1/16 miles (1986 and since 1988).

Year	Time	Jockey	Trainer	2nd place	3rd place
1984 **Outstandingly**	1:37 4/5	Walter Guerra	Pancho Martin	Dusty Heart	Fine Spirit
1985 **Twilight Ridge**	1:35 4/5	Jorge Velasquez	D. Wayne Lukas	Family Style	Steal A Kiss
1986 **Brave Raj**	1:43 1/5	Pat Valenzuela	Melvin Stute	Tappiano	Saros Brig
1987 **Epitome**	1:36 2/5	Pat Day	Phil Hauswald	Jeanne Jones	Dream Team
1988 **Open Mind**	1:46 3/5	Angel Cordero Jr.	D. Wayne Lukas	Darby Shuffle	Lea Lucinda
1989 **Go for Wand**	1:44 1/5	Randy Romero	Wm. Badgett, Jr.	Sweet Roberta	Stella Madrid
1990 **Meadow Star**	1:44	Jose Santos	LeRoy Jolley	Private Treasure	Dance Smartly
1991 **Pleasant Stage**	1:46 2/5	Eddie Delahoussaye	Chris Speckert	La Spia	Cadillac Women
1992 **Liza**	1:42 4/5	Pat Valenzuela	Alex Hassingfer	Educated Risk	Boots 'n Jackie
1993 **Phone Chatter**	1:43	Laffit Pincay Jr.	Richard Mandella	Sardula	Heavenly Prize
1994 **Flanders**	1:45 1/5	Pat Day	D. Wayne Lukas	Serena's Song	Stormy Blues
1995 **My Flag**	1:42 2/5	Jerry Bailey	Shug McGaughey	Cara Rafaela	Golden Attraction
1996 **Storm Song**	1:43 3/5	Craig Perret	Nick Zito	Love That Jazz	Critical Factor
1997 **Countess Diana**	1:42	Shane Sellers	Patrick Byrne	Career Collection	Primaly

Note: In 1984, winner Fran's Valentine was disqualified for interference in the stretch and placed 10th.

Sprint

Distance: six furlongs (since 1984).

Year	Time	Jockey	Trainer	2nd place	3rd place
1984 **Eillo**	1:10 1/5	Craig Perret	Budd Lepman	Commemorate	Fighting Fit
1985 **Precisionist**	1:08 2/5	Chris McCarron	L.R. Fenstermaker	Smile	Mt. Livermore
1986 **Smile**	1:08 2/5	Jacinto Vasquez	Scotty Schulhofer	Pine Tree Lane	Bedside Promise
1987 **Very Subtle**	1:08 4/5	Pat Valenzuela	Melvin Stute	Groovy	Exclusive Enough
1988 **Gulch**	1:10 2/5	Angel Cordero Jr.	D. Wayne Lukas	Play The King	Afleet
1989 **Dancing Spree**	1:09	Angel Cordero Jr.	Shug McGaughey	Safely Kept	Dispersal
1990 **Safely Kept**	1:09 3/5	Craig Perret	Alan Goldberg	Dayjur	Black Tie Affair
1991 **Sheikh Albadou**	1:09 1/5	Pat Eddery	Alexander Scott	Pleasant Tap	Robyn Dancer
1992 **Thirty Slews**	1:08 1/5	Eddie Delahoussaye	Bob Baffert	Meafara	Rubiano
1993 **Cardmania**	1:08 3/5	Eddie Delahoussaye	Derek Meredith	Meafara	Gilded Time
1994 **Cherokee Run**	1:09 2/5	Mike Smith	Frank Alexander	Soviet Problem	Cardmania
1995 **Desert Stormer**	1:09	Kent Desormeaux	Frank Lyons	Mr. Greeley	Lit de Justice
1996 **Lit de Justice**	1:08 3/5	Corey Nakatani	Jenine Sahadi	Paying Dues	Honour and Glory
1997 **Elmhurst**	1:08	Corey Nakatani	Jenine Sahadi	Hesabull	Bet On Sunshine

Mile

Year	Time	Jockey	Trainer	2nd place	3rd place
1984 **Royal Heroine**	1:32 3/5	Fernando Toro	John Gosden	Star Choice	Cozzene
1985 **Cozzene**	1:35	Walter Guerra	Jan Nerud	Al Mamoon	Shadeed
1986 **Last Tycoon**	1:35 1/5	Yves St.-Martin	Robert Collet	Palace Music	Fred Astaire
1987 **Miesque**	1:32 4/5	Freddie Head	Francois Boutin	Show Dancer	Sonic Lady
1988 **Miesque**	1:38 3/5	Freddie Head	Francois Boutin	Steinlen	Simply Majestic
1989 **Steinlen**	1:37 1/5	Jose Santos	D. Wayne Lukas	Sabona	Most Welcome
1990 **Royal Academy**	1:35 1/5	Lester Piggott	M.V. O'Brien	Itsallgreektome	Priolo
1991 **Opening Verse**	1:37 2/5	Pat Valenzuela	Dick Lundy	Val des Bois	Star of Cozzene
1992 **Lure**	1:32 4/5	Mike Smith	Shug McGaughey	Paradise Creek	Brief Truce
1993 **Lure**	1:33 2/5	Mike Smith	Shug McGaughey	Ski Paradise	Fourstars Allstar
1994 **Barathea**	1:34 2/5	Frankie Dettori	Luca Cumani	Johann Quatz	Unfinished Symph
1995 **Ridgewood Pearl**	1:43 3/5	John Murtagh	John Oxx	Fastness	Sayyedati
1996 **Da Hoss**	1:35 4/5	Gary Stevens	Michael Dickinson	Spinning World	Same Old Wish
1997 **Spinning World**	1:32 3/5	Cash Asmussen	Jonathan Pease	Geri	Decorated Hero

Note: In 1985, 2nd place finisher Palace Music was disqualified for interference and placed 9th.

Distaff

Distances: 1 1/4 miles (1984-87); 1 1/8 miles (since 1988).

Year	Time	Jockey	Trainer	2nd place	3rd place
1984 **Princess Rooney**	2:02 2/5	Eddie Delahoussaye	Neil Drysdale	Life's Magic	Adored
1985 **Life's Magic**	2:02	Angel Cordero Jr.	D. Wayne Lukas	Lady's Secret	DontstopThemusic
1986 **Lady's Secret**	2:01 1/5	Pat Day	D. Wayne Lukas	Fran's Valentine	Outstandingly
1987 **Sacahuista**	2:02 4/5	Randy Romero	D. Wayne Lukas	Clabber Girl	Oueee Bebe
1988 **Personal Ensign**	1:52	Randy Romero	Shug McGaughey	Winning Colors	Goodbye Halo
1989 **Bayakoa**	1:47 2/5	Laffit Pincay Jr.	Ron McAnally	Gorgeous	Open Mind
1990 **Bayakoa**	1:49 1/5	Laffit Pincay Jr.	Ron McAnally	Colonial Waters	Valay Maid
1991 **Dance Smartly**	1:50 4/5	Pat Day	Jim Day	Versailles Treaty	Brought to Mind
1992 **Paseana**	1:48	Chris McCarron	Ron McAnally	Versailles Treaty	Magical Maiden
1993 **Hollywood Wildcat**	1:48 1/5	Eddie Delahoussaye	Neil Drysdale	Paseana	Re Toss
1994 **One Dreamer**	1:50 3/5	Gary Stevens	Thomas Proctor	Heavenly Prize	Miss Dominique
1995 **Inside Information**	1:46	Mike Smith	Shug McGaughey	Heavenly Prize	Lakeway
1996 **Jewel Princess**	1:48 1/5	Corey Nakatani	Wallace Dollase	Serena's Song	Different
1997 **Ajina**	1:47 1/5	Mike Smith	Bill Mott	Sharp Cat	Escena

Breeders' Cup Championship (Cont.)

Turf

Distance: 1½ miles (since 1984).

Year	Time	Jockey	Trainer	2nd place	3rd place
1984 **Lashkari**	2:25⅕	Yves St.-Martin	de Royer-Dupre	All Along	Raami
1985 **Pebbles**	2:27	Pat Eddery	Clive Brittain	StrawberryRoad II	Mourjane
1986 **Manila**	2:25⅖	Jose Santos	Leroy Jolley	Theatrical	Estrapade
1987 **Theatrical**	2:24⅖	Pat Day	Bill Mott	Trempolino	Village Star II
1988 **Gt. Communicator**	2:35⅕	Ray Sibille	Thad Ackel	Sunshine Forever	Indian Skimmer
1989 **Prized**	2:28	Eddie Delahoussaye	Neil Drysdale	Sierra Roberta	Star Lift
1990 **In The Wings**	2:29⅗	Gary Stevens	Andre Fabre	With Approval	El Senor
1991 **Miss Alleged**	2:30⅘	Eric Legrix	Pascal Bary	Itsallgreektome	Quest for Fame
1992 **Fraise**	2:24	Pat Valenzuela	Bill Mott	Sky Classic	Quest for Fame
1993 **Kotashaan**	2:25	Kent Desormeaux	Richard Mandella	Bien Bien	Luazur
1994 **Tikkanen**	2:26⅖	Mike Smith	Jonathan Pease	Hatoof	Paradise Creek
1995 **Northern Spur**	2:42	Chris McCarron	Ron McAnally	Freedom Cry	Carnegie
1996 **Pilsudski**	2:30⅕	Walter Swinburn	Michael Stoute	Singspiel	Swain
1997 **Chief Bearhart**	2:23⅘	Jose Santos	Mark Frostad	Borgia	Flag Down

Classic

Distance: 1¼ miles (since 1984).

Year	Time	Jockey	Trainer	2nd place	3rd place
1984 **Wild Again**	2:03⅖	Pat Day	Vincent Timphony	Slew o' Gold	Gate Dancer
1985 **Proud Truth**	2:00⅘	Jorge Velasquez	John Veitch	Gate Dancer	Turkoman
1986 **Skywalker**	2:00⅖	Laffit Pincay Jr.	M. Whittingham	Turkoman	Precisionist
1987 **Ferdinand**	2:01⅖	Bill Shoemaker	C. Whittingham	Alysheba	Judge Angelucci
1988 **Alysheba**	2:04⅘	Chris McCarron	Jack Van Berg	Seeking the Gold	Waquoit
1989 **Sunday Silence**	2:00⅕	Chris McCarron	C. Whittingham	Easy Goer	Blushing John
1990 **Unbridled**	2:02⅕	Pat Day	Carl Nafzger	Ibn Bey	Thirty Six Red
1991 **Black Tie Affair**	2:02⅘	Jerry Bailey	Ernie Poulos	Twilight Agenda	Unbridled
1992 **A.P. Indy**	2:00⅕	Eddie Delahoussaye	Neil Drysdale	Pleasant Tap	Jolypha
1993 **Arcangues**	2:00⅘	Jerry Bailey	Andre Fabre	Bertrando	Kissin Kris
1994 **Concern**	2:02⅖	Jerry Bailey	Richard Small	Tabasco Cat	Dramatic Gold
1995 **Cigar**	1:59⅖	Chris McCarron	Ron McAnally	Freedom Cry	Carnegie
1996 **Alphabet Soup**	2:01	Chris McCarron	David Hofmans	Louis Quatorze	Cigar
1997 **Skip Away**	1:59	Mike Smith	Hubert Hine	Deputy Commander	Dowty

Note: In 1984, 2nd place finisher Gate Dancer was disqualified for interference and placed 3rd.

Breeders' Cup Leaders

The all-time money-winning horses and race winning jockeys in the history of the Breeders' Cup through 1997.

Top 10 Horses

		Sts	1–2–3	Earnings
1	Skip Away	1	1–0–0	$2,288,000
2	Alysheba	3	1–1–1	2,133,000
3	Alphabet Soup	1	1–0–0	2,080,000
4	Cigar	2	1–0–1	2,040,000
5	Unbridled	2	1–0–1	1,710,000
6	Black Tie Affair (IRE)	3	1–0–1	1,668,000
7	A.P. Indy	1	1–0–0	1,560,000
	Arcangues	1	1–0–0	1,560,000
	Concern	1	1–0–0	1,560,000
10	Six horses tied.			1,350,000

Top 10 Jockeys

		Sts	1–2–3	Earnings
1	Pat Day	76	9-13-8	$14,411,000
2	Chris McCarron	79	7-11-6	12,500,000
3	Jerry Bailey	44	6-4-5	9,467,000
4	Gary Stevens	63	4-11-8	8,130,680
5	Mike Smith	36	8-3-3	7,860,200
6	Eddie Delahoussaye	58	7-3-5	7,499,000
7	Laffit Pincay, Jr.	60	7-4-9	6,811,000
8	Angel Cordero Jr.	48	4-7-7	6,020,000
9	Jose Santos	41	5-1-4	4,435,000
10	Pat Valenzuela	32	6-0-1	4,202,000

Top 10 Trainers

		Sts	1–2–3	Earnings
1	D. Wayne Lukas	112	13-17-11	$12,656,000
2	Shug McGaughey	39	7-8-1	6,479,000
3	Bill Mott	23	4-4-4	6,430,000
4	Andre Fabre	26	2-4-5	5,384,000
5	Neil Drysdale	16	5-2-0	4,602,000
6	Charlie Whittingham	24	2-2-3	$4,298,000
7	Jack Van Berg	14	1-3-3	3,600,000
8	Ron McAnally	22	4-2-2	3,276,000
9	Scotty Schulhofer	22	2-2-4	2,726,000
10	Bobby Frankel	26	0-4-3	2,463,000

Annual Money Leaders

Horses

Annual money-leading horses since 1910, according to *The American Racing Manual.*

Multiple leaders: Round Table, Buckpasser, Alysheba and Cigar (2).

Year		Age	Sts	1st	Earnings
1910	Novelty	2	16	11	$72,630
1911	Worth	2	13	10	16,645
1912	Star Charter	4	17	6	14,655
1913	Old Rosebud	2	14	12	19,057
1914	Roamer	3	16	12	29,105
1915	Borrow	7	9	4	20,195
1916	Campfire	2	9	6	49,735
1917	Sun Briar	2	9	5	59,505
1918	Eternal	2	8	6	56,173
1919	Sir Barton	3	13	8	88,250
1920	Man o' War	3	11	11	166,140
1921	Morvich	2	11	11	115,234
1922	Pillory	3	7	4	95,654
1923	Zev	3	14	12	272,008
1924	Sarzen	3	12	8	95,640
1925	Pompey	2	10	7	121,630
1926	Crusader	3	15	9	166,033
1927	Anita Peabody	2	7	6	111,905
1928	High Strung	2	6	5	153,590
1929	Blue Larkspur	3	6	4	153,450
1930	Gallant Fox	3	10	9	308,275
1931	Gallant Flight	2	7	7	219,000
1932	Gusto	3	16	4	145,940
1933	Singing Wood	2	9	3	88,050
1934	Cavalcade	3	7	6	111,235
1935	Omaha	3	9	6	142,255
1936	Granville	3	11	7	110,295
1937	Seabiscuit	4	15	11	168,580
1938	Stagehand	3	15	8	189,710
1939	Challedon	3	15	9	184,535
1940	Bimelech	3	7	4	110,005
1941	Whirlaway	3	20	13	272,386
1942	Shut Out	3	12	8	238,872
1943	Count Fleet	3	6	6	174,055
1944	Pavot	2	8	8	179,040
1945	Busher	3	13	10	273,735
1946	Assault	3	15	8	424,195
1947	Armed	6	17	11	376,325
1948	Citation	3	20	19	709,470
1949	Ponder	3	21	9	321,825
1950	Noor	5	12	7	346,940
1951	Counterpoint	3	15	7	250,525
1952	Crafty Admiral	4	16	9	277,225
1953	Native Dancer	3	10	9	513,425
1954	Determine	3	15	10	328,700
1955	Nashua	3	12	10	$752,550
1956	Needles	3	8	4	440,850
1957	Round Table	3	22	15	600,383
1958	Round Table	4	20	14	662,780
1959	Sword Dancer	3	13	8	537,004
1960	Bally Ache	3	15	10	445,045
1961	Carry Back	3	16	9	565,349
1962	Never Bend	2	10	7	402,969
1963	Candy Spots	3	12	7	604,481
1964	Gun Bow	4	16	8	580,100
1965	Buckpasser	2	11	9	568,096
1966	Buckpasser	3	14	13	669,078
1967	Damascus	3	16	12	817,941
1968	Forward Pass	3	13	7	546,674
1969	Arts and Letters	3	14	8	555,604
1970	Personality	3	18	8	444,049
1971	Riva Ridge	2	9	7	503,263
1972	Droll Role	4	19	7	471,633
1973	Secretariat	3	12	9	860,404
1974	Chris Evert	3	8	5	551,063
1975	Foolish Pleasure	3	11	5	716,278
1976	Forego	6	8	6	401,701
1977	Seattle Slew	3	7	6	641,370
1978	Affirmed	3	11	8	901,541
1979	Spectacular Bid	3	12	10	1,279,334
1980	Temperence Hill	3	17	8	1,130,452
1981	John Henry	6	10	8	1,798,030
1982	Perrault (GB)	5	8	4	1,197,400
1983	All Along (FRA)	4	7	4	2,138,963
1984	Slew o' Gold	4	6	5	2,627,944
1985	Spend A Buck	3	7	5	3,552,704
1986	Snow Chief	3	9	6	1,875,200
1987	Alysheba	3	10	3	2,511,156
1988	Alysheba	4	9	7	3,808,600
1989	Sunday Silence	3	9	7	4,578,454
1990	Unbridled	3	11	4	3,718,149
1991	Dance Smartly	3	8	8	2,876,821
1992	A.P. Indy	3	7	5	2,622,560
1993	Kotashaan (FRA)	5	10	6	2,619,014
1994	Paradise Creek	5	11	8	2,610,187
1995	Cigar	5	10	10	4,819,800
1996	Cigar	6	8	5	4,910,000
1997	Skip Away	4	11	4	4,089,000

Jockeys

Annual money-leading jockeys since 1910, according to *The American Racing Manual.*

Multiple leaders: Bill Shoemaker (10); Laffit Pincay Jr. (7); Eddie Arcaro (6); Braulio Baeza (5); Chris McCarron and Jose Santos (4); Jerry Bailey, Angel Cordero Jr. and Earl Sande (3); Ted Atkinson, Laverne Fator, Mack Garner, Bill Hartack, Charles Kurtsinger, Johnny Longden, Mike Smith, Sonny Workman and Wayne Wright (2).

Year		Mts	Wins	Earnings
1910	Carroll Shilling	506	172	$176,030
1911	Ted Koerner	813	162	88,308
1912	Jimmy Butwell	684	144	79,843
1913	Merritt Buxton	887	146	82,552
1914	J. McCahey	824	155	121,845
1915	Mack Garner	775	151	96,628
1916	John McTaggart	832	150	155,055
1917	Frank Robinson	731	147	148,057
1918	Lucien Luke	756	178	201,864
1919	John Loftus	177	65	252,707
1920	Clarence Kummer	353	87	$292,376
1921	Earl Sande	340	112	263,043
1922	Albert Johnson	297	43	345,054
1923	Earl Sande	430	122	569,394
1924	Ivan Parke	844	205	290,395
1925	Laverne Fator	315	81	305,775
1926	Laverne Fator	511	143	361,435
1927	Earl Sande	179	49	277,877
1928	Linus McAtee	235	55	301,295
1929	Mack Garner	274	57	314,975

Year		Mts	Wins	Earnings
1930	Sonny Workman	571	152	$420,438
1931	Charley Kurtsinger	519	93	392,095
1932	Sonny Workman	378	87	385,070
1933	Robert Jones	471	63	226,285
1934	Wayne Wright	919	174	287,185
1935	Silvio Coucci	749	141	319,760
1936	Wayne Wright	670	100	264,000
1937	Charley Kurtsinger	765	120	384,202
1938	Nick Wall	658	97	385,161
1939	Basil James	904	191	353,333
1940	Eddie Arcaro	783	132	343,661
1941	Don Meade	1164	210	398,627
1942	Eddie Arcaro	687	123	481,949
1943	Johnny Longden	871	173	573,276
1944	Ted Atkinson	1539	287	899,101
1945	Johnny Longden	778	180	981,977
1946	Ted Atkinson	1377	233	1,036,825
1947	Douglas Dodson	646	141	1,429,949
1948	Eddie Arcaro	726	188	1,686,230
1949	Steve Brooks	906	209	1,316,817
1950	Eddie Arcaro	888	195	1,410,160
1951	Bill Shoemaker	1161	257	1,329,890
1952	Eddie Arcaro	807	188	1,859,591
1953	Bill Shoemaker	1683	485	1,784,187
1954	Bill Shoemaker	1251	380	1,876,760
1955	Eddie Arcaro	820	158	1,864,796
1956	Bill Hartack	1387	347	2,343,955
1957	Bill Hartack	1238	341	3,060,501
1958	Bill Shoemaker	1133	300	2,961,693
1959	Bill Shoemaker	1285	347	2,843,133
1960	Bill Shoemaker	1227	274	2,123,961
1961	Bill Shoemaker	1256	304	2,690,819
1962	Bill Shoemaker	1126	311	2,916,844
1963	Bill Shoemaker	1203	271	2,526,925
1964	Bill Shoemaker	1056	246	$2,649,553
1965	Braulio Baeza	1245	270	2,582,702
1966	Braulio Baeza	1341	298	2,951,022
1967	Braulio Baeza	1064	256	3,088,888
1968	Braulio Baeza	1089	201	2,835,108
1969	Jorge Velasquez	1442	258	2,542,315
1970	Laffit Pincay Jr.	1328	269	2,626,526
1971	Laffit Pincay Jr.	1627	380	3,784,377
1972	Laffit Pincay Jr.	1388	289	3,225,827
1973	Laffit Pincay Jr.	1444	350	4,093,492
1974	Laffit Pincay Jr.	1278	341	4,251,060
1975	Braulio Baeza	1190	196	3,674,398
1976	Angel Cordero Jr.	1534	274	4,709,500
1977	Steve Cauthen	2075	487	6,151,750
1978	Darrel McHargue	1762	375	6,188,353
1979	Laffit Pincay Jr.	1708	420	8,183,535
1980	Chris McCarron	1964	405	7,666,100
1981	Chris McCarron	1494	326	8,397,604
1982	Angel Cordero Jr.	1838	397	9,702,520
1983	Angel Cordero Jr.	1792	362	10,116,807
1984	Chris McCarron	1565	356	12,038,213
1985	Laffit Pincay Jr.	1409	289	13,415,049
1986	Jose Santos	1636	329	11,329,297
1987	Jose Santos	1639	305	12,407,355
1988	Jose Santos	1867	370	14,877,298
1989	Jose Santos	1459	285	13,847,003
1990	Gary Stevens	1504	283	13,881,198
1991	Chris McCarron	1440	265	14,456,073
1992	Kent Desormeaux	1568	361	14,193,006
1993	Mike Smith	1510	343	14,024,815
1994	Mike Smith	1484	317	15,979,820
1995	Jerry Bailey	1367	287	16,311,876
1996	Jerry Bailey	1187	298	19,465,376
1997	Jerry Bailey	1136	269	18,206,013

Trainers

Annual money-leading trainers since 1908, according to *The American Racing Manual.*

Multiple Leaders: D. Wayne Lukas (14); Sam Hildreth (9); Charlie Whittingham (7); Sunny Jim Fitzsimmons and Jimmy Jones (5); Laz Barrera, Ben Jones and Willie Molter (4); Hirsch Jacobs, Eddie Neloy and James Rowe Sr. (3); H. Guy Bedwell, Jack Gaver, John Schorr, Humming Bob Smith, Silent Tom Smith and Mesh Tenney (2).

Year		Wins	Earnings
1908	James Rowe Sr.	50	$284,335
1909	Sam Hildreth	73	123,942
1910	Sam Hildreth	84	148,010
1911	Sam Hildreth	67	49,418
1912	John Schorr	63	58,110
1913	James Rowe Sr.	18	45,936
1914	R.C. Benson	45	59,315
1915	James Rowe Sr.	19	75,596
1916	Sam Hildreth	39	70,950
1917	Sam Hildreth	23	61,698
1918	H. Guy Bedwell	53	80,296
1919	H. Guy Bedwell	63	208,728
1920	Louis Feustel	22	186,087
1921	Sam Hildreth	85	262,768
1922	Sam Hildreth	74	247,014
1923	Sam Hildreth	75	392,124
1924	Sam Hildreth	77	255,608
1925	G.R. Tompkins	30	199,245
1926	Scott Harlan	21	205,681
1927	W.H. Bringloe	63	216,563
1928	John Schorr	65	258,425
1929	James Rowe Jr.	25	314,881
1930	Sunny Jim Fitzsimmons	47	397,355
1931	Big Jim Healy	33	297,300
1932	Sunny Jim Fitzsimmons	68	266,650
1933	Humming Bob Smith	53	135,720
1934	Humming Bob Smith	43	$249,938
1935	Bud Stotler	87	303,005
1936	Sunny Jim Fitzsimmons	42	193,415
1937	Robert McGarvey	46	209,925
1938	Earl Sande	15	226,495
1939	Sunny Jim Fitzsimmons	45	266,205
1940	Silent Tom Smith	14	269,200
1941	Ben Jones	70	475,318
1942	Jack Gaver	48	406,547
1943	Ben Jones	73	267,915
1944	Ben Jones	60	601,660
1945	Silent Tom Smith	52	510,655
1946	Hirsch Jacobs	99	560,077
1947	Jimmy Jones	85	1,334,805
1948	Jimmy Jones	81	1,118,670
1949	Jimmy Jones	76	978,587
1950	Preston Burch	96	637,754
1951	Jack Gaver	42	616,392
1952	Ben Jones	29	662,137
1953	Harry Trotsek	54	1,028,873
1954	Willie Molter	136	1,107,860
1955	Sunny Jim Fitzsimmons	66	1,270,055
1956	Willie Molter	142	1,227,402
1957	Jimmy Jones	70	1,150,910
1958	Willie Molter	69	1,116,544
1959	Willie Molter	71	847,290

Year		Wins	Earnings
1960	Hirsch Jacobs	97	$748,349
1961	Jimmy Jones	62	759,856
1962	Mesh Tenney	58	1,099,474

Year		Sts	Wins	Earnings
1963	Mesh Tenney	192	40	$860,703
1964	Bill Winfrey	287	61	1,350,534
1965	Hirsch Jacobs	610	91	1,331,628
1966	Eddie Neloy	282	93	2,456,250
1967	Eddie Neloy	262	72	1,776,089
1968	Eddie Neloy	212	52	1,233,101
1969	Elliott Burch	156	26	1,067,936
1970	Charlie Whittingham	551	82	1,302,354
1971	Charlie Whittingham	393	77	1,737,115
1972	Charlie Whittingham	429	79	1,734,020
1973	Charlie Whittingham	423	85	1,865,385
1974	Pancho Martin	846	166	2,408,419
1975	Charlie Whittingham	487	3	2,437,244
1976	Jack Van Berg	2362	496	2,976,196
1977	Laz Barrera	781	127	2,715,848
1978	Laz Barrera	592	100	$3,307,164
1979	Laz Barrera	492	98	3,608,517
1980	Laz Barrera	559	99	2,969,151
1981	Charlie Whittingham	376	74	3,993,302
1982	Charlie Whittingham	410	63	4,587,457
1983	D. Wayne Lukas	595	78	4,267,261
1984	D. Wayne Lukas	805	131	5,835,921
1985	D. Wayne Lukas	1140	218	11,155,188
1986	D. Wayne Lukas	1510	259	12,345,180
1987	D. Wayne Lukas	1735	343	17,502,110
1988	D. Wayne Lukas	1500	318	17,842,358
1989	D. Wayne Lukas	1398	305	16,103,998
1990	D. Wayne Lukas	1396	267	14,508,871
1991	D. Wayne Lukas	1497	289	15,942,223
1992	D. Wayne Lukas	1349	230	9,806,436
1993	Bobby Frankel	345	79	8,933,252
1994	D. Wayne Lukas	693	147	9,247,457
1995	D. Wayne Lukas	837	194	12,834,483
1996	D. Wayne Lukas	1006	192	15,966,344
1997	D. Wayne Lukas	824	169	9,993,569

All-Time Leaders

The all-time money-winning horses and race-winning jockeys of North America through 1997, according to *Thoroughbred Racing Communications, Inc.* Records include all available information on races in foreign countries.

Top 35 Horses — Money Won

Note that horses who raced in 1997 are in **bold** type.

		Sts	1st	2nd	3rd	Earnings
1	Cigar	33	19	4	5	$9,999,815
2	**Skip Away**	29	11	10	5	6,876,360
3	Alysheba	26	11	8	2	6,679,242
4	John Henry	83	39	15	9	6,597,947
5	Singspiel	20	9	8	0	5,950,217
6	Best Pal	47	18	11	4	5,668,245
7	Taiki Blizzard	22	6	8	2	5,544,484
8	Sunday Silence	14	9	5	0	4,968,554
9	Easy Goer	20	14	5	1	4,873,770
10	Unbridled	24	8	6	6	4,489,475
11	**Pilsudski**	22	10	6	2	4,389,167
12	Spend A Buck	15	10	3	2	4,220,689
13	Creme Fraiche	64	17	12	13	4,024,727
14	Devil His Due	41	11	12	3	3,920,405
15	**Sandpit**	40	14	11	6	3,802,971
16	Ferdinand	29	8	9	6	3,777,978
17	Slew o' Gold	21	12	5	1	3,533,534
18	Precisionist	46	20	10	4	3,485,398
19	Lando	23	10	2	1	3,484,413
20	Strike the Gold	31	6	8	5	3,457,026
21	Paradise Creek	25	14	7	1	3,386,925
22	Snow Chief	24	13	3	5	3,383,210
23	Cryptoclearance	44	12	10	7	3,376,327
24	Black Tie Affair	45	18	9	6	3,370,694
25	Bet Twice	26	10	6	4	3,308,599
26	Steinlen	45	20	10	7	3,300,100
27	Serena's Song (f)	38	18	11	3	3,283,388
28	**Awad**	69	14	10	11	3,270,818
29	Dance Smartly (f)	17	12	2	3	3,263,836
30	Sky Classic	29	15	6	1	3,240,398
31	Bertrando	24	9	6	2	3,185,610
32	Paseana (f)	36	19	10	2	3,171,203
33	**Siphon**	25	12	6	2	3,158,619
34	Gulch	32	13	8	4	3,095,521
35	Concern	30	7	7	11	3,079,350

Top 35 Jockeys — Races Won

Note that jockeys active in 1997 are in **bold** type.

		Yrs	Wins	Earnings
1	Bill Shoemaker	42	8833	$123,375,524
2	**Laffit Pincay Jr.**	32	8497	194,212,231
3	**Pat Day**	25	7087	188,681,842
4	Angel Cordero Jr.	35	7057	164,561,227
5	David Gall	40	6997	22,791,959
6	**Jorge Velasquez**	33	6795	125,544,379
7	**Chris McCarron**	24	6558	213,851,293
8	**Sandy Hawley**	30	6442	88,463,806
9	Larry Snyder	35	6388	47,207,289
10	Carl Gambardella	39	6349	29,389,041
11	**Russell Baze**	24	6032	83,260,899
	John Longden	41	6032	24,665,800
13	**Earlie Fires**	33	5967	72,328,911
14	**E. Delahoussaye**	30	5867	163,300,374
15	Jacinto Vasquez	37	5231	80,764,853
16	Eddie Arcaro	31	4779	30,039,543
17	**Ron Ardoin**	25	4622	47,155,648
18	Don Brumfield	37	4573	43,567,861
19	Steve Brooks	34	4451	18,239,817
20	Walter Blum	22	4382	26,497,189
21	**Eddie Maple**	33	4367	104,447,663
22	Bill Hartack	22	4272	26,466,758
23	**Gary Stevens**	19	4268	161,563,531
24	**Craig Perret**	31	4178	98,158,663
25	**Jerry Bailey**	24	4172	151,262,458
26	**Randy Romero**	24	4166	72,300,187
27	Rodolfo Baez	23	4114	24,291,396
28	Avelino Gomez	34	4081	11,777,297
29	**Rick Wilson**	25	4043	52,598,363
30	Hugo Dittfach	33	4000	13,506,052
31	Phil Grove	30	3990	16,500,859
32	Jeffrey Lloyd	22	3888	28,824,382
33	Ted Atkinson	22	3795	17,449,360
34	David Whited	36	3784	25,067,466
35	Ralph Neves	21	3772	13,786,239

Eclipse Awards

The Eclipse Awards, honoring the Horse of the Year and other champions of the sport, are sponsored by the *Daily Racing Form*, the Thoroughbred Racing Associations and the National Turf Writers Assn.

The awards are named after the 18th century racehorse and sire, Eclipse, who began racing at age five and was unbeaten in 18 starts (eight wins were walkovers). As a stallion, Eclipse sired winners of 344 races, including three Epsom Derby champions.

Horses listed in CAPITAL letters won the Triple Crown that year. Age of horse in parentheses where necessary.

Multiple winners: (horses): Forego (8); John Henry (7); Affirmed and Secretariat (5); Cigar, Flatterer, Lonesome Glory, Seattle Slew and Spectacular Bid (4); Ack Ack, Susan's Girl and Zaccio (3); All Along, Alysheba, Bayakoa, Black Tie Affair, Cafe Prince, Conquistador Cielo, Desert Vixen, Favorite Trick, Ferdinand, Flawlessly, Go for Wand, Holy Bull, Housebuster, Kotashaan, Lady's Secret, Life's Magic, Miesque, Morley Street, Open Mind, Paseana, Riva Ridge, Skip Away, Slew o'Gold and Spend A Buck (2).

Multiple winners: (people): Laffit Pincay Jr. (5); Laz Barrera, Pat Day, John Franks and D. Wayne Lukas (4); Jerry Bailey, Steve Cauthen, Pat Day, Harbor View Farm, Fred W. Hooper, Nelson Bunker Hunt, Mr. & Mrs. Gene Klein, Dan Lasater, Ogden Phipps, Bill Shoemaker, Edward Taylor and Charlie Whittingham (3); Braulio Baeza, C.T. Chenery, Claiborne Farm, Angel Cordero Jr., Kent Desormeaux, John W. Galbreath, John & Betty Mabee, Chris McCarron, Paul Mellon, Bill Mott, Allen Paulson and Mike Smith (2).

Horse of the Year

Year		Year		Year		Year	
1971	Ack Ack (5)	1978	AFFIRMED (3)	1985	Spend A Buck (3)	1992	A.P. Indy (3)
1972	SECRETARIAT (2)	1979	Affirmed (4)	1986	Lady's Secret (4)	1993	Kotashaan (5)
1973	SECRETARIAT (3)	1980	Spectacular Bid (4)	1987	Ferdinand (4)	1994	Holy Bull (3)
1974	Forego (4)	1981	John Henry (6)	1988	Alysheba (4)	1995	Cigar (5)
1975	Forego (5)	1982	Conquistador Cielo (3)	1989	Sunday Silence (3)	1996	Cigar (6)
1976	Forego (6)	1983	All Along (4)	1990	Criminal Type (5)	1997	Favorite Trick (2)
1977	SEATTLE SLEW (3)	1984	John Henry (9)	1991	Black Tie Affair (5)		

Older Male

Year		Year		Year		Year	
1971	Ack Ack (5)	1978	Seattle Slew (4)	1985	Vanlandingham (4)	1992	Pleasant Tap (5)
1972	Autobiography (4)	1979	Affirmed (4)	1986	Turkoman (4)	1993	Bertrando (4)
1973	Riva Ridge (4)	1980	Spectacular Bid (4)	1987	Ferdinand (4)	1994	The Wicked North (4)
1974	Forego (4)	1981	John Henry (6)	1988	Alysheba (4)	1995	Cigar (5)
1975	Forego (5)	1982	Lemhi Gold (4)	1989	Blushing John (4)	1996	Cigar (6)
1976	Forego (6)	1983	Bates Motel (4)	1990	Criminal Type (5)	1997	Skip Away (4)
1977	Forego (7)	1984	Slew o' Gold (4)	1991	Black Tie Affair (5)		

Older Filly or Mare

Year		Year		Year		Year	
1971	Shuvee (5)	1978	Late Bloomer (4)	1985	Life's Magic (4)	1992	Paseana (5)
1972	Typecast (6)	1979	Waya (5)	1986	Lady's Secret (4)	1993	Paseana (6)
1973	Susan's Girl (4)	1980	Glorious Song (4)	1987	North Sider (5)	1994	Sky Beauty (4)
1974	Desert Vixen (4)	1981	Relaxing (5)	1988	Personal Ensign (4)	1995	Inside Information (4)
1975	Susan's Girl (6)	1982	Track Robbery (6)	1989	Bayakoa (5)	1996	Jewel Princess (4)
1976	Proud Delta (4)	1983	Amb. of Luck (4)	1990	Bayakoa (6)	1997	Hidden Lake (4)
1977	Cascapedia (4)	1984	Princess Rooney (4)	1991	Queena (5)		

Horse of the Year (1936-70)

In 1971, the *Daily Racing Form*, the Thoroughbred Racing Associations, and the National Turf Writers Assn. joined forces to create the Eclipse Awards. Before then, however, the *Racing Form* (1936-70) and the TRA (1950-70) issued separate selections for Horse of the Year. Their picks differed only four times from 1950-70 and are so noted. Horses listed in CAPITAL letters are Triple Crown winners; (f) indicates female.

Multiple winners: Kelso (5); Challedon, Native Dancer and Whirlaway (2).

Year		Year		Year		Year	
1936	Granville	1946	ASSAULT	1955	Nashua	1964	Kelso
1937	WAR ADMIRAL	1947	Armed	1956	Swaps	1965	Roman Brother (DRF)
1938	Seabiscuit	1948	CITATION	1957	Bold Ruler (DRF)		Moccasin (TRA)
1939	Challedon	1949	Capot		Dedicate (TRA)	1966	Buckpasser
1940	Challedon	1950	Hill Prince	1958	Round Table	1967	Damascus
1941	WHIRLAWAY	1951	Counterpoint	1959	Sword Dancer	1968	Dr. Fager
1942	Whirlaway	1952	One Count (DRF)	1960	Kelso	1969	Arts and Letters
1943	COUNT FLEET		Native Dancer (TRA)	1961	Kelso	1970	Fort Marcy (DRF)
1944	Twilight Tear (f)	1953	Tom Fool	1962	Kelso		Personality (TRA)
1945	Busher (f)	1954	Native Dancer	1963	Kelso		

3-Year-Old Colt or Gelding

Year		Year		Year		Year	
1971	Canonero II	1978	AFFIRMED	1985	Spend A Buck	1992	A.P. Indy
1972	Key to the Mint	1979	Spectacular Bid	1986	Snow Chief	1993	Prairie Bayou
1973	SECRETARIAT	1980	Temperence Hill	1987	Alysheba	1994	Holy Bull
1974	Little Current	1981	Pleasant Colony	1988	Risen Star	1995	Thunder Gulch
1975	Wajima	1982	Conquistador Cielo	1989	Sunday Silence	1996	Skip Away
1976	Bold Forbes	1983	Slew o' Gold	1990	Unbridled	1997	Silver Charm
1977	SEATTLE SLEW	1984	Swale	1991	Hansel		

3-Year-Old Filly

Year		Year		Year		Year	
1971	Turkish Trousers	1978	Tempest Queen	1985	Mom's Command	1992	Saratoga Slew
1972	Susan's Girl	1979	Davona Dale	1986	Tiffany Lass	1993	Hollywood Wildcat
1973	Desert Vixen	1980	Genuine Risk	1987	Sacahuista	1994	Heavenly Prize
1974	Chris Evert	1981	Wayward Lass	1988	Winning Colors	1995	Serena's Song
1975	Ruffian	1982	Christmas Past	1989	Open Mind	1996	Yanks Music
1976	Revidere	1983	Heartlight No. One	1990	Go for Wand	1997	Ajina
1977	Our Mims	1984	Life's Magic	1991	Dance Smartly		

2-Year-Old Colt or Gelding

Year		Year		Year		Year	
1971	Riva Ridge	1978	Spectacular Bid	1985	Tasso	1992	Gilded Time
1972	Secretariat	1979	Rockhill Native	1986	Capote	1993	Dehere
1973	Protagonist	1980	Lord Avie	1987	Forty Niner	1994	Timber Country
1974	Foolish Pleasure	1981	Deputy Minister	1988	Easy Goer	1995	Maria's Mon
1975	Honest Pleasure	1982	Roving Boy	1989	Rhythm	1996	Boston Harbor
1976	Seattle Slew	1983	Devil's Bag	1990	Fly So Free	1997	Favorite Trick
1977	Affirmed	1984	Chief's Crown	1991	Arazi		

2-Year-Old Filly

Year		Year		Year		Year	
1971	Numbered Account	1978	(tie) Candy Eclair	1984	Outstandingly	1991	Pleasant Stage
1972	La Prevoyante		& It's in the Air	1985	Family Style	1992	Eliza
1973	Talking Picture	1979	Smart Angle	1986	Brave Raj	1993	Phone Chatter
1974	Ruffian	1980	Heavenly Cause	1987	Epitome	1994	Flanders
1975	Dearly Precious	1981	Before Dawn	1988	Open Mind	1995	Golden Attraction
1976	Sensational	1982	Landaluce	1989	Go for Wand	1996	Storm Song
1977	Lakeville Miss	1983	Althea	1990	Meadow Star	1997	Countess Diana

Champion Turf Horse

Year		Year		Year		Year	
1971	Run the Gantlet (3)	1973	SECRETARIAT (3)	1975	Snow Knight (4)	1977	Johnny D (3)
1972	Cougar II (6)	1974	Dahlia (4)	1976	Youth (3)	1978	Mac Diarmida (3)

Champion Male Turf Horse

Year		Year		Year		Year	
1979	Bowl Game (5)	1984	John Henry (9)	1989	Steinlen (6)	1994	Paradise Creek (5)
1980	John Henry (5)	1985	Cozzene (4)	1990	Itsallgreektome (3)	1995	Northern Spur (4)
1981	John Henry (6)	1986	Manila (3)	1991	Tight Spot (4)	1996	Singspiel (4)
1982	Perrault (5)	1987	Theatrical (5)	1992	Sky Classic (5)	1997	Chief Bearhart (4)
1983	John Henry (8)	1988	Sunshine Forever (3)	1993	Kotashaan (5)		

Champion Female Turf Horse

Year		Year		Year		Year	
1979	Trillion (5)	1984	Royal Heroine (4)	1989	Brown Bess (7)	1994	Hatoof (5)
1980	Just A Game II (4)	1985	Pebbles (4)	1990	Laugh and Be Merry (5)	1995	Possibly Perfect (5)
1981	De La Rose (3)	1986	Estrapade (6)	1991	Miss Alleged (4)	1996	Wandesta (5)
1982	April Run (4)	1987	Miesque (3)	1992	Flawlessly (4)	1997	Ryafan (3)
1983	All Along (4)	1988	Miesque (4)	1993	Flawlessly (5)		

Eclipse Awards (Cont.)

Sprinter

Year		Year		Year		Year	
1971	Ack Ack (5)	1978	(tie) Dr. Patches (4) & J.O. Tobin (4)	1984	Eillo (4)	1991	Housebuster (4)
1972	Chou Croute (4)			1985	Precisionist (4)	1992	Rubiano (5)
1973	Shecky Greene (3)	1979	Star de Naskra (4)	1986	Smile (4)	1993	Cardmania (7)
1974	Forego (4)	1980	Plugged Nickle (3)	1987	Groovy (4)	1994	Cherokee Run (4)
1975	Gallant Bob (3)	1981	Guilty Conscience (5)	1988	Gulch (4)	1995	Not Surprising (4)
1976	My Juliet (4)	1982	Gold Beauty (3)	1989	Safely Kept (3)	1996	Lit de Justice (6)
1977	What a Summer (4)	1983	Chinook Pass (4)	1990	Housebuster (3)	1997	Smoke Glacken (3)

Steeplechase or Hurdle Horse

Year		Year		Year		Year	
1971	Shadow Brook (7)	1978	Cafe Prince (8)	1985	Flatterer (6)	1992	Lonesome Glory (4)
1972	Soothsayer (5)	1979	Martie's Anger (4)	1986	Flatterer (7)	1993	Lonesome Glory (5)
1973	Athenian Idol (5)	1980	Zaccio (4)	1987	Inlander (6)	1994	Warm Spell (6)
1974	Gran Kan (8)	1981	Zaccio (5)	1988	Jimmy Lorenzo (6)	1995	Lonesome Glory (7)
1975	Life's Illusion (4)	1982	Zaccio (6)	1989	Highland Bud (4)	1996	Correggio (5)
1976	Straight and True (6)	1983	Flatterer (4)	1990	Morley Street (6)	1997	Lonesome Glory (10)
1977	Cafe Prince (7)	1984	Flatterer (5)	1991	Morley Street (7)		

Outstanding Jockey

Year		Year		Year		Year	
1971	Laffit Pincay Jr.	1978	Darrel McHargue	1985	Laffit Pincay Jr.	1992	Kent Desormeaux
1972	Braulio Baeza	1979	Laffit Pincay Jr.	1986	Pat Day	1993	Mike Smith
1973	Laffit Pincay Jr.	1980	Chris McCarron	1987	Pat Day	1994	Mike Smith
1974	Laffit Pincay Jr.	1981	Bill Shoemaker	1988	Jose Santos	1995	Jerry Bailey
1975	Braulio Baeza	1982	Angel Cordero Jr.	1989	Kent Desormeaux	1996	Jerry Bailey
1976	Sandy Hawley	1983	Angel Cordero Jr.	1990	Craig Perret	1997	Jerry Bailey
1977	Steve Cauthen	1984	Pat Day	1991	Pat Day		

Outstanding Apprentice Jockey

Year		Year		Year		Year	
1971	Gene St. Leon	1978	Ron Franklin	1985	Art Madrid Jr.	1992	Rosemary Homeister
1972	Thomas Wallis	1979	Cash Asmussen	1986	Allen Stacy	1993	Juan Umana
1973	Steve Valdez	1980	Frank Lovato Jr.	1987	Kent Desormeaux	1994	Dale Beckner
1974	Chris McCarron	1981	Richard Migliore	1988	Steve Capanas	1995	Ramon B. Perez
1975	Jimmy Edwards	1982	Alberto Delgado	1989	Michael Luzzi	1996	Neil Poznansky
1976	George Martens	1983	Declan Murphy	1990	Mark Johnston	1997	Roberto Rosado & Philip Teator
1977	Steve Cauthen	1984	Wesley Ward	1991	Mickey Walls		

Outstanding Trainer

Year		Year		Year		Year	
1971	Charlie Whittingham	1978	Laz Barrera	1985	D. Wayne Lukas	1992	Ron McAnally
1972	Lucien Laurin	1979	Laz Barrera	1986	D. Wayne Lukas	1993	Bobby Frankel
1973	H. Allen Jerkens	1980	Bud Delp	1987	D. Wayne Lukas	1994	D. Wayne Lukas
1974	Sherill Ward	1981	Ron McAnally	1988	Shug McGaughey	1995	Bill Mott
1975	Steve DiMauro	1982	Charlie Whittingham	1989	Charlie Whittingham	1996	Bill Mott
1976	Laz Barrera	1983	Woody Stephens	1990	Carl Nafzger	1997	Bob Baffert
1977	Laz Barrera	1984	Jack Van Berg	1991	Ron McAnally		

Outstanding Owner

Year		Year		Year		Year	
1971	Mr. & Mrs. E.E. Fogleson	1979	Harbor View Farm	1986	Mr. & Mrs. Gene Klein	1994	John Franks
1972-73	No award	1980	Mr. & Mrs. Bertram Firestone	1987	Mr. & Mrs. Gene Klein	1995	Allen Paulson
1974	Dan Lasater	1981	Dotsam Stable	1988	Ogden Phipps	1996	Allen Paulson
1975	Dan Lasater	1982	Viola Sommer	1989	Ogden Phipps	1997	Carolyn Hine
1976	Dan Lasater	1983	John Franks	1990	Frances Genter		
1977	Maxwell Gluck	1984	John Franks	1991	Sam-Son Farms		
1978	Harbor View Farm	1985	Mr. & Mrs. Gene Klein	1992	Juddmonte Farms		
				1993	John Franks		

Outstanding Breeder

Year		Year		Year		Year	
1971	Paul Mellon	1978	Harbor View Farm	1985	Nelson Bunker Hunt	1992	William S. Farish
1972	C.T. Chenery	1979	Claiborne Farm	1986	Paul Mellon	1993	Allan Paulson
1973	C.T. Chenery	1980	Mrs. Henry Paxson	1987	Nelson Bunker Hunt	1994	William T. Young
1974	John W. Galbreath	1981	Golden Chance Farm	1988	Ogden Phipps	1995	Juddmonte Farms
1975	Fred W. Hooper	1982	Fred W. Hooper	1989	North Ridge Farm	1996	Farnsworth Farms
1976	Nelson Bunker Hunt	1983	Edward P. Taylor	1990	Calumet Farm	1997	Mr. & Mrs. John Mabee
1977	Edward P. Taylor	1984	Claiborne Farm	1991	Mr. & Mrs. John Mabee		

Outstanding Achievement

Year		Year	
1971	Charles Engelhard*	1972	Arthur B. Hancock Jr.*

*Awarded posthumously.

Man of the Year

Year		Year	
1972	John W. Galbreath	1974	William L. McKnight
1973	Edward P. Taylor	1975	John A. Morris

Award of Merit

Year		Year		Year		Year	
1976	Jack J. Dreyfus	1981	Bill Shoemaker	1988	John Forsythe	1992	Joe Hirsch & Robert P. Strub
1977	Steve Cauthen	1984	John Gaines	1989	Michael Sandler	1995	James E. Bassett III
1978	Dinny Phipps	1985	Keene Daingerfield	1990	Warner L. Jones	1997	Robert & Beverly Lewis
1979	Jimmy Kilroe	1986	Herman Cohen	1991	Fred W. Hooper		
1980	John D. Shapiro	1987	J.B. Faulconer				

Special Award

Year		Year		Year		Year	
1971	Robert J. Kleberg	1980	John T. Landry & Pierre E. Bellocq	1985	Arlington Park	1989	Richard Duchossois
1974	Charles Hatton	1984	C.V. Whitney	1987	Anheuser-Busch	1995	Russell Baze
1976	Bill Shoemaker			1988	Edward J. DeBartolo Sr.		

HARNESS RACING

Triple Crown Winners

PACERS

Eight 3-year-olds have won the Cane Pace, Little Brown Jug and Messenger Stakes in the same year since the Pacing Triple Crown was established in 1956. No trainer or driver has won it more than once. This chapter was closed before the Oct. 16, 1998 running of the Messenger Stakes where a victory by Shady Character would give him the Triple Crown. See the updates section for results.

Year		Driver	Trainer	Owner
1959	**Adios Butler**	Clint Hodgins	Paige West	Paige West & Angelo Pellillo
1965	**Bret Hanover**	Frank Ervin	Frank Ervin	Richard Downing
1966	**Romeo Hanover**	Bill Myer & George Sholty*	Jerry Silverman	Lucky Star Stables & Morton Finder
1968	**Rum Customer**	Billy Haughton	Billy Haughton	Kennilworth Farms & L.C. Mancuso
1970	**Most Happy Fella**	Stanley Dancer	Stanley Dancer	Egyptian Acres Stable
1980	**Niatross**	Clint Galbraith	Clint Galbraith	Niagara Acres, Niatross Stables & Clint Galbraith
1983	**Ralph Hanover**	Ron Waples	Stew Firlotte	Waples Stable, Pointsetta Stable, Grant's Direct Stable & P.J. Baugh
1997	**Western Dreamer**	Mike Lachance	Bill Robinson Stable	Matthew, Daniel and Patrick Daly

*Myer drove Romeo Hanover in the Cane, Sholty in the other two races.

TROTTERS

Six 3-year-olds have won the Yonkers Trot, Hambletonian and Kentucky Futurity in the same year since the Trotting Triple Crown was established in 1955. Stanley Dancer is the only driver/trainer to win it twice.

Year		Driver/Trainer	Owner
1955	**Scott Frost**	Joe O'Brien	S.A. Camp Farms
1963	**Speedy Scot**	Ralph Baldwin	Castleton Farms
1964	**Ayres**	John Simpson Sr.	Charlotte Sheppard
1968	**Nevele Pride**	Stanley Dancer	Nevele Acres & Lou Resnick
1969	**Lindy's Pride**	Howard Beissinger	Lindy Farms
1972	**Super Bowl**	Stanley Dancer	Rachel Dancer & Rose Hild Breeding Farm

Triple Crown Near Misses

PACERS

Seven horses have won the first two legs of the Triple Crown, but not the third. The Cane Pace (CP), Little Brown Jug (LBJ), and Messenger Stakes (MS) have not always been run in the same order so numbers after races won indicate sequence for that year.

Year		CP	LBJ	MS
1957	**Torpid**	won, 1	won, 2	DNF
1960	**Countess Adios**	won, 2	NE	won, 1
1971	**Albatross**	won, 2	2nd*	won, 1
1976	**Keystone Ore**	won, 1	won, 2	2nd*
1986	**Barberry Spur**	won, 1	won, 2	2nd*
1990	**Jake and Elwood**	won, 1	NE	won, 2
1992	**Western Hanover**	won, 1	2nd*	won, 2
1993	**Rijadh**	won, 1	2nd*	won, 2

TROTTERS

Seven horses have won the first two legs of the Triple Crown–the Yonkers Trot (YT) and the Hambletonian (Ham)–but not the third. The eventual winner of the Ky. Futurity (KF) is listed.

Year		YT	Ham	KF
1962	**A.C.'s Viking**	won	won	Safe Mission
1976	**Steve Lobell**	won	won	Quick Pay
1977	**Green Speed**	won	won	Texas
1978	**Speedy Somolli**	won	won	Doublemint
1987	**Mack Lobell**	won	won	Napoletano
1993	**American Winner**	won	won	Pine Chip
1996	**Continentalvictory**	won	won	Running Sea

Note: Green Speed (1977) not eligible for Ky. Futurity; Continentalvictory (1996) was withdrawn from the Ky. Futurity due to a leg injury.

***Winning horses:** Nansemond (1971), Windshield Wiper (1976), Amity Chef (1986), Fake Left (1992), Life Sign (1993).

Note: Torpid (1957) scratched before the final heat; Countess Adios (1960) not eligible for Messenger; Jake and Elwood (1990) not eligible for Little Brown Jug.

The Hambletonian

For three-year-old trotters. Inaugurated in 1926 and has been held in Syracuse, N.Y.; Lexington, Ky.; Goshen, N.Y.; Yonkers, N.Y.; Du Quoin, Ill.; and, since 1981 at The Meadowlands in East Rutherford, N.J.

Run at one mile since 1947. Winning horse must win two heats.

Drivers with most wins: John Campbell (5); Stanley Dancer, Billy Haughton and Ben White (4); Howard Beissinger, Del Cameron, and Henry Thomas (3).

Year		Driver	Fastest Heat
1926	**Guy McKinney**	Nat Ray	2:04¾
1927	**Iosola's Worthy**	Marvin Childs	2:03¾
1928	**Spencer**	W.H. Lessee	2:02½
1929	**Walter Dear**	Walter Cox	2:02¾
1930	**Hanover's Bertha**	Tom Berry	2:03
1931	**Calumet Butler**	R.D. McMahon	2:03¼
1932	**The Marchioness**	Will Caton	2:01¼
1933	**Mary Reynolds**	Ben White	2:03¾
1934	**Lord Jim**	Doc Parshall	2:02¾
1935	**Greyhound**	Sep Palin	2:02¼
1936	**Rosalind**	Ben White	2:01¾
1937	**Shirley Hanover**	Henry Thomas	2:01½
1938	**McLin Hanover**	Henry Tomas	2:02¼
1939	**Peter Astra**	Doc Parshall	2:04¼
1940	**Spencer Scott**	Fred Egan	2:02
1941	**Bill Gallon**	Lee Smith	2:05
1942	**The Ambassador**	Ben White	2:04
1943	**Volo Song**	Ben White	2:02½
1944	**Yankee Maid**	Henry Thomas	2:04
1945	**Titan Hanover**	Harry Pownall Sr.	2:04
1946	**Chestertown**	Thomas Berry	2:02½
1947	**Hoot Mon**	Sep Palin	2:00
1948	**Demon Hanover**	Harrison Hoyt	2:02
1949	**Miss Tilly**	Fred Egan	2:01⅖
1950	**Lusty Song**	Del Miller	2:02
1951	**Mainliner**	Guy Crippen	2:02⅗
1952	**Sharp Note**	Bion Shively	2:02⅗
1953	**Helicopter**	Harry Harvey	2:01⅗
1954	**Newport Dream**	Del Cameron	2:02⅘
1955	**Scott Frost**	Joe O'Brien	2:00⅗
1956	**The Intruder**	Ned Bower	2:01⅖
1957	**Hickory Smoke**	John Simpson Sr.	2:00⅕
1958	**Emily's Pride**	Flave Nipe	1:59⅘
1959	**Diller Hanover**	Frank Ervin	2:01⅕
1960	**Blaze Hanover**	Joe O'Brien	1:59⅗
1961	**Harlan Dean**	James Arthur	1:58⅖
1962	**A.C.'s Viking**	Sanders Russell	1:59⅗
1963	**Speedy Scot**	Ralph Baldwin	1:57⅗
1964	**Ayres**	John Simpson Sr.	1:56⅘
1965	**Egyptian Candor**	Del Cameron	2:03⅘
1966	**Kerry Way**	Frank Ervin	1:58⅘
1967	**Speedy Streak**	Del Cameron	2:00
1968	**Nevele Pride**	Stanley Dancer	1:59⅖
1969	**Lindy's Pride**	Howard Beissinger	1:57⅗
1970	**Timothy T**	John Simpson Jr.	1:58⅖
1971	**Speedy Crown**	Howard Beissinger	1:57⅖
1972	**Super Bowl**	Stanley Dancer	1:56⅖
1973	**Flirth**	Ralph Baldwin	1:57⅕
1974	**Christopher T**	Billy Haughton	1:58⅗
1975	**Bonefish**	Stanley Dancer	1:59
1976	**Steve Lobell**	Billy Haughton	1:56⅖
1977	**Green Speed**	Billy Haughton	1:55⅗
1978	**Speedy Somolli**	Howard Beissinger	1:55
1979	**Legend Hanover**	George Sholty	1:56⅕
1980	**Burgomeister**	Billy Haughton	1:56⅗
1981	**Shiaway St. Pat**	Ray Remmen	2:01⅕
1982	**Speed Bowl**	Tommy Haughton	1:56⅘
1983	**Duenna**	Stanley Dancer	1:57⅖
1984	**Historic Freight**	Ben Webster	1:56⅖
1985	**Prakas**	Bill O'Donnell	1:54⅗
1986	**Nuclear Kosmos**	Ulf Thoresen	1:55⅖
1987	**Mack Lobell**	John Campbell	1:53⅗
1988	**Armbro Goal**	John Campbell	1:54⅗
1989	**Park Avenue Joe**	Ron Waples	1:54⅗
	& **Probe**	Bill Fahy	
1990	**Harmonious**	John Campbell	1:54⅕
1991	**Giant Victory**	Jack Moiseyev	1:54⅘
1992	**Alf Palema**	Mickey McNichol	1:56⅖
1993	**American Winner**	Ron Pierce	1:53⅕
1994	**Victory Dream**	Mike Lachance	1:54⅕
1995	**Tagliabue**	John Campbell	1:54⅘
1996	**Continentalvictory**	Mike Lachance	1:52⅘
1997	**Malabar Man**	Mal Burroughs	1:55
1998	**Muscles Yankee**	John Campbell	1:52⅖

Note: In 1989, Park Avenue Joe and Probe finished in a dead heat in the race-off. They were later declared co-winners, but Park Avenue Joe was awarded 1st place money because his three-race summary (2-1-1) was better than Probe's (1-9-1).

The Little Brown Jug

Harness racing's most prestigious race for three-year-old pacers. Inaugurated in 1946 and held annually at the Delaware, Ohio County Fairgrounds. Winning horse must win two heats.

Drivers with most wins: Billy Haughton (5); Stanley Dancer and Mike Lachance (4); John Campbell, Frank Ervin and John Simpson Sr. (3); Adelbert Cameron, Herve Filion, Jack Moiseyev, Joe O'Brien, Bill O'Donnell, "Curly" Smart and Ron Waples (2).

Year		Driver	Fastest Heat
1946	**Ensign Hanover**	"Curly" Smart	2:02
1947	**Forbes Chief**	Adelbert Cameron	2:05
1948	**Knight Dream**	Frank Safford	2:07
1949	**Good Time**	Frank Ervin	2:03$\frac{2}{5}$
1950	**Dudley Hanover**	Delvin Miller	2:02$\frac{3}{5}$
1951	**Tar Heel**	Adelbert Cameron	2:00
1952	**Meadow Rice**	"Curly" Smart	2:01$\frac{3}{5}$
1953	**Keystoner**	Frank Ervin	2:02$\frac{1}{5}$
1954	**Adios Harry**	Morris MacDonald	2:02$\frac{2}{5}$
1955	**Quick Chief**	Billy Haughton	2:00
1956	**Noble Adios**	John Simpson, Sr.	2:00$\frac{4}{5}$
1957	**Torpid**	John Simpson, Sr.	2:00$\frac{4}{5}$
1958	**Shadow Wave**	Joe O'Brien	2:01
1959	**Adios Butler**	Clint Hodgkins	1:59$\frac{2}{5}$
1960	**Bullet Hanover**	John Simpson, Sr.	1:58$\frac{3}{5}$
1961	**Henry T. Adios**	Stanley Dancer	1:58$\frac{4}{5}$
1962	**Lehigh Hanover**	Stanley Dancer	1:58$\frac{4}{5}$
1963	**Overtrick**	John Patterson, Sr.	1:57$\frac{1}{5}$
1964	**Vicar Hanover**	Billy Haughton	2:00$\frac{4}{5}$
1965	**Bret Hanover**	Frank Ervin	1:57
1966	**Romeo Hanover**	George Sholty	1:59$\frac{3}{5}$
1967	**Best Of All**	Jim Hackett	1:59
1968	**Rum Customer**	Billy Haughton	1:59$\frac{3}{5}$
1969	**Laverne Hanover**	Billy Haughton	2:00$\frac{2}{5}$
1970	**Most Happy Fella**	Stanley Dancer	1:57$\frac{1}{5}$
1971	**Nansemond**	Herve Filion	1:57$\frac{2}{5}$
1972	**Strike Out**	Keith Waples	1:56$\frac{3}{5}$
1973	**Melvin's Woe**	Joe O'Brien	1:57$\frac{3}{5}$
1974	**Armbro Omaha**	Billy Haughton	1:57
1975	**Seatrain**	Ben Webster	1:56$\frac{4}{5}$
1976	**Keystone Ore**	Stanley Dancer	1:56$\frac{4}{5}$
1977	**Governor Skipper**	John Chapman	1:56$\frac{1}{5}$
1978	**Happy Escort**	Bill Popfinger	1:55$\frac{2}{5}$
1979	**Hot Hitter**	Herve Filion	1:55$\frac{3}{5}$
1980	**Niatross**	Clint Galbraith	1:54$\frac{4}{5}$
1981	**Fan Hanover** (f)	Glen Garnsey	1:56
1982	**Merger**	John Campbell	1:54$\frac{3}{5}$
1983	**Ralph Hanover**	Ron Waples	1:55$\frac{3}{5}$
1984	**Colt Fortysix**	Chris Boring	1:53$\frac{3}{5}$
1985	**Nihilator**	Bill O'Donnell	1:52$\frac{1}{5}$
1986	**Barberry Spur**	Bill O'Donnell	1:52$\frac{4}{5}$
1987	**Jaguar Spur**	Dick Stillings	1:54
1988	**B.J. Scoot**	Mike Lachance	1:52$\frac{3}{5}$
1989	**Goalie Jeff**	Mike Lachance	1:54$\frac{1}{5}$
1990	**Beach Towel**	Ray Remmen	1:53$\frac{3}{5}$
1991	**Precious Bunny**	Jack Moiseyev	1:53$\frac{4}{5}$
1992	**Fake Left**	Ron Waples	1:53$\frac{3}{5}$
1993	**Life Sign**	John Campbell	1:52
1994	**Magical Mike**	Mike Lachance	1:52$\frac{3}{5}$
1995	**Nick's Fantasy**	John Campbell	1:51$\frac{2}{5}$
1996	**Armbro Operative**	Jack Moiseyev	1:52$\frac{3}{5}$
1997	**Western Dreamer**	Mike Lachance	1:51$\frac{1}{5}$
1998	**Shady Character**	Ron Pierce	1:52$\frac{3}{5}$

All-Time Leaders

The all-time winning trotters, pacers and drivers through 1997 according to *The Trotting and Pacing Guide.* Purses for horses include races in foreign countries. Earnings and wins for drivers include only races held in North America.

Top 10 Horses — Money Won

		T/P	Sts	1st	Earnings
1	Peace Corps	T	42	35	$5,506,443
2	Ourasi (FRA)	T	N/A	32	4,010,105
3	Mack Lobell	T	86	65	3,917,594
4	Reve d'Udon	T	23	18	3,611,351
5	Nihilator	P	38	35	3,225,653
6	Sea Cove	T	N/A	N/A	3,138,986
7	Artsplace	P	49	37	3,085,083
8	Presidential Ball	P	38	26	3,021,363
9	Matt's Scooter	P	61	37	2,944,591
10	On the Road Again	P	61	44	2,819,102

Top 10 Drivers — Races Won

		Yrs	1st	Earnings
1	Herve Filion	35	14,783	$85,044,328
2	Mike Lachance	30	7,986	100,416,130
3	Dave Magee	25	7,833	54,939,716
4	Cat Manzi	30	7,618	64,742,570
5	John Campbell	26	7,579	155,360,161
6	Walter Case Jr.	20	7,214	28,197,404
7	Carmine Abbatiello	41	7,163	50,201,484
8	Jack Moiseyev	22	7,113	69,207,153
9	Doug Brown	25	6,943	69,106,441
10	Eddie Davis	34	6,592	31,890,783

Annual Awards

Harness Horse of the Year

Selected since 1947 by U.S. Trotting Association and the U.S. Harness Writers Association; age of winning horse is noted; (t) indicates trotter and (p) indicates pacer. USTA added Trotter and Pacer of the Year awards in 1970.

Multiple winners: Bret Hanover and Nevele Pride (3); Adios Butler, Albatross, Cam Fella, Good Time, Mack Lobell, Niatross and Scott Frost (2).

Year	
1947	Victory Song (4t)
1948	Rodney (4t)
1949	Good Time (3p)
1950	Proximity (8t)
1951	Pronto Don (6t)
1952	Good Time (6t)
1953	Hi Lo's Forbes (5p)
1954	Stenographer (3t)
1955	Scott Frost (3t)
1956	Scott Frost (4t)
1957	Torpid (3p)
1958	Emily's Pride (3t)
1959	Bye Bye Byrd (4p)
1960	Adios Butler (4p)
1961	Adios Butler (5p)
1962	Su Mac Lad (8t)
1963	Speedy Scot (3t)
1964	Bret Hanover (2p)
1965	Bret Hanover (3p)
1966	Bret Hanover (4p)

Year	
1967	Nevele Pride (2t)
1968	Nevele Pride (3t)
1969	Nevele Pride (4t)
1970	Fresh Yankee (7t)
1971	Albatross (3p)
1972	Albatross (4p)
1973	Sir Dalrai (4p)
1974	Delmonica Hanover (5t)
1975	Savoir (7t)
1976	Keystone Ore (3p)
1977	Green Speed (3t)
1978	Abercrombie (3p)
1979	Niatross (2p)
1980	Niatross (3p)
1981	Fan Hanover (3p)
1982	Cam Fella (3p)
1983	Cam Fella (4p)
1984	Fancy Crown (3t)
1985	Nihilator (3p)
1986	Forrest Skipper (4p)
1987	Mack Lobell (3t)
1988	Mack Lobell (4t)
1989	Matt's Scooter (4p)
1990	Beach Towel (3p)
1991	Precious Bunny (3p)
1992	Artsplace (4p)
1993	Staying Together (4p)
1994	Cam's Card Shark (3p)
1995	CR Kay Suzie (3t)
1996	Continentalvictory (3t)
1997	Malabar Man (3t)

Driver of the Year

Determined by Universal Driving Rating System (UDR) and presented by the Harness Tracks of America since 1968. Eligible drivers must have at least 1,000 starts for the season.

Multiple winners: Herve Filion (10); John Campbell and Michel Lachance (3); Walter Case Jr., Tony Morgan, Bill O'Donnell, Luc Ouellette and Ron Waples (2).

Year	
1968	Stanley Dancer
1969	Herve Filion
1970	Herve Filion
1971	Herve Filion
1972	Herve Filion
1973	Herve Filion
1974	Herve Filion
1975	Joe O'Brien
1976	Herve Filion
1977	Donald Dancer
1978	Carmine Abbatiello & Herve Filion
1979	Ron Waples
1980	Ron Waples
1981	Herve Filion
1982	Bill O'Donnell
1983	John Campbell
1984	Bill O'Donnell
1985	Michel Lachance
1986	Michel Lachance
1987	Michel Lachance
1988	John Campbell
1989	Herve Filion
1990	John Campbell
1991	Walter Case Jr.
1992	Walter Case Jr.
1993	Jack Moiseyev
1994	Dave Magee
1995	Luc Ouellette
1996	Tony Morgan & Luc Ouellette
1997	Tony Morgan

STEEPLECHASE RACING

Champion Horses

Annual horse of the year since 1956 based on vote of the National Turf Writers Association and other selected media.

Multiple Winners: Flatterer and Lonesome Glory (4); Bon Nouvel, Zaccio (3); Café Prince, Morley Street, Neji (2).

Year	
1956	Shipboard
1957	Neji
1958	Neji
1959	Ancestor
1960	Benguala
1961	Peal
1962	Barnaby's Bluff
1963	Amber Diver
1964	Bon Nouvel
1965	Bon Nouvel
1966	Tuscalee & Mako
1967	Quick Pitch
1968	Bon Nouvel
1969	L'Escargot
1970	Top Bid
1971	Shadow Brok
1972	Soothsayer
1973	Athenian Idol
1974	Gran Kan
1975	Life's Illusion
1976	Fire Control & Straight and True
1977	Café Prince
1978	Café Prince
1979	Martie's Anger
1980	Zaccio
1981	Zaccio
1982	Zaccio
1983	Flatterer
1984	Flatterer
1985	Flatterer
1986	Flatterer
1987	Inlander
1988	Jimmy Lorenzo
1989	Highland Bud
1990	Morley Street
1991	Morley Street
1992	Lonesome Glory
1993	Lonesome Glory
1994	Warm Spell
1995	Lonesome Glory
1996	Correggio
1997	Lonesome Glory

Champion Jockeys

Annual leading jockeys by races won since 1956, according to the National Steeplechase Association.

Multiple Winners: Joe Aitcheson Jr. (7); Jerry Fishback (5); John Cushman and Alfred P. Smithwick (4); Tom Skiffington and Jeff Teter (3); Ricky Hendriks, James Lawrence, Blythe Miller and Thomas Walsh (2).

Year	
1956	Alfred P. Smithwick
1957	Alfred P. Smithwick
1958	Alfred P. Smithwick
1959	James Murphy
1960	Thomas Walsh
1961	Joe Aitcheson Jr.
1962	Alfred P. Smithwick
1963	Joe Aitcheson Jr.
1964	Joe Aitcheson Jr.
1965	Doug Small Jr.
1966	Thomas Walsh
1967	Joe Aitcheson Jr.
1968	Joe Aitcheson Jr.
1969	Joe Aitcheson Jr.
1970	Joe Aitcheson Jr.
1971	Jerry Fishback
1972	Michael O'Brien
1973	Jerry Fishback
1974	Jerry Fishback
1975	Jerry Fishback
1976	Tom Skiffington
1977	Jerry Fishback
1978	Tom Skiffington
1979	Tom Skiffington
1980	John Cushman
1981	John Cushman
1982	John Cushman
1983	John Cushman
1984	Jeff Teter
1985	Bernie Houghton
1986	Ricky Hendriks
1987	Ricky Hendriks
1988	Jonathan Smart
1989	James Lawrence
1990	Jeff Teter
1991	Jeff Teter
1992	Craig Thornton
1993	James Lawrence
1994	Blythe Miller
1995	Blythe Miller
1996	Chip Miller
1997	Arch Kingsley Jr. & Jonathan Kiser

Tennis

The future of women's tennis became the present in 1998 as both **Venus Williams** (r) and younger sister **Serena** cracked the top 20 in the WTA rankings.

AP/Wide World Photos

An American Dream

Lindsay Davenport became the first American-born woman to win the U.S. Open since 1982, proving once and for all that she's not to be overlooked.

by
Sal Paolantonio

Lindsay Davenport could easily be bitter. Growing up as a tall, gangly teenager in Southern California, she heard whispers that the only reason she won junior tournaments was because she was bigger – not necessarily better – than the other girls.

She was taller than most of the boys too. "I didn't go out on many dates," she said.

And when the Women's Tennis Association launched a high-octane marketing campaign based on the so-called glam set of the women's game, Davenport was ignored.

She won't be ignored anymore. With a vicious forehand and a relentless serve, Davenport finished the 1998 season with a spectacular run of hardcourt victories, culminating in an impressive sweep of the U.S. Open.

Without dropping a set, Davenport beat the 1997 finalists back-to-back – Venus Williams in the semifinals, then defending Open champion Martina Hingis in the finals – to win her first Grand Slam title.

"As an American kid from California," said Davenport, "the U.S. Open was always the one I wanted to win more than any other tournament."

Similar to her idol, Mark McGwire, who tied Roger Maris' home run record on his father's birthday, Davenport won the U.S. Open on her mother's birthday. "I can't begin to say how much this means to me," she said. "To

Sal Paolantonio covers tennis for ESPN.

AP/Wide World Photos

No. 2 seeded **Lindsay Davenport** was close to perfect in the 1998 U.S. Open as the 22-year-old rolled through her competition without losing a single set to grab her first Grand Slam title.

win this tournament when the women's game is so tough is unbelievable."

ESPN tennis analyst Betsy Nagelsen, a former pro, says the women's game has never been deeper or more competitive. "There are some real rivalries developing like in the old days. But now, some of these quarterfinal matches look like finals."

Indeed, four different women won Grand Slam titles in 1998, the first time that's happened in eight years. The world's top-ranked player Martina Hingis won the Australian Open, Arantxa Sanchez Vicario won her third French Open, Jana Novotna, finally overcoming her personal fears, prevailed at Wimbledon for her first Grand Slam singles title, and of course, Davenport took the U.S. Open.

Add to that star-studded list the teen phenoms who finally broke through on the women's tennis circuit. Venus Williams won the Lipton Hardcourt Championships and reached the semis at the U.S. Open. Anna Kournikova of Russia proved that she's not just a pretty face, but has good looking strokes to match.

And don't forget the veterans. Monica Seles and Steffi Graf made strong comebacks in 1998, and with the added television money pouring into the game in 1999, they're not likely to quietly fade onto the Seniors Tour just yet.

On the men's side, the sport is reaching an imbalance – geographically speaking. Australian men, led by

AP/Wide World Photos

Australian **Patrick Rafter** successfully defended his U.S. Open title in 1998, becoming just the sixth player in history to do so. After edging top seed Pete Sampras in five sets in the semifinal round, Rafter defeated fellow Australian Mark Philippoussis for the championship.

Patrick Rafter, had won ten titles on the tour through late September. The last time the Aussies won that many was in 1975, when they won 12. Three years earlier, led by John Newcombe and Co., Australians won 26 titles.

Rafter successfully defended his U.S. Open title, becoming only the sixth man in the open era to repeat. He beat fellow countryman Mark Philippoussis in an All-Australian final – the first one in two decades at the U.S. Open.

Meanwhile, here in the northern hemisphere, there is a downturn in the American game. Yes, Pete Sampras won his fifth Wimbledon and needs only one more Grand Slam title to tie Roy Emerson's career singles record of 12. But he suffered through four injuries in 1998, including a leg pull that was instrumental in his losing to Rafter in the semis at the Open.

Ranked out of the top 100 in 1997, Andre Agassi had a remarkable comeback to climb back into the top 10. But Michael Chang's career appears to be on the downside and Jim Courier seems close to retirement. Of those four Americans, only Courier (who was injured) was on the U.S. team in Davis Cup competition in September and the Americans were pounded by Italy in the semifinals.

The next generation of American players – with Justin Gimelstob, Jan Michael Gimball, and Alex O'Brien leading the way – are simply not ready

AP/Wide World Photos

Winners of two of the four Grand Slam singles tournaments in 1998, **Martina Hingis** (l) and **Jana Novotna** (r) also teamed up to win three Grand Slam doubles championships (Wimbledon, the U.S. Open and here at the French Open). Hingis completed the sweep by winning the Australian Open with Mirjana Lucic.

to challenge an Australian invasion that seems poised to dominate men's tennis at least until the end of the century. ■

Sal Paolantonio's Top Ten Tennis Highlights of 1998

10. After getting bounced out of the U.S. Open in the fourth round by Karol Kucera, **Andre Agassi tells the USTA** that if they don't play the Davis Cup semis near his Las Vegas home (so he won't have to miss a charity event), he won't play. They don't. He doesn't. USA loses to Italy.

9. **The Williams sisters sweep** mixed doubles titles at the Grand Slams – Venus wins the Australian and French Opens, and Serena wins Wimbledon and the U.S. Open.

8. After nearly a year away from the game due to a knee injury and financial troubles, **Steffi Graf storms back** onto the women's tour.

7. **The men's tour experiments** with coaching during matches for the first time at some non-Grand Slam events. "It might elevate the level of the game," says Agassi.

6. At age 30, after laboring on the men's tour for 12 years, **Petr Korda** of the Czech Republic crushes Chile's Marcelo Rios in straight sets to win the Australian Open, his first Grand Slam title.
5. Spain's **Arantxa Sanchez Vicario wins** her third French Open title.
4. **Jana Novotna** erases her "choke" label by finally winning Wimbledon in her third finals attempt. It is her first Grand Slam singles title in her 11-year career.
3. **Australian Patrick Rafter** sweeps through the American hardcourt season and becomes only the sixth player to successfully defend his men's U.S. Open title.
2. **Pete Sampras wins** his fifth Wimbledon, tying Bjorn Borg and Rod Laver with 11 career Grand Slam titles.
1. **Lindsay Davenport wins** her first Grand Slam title by sweeping through the U.S. Open without losing a set. ■

INSIDE THE NUMBERS

by
Craig Wachs

SUCCEEDING **UNSEEDED**

Unseeded Mark Philippoussis made it to the Finals of the 1998 U.S. Open before finally succumbing to defending champ Patrick Rafter. Since the arrival of open tennis in 1968, seven unseeded players have won Grand Slam singles events.

1997	Gustavo Kuerten	French Open
1996	Richard Krajicek	Wimbledon
1994	Andre Agassi	U.S. Open
1985	Boris Becker	Wimbledon
1982	Mats Wilander	French Open
1978	Chris O'Neil*	Australian Open
1976	Mark Edmondson	Australian Open

*O'Neil is the only unseeded woman to win a Grand Slam title.

AGE IS JUST A NUMBER

Jana Novotna bucked the trend of young Grand Slam winners in 1998. Her Wimbledon victory made her the second-oldest Grand Slam singles titlist in the open era of tennis and the oldest first-time winner.

	Age	Event
Martina Navratilova	34	1990 Wimbledon
Jana Novotna	**29**	**1998 Wimbledon**
Steffi Graf	27	1996 U.S. Open
Steffi Graf	27	1996 Wimbledon

FINALS FRUITION

Of the top men's Grand Slam singles winners of all-time, Pete Sampras has the best winning percentage in the finals. His only losses came at the 1992 U.S. Open and the 1995 Australian Open. He currently holds a six-game finals winning streak.

	Record in Finals	Win Pct.
Roy Emerson	12-3	.800
Pete Sampras	**11-2***	**.846**
Bjorn Borg	11-5	.688
Rod Laver	11-6	.647
Bill Tilden	10-5	.667

■

TENNIS STATISTICS

THE SEASON IN REVIEW

1997-1998

MEN • WOMEN • LEADERS

Tournament Results

Winners of men's and women's pro singles championships from Nov. 2, 1997 through Sept. 27, 1998. See Updates for later results.

Men's ATP Tour

LATE 1997

Finals	Tournament	Winner	Earnings	Runner-Up	Score
Nov. 2	Paris Open	Pete Sampras	$393,000	J. Bjorkman	63 46 63 61
Nov. 2	Columbian Open (Bogota)	Francisco Clavet	43,000	N. Lapentti	63 63
Nov. 9	Stockholm Open	Jonas Bjorkman	112,000	J. Siemerink	36 76 62 64
Nov. 9	Kremlin Cup (Moscow)	Yevgeny Kafelnikov	157,400	P. Korda	76 64
Nov. 9	Chevrolet Cup (Santiago)	Julian Alonso	43,000	M. Rios	62 61
Nov. 16	ATP World Championship (Hannover)	Pete Sampras	1,340,000	Y. Kafelnikov	63 62 62
Nov. 23	ATP Doubles Champs. (Hartford)	Rick Leach/ Jonathan Stark	115,000	M. Bhupathi/ L. Paes	63 64 76

1998 (through Sept. 20)

Finals	Tournament	Winner	Earnings	Runner-Up	Score
Jan. 11	Qatar Open (Doha)	Petr Korda	$137,000	F. Santoro	60 63
Jan. 11	Australian Hardcourt (Adelaide)	Lleyton Hewitt	43,000	J. Stoltenberg	36 63 76
Jan. 11	Sydney International	Karol Kucera	340,000	T. Henman	75 64
Jan. 11	BellSouth Open (Auckland)	Marcelo Rios	45,000	R. Fromberg	46 64 76
Feb. 1	**Australian Open** (Melbourne)	Petr Korda	407,376	M. Rios	62 62 62
Feb. 8	Croatian Indoors (Split)	Goran Ivanisevic	54,000	G. Rusedski	76 76
Feb. 8	Marseille Open	Thomas Enqvist	72,000	Y. Kafelnikov	64 61
Feb. 15	St. Petersburg Open (Russia)	Richard Krajicek	45,000	M. Rosset	64 76
Feb. 15	Dubai Open	Alex Corretja	142,000	F. Mantilla	76 61
Feb. 15	Sybase Open (San Jose)	Andre Agassi	45,000	P. Sampras	62 64
Feb. 22	European Community Champs. (Antwerp)	Greg Rusedski	162,500	M. Rosset	76 36 61 64
Feb. 22	Kroger/St.Jude International (Memphis)	Mark Philippoussis	120,000	M. Chang	63 62
Mar. 1	Guardian Direct Cup (London)	Yevgeny Kafelnikov	128,000	C. Pioline	75 64
Mar. 1	Advanta Champs.(Philadelphia)	Pete Sampras	110,000	T. Enqvist	75 76
Mar. 8	ABN/AMRO World (Rotterdam)	Jan Siemerink	101,500	T. Johansson	76 62
Mar. 8	Franklin Templeton Classic (Scottsdale)	Andre Agassi	45,000	J. Stoltenberg	64 76
Mar. 15	Copenhagen Open	Magnus Gustafsson	30,000	D. Prinosil	36 61 61
Mar. 15	Champions Cup (Indian Wells)	Marcelo Rios	361,000	G. Rusedski	63 67 76 64
Mar. 29	Lipton Championships (Key Biscayne)	Marcelo Rios	360,000	A. Agassi	75 63 64
Mar. 29	Grand Prix Hassan II (Casablanca)	Andrea Gaudenzi	30,000	A. Calatrava	64 57 64
Apr. 12	Gold Flake Open (Chennai)	Patrick Rafter	58,000	M. Tillstrom	63 64
Apr. 12	Salem Open (Hong Kong)	Kenneth Carlsen	45,000	B. Black	62 60
Apr. 12	Estoril Open	Alberto Berasategui	84,000	T. Muster	36 61 63
Apr. 19	Japan Open (Tokyo)	Andrei Pavel	95,000	B. Black	63 64
Apr. 19	Open Seat - Godo (Barcelona)	Todd Martin	135,600	A. Berasategui	62 16 63 62
Apr. 26	Monte Carlo Open	Carlos Moya	361,000	C. Pioline	63 60 75
Apr. 26	US Clay Court Champs. (Orlando)	Jim Courier	37,500	M. Chang	73 36 75
May 3	BMW Open (Munich)	Thomas Enqvist	70,000	A. Agassi	67 76 63
May 3	AT&T Challenge (Atlanta)	Pete Sampras	45,000	J. Stoltenberg	67 63 76 74
May 3	Skoda Czech Open (Prague)	Fernando Meligeni	48,200	S. Dosedel	61 64
May 10	Panasonic German Open (Hamburg)	Albert Costa	361,000	A. Corretja	62 60 10 (ret.)
May 10	Red Clay Champs. (Coral Springs)	Andrew Ilie	34,800	D. Sanguinetti	75 64
May 17	Italian Open (Rome)	Marcelo Rios	350,000	A. Costa	Default
May 24	Peugeot World Team Cup (Dusseldorf)	Germany	500,000	Czech Republic	3-0
May 24	Raiffeisen Grand Prix (St. Polten)	Marcelo Rios	57,000	V. Spadea	62 60
June 7	**French Open** (Paris)	Carlos Moya	642,000	A. Corretja	63 75 63
June 14	Stella Artois Grass Court (London)	Scott Draper	85,000	L. Tieleman	76 64
June 14	Gerry Weber Open (Halle)	Yevgeny Kafelnikov	122,000	M. Larsson	64 64

Tournament Results (Cont.)

Finals	Tournament	Winner	Earnings	Runner-Up	Score
June 14	Tennis International (Carisbo)	Julian Alonso	$45,000	K. Alami	61 64
June 21	The Nottingham Open	Jonas Bjorkman	45,000	B. Black	63 62
June 21	Heineken Open (Rosmalen)	Patrick Rafter	66,400	M. Damm	76 62
July 5	**Wimbledon** (London)	Pete Sampras	727,146	G. Ivanisevic	67 76 64 36 62
July 12	Hall of Fame Championships (Newport)	Leander Paes	39,000	N. Godwin	63 62
July 12	Swedish Open (Bastad)	Magnus Gustafsson	45,000	A. Medvedev	62 63
July 12	Rado Swiss Open (Gstaad)	Alex Corretja	74,000	B. Becker	76 75 63
July 26	Mercedes Cup (Stuttgart)	Gustavo Kuerten	279,000	K. Kucera	46 62 64
July 26	Legg Mason Classic (Washington, D.C.)	Andre Agassi	95,000	S. Draper	62 60
Aug. 2	EA Generali Open (Kitzbühel)	Albert Costa	62,400	A. Gaudenzi	62 16 62 36 61
Aug. 2	Croatian Championship (Umag)	Bohdan Uihrach	54,000	M. Norman	63 76
Aug. 2	Mercedes-Benz Cup (Los Angeles)	Andre Agassi	45,000	T. Henman	64 64
Aug. 9	Grolsch Open (Amsterdam)	Magnus Norman	45,000	R. Fromberg	63 63 26 64
Aug. 9	du Maurier Open (Montreal)	Patrick Rafter	361,000	R. Krajicek	76 64
Aug. 16	San Marino Open	Dominik Hrbaty	39,000	M. Puerta	62 75
Aug. 16	ATP Championships (Cincinnati)	Patrick Rafter	361,000	P. Sampras	16 76 64
Aug. 23	RCA/U.S. Hardcourts (Indianapolis)	Alex Corretja	122,500	A. Agassi	26 62 63
Aug. 23	Pilot Pen International (New Haven)	Karol Kucera	122,500	G. Ivanisevic	64 57 62
Aug. 30	Waldbaum's Hamlet Cup (Long Island)	Patrick Rafter	45,000	F. Mantilla	76 62
Aug. 30	MFS Pro Champs. (Boston)	Michael Chang	45,000	P. Haarhuis	63 64
Sept. 13	**U.S. Open** (New York)	Patrick Rafter	700,000	M. Philippoussis	63 36 62 60
Sept. 20	President's Cup (Tashkent)	Tim Henman	66,400	Y. Kafelnikov	75 64
Sept. 20	Samsung Open (Bournemouth)	Felix Mantilla	54,000	A. Costa	63 75
Sept. 20	Romanian Open (Bucharest)	Francisco Clavet	45,000	A. DiPasquale	64 26 75

Women's WTA Tour

LATE 1997

Finals	Tournament	Winner	Earnings	Runner-Up	Score
Nov. 2	Ladies Kremlin Cup (Moscow)	Jana Novotna	$150,000	A. Sugiyama	63 64
Nov. 9	Ameritech Cup	Lindsay Davenport	79,000	N. Tauziat	60 75
Nov. 16	Advanta Championships (Philadelphia)	Martina Hingis	79,000	L. Davenport	75 67 76
Nov. 23	Volvo Open (Pattaya)	Henrieta Nagyova	17,700	D. Van Roost	75 67 75
Nov. 23	WTA Tour Championship (New York)	Jana Novotna	500,000	M. Pierce	76 62 63

1998 (through Sept. 27)

Finals	Tournament	Winner	Earnings	Runner-Up	Score
Jan. 10	ASB Bank Classic (Auckland)	Dominique van Roost	$17,000	S. Farina	46 76 75
Jan. 10	Gold Coast Classic (Australia)	Ai Sugiyama	27,000	M. Vento	75 60
Jan. 17	Sydney International	Arantxa Sanchez Vicario	339,500	V. Williams	61 63
Jan. 17	Tasmanian International (Hobart)	Patty Schnyder	17,700	D. van Roost	63 62
Feb. 1	**Australian Open** (Melbourne)	Martina Hingis	383,200	C. Martinez	63 63
Feb. 8	Pan Pacific Open (Tokyo)	Lindsay Davenport	150,000	M. Hingis	63 63
Feb. 15	Open Gaz de France (Paris)	Mary Pierce	79,000	D. van Roost	63 75
Feb. 22	Faber Grand Prix (Hannover)	Patty Schnyder	79,000	J. Novotna	60 26 75
Feb. 22	Copa Colsanitas (Bogota)	Paola Suarez	17,700	S. Jeyaseelan	63 64
Mar. 1	EA Generali (Linz)	Jana Novotna	79,000	D. van Roost	61 76
Mar. 1	IGA Classic (Oklahoma City)	Venus Williams	27,000	J. Kruger	63 62
Mar. 15	State Farm Evert Cup (Indian Wells)	Martina Hingis	205,000	L. Davenport	63 64
Mar. 28	Lipton Championships (Key Biscayne)	Venus Williams	235,000	A. Kournikova	26 64 61
Apr. 5	Family Circle Cup (Hilton Head)	Amanda Coetzer	150,000	I. Spirlea	63 64
Apr. 12	Bausch & Lomb Champs. (Amelia Island)	Mary Pierce	78,000	C. Martinez	67 60 62
Apr. 19	Japan Open (Tokyo)	Ai Sugiyama	27,000	C. Morariu	63 63
Apr. 19	Makarska Open	Kvetoslava Hrdlickova	17,700	F. Li	63 61
Apr. 26	Budapest Lotto Ladies Open	Virginia Ruano-Pascual	17,700	S. Farina	64 46 63
May 3	Rexona Cup (Hamburg)	Martina Hingis	79,000	J. Novotna	63 75
May 3	Croatian Bol Ladies Open	Mirjana Lucic	17,700	C. Morariu	62 64
May 10	Italian Open (Rome)	Martina Hingis	150,000	V. Williams	63 26 63
May 17	German Open (Berlin)	Conchita Martinez	150,000	A. Mauresmo	64 64
May 23	Internationaux de Strasbourg	Irina Spirlea	33,000	J. Halard-Decugis	76 63
May 23	Yellow Pages Open (Madrid)	Patty Schnyder	27,000	D. van Roost	36 64 60
June 7	**French Open** (Paris)	Arantxa Sanchez Vicario	605,600	M. Seles	76 06 62
June 14	DFS Classic (Birmingham)	Rain			
June 21	Direct Line Insurance Int'l. (Eastbourne)	Jana Novotna	79,000	A. Sanchez Vicario	61 75
June 21	Heineken Trophy (S'hertogenbosch)	Julie Halard-Decugis	27,000	M. Oremans	62 64

Finals	Tournament	Winner	Earnings	Runner-Up	Score
July 5	**Wimbledon** (London)	Jana Novotna	$626,400	N. Tauziat	64 76
July 12	Styrian Open (Austria)	Patty Schnyder	17,700	G.L. Garcia	62 46 63
July 12	Skoda Czech Open (Prague)	Jana Novotna	26,000	S. Testud	63 60
July 19	International Tournament at Palermo	Patty Schnyder	17,000	B. Schett	61 57 62
July 19	Warsaw Cup	Conchita Martinez	27,000	S. Farina	60 63
Aug. 2	Bank of the West Classic (Stanford)	Lindsay Davenport	79,000	V. Williams	64 57 64
Aug. 2	Polish Open (Sopot)	Henrieta Nagyova	17,700	E. Wagner	63 57 61
Aug. 9	Toshiba Classic (San Diego)	Lindsay Davenport	79,000	M. Pierce	63 61
Aug. 9	Enka Ladies Open (Istanbul)	Henrieta Nagyova	17,700	O. Barabanschikova	64 36 76
Aug. 16	Acura Classic (Los Angeles)	Lindsay Davenport	79,000	M. Hingis	46 64 63
Aug. 16	Boston Cup	Mariaan de Swardt	27,000	B. Schett	36 76 75
Aug. 23	du Maurier Open (Montreal)	Monica Seles	150,000	A. Sanchez Vicario	63 62
Aug. 29	Pilot Pen International (New Haven)	Steffi Graf	79,000	J. Novotna	64 61
Sept. 13	**U.S. Open** (New York)	Lindsay Davenport	700,000	M. Hingis	63 75
Sept. 27	Toyota Princess Cup (Tokyo)	Monica Seles	79,000	A. Sanchez Vicario	46 63 64

1998 Grand Slam Tournaments

Australian Open

MEN'S SINGLES

FINAL EIGHT— #1 Pete Sampras; #4 Jonas Bjorkman; #6 Petr Korda; #9 Marcelo Rios; plus unseeded Alberto Berasategui, Nicolas Escude, Nicolas Kiefer and Karol Kucera.

Quarterfinals

Kucera def. Sampras....................64 62 67(5) 63
Korda def. Bjorkman 36 57 63 64 62
Escude def. Kiefer 46 36 64 61 62
Rios def. Berasategui....................67(6) 64 64 60

Semifinals

Korda def. Kucera 61 64 16 62
Rios def. Escude 61 63 62

Final

Korda def. Rios 62 62 62

WOMEN'S SINGLES

FINAL EIGHT— #1 Martina Hingis; #2 Lindsay Davenport; #5 Mary Pierce; #7 Arantxa Sanchez Vicario; #8 Conchita Martinez; #9 Sandrine Testud; #10 Anke Huber; plus unseeded Venus Williams.

Quarterfinals

Hingis def. Pierce 62 63
Huber def. Sanchez Vicario ....76(7) 75
Martinez def. Testud....................63 62
Davenport def. Williams 16 75 63

Semifinals

Hingis def. Huber....................61 26 61
Martinez def. Davenport....................46 63 63

Final

Hingis def. Martinez 63 63

DOUBLES FINALS

Men— #5 Jonas Bjorkman & Jacco Eltingh def. #1 Mark Woodforde & Todd Woodbridge, 6-2, 5-7, 2-6, 6-4, 6-3.

Women— Martina Hingis & Mirjana Lucic def. #1 Lindsay Davenport & Natasha Zvereva, 6-4, 2-6, 6-3.

Mixed— Justin Gimelstob & Venus Williams def. #5 Cyril Suk & Helena Sukova, 6-2, 6-1.

French Open

MEN'S SINGLES

FINAL EIGHT— #3 Marcelo Rios; #12 Carlos Moya; #14 Alex Corretja; #15 Felix Mantilla; plus unseated Hicham Arazi, Filip Dewulf, Thomas Muster and Cedric Pioline.

Quarterfinals

Mantilla def. Muster....................64 62 46 63
Moya def. Rios 61 26 62 64
Corretja def. Dewulf....................75 64 63
Pioline def. Arazi....................36 62 76(6) 46 63

Semifinals

Moya def. Mantilla 57 62 64 62
Corretja def. Pioline....................63 64 62

Final

Moya def. Corretja....................63 75 63

WOMEN'S SINGLES

FINAL EIGHT— #1 Martina Hingis; #2 Lindsay Davenport; #3 Jana Novotna; #4 Arantxa Sanchez Vicario; #6 Monica Seles; #8 Venus Williams; #10 Iva Majoli; plus unseeded Patty Schnyder.

Quarterfinals

Hingis def. Williams....................63 64
Seles def. Novotna....................46 63 63
Sanchez Vicario def. Schnyder ....62 67(5) 60
Davenport def. Majoli 61 57 63

Semifinals

Seles def. Hingis....................63 62
Sanchez Vicario def. Davenport ....63 76(5)

Final

Sanchez Vicario def. Seles....................76(5) 06 62

DOUBLES FINALS

Men— #1 Paul Haarhuis & Jacco Eltingh def. Mark Knowles & Daniel Nestor, 6-3, 3-6, 6-3.

Women—#2 Martina Hingis & Jana Novotna def. #1 Lindsay Davenport & Natasha Zvereva, 6-1, 7-6 (7-4).

Mixed— Justin Gimelstob & Venus Williams def. Serena Williams & Luis Lobo, 6-4, 6-4.

Wimbledon

MEN'S SINGLES

FINAL EIGHT— #1 Pete Sampras; #3 Petr Korda; #9 Richard Krajicek; #12 Tim Henman; #14 Goran Ivanisevic; plus unseeded Mark Philippoussis, Davide Sanguinetti and Jan Siemerink.

Quarterfinals

Sampras def. Philippoussis ....76(5) 64 64
Henman def. Korda 63 64 62
Ivanisevic def. Siemerink.............76(10) 76(5) 76(6)
Krajicek def. Sanguinetti 62 63 64

Semifinals

Sampras def. Henman.....................63 46 75 63
Ivanisevic def. Krajicek............63 64 57 67(5) 15-13

Final

Sampras def. Ivanisevic............67(2) 76(9) 64 36 62

WOMEN'S SINGLES

FINAL EIGHT— #1 Martina Hingis; #2 Lindsay Davenport; #3 Jana Novotna; #5 Arantxa Sanchez Vicario; #6 Monica Seles; #7 Venus Williams; #16 Nathalie Tauziat; plus unseeded Natasha Zvereva.

Quarterfinals

Hingis def. Sanchez Vicario 63 36 63
Novotna def. Williams ....75 76(2)
Zvereva def. Seles ....76(4) 62
Tauziat def. Davenport...........................63 63

Semifinals

Novotna def. Hingis.............................64 64
Tauziat def. Zvereva ....16 76(1) 63

Final

Novotna def. Tauziat..........................64 76(2)

DOUBLES FINALS

Men— #1 Jacco Eltingh & Paul Haarhuis def. #2 Mark Woodforde & Todd Woodbridge, 2-6, 6-4, 7-6 (7-3), 5-7, 10-8.

Women— #1 Martina Hingis & Jana Novotna def. #2 Lindsay Davenport & Natasha Zvereva, 6-3, 3-6, 8-6.

Mixed— Max Mirnyi & Serena Williams def. #5 Mahesh Bhupathi & Mirjana Lucic, 6-4, 6-4.

U.S. Open

MEN'S SINGLES

FINAL EIGHT— #1 Pete Sampras, #3 Patrick Rafter, #9 Karol Kucera, #10 Carlos Moya, #12 Jonas Bjorkman; plus unseeded Thomas Johansson, Magnus Larsson and Mark Philippoussis.

Quarterfinals

Sampras def. Kucera 63 75 64
Rafter def. Bjorkman..........................62 63 75
Philippoussis def. Johansson.......46 63 67(3) 63 76(10)
Moya def. Larsson 64 63 63

Semifinals

Rafter def. Sampras..................67(8) 64 26 64 63
Philippoussis def. Moya....................61 64 57 64

Final

Rafter def. Philippoussis....................63 36 62 60

WOMEN'S SINGLES

FINAL EIGHT— #1 Martina Hingis; #2 Lindsay Davenport; #3 Jana Novotna; #4 Arantxa Sanchez Vicario, #5 Venus Williams, #6 Monica Seles, #11 Patty Schnyder and #13 Amanda Coetzer.

Quarterfinals

Hingis def. Seles...............................64 64
Novotna def. Schnyder 62 63
Williams def. Sanchez Vicario................26 61 61
Davenport def. Coetzer..........................60 64

Semifinals

Hingis def. Novotna..........................36 61 64
Davenport def. Williams 64 64

Final

Davenport def. Hingis 63 75

DOUBLES FINALS

Men— #15 Sandon Stolle & Cyril Suk def. #6 Mark Knowles & Daniel Nestor 4-6, 7-6 (10-8), 6-2.

Women— #1 Martina Hingis & Jana Novotna def. #2 Lindsay Davenport & Natasha Zvereva 6-3, 6-3.

Mixed— Serena Williams & Max Mirnyi def. #3 Lisa Raymond & Patrick Galbraith 6-2, 6-2.

1998 Fed Cup

Originally the Federation Cup and started in 1963 by the International Tennis Federation as the Davis Cup of women's tennis. Played by 32 teams over one week at one site through 1994. Tournament changed in 1995 to Davis Cup-style format of four rounds and home sides.

Quarterfinals

(April 17-19)

Winner	Loser
France 3	Belgium 2
Switzerland 4	Czech Republic 1
Spain 3	Germany 2
USA 5	Netherlands 0

Semifinals

Switzerland 5, France 0

at Sion, Switzerland (July 25-26)

Day One— Martina Hingis (SWI) def. Julie Halard-Decugis (FRA), 7-5, 6-1; Patty Schnyder (SWI) def. Amelie Mauresmo (FRA), 7-5, 2-6, 6-3.

Day Two— Hingis (SWI) def. Mauresmo (FRA), 6-7 (6-8), 6-4, 6-2; Schnyder (SWI) def. Halard-Decugis (FRA), 6-3, 6-2; Emmanuelle Gagliardi & Schnyder (SWI) def. Nathalie Tauziat & Alexandra Fusai (FRA), 2-6, 6-3, 6-3.

Spain 3, United States 2

at Madrid, Spain (July 25-26)

Day One— Arantxa Sanchez Vicario (SPA) def. Lisa Raymond (USA), 6-7 (4-7), 6-3, 6-0; Monica Seles (USA) def. Conchita Martinez (SPA), 6-3, 3-6, 6-1.

Day Two— Seles (USA) def. Sanchez Vicario (SPA), 6-4, 6-0; Martinez (SPA) def. Raymond (USA), 7-6 (7-1), 6-4; Sanchez Vicario & Martinez (SPA) def. Raymond & Mary Jo Fernandez (USA), 6-4, 6-7 (5-7), 11-9.

Finals

Spain 3, Switzerland 2

at Geneva, Switzerland (Sept. 19-20)

Day One— Arantxa Sanchez Vicario (SPA) def. Patty Schnyder (SWI), 6-2, 3-6, 6-2; Martina Hingis (SWI) def. Conchita Martinez (SPA), 6-4, 6-4.

Day Two— Hingis (SWI) def. Sanchez Vicario (SPA), 7-6 (7-5), 6-3; Martinez (SPA) def. Schnyder (SWI), 6-3, 2-6, 9-7; Sanchez Vicario & Martinez (SPA) def. Hingis & Schnyder (SWI), 6-0, 6-2.

Singles Leaders

Official Top 20 computer rankings and money leaders of men's and women's tours for 1997 and unofficial rankings and money leaders for 1998 (through Sept. 28), as compiled by the ATP Tour (Association of Tennis Professionals) and WTA (Women's Tennis Association). Note that money lists include doubles earnings.

Final 1997 Computer Rankings and Money Won

Listed are events won and times a finalist and semifinalist (Finish, 1-2-SF), match record (W-L), and earnings for the year.

MEN

		Finish 1-2-SF	W-L	Earnings
1	Pete Sampras	8-0-1	55-12	$6,498,311
2	Patrick Rafter	1-6-4	65-29	2,923,519
3	Michael Chang	5-0-5	57-21	2,541,830
4	Jonas Bjorkman	3-2-8	71-26	1,950,375
5	Yevgeny Kafelnikov	3-1-5	55-27	3,207,757
6	Greg Rusedski	2-4-5	53-23	1,515,473
7	Carlos Moya	1-5-4	56-30	1,137,400
8	Sergi Bruguera	0-4-2	49-28	1,227,428
9	Thomas Muster	2-1-3	46-24	2,166,590
10	Marcelo Rios	1-4-0	60-26	1,397,445
11	Richard Krajicek	3-1-1	49-19	1,434,564
12	Alex Corretja	3-2-2	49-22	1,182,807
13	Petr Korda	1-3-4	55-24	1,515,483
14	Gustavo Kuerten	1-2-1	36-25	1,586,753
15	Goran Ivanisevic	3-2-5	53-22	1,458,257
16	Felix Mantilla	5-1-1	53-22	1,105,593
17	Tim Henman	2-2-3	48-24	1,828,358
18	Mark Philippoussis	3-2-1	48-21	904,211
19	Albert Costa	2-0-4	44-22	864,684
20	Cedric Pioline	1-1-5	36-28	999,701

WOMEN

		Finish 1-2-SF	W-L	Earnings
1	Martina Hingis	12-1-2	75-5	$3,400,196
2	Jana Novotna	4-3-5	54-15	1,685,115
3	Lindsay Davenport	6-2-3	59-16	1,533,101
4	Amanda Coetzer	2-1-10	61-26	701,994
5	Monica Seles	3-4-1	45-13	914,020
6	Iva Majoli	3-0-4	45-23	1,227,332
7	Mary Pierce	1-4-1	45-15	881,639
8	Irina Spirlea	0-1-5	47-23	720,758
9	Arantxa Sanchez Vicario	0-2-4	47-24	890,512
10	Mary Joe Fernandez	1-0-4	40-18	769,132
11	Nathalie Tauziat	1-2-1	45-21	600,642
12	Conchita Martinez	0-2-3	37-19	528,544
13	Sandrine Testud	1-1-0	44-23	417,753
14	Anke Huber	0-2-2	36-23	411,315
15	Brenda Schultz-McCarthy	1-0-4	36-27	348,247
16	Sabine Appelmans	0-1-0	39-28	339,845
17	Lisa Raymond	0-2-2	31-21	450,070
18	Dominique van Roost	2-2-1	44-17	274,010
19	Ruxandra Dragomir	0-1-2	37-26	381,500
20	Ai Sugiyama	1-2-0	32-28	307,837

1998 Computer Rankings (through Sept. 28)

Listed are tournaments won and times a finalist and semifinalist (Finish, 1-2-SF), match record (W-L), and computer points earned (Pts).

MEN

ATP Tour singles rankings based on total computer points from each player's 14 best tournaments covering the last 12 months. Tournaments, titles and match won-lost records, however, are for 1998 only.

Rank 98	(97)		Finish 1-2-SF	W-L	Pts
1	(1)	Pete Sampras	3-2-1	44-12	4015
2	(2)	Patrick Rafter	6-0-2	54-16	3575
3	(10)	Marcelo Rios	5-1-3	51-13	3467
4	(13)	Petr Korda	2-0-0	33-15	2908
5	(7)	Carlos Moya	2-0-4	42-22	2858
6	(24)	Karol Kucera	2-1-4	45-20	2732
7	(12)	Alex Corretja	3-2-1	43-15	2626
8	(122)	Andre Agassi	4-3-2	53-13	2545
9	(11)	Richard Krajicek	1-1-4	39-19	2534
10	(5)	Yevgeny Kafelnikov	2-2-1	43-22	2508
11	(17)	Tim Henman	1-2-3	45-22	2366
12	(15)	Goran Ivanisevic	1-2-0	33-21	2203
13	(4)	Jonas Bjorkman	1-0-1	31-22	2115
14	(6)	Greg Rusedski	1-2-1	33-17	2091
15	(18)	Mark Philippoussis	1-1-0	28-16	1987
16	(19)	Albert Costa	2-2-0	46-18	1823
17	(23)	Alberto Berasategui	1-1-2	30-19	1793
18	(20)	Cedric Pioline	0-2-4	37-24	1766
19	(28)	Thomas Enqvist	2-1-0	32-11	1681
20	(78)	Jan Siemerink	1-0-2	35-20	1652

WOMEN

Corel WTA Tour singles ranking system based on total Round and Quality Points for each tournament played during the last 12 months. Tournaments, titles and match won-lost records, however, are for 1998 only.

Rank 98	(97)		Finish 1-2-SF	W-L	Pts
1	(1)	Martina Hingis	4-3-5	60-10	5496
2	(3)	Lindsay Davenport	5-1-5	56-11	5470
3	(2)	Jana Novotna	4-3-3	51-12	4819
4	(9)	Arantxa Sanchez Vicario	2-3-3	48-15	3743
5	(22)	Venus Williams	2-3-1	44-10	3015
6	(5)	Monica Seles	2-1-4	39-10	2855
7	(12)	Conchita Martinez	2-2-0	38-16	2404
8	(11)	Nathalie Tauziat	1-0-2	28-17	2301
9	(26)	Patty Schnyder	5-0-1	52-16	2274
10	(4)	Amanda Coetzer	1-0-2	27-17	1963
11	(7)	Mary Pierce	2-1-0	22-9	1948
12	(18)	Dominique van Roost	1-4-0	36-21	1926
13	(32)	Anna Kournikova	0-1-3	39-15	1917
14	(8)	Irina Spirlea	1-1-0	27-18	1893
15	(20)	Ai Sugiyama	2-0-1	33-16	1669
16	(17)	Lisa Raymond	0-0-2	25-19	1612
17	(25)	Natasha Zvereva	0-0-3	30-16	1569
18	(13)	Sandrine Testud	0-1-3	43-22	1454
19	(99)	Serena Williams	0-0-1	27-10	1418
20	(14)	Anke Huber	0-0-2	19-14	1317

1998 Money Winners

Amounts include singles and doubles earnings through Sept. 28.

MEN

	Earnings
1 Patrick Rafter	$2,085,807
2 Marcelo Rios	1,681,071
3 Pete Sampras	1,541,537
4 Carlos Moya	1,536,423
5 Alex Corretja	1,167,839
6 Petr Korda	1,027,213
7 Yevgeny Kafelnikov	956,422
8 Albert Costa	941,326
9 Goran Ivanisevic	882,922
10 Mark Philippoussis	$865,320
11 Karol Kucera	857,277
12 Andre Agassi	840,018
13 Jonas Bjorkman	822,344
14 Richard Krajicek	818,144
15 Tim Henman	790,420
16 Paul Haarhuis	661,377
17 Cedric Pioline	656,738
18 Gustavo Kuerten	646,904
19 Greg Rusedski	$631,237
20 Alberto Berasategui	620,760
21 Felix Mantilla	615,196
22 Mark Woodforde	568,537
23 Jacco Eltingh	567,560
24 Todd Woodbridge	550,779
25 Daniel Vacek	535,868

WOMEN

	Earnings
1 Martina Hingis	$2,391,971
2 Lindsay Davenport	1,944,443
3 Jana Novotna	1,819,675
4 Arantxa Sanchez Vicario	1,278,344
5 Venus Williams	913,346
6 Monica Seles	831,739
7 Conchita Martinez	695,982
8 Natasha Zvereva	675,415
9 Nathalie Tauziat	598,764
10 Patty Schnyder	$512,913
11 Amanda Coetzer	464,453
12 Anna Kournikova	448,748
13 Mary Pierce	359,162
14 Irina Spirlea	324,643
15 Lisa Raymond	322,853
16 Sandrine Testud	317,685
17 Dominique van Roost	316,224
18 Ai Sugiyama	282,190
19 Mirjana Lucic	$274,905
20 Serena Williams	273,261
21 Iva Majoli	271,141
22 Steffi Graf	253,527
23 Elena Likhovtseva	253,041
24 Virginia Ruano-Pascual	246,896
25 Silvia Farina	238,581

Davis Cup

Sweden romped to a 5-0 sweep of the United States in the 1997 Davis Cup Finals. It was the Swedes' sixth Davis Cup title overall and their fifth in the last 13 years. The Finals shutout was the first since Sweden blanked India in 1987. The Americans hadn't been shutout in the finals since 1973, when they were crushed by Australia.

1997 Final

Sweden 5, United States 0

at Goteborg, Sweden (Nov. 28-30)

Day One— Jonas Bjorkman (SWE) def. Michael Chang (USA), 7-5, 1-6, 6-3, 6-3; Magnus Larsson (SWE) def. Pete Sampras (USA), 3-6, 7-6 (1), 2-1 (def.).

Day Two— Bjorkman & Nicklas Kulti (SWE) def. Todd Martin & Jonathan Stark (USA), 6-4, 6-4, 6-4.

Day Three— Bjorkman (SWE) def. Stark (USA), 6-1, 6-1; Larsson (SWE) def. Chang (USA), 7-6(4), 6-7(6), 6-4.

1998 Early Rounds

FIRST ROUND

(April 3-5)

Winner	Loser
at United States 3	Russia 2
Sweden 3	at Slovakia 2
at Germany 5	South Africa 0
Spain 3	at Brazil 2
at Switzerland 3	Czech Republic 2
at Italy 4	India 1
Zimbabwe 3	at Australia 2
at Belgium 3	Netherlands 2

QUARTERFINALS

(July 17-19)

Winner	Loser
at United States 4	Belgium 1
Sweden 3	at Germany 2
at Spain 4	Switzerland 1
at Italy 5	Zimbabwe 0

SEMIFINALS

Italy 4, United States 1

at Milwaukee, Wisc. (Sept. 25-27)

Day One— Andrea Gaudenzi (ITA) def. Jan-Michael Gambill (USA), 6-2, 0-6, 7-6(0), 7-6(4); Davide Sanguinetti (ITA) def. Todd Martin (USA), 7-6(0), 6-3, 7-6(8).

Day Two— Diego Nargiso & Gaudenzi (ITA) def. Martin & Justin Gimelstob (USA), 6-4, 7-6(3), 5-7, 2-6, 6-3.

Day Three— Gianluca Pozzi (ITA) def. Gimelstob (USA), 7-6(4), 7-5; Gambill (USA) def. Sanguinetti (ITA), 4-6, 6-3, 6-3.

Sweden 4, Spain 1

at Stockholm, Sweden (Sept. 25-27)

Day One— Jonas Bjorkman (SWE) def. Alex Corretja (SPA), 6-3, 7-5, 6-7(5), 6-3; Thomas Johansson (SWE) def. Carlos Moya (SPA), 7-5, 7-6(4), 7-6(6).

Day Two— Bjorkman & Nicklas Kulti (SWE) def. Javier Sanchez & Julian Alonso (SPA), 6-2, 6-2, 6-2.

Day Three— Bjorkman (SWE) def. Moya (SPA), 6-3, 7-5; Alonso (SPA) def. Johansson (SWE), 6-1, 7-6(0).

FINAL

Italy plays host to the 1998 Davis Cup final from Dec. 4-6. Jonas Bjorkman will once again lead the Swedes against an Italian team searching for revenge. Sweden, the defending champion, defeated Italy, 4-1, in a 1997 semifinal match. Sweden has won the Davis Cup six times while the Italians' only win came in 1976.

TENNIS STATISTICS

THROUGH THE YEARS

1877-1998

MAJOR TITLES • LEADERS

Grand Slam Championships

Australian Open

MEN

Became an Open Championship in 1969. Two tournaments were held in 1977; the first in January, the second in December. Tournament moved back to January in 1987, so no championship was decided in 1986.

Surface: Synpave Rebound Ace (hardcourt surface composed of polyurethane and synthetic rubber).

Multiple winners: Roy Emerson (6); Jack Crawford and Ken Rosewall (4); James Anderson, Rod Laver, Adrian Quist, Mats Wilander and Pat Wood (3); Boris Becker, Jack Bromwich, Ashley Cooper, Jim Courier, Stefan Edberg, Rodney Heath, Johan Kriek, Ivan Lendl, John Newcombe, Pete Sampras, Frank Sedgman, Guillermo Vilas and Tony Wilding (2).

Year	Winner	Loser	Score
1905	Rodney Heath	A. Curtis	46 63 64 64
1906	Tony Wilding	H. Parker	60 64 64
1907	Horace Rice	H. Parker	63 64 64
1908	Fred Alexander	A. Dunlop	36 36 60 62 63
1909	Tony Wilding	E. Parker	61 75 62
1910	Rodney Heath	H. Rice	64 63 62
1911	Norman Brookes	H. Rice	61 62 63
1912	J. Cecil Parke	A. Beamish	36 63 16 61 75
1913	Ernie Parker	H. Parker	26 61 62 63
1914	Pat Wood	G. Patterson	64 63 57 61
1915	Francis Lowe	H. Rice	46 61 61 64
1916-18	Not held	World War I	
1919	A.R.F. Kingscote	E. Pockley	64 60 63
1920	Pat Wood	R. Thomas	63 46 68 61 63
1921	Rhys Gemmell	A. Hedeman	75 61 64
1922	James Anderson	G. Patterson	60 36 36 63 62
1923	Pat Wood	C.B. St. John	61 61 63
1924	James Anderson	R. Schlesinger	63 64 36 57 63
1925	James Anderson	G. Patterson	11-9 26 62 63
1926	John Hawkes	J. Willard	61 63 61
1927	Gerald Patterson	J. Hawkes	36 64 36 18-16 63
1928	Jean Borotra	R.O. Cummings	64 61 46 57 63
1929	John Gregory	R. Schlesinger	62 62 57 75
1930	Gar Moon	H. Hopman	63 61 63
1931	Jack Crawford	H. Hopman	64 62 26 61
1932	Jack Crawford	H. Hopman	46 63 36 63 61
1933	Jack Crawford	K. Gledhill	26 75 63 62
1934	Fred Perry	J. Crawford	63 75 61
1935	Jack Crawford	F. Perry	26 64 64 64
1936	Adrian Quist	J. Crawford	62 63 46 36 97
1937	Viv McGrath	J. Bromwich	63 16 60 26 61
1938	Don Budge	J. Bromwich	64 62 61
1939	Jack Bromwich	A. Quist	64 61 63
1940	Adrian Quist	J. Crawford	63 61 62
1941-45	Not held	World War II	
1946	Jack Bromwich	D. Pails	57 63 75 36 62
1947	Dinny Pails	J. Bromwich	46 64 36 75 86
1948	Adrian Quist	J. Bromwich	64 36 63 26 63
1949	Frank Sedgman	J. Bromwich	63 63 62
1950	Frank Sedgman	K. McGregor	63 64 46 61
1951	Dick Savitt	K. McGregor	63 26 63 61
1952	Ken McGregor	F. Sedgman	75 12-10 26 62
1953	Ken Rosewall	M. Rose	60 63 64
1954	Mervyn Rose	R. Hartwig	62 06 64 62
1955	Ken Rosewall	L. Hoad	97 64 64
1956	Lew Hoad	K. Rosewall	64 36 64 75
1957	Ashley Cooper	N. Fraser	63 9-11 64 62
1958	Ashley Cooper	M. Anderson	75 63 64
1959	Alex Olmedo	N. Fraser	61 62 36 63
1960	Rod Laver	N. Fraser	57 36 63 86 86
1961	Roy Emerson	R. Laver	16 63 75 64
1962	Rod Laver	R. Emerson	86 06 64 64
1963	Roy Emerson	K. Fletcher	63 63 61
1964	Roy Emerson	F. Stolle	63 64 62
1965	Roy Emerson	F. Stolle	79 26 64 75 61
1966	Roy Emerson	A. Ashe	64 68 62 63
1967	Roy Emerson	A. Ashe	64 61 61
1968	Bill Bowrey	J. Gisbert	75 26 97 64
1969	Rod Laver	A. Gimeno	63 64 75
1970	Arthur Ashe	D. Crealy	64 97 62
1971	Ken Rosewall	A. Ashe	61 75 63
1972	Ken Rosewall	M. Anderson	76 63 75
1973	John Newcombe	O. Parun	63 67 75 61
1974	Jimmy Connors	P. Dent	76 64 46 63
1975	John Newcombe	J. Connors	75 36 64 75
1976	Mark Edmondson	J. Newcombe	67 63 76 61
1977	Roscoe Tanner	G. Vilas	63 63 63
	Vitas Gerulaitis	J. Lloyd	63 76 57 36 62
1978	Guillermo Vilas	J. Marks	64 64 36 63
1979	Guillermo Vilas	J. Sadri	76 63 62
1980	Brian Teacher	K. Warwick	75 76 63
1981	Johan Kriek	S. Denton	62 76 67 64
1982	Johan Kriek	S. Denton	63 63 62
1983	Mats Wilander	I. Lendl	61 64 64
1984	Mats Wilander	K. Curren	67 64 76 62
1985	Stefan Edberg	M. Wilander	64 63 63
1986	Not held		
1987	Stefan Edberg	P. Cash	63 64 36 57 63
1988	Mats Wilander	P. Cash	63 67 36 61 86
1989	Ivan Lendl	M. Mecir	62 62 62
1990	Ivan Lendl	S. Edberg	46 76 52 (ret.)
1991	Boris Becker	I. Lendl	16 64 64 64
1992	Jim Courier	S. Edberg	63 36 64 62
1993	Jim Courier	S. Edberg	62 61 26 75
1994	Pete Sampras	T. Martin	76 64 64
1995	Andre Agassi	P. Sampras	46 61 76 64
1996	Boris Becker	M. Chang	62 64 26 62
1997	Pete Sampras	C. Moya	62 63 63
1998	Petr Korda	M. Rios	62 62 62

WOMEN

Became an Open Championship in 1969. Two tournaments were held in 1977, the first in January, the second in December. Tournament moved back to January in 1987, so no championship was decided in 1986.

Multiple winners: Margaret Smith Court (11); Nancye Wynne Bolton (6); Daphne Akhurst (5); Evonne Goolagong Cawley, Steffi Graf and Monica Seles (4); Jean Hartigan and Martina Navratilova (3); Coral Buttsworth, Martina Hingis, Chris Evert Lloyd, Thelma Long, Hana Mandlikova, Mall Molesworth and Mary Carter Reitano (2).

Year	Winner	Loser	Score
1922	Mall Molesworth	E. Boyd	63 10-8
1923	Mall Molesworth	E. Boyd	61 75
1924	Sylvia Lance	E. Boyd	63 36 64
1925	Daphne Akhurst	E. Boyd	16 86 64
1926	Daphne Akhurst	E. Boyd	61 63
1927	Esna Boyd	S. Harper	57 61 62
1928	Daphne Akhurst	E. Boyd	75 62
1929	Daphne Akhurst	L. Bickerton	61 57 62
1930	Daphne Akhurst	S. Harper	10-8 26 75
1931	Coral Buttsworth	M. Crawford	16 63 64
1932	Coral Buttsworth	K. Le Messurier	97 64
1933	Joan Hartigan	C. Buttsworth	64 63
1934	Joan Hartigan	M. Molesworth	61 64
1935	Dorothy Round	N. Lyle	16 61 63
1936	Joan Hartigan	N. Bolton	64 64
1937	Nancye Wynne	E. Westacott	63 57 64
1938	Dorothy Bundy	D. Stevenson	63 62
1939	Emily Westacott	N. Hopman	61 62
1940	Nancye Wynne	T. Coyne	57 64 60
1941-45	Not held	World War II	
1946	Nancye Bolton	J. Fitch	64 64
1947	Nancye Bolton	N. Hopman	63 62
1948	Nancye Bolton	M. Toomey	63 61
1949	Doris Hart	N. Bolton	63 64
1950	Louise Brough	D. Hart	64 36 64
1951	Nancye Bolton	T. Long	61 75
1952	Thelma Long	H. Angwin	62 63
1953	Maureen Connolly	J. Sampson	63 62
1954	Thelma Long	J. Staley	63 64
1955	Beryl Penrose	T. Long	64 63
1956	Mary Carter	T. Long	36 62 97
1957	Shirley Fry	A. Gibson	63 64
1958	Angela Mortimer	L. Coghlan	63 64
1959	Mary Reitano	T. Schuurman	62 63
1960	Margaret Smith	J. Lehane	75 62
1961	Margaret Smith	J. Lehane	61 64
1962	Margaret Smith	J. Lehane	60 62
1963	Margaret Smith	J. Lehane	62 62
1964	Margaret Smith	L. Turner	63 62
1965	Margaret Smith	M. Bueno	57 64 52 (ret)
1966	Margaret Smith	N. Richey	walkover
1967	Nancy Richey	L. Turner	61 64
1968	Billie Jean King	M. Smith	61 62
1969	Margaret Court	B.J. King	64 61
1970	Margaret Court	K. Melville	61 63
1971	Margaret Court	E. Goolagong	26 76 75
1972	Virginia Wade	E. Goolagong	64 64
1973	Margaret Court	E. Goolagong	64 75
1974	Evonne Goolagong	C. Evert	76 46 60
1975	Evonne Goolagong	M. Navratilova	63 62
1976	Evonne Cawley	R. Tomanova	62 62
1977	Kerry Reid	D. Balestrat	75 62
	Evonne Cawley	H. Gourlay	63 60
1978	Chris O'Neil	B. Nagelsen	63 76
1979	Barbara Jordan	S. Walsh	63 63
1980	Hana Mandlikova	W. Turnbull	60 75
1981	Martina Navratilova	C. Evert Lloyd	67 64 75
1982	Chris Evert Lloyd	M. Navratilova	63 26 63
1983	Martina Navratilova	K. Jordan	62 76
1984	Chris Evert Lloyd	H. Sukova	67 61 63
1985	Martina Navratilova	C. Evert Lloyd	62 46 62
1986	Not held		
1987	Hana Mandlikova	M. Navratilova	75 76
1988	Steffi Graf	C. Evert	61 76
1989	Steffi Graf	H. Sukova	64 64
1990	Steffi Graf	M.J. Fernandez	63 64
1991	Monica Seles	J. Novotna	57 63 61
1992	Monica Seles	M.J. Fernandez	62 63
1993	Monica Seles	S. Graf	46 63 62
1994	Steffi Graf	A.S. Vicario	60 62
1995	Mary Pierce	A.S. Vicario	63 62
1996	Monica Seles	A. Huber	64 61
1997	Martina Hingis	M. Pierce	62 62
1998	Martina Hingis	C. Martinez	63 63

French Open

MEN

Prior to 1925, entry was restricted to members of French clubs. Became an Open Championship in 1968, but closed to contract pros in 1972.

Surface: Red clay.

First year: 1891. **Most wins:** Max Decugis (8).

Multiple winners (since 1925): Bjorn Borg (6); Henri Cochet (4); Rene Lacoste, Ivan Lendl and Mats Wilander (3); Sergi Bruguera, Jim Courier, Jaroslav Drobny, Roy Emerson, Jan Kodes, Rod Laver, Frank Parker, Nicola Pietrangeli, Ken Rosewall, Manuel Santana, Tony Trabert and Gottfried von Cramm (2).

Year	Winner	Loser	Score
1925	Rene Lacoste	J. Borotra	75 61 64
1926	Henri Cochet	R. Lacoste	62 64 63
1927	Rene Lacoste	B. Tilden	64 46 57 63 11-9
1928	Henri Cochet	R. Lacoste	57 63 61 63
1929	Rene Lacoste	J. Borotra	63 26 60 26 86
1930	Henri Cochet	B. Tilden	36 86 63 61
1931	Jean Borotra	C. Boussus	26 64 75 64
1932	Henri Cochet	G. de Stefani	60 64 46 63
1933	Jack Crawford	H. Cochet	86 61 63
1934	Gottfried von Cramm	J. Crawford	64 79 36 75 63
1935	Fred Perry	G. von Cramm	63 36 61 63
1936	Gottfried von Cramm	F. Perry	60 26 62 26 60
1937	Henner Henkel	H. Austin	61 64 63
1938	Don Budge	R. Menzel	63 62 64
1939	Don McNeill	B. Riggs	75 60 63
1941-45	Not held	World War II	
1946	Marcel Bernard	J. Drobny	36 26 61 64 63
1947	Joseph Asboth	E. Sturgess	86 75 64
1948	Frank Parker	J. Drobny	64 75 57 86
1949	Frank Parker	B. Patty	63 16 61 64
1950	Budge Patty	J. Drobny	61 62 36 57 75
1951	Jaroslav Drobny	E. Sturgess	63 63 63
1952	Jaroslav Drobny	F. Sedgman	62 60 36 64
1953	Ken Rosewall	V. Seixas	63 64 16 62
1954	Tony Trabert	A. Larsen	64 75 61
1955	Tony Trabert	S. Davidson	26 61 64 62

Year	Winner	Loser	Score
1956	Lew Hoad	S. Davidson	64 86 63
1957	Sven Davidson	H. Flam	63 64 64
1958	Mervyn Rose	L. Ayala	63 64 64
1959	Nicola Pietrangeli	I. Vermaak	36 63 64 61
1960	Nicola Pietrangeli	L. Ayala	36 63 64 46 63
1961	Manuel Santana	N. Pietrangeli	46 61 36 60 62
1962	Rod Laver	R. Emerson	36 26 63 97 62
1963	Roy Emerson	P. Darmon	36 61 64 64
1964	Manuel Santana	N. Pietrangeli	63 61 46 75
1965	Fred Stolle	T. Roche	36 60 62 63
1966	Tony Roche	I. Gulyas	61 64 75
1967	Roy Emerson	T. Roche	61 64 26 62
1968	Ken Rosewall	R. Laver	63 61 26 62
1969	Rod Laver	K. Rosewall	64 63 64
1970	Jan Kodes	Z. Franulovic	62 64 60
1971	Jan Kodes	I. Nastase	86 62 26 75
1972	Andres Gimeno	P. Proisy	46 63 61 61
1973	Ilie Nastase	N. Pilic	63 63 60
1974	Bjorn Borg	M. Orantes	26 67 60 61 61
1975	Bjorn Borg	G. Vilas	62 63 64
1976	Adriano Panatta	H. Solomon	61 64 46 76
1977	Guillermo Vilas	B. Gottfried	60 63 60
1978	Bjorn Borg	G. Vilas	61 61 63
1979	Bjorn Borg	V. Pecci	63 61 67 64
1980	Bjorn Borg	V. Gerulaitis	64 61 62
1981	Bjorn Borg	I. Lendl	61 46 62 36 61
1982	Mats Wilander	G. Vilas	16 76 60 64
1983	Yannick Noah	M. Wilander	62 75 76
1984	Ivan Lendl	J. McEnroe	36 26 64 75 75
1985	Mats Wilander	I. Lendl	36 64 62 62
1986	Ivan Lendl	M. Pernfors	63 62 64
1987	Ivan Lendl	M. Wilander	75 62 36 76
1988	Mats Wilander	H. Leconte	75 62 61
1989	Michael Chang	S. Edberg	61 36 46 64 62
1990	Andres Gomez	A. Agassi	63 26 64 64
1991	Jim Courier	A. Agassi	36 64 26 61 64
1992	Jim Courier	P. Korda	75 62 61
1993	Sergi Bruguera	J. Courier	64 26 62 36 63
1994	Sergi Bruguera	A. Berasategui	63 75 26 61
1995	Thomas Muster	M. Chang	75 62 64
1996	Yevgeny Kafelnikov	M. Stich	76 75 76
1997	Gustavo Kuerten	S. Bruguera	63 64 62
1998	Carlos Moya	A. Corretja	63 75 63

WOMEN

Prior to 1925, entry was restricted to members of French clubs. Became an Open Championship in 1968, but closed to contract pros in 1972.

First year: 1897. **Most wins:** Chris Evert Lloyd (7) and Suzanne Lenglen (6).

Multiple winners (since 1920): Chris Evert Lloyd (7); Margaret Smith Court and Steffi Graf (5); Helen Wills Moody (4); Arantxa Sanchez Vicario, Monica Seles and Hilde Sperling (3); Maureen Connolly, Margaret Osborne duPont, Doris Hart, Ann Haydon Jones, Suzanne Lenglen, Simone Mathieu, Margaret Scriven, Martina Navratilova and Lesley Turner (2).

Year	Winner	Loser	Score
1925	Suzanne Lenglen	K. McKane	61 62
1926	Suzanne Lenglen	M. Browne	61 60
1927	Kea Bouman	I. Peacock	62 64
1928	Helen Wills	E. Bennett	61 62
1929	Helen Wills	S. Mathieu	63 64
1930	Helen Moody	H. Jacobs	62 61
1931	Cilly Aussem	B. Nuthall	86 61
1932	Helen Moody	S. Mathieu	75 61
1933	Margaret Scriven	S. Mathieu	62 46 64
1934	Margaret Scriven	H. Jacobs	75 46 61
1935	Hilde Sperling	S. Mathieu	62 61
1936	Hilde Sperling	S. Mathieu	63 64
1937	Hilde Sperling	S. Mathieu	62 64
1938	Simone Mathieu	N. Landry	60 63
1939	Simone Mathieu	J. Jedrzejowska	63 86
1940-45	Not held	World War II	
1946	Margaret Osborne	P. Betz	16 86 75
1947	Patricia Todd	D. Hart	63 36 64
1948	Nelly Landry	S. Fry	62 06 60
1949	Margaret duPont	N. Adamson	75 62
1950	Doris Hart	P. Todd	64 46 62
1951	Shirley Fry	D. Hart	63 36 63
1952	Doris Hart	S. Fry	64 64
1953	Maureen Connolly	D. Hart	62 64
1954	Maureen Connolly	G. Bucaille	64 61
1955	Angela Mortimer	D. Knode	26 75 10-8
1956	Althea Gibson	A. Mortimer	60 12-10
1957	Shirley Bloomer	D. Knode	61 63
1958	Susi Kormoczi	S. Bloomer	64 16 62
1959	Christine Truman	S. Kormoczi	64 75
1960	Darlene Hard	Y. Ramirez	63 64
1961	Ann Haydon	Y. Ramirez	62 61
1962	Margaret Smith	L. Turner	63 36 75
1963	Lesley Turner	A. Jones	26 63 75
1964	Margaret Smith	M. Bueno	57 61 62
1965	Lesley Turner	M. Smith	63 64
1966	Ann Jones	N. Richey	63 61
1967	Francoise Durr	L. Turner	46 63 64
1968	Nancy Richey	A. Jones	57 64 61
1969	Margaret Court	A. Jones	61 46 63
1970	Margaret Court	H. Niessen	62 64
1971	Evonne Goolagong	H. Gourlay	63 75
1972	Billie Jean King	E. Goolagong	63 63
1973	Margaret Court	C. Evert	67 76 64
1974	Chris Evert	O. Morozova	61 62
1975	Chris Evert	M. Navratilova	26 62 61
1976	Sue Barker	R. Tomanova	62 06 62
1977	Mima Jausovec	F. Mihai	62 67 61
1978	Virginia Ruzici	M. Jausovec	62 62
1979	Chris Evert Lloyd	W. Turnbull	62 60
1980	Chris Evert Lloyd	V. Ruzici	60 63
1981	Hana Mandlikova	S. Hanika	62 64
1982	Martina Navratilova	A. Jaeger	76 61
1983	Chris Evert Lloyd	M. Jausovec	61 62
1984	Martina Navratilova	C. Evert Lloyd	63 61
1985	Chris Evert Lloyd	M. Navratilova	63 67 75
1986	Chris Evert Lloyd	M. Navratilova	26 63 63
1987	Steffi Graf	M. Navratilova	64 46 86
1988	Steffi Graf	N. Zvereva	60 60
1989	A. Sanchez Vicario	S. Graf	76 36 75
1990	Monica Seles	S. Graf	76 64
1991	Monica Seles	A.S. Vicario	63 64
1992	Monica Seles	S. Graf	62 36 10-8
1993	Steffi Graf	M.J. Fernandez	46 62 64
1994	A. Sanchez Vicario	M. Pierce	64 64
1995	Steffi Graff	A.S. Vicario	76 46 60
1996	Steffi Graf	A.S. Vicario	63 61
1997	Iva Majoli	M. Hingis	64 62
1998	A. Sanchez Vicario	M. Seles	76 06 62

Wimbledon

MEN

Officially called "The Lawn Tennis Championships" at the All England Club, Wimbledon. Challenge round system (defending champion qualified for following year's final) used from 1877-1921. Became an Open Championship in 1968, but closed to contract pros in 1972.

Surface: Grass.

Multiple winners: Willie Renshaw (7); Bjorn Borg, Laurie Doherty and Pete Sampras (5); Reggie Doherty, Rod Laver and Tony Wilding (4); Wilfred Baddeley, Boris Becker, Arthur Gore, John McEnroe, John Newcombe, Fred Perry and Bill Tilden (3); Jean Borotra, Norman Brookes, Don Budge, Henri Cochet, Jimmy Connors, Stefan Edberg, Roy Emerson, John Hartley, Lew Hoad, Rene Lacoste, Gerald Patterson and Joshua Pim (2).

Year	Winner	Loser	Score
1877	Spencer Gore	W. Marshall	61 62 64
1878	Frank Hadow	S. Gore	75 61 97
1879	John Hartley	V. St. L. Gould	62 64 62
1880	John Hartley	H. Lawford	60 62 26 63
1881	Willie Renshaw	J. Hartley	60 62 61
1882	Willie Renshaw	E. Renshaw	61 26 46 62 62
1883	Willie Renshaw	E. Renshaw	26 63 63 46 63
1884	Willie Renshaw	H. Lawford	60 64 97
1885	Willie Renshaw	H. Lawford	75 62 46 75
1886	Willie Renshaw	H. Lawford	60 57 63 64
1887	Herbert Lawford	E. Renshaw	16 63 36 64 64
1888	Ernest Renshaw	H. Lawford	63 75 60
1889	Willie Renshaw	E. Renshaw	64 61 36 60
1890	William Hamilton	W. Renshaw	68 62 36 61 61
1891	Wilfred Baddeley	J. Pim	64 16 75 60
1892	Wilfred Baddeley	J. Pim	46 63 63 62
1893	Joshua Pim	W. Baddeley	36 61 63 62
1894	Joshua Pim	W. Baddeley	10-8 62 86
1895	Wilfred Baddeley	W. Eaves	46 26 86 62 63
1896	Harold Mahony	W. Baddeley	62 68 57 86 63
1897	Reggie Doherty	H. Mahony	64 64 63
1898	Reggie Doherty	L. Doherty	63 63 26 57 61
1899	Reggie Doherty	A. Gore	16 46 62 63 63
1900	Reggie Doherty	S. Smith	68 63 61 62
1901	Arthur Gore	R. Doherty	46 75 64 64
1902	Laurie Doherty	A. Gore	64 63 36 60
1903	Laurie Doherty	F. Riseley	75 63 60
1904	Laurie Doherty	F. Riseley	61 75 86
1905	Laurie Doherty	N. Brookes	86 62 64
1906	Laurie Doherty	F. Riseley	64 46 62 63
1907	Norman Brookes	A. Gore	64 62 62
1908	Arthur Gore	R. Barrett	63 62 46 36 64
1909	Arthur Gore	M. Ritchie	68 16 62 62 62
1910	Tony Wilding	A. Gore	64 75 46 62
1911	Tony Wilding	R. Barrett	64 46 26 62 (ret)
1912	Tony Wilding	A. Gore	64 64 46 64
1913	Tony Wilding	M. McLoughlin	86 63 10-8
1914	Norman Brookes	T. Wilding	64 64 75
1915-18	Not held	World War I	
1919	Gerald Patterson	N. Brookes	63 75 62
1920	Bill Tilden	G. Patterson	26 63 62 64
1921	Bill Tilden	B. Norton	46 26 61 60 75
1922	Gerald Patterson	R. Lycett	63 64 62
1923	Bill Johnston	F. Hunter	60 63 61
1924	Jean Borotra	R. Lacoste	61 36 61 36 64
1925	Rene Lacoste	J. Borotra	63 63 46 86
1926	Jean Borotra	H. Kinsey	86 61 63
1927	Henri Cochet	J. Borotra	46 46 63 64 75
1928	Rene Lacoste	H. Cochet	61 46 64 62
1929	Henri Cochet	J. Borotra	64 63 64
1930	Bill Tilden	W. Allison	63 97 64
1931	Sidney Wood	F. Shields	walkover
1932	Ellsworth Vines	H. Austin	64 62 60
1933	Jack Crawford	E. Vines	46 11-9 62 26 64
1934	Fred Perry	J. Crawford	63 60 75
1935	Fred Perry	G. von Cramm	62 64 64
1936	Fred Perry	G. von Cramm	61 61 60
1937	Don Budge	G. von Cramm	63 64 62
1938	Don Budge	H. Austin	61 60 63
1939	Bobby Riggs	E. Cooke	26 86 36 63 62
1940-45	Not held	World War II	
1946	Yvon Petra	G. Brown	62 64 79 57 64
1947	Jack Kramer	T. Brown	61 63 62
1948	Bob Falkenburg	J. Bromwich	75 06 62 36 75
1949	Ted Schroeder	J. Drobny	36 60 63 46 64
1950	Budge Patty	F. Sedgman	61 8-10 62 63
1951	Dick Savitt	K. McGregor	64 64 64
1952	Frank Sedgman	J. Drobny	46 62 63 62
1953	Vic Seixas	K. Nielsen	97 63 64
1954	Jaroslav Drobny	K. Rosewall	13-11 46 62 97
1955	Tony Trabert	K. Nielsen	63 75 61
1956	Lew Hoad	K. Rosewall	62 46 75 64
1957	Lew Hoad	A. Cooper	62 61 62
1958	Ashley Cooper	N. Fraser	36 63 64 13-11
1959	Alex Olmedo	R. Laver	64 63 64
1960	Neale Fraser	R. Laver	64 36 97 75
1961	Rod Laver	C. McKinley	63 61 64
1962	Rod Laver	M. Mulligan	62 62 61
1963	Chuck McKinley	F. Stolle	97 61 64
1964	Roy Emerson	F. Stolle	64 12-10 46 63
1965	Roy Emerson	F. Stolle	62 64 64
1966	Manuel Santana	D. Ralston	64 11-9 64
1967	John Newcombe	W. Bungert	63 61 61
1968	Rod Laver	T. Roche	63 64 62
1969	Rod Laver	J. Newcombe	64 57 64 64
1970	John Newcombe	K. Rosewall	57 63 62 36 61
1971	John Newcombe	S. Smith	63 57 26 64 64
1972	Stan Smith	I. Nastase	46 63 63 46 75
1973	Jan Kodes	A. Metreveli	61 98 63
1974	Jimmy Connors	K. Rosewall	61 61 64
1975	Arthur Ashe	J. Connors	61 61 57 64
1976	Bjorn Borg	I. Nastase	64 62 97
1977	Bjorn Borg	J. Connors	36 62 61 57 64
1978	Bjorn Borg	J. Connors	62 62 63
1979	Bjorn Borg	R. Tanner	67 61 36 63 64
1980	Bjorn Borg	J. McEnroe	16 75 63 67 86
1981	John McEnroe	B. Borg	46 76 76 64
1982	Jimmy Connors	J. McEnroe	36 63 67 76 64
1983	John McEnroe	C. Lewis	62 62 62
1984	John McEnroe	J. Connors	61 61 62
1985	Boris Becker	K. Curren	63 67 76 64
1986	Boris Becker	I. Lendl	64 63 75
1987	Pat Cash	I. Lendl	76 62 75
1988	Stefan Edberg	B. Becker	46 76 64 62
1989	Boris Becker	S. Edberg	60 76 64
1990	Stefan Edberg	B. Becker	62 62 36 36 64
1991	Michael Stich	B. Becker	64 76 64
1992	Andre Agassi	G. Ivanisevic	67 64 64 16 64
1993	Pete Sampras	J. Courier	76 76 36 63
1994	Pete Sampras	G. Ivanisevic	76 76 60
1995	Pete Sampras	B. Becker	67 62 64 62
1996	Richard Krajicek	M. Washington	63 64 63
1997	Pete Sampras	C. Pioline	64 62 64
1998	Pete Sampras	G. Ivanisevic	67 76 64 36 62

WOMEN

Officially called "The Lawn Tennis Championships" at the All England Club, Wimbledon. Challenge round system (defending champion qualified for following year's final) used from 1877-1921. Became an Open Championship in 1968, but closed to contract pros in 1972.

Multiple winners: Martina Navratilova (9); Helen Willis Moody (8); Dorothea Douglass Chambers and Steffi Graf (7); Blanche Bingley Hillyard, Billie Jean King and Suzanne Lenglen (6); Lottie Dod and Charlotte Cooper Sterry (5); Louise Brough (4); Maria Bueno, Maureen Connolly, Margaret Smith Court and Chris Evert Lloyd (3); Evonne Goolagong Cawley, Althea Gibson, Dorothy Round, May Sutton and Maud Watson (2).

Year	Winner	Loser	Score
1884	Maud Watson	L. Watson	68 63 63
1885	Maud Watson	B. Bingley	61 75
1886	Blanche Bingley	M. Watson	63 63
1887	Lottie Dod	B. Bingley	62 60
1888	Lottie Dod	B. Hillyard	63 63
1889	Blanche Hillyard	L. Rice	46 86 64
1890	Lena Rice	M. Jacks	64 61
1891	Lottie Dod	B. Hillyard	62 61
1892	Lottie Dod	B. Hillyard	61 61
1893	Lottie Dod	B. Hillyard	68 61 64
1894	Blanche Hillyard	E. Austin	61 61
1895	Charlotte Cooper	H. Jackson	75 86
1896	Charlotte Cooper	W. Pickering	62 63
1897	Blanche Hillyard	C. Cooper	57 75 62
1898	Charlotte Cooper	L. Martin	64 64
1899	Blanche Hillyard	C. Cooper	62 63
1900	Blanche Hillyard	C. Cooper	46 64 64
1901	Charlotte Sterry	B. Hillyard	62 62
1902	Muriel Robb	C. Sterry	75 61
1903	Dorothea Douglass	E. Thomson	46 64 62
1904	Dorothea Douglass	C. Sterry	60 63
1905	May Sutton	D. Douglass	63 64
1906	Dorothea Douglass	M. Sutton	63 97
1907	May Sutton	D. Chambers	61 64
1908	Charlotte Sterry	A. Morton	64 64
1909	Dora Boothby	A. Morton	64 46 86
1910	Dorothea Chambers	D. Boothby	62 62
1911	Dorothea Chambers	D. Boothby	60 60
1912	Ethel Larcombe	C. Sterry	63 61
1913	Dorothea Chambers	R. McNair	60 64
1914	Dorothea Chambers	E. Larcombe	75 64
1915-18	Not held	World War I	
1919	Suzanne Lenglen	D. Chambers	10-8 46 97
1920	Suzanne Lenglen	D. Chambers	63 60
1921	Suzanne Lenglen	E. Ryan	62 60
1922	Suzanne Lenglen	M. Mallory	62 60
1923	Suzanne Lenglen	K. McKane	62 62
1924	Kathleen McKane	H. Wills	46 64 64
1925	Suzanne Lenglen	J. Fry	62 60
1926	Kathleen Godfree	L. de Alvarez	62 46 63
1927	Helen Wills	L. de Alvarez	62 64
1928	Helen Wills	L. de Alvarez	62 63
1929	Helen Wills	H. Jacobs	61 62
1930	Helen Moody	E. Ryan	62 62
1931	Cilly Aussem	H. Kranwinkel	62 75
1932	Helen Moody	H. Jacobs	63 61
1933	Helen Moody	D. Round	64 68 63
1934	Dorothy Round	H. Jacobs	62 57 63
1935	Helen Moody	H. Jacobs	63 36 75
1936	Helen Jacobs	H.K. Sperling	62 46 75
1937	Dorothy Round	J. Jedrzejowska	62 26 75
1938	Helen Moody	H. Jacobs	64 60
1939	Alice Marble	K. Stammers	62 60
1940-45	Not held	World War II	
1946	Pauline Betz	L. Brough	62 64
1947	Margaret Osborne	D. Hart	62 64
1948	Louise Brough	D. Hart	63 86
1949	Louise Brough	M. duPont	10-8 16 10-8
1950	Louise Brough	M. duPont	61 36 61
1951	Doris Hart	S. Fry	61 60
1952	Maureen Connolly	L. Brough	75 63
1953	Maureen Connolly	D. Hart	86 75
1954	Maureen Connolly	L. Brough	62 75
1955	Louise Brough	B. Fleitz	75 86
1956	Shirley Fry	A. Buxton	63 61
1957	Althea Gibson	D. Hard	63 62
1958	Althea Gibson	A. Mortimer	86 62
1959	Maria Bueno	D. Hard	64 63
1960	Maria Bueno	S. Reynolds	86 60
1961	Angela Mortimer	C. Truman	46 64 75
1962	Karen Susman	V. Sukova	64 64
1963	Margaret Smith	B.J. Moffitt	63 64
1964	Maria Bueno	M. Smith	64 79 63
1965	Margaret Smith	M. Bueno	64 75
1966	Billie Jean King	M. Bueno	63 36 61
1967	Billie Jean King	A. Jones	63 64
1968	Billie Jean King	J. Tegart	97 75
1969	Ann Jones	B.J. King	36 63 62
1970	Margaret Court	B.J. King	14-12 11-9
1971	Evonne Goolagong	M. Court	64 61
1972	Billie Jean King	E. Goolagong	63 63
1973	Billie Jean King	C. Evert	60 75
1974	Chris Evert	O. Morozova	60 64
1975	Billie Jean King	E. Cawley	60 61
1976	Chris Evert	E. Cawley	63 46 86
1977	Virginia Wade	B. Stove	46 63 61
1978	Martina Navratilova	C. Evert	26 64 75
1979	Martina Navratilova	C. Evert Lloyd	64 64
1980	Evonne Cawley	C. Evert Lloyd	61 76
1981	Chris Evert Lloyd	H. Mandlikova	62 62
1982	Martina Navratilova	C. Evert Lloyd	61 36 62
1983	Martina Navratilova	A. Jaeger	60 63
1984	Martina Navratilova	C. Evert Lloyd	76 62
1985	Martina Navratilova	C. Evert Lloyd	46 63 62
1986	Martina Navratilova	H. Mandlikova	76 63
1987	Martina Navratilova	S. Graf	75 63
1988	Steffi Graf	M. Navratilova	57 62 61
1989	Steffi Graf	M. Navratilova	62 67 61
1990	Martina Navratilova	Z. Garrison	64 61
1991	Steffi Graf	G. Sabatini	64 36 86
1992	Steffi Graf	M. Seles	62 61
1993	Steffi Graf	J. Novotna	76 16 64
1994	Conchita Martinez	M. Navratilova	64 36 63
1995	Steffi Graf	A.S. Vicario	46 61 75
1996	Steffi Graf	A.S. Vicario	63 75
1997	Martina Hingis	J. Novotna	26 63 63
1998	Jana Novotna	N. Tauziat	64 76

U.S. Open

MEN

Challenge round system (defending champion qualified for following year's final) used from 1884-1911. Known as the Patriotic Tournament in 1917 during World War I. Amateur and Open Championships held in 1968 and '69. Became an exclusively Open Championship in 1970.

Surface: Decoturf II (acrylic cement).

Multiple winners: Bill Larned, Richard Sears and Bill Tilden (7); Jimmy Connors (5); John McEnroe, Pete Sampras and Robert Wrenn (4); Oliver Campbell, Ivan Lendl, Fred Perry and Malcolm Whitman (3); Don Budge, Stefan Edberg, Roy Emerson, Neale Fraser, Pancho Gonzales, Bill Johnston, Jack Kramer, Rene Lacoste, Rod Laver, Maurice McLoughlin, Lindley Murray, John Newcombe, Frank Parker, Patrick Rafter, Bobby Riggs, Ken Rosewall, Frank Sedgman, Henry Slocum Jr., Tony Trabert, Ellsworth Vines and Dick Williams (2).

Year	Winner	Loser	Score
1881	Richard Sears	W. Glyn	60 63 62
1882	Richard Sears	C. Clark	61 64 60
1883	Richard Sears	J. Dwight	62 60 97
1884	Richard Sears	H. Taylor	60 16 60 62
1885	Richard Sears	G. Brinley	63 46 60 63
1886	Richard Sears	R. Beeckman	46 61 63 64
1887	Richard Sears	H. Slocum Jr.	61 63 62
1888	Henry Slocum Jr.	H. Taylor	64 61 60
1889	Henry Slocum Jr.	Q. Shaw	63 61 46 62
1890	Oliver Campbell	H. Slocum Jr.	62 46 63 61
1891	Oliver Campbell	C. Hobart	26 75 79 61 62
1892	Oliver Campbell	F. Hovey	75 36 63 75
1893	Robert Wrenn	F. Hovey	64 36 64 64
1894	Robert Wrenn	M. Goodbody	68 61 64 64
1895	Fred Hovey	R. Wrenn	63 62 64
1896	Robert Wrenn	F. Hovey	75 36 60 16 61
1897	Robert Wrenn	W. Eaves	46 86 63 26 62
1898	Malcolm Whitman	D. Davis	36 62 62 61
1899	Malcolm Whitman	P. Paret	61 62 36 75
1900	Malcolm Whitman	B. Larned	64 16 62 62
1901	Bill Larned	B. Wright	62 68 64 64
1902	Bill Larned	R. Doherty	46 62 64 86
1903	Laurie Doherty	B. Larned	60 63 10-8
1904	Holcombe Ward	B. Clothier	10-8 64 97
1905	Beals Wright	H. Ward	62 61 11-9
1906	Bill Clothier	B. Wright	63 60 64
1907	Bill Larned	R. LeRoy	62 62 64
1908	Bill Larned	B. Wright	61 62 86
1909	Bill Larned	B. Clothier	61 62 57 16 61
1910	Bill Larned	T. Bundy	61 57 60 68 61
1911	Bill Larned	M. McLoughlin	64 64 62
1912	Maurice McLoughlin	W.F. Johnson	36 26 62 64 62
1913	Maurice McLoughlin	R. Williams	64 57 63 61
1914	Dick Williams	M. McLoughlin	63 86 10-8
1915	Bill Johnston	M. McLoughlin	16 60 75 10-8
1916	Dick Williams	B. Johnston	46 64 06 62 64
1917	Lindley Murray	N. Niles	57 86 63 63
1918	Lindley Murray	B. Tilden	63 61 75
1919	Bill Johnston	B. Tilden	64 64 63
1920	Bill Tilden	B. Johnston	61 16 75 57 63
1921	Bill Tilden	W. Johnson	61 63 61
1922	Bill Tilden	B. Johnston	46 36 62 63 64
1923	Bill Tilden	B. Johnston	64 61 64
1924	Bill Tilden	B. Johnston	61 97 62
1925	Bill Tilden	B. Johnston	46 11-9 63 46 63
1926	Rene Lacoste	J. Borotra	64 60 64
1927	Rene Lacoste	B. Tilden	11-9 63 11-9
1928	Henri Cochet	F. Hunter	46 64 36 75 63
1929	Bill Tilden	F. Hunter	36 63 46 62 64
1930	John Doeg	F. Shields	10-8 16 64 16-14
1931	Ellsworth Vines	G. Lott Jr.	79 63 97 75
1932	Ellsworth Vines	H. Cochet	64 64 64
1933	Fred Perry	J. Crawford	63 11-13 46 60 61
1934	Fred Perry	W. Allison	64 63 16 86
1935	Wilmer Allison	S. Wood	62 62 63
1936	Fred Perry	D. Budge	26 62 86 16 10-8
1937	Don Budge	G. von Cramm	61 79 61 36 61
1938	Don Budge	G. Mako	63 68 62 61
1939	Bobby Riggs	S.W. van Horn	64 62 64
1940	Don McNeill	B. Riggs	46 68 63 63 75
1941	Bobby Riggs	F. Kovacs	57 61 63 63
1942	Fred Schroeder	F. Parker	86 75 36 46 62
1943	Joe Hunt	J. Kramer	63 68 10-8 60
1944	Frank Parker	B. Talbert	64 36 63 63
1945	Frank Parker	B. Talbert	14-12 61 62
1946	Jack Kramer	T. Brown, Jr.	97 63 60
1947	Jack Kramer	F. Parker	46 26 61 60 63
1948	Pancho Gonzales	E. Sturgess	62 63 14-12
1949	Pancho Gonzales	F. Schroeder	16-18 26 61 62 64
1950	Arthur Larsen	H. Flam	63 46 57 64 63
1951	Frank Sedgman	V. Seixas	64 61 61
1952	Frank Sedgman	G. Mulloy	61 62 63
1953	Tony Trabert	V. Seixas	63 62 63
1954	Vic Seixas	R. Hartwig	36 62 64 64
1955	Tony Trabert	K. Rosewall	97 63 63
1956	Ken Rosewall	L. Hoad	46 62 63 63
1957	Mal Anderson	A. Cooper	10-8 75 64
1958	Ashley Cooper	M. Anderson	62 36 46 10-8 86
1959	Neale Fraser	A. Olmedo	63 57 62 64
1960	Neale Fraser	R. Laver	64 64 97
1961	Roy Emerson	R. Laver	75 63 62
1962	Rod Laver	R. Emerson	62 64 57 64
1963	Rafael Osuna	F. Froehling	75 64 62
1964	Roy Emerson	F. Stolle	64 62 64
1965	Manuel Santana	C. Drysdale	62 79 75 61
1966	Fred Stolle	J. Newcombe	46 12-10 63 64
1967	John Newcombe	C. Graebner	64 64 86
1968	Am-Arthur Ashe	B. Lutz	46 63 8-10 60 64
	Op-Arthur Ashe	T. Okker	14-12 57 63 36 63
1969	Am-Stan Smith	B. Lutz	97 63 61
	Op-Rod Laver	T. Roche	79 61 63 62
1970	Ken Rosewall	T. Roche	26 64 76 63
1971	Stan Smith	J. Kodes	36 63 62 76
1972	Ilie Nastase	A. Ashe	36 63 67 64 63
1973	John Newcombe	J. Kodes	64 16 46 62 63
1974	Jimmy Connors	K. Rosewall	61 60 61
1975	Manuel Orantes	J. Connors	64 63 63
1976	Jimmy Connors	B. Borg	64 36 76 64
1977	Guillermo Vilas	J. Connors	26 63 76 60
1978	Jimmy Connors	B. Borg	64 62 62
1979	John McEnroe	V. Gerulaitis	75 63 63
1980	John McEnroe	B. Borg	76 61 67 57 64
1981	John McEnroe	B. Borg	46 62 64 63
1982	Jimmy Connors	I. Lendl	63 62 46 64
1983	Jimmy Connors	I. Lendl	63 67 75 60
1984	John McEnroe	I. Lendl	63 64 61
1985	Ivan Lendl	J. McEnroe	76 63 64
1986	Ivan Lendl	M. Mecir	64 62 60
1987	Ivan Lendl	M. Wilander	67 60 76 64
1988	Mats Wilander	I. Lendl	64 46 63 57 64
1989	Boris Becker	I. Lendl	76 16 63 76
1990	Pete Sampras	A. Agassi	64 63 62
1991	Stefan Edberg	J. Courier	62 64 60
1992	Stefan Edberg	P. Sampras	36 64 76 62
1993	Pete Sampras	C. Pioline	64 64 63
1994	Andre Agassi	M. Stich	61 76 75
1995	Pete Sampras	A. Agassi	64 63 46 75
1996	Pete Sampras	M. Chang	61 64 76
1997	Patrick Rafter	G. Rusedski	63 62 46 75
1998	Patrick Rafter	M. Philippoussis	63 36 62 60

WOMEN

Challenge round system used from 1887-1918. Five set final played from 1887-1901. Amateur and Open Championships held in 1968 and '69. Became an exclusively Open Championship in 1970.

Multiple winners: Molla Mallory Bjurstedt (8); Helen Wills Moody (7); Chris Evert Lloyd (6); Margaret Smith Court and Steffi Graf (5); Pauline Betz, Mario Bueno, Helen Jacobs, Billie Jean King, Alice Marble, Elisabeth Moore, Martina Navratilova and Hazel Hotchkiss Wightman (4); Juliette Atkinson, Mary Browne, Maureen Connolly and Margaret Osborne duPont (3); Tracy Austin, Mabel Cahill, Sarah Palfrey Cooke, Darlene Hard, Doris Hart, Althea Gibson, Monica Seles and Bertha Townsend (2).

Year	Winner	Loser	Score
1887	Ellen Hansell	L. Knight	61 60
1888	Bertha Townsend	E. Hansell	63 65
1889	Bertha Townsend	L. Voorhes	75 62
1890	Ellen Roosevelt	B. Townsend	62 62
1891	Mabel Cahill	E. Roosevelt	64 61 46 63
1892	Mabel Cahill	E. Moore	57 63 64 46 62
1893	Aline Terry	A. Schultz	61 63
1894	Helen Hellwig	A. Terry	75 36 60 36 63
1895	Juliette Atkinson	H. Hellwig	64 62 61
1896	Elisabeth Moore	J. Atkinson	64 46 62 62
1897	Juliette Atkinson	E. Moore	63 63 46 36 63
1898	Juliette Atkinson	M. Jones	63 57 64 26 75
1899	Marion Jones	M. Banks	61 61 75
1900	Myrtle McAteer	E. Parker	62 62 60
1901	Elizabeth Moore	M. McAteer	64 36 75 26 62
1902	Marion Jones	E. Moore	61 10(ret)
1903	Elizabeth Moore	M. Jones	75 86
1904	May Sutton	E. Moore	61 62
1905	Elizabeth Moore	H. Homans	64 57 61
1906	Helen Homans	M. Barger-Wallach	64 63
1907	Evelyn Sears	C. Neely	63 62
1908	Maud B. Wallach	Ev. Sears	63 16 63
1909	Hazel Hotchkiss	M. Wallach	60 61
1910	Hazel Hotchkiss	L. Hammond	64 62
1911	Hazel Hotchkiss	F. Sutton	8-10 61 97
1912	Mary Browne	E. Sears	64 62
1913	Mary Browne	D. Green	62 75
1914	Mary Browne	M. Wagner	62 16 61
1915	Molla Bjurstedt	H. Wightman	46 62 60
1916	Molla Bjurstedt	L. Raymond	60 61
1917	Molla Bjurstedt	M. Vanderhoef	46 60 62
1918	Molla Bjurstedt	E. Goss	64 63
1919	Hazel Wightman	M. Zinderstein	61 62
1920	Molla Mallory	M. Zinderstein	63 61
1921	Molla Mallory	M. Browne	46 64 62
1922	Molla Mallory	H. Wills	63 61
1923	Helen Wills	M. Mallory	62 61
1924	Helen Wills	M. Mallory	61 63
1925	Helen Wills	K. McKane	36 60 62
1926	Molla Mallory	E. Ryan	46 64 97
1927	Helen Wills	B. Nuthall	61 64
1928	Helen Wills	H. Jacobs	62 61
1929	Helen Wills	P. Watson	64 62
1930	Betty Nuthall	A. Harper	61 64
1931	Helen Moody	E. Whitingstall	64 61
1932	Helen Jacobs	C. Babcock	62 62
1933	Helen Jacobs	H. Moody	86 36 30(ret)
1934	Helen Jacobs	S. Palfrey	61 64
1935	Helen Jacobs	S. Fabyan	62 64
1936	Alice Marble	H. Jacobs	46 63 62
1937	Anita Lizana	J. Jedrzejowska	64 62
1938	Alice Marble	N. Wynne	60 63
1939	Alice Marble	H. Jacobs	60 8-10 64
1940	Alice Marble	H. Jacobs	62 63
1941	Sarah Cooke	P. Betz	75 62
1942	Pauline Betz	L. Brough	46 61 64
1943	Pauline Betz	L. Brough	63 57 63
1944	Pauline Betz	M. Osborne	63 86
1945	Sarah Cooke	P. Betz	36 86 64
1946	Pauline Betz	P. Canning	11-9 63
1947	Louise Brough	M. Osborne	86 46 61
1948	Margaret duPont	L. Brough	46 64 15-13
1949	Margaret duPont	D. Hart	64 61
1950	Margaret duPont	D. Hart	64 63
1951	Maureen Connolly	S. Fry	63 16 64
1952	Maureen Connolly	D. Hart	63 75
1953	Maureen Connolly	D. Hart	62 64
1954	Doris Hart	L. Brough	68 61 86
1955	Doris Hart	P. Ward	64 62
1956	Shirley Fry	A. Gibson	63 64
1957	Althea Gibson	L. Brough	63 62
1958	Althea Gibson	D. Hard	36 61 62
1959	Maria Bueno	C. Truman	61 64
1960	Darlene Hard	M. Bueno	64 10-12 64
1961	Darlene Hard	A. Haydon	63 64
1962	Margaret Smith	D. Hard	97 64
1963	Maria Bueno	M. Smith	75 64
1964	Maria Bueno	C. Graebner	61 60
1965	Margaret Smith	B.J. Moffitt	86 75
1966	Maria Bueno	N. Richey	63 61
1967	Billie Jean King	A. Jones	11-9 64
1968	Am-Margaret Court	M. Bueno	62 62
	Op-Virginia Wade	B.J. King	64 62
1969	Am-Margaret Court	V. Wade	46 63 60
	Op-Margaret Court	N. Richey	62 62
1970	Margaret Court	R. Casals	62 26 61
1971	Billie Jean King	R. Casals	64 76
1972	Billie Jean King	K. Melville	63 75
1973	Margaret Court	E. Goolagong	76 57 62
1974	Billie Jean King	E. Goolagong	36 63 75
1975	Chris Evert	E. Cawley	57 64 62
1976	Chris Evert	E. Cawley	63 60
1977	Chris Evert	W. Turnbull	76 62
1978	Chris Evert	P. Shriver	75 64
1979	Tracy Austin	C. Evert Lloyd	64 63
1980	Chris Evert Lloyd	H. Mandlikova	57 61 61
1981	Tracy Austin	M. Navratilova	16 76 76
1982	Chris Evert Lloyd	H. Mandlikova	63 61
1983	Martina Navratilova	C. Evert Lloyd	61 63
1984	Martina Navratilova	C. Evert Lloyd	46 64 64
1985	Hana Mandlikova	M. Navratilova	76 16 76
1986	Martina Navratilova	H. Sukova	63 62
1987	Martina Navratilova	S. Graf	76 61
1988	Steffi Graf	G. Sabatini	63 36 61
1989	Steffi Graf	M. Navratilova	36 75 61
1990	Gabriela Sabatini	S. Graf	62 76
1991	Monica Seles	M. Navratilova	76 61
1992	Monica Seles	A.S. Vicario	63 63
1993	Steffi Graf	H. Sukova	63 63
1994	A. Sanchez Vicario	S. Graf	16 76 64
1995	Steffi Graf	M. Seles	76 06 63
1996	Steffi Graf	M. Seles	75 64
1997	Martina Hingis	V. Williams	60 64
1998	Lindsay Davenport	M. Hingis	63 75

Grand Slam Summary

Singles winners of the four Grand Slam tournaments–Australian, French, Wimbledon and United States–since the French was opened to all comers in 1925. Note that there were two Australian Opens in 1977 and none in 1986.

MEN

Three wins in one year: Jack Crawford (1933); Fred Perry (1934); Tony Trabert (1955); Lew Hoad (1956); Ashley Cooper (1958); Roy Emerson (1964); Jimmy Connors (1974); Mats Wilander (1988).

Two wins in one year: Roy Emerson and Pete Sampras (4 times); Bjorn Borg (3 times); Rene Lacoste, Ivan Lendl, John Newcombe and Fred Perry (twice); Boris Becker, Don Budge, Henri Cochet, Jimmy Connors, Jim Courier, Neale Fraser, Jack Kramer, John McEnroe, Alex Olmedo, Budge Patty, Bobby Riggs, Ken Rosewall, Dick Savitt, Frank Sedgman and Guillermo Vilas (once).

Year	Australian	French	Wimbledon	U.S.
1925	Anderson	Lacoste	Lacoste	Tilden
1926	Hawkes	Cochet	Borotra	Lacoste
1927	Patterson	Lacoste	Cochet	Lacoste
1928	Borotra	Cochet	Lacoste	Cochet
1929	Gregory	Lacoste	Cochet	Tilden
1930	Moon	Cochet	Tilden	Doeg
1931	Crawford	Borotra	Wood	Vines
1932	Crawford	Cochet	Vines	Vines
1933	Crawford	Crawford	Crawford	Perry
1934	Perry	von Cramm	Perry	Perry
1935	Crawford	Perry	Perry	Allison
1936	Quist	von Cramm	Perry	Perry
1937	McGrath	Henkel	Budge	Budge
1938	**Budge**	**Budge**	**Budge**	**Budge**
1939	Bromwich	McNeill	Riggs	Riggs
1940	Quist	–	–	McNeill
1941	–	–	–	Riggs
1942	–	–	–	Schroeder
1943	–	–	–	Hunt
1944	–	–	–	Parker
1945	–	–	-	Parker
1946	Bromwich	Bernard	Petra	Kramer
1947	Pails	Asboth	Kramer	Kramer
1948	Quist	Parker	Falkenburg	Gonzales
1949	Sedgman	Parker	Schroeder	Gonzales
1950	Sedgman	Patty	Patty	Larsen
1951	Savitt	Drobny	Savitt	Sedgman
1952	McGregor	Drobny	Sedgman	Sedgman
1953	Rosewall	Rosewall	Seixas	Trabert
1954	Rose	Trabert	Drobny	Seixas
1955	Rosewall	Trabert	Trabert	Trabert
1956	Hoad	Hoad	Hoad	Rosewall
1957	Cooper	Davidson	Hoad	Anderson
1958	Cooper	Rose	Cooper	Cooper
1959	Olmedo	Pietrangeli	Olmedo	Fraser
1960	Laver	Pietrangeli	Fraser	Fraser
1961	Emerson	Santana	Laver	Emerson
1962	**Laver**	**Laver**	**Laver**	**Laver**
1963	Emerson	Emerson	McKinley	Osuna
1964	Emerson	Santana	Emerson	Emerson
1965	Emerson	Stolle	Emerson	Santana
1966	Emerson	Roche	Santana	Stolle
1967	Emerson	Emerson	Newcombe	Newcombe
1968	Bowrey	Rosewall	Laver	Ashe
1969	**Laver**	**Laver**	**Laver**	**Laver**
1970	Ashe	Kodes	Newcombe	Rosewall
1971	Rosewall	Kodes	Newcombe	Smith
1972	Rosewall	Gimeno	Smith	Nastase
1973	Newcombe	Nastase	Kodes	Newcombe
1974	Connors	Borg	Connors	Connors
1975	Newcombe	Borg	Ashe	Orantes
1976	Edmondson	Panatta	Borg	Connors
1977	Tanner & Gerulaitis	Vilas	Borg	Vilas
1978	Vilas	Borg	Borg	Connors
1979	Vilas	Borg	Borg	McEnroe
1980	Teacher	Borg	Borg	McEnroe
1981	Kriek	Borg	McEnroe	McEnroe
1982	Kriek	Wilander	Connors	Connors
1983	Wilander	Noah	McEnroe	Connors
1984	Wilander	Lendl	McEnroe	McEnroe
1985	Edberg	Wilander	Becker	Lendl
1986	–	Lendl	Becker	Lendl
1987	Edberg	Lendl	Cash	Lendl
1988	Wilander	Wilander	Edberg	Wilander
1989	Lendl	Chang	Becker	Becker
1990	Lendl	Gomez	Edberg	Sampras
1991	Becker	Courier	Stich	Edberg
1992	Courier	Courier	Agassi	Edberg
1993	Courier	Bruguera	Sampras	Sampras
1994	Sampras	Bruguera	Sampras	Agassi
1995	Agassi	Muster	Sampras	Sampras
1996	Becker	Kafelnikov	Krajicek	Sampras
1997	Sampras	Kuerten	Sampras	Rafter
1998	Korda	Moya	Sampras	Rafter

WOMEN

Three in one year: Helen Wills Moody (1928 and '29); Margaret Smith Court (1962, '65, '69 and '73); Billie Jean King (1972); Martina Navratilova (1983 and '84); Steffi Graf (1989, '93, '95 and '96); Monica Seles (1991 and '92); and Martina Hingis (1997).

Two in one year; Chris Evert Lloyd (5 times); Helen Wills Moody and Martina Navratilova (3 times); Maria Bueno, Maureen Connolly, Margaraet Smith Court, Althea Gibson, Billie Jean King (twice); Cilly Aussem, Pauleen Betz, Louise Brough, Evonne Goolagong Cawley, Shirley Fry, Darlene Hard, Margaret Osborne duPont, Suzanne Lenglen, Alice Marble and Arantxa Sanchez Vicario (once).

Year	Australian	French	Wimbledon	U.S.
1925	Akhurst	Lenglen	Lenglen	Wills
1926	Akhurst	Lenglen	Godfree	Mallory
1927	Boyd	Bouman	Wills	Wills
1928	Akhurst	Wills	Wills	Wills
1929	Akhurst	Wills	Wills	Wills
1930	Akhurst	Moody	Moody	Nuthall
1931	Buttsworth	Aussem	Aussem	Moody
1932	Buttsworth	Moody	Moody	Jacobs
1933	Hartigan	Scriven	Moody	Jacobs
1934	Hartigan	Scriven	Round	Jacobs
1935	Round	Sperling	Moody	Jacobs
1936	Hartigan	Sperling	Jacobs	Marble
1937	Bolton	Sperling	Round	Lizana
1938	Bundy	Mathieu	Moody	Marble
1939	Westacott	Mathieu	Marble	Marble
1940	Bolton	–	–	Marble
1941	–	–	–	Cooke
1942	–	–	–	Betz
1943	–	–	–	Betz
1944	–	–	–	Betz

Year	Australian	French	Wimbledon	U.S.
1945	—	—	—	Cooke
1946	Bolton	Osborne	Betz	Betz
1947	Bolton	Todd	Osborne	Brough
1948	Bolton	Landry	Brough	du Pont
1949	Hart	du Pont	Brough	du Pont
1950	Brough	Hart	Brough	du Pont
1951	Bolton	Fry	Hart	Connolly
1952	Long	Hart	Connolly	Connolly
1953	**Connolly**	**Connolly**	**Connolly**	**Connolly**
1954	Long	Connolly	Connolly	Hart
1955	Penrose	Mortimer	Brough	Hart
1956	Carter	Gibson	Fry	Fry
1957	Fry	Bloomer	Gibson	Gibson
1958	Mortimer	Kormoczi	Gibson	Gibson
1959	Reitano	Truman	Bueno	Bueno
1960	Smith	Hard	Bueno	Hard
1961	Smith	Haydon	Mortimer	Hard
1962	Smith	Smith	Susman	Smith
1963	Smith	Turner	Smith	Bueno
1964	Smith	Smith	Bueno	Bueno
1965	Smith	Turner	Smith	Smith
1966	Smith	Jones	King	Bueno
1967	Richey	Durr	King	King
1968	King	Richey	King	Wade
1969	Court	Court	Jones	Court
1970	**Court**	**Court**	**Court**	**Court**
1971	Court	Goolagong	Goolagong	King
1972	Wade	King	King	King

Year	Australian	French	Wimbledon	U.S.
1973	Court	Court	King	Court
1974	Goolagong	Evert	Evert	King
1975	Goolagong	Evert	King	Evert
1976	Cawley	Barker	Evert	Evert
1977	Reid & Cawley	Jausovec	Wade	Evert
1978	O'Neil	Ruzici	Navratilova	Evert
1979	Jordan	Evert Lloyd	Navratilova	Austin
1980	Mandlikova	Evert Lloyd	Cawley	Evert Lloyd
1981	Navratilova	Mandlikova	Evert Lloyd	Austin
1982	Evert Lloyd	Navratilova	Navratilova	Evert Lloyd
1983	Navratilova	Evert Lloyd	Navratilova	Navratilova
1984	Evert Lloyd	Navratilova	Navratilova	Navratilova
1985	Navratilova	Evert Lloyd	Navratilova	Mandlikova
1986	–	Evert Lloyd	Navratilova	Navratilova
1987	Mandlikova	Graf	Navratilova	Navratilova
1988	**Graf**	**Graf**	**Graf**	**Graf**
1989	Graf	Vicario	Graf	Graf
1990	Graf	Seles	Navratilova	Sabatini
1991	Seles	Seles	Graf	Seles
1992	Seles	Seles	Graf	Seles
1993	Seles	Graf	Graf	Graf
1994	Graf	Vicario	Martinez	Vicario
1995	Pierce	Graf	Graf	Graf
1996	Seles	Graf	Graf	Graf
1997	Hingis	Majoli	Hingis	Hingis
1998	Hingis	Vicario	Novotna	Davenport

Overall Leaders

All-Time Grand Slam titleists including all singles and doubles championships at the four major tournaments. Titles listed under each heading are singles, doubles and mixed doubles. Players active in 1998 are in **bold** type.

MEN

		Career	Australian	French	Wimbledon	U.S.	S-D-M	Total Titles
1	Roy Emerson	1959-71	6-3-0	2-6-0	2-3-0	2-4-0	12-16-0	28
2	John Newcombe	1965-76	2-5-0	0-3-0	3-6-0	2-3-1	7-17-1	25
3	Frank Sedgman	1949-52	2-2-2	0-2-2	1-3-2	2-2-2	5-9-8	22
4	Bill Tilden	1913-30	*	0-0-1	3-1-0	7-5-4	10-6-5	21
5	Rod Laver	1959-71	3-4-0	2-1-1	4-1-2	2-0-0	11-6-3	20
6	Jack Bromwich	1938-50	2-8-1	0-0-0	0-2-2	0-3-1	2-13-4	19
7	Ken Rosewall	1953-72	4-3-0	2-2-0	0-2-0	2-2-1	8-9-1	18
	Neale Fraser	1957-62	0-3-1	0-3-0	1-2-0	2-3-3	3-11-4	18
	Jean Borotra	1925-36	1-1-1	1-5-2	2-3-1	0-0-1	4-9-5	18
	Fred Stolle	1962-69	0-3-1	1-2-0	0-2-3	1-3-2	2-10-6	18
11	John McEnroe	1977-93	0-0-0	0-0-1	3-5-0	4-4-0	7-9-1	17
	Jack Crawford	1929-35	4-4-3	1-1-1	1-1-1	0-0-0	6-6-5	17
	Adrian Quist	1936-50	3-10-0	0-1-0	0-2-0	0-1-0	3-14-0	17
14	Laurie Doherty	1897-1906	*	*	5-8-0	1-2-0	6-10-0	16
15	Henri Cochet	1922-32	*	4-3-2	2-2-0	1-0-1	7-5-3	15
	Vic Seixas	1952-56	0-1-0	0-2-1	1-0-4	1-2-3	2-5-8	15
	Bob Hewitt	1961-79	0-2-1	0-1-2	0-5-2	0-1-1	0-9-6	15

WOMEN

		Career	Australian	French	Wimbledon	U.S.	S-D-M	Total Titles
1	Margaret Court Smith	1960-75	11-8-2	5-4-4	3-2-5	5-5-8	24-19-19	62
2	Martina Navratilova	1974-95	3-8-0	2-7-2	9-7-2	4-9-2	18-31-6	55
3	Billie Jean King	1961-81	1-0-1	1-1-2	6-10-4	4-5-4	12-16-11	39
4	Margaret du Pont	1941-60	*	2-3-0	1-5-1	3-13-9	6-21-10	37
5	Louise Brough	1942-57	1-1-0	0-3-0	4-5-4	1-12-4	6-21-8	35
	Doris Hart	1948-55	1-1-2	2-5-3	1-4-5	2-4-5	6-14-15	35
7	Helen Wills Moody	1923-38	*	4-2-0	8-3-1	7-4-2	19-9-3	31
8	Elizabeth Ryan	1914-34	*	0-4-0	0-12-7	0-1-2	0-17-9	26
9	Suzanne Lenglen	1919-26	*	6-2-2	6-6-3	0-0-0	12-8-5	25
10	**Steffi Graf**	1982—	4-0-0	5-0-0	7-1-0	5-0-0	21-1-0	22
	Pam Shriver	1981-97	0-7-0	0-4-1	0-5-0	0-5-0	0-21-1	22
12	Chris Evert	1974-89	2-0-0	7-2-0	3-1-0	6-0-0	18-3-0	21
	Darlene Hard	1958-69	*	1-3-2	0-4-3	2-6-0	3-13-5	21
14	**Natasha Zvereva**	1989—	0-3-2	0-6-0	0-5-0	0-4-0	0-18-2	20
	Nancye Wynne Bolton	1935-52	6-10-4	0-0-0	0-0-0	0-0-0	6-10-4	20

The Calendar Year Grand Slam

The tennis Grand Slam has only been accomplished nine times in the same calendar year in either singles or doubles. And only two players have managed to do it twice– Rod Laver in singles (1962 and '69) and Margaret Smith Court in singles (1970) and doubles (1963).

Men's Singles

1938 .... Don Budge, USA
1962 .... Rod Laver, Australia
1969 .... Rod Laver, Australia

Men's Doubles

1951 .... Frank Sedgman, Australia & Ken McGregor, Australia

Mixed Doubles

1963 .... Ken Fletcher, Australia & Margaret Smith, Australia
1967 .... Owen Davidson and two partners

Women's Singles

1953 .... Maureen Connolly, USA
1970 .... Margaret Smith Court, Australia
1988 .... Steffi Graf, West Germany*
*Also won gold medal at Seoul Olympics.

Women's Doubles

1960 .... Maria Bueno, Brazil & two partners
1984 .... Martina Navratilova, USA & Pam Shriver, USA
1998 .... Martina Hingis, Slovakia & two partners

Note: In women's doubles, Bueno won Australia with Christine Truman, then took the French, Wimbledon and the U.S. with Darlene Hard. Hingis won Australia with Mirjana Lucic, then took the French, Wimbledon and the U.S. with Jana Novotna. In mixed Doubles, Davidson won Australia with Lesley Turner, then took the French, Wimbledon and the U.S. with Billie Jean King.

All-Time Grand Slam Singles Titles

Men and women with the most singles championships in the Australian, French, Wimbledon and U.S. championships, through 1998. Note that (*) indicates player never played in that particular Grand Slam event; and players active in singles play in 1998 are in **bold** type.

Top 15 Men

		Aus	Fre	Wim	US	Total
1	Roy Emerson	6	2	2	2	12
2	Bjorn Borg	0	6	5	0	11
	Rod Laver	3	2	4	2	11
	Pete Sampras	2	0	5	4	11
5	Bill Tilden	*	0	3	7	10
6	Jimmy Connors	1	0	2	5	8
	Ivan Lendl	2	3	0	3	8
	Fred Perry	1	1	3	3	8
	Ken Rosewall	4	2	0	2	8
10	Henri Cochet	*	4	2	1	7
	Rene Lacoste	*	3	2	2	7
	Bill Larned	*	*	0	7	7
	John McEnroe	0	0	3	4	7
	John Newcombe	2	0	3	2	7
	Willie Renshaw	*	*	7	*	7
	Dick Sears	*	*	0	7	7

Top 15 Women

		Aus	Fre	Wim	US	Total
1	Margaret Smith Court	11	5	3	5	24
2	**Steffi Graf**	4	5	7	5	21
3	Helen Wills Moody	*	4	8	7	19
4	Chris Evert	2	7	3	6	18
	Martina Navratilova	3	2	9	4	18
6	Billie Jean King	1	1	6	4	12
	Suzanne Lenglen	*	6	6	0	12
8	Maureen Connolly	1	2	3	3	9
	Monica Seles	4	3	0	2	9
10	Molla Bjurstedt Mallory	*	*	0	8	8
11	Maria Bueno	0	0	3	4	7
	Evonne Goolagong	4	1	2	0	7
	Dorothea D. Chambers	*	*	7	0	7
14	Nancy Bolton	6	0	0	0	6
	Louise Brough	1	0	4	1	6
	Margaret duPont	*	2	1	3	6
	Doris Hart	1	2	1	2	6
	Blanche Bingley Hillyard	*	*	6	*	6

Annual Number One Players

Unofficial world rankings for men and women determined by the *London Daily Telegraph* from 1914-72. Since then, official world rankings computed by men's and women's tours. Rankings included only amateur players from 1914 until the arrival of open (professional) tennis in 1968. No rankings were released during World Wars I and II.

MEN

Multiple winners: Bill Tilden (6); Jimmy Connors and Pete Sampras (5); Henri Cochet, Rod Laver, Ivan Lendl and John McEnroe (4); John Newcombe and Fred Perry (3); Bjorn Borg, Don Budge, Ashley Cooper, Stefan Edberg, Roy Emerson, Neale Fraser, Jack Kramer, Rene Lacoste, Ilie Nastase, Frank Sedgman and Tony Trabert (2).

Year	
1914	Maurice McLoughlin
1915-18	No rankings
1919	Gerald Patterson
1920	Bill Tilden
1921	Bill Tilden
1922	Bill Tilden
1923	Bill Tilden
1924	Bill Tilden
1925	Bill Tilden
1926	Rene Lacoste
1927	Rene Lacoste
1928	Henri Cochet
1929	Henri Cochet

Year	
1930	Henri Cochet
1931	Henri Cochet
1932	Ellsworth Vines
1933	Jack Crawford
1934	Fred Perry
1935	Fred Perry
1936	Fred Perry
1937	Don Budge
1938	Don Budge
1939	Bobby Riggs
1940-45	No rankings
1946	Jack Kramer
1947	Jack Kramer

Year	
1948	Frank Parker
1949	Pancho Gonzales
1950	Budge Patty
1951	Frank Sedgman
1952	Frank Sedgman
1953	Tony Trabert
1954	Jaroslav Drobny
1955	Tony Trabert
1956	Lew Hoad
1957	Ashley Cooper
1958	Ashley Cooper
1959	Neale Fraser
1960	Neale Fraser

Year	
1961	Rod Laver
1962	Rod Laver
1963	Rafael Osuna
1964	Roy Emerson
1965	Roy Emerson
1966	Manuel Santana
1967	John Newcombe
1968	Rod Laver
1969	Rod Laver
1970	John Newcombe
1971	John Newcombe
1972	Ilie Nastase
1973	Ilie Nastase

Year		Year		Year		Year	
1974	Jimmy Connors	1980	Bjorn Borg	1986	Ivan Lendl	1992	Jim Courier
1975	Jimmy Connors	1981	John McEnroe	1987	Ivan Lendl	1993	Pete Sampras
1976	Jimmy Connors	1982	John McEnroe	1988	Mats Wilander	1994	Pete Sampras
1977	Jimmy Connors	1983	John McEnroe	1989	Ivan Lendl	1995	Pete Sampras
1978	Jimmy Connors	1984	John McEnroe	1990	Stefan Edberg	1996	Pete Sampras
1979	Bjorn Borg	1985	Ivan Lendl	1991	Stefan Edberg	1997	Pete Sampras

WOMEN

Multiple winners: Helen Wills Moody (9); Steffi Graf (8); Margaret Smith Court and Martina Navratilova (7); Chris Evert Lloyd (5); Margaret Osborne duPont and Billie Jean King (4); Maureen Connolly and Monica Seles (3); Maria Bueno, Althea Gibson, Suzanne Lenglen (2).

Year		Year		Year		Year	
1925	Suzanne Lenglen	1948	Margaret duPont	1966	Billie Jean King	1984	Martina Navratilova
1926	Suzanne Lenglen	1949	Margaret duPont	1967	Billie Jean King	1985	Martina Navratilova
1927	Helen Wills	1950	Margaret duPont	1968	Billie Jean King	1986	Martina Navratilova
1928	Helen Wills	1951	Doris Hart	1969	Margaret Court	1987	Steffi Graf
1929	Helen Wills Moody	1952	Maureen Connolly	1970	Margaret Court	1988	Steffi Graf
1930	Helen Wills Moody	1953	Maureen Connolly	1971	Evonne Goolagong	1989	Steffi Graf
1931	Helen Wills Moody	1954	Maureen Connolly	1972	Billie Jean King	1990	Steffi Graf
1932	Helen Wills Moody	1955	Louise Brough	1973	Margaret Court	1991	Monica Seles
1933	Helen Wills Moody	1956	Shirley Fry	1974	Billie Jean King	1992	Monica Seles
1934	Dorothy Round	1957	Althea Gibson	1975	Chris Evert	1993	Steffi Graf
1935	Helen Wills Moody	1958	Althea Gibson	1976	Chris Evert	1994	Steffi Graf
1936	Helen Jacobs	1959	Maria Bueno	1977	Chris Evert	1995	Steffi Graf & Monica Seles
1937	Anita Lizana	1960	Maria Bueno	1978	Martina Navratilova	1996	Steffi Graf
1938	Helen Wills Moody	1961	Angela Mortimer	1979	Martina Navratilova	1997	Martina Hingis
1939	Alice Marble	1962	Margaret Smith	1980	Chris Evert Lloyd		
1940-45	No rankings	1963	Margaret Smith	1981	Chris Evert Lloyd		
1946	Pauline Betz	1964	Margaret Smith	1982	Martina Navratilova		
1947	Margaret Osborne	1965	Margaret Smith	1983	Martina Navratilova		

Annual Top 10 World Rankings (since 1968)

Year by year Top 10 world computer rankings for Men (ATP Tour) and Women (WTA Tour) since the arrival of open tennis in 1968. Rankings from 1968-72 made by Lance Tingay of the London Daily Telegraph. Since 1973, computerized rankings by ATP Tour (men) and WTA Tour (women).

MEN

	1968	1971	1974	1977
1	Rod Laver	John Newcombe	Jimmy Connors	Jimmy Connors
2	Arthur Ashe	Stan Smith	John Newcombe	Guillermo Vilas
3	Ken Rosewall	Rod Laver	Bjorn Borg	Bjorn Borg
4	Tom Okker	Ken Rosewall	Rod Laver	Vitas Gerulaitis
5	Tony Roche	Jan Kodes	Guillermo Vilas	Brian Gottfried
6	John Newcombe	Arthur Ashe	Tom Okker	Eddie Dibbs
7	Clark Graebner	Tom Okker	Arthur Ashe	Manuel Orantes
8	Dennis Ralston	Marty Riessen	Ken Rosewall	Raul Ramirez
9	Cliff Drysdale	Cliff Drysdale	Stan Smith	Ilie Nastase
10	Pancho Gonzales	Ilie Nastase	Ilie Nastase	Dick Stockton

	1969	1972	1975	1978
1	Rod Laver	Stan Smith	Jimmy Connors	Jimmy Connors
2	Tony Roche	Ken Rosewall	Guillermo Vilas	Bjorn Borg
3	John Newcombe	Ilie Nastase	Bjorn Borg	Guillermo Vilas
4	Tom Okker	Rod Laver	Arthur Ashe	John McEnroe
5	Ken Rosewall	Arthur Ashe	Manuel Orantes	Vitas Gerulaitis
6	Arthur Ashe	John Newcombe	Ken Rosewall	Eddie Dibbs
7	Cliff Drysdale	Bob Lutz	Ilie Nastase	Brian Gottfried
8	Pancho Gonzales	Tom Okker	John Alexander	Raul Ramirez
9	Andres Gimeno	Marty Riessen	Roscoe Tanner	Harold Solomon
10	Fred Stolle	Andres Gimeno	Rod Laver	Corrado Barazzutti

	1970	1973	1976	1979
1	John Newcombe	Ilie Nastase	Jimmy Connors	Bjorn Borg
2	Ken Rosewall	John Newcombe	Bjorn Borg	Jimmy Connors
3	Tony Roche	Jimmy Connors	Ilie Nastase	John McEnroe
4	Rod Laver	Tom Okker	Manuel Orantes	Vitas Gerulaitis
5	Arthur Ashe	Stan Smith	Raul Ramirez	Roscoe Tanner
6	Ilie Nastase	Ken Rosewall	Guillermo Vilas	Guillermo Vilas
7	Tom Okker	Manuel Orantes	Adriano Panatta	Arthur Ashe
8	Roger Taylor	Rod Laver	Harold Solomon	Harold Solomon
9	Jan Kodes	Jan Kodes	Eddie Dibbs	Jose Higueras
10	Cliff Richey	Arthur Ashe	Brian Gottfried	Eddie Dibbs

Annual Top 10 World Rankings (since 1968) (Cont.)

MEN

1980

1 Bjorn Borg
2 John McEnroe
3 Jimmy Connors
4 Gene Mayer
5 Guillermo Vilas
6 Ivan Lendl
7 Harold Solomon
8 Jose-Luis Clerc
9 Vitas Gerulaitis
10 Eliot Teltscher

1981

1 John McEnroe
2 Ivan Lendl
3 Jimmy Connors
4 Bjorn Borg
5 Jose-Luis Clerc
6 Guillermo Vilas
7 Gene Mayer
8 Eliot Teltscher
9 Vitas Gerulaitis
10 Peter McNamara

1982

1 John McEnroe
2 Jimmy Connors
3 Ivan Lendl
4 Guillermo Vilas
5 Vitas Gerulaitis
6 Jose-Luis Clerc
7 Mats Wilander
8 Gene Mayer
9 Yannick Noah
10 Peter McNamara

1983

1 John McEnroe
2 Ivan Lendl
3 Jimmy Connors
4 Mats Wilander
5 Yannick Noah
6 Jimmy Arias
7 Jose Higueras
8 Jose-Luis Clerc
9 Kevin Curren
10 Gene Mayer

1984

1 John McEnroe
2 Jimmy Connors
3 Ivan Lendl
4 Mats Wilander
5 Andres Gomez
6 Anders Jarryd
7 Henrik Sundstrom
8 Pat Cash
9 Eliot Teltscher
10 Yannick Noah

1985

1 Ivan Lendl
2 John McEnroe
3 Mats Wilander
4 Jimmy Connors
5 Stefan Edberg
6 Boris Becker
7 Yannick Noah
8 Anders Jarryd
9 Miloslav Mecir
10 Kevin Curren

1986

1 Ivan Lendl
2 Boris Becker
3 Mats Wilander
4 Yannick Noah
5 Stefan Edberg
6 Henri Leconte
7 Joakim Nystrom
8 Jimmy Connors
9 Miloslav Mecir
10 Andres Gomez

1987

1 Ivan Lendl
2 Stefan Edberg
3 Mats Wilander
4 Jimmy Connors
5 Boris Becker
6 Miloslav Mecir
7 Pat Cash
8 Yannick Noah
9 Tim Mayotte
10 John McEnroe

1988

1 Mats Wilander
2 Ivan Lendl
3 Andre Agassi
4 Boris Becker
5 Stefan Edberg
6 Kent Carlsson
7 Jimmy Connors
8 Jakob Hlasek
9 Henri Leconte
10 Tim Mayotte

1989

1 Ivan Lendl
2 Boris Becker
3 Stefan Edberg
4 John McEnroe
5 Michael Chang
6 Brad Gilbert
7 Andre Agassi
8 Aaron Krickstein
9 Alberto Mancini
10 Jay Berger

1990

1 Stefan Edberg
2 Boris Becker
3 Ivan Lendl
4 Andre Agassi
5 Pete Sampras
6 Andres Gomez
7 Thomas Muster
8 Emilio Sanchez
9 Goran Ivanisevic
10 Brad Gilbert

1991

1 Stefan Edberg
2 Jim Courier
3 Boris Becker
4 Michael Stich
5 Ivan Lendl
6 Pete Sampras
7 Guy Forget
8 Karel Novacek
9 Petr Korda
10 Andre Agassi

1992

1 Jim Courier
2 Stefan Edberg
3 Pete Sampras
4 Goran Ivanisevic
5 Boris Becker
6 Michael Chang
7 Petr Korda
8 Ivan Lendl
9 Andre Agassi
10 Richard Krajicek

1993

1 Pete Sampras
2 Michael Stich
3 Jim Courier
4 Sergi Bruguera
5 Stefan Edberg
6 Andrei Medvedev
7 Goran Ivanisevic
8 Michael Chang
9 Thomas Muster
10 Cedric Pioline

1994

1 Pete Sampras
2 Andre Agassi
3 Boris Becker
4 Sergi Bruguera
5 Goran Ivanisevic
6 Michael Chang
7 Stefan Edberg
8 Alberto Berasategui
9 Michael Stich
10 Todd Martin

1995

1 Pete Sampras
2 Andre Agassi
3 Thomas Muster
4 Boris Becker
5 Michael Chang
6 Yevgeny Kafelnikov
7 Thomas Enqvist
8 Jim Courier
9 Wayne Ferreira
10 Goran Ivanisevic

1996

1 Pete Sampras
2 Michael Chang
3 Yevgeny Kafelnikov
4 Goran Ivanisevic
5 Thomas Muster
6 Boris Becker
7 Richard Krajicek
8 Andre Agassi
9 Thomas Enqvist
10 Wayne Ferreira

1997

1 Pete Sampras
2 Patrick Rafter
3 Michael Chang
4 Jonas Bjorkman
5 Yevgeny Kafelnikov
6 Greg Rusedski
7 Carlos Moya
8 Sergi Bruguera
9 Thomas Muster
10 Marcelo Rios

WOMEN

1968

1 Billie Jean King
2 Virginia Wade
3 Nancy Richey
4 Maria Bueno
5 Margaret Court
6 Ann Jones
7 Judy Tegart
8 Annette du Plooy
9 Leslie Bowrey
10 Rosie Casals

1969

1 Margaret Court
2 Ann Jones
3 Billie Jean King
4 Nancy Richey
5 Julie Heldman
6 Rosie Casals
7 Kerry Melville
8 Peaches Bartkowicz
9 Virginia Wade
10 Leslie Bowrey

1970

1 Margaret Court
2 Billie Jean King
3 Rosie Casals
4 Virginia Wade
5 Helga Niessen
6 Kerry Melville
7 Julie Heldman
8 Karen Krantczke
9 Francoise Durr
10 Nancy R. Gunter

1971

1 Evonne Goolagong
2 Billie Jean King
3 Margaret Court
4 Rosie Casals
5 Kerry Melville
6 Virginia Wade
7 Judy Tagert
8 Francoise Durr
9 Helga N. Masthoff
10 Chris Evert

1972

1 Billie Jean King
2 Evonne Goolagong
3 Chris Evert
4 Margaret Court
5 Kerry Melville
6 Virginia Wade
7 Rosie Casals
8 Nancy R. Gunter
9 Francoise Durr
10 Linda Tuero

1973

1 Margaret S. Court
2 Billie Jean King
3 Evonne G. Cawley
4 Chris Evert
5 Rosie Casals
6 Virginia Wade
7 Kerry Reid
8 Nancy Richey
9 Julie Heldman
10 Helga Masthoff

1974

1 Billie Jean King
2 Evonne G. Cawley
3 Chris Evert
4 Virginia Wade
5 Julie Heldman
6 Rosie Casals
7 Kerry Reid
8 Olga Morozova
9 Lesley Hunt
10 Francoise Durr

1975

1 Chris Evert
2 Billie Jean King
3 Evonne G. Cawley
4 Martina Navratilova
5 Virginia Wade
6 Margaret S. Court
7 Olga Morozova
8 Nancy Richey
9 Francoise Durr
10 Rosie Casals

1976

1 Chris Evert
2 Evonne G. Cawley
3 Virginia Wade
4 Martina Navratilova
5 Sue Barker
6 Betty Stove
7 Dianne Balestrat
8 Mima Jausovec
9 Rosie Casals
10 Francoise Durr

1977

1 Chris Evert
2 Billie Jean King
3 Martina Navratilova
4 Virginia Wade
5 Sue Barker
6 Rosie Casals
7 Betty Stove
8 Dianne Balestrat
9 Wendy Turnbull
10 Kerry Reid

1978

1 Martina Navratilova
2 Chris Evert Lloyd
3 Evonne G. Cawley
4 Virginia Wade
5 Billie Jean King
6 Tracy Austin
7 Wendy Turnbull
8 Kerry Reid
9 Betty Stove
10 Dianne Balestrat

1979

1 Martina Navratilova
2 Chris Evert Lloyd
3 Tracy Austin
4 Evonne G. Cawley
5 Billie Jean King
6 Dianne Balestrat
7 Wendy Turnbull
8 Virginia Wade
9 Kerry Reid
10 Sue Barker

1980

1 Chris Evert Lloyd
2 Tracy Austin
3 Martina Navratilova
4 Hana Mandlikova
5 Evonne G. Cawley
6 Billie Jean King
7 Andrea Jaeger
8 Wendy Turnbull
9 Pam Shriver
10 Greer Stevens

1981

1 Chris Evert Lloyd
2 Tracy Austin
3 Martina Navratilova
4 Andrea Jaeger
5 Hana Mandlikova
6 Sylvia Hanika
7 Pam Shriver
8 Wendy Turnbull
9 Bettina Bunge
10 Barbara Potter

1982

1 Martina Navratilova
2 Chris Evert Lloyd
3 Andrea Jaeger
4 Tracy Austin
5 Wendy Turnbull
6 Pam Shriver
7 Hana Mandlikova
8 Barbara Potter
9 Bettina Bunge
10 Sylvia Hanika

1983

1 Martina Navratilova
2 Chris Evert Lloyd
3 Andrea Jaeger
4 Pam Shriver
5 Sylvia Hanika
6 Jo Durie
7 Bettina Bunge
8 Wendy Turnbull
9 Tracy Austin
10 Zina Garrison

1984

1 Martina Navratilova
2 Chris Evert Lloyd
3 Hana Mandlikova
4 Pam Shriver
5 Wendy Turnbull
6 Manuela Maleeva
7 Helena Sukova
8 Claudia Kohde-Kilsch
9 Zina Garrison
10 Kathy Jordan

1985

1 Martina Navratilova
2 Chris Evert Lloyd
3 Hana Mandlikova
4 Pam Shriver
5 Claudia Kohde-Kilsch
6 Steffi Graf
7 Manuela Maleeva
8 Zina Garrison
9 Helena Sukova
10 Bonnie Gadusek

1986

1 Martina Navratilova
2 Chris Evert Lloyd
3 Steffi Graf
4 Hana Mandlikova
5 Helena Sukova
6 Pam Shriver
7 Claudia Kohde-Kilsch
8 M. Maleeva-Fragniere
9 Zina Garrison
10 Claudia Kohde-Kilsch

1987

1 Steffi Graf
2 Martina Navratilova
3 Chris Evert
4 Pam Shriver
5 Hana Mandlikova
6 Gabriela Sabatini
7 Helena Sukova
8 M. Maleeva-Fragniere
9 Zina Garrison
10 Claudia Kohde-Kilsch

1988

1 Steffi Graf
2 Martina Navratilova
3 Chris Evert
4 Gabriela Sabatini
5 Pam Shriver
6 M. Maleeva-Fragniere
7 Natalia Zvereva
8 Helena Sukova
9 Zina Garrison
10 Barbara Potter

1989

1 Steffi Graf
2 Martina Navratilova
3 Gabriela Sabatini
4 Z. Garrison-Jackson
5 A. Sanchez Vicario
6 Monica Seles
7 Conchita Martinez
8 Helena Sukova
9 M. Maleeva-Fragniere
10 Chris Evert

1990

1 Steffi Graf
2 Monica Seles
3 Martina Navratilova
4 Mary Joe Fernandez
5 Gabriela Sabatini
6 Katerina Maleeva
7 A. Sanchez Vicario
8 Jennifer Capriati
9 M. Maleeva-Fragniere
10 Z. Garrison-Jackson

1991

1 Monica Seles
2 Steffi Graf
3 Gabriela Sabatini
4 Martina Navratilova
5 A. Sanchez Vicario
6 Jennifer Capriati
7 Jana Novotna
8 Mary Joe Fernandez
9 Conchita Martinez
10 M. Maleeva-Fragniere

1992

1 Monica Seles
2 Steffi Graf
3 Gabriela Sabatini
4 A. Sanchez Vicario
5 Martina Navratilova
6 Mary Joe Fernandez
7 Jennifer Capriati
8 Conchita Martinez
9 M. Maleeva-Fragniere
10 Jana Novotna

1993

1 Steffi Graf
2 A. Sanchez Vicario
3 Martina Navratilova
4 Conchita Martinez
5 Gabriela Sabatini
6 Jana Novotna
7 Mary Joe Fernandez
8 Monica Seles
9 Jennifer Capriati
10 Anke Huber

1994

1 Steffi Graf
2 A. Sanchez Vicario
3 Conchita Martinez
4 Jana Novotna
5 Mary Pierce
6 Lindsay Davenport
7 Gabriela Sabatini
8 Martina Navratilova
9 Kimiko Date
10 Natasha Zvereva

1995

1 Steffi Graf
Monica Seles
2 Conchita Martinez
3 A. Sanchez Vicario
4 Kimiko Date
5 Mary Pierce
6 Magdalena Maleeva
7 Gabriela Sabatini
8 Mary Joe Fernandez
9 Iva Majoli
10 Anke Huber

Annual Top 10 World Rankings (since 1968) (Cont.)

WOMEN

1996

1	Steffi Graf
2	Monica Seles
	A. Sanchez Vicario
3	Jana Novotna
4	Martina Hingis
5	Conchita Martinez
6	Anke Huber
7	Iva Majoli
8	Kimiko Date
9	Lindsay Davenport
10	Barbara Paulus

1997

1	Martina Hingis
2	Jana Novotna
3	Lindsay Davenport
4	Amanda Coetzer
5	Monica Seles
6	Iva Majoli
7	Mary Pierce
8	Irina Spirlea
9	A. Sanchez Vicario
10	Mary Joe Fernandez

All-Time Singles Leaders

Tournaments Won

All-time tournament wins from the arrival of open tennis in 1968 through 1997. Men's totals include ATP Tour, Grand Prix and WCT tournaments. Players active in singles play in 1998 are in **bold** type.

MEN

		Total
1	Jimmy Connors	109
2	Ivan Lendl	94
3	John McEnroe	77
4	Bjorn Borg	62
	Guillermo Vilas	62
6	Ilie Nastase	57
7	**Pete Sampras**	52
8	**Boris Becker**	49
9	Rod Laver	47
10	**Thomas Muster**	44
11	Stefan Edberg	41
12	Stan Smith	39
13	**Andre Agassi**	34
14	Arthur Ashe	33
	Mats Wilander	33
16	John Newcombe	32
	Manuel Orantes	32
	Ken Rosewall	32
19	Tom Okker	31
	Michael Chang	31
21	Vitas Gerulaitis	27
22	Jose-Luis Clerc	25
	Brian Gottfried	25
24	Yannick Noah	23
25	Eddie Dibbs	22
	Harold Solomon	22
27	Andres Gomez	21
28	Brad Gilbert	20
	Goran Ivanisevic	20
30	**Jim Courier**	19

WOMEN

		Total
1	Martina Navratilova	167
2	Chris Evert	157
3	**Steffi Graf**	103
4	E. Goolagong Cawley	88
5	Margaret Court	79
6	Billie Jean King	67
7	Virginia Wade	55
8	**Monica Seles**	41
9	Helga Masthoff	37
10	Olga Morozova	31
	Conchita Martinez	31
12	Tracy Austin	29
13	Hana Mandlikova	27
	Gabriela Sabatini	27
15	Nancy Richey	25
16	**A. Sanchez Vicario**	24
17	Kerry Melville Reid	22
18	Sue Barker	21
	Pam Shriver	21
20	Julie Heldman	20
	Jana Novotna	20
22	D. Fromholtz Balestrat	19
	M. Maleeva-Fragniere	19
24	Rosie Casals	18
25	Virginia Ruzici	17
	Regina Marsikova	17
27	Sue Barker	15
28	Peaches Bartkowicz	14
	Andrea Jaeger	14
	Sandra Cecchini	14
	Z. Garrison Jackson	14

Money Won

All-time money winners from the arrival of open tennis in 1968 through 1997. Totals include doubles earnings.

MEN

		Earnings
1	Pete Sampras	$32,060,658
2	Boris Becker	24,515,647
3	Ivan Lendl	21,262,417
4	Stefan Edberg	20,630,941
5	Michael Chang	16,286,739
6	Goran Ivanisevic	16,206,537
7	Jim Courier	13,322,569
8	Andre Agassi	13,206,463
9	Michael Stich	12,628,890
10	John McEnroe	12,539,622
11	Thomas Muster	$11,640,654
12	Sergi Bruguera	10,748,329
13	Yevgeny Kafelnikov	9,604,741
14	Petr Korda	9,039,709
15	Jimmy Connors	8,641,040
16	Mats Wilander	7,976,256
17	Richard Krajicek	6,835,339
18	Mark Woodforde	6,727,181
19	Todd Woodbridge	6,169,741
20	Wayne Ferreira	5,928,743
21	Jakob Hlasek	$5,784,225
22	Guy Forget	5,657,793
23	Paul Haarhuis	5,518,152
24	Brad Gilbert	5,508,745
25	Anders Jarryd	5,377,067
26	Emilio Sanchez	5,337,724
27	David Wheaton	5,155,434
28	Andrei Medvedev	5,042,085
29	Guillermo Vilas	4,923,882
30	Todd Martin	4,824,749

WOMEN

		Earnings
1	Mart. Navratilova	$20,344,061
2	Steffi Graf	20,076,565
3	A. Sanchez Vicario	12,523,488
4	Monica Seles	9,874,510
5	Chris Evert	8,896,195
6	Gabriela Sabatini	8,785,850
7	Jana Novotna	8,257,850
8	Conchita Martinez	6,877,810
9	Helena Sukova	6,308,521
10	Natasha Zvereva	6,082,686
11	Pam Shriver	$5,448,686
12	Martina Hingis	4,948,617
13	Mary Joe Fernandez	4,903,886
14	Gigi Fernandez	4,680,456
15	Z. Garrison Jackson	4,590,816
16	Lindsay Davenport	3,692,454
17	Larisa Neiland	3,533,154
18	Hana Mandlikova	3,340,959
19	Lori McNeil	3,284,785
20	M. Maleeva-Fragniere	3,244,811
21	Mary Pierce	$3,219,509
22	Iva Majoli	3,173,232
23	Anke Huber	3,119,900
24	Nathalie Tauziat	3,014,864
25	Wendy Turnbull	2,769,024
26	Amanda Coetzer	2,613,328
27	B. Schultz-McCarthy	2,501,489
28	Claudia Kohde-Kilsch	2,227,116
29	Katerina Maleeva	2,220,371
30	Tracy Austin	1,992,380

Year-end Tournaments

MEN

Masters/ATP Tour World Championship

The year-end championship of the ATP men's tour since 1970. Contested by the year's top eight players. Originally a round-robin, the Masters was revised in 1972 to include a round-robin to decide the four semifinalists then a single elimination format after that. The tournament switched from December to January in 1977-78, then back to December in 1986. Held at Madison Square Garden in New York from 1978-89. Replaced by ATP Tour World Championship in 1990 and held in Frankfurt, Germany since then.

Multiple Winners: Ivan Lendl (5); Ilie Nastase and Pete Sampras (4); Boris Becker and John McEnroe (3); Bjorn Borg (2).

Year	Winner	Runner-Up
1970	Stan Smith (4-1)	Rod Laver (4-1)
1971	Ilie Nastase (6-0)	Stan Smith (4-2)

Year	Winner	Loser	Score
1972	Ilie Nastase	S. Smith	63 62 36 26 63
1973	Ilie Nastase	T. Okker	63 75 46 63
1974	Guillermo Vilas	I. Nastase	76 62 36 36 64
1975	Ilie Nastase	B. Borg	62 62 61
1976	Manuel Orantes	W. Fibak	57 62 06 76 61
1978	Jimmy Connors	B. Borg	64 16 64
1979	John McEnroe	A. Ashe	67 63 75
1980	Bjorn Borg	V. Gerulaitis	62 62
1981	Bjorn Borg	I. Lendl	64 62 62
1982	Ivan Lendl	V. Gerulaitis	67 26 76 62 64
1983	Ivan Lendl	J. McEnroe	64 64 62
1984	John McEnroe	I. Lendl	63 64 64
1985	John McEnroe	I. Lendl	75 60 64
1986	Ivan Lendl	B. Becker	62 76 63
1986	Ivan Lendl	B. Becker	64 64 64
1987	Ivan Lendl	M. Wilander	62 62 63
1988	Boris Becker	I. Lendl	57 76 36 62 76
1989	Stefan Edberg	B. Becker	46 76 63 61
1990	Andre Agassi	S. Edberg	57 76 75 62
1991	Pete Sampras	J. Courier	36 76 63 64
1992	Boris Becker	J. Courier	64 63 75
1993	Michael Stich	P. Sampras	76 26 76 62
1994	Pete Sampras	B. Becker	46 63 75 64
1995	Boris Becker	M. Chang	76 60 76
1996	Pete Sampras	B. Becker	36 76 76 67 64
1997	Pete Sampras	Y. Kafelnikov	63 62 62

Note: In 1970, Smith was declared the winner because he beat Laver in their round-robin match (4-6, 6-3, 6-4).

WCT Championship (1971-89)

World Championship Tennis was established in 1967 to promote professional tennis and led the way into the open era. It's major singles and doubles championships were held every May among the top eight regular season finishers on the circuit from 1971 until the WCT folded in 1989.

Multiple winners: John McEnroe (5), Jimmy Connors, Ivan Lendl and Ken Rosewall (2).

Year	Winner	Loser	Score
1971	Ken Rosewall	R. Laver	64 16 76 76
1972	Ken Rosewall	R. Laver	46 60 63 67 76
1973	Stan Smith	A. Ashe	63 63 46 64
1974	John Newcombe	B. Borg	46 63 63 62
1975	Arthur Ashe	B. Borg	36 64 64 60
1976	Bjorn Borg	G. Vilas	16 61 75 61
1977	Jimmy Connors	D. Stockton	67 61 64 63
1978	Vitas Gerulaitis	E. Dibbs	63 62 61
1979	John McEnroe	B. Borg	75 46 62 76
1980	Jimmy Connors	J. McEnroe	26 76 61 62
1981	John McEnroe	J. Kriek	61 62 64
1982	Ivan Lendl	J. McEnroe	62 36 63 63
1983	John McEnroe	I. Lendl	62 46 63 67 76
1984	John McEnroe	J. Connors	61 62 63
1985	Ivan Lendl	T. Mayotte	76 64 61
1986	Anders Jarryd	B. Becker	67 61 61 64
1987	Miloslav Mercir	J. McEnroe	60 36 62 62
1988	Boris Becker	S. Edberg	64 16 75 62
1989	John McEnroe	B. Gilbert	63 63 76

WOMEN

WTA Tour Championship

Originally the Virginia Slims Championships from 1971-94. The WTA Tour's year-end tournament took place in March from 1972 until 1986 when the WTA decided to adopt a January-to-November playing season. Given the changeover, two championships were held in 1986. Held every year since 1979 at Madison Square Garden in New York.

Multiple winners: Martina Navratilova (8); Steffi Graf (5); Chris Evert (4); Monica Seles (3); Evonne Goolagong and Gabriela Sabatini (2).

Year	Winner	Loser	Score
1972	Chris Evert	K. Reid	75 64
1973	Chris Evert	N. Richey	63 63
1974	Evonne Goolagong	C. Evert	63 64
1975	Chris Evert	M. Navratilova	64 62
1976	Evonne Goolagong	C. Evert	63 57 63
1977	Chris Evert	S. Barker	26 61 61
1978	M. Navratilova	E. Goolagong	76 64
1979	M. Navratilova	T. Austin	63 36 62
1980	Tracy Austin	M. Navratilova	62 26 62
1981	M. Navratilova	A. Jaeger	63 76
1982	Sylvia Hanika	M. Navratilova	16 63 64
1983	M. Navratilova	C. Evert	62 60
1984	M. Navratilova	C. Evert	63 75 61
1985	M. Navratilova	H. Sukova	63 75 64
1986	M. Navratilova	H. Mandlikova	62 60 36 61
1986	M. Navratilova	S. Graf	76 63 62
1987	Steffi Graf	G. Sabatini	46 64 60 64
1988	Gabriela Sabatini	P. Shriver	75 62 62
1989	Steffi Graf	M. Navratilova	64 75 26 62
1990	Monica Seles	G. Sabatini	64 57 36 64 62
1991	Monica Seles	M. Navratilova	64 36 75 60
1992	Monica Seles	M. Navratilova	75 63 61
1993	Steffi Graf	A. S. Vicario	61 64 36 61
1994	Gabriela Sabatini	L. Davenport	63 62 64
1995	Steffi Graf	A. Huber	61 26 61 46 63
1996	Steffi Graf	M. Hingis	63 46 60 46 60
1997	Jana Novotna	M. Pierce	76 62 63

*Two tournaments in 1986 due to change in playing season.

Mike Powell/Allsport

The 1992 U.S. Davis Cup team that beat Switzerland in the final at Fort Worth, Texas (from left to right): singles players **Andre Agassi** and **Jim Courier**, doubles partners **John McEnroe** and **Pete Sampras**, and non-playing captain **Tom Gorman**. The Americans beat the Swiss, 3–1, for their 30th Davis Cup title since 1900.

Davis Cup

Established in 1900 as an annual international tournament by American player Dwight Davis. Originally called the International Lawn Tennis Challenge Trophy. Challenge round system until 1972. Since 1981, the top 16 nations in the world have played a straight knockout tournament over the course of a year. The format is a best-of-five match of two singles, one doubles and two singles over three days. Note that from 1900–24 Australia and New Zealand competed together as Australasia.

Multiple winners: USA (31); Australia (20); France (8); Australasia and Sweden (6); British Isles (5); Britain (4); Germany (3).

Challenge Rounds

Year	Winner	Loser	Score	Site
1900	USA	British Isles	3-0	Boston
1901	Not held			
1902	USA	British Isles	3-2	New York
1903	British Isles	USA	4-1	Boston
1904	British Isles	Belgium	5-0	Wimbledon
1905	British Isles	USA	5-0	Wimbledon
1906	British Isles	USA	5-0	Wimbledon
1907	Australasia	British Isles	3-2	Wimbledon
1908	Australasia	USA	3-2	Melbourne
1909	Australasia	USA	5-0	Sydney
1910	Not held			
1911	Australasia	USA	5-0	Christchurch,NZ
1912	British Isles	Australasia	3-2	Melbourne
1913	USA	British Isles	3-2	Wimbledon
1914	Australasia	USA	3-2	New York
1915-18	Not held	World War I		
1919	Australasia	British Isles	4-1	Sydney
1920	USA	Australasia	5-0	Auckland, NZ
1921	USA	Japan	5-0	New York
1922	USA	Australasia	4-1	New York
1923	USA	Australasia	4-1	New York
1924	USA	Australia	5-0	Philadelphia
1925	USA	France	5-0	Philadelphia
1926	USA	France	4-1	Philadelphia
1927	France	USA	3-2	Philadelphia
1928	France	USA	4-1	Paris
1929	France	USA	3-2	Paris
1930	France	USA	4-1	Paris
1931	France	Britain	3-2	Paris
1932	France	USA	3-2	Paris
1933	Britain	France	3-2	Paris
1934	Britain	USA	4-1	Wimbledon
1935	Britain	USA	5-0	Wimbledon
1936	Britain	Australia	3-2	Wimbledon
1937	USA	Britain	4-1	Wimbledon
1938	USA	Australia	3-2	Philadelphia
1939	Australia	USA	3-2	Philadelphia
1940-45	Not held	World War II		
1946	USA	Australia	5-0	Melbourne
1947	USA	Australia	4-1	New York
1948	USA	Australia	5-0	New York
1949	USA	Australia	4-1	New York
1950	Australia	USA	4-1	New York
1951	Australia	USA	3-2	Sydney
1952	Australia	USA	4-1	Adelaide
1953	Australia	USA	3-2	Melbourne

Year	Winner	Loser	Score	Site
1954	USA	Australia	3-2	Sydney
1955	Australia	USA	5-0	New York
1956	Australia	USA	5-0	Adelaide
1957	Australia	USA	3-2	Melbourne
1958	USA	Australia	3-2	Brisbane
1959	Australia	USA	3-2	New York
1960	Australia	Italy	4-1	Sydney
1961	Australia	Italy	5-0	Melbourne
1962	Australia	Mexico	5-0	Brisbane
1963	USA	Australia	3-2	Adelaide
1964	Australia	USA	3-2	Cleveland
1965	Australia	Spain	4-1	Sydney
1966	Australia	India	4-1	Melbourne
1967	Australia	Spain	4-1	Brisbane

Final Rounds

Year	Winner	Loser	Score	Site
1968	USA	Australia	4-1	Adelaide
1969	USA	Romania	5-0	Cleveland
1970	USA	W. Germany	5-0	Cleveland
1971	USA	Romania	3-2	Charlotte
1972	USA	Romania	3-2	Bucharest
1973	Australia	USA	5-0	Cleveland
1974	So. Africa	India	walkover	Not held
1975	Sweden	Czech.	3-2	Stockholm
1976	Italy	Chile	4-1	Santiago
1977	Australia	Italy	3-1	Sydney
1978	USA	Britain	4-1	Palm Springs
1979	USA	Italy	5-0	San Francisco
1980	Czech.	Italy	4-1	Prague
1981	USA	Argentina	3-1	Cincinnati
1982	USA	France	4-1	Grenoble
1983	Australia	Sweden	3-2	Melbourne
1984	Sweden	USA	4-1	Göteborg
1985	Sweden	W. Germany	3-2	Munich
1986	Australia	Sweden	3-2	Melbourne
1987	Sweden	India	5-0	Göteborg
1988	W. Germany	Sweden	4-1	Göteborg
1989	W. Germany	Sweden	3-2	Stuttgart
1990	USA	Australia	3-2	St. Petersburg
1991	France	USA	3-1	Lyon
1992	USA	Switzerland	3-1	Ft. Worth
1993	Germany	Australia	4-1	Dusseldorf
1994	Sweden	Russia	4-1	Moscow
1995	USA	Russia	3-2	Moscow
1996	France	Sweden	3-2	Malmo
1997	Sweden	United States	5-0	Göteborg

Note: In 1974, India refused to play the final as a protest against the South African government's policies of apartheid.

Fed Cup

Originally the Federation Cup and started in 1963 by the International Tennis Federation as the Davis Cup of women's tennis. Played by 32 teams over one week at one site through 1994. Tournament changed in 1995 to Davis Cup-style format of four rounds and home site.

Multiple winners: USA (15); Australia (7); Czechoslovakia and Spain (5); Germany (2).

Year	Winner	Loser	Score	Site
1963	USA	Australia	2-1	London
1964	Australia	USA	2-1	Philadelphia
1965	Australia	USA	2-1	Melbourne
1966	USA	W. Germany	3-0	Italy
1967	USA	Britain	2-0	W. Germany
1968	Australia	Holland	3-0	Paris
1969	USA	Australia	2-1	Athens
1970	Australia	Britain	3-0	W. Germany
1971	Australia	Britain	3-0	Perth
1972	So. Africa	Britain	2-1	Africa
1973	Australia	So. Africa	3-0	W. Germany
1974	Australia	USA	2-1	Italy
1975	Czech.	Australia	3-0	France
1976	USA	Australia	2-1	Philadelphia
1977	USA	Australia	2-1	Eastbourne
1978	USA	Australia	2-1	Melbourne
1979	USA	Australia	3-0	Spain
1980	USA	Australia	3-0	W. Germany
1981	USA	Britain	3-0	Tokyo
1982	USA	W. Germany	3-0	Santa Clara
1983	Czech.	W. Germany	2-1	Zurich
1984	Czech.	Australia	2-1	Brazil
1985	Czech.	USA	2-1	Japan
1986	US	Czech.	3-0	Prague
1987	W. Germany	USA	2-1	Vancouver
1988	Czech.	USSR	2-1	Melbourne
1989	USA	Spain	3-0	Tokyo
1990	USA	USSR	2-1	Atlanta
1991	Spain	USA	2-1	Nottingham
1992	Germany	Spain	2-1	Frankfurt
1993	Spain	Australia	3-0	Frankfurt
1994	Spain	USA	3-0	Frankfurt
1995	Spain	USA	3-2	Valencia
1996	USA	Spain	5-0	Atlantic City
1997	France	Netherlands	4-1	Nice, France
1998	Spain	Switzerland	3-2	Geneva

COLLEGES

NCAA team titles were not sanctioned until 1946. NCAA women's individual and team championships started in 1982.

Men's NCAA Individual Champions (1883-1945)

Multiple winners: Malcolm Chace and Pancho Segura (3); Edward Chandler, George Church, E.B. Dewhurst, Fred Hovey, Frank Guernsey, W.P. Knapp, Robert LeRoy, P.S. Sears, Cliff Sutter, Ernest Sutter and Richard Williams (2).

Year	
1883	J. Clark, Harvard (spring)
	H. Taylor, Harvard (fall)
1884	W.P. Knapp, Yale
1885	W.P. Knapp, Yale
1886	G.M. Brinley, Trinity, CT
1887	P.S. Sears, Harvard
1888	P.S. Sears, Harvard
1889	R.P. Huntington Jr, Yale
1890	Fred Hovey, Harvard
1891	Fred Hovey, Harvard
1892	William Larned, Cornell
1893	Malcolm Chace, Brown
1894	Malcolm Chace, Yale
1895	Malcolm Chace, Yale
1896	Malcolm Whitman, Harvard
1897	S.G. Thompson, Princeton
1898	Leo Ware, Harvard
1899	Dwight Davis, Harvard
1900	Ray Little, Princeton

Year		Year		Year	
1901	Fred Alexander, Princeton	1916	G.C. Caner, Harvard	1932	Cliff Sutter, Tulane
1902	William Clothier, Harvard	1917-1918	Not held	1933	Jack Tidball, UCLA
1903	E.B. Dewhurst, Penn	1919	Charles Garland, Yale	1934	Gene Mako, USC
1904	Robert LeRoy, Columbia	1920	Lascelles Banks, Yale	1935	Wilbur Hess, Rice
1905	E.B. Dewhurst, Penn	1921	Philip Neer, Stanford	1936	Ernest Sutter, Tulane
1906	Robert LeRoy, Columbia	1922	Lucien Williams, Yale	1937	Ernest Sutter, Tulane
1907	G.P. Gardner Jr, Harvard	1923	Carl Fischer, Phi. Osteo.	1938	Frank Guernsey, Rice
1908	Nat Niles, Harvard	1924	Wallace Scott, Wash.	1939	Frank Guernsey, Rice
1909	Wallace Johnson, Penn	1925	Edward Chandler, Calif.	1940	Don McNeill, Kenyon
1910	R.A. Holden Jr, Yale	1926	Edward Chandler, Calif.	1941	Joseph Hunt, Navy
1911	E.H. Whitney, Harvard	1927	Wilmer Allison, Texas	1942	Fred Schroeder, Stanford
1912	George Church, Princeton	1928	Julius Seligson, Lehigh	1943	Pancho Segura, Miami-FL
1913	Richard Williams, Harv.	1929	Berkeley Bell, Texas	1944	Pancho Segura, Miami-FL
1914	George Church, Princeton	1930	Cliff Sutter, Tulane	1945	Pancho Segura, Miami-FL
1915	Richard Williams, Harv.	1931	Keith Gledhill, Stanford		

NCAA Men's Division I Champions

Multiple winners (Teams): Stanford (16); UCLA and USC (15); Georgia and William & Mary (2). (Players): Alex Olmedo, Mikael Pernfors, Dennis Ralston and Ham Richardson (2).

Year	Team winner	Individual Champion	Year	Team winner	Individual Champion
1946	USC	Bob Falkenburg, USC	1973	Stanford	Alex Mayer, Stanford
1947	Wm. & Mary	Garner Larned, Wm.& Mary	1974	Stanford	John Whitlinger, Stanford
1948	Wm. & Mary	Harry Likas, San Francisco	1975	UCLA	Bill Martin, UCLA
1949	San Francisco	Jack Tuero, Tulane	1976	USC & UCLA	Bill Scanlon, Trinity-TX
1950	UCLA	Herbert Flam, UCLA	1977	Stanford	Matt Mitchell, Stanford
1951	USC	Tony Trabert, Cincinnati	1978	Stanford	John McEnroe, Stanford
1952	UCLA	Hugh Stewart, USC	1979	UCLA	Kevin Curren, Texas
1953	UCLA	Ham Richardson, Tulane	1980	Stanford	Robert Van't Hof, USC
1954	UCLA	Ham Richardson, Tulane	1981	Stanford	Tim Mayotte, Stanford
1955	USC	Jose Aguero, Tulane	1982	UCLA	Mike Leach, Michigan
1956	UCLA	Alex Olmedo, USC	1983	Stanford	Greg Holmes, Utah
1957	Michigan	Barry MacKay, Michigan	1984	UCLA	Mikael Pernfors, Georgia
1958	USC	Alex Olmedo, USC	1985	Georgia	Mikael Pernfors, Georgia
1959	Tulane & Notre Dame	Whitney Reed, San Jose St.	1986	Stanford	Dan Goldie, Stanford
1960	UCLA	Larry Nagler, UCLA	1987	Georgia	Andrew Burrow, Miami-FL
1961	UCLA	Allen Fox, UCLA	1988	Stanford	Robby Weiss, Pepperdine
1962	USC	Rafael Osuna, USC	1989	Stanford	Donni Leaycraft, LSU
1963	USC	Dennis Ralston, USC	1990	Stanford	Steve Bryan, Texas
1964	USC	Dennis Ralston, USC	1991	USC	Jared Palmer, Stanford
1965	UCLA	Arthur Ashe, UCLA	1992	Stanford	Alex O'Brien Stanford
1966	USC	Charlie Pasarell, UCLA	1993	USC	Chris Woodruff, Tennessee
1967	USC	Bob Lutz, USC	1994	USC	Mark Merklein, Florida
1968	USC	Stan Smith, USC	1995	Stanford	Sargis Sargisian, Ariz. St.
1969	USC	Joaquin Loyo-Mayo, USC	1996	Stanford	Cecil Mamiit, USC
1970	UCLA	Jeff Borowiak, UCLA	1997	Stanford	Luke Smith, UNLV
1971	UCLA	Jimmy Connors, UCLA	1998	Stanford	Bob Bryan, Stanford
1972	Trinity-TX	Dick Stockton, Trinity-TX			

NCAA Women's Division I Champions

Multiple winners (Teams): Stanford (9); Florida (3); Texas and USC (2). (Players): Sandra Birch, Patty Fendick and Lisa Raymond (2).

Year	Team winner	Individual Champion	Year	Team winner	Individual Champion
1982	Stanford	Alycia Moulton, Stanford	1991	Stanford	Sandra Birch, Stanford
1983	USC	Beth Herr, USC	1992	Florida	Lisa Raymond, Florida
1984	Stanford	Lisa Spain, Georgia	1993	Texas	Lisa Raymond, Florida
1985	USC	Linda Gates, Stanford	1994	Georgia	Angela Lettiere, Georgia
1986	Stanford	Patty Fendick, Stanford	1995	Texas	Keri Phoebus, UCLA
1987	Stanford	Patty Fendick, Stanford	1996	Florida	Jill Craybas, Florida
1988	Stanford	Shaun Stafford, Florida	1997	Stanford	Lilia Osterloh, Stanford
1989	Stanford	Sandra Birch, Stanford	1998	Florida	Vanessa Webb, Duke
1990	Stanford	Debbie Graham, Stanford			

Golf

Mark O'Meara reacts after sinking his birdie putt on the 18th green to win the 1998 Masters, the first major win of his career.

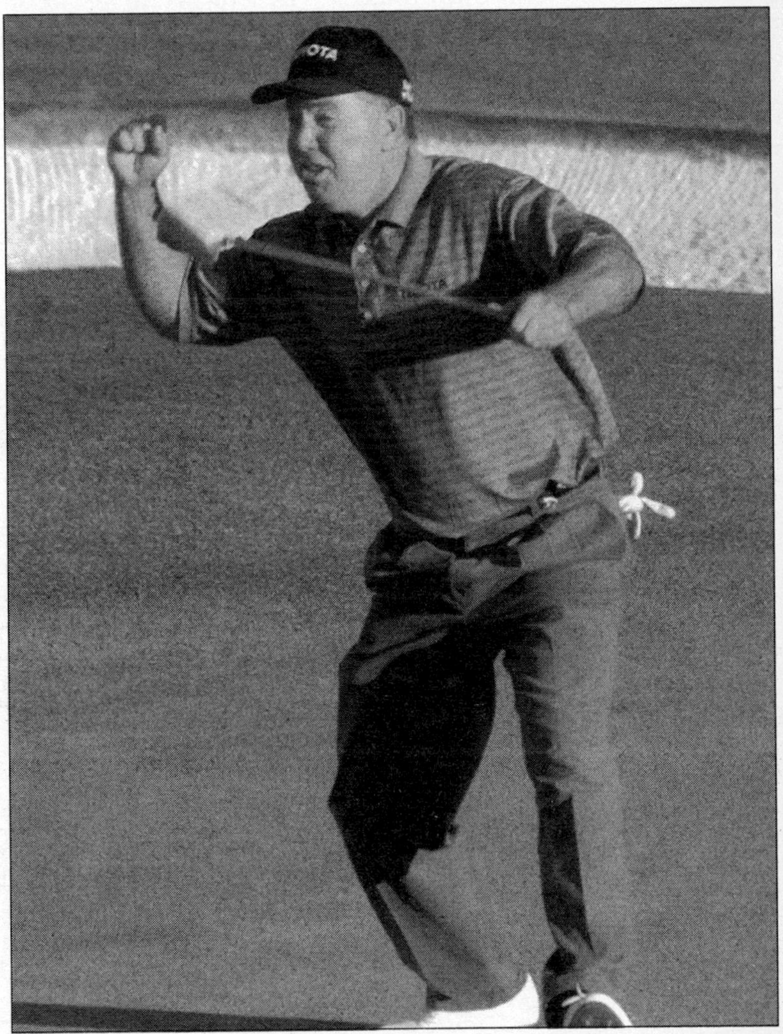

AP/Wide World Photos

Not So Fast

This was supposed to be the year for golf's next generation to take over, but the veterans showed they aren't going anywhere.

by
Mike Tirico

Television has become the element which defines, drives and sets the framework for our society. The clothes we wear, the way we act and the things we say are all influenced by what happens on the other end of that usually misplaced remote control. Who would have known that an otherwise forgettable ABC prime-time series of a decade ago would give us the genesis for the watch word in the 1998 golf season. *Thirty-something* begat *twenty-something*.

This was to be the year when the men's golfers who became the best in their sport in '97 simply dominated the game.

Have patience.

Perhaps driven by a sports cognoscente that does not understand the sport as well as the other stick and ball games, the anticipation that our five stars in their 20's would engage in intramural competitions at Augusta, Olympic, Royal Birkdale and Sahalee just was not realized.

Tiger Woods, Phil Mickelson, David Duval, Justin Leonard and Ernie Els did not have bad seasons, winning their share of events around the world. But in the events the world watches, the majors, they simply did not play their best golf. Duval's second-place showing at the Masters and Woods' sprint to finish third at the British Open were the only top three's for the young fab five.

Instead it was a year where experience prevailed. Mark O'Meara, 41, his game more aggressive from countless one-on-ones with neighbor and friend Woods, birdied Augusta's last two famous holes and had the infamous green jacket placed on him by Woods. Three months later, O'Meara's steady hand and hot Sunday back-nine putter led him to a win in the four-hole British Open playoff over Brian Watts.

Mike Tirico covers golf for ESPN.

AP/Wide World Photos

Mark O'Meara (l) grabbed the golf spotlight in 1998 with two major wins while his friend **Tiger Woods** (r) seemed to drift towards the background. Here the 1997 Masters champion Woods helps O'Meara don the green jacket after winning the 1998 tournament on April 12 at Augusta (Ga.) National Golf Club.

Watts, an American who makes his golf life on the Japanese tour, earned the respect of the world with his ability to play in the last group over the last two days and not fold under the pressure of a major. But the most memorable part of the British Open was Justin Rose. The pimple-faced English teen found himself in the final group on the final day and finished tied for fourth, the best amateur finish in the Open Championship in 42 years.

Unknowns and amateurs gave us golf's best moments in 1998. Korean Se Ri Pak, 20, turned the ladies tour on it's side by winning two majors, her U.S. Open win the result of surviving a classic 20-hole playoff with amateur Jenny Chuasiriporn, who this fall continued her college life at Duke University (for more, see the women's golf essay on page 853).

Matt Kuchar, the 19-year-old who redefined the engaging smile, thrilled crowds with his cheerleading father carrying his bag for a 21st-place finish at the Masters and a 14th-place showing at the U.S. Open.

Then there was Casey Martin, the 26-year-old with the leg disability that makes it virtually impossible to walk and play competitive golf. After suing for and receiving the right to use a cart, Martin qualified for the Nike Tour and won his first event but was unable to keep his game at that high level the rest of the season.

In all regards it was a year for the brand new, or the experienced.

O'Meara wasn't the only player over the age of 20 to prove that golfers

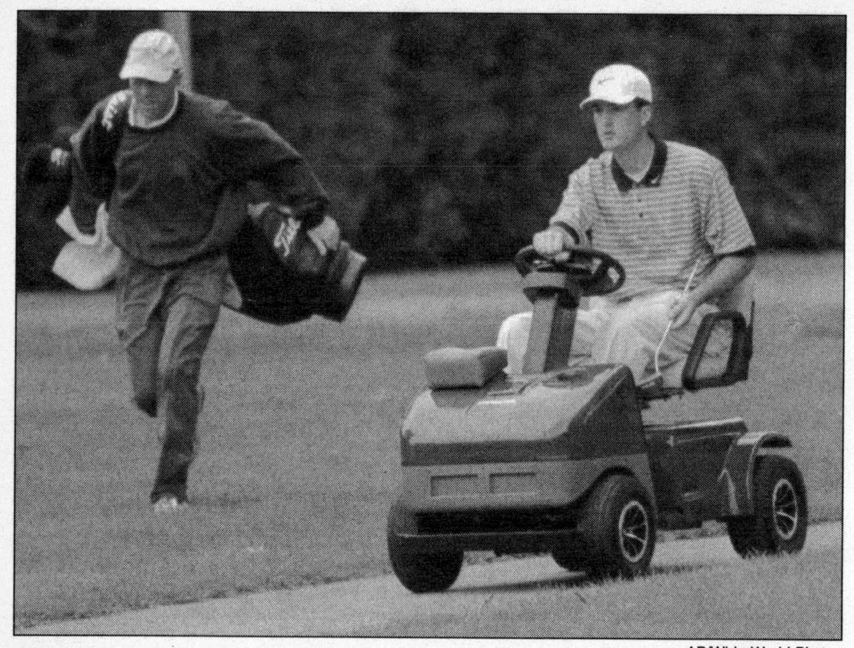

AP/Wide World Photos

Casey Martin (r) rides in his cart during a U.S. Open qualifier in Cincinnati while a caddy for another golfer jogs beside him. Martin, who suffers from a chronic leg disability, won a controversial decision in 1998 for the right to use the cart in all PGA Tour events.

get better with time. Payne Stewart's three days of U.S. Open dominance were erased when Lee Janzen passed him in the final round to win his second Open by one stroke. Vijay Singh's long worldwide career, defined by endless hours of practice, was finally rewarded with a win at the PGA Championship, his first major.

Still the "stop-the-world" moment came on Sunday at Augusta when 58-year-old Jack Nicklaus turned back the clock, coming within two strokes of the lead at the Masters. Often golfing with a hip that would keep many from their weekend match at the club, Jack proved that no matter how well Tiger fits Augusta, Georgia's greatest golf sod will be Jack's track forever. ■

Mike Tirico's Top Ten News Stories of the Year in Golf

10. **Greg Norman** is noticeably absent from the golf scene after having arthroscopic shoulder surgery in April.
9. **Fred Couples and David Duval** lose their leads on another unforgettable Sunday at Augusta, while Mark O'Meara birdies the last two holes to take the green jacket.
8. **The United States team**, led by the fiery and controversial Dottie Pepper, retains the Solheim Cup by beating Europe 16-12 in the biannual women's event.
7. **Tiger Woods**, although a top 10 regular on the money list and in

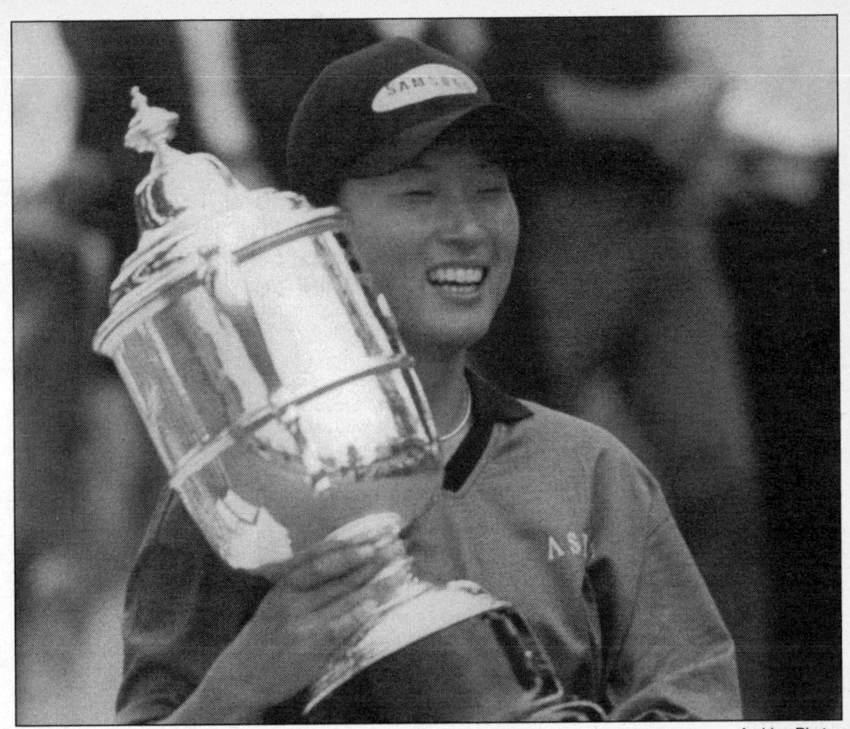

Archive Photos

LPGA rookie **Se Ri Pak** celebrates after finally defeating amateur Jenny Chuasiriporn on the 92nd hole at the U.S. Women's Open in Kohler, Wisc. It was the longest championship competition in women's golf history and the 20-year-old Pak's second major victory of the year.

tournament finishes, wins just one PGA Tour event since winning the Western Open in July 1997.

6. **Amateur Matt Kuchar** not only makes the cut, but draws perhaps the most attention at the Masters and U.S. Open.
5. **Hale Irwin** continues his dominance of the Senior PGA Tour, finishing in the top five for 19 straight events. For the second consecutive year, he shatters the $2 million earnings mark.
4. **Se Ri Pak and amateur Jenny Chuasiriporn** battle it out over 20 playoff holes at one of the most memorable U.S. Women's Opens in history.
3. **Casey Martin** wins the right to use a cart because of his leg disability and wins his first Nike Tour start. He qualifies for the U.S. Open and makes the cut, finishing in a tie for 23rd place.
2. **Se Ri Pak** explodes onto the women's golf scene by winning her first two majors.
1. **Mark O'Meara** emerges from the shadow of his friend Tiger Woods to win his first two career majors. ■

THE NUMBERS INSIDE

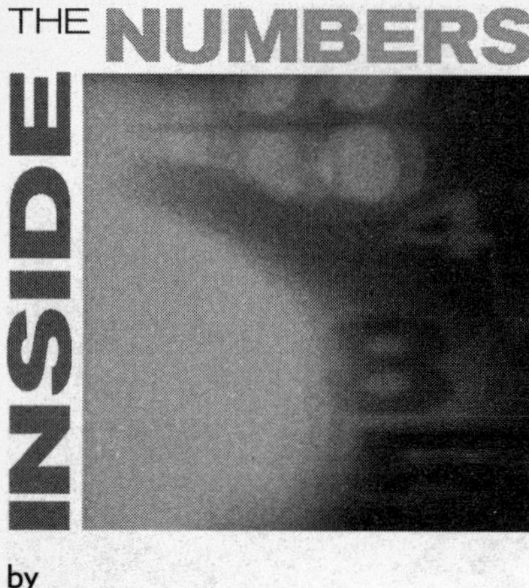

by
Steve Rutkowski

TWENTY-SOMETHINGS

Though Phil Mickelson has yet to win a major PGA tournament, he is still enjoying quite a successful run through his twenties. Below are the only four PGA players currently in their twenties to have at least six tour wins.

	Wins	Age*
Phil Mickelson	13	28
Tiger Woods	7	22
David Duval	6	26
Ernie Els	6	29

*as of Nov. 1, 1998

TAMED **TIGER**?

How tough is it to win on the PGA Tour? Just ask Tiger Woods. Through Oct. 4 of the 1998 season, Tiger had just one win, three shy of his total from last year. He has three more top-10 finishes than last year and is leading the tour in scoring but it just hasn't translated into victories.

	1998	1997
Wins	1	4
Top 3s	5	6
Top 10s	12	9
Scoring Rank	1st	2nd

COMPLETE **PAK**AGE

Se Ri Pak is the hottest young golfer to come around since you-know-who. Compare Pak's stats from her first 18 events of the 1998 LPGA season to Tiger Woods' stats from the first 18 events of 1997 (his first full year on the PGA Tour). And the similarities don't end there – each resides in Orlando, Fla.

	Pak 1998	Woods 1997
Age	20	21
Wins	4	4
Cuts Made	17	17
Stroke Average	71.1	69.6

SAY YOU, **SE RI**

With two major tournament victories in 1998, Se Ri Pak became one of the most successful rookies in LPGA history. Through Oct. 4, Pak had won four tournaments overall, good for a second-place tie on the all-time list of wins by a rookie.

	Wins	Events
Nancy Lopez, '77-78	9	24
Se Ri Pak, '98	**4**	**24**
Karrie Webb, '96	4	25
Juli Inkster, '83-84	3	26
Betsy Rawls, '51	2	n/a
Laura Davies, '88	2	21

MAJOR LETDOWN

From 1972 on, the PGA Championship has been the last of the four men's majors to be played. Six times, a player going into the PGA Championship had won two previous majors that year. Six times, that player has failed to win his third. In 1998, Mark O'Meara came the closest, tying for fourth.

	Year	PGA Champ. Finish
Mark O'Meara	**1998**	**t-4th**
Nick Faldo	1990	t-19th
Tom Watson	1982	t-9th
Tom Watson	1977	t-6th
Gary Player	1974	7th
Jack Nicklaus	1972	t-13th

■

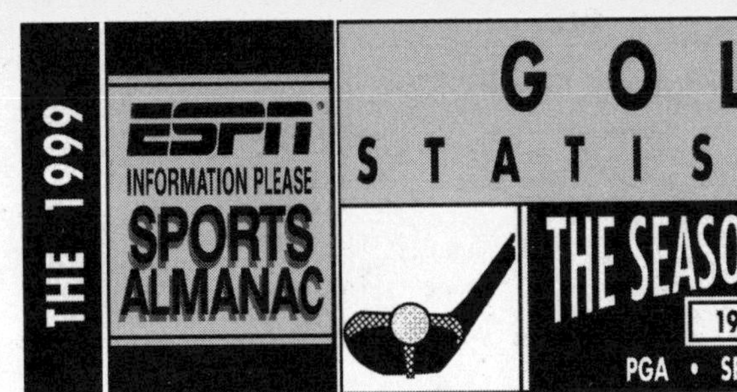

GOLF STATISTICS

THE SEASON IN REVIEW

1997-1998

PGA • SENIORS • LPGA

Tournament Results

Winners of PGA, European PGA, PGA Seniors and LPGA tournaments from Nov. 2, 1997 through Oct. 4, 1998.

PGA Tour

LATE 1997

Last Rd	Tournament	Winner	Earnings	Runner-Up
Nov. 2	The Tour Championship	David Duval (273)	$720,000	J. Furyk (274)
Nov. 9	Kapalua International	Davis Love III (268)	216,000	D. Toms (271)
Nov. 9	Sarazen World Open	Mark Calcavecchia (271)	360,000	L. Westwood (274)
Nov. 16	Shark Shootout	Bruce Lietzke/ Scott McCarron (187)	150,000 (each)	Duval/Hoch (188)
Nov. 23	World Cup of Golf	IRE—Padraig Harrington/ Paul McGinley (545)	200,000 (each)	SCOT—R. Russell/ C. Montgomerie (550)
Nov. 30	The Skins Game	Tom Lehman (10 skins)	300,000	M. O'Meara (5 skins)
Dec. 7	JC Penney Classic	Clarence Rose/ Amy Fruhwirth (264)	187,500 (each)	Clink/Klein & Forsman/Matthew (265)
Dec. 14	Diners Club Matches	Steve Elkington/ Jeff Maggert (2 & 1)	110,000 (each)	T. Lehman/ D. Waldorf

1998 (through Oct. 4)

Last Rd	Tournament	Winner	Earnings	Runner-Up
Jan. 11	Mercedes Championship	Phil Mickelson (271)	$306,000	M. O'Meara & T. Woods (272)
Jan. 18	Bob Hope Chrysler Classic	Fred Couples (332)*	414,000	B. Lietzke (332)
Jan. 25	Phoenix Open	Jesper Parnevik (269)	450,000	4-way tie (272)
Feb. 8	Buick Invitational	Scott Simpson (204)#*	378,000	S. Kendall (204)
Feb. 15	United Airlines Hawaiian Open	John Huston (260)	324,000	T. Watson (267)
Feb. 22	Tucson Chrysler Classic	David Duval (269)	360,000	J. Leonard & D. Toms (273)
Mar. 1	Nissan Open	Billy Mayfair (272)*	378,000	T. Woods (272)
Mar. 8	Doral-Ryder Open	Michael Bradley (278)	360,000	J. Huston & B. Mayfair (279)
Mar. 15	Honda Classic	Mark Calcavecchia (270)	324,000	V. Singh (273)
Mar. 22	Bay Hill Invitational	Ernie Els (274)	360,000	J. Maggert & B. Estes (278)
Mar. 29	The Players Championship	Justin Leonard (278)	720,000	T. Lehman & G. Day (280)
Apr. 5	Freeport-McDermott Classic	Lee Westwood (273)	306,000	S. Flesch (276)
Apr. 12	**The Masters** (Augusta)	Mark O'Meara (279)	576,000	F. Couples & D. Duval (280)
Apr. 19	MCI Classic	Davis Love III (266)	342,000	G. Day (273)
Apr. 26	Greater Greensboro Chrysler Classic	Trevor Dodds (276)*	396,000	S. Verplank (276)
May 3	Shell Houston Open	David Duval (276)	360,000	J. Maggert (277)
May 10	BellSouth Classic	Tiger Woods (271)	324,000	J. Don Blake (272)
May 17	GTE Byron Nelson Classic	John Cook (265)	450,000	3-way tie (268)
May 24	Mastercard Colonial	Tom Watson (265)	414,000	J. Furyk (267)
May 31	Memorial Tournament	Fred Couples (271)	396,000	A. Magee (275)
June 7	Kemper Open	Stuart Appleby (274)	360,000	S. Hoch (275)
June 14	Buick Classic	J.P. Hayes (201)#*	324,000	J. Furyk (201)
June 21	**U.S. Open** (San Francisco)	Lee Janzen (280)	535,000	P. Stewart (281)
June 28	Motorola Western Open	Joe Durant (271)	396,000	V. Singh (273)
July 5	Canon Greater Hartford Open	Olin Browne (266)*	360,000	S. Cink & L. Mize (266)
July 12	Quad City Classic	Steve Jones (263)	279,000	S. Gump (264)
July 19	**British Open** (Royal Birkdale)	Mark O'Meara (280)*	493,500	B. Watts (280)
July 19	Deposit Guaranty Classic	Fred Funk (270)	216,000	3-way tie (272)
July 26	CVS Charity Classic	Steve Pate (269)	270,000	S. Hoch & B. Hughes (270)
Aug. 2	FedEx St. Jude Classic	Nick Price (268)*	324,000	J. Sluman (268)
Aug. 9	Buick Open	Billy Mayfair (271)	324,000	S. Verplank (273)
Aug. 16	**PGA Championship** (Redmond)	Vijay Singh (271)	540,000	S. Stricker (273)
Aug. 17@	AT&T Pebble Beach Pro-Am	Phil Mickelson (202)	450,000	T. Pernice Jr. (203)

Tournament Results (Cont.)

Last Rd	Tournament	Winner	Earnings	Runner-Up
Aug. 23	Sprint International	Vijay Singh (47)†	$360,000	W. Wood & P. Mickelson (41)
Aug. 30	Greater Vancouver Open	Brandel Chamblee (265)	360,000	P. Stewart (268)
Aug. 30	NEC World Series of Golf	David Duval (269)	405,000	P. Mickelson (271)
Sept. 6	Greater Milwaukee Open	Jeff Sluman (265)	324,000	S. Stricker (266)
Sept. 13	Bell Canadian Open	Billy Andrade (275)*	396,000	B. Friend (275)
Sept. 20	B.C. Open	Chris Perry (273)	270,000	P. Jacobsen (276)
Sept. 27	Westin Texas Open	Hal Sutton (270)	306,000	J. Leonard & J. Haas (271)
Oct. 4	Buick Challenge	Steve Elkington (267)*	270,000	F. Funk (267)

(See Updates Chapter for later results.)
#Weather-shortened.
@The AT&T Pebble Beach Pro-Am began in January but rain postponed the final round until August 17.
†The scoring for the Sprint International was based on a modified Stableford system (8 points for a double eagle, 5 for an eagle, 2 for a birdie, 0 for a par, –1 for a bogey, –3 for double bogey or worse.
***Playoffs** (10): **Bob Hope**— Couples won on 1st hole; **Buick Invitational**— Simpson won on 1st hole; **Nissan**— Mayfair won on 1st hole; **Greater Greensboro**— Dodds won on 1st hole; **Buick Classic**— Hayes won on 1st hole; **GHO**— Browne won on 1st hole; **British**— O'Meara won by 2 strokes in a 4-hole playoff; **St. Jude**— Price won on 2nd hole; **Bell Canadian**— Andrade won on 1st hole; **Buick Challenge**— Elkington won on 1st hole.
Second place ties (3 players or more): 4-WAY—**Phoenix** (T. Armour III, B. Geiberger, S. Pate, T. Watson). 3-WAY—**Byron Nelson** (F. Couples, H. Sutton, H. Frazar); **Deposit Guaranty** (P. Goydos, F. Langham, T. Loustalot).

PGA Majors

The Masters

Edition: 62nd **Dates:** April 9–12
Site: Augusta National GC, Augusta, Ga.
Par: 36-36—72 (6925 yards) **Purse:** $3,200,000

		1 2 3 4	Tot	Earnings
1	Mark O'Meara	74-70-68-67	279	$576,000
2	Fred Couples	69-70-71-70	280	291,600
	David Duval	71-68-74-67	280	291,600
4	Jim Furyk	76-70-67-68	281	153,600
5	Paul Azinger	71-72-69-70	282	128,000
6	Jack Nicklaus	73-72-70-68	283	111,200
	David Toms	75-72-72-64	283	111,200
8	Darren Clarke	76-73-67-69	285	89,600
	Tiger Woods	71-72-72-70	285	89,600
	Justin Leonard	74-73-69-69	285	89,600
	Colin Montgomerie	71-75-69-70	285	89,600

Early round leaders: 1st— Couples (69); 2nd— Couples and Duval (139); 3rd— Couples (210).
Top amateur: Matt Kuchar (288).

British Open

Edition: 127th **Dates:** July 16–19
Site: Royal Birkdale GC, Southport, England
Par: 35-35—70 (7018 yards) **Purse:** $2,750,000

		1 2 3 4	Tot	Earnings
1	Mark O'Meara	72-68-72-68	280	$492,000
	Brian Watts	68-69-73-70	280	308,320
3	Tiger Woods	65-73-77-66	281	221,400
4	Jesper Parnevik	68-72-72-70	282	125,733
	Jim Furyk	70-70-72-70	282	125,733
	Justin Rose	72-66-75-69	282	amateur
	Raymond Russell	68-73-75-66	282	125,733
8	Davis Love III	67-73-77-68	285	81,180
9	Cosstantino Rocca	72-74-70-70	286	69,994
	Thomas Bjorn	68-71-76-71	286	69,994

Note: O'Meara won by 2 strokes in a 4-hole playoff.
Early round leaders: 1st— John Huston and Woods (65); 2nd— Watts (137); 3rd— Watts (210).
Top amateur: Rose (282).

U.S. Open

Edition: 98th **Dates:** June 18–21
Site: Lake Course at The Olympic Club, San Francisco, Calif.
Par: 35-35—70 (6797 yards) **Purse:** $3,000,000

		1 2 3 4	Tot	Earnings
1	Lee Janzen	73-66-73-68	280	$535,000
2	Payne Stewart	66-71-70-74	281	315,000
3	Bob Tway	68-70-73-73	284	201,730
4	Nick Price	73-68-71-73	285	140,957
5	Tom Lehman	68-75-68-75	286	107,392
	Steve Stricker	73-71-69-73	286	107,392
7	David Duval	75-68-75-69	287	83,794
	Jeff Maggert	69-69-75-74	287	83,794
	Lee Westwood	72-74-70-71	287	83,794
10	Jeff Sluman	72-74-74-68	288	64,490
	Phil Mickelson	71-73-74-70	288	64,490
	Stuart Appleby	73-74-70-71	288	64,490
	Stewart Cink	73-68-73-74	288	64,490

Early round leaders: 1st— Stewart (66); 2nd— Stewart (137); 3rd— Stewart (207).
Top amateur: Matt Kuchar (289).

PGA Championship

Edition: 80th **Dates:** Aug. 13–16
Site: Sahalee Country Club, Redmond, Wash.
Par: 35-35—70 (6906 yards) **Purse:** $3,000,000

		1 2 3 4	Tot	Earnings
1	Vijay Singh	70-66-67-68	271	$540,000
2	Steve Stricker	69-68-66-70	273	324,000
3	Steve Elkington	69-69-69-67	274	204,000
4	Mark O'Meara	69-70-69-68	276	118,000
	Frank Lickliter	68-71-69-68	276	118,000
	Nick Price	70-73-68-65	276	118,000
7	Billy Mayfair	73-67-67-70	277	89,500
	Davis Love III	70-68-69-70	277	89,500
9	John Cook	71-68-70-71	278	80,000
10	Tiger Woods	66-72-70-71	279	69,000
	Skip Kendall	72-68-68-71	279	69,000
	Kenny Perry	72-68-68-71	279	69,000

Early round leaders: 1st— Woods (66); 2nd— Singh (136); 3rd— Singh and Stricker (203).
Top Amateur: none.

European PGA Tour

Earnings listed in pounds sterling (£) unless otherwise indicated.

LATE 1997

Last Rd	Tournament	Winner	Earnings	Runner-Up
Nov. 2	Volvo Masters	Lee Westwood (200)#	£166,000	P. Harrington (203)
Nov. 9	Sarazen World Open	Mark Calcavecchia (271)	$360,000	L. Westwood (274)
Nov. 23	World Cup of Golf	IRE—Padraig Harrington/ Paul McGinley (545)	$200,000 (each)	SCOT—R. Russell/ C. Montgomerie (550)
Dec. 14	Johnnie Walker Super Tour	Jesper Parnevik (276)	$100,000	N. Faldo (280)

#Weather shortened

1998 (through Oct. 4)

Last Rd	Tournament	Winner	Earnings	Runner-Up
Jan. 25	Johnnie Walker Classic	Tiger Woods (279)*	£133,330	E. Els (279)
Feb. 1	Heineken Classic	Thomas Bjorn (280)	108,935	I. Woosnam (281)
Feb. 8	South African Open	Ernie Els (273)	71,465	D. Frost (276)
Feb. 16	Dunhill South Africa PGA	Tony Johnstone (271)	64,130	E. Els (273)
Mar. 1	Dubai Desert Classic	Jose Maria Olazabal (269)	130,000	S. Allan (272)
Mar. 8	Qatar Masters	Andrew Coltart (270)	101,006	A. Sherborne & P. Sjöland (272)
Mar. 15	Moroccan Open	Stephen Leaney (271)	58,330	R. Karlsson (279)
Mar. 22	Portugese Open	Peter Mitchell (274)	58,330	D. Gilford & J. Sandelin (275)
Apr. 19	Cannes Open	Thomas Levet (278)	50,000	3-way tie (279)
Apr. 26	Peugeot Spanish Open	Thomas Bjorn (267)	91,660	G. Chalmers & J.M. Olazabal (268)
May 3	Italian Open	Patrik Sjöland (195)#	81,854	J.M. Olazabal & J. Haeggman (198)
May 10	Turespaña Masters	Miguel Angel Jiménez (279)	58,330	M.A. Martin (281)
May 17	Benson & Hedges Intl. Open	Darren Clarke (273)	125,000	S. Luna (276)
May 25	Volvo PGA Championship	Colin Montgomerie (274)	200,000	3-way tie (275)
May 31	Deutsche Bank Open	Lee Westwood (265)	183,340	D. Clarke (266)
June 7	English Open	Lee Westwood (271)	108,330	G. Chalmers & O. Karlsson (273)
June 14	European Grand Prix	postponed due to rain		
June 21	Madeira Island Open	Mats Lanner (277)	50,000	S. Scahill (278)
June 28	Peugeot French Open	Sam Torrance (276)	83,330	4-way tie (278)
July 5	Murphy's Irish Open	David Carter (278)*	159,991	C. Montgomerie (278)
July 12	Loch Lomond World Invitational	Lee Westwood (276)	141,660	5-way tie (280)
July 20	**British Open** (Royal Birkdale)	Mark O'Meara (280)*	300,000	B. Watts (280)
July 26	TNT Dutch Open	Stephen Leaney (266)	133,330	D. Clarke (267)
Aug. 3	Volvo Scandinavian Masters	Jesper Parnevik (273)	133,330	D. Clarke (276)
Aug. 9	German Open	Stephen Allan (280)	116,660	4-way tie (281)
Aug. 23	Smurfit European Open	Mathias Grönberg (275)	208,300	M.A. Jiménez & P. Price (285)
Aug. 30	BMW International Open	Russell Claydon (270)	141,660	J. Spence (271)
Sept. 6	Canon European Masters	Sven Strüver (263)*	133,330	P. Sjöland (263)
Sept. 13	One 2 One British Masters	Colin Montgomerie (281)	125,000	P. Fulke & E. Romero (282)
Sept. 20	Lancome Trophy	Miguel Angel Jiménez (273)	133,330	4-way tie (275)
Sept. 27	Linde German Masters	Colin Montgomerie (266)	166,660	R. Karlsson & V. Singh (267)
Oct. 4	Belgacom Open	Lee Westwood (268)*	66,660	F. Jacobson (268)

(See Updates Chapter for later results.)

#Weather-shortened

***Playoffs** (5): **Johnnie Walker**— Woods won on 2nd hole; **Irish Open**— Carter won on 1st hole; **British Open**— O'Meara won by 2 strokes in a 4-hole playoff; **European Masters**— Strüver won on 1st hole; **Belgacom**— Westwood won on 1st hole.

Second place ties (3 players or more): 5-WAY— **Loch Lomond** (I. Woosnam, E. Romero, R. Allenby, D. Howell, D. Edlund). 4-WAY— **Peugeot French** (M. Florioli, O. Edmond, B. Langer, M. Goggin); **German** (P. Harrington, S. Webster, I. Garrido, M. Roe); **Lancome** (G. Turner, J. Sandelin, M. O'Meara, D. Duval). 3-WAY— **Cannes** (S. Strüver, G. Turner, P. Price); **Volvo PGA** (E. Els, G. Orr, P. Sjöland).

The Official World Golf Ranking

Begun in 1986, the Official World Golf Ranking (formerly the Sony World Ranking) combines the best golfers on the five PGA men's tours (U.S., Europe, South Africa, Japan and Australasia). Rankings are based on a rolling two-year period and weighted in favor of more recent results. Points are awarded after each worldwide tournament according to finish. Final point averages are determined by dividing a player's total points by the number of tournaments played over that two-year period (through Oct. 4, 1998).

		Avg
1	Tiger Woods, USA	11.91
2	David Duval, USA	10.77
3	Ernie Els, S. Afr.	9.98
4	Mark O'Meara, USA	9.90
5	Davis Love III, USA	9.29
6	Colin Montgomerie, Sco.	8.97
7	Nick Price, Zim.	8.90
8	Lee Westwood, Eng.	8.53
9	Vijay Singh, Fij.	8.27
10	Phil Mickelson, USA	8.14
11	Fred Couples, USA	8.05
12	Jumbo Ozaki, Jpn.	6.67
13	Greg Norman, Aus.	6.56
14	Steve Elkington, Aus.	6.32
15	Jim Furyk, USA	6.27

Tournament Results (Cont.)

Senior PGA Tour

LATE 1997

Last Rd	Tournament	Winner	Earnings	Runner-Up
Nov. 2	Ralphs Senior Classic	Gil Morgan (198)	$150,000	G. Archer (199)
Nov. 9	SENIOR TOUR Championship	Gil Morgan (272)	328,000	H. Irwin (274)

1998 (through Oct. 4)

Last Rd	Tournament	Winner	Earnings	Runner-Up
Jan. 18	MasterCard Championship	Gil Morgan (195)	$200,000	G. Gilbert & H. Irwin (201)
Jan. 25	Senior Skins Game	Raymond Floyd (11 skins)	300,000	H. Irwin (6)
Feb. 1	Royal Caribbean Classic	David Graham (202)*	127,500	D. Stockton (202)
Feb. 8	LG Championship	Gil Morgan (210)	180,000	D. Douglass & R. Floyd (212)
Feb. 15	GTE Classic	Jim Albus (207)	165,000	3-way tie (208)
Feb. 22	American Express Invitational	Larry Nelson (203)	180,000	D. Stockton (207)
Mar. 10	Senior Slam	Gil Morgan (134)	300,000	H. Irwin (140)
Mar. 15	Toshiba Classic	Hale Irwin (200)	165,000	H. Green (201)
Mar. 23	Liberty Mutual Legends of Golf	Charles Coody/ Dale Douglass (194)*	150,000 (each)	H. Baiocchi/ D. Graham (194)
Mar. 29	SW Bell Dominion	Lee Trevino (205)	150,000	M. McCullough (207)
Apr. 5	**The Tradition** (Scottsdale)	Gil Morgan (276)	210,000	T. Wargo (278)
Apr. 19	**PGA Seniors'** (Palm Beach Gardens)	Hale Irwin (275)	270,000	L. Nelson (282)
Apr. 26	Las Vegas Senior Classic	Hale Irwin (281)	210,000	V. Fernandez (282)
May 3	Bruno's Memorial Classic	Hubert Green (203)	172,500	H. Irwin (204)
May 10	Home Depot Invitational	Jim Dent (207)*	165,000	B. Charles (207)
May 17	Saint Luke's Classic	Larry Ziegler (208)	150,000	T. Shaw (209)
May 24	Bell Atlantic Classic	Jay Sigel (205)*	165,000	J.M. Canizares (205)
May 31	Pittsburgh Senior Classic	Larry Nelson (204)	165,000	B. Duval (209)
June 7	Nationwide Championship	John Jacobs (206)	202,500	H. Irwin (207)
June 14	BellSouth Classic at Opryland	Isao Aoki (198)	195,000	L. Nelson (200)
June 21	AT&T Canada Senior Open	Brian Barnes (277)	165,000	3-way tie (279)
June 28	Cadillac NFL Golf Classic	Bob Dickson (207)*	165,000	J. Colbert & L. Nelson (207)
July 5	State Farm Senior Classic	Bruce Summerhays (206)	187,500	W. Hall & H. Irwin (207)
July 12	**Senior Players Champs.** (Dearborn)	Gil Morgan (267)	300,000	H. Irwin (270)
July 19	Ameritech Senior Open	Hale Irwin (201)	195,000	L. Nelson (204)
July 26	**U.S. Senior Open** (Pacific Palisades)	Hale Irwin (285)	267,500	V. Fernandez (286)
Aug. 2	Utah Showdown	Gil Morgan (200)	150,000	I. Aoki & J. Mahaffey (204)
Aug. 9	Coldwell Banker Burnet Classic	Leonard Thompson (134)#*	225,000	I. Aoki (134)
Aug. 16	First of America Classic	George Archer (199)	150,000	J. Dent (204)
Aug. 23	Northville Long Island Classic	Gary Player (204)	150,000	J.C. Snead & W. Hall (205)
Aug. 30	BankBoston Classic	Hale Irwin (201)	150,000	J. Sigel (203)
Sept. 6	Emerald Coast Classic	Dana Quigley (200)	165,000	J. Colbert (201)
Sept. 13	Comfort Classic	Hugh Baiocchi (196)	172,500	B. Summerhays (198)
Sept. 20	Kroger Senior Classic	Hugh Baiocchi (133)#*	165,000	4-way tie (133)
Sept. 27	Boone Valley Classic	Larry Nelson (200)	195,000	G. Marsh (202)
Oct. 4	Vantage Championship	Gil Morgan (198)	225,000	H. Irwin (199)

(See Updates Chapter for later results.)

#Weather-shortened.

***Playoffs** (7): **Royal Caribbean**— Graham won on 10th hole; **Legends of Golf**— Coody/Douglass won on 2nd hole; **Home Depot**— Dent won on 2nd hole; **Bell Atlantic**— Sigel won on 3rd hole; **NFL Classic**— Dickson won on 1st hole; **Burnet Classic**— Thompson won on 2nd hole; **Kroger Classic**— Baiocchi won on 2nd hole.

Second place ties (3 players or more): 4-WAY— **Kroger Classic** (B. Charles, F. Conner, L. Nelson, B. Summerhays). 3-WAY— **GTE Classic** (J.M. Canizares, S. Hobday, K. Zarley); **Canada Open** (T. Jenkins, D. Quigley, B. Summerhays).

Senior PGA Majors

The Tradition

Edition: 10th **Dates:** Apr. 2–5
Site: Desert Mt. Cochise Course, Scottsdale, Ariz.
Par: 36-36—72 (6972 yards) **Purse:** $1,400,000

		1 2 3 4 Tot	Earnings
1	Gil Morgan	71-66-69-70—276	$210,000
2	Tom Wargo	68-67-69-74—278	123,200
3	Vicente Fernandez	71-70-69-69—279	100,800
4	Hale Irwin	69-69-74-68—280	84,000
5	Ray Floyd	73-68-69-72—282	67,200
6	Dave Stockton	73-70-73-67—283	50,400
	John Jacobs	71-72-70-70—283	50,400
	Mike McCullough	73-69-70-71—283	50,400
9	Bruce Summerhays	73-71-66-74—284	39,200
10	John Morgan	70-71-69-75—285	36,400

Early round leaders: 1st— Wargo (68); 2nd— Wargo (135); 3rd— Wargo (204).

PGA Seniors' Championship

Edition: 61st **Dates:** April 16–19
Site: PGA National GC, Palm Beach Gardens, Fla.
Par: 36-36—72 (6702 yards) **Purse:** $1,500,000

		1 2 3 4 Tot	Earnings
1	Hale Irwin	68-68-69-70—275	$270,000
2	Larry Nelson	69-71-70-72—282	162,000
3	Gil Morgan	69-72-70-72—283	102,000
4	Dave Stockton	73-73-73-68—287	63,500
	Dale Douglass	71-72-71-73—287	63,500
6	Jay Sigel	72-75-71-71—289	43,000
	Jack Nicklaus	68-74-75-72—289	43,000
	Walt Morgan	76-76-66-71—289	43,000
	Vicente Fernandez	75-72-70-72—289	43,000
	Dana Quigley	71-72-71-75—289	43,000

Early round leaders: 1st— Irwin and Nicklaus (68); 2nd— Irwin (136); 3rd— Irwin (205).

PGA Sr. Players Championship

Edition: 16th **Dates:** July 9–12
Site: TPC of Michigan, Dearborn, Mich.
Par: 36-36—72 (6966 yards) **Purse:** $2,000,000

		1 2 3 4 Tot	Earnings
1	Gil Morgan	69-64-68-66—267	$300,000
2	Hale Irwin	66-69-67-68—270	176,000
3	Isao Aoki	71-69-66-69—275	144,000
4	Jim Colbert	69-71-66-72—278	108,000
	Bob Murphy	67-72-64-75—278	108,000
6	Jack Nicklaus	67-70-72-70—279	80,000
7	Jose Maria Canizares	68-72-71-69—280	72,000
8	Lee Trevino	69-69-73-70—281	64,000
9	Mike McCullough	70-69-71-72—282	52,000
	J.C. Snead	72-66-69-75—282	52,000
	Kermit Zarley	71-71-69-71—282	52,000

Early round leaders: 1st— Irwin and John Jacobs (66); 2nd— Morgan (133); 3rd— Morgan (201).

U.S. Senior Open

Edition: 19th **Dates:** July 23–26
Site: Riviera CC, Pacific Palisades, Calif.
Par: 35-36—71 (6909 yards) **Purse:** $1,500,000

		1 2 3 4 Tot	Earnings
1	Hale Irwin	77-68-71-69—285	$267,500
2	Vicente Fernandez	73-71-74-68—286	157,500
3	Ray Floyd	70-70-73-74—287	101,537
4	Brian Barnes	72-72-75-69—288	64,040
	Isao Aoki	72-71-73-72—288	64,040
6	Dave Stockton	73-70-73-73—289	50,796
7	Dan Wood	75-73-72-70—290	39,122
	Jose Maria Canizares	73-72-74-71—290	39,122
	Gil Morgan	73-72-73-72—290	39,122
	Ed Dougherty	72-76-70-72—290	39,122
	Hugh Baiocchi	71-73-73-73—290	39,122

Early round leaders: 1st— Floyd (70); 2nd— Floyd (140); 3rd— Floyd (213).

LPGA Tour

LATE 1997

Last Rd	Tournament	Winner	Earnings	Runner-Up
Nov. 9	Toray Japan Queens Cup	Liselotte Neumann (205)	$112,500	L. Kane (206)
Nov. 23	ITT Tour Championship	Annika Sorenstam (277)*	160,000	L. Kane & P. Hurst (277)

***Playoffs** (1): **Tour Championship**— Sorenstam beat Hurst on 2nd hole and Kane on 3rd.

1998 (through Oct. 4)

Last Rd	Tournament	Winner	Earnings	Runner-Up
Jan. 18	HealthSouth Inaugural	Kelly Robbins (209)	$90,000	M. Mallon (211)
Jan. 24	Office Depot	Helen Alfredsson (277)	90,000	L. Neumann (279)
Feb. 15	Los Angeles Women's Championship	Dale Eggeling (141)#*	97,500	H. Kobayashi (141)
Feb. 21	Hawaiian Ladies Open	Wendy Ward (204)*	97,500	D. Dormann (204)
Mar. 1	Australian Ladies Masters	Karrie Webb (272)	105,000	H. Park & A. Sorenstam (277)
Mar. 15	Welch's/Circle K Championship	Helen Alfredsson (274)	75,000	L. Neumann & D. Dormann (275)
Mar. 22	Standard Register Ping	Liselotte Neumann (279)*	127,500	R. Jones (279)
Mar. 29	**Nabisco Dinah Shore** (Rancho Mirage)	Pat Hurst (281)	150,000	H. Dobson (282)
Apr. 5	Longs Drugs Challenge	Donna Andrews (278)	90,000	C. Koch (279)
Apr. 19	Myrtle Beach Classic	Karrie Webb (269)	90,000	M. Mallon (272)
Apr. 26	Chick-fil-A Charity Championship	Liselotte Neumann (202)	105,000	L. Kane & D. Pepper (205)
May 3	Mercury Titleholders Championship	Danielle Ammaccapane (276)	150,000	M. Estill (277)
May 10	Sara Lee Classic	Barb Mucha (205)*	112,500	3-way tie (205)
May 17	**McDonald's LPGA Championship** (Wilmington)	Se Ri Pak (273)	195,000	D. Andrews & L. Hackney (276)
May 24	Corning Classic	Tammie Green (268)	105,000	B. Burton & E. Klein (275)
May 24	Skins Game	Laura Davies (10 skins)	270,000	K. Webb (4 skins)
May 31	Rochester International	Rosie Jones (279)	105,000	J. Inkster (281)

LPGA Tour (Cont.)

Last Rd	Tournament	Winner	Earnings	Runner-Up
June 7	Michelob Light Classic	Annika Sorenstam (208)#*	$90,000	D. Andrews (208)
June 14	Oldsmobile Classic	Lisa Walters (265)	97,500	D. Andrews (271)
June 21	Friendly's Classic	Amy Fruhwirth (280)	90,000	K. Saiki & C. Sorenstam (282)
June 28	ShopRite Classic	Annika Sorenstam (196)	150,000	J. Inkster (200)
July 5	**U.S. Women's Open** (Kohler)	Se Ri Pak (290)*	267,500	a–J. Chuasiriporn (290)
July 12	Jamie Farr Kroger Classic	Se Ri Pak (261)	120,000	L. Hackney (270)
July 19	JAL Big Apple Classic	Annika Sorenstam (265)	116,250	J. Pitcock (273)
July 26	Giant Eagle LPGA Classic	Se Ri Pak (201)	120,000	D. Pepper (202)
Aug. 1	**du Maurier Classic** (Windsor)	Brandie Burton (270)	180,000	A. Sorenstam (271)
Aug. 9	Star Bank Classic	Meg Mallon (199)*	90,000	D. Pepper (199)
Aug. 16	Weetabix Women's British Open	Sherri Steinhauer (292)	162,000	S. Gustafson & B. Burton (293)
Aug. 23	Rainbow Foods LPGA Classic	Hiromi Kobayashi (206)*	90,000	T. Hanson (206)
Aug. 30	State Farm Rail Classic	Pearl Sinn (200)	105,000	M. Redman (201)
Sept. 6	SAFEWAY Open	Danielle Ammaccapane (204)	90,000	E. Klein (205)
Sept. 13	SAFECO Classic	Annika Sorenstam (273)	90,000	L. Davies & P. Sheehan (278)
Sept. 20	Solheim Cup (Dublin, Ohio)	USA (16)		Europe (12)
Sept 27	First Union Betsy King Classic	Rachel Hetherington (274)*	97,500	A. Sorenstam (274)

(See Updates Chapter for later results.)

Weather-shortened

***Playoffs** (9): **Los Angeles**— Eggeling won on 1st hole; **Hawaiian**— Ward won on 1st hole; **Standard Ping**— Neumann won on 3rd hole; **Sarah Lee**— Mucha won on 2nd hole; **Michelob Light**— Sorenstam won on 2nd hole; **U.S. Open**— Pak won on 2nd hole of sudden death after an 18-hole playoff; **Star Bank**— Mallon won on 1st hole; **Rainbow Foods**— Kobayashi won on 1st hole; **Betsy King**— Hetherington won on 1st hole.

Second place ties: (3 players or more): 3-WAY— **Sarah Lee** (D. Andrews, N. Lopez, J. Lidback).

LPGA Majors

Dinah Shore

Edition: 27th **Dates:** March 26–29
Site: Mission Hills CC, Rancho Mirage, Calif.
Par: 36-36—72 (6460 yards) **Purse:** $1,000,000

		1 2 3 4 Tot	Earnings
1	Pat Hurst	68-72-70-71—281	$150,000
2	Helen Dobson	70-74-71-67—282	93,093
3	Laura Davies	75-70-70-68—283	60,385
	Helen Alfredsson	70-73-70-70—283	60,385
5	Donna Andrews	71-72-71-70—284	38,998
	Liselotte Neumann	69-71-71-73—284	38,998
7	Annika Sorenstam	76-71-69-70—286	27,928
	Karrie Webb	71-72-70-73—286	27,928
9	Dottie Pepper	73-72-74-72—287	22,393
	Sherri Steinhauer	69-76-71-71—287	22,393

Early round leaders: 1st— Hurst and Rachel Hetherington (68); 2nd— Hurst and Neumann (140); 3rd— Hurst (210).

Top amateur: Beth Bauer (290).

LPGA Championship

Edition: 44th **Dates:** May 14–17
Site: DuPont CC, Wilmington, Del.
Par: 35-36—71 (6386 yards) **Purse:** $1,300,000

		1 2 3 4 Tot	Earnings
1	Se Ri Pak	65-68-72-68—273	$195,000
2	Donna Andrews	71-67-69-69—276	104,666
	Lisa Hackney	70-66-69-71—276	104,666
4	Karrie Webb	71-73-67-66—277	62,145
	Wendy Ward	71-67-69-70—277	62,145
6	Meg Mallon	71-69-68-70—278	39,467
	Chris Johnson	69-71-67-71—278	39,467
	Emilee Klein	72-67-68-71—278	39,467
9	Catrin Nilsmark	69-73-70-67—279	29,110
	Kelly Robbins	69-71-68-71—279	29,110

Early round leaders: 1st— Pak (65); 2nd— Pak (133); 3rd— Pak and Hackney (205).

Top amateur: None.

U.S. Women's Open

Edition: 53rd **Dates:** July 2–5
Site: Blackwolf Run Resort, Kohler, Wisc.
Par: 35-36—71 (6412 yards) **Purse:** $1,500,000

		1 2 3 4 Tot	Earnings
1	Se Ri Pak	69-70-75-76—290	$267,500
2	Jenny Chuasiriporn	72-71-75-72—290	amateur
3	Liselotte Neumann	70-70-75-76—291	157,500
4	Da. Ammaccapane	76-71-74-71—292	77,351
	Pat Hurst	69-75-75-73—292	77,351
	Chris Johnson	72-70-76-74—292	77,351
7	Stefania Croce	74-71-76-72—293	46,736
	Tammie Green	73-71-76-73—293	46,736
	Mhairi McKay	72-70-73-78—293	46,736
10	Trish Johnson	73-71-77-73—294	39,015

Note: Pak won on 2nd hole of sudden death after both players were tied after an 18-hole playoff on July 6.

Early round leaders: 1st— Laura Davies and Kim Williams (68); 2nd— Pak (139); 3rd— Pak (214).

Top amateur: Chuasiriporn (290).

du Maurier Classic

Edition: 26th **Dates:** July 30–Aug. 1
Site: Essex Golf & CC, Windsor, Ontario, Canada
Par: 36-36—72 (6359 yards) **Purse:** $1,200,000

		1 2 3 4 Tot	Earnings
1	Brandie Burton	68-64-66-72—270	$180,000
2	Annika Sorenstam	68-66-67-70—271	111,711
3	Betsy King	64-69-70-72—275	81,519
4	Gail Graham	70-70-68-68—276	44,804
	Dawn Coe-Jones	67-70-69-70—276	44,804
	Deb Richard	67-69-70-70—276	44,804
	Michelle Estill	69-69-66-72—276	44,804
	Meg Mallon	65-69-67-75—276	44,804
9	Sherri Steinhauer	70-71-69-67—277	26,871
	Hiromi Kobayashi	68-70-66-73—277	26,871

Early round leaders: 1st— King (64); 2nd— Burton and Pat Hurst (132); 3rd— Burton (198).

Top amateur: none.

LPGA: Pak'd with Emotion

by Linda Cohn

It was Monday, July 6, 1998. One of baseball's best seasons ever was in the midst of its All-Star break. The sports spotlight had an opening, and the LPGA not only lit the lamp, it shattered the bulb. Like most good things, it came when you least expected it, and you didn't need 20/20 vision to see it. You just had to be looking.

Twenty years after Nancy Lopez broke onto the tour in spectacular fashion with nine wins in her rookie season, there came an unforgettable battle of 20-year-olds. In one corner, we had the unfazed, trained-to-be-unemotional South Korean, Se Ri Pak and in the other was the bubbly, American-born, "just-happy-to-be-there" amateur from Duke University, Jenny Chuasiriporn. It was fitting that 20 extra holes were needed before Pak finally put an end to the "edge-of-your-seat" drama at Blackwolf Run.

I was fortunate enough to have a seat just off the green, watching these two warriors play their 92nd hole in the tour's most prestigious event. And I was fortunate enough to see Pak make history when she nailed an 18-footer to become the youngest player in history to win the U.S. Open, and the youngest woman to win two majors in the same year.

But it's not the historical significance of Pak's achievement that I remember most from that moment. It's the sound of her sobbing into the arms of her father and mother, the two people that raised her to be anything but emotional. We're talking about a dad who took her daughter on overnight camping trips in cemeteries to develop her mental toughness. The saying goes, "father knows best." In this case, maybe, maybe not. As for those unexpected tears, Pak said it was the first time she had ever cried.

Her season of fabulous firsts continued in the very next tour event, the Jamie Farr Kroger Classic in Toledo. Her second round, 61-stroke performance was the lowest 18-hole score in LPGA history. Her 23-under-par total tied the all-time LPGA mark for 72 holes. Oh yeah, she won the tournament.

It's not just the talent. It's her look. It's her presence. It's the impact she's made in such a short time. Lopez, who has become Pak's mentor, said, "She's just what the tour needs. She can carry us onward."

The Pak phenomenon even reached our Bristol headquarters. Just ask my ESPN colleague Kenny Mayne, who screamed out "Se Ri Pak!" as he coined a new home run call while doing baseball highlights on *SportsCenter*.

The surge of Pak was just fuel to the fire that burns Annika Sorenstam. The tour's most dominant player over the last three years stood up to the "Pak attack" and embraced the competition with style and sportsmanship.

But in a year dominated by a South Korean and a Swede, a group of players from the United States came together and beat what many believed was one of the strongest European teams ever, to capture their fourth Solheim Cup in five tries. It's just too bad that very few people outside the golf world noticed. With the event being played in September, the Solheim Cup had to compete with football and the historic home run race to get the attention of the average fan.

Here's a suggestion to the LPGA: take a look at the calendar. And here's a suggestion to the rabid golf fan (like me): don't dismiss the LPGA. In a sport that requires finesse, style and strength (just watch Laura Davies hit a ball 280 yards of the tee with a two-iron), the women golfers of the late 20th century are checked in and they're playing hard. See for yourself. And 20/20 vision is not necessary. ■

Linda Cohn is a *SportsCenter* anchor and covers women's golf for ESPN.

1998 Solheim Cup

The fifth Solheim Cup Tournament, Sept. 18-20, at Muirfield Village GC in Dublin, Ohio.

ROSTERS

Selections for the 1998 United States team were determined by a special Solheim Cup points ranking system based on wins and top-10 finishes over the past two years. The top 10 players were joined by two additional selections made by U.S. captain Judy Rankin.

The 1998 European squad was fielded via a similar points system based on top-10 finishes at ELPGA events. The top seven players were joined by five selections made by European captain Pia Nilsson.

United States: Qualifiers— Donna Andrews, Brandie Burton, Tammie Green, Pat Hurst, Juli Inkster, Chris Johnson, Betsy King, Meg Mallon, Dottie Pepper and Kelly Robbins; Captain's Selections— Rosie Jones and Sherri Steinhauer.

Europe: Qualifiers— Helen Alfredsson (Sweden), Laura Davies (England), Marie Laure de Lorenzi (France), Trish Johnson (England), Catriona Matthew (Scotland), Alison Nicholas (England), Annika Sorenstam (Sweden); Captain's Selections— Sophie Gustafson (Sweden), Lisa Hackney (Sweden), Liselotte Neumann (Sweden), Catrin Nilsmark (Sweden), Charlotta Sorenstam (Sweden).

First Day

Foursome Match Results

Winner	Score	Loser
Pepper/Inkster	3&1	Davies/T. Johnson
Mallon/Burton	3&1	Alfredsson/Nicholas
Robbins/Hurst	1-up	Hackney/Neumann
A. Sorenstam/Matthew	3&2	Andrews/Green

USA wins, 3-1

Four-Ball Match Results

Winner	Score	Loser
King/C. Johnson	halved	Davies/C. Sorenstam
Hurst/Jones	7&5	Hackney/Gustafson
Alfredsson/de Lorenzi	2&1	Robbins/Steinhauer
Pepper/Burton	2-up	A. Sorenstam/Nilsmark

USA wins, 2½-1½
(USA leads, 5½-2½)

Second Day

Foursome Match Results

Winner	Score	Loser
Andrews/Steinhauer	3&2	A. Sorenstam/Matthew
Davies/C. Sorenstam	3&2	Mallon/Burton
Pepper/Inkster	1-up	Alfredsson/de Lorenzi
Robbins/Hurst	1-up	Neumann/Nilsmark

USA wins, 3-1
(USA leads 8½-3½)

Four-Ball Match Results

Winner	Score	Loser
A. Sorenstam/Nilsmark	5&3	King/Jones
Davies/Hackney	2-up	C. Johnson/Green
Andrews/Steinhauer	4&3	de Lorenzi/Alfredsson
Mallon/Inkster	2&1	Neumann/Sorenstam

Teams tie, 2-2
(USA leads, 10½-5½)

Third Day

Singles Match Results

Winner	Score	Loser
Laura Davies	1-up	Pat Hurst
Helen Alfredsson	2&1	Juli Inkster
Annika Sorenstam	2&1	Donna Andrews
Liselotte Neumann	1-up	Brandie Burton
Dottie Pepper	3&2	Trish Johnson
Kelly Robbins	2&1	Charlotta Sorenstam
Marie-Laure de Lorenzi	1-up	Chris Johnson
Rosie Jones	6&4	Catrin Nilsmark
Tammie Green	1-up	Alison Nicholas
Sherry Steinhauer	3&2	Catriona Matthew
Lisa Hackney	6&5	Betsy King
Mag Mallon	halved	Sophie Gustafson

Europe wins day, 6½-5½

USA wins Solheim Cup, 16-12

Overall Records

Team and Individual match play combined

United States

	W-L-H
Dottie Pepper	4-0-0
Pat Hurst	3-1-0
Juli Inkster	3-1-0
Sherry Steinhauer	3-1-0
Kelly Robbins	3-1-0
Meg Mallon	2-1-1
Rosie Jones	2-1-0
Brandie Burton	2-2-0
Donna Andrews	2-2-0
Tammie Green	1-2-0
Betsy King	0-2-1
Chris Johnson	0-2-1

Europe

	W-L-H
Laura Davies	3-1-1
Annika Sorenstam	3-2-0
Lisa Hackney	2-2-0
Marie-Laure de Lorenzi	2-2-0
Helen Alfredsson	2-3-0
Charlotta Sorenstam	1-2-1
Catriona Matthew	1-2-0
Catrin Nilsmark	1-3-0
Liselotte Neumann	1-3-0
Sophie Gustafson	0-1-1
Trish Johnson	0-2-0
Alison Nicholas	0-2-0

Money Leaders

Official money leaders of PGA, European PGA, Senior PGA and LPGA tours for 1997 and unofficial money leaders for 1998 (through Oct. 4), as compiled by the PGA, European PGA and LPGA. All European amounts are in pound sterling (£).

PGA

Arnold Palmer Award standings: listed are tournaments played (TP); cuts made (CM); 1st, 2nd and 3rd place finishes; and earnings for the year.

Final 1997

	TP	CM	Finish 1-2-3	Earnings
1 Tiger Woods	21	20	4-1-1	$2,066,833
2 David Duval	29	21	3-2-0	1,885,308
3 Davis Love III	25	24	2-0-1	1,635,953
4 Jim Furyk	27	24	0-3-1	1,619,480
5 Justin Leonard	29	25	2-1-1	1,587,531
6 Scott Hoch	22	22	1-1-1	1,393,788
7 Greg Norman	15	13	2-2-1	1,345,856
8 Steve Elkington	17	14	2-0-1	1,320,411
9 Ernie Els	19	15	2-1-0	1,243,008
10 Brad Faxon	23	17	1-3-0	1,233,505

1998 (through Oct. 4)

	TP	CM	Finish 1-2-3	Earnings
1 David Duval	20	18	3-1-1	$2,122,408
2 Vijay Singh	24	22	2-2-0	1,764,998
3 Phil Mickelson	21	18	2-2-1	1,755,646
4 Tiger Woods	18	18	1-2-2	1,704,067
5 Mark O'Meara	17	14	2-1-1	1,687,359
6 Fred Couples	15	14	2-2-1	1,562,989
7 Jim Furyk	25	21	0-2-1	1,452,544
8 Justin Leonard	25	19	1-2-0	1,441,763
9 Steve Stricker	20	19	0-2-0	1,167,281
10 Glen Day	23	19	0-2-2	1,154,216

EUROPEAN PGA

Volvo Order of Merit standings: listed are tournaments played (TP); cuts made (CM); 1st, 2nd and 3rd place finishes; and earnings for the year.

Final 1997

	TP	CM	Finish 1-2-3	Earnings
1 Colin Montgomerie	22	22	2-2-1	£798,948
2 Bernhard Langer	20	16	4-0-0	692,398
3 Lee Westwood	25	20	1-2-2	588,718
4 Darren Clarke	25	21	0-2-2	537,409
5 Ian Woosnam	19	18	1-2-0	503,563
6 Ignacio Garrido	27	20	1-3-0	411,480
7 Retief Goosen	23	19	1-1-1	394,598
8 Padraig Harrington	30	28	0-1-0	388,982
9 José Maria Olazabal	19	18	1-1-2	385,649
10 Robert Karlsson	24	16	1-1-0	364,542

1998 (through Oct. 4)

	TP	CM	Finish 1-2-3	Earnings
1 Colin Montgomerie	16	13	3-1-0	£760,077
2 Lee Westwood	18	18	4-0-1	714,812
3 Darren Clarke	17	15	1-3-1	616,867
4 Patrik Sjöland	22	18	1-3-1	451,017
5 Miguel Angel Jiménez	23	18	2-1-0	444,920
6 Thomas Bjorn	19	16	2-0-1	429,498
7 José Maria Olazabal	19	17	1-2-1	389,133
8 Ernie Els	8	8	1-3-2	386,759
9 Mathias Grönberg	24	15	1-0-1	323,879
10 Stephen Leaney	19	14	2-0-0	276,068

SENIOR PGA

Final 1997

	TP	CM	Finish 1-2-3	Earnings
1 Hale Irwin	23	23	9-3-1	$2,343,364
2 Gil Morgan	25	25	6-4-2	2,160,562
3 Isao Aoki	28	28	1-5-4	1,410,499
4 Jay Sigel	31	31	2-2-1	1,294,838
5 David Graham	30	30	3-1-1	1,173,579
6 John Bland	33	33	0-3-2	1,169,707
7 Graham Marsh	29	29	2-0-1	1,128,578
8 Hugh Baiocchi	25	25	1-2-1	906,565
9 Larry Gilbert	23	23	1-1-3	902,816
10 Dave Stockton	29	28	1-1-2	854,611

1998 (through Oct. 4)

	TP	CM	Finish 1-2-3	Earnings
1 Hale Irwin	20	20	6-6-2	$2,499,420
2 Gil Morgan	23	23	6-0-3	1,903,447
3 Larry Nelson	21	21	3-5-0	1,389,398
4 Jay Sigel	28	28	1-1-4	1,028,412
5 Hugh Baiocchi	30	30	2-0-2	979,259
6 Bruce Summerhays	32	32	1-3-1	971,388
7 Isao Aoki	18	18	1-2-3	967,714
8 Dave Stockton	23	23	0-2-2	931,586
9 Dana Quigley	33	33	1-1-0	884,445
10 Jose Maria Canizares	26	26	0-2-2	874,775

LPGA

Final 1997

	TP	CM	Finish 1-2-3	Earnings
1 Annika Sorenstam	22	20	6-5-3	$1,236,789
2 Karrie Webb	25	25	3-4-4	987,606
3 Kelly Robbins	28	25	2-3-4	910,907
4 Chris Johnson	29	28	2-1-3	722,330
5 Tammie Green	25	21	2-3-1	595,077
6 Juli Inkster	24	24	1-1-3	557,988
7 Liselotte Neumann	27	25	2-1-0	497,841
8 Laura Davies	21	19	1-2-2	483,571
9 Nancy Lopez	16	14	1-1-1	470,386
10 Betsy King	30	27	1-0-3	469,632

1998 (through Oct. 4)

	TP	CM	Finish 1-2-3	Earnings
1 Annika Sorenstam	18	18	4-3-2	$956,698
2 Se Ri Pak	24	23	4-0-0	831,784
3 Donna Andrews	21	21	1-4-1	661,535
4 Liselotte Neumann	18	16	2-2-1	618,201
5 Karrie Webb	20	19	2-0-3	580,591
6 Meg Mallon	25	22	1-2-1	540,072
7 Brandie Burton	23	22	1-2-0	501,409
8 Pat Hurst	23	22	1-0-1	501,236
9 Dottie Pepper	22	19	0-3-1	457,109
10 Danielle Ammaccapane	26	20	2-0-0	449,209

Major Golf Championships

MEN

The Masters

The Masters has been played every year (except during World War II) since 1934 at the Augusta National Golf Club in Augusta, Ga. Both the course (6905 yards, par 72) and the tournament were created by Bobby Jones; (*) indicates playoff winner.

Multiple winners: Jack Nicklaus (6); Arnold Palmer (4); Jimmy Demaret, Nick Faldo, Gary Player and Sam Snead (3); Seve Ballesteros, Ben Hogan, Bernhard Langer, Byron Nelson, Horton Smith and Tom Watson (2).

Year	Winner	Score	Runner-up
1934	Horton Smith	284	Craig Wood (285)
1935	Gene Sarazen*	282	Craig Wood (282)
1936	Horton Smith	285	Harry Cooper (286)
1937	Byron Nelson	283	Ralph Guldahl (285)
1938	Henry Picard	285	Ralph Guldahl & Harry Cooper (287)
1939	Ralph Guldahl	279	Sam Snead (280)
1940	Jimmy Demaret	280	Lloyd Mangrum (284)
1941	Craig Wood	280	Byron Nelson (283)
1942	Byron Nelson*	280	Ben Hogan (280)
1943-45	Not held		World War II
1946	Herman Keiser	282	Ben Hogan (283)
1947	Jimmy Demaret	281	Frank Stranahan & Byron Nelson (283)
1948	Claude Harmon	279	Cary Middlecoff (284)
1949	Sam Snead	282	Lloyd Mangrum & Johnny Bulla (285)
1950	Jimmy Demaret	283	Jim Ferrier (285)
1951	Ben Hogan	280	Skee Riegel (282)
1952	Sam Snead	286	Jack Burke Jr. (290)
1953	Ben Hogan	274	Ed Oliver (279)
1954	Sam Snead*	289	Ben Hogan (289)
1955	Cary Middlecoff	279	Ben Hogan (286)
1956	Jack Burke Jr.	289	Ken Venturi (290)
1957	Doug Ford	283	Sam Snead (286)
1958	Arnold Palmer	284	Doug Ford, & Fred Hawkins (285)
1959	Art Wall Jr.	284	Cary Middlecoff (285)
1960	Arnold Palmer	282	Ken Venturi (283)
1961	Gary Player	280	Arnold Palmer & Charles R. Coe (281)
1962	Arnold Palmer*	280	Dow Finsterwald & Gary Player (280)
1963	Jack Nicklaus	286	Tony Lema (287)
1964	Arnold Palmer	276	Jack Nicklaus & Dave Marr (282)
1965	Jack Nicklaus	271	Arnold Palmer & Gary Player (280)
1966	Jack Nicklaus*	288	Gay Brewer Jr. & Tommy Jacobs (288)
1967	Gay Brewer Jr.	280	Bobby Nichols (281)
1968	Bob Goalby	277	Roberto DeVicenzo (278)
1969	George Archer	281	Billy Casper, George Knudson & Tom Weiskopf (282)
1970	Billy Casper*	279	Gene Littler (279)
1971	Charles Coody	279	Jack Nicklaus & Johnny Miller (281)
1972	Jack Nicklaus	286	Bruce Crampton, Bobby Mitchell & Tom Weiskopf (289)
1973	Tommy Aaron	283	J.C. Snead (284)
1974	Gary Player	278	Tom Weiskopf, & Dave Stockton (280)
1975	Jack Nicklaus	276	Johnny Miller & Tom Weiskopf (277)
1976	Ray Floyd	271	Ben Crenshaw (279)
1977	Tom Watson	276	Jack Nicklaus (278)
1978	Gary Player	277	Hubert Green, Rod Funseth & Tom Watson (278)
1979	Fuzzy Zoeller*	280	Ed Sneed & Tom Watson (280)
1980	Seve Ballesteros	275	Gibby Gilbert & Jack Newton (279)
1981	Tom Watson	280	Jack Nicklaus & Johnny Miller (282)
1982	Craig Stadler*	284	Dan Pohl (284)
1983	Seve Ballesteros	280	Ben Crenshaw, & Tom Kite (284)
1984	Ben Crenshaw	277	Tom Watson (279)
1985	Bernhard Langer	282	Curtis Strange, Seve Ballesteros & Ray Floyd (284)
1986	Jack Nicklaus	279	Greg Norman (280)
1987	Larry Mize*	285	Seve Ballesteros & Greg Norman (285)
1988	Sandy Lyle	281	Mark Calcavecchia (282)
1989	Nick Faldo*	283	Scott Hoch (283)
1990	Nick Faldo*	278	Ray Floyd (278)
1991	Ian Woosnam	277	J.M. Olazabal (278)
1992	Fred Couples	275	Ray Floyd (277)
1993	Bernhard Langer	277	Chip Beck (281)
1994	J.M. Olazabal	279	Tom Lehman (281)
1995	Ben Crenshaw	274	Davis Love III (275)
1996	Nick Faldo	276	Greg Norman (281)
1997	Tiger Woods	270	Tom Kite (282)
1998	Mark O'Meara	279	Fred Couples & David Duval (280)

***PLAYOFFS:**

1935: Gene Sarazen (144) def. Craig Wood (149) in 36 holes. **1942:** Byron Nelson (69) def. Ben Hogan (70) in 18 holes. **1954:** Sam Snead (70) def. Ben Hogan (71) in 18 holes. **1962:** Arnold Palmer (68) def. Gary Player (71) and Dow Finsterwald (77) in 18 holes. **1966:** Jack Nicklaus (70 def. Tommy Jacobs (72) and Gay Brewer (78) in 18 holes. **1970:** Billy Casper (69) def. Gene Littler (74) in 18 holes. **1979:** Fuzzy Zoeller (4-3) def. Ed Sneed (4-4) and Tom Watson (4-4) on 2nd hole of sudden death. **1982:** Craig Stadler (4) def. Dan Pohl (5) on 1st hole of sudden death. **1987:** Larry Mize (4-3) def. Greg Norman (4-4) and Seve Ballesteros (5) on 2nd hole of sudden death. **1989:** Nick Faldo (5-3) def. Scott Hoch (5-4) on 2nd hole of sudden death. **1990:** Nick Faldo (4-4) def. Raymond Floyd (4-x) on second hole of sudden death.

U.S. Open

Played at a different course each year, the U.S. Open was launched by the new U.S. Golf Association in 1895. The Open was a 36-hole event from 1895-97 and has been 72 holes since then. It switched from a 3-day, 36-hole Saturday finish to 4 days of play in 1965. Note that (*) indicates playoff winner and (a) indicates amateur winner.

Multiple winners: Willie Anderson, Ben Hogan, Bobby Jones and Jack Nicklaus (4); Hale Irwin (3); Julius Boros, Billy Casper, Ernie Els, Ralph Guldahl, Walter Hagen, Lee Janzen, John McDermott, Cary Middlecoff, Andy Norht, Gene Sarazen, Alex Smith, Curtis Strange and Lee Trevino (2).

Year	Winner	Score	Runner-up	Course	Location
1895	Horace Rawlins	173	Willie Dunn (175)	Newport GC	Newport, R.I.
1896	James Foulis	152	Horace Rawlins (155)	Shinnecock Hills GC	Southampton, N.Y.
1897	Joe Lloyd	162	Willie Anderson (163)	Chicago GC	Wheaton, Ill.
1898	Fred Herd	328	Alex Smith (335)	Myopia Hunt Club	Hamilton, Mass.
1899	Willie Smith	315	George Low, W.H. Way & Val Fitzjohn (326)	Baltimore CC	Baltimore
1900	Harry Vardon	313	J.H. Taylor (315)	Chicago GC	Wheaton, Ill.
1901	Willie Anderson*	331	Alex Smith (331)	Myopia Hunt Club	Hamilton, Mass.
1902	Laurie Auchterlonie	307	Stewart Gardner (313)	Garden City GC	Garden City, N.Y.
1903	Willie Anderson*	307	David Brown (307)	Baltusrol GC	Springfield, N.J.
1904	Willie Anderson	303	Gil Nicholls (308)	Glen View Club	Golf, Ill.
1905	Willie Anderson	314	Alex Smith (316)	Myopia Hunt Club	Hamilton, Mass.
1906	Alex Smith	295	Willie Smith (302)	Onwentsia Club	Lake Forest, Ill.
1907	Alec Ross	302	Gil Nicholls (304)	Phila. Cricket Club	Chestnut Hill, Pa.
1908	Fred McLeod*	322	Willie Smith (322)	Myopia Hunt Club	Hamilton, Mass.
1909	George Sargent	290	Tom McNamara (294)	Englewood GC	Englewood, N.J.
1910	Alex Smith*	298	Macdonald Smith & John McDermott (298)	Phila. Cricket Club	Chestnut Hill, Pa.
1911	John McDermott*	307	George Simpson & Mike Brady (307)	Chicago GC	Wheaton, Ill.
1912	John McDermott	294	Tom McNamara (296)	CC of Buffalo	Buffalo
1913	a-Francis Ouimet*	304	Harry Vardon & Ted Ray (304)	The Country Club	Brookline, Mass.
1914	Walter Hagen	290	a-Chick Evans (291)	Midlothian CC	Blue Island, Ill.
1915	a-John Travers	297	Tom McNamara (298)	Baltusrol GC	Springfield, N.J.
1916	a-Chick Evans	286	Jock Hutchinson (288)	Minikahda Club	Minneapolis
1917-18	Not held		World War I		
1919	Walter Hagen*	301	Mike Brady (301)	Brae Burn CC	West Newton, Mass.
1920	Ted Ray	295	Jock Hutchison, Jack Burke, Leo Diegel & Harry Vardon (296)	Inverness Club	Toledo, Ohio
1921	Jim Barnes	289	Walter Hagen & Fred McLeod (298)	Columbia CC	Chevy Chase, Md.
1922	Gene Sarazen	288	a-Bobby Jones & John Black (289)	Skokie CC	Glencoe, Ill.
1923	a-Bobby Jones*	296	Bobby Cruickshank (296)	Inwood CC	Far Rockaway, N.Y.
1924	Cyril Walker	297	a-Bobby Jones (300)	Oakland Hills CC	Birmingham, Mich.
1925	Willie Macfarlane*	291	a-Bobby Jones (291)	Worcester CC	Worcester, Mass.
1926	a-Bobby Jones	293	Joe Turnesa (294)	Scioto CC	Columbus, Ohio
1927	Tommy Armour*	301	Harry Cooper (301)	Oakmont CC	Oakmont, Pa.
1928	Johnny Farrell*	294	a-Bobby Jones (294)	Olympia Fields CC	Matteson, Ill.
1929	a-Bobby Jones*	294	Al Espinosa (294)	Winged Foot CC	Mamaroneck, N.Y.
1930	a-Bobby Jones	287	Macdonald Smith (289)	Interlachen CC	Hopkins, Minn.
1931	Billy Burke*	292	George Von Elm (292)	Inverness Club	Toledo, Ohio
1932	Gene Sarazen	286	Bobby Cruickshank & Phil Perkins (289)	Fresh Meadow CC	Flushing, N.Y.
1933	a-Johnny Goodman	287	Ralph Guldahl (288)	North Shore GC	Glenview, Ill.
1934	Olin Dutra	293	Gene Sarazen (294)	Merion Cricket Club	Ardmore, Pa.
1935	Sam Parks Jr.	299	Jimmy Thomson (301)	Oakmont CC	Oakmont, Pa.
1936	Tony Manero	282	Harry E. Cooper (284)	Baltusrol GC	Springfield, N.J.
1937	Ralph Guldahl	281	Sam Snead (283)	Oakland Hills CC	Birmingham, Mich.
1938	Ralph Guldahl	284	Dick Metz (290)	Cherry Hills CC	Denver
1939	Byron Nelson*	284	Craig Wood & Denny Shute (284)	Philadelphia CC	Philadelphia

U.S. Open (Cont.)

Year	Winner	Score	Runner-up	Course	Location
1940	Lawson Little*	287	Gene Sarazen (287)	Canterbury GC	Cleveland
1941	Craig Wood	284	Denny Shute (287)	Colonial Club	Ft. Worth
1942-45	Not held		World War II		
1946	Lloyd Mangrum*	284	Byron Nelson & Vic Ghezzi (284)	Canterbury GC	Cleveland
1947	Lew Worsham*	282	Sam Snead (282)	St. Louis CC	Clayton, Mo.
1948	Ben Hogan	276	Jimmy Demaret (278)	Riviera CC	Los Angeles
1949	Cary Middlecoff	286	Clayton Heafner & Sam Snead (287)	Medinah CC	Medinah, Ill.
1950	Ben Hogan*	287	Lloyd Mangrum & George Fazio (287)	Merion Golf Club	Ardmore, Pa.
1951	Ben Hogan	287	Clayton Heafner (289)	Oakland Hills CC	Birmingham, Mich.
1952	Julius Boros	281	Ed Oliver (285)	Northwood Club	Dallas
1953	Ben Hogan	283	Sam Snead (289)	Oakmont CC	Oakmont, Pa.
1954	Ed Furgol	284	Gene Littler (285)	Baltusrol GC	Springfield, N.J.
1955	Jack Fleck*	287	Ben Hogan (287)	Olympic CC	San Francisco
1956	Cary Middlecoff	281	Ben Hogan & Julius Boros (282)	Oak Hill CC	Rochester, N.Y.
1957	Dick Mayer*	282	Cary Middlecoff (282)	Inverness Club	Toledo, Ohio
1958	Tommy Bolt	283	Gary Player (287)	Southern Hills CC	Tulsa
1959	Billy Casper	282	Bob Rosburg (283)	Winged Foot GC	Marmaroneck, N.Y.
1960	Arnold Palmer	280	Jack Nicklaus (282)	Cherry Hills CC	Denver
1961	Gene Littler	281	Doug Sanders & Bob Goalby (282)	Oakland Hills CC	Birmingham, Mich.
1962	Jack Nicklaus*	283	Arnold Palmer (283)	Oakmont CC	Oakmont, Pa.
1963	Julius Boros*	293	Arnold Palmer & Jacky Cupit (293)	The Country Club	Brookline, Mass.
1964	Ken Venturi	278	Tommy Jacobs (282)	Congressional CC	Bethesda, Md.
1965	Gary Player*	282	Kel Nagle (282)	Bellerive CC	St. Louis
1966	Billy Casper*	278	Arnold Palmer (278)	Olympic CC	San Francisco
1967	Jack Nicklaus	275	Arnold Palmer (279)	Baltusrol GC	Springfield, N.J.
1968	Lee Trevino	275	Jack Nicklaus (279)	Oak Hill CC	Rochester, N.Y.
1969	Orville Moody	281	Al Geiberger, Deane Beman & Bob Rosburg (282)	Champions GC	Houston
1970	Tony Jacklin	281	Dave Hill (288)	Hazeltine National GC	Chaska, Minn.
1971	Lee Trevino*	280	Jack Nicklaus (280)	Merion GC	Ardmore, Pa.
1972	Jack Nicklaus	290	Bruce Crampton (293)	Pebble Beach GL	Pebble Beach, Calif.
1973	Johnny Miller	279	John Schlee (280)	Oakmont CC	Oakmont, Pa.
1974	Hale Irwin	287	Forest Fezler (289)	Winged Foot GC	Mamaroneck, N.Y.
1975	Lou Graham*	287	John Mahaffey (287)	Medinah CC	Medinah, Ill.
1976	Jerry Pate	277	Al Geiberger & Tom Weiskopf (279)	Atlanta AC	Duluth, Ga.
1977	Hubert Green	278	Lou Graham (279)	Southern Hills CC	Tulsa
1978	Andy North	285	Dave Stockton & J.C. Snead (286)	Cherry Hills CC	Denver
1979	Hale Irwin	284	Gary Player & Jerry Pate (286)	Inverness Club	Toledo, Ohio
1980	Jack Nicklaus	272	Isao Aoki (274)	Baltusrol GC	Springfield, N.J.
1981	David Graham	273	George Burns & Bill Rogers (276)	Merion GC	Ardmore, Pa.
1982	Tom Watson	282	Jack Nicklaus (284)	Pebble Beach GL	Pebble Beach, Calif.
1983	Larry Nelson	280	Tom Watson (281)	Oakmont CC	Oakmont, Pa.
1984	Fuzzy Zoeller*	276	Greg Norman (276)	Winged Foot GC	Mamaroneck, N.Y.
1985	Andy North	279	Dave Barr, T.C. Chen & Denis Watson (280)	Oakland Hills CC	Birmingham, Mich.
1986	Ray Floyd	279	Lanny Wadkins & Chip Beck (281)	Shinnecock Hills GC	Southampton, N.Y.
1987	Scott Simpson	277	Tom Watson (278)	Olympic Club	San Francisco
1988	Curtis Strange*	278	Nick Faldo (278)	The Country Club	Brookline, Mass.
1989	Curtis Strange	278	Chip Beck, Ian Woosnam & Mark McCumber (279)	Oak Hill CC	Rochester, N.Y.
1990	Hale Irwin*	280	Mike Donald (280)	Medinah CC	Medinah, Ill.
1991	Payne Stewart*	282	Scott Simpson (282)	Hazeline National GC	Chaska, Minn.
1992	Tom Kite	285	Jeff Sluman (287)	Pebble Beach GL	Pebble Beach, Calif.
1993	Lee Janzen	272	Payne Stewart (274)	Baltusrol GC	Springfield, N.J.

Year	Winner	Score	Runner-up	Course	Location
1994	Ernie Els*	279	Colin Montgomerie (279) & Loren Roberts (279)	Oakmont CC	Oakmont, Pa.
1995	Corey Pavin	280	Greg Norman (282)	Shinnecock Hills GC	Southampton, N.Y.
1996	Steve Jones	278	Davis Love III & Tom Lehman (279)	Oakland Hills CC	Bloomfield Hills, Mich.
1997	Ernie Els	276	Colin Montgomerie (277)	Congressional CC	Bethesda, Md.
1998	Lee Janzen	280	Payne Stewart (281)	Olympic Club	San Francisco

***PLAYOFFS:**

1901: Willie Anderson (85) def. Alex Smith (86) in 18 holes. **1903:** Willie Anderson (82) def. David Brown (84) in 18 holes. **1908:** Fred McLeod (77) def. Willie Smith (83) in 18 holes. **1910:** Alex Smith (71) def. John McDermott (75) & Macdonald Smith (77) in 18 holes. **1911:** John McDermott (80) def. Mike Brady (82) & George Simpson (85) in 18 holes. **1913:** Francis Ouimet (72) def. Harry Vardon (77) & Edward Ray (78) in 18 holes. **1919:** Walter Hagen (77) def. Mike Brady (78) in 18 holes. **1923:** Bobby Jones (76) def. Bobby Cruickshank (78) in 18 holes. **1925:** Willie Macfarlane (75-72—147) def. Bobby Jones (75-73—148) in 36 holes. **1927:** Tommy Armour (76) def. Harry Cooper (79) in 18 holes. **1928:** Johnny Farrell (70-73—143) def. Bobby Jones (73-71—144) in 36 holes. **1929:** Bobby Jones (141) def. Al Espinosa (164) in 36 holes. **1931:** Billy Burke (149-148) def. George Von Elm (149-149) in 72 holes. **1939:** Byron Nelson (68-70) def. Craig Wood (68-73) and Denny Shute (76) in 36 holes. **1940:** Lawson Little (70) def. Gene Sarazen (73) in 18 holes. **1946:** Lloyd Mangrum (72-72—144) def. Byron Nelson (72-73—145) and Vic Ghezzi (72-73—145) in 36 holes. **1947:** Lew Worsham (69) def. Sam Snead (70) in 18 holes. **1950:** Ben Hogan (69) def. Llyod Mangrum (73) & George Fazio (75) in 18 holes. **1955:** Jack Fleck (69) def. Ben Hogan (72) in 18 holes. **1957:** Dick Mayer (72) def. Cary Middlecoff (79) in 18 holes. **1962:** Jack Nicklaus (71) def. Arnold Palmer (74) in 18 holes. **1963:** Julius Boros (70) def. Jacky Cupit (73) & Arnold Palmer (76) in 18 holes. **1965:** Gary Player (71) def. Kel Nagle (74) in 18 holes. **1966:** Billy Casper (69) def. Arnold Palmer (73) in 18 holes. **1971:** Lee Trevino (68) def. Jack Nicklaus (71) in 18 holes. **1975:** Lou Graham (71) def. John Mahaffey (73) in 18 holes. **1984:** Fuzzy Zoeller (67) def. Greg Norman (75) in 18 holes. **1988:** Curtis Strange (71) def. Nick Faldo (75) in 18 holes. **1990:** Hale Irwin (74-3) def. Mike Donald (74-4) on 1st hole of sudden death after 18 holes. **1991:** Payne Stewart (75) def. Scott Simpson (77) in 18 holes. **1994:** Ernie Els (74-4-4) def. Loren Roberts (74-4-5) and Colin Montgomerie (78-x-x) on 2nd hole of sudden death after 18 holes.

British Open

The oldest of the Majors, The Open began in 1860 to determine "the champion golfer of the world." While only professional golfers participated in the first year of the tournament, amateurs have been invited ever since. Competition was extended from 36 to 72 holes in 1892. Conducted by the Royal and Ancient Golf Club of St. Andrews, The Open is rotated among select golf courses in England and Scotland. Note that (*) indicates playoff winner and (a) indicates amateur winner.

Multiple winners: Harry Vardon (6); James Braid, J.H. Taylor, Peter Thomson and Tom Watson (5); Walter Hagen, Bobby Locke, Tom Morris, Sr.; Tom Morris Jr.; and Willie Park (4); Jamie Anderson, Seve Ballesteros, Henry Cotton, Nick Faldo, Robert Ferguson, Bobby Jones, Jack Nicklaus and Gary Player (3); Harold Hilton, Bob Martin, Greg Norman, Arnold Palmer, Willie Park Jr.; and Lee Trevino (2).

Year	Winner	Score	Runner-up	Course	Location
1860	Willie Park	174	Tom Morris Sr. (176)	Prestwick Club	Ayrshire, Scotland
1861	Tom Morris Sr.	163	Willie Park (167)	Prestwick Club	Ayrshire, Scotland
1862	Tom Morris Sr.	163	Willie Park (176)	Prestwick Club	Ayrshire, Scotland
1863	Willie Park	168	Tom Morris Sr. (170)	Prestwick Club	Ayrshire, Scotland
1864	Tom Morris Sr.	167	Andrew Strath (169)	Prestwick Club	Ayrshire, Scotland
1865	Andrew Strath	162	Willie Park (164)	Prestwick Club	Ayrshire, Scotland
1866	Willie Park	169	David Park (171)	Prestwick Club	Ayrshire, Scotland
1867	Tom Morris Sr.	170	Willie Park (172)	Prestwick Club	Ayrshire, Scotland
1868	Tom Morris Jr.	157	Robert Andrew (159)	Prestwick Club	Ayrshire, Scotland
1869	Tom Morris Jr.	154	Tom Morris Sr. (157)	Prestwick Club	Ayrshire, Scotland
1870	Tom Morris Jr.	149	Bob Kirk (161)	Prestwick Club	Ayrshire, Scotland
1871	Not held				
1872	Tom Morris Jr.	166	David Strath (169)	Prestwick Club	Ayrshire, Scotland
1873	Tom Kidd	179	Jamie Anderson (180)	St. Andrews	St. Andrews, Scotland
1874	Mungo Park	159	Tom Morris Jr. (161)	Musselburgh	Musselburgh, Scotland
1875	Willie Park	166	Bob Martin (168)	Prestwick Club	Ayrshire, Scotland
1876	Bob Martin*	176	David Strath (176)	St. Andrews	St. Andrews, Scotland
1877	Jamie Anderson	160	Bob Pringle (162)	Musselburgh	Musselburgh, Scotland
1878	Jamie Anderson	157	Bob Kirk (159)	Prestwick Club	Ayrshire, Scotland
1879	Jamie Anderson	169	Andrew Kirkaldy & James Allan (172)	St. Andrews	St. Andrews, Scotland
1880	Bob Ferguson	162	Peter Paxton (167)	Musselburgh	Musselburgh, Scotland
1881	Bob Ferguson	170	Jamie Anderson (173)	Prestwick Club	Ayrshire, Scotland
1882	Bob Ferguson	171	Willie Fernie (174)	St. Andrews	St. Andrews, Scotland
1883	Willie Fernie*	159	Bob Ferguson (159)	Musselburgh	Musselburgh, Scotland
1884	Jack Simpson	160	David Rollan & Willie Fernie (164)	Prestwick Club	Ayrshire, Scotland
1885	Bob Martin	171	Archie Simpson (172)	St. Andrews	St. Andrews, Scotland
1886	David Brown	157	Willie Campbell (159)	Musselburgh	Musselburgh, Scotland
1887	Willie Park Jr.	161	Bob Martin (162)	Prestwick Club	Ayrshire, Scotland
1888	Jack Burns	171	David Anderson & Ben Sayers (172)	St. Andrews	St. Andrews, Scotland
1889	Willie Park Jr.*	155	Andrew Kirkaldy (155)	Musselburgh	Musselburgh, Scotland

British Open (Cont.)

Year	Winner	Score	Runner-up	Course	Location
1890	a-John Ball	164	Willie Fernie (167) & A. Simpson (167)	Prestwick Club	Ayrshire, Scotland
1891	Hugh Kirkaldy	166	Andrew Kirkaldy & Willie Fernie (168)	St. Andrews	St. Andrews, Scotland
1892	a-Harold Hilton	305	John Ball, Sandy Herd & Hugh Kirkaldy (308)	Muirfield	Gullane, Scotland
1893	Willie Auchterlonie	322	Johnny Laidlay (324)	Prestwick Club	Ayrshire, Scotland
1894	J.H. Taylor	326	Douglas Rolland (331)	Royal St. George's	Sandwich, England
1895	J.H. Taylor	322	Sandy Herd (326)	St. Andrews	St. Andrews, Scotland
1896	Harry Vardon*	316	J.H. Taylor (316)	Muirfield	Gullane, Scotland
1897	a-Harold Hilton	314	James Braid (315)	Hoylake	Hoylake, England
1898	Harry Vardon	307	Willie Park Jr. (308)	Prestwick Club	Ayrshire, Scotland
1899	Harry Vardon	310	Jack White (315)	Royal St. George's	Sandwich, England
1900	J.H. Taylor	309	Harry Vardon (317)	St. Andrews	St. Andrews, Scotland
1901	James Braid	309	Harry Vardon (312)	Muirfield	Gullane, Scotland
1902	Sandy Herd	307	Harry Vardon (308)	Hoylake	Hoylake, England
1903	Harry Vardon	300	Tom Vardon (306)	Prestwick Club	Ayrshire, Scotland
1904	Jack White	296	James Braid (297)	Royal St. George's	Sandwich, England
1905	James Braid	318	J.H. Taylor (323) & Rolland Jones (323)	St. Andrews	St. Andrews, Scotland
1906	James Braid	300	J.H. Taylor (304)	Muirfield	Gullane, Scotland
1907	Arnaud Massy	312	J.H. Taylor (314)	Hoylake	Hoylake, England
1908	James Braid	291	Tom Ball (299)	Prestwick Club	Ayrshire, Scotland
1909	J.H. Taylor	295	James Braid (299)	Deal	Deal, England
1910	James Braid	299	Sandy Herd (303)	St. Andrews	St. Andrews, Scotland
1911	Harry Vardon*	303	Arnaud Massy (303)	Royal St. George's	Sandwich, England
1912	Ted Ray	295	Harry Vardon (299)	Muirfield	Gullane, Scotland
1913	J.H. Taylor	304	Ted Ray (312)	Hoylake	Hoylake, England
1914	Harry Vardon	306	J.H. Taylor (309)	Prestwick Club	Ayrshire, Scotland
1915-19	Not held		World War I		
1920	George Duncan	303	Sandy Herd (305)	Deal	Deal, England
1921	Jock Hutchison*	296	Roger Wethered (296)	St. Andrews	St. Andrews, Scotland
1922	Walter Hagen	300	George Duncan & Jim Barnes (301)	Royal St. George's	Sandwich, England
1923	Arthur Havers	295	Walter Hagen (296)	Royal Troon	Troon, Scotland
1924	Walter Hagen	301	Ernest Whitcombe (302)	Hoylake	Hoylake, England
1925	Jim Barnes	300	Archie Compston & Ted Ray (301)	Prestwick Club	Ayrshire, Scotland
1926	a-Bobby Jones	291	Al Watrous (293)	Royal Lytham	Lytham, England
1927	a-Bobby Jones	285	Aubrey Boomer (291)	St. Andrews	St. Andrews, Scotland
1928	Walter Hagen	292	Gene Sarazen (294)	Royal St. George's	Sandwich, England
1929	Walter Hagen	292	Johnny Farrell (298)	Muirfield	Gullane, Scotland
1930	a-Bobby Jones	291	Macdonald Smith & Leo Diegel (293)	Hoylake	Hoylake, England
1931	Tommy Armour	296	Jose Jurado (297)	Carnoustie	Carnoustie, Scotland
1932	Gene Sarazen	283	Macdonald Smith (288)	Prince's	Prince's, England
1933	Denny Shute*	292	Craig Wood (292)	St. Andrews	St. Andrews, Scotland
1934	Henry Cotton	283	Sid Brews (288)	Royal St. George's	Sandwich, England
1935	Alf Perry	283	Alf Padgham (287)	Muirfield	Gullane, Scotland
1936	Alf Padgham	287	Jimmy Adams (288)	Hoylake	Hoylake, England
1937	Henry Cotton	290	Reg Whitcombe (292)	Carnoustie	Carnoustie, Scotland
1938	Reg Whitcombe	295	Jimmy Adams (297)	Royal St. George's	Sandwich, England
1939	Dick Burton	290	Johnny Bulla (292)	St. Andrews	St. Andrews, Scotland
1940-45	Not held		World War II		
1946	Sam Snead	290	Bobby Locke (294) & Johnny Bulla (294)	St. Andrews	St. Andrews, Scotland
1947	Fred Daly	293	Frank Stranahan & Reg Horne (294)	Hoylake	Hoylake, England
1948	Henry Cotton	284	Fred Daly (289)	Muirfield	Gullane, Scotland
1949	Bobby Locke*	283	Harry Bradshaw (283)	Royal St. George's	Sandwich, England
1950	Bobby Locke	279	Roberto de Vicenzo (281)	Royal Troon	Troon, Scotland
1951	Max Faulkner	285	Tony Cerda (287)	Royal Portrush	Portrush, Ireland
1952	Bobby Locke	287	Peter Thomson (288)	Royal Lytham	Lytham, England
1953	Ben Hogan	282	Frank Stranahan Dai Rees, Tony Cerda & Peter Thomson (286)	Carnoustie	Carnoustie, Scotland
1954	Peter Thomson	283	Sid Scott, Dai Rees & Bobby Locke (284)	Royal Birkdale	Southport, England

Year	Winner	Score	Runner-up	Course	Location
1955	Peter Thomson	281	Johny Fallon (283)	St. Andrews	St. Andrews, Scotland
1956	Peter Thomson	286	Flory Van Donck (289)	Hoylake	Hoylake, England
1957	Bobby Locke	279	Peter Thomson (282)	St. Andrews	St. Andrews, Scotland
1958	Peter Thomson*	278	Dave Thomas (278)	Royal Lytham	Lytham, England
1959	Gary Player	284	Flory Van Donck & Fred Bullock (286)	Muirfield	Gullane, Scotland
1960	Kel Nagle	278	Arnold Palmer (279)	St. Andrews	St. Andrews, Scotland
1961	Arnold Palmer	284	Dai Rees (285)	Royal Birkdale	Southport, England
1962	Arnold Palmer	276	Kel Nagle (282)	Royal Troon	Troon, Scotland
1963	Bob Charles*	277	Phil Rodgers (277)	Royal Lytham	Lytham, England
1964	Tony Lema	279	Jack Nicklaus (284)	St. Andrews	St. Andrews, Scotland
1965	Peter Thomson	285	Christy O'Connor & Brian Huggett (287)	Royal Birkdale	Southport, England
1966	Jack Nicklaus	282	Doug Sanders & Dave Thomas (283)	Muirfield	Gullane, Scotland
1967	Roberto de Vicenzo	278	Jack Nicklaus (280)	Hoylake	Hoylake, England
1968	Gary Player	289	Jack Nicklaus & Bob Charles (291)	Carnoustie	Carnoustie, Scotland
1969	Tony Jacklin	280	Bob Charles (282)	Royal Lytham	Lytham, England
1970	Jack Nicklaus*	283	Doug Sanders (283)	St. Andrews	St. Andrews, Scotland
1971	Lee Trevino	278	Lu Liang Huan (279)	Royal Birkdale	Southport, England
1972	Lee Trevino	278	Jack Nicklaus (279)	Muirfield	Gullane, Scotland
1973	Tom Weiskopf	276	Johnny Miller & Neil Coles (279)	Royal Troon	Troon, Scotland
1974	Gary Player	282	Peter Oosterhuis (286)	Royal Lytham	Lytham, England
1975	Tom Watson*	279	Jack Newton (279)	Carnoustie	Carnoustie, Scotland
1976	Johnny Miller	279	Seve Ballesteros & Jack Nicklaus (285)	Royal Birkdale	Southport, England
1977	Tom Watson	268	Jack Nicklaus (269)	Turnberry	Turnberry, Scotland
1978	Jack Nicklaus	281	Tom Kite, Ray Floyd, Ben Crenshaw & Simon Owen (283)	St. Andrews	St. Andrews, Scotland
1979	Seve Ballesteros	283	Jack Nicklaus & Ben Crenshaw (286)	Royal Lytham	Lytham, England
1980	Tom Watson	271	Lee Trevino (275)	Muirfield	Gullane, Scotland
1981	Bill Rogers	276	Bernhard Langer (280)	Royal St. George's	Sandwich, England
1982	Tom Watson	284	Peter Oosterhuis & Nick Price (285)	Royal Troon	Troon, Scotland
1983	Tom Watson	275	Hale Irwin & Andy Bean (276)	Royal Birkdale	Southport, England
1984	Seve Ballesteros	276	Bernhard Langer & Tom Watson (278)	St. Andrews	St. Andrews, Scotland
1985	Sandy Lyle	282	Payne Stewart (283)	Royal St. George's	Sandwich, England
1986	Greg Norman	280	Gordon J. Brand (285)	Turnberry	Turnberry, Scotland
1987	Nick Faldo	279	Paul Azinger & Rodger Davis (280)	Muirfield	Gullane, Scotland
1988	Seve Ballesteros	273	Nick Price (275)	Royal Lytham	Lytham, England
1989	Mark Calcavecchia*	275	Greg Norman & Wayne Grady (275)	Royal Troon	Troon, Scotland
1990	Nick Faldo	270	Payne Stewart & Mark McNulty (275)	St. Andrews	St. Andrews, Scotland
1991	Ian Baker-Finch	272	Mike Harwood (274)	Royal Birkdale	Southport, England
1992	Nick Faldo	272	John Cook (273)	Muirfield	Gullane, Scotland
1993	Greg Norman	267	Nick Faldo (269)	Royal St. George's	Sandwich, England
1994	Nick Price	268	Jesper Parnevik (269)	Turnberry	Turnberry, Scotland
1995	John Daly*	282	Costantino Rocca (282)	St. Andrews	St. Andrews, Scotland
1996	Tom Lehman	271	Mark McCumber & Ernie Els (273)	Royal Lytham	Lytham, England
1997	Justin Leonard	272	Jesper Parnevik & Darren Clarke (275)	Royal Troon	Troon, Scotland
1998	Mark O'Meara*	280	Brian Watts (280)	Royal Birkdale	Southport, England

***PLAYOFFS:**

1876: Bob Martin awarded title when David Strath refused playoff. **1883:** Willie Fernie (158) def. Robert Ferguson (159) in 36 holes. **1889:** Willie Park Jr. (158) def. Andrew Kirkaldy (163) in 36 holes. **1896:** Harry Vardon (157) def. John H. Taylor *161) in 36 holes. **1911:** Harry Bardon won when Arnaud Massy conceded at 35th hole. **1921:** Jack Hutchison (150) def. Roger Wethered (159) in 36 holes. **1933:** Denny Shute (149) def. Craig Wood (154) in 36 holes. **1949:** Bobby Locke (135) def. Harry Bradshaw (147) in 36 holes. **1958:** Peter Thomson (139) def. Dave Thomas (143) in 36 holes. **1963:** Bob Charles (140) def. Phil Rogers (148) in 36 holes. **1970:** Jack Nicklaus (72) def. Doug Sanders (73) in 18 holes. **1975:** Tom Watson (71) def. Jack Newton (72) in holes. **1989:** Mark Calcavecchia (4-3-3-3—13) def. Wayne Grady (4-4-4-4—16) and Greg Norman (3-3-4-x) in 4 holes. **1995:** John Daly (3-4-4-4—15) def. Costantino Rocca (4-5-7-3—19) in 4 holes. **1998:** Mark O'Meara (4-4-5-4—17) def. Brian Watts (5-4-5-5—19) in 4 holes.

PGA Championship

The PGA Championship began in 1916 as a professional golfers match play tournament, but switched to stroke play in 1958. Conducted by the PGA of America, the tournament is played on a different course each year.

Mulitple winners: Walter Hagen and Jack Nicklaus (5); Gene Sarazen and Same Snead (3); Jim Barnes, Leo Diegel, Raymond Floyd, Ben Hogan, Byron Nelson, Larry Nelson, Gary Player, Paul Runyan, Denny Shute, Dave Stockton and Lee Trevino (2).

Year	Winner	Score	Runner-up	Course	Location
1916	Jim Barnes	1-up	Jock Hutchison	Siwanoy CC	Bronxville, N.Y.
1917-18	Not held		World War I		
1919	Jim Barnes	6 & 5	Fred McLeod	Engineers CC	Roslyn, N.Y.
1920	Jock Hutchison	1-up	J. Douglas Edgar	Flossmoor CC	Flossmoor, Ill.
1921	Walter Hagen	3 & 2	Jim Barnes	Inwood CC	Far Rockaway, N.Y.
1922	Gene Sarazen	4 & 3	Emmet French	Oakmont CC	Oakmont, Pa.
1923	Gene Sarazen*	1-up/38	Walter Hagen	Pelham CC	Pelham, N.Y.
1924	Walter Hagen	2-up	Jim Barnes	French Lick CC	French Lick, Ind.
1925	Walter Hagen	6 & 5	Bill Mehlhorn	Olympia Fields CC	Matteson, Ill.
1926	Walter Hagen	5 & 3	Leo Diegel	Salisbury GC	Westbury, N.Y.
1927	Water Hagen	1-up	Joe Turnesa	Cedar Crest CC	Dallas
1928	Leo Diegel	6 & 5	Al Espinosa	Five Farms CC	Baltimore
1929	Leo Diegel	6 & 4	John Farrell	Hillcrest CC	Los Angeles
1930	Tommy Armour	1-up	Gene Sarazen	Fresh Meadow CC	Flushing, N.Y.
1931	Tom Creavy	2 & 1	Denny Shute	Wannamoisett CC	Rumford, R.I.
1932	Olin Dutra	4 & 3	Frank Walsh	Keller GC	St. Paul, Minn.
1933	Gene Sarazen	5 & 4	Willie Goggin	Blue Mound CC	Milwaukee
1934	Paul Runyan*	1-up/38	Craig Wood	Park CC	Williamsville, N.Y.
1935	Johnny Revolta	5 & 4	Tommy Armour	Twin Hills CC	Oklahoma City
1936	Denny Shute	3 & 2	Jimmy Thomson	Pinehurst CC	Pinehurst, N.C.
1937	Denny Shute*	1-up/37	Harold McSpaden	Pittsburgh FC	Aspinwall, Pa.
1938	Paul Runyan	8 & 7	Sam Snead	Shawnee CC	Shawnee-on-Del, Pa.
1939	Henry Picard*	1-up/37	Byron Nelson	Pomonok CC	Flushing, N.Y.
1940	Byron Nelson	1-up	Sam Snead	Hershey CC	Hershey, Pa.
1941	Vic Ghezzi*	1-up/38	Byron Nelson	Cherry Hills CC	Denver
1942	Sam Snead	2 & 1	Jim Turnesa	Seaview CC	Atlantic City, N.J.
1943	Not held		World War II		
1944	Bob Hamilton	1-up	Byron Nelson	Manito G & CC	Spokane, Wash.
1945	Byron Nelson	4 & 3	Sam Byrd	Morraine CC	Dayton, Ohio
1946	Ben Hogan	6 & 4	Porky Oliver	Portland GC	Portland, Ore.
1947	Jim Ferrier	2 & 1	Chick Harbert	Plum Hollow CC	Detroit
1948	Ben Hogan	7 & 6	Mike Turnesa	Norwood Hills CC	St. Louis
1949	Sam Snead	3 & 2	John Palmer	Hermitage CC	Richmond, Va.
1950	Chandler Harper	4 & 3	Henry Williams Jr.	Scioto CC	Columbus, Ohio
1951	Sam Snead	7 & 6	Walter Burkemo	Oakmont CC	Oakmont, Pa.
1952	Jim Turnesa	1-up	Chick Harbert	Big Spring CC	Louisville
1953	Walter Burkemo	2 & 1	Felice Torza	Birmingham CC	Birmingham, Mich.
1954	Chick Harbert	4 & 3	Walter Burkemo	Keller GC	St. Paul, Minn.
1955	Doug Ford	4 & 3	Cary Middlecoff	Meadowbrook CC	Detroit
1956	Jack Burke	3 & 2	Ted Kroll	Blue Hill CC	Boston
1957	Lionel Hebert	2 & 1	Dow Finsterwald	Miami Valley GC	Dayton, Ohio
1958	Dow Finsterwald	276	Billy Casper (278)	Llanerch CC	Havertown, Pa.
1959	Bob Rosburg	277	Jerry Barber & Doug Sanders (278)	Minneapolis GC	St. Louis Park, Minn.
1960	Jay Hebert	281	Jim Ferrier (282)	Firestone CC	Akron, Ohio
1961	Jerry Barber**	277	Don January (277)	Olympia Fields CC	Matteson, Ill.
1962	Gary Player	278	Bob Goalby (279)	Aronimink GC	Newtown Square, Pa.
1963	Jack Nicklaus	279	Dave Ragan (281)	Dallas AC	Dallas
1964	Bobby Nichols	271	Jack Nicklaus & Arnold Palmer (274)	Columbus CC	Columbus, Ohio
1965	Dave Marr	280	Jack Nicklaus & Billy Casper (282)	Laurel Valley GC	Ligonier, Pa.
1966	Al Geiberger	280	Dudley Wysong (284)	Firestone CC	Akron, Ohio
1967	Don January**	281	Don Massengale (281)	Columbine CC	Littleton, Colo.
1968	Julius Boros	281	Arnold Palmer & Bob Charles (282)	Pecan Valley CC	San Antonio
1969	Ray Floyd	276	Gary Player (277)	NCR GC	Dayton, Ohio
1970	Dave Stockton	279	Arnold Palmer & Bob Murphy (281)	Southern Hills CC	Tulsa
1971	Jack Nicklaus	281	Billy Casper (283)	PGA National GC	Palm Beach Gardens, Fla.
1972	Gary Player	281	Jim Jamieson & Tommy Aaron (283)	Oakland Hills GC	Birmingham, Mich.

Year	Winner	Score	Runner-up	Course	Location
1973	Jack Nicklaus	277	Bruce Crampton (281)	Canterbury GC	Cleveland
1974	Lee Trevino	276	Jack Nicklaus (277)	Tanglewood GC	Winston-Salem, N.C.
1975	Jack Nicklaus	276	Bruce Crampton (278)	Firestone CC	Akron, Ohio
1976	Dave Stockton	281	Don January & Ray Floyd (282)	Congressional CC	Bethesda, Md.
1977	Lanny Wadkins**	282	Gene Littler (282)	Pebble Beach GL	Pebble Beach, Calif.
1978	John Mahaffey**	276	Jerry Pate & Tom Watson (276)	Oakmont CC	Oakmont, Pa.
1979	David Graham**	272	Ben Crenshaw (272)	Oakland Hills CC	Birmingham, Mich.
1980	Jack Nicklaus	274	Andy Bean (281)	Oak Hill CC	Rochester, N.Y.
1981	Larry Nelson	273	Fuzzy Zoeller (277)	Atlanta AC	Duluth, Ga.
1982	Ray Floyd	272	Lanny Wadkins (275)	Southern Hills CC	Tulsa
1983	Hal Sutton	274	Jack Nicklaus (275)	Riviera CC	Los Angeles
1984	Lee Trevino	273	Lanny Wadkins & Gary Player (277)	Shoal Creek	Birmingham, Ala.
1985	Hubert Green	278	Lee Trevino (280)	Cherry Hills CC	Denver
1986	Bob Tway	276	Greg Norman (278)	Inverness Club	Toledo, Ohio
1987	Larry Nelson**	287	Lanny Wadkins (287)	PGA National	Palm Beach Gardens, Fla.
1988	Jeff Sluman	272	Paul Azinger 275)	Oak Tree GC	Edmond, Okla.
1989	Payne Stewart	276	Andy Bean, Mike Reid & Curtis Strange (277)	Kemper Lakes GC	Hawthorn Woods, Ill.
1990	Wayne Grady	282	Fred Couples (285)	Shoal Creek	Birmingham, Ala.
1991	John Daly	276	Bruce Lietzke (279)	Crooked Stick GC	Carmel, Ind.
1992	Nick Price	278	Nick Faldo, John Cook, Jim Gallagher & Gene Sauers (281)	Bellerive CC	St. Louis
1993	Paul Azinger**	272	Greg Norman (272)	Inverness Club	Toledo, Ohio
1994	Nick Price	269	Corey Pavin (275)	Southern Hills CC	Tulsa
1995	Steve Elkington**	267	Colin Montgomerie (267)	Riviera CC	Pacific Palisades, Calif.
1996	Mark Brooks**	277	Kenny Perry (277)	Valhalla GC	Louisville, Ky.
1997	Davis Love III	269	Justin Leonard (274)	Winged Foot GC	Mamaroneck, N.Y.
1998	Vijay Singh	271	Steve Stricker (273)	Sahalee CC	Redmond, Wash.

*While the PGA Championship was a match play tournament from 1916-57, the two finalists played 36 holes for the title. In the five years that a playoff was necessary, the match was decided on the 37th or 38th hole.

****PLAYOFFS:**

1961: Jerry Barber (67) def. Don January (68) in 18 holes. **1967:** Don January (69) def. Don Massengale (71) in 18 holes. **1977:** Lanny Wadkins (4-4-4) def. Gene Littler (4-4-5) on 3rd hole of sudden death. **1978:** John Mahaffey (4-3) def. Jerry Pate (4-4) and Tom Watson (4-5) on 2nd hole of sudden death. **1979:** David Graham (4-4-2) def. Ben Crenshaw (4-4-4) on 3rd hole of sudden death. **1987:** Larry Nelson (4) def. Lanny Wadkins (5) on 1st hole of sudden death. **1993:** Paul Azinger (4-4) def. Greg Norman (4-5) on 2nd hole of sudden death. **1995:** Steve Elkington (3) def. Colin Montgomerie (4) on 1st hole of sudden death. **1996:** Mark Brooks (4) def. Kenny Perry (5) on 1st hole of sudden death.

Major Championship Leaders

Through 1998; active PGA players in bold type.

	US Open	British Open	PGA	Masters	US Am	British Am	Total
Jack Nicklaus	4	3	5	6	2	0	**20**
Bobby Jones	4	3	0	0	5	1	**13**
Walter Hagen	2	4	5	0	0	0	**11**
Ben Hogan	4	1	2	2	0	0	**9**
Gary Player	1	3	2	3	0	0	**9**
John Ball	0	1	0	0	0	8	**9**
Arnold Palmer	1	2	0	4	1	0	**8**
Tom Watson	1	5	0	2	0	0	**8**
Harold Hilton	0	2	0	0	1	4	**7**
Gene Sarazen	2	1	3	1	0	0	**7**
Sam Snead	0	1	3	3	0	0	**7**
Harry Vardon	1	6	0	0	0	0	**7**
Nick Faldo	0	3	0	3	0	0	**6**
Lee Trevino	2	2	2	0	0	0	**6**

Tournaments: U.S. Open, British Open, PGA Championship, Masters, U.S. Amateur, and British Amateur.

Grand Slam Summary

The only golfer ever to win a recognized Grand Slam—four major championships in a single season—was Bobby Jones in 1930. That year, Jones won the U.S. and British Opens as well as the U.S. and British Amateurs.

The men's professional Grand Slam—the Masters, U.S. Open, British Open and PGA Championship—did not gain acceptance until 30 years later when Arnold Palmer won the 1960 Masters and U.S. Open. The media wrote that the popular Palmer was chasing the "new" Grand Slam and would have to win the British Open and the PGA to claim it. He did not, but then nobody has before or since.

Three wins in one year: Ben Hogan (1953). **Two wins in one year** (18): Jack Nicklaus (5 times); Ben Hogan, Arnold Palmer and Tom Watson (twice); Nick Faldo, Mark O'Meara, Gary Player, Nick Price, Sam Snead, Lee Trevino and Craig Wood (once).

Year	Masters	US Open	Brit. Open	PGA
1934	H. Smith	Dutra	Cotton	Runyan
1935	Sarazen	Parks	Perry	Revolta
1936	H. Smith	Manero	Padgham	Shute
1937	B. Nelson	Guldahl	Cotton	Shute
1938	Picard	Guldahl	Whitcombe	Runyan
1939	Guldahl	B. Nelson	Burton	Picard
1940	Demaret	Little	—	B. Nelson
1941	Wood	Wood	—	Ghezzi
1942	B. Nelson	—	—	Snead
1943	—	—	—	—
1944	—	—	—	Hamilton
1945	—	—	—	B. Nelson
1946	Keiser	Mangrum	Snead	Hogan
1947	Demaret	Worsham	F. Daly	Ferrier
1948	Harmon	Hogan	Cotton	Hogan
1949	Snead	Middlecoff	Locke	Snead
1950	Demaret	Hogan	Locke	Harper
1951	Hogan	Hogan	Faulkner	Snead
1952	Snead	Boros	Locke	Turnesa
1953	Hogan	Hogan	Hogan	Burkemo
1954	Snead	Furgol	Thomson	Harbert
1955	Middlecoff	Fleck	Thomson	Ford
1956	Burke	Middlecoff	Thomson	Burke
1957	Ford	Mayer	Locke	L. Hebert
1958	Palmer	Bolt	Thomson	Finsterwald
1959	Wall	Casper	Player	Rosburg
1960	Palmer	Palmer	Nagle	J. Hebert
1961	Player	Littler	Palmer	J. Barber
1962	Palmer	Nicklaus	Palmer	Player
1963	Nicklaus	Boros	Charles	Nicklaus
1964	Palmer	Venturi	Lema	Nichols
1965	Nicklaus	Player	Thomson	Marr
1966	Nicklaus	Casper	Nicklaus	Geiberger

Year	Masters	US Open	Brit. Open	PGA
1967	Brewer	Nicklaus	DeVicenzo	January
1968	Goalby	Trevino	Player	Boros
1969	Archer	Moody	Jacklin	Floyd
1970	Casper	Jacklin	Nicklaus	Stockton
1971	Coody	Trevino	Trevino	Nicklaus
1972	Nicklaus	Nicklaus	Trevino	Player
1973	Aaron	J. Miller	Weiskopf	Nicklaus
1974	Player	Irwin	Player	Trevino
1975	Nicklaus	L. Graham	T. Watson	Nicklaus
1976	Floyd	J. Pate	Miller	Stockton
1977	T. Watson	H. Green	T. Watson	L. Wadkins
1978	Player	North	Nicklaus	Mahaffey
1979	Zoeller	Irwin	Ballesteros	D. Graham
1980	Ballesteros	Nicklaus	T. Watson	Nicklaus
1981	T. Watson	D. Graham	Rogers	L. Nelson
1982	Stadler	T. Watson	T. Watson	Floyd
1983	Ballesteros	L. Nelson	T. Watson	Sutton
1984	Crenshaw	Zoeller	Ballesteros	Trevino
1985	Langer	North	Lyle	H. Green
1986	Nicklaus	Floyd	Norman	Tway
1987	Mize	S. Simpson	Faldo	L. Nelson
1988	Lyle	Strange	Ballesteros	Sluman
1989	Faldo	Strange	Calcavecchia	Stewart
1990	Faldo	Irwin	Faldo	Grady
1991	Woosnam	Stewart	Baker-Finch	J. Daly
1992	Couples	Kite	Faldo	Price
1993	Langer	Janzen	Norman	Azinger
1994	Olazabal	Els	Price	Price
1995	Crenshaw	Pavin	Daly	Elkington
1996	Faldo	S. Jones	Lehman	Brooks
1997	Woods	Els	Leonard	Love
1998	O'Meara	Janzen	O'Meara	Singh

Vardon Trophy

Awarded since 1937 by the PGA of America to the PGA Tour regular with the lowest adjusted scoring average. The award is named after Harry Vardon, the six-time British Open champion, who won the U.S. Open in 1900. A point system was used from 1937-41.

Multiple winners: Billy Casper and Lee Trevino (5); Arnold Palmer and Sam Snead (4); Ben Hogan, Greg Norman and Tom Watson (3); Fred Couples, Bruce Crampton, Tom Kite, Lloyd Mangrum and Nick Price (2).

Year		Pts
1937	Harry Cooper	.500
1938	Sam Snead	.520
1939	Byron Nelson	.473
1940	Ben Hogan	.423
1941	Ben Hogan	.494
1942-46	No award	

Year		Avg
1947	Jimmy Demaret	69.90
1948	Ben Hogan	69.30
1949	Sam Snead	69.37
1950	Sam Snead	69.23
1951	Lloyd Mangrum	70.05
1952	Jack Burke	70.54
1953	Lloyd Mangrum	70.22
1954	E.J. Harrison	70.41
1955	Sam Snead	69.86
1956	Cary Middlecoff	70.35
1957	Dow Finsterwald	70.30
1958	Bob Rosburg	70.11
1959	Art Wall	70.35

Year		Avg
1960	Billy Casper	69.95
1961	Arnold Palmer	69.85
1962	Arnold Palmer	70.27
1963	Billy Casper	70.58
1964	Arnold Palmer	70.01
1965	Billy Casper	70.85
1966	Billy Casper	70.27
1967	Arnold Palmer	70.18
1968	Billy Casper	69.82
1969	Dave Hill	70.34
1970	Lee Trevino	70.64
1971	Lee Trevino	70.27
1972	Lee Trevino	70.89
1973	Bruce Crampton	70.57
1974	Lee Trevino	70.53
1975	Bruce Crampton	70.51
1976	Don January	70.56
1977	Tom Watson	70.32
1978	Tom Watson	70.16
1979	Tom Watson	70.27

Year		Avg
1980	Lee Trevino	69.73
1981	Tom Kite	69.80
1982	Tom Kite	70.21
1983	Ray Floyd	70.61
1984	Calvin Peete	70.56
1985	Don Pooley	70.36
1986	Scott Hoch	70.08
1987	Dan Pohl	70.25
1988	Chip Beck	69.46
1989	Greg Norman	69.49
1990	Greg Norman	69.10
1991	Fred Couples	69.59
1992	Fred Couples	69.38
1993	Nick Price	69.11
1994	Greg Norman	68.81
1995	Steve Elkington	69.62
1996	Tom Lehman	69.32
1997	Nick Price	68.98

U.S. Amateur

Match play from 1895-64, stroke play from 1965-72, match play since 1972.

Multiple winners: Bobby Jones (5); Jerry Travers (4); Walter Travis and Tiger Woods (3); Deane Beman, Charles Coe, Gary Cowan, H. Chandler Egan, Chick Evans, Lawson Little, Jack Nicklaus, Francis Ouimet, Jay Sigel, William Turnesa, Bud Ward, Harvie Ward, and H.J. Whigham (2).

Year	
1895	Charles Macdonald
1896	H.J. Whigham
1897	H.J. Whigham
1898	Findlay Douglas
1899	H.M. Harriman
1900	Walter Travis
1901	Walter Travis
1902	Louis James
1903	Walter Travis
1904	H. Chandler Egan
1905	H. Chandler Egan
1906	Eben Byers
1907	Jerry Travers
1908	Jerry Travers
1909	Robert Gardner
1910	W.C. Fownes Jr.
1911	Harold Hilton
1912	Jerry Travers
1913	Jerry Travers
1914	Francis Ouimet
1915	Robert Gardner
1916	Chick Evans
1917-18	Not held
1919	Davidson Herron
1920	Chick Evans
1921	Jesse Guilford
1922	Jess Sweetser
1923	Max Marston
1924	Bobby Jones
1925	Bobby Jones
1926	George Von Elm
1927	Bobby Jones
1928	Bobby Jones
1929	Harrison Johnston
1930	Bobby Jones
1931	Francis Ouimet
1932	Ross Somerville
1933	George Dunlap
1934	Lawson Little
1935	Lawson Little
1936	John Fischer
1937	John Goodman
1938	William Turnesa
1939	Bud Ward
1940	Richard Chapman
1941	Bud Ward
1942-45	Not held
1946	Ted Bishop
1947	Skee Riegel
1948	William Turnesa
1949	Charles Coe
1950	Sam Urzetta
1951	Billy Maxwell
1952	Jack Westland
1953	Gene Littler
1954	Arnold Palmer
1955	Harvie Ward
1956	Harvie Ward
1957	Hillman Robbins
1958	Charles Coe
1959	Jack Nicklaus
1960	Deane Beman
1961	Jack Nicklaus
1962	Labron Harris
1963	Deane Beman
1964	Bill Campbell
1965	Bob Murphy
1966	Gary Cowan
1967	Bob Dickson
1968	Bruce Fleisher
1969	Steve Melnyk
1970	Lanny Wadkins
1971	Gary Cowan
1972	Vinny Giles
1973	Craig Stadler
1974	Jerry Pate
1975	Fred Ridley
1976	Bill Sander
1977	John Fought
1978	John Cook
1979	Mark O'Meara
1980	Hal Sutton
1981	Nathaniel Crosby
1982	Jay Sigel
1983	Jay Sigel
1984	Scott Verplank
1985	Sam Randolph
1986	Buddy Alexander
1987	Billy Mayfair
1988	Eric Meeks
1989	Chris Patton
1990	Phil Mickelson
1991	Mitch Voges
1992	Justin Leonard
1993	John Harris
1994	Tiger Woods
1995	Tiger Woods
1996	Tiger Woods
1997	Matt Kuchar
1998	Hank Kuehne

British Amateur

Match play since 1885.

Multiple winners: John Ball (8); Michael Bonallack (5); Harold Hilton (4); Joe Carr (3); Horace Hutchinson, Ernest Holderness, Trevor Homer, Johnny Laidley, Lawson Little, Peter McEvoy, Dick Siderowf, Frank Stranahan, Freddie Tait and Cyril Tolley (2).

Year	
1885	Allen MacFie
1886	Horace Hutchinson
1887	Horace Hutchinson
1888	John Ball
1889	Johnny Laidley
1890	John Ball
1891	Johnny Laidley
1892	John Ball
1893	Peter Anderson
1894	John Ball
1895	Leslie Balfour-Melville
1896	Freddie Tait
1897	Jack Allan
1898	Freddie Tait
1899	John Ball
1900	Harold Hilton
1901	Harold Hilton
1902	Charles Hutchings
1903	Robert Maxwell
1904	Walter Travis
1905	Arthur Barry
1906	James Robb
1907	John Ball
1908	E.A. Lassen
1909	Robert Maxwell
1910	John Ball
1911	Harold Hilton
1912	John Ball
1913	Harold Hilton
1914	J.L.C. Jenkins
1915-19	Not held
1920	Cyril Tolley
1921	William Hunter
1922	Ernest Holderness
1923	Roger Wethered
1924	Ernest Holderness
1925	Robert Harris
1926	Jesse Sweetser
1927	William Tweddell
1928	Thomas Perkins
1929	Cyril Tolley
1930	Bobby Jones
1931	Eric Smith
1932	John deForest
1933	Michael Scott
1934	Lawson Little
1935	Lawson Little
1936	Hector Thomson
1937	Robert Sweeny Jr.
1938	Charles Yates
1939	Alexander Kyle
1940-45	Not held
1946	James Bruen
1947	William Turnesa
1948	Frank Stranahan
1949	Samuel McCready
1950	Frank Stranahan
1951	Richard Chapman
1952	Harvie Ward
1953	Joe Carr
1954	Douglas Bachli
1955	Joe Conrad
1956	John Beharrell
1957	Reid Jack
1958	Joe Carr
1959	Deane Beman
1960	Joe Carr
1961	Michael Bonallack
1962	Richard Davies
1963	Michael Lunt
1964	Gordon Clark
1965	Michael Bonallack
1966	Bobby Cole
1967	Bob Dickson
1968	Michael Bonallack
1969	Michael Bonallack
1970	Michael Bonallack
1971	Steve Melnyk
1972	Trevor Homer
1973	Dick Siderowf
1974	Trevor Homer
1975	Vinny Giles
1976	Dick Siderowf
1977	Peter McEvoy
1978	Peter McEvoy
1979	Jay Sigel
1980	Duncan Evans
1981	Phillipe Ploujoux
1982	Martin Thompson
1983	Philip Parkin
1984	Jose-Maria Olazabal
1985	Garth McGimpsey
1986	David Curry
1987	Paul Mayo
1988	Christian Hardin
1989	Stephen Dodd
1990	Rolf Muntz
1991	Gary Wolstenholme
1992	Stephen Dundas
1993	Ian Pyman
1994	Lee James
1995	Gordon Sherry
1996	Warren Bledon
1997	Craig Watson
1998	Sergio Garcia

WOMEN

The U.S. Women's Open began under the direction of the defunct Women's Professional Golfers Assn. in 1946, passed to the LPGA in 1949 and to the USGA in 1953. The tournament used a match play format its first year then switched to stroke play; (*) indicates playoff winner and (a) indicates amateur winner.

Multiple winners: Betsy Rawls and Mickey Wright (4); Susie Maxwell Berning, Hollis Stacy and Babe Zaharis (3); JoAnne Carner, Donna Caponi, Betsy King, Patty Sheehan, Annika Sorenstam and Louise Suggs (2).

U.S. Women's Open

Year		Year		Year		Year	
1946	Patty Berg	1960	Betsy Rawls	1974	Sandra Haynie	1988	Liselotte Neumann
1947	Betty Jameson	1961	Mickey Wright	1975	Sandra Palmer	1989	Betsy King
1948	Babe Zaharias	1962	Murle Lindstrom	1976	JoAnne Carner*	1990	Betsy King
1949	Louise Suggs	1963	Mary Mills	1977	Hollis Stacy	1991	Meg Mallon
1950	Babe Zaharias	1964	Mickey Wright*	1978	Hollis Stacy	1992	Patty Sheehan*
1951	Betsy Rawls	1965	Carol Mann	1979	Jerilyn Britz	1993	Lauri Merten
1952	Louise Suggs	1966	Sandra Spuzich	1980	Amy Alcott	1994	Patty Sheehan
1953	Betsy Rawls*	1967	a-Catherine Lacoste	1981	Pat Bradley	1995	Annika Sorenstam
1954	Babe Zaharias	1968	Susie M. Berning	1982	Janet Anderson	1996	Annika Sorenstam
1955	Fay Crocker	1969	Donna Caponi	1983	Jan Stephenson	1997	Alison Nicholas
1956	Kathy Cornelius*	1970	Donna Caponi	1984	Hollis Stacy	1998	Se Ri Pak*
1957	Betsy Rawls	1971	JoAnne Carner	1985	Kathy Baker		
1958	Mickey Wright	1972	Susie M. Berning	1986	Jane Geddes*		
1959	Mickey Wright	1973	Susie M. Berning	1987	Laura Davies*		

*PLAYOFFS:

1953: Betsy Rawls (71) def. Jackie Pung (77) in 18 holes. **1956:** Kathy Cornelius (75) def. Barbara McIntire (82) in 18 holes. **1964:** Mickey Wright (70) def. Ruth Jessen (72) in 18 holes. **1976:** JoAnne Carner (76) def. Sandra Palmer (78) in 18 holes. **1986:** Jane Geddes (71) def. Sally Little (73) in 18 holes. **1987:** Laura Davies (71) def. Ayako Okamoto (73) and JoAnne Carner (74) in 18 holes. **1992:** Patty Sheehan (72) def. Juli Inkster (74) in 18 holes. **1998:** Se Ri Pak def. Jenny Chuasiriporn on the second sudden death hole after both players were tied after an 18-hole playoff.

LPGA Championship

Officially the McDonald's LPGA Championship since 1994 (Mazda sponsored from 1987-93), the tournament began in 1955 and has had extended stays at the Stardust CC in Las Vegas (1961-66), Pleasant Valley CC in Sutton, Mass. (1967-68, 70-74); the Jack Nicklaus Sports Center at Kings Island, Ohio (1978-89) and Bethesda CC in Maryland (since 1990); (*) indicates playoff winner.

Multiple winners: Mickey Wright (4); Nancy Lopez, Patty Sheehan and Kathy Whitworth (3); Donna Caponi, Laura Davies, Sandra Haynie, Mary Mills and Betsy Rawls (2).

Year		Year		Year		Year	
1955	Beverly Hanson	1966	Gloria Ehret	1977	Chako Higuchi	1988	Sherri Turner
1956	Marlene Hagge*	1967	Kathy Whitworth	1978	Nancy Lopez	1989	Nancy Lopez
1957	Louise Suggs	1968	Sandra Post*	1979	Donna Caponi	1990	Beth Daniel
1958	Mickey Wright	1969	Betsy Rawls	1980	Sally Little	1991	Meg Mallon
1959	Betsy Rawls	1970	Shirley Englehorn*	1981	Donna Caponi	1992	Betsy King
1960	Mickey Wright	1971	Kathy Whitworth	1982	Jan Stephenson	1993	Patty Sheehan
1961	Mickey Wright	1972	Kathy Ahern	1983	Patty Sheehan	1994	Laura Davies
1962	Judy Kimball	1973	Mary Mills	1984	Patty Sheehan	1995	Kelly Robbins
1963	Mickey Wright	1974	Sandra Haynie	1985	Nancy Lopez	1996	Laura Davies
1964	Mary Mills	1975	Kathy Whitworth	1986	Pat Bradley	1997	Chris Johnson*
1965	Sandra Haynie	1976	Betty Burfeindt	1987	Jane Geddes	1998	Se Ri Pak

*PLAYOFFS:

1956: Marlene Hagge def. Patti Berg in sudden death. **1968:** Sandra Post (68) def. Kathy Whitworth (75) in 18 holes. **1970:** Shirley Englehorn def. Kathy Whitworth in sudden death. **1997:** Chris Johnson def. Leta Lindley in sudden death.

Nabisco Dinah Shore

Formerly known as the Colgate Dinah Shore from 1972-81, the tournament become the LPGA's fourth designated major championship in 1983. Named after the entertainer, this tourney has been played at Mission Hills CC in Rancho Mirage, Calif., since it began; (*) indicates playoff winner.

Multiple winners: (as a major): Amy Alcott and Betsy King (3); Juli Inkster (2).

Year		Year		Year		Year	
1972	Jane Blalock	1979	Sandra Post	1986	Pat Bradley	1993	Helen Alfredsson
1973	Mickey Wright	1980	Donna Caponi	1987	Betsy King*	1994	Donna Andrews
1974	Jo Ann Prentice	1981	Nancy Lopez	1988	Amy Alcott	1995	Nanci Bowen
1975	Sandra Palmer	1982	Sally Little	1989	Juli Inkster	1996	Patty Sheehan
1976	Judy Rankin	1983	Amy Alcott	1990	Betsy King	1997	Betsy King
1977	Kathy Whitworth	1984	Juli Inkster*	1991	Amy Alcott	1998	Pat Hurst
1978	Sandra Post	1985	Alice Miller	1992	Dottie Mochrie*		

*PLAYOFFS:

1984: Juli Inkster def. Pat Bradley in sudden death. **1987:** Betsy King def. Patty Sheehan in sudden death. **1992:** Dottie Mochrie def. Juli Inkster in sudden death.

du Maurier Classic

Formerly known as La Canadienne in 1973 and the Peter Jackson Classic from 1974-83, this Canadian stop on the LPGA Tour became the third designated major championship in 1979; (*) indicates playoff winner.

Multiple winners (as a major): Pat Bradley (3); Brandie Burton (2).

Year		Year		Year		Year	
1973	Jocelyne Bourassa	1980	Pat Bradley	1987	Jody Rosenthal	1994	Martha Nause
1974	Carole Jo Skala	1981	Jan Stephenson	1988	Sally Little	1995	Jenny Lidback
1975	JoAnne Carner	1982	Sandra Haynie	1989	Tammie Green	1996	Laura Davies
1976	Donna Caponi	1983	Hollis Stacy	1990	Cathy Johnston	1997	Colleen Walker
1977	Judy Rankin	1984	Juli Inkster	1991	Nancy Scranton	1998	Brandie Burton
1978	JoAnne Carner	1985	Pat Bradley	1992	Sherri Steinhaur		
1979	Amy Alcott	1986	Pat Bradley*	1993	Brandie Burton*		

***PLAYOFFS:**

1986: Pat Bradley def. Ayako Okamoto in sudden death. **1993:** Brandie Burton def. Betsy King in sudden death.

Titleholders Championship (1937-72)

The Titleholders was considered a major title on the women's tour until it was discontinued after the 1972 tournament.

Multiple winners: Patty Berg (7); Louise Suggs (4); Babe Zaharis (3); Dorothy Kirby, Marilynn Smith, Kathy Whitworth and Mickey Wright (2).

Year		Year		Year		Year	
1937	Patty Berg	1947	Babe Zaharias	1955	Patty Berg	1963	Marilynn Smith
1938	Patty Berg	1948	Patty Berg	1956	Louise Suggs	1964	Marilynn Smith
1939	Patty Berg	1949	Peggy Kirk	1957	Patty Berg	1965	Kathy Whitworth
1940	Betty Hicks	1950	Babe Zaharias	1958	Beverly Hanson	1966	Kathy Whitworth
1941	Dorothy Kirby	1951	Pat O'Sullivan	1959	Louise Suggs	1967-71	Not held
1942	Dorothy Kirby	1952	Babe Zaharias	1960	Fay Crocker	1972	Sandra Palmer
1943-45	Not held	1953	Patty Berg	1961	Mickey Wright		
1946	Louise Suggs	1954	Louise Suggs	1962	Mickey Wright		

Western Open (1930-67)

The Western Open was considered a major title on the women's tour until it was discontinued after the 1967 tournament.

Multiple winners: Patty Berg (7); Louise Suggs and Babe Zaharis (4); Mickey Wright (3); June Beebe, Opal Hill, Betty Jameson and Betsy Rawls (2).

Year		Year		Year		Year	
1930	Mrs. Lee Mida	1940	Babe Zaharias	1950	Babe Zaharias	1960	Joyce Ziske
1931	June Beebe	1941	Patty Berg	1951	Patty Berg	1961	Mary Lena Faulk
1932	Jane Weiller	1942	Betty Jameson	1952	Betsy Rawls	1962	Mickey Wright
1933	June Beebe	1943	Patty Berg	1953	Louise Suggs	1963	Mickey Wright
1934	Marian McDougall	1944	Babe Zaharias	1954	Betty Jameson	1964	Carol Mann
1935	Opal Hill	1945	Babe Zaharias	1955	Patty Berg	1965	Susie Maxwell
1936	Opal Hill	1946	Louise Suggs	1956	Beverly Hanson	1966	Mickey Wright
1937	Betty Hicks	1947	Louise Suggs	1957	Patty Berg	1967	Kathy Whitworth
1938	Bea Barrett	1948	Patty Berg	1958	Patty Berg		
1939	Helen Dettweiler	1949	Louise Suggs	1959	Betsy Rawls		

Major Championship Leaders

Through 1998; active players in bold type.

	US Open	LPGA	duM	Dinah	Title	Western	US Am	Brit Am	Total
Patty Berg	1	0	0	0	7	7	1	0	**16**
Mickey Wright	4	4	0	0	2	3	0	0	**13**
Louise Suggs	2	1	0	0	4	4	1	1	**13**
Babe Zaharias	3	0	0	0	3	4	1	1	**12**
Betsy Rawls	4	2	0	0	0	2	0	0	**8**
JoAnne Carner	2	0	0	0	0	0	5	0	**7**
Kathy Whitworth	0	3	0	0	2	1	0	0	**6**
Pat Bradley	1	1	3	1	0	0	0	0	**6**
Juli Inkster	0	0	1	2	0	0	3	0	**6**
Betsy King	2	1	0	3	0	0	0	0	**6**
Patty Sheehan	2	3	0	1	0	0	0	0	**6**
Glenna C. Vare	0	0	0	0	0	0	6	0	**6**

Tournaments: U.S. Open, LPGA Championship, du Maurier Classic, Nabisco Dinah Shore, Titleholders (1937-72), Western Open (1937-67), U.S. Amateur, and British Amateur.

Grand Slam Summary

The Women's Grand Slam has consisted of four tournaments only 19 years. From 1955-66, the U.S. Open, LPGA Championship, Western Open and Titleholders tournaments served as the major events. Since 1983, the U.S. Open, LPGA, du Maurier Classic in Canada and Nabisco Dinah Shore have been the major events. No one has won a four-event Grand Slam on the women's tour.

Three wins in one year (3): Babe Zaharias (1950), Mickey Wright (1961) and Pat Bradley (1986).

Two wins in one year (16): Patty Berg and Mickey Wright (3 times); Louise Suggs (twice); Laura Davies, Sandra Haynie, Juli Inkster, Betsy King, Meg Mallon, Se Ri Pak, Betsy Rawls and Kathy Whitworth (once).

Year	LPGA	US Open	T'holders	Western
1937	—	—	Berg	Hicks
1938	—	—	Berg	Barrett
1939	—	—	Berg	Dettweiler
1940	—	—	Hicks	Zaharias
1941	—	—	Kirby	Berg
1942	—	—	Kirby	Jameson
1943	—	—	—	Berg
1944	—	—	—	Zaharias
1945	—	—	—	Zaharias
1946	—	Berg	Suggs	Suggs
1947	—	Jameson	Zaharias	Suggs
1948	—	Zaharias	Berg	Berg
1949	—	Suggs	Kirk	Suggs
1950	—	Zaharias	Zaharias	Zaharias
1951	—	Rawls	O'Sullivan	Berg
1952	—	Suggs	Zaharias	Rawls
1953	—	Rawls	Berg	Suggs
1954	—	Zaharias	Suggs	Jameson
1955	Hanson	Crocker	Berg	Berg
1956	Hagge	Cornelius	Suggs	Hanson
1957	Suggs	Rawls	Berg	Berg
1958	Wright	Wright	Hanson	Berg
1959	Rawls	Wright	Suggs	Rawls
1960	Wright	Rawls	Crocker	Ziske
1961	Wright	Wright	Wright	Faulk
1962	Kimball	Lindstrom	Wright	Wright
1963	Wright	Mills	M.Smith	Wright
1964	Mills	Wright	M.Smith	Mann
1965	Haynie	Mann	Whitworth	Maxwell
1966	Ehret	Spuzich	Whitworth	Wright
1967	Whitworth	a-LaCoste	—	Whitworth
1968	Post	Berning	—	—
1969	Rawls	Caponi	—	—
1970	Englehorn	Caponi	—	—
1971	Whitworth	Carner	—	—
1972	Ahern	Berning	Palmer	—
1973	Mills	Berning	—	—
1974	Haynie	Haynie	—	—
1975	Whitworth	Palmer	—	—
1976	Burfeindt	Carner	—	—
1977	Higuchi	Stacy	—	—
1978	Lopez	Stacy	—	—

Year	LPGA	US Open	duMaurier	D. Shore
1979	Caponi	Britz	Alcott	—
1980	Little	Alcott	Bradley	—
1981	Caponi	Bradley	Stephenson	—
1982	Stephenson	Anderson	Haynie	—
1983	Sheehan	Stephenson	Stacy	Alcott
1984	Sheehan	Stacy	Inkster	Inkster
1985	Lopez	Baker	Bradley	Miller
1986	Bradley	Geddes	Bradley	Bradley
1987	Geddes	Davies	Rosenthal	King
1988	Turner	Neumann	Little	Alcott
1989	Lopez	King	Green	Inkster
1990	Daniel	King	Johnston	King
1991	Mallon	Mallon	Scranton	Alcott
1992	King	Sheehan	Steinhaur	Mochrie
1993	Sheehan	Merten	Burton	Alfredsson
1994	Davies	Sheehan	Nause	Andrews
1995	Robbins	Sorenstam	Lidback	Bowen
1996	Davies	Sorenstam	Davies	Sheehan
1997	Johnson	Nicholas	Walker	King
1998	Pak	Pak	Burton	Hurst

Vare Trophy

The Vare Trophy for best scoring average by a player on the LPGA Tour has been awarded since 1937 by the LPGA. The award is named after Glenna Collett Vare, winner of six U.S. women's amateur titles from 1922-35.

Multiple winners: Kathy Whitworth (7); JoAnne Carner and Mickey Wright (5); Patty Berg, Nancy Lopez and Judy Rankin (3); Pat Bradley, Beth Daniel, Betsy King and Annika Sorenstam (2).

Year		Avg
1953	Patty Berg	75.00
1954	Babe Zaharias	75.48
1955	Patty Berg	74.47
1956	Patty Berg	74.57
1957	Louise Suggs	74.64
1958	Beverly Hanson	74.92
1959	Betsy Rawls	74.03
1960	Mickey Wright	73.25
1961	Mickey Wright	73.55
1962	Mickey Wright	73.67
1963	Mickey Wright	72.81
1964	Mickey Wright	72.46
1965	Kathy Whitworth	72.61
1966	Kathy Whitworth	72.60
1967	Kathy Whitworth	72.74
1968	Carol Mann	72.04
1969	Kathy Whitworth	72.38
1970	Kathy Whitworth	72.26
1971	Kathy Whitworth	72.88
1972	Kathy Whitworth	72.38
1973	Judy Rankin	73.08
1974	JoAnne Carner	72.87
1975	JoAnne Carner	72.40
1976	Judy Rankin	72.25
1977	Judy Rankin	72.16
1978	Nancy Lopez	71.76
1979	Nancy Lopez	71.20
1980	Amy Alcott	71.51
1981	JoAnne Carner	71.75
1982	JoAnne Carner	71.49
1983	JoAnne Carner	71.41
1984	Patty Sheehan	71.40
1985	Nancy Lopez	70.73
1986	Pat Bradley	71.10
1987	Betsy King	71.14
1988	Colleen Walker	71.26
1989	Beth Daniel	70.38
1990	Beth Daniel	70.54
1991	Pat Bradley	70.66
1992	Dottie Mochrie	70.80
1993	Betsy King	70.85
1994	Beth Daniel	70.90
1995	Annika Sorenstam	71.00
1996	Annika Sorenstam	70.47
1997	Karrie Webb	70.00

U.S. Women's Amateur

Stroke play in 1895, match play since 1896.

Multiple winners: Glenna Collett Vare (6); JoAnne Gunderson Carner (5); Margaret Curtis, Beatrix Hoyt, Dorothy Campbell Hurd, Juli Inkster, Alexa Stirling, Virginia Van Wie, Anne Quast Decker Welts (3); Kay Cockerill, Beth Daniel, Vicki Goetze, Katherine Harley, Genevieve Hecker, Betty Jameson, Kelli Kuehne and Barbara McIntire (2).

Year	Winner
1895	Mrs. C.S. Brown
1896	Beatrix Hoyt
1897	Beatrix Hoyt
1898	Beatrix Hoyt
1899	Ruth Underhill
1900	Frances Griscom
1901	Genevieve Hecker
1902	Genevieve Hecker
1903	Bessie Anthony
1904	Georgianna Bishop
1905	Pauline Mackay
1906	Harriot Curtis
1907	Margaret Curtis
1908	Katherine Harley
1909	Dorothy Campbell
1910	Dorothy Campbell
1911	Margaret Curtis
1912	Margaret Curtis
1913	Gladys Ravenscroft
1914	Katherine Harley
1915	Florence Vanderbeck
1916	Alexa Stirling
1917-18	Not held
1919	Alexa Stirling
1920	Alexa Stirling
1921	Marion Hollins
1922	Glenna Collett
1923	Edith Cummings
1924	Dorothy C. Hurd
1925	Glenna Collett
1926	Helen Stetson
1927	Miriam Burns Horn
1928	Glenna Collett
1929	Glenna Collett
1930	Glenna Collett
1931	Helen Hicks
1932	Virginia Van Wie
1933	Virginia Van Wie
1934	Virginia Van Wie
1935	Glenna Collett Vare
1936	Pamela Barton
1937	Estelle Lawson
1938	Patty Berg
1939	Betty Jameson
1940	Betty Jameson
1941	Elizabeth Hicks
1942-45	Not held
1946	Babe D. Zaharias
1947	Louise Suggs
1948	Grace Lenczyk
1949	Dorothy Porter
1950	Beverly Hanson
1951	Dorothy Kirby
1952	Jacqueline Pung
1953	Mary Lena Faulk
1954	Barbara Romack
1955	Patricia Lesser
1956	Marlene Stewart
1957	JoAnne Gunderson
1958	Anne Quast
1959	Barbara McIntire
1960	JoAnne Gunderson
1961	Anne Quast Decker
1962	JoAnne Gunderson
1963	Anne Quast Welts
1964	Barbara McIntire
1965	Jean Ashley
1966	JoAnne G. Carner
1967	Mary Lou Dill
1968	JoAnne G. Carner
1969	Catherine Lacoste
1970	Martha Wilkinson
1971	Laura Baugh
1972	Mary Budke
1973	Carol Semple
1974	Cynthia Hill
1975	Beth Daniel
1976	Donna Horton
1977	Beth Daniel
1978	Cathy Sherk
1979	Carolyn Hill
1980	Juli Inkster
1981	Juli Inkster
1982	Juli Inkster
1983	Joanne Pacillo
1984	Deb Richard
1985	Michiko Hattori
1986	Kay Cockerill
1987	Kay Cockerill
1988	Pearl Sinn
1989	Vicki Goetze
1990	Pat Hurst
1991	Amy Fruhwirth
1992	Vicki Goetze
1993	Jill McGill
1994	Wendy Ward
1995	Kelli Kuehne
1996	Kelli Kuehne
1997	Silvia Cavalleri
1998	Grace Park

British Women's Amateur Championship

Match play since 1893.

Multiple winners: Cecil Leitch and Joyce Wethered (4); May Hezlet, Lady Margaret Scott, Brigitte Varangot and Enid Wilson (3); Rhone Adair, Pam Barton, Dorothy Campbell, Elizabeth Chadwick, Helen Holm, Marley Spearman, Frances Stephens, Jessie Valentine and Michelle Walker (2).

Year	Winner
1893	Lady Margaret Scott
1894	Lady Margaret Scott
1895	Lady Maraaret Scott
1896	Amy Pascoe
1897	Edith Orr
1898	Lena Thomson
1899	May Hezlet
1900	Rhona Adair
1901	Mary Graham
1902	May Hezlet
1903	Rhona Adair
1904	Lottie Dod
1905	Bertha Thompson
1906	Mrs. W. Kennion
1907	May Hezlet
1908	Maud Titterton
1909	Dorothy Campbell
1910	Elsie Grant-Suttie
1911	Dorothy Campbell
1912	Gladys Ravenscroft
1913	Muriel Dodd
1914	Cecil Leitch
1915-19	Not held
1920	Cecil Leitch
1921	Cecil Leitch
1922	Joyce Wethered
1923	Doris Chambers
1924	Joyce Wethered
1925	Joyce Wethered
1926	Cecil Leitch
1927	Simone de la Chaume
1928	Nanette le Blan
1929	Joyce Wethered
1930	Diana Fishwick
1931	Enid Wilson
1932	Enid Wilson
1933	Enid Wilson
1934	Helen Holm
1935	Wanda Morgan
1936	Pam Barton
1937	Jessie Anderson
1938	Helen Holm
1939	Pam Barton
1940-45	Not held
1946	Jean Hetherington
1947	Babe Zaharias
1948	Louise Suggs
1949	Frances Stephens
1950	Lally de St. Sauveur
1951	Catherine MacCann
1952	Moira Paterson
1953	Marlene Stewart
1954	Frances Stephens
1955	Jessie Valentine
1956	Wiffi Smith
1957	Philomena Garvey
1958	Jessie Valentine
1959	Elizabeth Price
1960	Barbara McIntire
1961	Marley Spearman
1962	Marley Spearman
1963	Brigitte Varangot
1964	Carol Sorenson
1965	Brigitte Varangot
1966	Elizabeth Chadwick
1967	Elizabeth Chadwick
1968	Brigitte Varangot
1969	Catherine Lacoste
1970	Dinah Oxley
1971	Michelle Walker
1972	Michelle Walker
1973	Ann Irvin
1974	Carol Semple
1975	Nancy Roth Syms
1976	Cathy Panton
1977	Angela Uzielli
1978	Edwina Kennedy
1979	Maureen Madill
1980	Anne Quast Sander
1981	Belle Robertson
1982	Kitrina Douglas
1983	Jill Thornhill
1984	Jody Rosenthal
1985	Lillian Behan
1986	Marnie McGuire
1987	Janet Collingham
1988	Joanne Furby
1989	Helen Dobson
1990	Julie Wade Hall
1991	Valerie Michaud
1992	Bernille Pedersen
1993	Catriona Lambert
1994	Emma Duggleby
1995	Julie Wade Hall
1996	Kelli Kuehne
1997	Alison Rose
1998	Kim Rostron

Senior PGA

PGA Seniors' Championship

First played in 1937. Two championships played in 1979 and 1984.

Multiple winners: Sam Snead (6); Hale Irwin, Gary Player, Al Watrous and Eddie Williams (3); Julius Boros, Jock Hutchison, Don January, Arnold Palmer, Paul Runyan, Gene Sarazen and Lee Trevino (2).

Year	Year	Year	Year
1937 Jock Hutchison	1954 Gene Sarazen	1970 Sam Snead	1984 Peter Thomson
1938 Fred McLeod*	1955 Mortie Dutra	1971 Julius Boros	1985 Not held
1939 Not held	1956 Pete Burke	1972 Sam Snead	1986 Gary Player
1940 Otto Hackbarth*	1957 Al Watrous	1973 Sam Snead	1987 Chi Chi Rodriguez
1941 Jack Burke	1958 Gene Sarazen	1974 Roberto de Vicenzo	1988 Gary Player
1942 Eddie Williams	1959 Willie Goggin	1975 Charlie Sifford*	1989 Larry Mowry
1943-44 Not held	1960 Dick Metz	1976 Pete Cooper	1990 Gary Player
1945 Eddie Williams	1961 Paul Runyan	1977 Julius Boros	1991 Jack Nicklaus
1946 Eddie Williams*	1962 Paul Runyan	1978 Joe Jiminez*	1992 Lee Trevino
1947 Jock Hutchison	1963 Herman Barron	1979 Jack Fleck*	1993 Tom Wargo*
1948 Charles McKenna	1964 Sam Snead	1979 Don January	1994 Lee Trevino
1949 Marshall Crichton	1965 Sam Snead	1980 Arnold Palmer*	1995 Ray Floyd
1950 Al Watrous	1966 Fred Haas	1981 Miller Barber	1996 Hale Irwin
1951 Al Watrous*	1967 Sam Snead	1982 Don January	1997 Hale Irwin
1952 Ernest Newnham	1968 Chandler Harper	1983 Not held	1998 Hale Irwin
1953 Harry Schwab	1969 Tommy Bolt	1984 Arnold Palmer	

***PLAYOFFS:**

1938: Fred McLeod def. Otto Hackbarth in 18 holes. **1940:** Otto Hackbarth def. Jock Hutchison in 36 holes. **1946:** Eddie Williams def. Jock Hutchison in 18 holes. **1951:** Al Watrous def. Jock Hutchison in 18 holes. **1975:** Charlie Sifford def. Fred Wampler on 1st extra hole **1978:** Joe Jiminez def. Paul Harney on 1st extra hole. **1979:** Jack Fleck def. Bill Johnston on 1st extra hole. **1980:** Arnold Palmer def. Paul Harney on 1st extra hole. **1993:** Tom Wargo def. Bruce Crampton on 2nd extra hole.

U.S. Senior Open

Established in 1980 for senior players 55 years old and over, the minimum age was dropped to 50 (the PGA Seniors Tour entry age) in 1981. Arnold Palmer, Billy Casper, Orville Moody, Jack Nicklaus and Lee Trevino are the only golfers who have won both the U.S. Open and U.S. Senior Open.

Multiple winners: Miller Barber (3); Jack Nicklaus and Gary Player (2).

Year	Year	Year	Year
1980 Roberto deVicenzo	1985 Miller Barber	1990 Lee Trevino	1995 Tom Weiskopf
1981 Arnold Palmer*	1986 Dale Douglass	1991 Jack Nicklaus*	1996 Dave Stockton
1982 Miller Barber	1987 Gary Player	1992 Larry Laoretti	1997 Graham Marsh
1983 Bill Casper*	1988 Gary Player*	1993 Jack Nicklaus	1998 Hale Irwin
1984 Miller Barber	1989 Orville Moody	1994 Simon Hobday	

***PLAYOFFS:**

1981: Arnold Palmer (70) def. Bob Stone (74) and Billy Casper (77) in 18 holes. **1983:** Tied at 75 after 18-hole playoff, Casper def. Rod Funseth with a birdie on the 1st extra hole. **1988:** Gary Player (68) def. Bob Charles (70) in 18 holes. **1991:** Jack Nicklaus (65) def. Chi Chi Rodriguez (69) in 18 holes.

Senior Players Championship

First played in 1983 and contested in Cleveland (1983-86), Ponte Vedra, Fla. (1987-89), and Dearborn, Mich. (since 1990).

Multiple winners: Arnold Palmer and Dave Stockton (2).

Year	Year	Year	Year
1983 Miller Barber	1987 Gary Player	1991 Jim Albus	1995 J.C. Snead*
1984 Arnold Palmer	1988 Billy Casper	1992 Dave Stockton	1996 Ray Floyd
1985 Arnold Palmer	1989 Orville Moody	1993 Jim Colbert	1997 Larry Gilbert
1986 Chi Chi Rodriguez	1990 Jack Nicklaus	1994 Dave Stockton	1998 Gil Morgan

***PLAYOFF:**

1995: J.C. Snead def. Jack Nicklaus on 1st extra hole.

The Tradition

First played in 1989 and played every year since at the Golf Club at Desert Mountain in Scottsdale, Ariz.

Multiple winners: Jack Nicklaus (4); Gil Morgan (2).

Year	Year	Year	Year
1989 Don Bies	1992 Lee Trevino	1995 Jack Nicklaus*	1998 Gil Morgan
1990 Jack Nicklaus	1993 Tom Shaw	1996 Jack Nicklaus	
1991 Jack Nicklaus	1994 Ray Floyd*	1997 Gil Morgan	

***PLAYOFFS:**

1994: Ray Floyd def. Dale Douglas on 1st extra hole. **1995:** Jack Nicklaus def. Isao Aoki on 3rd extra hole.

Major Senior Championship Leaders

Through 1998. All players are still active.

		PGA Sr.	US Open	Senior Players	Trad	Total
1	Jack Nicklaus	1	2	1	4	**8**
2	Gary Player	3	2	1	0	**6**
3	Lee Trevino	2	1	0	1	**4**
	Hale Irwin	3	1	0	0	**4**
5	Arnold Palmer	1	0	2	0	**3**
	Miller Barber	0	2	1	0	**3**
	Gil Morgan	0	0	1	2	**3**
	Ray Floyd	1	0	1	1	**3**
9	Billy Casper	0	1	1	0	**2**
	Orville Moody	0	1	1	0	**2**
	Chi Chi Rodriguez	1	0	1	0	**2**
	Dave Stockton	0	0	2	0	**2**

Grand Slam Summary

The Senior Grand Slam has officially consisted of The Tradition, the PGA Senior Championship, the Senior Players Championship and the U.S. Senior Open since 1990. Jack Nicklaus won three of the four events in 1991, but no one has won all four in one season.

Three wins in one year: Jack Nicklaus (1991). **Two wins in one year:** Gary Player (twice); Hale Irwin, Gil Morgan, Orville Moody, Jack Nicklaus, Arnold Palmer and Lee Trevino (once).

Year	Tradition	PGA Sr.	Players	US Open
1983	—	—	M. Barber	Casper
1984	—	Palmer	Palmer	M. Barber
1985	—	Thomson	Palmer	M. Barber
1986	—	Player	Rodriguez	Douglass
1987	—	Rodriguez	Player	Player
1988	—	Player	Casper	Player
1989	Bies	Mowry	Moody	Moody
1990	Nicklaus	Player	Nicklaus	Trevino
1991	Nicklaus	Nicklaus	Albus	Nicklaus
1992	Trevino	Trevino	Stockton	Laoretti
1993	Shaw	Wargo	Colbert	Nicklaus
1994	Floyd	Trevino	Stockton	Hobday
1995	Nicklaus	Floyd	Snead	Weiskopf
1996	Nicklaus	Irwin	Floyd	Stockton
1997	Morgan	Irwin	Gilbert	Marsh
1998	Morgan	Irwin	Morgan	Irwin

Annual Money Leaders

Official annual money leaders on the PGA, European PGA, Senior PGA and LPGA tours. European PGA earnings listed in pounds sterling (£).

PGA

Multiple leaders: Jack Nicklaus (8); Ben Hogan and Tom Watson (5); Arnold Palmer (4); Greg Norman, Sam Snead and Curtis Strange (3); Julius Boros, Billy Casper, Tom Kite, Byron Nelson and Nick Price (2).

Year		Earnings
1934	Paul Runyan	$6,767
1935	Johnny Revolta	9,543
1936	Horton Smith	7,682
1937	Harry Cooper	14,139
1938	Sam Snead	19,534
1939	Henry Picard	10,303
1940	Ben Hogan	10,655
1941	Ben Hogan	18,358
1942	Ben Hogan	13,143
1943	No records kept	
1944	Byron Nelson	37,968
1945	Byron Nelson	63,336
1946	Ben Hogan	42,556
1947	Jimmy Demaret	27,937
1948	Ben Hogan	32,112
1949	Sam Snead	31,594
1950	Sam Snead	35,759
1951	Lloyd Mangrum	26,089
1952	Julius Boros	37,033
1953	Lew Worsham	34,002
1954	Bob Toski	65,820
1955	Julius Boros	63,122
1956	Ted Kroll	$72,836
1957	Dick Mayer	65,835
1958	Arnold Palmer	42,608
1959	Art Wall	53,168
1960	Arnold Palmer	75,263
1961	Gary Player	64,540
1962	Arnold Palmer	81,448
1963	Arnold Palmer	128,230
1964	Jack Nicklaus	113,285
1965	Jack Nicklaus	140,752
1966	Billy Casper	121,945
1967	Jack Nicklaus	188,998
1968	Billy Casper	205,169
1969	Frank Beard	164,707
1970	Lee Trevino	157,037
1971	Jack Nicklaus	244,491
1972	Jack Nicklaus	320,542
1973	Jack Nicklaus	308,362
1974	Johnny Miller	353,022
1975	Jack Nicklaus	298,149
1976	Jack Nicklaus	266,439
1977	Tom Watson	310,653
1978	Tom Watson	$362,429
1979	Tom Watson	462,636
1980	Tom Watson	530,808
1981	Tom Kite	375,699
1982	Craig Stadler	446,462
1983	Hal Sutton	426,668
1984	Tom Watson	476,260
1985	Curtis Strange	542,321
1986	Greg Norman	653,296
1987	Curtis Strange	925,941
1988	Curtis Strange	1,147,644
1989	Tom Kite	1,395,278
1990	Greg Norman	1,165,477
1991	Corey Pavin	979,430
1992	Fred Couples	1,344,188
1993	Nick Price	1,478,557
1994	Nick Price	1,499,927
1995	Greg Norman	1,654,959
1996	Tom Lehman	1,780,159
1997	Tiger Woods	2,066,833

Note: In 1944-45, Nelson's winnings were in War Bonds.

Senior PGA

Multiple leaders: Don January (3); Miller Barber, Bob Charles, Jim Colbert, Dave Stockton and Lee Trevino (2).

Year		Earnings
1980	Don January	$44,100
1981	Miller Barber	83,136
1982	Miller Barber	106,890
1983	Don January	237,571
1984	Don January	328,597
1985	Peter Thomson	386,724
1986	Bruce Crampton	$454,299
1987	Chi Chi Rodriguez	509,145
1988	Bob Charles	533,929
1989	Bob Charles	725,887
1990	Lee Trevino	1,190,518
1991	Mike Hill	1,065,657
1992	Lee Trevino	$1,027,002
1993	Dave Stockton	1,175,944
1994	Dave Stockton	1,402,519
1995	Jim Colbert	1,444,386
1996	Jim Colbert	1,627,890
1997	Hale Irwin	2,343,364

European PGA

Multiple leaders: Seve Ballesteros (6); Colin Montgomerie (5); Sandy Lyle (3); Gay Brewer, Nick Faldo, Bernard Hunt, Bernhard Langer, Peter Thomson and Ian Woosnam (2).

Year		Earnings	Year		Earnings	Year		Earnings
1961	Bernard Hunt	£4,492	1974	Peter Oosterhuis	£32,127	1987	Ian Woosnam	£439,075
1962	Peter Thomson	5,764	1975	Dale Hayes	20,507	1988	Seve Ballesteros	502,000
1963	Bernard Hunt	7,209	1976	Seve Ballesteros	39,504	1989	Ronan Rafferty	465,981
1964	Neil Coles	7,890	1977	Seve Ballesteros	46,436	1990	Ian Woosnam	737,977
1965	Peter Thomson	7,011	1978	Seve Ballesteros	54,348	1991	Seve Ballesteros	790,811
1966	Bruce Devlin	13,205	1979	Sandy Lyle	49,233	1992	Nick Faldo	1,220,540
1967	Gay Brewer	20,235	1980	Greg Norman	74,829	1993	Colin Montgomerie	798,145
1968	Gay Brewer	23,107	1981	Bernhard Langer	95,991	1994	Colin Montgomerie	920,647
1969	Billy Casper	23,483	1982	Sandy Lyle	86,141	1995	Colin Montgomerie	999,260
1970	Christy O'Connor	31,532	1983	Nick Faldo	140,761	1996	Colin Montgomerie	1,034,752
1971	Gary Player	11,281	1984	Bernhard Langer	160,883	1997	Colin Montgomerie	798,948
1972	Bob Charles	18,538	1985	Sandy Lyle	254,711			
1973	Tony Jacklin	24,839	1986	Seve Ballesteros	259,275			

LPGA

Multiple leaders: Kathy Whitworth (8); Mickey Wright (4); Patty Berg, JoAnne Carner, Betsy King and Nancy Lopez (3); Pat Bradley, Beth Daniel, Judy Rankin, Betsy Rawls, Annika Sorenstam, Louis Suggs and Babe Zaharis (2).

Year		Earnings	Year		Earnings	Year		Earnings
1950	Babe Zaharias	$14,800	1966	Kathy Whitworth	$33,517	1982	JoAnne Carner	$310,400
1951	Babe Zaharias	15,087	1967	Kathy Whitworth	32,937	1983	JoAnne Carner	291,404
1952	Betsy Rawls	14,505	1968	Kathy Whitworth	48,379	1984	Betsy King	266,771
1953	Louise Suggs	19,816	1969	Carol Mann	49,152	1985	Nancy Lopez	416,472
1954	Patty Berg	16,011	1970	Kathy Whitworth	30,235	1986	Pat Bradley	492,021
1955	Patty Berg	16,492	1971	Kathy Whitworth	41,181	1987	Ayako Okamoto	466,034
1956	Marlene Hagge	20,235	1972	Kathy Whitworth	65,063	1988	Sherri Turner	350,851
1957	Patty Berg	16,272	1973	Kathy Whitworth	82,864	1989	Betsy King	654,132
1958	Beverly Hanson	12,639	1974	JoAnne Carner	87,094	1990	Beth Daniel	863,578
1959	Betsy Rawls	26,774	1975	Sandra Palmer	76,374	1991	Pat Bradley	763,118
1960	Louise Suggs	16,892	1976	Judy Rankin	150,734	1992	Dottie Mochrie	693,335
1961	Mickey Wright	22,236	1977	Judy Rankin	122,890	1993	Betsy King	595,992
1962	Mickey Wright	21,641	1978	Nancy Lopez	189,814	1994	Laura Davies	687,201
1963	Mickey Wright	31,269	1979	Nancy Lopez	197,489	1995	Annika Sorenstam	666,533
1964	Mickey Wright	29,800	1980	Beth Daniel	231,000	1996	Karrie Webb	1,002,000
1965	Kathy Whitworth	28,658	1981	Beth Daniel	206,998	1997	Annika Sorenstam	1,236,789

All-Time Leaders

PGA, Senior PGA and LPGA leaders through 1997.

Tournaments Won

PGA

		No
1	Sam Snead	81
2	Jack Nicklaus	70
3	Ben Hogan	63
4	Arnold Palmer	60
5	Byron Nelson	52
6	Billy Casper	51
7	Walter Hagan	40
	Cary Middlecoff	40
9	Gene Sarazen	38
10	Lloyd Mangrum	36
11	Tom Watson	33
12	Horton Smith	32
13	Harry Cooper	31
	Jimmy Demaret	31
15	Leo Diegel	30
16	Gene Littler	29
	Paul Runyan	29
18	Lee Trevino	27
19	Henry Picard	26
20	Tommy Armour	24
	Macdonald Smith	24
	Johnny Miller	24

Senior PGA

		No
1	Lee Trevino	27
2	Miller Barber	24
3	Bob Charles	23
4	Don January	22
	Chi Chi Rodriguez	22
6	Bruce Crampton	20
7	Gary Player	18
	Mike Hill	18
	Jim Colbert	18
10	George Archer	17
11	Dave Stockton	14
12	Raymond Floyd	13
	Hale Irwin	13
14	Orville Moody	11
	Peter Thomson	11
	Dale Douglass	11
	Jim Dent	11
	Bob Murphy	11
19	Arnold Palmer	10
	Al Geiberger	10
	Jack Nicklaus	10

LPGA

		No
1	Kathy Whitworth	88
2	Mickey Wright	82
3	Patty Berg	57
4	Betsy Rawls	55
5	Louise Suggs	50
6	Nancy Lopez	48
7	JoAnne Carner	42
	Sandra Haynie	42
9	Carol Mann	38
10	Patty Sheehan	35
11	Beth Daniel	32
12	Pat Bradley	31
	Babe Zaharias	31
	Betsy King	31
15	Amy Alcott	29
	Jane Blalock	29
17	Judy Rankin	26
18	Marlene Hagge	25
19	Donna Caponi	24
20	Marilynn Smith	22

Note: Patty Berg's total includes 13 official pro wins prior to formation of LPGA in 1950.

Money Won

PGA

	Earnings
1 Greg Norman	$11,910,518
2 Tom Kite	10,286,177
3 Fred Couples	8,885,487
4 Nick Price	8,794,431
5 Mark O'Meara	8,506,774
6 Davis Love III	8,470,982
7 Payne Stewart	8,465,062
8 Tom Watson	8,307,277
9 Corey Pavin	8,130,356
10 Scott Hoch	$7,899,250
11 Mark Calcavecchia	7,612,931
12 Paul Azinger	7,451,410
13 Curtis Strange	7,147,752
14 Ben Crenshaw	7,064,604
15 Craig Stadler	6,870,877
16 Jay Haas	6,390,645
17 Steve Elkington	6,328,138
18 David Frost	6,299,819
19 Lanny Wadkins	$6,249,812
20 John Cook	6,109,117
21 Chip Beck	5,994,624
22 Hale Irwin	5,902,306
23 Bruce Lietzke	5,880,083
24 Brad Faxon	5,842,619
25 Tom Lehman	5,642,999

Senior PGA

	Earnings
1 Lee Trevino	$7,449,561
2 Bob Charles	7,244,675
3 Jim Colbert	7,126,797
4 Dave Stockton	6,636,029
5 Mike Hill	6,336,905
6 Chi Chi Rodriguez	6,068,903
7 George Archer	5,671,991
8 Ray Floyd	5,580,271
9 Jim Dent	5,492,510
10 Dale Douglass	$5,140,633
11 Isao Aoki	5,130,137
12 Hale Irwin	4,758,308
13 Bob Murphy	4,618,929
14 Gary Player	4,478,607
15 Bruce Crampton	4,391,178
16 Al Geiberger	4,103,795
17 J.C. Snead	4,023,511
18 Jim Albus	3,843,798
19 Miller Barber	$3,800,297
20 Tom Wargo	3,670,425
21 Rocky Thompson	3,620,980
22 Jay Sigel	3,591,156
23 Graham Marsh	3,494,620
24 Harold Henning	3,477,381
25 Charles Coody	3,401,799

European PGA

	Earnings
1 Colin Montgomerie	£6,778,611
2 Bernhard Langer	6,058,684
3 Ian Woosnam	5,482,574
4 Nick Faldo	5,271,101
5 Seve Ballesteros	4,514,691
6 Sam Torrance	4,049,589
7 José Maria Olazabal	3,553,580
8 Mark McNulty	3,208,808
9 Ernie Els	2,877,174
10 Mark James	£2,830,364
11 Barry Lane	2,819,114
12 Costantino Rocca	2,730,060
13 Ronan Rafferty	2,685,663
14 Fred Couples	2,552,064
15 Anders Forsbrand	2,539,652
16 Sandy Lyle	2,525,970
17 Gordon Brand Jr.	2,510,826
18 Frank Nobilo	2,420,288
19 Vijay Singh	£2,278,130
20 Rodger Davis	2,069,671
21 Howard Clark	2,049,633
22 Eduardo Romero	1,994,908
23 Darren Clarke	1,991,435
24 Miguel Angel Jiménez	1,971,319
25 Per-Ulrik Johansson	1,951,918

LPGA

	Earnings
1 Betsy King	$5,980,114
2 Pat Bradley	5,539,184
3 Patty Sheehan	5,310,390
4 Beth Daniel	5,207,209
5 Nancy Lopez	5,008,522
6 Dottie Pepper	3,977,769
7 Laura Davies	3,626,879
8 Jane Geddes	3,305,616
9 Rosie Jones	3,276,834
10 Amy Alcott	$3,261,334
11 Juli Inkster	3,083,805
12 Meg Mallon	3,046,591
13 JoAnne Carner	2,899,052
14 Annika Sorenstam	2,839,084
15 Tammie Green	2,803,295
16 Liselotte Neumann	2,793,109
17 Ayako Okamoto	2,743,175
18 Kelly Robbins	2,688,947
19 Chris Johnson	$2,677,209
20 Colleen Walker	2,666,353
21 Jan Stephenson	2,543,935
22 Michelle McGann	2,362,097
23 Deb Richard	2,214,632
24 Hollis Stacy	2,207,652
25 Val Skinner	2,185,732

Annual Awards

PGA of America Player of the Year

Awarded by the PGA of America; based on points scale that weighs performance in major tournaments, regular events, money earned and scoring average.

Multiple winners: Tom Watson (6); Jack Nicklaus (5); Ben Hogan (4); Julius Boros, Billy Casper, Arnold Palmer and Nick Price (2).

Year	
1948	Ben Hogan
1949	Sam Snead
1950	Ben Hogan
1951	Ben Hogan
1952	Julius Boros
1953	Ben Hogan
1954	Ed Furgol
1955	Doug Ford
1956	Jack Burke
1957	Dick Mayer
1958	Dow Finsterwald
1959	Art Wall
1960	Arnold Palmer
1961	Jerry Barber
1962	Arnold Palmer
1963	Julius Boros
1964	Ken Venturi
1965	Dave Marr
1966	Billy Casper
1967	Jack Nicklaus
1968	No award
1969	Orville Moody
1970	Billy Casper
1971	Lee Trevino
1972	Jack Nicklaus
1973	Jack Nicklaus
1974	Johnny Miller
1975	Jack Nicklaus
1976	Jack Nicklaus
1977	Tom Watson
1978	Tom Watson
1979	Tom Watson
1980	Tom Watson
1981	Bill Rogers
1982	Tom Watson
1983	Hal Sutton
1984	Tom Watson
1985	Lanny Wadkins
1986	Bob Tway
1987	Paul Azinger
1988	Curtis Strange
1989	Tom Kite
1990	Nick Faldo
1991	Corey Pavin
1992	Fred Couples
1993	Nick Price
1994	Nick Price
1995	Greg Norman
1996	Tom Lehman
1997	Tiger Woods

Annual Awards (Cont.)

PGA Tour Player of the Year

Award by the PGA Tour starting in 1990. Winner voted on by tour members from list of nominees. Winner receives the Jack Nicklaus Trophy, which originated in 1997.

Multiple winners: Fred Couples and Nick Price (2).

Year	Year	Year	Year
1990 Wayne Levi	1992 Fred Couples	1994 Nick Price	1996 Tom Lehman
1991 Fred Couples	1993 Nick Price	1995 Greg Norman	1997 Tiger Woods

PGA Tour Rookie of the Year

Awarded by the PGA Tour in 1990. Winner voted on by tour members from list of first-year nominees.

Year	Year	Year	Year
1990 Robert Gamez	1992 Mark Carnevale	1994 Ernie Els	1996 Tiger Woods
1991 John Daly	1993 Vijay Singh	1995 Woody Austin	1997 Stewart Cink

PGA Senior Player of the Year

Awarded by th PGA Seniors Tour starting in 1990. Winner voted on by tour members from list of nominees.

Multiple winner: Lee Trevino (3); Jim Colbert (2).

Year	Year	Year	Year
1990 Lee Trevino	1992 Lee Trevino	1995 Jim Colbert	1997 Hale Irwin
1991 George Archer & Mike Hill	1993 Dave Stockton	1996 Jim Colbert	
	1994 Lee Trevino		

PGA Senior Tour Rookie of the Year

Awarded by th PGA Tour starting in 1990. Winner voted on by tour members from list of first-year nominees.

Year	Year	Year	Year
1990 Lee Trevino	1992 Dave Stockton	1994 Jay Sigel	1996 John Bland
1991 Jim Colbert	1993 Bob Murphy	1995 Hale Irwin	1997 Gil Morgan

European Golfer of the Year

Officially, the Johnnie Walker Trophy; voting done by panel of European golf writers and tour members.

Multiple winners: Seve Ballesteros, Nick Faldo and Colin Montgomerie (3); Bernhard Langer (2).

Year	Year	Year	Year
1985 Bernhard Langer	1989 Nick Faldo	1993 Bernhard Langer	1997 Colin Montgomerie
1986 Seve Ballesteros	1990 Nick Faldo	1994 Ernie Els	
1987 Ian Woosnam	1991 Seve Ballesteros	1995 Colin Montgomerie	
1988 Seve Ballesteros	1992 Nick Faldo	1996 Colin Montgomerie	

LPGA Player of the Year

Awarded by the LPGA; based on performance points accumulated during the year.

Multiple winners: Kathy Whitworth (7); Nancy Lopez (4); JoAnne Carner, Beth Daniel and Betsy King (3); Pat Bradley, Judy Rankin and Annika Sorenstam (2).

Year	Year	Year	Year
1966 Kathy Whitworth	1974 JoAnne Carner	1982 JoAnne Carner	1990 Beth Daniel
1967 Kathy Whitworth	1975 Sandra Palmer	1983 Patty Sheehan	1991 Pat Bradley
1968 Kathy Whitworth	1976 Judy Rankin	1984 Betsy King	1992 Dottie Mochrie
1969 Kathy Whitworth	1977 Judy Rankin	1985 Nancy Lopez	1993 Betsy King
1970 Sandra Haynie	1978 Nancy Lopez	1986 Pat Bradley	1994 Beth Daniel
1971 Kathy Whitworth	1979 Nancy Lopez	1987 Ayako Okamoto	1995 Annika Sorenstam
1972 Kathy Whitworth	1980 Beth Daniel	1988 Nancy Lopez	1996 Laura Davies
1973 Kathy Whitworth	1981 JoAnne Carner	1989 Betsy King	1997 Annika Sorenstam

Official World Rankings

Begun in 1986, the Official World Golf Ranking (formerly the Sony World Ranking) combines the best golfers on the five PGA men's tours throughout the world. Rankings are based on a rolling two-year period and weighed in favor of more recent results. While annual winners are not announced, certain players reaching No. 1 have dominated each year.

Multiple winners (at year's end): Greg Norman (6); Nick Faldo (3); Seve Ballesteros (2).

Year	Year	Year	Year
1986 Seve Ballesteros	1990 Nick Faldo & Greg Norman	1993 Nick Faldo	1996 Greg Norman
1987 Greg Norman	1991 Ian Woosnam	1994 Nick Price	1997 Tiger Woods
1988 Greg Norman	1992 Fred Couples & Nick Faldo	1995 Greg Norman	
1989 Seve Ballesteros & Greg Norman			

National Team Competition

MEN

Ryder Cup

The Ryder Cup was presented by British seed merchant and businessman Samuel Ryder in 1927 for competition between professional golfers from Great Britain and the United States. The British team was expanded to include Irish players in 1973 and the rest of Europe in 1979. The United States leads the series 23-7-2 after 32 matches.

Year
1927 United States, 9½-2½
1929 Britain-Ireland, 7-5
1931 United States, 9-3
1933 Great Britain, 6½-5½
1935 United States, 9-3
1937 United States, 8-4
1939-45 Not held
1947 United States, 11-1
1949 United States, 7-5
1951 United States, 9½-2½
1953 United States, 6½-5½

Year
1955 United States, 8-4
1957 Britain-Ireland, 7½-4½
1959 United States, 8½-3½
1961 United States, 14½-9½
1963 United States, 23-9
1965 United States, 19½-12½
1967 United States, 23½-8½
1969 Draw, 16-16
1971 United States, 18½-13½
1973 United States, 19-13
1975 United States, 21-11

Year
1977 United States, 12½-13½
1979 United States, 17-11
1981 United States, 18½-9½
1983 United States, 14½-13½
1985 Europe, 16½-11½
1987 Europe, 15-13
1989 Draw, 14-14
1991 United States, 14½-13½
1993 United States, 15-13
1995 Europe, 14½-13½
1997 Europe, 14½-13½

Playing Sites

1927—Worcester CC (Mass.); **1929**—Moortown, England; **1931**—Scioto CC (Ohio); **1933**—Southport & Ainsdale, England; **1935**—Ridgewood CC (N.J.); **1937**—Southport & Ainsdale, England; **1939-45**—Not held. **1947**—Portland CC (Ore.); **1949**—Ganton GC, England; **1951**—Pinehurst CC (N.C.); **1953**—Wentworth, England; **1955**—Thunderbird Ranch &CC (Calif.); **1957**—Lindrick GC, England; **1959**—Eldorado CC (Calif.); **1961**—Royal Lytham & St. Annes, England; **1963**—East Lake CC (Ga.); **1965**—Royal Birkdale, England; **1967**—Champions GC (Tex.); **1969**—Royal Birkdale, England; **1971**—Old Warson CC (Mo.); **1973**—Muirfield, Scotland; **1975**—Laurel Valley GC (Pa.); **1977**—Royal Lytham & St. Annes, England; **1979**—Greenbrier; **1981**—Walton Heath GC, England; **1983**—PGA National GC (Fla.); **1985**—The Belfry, England; **1987**—Muirfield Village GC (Ohio); **1989**—The Belfry, England; **1991**—Ocean Course (S.C.); **1993**—The Belfry, England; **1995**—Oak Hill CC (N.Y.); **1997**—Valderrama, Costa del Sol, Spain.

Walker Cup

The Walker Cup was presented by American businessman George Herbert Walker in 1922 for competition between amateur golfers from Great Britain and the United States. The U.S. leads the series with a 31-4-1 record after 36 matches.

Year
1922 United States, 8-4
1923 United States, 6½-5½
1924 United States, 9-3
1926 United States, 6½-5½
1928 United States, 11-1
1930 United States, 10-2
1932 United States, 9½-2½
1934 United States, 9½-2½
1936 United States, 10½-1½
1938 Britain-Ireland, 7½-4½
1940-46 Not held
1947 United States, 8-4
1949 United States, 10-2

Year
1951 United States, 7½-4½
1953 United States, 9-3
1955 United States, 10-2
1957 United States, 8½-3½
1959 United States, 9-3
1961 United States, 11-1
1963 United States, 14-10
1965 Draw, 12-12
1967 United States, 15-9
1969 United States, 13-11
1971 Britain-Ireland, 13-11
1973 United States, 14-10
1975 United States, 15½-8½

Year
1977 United States, 16-8
1979 United States, 15½-8½
1981 United States, 15-9
1983 United States, 13½-10½
1985 United States, 13-11
1987 United States, 16½-7½
1989 Britain-Ireland, 12½-11½
1991 United States, 14-10
1993 United States, 19-5
1995 Britain-Ireland, 14-10
1997 United States, 18-6

WOMEN

Solheim Cup

The Solheim Cup was presented by the Karsten Manufacturing Co. in 1990 for competition between women professional golfers from Europe and the United States. The U.S. leads the series with a 4-1 record after five matches.

Year
1990 United States, 11½-4½
1992 Europe, 11½-6½

Year
1994 United States, 13-7
1996 United States, 17-11

Year
1998 United States, 16-12

Curtis Cup

Named after British golfing sisters Harriot and Margaret Curtis, the Curtis Cup was first contested in 1932 between teams of women amateurs from the United States and the British Isles.

Competed for every other year since 1932 (except during World War II). The U.S. leads the series with a 21-6-3 record after 30 matches.

Year
1932 United States, 5½-3½
1934 United States, 6½-2½
1936 Draw, 4½-4½
1938 United States, 5½-3½
1940-46 Not held
1948 United States, 6½-2½
1950 United States, 7½-1½
1952 British Isles, 5-4
1954 United States, 6-3
1956 British Isles, 5-4
1958 Draw, 4½-4½

Year
1960 United States, 6½-2½
1962 United States, 8-1
1964 United States, 10½-7½
1966 United States, 13-5
1968 United States, 10½-7½
1970 United States, 11½-6½
1972 United States, 10-8
1974 United States, 13-5
1976 United States, 11½-6½
1978 United States, 12-6
1980 United States, 13-5

Year
1982 United States, 14½-3½
1984 United States, 9½-8½
1986 British Isles, 13-5
1988 British Isles, 11-7
1990 United States, 14-4
1992 British Isles, 10-8
1994 Draw, 9-9
1996 British Isles, 11½-6½
1998 United States, 10-8

COLLEGES

Men's NCAA Division I Champions

College championships decided by match play from 1897-1964, and stroke play since 1965.

Multiple winners (Teams): Yale (21); Houston (16); Oklahoma St. (8); Stanford (7); Harvard (6); LSU and North Texas (4); Florida and Wake Forest (3); Arizona St., Michigan, Ohio St. and Texas (2).

Multiple winners (Individuals): Ben Crenshaw and Phil Mickelson (3); Dick Crawford, Dexter Cummings, G.T. Dunlop, Fred Lamphrecht and Scott Simpson (2).

Year	Team winner	Individual champion
1897	Yale	Louis Bayard, Princeton
1898	Harvard (spring)	John Reid, Yale
1898	Yale (fall)	James Curtis, Harvard
1899	Harvard	Percy Pyne, Princeton
1900	Not held	
1901	Harvard	H. Lindsley, Harvard
1902	Yale (spring)	Chas. Hitchcock Jr., Yale
1902	Harvard (fall)	Chandler Egan, Harvard
1903	Harvard	F.O. Reinhart, Princeton
1904	Harvard	A.L. White, Harvard
1905	Yale	Robert Abbott, Yale
1906	Yale	W.E. Clow Jr., Yale
1907	Yale	Ellis Knowles, Yale
1908	Yale	H.H. Wilder, Harvard
1909	Yale	Albert Seckel, Princeton
1910	Yale	Robert Hunter, Yale
1911	Yale	George Stanley, Yale
1912	Yale	F.C. Davison, Harvard
1913	Yale	Nathaniel Wheeler, Yale
1914	Princeton	Edward Allis, Harvard
1915	Yale	Francis Blossom, Yale
1916	Princeton	J.W. Hubbell, Harvard
1917-18	Not held	
1919	Princeton	A.L. Walker Jr., Columbia
1920	Princeton	Jess Sweetster, Yale
1921	Dartmouth	Simpson Dean, Princeton
1922	Princeton	Pollack Boyd, Dartmouth
1923	Princeton	Dexter Cummings, Yale
1924	Yale	Dexter Cummings, Yale
1925	Yale	Fred Lamprecht, Tulane
1926	Yale	Fred Lamprecht, Tulane
1927	Princeton	Watts Gunn, Georgia Tech
1928	Princeton	Maurice McCarthy, G'town
1929	Princeton	Tom Aycock, Yale
1930	Princeton	G.T. Dunlap Jr., Princeton
1931	Yale	G.T. Dunlap Jr., Princeton
1932	Yale	J.W. Fischer, Michigan
1933	Yale	Walter Emery, Oklahoma
1934	Michigan	Charles Yates, Ga.Tech
1935	Michigan	Ed White, Texas
1936	Yale	Charles Kocsis, Michigan
1937	Princeton	Fred Haas Jr., LSU
1938	Stanford	John Burke, Georgetown
1939	Stanford	Vincent D'Antoni, Tulane
1940	Princeton & LSU	Dixon Brooke, Virginia
1941	Stanford	Earl Stewart, LSU
1942	LSU & Stanford	Frank Tatum Jr., Stanford
1943	Yale	Wallace Ulrich, Carleton
1944	Notre Dame	Louis Lick, Minnesota
1945	Ohio State	John Lorms, Ohio St.
1946	Stanford	George Hamer, Georgia
1947	LSU	Dave Barclay, Michigan
1948	San Jose St.	Bob Harris, San Jose St.
1949	North Texas	Harvie Ward, N.Carolina
1950	North Texas	Fred Wampler, Purdue
1951	North Texas	Tom Nieporte, Ohio St.
1952	North Texas	Jim Vichers, Oklahoma
1953	Stanford	Earl Moeller, Oklahoma St.
1954	SMU	Hillman Robbins, Memphis St.
1955	LSU	Joe Campbell, Purdue
1956	Houston	Rick Jones, Ohio St.
1957	Houston	Rex Baxter Jr., Houston
1958	Houston	Phil Rodgers, Houston
1959	Houston	Dick Crawford, Houston
1960	Houston	Dick Crawford, Houston
1961	Purdue	Jack Nicklaus, Ohio St.
1962	Houston	Kermit Zarley, Houston
1963	Oklahoma St.	R.H. Sikes, Arkansas
1964	Houston	Terry Small, San Jose St.
1965	Houston	Marty Fleckman, Houston
1966	Houston	Bob Murphy, Florida
1967	Houston	Hale Irwin, Colorado
1968	Florida	Grier Jones, Oklahoma St.
1969	Houston	Bob Clark, Cal St.-LA
1970	Houston	John Mahaffey, Houston
1971	Texas	Ben Crenshaw, Texas
1972	Texas	Ben Crenshaw, Texas & Tom Kite, Texas
1973	Florida	Ben Crenshaw, Texas
1974	Wake Forest	Curtis Strange, W.Forest
1975	Wake Forest	Jay Haas, Wake Forest
1976	Oklahoma St.	Scott Simpson, USC
1977	Houston	Scott Simpson, USC
1978	Oklahoma St.	David Edwards, Okla. St.
1979	Ohio St.	Gary Hallberg, Wake Forest
1980	Oklahoma St.	Jay Don Blake, Utah St.
1981	Brigham Young	Ron Commans, USC
1982	Houston	Billy Ray Brown, Houston
1983	Oklahoma St.	Jim Carter, Arizona St.
1984	Houston	John Inman, N.Carolina
1985	Houston	Clark Burroughs, Ohio St.
1986	Wake Forest	Scott Verplank, Okla. St.
1987	Oklahoma St.	Brian Watts, Oklahoma St.
1988	UCLA	E.J. Pfister, Oklahoma St.
1989	Oklahoma	Phil Mickelson, Ariz. St.
1990	Arizona St.	Phil Mickelson, Ariz. St.
1991	Oklahoma St.	Warren Schuette, UNLV
1992	Arizona	Phil Mickelson, Ariz. St.
1993	Florida	Todd Demsey, Ariz. St.
1994	Stanford	Justin Leonard, Texas
1995	Oklahoma St.	Chip Spratlin, Auburn
1996	Arizona St.	Tiger Woods, Stanford
1997	Pepperdine	Charles Warren, Clemson
1998	UNLV	James McLean, Minnesota

Women's NCAA Division I Champions

College championships decided by stroke play since 1982.

Multiple winners (teams): Arizona St. (6); Florida, San Jose St. and Tulsa (2).

Year	Team winner	Individual champion
1982	Tulsa	Kathy Baker, Tulsa
1983	TCU	Penny Hammel, Miami
1984	Miami-FL	Cindy Schreyer, Georgia
1985	Florida	Danielle Ammaccapane, Ariz.St.
1986	Florida	Page Dunlap, Florida
1987	San Jose St.	Caroline Keggi, New Mexico
1988	Tulsa	Melissa McNamara, Tulsa
1989	San Jose St.	Pat Hurst, San Jose St.
1990	Arizona St.	Susan Slaughter, Arizona
1991	UCLA	Annika Sorenstam, Arizona
1992	San Jose St.	Vicki Goetze, Georgia
1993	Arizona St.	Charlotta Sorenstam, Ariz. St.
1994	Arizona St.	Emilee Klein, Ariz. St.
1995	Arizona St.	K. Mourgue d'Algue, Ariz. St.
1996	Arizona	Marisa Baena, Arizona
1997	Arizona St.	Heather Bowie, Texas
1998	Arizona St.	Jennifer Rosales, USC

Auto Racing

Homecoming king and queen? No, it's **Jeff Gordon**, shown here with his wife Brooke. Gordon was stellar in 1998, winning six out of seven races during one stretch of the NASCAR circuit.

AP/Wide World Photos

Finally!

On his 20th attempt, legend Dale Earnhardt captured his first Daytona 500 win.

by
Rece Davis

Nineteen times he'd tried. Nineteen times he'd failed. Four times, he'd lost the lead inside the final 10 laps. Cut tires in the final turn, scary yet spectacular end-over-end crashes, and cars that simply weren't stout enough to hold on, all bedeviled him. Finally, in his 20th try, Dale Earnhardt exorcised his Daytona demons by winning the Daytona 500.

In a scene that the "Days of Thunder" writers couldn't have dreamed up, Earnhardt's receiving line on his way to victory lane was virtually every member of every other team. They rushed to line pit road as Earnhardt drove slowly by and shook hands with each person. When they call you the "Intimidator," you don't cry, but Earnhardt admitted his eyes watered a little. NASCAR's 50th anniversary season was off to a golden start as the seven-time champion finally captured the lone jewel missing from his crown.

But any thoughts Earnhardt had of an unprecedented eighth championship were quickly vanquished by the reigning champ Jeff Gordon and Mark Martin. The duo owned victory lane. Others were just renting. After Daytona, Gordon and Martin combined to win 17 of the next 27 races.

Gordon reeled off a modern-era (since 1972) record-tying four straight wins at mid-season. Martin finished second in three of those races. Gordon was denied a record fifth straight win in Bristol, Tenn. by, who else, Martin, but he bounced back to win the next two races. During his torrid six-out-of-seven stretch, the driver of the No. 24 car also cashed a pair of million dollar bonus checks by winning the *No Bull* bonus at Indianapolis and Darlington. For the record, that made Gordon three-for-three in his career when driving for a million dollar bonus. He later failed to go four-for-four when Dale Jarrett won at Talladega, but talk about a money driver.

Rece Davis is the host of *RPM 2Night* on espn2.

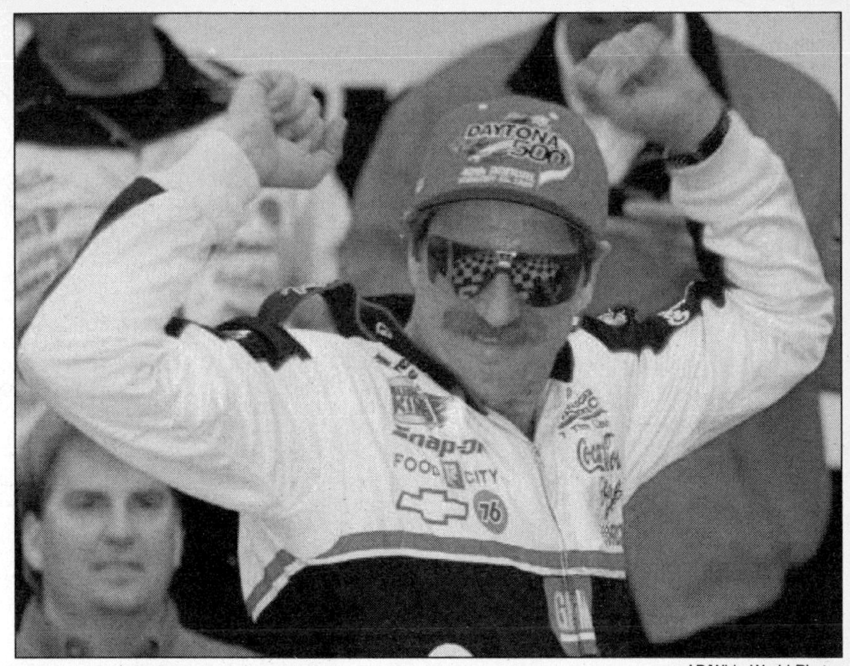

AP/Wide World Photos

Yeah baby! With victory lane reflected in his sunglasses, **Dale Earnhardt** celebrates his first Daytona 500 win on February 15.

CART

The CART season from A to Z was pretty much covered by the man with those initials, Alex Zanardi. The reigning PPG Cup champion ripped off a record-tying four straight wins during June and July. By that time, the question wasn't whether Zanardi would repeat as champion but whether he would jump to Formula One after the season. The answer is yes. The Italian officially wrapped up the championship in Vancouver and shortly thereafter announced he would join the Williams F-1 team next year. Many CART drivers likely volunteered to spring for a going away party. In just under three seasons, Zanardi's 14 wins placed him in the top-25 on CART's all-time win list. Zanardi's second straight crown made Target Chip Ganassi only the second team ever to win three straight championships. The CART season was marred, however, by a tragic accident at the US 500 at Michigan Speedway. Pole sitter Adrian Fernandez crashed into the wall sending a wheel from his car catapulting into the stands, killing three fans. Inexplicably, the race was not stopped.

IRL

Though continually plagued by poor crowds, the IRL still has the Indianapolis 500. Veteran Eddie Cheever Jr. took the checkered flag, becoming the first owner-driver to win at Indy since A.J. Foyt in 1977. Speaking of Foyt the owner, his driver Kenny Brack set a series record by winning

AP/Wide World Photos

Teammates **Jimmy Vasser** (l) and **Alex Zanardi** (r) had plenty of reason to smile in 1998. Zanardi ran away with the CART points championship for the second consecutive year and now plans to run away to the Formula One circuit. Vasser won two races himself and fought all year for the runner-up spot.

three straight races. Brack finished 10th in the IRL finale in Las Vegas to clinch the series championship by 40 points over Davey Hamilton.

Formula One

At the start of the season, F-1 results seemed a little more like WWF-1 results. Scripted. A script that kept starring Mika Hakkinen. He won four of the first six grand prixs. Once, he and McLaren teammate David Coulthard finished a full minute ahead of the field. Gradually, Michael Schumacher's Ferrari caught up with Hakkinen and at one point tied him in the Driver's Championship standings. With 15 of the 16 races finished, the dynamic duo had combined for 13 wins. Coulthard and Damon Hill were the only others who managed to sneak in victories. As of October, 1998, all the Flying Finn needed to do to clinch his first Driver's Championship was finish second in the Grand Prix of Japan, no matter how Schumacher fared. ■

Rece Davis' Top Ten 1998 Auto Racing Highlights

10. **Dale Jr. Wins Texas Busch race.** Earnhardt Jr.'s win at Texas is memorable because for the second time this season, it brought tears to the Intimidator's eyes and it signaled the arrival of a star. The "kid" beat Joe Nemechek with a veteran move. Dad, no doubt, realized he saw a chip off the old block.

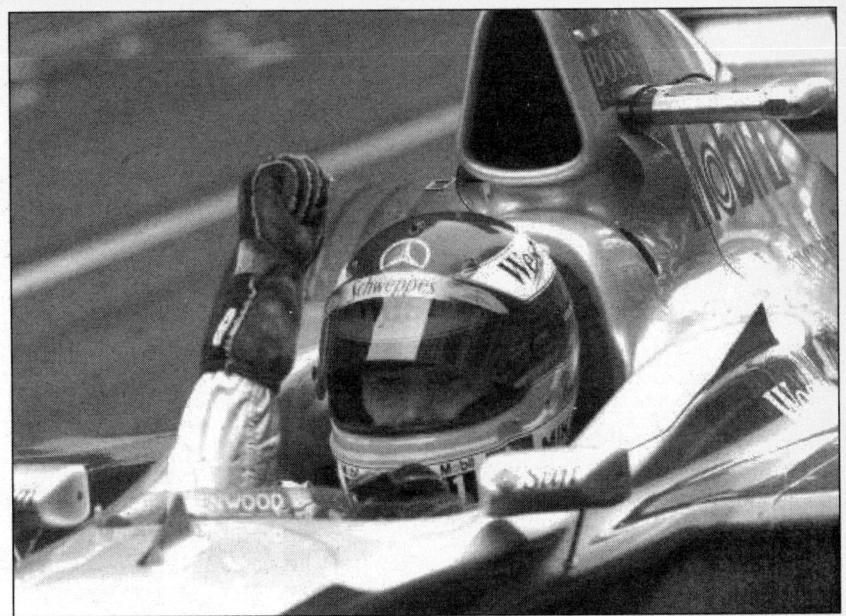

AP/Wide World Photos

Mika Hakkinen of Finland raises his fist in his McLaren-Mercedes after winning the Monaco Grand Prix on May 24. It was Hakkinen's fourth Formula One title in the first six races of the season as he battled Michael Schumacher for the overall championship.

9. **Farm Aid/CMT 300**— Jeff Gordon wins, but the post-race action is better. Frustrated that the 24 car had won by taking only two tires late, relegating his man Mark Martin to a fourth place finish, rival owner Jack Roush insinuates Gordon's team was cheating. Gordon's crew chief Ray Evernham gets into a shouting match with Roush in the garage. Exhaustive tests exonerates Gordon. No punches are thrown.
8. **Moore's Snacks 250**— Again, not so much the race, but the extracurricular activities. Michael Waltrip and Mike Dillon wreck, then wrestle on pit road. No pile drivers are successfully executed.
7. **Lone Star 500**— John Paul Jr. wins his first race in 15 years. This wasn't your run of the mill comeback. Paul's promising career had been derailed when he spent more than two years in prison on drug trafficking charges in the 80s.
6. **Mopar Nationals**— John Force goes 323.89 mph, faster than any human ever has in any type of dragster.
5. **Grand Prix of Belgium**— Amidst near-typhoon conditions, a massive crash at the start sends car parts flying. Twelve cars are wrecked. Drivers scurry through the rain to get to backup cars and they start the whole thing over. Michael Schumacher is cruising to

victory and the Driver's Championship lead when, blinded by the rain, he rear ends Hakkinen's teammate Coulthard and is knocked out of the race. Schumacher then goes after Coulthard in the garage area, apparently unaware that the insurance company always finds the rear-ending driver at fault.

4. **Exide 400**— For the second straight year, Gordon and Jeff Burton have a door handle to door handle finish. This time it's at Richmond. And this time, Burton wins. The hard finish is reminiscent of '97 when Gordon nosed out Burton at Darlington to win the Winston Million.
3. **Grand Prix of Long Beach**— Vintage Alex Zanardi. The champ comes back from 18th place and a lap down to win. Naturally, he passes Bryan Herta for the lead two laps from the finish.
2. **Grand Prix of Monterey**— After being denied his first victory at least three times over the last two years by Zanardi, Herta claims his first checkered flag by holding off Zanardi. Herta does so in the shadow of a billboard showing him "poster-ized." The giant board by the side of the track showed Herta as the victim of Zanardi's miraculous off-course, final lap pass in the famed corkscrew in '96. Afterward, Herta tells me, "If I hadn't beaten him this time, I couldn't have faced my crew."
1. **Dale Earnhardt wins the Daytona 500**— The race and the reaction. One of the greatest things I've ever seen in sports. ■

INSIDE THE NUMBERS

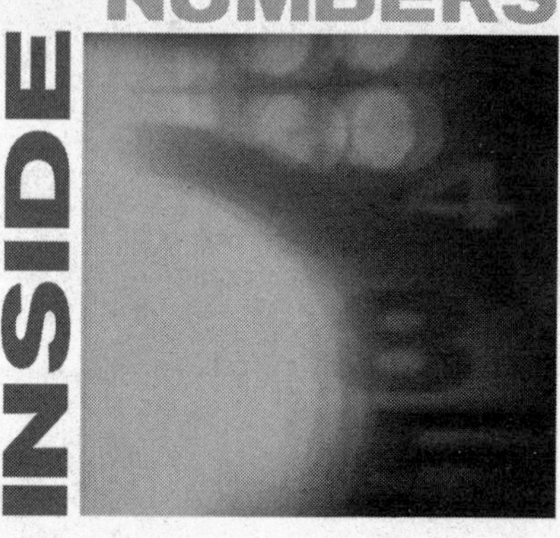

by
Paul Kinney

HE **EARN**ED IT

Dale Earnhardt removed the monkey from his back in 1998 by winning the Daytona 500. In doing so, he became the second-oldest driver in history to win the race.

	Year	Age
Bobby Allison	1988	50
Dale Earnhardt	**1998**	**46**
Lee Petty	1959	44
Bobby Allison	1982	44
Richard Petty	1981	43
Cale Yarborough	1984	43

Note: Earnhardt turned 47 in April, 1998. The race took place in February.

PETTY CASH

Oh, how times have changed. Richard Petty is one of the most heralded drivers in racing history, but you certainly wouldn't know it from his career earnings. In 1997, Jeff Gordon earned almost as much as Petty earned over his entire 34-year career.

	Petty (career)	Gordon (1997)
Starts	1,177	32
Wins	200	10
Poles	126	1
Earnings	$7.75M	$6.37M*
Earnings/Race	$7,000	$199,000

*Includes all bonuses. ■

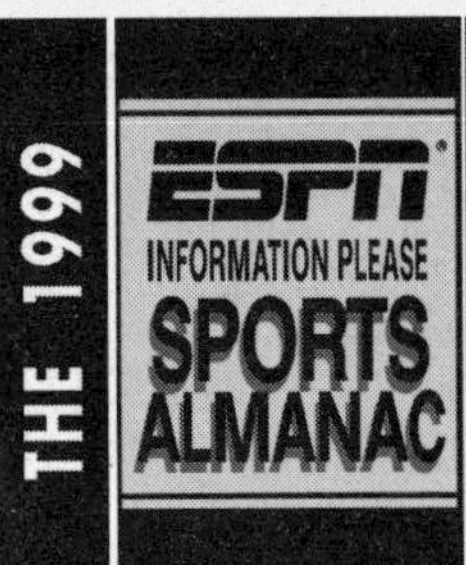

AUTO RACING STATISTICS

THE SEASON IN REVIEW

1997-1998

NASCAR •CART• IRL • F1

NASCAR RESULTS

Winston Cup Series

Winners of NASCAR Winston Cup races from Nov. 2, 1997 through Oct. 11, 1998 (see Updates chapter for later results).

LATE 1997

Date	Event	Location	Winner (Pos.)	Avg.mph	Earnings	Pole	Qual.mph
Nov. 2	Dura-Lube 500	Phoenix	Dale Jarrett (9)	110.824	$98,830	B. Hamilton	131.579
Nov. 16	NAPA 500	Atlanta	Bobby Labonte (21)	159.904	158,600	G. Bodine	197.478

Winning cars (for entire season): CHEVY MONTE CARLO (12)— Gordon 11, T. Labonte 1; FORD THUNDERBIRD (11)— Jarrett 7, Rudd 2, Irvan 1, Wallace 1; PONTIAC GRAND PRIX (2)— Hamilton, B. Labonte.

1998 SEASON (through Oct. 11)

Date	Event	Location	Winner (Pos.)	Avg.mph	Earnings	Pole	Qual.mph
Feb. 15	**Daytona 500**	Daytona	Dale Earnhardt (4)	172.712	$1,059,105	B. Labonte	192.415
Feb. 22	Goodwrench 400	Rockingham	Jeff Gordon (4)	117.065	90,090	R. Mast	156.361
Mar. 1	Las Vegas 400	Las Vegas	Mark Martin (7)	146.554	313,900	D. Jarrett	168.224
Mar. 9	Primestar 500	Atlanta	Bobby Labonte (14)	139.501	106,800	J. Andretti	192.956
Mar. 22	TranSouth 400	Darlington	Dale Jarrett (3)	127.962	110,035	M. Martin	168.665
Mar. 29	Food City 500	Bristol	Jeff Gordon (2)	82.850	90,860	R. Wallace	124.275
Apr. 5	Texas 500	Texas	Mark Martin (7)	136.771&	356,850	J. Mayfield	185.906
Apr. 19	Goody's 500	Martinsville	Bobby Hamilton (1)	70.709	227,025*	B. Hamilton	93.175
Apr. 26	Sears DieHard 500	Talladega	Bobby Labonte (1)	142.428	141,870	B. Labonte	195.728
May 3	California 500	Fontana	Mark Martin (3)	140.220	141,375	J. Gordon	181.772
May 16	*The Winston*	Concord	Mark Martin (5)	—	257,500	B. Elliott	142.084
May 24	**Coca-Cola 600**	Concord	Jeff Gordon (1)	136.424	429,950+*	J. Gordon	182.976
May 31	MBNA Platinum 400	Dover	Dale Jarrett (4)	119.522	89,950	R. Wallace	155.898
June 6	Pontiac 400	Richmond	Terry Labonte (16)	97.044	99,975	J. Gordon	125.558
June 14	Miller Lite 400	Brooklyn	Mark Martin (7)	158.695	92,375	W. Burton	181.561
June 21	Pocono 500	Long Pond	Jeremy Mayfield (3)	117.809	111,580+	J. Gordon	168.042
June 28	Save Mart/Kragen 350	Sonoma	Jeff Gordon (1)	72.387	160,675+*	J. Gordon	98.711
July 12	Jiffy Lube 300	Loudon	Jeff Burton (5)	102.996	128,575	R. Craven	128.394
July 26	Pennsylvania 500	Long Pond	Jeff Gordon (2)	134.650	165,495	W. Burton	168.805
Aug. 1	Brickyard 400	Indianapolis	Jeff Gordon (3)	126.770	1,637,625+**†	E. Irvan	179.394
Aug. 9	The Bud at the Glen	Watkins Glen	Jeff Gordon (1)	94.446	152,970+*	J. Gordon	120.331
Aug. 16	Pepsi 400	Michigan	Jeff Gordon (3)	151.995	120,302+	E. Irvan	183.416
Aug. 22	Goody's 500	Bristol	Mark Martin (4)	86.918	85,315	R. Wallace	123.554
Aug. 30	Farm Aid on CMT 300	Loudon	Jeff Gordon (1)	112.978	205,400+*	J. Gordon	129.033
Sept. 6	**Pepsi Southern 500**	Darlington	Jeff Gordon (5)	130.031	1,134,655+**	D. Jarrett	168.879
Sept. 12	Select 400	Richmond	Jeff Burton (3)	91.985	108,495	R. Wallace	125.377
Sept. 20	MBNA Gold 400	Dover	Mark Martin (1)	113.834	126,130*	M. Martin	155.966
Sept. 27	NAPA AutoCare 500	Martinsville	Ricky Rudd (2)	73.350	102,575	E. Irvan	93.608
Oct. 4	Quality 500	Concord	Mark Martin (2)	123.188	151,950	D. Cope	181.690
Oct. 11	**Winston 500**	Talladega	Dale Jarrett (3)	159.317	1,110,125**	K. Schrader	196.153

Note: *The Winston* (May 16) is 105-mile, non-points race.

&Race record.

†NASCAR/Motorsports record.

+Includes carryover Winston Cup leader bonus ($10,000 per race): **Coca Cola 600**— Gordon ($110,000); **Pocono 500**— Mayfield ($40,000); **Save Mart 350**— Gordon ($10,000); **Pennsylvania 500**— Gordon ($20,000); **Brickyard 400**— Gordon ($10,000); **Bud at the Glen**— Gordon ($10,000); **Pepsi 400**— Gordon ($10,000); **Farm Aid 300**— Gordon ($20,000); **Pepsi Southern 500**— Gordon ($10,000).

*Includes carryover Unocal 76 bonus ($7,600 per race) for winning race from the pole: **Goody's 500**— Hamilton ($106,400); **Die Hard 500**— Hamilton ($7,600); **Coca Cola 600**— Gordon ($15,200); **Save Mart 350**— Gordon ($38,000); **Bud at the Glen**— Gordon ($30,400); **Farm Aid 300**— Gordon ($22,800); **MBNA Gold 400**— Martin ($22,800).

**Includes $1 million Winston No Bull 5 program.

Winning Cars: FORD THUNDERBIRD (15)— Martin 8, Jarrett 3, J. Burton 2, Mayfield 1, Rudd 1; CHEVY MONTE CARLO (13)— Gordon 10, Earnhardt 1, Hamilton 1, T. Labonte 1; PONTIAC GRAND PRIX (2)— B. Labonte 2.

Remaining Races (4): Pepsi 400 in Daytona Beach (Oct. 17); Dura-Lube/Kmart 500 in Phoenix (Oct. 25); AC-Delco 400 in Rockingham (Nov. 1); NAPA 500 in Atlanta (Nov. 8).

1998 Race Locations

February— DAYTONA 500 at Daytona International Speedway in Daytona Beach, Fla.; GOODWRENCH 400 at North Carolina Motor Speedway in Rockingham, N.C. **March**— LAS VEGAS 400 at Las Vegas Motor Speedway; PRIMESTAR 500 at Atlanta International Speedway in Atlanta, Ga.; TRANSOUTH FINANCIAL 400 at Darlington (S.C.) International Raceway; FOOD CITY 500 at Bristol (Tenn.) Motor Speedway. **April**— TEXAS 500 at Texas Motor Speedway; GOODY'S HEADACHE POWDERS 500 at Martinsville (Va.) Speedway; SEARS DIEHARD 500 at Talladega (Ala.) Superspeedway. **May**— CALIFORNIA 500 by NAPA at California Speedway in Fontana, Calif.; COCA-COLA 600 at Charlotte Motor Speedway in Concord, N.C.; MBNA PLATINUM 500 at Dover Downs International Speedway. **June**— PONTIAC EXCITEMENT 400 at Richmond (Va.) International Speedway; MILLER LITE 400 at Michigan Speedway in Brooklyn, Mich.; POCONO 500 at Pocono International Raceway in Long Pond, Pa.; SAVE MART SUPERMARKETS 350K at Sears Point International Raceway in Sonoma, Calif. **July**— JIFFY LUBE 300 at New Hampshire International Speedway in Loudon, N.H.; PENNSYLVANIA 500 at Pocono. **August**— BRICKYARD 400 at Indianapolis (Ind.) Motor Speedway; THE BUD AT THE GLEN at Watkins Glen (N.Y.) International; DEVILBISS 400 at Michigan; GOODY'S HEADACHE POWDER 500 at Bristol; NEW HAMPSHIRE 300 at New Hampshire. **September**— MT. DEW 500 at Darlington; SELECT 400 at Richmond; GOLD 400 at Dover; AUTOCARE 500 at Martinsville. **October**— UAW-GM QUALITY 500 at Charlotte; WINSTON 500 at Talladega; PEPSI 400 at Daytona International Speedway in Daytona Beach, Fla.; DURA-LUBE 500 at Phoenix (Ariz.) International Raceway. **November**— AC-DELCO 400 at Rockingham; NAPA 500 at Atlanta.

1998 Daytona 500

Date— Sunday, Feb. 15 , 1998, at Daytona International Speedway. **Distance**— 500 miles; **Course**— 2.5 miles; **Field**— 43 cars; **Average speed**— 172.712 mph; **Margin of victory**— under caution; **Time of race**— 2 hours, 53 minutes, 42 seconds; **Caution flags**— 3 for 9 laps; **Lead changes**— 13 among 8 drivers; **Lap leaders**— D. Earnhardt (107), J. Gordon (56), B. Labonte (22), J. Nemechek (6), R. Wallace (4), M. Martin (2), T. Labonte (2), M. Skinner (1); **Pole sitter**— Bobby Labonte at 192.415; **Attendance**— 150,000 (estimated).

	Driver (start pos.)	Team	Car	Laps	Ended	Earnings
1	Dale Earnhardt (4)	GM Goodwrench	Chevrolet Monte Carlo	200	Running	$1,059,105
2	Bobby Labonte (1)	Interstate Batteries	Pontiac Grand Prix	200	Running	548,555
3	Jeremy Mayfield (13)	Mobil 1	Ford Thunderbird	200	Running	375,005
4	Ken Schrader (31)	Skoal	Chevrolet Monte Carlo	200	Running	312,780
5	Rusty Wallace (12)	Miller Lite	Ford Thunderbird	200	Running	232,005
6	Ernie Irvan (10)	Skittles	Pontiac Grand Prix	200	Running	204,500
7	Chad Little (21)	John Deere	Ford Thunderbird	200	Running	126,980
8	Mike Skinner (8)	Lowe's	Chevrolet Monte Carlo	200	Running	135,005
9	Michael Waltrip (6)	Citgo	Ford Thunderbird	200	Running	142,005
10	Bill Elliot (19)	McDonald's	Ford Thunderbird	200	Running	128,455
11	Kyle Petty (39)	Hot Wheels	Pontiac Grand Prix	200	Running	125,155
12	Bobby Hamilton (22)	Kodak	Chevrolet Monte Carlo	200	Running	117,455
13	Terry Labonte (2)	Kellogg's	Chevrolet Monte Carlo	200	Running	116,005
14	Ricky Craven (32)	Budweiser	Chevrolet Monte Carlo	200	Running	107,710
15	Jimmy Spencer (7)	Winston	Ford Thunderbird	200	Running	115,555
16	Jeff Gordon (29)	DuPont	Chevrolet Monte Carlo	200	Running	114,730
17	Lake Speed (16)	Cartoon Network	Ford Thunderbird	200	Running	96,005
18	John Andretti (17)	STP	Pontiac Grand Prix	200	Running	105,480
19	Kenny Irwin (38)	Texaco/Havoline	Ford Thunderbird	199	Running	106,580
20	Ted Musgrave (37)	PRIMESTAR	Ford Thunderbird	199	Running	101,030
21	Jerry Nadeau (26)	FIRSTPLUS Financial	Ford Thunderbird	199	Running	87,155
22	Sterling Marlin (3)	Coors Light	Chevrolet Monte Carlo	199	Running	121,305
23	Mike Wallace (23)	X1-R	Chevrolet Monte Carlo	199	Running	85,405
24	Brett Bodine (42)	Paychex	Ford Thunderbird	199	Running	94,855
25	Ward Burton (9)	MBNA America	Pontiac Grand Prix	199	Running	98,105
26	Joe Nemechek (28)	BellSouth	Chevrolet Monte Carlo	199	Running	92,380
27	Dick Trickle (34)	Heilig-Meyers/Simmons	Ford Thunderbird	198	Running	91,005
28	Steve Grissom (41)	Kodiak	Chevrolet Monte Carlo	198	Running	90,030
29	Andy Hillenburg (18)	Shoney's Inn	Chevrolet Monte Carlo	198	Running	79,505
30	Rick Mast (27)	Remington Arms	Ford Thunderbird	197	Running	78,355
31	Geoff Bodine (25)	Philips	Ford Thunderbird	197	Running	84,880
32	Robert Pressley (30)	Jasper Engines/Federal-Mogul	Ford Thunderbird	197	Running	76,355
33	Darrell Waltrip (43)	Speedblock/Builders Square	Chevrolet Monte Carlo	196	Running	82,005
34	Dale Jarrett (5)	Quality Care/Ford Credit	Ford Thunderbird	196	Running	110,805
35	Billy Standridge (36)	Fans Can Race	Ford Thunderbird	196	Running	73,305
36	Dave Marcis (35)	Realtree Camouflage	Chevrolet Monte Carlo	193	Running	72,230
37	Derrike Cope (11)	Gumout	Pontiac Grand Prix	191	Running	80,605
38	Mark Martin (15)	Valvoline	Ford Thunderbird	187	Running	87,505
39	Greg Sacks (24)	Thorn Apple Valley	Ford Thunderbird	173	Running	77,430
40	Jeff Burton (14)	Exide	Ford Thunderbird	160	Engine	89,205
41	Steve Park (33)	Pennzoil	Chevrolet Monte Carlo	158	Ignition	70,030
42	Ricky Rudd (40)	Tide	Ford Thunderbird	117	Ignition	86,480
43	Kevin Lepage (20)	Pionite	Chevrolet Monte Carlo	78	Engine	70,480

Winston Cup Point Standings

Official Top 10 NASCAR Winston Cup point leaders and Top 15 money leaders for 1997 and unofficial Top 10 point leaders and Top 15 money leaders for 1998 (through Oct. 11). Points awarded for all qualifying drivers (winner receives 175) and lap leaders. Earnings include bonuses. Listed are starts (Sts), Top 5 finishes (1-2-3-4-5), poles won (PW) and points (Pts).

FINAL 1997

		Sts	Finishes 1-2-3-4-5	PW	Pts
1	Jeff Gordon	32	10-3-2-4-3	1	4710
2	Dale Jarrett	32	7-4-4-2-3	3	4696
3	Mark Martin	32	4-2-4-2-4	3	4681
4	Jeff Burton	32	3-3-3-2-2	0	4285
5	Dale Earnhardt	32	0-4-1-1-1	0	4216
6	Terry Labonte	32	1-3-2-2-0	0	4177
7	Bobby Labonte	32	1-2-2-2-1	3	4101
8	Bill Elliott	32	0-1-0-3-1	1	3836
9	Rusty Wallace	32	1-3-2-0-2	1	3598
10	Ken Schrader	32	0-0-0-2-0	2	3576

1998 SEASON (through Oct. 11)

		Sts	Finishes 1-2-3-4-5	PW	Pts
1	Jeff Gordon	29	10-6-3-1-3	7	4632
2	Mark Martin	29	7-5-3-2-2	2	4344
3	Dale Jarrett	29	3-3-6-2-3	2	4098
4	Rusty Wallace	29	0-2-4-3-3	4	3883
5	Jeff Burton	29	2-4-2-3-4	0	3806
6	Jeremy Mayfield	29	1-1-3-1-5	1	3761
7	Bobby Labonte	29	2-2-2-4-0	2	3759
8	Dale Earnhardt	29	1-0-0-2-1	0	3357
9	Terry Labonte	29	1-1-2-1-0	0	3323
10	John Andretti	29	0-0-2-0-1	0	3278

Top 5 Finishing Order + Pole

1998 SEASON (through Oct. 11)

No.	Event	Winner	2nd	3rd	4th	5th	Pole
1	Daytona 500	D. Earnhardt	B. Labonte	J. Mayfield	K. Schrader	R. Wallace	B. Labonte
2	Goodwrench 400	J. Gordon	R. Wallace	M. Martin	J. Spencer	G. Bodine	R. Mast
3	Las Vegas 400	M. Martin	J. Burton	R. Wallace	J. Benson	J. Mayfield	D. Jarrett
4	Primestar 500	B. Labonte	D. Jarrett	J. Mayfield	R. Wallace	K. Irwin	J. Andretti
5	TranSouth 400	D. Jarrett	J. Gordon	R. Wallace	J. Mayfield	J. Burton	M. Martin
6	Food City 500	J. Gordon	T. Labonte	D. Jarrett	J. Burton	J. Benson	R. Wallace
7	Texas 500	M. Martin	C. Little	R. Pressley	J. Nemechek	J. Benson	J. Mayfield
8	Goody's 500	B. Hamilton	T. Musgrave	D. Jarrett	D. Earnhardt	R. Lajoie	B. Hamilton
9	Sears DieHard 500	B. Labonte	J. Spencer	D. Jarrett	T. Labonte	J. Gordon	B. Labonte
10	California 500	M. Martin	J. Mayfield	T. Labonte	J. Gordon	D. Waltrip	J. Gordon
11	Coca-Cola 600	J. Gordon	R. Wallace	B. Labonte	M. Martin	D. Jarrett	J. Gordon
12	MBNA 400	D. Jarrett	J. Burton	J. Gordon	B. Labonte	J. Mayfield	R. Wallace
13	Pontiac 400	T. Labonte	D. Jarrett	R. Wallace	K. Schrader	M. Martin	J. Gordon
14	Miller Lite 400	M. Martin	D. Jarrett	J. Gordon	J. Burton	J. Mayfield	W. Burton
15	Pocono 500	J. Mayfield	J. Gordon	D. Jarrett	J. Burton	M. Martin	J. Gordon
16	Save Mart 350	J. Gordon	B. Hamilton	J. Andretti	B. Labonte	R. Wallace	J. Gordon
17	Jiffy Lube 300	J. Burton	M. Martin	J. Gordon	R. Wallace	M. Skinner	R. Craven
18	Pennsylvania 500	J. Gordon	M. Martin	J. Burton	B. Labonte	D. Jarrett	W. Burton
19	Brickyard 400	J. Gordon	M. Martin	B. Labonte	M. Skinner	D. Earnhardt	E. Irvan
20	Bud at the Glen	J. Gordon	M. Martin	M. Skinner	R. Wallace	D. Jarrett	J. Gordon
21	Pepsi 400	J. Gordon	B. Labonte	D. Jarrett	M. Martin	J. Burton	E. Irvan
22	Goody's 500	M. Martin	J. Burton	R. Wallace	D. Jarrett	J. Gordon	R. Wallace
23	Farm Aid 300	J. Gordon	M. Martin	J. Andretti	D. Jarrett	J. Burton	J. Gordon
24	Pepsi Southern 500	J. Gordon	J. Burton	D. Jarrett	D. Earnhardt	J. Mayfield	D. Jarrett
25	Select 400	J. Burton	J. Gordon	M. Martin	K. Schrader	J. Andretti	R. Wallace
26	MBNA Gold 400	M. Martin	J. Gordon	J. Mayfield	B. Labonte	R. Wallace	M. Martin
27	AutoCare 500	R. Rudd	J. Gordon	M. Martin	R. Bickle	J. Burton	E. Irvan
28	Quality 500	M. Martin	W. Burton	J. Burton	B. Hamilton	J. Gordon	D. Cope
29	Winston 500	D. Jarrett	J. Gordon	T. Labonte	J. Spencer	J. Mayfield	K. Schrader

Money Leaders

FINAL 1997

		Earnings
1	Jeff Gordon	$4,201,227
2	Dale Jarrett	2,512,382
3	Terry Labonte	1,951,844
4	Bobby Labonte	1,943,239
5	Mark Martin	1,877,139
6	Ricky Rudd	1,863,040
7	Jeff Burton	1,858,234
8	Dale Earnhardt	1,663,019
9	Rusty Wallace	1,505,260
10	Ernie Irvan	1,492,739
11	Bill Elliott	1,377,607
12	Bobby Hamilton	1,350,335
13	Sterling Marlin	1,287,570
14	Ricky Craven	1,139,860
15	Ted Musgrave	1,128,404

1998 SEASON (through Oct. 11)

		Earnings
1	Jeff Gordon	$5,668,477
2	Mark Martin	3,042,675
3	Bobby Labonte	2,441,325
4	Dale Earnhardt	2,416,125
5	Dale Jarrett	2,095,070
6	Jeff Burton	1,908,675
7	Rusty Wallace	1,902,095
8	Jeremy Mayfield	1,819,481
9	Terry Labonte	1,651,260
10	Bobby Hamilton	1,596,895
11	Ken Schrader	1,565,456
12	John Andretti	1,479,415
13	Jimmy Spencer	1,464,696
14	Ernie Irvan	1,426,566
15	Ricky Rudd	1,402,160

CART RESULTS

Winners of CART races from Mar. 15 through Oct. 11, 1998.

FedEx Championship Series

1998 SEASON

Date	Event	Location	Winner (Pos.)	Time	Avg.mph	Pole	Qual.mph
Mar. 15	GP of Miami	Homestead	Michael Andretti (8)	1:33:39.268	144.339	G. Moore	217.541
Mar. 28	Budweiser 500	Motegi	Adrian Fernandez (2)	1:57:12.016	159.393	J. Vasser	217.964
Apr. 5	GP of Long Beach	Long Beach	Alex Zanardi (11)	1:51:29.113	88.946	B. Herta	111.226
Apr. 27	Bosch GP	Nazareth	Jimmy Vasser (5)	1:57:20.307	108.839	P. Carpentier	184.896
May 10	Rio 400	Rio de Janeiro	Greg Moore (7)	1:52:14.135	132.531	D. Franchitti	172.039
May 23	Motorola 300	Madison	Alex Zanardi (11)	2:23:02.140	125.725	G. Moore	177.505
May 31	Miller 200	West Allis	Jimmy Vasser (5)	1:34:17.011	131.349	P. Carpentier	185.500
June 7	Detroit GP	Detroit	Alex Zanardi (2)	1:41:17.673	100.052	G. Moore	114.859
June 21	Bud/G.I. Joe's 200	Portland	Alex Zanardi (5)	1:54:06.822	101.355	B. Herta	121.341†
July 12	GP of Cleveland	Cleveland	Alex Zanardi (3)	1:52:22.282	112.449	J. Vasser	134.385
July 19	Molson Indy	Toronto	Alex Zanardi (2)	1:52:24.080	87.274	D. Franchitti	105.558
July 26	**U.S. 500**	Brooklyn	Greg Moore (14)	3:00:48.785	165.913	A. Fernandez	229.519
Aug. 9	Miller Lite 200	Lexington	Adrian Fernandez (5)	1:53:39.270	98.428	D. Franchitti	123.766
Aug. 16	Texaco/Havoline 200	Elkhart Lake	Dario Franchitti (6)	1:35:30.767	127.145	M. Andretti	145.745
Sept. 6	Molson Indy	Vancouver	Dario Franchitti (1)	2:00:37.871	77.081	D. Franchitti	101.157
Sept. 13	Texaco/Havoline 300	Monterey	Bryan Herta (1)	1:55:13.472	96.726	B. Herta	118.229
Oct. 4	GP of Houston	Houston	Dario Franchitti (2)	1:36:30.024	66.051	G. Moore	92.377

†Track record.

Note: CART does not release per race winnings.

Winning cars: REYNARD/HONDA (11)— Zanardi 6, Franchitti 3, Vasser 2; REYNARD/MERCEDES-BENZ (2)— Moore 2; REYNARD/FORD COSWORTH (3)— Fernandez 2, Herta; SWIFT/FORD COSWORTH (1)— Andretti 1.

Remaining races (2): IndyCarnival Australia in Gold Coast, Queensland (Oct. 18); Marlboro 500 in Fontana, Calif. (Nov. 1).

1998 Race Locations

March— MARLBORO GRAND PRIX OF MIAMI Presented by Toyota at Metro-Dade Homestead Motorsports Complex at Homestead, Fla.; BUDWEISER 500 at Twin Ring Motegi, Motegi, Japan. **April**— TOYOTA GP OF LONG BEACH at Long Beach, Calif.; BOSCH SPARK PLUG GP Presented by Toyota at Nazareth (Pa.) Speedway. **May**— RIO 400 at Emerson Fittipaldi Speedway at Nelson Piquet International, Rio de Janeiro, Brazil; MOTOROLA 300 at Gateway International Raceway, Madison, Ill.; MILLER 200 at The Milwaukee Mile in West Allis, Wisc. **June**— ITT AUTOMOTIVE DETROIT GP at The Raceway on Belle Isle, Detroit, Mich.; BUDWEISER/G.I. JOE'S 200 Presented by Texaco/Havoline at Portland (Ore.) International Raceway. **July**— MEDIC DRUG GRAND PRIX OF CLEVELAND at Burke Lakefront Airport, Cleveland, Ohio; MOLSON INDY at Exhibition Place, Toronto, Ontario, Canada; U.S. 500 at Michigan International Speedway, Brooklyn, Mich. **August**— MILLER 200 at Mid-Ohio Sports Car Course in Lexington, Ohio; TEXACO/HAVOLINE 200 at Road America in Elkart Lake, Wisc. **September**—MOLSON INDY VANCOUVER (B.C.) at Concord Pacific Place; GRAND PRIX OF MONTEREY Featuring the Texaco/Havoline 300 at Laguna Seca Raceway, Monterey, Calif. **October**— TEXACO GRAND PRIX OF HOUSTON (Tex.); INDYCARNIVAL AUSTRALIA at Gold Coast, Queensland, Australia. MARLBORO 500 Presented by Toyota at the California Speedway, Fontana, Calif.

1998 U.S. 500

Date— Sunday, July 26, 1998, at Michigan International Speedway. **Distance**— 500 miles; **Course**— 2 mile oval; **Field**—28 cars; **Winner's average speed**— 165.913 mph; **Margin of victory**— 0.259 seconds; **Time of race**— 3 hours, 48.785 seconds; **Caution flags**— 8 for 55 laps; **Lead changes**— 62 by 9 drivers; **Lap leaders**—Zanardi (63 laps), Andretti (62), Moore (36), de Ferran (26), Tracy (22), Vasser (18), Hearn (11), Fernandez (9), Unser (3); **Pole Sitter**—Adrian Fernandez at 229.519; **Attendance**— 70,000.

	Driver (start pos.)	Country	Car	Laps	Ended
1	Greg Moore (14)	Canada	Reynard-Mercedes	250	Running
2	Jimmy Vasser (2)	United States	Reynard-Honda	250	Running
3	Alex Zanardi (7)	Italy	Reynard-Honda	250	Running
4	Scott Pruett (6)	United States	Reynard-Ford	250	Running
5	Richie Hearn (3)	United States	Swift-Ford	250	Running
6	Michael Andretti (8)	United States	Swift-Ford	250	Running
7	Bobby Rahal (12)	United States	Reynard-Ford	250	Running
8	Patrick Carpentier (21)	Canada	Reynard-Mercedes	250	Running
9	Paul Tracy (15)	Canada	Reynard-Honda	250	Running
10	Bryan Herta (5)	United States	Reynard-Ford	250	Running
11	Tony Kanaan (20)	Brazil	Reynard-Honda	249	Running
12	Helio Castro-Neves (24)	Brazil	Reynard-Mercedes	248	Running
13	Mauricio Gugelmin (17)	Brazil	Reynard-Mercedes	248	Running
14	Arnd Meier (18)	Germany	Lola-Ford	247	Running
15	Alex Barron (28)	United States	Reynard-Toyota	242	Running
16	Gil de Ferran (10)	Brazil	Reynard-Honda	240	Engine
17	Mark Blundell (19)	England	Reynard-Mercedes	240	Running
18	Michel Jourdain Jr. (26)	Mexico	Reynard-Ford	238	Running
19	Max Papis (22)	Italy	Reynard-Toyota	237	Electrical
20	J.J. Lehto (13)	Finland	Reynard-Mercedes	223	Contact
21	Dario Franchitti (16)	Scotland	Reynard-Honda	213	Engine

	Driver (start pos.)	Country	Car	Laps	Ended
22	Al Unser Jr. (4)	United States	Penske-Mercedes	194	Oil Leak
23	Adrian Fernandez (1)	Mexico	Reynard-Ford	174	Contact
24	P.J. Jones (27)	United States	Reynard-Toyota	111	Engine
25	Christian Fittipaldi (9)	Brazil	Swift-Ford	87	Overheating
26	Dennis Vitolo (25)	United States	Reynard-Ford	85	Contact
27	Robby Gordon (23)	United States	Reynard-Toyota	76	Contact
28	Andre Ribeiro (11)	Brazil	Penske-Mercedes	75	Oil Leak

Note: CART does not release earnings on a per-race basis.

CART Point Standings

Official Top 10 PPG Cup point leaders and Top 15 money leaders for 1997 and unofficial Top 10 point leaders and Top 15 money leaders for 1998 (through Oct. 11). Points awarded for places 1 to 12, fastest qualifier and overall lap leader. Listed are starts (Sts), Top 5 finishes, poles won (PW) and points (Pts).

FINAL 1997

		Sts	Finishes 1-2-3-4-5	PW	Pts
1	Alex Zanardi	17	5-1-1-4-0	4	195
2	Gil de Ferran	17	0-2-5-1-2	2	162
3	Jimmy Vasser	17	1-2-2-1-3	0	144
4	Mauricio Gugelmin	17	1-2-0-1-1	3	132
5	Paul Tracy	17	3-1-0-1-0	2	121
6	Mark Blundell	17	3-2-0-0-0	0	115
7	Greg Moore	17	2-3-0-1-1	0	111
8	Michael Andretti	17	1-3-1-1-0	0	108
9	Scott Pruett	17	1-0-2-0-3	2	102
10	Raul Boesel	17	0-0-1-2-1	1	91

1998 SEASON (through Oct. 11)

		Sts	Finishes 1-2-3-4-5	PW	Pts
1	Alex Zanardi	17	6-5-2-1-0	0	250
2	Jimmy Vasser	17	2-1-1-2-1	2	148
3	Dario Franchitti	17	3-1-1-3-0	4	143
4	Adrian Fernandez	17	2-1-1-0-2	1	134
5	Greg Moore	17	2-1-2-1-1	4	119
6	Michael Andretti	17	1-4-0-0-1	1	112
7	Scott Pruett	17	0-2-1-2-2	0	108
8	Bryan Herta	17	1-0-2-1-1	3	94
9	Tony Kanaan	17	0-0-2-2-1	0	86
10	Bobby Rahal	17	0-0-1-1-1	0	80

Top 5 Finishing Order + Pole
1998 Season

No.	Event	Winner	2nd	3rd	4th	5th	Pole
1	Miami GP	M. Andretti	G. Moore	A. Zanardi	C. Fittipaldi	S. Pruett	G. Moore
2	Budweiser 500	A. Fernandez	A. Unser Jr.	G. de Ferran	G. Moore	P. Tracy	J. Vasser
3	Long Beach	A. Zanardi	D. Franchitti	B. Herta	A. Fernandez	T. Kanaan	B. Herta
4	Bosch GP	J. Vasser	A. Zanardi	G. Moore	G. de Ferran	P. Tracy	P. Carpentier
5	Rio 400	G. Moore	A. Zanardi	A. Fernandez	B. Herta	M. Andretti	D. Franchitti
6	Motorola 300	A. Zanardi	M. Andretti	G. Moore	J. Vasser	S. Pruett	G. Moore
7	Miller 200	J. Vassar	H. Castro-Neves	A. Unser Jr.	D. Franchitti	B. Rahal	P. Carpentier
8	Detroit	A. Zanardi	A. Fernandez	G. de Ferran	D. Franchitti	G. Moore	G. Moore
9	Bud/G.I. Joe 200	A. Zanardi	S. Pruett	B. Herta	T. Kanaan	A. Unser Jr.	B. Herta
10	Cleveland	A. Zanardi	M. Andretti	D. Franchitti	S. Pruett	A. Fernandez	J. Vasser
11	Toronto	A. Zanardi	M. Andretti	J. Vasser	B. Rahal	B. Herta	D. Franchitti
12	**U.S. 500**	G. Moore	J. Vasser	A. Zanardi	S. Pruett	R. Hearn	A. Fernandez
13	Miller Lite 200	A. Fernandez	S. Pruett	B. Rahal	M. Gugelmin	P. Tracy	D. Franchitti
14	Texaco 200	D. Franchitti	A. Zanardi	C. Fittipaldi	T. Kanaan	A. Fernandez	M. Andretti
15	Vancouver	D. Franchitti	M. Andretti	S. Pruett	A. Zanardi	A. Unser Jr.	D. Franchitti
16	Monterey	B. Herta	A. Zanardi	T. Kanaan	D. Franchitti	J. Vasser	B. Herta
17	Houston	D. Franchitti	A. Zanardi	T. Kanaan	J. Vasser	M. Papis	G. Moore

Money Leaders

FINAL 1997

		Earnings
1	Alex Zanardi	$2,096,250
2	Gil de Ferran	1,355,250
3	Jimmy Vasser	1,133,500
4	Mauricio Gugelmin	1,045,250
5	Paul Tracy	977,250
6	Mark Blundell	949,750
7	Greg Moore	881,000
8	Scott Pruett	864,250
9	Michael Andretti	842,000
10	Bobby Rahal	636,500
11	Bryan Herta	627,500
12	Al Unser Jr.	606,250
13	Andre Ribeiro	567,250
14	Parker Johnstone	557,000
15	Patrick Carpentier	531,500

1998 SEASON (through Oct. 11)

		Earnings
1	Alex Zanardi	$1,069,250
2	Dario Franchitti	944,250
3	Jimmy Vasser	584,250
4	Adrian Fernandez	545,750
5	Greg Moore	519,250
6	Michael Andretti	485,250
7	Bryan Herta	425,000
8	Scott Pruett	421,750
9	Tony Kanaan	333,000
10	Bobby Rahal	328,500
11	Al Unser Jr.	300,250
12	Gil de Ferran	294,250
13	Paul Tracy	247,000
14	Mauricio Gugelmin	238,500
15	Richie Hearn	215,250

Note: The 1998 totals don't include Performance Award earnings.

INDY RACING LEAGUE RESULTS

Winners of Indy Racing League events in the 1998 season that ran from Jan. 24, 1998 through Oct. 11, 1998. The IRL now runs on a calendar-year basis, beginning with the 1998 season.

1998 SEASON

Date	Event	Location	Winner (Pos.)	Time	Avg.mph	Pole	Qual.mph
Jan. 24	Indy 200 at WDW	Orlando	Tony Stewart (1)	2:06:07	95.140	T. Stewart	—*
Mar. 22	Dura-Lube 200	Phoenix	Scott Sharp (8)	2:02:18	98.110	J. Ward	172.753†
May 24	**Indianapolis 500**	Indianapolis	Eddie Cheever Jr. (17)	3:26:40	145.155	B. Boat	223.503
June 6	True Value 500	Fort Worth	Billy Boat (2)	2:08:45	145.388	T. Stewart	224.448†
June 28	New England 200	Loudon	Tony Stewart (6)	1:51:30	113.861	B. Boat	162.146†
July 19	Pep Boys 400K	Dover	Scott Sharp (4)	2:29:49	99.318	T. Stewart	185.204†
July 25	Visionaire 500	Concord	Kenny Brack (3)	1:58:10	158.408	T. Stewart	220.498†
Aug. 16	Radisson 200	Fountain	Kenny Brack (5)	1:29:52	133.515	B. Boat	178.571†
Aug. 29	Atlanta 500 Classic	Atlanta	Kenny Brack (6)	2:17:15	140.026	B. Boat	224.145†
Sept. 20	Lone Star 500	Fort Worth	John Paul Jr. (14)	2:21:53	131.931	B. Boat	225.979†
Oct. 11	Las Vegas 500K	Las Vegas	Arie Luyendyk (14)	2:18:19	135.338	B. Boat	214.567†

†Track record for the new formula IRL cars.

Winning cars: DALLARA/OLDS AURORA (8)— Brack 3, Sharp 2, Boat 1, Cheever Jr. 1, Stewart 1; G-FORCE/OLDS AURORA (3)— Luyendyk 1, Paul Jr. 1, Stewart 1.

Note: In 1997 IRL drivers started using new cars; chassis by Dallara of Italy and G-Force of England and engines by Oldsmobile and Nissan.

*Qualifying day was cancelled due to rain. The first 20 positions were determined by 1996-97 entrant points, while final eight positions were done by practice speeds.

82nd Indianapolis 500

Date— Tuesday, May 24, 1998, at Indianapolis Motor Speedway. **Distance**— 500 miles; **Course**— 2.5 mile oval; **Field**— 33 cars; **Winner's average speed**— 145.155 mph; **Margin of victory**— 3.191 seconds; **Time of race**— 3 hours, 26 minutes, 40.524 seconds; **Caution flags**— 12 for 50 laps; **Lead changes**— 15 by 5 drivers; **Lap leaders**— Cheever (76), Paul Jr. (39), Brack (23), Lazier (20), Ray (18), Boat (12), Calkins (4), Luyendyk (4), Hamilton (3), Stewart (1); **Pole Sitter**— Billy Boat at 223.503 mph; **Attendance**— 375,000 (est.); **TV Rating**— 5.6 (ABC). Note that (r) indicates rookie driver.

	Driver (start pos.)	Country	Car	Laps	Ended	Earnings
1	Eddie Cheever Jr. (17)	United States	D/A/G	200	Running	$1,433,000
2	Buddy Lazier (11)	United States	D/A/G	200	Running	483,200
3	r-Steve Knapp (23)	United States	G/A/G	200	Running	338,750
4	Davey Hamilton (8)	United States	G/A/G	199	Running	301,650
5	r-Robby Unser (21)	United States	G/A/G	198	Running	209,400
6	Kenny Brack (3)	Sweden	D/A/G	198	Running	310,750
7	John Paul Jr. (16)	United States	D/A/F	197	Running	216,350
8	r-Andy Michner (19)	United States	D/A/G	197	Running	182,050
9	r-J.J. Yeley (13)	United States	D/A/F	197	Running	198,550
10	Buzz Calkins (18)	United States	G/A/G	195	Running	248,500
11	r-Jimmy Kite (26)	United States	D/A/G	195	Running	287,300
12	r-Jack Hewitt (22)	United States	G/A/G	195	Running	265,800
13	Jeff Ward (27)	United States	G/A/G	194	Running	242,050
14	Marco Greco (14)	Brazil	G/A/F	183	Engine	167,800
15	Mike Groff (32)	United States	G/A/F	183	Running	237,600
16	Scott Sharp (7)	United States	D/A/G	181	Gearbox	234,800
17	Stephan Gregoire (31)	France	G/A/G	172	Running	225,300
18	Greg Ray (2)	United States	D/A/F	167	Gearbox	175,400
19	Raul Boesel (30)	Brazil	G/A/G	164	Accident	221,300
20	Arie Luyendyk (28)	Netherlands	G/A/F	151	Gearbox	241,100
21	Jack Miller (15)	United States	D/I/F	128	Running	159,800
22	Roberto Guerrero (9)	United States	D/A/G	125	Running	165,300
23	Billy Boat (1)	United States	D/A/G	111	Drive Line	364,200
24	Scott Goodyear (10)	Canada	G/A/G	100	Clutch	253,300
25	Johnny Unser (25)	United States	D/A/G	98	Engine	136,300
26	Sam Schmidt (6)	United States	D/A/F	48	Accident	215,300
27	Mark Dismore (12)	United States	D/A/G	48	Accident	209,300
28	r-Stan Wattles (29)	United States	R/A/G	48	Accident	138,550
29	Jim Guthrie (20)	United States	G/A/G	48	Accident	133,300
30	Billy Roe (33)	United States	D/A/G	48	Accident	137,300
31	Robbie Buhl (5)	United States	D/A/F	44	Engine	222,300
32	r-Donnie Beechler (24)	United States	G/A/F	34	Engine	132,300
33	Tony Stewart (4)	United States	D/A/F	22	Engine	220,250

Car Legend: Chassis/Engine/Tires. D—Dallara; G (chassis)—G Force; R—Riley & Scott; A—Oldsmobile Aurora V-8; I—Nissan Infiniti V-8; F—Firestone; G (tires)—Goodyear.

Indy Racing League Point Standings

FINAL 1996-97

		Sts	Finishes 1-2-3-4-5	PW	Pts
1	Tony Stewart	10	1-1-0-0-2	4	278
2	Davey Hamilton	10	0-0-3-0-1	0	272
3	Marco Greco	10	0-0-0-1-0	1	230
	Eddie Cheever Jr.	10	1-0-0-1-0	0	230
5	Scott Goodyear	8	0-2-2-1-0	0	226
6	Arie Luyendyk	10	2-0-1-0-0	2	223
7	Roberto Guerrero	10	0-0-0-1-0	0	221
8	Buddy Lazier	10	1-0-0-1-1	0	209
9	Eliseo Salazar	8	1-0-0-1-0	0	208
10	Buzz Calkins	9	0-1-0-0-1	0	204

FINAL 1998

		Sts	Finishes 1-2-3-4-5	PW	Pts
1	Kenny Brack	11	3-0-1-0-1	0	332
2	Davey Hamilton	11	0-1-1-3-1	0	292
3	Tony Stewart	11	2-1-1-0-1	4	289
4	Scott Sharp	11	2-0-1-0-1	0	272
5	Buddy Lazier	11	0-2-1-0-0	0	262
6	Jeff Ward	11	0-2-1-0-1	1	252
7	Scott Goodyear	11	0-1-1-2-0	0	244
8	Arie Luyendyk	11	1-0-0-1-1	0	227
9	Eddie Cheever Jr.	11	1-0-1-0-1	0	222
10	Marco Greco	11	0-0-1-0-1	0	219

Top 5 Finishing Order + Pole

1998 Season

No.	Event	Winner	2nd	3rd	4th	5th	Pole
1	Indy 200 at WDW	T. Stewart	J. Ward	D. Hamilton	S. Gregoire	M. Dismore	T. Stewart
2	Dura-Lube 200	S. Sharp	T. Stewart	B. Boat	S. Gregoire	J. Ward	J. Ward
3	**Indianapolis 500**	E. Cheever Jr.	B. Lazier	S. Knapp	D. Hamilton	R. Unser	B. Boat
4	True Value 500	B. Boat	G. Ray	K. Brack	S. Goodyear	S. Sharp	T. Stewart
5	New England 200	T. Stewart	S. Goodyear	S. Sharp	D. Hamilton	A. Luyendyk	B. Boat
6	Pep Boys 400K	S. Sharp	B. Lazier	M. Greco	D. Hamilton	S. Gregoire	T. Stewart
7	VisionAire 500	K. Brack	J. Ward	S. Goodyear	A. Luyendyk	M. Greco	T. Stewart
8	Radisson 200	K. Brack	R. Buhl	T. Stewart	S. Gregoire	D. Hamilton	B. Boat
9	Atlanta 500 Classic	K. Brack	D. Hamilton	E. Cheever Jr.	S. Goodyear	T. Stewart	B. Boat
10	Lone Star 500	J. Paul Jr.	R. Unser	J. Ward	R. Guerrero	K. Brack	B. Boat
11	Las Vegas 500K	A. Luyendyk	S. Schmidt	B. Lazier	J. Paul Jr.	E. Cheever Jr.	B. Boat

Money Leaders

FINAL 1996-97 SEASON

		Earnings
1	Arie Luyendyk	$2,079,150
2	Tony Stewart	1,090,450
3	Scott Goodyear	953,350
4	Davey Hamilton	785,950
5	Buddy Lazier	736,550
6	Eddie Cheever Jr.	725,400
7	Jim Guthrie	627,200
8	Billy Boat	604,150
9	Roberto Guerrero	601,000
10	Buzz Calkins	599,750

FINAL 1998

		Earnings
1	Eddie Cheever Jr.	$1,811,200
2	Kenny Brack	1,096,700
3	Billy Boat	1,004,150
4	Tony Stewart	1,002,850
5	Buddy Lazier	984,850
6	Davey Hamilton	856,850
7	Jeff Ward	811,650
8	Scott Sharp	808,900
9	Scott Goodyear	761,450
10	Arie Luyendyk	746,100

FORMULA ONE RESULTS

Winners of Formula One Grand Prix races from Mar. 8 through Sept. 27, 1998. See Updates for later results.

1998 SEASON

Date	Grand Prix	Location	Winner (Pos.)	Time	Avg.mph	Pole	Qual.mph
Mar. 8	Australian	Melbourne	Mika Hakkinen (1)	1:31:45.996	124.958	M. Hakkinen	131.785
Mar. 29	Brazilian	Interlagos	Mika Hakkinen (1)	1:37:11.747	118.535	M. Hakkinen	124.542
Apr. 12	Argentine	Buenos Aires	Michael Schumacher (2)	1:48:36.175	105.304	D. Coulthard	110.971
Apr. 26	San Marino	Imola	David Coulthard (1)	1:34:24.593	120.619	D. Coulthard	128.259
May 10	Spanish	Barcelona	Mika Hakkinen (1)	1:33:37.621	122.288	M. Hakkinen	131.778
May 24	Monaco	Monte Carlo	Mika Hakkinen (1)	1:51:23.595	87.898	M. Hakkinen	90.794
June 7	Canadian	Montreal	Michael Schumacher (3)	1:40:57.355	112.654	D. Coulthard	126.445†
June 28	French	Magny-Cours	Michael Schumacher (2)	1:34:45.026	118.659	M. Hakkinen	126.880
July 12	British	Silverstone	Michael Schumacher (2)	1:47:02.450	107.379	M. Hakkinen	138.077
July 26	Austrian	A1-Ring	Mika Hakkinen (3)	1:30:44.086	126.001	G. Fisichella	107.831
Aug. 2	German	Hockenheim	Mika Hakkinen (1)	1:20:47.984	141.672	M. Hakkinen	149.873
Aug. 16	Hungarian	Budapest	Michael Schumacher (3)	1:45:25.550	108.157	M. Hakkinen	115.769
Aug. 30	Belgian	Spa-Francorchamps	Damon Hill (3)	1:43:47.407	110.127	M. Hakkinen	143.420
Sept. 13	Italian	Monza	Michael Schumacher (1)	1:17:09.672	147.632	M. Schumacher	151.334
Sept. 27	Luxembourg	Nuerburgring	Mika Hakkinen (3)	1:32:14.789	123.363	M. Schumacher	129.728

†Track record.

Winning Constructors: McLAREN-MERCEDES (8)— Hakkinen 7, Coulthard 1; FERRARI (6)— M. Schumacher 6; JORDAN-MUGEN HONDA (1)— Hill 1.

Remaining Races (1): Japanese GP at Suzuka (Nov. 1).

Formula One Point Standings

Official Top 10 Formula One World Championship point leaders for 1997 and unofficial Top 10 point leaders for 1998 (through Sept. 27). Points awarded for places 1 through 6 only (i.e., 10-6-4-3-2-1). Listed are starts (Sts), Top 6 finishes, poles won (PW) and points (Pts). **Note:** Formula One does not keep Money Leader standings.

FINAL 1997

		Sts	Finishes 1-2-3-4-5-6	PW	Pts
1	Jacques Villeneuve	17	7-0-1-1-2-1	10	81
2	Michael Schumacher*	17	5-3-0-2-1-3	3	78
3	Heinz-Harald Frentzen	17	1-2-3-2-0-1	1	42
4	David Coulthard	17	2-2-0-1-0-1	0	36
	Jean Alesi	17	0-4-1-0-2-3	1	36
6	Gerhard Berger	14	1-1-0-3-0-1	1	27
	Mika Hakkinen	16	1-0-3-2-1-1	1	27
8	Eddie Irvine	17	0-1-4-0-1-0	0	24
9	Giancarlo Fisichella	17	0-1-1-3-0-1	0	20
10	Olivier Panis	10	0-1-1-1-1-2	0	16

*Officially, Schumacher was stripped of his points and second-place finish in the standings following the season-ending European GP.

1998 SEASON (through Sept. 27)

		Sts	Finishes 1-2-3-4-5-6	PW	Pts
1	Mika Hakkinen	13	7-2-1-1-0-1	9	90
2	Michael Schumacher	15	6-2-3-0-1-0	2	86
3	David Coulthard	15	1-6-1-0-0-2	3	52
4	Eddie Irvine	15	0-2-5-3-0-0	0	41
5	Jacques Villeneuve	15	0-0-2-2-2-2	0	20
6	Alexander Wurz	14	0-0-0-5-1-0	0	17
	Damon Hill	14	1-0-0-2-0-1	0	17
8	Giancarlo Fisichella	15	0-2-0-0-1-2	1	16
9	Heinz-Harald Frentzen	15	0-0-1-1-4-0	0	15
10	Ralf Schumacher	13	0-1-1-0-1-2	0	14

Top 5 + Pole Finishing Order

No.	Event	Winner	2nd	3rd	4th	5th	Pole
1	Australia	M. Hakkinen	D. Coulthard	H. Frentzen	E. Irvine	J. Villeneuve	M. Hakkinen
2	Brazil	M. Hakkinen	D. Coulthard	M. Schumacher	A. Wurz	H. Frentzen	M. Hakkinen
3	Argentina	M. Schumacher	M. Hakkinen	E. Irvine	A. Wurz	J. Alesi	D. Coulthard
4	San Marino	D. Coulthard	M. Schumacher	E. Irvine	J. Villeneuve	H. Frentzen	D. Coulthard
5	Spain	M. Hakkinen	D. Coulthard	M. Schumacher	A. Wurz	R. Barrichello	M. Hakkinen
6	Monaco	M. Hakkinen	G. Fisichella	E. Irvine	M. Salo	J. Villeneuve	M. Hakkinen
7	Canada	M. Schumacher	G. Fisichella	E. Irvine	A. Wurz	R. Barrichello	D. Coulthard
8	France	M. Schumacher	E. Irvine	M. Hakkinen	J. Villeneuve	A. Wurz	M. Hakkinen
9	Britain	M. Schumacher	M. Hakkinen	E. Irvine	A. Wurz	G. Fisichella	M. Hakkinen
10	Austria	M. Hakkinen	D. Coulthard	M. Schumacher	E. Irvine	R. Schumacher	G. Fisichella
11	Germany	M. Hakkinen	D. Coulthard	J. Villeneuve	D. Hill	M. Schumacher	M. Hakkinen
12	Hungary	M. Hakkinen	D. Coulthard	J. Villeneuve	D. Hill	H. Frentzen	M. Hakkinen
13	Belgium	D. Hill	R. Schumacher	J. Alesi	H. Frentzen	P. Diniz	M. Hakkinen
14	Italy	M. Schumacher	E. Irvine	R. Schumacher	M. Hakkinen	J. Alesi	M. Schumacher
15	Luxembourg	M. Hakkinen	M. Schumacher	D. Coulthard	E. Irvine	H. Frentzen	M. Schumacher

Major 1998 Endurance Races

24 Hours of Daytona

Jan. 31-Feb. 1, at Daytona Beach, Fla.

Officially the Rolex 24 at Daytona and first held in 1962 (as a 3-hour race). An IMSA Camel GT race for exotic prototype sports cars and contested over a 3.56-mile road course at Daytona International Speedway. Listed are qualifying position, drivers, chassis, class and laps completed.

1 (2) Mauro Baldi, Arie Luyendyk, Gianpiero Moretti and Didier Theys; FERRARI 333 SP; Can-Am; 711 laps (2531.2 miles) at 105.40 mph; 5.287 second margin of victory.

2 (9) Uwe Alzen, Allan McNish, Dirk Mueller, Jorg Mueller and Danny Sullivan; PORSCHE 911; GT1; 703 laps.

3 (16) Andre Ahrle, Christophe Bouchut, Patrice Goueslard and Carl Rosenblad; PORSCHE 911; GT1; 667 laps.

4 (30) Peter Kitchak, Franz Konrad, Toni Seiler, Wido Roessler and Angelo Zadra; PORSCHE 911; GT2; 660 laps.

5 (37) John Graham, Duncan Huisman, Patrick Huisman and John Morton; PORSCHE 911; GT2; 659 laps.

Fastest lap: Max Papis (lap #518), FERRARI 333 SP; Can-Am; 127.465 mph. **Top qualifier:** Yannick Dalmas, 129.20 mph (1:39.195).

Weather: Sunny and hot. **Attendance:** 50,000 (est.).

24 Hours of Le Mans

June 6-7, at Le Mans, France

Officially the Le Mans Grand Prix d'Endurance and first held in 1923. Contested over the 8.451-mile Circuit de la Sarthe in Le Mans, France. Listed are qualifying position, drivers, car, and laps completed.

1 (5) Laurent Aiello, Allan McNish and Stephane Ortelli; PORSCHE GT1-98; 351 laps (2966.301 miles) at 123.856 mph

2 (4) Uwe Alzen, Jorg Muller and Bob Wollek; PORSCHE GT1-98; 350 laps.

3 (14) Kazuyoshi Hoshino, Takuya Kurosaka and Aguri Suzuki; NISSAN R390; 347 laps.

4 (24) Bill Auberlen, Steve O'Rourke and Tim Sugden; McLAREN BMW F1 GTR; 343 laps.

5 (10) Michael Krumm, Franck Lagorce and John Nielsen; NISSAN R390; 342 laps.

Fastest lap: Aiello/McNish/Ortelli; 137.207 mph. **Top qualifier:** Bernd Schneider, MERCEDES CLK-LM, 141.110 mph (3:35.544).

Weather: Mostly dry, some rain. **Attendance:** 200,000 (est.).

NHRA RESULTS

National Hot Rod Association Drag Racing champions in the Top Fuel, Funny Car and Pro Stock divisions from Feb. 1 through Oct. 11, 1998. All times are based on two cars racing head-to-head from a standing start over a straight line, quarter-mile course. Differences in reaction time account for apparently faster losing times. See updates for later results.

1998 Season

Date	Event	Event	Winner	Time	MPH	2nd Place	Time	MPH
Feb. 1	Winternationals	Top Fuel	Larry Dixon Jr.	4.752	251.18	J. Head	4.739	261.93
		Funny Car	Ron Capps	6.603	211.71	T. Wilkerson	(broke)	—
		Pro Stock	Jim Yates	6.968	197.49	J. Coughlin Jr.	6.989	198.32
Feb. 22	ATSCO Nationals	Top Fuel	Cory McClenathan	4.627	319.71	J. Head	4.656	311.52
		Funny Car	Chuck Etchells	4.944	312.82	R. Capps	8.630	92.40
		Pro Stock	Warren Johnson	6.974	197.49	J. Yates	7.020	196.80
Mar. 8	Gatornationals	Top Fuel	Kenny Bernstein	4.604	318.47	L. Dixon Jr.	4.734	288.73
		Funny Car	Cruz Pedregon	5.747	277.77	J. Force	6.416	217.81
		Pro Stock	Warren Johnson	6.873	200.66	J. Yates	6.935	198.10
Mar. 22	Pennzoil Nationals (TX)	Top Fuel	Cory McClenathan	4.559	320.74	D. Grubnic	4.743	261.24
		Funny Car	Tony Pedregon	4.847	316.67	J. Force	4.887	310.88
		Pro Stock	Warren Johnson	6.878	201.02	M. Thomas	6.926	198.01
Apr. 19	Fram Nationals	Top Fuel	Cory McClenathan	4.756	306.12	P. Dakin	5.944	147.13
		Funny Car	Cruz Pedregon	5.049	303.74	J. Force	5.109	284.27
		Pro Stock	Mark Osborne	6.996	198.10	B. Allen	7.015	197.02
Apr. 26	Pennzoil Nationals (VA)	Top Fuel	Cory McClenathan	4.723	302.01	J. Amato	11.589	82.39
		Funny Car	Chuck Etchells	6.019	238.79	T. Wilkerson	6.381	212.06
		Pro Stock	Warren Johnson	6.952	198.50	T. Martino	8.842	108.45
May 3	Lone Star Nationals	Top Fuel	Joe Amato	4.695	313.58	D. Kalitta	4.686	312.82
		Funny Car	Ron Capps	4.960	292.39	J. Force	6.463	146.93
		Pro Stock	Mike Edwards	7.024	195.56	K. Johnson	7.018	196.89
May 17	Mopar Nationals	Top Fuel	Joe Amato	4.614	319.90	C. McClenathan	4.660	314.39
		Funny Car	John Force	4.845	323.89	J. Elper	11.760	77.33
		Pro Stock	Jeg Coughlin Jr.	6.932	198.52	M. Edwards	8.280	115.04
May 31	Fram Rte. 66 Nationals	Top Fuel	Kenny Bernstein	5.586	265.43	G. Scelzi	(broke)	—
		Funny Car	Whit Bazemore	5.001	297.42	D. Warsham	7.683	113.47
		Pro Stock	Mike Thomas	7.075	196.39	W. Johnson	7.075	194.80
June 14	Pontiac Nationals	Top Fuel	Kenny Bernstein	4.687	310.66	B. Vandergriff	4.702	297.81
		Funny Car	Frank Pedregon	5.262	285.53	D. Skuza	8.697	96.19
		Pro Stock	Jeg Coughlin Jr.	7.022	193.03	J. Yates	7.066	195.14
June 28	Sears Craftsman Nat'ls.	Top Fuel	Gary Scelzi	4.711	300.60	K. Bernstein	4.858	288.73
		Funny Car	Frank Pedregon	5.295	232.07	C. Etchells	5.354	259.06
		Pro Stock	Kurt Johnson	7.056	195.31	J. Coughlin Jr.	7.169	194.25
July 19	Mile-High Nationals	Top Fuel	Cory McClenathan	4.926	297.52	J. Amato	5.242	270.92
		Funny Car	Tony Pedregon	5.417	282.30	R. Capps	5.399	279.93
		Pro Stock	Jeg Coughlin Jr.	7.468	184.31	W. Johnson	7.476	186.10
July 26	Autolite Nationals	Top Fuel	Doug Kalitta	4.802	306.43	B. Sarver	4.783	302.40
		Funny Car	Cruz Pedregon	5.073	300.80	W. Bazemore	5.268	289.38
		Pro Stock	Warren Johnson	7.135	196.24	V. Gaines	7.106	195.31
Aug. 2	Northwest Nationals	Top Fuel	Joe Amato	4.857	294.88	C. McClenathan	4.895	299.70
		Funny Car	Ron Capps	5.136	288.27	J. Force	5.253	274.72
		Pro Stock	Warren Johnson	6.967	198.45	K. Johnson	6.990	198.06
Aug. 23	Visionaire Northstar Nat'ls.	Top Fuel	Gary Scelzi	4.829	303.23	M. Dunn	5.273	259.96
		Funny Car	Ron Capps	5.098	291.16	D. Skuza	7.848	112.57
		Pro Stock	Tom Martino	7.165	191.81	M. Osborne	7.115	194.36
Sept. 7	U.S. Nationals	Top Fuel	Gary Scelzi	5.961	282.57	M. Dunn	8.456	100.21
		Funny Car	John Force	4.992	306.43	R. Anderson	5.041	290.13
		Pro Stock	Mike Edwards	7.034	194.46	W. Johnson	7.045	196.46
Sept. 20	Pioneer Nationals	Top Fuel	Gary Scelzi	4.637	305.37	M. Dunn	6.534	117.70
		Funny Car	Dean Skuza	5.039	288.55	J. Force	5.112	282.57
		Pro Stock	Kurt Johnson	6.984	196.63	M. Edwards	7.034	195.86
Oct. 11	Pennzoil Nationals (TN)	Top Fuel	Joe Amato	4.648	318.92	K. Bernstein	4.696	315.12
		Funny Car	Al Hofmann	5.172	280.43	C. Pedregon	16.584	64.88
		Pro Stock	Warren Johnson	6.901	199.20	K. Johnson	6.964	198.50

Winston Point Standings

First place finishers in parentheses.

1998 SEASON (through Oct. 11)

Top Fuel

		Pts
1	Gary Scelzi (4)	1369
2	Cory McClenathan (5)	1325
3	Joe Amato (4)	1321
4	Mike Dunn (0)	1113
5	Kenny Bernstein (3)	1089

Funny Car

		Pts
1	John Force (2)	1342
2	Ron Capps (4)	1232
3	Chuck Etchells (2)	1150
4	Cruz Pedregon (3)	1134
5	Tony Pedregon (2)	1058

Pro Stock

		Pts
1	Warren Johnson (7)	1587
2	Kurt Johnson (2)	1214
3	Jeg Coughlin Jr. (3)	1157
4	Jim Yates (1)	1090
5	Mark Osborne (1)	904

THROUGH THE YEARS

1911-1998

MAJOR RACES • LEADERS

NASCAR Circuit

The Crown Jewels

The four biggest races on the NASCAR circuit are the Daytona 500, the Winston 500, the Coca-Cola 600 and the Pepsi Southern 500. The Winston Cup Media Guide lists them as the richest (Daytona), the fastest (Winston), the longest (Coca-Cola) and the oldest (Southern). The only drivers to win three of the races in a single year are Lee Roy Yarbrough (1969), David Pearson (1976), Bill Elliott (1985) and Jeff Gordon (1997).

Daytona 500

Held early in the NASCAR season; 200 laps around a 2.5-mile high-banked oval at Daytona International Speedway in Daytona Beach, FL. First race in 1959, although stock car racing at Daytona dates back to 1936. Winning drivers who started from pole positions are in **bold** type.

Multiple winners: Richard Petty (7); Cale Yarborough (4); Bobby Allison (3); Bill Elliott, Dale Jarrett and Sterling Marlin (2). **Multiple poles:** Buddy Baker and Cale Yarborough (4); Bill Elliott, Fireball Roberts and Ken Schrader (3); Donnie Allison (2).

Year	Winner	Car	Owner	MPH	Pole Sitter	MPH
1959	Lee Petty	Oldsmobile	Petty Enterprises	135.521	Bob Welborn	140.121
1960	Junior Johnson	Chevrolet	Ray Fox	124.740	Cotton Owens	149.892
1961	Marvin Panch	Pontiac	Smokey Yunick	149.601	Fireball Roberts	155.709
1962	**Fireball Roberts**	Pontiac	Smokey Yunick	152.529	Fireball Roberts	156.999
1963	Tiny Lund	Ford	Wood Brothers	151.566	Fireball Roberts	160.943
1964	Richard Petty	Plymouth	Petty Enterprises	154.334	Paul Goldsmith	174.910
1965-**a**	Fred Lorenzen	Ford	Holman-Moody	141.539	Darel Dieringer	171.151
1966-**b**	**Richard Petty**	Plymouth	Petty Enterprises	160.627	Richard Petty	175.165
1967	Mario Andretti	Ford	Holman-Moody	149.926	Curtis Turner	180.831
1968	**Cale Yarborough**	Mercury	Wood Brothers	143.251	Cale Yarborough	189.222
1969	Lee Roy Yarbrough	Ford	Junior Johnson	157.950	Buddy Baker	188.901
1970	Pete Hamilton	Plymouth	Petty Enterprises	149.601	Cale Yarborough	194.015
1971	Richard Petty	Plymouth	Petty Enterprises	144.462	A.J. Foyt	182.744
1972	A.J. Foyt	Mercury	Wood Brothers	161.550	Bobby Isaac	186.632
1973	Richard Petty	Dodge	Petty Enterprises	157.205	Buddy Baker	185.662
1974-**c**	Richard Petty	Dodge	Petty Enterprises	140.894	David Pearson	185.017
1975	Benny Parsons	Chevrolet	L.G. DeWitt	153.649	Donnie Allison	185.827
1976	David Pearson	Mercury	Wood Brothers	152.181	Ramo Stott	183.456
1977	Cale Yarborough	Chevrolet	Junior Johnson	153.218	Donnie Allison	188.048
1978	Bobby Allison	Ford	Bud Moore	159.730	Cale Yarborough	187.536
1979	Richard Petty	Oldsmobile	Petty Enterprises	143.977	Buddy Baker	196.049
1980	**Buddy Baker**	Oldsmobile	Ranier Racing	177.602*	Buddy Baker	194.099
1981	Richard Petty	Buick	Petty Enterprises	169.651	Bobby Allison	194.624
1982	Bobby Allison	Buick	DiGard Racing	153.991	Benny Parsons	196.317
1983	Cale Yarborough	Pontiac	Ranier Racing	155.979	Ricky Rudd	198.864
1984	**Cale Yarborough**	Chevrolet	Ranier Racing	150.994	Cale Yarborough	201.848
1985	**Bill Elliott**	Ford	Melling Racing	172.265	Bill Elliott	205.114
1986	Geoff Bodine	Chevrolet	Hendrick Motorsports	148.124	Bill Elliott	205.039
1987	**Bill Elliott**	Ford	Melling Racing	176.263	Bill Elliott	210.364†
1988	Bobby Allison	Buick	Stavola Brothers	137.531	Ken Schrader	198.823
1989	Darrell Waltrip	Chevrolet	Hendrick Motorsports	148.466	Ken Schrader	196.996
1990	Derrike Cope	Chevrolet	Bob Whitcomb	165.761	Ken Schrader	196.515
1991	Ernie Irvan	Chevrolet	Morgan-McClure	148.148	Davey Allison	195.955
1992	Davey Allison	Ford	Robert Yates	160.256	Sterling Martin	192.213
1993	Dale Jarrett	Chevrolet	Joe Gibbs Racing	154.972	Kyle Petty	189.426
1994	Sterling Marlin	Chevrolet	Morgan-McClure	156.931	Loy Allen	190.158
1995	Sterling Marlin	Chevrolet	Morgan-McClure	141.710	Dale Jarrett	193.498
1996	Dale Jarrett	Ford	Robert Yates	154.308	Dale Earnhardt	189.510
1997	Jeff Gordon	Chevrolet	Rick Hendrick	148.295	Mike Skinner	189.813
1998	Dale Earnhardt	Chevrolet	Richard Childress	172.712	Bobby Labonte	192.415

*Track and race record for Winning Speed. †Track and race record for Qualifying Speed.

Notes: a–rain shortened 1965 to 332+ miles; **b**–rain shortened 1966 race to 495 miles; **c**–in 1974, race shortened 50 miles due to energy crisis. **Also:** Pole sitters determined by pole qualifying race (1959-65); by two-lap average (1966-68); by fastest single lap (since 1969).

Winston 500

Held at Talladega (Ala.) Superspeedway. **Multiple winners:** Bobby Allison, Davey Allison, Buddy Baker and David Pearson (3); Dale Earnhardt, Mark Martin Darrell Waltrip and Cale Yarborough (2).

Year		Year		Year		Year	
1970	Pete Hamilton	1978	Cale Yarborough	1986	Bobby Allison	1994	Dale Earnhardt
1971	Donnie Allison	1979	Bobby Allison	1987	Davey Allison	1995	Mark Martin
1972	David Pearson	1980	Buddy Baker	1988	Phil Parsons	1996	Sterling Marlin
1973	David Pearson	1981	Bobby Allison	1989	Davey Allison	1997	Mark Martin
1974	David Pearson	1982	Darrell Waltrip	1990	Dale Earnhardt	1998	Dale Jarrett
1975	Buddy Baker	1983	Richard Petty	1991	Harry Gant		
1976	Buddy Baker	1984	Cale Yarborough	1992	Davey Allison		
1977	Darrell Waltrip	1985	Bill Elliott	1993	Ernie Irvan		

Coca-Cola 600

Held at Charlotte (N.C.) Motor Speedway. **Multiple winners:** Darrell Waltrip (5); Bobby Allison, Buddy Baker, Dale Earnhardt, Jeff Gordon and David Pearson (3); Neil Bonnett, Fred Lorenzen, Jim Paschal and Richard Petty (2).

Year		Year		Year		Year	
1960	Joe Lee Johnson	1970	Donnie Allison	1980	Benny Parsons	1990	Rusty Wallace
1961	David Pearson	1971	Bobby Allison	1981	Bobby Allison	1991	Davey Allison
1962	Nelson Stacy	1972	Buddy Baker	1982	Neil Bonnett	1992	Dale Earnhardt
1963	Fred Lorenzen	1973	Buddy Baker	1983	Neil Bonnett	1993	Dale Earnhardt
1964	Jim Paschal	1974	David Pearson	1984	Bobby Allison	1994	Jeff Gordon
1965	Fred Lorenzen	1975	Richard Petty	1985	Darrell Waltrip	1995	Bobby Labonte
1966	Marvin Panch	1976	David Pearson	1986	Dale Earnhardt	1996	Dale Jarrett
1967	Jim Paschal	1977	Richard Petty	1987	Kyle Petty	1997	Jeff Gordon
1968	Buddy Baker	1978	Darrell Waltrip	1988	Darrell Waltrip	1998	Jeff Gordon
1969	Lee Roy Yarbrough	1979	Darrell Waltrip	1989	Darrell Waltrip		

Southern 500

Held at Darlington (S.C.) International Raceway. **Multiple winners:** Cale Yarborough (5); Bobby Allison and Jeff Gordon (4); Buck Baker, Dale Earnhardt, Bill Elliott, David Pearson and Herb Thomas (3); Harry Gant and Fireball Roberts (2).

Year		Year		Year		Year	
1950	Johnny Mantz	1963	Fireball Roberts	1976	David Pearson	1989	Dale Earnhardt
1951	Herb Thomas	1964	Buck Baker	1977	David Pearson	1990	Dale Earnhardt
1952	Fonty Flock	1965	Ned Jarrett	1978	Cale Yarborough	1991	Harry Gant
1953	Buck Baker	1966	Darel Dieringer	1979	David Pearson	1992	Darrell Waltrip
1954	Herb Thomas	1967	Richard Petty	1980	Terry Labonte	1993	Mark Martin
1955	Herb Thomas	1968	Cale Yarborough	1981	Neil Bonnett	1994	Bill Elliott
1956	Curtis Turner	1969	Lee Roy Yarbrough	1982	Cale Yarborough	1995	Jeff Gordon
1957	Speedy Thompson	1970	Buddy Baker	1983	Bobby Allison	1996	Jeff Gordon
1958	Fireball Roberts	1971	Bobby Allison	1984	Harry Gant	1997	Jeff Gordon
1959	Jim Reed	1972	Bobby Allison	1985	Bill Elliott	1998	Jeff Gordon
1960	Buck Baker	1973	Cale Yarborough	1986	Tim Richmond		
1961	Nelson Stacy	1974	Cale Yarborough	1987	Dale Earnhardt		
1962	Larry Frank	1975	Bobby Allison	1988	Bill Elliott		

All-Time Leaders

NASCAR's all-time Top 20 drivers in victories, pole positions and earnings based on records through 1997. Drivers active in 1998 are in **bold** type.

Victories

1	Richard Petty	200
2	David Pearson	105
3	**Darrell Waltrip**	84
	Bobby Allison	84
5	Cale Yarborough	83
6	**Dale Earnhardt**	70
7	Lee Petty	55
8	Ned Jarrett	50
	Junior Johnson	50
10	Herb Thomas	48
11	**Rusty Wallace**	47
12	Buck Baker	46
13	**Bill Elliott**	40
	Tim Flock	40
15	Bobby Isaac	37
16	Fireball Roberts	32
17	**Jeff Gordon**	29
18	Rex White	26
	Fred Lorenzen	26
20	Jim Paschal	24
	Joe Weatherly	24

Pole Positions

1	Richard Petty	126
2	David Pearson	113
3	Cale Yarborough	70
4	**Darrell Waltrip**	59
5	Bobby Allison	57
6	Bobby Isaac	51
7	**Bill Elliott**	49
8	Junior Johnson	47
9	Buck Baker	44
10	Buddy Baker	40
11	Herb Thomas	39
	Tim Flock	39
13	**Geoff Bodine**	37
14	Ned Jarrett	35
	Rex White	35
	Mark Martin	35
	Fireball Roberts	35
18	Fonty Flock	34
19	Fred Lorenzen	33
20	**Terry Labonte**	25

Earnings

1	**Dale Earnhardt**	$30,386,380
2	**Bill Elliott**	17,864,812
3	**Terry Labonte**	16,755,547
4	**Jeff Gordon**	16,702,462
5	**Darrell Waltrip**	16,140,730
6	**Rusty Wallace**	16,125,660
7	**Mark Martin**	14,450,692
8	**Ricky Rudd**	13,502,320
9	**Geoff Bodine**	11,537,284
10	**Dale Jarrett**	11,293,362
11	**Sterling Marlin**	10,242,027
12	**Ken Schrader**	10,148,078
13	**Ernie Irvan**	8,951,590
14	**Kyle Petty**	8,861,054
15	Harry Gant	8,456,104
16	**Morgan Shepard**	8,064,248
17	Richard Petty	7,755,409
18	Bobby Allison	7,102,233
19	Davey Allison	6,726,974
20	**Michael Waltrip**	6,516,271

AP/Wide World Photos

Richard Petty, in his infamous No. 43 car, waves to the crowd (ignoring the "both hands on the wheel" rule) after passing David Pearson at the Michigan Speedway on August 24, 1975. It is the 173rd of Petty's 200 NASCAR wins.

Winston Cup Champions

Originally the Grand National Championship, 1949-70, and based on official NASCAR (National Association for Stock Car Auto Racing) records.

Multiple winners: Dale Earnhardt and Richard Petty (7); David Pearson, Lee Petty, Darrell Waltrip and Cale Yarborough (3); Buck Baker, Tim Flock, Jeff Gordon, Ned Jarrett, Herb Thomas and Joe Weatherly (2).

Year	
1949	Red Byron
1950	Bill Rexford
1951	Herb Thomas
1952	Tim Flock
1953	Herb Thomas
1954	Lee Petty
1955	Tim Flock
1956	Buck Baker
1957	Buck Baker
1958	Lee Petty
1959	Lee Petty
1960	Rex White
1961	Ned Jarrett
1962	Joe Weatherly
1963	Joe Weatherly
1964	Richard Petty
1965	Ned Jarrett
1966	David Pearson
1967	Richard Petty
1968	David Pearson
1969	David Pearson
1970	Bobby Isaac
1971	Richard Petty
1972	Richard Petty
1973	Benny Parsons
1974	Richard Petty
1975	Richard Petty
1976	Cale Yarborough
1977	Cale Yarborough
1978	Cale Yarborough
1979	Richard Petty
1980	Dale Earnhardt
1981	Darrell Waltrip
1982	Darrell Waltrip
1983	Bobby Allison
1984	Terry Labonte
1985	Darrell Waltrip
1986	Dale Earnhardt
1987	Dale Earnhardt
1988	Bill Elliott
1989	Rusty Wallace
1990	Dale Earnhardt
1991	Dale Earnhardt
1992	Alan Kulwicki
1993	Dale Earnhardt
1994	Dale Earnhardt
1995	Jeff Gordon
1996	Terry Labonte
1997	Jeff Gordon

NASCAR Rookie of the Year

Award presented to rookie driver who accumulates the most Winston Cup points based on his best 15 finishes.

Year	
1958	Shorty Rollins
1959	Richard Petty
1960	David Pearson
1961	Woodie Wilson
1962	Tom Cox
1963	Billy Wade
1964	Doug Cooper
1965	Sam McQuagg
1966	James Hylton
1967	Donnie Allison
1968	Pete Hamilton
1969	Dick Brooks
1970	Bill Dennis
1971	Walter Ballard
1972	Larry Smith
1973	Lennie Pond
1974	Earl Ross
1975	Bruce Hill
1976	Skip Manning
1977	Ricky Rudd
1978	Ronnie Thomas
1979	Dale Earnhardt
1980	Jody Ridley
1981	Ron Bouchard
1982	Geoff Bodine
1983	Sterling Marlin
1984	Rusty Wallace
1985	Ken Schrader
1986	Alan Kulwicki
1987	Davey Allison
1988	Ken Bouchard
1989	Dick Trickle
1990	Rob Moroso
1991	Bobby Hamilton
1992	Jimmy Hensley
1993	Jeff Gordon
1994	Jeff Burton
1995	Ricky Craven
1996	Johnny Benson
1997	Mike Skinner

CART Circuit

PPG Cup Champions

Officially the PPG Indy Car World Series Championship since 1979 and based on official AAA (American Automobile Assn., 1909-55), USAC (U.S. Auto Club, 1956-79), and CART (Championship Auto Racing Teams, 1979-91) records. CART was renamed IndyCar in 1992 and then lost use of the name in 1997.

Multiple titles: A.J. Foyt (7); Mario Andretti (4); Jimmy Bryan, Earl Cooper, Ted Horn, Rick Mears, Louie Meyer, Bobby Rahal, Al Unser (3); Tony Bettenhausen, Ralph DePalma, Peter DePaolo, Joe Leonard, Rex Mays, Tommy Milton, Jimmy Murphy, Wilbur Shaw, Tom Sneva, Al Unser Jr., Bobby Unser, Rodger Ward and Alex Zanardi (2).

AAA

Year		Year		Year		Year	
1909	George Robertson	1920	Tommy Milton	1931	Louis Schneider	1942-45	No racing
1910	Ray Harroun	1921	Tommy Milton	1932	Bob Carey	1946	Ted Horn
1911	Ralph Mulford	1922	Jimmy Murphy	1933	Louie Meyer	1947	Ted Horn
1912	Ralph DePalma	1923	Eddie Hearne	1934	Bill Cummings	1948	Ted Horn
1913	Earl Cooper	1924	Jimmy Murphy	1935	Kelly Petillo	1949	Johnnie Parsons
1914	Ralph DePalma	1925	Peter DePaolo	1936	Mauri Rose	1950	Henry Banks
1915	Earl Cooper	1926	Harry Hartz	1937	Wilbur Shaw	1951	Tony Bettenhausen
1916	Dario Resta	1927	Peter DePaolo	1938	Floyd Roberts	1952	Chuck Stevenson
1917	Earl Cooper	1928	Louie Meyer	1939	Wilbur Shaw	1953	Sam Hanks
1918	Ralph Mulford	1929	Louie Meyer	1940	Rex Mays	1954	Jimmy Bryan
1919	Howard Wilcox	1930	Billy Arnold	1941	Rex Mays	1955	Bob Sweikert

USAC

Year		Year		Year		Year	
1956	Jimmy Bryan	1962	Rodger Ward	1968	Bobby Unser	1974	Bobby Unser
1957	Jimmy Bryan	1963	A.J. Foyt	1969	Mario Andretti	1975	A.J. Foyt
1958	Tony Bettenhausen	1964	A.J. Foyt	1970	Al Unser	1976	Gordon Johncock
1959	Rodger Ward	1965	Mario Andretti	1971	Joe Leonard	1977	Tom Sneva
1960	A.J. Foyt	1966	Mario Andretti	1972	Joe Leonard	1978	A.J. Foyt
1961	A.J. Foyt	1967	A.J. Foyt	1973	Roger McCluskey		

CART

Year		Year		Year		Year	
1979	Rick Mears	1984	Mario Andretti	1989	Emerson Fittipaldi	1994	Al Unser Jr.
1980	Johnny Rutherford	1985	Al Unser	1990	Al Unser Jr.	1995	Jacques Villeneuve
1981	Rick Mears	1986	Bobby Rahal	1991	Michael Andretti	1996	Jimmy Vasser
1982	Rick Mears	1987	Bobby Rahal	1992	Bobby Rahal	1997	Alex Zanardi
1983	Al Unser	1988	Danny Sullivan	1993	Nigel Mansell	1998	Alex Zanardi

All-Time CART Leaders

CART's all-time Top 20 drivers in victories, pole positions and earnings, based on records through 1997. Drivers active in 1998 are in **bold** type. Totals include victories, poles and earnings before CART was established in 1979.

Victories

1	A.J. Foyt	67
2	Mario Andretti	52
3	Al Unser	39
4	**Michael Andretti**	36
5	Bobby Unser	35
6	**Al Unser Jr.**	31
7	Rick Mears	29
8	Johnny Rutherford	27
9	Roger Ward	26
10	Gordon Johncock	25
11	Ralph DePalma	24
	Bobby Rahal	24
13	Tommy Milton	23
14	Tony Bettenhausen	22
	Emerson Fittipaldi	22
16	Earl Cooper	20
17	Jimmy Bryan	19
	Jimmy Murphy	19
19	Ralph Mulford	17
	Danny Sullivan	17

Pole Positions

1	Mario Andretti	67
2	A.J. Foyt	53
3	Bobby Unser	49
4	Rick Mears	40
5	**Michael Andretti**	30
6	Al Unser	27
7	Johnny Rutherford	23
8	Gordon Johncock	20
9	Rex Mays	19
	Danny Sullivan	19
11	**Bobby Rahal**	18
12	Emerson Fittipaldi	17
13	Tony Bettenhausen	14
	Don Branson	14
	Tom Sneva	14
16	Parnelli Jones	12
17	Rodger Ward	11
	Danny Ongais	11
	Paul Tracy	11
20	Johnny Thomson	10
	Dan Gurney	10
	Teo Fabi	10
	Nigel Mansell	10
	Alex Zanardi	10

Earnings

1	**Al Unser Jr.**	$18,342,156
2	**Bobby Rahal**	15,900,258
3	**Michael Andretti**	14,704,619
4	Emerson Fittipaldi	14,293,625
5	Mario Andretti	11,552,154
6	Rick Mears	11,050,807
7	Danny Sullivan	8,844,129
8	Arie Luyendyk*	7,732,188
9	**Raul Boesel**	6,971,887
10	Al Unser	6,740,843
11	**Jimmy Vasser**	6,554,994
12	**Paul Tracy**	5,968,020
13	A.J. Foyt	5,357,589
14	Teo Fabi	5,045,881
15	Scott Brayton	4,807,274
16	**Scott Pruett**	4,611,644
17	Scott Goodyear*	4,579,451
18	Roberto Guerrero*	4,275,163
19	Johnny Rutherford	4,209,232
20	Jacques Villeneuve†	4,097,732

*drivers active, but in IRL not CART.
†driver active, but in F-1 not CART.

CART Rookie of the Year

Award presented to rookie who accumulates the most PPG Cup points among first year drivers. Originally the CART Rookie of the Year; CART was renamed IndyCar in 1992 and then lost use of the name in 1997.

Year		Year		Year		Year	
1979	Bill Alsup	1984	Roberto Guerrero	1989	Bernard Jourdain	1994	Jacques Villeneuve
1980	Dennis Firestone	1985	Arie Luyendyk	1990	Eddie Cheever	1995	Gil de Ferran
1981	Bob Lazier	1986	Dominic Dobson	1991	Jeff Andretti	1996	Alex Zanardi
1982	Bobby Rahal	1987	Fabrizio Barbazza	1992	Stefan Johansson	1997	Patrick Carpentier
1983	Teo Fabi	1988	John Jones	1993	Nigel Mansell		

Indy Racing League Circuit

Indianapolis 500

Held every Memorial Day weekend; 200 laps around a 2.5-mile oval at Indianapolis Motor Speedway. First race was held in 1911. The Indy Racing League began in 1996 and made the Indianapolis 500 its cornerstone event. Winning drivers are listed with starting positions. Winners who started from pole position are in **bold** type.

Multiple wins: A.J. Foyt, Rick Mears and Al Unser (4); Louis Meyer, Mauri Rose, Johnny Rutherford, Wilbur Shaw and Bobby Unser (3); Emerson Fittipaldi, Gordon Johncock, Arie Luyendyk, Tommy Milton, Al Unser Jr., Bill Vukovich and Rodger Ward (2).

Multiple poles: Rick Mears (6); Mario Andretti and A.J. Foyt (4); Rex Mays, Duke Nalon and Tom Sneva (3); Billy Arnold, Bill Cummings, Ralph DePalma, Leon Duray, Walt Faulkner, Parnelli Jones, Jack McGrath, Jimmy Murphy, Johnny Rutherford, Eddie Sachs and Jimmy Snyder (2).

Year	Winner (Pos.)	Car	MPH	Pole Sitter	MPH
1911	Ray Harroun (28)	Marmon Wasp	74.602	Lewis Strang	–
1912	Joe Dawson (7)	National	78.719	Gil Anderson	–
1913	Jules Goux (7)	Peugeot	75.933	Caleb Bragg	–
1914	Rene Thomas (15)	Delage	82.474	Jean Chassagne	–
1915	Ralph DePalma (2)	Mercedes	89.840	Howard Wilcox	98.90
1916-**a**	Dario Resta (4)	Peugeot	84.001	John Aitken	96.69
1917-18	Not held	World War I			
1919	Howdy Wilcox (2)	Peugeot	88.050	Rene Thomas	104.78
1920	Gaston Chevrolet (6)	Monroe	88.618	Ralph DePalma	99.15
1921	Tommy Milton (20)	Frontenac	89.621	Ralph DePalma	100.75
1922	**Jimmy Murphy** (1)	Murphy Special	94.484	Jimmy Murphy	100.50
1923	**Tommy Milton** (1)	H.C.S. Special	90.954	Tommy Milton	108.17
1924	L.L. Corum & Joe Boyer (21)	Duesenberg Special	98.234	Jimmy Murphy	108.037
1925	Peter DePaolo (2)	Duesenberg Special	101.127	Leon Duray	113.196
1926-**b**	Frank Lockhart (20)	Miller Special	95.904	Earl Cooper	111.735
1927	George Souders (22)	Duesenberg	97.545	Frank Lockhart	120.100
1928	Louie Meyer (13)	Miller Special	99.482	Leon Duray	122.391
1929	Ray Keech (6)	Simplex Piston Ring Special	97.585	Cliff Woodbury	120.599
1930	**Billy Arnold** (1)	Miller-Hartz Special	100.448	Billy Arnold	113.268
1931	Louis Schneider (13)	Bowes Seal Fast Special	96.629	Russ Snowberger	112.796
1932	Fred Frame (27)	Miller-Hartz Special	104.144	Lou Moore	117.363
1933	Louie Meyer (6)	Tydol Special	104.162	Bill Cummings	118.530
1934	Bill Cummings (10)	Boyle Products Special	104.863	Kelly Petillo	119.329
1935	Kelly Petillo (22)	Gilmore Speedway Special	106.240	Rex Mays	120.736
1936	Louie Meyer (28)	Ring Free Special	109.069	Rex Mays	119.644
1937	Wilbur Shaw (2)	Shaw-Gilmore Special	113.580	Bill Cummings	123.343
1938	**Floyd Roberts** (1)	Burd Piston Ring Special	117.200	Floyd Roberts	125.681
1939	Wilbur Shaw (3)	Boyle Special	115.035	Jimmy Snyder	130.138
1940	Wilbur Shaw (2)	Boyle Special	114.277	Rex Mays	127.850
1941	Floyd Davis & Mauri Rose (17)	Noc-Out Hose Clamp Special	115.117	Mauri Rose	128.691
1942-45	Not held	World War II			
1946	George Robson (15)	Thorne Engineering Special	114.820	Cliff Bergere	126.471
1947	Mauri Rose (3)	Blue Crown Spark Plug Special	116.338	Ted Horn	126.564
1948	Mauri Rose (3)	Blue Crown Spark Plug Special	119.814	Duke Nalon	131.603
1949	Bill Holland (4)	Blue Crown Spark Plug Special	121.327	Duke Nalon	132.939
1950-**c**	Johnnie Parsons (5)	Wynn's Friction Proofing	124.002	Walt Faulkner	134.343
1951	Lee Wallard (2)	Belanger Special	126.244	Duke Nalon	136.498
1952	Troy Ruttman (7)	Agajanian Special	128.922	Fred Agabashian	138.010
1953	**Bill Vukovich** (1)	Fuel Injection Special	128.740	Bill Vukovich	138.392
1954	Bill Vukovich (19)	Fuel Injection Special	130.840	Jack McGrath	141.033
1955	Bob Sweikert (14)	John Zink Special	128.213	Jerry Hoyt	140.045
1956	**Pat Flaherty** (1)	John Zink Special	128.490	Pat Flaherty	145.596
1957	Sam Hanks (13)	Belond Exhaust Special	135.601	Pat O'Connor	143.948
1958	Jimmy Bryan (7)	Belond AP Parts Special	133.791	Dick Rathmann	145.974
1959	Rodger Ward (6)	Leader Card 500 Roadster	135.857	Johnny Thomson	145.908

Year	Winner (Pos.)	Car	MPH	Pole Sitter	MPH
1960	Jim Rathmann (2)	Ken-Paul Special	138.767	Eddie Sachs	146.592
1961	A.J. Foyt (7)	Bowes Seal Fast Special	139.130	Eddie Sachs	147.481
1962	Rodger Ward (2)	Leader Card 500 Roadster	140.293	Parnelli Jones	150.370
1963	**Parnelli Jones** (1)	Agajanian-Willard Special	143.137	Parnelli Jones	151.153
1964	A.J. Foyt (5)	Sheraton-Thompson Special	147.350	Jim Clark	158.828
1965	Jim Clark (2)	Lotus Ford	150.686	A.J. Foyt	161.233
1966	Graham Hill (15)	American Red Ball Special	144.317	Mario Andretti	165.899
1967-**d**	A.J. Foyt (4)	Sheraton-Thompson Special	151.207	Mario Andretti	168.982
1968	Bobby Unser (3)	Rislone Special	152.882	Joe Leonard	171.559
1969	Mario Andretti (2)	STP Oil Treatment Special	156.867	A.J. Foyt	170.568
1970	**Al Unser** (1)	Johnny Lightning Special	155.749	Al Unser	170.221
1971	Al Unser (5)	Johnny Lightning Special	157.735	Peter Revson	178.696
1972	Mark Donohue (3)	Sunoco McLaren	162.962	Bobby Unser	195.940
1973-**e**	Gordon Johncock (11)	STP Double Oil Filters	159.036	Johnny Rutherford	198.413
1974	Johnny Rutherford (25)	McLaren	158.589	A.J. Foyt	191.632
1975-**f**	Bobby Unser (3)	Jorgensen Eagle	149.213	A.J. Foyt	193.976
1976-**g**	**Johnny Rutherford** (1)	Hy-Gain McLaren/Goodyear	148.725	Johnny Rutherford	188.957
1977	A.J. Foyt (4)	Gilmore Racing Team	161.331	Tom Sneva	198.884
1978	Al Unser (5)	FNCTC Chaparral Lola	161.363	Tom Sneva	202.156
1979	**Rick Mears** (1)	The Gould Charge	158.899	Rick Mears	193.736
1980	**Johnny Rutherford** (1)	Pennzoil Chaparral	142.862	Johnny Rutherford	192.256
1981-**h**	**Bobby Unser** (1)	Norton Spirit Penske PC-9B	139.084	Bobby Unser	200.546
1982	Gordon Johncock (5)	STP Oil Treatment	162.029	Rick Mears	207.004
1983	Tom Sneva (4)	Texaco Star	162.117	Teo Fabi	207.395
1984	Rick Mears (3)	Pennzoil Z-7	163.612	Tom Sneva	210.029
1985	Danny Sullivan (8)	Miller American Special	152.982	Pancho Carter	212.583
1986	Bobby Rahal (4)	Budweiser/Truesports/March	170.722	Rick Mears	216.828
1987	Al Unser (20)	Cummins Holset Turbo	162.175	Mario Andretti	215.390
1988	**Rick Mears** (1)	Pennzoil Z-7/Penske Chevy V-8	144.809	Rick Mears	219.198
1989	Emerson Fittipaldi (3)	Marlboro/Penske Chevy V-8	167.581	Rick Mears	223.885
1990	Arie Luyendyk (3)	Domino's Pizza Chevrolet	185.981*	Emerson Fittipaldi	225.301
1991	**Rick Mears** (1)	Marlboro Penske Chevy	176.457	Rick Mears	224.113
1992	Al Unser Jr. (12)	Valvoline Galmer '92	134.477	Roberto Guerrero	232.482
1993	Emerson Fittipaldi (9)	Marlboro Penske Chevy	157.207	Arie Luyendyk	223.967
1994	**Al Unser Jr.** (1)	Marlboro Penske Mercedes	160.872	Al Unser Jr.	228.011
1995	Jacques Villeneuve (5)	Player's Ltd. Reynard Ford	153.616	Scott Brayton	231.604
1996	Buddy Lazier (5)	Reynard Ford	147.956	Tony Stewart	233.100&
1997	**Arie Luyendyk** (1)	G-Force Olds Aurora	145.827	Arie Luyendyk	218.263
1998	Eddie Cheever Jr. (17)	Dallara Olds Aurora	145.155	Billy Boat	223.503

*Track record for Winning Time.

& Scott Brayton won the pole position with an avg. mph of 233.718 but was killed in a practice run. Stewart was given pole position with the next fastest speed.

Notes: a–1916 race scheduled for 300 miles; **b**–rain shortened 1926 race to 400 miles; **c**–rain shortened 1950 race to 345 miles; **d**–1967 race postponed due to rain after 18 laps (May 30), resumed next day (May 31); **e**–rain shortened 1973 race to 332.5 miles; **f**–rain shortened 1975 race to 435 miles; **g**–rain shortened 1976 race to 255 miles; **h**–in 1981, runner-up Mario Andretti was awarded 1st place when winner Bobby Unser was penalized a lap after the race was completed for passing cars illegally under the caution flag. Unser and car-owner Roger Penske appealed the race stewards' decision to the U.S. Auto Club. Four months later, USAC overturned the ruling, saying that the penalty was too harsh and Unser should be fined $40,000 rather than stripped of his championship.

Indy 500 Rookie of the Year

Voted on by a panel of auto racing media. Award does not necessarily go to highest-finishing first-year driver. Graham Hill won the race on his first try in 1966, but the rookie award went to Jackie Stewart, who led with 10 laps to go only to lose oil pressure and finish 6th.

Father and son winners: Mario and Michael Andretti (1965 and 1984); Bill and Billy Vukovich (1968 and 1988).

Year		Year		Year		Year	
1952	Art Cross	1964	Johnny White	1977	Jerry Sneva	1988	Billy Vukovich III
1953	Jimmy Daywalt	1965	Mario Andretti	1978	Rick Mears & Larry Rice	1989	Bernard Jourdain & Scott Pruett
1954	Larry Crockett	1966	Jackie Stewart	1979	Howdy Holmes	1990	Eddie Cheever
1955	Al Herman	1967	Denis Hulme	1980	Tim Richmond	1991	Jeff Andretti
1956	Bob Veith	1968	Bill Vukovich	1981	Josele Garza	1992	Lyn St. James
1957	Don Edmunds	1969	Mark Donohue	1982	Jim Hickman	1993	Nigel Mansell
1958	George Amick	1970	Donnie Allison	1983	Teo Fabi	1994	Jacques Villeneuve
1959	Bobby Grim	1971	Denny Zimmerman	1984	Michael Andretti & Roberto Guerrero	1995	Christian Fittipaldi
1960	Jim Hurtubise	1972	Mike Hiss	1985	Arie Luyendyk	1996	Tony Stewart
1961	Parnelli Jones & Bobby Marshman	1973	Graham McRae	1986	Randy Lanier	1997	Jeff Ward
1962	Jimmy McElreath	1974	Pancho Carter	1987	Fabrizio Barbazza	1998	Steve Knapp
1963	Jim Clark	1975	Bill Puterbaugh				
		1976	Vern Schuppan				

IRL Champions

Year		Year		Year	
1996	Buzz Calkins/ Scott Sharp	1997	Tony Stewart	1998	Kenny Brack

IRL Rookie of the Year

Officially the Sprint PCS Rookie of the Year. Award presented to rookie driver who accumulates the most points in the IRL standings.

Year		Year		Year	
1996	none	1997	Jim Guthrie	1998	Robby Unser

Formula One Circuit

United States Grand Prix

There have been 54 official Formula One races held in the United States since 1950, including the Indianapolis 500 from 1950-60. FISA sanctioned two annual U.S. Grand Prix–USA/East and USA/West–from 1976-80 and 1983. Phoenix was the site of the U.S. Grand Prix from 1989-91.

Indianapolis 500

Officially sanctioned as Grand Prix race from 1950-60 only. See IRL Circuit for details.

U.S. Grand Prix–East

Held from 1959-80 and 1981-88 at the following locations: Sebring, Fla. (1959); Riverside, Calif. (1960); Watkins Glen, N.Y. (1961-80); and Detroit (1982-88). There was no race in 1981. Race discontinued in 1989.

Multiple winners: Jim Clark, Graham Hill and Ayrton Senna (3); James Hunt, Carlos Reutemann and Jackie Stewart (2).

Year		Car
1959	Bruce McLaren, NZE	Cooper Climax
1960	Stirling Moss, GBR	Lotus Climax
1961	Innes Ireland, GBR	Lotus Climax
1962	Jim Clark, GBR	Lotus Climax
1963	Graham Hill, GBR	BRM
1964	Graham Hill, GBR	BRM
1965	Graham Hill, GBR	BRM
1966	Jim Clark, GBR	Lotus BRM
1967	Jim Clark, GBR	Lotus Ford
1968	Jackie Stewart, GBR	Matra Ford
1969	Jochen Rindt, AUT	Lotus Ford
1970	Emerson Fittipaldi, BRA	Lotus Ford
1971	Francois Cevert, FRA	Tyrrell Ford
1972	Jackie Stewart, GBR	Tyrrell Ford
1973	Ronnie Peterson, SWE	Lotus Ford
1974	Carlos Reutemann, ARG	Brabham Ford
1975	Niki Lauda, AUT	Ferrari
1976	James Hunt, GBR	McLaren Ford
1977	James Hunt, GBR	McLaren Ford
1978	Carlos Reutemann, ARG	Ferrari
1979	Gilles Villeneuve, CAN	Ferrari
1980	Alan Jones, AUS	Williams Ford
1981	Not held	
1982	John Watson, GBR	McLaren Ford
1983	Michele Alboreto, ITA	Tyrrell Ford
1984	Nelson Piquet, BRA	Brabham BMW Turbo
1985	Keke Rosberg, FIN	Williams Honda Turbo
1986	Ayrton Senna, BRA	Lotus Renault Turbo
1987	Ayrton Senna, BRA	Lotus Honda Turbo
1988	Ayrton Senna, BRA	McLaren Honda Turbo

U.S. Grand Prix–West

Held from 1976-83 at Long Beach, Calif. Races also held in Las Vegas (1981-82), Dallas (1984) and Phoenix (1989-91). Race discontinued in 1992.

Multiple winners: Alan Jones and Ayrton Senna (2).

Long Beach

Year		Car
1976	Clay Regazzoni, SWI	Ferrari
1977	Mario Andretti, USA	Lotus Ford
1978	Carlos Reutemann, ARG	Ferrari
1979	Gilles Villeneuve, CAN	Ferrari
1980	Nelson Piquet, BRA	Brabham Ford
1981	Alan Jones, AUS	Williams Ford
1982	Niki Lauda, AUT	McLaren Ford
1983	John Watson, GBR	McLaren Ford

Las Vegas

Year		Car
1981	Alan Jones, AUS	Williams Ford
1982	Michele Alboreto, ITA	Tyrrell Ford

Dallas

Year		Car
1984	Keke Rosberg, FIN	Williams Honda Turbo

Phoenix

Year		Car
1989	Alain Prost, FRA	McLaren Honda
1990	Ayrton Senna, BRA	McLaren Honda
1991	Ayrton Senna, BRA	McLaren Honda

All-Time Leaders

The all-time Top 20 Grand Prix winning drivers, based on records through 1997. Listed are starts (Sts), poles won (Pole), wins (1st), second place finishes (2nd), and third (3rd). Drivers active in 1998 and career victories in **bold** type.

		Sts	Pole	1st	2nd	3rd
1	Alain Prost	199	33	**51**	35	20
2	Ayrton Senna	161	65	**41**	23	16
3	Nigel Mansell	187	32	**31**	17	11
4	Jackie Stewart	99	17	**27**	11	5
	M. Schumacher	102	17	**27**	17	10
6	Jim Clark	72	33	**25**	1	6
	Niki Lauda	171	24	**25**	20	9
8	Juan-Manuel Fangio	51	28	**24**	10	1
9	Nelson Piquet	204	24	**23**	20	17
10	**Damon Hill**	84	20	**21**	15	5
11	Stirling Moss	66	16	**16**	5	3
12	Jack Brabham	126	13	**14**	10	7
	Emerson Fittipaldi	144	6	**14**	13	8
	Graham Hill	176	13	**14**	15	7
15	Alberto Ascari	32	14	**13**	4	0
16	Mario Andretti	128	18	**12**	2	5
	Alan Jones	116	6	**12**	7	5
	Carlos Reutemann	146	6	**12**	13	20

	Sts	Pole	1st	2nd	3rd
19 **Jacques Villeneuve**	32	13	**11**	5	3
20 James Hunt	92	14	**10**	6	7
Gerhard Berger	212	12	**10**	17	21
Ronnie Peterson	123	14	**10**	10	6
Jody Scheckter	112	3	**10**	14	9

Note: The following five drivers either died or were killed in their final year of competition—Clark in a Formula Two race in West Germany in 1968; Graham Hill in a plane crash in 1975; Ascari in a private practice run in 1955; Peterson following a crash in the 1978 Italian GP; and Senna following a crash in the 1994 San Marino GP.

World Champions

Officially called the World Championship of Drivers and based on Formula One (Grand Prix) records through the 1997 racing season.

Multiple winners: Juan-Manuel Fangio (5); Alain Prost (4); Jack Brabham, Niki Lauda, Nelson Piquet, Ayrton Senna and Jackie Stewart (3); Alberto Ascari, Jim Clark, Emerson Fittipaldi, Graham Hill and Michael Schumacher (2).

Year		Car
1950	Guiseppe Farina, ITA	Alfa Romeo
1951	Juan-Manuel Fangio, ARG	Alfa Romeo
1952	Alberto Ascari, ITA	Ferrari
1953	Alberto Ascari, ITA	Ferrari
1954	Juan-Manuel Fangio, ARG	Maserati/Mercedes
1955	Juan-Manuel Fangio, ARG	Mercedes
1956	Juan-Manuel Fangio, ARG	Ferrari
1957	Juan-Manuel Fangio, ARG	Maserati
1958	Mike Hawthorn, GBR	Ferrari
1959	Jack Brabham, AUS	Cooper Climax
1960	Jack Brabham, AUS	Cooper Climax
1961	Phil Hill, USA	Ferrari
1962	Graham Hill, GBR	BRM
1963	Jim Clark, GBR	Lotus Climax
1964	John Surtees, GBR	Ferrari
1965	Jim Clark, GBR	Lotus Climax
1966	Jack Brabham, AUS	Brabham Repco
1967	Denis Hulme, NZE	Brabham Repco
1968	Graham Hill, GBR	Lotus Ford
1969	Jackie Stewart,GBR	Matra Ford
1970	Jochen Rindt, AUT	Lotus Ford
1971	Jackie Stewart, GBR	Tyrrell Ford
1972	Emerson Fittipaldi, BRA	Lotus Ford
1973	Jackie Stewart, GBR	Tyrrell Ford
1974	Emerson Fittipaldi, BRA	McLaren Ford
1975	Niki Lauda, AUT	Ferrari
1976	James Hunt, GBR	McLaren Ford
1977	Niki Lauda, AUT	Ferrari
1978	Mario Andretti, USA	Lotus Ford
1979	Jody Scheckter, SAF	Ferrari
1980	Alan Jones, AUS	Williams Ford
1981	Nelson Piquet, BRA	Brabham Ford
1982	Keke Rosberg, FIN	Williams Ford
1983	Nelson Piquet, BRA	Brabham BMW Turbo
1984	Niki Lauda, AUT	McL. TAG Porsche Turbo
1985	Alain Prost, FRA	McL. TAG Porsche Turbo
1986	Alain Prost, FRA	McL. TAG Porsche Turbo
1987	Nelson Piquet, BRA	Williams Honda Turbo
1988	Ayrton Senna, BRA	McLaren Honda Turbo
1989	Alain Prost, FRA	McLaren Honda
1990	Ayrton Senna, BRA	McLaren Honda
1991	Ayrton Senna, BRA	McLaren Honda
1992	Nigel Mansell, GBR	Williams-Renault
1993	Alain Prost, FRA	Williams-Renault
1994	Michael Schumacher, GER	Benetton Ford
1995	Michael Schumacher, GER	Benetton Renault
1996	Damon Hill, GBR	Williams-Renault
1997	Jacques Villeneuve, CAN	Williams-Renault

ENDURANCE RACES

The 24 Hours of Le Mans

Officially, the Le Mans Grand Prix d'Endurance. First run May 22-23, 1923, and won by Andre Lagache and Rene Leonard in a 3-litre Chenard & Walcker. All subsequent races have been held in June, except in 1956 (July) and 1968 (September). Originally contested over a 10.73-mile track, the circuit was shortened to its present 8.451-mile distance in 1932. The original start of Le Mans, where drivers raced across the track to their unstarted cars, was discontinued in 1970.

Multiple winners: Jacky Ickx (6); Derek Bell (5); Oliver Gendebien and Henri Pescarolo (4); Woolf Barnato, Luigi Chinetti, Yannick Dalmas, Hurley Haywood, Phil Hill, Al Holbert and Klaus Ludwig (3); Sir Henry Birkin, Ivoe Bueb, Ron Flockhart, Jean-Pierre Jaussaud, Gerard Larrousse, Andre Rossignol, Raymond Sommer, Hans Stuck, Gijs van Lennep and Jean-Pierre Wimille (2).

Year	Drivers	Car	MPH
1923	Andre Lagache & Rene Leonard	Chenard & Walcker	57.21
1924	John Duff & Francis Clement	Bentley	53.78
1925	Gerard de Courcelles & Andre Rossignol	La Lorraine	57.84
1926	Robert Bloch & Andre Rossignol	La Lorraine	66.08
1927	J.D. Benjafield & Sammy Davis	Bentley	61.35
1928	Woolf Barnato & Bernard Rubin	Bentley	69.11
1929	Woolf Barnato & Sir Henry Birkin	Bentley Speed 6	73.63
1930	Woolf Barnato & Glen Kidston	Bentley Speed 6	75.88
1931	Earl Howe & Sir Henry Birkin	Alfa Romeo	78.13
1932	Raymond Sommer & Luigi Chinetti	Alfa Romeo	76.48
1933	Raymond Sommer & Tazio Nuvolari	Alfa Romeo	81.40
1934	Luigi Chinetti & Philippe Etancelin	Alfa Romeo	74.74
1935	John Hindmarsh & Louis Fontes	Lagonda	77.85
1936	Not held		
1937	Jean-Pierre Wimille & Robert Benoist	Bugatti 57G	85.13
1938	Eugene Chaboud & Jean Tremoulet	Delahaye	82.36
1939	Jean-Pierre Wimille & Pierre Veyron	Bugatti 57G	86.86
1940-48	Not held	World War II	
1949	Luigi Chinetti & Lord Selsdon	Ferrari	82.28

AP/Wide World Photos

The Porsche driven by Allan McNish, Laurent Aiello and Stephane Ortelli drives past the checkered flag to win the 66th 24 Hours of Le Mans on June 7, 1998.

Year	Drivers	Car	MPH
1950	Louis Rosier & Jean-Louis Rosier	Talbot-Lago	89.71
1951	Peter Walker & Peter Whitehead	Jaguar C	93.50
1952	Hermann Lang & Fritz Reiss	Mercedes-Benz	96.67
1953	Tony Rolt & Duncan Hamilton	Jaguar C	98.65
1954	Froilan Gonzalez & Maurice Trintignant	Ferrari 375	105.13
1955	Mike Hawthorn & Ivor Bueb	Jaguar D	107.05
1956	Ron Flockhart & Ninian Sanderson	Jaguar D	104.47
1957	Ron Flockhart & Ivor Bueb	Jaguar D	113.83
1958	Oliver Gendebien & Phil Hill	Ferrari 250	106.18
1959	Roy Salvadori & Carroll Shelby	Aston Martin	112.55
1960	Oliver Gendebien & Paul Frăre	Ferrari 250	109.17
1961	Oliver Gendebien & Phil Hill	Ferrari 250	115.88
1962	Oliver Gendebien & Phil Hill	Ferrari 250	115.22
1963	Lodovico Scarfiotti & Lorenzo Bandini	Ferrari 250	118.08
1964	Jean Guichel & Nino Vaccarella	Ferrari 275	121.54
1965	Masten Gregory & Jochen Rindt	Ferrari 250	121.07
1966	Bruce McLaren & Chris Amon	Ford Mk. II	125.37
1967	A.J. Foyt & Dan Gurney	Ford Mk. IV	135.46
1968	Pedro Rodriguez & Lucien Bianchi	Ford GT40	115.27
1969	Jacky Ickx & Jackie Oliver	Ford GT40	129.38
1970	Hans Herrmann & Richard Attwood	Porsche 917	119.28
1971	Gijs van Lennep & Helmut Marko	Porsche 917	138.13
1972	Graham Hill & Henri Pescarolo	Matra-Simca	121.45
1973	Henri Pescarolo & Gerard Larrousse	Matra-Simca	125.67
1974	Henri Pescarolo & Gerard Larrousse	Matra-Simca	119.27
1975	Derek Bell & Jacky Ickx	Mirage-Ford	118.98
1976	Jacky Ickx & Gijs van Lennep	Porsche 936	123.49
1977	Jacky Ickx, Jurgen Barth & Hurley Haywood	Porsche 936	120.95
1978	Jean-Pierre Jaussaud & Didier Pironi	Renault-Alpine	130.60
1979	Klaus Ludwig, Bill Wittington & Don Whittington	Porsche 935	108.10
1980	Jean-Pierre Jaussaud & Jean Rondeau	Rondeau-Cosworth	119.23
1981	Jacky Ickx & Derek Bell	Porsche 936	124.94
1982	Jacky Ickx & Derek Bell	Porsche 956	126.85
1983	Vern Schuppan, Hurley Haywood & Al Holbert	Porsche 956	130.70
1984	Klaus Ludwig & Henri Pescarolo	Porsche 956	126.88
1985	Klaus Ludwig, Paolo Barilla & John Winter	Porsche 956	131.75
1986	Derek Bell, Hans Stuck & Al Holbert	Porsche 962	128.75
1987	Derek Bell, Hans Stuck & Al Holbert	Porsche 962	124.06
1988	Jan Lammers, Johnny Dumfries & Andy Wallace	Jaguar XJR	137.75
1989	Jochen Mass, Manuel Reuter & Stanley Dickens	Sauber-Mercedes	136.39
1990	John Nielsen, Price Cobb & Martin Brundle	Jaguar XJR-12	126.71
1991	Volker Weider, Johnny Herbert & Bertrand Gachof	Mazda 787B	127.31
1992	Derek Warwick, Yannick Dalmas & Mark Blundell	Peugeot 905B	123.89
1993	Geoff Brabham, Christophe Bouchut & Eric Helary	Peugeot 905	132.58
1994	Yannick Dalmas, Hurley Haywood & Mauro Baldi	Porsche 962LM	129.82
1995	Yannick Dalmas, J.J. Lehto & Masanori Sekiya	McLaren BMW	105.00

Year	Drivers	Car	MPH
1996	Davy Jones, Manuel Reuter & Alexander Wurz	TWR Porsche	124.65
1997	Michele Alberto, Stefan Johansson & Tom Kristensen	TWR Porsche	126.88
1998	Laurent Aiello, Allan McNish & Stephane Ortelli	Porsche 911 GT1	123.86

The 24 Hours of Daytona

Officially, the Rolex 24 at Daytona. First run in 1962 as a three-hour race and won by Dan Gurney in a Lotus 19 Ford. Contested over a 3.56-mile course at Daytona (Fla.) International Speedway. There have been several distance changes since 1962: the event was a three-hour race (1962-63); a 2,000-kilometer race (1964-65); a 24-hour race (1966-71); a six-hour race (1972) and a 24-hour race again since 1973. The race was canceled in 1974 due to a national energy crisis.

Multiple winners: Hurley Haywood (5); Peter Gregg, Pedro Rodriguez and Bob Wollek (4); Derek Bell and Rolf Stommelen (3); A.J. Foyt, Al Holbert, Ken Miles, Brian Redman, Lloyd Ruby and Al Unser Jr. (2).

Year	Drivers	Car	MPH
1962	Dan Gurney	Lotus Ford	104.101
1963	Pedro Rodriguez	Ferrari GTO	102.074
1964	Pedro Rodriguez & Phil Hill	Ferrari GTO	98.230
1965	Ken Miles & Lloyd Ruby	Ford GT	99.944
1966	Ken Miles & Lloyd Ruby	Ford Mk. II	108.020
1967	Lorenzo Bandini & Chris Amon	Ferrari 330	105.688
1968	Vic Elford & Jochen Neerpasch	Porsche 907	106.697
1969	Mark Donohue & Chuck Parsons	Lola Chevrolet	99.268
1970	Pedro Rodriguez & Leo Kinnunen	Porsche 917	114.866
1971	Pedro Rodriguez & Jackie Oliver	Porsche 917K	109.203
1972	Mario Andretti & Jacky Ickx	Ferrari 312P	122.573
1973	Peter Gregg & Hurley Haywood	Porsche Carrera	106.225
1974	Not held		
1975	Peter Gregg & Hurley Haywood	Porsche Carrera	108.531
1976	Peter Gregg, Brian Redman & John Fitzpatrick	BMW CSL	104.040
1977	Hurley Haywood, John Graves & Dave Helmick	Porsche Carrera	108.801
1978	Peter Gregg, Rolf Stommelen & Antoine Hezemans	Porsche Turbo	108.743
1979	Hurley Haywood, Ted Field & Danny Ongais	Porsche Turbo	109.249
1980	Rolf Stommelen, Volkert Merl & Reinhold Joest	Porsche Turbo	114.303
1981	Bobby Rahal, Brian Redman & Bob Garretson	Porsche Turbo	113.153
1982	John Paul Sr., John Paul Jr. & Rolf Stommelen	Porsche Turbo	114.794
1983	A.J. Foyt, Preston Henn, Bob Wollek & Claude Ballot-Lena	Porsche Turbo	98.781
1984	Sarel van der Merwe, Tony Martin & Graham Duxbury	March Porsche	103.119
1985	A.J. Foyt, Bob Wollek, Al Unser Sr. & Thierry Boutsen	Porsche 962	104.162
1986	Al Holbert, Derek Bell & Al Unser Jr	Porsche 962	105.484
1987	Al Holbert, Derek Bell, Chip Robinson & Al Unser Jr	Porsche 962	111.599
1988	Raul Boesel, Martin Brundle & John Nielsen	Jaguar XJR-9	107.943
1989	John Andretti, Derek Bell & Bob Wollek	Porsche 962	92.009
1990	Davy Jones, Jan Lammers & Andy Wallace	Jaguar XJR-12	112.857
1991	Hurley Haywood, John Winter, Frank Jelinski, Henri Pescarolo & Bob Wollek	Porsche 962-C	106.633
1992	Masahiro Hasemi, Kazuyoshi Hoshino & Toshio Suzuki	Nissan R-91	112.897
1993	P.J. Jones, Mark Dismore & Rocky Moran	Toyota Eagle	103.537
1994	Paul Gentilozzi, Scott Pruett, Butch Leitzinger & Steve Millen	Nissan 300 ZXT	104.80
1995	Jurgen Lassig, Christophe Bouchut, Giovanni Lavaggi & Marco Werner	Porsche Spyder	102.280
1996	Wayne Taylor, Scott Sharp & Jim Pace	Oldsmobile Arness MK-III	103.32
1997	Rob Dyson, James Weaver, Butch Leitzinger, Andy Wallace, John Paul Jr. Eliot Forbes-Robinson & John Schneider	Ford R&S MK-III	102.29
1998	Mauro Baldi, Arie Luyendyk, Gianpiero Moretti & Didier Theys	Ferrari 333 SP	105.40

NHRA Drag Racing

NHRA Winston Champions

Based on points earned during the NHRA Winston Drag Racing series. The series began for Top Fuel, Funny Car and Pro Stock in 1975.

Top Fuel

Multiple winners: Joe Amato (5); Don Garlits and Shirley Muldowney (3); Scott Kalitta (2).

Year		Year		Year		Year	
1975	Don Garlits	1981	Jeb Allen	1987	Dick LaHaie	1993	Eddie Hill
1976	Richard Tharp	1982	Shirley Muldowney	1988	Joe Amato	1994	Scott Kalitta
1977	Shirley Muldowney	1983	Gary Beck	1989	Gary Ormsby	1995	Scott Kalitta
1978	Kelly Brown	1984	Joe Amato	1990	Joe Amato	1996	Kenny Bernstein
1979	Rob Bruins	1985	Don Garlits	1991	Joe Amato	1997	Gary Scelzi
1980	Shirley Muldowney	1986	Don Garlits	1992	Joe Amato		

Funny Car

Multiple winners: John Force (7); Don Prudhomme, Kenny Bernstein (4); Raymond Beadle (3); Frank Hawley (2).

Year		Year		Year		Year	
1975	Don Prudhomme	1981	Raymond Beadle	1987	Kenny Bernstein	1993	John Force
1976	Don Prudhomme	1982	Frank Hawley	1988	Kenny Bernstein	1994	John Force
1977	Don Prudhomme	1983	Frank Hawley	1989	Bruce Larson	1995	John Force
1978	Don Prudhomme	1984	Mark Oswald	1990	John Force	1996	John Force
1979	Raymond Beadle	1985	Kenny Bernstein	1991	John Force	1997	John Force
1980	Raymond Beadle	1986	Kenny Bernstein	1992	Cruz Pedregon		

Pro Stock

Multiple winners: Bob Glidden (9); Lee Shepherd (4); Warren Johnson (3); Darrell Alderman and Jim Yates (2).

Year		Year		Year		Year	
1975	Bob Glidden	1981	Lee Shepherd	1987	Bob Glidden	1993	Warren Johnson
1976	Larry Lombardo	1982	Lee Shepherd	1988	Bob Glidden	1994	Darrell Alderman
1977	Don Nicholson	1983	Lee Shepherd	1989	Bob Glidden	1995	Warren Johnson
1978	Bob Glidden	1984	Lee Shepherd	1990	John Myers	1996	Jim Yates
1979	Bob Glidden	1985	Bob Glidden	1991	Darrell Alderman	1997	Jim Yates
1980	Bob Glidden	1986	Bob Glidden	1992	Warren Johnson		

All-Time Leaders

Career Victories (through Sept. 21, 1998)

Top Fuel

1	**Joe Amato**	45
2	Don Garlits	35
3	**Kenny Bernstein**	21
4	**Cory McClenathan**	21
5	Gary Beck	19

Funny Car

1	**John Force**	69
2	Don Prudhomme	35
3	**Kenny Bernstein**	30
4	**Cruz Pedregon**	20
5	Ed McCulloch	18
	Mark Oswald	18

Pro Stock

1	**Bob Glidden**	85
2	**Warren Johnson**	70
3	**Darrell Alderman**	27
4	Lee Shepherd	26
5	**Jim Yates**	20

National-Event Victories (pro categories)

Drivers active in 1998 season are in **bold** type.

Totals as of Sept. 21, 1998

1	**Bob Glidden**	85
2	**Warren Johnson**	70
3	**John Force**	69
4	**Kenny Bernstein**	51
5	**Don Prudhomme**	49
6	**Joe Amato**	45
7	**Dave Schultz**	42
8	Don Garlits	35
9	**John Myers**	33
10	**Darrell Alderman**	27
11	Lee Shepherd	26
12	Terry Vance	24
13	Ed McCulloch	22
14	**Cory McClenathan**	21
15	Mark Oswald	20
	Jim Yates	20
	Cruz Pedregon	20
18	Gary Beck	19
	Matt Hines	19
20	Shirley Muldowney	18
	Darrell Gwynn	18

Fastest Mile-Per-Hour Speeds

Fastest performances in NHRA major event history as of Sept. 21, 1998.

Top Fuel

MPH	
323.50	Joe Amato, 5/17/98
322.92	Cory McClenathan, 2/22/98
322.58	Joe Amato, 3/14/98
322.42	Kenny Bernstein, 5/16/98
321.88	Kenny Bernstein, 6/12/98

Funny Car

MPH	
323.89	John Force, 5/17/98
323.35	John Force, 5/15/98
321.35	John Force, 5/17/98
321.27	John Force, 5/17/98
319.14	Whit Bazemore, 5/17/98

Pro Stock

MPH	
201.20	Warren Johnson, 3/14/98
201.11	Warren Johnson, 3/13/98
201.11	Warren Johnson, 3/22/98
201.08	Warren Johnson, 3/22/98
200.80	Warren Johnson, 3/21/98

Boxing

Featherweight **Prince Naseem Hamed**, a heavyweight when it comes to self-promotion, is becoming boxing's biggest drawing card while Mike Tyson is suspended.

AP/Wide World Photos

Who's the Greatest?

Roy Jones Jr. and Oscar De La Hoya battled it out for the mythical title of pound-for-pound champion in 1998, too bad they'll never settle it in the ring.

by
Al Bernstein

Because there are so many different ruling organizations and weight divisions in professional boxing, the sport has become largely a personality-driven enterprise. It was a mixed bag for boxing's top personalities this year, and so it was an up and down year for the sport in general.

Perhaps boxing's biggest active name is Oscar De La Hoya. Despite a hand injury, he did defend his welterweight title several times including an exciting TKO win over fading legend Julio Cesar Chavez. The Golden Boy also showed his incredible drawing power by filling the El Paso Sun Bowl with fans for another title defense (against Patrick Charpentier), as he prepped for the tough former champion Ike Quartey. Felix Trinidad, the other welterweight star, battled Don King in court more than he battled in the ring. He looks forward to a De La Hoya superfight in 1999.

Featherweight champion Prince Naseem Hamed, perhaps boxing's most colorful performer, was inactive much of the year but did manage to unify part of the title by beating Wilfredo Vasquez. Hamed's theatrics have made him one of boxing's biggest TV and live draws.

The most unfortunate member of boxing's elite circle is Light Heavyweight champ Roy Jones Jr., who has no marquee opponent to fight in a big-money match—so he beat up ex-champ Virgil Hill and WBA champ

---

Al Bernstein has been ESPN's boxing analyst since 1980.

AP/Wide World Photos

Light Heavyweight **Roy Jones Jr.** connects with the head of Virgil Hill in their April 25 bout. Jones, thought by many to be the world's best prizefighter, has suffered from a lack of quality opponents. Rumors of him attempting a move up to the heavyweight ranks continue to circulate.

Lou Del Valle. He flirted with a move to the heavyweight division but turned down a match with Buster Douglas—and may have regretted that decision when Douglas promptly went out and lost in one round to Lou Savarese.

Since the heavyweight division always seems to take center stage, its big guns got plenty of attention this year, even though they never even fought each other. The WBA/IBF champion, Evander Holyfield, avoided the WBC champ, Lennox Lewis, like the plague despite a $20 million offer to box him. Holyfield was holding out for a guaranteed $25 million.

Instead, he had his June fight with towering contender Henry Akinwande cancelled after Akinwande tested positive for hepatitis-B. Then he labored through a successful IBF title defense with the lightly-regarded Vaughn Bean. Meanwhile, Lewis struggled with Shannon Briggs, who got his title shot after beating 48-year-old George Foreman in a controversial decision, before knocking him out in March. Lewis then had difficulty while outpointing the obscure Croatian Zejlko Mavroric.

The brightest new star in the sport appears to be IBF Lightweight Champ Shane Mosley, who defended his crown several times and dazzled boxing fans with his formidable speed and power.

The other young fighters who flourished in 1998 were the 12 members of the 1996 U.S. Olympic Team. As a group they continued an amazing

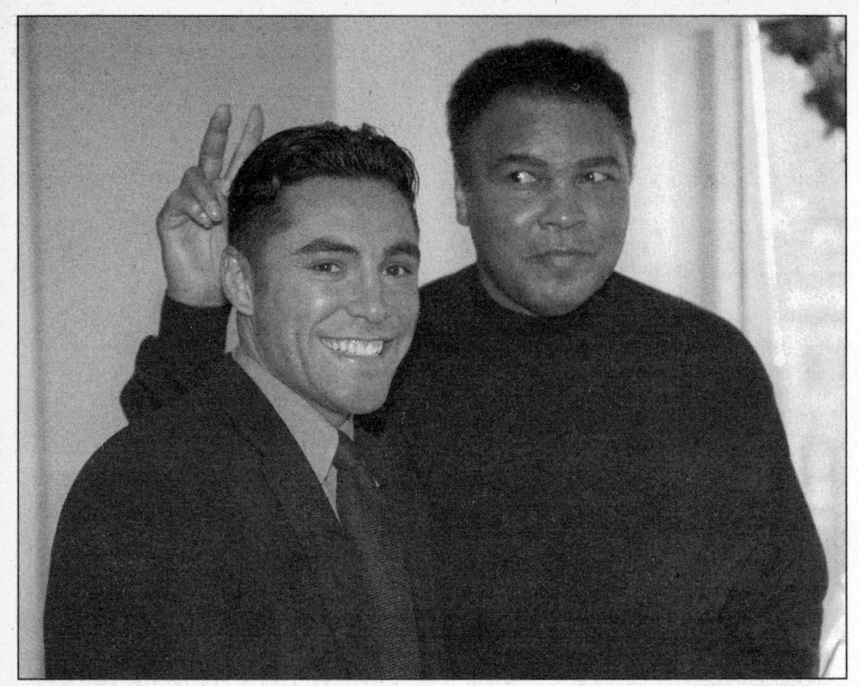

AP/Wide World Photos

Muhammad Ali shows he still has quick hands in his meeting with an unsuspecting **Oscar De La Hoya**. De La Hoya, the WBC welterweight champion, has been dominant in the ring but still has yet to face a big challenge. That challenge may come in 1999 in the shape of Ike Quartey.

story, tallying nearly 140 career wins and just a few losses among them. Bronze medalist Floyd Mayweather scored a TKO over Genaro Hernandez for the WBC super featherweight belt, while gold medalist David Reid looked like a superstar in the making.

The enigmatic Mike Tyson continued to make headlines in 1998 even though he'd been suspended from boxing since July 9, 1997 after biting the ears of Holyfield. Whether it was during an Aug. 31 fender-bender, where he allegedly threatened the driver of the other car, or in the ring as a "special enforcer" during a professional wrestling event, the media's fascination with the former undisputed heavyweight champion showed little sign of abatement.

Whether it's primarily financially-driven or not, Tyson apparently wants to return to the ring. He first applied for reinstatement with the New Jersey State Athletic Control Board before withdrawing his application at the 11th hour. He then tried his luck in Nevada where the Nevada Athletic Commission ordered Tyson to undergo an examination by a panel of six Boston doctors to determine if he was mentally fit to return to the ring.

The report that found Tyson "fit" to return to boxing said that he was extremely depressed when his bit Holyfield and was unlikely to commit such an act again. ■

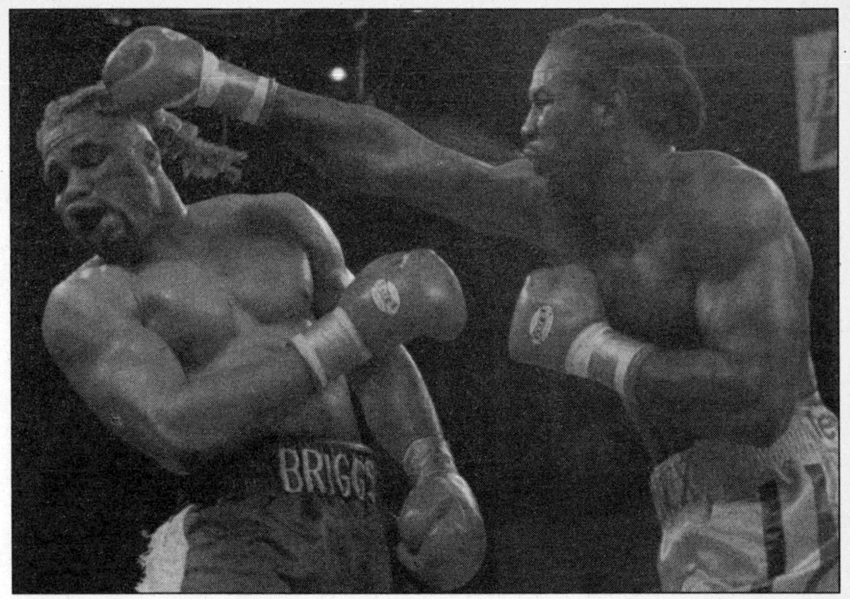

AP/Wide World Photos

WBC heavyweight champion **Lennox Lewis** defended his belt twice while he waited for Evander Holyfield to make a deal for a unification bout. Lewis didn't dazzle in 1998 but he TKO'd **Shannon Briggs** (above, left) and then decisioned Zeljko Mavrovic.

Al Bernstein's Ten Biggest Events of the Year

10. **Arturo Gatti vs. Angel Manfredy.** As always Gatti was in a war of attrition, but this time Manfredy prevailed with a late-fight TKO.

9. **Arturo Gatti vs. Ivan Robinson.** Gatti's other outing in 1998 was the fight of the year. Ivan Robinson shelved his slick boxing style and slugged it out with Arturo. It was a wild affair, and Robinson won a decision.

8. **Duran loses title bid.** The nearly 50-year-old Roberto Duran tried for yet another world title against WBA middleweight champ William Joppy. It was a sad sight. Duran lost by TKO in the fourth round and looked terrible. This appears to be Duran's swan song—finally.

7. **Johnson pulls an upset.** Former middleweight champ Reggie Johnson shocked light heavyweight "King" William Guthrie with a one-punch knockout in the biggest upset of the year.

6. **Roy Jones brings big-time boxing to the Gulf Coast.** Roy Jones Jr. defeated Virgil Hill easily with one big body shot in a battle of (then) ex-champs. But the big news was the 10,000-plus crowd and excitement that this match caused in Biloxi, Miss. It was that area's biggest match in years.

5. **De La Hoya fills the Sun Bowl.** Matinee idol Oscar De La Hoya took the city of El Paso, Texas by storm and filled the Sun Bowl with over 50,000 fight fans, despite boxing a relatively unknown

foreign challenger, Patrick Charpentier. Over half the crowd was female.

4. **Shane Mosley becomes a star.** With four title defenses, this IBF lightweight champ became boxing's biggest young star. This young Californian could have a breakout year in 1999.

3. **Holyfield goes home again.** While avoiding Lennox Lewis, Evander Holyfield did bring his title belts to his hometown of Atlanta for a defense against Vaughn Bean. The bout was lackluster but Evander drew 40,000 to the Georgia Dome and made tickets available to youngsters.

2. **De La Hoya beats Julio Chavez again.** It was thought by many to be a needless rematch, but De La Hoya-Chavez II turned out to be an exciting affair, even though Chavez tarnished it a bit by quitting on his stool after the eighth round.

1. **Dunphy passes away.** The voice of boxing was silenced when legendary broadcaster Don Dunphy died. Don broadcast more matches on radio and television than anyone who ever lived (see obituary on page 951). ■

INSIDE THE NUMBERS

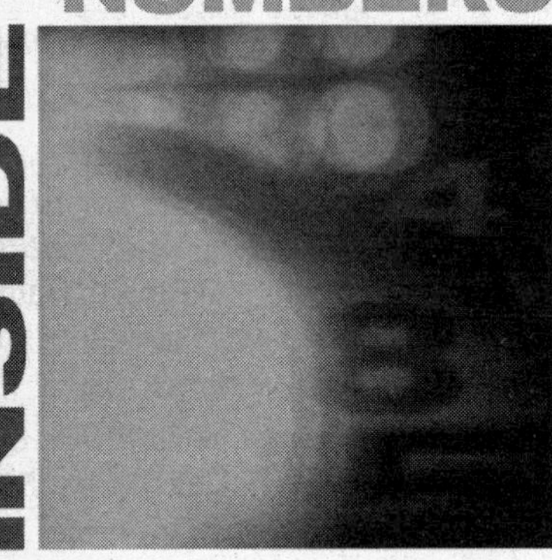

by
Todd Snyder

DE LA STROYA

On September 18, 1998, Oscar De La Hoya defeated Julio Cesar Chavez to successfully defend his WBC Welterweight crown for the fifth time. The Golden Boy is now 17-0 in title bouts. Breaking down his career by the weight classes he has fought at, one will notice that it's taken him a little longer to dispose of his opponents as he's gotten heavier, but in the overall scheme of things he has dominated at every level.

Division	Record	Average Round Per Bout
Welterweight	6-0	7.5
Jr. Welterweight	2-0	8.0
Lightweight	7-0	5.1
Jr. Lightweight	2-0	6.5

Note: De La Hoya has won four of his last five fights by knockout.

QUICKEST KNOCKOUTS

Lennox Lewis's first round knockout of Andrew Golota 95 seconds into their fight on Oct. 4, 1997, was the sixth-quickest knockout in Heavyweight title history. Mike Tyson is the only fighter to have two of the fastest five in history.

Year	Title Fight	Seconds
1900	James Jeffries def. Jack Finnegan	55
1982	Michael Dokes def. Mike Weaver	63
1908	Tommy Burns def. Jem Roche	88
1988	Mike Tyson def. Michael Spinks	91
1989	Mike Tyson def. Charles Williams	93
1997	Lennox Lewis def. Andrew Golota	95

■

BOXING STATISTICS

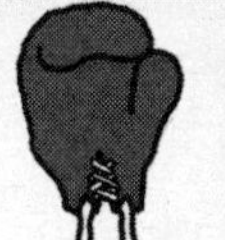

THE SEASON IN REVIEW

1997-1998

CHAMPIONS • TITLE BOUTS

Current Champions

WBA, WBC and IBF Titleholders (through Oct. 12, 1998)

The champions of professional boxing's 17 principal weight divisions, as recognized by the Word Boxing Association (WBA), World Boxing Council (WBC) and International Boxing Federation (IBF).

	Weight Limit	WBA Champion	WBC Champion	IBF Champion
Heavyweight	–	Evander Holyfield 36-3-0, 25 KOs	Lennox Lewis 34-1-0, 27 KOs	Evander Holyfield 36-3-0, 25 KOs
Cruiserweight	190 lbs	Fabrice Tiozzo 39-1-0, 25 KOs	Juan Carlos Gomez 24-0-0, 20 KOs	Imamu Mayfield 18-1-0, 14 KOs
Light Heavyweight	175 lbs	Roy Jones Jr. 37-1-0, 31 KOs	Roy Jones Jr.* 37-1-0, 31 KOs	Reggie Johnson 38-5-1, 24 KOs
Super Middleweight	168 lbs	Frank Liles 32-1-0, 19 KOs	Richie Woodhall 24-1-0, 15 KOs	Charles Brewer 32-5-0, 21 KOs
Middleweight	160 lbs	William Joppy 26-1-1, 20 KOs	Hassine Cherifi 25-2-1, 17 KOs	Bernard Hopkins* 34-2-1, 26 KOs
Jr. Middleweight	154 lbs	Laurent Boudouani 37-2-1, 31 KOs	Keith Mullings 16-4-1, 11 KOs	Yory Boy Campas 72-2-0, 62 KOs
Welterweight	147 lbs	Vacant	Oscar De La Hoya 29-0-0, 24 KOs	Felix Trinidad 33-0-0, 29 KOs
Jr. Welterweight	140 lbs	Sharmba Mitchell 43-2-0, 29 KOs	Vacant	Vince Phillips 39-3-1, 28 KOs
Lightweight	135 lbs	Jean-Baptiste Mendy 51-7-2, 31 KOs	Cesar Bazan 33-2-1, 23 KOs	Shane Mosley 29-0-0, 27 KOs
Jr. Lightweight	130 lbs	Takanori Hatakeyama 22-0-1, 17 KOs	Floyd Mayweather 18-0-0, 14 KOs	Roberto Garcia 30-0-0, 23 KOs
Featherweight	126 lbs	Antonio Cermeno 30-2-0, 18 KOs	Luisito Espinoza 43-7-0, 22 KOs	Manuel Medina 55-10-1, 25 KOs
Jr. Featherweight	122 lbs	Enrique Sanchez* 24-0-1, 17 KOs	Erik Morales 31-0-1, 25 KOs	Vuyani Bungu 35-2-0, 18 KOs
Bantamweight	118 lbs	Nana Yaw Konadu 39-3-1, 31 KOs	Joichiro Tatsuyoshi 17-4-1, 12 KOs	Tim Austin 18-0-1, 17 KOs
Jr. Bantamweight	115 lbs	Satoshi Iida 25-1-1, 11 KOs	Cho In-joo 13-0-0, 7 KOs	Johnny Tapia 44-0-2, 25 KOs
Flyweight	112 lbs	Hugo Soto* 50-5-2, 33 KOs	Chatchai Sasakul 33-1-0, 24 KOs	Mark Johnson 36-1-0, 26 KOs
Jr. Flyweight	108 lbs	Phichitnoi C. Siriwat 19-1-0, 11 KOs	Saman Sor Jaturong 38-2-1, 31 KOs	Vacant
Minimumweight	105 lbs	Rosendo Alvarez 24-0-1, 16 KOs	Ricardo Lopez* 46-0-1, 35 KOs	Zolani Petelo 13-2-2, 7 KOs

Note: The following weight divisions are also known by these names—**Cruiserweight** as Jr. Heavyweight; **Jr. Middleweight** as Super Welterweight; **Jr. Welterweight** as Super Lightweight; **Jr. Lightweight** as Super Featherweight; **Jr. Featherweight** as Super Bantamweight; **Jr. Bantamweight** as Super Flyweight; **Jr. Flyweight** as Light Flyweight; and **Minimum** as Strawweight.

*Graciano Rocchigiani (40-4-1, 19 KOs) is currently the interim WBC light heavyweight champion. Robert Allen (23-2-0, 17 KOs) is currently the interim IBF Middleweight champion. Carlos Barreto (13-0-1, 9 KOs) is currently the interim WBA Flyweight champion. Wande Chareon (22-3-0, 6 KOs) is currently the interim WBC Minimumweight champion.

Major Bouts, 1997-98

Division by division, from Oct. 1, 1997 through Oct. 12, 1998.

WBA, WBC and IBF champions are listed in **bold** type. Note the following Result columm abbreviations (in alphabetical order): **Disq.** (won by disqualification); **KO** (knockout); **MDraw** (majority draw); **NC** (no contest); **SDraw** (split draw); **TDraw** (technical draw); **TKO** (technical knockout); **TWs** (won by technical split decision); **TWu** (won by technical unanimous decision); **Wm** (won by majority decision); **Ws** (won by split decision) and **Wu** (won by unanimous decision).

Heavyweights

Date	Winner	Loser	Result	Title	Site
Oct. 4	**Lennox Lewis**	Andrew Golota	TKO 1	**WBC**	Atlantic City
Oct. 18	Zeljko Mavrovic	Vincenzo Cantatore	KO 4	EBU	Vienna, AUT
Nov. 1	Alonzo Highsmith	Sean Jegen	TKO 1	—	New York City
Nov. 1	Hasim Rahman	Obed Sullivan	Wm 12	USBA	New York City
Nov. 4	Oliver McCall	Brian Yates	TKO 8	—	Nashville, Tenn.
Nov. 7	Michael Grant	Jorge Luis Gonzalez	TKO 1	IBC	Las Vegas
Nov. 8	**Evander Holyfield**	**Michael Moorer**	TKO 8	**WBA/IBF**	Las Vegas
Nov. 22	David Tua	Jeff Lally	TKO 2	—	Atlantic City
Nov. 22	Shannon Briggs	George Foreman	Wm 12	—	Atlantic City
Nov. 29	Vaughn Bean	Bryant Smith	TKO 1	—	Vineland, N.J.
Dec. 13	Henry Akinwande	Orlin Norris	Wu 12	—	Pompano Beach, Fla.
Dec. 16	Oliver McCall	Mike DeVito	TKO 2	—	Nashville, Tenn.
Dec. 18	Vaughn Bean	Kimmuel Odum	TKO 2	—	Newark, N.J.
Jan. 17	Michael Grant	David Izonritei	TKO 5	—	Atlantic City
Jan. 22	Alonzo Highsmith	Jaime Munguia	KO 1	—	San Diego
Jan. 30	Vaughn Bean	Isaac Brown	TKO 2	—	Newark, N.J.
Jan. 31	Hasim Rahman	Jesse Ferguson	Wu 12	USBA	Atlantic City
Feb. 21	Ray Mercer	Leo Loiacono	KO 2	—	Miami
Feb. 24	Obed Sullivan	Keith McKnight	KO 7	—	Ledyard, Conn.
Feb. 28	Axel Schulz	Julius Francis	Wu 12	—	Dortmund, GER
Mar. 10	David Tua	Jeff Wooden	Wm 10	—	Pikesville, Md.
Mar. 28	**Lennox Lewis**	Shannon Briggs	TKO 5	**WBC**	Atlantic City
Apr. 14	Andrew Golota	Eli Dixon	KO 6	—	Aquisgranum, GER
Apr. 18	Herbie Hide	Damon Reed	TKO 1	WBO	Manchester, ENG
Apr. 18	Vaughn Bean	Lamont Burgin	TKO 3	—	Alexandria, Va.
Apr. 18	David Tua	Cleveland Woods	KO 3	—	San Francisco
Apr. 21	Hasim Rahman	Steve Panell	KO 2	—	Lake Charles, La.
May 2	Vitalij Klitschko	Dickie Ryan	TKO 3	—	Luebeck, GER
May 8	Andrew Golota	Jack Basting	TKO 3	—	Atlantic City
May 30	Michael Grant	Obed Sullivan	TKO 9	—	Atlantic City
June 25	Lou Savarese	Buster Douglas	TKO 1	—	Ledyard, Conn.
July 9	Ike Ibeabuchi	Tim Ray	KO 1	—	Marksville, La.
July 9	Hasim Rahman	Garing Lane	KO 3	—	Marksville, La.
July 14	Chris Byrd	Ross Purrity	Wu 10	—	Bay St. Louis, Miss.
July 21	Andrew Golota	Corey Sanders	Wu 10	—	Atlantic City
Aug. 11	Vitalij Klitschko	Ricardo Kennedy	TKO 1	—	Miami
Sept. 19	**Evander Holyfield**	Vaughn Bean	Wu 12	**WBA**	Atlanta, Ga.
Sept. 26	**Lennox Lewis**	Zeljko Mavrovic	Wu 12	**WBC**	Uncasville, Conn.
Sept. 26	Herbie Hide	Willi Fischer	KO 2	WBO	Norwich, ENG
Oct. 2	Andrew Golota	Tim Witherspoon	Wu 10	—	Wroclaw, POL

Cruiserweights (190 lbs)

(Jr. Heavyweights)

Date	Winner	Loser	Result	Title	Site
Oct. 4	Carl Thompson	Ralf Rocchigiani	Ws 12	WBO	Hanover, GER
Oct. 4	Juan C. Gomez	Mike Sedillo	KO 2	—	Hanover, GER
Oct. 18	Torsten May	Matthew Charleston	TKO 5	—	Vienna, AUT
Nov. 8	Imamu May	**Uriah Grant**	Wu 12	**IBF**	Las Vegas
Nov. 8	Fabrice Tiozzo	**Nate Miller**	Wu 12	**WBA**	Las Vegas
Feb. 21	Juan C. Gomez	**Marcelo Dominguez**	Wu 12	**WBC**	Mar del Plata, ARG
Mar. 28	**Imamu Mayfield**	Terry Dunstan	KO 11	**IBF**	Hull, York., ENG
Apr. 18	Carl Thompson	Chris Eubank	Wu 12	WBO	Manchester, ENG
May 2	**Fabrice Tiozzo**	Terry Ray	TKO 1	**WBA**	Villeurbanne, FRA
May 5	Vassiliy Jirov	Richard LaMontagne	Wu 12	—	Biloxi, Miss.
June 5	**Juan C. Gomez**	Guy Waters	TKO 6	**WBC**	Hamburg, GER
July 18	Carl Thompson	Chris Eubank	TKO 9	WBO	Sheffield, ENG
Oct. 3	**Juan C. Gomez**	Alexei Iliin	KO 2	**WBC**	Augsburg, GER
Oct. 10	Torsten May	Pascal Warusfel	Wu 10	—	Vienna, AUT

Light Heavyweights (175 lbs)

Date	Winner	Loser	Result	Title	Site
Oct. 4	D. Michalczewski	Nicky Piper	TKO 8	WBO	Hanover, GER
Oct. 4	Ole Klemetsen	Crawford Ashley	KO 2	—	London, ENG
Nov. 29	Montell Griffin	Vinson Durham	Wu 10	—	Las Vegas
Dec. 13	D. Michalczewski	Darren Zenner	TKO 7	WBO	Hamburg, GER
Dec. 26	Montell Griffin	Jesus J. Castaneda	TKO 8	—	Las Vegas
Jan. 17	Antonio Tarver	Boyor Chew	TKO 7	—	Atlantic City
Feb. 6	Reggie Johnson	**William Guthrie**	KO 5	**IBF**	Uncasville, Conn.
Feb. 27	Montell Griffin	Thomas Reid	Wu 10	—	Las Vegas
Mar. 20	D. Michalczewski	Andrew Magi	KO 4	WBO	Frankfurt, GER
Mar. 21	Graciano Rocchigiani	Michael Nunn	Ws 12	**WBC***	Berlin, GER
Mar. 28	Montell Griffin	Kenny Lopez	TKO 9	—	Atlantic City
Apr. 25	Roy Jones Jr.*	Virgil Hill	KO 4	—	Biloxi, Miss.
May 29	**Reggie Johnson**	Ole Klemetsen	Wu 12	**IBF**	Pesaro, ITA
June 23	Antonio Tarver	Jose Luis Rivera	TKO 4	—	Philadelphia
July 18	**Roy Jones Jr.**	**Louis Del Valle**	Wu 12	**WBC/WBA**	New York City
Sept. 19	D. Michalczewski	Mark Prince	KO 8	WBO	Oberhausen, GER
Oct. 9	David Telesco	Frank Tate	KO 4	—	Port Chester, N.Y.

*Graciano Rocchigiani won the vacant interim WBC light heavyweight title. Note that Roy Jones Jr.'s WBC title was not at risk for his April 25 bout with Virgil Hill.

Super Middleweights (168 lbs)

Date	Winner	Loser	Result	Title	Site
Oct. 11	Joe Calzaghe	Chris Eubank	Wu 12	WBO	Sheffield, ENG
Oct. 24	Antoine Byrd	Willie Monroe	TKO 8	USBA	Atlantic City
Oct. 28	Thomas Tate	Joseph Kiwanuka	KO 11	NABF	Philadelphia
Nov. 15	Roberto Duran	Dave Radford	Wu 8	—	Hammanskraal, S. Afr.
Dec. 2	**Charles Brewer**	Joey DeGrandis	Wu 12	**IBF**	Philadelphia
Dec. 19	Thulane Malinga	**Robin Reid**	Wu 12	**WBC**	Milwall, ENG
Jan. 24	Joe Calzaghe	Branko Sobot	TKO 3	WBO	Cardiff, Wales
Jan. 31	Roberto Duran	Felix Hernandez	Wu 10	—	Panama City
Mar. 27	Richie Woodhall	**Thulane Malinga**	Wu 12	**WBC**	Telford, ENG
Mar. 28	**Charles Brewer**	Herol Graham	TKO 10	**IBF**	Atlantic City
Apr. 3	**Frankie Liles**	Andrei Schkalikov	Wu 12	**WBA**	Bayamon, P.R.
Apr. 25	Joe Calzaghe	Juan Carlos Gimenez	TKO 9	WBO	Cardiff, Wales
June 5	Thulane Malinga	Fredrik Alvarez	TKO 11	WBF	Copenhagen, DEN
July 26	Vinny Pazienza	Glenwood Brown	Wm 10	—	Ledyard, Conn.
Aug. 22	**Charles Brewer**	Antoine Byrd	KO 3	**IBF**	Leipzig, GER
Sept. 5	**Richie Woodhall**	Glenn Catley	Wm 12	**WBC**	Telford, ENG

Middleweights (160 lbs)

Date	Winner	Loser	Result	Title	Site
Oct. 11	Ryan Rhodes	Yuri Epifantsev	TKO 2	—	Sheffield, ENG
Nov. 18	**Bernard Hopkins**	Andrew Council	Wu 12	**IBF**	Upper Marlboro, Md.
Dec. 5	**Keith Holmes**	Paul Vaden	TKO 11	**WBC**	Pompano Beach, Fla.
Dec. 6	Herol Graham	Vinny Pazienza	Wu 12	—	Webley, ENG
Dec. 13	Otis Grant	Ryan Rhodes	Wu 12	WBO	Sheffield, ENG
Jan. 17	Glenn Catley	Neville Brown	TKO 8	—	Bristol, ENG
Jan. 31	Robert Allen	Lloyd Bryan	TKO 3	—	Tampa, Fla.
Jan. 31	William Joppy	**Julio Cesar Green**	Wu 12	**WBA**	Tampa, Fla.
Jan. 31	**Bernard Hopkins**	Simon Brown	KO 6	**IBF**	Atlantic City
May 2	Hassine Cherifi	**Keith Holmes**	Wu 12	**WBC**	Villeurbanne, FRA
May 12	Otis Grant	Ernesto Sena	TWu 9	WBO	Kanata, Ont.
June 25	Dana Rosenblatt	Arthur Allen	Wu 10	—	Ledyard, Conn.
June 27	Silvio Branco	Rogerio Cacciatore	Wu 12	WBU	Messina, ITA
July 28	Antwun Echols	Urbano Gurrola	KO 6	NABF	Tunica, Miss.
Aug. 28	**William Joppy**	Roberto Duran	TKO 3	**WBA**	Las Vegas
Aug. 28	**Bernard Hopkins**	Robert Allen	NC 4*	**IBF**	Las Vegas
Sept. 19	Robert Allen*	Abdula Ramadan	TKO 1	**IBF**	Atlanta
Sept. 25	Dana Rosenblatt	Terry Norris	Wu 12	IBA	Ledyard, Conn.

*The Bernard Hopkins/Robert Allen fight was ruled a no contest after Hopkins fell out of the ring in the fourth round when referee Mills Lane was breaking up a clinch. Hopkins hurt his ankle and could not continue. Allen then won the vacant interim IBF Middleweight belt on Sept. 19.

Junior Middleweights (154 lbs)

(Super Welterweights)

Date	Winner	Loser	Result	Title	Site
Oct. 3	David Reid	Jorge Vaca	KO 1	—	Atlantic City
Oct. 7	Bronco McKart	Eric Holland	Wu 12	—	Auburn Hills, Mich.
Nov. 22	David Reid	Dan Connolly	TKO 5	—	Atlantic City
Dec. 6	Yory Boy Campas	**Raul Marquez**	TKO 8	**IBF**	Atlantic City
Dec. 6	Keith Mullings	**Terry Norris**	TKO 9	**WBC**	Atlantic City
Dec. 19	Ronald Wright	Adrian Dodson	TKO 6	WBO	Millwall, ENG
Jan. 31	David Reid	Robert Frazier	Wu 8	—	Atlantic City
Feb. 13	**Laurent Boudouani**	Guillermo Jones	MDraw 12	**WBA**	Albuquerque, N.M.
Mar. 14	**Keith Mullings**	Davide Ciarlante	TKO 5	**WBC**	Atlantic City
Mar. 23	**Yory Boy Campas**	Anthony Stephens	TKO 3	**IBF**	Ledyard, Conn.
May 9	David Reid	Nick Rupa	TKO 2	—	Atlantic City
May 22	Bronco McKart	Ron Weaver	Wu 12	IBA	Monroe, Mich.
May 30	**Laurent Boudouani**	Guillermo Jones	Ws 12	**WBA**	Las Vegas
June 5	**Yory Boy Campas**	Pedro Ortega	TKO 11	**IBF**	Tijuana, MEX
June 27	David Reid	Simon Brown	KO 4	—	Philadelphia
Aug. 11	Hector Camacho	Tony Menefee	Wu 12	IBC	Miami
Sept. 18	**Yory Boy Campas**	Larry Barnes	TKO 4*	**IBF**	Las Vegas
Sept. 25	Raul Marquez	Jose Flores	Wu 10	—	Ledyard, Conn.
Sept. 28	Rodney Jones	William Ruiz	TKO 9	NABO	Inglewood, Calif.

*The ringside physician stopped the fight between the third and fourth rounds.

Welterweights (147 lbs)

Date	Winner	Loser	Result	Title	Site
Oct. 17	Pernell Whitaker	Andrei Pastriaev	Wu 12	—	Ledyard, Conn.
Oct. 17	**Ike Quartey**	Jose Luis Lopez	Dm 12	**WBA**	Ledyard, Conn.
Oct. 18	Daniel Santos	Miguel A. Gonzalez	TKO 7	—	Primm, Nev.
Dec. 6	**Oscar De La Hoya**	Wilfredo Rivera	TKO 8	**WBC**	Atlantic City
Dec. 13	Vincent Pettway	Gerald Reed	Wu 10	—	Pompano Beach, Fla.
Feb. 14	Ahmed Katejev	Leonard Townsend	Wu 12	WBO	Stuttgart, GER
Mar. 27	Paul Nave	Greg Haugen	Wu 12	WBF	San Rafael, Calif.
Apr. 3	**Felix Trinidad**	Mahenge Zulu	KO 4	**IBF**	Bayamon, P.R.
Apr. 8	Patrick Charpentier	Rene Uranga	KO 2	—	S. Martin, Guad.
May 9	Jose Luis Lopez	Sammy Fuentes	TKO 2	—	Sacramento, Calif.
May 23	Ahmed Katejev	Paulo Sanchez	Wu 12	WBO	Offenburg, GER
May 30	Wilfredo Rivera	Carlos Palomino	Wu 10	—	Los Angeles
June 5	Soren Sondergaard	Carlos Baldomir	Wu 12	IBC	Copenhagen, DEN
June 13	**Oscar De La Hoya**	Patrick Charpentier	TKO 3	**WBC**	El Paso, Tex.
June 25	Julio Cesar Chavez	Ken Sigurani	TKO 3	—	Ledyard, Conn.
Aug. 3	Joey Gamache	Tim Scott	KO 3	—	Atlanta, Ga.
Aug. 4	Oba Carr	Alfred Ankamah	Wu 10	—	Auburn Hills, Mich.
Sept. 18	**Oscar De La Hoya**	Julio Cesar Chavez	TKO 9*	**WBC**	Las Vegas
Oct. 10	James Page	Andrei Pastriaev	KO 2	**WBA**†	Paris

*Chavez failed to answer the bell at the start of round nine.
†Quartey vacated his WBA Welterweight title for a Nov. 21, 1998 fight against WBC champion Oscar De La Hoya.

Junior Welterweights (140 lbs)

(Super Lightweights)

Date	Winner	Loser	Result	Title	Site
Oct. 4	Giovanni Parisi	Nigel Wenton	TKO 7	WBO	V. Valentia, ITA
Dec. 6	Giovanni Parisi	Jose M. Berdonce	Wu 12	WBO	Catanzaro, ITA
Dec. 6	Kostya Tszyu	Ismael Chaves	TKO 3	—	Townsville, AUS
Dec. 13	**Vincent Phillips**	Fred Pendleton	TKO 10	**IBF**	Pompano Beach, Fla.
Feb. 21	**Khalid Rahilou**	Jean-Baptiste Mendy	Wu 12	**WBA**	Bercy, FRA
Mar. 7	Miguel A. Gonzalez	Julio Cesar Chavez	SDraw 12	**WBC**	Mexico City
Mar. 14	**Vincent Phillips**	Alfonso Sanchez	KO 1	**IBF**	Atlantic City
Apr. 5	Kostya Tszyu	Calvin Grove	KO 1	—	Newcastle, NSW
May 29	Carlos Gonzalez	Giovanni Parisi	TKO 9	WBO	Pesaro, ITA
June 7	Diobelys Hurtado	Leonardo Mas	KO 3	—	Miami
June 19	Rafael Ruelas	Juan Baldwin	TKO 5	—	Atlantic City
July 11	Miguel A. Gonzalez	Alexis Perez	TKO 5	—	San Antonio, Tex.
July 21	Shea Neary	Naas Scheepers	Wu 12	—	Widnes, ENG
July 24	Diobelys Hurtado	Elias Quiroz	TKO 1	—	Miami, Fla.
Aug. 15	Kotsya Tszyu	Rafael Ruelas	KO 9	—	El Paso, Tex.
Sept. 4	Diobelys Hurtado	Darryl Tyson	KO 5	—	Miami, Fla.
Oct. 10	Sharmba Mitchell	**Khalid Rahilou**	Wu 12	**WBA**	Paris

Lightweights (135 lbs)

Date	Winner	Loser	Result	Title	Site
Oct. 4	**Orzubek Nazarov**	Oscar Lopez	KO 4	**WBA**	Villebon, FRA
Oct. 11	Artur Grigorian	David Armstrong	Wu 12	WBO	Cottbus, GER
Nov. 15	Cesar Bazan	Joel Perez	TD 1	NABF	Indio, Calif.
Nov. 25	**Shane Mosley**	Manuel Gomez	TKO 11	**IBF**	El Paso, Tex.
Jan. 17	Angel Manfredy	Artuto Gatti	TKO 8	—	Atlantic City
Jan. 20	Jesse James Leija	Joel Perez	Wu 12	—	San Antonio, Tex.
Feb. 6	**Shane Mosley**	Demetrio Ceballos	KO 8	**IBF**	Uncasville, Conn.
Feb. 28	**Steve Johnston**	George Scott	Wu 12	**WBC**	Atlantic City
Mar. 14	Artur Grigorian	Marco Rudolph	KO 6	WBO	Hamburg, GER
Apr. 8	**Orzubek Nazarov**	Freddy Cruz	Wu 8	**WBA**	S. Martin, Grad.
Apr. 25	Philip Holiday	Miguel Chavez Tellez	TKO 6	—	Cardiff, Wales
May 9	**Shane Mosley**	Juan Molina	TKO 8	**IBF**	Atlantic City
May 16	Jean-Baptiste Mendy	**Orzubek Nazarov**	Wu 12	**WBA**	Bercy, FRA
May 19	Tracy Harris Patterson	German Castro	KO 1	—	Corpus Christi, Tex.
June 13	Cesar Bazan	**Steve Johnston**	Ws 12	**WBC**	El Paso, Tex.
June 16	Angel Manfredy	Islander Lacen	TKO 7	—	Biloxi, Miss.
June 27	**Shane Mosley**	Wilfredo Ruiz	KO 5	**IBF**	Philadelphia
July 11	Gabriel Ruelas	Troy Dorsey	TKO 6	—	San Antonio, Tex.
July 11	Jesse James Leija	Azumah Nelson	Wu 12	IBA	San Antonio, Tex.
Aug 23	**Cesar Bazan**	Hiroyuki Sakamoto	Wu 12	**WBC**	Yokohama, JPN
Sept. 22	**Shane Mosley**	Eduardo Morales	TKO 5	**IBF**	New York City

Junior Lightweights (130 lbs)

(Super Featherweights)

Date	Winner	Loser	Result	Title	Site
Oct. 4	Julien Lorcy	Arnulfo Castillo	Ds 12	WBO	Villebon, FRA
Oct. 4	Jesus Chavez	Troy Dorsey	TKO 7	NABF	Atlantic City
Oct. 4	**Arturo Gatti**	Gabriel Ruelas	TKO 5	**IBF**	Atlantic City
Oct. 5	**Yong-Soo Choi**	Takanori Hatakeyama	SDraw 12	**WBA**	Tokyo
Oct. 14	Floyd Mayweather	Felipe Garcia	KO 6	—	Boise, Idaho
Nov. 20	Floyd Mayweather	Angelo Nunez	TKO 3	—	Los Angeles
Nov. 20	**Genaro Hernandez**	Carlos Hernandez	Wu 12	**WBC**	Los Angeles
Dec. 19	Barry Jones	Wilson Palacio	Wu 12	WBO	Milwall, ENG
Dec. 20	Tracy Harris Patterson	Manuel Chavez	KO 8	—	Reseda, Calif.
Jan. 9	Floyd Mayweather	Hector Arroyo	TKO 5	—	Biloxi, Miss.
Feb. 28	Floyd Mayweather	Sam Girard	KO 2	—	Atlantic City
Mar. 13	Roberto Garcia*	Harold Warren	Wu 12	**IBF**	Miami
Mar. 23	Floyd Mayweather	Miguel Melo	TKO 3	—	Ledyard, Conn.
Apr. 18	**Yong-Soo Choi**	Gilberto Serrano	TKO 9	**WBA**	Seoul, KOR
Apr. 18	Floyd Mayweather	Gustavo Cuello	Wu 10	—	Los Angeles, Calif.
Apr. 30	Tom Johnson	Javier Diaz	Wu 10	—	Ft. Lauderdale, Fla.
May 16	Anatoly Alexandrov	Julien Lorcy	Wm 12	WBO	Bercy, FRA
May 16	**Genaro Hernandez**	Carlos Gerena	Wu 12	**WBC**	Indio, Calif.
June 14	Floyd Mayweather	Tony Pep	Wu 10	—	Atlantic City
July 11	Gregorio Vargas	Tracy Harris Patterson	TKO 6	—	San Antonio, Tex.
Sept. 5	Takanori Hatakeyama	**Yong-Soo Choi**	Wm 12	**WBA**	Tokyo
Sept. 22	Angel Manfredy	John Brown	Wu 12	WBU	New York City
Oct. 3	Floyd Mayweather	**Genaro Hernandez**	TKO 9†	**WBC**	Las Vegas

*Garcia won the vacant IBF title.
†Hernandez failed to answer the bell at the start of round nine.

Featherweights (126 lbs)

Date	Winner	Loser	Result	Title	Site
Oct. 11	Paul Ingle	Johnjo Irwin	KO 9	—	Sheffield, ENG
Oct. 11	Naseem Hamed	Jose Badillo	TKO 7	WBO	Sheffield, ENG
Nov. 8	**Wilfredo Vazquez**	Genaro Rios	Wu 12	**WBA**	Las Vegas
Dec. 6	**Luisito Espinosa**	Carlos Rios	TKO 6	**WBC**	Koronadal, PHI
Dec. 12	Freddie Norwood	Benito Rodriguez	TKO 6	—	Tijuna, MEX
Dec. 13	Hector Lizarraga*	Welcome Ncita	TKO 11	**IBF**	Pompano Beach, Fla.
Dec. 19	Naseem Hamed	Kevin Kelley	KO 4	WBO	New York City
Mar. 21	Mbuelo Botile	Mustapha Hame	Wu 10	—	Hammanskraal. S. Afr.
Apr. 3	Freddie Norwood	Antonio Cermeno	Wu 12	**WBA**	Bayamon, P.R.
Apr. 18	Naseem Hamed	Wilfredo Vazquez	TKO 7	WBO	Manchester, ENG
Apr. 24	Manuel Medina	**Hector Lizarraga**	Wu 12	**IBF**	San Jose, Calif.
May 8	Kevin Kelley	Vincent Howard	Wu 10	—	Atlantic City
June 9	Paul Ingle	Moussa Sangare	Wu 12	—	Hull, York., ENG
June 13	**Freddie Norwood**	Genaro Rios	TKO 8	**WBA**	Atlantic City

Date	Winner	Loser	Result	Title	Site
June 20	Juan M. Marquez	Juan Cabrera	TKO 4	NABO	Las Vegas
July 10	**Freddie Norwood**	Luis E. Mendoza	Wu 12	**WBA**	Miami, Fla.
Aug. 8	Paul Ingle	Rakhim Mingaleev	KO 4	—	Scarborough, ENG
Aug. 15	**Luisito Espinosa**	Juan Carlos Ramirez	TWs 11	**WBC**	El Paso, Tex.
Sept. 22	**Freddie Norwood**	Koji Matsumoto	TKO 10	**WBA**	Tokyo
Sept. 25	Paul Ingle	Billy Hardy	KO 8	—	York, ENG
Oct. 3	Antonio Cermeno	Genaro Rios	KO 4	**WBA**	Caracas, VEN

Note: The WBA featherweight belt was passed around quite a bit in 1998. Wilfredo Vazquez was initially stripped of the belt in April. Freddie Norwood beat Antonio Cermeno for the vacant title on April 3, successfully defended it twice, but then lost the belt when he failed make his weight at the weigh-in of his Sept. 22 fight with Koji Matsumoto. Cermeno then won the vacant WBA title on Oct. 3.

*Lizarraga won the vacant IBF title.

Junior Featherweights (122 lbs)

(Super Bantamweights)

Date	Winner	Loser	Result	Title	Site
Oct. 5	Kennedy McKinney	Luigi Camputaro	TKO 5	—	Killeen, Tex.
Nov. 15	**Vuyani Bungu**	Arnel Barotillo	Wu 12	**IBF**	Hammanskraal, S. Afr.
Dec. 12	**Erik Morales**	John Lowey	TKO 8	**WBC**	Tijuana, MEX
Dec. 19	Kennedy McKinney	Junior Jones	TKO 4	WBO	New York City
Feb. 8	Enrique Sanchez*	Rafael del Valle	Wu 12	**WBA**	Lakes Charles, La.
Feb. 21	Carlos Navarro	Nicky Bentz	Wu 12	WBU	Indio, Calif.
Apr. 4	**Erik Morales**	Remigio Molina	TKO 6	**WBC**	Tijuana, MEX
May 16	**Vuyani Bungu**	Ernesto Grey	Ws 12	**IBF**	Hammanskraal, S. Afr.
May 16	**Erik Morales**	Jose Luis Bueno	KO 2	**WBC**	Indio, Calif.
May 19	Wayne McCullough	Juan Polo Perez	Ws 10	—	Corpus Christi, Tex.
July 5	Enrique Sanchez	Ricardo Medina	MDraw 10	—	Indio, Calif.
July 28	Mbulele Botile	Dino Olivetti	TKO 6	—	Hammanskraal, S. Afr.
Sept. 12	**Erik Morales**	Junior Jones	TKO 4	**WBC**	Tijuana, MEX
Oct. 3	Carlos Barreto†	Hector Acero-Sanchez	Wu 12	**WBA**	Caracas, VEN

*Sanchez won the vacant WBA title on Feb. 8.

†Barreto won the interim WBA title.

Bantamweights (118 lbs)

Date	Winner	Loser	Result	Title	Site
Oct. 3	Johnny Bredahl	Javier Campanario	KO 5	—	Copenhagen, DEN
Nov. 14	Johnny Bredahl	Willy Salazar	Wu 8	—	Copenhagen, DEN
Nov. 22	Joichiro Tatsuyoshi	**Siri. Singmanassak**	TKO 7	**WBC**	Osaka, JPN
Feb. 13	Johnny Bredahl	Cruz Carbajal	Wu 8	—	Copenhagen, DEN
Feb. 21	**Nana Yaw Konadu**	Abraham Torres	KO 2	**WBA**	Buenos Aires, ARG
Mar. 8	**Joichiro Tatsuyoshi**	Jose Rafael Sosa	Wu 12	**WBC**	Yokohama, JPN
Mar. 28	**Tim Austin**	Paul Lloyd	TKO 2	**IBF**	Hull, York., ENG
Apr. 3	Johnny Bredahl	Alexandre Yagupov	Wu 12	EBU	Holbaek, DEN
Apr. 3	Jorge E. Julio	Daniel Jimenez	TKO 9	WBO	Bayamon, P.R.
May 16	Paul Ayala	Antonio Ramirez	TKO 7	—	Indio, Calif.
May 30	Nana Yaw Konadu	Julio A. Salinas	Disq. 8	—	Las Vegas
May 30	**Tim Austin**	Andrian Kaspari	TKO 3	**IBF**	Las Vegas
June 5	Johnny Bredahl	Patrick Quka	TKO 5	WBU	Copenhagen, DEN
July 19	Danny Romero	Tomas Cordova	KO 1	—	Lake Charles, La.
Aug. 23	**Joichiro Tatsuyoshi**	Paul Ayala	TD 6	**WBC**	Yokohama, JPN
Aug. 29	Johnny Tapia*	Carlos Hernandez	Wu 10	—	Las Vegas

Junior Bantamweights (115 lbs)

(Super Flyweights)

Date	Winner	Loser	Result	Title	Site
Nov. 23	**Gerry Penalosa**	Young-Joo Cho	KO 10	**WBC**	Songnam, KOR
Nov. 29	Hugo Soto	Adrian Ochoa	KO 1	—	Buenos Aires, ARG
Dec. 13	**Johnny Tapia**	Andy Agosto	Wu 12	**IBF**/WBO	Pompano Beach, Fla.
Dec. 23	Satoshi Iida	**Yokthai Sith-Oar**	Wu 12	**WBA**	Nagoya, JPN
Feb. 13	**Johnny Tapia**	Rudolfo Blanco	Wu 12	**IBF**/WBO	Alburquerque, N.M.
Apr. 25	**Gerry Penalosa**	Joel Luna Zarate	TDraw 2	**WBC**	Pasay City, PHI
Apr. 29	**Satoshi Iida**	Hiroki Ioka	Wm 12	**WBA**	Nagoya, JPN
May 9	Eric Morel	Orlando Malone	TKO 8	—	Madison, Wisc.
July 26	**Satoshi Iida**	Julio Gamboa	Wu 12	**WBA**	Nagoya, JPN
Aug. 29	Cho In-Joo	**Gerry Penalosa**	Ws 12	**WBC**	Seoul, KOR

Flyweights (112 lbs)

Date	Winner	Loser	Result	Title	Site
Oct. 4	Will Grigsby	Jesus Lopez	Wu 8	USBA	Rochester, Minn.
Oct. 10	Carlos Salazar	Everardo Morales	Wu 12	WBO	Resistencia, ARG
Nov. 12	Chatchai Saskul	**Yuri Arbachakov**	Wu 12	**WBC**	Sapporo, JPN
Nov. 22	**Jose Bonilla**	Keiji Yamaguchi	TKO 6	**WBA**	Osaka, JPN
Feb. 13	Will Grigsby	Javier Cintron	Wu 12	USBA	Albuquerque, N.M.
Feb. 22	**Mark Johnson**	Arthur Johnson	KO 1	**IBF**	Washington, D.C.
Feb. 27	S. Sow Ploenchit	Nico Barque Bas	TKO 8	—	Koh Samui, THAI
Feb. 27	**Chatchai Sasakul**	Yong-Jin Kim	Wu 12	**WBC**	Koh Samui, THAI
Mar. 21	Carlos Salazar	Jose (Carnita) Lopez	Ws 12	WBO	Chaco, ARG
May 1	**Chatchai Saskul**	Young-Soon Chang	KO 5	**WBC**	Bangkok, THAI
May 29	Hugo Soto	**Jose Bonilla**	Ws 12	**WBA**	Las Vegas
July 26	**Mark Johnson**	Luis Rolon	Wu 12	**IBF**	Verona, N.Y.
Sept. 4	**Mark Johnson**	Jose Laureano	KO 6	**IBF**	Atlantic City
Oct. 3	Mauricio Pastrana*	Jose Bonilla	Wu 12	**WBA**	Caracas, VEN

*Pastrana won the interim WBA title.

Junior Flyweights (108 lbs)
(Light Flyweights)

Date	Winner	Loser	Result	Title	Site
Dec. 13	Mauricio Pastrana	**Manuel J. Herrera**	TKO 3	**IBF**	Pompano Beach, Fla.
Jan. 16	Juan D. Cordoba	Melchor Cob Castro	Wu 12	WBO	Santiago, ARG
Mar. 1	**P. Chor Siriwat**	Kaaj Chartbandit	Wu 12	**WBA**	Bangkok, THAI
Mar. 8	**Saman Sor Jaturong**	Shiro Yahiro	TKO 4	**WBC**	Yokohama, JPN
Apr. 30	**Mauricio Pastrana**	Anis Roga	KO 4	**IBF**	Ft. Lauderdale, Fla.
May 9	Juan D. Cordoba	Sandro Oviedo	Wu 12	WBO	Santiago, ARG
June 21	Joma Gamboa	Ramel Gevero	KO 6	—	Mandaue, PHI
July 4	Jacob Matlala	Ric Magramo	Wu 10	—	Hammanskraal, S. Afr.
Aug. 29	**Mauricio Pastrana***	Carlos Murillo	TKO 9	**IBF**	Ft. Lauderdale, Fla.

*Pastrana won the fight was lost his title when he failed to make weight at the weigh-in. He must fight the IBF number-one contender to reclaim the IBF title.

Minimumweights (105 lbs)
(Strawweights or Mini-Flyweights)

Date	Winner	Loser	Result	Title	Site
Dec. 19	Eric Jamili	Mickey Cantwell	TKO 8	WBO	Millwall, ENG
Dec. 27	Zolani Petelo	**R. Sow Voraphin**	TKO 4	**IBF**	Songkhla, THAI
Mar. 7	**Ricardo Lopez**	**Rosendo Alvarez**	TDraw 7	**WBA/WBC**	Mexico City
Mar. 22	**Zolani Petelo**	Faisol Akbar	Ws 12	**IBF**	Hammanskraal, S. Afr.
May 30	Kermin Guardia	Eric Jamili	TKO 5	WBO	Las Vegas
July 4	**Zolani Petelo**	Carmelo Caceres	TKO 7	**IBF**	Hammanskraal, S. Afr.

Top Fighters Records

The career pro records of Welterweight Oscar De La Hoya, Light Heavyweight Roy Jones Jr. and Heavyweights Evander Holyfield and Mike Tyson, as of Oct. 12, 1998.

Roy Jones Jr.

Born: Jan. 16, 1969 **Pro record:** 37-1-0, 31 KOs
Height: 5'11" **Promoter:** Murad Muhammad
Weight: 180
Olympic medal: 1988 Silver as a light middleweight.

No	Date	Opponent, location	Result
1	5/6/89	Ricky Randall, Pensacola, Fla.	KO 2
2	6/11/89	Stephan Johnson, Atlantic City	KO 8
3	9/3/89	Ron Amundsen, Pensacola, Fla.	KO 7
4	11/30/89	Dave McCluskey, Pensacola, Fla.	KO 3
5	1/8/90	Joe Edens, Mobile, Alabama	KO 2
6	2/28/90	Billy Mitchum, Pensacola, Fla.	TKO 2
7	3/28/90	Knox Brown, Pensacola, Fla.	KO 3
8	5/11/90	Ron Johnson, Pensacola, Fla.	KO 2
9	7/14/90	Tony Waddles, Pensacola, Fla.	KO 1
10	9/25/90	Rollin Williams, Pensacola, Fla.	KO 4
11	11/8/90	Reggie Miller, Pensacola, Fla.	KO 5
12	1/31/91	Ricky Stackhouse, Pensacola, Fla.	KO 1
13	4/13/91	Eddie Evans, Pensacola, Fla.	TKO 3
14	8/3/91	Kevin Daigle, Pensacola, Fla.	TKO 2
15	8/31/91	Lester Yarbrough, Pensacola, Fla.	KO 8
16	1/10/92	Jorge Vaca, New York City	KO 1
17	4/3/92	Art Serwano, Reno	KO 1
18	6/30/92	Jorge Castro, Pensacola, Fla.	Wu 12
19	8/18/92	Glenn Thomas, Pensacola, Fla.	KO 8
20	12/5/92	Percy Harris, Atlantic City	KO 4
21	2/13/93	Glenn Wolfe, Las Vegas	KO 1
22	5/22/93	Bernard Hopkins, Washington D.C. **(won IBF middleweight title)**	Wu 12
23	8/14/93	Thulane Malinga, St. Louis Bay, Miss.	KO 6
24	11/30/93	Fermin Chirino, Pensacola, Fla.	W 10
25	3/22/94	Daniel Garcia, Pensacola, Fla.	KO 6
26	5/27/94	Thomas Tate, Las Vegas	KO 2
27	11/18/94	James Toney, Las Vegas **(won IBF super middleweight title)**	Wu 12
28	3/18/95	Antoine Byrd, Pensacola, Fla.	TKO 1
29	6/24/95	Vinny Pazienza, Atlantic City	TKO 6
30	9/30/95	Tony Thornton, Pensacola, Fla.	TKO 2
31	1/12/96	Merqui Sosa, New York City	TKO 2
32	6/15/96	Eric Lucas, Jacksonville, Fla.	KO 11
33	8/4/96	Bryant Brannon, New York City	KO 2
34	11/22/96	Mike McCallum, Tampa, Fla. **(won interim WBC light heavyweight title)**	Wu 12
35	3/21/97	Montel Griffin, Atlantic City **(lost WBC light heavyweight title)**	L-DQ 9
36	8/21/97	Montel Griffin, Ledyard, Conn. **(won WBC light heavyweight title)**	KO 1
37	4/25/98	Virgil Hill, Biloxi, Miss.	KO 4
38	7/18/98	Lou Del Valle, New York City **(won WBA light heavyweight title)**	Wu 12

AP/Wide World Photos

A determined **Oscar De La Hoya** beat Julio Cesar Chavez in 1998 when Chavez failed to answer the bell to start the ninth round of their WBC Welterweight championship bout on Sept. 18, 1998.

Oscar De La Hoya

Born: Feb. 4, 1973
Height: 5′10½″
Weight: 145
Olympic medal: 1992 Gold as a lightweight
Pro record: 29-0, 24 KOs
Promoter: Bob Arum

No	Date	Opponent, location	Result
1	11/23/92	Lamar Williams, Inglewood, Calif.	KO 1
2	12/12/92	Cliff Hicks, Phoenix	KO 1
3	1/3/93	Paris Alexander, Hollywood	TKO 2
4	2/6/93	Curtis Strong, San Diego	TKO 4
5	3/13/93	Jeff Mayweather, Las Vegas	TKO 4
6	4/6/93	Mike Grable, Rochester, N.Y.	Wu 8
7	5/8/93	Frank Avelar, Lake Tahoe	TKO 4
8	6/7/93	Troy Dorsey, Las Vegas	TKO 1
9	8/14/93	Renaldo Carter, Bay St. Louis, Miss.	KO 6
10	8/27/93	Angelo Nunez, Beverly Hills	TKO 4
11	10/30/93	Narcisco Valenzuela, Phoenix	KO 1
12	3/5/94	Jimmi Bredahl, Los Angeles	TKO 10
13	5/27/94	Giogio Campenella, Las Vegas	KO 3
14	7/29/94	Jorge Paez, Las Vegas	KO 2
15	11/18/94	Carl Griffith, Las Vegas	KO 3
16	12/10/94	John Avila, Los Angeles	TKO 9
17	2/18/95	John John Molina, Las Vegas	Wu 12
18	5/6/95	Rafael Ruelas, Las Vegas	TKO 2
		(won IBF lightweight title)	
19	9/9/95	Genaro Hernandez, Las Vegas	TKO 6
20	12/15/95	James Leija, New York City	TKO 2
21	2/9/96	Darryl Tyson, Las Vegas	KO 2
22	6/7/96	Julio Cesar Chavez, Las Vegas	TKO 4
		(won WBC super lightweight title)	
23	1/18/97	Miguel Angel Gonzalez, Las Vegas	Wu 12
24	4/12/97	Pernell Whitaker, Las Vegas	Wu 12
		(won WBC welterweight title)	
25	6/14/97	David Kamau, San Antonio	KO 2
26	9/13/97	Hector Camacho, Las Vegas	Wu 12
27	12/6/97	Wilfredo Rivera, Atlantic City	TKO 8
28	6/13/98	Patrick Charpentier, El Paso, Texas	TKO 3
29	9/18/98	Julio Cesar Chavez, Las Vegas	TKO 8

Evander Holyfield

Born: Oct. 19, 1962 **Pro record:** 36-3-0, 25 KOs
Height: 6′ 2½″ **Weight:** 217
Olympic medal: 1984 Bronze as light heavyweight (disqualifed for controversial late knockout punch in semifinal against Kevin Barry of New Zealand)

No	Date	Opponent, location	Result
1	11/15/84	Lionel Byarm, New York	Wu 6
2	1/20/85	Eric Winbush, Atlantic City	Wu 6
3	3/13/85	Freddie Brown, Norfolk	KO 1
4	4/20/85	Mark Rivera, Corpus Christi	KO 2
5	7/20/85	Tyrone Booze, Norfolk	Wu 8
6	8/29/85	Rick Myers, Atlanta	KO 1
7	10/30/85	Jeff Meachem, Atlantic City	KO 5
8	12/21/85	Anthony Davis, Virginia Beach	KO 4
9	3/1/86	Chisanda Mutti, Lancaster, Pa	KO 3
10	4/6/86	Jesse Shelby, Corpus Christi	KO 3
11	5/28/86	Terry Mims, Metairie, LA	KO 5
12	7/20/86	Dwight M. Qawi, Atlanta	Ws 15
		(won WBA cruiserweight title)	
13	12/8/86	Mike Brothers, Paris	KO 3
14	2/14/87	Henry Tillman, Reno	TKO 7
15	5/15/87	Rickey Parkey, Las Vegas	TKO 3
		(won IBF cruiserweight title)	
16	8/15/87	Ossie Ocasio, St.Topez, France	TKO 11
17	12/4/87	Dwight M. Qawi, Atlantic City	TKO 4
18	4/9/88	Carlos DeLeon, Las Vegas	KO 8
		(won WBC cruiserweight title)	
19	7/16/88	James Tillis, Lake Tahoe	KO 5
20	12/9/88	Pinklon Thomas, Atlantic City	TKO 7
21	3/11/89	Michael Dokes, Las Vegas	TKO 10
22	7/15/89	Adilson Rodrigues, Lake Tahoe	KO 2
23	11/4/89	Alex Stewart, Atlantic City	TKO 8
24	6/1/90	Seamus McDonagh, Atlantic City	TKO 4
25	10/25/90	Buster Douglas, Las Vegas	KO 3
		(won undisputed heavyweight title)	
26	4/19/91	George Foreman, Atlantic City	Wu 12
27	11/23/91	Bert Cooper, Atlanta	TKO 7
28	6/19/92	Larry Holmes, Las Vegas	Wu 12
29	11/13/92	Riddick Bowe, Las Vegas	Lu 12
		(lost undisputed heavyweight title)	
30	6/26/93	Alex Stewart, Atlantic City	Wu 12
31	11/6/93	Riddick Bowe, Las Vegas	Wm 12
		(won IBF/WBA heavyweight titles)	
32	4/22/94	Michael Moorer, Las Vegas	Lm 12
		(lost IBF/WBA heavyweight titles)	
33	5/20/95	Ray Mercer, Atlantic City	Wu 10
34	11/4/95	Riddick Bowe, Las Vegas	TKO by 8
35	5/10/96	Bobby Czyz, New York	TKO 5
36	11/9/96	Mike Tyson, Las Vegas	TKO 11
		(won WBC heavyweight title)	
37	6/28/97	Mike Tyson, Las Vegas	W Disq. 3
38	11/8/97	Michael Moorer, Las Vegas	TKO 8
		(won IBF/WBA heavyweight titles)	
39	9/19/98	Vaughn Bean, Atlanta	Wu 12

Mike Tyson

Born: June 30, 1966 **Pro record:** 45-3-0, 39 KOs
Height: 5′11″ **Manager:** Rory Holloway
Weight: 218

No	Date	Opponent, location	Result
1	3/6/85	Hector Mercedes, Albany, N.Y.	KO 1
2	4/10/85	Trent Singleton, Albany, N.Y.	TKO 1
3	5/23/85	Don Halpin, Albany, N.Y.	KO 4
4	6/20/85	Rick Spain, Atlantic City	KO 1
5	7/11/85	John Anderson, Atlantic City	TKO 2
6	7/19/85	Larry Sims, Poughkeepsie, N.Y.	KO 3
7	8/15/85	Lorenzo Canady, Atlantic City	TKO 1
8	9/5/85	Michael Johnson, Atlantic City	KO 1
9	10/9/85	Donnie Long, Atlantic City	KO 1
10	10/25/85	Robert Colay, Atlantic City	KO 1
11	11/1/85	Sterling Benjamin, Latham, N.Y.	TKO 1
12	11/13/85	Eddie Richardson, Houston	KO 1
13	11/22/85	Conroy Nelson, Latham, N.Y.	KO 2
14	12/6/85	Sammy Scaff, New York City	KO 1
15	12/27/85	Mark Young, Latham, N.Y.	KO 1
16	1/10/86	Dave Jaco, Albany, N.Y.	TKO 1
17	1/24/86	Mike Jameson, Atlantic City	TKO 5
18	2/16/86	Jesse Ferguson, Troy, N.Y.	TKO 6
19	3/10/86	Steve Zouski, Uniondale, N.Y.	KO 3
20	5/3/86	James Tillis, Glens Falls, N.Y.	Wu 10
21	5/20/86	Mitchell Green, New York City	Wu 10
22	6/13/86	Reggie Gross, New York City	TKO 1
23	6/28/86	William Hosea, Troy, N.Y.	KO 1
24	7/11/86	Lorenzo Boyd, Swan Lake, N.Y.	KO 2
25	7/26/86	Marvis Frazier, Glens Falls, N.Y.	KO 1
26	8/17/86	Jose Ribalta, Atlantic City	TKO 10
27	9/6/86	Alfonzo Ratliff, Las Vegas	KO 2
28	11/22/86	Trevor Berbick, Las Vegas	KO 2
		(won WBC heavyweight title)	
29	3/7/87	Bonecrusher Smith, Las Vegas	Wu 12
		(won WBA heavyweight title)	
30	5/30/87	Pinklon Thomas, Las Vegas	TKO 6
31	8/1/87	Tony Tucker, Las Vegas	Wu 12
		(won IBF heavyweight title)	
32	10/16/87	Tyrell Biggs, Atlantic City	TKO 7
33	1/22/88	Larry Holmes, Atlantic City	KO 4
34	3/21/88	Tony Tubbs, Tokyo	TKO 2
35	6/27/88	Michael Spinks, Atlantic City	KO 1
36	2/25/89	Frank Bruno, Las Vegas	TKO 5
37	7/21/89	Carl Williams, Atlantic City	TKO 1
38	2/10/90	Buster Douglas, Tokyo	KO by 10
		(lost world heavyweight title)	
39	6/16/90	Henry Tillman, Las Vegas	KO 1
40	12/8/90	Alex Stewart, Atlantic City	TKO 1
41	3/18/91	Razor Ruddock, Las Vegas	TKO 7
42	6/28/91	Razor Ruddock, Las Vegas	Wu 12
43	8/19/95	Peter McNeeley, Las Vegas	W disq. 1
		(first fight since release from prison)	
44	12/16/95	Buster Mathis Jr., Philadelphia	KO 3
45	3/16/96	Frank Bruno, Las Vegas	TKO 3
		(won WBC heavyweight title)	
46	9/7/96	Bruce Seldon, Las Vegas	TKO 1
		(won WBA heavyweight title)	
47	11/9/96	Evander Holyfield, Las Vegas	TKO by 11
		(lost WBA heavyweight title)	
48	6/28/97	Evander Holyfield, Las Vegas	L Disq 3
		(disqualified for biting Holyfield's ears)	

World Heavyweight Championship Fights

Widely accepted world champions in **bold** type. Note following result abbreviations: KO (knockout), TKO (technical knockout), Wu (unanimous decision), Wm (majority decision), Ws (split decision), Ref (referee's decision), ND (no decision), Disq (won on disqualification).

Year	Date	Winner	Age	Wgt	Loser	Wgt	Result	Location
1892	Sept. 7	James J. Corbett	26	178	John L. Sullivan	212	KO 21	New Orleans
1894	Jan. 25	**James J. Corbett**	27	184	Charley Mitchell	158	KO 3	Jacksonville, Fla.
1897	Mar. 17	Bob Fitzsimmons	34	167	**James J. Corbett**	183	KO 14	Carson City, Nev.
1899	June 9	James J. Jeffries	24	206	**Bob Fitzsimmons**	167	KO 11	Coney Island, N.Y.
1899	Nov. 3	**James J. Jeffries**	24	215	Tom Sharkey	183	Ref 25	Coney Island, N.Y.
1900	Apr. 6	**James J. Jeffries**	24	NA	Jack Finnegan	NA	KO 1	Detroit
1900	May 11	**James J. Jeffries**	25	218	James J. Corbett	188	KO 23	Coney Island, N.Y.
1901	Nov. 15	**James J. Jeffries**	26	211	Gus Ruhlin	194	TKO 6	San Francisco
1902	July 25	**James J. Jeffries**	27	219	Bob Fitzsimmons	172	KO 8	San Francisco
1903	Aug. 14	**James J. Jeffries**	28	220	James J. Corbett	190	KO 10	San Francisco
1904	Aug. 25	**James J. Jeffries***	29	219	Jack Munroe	186	TKO 2	San Francisco
1905	July 3	Marvin Hart	28	190	Jack Root	171	KO 12	Reno, Nev.
1906	Feb. 23	Tommy Burns	24	180	**Marvin Hart**	188	Ref 20	Los Angeles
1906	Oct. 2	**Tommy Burns**	25	NA	Jim Flynn	NA	KO 15	Los Angeles
1906	Nov. 28	**Tommy Burns**	25	172	Phila. Jack O'Brien	163½	Draw 20	Los Angeles
1907	May 8	**Tommy Burns**	25	180	Phila. Jack O'Brien	167	Ref 20	Los Angeles
1907	July 4	**Tommy Burns**	26	181	Bill Squires	180	KO 1	Colma, Calif.
1907	Dec. 2	**Tommy Burns**	26	177	Gunner Moir	204	KO 10	London
1908	Feb. 10	**Tommy Burns**	26	NA	Jack Palmer	NA	KO 4	London
1908	Mar. 17	**Tommy Burns**	26	NA	Jem Roche	NA	KO 1	Dublin
1908	Apr. 18	**Tommy Burns**	26	NA	Jewey Smith	NA	KO 5	Paris
1908	June 13	**Tommy Burns**	26	184	Bill Squires	183	KO 8	Paris
1908	Aug. 24	**Tommy Burns**	27	181	Bill Squires	184	KO 13	Sydney
1908	Sept. 2	**Tommy Burns**	27	183	Bill Lang	187	KO 6	Melbourne
1908	Dec. 26	Jack Johnson	30	192	**Tommy Burns**	168	TKO 14	Sydney
1909	Mar. 10	**Jack Johnson**	30	NA	Victor McLaglen	NA	ND 6	Vancouver
1909	May 19	**Jack Johnson**	31	205	Phila. Jack O'Brien	161	ND 6	Philadelphia
1909	June 30	**Jack Johnson**	31	207	Tony Ross	214	ND 6	Pittsburgh
1909	Sept. 9	**Jack Johnson**	31	209	Al Kaufman	191	ND 10	San Francisco
1909	Oct. 16	**Jack Johnson**	31	205½	Stanley Ketchel	170¼	KO 12	Colma, Calif.
1910	July 4	**Jack Johnson**	32	208	James J. Jeffries	227	KO 15	Reno, Nev.
1912	July 4	**Jack Johnson**	34	195½	Jim Flynn	175	TKO 9	Las Vegas, N.M.
1913	Dec. 19	**Jack Johnson**	35	NA	Jim Johnson	NA	Draw 10	Paris
1914	June 27	**Jack Johnson**	36	221	Frank Moran	203	Ref 20	Paris
1915	Apr. 5	Jess Willard	33	230	**Jack Johnson**	205½	KO 26	Havana
1916	Mar. 25	**Jess Willard**	34	225	Frank Moran	203	ND 10	NYC (Mad.Sq. Garden)
1919	July 4	Jack Dempsey	24	187	**Jess Willard**	245	TKO 4	Toledo, Ohio
1920	Sept. 6	**Jack Dempsey**	25	185	Billy Miske	187	KO 3	Benton Harbor, Mich.
1920	Dec. 14	**Jack Dempsey**	25	188¼	Bill Brennan	197	KO 12	NYC (Mad. Sq. Garden)
1921	July 2	**Jack Dempsey**	26	188	Georges Carpentier	172	KO 4	Jersey City, N.J.
1923	July 4	**Jack Dempsey**	28	188	Tommy Gibbons	175½	Ref 15	Shelby, Montana
1923	Sept. 14	**Jack Dempsey**	28	192½	Luis Firpo	216½	KO 2	NYC (Polo Grounds)
1926	Sept. 23	Gene Tunney	29	189½	**Jack Dempsey**	190	Wu 10	Philadelphia
1927	Sept. 22	**Gene Tunney**	30	189½	Jack Dempsey	192½	Wu 10	Chicago
1928	July 26	**Gene Tunney****	31	192	Tom Heeney	203	TKO 11	NYC (Yankee Stadium)

*James J. Jeffries retired as champion on May 13, 1905, then came out of retirement to fight Jack Johnson for the title in 1910.
**Gene Tunney retired as undefeated champion in 1928.

Year	Date	Winner	Age	Wgt	Loser	Wgt	Result	Location
1930	June 12	Max Schmeling	24	188	Jack Sharkey	197	Foul 4	NYC (Yankee Stadium)
1931	July 3	**Max Schmeling**	25	189	Young Stribling	186½	TKO 15	Cleveland
1932	June 21	Jack Sharkey	29	205	**Max Schmeling**	188	Ws 15	Long Island City, N.Y.
1933	June 29	Primo Carnera	26	260½	**Jack Sharkey**	201	KO 6	Long Island City, N.Y.
1933	Oct. 22	**Primo Carnera**	26	259½	Paulino Uzcudun	229¼	Wu 15	Rome
1934	Mar. 1	**Primo Carnera**	27	270	Tommy Loughran	184	Wu 15	Miami
1934	June 14	Max Baer	25	209½	**Primo Carnera**	263¼	TKO 11	Long Island City, N.Y.
1935	June 13	James J. Braddock	29	193¾	**Max Baer**	209	Wu 15	Long Island City, N.Y.
1937	June 22	Joe Louis	23	197¼	**James J. Braddock**	197	KO 8	Chicago
1937	Aug. 30	**Joe Louis**	23	197	Tommy Farr	204¼	Wu 15	NYC (Yankee Stadium)
1938	Feb. 23	**Joe Louis**	23	200	Nathan Mann	193½	KO 3	NYC (Mad. Sq. Garden)
1938	Apr. 1	**Joe Louis**	23	202½	Harry Thomas	196	KO 5	Chicago
1938	June 22	**Joe Louis**	24	198¾	Max Schmeling	193	KO 1	NYC (Yankee Stadium)
1939	Jan. 25	**Joe Louis**	24	200¼	John Henry Lewis	180¾	KO 1	NYC (Mad. Sq. Garden)
1939	Apr. 17	**Joe Louis**	24	201¼	Jack Roper	204¾	KO 1	Los Angeles
1939	June 28	**Joe Louis**	25	200¾	Tony Galento	233¾	TKO 4	NYC (Yankee Stadium)
1939	Sept. 20	**Joe Louis**	25	200	Bob Pastor	183	KO 11	Detroit
1940	Feb. 9	**Joe Louis**	25	203	Arturo Godoy	202	Ws 15	NYC (Mad. Sq. Garden)
1940	Mar. 29	**Joe Louis**	25	201½	Johnny Paychek	187½	KO 2	NYC (Mad. Sq. Garden)
1940	June 20	**Joe Louis**	26	199	Arturo Godoy	201¼	TKO 8	NYC (Yankee Stadium)
1940	Dec. 16	**Joe Louis**	26	202¼	Al McCoy	180¾	TKO 6	Boston
1941	Jan. 31	**Joe Louis**	26	202½	Red Burman	188	KO 5	NYC (Mad. Sq. Garden)
1941	Feb. 17	**Joe Louis**	26	203½	Gus Dorazio	193½	KO 2	Philadelphia
1941	Mar. 21	**Joe Louis**	26	202	Abe Simon	254½	TKO 13	Detroit
1941	Apr. 8	**Joe Louis**	26	203½	Tony Musto	199½	TKO 9	St. Louis
1941	May 23	**Joe Louis**	27	201½	Buddy Baer	237½	Disq 7	Washington, D.C.
1941	June 18	**Joe Louis**	27	199½	Billy Conn	174	KO 13	NYC (Polo Grounds)
1941	Sept. 29	**Joe Louis**	27	202¼	Lou Nova	202½	TKO 6	NYC (Polo Grounds)
1942	Jan. 9	**Joe Louis**	27	206¾	Buddy Baer	250	KO 1	NYC (Mad. Sq. Garden)
1942	Mar. 27	**Joe Louis**	27	207½	Abe Simon	255½	KO 6	NYC (Mad. Sq. Garden)
1942-45 World War II								
1946	June 9	**Joe Louis**	32	207	Billy Conn	187	KO 8	NYC (Yankee Stadium)
1946	Sept. 18	**Joe Louis**	32	211	Tami Mauriello	198½	KO 1	NYC (Yankee Stadium)
1947	Dec. 5	**Joe Louis**	33	211½	Jersey Joe Walcott	194½	Ws 15	NYC (Mad. Sq. Garden)
1948	June 25	**Joe Louis***	34	213½	Jersey Joe Walcott	194¾	KO 11	NYC (Yankee Stadium)
1949	June 22	**Ezzard Charles**	27	181¾	Jersey Joe Walcott	195½	Wu 15	Chicago
1949	Aug. 10	**Ezzard Charles**	28	180	Gus Lesnevich	182	TKO 8	NYC (Yankee Stadium)
1949	Oct. 14	**Ezzard Charles**	28	182	Pat Valentino	188½	KO 8	San Francisco
1950	Aug. 15	**Ezzard Charles**	29	183¼	Freddie Beshore	184½	TKO 14	Buffalo
1950	Sept. 27	**Ezzard Charles**	29	184½	Joe Louis	218	Wu 15	NYC (Yankee Stadium)
1950	Dec. 5	**Ezzard Charles**	29	185	Nick Barone	178½	KO 11	Cincinnati
1951	Jan. 12	**Ezzard Charles**	29	185	Lee Oma	193	TKO 10	NYC (Mad. Sq. Garden)
1951	Mar. 7	**Ezzard Charles**	29	186	Jersey Joe Walcott	193	Wu 15	Detroit
1951	May 30	**Ezzard Charles**	29	182	Joey Maxim	181½	Wu 15	Chicago
1951	July 18	Jersey Joe Walcott	37	194	**Ezzard Charles**	182	KO 7	Pittsburgh
1952	June 5	**Jersey Joe Walcott**	38	196	Ezzard Charles	191½	Wu 15	Philadelphia
1952	Sept. 23	Rocky Marciano	29	184	**Jersey Joe Walcott**	196	KO 13	Philadelphia
1953	May 15	**Rocky Marciano**	29	184½	Jersey Joe Walcott	197¾	KO 1	Chicago
1953	Sept. 24	**Rocky Marciano**	30	185	Roland LaStarza	184¾	TKO 11	NYC (Polo Grounds)
1954	June 17	**Rocky Marciano**	30	187½	Ezzard Charles	185½	Wu 15	NYC (Yankee Stadium)
1954	Sept. 17	**Rocky Marciano**	31	187	Ezzard Charles	192½	KO 8	NYC (Yankee Stadium)
1955	May 16	**Rocky Marciano**	31	189	Don Cockell	205	TKO 9	San Francisco
1955	Sept. 21	**Rocky Marciano****	32	188¼	Archie Moore	188	KO 9	NYC (Yankee Stadium)
1956	Nov. 30	Floyd Patterson	21	182¼	Archie Moore	187¾	KO 5	Chicago
1957	July 29	**Floyd Patterson**	22	184	Tommy Jackson	192½	TKO 10	NYC (Polo Grounds)
1957	Aug. 22	**Floyd Patterson**	22	187¼	Pete Rademacher	202	KO 6	Seattle
1958	Aug. 18	**Floyd Patterson**	23	184½	Roy Harris	194	TKO 13	Los Angeles
1959	May 1	**Floyd Patterson**	24	182½	Brian London	206	KO 11	Indianapolis
1959	June 26	Ingemar Johansson	26	196	**Floyd Patterson**	182	TKO 3	NYC (Yankee Stadium)

*Joe Louis retired as undefeated champion on Mar. 1, 1949, then came out of retirement to fight Ezzard Charles for the title in 1950.

**Rocky Marciano retired as undefeated champion on Apr. 27, 1956.

Year	Date	Winner	Age	Wgt	Loser	Wgt	Result	Location
1960	June 20	Floyd Patterson	25	190	**Ingemar Johansson**	194¾	KO 5	NYC (Polo Grounds)
1961	Mar. 13	**Floyd Patterson**	26	194¾	Ingemar Johansson	206½	KO 6	Miami Beach
1961	Dec. 4	**Floyd Patterson**	26	188½	Tom McNeeley	197	KO 4	Toronto
1962	Sept. 25	Sonny Liston	30	214	**Floyd Patterson**	189	KO 1	Chicago
1963	July 22	**Sonny Liston**	31	215	Floyd Patterson	194½	KO 1	Las Vegas
1964	Feb. 25	Cassius Clay**	22	210½	**Sonny Liston**	218	TKO 7	Miami Beach
1965	Mar. 5	Ernie Terrell WBA	25	199	Eddie Machen	192	Wu 15	Chicago
1965	May 25	**Muhammad Ali**	23	206	Sonny Liston	215¼	KO 1	Lewiston, Me.
1965	Nov. 1	Ernie Terrell WBA	26	206	George Chuvalo	209	Wu 15	Toronto
1965	Nov. 22	**Muhammad Ali**	23	210	Floyd Patterson	196¾	TKO 12	Las Vegas
1966	Mar. 29	**Muhammad Ali**	24	214½	George Chuvalo	216	Wu 15	Toronto
1966	May 21	**Muhammad Ali**	24	201½	Henry Cooper	188	TKO 6	London
1966	June 28	Ernie Terrell WBA	27	209½	Doug Jones	187½	Wu 15	Houston
1966	Aug. 6	**Muhammad Ali**	24	209½	Brian London	201½	KO 3	London
1966	Sept. 10	**Muhammad Ali**	24	203½	Karl Mildenberger	194¼	TKO 12	Frankfurt, W. Ger.
1966	Nov. 14	**Muhammad Ali**	24	212¾	Cleveland Williams	210½	TKO 3	Houston
1967	Feb. 6	**Muhammad Ali**	25	212¼	Ernie Terrell WBA	212½	Wu 15	Houston
1967	Mar. 22	**Muhammad Ali**	25	211½	Zora Folley	202½	KO 7	NYC (Mad. Sq. Garden)
1968	Mar. 4	Joe Frazier	24	204½	Buster Mathis	243½	TKO 11	NYC (Mad. Sq. Garden)
1968	Apr. 27	Jimmy Ellis	28	197	Jerry Quarry	195	Wm 15	Oakland
1968	June 24	Joe Frazier NY	24	203½	Manuel Ramos	208	TKO 2	NYC (Mad. Sq. Garden)
1968	Aug. 14	Jimmy Ellis WBA	28	198	Floyd Patterson	188	Ref 15	Stockholm
1968	Dec. 10	Joe Frazier NY	24	203	Oscar Bonavena	207	Wu 15	Philadelphia
1969	Apr. 22	Joe Frazier NY	25	204½	Dave Zyglewicz	190½	KO 1	Houston
1969	June 23	Joe Frazier NY	25	203½	Jerry Quarry	198½	TKO 8	NYC (Mad. Sq. Garden)
1970	Feb. 16	Joe Frazier NY	26	205	Jimmy Ellis WBA	201	TKO 5	NYC (Mad. Sq. Garden)
1970	Nov. 18	Joe Frazier	26	209	Bob Foster	188	KO 2	Detroit
1971	Mar. 8	Joe Frazier	27	205½	**Muhammad Ali**	215	Wu 15	NYC (Mad. Sq. Garden)
1972	Jan. 15	**Joe Frazier**	28	215½	Terry Daniels	195	TKO 4	New Orleans
1972	May 26	**Joe Frazier**	28	217½	Ron Stander	218	TKO 5	Omaha, Neb.
1973	Jan. 22	George Foreman	24	217½	**Joe Frazier**	214	TKO 2	Kingston, Jamaica
1973	Sept. 1	**George Foreman**	24	219½	Jose (King) Roman	196½	KO 1	Tokyo
1974	Mar. 26	**George Foreman**	25	224¾	Ken Norton	212¾	TKO 2	Caracas, Venezuela
1974	Oct. 30	Muhammad Ali	32	216½	**George Foreman**	220	KO 8	Kinshasa, Zaire
1975	Mar. 24	**Muhammad Ali**	33	223½	Chuck Wepner	225	TKO 15	Cleveland
1975	May 16	**Muhammad Ali**	33	224½	Ron Lyle	219	TKO 11	Las Vegas
1975	July 1	**Muhammad Ali**	33	224½	Joe Bugner	230	Wu 15	Kuala Lumpur, Malaysia
1975	Oct. 1	**Muhammad Ali**	33	224½	Joe Frazier	215	TKO 15	Manila, Philippines
1976	Feb. 20	**Muhammad Ali**	34	226	Jean Pierre Coopman	206	KO 5	San Juan, P.R.
1976	Apr. 30	**Muhammad Ali**	34	230	Jimmy Young	209	Wu 15	Landover, Md.
1976	May 24	**Muhammad Ali**	34	220	Richard Dunn	206½	TKO 5	Munich, W. Ger.
1976	Sept. 28	**Muhammad Ali**	34	221	Ken Norton	217½	Wu 15	NYC (Yankee Stadium)
1977	May 16	**Muhammad Ali**	35	221¼	Alfredo Evangelista	209¼	Wu 15	Landover, Md.
1977	Sept. 29	**Muhammad Ali**	35	225	Earnie Shavers	211¼	Wu 15	NYC (Mad. Sq. Garden)
1978	Feb. 15	Leon Spinks	24	197¼	**Muhammad Ali**	224¼	Ws 15	Las Vegas
1978	June 9	Larry Holmes	28	209	Ken Norton WBC††	220	Ws 15	Las Vegas
1978	Sept. 15	Muhammad Ali†	36	221	**Leon Spinks**	201	Wu 15	New Orleans
1978	Nov. 10	Larry Holmes WBC	29	214	Alfredo Evangelista	208¼	KO 7	Las Vegas
1979	Mar. 23	Larry Holmes WBC	29	214	Osvaldo Ocasio	207	TKO 7	Las Vegas
1979	June 22	Larry Holmes WBC	29	215	Mike Weaver	202	TKO 12	NYC (Mad. Sq. Garden)
1979	Sept. 28	Larry Holmes WBC	29	210	Earnie Shavers	211	TKO 11	Las Vegas
1979	Oct. 20	John Tate	24	240	Gerrie Coetzee	222	Wu 15	Pretoria, S. Africa
1980	Feb. 3	Larry Holmes WBC	30	213½	Lorenzo Zanon	215	TKO 6	Las Vegas
1980	Mar. 31	Mike Weaver	27	232	John Tate WBA	232	KO 15	Knoxville, Tenn.
1980	Mar. 31	Larry Holmes WBC	30	211	Leroy Jones	254½	TKO 8	Las Vegas
1980	July 7	Larry Holmes WBC	30	214¼	Scott LeDoux	226	TKO 7	Minneapolis
1980	Oct. 2	Larry Holmes WBC	30	211½	Muhammad Ali	217½	TKO 11	Las Vegas
1980	Oct. 25	Mike Weaver WBA	28	210	Gerrie Coetzee	226½	KO 13	Sun City, Boph'swana

**After defeating Liston, Cassius Clay announced that he had changed his name to Muhammad Ali. He was later stripped of his title by the WBA and most state boxing commissions after refusing induction into the U.S. Army on Apr. 28, 1967.

† Muhammad Ali retired as champion on June 27, 1979, then came out of retirement to fight Larry Holmes for the title in 1980.

†† WBC recognized Ken Norton as world champion when Leon Spinks refused to meet Norton before Spinks' rematch with Muhammad Ali. Norton had scored a 15-round split decision over Jimmy Young on Nov. 5, 1977 in Las Vegas.

Year	Date	Winner	Age	Wgt	Loser	Wgt	Result	Location
1981	Apr. 11	**Larry Holmes**	31	215	Trevor Berbick	215½	Wu 15	Las Vegas
1981	June 12	**Larry Holmes**	31	212¼	Leon Spinks	200¼	TKO 3	Detroit
1981	Oct. 3	Mike Weaver WBA	29	215	Quick Tillis	209	Wu 15	Rosemont, Ill.
1981	Nov. 6	**Larry Holmes**	32	213¼	Renaldo Snipes	215¾	TKO 11	Pittsburgh
1982	June 11	**Larry Holmes**	32	212½	Gerry Cooney	225½	TKO 13	Las Vegas
1982	Nov. 26	**Larry Holmes**	33	217½	Randall (Tex) Cobb	234¼	Wu 15	Houston
1982	Dec. 10	Michael Dokes	24	216	Mike Weaver WBA	209¾	TKO 1	Las Vegas
1983	Mar. 27	**Larry Holmes**	33	221	Lucien Rodriguez	209	Wu 12	Scranton, Pa.
1983	May 20	Michael Dokes WBA	24	223	Mike Weaver	218½	Draw 15	Las Vegas
1983	May 20	**Larry Holmes**	33	213	Tim Witherspoon	219½	Ws 12	Las Vegas
1983	Sept. 10	**Larry Holmes**	33	223	Scott Frank	211¼	TKO 5	Atlantic City
1983	Sept. 23	Gerrie Coetzee	28	215	Michael Dokes WBA	217	KO 10	Richfield, Ohio
1983	Nov. 25	**Larry Holmes**	34	219	Marvis Frazier	200	TKO 1	Las Vegas
1984	Mar. 9	Tim Witherspoon*	26	220¼	Greg Page	239½	Wm 12	Las Vegas
1984	Aug. 31	Pinklon Thomas	26	216	Tim Witherspoon WBC	217	Wm 12	Las Vegas
1984	Nov. 9	**Larry Holmes** IBF	35	221½	Bonecrusher Smith	227	TKO 12	Las Vegas
1984	Dec. 1	Greg Page	26	236½	Gerrie Coetzee WBA	218	KO 8	Sun City, Boph'swana
1985	Mar. 15	**Larry Holmes**	35	223½	David Bey	233¼	TKO 10	Las Vegas
1985	Apr. 29	Tony Tubbs	26	229	Greg Page WBA	239½	Wu 15	Buffalo
1985	May 20	**Larry Holmes**	35	222¼	Carl Williams	215	Wu 15	Las Vegas
1985	June 15	Pinklon Thomas	27	220¼	Mike Weaver	221¼	KO 8	Las Vegas
1985	Sept. 21	Michael Spinks	29	200	**Larry Holmes** IBF	221½	Wu 15	Las Vegas
1986	Jan. 17	Tim Witherspoon	28	227	Tony Tubbs WBA	229	Wm 15	Atlanta
1986	Mar. 22	Trevor Berbick	33	218½	Pinklon Thomas WBC	222¾	Wu 15	Las Vegas
1986	Apr. 19	**Michael Spinks**	29	205	Larry Holmes	223	Ws 15	Las Vegas
1986	July 19	Tim Witherspoon WBA	28	234¾	Frank Bruno	228	TKO 11	Wembley, England
1986	Sept. 6	**Michael Spinks**	30	201	Steffen Tangstad	214¾	TKO 4	Las Vegas
1986	Nov. 22	Mike Tyson	20	221¼	Trevor Berbick WBC	218½	TKO 2	Las Vegas
1986	Dec. 12	Bonecrusher Smith	33	228½	Tim Witherspoon WBA	233½	TKO 1	NYC (Mad. Sq. Garden)
1987	Mar. 7	Mike Tyson WBC	20	219	Bonecrusher Smith WBA	233	Wu 12	Las Vegas
1987	May 30	Mike Tyson	20	218¾	Pinklon Thomas	217¾	TKO 6	Las Vegas
1987	May 30	Tony Tucker**	28	222¼	Buster Douglas	227¼	TKO 10	Las Vegas
1987	June 15	**Michael Spinks**	30	208¾	Gerry Cooney	238	TKO 5	Atlantic City
1987	Aug. 1	Mike Tyson	21	221	Tony Tucker IBF	221	Wu 12	Las Vegas
1987	Oct. 16	Mike Tyson	21	216	Tyrell Biggs	228¾	TKO 7	Atlantic City
1988	Jan. 22	Mike Tyson	21	215¾	Larry Holmes	225¾	TKO 4	Atlantic City
1988	Mar. 20	Mike Tyson	21	216¼	Tony Tubbs	238¼	KO 2	Tokyo
1988	June 27	Mike Tyson	21	218¼	**Michael Spinks**	212¼	KO 1	Atlantic City
1989	Feb. 25	**Mike Tyson**	22	218	Frank Bruno	228	TKO 5	Las Vegas
1989	July 21	**Mike Tyson**	23	219¼	Carl Williams	218	TKO 1	Atlantic City
1990	Feb. 10	Buster Douglas	29	231½	**Mike Tyson**	220½	KO 10	Tokyo
1990	Oct. 25	Evander Holyfield	28	208	**Buster Douglas**	246	KO 3	Las Vegas
1991	Apr. 19	**Evander Holyfield**	28	208	George Foreman	257	Wu 12	Atlantic City
1991	Nov. 23	**Evander Holyfield**	29	210	Bert Cooper	215	TKO 7	Atlanta
1992	June 19	**Evander Holyfield**	29	210	Larry Holmes	233	Wu 12	Las Vegas
1992	Nov. 13	Riddick Bowe	25	235	**Evander Holyfield**	205	Wu 12	Las Vegas
1993	Feb. 6	**Riddick Bowe**	25	243	Michael Dokes	244	TKO 1	NYC (Mad. Sq. Garden)
1993	May 8	Lennox Lewis WBC†	27	235	Tony Tucker	235	Wu 12	Las Vegas
1993	May 22	**Riddick Bowe**	25	244	Jesse Ferguson	224	TKO 2	Washington, D.C.
1993	Oct. 1	Lennox Lewis WBC	28	233	Frank Bruno	238	TKO 7	Cardiff, Wales
1993	Nov. 6	Evander Holyfield	31	217	**Riddick Bowe**	246	Wm 12	Las Vegas
1994	Apr. 22	Michael Moorer	26	214	**Evander Holyfield**	214	Wm 12	Las Vegas
1994	May 6	Lennox Lewis WBC	28	235	Phil Jackson	218	TKO 8	Atlantic City
1994	Sept. 25	Oliver McCall	29	231¼	**Lennox Lewis** WBC	238	TKO 2	London

*WBC recognized winner of Mar. 9, 1984 fight between Tim Witherspoon and Greg Page as world champion after Larry Holmes relinquished title in dispute. IBF then recognized Holmes.

**IBF recognized winner of May 30, 1987 fight between Tony Tucker and James (Buster) Douglas as world champion after Michael Spinks relinquished title in dispute.

† WBC recognized Lennox Lewis as world champion when Riddick Bowe gave up that portion of his title on Dec. 14, 1992, rather than fight Lewis, the WBC's mandatory challenger.

Year	Date	Winner	Age	Wgt	Loser	Wgt	Result	Location
1994	Nov. 5	George Foreman*	45	250	**Michael Moorer**	222	KO 10	Las Vegas
1995	Apr. 8	Oliver McCall WBC	29	231	Larry Holmes	236	Wu 12	Las Vegas
1995	Apr. 8	Bruce Seldon*	28	236	Tony Tucker	240	TKO 7	Las Vegas
1995	Apr. 22	**George Foreman***	46	256	Axel Schulz	221	Wm 12	Las Vegas
1995	Aug. 19	Bruce Seldon WBA	28	234	Joe Hipp	223	TKO 10	Las Vegas
1995	Sept. 2	Frank Bruno	33	248	Oliver McCall WBC	235	Wu 12	London
1995	Dec. 9	Frans Botha**	27	227	Axel Schulz	222	Wu 12	Stuttgart, GER
1996	Mar. 16	Mike Tyson	29	220	Frank Bruno WBC	247	TKO 3	Las Vegas
1996	June 22	Michael Moorer**	28	222	Axel Schulz	223	Ws 12	Dortmund, GER
1996	Sept. 7	Mike Tyson WBC†	30	219	Bruce Seldon WBA	229	TKO 1	Las Vegas
1996	Nov. 9	Evander Holyfield	34	215	Mike Tyson WBA	222	TKO 11	Las Vegas
1997	Feb. 7	Lennox Lewis†	31	251	Oliver McCall	237	TKO 5	Las Vegas
1997	Mar. 29	Michael Moorer IBF	29	212	Vaughn Bean	212	Wm 12	Las Vegas
1997	June 28	Evander Holyfield WBA‡	34	218	Mike Tyson	218	Disq. 3	Las Vegas
1997	July 12	Lennox Lewis WBC	31	242	Henry Akinwande	237½	Disq. 5	Stateline, Nev.
1997	Oct. 4	Lennox Lewis WBC	32	244	Andrew Golota	244	TKO 1	Atlantic City
1997	Nov. 8	Evander Holyfield WBA	35	214	Michael Moorer IBF	223	TKO 8	Las Vegas
1998	Mar. 28	Lennox Lewis WBC	32	243	Shannon Briggs	228	TKO 5	Atlantic City
1998	Sept. 19	Evander Holyfield WBA/IBF	35	217	Vaughn Bean	231	Wu 12	Atlanta
1998	Sept. 26	Lennox Lewis WBC	33	250	Zeljko Mavrovic	220	Wu 12	Uncasville, Conn.

*George Foreman won WBA and IBF championships when he beat Michael Moorer on Nov. 5, 1994. He was stripped of WBA title on Mar. 4, 1995, when he refused to fight No. 1 contender Tony Tucker, and he relinquished IBF title on June 29, 1995, rather than give Axel Schulz a rematch. Tucker lost to Bruce Seldon in their April 8 fight for vacant WBA title.

**Botha won the vacant IBF title with a controversial 12–round decision over Axel Schulz on Dec. 9, 1995, but after legal sparring was eventually stripped of the IBF belt for using anabolic steroids. Moorer then claimed the revacated title with his June 22 win over Schulz.

†Mike Tyson won the WBC belt from Frank Bruno on Mar. 16 and still held it at the time of his Sept. 7 win over Bruce Seldon (although it was not at risk for that fight) but was forced to relinquish title after the bout for not fighting mandatory challenge Lennox Lewis. Tyson also paid Lewis $4 million to step aside and allow the Tyson-Seldon bout to take place. Lewis then fought Oliver McCall for the vacant WBC belt. The fight was stopped 55 seconds into round 5 because, inexplicably, McCall was visibly distraught and stopped throwing punches.

‡Holyfield won the bout by disqualification and retained the WBA belt after Tyson spit out his mouthpiece and bit off a piece of Holyfield's ear. Tyson received a two-point deduction from referee Mills Lane and after a stern warning and a short delay the fight was allowed to continue. Shortly thereafter he bit Holyfield's other ear and Tyson was disqualified.

All-Time Heavyweight Upsets

Buster Douglas was a 50-1 underdog when he defeated previously-unbeaten heavyweight champion Mike Tyson on Feb. 10, 1990. That 10th-round knockout ranks as the biggest upset in boxing history. By comparison, 45-year-old George Foreman was only a 3-1 underdog before he unexpectedly won the title from Michael Moorer on Nov. 5, 1994.

Here are the best-known upsets in the annals of the heavyweight division. All fights were for the world championship except the Max Schmeling-Joe Louis bout.

Date	Winner	Loser	Result	KO Time	Location
9/7/1892	James J. Corbett	John L. Sullivan	KO 21	1:30	Olympic Club, New Orleans
4/5/1915	Jess Willard	Jack Johnson	KO 26	1:26	Mariano Race Track, Havana
9/23/26	Gene Tunney	Jack Dempsey	Wu 10	–	Sesquicentennial Stadium, Phila.
6/13/35	James J. Braddock	Max Baer	Wu 15	–	Mad.Sq.Garden Bowl, L.I.City
6/19/36	Max Schmeling	Joe Louis	KO 12	2:29	Yankee Stadium, New York
7/18/51	Jersey Joe Walcott	Ezzard Charles	KO 7	0:55	Forbes Field, Pittsburgh
6/26/59	Ingemar Johansson	Floyd Patterson	TKO 3	2:03	Yankee Stadium, New York
2/25/64	Cassius Clay	Sonny Liston	TKO 7	*	Convention Hall, Miami Beach
10/30/74	Muhammad Ali	George Foreman	KO 8	2:58	20th of May Stadium, Zaire
2/15/78	Leon Spinks	Muhammad Ali	Ws 15	–	Hilton Pavilion, Las Vegas
9/21/85	Michael Spinks	Larry Holmes	Wu 15	–	Riviera Hotel, Las Vegas
2/10/90	Buster Douglas	Mike Tyson	KO 10	1:23	Tokyo Dome, Tokyo
11/5/94	George Foreman	Michael Moorer	KO 10	2:03	MGM Grand, Las Vegas
11/9/96	Evander Holyfield	Mike Tyson	TKO 11	0:37	MGM Grand, Las Vegas

*Liston failed to answer bell for Round 7.

Muhammad Ali's Career Pro Record

Born Cassius Marcellus Clay, Jr. on Jan. 17, 1942, in Louisville; Amateur record of 100-5; won light-heavyweight gold medal at 1960 Olympic Games; Pro record of 56-5-0 with 37 KOs in 61 fights.

1960

Date	Opponent (location)	Result
Oct. 29	Tunney Hunsaker, Louisville	Wu 6
Dec. 27	Herb Siler, Miami Beach	TKO 4

1961

Date	Opponent (location)	Result
Jan. 17	Tony Esperti, Miami Beach	TKO 3
Feb. 7	Jim Robinson, Miami Beach	TKO 1
Feb. 21	Donnie Fleeman, Miami Beach	TKO 7
Apr. 19	Lamar Clark, Louisville	KO 2
June 26	Duke Sabedong, Las Vegas	Wu 10
July 22	Alonzo Johnson, Louisville	Wu 10
Oct. 7	Alex Miteff, Louisville	TKO 6
Nov. 29	Willi Besmanoff, Louisville	TKO 7

1962

Date	Opponent (location)	Result
Feb. 10	Sonny Banks, New York	TKO 4
Feb. 28	Don Warner, Miami Beach	TKO 4
Apr. 23	George Logan, Los Angeles	TKO 4
May 19	Billy Daniels, Los Angeles	TKO 7
July 20	Alejandro Lavorante, Los Angeles	KO 5
Nov. 15	Archie Moore, Los Angeles	KO 4

1963

Date	Opponent (location)	Result
Jan. 24	Charlie Powell, Pittsburgh	KO 3
Mar. 13	Doug Jones, New York	Wu 10
June 18	Henry Cooper, London	TKO 5

1964

Date	Opponent (location)	Result
Feb. 25	Sonny Liston, Miami Beach **(won World Heavyweight title)**	TKO 7

After the fight, Clay announces he is a member of the Black Muslim religious sect and has changed his name to Muhammad Ali.

1965

Date	Opponent (location)	Result
May 25	Sonny Liston, Lewiston, Me	KO 1
Nov. 22	Floyd Patterson, Las Vegas	TKO 12

1966

Date	Opponent (location)	Result
Mar. 29	George Chuvalo, Toronto	Wu 15
May 21	Henry Cooper, London	TKO 6
Aug. 6	Brian London, London	KO 3
Sept.10	Karl Mildenberger, Frankfurt	TKO 12
Nov. 12	Cleveland Williams, Houston	TKO 3

1967

Date	Opponent (location)	Result
Feb. 6	Ernie Terrell, Houston	Wu 15
Mar. 22	Zora Folley, New York	KO 7
Apr. 28	Refuses induction into U.S. Army and is stripped of world title by WBA and most state commissions the next day.	
June 20	Found guilty of draft evasion in Houston; fined $10,000 and sentenced to 5 years; remains free pending appeals, but is barred from the ring.	

1968-69 (Inactive)

1970

Date	Opponent (location)	Result
Feb. 3	Announces retirement.	
Oct. 26	Jerry Quarry, Atlanta	TKO 3
Dec. 7	Oscar Bonavena, New York	TKO 15

1971

Date	Opponent (location)	Result
Mar. 8	Joe Frazier, New York **(for World Heavyweight title)**	Lu 15
June 28	U.S. Supreme Court reverses Ali's 1967 conviction saying he had been drafted improperly.	
July 26	Jimmy Ellis, Houston **(won vacant NABF Heavyweight title)**	TKO 12
Nov. 17	Buster Mathis, Houston	Wu 12
Dec. 26	Jurgen Blin, Zurich	KO 7

1972

Date	Opponent (location)	Result
Apr. 1	Mac Foster, Tokyo	Wu 15
May 1	George Chuvalo, Vancouver	Wu 12
June 27	Jerry Quarry, Las Vegas	TKO 7
July 19	Al (Blue) Lewis, Dublin, Ire	TKO 11
Sept.20	Floyd Patterson, New York	TKO 7
Nov. 21	Bob Foster, Stateline, Nev	TKO 8

1973

Date	Opponent (location)	Result
Feb. 14	Joe Bugner, Las Vegas	Wu 12
Mar. 31	Ken Norton, San Diego **(lost NABF Heavyweight title)**	Ls 12
Sept.10	Ken Norton, Inglewood, Calif **(regained NABF Heavyweight title)**	Ws 12
Oct. 20	Rudi Lubbers, Jakarta, Indonesia	Wu 12

1974

Date	Opponent (location)	Result
Jan. 28	Joe Frazier, New York	Wu 12
Oct. 30	George Foreman, Kinshasa, Zaire **(regained World Heavyweight title)**	KO 8

1975

Date	Opponent (location)	Result
Mar. 24	Chuck Wepner, Cleveland	TKO 15
May 16	Ron Lyle, Las Vegas	TKO 11
June 30	Joe Bugner, Kuala Lumpur, Malaysia	Wu 15
Sept.30	Joe Frazier, Manila	TKO 14

1976

Date	Opponent (location)	Result
Feb. 20	Jean-Pierre Coopman, San Juan	KO 5
Apr. 30	Jimmy Young, Landover, Md	Wu 15
May 24	Richard Dunn, Munich	TKO 5
Sept.28	Ken Norton, New York	Wu 15

1977

Date	Opponent (location)	Result
May 16	Alfredo Evangelista, Landover	Wu 15
Sept.29	Earnie Shavers, New York	Wu 15

1978

Date	Opponent (location)	Result
Feb. 15	Leon Spinks, Las Vegas **(lost World Heavyweight title)**	Ls 15
Sept.15	Leon Spinks, New Orleans **(regained World Heavyweight title)**	Wu 15

1979

Date	
June 27	Announces retirement.

1980

Date	Opponent (location)	Result
Oct. 2	Larry Holmes, Las Vegas	TKO by 11

1981

Date	Opponent (location)	Result
Dec. 11	Trevor Berbick, Nassau (retires after fight)	Lu 10

Foreman and Frazier

The career pro records of George Foreman and Joe Frazier as of Oct. 12, 1998

George Foreman

Born: Jan. 10, 1949 in Marshall, Tex.
Pro record: 75-5-0, 68 KO

No	Date	Opponent, location	Result	
1	6/23/69	Don Waldhelm, New York	KO	3
2	7/1/69	Fred Ashew, Houston	KO	1
3	7/14/69	Sylvester Dullaire, Wash., D.C.	KO	1
4	8/18/69	Chuck Wepner, New York	TKO	3
5	9/18/69	John Carroll, Seattle	KO	1
6	9/23/69	Cookie Wallace, Houston	KO	2
7	10/7/69	Vernon Clay, Houston	TKO	2
8	10/31/69	Roberto Davila, New York	Wu	8
9	11/5/69	Leo Peterson, Scranton	KO	4
10	11/18/69	Max Martinez, Houston	KO	2
11	12/6/69	Bob Hazelton, Las Vegas	KO	1
12	12/16/69	Levi Forte, Miami Beach	Wu	10
13	12/18/69	Gary Wilder, Seattle	TKO	1
14	1/6/70	Charley Polite, Houston	KO	4
15	1/26/70	Jack O'Halloran, New York	KO	5
16	2/16/70	Gregorio Peralta, New York	Wu	10
17	3/31/70	Rufus Brassell, Houston	KO	1
18	4/17/70	James J. Woody, New York	TKO	3
19	4/29/70	Aaron Easting, Cleveland	TKO	4
20	5/16/70	George Johnson, Inglewood	TKO	7
21	7/20/70	Roger Russell, Philadelphia	TKO	1
22	8/4/70	George Chuvalo, New York	TKO	3
23	11/3/70	Lou Bailey, Oklahoma City	KO	3
24	11/18/70	Boone Kirkman, New York	TKO	2
25	12/19/70	Mel Turnbow, Seattle	TKO	1
26	2/8/71	Charlie Boston, St. Paul, Minn.	KO	1
27	4/3/71	Stanford Harris, Lake Geneva	KO	2
28	5/10/71	Gregorio Peralta, Oakland	TKO	10
29	9/14/91	Vic Scott, El Paso	KO	1
30	9/21/71	Leroy Caldwell, Beaumont, Tex.	KO	2
31	10/7/71	Ollie Wilson, San Antonio	TKO	2
32	10/29/71	Luis F. Pires, New York	TKO	5
33	2/29/72	Murphy Goodwin, Austin, Tex.	KO	2
34	3/7/72	Clarence Boone, Beaumont, Tex.	TKO	2
35	4/10/72	Ted Gullick, Inglewood	KO	2
36	5/11/72	Miguel A. Paez, Oakland	KO	2
37	10/10/72	Terry Sorrels, Salt Lake City	KO	2
38	1/22/73	Joe Frazier, Kingston, Jamaica	TKO	2
		(won World Heavyweight title)		
39	9/1/73	Jose Roman, Tokyo	KO	1
40	3/26/74	Ken Norton, Caracus, Venezuela	TKO	2
41	10/30/74	Muhammad Ali, Kinshasa, Zaire	KO by	8
		(lost World Heavyweight title)		
42	1/24/76	Ron Lyle, Las Vegas	KO	5
43	6/15/76	Joe Frazier, Uniondale, N.Y.	TKO	5
44	8/14/76	Scott Le Doux, Utica, N.Y.	KO	3
45	10/15/76	Dino Denis, Hollywood, Fla.	TKO	4
46	1/22/77	Pedro Agosto, Pensacola, Fla.	TKO	4
47	3/17/77	Jimmy Young, Hato Rey, P.R.	Lu	12
		(retired after fight)		
48	3/9/87	Steve Zouski, Sacramento	TKO	4
		(first fight of comeback)		
49	7/9/87	Charles Hostetter, Oakland	KO	3
50	9/15/87	Bobby Crabree, Springfield, Mo.	TKO	6
51	11/21/87	Tim Anderson, Orlando	TKO	4
52	12/18/87	Rocky Sekorski, Las Vegas	TKO	3
53	1/23/88	Tom Trimm, Orlando	TKO	1
54	2/5/88	Guido Trane, Las Vegas	TKO	5
55	3/19/88	Dwight Qawi, Las Vegas	TKO	7
56	5/21/88	Frank Williams, Anchorage	KO	3
57	6/26/88	Carlos Hernandez, Atlantic City	TKO	4
58	8/25/88	Ladislao Mijangos, Ft. Myers	TKO	2
59	9/10/88	Bobby Hitz, Auburn Hills, Mich.	KO	1
60	10/27/88	Tony Fulilangi, Marshall, Tex.	TKO	2
61	12/28/88	David Jaco, Bakersfield, Calif.	KO	1
62	1/26/89	Mark Young, Rochester, N.Y.	TKO	7
63	2/16/89	Manuel de Almeida, Orlando	TKO	3
64	4/30/89	J.B. Williamson, Galveston, Tex.	TKO	5
65	6/1/89	Bert Cooper, Phoenix	TKO	3
66	7/20/89	Everett Martin, Tucson	Wu	10
67	1/15/90	Gerry Cooney, Atlantic City	KO	2
68	4/17/90	Mike Jameson, Stateline, Nev.	TKO	4
69	6/16/90	Adilson Rodrigues, Las Vegas	KO	2
70	7/31/90	Ken Lakusta, Edmonton	KO	3
71	9/25/90	Terry Anderson, Millwall, England	KO	1
72	4/19/91	Evander Holyfield, Atlantic City	Lu	12
		(for World Heavyweight title)		
73	12/7/91	Jimmy Ellis, Reno, Nev.	TKO	3
74	4/11/92	Alex Stewart, Las Vegas	Wm	10
75	1/16/93	Pierre Coetzer, Reno, Nev.	TKO	8
76	6/7/93	Tommy Morrison, Las Vegas	Lu	12
77	11/5/94	Michael Moorer, Las Vegas	KO	10
		(won WBA/IBF Heavyweight titles)		
78	4/22/95	Axel Schulz, Las Vegas	Wm	12
79	11/3/96	Crawford Grimsley, Tokyo	Wu	12
80	11/22/97	Shannon Briggs, Atlantic City	Lm	12

Joe Frazier

Born: Jan. 12, 1944 in Beaufort, S.C.
Pro record: 32-4-1, 27 KO

No	Date	Opponent	Result	
1	8/16/65	Woody Gross	TKO	1
2	9/20/65	Michael Bruce	KO	3
3	9/28/65	Ray Staples	KO	2
4	11/11/65	Abe Davis	KO	1
5	1/17/66	Mel Turnbow	KO	1
6	3/4/66	Dick Wipperman	TKO	5
7	4/4/66	Charley Polite	TKO	2
8	4/28/66	Don Smith	KO	3
9	5/19/66	Chuck Leslie	KO	3
10	5/26/66	Memphis Jones	KO	1
11	7/25/66	Billy Daniels	TKO	6
12	9/21/66	Oscar Bonavena	Wu	10
13	11/21/66	Eddie Machen	TKO	10
14	2/21/67	Doug Jones	KO	5
15	4/11/67	Jeff Davis	KO	5
16	5/4/67	George Johnson	Wu	10
17	7/19/67	George Chuvalo	TKO	4
18	10/17/67	Tony Doyle	TKO	2
19	12/18/67	Marion Connors	KO	3
20	3/4/68	Buster Mathis	KO	11
21	6/24/68	Manuel Ramos	TKO	2
22	12/10/68	Oscar Bonavena	Wu	15
23	4/22/69	Dave Zyglewicz	KO	1
24	6/23/69	Jerry Quarry	TKO	7
25	2/6/70	Jimmy Ellis	TKO	5
		(won World Heavyweight title)		
26	11/18/70	Bob Foster	KO	2
27	3/8/71	Muhammad Ali	Wu	15
28	1/15/72	Terry Daniels	TKO	4
29	5/25/72	Ron Stander	TKO	5
30	1/22/73	George Foreman	TKO by	2
		(lost World Heavyweight title)		
31	7/2/73	Joe Bugner	Wu	12
32	1/28/74	Muhammad Ali	Lu	12
33	6/17/74	Jerry Quarry	TKO	5
34	4/1/75	Jimmy Ellis	TKO	9
35	9/30/75	Muhammad Ali	TKO by	14
		(for World Heavyweight title)		
36	6/15/76	George Foreman	KO by	5
37	3/12/81	Floyd Cummings	Draw	10

Major Titleholders

Note the following sanctioning body abbreviations: NBA (National Boxing Association), WBA (World Boxing Association), WBC (World Boxing Council), GBR (Great Britain), IBF (International Boxing Federation), plus other national and state commissions. Fighters who retired as champion are indicated by (*) and champions who abandoned or relinquished their titles are indicated by (†).

Heavyweights

Widely accepted champions in CAPITAL letters. Current champions in **bold** type (as of Oct. 12, 1998).

Note: that Muhammad Ali was stripped of his world title in 1967 after refusing induction into the Army (see Muhammad Ali's Career Pro Record). George Foreman was stripped of his WBA and IBF titles in 1995, but remained active as linear champion (see Boxing: Major Bouts 1996-97).

Champion	Held Title
JOHN L. SULLIVAN	1885-92
JAMES J. CORBETT	1892-97
BOB FITZSIMMONS	1897-99
JAMES J. JEFFRIES	1899-1905*
MARVIN HART	1905-06
TOMMY BURNS	1906-08
JACK JOHNSON	1908-15
JESS WILLARD	1915-19
JACK DEMPSEY	1919-26
GENE TUNNEY	1926-28*
MAX SCHMELING	1930-32
JACK SHARKEY	1932-33
PRIMO CARNERA	1933-34
MAX BAER	1934-35
JAMES J. BRADDOCK	1935-37
JOE LOUIS	1937-49*
EZZARD CHARLES	1949-51
JERSEY JOE WALCOTT	1951-52
ROCKY MARCIANO	1952-56*
FLOYD PATTERSON	1956-59
INGEMAR JOHANSSON	1959-60
FLOYD PATTERSON	1960-62
SONNY LISTON	1962-64
CASSIUS CLAY (MUHAMMAD ALI)	1964-70
Ernie Terrell (WBA)	1965-67
Joe Frazier (NY)	1968-70
Jimmy Ellis (WBA)	1968-70
JOE FRAZIER	1970-73
GEORGE FOREMAN	1973-74
MUHAMMAD ALI	1974-78
LEON SPINKS	1978
Ken Norton (WBC)	1978
Larry Holmes (WBC)	1978-80
MUHAMMAD ALI	1978-79*
John Tate (WBA)	1979-80
Mike Weaver (WBA)	1980-82
LARRY HOLMES	1980-85
Michael Dokes (WBA)	1982-83
Gerrie Coetzee (WBA)	1983-84
Tim Witherspoon (WBC)	1984
Pinklon Thomas (WBC)	1984-86
Greg Page (WBA)	1984-85
MICHAEL SPINKS	1985-87
Tim Witherspoon (WBA)	1986
Trevor Berbick (WBC)	1986
Mike Tyson (WBC)	1986-87
James (Bonecrusher) Smith (WBA)	1986-87
Tony Tucker (IBF)	1987
MIKE TYSON (WBC, WBA, IBF)	1987-90
BUSTER DOUGLAS (WBC, WBA, IBF)	1990
EVANDER HOLYFIELD (WBC, WBA, IBF)	1990-92
Riddick Bowe (WBA, IBF)	1992-93
Lennox Lewis (WBC)	1992-94
EVANDER HOLYFIELD (WBA, IBF)	1993-94
MICHAEL MOORER (WBA, IBF)	1994
Oliver McCall (WBC)	1994-95
GEORGE FOREMAN (WBA, IBF)	1994-95
Bruce Seldon (WBA)	1995-96
GEORGE FOREMAN	1995-96
Frank Bruno (WBC)	1995-96
Mike Tyson (WBC)	1996†
Mike Tyson (WBA)	1996
Michael Moorer (IBF)	1996-1997
Evander Holyfield (WBA, IBF)	1996—
Lennox Lewis (WBC)	1997—

Note: John L. Sullivan held the Bare Knuckle championship from 1882-85.

Light Heavyweights

Widely accepted champions in CAPITAL letters. Current champions in **bold** type.

Champion	Held Title
JACK ROOT	1903
GEORGE GARDNER	1903
BOB FITZSIMMONS	1903-05
PHILADELPHIA JACK O'BRIEN	1905-12*
JACK DILLON	1914-16
BATTLING LEVINSKY	1916-20
GEORGES CARPENTIER	1920-22
BATTLING SIKI	1922-23
MIKE McTIGUE	1923-25
PAUL BERLENBACH	1925-26
JACK DELANEY	1926-27†
Jimmy Slattery (NBA)	1927
TOMMY LOUGHRAN	1927-29
JIMMY SLATTERY	1930
MAXIE ROSENBLOOM	1930-34
George Nichols (NBA)	1932
Bob Godwin (NBA)	1933
BOB OLIN	1934-35
JOHN HENRY LEWIS	1935-38
MELIO BETTINA (NY)	1939
Len Harvey (GBR)	1939-42
BILLY CONN	1939-40†
ANTON CHRISTOFORIDIS (NBA)	1941
GUS LESNEVICH	1941-48
Freddie Mills (GBR)	1942-46
FREDDIE MILLS	1948-50
JOEY MAXIM	1950-52
ARCHIE MOORE	1952-62
Harold Johnson (NBA)	1961
HAROLD JOHNSON	1962-63
WILLIE PASTRANO	1963-65
Eddie Cotton (Mich.)	1963-64
JOSE TORRES	1965-66
DICK TIGER	1966-68
BOB FOSTER	1968-74*
Vicente Rondon (WBA)	1971-72
John Conteh (WBC)	1974-77
Victor Galindez (WBA)	1974-78
Miguel A. Cuello (WBC)	1977-78
Mate Parlov (WBC)	1978
Mike Rossman (WBA)	1978-79
Marvin Johnson (WBC)	1978-79
Matthew (Franklin) Saad Muhammad (WBC)	1979-81
Marvin Johnson (WBA)	1979-80

Champion	Held Title
Eddie (Gregory) Mustapha Muhammad (WBA)	1980-81
Michael Spinks (WBA)	1981-83
Dwight (Braxton) Muhammad Qawi (WBC)	1981-83
MICHAEL SPINKS	1983-85†
J.B.Williamson (WBC)	1985-86
Slobodan Kacar (IBF)	1985-86
Marvin Johnson (WBA)	1986-87
Dennis Andries (WBC)	1986-87
Bobby Czyz (IBF)	1986-87
Leslie Stewart (WBA)	1987
Virgil Hill (WBA)	1987-91
Prince Charles Williams (IBF)	1987-93
Thomas Hearns (WBC)	1987
Donny Lalonde (WBC)	1987-88
Sugar Ray Leonard (WBC)	1988
Dennis Andries (WBC)	1989
Jeff Harding (WBC)	1989-90
Dennis Andries (WBC)	1990-91
Jeff Harding (WBC)	1991-94
Thomas Hearns (WBA)	1991-92
Iran Barkley (WBA)	1992†
Virgil Hill (WBA)	1992-97
Henry Maske (IBF)	1993-96
Virgil Hill (WBA/IBF)	1996-97
Mike McCallum (WBC)	1994-95
Fabrice Tiozzo (WBC)	1995-96
Roy Jones Jr. (WBC)	1996
Montell Griffin (WBC)	1996
D. Michaelczewski (WBA/IBF)	1997†
William Guthrie (IBF)	1997-98
Lou Del Valle (WBA)	1997-98
Roy Jones Jr. (WBA, WBC)	1997–
Reggie Johnson (IBF)	1998–

Middleweights

Widely accepted champions in CAPITAL letters. Current champions in **bold** type.

Champion	Held Title
JACK (NONPAREIL) DEMPSEY	1884-91
BOB FITZSIMMONS	1891-97
CHARLES (KID) McCOY	1897-98
TOMMY RYAN	1898-1907
STANLEY KETCHEL	1908
BILLY PAPKE	1908
STANLEY KETCHEL	1908-10
FRANK KLAUS	1913
GEORGE CHIP	1913-14
AL McCOY	1914-17
Jeff Smith (AUS)	1914
Mick King (AUS)	1914
Jeff Smith (AUS)	1914-15
Lee Darcy (AUS)	1915-17
MIKE O'DOWD	1917-20
JOHNNY WILSON	1920-23
Wm. Bryan Downey (Ohio)	1921-22
Dave Rosenberg (NY)	1922
Jock Malone (Ohio)	1922-23
Mike O'Dowd (NY)	1922
Lou Bogash (NY)	1923
HARRY GREB	1923-26
TIGER FLOWERS	1926
MICKEY WALKER	1926-31†
GORILLA JONES	1931-32
MARCEL THIL	1932-37
Ben Jeby (NY)	1932-33
Lou Brouillard (NBA, NY)	1933
Vince Dundee (NBA, NY)	1933-34
Teddy Yarosz (NBA, NY)	1934-35
Babe Risko (NBA, NY)	1935-36
Freddie Steele (NBA, NY)	1936-38
FRED APOSTOLI	1937-39
Al Hostak (NBA)	1938
Solly Krieger (NBA)	1938-39
Al Hostak (NBA)	1939-40
CEFERINO GARCIA	1939-40
KEN OVERLIN	1940-41
Tony Zale (NBA)	1940-41
BILLY SOOSE	1941
TONY ZALE	1941-47
ROCKY GRAZIANO	1947-48
TONY ZALE	1948
MARCEL CERDAN	1948-49
JAKE LA MOTTA	1949-51
SUGAR RAY ROBINSON	1951
RANDY TURPIN	1951
SUGAR RAY ROBINSON	1951-52*
CARL (BOBO) OLSON	1953-55
SUGAR RAY ROBINSON	1955-57
GENE FULLMER	1957
SUGAR RAY ROBINSON	1957
CARMEN BASILIO	1957-58
SUGAR RAY ROBINSON	1958-60
Gene Fullmer (NBA)	1959-62
PAUL PENDER	1960-61
TERRY DOWNES	1961-62
PAUL PENDER	1962-63
Dick Tiger (WBA)	1962-63
DICK TIGER	1963
JOEY GIARDELLO	1963-65
DICK TIGER	1965-66
EMILE GRIFFITH	1966-67
NINO BENVENUTI	1967
EMILE GRIFFITH	1967-68
NINO BENVENUTI	1968-70
CARLOS MONZON	1970-77*
Rodrigo Valdez (WBC)	1974-76
RODRIGO VALDEZ	1977-78
HUGO CORRO	1978-79
VITO ANTUOFERMO	1979-80
ALAN MINTER	1980
MARVELOUS MARVIN HAGLER	1980-87
SUGAR RAY LEONARD	1987
Frank Tate (IBF)	1987-88
Sumbu Kalambay (WBA)	1987-89
Thomas Hearns (WBC)	1987-88
Iran Barkley (WBC)	1988-89
Michael Nunn(IBF)	1988-91
Roberto Duran (WBC)	1989-90*
Mike McCallum (WBA)	1989-91
Julian Jackson (WBC)	1990-93
James Toney (IBF)	1991-93†
Reggie Johnson (WBA)	1992-93
Roy Jones Jr. (IBF)	1993-94†
Gerald McClellan (WBC)	1993-95†
John David Jackson (WBA)	1993-94
Jorge Castro (WBA)	1994-97
Julian Jackson (WBC)	1995
Bernard Hopkins (IBF)	1995–
Quincy Taylor (WBC)	1995-96
Shinji Takehara (WBA)	1995-96
William Joppy (WBA)	1996-97
Keith Holmes (WBC)	1996-98
Julio Cesar Green (WBA)	1997-98
William Joppy (WBA)	1998–
Hassine Cherifi (WBC)	1998–

Welterweights

Widely accepted champions in CAPITAL letters. Current champions in **bold**type.

Champion	Held Title
PADDY DUFFY	1888-90
MYSTERIOUS BILLY SMITH	1892-94
TOMMY RYAN	1894-98
MYSTERIOUS BILLY SMITH	1898-1900
MATTY MATTHEWS	1900
EDDIE CONNOLLY	1900
JAMES (RUBE) FERNS	1900
MATTY MATHEWS	1900-01
JAMES (RUBE) FERNS	1901
JOE WALCOTT	1901-04
THE DIXIE KID	1904-05
HONEY MELLODY	1906-07
Mike (Twin) Sullivan	1907-08†
Harry Lewis	1908-11
Jimmy Gardner	1908
Jimmy Clabby	1910-11
WALDEMAR HOLBERG	1914
TOM McCORMICK	1914
MATT WELLS	1914-15
MIKE GLOVER	1915
JACK BRITTON	1915
TED (KID) LEWIS	1915-16
JACK BRITTON	1916-17
TED (KID) LEWIS	1917-19
JACK BRITTON	1919-22
MICKEY WALKER	1922-26
PETE LATZO	1926-27
JOE DUNDEE	1927-29
JACKIE FIELDS	1929-30
YOUNG JACK THOMPSON	1930
TOMMY FREEMAN	1930-31
YOUNG JACK THOMPSON	1931
LOU BROUILLARD	1931-32
JACKIE FIELDS	1932-33
YOUNG CORBETT III	1933
JIMMY McLARNIN	1933-34
BARNEY ROSS	1934
JIMMY McLARNIN	1934-35
BARNEY ROSS	1935-38
HENRY ARMSTRONG	1938-40
FRITZIE ZIVIC	1940-41
Izzy Jannazzo (Md.)	1940-41
Freddie (Red) Cochrane	1941-46
MARTY SERVO	1946*
SUGAR RAY ROBINSON	1946-51†
Johnny Bratton	1951
KID GAVILAN	1951-54
JOHNNY SAXTON	1954-55
TONY DeMARCO	1955
CARMEN BASILIO	1955-56
JOHNNY SAXTON	1956
CARMEN BASILIO	1956-57†
VIRGIL AKINS	1958
DON JORDAN	1958-60
BENNY (KID) PARET	1960-61
EMILE GRIFFITH	1961
BENNY (KID) PARET	1961-62
EMILE GRIFFITH	1962-63
LUIS RODRIGUEZ	1963
EMILE GRIFFITH	1963-66†
Charlie Shipes (Calif.)	1966-67
CURTIS COKES	1966-69
JOSE NAPOLES	1969-70
BILLY BACKUS	1970-71
JOSE NAPOLES	1971-75
Hedgemon Lewis (NY)	1972-73
Angel Espada (WBA)	1975-76
JOHN H. STRACEY	1975-76
CARLOS PALOMINO	1976-79
Pipino Cuevas (WBA)	1976-80
WILFREDO BENITEZ	1979
SUGAR RAY LEONARD	1979-80
ROBERTO DURAN	1980
Thomas Hearns (WBA)	1980-81
SUGAR RAY LEONARD	1980-82
Donald Curry (WBA)	1983-85
Milton McCrory (WBC)	1983-85
DONALD CURRY	1985-86
LLOYD HONEYGHAN	1986-87
JORGE VACA (WBC)	1987-88
LLOYD HONEYGHAN (WBC)	1988-89
Mark Breland (WBA)	1987
Marlon Starling (WBA)	1987-88
Tomas Molinares (WBA)	1988-89
Simon Brown (IBF)	1988-91
Mark Breland (WBA)	1989-90
MARLON STARLING (WBC)	1989-90
Aaron Davis (WBA)	1990-91
Maurice Blocker (WBC)	1990-91
Meldrick Taylor (WBA)	1991-92
Simon Brown (WBC)	1991
Maurice Blocker (IBF)	1991-93
Buddy McGirt (WBC)	1991-93
Crisanto Espana (WBA)	1992-94
Pernell Whitaker (WBC)	1993-97
Felix Trinidad (IBF)	1993–
Ike Quartey (WBA)	1994-98†
Oscar De La Hoya (WBC)	1997–

Lightweights

Widely accepted champions in CAPITAL letters. Current champions in **bold** type.

Champion	Held Title
JACK McAULIFFE	1886-94
GEORGE (KID) LAVIGNE	1896-99
FRANK ERNE	1899-02
JOE GANS	1902-04
JIMMY BRITT	1904-05
BATTLING NELSON	1905-06
JOE GANS	1906-08
BATTLING NELSON	1908-10
AD WOLGAST	1910-12
WILLIE RITCHIE	1912-14
FREDDIE WELSH	1915-17
BENNY LEONARD	1917-25*
JIMMY GOODRICH	1925
ROCKY KANSAS	1925-26
SAMMY MANDELL	1926-30
AL SINGER	1930
TONY CANZONERI	1930-33
BARNEY ROSS	1933-35†
TONY CANZONERI	1935-36
LOU AMBERS	1936-38
HENRY ARMSTRONG	1938-39
LOU AMBERS	1939-40
Sammy Angott (NBA)	1940-41
LEW JENKINS	1940-41
SAMMY ANGOTT	1941-42
Beau Jack (NY)	1942-43
Slugger White (Md.)	1943
Bob Montgomery (NY)	1943

Champion	Held Title
Sammy Angott (NBA)	1943-44
Beau Jack (NY)	1943-44
Bob Montgomery (NY)	1944-47
Juan Zurita (NBA)	1944-45
IKE WILLIAMS	1947-51
JAMES CARTER	1951-52
LAURO SALAS	1952
JAMES CARTER	1952-54
PADDY DeMARCO	1954
JAMES CARTER	1954-55
WALLACE (BUD) SMITH	1955-56
JOE BROWN	1956-62
CARLOS ORTIZ	1962-65
Kenny Lane (Mich.)	1963-64
ISMAEL LAGUNA	1965
CARLOS ORTIZ	1965-68
CARLOS TEO CRUZ	1968-69
MANDO RAMOS	1969-70
ISMAEL LAGUNA	1970
KEN BUCHANAN	1970-72
Pedro Carrasco (WBC)	1971-72
Mando Ramos (WBC)	1972
ROBERTO DURAN	1972-79†
Chango Carmona (WBC)	1972
Rodolfo Gonzalez (WBC)	1972-74
Ishimatsu Suzuki (WBC)	1974-76
Esteban De Jesus (WBC)	1976-78
Jim Watt (WBC)	1979-81
Ernesto Espana (WBA)	1979-80
Hilmer Kenty (WBA)	1980-81
Sean O'Grady (WBA,WAA)	1981
Alexis Arguello (WBC)	1981-82
Claude Noel (WBA)	1981
Andrew Ganigan (WAA)	1981-82
Arturo Frias (WBA)	1981-82
Ray Mancini (WBA)	1982-84
ALEXIS ARGUELLO	1982-83
Edwin Rosario (WBC)	1983-84
Choo Choo Brown (IBF)	1984
Livingstone Bramble (WBA)	1984-86
Harry Arroyo (IBF)	1984-85
Jose Luis Ramirez (WBC)	1984-85
Jimmy Paul (IBF)	1985-86
Hector Camacho (WBC)	1985-86
Edwin Rosario (WBA)	1986-87
Greg Haugen (IBF)	1986-87
Julio Cesar Chavez (WBA)	1987-88
Jose Luis Ramirez (WBC)	1987-88
JULIO CESAR CHAVEZ (WBC,WBA)	1988-89
Vinny Pazienza (IBF)	1987-88
Greg Haugen (IBF)	1988-89
Pernell Whitaker (IBF,WBC)	1989-90
Edwin Rosario (WBA)	1989-90
Juan Nazario (WBA)	1990
PERNELL WHITAKER (IBF, WBC, WBA)	1990-92†
Joey Gamache (WBA)	1992
Miguel A. Gonzalez (WBC)	1992-96
Tony Lopez (WBA)	1992-93
Dingaan Thobela (WBA)	1993
Fred Pendleton (IBF)	1993-94
Orzubek Nazarov (WBA)	1993-98
Rafael Ruelas (IBF)	1994-95
Oscar De La Hoya (IBF)	1995†
Phillip Holiday (IBF)	1995-97
Jean-Baptiste Mendy (WBC)	1996-97
Steve Johnston (WBC)	1997-98
Shane Mosley (IBF)	1997—
Cesar Bazan (WBC)	1998—
Jean-Baptiste Mendy (WBA)	1998—

Featherweights

Widely accepted champions in CAPITAL letters. Current champions in **bold** type.

Champion	Held Title
TORPEDO BILLY MURPHY	1890
YOUNG GRIFFO	1890-92
GEORGE DIXON	1892-97
SOLLY SMITH	1897-98
Ben Jordan (GBR)	1898-99
Eddie Santry (GBR)	1899-1900
DAVE SULLIVAN	1898
GEORGE DIXON	1898-1900
TERRY McGOVERN	1900-01
YOUNG CORBETT II	1901-04
JIMMY BRITT	1904
ABE ATTELL	1904
BROOKLYN TOMMY SULLIVAN	1904-05
ABE ATTELL	1906-12
JOHNNY KILBANE	1912-23
Jem Driscoll (GBR)	1912-13
EUGENE CRIQUI	1923
JOHNNY DUNDEE	1923-24†
LOUIS (KID) KAPLAN	1925-26†
Dick Finnegan (Mass.)	1926-27
BENNY BASS	1927-28
TONY CANZONERI	1928
ANDRE ROUTIS	1928-29
BATTLING BATTALINO	1929-32†
Tommy Paul (NBA)	1932-33
Kid Chocolate (NY)	1932-33
Freddie Miller (NBA)	1933-36
Baby Arizmendi (MEX)	1935-36
Mike Belloise (NY)	1936-37
Petey Sarron (NBA)	1936-37
HENRY ARMSTRONG	1937-38†
Joey Archibald (NY)	1938-39
Leo Rodak (NBA)	1938-39
JOEY ARCHIBALD	1939-40
Petey Scalzo (NBA)	1940-41
Jimmy Perrin (La.)	1940-41
HARRY JEFFRA	1940-41
JOEY ARCHIBALD	1941
Richie Lemos (NBA)	1941
CHALKY WRIGHT	1941-42
Jackie Wilson (NBA)	1941-43
WILLIE PEP	1942-48
Jackie Callura (NBA)	1943
Phil Terranova (NBA)	1943-44
Sal Bartolo (NBA)	1944-46
SANDY SADDLER	1948-49
WILLIE PEP	1949-50
SANDY SADDLER	1950-57*
HOGAN (KID) BASSEY	1957-59
DAVEY MOORE	1959-63
ULTIMINIO (SUGAR) RAMOS	1963-64
VICENTE SALDIVAR	1964-67*
Howard Winstone (GBR)	1968
Raul Rojas (WBA)	1968
Jose Legra (WBC)	1968-69
Shozo Saijyo (WBA)	1968-71
JOHNNY FAMECHON (WBC)	1969-70
VICENTE SALDIVAR (WBC)	1970
KUNIAKI SHIBATA (WBC)	1970-72
Antonio Gomez (WBA)	1971-72
CLEMENTE SANCHEZ (WBC)	1972
Ernesto Marcel (WBA)	1972-74

Champion	Held Title
JOSE LEGRA (WBC)	1972-73
EDER JOFRE (WBC)	1973-74
Ruben Olivares (WBA)	1974
Bobby Chacon (WBC)	1974-75
ALEXIS ARGUELLO (WBA)	1974-76†
Ruben Olivares (WBC)	1975
David (Poison) Kotey (WBC)	1975-76
DANNY (LITTLE RED) LOPEZ (WBC)	1976-80
Rafael Ortega (WBA)	1977
Cecilio Lastra (WBA)	1977-78
Eusebio Pedroza (WBA)	1978-85
SALVADOR SANCHEZ (WBC)	1980-82
Juan LaPorte (WBC)	1982-84
Wilfredo Gomez (WBC)	1984
Min-Keun Oh (IBF)	1984-85
Azumah Nelson (WBC)	1984-88
Barry McGuigan (WBA)	1985-86
Ki-Young Chung (IBF)	1985-86
Steve Cruz (WBA)	1986-87
Antonio Rivera (IBF)	1986-88
Antonio Esparragoza (WBA)	1987-91
Calvin Grove (IBF)	1988
Jorge Paez (IBF)	1988-91†
Jeff Fenech (WBC)	1988-90†
Marcos Villasana (WBC)	1990-91
Yung-Kyun Park (WBA)	1991-93
Troy Dorsey (IBF)	1991
Manuel Medina (IBF)	1991-93
Paul Hodkinson (WBC)	1991-93
Tom Johnson (IBF)	1993-97
Goyo Vargas (WBC)	1993
Kevin Kelley (WBC)	1993-95
Eloy Rojas (WBA)	1993-96
Alejandro Gonzalez (WBC)	1995
Manuel Medina (WBC)	1995-96
Wilfredo Vasquez (WBA)	1996-98†
Luisito Espinoza (WBC)	1995—
Naseem Hamed (IBF)	1997†
Hector Lizarraga (IBF)	1997-98
Freddie Norwood (WBA)	1998
Manuel Medina (IBF)	1998—
Antonio Cermeno (WBA)	1998—

Bantamweights

Widely accepted champions in CAPITAL letters. Current champions in **bold** type.

Champion	Held Title
TOMMY (SPIDER) KELLY	1887
HUGHEY BOYLE	1887-88
TOMMY (SPIDER) KELLY	1889
CHAPPIE MORAN	1889-90
Tommy (Spider) Kelly	1890-92
GEORGE DIXON	1890-91
Billy Plummer	1892-95
JIMMY BARRY	1894-99
Pedlar Palmer	1895-99
TERRY McGOVERN	1899-1900
HARRY HARRIS	1901-02
DANNY DOUGHERTY	1900-01
HARRY FORBES	1901-03
FRANKIE NEIL	1903-04
JOE BOWKER	1904-05
JIMMY WALSH	1905-06†
OWEN MORAN	1907-08
MONTE ATTELL	1909-10
FRANKIE CONLEY	1910-11
JOHNNY COULON	1911-14
Digger Stanley (GBR)	1910-12
Charles Ledoux (GBR)	1912-13
Eddie Campi (GBR)	1913-14
KID WILLIAMS	1914-17
Johnny Ertle	1915-18
PETE HERMAN	1917-20
Memphis Pal Moore	1918-19
JOE LYNCH	1920-21
PETE HERMAN	1921
JOHNNY BUFF	1921-22
JOE LYNCH	1922-24
ABE GOLDSTEIN	1924
CANNONBALL EDDIE MARTIN	1924-25
PHIL ROSENBERG	1925-27
Teddy Baldock (GBR)	1927
BUD TAYLOR (NBA)	1927-28†
Willie Smith (GBR)	1927-28
Bushy Graham (NY)	1928-29
PANAMA AL BROWN	1929-35
Sixto Escobar (NBA)	1934-35
BALTAZAR SANGCHILLI	1935-36
Lou Salica (NBA)	1935
Sixto Escobar (NBA)	1935-36
TONY MARINO	1936
SIXTO ESCOBAR	1936-37
HARRY JEFFRA	1937-38
SIXTO ESCOBAR	1938-39*
Georgie Pace (NBA)	1939-40
LOU SALICA	1940-42
MANUEL ORTIZ	1942-47
HAROLD DADE	1947
MANUEL ORTIZ	1947-50
VIC TOWEEL	1950-52
JIMMY CARRUTHERS	1952-54*
ROBERT COHEN	1954-56
Raul Macias (NBA)	1955-57
MARIO D'AGATA	1956-57
ALPHONSE HALIMI	1957-59
JOE BECERRA	1959-60*
Johnny Caldwell (EBU)	1961-62
EDER JOFRE	1961-65
MASAHIKO FIGHTING HARADA	1965-68
LIONEL ROSE	1968-69
RUBEN OLIVARES	1969-70
CHUCHO CASTILLO	1970-71
RUBEN OLIVARES	1971-72
RAFAEL HERRERA	1972
ENRIQUE PINDER	1972-73
ROMEO ANAYA	1973
Rafael Herrera (WBC)	1973-74
ARNOLD TAYLOR	1973-74
SOO-HWAN HONG	1974-75
Rodolfo Martinez (WBC)	1974-76
ALFONSO ZAMORA	1975-77
Carlos Zarate (WBC)	1976-79
JORGE LUJAN	1977-80
Lupe Pintor (WBC)	1979-83
JULIAN SOLIS	1980
JEFF CHANDLER	1980-84
Albert Davila (WBC)	1983-85
RICHARD SANDOVAL	1984-86
Satoshi Shingaki (IBF)	1984-85
Jeff Fenech (IBF)	1985
Daniel Zaragoza (WBC)	1985
Miguel (Happy) Lora (WBC)	1985-88
GABY CANIZALES	1986
BERNARDO PINANGO	1986-87
Wilfredo Vasquez (WBA)	1987-88
Kevin Seabrooks (IBF)	1987-88
Kaokor Galaxy (WBA)	1988

Champion	Held Title
Moon Sung-Kil (WBA)	1988-89
Kaokor Galaxy (WBA)	1989
Raul Perez (WBC)	1988-91
Orlando Canizales (IBF)	1988-94†
Luisito Espinosa (WBA)	1989-91
Greg Richardson	1991
Joichiro Tatsuyoshi (WBC)	1991-92
Israel Contreras (WBA)	1991-92
Eddie Cook (WBA)	1992
Victor Rabanales (WBC)	1992-93
Jorge Julio (WBA)	1992-93
Jung-Il Byun (WBC)	1993
Junior Jones (WBA)	1993-94
Yasuei Yakushiji (WBC)	1993-95
John M. Johnson (WBA)	1994
Daorung Chuvatana (WBA)	1994-95
Harold Mestre (IBF)	1995
Mbulelo Botile (IBF)	1995-97
Wayne McCullough (WBC)	1995-96
Veeraphol Sahaprom (WBA)	1995-96
Nana Yaw Konadu (WBA)	1996
Daorung Chuvatana (WBA)	1996-97
Nana Yaw Konadu (WBA)	1997–
Sirimongkol Singmanassak (WBC)	1996-97
Tim Austin (IBF)	1997–
Joichiro Tatsuyoshi (WBC)	1997–

Flyweights

Widely accepted champions in CAPITAL letters. Current champions in **bold** type.

Champion	Held Title
Sid Smith (GBR)	1913
Bill Ladbury (GBR)	1913-14
Percy Jones (GBR)	1914
Joe Symonds (GBR)	1914-16
JIMMY WILDE	1916-23
PANCHO VILLA	1923-25
FIDEL LaBARBA	1925-27*
FRENCHY BELANGER (NBA,IBU)	1927-28
Izzy Schwartz (NY)	1927-29
Johnny McCoy (Calif.)	1927-28
Newsboy Brown (Calif.)	1928
FRANKIE GENARO (NBA,IBU)	1928-29
Johnny Hill (GBR)	1928-29
SPIDER PLADNER (NBA,IBU)	1929
FRANKIE GENARO (NBA,IBU)	1929-31
Willie LaMorte (NY)	1929-30
Midget Wolgast (NY)	1930-35
YOUNG PEREZ (NBA,IBU)	1931-32
JACKIE BROWN (NBA,IBU)	1932-35
BENNY LYNCH	1935-38†
Small Montana (NY,Calif.)	1935-37
PETER KANE	1938-43
Little Dado (NBA,Calif.)	1938-40
JACKIE PATERSON	1943-48
RINTY MONAGHAN	1948-50*
TERRY ALLEN	1950
SALVADOR (DADO) MARINO	1950-52
YOSHIO SHIRAI	1953-54
PASCUAL PEREZ	1954-60
PONE KINGPETCH	1960-62
MASAHIKO (FIGHTING) HARADA	1962-63
PONE KINGPETCH	1963
HIROYUKI EBIHARA	1963-64
PONE KINGPETCH	1964-65
SALVATORE BURRINI	1965-66
Horacio Accavallo (WBA)	1966-68
WALTER McGOWAN	1966
CHARTCHAI CHIONOI	1966-69
EFREN TORRES	1969-70
Hiroyuki Ebihara (WBA)	1969
Bernabe Villacampo (WBA)	1969-70
CHARTCHAI CHIONOI	1970
Berkrerk Chartvanchai (WBA)	1970
Masao Ohba (WBA)	1970-73
ERBITO SALAVARRIA	1970-73
Betulio Gonzalez (WBC)	1972
Venice Borkorsor (WBC)	1972-73
VENICE BORKORSOR	1973
Chartchai Chionoi (WBA)	1973-74
Betulio Gonzalez (WBA)	1973-74
Shoji Oguma (WBC)	1974-75
Susumu Hanagata (WBA)	1974-75
Miguel Canto (WBC)	1975-79
Erbito Salavarria (WBA)	1975-76
Alfonso Lopez (WBA)	1976
Guty Espadas (WBA)	1976-78
Betulio Gonzalez (WBA)	1978-79
Chan-Hee Park (WBC)	1979-80
Luis Ibarra (WBA)	1979-80
Tae-Shik Kim (WBA)	1980
Shoji Oguma (WBC)	1980-81
Peter Mathebula (WBA)	1980-81
Santos Laciar (WBA)	1981
Antonio Avelar (WBC)	1981-82
Luis Ibarra (WBA)	1981
Juan Herrera (WBA)	1981-82
Prudencio Cardona (WBC)	1982
Santos Laciar (WBA)	1982-85
Freddie Castillo (WBC)	1982
Eleoncio Mercedes (WBC)	1982-83
Charlie Magri (WBC)	1983
Frank Cedeno (WBC)	1983-84
Soon-Chun Kwon (IBF)	1983-85
Koji Kobayashi (WBC)	1984
Gabriel Bernal (WBC)	1984
Sot Chitalada (WBC)	1984-88
Hilario Zapate (WBA)	1985-87
Chong-Kwan Chung (IBF)	1985-86
Bi-Won Chung (IBF)	1986
Hi-Sup Shin (IBF)	1986-87
Dodie Penalosa (IBF)	1987
Fidel Bassa (WBA)	1987-89
Choi Chang-Ho (IBF)	1987-88
Rolando Bohol (IBF)	1988
Yong-Kang Kim (WBC)	1988-89
Duke McKenzie (IBF)	1988-89
Dave McAuley (IBF)	1989-92
Sot Chitalada (WBC)	1989-91
Jesus Rojas (WBA)	1989-90
Yul-Woo Lee (WBA)	1990
Leopard Tamakuma (WBA)	1990-91
Muangchai Kittikasem (WBC)	1991-92
Yong-Kang Kim (WBA)	1991-92
Rodolfo Blanco (IBF)	1992
Yuri Arbachakov (WBC)	1992-97
Aquiles Guzman (WBA)	1992
Phichit Sithbangprachan (IBF)	1992-94†
David Griman (WBA)	1992-94
Saen Sor Ploenchit (WBA)	1994-96
Francisco Tejedor (IBF)	1995
Danny Romero (IBF)	1995-96
Mark Johnson (IBF)	1996–
Jose Bonilla (WBA)	1996-97
Chatchai Sasakul (WBC)	1997–
Hugo Soto (WBA)	1998–

Annual Awards

Ring Magazine Fight of the Year

First presented in 1945 by Nat Fleischer, who started *The Ring* magazine in 1922.

Multiple matchups: Muhammad Ali vs. Joe Frazier, Carmen Basilio vs. Sugar Ray Robinson and Graziano vs. Tony Zale (2).

Multiple fights: Muhammad Ali (6); Carmen Basilio (5); George Foreman and Joe Frazier (4); Rocky Graziano, Rocky Marciano and Tony Zale (3); Nino Benvenuti, Bobby Chacon, Ezzard Charles, Marvin Hagler, Thomas Hearns, Sugar Ray Leonard, Floyd Patterson, Sugar Ray Robinson and Jersey Joe Walcott (2).

Year	Winner	Loser	Result
1945	Rocky Graziano	Red Cochrane	KO 10
1946	Tony Zale	Rocky Graziano	KO 6
1947	Rocky Graziano	Tony Zale	KO 6
1948	Marcel Cerdan	Tony Zale	KO 12
1949	Willie Pep	Sandy Saddler	W 15
1950	Jake LaMotta	Laurent Dauthuille	KO 15
1951	Jersey Joe Walcott	Ezzard Charles	KO 7
1952	Rocky Marciano	Jersey Joe Walcott	KO 13
1953	Rocky Marciano	Roland LaStarza	KO 11
1954	Rocky Marciano	Ezzard Charles	KO 8
1955	Carmen Basilio	Tony DeMarco	KO 12
1956	Carmen Basilio	Johnny Saxton	KO 9
1957	Carmen Basilio	Sugar Ray Robinson	W 15
1958	Sugar Ray Robinson	Carmen Basilio	W 15
1959	Gene Fullmer	Carmen Basilio	KO 14
1960	Floyd Patterson	Ingemar Johansson	KO 5
1961	Joe Brown	Dave Charnley	W 15
1962	Joey Giardello	Henry Hank	W 10
1963	Cassius Clay	Doug Jones	W 10
1964	Cassius Clay	Sonny Liston	KO 7
1965	Floyd Patterson	George Chuvalo	W 12
1966	Jose Torres	Eddie Cotton	W 15
1967	Nino Benvenuti	Emile Griffith	W 15
1968	Dick Tiger	Frank DePaula	W 10
1969	Joe Frazier	Jerry Quarry	KO 7
1970	Carlos Monzon	Nino Benvenuti	KO 12
1971	Joe Frazier	Muhammad Ali	W 15
1972	Bob Foster	Chris Finnegan	KO 14
1973	George Foreman	Joe Frazier	KO 2
1974	Muhammad Ali	George Foreman	KO 8
1975	Muhammad Ali	Joe Frazier	KO 14
1976	George Foreman	Ron Lyle	KO 4
1977	Jimmy Young	George Foreman	W 12
1978	Leon Spinks	Muhammad Ali	W 15
1979	Danny Lopez	Mike Ayala	KO 15
1980	Saad Muhammad	Yaqui Lopez	KO 14
1981	Sugar Ray Leonard	Thomas Hearns	KO 14
1982	Bobby Chacon	Rafael Limon	W 15
1983	Bobby Chacon	C. Boza-Edwards	W 12
1984	Jose Luis Ramirez	Edwin Rosario	KO 4
1985	Marvin Hagler	Thomas Hearns	KO 3
1986	Stevie Cruz	Barry McGuigan	W 15
1987	Sugar Ray Leonard	Marvin Hagler	W 12
1988	Tony Lopez	Rocky Lockridge	W 12
1989	Roberto Duran	Iran Barkley	W 12
1990	Julio Cesar Chavez	Meldrick Taylor	KO 12
1991	Robert Quiroga	Akeem Anifowoshe	W 12
1992	Riddick Bowe	Evander Holyfield	W 12
1993	Michael Carbajal	Humberto Gonzalez	KO 7
1994	Jorge Castro	John David Jackson	TKO 9
1995	Saman Sorjaturong	Chiquita Gonzalez	KO 7
1996	Evander Holyfield	Mike Tyson	TKO 11
1997	Arturo Gatti	Gabriel Ruelas	KO 5

Ring Magazine Fighter of the Year

First presented in 1928 by Nat Fleischer, who started *The Ring* magazine in 1922.

Multiple winners: Muhammad Ali (5); Joe Louis (4); Joe Frazier, Evander Holyfield and Rocky Marciano (3); Ezzard Charles, George Foreman, Marvin Hagler, Thomas Hearns, Ingemar Johansson, Sugar Ray Leonard, Tommy Loughran, Floyd Patterson, Sugar Ray Robinson, Barney Ross, Dick Tiger and Mike Tyson (2)

Year	
1928	Gene Tunney
1929	Tommy Loughran
1930	Max Schmeling
1931	Tommy Loughran
1932	Jack Sharkey
1933	No award
1934	Tony Canzoneri & Barney Ross
1935	Barney Ross
1936	Joe Louis
1937	Henry Armstrong
1938	Joe Louis
1939	Joe Louis
1940	Billy Conn
1941	Joe Louis
1942	Sugar Ray Robinson
1943	Fred Apostoli
1944	Beau Jack
1945	Willie Pep
1946	Tony Zale
1947	Gus Lesnevich
1948	Ike Williams
1949	Ezzard Charles
1950	Ezzard Charles
1951	Sugar Ray Robinson
1952	Rocky Marciano
1953	Carl (Bobo) Olson
1954	Rocky Marciano
1955	Rocky Marciano
1956	Floyd Patterson
1957	Carmen Basilio
1958	Ingemar Johansson
1959	Ingemar Johansson
1960	Floyd Patterson
1961	Joe Brown
1962	Dick Tiger
1963	Cassius Clay
1964	Emile Griffith
1965	Dick Tiger
1966	No award
1967	Joe Frazier
1968	Nino Benvenuti
1969	Jose Napoles
1970	Joe Frazier
1971	Joe Frazier
1972	Muhammad Ali & Carlos Monzon
1973	George Foreman
1974	Muhammad Ali
1975	Muhammad Ali
1976	George Foreman
1977	Carlos Zarate
1978	Muhammad Ali
1979	Sugar Ray Leonard
1980	Thomas Hearns
1981	Sugar Ray Leonard & Salvador Sanchez
1982	Larry Holmes
1983	Marvin Hagler
1984	Thomas Hearns
1985	Donald Curry & Marvin Hagler
1986	Mike Tyson
1987	Evander Holyfield
1988	Mike Tyson
1989	Pernell Whitaker
1990	Julio Cesar Chavez
1991	James Toney
1992	Riddick Bowe
1993	Michael Carbajal
1994	Roy Jones Jr.
1995	Oscar De La Hoya
1996	Evander Holyfield
1997	Evander Holyfield

Note: Cassius Clay changed his name to Muhammad Ali after winning the heavyweight title in 1964.

All-Time Leaders

As compiled by *The Ring Record Book and Encyclopedia.*

Knockouts

		Division	Career	No
1	Archie Moore	Lt. Heavy	1936-63	130
2	Young Stribling	Heavy	1921-33	126
3	Billy Bird	Welter	1920-48	125
4	George Odwel	Welter	1930-45	114
5	Sugar Ray Robinson	Middle	1940-65	110
6	Sandy Saddle	Feather	1944-56	103
7	Sam Langford	Middle	1902-26	102
8	Henry Armstrong	Welter	1931-45	100
9	Jimmy Wilde	Fly	1911-23	98
10	Len Wickwar	Lt. Heavy	1928-47	93

Total Bouts

		Division	Career	No
1	Len Wickwar	Lt. Heavy	1928-47	463
2	Jack Britton	Welter	1905-30	350
3	Johnny Dundee	Feather	1910-32	333
4	Billy Bird	Welter	1920-48	318
5	George Marsden	n/a	1928-46	311
6	Maxie Rosenbloom	Lt. Heavy	1923-39	299
7	Harry Greb	Middle	1913-26	298
8	Young Stribling	Lt. Heavy	1921-33	286
9	Battling Levinsky	Lt. Heavy	1910-29	282
10	Ted (Kid) Lewis	Welter	1909-29	279

Former Champions Who Have Won Back Heavyweight Title

Only nine times since 1892 has the heavyweight championship been lost by a fighter who was able to win it back. Eight men have done it and Muhammad Ali and Evander Holyfield have done it twice.

	Lost To	Won Back From
Floyd Patterson	Johansson (1959)	Johansson (1960)
Muhammad Ali	Frazier (1970)	Foreman (1974)
Muhammad Ali	L Spinks (1978)	L Spinks (1978)
Tim Witherspoon	Thomas (1984)	Tubbs (1986)
Evander Holyfield	Bowe (1992)	Bowe (1993)
George Foreman	Ali (1974)	Moorer (1994)
Michael Moorer	Foreman (1994)	Schulz (1996)*
Mike Tyson	Douglas (1990)	Bruno (1996)
Evander Holyfield	Moorer (1994)	Tyson (1996)
Lennox Lewis	McCall (1994)	McCall (1997)

*Moorer won the vacant IBF title in a fight with Germany's Axel Schulz

Triple Champions

Fighters who have won widely-accepted world titles in more than one division. Henry Armstrong is the only fighter listed to hold three titles simultaneously. Note that (*) indicates title claimant.

Sugar Ray Leonard (5) WBC Welterweight (1979-80,80-82); WBA Jr. Middleweight (1981); WBC Middleweight (1987); WBC Super Middleweight (1988-90); WBC Light Heavyweight (1988).

Roberto Duran (4) Lightweight (1972-79); WBC Welterweight (1980); WBA Jr. Middleweight (1983-84); WBC Middleweight (1989-90).

Thomas Hearns (4) WBA Welterweight (1980-81); WBC Jr. Middleweight (1982-84); WBC Light Heavyweight (1987); WBA Light Heavyweight (1991); WBC Middleweight (1987-88).

Pernell Whitaker (4) IBF/WBC/WBA Lightweight (1989-92); IBF Jr. Welterweight (1992-93); WBC Welterweight (1993-97); WBC Jr. Middleweight (1995).

Alexis Arguello (3) WBA Featherweight (1974-77); WBC Jr. Lightweight (1978-80); WBC Lightweight (1981-83).

Henry Armstrong (3) Featherweight (1937-38); Welterweight (1938-40); Lightweight (1938-39).

Iran Barkley (3) WBC Middleweight (1988-89); IBF Super Middleweight (1992-93); WBA Light Heavyweight (1992).

Wilfredo Benitez (3) Jr. Welterweight (1976-79); Welterweight (1979); WBC Jr. Middleweight (1981-82).

Tony Canzoneri (3) Featherweight (1928); Lightweight (1930-33); Jr. Welterweight (1931-32,33).

Julio Cesar Chavez (3) WBC Jr. Lightweight (1984-87); WBA/WBC Lightweight (1987-89); WBC/IBF Jr. Welterweight (1989-91); WBC Jr. Welterweight (1991-94, 1994).

Oscar De La Hoya (3) IBF Lightweight (1995-96); WBC Super Lightweight (1996-97); WBC Welterweight (1997–).

Jeff Fenech (3) IBF Bantamweight (1985); WBC Jr. Featherweight (1986-88); WBC Featherweight (1988-90).

Bob Fitzsimmons (3) Middleweight (1891-97); Light Heavyweight (1903-05); Heavyweight (1897-99).

Wilfredo Gomez (3) WBC Super Bantamweight (1977-83); WBC Featherweight (1984); WBA Jr. Lightweight (1985-86).

Emile Griffith (3) Welterweight (1961,62-63,63-66); Jr. Middleweight (1962-63); Middleweight (1966-67,67-68).

Roy Jones Jr. (3) IBF Middleweight (1993-94); IBF Super Middleweight (1994-96); WBC Light Heavyweight (1996, 1997–).

Terry McGovern (3) Bantamweight (1889-1900); Featherweight (1900-01); Lightweight* (1900-01).

Barney Ross (3) Lightweight (1933-35); Jr. Welterweight (1933-35); Welterweight (1934, 35-38).

Miscellaneous Sports

East's **Chris Cardone**, of Toms River, NJ, is all smiles as he encounters a happy mob after hitting a two-run home run against the team from Kashima, Japan in the Little League World Series. Cardone's team won 12-9.

AP/Wide World Photos

CHESS

World Champions

PCA champion Garry Kasparov of Russia, fell to Deep Blue, IBM's RS-6000 supercomputer, 3½-2½ in a six-game match held in New York City during the first week of May 1997. It was the first time that a computer defeated a world chess champion in a multi-game match. Kasparov beat Deep Blue in a six-game match 15 months previous, but the computer had since been upgraded and its programmers had been assisted on strategic nuances by chess grandmasters. Even still, Kasparov and Deep Blue traded wins in the first two games before playing to draws in the next three.

In the final game it seemed that Kasparov blundered and was forced to resign after just one hour and 19 moves. Each of the first five games lasted around four hours. After game six, an irate Kasparov complained that the match was unfair because he was unable to see records of Deep Blue's past games, while Deep Blue was programmed with all of his. After calming down, Kasparov admitted that he was tired and that the computer was playing above his comprehension. "When I see something that is beyond my understanding," he said, "I'm scared."

The match, widely touted as something more than a simple chess match, was billed by many as a battle of man and machine. The man took home the $400,000 loser's share of the $1.1 million prize fund, while spokesmen for the machine said they would use the winner's purse to fund further research.

The 34-year-old Kasparov suggested that Deep Blue enter the world of competitive chess tournaments. "It's time for Deep Blue to start playing real chess," said Kasparov. I personally guarantee you I will tear it to pieces.

Unfortunately for Kasparov, he will never get that chance. IBM announced late in 1997 that it was retiring Deep Blue from chess to work on other projects.

Kasparov became the youngest man to win the world chess championship when he beat fellow Russian Anatoly Karpov in 1985 at age 22. In 1993, Kasparov and then-No. 1 challenger Nigel Short of England broke away from the established International Chess Federation (FIDE) to form the PCA. FIDE retaliated by stripping Kasparov of their world title and arranging a playoff that was won by Karpov, the former title-holder. Karpov has since successfully defended the FIDE title several times.

Years	
1866-94	Wilhelm Steinitz, Austria
1894-1921	Emanuel Lasker, Germany
1921-27	Jose Capablanca, Cuba
1927-35	Alexander Alekhine, France
1935-37	Max Euwe, Holland
1937-46	Alexander Alekhine, France
1948-57	Mikhail Botvinnik, USSR
1957-58	Vassily Smyslov, USSR
1958-59	Mikhail Botvinnik, USSR
1960-61	Mikhail Tal, USSR
1961-63	Mikhail Botvinnik, USSR
1963-69	Tigran Petrosian, USSR
1969-72	Boris Spassky, USSR
1972-75	Bobby Fischer, USA*
1975-85	Anatoly Karpov, USSR
1985—	Garry Kasparov, RUS

*Fischer defaulted the championship in 1975.

U.S. Champions

New Yorker Joel Benjamin, who served as the grandmaster "trainer" for IBM's Deep Blue team (see above), won the 1997 U.S. Chess Championships in the 14-player, round robin tournament that ran Aug. 22-Sept. 12 in Chandler, Ariz. Benjamin defeated Larry Christiansen, 3½-2½ in the "best-of-six" finals match, and won the $10,000 first prize. The 1998 U.S. Chess Championships were scheduled for Oct. 30-Nov. 19 in Denver, Colo.

Years	
1857-71	Paul Morphy
1871-76	George Mackenzie
1876-80	James Mason
1880-89	George Mackenzie
1889-90	Samuel Lipschutz
1890	Jackson Showalter
1890-91	Max Judd
1891-92	Jackson Showalter
1892-94	Samuel Lipschutz
1894	Jackson Showalter
1894-95	Albert Hodges
1895-97	Jackson Showalter
1897-1906	Harry Pillsbury
1906-09	Vacant
1909-36	Frank Marshall
1936-44	Samuel Reshevsky
1944-46	Arnold Denker
1946-48	Samuel Reshevsky
1948-51	Herman Steiner
1951-54	Larry Evans
1954-57	Arthur Bisguier
1957-61	Bobby Fischer
1961-62	Larry Evans
1962-68	Bobby Fischer
1968-69	Larry Evans
1969-72	Samuel Reshevsky
1972-73	Robert Byrne
1973-74	Lubomir Kavalek & John Grefe
1974-77	Walter Browne
1978-80	Lubomir Kabalek
1980-81	Larry Evans, Larry Christiansen & Walter Browne
1981-83	Walter Browne & Yasser Seirawan
1983	Roman Dzindzichashvili, Larry Christiansen & Walter Browne
1984-85	Lev Alburt
1986	Yasser Seirawan
1987	Joel Benjamin & Nick DeFirmian
1988	Michael Wilder
1989	Roman Dzindzichashvili, Stuart Rachels & Yasser Seirawan
1990	Lev Alburt
1991	Gata Kamsky
1992	Patrick Wolff
1993	Alexander Shabalov & Alex Yermolinsky
1994	Boris Gulko
1995	Alexander Ivanov
1996	Alexander Yermolinsky
1997	Joel Benjamin

DOGS

Iditarod Trail Sled Dog Race

Jeff King won his third Iditarod Trail Sled Dog Race in six years, reaching the finish line on Front Street in Nome in 9 days, 5 hours, 52 minutes and 26 seconds. King was neck and neck with Dee Dee Jonrowe before pulling away on the final day of the race and arriving in Nome in a terrible blizzard. King finished almost three hours ahead of runner-up Jonrowe, and posted the third-best time in race history.

"I ran the race the way I wanted, and it was anybody's race until the very end," said King, who ran his dogs in six-hour intervals instead of the usual four. "If anybody in the whole race would have beat me, I would have liked it to be DeeDee. If I couldn't win, I would have hoped I would have finished second to her." For his win, King collected a check for $50,000 and the keys to a new pickup truck.

In even-numbered years the trail follows the 1,151-mile Northern Route, while in odd-numbered years, it takes a slightly different 1,161-mile Southern Route.

Multiple winners: Rick Swenson (5); Susan Butcher (4); Martin Buser and Jeff King (3); Rick Mackey (2).

Year		Elapsed Time
1973	Dick Wilmarth	20 days, 00:49:41
1974	Carl Huntington	20 days, 15:02:07
1975	Emmitt Peters	14 days, 14:43:45
1976	Gerald Riley	18 days, 22:58:17
1977	Rick Swenson	16 days, 16:27:13
1978	Dick Mackey	14 days, 18:52:24
1979	Rick Swenson	15 days, 10:37:47
1980	Joe May	14 days, 07:11:51
1981	Rick Swenson	12 days, 08:45:02
1982	Rick Swenson	16 days, 04:40:10
1983	Rick Mackey	12 days, 14:10:44
1984	Dean Osmar	12 days, 15:07:33
1985	Libby Riddles	18 days, 00:20:17
1986	Susan Butcher	11 days, 15:06:00
1987	Susan Butcher	11 days, 02:05:13
1988	Susan Butcher	11 days, 11:41:40
1989	Joe Runyan	11 days, 05:24:34
1990	Susan Butcher	11 days, 01:53:23
1991	Rick Swenson	12 days, 16:34:39
1992	Martin Buser	10 days, 19:17:00
1993	Jeff King	10 days, 15:38:15
1994	Martin Buser	10 days, 13:02:39
1995	Doug Swingley	9 days, 02:42:19*
1996	Jeff King	9 days, 05:43:13
1997	Martin Buser	9 days, 08:31:45
1998	Jeff King	9 days, 05:52:26

*Course record.

Westminster Kennel Club

Best in Show

Ch. Fairewood Frolic, a norwich terrier, won Best in Show at the 122nd annual Westminster Kennel Club show on Feb. 17 at Madison Square Garden in New York. The bitch, who answers to the name Rocki, is owned by Sandina Kennels of Tuxedo Park, N.Y. and became the second Norwich Terrier in five years to win Best in Show honors. The Westminster show is the most prestigious dog show in the country, and one of America's oldest annual sporting events.

Multiple winners: Ch. Warren Remedy (3); Ch. Chinoe's Adamant James, Ch. Comejo Wycollar Boy, Ch. Flornell Spicy Piece of Halleston; Ch. Matford Vic, Ch. My Own Brucie, Ch. Pendley Calling of Blarney, Ch. Rancho Dobe's Storm (2).

Year		Breed
1907	Warren Remedy	Fox Terrier
1908	Warren Remedy	Fox Terrier
1909	Warren Remedy	Fox Terrier
1910	Sabine Rarebit	Fox Terrier
1911	Tickle Em Jock	Scottish Terrier
1912	Kenmore Sorceress	Airedale
1913	Strathway Prince Albert	Bulldog
1914	Brentwood Hero	Old English Sheepdog
1915	Matford Vic	Old English Sheepdog
1916	Matford Vic	Old English Sheepdog
1917	Comejo Wycollar Boy	Fox Terrier
1918	Haymarket Faultless	Bull Terrier
1919	Briergate Bright Beauty	Airedale
1920	Comejo Wycollar Boy	Fox Terrier
1921	Midkiff Seductive	Cocker Spaniel
1922	Boxwood Barkentine	Airedale
1923	No best-in-show award	
1924	Barberryhill Bootlegger	Sealyham
1925	Governor Moscow	Pointer
1926	Signal Circuit	Fox Terrier
1927	Pinegrade Perfection	Sealyham
1928	Talavera Margaret	Fox Terrier
1929	Land Loyalty of Bellhaven	Collie
1930	Pendley Calling of Blarney	Fox Terrier
1931	Pendley Calling of Blarney	Fox Terrier
1932	Nancolleth Markable	Pointer
1933	Warland Protector of Shelterock	Airedale
1934	Flornell Spicy Bit of Halleston	Fox Terrier
1935	Nunsoe Duc de la Terrace of Blakeen	Stan. Poodle
1936	St. Margaret Magnificent of Clairedale	Sealyham
1937	Flornell Spicy Bit of Halleston	Fox Terrier
1938	Daro of Maridor	English Setter
1939	Ferry v.Rauhfelsen of Giralda	Doberman
1940	My Own Brucie	Cocker Spaniel
1941	My Own Brucie	Cocker Spaniel
1942	Wolvey Pattern of Edgerstoune	W. Highland Terrier
1943	Pitter Patter of Piperscroft	Miniature Poodle
1944	Flornell Rarebit of Twin Ponds	Welsh Terrier
1945	Shieling's Signature	Scottish Terrier
1946	Hetherington Model Rhythm	Fox Terrier
1947	Warlord of Mazelaine	Boxer
1948	Rock Ridge Night Rocket	Bedling. Terrier
1949	Mazelaine's Zazarac Brandy	Boxer
1950	Walsing Winning Trick of Edgerstoune	Scot. Terrier
1951	Bang Away of Sirrah Crest	Boxer
1952	Rancho Dobe's Storm	Doberman
1953	Rancho Dobe's Storm	Doberman
1954	Carmor's Rise and Shine	Cocker Spaniel
1955	Kippax Fearnought	Bulldog
1956	Wilber White Swan	Toy Poodle
1957	Shirkhan of Grandeur	Afghan Hound
1958	Puttencove Promise	Standard Poodle
1959	Fontclair Festoon	Miniature Poodle
1960	Chick T'Sun of Caversham	Pekingese
1961	Cappoquin Little Sister	Toy Poodle
1962	Elfinbrook Simon	W. Highland Terrier
1963	Wakefield's Black Knight	English Springer Spaniel
1964	Courtenay Fleetfoot of Pennyworth	Whippet
1965	Carmichaels Fanfare	Scottish Terrier
1966	Zeloy Mooremaides Magic	Fox Terrier
1967	Bardene Bingo	Scottish Terrier
1968	Stingray of Derryabah	Lakeland Terrier
1969	Glamoor Good News	Skye Terrier
1970	Arriba's Prima Donna	Boxer
1971	Chinoe's Adamant James	E.S. Spaniel
1972	Chinoe's Adamant James	E.S. Spaniel
1973	Acadia Command Performance	Standard Poodle
1974	Gretchenhof Columbia River	German SH Pointer
1975	Sir Lancelot of Barvan	Old Eng. Sheepdog
1976	Jo Ni's Red Baron of Crofton	Lakeland Terrier
1977	Dersade Bobby's Girl	Sealyham
1978	Cede Higgens	Yorkshire Terrier
1979	Oak Tree's Irishtocrat	Irish Water Spaniel
1980	Sierra Cinnar	Siberian Husky
1981	Dhandy Favorite Woodchuck	Pug
1982	St. Aubrey Dragonora of Elsdon	Pekingese
1983	Kabik's The Challenger	Afghan Hound
1984	Seaward's Blackbeard	Newfoundland
1985	Braeburn's Close Encounter	Scottish Terrier
1986	Marjetta National Acclaim	Pointer
1987	Covy Tucker Hill's Manhattan	German Shepherd
1988	Great Elms Prince Charming II	Pomeranian
1989	Royal Tudor's Wild As The Wind	Doberman
1990	Wendessa Crown Prince	Pekingese
1991	Whisperwind on a Carousel	Stan. Poodle
1992	Lonesome Dove	Fox Terrier
1993	Salilyn's Condor	E.S. Spaniel
1994	Chidley Willum	Norwich Terrier
1995	Gaelforce Post Script	Scottish Terrier
1996	Clussex Country Sunrise	Clumber Spaniel
1997	Parsifal di Casa Netzer	Standard Schnauzer
1998	Fairewood Frolic	Norwich Terrier

FISHING

IGFA All-Tackle World Records

All-tackle records are maintained for the heaviest fish of any species caught on any line up to 130-lb (60 kg) class and certified by the International Game Fish Association. Records logged through Aug. 19, 1998. **Address:** 3000 East Las Olas Blvd., Ft. Lauderdale, FL, 33316. **Telephone:** 954-941-3474.

FRESHWATER FISH

Species	Lbs-Oz	Where Caught	Date	Angler
Barramundi	63-2	Queensland, Australia	Apr. 28, 1991	Scott Barnsley
Bass, Guadalupe	3-11	Lake Travis, TX	Sept. 25, 1983	Allen Christenson Jr.
Bass, largemouth	22-4	Montgomery Lake, GA	June 2, 1932	George W. Perry
Bass, redeye	8-12	Apalachicola River, FL	Jan. 28, 1995	Carl W. Davis
Bass, Roanoke	1-5	Nottoway River, VA	Nov. 11, 1991	Tom Elkins
Bass, rock	3-0	York River, Ontario	Aug. 1, 1974	Peter Gulgin
Bass, smallmouth	10-14	Dale Hollow, TN	Apr. 24, 1969	John T. Gorman
Bass, spotted	9-9	Pine Flat Lake, CA	Oct. 12, 1996	Kirk Sakamoto
Bass, striped (landlocked)	67-8	O'Neill Forebay, San Luis, CA	May 7, 1992	Hank Ferguson
Bass, Suwannee	3-14	Suwannee River, FL	Mar. 2, 1985	Ronnie Everett
Bass, white	6-13	Lake Orange, VA	July 31, 1989	Ronald L. Sprouse
Bass, whiterock	27-5	Greers Ferry Lake, AR	Apr. 24, 1997	Jerald C. Shaum
Bass, yellow	2-4	Lake Monroe, IN	Mar. 27, 1977	Donald L. Stalker
Bass, yellow hybrid	2-5	Kiamichi River, OK	Mar. 26, 1991	George Edwards
Bluegill	4-12	Ketona Lake, AL	Apr. 9, 1950	T.S. Hudson
Bowfin	21-8	Florence, SC	Jan. 29, 1980	Robert L. Harmon
Buffalo, bigmouth	70-5	Bussey Brake, Bastrop, LA	Apr. 21, 1980	Delbert Sisk
Buffalo, black	55-8	Cherokee Lake, TN	May 3, 1984	Edward H. McLain
Buffalo, smallmouth	82-3	Athens Lake, TX	June 6, 1993	Randy Collins
Bullhead, black	8-0	Lake Waccabuc, NY	Aug. 1, 1951	Kani Evans
Bullhead, brown	5-11	Cedar Creek, FL	Mar. 28, 1995	Robert Bengis
Bullhead, yellow	4-4	Mormon Lake, AZ	May 11, 1984	Emily Williams
Burbot	18-11	Angenmanelren, Sweden	Oct. 22, 1996	Margit Agren
Carp	75-11	Lac de St. Cassien, France	May 21, 1987	Leo van der Gugten
Catfish, blue	111-0	Wheeler's Reservoir, TN	July 5, 1996	William McKinley
Catfish, channel	58-0	Santee-Cooper Res., SC	July 7, 1964	W.B. Whaley
Catfish, flathead	91-4	Lake Lewisville, TX	Mar. 28, 1982	Mike Rogers
Catfish, flatwhiskered	9-4	Rio Paraquai, Brazil	Sept. 11, 1996	Cavour Pieranti
Catfish, gilded	85-8	Amazon River, Brazil	Nov. 15, 1986	Gilberto Fernandes
Catfish, redtail	97-7	Amazon River, Brazil	July 16, 1988	Gilberto Fernandes
Catfish, sharptoothed	79-5	Orange River, S. Africa	Dec. 5, 1992	Hennie Moller
Catfish, white	18-14	Inverness, FL	Sept. 21, 1991	Jim Miller
Char, Arctic	32-9	Tree River, Canada	July 30, 1981	Jeffery Ward
Crappie, black	4-8	Kerr Lake, VA	Mar. 1, 1981	L. Carl Herring Jr.
Crappie, white	5-3	Enid Dam, MS	July 31, 1957	Fred L. Bright
Dolly Varden	18-9	Mashutuk River, AK	July 13, 1993	Richard B. Evans
Dorado	51-5	Corrientes, Argentina	Sept. 27, 1984	Armando Giudice
Drum, freshwater	54-8	Nickajack Lake, TN	Apr. 20, 1972	Benny E. Hull
Gar, alligator	279-0	Rio Grande, TX	Dec. 2, 1951	Bill Valverde
Gar, Florida	21-3	Boca Raton, FL	June 3, 1981	Jeff Sabol
Gar, longnose	50-5	Trinity River, TX	July 30, 1954	Townsend Miller
Gar, shortnose	5-12	Rend Lake, Ill.	July 16, 1995	Donna K. Willmart
Gar, spotted	9-12	Lake Mevia, TX	Apr. 7, 1994	Rick Rivard
Goldfish	6-10	Lake Hodges, CA	Apr. 17, 1996	Florentino M. Abena
Grayling, Arctic	5-15	Katseyedie River, N.W.T.	Aug. 16, 1967	Jeanne P. Branson
Inconnu	53-0	Pah River, AK	Aug. 20, 1986	Lawrence E. Hudnall
Kokanee	9-6	Okanagan Lake, Brit. Columbia	June 18, 1988	Norm Kuhn
Muskellunge	67-8	Hayward, WI	July 24, 1949	Cal Johnson
Muskellunge, tiger	51-3	Lac Vieux-Desert, WI-MI	July 16, 1919	John A. Knobla
Peacock, butterfly	10-8	Raraima, Brazil	Mar. 21, 1994	Larry Larsen
Peacock, speckled	27-0	Rio Negro, Brazil	Dec. 4, 1994	Gerald (Doc) Lawson
Perch, Nile	213-8	Lake Nasser, Egypt	Dec. 18, 1997	Adrian Brayshaw
Perch, white	4-12	Messalonskee Lake, ME	June 4, 1949	Mrs. Earl Small
Perch, yellow	4-3	Bordentown, NJ	May, 1865	Dr. C.C. Abbot
Pickerel, chain	9-6	Homerville, GA	Feb. 17, 1961	Baxley McQuaig Jr.
Pickerel, grass	1-0	Dewart Lake, IN	June 9, 1990	Mike Berg
Pickerel, redfin	2-4	St. Pauls, NC	June 27, 1997	Edward C. Davis
Pike, northern	55-1	Lake of Grefeern, Germany	Oct. 16, 1986	Lothar Louis
Redhorse, greater	9-3	Salmon River, Pulaski, NY	May 11, 1985	Jason Wilson
Redhorse, silver	11-7	Plum Creek, WI	May 29, 1985	Neal D.G. Long
Salmon, Atlantic	79-2	Tana River, Norway	1928	Henrik Henriksen
Salmon, chinook	97-4	Kenai River, AK	May 17, 1985	Les Anderson
Salmon, chum	35-0	Edye Pass, Brit. Columbia	July 11, 1995	Todd Johansson

Species	Lbs-Oz	Where Caught	Date	Angler
Salmon, coho	33-4	Salmon River, Pulaski, NY	Sept. 27, 1989	Jerry Lifton
Salmon, lake	18-4	Lake Tanganyika, Zambia	Dec. 1, 1987	Steve Robinson
Salmon, pink	13-1	St. Mary's River, Ontario	Sept. 23, 1992	Ray Higaki
Salmon, sockeye	15-3	Kenai River, AK	Aug. 9, 1987	Stan Roach
Sauger	8-12	Lake Sakakawea, ND	Oct. 6, 1971	Mike Fischer
Shad, American	11-4	Conn. River, S. Hadley, MA	May 19, 1986	Bob Thibodo
Shad, gizzard	4-6	Lake Michigan, IN	Mar. 2, 1996	Mike Berg
Sturgeon, lake	168-0	Georgian Bay, Canada	May 29, 1982	Edward Paszkowski
Sturgeon, white	468-0	Benicia, CA	July 9, 1983	Joey Pallotta 3rd
Tigerfish, giant	97-0	Zaire River, Kinshasa, Zaire	July 9, 1988	Raymond Houtmans
Tilapia	6-5	Lake Arsenal, Costa Rica	Feb. 10, 1995	Marvin C. Smith
Trout, Apache	5-3	White Mountain, AZ	May 29, 1991	John Baldwin
Trout, brook	14-8	Nipigon River, Ontario	July, 1916	Dr. W.J. Cook
Trout, brown	40-4	Little Red River, AR	May 9, 1992	Rip Collins
Trout, bull	32-0	Lake Pond Orielle, ID	Oct. 27, 1949	N.L. Higgins
Trout, cutthroat	41-0	Pyramid Lake, NV	Dec., 1925	John Skimmerhorn
Trout, golden	11-0	Cooks Lake, WY	Aug. 5, 1948	Charles S. Reed
Trout, lake	72-0	Great Bear Lake, N.W.T.	Aug. 19, 1995	Lloyd E. Bull
Trout, rainbow	42-2	Bell Island, AK	June 22, 1970	David Robert White
Trout, tiger	20-13	Lake Michigan, WI	Aug. 12, 1978	Peter M. Friedland
Walleye	25-0	Old Hickory Lake, TN	Aug. 2, 1960	Mabry Harper
Warmouth	2-7	Guess Lake, Holt, FL	Oct. 19, 1985	Tony D. Dempsey
Whitefish, lake	14-6	Meaford, Ontario	May 21, 1984	Dennis M. Laycock
Whitefish, mountain	5-8	Elbow River, Manitoba	Aug. 1, 1995	Randy G. Woo
Whitefish, round	6-0	Putahow River, Manitoba	June 14, 1984	Allan J. Ristori
Zander	25-2	Trosa, Sweden	June 12, 1986	Harry Lee Tennison

SALTWATER FISH

Species	Lbs-Oz	Where Caught	Date	Angler
Albacore	88-2	Gran Canaria, Canary Islands	Nov. 19, 1977	Siegfried Dickemann
Amberjack, greater	155-10	Challenger Bank, Bermuda	June 24, 1981	Joseph Dawson
Amberjack, pacific	104-0	Baja Calif., Mexico	July 4, 1984	Richard Cresswell
Barracuda, great	85-0	Christmas Is., Rep. of Kiribati	Apr. 11, 1992	John W. Helfrich
Barracuda, Mexican	21-0	Phantom Island, Costa Rica	Mar. 27, 1987	E. Greg Kent
Barracuda, pickhandle	25-5	Scottburgh, South Africa	July 3, 1996	Demetrios Stamatis
Bass, barred sand	13-3	Huntington Beach, CA	Aug. 29, 1988	Robert Halal
Bass, black sea	9-8	Virginia Beach, VA	Jan. 9, 1987	Joe Mizelle Jr.
	9-8	Virginia Beach, VA	Dec. 22, 1990	Jack G. Stallings Jr.
Bass, European	20-11	Stes Maries de la Mer, France	May 6, 1986	Jean Baptiste Bayle
Bass, giant sea	563-8	Anacapa Island, CA	Aug. 20, 1968	J.D. McAdam Jr.
Bass, striped	78-8	Atlantic City, NJ	Sept. 21, 1982	Albert R. McReynolds
Bluefish	31-12	Hatteras, NC	Jan. 30, 1972	James M. Hussey
Bonefish	19-0	Zululand, South Africa	May 26, 1962	Brian W. Batchelor
Bonito, Atlantic	18-4	Faial Island, Azores	July 8, 1953	D. Gama Higgs
Bonito, Pacific	14-12	San Benitos Is., Baja Calif., Mexico	Oct. 12, 1980	Jerome H. Rilling
Cabezon	23-0	Juan de Fuca Strait, WA	Aug. 4, 1990	Wesley Hunter
Cobia	135-9	Shark Bay, W. Australia	July 9, 1985	Peter W. Goulding
Cod, Atlantic	98-12	Isle of Shoals, NH	June 8, 1969	Alphonse Bielevich
Cod, Pacific	32-0	Unalaska Bay, AK	June 29, 1997	Donald Boston
Conger	133-4	South Devon, England	June 5, 1995	Vic Evans
Dolphin	87-0	Papagallo Gulf, Costa Rica	Sept. 25, 1976	Manuel Salazar
Drum, black	113-1	Lewes, DE	Sept. 15, 1975	Gerald M. Townsend
Drum, red	94-2	Avon, NC	Nov. 7, 1984	David G. Deuel
Eel, marbled	36-1	Durban, S. Africa	June 10, 1984	Ferdie van Nooten
Eel, American	9-4	Cape May, NJ	Nov. 9, 1995	Jeff Pennick
Flounder, southern	20-9	Nassau Sound, FL	Dec. 23, 1983	Larenza Mungin
Flounder, summer	22-7	Montauk, NY	Sept. 15, 1975	Charles Nappi
Grouper, warsaw	436-12	Gulf of Mexico, Destin, FL	Dec. 22, 1985	Steve Haeusler
Haddock	14-15	Saltraumen, Germany	Aug. 15, 1997	Heike Neblinger
Halibut, Atlantic	255-4	Gloucester, MA	July 28, 1989	Sonny Manley
Halibut, California	53-4	Santa Rosa Island, CA	July 7, 1988	Russell J. Harmon
Halibut, Pacific	459-0	Dutch Harbor, AK	June 11, 1996	Jack Tragis
Jack, almaco (Pacific)	132-0	La Paz, Baja Calif., Mexico	July 21, 1964	Howard H. Hahn
Jack, crevalle	57-14	Southwest Pass, LA	Aug. 15, 1997	Leon D. Richard
Jack, horse-eye	24-8	Miami, FL	Dec. 20, 1982	Tito Schnau
Jewfish	680-0	Fernandina Beach, FL	May 20, 1961	Lynn Joyner
Kawakawa	29-0	Clarion Island, Mexico	Dec. 17, 1986	Ronald Nakamura
Lingcod	69-0	Langara Is., Brit. Columbia	June 16, 1992	Murray M. Romer
Mackerel, cero	17-2	Islamorada, FL	Apr. 5, 1986	G. Michael Mills
Mackerel, king	90-0	Key West, FL	Feb. 16, 1976	Norton I. Thomton

Species	Lbs-Oz	Where Caught	Date	Angler
Mackerel, Spanish	13-0	Ocracoke Inlet, NC	Nov. 4, 1987	Robert Cranton
Marlin, Atlantic blue	1402-2	Vitoria, Brazil	Feb. 29, 1992	Paulo R.A. Amorim
Marlin, black	1560-0	Cabo Blanco, Peru	Aug. 4, 1953	A.C. Glassell Jr.
Marlin, Pacific blue	1376-0	Kaaiwi Point, Kona, HI	May 31, 1982	Jay W. deBeaubien
Marlin, striped	494-0	Tutakaka, New Zealand	Jan. 16, 1986	Bill Boniface
Marlin, white	181-14	Vitoria, Brazil	Dec. 8, 1979	Evandro Luiz Coser
Permit	56-2	Ft. Lauderdale, FL	June 30, 1997	Thomas Sebestyen
Pollack	27-6	Salcombe, Devon, England	Jan. 16, 1986	Robert S. Milkins
Pollock	50-0	Salstraumen, Norway	Nov. 30, 1996	Thor-Magnus Ukang
Pompano, African	50-8	Daytona Beach, FL	Apr. 21, 1990	Tom Sargent
Roosterfish	114-0	La Paz, Baja Calif., Mexico	June 1, 1960	Abe Sackheim
Runner, blue	11-2	Dauphin Island, AL	June 28, 1997	Stacey M. Moiren
Runner, rainbow	37-9	Clarion Island, Mexico	Nov. 21, 1991	Tom Pfleger
Sailfish, Atlantic	141-1	Luanda, Angola	Feb. 19, 1994	Alfredo de Sousa Neves
Sailfish, Pacific	221-0	Santa Cruz Is., Ecuador	Feb. 12, 1947	C.W. Stewart
Seabass, white	83-12	San Felipe, Mexico	Mar. 31, 1953	L.C. Baumgardner
Seatrout, spotted	17-7	Ft. Pierce, FL	May 11, 1995	Craig F. Carson
Shark, blue	454-0	Martha's Vineyard, MA	July 19, 1996	Pete Bergin
Shark, great white	2664-0	Ceduna, S. Australia	Apr. 21, 1959	Alfred Dean
Shark, Geenland	1708-9	Trondheimsfjord, Norway	Oct. 18, 1987	Terje Nordtvedt
Shark, hammerhead	991-0	Sarasota, FL	May 30, 1982	Allen Ogle
Shark, shortfin mako	1115-0	Black River, Mauritius	Nov. 16, 1988	Patrick Guillanton
Shark, porbeagle	507-0	Pentland Firth, Scotland	Mar. 9, 1993	Christopher Bennet
Shark, bigeye thresher	802-0	Tutukaka, New Zealand	Feb. 8, 1981	Dianne North
Shark, tiger	1780-0	Cherry Grove, SC	June 14, 1964	Walter Maxwell
Snapper, cubera	121-8	Cameron, LA	July 5, 1982	Mike Hebert
Snapper, red	50-4	Gulf of Mexico, LA	June 23, 1996	Capt. Doc Kennedy
Snook	53-10	Parismina Ranch, Costa Rica	Oct. 18, 1978	Gilbert Ponzi
Spearfish, Mediterranean	90-13	Madeira Island, Portugal	June 2, 1980	Joseph Larkin
Swordfish	1182-0	Iquique, Chile	May 7, 1953	L. Marron
Tarpon	283-4	Sherbro Is., Sierra Leone	Apr. 16, 1991	Yvon Victor Sebag
Tautog	24-0	Wachapreague, VA	Aug. 25, 1987	Gregory R. Bell
Tuna, Atlantic bigeye	392-6	Gran Canaria, Puerto Rico	July 25, 1997	Dieter Vogel
Tuna, blackfin	45-8	Key West, FL	May 4, 1996	Sam J. Burnett
Tuna, bluefin	1496-0	Aulds Cove, Nova Scotia	Oct. 26, 1979	Ken Fraser
Tuna, longtail	79-2	Montague Is., NSW, Australia	Apr. 12, 1982	Tim Simpson
Tuna, Pacific bigeye	435-0	Cabo Blanco, Peru	Apr. 17, 1957	Dr. Russell Lee
Tuna, skipjack	45-4	Flathead Bank, Mexico	Nov. 16, 1996	Brian Evans
Tuna, southern bluefin	348-5	Whakatane, New Zealand	Jan. 16, 1981	Rex Wood
Tuna, yellowfin	388-12	San Benedicto Island, Mexico	Apr. 1, 1977	Curt Wiesenhutter
Tunny, little	35-2	Cape de Garde, Algeria	Dec. 14, 1988	Jean Yves Chatard
Wahoo	158-8	Loreto, Baja Calif., Mexico	June 10, 1996	Keith Winter
Weakfish	19-2	Jones Beach, Long Island, NY	Oct. 11, 1984	Dennis R. Rooney
	19-2	Delaware Bay, DE	May 20, 1989	William E. Thomas

BASS Masters Classic

Denny Brauer, 49, finally landed the big one on Aug. 10 when he won the 28th annual BASS Masters Classic Championship on High Rock Lake near Greensboro, N.C. The Camdenton, Mo. pro had won 10 B.A.S.S. tournaments and the 1987 B.A.S.S. Angler of the Year award but had never won the Classic. His three-day total of 46 pounds, 3 ounces changed all that, easily outdistancing runner-up George Cochran (36-4).

"After 16 years, you really don't know if it's ever going to happen," Brauer said. "And it finally happened. That's one question I won't have to answer anymore. You bet I won a Classic. Finally."

With his $151,000 payoff, Brauer passed Larry Nixon as the all-time B.A.S.S. money-winner with a career total of $1,355,801.

The BASS Masters Classic is fishing's version of the Masters golf tournament. Invitees to the three-day event include the 25 top-ranked pros on the B.A.S.S. tour and the five top-ranked anglers from each BASSMASTER Invitational circuit. Anglers may weigh only seven bass per day and each bass must be at least 12 inches long. Competitors are allowed only seven rods and reels and are limited to the tackle they can pack into two tournament-approved tackleboxes. Only artificial lures are permitted. The first Classic, held at Lake Mead, Nev. in 1971, was a $10,000 winner-take-all event.

Multiple winners: Rick Clunn (4); George Cochran, Bobby Murray and Hank Parker (2).

Year		Weight
1971	Bobby Murray, Hot Springs, Ark	43-11
1972	Don Butler, Tulsa, Okla	38-11
1973	Rayo Breckenridge, Paragould, Ark	52-8
1974	Tommy Martin, Hemphill, Tex.	33-7
1975	Jack Hains, Rayne, La	45-4
1976	Rick Clunn, Montgomery, Tex	59-15
1977	Rick Clunn, Montgomery, Tex.	27-7
1978	Bobby Murray, Nashville, Tenn	37-9
1979	Hank Parker, Clover, S.C	31-0
1980	Bo Dowden, Natchitoches, La	54-10

Year		Weight
1981	Stanley Mitchell, Fitzgerald, Ga	35-2
1982	Paul Elias, Laurel, Miss	32-8
1983	Larry Nixon, Hemphill, Tex.	18-1
1984	Rick Clunn, Montgomery, Tex.	75-9
1985	Jack Chancellor, Phenix City, Ala	45-0
1986	Charlie Reed, Broken Bow, Okla	23-9
1987	George Cochran, N. Little Rock, Ark	15-5
1988	Guido Hibdon, Gravois Mills, Mo.	28-8
1989	Hank Parker, Denver, N.C	31-6
1990	Rick Clunn, Montgomery, Tex.	34-5

Year		Weight
1991	Ken Cook, Meers, Okla	33-2
1992	Robert Hamilton Jr., Brandon, Miss	59-6
1993	David Fritts, Lexington, N.C	48-6
1994	Bryan Kerchal, Newtown, Conn	36-7
1995	Mark Davis, Mount Ida, Ark.	47-14
1996	George Cochran, Hot Springs, Ark.	31-14
1997	Dion Hibdon, Stover, Mo.	34-13
1998	Denny Brauer, Camdenton, Mo.	46-3

POWER BOAT RACING

APBA Gold Cup

Dave Villwock won the 95th edition of the APBA Gold Cup as he drove *Miss Budweiser* to victory July 12, 1998 on the Detroit River. The 43-year old Villwock outdistanced Steve David in *Miss Chrysler/Jeep* on the 2.5-mile course for his third straight win in the race. Villwock became the 11th driver to win three or more Gold Cup titles.

The American Power Boat Association Gold Cup for unlimited hydroplane racing is the oldest active motorsports trophy in North America. The first Gold Cup was competed for on the Hudson River in New York in June and September of 1904. Since then several cities have hosted the race, led by Detroit (29 times, including 1990) and Seattle (14). Note that (*) indicates driver was also owner of the winning boat.

Drivers with multiple wins: Chip Hanauer (10); Bill Muncey (8); Gar Wood (5); Dean Chenoweth (4); Caleb Bragg, Tom D'Eath, Lou Fageol, Ron Musson, George Reis, Dave Villwock and J.M. Wainwright (3); Danny Foster, George Henley, Vic Kliesrath, E.J. Schroeder, Bill Schumacher, Zalmon G. Simmons Jr., Joe Taggart, Mark Tate and George Townsend (2).

Year	Boat	Driver	Avg. MPH
1904	*Standard* (June)	Carl Riotte*	23.160
1904	*Vingt-Et-Un II* (Sept.)	W. Sharpe Kilmer*	24.900
1905	*Chip I*	J.M. Wainwright*	15.000
1906	*Chip II*	J.M. Wainwright*	25.000
1907	*Chip II*	J.M. Wainwright*	23.903
1908	*Dixie II*	E.J. Schroeder*	29.938
1909	*Dixie II*	E.J. Schroeder*	29.590
1910	*Dixie III*	F.K. Burnham*	32.473
1911	*MIT II*	J.H. Hayden*	37.000
1912	*P.D.Q. II*	A.G. Miles*	39.462
1913	*Ankle Deep*	C.S. Mankowski*	42.779
1914	*Baby Speed Demon II*	Jim Blackton & Bob Edgren	48.458
1915	*Miss Detroit*	Johnny Milot & Jack Beebe	37.656
1916	*Miss Minneapolis*	Bernard Smith	48.860
1917	*Miss Detroit II*	Gar Wood*	54.410
1918	*Miss Detroit II*	Gar Wood	51.619
1919	*Miss Detroit III*	Gar Wood*	42.748
1920	*Miss America I*	Gar Wood*	62.022
1921	*Miss America I*	Gar Wood*	52.825
1922	*Packard Chriscraft*	J.G. Vincent*	40.253
1923	*Packard Chriscraft*	Caleb Bragg	43.867
1924	*Baby Bootlegger*	Caleb Bragg*	45.302
1925	*Baby Bootlegger*	Caleb Bragg*	47.240
1926	*Greenwich Folly*	George Townsend*	47.984
1927	*Greenwich Folly*	George Townsend*	47.662
1928	Not held		
1929	*Imp*	Richard Hoyt*	48.662
1930	*Hotsy Totsy*	Vic Kliesrath*	52.673
1931	*Hotsy Totsy*	Vic Kliesrath*	53.602
1932	*Delphine IV*	Bill Horn	57.775
1933	*El Lagarto*	George Reis*	56.260
1934	*El Lagarto*	George Reis*	55.000
1935	*El Lagarto*	George Reis*	55.056
1936	*Impshi*	Kaye Don	45.735
1937	*Notre Dame*	Clell Perry	63.675
1938	*Alagi*	Theo Rossi*	64.340
1939	*My Sin*	Z.G. Simmons Jr.*	66.133
1940	*Hotsy Totsy III*	Sidney Allen*	48.295
1941	*My Sin*	Z.G. Simmons Jr.*	52.509
1942-45	Not held		
1946	*Tempo VI*	Guy Lombardo*	68.132
1947	*Miss Peps V*	Danny Foster	57.000
1948	*Miss Great Lakes*	Danny Foster	46.845
1949	*My Sweetie*	Bill Cantrell	73.612
1950	*Slo-Mo-Shun IV*	Ted Jones	78.216
1951	*Slo-Mo-Shun V*	Lou Fageol	90.871
1952	*Slo-Mo-Shun IV*	Stan Dollar	79.923
1953	*Slo-Mo-Shun IV*	Joe Taggart & Lou Fageol	99.108
1954	*Slo-Mo-Shun V*	Lou Fageol	92.613
1955	*Gale V*	Lee Schoenith	99.552
1956	*Miss Thriftway*	Bill Muncey	96.552
1957	*Miss Thriftway*	Bill Muncey	101.787
1958	*Hawaii Kai III*	Jack Regas	103.000
1959	*Maverick*	Bill Stead	104.481
1960	Not held		
1961	*Miss Century 21*	Bill Muncey	99.678
1962	*Miss Century 21*	Bill Muncey	100.710
1963	*Miss Bardahl*	Ron Musson	105.124
1964	*Miss Bardahl*	Ron Musson	103.433
1965	*Miss Bardahl*	Ron Musson	103.132
1966	*Tahoe Miss*	Mira Slovak	93.019
1967	*Miss Bardahl*	Bill Shumacher	101.484
1968	*Miss Bardahl*	Bill Shumacher	108.173
1969	*Miss Budweiser*	Bill Sterett	98.504
1970	*Miss Budweiser*	Dean Chenoweth	99.562
1971	*Miss Madison*	Jim McCormick	98.043
1972	*Atlas Van Lines*	Bill Muncey	104.277
1973	*Miss Budweiser*	Dean Chenoweth	99.043
1974	*Pay 'n Pak*	George Henley	104.428
1975	*Pay 'n Pak*	George Henley	108.921
1976	*Miss U.S.*	Tom D'Eath	100.412
1977	*Atlas Van Lines*	Bill Muncey*	111.822
1978	*Atlas Van Lines*	Bill Muncey*	100.412
1979	*Atlas Van Lines*	Bill Muncey*	100.765
1980	*Miss Budweiser*	Dean Chenoweth	106.932
1981	*Miss Budweiser*	Dean Chenoweth	116.387
1982	*Atlas Van Lines*	Chip Hanauer	120.050
1983	*Atlas Van Lines*	Chip Hanauer	118.507
1984	*Atlas Van Lines*	Chip Hanauer	130.175
1985	*Miller American*	Chip Hanauer	120.643
1986	*Miller American*	Chip Hanauer	116.523
1987	*Miller American*	Chip Hanauer	127.620
1988	*Miss Circus Circus*	Chip Hanauer & Jim Prevost	123.756
1989	*Miss Budweiser*	Tom D'Eath	131.209
1990	*Miss Budweiser*	Tom D'Eath	143.176
1991	*Winston Eagle*	Mark Tate	137.771
1992	*Miss Budweiser*	Chip Hanauer	136.282
1993	*Miss Budweiser*	Chip Hanauer	141.296
1994	*Smokin' Joe's*	Mark Tate	145.532
1995	*Miss Budweiser*	Chip Hanauer	149.160
1996	*Pico/American Dream*	Dave Villwock	149.328
1997	*Miss Budweiser*	Dave Villwock	129.366
1998	*Miss Budweiser*	Dave Villwock	140.704

PRO RODEO

All-Around Champion Cowboy

Dan Mortensen, of Manhattan, Mont. won two world titles at the 1997 National Finals Rodeo held Dec. 5-14 in Las Vegas. Mortensen had a huge lead in saddle bronc riding prior to the NFR and clinched the title of World Champion Saddle Bronc Rider early on, but the All-Around Cowboy Championship was a different story entirely. Heading into the NFR Mortensen's closest competitors for the all-around title were Cody Ohl and defending champ Joe Beaver. By the 10th round, Ohl and Beaver had made Mortensen's lead all but vanish. But Mortensen did not panic and rode his 10th-round horse Range Sheep to a tie for second place and $8,020–enough to clinch his first All-Around Cowboy Championship buckle.

The Professional Rodeo Cowboys Association (PRCA) title of All-Around World Champion Cowboy goes to the rodeo athlete who wins the most prize money in a single year in two or more events, earning a minimum of $2,000 in each event. Only prize money earned in sanctioned PRCA rodeos is counted. From 1929-44, All-Around champions were named by the Rodeo Association of America (earnings for those years is not available).

Multiple winners: Tom Ferguson, Larry Mahan and Ty Murray (6); Jim Shoulders (5); Lewis Feild and Dean Oliver (3); Joe Beaver, Everett Bowman, Louis Brooks, Clay Carr, Bill Linderman, Phil Lyne, Gerald Roberts, Casey Tibbs and Harry Tompkins (2).

Year		Year		Year		Year	
1929	Earl Thode	1934	Leonard Ward	1939	Paul Carney	1944	Louis Brooks
1930	Clay Carr	1935	Everett Bowman	1940	Fritz Truan	1945-46	No award
1931	John Schneider	1936	John Bowman	1941	Homer Pettigrew		
1932	Donald Nesbit	1937	Everett Bowman	1942	Gerald Roberts		
1933	Clay Carr	1938	Burel Mulkey	1943	Louis Brooks		

Year		Earnings
1947	Todd Whatley	$18,642
1948	Gerald Roberts	21,766
1949	Jim Shoulders	21,495
1950	Bill Linderman	30,715
1951	Casey Tibbs	29,104
1952	Harry Tompkins	30,934
1953	Bill Linderman	33,674
1954	Buck Rutherford	40,404
1955	Casey Tibbs	42,065
1956	Jim Shoulders	43,381
1957	Jim Shoulders	33,299
1958	Jim Shoulders	32,212
1959	Jim Shoulders	32,905
1960	Harry Tompkins	32,522
1961	Benny Reynolds	31,309
1962	Tom Nesmith	32,611
1963	Dean Oliver	31,329
1964	Dean Oliver	$31,150
1965	Dean Oliver	33,163
1966	Larry Mahan	40,358
1967	Larry Mahan	51,996
1968	Larry Mahan	49,129
1969	Larry Mahan	57,726
1970	Larry Mahan	41,493
1971	Phil Lyne	49,245
1972	Phil Lyne	60,852
1973	Larry Mahan	64,447
1974	Tom Ferguson	66,929
1975	Tom Ferguson	50,300
1976	Tom Ferguson	87,908
1977	Tom Ferguson	65,981
1978	Tom Ferguson	83,734
1979	Tom Ferguson	96,272
1980	Paul Tierney	105,568
1981	Jimmie Cooper	$105,861
1982	Chris Lybbert	123,709
1983	Roy Cooper	153,391
1984	Dee Pickett	122,618
1985	Lewis Feild	130,347
1986	Lewis Feild	166,042
1987	Lewis Feild	144,335
1988	Dave Appleton	121,546
1989	Ty Murray	134,806
1990	Ty Murray	213,772
1991	Ty Murray	244,231
1992	Ty Murray	225,992
1993	Ty Murray	297,896
1994	Ty Murray	246,170
1995	Joe Beaver	141,753
1996	Joe Beaver	166,103
1997	Dan Mortensen	184,559

LITTLE LEAGUE BASEBALL

World Series

Played annually in late August in Williamsport, Pa. at Original Field in Williamsport, Pa. from 1947-1958 and at Howard J. Lamade Stadium since 1959.

Multiple winners: Taiwan (16); California (5); Connecticut, New Jersey and Pennsylvania (4); Japan and Mexico (3); New York, South Korea and Texas (2).

Year	Winner	Score	Loser
1947	Williamsport, PA	16-7	Lock Haven, PA
1948	Lock Haven, PA	6-5	St. Petersburg, FL
1949	Hammonton, NJ	5-0	Pensacola, FL
1950	Houston, TX	2-1	Bridgeport, CT
1951	Stamford, CT	3-0	Austin, TX
1952	Norwalk, CT	4-3	Monongahela, PA
1953	Birmingham, AL	1-0	Schenectady, NY
1954	Schenectady, NY	7-5	Colton, CA
1955	Morrisville, PA	4-3	Merchantville, NJ
1956	Roswell, NM	3-1	Merchantville, NJ
1957	Monterrey, Mexico	4-0	La Mesa, CA
1958	Monterrey, Mexico	10-1	Kankakee, IL
1959	Hamtramck, MI	12-0	Auburn, CA
1960	Levittown, PA	5-0	Ft. Worth, TX
1961	El Cajon, CA	4-2	El Campo, TX
1962	San Jose, CA	3-0	Kankakee, IL
1963	Granada Hills, CA	2-1	Stratford, CT
1964	Staten Island, NY	4-0	Monterrey, Mex.
1965	Windsor Locks, CT	3-1	Stoney Creek, Can.
1966	Houston, TX	8-2	W. New York, NJ
1967	West Tokyo, Japan	4-1	Chicago, IL
1968	Osaka, Japan	1-0	Richmond, VA
1969	Taipei, Taiwan	5-0	Santa Clara,CA
1970	Wayne, NJ	2-0	Campbell, CA
1971	Tainan, Taiwan	12-3	Gary, IN
1972	Taipei, Taiwan	6-0	Hammond, IN
1973	Tainan City, Taiwan	12-0	Tucson, AZ
1974	Kao Hsiung, Taiwan	12-1	Red Bluff, CA
1975	Lakewood, NJ	4-3*	Tampa, FL
1976	Tokyo, Japan	10-3	Campbell, CA
1977	Li-Teh, Taiwan	7-2	El Cajon, CA
1978	Pin-Tung, Taiwan	11-1	Danville, CA
1979	Hsien, Taiwan	2-1	Campbell, CA
1980	Hua Lian, Taiwan	4-3	Tampa, FL
1981	Tai-Chung, Taiwan	4-2	Tampa, FL
1982	Kirkland, WA	6-0	Hsien, Taiwan
1983	Marietta, GA	3-1	Barahona, D. Rep.
1984	Seoul, S. Korea	6-2	Altamonte, FL
1985	Seoul, S. Korea	7-1	Mexicali, Mex.
1986	Tainan Park, Taiwan	12-0	Tucson, AZ

Year	Winner	Score	Loser
1987	Hua Lian, Taiwan	21-1	Irvine, CA
1988	Tai Ping, Taiwan	10-0	Pearl City, HI
1989	Trumbull, CT	5-2	Kaohsiung, Taiwan
1990	Taipei, Taiwan	9-0	Shippensburg, PA
1991	Taichung, Taiwan	11-0	Danville, CA
1992	Long Beach, CA	6-0	Zamboanga, Phil.
1993	Long Beach, CA	3-2	Panama
1994	Maracaibo, Venezuela	4-3	Northridge, CA
1995	Tainan, Taiwan	17-3	Spring, TX
1996	Taipei, Taiwan	13-3	Cranston, RI (called after 5th inn.)
1997	Guadalupe, Mexico	5-4	Mission Viejo, CA
1998	Toms River, NJ	12-9	Kashima, Japan

*Foreign teams were banned from the tournament in 1975, but allowed back in the following year.

Note: In 1992, Zamboanga City of the Philippines beat Long Beach, 15-4, but was stripped of the title a month later when it was discovered that the team had used several players from outside the city limits. Long Beach was then awarded the title by forfeit, 6-0 (one run for each inning of the game).

SOAP BOX DERBY

All-American Soap Box Derby

Twelve-year-old James Marsh, of Cleveland, won the Masters division at the 61st All-American Soap Box Derby in Akron, Ohio with a time of 28.52 seconds. The local favorite edged out Greg Patchen and Christina Vassallo in the championship run of a tournament that features more than 300 youngsters from around the world. Stacy Sharp of Kingman, Ariz. won the SuperStock title (28.79) and Hailey Simpson of Salem, Ore., beat out A.J. Sanders and Spencer Thulin for the Stock World Championship.

The All-American Soap Box Derby is a coasting race for small gravity-powered cars built by their drivers and assembled within strict guidelines on size, weight and cost. The Derby got its name in the 1930s when most cars were built from wooden soap boxes. Held every summer on the second Saturday of August at Derby Downs in Akron, the Soap Box Derby is open to all boys and girls from 9 to 16 years old who qualify.

There are three competitive divisions: 1. Stock (ages 9-16)— made up of generic, prefab racers that come from Derby-approved kits, can be assembled in four hours and don't exceed 200 pounds when driver, car and wheels are weighed together; 2. Super Stock (ages 10-16)— the same as Stock only with a weight limit of 220 pounds; 3. Masters (ages 11-16)— made up of racers designed by the drivers, but constructed with Derby-approved hardware. The racing ramp at Derby Downs is 953.75 feet with an 11 percent grade.

One champion reigned at the All-American Soap Box Derby each year from 1934-75; Junior and Senior division champions from 1976-87; Kit and Masters champions from 1988-91; Stock, Kit and Masters champions from 1992-94; Stock, Super Stock and Masters champions starting in 1995.

Year		Hometown	Age
1934	Robert Turner	Muncie, IN	11
1935	Maurice Bale Jr.	Anderson, IN	13
1936	Herbert Muench Jr.	St. Louis	14
1937	Robert Ballard	White Plains, NY	12
1938	Robert Berger	Omaha, NE	14
1939	Clifton Hardesty	White Plains, NY	11
1940	Thomas Fisher	Detroit	12
1941	Claude Smith	Akron, OH	14
1942-45	Not held		
1946	Gilbert Klecan	San Diego	14
1947	Kenneth Holmboe	Charleston, WV	14
1948	Donald Strub	Akron, OH	13
1949	Fred Derks	Akron, OH	15
1950	Harold Williamson	Charleston, WV	15
1951	Darwin Cooper	Williamsport, PA	15
1952	Joe Lunn	Columbus, GA	11
1953	Fred Mohler	Muncie, IN	14
1954	Richard Kemp	Los Angeles	14
1955	Richard Rohrer	Rochester, NY	14
1956	Norman Westfall	Rochester, NY	14
1957	Terry Townsend	Anderson, IN	14
1958	James Miley	Muncie, IN	15
1959	Barney Townsend	Anderson, IN	13
1960	Fredric Lake	South Bend, IN	11
1961	Dick Dawson	Wichita, KS	13
1962	David Mann	Gary, IN	14
1963	Harold Conrad	Duluth, MN	12
1964	Gregory Schumacher	Tacoma, WA	14
1965	Robert Logan	Santa Ana, CA	12
1966	David Krussow	Tacoma, WA	12
1967	Kenneth Cline	Lincoln, NE	13
1968	Branch Lew	Muncie, IN	11
1969	Steve Souter	Midland, TX	12
1970	Samuel Gupton	Durham, NC	13
1971	Larry Blair	Oroville, CA	13
1972	Robert Lange Jr.	Boulder, CO	14
1973	Bret Yarborough	Elk Grove, CA	11
1974	Curt Yarborough	Elk Grove, CA	11
1975	Karren Stead	Lower Bucks, PA	11
1976	JR: Phil Raber	Sugarcreek, OH	11
	SR: Joan Ferdinand	Canton, OH	14
1977	JR: Mark Ferdinand	Canton, OH	10
	SR: Steve Washburn	Bristol, CT	15
1978	JR: Darren Hart	Salem, OR	11
	SR: Greg Cardinal	Flint, MI	13
1979	JR: Russell Yurk	Flint, MI	10
	SR: Craig Kitchen	Akron, OH	14
1980	JR: Chris Fulton	Indianapolis	11
	SR: Dan Porul	Sherman Oaks, CA	12
1981	JR: Howie Fraley	Portsmouth, OH	11
	SR: Tonia Schlegel	Hamilton, OH	13
1982	JR: Carol A. Sullivan	Rochester, NH	10
	SR: Matt Wolfgang	Lehigh Val., PA	12
1983	JR: Tony Carlini	Del Mar, CA	10
	SR: Mike Burdgick	Flint, MI	14
1984	JR: Chris Hess	Hamilton, OH	11
	SR: Anita Jackson	St. Louis	15
1985	JR: Michael Gallo	Danbury, CT	12
	SR: Matt Sheffer	York, PA	14
1986	JR: Marc Behan	Dover, NH	9
	SR: Tami Jo Sullivan	Lancaster, OH	13
1987	JR: Matt Margules	Danbury, CT	11
	SR: Brian Drinkwater	Bristol, CT	14
1988	KIT: Jason Lamb	Des Moines, IA	10
	MAS: David Duffield	Kansas City	13
1989	KIT: David Schiller	Dayton, OH	12
	MAS: Faith Chavarria	Ventura, CA	12
1990	MAS: Sami Jones	Salem, OR	13
	KIT: Mark Mihal	Valparaiso, IN	12
1991	MAS: Danny Garland	San Diego, CA	14
	KIT: Paul Greenwald	Saginaw, MI	13
1992	MAS: Bonnie Thornton	Redding, CA	12
	KIT: Carolyn Fox	Sublimity, OR	11
	STK: Loren Hurst	Hudson, OH	10

Year		Hometown	Age
1993	MAS: Dean Lutton	Delta, OH	14
	KIT: D.M. Del Ferraro	Stow, OH	12
	STK: Owen Yuda	Boiling Springs, PA	10
1994	MAS: D.M. Del Ferraro	Akron, OH	13
	KIT: Joel Endres	Akron, OH	14
	STK: Kristina Damond	Jamestown, NY	13
1995	MAS: J. Fensterbush	Kingman, AZ	11
	SS: Darcie Davisson	Kingman, AZ	11
	STK: Karen Thomas	Jamestown, NY	11
1996	MAS: Tim Scrofano	Conneaut, OH	12
	SS: Jeremy Phillips	Charlestown, WV	14
	STK: Matt Perez	No. Canton, OH	12
1997	MAS: Wade Wallace	Elk Hart, IN	11
	SS: Dolline Vance	Salem, OR	13
	STK: Mark Stephens	Waynesboro, VA	13
1998	MAS: James Marsh	Cleveland, OH	12
	SS: Stacy Sharp	Kingman, AZ	14
	STK: Hailey Simpson	Salem, OR	10

SOFTBALL

Men's and women's national champions since 1933 in Major Fast Pitch, Major Slow Pitch and Super Slow Pitch (men only). Sanctioned by the Amateur Softball Association of America.

MEN

Major Fast Pitch

Multiple winners: Clearwater Bombers (10); Raybestos Cardinals (5); Sealmasters (4); Briggs Beautyware, Pay'n Pak and Zollner Pistons (3); Billard Barbell, Decatur Pride, Hammer Air Field, Kodak Park, National Health Care, Penn Corp and Peterbilt Western (2).

Year
1933 J.L. Gill Boosters, Chicago
1934 Ke-Nash-A, Kenosha, WI
1935 Crimson Coaches, Toledo, OH
1936 Kodak Park, Rochester, NY
1937 Briggs Body Team, Detroit
1938 The Pohlers, Cincinnati
1939 Carr's Boosters, Covington, KY
1940 Kodak Park
1941 Bendix Brakes, South Bend, IN
1942 Deep Rock Oilers, Tulsa, OK
1943 Hammer Air Field, Fresno, CA
1944 Hammer Air Field
1945 Zollner Pistons, Ft. Wayne, IN
1946 Zollner Pistons
1947 Zollner Pistons
1948 Briggs Beautyware, Detroit
1949 Tip Top Tailors, Toronto
1950 Clearwater (FL) Bombers
1951 Dow Chemical, Midland, MI
1952 Briggs Beautyware
1953 Briggs Beautyware
1954 Clearwater Bombers
1955 Raybestos Cardinals,
1956 Clearwater Bombers
1957 Clearwater Bombers
1958 Raybestos Cardinals
1959 Sealmasters, Aurora, IL
1960 Clearwater Bombers
1961 Sealmasters
1962 Clearwater Bombers
1963 Clearwater Bombers
1964 Burch Tool, Detroit
1965 Sealmasters
1966 Clearwater Bombers
1967 Sealmasters
1968 Clearwater Bombers
1969 Raybestos Cardinals
1970 Raybestos Cardinals
1971 Welty Way, Cedar Rapids, IA
1972 Raybestos Cardinals
1973 Clearwater Bombers
1974 Gianella Bros., Santa Rosa, CA
1975 Rising Sun Hotel, Reading, PA
1976 Raybestos Cardinals
1977 Billard Barbell, Reading, PA
1978 Billard Barbell
1979 McArdle Pontiac/Cadillac, Midland, MI
1980 Peterbilt Western, Seattle
1981 Archer Daniels Midland, Decatur, IL
1982 Peterbilt Western
1983 Franklin Cardinals, Stratford, CA
1984 California Kings, Merced, CA
1985 Pay'n Pak, Seattle
1986 Pay'n Pak
1987 Pay'n Pak
1988 TransAire, Elkhart, IN
1989 Penn Corp, Sioux City, IA
1990 Penn Corp
1991 Gianella Bros., Rohnert Park, CA
1992 National Health Care, Sioux City, IA
1993 National Health Care
1994 Decatur (IL) Pride
1995 Decatur Pride
1996 Green Bay All-Car, Green Bay, WI
1997 Tampa Bay Smokers, Tampa Bay, FL
1998 Meierhoffer-Fleeman, St. Joseph, MO

Super Slow Pitch

Multiple winners: Ritch's/Superior (4); Howard's/Western Steer and Steele's Sports (3); Lighthouse/Worth (2).

Year
1981 Howard's/Western Steer, Denver, NC
1982 Jerry's Catering, Miami
1983 Howard's/Western Steer
1984 Howard's/Western Steer
1985 Steele's Sports, Grafton, OH
1986 Steele's Sports
1987 Steele's Sports
1988 Starpath, Monticello, KY
1989 Ritch's Salvage, Harrisburg, NC
1990 Steele's Silver Bullets
1991 Sun Belt/Worth, Atlanta
1992 Ritch's/Superior, Windsor Locks, CT
1993 Ritch's/Superior
1994 Bellcorp., Tampa
1995 Lighthouse/Worth, Stone Mt., GA
1996 Ritch's/Superior
1997 Ritch's/Superior
1998 Lighthouse/Worth

Major Slow Pitch

Multiple winners: Gatliff Auto Sales, Riverside Paving and Skip Hogan A.C. (3); Campbell Carpets, Hamilton Tailoring and Howard's Furniture (2).

Year
1953 Shields Construction, Newport, KY
1954 Waldneck's Tavern, Cincinnati
1955 Lang Pet Shop, Covington, KY
1956 Gatliff Auto Sales, Newport, KY
1957 Gatliff Auto Sales
1958 East Side Sports, Detroit
1959 Yorkshire Restaurant, Newport, KY
1960 Hamilton Tailoring, Cincinnati
1961 Hamilton Tailoring
1962 Skip Hogan A.C., Pittsburgh
1963 Gatliff Auto Sales
1964 Skip Hogan A.C.
1965 Skip Hogan A.C.
1966 Michael's Lounge, Detroit
1967 Jim's Sport Shop, Pittsburgh

Year
1968 County Sports, Levittown, NY
1969 Copper Hearth, Milwaukee
1970 Little Caesar's, Southgate, MI
1971 Pile Drivers, Va. Beach, VA
1972 Jiffy Club, Louisville, KY
1973 Howard's Furniture, Denver, NC
1974 Howard's Furniture
1975 Pyramid Cafe, Lakewood, OH
1976 Warren Motors, J'ville, FL
1977 Nelson Painting, Okla. City
1978 Campbell Carpets, Concord, CA
1979 Nelco Mfg. Co., Okla. City

Year
1980 Campbell Carpets
1981 Elite Coating, Gordon, CA
1982 Triangle Sports, Minneapolis
1983 No.1 Electric & Heating, Gastonia, NC
1984 Lilly Air Systems, Chicago
1985 Blanton's Fayetteville, NC
1986 Non-Ferrous Metals, Cleveland
1987 Stapath, Monticello, KY
1988 Bell Corp/FAF, Tampa, FL
1989 Ritch's Salvage, Harrisburg, NC

Year
1990 New Construction, Shelbyville, IN
1991 Riverside Paving, Louisville
1992 Vernon's, Jacksonville, FL
1993 Back Porch/Destin (FL) Roofing
1994 Riverside Paving, Louisville
1995 Riverside Paving
1996 Bell II, Orlando, FL
1997 Long Haul TPS, Albertville, MN
1998 Chase Mortgage/Easton, Wilmington, NC

WOMEN

Major Fast Pitch

Multiple winners: Raybestos Brakettes (21); Orange Lionettes (9); Jax Maids (5); Arizona Ramblers and Redding Rebels (3); California Commotion, Hi-Ho Brakettes, J.J. Krieg's and National Screw & Manufacturing (2).

Year
1933 Great Northerns, Chicago
1934 Hart Motors, Chicago
1935 Bloomer Girls, Cleveland
1936 Nat'l Screw & Mfg., Cleveland
1937 Nat'l Screw & Mfg.
1938 J.J. Krieg's, Alameda, CA
1939 J.J. Krieg's
1940 Arizona Ramblers, Phoenix
1941 Higgins Midgets, Tulsa, OK
1942 Jax Maids, New Orleans
1943 Jax Maids
1944 Lind & Pomeroy, Portland, OR
1945 Jax Maids
1946 Jax Maids
1947 Jax Maids
1948 Arizona Ramblers
1949 Arizona Ramblers
1950 Orange (CA) Lionettes
1951 Orange Lionettes
1952 Orange Lionettes
1953 Betsy Ross Rockets, Fresno, CA
1954 Leach Motor Rockets,Fresno, CA
1955 Orange Lionettes

Year
1956 Orange Lionettes
1957 Hacienda Rockets, Fresno, CA
1958 Raybestos Brakettes, Stratford, CT
1959 Raybestos Brakettes
1960 Raybestos Brakettes
1961 Gold Sox, Whittier, CA
1962 Orange Lionettes
1963 Raybestos Brakettes
1964 Erv Lind Florists, Portland, OR
1965 Orange Lionettes
1966 Raybestos Brakettes
1967 Raybestos Brakettes
1968 Raybestos Brakettes
1969 Orange Lionettes
1970 Orange Lionettes
1971 Raybestos Brakettes
1972 Raybestos Brakettes
1973 Raybestos Brakettes
1974 Raybestos Brakettes
1975 Raybestos Brakettes
1976 Raybestos Brakettes
1977 Raybestos Brakettes

Year
1978 Raybestos Brakettes
1979 Sun City (AZ) Saints
1980 Raybestos Brakettes
1981 Orlando (FL) Rebels
1982 Raybestos Brakettes
1983 Raybestos Brakettes
1984 Los Angeles Diamonds
1985 Hi-Ho Brakettes, Stratford, CT
1986 So. California Invasion, LA
1987 Orange County Majestics, Anaheim, CA
1988 Hi-Ho Brakettes
1989 Whittier (CA) Raiders
1990 Raybestos Brakettes
1991 Raybestos Brakettes
1992 Raybestos Brakettes
1993 Redding (CA) Rebels
1994 Redding Rebels
1995 Redding Rebels
1996 California Commotion, Woodland Hills
1997 California Commotion
1998 California Commotion

Major Slow Pitch

Multiple winners: Spooks (5); Dana Gardens (4); Universal Plastics (3); Cannan's Illusions, Bob Hoffman's Dots and Marks Brothers Dots (2).

Year
1959 Pearl Laundry, Richmond, VA
1960 Carolina Rockets, High Pt., NC
1961 Dairy Cottage, Covington, KY
1962 Dana Gardens, Cincinnati
1963 Dana Gardens
1964 Dana Gardens
1965 Art's Acres, Omaha, NE
1966 Dana Gardens
1967 Ridge Maintenance, Cleveland
1968 Escue Pontiac, Cincinnati
1969 Converse Dots, Hialeah, FL
1970 Rutenschruder Floral, Cincinnati
1971 Gators, Ft. Lauderdale, FL
1972 Riverside Ford, Cincinnati
1973 Sweeney Chevrolet, Cincinnati

Year
1974 Marks Brothers Dots, Miami
1975 Marks Brothers Dots
1976 Sorrento's Pizza, Cincinnati
1977 Fox Valley Lassies, St. Charles, IL
1978 Bob Hoffman's Dots, Miami
1979 Bob Hoffman's Dots
1980 Howard's Rubi-Otts, Graham, NC
1981 Tifton (GA) Tomboys
1982 Richmond (VA) Stompers
1983 Spooks, Anoka, MN
1984 Spooks
1985 Key Ford Mustangs, Pensacola, FL

Year
1986 Sur-Way Tomboys, Tifton, GA
1987 Key Ford Mustangs
1988 Spooks
1989 Cannan's Illusions, Houston
1990 Spooks
1991 Cannan's Illusions, San Antonio
1992 Universal Plastics, Cookeville, TN
1993 Universal Plastics
1994 Universal Plastics
1995 Armed Forces, Sacramento
1996 Spooks
1997 Taylor's, Glendale, MD
1998 not held

TRIATHLON

World Championship

Contested since 1989, the Triathlon World Championship consists of a 1.5-kilometer swim, a 40-kilometer bike ride and a 10-kilometer run. The 1998 championship took place on August 29 in Lausanne, Switzerland

Multiple winners: MEN— Simon Lessing (4); Spencer Smith (2). WOMEN— Emma Carney, Michelle Jones and Karen Smyers (2).

MEN

Year		Time
1989	Mark Allen, United States	1:58:46
1990	Greg Welch, Australia	1:51:37
1991	Miles Stewart, Australia	1:48:20
1992	Simon Lessing, Great Britain	1:49:04
1993	Spencer Smith, Great Britain	1:51:20
1994	Spencer Smith, Great Britain	1:51:04
1995	Simon Lessing, Great Britain	1:48:29
1996	Simon Lessing, Great Britain	1:39:50
1997	Chris McCormack, Australia	1:48:29
1998	Simon Lessing, Great Britain	1:55:31

WOMEN

Year		Time
1989	Erin Baker, New Zealand	2:10:01
1990	Karen Smyers, United States	2:03:33
1991	Joanne Ritchie, Canada	2:02:04
1992	Michellie Jones, Australia	2:02:08
1993	Michellie Jones, Australia	2:07:41
1994	Emma Carney, Australia	2:03:19
1995	Karen Smyers, USA	2:04:58
1996	Jackie Gallagher, Australia	1:50:52
1997	Emma Carney, Australia	1:59:22
1998	Joanne King, Australia	2:07:25

Ironman Championship

Contested in Hawaii since 1978, the Ironman Triathlon Championship consists of a 2.4-mile swim, a 112-mile bike ride and 26.2-mile run. The race begins at 7 a.m. and continues all day until the course is closed at midnight. The 1998 Ironman Championship was scheduled for Oct. 3.

MEN

Multiple winners: Mark Allen and Dave Scott (6); Scott Tinley (2).

Year	Date	Winner	Time	Runner-up	Margin	Start	Finish	Location
I	2/18/78	Gordon Haller	11:46	John Dunbar	34:00	15	12	Waikiki Beach
II	1/14/79	Tom Warren	11:15:56	John Dunbar	48:00	15	12	Waikiki Beach
III	1/10/80	Dave Scott	9:24:33	Chuck Neumann	1:08	108	95	Ala Moana Park
IV	2/14/81	John Howard	9:38:29	Tom Warren	26:00	326	299	Kailua-Kona
V	2/6/82	Scott Tinley	9:19:41	Dave Scott	17:16	580	541	Kailua-Kona
VI	10/9/82	Dave Scott	9:08:23	Scott Tinley	20:05	850	775	Kailua-Kona
VII	10/22/83	Dave Scott	9:05:57	Scott Tinley	0:33	964	835	Kailua-Kona
VIII	10/6/84	Dave Scott	8:54:20	Scott Tinley	24:25	1036	903	Kailua-Kona
IX	10/25/85	Scott Tinley	8:50:54	Chris Hinshaw	25:46	1018	965	Kailua-Kona
X	10/18/86	Dave Scott	8:28:37	Mark Allen	9:47	1039	951	Kailua-Kona
XI	10/10/87	Dave Scott	8:34:13	Mark Allen	11:06	1380	1284	Kailua-Kona
XII	10/22/88	Scott Molina	8:31:00	Mike Pigg	2:11	1277	1189	Kailua-Kona
XIII	10/15/89	Mark Allen	8:09:15	Dave Scott	0:58	1285	1231	Kailua-Kona
XIV	10/6/90	Mark Allen	8:28:17	Scott Tinley	9:23	1386	1255	Kailua-Kona
XV	10/19/91	Mark Allen	8:18:32	Greg Welch	6:01	1386	1235	Kailua-Kona
XVI	10/10/92	Mark Allen	8:09:08	Cristian Bustos	7:21	1364	1298	Kailua-Kona
XVII	10/30/93	Mark Allen	8:07:45	Paulli Kiuru	6:37	1438	1353	Kailua-Kona
XVIII	10/15/94	Greg Welch	8:20:27	Dave Scott	4:05	1405	1290	Kailua-Kona
XIX	10/7/95	Mark Allen	8:20:34	Thomas Hellriegel	2:25	1487	1323	Kailua-Kona
XX	10/26/96	Luc Van Lierde	8:04:08	Thomas Hellriegel	1:59	1420	1288	Kailua-Kona
XXI	10/18/97	Thomas Hellriegel	8:33:01	Jurgen Zack	6:17	1534	1365	Kailua-Kona

WOMEN

Multiple winners: Paula Newby-Fraser (8); Erin Baker and Sylviane Puntous (2).

Year	Winner	Time	Runner-up
1978	No finishers		
1979	Lyn Lemaire	12:55.00	None
1980	Robin Beck	11:21:24	Eve Anderson
1981	Linda Sweeney	12:00:32	Sally Edwards
1982	Kathleen McCartney	11:09:40	Julie Moss
1982	Julie Leach	10:54:08	Joann Dahlkoetter
1983	Sylviane Puntous	10:43:36	Patricia Puntous
1984	Sylviane Puntous	10:25:13	Patricia Puntous
1985	Joanne Ernst	10:25:22	Liz Bulman
1986	Paula Newby-Fraser	9:49:14	Sylviane Puntous
1987	Erin Baker	9:35:25	Sylviane Puntous
1988	Paula Newby-Fraser	9:01:01	Erin Baker
1989	Paula Newby-Fraser	9:00:56	Sylviane Puntous
1990	Erin Baker	9:13:42	P. Newby-Fraser
1991	Paula Newby-Fraser	9:07:52	Erin Baker
1992	Paula Newby-Fraser	8:55:28	Julie Anne White
1993	Paula Newby-Fraser	8:58:23	Erin Baker
1994	Paula Newby-Fraser	9:20:14	Karen Smyers
1995	Karen Smyers	9:16:46	Isabelle Mouthon
1996	Paula Newby-Fraser	9:06:49	Natascha Badmann
1997	Heather Fuhr	9:31:43	Lori Bowden

Triathlon Added To Olympics

The triathlon will be held for the first time in an Olympic Games at Sydney in 2000. It was developed as a combination of the longest Olympic swimming distance, 1500 meters, the 40 kilometer cycling time trial, and the longest athletic track event of 10,000 meters. The triathlon will start and finish at the Sydney Opera House.

X GAMES

The ESPN Extreme Games, orginally envisioned as a biannual showcase for "alternative" sports, were first held June 24-July 1, 1995 in Newport and Providence, R.I. and Mt. Snow, Vermont. The success of the inaugural event prompted organizers to make it an annual competition. Newport would again serve as host for the redubbed X Games in 1996 before they moved to San Diego for 1997 and 1998. The X Games has evolved rapidly since its inception. New sports and events are added while others are dropped.

In 1997, the first Winter X Games were held at Snow Summit Mountain Resort in Big Bear Lake, Calif. before moving to Crested Butte, Colo. in 1998.

The 1999 Summer X Games will be held June 25-July 3 in San Francisco. The 1999 Winter X Games will again be held in Crested Butte, Colo. January 14-17.

Summer X Games

Bicycle Stunt

Year	Vert
1995	Matt Hoffman
1996	Matt Hoffman
1997	Dave Mirra
1998	Dave Mirra

Year	Dirt
1995	Jay Miron
1996	Joey Garcia
1997	T.J. Lavin
1998	Brian Foster

Year	Street
1996	Dave Mirra
1997	Dave Mirra
1998	Dave Mirra

Year	Flatland
1997	Trevor Meyer
1998	Trevor Meyer

Big-Air Snowboarding

Year	Men
1997	Peter Line
1998	Kevin Jones

Year	Women
1997	Tina Dixon
1998	Janet Matthews

Skysurfing

Year	
1995	Fradet/Zipser
1996	Furrer/Scmid
1997	Hartman/Pappadato
1998	Rozov/Burch

Skateboard

Year	Vert Singles
1995	Tony Hawk
1996	Andy Macdonald
1997	Tony Hawk
1998	Andy Macdonald

Year	Vert Doubles
1997	Hawk/Macdonald
1998	Hawk/Macdonald

Year	Street
1995	Chris Senn
1996	Rodil de Araujo Jr.
1997	Chris Senn
1998	Rodil de Araujo Jr.

Bungee Jumping

Year	
1995	Doug Anderson
1996	Peter Bihun
1997	event discontinued

Street Luge

Year	Dual
1995	Bob Pereyra
1996	Shawn Goular
1997	Biker Sherlock
1998	Biker Sherlock

Year	Mass
1995	Shawn Gilbert
1996	Biker Sherlock
1997	Biker Sherlock
1998	Rat Sult

Year	Super Mass
1997	Biker Sherlock
1998	Rat Sult

In-Line Skating

Year	Men's Vert
1995	Tom Fry
1996	Rene Hulgreen
1997	Tim Ward
1998	Cesar Mora

Year	Women's Vert
1995	Tash Hodgeson
1996	Fabiola da Silva
1997	Fabiola da Silva
1998	Fabiola da Silva

Year	Men's Street
1995	Matt Salerno
1996	Arlo Eisenberg
1997	Arron Feinberg
1998	Jonathan Bergeron

Year	Women's Street
1997	Sayaka Yabe
1998	Jenny Curry

Year	Vert Triples
1998	Malina/Fogarty/Popa

Year	Men's Downhill
1995	Derek Downing
1996	Dante Muse
1997	Derek Downing
1998	Patrick Naylor

Year	Women's Downhill
1995	Julie Brandt
1996	Gypsy Tidwell
1997	Gypsy Tidwell
1998	Julie Brandt

Sportclimbing

Year	Men's Difficulty
1995	Ian Vickers
1996	Arnaud Petit
1997	Francois Legrand
1998	Christian Core

Year	Women's Difficulty
1995	Robyn Erbersfield
1996	Katie Brown
1997	Katie Brown
1998	Katie Brown

Year	Men's Speed
1995	Hans Florine
1996	Hans Florine
1997	Hans Florine
1998	Vladimir Netsvetaev

Year	Women's Speed
1995	Elena Ovtchinnikova
1996	Cecile Le Flem
1997	Elena Ovtchinnikova
1998	Elena Ovtchinnikova

Watersports

Year	Barefoot Waterski Jumping
1995	Justin Seers
1996	Ron Scarpa
1997	Peter Fleck
1998	Peter Fleck

Year	Men's Wakeboarding
1996	Parks Bonifay
1997	Jeremy Kovak
1998	Darin Shapiro

Year	Women's Wakeboarding
1997	Tara Hamilton
1998	Andrea Gaytan

X-Venture Race

Year	
1995	Team Threadbo*
1996	Team Kobeer
1997	Team Presidio
1998	event discontinued

*In 1995, Team Threadbo won the Eco-Challenge which was held in conjunction with the ESPN Extreme Games.

AP/Wide World Photos

So-called "alternative" sports like snowboarding have found increased mass-market exposure thanks in part to ESPN's X Games. Above, **Ross Powers** of South Londonderry, Vt. busts a trick in the halfpipe at the 1998 Winter X Games in Crested Butte, Colo.

Winter X Games

CrossOver

Year	
1997	Brian Patch
1998	event discontinued

Free Skiing

Year	Skier X
1998	Dennis Rey

Ice Climbing

Year	Men's Difficulty
1997	Jaren Ogden
1998	Will Gadd

Year	Women's Difficulty
1997	Bird Lew
1998	Kim Csizmazia

Year	Men's Speed
1997	Jared Ogden
1998	Will Gadd

Year	Women's Speed
1997	Bird Lew
1998	Kim Csizmazia

Skiboarding

Year	
1998	Mike Nick

Snowboarding

Year	Men's Big Air
1997	Jimmy Halopoff
1998	Jason Borgstede

Year	Women's Big Air
1997	Barrett Christy
1998	Tina Basich

Year	Men's Boarder X
1997	Shaun Palmer
1998	Shaun Palmer

Year	Women's Boarder X
1997	Jennie Waara
1998	Tina Dixon

Year	Men's Halfpipe
1997	Todd Richards
1998	Ross Powers

Year	Women's Halfpipe
1997	Shannon Dunn
1998	Cara-Beth Burnside

Year	Men's Slopestyle
1997	Daniel Franck
1998	Ross Powers

Year	Women's Slopestyle
1997	Barrett Christy
1998	Jennie Waara

Snow Mountain Bike Racing

Year	Men's Downhill
1997	Shaun Palmer
1998	Andrew Shandro

Year	Women's Downhill
1997	Missy Giove
1998	Marla Streb

Year	Men's Speed
1997	Phil Tintsman
1998	Jurgen Beneke

Year	Women's Speed
1997	Cheri Elliott
1998	Elke Brutsaert

Snocross

Year	
1998	Toni Haikonen

Super-modified Shovel Racing

Year	
1997	Don Adkins
1998	event discontinued

YACHTING

The America's Cup

International yacht racing was launched in 1851 when England's Royal Yacht Squadron staged a 60-mile regatta around the Isle of Wight and offered a silver trophy to the winner. The 101-foot schooner *America*, sent over by the New York Yacht Club, won the race and the prize. Originally called the Hundred-Guinea Cup, the trophy was renamed The America's Cup after the winning boat's owners deeded it to the NYYC with instructions to defend it whenever challenged.

From 1870-1980, the NYYC successfully defended the Cup 25 straight times; first in large schooners and J-class boats that measured up to 140 feet in overall length, then in 12-meter boats. A foreign yacht finally won the Cup in 1983 when *Australia II* beat defender *Liberty* in the seventh and deciding race off Newport, R.I. Four years later, the San Diego Yacht Club's *Stars & Stripes* won the Cup back, sweeping the four races of the final series off Fremantle, Australia.

Then in 1988, New Zealand's Mercury Bay Boating Club, unwilling to wait the usual three- to four-year period between Cup defenses, challenged the SDYC to a match race, citing the Cup's 102-year-old Deed of Gift, which clearly stated that every challenge had to be honored. Mercury Bay announced it would race a 133-foot monohull. San Diego countered with a 60-foot catamaran. The resulting best-of-three series (Sept. 7-8) was a mismatch as the SDYC's catamaran *Stars & Stripes* won two straight by margins of better than 18 and 21 minutes. Mercury Bay syndicate leader Michael Fay protested the outcome and took the SDYC to court in New York State (where the Deed of Gift was first filed) claiming San Diego had violated the spirit of the deed by racing a catamaran instead of a monohull. N.Y. State Supreme Court judge Carmen Ciparick agreed and on March 28, 1989, ordered the SDYC to hand the Cup over to Mercury Bay. The SDYC refused, but did consent to the court's appointment of the New York Yacht Club as custodian of the Cup until an appeal was ruled on.

On Sept. 19, 1989, the Appellate Division of the N.Y. Supreme Court overturned Ciparick's decision and awarded the Cup back to the SDYC. An appeal by Mercury Bay was denied by the N.Y. Court of Appeals on April 26, 1990, ending three years of legal wrangling. To avoid the chaos of 1988-90, a new class of boat—75-foot monohulls with 110-foot masts—has been used by all competing countries since 1992.

The next America's Cup races will be held in New Zealand from Feb. 26-Mar. 11, 2000.

Note that (*) indicates skipper was also owner of the boat.

Schooners And J-Class Boats

Year	Winner	Skipper	Series	Loser	Skipper
1851	*America*	Richard Brown	—	—	—
1870	*Magic*	Andrew Comstock	1-0	*Cambria*, GBR	J. Tannock
1871	*Columbia* (2-1)	Nelson Comstock	4-0	*Livonia*, GBR	J.R. Woods
	& *Sappho* (2-0)	Sam Greenwood			
1876	*Madeleine*	Josephus Williams	2-0	*Countess of Dufferin*, CAN	J.E. Ellsworth
1881	*Mischief*	Nathanael Clock	2-0	*Atalanta*, CAN	Alexander Cuthbert*
1885	*Puritan*	Aubrey Crocker	2-0	*Genesta*, GBR	John Carter
1886	*Mayflower*	Martin Stone	2-0	*Galatea*, GBR	Dan Bradford
1887	*Volunteer*	Henry Haff	2-0	*Thistle*, GBR	John Barr
1893	*Vigilant*	William Hansen	3-0	*Valkyrie II*, GBR	Wm. Granfield
1895	*Defender*	Henry Haff	3-0	*Valkyrie III*, GBR	Wm. Granfield
1899	*Columbia*	Charles Barr	3-0	*Shamrock I*, GBR	Archie Hogarth
1901	*Columbia*	Charles Barr	3-0	*Shamrock II*, GBR	E.A. Sycamore
1903	*Reliance*	Charles Barr	3-0	*Shamrock III*, GBR	Bob Wringe
1920	*Resolute*	Charles F. Adams	3-2	*Shamrock IV*, GBR	William Burton
1930	*Enterprise*	Harold Vanderbilt*	4-0	*Shamrock V*, GBR	Ned Heard
1934	*Rainbow*	Harold Vanderbilt*	4-2	*Endeavour*, GBR	T.O.M. Sopwith
1937	*Ranger*	Harold Vanderbilt*	4-0	*Endeavour II*, GBR	T.O.M. Sopwith

12-METER BOATS

Year	Winner	Skipper	Series	Loser	Skipper
1958	*Columbia*	Briggs Cunningham	4-0	*Sceptre*, GBR	Graham Mann
1962	*Weatherly*	Bus Mosbacher	4-1	*Gretel*, AUS	Jock Sturrock
1964	*Constellation*	Bob Bavier & Eric Ridder	4-0	*Sovereign*, AUS	Peter Scott
1967	*Intrepid*	Bus Mosbacher	4-0	*Dame Pattie*, AUS	Jock Sturrock
1970	*Intrepid*	Bill Ficker	4-1	*Gretel II*, AUS	Jim Hardy
1974	*Courageous*	Ted Hood	4-0	*Southern Cross*, AUS	John Cuneo
1977	*Courageous*	Ted Turner	4-0	*Australia*	Noel Robins
1980	*Freedom*	Dennis Conner	4-1	*Australia*	Jim Hardy
1983	*Australia II*	John Bertrand	4-3	*Liberty*, USA	Dennis Conner
1987	*Stars & Stripes*	Dennis Conner	4-0	*Kookaburra III*, AUS	Iain Murray

60-FT CATAMARAN VS 133-FT MONOHULL

Year	Winner	Skipper	Series	Loser	Skipper
1988	*Stars & Stripes*	Dennis Conner	2-0	*New Zealand*, NZE	David Barnes

75-FT INTERNATIONAL AMERICA'S CUP CLASS

Year	Winner	Skipper	Series	Loser	Skipper
1992	*America*^{3}	Bill Koch* & Buddy Melges	4-1	*Il Moro di Venezia*, ITA	Paul Cayard
1995	*Black Magic*, NZE	Russell Coutts	5-0	*Young America*, USA	Dennis Conner & Paul Cayard

Other Champions

Championships decided in 1998, unless otherwise indicated.

LACROSSE

National Lacrosse League Final Standings

(*) denotes playoff qualifier.

	W	L	Pct	GF	GA
*Philadelphia Wings	9	3	.750	166	148
*Baltimore Thunder	8	4	.667	184	160
*Rochester Knighthawks	6	6	.500	168	159
*Buffalo Bandits	6	6	.500	166	171
Ontario Raiders	6	6	.500	165	157
New York Saints	5	7	.417	167	165
Syracuse Smash	2	10	.167	163	219

Semifinals

at Philadelphia 17 .... Buffalo 12
at Baltimore 15 .... Rochester 14

Finals (Best of 3)

	W-L	GF	GA
Philadelphia Wings	2-0	33	24
Baltimore Thunder	0-2	24	33

RESULTS: **April 26**–Philadelphia, 16-12; **April 28**–Philadelphia, 17-12.

ROLLER HOCKEY

Major League Roller Hockey Final Standings

(*) denotes division champion; (†) denotes playoff qualifier.

Teams receive three points for a win and one point for overtime losses (OTL).

Coastal Division

	W	L	OTL	Pts	GF	GA
Anaheim	19	0	1	39	263	84
Washington	9	11	0	18	138	216
New York	7	12	1	15	144	175
Philadelphia	6	14	0	12	92	248

Great Lakes Division

	W	L	OTL	Pts	GF	GA
Columbus	17	2	1	35	172	82
Buffalo	11	8	1	23	178	126
Port Huron	9	9	2	20	133	185
Toronto	5	13	2	12	136	178
Pennsylvania	5	15	0	10	101	193

Southern Division

	W	L	OTL	Pts	GF	GA
Orlando	18	1	1	37	237	93
Virginia	16	4	0	32	290	125
Tampa Bay	10	8	2	22	168	160
South Carolina	8	11	1	17	142	152
Carolina	0	19	1	1	81	258

Playoffs

Second Round

Aug. 20–at Anaheim 20, Washington 4
Aug. 20–at Columbus 7, Buffalo 6
Aug. 22–at Orlando 7, Virginia 6

Note: Brighton (ENG) won the UK division of MLRH and a Final Four berth.

Final Four

at the Arrowhead Pond, Anaheim

Aug. 25–at Anaheim 35, Brighton 2
Aug. 25–Orlando 5, Columbus 4

Championship Game

Aug. 26 at the Arrowhead Pond, Anaheim

Anaheim 5 .... Orlando 4

MVP: Bill Lund, Anaheim, 3 goals, 1 assist.

RUGBY

Five Nations

1998 Champion: France

	W	L	PF	PA	Pts
France	4	0	144	49	8
England	3	1	146	87	6
Wales	2	2	75	145	4
Scotland	1	3	66	120	2
Ireland	0	4	70	100	0

RESULTS: **Feb. 7**–France 24, England 17; Scotland 17, Ireland 16; **Feb. 21**–England 60, Wales 26; France 51, Scotland 16; **Mar. 7**–France 18, Ireland 16; Wales 19, Scotland 13; **Mar. 21**–Wales 30, Ireland 21; **Mar. 22**–England 34, Scotland 20; **Apr. 4**–England 35, Ireland 17; **Apr. 5**–France 51, Wales 0.

Tri-Nations

1998 Champion: South Africa

	W	L	PF	PA	Pts
South Africa	4	0	70	54	14
Australia	2	2	79	82	10
New Zealand	0	4	65	88	2

RESULTS: **July 11**–Australia 24, New Zealand 16; **July 18**–South Africa 14, Australia 13; **July 25**–South Africa 13, New Zealand 3; **Aug. 1**–Australia 27, New Zealand 23; **Aug. 15**–South Africa 24, New Zealand 23; **Aug. 22**–South Africa 29, Australia 15.

SURFING

1997 Assn. of Surfing Professionals World Tour Champions

Men .... Kelly Slater, Cocoa Beach, Fla.
Women .... Lisa Andersen, Ormond, Fla.

BEACH VOLLEYBALL

Association of Volleyball Professionals AVP Grand Slam events

Date	Event	Winners
Apr. 17-19	Players Championship	Kent Steffes & Jose Loiola
July 3-5	Chicago Open	Kent Steffes & Mike Whitmarsh
Aug. 14-16	U.S. Championship	Adam Johnson & Karch Kiraly
Aug. 28-30	AVP Tour Championship	Canyon Ceman & Mark Kerins

Deaths

World record holder **Florence Griffith Joyner**, shown here celebrating her victory in the 100-meter dash at the 1988 Olympic Summer Games in Seoul, Korea, succumbed to a heart seizure on Sept. 21.

AP/Wide World Photos

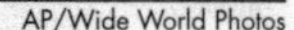

Eddie Arcaro

Washington St. Univ.

Leon Bender

Los Angeles Dodgers

Al Campanis

Lionel Aldridge, 57; former NFL defensive end who played on four of Green Bay's championship teams in the 1960s; played from 1963-71, winning two NFL championships and two Super Bowls; after a short stint in broadcasting Aldridge spent almost 20 years after his football career suffering from mental illness and homelessness before getting treatment and spending his last few years as an advocate for those with psychiatric problems; of natural causes; in Shorewood, Wisc., Feb. 12.

Ella Maria Gonzalez Alvarez, 93; a pioneer in women's tennis in Spain; better known as "Lili Alvarez", she ruled Spanish tennis in the 1920s, making it to three consecutive Wimbledon finals from 1926-28 and winning the French Open doubles in 1929; cause of death not given; in Madrid, July 8.

John Anderson, 65; former Brown football coach who led the school to its only Ivy League championship in 1976; compiled a record of 60-39-2 between 1973-83 and was named UPI New England Coach of the Year in 1976; of a heart attack; in Palm Coast, Fla., Jan. 14.

Eddie Arcaro, 81; only jockey in history to ride two Triple Crown champions, Whirlaway in 1941 and Citation in 1948; nicknamed "The Master," Arcaro rode 4,779 winners, including five Kentucky Derby titles and six victories in both the Preakness and Belmont stakes; the 5-foot-3 rider began his career in 1931 when he failed to win a single race on horses that earned a combined $200; after more than 24,000 career mounts and total earnings of $30,309,543, Arcaro became a network television racing analyst; of liver cancer; in Miami, Nov. 14, 1997.

Gene Autry, 91; owner of the Angels Major League Baseball franchise since its inception in 1961, but best known as Hollywood's first singing cowboy; the Angels won three American League pennants (1979,82,86) during Autry's 38 years of ownership, but never made an appearance in the World Series; had the number 26 retired in his honor as the team's 26th player in 1982; in May 1996 the Walt Disney Co. bought 25 percent interest in the team and renamed the California Angels, the Anaheim Angels in November 1996; acted in 91 musical westerns from 1935-53, starred in many radio shows, including Autry's Melody Ranch radio show, and was one of the most recognized faces during the golden age of television; of a lengthy illness; in Studio City, Calif., Oct. 2.

Morris (Red) Badgro, 95; four-time All-NFL end on defense and offense who caught the first touchdown pass of the first NFL championship game; three-sport star at USC, he spent time in pro football and minor league baseball until 1930 when he joined the NY Giants of the NFL; caught a 29-yard pass from Harry Newman in the 1933 title game despite losing to Chicago 23-21; hospitalized after a fall, but details of death not given; in Seattle, July 13.

Cliff Barker, 77; a member of Kentucky's "Fabulous Five" which went 36-3 and won the school's first NCAA men's basketball championship in 1948; later that summer Barker and his four teammates at Kentucky – Alex Groza, Ralph Beard, Kenny Rollins and Wally Jones – teamed with AAU champion Phillips Oilers and coach Adolph Rupp to win the Olympic gold medal in London; of natural causes; in Satsuma, Fla., March 17.

Emery Barnes, 68; defensive end with the Green Bay Packers who later became the first black to serve as speaker of the British Columbia parliament; captain of the Oregon football team, Barnes also shared the NCAA high jump title in 1954; drafted 18th overall by the Packers that fall and joined the team after a two-year stint in the U.S. Army; won Grey Cup in 1964 with British Columbia of the CFL; elected deputy speaker in 1991 and speaker two years later; of cancer; in British Columbia, Canada, on Canada Day, July 1.

Mark Belanger, 54; eight-time Gold Glove-winning shortstop with the Baltimore Orioles and key figure in the baseball players' union after his playing career ended in 1982; nicknamed "Blade," Belanger owned a career .977 fielding percentage, eighth all-time among shortstops at the time of his death; won four pennants and the 1970 World Series with Baltimore; longtime assistant to union head Donald Fehr; was instrumental in keeping players together through strikes in 1985 and 1990 as well as the strike that wiped out the 1994 season; of lung cancer; in Baltimore, Oct. 6.

Leon Bender, 22; defensive lineman at Washington St. and 1998 second round draft pick (31st overall) of the Oakland Raiders; 6-foot-5, 300-pound tackle started all but one game over the last two seasons for Washington St. and finished his college career at the Rose Bowl; cause of death is unknown; Bender who suffered from epilepsy, was found in the bathroom of his agent's home; in Marietta, Ga., May 30.

Jack Bowman, 61; Buffalo Sabres director of scouting since 1996 and a member of the organization since 1980; after a brief illness; in London, Ontario, Canada, June 22.

Jack Brickhouse, 82; was the voice of the Chicaco Cubs for four decades before being replaced by Harry Caray in 1982; also broadcast the Chicago Bears for 24 years; honored in 1979 at Wrigley Field for his 5,000th broadcast; retired in 1981; inducted into the National Sportscasters and Sportswriters Hall of Fame in 1983; underwent brain surgery March 3, 1998 to remove a small tumor; of cardiac arrest; in Chicago, Aug. 6.

Jack Bruen, 48; turned a struggling Colgate basketball team, which had endured 14 straight losing seasons, into a winner during his nine years (1989-98) as head coach; led the Red Raiders to a share of three Patriot League titles and their first NCAA tournaments in 1995 and 1996; twice named the league's Coach of the Year, his 1992-93 squad won a school record 18 games; won the last game he coached just six days before his long battle with pancreatic cancer ended; in Hamilton, N.Y., Dec. 19, 1997.

George Cafego, 82; "Bad News" was a two-time All-American tailback/safety at Tennessee during the 1930s and returned to the team as an assistant coach in 1966; worked with kickers and punters, including the NFL's Fuad Reveiz and Craig Colquitt; entered the College Football Hall of Fame in 1969; of natural causes; in Knoxville, Tenn., Feb. 9.

Al Campanis, 81; former Dodgers general manager who helped assemble teams that won four National League pennants and the 1981 World Series; is remembered more, however, for telling a national audience watching ABC's "Nightline" that blacks lacked "the necessities" to be managers and executives; although Campanis was responsible for signing minority stars like Roberto Clemente and Tommy Davis, it still wasn't enough to overshadow his racist comments; he spent almost a half century as a player scout and manager, serving as the team's GM from 1968-87; of coronary artery disease; in Fullerton, Calif., June 21.

Harry Caray, 78; legendary radio/TV broadcaster best remembered for his oversized, black-rimmed glasses and outgoing personality that earned him the title "Mayor of Rush Street" – a nightclub district in Chicago; spent 53 years broadcasting baseball games for St. Louis, Oakland, and most memorably the Chicago White Sox and Cubs; during his 27 years in Chicago (11 with the Sox, 16 with the Cubs) Caray made the seventh-inning stretch almost as interesting as the game, crooning "Take Me Out to the Ballgame" in his own off-key strain with the rest of the fans; a stroke in 1987 caused him to miss his first game and he sat out the first six weeks of the season; in 1989 he was inducted into the Baseball Hall of Fame; his son Skip broadcasts Braves games and grandson Chip is a studio host for Fox Sports; of cardiac arrest; in Rancho Mirage, Calif., Feb. 18.

Al Ciraldo, 76; the voice of Georgia Tech football and basketball from 1954-93, whose "toe meets leather" line before kickoffs became a college football trademark; after doing play-by-play for 416 football and 1,030 basketball games Ciraldo moved into the studio where he hosted pregame, halftime and postgame shows; of complications from congestive heart failure; in Atlanta, Nov. 7, 1997.

Lisa Coole, 23; the 1997 NCAA Woman of the Year and the most decorated swimmer ever at the University of Georgia where she earned 19 NCAA All-American honors; two-time NCAA champion: won the 100-yard butterfly in 1996 and was a member of the winning 200 freestyle relay in 1995; died in an automobile accident; in Champaign, Ill., May 16.

Bobby Cotton, 21; harness racer who had 67 career victories and earned $216,739 in his brief career; died from head and neck injuries sustained in an automobile accident; in Camden, N.J., Nov. 17, 1997.

J.W. (Wobble) Davidson, 79; a three-sport star at Mississippi who was an assistant football coach for 22 seasons under John Vaught; as an assistant from 1947-68 he saw the Rebels win 16 bowl games and all six of the school's Southeastern Conference championships; lettered in football, track and basketball; cause of death was not given; in Oxford, Miss., May 25.

Fred Davis, 84; former world snooker champion; of natural causes; in London, April 16.

Gardner Dickinson, 70; a founder of the Senior PGA Tour and prolific Ryder Cup player; was 9-1 as a member of the U.S. Ryder Cup teams in 1967 and 1971; posted a 5-0 record with teammate Arnold Palmer in Cup play; won seven times on the PGA tour; his last victory was over Jack Nicklaus in a sudden-death playoff at the 1971 Atlanta Classic; later taught the sport to players such as LPGA great JoAnne Carner, and his wife, Judy, who is a former player and president of the LPGA; after a long illness; in Tequesta, Fla., April 19.

Helena Mroczkowska Dow, 80; a four-time national fencing champion and former U.S. Olympic Team member who was part of what is believed to be the only mother-father-son trio in U.S. Olympic history (all fencers); she was an Olympian in 1948, her late husband Warren Dow was one in 1936, and her son Robert in 1972; coached the women's varsity team at Fairleigh-Dickinson University from 1967-69; of cancer; in New York, April 22.

Don Dunphy, 90; the undisputed "Voice of Boxing," who broadcast more than 2,000 fights, including 200 championship bouts for the Gillette Co. (1941-60) and ABC Television (1960-64); his first fight was the Joe Louis-Billy Conn heavyweight bout in 1941, which attracted a rating of 56.2, making it one of the most listened to radio broadcasts in history; retired in 1981; also appeared in six movies between 1970-81, including "Bananas" and "Raging Bull"; member of the National Broadcasters, International Boxing and World Boxing halls of fame; following heart surgery; in New York, July 22.

Irwin (Winn) Elliot, 83; longtime play-by-play man for the New York Rangers; also the voice of "Sports Central USA" on the CBS Radio Network where over a 50-year career he covered every major sport; cause of death not released; in Weston, Conn., Sept. 17.

Joey Embry, 21; University of Mississippi junior offensive tackle who played all 11 games as a freshman but missed the 1997 season because of a back injury; listed as the No. 2 right tackle going into spring practice in 1998; drowned in a golf course pond while apparently suffering a diabetic-related seizure retrieving lost golf balls; in Starkville, Miss., May 19.

Roy Evans, 88; longtime president of the International Table Tennis Federation who is credited with coming up with the idea of Ping-Pong Diplomacy, the 1971 initiative that paved the way for diplomatic relations between the U.S. and Communist China; during Evans' term he watched the sport of "table tennis" expand to include 180 countries which now have national teams and its elevation to an Olympic sport in 1988; his most notable accomplishment, however, was his suggestion to Chinese premier Zhou En-lai that he invite Western countries competing in the world table tennis championships in Japan to visit China on their way home; the Chinese obliged, and ultimately, the action spawned President Nixon's notorious trip in 1972; of natural causes; in Cardiff, Wales, May 18.

Justin Fashanu, 36; former English soccer star charged in Maryland with sexually assaulting a teenage boy; apparently fled police in Britain and hung himself from the rafters at a garage complex underneath a railroad bridge; in London, May 2.

Tim Flock, 73; pioneer of stock car racing who won 40 career NASCAR races, including Winston Cup titles in 1952 and 1955; set a NASCAR record with 19 poles in 1955; was recognized as one of NASCAR's top 50 drivers by the media early in 1998; retired in 1961 and held various positions with Charlotte Motor Speedway; of liver and throat cancer; in Charlotte, N.C., March 31.

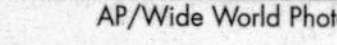
AP/Wide World Photos
Harry Caray

Archive Photos
Sid Luckman

AP/Wide World Photos
Jim Murray

Lawrence Gable, 48; a member of the Harlem Wizards, a Harlem Globetrotters-style exhibition basketball team that plays amateur teams at schools, camps and charity events; Gable entertained audiences for 31 years as a Wizard; he was also the longtime recreation coordinator for the Frederick Douglass Center-Children's AIDS Society in New York; of a heart attack during a performance at an elementary school; in Freehold, N.J., June 8.

Tom Gentry, 67; offshore speedboat racer who set several world records before a crash at the 1994 Key West World Offshore Championship left him hospitalized and in a coma; just a month before the crash, Gentry, who already owned the transatlantic speed record, captured a new world record, reaching an average speed of 157.4 mph; of respiratory failure; in Honolulu, Jan. 15.

Larry Gilbert, 55; three-time PGA Club Professional champion and winner of the 1997 Senior Players Championship; joined the Senior Tour in 1992 and won twice in 1994, capturing the Dallas Reunion Pro-Am and the Vantage Championship; one of three prominent Senior PGA Tour members to be diagnosed with cancer in 1997, joining Arnold Palmer and Jim Colbert, both of whom were found to have prostate cancer. Palmer and Colbert underwent surgery and returned to competition; Gilbert is a member of the Kentucky Golf and Middle Tennessee State University halls of fame; of lung cancer; in Lexington, Ky., Jan. 21.

Bob Green, 66; Associated Press writer whose career spanned four decades, including 26 years as a golf writer; covered six Olympics, five NCAA Final Fours, a World Series and more than 1,000 golf tournaments before retiring in 1995; former two-term president of the Golf Writers Association of America and one of the few American members of England's Association of Golf Writers; PGA of America presented him with a Lifetime Achievement award in 1994; of cancer; in Dallas, July 30.

Clarence Griffin, 49; men's basketball coach at Triton College in Illinois, who over 18 seasons established one of the best records in the country among junior colleges; "Griff" was named head coach in 1983; a three-time winner of Regional Coach of the Year honors, Griffin took Triton to the national tournament in 1985-86; of a heart attack; in River Grove, Ill., Jan. 31.

Pete Griffin, 81; former Florida A&M track coach who helped develop Olympic sprinter Bob Hayes; played center on A&M's undefeated and unscored-upon 1938 football team; of a lengthy illness; in Tallahassee, Fla., May 13.

Darrell Halloran, 47; head basketball coach at Pace University died during halftime of a game against American International College; Halloran, whose team won the ECAC Div. 2 title in 1990 and 1991, was stricken while conferring with his assistant coaches in preparation for the halftime pep talk; of heart failure; in New York, Jan. 3.

Steve Hamilton, 62; baseball relief pitcher who pitched in the 1963 and 1964 World Series with the New York Yankees and was remembered best for his "Folly Floater" pitch; he also played in the NBA with the Minneapolis Lakers before his baseball career began in 1961; a three-sport star at Morehead State University, Hamilton was baseball coach at the school from 1976-89 and athletic director at his alma mater since 1987; of colon cancer; in Morehead, Ky., Dec. 2, 1997.

Les Harrison, 93; NBA Hall of Famer who led the Rochester Royals to the NBA championship in 1951 as owner, general manager and coach; captured National Basketball League titles in 1946 and 1947 as well; coached three future Hall of Famers: Red Holzman, Bob Davies and Bobby Wanzer; tallied a 259-181 coaching record over seven seasons in the NBA, and a .620 winning percentage which ranked seventh all-time at his death; of natural causes; in Rochester, N.Y., Dec. 23, 1997.

Lewis W. Hays, 83; founder of Pony League baseball for 13 and 14-year-olds in 1951 and its president from 1965-80; former chairman of USA Baseball; of a heart attack, May 2.

Jim Hearn, 77; "Big Jim," who stood 6-foot-5, 205 pounds, pitched for 13 seasons with St. Louis, Philadelphia and the NY Giants; won Game 3 of the 1951 World Series after compiling a 17-9 record with the NL champion Giants; retired in 1959 with a career record of 109-89; opened the Jim Hearn Golf Center in 1961 and retired from that work 10 years ago, of Hodgkin's lymphoma; in Atlanta, June 10.

Viljo Akseli Heino, 84; the last of the track stars called the "Flying Finns"; established world records despite suffering from a leg injury during Finland's war with the Soviet Union in 1939; set the world record for the 10,000-meter run, and was given credit in the same race for setting a world six-mile record in 1944; cause of death not given; in Tempere, Finland, Sept. 15.

Chris Hitopoulos, 73; former coach for U.S. boxing teams that traveled to Poland and the Soviet Union in 1980 and Canada in 1990; a South Carolina boxing administrator for nearly 50 years, he retired as that state's chief commissioner in 1996; of natural causes; in Columbia, S.C., May 5.

Chandler (Buss) Hovey Jr., 83; disabled yachtsman who, with his family, raced boats in the America's Cup competitions of the 1930s and later helped build and campaign the 12-Meter yacht *Easterner*; the national trophy for the disabled, the Independence Cup, was named in his honor; of complications from multiple sclerosis; in Ocean Reef, Fla., April 9.

Chester (Red) Huff, 107; left-handed pitcher for the New York Highlanders from 1911-13 and the St. Louis Browns in 1915; lived longer than any other Major League Baseball player in history; claimed his first appearance was against Ty Cobb, whom he struck out on three pitches; pitched 83 innings over 23 major league games, compiling a 2.49 ERA before the outbreak of WWI ended his career; of natural causes; in Daytona Beach, Fla., Sept. 18.

Mary Fendrich Hulman, 93; chairman of the Indianapolis Motor Speedway since 1977 and traditionally responsible for the famous command "Gentlemen, start your engines," before each race; widow of Tony Hulman, who bought the struggling race track in 1945 and turned it into the richest auto race in the world; her daughter is now chairman of the board and her grandson, Tony George, is the president of the Speedway; of natural causes; in Indianapolis, Ind., April 10.

Anna May Hutchison, 72; professional baseball player who dazzled crowds during World War II and was immortalized in the 1992 motion picture "A League of Their Own"; "Hutch" broke in as a catcher with the Racine Belles of the All-American Girl's Professional Baseball League before switching to pitcher, a move that paid off during the 1946-47 season when she mastered the new side-arm delivery and won 53 games; she was a star for the league which formed during the war to provide entertainment for workers; she graduated from the University of Wisconsin-Parkside, and was an elementary teacher with Kenosha Unified Schools for 16 years before retiring in 1987; of natural causes; in Racine, Wis., Jan. 29.

Buddy Jeannette, 80; basketball star of the late 1930s and early 40s; played in Sheboygan, Fort Wayne and Baltimore for the National Basketball League, the American Basketball League and the Basketball Association of America, winning five championships; elected Most Valuable Player four times; enshrined into the Hall of Fame in 1994, Jeannette became a media favorite; he rode to the ceremony via Amtrak from Nashua, N.H. to Springfield and was a fixture there every year after; of a stroke; in Nashua, N.H., March 11.

Curtis Jones, 55; Missouri assistant football coach and father of the team's starting quarterback; played two seasons for Missouri (1966-67) before spending three seasons in the NFL with San Diego and Green Bay; his son Corby helped lead Missouri to its first winning season in 14 years and a trip to the Holiday Bowl in 1997; of a heart attack; in Columbia, Mo., July 26.

Florence Griffith Joyner, 38; triple gold medalist at the 1988 Olympics recognized around the world by her unusual running outfits and long, painted fingernails; won AP Female Athlete of the Year honors and the Sullivan Award in 1988 as the country's best amateur athlete; known simply as "FloJo," she smashed the world records for the 100 and 200-meter runs at Seoul, South Korea in 1988; she also won a gold medal anchoring the U.S. 4x100m relay team that year; her husband was 1984 Olympic triple-jump gold medalist Al Joyner and her sister-in-law was six-time Olympic medalist and world heptathlon record-holder Jackie Joyner-Kersee; served as co-chairman of the President's Council on Physical Fitness; suffered a seizure during an airline flight in 1996 and was hospitalized for one day; of a heart seizure; in Mission Viejo, Calif., Sept. 21.

Junius Kellogg, 71; college basketball player at CCNY-Manhattan who blew the top off a point-shaving scandal in the late 1940s which led to the arrest of seven players on City College's 1950 NCAA-NIT double-championship team; after the team captain approached Kellogg with the idea of shaving points, Kellogg told the head coach who then contacted the authorities. The investigation revealed that between 1947-50, 86 games had been fixed; Kellogg, who was a 6-10 center and the first black player in the school's history, finished school after serving in the Army during the Korean War; joined the Harlem Globetrotters in 1953; a year later was paralyzed in a car accident and spent four years in the hospital; he spent the rest of his life working for New York City agencies, coaching wheelchair athletes and making motivational speeches; of respiratory failure; in New York, Sept. 16.

Jamil Khan, 22; professional snowboarder who just missed qualifying for the U.S. Olympic team that competed in Nagano; died in an area called the "Poop Chute" when a 20-foot section of ice he was standing on gave way during a video shoot; of injuries sustained in the 300-foot fall; in Truckee, Calif., Feb. 11.

Northrup Knox, 69; with the help of his brother Seymour, brought the Sabres to Buffalo when the NHL expanded in 1969; served as Sabres chairman after his brother's death from cancer in 1996, and held the position until stepping aside in the spring of 1998 when the team was sold; after a lengthy illness; in East Aurora, N.Y., July 23.

Hal Laycoe, 75; first coach of the Vancouver Canucks, beginning in 1970-71; won three Stanley Cups as a player with the New York Islanders; of a brief illness; in Vancouver, April 28.

Buck Leonard, 90; Hall-of-Fame first baseman known as the "Black Lou Gehrig"; batted .340 and averaged 34 home runs a season during his 17-year career in the Negro Leagues; began his career with the Rocky Mount Black Swans in 1925; is best remembered for his years with the Homestead (Pa.) Grays from 1933-50, where batting after Josh Gibson, the Grays won nine straight league titles; elected to the Hall of Fame in 1972; from complications of a stroke he suffered in 1987; in Rocky Mount, N.C., Nov. 27, 1997.

Sid Luckman, 81; Chicago Bears all-time leader in career touchdowns thrown (137) and passing yards (14,686); named NFL MVP three times and All-Pro seven times; led Chicago to a 73-0 victory over Washington, which is still the most lopsided game in league history; after an All-American senior season at Columbia, Bears owner George Halas traded two players and a draft choice to Pittsburgh to acquire Luckman in 1939; spent 14 years as a part-time coach with the Bears and other teams after retiring in 1950, but never accepted a coaching salary from the Bears; after football he went to work for Cellu-Craft Inc. which makes wrapping materials for food companies; cause of death not given; in North Miami Beach, Fla., July 5.

Harry Lumley, 71; Hall of Fame goaltender with Detroit, Toronto and Boston; ranked ninth in career shutouts at the time of his death with 71; helped Detroit win the Stanley Cup in 1950; traded to Toronto in 1952 and won the Vezina Trophy after the 1953-54 season when he had a league best 1.86 GAA and 13 shutouts; retired in 1960 and inducted into the Hall of Fame 20 years later; of a heart attack; in London, Ontario, Canada, Sept. 13.

Sadie Magee, 65; Jackson State University assistant athletic director and coordinator of women's sports; coached women's basketball for 14 seasons, beginning in 1975 and is the Tigers all-time winningest coach at 271-154; of a lengthy illness; in Mount Olive, Miss., May 31.

AP/Wide World Photos

Helen Wills Moody

AP/Wide World Photos

Dan Quisenberry

AP/Wide World Photos

Doak Walker

Earl (The Goat) Manigault, 53; New York City playground legend who battled the likes of Lew Alcindor and Connie Hawkins in the 1960s; his heroin addiction cost him a professional basketball career; was featured in a 1996 HBO movie; his domination of players at the 98th Street courts was so well known that it became nicknamed "Goat Park"; played college ball at Johnson C. Smith University but fought with the coach about playing time and returned to the Harlem courts; was jailed in 1969-70 for drug possession and again in 1977-79 for a failed robbery; he later kicked his drug habit and had been working at a neighborhood recreation and counseling center; of heart failure; in New York City, May 15.

Jason McCray, 20; had 17 tackles in 10 games as a freshman defensive end on the Navy football team; died while playing basketball with other midshipmen at the First District Coast Guard Station; in Boston, June 5.

Bill Meek, 76; former SMU football coach who guided the Don Meredith-led Mustangs to the 1958 Cotton Bowl; coached SMU from 1957-61 after stints in Houston and Kansas State; finished his career with Utah, retiring in 1973; cause of death not given; in Dallas, May 29.

Warren Mehrtens, 77; one of only 10 jockeys to ride a Triple Crown winner when he rode Assault to victories in the Kentucky Derby, the Preakness and Belmont in 1946; retired from racing in 1952 and served as a steward at several tracks; cause of death not given; in Miami, Jan. 5.

Russ Meyer, 74; "Mad Monk" pitched 13 seasons in the majors and was a member of the Philadelphia Phillies "Whiz Kids" in the 1950s; pitched in three World Series—with the Phillies in 1949 and the Dodgers in 1953 and 1955; his career record was 94-73 with a 3.99 ERA, and he was a member of the Cubs, Red Sox and Athletics before retiring in 1959; spent 12 years coaching in the Yankees' organization, including a stint as Buck Showalter's bench coach in 1992; of congestive heart failure; in Oglesby, Ill., Nov. 16, 1997.

Cary Middlecoff, 77; prolific PGA golfer who won the U.S. Open in 1949 and 1956 as well as the 1955 Masters; won 40 professional golf tournaments and was the tour's leading money winner in the 1950s; began his career by winning the Tennessee Amateur four straight years, starting in 1940; back surgery forced him to retire in 1963; was elected to the PGA World Golf Hall of Fame in 1986; of heart failure; in Memphis, Sept. 1.

Christopher Midgett, 22; a junior reserve defensive end in 1997, he was a part of a Northeastern football team that posted an 8-3 record, the team's best in 34 years; of gun shot wounds while he refueled his car at a gas station; in Portsmouth, Va., March 26.

Rod Milburn, 47; won a gold medal in the 110-meter hurdles at the 1972 Munich Olympics; a track star at Southern University, Milburn went unbeaten in 27 consecutive finals the year before his Olympic victory; went pro in 1974 and later coached at Southern; carried the Olympic torch in 1996; was found dead in a rail car at the paper plant where he worked; cause of death unknown, but reportedly toxic gas was found in the car Milburn had been working; in Baton Rouge, La., Nov. 11, 1997.

Doug Miller, 28; San Diego Chargers linebacker from 1992-95 who appeared in Super Bowl XXIX; was struck by lightning twice while camping on the Colorado River; in Dotsero, Colo., July 21.

Glenn Montgomery, 31; former Houston Oilers and Seattle Seahawks defensive lineman who was diagnosed with amyotrophic lateral sclerosis, or Lou Gehrig's disease, in 1996; played eight years (114 games) in the NFL and had 13½ career sacks, including six in 1993; in Houston, June 28.

Helen Wills Moody, 92; women's tennis great who won eight Wimbledon singles titles in the 1920s and 1930s; won 31 major titles, including seven U.S. championships and four French titles over her illustrious career; garnered an Olympic gold medal in Paris in 1924; she won her first girl's national title at the age of 17, making her the youngest champion to that point; her serious demeanor earned her the nickname "Little Miss Poker Face"; was inducted to the International Tennis Hall of Fame in 1959 and was named AP Female Athlete of the Year in 1935; cause of death not given; in Carmel, Calif., Jan. 1.

Francis (Franny) Murray, 82; former All-American football and basketball star at the University of Pennsylvania and last surviving member of the Quakers' "Destiny Backfield", which also included Lew Elverson, Bill Kurlish and Eddie Warwick; most noted for his kicking, Murray averaged 67 yards per punt, including an 80-yard boot in 1936; also captain of the basketball team as a junior and co-captain as a senior; played halfback and punter for the Philadelphia Eagles in 1939-40; of complications from a stroke; in Boca Raton, Fla., June 28.

Jim Murray, 78; untouchable wit and an unmatched frankness in his writing distinguished Murray as one of the century's best sports columnists; his more than 50 years experience as a sports reporter spilled into newspaper columns, creating a distinct style which always gave the impression he was writing about the ballet from the usher's perspective; one of only four sportswriters to win the Pulitzer Prize for general commentary, the modest Murray said after receiving the award in 1990, he thought a winner should have "to bring down government or expose major graft or give advice to prime ministers. Correctly quoting Tommy

Lasorda shouldn't merit a Pulitzer Prize."; began his career as a campus correspondent for the *Hartford Times* in the 1940s; joined *Time* magazine in 1948 and became West Coast editor for *Sports Illustrated*, which he helped found in 1953; joined the *Los Angeles Times* staff in 1961 and battled through a loss of eyesight, the death of his wife and his son; of cardiac arrest; in Los Angeles, Aug. 16.

John Myers, 40; three-time NHRA Winston Pro Stock Motorcycle champion; won 33 NHRA national events with George Bryce's Star Racing Team; of injuries sustained in a non-racing motorcycle accident; in Tuscaloosa, Ala., Aug. 9.

Tom Neville, 36; a 350-pound NFL offensive lineman with Green Bay and San Francisco from 1986-92; was shot dead by police after escaping from a psychiatric hospital (where he had spent the last three days) and barricading himself in an apartment; in Fresno, Calif., May 9.

Ray Nitschke, 61; epitomized the grit and determination of the Vince Lombardi-era Green Bay Packers; a third round pick out of Illinois in 1958, Nitschke played linebacker and was the defensive captain of the Packers' teams that won five NFL titles and the first two Super Bowls; All-Pro (1964-66); MVP of the 1962 NFL title game; played in 190 games and had 25 interceptions for 385 yards and two touchdowns; of a brief illness; in Naples, Fla., Mar. 8.

Harry Ornest, 75; former owner of the St. Louis Blues and the Toronto Argonauts; owned the Blues 1983-86; sold Argonauts to Bruce McNall, Wayne Gretzky and the late John Candy in 1991; founded Vancouver Canadiens minor league baseball franchise in 1978; refereed in AHL and was a linesman in NHL; after a brief illness; in Los Angeles, July 21.

Murray (Muzz) Patrick, 83; lifelong member of the New York Rangers' family, serving as a player, coach and general manager; son of Hall of Famer Lester Patrick, Muzz's brother Lynn was also a player and coach, as were his nephews Craig and Glenn; took over for Rangers coach Frank Boucher in 1954 and moved up to general manager after the season; swung several memorable trades as a GM, but remembered as a player for his one-swing victory in a fight with Boston defenseman Eddie Shore at Madison Square Garden in 1939; he played four seasons as a defenseman for the Rangers, helping them to the Stanley Cup in 1940; worked in a variety of executive positions with the Rangers until his retirement in 1973; of a heart attack; in Riverside, Conn., July 23.

Gabe Paul, 88; renowned wheeling and dealing baseball executive partly responsible for building the Reds' teams of the 1960s and the Yankees' teams of the 1970s; briefly worked with the expansion Houston Astros before becoming GM of the Cleveland Indians; fused friendly relationship with George Steinbrenner and traded for the likes of Willie Randolph, Chris Chambliss and Lou Piniella; of natural causes; in Tampa, Fla., April 26.

Elijah Pitts, 60; scored first rushing touchdown in the Super Bowl as a running back for the Green Bay Packers where he spent nine seasons before becoming a longtime assistant coach in the NFL and CFL; spent 16 years as a Buffalo Bills assistant and in 1995 served as an interim head coach after Marv Levy was diagnosed with prostate cancer; a native of Mayflower, Ark., Pitts starred at Philander Smith College and was chosen in the 13th round of the 1961 draft by Green Bay; also played in Chicago, Los Angeles and New Orleans before retiring in 1971; began coaching career under Chuck Knox in Los Angeles in 1973; went to Buffalo, Houston and the Hamilton Tiger-Cats of the CFL before rejoining the Bills in 1985 as running backs coach; of abdominal cancer; in Buffalo, N.Y., July 10.

Sam Plumeri, 84; former Trenton, N.J. city official who in 1994 brought minor-league baseball back to the New Jersey capital for the first time in 45 years; helped oversee the move of the London Tigers from Ontario to Trenton in 1994; the Trenton Thunder, then a double-A affiliate of the Detroit Tigers, shifted to the Boston Red Sox a year later and became the first team in Eastern League history to draw more than 400,000 fans in a season; died while undergoing tests at Graduate Hospital; in Philadelphia, Sept. 9.

Shirley Povich, 92; Washington Post columnist who's first byline appeared in 1923 and last appeared the day he died; logged more than 15,000 columns over his 75-year career covering sports; he became the youngest sports editor in the country at the age of 20 in 1926; his "This Morning" column ran six days a week from 1926 to 1974; he saw it all, from the Senators' first World Series championship in 1924 to Cassius Clay's upset of Sonny Liston in 1964 to the terrorism at the 1972 Olympics in Munich and Cal Ripken's 2,131st consecutive game played; one of his sons is talk show host Maury Povich, of a heart attack; in Washington D.C., June 4.

Richie Powers, 67; NBA referee from 1956-79; worked 25 NBA Finals games including the triple overtime contest in 1976 between the Phoenix Suns and the Boston Celtics and three All-Star Games; after retirement became sportscaster on WABC-TV in New York, cause of death not given; in Allentown, Pa., July 31.

Dan Quisenberry, 45; submarine-throwing relief pitcher for the Kansas City Royals; a three-time all-star, "Quiz" led the league in saves five times during his career and helped the Royals garner two AL pennants and the 1985 World Series; got the save in the infamous "Pine Tar Game"; finished his career with 244 saves and a 2.76 ERA in 12 seasons; after eight years with the Royals he was released in 1988, spent a year-and-a-half with St. Louis and then retired after a brief stay with San Francisco; described as a "prankster" and "quick-witted" by teammates, who spent evenings as an audience to Quisenberry's nightly antics in the bullpen; diagnosed with brain cancer in December 1997; on May 30, 1998 an emotional crowd was on hand to see him inducted into the Royals' Hall of Fame; of a brain tumor; in Leawood, Kan., Sept. 30.

Claude Retherford, 72; former University of Nebraska basketball star who was named mayor of Tulare, Calif. in 1992; a native of French Lick, Ind., Retherford was named Big 7 MVP in 1949, leading the Cornhuskers to their only conference title; named to Nebraska Hall of Fame in 1989; of a heart-related illness; in Tulare, Calif., June 10.

Edwin (Chapo) Rosario, 34; three-time world champion boxer who won his first world title in 1983, defeating Jose Luis Ramirez for the WBC lightweight belt; after losing the title to Hector Camacho in 1986, later in the year, Rosario captured the WBA lightweight crown, and held it until 1990 when he was stopped in the 11th round by Julio Cesar Chavez; served a year in a Puerto Rican jail for drug charges, but spent the last year of his life on the comeback trail; from pulmonary edema, an excessive buildup of fluid in the lungs; in Toa Baja, Puerto Rico, Dec. 1, 1997.

Browning Ross, 74; formed the Philadelphia Road Runners Club in 1957 which expanded into a national organization a year later and became what is today the 180,000-member Road Runners Club of America; finished seventh in the steeplechase at the 1948 Olympics; won 1,500-meter race at 1951 Pan-Am Games; of a heart attack; in Woodbury, N.J., April 27.

Esco Sarkkinen, 79; All-American in 1939 on Ohio St. Big 10 championship team and assistant coach with the Buckeyes from 1946-78; cause of death not given; in Columbus, Ohio, Feb. 28.

Fernand Sastre, 74; co-president of the French World Cup organizing committee which led France's drive to host the tournament beginning in 1989; Sastre was also a longtime official with the French Football Federation; he died three days after the 1998 championship began; of lung cancer; in Paris, June 13.

Frank Scott, 80; negotiated endorsement deals and public appearances for baseball-star clients such as Mickey Mantle (bubble gum) and Yogi Berra (soft drink); became an agent after a stint as the Yankees' traveling secretary and later became an executive with the players' association; cause of death was not given; in Livingston, N.J., June 28.

Ray Scott, 78; the voice heard describing every moment of the Green Bay Packers' dynasty years of the 1960s was owned by Scott; paired with Pat Summerall to form CBS's number one duo after the AFL/NFL merger in 1967; broadcasted four Super Bowls; began his career as host of nationally syndicated radio show in Johnstown, Pa. in 1937; an illness forced his retirement from broadcasting in 1997; named National Sportscaster of the Year in 1968 and 1971; elected to National Sportswriters and Sportscasters Hall of Fame in 1982; of a long illness; in Minneapolis, March 23.

Cliff Shaw, 91; college football and basketball official whose call in the 1954 Cotton Bowl set a precedent still observed in the NCAA; when Alabama's Tommy Lewis came off the bench to tackle Rice halfback Dickie Moegle, Shaw awarded Rice a touchdown, causing the sport's rules committee to make the procedure a standard at their next meeting; once rated the top referee in the Southwest Conference, Shaw also co-hosted a weekly football highlight show for KARK-TV in Arkansas; of natural causes; in Little Rock, Ark., Jan 22.

Roland (Rolly) Schwartz, 85; active in amateur boxing for almost 60 years as coach, referee and administrator; manager and part-time coach of 1976 U.S. Olympic boxing team which won five gold medals, one silver and one bronze in 11 weight classes; officiated at 1968 and 1972 Olympics; helped shape international rules, including one that required amateur boxers to wear protective headwear; of renal failure; in Dayton, Ohio, April 7.

Joseph Sobek, 79; inventor of racquetball; developed the sport while working in a rubber manufacturing plant in Bridgeport, Conn. in 1950; single-handedly promoted the sport and founded the Paddle Rackets Association to generate interest; a group of racquetball players formed an association under the direction of Robert Kendler who headed the U.S. Handball Association in 1968 and the sport took off; Sobek took himself out of the picture shortly after and returned to his work as a tennis professional; of congestive heart failure; in Greenwich, Conn., March 27.

Benjamin Spock, 94; famed pediatrician who revolutionized baby care for the Baby Boom generation, and Olympic gold medalist; while studying at Yale University Spock was a member of the 1924 U.S. national crew that won a gold medal in Paris; cause of death not given; in San Diego, March 15.

Woody Stephens, 84; legendary thoroughbred racing trainer who won the Eclipse Award in 1983 as the nation's No. 1 trainer; his horses won five straight Belmont Stakes races in the 1980s; he won the Kentucky Derby with Canonade in 1974 and Swale in 1984 and the Preakness with Blue Man in 1952; elected to racing's Hall of Fame in 1976; of complications from chronic emphysema; in Miami, July 29.

Billy Sullivan, 82; founded the New England Patriots in 1959 and was president of the American Football League from 1961-64; moved the Patriots to Schaefer Stadium (now Foxboro Stadium) in 1969; named majority owner in 1975 and remained president until 1992; sued the NFL for $116 million in 1991, claiming its refusal to allow him to sell additional public stock forced him to sell the team at a low price of $84 million; he received an $11.5 million settlement in 1996; of cancer; in Atlantis, Fla., Feb. 23.

Rell Sunn, 47; international surfing champion who helped found the Women's Professional Surfing Association and established the first professional tour for women; one of the first five women inducted into the International Surfing Museum's Walk of Fame; Sunn was the top-ranked woman on the longboard in 1982 before being diagnosed with cancer the following year; of breast cancer; in Makaha on the island of Oahu, Hawaii, Jan. 2.

John Tate, 43; former WBA heavyweight champion and U.S. Olympian; won title in a decision over Gerrie Coetzee in South Africa in 1979; lost the belt five months later to Mike Weaver; won bronze at the 1976 Olympics; his career record was 34-3 with 23 knockouts; admitted to a cocaine habit during the 1980s and served time in prison for petty theft and assault before resorting to panhandling on the streets of Knoxville, Tenn.; of injuries sustained when he crashed his pickup truck into a utility pole; in Knoxville, Tenn., April 9.

Bill Tuttle, 69; outspoken critic of chewing tobacco, Tuttle was diagnosed with oral cancer in 1993 and had most of his jaw and cheek removed due to a 37-year chewing habit which began during his 11 years as a Major League Baseball player; played for Detroit, Kansas City and Minnesota before retiring in 1962; was actively involved in Oral Health America's National Spit Tobacco Education Program and said he wanted his cancer-ravaged face to serve as an example to youngsters; Oral Health America has named the Bill Tuttle Award in his honor, to be given to individuals or groups who distinguish themselves in the fight for tobacco awareness and education; of cancer; in Anoka, Minn., July 27.

Doak Walker, 71; 1948 Heisman Trophy winner and member of two NFL championship teams with the Detroit Lions; was involved in a skiing accident early in 1998 which left him paralyzed; his four years at SMU (1946-49) were legendary; Walker played running back, quarterback, receiver, punt/kick returner and defensive back during his years with the Mustangs; he was a three-time All-American whose popularity forced SMU to move from Ownby Stadium to the 47,000-seat Cotton Bowl in 1948. By his senior season the Cotton Bowl expanded to seat 75,000 and was called "The House that Walker Built"; high school and pro teammate Bobby Layne called him, "the greatest clutch player I've ever seen"; in six seasons as a pro with Detroit he scored an astonishing 534 points, including 34 touchdowns, 183 extra-points and 49 field goals; abruptly retired from football in 1956 to pursue business interests; is a member of both the college and pro football Halls of Fame; the award given annually to college football's best running back is named after him; of complications from paralysis; in Steamboat Springs, Colo., Sept. 27.

Todd Witsken, 34; Indianapolis Tennis Center director who was a three-time All-American at USC and first burst on the pro tennis scene by beating Jimmy Connors in the third round of the U.S. Open in 1986; earned $1.4 million in his pro career, ranking as high as fourth in doubles in 1989 and 43rd in singles; retired after the 1993 U.S. Open; of brain cancer; in Indianapolis, June 1.

Warren Woodson, 95; the most successful football coach in New Mexico State history; coached the Aggies from 1958-67 and led them to back-to-back Sun Bowl victories in 1959 and 1960; remains the only coach ever to have the nation's top individual rusher four years in a row; began his coaching career in 1927 at Texarkana Junior College and moved on to Arizona where he spent five years; he finished his career at Trinity College; compiled a 203-94-19 record overall; of colon cancer; in Las Cruces, N.M., Feb. 24.

RESEARCH MATERIAL

Many sources were used in the gathering of information for this almanac. Day to day material was almost always found in copies of *USA Today*, *The Boston Globe*, and *The New York Times* or online at various world wide web addresses (see below).

Several weekly and bi-weekly periodicals were also used in the past year's pursuit of facts and figures, among them— *Baseball America, International Boxing Digest, ESPN the Magazine, FIFA News* (Soccer), *The Hockey News, The NCAA News, On Track, Soccer America, Sports Illustrated, The Sporting News, Track & Field News*, and *USA Today Baseball Weekly*.

In addition, the following books provided background material for one or more chapters of the almanac.

Arenas & Ballparks

The Ballparks, by Bill Shannon and George Kalinsky; Hawthorn Books, Inc. (1975); New York.

Diamonds, by Michael Gershman; Houghton Mifflin Co. (1993); Boston.

Green Cathedrals (Revised Edition), by Philip Lowry; Addison-Wesley Publishing Co. (1992); Reading, Mass.

The NFL's Encyclopedic History of Professional Football, Macmillan Publishing Co. (1977); New York.

Take Me Out to the Ballpark, by Lowell Reidenbaugh; The Sporting News Publishing Co. (1983); St. Louis.

24 Seconds to Shoot (An Informal History of the NBA), by Leonard Koppett; Macmillan Publishing Co. (1968); New York.

Plus many major league baseball, NBA, NFL, NHL league and team guides, and college football and basketball guides.

Auto Racing

1997 IndyCar Media Guide, edited by Bob Andrew; Championship Auto Racing Teams; Troy, Mich.

Indy: 75 Years of Racing's Greatest Spectacle, by Rich Taylor; St. Martin's Press (1991); New York.

Marlboro Grand Prix Guide, 1950-96 (1997 Edition), compiled by Jacques Deschenaux and Claude Michele Deschenaux; Charles Stewart & Company Ltd; Brentford, England.

1997 Winston Cup Media Guide, compiled and edited by Chris Powell; NASCAR Winston Cup Series; Winston-Salem, N.C.

NASCAR Online, produced by Starwave Corp. http://www.nascar.com

CART Online, maintained by USAInternet Direct. http://www.cart.com

Baseball

The All-Star Game (A Pictorial History, 1933 to Present), by Donald Honig; The Sporting News Publishing Co. (1987); St. Louis.

1998 American League Red Book, published by The Sporting News Publishing Co.; St. Louis.

The Baseball Chronology, edited by James Charlton; Macmillian Publishing Co. (1991); New York.

The Baseball Encyclopedia (Ninth Edition), editorial director, Rick Wolff; Macmillan Publishing Co. (1993); New York.

The Complete 1996 Baseball Record Book, edited by Craig Carter; The Sporting News Publishing Co.; St. Louis.

1998 National League Green Book, published by The Sporting News Publishing Co.; St. Louis.

The Scrapbook History of Baseball by Jordan Deutsch, Richard Cohen, Roland Johnson and David Neft; Bobbs-Merrill Company, Inc. (1975); Indianapolis/New York.

1998 Sporting News Official Baseball Guide, edited by Craig Carter and Dave Sloan; The Sporting News Publishing Co.; St. Louis.

1998 Sporting News Official Baseball Register, edited by Mark Bonavita and Sean Stewart; The Sporting News Publishing Co.; St. Louis.

The Sports Encyclopedia: Baseball (1996 Edition), edited by David Neft and Richard Cohen; St. Martin's Press; New York.

Total Baseball (Fourth Edition), edited by John Thorn and Pete Palmer; HarperPerennial (1995); New York.

The Official Site of Major League Baseball, produced by Major League Baseball Properties, Inc. http://www.majorleaguebaseball.com

College Basketball

All the Moves (A History of College Basketball), by Neil D. Issacs; J.B. Lippincott Company (1975); New York.

College Basketball, U.S.A. (Since 1892), by John D. McCallum; Stein and Day (1978); New York.

Collegiate Basketball: Facts and Figures on the Cage Sport, by Edwin C. Caudle; The Paragon Press (1960); Montgomery, Ala.

The Encyclopedia of the NCAA Basketball Tournament, written and compiled by Jim Savage; Dell Publishing (1990); New York.

The Final Four (Reliving America's Basketball Classic), compiled by Billy Reed; Host Communications, Inc. (1988); Lexington, Ky.

1997 NCAA Final Four Records Book, compiled by Gary Johnson; edited by Stephen R. Hagwell; NCAA Books; Overland Park, Kan.

The Modern Encyclopedia of Basketball (Second Revised Edition), edited by Zander Hollander; Dolphins Books (1979); Doubleday & Company, Inc.; Garden City, N.Y.

1998 NCAA Men's Records Book, compiled by Gary Johnson, Richard Campbell, John Painter, Jenifer Scheibler, Sean Straziscar and James Wright; edited by Shawna Hansen; NCAA Books; Overland Park, Kan.

1998 NCAA Women's Records Book, compiled by Gary Johnson, Sean Straziscar; edited by Gary T. Brown; NCAA Books; Overland Park, Kan.

NCAA Online, produced by National Collegiate Athletic Association. http://www.ncaa.org

Plus many 1997-98 NCAA Division I conference guides from America East to the WAC.

Pro Basketball

The Official NBA Basketball Encyclopedia (Second Edition), edited by Alex Sachare; Villard Books (1994); New York.

1997-98 Sporting News Official NBA Guide, edited by Mark Broussard and Craig Carter; The Sporting News Publishing Co.; St. Louis.

1997-98 Sporting News Official NBA Register, edited by Mark Bonavita, Mark Broussard and Sean Stewart; The Sporting News Publishing Co.; St. Louis.

NBA Online, produced by Starwave Corp. http://www.nba.com

Bowling

1995 Bowlers Journal Annual & Almanac; Luby Publishing; Chicago.

1996 LPBT Guide, Ladies Pro Bowlers Tour; Rockford, Ill.

1996 PBA Media Guide; Professional Bowlers Association; Akron, Ohio.

PBA Online, produced by the Pro Bowlers Association and Cadmus Interactive, http://www.pba.org

PWBA Online, produced by Professional Women's Bowling Association, http://www.pwba.com

Boxing

The Boxing Record Book (1996), edited by Phill Marder; Fight Fax Inc.; Sicklerville, N.J.

The Ring 1985 Record Book & Boxing Encyclopedia, edited by Herbert G. Goldman; The Ring Publishing Corp.; New York.

The Ring: Boxing, The 20th Century, Steven Farhood, editor-in-chief; BDD Illustrated Books (1993); New York.

College Sports

1994-95 National Collegiate Championships, edited by Ted Breidenthal; NCAA Books; Overland Park, Kan.

1996-97 NAIA Championships History and Records Book; National Assn. of Intercollegiate Athletics; Tulsa, Okla.

1996-97 National Directory of College Athletics, edited by Kevin Cleary; Collegiate Directories, Inc.; Cleveland.

NCAA Online, produced by National Collegiate Athletic Association. http://www.ncaa.org

College Football

Football: A College History, by Tom Perrin; McFarland & Company, Inc. (1987); Jefferson, N.C.

Football: Facts & Figures, by Dr. L.H. Baker; Farrar & Rinehart, Inc. (1945); New York.

Great College Football Coaches of the Twenties and Thirties, by Tim Cohane; Arlington House (1973); New Rochelle, N.Y.

1997 NCAA College Football Records Book, compiled by Richard Campbell, John Painter and Sean Straziscar; edited by Ted Breidenthal; NCAA Books; Overland Park, Kan.

Saturday Afternoon, by Richard Whittingham; Workman Publishing Co., Inc. (1985); New York.

Saturday's America, by Dan Jenkins; Sports Illustrated Books; Little, Brown & Company (1970); Boston.

Tournament of Roses, The First 100 Years, by Joe Hendrickson; Knapp Press (1989); Los Angeles.

NCAA Online, produced by National Collegiate Athletic Association. http://www.ncaa.org

Plus numerous college football team and conference guides, especially the 1997 guides compiled by the Atlantic Coast Conference, Big 12 and Southeastern Conference.

Pro Football

1997 Canadian Football League Guide, compiled by the CFL Communications Dept.; Toronto.

The Football Encyclopedia (The Complete History of NFL Football from 1892 to the Present), compiled by David Neft and Richard Cohen; St. Martin's Press (1994); New York.

The Official NFL Encyclopedia, by Beau Riffenburgh; New American Library (1986); New York.

Official NFL 1996 Record and Fact Book, compiled by the NFL Communications Dept. and Seymour Siwoff, Elias Sports Bureau; edited by Chris McCloskey and Chuck Garrity Jr.; produced by NFL Properties, Inc.; Los Angeles.

The Scrapbook History of Pro Football, by Richard Cohen, Jordan Deutsch, Roland Johnson and David Neft; Bobbs-Merrill Company, Inc. (1976); Indianapolis/New York.

1997 Sporting News Football Guide, edited by Craig Carter and Dave Sloan; The Sporting News Publishing Co.; St. Louis.

1997 Sporting News Football Register, edited Mark Bonavita and Sean Stewart; The Sporting News Publishing Co.; St. Louis.

1995 Sporting News Super Bowl Book, edited by Tom Dienhart, Joe Hoppel and Dave Sloan; The Sporting News Publishing Co.; St. Louis.

NFL.Com, produced by Starwave Corp. http://www.nfl.com

CFL Online, produced by SLAM! Sports. http://www.cfl.ca

Golf

The Encyclopedia of Golf (Revised Edition), compiled by Nevin H. Gibson; A.S. Barnes and Company (1964); New York.

Guinness Golf Records: Facts and Champions, by Donald Steel; Guinness Superlatives Ltd. (1987); Middlesex, England.

The History of the PGA Tour, by Al Barkow; Doubleday (1989); New York.

The Illustrated History of Women's Golf, by Rhonda Glenn, Taylor Publishing Co. (1991); Dallas.

1998 LPGA Player Guide, produced by LPGA Communications Dept.; Ladies Professional Golf Assn. Tour; Daytona Beach, Fla.

1998 PGA Tour Guide, produced by PGA Tour Creative Services; Professional Golfers Assn. Tour; Ponte Vedra, Fla.

Official Guide of the PGA Championships; Triumph Books (1994); Chicago.

The PGA World Golf Hall of Fame Book, by Gerald Astor, Prentice Hall Press (1991); New York.

1998 Senior PGA Tour Guide, produced by PGA Tour Creative Services; Professional Golfers Assn. Tour; Ponte Vedra, Fla.

Pro-Golf 1998, PGA European Tour Media Guide, Virginia Water, Surrey, England.

The Random House International Encyclopedia of Golf, by Malcolm Campbell; Random House (1991); New York.

USGA Record Books (1895-1959, 1960-80 and 1981-90); U.S. Golf Association; Far Hills, N.J.

LPGA.com, produced by the LPGA and Black Dog Design, http://www.lpga.com

PGA.com, produced by the PGA of America, http://www.pgaonline.com

Hockey

Canada Cup '87: The Official History, No.1 Publications Ltd.; Toronto.

The Complete Encyclopedia of Hockey; edited by Zander Hollander; Visible Ink Press (1993); Detroit.

The Hockey Encyclopedia, by Stan Fischler and Shirley Walton Fischler; research editor, Bob Duff; Macmillan Publishing Co. (1983); New York.

Hockey Hall of Fame (The Official History of the Game and Its Greatest Stars), by Dan Diamond and Joseph Romain; Doubleday (1988); New York.

The National Hockey League, by Edward F. Dolan Jr.; W H Smith Publishers Inc. (1986); New York.

The Official National Hockey League 75th Anniversary Commemorative Book, edited by Dan Diamond; McClelland & Stewart, Inc. (1991); Toronto.

1997-98 Official NHL Guide & Record Book, compiled by the NHL Public Relations Dept.; New York/Montreal/Toronto.

1997-98 Sporting News Hockey Guide, edited by Craig Carter; The Sporting News Publishing Co.; St. Louis.

1997-98 Sporting News Hockey Register, edited by Mark Bonavita and Sean Stewart; The Sporting News Publishing Co.; St. Louis.

The Stanley Cup, by Joseph Romain and James Duplacey; Gallery Books (1989); New York.

The Trail of the Stanley Cup (Volumns I-III), by Charles L. Coleman; Progressive Publications Inc. (1969); Sherbrooke, Quebec.

NHL.com, produced by the NHL, http://www.nhl.com

Horse Racing

1997 American Racing Manual, compiled by the Daily Racing Form; Hightstown, N.J.

1997 Breeders' Cup Statistics; Breeders' Cup Limited; Lexington, Ky.

1996 Directory and Record Book, Thoroughbred Racing Associations of North America Inc.; Elkton, Md.

1996 Trotting and Pacing Guide, compiled and edited by John Pawlak; United States Trotting Association; Columbus, Ohio.

USTA online, produced by the USTA, http://www.ustrotting.com

International Sports

Athletics: A History of Modern Track and Field (1860-1990, Men and Women), by Roberto Quercetani; Vallardi & Associati (1990); Milan, Italy.

1998 International Track & Field Annual, Association of Track & Field Statisticians; edited by Peter Matthews; SportsBooks Ltd.; Surrey, England.

Track & Field News' Little Blue Book; Metric conversion tables; From the editors of Track & Field News (1989); Los Altos, Calif.

US Ski Team online, produced by US Ski Team and SportsLine USA, http://www.usskiteam.com

Miscellaneous

The America's Cup 1851-1987 (Sailing for Supremacy), by Gary Lester and Richard Sleeman; Lester-Townsend Publishing (1986); Sydney, Australia.

The Encyclopedia of Sports (Fifth Revised Edition), by Frank G. Menke; revisions by Suzanne Treat; A.S. Barnes and Co., Inc. (1975); Cranbury, N.J.

The Great American Sports Book, by George Gipe; Doubleday & Company, Inc. (1978); Garden City, N.Y.

The 1998 Information Please Almanac, edited by Borgna Brunner; Information Please, LLC; Boston.

1997 Official PRCA Media Guide, edited by Steve Fleming; Professional Rodeo Cowboys Association; Colorado Springs.

The Sail Magazine Book of Sailing, by Peter Johnson; Alfred A. Knopf (1989); New York.

Ten Years of the Ironman, Triathlete Magazine; October, 1988; Santa Monica, Calif.

The Ultimate Book of Sports Lists 1998, by Mike Meserole; DK Publishing (1997); New York.

Iditarod online, produced by the Iditarod Trail Committtee and GCI, http://www.iditarod.com

Ironman online, produced by SportsLine USA, http://ironman.sportsline.com

PRCA online, produced by the Pro Rodeo Cowboys Association, http://www.prorodeo.com

Olympics

All That Glitters Is Not Gold (An Irreverent Look at the Olympic Games); by William O. Johnson, Jr.; G.P. Putnam's Sons (1972); New York.

Barcelona/Albertville 1992; edited by Lisa H. Albertson; for U.S. Olympic Committee by Commemorative Publications; Salt Lake City.

Chamonix to Lillehammer (The Glory of the Olympic Winter Games); edited by Lisa H. Albertson; for U.S. Olympic Committee by Commemorative Publication (1994); Salt Lake City.

The Complete Book of the Olympics (1992 Edition); by David Wallechinsky; Little, Brown and Co.; Boston.

The Games Must Go On (Avery Brundage and the Olympic Movement), by Allen Guttmann; Columbia University Press (1984); New York.

The Golden Book of the Olympic Games, edited by Erich Kamper and Bill Mallon; Vallardi & Associati (1992); Milan, Italy.

Hitler's Games (The 1936 Olympics), by Duff Hart-Davis; Harper & Row (1986); New York/London.

An Illustrated History of the Olympics (Third Edition); by Dick Schaap; Alfred A. Knopf (1975); New York.

The Nazi Olympics, by Richard D. Mandell; Souvenir Press (1972); London.

The Official USOC Book of the 1984 Olympic Games, by Dick Schaap; Random House/ABC Sports; New York.

The Olympics: A History of the Games, by William Oscar Johnson; Oxmoor House (1992); Birmingham, Ala.

Pursuit of Excellence (The Olympic Story), by The Associated Press and Grolier; Grolier Enterprises Inc. (1979); Danbury, Conn.

The Story of the Olympic Games (776 B.C. to 1948 A.D.), by John Kieran and Arthur Daley; J.B. Lippincott Company (1948); Philadelphia/New York.

United States Olympic Books (Seven Editions): 1936 and 1948-88; U.S. Olympic Association; New York.

The USA and the Olympic Movement, produced by the USOC Information Dept.; edited by Gayle Plant; U.S. Olympic Committee (1988); Colorado Springs.

Soccer

The American Encyclopedia of Soccer, edited by Zander Hollander; Everest House Publishers (1980); New York.

The European Football Yearbook (1994-95 Edition), edited by Mike Hammond; Sports Projects Ltd; West Midlands, England.

The Guinness Book of Soccer Facts & Feats, by Jack Rollin; Guinness Superlatives Ltd. (1978); Middlesex, England.

History of Soccer's World Cup, by Michael Archer; Chartwell Books, Inc. (1978); Secaucus, N.J.

The Simplest Game, by Paul Gardner; Collier Books (1994); New York.

The Story of the World Cup, by Brian Glanville; Faber and Faber Limited (1993); London/Boston.

1998 MLS Official Media Guide, edited by the MLS Communications staff; Los Angeles.

1991-92 MSL Official Guide, Major (Indoor) Soccer League; Overland Park, Kan.

U.S. Soccer 1996 Media Guide, edited by Tom Lang; U.S. Soccer Federation; Chicago.

FIFA online, produced by FIFA, http://www.fifa.com

France98 online, produced by the France 98 Organizing Committee, http://www.france98.com

MLSnet, produced by Major League Soccer and Boxtop Interactive, http://www.mlsnet.com

Tennis

Bud Collins' Modern Encyclopedia of Tennis, edited by Bud Collins and Zander Hollander; Visible Ink Press (1994); Detroit.

The Illustrated Encyclopedia of World Tennis, by John Haylett and Richard Evans; Exeter Books (1989); New York.

Official Encyclopedia of Tennis, edited by the staff of the U.S. Lawn Tennis Assn.; Harper & Row (1972); New York.

1998 ATP Tour Player Guide, compiled by ATP Tour Communications Dept.; Association of Tennis Professionals; Ponte Vedra Beach, Fla.

1998 Corel WTA Tour Media Guide, compiled by WTA Public Relations staff; edited by Renee Bloch Shallouf, Doug Clery and Toni Woods; St. Petersburg, Fla.

ATP Tour online, produced by ATP Tour, Inc., http://www.atptour.com

Corel WTA Tour Site, produced by the Corel WTA Tour, http://www.corelwtatour.com

Who's Who

The Guiness International Who's Who of Sport, edited by Peter Mathews, Ian Buchanan and Bill Mallon; Guiness Publishing (1993); Middlesex, England

101 Greatest Athletes of the Century, by Will Grimsley and the Associated Press Sports Staff; Bonanza Books (1987); Crown Publishers, Inc.; New York.

The New York Times Book of Sports Legends, edited by Joseph Vecchione; Simon & Schuster (1991); New York.

Superstars, by Frank Litsky; Vineyard Books, Inc. (1975); Secaucus, N.J.

A Who's Who of Sports Champions (Their Stories and Records), by Ralph Hickok, Houghton Mifflin Co. (1995); Boston.

Other Reference Books/Sites

Facts & Dates of American Sports, by Gorton Carruth & Eugene Ehrlich; Harper & Row, Publishers, Inc. (1988); New York.

Sports Market Place 1997 (January edition), edited by Kevin J. Myers; Franklin Quest Sports; Phoenix, Ariz.

The World Book Encyclopedia (1988 Edition); World Book, Inc.; Chicago.

The World Book Yearbook (Annual Supplements, 1954-95); World Book, Inc.; Chicago.

ESPN.com, produced by ESPN and Starwave Corp., http://ESPN.com

CBS SportsLine, produced by CBS and SportsLine USA, http://www.sportsline.com